MW01001482

THE

STAR TREK® ENCYCLOPEDIA

A Reference Guide to the Future

UPDATED AND EXPANDED EDITION

BY

MICHAEL OKUDA
DENISE OKUDA

ILLUSTRATIONS BY: DOUG DREXLER
PHOTO EDITOR: MARGARET CLARK
RESEARCH CONSULTANT: ROBERT H. JUSTMAN

ADDITIONAL RESEARCH: CURT DANHAUSER
ADDITIONAL RESEARCH: S. J. CASEY BERNAY
RESEARCH CONSULTANT: GREG JEIN
RESEARCH CONSULTANT: BJO TRIMBLE
FIRST EDITION WITH DEBBIE MIREK

POCKET BOOKS
New York London Toronto Sydney Tokyo Singapore Alpha Centauri

POCKET BOOKS, a division of Simon & Schuster Inc.
1230 Avenue of the Americas, New York, NY 10020

This book is published by Pocket Books, a division of
Simon & Schuster Inc., under exclusive license from
Paramount Pictures.

ISBN: 0-671-03475-8
ISBN: 0-671-53609-5 (trade paperback)

Pocket Books revised hardcover printing October 1999
First Pocket Books trade paperback printing October 1999

10 9 8 7 6 5 4 3 2

Printed in the U.S.A.

INTRODUCTION

The *Star Trek* saga now spans more than three decades, far longer than anyone imagined when Gene Roddenberry's creation first hit the airwaves in 1966. *Star Trek* has indeed become an icon of 20th-century popular culture. Yet because of this extraordinary success, it has become increasingly difficult for those involved with the show (either as viewers or as writers and production staff) to remember the enormous body of details that has been created for the show. This book has been created to help keep track of all that stuff. This updated and expanded (1999) edition includes material partway through the 1996–1997 production seasons of *Star Trek: Deep Space Nine* and *Star Trek: Voyager*. **The special supplement at the end of this edition completes the 1996–97 season, as well as the entirety of the following year, and covers part of the 1998–1999 season.**

In compiling this material, we have assumed editorially that both authors and readers are residents of the future, a number of years after the current *Star Trek* adventures. This is our attempt to place everything in a historical perspective. Dates indicated in this work are drawn from our own *Star Trek Chronology: The History of the Future*, 1996 edition, published by Pocket Books.

We have stayed fairly strictly with material only from finished, aired versions of episodes and released versions of films. We have not used any material from the *Star Trek* novels or other publications. This isn't because we don't like those works (we're quite fond of many of them, and we hope this information will be useful to our writer friends), but as with the *Chronology,* we wanted to create a reference to the source material itself—that is, the episodes and the movies. This way, anyone building on this Encyclopedia can be reasonably sure that his or her work is directly based on actual *Star Trek* source material. In a related vein, this work adheres to Paramount studio policy that regards the animated *Star Trek* series as not being part of the "official" *Star Trek* universe, even though we count ourselves among that show's fans. Of course, the final decision as to the "authenticity" of the animated episodes, as with all elements of the show, must clearly be the choice of each individual reader.

Episode numbers. In the main listing for each episode, we have indicated an episode number. These are *not* Paramount's internal production numbers (which are sometimes confusing), but are simply the number of that episode within that series in order of production. In other words, "The Cage" (TOS), "Encounter at Farpoint, Part I" (TNG), "Emissary, Part I" (DS9), and "Caretaker, Part I" (VGR) are all episode #1 of their respective series. The suffix (TOS) indicates an episode of The Original Series, while (TNG) denotes an episode of *The Next Generation*, a title labeled (DS9) is from *Deep Space Nine*, and (VGR) is an episode of *Star Trek: Voyager*. (For those who simply *must* know: Episode numbers assigned to episodes of the Original Series are indeed the internal Desilu/Paramount numbers. Studio production numbers for *Next Generation* episodes can be determined by adding 100 to our episode number, so that "Encounter at Farpoint, Part I" is production number 101. The same numbering scheme was used for episodes of *Voyager*, as well. Add 400 to our episode numbers to get production numbers for *Deep Space Nine* episodes, so that "Emissary, Part I" is production number 401. To further complicate matters, the two-hour pilot movie versions of the three new shows were also assigned the production number 721. Don't ask us. It has something to do with studio accounting.)

Please note that **boldfaced** items indicate cross references to other entries in the Encyclopedia. If a word is boldfaced, it means there is an entry by that name containing related information.

ACKNOWLEDGEMENTS

Our thanks to the researchers who worked with us on this updated edition: Curt H. Danhauser, S.J. Casey Bernay, Alan Kobayashi, Anthony Fredrickson, Joshua Schroeder, George Brozak, David Hirsch, James Van Over, Jackie Edwards, Penny Juday, Judy Saul, D. Joseph Creighton, Kasey K.S. Chang, and Matthew F. Lyons. *Star Trek* producer Bob Justman served as a research consultant, offering his first-hand experiences from the original *Star Trek* and *Star Trek: The Next Generation* (as well as no small measure of the infamous Justman wit.) At Simon and Schuster Interactive, our gratitude to Keith Halper and Elizabeth Braswell, who produced the *Star Trek Omnipedia* CD-ROM, portions of which were incorporated into this work. Also, appreciation to Peter Mackey, Marshall Lefferts, Stephanie Triggiani, and the good people at Imergy who were our developers on the project. Assistance with the cast and crew appendices was lent by Ken Rowland, Mark C. Bernay, Suzanne F. Kovaks, Dennis H. Lotka, and Richard C. Rierdan, PhD.

Additional assistance in research for the first edition was lent by Rick Sternbach, Jeff Erdmann, Terry Erdmann, Paul Frenczli, Suzanne Gibson, Warren James, Wes Yokoyama, David Alexander, Larry Nemecek, and Shirley Maiewski of the *Star Trek* Welcommittee. We would like to thank Bjo Trimble for permission to use some of her cast list research from the original *Star Trek* series that was incorporated into our cast appendix. We want to acknowledge the significant contributions of Debbie Mirek, our collaborator on the first edition of this Encyclopedia, who has since moved onto other projects. Her absence from this edition is keenly felt.

At Pocket Books, we are deeply indebted to Margaret Clark, our editor, who also served as photo editor for this edition, a herculean task, indeed. Kevin Ryan was our editor on the first edition, and we thank him for inviting us to be involved with this project in the first place and for being a keeper of the flame. Our copy editors were Bernadette Bosky and Arthur D. Hlavaty, with the assistance of Kevin J. Maroney, Gary Farber, Avram Grumer, and Lisa V. Padol; we salute their diligence. This book was designed by Jackie Frant, and the supplement by David Stevenson. Thanks also to Judith Curr, Kara Welsh, Scott Shannon, Donna O'Neill, Donna Ruvituso, Paolo Pepe, John Ordover, Marco Palmieri, Robert Simpson, Erin Galligan, Lisa Feuer, Twisne Fan, Linda Dingler, and John Perrella.

Cover design by Bill Snebold of 5555 Communications; thanks to Jay Warner and Bryan D. Allen. Jay Roth of Electric Image, Adam "Mojo" Lebowitz and Ron Thornton of Foundation Imaging, and Anthony Fredrickson at Paramount provided some of the ship images. Additional cover photography by Lee Varis.

At Paramount Pictures, our thanks to: Rick Berman, Michael Piller, Jeri Taylor, Ira Steven Behr, David Livingston, Merri Howard, Steve Oster, Peter Lauritson, Robert della Santina, Brad Yacobian, Ronald D. Moore, Brannon Braga, Robert Wolfe, René Echevarria, Hans Beimler, Joe Menosky, Wendy Neuss, Steve Oster, Paula Block, Harry Lang, Bill Bertini, Dan Curry, Gary Hutzel, Ronald B. Moore, Judy Elkins, Marvin Rush, Jonathan West, Andre Bormanis, Benjamin Betts, Joe Longo, Alan Sims, Susan Sackett, Guy Vardaman, Heidi Smothers, Lolita Fatjo, Jana Wallace, Mary Allen, Robbin Slocum, Dave Rossi, April Rossi, Peter Lefabvre, Eddie Williams, and Deborah McRae.

Our colleagues and friends at the *Star Trek* art departments: Shawn Baden, Greg Berry, Tony Bro, Ricardo Delgado, Daren ("I Am Kirok!") Dochterman, Louise Dorton, Wendy Drapanas, Doug Drexler, John Eaves, Leslie Frankenheimer, Anthony Fredrickson, Kurt Hanson, Scott Herbertson, Greg Hooper, Matt Bekoff, Richard James, Walter M. Jefferies, John Josselyn, Penny Juday, Alan Kobayashi, Geoff Mandel, Michael Mayer, Jimmy Mees, Randy McIlvain, Richard F. McKenzie, Leslie Parsons, Andrew Probert, Andrew Reeder, Laura Richarz, Lisa Rich, Eugene W. Roddenberry, Jr., Tony Sears, Gary Speckman, Berndt Heidemann, Kim Spoerer, Rick Sternbach, James Van Over, Sandy Veneziano, Ron Wilkinson, Fritz Zimmerman, and Herman Zimmerman.

Many photographs in this volume were directly taken from film and video frames of the actual episodes and movies. As a result, the directors of photography of the shows should be credited: Jerry Finnerman and Al Francis (original *Star Trek* series), William E. Snyder ("The Cage" [TOS]), Ernest Haller ("Where No Man Has Gone Before" [TOS]), Richard H. Kline *(Star Trek: The Motion Picture),* Gayne Rescher *(Star Trek II: The Wrath of Khan),* Charles Correll *(Star Trek III: The Search for Spock),* Don Peterman *(Star Trek IV: The Voyage Home),* Andrew Laszlo *(Star Trek V: The Final Frontier),* Hiro Narita *(Star Trek VI: The Undiscovered Country)*, John Alonzo *(Star Trek Generations),* and Matt Leonetti *(Star Trek: First Contact)*. Ed Brown, Jr., Marvin Rush, and Jonathan West were directors of photography for *Star Trek: The Next Generation, Star Trek: Deep Space Nine,* and *Star Trek: Voyager.* Production stills by: Larry Barbier (original *Star Trek* series), Mel Traxel *(Star Trek I),* Bruce Birmelin *(Star Trek II, IV,* and *V),* John Shannon *(Star Trek III),* Gregory Schwartz *(Star Trek VI),* and Elliott Marks *(Star Trek Generations, Star Trek: First Contact*, and *Star Trek: Insurrection)*. *Star Trek: The Next Generation*, *Star Trek: Deep Space Nine,* and *Star Trek: Voyager* still photographers have included Gale M. Adler, Carin Baer, Byron J. Colten, Julie Dennis, Danny Feld, Kim Gottlieb-Walker, Peter Iovino, Michael Leshnov, Dianna Lynn, Wren Maloney, Lynn McAfee, Brian D. McLaughlin, Michael Paris, Robbie Robinson, Fred Sabine, Gregory Schwartz, Barry Slobin, Randy Tepper, Ron Tom, and Joseph Viles. ILM effects stills by Terry Chostner and Kerry Nordquist. Some ship photography and composites by Gary Hutzel. Photos of the original *Enterprise* model by Ed Miarecki.

Some photos are from the collections of Doug Drexler, Greg Jein, and Richard Barnett. Original-series props courtesy of Steve Horch and Mike Moore. Mars globe by Don Davis. Saturn photo courtesy Space Telescope Science Institute. Photo laboratory and digital services by Bob Brown at RGB Optical, Inc., Bob Pieschell at Composite Image Systems, and Patrick Donahue and Diana Penilla at The Photo Lab. At the Paramount Photo Lab, our appreciation to Sarah Francis, Shannon Foster, and Jeannine Giesregen. Thanks also to Bill George, John Goodson, and Alex Jaeger at Industrial Light and Magic, and the team at Blue Sky/VIFX.

This book was produced on Apple Macintosh computers using Microsoft Word software. Other resources included Adobe Photoshop, Adobe Illustrator, Adobe Dimensions, QuarkXPress, Adobe PageMaker, Microsoft Excel, Radius VideoVision, and Electric Image. We salute everyone who helped create these wonderful tools for the rest of us.

Thanks to our bug-catchers, who helped us fix mistakes from the first edition of the encyclopedia: William P. Aaron, Faisal Abou-Shahla, Isabel C. Acevedo, Dorothy Adrien, Jacob Agamao III, Sandra Agnew, Mark Alfred, Chris Allsop, Jessica Amos, Vance "Eagle Eyes" Anderson, Jeffrey C. Apparius, Brandon Argainas, Charles Askew, Allan P. Azcrieta, Frederick W. Babineaux, Elizabeth Bacher, Daniel Bagley, Danette Banning, Mr. Bateman, Charlotte Baumgartner, Holly Benton, Casey Bernay, Rod Alan Beskitt, Alan C. Bevington, Suzanne Bitterman, David Borowski, Dan Borton, Ward Botsford, Josh Brown, Padraic Brown, Dan Butler, Pamela Callum, Jennifer Campany, Ted Camus, Damon Carella, Mark A. Carlisle, Josh Carlson, Rick Carter, Marco Cassili, Antonio Celaya, G.J. Chacon, Lee Chambers, Benjamin Chee, Leslie K.L. Ching, Rob Chittenden, Mitch Christiansen, John D. Clayton, Ronald Cormier, Buddy Crowfoot, Jr., Curt Danhauser, Randy Delucchi, Michael A. Dexter, Harold J. Dollar, Jr., Greg Dolter, Daniel Dougherty, Patrick & Philip Duff, Bill Dwyer, Louann Emick, Ali Nabil Fakhouri, Amy & Samuel Falk, Norm K. Feldman, Todd Felton, Barry Fisher, Michael Fitzgerald, Cyrus Forman, Chris Foster, Doug Foulk, Robert S. Fowler, Alex Frank, Inga Frankenheimer, Mark A. Franklin, Stephanie Fox, Heather Frese, Mark Fukuchi, Mike Garcia, David Gianopoulos, Janette E. Gillespie, D. Glenn, Gayle Gregory, Kein Grover, Dennis R. Hollinger, David Hopkins, Eric Hughes, Li-Kuei Hung, Valerie Issac, Greg Jein, David E. Jones, Alexander Karl, Alayna-Joenic Kazimer, Barbara Kefford, Darren Kehrer, Stephen J. Kert, Jerry Kiewe, Matt, Jim & Pete Klanos, Eric Niel Koenig, Joseph D. Kolodski, Mark Edward Koltko, Kenneth Kong, W. Koslowsky, MD, Bill Kotis, Jill Krieg, Carsten Kurte, Jonah Kuttner, Steve La, Richard Laban, Johnson Lai, Stephen H. Lampen, Paulina Lee, Conor Lennon, Herb Lichtenstein, Troy Douglas Light, Daniel Loughn, Robert Lowndes, Alexander Lowry, P.H. Lubbe, Ian Lusignan, Tim Lynch, Matthew F. Lyons, Robert Magil, Jason Mah, Barbara Mahoney, Dennis Mangold, Marlene Mannella, Jack Mantz, Stephen Marlow, Wells P. Martin, Chris Matheis, Philip Maywah, Ed Mazur, Christopher McGlothlin, Ceven McGuire, Sandoval McNair, John McQuarrie, Christina McVety, Ana Maria Meca, Derek Mehl, Simon Mendelson, Paul Millar, Nora Mills, Derek B. Mirabel, Hiroko Miyahara, David W. Morris, Matthew S. Moyer, Doug & Heidi Nash, Madeline Neunueb, William Newsom, Lori Nicol, Patricia Niero, C.W. O'Keffe, Barry O'Mahoney, Donald M. O'Malley, Robert Oliver, Graham Ollis, Sean Padykula, Angel Perez, Timothy A. Povhe, Mel Powell & Myki Tsuchiyama, Shaun Pulsifer, Chris F. Puorro, Tim Randall, Robert James Rasmussen II, Robert Royce Riggs, Martin C. Risby, Judith P. Robinson, Audrey Ross, Paul Roth, Michael E. Rothman, Trevor Ruppe, Gary W. Sackett, Jeffrey Saks, Hartriono Sastrowardoyo, Christopher Scott, Trevor Shaffer, Don J. Shaw, Christine A. Sheil, Olive D. Shelton; Nicholas Shewmaker, Peter S. Shinozaki, Casey A. Smith, Larry Smith, Michael A Soria, Chris St. John, Randall Lee Stack, Mark B. Stalnaker, Jason Stefanich, Rick Steffens, Tarn Stephanos, Carol F. Stern, Rick "Tritanium" Sternbach, Janet Stevenson, Louise Pauline Sugiyama, Kurtis D. Taylor, M.A. Thomer, Cheryl Toliver, Alan Tonn, Patrick Tounley, Lynn Tucker, Jim Vail, Mark Valentino, Craig Verba, Dave Viands, Scott Washington, John Watker, Debra Westford, Thomas Whitmire, Greg Wilson, Kerry Wilson, Torren & Susan Wolfe, John Smallberries, John Zaepfel, and Sean Ziemer. Our appreciation to everyone who took the time to write.

Special thanks to Miriam Mita, Ralph Winter, Dorothy Fontana, Donna Drexler, Salvatore Capone, K. M. "Killer" Fish, Moja Richarz, Russ Galen, Helen Cohen, Bob Levinson, Paul Brodsky, Dr. Todd Hewitt, Dr. James Isaacs, Dr. Richard Wulfsberg, Stephen Poe, Judith and Gar Reeves-Stevens, Pat Repalone, Richard Arnold, Ernie Over, Dorothy Duder, Tamara Haack, Craig Okuda, Judy Saul, Todd Tathwell, and Annie Yokoyama. Love to Diane Pittman. Welcome to Kaci Yokoyama, who will see the future. Inspiration by Alice P. Liddell, Ford Prefect, Susan Calvin, Heywood Floyd, Jonas Grumby, Logan Five, Margaret O'Keefe, Elwood Blues, William Robinson, Mindy O'Connell, Edison Carter, Leia Organa, Dr. Benton Quest, Hugh Lockwood, Arthur Hoggitt, Alan Tracy, Henry Higgins, Alta Morbius, Howard Beale, Valentine Michael Smith, Tony Newman, Ray Kinsella, John Sheridan, and everyone at the Banzai Institute.

Once again, our thanks and love to Gene Roddenberry, who created a universe and let us all play in it.

—Michael Okuda
—Denise Okuda
Los Angeles,
1997, 1999

For our parents.

'audet IX. Planet. Site of a major Federation Medical Collection Station. The *Enterprise*-D was assigned to transport specimens of **plasma plague** from this station to Science Station **Tango Sierra** in hopes that a vaccine might be found. ("The Child" [TNG]).

A&A officer. Abbreviation for archaeology and anthropology specialist, a staff officer aboard the original *Starship Enterprise*. **Lieutenant Carolyn Palamas** was the A&A officer when the *Enterprise* visited planet **Pollux IV** in 2267. ("Who Mourns for Adonais" [TOS]).

A-koo-chee-moya. Native American term used in Chakotay's **vision quest** prayer. ("The Cloud" [VGR]).

A.F. An old aquaintance of Jean-Luc Picard. While Picard was at Starfleet Academy, he carved A.F.'s initials into **Boothby**'s prized elm tree on the parade grounds. Picard failed Organic Chemistry because of A.F. ("The Game" [TNG]).

Aaron, Admiral. (Ray Reinhardt). Starfleet official. Stationed at **Starfleet Headquarters** in San Francisco, Aaron had been taken over by the unknown alien intelligence that infiltrated Starfleet Command in 2364. ("Conspiracy" [TNG]).

"Abandoned, The." *Deep Space Nine* episode #52. Written by D. Thomas Maio & Steve Warnek. Directed by Avery Brooks. Stardate 48214.5. *First aired in 1994. A Jem'Hadar baby is discovered on Deep Space 9 and grows at an alarming rate into a warrior, genetically programmed to kill.* GUEST CAST: Bumper Robinson as Teenage Jem'Hadar; Jill Sayre as **Mardah**; Leslie Bevis as **Boslic freighter captain**; Matthew Kimborough as Alien high roller; Hassan Nicholas as Jem'Hadar boy. SEE: ***Constellation, U.S.S.;*** **Creole shrimp with Mandalay sauce; dom-jot; Founders; holodeck and holosuite programs; isogenic enzyme; Jem'Hadar, the; *karjinko*; Koran; Mardah; Odo; Okalar; Rionoj; Risa; Sarjeno; Sisko, Jake; Starbase 201.**

ablative armor. Starship protective skin that is designed to vaporize under weapons fire, thereby dissipating energy and protecting the ship's systems inside. In 2371, **chroniton particles** emitted by the **Romulan cloaking device** became lodged in the ***Starship Defiant***'s ablative armor matrix. ("Past Tense, Part I" [DS9]). Ablative armor technology was a closely-held secret, and until 2372, even Starfleet Operations did not know that the *Defiant* was so equipped. ("Paradise Lost" [DS9]).

Abrom. (William Wintersole). **Zeon** member of the underground on planet **Ekos** fighting against the Nazi oppression in 2268. Abrom, his brother Isak, and other members of the underground aided Kirk and Spock in locating Federation cultural observer **John Gill**. ("Patterns of Force" [TOS]).

absorbed. Term used to describe members of the society on planet **Beta III** who were controlled by the computer-generated entity known as **Landru**. When a person was absorbed, his or her individual will was stripped, and the person was forced to behave in a manner that the computer prescribed as being beneficial to society. ("Return of the Archons" [TOS]).

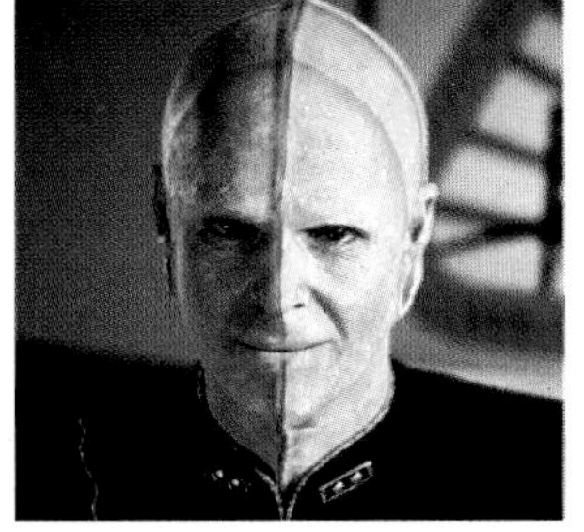

academy commandant. (Rudolph Willrich). Starfleet officer in charge of **Starfleet Academy**. In 2372 the academy commandant conspired with **Admiral Leyton** in his attempted coup of the Earth government. The commandant allowed the formation of **Red Squad**, an elite group of Starfleet Academy cadets that Leyton used in his plan. ("Paradise Lost" [DS9]).

Academy Flight Range. Located near **Saturn** in the Sol System, an area of space reserved for flight exercises by cadets from the **Starfleet Academy**. An accident at the Academy Flight Range in 2368 took the life of cadet Joshua Albert. ("The First Duty" [TNG]). SEE: **Crusher, Wesley; Kolvoord Starburst; Locarno, Cadet First Class Nicholas.**

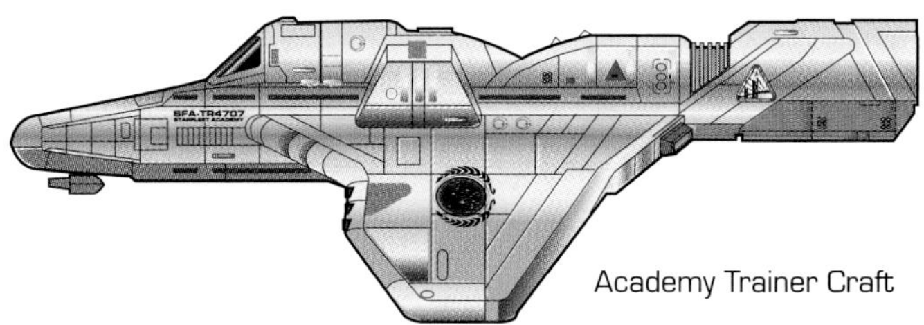

Academy Trainer Craft

academy range officer. Starfleet officer in charge of the **Academy Flight Range**, located near Saturn. ("The First Duty" [TNG]).

academy. SEE: **Starfleet Academy.**

Acamar III. Home planet of the **Acamarian** civilization. The *Enterprise*-D met Sovereign **Marouk**, an Acamarian leader, and her attendants there. ("The Vengeance Factor" [TNG]).

Acamar system. The location of the planet **Acamar III**. ("The Vengeance Factor" [TNG]).

Acamarians. Humanoid civilization from planet **Acamar III.** The Acamarians had enjoyed peace for the past century, with the exception of Acamar's nomadic **Gatherers**, who left their homeworld to become interstellar marauders. These people appeared largely human with the exception of a facial cleft in their foreheads. They are also notable for individualized decorative facial tattooing. Acamarian blood is based on an unusual iron and copper composite, making it readily identifiable. Within Acamarian culture, membership in a clan is considered of great social and political importance, and conflicts between the various clans often became violent. One such feud, between the **Lornaks** and the **Tralestas**, lasted some three centuries, and ended only after the last Tralesta was dead. The Acamarian government, headed by Sovereign **Marouk** (pictured), extended an offer of reconciliation to the renegade Gatherers in 2366. The negotiations, mediated by Jean-Luc Picard, were eventually successful. ("The Vengeance Factor" [TNG]). SEE: **Yuta.**

ACB. SEE: **annular confinement beam.**

accelerated critical neural pathway formation. Medical procedure that uses genetic recoding to alter the brain of a humanoid patient. Although it was banned in the Federation, physicians on planet **Adigeon Prime** used the technique to enhance the brain of **Julian Bashir** when he was almost seven years old. The procedure is illegal under laws dating back to the end of the **Eugenics Wars**. ("Doctor Bashir, I Presume?" [DS9]).

accelerometer. Instrument used to measure the direction and amount of velocity change. ("Twisted" [VGR]).

access terminal. Systems connector port used aboard **Borg** ships to allow individual Borg to link to their collective. ("I, Borg" [TNG]).

access tunnel. Series of passageways traversing Deep Space 9, filled with circuitry and other utilities that may be accessed for repairs. The device responsible for the **aphasia virus** was located in one of the access tunnels containing the food-replicator circuitry. ("Babel" [DS9]). *Similar to the **Jefferies tubes** used aboard Federation starships.*

"Accession." *Deep Space Nine* episode #89. Teleplay by Jane Espenson & René Echevarria. Story by Jane Espenson. Directed by Les Landau. No stardate given. *First aired in 1996. An ancient Bajoran ship emerges from the wormhole bearing an occupant who claims to be the Emissary of the Prophets, causing a resurgence of Bajoran fundamentalism and enmity for the Federation.* GUEST CAST: Rosalind Chao as **O'Brien, Keiko**; Robert Symonds as **Porta, Vedek**; Camille Saviola as **Opaka, Kai**; Hana Hatae as **O'Brien, Molly**; Richard Libertini as **Akorem Laan**; David Carpenter as **Onara**; Grace Zandarski as **Latara, Ensign**; Laura Jane Salvato as **Gia**. SEE: **Akorem Laan; Bajoran solar-sail vessel; Bajorans; Brak; *Call of the Prophets, The*; *D'jarra*; Emissary; *Gaudaal's Lament*; Gia; *ih'tanu* ceremony; *Ih'valla*; Imutta; Jatarn, Major; Kira Nerys; *Kitara's Song*; Latara, Ensign; O'Brien, Keiko; Onara; Opaka, Kai; Orb shadow; Porta, Vedek; Shakaar Edon; Spitfire; *te'nari*; United Federation of Planets; Winn; Yridian yak.**

Accolan. (Dan Mason). Citizen and artist on planet **Aldea** who would have helped raise **Harry Bernard, Jr.**, child of an *Enterprise*-D crew member, had Harry and other children remained on Aldea in 2364. ("When the Bough Breaks" [TNG]).

aceton assimilators. Weapon used by the ancient **Menthars** in their war with the **Promellians** a thousand years ago. Aceton assimilators could drain power from distant sources (such as an enemy ship), then use that power to generate deadly radiation to kill the ship's crew. The Menthars placed hundreds of thousands of these devices in the asteroid field near **Orelious IX,** thus trapping the Promellian cruiser ***Cleponji*** a millennium ago. The devices remained active for centuries and trapped the *Enterprise*-D there in 2366. ("Booby Trap" [TNG]).

acetylcholine. Biochemical substance, a neurotransmitter that promotes the propagation of electrical impulses from one nerve cell to another in carbon-based life. Spock performed an acetylcholine test on a huge spaceborne **amoeba** creature that destroyed the **Gamma 7A System** in 2268, although McCoy felt the test was improperly done. ("The Immunity Syndrome" [TOS]). Levels of acetylcholine in the **hippocampus** can quantify the amount of memory an individual has accumulated. ("All Good Things..." [TNG]). The clamps implanted in Akritirian prison inmates were designed to stimulate the production of acetylcholine in the hypothalamus to stimulate their aggressive tendencies, thus keeping them at each other's throats. ("The Chute" [VGR]).

Achilles. (Max Kelvin). Popular gladiator on planet Eight Ninety-Two IV. Achilles fought McCoy and Spock in the planet's televised arena in 2267. ("Bread and Circuses" [TOS]). SEE: **Eight Ninety-Two IV**.

acidichloride. Corrosive gaseous chemical, toxic to humanoid life. In 2372 while Thomas Paris was undergoing a mutative change, the Emergency Medical Hologram surrounded his patient with a force field containing nitrogen and acidichloride gas. ("Threshold" [VGR]).

actinides. Radioactive compounds often found in uranium ore. Actinides in the **Ikalian asteroid belt** made it difficult for sensors to determine the location of **Kriosian** rebels in the area in 2367. ("The Mind's Eye" [TNG]).

active tachyon beam. SEE: **tachyon detection grid**.

active-scan navigation. Navigation technique used when conventional passive sensors cannot be used. Active-scan navigation works by echolocation, such as when a modulated **tetryon** pulse is transmitted, so that a reflection off an object (such as a ship) will permit the object's location to be determined. ("Starship Down" [DS9]).

Adam. (Charles Napier). Follower of **Dr. Sevrin** who sought the mythical planet **Eden** in 2269. The musically inclined Adam died when he ate an acid-saturated fruit on a world he thought was Eden. ("The Way to Eden" [TOS]). *Charles Napier also played General Rex Denning in "Little Green Men" (DS9), and country-and-western singer Tucker McElroy in* The Blues Brothers.

Adams, Dr. Tristan. (James Gregory). Assistant director of the **Tantalus V** penal colony in 2266. Adams seized control of the colony after director **Simon Van Gelder** became insane from testing a neural neutralizer device. Adams later died from exposure to the unit. ("Dagger of the Mind" [TOS]).

adanji. Variety of incense used in the Klingon *Mauk-to'Vor* ritual. ("Sons of Mogh" [DS9]).

adaptive heuristic matrix. Extremely sophisticated computer memory architecture incorporated into the *Voyager*'s **Emergency Medical Hologram** and the Jupiter station EMH diagnostic program. ("The Swarm" [VGR]).

adaptive interface link. Computer connection used to exchange information between two computer systems of totally alien origin. An adaptive interface link was used to download information from an alien space probe of unknown origin to station Deep Space 9's computers on stardate 46925. ("The Forsaken" [DS9]). SEE: **Pup**.

Adele, Aunt. Jean-Luc Picard's relative, who taught him a number of home remedies for common ailments. These included ginger tea for the common cold ("Ensign Ro" [TNG]) and steamed milk with nutmeg to treat sleeplessness. ("Cause and Effect" [TNG]). *Aunt Adele was also mentioned in "Schisms" (TNG). She was named for* Star Trek *assistant director Adele Simmons.*

Adelman Neurological Institute. Biomedical research facility. **Dr. Toby Russell** served on staff at the Adelman Neurological Institute in 2368. ("Ethics" [TNG]).

Adelphi, U.S.S. Federation starship, *Ambassador* class, Starfleet registry NCC-26849, that conducted the disastrous first contact with the planet Ghorusda. Forty-seven people, including *Adelphi*'s **Captain Darson**, were killed in the incident, which later became known as the **Ghorusda disaster**. ("Tin Man" [TNG]).

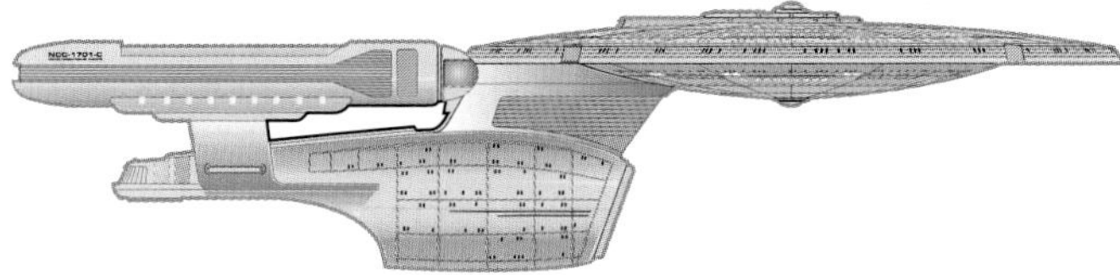

Adelphous IV. Planet. Destination of the *Enterprise*-D following its encounter with the Romulan warbird ***Devoras*** in 2367. ("Data's Day" [TNG]).

Adigeon Prime. Planet. Location of a medical facility where seven-year-old **Julian Bashir** was taken by his parents to have the structure of his brain altered for the enhancement of his physical and mental skills. ("Doctor Bashir, I Presume?" [DS9]).

Adin. (Anthony Crivello). Personal physician to the tyrant **Tieran** of the **Ilari** nation in the Delta Quadrant. Adin continued to minister to him even when Tieran's body died and his consciousness inhabited Kes's body in 2373. Adin warned Tieran to leave Kes's body because it was unstable due to her being an unwilling host, but Tieran wanted to keep Kes's body because of her unique mental abilities, and so he killed Adin. ("Warlord" [VGR]).

Admiral's Banquet. Annual Starfleet social function. Picard had avoided going to these tedious affairs for six years in a row. Picard finally had to agree to attend in 2370 when it was held at **Starbase 219**, although he somehow managed to escape anyway. ("Phantasms" [TNG]).

Adred. Ferengi entrepreneur. Father of **Ishka**, Quark's mother. ("Family Business" [DS9]).

adrenaline. Pharmaceutical based on the humanoid hormone epinephrine. Adrenaline was an accepted treatment for radiation illness right after the Atomic Age but was replaced as the preferred treatment after **hyronalin** was developed. In 2267, Dr. Leonard McCoy found adrenaline to be an effective treatment for a radiation-induced hyperaccelerated aging disease that affected several *Enterprise* crew members. ("The Deadly Years" [TOS]). SEE: **hyronalin; polyadrenaline**.

Advanced Tactical Training. Starfleet curriculum for specialized tactical and intelligence operations. Admission to Advanced Tactical Training required the recommendation of a superior officer. The course load was very difficult, and half of the members of each year's class failed to complete it. In 2370, Lieutenant Ro Laren graduated from Advanced Tactical Training, having been recommended by Captain Jean-Luc Picard. ("Preemptive Strike" [TNG]).

"Adversary, The." *Deep Space Nine* episode #72. Written by Ira Steven Behr & Robert Hewitt Wolfe. Directed by Alexander Singer. Stardate 48959.1. First aired in 1995. *A member of the Founders infiltrates the* U.S.S. Defiant *in a plot to disrupt the balance of power in the Alpha Quadrant. This was the last episode of the third season, and marks the first appearance of the* Defiant*'s engine room.* GUEST CAST: Lawrence Pressman as **Krajensky, Ambassador**; Kenneth Marshall as **Eddington, Michael**; Jeff Austin as Bolian; Majel Barrett as Computer voice. SEE: **Autarch; autodestruct; Barisa Prime; Bolians; Chateau Cleon; *Defiant, U.S.S.*; Dominion; Entebe, Captain; Founders; Helaspont Nebula; Krajensky, Ambassador; M'kemas III; Odo; phaser rifle; Risa; Sisko, Benjamin; Solais V; Tzenkethi; Tzenkethi war; *Ulysses, U.S.S.***

Aeon. Federation timeship from the 29th century, commanded by **Captain Braxton**. The *Aeon* made a forced landing on Earth in the year 1967, where it was captured by Earth native **Henry Starling**, and became a source of significant timeline contamination. The *Aeon* was equipped with subatomic disruptor weapons. ("Future's End, Part I" [VGR]). SEE: **temporal explosion**.

Agamemnon, U.S.S. Federation starship. The *Agamemnon* was part of task force three, under Captain Picard's indirect command during an expected **Borg** invasion of 2369. ("Descent, Part I" [TNG]). *The* Agamemnon *was named for the Greek mythological figure who was commander of the Greek forces during the Trojan War.*

Age of Ascension. Klingon rite of passage, marking a new level of spiritual attainment for a **Klingon** warrior. The ritual involves a recitation by the ascendee, proclaiming *"DaHjaj Suvwl'e' jIH. tlgwlj Sa'angNIS. Iw blQtlqDaq jljaH."* ("Today I am a Warrior. I must show you my heart. I travel the river of blood.") The warrior then strides between two lines of other Klingons, who subject him or her to **painstiks.** The warrior is expected to express his or her most profound feelings while under this extreme duress. ("The Icarus Factor" [TNG]). The first Rite of Ascension must take place before age 13 so that a Klingon youth can declare his intention to become a warrior. The rite involves testing one's fighting skills with ***bat'leth*** and other weapons. When Alexander approached his first Age of Ascension in 2370, he was unsure if he wanted to perform the ritual. ("Firstborn" [TNG]). **Worf** underwent his second Age of Ascension ritual at age 15 in 2355. Ten years later, in 2365, Worf

celebrated the anniversary of his Age of Ascension with his *Enterprise*-D crew mates ("The Icarus Factor" [TNG]). Worf's brother, **Kurn**, was not told that he was the son of **Mogh** until Kurn reached his Age of Ascension in 2360. Until that point, Kurn believed he was the son of **Lorgh** ("Sins of the Father" [TNG]).

Age of Decision. A **Talarian** rite of passage signaling the age of majority for a Talarian male at 14 years. SEE: **Jono.** ("Suddenly Human" [TNG]).

Agents 201 and 347. Humans raised on an unknown alien planet, then returned to Earth in the 1960s with a mission to protect humanity from its own self-destructive nature. Both agents were killed in an automobile accident before they could complete their task, so their mission fell to Supervisor 194, also known as **Gary Seven**. ("Assignment: Earth" [TOS]).

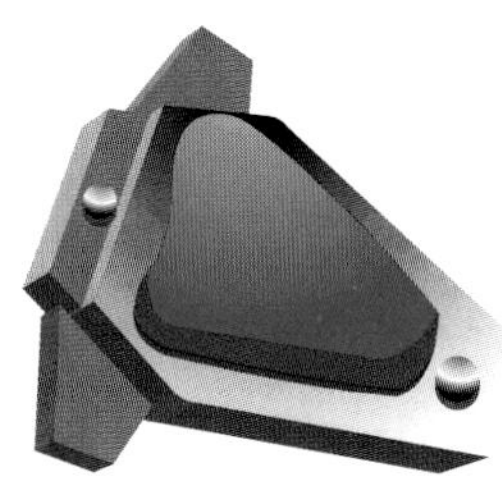

agonizer. Small device worn by each crew member on the ***I.S.S. Enterprise*** in the **mirror universe**. The agonizer was used for punishment and was extremely painful. ("Mirror, Mirror" [TOS]). Agonizers were still in use in the mirror universe in 2372. ("Shattered Mirror" [DS9]). *The Klingons used the same prop for discipline in "Day of the Dove" (TOS).*

agony booth. Torture device used to enforce discipline in the **mirror universe** aboard the ***I.S.S. Enterprise***. The mirror Chekov was subjected to the booth after an assassination attempt on Captain Kirk. ("Mirror, Mirror" [TOS]).

Ah-Kel. (Randy Ogelsby). Humanoid of the **Miradorn** species. Ah-Kel's twin, **Ro-Kel**, was killed by the fugitive **Croden** during a robbery in 2369. Ah-Kel's symbiotic relationship with his twin was severed and he vowed to kill Croden in retaliation. ("Vortex" [DS9]).

Ahab, Captain. Fictional sea captain who was the main character in Earth writer Herman Melville's 1851 classic novel *Moby-Dick*. Lily Sloane compared Captain Picard to Ahab because Picard seemed to want revenge on the Borg above all else. *(Star Trek: First Contact).*

Ahjess. Son of **Lela Dax**. Ahjess would crawl into bed with his mother for attention. ("To the Death" [DS9]).

ahn-woon. Vulcan weapon made of a single leather strip that could be used as a whip or noose. Spock appeared to strangle Kirk with the *ahn-woon* at the conclusion of their fight on **Vulcan** in 2267. ("Amok Time" [TOS]).

Ailis pâté. Hors d'oeuvre. Neelix prepared Ailis pâté aboard *Voyager*. ("The Cloud" [VGR]).

air police sergeant. (Hal Lynch). Security officer of Earth's 20th-century United States Air Force who was beamed aboard the *Enterprise* in 1969. He apprehended Kirk and Sulu trying to remove data from the **Omaha Air Base**, but was beamed up to the *Enterprise*, where he was detained under the watchful eye of Transporter Chief **Kyle**. ("Tomorrow is Yesterday" [TOS]).

air tram. Transit vehicle used in the **San Francisco** Bay area in the 23rd century. Admiral Kirk rode an air tram to Starfleet Headquarters prior to his meeting with Admiral Nogura regarding the **V'Ger** threat. *(Star Trek: The Motion Picture).*

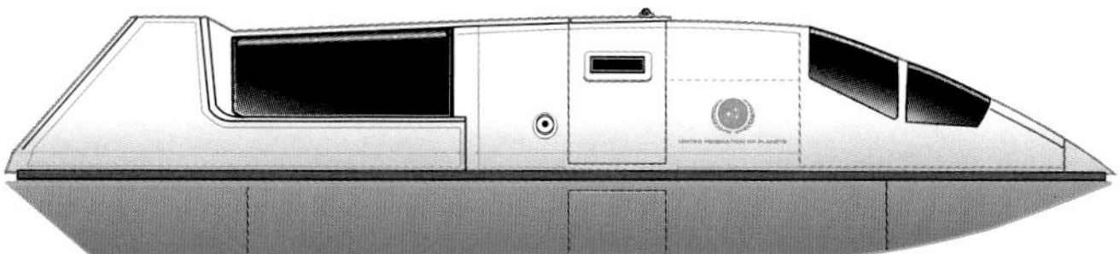

airlock. Aboard a spaceship or space station, an airlock is a chamber that permits personnel to pass from an area in which an atmosphere is maintained, into an area where no atmosphere, or a different atmosphere, exists. Typically, airlocks are used to exit a vehicle into the vacuum of space. Aboard station Deep Space 9, airlocks are also used as passageways to docked spacecraft. ("Captive Pursuit" [DS9]).

airponics bay. Compartment aboard the *Starship Voyager* dedicated to plant cultivation using a moist air medium rather than soil. The airponics bay was maintained by **Kes**, who used it to help supplement the crew's food supply. ("Elogium" [VGR]) Kes accidentally destroyed all the plants in the bay in early 2372 when she lost control of her psychokinetic powers. ("Cold Fire" [VGR]). SEE: **hydroponics bay**.

Ajax, U.S.S. Federation starship, *Apollo* class, Starfleet registry number NCC-11574. In 2327, the *Ajax* was Ensign Cortin **Zweller**'s first assignment after his graduation from Starfleet Academy ("Tapestry" [TNG]). In 2364, Starfleet propulsion specialist **Kosinski** tested an experimental warp drive upgrade on the *Ajax*, although it was later discovered that Kosinski's theories were baseless. ("Where No One Has Gone Before." [TNG]). In 2368, the *Ajax* served as part of the **tachyon detection grid**, part of Picard's blockade against Romulan interference during the **Klingon civil war**. ("Redemption, Part II" [TNG]). *Named for two heroes from Greek mythology who fought in the Trojan War, Ajax of Salamis and Ajax of Locris.*

Ajilon Prime. Federation Class-M planet. Site of a skirmish between Klingon and Federation forces in early 2373. Deep Space 9 personnel Dr. **Julian Bashir** and **Jake Sisko** went to Ajilon Prime to help in an emergency underground hospital during the battle. ("Nor the Battle to the Strong" [DS9]).

Ajur. (Karen Landry). Twenty-seventh-century **Vorgon** criminal who traveled backward in time to locate Captain Picard and the ***Tox Uthat***. ("Captain's Holiday" [TNG]).

"Ak'la bella doo." Klingon folk song. Jadzia Dax taught the song to the proprietor of the Klingon kiosk on DS9. He was amazed that she knew a Klingon song he had never heard. ("Playing God" [DS9]).

Ak'voh. Old Klingon tradition in which a fallen warrior's comrades stay with the body to keep away predators. This allowed the spirit to leave the body when it was time to make the journey to *Sto'vo'kor*. ("The Ship" [DS9]).

Akaar, Leonard James. Son of **Eleen** and **Teer Akaar** on planet **Capella IV**, born 2267. Leonard James Akaar was hereditary leader, or **teer**, of the Ten Tribes on that planet, and was named after Captain James Kirk and Chief Surgeon Leonard McCoy. Akaar's mother, Eleen, ruled as regent during his childhood. Eleen's decision to name the boy after the two Starfleet officers was believed to have made both of them insufferably proud for at least a month. ("Friday's Child" [TOS]).

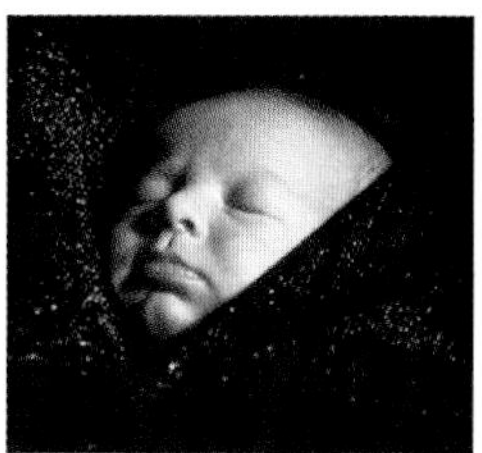

Akaar, Teer. (Ben Gage). High **teer** or leader of the Ten Tribes of planet **Capella IV**. Akaar was killed in 2267 by rival **Maab** in a power struggle for leadership of the ten tribes. Akaar was succeeded by his son, **Leonard James Akaar**, born of his widow **Eleen** shortly after the elder Akaar's death. ("Friday's Child" [TOS]).

Akadar, Temple of. Ancient ceremonial temple from which, centuries ago, the brothers **Krios** and **Valt** ruled a vast interstellar empire. In 2368, a holodeck re-creation of the temple served as the location of a **Ceremony of Reconciliation** between the peoples of two star systems that had taken the names of each of the brothers. ("The Perfect Mate" [TNG]).

Akagi, U.S.S. Federation starship, *Rigel* class, Starfleet registry number NCC-62158. The *Akagi* served in Picard's armada to blockade Romulan supply ships supplying the **Duras** family forces during the **Klingon civil war** in 2368. ("Redemption, Part II" [TNG]). *The* Akagi *was named for the Japanese carrier that fought the American warship* U.S.S. Hornet *in the bitter Battle of Midway in World War II. Episode writer Ron Moore thought it fitting that in* Star Trek*'s future, the* Akagi *would be serving alongside the* **Hornet**.

Akira*-class starship.** Type of Federation starship in use in the late 24th century. The *U.S.S.* ***Thunderchild was a ship of the *Akira* class. *(Star Trek: First Contact). The* Akira*-class starship was designed by Alex Jaegar at ILM. It was rendered as a computer-generated visual effect. Named for the animated fantasy film.*

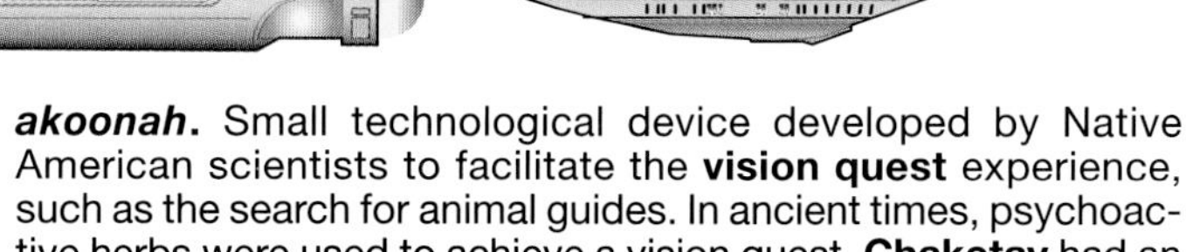

akoonah. Small technological device developed by Native American scientists to facilitate the **vision quest** experience, such as the search for animal guides. In ancient times, psychoactive herbs were used to achieve a vision quest. **Chakotay** had an *akoonah* in his **medicine bundle**. ("The Cloud" [VGR]).

Akorem Laan. (Richard Libertini). Renowned 22nd-century **Bajoran** poet. Akorem's works included ***Kitara's Song*** and ***Gaudaal's Lament***. Akorem Laan disappeared without a trace in 2172 when his traditional **Bajoran solar-sail vessel** encountered an ion storm. Two centuries later, he emerged from the **Bajoran wormhole**. Akorem, who had not aged at all, believed that his experience in discovering the wormhole and encountering the **Prophets** made him the **Emissary** of the Bajoran people. **Benjamin Sisko** willingly relinquished the title to Akorem, who immediately instituted a series of conservative religious reforms in Bajoran society. Unfortunately, certain traditional Bajoran values, such as the discriminatory ***D'jarra*** caste system, while comforting to Akorem, were no longer appropriate in modern Bajoran society, and even infringed on individual rights. Akorem returned to his own time after the Prophets made it clear that he was not the Emissary of Bajoran prophecy. Akorem's return to his own time caused a change in the timeline. Instead of disappearing in 2172, Akorem returned from his voyage to live out his life, even completing his epic poem, ***The Call of the Prophets***. (History had previously recorded that the poem was unfinished at the time of his disappearance.) Such alternations in time would ordinarily be undetectable to individuals within the affected timeline, but for some reason, **Kira Nerys** retained a memory of the changes, even though Akorem

evidently did not. She speculated that this was evidence of the Prophets' handiwork. ("Accession" [DS9]).

Akritiri. Technologically sophisticated civilization in the Delta Quadrant. The Akritiri had an oppressive government and a system of justice described by Starfleet observers as cruel and draconian. In 2373, Starfleet officers Harry Kim and Tom Paris were accused by Akritiri authorities of carrying out a terrorist bombing and imprisoned on the **Akritirian prison satellite**. Akritiri ambassador Liria refused to release Kim and Paris even after Captain Janeway had captured the actual persons behind the bombing. ("The Chute" [VGR]).

Akritirian freighter. Small cargo vessel of Akritirian registry, commanded by **Vel**. The ship had an ion-based propulsion system that used paralithium as fuel. The explosive device used to bomb the **Laktivia** Recreational Facility on Akritiri in 2373 was produced aboard Vel's ship by members of the **Open Sky** terrorist group. ("The Chute" [VGR]).

Akritirian patrol ship. Medium-sized blunt dart-shaped vessels used by the Akritirian militia. ("The Chute" [VGR]).

Akritirian prison satellite. Maximum security detention facility operated by the Akritiri government. In the Akritirian method of incarceration, prisoners were left without guards or medical services on a space station. The inmates were also fitted with clamps which stimulated their aggressive tendencies, effectively keeping them at each other's throats. ("The Chute" [VGR]).

Aktuh and Melota. A Klingon opera, a favorite of *Enterprise*-D lieutenant Worf. ("Unification, Part II" [TNG]).

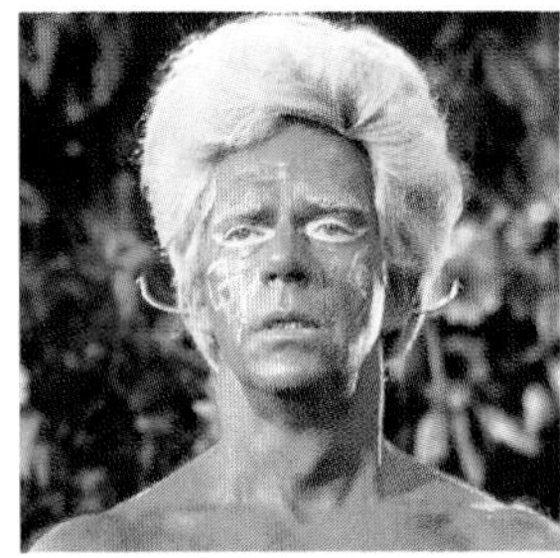

Akuta. (Keith Andes). Leader of the people who inhabited planet **Gamma Trianguli VI**. As leader of his people, he wore antennae so he could receive commands from **Vaal**, their god. Vaal felt that the *Enterprise* landing party was a threat and instructed Akuta how to kill them. Among his people, Akuta was known as "the eyes of Vaal." ("The Apple" [TOS]).

Al-Batani, U.S.S. Federation starship. Kathryn Janeway once served aboard the *Al-Batani* as science officer under the command of Captain Paris. ("Caretaker" [VGR]). SEE: **Paris, Admiral**.

Al-Leyan transport. Interstellar vessel of Al-Leyan registry. Professor **Richard Galen** had hoped to gain passage on an Al-Leyan transport from **Deep Space 4** to Caere as part of his quest in 2369 to learn about the first humanoids to live in our galaxy. ("The Chase" [TNG]).

Alameda. City on planet Earth, location of a 20th-century American naval base near San Francisco. The American aircraft carrier ***U.S.S. Enterprise*** was docked there in 1986, and Starfleet officers Chekov and Uhura broke into the facility to obtain high-energy photons. (*Star Trek IV: The Voyage Home*).

Alan-a-Dale. (LeVar Burton). In Earth mythology, a minstrel who was a member of **Robin Hood**'s band of outlaws in ancient England. Geordi La Forge was cast in this part by **Q** during a fantasy crafted for Captain Picard in 2367. Unfortunately, Geordi's musical skills were not quite up to the part. ("QPid" [TNG]).

Alans. (Whitney Rydbeck). Starfleet officer, a specialist in volcanology and geomechanics aboard the *Enterprise*-D. Alans assisted in the geological survey of planets in the **Selcundi Drema** sector in 2365. ("Pen Pals" [TNG]).

Alastria. Class-M planet in a binary system in the Delta Quadrant. At dawn on Alastria, almost 40,000 light-years from planet Sikaris, euphoric **erosene winds** blew across the surface. ("Prime Factors." [VGR]).

Alawanir Nebula. Stellar gas cloud. The Alawanir Nebula was investigated by the *Enterprise*-D in 2369. ("Rightful Heir" [TNG]).

Alba Ra. A contemporary (24th-century) **Talarian** music form. Electronic, discordant, and very loud, it was a favorite of **Jono**, although Jean-Luc Picard thought it somewhat less than wonderful. ("Suddenly Human" [TNG]).

Alben, Captain. (Christopher Carroll). Commander of the **Nasari** space vehicle *Nerada*. ("Favorite Son" [VGR]).

Albeni meditation crystal. A colorless sphere about 10 cm in diameter, producing a warm glow and a soft hum. Used as an aid to meditation. Riker presented an Albeni meditation crystal to **Beata** of planet **Angel One**. ("Angel One" [TNG]).

Albert, Joshua. Starfleet Academy cadet and part of the academy's **Nova Squadron**, killed in a flight accident in 2368. Although preliminary testimony pointed to pilot error on the part of Albert as the cause of his death, Cadet **Wesley Crusher** later testified that the squadron was attempting to perform a **Kolvoord Starburst** at the time of the accident. The attempt at the prohibited maneuver was blamed for the cadet's death. ("The First Duty" [TNG]).

Albert, Lieutenant Commander. (Ed Lauter). Starfleet officer and father of Cadet **Joshua Albert**. Commander Albert was present at the inquiry into his son's death in 2368. ("The First Duty" [TNG]).

Albino, the. (Bill Bolender). Notorious and powerful criminal who raided **Klingon** colonies. He was nearly apprehended in 2290 when three Klingon warships, commanded by **Kang**, **Koloth**, and **Kor**, were sent to stop the Albino and his band. The mission was successful, but the Albino escaped and later took revenge on the Klingon captains by using a **genetic virus** to kill each of their firstborn children. The three fathers, along with **Curzon Dax** (godfather to Kang's son), swore a blood oath of revenge, so the Albino spent decades in hiding. The four nearly caught up to him at planet **Galdonterre**, but the Albino's informants tipped him off, and he fled. In 2345, the Albino went to planet **Secarus IV**, where he remained in hiding until 2370, when Kang learned his whereabouts. The Albino offered a fair fight, but instead tried to booby-trap the four. The Albino's plan was unsuccessful, and he was killed by Kang. ("Blood Oath" [DS9]).

Alcia. (Marnie McPhail). First Prelate of the planet **Drayan II** in the Delta Quadrant. Alcia supported her culture's isolationist policy but visited the *Voyager* in 2372 because she was intrigued with the lost ship's plight. ("Innocence" [VGR]). *Marnie McPhail later portrayed Eiger in* Star Trek: First Contact.

Alcyones. Civilization. The Alcyones destroyed the last **Tarellian** plague vessel in 2356. ("Haven" [TNG]).

Aldabren Exchange. A strategy in **three-dimensional chess**. Commander Riker used the Aldabren Exchange to defeat **Nibor** during the **Trade Agreements Conference** in 2366. ("Ménage à Troi" [TNG]).

Aldara. Cardassian *Galor*-class warship commanded by **Gul Danar**. The *Aldara* pursued **Tahna Los** after the Bajoran terrorist stole an antimatter converter from the Cardassians in 2369. ("Past Prologue" [DS9]).

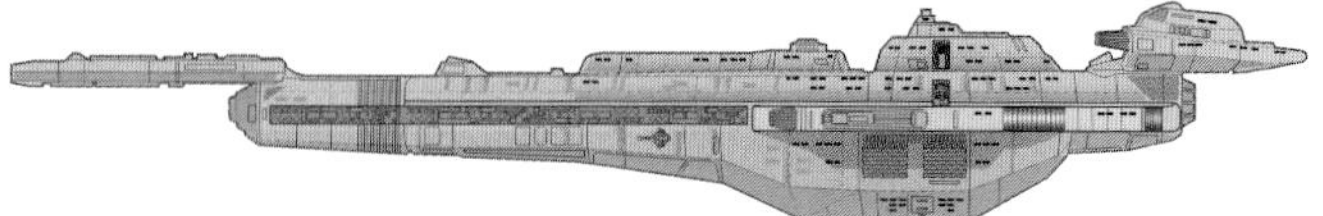

Aldea. Planet, long thought to be mere legend, discovered in 2364. Aldea was held to be a peaceful, advanced world where technology provided for every citizen to pursue intellectual and artistic endeavors. The legends had a basis in truth. The **Aldeans** had indeed achieved an idyllic existence, then used a powerful cloaking device to mask their planet from potential intruders. Over the centuries, the planet, located in the **Epsilon Mynos system**, faded into the obscurity of legend. Unfortunately, the planet's cloaking and shielding systems caused damage to the planet's **ozone** layer, resulting in widespread radiation poisoning to the Aldeans. Eventually, the Aldeans became sterile, unable to bear children. Finally, in the year 2364, they attempted to kidnap children from the *Enterprise*-D crew in a desperate bid to perpetuate their society. After the attempt failed, starship personnel assisted the Aldeans in dismantling their shielding systems so that the planet's ozone layer would have a chance to return to normal. ("When the Bough Breaks" [TNG]).

Aldeans. Humanoid inhabitants of planet **Aldea**. The Aldeans suffered long-term chromosomal damage from radiation exposure when their cloaking device caused a breakdown in the planet's **ozone** layer. ("When the Bough Breaks" [TNG]).

Aldebaran Music Academy. Prestigious school of the arts. Michael O'Brien hoped his son, **Miles O'Brien**, would attend the academy to become a concert cellist, but two days before he was to start, Miles signed up for Starfleet instead. ("Shadowplay" [DS9]).

Aldebaran serpent. A three-headed reptile from Aldebaran. **Q** appeared briefly in the form of such an animal during his second visit to the *Enterprise*-D. ("Hide and Q" [TNG]). *The Aldebaran serpent was a special visual effect created by Rob Legato.*

Aldebaran whiskey. A green-colored alcoholic beverage of considerable potency. Although most intoxicating beverages served aboard the *Enterprise*-D used **synthehol** instead of alcohol, Picard gave Guinan a bottle of Aldebaran whiskey that she kept behind the bar. ("Relics" [TNG]). *Data served some Aldebaran whiskey to Scotty after he expressed displeasure with synthehol-based Scotch. Data must have been unfamiliar with Aldebaran whiskey, because he described the drink by simply noting that "it is green," an homage by episode writer Ron Moore to Scotty's delivery of (nearly) the same line in "By Any Other Name" (TOS).* Aldebaran whiskey was available at **Quark's bar** on Deep Space 9. ("Prophet Motive" [DS9]). SEE: **Tomar**.

Aldebaran whiskey label

Aldebaran. Star system. Psychologist Dr. **Elizabeth Dehner** joined the *Enterprise* crew at the Aldebaran colony in 2265. ("Where No Man Has Gone Before" [TOS]). **Janet Wallace** and her husband, Theodore, performed experiments at planet Aldebaran III that used various carbohydrate compounds to slow the degeneration of plant life. Dr. Wallace suggested those experiments might be used to find a cure to the aging disease that afflicted several of the *Enterprise* crew in 2267. ("The Deadly Years" [TOS]). In 2371, **Belongo**, the nephew of Grand Nagus **Zek**, was held on Aldebaran III by Starfleet authorities. ("Past Tense, Part I" [DS9]).

Aldorian ale. Beverage. Aldorian ale was served in the Ten-Forward Lounge of the *Enterprise*-D at the request of the **Harodian miners** who were guests aboard the ship in 2368. ("The Perfect Mate" [TNG]).

Alenis Grem. (Freyda Thomas). **Bajoran** archivist. In 2371, Alenis Grem conducted a study on the **Elemspur Detention Center** for the **Bajoran Central Archives**. She contacted **Kira Nerys** on station **Deep Space 9** regarding Kira's supposed confinement at Elemspur during the Cardassian occupation. ("Second Skin" [DS9]). SEE: **Ghemor**, **Legate**.

Alexander. (Michael Dunn). Platonian citizen who, unlike other **Platonians**, lacked telekinetic powers. Alexander had a pituitary hormone deficiency, resulting in his short stature and his inability to absorb the chemical **kironide** from his planet's native food. Because he had no telekinetic powers, Alexander was forced to act as court buffoon to his fellow Platonians. Alexander befriended the *Enterprise* landing party in 2268 and eventually left with them. ("Plato's Stepchildren" [TOS]).

Alexander. SEE: **Rozhenko, Alexander**.

Alfa 117. Class-M planet. Alfa 117 was the site of a geological survey mission when a transporter malfunction created a partial duplicate of Captain Kirk in 2266. The transporter malfunction also stranded remaining members of the landing party on the planet's surface, threatening their survival when nighttime temperatures dropped to 120 degrees below zero. The survey team survived in part by using their phasers to heat rocks, which then served to warm team personnel. ("The Enemy Within" [TOS]).

Alfarian hair pasta. Food, very high in protein, made from the follicles of a mature Alfarian. The hair is harvested during shedding season in early fall. Neelix prepared Alfarian hair pasta in 2372 on the *Starship Voyager*. ("Parturition" [VGR]).

algae puffs. Small green pastries. Neelix baked algae puffs for the *Voyager* crew. ("Remember" [VGR]).

Algeron. SEE: **Treaty of Algeron**.

Algira sector. Volume of space in **Cardassian** territory. In 2371, the *Starship **Portland*** and a **Cardassian** cruiser searched the Algira sector for a Deep Space 9 **runabout**. ("The Die is Cast" [DS9]).

Algolian ceremonial rhythms. Percussive musical style. Algolian ceremonial rhythms were played during the closing reception of the **Trade Agreements Conference** aboard the *Enterprise*-D. Commander Riker later imitated the rhythms by modifying the warp field phase adjustment of the Ferengi ship ***Krayton***'s warp engines, thereby making it possible for *Enterprise*-D personnel to determine that he, Deanna Troi, and Lwaxana Troi were being held aboard the *Krayton*. ("Ménage à Troi" [TNG]).

Algorian mammoth. Large animal. **Dr. Julian Bashir** told **Garak** that 30cc's of **triptacederin** would anesthetize an Algorian mammoth. ("The Wire" [DS9]).

Alice in Wonderland. Old Earth children's story written by 19th-century English author Lewis Carroll. Two characters from this book, the **White Rabbit** and **Alice**, appeared on the

amusement park planet during an *Enterprise* landing party's visit in 2267. ("Shore Leave" [TOS]).

Alice series. (#1-250: Alyce Andrece, #251-500: Rhae Andrece). One of the many models of **androids** who populated the planet controlled by **Harcourt Fenton Mudd** in 2267. This brunette model was a particular favorite of Mudd's, who had 500 Alices made. ("I, Mudd" [TOS]). *Alyce Andrece and Rhae Andrece were able to portray their many roles because of a "split screen" optical film technique that was used to make additional copies of them, as well as the actors who played Harry Mudd's other androids.*

Alice. Character from the children's story, ***Alice in Wonderland***. Alice appeared on the **amusement park planet** after Dr. McCoy, on a landing party there in 2267, mentioned the world looked like something out of that fanciful book. ("Shore Leave" [TOS]).

Alixia. Sister to **Neelix**. Alixia often went exploring with her brother. The two visited the Caves of Touth, the equatorial dust shrouds and they even hunted arctic spiders together. Alixia died along with the rest of Neelix's family around 2356 during the Talaxian war with the **Haakonian Order**. ("Rise" [VGR]).

Alixus. (Gail Strickland). Technophobic leader of a colony that settled on planet **Orellius** in 2360. Alixus was a philosopher and a prolific writer who felt that technology had been the undoing of modern society. Her group had originally planned to colonize planet **Gemulon V**, but a systems malfunction forced their transport ship, the ***S.S. Santa Maria***, to land on Orellius. It was not learned until ten years later that Alixus had planned the forced landing in order to establish a society that conformed to her ideals. Alixus had selected Orellius because it was far from shipping lanes, and even went so far as to create a **duonetic field** around the colony site, to make it impossible for her followers to use any advanced technology. Although many of her followers seemed happy with this way of life, Alixus was responsible for several deaths because she also rejected any form of technologically-based medicine. After her colony was accidentally discovered in 2370 by Ben Sisko and Miles O'Brien, Alixus and her son, Vinod, were taken into custody for having permitted these deaths. ("Paradise" [DS9]).

alizine. Medical drug. Alizine is used to counter an allergic reaction. ("Darkling" [VGR]).

Alkar, Ambassador Ves. (Chip Lucia). Federation mediator. Alkar used his Lumerian empathic powers to surreptitiously transfer his negative emotions into another person, giving him the emotional strength to handle even the most difficult disputes. These "receptacles" (as Alkar described them) suffered from greatly accelerated aging and severe personality disorders, eventually dying. Alkar continued this practice for many years before Dr. Beverly Crusher discovered it during an investigation into the death of **Sev Maylor** in 2369. Maylor had been a victim of Alkar's abuse. He was in the process of subjecting Deanna Troi to the same treatment when he died after being cut off from access to her mind. ("Man of the People" [TNG]).

"All Good Things..." *Next Generation* episode #177 and 178. Written by Ronald D. Moore & Brannon Braga. Directed by Winrich Kolbe. Stardate 47988.1. *First aired in 1994. Mankind's existence hangs in the balance as Q causes Picard to travel between the past, present, and future to reconcile a space-time anomaly. "All Good Things..." was the last television episode of* Star Trek: The Next Generation. *It was originally produced as a two-hour movie for television, then separated into two hour-long episodes for subsequent airings. The adventures of Jean-Luc Picard and his crew aboard the* Enterprise-*D continued in the feature film* Star Trek Generations. GUEST CAST: John de Lancie as **Q**; Andreas Katsulas as **Tomalak**; Clyde Kusatsu as **Nakamura, Admiral**; Patti Yasutake as **Ogawa, Nurse Alyssa**; Denise Crosby as **Yar, Natasha**; Colm Meaney as **O'Brien, Miles**; Pamela Kosh as **Jessel**; Tim Kelleher as Gaines, Lieutenant; Alison Brooks as **Chilton, Ensign Nell**; Stephen Matthew as Garvin, Ensign; Majel Barrett as Computer voice. SEE: **acetylcholine; anti-time; anti-time (future); anti-time (past); anti-time (present); bacillus spray; Betazed; Black Sea at Night; *Bozeman, U.S.S.*; Cambridge University; Cataria, Lake; Chilton, Ensign Nell; cloaking device; *Concorde, U.S.S.*; Devron system, Earth Station McKinley; *Enterprise*-D, *U.S.S.*; *Galileo, shuttlecraft*; H'atoria; hippocampus; inverse tachyon beam; Irumodic Syndrome; Jessel; Klingon Empire; La Forge, Alandra; La Forge, Brett; La Forge, Leah; La Forge, Sydney; leaf miners; level-4 neurographic scan.; Lucasian Chair; mutual annihilation; Nakamura, Admiral; *Pasteur U.S.S.*; peridaxon; poker; Q; Romulan Neutral Zone; Satie, Rear Admiral Norah; Starbase 23; Starbase 247; static warp shell; temporal reversion; Terrellian plague; Tomalak; tomographic imaging scanner; tripamine; Wallace, Darian; warm milk with a dash of nutmeg; warp speed; *Yorktown, U.S.S.***

"All Our Yesterdays." Original Series episode #78. Written by Jean Lisette Aroeste. Directed by Marvin Chomsky. Stardate 5943.7. *First aired in 1969. Spock and McCoy are trapped in a planet's distant past, where Spock finds love with an exiled woman. Writer Jean Lisette Aroeste was a librarian at UCLA when Robert Justman read an unsolicited screenplay sent in by her. Her first* Star Trek *script was "Is There In Truth No Beauty?" (TOS).* GUEST CAST: Mariette Hartley as **Zarabeth**; Ian Wolfe as **Atoz, Mr.**; Kermit Murdock as Prosecutor, The; Ed Bakey as First fop, The; Anna Karen as Woman; Al Cavens as Second fop; Stan Barrett as Jailer, The; Johnny Haymer as Constable, The. SEE: **atavachron; Atoz, Mr.; Beta Niobe; Sarpeidon; Vulcans; Zarabeth; Zor Khan.**

allamaraine. Word in the **chula** game, shouted by **Falow** each time the players moved to another **shap**, or level. Also the basis of a nursery rhyme recited by a little girl named **Chandra** as part of the game. ("Move Along Home" [DS9]).

allasomorph. Shape-shifting species of intelligent life with the power to alter its molecular structure into that of other lifeforms. **Salia** and **Anya** of planet **Daled IV** were both allasomorphs. ("The Dauphin" [TNG]). SEE: **shape-shifter**.

"Allegiance." *Next Generation* episode #66. Written by Richard Manning & Hans Beimler. Directed by Winrich Kolbe. Stardate 43714.1. *First aired in 1990. Picard is kidnapped by unknown aliens, who lock him in a room with other humanoids in an effort to study the concept of authority. The aliens that kidnapped Picard are given no name or homeworld, so those lifeforms are described under* ***Haro, Mitena****, the identity they assumed in the episode.* GUEST CAST: Stephen Markle as **Tholl, Kova**; Reiner Schoener as **Esoqq**; Joycelyn O'Brien as **Haro, Mitena**; Jerry Rector as Alien #1; Jeff Rector as Alien #2. SEE: **Bolarus IX; Bolians; Browder IV; Chalna; Chalnoth; Cor Caroli V; Esoqq; Haro, Mitena; *Hood, U.S.S.*; Lonka Pulsar; Mizar II; Mizarians; Moropa; Ordek Nebula; Phyrox Plague; *Stargazer, U.S.S.*; Tholl, Kova; Wogneer creatures.**

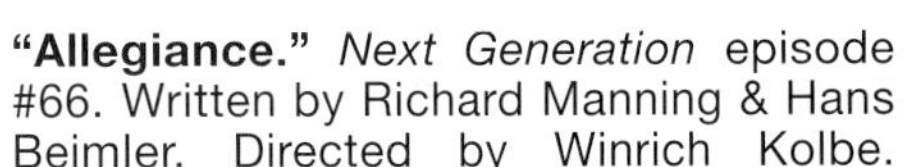

Allenby, Ensign Tess. (Mary Kohnert). Flight Control officer aboard the *Enterprise*-D, she piloted the ship during the mission at **Gamelan V** in 2367 ("Final Mission" [TNG]). Allenby was at the conn when the ship encountered a school of two-dimensional creatures while en route to planet **T'lli Beta** ("The Loss" [TNG]).

Graffiti symbol
Alliance for Global Unity

Alliance for Global Unity, The. Extremist Bajoran isolationist faction that sought to overthrow the **Bajoran provisional government** following the **Cardassian** withdrawal of 2369. The Alliance, also known as the Circle, was secretly led by conservative **Minister Jaro Essa**. Well organized and armed, the Alliance was often successful in confounding the provisional government. ("The Homecoming" [DS9]). SEE: **symbols.** Arms for the Circle were supplied by Cardassian operatives who sought to take advantage of the Circle's aim of ending **Bajor**'s association with the **Federation**. The Circle was not aware of the Cardassian involvement because the weapons were being shipped through **Kressari** intermediaries. ("The Circle" [DS9]). SEE: **Perikian peninsula**. Though the Circle briefly seized control of station **Deep Space 9**, they abandoned the takeover when Major Kira Nerys revealed the source of their weapons. The influence of the Circle, and Minister Jaro, evaporated shortly thereafter. SEE: **Day, Colonel**. ("The Siege" [DS9]).

Alliance. In the **mirror universe**, the political union formed by the Cardassians and the Klingons after they conquered the **Terran Empire**. Planet **Bajor** was an influential member of the Alliance. ("Crossover" [DS9]). By 2371, humans led by **Benjamin Sisko (mirror)** banded together in a fight to regain **Terran** freedom from the oppressive Alliance. ("Through the Looking Glass" [DS9]). By 2372, the **Terran resistance** had driven the Alliance from station **Terok Nor (mirror)**. ("Shattered Mirror" [DS9]).

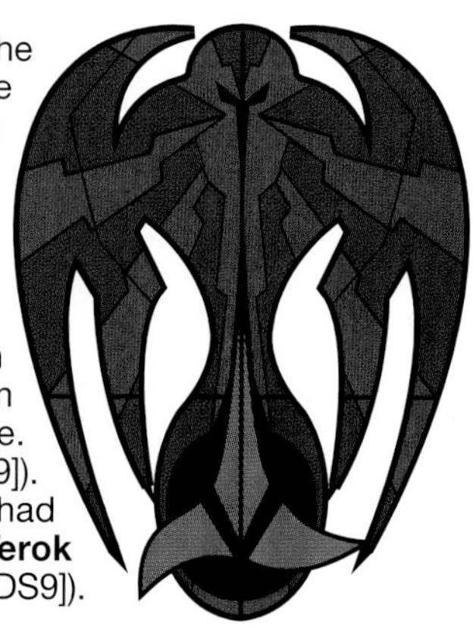

Alliance. One of the two main rival factions in control of the colony on planet **Turkana IV** following the collapse of the colonial government in 2337. In bitter competition with the **Coalition**, the Alliance captured the crew of the Federation freighter ***Arcos***, crashed on the planet in 2350. The Alliance hoped to trade the *Arcos* crew members for weapons from the *Enterprise*-D to use in their ongoing battle with the Coalition. ("Legacy" [TNG]).

"Alliances." *Voyager* episode #31. Written by Jeri Taylor. Directed by Les Landau. Stardate 49337.4. *First aired in 1996. In an effort to survive in the hazardous Delta Quadrant, the crew of the Voyager tries to forge an alliance with the sects of the Kazon Collective.* GUEST CAST: Charles O. Lucia as **Mabus**; Anthony DeLongis as **Culluh, Jal**; Martha Hackett as **Seska**; Raphael Sbarge as **Jonas**; Larry Cedar as **Tersa**; John Gegenhuber as **Surat**, **Jal**; Simon Billig as **Hogan**; Mirron E. Willis as **Rettick**. SEE: **Bendera, Kurt; Calogan dog; Chakotay; Culluh, Jal; dodecahedron; Hogan; icosahedron; impedrezene; Jonas, Michael; Kazon; Kazon-Hobii; Kazon-Mostral; Kazon-Nistrim; Kazon-Ogla; Kazon-Oglamar; Kazon-Pommar; Kazon-Relora; Loran, Jal; Mabus; Minnis; Rettick; Seska; Sobras; Surat, Jal; Takrit; Telfas Prime; Tersa, Jal; Trabe; Trabe police; Tuvok; Valek, Jal; Vulcan favinit plant; Vulcan spice tea.**

Almatha sector. Region of space in **Cardassian** territory. The *Starship* ***Defiant*** was sighted in the Almatha sector during **Thomas Riker**'s cat-and-mouse game with the Cardassian military in 2371. ("Defiant" [DS9]).

Alpha 441. Planetoid located in the **Badlands**. On stardate 46437, a Cardassian guided tactical missile, later dubbed Dreadnought, was launched on a mission to destroy a **Maquis** munitions base on planetoid Alpha 441. ("Dreadnought" [VGR]).

Alpha Carinae II. Class-M planet with two major land masses. Used in 2268 to test the **M-5** computer's performance in conducting routine planetary contact and survey operations. ("The Ultimate Computer" [TOS]). SEE: **Canopus Planet**.

Alpha Carinae V. Planet. Homeworld of the **drella**, a creature that derives its energy from the emotion of love. ("Wolf in the Fold" [TOS]).

Alpha Centauri. Star. One of the nearest stars to Earth's Solar system, some 4.3 light-years from Sol. In Earth's past, Kirk told United States Air Force officer **Fellini** that he was a little green man from Alpha Centauri and that it was a beautiful place to visit ("Tomorrow Is Yesterday" [TOS]). Alpha Centauri was home to noted scientist **Zefram Cochrane**, who invented warp drive in the 21st century ("Metamorphosis" [TOS]).

Alpha Cygnus IX. Planet. Federation Ambassador **Sarek** was credited for a treaty with Alpha Cygus IX, one of the many triumphs of his distinguished career. ("Sarek" [TNG]).

Alpha III, Statutes of. Landmark document in the protection of individual civil liberties, cited by **Samuel Cogley** when James Kirk was accused of murder in 2267 but denied the opportunity to face his accuser. ("Court Martial" [TOS]).

Alpha Majoris I. Planet. Homeworld of the **mellitus**, a creature that is gaseous when moving and becomes solid when it is dormant. ("Wolf in the Fold" [TOS]).

Alpha Moon. One of two satellites orbiting planet **Peliar Zel**. The inhabitants of Alpha Moon devised an ingenious system to generate power by tapping into the magnetic field of Peliar Zel. While this was of great benefit to the people on Alpha Moon, it had detrimental environmental effects on nearby **Beta Moon**, also orbiting Peliar Zel. The two moons, historically at odds, sought the mediation services of Ambassador **Odan** to resolve the conflict in 2367. ("The Host" [TNG]).

Alpha Omicron system. An uncharted system. The *Enterprise*-D passed the Alpha Omicron system en route to a mission in the **Guernica system** in 2367. A previously unknown life-form was discovered in the Alpha Omicron system, living in an asteroid belt. ("Galaxy's Child" [TNG]) SEE: **Junior**.

Alpha Onias III. An uninhabited Class-M planet, listed by Federation survey teams as barren and inhospitable. Subspace fluctuations detected in the system in 2367 suggested a possible Romulan base. While on Alpha Onias III to investigate this possibility, Commander Riker experienced an elaborate holodeck-type virtual reality devised by **Barash**. ("Future Imperfect" [TNG]).

Alpha Proxima II. Inhabited planet. Site of violent crimes where several women were knifed to death. The murders were reminiscent of those committed by Jack the Ripper. ("Wolf in the Fold" [TOS]).

Alpha Quadrant. One quarter of the entire Milky Way Galaxy. The region in which most of the **United Federation of Planets**, including **Earth**, is located. The galaxy is so huge that the majority of the Alpha Quadrant remains unexplored, even in the 24th century. Station **Deep Space 9** is located in Alpha Quadrant. ("Captive Pursuit" [DS9]). The Klingon and Romulan empires are located in **Beta Quadrant**. *The reason for splitting the Federation between Alpha and Beta Quadrants was to rationalize Kirk's line in* Star Trek II *that the* Enterprise *was the only starship in the quadrant.*

Alpha V, Colony. Federation settlement. **Charles Evans**'s nearest surviving relatives lived at Colony Alpha V in 2266. ("Charlie X" [TOS]).

alpha four seven authorization. Security code required to access Starfleet subspace secured channels aboard the *Starship Enterprise*-D on stardate 47653. Under the early influence of

Barclay's Protomorphosis Syndrome, Riker could no longer remember the code sequence. ("Genesis" [TNG]).

alpha search pattern. Standard Starfleet exploration scheme in which a group is divided into a number of smaller search teams and sent out in specific predetermined directions. ("Basics, Part I" [VGR]).

alpha-currant nectar. Priceless **Wadi** beverage offered by **Falow** as a wager in a **dabo** game at Deep Space 9 in 2369. Quark declined the bid after taking a drink of the nectar and finding it distasteful. ("Move Along Home" [DS9]).

alpha-wave inducer. Device used to enhance sleep in humanoids, but only meant for occasional use. **Kajada** told Dr. Bashir she was having difficulty sleeping so she used an alpha-wave inducer. ("The Passenger" [DS9]).

Alrik, Chancellor. (Mickey Cottrell). The head of the government of the **Valt Minor** system who, in 2368, conducted the historic **Ceremony of Reconciliation** between his star system and the **Krios** system, ending centuries of war. A stern and humorless man, Alrik was concerned only with the matters of the treaty between the two systems, and not with the ceremony or with the gift of the **empathic metamorph** named **Kamala**. ("The Perfect Mate" [TNG]).

Alsaurian resistance movement. Among the citizens of the **Mokra Order**, a group of freedom fighters committed to opposing the oppressive Mokra government. Members of the resistence included **Caylem** and his wife, and his daughter, **Ralkana**. ("Resistance" [VGR]).

Alsia. (K. Callan). Humanoid con artist. On Deep Space 9 in 2370, Alsia told **Martus Mazur** she wanted to mine the **Vlugta asteroid belt** but lacked the funds needed to finalize the transaction. Martus gave her 10,000 **isiks** but regretted his action when Odo arrested Alsia for fraud, learning the asteroid deal was worthless. ("Rivals" [DS9]).

Altair III. Third planet in the Altair system. Site of an away mission where *Starship **Hood*** executive officer **William Riker** refused to allow *Hood* captain **DeSoto** to transport to the surface. Riker felt the mission was too dangerous to expose the ship's captain to risk. The incident took place prior to Riker's assignment to the *Enterprise*-D. *The star Altair, also known as Alpha Aquila, is the brightest star in the constellation Aquila the Eagle, visible from Earth.* ("Encounter at Farpoint, Part I" [TNG]).

Altair IV. Federation planet. **Dr. Henri Roget,** winner of the **Carrington Award** in 2371, worked at the Central Hospital on Altair IV. ("Prophet Motive" [DS9]). *Planet Altair IV was the setting for the classic 1956 science fiction film* Forbidden Planet.

Altair VI. Planet. The inhabitants of Altair VI ended a long interplanetary conflict in 2267. The *Starship Enterprise* was scheduled to attend the inauguration of their new president shortly after the end of that war, but the visit was postponed when Spock diverted the ship to planet **Vulcan** because he was undergoing ***Pon farr*** ("Amok Time" [TOS]). Altair VI was mentioned in Starfleet Academy's notorious ***Kobayashi Maru*** training simulation. The incident involved a damaged ship near that planet. (*Star Trek II: The Wrath of Khan*).

Altair water. Beverage. Dr. McCoy ordered Altair water at a bar on Earth just before trying to book passage to the **Genesis Planet**. *(Star Trek III: The Search for Spock).*

Altairian Conference. Meeting at which Picard met **Captain Rixx** prior to 2364. ("Conspiracy" [TNG]).

Altarian encephalitis. A retrovirus that incorporated its DNA directly into the cells of its host. The virus can lie dormant for years, but activate without warning. Victims would be pyrexic and comatose and would suffer from widespread synaptic degradation. Long-term memory, usually from the moment of the infection, would be destroyed. In a virtual reality created by **Barash** on **Alpha Onias III**, Commander Riker was told he had contracted Altarian encephalitis in 2367, thus explaining a significant memory loss. ("Future Imperfect" [TNG]).

Altec. Class-M planet; along with **Straleb**, part of the **Coalition of Madena**. Although Altec was technically at peace with Straleb, relations between the two planets had been strained to the point that an interplanetary incident was created when it was revealed that **Benzan** of Straleb had been engaged to **Yanar** of Altec in 2365. ("The Outrageous Okona" [TNG]).

"Alter Ego." *Voyager* episode #55. Written by Joe Menosky. Directed by Robert Picardo. Stardate 50460.3. *First aired in 1997. Harry Kim falls in love with a beautiful holodeck character, then turns to Tuvok to help him eliminate his emotions. Unfortunately, Tuvok falls for her too, then learns that she is actually a lonely being living in a nearby nebula.* GUEST CAST: Sandra Nelson as **Marayna**; Alexander Enberg as **Vorik**; Shay Todd as Holowoman; Majel Barrett as Computer voice. SEE: **big daddy-O; holodeck and holosuite programs: Polynesian resort; hydrosail; inversion nebula; *k'oh-nar; kal-toh*; lei; Marayna; plasma strand; Polynesian resort; *shon-ha'lock; soo-lak; t'an; t'san s'at;* volleyball; Vorik.**

Alterian chowder. Soup. Benjamin Sisko ordered Alterian chowder at Quark's on Deep Space 9. ("Armageddon Game" [DS9]).

"Alternate, The." *Deep Space Nine* episode #32. Teleplay by Bill Dial. Story by Jim Trombetta and Bill Dial. Directed by David Carson. Stardate 47391.7. *First aired in 1993. Odo's humanoid "father" helps him track down a mysterious shapeshifting entity on Deep Space 9.* GUEST CAST: James Sloyan as **Mora Pol**, **Dr.**; Matt McKenzie as **Weld Ram**, **Dr.** SEE: **Bajoran Institute of Science; Deka tea; Ferengi Certificate of Dismemberment; Ferengi death rituals; Khofla II; Klingon opera; Krokan petri dish; L-S VI; L-S VI lifeform; Mora Pol, Dr.; Plegg; strip; Weld Ram, Dr.**

"Alternative Factor, The." Original Series episode #20. Written by Don Ingalls. Directed by Gerd Oswald. Stardate 3087.6. *First aired in 1967. A mysterious "rip" in space is opened between our universe and an antimatter universe, and a madman threatens the existence of both realities. John Barrymore, Jr. was originally cast as Lazarus but, when he failed to report for work on the first day of production, Robert Brown was hurriedly recast in the role.* GUEST CAST: Robert Brown as **Lazarus**; Janet MacLachlan as **Masters**, **Lieutenant**; Richard Derr as **Barstow**, **Commodore**; Arch Whiting as Assistant engineering officer; Christian Patrick as Transporter Chief; Eddie Paskey as **Leslie**, **Mr.**; Larry Riddle as Officer; Tom Lupo, Ron Veto, Bill Blackburn, and Vince Calenti, as Security guards; Gary Coombs as Kirk's stunt double; Al Wyatt, Bill Catching as Lazarus' stunt doubles; Frank Vinci, Carey Foster, Tom Steele, Crew stuntmen. SEE: **Barstow, Commodore; Code Factor 1; door in the universe; Lazarus; Leslie, Mr.; Masters, Lieutenant; Starbase 200**.

Altine Conference. Scientific conference attended by *Enterprise*-D Chief Medical Officer Beverly Crusher in 2369. She met **Dr. Reyga** while at the conference. ("Suspicions" [TNG]).

Altonian brain teaser. A holographic puzzle that responds to neural theta waves, the goal being to turn a floating multicolor sphere into a solid color. The **Dax symbiont** had been attempting to master the game for 140 years and, as of 2369, had yet to succeed. ("A Man Alone" [DS9]).

Altovar. A **Lethean** criminal. In 2371 on station **Deep Space 9**, Altovar attempted to steal **bio-mimetic gel** from the infirmary. When **Julian Bashir** caught him ransacking the supplies in search of the gel, Altovar attacked the doctor, causing a telepathically induced coma. ("Distant Voices" [DS9]).

Alture VII relaxation program. Holosuite program that first bathes you in a protein bath, then carries you off on a cloud of chromal vapor into a meditation chamber. Beverly Crusher wanted to try this program at Quark's bar when the *Enterprise*-D visited Deep Space 9. ("Birthright, Part I" [TNG]).

aluminum, transparent. SEE: **transparent aluminum.**

Alvanian beehive. Insect community known for its frenetic activity. ("Rapture" [DS9]).

Alvanian brandy. Alcoholic beverage. Dr. Bashir didn't like Alvanian brandy, so he donated a case of it to Quark's bar. ("Body Parts" [DS9]).

Alvanian cave sloth. Animal known for its deep slumbering. ("The Sword of Kahless" [DS9]).

Alvanian spine mite. Tiny parasitic insects that make their homes in humanoid spinal columns. Alvanian spine mites can cause the host organism to experience pain for many years. ("The Begotten" [DS9]).

Alverian dung beetle. Form of insect life. ("Apocalypse Rising" [DS9]).

Alvinian melons. Large green fruit. ("Return to Grace" [DS9]).

Amanda. (Jane Wyatt). Ambassador Sarek's human wife and mother to Spock. Amanda came aboard the *Enterprise* in 2267 with her husband, Sarek, who was attending the **Babel Conference** ("Journey to Babel" [TOS]). Amanda helped Spock reeducate himself following his ***fal-tor-pan*** refusion in 2285. She tried especially to help her son rediscover the human portion of his personality (*Star Trek IV: The Voyage Home*). *Amanda's first appearance was in "Journey To Babel" (TOS). A younger Amanda was played by Cynthia Blaise in* Star Trek V *for Spock's birth flashbacks. According to original* Star Trek *series story editor Dorothy Fontana, Amanda's maiden name was Grayson, although this was not established in a regular episode.*

Amanita muscaria. Poisonous mushroom native to Earth. The *Amanita muscaria* has a red or orange cap with white patches and if ingested, causes profuse sweating, convulsions, and even death. ("Heroes and Demons" [VGR]).

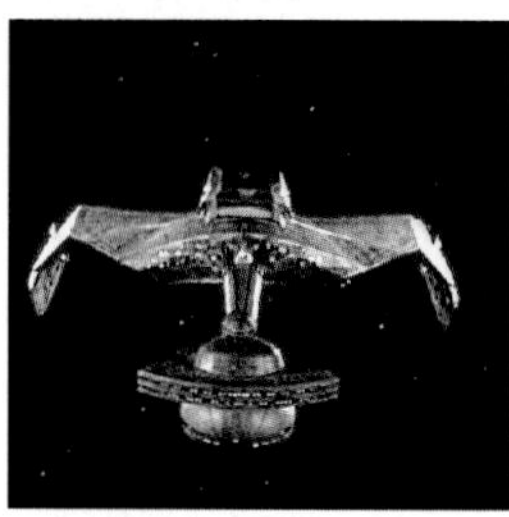

Amar, I.K.S. Klingon battle cruiser, *K't'inga* class, destroyed in 2271 while investigating the **V'Ger** machine lifeform. (*Star Trek: The Motion Picture*). *The new Klingon battle cruiser was closely based on the original battle cruiser designed by Matt Jefferies for the original* Star Trek *television series. This new version, built at Magicam and at Future General, incorporated much more elaborate surface detailing for a more realistic look. The commander of the* Amar *was played by Mark Lenard, who also played Spock's father, Sarek, and had been the Romulan commander in "Balance of Terror" (TOS).*

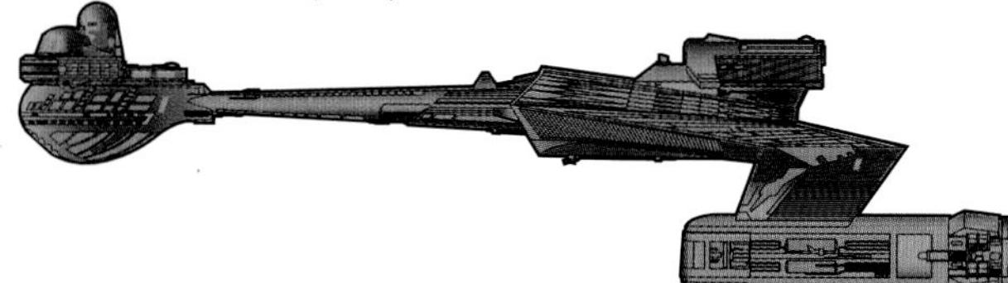

Amargosa Diaspora. Dense globular star cluster. The *Enterprise*-D investigated the Amargosa Diaspora in 2369. ("Schisms" [TNG]).

Amargosa Observatory. Small Federation science space station located in the **Amargosa** system. In 2371, the observatory was attacked by Romulans looking for **trilithium** stolen by Klingon outlaws **Lursa** and **B'Etor**. **Dr. Tolian Soran** was a scientist aboard the observatory, and in 2371 he used the station to launch a solar probe into the Amargosa sun. The probe destroyed the star in a quantum implosion and the resultant shock wave obliterated the observatory. *(Star Trek Generations).* SEE: **nexus**.

Amargosa. Yellow giant star. **Dr. Tolian Soran**, who had been studying the star from the **Amargosa Observatory**, destroyed the Amargosa star in 2371 with a **trilithium**-laden solar probe. The destruction of the star altered gravitational forces in the sector, steering the **nexus** ribbon toward the **Veridian system**. *(Star Trek Generations).*

Amarie. (Harriet Leider). A musician at a lounge on planet **Qualor II**. Amarie was the ex-wife of an arms smuggler whose ship attacked the *Enterprise*-D in 2368. She was uniquely qualified for her occupation as a keyboard artist, as she had four arms. ("Unification, Part II" [TNG]).

Amaros. (Tony Plana). Member of the **Maquis**. He was among the group that abducted **Gul Dukat** from **Deep Space 9** in 2370 and worked with Maquis leader **Calvin Hudson** to liberate **Federation** colonists from **Cardassian** control in the **Demilitarized Zone.** ("The Maquis, Parts I and II" [DS9]).

Amat'igan. (Andrew Hawkes). **Jem'Hadar** soldier. Amat'igan accompanied the **Founder Leader** on stardate 49962.4 aboard the *Starship Defiant* to escort Odo to the Founders' homeworld. Amat'igan took the conn during the trip. ("Broken Link" [DS9]).

Amazing Detective Stories. Pulp detective magazine published on early-20th-century Earth. The character **Dixon Hill** first appeared in a 1934 issue of this magazine. ("The Big Goodbye" [TNG]).

ambassador, Klingon. (John Schuck). Representative of the Klingon government in 2286. The ambassador attempted to secure the extradition of James Kirk so that he could be brought to trial for alleged crimes, including the theft of a Klingon spacecraft. The Klingon ambassador believed, mistakenly, that Kirk had participated in the development of **Project Genesis** with the intent of using it as a weapon against the Klingon people. (*Star Trek IV: The Voyage Home*). The Klingon ambassador vehemently opposed efforts to free James Kirk and Leonard McCoy from Klingon custody after the two had been arrested on charges of murdering **Chancellor Gorkon** in 2293. *(Star Trek VI: The Undiscovered Country). The character did not have a given name in dialog, or in the script.*

Ambassador*-class starship**. Type of Federation starship including the fourth *Starship Enterprise.* ("Yesterday's *Enterprise*" [TNG]). The prototype ship, the *U.S.S. Ambassador*, bore registry number NCC-10521. *Ambassador*-class ships have included the ***U.S.S. Adelphi (NCC-26849), the second ***U.S.S. Excalibur*** (NCC-26517), the ***U.S.S. Zhukov*** (NCC-26136), and the aforementioned ***U.S.S. Enterprise-C*** (NCC-1701C). *The* Ambassador-*class ship was designed by Rick Sternbach and Andrew Probert. The model, built by Greg Jein, was intended to suggest an* *intermediate step between the* Excelsior-*class and the* Galaxy-*class starships.*

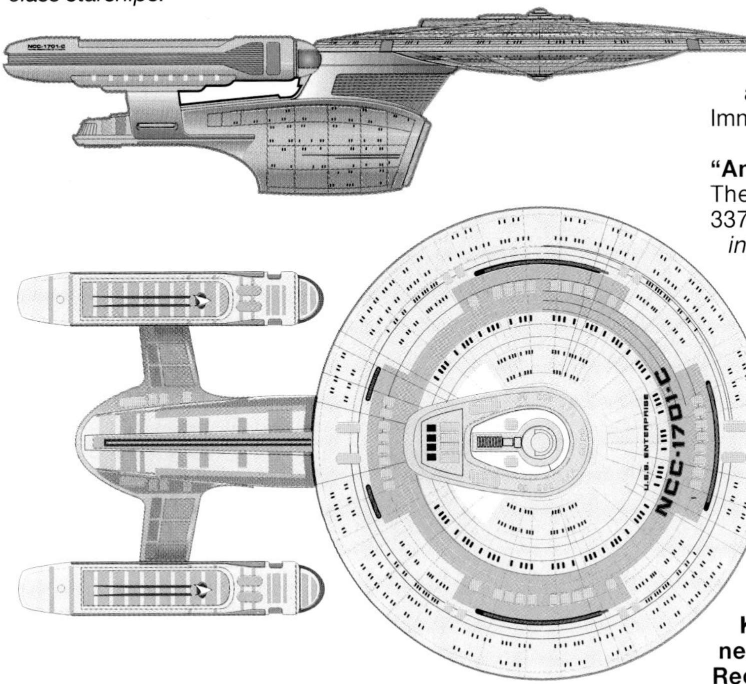

American Sign Language. A form of nonverbal communication developed on Earth in the United States for communication by the hearing impaired. ("Macrocosm" [VGR]).

Ameron. (Karl Wiedergott). Son of the Autarch of the **Ilari** nation in the Delta Quadrant. Ameron was second in line to become Autarch, after his older brother, **Demmas**. In 2373, **Tieran** killed the Autarch, gaining the title for himself. Tieran, whose consciousness inhabited Kes's body, intended to marry Ameron in order to solidify his power base. Although outraged at first, Ameron became seduced by the promise of power and joined in Tieran's plan. ("Warlord" [VGR]).

Amleth Prime. Cardassian planet located within an **emission nebula**. The Cardassians maintained a station on Amleth Prime. ("Return to Grace" [DS9]).

amniotic fluid. Also known as *liquor amnii* or the "waters," amniotic fluid is the albuminous liquid that surrounds the fetus during pregnancy in many mammalian species. The amniotic fluid of Spot's pregnancy protected her kittens from the influence of **Barclay's Protomorphosis Syndrome** in 2370; it was later found to have protected **Alyssa Ogawa**'s fetus as well. Data was able to extract some of the antibodies from Ogawa's amnion and use them to synthesize a **retrovirus** to combat the syndrome. ("Genesis" [TNG]).

amniotic scan. Sensor readings of the fluid contained within the amniotic sac of a mammalian pregnancy. Such a scan can provide a wealth of information about the fetus, including its sex. ("Genesis" [TNG]).

amoeba. A massive spaceborne single-celled organism that consumed the **Gamma 7A System** and the ***U.S.S. Intrepid*** in

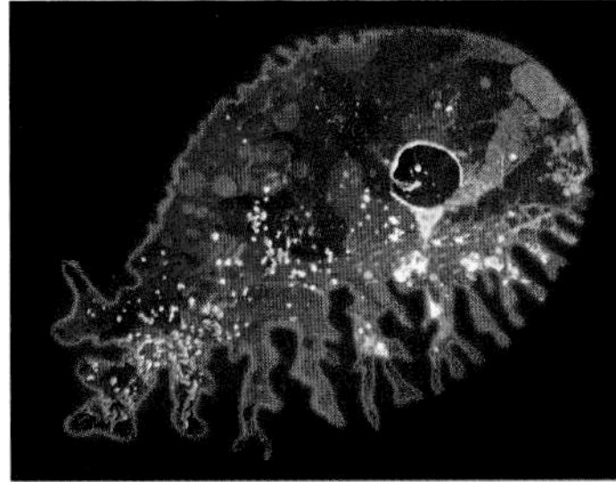

2268. The creature strongly resembled microscopic protozoans found on terrestrial planets, save for its enormous size. The spaceborne amoeba was some 18,000 kilometers long, and about 3,000 kilometers wide, surrounded by a large energy-absorbing field. The creature was believed to originate from outside our galaxy. The *Starship Enterprise* approached the organism shortly after stardate 4307 and was nearly crippled by the amoeba's energy-absorbing field, termed a "zone of darkness." The organism was destroyed by an antimatter bomb planted into the amoeba's nucleus with assistance from a shuttlecraft piloted by Spock. ("The Immunity Syndrome" [TOS]).

"Amok Time." Original Series episode #34. Written by Theodore Sturgeon. Directed by Joseph Pevney. Stardate 3372.7. *First aired in 1967. Spock experiences the Vulcan mating drive and must return home to take a wife, or die. This is the first episode in which the greetings "peace and long life" and "live long and prosper" were used. Also seen for the first time in this episode were the Vulcan hand salute (invented by Leonard Nimoy) and the planet Vulcan itself.* GUEST CAST: Celia Lovsky as **T'Pau**; Arlene Martel as **T'Pring**; Lawrence Montaigne as **Stonn**; Majel Barrett as **Chapel, Christine**; Byron Morrow as **Komack, Admiral**; Walker Edmiston as Space Central voice; Russ Peek as Vulcan executioner; Joe Paz, Charles Palmer, Mauri Russell, Gary Wright, Vulcan litter bearers; Mauri Russell, Frank Vinci, Vulcan bell carriers; Dave Perna as Spock's stunt double; Paul Baxley, Phil Adams as Kirk's stunt doubles. SEE: ***ahn-woon*; Altair VI; eel-birds; Federation Council; Finagle's law; *Kal-if-fee*; Komack, Admiral; *Koon-ut-kal-if-fee*; *Kroykah*; *lirpa*; neural paralyzer; *Plak-tow*; *plomeek* soup; *Pon farr*; Regulus V; Spock; Stonn; T'Pau; T'Pring; tri-ox compound; Vulcan; Vulcan lute; Vulcans; wedding.**

amphibian. A vertebrate animal capable of living both on land and in water. The reproductive cycles of amphibians often involve both aquatic and land-based phases. Deanna Troi's activated **introns** caused her to devolve into an amphibian when she suffered from **Barclay's Protomorphosis Syndrome** in 2370. ("Genesis" [TNG]).

AMU. Antimatter unit. In 2372, Torres extracted 0.75 AMUs of **antiproton** radiation from the *Starship Voyager*'s warp core in an attempt to cure Thomas Paris's mutative process. ("Threshold" [VGR]).

amusement park planet. Planet in the Omicron Delta region equipped with sophisticated subterranean equipment that could read the minds of visitors, then almost immediately create whatever it is that the visitor imagined. The original *Starship Enterprise* visited the amusement park planet in 2267. Members of an *Enterprise* landing party encountered a variety of images, from old lovers and school rivals to storybook characters. Although the images were fascinating, they were disturbing and even frightening until the landing party members understood what was happening. SEE: **Alice; black knight; Caretaker; Finnegan; Police Special; Ruth; tiger; White Rabbit.** ("Shore Leave" [TOS]). *The actual name for the planet was not given in the episode. The location filming for "Shore Leave" took place near Los Angeles at Vasquez Rocks and Africa USA. Vasquez Rocks was featured in several Original Series episodes, as well as in episodes of* Star Trek: The Next Generation. *It was also seen in "The Zanthi Misfits" episode of* The Outer Limits. *SEE:* ***Cestus III.*** *("Arena" [TOS]).*

analeptic. Pharmaceutical used as a restorative. ("Rise" [VGR]).

Anan 7. (David Opatoshu). Leader of the High Council of planet **Eminiar VII** in 2267. Anan 7 was his planet's military commander in the war between Eminiar and **Vendikar**. When the *Starship Enterprise* arrived at Eminiar VII in 2267, Anan tried to warn the ship to stay away. After the *Enterprise* ignored the warning, it was Anan's difficult task to enforce the declaration that the ship was a war casualty under the agreement between his

government and Vendikar. When *Enterprise* Captain Kirk refused to surrender his ship, Anan agreed to peace talks with the Vendikar government to avoid the possibility of real war. ("A Taste of Armageddon" [TOS]).

anapestic tetrameter. Syle of poetic meter. Commander Data employed anapestic tetrameter in a poem he once recited. ("Schisms" [TNG]).

anaphasic life-form. Noncorporeal, sentient, and extremely long-lived life-form that requires a corporeal host to maintain its molecular cohesion. The anaphasic life-form known as **Ronin** found a compatible biochemistry with the women of the Howard family. ("Sub Rosa" [TNG]). SEE: **Howard, Felisa**.

Anara. (Benita Andre). Apprentice engineer on **Deep Space 9**, who served on the station in 2369. A Bajoran national. ("The Forsaken" [DS9]).

Anaya, Ensign April. (Page Leong). An *Enterprise*-D crew member. Anaya was assigned to the conn during the *Enterprise*-D's encounter with a **Cytherian** probe in 2367. ("The Nth Degree" [TNG]).

anbo-jytsu. Considered by some to be the ultimate evolution in the martial arts, anbo-jytsu is derived from a number of Earth's Asian forms. The sport involves two opponents striking each other with three-meter-long staffs while blindfolded. A proximity detector at one end of each staff provides guidance on the opponent's location, while full-body armor protects each player. Points are scored for contact with the opponent, and for knocking the opponent outside of the playing ring. **Kyle Riker** played this highly competitive game with his son, **William Riker**, from the time William was eight years old. Although the elder Riker never lost to his son, William later learned that Kyle had been cheating since William had been 12 years old. ("The Icarus Factor" [TNG]).

Ancestral Spirits. Name given to the supernatural entities that were revered by members of the **Nechisti Order** on the **Nechani** homeworld. ("Sacred Ground" [VGR]).

Anchilles fever. Deadly disease capable of spreading rapidly in a planetary population and causing widespread and painful deaths in the millions. The disease struck planet **Styris IV** in 2364. ("Code of Honor" [TNG]).

Ancient Philosophies. A required course at Starfleet Academy. Cadet Wesley Crusher had difficulty mastering Ancient Philosophies. ("The Host" [TNG]).

Ancient West. Holodeck program created by **Alexander Rozhenko** and **Reginald Barclay**. Set in Earth's 19th century in the town of **Deadwood**, South Dakota, the program allowed participants to play the town sheriff, the sheriff's deputy, and **Durango**, the mysterious stranger. The holoprogram malfunctioned and the fantasy became a deadly reality. During the malfunction, information from Data's neural net became incorporated into the holodeck program. SEE: **Subroutine C-47; progressive memory purge; Spot**. ("A Fistful of Datas" [TNG]). *Deadwood was an actual town in South Dakota. The Western sequences were filmed on the back lot of Universal Studios in Los Angeles.*

"And the Children Shall Lead." Original Series episode #60. Written by Edward J. Lakso. Directed by Marvin Chomsky. Stardate: 5029.5. *First aired in 1968. Children who have survived the bizarre death of their parents are possessed by the evil spirit that killed their parents.* GUEST CAST: Craig Hundley as **Starnes, Tommy**; James Wellman as **Starnes, Professor**; Melvin Belli as **Gorgan**; Majel Barrett as **Chapel, Christine**; Pamelyn Ferdin as **Janowski, Mary**; Caesar Belli as **O'Connel, Steve**; Mark Robert Brown as Linden, Don; Brian Tochi as **Tsingtao, Ray**; Lou Elias as 1st Technician; Eddie Paskey as **Leslie, Mr.**; Dick Dial as Technician #2; Jay Jones as Crew stunt double. SEE: **cyalodin; Epsilon Indi; food slot; Gorgan; Janowski, Mary; lacunar amnesia; Marcos XII; O'Connel, Steve; Starbase 4; Starnes Expedition; Starnes, Professor; Starnes, Tommy; Triacus; Tsingtao, Ray; Wilkins, Professor.**

Andarian glass bead. Very valuable and beautiful gem. Even a small quantity of Andarian glass beads fetched a considerable price. **Hagath** gave some Andarian glass beads to Quark in 2373 while the two were partners in a series of arms sales. ("Business As Usual" [DS9]).

Andevian II. Second planet in the Andevian system. **Lwaxana Troi** felt the fourth moon orbiting Andevian II to be an ideal site for a romantic picnic. Ambassador Troi reserved a **holosuite** at **Quark's bar** on Deep Space 9 so that she could have such a picnic with **Odo** on a re-creation of Andevian II, although she neglected to ask Odo first. ("The Forsaken" [DS9]).

Andolian brandy. A special liqueur. Quark offered a bottle of Andolian brandy to the **Wadi** delegation at Deep Space 9 in 2369 after he was caught cheating at the **dabo** wheel. ("Move Along Home" [DS9]).

Andonian tea. Beverage. **Admiral Aaron** offered Andonian tea to Captain Picard when the latter was visiting **Starfleet Headquarters** in 2364. ("Conspiracy" [TNG]).

Andoria. Homeworld to the **Andorian** people, and a member of the **United Federation of Planets**. Chirurgeon Ghee P'Trell was from Andoria. ("Prophet Motive" [DS9]). *The Andorians were first seen in "Journey to Babel" (TOS), but their homeworld didn't get a name until "Prophet Motive" (DS9).*

Andorian ale. Beverage. Served at **Quark's bar**. ("Meridian" [DS9]).

Andorian amoeba. Variety of unicellular protozoan indigenous to planet Andoria. Andorian amoebae reproduce by means of **symbiogenesis**. ("Tuvix" [VGR]).

Andorian blues. Musical form. Popular with keyboardist **Amarie**. ("Unification, Part II" [TNG]). *The term was, of course, a gag based on the fact that Andorians have blue skin.*

Andorian transport. Spacecraft of Andorian registry. **Pel** booked passage to the Gamma Quadrant from station Deep Space 9 aboard an Andorian transport in 2370. ("Rules of Acquisition" [DS9]).

Andorian tuber root. Food. Jadzia Dax enjoyed Andorian tuber roots more than did Ben Sisko. ("Second Sight" [DS9]).

Andorians. Humanoid civilization from the planet **Andoria**. ("Prophet Motive" [DS9]). Andorians sometimes describe themselves as a passionate, violent people. Their appearance is characterized by beautiful blue skin and a pair of antennae on their heads. Members of the United Federation of Planets, an Andorian delegation journeyed to the **Babel Conference** of 2267 aboard the *Starship Enterprise*. The Andorian contingent included Ambassador **Shras** and staff member **Thelev**. SEE: **Orions**. ("Journey to Babel" [TOS]). Andorian marriages generally require groups of four people. ("Data's Day" [TNG]). *Andorians were also seen in "Whom Gods Destroy" (TOS), in the Federation Council chambers in* Star Trek IV, *and were glimpsed in "Captain's Holiday" (TNG), and "The Offspring" (TNG). Renegade Andorians were mentioned in "The Survivors" (TNG).*

Andrea. (Sherry Jackson). Beautiful female android creation of archaeologist **Roger Korby**. Andrea was built using technology left over from the ancient civilization that lived under the surface of planet **Exo III**. ("What Are Little Girls Made Of?" [TOS]).

android. According to *Webster's Twenty-Fourth-Century Dictionary, Fifth Edition*, an android is an automaton made to resemble a human being. ("The Measure of a Man" [TNG]). The **Old Ones** of planet **Exo III** developed highly sophisticated androids, but those androids eventually destroyed their civilization. Centuries later, Dr. Roger Korby built androids based on those ancient designs. ("What Are Little Girls Made Of?" [TOS]). The androids created by the **Makers** from the Andromeda Galaxy were programmed to perform the menial tasks of their society. ("I, Mudd" [TOS]). Androids were created by **Sargon**, **Thalassa**, and **Henoch** aboard the *Enterprise* so that their minds could be transferred into robot bodies. ("Return to Tomorrow" [TOS]). **Flint** attempted to create an immortal mate named **Rayna Kapec** but was unable to achieve his goal. ("Requiem for Methuselah" [TOS]). The android **Data** (pictured), who served aboard the *Enterprise*-D, strove to become more like his human shipmates ("Encounter at Farpoint" [TNG]). A legal decision handed down by Starfleet Judge Advocate General **Phillipa Louvois** in 2365 established that Data was indeed a sentient being, entitled to full constitutional protection as a citizen of the United Federation of Planets. ("The Measure of a Man" [TNG]). A significant advance in android technology was made in 2366 when Data used a new **submicron matrix transfer technology** to build an android daughter, whom he named **Lal** ("The Offspring" [TNG]). SEE: **Andrea; Annabelle series; Atoz, Mr.; Barbara series; Brown, Dr.; Data; Finnegan; Ilia; Lal; Lore; Maizie series; Norman; Ruk; Mudd, Stella; Trudy series.** SEE ALSO: **biomechanical maintenance program; bioplast sheeting; bitanium; Maddox, Commander Bruce; molybdenum-cobalt alloys; Omicron Theta; phase discriminator; positronic brain; Pralor Automated Personnel Unit; Soong, Dr. Noonien; Soong-type android; *Starfleet Cybernetics Journal*; tripolymer composites.**

Andromeda Galaxy. Large spiral galaxy, close neighbor to the **Milky Way Galaxy**, about one million light years away. Although Andromeda is home to many forms of life, scientists from the **Kelvan** empire believe that increasing levels of radiation will render it uninhabitable within the next ten millennia. ("By Any Other Name" [TOS]).

Andronesian encephalitis. A disease transmitted by airborne particles. *Enterprise*-D crew member Henessey suffered from Andronesian encephalitis in 2365 and was treated by Dr. Katherine Pulaski. ("The Dauphin" [TNG]).

anesthezine. Sedative gas used by Starfleet for emergency crowd control and to subdue dangerous persons. Captain Picard ordered one of the ship's cargo bays flooded with anesthezine in the hopes of subduing **Roga Danar**. ("The Hunted" [TNG]). Anesthezine was deemed unsuitable to subdue the **Ux-Mal** terrorists who attempted to commandeer the *Enterprise*-D on stardate 45571 because it would not have been effective against the android Data. ("Power Play" [TNG]). Anesthezine was also available for riot control aboard station Deep Space 9. ("The Siege" [DS9]).

Anetra. Holographic humanoid on planet **Yadera II.** Anetra, **Taya**'s mother, was one of several people who mysteriously disappeared in 2370 and were later found to be sentient holographic images. ("Shadowplay" [DS9]).

Angel Falls, Venezuela. Located in southeastern Venezuela on Earth, Angel Falls is the highest waterfall on that planet. William Riker and Deanna Troi considered taking shore leave there while the *Enterprise*-D was in drydock around Earth in 2367. ("Family" [TNG]).

Angel One. Class-M planet supporting carbon-based life-forms including an intelligent humanoid population. Ruled by a constitutionally run, elected matriarchy, the planet's society treated males as second-class citizens, although this may be expected to change over time since four survivors from the Federation freighter ***Odin*** took up residence there in 2364. Angel One is located fairly close to the Romulan Neutral Zone. SEE: **Beata; Ramsey**. ("Angel One" [TNG]).

"Angel One." *Next Generation* episode #15. Written by Patrick Barry. Directed by Michael Rhodes. Stardate 41636.9. *First aired in 1988. The* Enterprise-D *attempts to rescue crash survivors living on a planet where males are second-class citizens. In the unsold Warner Brothers television pilot* Planet Earth, *Gene Roddenberry also postulated a matriarchal society in which the males, known as "dinks," were used as laborers. Certain males were also selected to be used as "breeders."* GUEST CAST: Karen Montgomery as **Beata**; Sam Hennings as **Ramsey**; Patricia McPherson as **Ariel**; Leonard John Crofoot as **Trent**. SEE: **Albeni meditation crystal; Angel One; Ariel; Armus IX; Beata; *Berlin, U.S.S.*; Denubian Alps; Elected One, the; escape pod; Hesperan thumping cough; Mortania; Night-Blooming *throgni*; *Odin, S.S.*; Quazulu VIII; Ramsey; Trent.**

Angel, Friendly. SEE: **Gorgan**.

angla'bosque. Food. Neelix was proud of his recipe for *angla'bosque*. ("Caretaker" [VGR]).

Angosia III. Class-M planet whose government applied for Federation membership in 2366. The **Angosian** government was, at the time, experiencing civil unrest due to difficulties in repatriating their veterans from the recent **Tarsian War**. ("The Hunted" [TNG]).

Angosian transport vessel. A small sublight vessel used by the **Angosians** to ferry people within their system. It did not have warp capability or a cloaking device and it carried minimal weaponry. One of these vessels was hijacked in 2366 by **Roga Danar**, a prisoner escaping from the Angosian penal moon **Lunar V.** ("The Hunted" [TNG]). *The Angosian transport vessel model was a modification of the Straleb ship from "The Outrageous Okona" (TNG).*

Angosians. The humanoid residents of the planet **Angosia III.** Nonviolent by nature, the Angosians had dedicated their society to the development of the mind and the cultivation of the intellect. However, in order to fight their **Tarsian War** in the mid-24th century, the government chemically altered their military, converting them into "supersoldiers" who were able to survive at any cost. Unfortunately, when the war ended, the "improvements" made on the soldiers were found to be irreversible. These veterans were imprisoned on a penal moon, **Lunar V**, because they were

deemed too dangerous to return to Angosian society. The Angosian government applied for Federation membership in 2366, but the application was suspended by Jean-Luc Picard, pending resolution of civil unrest resulting from the Angosians' inability to repatriate the veterans. SEE: **Danar, Roga** (pictured). ("The Hunted" [TNG]). *The shirts worn by the members of the Angosian council were the turtlenecked men's shirts from the* Star Trek II *Starfleet officers' uniforms.*

animal guide. Native American concept of a spiritual companion. Native Americans used animal guides as counselors. These guides took the form of an animal that the individual encountered in a **vision quest**. Each person has a different animal guide. Animal guides merely choose to be with a particular individual; they do not define that individual. ("The Cloud" [VGR]).

anionic energy. Form of energy composed of quantum-level particles. Anionic energy was detected in the synaptic patterns of the *Enterprise*-D crew whose minds were controlled by **Ux-Mal** criminals from **Mab-Bu VI** in 2368. ("Power Play" [TNG]).

Anjoran biometic gel. Valuable substance. *Enterprise*-D executive officer William Riker traded one-half gram of Anjoran biometic gel to **Yog**, an Yridian entrepreneur, in exchange for 500 kilograms of **magnesite ore** in 2370. He later destroyed the ore in space to expose a cloaked ship belonging to **Lursa** and **B'Etor.** ("Firstborn" [TNG]).

Anna. (Barbara Williams). Human woman who survived the crash of a Terellian cargo freighter on a planet near the **Iyaaran homeworld** in 2363. Anna kept logs of her experiences following the crash, including details of a man who also crashed on the planet. She apparently nursed him back to health, and the two of them fell in love. Her logs would later be discovered by the Iyaarans; they were their first contact with humans. Curious about the many emotions that Anna detailed in her logs, the Iyaaran ambassador **Voval** took her form and tried to evoke a similar romantic response from Captain Picard. ("Liaisons" [TNG]).

Annabelle series. Type of **android** designed by Mudd the First, aka **Harcourt Fenton Mudd**, in 2267. ("I, Mudd" [TOS]).

Annel. Inhabitant of station Deep Space 9 in 2373. Annel would often babysit for the O'Brien family. ("Business As Usual" [DS9]).

annual physical. Routine medical examination required of all Starfleet personnel. ("Whispers" [DS9]). *Annual physicals have apparently been the bane of command officers for a long time, but they make a good excuse to examine someone who's suspected of some problem.*

annular confinement beam. Abbreviated as ACB. A cylindrical force field used to ensure that a person being transported remains within the beam. ("Power Play" [TNG]). Failure to remain within the confinement field can cause a dangerous release of beam energy, possibly fatally injuring the transport subject and those nearby. **Roga Danar**, during transport from a security holding area to an Angosian police ship, deliberately disrupted the ACB, causing a blast of energy that permitted him to escape. ("The Hunted" [TNG]). When Picard was trapped on the surface of planet **El-Adrel IV** in 2368, La Forge attempted to boost the ACB in an effort to penetrate the particle scattering field that surrounded the planet. ("Darmok" [TNG]).

anodyne relay. Power transfer device used aboard the *U.S.S. Voyager*. ("Prototype" [VGR], "Deadlock" [VGR]).

Ansata. Radical political group, also called the Ansata Separatist Movement, on the western continent of planet **Rutia IV**. The Ansata had demanded autonomy and self-determination for over a generation, but received no recognition from the **Rutian** government. The Ansata movement began in 2296, when the government denied an early bid for independence, and some of the Ansata turned to terrorist action. In 2366, the Ansata, led by **Kyril Finn**, engineered an incident in which they abducted *Enterprise*-D officers Jean-Luc Picard and Beverly Crusher in a successful bid to gain recognition by involving Federation interests in their struggle. ("The High Ground" [TNG]).

Anslem. Semi-autobiographical novel written by **Jake Sisko**. ("The Visitor" [DS9]). Sisko wrote the first draft of *Anslem* in 2372, with the assistance of a **noncorporeal life-form** known as **Onaya**. ("The Muse" [DS9]). (In an alternate future in which Ben Sisko was believed killed aboard the *Defiant* in 2372, Jake wrote *Anslem* in his Louisiana home sometime prior to 2391. According to Jake, the book got "generally positive" reviews, but **Melanie**, an aspiring writer, thought it brilliant. SEE: **Sisko, Jake.**) ("The Visitor" [DS9]).

Antarean brandy. Beverage. Antarean brandy was served at a dinner honoring **Dr. Miranda Jones** and her colleagues held aboard the *Enterprise* in 2268. ("Is There in Truth No Beauty?" [TOS]).

Antares, U.S.S. Federation science vessel whose crew rescued **Charles Evans** from planet **Thasus** in 2266. Commanded by **Captain Ramart**, the ship was destroyed when Evans caused a **baffle plate** on their energy pile to vanish. ("Charlie X" [TOS]). *Named for the brightest star (as seen from Earth) in the constellation Scorpius (the Scorpion). Although the* Antares *was not seen in "Charlie X,"* Star Trek: The Next Generation *writer/consultant Naren Shankar suggested that the Bajoran cargo vessels in "Ensign Ro" (TNG) be designated as* Antares-*class ships, a tip of the hat to "Charlie X."*

***Antares*-class carrier**. A common spacecraft design in use by many different cultures in the 24th century. The **Corvallen freighter** that had been contracted to smuggle Romulan **Vice-Proconsul M'ret** to Federation space in 2369 was an *Antares*-class vessel. ("Face of the Enemy" [TNG]). An *Antares*-class sublight ship was used to mislead **Cardassian** forces into attacking what they believed was a group of Bajoran terrorists traveling from Valo I to Valo III in 2368. The ship was empty, but its destruction provided evidence that **Admiral Kennelly** had been collaborating with the Cardassians. SEE: **Orta, Valo system.** ("Ensign Ro" [TNG]). *The Corvallen freighter seen in "Face of the Enemy" (TNG) was identified as an* Antares-*class ship. Since that ship was a re-use of the* **Batris** *from "Heart of Glory" (TNG), we speculate that other uses of that model were also* Antares-*class ships. We further wonder if this might be what the ship in "Charlie X" (TOS) looked like.*

Antarian Glow Water. Purportedly exotic substance. **Cyrano Jones** hawked the stuff, but it was only good for polishing **Spican flame gems**, at least according to the shopkeeper on **Deep Space Station K-7**. ("The Trouble with Tribbles" [TOS]).

Antede III. Class-M planet. In late 2365 the government of Antede III made a bid for Federation membership. Antede III is located some three days' warp travel from **Pacifica**. ("Manhunt" [TNG]).

Antedean ambassador. (Mick Fleetwood). Head of the Antedean delegation to the **Pacifica** conference of 2365. The ambassador was later found to be an assassin who had conspired to blow up the conference by smuggling large amounts of **ultritium** explosive to the planet. ("Manhunt" [TNG]). *Noted rock musician Mick Fleetwood played the Antedean ambassador, reportedly because he is a big* Star Trek *fan. (He must be, to have put up with all that makeup...)*

Antedean transport. Cargo vessel of Antedean registry. An Antedean transport, docked at Deep Space 9 in 2373, carried cargo requiring a health certificate to be issued by Dr. **Julian Bashir** before it could be released. ("Doctor Bashir, I Presume?" [DS9]).

Antedeans. A civilization of fishlike humanoids from planet Antede III. Antedeans find spaceflight extremely traumatic and survive the ordeal by entering a self-induced catatonic state. Upon revival at the end of a voyage, Antedeans require large amounts of food to replenish their bodies. SEE: **vermicula**. ("Manhunt" [TNG]).

anthracite strike of 1902. Labor dispute between management and coal miners that occurred in Pennsylvania on Earth in 1902. The strike was led by **Sean Aloysius O'Brien**. The bitter strike lasted eleven months until all of the miners' demands were met. Sean O'Brien did not live to see the dispute resolved. His bullet-ridden body was found in the Allegheny River a week before the strike's conclusion. Sean O'Brien was an ancestor of Starfleet Chief Miles O'Brien. ("Bar Association" [DS9]). *There was a real Pennsylvania coal strike in 1902, led by United Mine Workers' president John Mitchell. The dispute lasted five months.*

Anthraxic citrus. Delta Quadrant fruit not unlike Earth citrus fruits. ("Flashback" [VGR]).

Anthwara. (Tom Jackson). Leader of the tribal council of the Native American colonists on planet **Dorvan V**. Anthwara's grandfather, **Katowa,** had led this band from Earth the 2170s, in search of a new home among the stars. The group wandered the stars for nearly two centuries, searching for a suitable home, until Anthwara led his group to Dorvan V in 2350. When he arrived, the mountains, the rivers and the sky welcomed him. He refused to be moved from what he knew was his sacred land, despite pressure from the Federation government in 2370. Anthwara was able to convince both the Federation and the Cardassian Union that his people should be allowed to remain on Dorvan V under Cardassian jurisdiction. ("Journey's End" [TNG]).

anti-intoxicant. Medicine taken to allow one to drink alcoholic beverages without becoming inebriated. ("Apocalypse Rising" [DS9]).

anti-time (future). An alternate timeline apparently created by the **Q Continuum** in which Jean-Luc Picard from the year 2370 found himself 25 years in his future, the year 2395. (In **anti-time** future, Picard lived at his family vineyards in France, having retired from an ambassadorial post. In this reality, Beverly Crusher Picard had once been his wife, and was currently serving as captain of the Federation medical ship *Pasteur*. William Riker was, in this time, an admiral, and was the commander of **Starbase 247**. He had saved the *Enterprise*-D from being decommissioned, and was using her as his personal flagship. This *Enterprise*-D had been outfitted with a third warp nacelle, a cloaking device, and improved weaponry. In this time period, Deanna Troi had died in 2375. The incident had left Riker and Worf's relationship strained. They had not spoken for 20 years, both feeling that the other was at fault for the fact that neither one had established a permanent relationship with Deanna. Worf had returned to the Klingon Empire, where he had spent some time as a member of the **Klingon High Council**. By this 2395, he was serving as governor of the **H'atoria Colony**. Geordi La Forge, in this reality, had left Starfleet, had gotten married, and was raising three children along with his wife, Leah. He had acquired a set of cybernetic eyes, replacing his VISOR. This Geordi was an author; his wife was director of the **Daystrom Institute**. *If Geordi's wife in this future was the former Leah Brahms, it was not made clear what happened to Leah's former husband.* Finally, Data in this reality had also left Starfleet and

held the **Lucasian Chair** at **Cambridge University**. This Data had grown more at ease with his humanity, had gained the ability to use contractions, and had acquired a rather amazing collection of cats. In this reality, Picard collected his old crew and convinced them to travel to the **Devron system** to investigate a temporal anomaly there. This was made more difficult because the Picard of this time reality suffered from **Irumodic Syndrome** and his insistence that he was traveling through time was first dismissed as the ravings of a man gone senile from his disease.) ("All Good Things..." [TNG]). *We suspect that this future should be regarded as an alternate quantum reality, a possible future, but not necessarily the one that will unfold in the "real"* Star Trek *timeline. In particular, we don't know when or if the warp scale might be recalibrated again to make warp 13 speeds a reality.*

anti-time (past). An alternate timeline apparently created by the **Q Continuum** in which Jean-Luc Picard from the year 2370 found himself seven years in his past, the year 2364, just prior to his first arrival aboard the *Starship Enterprise*-D. (Picard found this **anti-time** past to differ somewhat from history as he remembered it. The mission to **Farpoint Station**, which was to be the *Enterprise*-D's first, was canceled, and the ship was ordered to the **Devron system** to investigate an anomaly there. Picard initially disobeyed these orders and took the ship to the point in space where the crew had originally encountered **Q** in 2364. When Q did not appear, the *Enterprise*-D continued to the Devron system, where the crew initiated the **inverse tachyon beam** (pictured) that apparently caused the anomaly.) ("All Good Things..." [TNG]). *Much of the original costuming and set dressing from* Star Trek: The Next Generation's *first season was used for the anti-time past sequences. Careful viewers will note the switch of conn and ops positions on the bridge that hearkens back to the pilot episode and that production designer Richard James even restored the sculptures of the first five* Starships Enterprise *to the ship's observation lounge. Data, however, is wearing Lieutenant Junior Grade pips, instead of the Lieutenant Commander pips he wore throughout the series. (This is a prime example of what happens when you let Q mess with the space-time continuum.) Note that we assume the anti-time past scenes are essentially "real" up to the point where Starfleet canceled the Farpoint mission. Even though the backstory of Tasha piloting Picard to the* Enterprise-D *contradicts some information established earlier, we felt the "All Good Things..." version was more widely accepted by both viewers and the show's writing staff.*

anti-time (present). An alternate timeline apparently created by the **Q Continuum** in 2370 in which Jean-Luc Picard found himself experiencing the effects of an **anti-time** anomaly in the **Devron system**. (In this alternate reality, Picard found himself shifting between the past [2364], present [2370] and future [2395]. Picard shared his experiences with his crew of this time, and Dr. Beverly Crusher was able to find evidence to support his story. SEE: **acetylcholine**. The *Enterprise*-D of this **anti-time** reality traveled to the **Devron system** and found a temporal anomaly. Attempting to learn more about its nature, the crew scanned the anomaly with an **inverse tachyon beam**. As in the other time periods, this beam amplified the temporal distortion, threatening to destroy humanity as we know it.) ("All Good Things..." [TNG]).

anti-time. An occurrence of multi-phasic temporal convergence. Anti-time is the opposite of time, in much the same manner as antimatter is the opposite of matter. If time and anti-time were to collide, they would annihilate each other, causing a rupture in the fabric of space. This phenomenon apparently occurred in the **Devron system**, where starships from three separate time periods—2364, 2370, and 2395—all began to scan a temporal anomaly with inverse tachyon beams. The anomaly was a temporal paradox apparently created by these beams. Within the paradox, Captain Jean-Luc Picard found himself traveling between the three time periods, acting and reacting as if he belonged in each one. The phenomenon was actually caused by the **Q Continuum**, who devised this as a test of mankind, to learn if humanity (as represented by Jean-Luc Picard) could stretch its mind to comprehend other levels of existence. Had Picard been unable to understand the paradox and fix the temporal rift, humanity's fate would have been sealed, but Picard was successful in restoring the timeline. ("All Good Things..." [TNG]). *We assume that the anti-time events in "All Good Things" (TNG) should be viewed as alternate quantum realities, but the fact that no one except Picard remembered any of the anti-time events might lead one to suspect that what we witnessed may have been created by Q, strictly for Picard's benefit. Even if the anti-time events were "real," it seems unlikely that the future will unfold in the same manner, since our heroes were determined to change things. Already, we know that the* Enterprise-*D will not exist in 2395, since we saw it destroyed in* Star Trek Generations.

Antica. One of two habitable planets in the **Beta Renner** star system. ("Lonely Among Us" [TNG]).

Anticans. Large, furry, sentient humanoids from planet Antica in the **Beta Renner** star system. Anticans are a carnivorous species who prefer to eat live meat. The Anticans applied for admission to the Federation in 2364. The *Enterprise*-D transported their delegates to planet **Parliament** to help resolve a long-standing dispute with sister planet **Selay** as part of the admission process. ("Lonely Among Us" [TNG]).

antichroniton. Antiparticle of the **chroniton**. Chroniton particles in the body can be eliminated by exposure to a precisely modulated field of antichroniton particles. ("Before and After" [VGR]).

antigen. In biology, any foreign substance in a body that triggers an immune response. A synthetic antigen developed by *Voyager's* Emergency Medical Hologram in 2373 was successful in combating the **macrovirus** infestation that threatened the ship's crew on stardate 50425. The antigen was delivered using a plasma grenade that Captain Janeway referred to as an antigen bomb. ("Macrocosm" [VGR]).

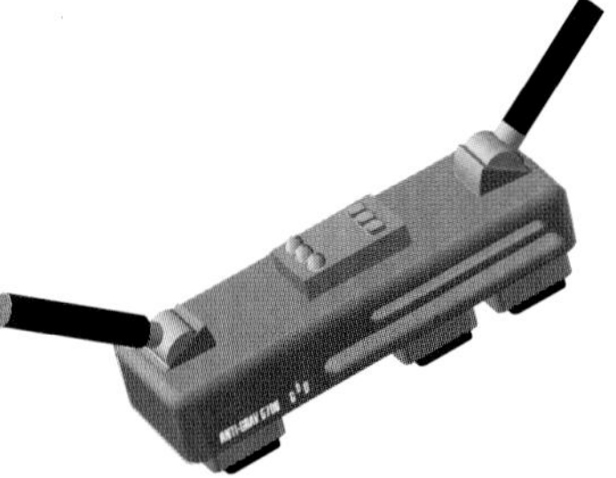

antigrav. Portable device used aboard Federation starships for handling cargo and other items too large for a single crew member to carry. Captain Kirk and **Ensign Garrovick** used an antigrav to carry an **antimatter** bomb on planet **Tycho IV** on stardate 3619. ("Obsession" [TOS]). Two antigravs were used to carry the deactivated **Nomad** to the transporter room just prior to that robot's destruction. ("The Changeling" [TOS]). Antigravs were also used for handling of Ambassador **Kollos**'s protective container aboard the *Enterprise*. ("Is There in Truth No Beauty?" [TOS]). Antigravs were also built into small equipment pallets used for handling cargo. A **graviton** inverter circuit was a key component of an antigrav. ("Hollow Pursuits" [TNG]). Antigravs can become unreliable in the presence of high radiation levels. ("Disaster" [TNG]). When a worker on station Deep Space 9 injured his back in 2369, Dr. Julian Bashir advised him to use an antigrav to avoid further problems. ("The Passenger" [DS9]). Starfleet shuttlecraft were equipped with antigrav thrusters for emergency landings. ("Coda" [VGR]).

antigraviton. Elemental particle that carries a charge and spin opposite to that of gravitons. Antigraviton particles are generated in a standard **tractor beam**. The presence of antigraviton particles in a transporter emitter coil would be indicative of a tractor beam's use on that transporter beam. ("Attached" [TNG]). SEE: **Kesprytt III; Kes; Lorin, Prytt Security Minister; Mauric, Ambassador; Prytt.**

antigravity generator. SEE: **antigrav**.

antilepton interference. Energetic particle field that can interfere with subspace communications. Shortly after the discovery of the **Bajoran wormhole** in 2369, the **Cardassians** flooded subspace with antileptons to prevent **Deep Space 9** from contacting Starfleet. ("Emissary" [DS9]).

antimatter containment. In **warp drive** propulsion systems, **antimatter** containment refers to the use of **magnetic seals** and **confinement fields** to prevent antimatter from physically touching the surface of the storage pod or any other part of the starship. Failure of antimatter containment is a catastrophic malfunction, generally resulting in total destruction of the spacecraft. The *Starship* ***Yamato*** was destroyed in 2365 when its antimatter containment failed because of the **Iconian computer weapon**. ("Contagion" [TNG]). SEE: **antimatter pod**. The *Enterprise*-D suffered several catastrophic losses of antimatter containment on stardate 45652 when it repeatedly impacted the *Starship* ***Bozeman*** while both vessels were trapped in a **temporal causality loop**. ("Cause and Effect" [TNG]). *The* Enterprise-*D almost lost antimatter containment in "11001001" (TNG), "Violations" (TNG), "Cost of Living" (TNG), "Disaster" (TNG), and "Force of Nature" (TNG).* The *Starship* ***Enterprise*-D** lost antimatter containment in 2371 in a combat situation with a Klingon vessel. No crew fatalities resulted due to a successful **saucer separation** maneuver, but the ship's **stardrive section** was destroyed in a warp core breach. *(Star Trek Generations).* In 2372, while the *Defiant* was in the Gamma Quadrant to observe a subspace inversion of the Bajoran wormhole, a power surge of the ship's warp core threatened to cause a breach. ("The Visitor" [DS9]).

antimatter converter assembly. Component of starship warp drive systems, including those used in *Constitution*-class vessels such as the original *U.S.S. Enterprise*.

antimatter mines. Explosive charges, often used as proximity bombs. In 2369, a shuttlecraft from the *Enterprise*-D used antimatter mines with magnetic targeting capabilities to threaten a Cardassian fleet concealed in the **McAllister C-5 Nebula**. ("Chain of Command, Part II" [TNG]).

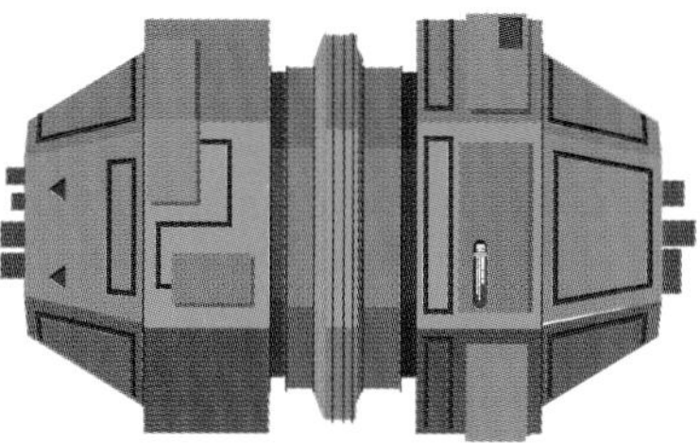

antimatter pod. Magnetic confinement bottle used for the storage of **antimatter** fuel in a Federation **starship**. Antimatter pods were designed to prevent the highly volitile antimatter from coming into physical contact with the structure of the spacecraft. In an emergency, antimatter pods could be ejected from the vehicle. ("The Apple" [TOS]). In late 2372, the crew of the *Starship Voyager* escaped from a **Vidiian** attack by ejecting an antimatter pod, then detonating it with a **photon torpedo**. The resulting explosion was successful in disabling the Vidiian ships. ("Resolutions" [VGR]).

antimatter spread. An impressive but harmless series of small explosive charges deployed from the saucer section of the *Enterprise*-D during its engagements with the **Borg** ship following the battle of **Wolf 359** in 2367. The charges were essentially fireworks used to cover the departure of a shuttlecraft from the saucer section. ("The Best of Both Worlds, Part II" [TNG]).

antimatter. Matter whose electrical charge properties are the opposite of "normal" matter. For example, a "normal" proton has a positive charge, but an antiproton has a negative charge. When a particle of antimatter is brought into contact with an equivalent particle of normal matter, both particles are annihilated, and a considerable amount of energy is released. The controlled annihilation of matter and antimatter is used as the power source for the **warp drive** systems used aboard Federation starships. ("The Naked Time" [TOS]). Because of the highly volatile nature of antimatter, it has to be stored in special magnetic containment vessels, also known as **antimatter pods**, to prevent the antimatter from physically touching the storage vessel or any part of the ship. ("The Apple" [TOS]).

antimonium. Mined substance. Quark owned some antimonium options, but they became worthless in 2373. ("Business As Usual" [DS9]).

antiproton. Subatomic particle of **antimatter** identical to a proton except that it has the opposite spin and electrical charge. Normal protons have a positive charge, but antiprotons have a negative charge. The **planet killer** (pictured) encountered by the *U.S.S. Constellation* in 2267 used a powerful antiproton beam to destroy entire planets. ("The Doomsday Machine" [TOS]). A faint residue of antiprotons was left behind in the wake of the **Crystalline Entity**, and the decay of those antiprotons left gamma radiation traces that provided a means whereby the entity could be tracked. ("Silicon Avatar" [TNG]). An antiproton beam could sometimes be used to detect a ship employing a **Romulan cloaking device**. ("Defiant" [DS9]). In 2372, aboard the *Starship Voyager*, antiproton radiation was used to destroy mutant DNA from Tom Paris's body, allowing his original genetic pattern to flourish. ("Threshold" [VGR]). In 2373, a female member of the Q Continuum showed *Voyager* personnel method in which antiproton beams could be used to increase the power of a Federation starship's shields by a factor of ten. The technique involved remodulating the shields to emit a beta-tachyon pulse, then emitting antiproton beams into the shield bubble. ("The Q and the Grey" [VGR]). The main **navigational deflector** dish on Federation starships are charged with antiprotons. If a dish so charged were directly hit with phaser fire, the ensuing explosion could destroy half of the starship. *(Star Trek: First Contact)*.

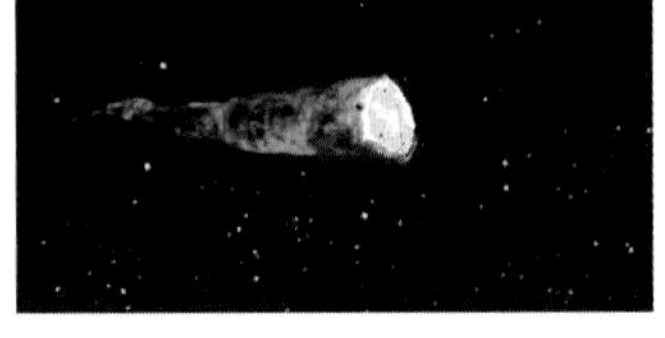

antithoron radiation. Energetic antiparticles. Antithoron bombardment is used to decontaminate a planetary crust before **polyferranide** can be excavated. ("Tattoo" [VGR]).

Antonia. (Lynn Salvatore). Woman who met **James T. Kirk** in 2282. Antonia and Kirk met at Kirk's uncle's farm in Iowa and became romantically involved, but the relationship ended unhappily when Kirk decided to return to Starfleet in 2285. Later, Kirk deeply regretted not having married Antonia. In the reality of the **nexus**, Kirk almost had a second chance to propose to her. *(Star Trek Generations).*

Antonio. (Joseph Palmas). An inhabitant of Earth who worked as a safari guide in the Central American rain forest during the mid-24th century. Antonio once guided **Kolopak** and **Chakotay**, in a search for the descendants of the **Rubber Tree People**. ("Tattoo" [VGR]).

Antos IV. Federation planet. Homeworld to benevolent and peaceful people who cared for Captain **Garth** after he suffered an accident. They taught him the art of **cellular metamorphosis** in the 2260s. ("Whom Gods Destroy" [TOS]). Antos IV was the home of a species of giant energy-generating worms. ("Who Mourns for Adonais" [TOS]).

Antwerp Conference. High-level meeting between the Federation and the Romulan Star Empire diplomats held in northern Belgium on Earth on stardate 49170.65. Also present at the talks was a Tholian observer. The Antwerp Conference was disrupted when a bomb placed by a changeling exploded, killing 27 people. The incident, the worst crime of its kind on Earth in over a century, triggered serious concerns for planetary security in view of the changeling threat. SEE: **Jaresh-Inyo; Leyton, Admiral**. ("Homefront" [DS9], "Paradise Lost" [DS9]).

Anya. (Paddi Edwards). Guardian of **Salia** of planet **Daled IV**. A shape-shifting **allasomorph**, Anya appeared to the *Enterprise*-D crew as an older human woman, although her natural appearance was not known. Originally from the third moon of Daled IV, Anya was protective of Salia in the extreme, and was reluctant to allow Salia to mingle with the *Enterprise*-D crew. *Anya's other forms were played by actors Mädchen Amick and Cindy Sorenson.* ("The Dauphin" [TNG]).

anyon emitter. Engineering device used aboard Federation starships. Lieutenant Commander Data modified an emitter to clear the *Enterprise*-D of **chroniton** particle contamination in 2368 when affected by a Romulan **interphase generator**. Coincidentally, the anyon emitter was also able to dephase Lieutenant Commander La Forge and Ensign Ro. ("The Next Phase" [TNG]).

Aolian Cluster. Stellar group. Site of archaeological research conducted by **Professor Richard Galen** while trying to learn about the first humanoid species to inhabit the galaxy. ("The Chase" [TNG]).

aorta. The main arterial trunk of the circulatory system in many humanoid species. Joseph Sisko, father of Starfleet captain Benjamin Sisko, developed progressive atherosclerosis, eventually necessitating that he be given a new aorta. ("Homefront" [DS9]).

Apella. (Arthur Bearnard). Leader of the villagers on **Tyree**'s planet. The Klingons gave Apella **flintlock** weapons to use against Tyree's followers, the **hill people,** in 2267, thus upsetting the balance of power in that society. ("A Private Little War" [TOS]).

Apgar, Dr. Nel. (Mark Margolis). **Tanugan** scientist who worked on development of a **Krieger Wave** converter on a science station in orbit around **Tanuga IV**. Apgar was killed under suspicious circumstances in the explosion of the science station in 2366. Commander **William Riker** was implicated in the case, but was eventually cleared when holodeck re-creation of the incident provided convincing evidence that Apgar himself was responsible for the fatal explosion, apparently while trying to kill Riker. ("A Matter Of Perspective" [TNG]).

Apgar, Mauna. (Gina Hecht). Widow to **Tanugan** scientist **Dr. Nel Apgar**. Mauna Apgar accused Commander **William Riker** of being responsible for the explosion that killed her husband in 2366. ("A Matter of Perspective" [TNG]).

aphasia device. Mechanism built by Bajoran terrorists, intended to distribute an **aphasia virus** into the food replicators of station Deep Space 9. The aphasia device was planted by the **Bajoran** underground when the station was under construction in 2351, as a weapon against the **Cardassians**. The device wasn't activated at that time, but was accidentally triggered when O'Brien repaired one of the replicators in 2369, after the Cardassian retreat from Bajor. The virus spread at first through the food, then became airborne, infecting a large part of the population. ("Babel" [DS9]).

aphasia virus. Virus created by Bajoran scientist **Dekon Elig**, intended to be used as a terrorist weapon against the Cardassians. The disease organism would have been delivered through an **aphasia device** planted in a food replicator by the Bajoran underground. Once contracted, the virus would find its way to temporal lobes and disrupt normal communication processes, causing a type of **aphasia**. As the virus spread, it attacked the autonomic nervous system, causing a coma, then death. The aphasia virus was accidentally unleashed on Deep Space 9 in 2369, ironically after the Cardassians had abandoned the station. ("Babel" [DS9]).

aphasia. Dysfunction of certain brain centers affecting the ability to communicate in a coherent manner. Different forms of aphasia exist, but the type that afflicted the members of Deep Space 9 in 2369 caused an inability of the brain to process audio and visual stimuli, making the victims incapable of understanding others or expressing themselves coherently. ("Babel" [DS9]). SEE: **aphasia device**.

Apnex Sea. Oceanic body on planet **Romulus**. Romulan admiral **Alidar Jarok**'s home was located near the Apnex Sea. ("The Defector" [TNG]).

"Apocalypse Rising." *Deep Space Nine* episode #99. Written by Ira Steven Behr & Robert Hewitt Wolfe. Directed by James L. Conway. No stardate given. *First aired in 1996. Sisko, Worf, Odo, and O'Brien masquerade as Klingons and infiltrate Gowron's Command Center on a mission to expose a shape-shifter within the empire. This was the first episode of the fifth season and it continued the storyline begun in "Broken Link."* GUEST CAST: Robert O'Reilly as **Gowron**; J.G. Hertzler as **Martok**; Marc Alaimo as **Dukat, Gul**; Casey Biggs as **Damar, Glinn**; Robert Budaska as Burly Klingon; Robert Zachar as Head guard; John Lendale Bennett as Towering Klingon; Tony Epper as Drunken Klingon; Ivor Bartels as Young Klingon. SEE: **Alverian dung beetle; anti-intoxicant; Archanis; *Armstrong, U.S.S.*; *Bat'leth,* Order of the; Benzites; blood screening; Damar, Glinn; *Drake, U.S.S.*; Founders; Gowron; H'Ta; Hall of Warriors; holo-filter; Huss; Jodmos; Klingons; Klingon bloodwine; Kodrak; Laporin, Captain; Martok, General; Mempa; Pahash; polaron; Rurik the Damned; Sisko, Benjamin; T'Vis; tachyon detection grid; Tellarites; tinghamut; Ty'Gokor; Vilix'pran; *Yan-Isleth*; Yndar.**

Apollinaire, Dr. (James Gleason). Physician at the **Sisters of Hope Infirmary** in 19th-century San Francisco on Earth. Not noted for tact in dealing with female nurses. ("Time's Arrow, Part II" [TNG]).

***Apollo* 11**. Early space exploration expedition launched from **Earth** by the **NASA** space agency in July 1969, the first mission to send humans to Earth's **moon**. The spacecraft was launched by a huge chemically-fueled rocket vehicle known as a *Saturn V. Apollo* 11 astronauts Neil Armstrong and Buzz Aldrin became the first humans to set foot on another world, describing the achievement as "one small step for [a] man, one giant leap for mankind." ("Tomorrow is Yesterday" [TOS]). Apollo *11 was not directly mentioned in the episode, but the radio broadcast picked up by the* Enterprise *referred to the impending launch of the first moon landing mission. A model of the* Apollo *11 command/service module could be seen in Wesley Crusher's quarters at Starfleet Academy in "The First Duty" (TNG). Harry Kim's San Francisco apartment in "Non Sequitur" (VGR) had a framed certificate on the wall, thanking Kim for his contribution to Starfleet's* Apollo *11 quadricentennial celebration.*

Apollo*-class starship**. Conjectural designation for a type of Federation starship. The ***U.S.S. Ajax, which was Ensign Cortin **Zweller**'s first assignment after Starfleet Academy, was an *Apollo*-class starship. *Named for the sun god in Earth's Greek mythology, as well as for the spacecraft that first carried humans to the moon.*

Apollo. (Michael Forest). Humanoid entity once worshiped as a god by the ancient Greeks on planet Earth. To the ancient Greeks, Apollo was the god of light and purity, skilled in the bow and on the lyre. He was the twin brother of Artemis, son of the god Zeus and Latona, a mortal. The extraterrestrial Apollo and his fellow "gods" had an extra organ in their chests that apparently gave them the ability to channel considerable energy, giving them godlike powers. After leaving ancient Earth, Apollo settled on planet **Pollux IV,** where he grew to miss the adulation he had received from the Greeks. In 2267, he attempted to capture the crew of the *Starship Enterprise*, inviting them to live on the planet and to worship him as a god. When it became clear that the *Enterprise* crew could not comply, he spread himself against the wind and disappeared. ("Who Mourns for Adonais?" [TOS]). SEE: **Palamas, Lieutenant Carolyn**.

Appalachia, U.S.S. Federation starship, ***Steamrunner*-class**, Starfleet registry number NCC-52136. The *Appalachia* was among the ships defending Sector 001 against the Borg incursion of 2373. *(Star Trek: First Contact).*

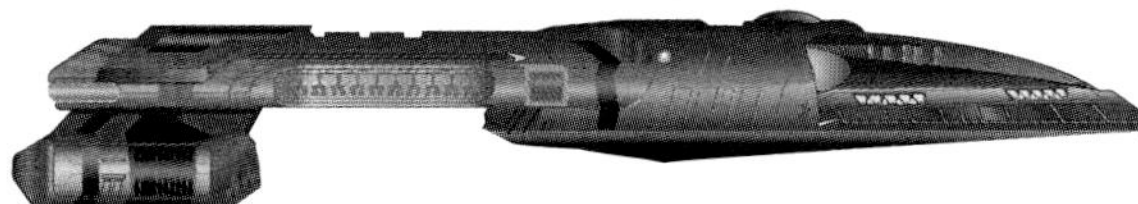

Appel, Ed. (Brad Weston). Chief processing engineer at the underground mining colony on planet **Janus VI** in 2267. Appel helped to defend the colony against an unknown adversary later learned to be a life-form known as a **Horta**. ("The Devil in the Dark" [TOS]).

"Apple, The." *Original Series* episode #38. Written by Max Ehrlich. Directed by Joseph Pevney. Stardate 3715.3. *First aired in 1967. The* Enterprise *encounters a primitive humanoid culture on an Eden-like planet controlled by a machine-god known as Vaal.* GUEST CAST: Keith Andes as **Akuta**; Celeste Yarnall as **Landon**, **Yeoman Martha**; David Soul as **Makora**; Jay Jones as **Mallory, Lieutenant**; Jerry Daniels as **Marple**; John Winston as **Kyle, Mr.**; Mal Friedman as **Hendorf, Ensign**; Dick Dial as **Kaplan, Lieutenant**; Shair Nims as **Sayana**; Julie Johnson as Landon's stunt double; Paul Baxley, Bobby Clark, Vince Deadrick, Ron Burke, Native stunt doubles. SEE: **Akuta; antimatter pod; antimatter; Gamma Trianguli VI; Hendorf, Ensign; Kaplan, Lieutenant; Kyle, Mr.; Landon, Yeoman Martha; Makora; Mallory, Lieutenant; Marple; Masiform D; saucer separation; Sayana; Vaal.**

April, Captain Robert T. First captain of the original ***Starship Enterprise***. April assumed command of the ship when it was launched in 2245 and helmed the *Enterprise*'s first five-year mission of deep-space exploration. April was succeeded as *Enterprise* commander by Christopher Pike and later by James T. Kirk. *April is, of course, totally conjectural, but is being included at Gene Roddenberry's suggestion. Gene had used the character name for the ship's commander in his first proposal for* Star Trek, *written in 1964.*

aquatic lab. Science facility devoted to the study of water-dwelling life-forms. Many of the crew of the *Enterprise*-D retreated to the ship's aquatic lab following their exposure to **Barclay's Protomorphosis Syndrome** in 2370. ("Genesis" [TNG]).

aqueduct systems. Network of canals and aboveground water conduits that provide water for drinking, sanitation, and agriculture. Ancient aqueducts provided water to part of planet **Bajor**, and Captain Jean-Luc Picard attended a conference on management of this system when the *Enterprise*-D visited Deep Space 9 late in 2369. ("Birthright, Part I" [TNG]).

"Aquiel." *Next Generation* episode #139. Teleplay by Brannon Braga & Ronald D. Moore. Story by Jeri Taylor. Directed by Cliff Bole. Stardate 46461.3. *First aired in 1993. A technician on a subspace relay station is believed to have been murdered.* GUEST CAST: Reneé Jones as **Uhnari, Lieutenant Aquiel**; Wayne Grace as **Torak**, **Governor**; Reg E. Cathey as **Morag**; Majel Barrett as Computer voice. SEE: **Batarael; Canar; coalescent organism; *Cold Moon Over Blackwater*; Deriben V; disruptor; *Fatal Revenge, The*; Halii; Horath; iced coffee; La Forge, Geordi; Maura; Morag; Muskan seed punch; *oumriel*; Pendleton, Chief; *Qu'Vat*; Relay Station 47; Relay Station 194; Rocha, Lieutenant Keith; Sector 2520; Shiana; Starbase 212; subspace technology; Torak, Governor; Triona system; Uhnari, Lieutenant Aquiel**.

Aquino, Ensign. Starfleet officer who served at station Deep Space 9. Aquino was killed in 2369 after investigating a security breach. **Neela**, who had planned to assassinate **Vedek Bareil**, was preparing her escape route when Ensign Aquino caught her in the act. Neela killed the ensign, then tried to conceal the crime by placing him into a conduit where energy bursts would reduce the body to ashes. ("In the Hands of the Prophets" [DS9]).

ARA scan. Medical scan that can be used to determine the truthfulness of a humanoid subject. ("Projections" [VGR]).

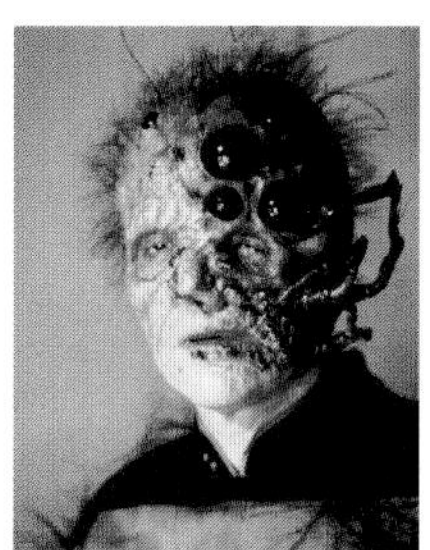

arachnid. Referring to any arthropod of the class Arachnida, including spiders, mites, ticks, and scorpions. Following his exposure to **Barclay's Protomorphosis Syndrome** in 2370, **Reginald Barclay** devolved into an arachnid. ("Genesis" [TNG]). SEE: **Christina; *palukoo*; Talarian hook spider**.

Arak'Taral. (Stephen Davies). **Jem'Hadar** soldier, second in command to **Goran'Agar**. In 2372, Goran'Agar brought his crew to Bopak III because he believed that the planet could cure his men of their addiction to **ketracel-white**. Arak'Taral was against Goran'Agar's idea of curing their addiction if it meant becoming "soft" like humans. Arak'Taral was killed around stardate 49066 by Goran'Agar when he refused to follow Goran'Agar's orders. ("Hippocratic Oath" [DS9]). *Arak'Taral's name was not mentioned in dialog, but is from the script.*

Arandis. (Vanessa Williams). Chief facilitator for the entire Temtibi Lagoon on the planet **Risa** in 2373. **Curzon Dax** had been a good friend of Arandis, and the two spent a lot of time together on his last trip to Risa in 2367. Curzon died while making love with Arandis. She termed it "death by ***jamaharon***." ("Let He Who Is Without Sin..." [DS9]). *We saw Curzon die in a flashback in "Emissary" (DS9), although Arandis was nowhere to be seen in that shot. We speculate that he suffered a serious heart attack in her presence, then died shortly after in a hospital room.*

Arawath Colony. A **Cardassian** settlement. **Obsidian Order** founder **Enabran Tain** retired there. ("The Wire" [DS9]).

Arbazan. Humanoid civilization that is a member of the **United Federation of Planets.** The Arbazan ambassador, **Taxco**, visited station **Deep Space 9** in 2369 on a fact-finding mission to the wormhole. Federation ambassador **Vadosia** expressed an opinion that Arbazan are sexually repressed, to which Taxco took great offense. ("The Forsaken" [DS9]).

Arbazon vulture. Type of predatory bird. In 2371, **Odo** briefly took the form of an Arbazon vulture while at the **Founders' homeworld**. ("The Search, Part II" [DS9]).

Arbiter of Succession. Under Klingon law, the individual responsible for administering the **Rite of Succession**, the procedures under which a new chancellor of the **Klingon High Council** is chosen. Jean-Luc Picard served as Arbiter of Succession following the death of **K'mpec** in 2367. Picard ruled **Gowron** to be the sole challenger for council leader. ("Reunion" [TNG]). Picard later rejected a last-minute bid by **Toral** for the council leadership on the grounds that Toral had not yet distinguished himself in the service of the empire. ("Redemption, Part I" [TNG]).

arbiter. Official in charge of judicial matters on station Deep Space 9. ("Little Green Men" [DS9], "Crossfire" [DS9]).

arboretum. Science lab aboard Federation starships devoted to study of plants. The arboretum aboard the *Enterprise*-D was located on deck 17, section 21-alpha. The flooring in the arboretum was covered with soil and planted with various vegetative species, both for scientific study and for the enjoyment of the crew. The arboretum was the primary workstation of **Keiko O'Brien**, prior to her transfer to DS9. In 2370, following the crew's exposure to **Barclay's Protomorphosis Syndrome**, much of the devolved crew were found in the ship's arboretum, taking advantage of the "natural" atmosphere. ("Genesis" [TNG]). *The arboretum has been seen in such episodes as "Data's Day" (TNG), "Imaginary Friend" (TNG) and "Dark Page" (TNG) and was mentioned in "Genesis" (TNG) and "The Nth Degree" (TNG).*

arch. An inner doorway in some **holodeck** entrances. When used, the arch can be a demarcation between the simulated world of the holodeck and the outside world of the *Enterprise*-D corridors. Some holodeck programs conceal the arch until it is made visible by a verbal command. ("Elementary, Dear Data" [TNG]).

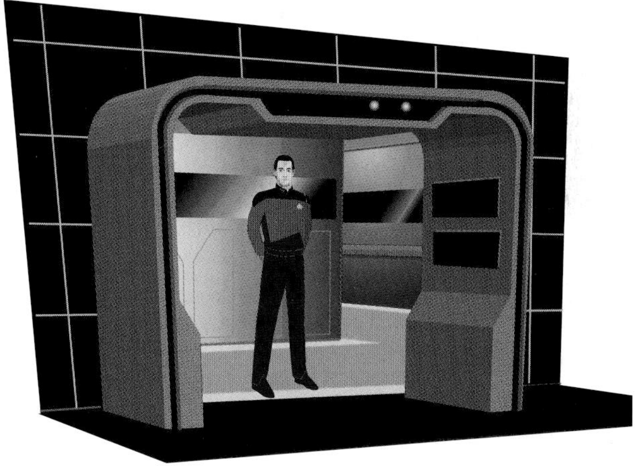

archaeology. Study of ancient civilizations and life-forms. Dr. **Roger Korby** made many significant medical discoveries through archaeology, becoming known as the "Pasteur of archaeological medicine." ("What Are Little Girls Made Of?" [TOS]). *Enterprise*-D captain **Jean-Luc Picard** was an enthusiast of archaeology since his academy days, having studied the ancient **Iconians**. ("Contagion" [TNG]). One of the most noted figures in the field of archaeology was **Professor Richard Galen**, who, in 2369, demonstrated that many species of **humanoid life** in the galaxy evolved from a common progenetor. ("The Chase" [TNG]). SEE: **A&A officer; Aster, Lieutenant Marla; Palamas, Carolyn; Stone of Gol.**

Archanis IV. Fourth planet orbiting Archanis. While under the influence of the **Beta XII-A entity** in 2268, **Pavel A. Chekov** said he had a brother named **Piotr** who was murdered by Klingons at the Archanis IV research outpost. Chekov had no such brother. ("Day of the Dove" [TOS]). The Klingons had an ancient claim to the planet that they relinquished in 2272. A century later, Klingon chancellor Gowron demanded that the Federation withdraw from Archanis IV and abandon all of the bases in the surrounding sector. ("Broken Link" [DS9]).

Archanis. Star. Sulu used Archanis as a navigational reference when the original *Enterprise* was thrown across the galaxy in 2267 by the advanced civilization known as the **Metrons**. ("Arena" [TOS]). The sector surrounding Archanis contained several Federation starbases and military installations. In 2372, Klingon chancellor Gowron demanded that the Federation withdraw from the sector and abandon all of its bases there. ("Broken Link" [DS9]). Shortly thereafter, Archanis was conquered by the Klingons. ("Apocalypse Rising" [DS9], "Nor the Battle to the Strong" [DS9]).

Archer IV (alternate). Planet. In the alternate timeline created when the ***Enterprise*-C** vanished from its "proper" place in 2344, Riker mentioned **Archer IV** as the site of a significant Klingon defeat at the hands of the Federation. ("Yesterday's *Enterprise*" [TNG]).

Archer IV. Planet. Destination of the *Enterprise*-D after its encounter with the **temporal rift** in 2366. ("Yesterday's *Enterprise*" [TNG]).

Archon, U.S.S. Early Federation starship that disappeared at planet **Beta III** in the year 2167. The ship was pulled from orbit by a planetary computer system called **Landru**. The surviving crew members were absorbed into Beta III society, becoming known as the **Archons**. ("Return of the Archons" [TOS]). *We speculate that the Archon was a* Daedalus*-class starship, since it was contemporary with the* U.S.S. Essex *from "Power Play" (TNG).*

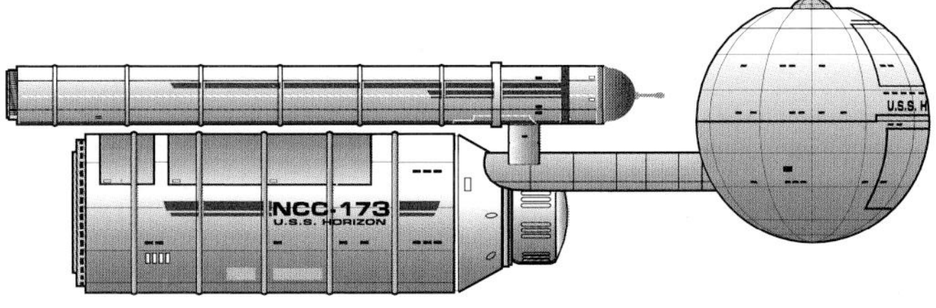

archon. Presiding officer of a Cardassian court. ("Tribunal" [DS9]). SEE: **Makbar**.

Archons. Name given by the humanoid inhabitants of planet **Beta III** to crew members of the *Starship* ***Archon***. The ship was destroyed in 2167 by the Beta III planetary computer called **Landru**. In the process, many *Archon* crew members were killed but others were absorbed into the planet's society and became part of the **Body**, a tranquil but stagnant population. ("Return of the Archons" [TOS]).

Arcos, U.S.S. Federation freighter that suffered a warp containment breach near planet **Turkana IV** in 2367. The *Arcos* crew evacuated when the ship exploded over Turkana IV. Their **escape pod** landed on the surface of the planet, whereupon they were captured by members of the **Alliance**. ("Legacy" [TNG]).

arctic spider. Cold climate animal life found on **Rinax**. **Neelix** once went arctic spider hunting with his favorite sister, **Alixia**. ("Rise" [VGR]).

Arcturian Fizz. A beverage with pleasure-enhancing qualities. Ambassador **Lwaxana Troi** offered to make one for **DaiMon Tog**, while being held captive aboard his ship in 2366. ("Ménage à Troi" [TNG]).

Arcybite. Planet in the Clarus system. A Ferengi entrepreneur named **Nava** took over the mining refineries at Arcybite. Nava was congratulated at a Ferengi trade conference on Deep Space 9 in 2369 by **Zek**, the **grand nagus**, for this accomplishment. ("The Nagus" [DS9]).

Ardana. Class-M planet, location of the cloud city **Stratos**. The *Starship Enterprise* visited Ardana in 2269 to pick up a consignment of **zenite**, but the delivery was delayed because of a dispute between the wealthy Ardanans who lived in Stratos, and the workers who lived on the surface below. Ardana is a Federation member. ("The Cloud Minders" [TOS]).

Ardra. (Marta DuBois). A mythic figure in the theology of planet **Ventax II**. According to Ventaxian legend, Ardra appeared a thousand years ago and promised the Ventaxian people a millennium of peace and prosperity. At the end of that time, Ardra promised to return and enslave the population. According to this mythology, Ardra's return was to be heralded by "the shaking of the cities" and other paranormal phenomena. These prophecies apparently came to pass in 2367 when a humanoid female appeared on Ventax II, identifying herself as Ardra. Investigation by *Enterprise*-D personnel determined, however, that this person was a con artist using various technological tricks to simulate Ventaxian prophecy. ("Devil's Due" [TNG]).

"Arena." Original Series episode #19. Teleplay by Gene L. Coon. From a story by Fredric Brown. Directed by Joseph Pevney. Stardate 3045.6. *First aired in 1967. A powerful civilization known as the Metrons puts Kirk and a Gorn captain on a planetoid where they are expected to resolve their differences by fighting to the death. "Arena" is the first episode in which the original* Enterprise*'s warp factor 6 maximum speed was established, and the first episode to show that you can't beam through shields.* GUEST CAST: Jerry Ayres as O'Herlihy, Lieutenant; Grant Woods as **Kelowitz, Lieutenant Commander**; Tom Troupe as Harold, Lieutenant; James Farley as **Lang, Lieutenant**; Carole Shelyne as **Metron**; Sean Kenney as **DePaul, Lieutenant**; Vic Perrin as The Metron's voice; Gary Coombs as Clark, Bobby; Vic Perrin as Gorn's voice; Dick Dial as Kirk's stunt double. SEE: **Archanis; Canopus; Cestus III; DePaul, Lieutenant; Gorn; gunpowder; Kelowitz, Lieutenant Commander; Lang, Lieutenant; Metron; shields; Sirius; transporter; Travers, Commodore; warp drive.**

Arethian flu. Viral disease. On stardate 48579, the *Voyager*'s **Emergency Medical Hologram** suspected that **Lieutenant Hargrove** might have Arethian flu. ("Eye of the Needle" [VGR]).

Argaya system. Planetary system near the border between the Federation and the Cardassian Union. It was in the Argaya system that the escape pod containing **Joret Dal** was retrieved by the *Enterprise*-D in 2370. ("Lower Decks" [TNG]).

Argelian massage facility. Massage parlor. After **Cardassian** exile **Elim Garak**'s shop was blown up in 2371, Quark wanted to use that space to open an Argelian massage facility. ("The Die is Cast" [DS9]). *Argelians were first introduced in "Wolf in the Fold" (TOS).*

Argelians. Peaceful humanoid civilization from planet **Argelius II**. Formerly a violent people, the Argelians underwent a social upheaval in 2067 they called their Great Awakening, in which their society turned to peace. In 2267, the *U.S.S. Enterprise* visited the planet for shore leave. During their stay, Montgomery Scott was extradited for the murder of two women. Having no current laws regarding murder, the Argelians were forced to rely on their brutal ancient codes established before the Great Awakening. ("Wolf in the Fold" [TOS]). SEE: **Jack the Ripper; Redjac**.

Argelius II. Planet whose location makes it a strategically important spaceport. Argelius II is home to a humanoid culture that is peaceful, hedonistic, and known for its hospitality. Argelian cultural traits make it necessary to hire administrative officers from other planets. ("Wolf in the Fold" [TOS]). SEE: **Hengist, Mr.; Redjac**.

argine. Explosive. Argine was used in a Ferengi **locator bomb** intended to kill Quark when he served as **grand nagus** in 2369. ("The Nagus" [DS9]).

Argolis Cluster. Area of space made up of six solar systems. In 2368, the *Enterprise*-D was charting the cluster as a prelude to colonization when it encountered a downed **Borg scout ship**. ("I, Borg" [TNG]). The Argolis Cluster was the location of the ecologically devastated planet **Tagra IV**. ("True-Q" [TNG]).

argonite. Potentially hazardous substance. ("Doctor Bashir, I Presume?" [DS9]).

Argos system. An uninhabited star system in Federation space. The Argos system was near the flight path of the **Crystalline Entity** after it destroyed the **Melona IV** colony in 2368. ("Silicon Avatar" [TNG]).

Argosian Sector. Area of space in the **Alpha Quadrant**. Star charts of the Argosian Sector were stored in the navigational computer on Deep Space 9. Major Kira requested star charts of the Argosian Sector on stardate 46423, but the Glessene Sector was displayed instead due to a computer malfunction caused by the **aphasia device**. ("Babel" [DS9]).

Argosian. Life-form. Many years ago, an Argosian threw a drink in **Benjamin Sisko**'s face. **Curzon Dax** stopped his friend from retaliating. Sisko recounted the story to **Jadzia Dax**, saying he still had a scar on his chin from Curzon's ring. ("Dax" [DS9]).

Argratha. Planet in the Gamma Quadrant. Homeworld to the **Argrathi** people. ("Hard Time" [DS9]).

Argrathi. Humanoid society native to planet **Argratha**. The Argrathi had an unusual form of punishment for criminals that involved implanting memories into the accused's brain. These memories would cause the criminal to have effectively experienced years of brutal incarceration, when in reality, no actual prison time was served, thereby saving the Argrathi government the cost of building and operating prisons. In 2372, Miles O'Brien was accused of espionage and implanted with the memory of a 20-year prison sentence. ("Hard Time" [DS9]).

Argus Array. A huge subspace radio telescope located three light-years from Cardassian space. ("Parallels" [TNG]). The Argus Array stopped transmitting data in 2367, and the *Enterprise*-D was sent to investigate. *Enterprise*-D personnel discovered that the array's fusion reactors had gone unstable and were threatening to overload. An alien probe, sent by the **Cytherians**, was later found to be responsible for the malfunctions. ("The Nth Degree" [TNG]). (In an alternate **quantum reality** visited by Worf during 2370, the Argus Array became the subject of an investigation by the *Enterprise*-D. The array had been tampered with, apparently by Cardassians, and reset to survey sensitive Starfleet installations and relay that data to a sector outside Federation space. In yet another quantum reality, the array was destroyed by Cardassians, and in a third, it was destroyed by Bajorans. In yet another, the array remained intact, but had ceased functioning because of a mechanical failure.) ("Parallels" [TNG]). *One of the images shown on Geordi's screen was a re-use of the Regula I space station from* Star Trek II, *and another was the* S.S. Birdseye *from "The Neutral Zone" (TNG). One of the planet images was an alien city designed by Anthony Fredrickson, and the other was a painting of the Utopia Planitia Fleet Yards surface facilities by Rick Sternbach and Mike Okuda.*

Argus River region. Location on planet **Rigel IV**. One of the weapons used in the serial murders on planet **Argelius II** in 2267 was manufactured by the hill people of the Argus River region. ("Wolf in the Fold" [TOS]).

Argus sector. Region of Federation space. The *Enterprise*-D was scheduled for a mission in the Argus sector in 2370. William Riker postponed the mission in order to conduct an investigation into Captain Picard's disappearance. ("Gambit, Part I" [TNG]).

Argyle, Lieutenant Commander. (Biff Yeager). A chief engineer of the *Enterprise*-D in 2364. Argyle worked with the **Traveler** and Mr. **Kosinski** during warp drive upgrade tests. ("Where No One Has Gone Before" [TNG]). Argyle also supervised the assembly and activation of Data's brother, **Lore**, in the *Enterprise*-D sickbay. ("Datalore" [TNG]).

Ari. (Billy Burke). Member of the **Cardassian underground movement**. In 2371, Ari was killed while attempting to help **Kira Nerys** escape from planet **Cardassia**. ("Second Skin" [DS9]). SEE: **Ghemor**, **Legate**.

Ariana. (Danitza Kingsley). One of the last eight survivors of the **Tarellian** plague and daughter of Tarellian leader **Wrenn**. Ariana had been in telepathic contact with **Wyatt Miller** for many years, and looked to his medical knowledge as being their hope for survival. Miller, attracted to the beautiful Ariana, chose to remain with her and the other Tarellian plague victims in the hopes of finding the means for their survival. ("Haven" [TNG]).

Ariannus. Planet vital as a transfer point for commercial traffic. In 2268, Ariannus was infected by a bacterial invasion that threatened to destroy all life. The *Starship Enterprise* conducted an orbital decontamination mission to save the planet. ("Let That Be Your Last Battlefield" [TOS]).

Arias Expedition. Mission carried out by the *Starship Al-Batani* under the command of Captain Paris. The *Al-Batani*'s science officer during the assignment was **Kathryn Janeway**. ("Caretaker" [VGR]).

Ariel. (Patricia McPherson). A member of the female-dominated ruling council on planet **Angel One** in 2364. Ariel secretly married ex-***Odin*** crew member **Ramsey**, a move viewed by the council as traitorous, since Ramsey advocated radical reforms to grant equal rights for men on the planet. ("Angel One" [TNG]).

Aries*, U.S.S.** Federation starship, *Renaissance* class, registry number NCC-45167. **William Riker** turned down a chance to command this ship in 2365. ("The Icarus Factor" [TNG]). The *Aries* was the last assignment of former ***Victory crew member **Mendez** before her disappearance in 2367. ("Identity Crisis" [TNG]). *The* Aries *was named for the constellation (the Ram) of the same name, as well as for the moon landing shuttle from the motion picture* 2001: A Space Odyssey.

Arissa. (Dey Young). Undercover Idanian intelligence agent. In 2371, Arissa was sent on a mission to collect evidence against **Draim**, a member of the **Orion Syndicate**. Because Draim routinely employed telepaths to scan all employees, Arissa's memories were removed and stored in a **data crystal**. While at station Deep Space 9 to recover the data crystal in 2373, Arissa fell in love with **Odo**. After her memories were restored, Arissa revealed that she was married. She told Odo that in a way she still loved him and that she would never forget him. ("A Simple Investigation" [DS9]). *Dey Young was seen previously as Hannah Bates in "The Masterpiece Society" (TNG).*

Arjin. (Geoffrey Blake). Trill **initiate** who became a host candidate because he hoped to fulfill his father's wishes. Arjin worked hard to attain the goal of joining, winning honors in astrophysics and even becoming a fifth-level pilot. Arjin did not, however, have a clear idea of what he would do with his life, if and when he were **joined**. His **field docent**, Jadzia Dax, pointed this out to him in 2370, during his initiate training. This was a difficult realization for Arjin, but it helped him find a greater sense of purpose. ("Playing God" [DS9]).

Arkaria Base. Federation facility located on the planet Arkaria. The station controlled the **Remmler Array.** ("Starship Mine" [TNG]).

Arkarian water fowl. Ornithoid species native to planet Arkaria. The birds' mating habits were regarded as interesting, at least according to **Commander Calvin Hutchinson**. ("Starship Mine" [TNG]).

Arlin, Lysia. Shopkeeper of the ***jumja*** kiosk on the Promenade of station Deep Space 9. A **Bolian** woman who may have been attracted to Odo. ("Shadowplay" [DS9]).

"Armageddon Game." *Deep Space Nine* episode # 33. Written by Morgan Gendel. Directed by Winrich Kolbe. No stardate given. *First aired in 1994. Dr. Bashir and Chief O'Brien are marked for death after helping two formerly warring peoples to eliminate their biological weapons.* GUEST CAST: Rosalind Chao as **O'Brien**, **Keiko**; Darleen Carr as **E'Tyshra**; Peter White as **Sharat**; Larry Cedar as **Nydom**, **Dr.**; Bill Mondy as Jakin. SEE: **Alterian chowder; Bashir, Julian**; **biomechanical gene disrupter**; **chambers coil**; **data clip**; **E'Tyshra; Ferengi Rules of Acquisition; *Ganges, U.S.S.*; harvesters; Kellerun; muon frequencies; nanobiogenic weapon; Nydom, Dr.; O'Brien, Miles; Palis, Delon; *Rio Grande, U.S.S.*; Sharat; T'Lani; T'Lani III; T'Lani munitions cruiser; T'Lani Prime; uttaberry crepes.**

Armens, Treaty of. Established in 2255 between the **Sheliak Corporate** and the United Federation of Planets, the treaty cedes several Class-H planets from the Federation to the Sheliak. A Federation colony was established on planet **Tau Cygna V** in the 2270s in violation of the Treaty of Armens. The Sheliak exercised their rights to order the colony removed in 2366. The treaty contained 500,000 words and took 372 Federation legal experts to draft. ("The Ensigns of Command" [TNG]).

armory. Weapons storage compartment aboard the *Starship Enterprise*. The **Beta XII-A entity,** which fed on hate and anger, transformed all weapons in the armory to swords while it held the *Enterprise* crew and Klingons captive in 2268. ("Day of the Dove" [TOS]).

Armstrong, Lake. Body of water located on Earth's **moon**. The lake was large enough that it could be seen from Earth on a clear day. *(Star Trek: First Contact). Presumably named for Apollo astronaut Neil Armstrong.*

Armstrong, Neil. Twentieth-century Earth explorer, commander of the **Apollo 11** lunar landing expedition in 1969. The first inhabitant of planet Earth to walk on that planet's moon. ("Threshold" [VGR]).

Armstrong, U.S.S. Federation starship. The *Armstrong* was ambushed by a Klingon battle group in 2373 and took heavy casualties. After the battle, the *Armstrong* docked at Deep Space 9 to receive medical aid. ("Apocalypse Rising" [DS9]). *Named for Apollo 11 astronaut Neil Armstrong, the first human to set foot on Earth's moon.*

Armus IX. Planet. Riker once had to wear a feathered costume on Armus IX for diplomatic reasons. ("Angel One" [TNG]).

Armus. (Mart McChesney). A malevolent life-form on planet **Vagra II**. Armus was formed when the inhabitants of Vagra II developed a means of ridding themselves of all that was evil within themselves. The Vagrans all departed from their home as creatures of dazzling beauty, leaving behind Armus, whose malevolence was compounded by the loneliness of having been abandoned. Armus resembled an oil slick, but was capable of forming himself into a humanoid shape, and could also generate force fields of considerable strength. Armus killed *Enterprise*-D security chief **Natasha Yar** when Yar was participating in a rescue mission on Vagra II. Armus had no apparent motive for the murder, except for his own amusement. Armus is believed to still exist on Vagra II. ("Skin of Evil" [TNG]).

Arneb. Star. Wesley Crusher once recognized Arneb when he gazed from Ten-Forward while discussing his future with Guinan. ("The Child" [TNG]).

Array. Large spaceborne installation located in the **Delta Quadrant**, created by the **Caretaker**. A millennium ago, the Caretaker created the Array to supply the **Ocampa** with energy, enabling the civilization to survive under their planet's ravaged surface. Toward the end of his life, the Caretaker used the Array to collect spacecraft from all over the galaxy in his search for life-forms compatible with his own, in hopes of producing an offspring who would continue to care for the Ocampa. When his quest was unsuccessful, the Caretaker realized that the Array, in the wrong hands, could be used against the Ocampa. After the Caretaker's death in 2371, *Voyager* captain Janeway used **tricobalt explosives** to destroy the Array to prevent it from being used by the **Kazon-Ogla**. ("Caretaker" [VGR]). SEE: **Suspiria's Array**.

Arriaga, Lieutenant. Starfleet junior officer assigned to station Deep Space 9. In 2372, under orders from **Admiral Leyton**, Arriaga attached a subspace modulator to the relay satellite on the far side of the Bajoran wormhole to create the appearance that cloaked ships were coming through, feeding Federation fears of an imminent **Dominion** invasion. When confronted, Arriaga confessed his role in Leyton's conspiracy. Leyton subsequently attempted unsuccessfully to destroy the *Starship Defiant* to prevent Arriaga from returning to Earth. ("Paradise Lost" [DS9]).

Arridor, Dr. (Dan Shor). Member of a Ferengi delegation sent to negotiate for the rights to the **Barzan wormhole** in 2366. Dr. Arridor was responsible for the distillation of a Ferengi **pyrocyte** which **DaiMon Goss** used to poison the Federation ambassador, **Dr. Mendoza**. Dr. Arridor was one of the crew of the **Ferengi shuttle** sent to investigate the Barzan wormhole; he was lost in the distant **Delta Quadrant** when one terminus of the wormhole changed location. ("The Price" [TNG]). Arridor and **Kol** became stranded in the Delta Quadrant when the other terminus of the Barzan wormhole also changed position. The two crash-landed on the **Takarian** homeworld and assumed the role of the Great Sages from Takarian mythology. In 2373, the *U.S.S. Voyager* happened upon the planet and forced Arridor and Kol to leave. When they attempted to return to the Takarian planet, their shuttle was pulled into the Barzan wormhole by a gravitational eddy. Their actions knocked the wormhole off of its subspace axis so that both of its endpoints jumped around erratically. The fate of Arridor and the shuttle remains unknown. ("False Profits" [VGR]).

"Arsenal of Freedom, The." *Next Generation* episode #21. Teleplay by Richard Manning & Hans Beimler. Story by Maurice Hurley & Robert Lewin. Stardate 41798.2. *First aired in 1988. The* Enterprise-*D is threatened by ancient weapons systems from a now-dead civilization.* GUEST CAST: Vincent Schiavelli as **Peddler, Minosian**; Marco Rodriguez as **Rice**, **Captain Paul**; Vyto Ruginis as **Logan**, **Chief Engineer**; Julia Nickson as **T'su**, **Lieutenant Lian**; George De La Pena as **Solis**, **Lieutenant (J.G.) Orfil**. SEE: **Arsenal of Freedom; Arvada III; Battle Bridge; Crusher, Dr. Beverly; *Drake, U.S.S.*; Echo Papa 607; Erselrope Wars; Howard, Felisa; Logan, Chief Engineer; Lorenze Cluster; Minos; Peddler, Minosian; photon torpedo; Rice, Captain Paul; Riker, William T.; saucer separation; Solis, Lieutenant Orfil; Starbase 103; T'Su, Ensign Lian.**

Arsenal of Freedom. Nickname that the people of planet **Minos** gave to their world to promote their role as (formerly) successful arms merchants. One of their sales slogans was "Peace through superior firepower." ("The Arsenal of Freedom" [TNG]).

Artemis, S.S. Federation ship that departed in 2274 on a mission to transport colonists to planet Septimus Minor, but went off course when the ship's navigation system failed. The ship actually delivered the colonists to planet **Tau Cygna V**. ("The Ensigns of Command" [TNG]).

artificial quantum singularity. Synthetically created microscopic **black hole**. Romulan warbird spacecraft used an artifical quantum singularity as a power source for their warp drive systems. While extremely efficient, the **quantum singularity** had the disadvantage that once enabled, it could not be deactivated. ("Face of the Enemy" [TNG], "Timescape" [TNG]).

artificial wormhole. The first known instance of an artificially-created **wormhole** was the **Bajoran Wormhole**, created by unknown entities in the Denorios Belt. Federation scientist Dr. **Lenara Kahn**, with the Trill ministry of science, worked for years to duplicate the feat. In 2372 she led a team of scientists to attempt to generate an artificial wormhole. The team used the *U.S.S. Defiant* and was successful in generating a stable wormhole that was open for 23.4 seconds, the first in Federation history. ("Rejoined" [DS9]).

Arton, Jeff. *Enterprise*-D crew member. Arton had, at one time, been romantically involved with **Lieutenant Jenna D'Sora**, prior to D'Sora's involvement with Data in 2367. ("In Theory" [TNG]).

Artonian laser. Coherent energy weapon. Stolen Artonian lasers were discovered in the **Gatherer** camp on **Gamma Hromi II**. ("The Vengeance Factor" [TNG]).

arva nodes. Term in an unknown alien language for machinery roughly equivalent to a **Bussard collector**. The arva nodes in **Tosk**'s ship were damaged prior to his visit to Deep Space 9 in 2369. ("Captive Pursuit" [DS9]). SEE: **ramscoop**.

Arvada III. Planet. Site of a colony where many people died in a terrible tragedy. Young **Beverly Crusher** (neé Howard) was one of the survivors there, along with her grandmother, Felisa Howard. Although her grandmother was not a physician, she was skilled in the medicinal uses of roots and herbs. She used this knowledge to help care for the colonists after regular medical supplies had been exhausted. Beverly Crusher credited her grandmother and this experience for her knowledge of such nontraditional pharmacopoeia. ("The Arsenal of Freedom" [TNG]). *Very few specifics have been established about the Arvada tragedy, even though it seems to have been an important chapter in Beverly's life. "Sub Rosa" (TNG) establishes her grandmother's name was Felisa Howard.*

"Ascent, The." *Deep Space Nine* episode #107. Written by Ira Steven Behr & Robert Hewitt Wolfe. Directed by Allan Kroeker. No stardate given. *First aired in 1996. As Odo escorts Quark to a Federation Grand Jury hearing, their sabotaged runabout crash-lands on a deserted planet, forcing them to rely on each other for survival.* GUEST CAST: Max Grodénchik as **Rom**; Aron Eisenberg as **Nog.** SEE: **Federation Grand Jury; fizzbin; Inferna Prime; Nog; Orion Syndicate; "Past Prologue"; planetary classification system: Class L planet; polynutrient solution; root beer; Sisko, Benjamin; Sisko, Jake; snail juice; Starbase 137; Vorian pterodactyl; *Vulcan Love Slave*.**

Aschelan V. Cardassian planet, site of a Cardassian fuel depot. On stardate 47582, B'Elanna Torres reprogrammed a Cardassian guided tactical missile to destroy the fuel depot on Aschelan V. ("Dreadnought" [VGR]).

Ashmore, Ensign. (Christine Delgado). Starfleet officer assigned to the engineering staff of the *Starship Voyager*. ("Learning Curve" [VGR], "Favorite Son" [VGR]).

Ashrok. (Don Stark). Business acquaintance of Quark's. In 2370, Ashrok contracted to purchase forty-two of the Rings of Paltriss from Quark. Unfortunately, Ashrok was killed while attempting to complete the transaction. ("Melora" [DS9]). SEE: **Paltriss, Ring of**.

Asimov, Dr. Isaac. Twentieth-century biochemist and writer (1920-1992). Asimov postulated robots that would employ sophisticated positronic computing devices in their brains. Cyberneticist **Noonien Soong** attempted to construct such devices, ultimately succeeding with the creation of the androids **Data** and **Lore**. ("Datalore" [TNG]). *In real life, science-fiction writer Isaac Asimov was a friend of* Star Trek *creator Gene Roddenberry and was a science consultant for* Star Trek: The Motion Picture. *Asimov was noted as the author of a series of novels and short stories in which robots operated according to what Asimov termed his three "Laws of Robotics." Asimov's laws suggested that robots would be built with programming to insure that they would 1) not harm human beings, 2) obey human commands, except for commands that would harm humans, and 3) protect their own existence, except when such protection would violate the other two laws.*

asinolyathin. Pharmaceutical used for pain relief. ("Visionary" [DS9]).

Asoth. (Bo Zenga). Customer at Quark's bar at Deep Space 9. Asoth once complained that the Kohlanese stew served there was unpalatable. Even Quark had to agree. ("Babel" [DS9]).

asparagus. Earth vegetable, the succulent, edible shoots of a cultivated variety of a perennial herb, *Asparagus officinalis.* Captain Kathryn Janeway liked asparagus for breakfast. Unfortunately, aboard the *Voyager*, asparagus was available only in **ration packs**. ("Phage" [VGR]). Tora Ziyal liked asparagus with *yamok* sauce. ("By Inferno's Light" [DS9]).

assay office. Area on the **Promenade** of station **Deep Space 9** where valuables were assessed and secured. Archaeologist **Vash** stored several artifacts brought back from the Gamma Quadrant at the assay office on stardate 46531, after being reassured that they were protected by a personal authorization code and a verified retinal print using a Cardassian **MK-12 scanner**. ("Q-Less" [DS9]).

"Assignment, The." *Deep Space Nine* episode #104. Teleplay by David Weddle & Bradley Thompson. Story by David R. Long & Robert Lederman. Directed by Allan Kroeker. No stardate mentioned. First aired in 1996. *An alien entity possesses Keiko O'Brien and plots to kill the life-forms who inhabit the Bajoran wormhole.* GUEST CAST: Rosalind Chao as **O'Brien, Keiko**; Max Grodénchik as **Rom**; Hana Hatae as **O'Brien**, **Molly**; Patrick B. Egan as Jiyar; Rosie Malek-Yonan as **Tekoa**; Judi Durand as Station computer voice; Majel Barrett as Computer voice. SEE: **Chroniton particles; eggs with bacon and corned beef hash; fire caves; Idran hybrids; Koss'moran; O'Brien, Keiko; orange juice; Pah-wraiths; pancakes; puree of beetle; Q'parol; Rom; Rudellian brain fever; slug liver; Tekoa; Tellurian mint truffles; Watley; whiskey.**

"Assignment: Earth." Original Series episode #55. Teleplay by Art Wallace. Story by Gene Roddenberry and Art Wallace. Directed by Marc Daniels. No stardate given. *First aired in 1968. The* Enterprise *travels back in time to 1968, where Kirk and Spock help a mysterious stranger named Gary Seven avert a nuclear crisis. "Assignment: Earth" was an unofficial pilot episode for a proposed television series that would have chronicled the present-day adventures of Gary Seven and Roberta Lincoln on Earth as they battled extraterrestrial invaders called Omegans.* GUEST CAST: Robert Lansing as **Seven, Gary**; Teri Garr as **Lincoln, Roberta**; Don Keefer as Cromwell, Mr.; Lincoln Demyan as Lipton, Sergeant; Morgan Jones as Nesvig, Colonel; Bruce Mars as First policeman; Ted Gehring as Second policeman; Paul Baxley as McKinley, Crewman; Eddie Paskey as **Leslie, Mr.**; Barbara Babcock as Isis's voice; Barbara Babcock as Exciever computer voice; Majel Barrett as Beta 5 computer voice. SEE: **Agents 201 and 347; Beta 5 computer; exceiver; Isis; light-speed breakaway factor; Lincoln, Roberta; McKinley Rocket Base; Omicron IV; Seven, Gary; Supervisor 194.**

astatine. Mineral found on planet **Orellius**. Colonists on the planet believed astatine deposits created a **duonetic field** found in the planet's atmosphere. ("Paradise" [DS9]).

Aster, Jeremy. (Gabriel Damon). Son of *Enterprise*-D officer Lieutenant **Marla Aster**. Jeremy was orphaned when his mother died on an away mission in 2366. His father had died five years earlier of a Rushton infection. After Marla Aster's death, energy-based life-forms known as **Koinonians** expressed regret at their accidental part in the incident and offered to care for Jeremy. Their care would have been delivered by a nearly identical replica of his late mother, in an environment that closely reproduced his home on Earth. Jeremy eventually found the courage to accept his mother's loss, and became a part of Worf's family through the Klingon ***R'uustai***, or bonding, ceremony. Jeremy later returned to Earth to be raised by his biological aunt and uncle. ("The Bonding" [TNG]).

Aster, Lieutenant Marla. (Susan Powell). *Enterprise*-D archaeologist, who was killed during an away team mission in the Koinonian ruins in 2366. Aster was killed by a bomb left over from an ancient **Koinonian** war. Koinonian energy-based life-forms later created a replica of Aster in an offer to care for her orphaned son, **Jeremy Aster**. ("The Bonding" [TNG]).

asteroid belt. Band of several thousand small bodies revolving around Earth's sun between the orbits of Mars and Jupiter. When Chakotay studied to be a pilot during his first year at Starfleet Academy, he spent some time training in the belt, learning how to dodge asteroids. ("Future's End, Part II" [VGR]).

asteroid gamma 601. Moon-sized asteroid located in the **Devolin system**. This asteroid was the final resting place of the *Starship* ***Pegasus*** after it was believed destroyed in 2358. In 2370, the hulk of the *Pegasus* was discovered inside the body of the asteroid, partially encased within the rock. The ship had apparently traveled through the asteroid in a phased state. Once inside, the **phasing cloak** failed, and the ship was trapped in the rock face. The salvage of the *Pegasus* involved the *Enterprise*-D also traveling inside the body of the asteroid, a first for any Federation starship. ("The *Pegasus*" [TNG]). SEE: **Pressman, Admiral Erik; Riker, William T.**

asteroid. Small, rocky celestial object, usually much smaller than a planet, often irregularly shaped. Asteroids often occur in orbital belts within a star system, sometimes the debris remaining from the formation of that system, other times the fragments remaining from the disintegration of a planet. Larger asteroids are sometimes called planetoids.

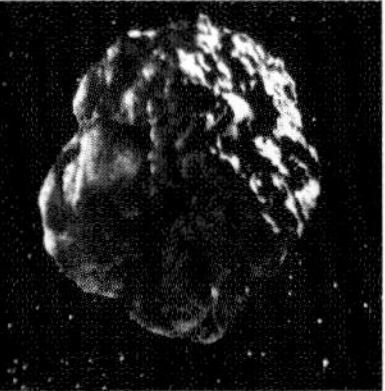

SEE: **actinides; Alpha Omicron system; asteroid gamma 601; Babel; Bre'el IV; Chamra Vortex; class-J cargo ship; co-orbital satellite; Companion; cutter; Deltived Asteroid Belt; Gamma II; Hanolin asteroid belt; Holberg 917G; Ikalian asteroid belt; Jeraddo; Junior; Kalandan outpost; Meltasion asteroid belt; Memory Alpha; Metron; Miramanee's planet; New Seattle; nitrium metal parasites; *Odin, S.S.*; Orelious IX; Pelloris Field; Penthara IV; Regula; Rousseau V; Rura Penthe; Selcundi Drema; Selebi Asteroid Belt; Tessen III; Vandor IX; Vlugta asteroid belt**; ***Yonada*** (pictured).

Astral Queen. Passenger spacecraft commanded by Captain **Jon Daily** in 2266. At the request of *Enterprise* captain James Kirk, Daily bypassed a scheduled stop at **Planet Q**, forcing the **Karidian Company of Players** to request passage aboard the *Enterprise*. ("The Conscience of the King" [TOS]).

Astral V annex. Historical museum and repository for classic spacecraft. Captain Picard suggested the Astral V annex might want to acquire the hulk of the **Promellian** cruiser ***Cleponji***, discovered near **Orelious IX** in 2366, although the Promellian ship was destroyed before this could happen. ("Booby Trap" [TNG]). *An early draft script for "Booby Trap" suggested the Astral V annex was part of the Smithsonian Institution.*

astrometric readings. A determination of the date by observing the apparent positions of the stars. ("Future's End, Part I" [VGR]).

Atalia VII. Planet. Location of a vital diplomatic conference in 2369. Captain Jean-Luc Picard was scheduled to be a mediator there, but was detained when **Professor Richard Galen** was killed. ("The Chase" [TNG]).

atavachron. Temporal portal developed on planet **Sarpeidon** to travel back through time. The atavachron altered a time traveler's cellular structure, making it possible to survive in earlier environments, but also making it impossible to return to the present without reversing the alteration. The people of Sarpeidon used the atavachron to escape into the past when their sun, **Beta Niobe**, went nova in 2269. ("All Our Yesterdays" [TOS]). SEE: **Atoz, Mr.**; **Zarabeth**.

Atheneum Vaults. A government building on planet **Ventax II.** The **Scrolls of Ardra** were stored there. ("Devil's Due" [TNG]).

atherosclerosis. A pathological condition in some humanoid species characterized by the hardening of the arteries and accompanied by the deposit of fat in the inner arterial walls. **Joseph Sisko** developed progressive atherosclerosis, eventually necessitating that he be given a new aorta. ("Homefront" [DS9]).

Atlantis Project. An ambitious 24th-century proposal to create a small continent in the middle of Earth's Atlantic Ocean. **Jean-Luc Picard** was offered directorship on the Atlantis Project when he took shore leave on Earth in 2367. Picard declined the opportunity, preferring to remain in Starfleet. Picard's boyhood friend, **Louis**, was a supervisor on the project. ("Family" [TNG]).

atmosphere conditioning pumps. Part of a starship's life-support system. Data, temporarily controlled by **Noonien Soong** in 2367, programmed the atmosphere conditioning pumps on the *Enterprise*-D's bridge to operate in negative mode, evacuating the air and rendering the bridge uninhabitable to air-breathing humanoids. Doing so required Data to override seven independent safety interlocks designed to prevent just such an occurrence. ("Brothers" [TNG]).

atmospheric dissipation. Rare and unpredictable phenomenon in which severe plasmonic energy bursts rapidly burn off the atmospheric layers of a planetary body. Once the process begins, it is unstoppable by any known means. In 2370, atmospheric dissipation struck planet **Boraal II**, rendering it uninhabitable in a matter of days. ("Homeward" [TNG]).

atomic bomb. Primitive weapon using explosive nuclear fission reactions in isotopes of uranium and plutonium. Early **Earth** nations stockpiled such weapons, despite the fact that their widespread use could have wiped out all life on their planet and contaminated their ecosphere for generations. ("Little Green Men" [DS9]). SEE: **World War III.**

Atoz, Mr. (Ian Wolfe). Last inhabitant on planet **Sarpeidon** before their sun, **Beta Niobe**, went nova in 2269. Mr. Atoz managed a vast library on Sarpeidon, part of his people's **atavachron** time-travel facility. For this task, Atoz had the assistance of numerous **android** copies of himself. The library allowed the people of Sarpeidon to select past eras to which they could travel to escape the explosion of their sun. Just prior to the detonation of Beta Niobe, Atoz mistook a landing party from the *Starship Enterprise* for Sarpeidon citizens seeking escape, and sent Kirk, Spock, and McCoy into his planet's past. They were returned to the present, just in time for Atoz to escape into his chosen past. SEE: **Zarabeth**. ("All Our Yesterdays" [TOS]). *An appropriate name for a librarian, Mr. A to Z. Ian Wolfe had previously played* ***Septimus*** *in "Bread and Circuses" (TOS).*

Atrea IV. Class-M planet. In 2370, it was discovered that the molten core of Atrea was cooling, causing dramatic seismic activity. Atrean scientists estimated the planet would become uninhabitable in 13 months. The *Enterprise*-D was dispatched to assist the Atrean government in their attempts to correct the problem. *Enterprise*-D officers Data and La Forge, working with Atrean scientists Dr. **Pran Tainer** and his wife **Dr. Juliana Tainer,** developed a means to reliquefy the core using **ferroplasmic infusion**, which injected sufficient heat into the planet to reliquefy the core for centuries. The technique used phasers to drill through the planet's crust, into pockets in the magma, where ferroplasmic infusion units injected plasma directly into the magma, triggering a chain reaction. ("Inheritance" [TNG]). *While we didn't see it occur, we are confident that Data and Geordi's plan was successful.*

"Attached." *Next Generation* episode #160. Written by Nicholas Sagan. Directed by Jonathan Frakes. Stardate 47304.2. *First aired in 1993. Picard and Crusher are kidnapped by an isolationist nation whose political enemy is petitioning for Federation membership.* GUEST CAST: Robin Gammell as **Mauric, Ambassador**; Lenore Kasdorf as **Lorin, Security Minister**; J.C. Stevens as Kes aide. SEE: **antigraviton; attack satellite; Balfour Lake; coffee; croissant; Crusher, Beverly, Crusher, Jack; Earth; Horath, Prime Minister; Kes; Kesprytt III; Kes Security Relation Station One; Kolrod Island; Lorin, Security Minister; *manta* leaves; Markson, Ensign; Mauric, Ambassador; methanogenic compound; multiphase pulse; Norris, Tom; Ogawa, Alyssa; Ohn-Kor; Picard, Jean-Luc; Prytt; Prytt Security Ministry; psi-wave device; transporter sensor log; transporter targeting components; United Federation of Planets; xenophobia.**

attack cruiser. SEE: **Klingon attack cruiser**.

attack satellite. Spaceborne weapons system. The **Prytt** nation on planet Kesprytt III feared the **Kes** could gain access to attack satellite technology in 2370 by aligning themselves with the Federation. ("Attached" [TNG]).

attack skimmer. Flying assault platform. In 2373, Quark sold 7,000 attack skimmers to the Proxcinian to be used in their war. ("Business As Usual" [DS9]).

Attendants. In the **Drayan** culture in the Delta Quadrant, the name given to the persons who aid elderly Drayans as they go through their final death ritual on the **crysata** moon. ("Innocence" [VGR]).

Atul. (Dennis Madalone). An agent of the **Klingon Intelligence** service. One of three agents sent to **Deep Space 9** in 2371 to observe and to take appropriate action against a **Romulan** delegation visiting the station. ("Visionary" [DS9]). *Dennis Madalone is stunt coordinator for* Star Trek: Deep Space Nine, *and* Star Trek: Voyager, *and has previously played numerous stunt roles including Chief Hendrick in "Identity Crisis" (TNG), and the one-eyed Terran in "Crossover" (DS9), "Through the Looking Glass" (DS9), and "Shattered Mirror" (DS9).*

atuta. SEE: ***Amanita muscaria***.

AU. Abbreviation for Astronomical Unit, a measure of length equal to the distance from the Earth to the Sun, some 150 million kilometers. The **V'Ger** cloud was described as being over 82 AUs in diameter, which is pretty darned big. *(Star Trek: The Motion Picture).*

Audubon Park. Nature preserve located in New Orleans on Earth. Members of the Sisko family often enjoyed Audubon Park. ("Homefront" [DS9]).

Augergine stew. Food. **Jadzia Dax** helped herself to a plateful of the stuff when Commander Sisko left the dinner table to look for his tardy son. ("The Nagus" [DS9]).

Augris. (Alan Scarfe). Third Magistrate of the oppressive, technologically advanced regime known as the **Mokra Order**. In 2372, the *Voyager* visited a planet controlled by the Mokra and during an away mission, crew members Tuvok and Torres were arrested by Mokra agents and were questioned by Augris. He was killed in a struggle with **Caylem** during Kathryn Janeway's attempt to rescue her officers from custody. ("Resistance" [VGR]). *Alan Scarfe previously played Admiral Mendak in "Data's Day" (TNG) and Tokath in "Birthright, Parts I and II" (TNG).*

Aurora. Space cruiser. The *Aurora* was stolen by **Dr. Sevrin** and his followers for their search for the mythical planet **Eden** in 2269. ("The Way to Eden" [TOS]). *The* Aurora *miniature was a modification of the* ***Tholian*** *ship from "The Tholian Web" (TOS).*

Australopithecine. Referring to protohuman life-forms that inhabited Earth some 4 to 5 million years ago. Australopithecine species include *Australopithecus afarensis*, *A. africanus*, *A. robustus*, and *A. boisei*. Following his exposure to **Barclay's Protomorphosis Syndrome** in 2370, Commander William Riker devolved into an Australopithecine protohuman. ("Genesis" [TNG]).

Autarch. Leader of the **Tzenkethi** homeworld. In 2371, Captain **Benjamin Sisko** was falsely informed of a coup d'état on the Tzenkethi homeworld and of a plot to overthrow the Autarch. ("The Adversary" [DS9]).

Autarch. SEE: **Ilari Autarch.**

authorization code. SEE: **security access code**.

auto-phaser interlock. A computer control subroutine that allowed for precise timing in the firing of ship-mounted phasers. ("A Matter of Time" [TNG]).

autodestruct. A command program in the main computer system of a *Galaxy*-class starship enabling the destruction of the vessel should the ship fall into enemy hands. Initiation of this program requires the verbal order (with dermal hand print identification verification) of the two most senior command officers on the ship. Once the computer has recognized the two officers, the senior officer gives the command to "set autodestruct sequence," whereupon the computer asks the other officer for verbal concurrence. Captain Picard and Commander Riker used the autodestruct sequence when the **Bynars** attempted to hijack the *Enterprise*-D. ("11001001" [TNG]). Picard and Riker again initiated the autodestruct sequence when **Nagilum** threatened the lives of half the *Enterprise*-D crew. ("Where Silence Has Lease" [TNG]). *The auto- destruct protocol was similar, but not identical to the* ***destruct sequence*** *for the original* Starship Enterprise. In 2371, Captain **Benjamin Sisko** and Major **Kira Nerys** initiated the ***U.S.S. Defiant***'s autodestruct sequence when a hostile **Founder** took control of the ship. ("The Adversary" [DS9]). Captain Jean-Luc Picard, Doctor Crusher, and Lieutenant Commander Worf set the *U.S.S. Enterprise*-E's autodestruct sequence in 2373 to prevent the **Borg** from taking over the ship. *(Star Trek: First Contact).*

Automated Personnel Unit. SEE: **Pralor Automated Personnel Unit**.

autonomic response analysis. Test of involuntary physiologic parameters used in law enforcement to evaluate the truthfulness of a witness. In 2371, Tuvok performed an ARA on Lieutenant Paris to determine if Paris had killed Professor **Tolen Ren**. ("Ex Post Facto" [VGR]). Autonomic response analysis works by comparing the subject's readings with a baseline reading for another member of the subject's species. ("Basics, Part I" [VGR]).

autonomous holo-emitter. Small device built with 29th-century technology that allowed the *Voyager's* **Emergency Medical Hologram** to exist outside of sickbay. When the *Voyager* visited Earth's past in 1996, **Henry Starling** fitted the EMH with the autonomous holo-emitter. When the *Voyager* returned to their own time of 2373, the doctor retained the holo-emitter and became able to leave sickbay thereafter. ("Future's End, Part II" [VGR]).

autosequencer. A subsystem of a starship's **transporter** that controls the actual transport process. Possible autosequencer malfunction was investigated following the apparent transporter-related death of **Ambassador T'Pel** in 2367. It was later found that T'Pel was not dead, and that **Subcommander Selok** (her real name) had faked the malfunction to cover her escape into Romulan hands. ("Data's Day" [TNG]).

autosuture. A medical instrument in use aboard the *Enterprise*-D, used for wound closures. ("Suddenly Human" [TNG]).

auxiliary control. Secondary command room on the original *Starship Enterprise*, also known as the emergency manual monitor and the auxiliary control center, serving as a backup to the ship's **bridge**. ("I, Mudd" [TOS], "The Doomsday Machine" [TOS], "The Changeling" [TOS], "Day of the Dove" [TOS], "The Way to Eden" [TOS]).

Avery III. Class-M planet in the Delta Quadrant. The **Vidiians** maintained an underground complex on Avery III, and Dr. **Sulan** conducted scientific experiments there. ("Faces" [VGR]).

Avesta. Governor of the **Prophet's Landing** colony in 2371. ("Heart of Stone" [DS9]).

Avidyne engines. A type of impulse engines utilized in old ***Constellation*-class** starships such as the ***U.S.S. Hathaway***. Although these units were considered obsolete by 2365, the *Hathaway* and her engines performed serviceably in a **Starfleet battle simulation**. *The term "avidyne" was devised by writer Melinda Snodgrass as a variation of "Yoyodyne," a reference to the cult s-f movie* Buckaroo Banzai, *whose writer borrowed it from Thomas Pynchon's novel* The Crying of Lot 49. ("Peak Performance" [TNG]).

away mission. Starfleet term for an assignment that takes a team away from a ship, such as a landing party sent to a planet's surface.

away team. Starfleet term for a specialized squad of personnel sent on an extravehicular **away mission**, usually to a planetary surface or another spacecraft. *The term was introduced in* Star Trek: The Next Generation. *During the original* Star Trek *series, the terms landing party and boarding party were used.*

Axanar. Planet that was the site of a major battle in which Starfleet captain **Garth** won a historic victory in the 2250s. James Kirk's first visit to Axanar was as a cadet on a peace mission. ("Whom Gods Destroy" [TOS]). Kirk was subsequently awarded the Palm Leaf of Axanar Peace Mission. ("Court Martial" [TOS]). *It was not established who the opponent was in Garth's victory. It has been speculated that it might have been the Romulans, although the history implied by "Balance of Terror" (TOS) indicates that there was no Federation contact with the Romulans during that time frame. Kirk noted that Garth's victory was instrumental in making it possible for Spock and him to work together as brothers, so the Axanar battle apparently had something to do with holding the Federation together.*

axionic chip. Component of an **exocomp**'s neural computing system. ("The Quality of Life" [TNG]).

axonal amplifier. Bioelectronic device of **Borg** origin, believed to be some type of **neuroprocessor**. ("Unity" [VGR]).

Ayala, Lieutenant. Member of the *Starship Voyager* crew. ("Initiations" [VGR]). Ayala missed his sons, who he left behind in the Alpha Quadrant. Ayala's quarters were on Deck 7. Ayala was temporarily in command of the *Voyager* in 2372 during the ship's encounter with a distortion ring being. ("Twisted" [VGR]).

Ayelborne. (Jon Abbott). Leader of the **Council of Elders** on planet **Organia**. Ayelborne, along with all Organians, welcomed representatives of both the Federation and the **Klingon Empire** to his planet in 2267. Ayelborne ignored strong warnings from Federation representative James Kirk that Klingon occupation would have potentially disastrous consequences to the technologically unsophisticated Organian people. It was later learned that the Organians were an incredibly advanced civilization of **noncorporeal life-forms** who had been masquerading in humanoid form in order to make it easier for the Klingon and Federation representatives to deal with them. Ayelborne predicted that the Federation and Klingon antagonists would become fast friends. ("Errand of Mercy" [TOS]). *Ayelborne's prediction has in fact largely come true by the time of* Star Trek: The Next Generation.

Azetbur. (Rosana DeSoto). Daughter of Klingon **Chancellor Gorkon**, Azetbur ascended to lead the Klingon High Council after the assassination of her father in 2293. As chancellor, Azetbur continued Gorkon's peace initiative with the Federation, concluding with the historic **Khitomer** peace accords. *(Star Trek VI: The Undiscovered Country). Interestingly, although Azetbur led the Klingon High Council after her father's death, the episode "Redemption, Part II" (TNG) established that a under Klingon law, a woman could not head the council.*

Azin, Minister. Official of the Bajoran Commerce Ministry. In 2372, Minister Azin hired **Kasidy Yates** to captain a freighter for the Commerce Ministry. ("Indiscretion" [DS9]).

azna. Food. A favorite meal of Jadzia Dax, who told Benjamin Sisko it would put years on his life. ("A Man Alone" [DS9]).

Azure Nebula. Interstellar gas cloud located near the border of Klingon and Federation space. The Azure Nebula was a type-11 nebula, cobalt blue in color, and contained **sirillium** gas. In 2293, it was the site of an encounter between the *U.S.S. Excelsior* and several Klingon battle cruisers, one of which was commanded by **Kang**. ("Flashback" [VGR]).

***B'aht Qul* challenge.** A traditional Klingon game of strength in which one contestant holds both arms forward, while the other places his or her arms between the first, wrists touching. The first contestant attempts to press the arms together, while the second attempts to force them apart. ("The Chase" [TNG]).

B'Etor. (Gwynyth Walsh). A member of the Klingon Empire's politically influential **Duras** family, B'Etor was the younger of Duras's two sisters. Following the death of Duras in 2367, B'Etor plotted unsuccessfully with her sister, **Lursa**, to seat Duras's illegitimate son, **Toral**, as leader of the **Klingon High Council**, plunging the empire into a **Klingon civil war**. ("Redemption, Parts I and II" [TNG]). B'Etor subsequently dropped out of sight for two years until she and her sister attempted to raise capital for their armies by selling **bilitrium** explosives to the **Kohn-ma**, a Bajoran terrorist organization in 2369. ("Past Prologue" [DS9]). In 2370 she and her sister illegally mined a **magnesite ore** deposit on **Kalla III** that belonged to the **Pakleds**. They later tried to sell the ore to the **Yridians**. ("Firstborn" [TNG]). In 2371, B'Etor and Lursa obtained **trilithium** weapons technology from **Dr. Tolian Soran**, in hopes of making another attempt to reconquer the Klingon Empire. When the *Starship* ***Enterprise*-D** stumbled upon their activities with Soran at the **Amargosa Observatory**, B'Etor and Lursa attacked the *Enterprise*-D. B'Etor was killed when the *Enterprise*-D returned fire, destroying her bird-of-prey spacecraft. *(Star Trek Generations).*

B'hala. Legendary ancient city on planet Bajor that disappeared some 20,000 years ago. Bajoran archaeologists searched for B'hala for the past ten millennia, but it was not until **Benjamin Sisko**, the **Emissary** of Bajoran prophecy, experienced ***pagh'tem'far***, that the ruins of B'hala were uncovered in 2373. Up until that point, one of the few records of the sacred city was an ancient icon painting that showed the city 20 millennia ago. The painting showed a **bantaca** at the center of the city. ("Rapture" [DS9]). SEE: **Zocal's Third Prophecy.** *The painting of B'hala was done by scenic artists Doug Drexler and Mike Okuda.*

B'iJik. (Erick Avari). Minor bureaucrat serving the **Klingon High Council** in 2368. B'iJik was reluctant to convey a request from Captain Jean-Luc Picard to High Council leader **Gowron** in 2368 when Picard requested the loan of a Klingon bird-of-prey. B'iJik eventually relented when Picard's arguments proved highly persuasive. ("Unification, Part I" [TNG]). *Erick Avari also appeared as Vedek Yarka in "Destiny"(DS9).*

***B'Nar*.** A **Talarian** mourning ritual. The *B'Nar* is a rhythmic high-pitched wail that is expressed for hours at a time. The Talarian boys rescued from a damaged observation craft in 2367 made the *B'Nar* in protest for being held aboard the *Enterprise*-D. ("Suddenly Human" [TNG]).

B'rel*-class bird-of-prey.** Small **Klingon bird-of-prey** with a crew of about a dozen, commonly used as a scout ship. ("Rascals" [TNG]). *We assume that the bird-of-prey in* Star Trek III *was a* B'rel-*class ship, while the larger versions of that ship sometimes seen on* Star Trek: The Next Generation *were* **K'Vort-*class *vessels. There was no difference in the design of the two ship types, since the same model was used for visual effects photography. The two names were created, in part, simply to acknowledge that the ship had different apparent sizes in different episodes.* ("Yesterday's *Enterprise*" [TNG]).

B'tardat. (Terence McNally). Science minister of planet **Kaelon II**. In 2367, B'tardat initiated hostile action against the *Enterprise*-D when **Dr. Timicin** requested asylum aboard the ship in defiance of his planet's laws. ("Half a Life" [TNG]).

B'Zal. Ferengi signal code that used alternating patterns of light and dark to transmit simple text messages. In 2370, **Bok** exploded a probe near the *Enterprise*-D, which created a series of light patterns. In B'Zal, these translated as, "My revenge is at hand." ("Bloodlines" [TNG]).

B-Type warbird. Federation Starfleet designation for the Romulan ***D'deridex*-class warbird** spacecraft. ("The Defector" [TNG]).

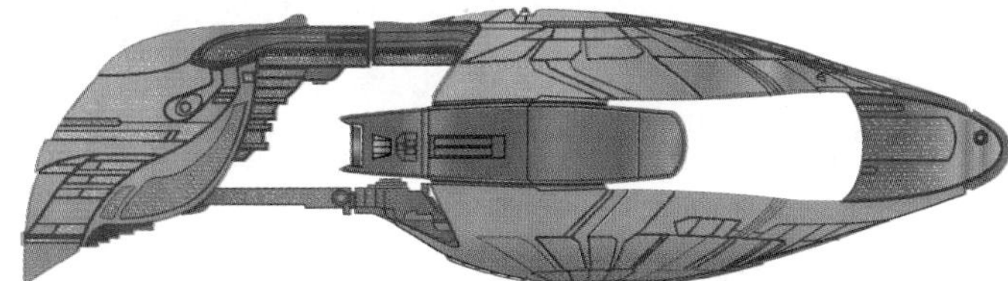

Ba'el. (Jennifer Gatti). Daughter of a Klingon woman, **Gi'ral**, and Romulan officer **Tokath**. Ba'el was born and raised at the Romulan prison camp in the **Carraya system**, and thus had an unusual sense of tolerance toward both cultures. Although the existence of the camp remains a secret from the **Klingon Homeworld**, Ba'el did once meet a Klingon from the outside when **Worf** discovered the camp in 2369. The two became romantically involved, but Ba'el felt she could not leave Carraya because of the racial intolerance she would experience in either the Romulan or Klingon empires. ("Birthright, Parts I and II" [TNG]).

Balt'masor Syndrome. Disease. Klingon exobiologist **J'Ddan** suffered from Balt'masor Syndrome. He required regular treatments, given by injection, for the condition. ("The Drumhead" [TNG]).

baakonite. Type of metal. The blades of a modern ***bat'leth*** sword are made of *baakonite*. ("Blood Oath" [DS9]).

Babel Conference. Interstellar meeting held on planetoid Babel in 2267 to consider the admission of the **Coridan** planets to the United Federation of Planets. Among the attendees at the conference were representatives from the **Andorian**, **Tellarite**, and **Vulcan** governments. ("Journey to Babel" [TOS]). Vulcan ambassador **Sarek** spoke in favor of the Coridan admission, and is credited with passage of the measure. ("Sarek" [TNG]).

Babel. Code name of a neutral planetoid, site of the **Babel Conference** in 2267. ("Journey to Babel" [TOS]).

"Babel." *Deep Space Nine* episode #5. Teleplay by Michael McGreevey and Naren Shankar. Story by Sally Caves and Ira Steven Behr. Directed by Paul Lynch. Stardate 46423.7 *First aired in 1993. A virus infects the population of Deep Space 9, making everyone unable to speak coherently.* GUEST CAST: Jack Kehler as **Jaheel, Captain**; Matthew Faison as **Surmak Ren**; Ann Gillespie as **Jabara**; Geraldine Farrell as **Galis Blin**; Bo Zenga as **Asoth**; Kathleen Wirt, Lee Brooks, Aphasia victims; Richard Ryder as Bajoran deputy; Frank Novak as Businessman; Todd Feder as Federation male. SEE: **access tunnel; aphasia device; aphasia virus; aphasia; Argosian Sector; Asoth; corophizine; Deep Space 9; Dekon Elig; diboridium core; Ferengi; Galis Blin; Higa Metar; I'danian spice pudding; Jabara; Jaheel, Captain; Kohlanese stew; Kran-Tobal Prison; Largo V; mooring clamps; neural imaging scan; Odo; Quark; Sahsheer; security clearance; stardrifter; Surmak Ren; Terok Nor; Velos VII Internment Camp**.

baccarat. An old Earth gambling game in which winnings were decided by comparing cards held by the banker with those held by the players. Julian Bashir's **secret agent** holosuite character was an exceptionally good baccarat player. ("Our Man Bashir" [DS9]).

bacillus spray. Organic pesticide, whose major component is one of a number of rod-shaped bacteria, usually B. *thuringiensis*. The pesticide works by infecting plant parasites with a fatal dose of the bacterium. ("All Good Things..." [TNG]).

Badar N'D'D. (Marc Alaimo). Chief delegate of the **Antican** contingent to the Parliament Conference of 2364. ("Lonely Among Us" [TNG]). *This was Marc Alaimo's first role in* Star Trek. *He also played Commander Tebok ("The Neutral Zone" [TNG]), Gul Macet ("The Wounded" [TNG]), the gambler Frederick La Rouque ("Time's Arrow, Part I" [TNG]), and the recurring role of Gul Dukat in* Star Trek: Deep Space Nine.

Badlands. Region of space near the **Cardassian** border. Populated with dangerous **plasma storm**s, the Badlands were considered extremely dangerous for space travel. Numerous ships have been lost there. ("The Maquis, Part I" [DS9]). During the occupation of Bajor, Kira Nerys and other Bajoran resistance members used to hide in the Badlands to evade Cardassian ships. ("Starship Down" [DS9]). A **Maquis** interceptor, used by the **Founder Leader** to lure **Deep Space 9** Chief of Security **Odo** and **Kira Nerys**, ducked into the Badlands so that the plasma fields would disrupt their **runabout**'s sensors. ("Heart of Stone" [DS9]). In 2371, **Thomas Riker** ordered the hijacked ***U.S.S. Defiant*** to the Badlands before changing course for the **Orias system**. ("Defiant" [DS9]). Even in the **mirror universe**, the Badlands served as a haven in which the **Terran resistance** found safety in its fight against the **Alliance**. ("Through the Looking Glass" [DS9]). In 2371, **Chakotay** and his **Maquis** crew fled Gul Evek's *Galor*-class warship by entering the Badlands. While there, the **U.S.S. Voyager** and Chakotay's ship were propelled into the Delta Quadrant by a displacement wave created by the Caretaker's **Array**. ("Caretaker" [VGR]).

baffle plate. A crucial component of the ***U.S.S. Antares***'s propulsion system. The *Antares* was destroyed when **Charles Evans** caused the baffle plate to disappear, but Evans rationalized that the plate had been warped and it was just a matter of time before the ship would have exploded anyway. ("Charlie X" [TOS]).

BaH. Klingon term for "fire," as in the command to fire weapons. ("Redemption, Part I" [TNG]).

bahgol. Beverage. Best served warm. **Kor**, **Kang**, **Koloth**, and **Curzon Dax** once drank *bahgol* at the **Korvat colony**. ("Blood Oath" [DS9]).

Bahrat. (Carlos Carrasco). Manager of the **Nekrit Supply Depot** on the border of the Nekrit Expanse. Bahrat was obsessive about law and order on his station, and imposed heavy punishment on those found guilty of criminal activity. Punishment ranged from fines to imprisonment in a **cryostatic chamber**. Bahrat also demanded a 20 percent commission for trading on his station. ("Fair Trade" [VGR]).

Bailey, Lieutenant David. (Anthony Hall). Junior navigator on the original *U.S.S. Enterprise* during the early days of Kirk's first mission. Although an inexperienced junior officer, Bailey was assigned by Kirk in 2266 to special duty as a cultural envoy to the flagship ***Fesarius*** of the **First Federation**. ("The Corbomite Maneuver" [TOS]).

Bajor (mirror). In the **mirror universe**, a Class-M planet that was once a territory of the **Terran Empire**. After the empire fell, Bajor became an influential member of the **Alliance**. ("Crossover" [DS9]). SEE: **Kira Nerys (mirror)**.

Bajor VIII. Eighth planet in the **Bajoran** star system. It contained six colonies. In 2369, the **Duras** sisters delivered a cylinder of **bilitrium** explosive to **Tahna Los** on the dark side of Bajor VIII's lower moon. ("Past Prologue" [DS9]).

Bajor. Class-M planet, homeworld to the **Bajoran** people. Located near the **Cardassian** border, Bajor was valued by the Cardassians for its rich natural resources. ("Emissary" [DS9]). SEE: **uridium**. The oceans on Bajor are greener than those of Earth. ("Past Tense, Part I" [DS9]). Bajor has several moons, the fifth of which is a Class-M planetoid named **Jeraddo**. In 2369, shortly after the end of the Cardassian occupation, Jeraddo's molten core was tapped as an energy source for Bajor. Although this new energy source was badly needed on Bajor, tapping the core made life on Jeraddo impossible due to the toxic gases released during the procedure, making it necessary to evacuate that moon. *The fact that Jeraddo is the fifth moon of Bajor establishes that Bajor has at least five moons.* ("Progress" [DS9]), *although Nog's text in "The Nagus" (DS9) says it only has three moons.* SEE: **Mullibok**. *"The Nagus" also established that the Bajoran system contains 14 planets, of which at least two are habitable (Bajor is one; Bajor VIII, established in "Past Prologue" [DS9] is the other.)* The provisional government of Bajor applied for membership in the **United Federation of Planets** in 2369. ("Emissary" [DS9]). The **Federation Council** voted in 2373 to accept Bajor's application, but the **Bajoran Chamber of Ministers** subsequently elected to defer admission, following the recommendation of **Benjamin Sisko**, the **Emissary** of Bajoran prophecy. ("Rapture" [DS9]).

Bajora. SEE: **Bajorans**.

Bajoran assault vessel. Interplanetary spacecraft capable of carrying multi-person assault teams. Three of these vessels docked at station Deep Space 9 in 2370, part of the attempted coup staged by the **Alliance for Global Unity**. ("The Siege" [DS9]).

Bajoran Central Archives. Information repository for the Bajoran government. In 2370, **Kira Nerys** accessed the Vedek Assembly files through the Bajoran Central Archives, attempting to find the person responsible for the **Kendra Valley massacre**. ("The Collaborator" [DS9]).

Bajoran Chamber of Ministers. Legislative body of the **Bajoran provisional government**. In 2370, the Chamber of Ministers was highly factionalized by a variety of groups that opposed accepting Federation aid for planetary reconstruction after the Cardassian occupation. Because of such factionalism, the Council of Ministers refused to sanction the rescue of war hero **Li Nalas** from planet Cardassia IV. ("The Homecoming" [DS9]). Later that year, the Bajoran Chamber of Ministers and the **Vedek Assembly** denied the refugee **Skrreea's** request to colonize on planet Bajor. ("Sanctuary" [DS9]). When the **Federation Council** voted in 2373 to admit Bajor to the Federation, the chamber elected to delay admission. The ministers took this unusual action on the advice of **Benjamin Sisko**, the **Emissary** of Bajoran prophecy, who had undergone ***pagh'tem'far***, and experienced visions convincing him that admission at this time would be unwise. ("Rapture" [DS9]).

Bajoran communicator. Personal communications device incorporated into a decorative pin worn by Bajoran personnel. Similar in operation to a Starfleet **communicator**.

Bajoran Days of Atonement. Holy festival. Former **Shakaar resistance cell** member **Latha Mabrin** was murdered at the **Calash Retreat** in 2373 while preparing for the Days of Atonement. ("The Darkness and the Light" [DS9]).

Bajoran death chant. Funeral ritual of the **Bajoran** people. It was reputed to be over two hours long. ("The Next Phase" [TNG]).

Bajoran First Minister. Secular head of the **Bajoran Chamber of Ministers**. The First Minister was elected for a term of six years. **Kalem Apren** served as first minister until his death in late 2371. Kai **Winn** served the remainder of Kalem's term until the next election, for which former resistance leader **Shakaar Edon** was a leading contender. ("Shakaar" [DS9]). Shakaar won the election, and served as first minister. ("Crossfire" [DS9]).

Bajoran Gratitude Festival. Annual **Bajoran** celebration, of great importance to the Bajoran people. ("The Nagus" [DS9]). During the holiday, participants wrote down their problems on **Renewal Scrolls**, then placed them to be burned in a special brazier so that their troubles could symbolically turn to ashes. Station **Deep Space 9** hosted its third annual celebration of the Gratitude Festival in 2371. ("Fascination" [DS9]). In 2369, Sisko had hoped to make a three-day trip to planet Bajor with his son Jake to attend the Gratitude Festival and visit the fire caves. ("The Nagus" [DS9]). ***Bateret* leaves** were traditionally burned during the festival. The celebration was also called the Peldor Festival, and had been celebrated as far back as 20,000 years ago. ("Rapture" [DS9]).

Bajoran impulse ship. Small piloted spacecraft used to defend the high orbit of planet Bajor. Two Bajoran impulse ships, flown by forces loyal to the **Circle**, were encountered by Deep Space 9 officers Kira and Dax as they attempted to reach the **Bajoran Chamber of Ministers** in 2370. ("The Siege" [DS9]).

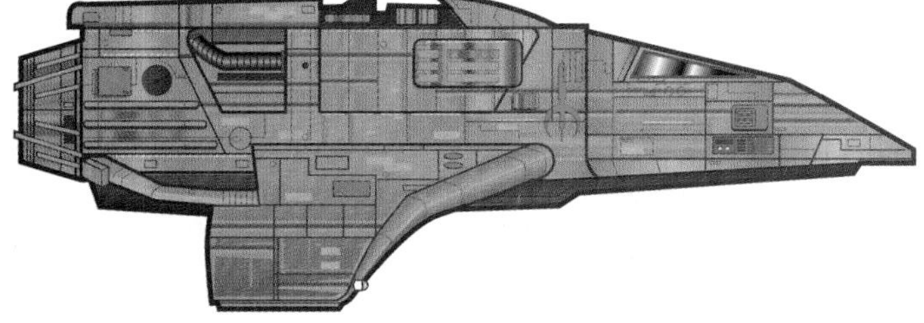

Bajoran Institute of Science. Bajoran research center. **Dr. Mora Pol** studied **Odo** at the Bajoran Institute of Science during the years immediately after Odo's discovery in the Denorios Belt. Odo left the institute in 2365 for the Cardassian space station, **Terok Nor**. ("The Alternate" [DS9]).

Bajoran Military Academy. Armed forces institute on planet **Bajor**. ("Meridian" [DS9]).

Bajoran Militia. The armed service of the **Bajoran** provisional government. **Kira Nerys** was a major in the Bajoran Militia. ("The Darkness and the Light" [DS9]).

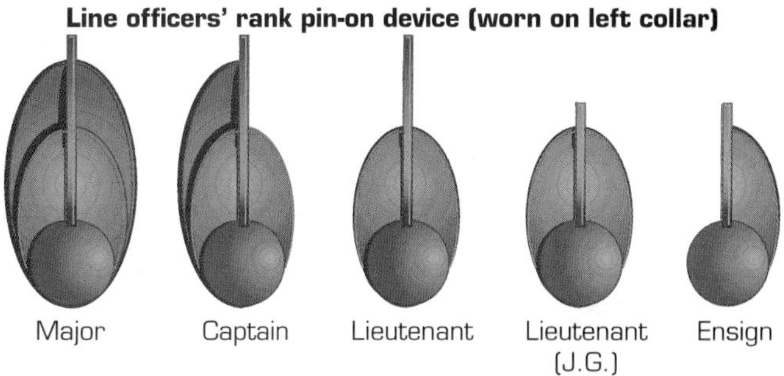

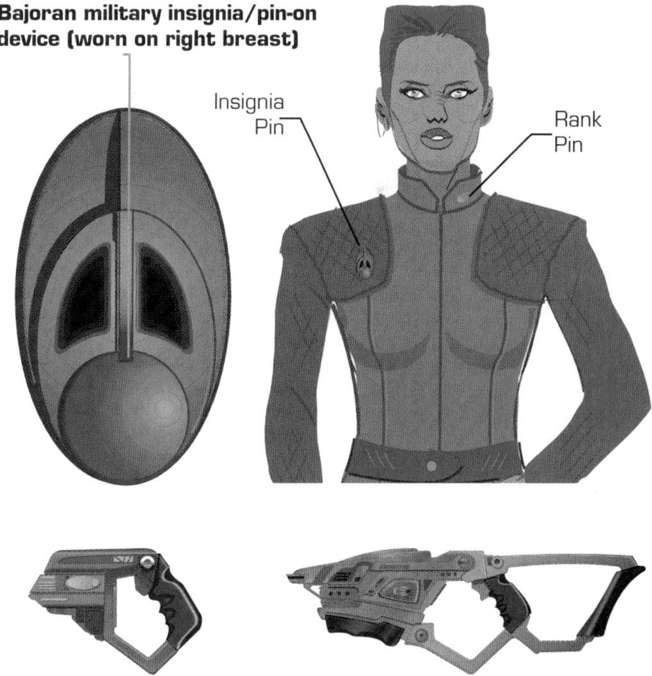

Bajoran phaser pistol

Bajoran phaser rifle

Bajoran provisional government. Loose coalition of Bajoran factions that assumed the role of planetary leadership following the Cardassian withdrawal in 2369. The provisional government was headed by the **Chamber of Ministers**, which was bitterly divided into many factions, each seeking dominance. One of the first actions of the provisional government was to request Federation assistance, a move that was opposed by isolationist factions. This aid included Starfleet operation of station Deep Space 9. ("Emissary" [DS9]). The Bajoran provisional government refused to sanction the rescue of **Li Nalas** from planet Cardassia IV. When Kira Nerys proceeded with the rescue despite their refusal, they retaliated by removing her from her position on station Deep Space 9. ("The Homecoming" [DS9]). SEE: **Jaro, Minister Essa.**

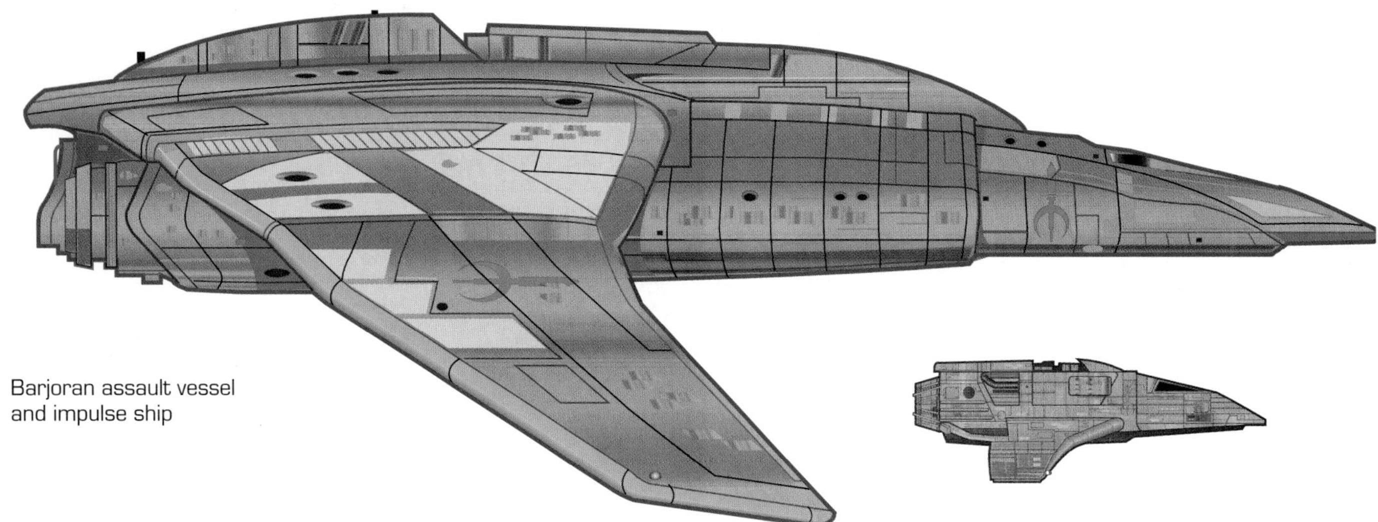

Barjoran assault vessel and impulse ship

Bajoran solar-sail vessel. Spacecraft used by ancient **Bajorans**, propelled by light pressure from Bajor's sun. Solar-sail vessels, also known as lightships, had no impulse reaction or warp propulsion system, but rather had enormous reflective sails that caught the tenuous solar wind. Crew accommodations were minimal in order to conserve mass. Such ships were used eight centuries ago to explore the Bajor system. Some ancient solar sailers even reached **Cardassia**. Until recently, Cardassian scholars scoffed at the suggestion that Bajorans crossed interstellar space so long ago, but such a transit was demonstrated in 2371 by **Benjamin Sisko**, who built a solar sailer from ancient plans. Sisko's craft was caught by **tachyon eddies** in the **Denorios Belt**, sweeping it at faster-than-light speeds to Cardassia. Shortly after Sisko's arrival, Cardassian archaeologists reported they had found ancient wreckage of such a ship on Cardassia. ("Explorers" [DS9]). Bajoran poet **Akorem Laan** piloted a traditional solar sailer in 2172. That particular craft was a hundred years old at the time of his flight. ("Accession" [DS9]). *The solar sailer was designed by Jim Martin, under the supervision of production designer Herman Zimmerman. The ship-in-flight scenes were computer-generated images created by John Knoll, under the direction of visual effects supervisor Glen Neufeld.*

Bajoran system. Star system in which is located the planet **Bajor**, homeworld to the Bajoran people. The system has 14 planets, of which Bajor is the largest. Also located in the Bajoran system is the **Denorios Belt**, where the **Bajoran wormhole** was discovered in 2369. ("The Nagus" [DS9]).

Bajoran Time of Cleansing. Bajoran ritual in which the participants abstain from worldly pleasures. In 2372, Quark used the fact that his revenues were down during the monthlong Time of Cleansing as an excuse to impose drastic reductions in pay and working conditions. ("Bar Association" [DS9]).

Bajoran wormhole. Artificially generated stable passageway to the **Gamma Quadrant** located in the **Denorios Belt** in the Bajoran star system. ("Emissary" [DS9]). The wormhole was formed by **verteron** particles that allow a vessel to pass through on impulse power. Bajoran religious faith interpreted the safe passage as evidence of guidance by the **Prophets**, so some conservative religious leaders objected strongly to the teaching of such scientific concepts. ("In the Hands of the Prophets" [DS9]). In the Bajoran religion, the wormhole is the **Celestial Temple**, home of the **Prophets** who sent the **Orbs** to the people of **Bajor**. In 2369, Commander **Benjamin Sisko** and science officer **Dax** discovered the Bajoran wormhole and came in contact with the aliens occupying the space. **Deep Space 9** was subsequently moved to the mouth of the Bajoran wormhole. ("Emissary" [DS9]). One travels almost 70,000 light-years when coming through the wormhole from the Gamma Quadrant. ("Battle Lines" [DS9]). *(The length of the wormhole was established as 90,000 light-years in "Captive Pursuit" [DS9], although subsequent episodes changed it to 70,000.)* Sensors read elevated neutrino levels when an object comes through the wormhole. ("Dramatis Personae" [DS9]). SEE: **Hawking, Professor Stephen; quantum fluctuation; wormhole**. The opening of the wormhole was a beautiful sight, inspiring some to adopt a superstition that making a wish when seeing the wormhole open would cause that wish to come true. ("Crossfire" [DS9]). Use of warp drive in the wormhole can be unpredictable and dangerous. In 2370, officers of station Deep Space 9 exposed the wormhole to warp energies, creating a momentary bridge to the same **mirror universe** discovered by the crew of the original *U.S.S. Enterprise* in 2267. ("Crossover" [DS9]). In 2371, **Cardassian** scientists and Deep Space 9 personnel collaborated to test a **subspace relay** that would provide communications between the Alpha and Gamma Quadrants through the Bajoran wormhole. Serendipitously, during the test, a comet near the wormhole broke up, leaving behind a trail of **silithium** particles in the wormhole. These particles created a subspace filament that facilitated the propagation of radio signals across the wormhole. ("Destiny" [DS9]). The Bajoran wormhole undergoes a subspace inversion every fifty years. It underwent one in 2372. ("The Visitor" [DS9]). In 2373, in response to an imminent **Dominion** attack, the staff of Deep Space 9 attempted to permanently close the Bajoran wormhole by using the station's graviton emitters to send out phase conjugate graviton beams at the terminus to collapse the wormhole's spatial matrix. ("In Purgatory's Shadow" [DS9]). The plan to seal the wormhole failed because the station's equipment was sabotaged by a **Founder** in the guise of **Dr. Julian Bashir**. The result was that the wormhole's spatial matrix was made even more stable. Even **trilithium** explosives would not be able to destroy it. ("By Inferno's Light" [DS9]).

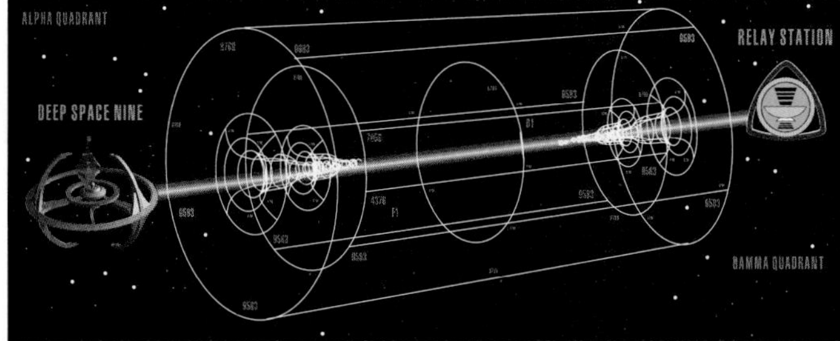

Bajorans. Humanoid civilization from the planet **Bajor**. Bajoran culture flourished a half-million years ago, when humans on Earth were not yet standing erect. The Bajoran people are deeply spiritual, but their history also recorded many great architects, artists, builders, and philosophers. Bajoran culture declined seriously during decades of **Cardassian** occupation in the 24th century, during which most Bajorans were driven from their homeworld. ("Ensign Ro" [TNG]). Bajorans traveled in space at least eight centuries ago, using **Bajoran solar-sail vessels** to explore their star system. Some ancient Bajoran space travelers even made it all the way to **Cardassia**. ("Explorers" [DS9]). SEE: **First Republic**. As recently as the 22nd century, Bajoran society was strictly divided into ***D'jarra*s**, or castes. A family's *D'jarra* determined its status in society, as well as what occupation its workers could hold. ("Accession" [DS9]). Under Bajoran custom, a person's family name is first, followed by the given name. Most Bajorans wear an ornamental earring, a symbol of their spiritual devotion. SEE: **Ro Laren**. ("Ensign Ro" [TNG]). Bajoran women carry their children for less than five months. Because they have a relatively short gestation period, they vascularize very quickly. Mother and child form a complex interconnecting network of blood vessels. Bajoran women often have fits of uncontrollable sneezing while pregnant. ("Body Parts" [DS9], "Looking for *par'Mach* in All the Wrong Places" [DS9]). In Bajoran childbirth, relaxation of the mother is essential. Participants at the birthing ceremony play rhythmic instruments to help her reach a fully relaxed state. When the child arrives, all present verbally welcome the child into the world. ("The Begotten" [DS9]).

Bajor was claimed as Cardassian territory from about 2328. ("Ensign Ro" [TNG]). The *D'jarra* caste system was abolished in the 24th century when all Bajorans, regardless of *D'jarra*, were called upon to fight Cardassian oppression. ("Accession" [DS9]). The Cardassians formally annexed Bajor in 2339, and occupied the planet until 2369, when Bajoran resistance fighters finally drove them away. ("Emissary" [DS9]). A **Bajoran provisional government** assumed authority for planetary government, led by the **Bajoran Chamber of Ministers**, which was headed by the **Bajoran First Minister**. ("The Homecoming" [DS9]). Also highly influential in governmental affairs is the religious **Vedek Assembly**, led by the **kai**. ("In the Hands of the Prophets" [DS9]). Upon the departure of the Cardassians, the Bajoran provisional government requested Federation assistance in operating the former Cardassian space station Terok Nor, now designated **Deep Space 9**. ("Emissary" [DS9]). After the Cardassian occupation, the Federation Council agreed to provide the provisional government with two industrial **replicators** to help them rebuild their economic base. ("For the Cause" [DS9]).

A deeply religious people, Bajorans look to their spiritual leader, the **kai**, for leadership and guidance. ("Emissary" [DS9]). The Bajoran religious faith was a powerful force in their society, and helped give the Bajoran people the spiritual strength to survive the brutal Cardassian oppression. ("In the Hands of the Prophets" [DS9]). The Bajoran religion believes that ships are safely guided through the **wormhole** by the **Prophets** and that the **Celestial Temple** dwells within the passage. SEE: **Orb**. Some conservative Bajoran religious leaders, notably **Winn**, tried to suppress scientific theories of the wormhole's creation, believing that the teaching of science lessened the religious leaders' political power. ("In the Hands of the Prophets" [DS9]). In 2371, newly elected Kai Winn began the process of healing her people's wounds with the signing of a historic peace accord with the Cardassians. The news of the treaty sent shock waves throughout the entire quadrant. ("Life Support" [DS9]).

An old Bajoran saying holds that "The land and the people are one." Major Kira Nerys mentioned this to Commander Sisko regarding the dispute between the Bajoran factions, the **Paqu** and the **Navot**. ("The Storyteller" [DS9]). Traditional Bajoran beliefs hold that the soul of the dead is far more important than the physical remains. ("Indiscretion" [DS9]). (In an alternate **quantum reality**, the Bajorans overpowered the neighboring Cardassians, and became increasingly hostile towards the Federation as well. In this alternate reality, a Bajoran ship fired upon the *Enterprise*-D as it was investigating a **quantum fissure** the crew discovered in 2370. The energy discharge caused the fissure to destabilize and allow incursions from other quantum realities into that one.) ("Parallels" [TNG]).

military military general prylar kai vedek kai

baked potato. Edible tuber of the *Solanum tuberosum* plant, baked and served as a side dish, often garnished with butter or sour cream and chives. ("The Chute" [VGR]).

baked Risan beans. Seeds from a leguminous plant indigenous to Risa, baked and served as a side dish. ("The Chute" [VGR]).

baktag. A Klingon insult. ("Redemption, Part II" [TNG]).

baktun. Measure of time used by the now-extinct **Tkon Empire**. A *baktun* was a large number of years, possibly centuries or millennia. ("The Last Outpost" [TNG]).

"Balance of Terror." Original Series episode #9. Written by Paul Schneider. Directed by Vincent McEveety. Stardate 1709.2. *First broadcast in 1966. Kirk matches wits with the commander of an invisible Romulan spaceship. This episode features the first appearance of the Romulans and their cloaking device.* GUEST CAST: Mark Lenard as **Romulan commander**; Paul Comi as **Stiles, Lieutenant**; Lawrence Montaigne as **Decius**; Grace Lee Whitney as **Rand, Janice**; Stephen Mines as **Tomlinson, Lieutenant Robert**; Barbara Baldavin as **Martine, Ensign Angela**; Garry Walberg as **Hansen, Commander**; John Warburton as **Centurion**; John Arndt as Fields, Engineer; Robert Chadwick as Romulan scanner operator; Walter Davis, Vince Deadrick, Sean Morgan, Romulan crewmen. SEE: **Centurion; cloaking device, Romulan; Decius; Hanson, Commander; Icarus IV; Martine, Ensign Angela; Neutral Zone Outposts; Praetor; Remus; rodinium; Romulan Bird-of-Prey; Romulan Commander; Romulan Neutral Zone; Romulan Star Empire; Romulans; Romulus; Stiles, Lieutenant; Tomlinson, Robert.**

Baldoxic vinegar. A salad dressing. Neelix used Baldoxic vinegar on a salad of orchids. ("Tattoo" [VGR]).

Balduk warriors. A fierce group. **Worf**, however, found them not as frightening as a small angry child. ("New Ground" [TNG]).

Balfour Lake. Body of water. Location where Jack and Beverly Crusher took their young son Wesley on his first camping trip. The boy entertained himself by throwing *manta* leaves into the fire. ("Attached" [TNG]).

Ballard, Lieutenant. (Judyann Elder). *Enterprise*-D crew member and teacher at the ship's primary school when Data's daughter, **Lal**, briefly attended class in 2366. ("The Offspring" [TNG]).

Balok. (Clint Howard). Commander of the **First Federation** flagship ***Fesarius***. Balok conducted his people's first contact with the **United Federation of Planets** in 2266. In an effort to ascertain the sincerity of Federation offers of friendship, Balok staged an incident in which he first threatened the *Enterprise*, then later claimed his ship had suffered severe damage. ("The Corbomite Maneuver" [TOS]). *Nearly 30 years after "The Corbomite Maneuver," Clint Howard portrayed Grady in "Past Tense, Part II" (DS9). Howard also played NASA mission control technician Sy Liebergot in the 1995 feature film* Apollo 13.

Balosnee VI. Planet where the harmonies of the tides can cause stimulating hallucinations. **Grand Nagus Zek** couldn't decide if he wanted to spend his first vacation in 85 years at **Risa** or Balosnee VI. ("The Nagus" [DS9]).

***balso* tonic**. Drink. Federation **Ambassador Odan** was fond of *balso* tonic. The *Enterprise*-D food replicator was, unfortunately, unable to manufacture it. ("The Host" [TNG]).

Balthus, Dr. Scientist. A botanist aboard the *Enterprise*-D and a colleague of **Keiko O'Brien.** ("Night Terrors" [TNG]).

Baltrim. (Terrence Evans). Resident of **Jeraddo**, a moon orbiting planet **Bajor**. Baltrim, a Bajoran national, was made mute by the **Cardassians**, during the Cardassian occupation of Bajor. Baltrim escaped to Jeraddo with his companion, **Keena**, in 2351 and started a new life. Teaming up with farmer **Mullibok**, they lived peacefully until an energy-transfer project in 2369 forced the evacuation of Jeraddo. ("Progress" [DS9]).

banana split. Earth dessert made from ice cream, various sweet toppings, and a sliced banana. Wesley Crusher described it to **Jono** as "maybe the best thing there is in the universe." ("Suddenly Human" [TNG]).

Bandi. Humanoid civilization native to planet **Deneb IV**. The Bandi, desiring to become a member of the Federation, offered Starfleet the use of a newly constructed starbase called **Farpoint Station**. It was later learned that Farpoint Station had not been built by the Bandi, but was in fact a shape-shifting spaceborne life-form. The life-form had been captured by the Bandi and coerced into assuming the form of the station. Investigation by *Enterprise*-D personnel uncovered the coercion, and the life-form was allowed to return to space. ("Encounter at Farpoint, Parts I and II" [TNG]).

Baneans. Spacefaring civilization from the Delta Quadrant. The Baneans were at war with a neighboring culture, the **Numiri**, even though the two once coexisted on one planet. In 2371, *Starship Voyager* crew members Thomas Paris and Harry Kim visited the Baneans, on a mission to request assistance in repairing *Voyager*'s navigational array. During the visit, Paris was accused and found guilty of having murdered Professor **Tolen Ren** (*pictured*), the inventor of Banean warship technology. Paris was later found to have been framed by a Numiri operative *(played by Aaron Lustig)* who had sought to use Paris as a courier for Banean military secrets. ("Ex Post Facto" [VGR]). *The exterior shot of the Banean city was a re-use of a matte painting first done for "Angel One" (TNG).*

Baneriam hawk. Predatory bird. **Quark** told **Odo** that he resembled a Baneriam hawk looking for prey, when the security chief was observing patrons at the bar on stardate 46853. ("If Wishes Were Horses" [DS9]).

banjo man. SEE: **Caretaker**.

bantaca. Large stone spire built at the center of ancient **Bajoran** cities, said to mark the city's place in the cosmos. *Bantacas* were about 11 meters tall, made of hundreds of stones fitted together so tightly that they didn't require mortar. An ancient icon painting of **B'hala** showed a *bantaca*. Symbols carved into the spire helped provide clues leading to the discovery of the city in 2373. ("Rapture" [DS9]). *The* bantaca *spire was designed by John Eaves and Fritz Zimmerman.*

bantan. Spicy vegetable dish. One of Neelix's specialties. ("The Cloud" [VGR]).

"Bar Association." *Deep Space Nine* episode #88. Teleplay by Robert Hewitt Wolfe & Ira Steven Behr. Story by Barbara J. Lee & Jenifer A. Lee. Directed by LeVar Burton. No stardate given. *First aired in 1996. Quark's heavy-handed management is more than his employees can stand, so with Rom's leadership they form a union and go on strike.* GUEST CAST: Max Grodénchik as **Rom**;

Chase Masterson as **Leeta**; Jason Marsden as **Grimp**; Emilio Borelli as **Frool**; Jeffrey Combs as **Brunt**. SEE: **anthracite strike of 1902; Bajoran Time of Cleansing; Battle of Clontarf; Boru, King Brian; Briok; Brunt; Ferengi; Ferengi Rules of Acquisition; Frool; Grimp; Guild of Restaurant and Casino Employees; holodeck and holosuite programs; holographic waiter; Kar-telos system; Lissepians; Nausicaans; O'Brien, Miles; O'Brien, Sean Aloysius; Quark; Quark's bar; Rom; snail juice; Worf.**

Barak-Kadan. Klingon opera singer. **Worf** liked Barak-Kadan's strong intonations and traditional style, but **Jadzia Dax** thought Barak-Kadan was boring because he never varied his performances. ("Looking for *par'Mach* in All the Wrong Places" [DS9]).

Baran, Arctus. (Richard Lynch). Shrewd and ruthless captain of a mercenary vessel in 2370. Baran's crew of some 12 mercenaries raided archaeological artifacts from several star systems, searching for artifacts with a particular **terikon** decay profile. Baran's ship was equipped with an energy sheath that rendered it undetectable on long-range sensors. It was armed with disruptors, and its maximum speed was warp factor 8.7. Baran controlled his crew with **neural servo** implants, which had been given to the crew by Baran's predecessor. In 2370, Baran was hired by agents of the **Vulcan isolationist movement** who sought to obtain ancient fragments of the **Stone of Gol**. Baran's search attracted the attention of *Enterprise*-D captain Jean-Luc Picard, who, under the name Galen, infiltrated Baran's crew along with William Riker. Baran was killed before all the fragments could be assembled. ("Gambit, Parts I and II" [TNG]).*The miniature used for Baran's vessel was a re-use of the Miradorn ship designed by Ricardo F. Delgado for "Vortex" (DS9).*

Barash. (Chris Demetral). A humanoid child who was forced to leave his home planet when it was attacked in the late 2350s or early 2360s. Fearing for his safety, Barash's mother hid him in a cavern on **Alpha Onias III**. The cavern was equipped for his survival and included specialized neural scanners that were able to transform matter into any form imagined, so that he could live his life in safety. In 2367, Barash used this equipment to lure Commander William Riker into a fantasy world in which Barash hoped Riker would remain as a playmate. In this virtual reality, some 16 years had passed, during which Riker had been promoted to captain of the *Enterprise*-D, Picard had become an admiral, and there was some rapprochement with the Romulans. Also in this fantasy, Riker had married **Minuet**, and they had a 10-year-old son named **Jean-Luc Riker**. This "son" was actually Barash, who hoped Riker would play with him in this artificial environment. Riker eventually saw through the pretense, and Barash revealed the true nature of the cavern and his true form as well. Unwilling to leave the child behind alone, Riker returned with him to the *Enterprise*-D. ("Future Imperfect" [TNG]).

Barbara series. (Maureen and Colleen Thornton). **Android** model designed by Mudd the First, aka **Harcourt Fenton Mudd**, in 2267. ("I, Mudd" [TOS]).

barber shop. Service establishment dedicated to cosmetic care of humanoid hair. Aboard the *Starship Enterprise*-D, the province of Mr. **Mot**, who provided stylish hair and beauty treatments to ship's personnel. ("Data's Day" [TNG]). *The* Enterprise-D *barber shop was first seen in "Data's Day" (TNG).*

Barbo. Quark's cousin. Barbo was released from the **Tarahong** detention center in 2369. At a Ferengi trade conference held on Deep Space 9, **Zek**, the **grand nagus**, recounted how **Quark** and his cousin sold defective warp drives to the Tarahong government. Zek praised Quark for betraying Barbo to the authorities and leaving him at the **Tarahong detention center** while Quark kept all the profits, an honorable act in the Ferengi system of values. ("The Nagus" [DS9]).

Barclay's Protomorphosis Syndrome. An **intron virus** that causes humanoids and other animals to develop structural and behavioral characteristics of earlier evolutionary forms. Accidentally developed in 2370 when a routine synthetic T-cell treatment became mutated. The virus exhibited airborne transmission and worked by invading the host's **DNA** and activating introns. Discovered by Dr. Beverly Crusher of the *U.S.S. Enterprise*-D, named for **Reginald Barclay**, the first patient known to have contracted the virus. ("Genesis" [TNG]).

Barclay, Reginald (Dwight Schultz). Starfleet systems diagnostic engineer. Barclay transferred to the *U.S.S. Enterprise*-D from the **U.S.S. Zhukov** in 2366. Lieutenant Barclay was an extremely talented engineer, but was timid and awkward in social situations. Noted as having reclusive tendencies, Barclay compensated for his shyness by devising a rich fantasy life inside the *Enterprise*-D **holodeck**. In these fantasies, Barclay would re-create images of those crew mates in bizarre settings that he controlled. Engineer Geordi La Forge helped Barclay overcome the need for such escapes by encouraging Barclay's sense of self-worth. ("Hollow Pursuits" [TNG]). In 2367, Barclay was exposed to a broad-spectrum emission from a **Cytherian** probe. The signal from the probe caused a dramatic increase in Barclay's neurochemical activity, increasing his I.Q. to at least 1200. With this newly enhanced intelligence, Barclay designed and built an innovative new computer interface system, as well as an incredibly fast new warp drive. It was learned that the Cytherians were reluctant to explore space themselves, so they resorted to this technique to give others the ability to reach them. Although the *Enterprise*-D contact with the Cytherians yielded valuable cultural and scientific exchanges, Barclay's enhanced intelligence faded, and with it the advanced warp drive technology was also lost. ("The Nth Degree" [TNG]). Barclay had a strong phobia of traveling by **transporter**. He described his "mortal terror" of being dematerialized. Barclay concealed this fear to avoid jeopardizing his Starfleet career, but he spent many hours traveling aboard shuttlecraft in order to avoid being beamed. He ultimately faced his greatest fears during a rescue mission to the ***U.S.S. Yosemite*** in 2369, when Barclay was threatened by **quasi-energy microbes** actually living in the transporter beam. ("Realm of Fear" [TNG]). Barclay helped Worf's son, **Alexander Rozhenko**, create a holodeck program called **Ancient West** just prior to stardate 46271. ("A Fistful of Datas" [TNG]). Barclay was part of the engineering team that attempted to solve the problem of how to give the computer-generated intelligence, **Professor James Moriarty**, physical reality, when Moriarty held the ship hostage in 2369. ("Ship in a Bottle" [TNG]). Fond of investigating the **Starfleet Medical Database**, Barclay often convinced himself that he had contracted some rare and fatal disease. In 2370, he visited sickbay, convinced that he was suffering from **Terellian Death Syndrome**. Dr. Crusher assured him that he only had a mild case of the **Urodelean flu**, and prescribed a synthetic T-cell to allow his body to fight the infection naturally. Unfortunately, the **T-cell** caused some of Barclay's **introns** to mutate. These mutated introns, once airborne, affected the entire crew, causing them to revert to earlier evolutionary forms. Once the cause and cure of the disease was found, Dr. Crusher named the syndrome after its first case. SEE: **Barclay's Protomorphosis Syndrome**. Barclay was one of the few persons aboard the *Enterprise*-D, besides Data, that **Spot** seemed to like. ("Genesis" [TNG]). Lieutenant Barclay left the *Enterprise*-D and transferred to the

Holoprogramming Center at Starfleet's **Jupiter Station**. He worked with **Dr. Lewis Zimmerman** on the engineering team that designed Starfleet's **Emergency Medical Hologram** program. Barclay tested the holographic doctor's interpersonal skills. In 2372, the holographic doctor aboard the *Starship Voyager* encountered a holographic representation of Barclay. ("Projections" [VGR]). Barclay later transferred onto the new *Enterprise*-E and was on the ship in 2373 during its encounter with the Borg in Earth's past. **Zefram Cochrane** was one of Barclay's heroes, and Barclay became starstruck when he met the scientist while in Montana in 2063. *(Star Trek: First Contact). Reg Barclay was first seen in "Hollow Pursuits" (TNG).*

Bardakian pronghorn moose. An animal life-form. Known for its loud and horrible call. ("Unification, Part II" [TNG]).

Bardeezan merchant ship. Trading vessel. In 2370, a Bardeezan vessel departing Deep Space 9 was briefly suspected of carrying the abducted **Gul Dukat,** but was later cleared. ("The Maquis, Part I" [DS9]).

Bare, Professor Honey. (Terry Farrell). A character in Julian Bashir's **secret agent** holosuite program. Professor Honey Bare was one of Earth's leading seismologists in 1964. A holosuite malfunction in 2372 caused the character to look exactly like Jadzia Dax. ("Our Man Bashir" [DS9]).

Bareil, Vedek. (Philip Anglim). Bajoran spiritual leader who was a leading candidate to become the next **kai** after the departure of **Kai Opaka** in 2369. ("In the Hands of the Prophets." [DS9]). Bareil was interned at the brutal Relegeth refugee camp during the Cardassian occupation. ("Shadowplay" [DS9]). Bareil started his spiritual service as a gardener at a monastery, and although he became an influential religious leader, he still enjoyed tending the grounds. Bareil was opposed in his bid to become kai by political rival Vedek **Winn**, who attempted to have Bareil assassinated. Winn engineered an incident on **Deep Space 9**, sparking protests about the teaching of science in **Keiko O'Brien**'s schoolroom, an effort to draw Bareil to the station, where he was the target of Winn's assassination plot. Fortunately, the plan failed and Vedek Bareil survived to continue his bid for kai and continue the cooperative Bajoran/Federation relationship. ("In the Hands of the Prophets." [DS9]). *Bareil's monastery scenes were filmed at Ferndale, near Griffith Park in Los Angeles, also used for the holodeck sequence in "Encounter at Farpoint" (TNG).* Bareil became romantically involved with **Kira Nerys** in 2370. ("Shadowplay" [DS9]). He was favored to become the new **kai** in 2370, but withdrew from the election when he became tied to the infamous **Kendra Valley massacre**. No one knew that Bareil's sudden withdrawal from the election was because he had been covering up the role of then-**Kai Opaka** in the massacre. Bareil knew that Opaka had allowed the Cardassians to kill 42 Bajorans (including her own son) to prevent them from killing over a thousand other Bajorans in the Kendra Valley. Bareil kept the secret for years and willingly sacrificed his political ambitions to protect Opaka's memory when then-Vedek **Winn** re-opened the investigation in 2370. Once Winn and Kira learned the truth, both appeared likely to preserve the secret. ("The Collaborator" [DS9]). SEE: **Bek, Prylar**. Bareil refused to let his defeat stop him, and in 2371 he accepted the opportunity to become a key advisor to the newly elected Kai Winn. As Winn's representative, Bareil conducted five months of negotiations with **Legate Turrel**, laying the groundwork for the historic peace treaty between the Bajorans and the Cardassians. Just prior to the signing of the treaty, Bareil was critically injured in an explosion aboard a Bajoran transport ship. At station Deep Space 9, Bareil refused extraordinary life-prolonging measures so that he could advise Kai Winn during the critical final stages of the talks. Bareil believed it was the will of the **Prophets** that he had been spared death in the explosion so that he could ensure the success of the peace talks. Bareil died shortly after the signing of the historic peace treaty. ("Life Support" [DS9]).

Baris, Nilz. (William Schallert). Federation Undersecretary in charge of Agricultural Affairs, sent from Earth to **Deep Space Station K-7** to oversee the development project for **Sherman's Planet** in 2267. In that capacity, he summoned the *Starship Enterprise* to protect several storage containers of the valuable grain, **quadrotriticale**. It was discovered that his assistant, **Arne Darvin**, was a Klingon spy who had poisoned the grain. ("The Trouble with Tribbles" [TOS]). *William Schallert also played Varani in "Sanctuary" (DS9).*

Barisa Prime. Planet. Site of a Federation settlement, Barisa Prime is located near the Federation border with the **Tzenkethi**. In late 2371, a **Founder** posing as **Ambassador Krajensky** faked a distress call from Barisa Prime, claiming the Tzenkethi had attacked the settlement. In reality, no attack occurred. ("The Adversary" [DS9]).

baristatic filter. Device used in a planet's atmosphere to remove air pollution on a large scale. A thousand baristatic filters were used on planet **Tagra IV** to clean the air. ("True-Q" [TNG]).

barium. Chemical element with atomic number 56. Until the late 21st century, barium was administered to patients with gastrointestinal disorders to facilitate the imaging of the intestinal lining with X-rays. ("Tuvix" [VGR]).

Barkon IV. Class-M planet supporting a society of humanoids. A Federation deep space probe went off course and crashed on Barkon IV in 2370. Some materials in the probe's casing were radioactive, and *Enterprise*-D officer Data was dispatched to retrieve the probe's remains before it could contaminate the planet's biosphere. When Data found the probe, a power surge overloaded his positronic matrix, giving him amnesia. Data wandered into a Barkon village carrying the radioactive casing fragments, and was taken in by **Garvin**. The fragments caused radiation poisoning in the village. The **Barkonians** understandably attributed this phenomenon to Data, who was mobbed by people who did not understand why they were becoming sick. Data was able to introduce medication into the village's water supply to counteract the radiation poisoning. ("Thine Own Self" [TNG]).

Barkonians. Humanoid inhabitants of planet **Barkon IV**. The Barkonians have purple-colored symmetrical forehead markings. In 2370, their civilization was in a pre-industrial stage. ("Thine Own Self" [TNG]).

Barnaby, Lieutenant. (James Horan). Starfleet tactical officer aboard the *Enterprise*-D. He served under Dr. Crusher during the encounter with the self-aware **Borg** in 2370. ("Descent, Part II" [TNG]). *James Horan also portrayed Jo'Bril in "Suspicions" (TNG).*

Barnhart. *Enterprise* crew member. Barnhart was killed in 2266 by the **M-113 creature**, who had been masquerading as **Crewman Green**. Barnhart's body was found on Deck 9. ("The Man Trap" [TOS]).

Barnum. P. T. Phineas Taylor Barnum (1810-1891), an American showman and businessman noted for creating "The Greatest

Show on Earth." Captain Picard quoted P. T. Barnum's saying, "There's a sucker born every minute," when referring to techniques used by **Ardra** at planet **Ventax II** in 2367. ("Devil's Due" [TNG]).

barokie. Twenty-fourth-century game. Ensign **Cortin Zweller** preferred barokie to **dom-jot**, saying barokie was "more of a challenge." ("Tapestry" [TNG]).

Barolian freighter. Space vessel that, in 2368, received a deflector array later found to have been stolen from the Vulcan ship ***T'Pau***. ("Unification, Part II" [TNG]).

Barolians. Civilization whose government entered into trade negotiations with the Romulans in 2364. Romulan **Senator Pardek** took part in the conference. ("Unification, Part I" [TNG]).

Baroner. Pseudonym adopted by Captain Kirk on planet **Organia** when the *Enterprise* was sent to Organia in 2267 to protect the planet from possible **Klingon** invasion. The Klingons did arrive, and Kirk disguised himself as an Organian citizen named Baroner. ("Errand of Mercy" [TOS]).

Barradas III. Uninhabited planet used as an outpost by the **Debrune** some 2000 years ago. A Federation archaeological survey has studied the planet and has cataloged numerous ruins on the surface. In 2370, these ruins were the target of mercenary **Arctus Baran**, who was working for the **Vulcan isolationist movement**, searching for fragments of the ancient **Stone of Gol**. ("Gambit, Part I" [TNG]).

Barradas system. Solar system containing planet Barradas III. ("Gambit, Part I" [TNG]).

barrier, galactic. Powerful energy field at the perimeter of the Milky Way Galaxy. First discovered around 2065 by the exploratory vessel ***S.S. Valiant***, the barrier was later crossed by the *Starship Enterprise* in 2265. Certain members of both ships' crews became endowed with dramatically amplified ESP and psychokinetic powers, and in both cases these mutated crew members became a threat to their ships. ("Where No Man Has Gone Before" [TOS]). The *Enterprise* crossed the barrier a second time in 2268, when the ship was hijacked by **Kelvans** attempting to return to their home in the **Andromeda Galaxy**. The barrier had also been responsible for the earlier destruction of their ship when they entered our galaxy. ("By Any Other Name" [TOS]). The *Enterprise* once again crossed the barrier later that year when designer **Laurence Marvick**, stricken by insanity, drove the ship across the barrier at warp 9.5. ("Is There In Truth No Beauty?" [TOS]).

Barron, Dr. (James Greene). Federation anthropologist assigned to planet **Mintaka III** to study the proto-Vulcan culture in 2366. ("Who Watches the Watchers?" [TNG]).

Barros Inn. A bar located on one of the Rigel planets. The Barros Inn was known as one of the wildest bars in the Rigel system. **Curzon Dax** was once thrown out of the Barros Inn for setting fire to the place. ("Rejoined" [DS9]).

Barrows, Yeoman Tonia. (Emily Banks). Member of the crew of the original *Starship Enterprise*. Barrows was part of the landing party to the **amusement park planet** in 2267. Unaware that the planet's equipment would instantly fabricate nearly anything she imagined, Barrows conjured up a replica of Don Juan. When she found herself alone with Dr. McCoy, she imagined herself a fairy-tale princess with a long flowing gown, and created a **black knight** from which McCoy needed to protect her. ("Shore Leave" [TOS]).

Barson II. Inhabited planet. The population of Barson II suffered a medical emergency around stardate 47623. The *Enterprise*-D picked up viral medicines on **Starbase 328** and was authorized to exceed warp speed limitations when transporting them to Barson II. ("Eye of the Beholder" [TNG]).

Barstow, Commodore. (Richard Derr). Starfleet official. Barstow contacted the *Enterprise* after a galaxy-wide time warp distortion was detected in 2267. Barstow ordered the *Enterprise* to investigate and determine if this phenomena was a prelude to invasion by an unknown force. ("The Alternative Factor" [TOS]).

Bartel, Engineer. (Stacie Foster). Crew member aboard the *Enterprise*-D at the time the ship encountered the **Dyson Sphere** near Norpin V. ("Relics" [TNG]).

Barthalomew, Countess Regina. (Stephanie Beacham). Fictional character inspired by the **Sherlock Holmes** stories of **Sir Arthur Conan Doyle**. The countess was the love of **Professor James Moriarty**, and a holographic representation of her was created by Moriarty within the *Enterprise*-D **holodeck** computer in 2369. ("Ship in a Bottle" [TNG]). *Stephanie Beacham also played Dr. Kristin Westphalen during the first season of* seaQuest DSV.

Bartlett. Starfleet officer assigned to Deep Space 9. In 2372, Bartlett was killed aboard the *Starship Defiant* during a battle with the *U.S.S. Lakota*. ("Paradise Lost" [DS9]).

Barton. Twenty-third century Earth playwright. Bashir felt that Earth writers after Barton's time were too derivative of alien drama. ("The Die is Cast" [DS9]).

baryon particles. Any member of a class of heavy fundamental particles. Baryons build up on starship superstructures as a result of warp travel, requiring periodic decontamination. SEE: **Remmler Array**. ("Starship Mine" [TNG]). An increase in baryon particles was detected with the malfunction of the **metaphasic shield** test of 2369. The increase in cabin baryons was believed to be partially responsible for the death of **Jo'Bril**. ("Suspicions" [TNG]). Highly energetic baryons were present in great abundance at the beginning of the universe. ("Death Wish" [VGR]).

baryon sweep. High-frequency plasma field used for removal of **baryon particle** contamination from starships. The process is dangerous to living tissue and requires complete evacuation of starship personnel. ("Starship Mine" [TNG]).

Barzan wormhole. A transdimensional conduit, initially believed to be stable, with one terminus near planet Barzan and the other some 70,000 light-years distant, in the **Gamma Quadrant**. In 2366, the Barzan government sold rights to the wormhole to the **Chrysalians**. Later investigation by an *Enterprise*-D shuttle and a **Ferengi shuttle** indicated that the wormhole was only partially stable, and that both ends would eventually shift location. The Ferengi ship was lost in the **Delta Quadrant** after just such a location shift. ("The Price" [TNG]). At that time, one terminus was relatively fixed in the Alpha Quadrant, but the other end shifted rapidly in the Delta Quadrant. A graviton pulse emitted by the Ferengi shuttle in 2373 further destabilized the wormhole. The pulse knocked the wormhole off of its subspace axis so that both of its endpoints jumped around erratically. ("False Profits" [VGR]). SEE: **quantum fluctuations**. *Not to be confused with the Bajoran wormhole.*

Barzans. Humanoid inhabitants of the planet Barzan. These vaguely catlike humanoids wore breathing devices when in a standard Class-M atmosphere; their society reportedly did not yet have space travel. **Premier Bhavani** of the planet Barzan visited the *Enterprise*-D in 2366 for a trade conference in which the Barzans hoped to benefit by selling rights to a wormhole discovered in their solar system. Rights to use the Barzan wormhole, believed to be a stable passageway to the **Delta Quadrant** of the galaxy, were the topic of a conference held aboard the *Enterprise*-D in 2366. Being politically neutral, the Barzans were concerned that favoring any one delegation might involve them in disputes with other parties. The question was later made moot when the wormhole was found to be unstable. ("The Price" [TNG]).

Basai Master. Honorific applied to great Klingon poets. ("Looking for *par'Mach* in All the Wrong Places" [DS9]).

baseball. Team sport that was once regarded as the national pastime of the Americas on **Earth**. After enjoying planetwide popularity for over a century, professional baseball died shortly after 2042, victim of a society that had no time for such diversions. ("Evolution" [TNG]). One of baseball's last great heroes was a player for the **London Kings** named **Buck Bokai**, who broke **Joe DiMaggio**'s record for hits in consecutive games in 2026. ("The Big Goodbye" [TNG]). Bokai did well for the Kings during 2015, his rookie year. ("Past Tense, Part II" [DS9]). The end of professional baseball came shortly after only 300 spectators attended the last game of the 2042 World Series, in which the Kings won. ("If Wishes Were Horses" [DS9]). Deep Space 9 commander **Ben Sisko** was a baseball fan and enjoyed watching replays of old games, as well as playing with holodeck re-creations of famous players. ("Emissary" [DS9], "The Storyteller" [DS9], "If Wishes Were Horses" [DS9]). Sisko even once invited Kira Nerys to watch a holographic baseball game with him. ("Starship Down" [DS9]). Noted scientist **Dr. Paul Stubbs** was also a fan of baseball, although he eschewed holodeck re-creations in favor of the power of his own imagination. ("Evolution" [TNG]). SEE: **Gibson, Bob; Maris, Roger; Newson, Eddie; Yankees**. Baseball, however, did survive in some form until the year 2071. The sport enjoyed a small renaissance in 2371 when Federation colonists on planet **Cestus III** formed a league of their own. ("Family Business" [DS9]). SEE: **Cestus Comets; Dodger Stadium; Pike City Pioneers; Yates, Kasidy**.

Bashir, Amsha. (Fadwa El Guindi). Earth citizen. Amsha Bashir conspired with her husband, **Richard Bashir**, to have illegal genetic enhancement performed on their child, **Julian Bashir**, when Julian was seven years old. ("Doctor Bashir, I Presume?" [DS9]).

Bashir, Dr. Julian. (Alexander Siddig). Starfleet medical officer, born 2341 ("Distant Voices" [DS9]), assigned to station **Deep Space 9** in 2369, shortly after the **Cardassian** withdrawal from the **Bajoran** system. ("Emissary" [DS9]). Dr. Julian Bashir's middle name was Subatoi. ("The Wire" [DS9]). His parents were **Richard** and **Amsha Bashir.** ("Doctor Bashir, I Presume?" [DS9]).

Julian was born with serious learning disabilities and did poorly at early school. When he was six years old, Julian's parents took him to planet Adigeon Prime, where he underwent genetic resequencing. The procedure, illegal under Federation law, greatly enhanced his intellectual and physical abilities. When Julian learned what his parents had done, he began to feel unnatural, as if he were an artificial replacement for a defective child. Bashir's parents went to great lengths to conceal this alteration, until their secret was uncovered in 2373 by **Dr. Lewis Zimmerman**. ("Doctor Bashir, I Presume?" [DS9]).

In 2352, young Julian and his father, who was a diplomat, were stranded during a planetary ion storm on planet Invernia II. Father and son were forced to watch one of the local inhabitants succumb to a disease which could have been treated with a local herb. The incident left a lasting impression on Julian, and was in part responsible for his decision later to study medicine. ("Melora" [DS9]). As a child of five, Julian performed his first surgery when he stitched the leg of **Kukalaka** (*pictured*), his beloved teddy bear. Julian was so fond of Kukalaka that he kept him on a shelf in his room, even after he'd grown up. ("The Quickening" [DS9]). In addition to his medical training, Bashir took engineering extension courses at Starfleet Medical. While studying to become a physician he fell in love with Delon Palis, a ballet dancer whom he never forgot ("Armageddon Game" [DS9]). Bashir was a brilliant physician, having graduated second in his class. He would have graduated first had he not mistaken a preganglionic fiber for a postganglionic nerve. Fancying himself to be an adventurer, he requested posting to Deep Space 9 because he wanted to experience the excitement of the frontier. ("Emissary" [DS9]). Bashir was first in his class in pediatric medicine. ("To the Death" [DS9]).

As a young man on Deep Space 9, Bashir found himself attracted to the beautiful **Jadzia Dax**. Unfortunately, Dax did not return the affection, although the two had a good professional working relationship and eventually became close friends. Bashir's interest in Dax became a source of embarrassment on stardate 46853, when unknown aliens from the Gamma Quadrant, seeking to study humanoid life, created a replica of Dax who was as attracted to Bashir as he was to her. ("If Wishes Were Horses" [DS9]). Bashir became romantically involved with Ensign **Melora Pazlar** when he helped her to adapt to Deep Space 9's gravity in 2370. ("Melora" [DS9]). Bashir became romantically involved with **Leeta** for a few months, until they performed the Bajoran **Rite of Separation** on **Risa** in 2373, ending their relationship. ("Let He Who Is Without Sin..." [DS9]). Bashir enjoyed playing racquetball and was the captain of the racquetball team at Starfleet Medical Academy. He sometimes played racquetball on Deep Space 9 with Miles O'Brien. ("Rivals" [DS9]). He befriended **Elim Garak**, and despite his initial distrust, Bashir began to respect Garak's insights. ("Cardassians" [DS9]). Bashir's fantasy life included indulging in a holosuite adventure in which he played a colorful **secret agent** who worked for the British government in 1960's era Earth. ("Our Man Bashir" [DS9]). Bashir suspected he was experiencing a **predestination paradox** when he traveled back in time to 2267 and met **Lieutenant Watley**, a woman he thought might have been his great-grandmother, aboard the original *Starship Enterprise*. ("Trials and Tribble-ations" [DS9]).

Bashir worked hard to relieve suffering on many worlds, often at great personal risk to himself. He spent several weeks in 2372 trying unsuccessfully to find a cure for the addiction to ketracel-white that kept the Jem'Hadar under Dominion control. ("Hippocratic Oath" [DS9]). He also sought to discover a cure for the **Teplan blight** that plagued the entire population of a planet in the **Teplan system**, and was successful in identifying and developing an inoculation against a deadly pathogen that had taken thousands of lives on **Boranis III**. ("The Quickening" [DS9]).

In 2371, Bashir's research in biomolecular replication was recognized when he was nominated for that year's **Carrington Award**, becoming the youngest nominee in the history of the prize. ("Prophet Motive" [DS9]).

In 2373, while attending a burn treatment conference on Meezan IV, Bashir was abducted by the **Dominion** and replaced by a **Founder**. The changeling infiltrator hijacked the runabout *Yukon* and attempted to destroy the Bajoran sun with a **trilithium** explosive. Bashir, meanwhile, was held captive by the Jem'Hadar at **Dominion internment camp 371**, on an asteroid in the

Gamma Quadrant. ("In Purgatory's Shadow" [DS9], "By Inferno's Light" [DS9]).

Bashir was first seen in "Emissary" (DS9). Alexander Siddig was originally listed as "Siddig El Fadil" during the first three seasons of Star Trek: Deep Space Nine. *He changed his screen credit to Alexander Siddig at the beginning of the show's fourth season.*

Bashir, Julian (mirror). (Alexander Siddig). In the **mirror universe**, Julian Bashir resided on station **Terok Nor (mirror)**, and was an argumentative member of the **Terran resistance**. ("Crossover" [DS9], "Through the Looking Glass" [DS9]). By 2372, Bashir (mirror) had become a captain in the resistance, and as pilot of a **Rebel raider ship**, he helped fend off an **Alliance** fleet that threatened the rebel-held Terok Nor (mirror). ("Shattered Mirror" [DS9]).

Bashir, Richard. (Brian George). Husband to **Amsha Bashir** and father of **Julian Bashir**. Bashir held a wide variety of jobs during his life, ranging from serving as a ship's steward ("Doctor Bashir, I Presume?" [DS9]) to a stint in the diplomatic corps. ("Melora" [DS9]). Bashir and his wife were deeply concerned when their young son, Julian, exhibited serious learning disabilities. When Julian was six years old, Richard took him to planet **Adigeon Prime** to undergo an illegal genetic engineering procedure. While the DNA resequencing greatly enhanced Julian's intellectual and physical abilities, it led to a rift between father and son because Julian felt himself to be an unnatural replacement for a defective child. Although the Bashir family was successful in maintaining the secret of Julian's alteration for many years, the truth was revealed in 2373. Richard Bashir pled guilty to illegal genetic engineering and accepted a two-year sentence at the **Federation Penal Settlement** in New Zealand. Under the terms of his guilty plea, Julian Bashir was permitted to retain his Starfleet commission and his medical degree, since he was not responsible for his father's actions. ("Doctor Bashir, I Presume?" [DS9]).

Basic Warp Drive. A required engineering course taught at Starfleet Academy. The first chapter of the course's text was entitled "**Zefram Cochrane**." *(Star Trek: First Contact).*

"Basics, Part I." *Voyager* episode #43. Written by Michael Piller. Directed by Winrich Kolbe. No stardate given. *First aired in 1996. The Kazon-Nistrim take control of* Voyager *via an elaborate trap involving Seska's infant who is purported to be Chakotay's son. This episode, the last of the second season, was a cliff-hanger that was resolved in the opening episode of the third season.* GUEST CAST: Brad Dourif as **Suder, Lon**; Anthony DeLongis as **Culluh, Jal**; John Gegenhuber as **Tierna**; Martha Hackett as **Seska**; Henry Darrow as **Kolopak**. SEE: **alpha search pattern; autonomic response analysis; Ce Acatl; Culluh, Jal; echo displacement; floriculture; Gema IV; gene splicing; Hanon IV; Kolopak; *leola* root; nitrogen tetroxide; polycythemia; Prema II; pulmozine; security access code; Seska; Suder, Lon; Tenarus cluster; Tierna; Tuvok orchid.**

"Basics, Part II." *Voyager* episode #46. Written by Michael Piller. Directed by Winrich Kolbe. Stardate 50032.7. *First aired in 1996. The crew of the* Voyager, *stranded on a primitive world, struggles for survival while Paris, Suder, and the Doctor plot to wrest control of their ship back from the Kazon. This episode was actually the last episode filmed for* Voyager's *second season, although it was aired as the first episode of the third season. "Basics, Part II" resolved the cliff-hanger final episode of the second season. Seska and Suder die in this episode.* GUEST CAST: Brad Dourif as **Suder, Lon**; Anthony DeLongis as **Culluh, Jal**; Martha Hackett as **Seska**; Nancy Hower as **Wildman, Samantha**; Simon Billig as **Hogan**, Scott Haven as Kazon; David Cowgill as Hanonian; Michael Bailey Smith as Hanonian; John Kenton Shull as Kazon. SEE: **Culluh, Jal; Hanon IV; Hanonian land eel; Hogan; improvoline; Paxim; phaser power coupling; security access code; Seska; stasis unit; Suder, Lon; Talaxian fighter; thoron; Torres, B'Elanna; tricorder; Tuvok; Vulcan Institute of Defensive Arts.**

basilar arterial scan. Medical diagnostic test. A basilar arterial scan evaluates the arteries in the brainstem. ("Visionary" [DS9]).

Basotile. A two-meter-high, metallic abstract sculpture that was hundreds of years old. The rare art piece was owned by 24th-century collector **Kivas Fajo**. ("The Most Toys" [TNG]).

***bat'leth* competition.** Klingon martial arts contest. A *bat'leth* competition was held on planet **Forcas III** in 2370. Worf took shore leave in order to compete in the contest, and won Champion Standing, returning to the *Enterprise*-D with an impressive trophy. (In some alternate **quantum realities** visited by Worf, he did not in fact take Champion Standing, but ninth place. In yet another reality, Worf did not attend at all, but sent his brother, **Kurn**, in his stead.) ("Parallels" [TNG]).

***Bat'leth,* Order of the.** Elite group of Klingon warriors honored for their courage and strength. Members of the order were inducted at a ceremony at which they were presented a medal by the chancellor of the empire. Before the induction ceremony, the warriors gathered in the **Hall of Warriors** at **Ty'Gokor** and underwent an initiation rite that was an endurance test as much as it was a celebration. ("Apocalypse Rising" [DS9]).

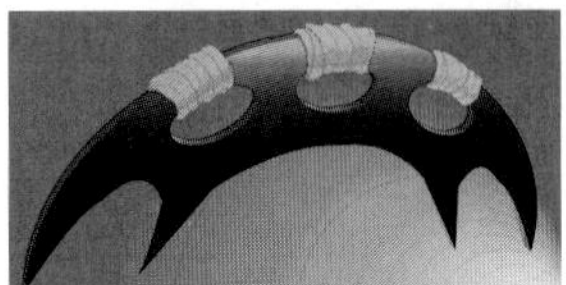

bat'leth. The traditional Klingon "sword of honor," resembling a meter-long two-ended scimitar. The *bat'leth* was carried along the inside of the arm and controlled by handholds located on the outside edge of the weapon. ("Reunion" [TNG]). Oral history holds that the first *bat'leth* was forged about 1,500 years ago when **Kahless the Unforgettable** dropped a lock of his hair in the lava from the **Kri'stak Volcano** and then plunged the burning lock into the lake of **Lursor** and twisted it into a blade. After forging the weapon, he used it to kill the tyrant **Molor** and named it the "*bat'leth,*" or sword of honor. This tale of the sword was never recorded in the sacred texts, but was passed down verbally among the high clerics. The retelling of the tale was to be a test of Kahless's return, as only he and the high clerics would know the story. SEE: **Story of the Promise, The.** ("Rightful Heir" [TNG]). The **Sword of Kahless** was stolen about five centuries after Kahless's death by **Hur'q** invaders, who plundered the Homeworld. ("The Sword of Kahless" [DS9]). Worf owned a *bat'leth* that had been in his family for ten generations. He used this weapon to kill **Duras**, after Duras had murdered **K'Ehleyr**. ("Reunion" [TNG]). Worf also instructed Dr. Beverly Crusher in the use of the *bat'leth*. ("The Quality of Life" [TNG]). A modern *bat'leth* is typically 116 centimeters long, composed of *baakonite* metal, weighing 5.3 kilograms. ("Blood Oath" [DS9]). *The* bat'leth *was designed by martial-arts expert (and* Star Trek *visual effects producer) Dan Curry, who also helped develop the intricate dancelike movements associated with its use.*

Batai (young). (Daniel Stewart, Logan White). A native of the planet **Kataan** and son of the ironweaver **Kamin**. Young Batai was named after Kamin's friend, council leader of the **Ressik** community a thousand years ago, prior to the explosion of the star Kataan. Memories of him were preserved aboard a space probe launched from Kataan. The probe encountered the *Starship Enterprise*-D in 2368, transferring its memories, including the memory of Batai, to Jean-Luc Picard. ("The Inner Light" [TNG]). *Daniel Stewart,*

pictured, is actor Patrick Stewart's son, an appropriate bit of casting since the elder Stewart played Batai's father.

Batai. (Richard Riele). A native of the planet **Kataan** and the council leader of the **Ressik** community. He was a good friend of **Kamin**, who named his son after Batai. ("The Inner Light" [TNG]).

Batanides, Marta. (J. C. Brandy). Starfleet officer and an academy classmate of **Jean-Luc Picard**. Batanides and Picard graduated together in 2327, after which the two young ensigns were transferred to **Starbase Earhart**, awaiting their first deep-space assignments. When Q allowed Picard to relive this portion of his life many years later, Picard acted on a long-held desire to be more than "just friends" with Marta. Unfortunately, the liaison strained their friendship. ("Tapestry" [TNG]).

Bataraei. Traditional celebration observed on **Halii**, Aquiel's homeworld. At the Bataraei, **Aquiel Uhnari** would sing the **Horath**, a beautiful song. ("Aquiel" [TNG]).

***bateret* leaves.** Form of Bajoran incense used in celebration of the **Bajoran Gratitude Festival.** ("Rapture" [DS9]).

Bates, Hannah. (Dey Young). A member of the isolated **Genome Colony** on planet **Moab IV**. Bates was genetically engineered to be a scientist and was the colony's expert on their biosphere and maintaining its environment. Bates worked with Commander La Forge to develop a solution to the problem of an approaching **stellar core fragment** in 2368. After her exposure to people outside the closed society of the colony, Bates was unwilling to remain in the isolated community. She asked for and was granted asylum aboard *the Enterprise*-D, despite fears from colony leaders that her absence and the absence of others would damage the carefully designed society. ("The Masterpiece Society" [TNG]). *Dey Young also played Arissa in "A Simple Investigation" (DS9).*

Bateson, Captain Morgan. (Kelsey Grammer). Commanding officer of the Federation *Starship* **Bozeman**. Bateson, along with the rest of his crew, was trapped in a **temporal causality loop** for 90 years, emerging in 2368. ("Cause and Effect" [TNG]). *Kelsey Grammer starred in* Cheers *and* Frasier, *both filmed at Paramount Pictures.*

Batris. A **Talarian** freighter ship. The *Batris* was hijacked by renegade Klingons in 2364. The ship exploded shortly after three of the hijackers were rescued by an away team from the *Starship Enterprise*-D. SEE: **Korris, Captain**. ("Heart of Glory" [TNG]). *The* Batris *was a modification of a Visitor freighter from the miniseries* V. *The* Batris *itself was further modified and seen as a variety of other freighters in later episodes, presumably suggesting that it is a design in use by many different planets. The* Batris *was built by Greg Jein. SEE:* **Antares-class carrier**.

Battle Bridge. Secondary control center on ***Galaxy*-class starships** from which battle operations can be controlled. Located in the **stardrive** (or **battle**) **section** of the starship, the Battle Bridge is normally used when the **Saucer Module** (containing the main bridge) is separated from the ship. ("Encounter at Farpoint, Part I" [TNG]). *The Battle Bridge was also seen in "The Arsenal of Freedom" (TNG) and "The Best of Both Worlds, Part II" (TNG).*

"Battle Lines." *Deep Space Nine* episode #13. Teleplay by Richard Danus and Evan Carlos Somers. Story by Hilary D. Bader. Directed by Paul Lynch. No stardate given. *First aired in 1993. Bajoran spiritual leader Kai Opaka is killed, then resurrected on a planet of eternal war.* GUEST CAST: Camille Saviola as **Opaka, Kai**; Paul Collins as **Zlangco**; Jonathan Banks as **Shel-La, Golin**; Majel Barrett as Computer voice. SEE: **Bajoran wormhole; delta radiation; differential magnetomer; Ennis; Idran; Kira Nerys; mutual induction field; Nol-Ennis; Opaka, Kai; *Rio Grande, U.S.S.*; Shel-la, Golin; *Yangtzee Kiang, U.S.S.*; Zlangco.**

Battle of Britain. Series of aerial attacks directed against Great Britain by the German Air Force during Earth's second world war. The battle, which employed primitive slower-than-light aircraft, raged from June, 1940 until about April, 1941. Julian Bashir and Miles O'Brien enjoyed a holosuite program of the Battle of Britain on station Deep Space 9 in 2372. ("Homefront" [DS9], "Accession" [DS9]). SEE: **Spitfire**.

Battle of Cheron. SEE: **Cheron, Battle of.**

Battle of Clontarf. Historic conflict between a thousand Irish warriors and a horde of ravening Vikings that took place on Earth in 1014. The battle was a disastrous defeat for the Irish, led by **King Brian Boru**. Chief Miles O'Brien owned a holosuite re-creation of the battle. ("Bar Association" [DS9]).

Battle of *HarOs*, the. Glorious Klingon campaign. The Battle of *HarOs* was depicted in an abstract painting done by Commander Data for Worf's 30th birthday. ("Parallels" [TNG]).

Battle of Wolf 359. SEE: **Wolf 359**.

battle cruiser. SEE: **Klingon battle cruiser**.

battle section. Alternate term for **stardrive section.** The portion of a ***Galaxy*-class** starship remaining after the **Saucer Module** has been separated. ("Encounter at Farpoint, Part I" [TNG]). SEE: **Battle Bridge**.

battle simulation, Starfleet. A combat exercise conducted in 2365 between the *U.S.S. Enterprise*-D and the *Starship Hathaway*. The war game was an effort to assess Starfleet readiness. *Enterprise*-D captain Jean-Luc Picard initially opposed this exercise on the grounds that Starfleet's primary mission is not military, but relented because of the need to prepare for the **Borg** threat. ("Peak Performance" [TNG]).

"Battle, The." *Next Generation* episode #10. Teleplay by Herbert J. Wright. Story by Larry Forrester. Directed by Rob Bowman. Stardate 41723.9. *First aired in 1987. A Ferengi commander offers Picard a gift: the hulk of his old ship, the* U.S.S. Stargazer. GUEST CAST: Frank Corsentino as **Bok, DaiMon**; Doug Warhit as **Kazago**; Robert Towers as **Rata**. SEE: **Bok, DaiMon; *Constellation*-class starship; cold, common; escape pod; Kazago; Maxia Zeta Star System; Maxia, Battle of; Picard, Jean-Luc; Picard Maneuver; Rata; *Stargazer, U.S.S.*; thought maker; Vigo; Xendi Sabu star system; Xendi Starbase 9.**

Baxter, Lieutenant. (Tom Virtue). Starfleet officer on the *U.S.S. Voyager*. Prior to stardate 48579, he complained of exercise-related injuries. ("Eye of the Needle" [VGR]). Baxter was a frequent user of the *Starship Voyager's* **gymnasium**. ("Twisted" [VGR]).

Baytart, Pablo. Officer aboard the *U.S.S. Voyager*. Ensign Baytart was an exceptional pilot who once instructed Neelix on basic **shuttlecraft** operations. ("Parturition" [VGR]). Baytart was quite adept at juggling; he was scheduled to demonstrate this talent on *A Briefing With Neelix* ("Investigations" [VGR]). Baytart's quarters were adjacent to Ensign Kim's. ("The Thaw" [VGR]).

Beach, Commander. (Paul Kent). Officer on the *Starship* ***Reliant*** under the command of Captain **Clark Terrell** in 2285. *(Star Trek II: The Wrath of Khan).*

Beagle, S.S. Small class-IV stardrive survey vessel with a crew of 47, commanded by Captain **R. M. Merrick**. The *S.S. Beagle* was exploring star system Eight Ninety-Two in 2261, when it was damaged by meteors and drifted toward the fourth planet of that system. The crew of the *Beagle* was eventually captured by the inhabitants of planet Eight Ninety-Two-IV. ("Bread and Circuses" [TOS]). SEE: **Eight Ninety-Two-IV**.

beam. Colloquial term for travel by matter-energy transport, as in "Beam me up." SEE: **transporter**. *Ironically, the catch-phrase "Beam me up, Scotty" was never actually spoken by Captain Kirk in any episode of the original series.*

beans. Traditional Earth culinary delicacy. Dr. Leonard McCoy, a native of Earth, was proud of his recipe for beans. McCoy's dish involved simmering bipodal seeds in sauce prepared from an old Southern recipe handed down from his father. McCoy, who served the dish to Kirk and Spock when the three of them camped in Yosemite in 2287, was particularly proud of the secret ingredient, Tennessee whiskey. *(Star Trek V: The Final Frontier).*

bearing. In celestial navigation, a mathematical expression describing a direction in space with relationship to a space vehicle. A bearing measures the angular difference between the current forward direction of the spacecraft and the direction being described. The first number in a bearing describes an azimuth in degrees, and the second describes an elevation. For example, a bearing of 000 mark 0 describes a direction directly ahead of the vessel. A bearing of 330 mark 15 describes a direction to the port side (left) of the ship, somewhat above the centerline of the vessel. SEE: **heading**.

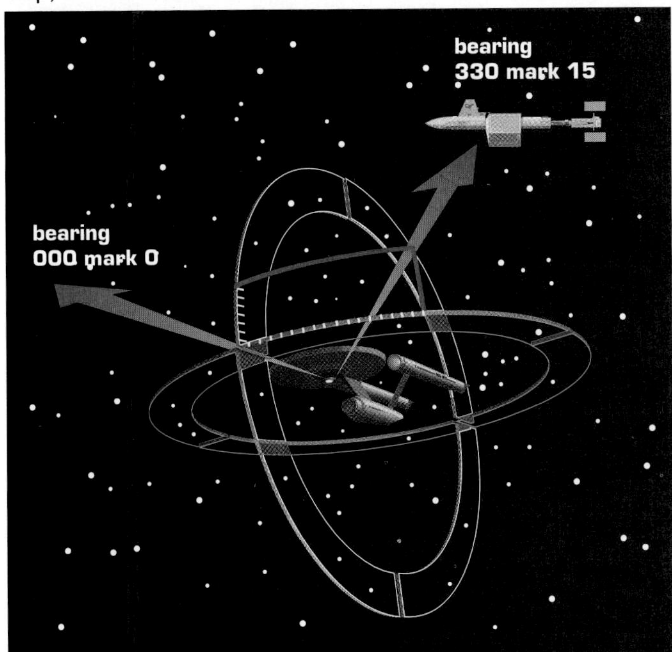

Beata. (Karen Montgomery). Leader of the government on planet **Angel One** in 2364. Beata, who carried the title of **The Elected One**, attempted to maintain the planet's tradition of treating their males as second-class citizens, although she acknowledged that this might eventually change over time. ("Angel One" [TNG]).

Beauregard. Nickname given by Sulu to an unusual plant in the *Enterprise*'s botany lab in 2266. Beauregard—who Sulu insisted should be called Gertrude—seemed to be fond of Janice Rand, almost purring in her presence. ("The Man Trap" [TOS]). *Notes Bob Justman, "I'd purr, too." Beauregard was a hand puppet operated by Bob Baker. He may have been named for* Star Trek *makeup artist Fred Phillips, whose middle name was Beauregard.*

Beck. Obstetrical nurse assigned to the *Enterprise*-D medical section after leaving Starbase 218 in 2369. ("Lessons" [TNG]). *Named for Don Beck, who produced promotional preview commercials for* Star Trek: The Next Generation *and* Star Trek: Deep Space Nine.

"Before and After." Voyager episode #63. Written by Kenneth Biller. Directed by Allan Kroeker. No stardate given. *First aired in 1997. In the future, when Kes undergoes treatment to extend her lifespan, she is sent out of temporal synch. She then travels back and forth through time glimpsing the future of the Voyager's crew.* GUEST CAST: Jessica Collins as **Paris, Linnis;** Michael L. Maguire as **Benaren**; Christopher Augilar as **Kim, Andrew**; Janna Michaels as young Kes; Rachel Harris as **Martis**. SEE: **antichroniton; Benaren; bio-temporal chamber; Carey, Joseph; chroniton torpedo; chroniton; Emergency Medical Hologram; entropy; Kes; Krenim; Martis; MEV; morilogium; Mozart, Wolfgang Amadeus; Paris, Linnis; Paris, Thomas; roentgen; Yattho.**

"Begotten, The." *Deep Space Nine* episode #110. Written by René Echevarria. Directed by Jesús Salvador Trevio. No stardate given. *First aired in 1996. Odo becomes the guardian of an infant changeling, and Kira gives birth to Miles and Keiko O'Brien's child. Odo becomes a shape-shifter again in this episode.* GUEST CAST: Rosalind Chao as **O'Brien, Keiko**; Duncan Regehr as **Shakaar Edon**; Peggy Roeder as **Y'Pora**; James Sloyan as **Mora Pol, Dr.** SEE: **Alvanian spine mite; Bajorans; biomimetic fluctuation; champagne; changeling infant; endorphins; Filian python; Founders; holodeck and holosuite programs; Kira Nerys; Mora Pol, Dr.; morphogenic matrix; O'Brien, Keiko; O'Brien, Kirayoshi; O'Brien, Miles; Odo; Orion animal women; Shakaar Edon; Tarkalean hawk; tetryon; Y'Pora; zero-grav tumbling.**

behavioral nodes. Program artifacts in Data's positronic net created by exposure to the **D'Arsay archive** in 2370. The nodes used Data to recreate D'Arsan mythological characters from the archive, much as it was using the replicators of the *Enterprise*-D to create artifacts from that civilization. ("Masks" [TNG]). SEE: **D'Arsay; Ihat; Korgano; Masaka.**

Bek, Prylar. (Tom Villard). Bajoran monk who was a liaison between the **Cardassians** and the **Vedek Assembly** during the occupation of Bajor, when **Kubus Oak** was Secretary to the occupational government. Bek was believed to have collaborated with the Cardassians, providing them with information leading to the infamous **Kendra Valley massacre**. Bek committed suicide after the incident, hanging himself on the **Promenade** of station **Terok Nor**, and leaving behind a full confession. It was not known that Bek was, in fact, innocent, and that he had been covering up for **Kai Opaka**'s involvement in the massacre. ("The Collaborator" [DS9]). *Also named for Don Beck.* SEE: **Beck**.

Belak. **Romulan** *warbird.* The *Belak* was part of the fleet assembled by the **Tal Shiar** and **Obsidian Order** in 2371 that was lost in a strike against the Founders' homeworld. ("The Die is Cast" [DS9]).

belaklavion. Traditional Bajoran musical instrument. **Ro Laren**'s father played the belaklavion for her during her childhood. **Macias** also played the belaklavion, saying he enjoyed the challenge. ("Preemptive Strike" [TNG]).

Belar, Joran. (Jeff Magnus McBride). Composer, born 2264 and died 2285. Belar applied and was accepted to the Trill **initiate** program. Official Trill records report that in 2285, during the second year of his initiate training, Belar murdered a physician with the **Trill Symbiosis Commission** who had recommended that Belar be dropped from the program. Belar was killed trying to flee the murder scene. ("Equilibrium" [DS9]). SEE: **Dax, Joran**.

Belar, Yolad. (Harvey Vernon). Composer, brother to **Joran Belar**. In 2371, Yolad was questioned by Deep Space 9 personnel about his memories regarding the death of his brother. ("Equilibrium" [DS9]).

Belar. (Victor Bevine). Bajoran man who was a resistance fighter during the occupation. In 2367 he was present on station **Terok Nor** during the time that **Ishan Chaye**, **Jillur Gueta**, and **Timor Landi** were wrongly accused of attempting to assassinate Gul Dukat. ("Things Past" [DS9]). *Victor Bevine also played a guard in* Star Trek: First Contact*.*

Bele. (Frank Gorshin). Chief officer of the Commission on Political Traitors from the planet **Cheron**. Bele pursued an accused criminal named **Lokai** across the galaxy for fifty thousand years. White on the left side of his body and black on the right, Bele harbored racial prejudice against those of his people who were of opposite coloring. In 2268 Bele commandeered the *Enterprise* to take him and his prisoner back to Cheron, but learned that racial hatred had long since destroyed their homeworld. ("Let That Be Your Last Battlefield" [TOS]). *Bele's scout ship was conveniently invisible, a clever way for the show to save money on visual effects.*

Bell Riots. Watershed event in American history on Earth, in which internees of **San Francisco**'s infamous **Sanctuary District** A took several government employees hostage in early September 2024. The ensuing riots, which were among the most violent civil uprisings in American history, were triggered by years of inhumane treatment by the American government of homeless, unemployed, and mentally ill people. Hundreds of protesters were killed when the government quelled the disturbance, but thanks to **Gabriel Bell**, no hostages were harmed. The event made the American people aware of the injustice of the Sanctuary Districts, leading to much-needed social reforms and the closing of the Sanctuaries. Named for protest leader **Gabriel Bell**, who was killed protecting the hostages. ("Past Tense, Parts I and II" [DS9]). SEE: **Brynner, Christopher.** *Twenty-first century history did not record the fact that Bell was actually killed shortly before the riots, and that Benjamin Sisko assumed his identity so that history could follow its proper course.*

Bell, Gabriel. (John Lendale Bennett, Avery Brooks). Resident of **Sanctuary District A** in San Francisco on **Earth** in 2024, regarded as the man responsible for the relatively peaceful resolution of the violent **Bell Riots**. During the riots, Bell guarded government hostages held by the rebellious residents in a district processing center. When government troops stormed the place, killing hundreds of residents, Bell gave his life to protect the hostages. His sacrifice made the **Bell Riots** one of the watershed events of the 21st century and led to the closure of the Sanctuary Districts throughout the United States. In 2371, a transporter accident deposited Commander **Benjamin Sisko**, and other *Starship Defiant* personnel, in San Francisco in 2024. While there, they inadvertently precipitated the death of Gabriel Bell *before* the riots. Benjamin Sisko was forced to take Bell's place to ensure that the Bell Riots would have the necessary effect on the social policy of 21st-century America. Accordingly, in the current timeline, historical photos of Gabriel Bell are now the image of Benjamin Sisko. ("Past Tense, Parts I and II" [DS9]). Oddly enough, Nog, studying a text on Earth history, did notice a resemblance between Bell and Sisko, although Quark said it was because he thought that all humans look alike to Ferengi. ("Little Green Men" [DS9]). *John Lendale Bennett, who played the original Bell, has also portrayed Kozak in "House of Quark" (DS9).*

Bell, Lieutenant Dan. (William Boyett). Fictional character from the **Dixon Hill** detective stories. Bell was a gruff career police officer who interrogated Hill after the murder of **Jessica Bradley**. A holographic version of Bell was part of the Dixon Hill **holodeck** programs. ("The Big Goodbye" [TNG]).

Belongo. Nephew of the Ferengi Grand Nagus **Zek**. In 2371, Belongo was held by Starfleet authorities on **Aldebaran** III for some minor transgression. ("Past Tense, Part I" [DS9]).

Beloti Sector. Region of space. Destination of the *U.S.S. Denver* in 2368, just before the ship hit a **gravitic mine**. ("Ethics" [TNG]).

Beltane IX. Planet that serves as a center for commercial-shipping space travel. **Jake Kurland** once threatened to run away to Beltane IX to sign onto a freighter. ("Coming of Age" [TNG]).

Belzoidian flea. Life-form. **Q** claimed he could have chosen to become a Belzoidian flea when he was stripped of his powers in 2366. For some reason, he instead chose to become human. ("Deja Q" [TNG]).

Bemar. Security chief of the **Prophet's Landing** colony in 2371. ("Heart of Stone" [DS9]).

Ben. (Bruce Beatty). Waiter who worked in the *Enterprise*-D's **Ten-Forward Lounge**. He sometimes played poker with the junior officers and with the senior officers on the ship. ("Lower Decks" [TNG]).

Benaren. (Michael L. Maguire). Ocampa man, father of **Kes**. ("Dreadnought" [VGR]). Benaren was married to a woman named **Martis**. ("Before and After" [VGR]). Benaren died in 2371, when his daughter, Kes, was one year old. ("Resolutions" [VGR]). *Benaren was first seen in "Before and After" (VGR). Michael Maguire won a Tony award for his portrayal of Enjolras in the Broadway production of* Les Misérables.

Benbeck, Martin. (Ron Canada). Member of the isolated **Genome colony** on planet **Moab IV**. Benbeck was genetically engineered for his function as the interpreter of the society's laws. Benbeck advised strongly against allowing the crew of the *Enterprise*-D to visit their colony in 2368, despite the fact that outside assistance was required to prevent the close passage of a massive **stellar core fragment** from destroying the colony. ("The Masterpiece Society" [TNG]). *Ron Canada also played Ch'Pok in "Rules of Engagement" (DS9).*

Bender, Slade. (Robert Costanza). Character in the **Dixon Hill** detective novels. In one such story, Bender tried to shoot Hill. The Dixon Hill **holodeck** program included a holographic representation of Bender. ("Manhunt" [TNG]).

Bendera, Kurt. (K. Gruz). *Voyager* crew member who served in engineering. A former member of the **Maquis**, Bendera met *Starship Voyager*'s commander Chakotay in a mining community on the planet **Telfas Prime**. Bendera was killed in 2372 in a Kazon attack. ("Alliances" [VGR]).

Bendii Syndrome. Rare illness that sometimes affects **Vulcans** over the age of 200. The disease is characterized by gradual loss of emotional control; victims exhibit sudden bursts of emotion and irrational anger. Diagnosis is made by culturing tissue from the patient's metathalamus. A dangerous side effect of Bendii Syndrome is that the loss of emotional control can be telepathically projected to others. Ambassador **Sarek** was afflicted with Bendii Syndrome at the age of 202, endangering his last diplomatic mission. ("Sarek" [TNG]). Sarek eventually succumbed to Bendii Syndrome at his home on **Vulcan**, in 2368. ("Unification, Part I" [TNG]).

Benecia Colony. Federation settlement. The **Karidian Company of Players** had been scheduled to perform at the Benecia Colony following their engagement at **Planet Q** in 2266. ("The Conscience of the King" [TOS]). Dr. **Janice Lester** had hoped to send her former self, when it imprisoned the mind of James Kirk, to the Benecia Colony in 2269. Benecia's medical facilities were limited, so the chances of Lester's theft of Kirk's body being discovered were minimal. ("Turnabout Intruder" [TOS]).

Benev Selec. One of the star systems in the **Selcundi Drema** sector. Wesley Crusher ordered Ensign Davies to conduct an **icospectrogram** on the Benev Selec system. ("Pen Pals" [TNG]).

Benil, Gul. (Christopher Carroll). Captain of a ***Galor*-class Cardassian warship**. In 2371, Benil's ship intercepted the Federation starship *Defiant* on a rescue mission to planet **Cardassia**. ("Second Skin" [DS9]). SEE: **holo-filter**.

benjisidrine. Drug. Vulcan physicians prescribed benjisidrine for treatment of Ambassador **Sarek**'s heart condition. ("Journey to Babel" [TOS]).

Bennet, Ensign. (Richard Garon). Crew member aboard the *Starship Voyager*. Bennet was killed in a shuttlecraft crash in 2372 during a geological survey mission to one of the moons of planet **Drayan II**. ("Innocence" [VGR]).

Bennett, Admiral Robert. (Harve Bennett). Starfleet chief-of-staff in 2287. Bennett assigned Kirk and the *Enterprise*-A to rescue Federation Representative **St. John Talbot** at planet **Nimbus III**, despite the fact that the *Enterprise* was far from operational at the time. (*Star Trek V: The Final Frontier*). *This character, whom Kirk addressed as "Bob," had no last name in the movie or the script, but we're calling him Admiral Bennett because he was played by* Star Trek *feature film writer-producer Harve Bennett, making a cameo appearance.*

Bennett, Rear Admiral. (J. Patrick McCormack). Starfleet official. Bennett was part of Starfleet's **Judge Advocate General** and presided in the 2373 case of **Richard Bashir** for illegal genetic engineering. Bennett sentenced Bashir to two years at the **Federation Penal Settlement** in New Zealand. ("Doctor Bashir, I Presume?" [DS9]).

Bensen, Bjorn. (Gerard Prendergast). Chief engineer of the unsuccessful **terraforming** project at planet **Velara III** in 2364. ("Home Soil" [TNG]).

Benteen, Erika. (Susan Gibney). Starfleet officer. Benteen served at Starfleet Command as adjutant to **Admiral Leyton** in 2372. ("Homefront" [DS9]). Around stardate 49170, Leyton promoted Benteen to the rank of captain and assigned her to command the *U.S.S. Lakota*. Although Benteen was loyal to Leyton and supported his attempted coup of the Earth government, she refused to obey an order from Leyton to destroy the starship *Defiant*. ("Paradise Lost" [DS9]). *Susan Gibney previously portrayed Dr. Leah Brahms in "Booby Trap" (TNG) and "Galaxy's Child" (TNG). Benteen's first name was not mentioned in dialog, but is from the script.*

Benton. (Seamon Glass). One of the three miners at the **Rigel XII** lithium-mining station in 2266. ("Mudd's Women" [TOS]).

Benzan. (Kieran Mulroney). Son of Secretary **Kushell** of the planet **Straleb**. Benzan had been secretly engaged to marry **Yanar** of the planet **Altec**, and was the father of her child. Benzan nearly triggered an interplanetary incident in 2365 after giving Yanar the **Jewel of Thesia** as a pledge of marriage. ("The Outrageous Okona" [TNG]).

Benzar. Homeworld to the **Benzites**. ("Coming of Age" [TNG]). Benzar, a recent member of the Federation, has an atmosphere similar to Class-M norms, but Benzites in a Class-M environment need a respiration device to provide supplemental gases for them to breathe. ("A Matter of Honor" [TNG]).

Benzites. Humanoid inhabitants of the planet **Benzar**. Ensign **Mendon** served briefly aboard the *Enterprise*-D as part of an **Officer Exchange Program** in 2365. Benzites from the same geostructure often look identical to a non-Benzite. ("A Matter of Honor" [TNG]). Captain Laporin, the commander of a Federation starship that was stormed by Klingons in 2372, was of Benzite ancestry. Benzites are sometimes called Benzenites. ("Apocalypse Rising" [DS9]). By 2372, advances in Benzite medical technology made it unnecessary for Benzites to use a respiration device in a Class-M atmosphere. ("The Ship" [DS9]).

benzocyatizine. Medication used to adjust the levels of **isoboramine** in joined **Trill**. A benzocyatic regimen generally involves frequent doses of benzocyatizine. ("Equilibrium" [DS9]).

Beowulf. Ancient English epic poem. Probably written in Earth's eighth century, *Beowulf* drew from Scandinavian history and folklore. The poem recounted Beowulf's fight with the water monster, Grendel, his victory over a dragon, and his later death and funeral. In 2371, Harry Kim participated in a **holonovel** reenactment of the epic poem on the *Starship Voyager*. While running the program, **photonic being**s from a nearby protostar entered the ship, resulting in the temporary loss of three *Voyager* crew members. The *Beowulf* program became the setting for **Emergency Medical Hologram**'s first away mission, as he was dispatched to investigate the disappearance of those personnel. ("Heroes and Demons" [VGR]).

Beratis. Name given to an unidentified mass murderer of women on planet **Rigel IV**. SEE: **Redjac**. ("Wolf in the Fold" [TOS]).

Berel. (George Hearn). Physician on planet **Malcor III**, and head of the **Sikla Medical facility**. In 2367, Berel cared for the injured Malcorian **Rivas Jakara**, later found to be Starfleet officer William Riker on a covert surveillance mission on the planet. Berel was relieved as head of the medical facility when he refused to endanger Riker's life for questioning by Malcorian security. ("First Contact" [TNG]).

Berellians. Society that is a member of the Federation. Berellians are not known for engineering skills, although this might be an unfair characterization. ("Redemption, Part II" [TNG]).

Berengaria VII. Planet. Dragons are an indigenous life-form on Berengaria VII. Spock told **Leila Kalomi** he'd once seen a dragon on Berengaria VII. ("This Side of Paradise" [TOS]).

Berik. (Tracey Walter). One of the renegade Ferengi who took over the *Enterprise* in 2369. ("Rascals" [TNG]).

Bering Sea. Northern region of Earth's Pacific Ocean. Two humpback whales, **George and Gracie**, were released in the Bering Sea by the **Cetacean Institute** in 1986. *(Star Trek IV: The Voyage Home).*

beritium. Metallic substance. Some **Bajoran** earrings were made out of **diamide**-laced beritium. ("The Search, Part I" [DS9]).

Berlin, Karyn. (Brenda Jean). Colonist on the former **Briori** homeworld in the Delta Quadrant. Karyn Berlin was a defense soldier who fought with **John Evansville** against the *Voyager* crew when they thought the Starfleet people were working for the Briori. ("The 37's" [VGR]).

Berlin, U.S.S. Federation starship, *Excelsior* class, Starfleet registry number NCC-14232, stationed near the **Romulan Neutral Zone** in 2364 just prior to the first Romulan violation of the zone since the **Tomed Incident**. ("Angel One" [TNG]).

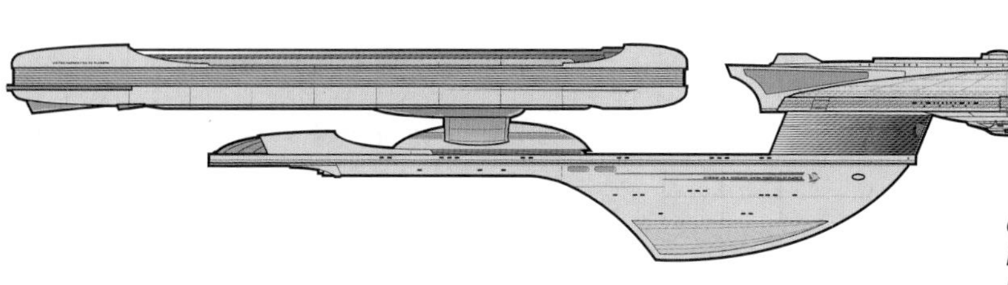

Berlioz, Hector. (1803-1869). French composer of Earth music. Captain Jean-Luc Picard listened to Berlioz in his ready room on the *Enterprise*-E in 2373. *(Star Trek: First Contact).*

Bernard, Dr. Harry, Sr. (Dierk Torsek). An oceanographer aboard the ***Starship Enterprise*-D**, and father of **Harry Bernard, Jr.** ("When the Bough Breaks" [TNG]).

Bernard, Harry, Jr. (Phillip N. Waller). Son to *Enterprise*-D crew member **Dr. Harry Bernard, Sr.** The younger Bernard, born in 2354, was kidnapped in 2364 by the **Aldeans,** who wanted to use the child to revitalize their dying race. Harry was not fond of having to study math, but his father reminded him that a basic understanding of **calculus** was expected of all children his age. ("When the Bough Breaks" [TNG]).

Bersallis firestorms. Deadly phenomena in the atmosphere of planet **Bersallis III** that occur every seven years, caused by particle emissions from the planet's sun. The storms can reach temperatures of 300 degrees Centigrade and wind velocities of over 200 kilometers per hour. In 2369, a fierce firestorm hit the planet and the *Enterprise*-D was summoned to assist with the evacuation of a Federation outpost located there. A rescue team headed by *Enterprise*-D crew member **Neela Daren** deployed a series of **thermal deflector** units to deflect some of the heat from the outpost. The intensity of the storm necessitated team members to remain to operate the defectors manually. All 643 colonists were saved, but eight *Enterprise*-D crew members lost their lives. ("Lessons" [TNG]).

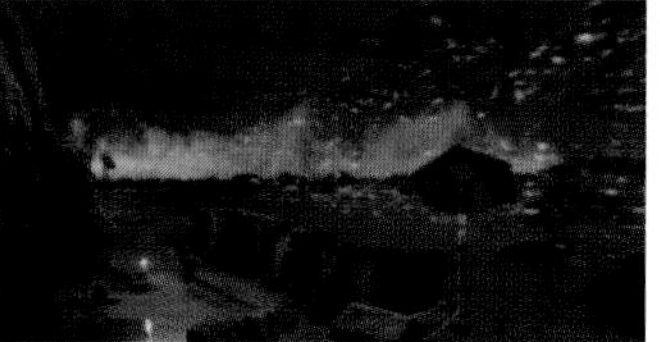

Bersallis III. Planet. Site of deadly firestorms that threatened to destroy all life at a **Federation** outpost stationed there in 2369. ("Lessons" [TNG]).

berserker cat. Wild animal known for its courage. ("Let He Who Is Without Sin..." [DS9]).

berthold rays. Deadly radiation that causes disintegration of carbon-based animal tissue, including humanoid flesh. Planet **Omicron Ceti III**, which was bombarded with berthold rays, was colonized prior to the discovery of the radiation. As a result, many members of the expedition led by **Elias Sandoval** to colonize that planet died from berthold-ray exposure in 2264. Approximately one-third of the colonists survived because they had been infected by a previously undiscovered form of alien spores. ("This Side of Paradise" [TOS]). SEE: **spores, Omicron Ceti III**. The **Calamarain** were found to emit berthold rays when they scanned the *Enterprise*-D during their encounter with that ship in 2366. ("Deja Q" [TNG]).

Bertram. Starfleet officer assigned to Deep Space 9. On stardate 50049, Bertram, Hoya and Rooney were killed when their runabout was destroyed by the Jem'Hadar at **Torga IV**. ("The Ship" [DS9]).

berylite scan. Medical procedure used aboard Federation starships. ("A Matter of Time" [TNG]).

"Best of Both Worlds, Part I, The." *Next Generation* episode #74. Written by Michael Piller. Directed by Cliff Bole. Stardate 43989.1. *First aired in 1990. Captain Picard is captured by the Borg as the long-feared confrontation between the Borg and the Federation begins. This episode, the last of the third season, was a cliff-hanger that was resolved in the opening episode of the fourth season. Picard's assimilation was later seen in greater detail in* Star Trek: First Contact. GUEST CAST: Elizabeth Dennehy as **Shelby, Lieutenant Commander**; George Murdock as **Hanson, Admiral J.P.**; Colm Meaney as **O'Brien, Miles**; Whoopi Goldberg as **Guinan**. SEE: **Borg; Borg collective; Borg queen; EM base frequencies; Hanson, Admiral J. P.; Honorius; Jouret IV; *Lalo, U.S.S.*; Locutus of Borg; magnetic resonance traces; navigational deflector; *Melbourne, U.S.S.*; Nelson, Lord Horatio; New Providence; Paulson Nebula; Picard, Jean-Luc; Riker, William T.; Sector 001; Sentinel Minor IV; shields; Shelby, Lieutenant Commander; shield nutation; Starbase 157; Starbase 324; System J-25; *Victory, H.M.S.*; Zeta Alpha II.**

"Best of Both Worlds, Part II, The." *Next Generation* episode #75. Written by Michael Piller. Directed by Cliff Bole. Stardate 44001.4. *First aired in 1990. The Borg ship decimates a Starfleet armada and threatens Earth as Riker tries to rescue Picard. The first of the fourth season, this episode resolved the cliff-hanger from Part I, but the story of Picard's rehabilitation was continued in "Family" (TNG). We saw the aftermath of the battle of Wolf 359 in this episode, although we didn't see the battle itself until the flashback scenes in "Emissary" (DS9).* Guest cast Elizabeth Dennehy as **Shelby, Lieutenant Commander**; George Murdock as **Hanson, Admiral J.P.**; Colm Meaney as **O'Brien, Miles**; Whoopi Goldberg as **Guinan**; Todd Merrill as **Gleason, Ensign.** SEE: **antimatter spread; Battle Bridge; Borg; Danula II; Earth Station McKinley; Earth; Gleason, Ensign; emergency transporter armbands; Hanson, Admiral J. P.; heavy graviton beam; Jupiter Outpost 92; *Kyushu, U.S.S.*; Locutus of Borg; Mars Defense Perimeter; *Melbourne, U.S.S.*; microcircuit fibers; multimodal reflection sorting; nanites; navigational deflector; Picard, Jean-Luc; Riker, William T.; saucer separation; Sector 001; Shelby, Lieutenant Commander; shuttle escape transporter; Starfleet Academy marathon; *Tolstoy, U.S.S.*; Wolf 359.**

Bestri Woods. Forest on planet **Bajor**. During the **Cardassian** occupation, **Kira Nerys** killed a **hara cat** in the Bestri Woods, mistaking the animal for a Cardassian soldier. ("Second Skin" [DS9]).

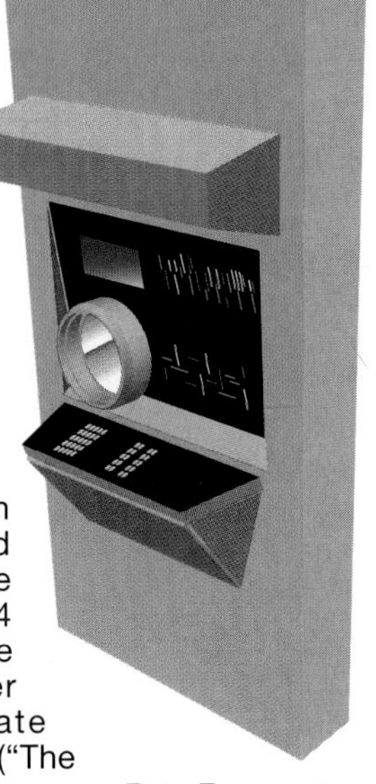
Beta 5 computer

Beta 5 computer. (Voice of Majel Barrett). Computer of extraterrestrial origin, used by Gary Seven to support operations on Earth in 1968. While a highly efficient tool, the computer, Seven felt, had a snobbish personality. ("Assignment Earth" [TOS]).

Beta Agni II. Class-M planet, site of a Federation colony. The Beta Agni II colony experienced a sudden **tricyanate** contamination of its water supply in 2366. The contamination was neutralized with the assistance of the *Enterprise*-D, which obtained an adequate supply of **hytritium**, and delivered it into the planet's subsurface water supply by means of a class-4 probe. The incident turned out to have been engineered by **Zibalian** trader **Kivas Fajo**, as part of an elaborate scheme to capture the android Data. ("The Most Toys" [TNG]).

Beta Antares IV. Planet. Origin of the card game **fizzbin**, at least according to Captain James T. Kirk. ("A Piece of the Action" [TOS]).

Beta Aurigae. Binary star system. The original *Starship Enterprise* was to rendezvous with the *U.S.S. Potemkin* at the Beta Aurigae system for a gravitational-phenomena study. While en route, Dr. Janice Lester, in Captain Kirk's body, ordered the ship's course changed to the **Benecia Colony**. ("Turnabout Intruder" [TOS]).

Beta Cassius. SEE: **Haven**. ("Haven" [TNG]).

Beta Geminorum system. Star system that contained planets **Pollux IV** and **V**. The *Enterprise* investigated the Beta Geminorum system in 2267 when the entity named **Apollo** stopped the ship and demanded the crew beam down to Pollux IV. ("Who Mourns for Adonais?" [TOS]).

Beta III. Class-M planet located in star system **C-111**. The humanoid inhabitants of Beta III once had a technologically advanced, but war-ridden society. Some 6,000 years ago, a great leader named **Landru** united these people by returning them to a simpler time. Upon his death, Landru's leadership was continued by a sophisticated computer system that governed the people. The computer interpreted Landru's philosophies very literally, resulting in the creation of an oppressive society with virtually no individual freedom. This Landru destroyed the *Starship Archon* and absorbed its crew in 2167. The computer's rule continued until 2267, when Landru was destroyed while attempting to absorb the crew of the *Starship Enterprise*. ("Return of the Archons" [TOS]).

Beta Kupsic. Planet. Destination of the *Enterprise*-D after its layover at **Starbase Montgomery** in 2365. ("The Icarus Factor" [TNG]).

Beta Lankal. Planetary system in Klingon space. Forces loyal to **Gowron** were forced to retreat and regroup there following their defeat in the **Mempa system** during the **Klingon civil war** in 2368. ("Redemption, Part II" [TNG]).

Beta Magellan. Star system in which the planet **Bynaus** is located. The system's star went nova in 2364, threatening the society living on planet Bynaus. ("11001001" [TNG]). SEE: **Bynars**.

Beta Moon. One of two inhabited satellites orbiting planet **Peliar Zel**. The population of Beta Moon suffered detrimental environmental effects when **Alpha Moon** used Peliar Zel's magnetic field as a power source. The two moons, historically at odds, sought the mediation services of **Ambassador Odan** to resolve the conflict in 2367. ("The Host" [TNG]).

Beta Niobe. Star that went nova in 2269, destroying the Class-M planet **Sarpeidon**, its only satellite. ("All Our Yesterdays" [TOS]).

Beta Portolan system. Home of an ancient civilization whose population was wiped out centuries ago by what were later called **Denevan neural parasites**. Archaeological evidence indicated the inhabitants of the Beta Portolan system were the first victims of these creatures. The parasites later left Beta Portolan, traveling in a line across the galaxy toward planet **Levinius V**. ("Operation— Annihilate!" [TOS]). SEE: **Deneva**.

Beta Quadrant. One quarter of the entire Milky Way Galaxy. The region in which most of the **Klingon Empire** and the **Romulan Star Empire**s are located. Parts of the **United Federation of Planets** also spill over into Beta Quadrant, although the majority of this area remains unexplored. The *Starship* **Excelsior** was conducting a scientific mission in Beta Quadrant when it detected the explosion of **Praxis** in 2293. *(Star Trek VI: The Undiscovered Country).* SEE: **quadrant**.

Beta Renner cloud. An intelligent, spaceborne entity. The *Enterprise*-D encountered the life-form near the Beta Renner star system in 2364. This entity came aboard the starship and entered the neural systems of several *Enterprise*-D crew members, including Captain Picard, in an attempt to establish communications with life-forms it considered extremely alien. ("Lonely Among Us" [TNG]). *The cloud did not have a formal name in the episode.*

Beta Renner system. Star system where the home planets of the **Anticans** and **Selay** are located. The two worlds applied for admission to the Federation in 2364. ("Lonely Among Us" [TNG]).

Beta Stromgren. Former red giant star located 23 parsecs beyond Starfleet's farthest manned explorations as of 2366. In the final alternating stages of expansion and collapse when the entity code-named **Tin Man** was discovered by the **Vega IX probe**, Beta Stromgren went nova shortly thereafter. ("Tin Man" [TNG]).

Beta Thoridar. Planet located in the Klingon sphere of influence. Beta Thoridar was used as a staging area for the forces loyal to **Duras** during the **Klingon civil war** of 2368. ("Redemption, Part I" [TNG]).

Beta VI. Planet, location of a Federation colony. While en route to deliver supplies to Beta VI in 2267, the *Starship Enterprise* was detained by the alien known as **Trelane**. ("The Squire of Gothos" [TOS]).

Beta XII-A entity. Alien life-form of unknown origin, composed of pure energy, that thrived on the energy of negative emotions. The entity, first encountered at planet **Beta XII-A**, was capable of manipulating matter and the minds of its victims. It created a confrontation between crew members of a Klingon ship and the *Starship Enterprise* in 2268. Pitting these longtime enemies against each other, the entity fed on their anger, growing stronger as their hatred increased. The entity was defeated by a peaceful collaboration between the Klingons and the *Enterprise* crew. ("Day of the Dove" [TOS]). SEE: **Kang; Mara; noncorporeal life.** *Note that the entity was not given a name in the episode, and we're not even sure it came from planet Beta XII-A. The entity's special visual effects were designed by Mike Minor.*

Beta XII-A. Class-M planet. The **Beta XII-A entity** sent fake distress calls from Beta XII-A in 2268, luring both the *Enterprise* and a Klingon vessel to a violent encounter. ("Day of the Dove" [TOS]).

beta-tachyon. Form of particle that can exist only at faster-than-light velocities. In 2373, a female member of the **Q Continuum** showed the *Voyager* crew a method to increase shield power by a factor of ten by remodulating the shields to emit a beta-tachyon pulse, then emitting a series of antiproton beams into the shield bubble. ("The Q and the Grey" [VGR]).

Betar Prize. Annual literary award. (In an alternate future in which Ben Sisko was believed killed aboard the *Defiant* in 2372, Jake Sisko won the 2391 Betar Prize for his second book, *Collected Stories.* SEE: **Sisko, Jake.**) ("The Visitor" [DS9]).

Betazed, Holy Rings of. Relics of great significance in **Betazoid** culture. **Lwaxana Troi** was the holder of the Holy Rings of Betazed. ("Haven" [TNG]).

Betazed. Class-M planet; a member of the United Federation of Planets. Homeworld to **Deanna Troi**. ("Haven" [TNG]). As a young lieutenant, **William Riker** was once stationed on Betazed, where he became romantically involved with psychology student (and future *Enterprise*-D crew member) Deanna Troi. ("Encounter at Farpoint" [TNG], "Ménage à Troi" [TNG]). The biennial **Trade Agreements Conference** was held on Betazed in 2366. Commander Riker and Counselor Troi took shore leave there following the conference. Riker, Troi, and Lwaxana Troi were subsequently kidnapped from the surface of Betazed by the **Ferengi, DaiMon Tog**. ("Ménage à Troi" [TNG]). Archaeologist **Vash** was *persona non grata* on Betazed. ("Q-Less" [DS9]). Lake Cataria was one of Deanna Troi's favorite places on Betazed. She had devised a holodeck recreation of the locale on the *Enterprise*-D. ("All Good Things..." [TNG]).

Betazoids. Civilization of humanoid telepaths from the Federation planet **Betazed**. ("Haven" [TNG]). Most Betazoids develop their telepathic abilities in adolescence, although a few individuals are born with their telepathy fully functional. These troubled individuals generally require extensive therapy to survive in society, since they lack the ability to screen out the telepathic noise of other people. **Tam Elbrun** was one such person. ("Tin Man" [TNG]). Betazoids are, however, incapable of reading **Ferengi, Breen,** or **Dopterian** minds, possibly a result of the unusual four-lobed construction of their brains. ("Ménage à Troi" [TNG], ("The Forsaken" [DS9]). Betazoids are also unable to read **Ullians** ("Violations" [TNG]). The normal gestation period of a Betazoid is ten months. ("The Child" [TNG]). Sometimes pregnant Betazoid women can sense the thoughts of their unborn babies. ("The Muse" [DS9]).

Beth Delta I. Planet. Location of the city of **New Manhattan**. **Dr. Paul Stubbs** jokingly promised to take Deanna Troi there for champagne. ("Evolution" [TNG]).

Betreka Nebula Incident. An 18-year-long conflict that occurred several years ago between the Klingon Empire and the Cardassian Union. ("The Way of the Warrior" [DS9]).

Beumont, Neffie. Young lady whom a youthful Benjamin Sisko once had an intense crush on. ("Paradise Lost" [DS9]).

beverages. SEE: **food and beverages.**

"Beyond Antares." Love song. **Uhura** sang it for **Kevin Riley** when he was feeling depressed; she also gained **Nomad**'s attention by humming it on the bridge. ("Conscience of the King" [TOS], "The Changeling" [TOS]). *Music by Wilbur Hatch, lyrics by Gene L. Coon, performed by Nichelle Nichols.*

Bhavani, Premier. (Elizabeth Hoffman). The head of the **Barzan** government. Because of her planet's inhospitable nature, Premier Bhavani asked to use the *Enterprise*-D as a place to hold negotiations for rights to the **Barzan wormhole** in 2366. ("The Price" [TNG]).

bicaridine treatment. Regenerative therapy for fracture patients. It is used for patients who are allergic to **metorapan**. Beverly Crusher recommended bicaridine when her son, Wesley, was injured in an accident at the **Academy Flight Range** in 2368. ("The First Duty" [TNG]).

Big Bang. A massive explosion, about 15 billion years ago, in which the present universe and everything in it is believed to have been formed. At least two members of the omnipotent **Q Continuum** took refuge in the first moments of the cosmos. One of them, who would later be known as **Quinn**, also tried to hide the *Starship Voyager* in the maelstrom of creation. ("Death Wish" [VGR]).

"Big Goodbye, The." *Next Generation* episode #13. Written by Tracy Tormé. Directed by Joseph L. Scanlan. Stardate 41997.7. *First aired in 1988. Picard and company are trapped in a holodeck simulation of fictional gumshoe detective Dixon Hill. This is the first episode to feature Picard's fascination with the adventures of Dixon Hill. At one point, this episode had been scheduled for production after "11001001" (TNG). If this had indeed happened, the computer modifications of the Bynars would have served to explain the holodeck malfunctions in this episode. Robert Justman scoured the Paramount studio music archives and selected a nostalgic song, "You Came to Me From Out of Nowhere" for composer Dennis McCarthy to arrange, using a female singer for this episode.* Star Trek *producers Gene Roddenberry, Rick Berman, Robert H. Justman, and writer Tracy Tormé received a Peabody Award for this episode.* GUEST CAST: Lawrence Tierney as **Redblock**, **Cyrus**; Harvey Jason as **Leech**, **Felix**; William Boyett as **Bell**, **Lieutenant Dan**; David Selburg as **Whalen**; Gary Armagnac as **McNary**; Mike Genovese as Desk sergeant; Dick Miller as Vendor; Carolyn Allport as **Bradley**, **Jessica**; Rhonda Aldrich as Secretary; Erik Cord as Thug. SEE: ***Amazing Detective Stories*; baseball; Bell, Lieutenant Dan; "Big Goodbye, The"; Bokai, Buck; Bradley, Jessica; DiMaggio, Joe; Hill, Dixon; Jarada; Leech, Felix; London Kings; *Long Dark Tunnel, The*; McNary; Madeline; Redblock, Cyrus; Torona IV; Whalen.**

"Big Goodbye, The." Short story featuring the first adventures of fictional San Francisco gumshoe detective **Dixon Hill**. Published 1934 on Earth in *Amazing Detective Stories* magazine. ("The Big Goodbye" [TNG]).

big daddy-O. Twentieth-century American slang expression, referring to a subculture of beach and surf popular in the states of Hawai'i and California. When Neelix held a luau in his **Polynesian resort** program on the *Voyager's* holodeck, **Tom Paris** wore a Hawaiian-style shirt that he said was an exact re-creation of the 1962 "big daddy-O" surf special, an American classic. ("Alter Ego" [VGR]).

Biko, U.S.S. Federation supply ship *Olympic* Class, Starfleet registry number NCC-50331. The *Biko* was scheduled to rendezvous with the *Enterprise*-D on stardate 46271 at planet **Deinonychus VII**. ("A Fistful of Datas" [TNG]). *Named for Steven Biko, South African civil rights activist, martyred in 1977.*

Bilana III. Federation Class-M planet. Site where **soliton wave** based propulsion was developed by **Dr. Ja'Dar**. In 2368, the *Enterprise*-D participated in the first practical test of the new technology. The soliton wave was generated by an array of massive generators on the surface of Bilana III and projected toward a sister facility on the planet **Lemma II**. ("New Ground" [TNG]).

Bilar. (Ralph Maurer). Citizen of the society on planet **Beta III** who was under the control on the machine entity **Landru**. When an

Enterprise landing party arrived on the planet in 2267, Bilar asked if they had found accommodations to sleep after the **Red Hour**. ("Return of the Archons" [TOS]).

Bilaren system. Star system. Location of **Amanda Rogers**'s adoptive parents' homeworld. ("True-Q" [TNG]).

Bilecki, Lieutenant. Starfleet officer assigned to station **Deep Space 9** in 2369. During her tour on the station she became engaged to a young man from Bajor. Bilecki was among the Starfleet personnel who remained aboard the station during the **Circle**'s attempted coup in 2370. ("The Siege" [DS9]).

bilitrium. Crystalline compound that is an extremely rare energy source. When used in conjunction with an antimatter converter, it becomes a powerful explosive. **Kohn-ma** terrorist **Tahna Los** attempted to destroy one side of the **Bajoran wormhole** in 2369 using bilitrium and an antimatter converter. ("Past Prologue" [DS9]).

bio-neural circuitry. Advanced computer technology using synthetic neural cells for data processing. Bio-neural circuitry could organize and process complex information faster and more efficiently than traditional optical processors. The computer systems on the *Starship* ***Voyager*** used bio-neural gel packs to supplement its optical data network. ("Caretaker" [VGR]). In fact, the *U.S.S. Voyager* was the first Federation starship to have bio-neural fibers incorporated into its systems. ("State of Flux" [VGR]). SEE: **bio-neural gel pack**.

bio-neural energy. Electrical activity generated by an organic life-form's nervous system, absence of which generally constitutes death. In 2371, Commander Chakotay's bio-neural energy was displaced by **trianic energy being**s known as the **Komar**. Although *Voyager*'s **Emergency Medical Hologram** pronounced **Chakotay** brain-dead, his now-disembodied consciousness remained intact, able to navigate and infiltrate other life-forms. ("Cathexis" [VGR]).

bio-neural gel pack. Component of a bio-neural computer system consisting of a flexible, liquid-tight package containing synthetic neural cells in an gelatinous organic medium. The gel packs were designed for convenient management of **bio-neural circuitry**, and could be easily swapped out as needed. The *Starship Voyager* initially carried 47 replacement gel packs in its inventory. Bio-neural processors were vulnerable to viral and other infections, which could adversely affect system performance. A virus infected the bio-neural gel packs aboard the *Voyager* on stardate 48846. The virus, which threatened to cause a major systems malfunction, was successfully eradicated by heating the ship's systems, in much the same way that a biological organism might run a fever to fight an infection. ("Learning Curve" [VGR]). SEE: **schplict.**

bio-temporal chamber. Medical device created by the Emergency Medical Hologram aboard the Voyager in 2379. The chamber was to be used to stave off **morilogium** in Kes and extend her life by as much as a year. The chamber used a bio-temporal field to push her cells into an earlier stage of entropic decay. ("Before and After" [VGR]).

biochips. Cybernetic implants such as those surgically imbeded into bodies of the **Borg**. They serve to enhance their physical abilities and synthesize any organic molecules needed by their biological tissues. The Borg are dependent on the implants, and will die if the biochips are removed. ("I, Borg" [TNG]).

biocontainment field. Force field used for containment of infectious material aboard Federation starships. A level 4 quarantine involved the use of a biocontainment field. ("Macrocosm" [VGR]). SEE: **quarantine seal**.

bioenzymatic supplements. Small, bland yellow wafers that comprise the normal diet of the **Iyaarans**. ("Liaisons" [TNG]).

biofilter, transporter. A subsystem of the **transporter** designed to scan an incoming transporter beam prior to materialization and remove potentially harmful disease and virus contamination. The biofilter could be programmed against a wide range of disease organisms, but was effective only against organisms so programmed. *The biofilter was not only a very ingenious idea, but a very logical one in terms of the technology theoretically available to Starfleet, especially considering the risks entailed in exploring unknown planets. Unfortunately, one of the things that* Star Trek's *writers discovered was that the biofilter made it difficult to tell certain kinds of stories. As a result, they invented the theory that the biofilter was effective only against known organisms, thus making it possible for the occasional unknown virus to wreak havoc aboard the ship.*

biogenic field. Form of naturally occurring energy. A biogenic field of 800 megajoules surrounded a **Nechisti shrine** on the Nechani homeworld. ("Sacred Ground" [VGR]).

biogenic weapon. Extremely deadly biological armament, illegal under interstellar treaties. The components necessary to create biogenic weapons include **biomimetic gel**, **retroviral vaccines**, **isomiotic hypos**, and **plasma flares**. In 2370, Maquis intelligence believed the Cardassians to be stockpiling these supplies near the Demilitarized Zone. ("Preemptive Strike" [TNG]). **Cobalt diselenide** is a biogenic weapon. In 2373, the Maquis, led by Michael Eddington, used cobalt diselenide against planets Veloz Prime and Quatal Prime. ("For the Uniform" [DS9]).

bioimplant. Artificial organic material that can be surgically implanted into person's body to replace damaged tissue. Noted soccer player **Golanga** had a bioimplant replacement for his knee. ("Paradise" [DS9]). SEE: **parthenogenic implant**.

biomechanical gene disrupter. Deadly **nanobiogenic weapon** used by both the **T'Lani** and the **Kellerun** during a war that lasted for centuries. Also known as **harvesters**. ("Armageddon Game" [DS9]).

biomechanical maintenance program. Software incorporated into Commander **Data**'s positronic network. It kept him physically healthy and rarely in need of Dr. Crusher's professional services. ("Data's Day" [TNG]).

biomimetic fluctuation. Medical reading in **Founders** that are indicative of dangerous instability of the morphogenic matrix. ("The Begotten" [DS9]).

biomimetic gel. A dangerous and highly illegal substance. Biomimetic gel is necessary for the creation of biogenic weapons. ("Preemptive Strike" [TNG]). Starfleet issue L-647-X-7 containers were recommended for transport of biomimetic gel. ("Fair Trade" [VGR]). Biomimetic gel was one of the principal cargoes of the *U.S.S. Fleming*. It was feared that the *Fleming*'s disappearance in 2370 might have been due to this rare substance. ("Force of Nature" [TNG]). Biomimetic gel is a restricted substance and can be very hazardous if not handled correctly. The sale of biomimetic gel was forbidden by Federation law, and an unauthorized attempt to obtain the substance was a felony. ("Distant Voices" [DS9]).

biomolecular physiologist. (Tzi Ma). Specialized surgeon. A biomolecular physiologist was called in when Picard's life was threatened by complications in a routine cardiac replacement procedure in 2365, but Dr. Katherine Pulaski had to be brought in to save the captain. ("Samaritan Snare" [TNG]).

bioplast sheeting. Material used in the construction of the android **Data**, who had about 1.3 kilograms of the stuff in his body. ("The Most Toys" [TNG]).

bioregenerative field. Radiated energy used in biomedical applications to accelerate cellular growth. Dr. Bashir used a bioregenerative field to accelerate cells found in Ibudan's quarters that later developed into a clone of **Ibudan.** ("A Man Alone" [DS9]).

biospectral analysis. Sensor study used to evaluate organic life-forms or material. ("Sub Rosa" [TNG], "Genesis" [TNG]).

bipolar torch. Powerful cutting tool. Used aboard station Deep Space 9. A bipolar torch was used to cut through **toranium** metal inlay on a station door on stardate 46925. ("The Forsaken" [DS9]).

bird-of-prey. SEE: **Klingon bird-of-prey; Romulan bird-of-prey**.

Birta, DaiMon. (Peter Slutsker). Ferengi government official. Birta responded to an inquiry made by *Enterprise*-D captain Jean-Luc Picard in 2370 regarding the status of former DaiMon **Bok**. Birta confirmed that Bok had in fact been stripped of his DaiMon title, but added that Bok had bought his way out of **Rog Prison** in 2368, and that he was last seen somewhere in the **Dorias Cluster**. ("Bloodlines" [TNG]). *Peter Slutsker also played Nibor in "Ménage à Troi" (TNG) and Dr. Reyga in "Suspicions" (TNG).*

birthday cake. Baked confection made in a loaf or layer form and used as part of a traditional human celebration to mark the anniversary of a person's day of birth. (In 2370, a birthday cake made for Worf became one of the first signs of Worf's shifting between **quantum realities**. The cake first appeared as chocolate, then was yellow.) ("Parallels" [TNG]).

"Birthright, Part I." *Next Generation* episode #142. Written by Brannon Braga. Directed by Winrich Kolbe. Stardate 46578.4. *First aired in 1993. At Deep Space 9, Worf finds evidence that his father may still be alive in a secret Romulan prison camp. Data dreams. Along with "Emissary" (DS9) and "Defiant" (DS9), this was one of the few "crossover" episodes using characters from both* Star Trek: The Next Generation *and* Star Trek: Deep Space Nine. GUEST CAST: Siddig El Fadil as **Bashir, Dr. Julian**; James Cromwell as **Shrek, Jaglom**; Cristine Rose as **Gi'ral**; Jennifer Gatti as **Ba'el**; Richard Herd as **L'Kor**. SEE: **Alture VII relaxation program; aqueduct systems; Ba'el; Carraya System; Data; Gi'ral; hammer; Khitomer; Ktaran antiques; L'Kor; Lopez, Ensign; *MajQa*, Rite of; Mogh; No'Mat; painting; pasta al fiorella; Rudman, Commander; Shrek, Jaglom; Soong, Dr. Noonien; *Starfleet Cybernetics Journal*; Tokath; Toq; Worf; Yridians.**

"Birthright, Part II." *Next Generation* episode #143. Written by René Echevarria. Directed by Dan Curry. Stardate 46759.2. *First aired in 1993. At the secret Romulan prison camp, Worf tries to help Klingon prisoners rediscover what it is to be truly Klingon. This episode was directed by visual effects producer Dan Curry.* GUEST CAST: Cristine Rose as **Gi'ral**; James Cromwell as **Shrek, Jaglom**; Sterling Macer, Jr. as **Toq**; Alan Scarfe as **Mendak, Admiral**; Jennifer Gatti as **Ba'el**; Richard Herd as **L'Kor**. SEE: **Ba'el; boridium pellet; Carraya System; *d'k tahg*; Gi'ral; *jinaq*; Kahless the Unforgettable; Khitomer; L'Kor; *Mok'bara*; Nequencia system; *qa'vak*; Shrek, Jaglom; Tokath; Toq; Worf.**

bitanium. Exotic metal compound. Bitanium was used in Commander Data's neural pathways. ("Time's Arrow, Part I" [TNG]).

bitrious filaments. Mineral traces found in the soil on **Melona IV** in 2368 and on three other planets attacked by the **Crystalline Entity**. Bitrium was apparently produced when the entity absorbed living matter. ("Silicon Avatar" [TNG]).

bitters. A sharp-tasting beer made with hops, favored by Britons on Earth. Dr. Bashir ordered bitters for O'Brien shortly after completing their **Battle of Britain** holosuite simulation. ("Homefront" [DS9]).

Bizet, Georges. (1838-1875). French composer of Earth music. When Captain Jean-Luc Picard listened to Berlioz in his ready room on the *Enterprise*-E in 2373, Riker mistook the music for the work of Bizet. *(Star Trek: First Contact).*

Black Cluster. An astronomical formation created some nine billion years ago when hundreds of proto-stars collapsed in close proximity to each other. The resulting formation is fraught with violent, unpredictable gravitational wavefronts. The phenomena, which can absorb energy, are extremely dangerous to spacecraft systems. The Federation science vessel *Vico* was destroyed in the Black Cluster in 2368, and the *Enterprise*-D, investigating the disappearance of the *Vico*, nearly suffered the same fate. ("Hero Worship" [TNG]).

black hole. Celestial phenomenon caused by the collapse of a neutron star. The gravity well generated by the star's collapse becomes so great that neither **space-normal** matter nor light can escape. Extremely small black holes are known as quantum singularities. ("Timescape" [TNG]). SEE: **black star; quantum singularity**.

Black Hole. Ferengi beverage. The drink took its name from its opaque black color, as well as from its pungent odor. Jadzia Dax enjoyed Black Holes. ("Playing God" [DS9], "Hard Time" [DS9]). The beverage was also a favorite of a certain **Boslic freighter captain.** ("The Homecoming" [DS9]).

black knight. (Paul Baxley). Medieval dark horseman brought to life by **Yeoman Tonia Barrows** on the **amusement park planet** in 2267. The black knight and other beings imagined by the *Enterprise* landing party were made from cellular castings manufactured beneath the planet. The inhabitants of this world created the images to fulfill visitors' daydreams, but some of the dreams turned into nightmares, like the black knight who nearly killed Dr. McCoy. ("Shore Leave" [TOS]).

Black Sea at Night. Romantic holodeck program, complete with moonlight and balalaikas. ("All Good Things..." [TNG]).

black star. Alternate term for a **black hole**. In 2267, the original *Starship Enterprise* nearly collided with a black star in a maneuver that propelled them back in time to 1969. ("Tomorrow is Yesterday" [TOS]). SEE: **quantum singularity; slingshot effect.**

blackened redfish. Prepared dish of a variety of fish found in the bayous of Louisiana on Earth. ("The Visitor" [DS9]).

Blackjack. Code name for the **Omaha Air Base,** which dispatched a jet to photograph and intercept a **UFO** in 1969. The jet was piloted by **Captain John Christopher** and the UFO was the *Starship Enterprise*. ("Tomorrow Is Yesterday" [TOS]). SEE: **Bluejay 4.**

Blackwell, Admiral Margaret. (Nancy Vawter). Starfleet official. Blackwell suspended the *Enterprise*-D's mission to map the Merkoria Quasar and ordered the ship to rendezvous with the *U.S.S. Crazy Horse* in sector 1607. She suspended warp speed limitations for the duration of the mission. ("The *Pegasus*" [TNG]).

Blessed Exchequer. In **Ferengi** mythology, the accountant who presides over the **Divine Treasury**, the part of the afterlife reserved for those who have made a profit in their mortal lives. ("Little Green Men" [DS9]).

blight. SEE: **Teplan blight.**

blind beam-out. Transporter technique usually employed as an emergency measure, in which all life-forms in a given area are transported as a group instead of each pattern being isolated before transport. ("Emanations" [VGR]). SEE: **transporter**.

"Blood Fever." *Voyager* episode #57. Written by Lisa Klink. Directed by Andrew Robinson. Stardate 50537.2. First aired in 1997. *A Vulcan crew member undergoes* Pon farr, *the Vulcan mating drive, and he selects B'Elanna Torres as his mate.* GUEST CAST: Alexander Enberg as **Vorik**; Bruce Bohne as **Ishan**; Deborah Levin as **Lang.** SEE: **Borg; gallicite; holodeck and holosuite programs: *Pon farr* therapy; Ishan; Kal-if-fee; *Koon-ut so'lik*; Lang; Neelix; neurochemical imbalance; Paris, Thomas; *Pon farr*; Sakari; T'Pera; Torres, B'Elanna; Vorik; wedding: Klingons.**

"Blood Oath." *Deep Space Nine* episode #39. Television story and teleplay by Peter Allan Fields. Directed by Winrich Kolbe. No stardate given. *First aired in 1994. Dax is bound by an 80-year-old oath to help three elderly Klingons avenge the deaths of their children. This episode features the reunion of three of the first Klingons from the original* Star Trek *series.* GUEST CAST: John Colicos as **Kor**; Michael Ansara as **Kang**; William Campbell as **Koloth**; Bill Bolender as **Albino, the**; Christopher Collins as Head guard. SEE: **Albino, the; *baakonite*; *bahgol*; *bat'leth*; blood oath; brestanti ale; calisthenics program, Klingon; *Dahar* Master; *D'akturak*; Dayos IV; Dax, Curzon; Dax, Jadzia; Dax, son of Kang; Galdonterre; genetic virus; *ghoptu*; gravitic mine; holodeck and holosuite programs; ice man; *kajanpak't*; Kahless the Unforgettable; Kang; Klach D'kel Brakt, Battle of; Klingon death ritual; Klingon Empire; Koloth; Kor; Korvat colony; kuttars; *kyamo*; Mara; *N'yengoren* strategy; *QiVon*; riddinite; Secarus IV; scorcher; tetryon; Trill.**

blood oath. In the **Klingon** culture, a promise of vengeance that once sworn, can never be broken. **Kang**, **Koloth**, and **Kor** swore a blood oath against the **Albino** for murdering their firstborn children. ("Blood Oath" [DS9]).

blood screening. Medical test used by **Federation** personnel to identify shape-shifters. This was considered necessary because of the possibility that shape-shifting **Founders** had taken humanoid form and infiltrated the Federation and other Alpha Quadrant powers. The test involved removing a small sample of blood from an individual's body. If the individual was a **changeling**, the blood would revert to a gelatinous orange liquid. Captain Sisko ordered blood screenings on Gul Dukat and the Detapa Council members after rescuing them from the Klingons in 2372. ("The Way of the Warrior" [DS9]). Blood screenings, along with phaser sweeps, were employed as security measures on Earth in 2372 shortly after the bombing of the **Antwerp Conference** by a changeling. ("Homefront" [DS9]). In 2373, the Klingon Empire became obsessive about doing blood screenings to prevent infiltration of the empire by Founders. ("Apocalypse Rising" [DS9]).

blood-gas infuser. Medical instrument used to stabilize oxygen levels of a patient in respiratory distress. The Emergency Medical Hologram aboard the *Starship Voyager* used a blood-gas infuser on Neelix in 2371 when his lungs were stolen by Vidiians. ("Phage" [VGR]).

"Bloodlines." *Next Generation* episode #174. Written by Nicholas Sagan. Directed by Jonathan West. Stardate 47829.1. *First aired in 1994. A renegade Ferengi promises revenge on Picard by threatening to kill a son Picard never knew he had. This episode is something of a sequel to "The Battle" (TNG).* GUEST CAST: Ken Olandt as **Vigo**, **Jason**; Lee Arenberg as **Bok, DaiMon**; Peter Slutsker as **Birta, DaiMon**; Amy Pietz as **Rhodes, Sandra**; Michelan Sisti as Tol; Majel Barrett as Computer voice. SEE: **Birta, DaiMon; Bok; B'Zal; Camor V; Camorites; Dichromic Nebula; Dorias Cluster; Forrester-Trent syndrome; Gorlan prayer stick; New Gaul; Picard, Jean-Luc; Rhodes, Sandra; Rog Prison; Saurian brandy; subspace technology; Vigo, Jason; Vigo, Miranda; Xendi Sabu system.**

bloodwine. SEE: **Klingon bloodwine**.

bloodworms. Animal life-form. ("State of Flux" [VGR]).

Bloom sisters. Acquaintances of **Jean-Luc Picard** and his friend, **Louis**. When they were both young, Picard warned Louis not to take a bicycle trip with the Bloom sisters, but apparently Louis did not heed his warning. Louis ended up breaking a leg on the trip. He also ended up getting married, twice. ("Family" [TNG]).

Blue Horizon. Planet. Site of a terraforming project by **Professor Seyetik** and reputed to be an incredibly beautiful sight. Commander Benjamin Sisko and his son Jake visited Blue Horizon on their way to **Deep Space 9** in 2369. ("Second Sight" [DS9]).

Blue Parrot Cafe. A club on planet Sarona VIII. Riker recalled that exotic blue drinks were served at the Blue Parrot Cafe. Picard said Troi should buy everyone drinks there when the *Enterprise*-D went to Sarona VIII for shore leave in 2364. ("We'll Always Have Paris" [TNG]).

blue alert. Aboard Federation starships with the ability of planetfall, blue alert is a state of readiness for landing operations. Blue alert notifies the ship's crew to occupy Code Blue stations, and is ordered prior to the starship's landing on a planet and prior to liftoff. A starship commander should not order the start of descent until all decks report that condition blue has been set. ("The 37's" [VGR]).

Bluejay 4. Radio call sign given to United States Air Force **Captain John Christopher**'s F-104 air vehicle in 1969. ("Tomorrow Is Yesterday" [TOS]).

Bo'rak. (Bob Minor). An agent of the **Klingon Intelligence** service. One of three agents sent to **Deep Space 9** in 2371 to observe and to take appropriate action against a **Romulan** delegation visiting the station. Bo'rak was under direct orders from the Klingon High Council. ("Visionary" [DS9]).

Bochra, Centurion. (John Snyder). Romulan officer. Bochra was marooned with Commander La Forge on planet **Galorndon Core** in 2366. Bochra at first attempted to capture La Forge and hold him prisoner, but later cooperated with him for their mutual survival when they suffered neural damage from the magnetic fields on the surface. ("The Enemy" [TNG]). *John Snyder also played Aaron Conor in "The Masterpiece Society" (TNG).*

Boday, Captain. Commander of a **Gallamite** vessel. Jadzia Dax had dinner with Boday in 2370. ("The Maquis, Part I" [DS9]). Jadzia Dax and Boday were lovers for a time. Years later, Dax had lunch with Boday in 2373, although Worf did not like her associating with a past flame. ("Let He Who Is Without Sin..." [DS9]).

"Body Parts." *Deep Space Nine* episode #97. Teleplay by Hans Beimler. Story by Louis P. DeSantis & Robert J. Bolivar. Directed by Avery Brooks. No stardate given. *First aired in 1996. Quark, thinking he is about to die of a deadly disease, agrees to sell his remains to raise money, only to learn his diagnosis was in error. Keiko is injured and her baby is placed in Kira's body.* GUEST CAST: Rosalind Chao as **O'Brien, Keiko**; Max Grodénchik as **Rom**; Hana Hatae as **O'Brien, Molly**; Jeffrey Combs as **Brunt**; Andrew Robinson as **Garak, Elim**. SEE: **Alvanian brandy; Bajorans; Brunt; Divine Treasury; Dorek syndrome; Ferengi; Ferengi Futures Exchange; Ferengi Rules of Acquisition; Gaila; Gint; Gorad; Kira Nerys; latinum; Nagus, Grand; O'Brien, Keiko; Orpax, Dr.; Quark; Quark's bar; Registrar; slip; snail juice; strip; tesokine; Torad IV; Undalar; vole bellies; *Volga, U.S.S.***

Body. Term describing the whole of society on planet **Beta III** under the rule of **Landru**. The population on Beta III was controlled by Landru and made to act simply, in peace and tranquillity, but they became totally stagnant and nonproductive. The good of the Body was the prime directive and anyone who disturbed the peace of the Body was absorbed into the Body or destroyed. ("Return of the Archons" [TOS]).

Bogrow, Paul. An old friend of former *U.S.S. Victory* crew members Geordi La Forge and **Susanna Leijten**. Leijten said she almost married Bogrow. ("Identity Crisis" [TNG]).

Boheeka. (Jimmie F. Skaggs). **Cardassian** officer. Boheeka's career was placed in jeopardy in 2370 when he accepted a bribe from Quark to order a **cranial implant** device for Garak. Boheeka did not realize that the device was so secret that even inquiring about it would attract the attention of the **Obsidian Order**. ("The Wire" [DS9]).

Bok'Nor. Freighter ship of **Cardassian** registry. In 2370, the *Bok'Nor* was blown up at **Deep Space 9** by the **Maquis**, resulting in the death of the 78 **Cardassians** aboard. The Maquis believed that it was carrying weapons to Cardassian colonies in the **Demilitarized Zone**. ("The Maquis, Parts I and II" [DS9]). *The* Bok'Nor *model was a re-use of the* **Merchantman** *ship first seen in* Star Trek III.

Bok, DaiMon. (Frank Corsentino, Lee Arenberg). Ferengi officer and father to the commander of a **Ferengi** ship destroyed in 2355 in a battle with the *U.S.S.* ***Stargazer***. Bok blamed *Stargazer* captain **Jean-Luc Picard** for his son's death. Years later, in 2364, Bok sought to exact revenge on Picard by attempting to discredit the captain by falsifying evidence suggesting that Picard had attacked without provocation. Bok was later demoted by his first officer, **Kazago**, when Bok's plan for revenge was discovered. SEE: **Maxia, Battle of; thought maker.** ("The Battle" [TNG]). Bok was subsequently stripped of his title of DaiMon, relieved of command, and sent to Rog Prison; he was able to buy his freedom in 2368. In 2370, he again attempted to take revenge on Picard first by convincing him that **Jason Vigo** was his son, and then threatening to kill the boy. Jason was not Picard's son, but Bok had secretly resequenced his DNA to make it appear that he was. When Bok's plans were revealed, he was turned over to Ferengi authorities. ("Bloodlines" [TNG]). *Bok was portrayed by Frank Corsentino in "The Battle" (TNG) and by Lee Arenberg in "Bloodlines" (TNG).*

Bokai, Buck. (Keone Young). Also known as Harmon Bokai. One of professional baseball's greatest players, Buck Bokai broke **Joe DiMaggio**'s record for hits in consecutive games in 2026. ("The Big Goodbye" [TNG]). Buck Bokai played his rookie year with the **London Kings** in 2015. ("Past Tense, Part II" [DS9]). Initially a shortstop, Bokai later switched to third base. Bokai hit the winning home run in the 2042 **World Series**, just before the demise of the sport. SEE: **Newson, Eddie**. ("If Wishes Were Horses" [DS9]). A holographic version of Bokai was part of a holodeck program that **Ben Sisko** brought with him to **Deep Space 9**. Ben and his son, Jake, enjoyed playing with Bokai and other baseball greats. ("The Storyteller" [DS9]). This holographic Buck Bokai came to life in 2369 when unknown aliens from the **Gamma Quadrant** used images of Bokai and a variety of fantasy figures to learn more about human beings. Despite himself, Ben Sisko became quite fond of this image of Bokai. ("If Wishes Were Horses" [DS9]). *The player who broke DiMaggio's record in 2026 was mentioned in "The Big Goodbye" (TNG), but he remained nameless until "If Wishes Were Horses" (DS9). The character's name actually originated in a baseball card proposed by* Star Trek: Deep Space Nine *illustrator (and baseball fan) Ricardo Delgado as a decorative prop for Ben Sisko's quarters. Fellow baseball fan (and executive producer) Michael Piller suggested the card feature a 21st-century player, which would make it a valuable collectors' item to the 24th-century Ben Sisko.* Star Trek *model maker Greg Jein (yet another baseball fan) got into the act at this point, providing photos of himself in a baseball jersey that the art department converted into the prop card. Greg also provided the fictional "history" of his character and the statistics that appeared on the card. Bokai, whose name was a vague allusion to Buckaroo Banzai, from the movie of the same name, was mentioned in "The Storyteller" (DS9), but not actually seen until "If Wishes Were Horses," in which Bokai was played by actor Keone Young, who bore an uncanny resemblance to Jein. The prop baseball card, which was revised after the episode, has Young's photo on the front, but still shows Jein on the back.*

Bolarus IX. Home planet of the **Bolian** people. ("Allegiance" [TNG]).

Boldaric masters. School of 22nd-century Bajoran composers. Dr. Julian Bashir considered the music of a modern composer, Tor Jolan, to be derivative of their work. ("Crossover" [DS9]).

Bolian cuisine. Bolian cuisine makes use of meat that has been allowed to partially decay. ("Crossfire" [DS9]).

Bolian currency. Medium of monetary exchange. ("Starship Down" [DS9]).

Bolian restaurant. In 2372, a Bolian restaurant opened on station Deep Space 9. ("Crossfire" [DS9]).

Bolian tonic water. A refreshing beverage of Bolian origin. ("Paradise Lost" [DS9]).

Bolians. Civilization of humanoids native to planet Bolarus IX ("Allegiance" [TNG]) and distinguished by a light blue skin and a bifurcated ridge running down the center of the face. Their blood is blue. ("The Adversary" [DS9]). Bolians have very different blood chemistry from **Vulcans**. A blood transfusion from a Vulcan to a Bolian would be fatal for the Bolian. ("Prototype" [VGR]). Bolians have a cartilaginous lining on their tongues. ("Flashback" [VGR]). The Bolians have a principle of assisted suicide that dates back to their middle ages. This was termed the double effect principle, and it deemed ethical any action that relieved suffering, even if that same action had the secondary effect of causing death. ("Death Wish" [VGR]). Captain **Rixx**, commander of the *Starship* ***Thomas Paine***, was Bolian ("Conspiracy" [TNG]), as was Starfleet cadet **Mitena Haro** ("Allegiance" [TNG]), *Enterprise*-D barber **Mr. Mot**, Ambassador **Vadosia** ("The Forsaken" [DS9]), and the tactical officer aboard the *Starship* ***Saratoga***, destroyed in the battle of **Wolf 359.** ("Emissary" [DS9]). *Bolians were named for director Cliff Bole, who directed "Conspiracy" (TNG), the first episode in which these people were seen. The unnamed* Saratoga *tactical officer was played by Stephen Davies.*

Boma, Lieutenant. (Don Marshall). Starfleet officer. Member of the **shuttlecraft Galileo** crew when it crashed on planet **Taurus II** in 2267. ("The *Galileo* Seven" [TOS]).

Bonaparte, Napoleon. (1769-1821). Military leader and emperor of France from 1804 to 1814. **Trelane** of Gothos fancied himself a student of Napoleon Bonaparte. ("The Squire of Gothos" [TOS]).

bonding gifts. Betazoid term for wedding presents. SEE: **gift box, Betazoid.** ("Haven" [TNG]).

"Bonding, The." *Next Generation* episode #53. Written by Ronald D. Moore. Directed by Winrich Kolbe. Stardate 43198.7. *First aired in 1989. When an* Enterprise-*D crew member is killed on an away mission, a planet's inhabitants attempt to make amends by providing a "perfect" life for her orphaned son. This was the first script written by Ronald D. Moore, who went on to become a staff writer and producer on* Star Trek: The Next Generation *and* Star Trek: Deep Space Nine, *as well as a writer for the* Star Trek *feature films.* GUEST CAST: Susan Powell as **Aster, Lieutenant Marla**; Gabriel Damon as **Aster, Jeremy**; Colm Meaney as **O'Brien, Miles**. SEE: **Aster, Jeremy; Aster, Lieutenant Marla; computer core; *d'k tahg*; Klingons; Koinonians; noncorporeal life; Patches; *R'uustai*; Rushton infection; subspace technology; tricorder; Worf.**

Bonestell Recreation Facility. A seamy bar at **Starbase Earhart**, filled with unruly galactic cutthroats. **Jean-Luc Picard** was stabbed through the heart in 2327 (shortly after his graduation from the academy) by a **Nausicaan** who picked a fight with Picard and his classmates at the Bonestell Facility. Picard's injuries in the incident required him to undergo cardiac replacement surgery. ("Samaritan Snare" [TNG]). Picard regretted his impulsiveness in that incident for years, but in 2369, when **Q** gave him a chance to relive that moment, Picard found that he had indeed made the right choice. ("Tapestry" [TNG]). *The Bonestell Facility was named for classic astronomical artist Chesley Bonestell.* SEE: **barokie; dom-jot; *guramba*; *undari*.**

"Booby Trap." *Next Generation* episode #54. Teleplay by Ron Roman and Michael Piller & Richard Danus. Directed by Gabrielle Beaumont. Stardate 43205.6. *First aired in 1989. The* Enterprise-*D investigates a derelict warship and becomes caught in an ancient booby trap. Geordi enlists the help of a holographic image of Dr. Leah Brahms.* GUEST CAST: Susan Gibney as **Brahms, Dr. Leah**; Colm Meaney as **O'Brien, Miles**; Whoopi Goldberg as **Guinan**; Albert Hall as **Galek Sar**; Julie Warner as **Henshaw, Christi**. SEE: **aceton assimilators; Astral V Annex; Brahms, Dr. Leah; *Cleponji*; Daystrom Institute of Technology; dilithium crystal chamber; Drafting Room 5; Galek Sar; Henshaw, Christi; *Kavis Teke* elusive maneuver; La Forge, Geordi; Lang cycle fusion engines; Mars; Martian Colonies; Menthars; Orelious IX; Outpost Seran-T-One; Picard, Jean-Luc; Promellian/Menthar war; Promellians; Theoretical Propulsion Group; Utopia Planitia Fleet Yards.**

Book of the People, Fabrini. SEE: **Fabrini Book of the People**.

Book, The. Term used by the inhabitants of planet Sigma Iotia II for a copy of *Chicago Mobs of the Twenties*, a book left behind on that planet by the crew of the ***U.S.S. Horizon*** in 2168. The Iotians used The Book as the pattern for their society, and revered it, almost as a holy relic. ("A Piece of the Action" [TOS]).

Boone, Raymond. (John Beck). Starfleet officer who was a member of the crew of the ***U.S.S. Rutledge*** during the **Setlik III** massacre of 2347. Boone was taken prisoner during the fighting and was killed while in **Cardassian** captivity. Unknown to Starfleet authorities, a Cardassian agent was surgically altered to resemble Boone, and this duplicate was released, posing as the original. The duplicate Boone took up residence on planet **Volon III**. The ruse was largely successful for many years, although his wife did notice behavioral changes and the marriage subsequently ended. The duplicate Boone was a key part of a Cardassian plot in 2370 to falsely implicate former *Rutledge* crew member **Miles O'Brien** in **Maquis** activity. The frame-up would have succeeded, except that Boone's replacement was discovered by **Odo**, and the Cardassian government dropped the charges to avoid having its actions made public. ("Tribunal" [DS9]).

Boothby. (Ray Walston). The groundskeeper at **Starfleet Academy**. Boothby was something of a fixture at the academy, having worked there since **Jean-Luc Picard** was a cadet in the 2320s. During those days, Picard regarded the irascible Boothby as "a mean-spirited, vicious old man." Boothby nevertheless helped guide Picard through a particularly difficult time when the young cadet had committed a serious offense. Boothby later recalled that he had simply helped Picard listen to himself. Boothby, for his part, followed Picard's career with some satisfaction. ("The First Duty" [TNG]). Years later, Picard came to understand Boothby more clearly, and regarded the old groundskeeper as one of the wisest men he had ever known. When **Wesley Crusher** entered Starfleet Academy in 2367, Picard advised him to seek out Boothby's advice. ("Final Mission" [TNG]). *Picard never did describe the nature of his transgression. Picard first mentioned Boothby to Wesley in "Final Mission" (TNG), then again in "The Game" (TNG). We finally got to meet the character in "The First Duty" (TNG). Ray Walston gained popularity in the 1960s as Uncle Martin in* My Favorite Martian.

Bopak III. Uninhabited Class-M world in the Gamma Quadrant. In 2368, **Jem'Hadar** soldier **Goran'Agar** was the only survivor of a ship that crashed on Bopak III. After his supply of **ketracel-white** ran out, he learned that he was not dependent on the drug. He believed that something in the environment on Bopak III was responsible for curing him, so four years later he brought his men to the planet in order for them to be similarly cured. ("Hippocratic Oath" [DS9]).

Bopak system. Red giant star system in the Gamma Quadrant. The third planet, Bopak III, was an uninhabited Class-M world. ("Hippocratic Oath" [DS9]).

Boraal II. Homeworld to the **Boraalans**. In 2370, the planet's atmosphere suddenly dissipated, rendering it uninhabitable. ("Homeward" [TNG]).

Boraal II/Vacca VI transformation. Holodeck program devised by Dr. **Nikolai Rozhenko**, re-creating the surface of planet Boraal II. The program was designed to recreate a long cross-country journey, with the topography slowly changing to match the surface of planet Vacca VI ("Homeward" [TNG]).

Boraalan chronicle. Pictorial history of a **Boraalan** village; it was also the name given to the individual who kept this record. **Vorin** kept the chronicle of his village. Following his death in 2370, he was succeeded by **Nikolai Rozhenko**, an offworlder who had saved Vorin's village. ("Homeward" [TNG]).

Boraalan seer. Spiritual and secular guide of a **Boraalan** village. The seer studied by **Nikolai Rozhenko** was killed during the storms generated by atmospheric dissipation. Rozhenko told the villagers that Worf, who had been altered to pass as a Boraalan, was a seer, who had come to lead them to safety. ("Homeward" [TNG]).

Boraalans. Humanoid inhabitants of planet **Boraal II,** who lived on a technological level similar to Earth's medieval period. The Boraalans had a rich and deep spiritual life, and were the subject of a cultural study by **Nikolai Rozhenko**. The entire population of Boraal II, with the exception of one village, was lost in 2370, when the planet was subjected to sudden **atmospheric dissipation**. ("Homeward" [TNG]). SEE: **Boraalan chronicle; Boraalan seer.**

Boradis system. Star system. A Federation outpost was established on Boradis III in 2331. By 2365, three other planets in that system had been colonized. The *Enterprise*-D was ordered to a point near the Boradis system to meet Federation Emissary **K'Ehleyr** from **Starbase 153**. ("The Emissary" [TNG]).

Boranis III. Planet. The population of Boranis III was infected with a plague that consumed thousands of lives. Dr. Julian Bashir was able to identify the pathogen and inoculate the entire population. ("The Quickening" [DS9]).

Borath. (Dennis Christopher). **Vorta** analyst. Borath conducted an experiment on the captured senior crew of the *U.S.S. Defiant* in 2371. Borath caused the *Defiant*'s command crew to experience an illusory invasion of the **Dominion** into the Alpha Quadrant. This was a test to see how much resistance the Dominion might encounter if they were to conduct an actual invasion. Borath and the **Founders** learned that Ben Sisko and his staff were willing to risk their careers and their lives to destroy the **Bajoran wormhole**, in order to keep the Dominion on their side of the galaxy. ("The Search, Part II" [DS9]).

borathium. An experimental rybotherapy medication developed by **Dr. Toby Russell** as a potential replacement for leporazine and morathial. The drug was still in an experimental stage in 2368 when Russell used it unsuccessfully to treat a crash victim from the transport ship **Denver**. Dr. Beverly Crusher believed that Russell's use of borathium in that case was a violation of medical ethics, since conventional leporazine therapy might have been effective. ("Ethics" [TNG]).

Boratus. (Michael Champion). A **Vorgon** criminal who traveled backward in time to locate Captain Picard and the **Tox Uthat**. ("Captain's Holiday" [TNG]).

Boreal III. Planet. Home port of the transport ship **Kallisko**, which was attacked by the **Crystalline Entity** in 2368. ("Silicon Avatar" [TNG]).

Boreth. Class-M planet located in Klingon space. Klingon legend has it that Boreth was the planet where the Klingon messiah, **Kahless the Unforgettable**, promised to return following his death on the Klingon Homeworld some 1500 years ago. The followers of Kahless established a monastery on the planet to await his return. To the Klingons, there is no more sacred place. SEE: **Story of the Promise, The.** Clerics on Boreth, fearing that political infighting in the Klingon High Council signaled a loss of honor in the empire, conspired in 2369 to provide new leadership for the Klingon people by creating a clone of Kahless, using his actual genetic material, thereby attempting to fulfill Kahless's promise. **Worf** made a pilgrimage to Boreth in that year, where he was the first to meet the clone of Kahless. Although the clerics' deception was soon discovered, Kahless's clone was installed as the ceremonial Emperor of the Klingon people. ("Rightful Heir" [TNG]). SEE: **Gowron**. After the destruction of the *Enterprise*-D in 2371, Worf returned to study at Boreth. Worf left the monastery a year later, on stardate 49011, to accept an assignment at Deep Space 9. ("The Way of the Warrior" [DS9]). *The exterior of the Boreth monastery was a matte painting designed by Dan Curry.*

Borg collective. Term used to describe the group consciousness of the **Borg** civilization. Each Borg individual was linked to the collective by a sophisticated subspace network that insured each member was given constant supervision and guidance. ("Best of Both Worlds, Part I" [TNG], "I, Borg" [TNG]). Being part of the collective offered significant biomedical advantages to individual members. The mental energy of the group consciousness could help an injured individual to heal or regenerate damaged body parts. A group of former Borg drones, living in the **Nekrit Expanse** of the Delta Quadrant, sought to reestablish the collective link to bring peace and order to their new society, thus creating a New Cooperative consciousness. ("Unity" [VGR]).

Borg queen. (Alice Krige). Central locus of the **Borg collective**. The Borg queen brought order to the multitude of voices within the Borg shared consciousness. She was the "one who was many," in that she embodied elements of individuality as well as being the central node in a vast group mind. When the Borg invaded the Federation in late 2366, the Borg queen wanted a counterpart, a human being with a mind of his own who could bridge the gulf between humanity and the Borg. Captain Jean-Luc Picard as **Locutus** was to have fulfilled this role. The Borg queen wanted Picard to give himself freely to the Borg. She wanted more than just another Borg drone, but he resisted and was forced into the collective. When the Borg attempted to take over the ***U.S.S. Enterprise*-E** in 2373, the Borg queen attempted to seduce Lieutenant Commander Data by giving him organic components and by appealing to his emotions. She and all the Borg on the *Enterprise*-E were killed when plasma coolant released by Data liquefied their organic components. With the death of the Borg queen, the Borg apparently lost the basic structure of their collective. *(Star Trek: First Contact).* Star Trek: First Contact *establishes that the Borg queen was an unseen part of Picard's assimilation in "The Best of Both Worlds, Part I" (TNG).*

Borg scout ship. Small Borg vessel, cubical in shape, with a mass of 2.5 million metric tons. The ship generally carried a crew of five. One such ship was discovered crashed on a moon in the **Argolis Cluster** in 2368. SEE: **Hugh**. ("I, Borg" [TNG]).

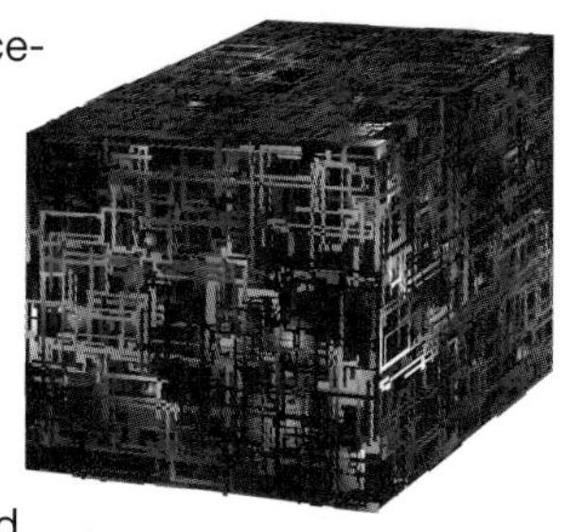

Borg ship. Huge cube-shaped spacecraft, operated by the Borg collective. The first known Federation encounter with a Borg ship was by the *Enterprise*-D near **System J-25** in 2365. The Borg vessel had a highly decentralized design, and *Enterprise*-D personnel reported finding no specific bridge, engineering, or living areas. Combat experience showed the ship to be equipped with powerful energy weapons and capable of repairing major damage almost immediately, including the impact of direct phaser hits. *Model concept by Maurice Hurley, design by Rick Sternbach, built by Kim Bailey.* ("Q Who?" [TNG]). A Borg cube ship made its way into Federation space in 2373 and proceeded to Earth on stardate 50893. It was destroyed by a Starfleet armada, but was able to launch a small Borg sphere that traveled into Earth's past on a mission to prevent Zefram Cochrane's first warp flight in 2063. *(Star Trek: First Contact).* A Borg vessel of a totally different design was used in the Borg incursion of 2369, in which a **transwarp conduit** was used to reach the Alpha Quadrant much more rapidly than was possible with normal warp travel. ("Descent, Part I" [TNG]). This ship was destroyed by a solar fusion eruption caused by *Enterprise*-D. ("Descent, Part II" [TNG]). *The Type-2 Borg ship was designed by Dan Curry and built by Greg Jein.*

Borg sphere. Small spherical **Borg** vessel capable of creating a **temporal vortex**. A Borg sphere was a timeship launched from a special bay on the surface of larger Borg ships. A Borg cube ship made its way into Federation space in 2373 and proceeded to **Earth** on stardate 50893. It was destroyed by a Starfleet armada, but not before it launched a timeship that traveled into Earth's past in an attempt to prevent **Zefram Cochrane**'s first warp flight in 2063. *(Star Trek: First Contact)*.

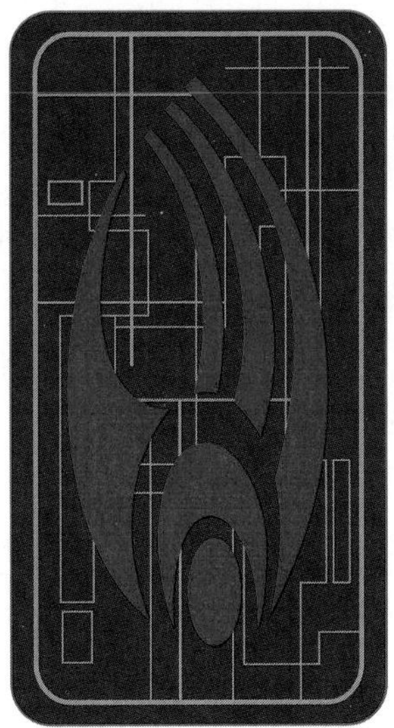

Borg. An immensely powerful civilization of enhanced humanoids from the **Delta Quadrant** of the galaxy. The Borg implant themselves with cybernetic devices, giving them great technological and combat capabilities. Different Borg are equipped with different hardware for specific tasks. Each Borg is tied into a sophisticated subspace communications network, forming the **Borg collective**, a shared consciousness in which the idea of the individual was nearly a meaningless concept. The Borg exhibit a high degree of intelligence and adaptability in their tactics. Most means of defense or offense against them were found to work only once, almost immediately after which the Borg developed a countermeasure. ("Q Who?" [TNG]). The Borg operated by conquering entire worlds, assimilating the civilizations and technology thereon. Individual members of assimilated races were implanted with sophisticated cybernetic implants, permitting each individual to perform a specific task as required by the collective. Thousands of worlds across the galaxy were conquered in this fashion. *(Star Trek: First Contact)*. The Borg were responsible for the near-extinction of the **El-Aurian** people in the late 23rd century. SEE: **Guinan**. *(Star Trek Generations)*. The first known contact between the Borg and the Federation was in 2365, when **Q** transported the *Enterprise*-D out of Federation space into the flight path of a Borg vessel heading toward Alpha Quadrant. ("Q Who?" [TNG]). Following this first contact, Starfleet began advance planning for a potential Borg offensive against the Federation. **Lieutenant Commander Shelby** was placed in charge of this project to develop a defense strategy. ("The Best of Both Worlds, Part I" [TNG]). One of the weapons systems developed to help meet the Borg threat was the new ***U.S.S. Defiant***, a heavily armed starship prototype. ("The Search, Part I" [DS9]).

The anticipated Borg attack came in late 2366, when a Borg vessel entered Federation space, heading for Earth. Starfleet tactical planners had expected at least several more months before the Borg arrival, and thus were caught unprepared. *Enterprise*-D captain **Jean-Luc Picard** was captured by the Borg at the beginning of this offensive. He was assimilated into the Borg collective consciousness and became known as **Locutus of Borg**, providing crucial guidance to the Borg in their attack. ("The Best of Both Worlds, Part I" [TNG]).

Starfleet massed an armada of some 40 starships in hopes of stopping the Borg ship at **Wolf 359**, but the fleet was decimated with the loss of 39 ships and 11,000 lives ("The Drumhead" [TNG]), including the ***U.S.S. Saratoga***. ("Emissary" [DS9]). As Locutus, Picard explained that the Borg purpose

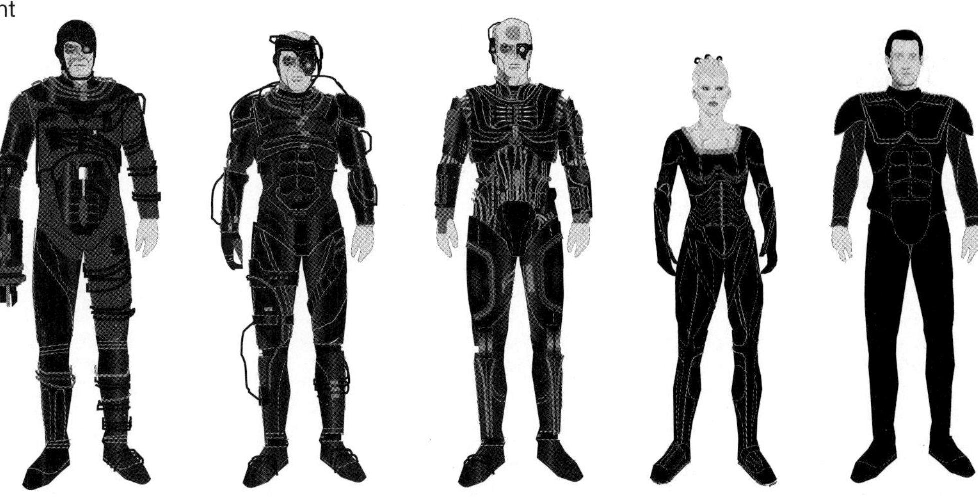

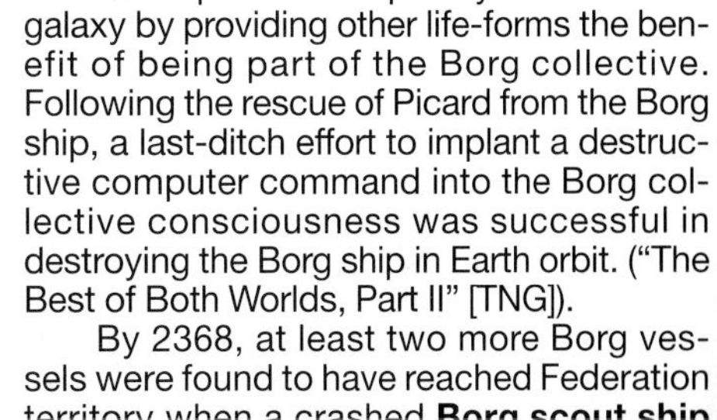

was to improve the quality of life in the galaxy by providing other life-forms the benefit of being part of the Borg collective. Following the rescue of Picard from the Borg ship, a last-ditch effort to implant a destructive computer command into the Borg collective consciousness was successful in destroying the Borg ship in Earth orbit. ("The Best of Both Worlds, Part II" [TNG]).

By 2368, at least two more Borg vessels were found to have reached Federation territory when a crashed **Borg scout ship** was discovered on the surface of a moon in the **Argolis Cluster**. One surviving Borg, designated Third of Five, was rescued from the crash by *Enterprise*-D crew personnel. This Borg, named **Hugh** *(pictured)* by the *Enterprise*-D crew, was nursed back to health. During Hugh's convalescence, *Enterprise*-D personnel developed what they termed an **invasive program**, which, when introduced into the Borg collective consciousness, was designed to cause a fatal overload in the entire collective. In the process, Hugh befriended Geordi La Forge, a friendship that provided an argument that this invasive program, effectively a weapon of mass murder, should not be used. Hugh was then returned to the Argolis crash site, where he was rescued by another Borg scout ship. ("I, Borg" [TNG]). Following the return of Hugh, Hugh's new sense of individuality began to permeate a portion of the collective. The results were dramatic: Deprived of their group identity, individual Borg were unable to function as a unit. The unexpected arrival of the android, **Lore**, changed this. Lore appointed himself the leader of those Borg, and promised them he would provide them with the means to become completely artificial life-forms, free of dependence on organic bodies. ("Descent, Parts I and II" [TNG]).

In 2369, Lore led the Borg in launching a major new offensive against the Federation. Utilizing transwarp conduits, they entered Federation space in a ship of an unfamiliar design and attacked a Federation outpost at **Ohniaka III**. During this offensive, the Borg attacked with uncharacteristic anger, later found to be due to Lore's influence. The offensive was halted when Lore was dismantled by his brother, **Data**. ("Descent, Parts I and II" [TNG]).

In 2373, the Borg launched a second attempt to assimilate Earth. Although the Federation Starfleet was successful in stopping the Borg attack, a single **Borg sphere** escaped into a **temporal vortex**, to Earth's 21st century. In the past, the Borg attempted to prevent space pioneer **Zefram Cochrane** from making Earth's first faster-than-light flight in 2063. The crew of the *Starship Enterprise*-E, following the Borg sphere into the past, ensured that Cochrane was able to make the critical first warp flight. In doing so, the *Enterprise*-E crew destroyed the **Borg queen**, the central nexus of the **Borg collective**. *(Star Trek: First Contact)*.

On stardate 50541, the crew of the ***U.S.S. Voyager*** discovered a Borg corpse on a planet in the **Delta Quadrant** while trading with **Sakari** colonists for the mineral **gallicite**. ("Blood Fever" [VGR]). A few weeks later, in the **Nekrit Expanse**, the *Starship*

Voyager discovered a planet of former Borg drones that had somehow broken away from the collective five years ago. Unfortunately, in a free society, the former drones reverted to destructive ethnic warfare. The survivors asked *Voyager* personnel to help them reactivate a derelict Borg cube ship in order that a new collective could restore harmony to their society. ("Unity" [VGR]).

(In an alternate **quantum reality** visited by Worf in 2370, the crew of the *Enterprise*-D did not recover Captain Picard from the Borg. In yet another reality, the Borg had taken over most of the Federation, with a heavily damaged *Enterprise*-D being one of the few ships remaining. ("Parallels" [TNG]).

Writer Maurice Hurley derived the name Borg from the term cyborg (cybernetic organism), although it seems unlikely that a people living on the other side of the galaxy would know of the term. The Borg were first seen in "Q Who" (TNG).

Borgia plant. Plant form indigenous to planet **M-113**. Described as Carbon Group III vegetation, it is mildly toxic. **Professor Robert Crater** tried to convince Kirk and McCoy that **Crewman Darnell** had died from eating a **Borgia plant**. ("The Man Trap" [TOS]).

Borgolis Nebula. Blue-tinged gaseous cloud. The Borgolis Nebula was studied by *Enterprise*-D personnel in 2369. **Neela Daren** recommended that the **Spectral Analysis Department** have more sensor observation time to examine the Borgolis Nebula, but sensor-array usage was allocated to Engineering. ("Lessons" [TNG]).

borhyas. In the **Bajoran** culture, a term for ghost or spirit. ("The Next Phase" [TNG]).

boridium pellet. Small object planted subcutaneously by Romulan security forces into prisoners, enabling such prisoners to be located by use of the pellet's energy signature in a manner similar to that used in a Federation **emergency transponder**. ("Birthright, Part II" [TNG]).

boridium power converter. Component of an **exocomp**, used to provide energy for the device's internal functions. ("The Quality of Life" [TNG]).

Borka VI. Planet. Deanna Troi attended a neuropsychology seminar on Borka VI in 2369. Troi was abducted from the seminar by Romulan underground operatives who used her in an elaborate plot to help Romulan **Vice Proconsul M'ret** defect to the Federation. ("Face of the Enemy" [TNG]). SEE: **N'Vek, Subcommander**.

Bortas, I.K.S. Klingon ***Vor'cha*-class** attack cruiser. The *Bortas* conveyed Captain Picard's request for Klingon assistance at planet **Nelvana III** when the *Enterprise*-D investigated reports of a secret Romulan base there. The three Klingon vessels that responded to Picard's request made it possible for the *Enterprise*-D to escape without provoking an interstellar war, despite the hopes of the Romulans. ("The Defector" [TNG]). The *Bortas* served as **Gowron**'s flagship during the **Klingon civil war** of 2367-68. **Worf** served as weapons officer aboard the *Bortas* during the early part of that conflict. ("Redemption, Part I" [TNG]).

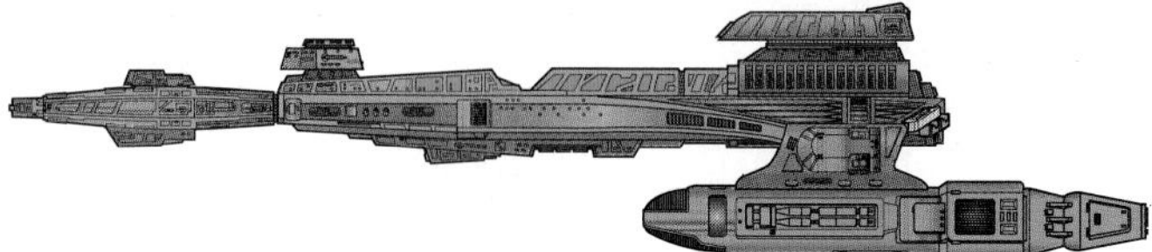

Boru, King Brian. Irish king during the time of the **Battle of Clontarf**. Miles O'Brien claimed to be a direct descendant of King Boru and played the role of Boru in a holosuite re-creation of the famous battle. ("Bar Association" [DS9]).

Borum. (Michael Bell). Internee at the **Hutet labor camp**. Borum arranged to have **Li Nalas**'s earring smuggled back to planet **Bajor** in 2370, thereby alerting outsiders to the fact that Li was still alive. ("The Homecoming" [DS9]). *This character's name was never given on air and is from the script.*

Boslic freighter captain. SEE: **Rionoj**.

Boslics. Humanoid spacefaring civilization. A Boslic freighter docked at station Deep Space 9 in 2372 and contraband was found aboard the vessel by security officer Kurn. The Boslic freighter captain pulled out a disruptor pistol and shot Kurn, injuring him. ("Sons of Mogh" [DS9]).

Botany Bay, S.S. Ancient **DY-100** space vessel launched from Earth in 1996. The *Botany Bay* was a **sleeper ship** carrying the former dictator **Khan Noonien Singh** and his followers, who had escaped from Earth after the terrible **Eugenics Wars**. The *Botany Bay* traveled for some 300 years with most of its passengers preserved in suspended animation before being discovered by the *Starship Enterprise* near the **Mutara Sector** in 2267. ("Space Seed" [TOS]). *The* Botany Bay *miniature was also used as the freighter* **Woden** *in "The Ultimate Computer" (TOS). The model was displayed at the Smithsonian National Air and Space Museum in Washington, D.C. A conjectural model of the* Botany Bay, *built by Greg Jein for a photograph in the* Star Trek Chronology, *was equipped with several space shuttle-style solid rocket strap-on boosters, suggesting how the 1996-vintage spacecraft might have gotten into orbit. The model was seen as a desktop decoration in Rain Robinson's SETI laboratory in the 1996 scenes of "Future's End, Parts I and II" (VGR).*

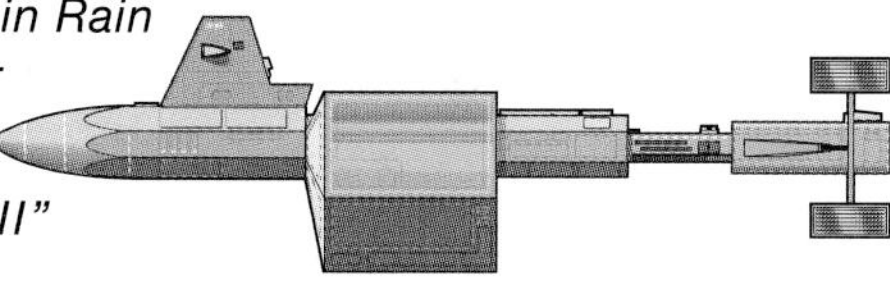

Botha. A people who occupy a sector of the **Delta Quadrant** known as **Bothan** space. ("Persistence of Vision" [VGR]).

Bothan. A member of the **Botha** civilization. Bothans are regarded as a fiercely territorial society and are endowed with extraordinary telepathic abilities. Using bio-electric energy fields, their psionic skills can cause mass delusions leading to catatonic states. Individuals so affected live out secret desires that are normally suppressed deep within their minds. ("Persistence of Vision" [VGR]). *No relation to those who stole the plans to the second Death Star. (Oops, wrong universe!)*

Bounty, H.M.S. Eighteenth-century British sailing ship famous for the mutiny of its crew in 1789. Dr. Leonard McCoy gave the name *"H.M.S. Bounty"* to the captured Klingon ship that he and his shipmates planned to return to Earth in after having disobeyed Starfleet orders to save Spock. *(Star Trek IV: The Voyage Home).*

Boyce, Dr. Phillip. (John Hoyt). **Chief medical officer** on the original *Starship Enterprise* under the command of Captain **Christopher Pike** in 2254. Boyce, noting that Pike was suffering from exhaustion following a mission to **Rigel VII**, urged Pike to relax a bit to avoid burnout. Boyce was of the opinion that there are things a man will tell his bartender that he would never tell his doctor. ("The Cage" [TOS], "The Menagerie, Part I" [TOS]).

Boyce. Starfleet officer assigned to station Deep Space 9. In 2372, while serving on the bridge of the *U.S.S. Defiant*, Boyce was killed during a Jem'Hadar attack. ("Starship Down" [DS9]). *Boyce was named as a tip of the hat to the* Enterprise *doctor in "The Cage" (TOS), the first* Star Trek *pilot episode.*

Boylen, Lieutenant. Starfleet officer. Crewmember aboard the *U.S.S. Pegasus* who died in the tragic loss of that ship in 2358. He referred to then-Ensign **William Riker** as "Ensign Babyface."

Bozeman, U.S.S. Federation starship, ***Soyuz* class**, Starfleet registry NCC-1941, commanded by Captain **Morgan Bateman**. The *Bozeman* was three weeks out of its home starbase when it disappeared near the **Typhon Expanse** in 2278, where it remained until 2368. During those 90 years, those aboard the *Bozeman* experienced the passage of only a brief period of time. Unknown to them, they were in a recursive **temporal causality loop**, so they experienced that same brief period over and over, *ad infinitum,* until the loop was disrupted by the *Enterprise*-D, with which it nearly collided. ("Cause and Effect" [TNG]). The *Bozeman* was subsequently recertified for Starfleet service. (During the **anti-time** occurrence created by the **Q Continuum**, Admiral Nakamura deployed the *Bozeman*, along with 15 other starships, to the **Romulan Neutral Zone** to investigate a Romulan military buildup on their side of the zone.) ("All Good Things..." [TNG]). The *Bozeman* was required to make a minor course correction in 2371 after the **Amargosa** star's destruction altered gravitational forces in an entire sector. *(Star Trek Generations).* The *Bozeman* was later part of the Starfleet armada that intercepted a Borg ship at Earth on stardate 50893. *(Star Trek: First Contact). Named for the city of Bozeman, Montana, hometown of "Cause and Effect" writer Brannon Braga, who also co-wrote "All Good Things...",* Star Trek Generations, *and* Star Trek: First Contact. *The registry number was an homage to Steven Spielberg's movie* 1941, *for which* Star Trek *model maker Greg Jein provided miniatures.*

Bracas V. Planet. Lieutenant Commander La Forge once took a vacation and went skindiving on Bracas V. La Forge compared the appearance of the **two-dimensional creatures** discovered in 2367 to a school of fish he had seen while diving on a coral reef on Bracas V. ("The Loss" [TNG]).

Brack, Mr. Alias used by **Flint** in 2239 to purchase planet Holberg 917G. ("Requiem for Methuselah" [TOS]).

Brackett, Fleet Admiral. (Karen Hensel). Starfleet official. Brackett met with Captain Picard at Starbase 234 in 2368 to discuss the sudden disappearance of Ambassador **Spock**. On Brackett's orders, the *Enterprise*-D proceeded to planet Vulcan to obtain more information about Spock's whereabouts and motives. ("Unification, Part I" [TNG]).

Bractor. (Armin Shimerman). Commander of the **Ferengi** attack vessel ***Kreechta***. When the *Kreechta* stumbled into a **Starfleet battle simulation** in 2365, Bractor misinterpreted the situation, believing the derelict ***U.S.S. Hathaway*** to be of some secret strategic importance, when in fact it was merely engaging in war games with the *Enterprise*-D. ("Peak Performance" [TNG]). *Actor Armin Shimerman would later play the part of Quark in* Star Trek: Deep Space Nine. *He also played Letek in "The Last Outpost" (TNG), one of the first Ferengi ever seen.*

Bradbury, U.S.S. Federation starship, Starfleet registry number NX-72307. Upon his acceptance to Starfleet Academy in 2366, **Wesley Crusher** was scheduled for transport aboard the *Bradbury* from the *Enterprise*-D to Starfleet Academy on Earth. Wesley unfortunately missed the transport while assisting with the recovery of Ambassador Troi, Commander Riker, and Counselor Troi from a Ferengi ship. ("Ménage à Troi" [TNG]). *The* Bradbury *was named for s-f/fantasy writer Ray Bradbury, a friend of the late Gene Roddenberry's. Based on the ship's registry number, we suspect it is an experimental vessel, the first of its class.*

Bradley, Jessica. (Carolyn Allport). A fictional character from the **Dixon Hill** detective stories. Picard encountered a holographic representation of Bradley, a wealthy, beautiful socialite, in his Dixon Hill holodeck adventures, during which she was "murdered" by persons unknown, although Picard (as Hill) suspected the work of **Cyrus Redblock**. ("The Big Goodbye" [TNG]).

Brahms, Dr. Leah. (Susan Gibney). A graduate of the **Daystrom Institute of Technology**, Dr. Leah Brahms was part of an engineering design team on the ***Galaxy*-Class Starship Development Project** at the **Utopia Planitia Fleet Yards** in 2358. Brahms made major contributions to the **Theoretical Propulsion Group**, far beyond her official role as a junior team member, and was responsible for much of the warp engine design on the *Starship* ***Enterprise*-D**. At the time, Brahms resided in the **Martian Colonies**. In an attempt to learn more about the engine design of the *Enterprise*-D, Commander La Forge re-created Dr. Brahms's image in the holodeck. While he did learn a great deal about the engines, Commander LaForge also, unfortunately, developed a real attraction for Dr. Brahms's image. ("Booby Trap" [TNG]). By 2367, Brahms was married and had been promoted to senior design engineer of the Theoretical Propulsion Group. Brahms visited the *Enterprise*-D in that year, to inspect the field modifications made to that ship's engines by Chief Engineer Geordi La Forge. Much to La Forge's dismay, Brahms was highly critical of La Forge's work. Brahms also strongly objected to La Forge's having programmed a holographic replica of herself, noting that doing so without her permission constituted an invasion of privacy. Nevertheless, the two engineers pulled together in a crisis and became friends. SEE: **Junior**. ("Galaxy's Child" [TNG]). *In the anti-time future visited by Picard in "All Good Things..." (TNG), Geordi La Forge was married to a woman named Leah. It was not made clear if, in this alternate timeline, Leah Brahms had married Geordi, but it seems to be likely. In an early draft of "Booby Trap," Brahms was named Navid Daystrom, presumably a descendant of Dr. Richard Daystrom. Unfortunately, the casting department did not realize that this would require a Black actress to play the part until after Susan Gibney had been hired. At the suggestion of script coordinator Eric A. Stillwell, the character was renamed, but the Daystrom tie-in was kept by adding a line stating that she had graduated from the Daystrom Institute. Susan Gibney was a strong contender for the part of Captain Janeway in* Star Trek: Voyager. *She also played Erika Benteen in "Paradise Lost" (DS9).*

brain-circuitry pattern. Medical diagnostic image mapping neural activity in a humanoid brain. The BCP of each individual is unique, and thus serves as a positive means of identification. **Mira Romaine** was given a BCP diagnostic exam in 2269 during the battle with the **Zetarians**. The test revealed the fact that her brain-wave patterns were changing to match those of the aliens. ("The Lights of Zetar" [TOS]).

brak'lul. Klingon term for a characteristic redundancy in **Klingon** physiology. All vital bodily functions are protected by a redundant organ or system. For example, Klingons possess two livers, an eight-chambered heart (double the four chambers found in many other humanoids), and 23 ribs, unlike the ten pairs found in humans. ("Ethics" [TNG]).

Brak. Character in Ferengi children's books. ("Accession" [DS9]). *Quark quoted from such a book: "See Brak acquire. Acquire, Brak. Acquire!"*

Branch, Commander. (David Gautreaux). Commander of the **Epsilon IX monitoring station** that was destroyed when the **V'Ger** probe returned to Federation space. (*Star Trek: The Motion Picture*). *Commander Branch was never referred to by name in the film, but his name was in the credits. Just before* Star Trek I *began production, actor David Gautreaux had been cast in the role of Commander Xon, science officer aboard the* Enterprise *for the proposed television series* **Star Trek II**. *When the first episode of this series became* Star Trek: The Motion Picture, *the character of Xon was eliminated and Gautreaux was recast as Branch.*

Brand, Admiral. (Jacqueline Brookes). Superintendent of **Starfleet Academy** in 2368. Brand presided over the **Nova Squadron** inquiry following the death of cadet **Joshua Albert** in that year. ("The First Duty" [TNG]). SEE: **Kolvoord Starburst; Locarno, Cadet First Class Nicholas.** Beverly Crusher contacted Admiral Brand in 2370, and was dismayed to learn that Wesley was in danger of washing out of the academy. ("Journey's End" [TNG]).

Braslota system. Planetary system. A **Starfleet battle simulation** was held involving the *U.S.S. Enterprise*-D and the ***U.S.S. Hathaway*** in 2365 in the Braslota system. ("Peak Performance" [TNG]).

Brathaw. (John Prosky). Engineer aboard the cargo ship ***Xhosa*** in 2372. ("For the Cause" [DS9]). *Brathaw was Bolian. His name was not mentioned in dialog, but is from the script.*

Brattain, U.S.S. Federation *Miranda*-class science vessel, Starfleet registry number NCC-21166, commanded by Captain Chantal Zaheva. The *Brattain* mysteriously disappeared in 2367 and was found trapped in a **Tyken's Rift** near a binary star system by *Enterprise*-D personnel. All but one of the *Brattain* crew were discovered dead, apparently having brutally killed each other. Autopsies conducted by Dr. Beverly Crusher revealed unusual chemical imbalances in their brains, apparently due to severe **REM sleep** deprivation, believed to be the cause of the bizarre violence. The REM sleep loss was found to be a side effect of an attempt by an alien ship to communicate from the Tyken's Rift. The alien intelligence had apparently been trying to enlist the *Brattain* crew to help both ships escape the rift. ("Night Terrors" [TNG]). *The dedication plaque on the* Brattain*'s bridge said that the ship had been built by Yoyodyne Propulsion Systems, and bore the motto, "...a three hour tour, a three hour tour." The ship's name on the model was spelt "Brittain" by mistake. The model was a re-use of the* U.S.S. Reliant *from* Star Trek II: The Wrath of Khan, *with minor modifications.*

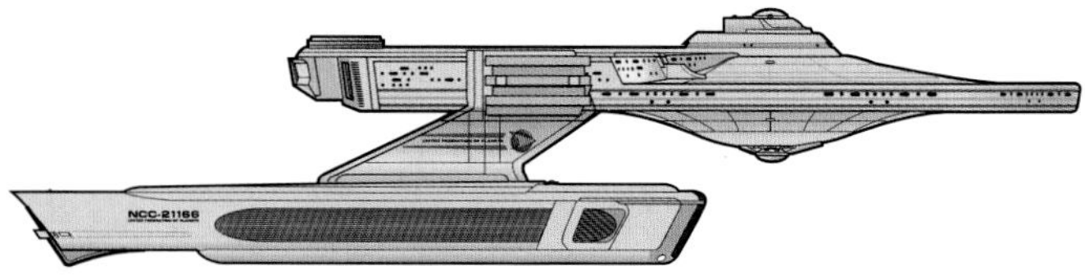

Brax. Planet. According to archaeologist **Vash**, **Q** is known as "The God of Lies" to the inhabitants of Brax. ("Q-Less" [DS9]).

Braxton, Captain. (Allan G. Royal). Native of the 29th century, pilot of the Federation *Timeship* ***Aeon***. Braxton traveled to the Delta Quadrant in 2373 to destroy the *Starship Voyager,* which he believed would be responsible for a 29th-century **temporal explosion** that would destroy Earth's solar system. In confronting *Voyager*, Braxton's ship was thrown back in time, where it crash-landed on Earth in 1967. Braxton survived the crash, but became separated from his ship. Stranded in the past, Braxton watched helplessly while Earth native **Henry Starling** salvaged the *Aeon* and exploited its technology over the next three decades. In 1996, Braxton was homeless and destitute. In that year, another ship from the future, the *U.S.S. Voyager* from 2373, arrived and destroyed the *Aeon*, preventing Starling from traveling into the future. This action, which prevented the 29th century temporal explosion, resulted in the creation of an alternate 29th century in which Braxton was not trapped in the 20th century. This Braxton escorted *Voyager* back to the Delta Quadrant in 2373. ("Future's End, Parts I and II" [VGR]). *It is not entirely clear what happened to the original Braxton in the altered timeline. The episode seems to suggest that the original Braxton, along with all the technological changes wrought by Starling, disappeared when* Voyager *destroyed the* Aeon *in 1996. However, the holographic doctor's autonomous holoemitter did* not *disappear, suggesting that some effects of Braxton's 1967 crash remained, even in the altered timeline.*

Bre'el IV. A Federation member planet whose asteroidal moon was knocked out of its normal orbit in 2366 by the nearby passage of a black hole or other celestial object. The moon's new orbit began to decay rapidly and soon threatened to collide with the planet's surface. Bre'el IV was heavily populated by a humanoid civilization that might have been wiped out if the moon did indeed hit the planet. The *Enterprise*-D made repeated attempts to return the moon to its proper orbit, but was unable to do so. The planet was finally saved by a magnanimous gesture from Q, who returned the moon to a nearly circular, 55,000-kilometer orbit. ("Deja Q" [TNG]).

"Bread and Circuses." Original Series episode #43. Written by Gene Roddenberry and Gene L. Coon. Directed by Ralph Senensky. Stardate 4040.7. *First aired in 1967. Kirk, Spock, and McCoy are captured on an Earthlike planet on which the Roman Empire never fell.* GUEST CAST: William Smithers as **Merrick, R. M.**; Logan Ramsey as **Marcus, Claudius**; Ian Wolfe as **Septimus**; William Bramley as Policeman; Rhodes Reason as **Flavius**; Bart LaRue as Announcer; Jack Perkins as Master of the Games; Max Kelvin as **Achilles**; Lois Jewell as **Drusilla**; Bob Orrison as Policeman and guard; Paul Baxley as Policeman and McCoy's stunt double; Allen Pinson as Spock's stunt double; Tom Steele, Gil Perkins, Stunt slaves. SEE: **Achilles; *Beagle, S.S.*; Children of the Sun; Condition Green; Drusilla; Eight ninety-two-IV; Flavius; Harrison, William B.; Hodgkins's Law of Parallel Planet Development; Jupiter 8; Marcus, Cladius; Merrick, R. M.; *Name the Winner!*; Prime Directive; Septimus; transponder, emergency; World War III.**

bread pudding soufflé. Light, fluffy, baked dessert dish. Bread pudding soufflé was a specialty at **Sisko's** in New Orleans on Earth. ("Homefront" [DS9]).

Brechtian Cluster. Star system with two inhabited planets. The **Crystalline Entity** was destroyed in 2368 while en route to the Brechtian Cluster. ("Silicon Avatar" [TNG]).

Breen. Humanoid civilization. ("Hero Worship" [TNG]). Owing to the extremely cold climate of their homeworld, Breen do not have blood. ("In Purgatory's Shadow" [DS9]). The Breen had outposts near the **Black Cluster** that were investigated by the *Enterprise*-D in 2368. The Breen utilized cloaking technology and their ships were armed with disruptor-type weapons. The Breen, politically nonaligned, were considered but dismissed as a possible explanation for the destruction of the ***S.S. Vico*** in the Black Cluster. ("Hero Worship" [TNG]). In 2370, a Breen pilot participated in the palio on **Deep Space 3.** ("Interface" [TNG]). The Breen were not empathically detectable by Betazoids. ("The Loss" [TNG]). The Breen were one of the civilizations who used type-3 disruptor weapons. *(Star Trek Generations).* The Breen homeworld was a frozen wasteland. ("Crossfire" [DS9]). Among the Breen, pregnancy at a young age was a common occurrence. ("Elogium" [VGR]). In 2366, two Breen warships attacked the Cardassian ship *Ravinok*. The Breen ships chased the *Ravinok* to planet Dozaria and forced it to crash. The Breen used the survivors from the *Ravinok* to mine dilithium on Dozaria. To protect themselves from the heat of Dozaria, the Breen guards wore completely sealed, refrigerated suits. ("Indiscretion" [DS9]). Breen privateers attacked the Bajoran colony of Free Haven in early 2372. ("To the Death" [DS9]). The Romulans have a saying: "Never turn your back on a Breen." ("By Inferno's Light" [DS9]).

***bregit* lung.** A traditional **Klingon** dish. Riker said he enjoyed *bregit* lung when it was served aboard the Klingon vessel *Pagh*. ("A Matter of Honor" [TNG]).

***brek'tal* ritual.** Klingon ceremony in which a warrior who slays the head of a **House** in honorable combat becomes the new head of the House. The victor of the battle is invited to take the loser's place, both in his House and with his wife. The *brek'tal* ritual was performed in 2371 by **Grilka**, following the death of her husband, **Kozak**. ("The House of Quark" [DS9]).

Brekka. The fourth planet in the **Delos** star system, home to an intelligent humanoid species, the **Brekkians**. ("Symbiosis" [TNG]).

Brekkians. Humanoid species from the planet **Brekka**. The Brekkians had only one industry, that of producing the narcotic **felicium**, which the Brekkians traded with their neighbors, the **Ornarans**, in exchange for all the Brekkians' needs. Brekkians possess the natural ability to generate electrical discharges with their bodies. ("Symbiosis" [TNG]).

Brel, Jor. (Eugene Roche). **Enaran** citizen who, in 2373, was part of a group transported aboard the *U.S.S. Voyager* to Enara Prime from a colony in the Fima system. Jor Brel was a musician. Brel expressed disbelief at accusations that his people had, decades ago, deliberately exterminated the people known as the **Regressives**. ("Remember" [VGR]). *"Jor" was a title of address prefixed to the names of an elder Enaran man.*

Brentalia. A protected planet that, during the 24th century, was used as a wildlife preserve. In 2368, two rare **Corvan gilvos** were being transported to Brentalia in the hopes that they would reproduce there and replenish the species. ("New Ground" [TNG]). Lieutenant Worf took his son, Alexander, to the zoo on Brentalia to see the Kryonian tigers. ("Imaginary Friend" [TNG]).

brestanti ale. Intoxicating beverage. ("Blood Oath" [DS9]).

Brevelle, Ensign. (Paul Tompkins). Starfleet officer who was a crew member on the *U.S.S. Victory*, and who participated in an investigation on the planet **Tarchannen III** in 2362. In 2367, Brevelle was compelled to return to Tarchannen III, where he was transformed into a reptilian life-form native to that planet. ("Identity Crisis" [TNG]).

Briam, Ambassador. (Tim O'Connor). Representative of the **Krios** government, assigned to the historic **Ceremony of Reconciliation** between Krios and the **Valt Minor** system, held aboard the *Starship Enterprise*-D in 2368. Briam's mission was to escort **Kamala**, a Kriosian **empathic metamorph**, to the ceremony so that she could be married to **Chancellor Alrik** of Valt. This marriage would seal the peace treaty. Briam had been selected for this assignment in part because he was 200 years old and might therefore be less likely to succumb to Kamala's considerable charms. Briam was injured by a Ferengi named Par Lenor just prior to the ceremony, but Captain Picard was able to serve in his place. ("The Perfect Mate" [TNG]).

Brianon, Kareen. (Barbara Alyn Woods). Assistant to **Dr. Ira Graves** during the final years of his life. Just prior to his death, Brianon secretly sent a distress call in an effort to get medical attention for the ailing Graves. Brianon, an attractive woman, later admitted she had been attracted to Graves, and regretted she was so much younger than he was. ("The Schizoid Man" [TNG]).

***Bride of the Corpse*.** Entertainment program produced on **Earth** in the mid-20th century. *Bride of the Corpse* was a low-budget horror motion picture, a sequel to *Orgy of the Walking Dead*. Astronomer **Rain Robinson** and Starfleet officer **Tom Paris** were both fans of these classic films. ("Future's End, Part I" [VGR]).

Bridge Officer Examination, Starfleet. Battery of tests required in order to qualify to serve as a line officer in the Federation **Starfleet**. The examination is a requirement to earn the rank of full commander. The tests include qualifications in diplomatic law, first-contact procedures, **bridge** operations, and engineering. Unbeknownst to candidates, the exam also included measures of command ability, including the ability to order personnel into situations where they might be killed. An officer must pass this test in order to serve as commander or duty officer aboard a starship. ("Thine Own Self" [TNG]).

bridge. Primary command center for **starship**s and other spacecraft. On most Federation starships, the bridge is located on Deck 1, at the top of the **Primary Hull**. *The* Enterprise *bridge was first designed by original* Star Trek *series art director Matt Jefferies. The first motion picture version was designed under the supervision of Harold Michelson (based on an earlier* Star Trek II *television version developed by Joseph R. Jennings and Mike Minor), while Herman Zimmerman designed the* Star Trek V *and* Star Trek VI *versions for the* Enterprise-*A, as well as the* Enterprise-*B bridge from* Star Trek Generations. *Zimmerman also developed the* Enterprise-*D bridge for* Star Trek: The Next Generation, *based on designs by Andrew Probert, as well as the* Defiant *bridge for Star Trek: Deep Space Nine, and the* Enterprise-*E bridge for* Star Trek: First Contact. *Numerous other starship bridge sets seen on* Star Trek: The Next Generation *(including the* Enterprise-C *bridge) were created by production designer Richard James, who also designed the bridge of the* starship Voyager. *The bridge of the* Enterprise-*D featured a beautiful curved railing that served as the ship's tactical console. Gene Roddenberry insisted that the railing be made of wood, rather than metal, saying that the use of the natural material would help the command center to retain a certain "humanity." The* Enterprise *bridge has been studied numerous times by various defense and aerospace organizations as a model for an efficient futuristic control room. At least one such computerized command center has actually been built, closely based on the design of the* Enterprise *bridge.* SEE: **auxiliary control; conn; dedication plaque; engineering; helm; library computer; navigator; operations manager; science officer; turbolift; viewer**.

Briefing With Neelix, A. Audiovisual program produced by *Starship Voyager* morale officer Neelix for the ship's crew. The show, hosted by Neelix, included such features as news, interviews with crew members, musical performances, recommendations for new holodeck programs, fascinating medical information, gossip, and previews of upcoming meals. ("Investigations" [VGR]).

brig. Security detention area, used to detain individuals believed to have committed serious criminal offenses or for individuals believed to pose a serious danger to other people or to the ship itself. Secure entrance to starship brigs is often provided by a force field door.

U.S.S. Enterprise

U.S.S. Enterprise-refit (STII)

U.S.S. Enterprise-B

U.S.S. Enterprise-D

U.S.S. Defiant

U.S.S. Voyager

U.S.S. Enterprise-E

Briggs, Bob. (Scott DeVenney). Director of the **Cetacean Institute** on Earth during the late 20th century. Briggs supervised the return of two **humpback whale**s, **George and Gracie**, to the open ocean in 1986 because the institute could no longer afford to feed them. *(Star Trek IV: The Voyage Home).*

Brilgar. (Christian Conrad). Security officer on station Deep Space 9. On stardate 50416.2, Lieutenant Brilgar was assigned to protect Major **Kira Nerys** after members of the **Shakaar resistance cell** were murdered. ("The Darkness and the Light" [DS9]).

brill cheese. Solid dairy food made from creamy pale green cheese. Neelix made brill cheese from some **schplict** he had obtained from the planet **Napinne**. He made the cheese for Ensign Ashmore, who had asked Neelix to prepare macaroni and cheese. ("Learning Curve" [VGR]).

Brin Tusk. Bajoran national. Brin was arrested on station Terok Nor in 2367 for a crime and sentenced to five years hard labor for the offense. ("Things Past" [DS9]).

Bringloid V. Class-M planet in the **Ficus Sector**. Bringloid V was settled by human colonists from the ***S.S. Mariposa***. The planet (and the colonists) were threatened in 2365 by massive solar flares from the system's star. ("Up the Long Ladder" [TNG]).

Bringloidi. Colonists from Earth who settled **Bringloid V**. The Bringloidi, under the leadership of colony head **Danilo Odell**, were Irish descendants who had rejected advanced technology in favor of a more agrarian lifestyle. By 2365, the Bringloidi were threatened by solar flares, so the colonists relocated on planet **Mariposa** with the assistance of *Enterprise*-D personnel. ("Up the Long Ladder" [TNG]).

Brink. First officer of the ***U.S.S. Brattain***. Brink died violently, along with most of the *Brattain* crew, in 2367 when the ship was trapped in a **Tyken's Rift**, and all ship's personnel suffered from severe **REM sleep** deprivation. ("Night Terrors" [TNG]).

Briok. Ferengi waiter who worked at Quark's bar on Deep Space 9 in 2372. ("Bar Association" [DS9]).

Briori. Humanoid civilization native to the Delta Quadrant. The Briori abducted over 300 humans from **Earth** in 1937 and transported them 70,000 light years to their homeworld, a Class-L planet in the Delta Quadrant, to work as slaves. Eventually, the slaves revolted, killed the Briori, took their technology and weapons, and established a civilization on the former Briori homeworld. The *Starship Voyager* visited the planet in late 2371. ("The 37's" [VGR]). SEE: **Thirty-Sevens**.

Bristow, Fred. Starfleet officer assigned to the *Starship Voyager*. In 2373 Ensign Bristow had a crush on Lieutenant B'Elanna Torres, but she thought of him as a child. Torres and Bristow had played a match of parrisses squares once, with Torres being the easy victor. ("The Swarm" [VGR]).

brizeen nitrate. Chemical substance used as a soil enhancer on Bajor. Grand Nagus **Zek** gifted 50,000 kilograms to Kira Nerys in exchange for permission to conduct business negotiations with the **Dosi** aboard station Deep Space 9. ("Rules of Acquisition" [DS9]).

broad-spectrum warp field. Subspace bubble, also referred to as an inverse warp field, capable of interfering with the structure of a quantum fissure. A broad-spectrum field was emitted by the **Shuttlecraft Curie** to seal a **quantum fissure** in 2370. ("Parallels" [TNG]).

"Broccoli". A nickname given by Ensign Crusher to Lieutenant **Reginald Barclay**. It was not meant kindly, and was unfortunately used at the most inopportune moments. ("Hollow Pursuits" [TNG]).

"Broken Link." *Deep Space Nine* episode #98. Teleplay by Robert Hewitt Wolfe & Ira Steven Behr. Story by George Brozak. Directed by Les Landau. Stardate 49962.4. *First aired in 1996. Odo returns to the Founders' homeworld to find a cure for a strange debilitating disease and is judged by the Great Link for his killing a changeling. Odo becomes a human in this episode, the last of* Star Trek: Deep Space Nine's *fourth season.* GUEST CAST: Salome Jens as **Founder Leader**; Robert O'Reilly as **Gowron**; Jill Jacobson as **Aroya**; Leslie Bevis as **Rionoj**; Andrew Robinson as **Garak, Elim**; Andrew Hawkes as **Amat'igan**. SEE: **Amat'igan; Archanis; Archanis IV; Cardassian embassy on Romulus; Celestial Cafe; Chalan Aroya; Edosian orchid; Falangian diamond; Founder Leader; Garak, Elim; Gowron; Great Link; Inkarian wool; Merrok, Proconsul; Mora Pol, Dr.; Odo; quantum torpedo; Rionoj; Ustard, Subcommander.**

Brooks, Admiral. Starfleet officer. Brooks was to head the inquiry into Dr. Beverly Crusher's activities following the death of **Dr. Reyga** in 2369. ("Suspicions" [TNG]). Following the *Enterprise*-D's encounter with Third of Five, the Borg individual the crew named **"Hugh,"** Captain Picard sent a detailed report to Admiral Brooks. The report detailed Hugh's reactions to captivity, his development of self-awareness, as well as Picard's decision not to use an invasive program designed to destroy the Borg collective. The report to Brooks would later cause Picard trouble with **Admiral Alynna Necheyev**, who criticized Picard's choice to return Hugh to the collective. ("Descent, Part I" [TNG]).

Brooks, Ensign Janet. (Kim Braden). Starfleet officer. Brooks was an *Enterprise*-D crew member whose husband, **Marc Brooks**, died in 2366. Brooks was under the care of Counselor **Deanna Troi** following her husband's death. Despite the fact that Troi had temporarily lost her empathic powers at the time, Brooks felt that Troi helped her to deal realistically with Marc's death. ("The Loss" [TNG]). *Kim Braden also portrayed Jean-Luc Picard's wife in the nexus sequence of* Star Trek Generations.

Brooks, Marc. An *Enterprise*-D crew member who was killed in an accident in late 2366, five months before his 38th birthday. Marc's widow, **Janet Brooks**, was also an *Enterprise*-D officer. ("The Loss" [TNG]).

Brossmer, Chief. (Shelby Leverington). *Enterprise*-D transporter technician. She was at the transporter controls when Ro Laren and Geordi La Forge disappeared in an apparent transporter accident in 2368. ("The Next Phase" [TNG]).

"Brothers." *Next Generation* episode #77. Written by Rick Berman. Directed by Robert Bowman. Stardate 44085.7. *First aired in 1990. Data and his brother, Lore, are both summoned to a secret location by their creator, Dr. Noonien Soong. This was the first episode written by producer-writer Rick Berman, who went on to co-create* Star Trek: Deep Space Nine. *and* Star Trek: Voyager. GUEST CAST: Cory Danziger as **Potts, Jake**; Colm Meaney as **O'Brien, Miles**; Adam Ryen as **Potts, Willie**; James Lashly as **Kopf, Ensign**; Brent Spiner as **Lore** and **Soong, Noonien**. SEE: **atmosphere conditioning pumps; Casey; cove palm; Data; dilithium vector calibrations; emotion chip; Kopf, Ensign; Lore; Ogus II; Pakleds; Potts, Jake; Potts, Willie; site-to-site transport; Soong, Noonien; Starbase 416.**

Browder IV. Planet. The *U.S.S. Hood* and the *U.S.S. Enterprise*-D were assigned to Browder IV for a terraforming mission on stardate 43714.1. ("Allegiance" [TNG]).

Brower, Ensign. (David Coburn). An *Enterprise*-D staff engineer. Brower was on duty when the *Enterprise*-D saved the **Argus Array** in 2367. ("The Nth Degree" [TNG]).

brown dwarf. Small celestial object similar to a star, but with insufficient mass to generate a star's powerful nuclear reactions.

Because a brown dwarf might glow with only feeble infrared light, it can be difficult to detect across interstellar distances. Data once commented that some brown dwarfs have anomalous chemical compositions including unusual depletion of europium. ("Manhunt" [TNG]).

Brown, Doc. Pediatrician. Childhood physician of Lieutenant Thomas Paris. Brown had lollipops and the latest holocomic books in his waiting room, a contrast to *Voyager*'s Emergency Medical Holo-gram, at least according to Paris. ("Cathexis" [VGR]).

Brown, Dr. (Harry Basch). Assistant to archaeologist **Roger Korby**. Brown may have originally been a human member of Korby's staff, but by the time the *Starship Enterprise* arrived on a rescue mission, Brown was actually a sophisticated **android** built with the technology left over from the ancient civilization that lived under the surface of planet **Exo III**. The technology used to create Brown was also used to create Korby's android body. ("What Are Little Girls Made Of?" [TOS]).

Brull. (Joey Aresco). A leader of the **Gatherer** group on **Gamma Hromi II**. Proud of his maurauding lifestyle, Brull nevertheless hoped for a better life for his two sons. He agreed to conduct the *Enterprise*-D, and Acamarian Sovereign **Marouk** to talks with the leader of the Gatherers, **Chorgan**. ("The Vengeance Factor" [TNG]).

Brun. Former enemy of **Enabran Tain**. In 2373, Garak intimated that he was responsible for Brun's death. ("In Purgatory's Shadow" [DS9]).

Brunt. (Jeffrey Combs). **Liquidator** from the **Ferengi Commerce Authority** (FCA). Brunt was assigned the case of Quark's mother **Ishka**, who was charged in 2371 with breaking **Ferengi** law by earning profit. ("Family Business" [DS9]). In 2372, the FCA sent Liquidator Brunt to Deep Space 9 to investigate allegations that Ferengi workers at Quark's bar had formed a labor union. ("Bar Association" [DS9]). Brunt's dislike of Quark was considerable. When Quark thought he was dying of **Dorek syndrome** later that year, Brunt bid the enormous sum of 500 bars of **latinum** on the **Ferengi Futures Exchange** for Quark's vacuum-desiccated remains. SEE: **Ferengi death rituals**. Shortly thereafter, when Quark learned that he was not terminally ill, Brunt demanded the fulfillment of the sale, forcing Quark to break the contract. Brunt used this serious violation of Ferengi law to justify the seizure of Quark's assets and the revocation of his Ferengi business licence. ("Body Parts" [DS9]). *Jeffrey Combs previously played Tiron in "Meridian" (DS9).*

Bryma. Planet located in the **Demilitarized Zone**, colonized by **Cardassians**. The Cardassian military maintained a secret weapons depot there. In 2370, the **Maquis** sent two attack ships to destroy the depot, but three **runabouts** from **Deep Space 9** intercepted and prevented the attack. Starfleet feared that an attack by Federation citizens on a civilian Cardassian target might have triggered a full-scale war. ("The Maquis, Part II" [DS9]).

Brynner Information Systems. Business that operated in **San Francisco** on **Earth** in the early 21st century. The company was owned and operated by entrepreneur **Christopher Brynner** and dealt with the operation of Channel 90 of the **Net**. ("Past Tense, Part I" [DS9]).

Brynner, Christopher. (Jim Metzler). Entrepreneur in **San Francisco** on **Earth** in the 21st century. Chris Brynner owned **Brynner Information Systems**, a firm that operated Channel 90 of the **Net**. During the **Bell Riots**, Brynner risked government reprisals by using his Interface access to make it possible for the world to learn the plight of the **Sanctuary District** residents. ("Past Tense, Parts I and II" [DS9]).

***Budapest*, U.S.S.** Federation starship, *Norway*-class, Starfleet registry number NCC-64923. The *Budapest* was among the ships defending Sector 001 against the Borg incursion of 2373. *(Star Trek: First Contact). Named for the European city.*

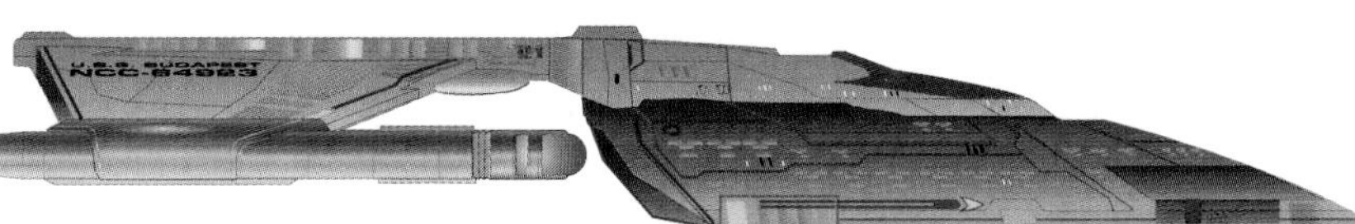

Budrow, Admiral. Commander of Starbase 29 in 2369. While being brainwashed on planet **Tilonus IV**, Commander William Riker was told by his captors that Admiral Budrow had no record of a Starfleet officer matching his description. ("Frame of Mind" [TNG]).

buffer. Cybernetic device used by the **Bynars** to aid in the transfer of information to one another. The Bynars' buffers were small rectangular units worn on their belts. ("11001001" [TNG]).

Builders. Name used by the **Cravic** and the **Pralor Automated Personnel Units** to refer to their creators. ("Prototype" [VGR]).

Bularian canapés. Hors d'oeuvre. Favorite dish of Admiral **Alynna Necheyev**, who thought they were fattening. ("Journey's End" [TNG], "Preemptive Strike" [TNG]).

Bulgallian rat. A frightening animal. Wesley Crusher considered re-creating a Bulgallian rat on the holodeck to prepare himself for the **Psych Test** portion of the Starfleet Academy entrance exam. ("Coming of Age" [TNG]).

bunny rabbit. Terrestrial life-form. Data claimed to have imagined a bunny rabbit in the clouds of the **FGC-47** nebula. Guinan, on the other hand, said she saw a Samarian coral fish. ("Imaginary Friend" [TNG]).

***Buran*, U.S.S.** Federation starship, *Challenger*-class, Starfleet registry number NCC-57580. The *Buran* was one of the 39 starships destroyed by the **Borg** in the battle of **Wolf 359**. ("The Best of Both Worlds, Part II" [TNG]). *The* Buran *was a "kit bashed" study model barely glimpsed among the wreckage of the "graveyard" scene in that episode. The ship was named for the Russian space shuttle, which was in turn named for the Russian word for "snowstorm."*

Buranian. Archaeological period classification on planet **Marlonia.** Picard mentioned that the pottery from planet Marlonia was very similar to early **Taguan** designs but was probably closer to the Buranian period instead. ("Rascals" [TNG]).

Bureau of Planetary Treaties. Branch of the Federation government that deals with interstellar agreements. When Captain James Kirk disappeared mysteriously on a diplomatic mission to planet **Gideon** in 2268, neither the Bureau of Planetary Treaties nor any other bureaucratic agency was of much help. ("The Mark of Gideon" [TOS]).

Burke, John. Chief astronomer of **Earth**'s Royal Academy in England. Burke first mapped the area of space around **Sherman's Planet**. For some reason, Chekov remembered him as Ivan Burkoff. ("The Trouble with Tribbles" [TOS]).

Burke, Lieutenant. (Glenn Morshower). Tactical officer aboard the *U.S.S. Enterprise*-D during the Starfleet **battle simulation** exercise in 2365. Burke unwittingly allowed Wesley Crusher to smuggle a small quantity of antimatter from the *Enterprise*-D to the *Hathaway*, giving the *Hathaway* an advantage in the war game. ("Peak Performance" [TNG]). *Glenn Morshower also portrayed Mr. Orton in "Starship Mine" (TNG) and was the navigator of the* U.S.S. Enterprise-B *in* Star Trek Generations.

Burke, Yeoman. Crew member aboard the *Starship Enterprise*-A who was one of two "hit men" who carried out the assassination of Klingon **Chancellor Gorkon** in 2293. Burke was later murdered, apparently by **Valeris**, in order to protect others involved with the conspiracy. (*Star Trek VI: The Undiscovered Country*).

Burke. (Danny Goldring). Starfleet officer who fought and died on Ajilon Prime in 2373 during a minor skirmish with the Klingons. Lieutenant Burke gave his life so that the rest of his squad could escape up the ramp of a hopper. ("Nor the Battle to the Strong" [DS9]). *Danny Goldring previously played Legate Kell in "Civil Defense" (DS9).*

Burleigh, Beatrice. (Lindsey Haun). **Holonovel** character, the Lady Beatrice Flora. Beatrice Burleigh, the young daughter of **Lord Burleigh**, was to be looked after by governess **Lucille Davenport**, played by *Voyager* captain Kathryn Janeway. ("Cathexis" [VGR]). Beatrice resented the presence of Mrs. Davenport in the Burleigh home, part of Beatrice's difficulty in accepting the recent death of her mother. Beatrice had a younger brother, Henry ("Learning Curve" [VGR]) and enjoyed playing the piano. When a Bothan attacked the *Starship Voyager* in 2372, Janeway hallucinated that she saw young Beatrice on the ship, not just on the holodeck. ("Persistence of Vision" [VGR]). SEE: **Janeway Lambda-1.**

Burleigh, Henry. (Thomas Dekker). **Holonovel** character, the Viscount Timmins. Son of **Lord Burleigh**, young Henry, with his older sister, Beatrice, was cared for by a governess after the death of their mother. ("Cathexis" [VGR], "Learning Curve" [VGR]). Henry had a talent for mathematics and disapproved of his father's romantic interest in **Lucille Davenport**. ("Persistence of Vision" [VGR]). SEE: **Janeway Lambda-1.**

Burleigh, Lord. (Michael Cumpsty). **Holonovel** character. After the death of his wife, Lord Burleigh hired Mrs. Lucille Davenport (played by *Voyager* captain **Kathryn Janeway**) as governess to his children, Beatrice and Henry. ("Cathexis" [VGR]). Eventually, Burleigh fell in love with Lucille, to the dismay of Henry and Beatrice. ("Persistence of Vision" [VGR]). SEE: **Janeway Lambda-1.** *Lord Burleigh was first seen in "Cathexis" (VGR).*

Buruk, I.K.S. **Klingon bird-of-prey** spacecraft that transported **Gowron** to the rendezvous with the *Enterprise*-D in 2367. ("Reunion" [TNG]).

"Business As Usual." Deep Space Nine episode #116. Written by Bradley Thompson & David Weddle. Directed by Siddig El Fadil. No stardate given. *First aired in 1997. Quark becomes an arms dealer in an effort to finally erase his debts. This was the first episode directed by actor Siddig El Fadil.* GUEST CAST: Josh Pais as **Gaila**; Tim Halligan as **Farrakk**; Steven Berkoff as **Hagath**; Lawrence Tierney as **Regent of Palamar**; Charlie Curtis as **Talura**; Eric Cadora as Customer. SEE: **Andarian glass bead; Annel; antimonium; attack skimmer; clavisoa berry; Farrakk; feldomite; Gaila; gigajoule; Hagath; Manchovites; Matopin rock fungi; Metron Consortium; Minnobia; moon grass; mutagenic retrovirus; Nassuc, General; neural modulator; Palamarian Freedom Brigade; Palamarian sea urchin; Parsion III; powdered newt; prion; Proxcinian War; Proxcinians; purification squad; quadrotriticale; Quark; reactive armor; Regent of Palamar; Sepian Commodities Exchange; Talura; tartoc; Varaxian LM-7; Vek; Verillians; Vilix'pran; Wentlian condor snake.**

Bussard collectors. Large electromagnetic devices located at the front of the warp drive nacelles of some Federation starships. The Bussard collectors created a large magnetic field used to attract interstellar hydrogen gas that could be used as fuel by the ship's fusion reactors. The *Enterprise*-D's Bussard collectors were back-flushed with hydrogen to create a dramatic but harmless pyrotechnic display that was successful in frightening the **Pakleds** when Geordi La Forge was held captive aboard the *Mondor*. ("Samaritan Snare" [TNG]). The Bussard ramscoop was again back-flushed to release a stream of hydrogen into the **Tyken's Rift** where the *Enterprise*-D was trapped in 2367. An alien ship, also trapped in the rift, was able to utilize the hydrogen to produce an explosion large enough to rupture the anomaly and allow both ships to escape. ("Night Terrors" [TNG]). *The concept of electromagnetic ramscoops being used to gather fuel for an interstellar vehicle was proposed in 1960 by physicist Robert W. Bussard, after whom the device is named.*

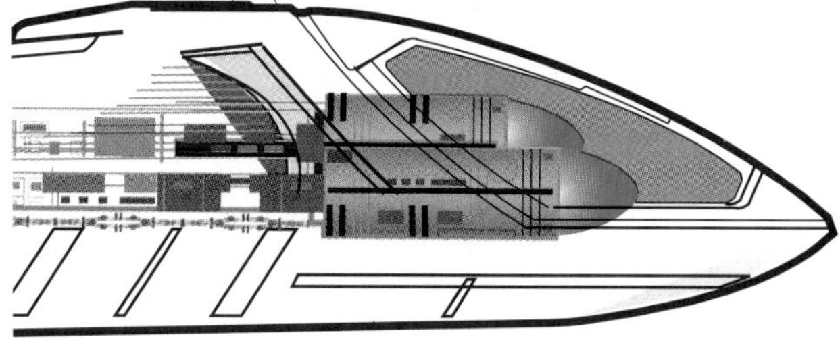

Butch. (Brent Hinkley). Citizen of the American nation on 20th century Earth. Butch was a member of an antigovernment militia cell located in a house 30 kilometers northeast of Phoenix in 1996. ("Future's End, Part II" [VGR]).

Butcher of Bozeman, The. SEE: **Hollander, Eli.**

"Butcher of Gallitep, The." Nickname given to **Gul Darhe'el**, brutal Cardassian commander of the infamous **Gallitep** labor camp on Bajor. ("Duet" [DS9]). SEE: **Marritza, Aamin.**

Butler. James Kirk's pet Great Dane. Butler died in 2286. In the reality of the **nexus**, Kirk got to see Butler again several years after his death. *(Star Trek Generations).*

"By Any Other Name." Original Series episode #50. Teleplay by D. C. Fontana and Jerome Bixby. Story by Jerome Bixby. Directed by Marc Daniels. Stardate 4657.5. *First aired in 1968. Aliens from the Andromeda Galaxy hijack the* Enterprise*, but they are unfamiliar with the human forms they have assumed for this mission.* GUEST CAST: Warren Stevens as **Rojan**; Barbara Bouchet as **Kelinda**; Majel Barrett as **Chapel, Christine**; Stewart Moss as **Hanar**; Robert Fortier as **Tomar**; Lizlie Dalton as **Drea**; Carl Byrd as **Shea, Lieutenant**; Julie Cobb as **Thompson, Yeoman Leslie**. SEE: **Andromeda Galaxy; barrier, galactic; Drea; formazine; Hanar; Kelinda; Kelva; Kelvans; paralysis field; Rigelian Kassaba fever; Rojan; Sahsheer; Saurian brandy; Shea, Lieutenant; stokaline; Thompson, Yeoman Leslie; Tomar; Vulcan mind-meld; warp drive.**

"By Inferno's Light." Deep Space Nine episode #113. Written by Ira Steven Behr & Robert Hewitt Wolfe. Directed by Les Landau. Stardate 50564.2. *First aired in 1997. Bashir, Worf and Garak break out of the Jem'Hadar prison; Sisko and Gowron combine forces to face an impending Dominion attack. This episode was the second of two parts, concluding the storyline begun in "In Purgatory's Shadow" (DS9). In this episode, the Federation and the Klingon Empire become allies again and the Cardassian Union joins the Dominion.* GUEST CAST: Andrew Robinson as **Garak, Elim**; Ray Buktenica as **Deyos**; Marc Alaimo as **Dukat, Gul**; James Horan as **Ikat'ika**; Melanie Smith as **Tora Ziyal**; Carrie Stauber as Female Romulan; Don Fischer as Jem'Hadar guard; Barry Wiggins as Jem'Hadar officer; Roger Loesch as Male Romulan. SEE: **asparagus; Bajoran wormhole; Bashir, Julian; Cardassians; Ch'Par; claustrophobia; Deep Space 9; Deyos; Dominion internment camp 371; Dominion; Dukat, Gul; duridium alloy; Founders; Gilhouly, Admiral; Gowron; Ikat'ika; Imperial Plaza; Jem'Hadar; Keedera; Khitomer Accords; Klingon Empire; Martok, General; protomatter; reverse-ratcheting router; Romulans; self-sealing stem bolt; tekasite; Tora Ziyal; trilithium; Tzenketh; *Volga, U.S.S.*; warp drive; Y'tem; *yamok* sauce; *Yukon, U.S.S.***

Byleth. (Michael Harris). **Iyaaran** ambassador. Byleth was assigned to experience antagonism during the cultural exchange between the Iyaarans and the crew of the *Enterprise*-D in early 2370. Byleth accomplished this by provoking Lieutenant Worf, with spectacular results. ("Liaisons" [TNG]).

Bynars. Humanoid civilization from planet Bynaus. The Bynars are heavily integrated with a sophisticated planetary computer network that serves as the framework of their society. Bynars usually live and work in pairs that are electronically connected for rapid exchange of binary data. The star **Beta Magellan**, around which Bynaus orbited, went nova in 2364, severely damaging the Bynars' planetary computer system. The Bynars attempted to steal the *Enterprise*-D in an effort to use the ship's computers to restart their own system. ("11001001" [TNG]). SEE: **buffer; Starbase 74.**

Bynaus. Planet located in the **Beta Magellan** star system, home to the **Bynars**. ("11001001" [TNG]).

Byrd, Daniel. Starfleet officer. Friend of **Harry Kim** when they attended Starfleet Academy together. In an alternate reality created in 2372 when Kim's shuttle intersected a timestream, Ensign Byrd took Kim's place as operations officer aboard the ***U.S.S. Voyager***. ("Non Sequitur" [VGR]). *We never saw Byrd.*

Byron, Lord. (Christopher Clarke). 1788-1824. Influential English romantic poet from planet **Earth**. Lord Byron's flamboyant and passionate lifestyle brought forth great poetry but also led to scandal, forcing him to leave England and live in exile until his death in 1824. In 2373, *Voyager's* **Emergency Medical Hologram** incorporated segments of Lord Byron's personality into his personality improvement project. ("Darkling" [VGR]).

Byzallians. Spacefaring life-forms. Representatives of the Byzallian government were scheduled to hold a conference at **Deep Space 9** in 2371. ("Defiant" [DS9]).

Byzatium transports. Cargo ships. Byzatium transports were scheduled to offload their cargo at **Deep Space 9** in 2371. ("Defiant" [DS9]).

C-111 Star system. Location of planet **Beta III**. ("Return of the Archons" [TOS]).

caber toss. Ancient Scottish sport which involves throwing a heavy three-meter-long wooden pole. The pole is tossed end over end as a show of strength. ("Sub Rosa" [TNG]).

Cabot, Ensign. *Enterprise*-D crew member. Cabot wanted to transfer from Quantum Mechanics to the **Stellar Cartography** department in 2369. Stellar Cartography head Neela Daren offered Ensign Cabot such a transfer without getting prior approval from Executive Officer William Riker, a significant breach of operating protocol. ("Lessons" [TNG]).

Cabral sector. Area of Federation space containing the planet **Vacca VI**. ("Homeward" [TNG]).

cabrodine. Common chemical explosive. A combination of cabrodine and infernite was used by **Neela** on Deep Space 9 to destroy Keiko O'Brien's schoolroom in 2369. ("In the Hands of the Prophets" [DS9]).

Cafe des Artistes. Outdoor cafe in the city of **Paris** on Earth. **Jean-Luc Picard** and the future Mrs. **Jenice Manheim** once had planned to meet there in April 2342 so that they could say goodbye, ending their romantic relationship. Picard failed to keep the rendezvous, but years later, the two re-created the cafe on the *Enterprise*-D holodeck so that they could properly bid each other adieu. ("We'll Always Have Paris" [TNG]). *The futuristic Paris skyline seen from the Cafe des Artistes was also used outside the Federation President's office in* Star Trek VI *and "Paradise Lost" (DS9). The menu at the cafe (handed out by waiter Edouard but never legible on television) included such delicacies as Croissants Dilithium, Klingon Targ ala Mode, and for dessert, L'antimatter Flambe!*

"Cage, The." Original Series episode #1. Written by Gene Roddenberry. Directed by Robert Butler. No stardate mentioned. *Captain Pike is captured by the illusion-creating Talosians, who want Pike to help them create a community of humans in hopes of revitalizing the Talosian civilization. This was the first pilot for* Star Trek. *It was produced in 1964 and was rejected by the network. It had a significantly different cast from the series, featuring Jeffrey Hunter as Captain Christopher Pike. A second pilot episode ("Where No Man Has Gone Before" [TOS]) was produced the following year, starring William Shatner as Captain Kirk. In fact, the only character from "The Cage" to carry over into* Star Trek's *first season was Mr. Spock, portrayed by Leonard Nimoy. Robert C. Johnson, who provided the "1st Talosian" voice, gained fame as the tape-recorded assignment voice in* Mission: Impossible. *Bob Justman, who was associate producer on the pilot of* Mission: Impossible, *was responsible for selecting Johnson for both roles. Portions of "The Cage" were later incorporated into flashback scenes in the two-part episode "The Menagerie" (TOS). Years later, a restored version of "The Cage" was released for home video and syndicated broadcast. "The Menagerie" won the World Science Fiction Society's Hugo Award for Best Dramatic Presentation in 1967.* GUEST CAST: Jeffrey Hunter as **Pike, Christopher**; Susan Oliver as **Vina**; M. Leigh Hudec (Majel Barrett Roddenberry) as **Number One**; John Hoyt as **Boyce, Dr. Phillip**; Peter Duryea as **Tyler, José**; Laurel Goodwin as **Colt, Yeoman J.M.**; Clegg Hoyt as Pitcairn, Transporter Chief; Meg Wyllie as **Keeper, The**; Malachi Throne as Keeper's voice, The; Georgia Schmidt as 1st Talosian; Robert C. Johnson as 1st Talosian's voice; Sande Serena as 2nd Talosian; Barker as Talosian female; Jon Lormer as **Haskins, Dr. Theodore**; Leonard Mudie as Survivor #2; Anthony Jochim as Survivor #3; Ed Madden as Geologist; Robert Phillips as Space officer (Orion); Joseph Mell as Earth trader; Mike Dugan as **Kaylar**; Robert Herron as Pike's stunt double and stunt captain; Adam Roarke as C.P.O. Garrison and First crewman; Janos Prohaska as Anthropoid ape and Humanoid bird; Frank Vinci as Stunt double. SEE: **Boyce, Dr. Phillip; Class-M planet; Colt, Yeoman J.M.; *Columbia, S.S.*; *Enterprise, U.S.S.*; Haskins, Dr. Theodore; Kaylar; Keeper, The; laser weapons; Mojave; Number One; Orion animal women; Pike, Christopher; planetary classification system; Rigel VII; Spock; Starbase 11; Talos IV; Talos Star Group; Talosians; Tango; transporter; Tyler, José; Vega Colony; Vina.**

Cairn. Humanoid society. The Cairn communicate telepathically and have no concept of spoken language. They applied for admission to the Federation in 2370. The Cairn exchange information telepathically, but unlike many other telepathic species, their communications involved sending images instead of words. Like **Betazoids**, they could communicate telepathically only with other telepaths. The Cairn sent a diplomatic mission to the Federation *Starship Enterprise*-D in 2370. Betazoid ambassador **Lwaxana Troi** accompanied the Cairn delegation so that she could use her telepathic abilities to help overcome the communication barrier. ("Dark Page" [TNG]). SEE: **Hedril; Maques** (*pictured*).

Cairo, U.S.S. Federation starship, *Excelsior* class, commanded by **Captain Edward Jellico**. The *Cairo* transported **Vice-Admiral Necheyev** to a rendezvous with the *Enterprise*-D in 2369 when it was feared Cardassians were developing a metagenic weapon. ("Chain of Command, Part I" [TNG]).

Cal Tech. California Polytechnical Institute. Educational institution located in Pasadena, California, on Earth, founded in 1891. ("Future's End, Part I" [VGR]).

Calaman sherry. Drink. **Lieutenant Jenna D'Sora**, a crew member aboard the *Enterprise*-D, enjoyed the stuff. ("In Theory" [TNG]).

Calamarain. An intelligent spaceborne civilization that exists as energetic clouds of ionized gas. The Calamarain had some kind of prior experience with **Q**, and though he denied doing anything "bizarre" or "grotesque" to them, they came seeking vengeance on Q when he sought refuge on the *Enterprise*-D after he became mortal in 2366. Commander **Data** was seriously injured while protecting Q from their attack. The Calamarain can emit **berthold rays**. ("Deja Q" [TNG]).

Calash Retreat. A gathering place for **Bajoran** monks. **Vedek Latha Mabrin** was murdered at the Calash Retreat in 2373 during preparations for the **Bajoran Days of Atonement.** ("The Darkness and the Light" [DS9]).

calculus. Branch of higher mathematics first devised on Earth by **Isaac Newton**. Aboard the *Starship Enterprise*-D, a basic understanding of calculus was regarded as essential for all children. ("When the Bough Breaks" [TNG]).

Calder II. Planet. Calder II was the site of the Sakethan burial mounds, built by ancient Romulans. The Federation maintained a small science outpost there. In 2370, the outpost was the target of mercenary Arctus Baran, who was working for the **Vulcan isolationist movement**, searching for fragments of the ancient **Stone of Gol**. ("Gambit, Part I" [TNG]).

Caldonians. Humanoid civilization. The Caldonians bid for rights to use the **Barzan wormhole** in 2366. The Caldonians were large, bi-fingered humanoids with a love of pure research. **Leyor** (pictured). represented his people in the negotiations for rights to the wormhole. ("The Price" [TNG]).

Caldorian eel. Animal life-form. **Klim Dokachin** once discovered a Caldorian eel in a storage locker on a freighter ship. The animal, which was four meters in length, became a pet. ("Unification, Part I" [TNG]).

Caldos colony. Federation settlement. Caldos was terraformed in 2271, one of the oldest **terraforming** projects undertaken by the Federation. The colony was patterned after the highlands of Scotland on Earth; each of the colony buildings contained a cornerstone from a Scottish building. In 2370, the colony experienced trouble with its **weather control matrix**, and the *Enterprise*-D, in orbit of the planet, was asked to assist. **Felisa Howard** was a resident of Caldos colony. ("Sub Rosa" [TNG]).

Calgary. City in Alberta, Canada, on Earth. Noted for its suitability for winter sports. **Wesley Crusher** and **Joshua Albert** took a weekend trip there in 2368. ("The First Duty" [TNG]).

calisthenics program, Klingon. A holodeck simulation program re-creating a primitive jungle setting in which the participant engages in mortal hand-to-hand combat with a number of powerful humanoid adversaries of various species. **Worf** spent much of his off-duty time honing his combat skills with this program. ("Where Silence Has Lease" [TNG]). After one particularly strenuous session with this program, Worf and **K'Ehleyr** spent a night of passion together, resulting in the conception of their child, Alexander. ("The Emissary" [TNG]). Alexander even tried the program, once he was big enough to lift a ***bat'leth*** sword ("New Ground" [TNG]). **Jadzia Dax** also practiced with the program and was quite skilled in Klingon combat. ("Blood Oath" [DS9]). *One of the creatures in Worf's calisthenics program used the mask of the character Skeletor from the movie* Masters of the Universe. Star Trek *makeup designer Michael Westmore also did makeup work for that film.* Star Trek *stunt coordinator Dennis Madalone played the skull monster.*

Call of the Prophets, The. Poem written by renowned Bajoran poet Akorem Laan more than 200 years ago. This poem was one of Kira Nerys's favorites and was over twelve stanzas in length. ("Accession" [DS9]).

Callas, Maria. (1923-1977). Operatic soprano from Earth who revived classical coloratura roles in the mid-20th century with her lyrical and dramatic versatility. In 2373, the *Voyager's* Emergency Medical Hologram performed the operatic duet "O soave fanciulla" from Puccini's *La Bohème* with a holodeck re-creation of **Giuseppina Pentangeli**. After bumping into her large ego, the doctor planned on performing the duet with a holographic version of Maria Callas the next time. ("The Swarm" [VGR]).

Calloway, Maddy. (Johanna McCloy). Medical technician assigned to the *Enterprise*-D in 2370. She was romantically involved with **Daniel Kwan** before his death. ("Eye of the Beholder" [TNG]).

Calogan dog. Obedient animal. ("Initiations" [VGR], "Alliances" [VGR]).

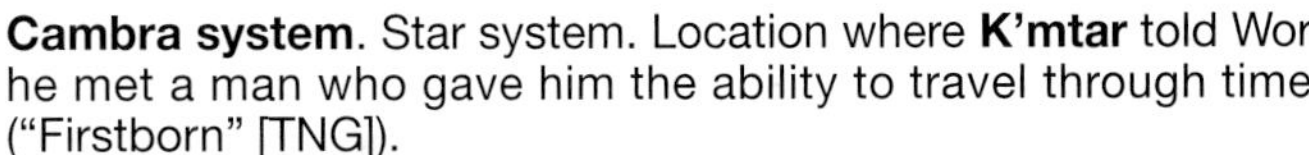

Cambra system. Star system. Location where **K'mtar** told Worf he met a man who gave him the ability to travel through time. ("Firstborn" [TNG]).

Cambridge University. Educational institution, located on Earth, founded in the early 12th century in Great Britain. Cambridge has been a major center for the sciences since the Renaissance. Much important work has been done there, including theories of physics and mathematics including **Isaac Newton**'s *Opticks*, Dirak's theories on the existence of positrons and **Stephen Hawking**'s quantum theory of gravity. (In the **anti-time future** created by Q, Data held the **Lucasian Chair** for physics at Cambridge in 2395.) ("All Good Things..." [TNG]).

camellia. Evergreen shrubs of the Earth genus *Camellia*. These plants produce large flattened blossoms that are red, white, or pink in color. This was **Felisa Howard**'s favorite flower. Following her death in 2370, **Ronin** covered her grave and filled her home with the blossoms, as a signal to Beverly Crusher of his presence. ("Sub Rosa" [TNG]).

Camor V. Class-M planet. The inhabitants of Camor V suffered greatly during the Cardassian war in the 2350s. In 2358, **Miranda Vigo** and her son, Jason, went to live on Camor V because Miranda wanted to help care for Camor's war orphans. ("Bloodlines" [TNG]).

Camorites. Inhabitants of **Camor V**. Camorites are physiologically different enough from humans to be easily distinguished via sensor readings from space. ("Bloodlines" [TNG]).

camouflage field. Technological device that can generate false sensor readings. Camouflage fields were used to mask the signatures of contraband materials when scanned by cargo inspectors. ("For the Cause" [DS9]).

Camp Khitomer. Near the Romulan border, the site of the historic peace conference between the Klingons and the Federation in 2293. (*Star Trek VI: The Undiscovered Country*). SEE: **Khitomer**. *The Camp Khitomer scenes in* Star Trek VI *were filmed at the Brandes Institute religious retreat in Simi Valley, California. The Brandes Institute was also used as the location for the Borg hall exteriors in "Descent, Parts I and II" (TNG).*

Campio, Minister. (Tony Jay). Third minister of planet **Kostolain**'s Conference of Judges. Minister Campio was engaged to marry Ambassador **Lwaxana Troi** of planet **Betazed** in 2368. Their courtship was conducted entirely by subspace radio, and they had planned to meet aboard the *Enterprise*-D just prior to their wedding. Upon meeting the ambassador, Campio found Troi's disdain for protocol to be unacceptable. Campio abandoned the wedding when the ambassador arrived at the ceremony nude, as is required by Betazoid custom. ("Cost of Living" [TNG]). SEE: **Erko**.

Camus II. Planet that was once home to a technologically advanced society. Dr. Janice Lester and Dr. Arthur Coleman were the only two survivors of a disastrous Federation archaeological expedition to Camus II in 2269. In one of the dig sites, Lester discovered an extraordinary life-energy transfer device that she used to exchange bodies with Captain James T. Kirk. SEE: **celebium**. ("Turnabout Intruder" [TOS]). The *Enterprise*-D was scheduled to conduct an archaeological survey mission to Camus II in 2367, but had to bypass the planet when it received a distress call from the Federation freighter ***U.S.S. Arcos.*** ("Legacy" [TNG]). *Captain Picard's reference to bypassing an archaeological survey of Camus II in the opening captain's log of "Legacy" was an "in-joke" devised by Rick Berman, Jonathan Frakes, and Eric Stillwell. It's a tip of the hat to "Turnabout Intruder" (TOS), the 79th and last episode of the original Star Trek series, which involved an archaeological mission to Camus II. "Legacy" (TNG) was the 80th episode of* Star Trek: The Next Generation.

Canar. A **Haliian** crystal artifact used to help focus thoughts. Haliians, a partially telepathic species, also use the Canar to establish a stronger emotional link during love. ("Aquiel" [TNG]).

Canopus Planet. Planet. Poet **Phineas Tarbolde**, a resident of the Canopus Planet, wrote **"Nightingale Woman"** there in 1996, considered to be one of the most passionate love sonnets written in the past couple of centuries. ("Where No Man Has Gone Before" [TOS]). *The star Canopus, also known as **Alpha Carinae**, is a red supergiant visible from Earth. The* Enterprise *visited the Alpha Carinae system in "The Ultimate Computer" (TOS).*

Canopus. Red supergiant star, also known as **Alpha Carinae**. Canopus was used by Sulu as a navigational reference when the original *Enterprise* was thrown across the galaxy in 2267 by the advanced civilization known as the **Metrons**. ("Arena" [TOS]). *In real life, Canopus was used by* Voyager *and other NASA spacecraft as a navigational reference.*

Capella IV. Class-M planet. Capella IV is a rich source of the rare mineral **topaline**, vital to the life-support systems of many Federation colonies. The original *Starship Enterprise* was sent to planet Capella IV in 2267 to obtain a mining agreement with the **Capellans**. The agreement was secured, although a Klingon officer attempted to gain mining rights for the Klingon Empire. ("Friday's Child" [TOS]). *Exterior planet scenes were filmed at the familiar Vasquez Rocks, located North of Los Angeles.*

Capellans. Humanoid inhabitants of planet **Capella IV**. Relatively primitive by Federation technological standards, the Capellans had a strong tribal government and a strict set of warrior mores. They considered combat more interesting than love, and did not believe in medicine, feeling that the weak should die. Their tribal government was led by a ruler called a **teer**, who headed the Ten Tribes of Capella. A significant power struggle in 2267 resulted in the death of High **Teer Akaar** at the hands of rival **Maab**, with the support of Klingon operatives who sought to influence the outcome of **topaline** negotiations with the Federation. Maab was himself later killed, and leadership of the Ten Tribes was assumed by **Leonard James Akaar**, infant son of the late Teer Akaar. While the child was growing, Leonard James's mother, **Eleen**, ruled the Ten Tribes as regent. ("Friday's Child" [TOS]).

Caprice. (Melissa Young). Very attractive young woman who was a character in Julian Bashir's **secret agent** holosuite program. ("Our Man Bashir" [DS9]).

Captain Picard Day. Annual school activity aboard the *Enterprise*-D. The children participated in a contest to fashion the best likeness of Captain Picard. Paul Menegay, age 7, was the winner of the contest in 2370. ("The *Pegasus*" [TNG]). SEE: **Commander Riker Day**.

"Captain's Holiday." *Next Generation* episode #67. Written by Ira Steven Behr. Directed by Chip Chalmers. Stardate 43745.2. *First aired in 1990. Captain Picard, on vacation at a resort planet, becomes involved in archaeological intrigue with a beautiful woman named Vash. This episode marks the first reference to (and visit to) Risa.* GUEST CAST: Jennifer Hetrick as **Vash**; Karen Landry as **Ajur**; Michael Champion as **Boratus**; Max Grodénchik as **Sovak**; Dierdre Impershein as **Joval**. SEE: **Ajur; Andorians; Boratus; Dachlyds; Dano, Kal; Daystrom Institute of Technology; *Ethics, Sophistry and the Alternate Universe*; Gemaris V; *Horga'hn*; hoverball; Icor IX; *jamaharon*; Joval; quantum phase inhibitor; Risa; Sarthong V; Sovak; Starbase 12; *Tox Uthat*; Transporter Code 14; *Ulysses*; Vash; Vorgons; Zytchin III.**

captain's yacht. Large shuttle vehicle carried by *Galaxy*-class starships. The captain's yacht was intended for transport of dignitaries and other diplomatic functions. The yacht was a large elliptical vessel that docked at an external port on the underside of the *Galaxy*-class starship's Saucer Module. *Patrick Stewart informs us that the unseen captain's yacht aboard the* Enterprise-*D was called the* Calypso. *We believe him.*

"Captive Pursuit." *Deep Space Nine* episode #6. Teleplay by Jill Sherman Donner and Michael Piller. Story by Jill Sherman Donner. Directed by Corey Allen. No stardate given. *First aired in 1993. Hunters descend on the station in search of their humanoid quarry, an individual named Tosk who is befriended by O'Brien.* GUEST CAST: Gerrit Graham as Hunter; Scott MacDonald as **Tosk**; Kelly Curtis as **Sarda**, **Miss**. SEE: **airlock; Alpha Quadrant; arva nodes; Bajoran wormhole; coladrium flow; dabo girl; Deep Space 9; duranium; graviton; Hunters; neutrino; plasma injector; ramscoop; Sarda, Miss; security clearance; security sensor; Tosk.**

carbon reaction chambers. Engineering term used to describe carbon-lined containment vessels used in Cardassian nuclear **fusion reactors**, including those on **Deep Space 9**. ("The Forsaken" [DS9]).

carbon units. Term used by the machine life-form **V'Ger** to describe humanoid biochemical life-forms. V'Ger believed carbon units to be an inferior form of life. (*Star Trek: The Motion Picture*).

Cardassia Prime. SEE: **Cardassia**.

Cardassia. Homeworld of the Cardassian Union, ("The Wounded" [TNG]) the planet is also referred to as Cardassia Prime. ("Tribunal" [DS9]). Cardassia is a planet poor in natural resources, but in ancient times was home to a splendid civilization whose legendary ruins are still considered some of the most remarkable in the galaxy. Most of the archaeological treasures were plundered by starving Cardassians, as well as by the Cardassian military, which sought funds for their war against the Federation. SEE: **First Hebitian civilization**. ("Chain of Command, Part II" [TNG]). Cardassia was believed to have been visited some 800 years ago by ancient **Bajoran** explorers. Until recently, Cardassian scholars scoffed at such theories, but in 2371, Cardassian archaeologists reported finding wreckage of an ancient **Bajoran solar-sail vessel** on Cardassia. ("Explorers" [DS9]).

Cardassian Central Command. Government of the Cardassian Union, in control of the Cardassian military. ("The Maquis, Part I" [DS9]). The Central Command has traditionally been under the direct control of the **Detapa Council**, but in practice operated with virtual autonomy. The Central Command has often been at odds with the **Obsidian Order**. ("Defiant" [DS9]). In 2372, a civilian uprising successfully overthrew the Central Command, placing power into the hands of the Detapa Council. After the *coup*, **Gul Dukat** became chief military advisor to the Detapa Council. ("The Way of the Warrior" [DS9]).

Cardassian Embassy on Romulus. Cardassian intelligence operative **Elim Garak** worked as a gardener at the Cardassian Embassy on Romulus during the time that Proconsul Merrok was assassinated. Apparently, several Romulan dignitaries died unexpectedly that year. ("Broken Link" [DS9]).

Cardassian Federation treaty. SEE: **Federation-Cardassian treaty.**

Cardassian neck trick. Stunt that Odo performed for members of the Cardassian High Command in 2363. It was a rousing success. ("Necessary Evil" [DS9], "Improbable Cause" [DS9]). *Unfortunately, we don't know just what the "neck trick" was. On the other hand, judging from Odo's reaction to mention of the trick, we probably don't* want *to know.*

Cardassian operation guidelines. Specifications used by the **Cardassians** providing instructions on operating procedures for station **Deep Space 9**. The station's main computer advised

Chief **Miles O'Brien** to review Cardassian operational guidelines, paragraph 254-A, when increasing the **deuterium** flow to reaction chamber 2 on stardate 46925. ("The Forsaken" [DS9]).

Cardassian phase-disruptor rifle. Standard issue Cardassian field weapon. The Cardassian phase-disruptor rifle had a 4.7 megajoule power capacity, three millisecond recharge and two beam settings. ("Return to Grace" [DS9]).

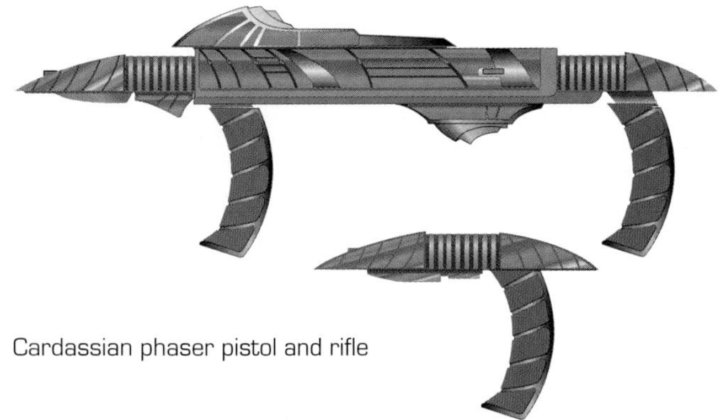
Cardassian phaser pistol and rifle

Cardassian riding hound. Medium-sized Cardassian draft animal used primarily for transportation. ("In Purgatory's Shadow" [DS9]).

Cardassian underground movement. Dissident political movement that opposed military dominance of the **Cardassian** government. The Cardassian Central Command regarded members of the underground as dangerous terrorists, and sought to silence them through any means necessary, including murder. Three of the movement's most influential leaders in 2371 were **Rekelen**, **Hogue**, and Professor **Natima Lang**. ("Profit and Loss" [DS9]). Also in 2371, the **Obsidian Order** devised a ruse to expose **Legate Ghemor**, a prominent member of the Central Command, as a member of the dissident movement. ("Second Skin" [DS9]).

Cardassians. Technologically advanced, humanoid civilization. ("The Wounded" [TNG]). In the past, the Cardassians were a peaceful and spiritual people. But because their planet was resource-poor, starvation and disease were rampant, and people died by the millions. With the rise of the military to power, new territories and technology were acquired by violence, at the cost of millions of lives sacrificed to the war effort. ("Chain of Command, Part II" [TNG]).

In Cardassian society, the criminal justice system served to enforce cultural norms, while reassuring the public with the comforting notion that good did triumph over evil. Accordingly, no criminal was brought to trial until authorities had already found the defendant guilty. ("Maquis, Part II" [DS9]). Trials were broadcast for viewing by the public, serving as a dramatic demonstration of the futility of violating society's norms. Under the Cardassian system of jurisprudence, a defendant could not present evidence until the trial was under way—in other words, until after a verdict of guilty had already been rendered. Further, such defendants were required to testify against themselves. Cardassian citizens were required to have one of their molars extracted at age ten so that they could be kept on file by the Cardassian bureau of identification. ("Tribunal" [DS9]). SEE: **archon**; **conservator**; **nestor**.

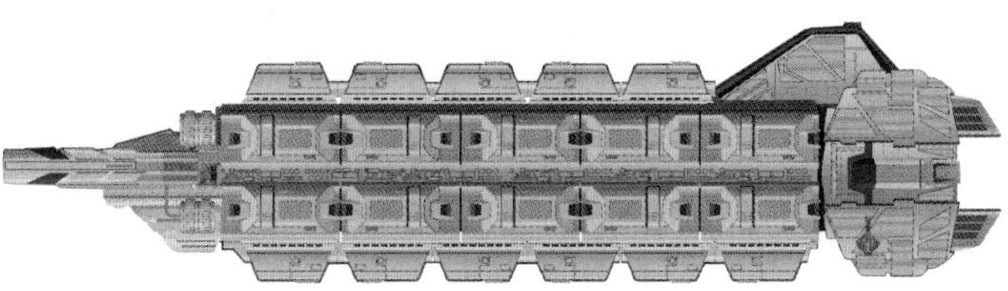
Cardassian freighter

In Cardassian culture, advanced age is viewed as a sign of power and dignity. ("Distant Voices" [DS9]). Cardassian men and women sometimes exhibit overt irritability toward each other as an overture to a sexual relationship. ("Destiny" [DS9]). Family is very important to the Cardassians, with some households being multi-generational. Intense mind-training programs are given to their children as early as four years of age, perhaps contributing to the famous Cardassian photographic memories. ("The Maquis, Part I" [DS9]). Cardassian funeral rites are very strict. They considered it a dishonor to the deceased if a non-Cardassian views the remains. ("Indiscretion" [DS9]). Cardassians dislike cold temperatures. It is traditional in Cardassian culture that the commanding officer of a ship should entertain guests when they travel aboard his or her ship. It was also traditional for a freighter captain to take a percentage of the cargo's worth for himself. ("Return to Grace" [DS9]). A favorite morning beverage of Cardassians is hot fish juice. ("Trials and Tribble-ations" [DS9]).

The Cardassians were involved in a bitter, extended conflict with the **United Federation of Planets**. An uneasy truce between the two adversaries was finally reached in 2366. During the negotiations, Ambassador Spock publicly disagreed with his father, Ambassador Sarek, on the treaty. ("Unification, Part I" [TNG]).

The following year, the treaty was violated by Starfleet **Captain Benjamin Maxwell**, commanding the *Starship* ***Phoenix***. Although Maxwell's actions were illegal, Starfleet authorities believed his suspicions of illicit Cardassian military activity were correct. Captain Picard recalled that while in command of the ***U.S.S. Stargazer*** in 2355, he had fled from a Cardassian warship, barely escaping with his ship and crew intact. ("The Wounded" [TNG]).

In 2367, a historic peace treaty established a fragile armistice between the Federation and the Cardassian Union. Starfleet **Captain Edward Jellico** was partially credited for the negotiations. Among other things, the treaty provided that captives of either government would be allowed to see a representative from a neutral planet following their incarceration. ("Chain of Command, Part II" [TNG]).

The Cardassians annexed planet **Bajor** around 2328, and over the next several decades systematically stripped the planet of resources and forced most **Bajorans** to resettle on other worlds. ("Ensign Ro" [TNG]). During the occupation, the Cardassians arrested any Bajorans that were caught teaching the word of the **Prophets**. They were imprisoned and often received repeated beatings for their beliefs. ("Rapture" [DS9]).

In 2369, it was believed that Cardassia was developing a **metagenic weapon** and planning to use it in conjunction with an incursion into Federation space. *Enterprise*-D Captain Jean-Luc Picard, along with Chief Medical Officer Beverly Crusher

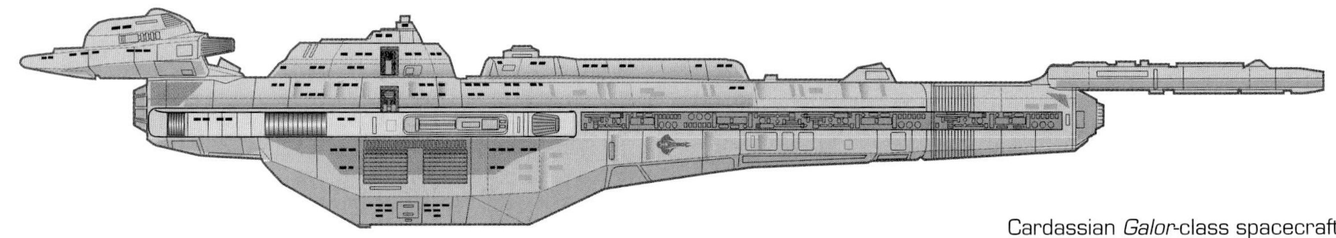
Cardassian *Galor*-class spacecraft

and Security Officer Worf, was sent covertly into Cardassian space to investigate. The reports were found to be a ruse, designed to lure Captain Picard into Cardassian captivity. ("Chain of Command, Part I & II" [TNG]). Also in 2369, the Bajoran resistance movement had forced the Cardassians from Bajor after years of terrorist activity. In their retreat, they abandoned **Terok Nor**, an old Cardassian mining station orbiting Bajor. SEE: **Deep Space 9**. This proved to be a major misstep for the Cardassians, as the station became of major strategic, scientific, and commercial value when the Bajoran wormhole was discovered shortly thereafter. ("Emissary, Parts I and II" [DS9]). Many Cardassian war orphans were left behind on planet Bajor when the occupation ended. In Cardassian society, orphans are shunned and not acknowledged by the populace. ("Cardassians" [DS9]).

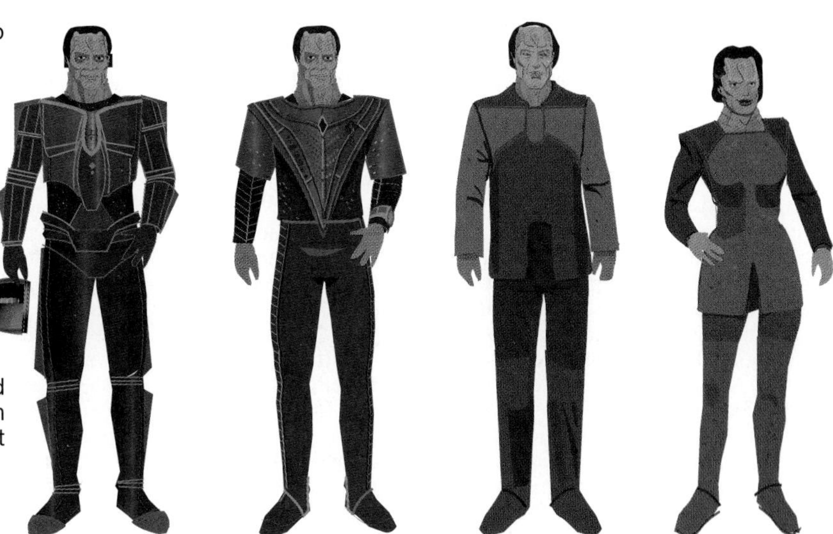

The Cardassian withdrawal included an agreement to release all Bajoran political prisoners, per Supreme Directive 2645, although some prisoners remained at the **Hutet labor camp** on Cardassia IV for nearly a year. SEE: **Li Nalas**. ("The Homecoming" [DS9]). In 2371, the Cardassian government, represented by **Legate Turrel**, concluded a historic peace treaty with Bajoran leader Kai **Winn**. ("Life Support" [DS9]).

In 2372, a civilian uprising overthrew the Cardassian Central Command, placing power into the hands of the **Detapa Council**. Suspecting that the Council had been replaced by shape-shifting agents of the **Dominion**, the Klingon Empire subsequently invaded Cardassia Prime, and was nearly successful in eliminating the Detapa Council. **Gul Dukat** helped the Council flee the Klingon invasion fleet by evacuating them aboard the *Prakesh*. Dukat, with assistance from Starfleet personnel, was able to ascertain that the Council had not been replaced by the **Founders**. ("The Way of the Warrior" [DS9]). The Klingon invasion destroyed the industrial capability of dozens of Cardassian worlds, devastating the Cardassian economy. The **Federation Council**, eager to maintain ties to the Cardassians, agreed to provide twelve industrial replicators to the Cardassian government. The replicators were hijacked by members of the **Maquis** led by Lieutenant Commander **Eddington**. ("For the Cause" [DS9]).

Humiliated by its dealings with the Federation and stung by the Klingon attack, the Cardassian government entered into an alliance with the **Dominion** in 2373. The pact had been secretly negotiated by **Gul Dukat** (*pictured*), who thereafter assumed leadership of the Cardassian Union. Dukat promised to return the Cardassians to their former glory. ("By Inferno's Light" [DS9]).

(In one of the **quantum realities** visited by Worf in 2370, the Cardassians tampered with the **Argus Array**, using it to spy on Federation facilities. In yet another, the Cardassians and the Federation had reached some degree of rapprochement, as evidenced by the Cardassian conn officer found in this universe.) ("Parallels" [TNG]).

The Cardassians first appeared in "The Wounded" (TNG), although the backstory established in that episode suggests that hostilities with them go back to at least the 2350s. The Cardassians recurred in several episodes and became major adversaries in Star Trek: Deep Space Nine.

"Cardassians." *Deep Space Nine* episode #25. Teleplay by James Crocker. Story by Gene Wolande & John Wright. Directed by Cliff Bole. Stardate 47177.2. *First aired in 1993. When a young Cardassian orphan arrives at DS9, Dr. Bashir and Garak become embroiled in political intrigue involving the boy's father and Gul Dukat.* GUEST CAST: Rosalind Chao as **O'Brien**, **Keiko**; Andrew Robinson as **Garak, Elim**; Robert Mandan as **Pa'Dar**, **Kotran**; Terrence Evans as **Proka Migdal**; Vidal Peterson as **Rugal**; Dion Anderson as **Zolan**; Marc Alaimo as **Dukat**; Sharon Conley as **Jomat**, **Luson**; Karen Hensel as **Deela**; Jillian Ziesmer as Asha. SEE: **Bajorans; Bashir, Dr. Julian; Cardassians; Deela; Deep Space Nine; Dukat, Gul; Garak; Jomat Luson; Pa'Dar, Kotran; Proka Migdal; Rokassa juice; Rugal; tarkalean tea; Terok Nor; Tozhat Resettlement Center;** ***zabo*** **meat; Zolan.**

Cardaway leaves, stuffed. Hors d'oeuvres. One of Neelix's specialties. ("The Cloud" [VGR]).

cardiac induction. Emergency medical resuscitative measure. Cardiac induction was used on Jean-Luc Picard on stardate 45944, following his exposure to the **Kataan probe**. ("The Inner Light" [TNG]).

cardiac replacement. Surgical procedure in which a patient's diseased or injured heart is replaced by an artificial device. The technique was developed by **Dr. Van Doren**. Captain **Jean-Luc Picard** underwent a cardiac replacement procedure in 2327 and again in 2365. ("Samaritan Snare" [TNG]).

Cardies. Racist term for **Cardassians**. ("The Wounded" [TNG], "Emissary" [DS9]).

cardiostimulator. Medical instrument. Dr. McCoy used a cardiostimulator when Ambassador **Sarek** suffered cardiac arrest aboard the *Enterprise* in 2267. The cardiostimulator revived the ambassador, allowing McCoy to continue lifesaving surgery. ("Journey to Babel" [TOS]). SEE: **benjisidrine**; **cryogenic open-heart procedure**; **T-negative**. *Voyager*'s Emergency Medical Hologram used a cardiostimulator to revive Commander Chakotay after his **bio-neural energy** was displaced by the **Komar** on stardate 48734. ("Cathexis" [VGR]).

Carema III. Planet. Carema III was considered by Starfleet to be a candidate for the **particle fountain** mining technology developed by **Dr. Farallon** in 2369. ("The Quality of Life" [TNG]).

"Caretaker, Parts I and II." *Voyager* episode #1 & 2. Teleplay by Michael Piller & Jeri Taylor. Story by Rick Berman & Michael Piller & Jeri Taylor. Directed by Winrich Kolbe. Stardate 48315.6. *First aired in 1995. While searching for a missing Maquis ship, the* U.S.S. Voyager *is transported to the distant unexplored Delta Quadrant of the galaxy along with the Maquis ship. The Maquis members join the crew of the* Voyager *when their ship is destroyed. This was the two-hour long first episode of the* Star Trek: Voyager *series, and introduces the* Starship Voyager *and her crew, including Captain Kathryn Janeway. Originally produced as a two-hour made-for-television movie, "Caretaker" was later aired as two one-hour segments. Armin Shimerman made a cameo appearance as Quark in this episode.* GUEST CAST: Basil Langton as **Caretaker** and **Banjo man**; Gavan O'Herlihy as **Jabin**; Angela Paton as Adah Reh, Aunt; Armin Shimerman as **Quark**; Alicia

Cappola as **Stadi, Lieutenant**; Bruce French as Ocampa doctor; Jennifer Parsons as Ocampa nurse; David Selburg as **Toscat**; Jeff McCarthy as Human doctor; Stan Ivar as **Mark**; Scott MacDonald as **Rollins, Ensign**; Josh Clark as **Carey, Joseph**; Richard Poe as **Evek, Gul**; Keely Sims as Farmer's daughter; Eric David Johnson as **Daggin**; Majel Barrett as Computer voice. SEE: ***Al-Batani, U.S.S.***; ***angla'bosque***; **antimatter containment; Arias Expedition; Array; Badlands; bio-neural circuitry; Caldik Prime; Caretaker; Carey, Joseph; Cavit, Lieutenant Commander; Chakotay; Class-M planet; cormaline; Daggin; Delta Quadrant; displacement wave; Emergency Medical Hologram; Evek, Gul; Federation Penal Settlement; *Intrepid*-class starship; Jabin; Janeway, Kathryn; Julliard Youth Symphony; Kazon Collective; Kazon spacecraft; Kazon-Ogla; Kazon; Kes; Kim, Harry; Koladan diamond; lek; Lobi crystal; maje; Maquis; Maquis ships; Mark; mess hall; Moriya system; Nacene; Neelix; nucleogenic particles; Ocampa planet; Ocampa; Paris, Admiral; Paris, Thomas; phaser rifle; planetary classification system; Rollins, Ensign; security anklet; Stadi, Lieutenant; Terikof Belt; tetryon; tomato soup; Torres, B'Elanna; Toscat; trianoline; tricobalt explosive; Tuvok; *Vetar;* Volnar Colony; *Voyager, U.S.S.;* warp factor; warp field effect; Zakarian, Commander.**

Caretaker. (Basil Langton). Highly advanced **noncorporeal life-form** ("Caretaker" [VGR]) based on **sporocystian energy**. The Caretaker's people were extradimensional explorers from another galaxy who called themselves the **Nacene**. ("Cold Fire" [VGR]). About 1,000 years ago, they accidentally devastated the atmosphere of the **Ocampa planet**, rendering the surface a desert. The Caretaker was one of two travelers who remained behind to care for the **Ocampa**. With the planet's surface all but uninhabitable, the Caretaker created a subterranean city for the Ocampa, and supplied them with energy by using his spaceborne **Array**. ("Caretaker" [VGR]). The Caretaker's mate, a female named **Suspiria** ("Cold Fire" [VGR]), went off to look for more interesting places. By 2371, the Caretaker was dying. He searched the galaxy for life-forms with a compatible bio-molecular pattern in order to procreate, hoping an offspring would continue to care for the Ocampa. While searching for compatible life-forms, the Caretaker abducted more than 50 ships from across the galaxy, including the ***Voyager*** and Chakotay's Maquis vessel. The Caretaker's search proved fruitless, and he died shortly thereafter without leaving an offspring. His final act to protect the Ocampa was to persuade *Voyager* Captain Janeway to destroy his Array to prevent it from falling into the hands of the **Kazon-Ogla**. ("Caretaker" [VGR]). Ten months after his death near the Ocampa homeworld, the Caretaker's remains reacted to a sporocystian energy field, making it possible for the Voyager crew to determine the location of Suspiria, the Caretaker's mate. ("Cold Fire" [VGR]). *The Caretaker took the form of an old grizzled man with a banjo, listed in the episode's credits as the Banjo Man. Not to be confused with the Caretaker who supervised the amusement park planet in "Shore Leave" (TOS).*

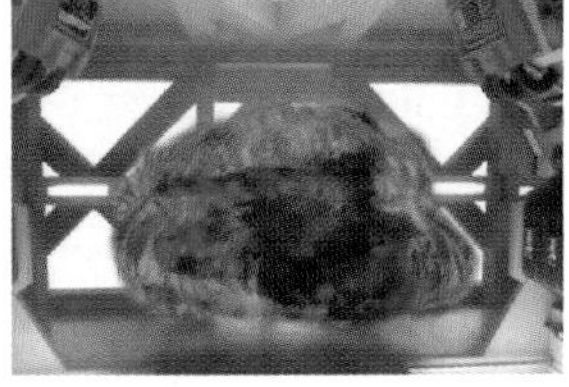

Caretaker. (Oliver McGowan). Supervisor of a sophisticated **amusement park planet** in the Omicron Delta region when a landing party from the *U.S.S. Enterprise* visited in 2267. The planet had advanced hardware that could read the minds of visitors, then manufacture whatever it was they imagined. It was the Caretaker's responsibility to coordinate such activities and make sure things ran smoothly. When it was apparent his guests were not enjoying themselves, he appeared to the *Enterprise* personnel, explaining that this was an amusement park where beings could visit and play. The Caretaker agreed that the more sophisticated the mind, the greater the need for the simplicity of play. ("Shore Leave" [TOS]). SEE: **Finnegan; Police Special; Ruth; tiger; White Rabbit.** *Not to be confused with the Caretaker encountered in the Delta Quadrant in "Caretaker" (VGR).*

Carey, Joseph. (Josh Clark). Starfleet officer. Engineer aboard the ***U.S.S. Voyager*** at the time the ship was lost in 2371. Carey became acting chief engineer after the chief engineer was killed during the ship's violent passage to the **Delta Quadrant**. ("Caretaker" [VGR]). Carey was disappointed when Captain Janeway later promoted **B'Elanna Torres** for the position of chief engineer, but soon recognized Torres's superior qualifications. ("Parallax" [VGR]). Lieutenant Carey had a wife and two small sons. He helped Torres and Seska in their unauthorized attempt to employ **trajector** technology on the *Voyager*. ("Prime Factors." [VGR]). In a possible future visited by Kes, Carey and several others aboard the *Voyager* died in an attack by a Krenim ship. ("Before and After" [VGR]). *Carey got a first name in "Before and After" (VGR). Carey was also seen in "State of Flux" (VGR). He was first seen in "Caretaker" (VGR).*

cargo bay. Storage area aboard a space vehicle for freight, supplies, and other payload stored for shipment. Cargo bays aboard the *Galaxy*-class *Starship Enterprise*-D were located on Decks 4, 38, and 39. Aboard the *Intrepid*-class *U.S.S. Voyager*, cargo bays were located on Decks 4 and 10. ("Macrocosm" [VGR]).

cargo module. A variety of different storage containers used by Starfleet and other agencies for safe shipping and handling of freight and payload. *Illustrations: Miscellaneous cargo module labels from Deep Space 9.*

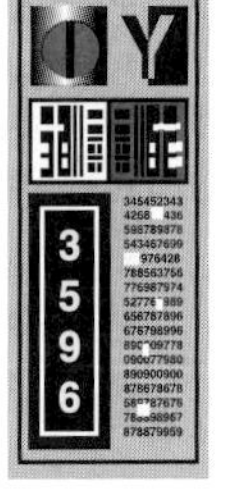

Carlson, Jeff. (Conor O'Farrell). Scientist on 20th century Earth. Professor Carlson assisted the Army Air Corps in trying to communicate with Quark, Rom, and Nog after they crash-landed on Earth in the year 1947. Upon learning of the Ferengis' situation and (relatively) benevolent intent, Carlson and his fiancée, **Faith Garland**, helped them escape. ("Little Green Men" [DS9]).

Carmichael, Mrs. (Pamela Kosh). Landlady in 19th-century San Francisco on Earth who had the misfortune of renting an apartment to an itinerant theater group headed by a "Mr. Pickerd." The group was terribly late with its rent. ("Time's Arrow, Part II" [TNG]). *Samuel Clemens did say he would make good on the rent. We are confident that he kept his word.*

carnivorous rastipod. Animal life-form. Not known for its grace or style. ("Progress" [DS9]).

Carolina, U.S.S. Federation starship. The *Carolina* apparently sent an emergency signal to the *Enterprise* on stardate 3497. The transmission turned out to be a hoax, a Klingon attempt to prevent the *Enterprise* from returning to planet **Capella IV**. ("Friday's Child" [TOS]). SEE: ***Dierdre, S.S.***

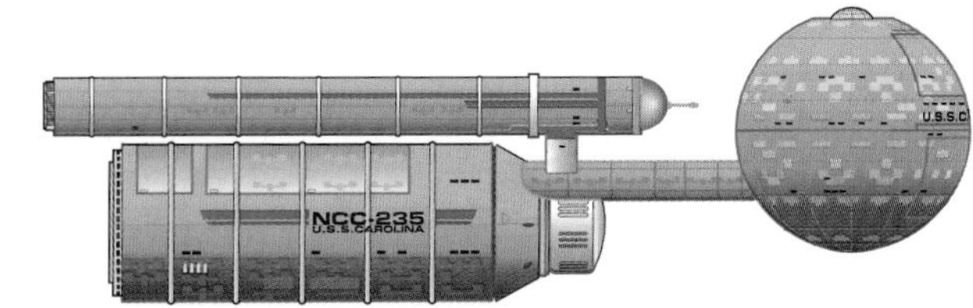

Carraya System. Near the Romulan/Klingon border, the location of a secret Romulan prison camp. This camp, established several months after the **Khitomer massacre** in 2346, imprisoned nearly a hundred Klingon prisoners who had been captured, unconscious, from a perimeter outpost. Romulan officer **Tokath** sacrificed his military career in a humanitarian gesture to establish the Carraya camp where these prisoners could be incarcerated so that the Romulan government would not execute them. In the years that followed, a peaceful coexistence developed between the Romulan jailers and their captives, whose Klingon warrior ethic would not permit them to return to their homeworld after having been captured in battle. Commander Tokath even took a Klingon woman, **Gi'ral**, as his wife, and they had a daughter named **Ba'el**, and other Klingon captives had children as well. **Worf** discovered the camp in 2369 while investigating rumors that his father might not have been killed at Khitomer. Discovering the reports to be untrue, Worf escorted some of the Klingon children, by then having reached adulthood, back to the Klingon Empire. Worf and the children all agreed never to reveal the existence of the camp to the outside world. ("Birthright, Parts I and II" [TNG]). *Worf's promise means that neither Starfleet nor the Klingon government is likely to have any record of the camp at Carraya. The exterior of the prison camp was designed by Richard James, from which a model was built that was the basis for a matte painting executed by Dan Curry. (Production designer James was, of course, also responsible for the full-size interior sets, as well.)*

Carrington Award. Prestigious scientific award given annually by the Federation Medical Council, honoring outstanding work in the field of medicine. Generally regarded as a lifetime achievement award, the Carrington in 2371 was awarded to **Dr. Henri Roget**. Also nominated that year was Dr. **Julian Bashir**, the youngest nominee in the history of the award. ("Prophet Motive" [DS9]). *The Federation official who presented the Carrington Award, listed as "Medical Big Shot" in the episode's credits, was played by Bennet G. Suillory.* SEE: **P'Trell, Chirurgeon Ghee; Senva, Healer; Wade, Dr. April.**

Carson, Ensign. (Sara Mornell). Starfleet officer assigned to station Deep Space 9. In 2372, she was stationed on the bridge of *Starship Defiant* when the ship came under Jem'Hadar attack during a trade conference with the Karemma. ("Starship Down" [DS9]).

Carstairs, Ensign. Geologist aboard the original *Starship Enterprise*. The **M-5** multitronic computer, when being tested aboard the *Enterprise*, chose Ensign Carstairs for landing party duty on stardate 4729 to planet **Alpha Carinae II**. M-5 picked Carstairs over Senior Geologist Rawlens because the ensign had surveyed geologically similar planets for a mining company while serving in the merchant marine. ("The Ultimate Computer" [TOS]).

Cartalian fever. A deadly viral plague. ("Nor the Battle to the Strong" [DS9]).

Cartwright, Admiral. (Brock Peters). Starfleet Command officer. Cartwright presided over emergency operations from Starfleet Headquarters in San Francisco when an alien **probe** threatened the Earth in 2286. *(Star Trek IV: The Voyage Home)*. Politically conservative and extremely wary of the Klingon government, Cartwright opposed the peace initiative of Klingon **Chancellor Gorkon**, and participated in the conspiracy with Klingon **General Chang** for Gorkon's assassination in 2293. *(Star Trek VI: The Undiscovered Country)*. SEE: **Klingon Empire**.

cascade anomaly. Progressive and escalating failure within a complex system such as a positronic matrix. A cascade anomaly was suspected in the failure of the android, **Juliana Tainer**, to regain consciousness after an accident on Atrea IV in 2370. This was later discovered to be untrue; Juliana's unconsciousness was a part of a program to protect her from discovering she was not human. ("Inheritance" [TNG]).SEE: **positronic brain.** *A cascade failure was responsible for the death of Data's daughter, **Lal**.*

cascade virus. Sophisticated computer software weapon. In 2373, Maquis leader **Michael Eddington** placed a cascade virus in the systems of the *U.S.S. Defiant*. The virus affected all of the computer memory cores aboard the ship, necessitating that the vessel be towed back to Deep Space 9. ("For the Uniform" [DS9]).

Casey. *Enterprise*-D security officer. Casey helped Riker and Worf break onto the bridge following the lockout by Data, when Data was under Dr. **Noonien Soong**'s control in 2367. ("Brothers" [TNG]).

Cassandra. (Julia Nickson). Colonist who settled on planet **Orellius** in 2360. **Alixus** sent Cassandra to seduce Deep Space 9 officer Benjamin Sisko in the hopes that he would want to live there. Cassandra believed in Alixus's teachings and, when offered passage off-planet, chose to remain with the colony. ("Paradise" [DS9]). *Julia Nickson also played Ensign Lian T'su in "The Arsenal of Freedom" (TNG).*

Castal I. Planet. Site of a conflict between Federation and **Talarian** forces in the 2350s. Talarian Captain **Endar**'s only son was killed in the conflict. ("Suddenly Human" [TNG]).

Caster. Noted writer. Caster was the author of the 17-volume work *Down the River Light*. ("Nor the Battle to the Strong" [DS9]).

Castillo, Lieutenant Richard. (Christopher McDonald). The helm officer of the ***Enterprise*-C**. He was injured in 2344 in the battle with Romulans at **Narendra III**. During the battle, Castillo was transported along with his ship into the future, to the year 2366, when a torpedo explosion opened up a **temporal rift**. With the disappearance of the *Enterprise*-C from its "proper" time frame, history developed in a dramatically altered manner. In this altered future, Castillo served as liaison between the *Enterprise*-C and *Enterprise*-D, working closely with tactical officer **Natasha Yar (alternate)**, with whom he became romantically involved. When it was learned that the *Enterprise*-C had to return to the past to restore the "proper" flow of history, Castillo volunteered to command the ship after the death of **Captain Rachel Garrett**. Castillo understood that returning to the past to repair history was a virtual suicide mission. ("Yesterday's *Enterprise*" [TNG]).

Cataria, Lake. Picturesque lake on the planet **Betazed**. A holodeck simulation of the locale was available on the *Enterprise*-D. ("All Good Things..." [TNG]).

cateline. Drug. Cateline simulates aphylactic shock. ("Darkling" [VGR]).

"Cathexis" *Voyager* episode #13. Teleplay by Brannon Braga. Story by Brannon Braga & Joe Menosky. Directed by Kim Friedman. Stardate 48734.2 *First aired in 1995. Chakotay's disembodied consciousness tries to warn his fellow crew members against entering a dangerous nebula, but the* Voyager *crew mistakes him for an alien presence.* GUEST CAST: Brian Markinson as **Durst, Peter**; Michael Cumpsty as **Burleigh, Lord**; Carolyn Seymour as **Templeton, Mrs.**; Majel Barrett as Computer voice. SEE: **bio-neural energy; Brown, Doc; Burleigh, Beatrice;**

Burleigh, Henry; Burleigh, Lord; cardiostimulator; Chakotay; cortical stimulator; Coyote Stone; dark-matter nebula; Davenport, Lucille; Durst, Peter; Emergency Medical Hologram; engram; garlic soup; gigaquad; holocomic books; holodeck and holosuite programs; holonovel; Ilidarians; Janeway Lambda-1; Janeway, Kathryn; Komar; magneton scan; matter/antimatter reaction chamber; medicine wheel; Mountains of the Antelope Women; noncorporeal life; Parsons, Ensign; pejuta; security access code; Templeton, Mrs.; trianic energy beings; Tuvok; *Voyager*, *U.S.S.*; Vulcan mind-meld; Vulcan nerve pinch.

"Catspaw." Original Series episode #30. Written by Robert Bloch. Directed by Joseph Pevney. Stardate 3018.2. *First aired in 1967. The* Enterprise *crew finds witches, black cats, and haunted castles on planet Pyris VII. This was the first episode produced for the original series' second season, and the first appearance of Pavel Chekov.* GUEST CAST: Antoinette Bower as **Sylvia**; Theo Marcuse as **Korob**; Michael Barrier as **DeSalle, Lieutenant**; John Winston as **Kyle, Mr.**; Rhodie Cogan as First witch; Gail Bonney as Second witch; Maryesther Denver as Third witch; Jimmy Jones as **Jackson**; Mike Howden as Rowe, Lieutenant; Frank Vinci as Kirk's stunt double; Jim Jones as McCoy's stunt double; Vic Toyota as Sulu's stunt double; Bob Fass as Scotty's stunt double; Carl Saxe as Korob's stunt double. SEE: **Chekov, Pavel A.; DeSalle, Lieutenant; Jackson; Korob; Kyle, Mr.; Old Ones; Pyris VII; Starbase 9; Sylvia; transmuter.**

Catualla. Planet that applied for Federation membership in 2269. Catualla was home to **Tongo Rad**, a follower of **Dr. Sevrin**. ("The Way to Eden" [TOS]).

Catullus. Famous artist whose creativity was unlocked by the ageless noncorporeal entity known as **Onaya**. ("The Muse" [DS9]).

causality loop. SEE: **temporal causality loop**.

"Cause and Effect." *Next Generation* episode #118. Written by Brannon Braga. Directed by Jonathan Frakes. Stardate 45652.1. *First aired in 1992. The* Enterprise-D *is caught in a time loop, doomed to explode again and again unless a way can be found to escape.* GUEST CAST: Michelle Forbes as **Ro Laren**; Patti Yasutake as **Ogawa, Nurse Alyssa**; Kelsey Grammer as **Bateson, Captain Morgan**. SEE: **Adele, Aunt; Bateson, Captain Morgan; *Bozeman*, *U.S.S.*; *déjà vu*; dekyon; *Enterprise*-D, *U.S.S.*; escape pod; Fletcher, Ensign; flux spectrometer; graviton polarimeter; inertial dampers; main shuttlebay; *nIb'poH*; Ogawa, Nurse Alyssa; Ro Laren; shuttlebay; *Soyuz*-class starship; temporal causality loop; Typhon Expanse; vertazine.**

cave-rat. Small furry animal found in the caves of some Class-M worlds. ("The Sword of Kahless" [DS9]).

caviar. Earth food. The unhatched eggs of a large scaleless Earth fish. Considered a culinary delicacy by some humans, and a personal favorite of Captain Picard. The captain felt that replicated caviar was not as good as the real thing, and had a few cases of real caviar from Earth stored aboard his ship for special occasions. ("Sins of the Father" [TNG]).

Cavit, Lieutenant Commander. (Scott Jaeck). Starfleet officer aboard the *Starship Voyager*. Cavit was fatally injured on the bridge during the ship's violent passage to the **Delta Quadrant** in 2371. ("Caretaker" [VGR]).

Caylem. (Joel Grey). Member of the **Alsaurian resistance movement** on a planet of the **Mokra Order** in the Delta Quadrant. Caylem's wife was caught by the Mokra after she led a raid on a Mokra supply center, and in 2360, she died in prison. Their daughter, **Ralkana**, was killed while trying to rescue her mother. Caylem was a gentle man who was so affected by these tragedies that he blocked the memories of them out of his mind. He spent the rest of his life believing that his wife and daughter were still alive, conducting quixotic missions to rescue them from the Mokra. In 2372, during an away-team mission to Caylem's planet, Captain **Kathryn Janeway** was seriously injured. Caylem, who was delusional, nursed Janeway's injuries, believing her to be his daughter, Ralkana. Caylem was killed helping Janeway free two of her officers from Mokra imprisonment. In doing so, he ultimately gave his life for the cause of the resistance movement. ("Resistance" [VGR]). SEE: **Darod**.

Ce Acatl. Ancestor of **Chakotay** of the *Starship Voyager*. Ce Acatl was born centuries ago on Earth. ("Basics, Part I" [VGR]).

celebium. Source of hazardous radiation. Celebium radiation killed all but two of the scientific team on planet **Camus II** in 2269. The two survivors were **Dr. Janice Lester** and **Dr. Arthur Coleman**. Lester may have deliberately sent the other members of the team into an area where the celebium shielding was weak. ("Turnabout Intruder" [TOS]).

Celestial Auction. In **Ferengi** mythology, after death, a Ferengi enters the **Divine Treasury**, where he can bid on a new life in a Celestial Auction. ("Little Green Men" [DS9]).

Celestial Cafe. A Bajoran restaurant overlooking the **Promenade** on Deep Space 9. The Celestial Cafe was owned by Chalan Aroya. ("Broken Link" [DS9]).

Celestial Temple. In the **Bajoran** religion, the Celestial Temple is a region of space where their spiritual **Prophets** reside. Some Bajorans believe the Celestial Temple is actually the **Bajoran wormhole**, and thus feel the wormhole to be sacred. Bajoran tradition holds that the Temple is the source of the nine **Orbs** sent by the Prophets to help teach the Bajoran people how to lead their lives. ("Emissary" [DS9]).

cellular disruption. Technique used to kill intruders by the image of **Losira**, defending the **Kalandan outpost** in 2268. Losira would touch her intended victim, causing individual cells to explode from within, resulting in a painful death. ("That Which Survives" [TOS]).

cellular metamorphosis. Process allowing an individual to assume another's form. After Captain **Garth** suffered an accident in the 2260s, he went to planet **Antos IV,** where the people taught him cellular metamorphosis to restore his health. He then used those techniques to take the shape of anyone he chose, giving him dangerous power in his mentally unstable state. ("Whom Gods Destroy" [TOS]). SEE: **shape-shifter**.

cellular peptides. Biochemical substance involved in maintaining cellular cohesion in the human body. The **interphasic organisms** that plagued the *Enterprise*-D consumed the cellular peptides from their host's bodies. At about the same time, Data began having nightmares that included Worf taking a bite out of a cellular peptide cake with mint frosting made in the image of Troi. Data later learned that this dream was symbolic of the interphasic organisms extracting the cellular peptides from the crew members of the *Enterprise*-D. ("Phantasms" [TNG]). The **memory virus** discovered by *Voyager* personnel in 2373 thrived on peptides generated by its host's brain. ("Flashback" [VGR]).

cellular toxicity. Measurement of biological waste products accumulating within a life-form's cells. Neelix's cellular toxicity level rose after his lungs were removed in 2371, due to his body's inability to oxygenate and remove wastes from his bloodstream. ("Phage" [VGR]).

Celtris III. Barren, uninhabited, Class-M planet located in **Cardassian** space. In 2369, Cardassian disinformation that a new **metagenic weapon** was being developed tricked Starfleet into sending a covert Starfleet team to Celtris III. There, Captain Jean-Luc Picard was captured. ("Chain of Command, Part I" [TNG]).

cenotaph. Coffin-like enclosure used in the **Vhnori transference ritual**. The cenotpath was designed to painlessly end a person's life, so that he or she could pass into the **Next Emanation**. ("Emanations" [VGR]).

center seat. Starfleet slang term referring to the captain's chair on the bridge of a starship, and by extension, the job of starship command. *(Star Trek: The Motion Picture).*

Central Bureau of Penology, Stockholm. Earth institution dealing with the rehabilitation of criminals. The *U.S.S. Enterprise* transported research materials from the Central Bureau of Penology to the **Tantalus V** penal colony in 2266. ("Dagger of the Mind" [TOS]). *A few cargo modules glimpsed in the cargo bay of Deep Space 9 bore cargo labels suggesting that they had been sent from the bureau to Dr. Van Gelder at the Tantalus colony, a tip of the hat to "Dagger of the Mind."*

Central Command, Cardassian. SEE: **Cardassian Central Command.**

central control complex. Device used by the android **Norman** to control and direct the 207,809 **androids** on a planet ruled by Harry Mudd in 2267. ("I, Mudd" [TOS]). SEE: **Mudd, Harcourt Fenton.**

Centurion. (John Warburton). Officer aboard the **Romulan bird-of-prey** that crossed the **Romulan Neutral Zone** in 2266. Older and more experienced than most members of the crew, the centurion counseled a cautious strategy in confronting the *Enterprise* but was overruled when the politically ambitious **Decius** advocated a more provocative approach. ("Balance of Terror" [TOS]). *Centurion was a rank in the Romulan guard, approximately equivalent to a captain in the Federation Starfleet.*

Cerebus II. Planet. The natives of Cerebus II developed a treatment that reverses the aging process in humans. The process, involving herb and drug combinations, was very painful and had a high mortality rate. **Admiral Mark Jameson** obtained the treatment in exchange for having negotiated a treaty for that planet's government. Although the process was initially successful, Jameson eventually died of the side effects. ("Too Short A Season" [TNG]).

Ceremony of Reconciliation. A historic ceremony ending centuries of war between the star systems **Krios** and **Valt Minor**, conducted aboard the *Starship Enterprise*-D in 2368. The ceremony, which was performed in a holodeck simulation of the ancient **Temple of Akadar**, involved presentation to Valtese **Chancellor Alrik** of the empathic metamorph **Kamala** to become his wife. The ceremony was almost disrupted when Kriosian **Ambassador Briam** was injured, but Captain Picard was able to fulfill Briam's duties. ("The Perfect Mate" [TNG]).

Certificate of Dismemberment. SEE: **Ferengi Certificate of Dismemberment.**

cervaline. Antirejection drug. In 2372, the **Emergency Medical Hologram** ordered cervaline to be administered to **Danara Pel** to fend off rejection of Klingon tissue implanted into her brain. ("Lifesigns" [VGR]).

Cestus Comets. One of the six **baseball** teams organized in mid 2371 on **Cestus III**. ("Family Business" [DS9]).

Cestus III. Planet. Location of a Federation outpost destroyed by a reptilian civilization known as the **Gorn** in 2267. The Federation had at the time been unaware that Cestus III was in space the Gorn considered to be their own territory, and that the Gorn had been protecting their own sovereignty. Unfortunately, the Gorn attack on the Federation outpost left only a single survivor. ("Arena" [TOS]). Misunderstandings with the Gorn were eventually resolved, and the planet was colonized by Federation settlers. In mid-2371, the colonists on Cestus III formed a league of six **baseball** teams. Two of the teams were the Cestus Comets and the **Pike City Pioneers**. ("Family Business" [DS9]). Cestus III is eight weeks' travel from the Bajor sector at maximum warp. ("The Way of the Warrior" [DS9]). *The location for filming Cestus III as well as for the Metrons' planetoid in "Arena" was Vasquez Rocks, near Los Angeles, which was used for various television and feature productions. Other* Star Trek *episodes filmed there include "Shore Leave" (TOS), "The Alternative Factor" (TOS), "Friday's Child" (TOS), "Who Watches the Watchers?" (TNG), "The Homecoming" (DS9), and one shot in* Star Trek IV. *The Cestus III outpost was actually a fort constructed for the feature* The Alamo, *produced in the 1930s. The fort was demolished in the late 1960s because it was thought to be in danger of collapse.*

Cetacean Institute. Aquarium and marine-biology research facility located in Sausalito on Earth in the 20th century. Kirk and Spock, traveling back in time, visited the Cetacean Institute to find two **humpback whale**s in hopes of repopulating that species in Earth's 23rd century. (*Star Trek IV: The Voyage Home*). SEE: **Taylor, Dr. Gillian**. *The Cetacean Institute scenes in* Star Trek IV *were filmed at the Monterey Bay Aquarium, which looks a lot like the Cetacean Institute except that it doesn't have a big whale tank (which was added with a bit of visual effects magic by ILM). The name had to be changed to the Cetacean Institute because it was necessary, for plot reasons, to move the location of the aquarium to Sausalito. The Cetacean Institute symbol is actually the logo of the Monterey Bay Aquarium, even though the name was changed to protect the innocent.*

Ceti Alpha V. Fifth planet in the Ceti Alpha star system. **Khan Noonien Singh** and his followers, along with *Enterprise* historian **Marla McGivers,** were exiled to Ceti Alpha V following their attempt to commandeer the *Enterprise* in 2267. The world was described as a bit savage, somewhat inhospitable, but livable. ("Space Seed" [TOS]). Following the explosion of sister planet **Ceti Alpha VI** later that year, Ceti Alpha V became nearly uninhabitable. During the following years, twenty of Khan's followers, including Marla McGivers, were killed by deadly **Ceti eels**. Khan and his surviving followers escaped in 2285 when the planet was being surveyed by the ***U.S.S. Reliant*** as a possible test site for the **Genesis Project**. (*Star Trek II: The Wrath of Khan*).

Ceti Alpha VI. Sixth planet in the Ceti Alpha star system. Ceti Alpha VI exploded some six months after **Khan Noonien Singh** had been marooned on **Ceti Alpha V** in 2267. The explosion disrupted the orbit of Ceti Alpha V. (*Star Trek II: The Wrath of Khan*).

Ceti eel. The last surviving life-form indigenous to planet **Ceti Alpha V**, following the explosion of planet **Ceti Alpha VI**. Ceti eels were mollusk-like creatures whose young incubated inside the brains of humanoid life-forms. These parasites caused the host considerable pain and left the host susceptible to external suggestion. Twenty of **Khan**'s followers were killed by Ceti eels, and Khan used the creatures to gain the cooperation of Captain Terrell and Commander Chekov. *(Star Trek II: The Wrath of Khan).*

CFI replicator. SEE: **replicator.**

Ch'Par. Officer in the Klingon military service. Ch'Par was an engineer assigned to a bird-of-prey that was docked at station Deep Space 9 for repairs in 2373. ("By Inferno's Light" [DS9]).

Ch'Pok. (Ron Canada). **Advocate** from the Klingon Empire. In 2372, Ch'Pok prosecuted an extradition hearing on station Deep Space 9 when **Lieutenant Commander Worf** was accused of firing on an unarmed Klingon transport vessel. ("Rules of Engagement" [DS9]). *Ron Canada also appeared as Martin Benbeck in "Masterpiece Society" (TNG).*

"Cha* Worf *Toh'gah-nah lo Pre'tOk." Klingon translation of an ancient Earth tune, "For He's a Jolly Good Fellow," a song typically sung at birthday celebrations. The lyrics were difficult to translate, as there is no Klingon word for "jolly." ("Parallels" [TNG]).

cha'DIch. Klingon term for a "second," or a person who stands with a warrior during a ceremonial challenge or trial. The duty of the *cha'DIch* is to defend the one challenged, since the one challenged is denied the right of combat while accused. **Worf** chose his brother, **Kurn**, as *cha'DIch* when their late father, **Mogh**, was accused of treason. When Kurn was the target of attempted murder, Worf asked Captain Picard to serve as *cha'DIch*. ("Sins of the Father" [TNG]). *The ritual knife given to Picard as* cha'DIch *can be seen on the desk in his quarters during "Suddenly Human" (TNG).* ***Jono*** *used the knife to stab Captain Picard.*

CHAH-mooz-ee. Among some ancient Native American cultures from Earth, an ancient healing symbol resembling a spiral trisected by a "V". Often seen accompanied by other spirals with linear elements, it is sometimes used as a blessing to the land. The symbol is believed to be of extraterrestrial origin and has been associated with the ancient **Rubber Tree People**, as well as on a planet near the Cardassian border, and among a civilization in the **Delta Quadrant.** The latter usages were discovered by the crew of the *Starship Voyager* in 2372, who left it on a moon and on their planet which were visited by the ***U.S.S. Voyager***. SEE: **Chakotay; Sky Spirits.** ("Tattoo" [VGR]). The *CHAH-mooz-ee* symbol was engraved onto a river rock in Chakotay's **medicine bundle**. ("The Cloud" [VGR]). Voyager *senior illustrator Rick Sternbach designed the* CHAH-mooz-ee *symbol. Rick says he based the design on a map of the Milky Way galaxy, and the V lines may—or may not—suggest the paths of various wormholes and other spatial phenomena across the galaxy.*

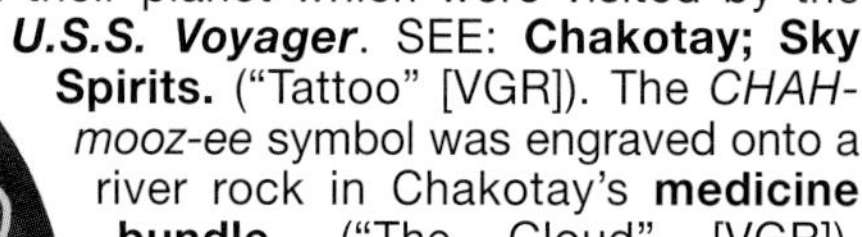

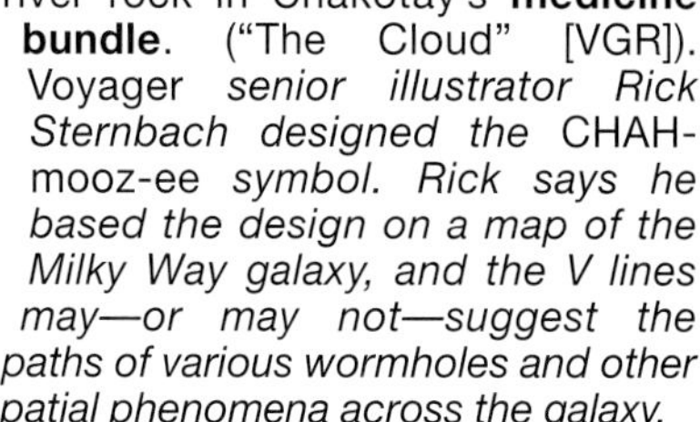

"Chain of Command, Part I." *Next Generation* episode #136. Teleplay by Ronald D. Moore. Story by Frank Abatemarco. Directed by Robert Scheerer. Stardate 46357.4. *First aired in 1993. Picard is relieved of command and replaced with a by-the-book officer who is intent on confronting the Cardassians.* GUEST CAST: Ronny Cox as **Jellico, Captain Edward**; Natalia Nogulich as **Necheyev, Alynna**; John Durbin as **Ssestar**; Lou Wagner as **Krax**; David Warner as **Madred, Gul**; Majel Barrett as Computer voice. SEE: ***Cairo, U.S.S.*; Cardassians; Celtris III; class-5 probe; Corak, Glinn; *Enterprise*-D, *U.S.S.*; *Feynman, Shuttlecraft*; fusing pitons; Jellico, Captain Edward; Lemec, Gul; *lynars*; Madred, Gul; metagenic weapon; Necheyev, Alynna; Picard, Jean-Luc; *Reklar*; Riker, William T.; security access code; Solok, DaiMon; Tajor, Glinn; Torman V.**

"Chain of Command, Part II." *Next Generation* episode #137. Written by Frank Abatemarco. Directed by Les Landau. Stardate 46360.8. *First aired in 1993. Picard, held captive by a brutal Cardassian, is the victim of psychological and physical torture.* GUEST CAST: Ronny Cox as **Jellico, Captain Edward**; David Warner as **Madred, Gul**; Heather L. Olson as **Orra, Jil**; Majel Barrett as Computer voice. SEE: **antimatter mines; Cardassia; Cardassians; First Hebitian civilization; Gessard, Yvette; *gettle*; Jellico, Captain Edward; jevonite; Jovian run; La Forge, Geordi; Lakat; Lyshan System; Madred, Gul; McAllister C-5 Nebula; Minos Korva; Orra, Jil; Picard, Jean-Luc; Picard, Maurice; Picard, Yvette Gessard; security access code; Seldonis IV Convention; taspar egg; Titan's Turn; Tohvun III; wompat.**

Chakotay. (Robert Beltran). First officer of the ***Starship Voyager*** and former member of the **Maquis** resistance group. ("Caretaker" [VGR]). Chakotay was of Native American descent and fiercely proud of his ancestry. As a child, however, Chakotay rebelled against his heritage. At the age of 15, Chakotay traveled with his father, **Kolopak** (*pictured below*), to Earth in search of the ancient **Rubber Tree People**. During the expedition, Chakotay hurt his father deeply by announcing that he was leaving his people to attend Starfleet Academy. Kolopak accepted his son's rebellion, noting that Chakotay had been a breech birth, indicating a problem child. Chakotay's application to the academy had been sponsored by Captain **Sulu**. ("Tattoo" [VGR]). *It is not clear if this Captain Sulu is the same person who appeared in the original* Star Trek *series, but this does seem to be the intent of the episode. In "Tattoo," Chakotay at 15 years old was played by Douglas Spain.* After his father's death, Chakotay came to recognize the importance of his people's heritage, and he tattooed his forehead in honor of his father and their ancestors. ("Tattoo" [VGR]). One of his ancestors was a school teacher in Arizona on Earth in the 20th century. ("Future's End, Part I" [VGR]).

During Chakotay's first year at Starfleet Academy, he trained as a pilot over Earth's North American continent and spent a couple of months on Venus learning how to handle atmospheric storms. He later learned to dodge asteroids in that system's asteroid belt. Chakotay had an interest in archaeology. ("Future's End, Part II" [VGR]). After Chakotay graduated from the academy, he was a member of the Starfleet team that made first contact with the **Tarkannans**. ("Innocence" [VGR]). He later left Starfleet to join the Maquis in defense of his homeworld against the **Cardassians**. He commanded a Maquis ship that was lost in the **Badlands** in 2371 while fleeing from a Cardassian ship. Chakotay and his crew were swept into the distant Delta Quadrant by the **Caretaker**, where they were trapped when their ship was destroyed by the **Kazon-Ogla**. Chakotay and his fellow Maquis subsequently accepted an invitation to join the crew of the *Starship Voyager* under the command of Captain **Kathryn Janeway**. Under this arrangement, Chakotay became the ship's first officer, replacing Lieutenant Commander Cavit. ("Caretaker"

[VGR]). The difficult conditions in the Delta Quadrant led Chakotay to question whether Starfleet's idealism was appropriate in this distant part of the galaxy, wondering if the expediency of Maquis techniques might be wiser. ("Alliances" [VGR]).

Chakotay practiced his people's **vision quest** rituals, seeking direction from his **animal guide**. He used his **medicine bundle** to help invoke these rituals. Chakotay would occasionally help those close to him experience the vision quest in search of their own animal guides. ("The Cloud" [VGR]). Chakotay honored his people's traditional medical practices, including the use of a **medicine wheel** to help guide his spirit back to his body when it was displaced by **trianic energy beings** on stardate 48734. ("Cathexis" [VGR]).

While in the Maquis, Chakotay was romantically involved with **Seska** (*pictured*), unaware that she was a Cardassian agent who had been surgically altered to appear Bajoran. ("State of Flux" [VGR], "Caretaker" [VGR]). Seska, who later defected to the **Kazon**, subsequently deceived Chakotay, telling him that she had impregnated herself with a sample of his DNA. ("Maneuvers" [VGR]).

Chakotay became afflicted with a potentially fatal viral disease in 2372 after exposure to an insectoid life-form on a planet in the Delta Quadrant. Extensive research determined that the condition could remain benign as long as he remained on the planet, but that he could not survive if he left. *Voyager* Captain **Kathryn Janeway** was also stricken with the disease. Determined that her people should not sacrifice their chance to return home, Janeway ordered her ship to continue their voyage, leaving Chakotay and Janeway behind. On the planet, Chakotay's wilderness skills that he learned as a boy from **Kolopak**, his father, proved invaluable. After several weeks, *Voyager's* crew, with the aid of **Vidiian** physician **Danara Pel**, was able to obtain an antiviral medication, and returned to successfully treat Chakotay and Janeway. Chakotay and Janeway grew closer during their time alone together on the planet. ("Resolutions" [VGR]).

In 2373, Chakotay was temporarily assimilated into a **Borg** collective while on a mission of exploration into the **Nekrit Expanse**. His brief exposure to the Borg group consciousness helped heal him from a serious injury. Chakotay later assisted a group of former Borg drones to reestablish a group consciousness, which they felt necessary to a life of harmony. ("Unity" [VGR]).

Chakotay's first appearance was in "Caretaker" (VGR).

Chalan Aroya. (Jill Jacobson). Bajoran national who owned the Celestial Cafe, a Bajoran restaurant overlooking the Promenade on Deep Space 9. Chalan was attracted to security chief Odo. ("Broken Link" [DS9]).

***Challenger*.** Early space ship, destroyed in 1986 in a tragic explosion that claimed the lives of seven astronauts shortly after launch from planet Earth. *The film* Star Trek IV: The Voyage Home, *released in 1986, bore the following dedication: "The cast and crew of* Star Trek *wish to dedicate this film to the men and women of the spaceship* Challenger, *whose courageous spirit shall live to the 23rd century and beyond...." One of the shuttlepods carried aboard the* Enterprise-D *was named for* Challenger *astronaut Ellison Onizuka ("The Ensigns of Command" [TNG]).*

Chalna. Planet that was home to the people known as the **Chalnoth**. The ***U.S.S. Stargazer***, under the command of Captain Picard, visited Chalna in 2354. ("Allegiance" [TNG]).

Chalnoth. The humanoid civilization that inhabited planet **Chalna**. The Chalnoth were very large and lupine in appearance, and anarchists by nature. Their people had no use for laws or governments; they existed by murdering those who threatened them. **Esoqq** was Chalnoth. ("Allegiance" [TNG]).

Chaltok IV. Planet. A Romulan research colony located on Chaltok IV was nearly destroyed during the testing of a polaric ion device. The incident led to the **Polaric Test Ban Treaty** of 2268. ("Time and Again" [VGR]). See: **polaric ion energy.**

Chamber of Ministers. See: **Bajoran Chamber of Ministers**.

chambers coil. Component of a starship's communications system. (*Star Trek II: The Wrath of Khan*). In 2370 on planet **T'Lani III**, Chief Miles O'Brien attempted to activate a communication system by resetting the actuators on the chambers coil. ("Armageddon Game" [DS9]).

chameleon rose. Flower from planet **Betazed** that changes color with the mood of its owner. **Wyatt Miller** gave **Deanna Troi** a chameleon rose before their planned wedding. ("Haven" [TNG]).

chameloid. Shape-shifting life-form. **Martia**, an inmate at **Rura Penthe**, was a chameloid who seemed to enjoy taking the form of a high fashion model. *(Star Trek VI: The Undiscovered Country).* SEE: **shape-shifter**.

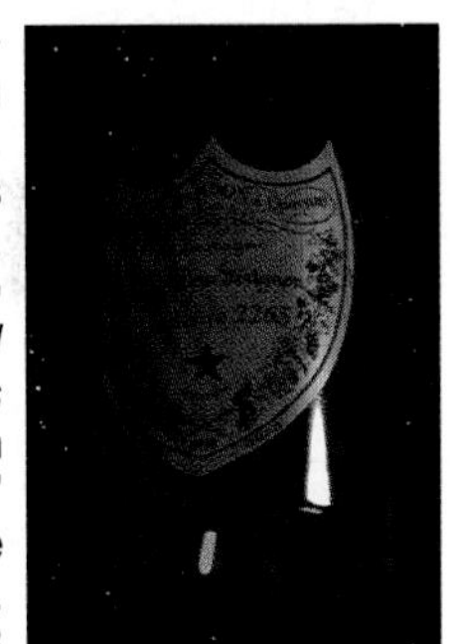

champagne. Effervescent alcoholic beverage made from an ancient process involving the double fermentation of Earth grapes. Lore shared a champagne toast with his brother, Data, but Lore spiked the drink. *Lore's bottle bore a label that read Altairian Grand Premier, which could be abbreviated as AGP, not coincidentally the same initials as first-season* Star Trek: The Next Generation *illustrator Andrew G. Probert.* ("Datalore" [TNG]). Worf served replicated champagne to Counselor Troi on his birthday in 2370. ("Parallels" [TNG]). The *U.S.S. Enterprise*-B was christened in 2293 by a bottle of Dom Pérignon brand champagne, vintage 2265. *(Star Trek Generations).* In Julian Bashir's **secret agent** holosuite program, Bashir used the cork of a bottle of 1945 Dom Pérignon as a projectile to knock out the Falcon. ("Our Man Bashir" [DS9]). SEE: **Chateau Cleon.** Odo and Dr. Mora drank champagne in 2373 to celebrate their success in training a **changeling infant**. ("The Begotten" [DS9]). After surviving a near-fatal injury in 2373, Kathryn Janeway felt like celebrating with Chakotay with champagne and a moonlight sail on **Lake George** in *Voyager*'s holodeck. ("Coda" [VGR]).

Champion Standing. Rank awarded to the most outstanding competitors in ***bat'leth*** competition. Worf earned Champion Standing at the *bat'leth* competition on Forcas III in 2370. ("Parallels" [TNG]).

Champs Elysees. A landmark of the Earth city of Paris. The Champs Elysees is a street in the old city, known for its beautiful gardens. **Nurse Alyssa Ogawa** told Beverly Crusher that she visted a holodeck re-creation of the Champs Elysees with a gentleman friend. ("Imaginary Friend" [TNG]).

Chamra Vortex. Nebula in the **Gamma Quadrant** containing millions of asteroids. **Croden** of the planet **Rakhar** hid his daughter, **Yareth**, on one of of the asteroids, where she survived in a stasis chamber. Croden returned to the Chamra Vortex in 2369 with Odo on a runabout from Deep Space 9, when they revived Yareth. ("Vortex" [DS9]). SEE: ***toh-maire***.

chancellor. Title given to the leader of the **Klingon High Council**. Past chancellors have included **Gorkon** and **Azetbur**. *(Star Trek VI: The Undiscovered Country). High Council leaders in episodes of* Star Trek: The Next Generation *did not use this title, instead being described as "council leader." Gowron was finally addressed as chancellor in "The Way of the Warrior" (DS9).* SEE: **Gowron; K'mpec**.

Chandra V. Planet. **Tam Elbrun** was assigned to Chandra V prior to the **Tin Man** encounter in 2366. Elbrun described the

Chandrans as beautiful, peaceful, nonhumanoid creatures, who had a three-day ritual for saying hello. ("Tin Man" [TNG]).

Chandra, Captain. Starship commander. Chandra was one of the board members who sat in judgment at James Kirk's court-martial at **Starbase 11** in 2267. ("Court Martial" [TOS]).

Chandra. (Clara Bryant). Little girl, part of the **Wadi** game of **chula**. Chandra sang a song and played hopscotch on **Wadi** symbols built into the floor of the game's maze. A player in chula could only move onto the third *shap*, or level, by imitating her apparently nonsensical children's song and hopscotch step. ("Move Along Home" [DS9]). SEE: ***allamaraine***.

Chang, General. (Christopher Plummer). Chief of staff to Klingon **Chancellor Gorkon**. A proud warrior, Chang was also fond of quoting **William Shakespeare** and other luminaries. Chang feared the changes that peace would bring and conspired with Starfleet **Admiral Cartwright** and others to assassinate Gorkon in an effort to block Gorkon's peace initiative. Chang was killed at **Khitomer** when attempting to disrupt the peace conference there in 2293. *(Star Trek VI: The Undiscovered Country). In addition to Chang's numerous Shakespearean quotes, his demand in court that Kirk answer a question without waiting for a translation is a paraphrase of American Ambassador Adlai Stevenson, who made the same demand of Soviet Ambassador Valerian Zorin at the United Nations during the Cuban missile crisis in 1962.*

Chang, Tac Officer. (Robert Ito). Starfleet officer. Chang was in charge of **Starfleet Academy** entrance examinations at the Starfleet facility on planet **Relva VII**. Chang supervised Wesley Crusher's first attempt to gain entrance to the academy in 2364. ("Coming of Age" [TNG]). *Actor Robert Ito also played Professor Toichi Hikita in the cult classic motion picture* The Adventures of Buckaroo Banzai.

changeling infant. A young member of the **Founders** of the **Dominion** that was found on station Deep Space 9 in 2373. Station security chief and fellow Founder **Odo** assumed care for the infant. Odo, who had resented the way he had been raised by solids, was determined to treat this surrogate child in a more compassionate manner. Odo's approach was successful. Over the course of several days, the infant learned to form simple shapes and even mimicked Odo's face. Unfortunately, the infant had suffered irreversible tetryon radiation exposure while in space, and died while in Odo's care. Just as it expired in Odo's hands, the changeling infant infused itself into Odo's humanoid body, transforming Odo back into a shape-shifter. ("The Begotten" [DS9]). SEE: **Mora Pol, Dr.**

"Changeling, The." Original Series episode #37. Written by John Meredyth Lucas. Directed by Marc Daniels. Stardate 3541.9. *First aired in 1967. An ancient space probe launched from Earth centuries ago returns to Federation space on a bizarre mission to search for "perfect" life.* GUEST CAST: Majel Barrett as **Chapel, Christine**; Makee Blaisdel as **Singh, Mr.**; Barbara Gates as Astrochemist; Meade Martin as Engineer; Arnold Lessing as Carlisle, Lieutenant and voice of Security guard #1; Vic Perrin as **Nomad,** voice of; Jay Jones as Scott's stunt double. SEE: **antigrav; "Beyond Antares"; changeling; Malurians; Malurian system; Manway, Dr.; *Nomad*; Roykirk, Jackson; Scott, Montgomery; Singh, Mr.; Symbalene blood burn; *Tan Ru*; Uhura; Vulcan mind-meld; warp drive.**

changeling. Ancient Earth legend of a fairy child that was left in place of a stolen human baby. The changeling took the identity of the human child. Kirk compared the space probe ***Nomad*** to a changeling. ("The Changeling" [TOS]). **Croden** used the term, in a different context, as a nickname for the shape-shifting **Odo**. ("Vortex" [DS9]). The term "changeling" was originally a derogatory name given to shape-shifters by **solids**, although the **Founders** of the **Dominion** adopted the term for their own. ("The Search, Part II" [DS9]).

Channing, Dr. Federation scientist who studied warp physics. Wesley Crusher once cited Channing's belief that it might be possible to force **dilithium** to recrystallize in configurations able to better control the reactions between matter and antimatter. ("Lonely Among Us" [TNG]).

Chapel, Christine. (Majel Barrett). Nurse aboard the original *U.S.S. Enterprise* under Chief Medical Officer Leonard McCoy. Chapel gave up a promising career in bioresearch to sign aboard a starship in the hopes of finding her lost fiancé, **Dr. Roger Korby**. Chapel found Korby on planet **Exo III** in 2266, but learned he had transferred his consciousness into an android body. Korby was destroyed by another android on that planet. ("What Are Little Girls Made Of?" [TOS]). Chapel admitted she was in love with Mr. Spock while under the influence of the **Psi 2000 virus**, although Spock did his best to ignore this. ("The Naked Time" [TOS]). Following the return of the *Enterprise* to Earth in 2270, Chapel earned a medical degree, and later returned to the *Enterprise* as a staff physician. (*Star Trek: The Motion Picture*). Chapel directed emergency operations at **Starfleet Command** when Earth was threatened in 2286 with ecological disaster by an alien space probe of unknown origin. *(Star Trek IV: The Voyage Home). Chapel's first appearance was in "The Naked Time" (TOS). Majel Barrett, real-life widow of* Star Trek *creator Gene Roddenberry, also played* ***Number One****, second-in-command of the* Enterprise *in "The Cage" (TOS), as well as the recurring character* ***Lwaxana Troi*** *in* Star Trek: The Next Generation. *Barrett lent her voice to computers on the original* Star Trek, Star Trek: The Next Generation, Star Trek: Deep Space Nine, *and* Star Trek: Voyager. *Barrett also provided the voice for the* ***Beta 5 computer*** *("Assignment: Earth" [TOS]), and M'Ress in the animated* Star Trek. *A nurse aboard the* Enterprise*-D in "Transfigurations" (TNG) was referred to in the script as Nurse Temple (played by Patti Tippo), sort of an homage to Nurse Chapel.*

Chapman, Professor. Instructor at Starfleet Academy. Professor Chapman was one of B'Elanna Torres's teachers at the academy, and although they often disagreed, he thought she was one of the most promising cadets he'd ever taught. ("Parallax" [VGR]).

Chardis. (Steve Houska). Occupant of a Mislen freighter that was attacked five parsecs from their homeworld in 2373. The Delta Quadrant civilization known as the **Swarm** attacked Chardis's freighter with neuroelectric weapons, killing all aboard. ("The Swarm" [VGR]). *This character's name was not mentioned in dialog but is from the end credits.*

Charleston, U.S.S. Federation starship, *Excelsior* class, Starfleet registry number NCC-42285, that ferried three revived

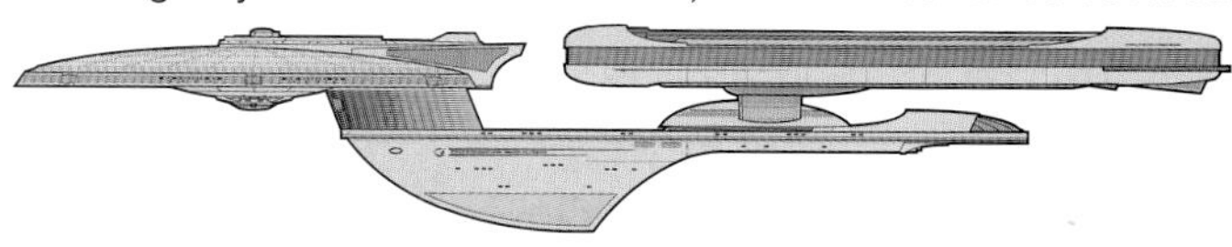

20th-century cryonic survivors back to Earth in 2364. ("The Neutral Zone" [TNG]). SEE: **cryonics**; **cryosatellite**.

"Charlie X." Original Series episode #8. Teleplay by D. C. Fontana. Story by Gene Roddenberry. Directed by Lawrence Dobkin. Stardate 1533.6. *First aired in 1966. An adolescent human boy, raised among aliens who have given him supernatural powers, finds it impossible to return to normal human society.* GUEST CAST: Robert Walker Jr. as **Evans, Charles**; Grace Lee Whitney as **Rand, Janice**; Charles J. Stewart as **Ramart, Captain**; Dallas Mitchell as Nellis, Tom; Don Eitner as Navigator; Patricia McNulty as **Lawton, Yeoman Tina**; John Bellah as Crewman 1; Garland Thompson as Crewman 2; Abraham Sofaer as Thasian, The; Laura Wood as Old lady; Frank da Vinci as Security guard; Beau Vandenecker as Sam; Gene Roddenberry as Galley chef's voice; Loren Janes as Kirk's stunt double; John Lindesmith as Helmsman; Robert Herron as Crewman in gym. SEE: **Alpha V, Colony; *Antares, U.S.S.*; baffle plate; Evans, Charles; gymnasium; Lawton, Yeoman Tina; noncorporeal life; Ramart, Captain; Rand, Janice; Thanksgiving; Thasians; Thasus; Uhura; United Earth Space Probe Agency; Vulcan lute**.

Charybdis*.** Early 21st-century space vehicle launched from Earth by **NASA** on July 23, 2037, under the command of **Colonel Stephen Richey**. The *Charybdis* was the third manned attempt to travel beyond Earth's solar system. The ship suffered a telemetry failure and its fate was unknown until 2365, when the remains of the *Charybdis* were discovered in orbit around a planet in the **Theta 116** system. ("The Royale" [TNG]). *In Greek mythology, Charybdis is one of two sea monsters who lived in a cave near the Straits of Messina. The other monster was* ***Scylla*, mentioned in "Samaritan Snare" (TNG).* SEE: **Richey, Colonel Stephen**.

"Chase, The." *Next Generation* episode #146. Story by Ronald D. Moore & Joe Menosky. Teleplay by Joe Menosky. Directed by Jonathan Frakes. Stardate 46731.5. *First aired in 1993. Picard's old archaeology professor sends the captain on a quest to solve a four-billion-year-old mystery, a message from the first humanoid people in this part of the galaxy. This episode was in part intended to answer the question of why* Star Trek *showed so many aliens that were humanoid.* GUEST CAST: Salome Jens as Humanoid; John Cothran, Jr. as **Nu'Daq**; Linda Thorson as **Ocett, Gul**; Norman Lloyd as **Galen, Professor Richard**; Majel Barrett as Computer voice. SEE: **Al-Leyan transport; Aolian Cluster; Atalia VII; *B'aht Qul* challenge; Data; Deep Space 4; DNA; Galen, Professor Richard; humanoid life; Indri VIII; Kea IV; Kurl; Kurlan *naiskos*; Loren III; macchiato; *Maht-H'a, I.K.S.*; Mot; M'Tell; Nu'Daq; Ocett, Gul; Picard, Jean-Luc; Rahm-Izad system; Ruah IV; Satarrans; Sothis III; Tarquin Hill, The Master of; Vilmor II; Volterra nebula; Ya'Seem; Yash-El, night blessing of; Yridians**.

Chateau Cleon. A type of **champagne**. On stardate 48959, **Quark** served Chateau Cleon, vintage 2303, to celebrate **Benjamin Sisko**'s promotion to captain. ("The Adversary" [DS9]).

Chateau Coeur. A variety of French **champagne**. ("Future's End, Part I" [VGR]).

Chateau Lafite Rothschild. Full-bodied, aged fine red wine from the Bordeaux region of France on Earth. While incarcerated in an Akritirian prison satellite, Tom Paris dreamed of having crown roast of lamb dinner with a 2296 vintage Chateau Lafite Rothschild when he was free again. ("The Chute" [VGR]). *Also one of* Star Trek *producer Bob Justman's favorites of the 1959 vintage.*

Chateau Picard. A fine wine produced at the Picard family vineyards in **Labarre, France**. **Robert Picard** gave his brother, Jean-Luc, a bottle of 2347 Chateau Picard following Jean-Luc's visit home in 2367. ("Family" [TNG]).

***chech'tluth*.** Klingon alcoholic beverage. Worf ordered some *chech'tluth* for **Bringloidi** colony leader **Danilo Odell**, who found it sufficiently potent. ("Up the Long Ladder" [TNG]).

***chee'lash*.** Fruit. In the **Argrathi** artificial reality prison program, *chee'lash* was a type of food given to prisoners. ("Hard Time" [DS9]).

***CHEGH-chew jaj-VAM jaj-KAK*.** Klingon expression meaning "It is a good day to die." ("The Way of the Warrior" [DS9]).

Chekote, Admiral. (Bruce Gray). Starfleet official attached to **Starbase 227.** He gave William Riker permission to delay a previously scheduled mission and investigate Captain Picard's apparent death at planet Dessica II in 2370, placing the *Enterprise*-D on detached duty for this investigation. ("Gambit, Part I" [TNG]). Chekote ordered the evacuation of station Deep Space 9, despite evidence that the **Circle**'s activities were backed by the Cardassians. ("The Circle" [DS9]). *Apparently no relation to Chakotay, from* Star Trek: Voyager.

Chekov, Pavel A. (Walter Koenig). Navigator on the original *Starship Enterprise* under the command of Captain James Kirk. Born in 2245 ("Who Mourns for Adonais?" [TOS]), Chekov held the rank of ensign during his first mission aboard the ship. ("Catspaw" [TOS]). His Starfleet serial number was 656-5827B. *(Star Trek IV: The Voyage Home).* Pavel Andreievich Chekov was an only child, although he once ima-gined he had a brother named Piotr while under the influence of the **Beta XII-A entity**. ("Day of the Dove" [TOS]). While at Starfleet Academy, Chekov became involved with a young woman named **Irina Galliulin**, but the relationship did not last because Galliulin was uncomfortable with the structured way of life required by Starfleet. Years later, the two met again when Galliulin sought the mythical planet **Eden** with **Dr. Sevrin**. ("The Way to Eden" [TOS]). In 2267, Chekov was the only member of an *Enterprise* landing party to Gamma Hydra IV who was not affected with an aging disease. During the mission, Chekov became startled at the sight of a dead colonist. The surge of adrenaline protected him from radiation sickness that caused the aging process. ("The Deadly Years" [TOS]). Chekov was promoted to lieutenant and assigned as security chief aboard the *Enterprise* following the conclusion of Kirk's first five-year mission. *(Star Trek: The Motion Picture).* Chekov later served aboard the ***U.S.S. Reliant*** as first officer under Captain **Clark Terrell**, before returning to the *Enterprise* after the *Reliant* was destroyed at the **Mutara Nebula** by **Khan**. *(Star Trek II: The Wrath of Khan).* Chekov was an honored guest during the maiden voyage of the *U.S.S.* ***Enterprise*-B** in 2294. *(Star Trek Generations). Chekov joined the* Star Trek *cast in "Catspaw" (TOS) at the beginning of the second season, although Khan claimed to have remembered him from "Space Seed" (TOS), filmed before the character was created. Walter Koenig's wife, actor Judy Levitt, played several roles in the* Star Trek *movies. These included a doctor at Mercy Hospital in* Star Trek IV, *and a Starfleet Command officer in* Star Trek VI. *Walter Koenig also played Bester, the psi cop, in* Babylon 5.

Chekov, Piotr. Imaginary brother to **Pavel A. Chekov**. Pavel, who was an only child, believed he had a brother while under the influence of the **Beta XII-A entity** in 2268. Chekov believed this brother had been murdered by Klingons at the Archanis IV research outpost and vowed to avenge his brother's death. ("Day of the Dove" [TOS]).

Chell. (Derek McGrath). **Maquis** resistance fighter who joined the crew of the ***Voyager***. During the first few weeks after the ship was lost in the Delta Quadrant in 2371, Chell became regarded as a disruptive and unreliable worker. Accordingly, Chell was among several Maquis crew members assigned to Lieutenant Tuvok for **field training**. ("Learning Curve" [VGR]).

Chen, Governor. Chief executive of the State of California on **Earth** in 2024. During the **Bell Riots**, Governor Chen believed rumors that government hostages had been killed, so he ordered government troops to storm the **Sanctuary District**, resulting in the death of hundreds of Sanctuary residents. ("Past Tense, Part II" [DS9]).

Cheney, Ensign. *Enterprise*-D crew member. Cheney played the cello, accompanying Data and **Neela Daren** in a concert in the Ten-Forward Lounge on stardate 46693. ("Lessons" [TNG]).

***cherel* sauce.** Drayan condiment sometimes served over ***takka* berries**. ("Innocence" [VGR]).

Cheron, Battle of. A crucial defeat for the **Romulan Star Empire**, ending the Romulan wars in 2160. Following this conflict, Earth authorities concluded peace with the Romulans and established the **Romulan Neutral Zone**. The Romulan government viewed the Battle of Cheron as a humiliating defeat. ("The Defector" [TNG]). *It is unclear if this battle involved the planet seen in "Let That Be Your Last Battlefield" (TOS) since the battle took place over a century prior to that episode, yet Spock was unfamiliar with Cheron in that episode.*

Cheron. Class-M planet located in the southernmost part of the galaxy, formerly home to an intelligent humanoid species. The inhabitants of Cheron, torn by racial hatreds, destroyed themselves and all life on the planet. ("Let That Be Your Last Battlefield" [TOS]). SEE: **Bele**; **Lokai**.

cherry pie. Dessert food consisting of a compote of Earth cherries baked in a flaky crust. Tom Paris liked cherry pie. ("The Chute" [VGR]).

Ches'sarro. (Dan Curry). Bajoran mining engineer who collaborated with the Cardassians during the Bajoran occupation. In 2370, **Pallra** discovered evidence of his collaboration and used it to blackmail him. Shortly after the evidence was uncovered, Ches'sarro's body was discovered, in a pond on his property. ("Necessary Evil" [DS9]). *It was not made clear who was responsible for Ches'sarro's death. The face of Ches'sarro was that of* Star Trek *visual effects producer Dan Curry, a re-use of the photo of Curry as Dekon Elig from "Babel" (DS9).*

chess. SEE: **three-dimensional chess.**

Chevy. Slang name for Chevrolet, a brand of internal-combustion powered wheeled land vehicle popular on 20th-century **Earth**. *Voyager* officer **Tom Paris**'s idea of a perfect date was a visit to the hills overlooking **Utopia Planitia** on **Mars**, in a 1957 model Chevy. ("Lifesigns" [VGR]).

Chez Sandrine. Wharf-side bistro, owned by a woman named **Sandrine**, in the city of Marseilles, France, on Earth. The bistro, which featured a traditional **pool** table, had been in Sandrine's family for over 600 years. **Thomas Paris** frequented Chez Sandrine when he was a cadet at Starfleet Academy. After the *Starship Voyager* was swept into the Delta Quadrant in 2371, Paris created a replica of Chez Sandrine on the ship's holodeck. ("The Cloud" [VGR], "Jetrel" [VGR], "Learning Curve" [VGR]). Sandrine's was the site where Paris held his **radiogenic sweepstakes**, strictly against regulations, until Chakotay ordered the gambling pool discontinued. ("Meld" [VGR]). SEE: **Daliwakan; Gaunt Gary; Ricky.** *Chez Sandrine was first seen in "The Cloud" [VGR]. We saw the "real" Chez Sandrine, albeit in an alternate reality, in "Non Sequitur" (VGR).*

Chicago Mobs of the Twenties. Book published in New York on Earth in 1992. A copy of *Chicago Mobs of the Twenties* was left on planet **Sigma Iotia II** in 2168 by the crew of the ***U.S.S. Horizon***. The Iotians used this document as the pattern for their society, revering it as **The Book**. ("A Piece of the Action" [TOS]).

chicken à la Sisko. Culinary dish that was a specialty of Benjamin Sisko and his son Jake. ("Shattered Mirror" [DS9]).

chief engineer. Aboard a Federation starship, the officer charged with responsibility for the operation and maintenance of the ship's power, environmental, and other key systems. The engineering officer was usually designated as third in command of a starship, after the captain and the first officer. **Montgomery Scott** was chief engineer of the original *Starship Enterprise*. **Geordi La Forge** held the position aboard the *Enterprise*-D, while **B'Elanna Torres** was appointed acting chief engineer of the *Starship Voyager* after the ship was lost in the Delta Quadrant in 2371.

chief medical officer. Aboard a Federation starship, the officer charged with responsibility for the health and well-being of the ship's crew. Under certain circumstances, the CMO is authorized to certify a ship's captain as unfit for command. Chief medical officers on the original *U.S.S. Enterprise* included **Dr. Phillip Boyce**, **Dr. Mark Piper**, and **Dr. Leonard McCoy** (*pictured*), while **Dr. Beverly Crusher** and **Dr. Katherine Pulaski** held that post on the *Enterprise*-D. **Dr. Julian Bashir** served as chief medical officer aboard station Deep Space 9, while the **Emergency Medical Hologram** program filled that post aboard the *Starship Voyager*.

"Child, The." *Next Generation* episode #27. Written by Jaron Summers & Jon Povill and Maurice Hurley. Directed by Rob Bowman. Stardate 42073.1. *First aired in 1988. Deanna Troi bears a child, the offspring of a mysterious alien life-form attempting to learn more about humanoid life. This episode, the first of* Star Trek: The Next Generation*'s second season, marked the first appearances of Guinan and Dr. Katherine Pulaski, and the promotion of Geordi to chief engineer, Worf to security chief, and Wesley to a regular bridge officer. It had the first scenes in the shuttlebay and the Ten-Forward Lounge. "The Child" was originally written for the proposed* **Star Trek II** *television series in the late 1970s.* GUEST CAST: Diana Muldaur as **Pulaski, Dr. Katherine**; Seymour Cassel as **Dealt, Lieutenant Commander Hester**; Whoopi Goldberg as **Guinan**; R.J. Williams as **Troi, Ian Andrew (junior)**; Colm Meaney as **O'Brien, Miles**; Dawn Arnemann as **Gladstone, Miss**; Zachary Benjamin as **Troi, Ian Andrew (junior)**; Dore Keller as Crewman. SEE: **'audet IX; Arneb; Betazoid; cyanoacrylates; Dealt, Lieutenant Commander Hester; Delovian souffle, Eichner radiation; Epsilon Indi; Gladstone, Miss; Guinan; La Forge, Geordi; Lorenze Cluster; Mareuvian tea; Morgana Quadrant; noncorporeal life; plasma plague; Pulaski, Dr. Katherine; Rachelis system; *Repulse*, *U.S.S.*; subspace technology; Tango Sierra, Science Station; Ten-Forward; Troi, Deanna; Troi, Ian Andrew (junior); Troi, Ian Andrew (senior).**

Children of Tama. Name used by the **Tamarians** to describe themselves. ("Darmok" [TNG]).

Children of the Sun. Religious sect that resisted the culture and social mores of the Roman order on planet Eight Ninety-Two-IV. Banding together and living in caves, members of this underground movement called themselves the Children of the Sun, preaching brotherhood, and rejecting the 20th-century imperial Roman culture that dominated the planet. After monitoring radio transmissions from the planet, Lieutenant Uhura noted that the reference to the sun referred not to the star which the planet orbited, but to the son of God. ("Bread and Circuses" [TOS]). SEE: **Eight Ninety-Two, Planet IV**.

Children's Center. Child-care facility and educational center for small children aboard the *Enterprise*-D. Activities there included ceramics classes. **Clara Sutter** met **Alexander Rozhenko** there. ("Imaginary Friend" [TNG]).

Childress, Ben. (Gene Dynarski). One of three miners on planet **Rigel XII** who attempted to swap **lithium crystal**s for Mudd's women in 2266. ("Mudd's Women" [TOS]). *Actor Gene Dynarski would again be seen in "11001001" (TNG) as* ***Commander Quinteros****.*

chili burrito. A highly seasoned dish of meat, chili, and beans wrapped in a flour tortilla, popular on 20th-century Earth. ("Future's End, Part II" [VGR]).

Chilton, Ensign Nell. (Alison Brooks). Starfleet officer who existed in the **anti-time future** created by **Q**. She stood watch at the helm console on the bridge of the ***U.S.S. Pasteur*** in this version of the year 2395. She was killed during an attack on the *Pasteur* by enemy Klingon warships. ("All Good Things..." [TNG]).

chime, Betazoid. A small, flat crystalline gong, traditionally used by certain members of **Betazoid** society as a means of expressing thanks for food being eaten. Unfortunately, some non-Betazoids find the use of the chime at mealtime to be quite annoying. ("Haven" [TNG], "Manhunt" [TNG]).

Chiraltan tea. Beverage. Benjamin Sisko once ordered Chiraltan tea instead of his usual ***raktajino***. ("Second Sight" [DS9]).

chlorinide. An extremely hazardous, corrosive substance. Several cargo modules of chlorinide were being transported aboard the *Enterprise*-D on stardate 45587. A leak developed in one of the containers, dissolving part of the support shelving. Several containers fell and severely injured Lieutenant **Worf**. ("Ethics" [TNG]).

chlorobicrobes. Agricultural spray applied to a **Bajoran** bean crop to increase production. Major Kira Nerys told Bajoran farmer **Mullibok** that her father said if you wanted a bigger **katterpod bean**, you should spray the crop with chlorobicrobes. ("Progress" [DS9]).

chloromydride. A second-line pharmaceutical, used if **inaprovaline** is ineffective. ("Ethics" [TNG]).

chloroplast. In botany, an organelle containing chlorophyll, found in a plant cell. ("Tuvix" [VGR]).

chocolate truffle. Small, rich, chocolate-covered confection with flavored filling. ("The Q and the Grey" [VGR]).

chocolate. Confection made from roasted and ground cacao beans. Chocolate was one of **Deanna Troi**'s great passions. She preferred real chocolate to the dietetic substitutes provided by the ship's replicators. ("The Price" [TNG]). Troi never met a chocolate she didn't like. ("The Game" [TNG]). SEE: **Thalian chocolate mousse**.

cholera. Acute infectious enteritis, common on **Earth** in the 19th and 20th centuries, caused by the organism *Vibrio cholerae*. A cholera epidemic in late-19th-century San Francisco was used as a cover for a group of time-travelers from **Devidia II**. The **Devidians** used the disease to conceal their murder of many humans so that they could steal their neural energy as food. ("Time's Arrow, Parts I and II" [TNG]).

cholic acid. Substance formed within a humanoid liver from systemic cholesterol. It plays an important role in digestion. When members of the *Enterprise*-D crew suffered from **Barclay's Protomorphosis Syndrome** in 2370, high levels of cholic acid were found around certain damaged bulkheads aboard the *Enterprise*-D. The acidic damage was linked to Worf's reversion into an earlier Klingon form. That form excreted a bioacidic venom from sacs located within its mandibles. ("Genesis" [TNG]).

Chopin's Trio in G Minor. Musical work by noted 19th-century Earth composer Frédéric-François Chopin (1810-1849). Data, **Neela Daren,** and **Ensign Cheney** performed Chopin's Trio in G Minor in the Ten-Forward Lounge on the *Enterprise-D* on stardate 46693. ("Lessons" [TNG]).

Chorgan. (Stephen Lee). The leader of the **Gatherers** from planet **Acamar III**, and a member of the **Lornak** clan. Chorgan accepted Acamarian Sovereign Marouk's offer of amnesty in 2366, ending nearly a century of interstellar piracy by the Gatherers. During the negotiations, **Yuta** of the rival clan Tralesta attempted to assassinate Chorgan. He was saved by Commander Riker's actions and later agreed to a Gatherer truce. ("The Vengeance Factor" [TNG]).

chorus. A team of aides who provide hearing and speech for members of the ruling family of planet **Ramatis III** who are genetically incapable of hearing. The chorus communicates telepathically with their assigned family member, with each member of the chorus representing a different part of the family member's personality. The Chorus that served mediator **Riva** was killed during peace talks at planet **Solais V** in 2365. ("Loud as a Whisper" [TNG]). SEE: **Scholar/Artist; Warrior/Adonis; Woman**.

Chow-yun. Twenty-third century Earth playwright. Bashir felt that Earth writers after Chow-yun's time were too derivative of alien drama. ("The Die is Cast" [DS9]).

Christina. Lycosa tarantula that **Miles O'Brien** found on planet Titus IV, and kept as a pet. ("Realm of Fear" [TNG]).

Christopher, Captain John. (Roger Perry). Aircraft pilot, serial number 4857932, in the United States Air Force on Earth during the 1960s. Christopher was assigned to intercept an unidentified flying object detected above the **Omaha Air Base** in mid-July 1969. The **UFO** was the *Starship Enterprise*, which had been propelled back in time to that period. Christopher was beamed to the *Enterprise* when his aircraft was accidentally destroyed by a tractor beam. It was not realized until after he was aboard that his exposure to 23rd-century technology would be a possible source for historical contamination. The dilemma was made worse when it was learned that Christopher would father a child who would command the historically significant first **Earth-Saturn probe**. A means was later found to return Christopher to Earth without leaving any trace of the *Enterprise*'s presence. ("Tomorrow Is Yesterday" [TOS]).

Christopher, Colonel Shaun Geoffrey. Commander of the first successful **Earth-Saturn probe** and son of **Captain John Christopher**. Shaun Christopher had not yet been conceived when his father was beamed aboard the *Enterprise* in 1969 when that ship was accidentally back in the 20th century. His unborn son was the primary reason John Christopher had to be returned to Earth; failure to do so would have caused significant changes to the course of history. ("Tomorrow Is Yesterday" [TOS]). *Captain*

John Christopher's son was named after Star Trek *writer John D.F. Black's three sons: Shaun, Geoffrey, and Christopher.*

Christopher, Dr. (John S. Ragin). Subspace theoretician and husband to Vulcan Science Academy director **Dr. T'Pan**. Christopher accompanied his wife aboard the *Enterprise*-D in 2369, to view the test of **Dr. Reyga**'s metaphasic shield. ("Suspicions" [TNG]).

chromodynamic power module. Power system employed by **Pralor Automated Personnel Units**. Chromodynamic power module receptacles were energized by tripolymer plasma. Chromodynamic modules were installed in **Pralor** and **Cravic** Automated Personnel Units as power sources and were designed to be impossible to replicate, thereby making the automated robots incapable of replicating themselves without the assistance of their builders. ("Prototype" [VGR]).

chromolinguistics. Form of nonverbal communication. Captain Janeway was familiar with chromolinguistics. ("Macrocosm" [VGR]).

chrondite. Mineral compound. Chrondites were found in the core of an asteroid that nearly impacted on planet **Tessen III** in 2368. ("Cost of Living" [TNG]).

chroniton torpedo. Tactical weapon used by the **Krenim** of the Delta Quadrant. Chroniton torpedoes were able to penetrate defensive shields because they were in a constant state of temporal flux. ("Before and After" [VGR]).

chroniton. Subatomic particle that transmits temporal quanta. Chroniton particles were generated as a waste product by an experimental **interphase generator**-based Romulan **cloaking device**. Damage to the cloaking device would cause it to emit the particles. ("The Next Phase" [TNG]). Chroniton particles are normally emitted in small quantities through the normal operation of a Romulan cloaking device. In 2371, chroniton particles accumulated in the hull of the *Starship* ***Defiant*** and became lodged in the ship's **ablative armor** matrix. The accumulation caused a transporter beam to be deflected almost 350 years into Earth's past. ("Past Tense, Part I" [DS9]). SEE: **quantum singularity**. A massive surge in chroniton radiation accompanied the timeshifting phenomenon produced by the Bajoran **Orb of Time**. ("Trials and Tribble-ations" [DS9]). In 2373, a **Pah-wraith** plotted to send a beam of chroniton particles from station Deep Space 9 to the **Bajoran wormhole** with the intent of killing the **Prophets**. Fortunately, the plan failed and the Pah-wraith was killed by the chroniton beam intended for its enemies. ("The Assignment" [DS9]). Chroniton radiation is deleterious to living tissue, but it is possible to inoculate against its effects. ("Before and After" [VGR]). SEE: **antichroniton; chronometric particles**.

chronometric data. Temporal measurements of the space-time continuum, particularly those pertaining to time travel. ("Future's End, Part I" [VGR]).

chronometric particles. Temporal subatomic quanta related to **chroniton**s. In 2373, a **Borg sphere** ship emitted chronometric particles while forming a temporal vortex. The Borg used this vortex to travel into Earth's past to the year 2063. *(Star Trek: First Contact).*

Chronowerx. Business corporation on 20th-century **Earth**. Chronowerx was responsible for a remarkable number of extraordinary technological innovations in computer technology, including the introduction of the first **isograted circuit** in 1969 and the HyperPro PC in 1996. It was not realized that Chronowerx founder **Henry Starling** had captured the ***Aeon***, a Federation timeship from the 29th century in 1967, and was using technology from the *Aeon* as the basis for his products. ("Future's End, Parts I and II" [VGR]).

Chrysalians. Politically neutral civilization that reportedly had enjoyed peace for the past ten generations. The Chrysalians were interested in gaining rights to the **Barzan wormhole** in 2366 and retained the services of professional negotiator **Devinoni Ral** for these talks. Ral was successful in winning rights to the wormhole for the Chrysalians, but shortly thereafter, the wormhole was found to be unstable and therefore commercially worthless. ("The Price" [TNG]).

chrysanthemum. Perennial Earth flower. In 2372, Paris and Torres experimented with a chrysanthemum and two other plants in order to find a way to separate Tuvok and Neelix, who had become merged by a transporter accident. ("Tuvix" [VGR]).

chula. Multilevel board game played by the **Wadi**, first introduced in the **Alpha Quadrant** at Quark's bar on Deep Space 9 in 2369, shortly after first contact with the Wadi. The game required live players to navigate an elaborate labyrinth of tests, as the primary player moved onyx figurines representing those players around the game board. Sisko, Kira, Dax, and Dr. Bashir were chosen to run the maze, moving into dangerous scenarios through different ***shaps***, or levels, under Quark's overall control. The second *shap* featured a powerful force field that could only be traversed by playing hopscotch with a little girl. The third *shap* had a deadly Wadi cocktail party where poisonous gas threatened to suffocate the players unless they discovered the beverages were an antidote. In *shap* four, Bashir was eliminated as a player by a bolt of energy. *Shap* five injured Dax's leg in a cavern with falling rocks, and *shap* six saw the three players falling into a deep crevasse. The fall brought them back to Quark's, where **Falow** revealed they were never in any danger and that it was all a game. SEE: **Chandra**. ("Move Along Home" [DS9]).

Chulak. Romulan officer who suffered a defeat at **Galorndon Core**. ("The Thaw" [VGR]).

"Chute, The." *Voyager* episode #48. Teleplay by Kenneth Biller. Story by Clayvon C. Harris. Directed by Les Landau. Stardate 50156.2. *First aired in 1996. Kim and Paris are convicted of terrorism by the Akritiri and are thrown into a hellish prison where devices attached to the inmates' necks slowly drive them insane.* GUEST CAST: Don McManus as **Zio**; Robert Pine as **Liria**; James Parks as **Vel**; Ed Trotta as **Pit**; Beans Morocco as **Rib**; Rosemary Morgan as **Piri**. SEE: **Akritirian prison satellite; Akritiri; Akritirian freighter; Akritirian patrol ship; baked potato; baked Risan beans; Chateau Lafite Rothschild; cherry pie; crown roast of lamb; Delaney Sisters; Delaney, Megan; fire ants; flambé noodles; fudge ripple pudding; grilled mushrooms; Heva VII; Laktivia; Liria; onion rings; Open Sky; paralithium; Piri; Pit; pulse gun; Rib; shrimp with fettran sauce; trilithium; Vel; Zio.**

Cing'ta. Federation informant within the **Maquis**. On stardate 50485.2, Benjamin Sisko went to a Maquis camp on **Marva IV** to meet with Cing'ta and obtain information about **Michael Eddington**. The Maquis discovered Cing'ta's betrayal and stranded him on an inhospitable planet in the **Badlands**. ("For the Uniform" [DS9]).

Circassian cat. A domesticated animal. **Geordi La Forge**'s first childhood pet was a Circassian cat. Geordi fondly described his pet as "funny-looking." ("Violations" [TNG]).

Circassian fig. Fruit. ("Learning Curve" [VGR]).

Circle, the. SEE: **Alliance for Global Unity**.

"Circle, The." *Deep Space Nine* episode #22. Written by Peter Allan Fields. Directed by Corey Allen. No stardate given. First aired in 1993. *Kira returns to Bajor while Minister Jaro furthers his plan to use the Circle to overthrow the provisional government. This episode continues the story begun in "The Homecoming" (DS9).* GUEST CAST: Richard Beymer as **Li Nalas**; Stephen Macht as **Krim**, **General**; Bruce Gray as **Chekote**, **Admiral**; Philip Anglim as **Bariel**, **Vedek**; Louise Fletcher as **Winn**; Mike Genovese as **Zef'No**; Eric Server as Peace officer; Anthony Guidera as Cardassian. SEE: **Alliance for Global Unity, The; Chekote, Admiral; Jaro, Minister Essa; Kira Nerys; Kressari; Krim, General; Navarch; Orb; Perikian peninsula; Winn; Zef'No.**

Cirl the Knife. Mobster on planet **Sigma Iotia II** loyal to **Jojo Krako** in 2268. At Krako's word, Cirl would use his collection of blades to persuade Krako's enemies to cooperate. ("A Piece of the Action" [TOS]).

Cirrus IV. Planetary location of the **Emerald Wading Pool**, which may not be a great spot for diving, but is known for its safety. ("Conundrum" [TNG]).

citrus blend. Common foodstuff consumed by **Trill**. The replicators on Deep Space 9 were able to produce a decent copy of it. ("Playing God" [DS9]).

"City on the Edge of Forever, The." Original Series episode #28. Written by Harlan Ellison. Directed by Joseph Pevney. No stardate given in episode. *First aired in 1967. McCoy, suffering from an accidental drug overdose, flees through a time portal into Earth of the 1930s, where he causes serious damage to the flow of history. Kirk must allow the woman he loves to die in order to restore the timeline. This episode won the Hugo Award for Best Dramatic Presentation in 1968. Ellison's original version of the script also won the Writers' Guild of America Award.* GUEST CAST: Joan Collins as **Keeler**, **Edith**; John Harmon as Rodent; Hal Baylor as Policeman; David L. Ross as **Galloway**, **Lieutenant**; John Winston as Transporter chief; Bart La Rue as Guardian voice; Michael Barrier as Guard #1 and **DeSalle**, **Lieutenant**; Mary Statier as Edith's stunt double; David Perna as McCoy's stunt double; Bobby Bass as Scott's stunt double; Carey Loftin as Truck driver. SEE: **cordrazine; flop; Gable, Clark; Great Depression; Guardian of Forever; Keeler, Edith; Kirk, James T.; Kyle, Mr.; "Let me help"; McCoy, Dr. Leonard H.; mechanical rice picker; mnemonic memory circuit; Twenty-First Street Mission.**

"Civil Defense." *Deep Space Nine* episode #53. Written by Mike Krohn. Directed by Reza Badiyi. No stardate given. *First aired in 1995. When Jake Sisko accidentally activates an old Cardassian security program, the station is locked down and threatened with self-destruction.* GUEST CAST: Andrew Robinson as **Garak**, **Elim**; Marc Alaimo as **Dukat**; Danny Goldring as **Kell**, **Legate**. SEE: **counterinsurgency program; dampening field; Deep Space 9; Dukat, Gul; Ferengi Rules of Acquisition; Frin; Gaila; Garak, Elim; Keldar; Kell, Legate; laser fusion initiator; main fusion reactor; maintenance conduit; neurocine gas; neutralization emitters; reaction stabilizers; red leaf tea; self-destruct sequence; Terok Nor; Tye, DaiMon; uridium.**

Claiborne, Billy. (Walter Koenig). Outlaw from Earth's ancient American west who fought on the side of the Clantons at the historic gunfight at **OK Corral** in 1881. Pavel Chekov portrayed Billy Claiborne in a bizarre charade created by the **Melkotians** in 2268. In actual history, Billy Claiborne survived the fight, but Chekov as Claiborne was killed by **Morgan Earp** in the Melkotian re-creation, proving that history need not repeat itself. ("Spectre of the Gun" [TOS]).

Clancy. (Anne Elizabeth Ramsay). Engineering officer aboard the *Enterprise*-D. Geordi La Forge left her in charge when Data and he went to the holodeck to run a **Sherlock Holmes** simulation. ("Elementary, Dear Data" [TNG]). She also served as conn on the bridge during the ***T'Ong*** crisis. ("The Emissary" [TNG]).

Clanton, Billy. (James Doohan). Outlaw from Earth's ancient American west, and a member of the Clanton family who died at the famous gunfight at the **OK Corral** in 1881. Mr. Scott represented Billy Clanton in the bizarre charade created by the **Melkotians** in 2268. ("Spectre of the Gun" [TOS]).

Clanton, Ike. (William Shatner). Historic outlaw from the American west, and a member of the Clanton family that fought the Earps at the famous gunfight in **Tombstone, Arizona,** in 1881. Kirk was cast as Ike Clanton in the Western scenario masterminded by the **Melkotians** in 2268 as the means for his death. ("Spectre of the Gun" [TOS]).

clarinet. Wind instrument used by Earth musicians. Harry Kim played the clarinet. In 2372, he even spent a week's worth of **replicator rations** to replicate a clarinet so that he could stay in practice. ("Parturition" [VGR]).

Clark, Dr. Howard. (Paul Lambert). Anthropologist and head of the Federation science station on **Ventax II**. Dr. Clark transmitted a distress call to the *Enterprise*-D when civil unrest on the planet threatened the crew of the science station in 2367. ("Devil's Due" [TNG]).

Clarus System. Location of planet Archybite. **Nava** took over the mining refineries in the Clarus System. ("The Nagus" [DS9]).

class-1 sensor probe. An instrumented torpedo launched from Federation starships for investigation into areas that one might not wish to take the starship. The class-1 probe carries a very wide range of scientific sensing equipment. A class-1 probe was used by *Enterprise*-D personnel to investigate the "hole in space" created by **Nagilum** in 2365. ("Where Silence Has Lease" [TNG]). Another class-1 probe was launched into the temporal rift discovered near **Archer IV** in 2366. ("Yesterday's *Enterprise*" [TNG]).

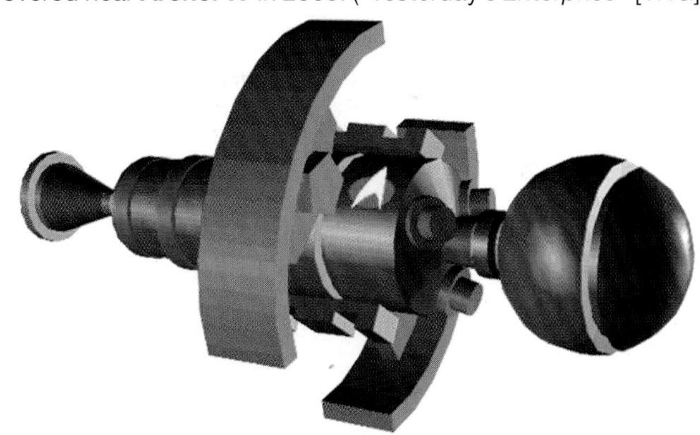

class-4 probe. Starfleet scientific instrument used for remote sensing studies. A class-4 probe was sent into a subspace disruption near station **Deep Space 9** on stardate 46853. It was later learned this subspace disruption was a product of Jadzia Dax's imagination, generated by aliens from the **Gamma Quadrant**. ("If Wishes Were Horses" [DS9]).

class-5 intelligence drone. Small automated sensor platform. **Starfleet** often used class-5 drones to monitor spacecraft activity in remote regions without the need to deploy starship assets. In 2373, two class-5 intelligence drones stationed near the **Breen** settlement of planet Portas V alerted Benjamin Sisko of the presence of a **Maquis** freighter there. ("For the Uniform" [DS9]).

class-5 probe. Medium-range reconnaissance probe, equipped with passive sensors and recording systems. In 2369, a class-5 probe was launched by the *Enterprise*-D to investigate a **Cardassian** research facility believed to be located on planet **Celtris III**. ("Chain of Command, Part I" [TNG]). The *U.S.S. Voyager* launched a class-5 probe in 2373 to gather information about the people on the **Takarian** homeworld. ("False Profits" [VGR]).

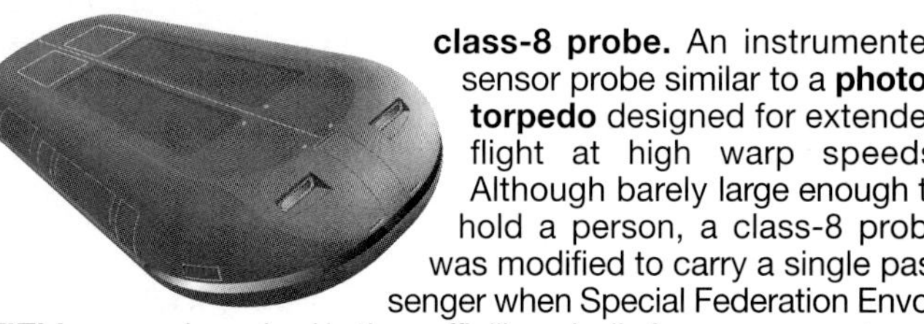

class-8 probe. An instrumented sensor probe similar to a **photon torpedo** designed for extended flight at high warp speeds. Although barely large enough to hold a person, a class-8 probe was modified to carry a single passenger when Special Federation Envoy **K'Ehleyr** was launched in the coffinlike missile for emergency transport to the *Enterprise*-D in 2365. ("The Emissary" [TNG]).

class-J cargo ship. A small, antiquated cargo vessel. **Harcourt Fenton Mudd** was piloting a class-J ship when he became caught in an asteroid belt before being rescued by the *Enterprise* in 2266. ("Mudd's Women" [TOS]).

Class-K planet. Planet adaptable for humans by the use of pressure domes and life-support systems. After the *Enterprise* was sabotaged by the android **Norman** in 2267, the starship was brought to a K-type world informally known as the planet **Mudd.** ("I, Mudd" [TOS]). SEE: **planetary classification system.**

Class-L planet. A barely inhabitable planet, with a thin atmosphere and extreme temperatures. Odo and Quark, after the sabotage of their runabout, were forced down on a Class-L planet. ("The Ascent" [DS9]).

Class-M planet. Designation for small, rocky terrestrial worlds with oxygen-nitrogen atmospheres.("The Cage" [TOS]). SEE: **planetary classification system.** A Class-M planet generally has nucleogenic particles in its atmosphere; lack of nucleogenic particles would result in an absence of precipitation and surface water. ("Caretaker" [VGR]). *The* Star Trek *format calls for most stories to involve missions to Class-M planets, since showing non-Earthlike planets would be far more costly. While this is probably unrealistic from a scientific point of view, it is a key reason for making the production of* Star Trek *practical on a television budget.*

class. Ancient naval term used to describe a group of ships sharing a basic design. Generally, a class of ships is named by **Starfleet** after the first ship of that type built. For example, the ***Constitution* class** (to which the original ***Enterprise*** belonged) was named after the *Starship Constitution*. Other classes of Starfleet ships have included ***Galaxy* class**, ***Excelsior* class**, ***Miranda* class**, ***Oberth* class**, ***Nebula* class**, ***Sovereign* class**, ***Soyuz* class**, ***Daedalus* class**, and ***Ambassador* class**. The most recent ship to bear the name *Enterprise* has been designated a ***Sovereign*-class** starship. *Note that several graphics, readouts, and charts used in various episodes and movies have listed numerous other ship classes in an subtle effort to suggest that Starfleet has a wider range of ship designs than the studio can actually afford to build and photograph for the show. Unfortunately, models or blueprints do not exist for most of these (since they haven't been seen), although an occasional conjectural design will show up in graphic readouts or as a desktop display model, used as set decoration. Several such designs, in the form of "study models," were used in the "graveyard" scene in "The Best of Both Worlds, Part II" (TNG), and in the junkyard of "Unification, Part I" (TNG). Some conjectural class designations include* Apollo, Cheyenne, Deneva, Freedom, Hokule'a, Istanbul, Korolev, Merced, New Orleans, Niagara, Renaissance, Rigel, Wambundu, *and* Yorkshire. SEE: **starships; planetary classification system**.

claustrophobia. Morbid fear of enclosed or confined spaces. **Elim Garak** suffered from an acute case of claustrophobia. ("By Inferno's Light" [DS9]).

clavisoa berry. Small succulent fruit sometimes used as a seasoning on salads. ("Business As Usual" [VGR]).

claymore. Two-handed sword with a double-edged blade, used by Scottish Highlanders in the 16th century on Earth. Chief Engineer Montgomery Scott found a claymore in the armory when all the phasers were changed to swords by the **Beta XII-A entity**. ("Day of the Dove" [TOS]).

cleaning processor. Part of a starship's solid-waste-recycling system. The processor was used for sterilization and recycling of clothing. ("In Theory" [TNG]).

Cleary. (Michael Rougas). Engineering technician aboard the refitted *Starship Enterprise* when the ship intercepted the **V'Ger** entity in 2271. (*Star Trek: The Motion Picture*).

clematis. Perennial flowering vine originating on Earth. In 2372 Paris and Torres experimented with a clematis and two other plants in order to find a way to separate Tuvok and Neelix, who had become merged by a transporter accident. ("Tuvix" [VGR]).

Clemens, Samuel Langhorne. (Jerry Hardin). (1835-1910). Noted 19th-century American author and humorist, famous for many classic novels written under the pen name Mark Twain. **Data**, traveling in Earth's past, met Clemens at a literary reception hosted by **Guinan**, who spent some time on Earth during her younger days. ("Time's Arrow, Part I" [TNG]). Clemens was noted for his bitingly satiric pessimism toward humanity, but this attitude may have been softened somewhat when he briefly visited the 24th century and witnessed the future of humanity as exemplified by the crew of the *Starship Enterprise*-D. ("Time's Arrow, Part II" [TNG]). *The book about time travel that Clemens describes to the reporter is* A Connecticut Yankee in King Arthur's Court, *first published in 1889.*

Clement, U.S.S. Federation starship, *Apollo* class, Starfleet registry number NCC-12537. A rendezvous with the *Clement* and the *Enterprise*-D in 2370 was canceled when the *Enterprise*-D was ordered to the **Argaya system**. ("Lower Decks" [TNG]).

Clemonds, Sonny. (Leon Rippy). Country-and-western singer from late 20th-century Earth. Clemonds died of emphysema and extensive liver damage, but had arranged for his body to be cryogenically stored aboard an orbital satellite. He was revived in the year 2364 aboard the *Enterprise*-D and later returned to Earth aboard the ***U.S.S. Charleston***. ("The Neutral Zone" [TNG]). SEE: **cryonics**; **cryosatellite**.

Clendenning, Dr. A resident of the **Omicron Theta** colony, killed by the **Crystalline Entity**'s attack in 2336. Clendenning used gamma radiation scans to detect decay by-products from the entity's antiproton trail. **Data**, who had records and memories from Clendenning and the other colonists, was able to build upon Clendenning's work when searching for the entity in 2368. ("Silicon Avatar" [TNG]).

Cleponji. An ancient **Promellian** battle cruiser discovered intact in the asteroid belt near **Orelious IX** by the *Enterprise*-D in 2366. Although the war between the Promellians and the **Menthars** had destroyed both civilizations a thousand years ago, the *Cleponji* survived in nearly perfect condition, surrounded by the deadly **aceton assimilators** that killed its crew. The *Cleponji* was destroyed by the *Enterprise*-D in a torpedo spread designed to destroy the aceton assimilators. ("Booby Trap" [TNG]). *The Promellian battle cruiser was designed by Steve Burg and built by Ron Thornton for* The Night of the Creeps.

Cliffs of Heaven. Location on planet Sumiko III that is renowned as a spot for diving. Holodeck program 47-C is a simulation of this spectacular site. Enterprise-D crew member **Kristin** *(no last name given)* hurt herself twice in this program, so Dr. Crusher recommended she tackle the **Emerald Wading Pool** on Cirrus IV instead. ("Conundrum" [TNG]).

Cliffs of Bole. Scenic spot. **Benjamin Sisko** and **Curzon Dax** took a memorable trip there once. ("Invasive Procedures" [DS9]). *The Cliffs of Bole were named after* Star Trek *director Cliff Bole.*

cloaking device, Aldean. An immensely powerful force field that effectively rendered the entire planet of **Aldea** invisible from space. Used to isolate the peaceful inhabitants of that planet, the Aldean cloaking device worked for millennia before defensive shields caused damage to the planet's **ozone** layer. ("When the Bough Breaks" [TNG]). SEE: **Aldea**.

cloaking device, Klingon. The Klingons apparently obtained basic cloaking technology from the **Romulans** around 2268, when an alliance existed between the Klingons and the Romulans. Many Klingon ships, including their birds-of-prey (apparently also based on Romulan technology, judging from the name), were equipped with cloaking devices. *(Star Trek III: The Search for Spock).* An experimental **Klingon bird-of-prey** was developed, circa 2292, which had the ability to fire torpedoes while still cloaked. This would have provided a significant tactical advantage, had means not been developed to detect a ship so equipped. *(Star Trek VI: The Undiscovered Country).* Cloaking devices on old D-12-class birds-of-prey were equipped with defective plasma coils, rendering the ship vulnerable. *(Star Trek Generations).* Klingon-style cloaking devices will not operate within emission nebulae. ("Return to Grace" [DS9]). *We assume that cloaking devices are continually being improved, as are the sensor systems used to detect them. For this reason, any advance in either cloaking or sensing technologies seems to provide only a brief advantage until the other side catches up.*

cloaking device, Romulan. The first known example of a practical cloaking device was on a **Romulan bird-of-prey** spacecraft that crossed the **Romulan Neutral Zone** in 2266. ("Balance of Terror" [TOS]). An improved cloaking device used by Romulan warships in 2268 was of sufficient concern to the Federation that Kirk and Spock were sent on a covert mission into Romulan territory to steal one such unit for analysis by Starfleet scientists. ("The *Enterprise* Incident" [TOS]). SEE: **Romulan commander**. Although the Romulans continually improved their cloaking technology, Federation innovations such as the **tachyon detection grid** technique developed by Geordi La Forge in 2368 served to reduce the tactical effectiveness of cloaked ships. ("Redemption, Part II" [TNG]). Vessels employing a Romulan cloaking device could sometimes be detected with an **antiproton** beam. ("Defiant" [DS9]). A cloaked ship radiated a slight subspace variance that was sometimes detectable at warp speeds. Before transporting or using weapons, the cloaking device had to be deactivated. ("Balance of Terror" [TOS], "The Search, Parts I and II" [DS9]). Defensive shields were also inoperative when a ship was cloaked. ("Face of the Enemy" [TNG]). An experimental cloaking device, based on an **interphase generator**, was developed by Romulan scientists and tested in 2368. ("The Next Phase" [TNG]). Possession of a cloaking device is illegal under Bajoran law. Despite this, Quark offered a small cloaking device for sale in 2370, but eventually gave it to Professor Natima Lang so that she and her colleagues could escape capture by Cardassian authorities ("Profit and Loss" [DS9]). In early 2371, the Federation and the Romulan Empire entered into an agreement granting Starfleet the use of a single Romulan cloaking device for use aboard the ***Starship Defiant***. Use of this cloaking device was restricted to the **Gamma Quadrant** and then only in exchange for all of Starfleet's intelligence reports on the **Dominion**. SEE: **T'Rul**. ("Defiant" [DS9]). SEE: **tetryon**. *"The* Pegasus" *(TNG) establishes that the Federation relinquished the right to develop or use such devices under the* ***Treaty of Algeron***. *Additionally, Gene Roddenberry once indicated that "our people are scientists and explorers—they don't go sneaking around." We therefore assume Starfleet has a policy against such things.*

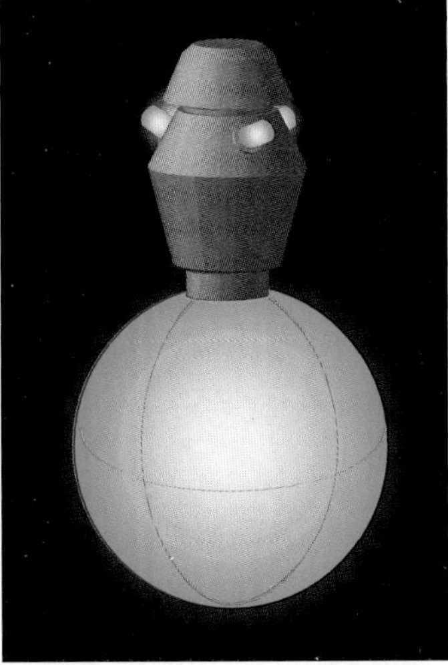

cloaking device. An energy screen generator used to render an object (typically, a space vehicle) invisible to the eye and to most sensor systems. Most cloaking devices require so much power that a vessel so equipped cannot use weapons systems without decloaking. ("Balance of Terror" [TOS]). Romulan and Klingon spacecraft are often equipped with cloaking devices, although Federation ships are prohibited from doing so under the terms of the **Treaty of Algeron** ("Pegasus" [TNG]), except for the Federation starship ***Defiant***, by special arrangement with the Romulan government. ("Defiant" [DS9]). (In the **anti-time future** created by Q, some Federation starships were equipped with cloaking devices, including the upgraded *Enterprise*-D, commanded by Admiral Riker in this future. The *Pasteur*, a medical ship, was not so equipped.) ("All Good Things..." [TNG]).

clone. Asexual reproduction technique in which the DNA of a parent organism is used to grow a genetically identical copy of that organism. Cloning was used to populate the **Mariposa** colony because their initial population base was too small to form an effective gene pool. ("Up the Long Ladder" [TNG]). SEE: **replicative fading**. In 2369, a man named **Ibudan** created a clone of himself, then killed it to frame Deep Space 9 security chief **Odo** for murder. ("A Man Alone" [DS9]).

"Cloud Minders, The." Original Series episode #74. Teleplay by Margaret Armen. Story by David Gerrold and Oliver Crawford. Directed by Jud Taylor. Stardate 5818.4. *First aired in 1969. Kirk and Spock must deal with terrorists striking at the beautiful cloud city Stratos.* GUEST CAST: Jeff Corey as **Plasus**; Diana Ewing as **Droxine**; Charlene Polite as **Vanna**; Kirk Raymone as Cloud Guard #1; Jimmy Fields as Cloud Guard #2; Ed Long as **Midro**; Fred Williamson as Anka; Garth Pillsbury as Prisoner; Harv Selsby as Security guard; Walter Scott as Cloud guard; Roger Holloway as **Lemli, Mr.**; Marvin Walters, Lou Elias,Troglytes; Jay Jones as Prisoner #1; Richard Geary as Cloud City sentinel #1; Bob Miles as Cloud City sentinel #2; Paul Baxley as Kirk's stunt double; Ralph Garrett as Troglyte stunt double; Donna Garrett as Vanna's stunt double. SEE: **Ardana; Disrupters; Droxine; filter masks; Merak II; Midro; mortae; Plasus; protectors; Stratos; Troglytes; Vanna; zenite.**

Cloud William. (Roy Jenson). Leaders of the **Yangs** on planet **Omega IV** in 2268, known among his people as the son of chiefs, guardian of the holies, and speaker of the holy words. ("The Omega Glory" [TOS]).

cloud creatures. SEE: **Beta Renner cloud; Calamarain; Companion; Dal'Rok; dikironium cloud creature; mellitus; Nagilum; noncorporeal life; nucleogenic cloud being.**

"Cloud, The." *Voyager* episode #6. Teleplay by Tom Szollosi and Michael Piller. Story by Brannon Braga. Directed by David Livingston. Stardate 48546.2. *First aired in 1995. While searching for fuel in what they believe to be a nebula, the crew of* Voyager *discovers that they have injured a new life-form.* GUEST CAST: Angela Dohrmann as **Ricky**; Judy Geeson as **Sandrine**; Larry A.

Hankin as **Gaunt Gary**; Luigi Amodeo as Gigolo, The. SEE: **Ailis pâté; *A-koo-chee-moya*; *akoonah*; animal guide; bantan; Cardaway leaves, stuffed; Chakotay; *CHAH-mooz-ee;* Chez Sandrine; coffee; Daliwakan; deuterium; Felada onion crisps; Gaunt Gary; holodeck and holosuite programs; Janeway, Kathryn; Jung, Carl; Jupiter Station; MacAllister, James Mooney; Marseilles, France; medicine bundle; Neelix; *nuan-ka*; nucleogenic cloud being; omicron particles; Paris, Thomas; pool; quantum chemistry; replicator rations; Ricky; Saint Emilion; Sandrine; Takar loggerhead eggs; vision quest; *Voyager, U.S.S.*; Zimmerman, Lewis.**

Clown. (Michael McKean). Malevolent character inhabiting the virtual reality created for the five hibernating survivors of the **Kohl settlement**. The Clown was created by the **Kohl hibernation system**'s control computer, which read the minds of the sleepers and translated their fears into an embodiment of evil. The Clown held the hibernating settlers captive and killed three of them, before the remaining two could be rescued by the crew of the *Voyager* in 2372. The Clown ceased to exist after the last survivor's mind was disconnected from the hibernation system. ("The Thaw" [VGR]).

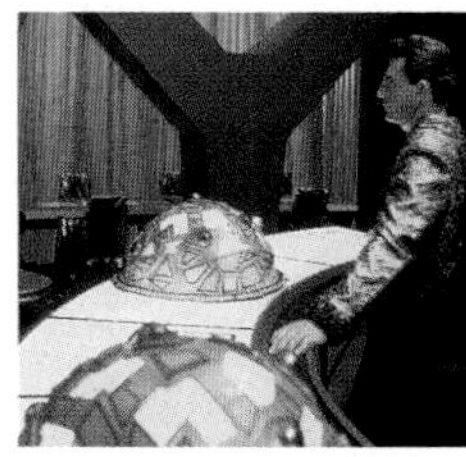

Club Martus. Casino on the **Promenade** of station Deep Space 9, opened by **Martus Mazur** in 2370. The club boasted several **gambling devices** and was located across from Quark's bar. It drew away most of Quark's customers, but was only in business for a few days until it was forced to close by a run of bad luck. ("Rivals" [DS9]).

"Clues." *Next Generation* episode #88. Teleplay by Bruce D. Arthurs and Joe Menosky. Story by Bruce D. Arthurs. Directed by Les Landau. Stardate 44502.7. *First aired in 1991. When the* Enterprise-*D falls through a wormhole, a lot of little clues just don't add up.* GUEST CAST: Colm Meaney as **O'Brien**, **Miles**; Pamela Winslow as **McKnight**, **Ensign**; Rhonda Aldrich as **Madeline**; Whoopi Goldberg as **Guinan**; Patti Yasutake as **Ogawa**, **Nurse Alyssa**; Thomas Knickerbocker as Gunman. SEE: **Data; Diomedian scarlet moss; Evadne IV; Gloria; Harrakis V; Hill, Dixon; Locklin, Ensign; Madeline; McKnight, Ensign; Ngame Nebula; Ogawa, Nurse Alyssa; Paxans; T-tauri type star system; Tethys III; *Trieste, U.S.S.*; Underhill, Pell.**

Cluster NGC 321. Location of planets **Eminiar VII** and **Vendikar**. The *Enterprise* was sent there to open diplomatic relations with Eminiar VII in 2267. ("A Taste of Armageddon" [TOS]). *NGC stands for New General Catalog of nebulae and star clusters, an actual list of objects visible from Earth, compiled in the late 19th century by astronomer J.L.E. Dreyer.*

CMO. SEE: **chief medical officer**.

co-orbital satellites. A pair of objects (such as planetoids) whose orbits are very close to each other. Under certain circumstances, a near collision between the two bodies can result in each object assuming the orbit previously occupied by the other. In other words, the two objects trade orbits. Data described the phenomenon to Picard and Lwaxana Troi. ("Manhunt" [TNG]).

CO. Abbreviation for commanding officer. ("Paradise Lost" [DS9]).

coalescent organism. Rare microscopic life-forms that absorb other organisms, then assume the form of the organism they've absorbed, right down to the cellular level. On a larger scale, this is essentially a type of **shape-shifter**. Lieutenant **Keith Rocha** was apparently killed by a coalescent organism just prior to his assignment to **Relay Station 47** in 2369. The organism assumed Rocha's form, and later threatened **Lieutenant Aquiel Uhnari**, and killed her dog, Maura. ("Aquiel" [TNG]).

Coalition. One of the two main rival factions in control of the colony on planet **Turkana IV** following the collapse of the colonial government in 2337. Led by **Hayne**, the Coalition offered assistance to the *Enterprise*-D crew in their mission to rescue the crew of the freighter ***Arcos*** in 2367. **Ishara Yar** was a member of the Coalition. ("Legacy" [TNG]).

cobalt diselenide. Biochemical substance used as a **biogenic weapon**. A nerve agent deadly to **Cardassians**, but harmless to many other humanoids. In 2373, the **Maquis**, lead by Michael Eddington, used cobalt diselenide against the Cardassian colony on **Veloz Prime**. They used three stratospheric torpedoes to spread the substance throughout the planet's biosphere. They later poisoned the atmosphere of **Quatal Prime**. Cobalt diselenide was very unstable and required refrigerated storage. ("For the Uniform" [DS9]).

cobalt-thorium device. Weapon. In 2370 **Maquis** operative **Sakonna** purchased cobalt-thorium devices from Quark. ("The Maquis, Part I" [DS9]).

Cochrane deceleration maneuver. Classic battle tactic used by the *Enterprise* to defeat the Romulans at Tau Ceti. When Captain **Garth** impersonated Kirk at the **Elba II** penal colony in 2268, Spock asked the two to identify the maneuver in hopes of differentiating the two. The attempt was unsuccessful because the maneuver was so well known that any starship captain would know of it. ("Whom Gods Destroy" [TOS]). *It is possible that this Romulan defeat may have been the incident depicted in "Balance of Terror" (TOS), but this is unclear.*

Cochrane distortion. A characteristic fluctuation in the phase of a subspace field generated by a starship's warp engines. ("Ménage à Troi" [TNG]).

Cochrane Medal of Excellence. Starfleet commendation for outstanding research in warp theory. In an alternate reality, Ensign **Harry Kim** received the Cochrane Medal of Excellence while attending Starfleet Academy. ("Non Sequitur" [VGR]).

***Cochrane*, Shuttlecraft**. In 2372, *U.S.S. Voyager Shuttlecraft Cochrane* under the command of Lieutenant **Thomas Paris** broke the **warp 10** barrier. ("Threshold" [VGR]). *Named after the inventor of warp drive, Zefram Cochrane.*

Cochrane, Zefram. (Glenn Corbett, James Cromwell). Discoverer of the space warp (2030-2117?). Cochrane became one of history's most renowned scientists when he revolutionized space travel in 2063 with the invention of the **warp drive**, making faster-than-light travel possible. ("Metamorphosis" [TOS]).

Cochrane worked with an engineer named **Lily Sloane**, constructing his warp ship, the ***Phoenix***, in an abandoned missile complex in central Montana on the North American continent. Ironically, the booster stage of the *Phoenix* was originally built as a nuclear weapon of mass destruction. Despite interference from a **Borg** attack from the future, Cochrane conducted the first warp flight on April 4, 2063. That historic flight was detected by a passing **Vulcan** ship, and was therefore directly responsible for humanity's first contact with the interstellar community on the following day. Cochrane's motivation for building the *Phoenix* had been purely commercial, and he was uncomfortable with the fame and adulation that was subsequently his, but he later realized that it was his individuality that made his extraordinary achievement possible. A decade after his historic flight, Cochrane said "Don't try to be a great man, just be a man, and let history make its own judgments." *(Star Trek: First Contact).* In later years, Cochrane's name became revered throughout the known galaxy; planets, great universities, and cities were later named after him. Zefram Cochrane disappeared from Alpha Centauri in 2117 at the age of 87 and is presumed to have died in space. ("Metamorphosis" [TOS]). The area of Montana that was once the *Phoenix*'s launch facility became a historical monument. A 20-meter marble statue was erected there, showing Cochrane reaching toward the future. *(Star Trek: First Contact). In 2267, Cochrane was discovered by Captain Kirk to be living on an planetoid in the* ***Gamma Canaris region*** *with the cloud creature known as the* ***Companion****, who loved him. Traveling along with Kirk was Federation* ***Commissioner Nancy Hedford****, dying of* ***Sakuro's disease****. Hedford merged with the Companion, choosing to remain with Cochrane, where they would both live the remainder of a normal human life span. Kirk promised never to reveal Cochrane's fate, so the main body of this entry indicates uncertainty about what happened to the famous scientist.* ("Metamorphosis" [TOS]). SEE: **millicochrane**. The first test of **soliton wave** based propulsion in 2368 was likened to Cochrane's breakthrough. ("New Ground" [TNG]). *Cochrane was portrayed by Glenn Corbett in "Metamorphosis" (TOS) and James Cromwell in* Star Trek: First Contact. *James Cromwell previously portrayed Nayrok in "The Hunted" (TNG) and Jaglom Shrek in "Birthright, Parts I and II" (TNG). We theorize that when the Companion restored Cochrane's youth, she reversed the effects of radiation poisoning, making him look like Glenn Corbett. Either that, or she simply restored Cochrane to an idealized self-image.*

"Coda." Voyager episode #58. Written by Jeri Taylor. Directed by Nancy Malone. Stardate 50518.6. *First aired in 1997. Janeway is involved in a near-fatal shuttle crash and an alien presence in her mind takes the form of her dead father and tries to convince her that she is in the afterlife.* GUEST CAST: Len Cariou as **Janeway, Admiral**. SEE: **antigrav; champagne; consciousness parasite; holodeck and holosuite programs: *Lake George;* hydrazine; Janeway, Admiral; Janeway, Kathryn; Lake George; magnetic storm; nitrogenase compound; Sacajawea; security access code; tachyon; talent night; Tau Ceti Prime; thoron.**

Code 1 Emergency. Federation signal for a total disaster, requiring an immediate response, also designated as a Priority 1 call. **Nilz Baris** sent a Code 1 Emergency call to the *U.S.S. Enterprise* from **Deep Space Station K-7** in 2267. ("The Trouble with Tribbles" [TOS]).

Code 1. Starfleet designation for a declaration of war. In 2267 the *Enterprise* received a Code 1 message from Starfleet Command stating they were at war with the Klingon Empire. The starship then proceeded to planet **Organia,** where the Klingons were expected to strike. ("Errand of Mercy" [TOS]). SEE: **Code Factor 1.**

Code 2. Starfleet encryption protocol. By 2267, the Romulans were able to decrypt Code 2. While under the effects of the aging disease acquired on planet **Gamma Hydra IV**, Kirk ordered a message sent using Code 2, forgetting that Romulan intelligence had broken that code. After he was cured of the illness, he again used Code 2, but intended the Romulans to understand what he was saying. ("The Deadly Years" [TOS]). SEE: **corbomite**.

Code 47. Term designating a Starfleet subspace communiqué of extremely high sensitivity or secrecy. Code 47 messages are intended only for the eyes of a starship captain, and voiceprint identification is required. Further, no computer records are maintained of Code 47 transmissions. **Walker Keel**'s message to Picard requesting a meeting at planet **Dytallix B** was a Code 47 signal, although the conspirators got wind of it anyhow. ("Conspiracy" [TNG]).

Code 710. Interstellar code prohibiting a spacecraft from approaching a planet. The *Enterprise* received a Code 710 from planet **Eminiar VII** in 2267. ("A Taste of Armageddon" [TOS]).

Code Factor 1. Starfleet code meaning invasion status. An unexplained time-warp distortion that swept across the galaxy in 2267 caused Starfleet Command to issue a Code Factor 1. ("The Alternative Factor" [TOS]). SEE: **Lazarus**.

"Code of Honor." *Next Generation* episode #4. Written by Katharyn Powers & Michael Baron. Directed by Russ Mayberry. Stardate 41235.25. *First aired in 1987. Tasha Yar is kidnapped in a planetary struggle for political power. Music for this episode was provided by talented composer Fred Steiner, who scored many episodes of the original* Star Trek *series.* GUEST CAST: Jessie Lawerence Ferguson as **Lutan**; Karole Selmon as **Yareena**; James Louis Watkins as **Hagon**; Michael Rider as Transporter chief. SEE: **Anchilles fever; First One; *glavin*; Hagon; Ligon II; Ligonians; Lutan; Starbase 14; Styris IV; Yareena.**

Code One Alpha Zero. Signal indicating the discovery of space vehicle in distress. Riker issued a Code One Alpha Zero following the detection of an automated distress signal from the ***U.S.S. Jenolen***. ("Relics" [TNG]).

coded transponder frequency. A specific subspace frequency and code that activated a starship's transponder to send back its identifying code, permitting allied vessels and authorities to accurately track the ship. When **Captain Benjamin Maxwell**, commanding the ***U.S.S. Phoenix***, made an unauthorized attack on a **Cardassian** ship in 2367, **Gul Macet** asked for the *Phoenix*'s coded transponder frequency so that other Cardassian ships could track the *Phoenix*. Ironically, the Federation Starfleet already possessed the ability to track Cardassian ships using Cardassian transponder codes. ("The Wounded" [TNG]). *One would assume the Cardassians changed all their transponder codes after this.*

coffee ice cream. Frozen Earth dairy confection made with **coffee** flavoring. Kathryn Janeway was particularly fond of coffee ice cream. ("Persistence of Vision" [VGR]).

coffee. Aromatic beverage made from ground, roasted seeds of an Earth tree of genus *Coffea*. Often served hot, sometimes with cream and sugar. *Starship Enterprise* captain James T. Kirk enjoyed coffee ("The Corbomite Maneuver" [TOS], "The Trouble with Tribbles" [TOS]), as did Dr. Leonard McCoy. ("City on the Edge of Forever" [TOS]). Miles O'Brien preferred a Jamaican blend of coffee, double strong, double sweet. ("Whispers" [DS9]). Geordi La Forge liked his coffee iced. ("Aquiel" [TNG]). Coffee was *Voyager* captain Kathryn Janeway's favorite drink. ("The Cloud" [VGR]). SEE: **iced coffee; macchiato; *raktajino*; Vulcan mocha.** *Members of the* Star Trek *art departments recognize coffee as the true power source for the* Starships Enterprise *and* Voyager, *as does producer Bob Justman.*

"Cogito ergo sum." "I think, therefore I am." A truism devised by Earth philosopher Descartes. The computer intelligence version of **Professor James Moriarty** quoted Descartes before attempting to exit the holodeck on his own volition. ("Ship in a Bottle" [TNG]).

Cogley, Samuel T. (Elisha Cook, Jr.). Attorney. Cogley successfully defended **James Kirk** in 2267 when Kirk was accused of the murder of **Ben Finney**. At the court-martial on **Starbase 11**, Cogley petitioned to hold the trial on the *Starship Enterprise*, on the grounds that Kirk had the right to face his accuser, in this case the *Enterprise* computer. Cogley proved that a computer malfunction, deliberately caused by Finney, had wrongly implicated Kirk. Cogley had a love of old books, and shunned the use of computers whenever possible. Cogley later defended Ben Finney. ("Court Martial" [TOS]). *Actor Elisha Cook, Jr. achieved fame for his portrayal of a near-out-of-control gunsel who menaced Humphrey Bogart in the classic film* The Maltese Falcon.

coherent graviton pulse. Energy waves that can neutralize **tetryon** emissions. ("Schisms" [TNG]).

coherent tetryon beam. SEE: **tetryon**.

coladrium flow. Term in an unknown alien language for tenuous space matter collected by **arva nodes** in **Tosk**'s ship converting the interstellar hydrogen into usable fuel. ("Captive Pursuit" [DS9]). SEE: **ramscoop**.

"Cold Fire." *Voyager* episode #26. Teleplay by Brannon Braga. Story by Anthony Williams. Directed by Cliff Bole. No stardate mentioned. *First aired in 1995. The* Voyager *crew encounters the Caretaker's mate, a malevolent entity who has enslaved hundreds of Ocampa, while Kes discovers the incredible power of her latent telekinetic powers. Opening narration establishes this episode to be set ten months after "Caretaker" (VGR), the show's pilot movie.* Gary Graham as **Tanis**; Lindsay Ridgeway as Girl; Norman Large as Ocampa; Majel Barrett as Narrator. SEE: **airponics bay; Caretaker; Exosia; hexiprismatic field; Kes; Nacene; noncorporeal life; Ocampa; sporocystian; Suspiria's Array; Suspiria; Tanis.**

Cold Moon Over Blackwater. Gothic novel enjoyed by **Lieutenant Aquiel Uhnari**. ("Aquiel" [TNG]).

cold, common. An infection of the upper respiratory tract caused by any of over 200 viruses in many humanoid species. By the 24th century, the common cold was a curable ailment. ("The Battle" [TNG]). *McCoy noted in "The Omega Glory" (TOS) that the common cold had not yet been cured by that point in the 23rd century.*

coleibric hemorrhage. A fatal condition in Cardassian physiology. Cause of death of the infamous **Gul Darhe'el**, who died in 2363. ("Duet" [DS9]).

Coleman, Dr. Arthur. (Harry Landers). Physician who was one of two survivors of a disastrous scientific expedition to planet **Camus II** in 2269. Shortly after the death of his colleagues, Coleman conspired with Dr. **Janice Lester**, the other survivor, to use a life-energy transfer device to place Lester's mind into the body of Captain James Kirk, and to trap Kirk's mind in Lester's body. Coleman, who was in love with Lester, indicated he would care for her after it was discovered she was insane at the time she caused the deaths on Camus II. ("Turnabout Intruder" [TOS]).

Coleridge, Biddle "B.C." (Frank Military). Resident of **Sanctuary District** A in **San Francisco** on **Earth** in 2024, and a leader in the **Bell Riots**. Coleridge was a violent, troublesome individual, who in the slang of the era, would be called a **ghost**. During the riots, B.C. was a guard of the hostages that were held in the District **Processing Center**. He was killed when government troops stormed the District. ("Past Tense, Parts I and II" [DS9]).

colgonite astringent. Beauty treatment offered in the barber shop aboard the *Enterprise*-D. Beverly Crusher enjoyed an occasional application of colgonite astringent. ("The Host" [TNG]).

"Collaborator, The." *Deep Space Nine* episode #44. Teleplay by Gary Holland and Ira Steven Behr & Robert Hewitt Wolfe. Story by Gary Holland. Directed by Cliff Bole. No stardate given. *First aired in 1994. Major Kira discovers that the cover-up of a massacre on Bajor involves Vedek Bareil, who is favored to be elected as the Bajoran spiritual leader.* GUEST CAST: Philip Anglim as **Bareil**, **Vedek**; Bert Remsen as **Kubus Oak**; Camille Saviola as **Opaka**, **Kai**; Louise Fletcher as **Winn**; Charles Parks as **Eblan**; Tom Villard as **Bek**, **Prylar**. SEE: **Bajoran Central Archives**; **Bareil, Vedek; Bek, Prylar; Cardassian occupational government; Dakeen Monastery; Eblan; Ferengi Rules of Acquisition; Ilvian Proclamation; kai; Kendra Valley massacre; Kubus Oak; Opaka, Kai; prylar; retinal scan; Sacred Texts; Tolena, Vedek; Winn.**

collar of obedience. Neck bands worn by the **drill thralls** on planet **Triskelion** that tightened when the thrall disobeyed an order. Each collar was coded with a color that signified which **Provider** owned that particular drill thrall. ("The Gamesters of Triskelion" [TOS]).

Collected Stories. (In an alternate future in which Ben Sisko was believed killed aboard the *Defiant* in 2372, *Collected Stories* was a book of short stories written by **Jake Sisko**. *Collected Stories* won the Betar Prize in 2391. SEE: **Sisko, Jake.**) ("The Visitor" [DS9]).

collective consciousness. SEE: **Borg; Borg collective**.

Collins, Ensign. (Harley Venton). Transporter technician aboard the *Enterprise*-D. Collins was on duty when an away team beamed down to meet **Bajoran** leader **Orta** in 2368. ("Ensign Ro" [TNG]).

Colt Firearms. Nineteenth-century Earth weapons manufacturing company, founded in 1847 by Samuel Colt. The company was famous for handheld firearms, including the double-action cavalry pistol discovered in 2368 in a cavern on Earth. ("Time's Arrow, Part I" [TNG]).

Colt, Yeoman J.M. (Laurel Goodwin). Officer aboard the original *Starship Enterprise* under the command of Captain **Christopher Pike**. After their mission to planet **Talos IV**, Colt wondered who Pike would have chosen to become his "Eve." ("The Cage" [TOS]).

Coltar IV. Planet. Coltar IV was home to a farming colony that experienced a "hiccough" in time that was found to be the result of **Dr. Paul Manheim**'s time/gravity experiments at **Vandor IX** in 2364. ("We'll Always Have Paris" [TNG]).

***coltayin* roots.** Edible plant form. The image of **Anna** prepared a meal of *coltayin* roots, mixed with some Terellian spices, for

Captain Picard during the time they were marooned together. ("Liaisons" [TNG]).

Colti, Admiral. Senior Starfleet officer. In 2373, Admiral Colti attended what was to have been a signing ceremony at Deep Space 9 for Bajor's entrance into the Federation. ("Rapture" [DS9]).

Columbia, S.S. Federation science vessel. The *Columbia* made a forced landing on planet **Talos IV** in 2254. The only survivor was a crew member named **Vina**, who was cared for by the natives of that planet. ("The Cage," "The Menagerie, Part I" [TOS]).

Columbia, U.S.S. Scout vessel, Starfleet registry number NCC-621. *The* Columbia *was not seen, but was mentioned in a Starfleet communique overheard at the **Epsilon IX Monitoring Station,** ordered to rendezvous with the* U.S.S. Revere *by Commodore Probert, a gag reference to production illustrator Andrew Probert. (Star Trek: The Motion Picture).*

Columbus, Shuttlecraft. Registry number NCC-1701-2. Shuttle attached to the original *Starship Enterprise*. This vehicle participated in a visual search for the ***Shuttlecraft Galileo***, after the *Galileo* crashed on planet **Taurus II** in 2267. ("The *Galileo* Seven" [TOS]). *Named for terrestrial explorer Christopher Columbus (1451-1506).*

Colyus. (Kenneth Mars). A sentient holographic life-form, and the law enforcement authority on planet **Yadera II.** As the Protector of his village, Colyus investigated the disappearance of 22 villagers in 2370. In fact, all of the villagers were living holograms, and the disappearances were the result of a malfunction in the **hologenerator**. ("Shadowplay" [DS9]). SEE: **Rurigan.**

combadge. Personal **communicator**, incorporated into the Starfleet emblem worn on the uniforms of Starfleet personnel. ("Encounter at Farpoint" [TNG]). Combadges were capable of broadcasting a subspace beacon. Starfleet combadges were programmed to activate automatically when the casing was destroyed, a feature designed to help rescuers locate a seriously injured person. ("Time and Again" [VGR]).

combat rations. Starfleet emergency food provisions. The brown flattened ovoids were packaged in a silver plastic wrapper and were designed to provide a timed release formula of all the nutrients needed by a humanoid body for three days. Unfortunately, few Starfleet personnel found them especially palatable. ("The Siege" [DS9]). *For some reason, Miles O'Brien liked them.*

Comic, The. (Joe Piscopo). An unnamed 20th-century comedian re-created on the holodeck of the *Enterprise*-D by Data, who had hoped to learn the concept of humor. Although The Comic tutored Data in stand-up comedy, the android found the concept difficult to grasp. The Comic's holodeck program was RW-93216. ("The Outrageous Okona" [TNG]). *The holodeck program menu used by Data to select this simulation identified the comic's name as Ron Moore. By amazing coincidence, Visual Effects Coordinator Ronald B. Moore was one of the people who assembled the computer graphic on that holodeck readout.*

"Coming of Age." *Next Generation* episode #19. Written by Sandy Fries. Directed by Mike Vejar. Stardate 41416.2. *Originally aired in 1988. Wesley Crusher fails his first attempt to gain entry into Starfleet Academy. "Coming of Age" marks the first appearance of a shuttlecraft in* Star Trek: The Next Generation. GUEST CAST: Ward Costello as **Quinn**, **Admiral Gregory**; Robert Schenkkan as **Remmick**, **Dexter**; John Putch as **Mordock**; Robert Ito as **Chang**, **Tac Officer**; Stephen Gregory as **Kurland**, **Jake**; Tasia Valenza as **T'Shanik**; Estee Chandler as **Mirren, Oliana**; Brendan McKane as Technician #1; Wyatt Knight as Technician #2; Daniel Riordan as **Rondon**. SEE: **Beltane IX; Benzar; Bulgallian rat; Chang, Tac Officer; Crusher, Wesley; hyperspace physics test; Kurland, Jake; Mirren, Oliana; Mordock Strategy; Mordock; Picard, Jean-Luc; Psych Test; Quinn, Admiral Gregory; Relva VII; Remmick, Dexter; Rondon; Shuttlecraft 13; T'Shanik; Vulcana Regar; Zaldans.**

Commander Riker Day. Proposed school activity for the children of the *Enterprise*-D. Captain Picard suggested the activity in response to Riker's enjoyment of **Captain Picard Day**. ("The *Pegasus*" [TNG]).

commodore. Title formerly given to high-ranking Starfleet officers such as those in charge of a starbase. *The term commodore, used in the original* Star Trek *series, has fallen into disuse since* Star Trek: The Next Generation.

communicator. Personal communications device used by **Starfleet** personnel. Communicators provided voice transmission from a planetary surface to an orbiting spacecraft, and

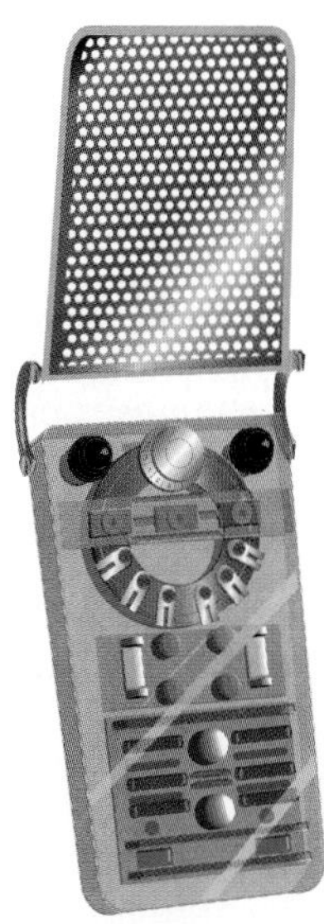

Starfleet communicator circa 2250

Starfleet communicator circa 2266

Starfleet wrist communicator circa 2271

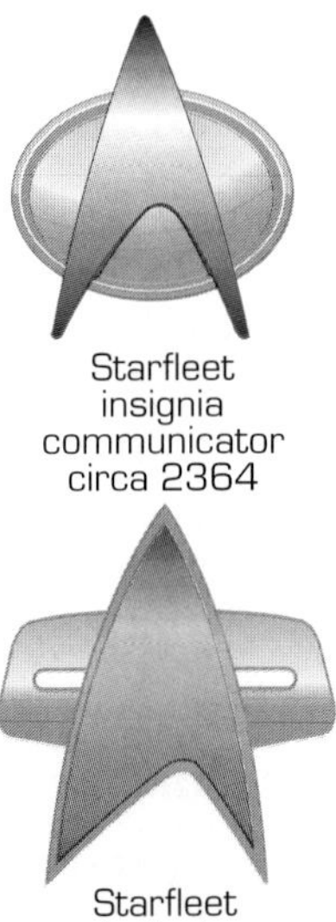

Starfleet insignia communicator circa 2364

Starfleet insignia communicator circa 2371

between members of a landing party. Communicators also provided a means for a ship's **transporter** system to determine the exact coordinates of a crew member for transport back to the ship. Early versions of the communicator were compact handheld units with a flip-up antenna grid. *When the communicator was first "invented" in 1964, it seemed incredibly compact and amazingly advanced. Few would have believed back then that* Star Trek *would still be on the air when portable cellular telephones, the same size as those original props, became a reality.* Starfleet briefly used wrist communicators, but more recent units have been incorporated into the Starfleet insignia worn on each crew member's uniform and have a dermal sensor that can be used to restrict usage to one authorized individual only. **Roga Danar**, fleeing from security confinement aboard the *Enterprise*-D, successfully bypassed this restriction by using an unconscious security officer's own finger to activate his communicator. ("The Hunted" [TNG]). The device is constructed of a crystalline composite of silicon, beryllium, carbon-70, and gold. ("Time's Arrow, Part I" [TNG]). SEE: **combadge**.

Companion. (Voice of Elizabeth Rogers). Cloudlike life-form that lived on a planetoid in the **Gamma Canaris region**. In 2117, the Companion discovered aged scientist **Zefram Cochrane** drifting in space, near death. The Companion brought Cochrane to her planetoid and cared for him, rejuvenating his body, giving him effective immortality, but subjecting him to extreme loneliness. Over time, the Companion grew to love Cochrane. In 2267, the Companion abducted Kirk, Spock, McCoy, and Federation **Commissioner Nancy Hedford** from the *Enterprise* **shuttlecraft *Galileo*** to live with Cochrane to alleviate his isolation. Hedford, terminally ill with **Sakuro's disease**, agreed to merge with the Companion, becoming a single, human individual. The resulting individual, still in love with Cochrane, remained with Cochrane on the planetoid for the rest of a normal human lifetime. ("Metamorphosis" [TOS]). *The Federation remained unaware of Cochrane's fate and of the existence of the Companion because of Kirk's promise to Cochrane. The Companion was designed by future* Star Wars *Oscar-winner Richard Edlund at Westheimer photographic effects company.*

compressed tetryon beam. Energy weapon. A compressed **tetryon** beam was used by the **Lenarians** to attack an *Enterprise*-D away team in 2369. Captain **Jean-Luc Picard** caught the full effect of the weapon, which fused the bio-regulator in his artificial heart, damaged his spleen and liver, and nearly killed him. ("Tapestry" [TNG]). Security scanners on station Deep Space 9 do not normally detect such weapons. A compressed tetryon beam weapon was used to attack Quark in 2370. ("Necessary Evil" [DS9]).

compression phaser rifle. SEE: **phaser rifle**.

Compton. (Geoffrey Binney). Starship *Enterprise* crew member who was subjected to biochemical **hyperacceleration** on planet **Scalos** in 2268 when exposed to Scalosian water. Because the **Scalosian** males were sterile, Compton was to be used for reproduction, but he quickly sustained cellular damage, resulting in his death. ("Wink of an Eye" [TOS]).

computer core. One of three large, redundant cylindrical chambers aboard a *Galaxy*-class starship, housing the ship's primary computer hardware. The upper core of the *Enterprise*-D was taken over by sentient **nanites** when that newly created life-forms explored the ship in 2366. ("Evolution" [TNG]). *The computer core set was also used in "The Bonding" (TNG) for Worf and Troi's talk.*

***comra*.** Ocampa term for soul or spirit. ("Emanations" [VGR]).

***Concorde*, U.S.S.** Federation starship, *Freedom* class, Starfleet registry number NCC-68711. (During the **anti-time** occurrence created by the Q Continuum, Admiral Nakamura deployed the *Concorde*, along with 15 other starships, to the **Romulan Neutral Zone** to investigate a Romulan military buildup on their side of the zone. ["All Good Things..." (TNG)].)

Condition Green. Covert **Starfleet** code used to secretly indicate on a clear channel that the speaker is being held captive. Captain Kirk relayed a Condition Green signal to Mr. Scott when Kirk was being held captive on planet Eight Ninety-Two-IV in 2267. Condition Green also prohibits the listener from taking any action such as a rescue mission. ("Bread and Circuses" [TOS]).

condition blue. SEE: **blue alert.**

conference lounge. SEE: **observation lounge.**

confinement beam. SEE: **annular confinement beam.**

confinement mode. SEE: **isolation protocol.**

Conklin, Captain. Starfleet officer. Commander of the Federation starship ***Magellan***. ("Starship Mine" [TNG]).

conn. Abbreviation for **flight controller**.

Conor, Aaron. (John Snyder). The leader of the isolated **Genome Colony** on **Moab IV**. Like everyone in the carefully planned colony, Conor was genetically engineered and trained for his specific job. When tidal forces from a **stellar core fragment** threatened to disrupt the planet and destroy his colony in 2368, Conor was faced with an impossible choice. If he accepted an offer of help from engineers aboard the *Enterprise*-D, he risked serious cultural contamination of his totally isolated colony. The alternative of rejecting outside help would have led to near-certain destruction of the colony. Conor chose to allow the *Enterprise*-D to help, but had to deal with the social consequences of their aid. ("The Masterpiece Society" [TNG]). SEE: **Bates, Hannah**; **Benbeck, Martin**. *John Snyder also played Centurion Bochra in "The Enemy" (TNG).*

"Conscience of the King, The." Original Series episode #13. Written by Barry Trivers. Directed by Gerd Oswald. Stardate: 2817.6. *First aired in 1966. Kirk suspects that a distinguished Shakespearean actor may have been an infamous mass murderer many years ago. The episode's title is a quote from Shakespeare's* Hamlet. GUEST CAST: Arnold Moss as **Karidian, Anton**; Barbara Anderson as **Karidian, Lenore**; Grace Lee Whitney as **Rand, Janice**; William Sargent as **Leighton, Dr. Thomas**; Natalie Norwick as **Leighton, Martha**; Troy David as Maston, Larry; Karl Bruck as King Duncan; Marc Adams as Hamlet; Bruce Hyde as **Riley, Kevin Thomas**; Eddie Paskey as **Leslie, Mr.**; Frank Vince as **Daily, Jon** (voice); Majel Barrett as Computer voice. SEE: ***Astral Queen*; Benecia Colony; "Beyond Antares"; Cygnia Minor; Daily, Jon; *Hamlet*; Karidian Company of Players; Karidian, Anton; Karidian, Lenore; Leslie, Mr.; Kirk, James T.; Kodos the Executioner; Leighton, Dr. Thomas; Leighton, Martha; Molson, E.; Q, Planet; Riley, Kevin Thomas; Saurian brandy; Shakespeare, William; Tarsus IV; tetralubisol; Uhura; Vulcan lute**.

consciousness parasite. Noncorporeal life-form that enters a host consciousness just before the moment of death. Once in the mind of the individual, the parasite attempts to coerce the host's consciousness into a matrix where it can be slowly be consumed to sustain the parasite. In 2373, following a near-fatal shuttle crash injury, Kathryn Janeway's cerebral cortex was inhabited by an alien entity. The entity fed a false reality to Janeway, and took the form of her long-dead father in the reality. The entity attempted to convince Janeway to let go of life and enter the matrix in which his kind lived. They nourished themselves for a long time on the life force of persons who die. ("Coda" [VGR]).

conservator. SEE: **public conservator.**

"Conspiracy." *Next Generation* episode #25. Story by Robert Sabaroff. Teleplay by Tracy Tormé. Directed by Cliff Bole. Stardate 41775.5. *First aired in 1988. Starfleet Command is infiltrated by alien parasites. The conspiracy in this episode was first alluded to in "Coming of Age" (TNG). "The Drumhead" (TNG) established that Admiral Norah Satie helped uncover the conspiracy. Writer Robert Sabaroff also wrote "The Immunity Syndrome" (TOS) and "Home Soil" (TNG).* GUEST CAST: Henry Darrow as **Savar**, **Admiral**; Ward Costello as **Quinn**, **Admiral Gregory**; Robert Schenkkan as **Remmick**, **Dexter**; Ray Reinhardt as **Aaron**; Jonathan Farwell as **Keel**, **Walker**; Michael Berryman as **Rixx**, **Captain**; Ursaline Bryant as **Scott**, **Tryla**. SEE: **Aaron, Admiral; Altarian Conference; Andonian tea; Bolians; Code 47; Crusher, Dr. Beverly; Delaplane, Governor; Dytallix B; *Horatio*, *U.S.S.*; Karapleedeez, Onna; Keel, Walker; McKinney; Mira system; Pacifica; Quinn, Admiral Gregory; Remmick, Dexter; *Renegade*, *U.S.S.*; Rixx, Captain; Satie, Admiral Norah; Savar, Admiral; Scott, Tryla; Sipe, Ryan; Starbase 12; Starfleet Headquarters; Tau Ceti III; *Thomas Paine*, *U.S.S.***

Constable. Affectionate nickname for **Deep Space 9** Security Chief **Odo**. ("Emissary" [DS9]).

Constantinople*, *U.S.S. Federation starship, *Istanbul* class, registry number NCC-34852. The *Constantinople* suffered a hull breach near **Gravesworld** while carrying some 2012 colonists in 2365. *Enterprise*-D conducted a rescue mission to save that ship's crew. ("The Schizoid Man" [TNG]). *Named for the Turkish city also known as Istanbul.*

Constantinople. City in Europe on planet **Earth** where, in 1334, the bubonic plague decimated the population. The (nearly) immortal **Flint** was in Constantinople at the time of that tragedy. ("Requiem For Methuselah" [TOS]).

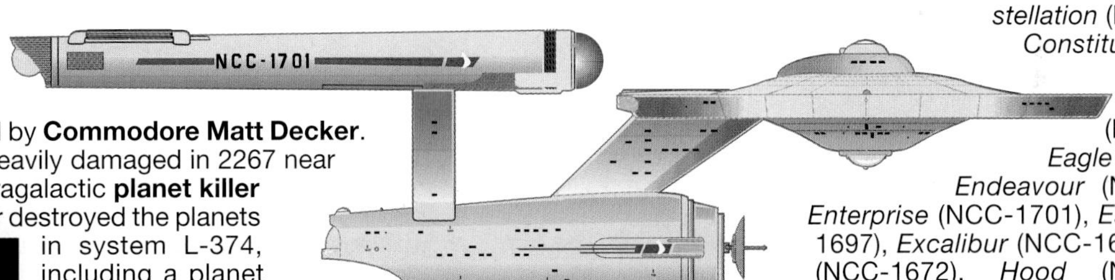

Constellation*, *U.S.S. Federation starship, *Constitution* class, Starfleet registry number NCC-1017, commanded by **Commodore Matt Decker**. The *Constellation* was heavily damaged in 2267 near system **L-374** by an extragalactic **planet killer** weapon. The planet killer destroyed the planets in system L-374, including a planet where the crew of the *Constellation* had taken refuge. *Enterprise* personnel programmed the hulk of the *Constellation* to self-destruct its **impulse drive** inside the planet killer, destroying the robotic weapon. ("The Doomsday Machine" [TOS]). *The miniature* Constellation, *identical in design to the original* Enterprise, *was an AMT plastic* Enterprise *model kit, appropriately burnt and scorched. The* Starship Constellation *was presumably replaced by a starship of a new design that was the prototype for the* Constellation *class, of which Picard's* **U.S.S. Stargazer** *was a member.*

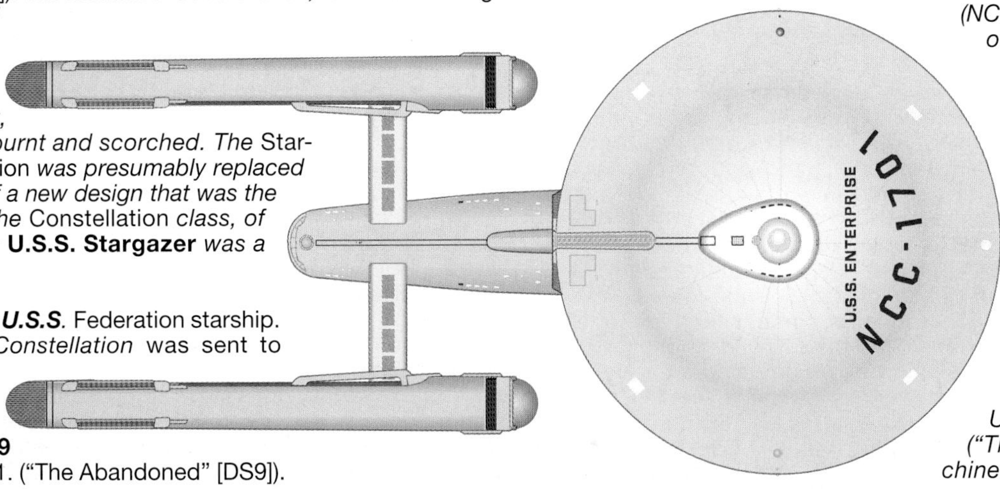

Constellation*, *U.S.S. Federation starship. In 2371, the *Constellation* was sent to transport the **Jem'Hadar** abandoned on **Deep Space 9** to Starbase 201. ("The Abandoned" [DS9]).

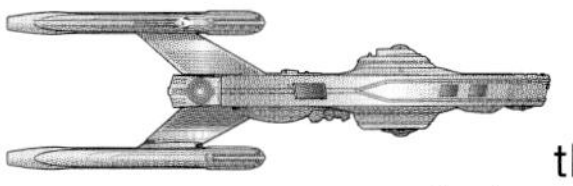

Constellation*-class starship.** Type of Federation spacecraft to which Picard's former command, the ***Stargazer, belonged. Similar in overall size to the *Constitution*-class ship, the *Constellation*-class ships were equipped with four warp nacelles and were thus suited for deep-space exploration and defensive patrol duties. Ships of this type have included the ***Stargazer***, ***Hathaway***, ***Victory***, and the *Constellation*, after which the class is named. ("The Battle" [TNG]). *The first* Constellation-*class ship seen,* Stargazer *was originally planned to be a* **Constitution-*class*** *ship, allowing our visual effects staff to make use of the existing movie* Enterprise *model. Our producers did not make the decision to build a new model for the* Stargazer *until after the episode was filmed with LeVar Burton calling it a* Constitution-*class ship. The choice of the name* Constellation *was based largely on the fact that it could be dubbed over Geordi's line since the two words are so similar. One might conjecture that this* U.S.S. Constellation *was named in honor of* ***Matt Decker****'s ship, destroyed in "The Doomsday Machine" (TOS).*

Constitution of the United Federation of Planets. Historic document framed in 2161, outlining the framework by which the Federation is governed for the mutual benefit and protection of member planets and individual citizens. Among the assurances of individual civil liberties contained in the Constitution is the **Seventh Guarantee**, protecting citizens against self-incrimination. ("The Drumhead" [TNG]). All persons aboard a Federation starship are guaranteed these fundamental individual rights under the Constitution. ("The Perfect Mate" [TNG]).

***Constitution*-class starship.** One of Starfleet's most famous types of vehicle, the *Constitution*-class starships included the acclaimed original *U.S.S. Enterprise*. During the time of Captain **James T. Kirk**'s celebrated first five-year mission of exploration, only 12 of these ships were in existence. ("Tomorrow is Yesterday" [TOS]). *Constitution*-class starships commissioned by Starfleet included: *Constellation* (NCC-1017), *Constitution* (NCC-1700), *Defiant* (NCC-1764), *Eagle* (NCC-956), *Endeavour* (NCC-1895), *Enterprise* (NCC-1701), *Essex* (NCC-1697), *Excalibur* (NCC-1664), *Exeter* (NCC-1672), *Hood* (NCC-1703), *Intrepid* (NCC-1831), *Lexington* (NCC-1709), *Potemkin* (NCC-1657), *Republic* (NCC-1371), and *Yorktown* (NCC-1717). *Constitution*-class ships used **duotronic** computers, based on designs developed by **Dr. Richard Daystrom** in 2243. ("The Ultimate Computer" [TOS]). *The registry number of the* Constitution *(NCC-1700) is from one of Scotty's technical manual screens in "Space Seed" (TOS). Since the class ship has a 1700 number, it would seem only reasonable that the other ships of the class would have higher, possibly even sequential numbers. Unfortunately, the* U.S.S. Constellation *("The Doomsday Machine" [TOS]), bore a*

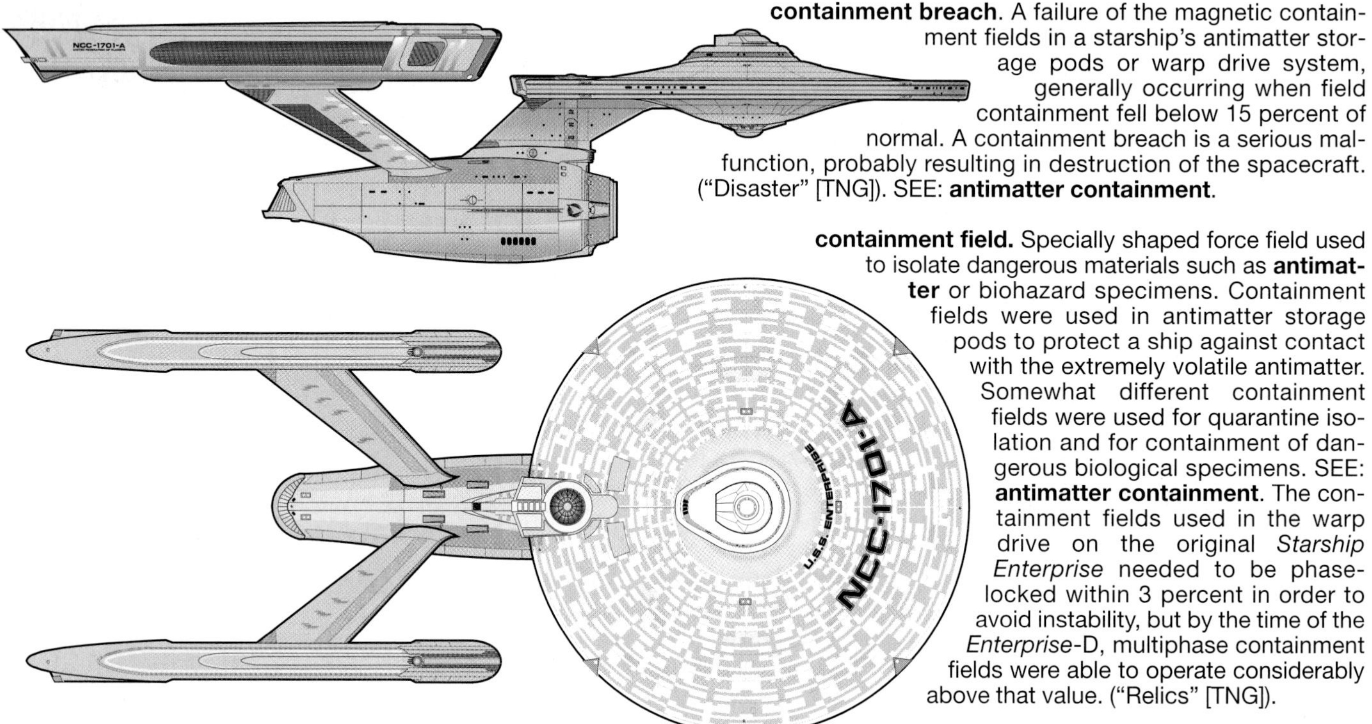

Constitution class starship
Refit configuration

much lower number, NCC-1017, (obviously because it was a simple rearrangement of the decal sheet from the AMT Enterprise *model kit) and the* Republic *was designated as NCC-1371. These data points suggest the* Constitution-*class ships had registry numbers that not only varied widely in range, but also could* not *be sequential. Modelmaker Greg Jein (through an amazingly complex and admittedly only barely logical means) managed to match up the various* Constitution *ships with the starship status chart in Commodore Stone's office in Starbase 11, seen in "Court Martial" (TOS). Most of these registry numbers are from Greg's conjectural list, although several are from various Starfleet charts and readouts in* Star Trek VI. *A few of the* Constitution-*class ships listed above are not from any episode or movie, but are from the original* Star Trek *production office's starship list in Stephen Whitfield's book,* The Making of Star Trek.

construction module. Remotely controlled robotic device used for construction in free space. Construction modules were used in 2367 to attach small propulsion units to a dangerously radioactive spacecraft in orbit of **Gamelan V** in the hopes that they could push the craft into the Gamelan sun. The attempt, engineered by *Enterprise*-D personnel, was unsuccessful. ("Final Mission" [TNG]).

"Contagion." *Next Generation* episode #37. Written by Steve Gerber & Beth Woods. Directed by Joseph L. Scanlan. Stardate 42609.1. *First aired in 1989. An ancient computer software weapon destroys the* Starship Yamato *and threatens the* Enterprise-*D and a Romulan ship. Picard first orders "Tea, Earl Grey, hot" in this episode.* GUEST CAST: Diana Muldaur as **Pulaski, Dr. Katherine**; Thalmus Rasulala as **Varley, Captain Donald**; Carolyn Seymour as **Taris, Subcommander**; Dana Sparks as Williams; Colm Meaney as **O'Brien, Miles**; Folkert Schmidt as Doctor. **SEE: antimatter containment; archaeology; "Demons of Air and Darkness"; Denius III; Dewan; Dinasian; *Galaxy*-class starship; *Haakona*; Iccobar; Iconia; Iconian computer weapon; Iconian gateway; Iconians; magnetic seals; Picard, Jean-Luc; Ramsey, Dr.; Romulan Neutral Zone; Taris, Subcommander; Varley, Captain Donald; *Yamato*, *U.S.S.***

containment breach. A failure of the magnetic containment fields in a starship's antimatter storage pods or warp drive system, generally occurring when field containment fell below 15 percent of normal. A containment breach is a serious malfunction, probably resulting in destruction of the spacecraft. ("Disaster" [TNG]). SEE: **antimatter containment**.

containment field. Specially shaped force field used to isolate dangerous materials such as **antimatter** or biohazard specimens. Containment fields were used in antimatter storage pods to protect a ship against contact with the extremely volatile antimatter. Somewhat different containment fields were used for quarantine isolation and for containment of dangerous biological specimens. SEE: **antimatter containment**. The containment fields used in the warp drive on the original *Starship Enterprise* needed to be phase-locked within 3 percent in order to avoid instability, but by the time of the *Enterprise*-D, multiphase containment fields were able to operate considerably above that value. ("Relics" [TNG]).

Contract of Ardra. A thousand-year-old agreement that, according to legend, was made between the ancient Ventaxians and the mythical figure, **Ardra**. The contract promised a millennium of peace and prosperity for the people of **Ventax II** in exchange for the population delivering itself into slavery at the end of the thousand years. ("Devil's Due" [TNG]).

control interface. User-operated panel permitting input into a computer or other system. A control interface, such as those found on a Starfleet food **replicator**, generally permits display of feedback information to show the results of the inputted command. Control interfaces varied very widely with different cultures (based heavily on their technological capabilities and system needs) and could include vocal, visual, and sensor-based commands and output. ("Fair Trade" [VGR]). SEE: **LCARS**.

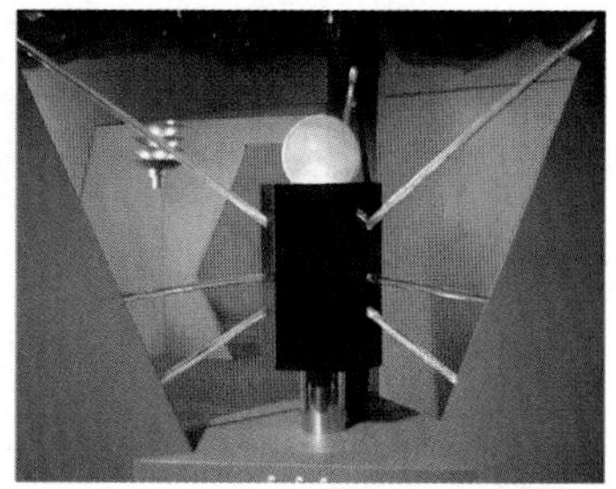

Controller. Sophisticated computer system that controlled the subterranean environmental for **Eymorg** women of planet **Sigma Draconis VI.** The heart of the Controller was a biological humanoid brain, which required periodic replacement. Spock's brain was stolen by the inhabitants of Sigma Draconis VI in 2268 to be used as the new Controller. When Spock's brain was returned to his body, the Controller was no longer able to regulate the environment and the population had to move to the surface. ("Spock's Brain." [TOS]). SEE: **Teacher**.

"Conundrum." *Next Generation* episode #114. Teleplay by Barry Schkolnick. Story by Paul Schiffer. Directed by Les Landau. Stardate 45494.2. *First aired in 1992. Contact with an alien probe leaves the* Enterprise-*D crew with amnesia, so they have no way of knowing if Starfleet orders to attack a space station are genuine.* GUEST CAST: Erich Anderson as **MacDuff, Commander Keiran**; Michelle Forbes as **Ro Laren**; Liz Vassey as **Kristin**; Erick Weiss as Crewman; Majel Barrett as Computer voice. SEE: **Cirrus IV; Cliffs of Heaven; crew manifest; el-Mitra Exchange; Emerald Wading Pool; Epsilon Silar system; hippocampus; Kriskov Gambit; La Forge, Edward M.; Lysia; Lysian Central Command; Lysian Destroyer; MacDuff, Commander Keiran; *Ode to Psyche*; photon torpedo; Ro**

Control interfaces, Starfleet and other cultures

Sensor probe telemetry readout, Tactical II—*U.S.S. Defiant* bridge.

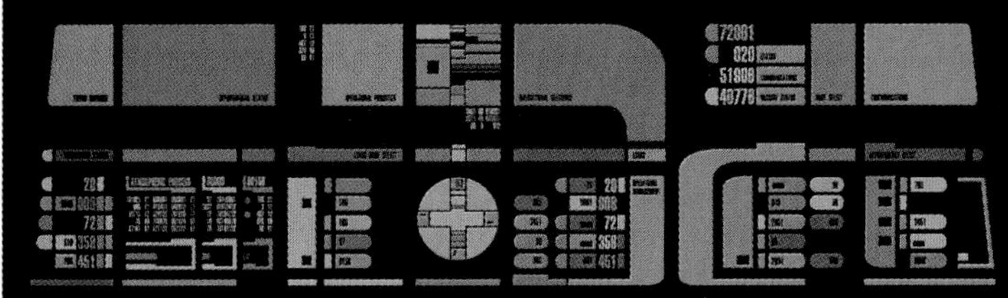

Operations manager console (ops)—*U.S.S. Enterprise*-D bridge.

Klingon interface. Bridge of a *K'Vort*-class.

Bird-of-Prey.

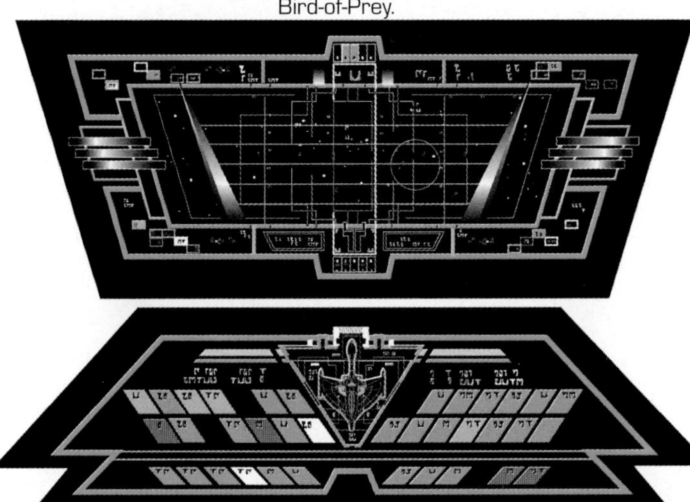

Romulan interface. Bridge of a warbird.

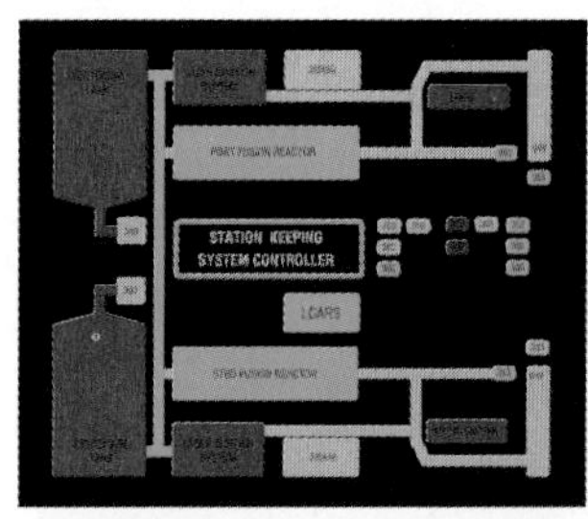

Engineering readout. *Constitution*-class *U.S.S. Enterprise*.

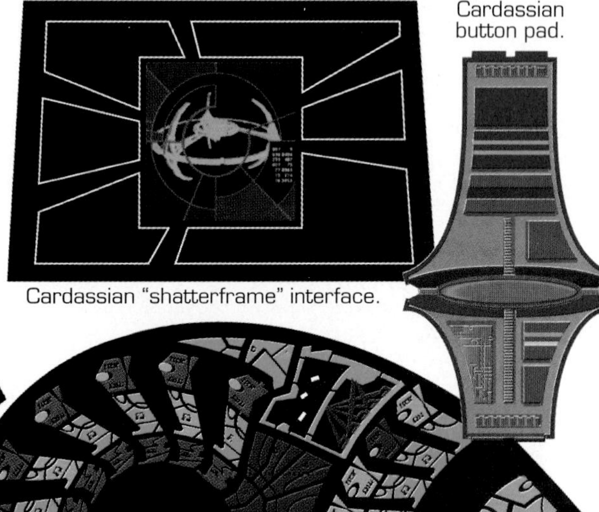

Cardassian button pad.

Cardassian "shatterframe" interface.

Cardassian interface. Operations—Deep Space 9.

Dominion interface—Jem'Hadar warship.

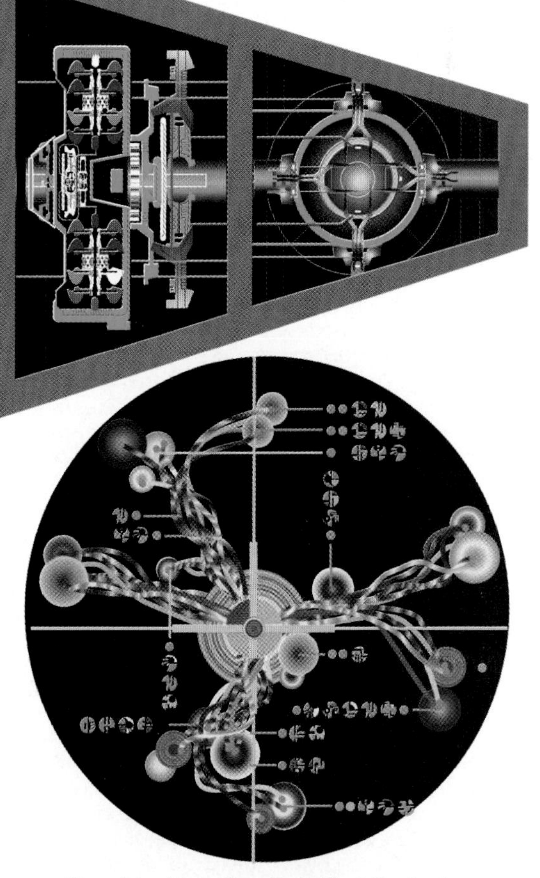

Borg interface. *Star Trek: First Contact*.

Laren; Samarian Sunset; Satarrans; Starbase 301; Troi, Deanna.

Copernicus*, *Shuttlecraft*.** Shuttle #3, attached to *U.S.S. Enterprise*-A. Kirk, Spock, McCoy, and Sybok transported down aboard the *Copernicus* to the planet that **Sybok** believed was ***Sha Ka Ree in search of Sybok's vision of God. (*Star Trek V: The Final Frontier*). *The* Copernicus *miniature was a re-use of the* Galileo *model made for* Star Trek V, *although two full-sized exterior mockups were also built.*

Cor Caroli V. Planet. The *Enterprise*-D was successful in eradicating the Phyrox Plague at Cor Caroli V in 2366. Starfleet Command classified the incident as Secret. ("Allegiance" [TNG]).

Corado I Transmitter Array. Subspace communications relay and booster facility near **Deep Space 9.** Station science officer **Jadzia Dax** ordered a subspace link established to the Corado I Array while trying to overload the station's computers when the software life-form called **Pup** was threatening station operation in 2369. ("The Forsaken" [DS9]).

Corak, Glinn. (Tom Morga). Aide to **Gul Lemec** during talks aboard the *Starship Enterprise*-D in 2369. ("Chain of Command, Part I" [TNG]). *Tom Morga also played a Nausicaan in "Tapestry" (TNG) and was a stunt player in* Star Trek III.

Corbin, Tom. An *Enterprise*-D crew member, scientist, and colleague of Keiko O'Brien. ("Night Terrors" [TNG]).

"Corbomite Maneuver, The." *Original Series* episode #3. Written by Jerry Sohl. Directed by Joseph Sargent. Stardate 1512.2. *First aired in 1966. A powerful ship captures the* Enterprise, *but it is just a test to learn the Federation's intentions. This was the first regular episode produced for the original* Star Trek *series after the two pilot episodes. It features the first appearances of McCoy, Uhura, and Rand. Numerous costume and set designs seen in this episode were changed from the way they originally appeared in* Star Trek*'s two pilot episodes.* GUEST CAST: Anthony Call as **Bailey, Lieutenant David**; Clint Howard as **Balok**; Grace Lee Whitney as **Rand, Janice**; Ted Cassidy as **Balok** (voice of puppet); Victor H. Perrin as **Balok** (Clint Howard's voice); Mittie Lawrence, Ena Hartman, Gloria Calomee, Crew women; Bruce Mars, John Gabriel, Jonathan Lippe, Stewart Moss, George Bochman, Crewmen. SEE: **Bailey, Lieutenant David; Balok; corbomite; *Fesarius*; First Federation; McCoy, Dr. Leonard H.; poker; Rand, Janice; recorder marker; sickbay; Sulu, Hikaru; *tranya*; Uhura.**

corbomite. A nonexistent substance, part of a bluff devised by James Kirk. When threatened by **Balok** of the ***Fesarius*** in 2266, Kirk claimed his ship's hull contained a substance called corbomite that would cause the destruction of any vessel attacking his ship. ("The Corbomite Maneuver" [TOS]). Kirk used a corbomite bluff a second time in 2267 when he escaped from the Romulan Neutral Zone by claiming that the ship had a "corbomite device" that would explode, destroying all matter in a 200,000-kilometer radius. ("The Deadly Years" [TOS]).

Cordannas system. Location of a white dwarf star. The *Enterprise*-D's **emergent life-form** attempted to reach the Cordannas system to obtain **vertion** particles from the white dwarf in 2370. ("Emergence" [TNG]).

cordrazine. Powerful pharmaceutical stimulant used by Federation medical personnel. Dr. McCoy prescribed 2 milliliters of cordrazine to Lieutenant Sulu, who suffered serious electrical burns when the ship was investigating time-distortion waves in 2267 near the **Guardian of Forever**. Another time wave caused McCoy to receive an accidental overdose of cordrazine, whereupon he experienced extreme paranoid delusions and fled to a planet's surface. ("The City on the Edge of Forever" [TOS]). McCoy also used cordrazine to revive **Ensign Rizzo** when he was attacked by the **dikironium cloud creature**. ("Obsession" [TOS]). Dr. Beverly Crusher used 25 milliliters of cordrazine in a last-ditch effort to save Worf's life when his body rejected **genetronic replicator** therapy in 2368. ("Ethics" [TNG]). SEE: **tricordrazine**. In 2371, Dr. Julian Bashir used cordrazine when fighting to save Vedek Bareil's life after Bareil was injured in an explosion aboard a Bajoran transport. ("Life Support" [DS9]). The *Voyager*'s **Emergency Medical Hologram** used two milliliters of cordrazine to revive Harry Kim after he died on the Vhnori homeworld in 2371. ("Emanations" [VGR]). In 2372, Neelix suggested administering cordrazine to an ailing reptilian infant life-form, but Lieutenant Tom Paris rejected the idea as too dangerous. ("Parturition" [VGR]). The *Voyager*'s holographic doctor administered 50 milligrams of cordrazine to Tuvok in 2373 when he almost entered a coma due to a sudden disruption in the **hippocampus** during a **mind-meld**. ("Flashback" [VGR]). *Cordrazine was also mentioned in "Distant Voices" (DS9), "The Quickening" (DS9), and numerous other episodes of* Star Trek: Deep Space Nine *and* Star Trek: Voyager.

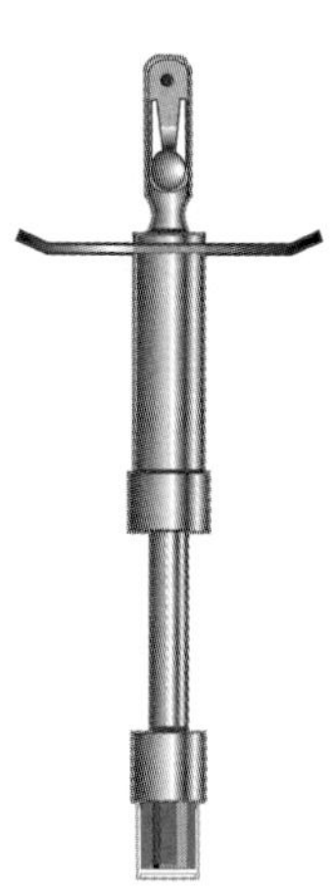

core behavior. Term coined by philosopher **Alixus** to describe humanity's essence, which would be released when people were free of technology. ("Paradise"[DS9]).

core breach. SEE: **antimatter containment.**

Corelki. *Enterprise*-D security officer. Corelki was assigned to the away team that investigated the attack on the **Ohniaka III** Outpost in 2368. She was killed in a **Borg** attack during the mission. ("Descent, Part I" [TNG]).

Coridan. Mineral-rich planet admitted to the **United Federation of Planets** in 2267. Coridan is rich in **dilithium** crystals, making the planet susceptible to illegal mining operations, which gave some motive to denying Coridan membership in the Federation during the Babel Conference, held in 2267 to consider Coridan's application to the Federation. ("Journey to Babel" [TOS]). The vote was affirmative, and Federation ambassador **Sarek** was credited with the Coridan admission. ("Sarek" [TNG]).

Corin. (Tahj D. Mowry). **Drayan** individual that, despite his advanced age, looked and acted like a young child. In 2372, Corin and several other elder Drayans traveled to one of the Drayan moons in order to carry out their **final ritual**. Their shuttle crashed on the moon and all of their **Attendants** died, leaving the elders alone. Lieutenant Tuvok, whose shuttle had also crashed there, comforted and took care of the easily confused Drayans. Corin died of natural causes on the **crysata** moon shortly thereafter. ("Innocence" [VGR]).

Corinth IV. Planet on which was located a Starfleet facility. When the *Enterprise* was delayed at planet **M-113**, the Starship Base on Corinth IV requested an explanation. ("The Man Trap" [TOS]).

cormaline. Mineral substance. The **Kazon-Ogla** mined cormaline. The crust of the **Ocampa planet** had rich deposits of the substance. ("Caretaker" [VGR]). Starfleet also mined cormaline. Rich deposits of cormaline were found on planet Torga IV in the Gamma Quadrant. ("The Ship" [DS9]).

corn salad. Dish made with kernels of an Earth grain. Neelix prepared corn salad for Chakotay. ("Faces" [VGR]).

Cornelian star system. Planetary system. Riker ordered the *Enterprise*-D toward the Cornelian star system in an attempt to escape the "hole" in space created by **Nagilum**. ("Where Silence Has Lease" [TNG]).

corophizine. Antibiotic. Corophizine was prescribed to Miles O'Brien to prevent secondary infection when he was critically ill due to the **aphasia virus** in 2369. ("Babel "[DS9]).

Correllium fever. Disease. Correllium fever broke out on planet **Nahmi IV** in 2366. ("Hollow Pursuits" [TNG]).

Corrigan. Starfleet officer. A member of James Kirk's graduating class from the academy. They met again at a bar at **Starbase 11** when the *Enterprise* was docked for repairs after an **ion storm** in 2267. The meeting was less than cordial because Corrigan believed Kirk had been responsible for the death of **Ben Finney**. ("Court Martial" [TOS]).

cortical analeptic. Pharmaceutical used to reinvigorate the tissues of the cerebral cortex. ("The Swarm" [VGR]).

cortical stimulator. Medical instrument used to revitalize neural activity in a humanoid nervous system. Used aboard Federation starships. Captain Jean-Luc Picard was treated with a cortical stimulator following his exposure to the **Kataan probe** on stardate 45944. ("The Inner Light" [TNG]). In 2371, *U.S.S. Voyager*'s Emergency Medical Hologram used two cortical simulators to return Commander Chakotay's **bio-neural energy** to his body. ("Cathexis" [VGR]). The holographic doctor also used a cortical stimulator on Tuvok when he suffered from a ***t'lokan* schism** ("Flashback" [VGR]) and to revive Kathryn Janeway following a near-fatal injury. ("Coda" [VGR]).

cortolin. Resuscitative drug. Used on station Deep Space 9. ("Necessary Evil" [DS9]).

corundium alloy. Material used in the construction of an alien probe that came through the **Bajoran** wormhole in 2369. ("The Forsaken" [DS9]). *The unnamed alien probe in "The Forsaken" was a modification of the* **Cytherian** *probe model originally built for "The Nth Degree" (TNG), with outboard antenna paddles added.*

Corvallan trader. Interstellar entrepreneur. A Corvallan trader served as one of the witnesses to the marriage of Juliana O' Donnell and **Dr. Noonien Soong** in 2332. ("Inheritance" [TNG]). Corvallan traders supposedly supplied the Yridian merchant Yog with **magnesite** ore in 2370. In truth, the Yridian was right in the middle, receiving the stolen ore from the **Duras sisters**. ("Firstborn" [TNG]).

Corvallen freighter. Cargo vessel of Corvallen registry. An *Antares*-class Corvallen freighter had been contracted to rendezvous with the Romulan warbird ***Khazara*** in 2369, part of the plan to enable Romulan **Vice-Proconsul M'ret** to defect to the Federation. The ship was destroyed by **Subcommander N'Vek** when it was believed that the captain of that ship did not intend to fulfill the contract and that the plan for M'ret's escape was therefore in jeopardy. ("Face of the Enemy" [TNG]). *The Corvallen freighter was another re-use of the* Batris *from "Heart of Glory" (TNG). One might therefore conjecture that other uses of this model represented* Antares-*class ships, and that perhaps this was also the design of the freighter blown up in "Charlie X" (TOS).*

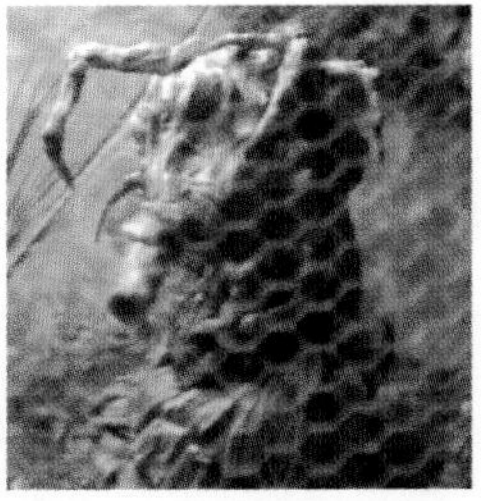

Corvan gilvos. A stick-like animal indigenous to the rainforests of **Corvan II**. The gilvos were uniquely suited to live in trees, as they closely resembled a tree branch. Their habitat was threatened by industrial pollutants on Corvan II, and by 2368, only 14 specimens remained. The *Enterprise*-D transported two gilvos to the protected planet of **Brentalia**. The gilvos were momentarily threatened by a fire that broke out aboard the *Enterprise*-D during their transport, but quick action by Commander Riker saved the animals. ("New Ground" [TNG]). *The gilvos was a hand puppet designed by makeup supervisor Michael Westmore. The same puppet (perhaps another surviving gilvos) was Grand Nagus Quark's pet in "The Nagus" (DS9).*

Corvan II. Federation planet whose ecosystem was threatened by industrial pollutants in the planetary atmosphere. The **Corvan gilvos** were among the animals threatened by the loss of rainforest habitat on that planet. ("New Ground" [TNG]).

Cory, Governor Donald. (Keye Luke). Governor and administrator of the Federation penal colony on planet **Elba II** who was violently overthrown by **Garth of Izar**, one of the inmates. ("Whom Gods Destroy" [TOS]).

Cos. (Albert Henderson). Humanoid who had suffered a long string of bad luck due to an unusual **gambling device**. In 2370, Cos shared a detention cell on Deep Space 9 with **Martus Mazur**. When Cos died, Martus took the gambling device. ("Rivals" [DS9]).

Cosimo. (Louis Giambalvo). A coffee shop owner in 24th-century San Francisco. An extradimensional intelligence posed as Cosimo in an alternate reality created when Ensign **Harry Kim**'s shuttle intersected one of Cosimo's **time stream**s in 2372. Cosimo was sent to watch Kim in the alternate reality, and eventually aided Kim in returning to the *U.S.S. Voyager*. Cosimo's civilization exists in a temporal inversion fold in the space-time matrix. ("Non Sequitur" [VGR]).

cosmic string fragment. An almost infinitely thin filament of almost infinitely dense matter. Although a string fragment can exhibit a gravitational pull of a hundred stars, it is no wider than a proton. Cosmic strings emanate a characteristic set of subspace frequencies which are caused by the decay of atomic particles along the string's event horizon. In 2367, the crew of the *Enterprise*-D used these harmonics to help guide a school of **two-dimensional creatures** back to their home in a cosmic string fragment. ("The Loss" [TNG]).

"Cost of Living." *Next Generation* episode #120. Written by Peter Allan Fields. Directed by Winrich Kolbe. Stardate 45733.6. *First aired in 1992. A planetary dignitary visits the* Enterprise-*D to be married to Lwaxana Troi, but he doesn't count on her being such a free spirit..* GUEST CAST: Majel Barrett as **Troi, Lwaxana**; Brian Bonsall as **Rozhenko, Alexander**; Tony Jay as **Campio, Minister**; Carel Struycken as **Homn**; David Oliver as Young humanoid man; Albie Selznick as Juggler; Patrick Cronin as **Erko**; Tracey D'Arcy as Young woman; George Ede as Poet; Christopher Halsted as 1st Learner; Majel Barrett as Computer voice. SEE: **antimatter containment; Campio, Minister; chrondite; Erko; exanogen gas; Jestral tea; Laughing Hour; Moselina system; nitrium; nitrium metal parasites; Parallax Colony; Pelloris Field; petrokian sausage; Shiralea VI; Tessen III; Troi, Lwaxana; wedding.**

Costa, Lieutenant. Member of the *Enterprise*-D engineering staff. ("The Mind's Eye" [TNG], "Hollow Pursuits" [TNG]).

Council of Elders. Group of **Organian** leaders who appeared to govern their planet. The actual nature of Organian government remains unknown because the Organians, contrary to the image that they chose to project to Federation and Klingon representatives, were incredibly advanced **noncorporeal life**-forms who shared little in common with their distant humanoid ancestors. For this reason, the Council of Elders expressed little concern when the Klingon occupational forces, led by **Commander Kor**, committed apparently horrific acts of oppression against the Organians in 2267. ("Errand of Mercy" [TOS]).

counselor. Starship officer responsible for the emotional well-being of the ship's crew. A counselor's duties included providing individual guidance and advice to crew members, as well as periodic crew performance evaluations, usually performed with the ship's executive officer or other department heads. A counselor is also expected to provide advice to the ship's captain on command decisions. **Deanna Troi** (pictured) was the counselor on the *Enterprise*-D. ("Man of the People" [TNG]).

counterinsurgency program. Security program installed into the computer system on station **Terok Nor** while the facility was still a **Cardassian** station. The counterinsurgency program was designed to activate automatically in case of a revolt by the station's **Bajoran** ore processing workers. It broadcast throughout the station a series of recorded visual messages of **Gul Dukat** entreating rebellious workers to surrender or face a series of escalating consequences, up to the destruction of the station. The counterinsurgency program was accidentally triggered in 2371, long after the station was no longer under Cardassian control. ("Civil Defense" [DS9]).

"Court Martial." Original Series episode #15. Teleplay by Don M. Mankiewicz and Steven W. Carabatsos. Story by Don M. Mankiewicz. Directed by Marc Daniels. Stardate 2947.3. *First aired in 1967. Kirk's career is jeopardized when he is put on trial for apparently causing the death of an* Enterprise *crew member.* GUEST CAST: Percy Rodriguez as **Stone, Commodore**; Elisha Cook as **Cogley, Samuel T.**; Joan Marshall as **Shaw, Areel**; Richard Webb as **Finney, Ben**; Hagan Beggs as **Hansen, Mr.**; Winston De Lugo as Timothy; Alice Rawlings as **Finney, Jamie**; Nancy Wong as Personnel officer; Bart Conrad as **Kransnowsky**; William Meader as **Lindstrom**, Space Command representative; Reginald Lal Singh as Chandra, Captain; Tom Curtis as **Corrigan**; Chuck Clow as Kirk's stunt double; Troy Melton as Finney's stunt double; Majel Barrett as Starbase recorder computer voice and Computer voice. SEE: **Alpha III, Statutes of; Chandra; Cogley, Samuel T.; Corrigan; Finney, Ben; Finney, Jamie; Hammurabi, Code of; Hanson, Mr.; *Intrepid*, *U.S.S.*; ion storm; Justinian Code; Kirk, James T.; Kransnowsky; Lindstrom; Magna Carta; Martian Colonies, Fundamental Declarations of the; Martian Colonies; McCoy, Leonard H.; Phase 1 Search; *Republic*, *U.S.S.*; Shaw, Areel; Spock; Starbase 11; Starfleet Command; Stone, Commodore; United States Constitution**.

***Cousteau*, Shuttlepod.** A shuttle vehicle from the *Starship Aries*. In 2367, the *Cousteau* was stolen by **Mendez** and abandoned on **Tarchannen III.** ("Identity Crisis" [TNG]). *The* Cousteau *was named for 20th-century oceanographer Jacques Cousteau.*

Coutu. (Philip LeStrange). Leader in the rebel faction on planet **Parada II** in 2370. Coutu discovered a Paradan government plot to sabotoge peace talks with the rebels using an exact replica of Miles O'Brien. Coutu was also responsible for rescuing the real O'Brien from government forces. ("Whispers" [DS9]). SEE: **Paradas**.

cove palm. A plant indigenous to planet **Ogus II**. The fruit of the plant contains a highly infectious parasite. **Willie Potts**, the child of an *Enterprise*-D crew member, accidently ate a cove palm fruit in 2367, requiring emergency treatment at a starbase. ("Brothers" [TNG]).

"cowboy diplomacy." Slang term that referred to actions taken impulsively by an individual on behalf of a government, without that government's sanction. Captain Picard accused Ambassador **Spock** of "cowboy diplomacy" in coming to **Romulus** in 2368 without the sanction of the Federation or Vulcan governments. ("Unification, Part II" [TNG]).

Coyote Stone. Icon placed on a Native American **medicine wheel**. In 2371, when **Commander Chakotay** was declared brain-dead after his **bio-neural energy** was displaced by the **Komar**, the Coyote Stone was one of several markers placed on the medicine wheel to guide Chakotay's soul back into his body, although placement at the crossroads of the fifth and sixth realms might divert his soul into the **Mountains of the Antelope Women**. ("Cathexis" [VGR]).

CPK enzymatic therapy. Medical treatment to limit the extent of spinal injury. ("Ethics" [TNG]).

CPK levels. A medical test performed aboard Federation starships. CPK, or creatinine phosphokinase, is a marker of muscular damage. It is mostly used to diagnose cardiac damage. ("Violations" [TNG]).

Crabtree, Susie. Former girlfriend to **Thomas Paris** during his first year at Starfleet Academy. In 2372, Paris told the **Emergency Medical Hologram** that he was depressed for almost a year after breaking up with Crabtree. ("Lifesigns" [VGR]).

cranial implant. Highly classified **Cardassian** biotechnological device used by the **Obsidian Order**. The implants, which were placed into the skulls of the order's operatives, were designed to stimulate the pleasure centers of the brain. This would release large quantities of **endorphins**, making the operative impervious to pain in the event the operative were tortured by an enemy. **Garak** volunteered to receive a cranial implant while in the **Obsidian Order**. The device was never designed for continuous operation for any length of time, so when Garak left it on for two years straight, it failed, causing excruciating pain. ("The Wire" [DS9]).

Crater, Nancy. (Jeanne Bal). The wife of archaeologist **Robert Crater**, Nancy Crater was killed some years prior to 2266 by the last surviving member of the civilization there. This creature had remarkable hypnotic abilities, able to masqurade as anyone, and chose to appear to Robert Crater in the image of his late wife. Prior to her marriage to Crater, Nancy had been romantically involved with **Leonard McCoy**. ("The Man Trap" [TOS]). SEE: **M-113 creature**.

Crater, Professor Robert. (Alfred Ryder). Reclusive archaeologist who studied the ruins on planet **M-113**. After his wife, **Nancy Crater**, was killed by the last surviving creature on that planet, Crater was unable to bring himself to kill that individual, choosing instead to befriend it. ("The Man Trap" [TOS]). *Actor Alfred Ryder suffered a severe arm injury just prior to filming. The injury was so painful he could not use his arm, but despite this, he performed his role without complaint.*

Cravic Automated Personnel Unit 122. (Rick Worthy). Humanoid automaton built by the **Cravic** people to fight in a war against robots built by the **Pralor**. Unit 122 commanded a Cravic vessel that encountered the *U.S.S. Voyager* in 2372. ("Prototype" [VGR]). SEE: **Pralor automated personnel unit**.

Cravic. Technologically sophisticated Delta Quadrant civilization that became extinct in a war with the **Pralor** people. The Cravic created sophisticated humanoid androids to fight their war with the Pralor. Later the entire Cravic society was destroyed when they attempted to deactivate these robotic soldiers. ("Prototype" [VGR]). SEE: **Pralor automated personnel unit**.

crayon. Children's drawing implement, generally containing wax-based pigment used to draw on paper. Guinan once noted that with a child's imagination, crayons can take you to more places than a starship can. ("Rascals" [TNG]).

Crazy Horse, U.S.S. Federation starship, *Excelsior* class. The *Crazy Horse* was part of task force 3, under Captain Picard's indirect command during an expected **Borg** invasion of late 2369. ("Descent, Part I" [TNG]). The *Enterprise*-D was ordered to rendezvous with the *Crazy Horse* in 2370 in order to pick up **Admiral Erik Pressman**. ("The *Pegasus*" [TNG]). *The* Crazy Horse *was named for the Oglala Sioux chief, who was one of the most important Native American leaders at the Battle of Little Bighorn in 1876.*

Creator. Term used by the machine life-form **V'Ger** to describe the agency responsible for its origin. In fact, V'Ger, originally known as ***Voyager VI***, had been created by humans on Earth in the late 20th century, although the immensely powerful and sophisticated V'Ger found it difficult to believe it had originated with such amazingly primitive creatures. *(Star Trek: The Motion Picture).*

Creators, Fabrini. SEE: **Fabrini Creators**.

credit chip. Instrument of monetary exchange used in the early 21st-century **United States** on **Earth**. ("Past Tense, Part I" [DS9]).

credit. Unit of monetary exchange used in the Federation. **Cyrano Jones** offered **tribble**s for sale at ten credits each, although he eventually settled for six credits. ("The Trouble With Tribbles" [TOS]). SEE: **monetary units**.

Creole food. Traditional style of Earth food cooked with a savory sauce containing peppers, tomatoes, onions, and the like. **Sisko's**, a restaurant in New Orleans on Earth, specialized in Creole food. ("Homefront" [DS9]).

Creole shrimp with Mandalay sauce. Spicy entrée made with shrimp and sautéed tomatoes. Benjamin Sisko prepared Creole shrimp from his father's recipe. ("The Abandoned" [DS9]).

crew manifest. A computer file containing biographical and Starfleet data on crew members aboard a Federation starship. ("Conundrum" [TNG]). *The bridge crew manifest in "Conundrum" contained numerous biographic details about our series regulars. Some of these data points were based on information established in earlier shows, but much was somewhat conjectural. For the most part, we're assuming this information is accurate, unless contradicted by information in an episode.*

CRM 114. Large portable hand cannon made by the **Breen**. The CRM-114 was designed to destroy moving vessels and surface emplacements, and was guaranteed to cut through reactive armor in the 6 to 15 centimeter range. It could also penetrate shields up to 4.6 gigajoules in strength. ("Business As Usual" [DS9]).

Crockett, U.S.S. Federation starship. The *Crockett* conveyed **Admiral Mitsuya** to station Deep Space 9 in 2370. ("Paradise" [DS9]). *The* Crockett *was named after Davey Crockett, American frontiersman and politician.*

Croden. (Cliff De Young). Fugitive from the planet **Rakhar** in the **Gamma Quadrant**. He was picked up in a damaged shuttlecraft and brought to Deep Space 9 in 2369. In a botched robbery attempt, Croden killed the **Miradorn** Ro-Kel, which caused his twin brother, **Ah-Kel,** to vow revenge. While in **Odo**'s jail, Croden told the shape-shifter he'd met others of his kind and offered as proof a unique necklace whose contents changed form. While Odo was returning Croden to his homeworld, Odo learned that Croden's "crime" was having spoken out against his government. For punishment, most of his family was killed. Croden fled from the government, but was able to save only one member of his family, his daughter, **Yareth**, whom he hid on an asteroid in the **Chamra Vortex**. Odo returned Croden to the asteroid, where the necklace served as a key to unlock a stasis chamber in which Yarneth was hidden. Odo then allowed Croden and his daughter to leave on a Vulcan transport ship to start a new life. ("Vortex" [DS9]). SEE: **toh-maire**.

croissant. Type of bread developed in the nation of France on planet Earth. The croissant was baked from a flaky wheat-based dough that was rolled into crescent-shaped pieces. It was a favorite breakfast food of *Enterprise*-D captain Jean-Luc Picard and Chief Medical Officer Beverly Crusher. ("Attached" [TNG]).

Crosis. (Brian Cousins). One of the self-aware, fanatical **Borg** who began attacking Federation colonies in 2369. Crosis beamed aboard the *Enterprise*-D as part of a diversion to allow a Borg ship to escape. He was captured and was confined in the ship's brig. Crosis revealed himself to be one of a group of followers of a persona called "**The One**." While there, he was able to convince Commander **Data** to release him and they left the ship in a stolen shuttlecraft. Crosis took Data back to the base of these new Borg. Once there, Data was reunited with his brother, **Lore**. ("Descent, Parts I and II" [TNG]).

"Crossfire." *Deep Space Nine* episode #85. Written by René Echevarria. Directed by Les Landau. No stardate given. *First aired in 1996. Odo's hidden feelings for Kira interfere with his duty to protect the Bajoran First Minister.* GUEST CAST: Duncan Regehr as **Shakaar Edon**; Bruce Wright as **Sarish**; Charles Tentindo as **Jimenez**. SEE: **arbiter; Bajoran First Minister; Bajoran wormhole; Bolian cuisine; Bolian restaurant; Breen; Ijarna; Jimenez, Ensign; *kava*; Kira Nerys; Odo; Oguy Jel; Rafalian mouse; *raktajino*; Sarish Rez; Shakaar Edon; Takaran wildebeest; *targ*; Tonsa, Vedek; Trellan crocodile; True Way, The.**

"Crossover." *Deep Space Nine* episode #43. Teleplay by Peter Allan Fields & Michael Piller. Story by Peter Allan Fields. Directed by David Livingston. No stardate given. *First aired in 1994. Bashir and Kira find themselves in a mirror universe where the Klingons and Cardassians have formed an alliance and have conquered humans. This episode continues the story begun in "Mirror, Mirror" (TOS).* GUEST CAST: Andrew Robinson as **Garak, Elim**; John Cothran Jr. as **Telok**; Stephen Gevedon as Klingon #1; Jack R. Orend as Human; Dennis Madalone as Marauder. SEE: **Alliance; Bajor (mirror); Bajoran wormhole; Boldaric masters; Deep Space 9; Drathan puppy lig; Fowla system; Garak (mirror); Helewa, Isam; Intendant; *jumja* tea; Kira Nerys (mirror); lambda designation; mirror universe; New Bajor; O'Brien, Miles (mirror); Odo (mirror); plasma injector; Quark (mirror); Sisko, Benjamin (mirror); Spock (mirror); Telok; Terok Nor (mirror); Terran Empire; Terran; theta designation; thorium; Tor Jolan.**

crown roast of lamb. Culinary main course consisting of a rack of lamb formed into a circle and roasted. While incarcerated in an Akritirian prison satellite, Tom Paris dreamed of having crown roast of lamb when he was free again. ("The Chute" [VGR]).

Cruses System. The last known location of a Tarkanian diplomat who was believed to be a co-conspirator of **J'Dan** in the theft of Federation technological secrets in 2367. ("The Drumhead" [TNG]).

Crusher, Dr. Beverly. (Gates McFadden). **Chief medical officer** aboard the *Enterprise*-D under the command of **Jean-Luc Picard**. Crusher was born Beverly Howard in 2324, and graduated from medical school in 2350. She was at the **Arvada III** colony, and helped her grandmother, Felisa Howard ("Sub Rosa" [TNG]) care for the survivors of that terrible tragedy. Although her grandmother was not a physician, she taught Beverly much about the

medicinal uses of herbs and roots to help care for the sick and wounded after regular medical supplies had been exhausted. ("The Arsenal of Freedom" [TNG]).

Beverly was introduced to her future husband, Starfleet officer **Jack Crusher**, by their mutual friend **Walker Keel**. ("Conspiracy" [TNG]). She married Jack in 2348, and the two had a child, **Wesley Crusher**, the following year. As a young married couple, Beverly and her husband Jack spent a great deal of time with Jean-Luc Picard. She did not learn until many years later that Picard had fallen in love with her, but he didn't act on his feelings in order to not betray his friend. ("Attached" [TNG]). Crusher did her internship on planet Delos IV under the tutelage of **Dr. Dalen Quaice** in 2352. ("Remember Me" [TNG]). Following her husband's death in 2354, Beverly continued to pursue her Starfleet career, attaining the position of chief medical officer aboard the *Enterprise*-D in 2364. ("Encounter at Farpoint" [TNG]). Crusher left the *Enterprise*-D in 2365 to accept a position as head of Starfleet Medical, but returned to the ship a year later, and was reunited with her son, Wesley. ("Evolution" [TNG]). In 2366, Crusher became romantically interested in a man from planet **Zalkon** whom she had named **John Doe**. ("Transfigurations" [TNG]). The following year, she became involved with a **Trill** named **Ambassador Odan**. Although the two were very much in love, Beverly found it difficult to accept her lover inhabiting a different body. ("The Host" [TNG]). Beverly's grandmother, **Felisa Howard**, died in 2370, and Beverly returned to her grandmother's home at the **Caldos Colony** to speak at the funeral. Beverly discovered her grandmother had taken a lover, apparently a 34-year-old man named **Ronin**, who was actually an **anaphasic life-form** that had been a "spirit lover" of Howard women for 20 generations. Beverly was at first taken in by Ronin, and even went so far as to resign from Starfleet to remain on Caldos with him, before Beverly was forced to kill him in order to protect her friends. ("Sub Rosa" [TNG]).

Although a physician aboard a starship is not normally regarded as a line officer, Crusher was left in command of the *Enterprise*-D when virtually the entire crew was transported to the surface of a planet to search for Data in early 2369. Crusher employed the **metaphasic shield** technology which the ship had aquired from **Dr. Reyga** in order to escape a pursuing **Borg ship** and rescue the crew on the surface. ("Descent, Part II" [TNG]). Later that year, Crusher was severely injured by Worf, who was under the influence of **Barclay's Protomorphosis Syndrome**. She was placed in stasis and required reconstructive surgery. ("Genesis" [TNG]). *Crusher's stint in stasis helped facilitate the fact that Gates McFadden was directing this episode.*

Beverly was quite an accomplished dancer. Her colleagues named her "The Dancing Doctor," a nickname she disliked, so aboard the *Enterprise*-D she did her best to avoid demonstrating her skills. Nevertheless, the fact that she had won first place in a dance competition in St. Louis was part of her Starfleet record, so Data asked her to help him learn to dance for the wedding of **Miles O'Brien** and **Keiko Ishikawa** in 2367. ("Data's Day" [TNG]). Beverly also had a strong interest in amateur theatrics and was director of a successful theater company aboard the *Enterprise*-D. Among the productions performed by her company in 2367 was ***Cyrano de Bergerac***. ("The Nth Degree" [TNG]). Several months later, her troupe performed Gilbert and Sullivan's ***The Pirates of Penzance***. ("Disaster" [TNG]). Crusher wrote a play for her troupe, called *Something for Breakfast*. ("A Fistful of Datas" [TNG]). Another play written by Crusher was entitled ***Frame of Mind***. ("Frame of Mind" [TNG]).

Beverly's maiden name, Howard, is from her biographical computer screen in "Conundrum" (TNG), named for Star Trek: The Next Generation *producer Merri Howard, although the name was used for her maternal grandmother. Gates McFadden left the* Star Trek *cast in the second season, during which the chief medical officer was played by Diana Muldaur as* Dr. Katherine Pulaski *(which is why Crusher left the ship to become head of Starfleet Medical during that year). McFadden and Crusher returned to the* Enterprise-*D during the third and subsequent seasons. Beverly Crusher first appeared in "Encounter at Farpoint" (TNG).*

Crusher, Jack R. (Doug Wert). Starfleet officer, husband to **Beverly Crusher**, and father to **Wesley Crusher**. Jack Crusher, a close friend to Captain **Jean-Luc Picard**, married medical student Beverly Howard in 2348. Crusher had proposed to Beverly by giving her a gag gift, a book entitled *How to Advance Your Career Through Marriage.* Their son, Wesley, was born a year later. ("Family" [TNG]). During their marriage, Crusher and his wife spent extended periods of time with his friend, Jean-Luc Picard. Crusher was never aware that his friend, Picard, was strongly attracted to Beverly. When Wesley was young, Jack and Beverly took him on a camping trip to Balfour Lake. ("Attached" [TNG]). Lieutenant Commander Jack Crusher served aboard the ***U.S.S. Stargazer*** under the command of Captain Picard and was killed on an away mission in 2354, when his son was only five years old. ("Encounter at Farpoint, Parts I and II" [TNG]). Shortly after Wesley's birth, Jack recorded a holographic message to his infant son, intended for playback when Wesley reached adulthood. Jack hoped this would be the first in a series of such messages, but it was the only one he made. Wesley played the message some 18 years later, in 2367. ("Family" [TNG]). *Even though Jack Crusher died several years before the first season of* Star Trek: The Next Generation*, we've seen him three times. The first was in Wesley's holographic message in "Family" (TNG), and then briefly again in Beverly's* ***telepathic memory invasion*** *flashback in "Violations" (TNG), and in Wesley's vision in "Journey's End" (TNG).*

Crusher, Wesley. (Wil Wheaton). Son of Starfleet officers **Jack Crusher** and **Beverly Crusher**. Wesley was born in 2349 and was raised by his mother following the death of his father, Jack, in 2354 when Wesley was five years old ("True Q" [TNG]). Wesley went to live on the *Starship Enterprise*-D in 2364, when his mother was assigned to that ship as chief medical officer. ("Encounter at Farpoint, Parts I and II" [TNG]). Wesley spent little time with his father before his death, but recalled that Jack taught him to play baseball. ("Evolution" [TNG]).

Wesley showed a keen interest in science and technology, and had an extraordinary ability to visualize complex mathematical concepts, an ability that the **Traveler** once urged Captain Picard to nurture. Perhaps in response, Picard commissioned Crusher an acting ensign on stardate 41263.4 in recognition of Wesley's key role in returning the *Enterprise*-D to Federation space after it was stranded by **Kosinski**'s failed warp-drive experiments. ("Where No One Has Gone Before" [TNG]).

As a member of an away team to planet **Rubicun III**, Crusher inadvertently broke a local law and was sentenced to death by the planetary government. Crusher was later freed by *Enterprise*-D captain Picard, although Picard acknowledged that the act violated the Prime Directive. ("Justice" [TNG]). Wesley's first experience with command was when Commander Riker assigned him the task of supervising geological surveys of the planets in the **Selcundi Drema** sector in 2365. Although Crusher initially found it difficult to supervise people older than himself, he eventually found that the experience built self-confidence, and Crusher's leadership led to scientifically important discoveries. ("Pen Pals" [TNG]). Crusher conducted a test using medical **nanites** in 2366, accidentally resulting in the creation of an enhanced version of the tiny robots, possessing enough intelligence to be considered a legitimate life-form. The nanites were so recognized and granted colonization rights on planet **Kavis Alpha IV**. ("Evolution" [TNG]).

Wesley's first romantic interest was with the lovely young **Salia**, leader of planet **Daled IV**. Although not human, Salia was a shape-shifting **allasomorph** who appeared as a teenaged human girl whose keen intelligence and wit captured his interest. ("The Dauphin" [TNG]).

Wesley first attempted to gain entrance to **Starfleet Academy** in 2364 at age 15. ("Coming of Age" [TNG]). Although he did not win admission at that time, he continued his studies and gained academic credit for his work aboard the *Enterprise*-D. ("Evolution" [TNG], "Samaritan Snare" [TNG]). Wesley was accepted to Starfleet Academy in 2366, but missed his transport to the academy because he was participating in a rescue mission after William Riker, Deanna Troi, and Lwaxana Troi had been kidnapped by Ferengi DaiMon Tog. In recognition of his sacrifice, Captain Picard granted Wesley a field promotion to the rank of ensign shortly after the incident. ("Ménage à Troi" [TNG]). Wesley finally entered **Starfleet Academy** in 2367 when a position opened up mid-term in the current class. His final assignment as part of the *Enterprise*-D crew was to accompany Captain Picard on a diplomatic mission to planet **Pentarus V**. The mission was interrupted when their transport shuttle, the ***Nenebek***, crashed on **Lambda Paz**, after which Captain Picard became critically injured. Crusher cared for Picard until a rescue party arrived. ("Final Mission" [TNG]).

Crusher's first year at the academy went well, and he even gained entry into the academy's elite **Nova Squadron** flight team. ("The First Duty" [TNG]). Wesley returned to the *Enterprise*-D for a brief visit on stardate 45208, where he became very fond of Mission Specialist **Robin Lefler**. ("The Game" [TNG]). Crusher's sophomore year was marred by a serious incident in which he and other members of Nova Squadron attempted a prohibited maneuver, and Cadet **Joshua Albert** died in the resulting accident. Although initial testimony by members of the squadron suggested Albert was responsible for the accident, Crusher later came forward with the truth. A reprimand was entered into Crusher's academic record, and he was forced to repeat his sophomore year. ("The First Duty" [TNG]).

Wesley Crusher became disenchanted with his studies at Starfleet and resigned his commission to the academy in 2370, choosing instead to live among the Native American colonists on planet Dorvan V, a world currently under Cardassian jurisdiction. Crusher's decision to leave Starfleet in favor of self-exploration was a difficult one, aided by insight offered by the Traveler. ("Journey's End" [TNG]). SEE: **Kolvoord Starburst; Locarno, Cadet First Class Nicholas.**

(In an alternate **quantum reality** visited by Worf in 2370, Wesley Crusher had not left the *Enterprise*-D but had remained, achieved the rank of Lieutenant, and was assigned to tactical. ["Parallels" (TNG)].)

Wesley Crusher first appeared in "Encounter at Farpoint." Wesley left the series during the fourth season (in "Final Mission" [TNG]), although he has since returned for "The Game" (TNG) ,"The First Duty" (TNG), "Parallels" (TNG), and "Journey's End" (TNG). At one point early in preproduction for Star Trek: The Next Generation, *supervising producer Bob Justman had convinced Roddenberry to make the character Wesley into Leslie, a female teenager. Wesley was named for* Star Trek *creator Gene Roddenberry, whose middle name was Wesley.*

cryogenic open-heart procedure. Surgical procedure used to repair damaged cardiac tissue using temperatures near absolute zero. *Enterprise* chief surgeon Leonard McCoy used a cryogenic open-heart procedure to repair a damaged heart valve of Vulcan Ambassador **Sarek** in 2267. This procedure required a large amount of the rare **T-negative** blood type, donated by his son, Spock. ("Journey to Babel" [TOS]).

cryonetrium. Substance that remains gaseous at cryogenic temperatures near absolute zero. The *Enterprise*-D warp drive systems were flooded with gaseous cryonetrium in 2366 to halt the effects of **invidium** contamination. ("Hollow Pursuits" [TNG]).

cryonics. Old practice of cryogenically freezing a human just after death in the hopes that future medical advances would render their sickness curable. Some cryogenically frozen bodies were actually sent into space in orbiting satellites for long-term storage. One such **cryosatellite** was discovered in 2364 by the Starship *Enterprise*-D. Cryonics was something of a fad in the late 20th century but fell into disuse by the mid-21st century. ("The Neutral Zone" [TNG]).

cryosatellite. An ancient space vessel launched in the late 20th century carrying a cargo of cryogenically preserved humans from Earth. These individuals had all died in the late 20th century, but their bodies had been frozen and sent into space. The **cryosatellite** drifted in space for some 300 years before being discovered near the **Kazis Binary** star system by the *Enterprise*-D. Although most of the satellite's storage modules had failed, three individuals were revived: **Claire Raymond**, **Sonny Clemonds**, and **Ralph Offenhouse**. All three were later returned to Earth on the *Starship* ***Charleston***. ("The Neutral Zone" [TNG]). SEE: **cryonics; sleeper ship**. *The cryosatellite was designed by Rick Sternbach and Mike Okuda. Extremely close examination of the model might have revealed tiny letters reading* "S.S. Birdseye" *inscribed on the hull. The model was later modified and used as Subspace Relay Station 47 in "Aquiel" (TNG).*

cryostasis chamber. Storage device used to preserve living beings at cryogenic temperatures for later revival. Over 300 people including Amelia Earhart were abducted from Earth in 1937 and brought to the **Briori** homeworld in the Delta Quadrant to work as slaves. Noted Earth aviator **Amelia Earhart** and seven others remained in cryostasis on the planet until they were revived by the crew of the *U.S.S. Voyager* in 2371. ("The 37's" [VGR]).

cryostasis. Medical procedure used to slow down biological functions in a critically injured patient, allowing the physician more time to correct the malady. Dr. Julian Bashir wanted to put **Hon'Tihl**, the critically injured first officer of a Klingon vessel, into cryostasis on stardate 46922, but the patient died shortly after transport to Deep Space 9. ("Dramatis Personae" [DS9]).

cryostatic chamber. Device used to sterilize foods by subjecting them to extremely cold temperatures. ("Flashback" [VGR]).

cryostatic suspension. A method of suspended animation used by manager **Bahrat** to punish criminals on the **Nekrit Supply Depot station** in the Delta Quadrant. The punishment for trafficking in illicit substances was 50 years of cryostatic imprisonment. ("Fair Trade" [VGR]).

cryptobiolin. One of several chemicals used by the **Angosians** during the **Tarsian War** to "improve" their soldiers, making them more effective in combat. Unfortunately, the effects of cryptobiolin were irreversible. ("The Hunted" [TNG]). SEE: **Danar, Roga**.

crysata. A place considered sacred by the **Drayan** people of the Delta Quadrant. One of the moons around planet Drayan II was a crysata used for the **final ritual**. ("Innocence" [VGR]).

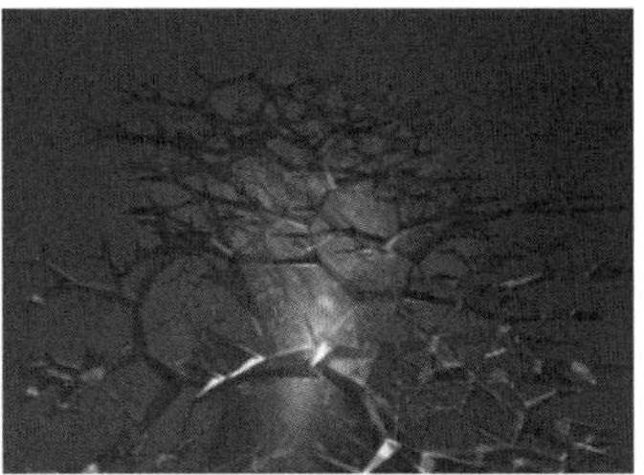

Crystalline Entity. A spaceborne life-form of unknown origin whose structure resembled a large snowflake, hundreds of meters across. The Crystalline Entity apparently thrived by absorbing the energy of biological life-forms on planets, leaving behind devastated planetary surfaces. The Crystalline Entity was responsible for the destruction of the **Omicron Theta** colony (including all inhabitants) in 2336. The androids **Data** and **Lore**, who were dormant underground at the time of the attack, escaped harm. It was believed that Lore had betrayed the colonists to the entity just prior to the attack. ("Datalore" [TNG]). Colony residents **Dr Noonien** and **Dr. Juliana Soong** both fled during the attack aboard an escape pod, although Juliana Soong was severely injured. ("Inheritance" [TNG]). In subsequent years, **Dr. Kila Marr**, whose son died at Omicron Theta, studied the entity, examining 12 attack sites, including planet **Forlat III**. The entity's last attack was in 2368 at the **Melona IV** colony. Shortly thereafter, Marr destroyed the entity with a modulated **graviton** beam. ("Silicon Avatar" [TNG]).

crystalline emiristol. Solid chemical rocket propellant used in the ancient space probe launched from the **Kataan** system a thousand years ago. It left a radioactive trail that allowed the *Enterprise*-D to trace the probe's point of origin. ("The Inner Light" [TNG]).

crystilia. Species of flowering plant found on planet Telemarius III. **Data** presented a bunch of orange and yellow crystilia to Lieutenant **Jenna D'Sora**. ("In Theory" [TNG]).

Cuellar system. A star system located in **Cardassian** space. The Cuellar system was the location of a Cardassian science station that was destroyed by the ***U.S.S. Phoenix*** in 2367. *Phoenix* captain Benjamin Maxwell believed the station to be a military installation. ("The Wounded" [TNG]).

Culluh, Jal. (Anthony DeLongis). First **maje** of the **Kazon-Nistrim**. In 2371, Culluh helped set up a deal with *Voyager* crew member **Seska**, in which Seska agreed to provide Federation replicator technology to the Kazon-Nistrim. When *Voyager* personnel discovered Seska's scheme, she transported over Culluh's ship and escaped. ("State of Flux" [VGR]). Later, with the assistance of **Seska**, Culluh conducted a raid on the ***U.S.S. Voyager***, using a Kazon shuttlecraft to pierce the hull of the *Voyager*. The purpose of the attack was to steal a **transporter** module, so that the Nistrim would then have transporter technology, and thereby gain an advantage over other Kazon sects. Although the raid was successful, the transporter module was later destroyed. Culluh's grandfather was first maje of the Nistrim when it was powerful, but the sect grew weak under Culluh's leadership. ("Maneuvers" [VGR]). In 2372 Culluh accepted a proposal by *Starship Voyager* Captain Kathryn Janeway to form an alliance, but demanded an exchange of crew, therefore negating the Federation offer. Shortly after that, he reluctantly attended a peace conference on planet **Sobras** organized by Janeway and **Trabe** leader **Mabus**. The meeting proved to be a trap devised by Mabus to eliminate the Kazons. ("Alliances" [VGR]). In late 2372, Maje Culluh and Seska were successful in capturing the *Starship Voyager* by convincing Chakotay that Seska's child was his and that it was in danger. Culluh and his forces stranded the *Voyager* crew on planet **Hanon IV**. ("Basics, Part I" [VGR]). Seska's newborn son was actually fathered by Culluh, not Chakotay. After Seska was killed in an explosion, and Talaxian forces, led by Tom Paris, retook the *Voyager,* Culluh took his infant son and ordered the Kazon to flee. ("Basics, Part II" [VGR]).

cultural database. Archive of information stored in computers on Federation starships. The cultural database contained information pertaining to the rites and customs of all civilizations known to the Federation. ("Sacred Ground" [VGR]).

Cumberland, Acts of. Twenty-first-century legal document relating to property rights. Judge Advocate General **Phillipa Louvois** cited the Acts of Cumberland in her initial ruling in 2365 that the android Data was the property of Starfleet and therefore could not resign or refuse to cooperate in proposed experiments. ("The Measure of a Man" [TNG]).

Curie, Marie. Earth physicist (1867-1934), co-discoverer (with Pierre Curie) of radium and polonium. Marie Sklodowska Curie earned two Nobel Prizes for her study of radioactivity. In 2373, *Voyager's* **Emergency Medical Hologram** incorporated segments of Marie Curie's personality into his personality improvement project. ("Darkling" [VGR]).

Curie, Shuttlecraft. Type-6 personnel shuttle assigned to the *U.S.S. Enterprise*-D. In 2370, Lieutenant Worf took the *Curie* to Forcas III to compete in the *bat'leth* competition there. During his return trip, Worf encountered a **quantum fissure** and caused himself to be propelled into a series of alternate **quantum realities**. When Worf's quantum shifting was finally discovered, the *Curie* was used to seal the quantum fissure, by sending the ship back through the rift and emitting a **broad-spectrum warp field**. ("Parallels" [TNG]). Later that same year, **Joret Dal** was sent back across the Cardassian border in the *Curie*. The ship was not returned. ("Lower Decks" [TNG]). *Named for physicist Marie Sklodowska Curie.*

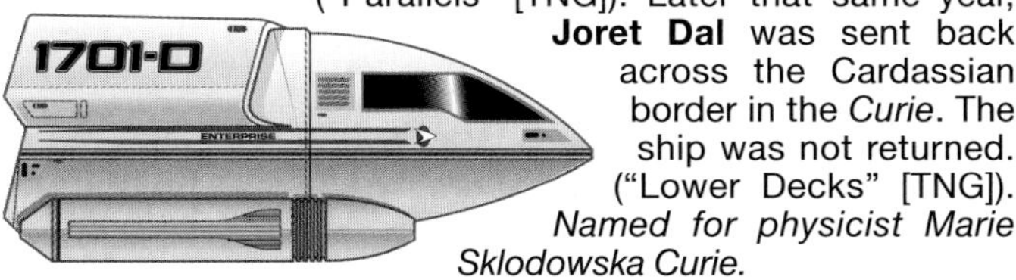

Curtis Creek program. A holodeck program that simulated a mountain stream on planet Earth. The program was mentioned during a virtual reality engineered by **Barash** on Alpha Onias III. Barash, as **Jean-Luc Riker**, told his "father," William Riker, that they used to fish in the Curtis Creek program. ("Future Imperfect" [TNG]).

Custodian, The. Sophisticated computer system built and programmed hundreds of centuries ago by the **Progenitors** of planet **Aldea**. The custodian provided for virtually all the needs of the citizens of Aldea, freeing them to pursue lives of artistic endeavor. ("When the Bough Breaks" [TNG]).

cutter. Slang term used to refer to a member of an asteroid mining team. Cutters split asteroids with phasers so that excavators could gain access to the asteroid's interior. ("Nor the Battle to the Strong" [DS9]).

cyalodin. Poison. The adult members of the **Starnes Expedition** used cyalodin in their mass suicide on planet **Triacus** in 2268. ("And the Children Shall Lead" [TOS]).

cyanoacrylates. Substances capable of generating low levels of **eichner radiation**. Cyanoacrylates, which could also stimulate growth of some strains of plasma plague, were not normally found aboard *Galaxy*-class starships. ("The Child" [TNG]). *Cyanoacrylate is actually a chemical term used to describe several types of fast-bonding adhesives, notably the stuff sold under the brand name "Krazy Glue." The use of this term here was scientifically inappropriate, but was apparently intended as a gag.*

cybernetic regeneration. Medical treatment. *Enterprise*-D chief medical officer Beverly Crusher conducted some research into cybernetic regeneration. ("11001001" [TNG]). Dr. Crusher published a paper on the subject during her tenure aboard the *Enterprise*-D. While the paper was not widely known, it did spark the interest of neurogeneticist **Dr. Toby Russell**. ("Ethics" [TNG]).

Cygnet XIV. Planet. Cygnet XIV's government was dominated by women when the original *Starship Enterprise* docked there for general repair and maintenance of the ship's computer system in 2267. The technicians on Cygnet XIV felt the computers lacked a personality and gave them one—female, with a tendency to flirt and giggle. ("Tomorrow is Yesterday" [TOS]).

Cygnia Minor. Planet. Location of an Earth colony threatened by famine in 2266 that a new synthetic food supposedly created by **Dr. Thomas Leighton** would have helped. Unfortunately, the report of a synthetic food was a ruse to summon the *Enterprise* to **Planet Q** with the hopes of confronting the actor **Anton Karidian**. ("The Conscience of the King" [TOS]).

Cygnian Respiratory Diseases, A Survey of. A computer disk in the medical library of the original *Starship Enterprise*. When **Ensign Garrovick** refused food shortly after stardate 3619, Nurse Chapel showed him the disk, telling him that it contained an order from Dr. McCoy to eat. ("Obsession" [TOS]). Dr. Julian Bashir studied a 24th-century edition of the publication in 2371 while preparing for a visit by his medical school class valedictorian, Dr. Elizabeth Lense. ("Explorers" [DS9]).

Cyprion cactus. Plant species notable for sharp spines, six to 12 centimeters in length. Cyprion cacti were cultivated in the *Enterprise*-D **arboretum**. Commander Riker accidentally rolled over on one during a visit to the arboretum with Tactical Officer Smith just prior to stardate 47653. ("Genesis" [TNG]).

Cypriprdium. Flowering plant native to Earth. Cypriprdium is an orchid of the Asiatic genus *Paphiopedilum* and has also been seen on a Class-M planet in the **Delta Quadrant**. The common Earth name is Lady's slipper or Moccasin flower. ("Tattoo" [VGR]).

Cyrano De Bergerac. French play by Edmond Rostand, first performed on Earth in 1897. Dr. Beverly Crusher's acting workshop, held aboard the *Enterprise*-D, performed *Cyrano* in 2367. Lieutenant **Reginald Barclay** played the title role. ("The Nth Degree" [TNG]).

Cyrillian microbe. Single-celled organism. ("The Q and the Grey" [VGR]).

Cytherians. Humanoid civilization that resides on a planet near the center of the galaxy. The Cytherians made outside contact, not by traveling through space, but by bringing space travelers to them. The Cytherians sent out specially designed probes that would reprogram some types of computers with instructions to bring travelers to the Cytherians. The *Enterprise*-D encountered one such probe in 2367. The Cytherian probe had attempted to reprogram the computers on the **Argus Array** and then attempted to reprogram an *Enterprise*-D shuttlecraft onboard computer. The probe was finally able to program Lieutenant **Reginald Barclay**'s mind to bring the *Enterprise*-D to the Cytherians. The *Enterprise*-D spent ten days in the company of the Cytherians, exchanging a great deal of cultural and scientific information. ("The Nth Degree" [TNG]). *The Cytherian probe model was later modified and reused in "The Forsaken" (DS9).*

cytoplasmic protein. Biochemical compounds contained in the jellylike cytoplasm of plant cells. ("Tuvix" [VGR]).

cytoplasmic stimulator. Medical instrument. A cytoplasmic stimulator was used to stabilize cellular toxicity levels in Neelix after his lungs were removed by the **Vidiians** in 2371. ("Phage" [VGR]).

d'akturak. Klingon word for ice man. Curzon Dax used it in 2289 to describe **Koloth**, who was an unyielding negotiator for his people. ("Blood Oath" [DS9]).

D'Amato, Lieutenant. (Arthur Batanides). *Enterprise* senior geologist killed in 2268 on a landing party to the mysterious **Kalandan outpost**. D'Amato was killed by **cellular disruption** caused by a mechanism devised to protect the planetoid. ("That Which Survives" [TOS]). SEE: **Losira.**

D'Arsay. Ancient humanoid civilization. Little is known about the D'Arsay, except that they flourished nearly a hundred million years ago, and that they had both spaceflight capability and a culture rich in mythology. The fate of the D'Arsay is unknown. ("Masks" [TNG]). SEE: **D'Arsay archive**.

D'Arsay archive. Spaceborne data-storage facility launched over 87 million years ago by a civilization known as the **D'Arsay**. The archive was discovered by the crew of the *Enterprise*-D in the center of a **rogue comet** in 2370. The archive contained records of artifacts and personalities from D'Arsay mythology. Using the ship's replicator, the archive transformed part of the ship into the setting of an epic drama involving Masaka, a sun goddess. The archive also altered the positronic programming of Commader Data to portray several characters from the Masaka myth. Among the D'Arsay characters portrayed by Data were a D'arsay boy, **Ihat**, **Masaka**, a victim, and an elder who was Masaka's father. The archive transformed parts of the Enterprise-D into an aqueduct, a swamp, and a temple. It also filled a photon torpedo with snakes, and turned Engineering into a fiery inferno. Captain Picard portrayed himself as **Korgano**, another D'Arsay mythic figure, in order to convince the archive to return the ship and Data back to their normal states. ("Masks" [TNG]).

D'Arsay symbols. Pictograms from ancient **D'Arsay** mythology representing characters and events from those stories. D'Arsay symbols were loaded into the *Enterprise*-D's computer by the **D'Arsay archive**. The icon believed to be **Masaka**'s symbol was also interpreted by Data to mean "death." ("Masks" [TNG]). *The symbols used in this episode were designed by Wendy Drapanas and Jim Magdaleno, loosely based on ancient Aztec and Mayan designs.*

d'blok. Klingon animal. ("The Way of the Warrior" [DS9]).

***D'deridex*-class warbird.** Designation for a massive Romulan spacecraft. These ships, significantly larger than a *Galaxy*-class starship, are believed to have greater firepower, but a slightly lower sustainable warp speed. ("Tin Man" [TNG]). Starfleet at one time designated these ships as B-Type warbirds. ("The Defector" [TNG]). *The* D'deridex-*class warbird was designed by Andrew Probert and first seen in "The Neutral Zone" (TNG).*

D'Ghor. (Carlos Carrasco). Head of a wealthy **Klingon** family. From 2366 through 2371, D'Ghor systematically attacked the financial assets of the **House** of **Kozak**, with the intention of acquiring the Kozak's wealth for himself. This would have made D'Ghor powerful enough to gain a seat on the **Klingon High Council**. After Kozak's death in 2371, D'Ghor's plans were thwarted by intervention from Kozak's widow, **Grilka**, and her new husband, **Quark**. D'Ghor's financial machinations resulted in his being shamed by the High Council. ("The House of Quark" [DS9]).

D'jarra. In **Bajoran** society, the *D'jarras* were once a system of castes. A family's *D'jarra* dictated social status as well as what occupation its members could hold. Members of one *D'jarra* were not permitted to associate with members of a lesser *D'jarra*. The *D'jarra* system was abolished around 2328, when all Bajorans were called upon to fight Cardassian oppression, regardless of caste. The experience of working together for that common goal helped Bajorans understand that all people are created equal. ("Accession" [DS9]). SEE: **Akorem Laan.**

d'k tahg. Traditional Klingon warrior's knife. A vicious, three-bladed weapon, the *d'k tahg* is commonly used in hand-to-hand combat, and has great ceremonial value in Klingon culture. *(Star Trek III*, "The Bonding" [TNG], "Redemption, Part I [TNG], "Birthright, Part II" [TNG], "The Way of the Warrior" [DS9]). *The Klingon knife, first used to kill* ***David Marcus*** *in* Star Trek III, *was designed by Phil Norwood. It was also seen in "The Bonding" (TNG) and several later episodes. It was given a name in "Birthright, Part II" (TNG). When it was used for the* Next Generation, *the original prop was not available, so Rick Sternbach duplicated the design for the show's prop makers, using a* Star Trek *trading card for reference.*

***D'Kora* class.** Class designation of a **Ferengi** maurauder ship. *D'Kora*-class ships typically carried a crew of 450. ("Force of Nature" [TNG]). *The term* D'Kora *class was first used in "Force of Nature," but we assume that previous Ferengi marauder ships were also* D'Kora-*class vessels.*

D'Sora, Lieutenant Jenna. (Michele Scarabelli). Security officer aboard the *Enterprise*-D. Lieutenant D'Sora pursued a brief romantic relationship with Lieutenant Commander **Data** in late 2367, shortly after she broke up with **Jeff Arton**. The relationship did not prove successful. ("In Theory" [TNG]).

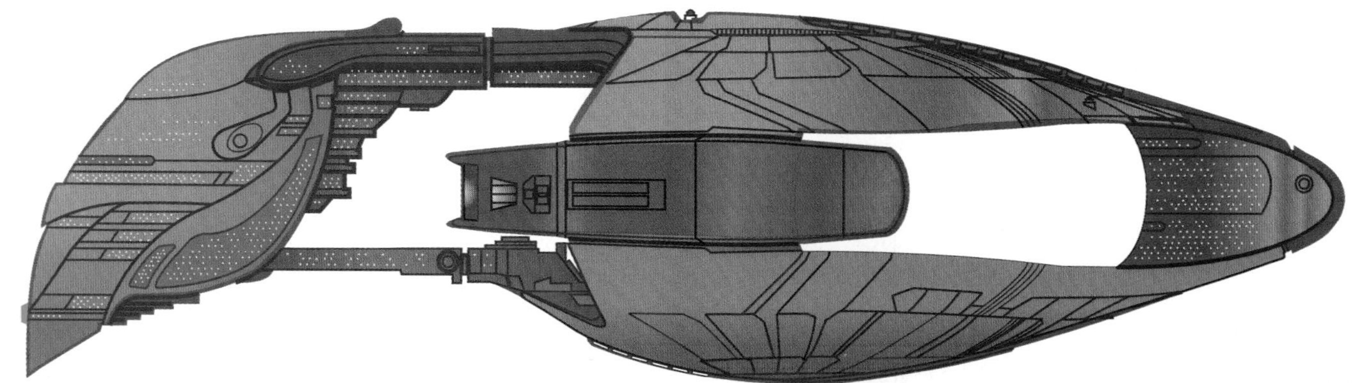

D'Tan. (Vidal Peterson). Romulan citizen, born in 2356, raised as a member of the Romulan reunification underground. As a youth, D'Tan was a friend of Ambassador **Spock**. ("Unification, Part II" [TNG]).

D7. SEE: **Klingon battle cruiser**.

da Vinci, Leonardo. (1452-1519). Influential artist, inventor, and scientific theorist of planet Earth's Renaissance period. Leonardo da Vinci's interests and achievements were numerous and diverse. His masterly paintings of the Last Supper and Mona Lisa are but two of his wondrous works. Da Vinci's visionary thinking postulated the possibilities of flying machines and automation. In 2373, *Voyager's* **Emergency Medical Hologram** incorporated segments of Leonardo da Vinci's personality into his personality improvement project. ("Darkling" [VGR]).

dabo girl. Beautiful women of various species who were employed as **dabo** game operators by **Quark** at his bar on Deep Space 9. Quark correctly believed that scantily-clad dabo girls significantly enhanced his revenues. ("Captive Pursuit" [DS9]). SEE: **Mardah; Leeta; Sarda, Miss**.

dabo. Game of chance played on a roulette-like wheel located in **Quark's bar** on the **Promenade** of station **Deep Space 9**. ("Emissary" [DS9]). "Double down" and "triple over" were among the wagers that could be made in dabo. "Pass 5" was a possible outcome. ("Starship Down" [DS9]).

Dachlyds. Civilization. During the mid-24th century, Dachlyds were involved in a trade dispute with their nearest neighbors, the Gemarians. Captain Jean-Luc Picard helped mediate the dispute in 2366 to help both parties arrive at a mutually beneficial solution. ("Captain's Holiday" [TNG]).

Daedalus*-class starship.** One of the first types of starships commissioned and operated under the auspices of the United Federation of Planets. These ships were among the first to demonstrate the primary/secondary hull and warp nacelle designs that would become characteristic of **Starfleet** vessels. The ***U.S.S. Essex, destroyed in 2167 at **Mab-Bu VI**, was a *Daedalus*-class starship. The *Daedalus* class was retired from service in 2196. ("Power Play" [TNG]). *We speculate that the* **U.S.S. Horizon** *("A Piece of the Action" [TOS]) and the* **U.S.S. Archon** *("Return of the Archons" [TOS]) were also of the* Daedalus *class. A conjectural design for this class, based on an early* Enterprise *design by Matt Jefferies and built by Greg Jein, is pictured here. This model has been seen as a desktop display in* Star Trek: Deep Space Nine.

"Dagger of the Mind." Original Series episode #11. Written by S. Bar-David. Directed by Vincent McEveety. Stardate 2715.1. *First aired in 1966. The* Enterprise *investigates a revolutionary treatment for the criminally insane, but the new device kills with loneliness. Spock first performs the Vulcan mind-meld in this episode. S. Bar-David was the pen name of writer Shimon Wincelberg, who also wrote "The Galileo Seven" and episodes of* Lost in Space *using the same pen name.* GUEST CAST: James Gregory as **Adams, Dr. Tristam**; Morgan Woodward as **Van Gelder, Dr. Simon**; Marianne Hill as **Noel, Dr. Helen**; Susanne Wasson as **Lethe**; John Arndt as First crewman; Larry Anthony as Transportation man; Ed McCready as Inmate; Eli Behar as Therapist; Walter Davis as Therapist; Irene Sale as Dr. Noel's stunt double. SEE: **Adams, Dr. Tristam; Central Bureau of Penology, Stockholm; Lethe; neural neutralizer; Noel, Dr. Helen; Tantalus V; Van Gelder, Dr. Simon; Vulcan mind-meld**.

Daggin. (Eric David Johnson). Gardener who worked in a botanical garden in the Ocampas' subterranean complex at the time of the **Caretaker**'s death. ("Caretaker" [VGR]).

DaH! Klingon for "Now!" ("Redemption, Part II" [TNG]).

***Dahar* Master**. Highly honored title bestowed upon only the greatest of **Klingon** warriors. Kor was a *Dahar* Master. ("Blood Oath" [DS9]).

Dahkur Hills. Locale on planet **Bajor**. In 2361, during the Cardassian occupation, **Kira Nerys** and members of the **Shakaar** spent a winter in the Dahkur Hills, hounded by Cardassian troops. ("Second Skin" [DS9]).

Dahkur Province. Geographical subdivision of the planet **Bajor**. Dahkur was the home province of **Kira Nerys** ("Second Skin" [DS9]), as well as other members of the **Shakaar resistance cell**. Resistance members utilized the mountainous terrain of Dahkur to hide from the Cardassians during the occupation. In 2371, Dahkur Province became the site of a minor political struggle over the possession of two **soil reclamators**. ("Shakaar" [DS9]). A Cardassian records office was located in Dahkur during the occupation. Shakaar cell member **Trentin Fala** worked at the records office, cleaning floors, and serving as an informant to the resistance. ("The Darkness and the Light" [DS9]).

Daily, Jon. Captain of the passenger vessel ***Astral Queen***. At the request of *Enterprise* Captain James Kirk, Daily bypassed a scheduled stop at **Planet Q**, forcing the **Karidian Company of Players** to request passage aboard the *Enterprise*. ("The Conscience of the King" [TOS]).

DaiMon. Title given to **Ferengi** leaders, approximately equivalent in rank to a Starfleet captain. ("The Last Outpost" [TNG]).

Dakar, Senegal. City in French West Africa on planet Earth where **nanites** were manufactured. ("Evolution" [TNG]).

Dakeen Monastery. Religious temple on planet **Bajor**. During the week prior to the **Kendra Valley Massacre**, religious leader **Vedek Bareil** was on retreat at the Dakeen Monastery. ("The Collaborator" [DS9]).

Dal'Rok. Cloudlike energy creature that threatened a Bajoran village for five nights every year. The village was saved each time by the **Sirah**, who would tell heroic tales of the village people, repelling the evil entity. In actual fact, the Dal'Rok was an illusion created from the fears of the villagers by the Sirah, who used a small fragment of an **Orb** from the **Celestial Temple** to create a common enemy that would unite the people of the village. ("The Storyteller" [DS9]).

Dal, Joret. (Don Reilly). Member of the Cardassian military. Dal was also a Federation operative who provided Starfleet with invaluable information about Cardassian strategic intentions. In 2370, he returned to Cardassian space in the ***Shuttlecraft Curie*** with **Ensign Sito,** who was posing as a Bajoran terrorist. ("Lower Decks" [TNG]).

Dalby, Kenneth. (Armand Schultz). **Maquis** resistance fighter who joined the crew of the ***Voyager***. Dalby spent his troubled youth on the **Bajoran** frontier, settling down for a time when he fell in love. His anger returned when the woman he loved was raped and murdered by **Cardassians**, and Dalby subsequently joined the **Maquis**. During the first few weeks after the *Starship Voyager* was lost in the Delta Quadrant in

2371, Dalby became regarded as a disruptive and unreliable worker. Accordingly, Dalby was among several Maquis crew members assigned to Lieutenant Tuvok for **field training**. ("Learning Curve" [VGR]).

Daled IV. Planet that revolves only once every planetary year, so that one hemisphere is always in light, while the other is in eternal night. For centuries, Daled IV had been torn by civil war between inhabitants of the two hemispheres. In the late 2340s, two parents from opposite sides conceived a child named **Salia**, and sent her to the nearby planet **Klavdia III** to be raised in a neutral environment. Salia returned to Daled IV at age 16 in the hopes of uniting the factions and bringing peace to her world. Daled IV was not a member of the Federation. ("The Dauphin" [TNG]).

Daliwakan. Humanoid life-form. A holographic character of a gigolo who frequented **Chez Sandrine** in a Tom Paris holodeck simulation was half-human and half-Daliwakan *(and played by Luigi Amodeo)*. ("The Cloud" [VGR]).

Dalvin hissing beetle. Insectoid life-form. Alexander Rozhenko kept a Dalvan hissing beetle as a pet. Counselor Troi agreed to care for the animal while Alexander was visiting his grandparents in 2370. ("Parallels" [TNG]).

Damar, Glinn. (Casey Biggs). Cardassian officer. Damar was assigned to the freighter *Groumall* in 2372, under the command of Gul Dukat. Damar went with Dukat after he commandeered a Klingon bird-of-prey and began a one-ship offensive against the Klingons. ("Return to Grace" [DS9], "Apocalypse Rising" [DS9]). *Rank (glinn) is from the script.*

dampening field. Energy field that inhibits transmission of most forms of energy, including communications. In 2371, a dampening field was activated on Deep Space 9 as part of a Level-1 counter-insurgency protocol. The dampening field remained in effect until the station staff were able to overload the station's power grid. ("Civil Defense" [DS9]).

Danar, Gul. (Vaughn Armstrong). Commander of the Cardassian warship ***Aldara***. Gul Danar demanded the return of the Bajoran terrorist **Tahna Los,** whom Commandar Sisko had given asylum on Deep Space 9 in 2369. ("Past Prologue" [DS9]).

Danar, Roga. (Jeff McCarthy). A male native of **Angosia III**, Danar volunteered for duty as a soldier in his planet's **Tarsian War**. His government put Danar through extensive psychological manipulation and biochemical modifications, making him extremely aggressive in combat, and programming him to be the perfect warrior. He served in many campaigns during that conflict and received two promotions to the rank of subhadar. In 2366, Danar became a leader of a veterans' uprising that forced the Angosian government to reconsider the plight of their ex-soldiers. ("The Hunted" [TNG]).

"Dancing Doctor, The." A nickname that **Dr. Beverly Crusher** acquired after winning a dance competition at a Saint Louis dance academy. Aboard the *Enterprise*-D, she did her best to hide her talent in dance to avoid the moniker. ("Data's Day" [TNG]).

Daneeka. Starfleet officer who was assigned to the ***U.S.S. Okinawa*** at the time Benjamin Sisko was the vessel's executive officer. In 2372, Daneeka and several other former *Okinawa* officers were reassigned to Earth and nearby starships by **Admiral Leyton** in preparation for Leyton's planned military coup of Earth's government. ("Paradise Lost" [DS9]).

Dano, Kal. A 27th-century scientist who invented the ***Tox Uthat***, a device with enormous weapons potential. Fearful that the device would be stolen, Dano fled to the 22nd century, where he hid the *Uthat* on planet **Risa**. ("Captain's Holiday" [TNG]).

Danula II. Planet; the site of a **Starfleet Academy marathon** in 2323. Freshman cadet **Jean-Luc Picard** managed to overtake two upperclassmen on the final hill of that 40-kilometer run to become the only freshman ever to win the Starfleet Academy marathon. ("The Best of Both Worlds, Part II" [TNG]).

Dar, Caithlin. (Cynthia Gouw). Romulan representative to the **Paradise City** settlement on planet **Nimbus III**, assigned in 2287. An idealistic young woman, Dar believed the colony might still serve as a catalyst for galactic peace, despite the failure of the project for the past two decades. Under the mental influence of Sybok, Dar joined **Sybok**'s quest for the mythical planet ***Sha Ka Ree***. *(Star Trek V: The Final Frontier).*

Dara. (Michelle Forbes). Daughter to noted Kaelon scientist **Timicin**, and the mother of his only grandson. Dara visited Timicin aboard the *Enterprise*-D in 2367 to plead with him to return home and carry out his **Resolution**. ("Half a Life" [TNG]). *Michelle Forbes would later return as Ensign Ro Laren.*

Daran V. Inhabited planet. Daran V had a population of 3,724,000, and was directly in the path of the **Fabrini** spaceship ***Yonada*** in 2268. Assistance by *Enterprise* personnel diverted *Yonada* from its collision course, sparing the inhabitants of both worlds. ("For the World Is Hollow and I Have Touched the Sky" [TOS]).

Daras. (Valora Noland). **Ekosian** resistance fighter who was presented the Iron Cross award by Deputy Fuhrer **Melakon** for apparently betraying her father to her planet's Nazi party in 2268. Daras's actions were actually part of the Ekosian underground's efforts to discredit Melakon and the Nazi party. ("Patterns of Force" [TOS]).

Daren, Neela. (Wendy Hughes). *Enterprise*-D scientist who headed the ship's **Stellar Cartography department** in 2369. An accomplished pianist, Lieutenant Commander Neela Daren discovered that Captain **Jean-Luc Picard** played a **Ressikan flute,** and the two enjoyed playing duets together. Their mutual appreciation for music soon blossomed into a romantic relationship. When a fierce firestorm threatened lives on planet **Bersallis III**, Neela Daren was chosen to supervise installation of **thermal deflector** units to protect the outpost. Daren and several other crew members risked their lives by operating the deflectors manually so all colonists could be safely transported to the ship. After the incident, it became obvious to both that it would be extremely difficult to continue their relationship because Picard would hesitate to place her in danger again. Each refusing to give up their professions, Neela Daren requested a transfer off the *Enterprise*-D. ("Lessons" [TNG]).

Darhe'el, Gul. (Harris Yulin). Cardassian commander of the infamous **Gallitep** labor camp on planet **Bajor**. Under Darhe'el's authority, thousands of **Bajorans** were tortured and killed while working under brutal conditions. Also known as **The Butcher of Gallitep**, Darhe'el committed acts of violence against the people of Bajor that won him admiration from his superiors and earned him the Proficient Service Medallion. When ordered to leave Gallitep, Darhe'el ordered all the Bajoran laborers be slaughtered, although several did escape. Darhe'el died in his sleep in 2363 from a massive

coleibric hemorrhage, and was buried under one of the largest military monuments on Cardassia with full honors. In 2369, Darhe'el's file clerk from Gallitep, a man named **Aamin Marritza**, impersonated Darhe'el in hopes of exposing the atrocities that had been committed at Gallitep. ("Duet" [DS9]). SEE: **Kalla-Nohra Syndrome**. *Okay, maybe Harris Yulin didn't actually play Gul Darhe'el. But he played a guy who looked exactly like him.*

"Dark Page." *Next Generation* episode #159. Written by Hilary J. Bader. Directed by Les Landau. Stardate 47254.1. *First aired in 1993. Counselor Troi enters her mother's mind to bring her out of a coma and learns of a sister that she never knew she had.* GUEST CAST: Majel Barrett as **Troi, Lwaxana**; Norman Large as **Maques**; Kirsten Dunst as **Hedril**; Amick Byram as **Troi, Ian Andrew (senior)**; Andreana Weiner as **Troi, Kestra**. SEE: **Cairn; Folnar III, Folnar jewel plant; Hedril; Maques; metaconscious; paracortex; psilosynine; Troi, Deanna; Troi, Ian Andrew (senior); Troi, Kestra; Troi, Lwaxana.**

dark-matter nebula. Interstellar gas or dust cloud that emits or reflects little or no detectable light or other energy. In 2371 trianic energy beings known as the **Komar,** inhabiting a dark-matter nebula in the Delta Quadrant, unsuccessfully attempted to absorb the **bio-neural energy** from the crew of the *Starship Voyager*. ("Cathexis" [VGR]). Neelix once lost a warp nacelle on a ship that he piloted through a dark-matter nebula. ("Threshold" [VGR]).

"Darkling." *Voyager* episode #61. Teleplay by Joe Menosky. Story by Brannon Braga & Joe Menosky. Directed by Alex Singer. Stardate 50693.2. *First aired in 1997. The Emergency Medical Hologram incorporates personalities from several historical figures with disastrous results.* GUEST CAST: Christopher Clarke as **Byron, Lord**; Noel de Souza as **Gandhi, Mahatma**; Stephen Davies as **Nakahn**; David Lee Smith as **Zahir**. SEE: **Byron, Lord; cateline; Curie, Maria; da Vinci, Leonardo; Emergency Medical Hologram; Gandhi, Mahatma; H'ohk, Professor; Hippocratic Oath; holodeck and holosuite programs: EMH program 4-C; Polynesian resort; intraspinal inhibitor; *kal-toh*; Kes; Mikhal Travelers; Nakahn; Socrates; Sylleran Rift; T'Pau; Tarkan; vorilium; Zahir.**

"Darkness and the Light, The." *Deep Space Nine* episode #109. Teleplay by Ronald D. Moore. Story by Bryan Fuller. Directed by Michael Vejar. Stardate 50416.2. First aired in 1997. *Members of Kira's old Shakaar resistance cell begin turning up dead, systematically picked off by an unknown assailant who taunts the major after each killing. Despite her pregnancy, she is unable to remain helpless, and travels alone into the Demilitarized Zone to track down the one responsible.* GUEST CAST: Randy Oglesby as **Silaran, Prin**; William Lucking as **Furel**; Diane Salinger as **Lupaza**; Jennifer Savidge as **Trentin Fala**; Aron Eisenberg as **Nog**; Matt Roe as **Latha Mabrin**; Christian Conrad as **Brilgar**; Scott McElroy as Guard; Judi Durand as Station computer voice. SEE: **Bajoran Days of Atonement; Bajoran militia; Brilgar; Calash Retreat; Dahkur Province; Demilitarized Zone; Feregi Rules of Acquisition: #111; Furel; Hathon; hunter probe; Kira Nerys; Latha Mabrin; Lupaza; *makara* herb; merfadon; Mobara; Musilla Province; Pirak; plasma charge; polaron; Prin, Silaran; Ramirez, Captain; remat detonator; security access code; Shakaar resistance cell; sinoraptor; skimmer; Starbase 63; Talavian freighter; *tongo*; Trentin Fala.**

"Darmok and Jalad at Tanagra." A **Tamarian** phrase that referred to a mythological hunter on planet Shantil III and his companion Jalad, who met and shared a danger at the mythical island of Tanagra. In the Tamarian metaphorical language, the phrase indicated an attempt to understand another by sharing a common experience. ("Darmok" [TNG]).

"Darmok." *Next Generation* episode #102. Teleplay by Joe Menosky. Story by Philip LaZebnik and Joe Menosky. Directed by Winrich Kolbe. Stardate 45047.2. *First aired in 1991. An alien ship captain strands himself and Captain Picard on a planet in hopes of helping Picard understand a language based entirely on metaphors. This episode marked the first appearance of the new midsized shuttlecraft.* GUEST CAST: Richard Allen as **Kentor**; Colm Meaney as **O'Brien, Miles**; Paul Winfield as **Dathon**; Ashley Judd as **Lefler, Ensign Robin**; Majel Barrett as Computer voice. SEE: **annular confinement beam; Children of Tama; "Darmok and Jalad at Tanagra"; Dathon; El-Adrel IV; El-Adrel system; Enkidu; Gilgamesh; Homeric hymns; Lefler, Ensign Robin; *Magellan, Shuttlecraft*; "Shaka, when the walls fell"; *Shiku Maru;* Silvestri, Captain; "Sokath, his eyes uncovered!"; Tamarians.**

Darnay's disease. A deadly ailment that attacks the brain and nervous system of its victims. **Dr. Ira Graves** died of Darnay's disease in 2365. ("The Schizoid Man" [TNG]).

Darnell, Crewman. (Michael Zaslow). *Enterprise* security officer killed in 2266 by the **M-113 creature**. ("The Man Trap" [TOS]).

Daro, Glinn. (Tim Winters). **Cardassian** aide to **Gul Macet**. Daro was aboard the *Enterprise*-D as an observer, as the *Enterprise*-D searched for the renegade *Starship* ***Phoenix*** in 2367. Daro made friendly overtures to Chief **Miles O'Brien**, but O'Brien found it difficult to be cordial to an ex-enemy. ("The Wounded" [TNG]).

Darod. (Tom Todoroff). Member of the **Alsaurian resistance movement** on a planet of the **Mokra Order** in the Delta Quadrant. In 2372, Darod helped the crew of the *Starship Voyager* obtain tellerium. When Tuvok and Torres were captured by the Mokra Order, Darod helped Kathryn Janeway and Caylem rescue them from prison. Darod had thought Caylem to be a coward, but later after witnessing his bravery, Darod swore that he would spread the word of Caylem's heroism. ("Resistance" [VGR]).

darseks. Unit of monetary exchange at the Klingon outpost on **Maranga IV**. ("Firstborn" [TNG]).

Darson, Captain. Commanding officer of the Federation starship ***Adelphi***. Darson was among 47 people killed in the notorious first-contact mission at Ghorusda. Darson was later found responsible for the **Ghorusda disaster**. ("Tin Man" [TNG]).

Darthen. Coastal city on planet **Rekag-Seronia**. Darthen had been neutral throughout the bitter wars on that planet, and served as the site of a peace conference in 2369 conducted by Federation mediator **Alkar**. ("Man of the People" [TNG]).

darts. Indoor game of skill involving the throwing of pointed projectiles at a circular target. The game originated on **Earth** during the middle ages and became very popular on that planet during the 19th and 20th centuries. In 2371 Chief **O'Brien** installed a dartboard in one of the cargo bays on station **Deep Space 9.** ("Prophet Motive" [DS9]). A few weeks later, he convinced **Quark** to put up the dartboard in his bar. ("Visionary" [DS9]). O'Brien even enjoyed a remarkable 46-game winning streak in late 2371, during which he felt he was "in the zone." ("Shakaar" [DS9]). Chief Miles O'Brien and Doctor Julian Bashir played a regular weekly game of darts. ("Hippocratic Oath" [DS9]).

Darvin, Arne. (Charlie Brill). Klingon agent who posed as a Federation bureaucrat in the late 23rd century. Darvin was an assistant to **Nilz Baris**, who was in charge of the development project for **Sherman's Planet**. Darvin, who had been surgically altered to appear human, was arrested for having poisoned the **quadrotriticale** stored at **Deep Space Station K-7** to sabotage

the Federation's development project on Sherman's Planet in 2267. ("The Trouble with Tribbles" [TOS]). The diplomatic embarrassment to the Klingon government over the Sherman's Planet incident marked the end of his career in Klingon Intelligence. Darvin spent the next hundred years eking out a meager existence, posing as a human merchant named Barry Waddle. When the Cardassian government returned the **Orb of Time** to the Bajoran government in early 2373, Darvin seized the opportunity to use the Orb to send him and the *Starship Defiant* back in time to 2267. In the past, Darvin unsuccessfully tried to murder Captain **James T. Kirk**, whom he blamed for his fall from grace. Darvin believed that Kirk's death would change the outcome of the Sherman's Planet incident, so that his younger self would not live his life in disgrace. Darvin had hoped that killing Kirk would have earned him a statue in the **Hall of Warriors**. ("Trials and Tribble-ations" [DS9]).

***darvot* fritters.** Breakfast food. Neelix made *darvot* fritters from vegetables from *Voyager*'s hydroponics bay. To be properly prepared, *darvot* fritters should be rotated every ten minutes until they turn a deep chartreuse. ("Phage" [VGR]). *"Never, never rotate the chef every ten minutes," cautions Bob Justman. "He'll turn chartreuse, the fritters will turn puce, and I'll turn and run." Promises, promises....*

Darwin Genetic Research Station. Federation science facility located on planet **Gagarin IV**, headed by **Dr. Sara Kingsley**. In the late 2350s and 2360s, a research project at the Darwin Station developed human children who had an aggressive immune system, capable of attacking disease organisms before they entered a human body. The children's antibodies were also capable of attacking human beings, a fact not discovered until 2365, when the entire crew of the ***U.S.S. Lantree*** was killed after exposure to the children. The scientific staff of the Darwin Station were also afflicted by the antibodies and suffered symptoms resembling hyperaccelerated aging, but a transporter-based technique was successful in restoring all station personnel to normal. ("Unnatural Selection" [TNG]). *The Darwin Station was named for naturalist Charles Darwin (1809-1882), who postulated the theory of evolution. The exterior of the station was a matte painting created by Illusion Arts. The painting was later re-used in other episodes, including as the science station in "Descent, Part I" (TNG).*

Darwin, Frank. *Starship Voyager* engineer. In 2372, Darwin was murdered while at his engineering post by fellow crew member **Lon Suder**. ("Meld" [VGR]).

data clip. Handheld information storage device. In 2370, command personnel from **Deep Space 9** reviewed information from a **Kellerun** data clip relating to the supposed death of **Dr. Julian Bashir** and **Miles O'Brien**. ("Armageddon Game" [DS9]).

data crystal. Small and very sophisticated information storage device. The **Idanian** intelligence agency used a data crystal to store **Arissa**'s memories. The data crystal was equipped with security features that prevented unauthorized access to the information contained inside. ("A Simple Investigation" [DS9]).

"Data's Day." *Next Generation* episode #85. Teleplay by Harold Apter and Ronald D. Moore. Story by Harold Apter. Directed by Robert Wiemer. Stardate 44390.1. *First aired in 1991. A typical day in the life aboard the* Enterprise-*D as seen through the eyes of Data. This is the episode in which we first meet Keiko, who marries Miles O'Brien. We also see the* Enterprise-*D barber shop and Data's cat for the first time.* GUEST CAST: Rosalind Chao as **O'Brien**, **Keiko**; Colm Meaney as **O'Brien**, **Miles**; Sierra Pecheur as **T'Pel**, **Ambassador**; Alan Scarfe as **Mendak**, **Admiral**; Shelly Desai as **V'Sal**; April Grace as Transporter technician. SEE: **Adelphous IV; Andorians; autosequencers; barber shop; bio-mechanical maintenance program; Crusher, Dr. Beverly; "Dancing Doctor, The"; Data; Daystrom Institute of Technology; *Devoras*; *Enterprise*-D, *U.S.S.*; feline supplement 74; Galvin V; Hindu Festival of Lights; Juarez, Lieutenant; Maddox, Commander Bruce; Mendak, Admiral; Mot; Murasaki Effect; O'Brien, Keiko; O'Brien, Miles; phase transition coils; Replicating Center; Selok, Subcommander; Spot; T'Pel, Ambassador; transporter carrier wave; transporter ID trace; Umbato, Lieutenant; wedding; *Zhukov*, *U.S.S.***

Data. (Brent Spiner). A humanoid android so sophisticated that he was regarded as a sentient life-form with full civil rights. Data was a Starfleet officer who served as operations manager under the command of Captain Jean-Luc Picard aboard the *Starship Enterprise*-D ("Encounter at Farpoint, Part II" [TNG]) and later, aboard the *Starship Enterprise*-E *(Star Trek: First Contact)*.

Creation. Data was built around 2335 by the reclusive scientist **Noonien Soong** (pictured) and his wife, **Juliana Soong**, at the **Omicron Theta** colony. Data was actually the fifth **positronic** android constructed by Soong; the first three were unsuccessful. ("Inheritance" [TNG]). The fourth, the first to become functional, was known as **Lore**. ("Datalore" [TNG]). SEE: **Soong-type android**. Lore exhibited dangerous behavior, forcing Soong to disassemble him. Soong thereafter pursued the idea of building an android free of emotions. Soong hoped this new android would not exhibit the cruelty shown by Lore. Juliana had wanted Data to have a female form, but Noonien, as before, created Data in his own image. Following his activation, Data was much like a baby, though he was made in the form of a full-grown adult. Data had difficulty learning basic social skills, and "social niceties" had to be built into his programming. SEE: **modesty subroutine**. In addition, a creative capacity was also programmed into Data by Mrs. Soong, who reasoned that, without emotions, the android would need another way to express himself. After this initial period, Data was thought unsuccessful and was deactivated. ("Inheritance" [TNG]). He was programmed with the logs and journals of the Omicron Theta colonists in an effort to help Data function better in human society. ("Datalore" [TNG], "Silicon Avatar" [TNG]). Unfortunately, before Data could be reactivated, the **Crystalline Entity** attacked the colony, and Soong and his wife, Juliana, were forced to abandon their work. Fearing that, when reactivated, Data might behave as Lore did, Juliana made Dr. Soong leave Data at the colony site. ("Inheritance" [TNG]). Data remained in a dormant condition underground, where he was discovered in 2338 by the crew of the *Starship* ***Tripoli***. Data subsequently joined the Starfleet and eventually became **operations manager** aboard the *Enterprise*-D. ("Datalore" [TNG]).

Form and function. Data was based on a sophisticated positronic brain developed by Soong, from concepts first postulated in the 20th century by **Dr. Isaac Asimov**. ("Datalore" [TNG]). Data's body closely mimicked humanoid form, and contained approximately 24.6 kilograms of tripolymer composites, 11.8 kilograms of molybdenum-cobalt alloys, and 1.3 kilograms of bioplast sheeting. ("The Most Toys" [TNG]). His upper spinal support was polyalloy, while his skull was composed of cortenide and **duranium**. ("The Chase" [TNG]). Soong went to extraordinary lengths to create a naturalistic human appearance in Data. He gave Data a functional respiration system, although its purpose was primarily for thermal regulation. (Data was in fact capable of functioning for extended periods in a vacuum. ["Brothers" (TNG)].) He gave Data a pulse and a circulatory system that distributed biochemical lubricants and regulated microhydraulic power throughout Data's body. Data's hair was even capable of growth at a controllable rate. ("Birthright, Part I" [TNG]). Data did not require food; he occasionally ingested a semi-organic nutrient suspension in a silicon-based liquid medium. ("Déjà Q" [TNG]). Although Data's systems were primarily mechanical, cybernetic, and positronic, sufficient biological components were present to allow him to become infected by the **Psi 2000 virus** in 2364. While under the influence of the inhibition-stripping effects of that disease, Data became intimate with *Enterprise*-D security chief **Tasha Yar** (pictured). ("The Naked Now" [TNG]). Data's basic programming included a strong inhibition against harming living beings, but he nevertheless had the ability to use deadly force to protect others. ("The Most Toys" [TNG]).

Data in Starfleet. Prior to his assignment to the *Enterprise*-D, Data served aboard the ***U.S.S. Trieste***. During this tour-of-duty, the *Trieste* once fell through a **wormhole**. ("Clues" [TNG]). Aboard the *Enterprise*-D, Data served as operations manager, and was in charge of coordinating the many departments aboard the ship. ("Encounter at Farpoint" [TNG]). In 2366, Commander Data was seriously injured trying to save Q from an attack by gaseous creatures called the **Calamarain**. In gratitude, Q gave Data the gift of allowing Data to experience human laughter for a brief time. ("Déjà Q" [TNG]). Data served as father of the bride for the wedding of **Miles O'Brien** and **Keiko Ishikawa** in 2367, and found it necessary to learn to dance to fulfill this ceremonial function. ("Data's Day" [TNG]). Data's first opportunity to command a starship came during the Federation blockade during the **Klingon civil war** of 2368. Data was assigned temporary command of the *Starship* ***Sutherland*** in Picard's armada. As an android, Data encountered a small amount of prejudice among his human crew, but was nevertheless able to lead effectively. ("Redemption, Part II" [TNG]). In late 2368, when bizarre evidence was found suggesting that he had died some 500 years ago, Data traveled back in time to old **San Francisco**. The evidence was Data's severed head, unearthed from beneath the city of San Francisco, where it had been buried for five centuries. ("Time's Arrow, Part I" [TNG]). Traveling back in time to the year 1893, Data uncovered a plot by aliens from the planet **Devidia II** who were using the **cholera** plague of the time to conceal their murder of humans. While attempting to stop the **Devidians**, Data's head was severed, and his body was sent forward in time, back to 2368. Aboard the *Enterprise*-D, Geordi La Forge was successful in reattaching Data's head to his body. ("Time's Arrow, Part II" [TNG]). Following the destruction of the *Enterprise*-D in 2371, Data accepted an assignment the following year to the sixth *Enterprise*, also under the command of Captain Jean-Luc Picard. *(Star Trek: First Contact).*

Data and Lore. Upon returning to the **Omicron Theta** colony site in 2364, Data participated in the discovery and activation of his android brother, **Lore**. Physically identical to Data, Lore had radically different personality programming, and attempted to commandeer the *Enterprise*-D before he was beamed into space. ("Datalore" [TNG]). Although Noonien Soong was believed to have died at Omicron Theta, he was discovered to have escaped the colony when, in 2367, he remotely gained control of Data, commanding his creation to visit him in his new secret laboratory. There, Soong attempted to install a new chip in Data's positronic brain that would have given Data the ability to experience human emotions. Unfortunately, Lore also responded to Soong's call, and stole the **emotion chip** from Soong's lab. Dr. Soong died shortly thereafter. ("Brothers" [TNG]). Data began to experience emotions in 2369 when Lore secretly bombarded Data with signals that triggered negative emotions in his positronic brain. Lore used these negative emotions to guide Data into joining him and the **Borg** against the Federation. When Data realized that Lore was manipulating him and harming the Borg, he was forced to deactivate Lore. Data kept Soong's emotion chip, but was reluctant to install it for fear of causing further harm to his friends. ("Descent, Parts I and II" [TNG]).

Efforts to understand humanity. Data's attempts to understand human nature once included an effort to learn about the concept of humor, which he studied with the assistance of Guinan and a **holodeck**-created comedian. ("The Outrageous Okona" [TNG]). SEE: **Comic, The**. Data even tried a beard once, to the considerable amusement of his shipmates even learned to dance. ("The Schizoid Man" [TNG]). Aboard the *Enterprise*-D, Data shared his living quarters with a cat that he named **Spot**. Data tried to provide for Spot's well-being, but found it difficult to predict the cat's preferences in food. ("Data's Day" [TNG]). One of Data's more challenging efforts to experience humanity was his attempt to pursue a romantic relationship with *Enterprise*-D Security Officer **Jenna D'Sora** in late 2367. Although D'Sora was attracted to Data, he was unable to return the affection, at least in a manner that she wanted. ("In Theory" [TNG]). Data began to experience dreams in 2369 as a result of an accidental plasma shock received during an experiment. It was later learned that the shock had triggered a program designed for this purpose by Soong, who had hoped the program would be activated when Data reached a certain level of development. Data's initial dreams were of Soong as a blacksmith, incongruously forging the wings of a bird, which Data believed represented himself. ("Birthright, Part I" [TNG]). SEE: **painting**. Those dreams turned to nightmares while under the influence of interphasic organisms in 2370. ("Phantasms" [TNG]). Later that year, following the *Enterprise*-D's discovery of the **D'Arsay archive**, Data's own personality became completely submerged by a series of personas, enacting the mythology of a long-dead civilization. Following the experience, Captain Picard commented that even if Data never become human, he had transcended the human condition by becoming an entire civilization. ("Masks" [TNG]). SEE: **Masaka**. One of Data's most noteworthy efforts in his quest for humanity was his construction of an android daughter in 2366. Data employed a new **submicron matrix transfer technology** to allow his own neural pathways to be duplicated in another positronic brain, which he used as the basis for his child. His daughter, whom he named **Lal** ("beloved" in Earth's Hindi language), developed at a remarkable rate and showed evidence of growth potential beyond that of her father, even experiencing emotions. Lal died after having lived little more than two weeks, when she experienced a serious failure in her positronic brain. ("The Offspring" [TNG]). In 2371, Data finally decided to install the **emotion chip** that Dr. Soong had created for him. Although Data had initial difficulty coping with the resulting flood of emotions—a problem made worse when the chip became fused into his neural net—the chip represented a significant step in his quest to become more human. *(Star Trek Generations).* By 2373 Data was able to turn his emotion chip on and off at will. During the **Borg** invasion of that year, the **Borg queen** used Data's quest to become human against him. She had organic components integrated onto his body, allowing him to experience tactile sensations, in an effort to seduce him to the Borg collective. Her efforts were remarkably successful, and Data later reported being tempted by her offer for

0.68 seconds. Data nevertheless destroyed the Borg queen and the collective by exposing them to highly toxic plasma coolant. His efforts not only saved the *Enterprise*-E and his shipmates, but blocked a time-traveling Borg effort to prevent **Zefram Cochrane**, in the year 2063, from making his historic first warp flight. *(Star Trek: First Contact).*

Android rights. The question of Data's sentience, and more specifically whether Data was entitled to civil rights as a citizen under the **Constitution of the United Federation of Planets**, was addressed in a number of important legal decisions. The first, in 2341, was rendered by a **Starfleet Academy** entrance committee that permitted Data to enter the academy and serve as a member of **Starfleet**. Several years later, the question was more definitively addressed when Judge Advocate General **Phillipa Louvois** ruled that Data was indeed a sentient being and therefore entitled to civil rights, including the right to resign from Starfleet if he so chose. As of stardate 42527, Data had been decorated by Starfleet Command for gallantry and had received the Medal of Honor with clusters, the Legion of Honor, and the Star Cross. ("The Measure of a Man" [TNG]). *Data first appeared in "Encounter at Farpoint" (TNG). Many fans have noticed similarities between Data and the character, Questor, from Gene Roddenberry's 1974 television movie/pilot* The Questor Tapes, *which featured Robert Foxworth as a humanoid android who searched for his creator while seeking to be human.*

"Datalore." *Next Generation* episode #14. Teleplay by Robert Lewin and Gene Roddenberry. Story by Robert Lewin and Maurice Hurley. Directed by Rob Bowman. Stardate 41242.4. *First aired in 1988. Investigating the planet where Data was found, the* Enterprise-D *discovers Data's twin brother, an android named Lore. This was the last* Star Trek *episode to carry Gene Roddenberry's name in the writing credits.* GUEST CAST: Biff Yeager as **Argyle, Lieutenant Commander**. SEE: **Argyle, Lieutenant Commander; Asimov, Dr. Isaac; champagne; Crystalline Entity; Data; Lore; Omicron Theta; positronic brain; Soong, Noonien; *Tripoli*, U.S.S.**

dataport. Computer interface implanted into a person's brain. A dataport allowed a person to directly interface with computer systems. **Arissa** was fitted with a dataport. ("A Simple Investigation" [DS9]).

Dathan. (Charles Esten). **Enaran** citizen and member of the ethnic group known to Enaran society as the **Regressives**. Dathan and his people were systematically exterminated by the Enaran government in the mid-24th century. Before his death, Dathan was romantically involved with **Korenna Mirell**. ("Remember" [VGR]). *Charles Esten previously played Divok in "Rightful Heir" (TNG).*

Dathon. (Paul Winfield). Captain of a **Tamarian** starship who made a heroic attempt to establish communication with the Federation in 2368. When his people were unable to establish communication with the Federation, despite several contacts over the course of a century, Dathon isolated himself and *Enterprise*-D Captain Picard on the surface of planet **El-Adrel IV**. There, he hoped that face-to-face contact and a shared danger would enable Picard to grasp the unusual nature of Tamarian speech. Although Dathon died from wounds inflicted by a beast on El-Adrel IV, Dathon was ultimately successful in his quest as Picard came to understand the fact that Tamarian speech was based entirely on metaphors. ("Darmok" [TNG]). *Paul Winfield also played Captain Terrell in* Star Trek II.

"Dauphin, The." *Next Generation* episode #36. Written by Scott Rubenstein & Leonard Mlodinow. Directed by Robert Bowman. Stardate 42568.8. *First aired in 1989. A young girl, sequestered on a distant planet, is returned to her homeworld, where it is hoped she can bring peace to warring peoples. The term dauphin comes from the title given in the 14th-19th centuries to the heir apparent to the French throne.* GUEST CAST: Diana Muldaur as **Pulaski, Dr. Katherine**; Paddi Edwards as **Anya**; Jamie Hubbard as **Salia**; Whoopi Goldberg as **Guinan**; Colm Meaney as **O'Brien, Miles**; Peter Neptune as Aron; Mädchen Amick as Teenage girl; Cindy Sorensen as Furry animal; Jennifer Barlow as Gibson, Ensign. SEE: **allasomorph; Andronesian encephalitis; Anya; Crusher, Wesley; Daled IV; deuterium control conduit; Klavdia III; love poetry, Klingon; Rousseau V; Salia; SCM Model 3; Thalian chocolate mousse; Thalos VII.**

Davenport, Lucille. (Kate Mulgrew). **Holonovel** character in an English gothic romance story, portrayed by *Voyager* Captain Kathryn Janeway. Mrs. Davenport was a woman hired to work as the governess for **Lord Burleigh**'s children. ("Cathexis" [VGR], "Learning Curve" [VGR]). The story took a dramatic turn when Burleigh fell in love with Lucille, to the dismay of Henry and Beatrice. ("Persistence of Vision" [VGR]). SEE: **Janeway Lambda-1.**

Davies, Ensign. (Nicholas Cascone). Geologist aboard the *Enterprise*-D. Davies participated in the geological survey of planets in the **Selcundi Drema** sector in 2365. The survey was supervised by Acting Ensign **Wesley Crusher**. Davies attempted to assist Crusher in the project, but his offers of help served to undermine young Crusher's confidence. ("Pen Pals" [TNG]).

Davila, Carmen. (Susan Diol). Colony engineer killed by the **Crystalline Entity** at planet **Melona IV** in 2368. She had been helping to prepare a colony site at the time. Davila was a friend of William Riker. ("Silicon Avatar" [TNG]).

DaVinci Falls. Waterfalls on terraformed planet **Blue Horizon.** ("Second Sight" [DS9]).

Davis, Ensign. (Craig Benton). Member of the *Enterprise*-D engineering staff. Davis was present when an **antimatter containment** failure occurred in Engineering. He was one of the last of the engineering crew to escape the matter/antimatter core area before the breach forced closure of the isolation doors. ("Violations" [TNG]). SEE: **Keller, Ensign.**

Davlos III. Planet located on the **Klingon** border. In the latter half of the 24th century, inhabitants of Davlos III did over 90 percent of their trade with the Klingon Empire. ("Visionary" [DS9]).

Dax (symbiont). Trill parasitic lifeform. As is normal for the **Trill** joined species, Dax lived in symbiosis with a succession of humanoid hosts. Each joined pair of the Dax symbiont and a host was a new individual, each sharing knowledge and memories from earlier joinings. Over a two hundred year period, the Dax symbiont served as a **field docent** to numerous Trill **initiates**, becoming somewhat notorious for recommending the rejection of 57 host candidates from the program. ("Playing God" [DS9]). Hosts of the Dax symbiont have been a father more than once. ("Explorers" [DS9]). As of 2371, Dax had been joined seven times prior to Jadzia. ("Meridian" [DS9]). First host: **Lela Dax**, the first woman to serve on the Trill council. Second host: **Tobin Dax**, a shy, scientifically knowledgeable man. Third host:

Emony Dax, a professional gymnast. Fourth host: **Audrid Dax**, a member of the **Trill Symbiosis Commission**, and mother of at least two children; died in 2284. Fifth host: **Torias Dax** was joined for less than a year before he suffered a fatal shuttle accident in 2285. Sixth host: **Joran Dax** was an unbalanced individual who was joined for only six months before committing a murder. All records of Joran's existence were suppressed by the Symbiosis Commission. Seventh host: **Curzon Dax**, a noted diplomat and friend to Benjamin Sisko. Died 2367. Eighth host: **Jadzia Dax**, science officer at station Deep Space 9. ("Equilibrium" [DS9], "Facets" [DS9]).

Dax, Audrid. Fourth host to the **Dax (symbiont)**, succeeding **Emony Dax**. Audrid was head of the **Trill Symbiosis Commission**, as well as a loving mother to at least two children. Died in 2284. ("Facets" [DS9]). Audrid had a daughter named Neema. At age six, Neema spent two weeks in the hospital with Rugalan fever. During her stay, Audrid read all seventeen volumes of *Down the River Light* to Neema, even though the child was unconscious at the time. Fifteen years later Audrid and her daughter were not on speaking terms and would not be for another eight years. ("Nor the Battle to the Strong" [DS9]).

Dax, Curzon. (Frank Owen Smith). **Trill** host to the **Dax (symbiont)** prior to **Jadzia Dax**. ("Emissary" [DS9]). Curzon Dax was a noted diplomat. In 2289, some years before the **Khitomer** accords, Curzon Dax walked out on a speech by **Kang** at the **Korvat colony**, angering Kang, but opening the door for understanding. Dax eventually won the respect of his Klingon colleagues and was deeply honored when Kang named his firstborn son for Dax, and made Dax the child's godfather. When the boy was murdered by the **Albino**, Dax swore a **blood oath** to avenge the death. Although Curzon Dax did not live to fulfill the promise, Jadzia Dax did so in 2370. ("Blood Oath" [DS9]). *(One might suspect that Curzon participated in the Khitomer talks seen in* Star Trek VI.)

Dax served as a Federation mediator on **Klaestron IV** during that planet's civil war in the 2330s. He became friends with **General Ardelon Tandro** and his family while stationed on the planet. Unknown to Tandro, Dax was also engaged in a love affair with Tandro's wife, **Enina**. Thirty years later, when Jadzia Dax was accused of Tandro's murder, Enina testified that at the time of her husband's death, Curzon Dax was in her bed. ("Dax" [DS9]). Curzon was usually not punctual. He was even late for his 100th birthday party. Curzon Dax was once thrown out of the infamous Barros Inn for setting fire to the place. ("Rejoined" [DS9]).

Curzon Dax and **Benjamin Sisko** were good friends when Sisko was an ensign, a friendship that they maintained for nearly two decades. ("Emissary" [DS9]). Curzon first met Ben Sisko at the Palios Station. They served together aboard the ***U.S.S. Livingston***. ("Invasive Procedures" [DS9]). Curzon Dax knew Benjamin Sisko from before Jake's birth. ("Explorers" [DS9]). He also was friends with Starfleet officer turned Maquis sympathizer, **Calvin Hudson**. ("The Maquis, Part I" [DS9]). Curzon used to assign Ben Sisko to guide VIP guests while under his command so the Trill wouldn't have to deal with them. ("The Forsaken" [DS9]).

Curzon acted as Jadzia's **field docent** and recommended she be dropped from the **initiate** program, noting that he felt she lacked a sense of purpose. She did not realize until years later that Curzon's harsh evaluation had spurred her to re-examine her purpose so that she eventually did win the opportunity for joining. Despite his early opinion of Jadzia, Curzon did not object when, at the end of Curzon's life, Jadzia asked to become the next host of the Dax symbiont. ("Playing God" [DS9]). In 2371, Jadzia learned that the true reason for Curzon's recommendation was that he had fallen in love with Jadzia during the young woman's initiate program. Unable to deal with these inappropriate feelings, and unwilling to admit them to Jadzia, Curzon recommended that she be dropped from the program. Curzon would later admit to feeling so guilty about his actions that he nearly retired from the **Trill Symbiosis Commission**. Four years after Curzon's death, Curzon's personality reluctantly admitted his feelings toward Jadzia through her ***zhian'tara*** ceremony. ("Facets" [DS9]).

When **Dax (symbiont)** became Jadzia, Sisko was fond of calling her "old man," despite the fact that Dax's new host was a young woman. ("Emissary" [DS9]). Curzon had learned to play ***tongo,*** and was fond of the game, a fondness that Jadzia retained. ("Rules of Acquisition" [DS9]).

Curzon Dax died in 2367. ("Dax" [DS9]). At the time of his death, he had been on planet **Risa**, making love with a beautiful woman named **Arandis**, who termed the experience "death by ***jamaharon.***" ("Let He Who Is Without Sin..." [DS9]). The Dax symbiont was subsequently implanted into Jadzia Dax. ("Emissary" [DS9]). *Curzon Dax, as played by Frank Owen Smith, was seen briefly in a flashback scene in "Emissary" (DS9).*

Dax, Emony. Third host to the **Dax (symbiont)**, succeeding **Tobin Dax**. Emony was a gymnast who discovered that her coordination improved following her joining. ("Facets" [DS9]). Emony was on Earth around 2245 to judge a gymnastics competition. While there, she met and had a romance with **Leonard McCoy** while he was a student at the University of Mississippi. ("Trials and Tribble-ations" [DS9]). *Since Dax didn't know that McCoy became a surgeon, it seems likely that he met Emony early in his college days, suggesting that their romance took place around 2245.*

Dax, Jadzia (mirror). (Terry Farrell). **Mirror universe** counterpart to **Jadzia Dax**. This Dax was an aggressive leader of the **Terran rebellion**. She was also the lover of **Benjamin Sisko (mirror)**. ("Through the Looking Glass" [DS9]).

Dax, Jadzia. (Terry Farrell). Starfleet science officer assigned to **Deep Space 9** in 2369, shortly after Starfleet took over the station. Jadzia Dax was a member of the **Trill** joined species. ("Emissary" [DS9]).

Jadzia had wanted to become a host to a Trill symbiont since she was a child and worked very hard at winning the honor. Neither of her parents nor her sister underwent symbiosis. ("Invasive Procedures" [DS9]). Before joining with the **Dax (symbiont)**, Jadzia was a brilliant but shy young woman. She did extremely well in the **initiate** program, winning Premier Distinctions in exobiology, zoology, astrophysics, and exoarchaeology ("Dax" [DS9]), and even won a third-level pilot certificate. Nevertheless, her training under **Curzon Dax**, her **field docent**, went poorly, and Curzon recommended she be rejected for joining. Curzon's harsh evaluation helped Jadzia realize she needed to find her purpose in life before she could be a successful Trill host. ("Playing God" [DS9]). Jadzia did not realize that the reason for Curzon's harshness was the fact that he was in love with her, a most inappropriate situation given their teacher-student relationship. ("Facets" [DS9]). Curzon felt guilty over his treatment of Jadzia, and later consented for her to become the Dax symbiont's next host upon his death in 2367. ("Playing God" [DS9]).

As Jadzia, Dax had been a close friend of **Benjamin Sisko**, but she noted that such friendships are often difficult to maintain when a Trill has a new host, particularly one of a different gender. ("Emissary" [DS9]). As is characteristic of Trills, Dax's hands are cold. ("A Man Alone" [DS9]).

Although Jadzia believed she was Dax's seventh host, she learned in 2371 of a previously unknown joining. This deeply held secret was revealed when Jadzia began experiencing vivid hallucinations and a dangerous drop in her **isoboramine** levels. These symptoms were found to have been caused by the deterioration of a memory block created by the **Trill Symbiosis Commission** in 2285 in hopes of suppressing knowledge of the existence of **Joran Dax**. ("Equilibrium" [DS9]). *Jadzia and her friends subsequently agreed to keep Joran Dax's existence a secret.*

In 2370 Jadzia almost died when a Trill named **Verad** briefly stole her symbiont. ("Invasive Procedures" [DS9]). Later that year,

Jadzia honored **Curzon**'s **blood oath** of vengeance against the **Albino** and accompanied **Kor**, **Kang**, and **Koloth** to **Secarus IV** to kill him. She battled the Albino, but could not bring herself to kill him. ("Blood Oath" [DS9]).

As an attractive woman, Dax drew the attentions of many men, including Dr. **Julian Bashir**. Dax considered herself above such interests, although she once admitted that she thought **Morn** was cute. ("Progress" [DS9]). **Captain Boday** was once her lover. ("Let He Who Is Without Sin..." [DS9]). As of 2369, Dax had been attempting to master the **Altonian brain teaser** for 140 years. ("A Man Alone" [DS9]). Jadzia Dax liked **icoberry juice**, but drinking it always made her spots itch. ("Let He Who Is Without Sin..." [DS9]).

Jadzia was regarded by her friends as something of a night owl. ("Playing God" [DS9]). She often threw surprise birthday parties for her friends at Deep Space 9. ("Distant Voices" [DS9]). Jadzia had several hobbies, including **Galeo-Manada style wrestling**, and collecting the music of lost composers. She and Ben Sisko played Earth chess together. Jadzia enjoyed the game of ***tongo***. Perhaps as a result of the Dax symbiont's many lifetimes of experience, Jadzia Dax disliked what she regarded as blind compliance to society's norms, and she occasionally enjoyed indulging in "inappropriate" behavior (such as playing *tongo*) for its shock value. Like Curzon, she had great fondness for Klingon food and Klingon music. ("Playing God" [DS9]). She enjoyed playing practical jokes on her colleagues. On several occasions in early 2372, she broke into Odo's quarters while he was regenerating, and moved all of his furniture very slightly, just to annoy him. ("Homefront" [DS9]).

Dax learned a great deal about her past in 2371 when she underwent her ***zhian'tara*** ceremony. In the *zhian'tara*, a Trill's friends embody the personalities of the symbiont's earlier hosts, giving the joined Trill the opportunity to meet his or her earlier selves. ("Facets" [DS9]). SEE: **Dax (symbiont)**.

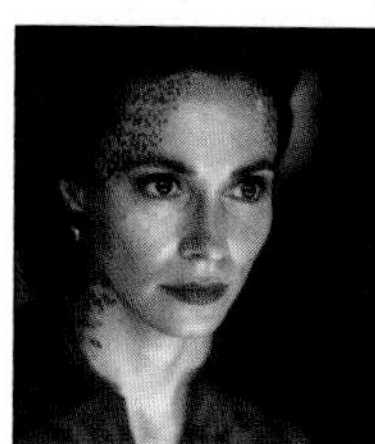

When Jadzia Dax was reunited with **Lenara Kahn** (pictured) in 2372, the two felt a great desire to continue the relationship started by their previous hosts, **Torias Dax** and **Nilani Kahn**. Though Jadzia felt strongly enough to go against **Trill** taboo, Lenara didn't wish to risk exile for reassociating with Dax. Lenara Kahn returned to Trill to continue her work. ("Rejoined" [DS9]). SEE: **reassociation**.

Jadzia found herself strongly attracted to Strategic Operations Officer **Worf**. Dax's familarity with Klingon culture was helpful in winning his attentions in 2373, although the process proved hazardous to both. ("Looking for *par'Mach* in All the Wrong Places" [DS9]). *Jadzia Dax was first seen in "Emissary" (DS9).*

Dax, Joran. Sixth host to the **Dax (symbiont)**, succeeding **Torias Dax**. Joran was deemed unsuitable for joining, but he was mistakenly accepted as an initiate by the **Trill Symbiosis Commission**. When Joran's body rejected the Dax symbiont in 2285, six months after being joined, the commission moved quickly to cover up the incident because it illustrated that about half of the humanoid **Trill** population could be joined. The commission had maintained publicly that only a tenth of a percent of the population could be joined, and that joining with an unsuitable host would result in death in only a few days. After Joran's death, official Symbiosis Commission records were altered to suggest that Joran had never been joined, and that Joran had been killed after he murdered a doctor that had recommended Joran be dropped from the initiate program. Commission records also suggested that following **Torias Dax**'s death in 2285, that the Dax symbiont was implanted directly into **Curzon**. Memories of Joran were even biochemically erased from Dax's mind. The commission was largely successful in maintaining this fiction until 2371, when the memory block deteriorated and friends of **Jadzia Dax** uncovered the truth while trying to save her life. ("Equilibrium" [DS9]). SEE: **Belar, Joran.** *Jadzia and her friends subsequently agreed not to reveal the truth, so the information in this entry presumably did not become public knowledge.* In 2371 during Jadzia's ***zhian'tara***, Benjamin Sisko volunteered to embody the memories of Joran Dax. ("Facets" [DS9]).

Dax, Lela. First host to the **Dax (symbiont)**. Lela was a legislator, one of the first women to be named as a council member. ("Facets" [DS9], "Playing God" [DS9]). Lela had a son named Ahjess. Jadzia recalled that after Ahjess was tucked into bed at night, he would climb into his mother's bed two hours later for attention. ("To the Death" [DS9]). *No dates have yet been established for Lela's life, but it seems possible that she could have been joined as far back as the middle of Earth's 21st century. We know from "Playing God" that Dax (although not necessarily Lela) had first served as a field docent around 2171.*

Dax, son of Kang. Firstborn son of Klingon warrior **Kang** and godson of **Curzon Dax.** Dax, son of Kang, was murdered as a child by the **Albino**. ("Blood Oath" [DS9]).

Dax, Tobin. Second host to the **Dax (symbiont)**. ("Invasive Procedures" [DS9]). Tobin Dax had a child named Raifi, who caused Tobin some difficulty over the years. ("Nor the Battle to the Strong" [DS9]). Though Tobin was socially inept and unimaginative (at least according to Jadzia), he was renowned for his knowledge of phase coil inverters. ("The Siege" [DS9]). Tobin was the only Dax host to try his hand at botany, but didn't have much success. ("The Wire" [DS9]). While on **Vulcan**, Tobin Dax met noted Cardassian poet **Iloja of Prim**. ("Destiny" [DS9]). Tobin used to dabble in sleight-of-hand magic. ("Rejoined" [DS9]). Prior to his death, Tobin worked on a new proof of **Fermat's last theorem**. ("Facets" [DS9]).

Dax, Torias. Fifth host to the **Dax (symbiont)**, succeeding **Audrid Dax**. ("Equilibrium" [DS9]). Torias was married to a joined Trill woman, **Nilani Kahn**. ("Rejoined" [DS9]). Torias hosted the Dax symbiont for less than a year before he was critically injured in a shuttle accident in 2285 and, according to official Trill records, remained comatose for six months following the accident. Despite the efforts of the Trill physicians caring for him, Torias's **isoboramine** concentrations fell below acceptable levels and the Dax symbiont was removed. Torias's death was recorded on stardate 8615.2. *Official Trill records show that the Dax symbiont was subsequently implanted into Curzon; the fact that it was first implanted into Joran is not reflected in commission records.* ("Equilibrium" [DS9], "Facets" [DS9]). *Sisko's discovery that the Dax symbiont was placed into Joran Belar following Torias's injury seems to place Torias's death six months earlier than his "official" date of death.* SEE: **Belar, Joran; Dax, Curzon; Dax, Joran.**

Dax. (Michael Snyder). Crew member aboard the *Starship Enterprise*-A in 2293. Incriminating evidence, **magnetic boots**, were planted in Dax's personal locker, implicating him in the murder of **Chancellor Gorkon**, but Dax's foot structure was clearly unable to fit boots designed for humans. (*Star Trek VI: The Undiscovered Country*). *It has been suggested that this Dax may have been an earlier host of the Trill that later served on Deep Space 9. The symbiont character in* Deep Space Nine *is certainly old enough for this to be possible, but in 2293, the Dax symbiont's host was either Emony or Audrid, both women. Michael Snyder also played Morta in "Rascals" (TNG) and Qol in "The Perfect Mate" (TNG).*

"Dax." *Deep Space Nine* episode #8. Teleplay by D. C. Fontana and Peter Allan Fields. Story by Peter Allan Fields. Directed by David Carson. Stardate 46910.1. *First aired in 1993. After thirty years, the son of a murdered Bajoran general claims that Dax's previous host is the murderer. This episode was written by D. C. Fontana, story editor of the original* Star Trek *television series.* GUEST CAST: Gregory Itzin as **Tandro, Ilon**; Anne Haney as **Uxbridge, Rishon**; Richard Lineback as **Peers, Selin**; Fionnula Flanagan as **Tandro, Enina**. SEE: **Argosian; Dax, Curzon; Dax, Jadzia; Klaestron IV; O'Brien, Keiko; Peers, Selin; Renora; Sisko, Benjamin; symbiont; Tandro, Enina; Tandro, General Ardelon; Tandro, Ilon; Trill.**

"Day of the Dove." Original Series episode #66. Written by Jerome Bixby. Directed by Marvin Chomsky. No stardate given. *First aired in 1968. The* Enterprise *crew and a group of Klingons* *are trapped by an energy creature that feeds on hatred. Kang, the Klingon commander, later returned in "Blood Oath" (DS9).* GUEST CAST: Michael Ansara as **Kang**; Susan Howard as **Mara**; David L. Ross as **Johnson**, **Lieutenant**; Mark Tobin as Klingon; Majel Barrett as Computer voice. SEE: **agonizer; Archanis IV; armory; auxiliary control; Beta XII-A entity; Beta XII-A; Chekov, Pavel A.; Chekov, Piotr; claymore; Devil; intraship beaming; Johnson, Lieutenant; Kang; Klingon Empire; Klingons; Mara; Organian Peace Treaty.**

Day, Colonel. (Steven Weber). Bajoran military officer who was secretly a member of **the Alliance for Global Unity**. Day participated in the takeover of station Deep Space 9 in 2370. Day was under the titular command of **General Krim**, but actually followed orders from **Minister Jaro**. Day tried to prevent Starfleet personnel from informing Krim that the **Circle** was receiving covert Cardassian support. When Krim did learn of the Circle's Cardassian backing, Day resisted Krim's order to return the station to Starfleet control. In the ensuing fray, Day tried to kill Commander Benjamin Sisko, but instead killed Bajoran resistance hero **Li Nalas**. ("The Siege" [DS9]).

Dayos IV. Planet. **Kang** found one of the **Albino**'s discarded wives on Dayos IV in 2363. ("Blood Oath" [DS9]).

Daystrom Institute. Major center for science and technology in the 24th century. Named for 23rd-century computer scientist **Richard Daystrom**. In 2365, **Commander Bruce Maddox** served as Chair of Robotics at the Daystrom Institute, and also worked with the Cybernetics Division. ("The Measure of a Man" [TNG], "Data's Day" [TNG]). *Enterprise*-D designer Dr. Leah Brahms was a graduate of the Daystrom Institute. ("Booby Trap" [TNG]). Archaeologist **Vash**, who continued Dr. Samuel Estragon's work to locate the fabled ***Tox Uthat*** after his death in 2366, promised Estragon that she would present the *Uthat* to the Daystrom Institute if she did find it. ("Captain's Holiday" [TNG]). In 2369, **Vash** was invited to speak at the Daystrom Institute concerning her travels in the **Gamma Quadrant**. This came as quite a surprise, since her membership to the Institute's Archaeological Council had been suspended twice for illegally selling artifacts. Vash declined the offer so that she could continue exploring archeological ruins throughout the galaxy. ("Q-Less" [DS9]). An annex of the Daystrom Institute was located on planet **Galor IV**. ("The Offspring" [TNG]). *The Daystrom Institute was, of course, a tip of the hat to "The Ultimate Computer" (TOS).*

Daystrom, Dr. Richard. (William Marshall). Brilliant 23rd-century computer scientist, inventor of comptronic and **duotronic** systems, born 2219. Daystrom won the prestigious **Nobel Prize** and the **Zee-Magnees Prize** in 2243 at the age of 24 for his breakthrough in duotronics, which became the basis for computer systems aboard Federation starships for over 80 years. Daystrom's early successes resulted in personal troubles, and he spent many years trying to live up to his reputation as a "boy wonder." In the 2260s, Daystrom tried to develop a concept he called **multitronic**s. This new system involved imprinting human neural **engram**s upon computer circuits, causing them to mimic the synapses of the brain. It was hoped the process would give a computer the ability to think and to reason like a human. Unfortunately, when tested, Daystrom's multitronic system also mimicked the unstable portions of his personality, resulting in a disaster in which nearly 500 Starfleet personnel were killed. The failure of his creation pushed Daystrom over the edge of insanity, and he was committed to a rehabilitation center for treatment. ("The Ultimate Computer" [TOS]). SEE: ***Excalibur, U.S.S.***; ***Lexington, U.S.S.***; **M-5**.

de Laure belt. Location of planet **Tau Cygna V**. ("The Ensigns of Command" [TNG]).

"Deadlock." *Voyager* episode #38. Written by Brannon Braga. Directed by David Livingston. Stardate 49548.7. *First aired in 1996. The* Voyager *and its crew are duplicated, and one Janeway must sacrifice herself and her ship so that the other can evade the Vidiians.* GUEST CAST: Nancy Hower as **Wildman, Samantha**; Simon Billig as **Hogan**; Bob Clendenin as Vidiian surgeon; Ray Proscia as Vidiian commander; Keythe Farley as Vidiian #2; Chris Johnston as Vidiian #1; Majel Barrett as Computer voice. SEE: **anodyne relay; dermaline gel; destruct sequence; fire suppression system; hemocythemia; hyperthermic charge; Janeway, Kathryn; Kent State University; Kim, Harry; Ktarians; molecular signature; mutual annihilation; osmotic pressure therapy; phase discriminator; security access code; spatial scission; *Voyager, U.S.S.*; Wildman, Samantha.**

"Deadly Years, The." Original Series episode #40. Written by David P. Harmon. Directed by Joseph Pevney. Stardate 3478.2. *First aired in 1967. Exposure to an unknown form of radiation causes* Enterprise *crew members to age at an incredible rate. William Shatner reportedly threatened producer Bob Justman with bodily harm after enduring many torturous hours during the old-age makeup process. "Who's afraid of such a wrinkled, feeble old coot?" scoffed Justman, derisively. Nevertheless, Bob locked his office door and hid under his desk until the episode finished shooting.* GUEST CAST: Charles Drake as **Stocker, Commodore**; Sarah Marshall as **Wallace**, **Dr. Janet**; Majel Barrett as **Chapel**, **Christine**; Felix Locher as **Johnson**, **Robert**; Carolyn Nelson as Arkins, Doris; Laura Wood as **Johnson**, **Elaine**; Beverly Washburn as **Galway**, **Arlene**; Majel Barrett as Computer voice. SEE: **adrenaline; Aldebaran; Chekov, Pavel A.; Code 2; corbomite; Galway, Lieutenant; Gamma Hydra IV; hyronalin; Johnson, Elaine; Johnson, Robert; Kirk, James T.; Romulan Neutral Zone; Scott, Montgomery; Starbase 10; Stocker, Commodore; Sulu, Hikaru; Wallace, Dr. Janet; Wallace, Dr. Theodore.**

Deadwood. American Western town in South Dakota on Earth, re-created in **Alexander Rozhenko**'s holodeck program, ***Ancient West***. ("A Fistful of Datas" [TNG]).

Dealt, Lieutenant Commander Hester. (Seymour Cassel). Medical trustee of the Federation Medical Collection Station on planet **'audet IX**. Dealt supervised the transport of plasma plague specimens aboard the *Enterprise*-D to Science Station **Tango Sierra** to help combat the plague outbreak in the Rachelis system in 2365. ("The Child" [TNG]).

Dean, Lieutenant. (Dan Kern). *Enterprise*-D crew member who was an accomplished swordsman, and who enjoyed fencing with Captain Picard in the ship's gymnasium. ("We'll Always Have Paris" [TNG]). *Lieutenant Dean was named for episode co-writer Deborah Dean Davis.*

"Death Wish." *Voyager* episode #30. Teleplay by Michael Piller. Story by Shawn Piller. Directed by James L. Conway. Stardate 49301.2. *First aired in 1996. A member of the Q Continuum asks Captain Janeway to grant him asylum, so that he can commit suicide. This episode marked the first appearance of Q on* Star Trek: Voyager. *Jonathan Frakes made a cameo appearance as Will Riker, the first crossover with* Star Trek: The Next Generation. SEE: **baryon particles; Big Bang; Bolians; Ginsberg, Maury; Gorokian midwife toad; Kylerian goat's milk; New Era; Newton, Isaac; Nogatch hemlock; Q; Q Continuum; Quinn; replicator; Riker, Thaddius; Riker, William T.; Romulan Star Empire; Vulcans; Welsh rabbit; Woodstock.**

Debin. (Douglas Rowe). Leader from the planet **Altec**, father to **Yanar**. ("The Outrageous Okona" [TNG]).

Debrune. Ancient offshoot of the Romulan people. Two millenia ago, the Debrune used planet **Barradas III** as an outpost, and left numerous archeological ruins on the planet's surface. In 2370, the Debrune ruins were the target of mercenary **Arctus Baran**, who was working for the **Vulcan isolationist movement**, searching for fragments of the ancient **Stone of Gol**. ("Gambit, Part I" [TNG]).

Decius. (Lawrence Montaigne). Officer aboard the **Romulan bird-of-prey** that crossed the **Romulan Neutral Zone** into Federation space in 2266. Although a junior officer aboard that vessel, he had relatives in high places in the Romulan government, and thus carried possibly undue influence. Decius used his influence to steer his commander into a more aggressive strategy when confronting the *Enterprise*. ("Balance of Terror" [TOS]). *Lawrence Montaigne also played Stonn in "Amok Time" (TOS). Along with Mark Lenard, Montaigne was a leading contender to replace Leonard Nimoy just prior to the original* Star Trek's *second season.*

Decius. A Romulan warbird, encountered by the *Enterprise*-D and "Captain" Riker during a virtual reality engineered by **Barash** on **Alpha Onias III** in 2367. In this fantasy, the *Decius* transported "Admiral" Picard, Counselor Troi, and "Ambassador" Tomalak to a rendezvous with the *Enterprise*-D. ("Future Imperfect" [TNG]).

Decker, Commodore Matt. (William Windom). Commander of the ***U.S.S. Constellation***. Decker's ship was attacked by a robotic **planet killer** weapon in 2267. During the attack, Decker sent his crew down to the third planet in the **L-374** system, but shortly thereafter, the planet killer destroyed all the planets in that system, leaving Decker aboard his ship as the only survivor. Decker later commandeered an *Enterprise* shuttlecraft on a suicide attack against the planet killer. The attack was unsuccessful, but his actions paved the way to the planet killer's destruction. ("The Doomsday Machine" [TOS]).

Decker, Willard. (Stephen Collins). Captain of the *Starship Enterprise* during the ship's refitting in 2270–2271. Decker, who had been assigned to the *Enterprise* at Kirk's recommendation, was replaced by Kirk and downgraded to executive officer when the ship intercepted the **V'Ger** entity near Earth in 2271. Decker was the son of Commodore **Matt Decker** and was apparently killed when he physically joined with V'Ger to help dissuade that entity from destroying the Earth. Decker was listed as "missing in action." Before his assignment to the *Enterprise*, Decker had been stationed on planet **Delta IV**, and was romantically involved with future *Enterprise* navigator **Ilia**. *(Star Trek: The Motion Picture). Paramount publicity materials suggested that Will Decker was the son of Commodore Matt Decker, but this was not confirmed by the movie itself.*

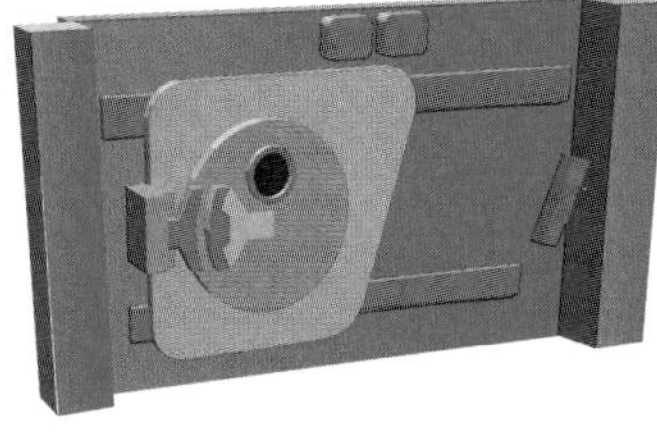

decompression chamber. Medical treatment facility aboard Federation starships for patients requiring exposure to atmospheric pressures other than Class-M normal. ("Space Seed" [TOS], "The Empath" [TOS], "The Lights of Zetar" [TOS]).

DeCurtis, Ensign. (Todd Waring). Starfleet officer assigned to station Deep Space 9. DeCurtis assisted command personnel in isolating the replicant O'Brien from sensitive areas of the station. ("Whispers" [DS9]).

Dedestris. Planet in the Delta Quadrant. A very delicate fabric spun from the petals of a flower that blooms only in moonlight was imported from Dedestris by the Sikarians. ("Prime Factors." [VGR]).

USS ENTERPRISE
STARSHIP CLASS
SAN FRANCISCO, CALIF.

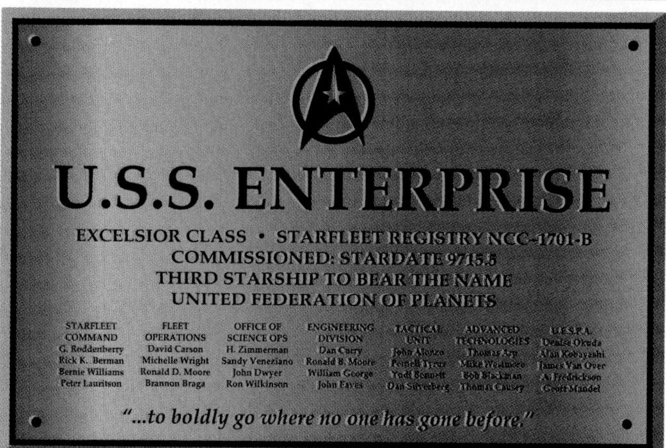

dedication plaque. Commemorative plate located on the bridge of Federation starships.

Deela. (Karen Hensel) **Bajoran** national who helped care for Cardassian war orphans at the **Tozhat Resettlement Center** in 2370. Deela was a member of the Bajoran underground during the Cardassian occupation of her homeworld. ("Cardassians" [DS9]). *Deela's name was never mentioned in the aired episode and only appeared in the script.*

Deela. (Kathie Browne). Queen of the Scalosian civilization who commandeered the *Starship Enterprise* in 2268, intending to procure a supply of fertile males for the perpetuation of her people. Like all **Scalosians**, Deela's biochemistry had undergone **hyperacceleration**, so one hour for her was like one of our seconds. Deela was attracted to James Kirk, and accelerated him to her level. Kirk thwarted her plans, and Deela subsequently returned to **Scalos** with her people. ("Wink of an Eye" [TOS]).

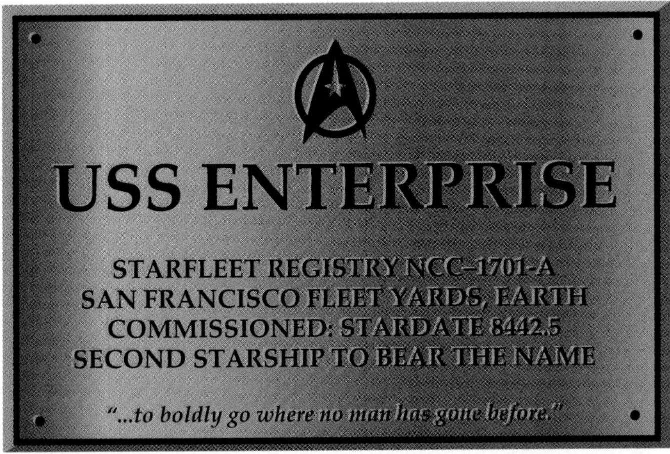

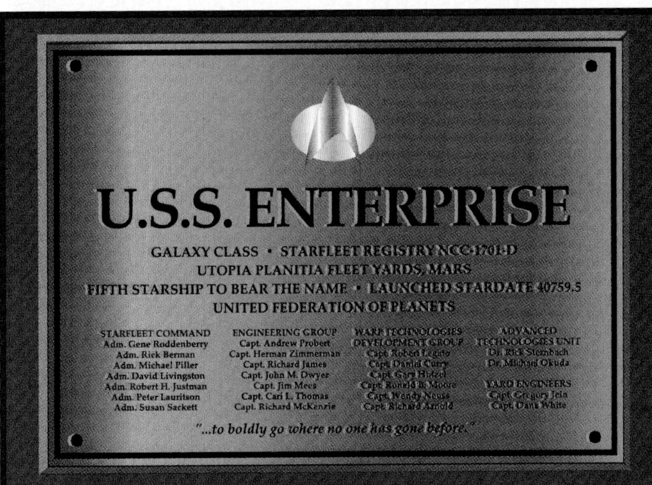

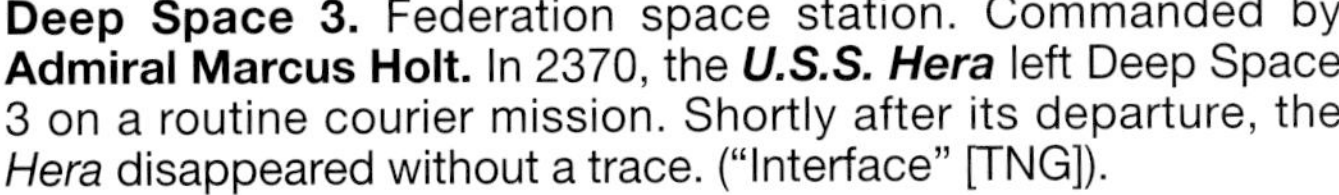

Deep Space 3. Federation space station. Commanded by **Admiral Marcus Holt.** In 2370, the ***U.S.S. Hera*** left Deep Space 3 on a routine courier mission. Shortly after its departure, the *Hera* disappeared without a trace. ("Interface" [TNG]).

Deep Space 4. Federation space station. Archaeologist **Richard Galen** hoped to gain passage at Deep Space 4 on an **Al-Leyan** transport to Caere as part of his quest to learn about the first humanoids to live in our galaxy. ("The Chase" [TNG]).

Deep Space 5. Federation base. (In an alternate **quantum reality** visited by Worf in 2370, Deep Space 5 was the object of covert surveillance by the Cardassians, who had reprogrammed the Argus Array to observe the station, as well as other Federation installations.) ("Parallels" [TNG]). Deep Space 5 was located near planet Ivor Prime. The staff of Deep Space 5 informed Starfleet command about the destruction of the Federation colony on Ivor Prime by the Borg in 2373. *(Star Trek: First Contact).*

Deep Space 9. Old **Cardassian** mining station built in orbit of planet **Bajor** during the Cardassian occupation. ("Emissary" [DS9]). Deep Space 9 was built in 2351 ("Babel" [DS9]) by the Cardassians, who called the station **Terok Nor**, to exploit Bajor's rich **uridium** deposits.

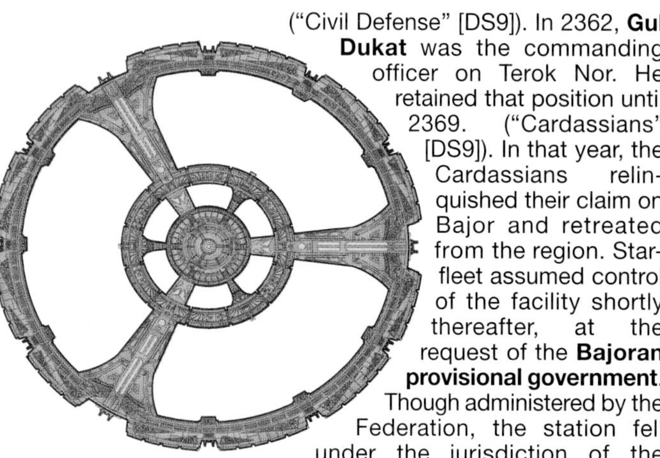

("Civil Defense" [DS9]). In 2362, **Gul Dukat** was the commanding officer on Terok Nor. He retained that position until 2369. ("Cardassians" [DS9]). In that year, the Cardassians relinquished their claim on Bajor and retreated from the region. Starfleet assumed control of the facility shortly thereafter, at the request of the **Bajoran provisional government**. Though administered by the Federation, the station fell under the jurisdiction of the Bajoran government and was subject to its laws. ("Profit and Loss" [DS9]).

Starfleet officer **Benjamin Sisko** was placed in charge of the station, and his staff included Bajoran Liaison **Kira Nerys**, Security Officer **Odo**, Chief Medical Officer **Julian Bashir**, Science Officer **Jadzia Dax**, and Chief of Operations **Miles O'Brien**. Shortly thereafter, the station assumed great commercial, scientific, and strategic importance when the **Bajoran wormhole** was discovered, linking the Bajor system with the distant **Gamma Quadrant**. Commander Sisko ordered the station moved near the wormhole in order to solidify the Bajoran claim on this remarkable phenomenon. ("Emissary" [DS9]). This placed the station three hours from planet Bajor. ("The House of Quark" [DS9]).

Major features of the station include the **Operations Center** (from which all station functions are managed), the **Promenade** (a main thoroughfare containing numerous service facilities and stores, including **Quark's bar**), three massive docking towers, and several smaller docking ports on an outer docking ring. ("Emissary" [DS9]). Incorporated into the docking towers were several massive ore processing facilities designed to refine **uridium** ore. ("Crossover" [DS9], "Civil Defense" [DS9]). The extent of the defensive shields around the station was almost 300 meters. ("The Search, Part I" [DS9]). There are normally about 300 permanent residents on the station, not counting visitors and crews of ships docked at the station. Weapons are stored in the Habitat Ring, Level 5, Section 3. ("Captive Pursuit" [DS9]). The station has the capacity to accommodate about 7000 people. ("Sanctuary" [DS9]). Access conduits on the station were shielded with **duranium** composites, making the interior of the conduits impervious to sensors. ("The Siege" [DS9]). All Federation and non-Bajoran personnel were briefly evacuated from Deep Space 9 in early 2370 when **Circle** forces threatened the station's safety. ("The Siege" [DS9]). In 2370, Commander Riker contacted Quark at the station, concerning the whereabouts of the Duras Sisters. ("Firstborn" [TNG]).

In 2371, Ben Sisko began a major program of upgrading the station's defensive systems in anticipation of a feared **Dominion** invasion. These preparations paid off handsomely a year later when they enabled Deep Space 9 to defend itself against a massive Klingon fleet, when Chancellor **Gowron** suspected that Dominion agents were controlling the Cardassian government. ("The Way of the Warrior" [DS9]). On stardate 49904.2, upper docking pylon three was severely damaged in an attack by renegade **Jem'Hadar**. ("To the Death" [DS9]). *The pylon was subsequently repaired.*

In 2373, a new treaty between the Federation and the Klingon Empire resulted in the assignment of a detachment of Klingon warriors to Deep Space 9 to help defend against **Dominion** aggression. The move was designed to counter the alliance of the Dominion with the Cardassian Union. **General Martok** commanded the detachment. ("By Inferno's Light" [DS9]).

The station model was designed at the Star Trek: Deep Space Nine *art department by Herman Zimmerman and Rick Sternbach. Contributing artists included Ricardo Delgado, Joseph Hodges, Nathan Crowley, Jim Martin, Rob Legato, Gary Hutzel, Mike Okuda, and executive producer Rick Berman. The miniature was fabricated by Tony Meininger.*

Deep Space Station K-7. Federation outpost near **Sherman's Planet**, located one parsec from the nearest Klingon outpost. A Federation development project for Sherman's Planet in 2267 was threatened when some 1,771,561 tribbles infested storage bins of **quadrotriticale** intended for the project. ("The Trouble with Tribbles" [TOS]). SEE: **Baris, Nilz**. Most of K-7 consisted of storage areas and industrial fabrication facilites, and relatively little was habitable. Unknown to anyone at the time, a former Klingon agent named **Arne Darvin**, from the year 2373, traveled back to station K-7 in 2267 in an attempt to change the outcome of the Sherman's Planet incident. Starfleet personnel from 2373 prevented Darvin from changing history. ("Trials and Tribble-ations" [DS9]). *Stock footage of K-7 was later reused in "The Ultimate Computer" (TOS), although it represented another station.*

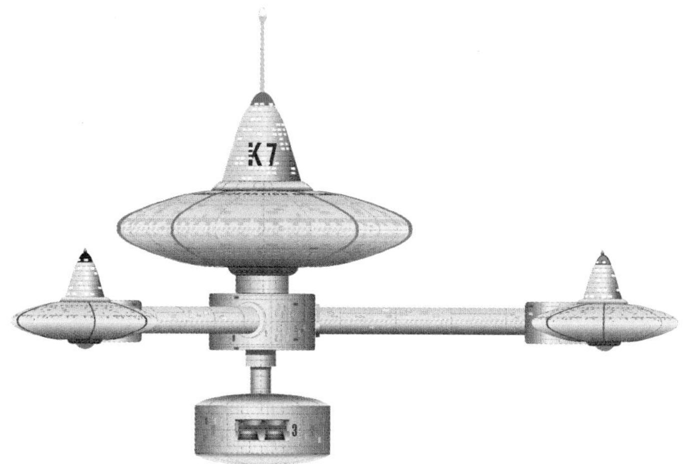

deep tissue scan. Medical scan done as part of a post mortem investigation. ("Sub Rosa" [TNG]).

"Defector, The." *Next Generation* episode #58. Written by Ronald D. Moore. Directed by Robert Scheerer. Stardate

43462.5. *First aired in 1990. A Romulan defector crosses the Neutral Zone with a terrifying report of a planned Romulan attack on Federation space.* GUEST CAST: James Sloyan as **Jarok, Alidar**; Andreas Katsulas as **Tomalak**; John Hancock as **Haden, Admiral**; S. A. Templeman as Bates. SEE: **Apnex Sea; B-Type Warbird; *Bortas, I.K.S.*; Cheron, Battle of; Gal Gath'thong; Haden, Admiral; *Henry V; Hood, U.S.S.*; Jarok, Alidar; *Monitor, U.S.S.*; Nelvana III; Neutral Zone, Romulan; Norkan outposts; onkians; Outpost Sierra VI; *pahtk*; Romulus; scout-ship, Romulan; Setal, Sublieutenant; Shakespeare, William; Starbase Lya III; *tohzah*; Tomalak; Treaty of Algeron; Valley of Chula; *veruul*.**

***Defiant* (mirror).** Starship constructed by the **Terran resistance** in the **mirror universe** for their struggle against the **Alliance**. The *Defiant* (mirror) was a close copy of the Federation starship of the same name from our universe, and was built using technical information downloaded by **Miles O'Brien (mirror)** during his visit to this universe's starbase Deep Space 9 in 2371. The mirror *Defiant* was launched in 2372. Piloted by Benjamin Sisko, this *Defiant* led the Terran resistance in fending off an Alliance fleet led by Regent **Worf (mirror)**. ("Shattered Mirror" [DS9]).

Defiant, U.S.S. Federation starship, ***Constitution* class**, Starfleet registry number NCC-1764. The *Defiant* disappeared in 2268 near **Tholian** territory into what was believed to be a **spatial interphase**. This interphase had an adverse effect on humanoid neurophysiology and caused mass insanity among the crew prior to the disappearance of the ship. The *Defiant* was last seen shimmering, suspended between two dimensions, until it faded into interspace. ("The Tholian Web" [TOS]).

Defiant, U.S.S. Federation starship, Starfleet registry number NX-74205. Prototype for the proposed *Defiant* class, the second starship to bear the name. The *Defiant* was officially classified as an escort, but began development in 2366 as a small, highly-powered, heavily-armed starship intended to defend the Federation against the **Borg**. The *Defiant* was the first of what was to be a new Federation battle fleet. Starfleet abandoned the project when the Borg threat became less urgent and after design flaws turned up during the *Defiant*'s shakedown cruise. In 2371, the *Defiant* was assigned to Deep Space 9 to help counter the threat posed by the **Jem'Hadar**, and was equipped with a **cloaking device** on loan from the **Romulans**. ("The Search, Part I" [DS9]). Later that year, **Maquis** member **Thomas Riker** hijacked the *Starship Defiant* from **Deep Space 9** to investigate a suspected **Cardassian** military buildup in the **Orias system**. ("Defiant" [DS9]). The ship had minimal crew accommodations, a small sickbay, and no provisions for families. ("The Search, Part I" [DS9]). The *Defiant* carried at least two shuttlecraft. ("The Search, Part II" [DS9]). In 2372, the *Starship Defiant* was flown to the Gamma Quadrant to observe a subspace inversion of the Bajoran wormhole. During the mission, an engine-room accident almost pulled Benjamin Sisko into subspace. ("The Visitor" [DS9]). SEE: **Sisko, Jake**. Shortly afterward, the *Defiant* battled the Federation starship *Lakota* when the *Defiant* transported Lieutenant Arriaga, a key witness in the case against **Admiral Leyton** in Leyton's attempted coup, to Earth. ("Paradise Lost" [DS9]). In 2373, the *Defiant*, under the command of Lieutenant Commander Worf, was part of the Starfleet armada that intercepted a **Borg** cube at Earth on stardate 50893. The *Defiant* was seriously damaged and the surviving crew

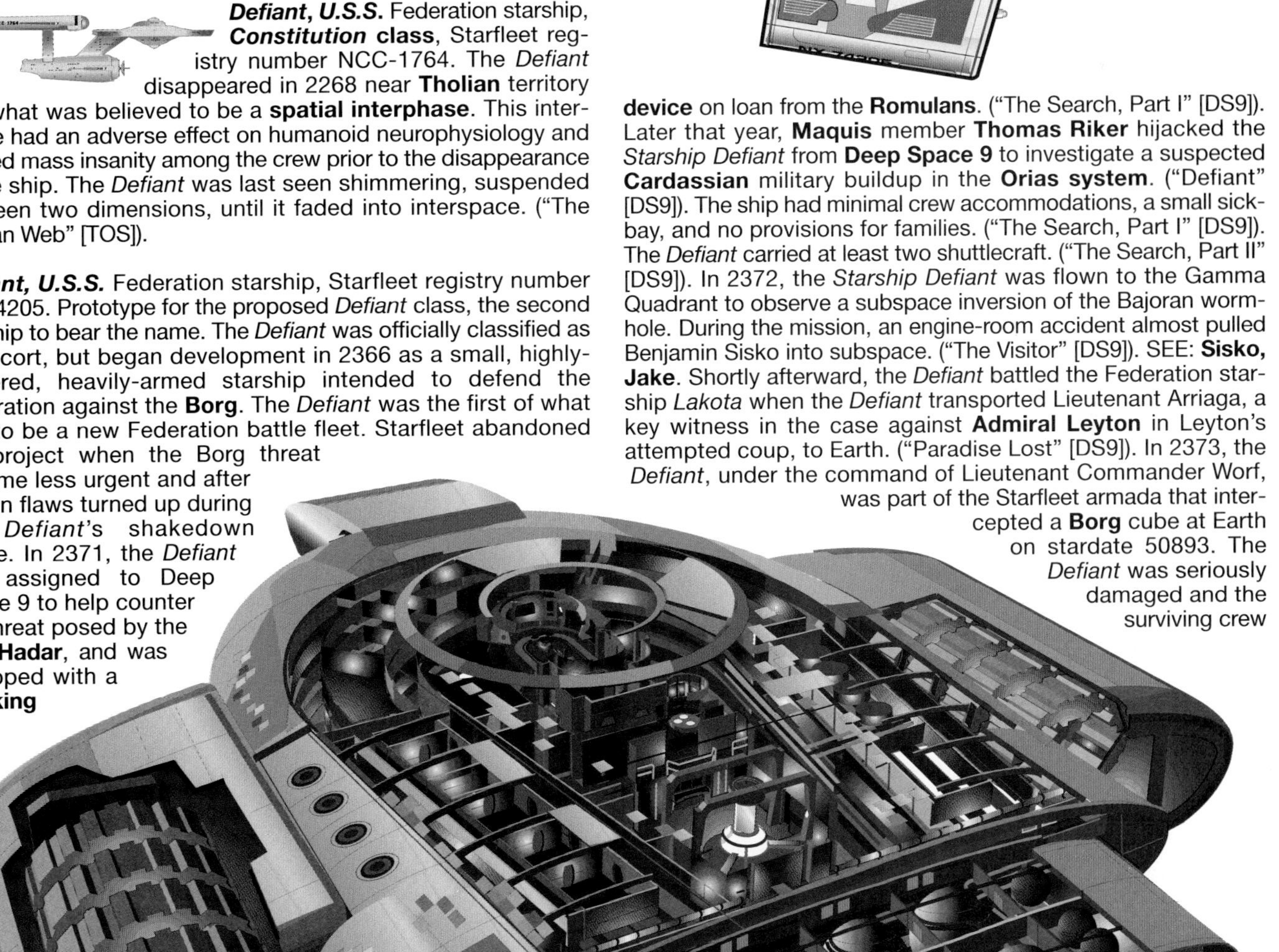

members were beamed aboard the *U.S.S. Enterprise*-E. *(Star Trek: First Contact). Fortunately, the* Defiant *was repaired in time for the next episode of* Star Trek: Deep Space Nine. *The* Defiant *was named after the ship from "The Tholian Web" (TOS) and was first seen in "The Search, Part I" (DS9). The model was designed by James Martin under the direction of Herman Zimmerman and Gary Hutzel. It was built by Tony Meininger. Interior sets supervised by Herman Zimmerman. The* Defiant *was originally to have been named the* Valiant. *When the ship was renamed* Defiant *prior to filming of "The Search, Part I" (DS9), some concept drawings for the ship suggested that it was a* Valiant*-class vessel. This notion was dropped after a revision of the script for "The Search, Part I" made it clear that the* Defiant *was the first starship of its type. The* Defiant's *engine room was first seen in "The Adversary" (DS9).*

"Defiant." *Deep Space Nine* episode #55. Written by Ronald D. Moore. Directed by Cliff Bole. Stardate 48467.3. *First aired in 1995. Thomas Riker arrives on DS9 and hijacks the* Defiant *for a Maquis mission deep within Cardassian territory. This was the first guest appearance of a* Next Generation *cast member after the end of* Star Trek: The Next Generation. GUEST CAST: Marc Alaimo as **Dukat**; Tricia O'Neil as **Korinas**; Shannon Cochran as **Kalita**; Robert Kerbeck as Cardassian soldier; Michael Canavan as **Tamal**; Jonathan Frakes as **Riker**, **Thomas**; Majel Barrett as Computer voice SEE: **Almatha sector; antiprotons; Badlands; Byzallians; Byzatium transports; Cardassian Central Command; cloaking device, Romulan; *Defiant, U.S.S.*; Detapa Council; docking clamps; Dukat, Gul; *Gandhi, U.S.S.*; *jumja*; Kalita; *karvino* juice; *Keldon*-class warship; Korinas; *Kraxon*; Lakarian City; Lazon II; Lorvan crackers; Maquis; Mekor; Ministry of Justice; Obsidian Order; Omekla III; Orias III; quantum torpedoes; Ranor, Gul; Riker, Thomas; Risa; Second Order; Sisko, Benjamin; Sixth Order; Tamal; Toran, Gul.**

deflector dish. SEE: **navigational deflector**.

deflectors. Energy field used to protect starships and other vessels from harm resulting from natural hazards or enemy attack. SEE: **shields**.

Degebian mountain goat. Animal known for its rock-climbing ability. ("The Sword of Kahless" [DS9]).

Dehner, Dr. Elizabeth. (Sally Kellerman). Psychologist assigned to the *Enterprise* in 2265 to study the crew's reactions to crisis situations. Dehner became mutated, along with Lieutenant Commander **Gary Mitchell**, into a godlike being. Dehner and Mitchell were later killed when *Enterprise* captain Kirk sought to quarantine them on planet **Delta Vega**. Both were later listed as having given their lives in the line of duty. ("Where No Man Has Gone Before" [TOS]).

Deinonychus VII. Planet. The *Starship Enterprise*-D was to rendezvous with the supply ship ***U.S.S. Biko*** at Deinonychus VII on stardate 46271. ("A Fistful of Datas" [TNG]).

"Déjà Q." *Next Generation* episode #61. Written by Richard Danus. Directed by Les Landau. Stardate 43539.1. *First aired in 1990. Q loses his powers and takes refuge on the* Enterprise*-D.* GUEST CAST: John de Lancie as **Q**; Whoopi Goldberg as **Guinan**; Richard Cansino as **Garin, Dr.**; Betty Muramoto as Scientist. SEE: **Belzoidian flea; berthold rays; Bre'el IV; Calamarain; Data; Deltived Asteroid Belt; Garin; Markoffian sea lizard; Q Continuum; Q; Q2; *Sakharov*, *Shuttlecraft*; Station Nigala IV; subspace phenomena; warp field.**

***déjà vu*.** French-language term from Earth referring to a perception that a current experience is a repetition of a previous one. An intense feeling of *déjà vu* experienced by several *Enterprise*-D crew members in 2368 was found to be due to the passage of the ship into a **temporal causality loop**. ("Cause and Effect" [TNG]).

Dejar. (Jessica Hendra). Operative of the **Obsidian Order**. In 2371 Dejar posed as a scientific colleague of **Ulani** and **Gilora** and attempted to sabotage a joint Cardassian-Bajoran scientific effort to place a subspace relay in the **Gamma Quadrant**. ("Destiny" [DS9]).

Deka tea. Hot beverage. Served at Quark's bar. ("The Alternate" [DS9]).

Dekon Elig. (Dan Curry). Bajoran geneticist who invented an **aphasia virus**, intended for use as a terrorist weapon against the **Cardassian** occupation forces. Dekon Elig, who was a member of the Bajoran **Higa Metar** underground, died while attempting escape from the Cardassians at the **Velos VII Internment Camp** in 2360. Dekon's aphasia virus was accidentally unleashed at Deep Space 9 in 2369, after the Cardassian retreat from **Bajor**. ("Babel" [DS9]). SEE: **Surmak Ren**. *The face of Dekon Elig, seen only as a mug shot in a computer screen, was provided by* Star Trek *visual effects producer Dan Curry.*

Dekora Assan. Person murdered on planet **Japori II** in 2371. **Retaya**, a Flaxian assassin, was accused of the murder, but later cleared of the charge. ("Improbable Cause" [DS9]).

dekyon. Subatomic particle with subspace and temporal properties. Dekyons can travel across a **temporal causality loop**. A dekyon field was used to interact with **positronic** subprocessors in Data's brain, permitting the transmission of a simple message to the next iteration of a causality loop when the *Enterprise*-D was trapped in such a loop in 2368. ("Cause and Effect" [TNG]). In 2371 the *U.S.S. Voyager* used a dekyon beam to escape the **event horizon** of a type-4 **quantum singularity**. ("Parallax" [VGR]).

delactovine. Systemic stimulant drug. Used aboard the *Enterprise*-D. ("The Inner Light" [TNG]).

Delaney sisters. Reference to two siblings, Megan and Jenny Delaney, who were scientists assigned to the stellar cartography department of the *Starship Voyager*. Shortly after the ship was lost in the Delta Quadrant, **Tom Paris** attempted to arrange a date with Jenny Delaney for **Harry Kim**. ("Time and Again" [VGR], "The Chute" [VGR]). Prior to visiting planet Sikaris in 2371, Tom Paris, Harry Kim, and the Delaney sisters shared a holodeck experience set in Venice. ("Prime Factors." [VGR]).

Delaney, Jenny. Starfleet officer onboard the *U.S.S. Voyager*. One of the Delaney sisters. Jenny Delaney and Harry Kim went on a holodeck date just prior to stardate 48642, sharing a gondola in the Venice holodeck program. During the date, Harry fell over the side of the boat. ("Prime Factors." [VGR]).

Delaney, Megan. Starfleet officer onboard the *U.S.S. Voyager.* One of the **Delaney sisters**. Megan Delaney dated Lieutenant Tom Paris while her sister, Jenny, went out with Ensign Harry Kim. ("The Chute" [VGR]).

Delaplane, Governor. Leader of the planet **Pacifica**. Delaplane sent a message to Starfleet Command when Picard canceled a scheduled visit there in 2364. ("Conspiracy" [TNG]).

Delavian chocolates. Rare and exotic confection. In 2371, **Garak** offered to share his Delavian chocolates with Dr. **Julian Bashir**. ("Improbable Cause" [DS9]).

Delb II. Planet. Homeworld of **Nellen Tore**, assistant to Starfleet **Admiral Norah Satie**. ("The Drumhead" [TNG]).

Delinia II. Planet where **transporter psychosis** was first diagnosed in 2209. ("Realm of Fear" [TNG]).

Delios VII. Planet that was the home to the Karis Tribe. ("Sacred Ground" [VGR]).

Delos IV. Planet on which **Dr. Beverly Crusher** did her medical internship under **Dr. Dalen Quaice** in 2352. ("Remember Me" [TNG]).

Delos. Star system in which two inhabited planets are located, **Ornara** and **Brekka**. The star Delos underwent a period of large-scale magnetic field changes in 2364. The *Enterprise*-D was assigned to study the phenomenon and accidentally became embroiled in an ongoing dispute between the two planets. ("Symbiosis" [TNG]).

Delovian souffle. An ice-cream-like dessert served by Guinan in the **Ten-Forward Lounge** aboard the *Enterprise*-D. ("The Child" [TNG]).

Delphi Ardu. Planetary system in which was located the last outpost of the now-defunct **Tkon Empire**. The *Starship Enterprise*-D and a **Ferengi Marauder** spacecraft were detained there by the Tkon outpost in 2364 when the Federation made first contact with both the Ferengi and the surviving Tkon outpost. ("The Last Outpost" [TNG]). SEE: **Portal**.

Delta IV. Homeworld to the Deltan civilization. Starfleet officer **Will Decker** once served on this planet, where he met future shipmate **Ilia**, a native of Delta IV. (*Star Trek: The Motion Picture*).

Delta Quadrant. One-quarter of the entire Milky Way Galaxy. Virtually nothing is known about this quadrant, as its closest point is some 40,000 light-years from the Federation. It is believed that the **Borg** homeworld is somewhere deep in Delta Quadrant. The **Barzan wormhole** (not to be confused with the Bajoran wormhole), at one time believed to be stable, had one terminus at least briefly in the Delta Quadrant, although that endpoint was later found to move unpredictably. ("The Price" [TNG]). **Q** offered to take **Vash** to explore Delta Quadrant, but the archaeologist declined. ("Q-Less" [DS9]). Dozens of ships from all over the galaxy were transported to Delta Quadrant in 2371 by the **Caretaker**, who was searching for life-forms with bio-molecular patterns compatible with his. Among these ships were the ***U.S.S. Voyager*** and a Maquis ship, transported from the **Badlands** in the Alpha Quadrant, some 70,000 light-years away. The destruction of the Caretaker's **Array** meant that the joint *Voyager*-Maquis crew was virtually stranded and some 70 years' travel time from home. ("Caretaker" [VGR]).

Gamma Quadrant

Delta Quadrant

Alpha Quadrant

Beta Quadrant

Delta Rana IV. Class-M planet that was home to a Federation colony which was destroyed by the **Husnock** in 2361. All but one of the 11,000 colonists were killed and the planet surface was ravaged. The one survivor, actually a **Douwd** traveling under the name of **Kevin Uxbridge**, used his enormous powers to destroy the entire Husnock race in retribution. Later, Uxbridge remained in self-imposed isolation on Delta Rana IV. Delta Rana IV has three moons. ("The Survivors" [TNG]).

Delta Rana star system. Planetary system. The location of planet **Delta Rana IV**. ("The Survivors" [TNG]).

Delta Vega. Distant Class-M planet near the galaxy's edge. Location of an automated **lithium** cracking station. Captain James Kirk attempted to maroon the mutated **Gary Mitchell** there in 2265 because, while habitable, the planet was visited only every 20 years by cargo freighters. ("Where No Man Has Gone Before" [TOS]). *The matte painting used to establish the huge exterior of the Delta Vega lithium cracking station was done by noted visual effects artist Albert Whitlock. The painting was later modified and re-used as the surface portion of the Tantalus penal colony in "Dagger of the Mind" (TOS).*

delta radiation. Form of hazardous energy. Fleet Captain **Christopher Pike** suffered severe delta-ray exposure following an accident aboard a class-J training ship in 2266. ("The Menagerie, Part I" [TOS]). Delta radiation emitted from a star can interfere with a ship's sensors, as when the ***Rio Grande*** searched for the downed ***Yangtzee Kiang*** in the Gamma Quadrant in 2369. ("Battle Lines" [DS9]).

delta wave frequency. Energy pattern. The bio-electric field generated by **Bothan** ships used delta wave frequencies. ("Persistence of Vision" [VGR]).

delta wave inducer. Medical instrument used to induce sleep. ("Invasive Procedures" [DS9]).

delta-series radioisotopes. Category of radioactive elements that are toxic to humans. In 2371, **Deep Space 9** Chief of Operations **Miles O'Brien** accidentally received a dose of delta-series radioisotopes. The **quantum singularity** in the engine of a nearby **Romulan warbird** affected the radioisotopes in O'Brien's body, causing him to timeshift into the future several times. ("Visionary" [DS9]).

Deltans. Humanoid species native to planet **Delta IV**. Deltans exhibit a characteristically bald head, except for eyebrows, and are known for their highly developed sexuality. *Enterprise* navigator **Ilia** was Deltan. (*Star Trek: The Motion Picture*).

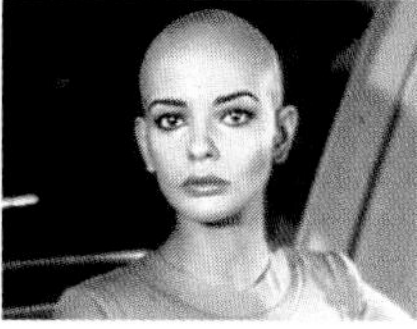

Deltived Asteroid Belt. An astronomical formation misplaced by **Q2**, who wasn't too proud of the mishap. ("Déjà Q" [TNG]).

Delvin fluff pastries. Confection. Delvin fluff pastries should not be eaten for breakfast. ("Facets" [DS9]).

Delvok. Composer of **Vulcan** études. Jadzia Dax felt his music too emotional for a Vulcan. ("Melora" [DS9]).

Demalos. Enaran citizen. Demalos, a member of the group called the **Regressives**, was murdered, along with the rest of his people as part of the horrific **resettlement** on Enara Prime. ("Remember" [VGR]).

Demilitarized Zone. Region of space along the border between **Cardassian** and **Federation** space, established as a buffer by the treaty signed between the two powers in 2370. Also known as the DMZ. Neither side was permitted to place military outposts, conduct fleet exercises, or station warships anywhere in the demilitarized area. As part of the treaty, territorial borders were redrawn, resulting in several Federation colonies becoming Cardassian property and some Cardassian colonies being placed within Federation territory. ("Journey's End" [TNG]). The peace was fragile at best. Federation colonists, believing their government had abandoned them, banded together to form the **Maquis** terrorist organization, while the **Cardassian Central Command** secretly supplied weapons to Cardassian colonists in the zone. ("Preemptive Strike" [TNG], "The Maquis, Parts I and II" [DS9]). **Silaran Prin** lived on a planet located near the Demilitarized Zone. ("The Darkness and the Light" [DS9]).

Demmas. (Brad Greenquist). Eldest son of the Autarch of **Ilari**. Demmas was next in line to become Autarch in 2373, when the centuries-old consciousness of the deposed tyrant **Tieran** killed the Autarch and staged a coup. Demmas fled the planet and enlisted the aid of the *Voyager* crew in thwarting Tieran's plans to take over his homeworld. ("Warlord" [VGR]).

"Demons of Air and Darkness." Name given to the ancient **Iconians** in ancient texts, referring to the Iconians' legendary ability to travel without spacecraft, using an advanced technology to transport between planets. ("Contagion" [TNG]).

Denar. Geographical and administrative province on planet **Ilari**. In 2373, the Viceroy of Denar Province pledged his support for **Tieran** in exchange for more territory. ("Warlord" [VGR]).

Deneb II. Planet where an unknown entity known as **Kesla** murdered several women. The same evil energy force continued its murderous deeds on planet **Argelius II** in 2267. ("Wolf in the Fold" [TOS]).

Deneb IV. Class-M planet inhabited by a humanoid civilization called the **Bandi**. *The star Deneb is part of the constellation Cygnus (the Swan) visible from Earth.* ("Encounter at Farpoint, Parts I and II" [TNG]).

Deneb V. Homeworld to the Denebians. ("I, Mudd" [TOS]).

Denebian slime devil. Nasty creature that the Klingon **Korax** thought bore a strong resemblance to Captain Kirk. ("The Trouble with Tribbles" [TOS]). *"A resemblance, perhaps. But not a strong one," says an unnamed source whose initials are R.H.J.*

Denebians. Humanoid civilization. The Denebians purchased all rights to a Vulcan fuel synthesizer from confidence man Harry Mudd in 2267. The Denebians contacted the Vulcans and found the sale a ruse. Mudd was arrested and given several colorful choices of execution, none of which appealed to Mudd. ("I, Mudd" [TOS]). SEE: **Mudd, Harcourt Fenton.**

Deneva. Federation planet, considered by many to be one of the most beautiful in the galaxy, boasting a population of over 1 million. Deneva was colonized in the 22nd century, and served as a base for interstellar freighting. The planet was infected by alien neural parasites in 2267, resulting in the deaths of many of the colonists. One infested colonist flew a small spacecraft directly into the Denevan sun. The sun's intense radiation drove the parasite from his body, just before the ship was incinerated by the sun. His attempt led science personnel from the *Starship Enterprise* to learn that the parasites were adversely affected by ultraviolet radiation. *Enterprise* personnel placed a series of satellites around the planet, bombarding the surface with sufficient ultraviolet radiation to eradicate the parasites. Among the colonists killed in 2267 were **Aurelan** and **George Samuel Kirk**. They were survived by their son **Peter Kirk**. ("Operation—Annihilate!" [TOS]). SEE: **Denevan neural parasites**; **Ingraham B**. *The city exteriors for Deneva were shot on location at TRW near Los Angeles. The establishing shot of Kirk's brother's lab was a building on the campus of UCLA, and the entrance to the building was the cafeteria at TRW.*

Denevan neural parasite. Origin unknown, an irregularly shaped gelatinous life-form analogous in structure to an oversized brain cell. The entire population of these parasites were somehow linked together to form a collective intelligence. In their young form, the parasites were mobile, capable of flight. They would latch themselves onto a humanoid life-form, infiltrating the humanoid nervous system, gaining control of both autonomic and higher functions, and inflicting severe pain on the victim. These parasites were so virulent that they were capable of infesting an entire planet's population, at which point they would reach across interstellar distances to another planet. The neural parasites appeared to have come from outside the Milky Way Galaxy, attacking the ancient Beta Portolan system, then infesting **Levinius V**, **Theta Cygni XII**, **Ingraham B,** and, in 2267, planet **Deneva**. Among the parasites' victims at Deneva were **Aurelan** and **George Samuel Kirk**, brother and sister-in-law to Captain James Kirk. Also infested was Science Officer Spock, although he was freed by exposure to intense light, an experiment that provided the means to destroy the remaining parasites on Deneva. The actual eradication was accomplished by placing 210 satellites in orbit around Deneva, bombarding the surface with powerful ultraviolet radiation. ("Operation— Annihilate!" [TOS]). SEE: **Denevan ship.**

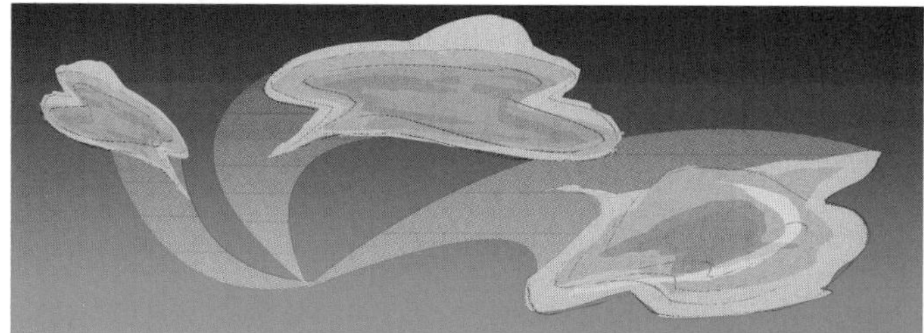

Denevan ship. Small one-person spacecraft. A Denevan ship was flown by a colonist from planet **Deneva** in 2267. The pilot had been infested by the **Denevan neural parasites**, and in desperation, he flew the ship directly into the Denevan sun. Just prior to the ship's incineration, the pilot was freed from the parasites, which apparently were unable to tolerate the intense levels of ultraviolet radiation. The pilot's death provided valuable information for the control and eradication of the parasites from Deneva. ("Operation—Annihilate!" [TOS]).

Deng. *Enterprise*-D crew member who assisted in setting up the **thermal deflectors** against a fierce firestorm on planet **Bersallis III** in 2369. ("Lessons" [TNG]).

Denius III. Planet. Visited by the ***U.S.S. Yamato*** under the command of **Captain Donald Varley** and **Dr. Ramsey** in 2365. Artifacts recovered from Denius III included an unknown instrument that displayed a star map, making it possible to determine the location of the legendary planet **Iconia**. ("Contagion" [TNG]).

denkir. Unit of volume measure used by **Zibalians**. One hundred denkirs is about equal to 200 milliliters. ("The Most Toys" [TNG]).

Denkiri Arm. Located mostly in the **Gamma Quadrant**, the Denkiri Arm is one of the massive spiral-shaped arms that make up the Milky Way Galaxy. The **Barzan wormhole**, previously thought to be stable, had one terminus that was located in the Denkiri Arm, some 70,000 light-years from Federation space. ("The Price" [TNG]).

Denning, General Rex. (Charles Napier). Military officer with the United States Army Air Corps on 20th century **Earth**. Denning investigated the crash of an extraterrestrial spacecraft near **Roswell**, New Mexico, on Earth in 1947. Denning, who was the veteran of two world wars, was deeply concerned for his nation's security, and about the potential risk that extraterrestrials might pose. Denning's investigation was conducted under the direct orders of American President **Harry S Truman**. ("Little Green Men" [DS9]). *Denning's first name was not in dialog, but is from the script. Charles Napier previously portrayed Adam in "The Way to Eden" (TOS).*

Denorios Belt. Charged plasma field in the **Bajor system** where at least five of the mystical Bajoran **Orbs** were discovered. The stable **Bajoran wormhole**, discovered in 2369, was located in the Denorios Belt. Bajoran religious beliefs held that the **Celestial Temple**, home of the **Prophets**, was in the belt, and many Bajorans interpreted the wormhole as being a manifestation of the temple itself. The Denorios Belt was characterized by unusually severe neutrino disturbances. ("Emissary" [DS9]). Ships have always avoided the Denorios Belt. ("If Wishes Were Horses" [DS9]). The Denorios Belt also contains numerous **tachyon eddies**. Such eddies were believed to have propelled ancient **Bajoran solar-sail vessels** across interstellar distances at warp speeds to Cardassia. ("Explorers" [DS9]).

dentarium. Metal alloy, used in Vulcan spacecraft such as the ***T'Pau***. ("Unification, Part I" [TNG]).

Denubian Alps. Nonterrestrial mountain range known for excellent skiing conditions. Denubian Alps skiing runs are among the **holodeck** programs available on the *Enterprise*-D. ("Angel One" [TNG]).

denucleation. Process by which genetic material is removed from the nuclei of an organism's cells. The women of **Taresia** used denucleation to harvest genetic material from cells of male humanoids as part of their procreation. Unfortunately for the males, this process was fatal. ("Favorite Son" [VGR]).

Denver, U.S.S. Federation transport ship. Crew complement of 23. In 2368, the *Denver* was transporting 517 colonists to the Beloti Sector when the ship struck a gravitic mine left over from the Cardassian wars. The *Denver* sustained heavy damage, crashing in the Mericor system. The *Enterprise*-D was called in to assist with the survivors. ("Ethics" [TNG]).

deoxyribonucleic acid. SEE: **DNA**.

deoxyribose suspensions. A fluid derived from deoxyribonucleic acid (**DNA**). **J'Dan** used deoxyribose suspensions to encode stolen *Enterprise*-D schematics into amino acid sequences, and injected them into his bloodstream, making his body an undetectable carrier of the secret information. ("The Drumhead" [TNG]).

DePaul, Lieutenant. (Sean Kenney). Crew member aboard the original *Starship Enterprise* who sometimes served as navigator and helm officer. ("Arena" [TOS], "A Taste of Armageddon" [TOS]). *Sean Kenney also played the disfigured Captain Pike in "The Menagerie, Parts I and II" (TOS).*

Deral. (Brett Cullen). Inhabitant of planet **Meridian**. In 2371, while Meridian was in its corporeal state, Deral worked with the crew of the ***U.S.S. Defiant***, attempting to stabilize the planet's dimensional shifts. During this period, he and **Jadzia Dax** became romantically involved. The two were separated when the planet shifted back into a noncorporeal state. ("Meridian" [DS9]).

Dereth. (Cully Fredericksen). Citizen of the **Vidiian Sodality**. Dereth served as ***honatta*** for **Motura**, a fellow **Vidiian**, and in that capacity he was responsible for finding replacement organs for Motura, when the **phage** caused Motura's own organs to fail. In 2371, Dereth abducted *Voyager* crew member **Neelix**, removing Neelix's lungs to be implanted into Motura's body. ("Phage" [VGR]).

Deriben V. Planet. Location of **Lieutenant Aquiel Uhnari**'s last posting prior to her assignment to **Relay Station 47** in 2368. She did not get along with her commanding officer at Deriben. ("Aquiel" [TNG]).

dermal dysplasia. Medical skin disorder caused by an overexposure of the epidermis to hazardous levels of thermal and ultraviolet radiation. ("Future's End, Part I" [VGR]).

dermal osmotic sealant. Medicinal skin application used as a protection against epidermal irritation, such as that caused by exposure to **trigemic vapors**. ("Parturition" [VGR]).

dermal regenerator. Starfleet medical instrument used to repair damaged epidermal tissue. ("The Homecoming" [DS9], "State of Flux" [VGR]).

dermal residue. Substance left behind on inanimate objects after contact with humanoid skin. Dermal residue left on a Bajoran earring permitted Deep Space 9 personnel to identify the earring's owner as the Bajoran resistance fighter **Li Nalas.** ("The Homecoming" [DS9]).

dermaline gel. Medicinal material used in the treatment of burns. ("Deadlock" [VGR]).

dermatiraelian plastiscine. Medication used to maintain the effects of cosmetic surgery. **Aamin Marritza** took it for five years after altering his face to that of **Gul Darhe'el.** ("Duet" [DS9]).

Dern, Ensign. (Carlos Ferro). *Enterprise*-D systems engineer. Lieutenant Reginald Barclay suggested Dern to serve on an away team to the *U.S.S. Yosemite*, but Geordi wanted Barclay to come along. ("Realm of Fear" [TNG]). Assigned to conn in 2370. He was killed by another member of the *Enterprise*-D crew, who was under the influence of **Barclay's Protomorphosis Syndrome**. ("Genesis" [TNG]). *Dern's name was never mentioned on air and is from the script.*

DeSalle, Lieutenant. (Michael Barrier). Crew member aboard the *Starship Enterprise* who served as navigator, and later as an assistant chief engineer. ("The Squire of Gothos" [TOS], "This Side of Paradise" [TOS], "Catspaw" [TOS]).

"Descent, Part I." *Next Generation* episode #152. Story by Jeri Taylor. Teleplay by Ronald D. Moore. Directed by Alexander Singer. Stardate 46982.1. *First aired in 1993. The* Enterprise-D *encounters a group of self-aware fanatical Borg who are followers of Data's evil brother, Lore. This was the cliff-hanger last episode of the sixth season. Noted physicist Stephen Hawking made a cameo appearance in this episode.* GUEST CAST: John Neville as **Newton, Issac**; Jim Morton as **Einstein, Albert**; Natalie Nogulich as **Necheyev, Alynna**; Brian Cousins as **Crosis**; Professor Stephen Hawking as **Hawking, Dr. Stephen William**; Richard Gilbert as Hill, Bosus; Stephen James Carver as Tayar. SEE: ***Agamemnon, U.S.S.*; Borg; Borg ship; Brooks, Admiral; Corelki; *Crazy Horse, U.S.S.*; Crosis; Data; Einstein, Albert; *El-Baz, Shuttlepod*; Ferengi trading vessel; forced plasma beam; Gates, Ensign; *Gorkon, U.S.S.*; Hawking, Dr. Stephen William; Hugh; level-2 security alert; Lore; luvetric pulse; MS 1 Colony; Necheyev, Vice-Admiral Alynna; New Berlin Colony; Newton, Isaac; Ohniaka III; One, The; quantum fluctuations; ship recognition protocols; Torsus; Towles; transwarp; Wallace, Darian.**

"Descent, Part II." Next Generation episode #153. Written by René Echevarria. Directed by Alexander Singer. Stardate 47025.4. *First aired in 1993. The* Enterprise-D *resolves the situation with the fanatical group of self-aware Borg by restoring Data's ethical programming and disassembling Lore. This was the first episode of the seventh season.* GUEST CAST: Jonathan Del Arco as **Hugh**; Alex Datcher as **Taitt, Ensign**; James Horan as **Barnaby, Lieutenant**; Brian Cousins as **Crosis**; Benito Martinez as **Salazar**; Michael Reilly Burke as **Goval**. SEE: **Barnaby, Lieutenant; Borg; Borg ship; Crosis; Crusher, Dr. Beverly; Data; Devala Lake; ethical program; Emotion chip; Goval; Hugh; kedion; Lore; metaphasic shield; Ohniaka III; Salazar; Starbase 295; Taitt, Ensign; transwarp; Wallace, Darian.**

desealer rod. Device used to unlock a pulsatel lockseal. ("Necessary Evil" [DS9]).

desegranine. Cardassian drug used to reverse memory loss. ("Second Skin" [DS9]).

DeSeve, Ensign Stefan. (Barry Lynch). Starfleet officer who renounced his Federation citizenship in 2349 to live on **Romulus**. DeSeve later recalled that he found the simplicity of the Romulan system of absolute values and their strong sense of purpose to be appealing. He noted that in later years, he began to realize that right and wrong is a more ambiguous matter. After 20 years on Romulus, DeSeve returned to Federation custody in 2369 to help arrange the defection of Romulan **Vice-Proconsul M'ret** to the Federation. ("Face of the Enemy" [TNG]).

DeSoto, Captain Robert. (Michael Cavanaugh). Commanding officer of the ***U.S.S. Hood.*** Future *Enterprise*-D Executive Officer **William T. Riker** served under DeSoto aboard the *Hood* after Riker's assignment to the *U.S.S. Potemkin*. DeSoto spoke very highly of Riker, despite an incident in which Riker refused to let DeSoto beam into a hazardous situation. ("Encounter at Farpoint, Parts I and II" [TNG]). In 2366, DeSoto and the *Hood* were assigned to transport mission specialist **Tam Elbrun** for a priority rendezvous with the *Enterprise*-D. ("Tin Man" [TNG]). *DeSoto was mentioned in "Encounter at Farpoint" (TNG), but not actually seen until "Tin Man" (TNG).*

Dessica II. Planet containing ruins of **Romulan** origin. In 2370, these ruins were the target of mercenary **Arctus Baran**, who was working for the **Vulcan isolationist movement**, searching for fragments of the ancient **Stone of Gol**. Baran's activities had caught the attention of *Enterprise*-D Captain Jean-Luc Picard (an amateur archaeologist), who was captured by Baran's crew at a Dessican bar. ("Gambit, Part I" [TNG]).

Dessican bartender. (Stephen Lee). Proprietor of a bar on planet **Dessica II**. He was reluctant to allow **Yranac** to share information about Captain Picard with an *Enterprise*-D away team, led by Commander Riker in 2370. ("Gambit, Part I" [TNG]). *This character was never given a name.*

"Destiny." *Deep Space Nine* episode #61. Written by David S. Cohen & Martin A. Winer. Directed by Les Landau. Stardate 48543.2. *First aired in 1995. The arrival of Cardassian scientists on DS9 appears to fulfill an ancient Bajoran prophecy—one that also predicts the destruction of the station.* GUEST CAST: Tracy Scoggins as **Gilora Rejal**; Wendy Robie as **Ulani Belor**; Erick Avari as **Yarka**; Jessica Hendra as **Dejar**. SEE: **Bajoran wormhole; Cardassians; Dax, Tobin; Dejar; Ferengi Rules of Acquisition; Gilora Rejal; Iloja of Prim; Janir; *kanar*; Kira Nerys; Obsidian Order; Orb of Change; Qui'al Dam; Regova eggs; shuttlepod; silithium; Starfleet General Orders and Regulations; subspace technology; tojal in yamok sauce; Trakor; Trakor's Third Prophecy; Trakor's Fourth Prophecy; Ulani Belor; vole; Vulcan; Yarka.**

destruct sequence. A command program incorporated into the main computer of Federation starships, intended to facilitate destruction of the ship to prevent it from falling into enemy hands. The *U.S.S. Enterprise* destruct sequence required voice authorization from the commanding officer and two other senior officers. After voiceprint confirmation of each officer's identity, the commanding officer would verbally enter the command, "Destruct sequence one, code one, one A." The computer would verify the command; then the second officer would verbally enter, "Destruct sequence two, code one, one-A, two-B," which would then be verified by the computer. The third officer would give the code, "Destruct sequence three, code one-B, two-B, three." The actual destruct countdown would be initiated by the command from the captain: "Code zero, zero, zero, destruct zero." The computer would then give a countdown to destruction. The destruct countdown could be aborted until minus five seconds by the command "Code one two three continuity, abort destruct order." The destruct sequence was entered but not executed when **Lokai** and **Bele** attempted to commandeer the *Enterprise* in 2269. ("Let That Be Your Last Battlefield" [TOS]). The same sequence was later used to destroy the *Enterprise* at the **Genesis Planet** when the ship was about to be seized by a Klingon boarding party in 2285. *(Star Trek III: The Search for Spock).* In 2372, Captain Kathryn Janeway initiated the *U.S.S. Voyager*'s destruct sequence in order to halt an automated Cardassian missile from attacking planet Rakosa V. Janeway aborted the destruct order after *Voyager* chief engineer B'Elanna Torres successfully destroyed the rogue missile. SEE: **Dreadnought**. ("Dreadnought" [DS9]). A duplicate Captain Kathryn Janeway of a duplicate *Voyager* used the destruct sequence to destroy her ship to prevent it from being taken over by Vidiians in 2372. ("Deadlock" [VGR]). SEE: **autodestruct**.

Detapa Council. Ruling body of the **Cardassian** government, established some five centuries ago. Both the military **Cardassian Central Command** and the **Obsidian Order** intelligence agency were under direct control of the Detapa Council, although in actual practice, both operated with virtual autonomy. ("Defiant" [DS9]). The Detapa Council won control of the Cardassian government in 2372 when a civilian uprising overthrew the Central Command. The **Klingon High Council** interpreted this *coup* as proof that the Cardassian government had been taken over by the Dominion, possibly by shape-shifters that could have replaced council members. Shortly thereafter, the Klingons invaded Cardassia in order to protect the Alpha Quadrant. They intended to execute the Detapa Council and install an imperial overseer to put down any further resistance. **Gul Dukat** helped the council flee the Klingon invasion fleet by evacuating them from Cardassia Prime aboard the ***Prakesh***, providing convincing evidence that the council had not been replaced by agents of the Dominion. ("The Way of the Warrior" [DS9]).

Detrian system. Star system that experienced a collision of two gas-giant planets in 2369. The combined mass of the two planets was sufficient to cause a self-sustaining fusion reaction; that is, the resulting object became a small star. The *Enterprise*-D recorded the event for scientific posterity. ("Ship in a Bottle" [TNG]).

detronal scanner. Medical instrument used to read and encode the DNA patterns of living tissue. ("Ethics" [TNG]).

deuridium. Rare substance used by the **Kobliad** people to stabilize their cell structures to prolong their lives. A shipment of deuridium from the Gamma Quadrant was delivered to Deep Space 9 in 2369. ("The Passenger" [DS9]). SEE: **Vantika, Rao**.

deuterium control conduit. An integral part of a starship's warp propulsion system. Geordi La Forge and Wesley Crusher were making routine adjustments on the deuterium control conduit on the *Enterprise*-D when the ship was assigned to transport **Salia** to her homeworld of **Daled IV**. ("The Dauphin" [TNG]).

deuterium maintenance. A technical support repair crew aboard a Federation starship responsible for the ship's supply of slush deuterium fuel. Captain Janeway ordered Neelix to serve two weeks scrubbing the exhaust manifolds in 2373. ("Fair Trade" [VGR]).

deuterium. Isotope of hydrogen consisting of one proton and one neutron in the nucleus, around which circles a single electron. Cryogenic (extremely cold) deuterium was the primary fuel source for the fusion impulse-engine reactors in Federation starships. Deuterium was also used as one of the reactants in the matter/**antimatter** reaction system in those ships' **warp drive**. The deuterium was the matter, and anti-hydrogen served as the antimatter. ("Relics" [TNG]). Deuterium was also used as fuel in the fusion reactors of the **impulse drive** as well as the reaction-control thrusters of Federation starships. ("The Cloud" [VGR]).

Devala Lake. Aquatic body. Geordi and Data once shared a sailing adventure at Devala Lake. Data decided to go swimming, but because he lacked buoyancy, he sank straight to the bottom. Data was forced to walk more than a kilometer along the bottom to reach shore. It required nearly two weeks to completely get all the water out of his servos. ("Descent, Part II" [TNG]).

Devidia II. Class-M planet located in the **Marrab sector**. The occupants existed on the surface, but in a slightly different time continuum from the *Enterprise*-D. The **Devidians** used their time-travel abilities to go back to 19th-century Earth. ("Time's Arrow, Part I" [TNG]). SEE: **LB10445.**

Devidian nurse. (Mary Stein). Shape-shifting person from **Devidia II**. This individual took human form in order to steal neural energy from humans on 19th-century Earth. ("Time's Arrow, Part II" [TNG]). SEE: **neural depletion.**

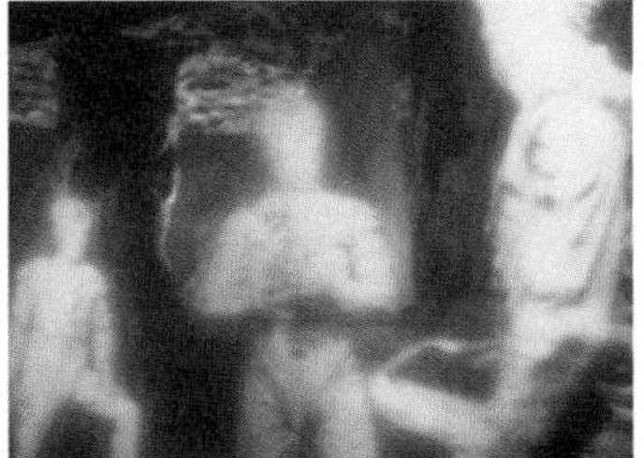

Devidians. Intelligent life-forms native to planet **Devidia II**. The Devidians existed in a slightly different time continuum from "normal" matter, and thus were only barely detectable to an observer in "normal" time. The Devidians thrived on neural energy that they stole from dying life-forms. In 2368, the Devidians sent an expedition back in time to 19th-century Earth, where they attempted to extract large amounts of neural energy from victims of the **cholera** epidemic in the city of San Francisco. They were prevented from doing so by members of the *Enterprise*-D crew who also traveled back in time. ("Time's Arrow, Parts I and II" [TNG]).

"Devil in the Dark, The." Original Series episode #26. Written by Gene L. Coon. Directed by Joseph Pevney. Stardate 3196.1. *First aired in 1967. A terrifying subterranean creature is found to be simply a mother protecting her eggs. Stuntman Janos Prohaska not only played the Horta, he designed and built the creature.* GUEST CAST: Ken Lynch as **Vanderberg**, **Chief Engineer**; Brad Weston as **Appel**, **Ed**; Biff Elliott as **Schmitter**; George E. Allen as Engineer #1; Jon Cavett as Guard; Barry Russo as **Giotto**, **Lieutenant Commander**; Dick Dial as Sam; Janos Prohaska as **Horta**; Eddie Paskey as Security guard; Frank da Vinci as Osborne, Lieutenant; Davis Roberts as Lewis. SEE: **Appel, Ed; Giotto, Commander; Horta; Janus VI; pergium; phaser type-1; phaser type-2; PXK reactor; Schmitter; silicon-based life; silicon nodule; thermoconcrete; Vanderberg, Chief Engineer; Vault of Tomorrow; Vulcan mind-meld.**

"Devil's Due." *Next Generation* episode #87. Teleplay by Philip LaZebnik. Story by Philip LaZebnik and William Douglas Lansford. Directed by Tom Benko. Stardate 44474.5. *First aired in 1991. A planet that has enjoyed a thousand years of peace by signing a pact with the devil now has to make good on the deal. "Devil's Due" was originally written for the proposed* **Star Trek II** *television series that had been planned in the late 1970s. A very early version of this story was part of Gene Roddenberry's first-draft proposal for* Star Trek *in the early 1960s.* GUEST CAST: Marta DuBois as **Ardra**; Paul Lambert as **Melian**; Marcello Tubert as **Jared**, **Acost**; Thad Lamey as Devil monster; Tom Magee as Klingon monster. SEE: **Ardra; Atheneum Vaults; Barnum, P. T.; Clark, Dr. Howard; Contract of Ardra; Data; Devil; *Fek'lhr*; *Gre'thor*; Jared, Acost; Klingons; Ligillium, ruins of; Mendora; Scrolls of Ardra; Scrooge, Ebenezer; Torak; Ventax II; Zaterl emerald.**

Devil. (Thad Lamey). A mythic figure in several Earth cultures. The Devil, or Satan, was an angel who fell from grace with God and came to rule the underworld, where the sinful would be punished for all eternity. In 2367, **Ardra** appeared on planet **Ventax II** as the Devil, while trying to impress the Ventaxians with her allegedly supernatural powers. ("Devil's Due" [TNG]). There is no devil in Klingon mythology ("Day of the Dove" [TOS]), although a demonic figure named ***Fek'lhr*** was held to be the guardian of ***Gre'thor***. ("Devil's Due" [TNG]).

Devolin system. Solar system located in politically neutral space. The system had no discrete planets, but was rather a large mass of dust and rocks, some of them as large as moons. In 2370, the hulk of the *U.S.S. Pegasus* was discovered inside of one of the larger asteroids in the Devolin system. ("The *Pegasus*" [TNG]). SEE: **asteroid gamma 601**.

Devor. (Tim Russ). Member of a group of terrorists who attempted to steal **trilithium** from the *Enterprise*-D in 2369. Devor intercepted Captain Picard as he was returning to the ship to fetch his **saddle**. Picard overpowered Devor and left him in the ship's sickbay. Devor was later killed by the **baryon sweep**. ("Starship Mine" [TNG]). SEE: **Remmler Array.** *Tim Russ also played T'Kar in "Invasive Procedures" (DS9), a lieutenant on the bridge of the* U.S.S. Enterprise-*B in* Star Trek Generations, *and Tuvok in* Star Trek: Voyager.

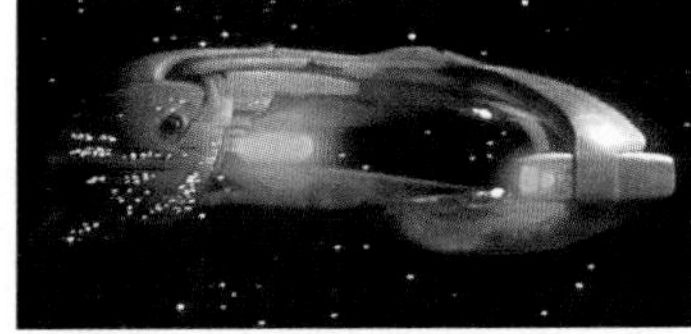

Devoras. A Romulan warbird, commanded by **Admiral Mendak**. The Devoras met the *Enterprise*-D inside the Romulan Neutral Zone, ostensibly to transfer Federation **Ambassador T'Pel** aboard the *Devoras* for treaty negotiations, in 2367. In actuality, T'Pel was a Romulan agent named **Subcommander Selok**, and the transfer was her means of escape into Romulan hands. ("Data's Day" [TNG]).

Devos, Alexana. (Kerrie Keane). Chief of security for the **Rutia IV** government in 2366. Devos was in charge of investigating an incident in which *Enterprise*-D officers Beverly Crusher and Jean-Luc Picard were kidnapped by **Ansata** terrorists. The abduction was a successful bid by the Ansata to force Rutian government recognition of the Ansata demands for independence. Embittered by the atrocities she had seen during her six-month tenure in that sector, Devos had little sympathy for the Ansata movement, but nevertheless agreed to work with the *Enterprise*-D crew in order to locate and rescue Crusher and Picard. ("The High Ground" [TNG]).

Devron system. Planetary system in the **Romulan Neutral Zone.** In the **anti-time** reality created by the **Q Continuum**, a **temporal anomaly** originated in this system. ("All Good Things..." [TNG]) SEE: **inverse tachyon beams**.

Dewan. Ancient language, along with **Dinasian** and **Iccobar**, believed to have historic roots from the **Iconian** language. ("Contagion" [TNG]).

dexalin. Medication used aboard Federation starships to treat oxygen deprivation. Dexalin was used to treat the survivors of the **J'naii** shuttle ***Taris Murn*** rescued by the *Enterprise*-D on stardate 45614. ("The Outcast" [TNG]).

Deyos. (Ray Buktenica). **Vorta** official in charge of **Dominion internment camp 371** in 2373 while Dr. Bashir, Worf, Elim Garak, Enabran Tain, and General Martok were imprisoned there. ("By Inferno's Light" [DS9]).

diagnostic. Engineering analysis programs used aboard Federation starships, intended to permit automated determination of system performance and identification of any malfunctions. Most key systems had a number of such programs available, ranging from level-5 diagnostics (the fastest, most automated) to level-1 diagnostics (the most thorough, but the slowest, requiring the most manual labor).

diamide. Metallic substance. Some Bajoran earrings were made out of diamide-laced **beritium**. ("The Search, Part I" [DS9]).

diamond slot formation. An aerobatic maneuver requiring five single-pilot spacecraft. The outer four craft form up in a diamond shape, with the fifth craft inserting itself into the center or slot of the diamond. The maneuver was used as a demonstration of piloting prowess by cadets at **Starfleet Academy**. ("The First Duty" [TNG]).

diboridium core. Small power-generation unit used in Cardassian technology. A diboridium core was part of the **aphasia device** found in the food replicators on Deep Space 9 in 2369. ("Babel" [DS9]).

diburnium-osmium alloy. Metal used by the **Kalandans** to construct artificial planets. ("That Which Survives" [TOS]). SEE: **Kalandan outpost**.

Dichromic Nebula. Interstellar gas cloud. A robotic probe sent by **Bok** in 2370 passed through the Dichromic Nebula, where it was exposed to intensive gravimetric distortion on the way to the *Starship Enterprise*-D. ("Bloodlines" [TNG]).

Dickerson, Lieutenant. (Arell Blanton). Security officer aboard the original *Starship Enterprise*. Dickerson piped the bos'n whistle to welcome the **Excalbian** re-creation of President **Abraham Lincoln** aboard the ship in 2269. ("The Savage Curtain" [TOS]).

dicosilium. Substance used by **Dr. Nel Apgar** to create reflective coils for the **Krieger-wave** converter he was trying to develop at the time of his death in 2366. The *Enterprise*-D delivered a shipment of dicosilium to Apgar at the **Tanuga IV** science station just before his death. ("A Matter of Perspective" [TNG]).

"Die is Cast, The." *Deep Space Nine* episode #67. Written by Ronald D. Moore. Directed by David Livingston. No stardate given. *First aired in 1995. After Garak is picked up by the renegade attack fleet of Romulan and Cardassian ships, his loyalties are tested when he must torture Odo for information about the Founders. "The Die is Cast" was filmed after "Through the Looking Glass" (DS9), but aired first, because it is the conclusion to the storyline begun in "Improbable Cause" (DS9).* GUEST CAST: Andrew Robinson as **Garak**, **Elim**; Leland Orser as **Lovok**, **Colonel**; Kenneth Marshall as **Eddington**, **Michael**; Leon Russom as **Toddman**, **Vice Admiral**; Paul Dooley as **Tain**, **Enebran**; Wendy Schenker as Romulan pilot. SEE: **Algira sector; Argelian massage facility; Barton; *Belak*; Chow-yun; Dominion; Eddington, Michael; Founders; Founders' homeworld; Garak, Elim; Jem'Hadar; *Keldon*-class warships; *Koranak*; Lovok, Colonel; *Makar*; *Mekong, U.S.S.;* Mila; Obsidian Order; Parmak, Dr.; *plomeek* soup; Porania, Legate; *Portland, U.S.S.*; Romulans; shape-shift inhibitor; Tain, Enabran; Tal Shiar; tetryon; Toddman, Vice Admiral; Vicarian razorback; Willemheld.**

Dieghan, Liam. Neo-Transcendentalist philosopher of Earth's early 22nd century who advocated a simple life in harmony with nature. ("Up the Long Ladder" [TNG]).

dielectric field. A semipolarized electromagnetic field. Interplanetary spacecraft used by the inhabitants of planet **Drayan II** employed a dielectric field to protect it from the kind of electrodynamic turbulence found in the atmospheres of some Drayan moons. ("Innocence" [VGR]).

diencephalon. Part of a humanoid brain, posterior to the forebrain. The hypothalamus, thalamus, and epithalamus are contained in the diencephalon. Unusual levels of neurotransmitters were discovered in the diencephalons of the three *Enterprise*-D officers who were victims of telepathic memory-invasion rape by Ullian researcher **Jev** in 2368. ("Violations" [TNG]).

Dierdre, S.S. Freighter spacecraft. The *Dierdre* supposedly sent a distress call to the *Starship Enterprise* on stardate 3497. The signal was a hoax sent by a Klingon vessel, the second Klingon attempt to prevent the *Enterprise* from returning to planet **Capella IV**. Upon receipt of the fraudulent message, Chief Engineer Scott succinctly commented, "Fool me once, shame on you. Fool me twice, shame on me." ("Friday's Child" [TOS]). SEE: ***Carolina, U.S.S.***

DiFalco, Chief. (Marcy Lafferty). Starfleet officer. DiFalco served as relief navigator aboard the *Enterprise* when it intercepted the **V'Ger** entity. She replaced **Ilia** on the bridge after Ilia was abducted by V'Ger. *(Star Trek: The Motion Picture). Actor Marcy Lafferty was the wife of William Shatner.*

differential magnetometer. Sensor device. Differential magnetometers were used on several probes launched from the runabout ***Rio Grande*** while searching for the downed ***Yangtzee Kiang*** in the Gamma Quadrant in 2369. The magnetometers were able to detect the presence of the *Yangtzee Kiang*'s hull on a moon. ("Battle Lines" [DS9]).

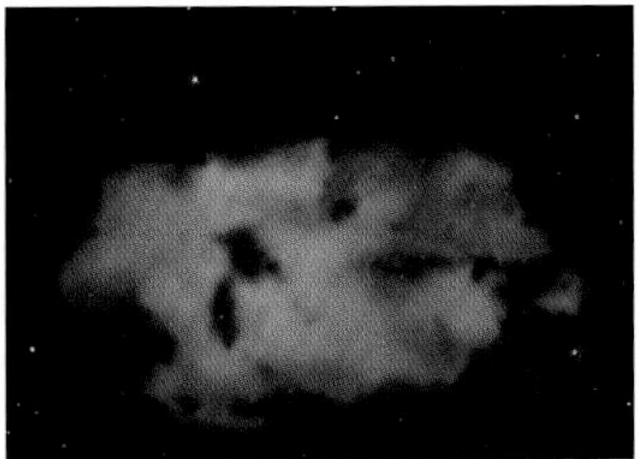

dikironium cloud creature. Gaseous entity that could change its molecular form, was capable of traveling across interstellar space, and could be recognized by a characteristic sickly-sweet smell. The cloud creature fed on the red blood cells of humanoid life-forms and was able to camouflage itself by momentarily throwing itself out of time sync, permitting it to be two places at once. This creature attacked the ***U.S.S. Farragut*** in 2257, killing the ship's captain and 200 of the crew. Lieutenant **James T. Kirk**, a crew member aboard the *Farragut* at the time, fired on the creature, with no effect. Years later, in 2268, the *Starship Enterprise*, with Captain James Kirk in command, encountered the same entity. Kirk followed the creature to planet **Tycho IV**, where he destroyed it with an antimatter blast. ("Obsession" [TOS]). SEE: **noncorporeal life**.

dikironium. Rare gaseous substance, formerly thought to be merely a laboratory curiosity. It was found to be a component in the **dikironium cloud creature** that killed 200 ***U.S.S. Farragut*** personnel at planet **Tycho IV** in 2257. ("Obsession" [TOS]).

Dikon alpha. Class 9 pulsar. Geordi La Forge studied Dikon alpha as a possible source for **vertion** particles that the **emergent life-form** needed to survive in 2370. ("Emergence" [TNG]).

dilithium chamber hatch. Outer door of the matter/**antimatter** reaction chamber in a starship's warp engine. The hatch permitted access to the **dilithium crystal articulation frame** for servicing and crystal replacement. The dilithium chamber hatch on the *Enterprise*-D failed in early 2367, resulting in a massive explosion in the ship's engine room. Although sabotage was initially suspected, it was later found that undetectable submicron fractures had existed in a defective hatch installed on the ship at **Earth Station McKinley** earlier that year. ("The Drumhead" [TNG]).

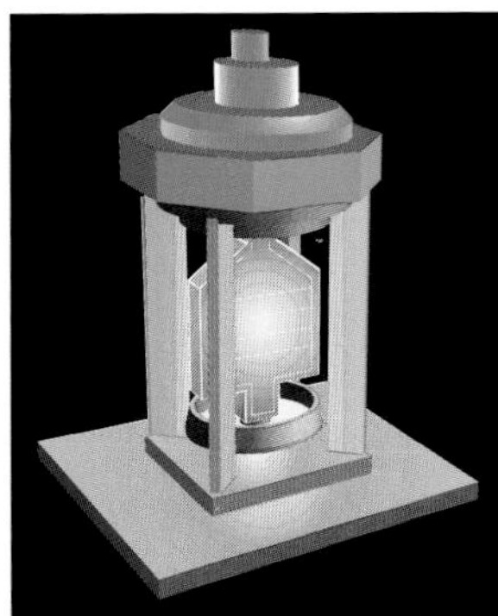

dilithium crystal articulation frame. Part of a starship's **warp drive** system, a device that held **dilithium crystal**s in the matter/antimatter stream so that the crystals could control the reaction in the chamber. Collapse of the articulation frame was thought to be the cause of a dilithium chamber explosion aboard the *Enterprise*-D in 2367. It was believed that sabotage was responsible for the explosion, a supposition supported by the discovery that plans for the articulation frame had been transmitted to the Romulans. The explosion was nevertheless later found to be accidental, the result of a materials defect in the **dilithium chamber hatch**. ("The Drumhead" [TNG]). SEE: **J'Dan; neutron fatigue.**

dilithium crystal chamber. Component of a starship's warp propulsion system. Located in the matter/antimatter reaction chamber, the dilithium crystal chamber controlled the reactions and routed the power flow to the warp nacelles. Within the chamber, the dilithium crystal was mounted within a device called an articulation frame. A prototype of *Enterprise*-D's chamber was developed at Seran T-One on stardate 40052. An improved version of the chamber, one which would permit adjustment of the crystal lattice direction, was under development for incorporation into the next class of starship. ("Booby Trap" [TNG]).

dilithium vector calibrations. Routine maintenance performed on a starship's warp engines. Following dilithium vector calibrations, it was necessary to increase warp speed slowly so the realignment progression could be maintained. ("Brothers" [TNG]).

dilithium. Crystalline substance used in warp propulsion systems aboard starships. Dilithium regulates the matter/antimatter reactions that provide the energy necessary to warp space and travel faster than light. Naturally occurring dilithium is extremely rare and is mined on only a few planets. Until the advent of recrystallization techniques that permitted the production of synthetic dilithium, the crystals were among the most valuable substances in the galaxy. This breakthrough occurred in 2286 when Spock (who had traveled back in time to 1986), devised a means whereby dilithium crystals could be recrystallized by exposure to gamma radiation (high-energy photons) that were by-products of nuclear fission reactions. *(Star Trek IV: The Voyage Home).* In later years, theta-matrix compositing techniques permitted even more efficient recrystallization. ("Family" [TNG]). By the late 2360s, recrystallization techniques had advanced to the point that crystals could be recomposited while still inside the articulation frame of the dilithium chamber, extending the useful life of the crystals even further. ("Relics" [TNG]). Dilithium was abundant on planet **Coridan**, admitted to the Federation in 2267. ("Journey to Babel" [TOS]). The planet **Troyius** is also a rich source of naturally-occurring dilithium crystals. ("Elaan of Troyius" [TOS]). The Breen employed forced labor at their dilithium mines on **Dozaria** ("Indiscretion" [DS9]) as did the Klingons at **Rura Penthe** *(Star Trek VI: The Undiscovered Country)*. In 2372, *U.S.S. Voyager* personnel discovered a new form of dilithium that remained stable at a much higher warp frequency. The new form of dilithium, installed aboard the *Shuttlecraft Cochrane*, made possible the first human flight at **transwarp** velocities. ("Threshold" [VGR]). SEE: **lithium crystals**.

dill weed. Earth seasoning made from the ground leaves of an aromatic herb *Anethum graveolens* native to Eurasia. When Neelix prepared Porakan eggs as a breakfast food on the *Voyager*, he added a little dill weed and a touch of *rengazo*. ("Flashback" [VGR]).

dim. Early 21st-century **Earth** slang, referring to a **Sanctuary District** resident who was mentally ill. ("Past Tense, Parts I and II" [DS9]). SEE: **gimme**.

DiMaggio, Joe. Twentieth-century baseball player (1914-), also known as Joltin' Joe and the Yankee Clipper. Arguably **baseball**'s greatest center fielder, DiMaggio scored hits in 56 consecutive games, a record that stood until 2026, when it was broken by **Buck Bokai**, a shortstop from the **London Kings**. ("The Big Goodbye" [TNG], "If Wishes Were Horses" [DS9]).

Dimorus. Planet. James Kirk and **Gary Mitchell** once visited Dimorus prior to their service aboard the *U.S.S. Enterprise*. While there, Mitchell saved Kirk's life by blocking a poison dart thrown by a native rodent creature. Mitchell almost died as a result. ("Where No Man Has Gone Before" [TOS]).

Dinasian. Ancient language, along with Dewan and Iccobar, believed to have historic roots in the **Iconian** language. This similarity is viewed by some as evidence that at least some of the ancient Iconians escaped the destruction of their home planet, settling elsewhere in the galaxy. ("Contagion" [TNG]).

Diomedian scarlet moss. Bright red, featherlike plant. Dr. Crusher cultivated Diomedian scarlet moss as part of her study of ethnobotany in 2367. She had collected spores from several different sources in the Diomedian system. ("Clues" [TNG]).

dirak. Monetary unit used by the **Karemma**. ("The Search, Part I" [DS9]).

direct reticular stimulation. Medical procedure in which electrical energy is applied directly to the nervous system of a humanoid patient in an attempt to revive neural activity. A device called a **neural stimulator** is used in this procedure. Direct reticular stimulation was unsuccessfully attempted when **Natasha Yar** was critically wounded by **Armus**. ("Skin of Evil" [TNG]).

direct transport. SEE: **site-to-site transport**.

directional sonic generator. Hand-held directional audio frequency emitter. Chief O'Brien tried to use one to combat an infestation of **vole**s aboard station Deep Space 9 in 2370. ("Playing God" [DS9]).

Dirgo. (Nick Tate). A native of **Pentarus V** and captain of the mining shuttle ***Nenebek***. Captain Dirgo was assigned to transport Captain Picard and Ensign Crusher from the *Enterprise*-D to a conference on **Pentarus V**. When the shuttle malfunctioned and was forced to crash-land on a Pentaran moon, Dirgo was reluctant to accept Captain Picard's leadership in what became a struggle for survival on the desert planet. Despite this, Dirgo continued to act impulsively and caused his own death. ("Final Mission" [TNG]). SEE: **sentry**. *Nick Tate also played astronaut Alan Carter on the series* Space: 1999. *Alan Carter was obviously a better pilot.*

"Disaster." *Next Generation* episode #105. Teleplay by Ronald D. Moore. Story by Ron Jarvis & Philip A. Scorza. Directed by Gabrielle Beaumont. Stardate 45156.1. *First aired in 1991. The* Enterprise-*D crew copes with a shipboard disaster, trapping Picard in a turbolift and placing Deanna Troi in command.* GUEST CAST: Rosalind Chao as **O'Brien**, **Keiko**; Colm Meaney as **O'Brien**, **Miles**; Michelle Forbes as **Ro Laren**; Erika Flores as **Flores**, **Marissa**; John Christian Graas as **Gordon**, **Jay**; Max Supera as **Supera**, **Patterson**; Cameron Arnett as **Mandel**, **Ensign**; Jana Marie Hupp as **Monroe**, **Lieutenant**. SEE: **antigravs; containment breach; emergency hand actuator; Emergency Procedure Alpha 2; Flores, Marissa; "Frere Jacques"; Gonal IV; Gordon, Jay; hyronalin; internal power grid; Ishikawa, Hiro; isolation protocol; "Laughing Vulcan and His Dog, The"; Mandel, Ensign; Monroe, Lieutenant; Mudor V; O'Brien, Keiko; O'Brien, Michael; O'Brien, Miles; O'Brien, Molly; *Pirates of Penzance, The*; plasma fire; polyduranide; quantum filament; quartum; Starfleet Emergency Medical course; Supera, Patterson; tripolymer composites; Troi, Deanna; turboshaft.**

discommendation. Klingon ritual shaming. An individual who receives discommendation is treated as nonexistent in the eyes of Klingon society. The individual's family is also disgraced for seven generations. **Worf** accepted a humiliating discommendation from the **Klingon High Council** in 2366 when his late father, **Mogh**, was accused of having committed treason at Khitomer in 2346, despite the fact that council leader **K'mpec** knew the charges to be unfounded. ("Sins of the Father" [TNG]). Worf's discommendation was reversed in 2367 by Council leader **Gowron**, shortly after Gowron assumed the office of Council leader. ("Redemption, Part I" [TNG]).

diseases. SEE: **Anchilles fever; Andronesian encephalitis; Arethian flu; atherosclerosis; Ba'ltmasor Syndrome; Barclay's Protomorphosis Syndrome; Bendii Syndrome; cold, common; dermal dysplasia; Dorek syndrome; hemocythemia; Hesperan thumping cough; HTDS; Irumodic Syndrome; Iverson's disease; Kalla-Nohra Syndrome; Levodian flu; memory virus; Mendakan pox; neurochemical imbalance; Orkett's disease; phage; Phyrox Plague; plasma plague; Pottrik Syndrome; Psi 2000 virus; Rigelian fever; Rigelian Kassaba fever; *rop'ngor;* Rudellian brain fever; Rudellian plague; Rugalan fever; Rushton infection; Sakuro's disease; schizophrenia; Symbalene blood burn; *Synthococcus novae;* Telurian plague; Teplan blight; Terellian Death Syndrome; Terrellian plague; Thelusian Flu; transporter psychosis; transporter shock; Vegan choriomeningitis; xenopolycythemia; Zanthi fever.** SEE ALSO: **drugs.**

displacement wave. Spatial phenomenon characterized by a polarized magnetic variation of space. In 2371, displacement waves generated by the **Caretaker** transported Chakotay's Maquis ship and later the *U.S.S. Voyager* more than 70,000 light-years to the **Delta Quadrant**. ("Caretaker" [VGR]).

Disrupters. Organized underground of discontented **Troglytes** on planet **Ardana** who sought economic and social equality with those who dwelled in the cloud city of **Stratos.** In 2269, in order to dramatize their plight, the Disrupters stole a badly needed consignment of **zenite** designated for pickup by the *Starship Enterprise*. ("The Cloud Minders" [TOS]).

disruptor. Directed-energy weapon used by Romulans, Klingons, ("Tin Man" [TNG]) and the Breen *(Star Trek Generations).* The Klingon disruptor was also known as a **phase disruptor**. ("Aquiel" [TNG]). SEE: **Klingon weapons.** Romulan disruptor fire can be identified by a high residue of antiprotons that can linger for several hours after the weapon has been used. ("Face of the Enemy" [TNG]). Disruptors were also used as ship-mounted weapons aboard Cardassian warships. ("Profit and Loss" [DS9]).

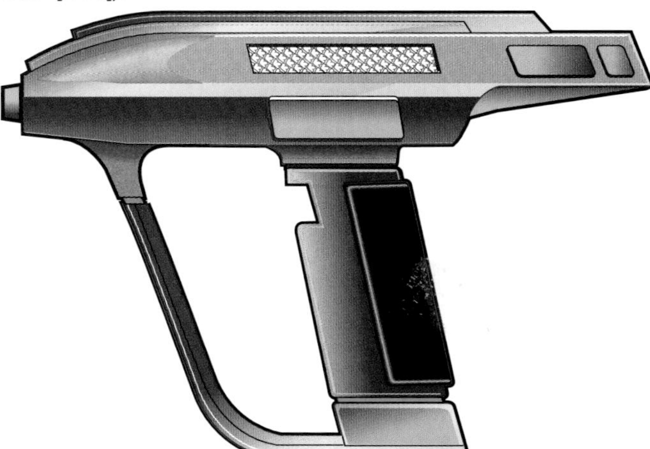

Romulan disruptor pistol

disruptors, system 5. Type of large **Cardassian** weaponry used for planetary emplacements. System 5 disruptors were installed at the outpost on Korma. In 2372, Gul Dukat and Kira Nerys removed the weapons from Korma, installed them on the *Groumall*, and then used them to disable K'Temang's bird-of-prey. ("Return to Grace" [DS9]).

"Distant Voices." *Deep Space Nine* episode #64. Teleplay by Ira Steven Behr & Robert Hewitt Wolfe. Story by Joe Menosky. Directed by Alexander Singer. No stardate given. *First aired in 1995. Comatose and dying after an alien attack, Bashir must access different parts of his personality, which take the form of crew members, to save his life.* GUEST CAST: Andrew Robinson as **Garak, Elim**; Victor Rivers as **Altovar**; Ann Gillespie as Bajoran nurse; Nichole Forester as dabo girl. SEE: **Altovar; Bashir, Julian; bio-mimetic gel; Cardassians; cordrazine; Dax, Jadzia; holodeck and holosuite programs; inpedrezine; Lethean; osteogenic stimulator; Shoggoth; Tarkalean tea; Yigrish cream pie.**

distortion field. Phenomenon present in the atmosphere of planet **Nervala IV**. The field prevented the use of transporters or shuttlecraft, effectively isolating the planet. The field was present during the majority of its eight-year orbit around Nervala, but during the planet's perihelion the field would temporarily dephase enough to allow for transport to the surface. ("Second Chances" [TNG]).

distortion ring being. A **noncorporeal life**-form that was a sentient spatial phenomenon capable of literally changing the shape of space. In 2372, the *U.S.S. Voyager* encountered a distortion ring being in the **Delta Quadrant**. In an attempt at communication, the anomaly immobilized the ship, disrupted communications and computer control, and caused the ship's physical arrangement to change. Only after the distortion wave had passed did the *Voyager* crew realize that the phenomenon was a sentient, intelligent being. During its encounter with *Voyager*, the distortion ring being deposited some twenty million gigaquads of information into the starship's computer memory banks. ("Twisted" [VGR]).

Divine Treasury. In **Ferengi** mythology, the place in the afterlife where financially successful Ferengi go after death. ("Little Green Men" [DS9]). The **Registrar** awaits the recently deceased at the entrance to the Divine Treasury. If the new arrival is worthy to enter, the Registrar will accept a bribe and then usher him inside. ("Body Parts" [DS9]). The Divine Treasury is believed to be made of pure **latinum** and it is where the **Blessed Exchequer** presides. In the Divine Treasury, Celestial Auctioneers allow the dead to bid for new lives through the Celestial Auction. Ferengi who did not earn a profit in their mortal lives are thought to be doomed to the **Vault of Eternal Destitution**. ("Little Green Men" [DS9]).

Division of Planetary Operations. Section of Starfleet tasked with Earth-based functions and operations. DPO headquarters was located in Lisbon, Portugal on Earth. ("Paradise Lost" [DS9]).

Divok. (Charles Esten). Young follower of the Klingon messiah **Kahless the Unforgettable**. Divok was present on the planet **Boreth** during Worf's visit to the monastery in 2369. Divok received a vision of Kahless and was present when Kahless's clone first appeared. ("Rightful Heir" [TNG]).

divorce, Klingon. Dissolution of Klingon marriage is accomplished by the simple declaration of "*N'Gos tlhogh cha!*" (our marriage is done!). There is then a ritual striking and expectorating on the individual being divorced. ("The House of Quark" [DS9]).

DMZ. SEE: **Demilitarized Zone.**

DNA reference scan. Medical test to confirm an individual's identity by matching DNA patterns. **Kobliad** security officer **Kajada** asked Dr. Julian Bashir to order a DNA reference scan to confirm the identity of a body believed to be that of her prisoner, **Rao Vantika**. ("The Passenger" [DS9]).

DNA. Acronym for deoxyribonucleic acid, a complex chemical chain containing the genetic codes enabling the reproduction of life on many planets. Virtually every individual life-form on such planets has a DNA code, which contains information common to that species, as well as distinguishing information unique to that individual. Because of this, DNA sequencing can be used as a means of positively identifying an individual, although it cannot distinguish between the individual and a clone. Many humanoid species throughout the galaxy share a common DNA structure, a characteristic that was recently discovered to be due to a humanoid species that lived some four billion years ago and "seeded" many planets with primordial genetic material. ("The Chase" [TNG]). SEE: **cloning; humanoid life.**

Dobara. (Penny Johnson). Native of **Boraal II.** Dobara was a resident of the village under study by **Nikolai Rozhenko** in 2370. Dobara became pregnant with Dr. Rozhenko's child, and lived with him after Rozhenko chose to remain with her people on **Vacca VI**. ("Homeward" [TNG]). *Penny Johnson later played Kasidy Yates on* Star Trek: Deep Space Nine.

docking clamps. Large mechanical devices that physically lock a docked ship to the exterior of a space station, such as Deep Space 9. ("Defiant" [DS9]).

"Doctor Bashir, I Presume?" Deep Space Nine episode #114. Teleplay by Ronald D. Moore. Story by Jimmy Diggs. Directed by David Livingston. No stardate given. *First aired in 1997. When Lewis Zimmerman arrives to make a "template" of Doctor Bashir for Starfleet's latest version of the holographic doctor program, Bashir's estranged parents reveal a terrible family secret that could end his Starfleet career. Meanwhile, Rom attempts to find the courage to reveal his feelings for Leeta before she leaves for good.* GUEST CAST: Robert Picardo as **Zimmerman, Lewis**; Max Grodénchik as **Rom**; Chase Masterson as **Leeta**; Fadwa El Guindi as **Bashir, Amsha**; Brian George as **Bashir, Richard**; J. Patrick McCormack as **Bennett, Rear Admiral**; SEE: **accelerated critical neural pathway formation; Adigeon Prime; argonite; Bashir, Amsha; Bashir, Julian; Bashir, Richard; Bennett, Rear Admiral; dom-jot; Emergency Medical Hologram; Eugenics Wars; Federation Penal Settlement; Federation Supreme Court; holodeck and holosuite programs: *Vulcan Love Slave, Part II, The Revenge*; Judge Advocate General; Jupiter station; Kama Sutra; Khan; Leeta; Longterm Medical Hologram; Nog; prayko; prion replication in ganglionic cell clusters; Prinadora; Rom; *Vulcan Love Slave Part II: The Revenge*; Zimmerman, Lewis.**

Doctor, the. SEE: **Emergency Medical Hologram**.

dodecahedron. Twelve-sided geometric solid. ("Alliances" [VGR]).

Dodger Stadium. Large open-air arena building located in **Los Angeles** on Earth, used to host athletic competitions, especially **baseball**. Named for the Los Angeles Dodgers, a baseball team that existed on Earth in the 20th and 21st centuries. ("Future's End, Part II" [VGR]). *"What about the* Brooklyn *Dodgers?" complains Brooklyn-born producer Bob Justman.*

Doe, John. (Mark LaMura). A Zalkonian male discovered by the *Enterprise*-D crew in a crashed escape pod on a planet in the **Zeta Gelis** system in 2366. Suffering from serious injuries, "Doe" (so designated by Dr. Beverly Crusher, with whom Doe became romantically involved) was treated aboard the *Enterprise*-D, where he astounded the medical staff with his extremely rapid recovery. Doe was later found to be a member of a persecuted minority of Zalkonian society, a

group that was undergoing a metamorphosis from humanoid forms into noncorporeal beings. Doe had fled into space to escape the Zalkonian government's attempts to destroy all who exhibited these traits. He completed his transfiguration aboard the *Enterprise*-D, and was last seen flying off into space, a being of pure energy. ("Transfigurations" [TNG]).

Dohlman. Leader of the planet Elas. **Elaan** was the Dohlman of **Elas** in 2268. ("Elaan of Troyius" [TOS]).

Dokachin, Klim. (Graham Jarvis). The quartermaster of the Starfleet surplus depot in orbit around planet **Qualor II.** An officious **Zakdorn**, Dokachin reluctantly agreed to help the crew of the *Enterprise*-D locate the ***T'Pau*** when the *Enterprise*-D visited Qualor in 2368. Dokachin was shocked to discover the *T'Pau* gone from its assigned berth at the surplus depot. ("Unification, Part I" [TNG]).

Dokkaran temple. An ancient structure of Kural-Hanesh, known for its harmonious architecture. The structure contained a great archway, large windows, and an altar. Children in the *Enterprise*-D primary school studied and built models of this historic building. ("Hero Worship" [TNG]).

Dolak, Gul. (Frank Collison). A member of the Cardassian militia, unit 41. Dolak was in command of the **Cardassian warships** that attacked and destroyed a Bajoran ***Antares*-class carrier** in an effort to kill Bajoran leader Orta in 2368. ("Ensign Ro" [TNG]). SEE: **Kennelly, Admiral**.

dolamide. Chemical energy source used in a wide variety of applications such as for power generators, for reactors, and, in an extremely pure form, for weapons. The **Valerians** made weapons for the **Cardassians** with dolamide during the occupation of **Bajor**. When a Valerian vessel docked at Deep Space 9 in 2369, Major Kira was denied permission to search the ship for evidence of dolamide on grounds of lack of probable cause. ("Dramatis Personae" [DS9]). SEE: ***Sherval Das***.

Dolbargy sleeping trance. Voluntarily induced deep coma. **Zek**, the Ferengi **grand nagus**, used the technique to fake his own death in 2369 when he wanted to test the readiness of his son, **Krax**, to serve as nagus. Zek's servant, **Maihar'du,** had taught him the technique. ("The Nagus" [DS9]).

dollar. Unit of monetary exchange used on Earth as late as the 2060s. *(Star Trek: First Contact).*

Dom Pérignon. SEE: **champagne**.

dom-jot. Billiards-like game with an irregularly shaped table, popular at the **Bonestell Recreational Facility** at **Starbase Earhart**. Ensign **Cortin Zweller** was fond of the game, as were a couple of **Nausicaans**. ("Tapestry" [TNG]). **Jake Sisko**'s girlfriend, **Mardah,** said that Jake played the game well. ("The Abandoned" [DS9]). **Leeta** thought dom-jot was a better game than **dabo**. She thought Quark's bar should have at least three dom-jot tables. ("Doctor Bashir, I Presume?" [DS9]). *Dom-jot was also mentioned in "Life Support" (DS9).*

Dominion internment camp 371. Asteroid-based prison facility located in the **Gamma Quadrant** and guarded by a detachment of **Jem'Hadar**. The former site of an **ultritium** mine, the asteroid had no atmosphere and was rendered habitable by means of a atmospheric dome. **Cardassian** and **Romulan** survivors of the failed **Obsidian Order** and **Tal Shiar** attack on the **Founders' homeworld** were imprisoned at Dominion internment camp 371. Also held captive there were **Klingon** official **General Martok** and Starfleet officers **Julian Bashir** and **Worf**. ("In Purgatory's Shadow" [DS9]). The camp was run by **Deyos**, a **Vorta**. ("By Inferno's Light" [DS9]). *The exterior miniature of the internment camp was a model designed by illustrator John Eaves.*

Dominion. Powerful alliance of planetary groups in the **Gamma Quadrant**. ("Rules of Acquisition" [DS9]). The Dominion was established two millenia ago ("To the Death" [DS9]) by the reclusive **Founders** who controlled hundreds of planets. Although the Founders themselves were almost never seen, Dominion power was brutally exercised by the **Jem'Hadar**, insuring compliance with the Founders' rule. ("The Jem'Hadar" [DS9], "The Search, Parts I and II" [DS9]). For example, when a planet in the **Teplan** system resisted Dominion control in 2172, the Jem'Hadar punished the planet's population by unleashing a disease, called the blight, that caused terrible suffering for centuries. SEE: **Teplan blight.** ("The Quickening" [DS9]). In 2340, the Dominion invaded and conquered planet **Yadera Prime** ("Shadowplay" [DS9]) and the **T-Rogorans** in 2370. ("Sanctuary" [DS9]). The Dominion planted agents in the Alpha Quadrant, so by late 2370, these agents provided the Dominion with tactical intelligence on the Federation and other Alpha Quadrant powers. SEE: **Eris; Krajensky, Ambassador; Lovok, Colonel.** Such agents, often Founders posing as members of other species, also worked to destabilize the Alpha Quadrant, apparently as an ongoing prelude to a Dominion invasion. ("The Die is Cast" [DS9], "The Adversary" [DS9]). The Dominion objected to the incursion of Alpha Quadrant cultures into the Gamma Quadrant. In late 2370, they made their displeasure known by destroying a number of ships and wiping out the **New Bajor** colony. ("The Jem'Hadar" [DS9]). Dominion operatives captured several members of the *Starship Defiant* command crew in 2371 in an effort to learn how strongly life-forms in the **Alpha Quadrant** would resist a Dominion incursion into that part of the galaxy. ("The Search, Parts I and II" [DS9]). In 2373, the Dominion entered into an alliance with the **Cardassian Union**, giving the Founders a significant stronghold in the Alpha Quadrant. **Gul Dukat** brokered the agreement after secret talks. ("By Inferno's Light" [DS9]). SEE: **Vorta.** *The Dominion was first mentioned in "Rules of Acquisition" (DS9).*

Donaldson. *Enterprise*-D crew member. Donaldson was part of Commander La Forge's engineering staff during the **soliton wave** rider test in 2368. ("New Ground" [TNG]).

Donatu V, Battle of. Conflict that occurred in 2242 near **Sherman's Planet** in a region under dispute by the Klingon Empire and the United Federation of Planets. ("The Trouble with Tribbles" [TOS]).

"Doomsday Machine, The." Original Series episode #35. Written by Norman Spinrad. Directed by Marc Daniels. No stardate given in episode. *First aired in 1967. An ancient weapon that destroyed the civilization that invented it is now destroying planets in Federation space. "The Doomsday Machine" was nominated for a Hugo Award for Best Dramatic Presentation at the 1968 World Science Fiction Convention.* GUEST CAST: William

Windom as **Decker, Commodore Matt**; Elizabeth Rogers as **Palmer, Lieutenant**; John Winston as **Kyle, Mr.**; Richard Compton as **Washburn**; John Copage as Elliot; Tim Burns as Russ; Jerry Catron as Montgomery, Security guard; Vince Deadrick as Decker's stunt double. SEE: **antiprotons; *Constellation*, *U.S.S.*; Decker, Commodore Matt; impulse drive; Kyle, Mr.; L-370; L-374; Masada; neutronium; Palmer, Lieutenant; planet killer; Starfleet General Orders and Regulations; Washburn.**

doomsday machine. SEE: **planet killer**.

door in the universe. Term used to describe an interdimensional passageway created by **Lazarus**, connecting our universe with an antimatter continuum. ("The Alternative Factor" [TOS]).

Doosodarians. Ancient civilization. Doosodarian art included an unusual form of poetry that contained empty spaces, or **lacunae**, during which the poet and audience were encouraged to acknowledge the emptiness of the experience. Data learned of these ancient people and their works during his study of poetry. ("Interface" [TNG]).

Dopa system. Planetary system located within the Cardassian Union. ("Return to Grace" [DS9]).

Dopterians. Humanoid species whose brains have certain structural similarities to the **Ferengi**. One characteristic of the Dopterians is that neither they nor the Ferengi can be empathically sensed by a Betazoid. A Dopterian stole **Lwaxana Troi**'s precious latinum hair-brooch on station Deep Space 9 in 2369, but she was unable to sense any feeling of guilt from the thief, for this reason. ("The Forsaken" [DS9]). **Gorta** was a Dopterian accomplice to the Duras sisters' **magnesite ore** mining operation on Kalla III in 2370. ("Firstborn" [TNG]).

Doraf I. Planet in Federation space. The *Enterprise*-D was assigned to a terraforming project at Doraf I in 2368. The mission was canceled when the ship was recalled to **Starbase 234** to receive orders to investigate the disappearance of Ambassador **Spock**. ("Unification, Part I" [TNG]).

dorak. Monetary unit used by the inhabitants of the village on **Barkon IV**. ("Thine Own Self" [TNG]).

Dorek syndrome. A very rare and incurable disease that afflicts one out of every five million **Ferengi**. In 2372, Dr. Orpax misdiagnosed **Quark** with Dorek syndrome during Quark's annual insurance physical. ("Body Parts" [DS9]).

Dorian. Transport vessel attacked near planet **Rekag-Seronia** in 2369 while attempting to deliver **Ambassador Ves Alkar** to that planet in hopes of mediating peace there. ("Man of the People" [TNG]). *The* Dorian *was a re-dress of the* ***Straleb*** *transport ship originally built for "The Outrageous Okona" (TNG).*

Dorias Cluster. Cluster of some 20 star systems near the Dichromic Nebula. In 2370, Ferengi government officials reported that former DaiMon **Bok** had been sighted in the Dorias Cluster. ("Bloodlines" [TNG]). SEE: **Vigo, Jason**.

Dorvan V. Class-M planet located in the border area between Federation and Cardassian space. A group of North American Indians from Earth settled there in 2350 and established a village in a small valley on the southern continent. These people had originally left Earth 200 years ago in order to preserve their cultural identity. In 2370 the **Federation-Cardassian treaty** placed Dorvan V under Cardassian jurisdiction. As a result, *Enterprise*-D captain Picard was ordered by **Admiral Necheyev** to evacuate the colonists by any means necessary. The settlers refused to leave, but succeeded in convincing Starfleet to allow them to renounce their Federation citizenships. In doing so, the colonists willingly placed themselves under Cardassian rule. ("Journey's End" [TNG]). SEE: **Anthwara.**

Dosi. Humanoid civilization from the Gamma Quadrant. The Ferengi attempted to purchase a large amount of tulaberry wine from the Dosi in 2370. It was believed that the Dosi had some ties to the **Dominion**. ("Rules of Acquisition" [DS9]). SEE: **Inglatu**; **Zyree**.

Douwd. A little-known civilization of sentient energy beings capable of assuming the appearance of other life-forms. Possessing awesome powers of creation and destruction, the Douwd considered themselves to be immortal beings of disguises and false surroundings. One member of the Douwd assumed a human identity around 2312, named himself **Kevin Uxbridge**, and settled on planet **Delta Rana IV** in 2361. ("The Survivors" [TNG]).

Down the River Light. Literary work in 17 volumes written by Caster. **Audrid Dax** once read the entire work to her daughter, Neema. ("Nor the Battle to the Strong" [DS9]).

Doyle, Sir Arthur Conan. Novelist (1859-1930) from old England on Earth, writer of the classic **Sherlock Holmes** adventures. *Enterprise*-D operations manager Data was a fan of Doyle's work, the Sherlock Holmes character in particular. ("Elementary, Dear Data" [TNG], "Ship in a Bottle" [TNG]). SEE: **Moriarty, Professor James**.

Dozaria. Class-M world with a hot desert-like climate. The Cardassian ship ***Ravinok*** was forced to crash-land on Dozaria in 2366 after being attacked by two **Breen** warships. The surviving crew and passengers of the ship were forced by the Breen to labor in their **dilithium** mines on Dozaria. The laborers were rescued in 2372 by Kira Nerys and Gul Dukat. ("Indiscretion" [DS9]). *The Dozaria exterior scenes were filmed at a rock quarry in Soledad Canyon, north of Los Angeles.*

Drabian love sonnet. Poetry. In 2373, Q used Drabian sonnets in an unsuccessful bid to convince Kathryn Janeway to have his child. ("The Q and the Grey" [VGR]).

Draco lizards. Species of flying reptile indigenous to southeast Asia on planet Earth. The Draco lizard was extinct by the year 2000. ("New Ground" [TNG]).

Draebidium calimus. Type of plant. Keiko O'Brien carried a specimen of *Draebidium calimus* with her when the ***Shuttlecraft Fermi*** passed through an energy cloud in 2369. When the shuttle crew transported back to the *Enterprise*-D, the plant was reduced to a seedling. ("Rascals" [TNG]).

Draebidium froctus. Type of plant. Upon returning to the *Enterprise*-D from planet Marlonia, Ensign Ro mistook a ***Draebidium calimus*** for a *Draebidium froctus*. ("Rascals" [TNG]).

Drafting Room 5. Part of Starfleet's **Utopia Planitia Fleet Yards** on Mars, where the ***Galaxy*-class** *U.S.S. Enterprise*-D was designed. This was the workplace of **Dr. Leah Brahms.** Geordi La Forge re-created Drafting Room 5 on the *Enterprise*-D holodeck when trying to escape an ancient **Menthar** booby trap in 2366. ("Booby Trap" [TNG]).

drag coefficient. Measurement of the frictional force on a body traveling through a fluid medium such as air or water relative to the body's speed in that medium. The drag coefficient on the *Enterprise*-D through the tenuous interstellar dust and gas of nebula **FGC-47** increased inexplicably when the ship explored the nebula in 2368. This increase was later found to be due to a life-form living in FGC-47. ("Imaginary Friend" [TNG])

Draim. Powerful member of the **Orion Syndicate**. Draim specialized in blackmail and extortion from his base of operations on Finnea Prime. ("A Simple Investigation" [DS9]). SEE: **Arissa**.

Drake Equation. Twentieth-century Earth scientific concept for estimating the number of technologically-sophisticated civilizations in the galaxy. Postulated by Earth astronomer Frank Drake before his planet's first contact with explorers from planet **Vulcan**, the Drake Equation was based on estimates of the total number of stars in the galaxy, the fraction of those stars that had planetary systems, the fraction of those planets that could support life, and so on. A copy of the Drake Equation was posted on the wall of the **SETI** laboratory where astronomer **Rain Robinson** worked in 1996. ("Future's End, Part I" [VGR]). *The Drake Equation was also part of Gene Roddenberry's first outline for the original* Star Trek *series, written in 1964. Roddenberry wanted to use the equation to show that the idea of alien civilizations on other worlds was within the realm of scientific possibility. Unfortunately, while Roddenberry knew of the Drake Equation, he did not have an actual copy of the formula. Under pressure of a deadline, Roddenberry simply made up a plausible-looking version of what he thought it might look like. Once he was successful in selling the* Star Trek *concept to Desilu Studios and NBC, he never got around to "correcting" the outline. The formula posted in Rain Robinson's lab, shown here, incorporates both versions. The top line is Dr. Drake's version, and the second line is the Drake Equation according to Gene Roddenberry. Dr. Drake has gently pointed out that a value raised to the first power is merely the value itself.*

$$N = R_* \text{ x } f_p \text{ x } n_e \text{ x } f_l \text{ x } f_i \text{ x } f_c \text{ x } L$$

$$Ef^2(MgE) - C^1Ri^1 \text{ x } M = L/So^*$$

***Drake*, Shuttlecraft.** Auxiliary vehicle attached to the *Starship Voyager*. Ensign **Harry Kim** piloted the *Drake* in 2372 when the shuttle intersected a **timestream**, sending Kim into an alternate reality. ("Non Sequitur" [VGR]).

***Drake*, U.S.S.** Federation starship, *Wambundu* class, registry number NCC-20381, that disappeared in the Lorenze Cluster. The *Drake* had been under the command of **Captain Paul Rice** when it was destroyed, apparently by an ancient weapons system still operational at planet **Minos** in 2364. **William Riker** had been offered the command of the *Drake*, but he turned it down to serve aboard the *Enterprise*-D. ("The Arsenal of Freedom" [TNG]). The *Drake* was ambushed by a Klingon battle group in 2373 and took heavy casualties. After the battle, the *Drake* docked at Deep Space 9 to receive medical aid. ("Apocalypse Rising" [DS9]). *The ship was named after the English admiral Sir Francis Drake, who commanded the first British ship to circumnavigate planet Earth.*

Draken IV. Planet located in the **Taugan** sector. It was the location of the nearest Stafleet base to the Kaleb sector. **Subcommander N'Vek** attempted to take the Romulan warbird ***Khazara*** there in 2369 as part of a plan for the defection of Romulan **Vice-Proconsul M'ret** to the Federation. ("Face of the Enemy" [TNG]). The planet possessed ruins of **Romulan** origin which made it a potential target of the band of archaeological raiders led by **Arctus Baran**. ("Gambit, Parts I and II" [TNG]).

Drakina Forest dwellers. Tribe with paranormal attributes, native to a planet in the **Delta Quadrant**. Neelix told Kes of the Drakina Forest dwellers when discussing her telepathic abilities. ("Time and Again" [VGR]).

"Dramatis Personae." *Deep Space Nine* episode #18. Written by Joe Menosky. Directed by Cliff Bole. Stardate 46922.3. *First aired in 1993. Unknown intelligences take over the minds of Deep Space 9 personnel, forcing them to act out an alien drama.* GUEST CAST: Tom Towles as **Hon'Tihl**; Stephen Parr as Valerian; Randy Pflug as Guard; Jeff Pruitt as Ensign. SEE: **Bajoran wormhole; cryostasis; dolamide; duranium; Fahleena III; Hon'Tihl; Kee'Bhor; Lasuma; Mariah IV; Modela aperitif; phoretic analyzer; Rochani III; Saltah'na clock; Saltah'na energy sphere; Saltah'na; *Sherval Das*; subspace technology; Tel'Peh; thalmerite; *Toh'Kaht, I.K.S.* ; Ultima Thule; Valerians.**

Drathan puppy lig. Animal life-form kept as a pet. ("Crossover" [DS9]).

Drayan II. Class-M planet in the Delta Quadrant with several moons; homeworld to the **Drayans**. ("Innocence" [VGR]).

Drayans. Civilization of technologically advanced humanoids from the planet Drayan II in the Delta Quadrant. The Drayan life cycle was the reverse of that of many other humanoid species. Drayans are born in an adult state and proceed to grow smaller and more innocent as they get older. Very old Drayans appear as small children. About three generations ago, the culture on Drayan II underwent a reformation in which they shifted their focus away from technology. During this time they also adopted an isolationist attitude toward outside cultures. In 2372, **Alcia** was the First **Prelate** of the Drayan nation. ("Innocence" [VGR]).

Draygo IV. Class-M world in Federation space. Draygo IV was studied as a potential new home for the **Boraalans** in 2370. While it had an unusually large temperate zone, the planet was discarded from consideration because it was within three light-years of Cardassian space. ("Homeward" [TNG]).

Draylon II. Class-M planet in the Alpha Quadrant. Site where the **Skrreea** settled in 2370. ("Sanctuary" [DS9]).

Drazman, Admiral. Starfleet official in command of the **Proxima Maintenance Yards**. Admiral Drazman was a long-winded and generally uninteresting conversationalist, earning him the nickname "Droner" Drazman. ("Past Tense, Part I" [DS9]).

Drea. (Lezlie Dalton). **Kelvan** who assisted in the capture of the *Enterprise* landing party in 2268 and forced the *Enterprise* crew to set a course for the **Andromeda Galaxy**. ("By Any Other Name" [TOS]).

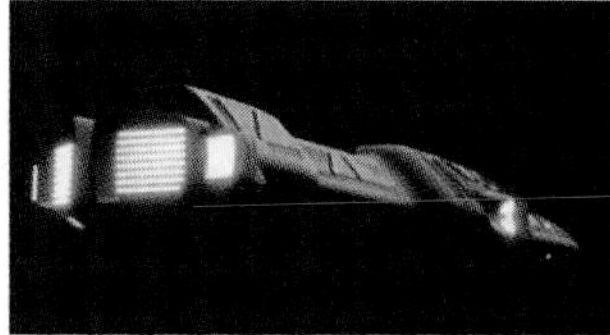

Dreadnought. Maquis designation for an experimental **Cardassian** tactical missile weapon that was launched around stardate 46437. The Dreadnought was programmed to destroy a Maquis munitions base on planetoid **Alpha 441** in the **Badlands**. The weapon carried a charge of a thousand kilograms of matter and an equal amount of **antimatter**, enough explosive power to destroy a small moon. Dreadnought was controlled by a sophisticated computer system that was highly adaptable, capable of evasion, and equipped with advanced defensive weaponry. The Dreadnought failed to detonate at its target and was subsequently captured by the **Maquis**, who reprogrammed it to destroy a Cardassian fuel depot on planet **Aschelan V**. The reprogramming was accomplished by Maquis member **B'Elanna Torres**. One day after the Dreadnought was launched toward Aschelan V, it was captured by the **Caretaker** and brought into the **Delta Quadrant**. In this unfamiliar environment, the Dreadnought's control computer locked onto planet **Rakosa V**, threatening Rakosa's two million inhabitants. B'Elanna Torres, now aboard the *Starship Voyager*, intercepted the Dreadnought in early 2372 and was successful in destroying it before it could reach Rakosa V. ("Dreadnought" [VGR]). *The Dreadnought missile model was designed by Rick Sternbach.*

"Dreadnought." *Voyager* episode #34. Written by Gary Holland. Directed by LeVar Burton. Stardate 49447. *First aired in 1996. A Cardassian automated missile that B'Elanna had reprogrammed for the Maquis turns up in the Delta Quadrant and she must deactivate it before it destroys an inhabited planet.* GUEST CAST: Raphael Sbarge as **Jonas**; Nancy Hower as **Wildman, Samantha**; Michael Spound as **Lorrum**; Dan Kern as **Kellan**; Majel Barrett as Computer voice. SEE: **Alpha 441; Aschelan V; Benaren; destruct sequence; Dreadnought; duritanium polyalloy; Elrem; Greskrendtregk; Kellan; Kes; kinetic detonator; Ktarian; Lorrum; photon torpedo; quantum torpedo; Rakosa V; Rakosan fighters; Rollins; Sakura Prime; security access code; Sural; Wildman, Samantha.**

Dream of the Fire, The. A classic work of Klingon literature by K'Ratak. Worf gave Data a leather-bound copy of *The Dream of the Fire* when Data was preparing to resign Starfleet rather than submit to disassembly by **Commander Bruce Maddox** in 2365. ("The Measure of a Man" [TNG]).

drechtal beam. Surgical device used to sever neural connections. ("Ethics" [TNG]).

drella. Entity from planet Alpha Carinae V that derives energy from the emotion of love. Spock mentioned the drella in relation to the entity on planet **Argelius II**, which gained strength from the emotion of terror. ("Wolf in the Fold" [TOS]). SEE: **Redjac**.

Drema IV. Fourth planet in the **Selcundi Drema** system, home to a humanoid civilization. Drema IV possesses the largest deposits of **dilithium** ore ever recorded. This ore is laid down in unusually aligned lattices that converted the planet's geologic heat into mechanical stress, thus resulting in significant tectonic instabilities that nearly destroyed the planet. While possessing some advanced technology, this planet was still under Prime Directive protection in 2365, and thus the discovery that *Enterprise*-D officer Data had been in radio contact with an inhabitant of the planet presented a significant problem. While the **Prime Directive** prohibited contact with the inhabitants, humanitarian considerations demanded a means of assistance that avoided cultural contamination. Such a means was found, and the geological instabilities were neutralized by the use of **resonator** probes launched from orbit without the knowledge of the planet's inhabitants. ("Pen Pals" [TNG]).

Dreon VII. Planet; site of a Bajoran colony. The freighter *Xhosa,* piloted by Kasidy Yates, made cargo runs between Bajor and the colony on Dreon VII. ("For the Cause" [DS9]).

dresci. An alcoholic beverage from planet **Pentarus V**. Captain **Dirgo** hid a bottle of *dresci* on his person following the crash of the shuttle ***Nenebek.*** ("Final Mission" [TNG]).

Drex. (Obi Ndefo). Klingon warrior. Drex, who was the son of **General Martok**, had a reputation for being an exceedingly belligerent warrior. Drex was part of the massive Klingon invasion force at station Deep Space 9 on stardate 49011. During their visit to the station, Drex and four other Klingons attacked **Garak** in his tailor shop, breaking seven of his transverse ribs and fracturing his clavicle. ("The Way of the Warrior" [DS9]).

drill thralls. Beings captured throughout the galaxy and brought to planet **Triskelion** by a group of disembodied brains known as the **Providers**. These unfortunate captives, called drill thralls, were branded by one of the three Providers and trained to fight. They spent the rest of their lives in competition to amuse their masters, until James Kirk persuaded the Providers to free the thralls in 2267. ("The Gamesters of Triskelion" [TOS]).

driver coil assembly. Component of a shuttlecraft's impulse propulsion system. ("Parturition" [VGR]).

Drofo Awa. (Michael Bell). Captain of a **Xepolite** freighter. In 2370, Ben Sisko and **Gul Dukat** apprehended Awa carrying weapons into the **Demilitarized Zone.** ("The Maquis, Part II" [DS9]). SEE: **Hetman.** *Michael Bell also portrayed Groppler Zorn in "Encounter at Farpoint" (TNG).*

Drovna, I.K.S. Klingon warship, *Vor'cha* class. In 2372 the *Drovna* illegally mined the Bajoran system with cloaked explosives. An accidental detonation of one of the mines caused severe damage to the *Drovna*. The *Starship Defiant* subsequently towed the damaged vessel to Deep Space 9 to provide medical aid to the ship's crew. While the *Drovna* was docked at the station, Worf and Kurn covertly obtained the detonation codes and locations of the cloaked Klingon mines. ("Sons of Mogh" [DS9]).

Droxine. (Diana Ewing). **Stratos** city dweller and daughter to city official **Plasus**. Protected by her father from the harsh realities of her society, Droxine was unaware of the bitter life led by the **Troglytes** who toiled on the planet's surface to support her life in the clouds. Droxine seemed fascinated by Mr. Spock and inquired if the ***Pon farr*** mating cycle could be broken. ("The Cloud Minders" [TOS]).

drugs. SEE: **adrenaline; alizine; analeptic; anesthezine; anti-intoxicant; asinolyathin; benjisidrine; benzocyatizine; borathium; cateline; cervaline; chloromydride; cordrazine; corophizine; cortical analeptic; cortolin; cryptobiolin; cyalodin; delactovine; deoxyribose suspensions; dermaline gel; dermatiraelian plastiscine; desegranine; deuridium; dexalin; dylamadon; Elasian tears; felicium; formazine; glucajen; hydrocortilene; hyperzine; hyronalin; hyvroxilated quint-ethyl metacetamine; immunosuppressant; impedrezene; improvoline; inaprovaline; inpedrezine; kayolane; kelotane; ketracel-white; kironide ; lectrazine; leporazine; lexorin; macrospentol; mahko root; makara herb; maraji crystals; Masiform D; melorazine; merfadon; metabolic reduction injection; metorapan treatments; metrazene; metremia; morathial series; morphenolog; neodextraline solution; netinaline; neural paralyzer; neurotransmitter; Nogatch hemlock; norep; norepinephrine; PCS; peridaxon; polyadrenaline; polynutrient solution; psychoactive drug; pulmozine; quadroline; Retnax V; retroviral vaccines; Rhuludian crystals; ryetalyn; serotonin; stokaline; terakine; tesokine; theragen; tri-ox compound; trianoline; triclenidil; tricordrazine; triptacederin; tryptophan-lysine distillates; vasokin; Venus drug; Veridium Six; vertazine; white.** SEE ALSO: **diseases.**

"Drumhead, The." *Next Generation* episode #95. Written by Jeri Taylor. Directed by Jonathan Frakes. Stardate 44769.2. *First aired in 1991. An overzealous admiral searches for evidence of a subversive conspiracy, but fails to see that her witch-hunting tactics are themselves subversive of the Federation Constitution.* GUEST CAST: Bruce French as **Genestra**, **Sabin**; Spencer Garrett as **Tarses**, **Crewman Simon**; Henry Woronicz as **J'Dan**; Earl Billings as **Henry**, **Admiral Thomas**; Jean Simmons as **Satie**, **Admiral Norah**; Ann Shea as **Tore, Nellen**. SEE: **Ba'ltmasor Syndrome; Borg; Constitution of the United Federation of Planets; Cruses System; Delb II; deoxyribose suspensions; dilithium chamber hatch; dilithium crystal articulation frame; Earth Station McKinley; encephalographic polygraph scan; *Enterprise*-D, *U.S.S.*; Genestra, Sabin; Henry, Admiral Thomas; J'Dan; Martian Colonies; microtomographic analysis; neutron fatigue; Officer Exchange Program; Satie, Admiral Norah; Satie, Judge Aaron; Seventh Guarantee;**

Tarses, Crewman Simon; Tore, Nellen, Uniform Code of Justice; Wolf 359.

Drusilla. (Lois Jewell). Slave of Proconsul **Claudius Marcus** on planet Eight Ninety-Two-IV. Drusilla was given to James Kirk for the night prior to his scheduled execution there in 2267. Drusilla and Kirk probably did not play chess. SEE: **Eight Ninety-Two, Planet IV**. ("Bread and Circuses" [TOS]).

drydock. Large orbital service structure used for construction and major maintenance of starships and other space vehicles. The original *Starship* ***Enterprise*** underwent a major overhaul at the **San Francisco Yards** drydock in Earth orbit following its five-year mission under the command of James Kirk. (*Star Trek: The Motion Picture*). The *U.S.S.* ***Enterprise*-B** was launched from a drydock in Earth orbit in late 2293. *(Star Trek Generations)*. SEE: **Spacedock**. *The drydock seen in* Star Trek Generations *was, in fact, a refurbished version of the model originally built for* Star Trek: The Motion Picture.

dryworm. Giant creature on planet Antos IV that can generate and control energy with no harm to itself. ("Who Mourns for Adonais?" [TOS]).

DS9. Abbreviation for space station **Deep Space 9**. ("Emissary" [DS9]).

Du'cha. Klingon language term meaning to put an audio signal "on speakers." *(Star Trek Generations)*.

dualitic inverter. Tool used by Starfleet engineers. ("Starship Down" [DS9]).

Duana. (Ivy Bethune). An older citizen on planet **Aldea**, Duana was a key figure in her planet's attempt to abduct children from the *Enterprise*-D in an effort to repopulate her world, in 2364. When the plan failed, Duana accepted technological assistance from starship personnel. ("When the Bough Breaks" [TNG]).

Dublin. City in Ireland on Earth, home to Miles O'Brien and his family. ("Homefront" [DS9]).

Duchamps. (Michael Dorn). Character in Julian Bashir's **secret agent** holosuite program. Duchamps was an associate of **Dr. Hippocrates Noah**. A holosuite malfunction in 2372 caused the character to look exactly like Worf. ("Our Man Bashir" [DS9]).

duck blind. Nickname given to a holographic image generator used to disguise the anthropological field research station on **Mintaka III**. The **hologenerator** created the image of a rocky hillside, thus concealing the station. ("Who Watches the Watchers?" [TNG]). SEE: **Liko**.

"Duet." *Deep Space Nine* episode #19. Teleplay by Peter Allan Fields. Story by Lisa Rich & Jeanne Carrigan-Fauci. Directed by James L. Conway. No stardate given in episode. *First aired in 1993. Kira arrests a Cardassian on Deep Space 9 for having committed atrocities during the Bajoran occupation, but the Cardassian is not what he seems to be.* GUEST CAST: Marc Alaimo as **Dukat**; Robin Christopher as **Neela**; Norman Large as Lissepian Captain; Tony Rizzoli as **Kainon**; Ted Sorel as **Kaval**; Harris Yulin as **Marritza, Aamin**. SEE: **"Butcher of Gallitep, The"; coleibric hemorrhage; Darhe'el, Gul; dermatiraelian plastiscine; Dukat, Gul; Gallitep; Kainon; Kalevian montar; Kalla-Nohra Syndrome; Kaval; Kira Nerys; Kora II; Maraltian *seev*-ale; Marritza, Aamin; Neela; Pottrik Syndrome; Proficient Service Medallion; *Rak-Miunis*; *sem'hal* stew; Shakaar resistance cell; Viterian, Captain; yamok sauce.**

Duffy, Lieutenant. (Charley Lang). An engineering technician aboard the *Enterprise*-D. In 2366, Duffy accidentally helped spread a dangerous **invidium** contamination through the ship. ("Hollow Pursuits" [TNG]).

Dukat, Gul. (Marc Alaimo). Cardassian military official who, as a **gul**, was the last prefect in charge of **Bajor**, just prior to the **Cardassian** retreat from that planet in 2369. ("Emissary" [DS9]). At that time, Deep Space 9 was a mining facility known by the Cardassians as **Terok Nor**. ("Cardassians" [DS9]). Since Dukat was commander of Terok Nor during the occupation, the Bajoran resistance made several attempts to assassinate him. ("Things Past" [DS9]). Dukat still commanded Terok Nor in 2362 and was strongly opposed the Cardassian withdrawal from Bajor in 2369, a move supported by **Pa'Dar**. In 2370, Dukat attempted to disgrace Pa'Dar by revealing that Pa'Dar's son, **Rugal**, who was believed killed in a terrorist attack, was in fact alive. Dukat had previously arranged for Rugal to be placed in the **Tozhat Resettlement Center**, a disgrace in Cardassian society. Dukat's ploy failed when his role in the affair was revealed. ("Cardassians" [DS9]).

Although Dukat was physically removed from the station, he still kept close tabs on his former command. In 2369, Dukat filed a complaint with Sisko when Cardassian citizen **Aamin Marritza** was being detained at the station, accused of being **Gul Darhe'el**, also known as **"The Butcher of Gallitep."** ("Duet" [DS9]).

He was the commander of the Second Order, security identification ADL-40. ("The Maquis, Part I" [DS9]) Dukat fell under suspicion of violating the **Federation-Cardassian treaty** in 2370 when he was implicated as being responsible of supplying illegal weapons to Cardassian colonists in the **Demilitarized Zone**. In fact, Dukat was innocent, but Legate **Parn** had blamed Dukat to try to divert suspicion from the **Cardassian Central Command**. Nevertheless **Maquis** terrorists believed Dukat guilty and abducted him, until he was rescued by Ben Sisko. ("The Maquis, Parts I and II" [DS9]).

In 2372, after a civilian uprising successfully overthrew the Cardassian Central Command, Dukat acted to defend the **Detapa Council** from Klingon invaders, and was instrumental in proving that council members had not been replaced by shape-shifting agents of the **Dominion**. Dukat was subsequently made chief military advisor to the Detapa Council. ("The Way of the Warrior" [DS9]).

Dukat's father had been arrested and executed under the Cardassian system of justice. Dukat blamed **Elim Garak** for his father's execution. ("The Wire" [DS9], "Civil Defense" [DS9], "Improbable Cause" [DS9], and "The Die is Cast" [DS9]).

Dukat was married ("Civil Defense" [DS9]) and had seven children ("The Maquis, Part I" [DS9]) including an 11-year-old son, **Mekor**. ("Defiant" [DS9]).

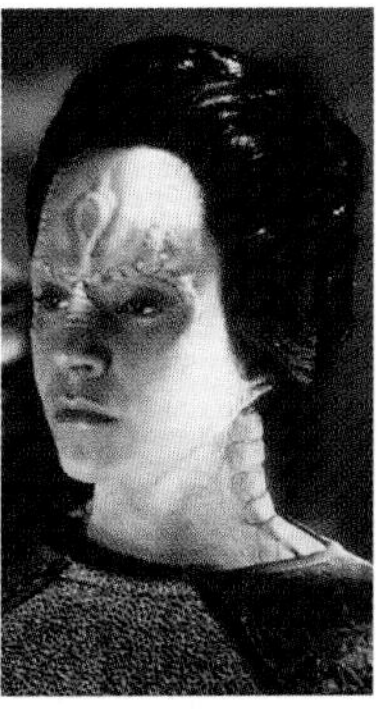

During the occupation of Bajor, Dukat fell in love with a Bajoran woman named **Tora Naprem**, and in 2353 the two had a daughter, **Tora Ziyal** (pictured). Since public revalation of this illicit affair would have ended his career, Dukat sent Tora Naprem and their daughter away in 2366, to **Lissepia** aboard the ***Ravinok***. The *Ravinok* was attacked by two **Breen** warships and forced to crash-land on **Dozaria**. Tora Naprem died in the crash, but her daughter survived. In 2372, Kira Nerys and Gul Dukat went on an expedition to search for the *Ravinok*, eventually rescuing several survivors from a Breen forced-labor dilithium mine on Dozaria. Dukat rescued Tora Ziyal and brought her home with him to Cardassia to live with his family. ("Indiscretion" [DS9]). Although a noble gesture by Earth standards, Dukat's admission drew swift reaction. His mother disowned him and his wife left him, taking their children with her. Gul Dukat was demoted and given command of the military freighter ***Groumall***. His daughter found herself ostracized from Cardassian society, and she went to live with her father on the *Groumall*. Dukat was nevertheless determined to regain his status in Cardassian society. Enlisting the aid of his former adversary, **Kira Nerys**, Dukat used the *Groumall* to capture a Klingon bird-of-prey spacecraft. ("Return to Grace" [DS9]).

In 2373, Dukat conducted secret negotiations with the **Dominion**, leading to an alliance between the Cardassian Union and the Dominion. The move dramatically shifted the balance of power in the Alpha Quadrant, and resulted in Dukat becaming the head of the Cardassian government, pledging to return Cardassia to its former greatness. ("By Inferno's Light" [DS9]).

Gul Dukat was first seen in "Emissary" (DS9).

Dulisian IV. Planet. Site of a Federation colony that transmitted a Priority-1 distress call to the *Enterprise*-D while it was in orbit around **Galorndon Core** in 2368. The colony reported massive failure of its environmental support systems. The distress call was later found to be a ruse sent in the hopes of dissuading the *Enterprise*-D from interfering with the Romulan invasion of planet Vulcan. ("Unification, Part II" [TNG]).

Dulmer. (Jack Blessing). Agent of the **Federation Department of Temporal Investigations**. In 2373, agents Dulmer and Lucsly traveled to Deep Space 9 to investigate the *U.S.S. Defiant*'s accidental trip back in time 105 years to stardate 4523. ("Trials and Tribble-ations" [DS9]). *Dulmer and Lucsly were anagrams for Mulder and Scully, a tip of the hat to Fox's popular fantasy show,* The X-Files.

Dumont, Ensign Suzanne. Crew member aboard the *Starship Enterprise*-D. Wesley's date on the night of the Mozart concert aboard the *Enterprise*-D in honor of Ambassador Sarek in 2366. They did not attend the concert, but went to the **arboretum** instead. ("Sarek" [TNG]).

Dunbar. (Christian R. Conrad). Employee of **Chronowerx**, an Earth corporation in 1996. Dunbar was in charge of security and worked directly for Chronowerx chief executive officer **Henry Starling**. ("Future's End, Parts I and II" [VGR]).

Dunlap, Nigel. Character in *The Queen's Gambit* holosuite adventure. In the story, Dunlap was a 20th-century former **secret agent** who came out of retirement to help foil a diabolical plot to assassinate the Queen of England. ("A Simple Investigation" [DS9]).

dunsel. Term used by midshipmen at Starfleet Academy for an item that serves no useful purpose. **Commodore Robert Wesley** referred to James Kirk as Captain Dunsel after a successful test of the **M-5** multitronic computer in 2268. ("The Ultimate Computer" [TOS]).

duonetic field. Form of energy that inhibits flow of electromagnetic radiation. Duonetic fields prevent operation of most technological devices. Planet **Orellius** had a duonetic field that colonists there thought was a natural phenomenon. Investigation by Starfleet personnel in 2370 found the field to be artificially generated. ("Paradise" [DS9]). SEE: **Alixus**.

duotronic enhancers. SEE: **duotronics; isolinear optical chips**.

duotronic probe. Engineering tool. B'Elanna used a duotronic probe to regulate plasma flow, although Ensign Vorik thought a gravitic caliper was more suited for the task. ("Fair Trade" [VGR]).

duotronics. Revolutionary computer technology invented by **Dr. Richard Daystrom** in 2243. Duotronics became the basis of the computers used aboard all Federation starships for over 80 years, including the main computers aboard the original *Starship Enterprise*. ("The Ultimate Computer" [TOS]). The *Enterprise* also used duotronic elements in its sensor arrays. ("Trials and Tribble-ations" [DS9]). Duotronic enhancers were finally replaced by **isolinear optical chips** in 2329. ("Relics" [TNG]).

Durango. Name for Counselor Troi's holodeck character in Alexander Rozhenko's holodeck program, ***Ancient West***. It was Troi's chance to play the part of a "mysterious stranger." ("A Fistful of Datas" [TNG]).

duranium. Metal alloy. Extremely strong, duranium is commonly used in spacecraft construction such as in the hulls of Starfleet **shuttlecraft**. ("The Menagerie, Part I" [TOS], "Threshold" [VGR]). The **Cardassians** built the access conduits such as those above Quark's bar on Deep Space 9 with a two-meter-thick duranium composite, making the area impervious to most scanning devices. Unfortunately, the **Hunters'** instruments were advanced enough to scan the access tube and locate the fleeing O'Brien and **Tosk**. ("Captive Pursuit" [DS9], "The Siege" [DS9]). Duranium composite was used in the skin of Starfleet **runabouts**, making them difficult to cut into. ("Q-Less" [DS9]). Klingon birds-of-prey were partially built of duranium. ("Dramatis Personae" [DS9]). Duranium was also used in the structure of some **Kazon** vessels, as well. ("Initiations" [VGR]).

duranja. Bajoran ceremonial lamp for the dead; a one-meter-high ornate candleholder in which a flame was kept continually lit in memory of a recently deceased loved one. Ritual prayers were said over the lamp, entreating the **Prophets** to guide the deceased into heaven. **Kira** lit a *duranja* for **Bareil**. ("Shakaar" [DS9]).

Duras sisters. SEE: **Lursa; B'Etor.**

Duras. (Patrick Massett). A member of a politically powerful Klingon family and member of the **Klingon High Council**. In 2366, Duras sought to conceal evidence that his father, **Ja'rod**, had committed treason during the **Khitomer massacre** in 2346. Duras fabricated evidence implicating **Mogh**, father of **Worf**, as the guilty party. Duras was initially successful in forcing the council to rule against Mogh's family, although council leader **K'mpec** was aware of Duras's treachery. ("Sins of the Father" [TNG]). Following the murder of council leader K'mpec in 2367, Duras sought to win K'mpec's position. Duras was one of two contenders for the leadership, and he used a bomb in an attempt to ensure his selection by eliminating Gowron, his competitor. It was also suspected that Gowron was responsible for K'mpec's death by poison. During the rite of succession, Duras also killed **K'Ehleyr**, Worf's mate, when she was on the verge of discovering the truth about Duras's cover-up of his father's crimes. Duras was subsequently killed by Worf, who sought the right of vengeance under Klingon law. ("Reunion" [TNG]). Following Duras's death, his family continued to play a significant role in Klingon politics. ("Redemption, Parts I and II" [TNG], "Past Prologue" [DS9]). SEE: **Lursa; B'Etor; Toral**.

Durenia IV. Planet. Destination of the *Enterprise*-D in early 2367 when a warp field experiment by Ensign Crusher went awry, trapping Dr. Beverly Crusher in a **static warp bubble**. The *Enterprise*-D was forced to abandon its mission and return to Starbase 133. ("Remember Me" [TNG]).

Durg. (Christopher Collins). Alien mercenary hired to help **Rao Ventika** steal a shipment of **deuridium** being transferred from the Gamma Quadrant to station Deep Space 9 in 2369. Durg was killed by Ventika when he failed to carry out an order. ("The Passenger" [DS9]).

duridium alloy. Metallic material used in the construction of throwing **darts**. ("By Inferno's Light" [DS9]).

duritanium polyalloy. Metallic composite alloy. Used in the fabrication of starship hulls. ("Dreadnought" [VGR]).

Durken, Chancellor Avel. (George Coe). The head of state on planet **Malcor III** in 2367. Durken led his people during the time when Malcorian advances in spaceflight technology promised great benefits to his people. Unfortunately, more conservative elements in his government greatly feared the cultural risks of contact with extraterrestrial life. The discovery that Federation operatives had been conducting covert surveillance on his planet as a possible prelude to **first contact** provoked a violent reaction from these conservative elements, leading Durken to scale back the Malcorian space program. Durken also asked Captain Picard to postpone indefinitely any plans for Federation contact with the Malcorians. ("First Contact" [TNG]). SEE: **Krola; Yale, Mirasta**. *George Coe also played the head of Network 23 in the television series* Max Headroom.

Durst, Peter. (Brian Markinson). Starfleet officer assigned to the *U.S.S. Voyager*. ("Cathexis" [VGR]). Durst was killed in 2371 while on an away mission to planet **Avery III** for inspection of magnesite formations. Durst was captured by **Vidiian**s, who harvested his organs to save the lives of more than a dozen Vidiians suffering from the **phage**. Vidiian doctor **Sulan** took Durst's face and had it grafted onto his own so that the full-Klingon Torres he created might find his new appearance more pleasing. ("Faces" [VGR]). *Brian Markinson played both Durst and Sulan. Lieutenant Durst was first seen in "Cathexis" (VGR). Brian Markinson previously played Vorin in "Homeward" (TNG).*

dust shrouds. Natural phenomenon located near the equator of planet **Rinax**. Neelix once visited the equatorial dust shrouds with his favorite sister, **Alixia**. ("Rise" [VGR]).

Dvorak, Antonín. Earth musical composer (1841-1904) known for his adaptations of Bohemian folk music. Dvorak's works, including "The Slavonic Dances," were among the music that Data studied in 2369. ("A Fistful of Datas" [TNG]).

DY-100. Ancient type of interplanetary space vehicle built on Earth in the late 20th century. DY-100 vessels used nuclear-powered engines and were equipped with suspended-animation facilities for extended voyages. The ***S.S. Botany Bay***, launched from Earth in 1996, was a DY-100-class ship. Sleeper ships like the DY-100 fell from general use by 2018 because of significant improvements in sublight propulsion technology. ("Space Seed" [TOS]). *A conjectural model of the* Botany Bay, *built by Greg Jein for a photograph in the* Star Trek Chronology, *was equipped with several space shuttle-style solid rocket strap-on boosters, suggesting how the 1996-vintage spacecraft might have gotten into orbit. The model was seen as a desktop decoration in Rain Robinson's SETI laboratory in the 1996 scenes of "Future's End, Parts I and II" (VGR).*

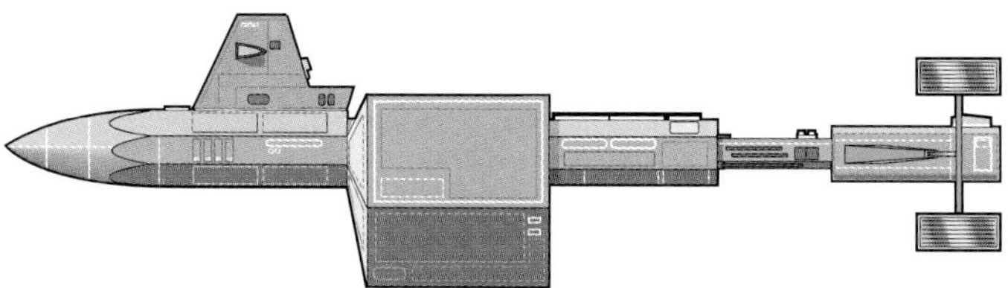

DY-500. Interplanetary vessel, relatively primitive by 23rd-century standards, but considerably more advanced than the older **DY-100** ships. ("Space Seed" [TOS]). The ***S.S. Mariposa***, launched from Earth in 2123, was a DY-500 ship. ("Up the Long Ladder" [TNG]).

dylamadon. Drug used in euthanasia for humanoid patients. Though deadly, dylamadon was believed to be painless. ("Man of the People" [TNG]).

dynametric array. Scientific analytical tool. Used aboard station Deep Space 9. ("Playing God" [DS9]).

dynoscanner. Sensor device used to detect low-level molecular activity. (*Star Trek II: The Wrath of Khan*, "Ethics" [TNG]).

Dyson Sphere. A gigantic artificial structure designed to completely enclose a star in a hollow sphere some 200 million kilometers in diameter. The interior surface of such a sphere, if constructed to provide a life-supporting environment, could theoretically provide the surface area of literally hundreds of millions of planets. Dyson Spheres were long believed to be impractical to build, due to their extreme size and the astronomical amount of raw materials required for construction. Nevertheless, a Dyson Sphere was discovered near **Norpin Colony** when the *Enterprise*-D found the transport ship ***Jenolen***, which had crashed on the sphere's surface in 2294. This object was built by an unknown civilization around a G-type star, and supported a Class-M atmosphere that clung to the interior surface of the sphere. The shell was composed of carbon-neutronium, with an interior surface area of some 10^{16} square kilometers. No signs of current habitation were found on that interior surface, apparently because the star was undergoing severe bursts of radiation. ("Relics" [TNG]). *The basic concept was first proposed in the 1960s by Earth scientist Freeman Dyson, after whom the sphere is named.*

Dyson. Starfleet officer assigned to the *Enterprise*-E in 2373. *(Star Trek: First Contact).*

Dytallix B. Planet in the Mira star system, one of seven worlds owned by the Dytallix Mining Corporation. Although the mines were long abandoned by 2364, the planet was the site of a covert meeting where Captain **Walker Keel** warned Jean-Luc Picard of his suspicions of an alien infiltration of Starfleet in that year. ("Conspiracy" [TNG]).

E'Tyshra. (Darleen Carr). **T'Lani** ambassador who helped negotiate the end of her people's war with the **Kellerun** in 2370. E'Tyshra collaborated with **Sharat**, the Kellerun ambassador, to destroy all information of the **harvester** technology and also to kill everyone who had technical knowledge of their manufacture, including Deep Space 9 personnel **Dr. Julian Bashir** and **Miles O'Brien**. ("Armageddon Game" [DS9]).

E-band emissions. Electromagnetic signals sometimes emitted by collapsing protostars. E-band emissions were used by Romulan operatives in late 2367 as a means of secretly transmitting commands to Geordi La Forge through his VISOR. Those signals were delta-compressed on a frequency similar to that of humanoid brainwaves. ("The Mind's Eye" [TNG]). SEE: **neural implants; Taibak; VISOR.**

E-mail. Electronic mail. The transmission of data and messages electronically from one computer to another. E-mail became commonplace on Earth in the late 20th century and continued to be used on the **Net** throughout the early 21st century. ("Past Tense, Part II" [DS9]). **SETI** astronomer **Rain Robinson** used E-mail to notify her colleagues when she discovered evidence of the *Starship Voyager* orbiting Earth in 1996. ("Future's End, Part I" [VGR]).

ear receiver. Small electronic device used by Starfleet personnel for personal monitoring of audio information without the inconvenience of a loudspeaker that might interfere with nearby personnel. *Uhura used this a lot on the bridge, although it was sometimes mistaken for a fancy earring. Spock used it, too.*

Earhart, Amelia. (Sharon Lawrence). Noted aviator, the first woman to fly alone across **Earth**'s Atlantic Ocean, born in 1898. Earhart disappeared without a trace in 1937 while piloting a **Lockheed Electra** aircraft in an attempt to fly around the Earth. Unknown to 20th-century Earth authorities, Earhart and her navigator, **Fred Noonan**, were among some three hundred humans abducted from the planet and taken some 70,000 light-years to the **Briori** homeworld in the Delta Quadrant. Earhart, Noonan, and six other abductees were kept in **cryostasis** for centuries until they were revived in 2371 by Starfleet personnel from the *Starship Voyager*. Earhart and Noonan both elected to remain on the former Briori homeworld, along with a colony of descendents from the original abductees. *Voyager* Captain **Kathryn Janeway** noted that Earhart had been an inspiration that had led her to a career in Starfleet. ("The 37's" [VGR]). SEE: **Thirty-Sevens.**

Earl Grey tea. A blended black tea flavored with bergamot or lavender oil. A favorite beverage of Jean-Luc Picard, who often ordered it through the ship's food **replicator**. He liked it hot. ("Contagion" [TNG]).

early French impressionists. School of painters on Earth who worked during the 1870s. These artists included Edouard Manet, Edgar Degas, Auguste Renoir, and Claude Monet. Data, as part of his exploration of painting, did several pieces emulating the styles of these artists. ("Inheritance" [TNG]).

Earp, Morgan. (Rex Holman). Law enforcement official from Earth's ancient American West, who fought against the Clanton family in 1881 at the famous gunfight at the **OK Corral**. A replica of Earp was created by the **Melkotians** in 2268 as part of a bizarre drama intended to kill Kirk and members of his crew. ("Spectre of the Gun" [TOS]). *Rex Holman also played J'Onn in* Star Trek V: The Final Frontier.

Earp, Virgil. (Charles Maxwell). Brother to **Morgan** and **Wyatt Earp**, who fought in the legendary gunfight at the **OK Corral** in **Tombstone, Arizona**. A replica of Virgil was part of the scenario created by the **Melkotians** in 2268 for the execution of Kirk and members of his crew. ("Spectre of the Gun" [TOS]).

Earp, Wyatt. (Ron Soble). Legendary law enforcement official from Earth's ancient American West, who fought members of the Clanton family at the famous gunfight at the **OK Corral** on October 26, 1881. The **Melkotians** re-created Earp for their drama intended to cause the deaths of Kirk and members of his crew. ("Spectre of the Gun" [TOS]).

Earth Colony 2. Settlement. Captain Kirk's brother, **George Samuel Kirk**, had hoped to be transferred to the research station at Earth Colony 2 prior to his death in 2267. ("What Are Little Girls Made Of?" [TOS]).

Earth guidebook. Padd containing an interactive program detailing **Earth**'s customs, culture, history and geography. In 2372, Dr. Julian Bashir gave an Earth guidebook padd to Nog to use while he was at Starfleet Academy. ("Little Green Men" [DS9]).

Earth Station Bobruisk. Transport facility located in Europe on planet Earth. Site from which Worf's adoptive parents, **Sergey and Helena Rozhenko,** transported to the *Enterprise*-D when the ship was at **Earth Station McKinley** in 2367. ("Family" [TNG]). *Bobruisk is a city in Belarus, the site of a major battle in the Second World War.*

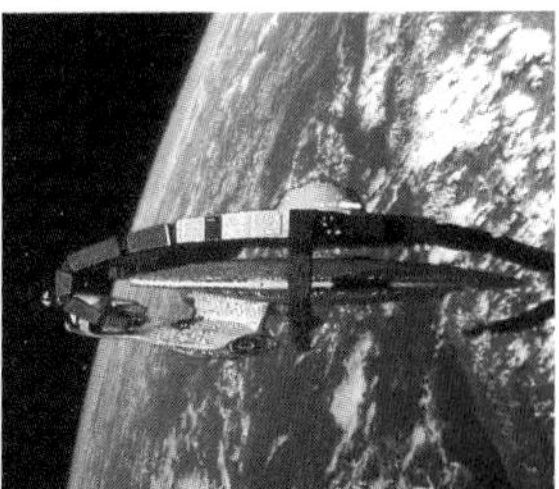

Earth Station McKinley. Starfleet shipbuilding and repair facility in **Earth** orbit. McKinley Station was a large orbital platform supporting several large articulated work arms, designed to service even the largest starships. The ***Enterprise*-D** docked there for six weeks following the defeat of the **Borg** ship in 2367. ("The Best of Both Worlds, Part II," "Family" [TNG]). Unknown to anyone at the time, a defective **dilithium chamber hatch** was installed in the *Enterprise*-D warp-drive system at McKinley Station. The hatch contained undetectable submicron fractures that were responsible for a serious explosion in the engine room later that year. ("The Drumhead" [TNG]). (In Q's **anti-time future**, the ***U.S.S. Pasteur*** canceled a scheduled stop at McKinley Station to proceed to the **Devron system**.) ("All Good Things..." [TNG]).

Earth-Saturn probe. The first successful piloted mission from Earth to **Saturn**. The flight was commanded in the early 21st century by **Colonel Shaun Geoffrey Christopher**, son of **Captain John Christopher**. ("Tomorrow Is Yesterday" [TOS]).

Earth. Third planet in the Sol system, a Class-M world located in Sector 001. ("The Best of Both Worlds, Part II" [TNG]). Homeworld to the human civilization, and location of the **Federation Council** and the **Federation President**'s office, as well as **Starfleet Command**. *(Star Trek IV: The Voyage Home, Star Trek VI: The Undiscovered Country).* Although humans did not make official contact with extraterrestrial intelligence until the 21st century, the planet received several visitors from space before then. Among these was a small Ferengi vessel that landed near **Roswell**, New Mexico, in July 1947. ("Little Green Men" [DS9]). In the past, social inequities plagued Earth. Symptomatic were 21st-century relocation camps called **Sanctuary Districts**, established in American cities, isolating the homeless, the unemployed, and the mentally ill from the rest of society. The Sanctuary Districts bred one of the most violent civil uprisings in American history, known as the **Bell Riots**, in September of 2024. This bloody revolt changed American public opinion about the Sanctuaries and forced the people of the United States to finally begin dealing with their social problems. ("Past Tense, Part I" [DS9]). SEE: **Bell, Gabriel; gimme**. A very sad chapter in Earth history was written when the planet suffered its last world war, in 2053. During **World War III**, millions of people perished in a massive nuclear exchange that destroyed most of the major cities on Earth and eliminated most national governments. A dark decade ensued, during which most of the planet reverted to barbarism. This **postatomic horror** began to ease on April 4, 2063, when space pioneer **Zefram Cochrane** conducted his planet's first faster-than-light spaceflight. Cochrane's flight was directly responsible for Earth's **first contact** with an extraterrestrial civilization, the **Vulcans**, on the following day. The event gave humanity the perspective it needed to begin a remarkable renaissance, bringing a virtual end to war, poverty, and disease over the next five decades. *(Star Trek: First Contact).*Earth's first world government was established only a few decades later, in 2150. ("Attached" [TNG]). In the 24th century, Earth is virtually a paradise, with no poverty, crime, or war. ("The Maquis, Part II" [DS9]). SEE: **Paris; San Francisco**. *Mostly harmless.*

Eastern Coalition. Loose alliance of eastern powers that existed on **Earth** after that planet's **World War III**. The Eastern Coalition was often adversarial towards the powers controlling North America. *(Star Trek: First Contact).*

Eblan. (Charles Parks). **Bajoran** national who resided at station **Deep Space 9** in 2370. Eblan recognized **Kubus Oak** on DS9 when Kubus sought to return to Bajor. ("Collaborator" [DS9]). *Eblan's name was not mentioned in dialog, but appeared only in the script.*

Echo Papa 607. An automated weapons drone system created by the now-dead arms merchants of planet **Minos**, built for use during the ancient **Erselrope Wars**. Billed by the Minosians as the ultimate in weapons system technology, the Echo Papa 607 was a small free-flying unit with a powerful energy projector and a cloaking device. The 607 was designed to be effective against ground personnel as well as deep-space vehicles, and could also be programmed for information gathering. Most significantly, the 607 embodied dynamic adaptive design, enabling it to learn during combat situations so that mistakes would not be repeated. An ancient Echo Papa 607 system was still active on Minos in 2364, when the *Enterprise*-D investigated the disappearance of the *U.S.S. Drake* there. The weapon, apparently also responsible for the destruction of the ***U.S.S. Drake***, threatened the *Enterprise* and an away team on the planet's surface. ("The Arsenal of Freedom" [TNG]). *The miniature of the Echo Papa 607 was built by visual effects supervisor Dan Curry, using an old L'Eggs pantyhose container and a discarded shampoo bottle.*

echo displacement. Tactical deception technique using a starship's deflector grid to project false sensor readings to convince an enemy that other spacecraft are present. In late 2372, the *U.S.S. Voyager* employed an echo displacement tactic to temporarily give the **Kazon** the impression that several Talaxian ships were present. ("Basics, Part I" [VGR]).

ECON. Abbreviation for **Eastern Coalition**. *(Star Trek: First Contact).*

Eddie. (C.J. Bau). Fictitious character, a bartender in a 1930s-1940s nightclub featured in the Dixon Hill stories and holodeck representations. *(Star Trek: First Contact). This character's name is from the script.*

Eddington, Michael. (Kenneth Marshall). **Starfleet** Security officer who defected to the **Maquis**. Lieutenant Commander Michael Eddington was assigned to **Deep Space 9** in 2371 because Starfleet Command did not have full confidence in **Odo**. ("The Search, Parts I and II" [DS9]). When Commander Sisko defied **Admiral Toddman**'s orders and embarked upon a rescue mission in 2371 during the joint Romulan and Cardassian attack on the Founders' homeworld, Eddington sabotaged the *Defiant*'s cloaking device. He explained that he was working under Toddman's direct orders to prevent an unauthorized expedition. ("The Die is Cast" [DS9]). In 2372, Eddington was discovered to be an agent of the Maquis when he hijacked 12 Federation industrial replicators destined for Cardassia. ("For the Cause" [DS9]). Eddington subsequently fled Starfleet authorities and, in 2373, organized a Maquis offensive using **biogenic weapons** against the Cardassian colonies on **Veloz Prime** and Quatal Prime. Eddington was also responsible for an attack that disabled the *Starship* ***Malinche***. Benjamin Sisko, determined to stop his former friend, scattered toxic **trilithium** resin into the atmosphere of Solosos III, rendering it uninhabitable. Eddington surrendered to Starfleet authorities when Sisko threatened to do the same to Tracken II. As a leader of the Maquis, Eddington envisioned himself as **Valjean**, the heroic character of a novel entitled ***Les Misérables***, which was Eddington's favorite book. (Eddington saw his former friend Sisko as **Javert**, the inflexible police inspector in the same book.) ("For the Uniform" [DS9]). *Eddington first appeared in "The Search, Part I" (DS9).*

Eden. In Earth mythology, a beautiful garden at the beginning of time. *(Star Trek V: The Final Frontier).* SEE: ***Sha Ka Ree.*** Others held Eden to be a mythical planet of extraordinary beauty and peace. Noted scientist **Dr. Sevrin** led a group of followers on a quest in 2269 to find planet Eden. They found a planet matching this description in Romulan space, but later found the plant life on the planet to be permeated with deadly acid. ("The Way to Eden" [TOS]).

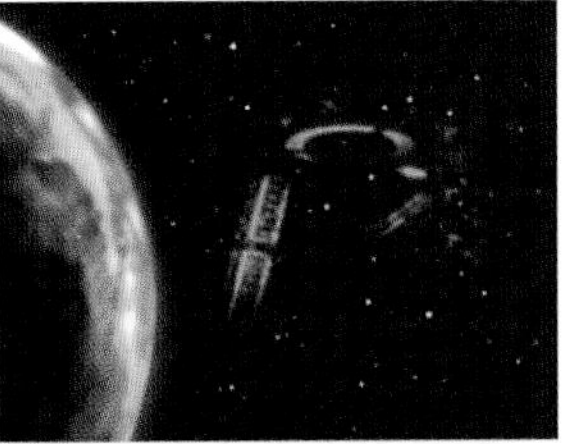

Edo god. Powerful spaceborne life-form (or forms) discovered near the Rubicun star system. This immensely powerful, transdimensional entity cares for and protects the humanoid species on planet **Rubicun III**. When the *Starship Enterprise*-D attempted to make contact with the inhabitants of that planet in 2364, the Edo god warned the ship to leave without interfering with the humanoids it called its "children." The Edo god also requested removal of a Federation colony established in the nearby **Strnad star system**. ("Justice" [TNG]).

Edo. Civilization of humanoids who inhabit planet **Rubicun III.** Known for a curious mixture of hedonistic sexuality and almost puritanical respect for their law, the Edo are governed and protected by a transdimensional entity they call their god. SEE: **Edo god**. Many years ago, Edo society was lawless and dangerously violent. They eventually adopted a system in which laws were enforced by a very small number of mediators (law enforcement officials) who monitored randomly selected areas called **punishment zones**. Violation of any law in a punishment zone would result in immediate death. Since no one except the mediators would know which area had been selected as a punishment zone, the system served as a strong incentive to obey all laws. ("Justice" [TNG]).

Edosian orchid. Type of exotic flowering plant. Garak was an experienced gardener, and his specialty was Edosian orchids. ("Broken Link" [DS9]).

Edouard. (Jean-Paul Vignon). A holodeck character, the understanding waiter at the **Cafe des Artistes** in Paris. ("We'll Always Have Paris" [TNG]).

Edwell, Captain. Federation officer, native of planet Gaspar VII. ("Starship Mine" [TNG]).

Ee'Char. (Craig Wasson). Character in an artificial reality program created by the **Argrathi** government for the punishment of convicted criminals. In the program, Ee'Char was a cell mate who shared a 20-year prison sentence with the convicted criminal. In 2372, Miles O'Brien, sentenced to the Argrathi punishment, experienced incarceration with Ee'Char. ("Hard Time" [DS9]).

eel-birds. Creatures from planet Regulus V that must return to the caverns where they hatched to mate every 11 years. Spock mentioned the mating habits of the eel-birds to Kirk in attempting to explain the Vulcan mating drive, ***Pon farr***. ("Amok Time" [TOS]).

Egg. An instrumented sensor probe, designed by **Dr. Paul Stubbs** to record the decay of neutronium expelled during a stellar explosion. Dr. Stubbs, who nicknamed his brainchild "the Egg," worked on it for twenty years before successfully launching it from the *Enterprise*-D at the **Kavis Alpha Sector** in 2366. ("Evolution" [TNG]). *The full-scale egg prop was a modification of the virus containment device originally built for "The Child" (TNG).*

eggs benedict. Traditional Earth breakfast made with cooked chicken eggs. Although limited to ration packs, Captain Janeway dreamed of having eggs benedict for breakfast. ("Phage" [VGR]). *Besides chicken eggs, it also contains a slice of smoked porcine flesh, both sitting atop a toasted, round, pasty, ground-grain product known as an "English muffin," the whole of which is smothered under a thick, white blanket of gooey viscous liquid known as "Hollandaise sauce," lightly dusted on top with a pungent red-colored spice. "And we call ourselves civilized?" asks Bob Justman.*

eggs with bacon and corned beef hash. Traditional Earth breakfast foods high in fat. Miles O'Brien enjoyed two eggs over easy, three strips of bacon, and a side of corned beef hash for breakfast. ("The Assignment" [DS9]).

eichner radiation. Form of radiation found to stimulate growth of certain strains of **plasma plague**. Eichner radiation can be created by a **subspace field inverter**, and it is also emitted by certain **cyanoacrylates**. ("The Child" [TNG]).

eidetic memory. Psychological term referring to an ability to recall images in near-photographic detail. **Kes** had an eidetic memory. ("Eye of the Needle" [VGR]).

Eiger. (Marnie McPhail). Starfleet officer assigned to the Engineering section of the *U.S.S. Enterprise*-E. In 2373, Eiger was captured and assimilated by the **Borg** and later died when the ship was retaken. *(Star Trek: First Contact). Marnie McPhail previously portrayed Alcia in "Innocence" (VGR).*

Eight ninety-two, Planet IV. Fourth planet of the Eight Ninety-Two solar system; a Class-M world where the survivors of the survey vessel ***S.S. Beagle*** beamed down after their ship was damaged in 2261. The planet's society was a 20th-century version of Earth's ancient Rome, with video communications, power transportation, and an imperial government. By 2267, slavery had existed for two thousand years, and a slave caste developed into a stratum of society with specified rights under the law. SEE: **Children of the Sun**; **Marcus, Claudius**; **Merrick, R. M.** ("Bread and Circuses" [TOS]).

Einstein, Albert. (Jim Morton). Nobel Prize-winning theoretical physicist (1879-1955), regarded as one of the greatest scientific minds of 20th-century Earth. Einstein postulated the theory of relativity and spent much of his later life attempting to unify relativity with quantum mechanics. **Reginald Barclay**, using his **Cytherian**-enhanced intelligence, spent a night in 2367 discussing grand unification theories with a holodeck simulation of Albert Einstein. ("The Nth Degree" [TNG]). The holographic Einstein was later enlisted by Data in a customized holodeck program that allowed him to play poker with such scientific luminaries as Einstein, **Sir Isaac Newton**, and **Professor Stephen Hawking**. ("Descent, Part I" [TNG]).

EJ7 interlock. Engineering tool used to open critical system access panels on **Deep Space 9**. **Neela** stole the interlock from Chief O'Brien's tool kit to access restricted areas on the station, in an attempt to escape after the planned assassination of **Vedek Bareil.** ("In the Hands of the Prophets" [DS9]).

Ekina. Cargo ship. The *Ekina* brought **Verad** and his band of thieves to station Deep Space 9 in 2370. ("Invasive Procedures" [DS9]).

Ekoria. (Ellen Wheeler). Inhabitant of a planet in the Teplan system located in the Gamma Quadrant. Like all on her planet, Ekoria was infected with a deadly disease known as the blight. SEE: **Teplan blight.** Ekoria's husband was an artist. Before his death in 2371, he painted a mural on a city building depicting life in happier and healthier times, before the blight devastated the Teplan civilization. In

2372, Dr. Julian Bashir saved the life of her unborn child by developing a vaccine that was effective if administered before birth. Ekoria died shortly following childbirth. ("The Quickening" [DS9]). *The mural of Ekoria's city was painted by scenic artist Doug Drexler.*

Ekos. Inner planet in star system M43 Alpha, homeworld to the **Ekosians** and sister world to planet **Zeon**. ("Patterns of Force" [TOS]).

Ekosians. Humanoid inhabitants of planet **Ekos**. The Ekosians were the victims of a terrible miscalculation by Federation sociologic observer **John Gill**, who tried to bring peace to the planet by introducing a government patterned after Earth's Nazi Germany. The plan initially worked, but Gill was unable to avoid the brutal excesses of the ancient Nazis. Gill became the puppet of ambitious Ekosians seeking to gain power for themselves by creating a repressive regime and seeking to exterminate the citizens of neighboring planet **Zeon**. In 2268, the *Starship Enterprise*, investigating the planet, allowed Gill to denounce the Nazi movement, paving the way for the resumption of peaceful relations with the Zeons. ("Patterns of Force" [TOS]). SEE: **Melakon**.

El Capitan. A massive monolithic mountain in **Yosemite National Park** on Earth. Formed by glaciers during a recent Ice Age, El Capitan has a sheer granite face, a kilometer high, considered by many to be among Earth's greatest challenges for rock climbers. James Kirk enjoyed the sport of free-climbing El Capitan, although he was nearly killed in an accident there in 2287. (*Star Trek V: The Final Frontier*).

El-Adrel IV. Planet in the El-Adrel star system. Site where Tamarian captain **Dathon** and *Enterprise*-D Captain Picard met in 2368. An indigenous beast there provided a significant threat to both men on the planet. Dathon hoped that the shared danger would help Picard understand the nature of his people's metaphoric language. Dathon was ultimately successful, but at the cost of his life. ("Darmok" [TNG]).

El-Adrel system. Star system located midway between Federation and Tamarian space. ("Darmok" [TNG]).

El-Aurians. Humanoid civilization nearly made extinct in the late 23rd century when their homeworld was destroyed by the **Borg**. *(Star Trek Generations).* Very few El-Aurians escaped this holocaust; the few who survived were spread thinly across the galaxy. ("Q Who?" [TNG]). El-Aurians were reputed to be good listeners. **Martus Mazur** was an El-Aurian, and he used his listening ability to cheat money from people. ("Rivals" [DS9]). SEE: **Guinan; *Lakul, S.S.*; Soran, Tolian**.

El-Baz, Shuttlepod. Shuttlepod 05, carried aboard *U.S.S. Enterprise*-D. This ship was discovered floating derelict near the **Endicor system**, carrying a future version of Captain Picard in 2365. ("Time Squared" [TNG]). *The vehicle was also seen in the shuttlebay in "Transfigurations" (TNG). Data stole the* El-Baz *while under the control of Lore, and it was seen on the planet's surface in "Descent, Parts I and II" (TNG). Designed by Rick Sternbach and Richard McKenzie under the direction of production designer Richard James, miniature built by Tony Meininger. The* El-Baz *was the first shuttle of this type seen; subsequent shuttlepods were re-dresses of the* El-Baz*. The shuttlepod was smaller than the shuttlecraft, and was used because it was impractical at the time to build a full exterior of the larger shuttlecraft. The* El-Baz *was named for former NASA planetary geoscientist Farouk El-Baz, currently on the faculty at Brown University.*

el-Mitra Exchange. A classic strategy in three-dimensional chess. It was considered a strong response to the **Kriskov Gambit**. When Data and Troi played the game on stardate 45494, Data expected Troi to employ the el-Mitra Exchange, but she surprised him. ("Conundrum" [TNG]).

"Elaan of Troyius." Original Series episode #57. Written by John Meredyth Lucas. Directed by John Meredyth Lucas. Stardate *4372.5. First aired in 1968. The* Enterprise *must transport Elaan, the beautiful Dohlman of Elas, to an arranged marriage on planet Troyius. Unfortunately, Elaan is uninterested in her duty, and instead causes Kirk to fall in love with her.* GUEST CAST: France Nuyen as **Elaan**; Jay Robinson as **Petri**; Tony Young as **Kryton**; Majel Barrett as **Chapel, Christine**; Lee Duncan as Evans; Victor Brandt as Watson; Dick Durock as Elasian guard #1; Charles Beck as Elasian guard #2; K.L. Smith as Klingon. SEE: **dilithium; Dohlman; Elaan; Elas; Elasian tears; Elasians; Kryton; Petri; radans; Tellun star system; Troyians; Troyius.**

Elaan. (France Nuyen). The **Dohlman** of planet **Elas**. Elaan married the leader of planet **Troyius** in 2268, an arranged marriage intended to bring peace to the two warring planets. Elaan was shuttled from Elas to Troyius aboard the *Starship Enterprise*. The flight was deliberately slowed in the hopes that Elaan would take the extra time to learn more of Troyan culture. The willful Elaan at first strongly resisted having a new culture forced upon her, but later accepted the responsibility. ("Elaan of Troyius" [TOS]). SEE: **Elasian tears.**

Elamos the Magnificent. A mythological figure who ruled the land of Tagas. Elamos was a topic of study in the *Enterprise*-D primary school during the 2360s. Elamos proclaimed that no children would be tolerated within his kingdom, but a girl named Dara and her brother defied him. ("Hero Worship" [TNG]).

Elani. (Sarah Rayne). **Drayan** individual who, despite her advanced age, looked and acted like a young child. In 2372, Elani and several other elder Drayans traveled to one of the Drayan moons in order to carry out their **final ritual**. Their shuttle crashed on the moon and all of their **Attendants** died, leaving the elders alone. Lieutenant Tuvok, whose shuttle had also crashed there, comforted and took care of the easily confused Drayans. Elani died of natural causes on the **crysata** moon shortly thereafter. ("Innocence" [VGR]).

Elanian singer stone. An artifact that emits beautiful musical sounds when held by a living being. **Dr. Katherine Pulaski** had a singer stone on her desk, but Data gave it to **Sarjenka** of planet **Drema IV**. ("Pen Pals" [TNG]). *The singer stone was loosely adapted from the* Star Trek *novel,* Tears of the Singers*. Both the book and "Pen Pals" were written by Melinda Snodgrass.*

Elas. Inner planet in the **Tellun star system** and home to the **Elasian** civilization of humanoids. ("Elaan of Troyius" [TOS]).

Elasian tears. The tears of women from the planet **Elas** contain an unusual biochemical compound that serves as a powerful love potion. Any man who comes into contact with an **Elasian** woman's tears will fall in love with her. Kirk brushed aside a tear from the **Dohlman** of Elas in 2268 and became obsessed with her until his true love, the *Enterprise*, cured him of her spell. ("Elaan of Troyius" [TOS])

Elasians. Proud warrior civilization of people from the planet **Elas** who had been at war with their neighbor **Troyius** for many years. Eventually, both planets gained the ability to destroy each other, and a marriage between the ruler of Troyius and the **Dohlman** of Elas was arranged in 2268 in the hope of bringing peace to the two worlds. ("Elaan of Troyius" [TOS]).

Elaysians. Humanoid civilization. The Elaysian homeworld had such low surface gravity that the Elaysians were able to fly in their atmosphere. Because they were adapted to these unusual conditions, Elaysians found living in a standard Class-M gravity field to be extremely challenging. For this reason, very few Elaysians left their homeworld. ("Melora" [DS9]). SEE: **Pazlar, Melora.**

Elba II. Planet with a poisonous atmosphere on which was located one of the few Federation penal colonies for the criminally insane. The Elba II facility, managed by **Governor Cory**, was home to 15 inmates in 2268, including Captain **Garth** of Izar, who became mentally unstable after an accident. ("Whom Gods Destroy" [TOS]). *The dove and hand symbol that adorned the medical jumpsuits on Elba II was originally used in the* ***Tantalus V*** *colony in "Dagger of the Mind" (TOS).*

Elbrun, Tam. (Harry Groener). A **Betazoid** specialist in **first contact** with new life-forms. Elbrun was a telepath of extraordinary talent, but he lacked the ability to screen out the normal telepathic "noise" emanating from other humanoids' thoughts. This caused Elbrun great emotional stress, for which he was hospitalized repeatedly. While a patient at the **University of Betazed**, Elbrun was cared for by psychology student **Deanna Troi**. As a first-contact specialist, Elbrun participated in the notorious **Ghorusda disaster**, and later served as Federation representative to **Chandra V**. In 2366, Elbrun was assigned to the *Enterprise*-D for the strategically significant **Tin Man** first contact. Elbrun, who had lived all his life desperately seeking isolation, found the living spacecraft Tin Man to be a kindred spirit. ("Tin Man" [TNG]).

Elected One, The. Head of the parliamentary body governing planet **Angel One**. The Elected One is one of six females who lead the constitutional oligarchy. **Beata** was the Elected One in 2364. ("Angel One" [TNG]).

electroceramic. Structural material used as component of Kazon spacecraft. ("Initiations" [VGR]).

electrodynamic turbulence. Strong and unpredictable currents in the upper atmosphere of some planetoids. Electrodynamic turbulence can pose a hazard to aircraft and shuttlecraft flight. Electrodynamic forces in the ionosphere of one of the moons around **Drayan II** caused a *Voyager* shuttlecraft piloted by Lieutenant Tuvok and **Ensign Bennet** to crash in 2372. ("Innocence" [VGR]).

electrophoretic activity. Slow movement of electrically charged colloidal particles dispersed in a fluid under the influence of an electric field. The **swarm** that obstructed *Voyager*'s path in 2372 caused increased levels of electrophoretic activity in the ship's atmosphere, causing the onset of early ***elogium*** in Kes. ("Elogium" [VGR]). Heightened cellular electrophoretic activity can be indicative of **Urodelean flu**. ("Genesis" [TNG]).

electrophoretic analysis. Standard medical test run to analyze cellular components. Dr. Julian Bashir ran an electrophoretic analysis on cells found in **Ibudan**'s quarters to help determine their origin. ("A Man Alone" [DS9]).

electroplasma system taps. Components of a Federation starship's warp-drive system used to divert a small amount of the drive plasma so that it can be used to generate electrical power for shipboard use. The **EPS** taps are located on the power transfer conduits. ("A Matter of Time" [TNG]). SEE: **electroplasma system.**

electroplasma system. Often abbreviated EPS. Power-distribution network used aboard Federation starships, as well as in Cardassian facilities like **Deep Space 9**. ("The Forsaken" [DS9]). Renegade Jem'Hadar soldiers stole EPS power stabilizers from Deep Space 9 in 2372 to help reactivate the Iconian gateway found on planet Vandros IV. ("To the Death" [DS9]). In 2372, *Voyager* Engineer **Lon Suder** murdered fellow crew member Frank Darwin and placed Darwin's body in an EPS conduit, hoping to vaporize the corpse. ("Meld" [VGR]).

Eleen. (Julie Newmar). Mother to High Teer **Leonard James Akaar** of planet **Capella IV**. Eleen's husband, High **Teer Akaar**, was killed in a local power struggle in 2267, whereupon Eleen accepted the necessity of her own death under **Capellan** law, since she carried the unborn child who would be **teer**. Her execution was prevented by personnel from the *Starship Enterprise.* Upon the birth of her son, Eleen became regent, ruling the Ten Tribes until Leonard James came of age. Eleen named her son Leonard James in honor of the two *Enterprise* officers who prevented Klingon outsiders from overthrowing her government, a distinction that probably caused James Kirk and Leonard McCoy to become insufferably pleased with themselves for at least a month. ("Friday's Child" [TOS]).

element 247. Stable transuranic element with an atomic number of 247. Element 247 was discovered by the crew of the *Starship Voyager* in 2371 in the ring system of a **Class-D planet** in the Delta Quadrant. The element emanated from the bodies of dead members of the **Vhnori** species as a natural byproduct of decomposition. ("Emanations" [VGR]). *Of course, the discovery of element 247 would not be known to the rest of the Federation until and unless the* Voyager *makes it back home.*

Elementary Temporal Mechanics. Course taught at Starfleet Academy. ("Trials and Tribble-ations" [DS9]). SEE: **predestination paradox.**

"Elementary, Dear Data." *Next Generation* episode #29. Written by Brian Alan Lane. Directed by Rob Bowman. Stardate 42286.3. *First aired in 1988. A holodeck malfunction during a Sherlock Holmes simulation causes the character of Moriarty to take on a life of his own. Moriarty later returned in "Ship in a Bottle" (TNG).* GUEST CAST: Diana Muldaur as **Pulaski**, **Dr. Katherine**; Daniel Davis as **Moriarty**, **Professor James**; Alan Shearman as **Lestrade**, **Inspector**; Biff Manard as Ruffian; Diz White as Prostitute; Anne Elizabeth Ramsay as **Clancy**, **Assistant Engineer**; Richard Merson as Pie man. SEE: **arch; Clancy; Doyle, Sir Arthur Conan; Holmes, Sherlock; holodeck matter; La Forge, Geordi; Lestrade, Inspector; Moriarty, Professor James; mortality fail-safe; particle stream; *Victory*, *H.M.S.*; *Victory*, *U.S.S.***

Elemspur Detention Center. Prison on planet **Bajor** during the Cardassian occupation. ("Second Skin" [DS9]). SEE: **Alenis Grem**.

Elgol-red. Message encryption protocol used by the **Cardassians**. ("In Purgatory's Shadow" [DS9]).

Eliann. (Cari Shayne). **Taresian** woman present when Harry Kim visited Taresia in 2373. Eliann was interested in becoming one of Harry Kim's wives and pursued him to that end. She wanted to use his cells' genetic material to conceive offspring. ("Favorite Son" [VGR]). SEE: **denucleation**.

Elim Garak. SEE: **Garak, Elim**.

Eline. (Margot Rose). Native of the now-dead planet **Kataan** and the beloved wife of the ironweaver **Kamin**. Eline lived over a thousand years ago in the village of **Ressik**. Memories of her life were preserved aboard a space probe launched from Kataan. The probe encountered the *Starship Enterprise*-D in 2368, transferring its memories, including the memory of Eline, to Jean-Luc Picard. ("The Inner Light" [TNG]).

elogium*.** The time of sexual maturation in **Ocampa** females when the body prepares for fertilization. During *elogium* a **mitral sac** develops on the Ocampa female's back and the ***ipasaphor appears on the palms of their hands. *Elogium* usually occurs between the ages of four and five years. **Kes** (*pictured*) underwent a premature partial *elogium* in early 2372 when exposed to electrophoretic activity caused by the **swarm**. ("Elogium" [VGR]).

"Elogium." *Voyager* episode #18. Teleplay by Kenneth Biller and Jeri Taylor. Story by Jimmy Diggs & Steve J. Kay. Directed by Winrich Kolbe. Stardate 48921.3. *First aired in 1995. When* Voyager *encounters a swarm of space-dwelling life-forms, Kes's reproductive process speeds up, jeopardizing her only chance to have a child. "Elogium" was filmed during the first season of* Star Trek: Voyager, *but was held back for airing during the second season.* GUEST CAST: Nancy Hower as **Wildman, Samantha**; Gary O'Brien as Crew member; Terry Correll as N.D. crew member. SEE: **airponics bay; Breen; electrophoretic activity; *elogium*; fraternization; *gabosti* stew; Gree; ground assault vehicles; *ipasaphor*; Kes; mashed potatoes with butter; mitral sac; Oblissian cabbage; plasma residue; *rolisisin*; Scathos; spawn beetle; swarm; *targ* scoop; Tuvok; *Voyager, U.S.S.*; Wildman, Samantha.**

Elrem. Ocampa man, uncle of **Kes**. ("Dreadnought" [VGR]).

Elway Theorem. Scientific treatise that proposed transport through a spatial fold as an alternative to matter-energy transport. Although the concept was initially very promising, development of interdimensional folded space transport was abandoned by the mid-23rd century when it was found that each use of the process caused cumulative and irreversible damage to the transport subject. The **Ansata** terrorists of planet **Rutia IV** made use of this technique with a device called an **inverter** to provide a nearly undetectable means of transport, despite the terrible cost to those being transported. ("The High Ground" [TNG]). The people of planet **Sikaris** in the Delta Quadrant were able to implement **folded-space transport** across distances of many light-years ("Prime Factors" [VGR]). SEE: **trajector**.

EM base frequencies. Engineering term used in measuring a **phaser** beam's component electromagnetic wavelengths. During the **Borg** offensive of 2366-2367, an attempt was made by *Enterprise*-D personnel to make phaser weapons more effective by retuning the phasers' base frequencies. The attempt was partially successful, but the Borg were able to quickly compensate for the adjustment. ("The Best of Both Worlds, Parts I and II" [TNG]).

"Emanations." *Voyager* episode #9. Teleplay by Brannon Braga. Directed by David Livingston. Stardate 48623.5. *First aired in 1995. While exploring an alien civilization's burial ground, Harry Kim is transported to a planet in another dimension, whose inhabitants believe Kim has arrived from beyond the grave.* GUEST CAST: Jerry Hardin as **Neria, Dr.**; Jefrey Alan Chandler as **Garan, Hatil**; Cecile Callan as **Ptera**; Martha Hackett as **Seska**; Robin Groves as Garan, Araya; John Cirigliano as Alien #1. SEE: **antimatter containment; blind beam-out; cenotaph; *comra*; cordrazine; element 247; Garan, Araya; Garan, Hatil; *garili* tree; Klingon; Ktaria VII; Neria, Dr.; netinaline; Next Emanation; Ocampa; Paffran; Ptera; Ranora, Dr.; spectral rupture; planetary classification system; postmortem resuscitation technique; Seska; subspace phenomena; thanatologist; transponder, emergency; Vhnori; Vhnori transference ritual.**

Emerald Wading Pool. A vacation spot on the planet Cirrus IV considered to be very safe, certainly safer than the **Cliffs of Heaven** on Sumiko III. This location was available as a holodeck simulation on the *Enterprise*-D. ("Conundrum" [TNG]).

"Emergence." *Next Generation* episode #175. Teleplay by Joe Menosky. Story by Brannon Braga. Directed by Cliff Bole. Stardate 47869.2. *First aired in 1994. The* Enterprise-*D's computer systems develop sentience and give birth to a new cybernetic life-form, taking over the ship in the process. The emergence of this new life-form causes a lot of strange images on the holodeck.* GUEST CAST: David Huddleston as Conductor; Vinny Argiro as Hitman; Thomas Kopache as Engineer; Arlee Reed as Hayseed. SEE: **Cordannas system; Dikon alpha; emergent life-form; emergent life-form holodeck sequence; magnascopic storm; MacPherson Nebula; Mekorda sector; Orient Express; Shakespeare, William; Tambor Beta VI; *Tempest, The*; theta flux distortion; vertion.**

Emergency Procedure Alpha 2. Emergency protocol used aboard Federation starships. Alpha 2 disengaged all shipboard computer control and placed the ship's systems on manual override. Counselor Troi, in command following the ship's collision with a **quantum filament** on stardate 45156, ordered this procedure put in effect. ("Disaster" [TNG]).

emergency hand actuator. Aboard Federation starships, a small hand crank located in an access panel on one side of an automatic door. The actuator can be used to open a door should the normal computer-driven system be inoperative. ("Disaster" [TNG]).

emergency manual monitor. Auxiliary control facility aboard the *Starship Enterprise*. Scotty attempted to disengage the **M-5** computer on stardate 4729 by removing the M-5's hookups at the emergency manual monitor. ("The Ultimate Computer" [TOS]). SEE: **auxiliary control**.

Emergency Medical Hologram. (Robert Picardo). Holographic program available on some Federation starships, including the *U.S.S. Voyager*, intended as a short-term supplement to medical personnel in emergency situations. The EMH manifested himself as a humanoid physician, and could treat virtually any injury or known disease, but could function only in areas equipped with holographic projectors. ("Caretaker" [VGR]). The Emergency Medical Hologram was developed at Starfleet's **Jupiter Station** and was designed by **Dr. Lewis Zimmerman**. Lieutenant **Reginald Barclay** was a member of Zimmerman's development team, in charge of testing the EMH's interpersonal skills. ("Projections" [VGR]). The EMH program caused holographic projectors not only to generate an image of a person, but also to create a magnetic containment field, within which electromagnetic energy was trapped, thereby giving the Doctor the ability to physically manipulate real objects such as patients and medical instruments. ("Phage" [VGR]). The *Sovereign*-class *Starship Enterprise*-E, launched in 2372, was also equipped with an Emergency Medical Hologram. *Enterprise*-E chief medical officer **Beverly Crusher** was not fond of the EMH program, although he proved useful in protecting the ship's medical staff during the Borg invasion of 2373. *(Star Trek: First Contact). Robert Picardo made a cameo appearance as the holographic doctor in* Star Trek: First Contact. Zimmerman's team also worked to develop a more sophisticated version, called the long-term medical hologram (LMH). ("Doctor Bashir, I Presume?" [DS9]).

After the entire medical staff of the ***U.S.S. Voyager*** were killed in 2371 during the ship's rough passage to the **Delta Quadrant**, the ship's Emergency Medical Hologram became the only source of medical treatment for the crew. ("Caretaker" [VGR]).

The Doctor was programmed with over five million possible treatments, with contingency options and adaptive programs ("Ex Post Facto" [VGR]) utilizing sophisticated **multitronic** pathway programming. ("The Swarm" [VGR]). He was programmed with information from 2,000 medical references and the experience of 47 physicians. ("Parallax" [VGR]). The EMH program, which was first activated on stardate 48308, consisted of more than fifty million **gigaquad**s of computer data and was equipped with the medical knowledge of more than three thousand cultures. ("Lifesigns" [VGR]). His knowledge of medical treatments included those based on psychospiritual beliefs such as those employed by some of Earth's Native Americans. ("Cathexis" [VGR]). The EMH's programming was extremely sophisticated, permitting him to learn from new data and experiences, and even to be creative. Shortly after stardate 48532, when crew member **Neelix**'s lungs were removed, the doctor saved Neelix's life by devising a means of creating a pair of holographic lungs, using the holographic emitters in sickbay. ("Phage" [VGR]). The EMH was definitely capable of independent thought. In 2372, he refused a direct order to separate Tuvix into Tuvok and Neelix. He did so because obeying the order would have required him to take a life, violating his doctor's oath to do no harm. ("Tuvix" [VGR]).

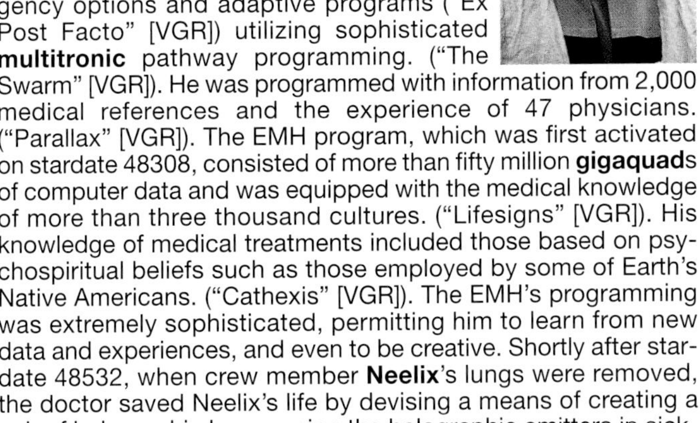

So sophisticated was the holographic doctor's program that he was a sentient life-form. He therefore found it frustrating when some members of the *Voyager* crew treated him as an inanimate computer program. Captain Janeway ordered that the EMH be given control over his own deactivation sequence, in order to avoid the indignity of his being deactivated by others. ("Eye of the Needle" [VGR]). The Doctor's role as sole medical professional on the ship caused him to undergo significant growth as a sentient life-form. One of his early steps in this growth process was his search for a name for himself. Among the names he considered were **Benjamin Spock** and **Jonas Salk**. ("Ex Post Facto" [VGR]). He also thought about **Albert Schweitzer**. ("Heroes and Demons" [VGR]). Vidiian physician **Danara Pel** (*pictured*) suggested **Shmullus**, after her beloved uncle. ("Lifesigns" [VGR]). (In one possible future visited by Kes, the holographic doctor aboard the *Voyager* decided on the name Dr. van Gogh, after being known as Dr. Mozart for a time.) ("Before and After" [VGR].) The doctor was not programmed to bleed or to feel pain. ("Projections" [VGR]). When activated, the Emergency Medical Hologram established communication links with all key areas of the *Starship Voyager*. He sometimes used this ability to surreptitiously listen to conversations throughout the ship, until Captain Janeway ordered him to refrain from eavesdropping. ("Parturition" [VGR]). The Doctor was sensitive to criticisms that, as a synthetic life-form, he would have difficulties empathizing with the suffering of an organic patient. In order to address this potential weakness, he once programmed himself with a holographic simulation of the 29-hour **Levodian flu** so that he could experience the disease process. ("Tattoo" [VGR]). His programming did not include the ability to cry. ("Threshold" [VGR]).

The EMH undertook his first away mission on stardate 48693. He was dispatched to the ship's holodeck to investigate the disappearance of three *Voyager* crew members. He was successful in interacting with a **photonic being** that had taken up residence on the holodeck and in gaining the return of the missing crew. His actions during this **first contact** mission gained him a special commendation from *Voyager* Captain Janeway. ("Heroes and Demons" [VGR]). On stardate 48892, a surge of kinoplastic radiation caused a malfunction in *Voyager's* holodeck circuits, trapping the Doctor in a delusional reality in which he briefly believed he was a real person named **Lewis Zimmerman**. In this fantasy, the Doctor imagined he was married to a human woman named Kes Zimmerman. ("Projections" [VGR]). In 2372, he fell in love with Vidiian **Danara Pel**. ("Lifesigns" [VGR]).

The holographic doctor was designed as a short-term supplement for medical personnel, not to be used for more than 1,500 hours. By stardate 50252.3, this limit had been greatly exceeded, and the EMH suffered level-4 memory fragmentation, resulting in rapid deterioration of program function. Rather than re-initialize the EMH, which would caused him to forget everything he had learned, including growth of personality, the *Voyager* crew instead decided to merge the EMH's program matrix with that of the Jupiter Station EMH diagnostic program. The matrix overlay process worked to maintain the integrity of the EMH, but his memory was not fully restored. ("The Swarm" [VGR]). When the *Voyager* visited Earth's past of 1996, **Henry Starling** fitted the EMH with an **autonomous holo-emitter**. When the *Voyager's* crew returned to their own time period, the doctor retained the holo-emitter, which gave him the ability to operate outside of sickbay, even in areas without holographic emitters. ("Future's End, Part II" [VGR]).

In 2373, the Emergency Medical Hologram created a personality-improvement holographic program that incorporated several historic characters' personalities into his subroutines. Unfortunately, the unsavory side of these characters turned the EMH to evil until **B'Elanna Torres** purged the personalities from his memory. ("Darkling" [VGR]).

The holographic doctor's first appearance was in "Caretaker" (VGR). During the early days of Star Trek: Voyager, *the show's producers had planned for the Doctor to choose the name Zimmerman for himself, and scripts for the show's first season referred to the character as Dr. Zimmerman. By the end of the first season, this plan was changed, and later scripts referred to the character simply as the Doctor, although the scientist who developed the program became known as Lewis Zimmerman, who was also played by Robert Picardo. The holographic doctor's eventual name, if any, remains a mystery at this writing.*

emergency saucer separation. SEE: **saucer separation**.

emergency transponder. SEE: **transponder, emergency.**

emergency transporter armbands. Devices used by Starfleet personnel for remote activation of the transporter in situations where there might not be sufficient time to contact the ship for transport orders. Emergency transport armbands were also used by members of the *Enterprise*-D crew to establish individual subspace force fields, to protect the wearers from the effects of a **temporal disturbance**. ("The Best of Both Worlds, Part II" [TNG], "Timescape" [TNG]).

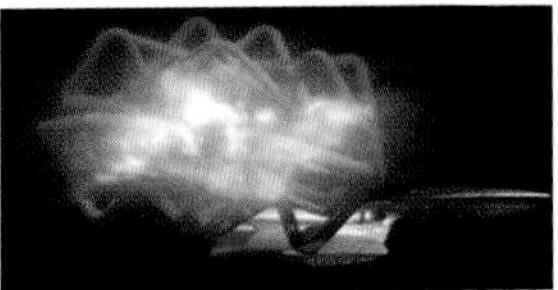

emergent life-form holodeck sequence. The **emergent life-form** created when the *Enterprise*-D computers in 2370 produced characters from several holodeck programs, symbolically re-creating the entity's struggle to survive. This holodeck sequence was based on Beverly Crusher's program, **Orient Express**, but incorporated characters from many other programs who were all journeying to Vertiform City. The *Enterprise*-D crew interfaced with the emergent life-form by dealing with the characters present in this holodeck program. In reality, "Vertiform City" was a white dwarf star that would provide the **vertion** particles the emergent life-form needed to survive and grow. ("Emergence" [TNG]).

emergent life-form. Self-determinant intelligence that served as a mechanism of procreation for a semiorganic spaceborne life-form. The main computer systems of the *Enterprise*-D became an emergent life-form in 2370 after the ship passed through a **magnascopic storm** in the **Mekorda sector**. The storm evidently caused the ship's computer systems to link together through emergent circuit nodes, forming a neural network that originated under Holodeck 3. The emergent life-form manifested different facets of its personality through characters from existing holodeck programs, which it combined on Holodeck 3. As the emergent life-form became more complex over a period of hours, it created a semiorganic offspring that needed **vertion** particles to survive. The emergent life-form therefore used its body, the *Enterprise*-D, to seek out a source of vertions so that its offspring could grow. Once the offspring reached an adequate level of development, the life-form departed the ship and ventured into space. ("Emergence" [TNG]).

EMH: SEE: **Emergency Medical Hologram**.

Emi. (Juliana Donald). Humanoid entrepreneur. In 2371, Emi wanted to buy some **self-sealing stem** bolts from Quark. Grand Nagus **Zek** spoiled Quark's deal by telling Emi where she could obtain stem bolts at wholesale prices. ("Prophet Motive" [DS9]).

Emila II. Planet. Destination of the *Enterprise*-D following the mission at **Tanuga IV** in 2366. ("A Matter of Perspective" [TNG]).

Eminiar disrupter pistol

Eminiar VII. Class-M planet in star **Cluster NGC 321**. Eminiar VII maintained a state of war with neighboring planet **Vendikar** for some 500 years. The governments of the two worlds agreed to a computer-based conflict in which attacks were launched mathematically, but in which any citizens declared as "casualties" would voluntarily report to disintegration stations so that their deaths could be recorded. Eminiar officials defended the arrangement as one that preserved the infrastructure of society despite the protracted, bitter war. The Federation starship ***Valiant*** was destroyed at Eminiar VII in 2217 when it was declared a casualty in the war. Fifty years later, the original *Starship Enterprise* nearly suffered the same fate, before Captain Kirk and **Ambassador Robert Fox** were able to persuade the Eminiar VII council to begin peace talks with Vendikar. Fox and the *Enterprise* had been sent to Eminiar to establish diplomatic relations in hopes of establishing a treaty port. ("A Taste of Armageddon" [TOS]). SEE: **Anan 7**. *The Eminiar city matte painting was later re-used for a city on planet Scalos in "Wink of an Eye" (TOS).*

"Emissary, Parts I and II." *Deep Space Nine* episodes #1 and 2. Teleplay by Michael Piller. Story by Rick Berman & Michael Piller. Directed by David Carson. Stardate 46379.1. *First aired in 1993. Benjamin Sisko takes command of station Deep Space 9, putting him in the midst of an ongoing conflict between the Bajorans and the Cardassians. Shortly thereafter, Sisko discovers the existence of the wormhole, and inadvertently becomes the Emissary, a major figure in the Bajoran religion. Flashback scenes show some of the terrible battle of Wolf 359, originally alluded to in "The Best of Both Worlds, Part II" (TNG). "Emissary, Parts I and II" (not to be confused with "The Emissary" [TNG]), was the first episode of* Star Trek: Deep Space Nine, *originally produced as a two-hour made-for-television movie, then divided into two hour-long episodes for later airings.* GUEST CAST: Camille Saviola as **Opaka**, **Kai**; Felecia M. Bell as **Sisko**, **Jennifer**; Marc Alaimo as **Dukat**; Joel Snetow as **Jasad**, **Gul**; Aron Eisenberg as **Nog**; Stephen Davies as Tactical officer; Max Grodénchik as Ferengi pit boss; Steve Rankin as Cardassian officer; Lily Mariya as Ops officer; Cassandra Byram as Conn officer; John Noah Hertzler as Vulcan captain; April Grace as Transporter chief; Kevin McDermott as Alien batter; Parker Whitman as Cardassian officer; William Powell-Blair as Cardassian officer; Frank Owen Smith as **Dax**, **Curzon**; Lynnda Ferguson as Doran; Megan Butler as Lieutenant; Stephen Rowe as Chanting monk; Thomas Hobson as Young Jake; Donald Hotton as Monk #1; Gene Armor as Bajoran bureaucrat; Diana Cignoni as Dabo girl; Judi Durand as Computer voice; Majel Barrett as Computer voice. SEE: **antilepton interference; Bajor; Bajoran wormhole; Bajorans; baseball; Bashir, Dr. Julian; Bolians; Borg; Cardassians; Cardies; Celestial Temple; Constable; dabo; Dax, Curzon; Dax, Jadzia; Deep Space 9; Denorios Belt; DS9; Dukat, Gul; Emissary; escape pod; Ferengi; Fourth Order; Frunalian; *Gage*, *U.S.S.*; Gamma Quadrant; Gilgo Beach; holosuite; Idran; infirmary; Jasad, Gul; kai; Kira Nerys; Kumomoto; Locutus of Borg; Morn; Nog; O'Brien, Keiko; O'Brien, Miles; O'Brien, Molly; ODN; Odo; Opaka, Kai; Operations Center; ops; Orb; *pagh*; Promenade; Prophets; pulse compression wave; Quadros-1 probe; Quark's bar; Quark; *Rio Grande*, *U.S.S.*; Roladan Wild Draw; Rom; runabout; *Saratoga*, *U.S.S.*; Setlik III; Sisko, Benjamin; Sisko, Jake; Sisko, Jennifer; synthale; Taluno, kai; thoron; Trill; Utopia Planitia Fleet Yards; Wolf 359; *Yangtzee Kiang*, *U.S.S.***

"Emissary, The." *Next Generation* episode #46. Television story and teleplay by Richard Manning & Hans Beimler. Based on an unpublished story by Thomas H. Calder. Directed by Cliff Bole. Stardate 42901.3. *First aired in 1989. Special emissary K'Ehleyr visits the* Enterprise-D *on a mission to destroy a Klingon warship returning from a 75-year mission of exploration. During the assignment, K'Ehleyr renews her romantic relationship with Worf. This episode introduced the character of K'Ehleyr, who later appeared (and died) in "Reunion" (TNG).* GUEST CAST: Diana Muldaur as **Pulaski**, **Dr. Katherine**; Suzie Plakson as **K'Ehleyr**; Lance le Gault as **K'Temoc**; Georgann Johnson as **Gromek**, **Admiral**; Colm Meaney as **O'Brien**, **Miles**; Anne Elizabeth Ramsay as **Clancy**, **Ensign**; Dietrich Bader as Tactical crewman. SEE: **Boradis system; calisthenics program, Klingon; Clancy; Class-8 probe; Gromek, Admiral; Iceman; K'Ehleyr; K'Temoc; Oath, Klingon; *P'Rang*, *I.K.S.*; Starbase 153; Starbase 336; *T'Ong*, *I.K.S.*; *Tlhlngan jIH*; wedding.**

Emissary. In the **Bajoran** religion, the Emissary was the person prophesied to save the Bajoran people and unite the planet by finding the mysterious **Celestial Temple**. Starfleet officer **Benjamin Sisko** (*pictured*), in command of station **Deep Space 9**, discovered the **Bajoran wormhole** in 2369, thereby becoming the Emissary in the eyes of the Bajoran people. Sisko was uncomfortable with this role, but his Starfleet duties demanded that he respect Bajoran religious beliefs. ("Emissary" [DS9]). The Bajoran people celebrated the arrival of the Emissary with an annual holiday called ***Ha'mara***. ("Starship Down" [DS9]). Sisko briefly relinqished the role of Emissary in 2372 to poet **Akorem Laan** until the Prophets made it clear that Sisko was indeed the true Emissary. ("Accession" [DS9]).

emission nebula. Interstellar dust cloud that is also a source of electromagnetic radiation. Emission nebulas can prevent cloaking devices from functioning. ("Return to Grace" [DS9]).

emitter crystal. Component of a subspace transceiver. ("Whispers" [DS9]).

emotion chip. Specialized positronic program module designed to permit a **Soong-type android** to experience human emotions. The one-of-a-kind chip, designed by Dr. **Noonien Soong**, contained basic emotions as well as memories that Soong intended for **Data**. Soong never installed the chip into Data's **positronic brain**, and the chip was stolen by **Lore** in 2367 ("Brothers" [TNG]), and not recovered until 2370, when Data disassembled Lore. ("Descent, Part II" [TNG]). Later, Data considered installing the emotion chip to find if it contained memories of his early "childhood" with Dr. Soong, but chose not to. Soong apparently created the chip to compensate for having originally built Data without emotions. ("Inheritance" [TNG]). In 2371 Data decided to install the emotion chip. Once installed, the chip functioned perfectly and Data experienced humor, but while on an away mission to the Amargosa Observatory the chip overloaded his positronic relays, became fused into his neural net, and thereafter could not be removed. *(Star Trek Generations).* By 2373 Data was able to turn his emotion chip on and off at will. When the **Borg** attempted to take over the *U.S.S. Enterprise*-E in 2373, the **Borg queen** reactivated Data's emotion chip against his will and attempted to seduce him by giving him organic components and by appealing to his emotions. *(Star Trek: First Contact).*

"Empath, The." Original Series episode #63. Written by Joyce Muskat. Directed by John Erman. Stardate 5121.5. *First aired in 1968. While investigating the disappearance of a Federation science team, Kirk, Spock, McCoy, and an alien woman are brutally tortured in a test of the woman's worthiness to have her race saved from an exploding star.* GUEST CAST: Kathryn Hays as **Gem**; Alan Bergmann as **Lal**; Davis Roberts as **Ozaba**; Jason Wingreen as **Linke**, **Dr.**; Willard Sage as **Thann**; Paul Baxley as McCoy's stunt double; Jay Jones as Kirk's stunt double. SEE: **decompression chamber; energy transfer device; Gamma Vertis IV; Gem; Lal; Linke, Dr.; Minara II; Minaran empath; Minaran star system; Ozaba; Ritter scale; sand bats; Thann; Vians.**

empath. Life-form capable of sharing the feelings of others. SEE: **Betazoid; empathic metamorph; Gem; Kamala; Minaran empath; Troi, Deanna; Troi, Lwaxana**.

empathic metamorph. A rare type of genetically mutated individual in the Kriosian and Valtese species. An empathic metamorph has the ability to sense what a potential mate wants and needs, and then to assume those behavioral traits. Male empathic metamorphs are relatively common, but females with this mutation occur only once in seven generations, and thus are extremely rare. Empathic metamorphs have a long and complex three-stage sexual maturing process. At the end of the final step, known as ***Finiis'ral***, the metamorph permanently bonds with his or her life mate. Prior to that point, the metamorph can mold him or herself to any potential mate. Centuries ago, an empathic metamorph named **Garuth** was the object of affection of two brothers named **Krios** and **Valt**, and became the cause of a centuries-long war between two star systems that bore the names of the two brothers. In 2368, another metamorph, named **Kamala,** helped to heal the rift between the two systems by bonding herself to Valtese **Chancellor Alrik**. ("The Perfect Mate" [TNG]).

emulator module. Component of the computer systems on **Deep Space 9** that allows the station's computers to access alien computer systems by matching the operating configuration of the alien system. ("The Forsaken" [DS9]). SEE: **Pup**.

enantiodromia. Psychological term that literally means conversion into the opposite. ***Vico*** survivor **Timothy** was diagnosed as suffering from enantiodromia following the death of his parents in 2368. ("Hero Worship" [TNG]).

Enara Prime. Homeworld to the **Enaran** civilization in the Delta Quadrant. ("Remember" [VGR]).

Enarans. Technologically sophisticated Delta Quadrant civilization that lived on Enara Prime and on a colony in the Fima system. In the mid-24th century, the Enaran government systematically exterminated the minority ethnic group called the **Regressives**. In later years, knowledge of this holocaust was kept from younger Enarans, until it had virtually disappeared from memory. ("Remember" [VGR]).

encephalographic polygraph scan. A brainwave scan used to determine truthfulness during questioning. ("The Drumhead" [TNG]).

"Encounter at Farpoint, Parts I and II." *Next Generation* episodes #1 and #2. Written by D. C. Fontana and Gene Roddenberry. Directed by Corey Allen. Stardate 41153.7. *First aired in 1987. The entity known as Q first harasses the crew of the* Enterprise-*D as they attempt to solve the mystery of Farpoint Station. This was the first episode of* Star Trek: The Next Generation. *"Farpoint," set some 95 years after the end of the first* Star Trek *series, introduces the* Starship Enterprise-*D and its crew, including Captain Jean-Luc Picard. This episode was originally produced as a two-hour made-for-TV movie, although for later airings it was divided into two hour-long segments. Q later returned in several other episodes, including "All Good Things..." (TNG), which was the last television episode of* Star Trek: The Next Generation. GUEST CAST: John de Lancie as **Q**; Michael Bell as **Zorn**, **Groppler**; Colm Meaney as **O'Brien**, **Miles**; Cary Hiroyuki as **Mandarin Balliff**; Timothy Dang as Main bridge security; David Erskine as Bandi shopkeeper; Evelyn Guerrero as Young female ensign; Chuck Hicks as Military officer; Timmy Ortega as **Torres, Lieutenant**. SEE: **Altair III; Bandi; battle bridge; battle section; Betazed; chief medical officer; combadge; Crusher, Dr. Beverly; Crusher, Jack R.; Crusher, Wesley; Data; Deneb IV; DeSoto, Captain Robert; *Enterprise*-D, *U.S.S.*; exobiology; Farpoint Station; *Galaxy*-class starship; Groppler; holodeck; *Hood*, *U.S.S.*; *Imzadi*; La Forge, Geordi; Library Computer Access and Retrieval System; McCoy, Dr. Leonard H.; Picard, Jean-Luc; postatomic horror; probability mechanics; Q; Q Continuum; Riker, William T.; Saucer Module; saucer separation; stardrive section; Torres, Lieutenant; Troi, Deanna; United Nations, New; VISOR; Worf; World War III; Yar, Natasha; Zorn, Groppler.**

encryption lockout. Computer security protocol intended to prevent unauthorized access to sensitive information. ("A Simple Investigation" [VGR]).

Endar. (Sherman Howard). Captain of the **Talarian** warship ***Q'Maire.*** Endar served in the Talarian militia and lost his only son in a conflict between the Federation and Talarian forces at **Castal I** in the 2350s. Endar was involved in another skirmish with Federation forces at **Galen IV** in 2356. After that battle, Endar discovered a three-year-old human male named **Jeremiah Rossa** near the body of the boy's dead mother. In accordance with Talarian custom that allows a warrior to claim the son of a slain enemy in replacement of his own dead son, Endar took the child, whom he named **Jono**, and raised him as his own son. ("Suddenly Human" [TNG]).

Endeavour, U.S.S. Federation starship, *Nebula* class, Starfleet registry number NCC-71805. It served in Picard's armada to blockade Romulan supply ships supplying the **Duras** family forces during the **Klingon civil war** of 2367-2368. ("Redemption,

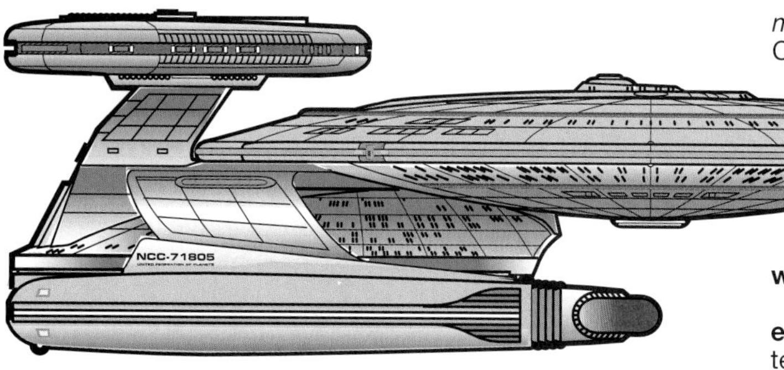

Part II" [TNG]). The *Endeavour* was stationed in the Cleon Sector later in 2368 when *Enterprise*-D crew members were controlled by **Ktarian** operatives seeking to gain control of Starfleet. Commander William Riker was ordered to pilot a shuttle to the *Endeavour* to spread the Ktarian takeover. ("The Game" [TNG]). The *Endeavor* was part of the Starfleet armada that intercepted a **Borg** cube at Earth on stardate 50893. *(Star Trek: First Contact). The* Starship Endeavour *was named in honor of British explorer James Cook's flagship and for NASA's space shuttle.*

Endicor system. Star system. Destination of the *Enterprise*-D on stardate 42679 when an unexplained energy vortex was encountered, in 2365. That energy vortex was responsible for the creation of an alternate version of Captain Picard from some six hours in the future. ("Time Squared" [TNG]).

endive salad. Dish made with leaves of the Earth plant *Cichorium endivia*. ("Whispers" [DS9]).

endorphins. Naturally occurring neurochemicals found in many humanoids and other vertebrate species. Endorphins are opiate peptides similar to the drug morphine, and can act upon the nervous system to affect sensations of pain and pleasure. Levels of endorphins in William Riker's bloodstream were found to control his response to alien neurotoxins when Riker was injured on an away mission to planet **Surata IV.** ("Shades of Gray" [TNG]). Endorphins can be released into the bloodstream by a Betazoid technique called **plexing**. ("Realm of Fear" [TNG]). Agents of the Obsidian Order were sometimes given a **cranial implant** that could stimulate the production of natural endorphins, making the agent better able to resist torture. SEE: **Garak**. ("The Wire" [DS9]). Endorphins are important in the Bajoran birthing process. They relax the mother so that the child can be born. ("The Begotten" [DS9]).

Eneg. (Patrick Horgan). Member of the **Zeon** underground on **Ekos** who infiltrated that planet's Nazi party and served as chairman at the time of the fall of the **John Gill** regime in 2268. ("Patterns of Force" [TOS]). *Eneg is Gene spelled backwards.*

"Enemy Within, The." Original Series episode #5. Written by Richard Matheson. Directed by Leo Penn. Stardate 1672.1. *First aired in 1966. A transporter malfunction splits Kirk into two people, each with half of his personality. Spock and McCoy work to reunite Kirk's halves, while Sulu and a landing party are trapped on the surface of a freezing planet. This episode marks Spock's first use of the Vulcan nerve pinch.* Grace Lee Whitney as **Rand, Janice**; Edward Madden as **Fisher, Geological Technician**; Garland Thompson as **Wilson, Transporter Technician**; Jim Goodwin as **Farrell, Lieutenant John**; Don Eitner as Kirk's stunt double; Eddie Paskey as Conners. SEE: **Alfa 117; Farrell, Lieutenant John; Fisher, Geological Technician; FSNP; ionizer, transporter; Kirk, James T.; Rand, Janice; Saurian brandy; Vulcan nerve pinch; Wilson, Transporter Technician.**

enemy's blood. A **Kazon** beverage. "Enemy's blood" is the translation of the Kazon name. ("Maneuvers" [VGR]).

"Enemy, The." *Next Generation* episode #55. Written by David Kemper and Michael Piller. Directed by David Carson. Stardate 43349.2. *First aired in 1989. Geordi La Forge and a Romulan officer must cooperate in order to survive on a hostile planet.* GUEST CAST: John Snyder as **Bochra, Centurion**; Andreas Katsulas as **Tomalak**; Colm Meaney as **O'Brien, Miles**; Steve Rankin as **Patahk**. SEE: **Bochra, Centurion; Galorndon Core; Neutral Zone, Romulan; Patahk; *Pi*; ribosome infusion; Romulans; Scoutship, Romulan; Station Salem One; Tomalak; tricorder; ultritium; VISOR; warbird, Romulan.**

energy containment cell. Device used to hold the neural patterns or consciousness of **Rao Vantika** on station Deep Space 9 in 2369. SEE: **Vantika, Rao; glial cells**. ("The Passenger" [DS9]).

energy ribbon. SEE: **nexus**.

energy transfer device. Handheld mechanism used by the **Vians** to perform various tasks from teleportation to physical manipulation. The unit was controlled by the user's mental impulses, and was programmed to respond to one user only. ("The Empath" [TOS]).

energy transfer matrix. Critical component of a **ferroplasmic infusion** device. An energy transfer matrix required priming following damage to a ferroplasmic infusion unit used on planet **Atrea IV**. ("Inheritance" [TNG]).

energy vortex. Unexplained time-space disturbance near the Endicor system, responsible for destroying an alternate version of the *Enterprise*-D in 2365 and sending an alternate version of Captain Picard some six hours back in time. The existence of the alternate Picard warned the crew of the *Enterprise*-D to avoid the ship's destruction by piloting the starship directly into the center of the vortex. ("Time Squared" [TNG]). *At one point, producer/writer Maurice Hurley had intended to follow "Time Squared" with an episode in which we would learn that the mysterious vortex had been caused by the mischievous entity Q. Although the second episode was indeed produced ("Q Who" [TNG]), the reference to Q having caused the vortex was deleted.*

engineering hull. The secondary hull of many Federation **starships**, where components of the warp drive system are generally located. Also called the stardrive section or the secondary hull. SEE: **engineering**.

engineering. Aboard Federation **starships**, the department responsible for the operation and maintenance of the ship's systems, including the **warp drive** and **impulse drive** propulsion systems, under the auspices of the ship's **chief engineer**. Most engineering functions were controlled from an engine room, usually located in the engineering hull, although the ship's **bridge** generally had an engineering monitor and control station as well. The engine room aboard the original *Constitution*-class *Starship Enterprise* was located on Deck 19. Aboard the *Galaxy*-class *Enterprise*-D, main engineering was located on Deck 36. The engine room of the *Starship Voyager* was on Deck 11, while the *Defiant's* engine room was on Deck 2.

engram. In neurophysiology, a specific complex memory. Computer scientist **Dr. Richard Daystrom** implanted his engrams into the experimental **M-5** computer in 2268, in an effort to give the machine the ability to reason like a human. ("The Ultimate Computer" [TOS]). Study of an individual's memory engrams could be used to analyze brain activity. ("Cathexis" [VGR]). The **Banean** people of the Delta Quadrant punished convicted murderers by implanting engrams from the victim into the murderer, thereby forcing the murderer to experience the last few minutes of the victim's life. **Thomas Paris** was subjected to this punishment when he was unjustly convicted of murdering **Tolen Ren** in 2371. ("Ex Post

Facto" [VGR]). By 2372, technology existed to permit a person's engrams to be selectively erased. ("Sons of Mogh" [DS9]). SEE: **Kurn**. *This worked with Klingon memories; we don't know if can work on other species.* In 2373, *Voyager* scientists discovered a **memory virus** parasite that was able to evade the body's immune system by disguising itself as an engram, thriving on the peptides generated by the host's brain. ("Flashback" [VGR]).

Enkidu. In ancient Earth mythology, a wild man, raised among animals, who was the friend of the warrior king **Gilgamesh.** ("Darmok" [TNG]).

Ennan VI. Planet. Location where Dr. Katherine Pulaski obtained some ale that she shared with William Riker and friends when Riker tried his hand at omelet making. ("Time Squared" [TNG]).

Ennis. Nation from a humanoid civilization in the Gamma Quadrant; the ancient enemies of the **Nol-Ennis**, whom they have fought for many generations. The leaders of their planet were unable to mediate a peace, so both factions were sent to a moon and stranded as an example to the rest of the civilization. A defensive net of artificial satellites was created to keep out unwelcome visitors. The planet's leaders also constructed artificial microbes that repaired the prisoners' biological functions at a cellular level, preventing death but making the prisoners unable to leave the moon. If a prisoner was removed from the moon, the microbes would stop functioning and the body would die. Thus the horrific cycle of death and life continued, with only hate and vengeance to sustain the combatants. ("Battle Lines" [DS9]).

"Ensign Ro." *Next Generation* episode #103. Teleplay by Michael Piller. Story by Rick Berman & Michael Piller. Directed by Les Landau. Stardate 45076.3. *First aired in 1991. Ensign Ro Laren joins the* Enterprise-D *crew for a special mission to locate a Bajoran terrorist. This episode introduced the Bajorans as well as the recurring character, Ro Laren.* GUEST CAST: Michelle Forbes as **Ro Laren**; Scott Marlowe as **Keeve Falor**; Frank Collison as **Dolak, Gul**; Jeffery Hayenga as **Orta**; Harley Venton as **Collins, Ensign**; Ken Thorley as **Mot**; Cliff Potts as **Kennelly, Admiral**; Whoopi Goldberg as **Guinan**; Majel Barrett as Computer voice. SEE: **Adele, Aunt; *Antares*-class carrier; Bajor; Bajorans; Cardassians; Collins, Ensign; Dolak, Gul; *Galor*-class Cardassian warship; Garon II; ginger tea; Jaros II; Jaz Holza; Keeve Falor; Kennelly, Admiral; Lya Station Alpha; molecular displacement traces; Mot; Orta; Ro Laren; Sector 21305; Solarion IV; Valo system; *Wellington, U.S.S.***

"Ensigns of Command, The." *Next Generation* episode #49. Written by Melinda M. Snodgrass. Directed by Cliff Bole. No stardate given in episode. *First aired in 1989. Data must persuade colonists to move away from the planet that has been their home for generations. This was the first episode produced during the third season, although "Evolution" (TNG) was aired first. This is the first episode in which Data plays the violin (except for "Elementary, Dear Data" [TNG], in which he played the violin as Sherlock Holmes).* GUEST CAST: Eileen Seeley as **McKenzie, Ard'rian**; Mark L. Taylor as **Haritath**; Richard Allen as **Kentor**; Colm Meaney as **O'Brien, Miles**; Mart McChesney as Sheliak. SEE: **Armens, Treaty of; *Artemis, S.S.*; de Laure Belt; Gosheven; Grisella; Haritath; hyperonic radiation; McKenzie, Ard'rian; O'Brien, Miles; *Onizuka, Shuttlepod*; planetary classification system: Class-H; Septimus Minor; Shelia star system; Sheliak Corporate; Sheliak Director; Sheliak; Tau Cygna V**.

Entebe, Captain. Commander of the *U.S.S. Ulysses*. In 2371, Entebe and her crew studied protoplanetary masses in the **Helaspont Nebula**. ("The Adversary" [DS9]).

Entek. (Gregory Sierra). **Obsidian Order** operative. In 2371, Entek was in charge of the ruse to expose **Legate Ghemor** as a member of the **Cardassian underground movement**. He questioned **Kira Nerys** after she had been surgically altered to pass as Cardassian. Entek was killed by **Garak** when **Deep Space 9** personnel entered Cardassian space to rescue Kira. ("Second Skin" [DS9]).

***"Enterprise* Incident, The."** Original Series episode #59. Written by D. C. Fontana. Directed by John Meredyth Lucas. Stardate: 5027.3. *First aired in 1968. Kirk, Spock, and the* Enterprise *are captured by the Romulans while on a secret mission to steal a new Romulan cloaking device.* GUEST CAST: Joanne Linville as **Romulan commander**; Jack Donner as **Tal**; Majel Barrett as **Chapel, Christine**; Richard Compton as Romulan technical officer; Robert Gentile as Romulan technician; Mike Howden as Romulan guard; Gordon Coffey as Romulan soldier. SEE: **cloaking device, Romulan; Klingon Empire; physiostimulator; Romulan battle cruiser; Romulan commander; Romulan Neutral Zone; Romulan Right of Statement; Tal; Vulcan death grip.**

Enterprise, I.S.S. Starship in the parallel **mirror universe**, serving the brutal **Terran Empire**. A landing party from the *U.S.S. Enterprise's* was accidentally transported to the *I.S.S. Enterprise* during a severe **ion storm** in 2267. The mirror universe's crew were savage and, in many ways, opposite to the *U.S.S. Enterprise* crew; their mission was to conquer and control worlds for the empire. Subtle but disturbing differences existed in the *I.S.S. Enterprise,* including daggers painted on doors and henchmen guarding the corridors. ("Mirror, Mirror" [TOS]).

Enterprise, S.S. Early spacecraft, one of the first space vehicles to bear the name *Enterprise*. An image of this historical vehicle was displayed on the rec deck of the refitted original ***Starship Enterprise***. *(Star Trek: The Motion Picture). This ship was designed by Matt Jefferies for a television series project developed by Gene Roddenberry after the run of the original Star Trek. Unfortunately, the series was never produced, and this remains the only appearance of the design.*

Enterprise, Space Shuttle. Early Earth orbital test vehicle, the prototype for that planet's first reusable spacecraft. An image of this ship, the first spacecraft to bear the name *Enterprise*, was displayed on the rec deck of the refitted original *Starship Enterprise. (Star Trek: The Motion Picture). In real life, the orbiter* Enterprise *was named by American President Gerald Ford after many* Star Trek *fans wrote to NASA, urging that the first space shuttle be named for* Star Trek's *starship. Gene Roddenberry and several members of the* Star Trek *cast were honored guests at the rollout of the* Enterprise *in September, 1976.*

***Enterprise, U.S.S.* (aircraft carrier).** Massive oceangoing ship, naval registry number CVN-65, part of the American Navy in the 20th century on Earth. This warship was a nuclear-powered aircraft carrier from which Starfleet officers Chekov and Uhura "borrowed" high-energy photons in order to recrystallize some **dilithium** so that they could return to the 23rd century. During that covert operation, Chekov was captured by Navy personnel, but he eventually escaped. The *Enterprise* was docked at the Alameda Naval Base at the time. *(Star Trek IV: The Voyage Home). The aircraft carrier* U.S.S. Ranger *actually stood in for the* Enterprise *for filming during* Star Trek IV, *since the real* Enterprise *was at sea at the time.*

Enterprise, U.S.S. Perhaps the most famous spacecraft in the history of space exploration, the original *U.S.S. Enterprise* was a ***Constitution*-class** vessel, registry number NCC-1701. Launched in 2245 from the San Francisco Yards orbiting Earth, the *Enterprise* was first commanded by **Captain Robert April**, then by Captain **Christopher Pike** ("The Cage" [TOS]). Superbly equipped for research in deep space, the *Enterprise* had 14 science labs. ("Operation—Annihilate!" [TOS]). The ship achieved legendary status during the five-year mission com-

Illustration: The six starships *Enterprise,* shown to approximate scale

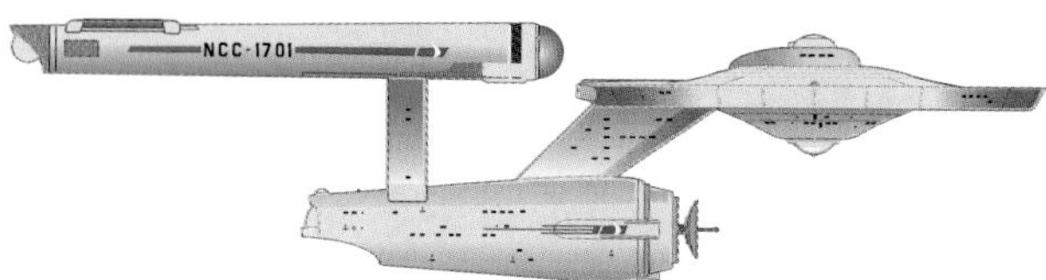

Original *Starship Enterprise, Constitution*-class, overall length 289 meters

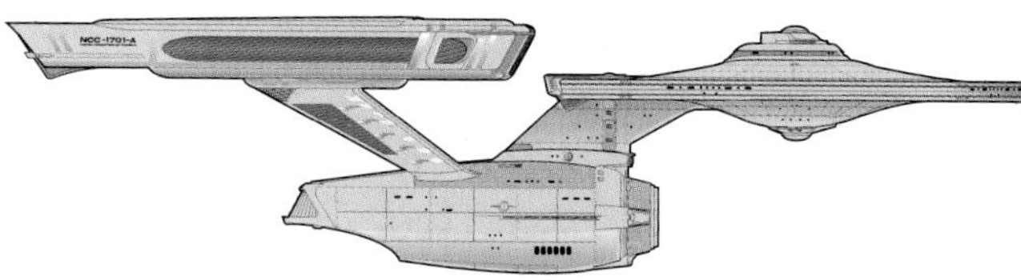

Starship Enterprise-A, *Constitution*-class refit, overall length 305 meters

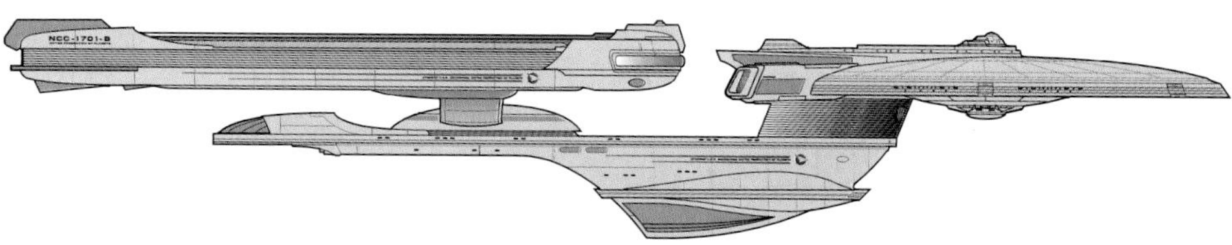

Starship Enterprise-B, *Excelsior*-class, overall length 467 meters

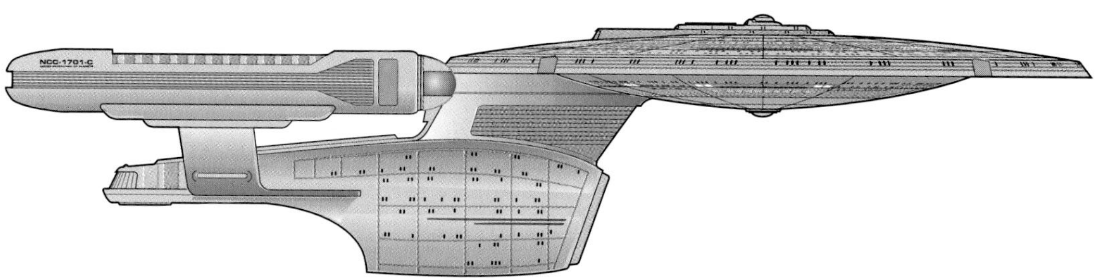

Starship Enterprise-C, *Ambassador*-class, overall length 526 meters

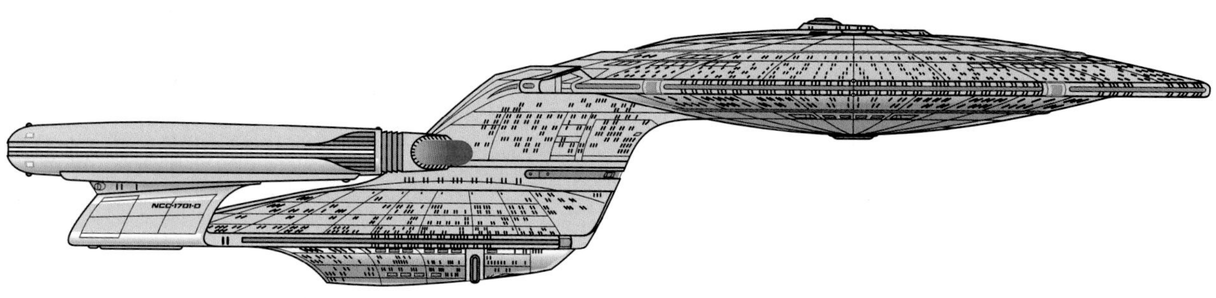

Starship Enterprise-D, *Galaxy*-class, overall length 641 meters

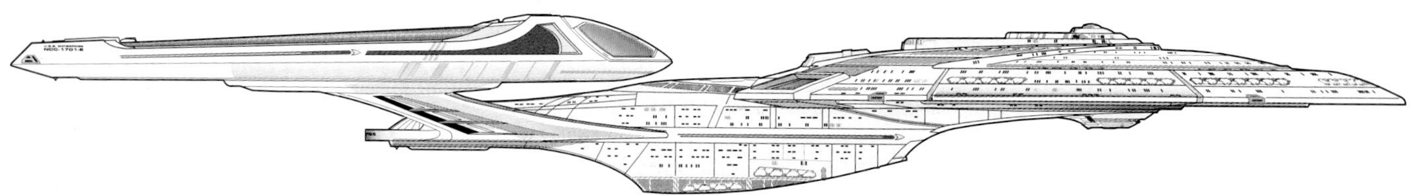

Starship Enterprise-E, *Sovereign*-class, overall length 680 meters

manded by Captain **James T. Kirk** from 2264 to 2269. *(Star Trek: The Original Series).* The original *Starship Enterprise* was refitted several times during its lifetime, most notably in 2270, when virtually every major system was upgraded, a new bridge module was installed, and the warp-drive nacelles were replaced. *(Star Trek: The Motion Picture).* The ship was destroyed by James Kirk in 2285, just prior to its scheduled retirement, in order to prevent the ship from falling into Klingon hands during a rescue mission to recover the body of Captain Spock. *(Star Trek III: The Search for Spock). The original* Starship Enterprise *was designed by series art director Matt Jefferies. The motion picture version was designed by Mike Minor, Joe Jennings, Andrew Probert, Douglas Trumbull, and Harold Michelson, based on the concepts of Matt Jefferies. We conjecture that Pike commanded two five-year missions of the* Enterprise *before Kirk's tenure at the helm, and that Captain April commanded a five-year mission before Pike. This is reasonably consistent with a commissioning date of 2245.*

Enterprise*-A, *U.S.S. The second Federation starship to bear the name, the *Enterprise*-A was a ***Constitution*-class** vessel, registry number NCC-1701-A. Launched in 2286, the *Enterprise*-A was placed under the command of Captain **James T. Kirk** by the **Federation Council** and Starfleet Command in appreciation for Kirk's role in saving planet Earth from the destructive effects of an alien space probe. (*Star Trek IV: The Voyage Home*). SEE: ***Yorktown, U.S.S.*** Although shakedown tests and systems installation under the aegis of Captain **Montgomery Scott** had not been completed, the *Enterprise*-A was rushed into service in early 2287 to intervene in a hostage situation at planet **Nimbus III**. (*Star Trek V: The Final Frontier*). The ship, under the reluctant command of Captain Kirk, was pressed back into service to escort Klingon **Chancellor Gorkon** to Earth for a peace conference. Although the scheduled talks were canceled after the assassination of Gorkon, the *Enterprise*-A and her crew were instrumental in the success of the historic **Khitomer** peace conference shortly thereafter. The *Enterprise*-A was scheduled to be decommissioned shortly after the Khitomer conference. (*Star Trek VI: The Undiscovered Country*). *The* Enterprise-*A's exterior was virtually identical to the upgraded original* Enterprise *first seen in* Star Trek: The Motion Picture, *although many of the interiors were redesigned for* Star Trek V *and* VI.

Enterprise*-B, *U.S.S. Federation starship, *Excelsior* class, Starfleet registry number NCC-1701-B, the third starship to bear the name. The *U.S.S. Enterprise*-B was launched from a **Spacedock** orbiting Earth in 2293, with Captain **John Harriman** in command. Its maiden voyage was planned as a publicity junket consisting of a brief trip out past Pluto. Dignitaries aboard the *Enterprise*-B for the occasion included Captain **James T. Kirk**, Captain **Montgomery Scott**, and Commander **Pavel Chekov**. During this flight, the *Enterprise*-B responded to an emergency distress call from two **El-Aurian** transport ships en route to Earth. The ships were trapped in the **nexus** energy ribbon and were on the verge of structural collapse. Problems with *Enterprise*-B equipment prevented the rescue of one El-Aurian ship, but some 47 passengers from the second ship, the ***S.S. Lakul***, were transported to safety just before the *Lakul* exploded. Among those rescued were scientist **Dr. Tolian Soran** and future *Enterprise*-D crew member **Guinan**. Captain James T. Kirk was missing and believed killed in the incident. Kirk had been making emergency modifications to the *Enterprise*-B deflector system, permitting the ship to escape the ribbon. It was later learned that Kirk had not been killed, but rather had been swept into the nexus. *(Star Trek Generations). The* Enterprise-*B miniature was a modification of the* Excelsior *model, originally designed by Bill George for* Star Trek III. *The* Enterprise-*B modifications were designed by John Eaves under the supervision of production designer Herman Zimmerman. The dedication plaque on the* Enterprise-*B bridge suggested that the ship had been launched on stardate 9715. We don't know when (or how) the* Enterprise-*B was retired or destroyed, but it had to have happened well before the destruction of the* Enterprise-*C in 2344.*

Enterprise*-C, *U.S.S. The fourth Federation starship to bear the name *Enterprise*, an ***Ambassador*-class** vessel, registry number NCC-1701-C. The *Enterprise*-C was lost and presumed destroyed near **Narendra III** in 2344. In that year, this ship, commanded by **Captain Rachel Garrett**, responded to a distress call from the Klingon outpost on Narendra III. The outpost was under a massive Romulan attack. During the battle, a torpedo explosion opened a **temporal rift**, and the *Enterprise*-C was sent some 22 years forward in time. This proved to be a focal point in history. With the *Enterprise*-C gone from the "normal" timeline, an alternate timeline was formed, in which the Federation and the Klingon Empire engaged in an extended war. The Federation was near defeat by 2366, when the *Enterprise*-C emerged from the rift, encountering the *Enterprise*-D. It was soon realized that the *Enterprise*-C had to return to its proper time if history was to be restored and the terrible war with the Klingons was to be averted. The tragedy of the war was emphasized when a Klingon attack resulted in the death of Captain Garrett, after which *Enterprise*-C officer **Lieutenant Richard Castillo** agreed to assume command of his ship and return it to 2344. *Enterprise*-D officer **Natasha Yar (alternate)**, who was still alive in this timeline, volunteered to return with Castillo to help defend Narendra III against the Romulans. All *Enterprise*-C personnel understood that returning to the past was a virtual suicide mission because of the intensity of the Romulan attack on Narendra III. Once the *Enterprise*-C returned through the temporal rift, the time flow returned to normal, and history was restored to its proper shape. ("Yesterday's *Enterprise*" [TNG]). SEE: **Sela**. *The* Enterprise-*C model was designed by Rick Sternbach and Andrew Probert. Interior supervised by Richard James.*

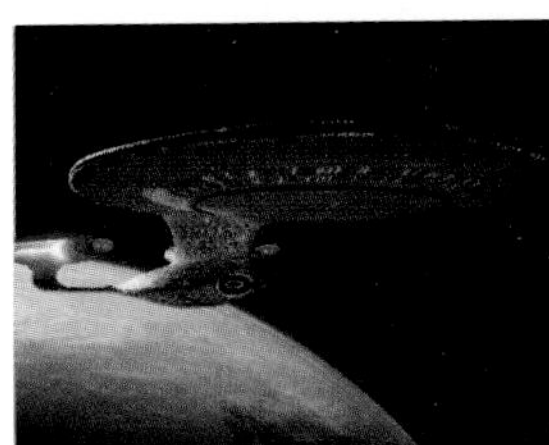

Enterprise*-D, *U.S.S. The fifth Federation starship to bear the name. ("Encounter at Farpoint, Part I" [TNG]). This ship, a ***Galaxy*-class** vessel, Starfleet registry number NCC-1701-D, was launched in 2363 ("Lonely Among Us" [TNG]) from Starfleet's **Utopia Planitia Fleet Yards** orbiting Mars and placed under the command of Captain **Jean-Luc Picard** on a mission of deep-space exploration and diplomacy. ("Encounter at Farpoint, Part I" [TNG]). The ship was severely damaged in the **Borg** encounter of early 2367, and had to undergo six weeks of repair work at **Earth Station McKinley**. ("Family" [TNG]). A **dilithium chamber hatch** installed at McKinley station was defective, resulting in a severe explosion in the ship's warp-drive system that crippled the *Enterprise*-D for two weeks. Although sabotage was initially suspected, it was later learned that undetectable flaws in the hatch were responsible. ("The Drumhead" [TNG]). The *Enterprise*-D was repeatedly destroyed in 2368, when the ship was trapped in a **temporal causality loop** near the **Typhon Expanse**. ("Cause and Effect" [TNG]). The *Enterprise*-D was briefly commanded by **Captain Edward Jellico** in early 2369 when Captain Picard was assigned to a covert Starfleet mission on planet **Celtris III**. ("Chain of Command, Part I" [TNG]). The *Starship Enterprise*-D was destroyed in 2371 during a mission to prevent a deranged scientist from destroying the **Veridian system**. During the mission, the *Enterprise*-D took a direct hit from a Klingon bird-of-prey, causing a loss of **antimatter containment**. Executive Officer William T. Riker ordered an emergency **saucer separation**, and Commander Deanna Troi was successful in maneuvering the **Saucer Module** to a relatively safe distance, just before the ship's **stardrive section** exploded. The resulting concussion knocked the saucer module out of orbit, but Troi was successful in piloting the vessel to a soft landing on the surface of planet **Veridian III**. Although the spacecraft was deemed a total loss, there were no fatalities in the emergency landing. (In the **anti-time future** created by the Q Continuum, the *Enterprise*-D was not destroyed at Veridian III, but remained in service until at least 2395, when Admiral Will Riker had saved the ship from being decommissioned, by making it his personal flagship. In this future, the *Enterprise*-D had undergone significant modifications, including the addition of a third warp **nacelle**. ["All Good Things" (TNG)]. *Q's anti-time future is not likely to come to pass, if only because the* Enterprise-D *was destroyed in* Star Trek Generations.*) The* Enterprise-D *model was designed by Andrew Probert. Interior sets were supervised by Herman Zimmerman and Richard James.*

***Enterprise*-E, U.S.S.** Federation starship, *Sovereign* class, the sixth ship to bear the name. The *U.S.S. Enterprise*-E was launched in 2372 under the command of Captain **Jean-Luc Picard** and was the most advanced starship in the fleet at the time. The *Enterprise*-E was almost 700 meters in length and had 24 decks. In 2373, the ship was partially assimilated by the Borg. *(Star Trek: First Contact). The* Starship Enterprise-E *was designed by production designer Herman Zimmerman with illustrator John Eaves. Rick Sternbach did the working construction drawings of the model, which was built at Industrial Light and Magic.*

***Enterprise*.** Three-masted 19th-century sailing frigate. A holographic representation of this *Enterprise* was used by the crew of the *Starship Enterprise-D* as the setting for the promotion ceremony held for Worf in 2371, when he became a lieutenant commander. *(Star Trek Generations). The* Enterprise *frigate was a re-dress of the* Lady Washington *sailing out of Marina Del Rey, California*.

entomology. Study of insect life-forms. Entomology was one of Jake Sisko's better subjects. ("Playing God" [DS9]). SEE: **Mardah**.

entropy. Tendency of matter and energy to become increasingly random over time. A decrease in local entropy can be evidence of life. ("Playing God" [DS9]). (In one possible future visited by Kes, the holographic doctor aboard the *Voyager* attempted to slow down Kes's aging process. The procedure involved exposing her to a **bio-temporal field** in order to push her cells back into an earlier stage of entropic decay.) ("Before and After" [VGR].)

environmental suit. Protective garments worn by Starfleet personnel when exploring inhospitable environments. ("The Naked Time" [TOS], "The Tholian Web" [TOS]). Environmental suits were also used by personnel at the **Elba II** penal colony when working in that planet's poisonous atmosphere. ("Whom Gods Destroy" [TOS]). *The space suits used by Kirk and Spock in* Star Trek: The Motion Picture*, by Terrell and Chekov in* Star Trek II, *and by Picard and company in* Star Trek: First Contact *might also be called environmental suits.* SEE: **thruster suit**.

eosinophilia. Medical condition. An abnormally high count of serum eosinophils, a type of white blood cell in humanoids. ("The Host" [TNG]).

EPI capacitor. Device used to open a **runabout** hatch in an emergency, bypassing the normal door actuation servos. ("Q-Less" [DS9]).

Epran. (Dylan Haggerty). Inhabitant of a planet in the Teplan system located in the Gamma Quadrant. Epran died in 2372 from a deadly disease known as the **blight** while under the care of Dr. Julian Bashir. SEE: **Teplan blight.** ("The Quickening" [DS9]).

EPS discharge. Power release from the **electroplasma system** of a starship. Such a discharge, focused through the impulse reactor, was suggested as a possible means of escape from the **subspace rift** which trapped the *Enterprise*-D in 2370. The plan was deemed unworkable because Commander Data felt the discharge would pose an unacceptable safety hazard to the saucer section. ("Force of Nature" [TNG]).

EPS. SEE: **electroplasma system**.

Epsilon 119. Dead star. **Professor Gideon Seyetik** re-ignited Epsilon 119 in 2370 by piloting a shuttlepod carrying a **protomatter** payload into the star. Although the ambitious experiment was a spectacular success, Seyetik lost his life in the process. ("Second Sight" [DS9]).

Epsilon Canaris III. Planet. **Commissioner Nancy Hedford** was sent to Epsilon Canaris III to prevent a war in 2267. She was forced to leave before her job was completed when she contracted rare and deadly **Sakuro's disease**. ("Metamorphosis" [TOS]).

Epsilon Hydra VII. Planet where archaeologist **Vash** was barred from the Royal Museum. ("Q-Less" [DS9]).

Epsilon Indi. Planetary system. Centuries ago, marauders from the planet **Triacus** in the Epsilon Indi system waged war. One such marauder apparently survived into the 23rd century, where it caused the death of all the adult members of the **Starnes Expedition**. ("And the Children Shall Lead" [TOS]). Wesley Crusher recognized Epsilon Indi when he gazed from **Ten-Forward** while discussing his future with Guinan. ("The Child" [TNG]).

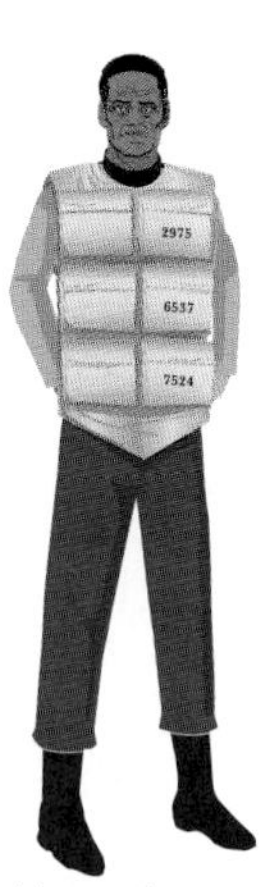

Hazard vest (TOS)

Environmental suit (TOS)

Protective garment (TOS)

Engineering suit (ST:TMP, et al)

Environmental suit (ST:TMP, et al)

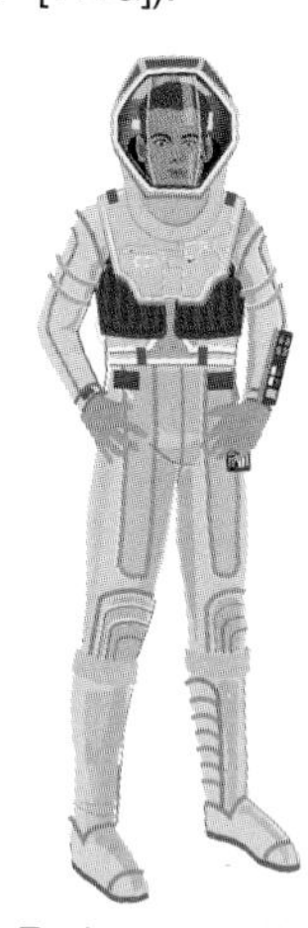
Environmental suit (ST:TFC, DS9)

Epsilon IX monitoring station. Starfleet space station located near the Klingon border. The facility was destroyed in 2271 by the **V'Ger** machine life-form, which was returning to Earth. (*Star Trek: The Motion Picture*).

Epsilon IX Sector. Region of space. Mission site where *U.S.S. Enterprise*-D was assigned to perform an astronomical survey of a new pulsar cluster shortly after stardate 42723. The Epsilon IX Sector is located near the **Scylla Sector**. ("Samaritan Snare" [TNG]). *The Epsilon IX Sector may have been the location of the Epsilon IX monitoring station seen in* Star Trek: The Motion Picture.

Epsilon Mynos system. Location of **Aldea**, a planet long believed to be merely legend until discovered by the *Enterprise*-D in 2364. ("When the Bough Breaks" [TNG]).

Epsilon Pulsar Cluster. Astronomical phenomenon located in the **Epsilon IX Sector**. ("Samaritan Snare" [TNG]).

Epsilon Silar system. Location where the *U.S.S. Enterprise*-D was attacked by a **Satarran** space probe that caused disruption of the *Enterprise*-D's computer systems and damaged the crew's short-term memories. The attack was an effort to obtain the use of the *Enterprise*-D in the Satarrans' war against the people of **Lysia**. ("Conundrum" [TNG]).

Epstein, Dr. Terence. A leading 24th-century authority on cybernetics. Epstein lectured at Beverly Crusher's medical school, and she said she was looking forward to meeting him when the *Enterprise*-D docked at Starbase 74 in 2364. ("11001001" [TNG]).

"Equilibrium." *Deep Space Nine* episode #50. Story by Christopher Teague. Teleplay by René Echevarria. Directed by Cliff Bole. No stardate given. *First aired in 1994. Dax learns she was once hosted by a murderer.* GUEST CAST: Lisa Banes as **Renhol, Dr.**; Jeff Magnus McBride as **Belar, Joran**; Nicholas Cascone as **Timor**; Harvey Vernon as Yolad. SEE: **Belar, Joran; Belar, Yolad; benzocyatizine; Dax (symbiont); Dax, Jadzia; Dax, Torias; Guardians; isoboramine; Mak'ala, caves of; Renhol, Doctor; sautéed beets; symbiont; Timor; Trill; Trill homeworld; Trill Symbiosis Commission.**

Erabus Prime. Planet. **Q** once saved **Vash** from illness when she was stung by a particularly nasty bug on Erabus Prime. ("Q-Less" [DS9]).

Erib. Friend of **Julian Bashir** from his Starfleet Medical School days. Julian Bashir and Erib, an Andorian, went to **Bruce Lucier**'s 2368 New Year's Eve party. At the party Erib was mistakenly pointed out to **Elizabeth Lense** as Julian Bashir. As a result, Lense thought Bashir was Andorian until she met him on **Deep Space 9** in 2371. ("Explorers" [DS9]).

Eric. (Rickey D'shon Collins). Child of an *Enterprise*-D crew member. Eric was the first child encountered by **Iyaaran** ambassador **Loquel** aboard the ship in 2370. ("Liaisons" [TNG]). Eric participated in a sculpting class aboard the ship, along with Commander Data. ("Masks" [TNG]).

Eris. (Molly Hagen). **Dominion** agent. Eris encountered Commander Benjamin Sisko on a planet in the Gamma Quadrant in 2370. Eris, a member of the **Vorta**, posed as a fugitive from the **Jem'Hadar** and was held by a small group of Jem'Hadar soldiers. When Sisko and his companion, Quark, were also captured, she helped them escape. Upon their return to station Deep Space 9, Eris was found to be a spy, but she escaped from the station before she could be questioned further. ("The Jem'Hadar" [DS9], "The Search, Part II" [DS9]). SEE: **telekinetic suppression collar.**

Erko. (Patrick Cronin). Protocol Master for **Minister Campio** of planet **Kostolain**. Erko strongly disapproved of Campio's decision to marry Ambassador **Lwaxana Troi** in 2368, correctly maintaining that Troi's disregard of protocol would strongly offend Kostolain sensibilities. ("Cost of Living" [TNG]).

ermanium. A metallic alloy used in Starfleet shuttlecraft. ("Final Mission" [TNG]).

Ermat Zimm. A **Bajoran** artist. The latinum-plated **Renewal Scroll** inscription pens that **Quark** was selling in 2371 featured a portrait of **Deep Space 9** by Ermat Zimm. ("Fascination" [DS9]). *Ermat Zimm was named after DS9 production designer Herman Zimmerman.*

erosene winds. Delightful euphoria-inducing winds that occur on planet **Alastria** at the break of dawn. Also called the dawn zephyr. ("Prime Factors." [VGR]).

"Errand of Mercy." *Original Series* episode #27. Written by Gene L. Coon. Directed by John Newland. Stardate 3198.4. *First aired in 1967. The* Enterprise *tries to protect Organia, an apparently primitive planet, from the Klingons, but appearances can be deceiving, and the Organians neither want nor need assistance. This episode features the first appearance of the Klingons in* Star Trek. *The Klingons seen here are much simpler in design than the elaborately made-up Klingons in the* Star Trek *features and in the* Star Trek *spinoff series.* GUEST CAST: Jon Abbott as **Ayelborne**; John Colicos as **Kor**; Peter Brocco as Claymare; Victor Lundin as Klingon Lieutenant #1; David Hillary Hughes as **Trefayne**; Walt Davis as Klingon soldier; George Sawaya as Second soldier; Gary Coombs, Bobby Bass, Klingon guards. SEE: **Ayelborne; Baroner; Code 1; Council of Elders; kevas; Klingon Empire; Klingons; Kor; mind-sifter; noncorporeal life; Organia; Organian Peace Treaty; Organians; Richter scale of culture; Trefayne; trillium.**

Errikang VII. Planet. **Vash** said **Q** almost got her killed on Errikang VII. ("Q-Less" [DS9]).

Erselrope Wars. Ancient conflict during which the arms merchants of planet **Minos** gained notoriety by selling sophisticated weapons systems to both sides. ("The Arsenal of Freedom" [TNG]). *Neither the date nor the adversaries of the Erselrope Wars were established, but the* Enterprise-*D people seemed to know a fair amount about them, so we might speculate they were not that long ago in historical terms.*

Erstwhile. A small class-9 interplanetary cargo vessel piloted by **Thadiun Okona**; armed with lasers only. The *Starship Enterprise*-D lent assistance to the *Erstwhile* when Okona's ship experienced a hardware malfunction near the **Omega Sagitta** system. ("The Outrageous Okona" [TNG]). *The* Erstwhile *was a re-use of the* Merchantman *miniature originally built for* Star Trek III.

escape pod. Small lifeboat that could be ejected from a starship or other space vehicle after a catastrophic accident. (*Star Trek II: The Wrath of Khan*, "Cause and Effect" [TNG]). The crew of the ***U.S.S. Stargazer*** used escape pods to survive following the **Battle of Maxia** in 2355. Escape pods from the ***S.S. Odin*** drifted

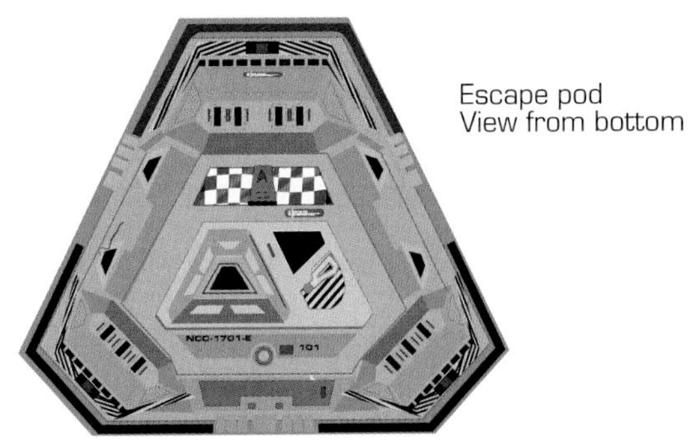

Escape pod
View from bottom

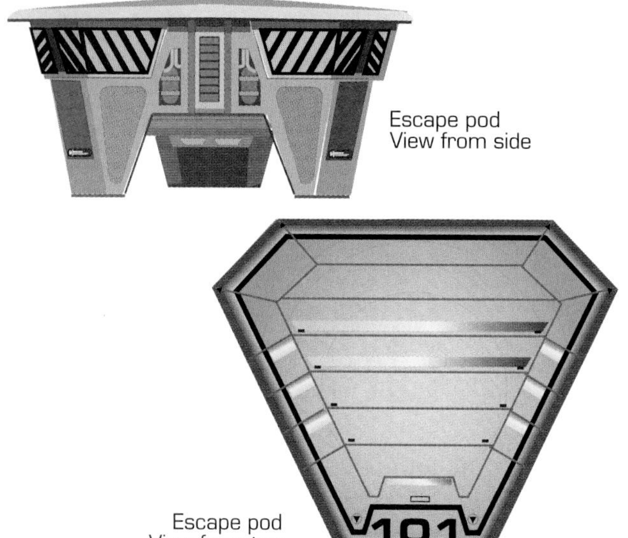

Escape pod
View from side

Escape pod
View from top

for five months before landing on planet **Angel One** in 2357. ("Angel One" [TNG]). Escape pods were also used by the crew of the ***U.S.S. Arcos*** when they abandoned ship above planet **Turkana IV** in 2367. ("Legacy" [TNG]). Following the destruction of the ***U.S.S. Saratoga*** at the battle of **Wolf 359** in 2367, many *Saratoga* personnel, including Commander **Benjamin Sisko** and his son, **Jake Sisko**, fled the ship aboard escape pods. ("Emissary, Part I" [DS9]). *The* Saratoga *escape pod model was designed by James Martin and built by Greg Jein. (Pictured escape pods from* Sovereign-*class starship.)*

eseekas. Geometric patterns, an **Argrathi** art form. During the Argrathi artificial reality program, **Ee'Char** drew *eseekas* in the dirt of a prison cell he and Miles O'Brien shared as a form of relaxation and diversion. ("Hard Time" [DS9]).

Eskarian egg. Edible egg found in the Delta Quadrant. ("Investigations" [VGR]).

Esoqq. (Reiner Schoener). Member of the people known as the **Chalnoth**. Esoqq was imprisoned with Captain Picard during an alien experiment in 2366. Esoqq had been kidnapped from Chalna by unknown life-forms, and he was replaced by a near-identical copy of himself, also part of this experiment. SEE: **Haro, Mitena**. ("Allegiance" [TNG]).

ESP. SEE: **extrasensory perception**.

Essex, U.S.S. Federation starship, ***Daedalus* class**, Starfleet registry NCC-173. Commanded by **Captain Bryce Shumar**, and under the sector command of **Admiral Uttan Narsu** at Starbase 12, the *Essex* was reported lost in 2167. The *Essex* was caught in an electromagnetic storm in the atmosphere of a Class-M moon of planet **Mab-Bu VI**. The storm had been caused by noncorporeal criminal life-forms from the **Ux-Mal** system who had hoped to escape aboard the *Essex*. The ship was destroyed and all 229 members of the crew were killed. In 2368, the *Enterprise*-D encountered beings who claimed to be members of the *Essex* crew, marooned there since 2167. These beings were in fact the Ux-Mal criminals, who sought to escape by commandeering the *Enterprise*-D. ("Power Play" [TNG]).

Esteban, Captain J. T. (Phillip Richard Allen). Commanding officer of the ***U.S.S. Grissom***, in charge of investigating the **Genesis Planet**. A conservative, by-the-book officer, Esteban was killed along with the rest of the *Grissom* crew when the ship was destroyed by a Klingon ship during the investigation. (*Star Trek III: The Search for Spock*).

Etanian Order. Delta Quadrant civilization of technologically sophisticated, imperialistic humanoids. The Etanian Order invaded other worlds by first creating what appeared to be a natural disaster such as an asteroid bombardment. Once the population had evacuated their homeworld, the Etanians would arrive in number and stake a claim. **Goth** was Etanian. ("Rise" [VGR]). SEE: **Nezu**.

Ethan. (Chris Demetral). Another name used by **Barash** of planet **Alpha Onias III**. ("Future Imperfect" [TNG]).

ethical program. Portion of **Data**'s software that enabled him to evaluate his behavior on the basis of real or potential harm to others. This section of his program was disabled by Lore during Data's encounter with him in 2370. ("Descent, Part II" [TNG]). SEE: **Asimov, Dr. Isaac**.

***Ethics, Sophistry and the Alternate Universe*.** Book written by Ving Kuda; not exactly light reading. Captain Picard took a copy along with him on his vacation to Risa. ("Captain's Holiday" [TNG]).

"Ethics." *Next Generation* episode #116. Teleplay by Ronald D. Moore. Story by Sara Charno & Stuart Charno. Directed by Chip Chalmers. Stardate 45587.3. *First aired in 1992. Worf is seriously injured, and his only hope for life is a dangerous experimental procedure proposed by a researcher, which Dr. Crusher believes to be making unethical use of Worf's vulnerability.* GUEST CAST: Caroline Kava as **Russell**, **Dr. Toby**; Brian Bonsall as **Rozhenko**, **Alexander**; Patti Yasutake as **Ogawa**, **Nurse Alyssa**. SEE: **Adelman Neurological Institute; Beloti Sector; borathium; *brak'lul*; chlorinide; chloromydride; cordrazine; CPK enzymatic therapy; cybernetic regeneration; *Denver*, *U.S.S.*; drechtal beams; dynoscanner; exoscalpel; Fang-lee; genetronic replicator; gravitic mine; *Hegh'bat* ceremony; inaprovaline; Klingons; leporazine; Mericor system; morathial series; neural metaphasic shock; neural transducers; neurogenetics; Ogawa, Nurse Alyssa; poker; polyadrenaline; *Potemkin*, *U.S.S.*; Russell, Dr. Toby; Sandoval; Sector 37628; *VeK'tal* response; Worf.**

Eudana. (Yvonne Suhor). Native of the planet **Sikaris** in the Delta Quadrant. Eudana was a woman whom Ensign Harry Kim met on Sikaris. ("Prime Factors." [VGR]).

Eugenics Wars. A terrible conflict on **Earth** during the 1990s, caused by a group of genetically engineered "supermen" who were the result of an ambitious selective-breeding program. The "supermen" believed their superior abilities gave them the right to rule the remainder of humanity, and in 1992 one such individual, **Khan Noonien Singh**, (*pictured*) rose to rule one-fourth of the entire planet. Within a year, his fellow supermen seized power in 40 nations. Terrible wars ensued, in part because the supermen fought among themselves. Entire populations were bombed out of existence, and Earth was on the verge of a new dark age. By 1996, the supermen were overthrown. Khan Noonien Singh escaped into space with several of his followers aboard the ***S.S. Botany Bay***. ("Space Seed" [TOS]). SEE: **Los Angeles**. Following the Eugenics Wars, Earth's governments outlawed genetic engineering procedures such as DNA resequencing, for fear of creating another man like Khan. These laws remained in effect even into the 24th century. ("Doctor Bashir, I Presume?" [DS9]). *Admiral Bennett referred to the Eugenics Wars as having taken place 200 years before the episode, but given a 1996 date for the wars, and a 2373 date for "Doctor Bashir, I Presume?" (DS9), Bennett would seem to have been off by about 200 years. The Eugenics Wars were apparently*

not the conflict mentioned in several episodes as World War III, since the Eugenics Wars were concluded by 1996, but World War III took place in the mid-21st century.

European Hegemony. A loose political alliance on 22nd-century **Earth**. The European Hegemony was considered to be among the beginnings of a world government on that planet. ("Up the Long Ladder" [TNG]).

Evadne IV. Destination of the *Enterprise*-D following the ship's encounter with an unstable wormhole in the **Ngame Nebula** in 2367. ("Clues" [TNG]).

Evans, Charles. (Robert Walker, Jr.). The sole survivor of a transport crash on planet **Thasus** in 2252. Charlie, who was only three years old at the time, was raised by the **Thasians**, a **noncorporeal** species. Charlie claimed to have survived by learning from the ship's computer tapes, but it was later found that the Thasians gave Charlie extraordinary mental powers in order for him to survive on Thasus. Charlie was rescued at age 17 by the crew of the science vessel ***Antares***, but his inexperience with living in human society, combined with his mental powers, made him too dangerous to live with humans, and the Thasians took him back to live on Thasus. ("Charlie X" [TOS]).

Evansville, John. (John Rubinstein). Twenty-fourth century inhabitant of the human settlement on the former **Briori** homeworld in the Delta Quadrant. Evansville's civilization numbered more than 100,000, the descendants of 300 persons abducted from Earth in 1937 by the Briori. Evansville invited the *Voyager* crew to stay and live with his people on their world. ("The 37's" [VGR]). SEE: **Thirty-Sevens**.

evasive pattern. Any of numerous Starfleet tactical maneuvers used to avoid enemy attack in combat situations. Evasive patterns were usually designated by a combination of Greek letters and numbers. Evasive pattern Beta 140 was employed by the *Starship Voyager* in 2371 when encountering a Numiri ship. ("Ex Post Facto" [VGR]).

Evek, Gul. (Richard Poe). Cardassian officer, commander of the ***Vetar***, a ***Galor*-class** warship. In 2370, he led a mission to planet **Dorvan V** to survey the buildings and equipment that would be left behind when the Native American settlers evacuated. When the colonists refused to leave, it appeared an armed conflict would ensue. Evek, who had lost two of his three sons in the war with the Federation, agreed to withdraw his troops from the surface until some solution could be reached. ("Journey's End" [TNG]). Following the incident at Dorvan V, Gul Evek remained in the Demilitarized Zone. Later that year, Evek's ship came under attack by **Maquis** ships. The *Enterprise*-D intervened and was able to halt the Maquis attack. ("Preemptive Strike" [TNG]). When **Deep Space 9** personnel contacted Evek for advice on eradicating a **vole** infestation, Evek wryly suggested that a Federation withdrawal from Bajor might help. ("Playing God" [DS9]). Evek interrogated suspected Maquis terrorist **William Samuels**. He later confronted a group of Federation colony leaders on **Volon III**, accusing them of taking part in a Starfleet plot to arm the colonists in the **Demilitarized Zone**, in violation of the new **Federation-Cardassian Treaty**. ("The Maquis, Part I" [DS9]). Evek was responsible for the arrest of Starfleet officer **Miles O'Brien** in 2370. Evek later testified against O'Brien during his trial. ("Tribunal" [DS9]). Gul Evek commanded the *Galor*-class warship that pursued Chakotay's Maquis craft into the **Badlands** in 2371, where Evek was believed killed. ("Caretaker" [VGR]).

event horizon. Gravitational boundary surrounding a **quantum singularity**, from which no light or **space-normal** object can escape. In 2371, the *Voyager* became trapped within the event horizon of a type-4 quantum singularity. The crew found a small rupture in the event horizon and were able escape using a **dekyon** beam. ("Parallax" [VGR]).

Everest, Mount. A peak in the Himalaya mountain range in eastern Nepal, the highest known point on the Earth's surface, measuring some 8,800 meters high. In Julian Bashir's **secret agent** holosuite program, **Dr. Hippocrates Noah** maintained a stronghold near the top of Mount Everest. ("Our Man Bashir" [DS9]).

"Evolution." *Next Generation* episode #50. Teleplay by Michael Piller. Story by Michael Piller and Michael Wagner. Directed by Winrich Kolbe. Stardate 43125.8. *First aired in 1989. A lab accident causes microscopic robots to evolve into an intelligent lifeform. This was the second episode filmed for the third season, although it was the first episode aired for that season; thus it marked the return of Dr. Beverly Crusher. "Evolution" was the first episode written by Michael Piller, who would later serve as executive producer of* Star Trek: The Next Generation *and co-creator of* Star Trek: Deep Space Nine *and* Star Trek: Voyager. GUEST CAST: Ken Jenkins as **Stubbs**, **Dr. Paul**; Whoopi Goldberg as **Guinan**; Mary McCusker as Nurse; Randal Patrick as Crewman #1. SEE: **baseball; Beth Delta I; computer core; Crusher, Dr. Beverly; Crusher, Wesley; Dakar, Senegal; Egg; gamma radiation; Guinan; Kavis Alpha IV; Kavis Alpha Sector; La Forge, Geordi; linear memory crystal; nanites; nanotechnology; neutron star; neutronium; New Manhattan; Stubbs, Dr. Paul; universal translator.**

"Ex Post Facto." *Voyager* episode #8. Teleplay by Evan Carlos Somers and Michael Piller. Story by Evan Carlos Somers. Directed by LeVar Burton. No stardate given. *First aired in 1995. Paris is wrongly convicted of murder on an alien world and as a punishment must repeatedly relive the last moments of the victim's life.* GUEST CAST: Robin McKee as **Ren**, **Lidell**; Francis Guinan as **Kray**, **Minister**; Aaron Lustig as Doctor; Ray Reinhardt as **Ren**, **Tolan**; Henry Brown as Numiri captain. SEE: **autonomic response analysis; Baneans; Emergency Medical Hologram; engram; evasive pattern; Galen; Kray, Minister; LN_2 exhaust conduits; *Marob* root tea; Neeka; neodextraline solution; Numiri; phase emitters; Ren, Lidell; Ren, Tolen; rolk; Salk, Dr. Jonas Edward; Spock, Dr. Benjamin McLane; Teluridian IV; thalmerite; Tuvok; Vulcan mind-meld.**

exanogen gas. An extremely cold gaseous compound. Exanogen can be used to retard the feeding and growth of **nitrium metal parasites**. ("Cost of Living" [TNG]).

Exarch. Official from the Nehelik Province of planet **Rakhar**. In 2369, he demanded that the Rakhari fugitive **Croden** be extradited from Deep Space 9. ("Vortex" [DS9]).

Excalbia. Uncharted planet whose surface was molten lava and the atmosphere poisonous. The original *Starship Enterprise* visited there in 2269. ("The Savage Curtain" [TOS]). SEE: **Excalbian**.

Excalbian. Life-form indigenous to planet **Excalbia**. These rock-based, intelligent entities possess ethics and values dramatically different from those of many humanoid species. They are intensely curious about other life-forms and have captured such forms, to observe their behavior in dramatic situations created by the Excalbians. They were **shape-shifters** and used their ability to alter their molecular form to remake themselves into characters to support such dramas. One such experiment, conducted in 2269, involved the capture of Kirk and Spock, who were placed into a conflict with various historical figures including **Abraham Lincoln**, **Kahless the Unforgettable**, and **Surak of Vulcan**. ("The Savage Curtain" [TOS]). SEE: **Yarnek**.

Excalibur, U.S.S. *Constitution*-class Federation starship, Starfleet registry number NCC-1664, commanded by **Captain Harris**. The *Excalibur* was severely damaged and all crew personel killed in 2268 during a disastrous war-game drill with the **M-5** computer. ("The Ultimate Computer" [TOS]).

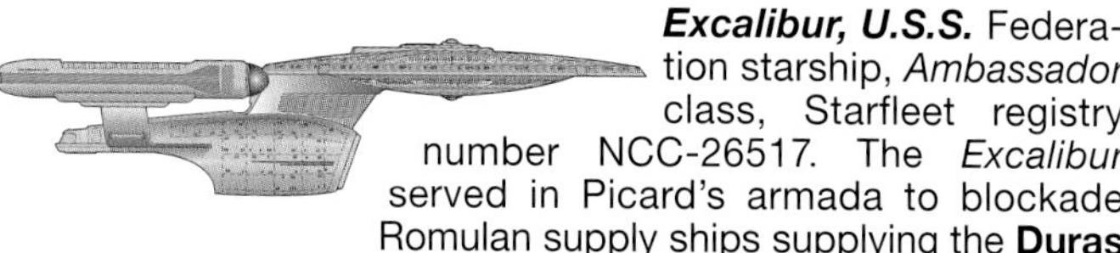

Excalibur, U.S.S. Federation starship, *Ambassador* class, Starfleet registry number NCC-26517. The *Excalibur* served in Picard's armada to blockade Romulan supply ships supplying the **Duras** family forces during the **Klingon civil war** in 2367-2368. During this assignment, Commander William Riker served as its captain and Commander La Forge was his first officer. ("Redemption, Part II" [TNG]). *The* Excalibur *was a re-use of the* Enterprise-C *model.*

exceiver. Alien device used by **Gary Seven** when assigned to Earth in 1968. ("Assignment: Earth" [TOS]).

Excelsior, U.S.S. The first starship of the *Excelsior* class, launched in 2284 with the registry number NX-2000. The ship served under the command of **Captain Styles** as the testbed vehicle for the unsuccessful **transwarp** drive development project. *(Star Trek III: The Search for Spock).* SEE: ***Excelsior*-class starship**. Under the command of Captain **Hikaru Sulu**, the ship began a three-year research mission in 2290, cataloging planetary atmospheric anomalies. Upon successful completion of this mission, Sulu and the *Excelsior* played a key role in the Khitomer peace conference of 2293. Once the ship was awarded operational status, her registry number was changed to NCC-2000. *(Star Trek VI: The Undiscovered Country).* Just prior to the Khitomer peace conference, Captain Sulu took the *Excelsior* on an unauthorized mission to rescue Captain Kirk and Dr. McCoy. On the way to **Qo'noS**, the *Excelsior* encountered several Klingon battle cruisers and sustained heavy damage and casualties, prompting Sulu to abort the rescue attempt. Serving aboard the *Excelsior* during the Khitomer incident was future *Voyager* crew member **Tuvok**. ("Flashback" [VGR]). *The* Excelsior *helm officer was portrayed by Boris Krutonog in* Star Trek VI: The Undiscovered Country *and "Flashback" (VGR).* In 2370, along with the ***U.S.S. Nobel*** , the *Excelsior* took part in a search and rescue mission for the ***U.S.S. Hera.*** ("Interface" [TNG]). *The* Excelsior *was designed by Bill George and built at ILM. Although this was never made clear on film, it is generally assumed that the transwarp drive being tested in* Star Trek III *was a failure, and that the ship was later outfitted with a more conventional warp drive. The* Excelsior's *bridge control panels and computer readout displays seen in* Star Trek VI *tend to support this theory. We assume that the Excelsior mentioned in "Interface" was the same ship first seen in* Star Trek III *because there is no evidence to suggest otherwise. (By contrast, we know that one* U.S.S. Intrepid *[presumably a* Constitution-*class vessel) was destroyed in "The Changeling" (TOS), and that an* Excelsior-*class* Intrepid *was Sergey Rozhenko's ship mentioned in "Family" (TNG). There had to be at least one more* Intrepid *to serve as the prototype for the* U.S.S. Voyager.*)*

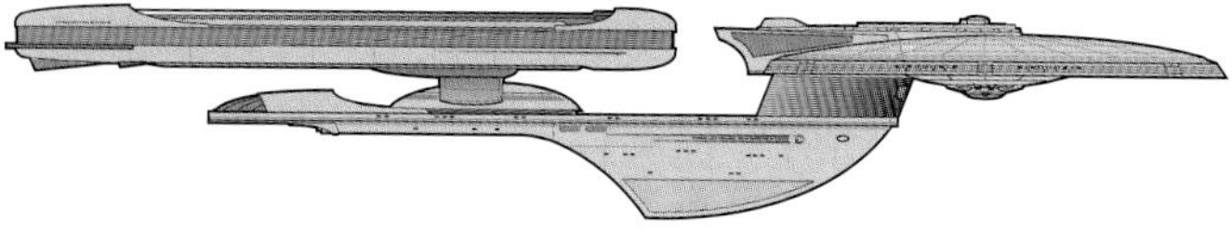

Excelsior*-class starship.** Dubbed "the Great Experiment," the first *Excelsior*-class vessel was launched in 2285 as a testbed for the unsuccessful **transwarp** drive development project. The ship, later refitted with a standard warp drive, became the prototype for the numerous *Excelsior*-class starships built over the next several decades. Among these ships was the ***U.S.S. Enterprise*-B**, the third Federation starship to bear that name. Other *Excelsior*-class starships have included the ***Hood ("Encounter at Farpoint" [TNG]), the ***Repulse*** ("The Child" [TNG]), the ***Intrepid*** ("Sins of the Father" [TNG]), and the ***Gorkon*** ("Descent, Part I" [TNG]).

Exeter, U.S.S. Federation ***Constitution*-class starship**, Starfleet registry number NCC-1672. Commanded by **Captain Ronald Tracey** in 2268 when the ship was found orbiting planet **Omega IV**, its entire crew reduced to dehydrated crystals by an ancient bacteriological warfare agent from the planet. ("The Omega Glory" [TOS]).

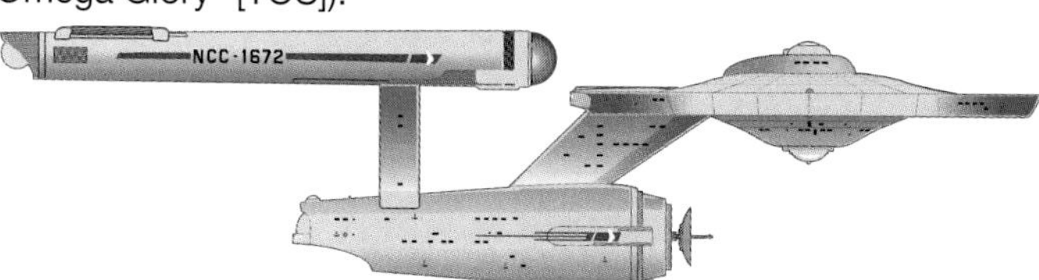

Exeter, U.S.S. Federation starship. **Thomas Paris** served aboard the *Exeter* prior to his stay in the New Zealand Penal Settlement. ("Non Sequitur" [VGR]). *There was also a* Constitution-*class* Exeter. *("The Omega Glory" [TOS]).*

Exo III. A barely habitable planet whose sun had been fading for a half-million years, once the home of a technically advanced humanoid civilization. Exo III's inhabitants moved underground as their sun dimmed. In doing so, they fostered a mechanistic, dehumanized society. Eventually, they began to fear the sophisticated **androids** they had built, but by that time the androids had become advanced enough to develop the instinct for self-preservation, so they eventually destroyed their makers. Noted archaeologist **Roger Korby** disappeared there, and two expeditions failed to find him prior to the *Enterprise* rescue mission of 2266. ("What Are Little Girls Made Of?" [TOS]).

exobiology. The study of alien life. An area of study in which the android **Data** excelled during his studies at **Starfleet Academy**. ("Encounter at Farpoint, Part I" [TNG]). Wesley Crusher also garnered honors in the subject. ("The Host" [TNG]).

Exochemistry. Required class at **Starfleet Academy**. ("Time's Arrow, Part I" [TNG]).

exocomp. Experimental servomechanism developed by **Dr. Farallon** for use in hazardous engineering applications. The exocomps incorporated an advanced microreplication system, providing the device with the ability to fabricate specialized tools for virtually any task, and ample onboard intelligence to make realtime repair decisions. The exocomps were later found to have a sufficient degree of intelligence to qualify as sentient life-forms. ("The Quality of Life" [TNG]). *The exocomps, designed by Rick Sternbach, were inspired by the character Nammo from the animated s-f series* The Dirty Pair.

exoscalpel. Surgical instrument used by Starfleet medical personnel to incise the skin and expose underlying tissue. ("Ethics" [TNG]).

Exosia. To the **Nacene** civilization of extradimensional **sporocystian** life-forms, Exosia is a **subspace** domain. **Tanis**, an inhabitant of **Suspiria's Array**, described it as a place of pure thought, pure energy, a place of the mind. **Suspiria** routinely traveled there and sometimes took **Ocampa** from the Array. ("Cold Fire" [VGR])

exothermal inversion. A dramatic upheaval in a planet's atmosphere caused by an external energy source. A cascading exothermal inversion was a real possibility at planet **Penthara IV** in 2368 if a plan to vaporize large amounts of volcanic dust in the planet's atmosphere failed. ("A Matter of Time" [TNG]).

"Explorers." *Deep Space Nine* episode #68. Written by René Echevarria. Story by Hilary J. Bader. Directed by Cliff Bole. No stardate given. *First aired in 1995. Sisko builds a replica of an ancient Bajoran solar-sail spacecraft, in which Jake and he voyage to Cardassia. Dr. Bashir encounters an old classmate from Starfleet Medical School.* GUEST CAST: Marc Alaimo as **Dukat**; Bari Hochwald as **Lense, Dr. Elizabeth**; Chase Masterson as **Leeta**. SEE: **Bajoran solar-sail vessel; Bajorans; Cardassia; *Cygnian Respiratory Diseases, A Survey of*; Dax, Curzon; Dax (symbiont); Denorios Belt; Erib; Fanalian toddy; First Republic; gravity net; Leeta; Lense, Dr. Elizabeth; *Lexington, U.S.S.*; Lucier, Bruce; Pennington School; Sisko, Benjamin; Sisko, Jake; Sisko, Joseph; tachyon eddies.**

Expressionistic phase. School of art. One of the many styles that Data attempted to emulate in his attempt to master all known styles of painting. Expressionism, which emphasized the artist's emotions rather than actual representation of objects, was popular on Earth during the early 1900s. Data executed a painting of the Battle of HarOs in this style and gave it to Lieutenant Worf for his birthday in 2370. Worf felt the painting made him "dizzy." ("Parallels" [TNG]).

extrasensory perception. Various mental and telekinetic powers, currently inexplicable by conventional science. Certain members of the *Valiant* and *Enterprise* crews exhibited dramatically enhanced ESP powers after contact with the barrier at the edge of the galaxy. ("Where No Man Has Gone Before" [TOS]). SEE: **Mitchell, Gary**.

"Eye of the Beholder." Next Generation episode # 170. Teleplay by René Echevarria. Story by Brannon Braga. Directed by Cliff Bole. Stardate 47623.2. *First aired in 1994. During the investigation of a crew member's mysterious suicide, Troi experiences a series of disturbing hallucinations.* GUEST CAST: Mark Rolston as **Pierce**, **Walter J.**; Nancy Harewood as **Nara**, **Lieutenant**; Tim Lounibos as **Kwan**, **Daniel L.**; Johanna McCloy as **Calloway**, **Maddy**; Nora Leonhardt as **Finn**, **Marla E.**; Dugan Savoye as Man; Majel Barrett as Computer voice. SEE: **Barson II; Calloway, Maddy; Finn, Marla E.; Kwan, Daniel L.; nacelle; Napean; Nara, Lieutenant; Pierce, Walter J.; psilosynine; Starbase 328; Til'amin froth; Utopia Planitia Fleet Yards; Wallace, Darian; Yridian tea.**

"Eye of the Needle." Voyager episode #7. Teleplay by Bill Dial and Jeri Taylor. Story by Hilary J. Bader. Directed by Winrich Kolbe. Stardate 48579.4. *First aired in 1995. The* Voyager *discovers a small wormhole, through which it makes contact with a Romulan vessel in the Alpha Quadrant.* GUEST CAST: Vaughn Armstrong as **Telek**; Tom Virtue as **Baxter**, **Lieutenant**. SEE: **Arethian flu; Baxter, Lieutenant; eidetic memory; Emergency Medical Hologram; Federation Astronomical Committee; gravitational eddy; Hargrove, Lieutenant; Kes; Kim, Harry; Kyoto, Ensign; microprobe; micro-wormhole; R'Mor, Telek; Romulan Astrophysical Academy; Romulan Senate; sector 1385; spinach juice; *Talvath*; Torres, B'Elanna; vegetable bouillon; verteron.**

Eye of the Universe. Translation of the **Skrreea**n term for the **Bajoran wormhole**. In 2370 Skrreeans fled from the Gamma Quadrant, which they called the *creshnee* side, to the Alpha Quadrant, where Skrreean legend said their homeworld of **Kentanna** was to be found. ("Sanctuary" [DS9]). SEE: **Haneek**.

"Eyes in the dark." A telepathic message sent to Counselor Troi by an alien vessel trapped with the *Enterprise*-D in a **Tyken's Rift** in 2367. The message referred to the binary star system where the rift was located. ("Night Terrors" [TNG]).

Eymorg. Female inhabitants of planet **Sigma Draconis VI** who lived beneath the surface in the reminants of a highly advanced culture. The male population, called the **Morgs**, lived aboveground in primitive conditions in a wintery environment, existed only to mate with the women, calling them the "givers of pain and delight." The Eymorgs were forced to return to the surface to live with the Morgs when they were unable to find a humanoid brain to serve in their **Controller**. ("Spock's Brain" [TOS]).

Fabrina. Star system containing eight planets that were destroyed 10,000 years ago when the star of the same name became a nova and exploded. ("For the World Is Hollow and I Have Touched the Sky" [TOS]). SEE: **Fabrini**; ***Yonada.***

Fabrini Book of the People. Massive printed text containing all the knowledge of the **Fabrini** people, provided by their creators, to be read when the asteroid/ship ***Yonada*** reached its final destination. ("For the World Is Hollow and I Have Touched the Sky" [TOS]).

Fabrini creators. Inhabitants of the star system **Fabrina** who, just prior to their sun going nova, constructed a massive space ark inside an asteroid so that some of their people could escape to resettle on another world. The passengers on the asteroid ship, called ***Yonada***, revered their creators for having literally built their world and established their society. ("For the World Is Hollow and I Have Touched the Sky" [TOS]). SEE: **Fabrini**.

Fabrini. Humanoids from the star system **Fabrina.** The Fabrini constructed a ship disguised as an asteroid to carry some of their people to safety before their star exploded 10,000 years ago. The creators of the asteroid/ship devised a religion intended to guide their descendants in their lives aboard the mobile world they called ***Yonada***. The Yonadan religion was enforced by a powerful computer called the **Oracle**, which attempted to provide as normal an environment as possible for the people, concealing from them the fact that they were living on a spaceship. ("For the World Is Hollow and I Have Touched the Sky" [TOS]). SEE: **Natira**. *The Fabrini apparently disembarked at their promised land sometime in 2269.*

"Face of the Enemy." *Next Generation* episode #140. Teleplay by Naren Shankar. Story by René Echevarria. Directed by Gabrielle Beaumont. Stardate 46519.1. *First aired in 1993. Deanna Troi is kidnapped and must masquerade as a Romulan intelligence officer to avoid being killed.* GUEST CAST: Scott MacDonald as **N'Vek, Subcommander**; Carolyn Seymour as **Toreth, Commander**; Barry Lynch as **DeSeve, Ensign Stefan**; Robertson Dean as Pilot; Dennis Cockrum as Alien captain; Pamela Winslow as **McKnight, Ensign**; Majel Barrett as Computer voice. SEE: ***Antares*-class freighter; artificial quantum singularity; Borka VI; cloaking device, Romulan; Corvallen freighter; DeSeve, Ensign Stefan; disruptors; Draken IV; gravitic sensor net; Imperial Senate, Romulan; Kaleb Sector; *Khazara*; Konsab, Commander; McKnight, Ensign; M'ret, Vice-Proconsul; N'Vek, Subcommander; nullifier core; Rakal, Major; Research Station 75; Romulan Warbird; Sotarek Citation; Spock; Tal Shiar; Toreth, Commander; *viinerine*.**

"Faces." *Voyager* episode #14. Teleplay by Kenneth Biller. Story by Jonathan Glassner and Kenneth Biller. Directed by Winrich Kolbe. Stardate 48784.2. *First aired in 1995. B'Elanna Torres is captured by the Vidiians and split into two separate beings—one Klingon, the other human. This was the second appearance of the Vidiians, first introduced in "Phage" (VGR).* GUEST CAST: Brian Markinson as **Durst**, **Peter** and **Sulan**; Rob LaBelle as Vidiian guard #1; Barton Tinapp as Talaxian. SEE: **Avery III; corn salad; Durst, Peter; genotron; Kessik IV; peanut butter and jelly sandwich; phage; *plomeek* soup à la Neelix; *plomeek* soup; Sulan; *Tika* cat; Torres, B'Elanna; transponder, emergency; Vidiian Sodality; Vidiians.**

"Facets." *Deep Space Nine* episode #71. Written by René Echevarria. Directed by Cliff Bole. No stardate given. *First aired in 1995. Dax undergoes a Trill ritual that lets her meet her previous hosts.* GUEST CAST: Jefrey Alan Chandler as Guardian; Max Grodénchik as **Rom**; Aron Eisenberg as **Nog**; Chase Masterson as **Leeta**; Majel Barrett as Computer voice. SEE: **Dax, Audrid; Dax, Curzon; Dax, Emony; Dax, Jadzia; Dax, Joran; Dax, Lela; Dax (symbiont); Dax, Tobin; Dax, Torias; Delvin fluff pastries; Guardians; Leeta; Lonzo; Nog; Odo; Program delta 5 9; root beer; runabout simulation; spatial orientation test; Starfleet Academy Preparatory Program; *tranya*; Trill Symbiosis Commission; *zhian'tara.***

Fahleena III. Planet. The Valerian vessel ***Sherval Das*** visited Fahleena III when delivering **dolamide** to the **Cardassians**. ("Dramatis Personae" [DS9]).

"Fair Trade." *Voyager* episode #56. Teleplay by André Bormanis. Story by Ronald Wilkerson & Jean Louise Matthias. Directed by Jesús Salvador Trevino. No stardate mentioned. *First aired in 1997. Upon encountering the Nekrit Expanse, an uncharted region of space, Voyager stops at a Supply Depot administrated by an unknown alien called Bahrat. While searching the station for materials needed for Voyager, Neelix encounters his old friend, Wix. To repay a debt to Wix for not reporting Neelix's involvement during an incident with the Ubeans, Wix convinces Neelix to help him smuggle illicit narcotics for the race known as the Kolaati.* GUEST CAST: James Nardini as **Wixiban**; Carlos Carrasco as **Bahrat**; Alexander Enberg as **Vorik**; Steve Kehela as **Sutok**; James Horan as **Tosin**; Eric Sharp as Map vendor. SEE: **Bahrat; biomimetic gel; control interface; cryostatic suspension; deuterium maintenance; duotronic probe; fire snakes; gravitic caliper; isonucleic residue; Kolaati Traders; magnetic spindle bearings; Neelix; Nekrit Expanse; Nekrit Supply Depot; Orillian lung maggot; Paris, Thomas; pergium; plasma canister; Rhuludian crystals; spectral analysis; Sutok; *Toffa* Ale; Tosin; Ubean prison; Vorik; warp plasma particles; Wixiban.**

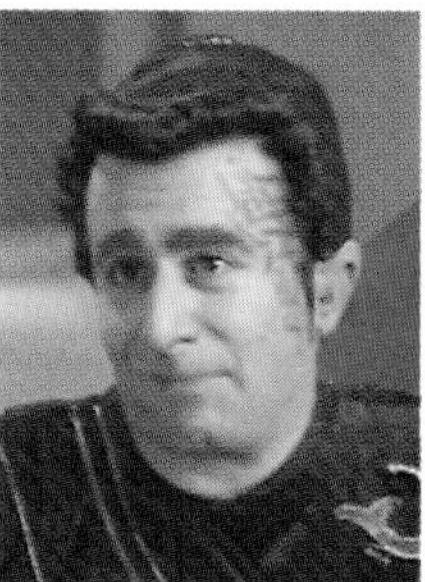

Fajo, Kivas. (Saul Rubinek). A **Zibalian** trader and an unscrupulous member of the Stacius Trade Guild, Fajo was owner of the trade ship ***Jovis***. Fajo was known for his fondness for such unique collectible items as the **Rejac Crystal**, Van Gogh's "Starry Night," and the only existing 1962 **Roger Maris** baseball card. In 2366, Fajo attempted to abduct the android Data for his collection. Data managed to escape Fajo's capture, but in the process, Fajo murdered his assistant, a woman named **Varria**. Fajo was subsequently placed under arrest and his collection confiscated. ("The Most Toys" [TNG]). SEE: **Beta Agni II; Starry Night.**

fal-tor-pan*.** Ancient **Vulcan** ritual, also called the refusion, intended to reunite an individual's ***katra (living spirit) to that person's body. Until 2285, the ceremony had not been performed for centuries, since in most cases a Vulcan's *katra* is returned home after the death of the body. **Sarek** requested the *fal-tor-pan* for his son, **Spock**, whose body had been regenerated at the Genesis Planet following his death there in 2285. High priestess **T'Lar** noted that the *fal-tor-pan* had not been attempted since "ages past," and then only in legend. Nevertheless, the ritual was successful in reuniting Spock's body and soul. *(Star Trek III: The Search for Spock).*

Falangian diamond. Precious stone. In 2372, Odo suspected Rionoj of trafficking in stolen Falangian diamonds. ("Broken Link" [DS9]).

Falcon. (Colm Meaney). A character in Julian Bashir's **secret agent** holosuite program. Falcon was a deadly assassin that had been trying to kill Julian's secret agent character for nine years. A holosuite malfunction in 2372 caused the character to look exactly like Miles O'Brien. ("Our Man Bashir" [DS9]). Falcon was also a character in ***The Queen's Gambit*** holosuite program. ("A Simple Investigation" [VGR]).

Fall of Kang, The. Klingon poem by **G'Trok**. Commander Benjamin Sisko and **Professor Seyetik** quoted from the poem: "So honor the valiant who die 'neath your sword/ But pity the warrior who slays all his foes." ("Second Sight" [DS9]). *It's not clear what, if any, connection the poem has to the character from "Day of the Dove" (TOS) and "Blood Oath" (DS9).*

Falling Hawk, Joe. (Sheldon P. Wolfchild). Gambling partner to **Frederick La Rouque**. ("Time's Arrow, Part I" [TNG]).

Fallit Kot. (Peter Crombie). Former business associate of Quark's. In 2362, Kot and **Quark** attempted to hijack a shipment of **Romulan ale**. Kot spent eight years in a Romulan labor camp for the crime, after Quark escaped prosecution by turning Kot in. In 2370, Kot was released and went to station Deep Space 9 to kill Quark. The murder attempt was unsuccessful, and Kot abducted Quark and two Starfleet officers while fleeing the station. His escape was foiled by Ensign Melora Pazlar, and he was returned to Federation custody. ("Melora" [DS9]).

"Falor's Journey." Traditional **Vulcan** folk song. "Falor's Journey" is a tale of enlightenment consisting of 348 verses. Falor was a prosperous merchant who went on a journey to gain greater awareness. **Tuvok**'s youngest son was fond of "Falor's Journey." ("Innocence" [VGR]).

Falow. (Joel Brooks). Leader of the **Wadi** delegation who visited Deep Space 9 in 2369, the first diplomatic mission from the Gamma Quadrant. Tall in stature, Falow introduced himself as **Master Surchid** of the Wadi when he took command of the games played at Quark's bar. ("Move Along Home" [DS9]).

"False Profits." *Voyager* episode #44. Teleplay by Joe Menosky. Story by George A. Brozak. Directed by Cliff Bole. Stardate 50074.3. *First aired in 1996. The two Ferengi lost into the Barzan wormhole seven years earlier are found acting as the Holy Sages to a planet's inhabitants. This episode continued the story begun in "The Price" (TNG). Episode co-writer George A. Brozak was one of the researchers on* The Star Trek Encyclopedia. GUEST CAST: Dan Shor as **Arridor**; Leslie Jordan as **Kol**; Michael Ensign as Bard; Rob LaBelle as **Kafar**; Alan Altshuld as sandal maker; John Walter Davis as Merchant. SEE: **Arridor; Barzan wormhole; class-5 probe; Ferengi; Ferengi Rules of Acquisition: Ferengi shuttle; frang; Ga'nah; grand proxy; graviton; Great Sages; Holy Pilgrim; Kafar; Kol; Murphy, Ensign; "Song of the Sages"; Takar; Takarian bard; Takarian merchant; Takarian sandal maker; Takarian temple; Takarians; verteron.**

"Family Business." *Deep Space Nine* episode #69. Written by Ira Steven Behr & Robert Hewitt Wolfe. Directed by René Auberjonois. No stardate given. *First aired in 1995. Quark and Rom return to their homeworld when their mother, Ishka, is accused of breaking Ferengi law; Sisko meets a friend of Jake's.* GUEST CAST: Penny Johnson as **Yates, Kasidy**; Max Grodénchik as **Rom**; Jeffrey Combs as **Brunt**; Andrea Martin as **Ishka**; Mel Green as Secretary. SEE: **Adred; baseball; Brunt; Cestus III; Cestus Comets; FCA; Ferengi Commerce Authority; Ferengi Trade By-Laws; Ferengi welcoming ceremony; Ferenginar; Gorn; Ishka; Keldar; latinum; Liquidator; Moogie; Peljenite; Petarian; Pike City; Pike City Pioneers; Quark; Rom; *Rubicon, U.S.S.*; Sisko, Benjamin: Sacred Marketplace; Stol; tooth sharpener; Tower of Commerce; transporter; tube grubs; Writ of Accountability; Yates, Kasidy.**

"Family." *Next Generation* episode #78. Written by Ronald D. Moore. Directed by Les Landau. Stardate 44012.3. *First aired in 1990. Picard returns to his hometown of Labarre, France, to recover from his experiences with the Borg. This episode, the second aired for the fourth season, was actually the fourth produced for that year, but was a direct continuation of "The Best of Both Worlds, Part II" (TNG). The episode was based in part on a premise by Susanne Lambdin & Bryan Stewart.* GUEST CAST: Jeremy Kemp as **Picard, Robert**; Samantha Eggar as **Picard, Marie**; Theodore Bikel as **Rozhenko, Sergey**; Georgia Brown as **Rozhenko, Helena**; Dennis Creaghan as **Louis**; Colm Meaney as **O'Brien, Miles**; Whoopi Goldberg as **Guinan**; David Tristan Birkin as **Picard, René**; Doug Wert as **Crusher, Jack**. SEE: **Angel Falls, Venezuela; Atlantis Project; Bloom sisters; Chateau Picard; Crusher, Jack R.; discommendation; Earth Station Bobruisk; Earth Station McKinley; *Enterprise*-D, *U.S.S.*; *How to Advance Your Career Through Marriage*; *Intrepid, U.S.S.*; Labarre, France; Louis; O'Brien, Miles Edward; Picard, Jean-Luc; Picard, Marie; Picard, René; Picard, Robert; *rokeg* blood pie; Rozhenko, Helena; Rozhenko, Sergey; synthehol; tectonic plates; theta-matrix compositer; Worf.**

Fanalian toddy. Hot alcoholic beverage. **Julian Bashir** ordered one at **Quark's bar** in 2371 as a remedy for a cough Leeta pretended to have. ("Explorers" [DS9]).

Fang-lee. *Enterprise*-D crew member who was killed while under Worf's command. ("Ethics" [TNG]).

Farallon, Dr. (Ellen Bry). Scientist. Inventor of an experimental **particle fountain** mining technology tested at planet Tyrus VIIA in 2369. Farallon also developed highly sophisticated robotic tools called **exocomps**, inadvertently endowing them with sufficient intelligence for them to become sentient life-forms. ("The Quality of Life" [TNG]).

Farek, Dr. (Ethan Phillips). A member of the crew of the Ferengi vessel ***Krayton***. Farek was present with **DaiMon Tog** at the **Trade Agreements Conference** on **Betazed** in 2366. ("Ménage à Troi" [TNG]). *Ethan Phillips later portrayed Neelix on* Star Trek: Voyager *and made a cameo appearance in* Star Trek: First Contact *as a holographic nightclub maître d'.*

Faren Kag. (Jim Jansen). Magistrate of a **Bajoran** village. Faren requested medical help from Deep Space 9 in 2369 when their storyteller, the **Sirah**, fell ill. ("The Storyteller" [DS9]).

Farius Prime. Planet. The flight plan of a **Galador freighter** listed Farius Prime as its destination. ("The Maquis, Part I" [DS9]).

Farn. Humanoid civilization in the **Delta Quadrant**. The Farn were once part of the **Borg collective**, but managed to break free around 2368. Unfortunately, once freed of **Borg** control, the Farn resumed an old ethnic conflict with the **Parein**. ("Unity" [VGR]).

Farpoint Station. Originally believed to be a large, advanced spaceport facility on planet **Deneb IV**. The **Bandi** people, natives of Deneb IV, claimed to have built Farpoint Station and offered it for Starfleet's use in 2364. It was later discovered that the station was actually a shapeshifting spaceborne life-form that had been coerced by the Bandi into assuming the form of the starbase. The creature was eventually allowed to return to space. An agreement with the Bandi for the use of a rebuilt Farpoint Station was concluded shortly after the departure of the creature. ("Encounter at Farpoint, Parts I and II" [TNG]). *The spaceborne life-forms, designed by Rick Sternbach and created by Industrial Light and Magic, were never given a name in the episode.*

Farragut, U.S.S. Federation starship, *Constitution* class, Starfleet registry number NCC-1647, commanded by **Captain Garrovick**. The *Farragut* was Lieutenant **James T. Kirk**'s first assignment after leaving Starfleet Academy. In 2257, 200 members of the *Farragut* crew, including Captain Garrovick, were killed by the **dikironium cloud creature** discovered at planet **Tycho IV**. ("Obsession" [TOS]). *Named for American naval officer David Glasgow Farragut, who commanded Union ships during the American Civil War, famous for his rallying cry, "Damn the torpedoes, full speed ahead!"*

Farragut, U.S.S. Federation starship, *Nebula* class, Starfleet registry number NCC-60591, second ship to bear the name. The *Farragut* was one of the three starships that transported the crew of the *Starship Enterprise*-D from **Veridian III** after the *Enterprise*-D saucer section crash-landed there in 2371. *(Star Trek Generations).* The *Farragut* was destroyed by Klingon forces in 2373 near the Lembatta cluster. The *Farragut* had been assigned to evacuate Federation colonists on **Ajilon Prime** during the Klingon offensive. ("Nor the Battle to the Strong" [DS9]).

Farrakk. (Tim Halligan). Former business associate of arms dealer **Hagath**. In 2373, after a relatively minor betrayal, Hagath had Farrakk killed by sabotaging his ship's **warp core**. ("Business As Usual" [DS9]).

Farran. Enaran citizen. Farran was a member of the group called the **Regressives**. Farran was murdered, along with the rest of his people as part of the horrific **resettlement** on Enara Prime. ("Remember" [VGR]).

Farrell (mirror). (Pete Kellett). Crew member on the **mirror universe** *Enterprise* who saved Captain Kirk from Chekov's assassination attempt. In the tradition of the alternate universe, Farrell expected that his betrayal of Chekov would earn him favor with the captain. ("Mirror, Mirror" [TOS])

Farrell, Lieutenant John. (Jim Goodwin). Crew member aboard the original *Starship Enterprise*. ("The Enemy Within" [TOS], "Mudd's Women" [TOS], "Miri" [TOS]).

Farrell, Lieutenant. (Dendrie Taylor). Starfleet officer assigned to the engineering section of the *Starship Enterprise*-D in 2371. *(Star Trek Generations).*

Farspace Starbase Earhart. SEE: **Starbase Earhart**.

"Fascination." *Deep Space Nine* episode #56. Teleplay by Philip LaZebnik. Story by Ira Steven Behr & James Crocker. Directed by Avery Brooks. No stardate given. *First aired in 1994. During a Bajoran celebration on the station, Lwaxana Troi suffers from an unusual illness that causes an epidemic of romantic attractions among the crew.* GUEST CAST: Majel Barrett as **Troi, Lwaxana**; Philip Anglim as **Bareil, Vedek**; Rosalind Chao as **O'Brien, Keiko**; Hana Hatae as **O'Brien, Molly**. SEE: **Bajoran Gratitude Festival; Ermat Zimm; I'danian spice pudding; Mardah; O'Brien, Keiko; Odo; *peldor joi*; Redab, Vedek; Regulus III; Renewal Scroll; Sebarr; Troi, Lwaxana; Zanthi fever.**

Fatal Revenge, The. Gothic novel. **Lieutenant Aquiel Uhnari** enjoyed it. ("Aquiel" [TNG]).

"Favorite Son." Voyager episode #62. Written by Lisa Klink. Directed by Marvin V. Rush. Stardate 50732.4. *First aired in 1997. Harry Kim receives genetic memories from a retrovirus and guides the ship to a planet where the female inhabitants greet him as a long-lost son, but he is wanted only as a donor of genetic material.* GUEST CAST: Christopher Carroll as **Alben, Captain**; Christine Delgado as **Ashmore, Ensign**; Cari Shayne as **Eliann**; Irene Tsu as Harry's mother; Deborah May as **Lyris**; Kristanna S. Loken as **Malia**; Kelli Kirkland as **Rinna**; Patrick Fabian as **Taymon**. SEE: **Alben, Captain; denucleation; Eliann; hatana; Kim, Harry; Lyris; Malia; Mendakan pox; Nasari; Nerada; pulmozine; retrovirus; rikka; Rinna; Taresia; Taresians; Taymon; vorillium.**

Fayla. Elderly Drayan who died of natural causes in 2372. A shuttle carried Fayla and several others destined for their **final ritual** on one of the moons of planet Drayan II. The shuttle crashed on the moon and Fayla died shortly thereafter. ("Innocence" [VGR]).

FCA. Abbreviation for **Ferengi Commerce Authority.** ("Family Business" [DS9]).

Fearless, U.S.S. Federation ***Excelsior*-class** starship, Starfleet registry number NCC-4598. Starfleet propulsion specialist **Kosinski** performed an unsuccessful series of experimental engine software upgrades on the *Fearless* in 2364. The *Fearless* later transported Kosinski and his assistant to the *Enterprise*-D, where similar upgrades were attempted. ("Where No One Has Gone Before" [TNG]).

Federal Employment Act. Legislation enacted in the **United States** on **Earth** in 1946. The Employment Act declared that it was the policy and responsibility of the American government to promote maximum employment, production, and purchasing power. The Act was repealed sometime before the establishment of **Sanctuary District**s throughout the United States in the 2020's. One of the demands made by the Sanctuary residents during the **Bell Riots** of 2024 was the reinstatement of the Federal Employment Act. ("Past Tense, Part II" [DS9]).

Federation Archaeology Council. Organization of Federation archaeologists. **Jean-Luc Picard** was asked to give the keynote address at the council's symposium, held aboard the *Enterprise*-D, in 2367. ("QPid" [TNG]).

Federation Astronomical Committee. Agency of the government of the **United Federation of Planets** whose responsibilities included naming celestial objects. ("Eye of the Needle" [VGR]).

Federation Astrophysical Survey. Federation governmental entity that was charged with maintaining current celestial navigation information. ("Masks" [TNG]).

Federation-Cardassian treaty. Agreement that ended hostilities between the **United Federation of Planets** and the **Cardassian Union** in 2370. Negotiations for the treaty were begun in 2367 and lasted for three years. The treaty established new boundaries between Federation and Cardassian space and created a **Demilitarized Zone** between the borders. ("Journey's End" [TNG]). *This is consistent with Captain Jellico's negotiation of the armistice between the Cardassians and the Federation in 2367.*

Federation Code of Justice. Laws governing citizens of the **United Federation of Planets**. The code includes provisions insuring that a defendant is innocent until proven guilty, and if innocent, will be set free. ("The Maquis, Part II" [DS9]). SEE: **Seventh Guarantee; Constitution of the United Federation of Planets; law**.

Federation Constitution. SEE: **Constitution of the United Federation of Planets**.

Federation Council. Governing body consisting of representatives of the member nations of the **United Federation of Planets**. ("Amok Time" [TOS]). The council chambers are located in the city of **San Francisco** on planet **Earth**. The Federation council met to consider Kirk's violation of Starfleet orders, and his theft and destruction of the *U.S.S. Enterprise* was a matter of sufficient gravity that the Council itself deliberated Kirk's fate.

Despite a strong protest from the Klingon government, the Council not only dismissed all but one charge, but also reinstated Kirk as captain of the new ***Starship Enterprise***, NCC-1701-A. *(Star Trek IV: The Voyage Home).* In 2370, in the face of evidence that warp travel was damaging the fabric of space, the Council imposed a warp 5 "speed limit" on all Federation vessels. ("Force of Nature" [TNG]). In 2372, Klingon Chancellor **Gowron** sought Federation support in an invasion of **Cardassia**. Gowron explained that the invasion was necessary because he believed the **Dominon** had gained control of the Cardassian government. The Federation Council condemned Gowron's actions, and Gowron unilaterally cancelled the **Khitomer Accords**, expelled all Federation citizens from the empire and recalled his ambassadors. ("The Way of the Warrior" [DS9]). Shortly thereafter, the Federation Council granted a Cardassian request for economic aid. The council agreed to provide 12 industrial **replicators** to help rebuild the devastated Cardassian industrial base. ("For the Cause" [DS9]). Membership in the council was a considerable honor, and **T'Pau** of Vulcan was the only person to have refused a seat in that august body. ("Amok Time" [TOS]). SEE: **Federation President**.

Federation Day. A holiday celebrating the founding of the **United Federation of Planets** in 2161. ("The Outcast" [TNG]).

Federation Department of Temporal Investigations. Federation governmental agency. Temporal Investigations concerned itself with assessing potential damage to the flow of history caused by time travelers. Agents of the Department of Temporal Investigations included **Dulmer** and **Lucsly**, who investigated an incident in which the *Starship Defiant* traveled from the year 2373 back to 2267. ("Trials and Tribble-ations" [DS9]).

Federation Grand Jury. Panel of citizens who evaluated judicial cases to determine if evidence warranted an indictment. In 2373, a Federation Grand Jury hearing was to have convened on planet Inferna Prime. At the hearing, Ferengi entrepreneur Quark was to have given testimony against the **Orion Syndicate**, as he was a witness to their activities. ("The Ascent" [DS9]).

Federation Penal Settlement. Institution located in New Zealand on Earth where criminals were rehabilitated. **Thomas Paris** was a prisoner there in 2371, until released by special arrangement with Captain Kathryn Janeway. ("Caretaker" [VGR]). **Richard Bashir** was sentenced to two years at the facility after pleading guilty in 2373 to illegal genetic engineering. ("Doctor Bashir, I Presume?" [DS9]).

Federation President. (Robert Ellenstein; Kurtwood Smith; Herschel Sparber). Leader of the representative council governing the **United Federation of Planets.** The Federation president *(played by Robert Ellenstein)* warned all spaceships to stay away from Earth when that planet's environment was being devastated by an alien space probe in 2286. *(Star Trek IV: The Voyage Home).* A later president *(played by Kurtwood Smith)* was in office when a massive ecological disaster forced the Klingon government to make unprecedented peace overtures to the Federation. These initiatives were disrupted by forces seeking to maintain the status quo, but the president avoided degeneration of the situation by adhering to the articles of interstellar law. An attempt was made on the president's life at the Khitomer conference by Starfleet **Colonel West**, but the president was saved by Captain Kirk. The Federation president's office is located in the city of Paris on planet Earth. *(Star Trek VI: The Undiscovered Country).* The Federation president in 2372 was **Jaresh-Inyo**, whose administration was marked by fears of possible infiltration by **Founders**, and an attempted coup by Starfleet **Admiral Leyton**. ("Homefront" [DS9], "Paradise Lost" [DS9]). *The Federation president in* Star Trek VI *had makeup identical to that of the navigator aboard the ill-fated* U.S.S. **Saratoga** *in* Star Trek IV, *so one might assume that both individuals were members of the same species. Robert Ellenstein, who played the president in* Star Trek IV, *also played* ***Steven Miller*** *in "Haven" (TNG). Kurtwood Smith served in* Star Trek VI, *while Herschel Sparber* (pictured) *was the president in "Homefront" (DS9) and "Paradise Lost" (DS9).*

Federation Science Council. Governmental entity charged with advising the Federation on scientific matters. In 2366, Hekaran scientists **Rabal** and **Serova** submitted preliminary research, theorizing that long-term use of warp-speed space travel was damaging the fabric of space. At that time, the Council found insufficient evidence to support Rabal and Serova's theory. ("Force of Nature" [TNG]).

Federation signal buoy. Deep-space beacon used to designate specific areas of Federation space. The **verteron mines** placed in the Hekaras Corridor in 2370 by Hekaran scientists Rabal and Serova were at first thought to be signal buoys. ("Force of Nature" [TNG]).

Federation Supreme Court. Highest judicial body in the Federation. When **Richard Bashir** was accused of illegal genetic engineering in 2373, he wanted to test the law by appealing to the Federation Supreme Court. ("Doctor Bashir, I Presume?" [DS9]).

Federation. SEE: **United Federation of Planets.**

Fek'lhr. (Tom Magee). A mythical **Klingon** beast that was the guardian of ***Gre'thor***. In 2367, **Ardra** appeared on planet **Ventax II** as *Fek'lhr* while trying to convince *Enterprise*-D personnel of her allegedly supernatural powers. Worf was not impressed. ("Devil's Due" [TNG]). SEE: ***Sto-Vo-Kor***. *Kang, in "Day of the Dove" (TOS), noted that the Klingon culture has no devil, so* Fek'lhr *would seem to have a different role in Klingon mythology. Either that, or Ardra didn't know everything about Klingons.*

Felada onion crisps. Hors d'oeuvres. One of Neelix's specialties. ("The Cloud" [VGR]).

Felaran rose. Flowering plant native to a planet in the Delta Quadrant. ("Parturition" [VGR]).

feldomite. Mineral substance. Unfortunately for Quark's finances, a mine on Parsion III struck feldomite in 2373. ("Business As Usual" [DS9]).

felicium. A narcotic substance produced from plants on the planet **Brekka**. Felicium has other medicinal properties, and was used, centuries ago, to cure a deadly plague on neighboring planet **Ornara**. Once the plague was ended, all the people on Ornara were addicted to the drug, and the people of Brekka continued to provide it, for a significant price. ("Symbiosis" [TNG]).

feline supplements, 25, 74, & 221. Cat food designed for **Spot**. Data believed number 25 to be Spot's favorite, but it was hard to tell. ("Data's Day" [TNG], "Force of Nature" [TNG], "Phantasms" [TNG]).

Fellini, Colonel. (Ed Peck). United States Air Force officer who interrogated Captain Kirk when Kirk was arrested at the **Omaha Air Base** on **Earth** in 1969. Kirk was on a covert mission to eliminate records of the *Enterprise*'s accidental presence in Earth's past to avoid the possible contamination of history. Fellini became frustrated with Kirk (who could not answer any questions for fear of causing further contamination), and threatened to lock the captain up for 200 years. Kirk thought that was just about right. ("Tomorrow Is Yesterday" [TOS]). *We assume that the original* Star Trek *series was actually set some 300 years in the future.*

Felton, Ensign. (Shelia Franklin). Conn officer aboard the *Enterprise*-D in 2368. ("A Matter of Time" [TNG], "New Ground"

[TNG], "Hero Worship" [TNG], "Masterpiece Society" [TNG], "Imaginary Friend" [TNG]).

female shape-shifter. SEE: **Founder Leader**.

fencing. Ancient art and sport of swordplay with foils. A hobby of *Enterprise* helm officer **Hikaru Sulu** ("The Naked Time" [TOS]). Jean-Luc Picard enjoyed fencing in the gymnasium of the *Enterprise*-D. ("We'll Always Have Paris" [TNG]).

Fendaus V. Planet. The government on Fendaus V was led by a family whose members have no limbs due to an inbred genetic defect. Data compared this family to the leaders of **Ramatis III**, who are incapable of hearing for similar reasons. ("Loud as a Whisper" [TNG]).

Fenna. (Salli Elise Richardson). Psycho-projective alter ego inadvertently created by **Nidell**, wife of **Professor Gideon Seyetik**. When Nidell experienced deep emotional distress and lost control of her special telepathic abilities, Fenna was the result. Fenna, who was composed of pure energy and looked exactly like Nidell, sought the happiness that Nidell couldn't have. When Nidell met Benjamin Sisko at Deep Space 9 in 2370, the two fell in love. Unfortunately for Sisko, when Nidell's emotional problems were resolved, Fenna ceased to exist. ("Second Sight" [DS9]).

Fento. (John McLiam). An elderly male on planet **Mintaka III**. Fento related many of his people's old legends about an **"Overseer,"** their equivalent of a God, when his people struggled to understand otherwise inexplicable experiences with advanced Federation technology. Fento was left to guard the injured **Dr. Palmer**, and Commander Riker was forced to overpower him to escape with Palmer. ("Who Watches the Watchers?" [TNG]).

***feragoit* goulash**. Vegetable stew. One of Neelix's specialties. ("Parallax" [VGR]).

Ferengi Alliance. Formal name of the Ferengi government.

Ferengi Attainment Ceremony. Ferengi ceremony in which a boy becomes an adult. In 2371 **Nog** completed the Attainment Ceremony. ("Heart of Stone" [DS9]).

Ferengi Benevolent Association. Philanthropic organization established by Grand Nagus **Zek** in 2371 while he was under the influence of the Bajoran **Prophets**, who had removed Zek's acquisitive drives. The organization was funded by Zek's own personal fortune to spread wealth and good fortune to those less fortunate. The association was dissolved after the Prophets restored Zek's original personality. ("Prophet Motive" [DS9]).

Ferengi cargo shuttle. A transport used by the Ferengi Alliance. One of these craft was discovered crashed in the **Hanolin asteroid belt** in early 2368. Remains of the cargo were discovered scattered over one hundred square kilometers. The remains of the Vulcan ship ***T'Pau***'s navigational deflector were found amid the debris, in crates marked "Medical Supplies." ("Unification, Part I" [TNG]).

Ferengi Certificate of Dismemberment. Document certifying the identity of Ferengi remains, accompanying pieces of the deceased's body that are sold as valuable souvenirs. In 2370, Quark tried to sell counterfeit remains of **Plegg**, offering faked Certificates of Dismemberment as proof of authenticity. ("The Alternate" [DS9]). See: **Ferengi death rituals.**

Ferengi Code. A set of ethical guidelines governing behavior of **Ferengi** citizens. Among its provisions is a clause requiring the lives of subordinates be offered in payment for a superior's dishonorable deeds. ("The Last Outpost" [TNG]). Ferengi By-Laws section 105, subparagraph 10 states, "Upon reaching adulthood, Ferengi males must purchase an apprenticeship from a suitable role model." ("Heart of Stone" [DS9]). SEE: **Ferengi Rules of Acquisition; Ferengi Salvage Code; Ferengi Trade By-Laws**

Ferengi Commerce Authority. Agency of the **Ferengi** government concerned with business practices and the enforcement of trade laws. The offices of the agency were located on the 40th floor of the **Tower of Commerce** on **Ferenginar**. Abbreviated as FCA. ("Family Business" [DS9]). SEE: **Liquidator; Writ of Accountability**.

Ferengi death rituals. Customs associated with the treatment of the body of a deceased **Ferengi**. Autopsy is strictly prohibited. ("Suspicions" [TNG]). To honor the dead, the deceased's body was cut into small pieces that were sealed into disk-shaped souvenir containers, then sold. These disks became valuable collector's items if the dead Ferengi was a personage of note. A **Ferengi Certificate of Dismemberment** accompanied the souvenir, attesting to the identity of the remains. ("The Alternate" [DS9], "Melora" [DS9]). Ferengi believe that those who have earned a profit during their mortal lives can enter the **Divine Treasury** after death. There, under the guidance of the Blessed Exchequer, the Celestial Auctioneers allow them to bid on new lives. Those who have not earned a profit are thought to be doomed to the **Vault of Eternal Destitution**. ("Little Green Men" [DS9]).

Ferengi Futures Exchange. Market based on **Ferenginar**, facilitating sale of commodities and securities upon agreement of future delivery. While under the impression that he was dying of Dorek syndrome in 2372, Quark put 52 disks of his vacuum-desiccated remains on the Ferengi Futures Exchange. SEE: **Ferengi death rituals**. ("Body Parts" [DS9]).

Ferengi lobes. Reference to the ears of a **Ferengi**, a Ferengi male in particular, and to his business prowess. If a Ferengi is not good at a business-related skill, it is said that "he doesn't have the lobes for it." This is considered to be a sexist remark, since Ferengi females generally have smaller ears than males. ("Heart of Stone" [DS9]). When a Ferengi displays exceptionally keen business skills, it is said that "He has the lobes." ("Starship Down" [DS9]). A Ferengi's lobes are considered to be highly erogenous. ("Ménage à Troi" [TNG]). SEE: ***oo-mox***.

Ferengi Marauder. Starship type used by the **Ferengi Alliance**. Sophisticated vessels, some Marauders were equipped with the ability to fire a powerful plasma energy burst, capable of disabling a *Galaxy*-class starship. First encounter with the Federation was in 2364 near planet **Gamma Tauri IV**. ("The Last Outpost" [TNG]). This ship was designated as a *D'Kora*-class vessel, with a crew of 450. ("Force of Nature" [TNG]). *The Ferengi ship was designed by Andrew Probert and built by Greg Jein. The Marauder made its first appearance in "The Last Outpost" and was also seen in "The Battle" (TNG), "Peak Performance" (TNG), "The Price" (TNG), "Ménage à Troi" (TNG), and "Rascals" (TNG).*

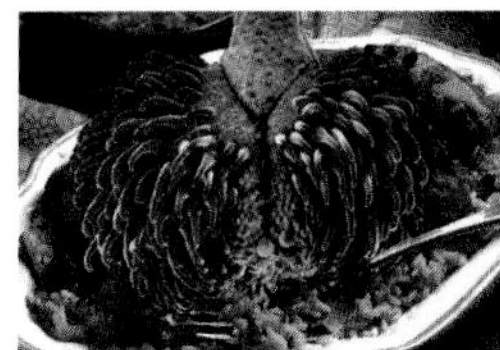

Ferengi spore pie. Delicacy available at the **Replimat** on station Deep Space 9. *The spore pie was never mentioned in dialog, but a photo of this delicious dish, created by scenic artist Doug Drexler, was seen on the wall of the Replimat.*

Ferengi Rules of Acquisition, Revised. An antithetically benevolent version of the **Ferengi Rules of Acquisition**, revised for the modern **Ferengi**, devised by Grand Nagus **Zek** in 2371 after his encounter with the Bajoran **Prophets**. Some of these radically altered rules included: Revised Rule #1: "If they want their money back, give it to them." Revised Rule #10: "Greed is dead." Revised Rule #21: "Never place profit before friendship." Revised Rule #22: "Latinum tarnishes, but family is forever." Revised Rule #23: "Money can never replace dignity." Revised Rule #285: "A good deed is its own reward." These rules were rescinded and all copies were destroyed shortly after the Prophets restored Zek's original personality. ("Prophet Motive" [DS9]).

Ferengi Rules of Acquisition. Words to live by in the **Ferengi** culture. Male Ferengi children are expected to memorize these pearls of wisdom and repeat them on command. ("The Nagus" [DS9]). Ferengi females are, however, forbidden to quote from the rules, due to their status as second-class citizens. There are 285 Rules of Acquisition. ("Rules of Acquisition" [DS9]). They were written tenmillennia ago by **Gint**, the first grand nagus, and his cronies. ("Body Parts" [DS9]).

The First Rule of Acquisition: "Once you have their money, you never give it back." ("The Nagus" [DS9]).

3rd Rule: "Never spend more for an acquisition than you have to." (The Maquis, Part II" [DS9]).

6th Rule: "Never allow family to stand in the way of opportunity." ("The Nagus" [DS9]).

7th Rule: "Keep your ears open." ("In the Hands of the Prophets" [DS9]).

9th Rule: "Opportunity plus instinct equals profit." ("The Storyteller" [DS9]).

10th Rule: "Greed is eternal." ("Prophet Motive" [DS9]).

16th Rule: "A deal is a deal." ("Melora" [DS9]).

17th Rule: "A contract is a contract is a contract. But only between Ferengi." ("Body Parts" [DS9]).

18th Rule: "A Ferengi without profit is no Ferengi at all." ("Heart of Stone" [DS9]).

21st Rule: "Never place friendship above profit." ("Rules of Acquisition" [DS9]).

22nd Rule: "A wise man can hear profit in the wind." ("Rules of Acquisition" [DS9]).

31st Rule: "Never make fun of a Ferengi's mother." ("The Siege" [DS9]).

33rd Rule: "It never hurts to suck up to the boss." ("Rules of Acquisition" [DS9]).

34th Rule: "War is good for business." ("Destiny" [DS9]).

35th Rule: "Peace is good for business." ("Destiny" [DS9]).

47th Rule: "Don't trust a man wearing a better suit than your own." ("Rivals" [DS9]).

48th Rule: "The bigger the smile, the sharper the knife." ("Rules of Acquisition" [DS9]).

57th Rule: "Good customers are as rare as latinum. Treasure them." ("Armageddon Game" [DS9]).

59th Rule: "Free advice is seldom cheap." ("Rules of Acquisition" [DS9]).

62nd Rule: "The riskier the road, the greater the profit." ("Rules of Acquisition" [DS9]).

75th Rule: "Home is where the heart is, but the stars are made of latinum." ("Civil Defense" [DS9]).

76th Rule: "Every once in a while, declare peace. It confuses the hell out of your enemies!" ("The Homecoming" [DS9]).

95th Rule: "Expand or die." ("False Profits" [VGR]).

102nd Rule: "Nature decays, but latinum lasts forever" ("The Jem'Hadar" [DS9]).

103rd Rule: "Sleep can interfere with..." ("Rules of Acquisition" [DS9]). *Unfortunately, Pel was interrupted before she could finish reciting this particular rule, so we don't know exactly what it is that sleep interferes with.*

109th Rule: "Dignity and an empty sack is worth a sack." ("Rivals" [DS9]).

111th Rule: "Treat people in your debt like family. Exploit them." ("Past Tense, Part I" [DS9], "The Darkness and the Light" [DS9]).

112th Rule: "Never have sex with the boss's sister." ("Playing God" [DS9]).

139th Rule: "Wives serve, brothers inherit." ("Necessary Evil" [DS9]).

194th Rule: "It's always good business to know about your customers before they walk in your door." ("Whispers" [DS9]).

203rd Rule: "New customers are like razor-toothed gree-worms. They can be succulent, but sometimes they bite back." ("Little Green Men" [DS9]).

211th Rule: "Employees are the rungs on the ladder of success. Don't hesitate to step on them." ("Bar Association" [DS9]).

214th Rule: "Never begin a business negotiation on an empty stomach." (The Maquis, Part I" [DS9]).

217th Rule: "You can't free a fish from water." ("Past Tense, Part I" [DS9]).

239th Rule: "Never be afraid to mislabel a product." ("Body Parts" [DS9]).

263rd Rule: "Never allow doubt to tarnish your lust for latinum." ("Bar Association" [DS9]).

285th Rule: "No good deed ever goes unpunished." ("The Collaborator" [DS9]).

The rules were the brainchild of executive producer-writer Ira Steven Behr, who elucidated further on these pearls in his books, The Rules of Acquisition *and* The Legends of the Ferengi, *published by Pocket Books. Ira insists that his books are a considerable bargain, worth many times their purchase price. The rules were first mentioned in "The Nagus" (DS9). Early in 2371, Quark suggested that a 286th rule be added to the list: "When Morn leaves, it's all over." ("House of Quark" [DS9]). One rule, whose number was not given, states: "Exploitation begins at home." In 2373, while posing as the grand proxy, Neelix told Arridor and Kol that Rule #299 was "When you exploit someone, it never hurts to thank them." ("False Profits" [VGR]).*

Ferengi Salvage Code. One of several Ferengi codes. The Salvage Code states that anything found abandoned is open to claim by those who find it. The Ferengi who took over the *Enterprise*-D in 2369 claimed it under the Ferengi Salvage Code. ("Rascals" [TNG]).

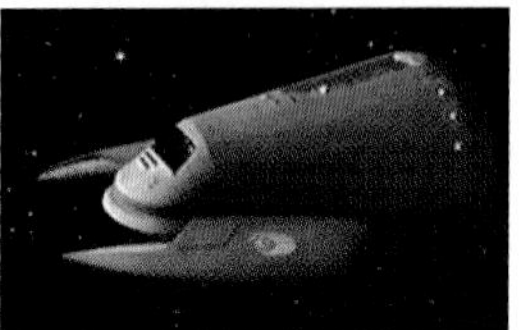

Ferengi shuttle. Small two-person vessel used for short-range transport, also known as a Ferengi pod. Once such a shuttle, carried aboard a Ferengi Marauder ship and piloted by **Dr. Arridor** and **Kol** into the **Barzan wormhole**, was lost when the pilot activated the shuttle's warp drive, causing the wormhole's terminus to move unexpectedly. ("The Price" [TNG]). Shortly thereafter, Arridor and Kol became stranded on the **Takarian** homeworld in the Delta Quadrant. Several years later, Arridor and Kol left the planet under pressure from the crew of the *U.S.S. Voyager*. When Arridor and Kol tried to return to the Takarian planet, they accidentally destabilized the Barzan wormhole, knocking it off its subspace axis. The fate of the shuttle remains unknown. ("False Profits" [VGR]). In 2368, the *Enterprise*-D rescued the crew of a Ferengi shuttle that reported a serious containment breach. The "accident" was later found to be a ruse by the crew, members of a **Ferengi Trade Mission**, so they could make their way aboard the *Enterprise*-D. ("The Perfect Mate" [TNG]). SEE: **Lenor, Par**.

military uniform military uniform civilian civilian civilian grand nagus civilian

Ferengi Trade By-Laws. Law pertaining to **Ferengi** business practices. Subsection 1027, paragraph 3 of the By-Laws pertained to the improper supervision of a family member. **Quark** was charged with violation of that article when his mother was accused by the **Ferengi Commerce Authority** of earning profit. ("Family Business" [DS9]).

Ferengi Trade Mission. A Ferengi diplomatic team intended to further Ferengi business interests. **Par Lenor** and **Qol** were members of this mission in 2368. ("The Perfect Mate" [TNG]).

Ferengi trading vessel. Starship operating under the auspices of the Ferengi Alliance. In late 2369, one of these vessels was mistaken for an attacking **Borg** ship when it entered the **New Berlin** system. ("Descent, Part I" [TNG]).

Ferengi welcoming ceremony. Traditional exchange spoken when a guest enters a Ferengi home. The exchange goes as follows. Host: "Welcome to our home. Place your imprint on the legal waivers and deposit your admission fee in the box by the door. Remember, my house is my house." Guest: "As are its contents." ("Family Business" [DS9]).

Ferengi whip. Handheld **Ferengi** weapon used to fire high-energy plasma discharges at a target. ("The Last Outpost" [TNG]). *The Ferengi whip fell into disuse after "The Last Outpost," and later episodes showed the Ferengi armed with a variety of phaser-like handheld pistol weapons.*

Ferengi. Technologically sophisticated humanoid civilization that was long a complete mystery to the Federation prior to first contact at planet **Delphi Ardu** in 2364 ("The Last Outpost" [TNG]). Originally from the planet **Ferenginar**, by the 24th century, the Ferengi were an interstellar culture. ("Family Business" [DS9]). It took the Ferengi 10,000 years from the time they first started using currency to establish the Ferengi Alliance. The Ferengi extended their culture on an interstellar scale by buying warp drive technology. ("Little Green Men" [DS9]). *We don't know from whom they bought warp drive.* Possessing a strict code of honor, Ferengi philosophy ruthlessly embraces the principles of capitalism. Ferengi culture finds the concept of organized labor to be abhorrent, since such things can interfere with the exploitation of workers. Similarly, Ferengi labor contracts never provide for sick leave, vacations, or paid overtime for employees. ("Bar Association" [DS9]). SEE: **Ferengi Rules of Acquisition**. Ferengi consider the sanctity of a contract to be a cornerstone of their civilization. Breaking a contract is unthinkable, and will generally result in the offender having his Ferengi business license revoked and all of his assets seized, and him becoming a pariah in Ferengi society. ("Body Parts" [DS9]). The Ferengi are sexist in the extreme, and do not allow their females the honor of clothing. ("The Last Outpost" [TNG]). In addition, Ferengi females are kept house-bound, uneducated, and wholly dependent on their male counterparts. It is illegal for Ferengi females to earn profit, or to quote from the Rules of Acquisition. ("Rules of Acquisition" [DS9]). They are also forbidden to travel or to talk to strangers. Ferengi tradition requires the females of the family to prepare and serve meals, and to soften the food for the males by chewing it for them. ("Family Business" [DS9]). SEE: ***oo-mox***. Interestingly, Ferengi males often find human females very attractive. ("The Last Outpost" [TNG]). Ferengi consider pregnancy to be a rental, with the father being termed the lessee. ("Nor the Battle to the Strong" [DS9]). When a young Ferengi reaches adulthood and prepares to leave home, he traditionally raises capital by auctioning his boyhood treasures. ("Little Green Men" [DS9]). Betazoids are incapable of empathically reading Ferengi minds. This may be due to the unusual four-lobed design of Ferengi brains. ("Ménage à Troi" [TNG], "The Loss" [TNG]). Dopterians, whose brains are structurally similar to those of the Ferengi, are similarly unreadable by Betazoids. ("The Forsaken" [DS9]). Ferengi have ascending ribs and an upper and lower lung. ("Bar Association" [DS9]). Shortly after first contact with the Federation, Ferengi entrepreneurs saw new opportunities and quickly assimilated themselves into Federation commerce, such as **Quark**, a Ferengi who established a bar at Deep Space 9. ("Emissary" [DS9]). The Ferengi are not members of the Federation. ("False Profits" [VGR]). Ferengi entrepreneurs served as intermediaries for the **Karemma** in commerce with the Federation. The Karemma sought this arrangement because the Dominion would not have tolerated direct trade with the Federation. ("Starship Down" [DS9]). One Ferengi quotation says, "Never ask when you can take." ("Babel" [DS9]). Another Ferengi saying is, "Good things come in small packages." ("Move Along Home" [DS9]). SEE: **Ferengi death rituals**. *Although the first known contact between the Federation and the Ferengi took place in 2364 ("The Last Outpost" [TNG]), Picard and the* Stargazer *were attacked some years earlier at Zeta Maxia by a ship that they did not realize was Ferengi. ("The Battle" [TNG]). The Ferengi were first seen in "The Last Outpost" (TNG). Their makeup was first designed and sketched by Andrew Probert, then refined and produced by Michael Westmore.*

Ferenginar. Class-M planet. **Ferengi** homeworld and center of the **Ferengi Alliance**. Ferenginar was the location of the **Sacred Marketplace** and the **Tower of Commerce**.

("Family Business" [DS9]). Ferenginar has an extremely wet climate, so much so that the Ferengi language has 178 different words for rain. They also have no word for crisp. ("Let He Who Is Without Sin..." [DS9]). A terrible financial decline struck Ferenginar in the mid-24th century, causing rampant inflation and currency devaluation. This catastrophe became known as the Great Monetary Collapse. ("Homefront" [DS9]).

Fermat's last theorem. A mathematical puzzle devised by 17th-century French mathematician Pierre de Fermat (1601-1665), who claimed to have developed a proof for the theorem that there is no whole number N where X to the Nth power, plus Y to the Nth, equals Z to the Nth, where N is greater than 2. Following Fermat's death, his notes indicated he had devised a "remarkable proof" of the theorem, but no one has yet been able to figure out what it might have been, including amateur scientist Jean-Luc Picard. ("The Royale" [TNG]). *After the episode was produced in 1989, a Princeton University professor, Andrew Wiles, developed a proof of Fermat's theorem.*

***Fermi*, Shuttlecraft.** *Enterprise*-D shuttlecraft #09, destroyed in 2369 after being enveloped by a molecular reversion field that reduced its crew to children. ("Rascals" [TNG]). *Named for Enrico Fermi, the 20th-century Italian-American physicist who developed the first nuclear fission reactor.*

Ferris, Galactic High Commissioner. (John Crawford). Federation bureaucrat who was assigned to the *Enterprise* to oversee the delivery of medical supplies to planet **Makus III** for transfer to the **New Paris colonies** in 2267. Ferris opposed a scientific shuttle mission just prior to the transfer, on the grounds that it might delay the transfer. Ferris's objections were borne out when the shuttlecraft was lost during the investigation, but the *Enterprise* was able to make the Makus III rendezvous after recovering most of the shuttle's crew. ("The *Galileo* Seven" [TOS]).

ferroplasmic infusion. Procedure by which high energy plasma, directed through an infusion device, is injected into a planetary body. Ferroplasmic infusion was used by the crew of the *Enterprise*-D in 2370 in order to re-liquefy the mantle core of planet **Atrea IV**. ("Inheritance" [TNG]).

***Fesarius*.** Flagship of the **First Federation**, commanded by **Balok**. Following first contact with the *Fesarius* by the original *Enterprise* in 2266, crew member **Lieutenant Bailey** remained with *Fesarius* Commander Balok as a cultural envoy. ("The Corbomite Maneuver" [TOS]). *Miniature designed by Matt Jefferies.*

Festival of Lights. Celebration held during ***Ha'mara***, the Bajoran holiday held on the anniversary of the **Emissary**'s arrival. ("Starship Down" [DS9]).

Festival. Also known as the **Red Hour** on planet **Beta III**. ("Return of the Archons" [TOS]).

***Feynman*, Shuttlecraft.** *Enterprise*-D shuttlecraft. The *Feynman* was taken by Captain Picard, Dr. Crusher, and Lieutenant Worf to planet **Torman V**. ("Chain of Command, Part I" [TNG]). *The shuttlecraft* Feynman *was named for Dr. Richard Feynman (1918-1988), noted Nobel physicist and bongo player. The name was misspelled as* Feyman *on the shuttle's exterior because of a mistake made in the art department.*

FGC-13 cluster. Stellar cluster near the Amargosa Diaspora. The *Enterprise*-D charted FGC-13 in 2369. ("Schisms" [TNG]).

FGC-47. Nebula that is home to a life-form based on cohesive plasma strands that feed on the gravity fields generated by the neutron star at the center of the nebula. The *Enterprise*-D explored FGC-47 in 2368, when it made contact with the life-forms living there. ("Imaginary Friend" [TNG]). SEE: **Isabella**. *FGC probably stands for* Federation General Catalog, *a variation of a real astronomical text, the* New General Catalogue (NGC), *by J. L. E. Dreyer, first published in 1888.*

Ficus Sector. Destination of the colony ship ***S.S. Mariposa***, launched from Earth in 2123. The *Mariposa* settled colonists on planet **Bringloid V** and later crashed on the planet **Mariposa** while settling a second group of colonists. ("Up the Long Ladder" [TNG]).

field coils. SEE: **warp field coils.**

field diverters. Device utilized to isolate areas of starships from the decontaminating plasma field of a **baryon sweep.** Field diverters were used to protect the ship's computer core and bridge. Multiple diverters on a starship required synchronization in order to be effective. ("Starship Mine" [TNG]).

field docent. In the Trill **initiate** program, a joined **Trill** who shepherded a host candidate through a field training program, allowing the candidate to observe the activities of a joined Trill over a two-week period. ("Playing God" [DS9]). SEE: **Arjin; Dax, Curzon; Dax, Jadzia**.

field training. Educational class taught in a real work environment, not in a classroom. Lieutenant Tuvok offered field training to former Maquis members of the *Voyager* crew in late 2371. The class was intended to help those crew members adjust to Starfleet discipline. The course included physical training, academic studies, and simulated tactical situations. Four former Maquis crew members took the course: **Kenneth Dalby**, **Mariah Henley**, **Gerron,** and **Chell**. ("Learning Curve" [VGR]).

Fifth House of Betazed. A family that is still considered something of royalty to the inhabitants of **Betazed**. Ambassador **Lwaxana Troi** was a daughter of the Fifth House. ("Haven" [TNG]).

Filian python. Type of large snake that burrows in the ground. ("The Begotten" [DS9]).

filter masks. Protective breathing device intended to protect against the debilitating effects of the **zenite** gas found in the mines on planet **Ardana**. ("The Cloud Minders" [TOS]).

Fima system. Planetary system in the Delta Quadrant. The **Enaran** people maintained a colony in the Fima system. ("Remember" [VGR]).

Fina Prime. Planet in the Delta Quadrant. An outbreak of the deadly Viidian **phage** struck planet Fina Prime in 2372. ("Lifesigns" [VGR]).

Finagle's Folly. Beverage concocted by Dr. McCoy, who claimed he was famous for the libation "from here to Orion." ("The Ultimate Computer" [TOS]).

Finagle's Law. "Any home port the ship makes will be somebody else's ... not mine." Kirk quoted Finagle's Law to Spock when they received a message diverting them from Vulcan to planet **Altair VI**. ("Amok Time" [TOS]).

"Final Mission." *Next Generation* episode #83. Teleplay by Kasey Arnold-Ince and Jeri Taylor. Story by Kasey Arnold-Ince. Directed by Corey Allen. Stardate 44307.3. *First aired in 1990. Wesley Crusher must care for Captain Picard when the two are stranded on a desert planet by a shuttle crash. This was the episode in which Wil Wheaton as Wesley Crusher left the series as a regular.* GUEST CAST: Nick Tate as **Dirgo**; Kim Hamilton as **Songi, Chairman**; Mary Kohnert as **Allenby, Ensign Tess**. SEE: **Allenby, Ensign Tess; Boothby; construction module; Crusher, Wesley; Dirgo; *dresci*; ermanium; Gamelan V; hyronalin; Lambda Paz; Meltasion asteroid belt; *Nenebek*; noncorporeal life; Pentarus II; Pentarus V; salenite miners; sentry; Songi, Chairman; sonodanite.**

final ritual. Drayan ceremony in which elderly **Drayans** near death are taken to a sacred moon on which they may die in peace. ("Innocence" [VGR]).

Finding and Winning Your Perfect Mate. Book written by Dr. Jennings Rain, an expert in humanoid interpersonal relationships. ("In Purgatory's Shadow" [DS9]).

Finiis'ral. Kriosian term for the final stage in the sexual maturation of an **empathic metamorph**. During *Finiis'ral*, the metamorph produces an elevated level of sexual **pheromones** and is extremely vulnerable to the empathic emanations of the opposite sex. The empath's behavior can change frequently to suit the needs of potential mates. **Kamala**, an empathic metamorph, was in the final stages of the *Finiis'ral* when she traveled aboard the *Enterprise*-D in 2368 for the **Ceremony of Reconciliation** between **Krios** and **Valt**. Her effect on the male members of the crew was, to say the least, interesting. ("The Perfect Mate" [TNG]).

Finn, Kyril. (Richard Cox). The charismatic leader of the **Ansata** terrorists on planet **Rutia IV** in 2366. Finn abducted Dr. Crusher and Captain Picard of the Federation starship *Enterprise*-D in 2366, hoping to force the Federation into becoming involved in the Ansata struggle for independence. A complicated man, Finn twisted the efforts of the crew to rescue Crusher into threats to his cause, and began to make Dr. Crusher doubt her beliefs about the Federation position on **Rutia IV**. Finn was killed in 2366 by **Alexana Devos** when **Rutian** security forces located the Ansata base with help from *Enterprise*-D personnel. ("The High Ground" [TNG]).

Finn, Marla E. (Nora Leonhardt). Starfleet officer who helped build the *Enterprise*-D at **Utopia Planitia Fleet Yards** in 2363. She was romantically involved with Lieutenant **Walter Pierce**, but also had an affair with another man. Starfleet believed Finn had been killed in a plasma explosion at Utopia Planitia on stardate 40987.2, about a year prior to the ship's launch. It was not learned until years later that she and her male friend had been killed by Pierce, who had caused the plasma explosion out of jealousy. ("Eye of the Beholder" [TNG]). *Nora Leonhardt was a regular stand-in and extra on* Star Trek: The Next Generation. *She worked as Marina Sirtis's stand-in, and could occasionally be seen as a background* Enterprise-*D crew member. Of course, when Nora was seen on the ship, she could not have been Marla Finn, since Finn was killed before the first episode of the show.*

Finnea Prime. A non-Federation world. **Orion Syndicate** member **Draim** had his base of operations on Finnea Prime. ("A Simple Investigation" [DS9]).

Finnegan. (Bruce Mars). Starfleet officer. Finnegan was an upperclassman and arch rival of James Kirk during his academy days in 2252. Finnegan delighted in playing practical jokes on Kirk. A replica of Finnegan was created on the **amusement park planet** in 2267, giving Kirk the chance to finally best his nemesis. ("Shore Leave" [TOS]). *Actor Bruce Mars also played a New York police officer in "Assignment: Earth" (TOS).*

Finney, Ben. (Richard Webb). Starfleet officer. Finney was an instructor at Starfleet Academy when **James Kirk** was a midshipman. The two men were good friends, and Ben Finney's daughter, Jamie, was named after Kirk. Later, when both were assigned to the ***U.S.S. Republic***, Ensign Kirk relieved Finney on watch and found a circuit open to the atomic matter piles that might have blown up the ship if it had not been closed. Kirk closed the switch and logged the incident, causing Finney to draw a reprimand and then be moved to the bottom of the promotion list. Finney was bitter about the incident for years, although he later accepted a position as records officer aboard the *Enterprise* under Kirk's command. In 2267, Finney staged his own death in an unsuccessful attempt to frame Kirk for murder. ("Court Martial" [TOS]). SEE: **ion storm**.

Finney, Jamie. (Alice Rawlings). **Ben Finney**'s daughter, named after **James T. Kirk**. ("Court Martial" [TOS]).

finoplak. A colorless liquid solvent, capable of dissolving Starfleet-issue fabrics, but harmless to **bioplast** sheeting. **Kivas Fajo** used one hundred **denkirs** of finoplak to melt Data's uniform. ("The Most Toys" [TNG]).

Fire Plains. Particularly inhospitable stretch of land on planet **Vulcan**. ("Innocence" [VGR]).

fire ants. Destructive and venomous mound-building red ants, *Solenopsis saevissima*, native to Earth, whose bites are particularly irritating to humanoids. ("The Chute" [VGR]).

fire beast of Sullus. Creature from **Drayan** folklore. A popular Drayan folktale told of the fire beast of Sullus. ("Innocence" [VGR]).

fire caves. Location on planet **Bajor** where **Pah-wraiths** were imprisoned. ("The Assignment" [DS9]). Ben Sisko hoped to take his son, Jake, to see the fire caverns in 2369 after the Bajoran Gratitude Festival. ("The Nagus" [DS9]).

fire snakes. Reptilian species. Wixiban told Neelix that the **Kolaati** were as mean as fire snakes. ("Fair Trade" [VGR]).

fire suppression system. System aboard starships that automatically extinguishes flames. ("Deadlock" [VGR]).

fireboxes. Term used by the inhabitants of planet **Omega IV** to describe Starfleet **phaser**s. ("The Omega Glory" [TOS]).

firefighting. Aboard Federation starships, a variety of systems were used to combat fires. Most habitable areas were equipped with containment field generators used to create a small force field around any fires. This would deprive the fire of atmospheric oxygen, extinguishing it. Handheld extinguishers were also available. In an extreme emergency, some parts of a ship could also be vented into the vacuum of space. ("Up the Long Ladder" [TNG], "New Ground" [TNG]).

firomactal drive. Fictional computer device that Riker made up to confuse the Ferengi who took over the *Enterprise*-D in 2369. ("Rascals" [TNG]).

First City. Seat of government for the Klingon Empire. Located on the **Klingon Homeworld**, site of the **Great Hall**. Worf and Picard visited the First City in 2366 to defend Worf's late father against charges brought by council member **Duras**. ("Sins of the Father" [TNG]). Worf returned to the First City a year later to support the **Gowron** regime during the Klingon civil war. ("Redemption, Parts I and II" [TNG]). *The skyline of the First City was a matte painting created by Illusion Arts.*

"First Contact." *Next Generation* episode #89. Teleplay by Dennis Russell Bailey & David Bischoff and Joe Menosky & Ronald D. Moore and Michael Piller. Story by Marc Scott Zicree. Directed by Cliff Bole. No stardate given in episode. *First aired in 1991. Riker is captured by the paranoid inhabitants of a technologically emerging planet, jeopardizing future relations with the Federation. Not to be confused with the feature film* Star Trek: First Contact. GUEST CAST: George Coe as **Durken, Chancellor Avel**; Carolyn Seymour as **Yale, Mirasta**; George Hearn as **Berel**; Michael Ensign as **Krola**; Steven Anderson as **Nilrem**; Sachi Parker as **Tava**; Bebe Neuwirth as **Lanel**. SEE: **Berel; Durken, Chancellor Avel; first contact; Garth system; Jakara, Rivas; Klingon Empire; Krola; Lanel; Malcor III; Malcorians; Marta community; Nilrem; quadroline; Sikla Medical Facility; Tava; telencephalon; terminus; Yale, Mirasta.**

"First Duty, The." *Next Generation* episode #119. Written by Ronald D. Moore & Naren Shankar. Directed by Paul Lynch. Stardate 45703.9. *First aired in 1992. An accident at Starfleet Academy leaves one of Wesley Crusher's classmates dead, and Wesley is pressured to participate in a cover-up.* GUEST CAST: Ray Walston as **Boothby**; Robert Duncan McNeill as **Locarno, Cadet First Class Nicholas**; Ed Lauter as **Albert, Lieutenant Commander**; Richard Fancy as **Satelk, Captain**; Jacqueline Brookes as **Brand, Admiral**; Wil Wheaton as **Crusher, Wesley**; Walker Brandt as **Hajar, Cadet Second Class Jean**; Shannon Fill as **Sito Jaxa**. SEE: **academy flight range; academy range officer; Albert, Joshua; Albert, Lieutenant Commander; *Apollo* 11; bicaridine treatments; Boothby; Brand, Admiral; Calgary; Crusher, Wesley; diamond slot formation; Hajar, Cadet Second Class Jean; Immelmann turn; Kolvoord Starburst; Locarno, Cadet First Class Nicholas; metorapan treatments; Mimas; Nova Squadron; Picard, Jean-Luc; Satelk, Captain; Saturn NavCon; Saturn; Sito Jaxa; Starfleet Academy; Statistical Mechanics; Titan; Yeager Loop.**

First Federation. Interstellar political entity under whose aegis the spacecraft ***Fesarius*** was operated under the command of **Balok**. First contact with the United Federation of Planets was made with the *Starship Enterprise* in 2266, at which time *Enterprise* **Lieutenant Bailey** remained aboard the *Fesarius* as a cultural envoy. ("The Corbomite Maneuver" [TOS]).

First Hebitian civilization. Ancient people of **Cardassia**. The burial vaults of the Hebitians were uncovered on Cardassia in the late 2160s. The tombs were said to be magnificent and were reputed to have been filled with many jeweled artifacts, symbols of ancient Cardassian glory. ("Chain of Command, Part II" [TNG]).

First Meal. Celebration on planet **Meridian**, commemorating the Meridian inhabitants' brief return to corporeal form every 60 years. In 2371, Commander **Benjamin Sisko** and the crew from the ***Starship Defiant*** shared First Meal with the Meridians ("Meridian" [DS9]).

First One. On planet **Ligon II**, title given to a spouse, male or female. **Ligonian** culture permits polygamous relationships, and a second spouse was called a "Second One." ("Code of Honor" [TNG]). SEE: **Lutan**.

First Republic. Ancient **Bajoran** government. An old library on Bajor containing manuscripts that dated from before the fall of the First Republic was reopened in 2371. ("Explorers" [DS9]). *It was not clear if the 800-year-old plans for Sisko's* ***Bajoran solar-sail vessel*** *were an artifact of the First Republic. It is possible that the First Republic was very much older, since "Ensign Ro" (TNG) implies that Bajoran civilization flourished some 25 millennia ago, and "Rapture" (DS9) establishes that B'hala city disappeared some 20 millennia ago.*

First Rule of Acquisition. SEE: **Ferengi Rules of Acquisition.**

first contact. Sociological term for a civilization's initial meeting with extraterrestrial life, often referring to first contact with representatives of the **United Federation of Planets**. First contact is perhaps the most risky and unpredictable of all of Starfleet's missions, because of the enormous risk of sociological impact for the civilization being contacted. Numerous Federation and Starfleet policies govern the conduct of first contacts. Among these are the **Prime Directive**, which prohibits interference with the normal development of any society, particularly a culture less technologically advanced than the Federation. ("Tin Man" [TNG]). Under the Prime Directive, first contact is generally avoided until a civilization has attained significant spaceflight capabilities. Another policy calls for covert surveillance of many cultures prior to first contact, enabling Federation sociologists to anticipate probable reactions. This directive was instituted after the disastrous initial contact with the **Klingon Empire** led to decades of war. ("First Contact" [TNG]). Starfleet's current first-contact guidelines were written by **Captain McCoullough**. ("Move Along Home" [DS9]). The first diplomatic first-contact mission from the **Gamma Quadrant** to pass through the **Bajoran wormhole** into the **Alpha Quadrant** was the **Wadi** gaming delegation that visited station Deep Space 9 in 2369. ("Move Along Home" [DS9]). **Earth**'s first official contact with extraterrestrial life took place on April 5, 2063. Space pioneer **Zefram Cochrane**, who had just completed his world's first faster-than-light spaceflight, had attracted the attention of a passing **Vulcan** survey ship. The ship followed Cochrane back to Earth, landing in the state of Montana in the North American continent, where Cochrane became the first human to officially greet beings from another world (*pictured*). This first contact spawned a new age of peace and progress for Cochrane's war-torn planet. *(Star Trek: First Contact). Other* Star Trek *episodes and movies have established other alien landings on Earth that predated Cochrane's contact, but his was the pivotal first contact that changed history.*

first maje. SEE: **maje**.

"Firstborn." *Next Generation* episode #173. Story by Mark Kalbfeld. Teleplay by René Echevarria. Directed by Jonathan West. Stardate 47779.4. *First aired in 1994. An enigmatic family friend gives Worf some unexpected help in teaching his son to* *be a Klingon warrior.* James Sloyan as **K'mtar**; Brian Bonsall as **Rozhenko, Alexander**; Gwynyth Walsh as **B'Etor**; Barbara March as **Lursa**; Joel Swetow as **Gorta**; Colin Mitchell as **Yog**; Armin Shimerman as **Quark**; Michael Danek as Singer; John Kenton Shull as **Molor**; Rickey D'shon Collins as **Eric**; Majel Barrett as Computer voice. SEE: **Age of Ascension; Anjoran biomimetic gel; B'Etor; Cambra system, Corvallan trader; darseks; Deep Space 9; Dopterian; fullerenes; *gin'tak*; Gorta; Hatarian system; Kalla III; *Kearsarge, U.S.S.*; Klingon opera; K'mtar; K'mtar Alpha-one; *kor'tova* candles; *Kot'baval* Festival; Lursa; magnesite; Maranga IV; Molor; Ogat Training Academy; Pakled; Rozhenko, Alexander; Ufandi III; Vodrey Nebula; *ya'nora kor*; Yog; Yridian; Yridian freighter.**

fish juice. Beverage. Cardassians often enjoyed hot fish juice as a morning drink. ("Trials and Tribble-ations" [DS9]).

Fisher, Geological Technician. (Edward Madden). Scientist aboard the original *Starship Enterprise*. Member of the scientific survey mission at planet **Alfa 117** in 2266. While on the survey, Fisher fell and bruised himself and had to be transported back to the *Enterprise*. Unknown to anyone at the time, Fisher's uniform was covered with a magnetic ore that caused a transporter malfunction, resulting in the accidental creation of a partial duplicate of Captain James Kirk. ("The Enemy Within" [TOS]).

"Fistful of Datas, A." *Next Generation* episode #134. Teleplay by Robert Hewitt Wolfe and Brannon Braga. Story by Robert Hewitt Wolfe. Directed by Patrick Stewart. Stardate 46271.5. *First aired in 1992. A holodeck malfunction traps Alexander, Worf, and Troi in the ancient American West, where everyone else is a replica of Data.* GUEST CAST: Brian Bonsall as **Rozhenko, Alexander**; John Pyper-Ferguson as **Hollander, Eli**; Joy Garrett as **Meyers, Annie**; Jorge Cervera, Jr as Bandito; Majel Barrett as Computer voice. SEE: ***Ancient West*; Barclay, Reginald; *Biko, U.S.S.*; Crusher, Dr. Beverly; Deadwood; Deinonychus VII; Durango; Dvorak, Antonín; Hollander, Eli; Hollander, Frank; Meyers, Annie; Mozart, Wolfgang Amadeus; "Ode to Spot"; Picard Mozart trio, program 1; progressive memory purge; Ressikan flute; *Something for Breakfast*; Spot; Starbase 118; Subroutine C-47; telegraph; Troi, Deanna; Winchester.**

fistrium. Refractory metal found in caves on planet **Melona IV**. Data speculated the presence of fistrium and kelbonite made it impossible for the **Crystalline Entity** to scan into the caves where the colonists hid. ("Silicon Avatar" [TNG]).

fizzbin. Fictitious card game, supposedly played on planet Beta Antares IV, but in actuality a product of James Kirk's imagination. Kirk fabricated the game to confuse the guards holding the landing party on planet **Sigma Iotia II**, allowing the landing party to escape. According to Kirk, fizzbin was played with a standard terrestrial deck of cards, but had terribly complicated rules that changed on Tuesdays and involved such things as half-fizzbins, sralks, and, of course, the astronomically improbable royal fizzbin. ("A Piece of the Action" [TOS]). SEE: **corbomite, Iotians**. Ferengi entrepreneur Quark tried to entice Deep Space 9 security chief Odo into playing the fictitious game in 2373. ("The Ascent" [DS9]). *It seems unusual that Quark would know of Kirk's bluff, but then again, maybe Quark (like Sisko) was a fan of the legendary starship captain.*

Flaherty, Commander. First officer of the ***U.S.S. Aries***. Flaherty possessed uncanny linguistic skills, speaking over forty languages, including Klingon, Romulan, Giamon, and Stroyerian. Flaherty would have been Riker's first officer if he had accepted command of the *Aries* in 2365. ("The Icarus Factor" [TNG]).

flaked blood fleas. Ferengi delicacy. A favorite of Grand Nagus **Zek**. ("Rules of Acquisition" [DS9]).

flambé noodles. Side dish of long thin pasta served flaming. ("The Chute" [VGR]).

flan. Earth dessert comprised of a molded custard topped with caramel syrup. ("Whispers" [DS9]).

"Flashback." *Voyager* episode #45. Written by Brannon Braga. Directed by David Livingston. Stardate 50126.4. *First aired in 1996. What appears to be a repressed memory resurfaces in Tuvok, and Janeway must mind-meld with him in order to prevent brain damage. The mind-meld takes them back to Tuvok's first assignment aboard the* U.S.S. Excelsior*, commanded by Captain Sulu. This episode was produced as* Star Trek: Voyager's *tribute to the 30th anniversary of the original* Star Trek *series, featuring original series cast members George Takei, Grace Lee Whitney, and Michael Ansara. Also re-creating their roles from* Star Trek VI: The Undiscovered Country *were Jeremy Roberts and Boris Krutonog.* GUEST CAST: Grace Lee Whitney as **Rand, Janice**; Jeremy Roberts as **Valtane, Dmitri**; Boris Krutonog as *Excelsior* helmsman; Michael Ansara as **Kang**; George Takei as **Sulu, Hikaru**. SEE: **Anthraxic citrus; Azure Nebula; Bolians; cellular peptides; cordrazine; cortical stimulator; cryostatic chamber; dill weed; engram; *Excelsior, U.S.S.;* Golwat, Ensign; holodeck; Kang; *keethara*; *Kolinahr*; memory virus; neurocortical monitor; orange juice; *papalla* juice; plasma weapons; *Pon farr*; Porakan eggs; positron beam; Praxis; *pyllora*; Rand, Janice; *rengazo*; replicator; sirillium; Sulu, Hikaru; *t'lokan* schism; T'Pel; tachyon; Talaxians; tea; telepathic cortex; theta-xenon; thoron; Tuvok; Valtane, Dmitri; *Wyoming, U.S.S.*; *Yorktown, U.S.S.***

Flavius. (Rhodes Reason). Popular gladiator in the brutal televised Roman arena battles on planet Eight Ninety-Two-IV. Known in the arena as Flavius Maximus, he rejected the Roman culture of the planet and refused to kill when he heard the words of the **Children of the Sun**, choosing to live in a cave along with other believers. He was captured in 2267, along with the *Enterprise* landing party investigating the fate of the ***S.S. Beagle*** crew. Flavius was killed trying to prevent the televised execution of James Kirk. ("Bread and Circuses" [TOS]). SEE: **Eight Ninety-Two-IV, Planet**.

Flaxian assassins. Professional killers, sometimes employed by the **Tal Shiar**. ("Improbable Cause" [DS9]).

Fleet Museum. Starfleet facility honoring the people and vehicles that went boldly where none had gone before. One of the great ships on exhibit there is a *Constitution*-class vessel, a near duplicate of the original *Starship Enterprise*. ("Relics" [TNG]).

fleet captain. Starfleet rank. **Christopher Pike** was promoted to fleet captain after the end of his tenure as *Enterprise* commander. ("The Menagerie, Parts I and II" [TOS]). Captain **Garth of Izar** also served as fleet captain. ("Whom Gods Destroy" [TOS]).

Fleming, U.S.S. Federation medical transport, *Wambundu* class, Starfleet registry number NCC-20316. The *Fleming* disappeared in the Hekaras Corridor in 2370. At the time of her disappearance, the *Fleming* was carrying a rare and valuable **biomimetic gel**. It was initially feared that the *Fleming* might have been hijacked for this cargo, but the ship was discovered within the Corridor, disabled by a Hekaran **verteron mine**. Unfortunately, almost immediately following its discovery, a **subspace rift** formed within the Corridor, and the *Fleming* was trapped within the rift. The crew of the *Enterprise*-D was able to beam the *Fleming* personnel onto the *Enterprise*-D, but the ship itself was lost. ("Force of Nature" [TNG]). *The* Fleming *was named for Sir Alexander Fleming, the British bacteriologist who discovered penicillin.*

Fletcher, Ensign. *Enterprise*-D engineering crew member. During the ship's mission to the **Typhon Expanse** in 2368, Fletcher was working with Commander Geordi La Forge on a catwalk over the warp core when La Forge became dizzy. Fletcher caught La Forge before he tumbled off the catwalk. ("Cause and Effect" [TNG]).

flight controller. Aboard more recent Starfleet vessels, the control station and officer responsible for both **helm** and **navigator** functions. The flight controller (or conn) is the pilot of the ship.

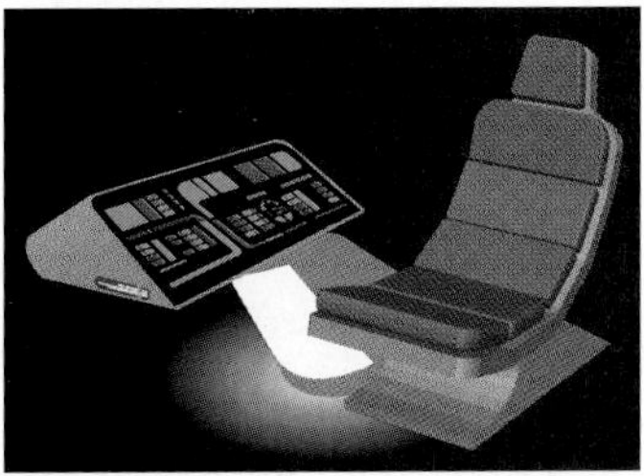

Conn is one of two freestanding consoles located ahead of the captain's chair on many starship bridges. ***Geordi La Forge** served as conn aboard the* Enterprise-*D during* Star Trek: The Next Generation*'s first season, to be replaced by **Wesley Crusher** during the second and third seasons. Since then, a variety of supernumeraries and guest performers filled that duty. On* Star Trek: Voyager ***Thomas Paris** filled the duties of conn.*

flight recorder. Data storage system aboard starships that records critical information and images from various locations in the ship, intended for use after a major accident, to reconstruct the events leading up to the incident. Spock's death in 2285 was recorded by the *U.S.S. Enterprise* flight recorder, and the playback of those images led Sarek and Kirk to believe Spock had placed his ***katra*** in McCoy's consciousness. (*Star Trek III: The Search for Spock*). In earlier ships, the flight recorder was also called a **recorder marker**. *The* Enterprise *flight recorder computer voice in* Star Trek III *was provided by producer-writer Harve Bennett.*

Flint. (James Daly). A nearly immortal human from planet **Earth**, born in Mesopotamia in 3834 BC. Flint was blessed with instant tissue regeneration, which allowed him to live through disease, war, accidents, and other calamities that killed other men. Flint soon learned to conceal his nature, living part of a life, marrying, pretending to age, then moving on before his immortality was suspected. During his life, his identities included Solomon, Alexander, Lazarus, Methuselah, and Johannes Brahms. In 2239, under the name of Brack, Flint purchased planet **Holberg 917G**, on which he built a castle where he could live undisturbed. Flint grew weary of his solitude and sought a companion who would be as immortal as he. His solution was to construct an android who would be his perfect woman. After several attempts, Flint created an android he called **Rayna Kapec**. When the *Starship Enterprise* visited Flint's world in 2269, Flint deliberately allowed Rayna to interact with James Kirk, in hopes that Kirk would stir emotions in Rayna that would permit her to love Flint. Unfortunately, he was too successful. Rayna fell in love with Kirk, then died because she could not bear to hurt Flint. Shortly thereafter, Flint learned that he, too, was slowly dying because he had left the complex balance of Earth's environment. Flint said he would devote the remaining portion of his life to the betterment of the human condition. ("Requiem for Methuselah" [TOS]).

flintlock. Primitive, muzzle-loading weapon that used an explosive charge to propel a small projectile. Klingon agents gave several flintlocks to the village people on **Tyree**'s planet in 2267, upsetting the balance of power in that society until *Enterprise* personnel provided similar weapons to Tyree's **hill people**. ("A Private Little War" [TOS]).

flitterbird. Avian life-form indigenous to planet **Rhymus Major**. ("Profit and Loss" [DS9]).

floater. Small hovercraft used for recreational transportation. Floaters were popular on planet **Risa**. ("Let He Who Is Without Sin..." [DS9]).

flop. Slang expression for a place to sleep, used by workers during Earth's **Great Depression** of the 1930s. ("The City on the Edge of Forever" [TOS]).

Flores, Marissa. (Erika Flores). Daughter of an *Enterprise*-D crew member. Marissa was one of the winners of the primary-school science fair held aboard the ship in 2368. As a prize for her accomplishment, Marissa was awarded a tour of the *Enterprise*-D, personally conducted by Captain Picard. Marissa's tour was delayed when she was trapped in a turbolift with the captain when the starship struck a **quantum filament**. Picard gave Marissa the honorary title of "Number One" during their escape. ("Disaster" [TNG]). SEE: **Gordon, Jay; Supera, Patterson**. *Marissa's last name was not given in dialog, but was printed on the plaque that the kids gave the captain.*

floriculture. Cultivation of flowers or ornamental plants. Former Maquis crew member Lon Suder acquired an appreciation of floriculture from his brief mind-meld with Lieutenant Tuvok. ("Basics, Part I" [VGR]). SEE: **Tuvok orchid.**

flux capacitance. A measurable physical property of energy flow. ("Prototype" [VGR]). *This is a tip-of-the-hat reference to the flux capacitor, the key component in the time-traveling DeLorean automobile from Universal's* Back to the Future *movies.*

flux generator. Science and engineering instrument. A flux generator was located in the science lab on station Deep Space 9. ("Second Sight" [DS9]).

flux spectrometer. Sensor device used aboard Federation starships. ("Cause and Effect" [TNG]).

foil. Ancient weapon used in the Earth sport of **fencing**, it has a flexible, rectangular blade about one meter in length and a bell guard to protect the hand. Lieutenant **Hikaru Sulu** owned a foil, much to the chagrin of his fellow *Enterprise* crew members. ("The Naked Time" [TOS]). Captain Picard enjoyed the sport and instructed Guinan in the use of the foil during the *Enterprise*-D's mission in the Argolis Cluster in 2368. ("I, Borg" [TNG]).

folded-space transport. Technology by which objects of almost any size could be transported across incredible distances almost instantaneously. The **Sikarians** used this technique in their spatial **trajector**, which permitted instantaneous travel across distances as great as 40,000 light-years. ("Prime Factors." [VGR]). The **Ansata** terrorists of planet **Rutia IV** developed a cruder implementation of folded-space transport based on the **Elway Theorem**. ("The High Ground" [TNG]).

Folnar III. Planet. Origin of the **Folnar jewel plant**. ("Dark Page" [TNG]).

Folnar jewel plant. Plant from planet **Folnar III** that secretes a resin which hardens into a gem. A Folnar jewel plant could be found in the *Enterprise*-D **arboretum**. ("Dark Page" [TNG])

food and beverages. SEE: **Ailis pâté; Aldebaran whiskey; Aldorian ale; Alfarian hair pasta; algae puffs; Altair water; Alterian chowder; Alvanian brandy; Alvinian melons; Andonian tea; Andorian tuber root; *angla'bosque*; Antarean brandy; Anthraxic citrus; Arcturian Fizz; asparagus; Augergine stew; azna; *bahgol*; baked potato; baked Risan beans; Baldoxic vinegar; *balso* tonic; banana split; bantan; beans; birthday cake; bitters; black hole; blackened redfish; Bolian tonic water; bread pudding soufflé; *bregit* lung; brestanti ale; brill cheese; Bulgarian canapé; Calaman sherry; Cardaway leaves, stuffed; caviar; champagne; Chateau Cleon; Chateau Coeur; Chateau Lafite Rothschild; Chateau Picard; *chech'tluth*; chee'lash; cherel sauce; cherry pie; chicken à la Sisko; chili burrito; Chiraltan tea; chocolate; chocolate truffle;**

Circassian fig; citrus blend; coffee; coffee ice cream; *coltayin* roots; combat rations; corn salad; Creole food; Creole shrimp with Mandalay; croissant; crown roast of lamb; *darvot* fritters; Delavian chocolates; Delovian soufflé; Delvin fluff pastries; dill weed; *dresci*; Earl Grey tea; eggs with

bacon and corned beef hash; endive salad; enemy's blood; Eskarian egg; Fanalian toddy; Felada onion crisps; feline Supplements 25, 74 & 221; *feragoit* goulash; Finagle's Folly; fish juice; flambé noodles; flan; *Foraiga;* French onion soup; fricandeau stew; fruit cocktail; fudge ripple pudding; fungilli; *gabarosti* stew; *gagh*; Gallia nectar; Gamzain wine; garlic soup; Gavaline tea; *gladst*; glop-on-a-stick; Gramilian sand peas; green beans; greenbread; grilled mushrooms; gumbo; haggis; *hasperat*; *hatana*; heart of *targ*; Hlaka soup; hot dog; I'danian spice pudding; iced coffee; icoberry torte; jambalaya; Jell-O; Jestral tea; Jibalian omelette; Jimbalian fudge; jumbo Romulan mollusks; *jumja*; *jumja* tea; Kaferian apple; Kai Winn soufflé; Kalavian biscuits; *kanar*; Kandora champagne; *karvino* juice; *kaylo*; Klingon bloodwine; Kohlanese stew; Ktarian chocolate puff; Ktarian eggs; Kylerian goat's milk; I'maki nut; Landras blend; Lapsang suchong tea; *larish* pie; Laurelian pudding; *leola* root; *lokar* beans; Lorvan crackers; macchiato; Mantickian Paté; Maporian ale; Maraltian seev-ale; Mareuvian tea; Marob root tea; mashed potatoes with butter; Matopin rock fungi; millipede juice; mint julep; mint tea; moba fruit; Modela aperitif; moon grass; mushroom soup; muskan seed punch; Nimian sea salt; oatmeal; Oblissian cabbage; Ongilin caviar; onion rings; orange juice; *oskoid*; *Owon* eggs; Palamarian sea urchin; pancakes; papalla juice; Paris delight; parthas à la Yuta; pasta al fiorella; pasta boudin; pazafer; PCS; peach cobbler; peanut butter and jelly sandwich; pecan pie; *pejuta*; Pendrashian cheese; Petrokian sausage; *Pipius* claw; pizza; plankton loaf; *plomeek* soup; *plomeek* soup à la Neelix; Porakan eggs; pot roast; Potak cold fowl; potato casserole; potatoes, mashed; prime rib; prishic; prune juice; puree of beetle; purple omelets; *putillo*; Pyrellian ginger tea; *q'lava*; *Q'parol*; quadrotriticale; *racht*; raktajino; *ratamba* stew; red leaf tea; Rekarri starburst; rengazo; Rokassa juice; *rokeg* blood pie; rolk; Romulan ale; root beer; Saint Émilion; Samarian Sunset; Saurian Brandy; sautéed beets; schplict; *Sem'hal* stew; Senarian egg broth; shrimp Creole; shrimp with fettran sauce; Silmic wine; slug liver; snail juice; spinach juice; spinach, creamed; spiny lobe-fish; Spith basil; spring wine; Stardrifter; strawberries and cream; suck salt; Synthale; synthehol; Takana root tea; Takar loggerhead eggs; Takarian mead; takka berries; Talaxian tomato; Tamarian Frost; tarin juice; Tarkalean tea; tartoc; Tarvokian pound cake; Tarvokian powder cake; Taspar egg; tea; Telluridian synthale; tequila; Terellian spices; Thalian chocolate mousse; Til'amin Froth; TKL ration; Toffa ale; tojal in *yamok* sauce; tomato soup; Traggle nectar; Trakian ale; *tranya*; Trellan crepes; Trixian bubble juice; tube grubs; tulaberry wine; Tzartak aperitif; uttaberries; uttaberry crepes; Vak clover soup; Valerian root tea; varmeliate fiber; vegetable bouillon; vermicula; *viinerine*; Vulcan mocha; Vulcan mollusks; Vulcan port; Vulcan spice tea; warm milk with dash of nutmeg; *warnog*; watercress sandwiches; Welsh rabbit; whiskey; *yamok* sauce; Yigrish cream pie; Yridian brandy; Yridian tea; *zabee* nuts; *zabo* meat; *zilm'kach*.

food replicator. SEE: **replicator**.

food slot. Part of a food delivery system aboard older Federation starships. Food slots were available in crew recreation and dining facilities, as well as some work areas. ("Tomorrow is Yesterday" [TOS], "The Trouble With Tribbles" [TOS], "And the Children Shall Lead" [TOS]). *"Flashback" (VGR) establishes that the food slots in Captain Kirk's day were* not ***replicators****.*

foolie. Slang on **Miri**'s planet for a game or a practical joke. ("Miri" [TOS]).

"For the Cause." *Deep Space Nine* episode #94. Teleplay by Ronald D. Moore. Story by Mark Gehred-O'Connell. Directed by James L. Conway. No stardate given. *First aired in 1996. Kasidy Yates and Lieutenant Commander Eddington are revealed to be Maquis members; Garak and Gul Dukat's daughter come to an understanding about each other. The game of springball is first seen in this episode.* GUEST CAST: Penny Johnson as **Yates, Kasidy**; Kenneth Marshall as **Eddington**, **Michael**; Tracy Middendorf as **Ziyal**; John Prosky as **Brathaw**; Stephen Vincent Leigh as **Reese, Lt.**; Andrew Robinson as **Garak**, **Elim**. SEE: **Bajorans; Brathaw; camouflage field; Cardassians; Dreon VII; Eddington, Michael; Federation Council; Garak, Elim; holodeck and holosuite programs; Kavarian tiger-bat; Maquis; oatmeal; *ratamba* stew; Reese, Lieutenant; replicator; Rolor Nebula; Sisko, Benjamin; springball; Temecklian virus; Tholian freighter; Tora Ziyal; *Xhosa*; Yates, Kasidy.**

"For the Uniform." Deep Space Nine episode #111. Written by Peter Allan Fields. Directed by Victor Lobl. Stardate 50485.2. *First aired in 1996. Sisko takes the* Defiant *into Maquis territory on a mission to apprehend a Starfleet officer turned Maquis leader, Michael Eddington. This episode continued the storyline begun in "For the Cause" (DS9).* GUEST CAST: Kenneth Marshall as **Eddington, Michael**; Eric Pierpoint as **Sanders, Captain**. SEE: **biogenic weapon; cascade virus; Cing'ta; class-5 intelligence drone; Eddington, Michael; Gamma 7 outpost; holocommunicator; Hugo, Victor; *Hunchback of Notre Dame, The;* Javert; *Les Misérables; Malinche, U.S.S.;* Maquis ships; Marva IV; neutrino; Panora; plasma fields; Portas V; quantum torpedo; Quatal Prime; rhodium nitrite; Salva II; Sanders, Captain; selenium; Solosos III; stratospheric torpedoes; Tracken II; trilithium; Valjean; Veloz Prime.**

"For the World Is Hollow and I Have Touched the Sky." Original Series episode #65. Written by Rik Vollaerts. Directed by Tony Leader. Stardate: 5476.3. *First aired in 1968. Dr. McCoy, stricken with a fatal disease, finds love with the leader of a doomed asteroid spaceship.* GUEST CAST: Kate Woodville as **Natira**; Majel Barrett as **Chapel**, **Christine**; Byron Morrow as Westervliet, Admiral; Jon Lormer as Old man; James Doohan as the **Oracle**, voice of. SEE: **Daran V; Fabrina; Fabrini Book of the People; Fabrini creators; Fabrini; Instrument of Obedience; McCoy, Dr. Leonard H.; Natira; Oracle; xenopolycythemia; *Yonada*.**

***foraiga*.** A difficult-to-obtain Bajoran delicacy. A buffet held aboard the *Enterprise*-D on stardate 47941 in honor of **Lieutenant Ro Laren** featured real *foraiga*. ("Preemptive Strike" [TNG]).

foramen magnum. In humanoid anatomy, the large opening at the base of the skull through which the spinal cord passes and joins with the medulla oblongata. The foramen magnum is considered by some to be the focal point of the body's bio-electric field. ("The Muse" [DS9]).

Forcas III. Planet. Site where a ***bat'leth*** competition was held in 2370. Lieutenant Worf won Champion Standing at the competition in that year. ("Parallels" [TNG]). Data found the taste of a beige-colored drink from Forcas III to be "revolting." *(Star Trek Generations).*

"Force of Nature." *Next Generation* episode #161. Written by Naren Shankar. Directed by Robert Lederman. Stardate 47310.2. *First aired in 1993. The* Enterprise-D *is disabled by two scientists trying to prove that warp drive is damaging the very fabric of space. This episode established a Federation-wide "speed limit" of warp 5.* GUEST CAST: Michael Corbett as **Rabal**, **Dr.**; Margaret Reed as **Serova**, **Dr.**; Lee Arenberg as **Prak**, **DaiMon**; Majel Barrett as Computer voice. SEE: **antimatter containment; biomimetic gel; *D'Kora*-class; EPS discharge; Federation Council; Federation Science Council; Federation signal buoy; feline supplement 221; *Fleming, U.S.S.*; Hekaras Corridor; Hekaras II; high-energy distortion wave; high-intensity warp pulse; hull stress; *Intrepid, U.S.S.*; junction A-9; junction C-12; Kaplan, Commander Donald; La Forge, Ariana; phase**

buffer; plasma grid; polycomposite; power conversion level; Prak, DaiMon; Rabal, Dr.; reconnaissance probe; second officer; Serova, Dr.; ship's log recorder; Spot; structural breach; subspace phenomena; tetryon; thermal stabilizers; verteron mines; warp field coils; warp field effect; warp speed; weather control matrix.

forced neutrino inverter. Explosive device. In 2371, a forced neutrino inverter was used in the bomb that destroyed **Retaya**'s ship. ("Improbable Cause" [DS9]).

forced plasma beam. Destructive energy source used in Borg and Ferengi handheld weapons. ("Descent, Part I" [TNG]).

Ford pickup truck. Ancient wheeled, internal-combustion vehicle used on **Earth** during the 20th century. Manufactured by the Ford Motor Company of North America, used to transport small to medium payloads across land distances of several kilometers, often for light industrial or agricultural applications. A Ford pickup truck, manufactured in 1936 and owned by **Jack Hayes**, was captured in 1937 by the **Briori**, who transported the vehicle and Hayes to the Briori homeworld in the Delta Quadrant. Hayes's vehicle was abandoned in orbit above the Briori planet, where it was discovered by the *Starship Voyager* in 2371. ("The 37's" [VGR]).

Forlat III. Class-M planet that was attacked by the **Crystalline Entity**. Colonists on the planet fled into caves in an attempt to escape the entity, but that did not protect them. ("Silicon Avatar" [TNG]).

formazine. Federation standard stimulant, often administered by hypospray. After the *Enterprise* was commandeered by the **Kelvans** in 2268, Dr. McCoy convinced **Hanar** that his body required vitamin injections, but instead delivered doses of formazine, causing all-too-human emotional irritation. ("By Any Other Name" [TOS]).

Forrester-Trent Syndrome. Degenerative neurological disorder. It is very rare, but if left untreated, can result in paralysis and even death. The syndrome is usually hereditary but can be activated by a random mutation. A neurostabilization regimen can stabilize or reverse the disease. **Jason Vigo** was diagnosed as having Forrester-Trent in 2370, caused when **Bok** secretly resequenced Vigo's DNA to make him appear to be Picard's genetic progeny. ("Bloodlines" [TNG]).

"Forsaken, The." *Deep Space Nine* episode #17. Teleplay by Don Carlos Dunaway and Michael Piller. Story by Jim Trombetta. Directed by Les Landau. Stardate 46925.1. First aired in 1993. *Ambassador Lwaxana Troi visits Deep Space 9 and takes a fancy to Security Chief Odo.* GUEST CAST: Majel Barrett as **Troi, Lwaxana**; Constance Towers as **Taxco**; Michael Ensign as **Lojal**; Jack Shearer as **Vadosia**; Benita Andre as **Anara**. SEE: **adaptive interface link; Anara; Andevian II; Arbazan; Betazoids; bipolar torch; carbon reaction chambers; Cardassian operation guidelines; Corado I Transmitter Array; corundium alloy; Dax, Curzon; Dopterian; electroplasma system; emulator module; Ferengi; fusion reactor; isolinear rods; laser-induced fusion; Lojal; Nehru Colony; New France Colony; Odo; Pup; recalibration sweep; root canal; Taxco; toranium; Troi, Lwaxana; turbolift; Vadosia; Wanoni tracehound.**

fortanium. Substance used in construction of the **D'Arsay Archive.** ("Masks" [TNG]).

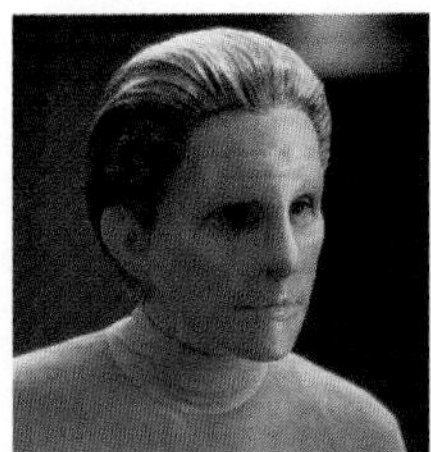

Founder Leader. (Salome Jens). Member of the **Founders**. This metamorphic individual assumed a female humanoid form in 2371 to greet **Odo** when he returned to the **Founders' homeworld**. She instructed him in the ways and history of her people. She also told Odo of his origin. ("The Search, Parts I and II" [DS9]). To learn why Odo chose to live among the solids rather than his own people, on stardate 48521 she impersonated **Kira Nerys** and pretended to be trapped on a distant moon with Odo. ("Heart of Stone" [DS9]). She boarded the *Starship Defiant* on stardate 49962.4 to escort Odo to the Founders' homeworld to be judged by the Great Link. The Great Link judged him and made him a human being. ("Broken Link" [DS9]). *Salome Jens previously portrayed the ancient humanoid in "The Chase" (TNG).*

Founders' homeworld. Sunless Class-M planet located somewhere in the **Omarion Nebula** in the **Gamma Quadrant**. The planet was the home of the reclusive civilization of shape-shifters known as the **Founders** and the central planet of the **Dominion**. ("The Search, Part I" [DS9]). In 2371, the **Tal Shiar** and **Obsidian Order** launched a massive attack against the Founders' homeworld, bombarding the planet's surface with a fleet of 20 starships. Neither attacker realized that the Founders had evacuated the planet, or that they had a fleet of 150 Jem'Hadar ships waiting to destroy the invaders. ("The Die is Cast" [DS9]). SEE: **Lovok, Colonel; Tain, Enabran.**

Founders. Ancient civilization of **shape-shifters**, the architects of the **Dominion** in the **Gamma Quadrant**. Long ago, the Founders explored the galaxy, but found themselves to be feared, hunted and killed by the **solids**, their term for non-shape-shifters. Out of self-defense, the Founders retreated to a planet in the **Omarion Nebula**. From this location, the Founders established the Dominion, through which they controlled hundreds of planets throughout the Gamma Quadrant, imposing order through ruthless violence and fear. Although isolated, the Founders did not lose their curiosity about the universe. They sent a hundred infant members of their species across the galaxy, implanting in each a powerful desire to return home, so that the Founders could learn about distant places. **Deep Space 9** security chief **Odo** was one of these infants. The Founders had a strong family link to each member of their species, and it has been said that no shape-shifter has ever killed another. ("The Search, Parts I and II" [DS9]). Another of these changeling infants ended up on Deep Space 9 in 2373. Odo began to rear the infant, until it died of radiation that it had been exposed to while in space. SEE: **changeling infant**. ("The Begotten" [DS9]). The Founders' ability to assume the shape of an object is so complete that a Founder in the guise of an individual of another species is virtually undetectable, even with sophisticated scanning equipment. Should, however, a piece of a Founder's body be separated from the main body mass, the separated piece reverts to its normal gelatinous state. ("The Adversary" [DS9]). Starfleet phasers set to a force of 3.5 were sufficient to force a Founder to revert to a gelatinous state. ("Homefront" [DS9]). Founders also revert to a gelatinous state upon death. ("Apocalypse Rising" [DS9]). SEE: **morphogenic enzyme.**

The Founders used a warrior species called the **Jem'Hadar** to force compliance of the various members of the Dominion. ("The Jem'Hadar" [DS9]). The Founders maintained control of the powerful Jem'Hadar through the use of genetic engineering, altering Jem'Hadar physiology to be dependent on **ketracel-white** (also known simply as "white," an **isogenic enzyme**), a drug that only the Founders could supply, through their agents, the **Vorta**. ("The Abandoned," et al. [DS9]). Some Vorta agents suspected that even this extreme measure may not have been sufficient to control the Jem'Hadar's powerfully violent tendencies. ("To the Death" [DS9]). Most Jem'Hadar spent their entire lives without meeting a Founder. To them, the Founders were thought of as myths ("Hippocratic Oath" [DS9]) or even gods. ("To the Death" [DS9]). On stardate 50049.3, a Founder was mortally injured when a Jem'Hadar ship crash-landed on planet Torga IV.

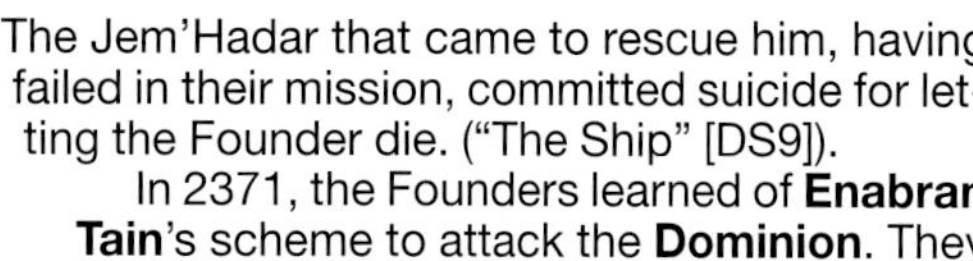

The Jem'Hadar that came to rescue him, having failed in their mission, committed suicide for letting the Founder die. ("The Ship" [DS9]).

In 2371, the Founders learned of **Enabran Tain**'s scheme to attack the **Dominion**. They took advantage of the situation, staging an ambush in the **Omarion Nebula** that virtually annihilated the armed forces of the **Obsidian Order** and the **Tal Shiar**. The incident substantially reduced the ability of the Alpha Quadrant powers to resist a potential Dominion invasion. ("The Die is Cast" [DS9]). SEE: **Lovok, Colonel.** The Founders also tried to initiate a war between the **Federation** and the **Tzenkethi**, hoping to make the Alpha Quadrant more susceptible to Dominion attacks. ("The Adversary." [DS9]). Sometime before 2373, the Founders replaced Klingon **General Martok,** in hopes the Dominion could gain control over the **Klingon Empire**. In order to reduce suspicions of the ersatz Martok, the Founders, through the Great Link, caused Odo to believe that **Gowron**, not Martok, had been replaced by a changeling. ("Apocalypse Rising" [DS9]).

In 2373, the Founders entered into an alliance with the **Cardassian** Union, giving the Dominion a significant foothold in the Alpha Quadrant. The agreement was a source of great concern to many Alpha Quadrant powers, and resulted in the reinstatement of the **Khitomer Accords**. ("By Inferno's Light" [DS9]).

Fourier series. Mathematical method derived by Jean Baptiste Joseph Fourier (1768-1830). The system can define any periodic function as a sum of sine and cosine waves. **Dr. Noonien Soong** utilized a Fourier system to give an appearance of randomness to the eye-blink pattern of his androids. ("Inheritance" [TNG]). Twentieth-century astronomer **Rain Robinson** used Fourier spectral analysis in her investigation of an extraterrestrial radio source in 1996, although Tom Paris thought her curves didn't look so good. ("Future's End, Part I" [VGR]).

Fourth Order. Cardassian military division posted near **Bajor** shortly after the Cardassian retreat from that planet in 2369. The Fourth Order was not close enough to prevent Starfleet personnel from claiming the **Bajoran wormhole** for the people of Bajor. ("Emissary" [DS9]).

Fowla system. In the **mirror universe**, star system that was under the jurisdiction of **Terok Nor (mirror)** in 2370. ("Crossover" [DS9]).

Fox, Ambassador Robert. (Gene Lyons). Federation ambassador sent aboard the *Enterprise* on a diplomatic mission to establish contact with planet **Eminiar VII** in 2267. Fox disregarded a signal from the planet warning the *Enterprise* to stay away. When it was learned that Eminiar had been embroiled in a bitter war with neighboring planet **Vendikar** that had lasted for five centuries, Fox offered his services as mediator. ("A Taste of Armageddon" [TOS]).

fractal encryption. Very sophisticated, virtually unbreakable computer encryption technique. Lieutenant Commander Data used a fractal encryption code to deny the Borg access to the *Enterprise*-E main computer when they attempted to take over the ship in 2373. *(Star Trek: First Contact).*

Frame of Mind. Theatrical play written and directed by Beverly Crusher in 2369 and performed by her theatre company aboard the *Enterprise*-D. The play featured a character, played by William Riker, who had been assigned to a psychiatric hospital after committing a brutal murder. While the play was in production, Riker was captured on planet **Tilonus IV** and subjected to brutal psychological torture. The play became a focal point in Riker's mind, and he was soon unable to tell the difference between nightmares of being trapped in the play's story, and his actual mistreatment by his captors. After he had been rescued from his captivity, Counselor Troi theorized that Riker had used the play to support his unconscious mind with elements from his real life to keep him sane. ("Frame of Mind" [TNG]).

"Frame of Mind." *Next Generation* episode #147. Written by Brannon Braga. Directed by James L. Conway. Stardate 46778.1. *First aired in 1993. Commander Riker is captured and tortured on planet Tilonus IV, and he's not sure what is reality, and what is a nightmare.* GUEST CAST: David Selburg as **Syrus, Dr.**; Andrew Prine as **Suna**; Gary Werntz as **Mavek**; Susanna Thompson as **Varel**; Allan Dean Moore as Wounded crew member. SEE: **Budrow, Admiral; Crusher, Dr. Beverly; *Frame of Mind*; Jaya; Jung, Carl Gustav; Mavek; neurosomatic technique; *nisroh*; pattern enhancer; phaser; plasma torch; reflection therapy; spiny lobe-fish; Suna; synaptic reconstruction; Syrus, Dr.; Tilonus Institute for Mental Disorders; Tilonus IV.**

frang. Monetary unit used by the **Takarian** people in the Delta Quadrant. ("False Profits" [VGR]).

Franklin, Ensign Matt. Starfleet officer. Engineer aboard the ***U.S.S. Jenolen*** at the time it crashed into a **Dyson Sphere** in 2294. Franklin and **Montgomery Scott** survived the crash and attempted to keep themselves alive until a rescue ship arrived by suspending themselves in a transporter **pattern buffer**. The attempt was partially successful: Scott survived for 75 years, but Franklin died when his pattern degraded beyond recovery. ("Relics" [TNG]).

fraternization. Intimate association between members of Starfleet. It was Starfleet's policy not to interfere with the personal lives of its personnel, so fraternization is not prohibited, so long as it was voluntary and desired by both parties. ("Elogium" [VGR]).

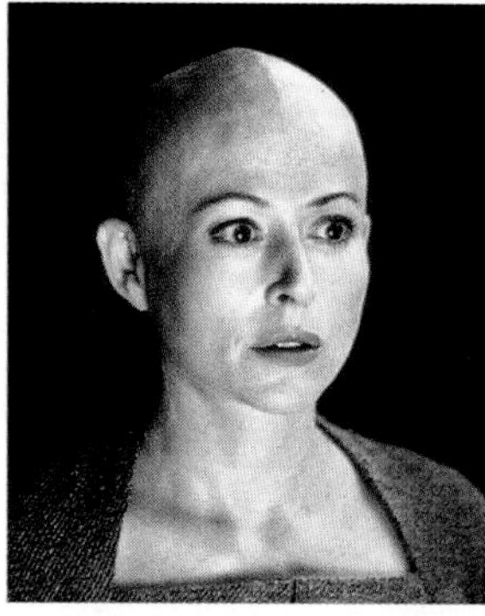

Frazier, Riley. (Lori Hallier). Starfleet science officer who served aboard the *Starship Roosevelt* at the battle of **Wolf 359**. Frasier was assimilated by the Borg when the Roosevelt was destroyed, and was taken to the Delta Quadrant aboard a **Borg** ship. She managed to escape when the Borg vessel was disabled in an electrokinetic storm. Dr. Frasier and her fellow survivors eventually reverted to their original personalities, and colonized a planet in the **Nekrit Expanse**. ("Unity" [VGR]).

freakasaurus. Late 20th-century slang term meaning a person whose dress or demeanor was out of the ordinary but in a good sort of way. Rain Robinson classified Tuvok as a definite freakasauraus. ("Future's End, Part II" [VGR]).

Free Haven. Bajoran colony. Free Haven was attacked by **Breen** privateers in early 2372. The *Defiant* was assigned to protect the colony. ("To the Death" [DS9]).

Freeman, Ensign. (Paul Baxley). *Enterprise* crew member who did not start the fight on **Deep Space Station K-7** with the Klingons in 2267. ("The Trouble with Tribbles" [TOS]). *Episode writer David Gerrold intended the character of Ensign Freeman as a walk-on part for himself, but the role went to Paul Baxley. Gerrold finally got to be part of the original* Enterprise *crew nearly 30 years later, in 1996, when he played a background security officer in "Trials and Tribble-ations" (DS9). (Gerrold also played an*

Enterprise *crew member in 1979 when he was an extra in the recreation deck scene in the first* Star Trek *movie.)*

French onion soup. Earth delicacy made from a sautéed root and meat broth. ("The Siege" [DS9]).

Frenchotte. Self-exiled Romulan composer of soothing, almost ethereal music. His compositions never attained wide popularity. By 2370, Jadzia Dax had added his music to her collection of forgotten composers. ("Playing God" [DS9]).

Freni, Mirella. One of the outstanding operatic sopranos of late-20th century Earth. To learn about opera, the *Voyager's* Emergency Medical Hologram studied recordings of Puccini's *La Bohème* featuring Freni in the role of Mimi. ("The Swarm" [VGR]).

"Frere Jacques." An old French folksong, favorite of *Enterprise*-D Captain Picard, who sung it with several children who were trapped with him in a **turboshaft** on stardate 45156. ("Disaster" [TNG]). Picard also played it as a duet with Nella Daren, with Picard on his Ressikan flute and Daren on her piano. ("Lessons" [TNG]).

Freud, Dr. Sigmund. (Bernard Kates). (1856-1939). Earth neurologist and founder of psychoanalysis. When Data began to have nightmares in 2370, he consulted a holodeck re-creation of the legendary psychoanalyst. ("Phantasms" [TNG]).

Freya. (Marjorie Monaghan). Character in the holonovel ***Beowulf***. A shield-maiden and daughter to **King Hrothgar,** Freya boasted about her victories with Scyld the Gar-Dane and her campaign against the heatho-bards. She was instrumental in assisting the **Emergency Medical Hologram** during his first away mission. ("Heroes and Demons" [VGR]). *In Norse mythology, Freya was the goddess of love and beauty. Friday is named after her.*

Friar Tuck. (Brent Spiner). In Earth mythology, the priest who was one of the members of **Robin Hood**'s band of outlaws in ancient England. Data was cast as Friar Tuck by **Q** in a fantasy he designed for Captain Picard's benefit in 2367. ("QPid" [TNG]).

fricandeau stew. Earth dish made with braised veal and root vegetables. It was one of Chief Miles O'Brien's favorite foods. ("Whispers" [DS9]). *This was, of course, replicated veal....*

"Friday's Child." Original Series episode #32. Written by D. C. Fontana. Directed by Joseph Pevney. Stardate 3497.2. *First aired in 1967. The* Enterprise *crew becomes embroiled in a local power struggle on planet Capella IV when Klingons attempt to gain mining rights there. "Ah, Capella," exclaimed Bob Justman, who burst into song after receiving the script.* GUEST CAST: Julie Newmar as **Eleen**; Tige Andrews as **Kras**; Michael Dante as **Maab**; Cal Bolder as **Keel**; Ben Gage as **Akaar**, **Teer**; Kirk Raymone as Duur; Robert Bralver as **Grant**; Jim Jones as Kras's stunt double; Dick Dial as Warrior's stunt double; Chuck Clow as Kirk's stunt double. SEE: **Akaar, Leonard James; Akaar, Teer; Capella IV; Capellans; *Carolina, U.S.S.*; *Dierdre, S.S.*; Eleen; Grant; *kligat*; Keel; Kras; Maab; magnesite-nitron tablet; teer; Ten Tribes; topaline.**

Friendly Angel. SEE: **Gorgan**.

Frin. Successful **Ferengi** entrepreneur who owned 30 taverns; uncle to **Quark**. ("Civil Defense" [DS9]).

frontal lobe. The anterior portion of the cerebral hemisphere in humanoid brains. The effects of the **Ktarian game**, introduced to the *Enterprise*-D crew in 2368, were centered in the frontal lobe. ("The Game" [TNG]).

Frool. (Emilio Borelli). Ferengi waiter who was employed at Quark's bar in 2372. Although Frool shared the Ferengi cultural dislike of labor unions, he joined the **Guild of Restaurant and Casino Employees** in 2372 to oppose Quark's exploitation of his employees. ("Bar Association" [DS9]).

fruit cocktail. Dessert or side dish consisting of chopped fruit pieces served in a thin syrup. Neelix prepared Jell-O with fruit cocktail for the Thirty-Sevens during their brief visit to the *Voyager* in 2371. ("The 37's" [VGR]).

Frunalians. Spacefaring civilization. Three Frunalian science vessels requested permission to dock at station **Deep Space 9** shortly after the discovery of the wormhole in 2369. ("Emissary" [DS9]).

FSNP. Star Trek *(TOS) writing staff's gag term for the Famous Spock Nerve Pinch, also known as the Vulcan nerve pinch or the neck pinch, first used in "The Enemy Within" (TOS). The abbreviation FSNP appeared in some later scripts calling for the use of the nerve pinch, although the term was never used in dialog.* SEE: **Vulcan nerve pinch**.

fudge ripple pudding. A sweetened dessert made from milk, a thickening agent, and chocolate flavoring. Harry Kim liked fudge ripple pudding. ("The Chute" [VGR]).

fullerenes. Shortened name for buckminsterfullerenes, macroscopic carbon molecules with a spherical lattice structure. **Alexander Rozhenko** and his schoolmates made fullerenes in a chemistry class aboard the *Enterprise*-D on stardate 47779. He and a friend filled them with water and threw them like water balloons. ("Firstborn" [TNG]). *Buckminsterfullerenes are real and were named after 20th-century architect R. Buckminster Fuller, inventor of the geodesic dome.*

Fullerton, Pascal. (Monte Markham). Chairman of the **New Essentialists Movement**. In 2373, Fullerton and several members of the New Essentialists Movement journeyed to **Risa** to hold rallies, protesting Risa as an example of what he saw as serious decay in the moral fiber of the Federation. Fullerton subsequently sabotaged the planet's weather control system in order to make their point that Federation citizens were becoming too complacent. ("Let He Who Is Without Sin..." [DS9]). *Fullerton's Bolian aide was played by Frank Kopyc.*

fungilli. One of **Dr. Leah Brahms**'s favorite foods. Geordi La Forge was also fond of it. ("Galaxy's Child" [TNG]).

Furel. (William Lucking). Member of the **Shakaar resistance cell** during the Cardassian occupation of Bajor. During the occupation, Furel rescued fellow cell members **Shakaar, Lupaza,** and **Kira Nerys** from a Cardassian interrogation center. While the rescue was a success, Furel lost his left arm during the fight. He refused to have it replaced, fearing it would be ungrateful to the **Prophets,** whom he believed allowed him to rescue his friends. After the occupation, Furel settled on a farm in his home province of **Dahkur**. ("Shakaar" [DS9]). Furel was killed in 2373 when **Silaran Prin**, a Cardassian who had been injured by the Shakaar resistance cell, sought to win revenge on former members of the Shakaar group. Furel, who had traveled to **Deep Space 9** to protect Kira Nerys, was killed along with Lupaza by a hunter probe. ("The Darkness and the Light" [DS9]).

fusing pitons. Self-setting anchor used for rappelling on sheer rock surfaces. ("Chain of Command, Part I" [TNG]).

fusion bomb. Weapon of mass destruction that generates a massive nuclear explosion from the fusion of hydrogen isotopes into helium. The inhabitants of planets **Vendikar** and **Eminiar VII** developed such weapons, but both peoples feared their awesome destructive power. Mathematical simulations of fusion bombs were used in a computer war fought between the two planets for five centuries, ending in 2267. The mathematical weapons were routinely used for attacks on both planets' population centers. These data were used to determine casualties, and the individuals so declared were given 24 hours to report to disintegration stations so that their deaths could be recorded. ("A Taste of Armageddon" [TOS]). *Earth, of course, has had fusion bombs in its arsenals for several decades, although to this point, we've had the good sense not to use them.*

fusion reactor. Energy-generation device employing nuclear fusion of hydrogen isotopes into helium. Fusion reactors are employed in the impulse drive systems of Federation starships. Station Deep Space 9 uses fusion reactors of Cardassian design. ("The Forsaken" [DS9]).

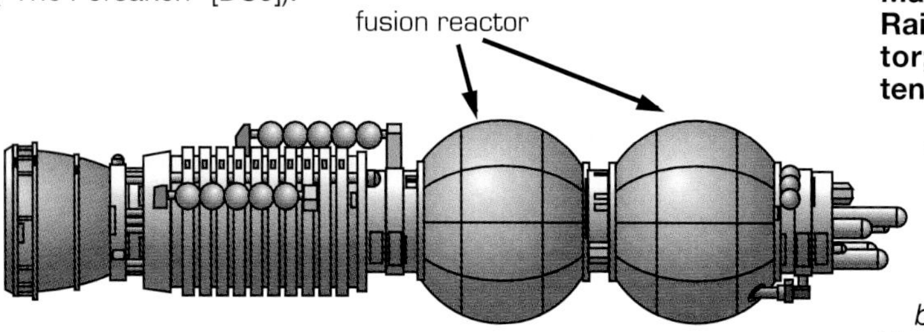

"Future Imperfect." *Next Generation* episode #82. Written by J. Larry Carroll & David Bennett Carren. Directed by Les Landau. Stardate 44286.5. *First aired in 1990. Riker wakes up, apparently suffering from amnesia, 16 years in the future, having lost all memory of the past 16 years.* GUEST CAST: Andreas Katsulas as **Tomalak**; Chris Demetral as **Barash**; Carolyn McCormick as **Minuet**; Patti Yasutake as **Ogawa, Nurse Alyssa**; Todd Merrill as Gleason; April Grace as **Hubbell**, **Chief**; George O'Hanlon, Jr. as Transporter chief. SEE: **Alpha Onias III; Altarian encephalitis; Barash; Curtis Creek program; *Decius*; Ethan; Hubble, Chief; Minuet; Miridian VI; Ogawa, Nurse Alyssa; Onias Sector; Outpost 23; Riker, Jean-Luc; Tomalak.**

"Future's End, Part I." *Voyager* episode #50. Written by Brannon Braga & Joe Menosky. Directed by David Livingston. No stardate given. *First aired in 1996.* Voyager *is thrown back in time to Los Angeles in 1996, where Janeway must locate a megalomaniac who has stolen a 29th-century Federation timeship, in order to prevent a catastrophe that will destroy the future.* GUEST CAST: Sarah Silverman as **Robinson**, **Rain**; Allan G. Royal as **Braxton, Captain**; Ed Begley, Jr. as **Starling**, **Henry**; Susan Patterson as **Kaplan**, **Ensign**; Barry Wiggins as Policeman; Christian R. Conrad as **Dunbar**. SEE: ***Aeon*; astrometric readings; *Botany Bay, S.S.;* Braxton, Captain; *Bride of the Corpse*; Cal Tech; Chakotay; Chateau Coeur; chronometric data; Chronowerx; dermal dysplasia; Drake Equation; Dunbar; E-mail; Fourier series; graviton matrix; Griffith Observatory; groovy; Hermosa Quake; High Sierras; holodeck and holosuite programs: Novice tennis tournament; HyperPro PC; isograted circuit; Janeway, Kathryn; Kaplan, Ensign; Los Angeles; Mars; Nixon, Richard M.; Paris, Thomas; polaron; Robinson, Rain; SETI greeting; SETI; Starling, Henry; subatomic disruptor; *Technology Future;* temporal explosion; temporal rift; tennis; timeship; transporter, emergency.**

"Future's End, Part II." *Voyager* episode #51. Written by Brannon Braga & Joe Menosky. Directed by Cliff Bole. Stardate 50312.5. *First aired in 1996. Still in 1996, Starling and Janeway match wits over the 29th-century timeship, while Chakotay and Torres are captured by militiamen who believe the two are a part of a government conspiracy.* Voyager's *holographic doctor gained the ability to leave sickbay at the end of this episode.* GUEST CAST. Sarah Silverman as **Robinson, Rain**; Allan G. Royal as **Braxton, Captain**; Brent Hinkley as Militiaman; Clayton Murray as Militiaman; Ed Begley, Jr. as **Starling, Henry**. SEE: **asteroid belt; autonomous holo-emitter; *Botany Bay, S.S.;* Braxton, Captain; Butch; Chakotay; chili burrito; Chronowerx; Dodger Stadium; Dunbar; Emergency Medical Hologram; freakasaurus; hyper-impulse; interferometric dispersion; Kaplan, Ensign; Los Angeles; Metro Plaza; *Mission: Impossible*; Porter; Robinson, Rain; SATCOM 47; Starling, Henry; Temporal Integrity Commission; Temporal Prime Directive; temporal explosion; timeship; tricorder uplink; UFO; Venus.**

Fuurinkazan battle strategies. Tactics developed by **Kyle Riker** at the **Tokyo Base** prior to his work for Starfleet as a tactical advisor. ("The Icarus Factor" [TNG]).

G'now juk Hol pajhard. Klingon law of heredity. A son shall share in the honors or crimes of his father. The law required **Worf**'s **discommendation** when the council accused his father, **Mogh**, of allowing the 2346 Romulan attack on the **Khitomer** outpost. ("Redemption, Part I" [TNG]).

G'Trok. Klingon poet and writer of ***The Fall of Kang***. ("Second Sight" [DS9]).

Ga'nah. Province of the **Takarian** nation on a Class-M world in the Delta Quadrant. ("False Profits" [VGR]).

***gabosti* stew.** Food native to the Delta Quadrant. Neelix prepared *gabosti* stew aboard the *Voyager*. The dish is sometimes served with a special pepper sauce. ("Elogium" [VGR]).

Gable, Clark. Entertainment personality popular during Earth's 20th century. **Edith Keeler** was one of Gable's legion of fans during the 1930s. She invited James Kirk to go with her to see one of his motion pictures. ("The City on the Edge of Forever" [TOS]).

Gabrielle. (Isabel Lorca). A **holodeck** character, the image of a lovely young French woman who was a patron at the **Cafe des Artistes** in Paris. ("We'll Always Have Paris" [TNG]).

Gaetano, Lieutenant. (Peter Marko). Starfleet officer. Gaetano was a member of the ***Shuttlecraft Galileo*** crew when it crashed on planet **Taurus II** in 2267. Gaetano was killed by the humanoid creatures on the planet. ("The *Galileo* Seven" [TOS]).

Gagarin IV. Planet. Location of the **Darwin Genetic Research Station**, a Federation science facility that produced genetically engineered human children whose immune systems actively sought out and attacked potential sources of disease, including other humans. Those so attacked suffered symptoms closely resembling hyperaccelerated aging. ("Unnatural Selection" [TNG]). *Gagarin IV was named for cosmonaut Yuri Gagarin (1934-1968), the first human to travel in space.*

Gage, U.S.S. Federation starship, *Apollo* class, Starship registry number NCC-11672. One of the 39 Federation ships destroyed by the **Borg** during the battle of **Wolf 359.** ("Emissary" [DS9]).

***gagh*.** Serpent worms, a Klingon culinary delicacy. Connoisseurs of Klingon cuisine claim that *gagh* is best served very fresh, i.e. live. *Gagh* is also served stewed. Both Riker and Picard claimed to have developed a taste for the dish. ("A Matter of Honor" [TNG], "Unification, Part I" [TNG]).

Gaila. (Josh Pais). Successful **Ferengi** entrepreneur who owned a small moon on which he lived; cousin to **Quark**. ("Civil Defense" [DS9]). Gaila was an arms merchant. ("The Way of the Warrior" [DS9]). He was a cool character who thought nothing of selling weapons that could be used to kill millions of innocent people. He was only interested in the profit that could be made from such a sale. ("Business As Usual" [VGR]). Quark once loaned Gaila the latinum to start his munitions business, with the promise that if he became a success, he would buy Quark his own ship. Gaila made good on his promise in 2372, with a ship that Quark dubbed ***Quark's Treasure***. Unfortunately, a malfunction (possibly caused by sabotage) caused the ship to crash on Earth in 1947, and the vessel was later sold as scrap. ("Little Green Men" [DS9]). By late 2372, Quark owed Gaila a large sum of money. ("Body Parts" [DS9]). Gaila started in the weapons business in 2333, and in 2373 he was ready to retire. Gaila traveled to Deep Space 9 to groom his cousin Quark to take over his business. After an arms deal with the **Regent of Palamar** went terribly wrong, **General Nassuc**, the regent's enemy, sent a purification squad after Gaila. ("Business As Usual" [DS9]).

Gal Gath'thong. Location on planet **Romulus** known for its great natural beauty and spectacular firefalls. **Alidar Jarok,** after defecting from the **Romulan Star Empire**, mourned the fact that he would never see Gal Gath'thong again. ("The Defector" [TNG]).

galactic barrier. SEE: **barrier, galactic**.

Galador freighter. Transport ship. In 2370, it supposedly operated on a trade route between **Galador II** and **Farius Prime**. In actuality, it was a **Maquis** ship with a falsified registration. ("The Maquis, Part I" [DS9]).

Galador II. Planet. Homeworld to **Galador freighter**s. ("The Maquis, Part I" [DS9]).

Galaxy M33. The 33rd object in Messier's catalog of nebulae and galaxies. In 2364, the *Enterprise*-D was hurled some 2,700,000 light-years to M33, with the help of the **Traveler**. ("Where No One Has Gone Before" [TNG]).

"Galaxy's Child." *Next Generation* episode #90. Teleplay by Maurice Hurley. Story by Thomas Kartozian. Directed by Winrich Kolbe. Stardate 44614.6. *First aired in 1991. The* Enterprise-D *accidentally kills a large spaceborne life-form, then must care for the creature's unborn child.* GUEST CAST: Susan Gibney as **Brahms**, **Dr. Leah**; Lanei Chapman as **Rager**, **Ensign**; Jana Marie Hupp as **Pavlick**, **Ensign**; Whoopi Goldberg as **Guinan**; April Grace as Transporter technician. SEE: **Alpha Omicron system; Brahms, Dr. Leah; fungilli; Guernica system; holodeck; Junior; kph; La Forge, Geordi; mid-range phase adjuster; Pavlick, Ensign; Rager, Ensign; Starbase 313; Theoretical Propulsion Group.**

Galaxy, U.S.S. Federation starship, prototype for the ***Galaxy*-class** series of deep-space exploratory starships. *The* U.S.S. Galaxy *has not (yet) been seen on any episode, but its existence is implied by the term,* Galaxy *class, used to designate the* Enterprise-D *and its sister ships. We conjecture that the Starfleet registry number of the* U.S.S. Galaxy *was NX-70637.*

***Galaxy*-Class Starship Development Project.** Starfleet project based at the **Utopia Planitia Fleet Yards** on Mars for the design and construction of the ***Galaxy*-class** starships, including the ***Enterprise*-D**. Among the engineers working on this project was **Dr. Leah Brahms** of the **Theoretical Propulsion Group.** Although a junior member of the team, Brahms made major contributions to the design of the ships' warp propulsion systems. ("Booby Trap" [TNG]). The actual assembly of the *Enterprise*-D was supervised by Commander Orfil Quinteros. ("11001001" [TNG]).

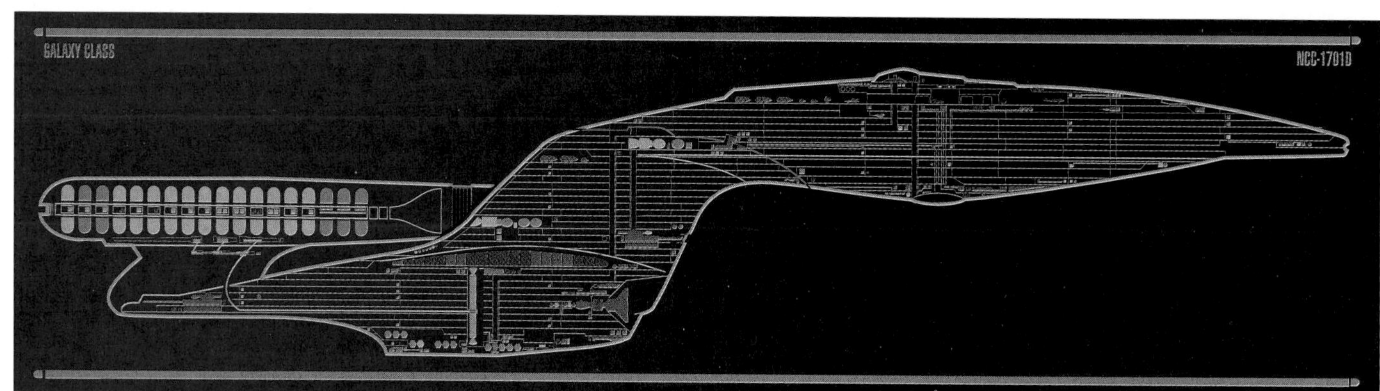

Galaxy*-class starship.** Among the most advanced and most powerful vessels in the Federation **Starfleet** during the late 24th century. The ***U.S.S. Enterprise*-D**, launched in 2363, was one of the first starships of this class, as was the ***U.S.S. Galaxy, after which the class was named. ("Encounter at Farpoint, Part I" [TNG]). The ***U.S.S. Yamato*** (registry number NCC-71807), destroyed in 2365, was another *Galaxy*-class starship ("Contagion" [TNG], as was the ***U.S.S. Odyssey***, NCC-71832 (destroyed in "The Jem'Hadar" [DS9]) and the ***U.S.S. Venture*** ("Way of the Warrior" [DS9]). *Gene Roddenberry once speculated that there were only six* Galaxy*-class ships built, but this has not been firmly established in an episode, and Starfleet has undoubtedly built others since "Encounter at Farpoint."*

Galdonterre. Planet. Former hiding place of the **Albino**. ("Blood Oath" [DS9]).

Galek Sar. (Albert Hall). Captain of the **Promellian** battle cruiser ***Cleponji***. Sar's ship was disabled in battle with the **Menthars** a thousand years ago. Prior to his death, Galek Sar left behind a recorded message in which he commended his crew and accepted all responsibility for the fate of his ship. ("Booby Trap" [TNG]).

Galen border conflicts. A series of skirmishes during the 2350s between the **Talarians** and the Federation over the Galen system, in which Federation colonies had been established. During the conflict, it was a common Talarian tactic to abandon observation spacecraft that had been rigged to self-destruct when boarded. The conflicts reached their peak in the Talarian attack on **Galen IV**, after which a peace accord was reached. ("Suddenly Human" [TNG]). SEE: **Endar; Jono; Rossa, Jeremiah.**

Galen IV. Class-M planet, site of a Federation colony. In 2356, the colony was attacked and destroyed by **Talarian** forces. The Talarians claimed the Federation was intruding on Talarian territory. ("Suddenly Human" [TNG]). SEE: **Endar**; **Jono**.

Galen, Professor Richard. (Norman Lloyd). Possibly the greatest archaeologist of the 24th century. Galen spent the last decade of his life attempting to confirm an extraordinary theory that numerous humanoid species in the galaxy had a common genetic heritage, born from the fact that some species apparently had "seeded" the primordial oceans of many worlds. Galen spent years gathering genetic information from at least 19 planets across the quadrant in an effort to confirm his theory. Galen's greatest discovery was that the genetic codes on these planets could be assembled to form a computer program containing a message of peace from those ancient progenitors. Among Galen's students was **Jean-Luc Picard**, whom Galen hoped would also become an archaeologist. Although Picard instead chose to pursue a career in Starfleet, he was instrumental in completing Galen's last work. ("The Chase" [TNG]). SEE: **archaeology; humanoid life**. *Galen's first name is from the script and was not mentioned on the air.*

Galen. (Patrick Stewart). Persona assumed by Jean-Luc Picard after his abduction by **Arctus Baran** in 2370. Picard told Baran's crew that Galen was a smuggler, who had been visiting the **ruins of Nafir** on planet Dessica II. Picard presumably chose the name in honor of his archaeology professor, **Dr. Richard Galen**. ("Gambit, Parts I and II" [TNG]).

Galen. Ancient Greek physician and writer from Earth who postulated that human arteries carried blood, not air as had been previously thought. Galen was among the names that *Voyager*'s **Emergency Medical Hologram** considered in 2371 when searching for a name to adopt as his own. ("Ex Post Facto" [VGR]).

Galeo-Manada style wrestling. Form of athletic competition. Jadzia Dax said it was a great way to start a day. ("Playing God" [DS9]). SEE: **Trajok.**

galicite. Mineral substance. A galicite excavation existed on a **Nezu** colony world in the Delta Quadrant. ("Rise" [VGR]).

***Galileo* 5, Shuttlecraft.** Shuttle #5, attached to *U.S.S. Enterprise*-A. Uhura picked up Kirk and company from **Yosemite National Park** in this shuttle when Kirk "accidentally" forgot to bring his communicator. The *Galileo* 5 crash-landed in the *Enterprise*-A **hangar deck** after being commandered by **Sybok** at **Nimbus III**. (*Star Trek V: The Final Frontier*). *The* Galileo 5 *was of a different (and presumably more advanced) design from the original* Galileo *and* Galileo II *seen in the first* Star Trek *series. The ship was designed by Nilo Rodis and*

Andy Neskoromny. The miniature was built by Greg Jein. Two full-scale exterior mockups were built for the film, one of which was later modified and used as a shuttle on Star Trek: The Next Generation.

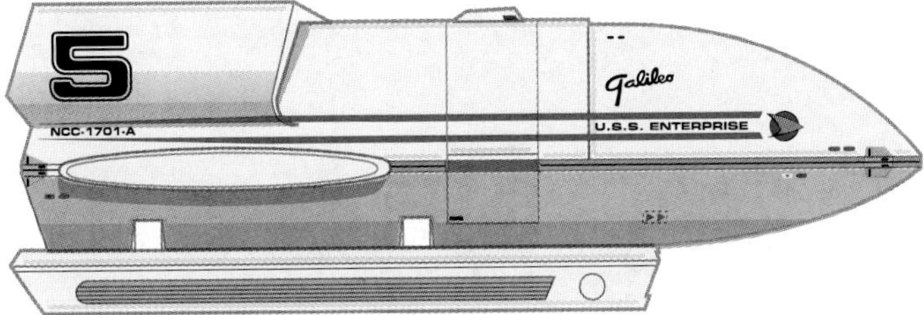

Galileo II*, Shuttlecraft.** Replacement for the original shuttlecraft ***Galileo aboard the *U.S.S. Enterprise*. **Dr. Sevrin** and his followers stole the *Galileo II* in their quest for the mythical planet **Eden** in 2269. ("The Way to Eden" [TOS]). *The* Galileo II *was, of course, the same mockup used for the original* Galileo, *with the simple addition of a "II" in the name. This was presumably because the first* Galileo *was destroyed in "The* Galileo *Seven" (TOS), although it was later seen in other episodes, an oversight on the part of the show's producers.*

"*Galileo* Seven, The." Original Series episode #14. Teleplay by Oliver Crawford and S. Bar-David. Story by Oliver Crawford. Directed by Robert Gist. Stardate 2821.5. *First aired in 1967. A shuttlecraft piloted by Spock crashes on planet Taurus II, forcing him to grapple with the life-and-death responsibilities of command. S. Bar-David was the pen name of dramatist Shimon Wincelberg, who also wrote "Dagger of the Mind" (TOS). The* Enterprise *shuttlecraft made its first appearance in this episode. Earlier episodes (like "The Enemy Within" [TOS]) did not use the shuttle because it had not been built until this point. Stephen Whitfield represented model toy manufacturer AMT and negotiated the deal to market the original* Enterprise *model kit. He also made a deal for the studio for AMT to fund construction of the full-sized* Galileo *mockup for filming in return for the rights to market the shuttlecraft model kit. With Gene Roddenberry, Whitfield wrote* The Making of Star Trek. *Now known as Stephen Poe, he has written many books, videos, and films.* GUEST CAST: Don Marshall as **Boma, Lieutenant**; John Crawford as **Ferris, Galactic High Commissioner**; Peter Marko as **Gaetano, Lieutenant**; Phyllis Douglas as **Mears, Yeoman**; Reese Vaughn as **Latimer, Lieutenant**; Grant Woods as **Kelowitz, Lieutenant Commander**; Buck Maffei as Creature; David L. Ross as Transporter chief; Gary Coombs as Latimer stunt double; Frank Vinci as Spock's stunt double; Majel Barrett as Computer voice. SEE: **Boma, Lieutenant; *Columbus*, Shuttlecraft; Ferris, Galactic High Commissioner; Gaetano, Lieutenant; *Galileo*, Shuttlecraft; Hansen's Planet; Immamura, Lieutenant; Kelowitz, Lieutenant Commander; Latimer, Lieutenant; Makus III; Mears, Yeoman; Murasaki 312; New Paris colonies; O'Neill, Ensign; quasars; space-normal; Taurus II**.

***Galileo*, Shuttlecraft.** Registry number NCC-1701-7. Shuttle attached to the original *Starship Enterprise*. In 2267, the *Galileo* was lost near planet **Taurus II** while investigating the **Murasaki Effect**. ("The *Galileo* Seven" [TOS]). The *Galileo* transported Kirk, Spock, McCoy, and **Commissioner Nancy Hedford** from planet **Epsilon Canaris III** to the *Enterprise* on stardate 3219. The shuttle was pulled off course by an electromagnetic storm in the **Gamma Canaris region**. ("Metamorphosis" [TOS]). SEE: **Cochrane, Zefram.** Spock piloted the *Galileo* into a huge spaceborne **amoeba** creature that destroyed the **Gamma 7A System** on stardate 4307. ("The Immunity Syndrome" [TOS]). *The latter two episodes were filmed after "The* Galileo *Seven" (TOS), in which the* Galileo *was destroyed at Taurus II. The* Galileo *was also glimpsed in "Journey to Babel" (TOS) and "Let That Be Your Last Battlefield" (TOS). Named for mathematician and astronomer Galileo Galilei (1564-1642).* SEE: ***Galileo II*, Shuttlecraft**.

***Galileo*, Shuttlecraft.** Type-6 personnel shuttle attached to the *U.S.S. Enterprise*-D. In 2364, Lieutenant Tasha Yar piloted the *Galileo* to transport Captain **Jean-Luc Picard** over to the ***Enterprise*-D** when he first accepted command of the vessel. ("All Good Things..." [TNG]). *Naturally, the writers of "All Good Things..." named this* Galileo *in homage to the* Galileo *that served aboard the first* Starship Enterprise.

Galipotans. Civilization whose concept of time is much different from that of many other humanoid species, at least according to Garak. A Galipotan freighter docked at **Deep Space 9** in 2370 with cargo for Garak. ("The Wire" [DS9]).

Galis Blin. Bajoran official. Major Kira Nerys contacted Galis Blin on stardate 46423, hoping she could shed light on who created the **aphasia virus** that infected Deep Space 9 in 2369. ("Babel" DS9]).

Gallamite. Species of humanoids with transparent skulls and brains twice human size. **Captain Boday** was Gallamite. ("The Maquis, Part I" [DS9]).

***Gallia* nectar.** Delicious pale yellow colored drink made from a blossom which grows near a certain lake on **Paxau**. The blossom blooms only once every six years. ("Warlord" [VGR]).

gallicite. Rare mineral substance used in the construction of **warp coils** on Federation starships. Routine scans detected a kiloton on a planet, which would be enough to completely refit ***U.S.S. Voyager's*** overworked system by stardate 50541.6. ("Blood Fever" [VGR]).

Gallitep. Infamous labor camp on planet **Bajor** during the **Cardassian** occupation. Numerous unspeakable atrocities against Bajoran citizens were committed there by the Cardassians under the command of **Gul Darhe'el**. Gallitep was liberated in 2357 by the Bajoran **Shakaar** resistance group, including future Deep Space 9 officer **Kira Nerys**. ("Duet" [DS9]). Among those liberated at Gallitep was the brother of Colonel **Lenaris Holem**. ("Shakaar" [DS9]). One of the Cardassians at Gallitep was a file clerk named **Aamin Marritza,** who saw the atrocities committed by his countrymen and felt intense guilt over his inability to prevent them. Many years later, Marritza tried to atone for the Bajoran deaths by posing as Darhe'el, hoping that a public trial would expose the Cardassian crimes. ("Duet" [DS9]).

Galliulin, Irina. (Mary-Linda Rapelye). Follower of renegade scientist **Dr. Sevrin**, who sought the mythical planet **Eden** in 2269. Galliulin had a romantic relationship with **Pavel Chekov** when both attended Starfleet Academy, but they broke up because they had differing life philosophies. ("The Way to Eden" [TOS]).

Galloway, Lieutenant. (David L. Ross). Crew member from the original *Starship Enterprise* who was part of the landing party to **Eminiar VII** in 2267. ("A Taste of Armageddon" [TOS]). Lieutenant Galloway was also a security officer killed in 2268 at planet **Omega IV** by **Captain Ronald Tracey**. ("The Omega Glory" [TOS]). *David L. Ross was one of the regular extras on the Original Series, also appearing as Lieutenant Galloway in "Miri" (TOS) and "City on the Edge of Forever" (TOS). He also played Lieutenant Johnson in "Day of the Dove" (TOS).*

Galor IV. Planet. The location of an annex to the **Daystrom Institute of Technology**. **Admiral Haftel**, upon learning that Data had constructed a daughter android in 2366, strongly advocated that the new android be placed at the Galor IV annex for programming and study. ("The Offspring" [TNG]).

***Galor*-class Cardassian warship.** Powerful military spacecraft operated by the **Cardassian** Union. Two Type-3 *Galor*-class ships, the most powerful in their fleet, were dispatched to the

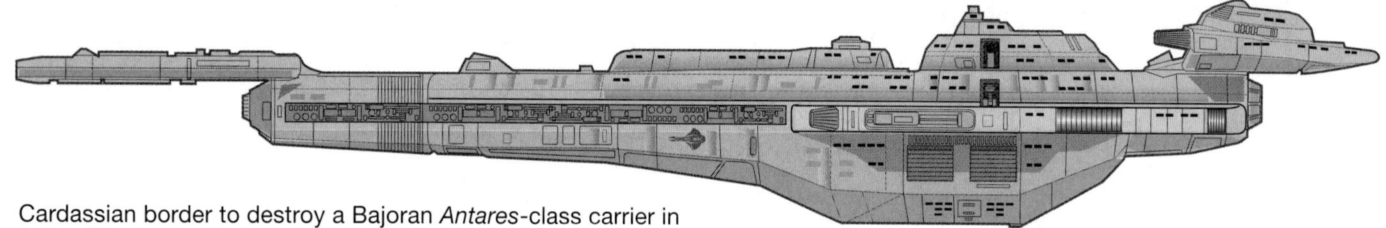

Cardassian border to destroy a Bajoran *Antares*-class carrier in 2368. ("Ensign Ro" [TNG]). *The Galor-class ship was designed by Rick Sternbach and built by Ed Miarecki. It was first seen in "The Wounded" (TNG).*

***Galor*-class plasma banks**. Heavy weapons array designed for Cardassian *Galor*-class warships. In 2370, Cardassian authorities secretly installed *Galor*-class plasma banks on small Cardassian shuttles to fight Federation colonists in the **Demilitarized Zone**. ("The Maquis, Part I" [DS9]).

Galorda Prime. Planet. In 2372, a Klingon civilian transport crashed on Galorda Prime, killing all 441 persons on-board. ("Rules of Engagement" [DS9]).

Galorndon Core. A barely-habitable planet in Federation space, one-half light-year from the **Romulan Neutral Zone**. The atmosphere of the planet was plagued by severe electromagnetic storms, which made transport difficult and rendered sensors inoperable. A **Romulan scoutship** landed there in 2366 and was destroyed by its crew to prevent the ship's capture. One crew member, **Centurion Bochra,** was marooned there with Commander **Geordi La Forge** for several hours. Both men suffered progressive breakdown of their synaptic connections, which La Forge speculated was a result of the "electromagnetic soup" in the planet's atmosphere. ("The Enemy" [TNG]). In 2368, Galorndon Core served as a rendezvous site for the delivery of a stolen deflector array to a **Barolian freighter**. ("Unification, Part II" [TNG]). Galorndon Core was also the site at which **Chulak** of Romulus experienced a crushing defeat. ("The Thaw" [VGR]). *We don't know who Chulak was defeated by, or when.*

Galt. (Joseph Ruskin). Master of the **drill thralls** on planet **Triskelion**. He was responsible for training newly captured aliens, including crew members from the *U.S.S. Enterprise* who were captured in 2268. Galt answered only to the rulers of the planet, the **Providers**. ("The Gamesters of Triskelion" [TOS]). *Joseph Ruskin also played Tumek in "House of Quark" (DS9) and "Looking for* par'Mach *in All the Wrong Places" (DS9), and the voice of an informant in "Improbable Cause" (DS9).*

Galvin V. Planet. Among the inhabitants of Galvin V, a marriage is considered successful only if children are produced in the first year. ("Data's Day" [TNG]).

Galway, Lieutenant. (Beverly Washburn). *Enterprise* crew member who was part of the landing party to planet **Gamma Hydra IV** in 2267. Galway contracted a radiation illness that sped the aging process. Though she was ten years younger than Kirk, she succumbed to the disease, dying of old age. ("The Deadly Years" [TOS]).

"Gambit, Part I." *Next Generation* episode #156. Teleplay by Naren Shankar. Story by Christopher Hatton and Naren Shankar. Directed by Peter Lauritson. Stardate 47135.2. *First aired in 1993. Picard and Riker infiltrate a band of mercenaries that are raiding archaeological sites on several planets.* GUEST CAST: Richard Lynch as **Baran**, **Arctus**; Robin Curtis as **Tallera**; Caitlin Brown as **Vekor**; Cameron Thor as **Narik**; Alan Altshuld as **Wranac**; Bruce Gray as **Chekote**, **Admiral**; Sabrina LeBeauf as **Giusti**, **Ensign**; Stephen Lee as Bartender; Derek Webster as Sanders, Lt. SEE: **Argus sector; Baran, Arctus; Barradas III; Barradas system; Calder II; Chekote, Admiral; Debrune; Dessica II; Dessican bartender; Draken IV; Galen; Giusti, Ensign; Nafir, ruins of; Narik; neural servo; Tallera; Taugan sector; terikon particle decay; T'Paal; V'Shar; Vekor; Yadalla Prime; Yranac.**

"Gambit, Part II." *Next Generation* episode #157. Teleplay by Ronald D. Moore. Story by Naren Shankar. Directed by Alexander Singer. Stardate 47160.1. *First aired in 1993. Picard discovers that Vulcan extremists are trying to steal an ancient weapon of enormous power.* Richard Lynch as **Baran**, **Arctus**; Robin Curtis as **Tallera**; Caitlin Brown as **Vekor**; Cameron Thor as **Narik**; James Worthy as **Koral**; Sabrina LeBeauf as **Giusti**, **Ensign**; Martin Goslins as **Satok**, **Security Minister**. SEE: **Baran, Arctus; Health and Safety inspection; Hyralan sector; *Justman, Shuttlecraft*; Klingon bloodwine; Koral; psionic resonator; Riker, William T.; Satok, Security Minister; Starbase 227; Stone of Gol; Surak; T'Karath Sanctuary; Time of Awakening; *Toron*-class shuttlecraft; Vulcan isolationist movement; Vulcans.**

gambling device. Spherical game mechanism of unknown origin, a game of chance that many players found irresistible. **Martus Mazur** obtained such a device in 2370 from a person named **Cos**. It was not until later that Martus realized that the device actually altered the laws of probability, initially bringing him good fortune, but later causing bad and even dangerous occurences, forcing Deep Space 9 personnel to destroy the devices. ("Rivals" [DS9]). SEE: **Club Martus**.

"Game, The." *Next Generation* episode #106. Teleplay by Brannon Braga. Story by Susan Sackett & Fred Bronson, and Brannon Braga. Directed by Corey Allen. Stardate 45208.2. *First aired in 1991. An addictive computer game leaves the* Enterprise-D *crew open for conquest. This episode featured Wesley Crusher's first appearance on* Star Trek: The Next Generation *since "Final Mission" (TNG).* GUEST CAST: Ashley Judd as **Lefler**, **Ensign Robin**; Katherine Moffat as **Jol**, **Etana**; Colm Meaney as **O'Brien**, **Miles**; Patti Yasutake as **Ogawa**, **Nurse Alyssa**; Wil Wheaton as **Crusher**, **Wesley**; Diane M. Hurley as Woman; Majel Barrett as Computer voice. SEE: **A.F.; Boothby; chocolate; Crusher, Wesley; *Endeavour, U.S.S.*; frontal lobe; Horne, Walter; Jol, Etana; Ktarian game; Ktarian vessel; Ktarians; Lefler's Laws; Lefler, Ensign Robin; *Merrimack, U.S.S.*; Novakovich; O'Brien, Molly; Oceanus IV; Ogawa, Nurse Alyssa; Phoenix Cluster; reticular formation; Risa; Sadie Hawkins Dance; septal area; serotonin; site-to-site transport; Starbase 67; Starbase 82; Tarvokian pound cake; Troi, Deanna; *Zhukov, U.S.S.***

Gamelan V. Class-M planet. Gamelan V experienced a dramatic increase in atmospheric radiation in 2367. The incident was found to be the result of an unidentified space vehicle that had entered the orbit of the planet. The ship, apparently adrift for at least three centuries, was carrying large amounts of dangerous radioactive waste that was leaking into Gamelan V's upper atmosphere. The *Enterprise*-D responded to Gamelan chairman **Songi**'s distress call, and was successful in towing the waste barge into the Gamelan sun. ("Final Mission" [TNG]).

"Gamesters of Triskelion, The." Original Series episode #46. Written by Margaret Armen. Directed by Gene Nelson. Stardate 3211.7. *First broadcast in 1968.* Enterprise *crew members are abducted and forced to fight to the death for the amusement of gamesters who gamble on the results. Director Gene Nelson first found fame as a dancer and actor in movie musicals.* GUEST

CAST: Joseph Ruskin as **Galt**; Angelique Pettyjohn as **Shahna**; Steve Sandor as **Lars**; Jane Ross as **Tamoon**; Victoria George as **Haines, Ensign**; Dick Crockett as Andorian thrall; Mickey Morton as **Kloog**; Bob Johnson as Provider voice #1; Paul Baxley as Kirk's stunt double. SEE: **collar of obedience; drill thralls; Galt; Gamma II; Haines, Ensign; Kloog; Lars; M24 Alpha; Providers; quatloo; Shahna; Tamoon; trisec; Triskelion.**

Gamma 7 outpost. Federation outpost colony located near the **Demilitarized Zone**. ("For the Uniform" [DS9]).

Gamma 7 Sector. Region of space. Assigned service area of the ill-fated ***U.S.S. Lantree*** as of stardate 42494. ("Unnatural Selection" [TNG]).

Gamma 7A System. Solar system with a fourth-magnitude star located in Sector 39J, containing billions of inhabitants. The system was destroyed and all inhabitants were believed killed in 2268 by a massive spaceborne **amoeba** creature. The same organism also destroyed the *Starship* ***Intrepid***, sent to investigate the incident. ("The Immunity Syndrome" [TOS]).

Gamma 400 star system. Location of **Starbase 12**, which was the command base in that sector of space. ("Space Seed" [TOS]).

Gamma Arigulon System. Planetary system in which the *U.S.S. LaSalle* reported a series of radiation anomalies just prior to stardate 44246.3. ("Reunion" [TNG]).

Gamma Canaris region. Area of space near system Epsilon Canaris. The ***Shuttlecraft Galileo*** was on course for the *Enterprise* from **Epsilon Canaris III** on stardate 3219 when it was pulled off course to a planet in the Gamma Canaris region by an electromagnetic disturbance. ("Metamorphosis" [TOS]). *That disturbance was later found to be the* ***Companion****, the life-form who cared for scientist* ***Zefram Cochrane****, who was living on a planetoid in this region. This information was not revealed by Kirk and company after the mission. Cochrane's fate remains unknown to the rest of the Federation.*

Gamma Erandi Nebula. An interstellar gaseous cloud. The *Enterprise*-D was assigned to study the Gamma Erandi Nebula following the **Trade Agreements Conference** on Betazed in 2366. Because of the tremendous subspace interference generated by the nebula, *Enterprise*-D communications were blocked for two days. ("Ménage à Troi" [TNG]).

Gamma Eridon. A star system in Klingon space. Picard's armada retreated there to regroup, following the disabling of their **tachyon detection grid** in 2368. ("Redemption, Part II" [TNG]).

Gamma Hromi II. Planet. Location of a **Gatherer** camp, where the first negotiations to reunite the Acamarians and the Gatherers took place. ("The Vengeance Factor" [TNG]).

Gamma Hydra IV. Class-M planet in the Gamma Hydra system; the location of experimental colony where all six of its members, none of them over 30 years of age, died in 2267 of a radiation-induced hyperaccelerated-aging disease. The disease later afflicted members of an *Enterprise* landing party that investigated the incident. Analysis of a comet in the Gamma Hydra system showed that radiation on the extreme lower range of the scale might have caused the disease. ("The Deadly Years" [TOS]).

Gamma Hydra. Star system. In Starfleet Academy's ***Kobayashi Maru*** training simulation, Gamma Hydra was the location of the *Kobayashi Maru* when it sent its distress call. (*Star Trek II: The Wrath of Khan*).

Gamma II. Planetoid, site of an automatic communication and astrogation station. In 2268, a landing party from the *Starship Enterprise* was scheduled to perform a routine check on the station when the **Providers** of **Triskelion** transported them to their planet. ("The Gamesters of Triskelion" [TOS]).

Gamma Quadrant. One-quarter of the entire **Milky Way Galaxy**, the portion most distant from the United Federation of Planets. At its closest point, the Gamma Quadrant is some 40,000 light-years from Federation space. In 2369, a stable wormhole was discovered near the planet **Bajor**, enabling the free flow of traffic to and from that distant part of the galaxy. ("Emissary" [DS9]). Even without benefit of the **Bajoran wormhole**, archaeologist **Vash** explored the Gamma Quadrant for two years, thanks to **Q**. In the Gamma Quadrant, she discovered some remarkable civilizations, including cultures whose histories date back millions of years. ("Q-Less" [DS9]).

Gamma Quadrant
Delta Quadrant
Alpha Quadrant
Earth
Beta Quadrant

Gamma Tauri IV. Planet. Location of an unmanned Federation monitoring post. **Ferengi** agents stole a T-9 energy converter from the Gamma Tauri IV station in 2364, just prior to first contact with the Federation. ("The Last Outpost" [TNG]).

Gamma Trianguli VI. Idyllic Class-M planet with a tropical climate. The atmosphere of Gamma Trianguli VI has no harmful bacteria and it even completely screens out any negative effects from the sun. The humanoid inhabitants of the planet worshipped a sophisticated computer they called **Vaal**, which provided for the people by controlling the planet's weather. Individuals on this planet had a life expectancy of approximately ten thousand years. The need for procreation was thus eliminated (or at least greatly postponed), making the concept of children an unknown. All this changed in 2267 when Vaal was destroyed by the *Starship Enterprise,* forcing the inhabitants of Gamma Triangulai VI to resume a more normal society. ("The Apple" [TOS]).

Gamma Vertis IV. Planet. The entire population of Gamma Vertis IV is unable to speak. ("The Empath" [TOS]).

gamma radiation. Highly energetic electromagnetic radiation with wavelengths less than 10^{-10} meters, associated with nuclear processes. Modulated gamma bursts were detected in **Meridian**'s sun Trialus by the ***U.S.S Defiant*** in 2371, prior to the planet Meridian's shift into a corporeal state. ("Meridian" [DS9]). **Dr. Paul Stubbs** used bursts of gamma radiation in an attempt to eradicate the **nanites** that inhabited the *Enterprise*-D computer core in 2366. ("Evolution" [TNG]). Damage to a starship's warp core can sometimes cause it to leak gamma radiation. ("Warlord" [VGR]).

Gamzian wine. Intoxicating beverage. Gamzian wine was served at **Quark's bar** on Deep Space 9. Quark commented to archaeologist **Vash** that he didn't know what was more intoxicating, her negotiating skills or his Gamzian wine. ("Q-Less" [DS9], "The Storyteller" [DS9]). **Alsia** blamed the Gamzian wine for her telling **Martus** about her investment plans. (Rivals" [DS9]).

Ganalda IV. Planet. In a battle with the Federation in 2373, Klingon forces were forced to retreat from Ganalda IV. ("Nor the Battle to the Strong" [DS9]).

Gandhi, Mahatma. (Noel de Souza). 1869-1948. Great spiritual leader on planet **Earth** during the 20th century. A native of the nation of India, Gandhi fought for political independence from the British government, but did so with a radical philosophy of nonviolence. Gandhi also strived to improve the quality of life for the lowest classes of society, preaching the benefits of manual labor and simple living. In 2373, *Voyager*'s **Emergency Medical Hologram** incorporated segments of Gandhi's personality into his personality improvement project. ("Darkling" [VGR]).

Gandhi, U.S.S. Federation starship *Ambassador* class, Starfleet registry number NCC-26632. Lieutenant **Thomas Riker**, with some assistance from Captain Picard, was assigned to the *Gandhi* in 2369 after his rescue from planet **Nervala IV**. He transferred to the ship just prior to its departure for a terraforming mission in the Lagana sector. ("Second Chances" [TNG]). Thomas Riker was serving aboard the ***Gandhi*** when he began to express pro-Maquis sentiments. By 2371 Thomas Riker deserted his post aboard the *Gandhi* to become a member of the **Maquis**. ("Defiant" [DS9]). *Named for Mohandas Karamchand Gandhi (1869-1948), leader of the Indian nationalist movement, an influential philosopher who advocated nonviolent confrontation and civil disobedience as a means of fostering political change on Earth.*

Ganges, U.S.S. Starfleet *Danube*-class **runabout**, registry number NCC-72454, one of three runabouts assigned to station Deep Space 9. ("Past Prologue." [DS9]). *The* Ganges *was first seen in "Past Prologue" (DS9). In that episode, it sported a "roll bar" that contained sensor equipment. From a visual-effects standpoint, the purpose of the roll bar was to make it easier to tell the* Ganges *from the* Yangtzee Kiang *in that episode's chase sequence. The* Ganges *was also seen in "Q-Less" (DS9), "Vortex" (DS9) and* "The Siege" (DS9). *The* Ganges *was destroyed by a* ***T'Lani munitions cruiser*** *in 2370.* ("Armageddon Game" [DS9]). *The ship was named after the river in northern India and eastern Pakistan that flows 1560 miles from the Himalayas to the Bay of Bengal.*

ganglion. A mass of nerve tissues that join each other outside the brain or spinal cord. **Dr. Julian Bashir** said he would have been valedictorian instead of salutatorian in his graduating class if he hadn't mistaken a pre-ganglionic fiber for a post-ganglionic nerve. ("Q-Less" [DS9]). *An understandable mistake...*

Garadius system. Planetary system. The *Enterprise*-D visited the Garadius system on a diplomatic mission following its encounter with a Romulan science vessel in 2368. ("The Next Phase" [TNG]).

Garak (mirror). (Andrew Robinson). In the **mirror universe**, first officer of station **Terok Nor** in 2370. ("Crossover" [DS9]). In 2371, this Garak tortured and killed **Rom (mirror)** after Rom revealed a **Terran rebellion** plan to get **Jennifer Sisko (mirror)** away from **Terok Nor (mirror)**. ("Through the Looking Glass" [DS9]).

Garak, Elim. (Andrew Robinson). Former agent of the powerful Cardassian **Obsidian Order** intelligence service until he was exiled to space station **Terok Nor** in 2368. ("The Wire" [DS9]). Garak was the only Cardassian citizen left on the station after the Cardassian retreat from the Bajoran system in 2369, at which time the station became known as **Deep Space 9**. While in exile, Garak opened a clothing shop on the station's **Promenade** and worked as a tailor. Garak made no references to his past, calling himself just "plain, simple Garak," but some people on the station still regarded him as a spy, including Dr. **Julian Bashir**, although the two eventually became friends. ("Past Prologue" [DS9]). Despite his protestations to Bashir, Garak maintained some contact with Cardassian intelligence. ("Cardassians" [DS9]). Garak enjoyed raising **Edosian orchids** as a hobby. His experience with plants proved to be of value when he served as a gardener at the **Cardassian Embassy on Romulus**. Oddly enough, there were an unusual number of accidental deaths among high-ranking Romulan officials while Garak served on Romulus. ("Broken Link" [DS9]).

While still a member of the Obsidian Order, Garak had volunteered to have a **cranial implant** placed into his skull, to help him resist torture if captured by an enemy. Garak found exiled life on Terok Nor (later Deep Space 9) to be intolerable, so he activated the cranial implant and left it on. The implant served as a powerful narcotic on which Garak became physically dependent until 2370, when the unit malfunctioned, nearly costing Garak his life. Dr. Bashir was able to remove the device. ("The Wire" [DS9]).

Even in exile, Garak never gave up hope of eventual political rehabilitation. ("Profit and Loss" [DS9]). Although **Enabran Tain** had been responsible for Garak's exile and even tried to have Garak killed, Garak found isolation so bitter that in 2371 he jumped at the opportunity to serve again with Tain. Garak participated in Tain's disastrous joint attack by the Obsidian Order and the Romulan **Tal Shiar** against the **Founders** of the **Dominion**. Garak was the only apparent Cardassian survivor of that battle. ("Improbable Cause" [DS9], "The Die is Cast" [DS9]).

Elim Garak distrusted **Gul Dukat** ("The Wire" [DS9], "Civil Defense" [DS9], "Improbable Cause" [DS9], and "The Die is Cast" [DS9]), because Garak had played a part in the downfall and execution of Dukat's father. ("Civil Defense" [DS9]). Garak nevertheless fought alongside Dukat to defend the **Detapa Council** in 2372, when Klingon warriors attempted to abduct the Council. ("The Way of the Warrior" [DS9]). Even more ironically, Garak found himself attracted to Dukat's daughter, **Tora Ziyal**, when she took up residence on Deep Space 9 in 2372. ("For the Cause" [DS9]).

Garak returned briefly to **Cardassia** in 2371 to help rescue **Kira Nerys**, who had been taken prisoner by the Obsidian Order. ("Second Skin" [DS9]). As a passenger on the *Defiant* while the ship was at the **Founders' homeworld** in 2372, Garak attempted to obliterate the planet by overriding the launch controls for the ship's quantum torpedoes. Had Garak been successful, he would have killed all of the Founders. For his actions, Captain Sisko ordered that Garak be imprisoned for six months in a holding cell. ("Broken Link" [DS9]).

Garak was the son of **Obsidian Order** chief Tain. Ironically, it was Tain who gave the order to have Garak exiled to **Terok Nor**. Garak spent much of his life desperately trying to please his father, although Tain kept his son at arm's length. It was only in 2373, when Tain was on his deathbed in a Jem'Hadar prison camp, that he confessed to Garak that he was proud of his son. ("In Purgatory's Shadow" [DS9]).

Garak's quarters on DS9 were Chamber 901, Habitat Level H-3. ("The Wire" [DS9]). *Garak was first seen in "Past Prologue" (DS9).*

Garan miner. (Michael Fiske). Administrator for the Garan mining colony in the Delta Quadrant. The miner, along with the rest of his colony, was killed in 2373 when the **Tak Tak consul** "purified" him of the **macrovirus** infection. ("Macrocosm" [VGR]).

Garan mining colony. Settlement on a planet in the Delta Quadrant. The colony was destroyed in 2373 by a **Tak Tak consul** in an attempt to stop the spread of the **macrovirus**. ("Macrocosm" [VGR]).

Garan, Araya. (Robin Groves). Native of the **Vhnori** homeworld and wife of **Hatil Garan**. Araya wanted Hatil to undergo the **Vhnori transference ritual** when he became a burden on the family after a debilitating accident. She felt his choice to die in 2371 was a selfless gift to his family. ("Emanations" [VGR]).

Garan, Hatil. (Jefrey Alan Chandler). Native of the **Vhnori** homeworld. Hatil suffered a debilitating accident and, in 2371, chose to undergo the **Vhnori transference ritual** since he had become a burden on his family. After meeting Harry Kim, Hatil began to have doubts about his beliefs concerning the afterlife. Hatil decided not to undergo the ritual, but instead fled to live in the Cararian Mountains with friends. ("Emanations" [VGR]). *Jefrey Alan Chandler also played the Trill guardian in "Facets" (DS9).*

Garanian bolites. Small creatures that, when applied to a person's body, cause extreme itching and brief skin discoloration. Jake Sisko and Nog played a practical joke by sprinkling Garanian bolites on two unsuspecting Bajorans on the Promenade at station Deep Space 9 in 2369. ("A Man Alone" [DS9]).

Garcia, Henry. (Daniel Zacapa). Resident of **Sanctuary District** A on **Earth** from 2022 to 2024. Garcia had been an employee of a **San Francisco** brewery, but ended up in the Sanctuary District after he lost his job. ("Past Tense, Part II" [DS9]).

***garili* tree.** Blooming tree found on the **Vhnori** homeworld. ("Emanations" [VGR]).

Gariman Sector. Area of Federation space. The *Enterprise*-D surveyed the Gariman Sector in 2369. ("Rightful Heir" [TNG]).

Garin. (Richard Cansino). Scientist from planet **Bre'el IV**. Garin was on duty in the planetary emergency center during the *Enterprise*-D's mission to restore the Bre'el IV moon to its normal orbit. ("Déjà Q" [TNG]). *Garin's name is never spoken in the dialog of "Déjà Q," and his name is only from the script.*

Garland, Faith. (Megan Gallagher). Military officer who served as a nurse with the Woman's Army Corps on Earth in the 20th century. Garland, who was stationed at Wright Field, was part of a team that investigated an extraterrestrial spacecraft of Ferengi origin that crashed on Earth near **Roswell**, New Mexico, in July 1947. Garland was something of a dreamer who foresaw a time when humanity would reach to the stars, forming a vast federation of planets. Garland was engaged to Professor **Jeff Carlson**. ("Little Green Men" [DS9]). *This character's first name was not mentioned in dialog, but is from the script. Megan Gallagher also played Mareel in "Invasive Procedures" (DS9).*

garlanic tree. Plant form indigenous to the **Elaysian** homeworld. Ensign **Melora Pazlar** carried a cane made from the wood of a garlanic tree. ("Melora" [DS9]).

garlic soup. Broth made with the cloves of an onionlike Earth plant. Tom Paris said that Doc Brown made garlic soup for his patients. ("Cathexis" [VGR]).

garnesite. Mineral substance. Garnesite can be heated with phaser fire to give off warmth and a dim orange light. ("Parturition" [VGR]).

Garon II. Planet. Site of a disastrous away mission involving crew members from the ***U.S.S. Wellington***. Ensign **Ro Laren** disobeyed orders during that mission, and eight people died. ("Ensign Ro" [TNG]).

Garrett, Captain Rachel. (Tricia O'Neil). Captain of the ***U.S.S. Enterprise*-C**. Garrett, along with the *Enterprise*-C, vanished from her "proper" timeline in 2344, when a torpedo explosion near

Narendra III opened up a **temporal rift**, emerging in 2366. This disappearance created an alternate timeline in which the Klingon Empire was at war with the Federation. In this altered future, Garrett was killed in a Klingon attack. **Lieutenant Richard Castillo** subsequently assumed command of the *Enterprise*-C, returning it to its proper time so that history could be restored. ("Yesterday's *Enterprise*" [TNG]). *Tricia O'Neil also played* ***Kurak*** *in "Suspicions" (TNG).*

Garrovick, Captain. Commanding officer of the ***U.S.S. Farragut*** who was killed, along with 200 other crew members, by the **dikironium cloud creature** at planet **Tycho IV** in 2257. **James T. Kirk** recalled Garrovick as one of the finest men he had ever known and carried the memory of his death through the years. Garrovick's son confronted the same creature aboard the *U.S.S. Enterprise* in 2268 under the command of Captain James T. Kirk. ("Obsession" [TOS]).

Garrovick, Ensign. (Stephen Brooks). Son of **Captain Garrovick**. Ensign Garrovick served as a security officer aboard the *Starship Enterprise*. In 2268, Garrovick encountered the same deadly **dikironium cloud creature** that had killed his father years before. Like Kirk in 2257, Ensign Garrovick paused briefly before firing at the creature, and believed his hesitation caused the death of several people. Later, the crew learned that phaser fire had no effect upon the creature, absolving Garrovick and Kirk of guilt. ("Obsession" [TOS]).

Garth of Izar. (Steve Ihnat). Famous 23rd-century starship fleet captain whose exploits are required reading at Starfleet Academy. Garth's achievements included the historic victory at **Axanar** in the 2250s that helped preserve the Federation. In the 2260s, Garth became seriously injured in a terrible accident. He recovered with the help of the inhabitants of planet **Antos IV**. The people of Antos IV repaired his body by teaching him the art of **cellular metamorphosis**, but did not realize that the accident had rendered him criminally insane. Garth ordered the crew of his starship to destroy Antos IV, after which he was committed to the Federation rehab colony on planet **Elba II**. In 2268, Garth managed to overpower the colony's keepers, proclaimed himself Lord Garth, master of the universe, and attempted to commandeer the *Starship Enterprise*, which was visiting the colony. Garth's escape attempt was aided by the Antos cellular-metamorphosis process, which allowed him to change his shape to become any person he wished. After Garth was recaptured, colony administrator **Donald Cory** indicated optimism that new experimental medications might be able to restore Garth to sanity. ("Whom Gods Destroy" [TOS]).

Garth system. Malcorian name for a solar system near planet **Malcor III**. It was to have been the destination of the first Malcorian warp-speed space flight in 2368. ("First Contact" [TNG]).

Garuth. A figure in ancient Kriosian and Valtese history. Garuth was an empathic metamorph, who was loved by two brothers, **Krios** and **Valt**. Garuth was kidnapped by Krios and taken away to a neighboring system, triggering a war that lasted for centuries. ("The Perfect Mate" [TNG]).

Garvin. (Michael Rothhaar). Inhabitant of planet **Barkon IV**. Garvin was a town magistrate and the widower father of **Gia**. He took Data into his home when the android wandered into his village with amnesia in 2370. Garvin developed radiation poisoning from exposure to fragments from a Federation deep space probe. He was cured of the radiation sickness by Data. ("Thine Own Self" [TNG]).

Gary 7. SEE: **Seven, Gary.**

Gasko. Romulan vessel. The *Gasko* reported sighting the runabout ***Rio Grande*** flying without a pilot around stardate 47573. ("Paradise" [DS9]).

gasoline. Chemical fossil fuel used on Earth during the 19th through the 21st centuries. A volatile, flammable liquid hydrocarbon used in internal combustion engines. ("The 37's" [VGR]).

Gaspar VII. Planet. Homeworld of Starfleet Captain **Edwell**. ("Starship Mine" [TNG]).

Gates, Ensign. (Joyce Robinson). Bridge officer aboard the *Enterprise*-D in 2370. Gates was on duty when the ship was en route to Starbase 219. ("Phantasms" [TNG]). She operated conn during the search for the ***U.S.S. Pegasus*** in the **Devolin system.** ("The Pegasus" [TNG]). **Lieutenant Ro Laren** relieved her at the conn when she visited the *Enterprise*-D on stardate 47941. ("Preemptive Strike" [TNG]). *Ensign Gates was first seen in "Descent, Part I" (TNG) and was in several seventh-season episodes. She was present at Worf's surprise 30th birthday party in "Parallels" (TNG).*

Gatherers. Nomadic marauders from planet **Acamar III.** Believed to have been responsible for numerous raids on various outposts and ships in sectors near Acamar III, the Gatherers were genetically identical to the **Acamarians** who remained on their homeworld. The Gatherers split from the more conservative Acamarians a century ago when they refused to accept a peace settlement in that planet's brutal clan warfare, but agreed to return home in 2366 as part of an accord negotiated by Jean-Luc Picard and Acamarian Sovereign **Marouk**. ("The Vengeance Factor" [TNG]). *The Federation science outpost attacked by the Gatherers just prior to the episode used a large scenic background painting originally from the classic 1956 movie* Forbidden Planet. *The painting is a planetscape seen through the window of the station.*

Gaudaal's Lament. Poem written by renowned Bajoran poet **Akorem Laan** more than 200 years ago. In the 24th century, Bajoran schoolchildren were required to memorize *Gaudaal's Lament*. ("Accession" [DS9]).

Gaullists. Dominant party within the French National Assembly on **Earth** prior to the **Neo-Trotskyists** of the 2020's. ("Past Tense, Part I" [DS9]).

Gault. Planet. Location of a farming colony where young **Worf** spent his formative years, cared for by his adoptive parents, Sergey and Helena Rozhenko. ("Heart of Glory" [TNG], "Sins of the Father" [TNG]). Gault was a sparsely populated world with only about 20,000 inhabitants. ("Let He Who Is Without Sin..." [DS9]).

Gaunt Gary. (Larry A. Hankin). Famous pool player from mid-20th century Earth. Gaunt Gary hustled the great Willie Mosconi in Ames Pool Hall, New York in 1953. Tom Paris programmed Gaunt Gary into his holodeck recreation of **Chez Sandrine**. ("The Cloud" [VGR]). During the *Voyager*'s encounter with a distortion ring in 2372, Gaunt Gary was not interested in the dangerous phenomenon at all; he just wanted someone to play pool with him. ("Twisted" [VGR]).

Gav. (John Wheeler). **Tellarite** ambassador with a distinguished snout and an attitude. Gav was murdered with a Vulcan technique called ***tal-shaya*** while en route to the historic **Babel Conference** of 2267. ("Journey to Babel" [TOS]).

Gavaline tea. Beverage. Lwaxana Troi enjoyed Gavaline tea while visiting Deep Space 9 in 2372. ("The Muse" [DS9]).

Gavara system. Star system located in the Gamma Quadrant. In 2372, Kira Nerys, Dr. Julian Bashir, and Jadzia Dax piloted a runabout to the Gavara system on a planet survey mission. ("The Quickening" [DS9]).

Gedana post. Trill base. Location where **Arjin**'s father served as a pilot instructor for 40 years. ("Playing God" [DS9]).

Gem. (Kathryn Hays). Native of one of the planets in the **Minaran** star system. Gem was selected by the **Vians** and tested in 2268 to see if her people would be spared the destruction of the impending nova. Kirk, Spock, and Dr. McCoy were also captured and subjected to various forms of torture while Gem watched, observing their compassion and willingness to sacrifice their lives for one another. The Vians then observed Gem's reaction, and judged whether Gem learned the sense of compassion and sacrifice. Gem was a **Minaran empath** and was willing to give her life to save Dr. McCoy from his injuries, which were inflicted by the Vians. This action convinced the Vians that her civilization was the one to be saved from extinction. ("The Empath" [TOS]).

Gema IV. Planet in the Delta Quadrant controlled by the **Kazon-Nistrim**. Gema IV possessed a defense force. ("Basics, Part I" [VGR]).

Gemaris V. Planet. The *Enterprise*-D visited Gemaris V in 2366, when Captain Picard mediated a trade dispute between the Gemarians and their neighbors, the Dachlyds. ("Captain's Holiday" [TNG]).

Gemulon V. Habitable planet. Original destination of colony ship ***S.S. Santa Maria***. ("Paradise" [DS9]).

gene splicing. Genetic engineering technique. Late in 2372, **Lon Suder** developed a new gene splicing technique and tested it on orchids. He hoped to later apply his techniques to make the *Voyager's* airponic vegetable garden more productive. ("Basics, Part I" [VGR]). SEE: **Tuvok orchid**.

General Orders, Starfleet. SEE: **Starfleet General Orders and Regulations.**

Genesis Device. Short-range torpedo intended to test the **Project Genesis** terraforming process. The Genesis Device was prematurely activated in 2285 after being stolen by **Khan Noonien Singh**. *(Star Trek II: The Wrath of Khan).*

Genesis Planet. Class-M world formed from the gaseous matter in the **Mutara Nebula** by the **Genesis Device** in 2285. The planet appeared to have an almost idyllic environment, but it was later learned that dangerously unstable **protomatter** used in the Genesis process caused the planet itself to become dangerously unstable and eventually explode. *(Star Trek III: The Search for Spock).*

Genesis. SEE: **Project Genesis**.

"Genesis." *Next Generation* episode #171. Written by Brannon Braga. Directed by Gates McFadden. Stardate 47653.2. *First* *aired in 1994. A cure for a simple flu becomes a disease that causes the crew to regress into their evolutionary forbearers.* GUEST CAST: Patti Yasutake as **Ogawa, Nurse Alyssa**; Dwight Schultz as **Barclay, Reginald**; Carlos Ferro as **Dern, Ensign**; Majel Barrett as Computer voice. SEE: **alpha four seven authorization; amniotic fluid; amniotic scan; amphibian; aquatic lab; arachnid; arboretum; Australopithecine; Barclay's Protomorphosis Syndrome; Barclay, Reginald; biospectral analysis; cholic acid; Crusher, Beverly; Cyprion cactus; Dern, Ensign; electrophoretic activity; Hacopian, Dr.; Hayes, Lieutenant; hypothalmic series; iguana; intravascular pressure; introns; K-3 cell count; lemur; microcellular scan; nictitating membrane; Ogawa, Alyssa; Ongilin caviar; pheromone; Powell, Lieutenant Andrew; pygmy marmoset; retrovirus; ribocyatic flux; Selar, Dr; Smith, Rebecca; Spot; spread pattern delta nine four; Starfleet Medical Database; Symbalene Blood Burn; T-cell; Terellian Death Syndrome; Urodelean flu; Worf.**

Genestra, Sabin. (Bruce French). Aide to Starfleet **Admiral Norah Satie.** Genestra came aboard the *Enterprise*-D with Satie in 2367 for the purpose of investigating a suspected security breach. Genestra accused *Enterprise*-D crew member **Tarses** of being a coconspirator in the theft of *Enterprise*-D engine schematics by Romulan operatives. Genestra, a **Betazoid**, sensed guilt in Tarses, but was incorrect in his accusation. Tarses had been hiding the fact that his ancestry included Romulan blood, but Tarses had nothing to do with the espionage being investigated. ("The Drumhead" [TNG]).

genetic bonding. In **Betazoid** culture, a term for ritual telepathic joining of children at an early age as a prelude to eventual marriage. **Deanna Troi** was genetically bonded to **Wyatt Miller** when both were children, although they eventually chose not to marry. ("Haven" [TNG]).

genetic virus. Deadly biological weapon. ("Blood Oath" [DS9]). See: **Albino**

genetronic replicator. Experimental medical device, developed by neurogeneticist **Dr. Toby Russell**, designed to translate the genetic code into a specific set of replication instructions, allowing the device to "grow" a replacement organ at an accelerated rate. Starfleet Medical turned down three requests by Russell to test the device on humanoid patients, prior to her successful implementation of the technique on Lieutenant Worf in 2368. ("Ethics" [TNG]).

Genghis Khan. (Nathan Jung). Warrior leader on planet Earth (c.1162-1227), conqueror of much of Earth's Asian continent. An image of Genghis Khan was re-created by the inhabitants of the planet **Excalbia** as part of a study conducted in 2269 to examine the human philosophies of "good" and "evil." ("The Savage Curtain" [TOS]). SEE: **Yarnek.**

Genome Colony. A self-contained society of humans founded in 2168 on planet **Moab IV**. The colony founders built a sealed biosphere on the planet, in which they tried to establish a perfectly engineered society. Every member of the colony was genetically designed and trained from birth to perform a specific task. In 2368, the Genome Colony was endangered by an approaching **stellar core fragment** that threatened to disrupt the planet. In order to avoid destruction, colony leader **Aaron Conor** allowed a group of engineers from the *Enterprise*-D to assist in fortifying the biosphere. The acceptance of outside aid was strongly opposed by colony member **Martin Benbeck**, who was greatly concerned about exposure to outsiders. Benbeck's fears were realized when 23 members of the colony chose to leave with the *Enterprise*-D, leaving irreparable gaps in the genetic makeup of the colony. SEE: **Bates, Hannah**. ("The Masterpiece Society" [TNG]).

genotron. Medical device used by **Vidiian** scientists to reconstruct a person's entire genome. In 2371, Dr. **Sulan** used a genotron to extract **B'Elanna Torres**'s Klingon DNA to produce a fully Klingon version of herself. In the process, a fully human Torres was also created. ("Faces" [VGR]).

George and Gracie. Two humpback whales, species *Megaptera novaeangliae*, that wandered into San Francisco Bay on Earth during the 1980s. They were raised in captivity at the **Cetacean Institute** in Sausalito, before being released into the open ocean because the institute could not afford to feed them. George and Gracie, both highly intelligent individuals, agreed to travel to the 23rd century, where they saved Earth from the effects of an alien space probe, and later began the repopulation of their species on Earth. (*Star Trek IV: The Voyage Home*). SEE: **Probe, the**. *The full-sized whales seen on the surface were supervised by Michael Lantieri, intercut with a couple of shots of real humpbacks in the ocean near Maui that were filmed by John Ferrari. The underwater versions of George and Gracie were models created by Walt Conti, who was also responsible for Ensign Darwin on* seaQuest DSV.

Gerron. (Kenny Morrison). **Maquis** resistance fighter who joined the crew of the *Voyager.* Gerron was regarded as being shy and withdrawn, and in late 2371, Commander Chakotay felt Tuvok's **field training** might help Gerron feel better about himself by teaching him new skills and helping him to set and accomplish goals. ("Learning Curve" [VGR]).

Gessard, Yvette. (Herta Ware). Mother of *Enterprise*-D Captain **Jean-Luc Picard**. ("Chain of Command, Part II" [TNG]). *Picard's mother was briefly seen in a fantasy sequence in "Where No One Has Gone Before" (TNG).* SEE: **Picard, Yvette Gessard.**

gettle. Wild herd animal, native to the planet **Cardassia**. ("Chain of Command, Part II" [TNG]).

Gettor, Minister. Member of the **Bajoran Chamber of Ministers** on Bajor. In 2372, Minister Gettor visited Deep Space 9 in order to elicit the Emissary's support for his land reform program. ("Shattered Mirror" [DS9]).

Gettysburg, U.S.S. Federation starship, *Constellation* class, Starfleet registry number NCC-3890, formerly commanded by Captain **Mark Jameson** prior to his promotion to admiral. The *Gettysburg* was the last ship Jameson commanded. ("Too Short a Season" [TNG]).

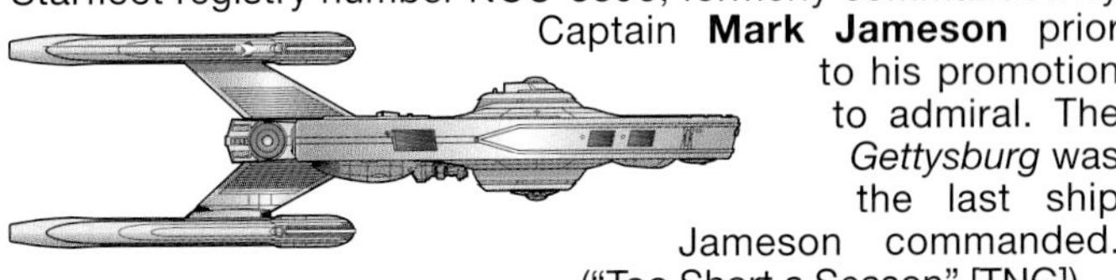

Ghemor, Legate. (Lawrence Pressman). Prominent member of the **Cardassian Central Command**. In 2371, Legate Ghemor was suspected by the **Obsidian Order** of being a member of the **Cardassian underground movement.** In an effort to expose his true sympathies, Ghemor was told that his daughter, **Iliana**, had returned from a ten-year covert mission where she had assumed the identity of a Bajoran terrorist. In fact, Iliana had not returned, and the Obsidian Order had substituted **Kira Nerys**, surgically altered to resemble his daughter, in an elaborate ruse to expose him. Ghemor was led to believe that his daughter had undergone mind conditioning, and that she was in danger of being killed by the Obsidian Order. Seeking to protect his daughter, Ghemor contacted his friends in the dissident movement to help her escape government interrogation. In doing this, Ghemor's ties to the dissident movement were exposed, but he was able to escape Cardassia with the help of **Garak** and **Deep Space 9** personnel. Ghemor reportedly accepted asylum with the Mathenites. ("Second Skin" [DS9]).

ghojmok. Klingon term for nursemaid. **Kahlest** was **Worf**'s *ghojmok*, having helped raise him as a small child when his family lived briefly on **Khitomer**. ("Sins of the Father" [TNG]).

***ghoptu*.** Klingon word for hand. ("Blood Oath" [DS9]).

Ghorusda disaster. A first-contact mission gone awry. The ***U.S.S. Adelphi*** was assigned to make first contact with the Ghorusdans. The mission was a failure, and 47 people, including **Captain Darson** and two of Commander Riker's friends from his academy class, were killed. A Starfleet Board of Inquiry later found Darson responsible for the incident because of carelessness in handling Ghorusdan cultural taboos, but a failure of mission specialist **Tam Elbrun** to warn Darson of Ghorusdan hostility may also have been a factor. ("Tin Man" [TNG]).

GhoS! Klingon for "Make it so!" ("Redemption, Part II" [TNG]). *Producer Bob Justman wrote the line "Make it so!" for Patrick Stewart to speak at the end of "The Last Outpost" (TNG) in tribute to Captain Horatio Hornblower, who uttered the same command in novels written by C.S. Forrester. Hornblower was one of the literary characters upon whom Gene Roddenberry modeled Captain Kirk.*

ghost. Ancient Earth term for a disembodied spirit of a deceased being that walks among the living. **Ronin** was believed to be the Howard family ghost. ("Sub Rosa" [TNG]). SEE: ***borhyas; Jat'yln.***

ghost. Early 21st century **Earth** slang, referring to a **Sanctuary District** resident who didn't integrate into the Sanctuary society. Ghosts were often dangerous and tended to prey on other residents. ("Past Tense, Parts I and II" [DS9]). SEE: **Coleridge, Biddle "B.C."; gimme.**

Gi'ral. (Christine Rose). Klingon warrior believed killed at a perimeter outpost in the **Khitomer massacre** of 2346. Gi'ral was held captive at the secret Romulan prison camp in the **Carraya System**. There, she married Romulan prison camp commander **Tokath**, and they had a daughter, **Ba'el**. Although Gi'ral accepted her lot as a prisoner, she later supported the wishes of some of the children in the camp to go free. ("Birthright, Parts I and II" [TNG]).

Gia. (Kimberly Cullum). Young girl who lived in a village on planet **Barkon IV**. She and her father, **Garvin**, took Data into their home when he stumbled into their village suffering from amnesia in 2370. As Data could not remember his name, Gia called him **Jayden**. ("Thine Own Self" [TNG]).

Gia. (Laura Lane Salvato). Bajoran woman who resided on station Deep Space 9 in 2372. ("Accession" [DS9]). *Gia's name was never mentioned in dialog but comes from the end credits.*

Giamon. A spoken language. Giamon was one of the forty-plus languages spoken by *U.S.S. Aries* First Officer Flaherty. ("The Icarus Factor" [TNG]).

Gibson, Bob. Professional **baseball** player and Hall of Fame member who played for the St. Louis Cardinals on Earth from 1959 to 1975. During his career, Gibson struck out a total of 3,117 players and won the Cy Young Award as best pitcher in 1968 and 1970. ("The Homecoming" [DS9]).

Giddings, Dianna. (Lorine Mendell). Crew member aboard the *Enterprise*-D. Giddings was one of the beautiful women who attracted the attentions of **Thadiun Okona**. ("The Outrageous Okona" [TNG]). *Although Giddings was not given a name in dialog, her name comes from the sign on the door to her quarters. Lorine Mendell was an extra and a stand-in on* Star Trek: The Next Generation, *and she was seen in the background of numerous episodes. She was featured as Keiko O'Brien's friend in "Power Play" (TNG).*

Gideon. Class-M planet. Gideon had a germ-free atmosphere and was once considered to be a paradise, but a spiritual inability to practice birth control resulted in a terrible population explosion, causing serious deterioration of the planet's environment. The government of Gideon applied for membership in the United Federation of Planets in 2268. During the admission review process, **Hodin**, leader of the high council of Gideon, engineered an elaborate plan whereby *Enterprise* Captain James T. Kirk was captured and placed on an exact copy of his ship, in an effort to confuse and disorient him. In this ersatz *Enterprise*, Kirk was introduced to **Odona**, Hodin's daughter, so that she would contract **Vegan choriomeningitis**, a disease carried in Kirk's bloodstream. Odona had volunteered to die from the disease in the hope that her death would inspire others of her world to follow her example. *Enterprise* personnel located Kirk and Odona, successfuly treating her, but she did return to her planet to carry out the deadly plan of exposing other volunteers to lower her population. ("The Mark of Gideon" [TOS]).

gift box, Betazoid. A traditional **Betazoid** means of presenting gifts of great value or importance, these ornate containers were decorated with the sculpted image of a humanoid face. In the presence of the intended recipient, the face on the gift box would briefly come to life, delivering a message or greeting before the box would open. **Wyatt Miller**'s family sent **Deanna Troi**'s bonding gifts to her in such a box. ("Haven" [TNG]). *The face on Deanna's gift box was played by Armin Shimerman, who would later portray various Ferengi, most notably* **Quark** *in* Star Trek: Deep Space Nine.

gigajoule. Unit of energy measure, one billion joules. ("Business As Usual" [VGR]).

gigaquad. Unit of computer memory storage, one billion quads. ("Cathexis" [VGR], "Threshold" [VGR]). During the *U.S.S. Voyager's* brief encounter with a **distortion ring being**, 20 million gigaquads of new information was input into the starship's computer memory banks. ("Twisted" [VGR]). By 2373, the computer memory used by *Voyager's* Emergency Medical Hologram grew to more than 15,000 gigaquads. This caused a level-4 memory fragmentation. ("The Swarm" [VGR]). SEE: **kiloquad**.

gik'tal* challenge.** Fictitious Klingon testing ritual. Worf told Ensign **Sito Jaxa** that she had to undergo the *gik'tal* challenge in order to qualify for his advanced ***Mok'bara class. The ritual supposedly required the subjects to defend themselves while blindfolded. In actuality, *gik'tal* in Klingonese meant "to the death." Worf concocted the ritual in order to test Sito's mettle as she was being considered for a dangerous covert mission into Cardassian space. ("Lower Decks" [TNG]).

Giles Belt. An asteroid belt. A possible destination of the ***Jovis***, following the kidnapping of Data by Kivas Fajo in 2366. ("The Most Toys" [TNG]).

Gilgamesh. Mythic figure of Earth's ancient Mesopotamia; a warrior king whose adventures were related on 12 incomplete stone tablets. Captain Picard shared one of the stories of Gilgamesh with **Tamarian** Captain **Dathon**, while the two of them were together on El-Adrel IV. ("Darmok" [TNG]).

Gilgo Beach. Seaside park on Earth. **Benjamin Sisko** met his future wife, Jennifer, at Gilgo Beach, shortly after graduating from **Starfleet Academy**. ("Emissary" [DS9]).

Gilhouly, Admiral. Senior Starfleet officer. In 2373, Admiral Gilhouly commanded a task force that positioned itself at Deep Space 9 in anticipation of a Dominion invasion. ("By Inferno's Light" [DS9]).

Gill, John. (David Brian). Federation cultural observer and noted professor of history. As a historian, Gill emphasized the study of causes and motivations rather than dates and events. He was an instructor at **Starfleet Academy** whose students included future *Enterprise* Captain James T. Kirk. In the late 2260s, Gill was stationed on planet **Ekos**, where he conducted a disastrous cultural experiment in which he violated the **Prime Directive** in an effort to give the planet a more efficient form of govern-ment, patterned after Earth's Nazi Germany, but based on more compassionate principles. The experiment failed terribly when those near him were corrupted by power and sought to create racial hatred against neighboring planet **Zeon**. Deputy Fuhrer **Melakon** murdered Gill in 2268 when Gill sought to discredit the program of genocide launched against Zeon. ("Patterns of Force" [TOS]).

Gillespie, Chief. (Duke Moosekian). An *Enterprise*-D crew member and friend of Miles O'Brien. Suffering from paranoia induced by a **REM sleep**-deprived state when the ship was trapped in a **Tyken's Rift** in 2367, Gillespie nearly incited a riot in the ship's Ten-Forward Lounge. ("Night Terrors" [TNG]).

Gilora Rejal. (Tracy Scoggins). Scientist from the **Cardassian** Ministry of Science. In 2371, Gilora and her colleague, **Ulani Belor,** worked with Starfleet personnel at Deep Space 9 to test a **subspace radio** relay station. This experiment was intended to allow communication between the **Alpha** and **Gamma Quadrants** through the **Bajoran wormhole**. While working with Chief O'Brien on the project, Gilora mistook O'Brien's overt display of irritation toward her as an overture to mating, as is Cardassian custom. ("Destiny" [DS9]).

gilvos. SEE: **Corvan *gilvos***.

gimme. Early 21st century Earth slang, referring to a **Sanctuary District** resident who was mentally and physically fit and was looking for a job or a place to live. Unlike **ghosts** or **dims**, gimmes were genuinely in search of work. ("Past Tense, Parts I and II" [DS9]).

gin rummy. Traditional Earth card game. Tuvok and Chakotay played gin rummy aboard the *Starship Voyager*, and Tuvok emerged the more skillful player. ("State of Flux" [VGR]).

gin'tak. Klingon term for an advisor so trusted as to become part of the family. The **Alexander Rozhenko** from 2410 posed as **K'mtar**, *gin'tak* to the house of Mogh when he visited Worf in 2370. ("Firstborn" [TNG]).

ginger tea. Beverage made from the root of the reedlike plant *Zingiber officinale*. Captain Picard's **Aunt Adele** served hot ginger tea to treat the common cold. ("Ensign Ro" [TNG]).

Ginsberg, Maury. (Maury Ginsberg). Spotlight operator at **Woodstock**, an outdoor music festival held on Earth in 1969. With the help of **Quinn**, a member of the **Q Continuum**, Ginsberg was able to notice an electrical problem that, if not discovered, might have shut down the concert for days. Ginsberg, who was not aware of the extradimensional intervention at Woodstock, later became an orthodontist in the North American city of Scarsdale. He married and had four children. ("Death Wish" [VGR]). *This character had a different name in early drafts of the script, but according to executive producer Michael Piller, once actor Maury Ginsberg was cast, everyone liked his name so much that they named the character after the actor.*

Gint. (Max Grodénchik, sort of). The first Ferengi **grand nagus**. Long ago, Gint was one of the original authors of the **Ferengi Rules of Acquisition**. Quark dreamed that he met Gint in 2372 and Gint advised him that life was more important than fulfilling a contract. Oddly enough, in Quark's dream, Gint looked a lot like Rom. ("Body Parts" [DS9]).

Giotto, Lieutenant Commander. (Barry Russo). *Enterprise* security officer who worked with **Janus VI** mining colony personnel to locate the **Horta**, responsible for several deaths on the planet prior to stardate 3196. ("The Devil in the Dark" [TOS]). *Actor Barry Russo also played Commodore Wesley in "The Ultimate Computer" (TOS). Giotto's uniform had a commander's braid.*

Giusti, Ensign. (Sabrina LeBeauf). Starfleet officer assigned to the *Enterprise*-D in early 2370. She operated the ops station on the bridge during the ship's encounter with a band of mercenaries led by **Arctus Baran**. ("Gambit, Parts I and II" [TNG]). *Giusti's name was not mentioned in dialogue, but appeared in the show's end credits. Sabrina LeBeauf is well known for her role as Sondra Huxtable on* The Cosby Show.

gladst. Leafy brown **Klingon** foodstuff. ("Melora" [DS9]). *No sauce, please.*

Gladstone, Miss. (Dawn Arnemann). A primary-school teacher aboard the *Enterprise*-D. ("The Child" [TNG]).

glavin. A traditional weapon of the people of planet **Ligon II**, used in ritual combat. Resembling a gauntlet-length oversized glove, the *glavin* has a large, vicious hook at the end and is covered with poison-tipped spines. Tasha Yar fought **Yareena** with *glavins*. ("Code of Honor" [TNG]).

Gleason, Captain. Commanding officer of the ***U.S.S. Zhukov***. Gleason recorded satisfactory reports for Lieutenant **Reginald Barclay** and spoke very highly of his performance on the *Zhukov*, just prior to Barclay's transfer to the *Enterprise*-D in 2366. ("Hollow Pursuits" [TNG]).

Gleason, Ensign. (Todd Merrill). *Enterprise*-D officer assigned to battle bridge ops in early 2367 during the rescue of Captain Picard from the **Borg** ship. ("The Best of Both Worlds, Part II" [TNG]).

glebbening. Ferengi word that referred to a severe downpour of rain. ("Let He Who Is Without Sin..." [DS9]).

glial cells. More specifically known as neuroglial tissue that forms the supporting elements of the nervous system, which play an important role in reacting to injury or infection. Kobliad **Rao Vantika** placed his neural patterns or consciousness in a microscopic generator. He used a weak electrical charge as a bio-coded message, placing it under his fingernails. When Dr. Bashir found Vantika injured, the **Kobliad** scratched the physician and introduced the microscopic generator into Bashir's skin. The bio-coded message was then transferred to Bashir's neuroglial cells and straight to his brain, where Vantika's consciousness was stored. ("The Passenger" [DS9]). SEE: **microscopic generator.**

glinn. A rank in the **Cardassian** militia, lower in stature than a **gul**. ("The Wounded" [TNG]).

***glob* fly.** Klingon insect, half the size of an Earth mosquito. The *glob* fly has no sting, but has a characteristic loud buzzing sound. ("The Outrageous Okona" [TNG]).

global power grid. Utility network on 24th-century Earth that controlled the distribution of power throughout the planet. In 2372, Earth's global power grid was sabotaged by **Red Squad** under orders from **Admiral Leyton**. ("Paradise Lost" [DS9]).

global warming. A gradual increase of a planet's mean atmospheric temperature, eventually resulting in catastrophic environmental damage. The **magnetospheric energy tap** of **Alpha Moon** of planet **Peliar Zel** caused global warming on **Beta Moon** in 2367. ("The Host" [TNG]). SEE: **greenhouse effect; Odan, Ambassador.**

glop-on-a-stick. Star Trek *production staff nickname for* ***jumja****, a food sold on the Promenade on Deep Space 9.* ("A Man Alone" [DS9]).

Gloria. (Whoopi Goldberg). **Guinan**'s persona when she participated in one of Captain Picard's **Dixon Hill** holodeck programs. Picard, as Hill, identified Gloria as his cousin from Cleveland. Guinan, as Gloria, had a great deal of trouble with the female accoutrements (i.e., stockings) of old Earth culture. ("Clues" [TNG]).

glucajen. Pharmaceutical used on **Earth** in the 21st century as a treatment for hypoglycemia. ("Past Tense, Part II" [DS9]).

Glyrhond. River on planet **Bajor** that defined the border between two villages, the **Paqu** and the **Navot**. A treaty signed in 2279 established the river Glyrhond as the boundary between the two rival peoples. During the **Cardassian** occupation of Bajor, the river was diverted for mining operations, setting the stage for a bitter dispute over whether the boundary should be the river's former course or its new path. ("The Storyteller" [DS9]). SEE: **Varis Sul**.

Goddard*, *Shuttlecraft*.** Vehicle technically assigned to the *Starship Enterprise*-D, actually on extended loan to Captain **Montgomery Scott**. Captain Picard presented the shuttle to Scott in 2369 after Scott's own ship, the ***Jenolen, was destroyed while saving the *Enterprise*-D. ("Relics" [TNG]). *The* Goddard *was named for American rocket scientist Robert H. Goddard (1882-1945), inventor of the liquid-fueled rocket.*

Goddard*, *U.S.S. Federation starship, *Korolev* class, Starfleet registry NCC-59621, scheduled for a rendezvous with the *Enterprise*-D shortly after stardate 43421. The rendezvous was postponed after the signing of the **Acamarian** truce. ("The Vengeance Factor" [TNG]). The *Goddard* was part of the **tachyon detection grid** during the **Klingon civil war** of 2367-2368. ("Redemption, Part II" [TNG]). *The* Korolev *class was named for spacecraft designer Sergey Pavlovich Korolev, a key figure in the early Russian space program.*

"Goddess of Empathy." A **holodeck** facsimile of Counselor **Deanna Troi**, created by **Reginald Barclay** in violation of protocols against the simulation of real people without their consent. ("Hollow Pursuits" [TNG]).

gods, Greek. In Earth's ancient Greek culture, a pantheon of dieties and heroic mortals responsible for the creation of the universe and for the primal forces of nature. According to the powerful extraterrestrial who called himself **Apollo**, the mythical figures Agamemnon, Hector, Ulysses, Zeus, Latona, Artemis, Pan, Athena, and Aphrodite were also extraterrestrials who lived on Earth some 5,000 years ago, where they were regarded as gods and heroic figures by the ancient Greeks. ("Who Mourns for Adonais?" [TOS]).

Gol, Stone of. Ancient **Vulcan** artifact, a powerful weapon dating back to the **Time of Awakening,** some 2,000 years ago. Long thought to be mere legend, the stone was a psionic resonator that operated by focusing and amplifying telepathic energy, enabling its bearer to kill by telepathy, turning an opponent's violent thoughts and emotions against him. The Stone of Gol was actually three interlocking artifacts covered with ancient Vulcan glyphs and symbols. These writings mostly warned of death to anyone who opposed the stone, but one set of three glyphs showed the symbol for war and the symbol of the god of death, separated by the symbol for peace. According to legend, it was destroyed by the gods when the Vulcan people found the way of peace. The stone had, in fact, been dismantled, with one piece placed in a Vulcan museum. The remaining two pieces were lost and presumed destroyed. In 2369, extremists from the **Vulcan isolationist movement** stole the first fragment and hired **Arctus Baran** to find the two remaining pieces. Baran raided numerous **Romulan** archaeological sites throughout the quadrant, and by early 2370, had located all three pieces. Baran's employers were prevented from using the device, and later, Vulcan authorities vowed that they would destroy the three pieces of the resonator once and for all. ("Gambit, Part II" [TNG]).

Golanga. Noted soccer player during the 2360's. He injured his knee in 2366, and though it was replaced with a **bioimplant**, his career suffered. ("Paradise" [DS9]).

gold-pressed latinum. SEE: **latinum**.

golside ore. Mineral. The **Cardassian Central Command** maintained that the freighter ***Bok'Nor*** was carrying 14 metric tons of golside ore in late 2370, when in fact it had been carrying illegal weapons to **Cardassian** colonies in the **Demilitarized Zone**. ("The Maquis, Part I" [DS9]).

Golwat, Ensign. Starfleet officer aboard the *U.S.S. Voyager* in 2373. ("Flashback" [VGR]). *Golwat was Bolian.*

Gomez, Ensign Sonya. (Lycia Naff). Young engineering officer assigned to *Enterprise*-D at **Starbase 173**. An attractive young woman, Gomez specialized in antimatter operations. ("Q Who?" [TNG]). Gomez helped devise a means of using the ship's **Bussard collectors** to create a harmless pyrotechnic display when Geordi La Forge was being held captive aboard the ***Mondor*** in 2365. ("Samaritan Snare" [TNG]). *Although Gomez was first in "Q Who" (TNG), she apparently transferred to the* ship *at Starbase 173 during "The Measure of a Man" (TNG).*

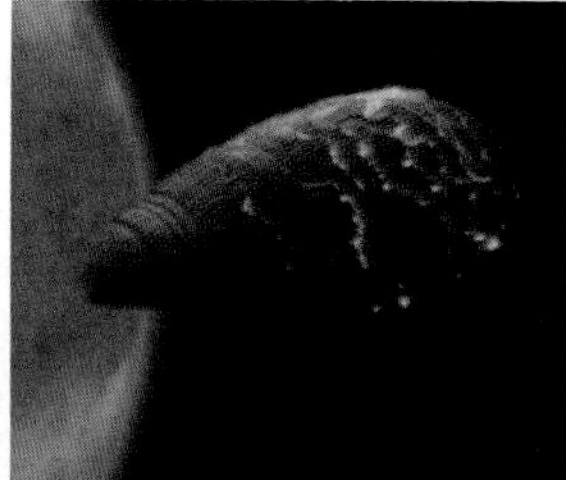

Gomtuu. An ancient, spaceborne organism, the last of a species of living spacecraft that shared symbiotic relationships with their crews. Gomtuu's crew died when radiation from an explosion penetrated its skin. Gomtuu was a social being, and with no fellow creatures remaining and with no crew to care for, it became lonely. Wandering aimlessly for millennia, Gomtuu finally decided to die at **Beta Stromgren**. **First-contact** specialist **Tam Elbrun**, sent to establish relations with Gomtuu (code-named **Tin Man** by Starfleet), found the living spaceship to be a kindred spirit, and the two new friends went off into the unknown together. ("Tin Man" [TNG]).

Gonal IV. Planet. Homeworld of the swarming moths that were the subject of *Enterprise*-D science fair winner **Jay Gordon**'s project in 2368. ("Disaster" [TNG]).

Gorad. Uncle of Quark. Quark owed Gorad a large sum of money. ("Body Parts" [DS9]).

Goran'Agar. (Scott MacDonald). **Jem'Hadar** soldier whose genetic makeup included a random mutation that made him able to survive without **ketracel-white**, a drug on which all other Jem'Hadar were dependent. In 2368, Goran'Agar was the only survivor of a ship that crashed on planet Bopak III. After his supply of ketracel-white ran out, he learned that he was not dependent on the drug. He believed that something in the environment on Bopak III had cured him, so four years later, he brought his men to the planet to be similarly cured. When his men remained addicted, Goran'Agar forced the *Runabout Rubicon* to land on the planet and coerced Dr. Julian Bashir to seek a medical cure for their addiction. When Arak'Taral and the rest of his men rebelled, Goran'Agar released Bashir and Chief O'Brien, and decided to remain on the planet to deal with his men. ("Hippocratic Oath" [DS9]). *Scott MacDonald has previously portrayed Subcommander N'Vek in "Face of the Enemy" (TNG), Tosk in "Captive Pursuit" (DS9), and Ensign Rollins in "Caretaker" (VGR).*

Gordon, Jay. (John Christian Graas). One of the winners of the primary-school science fair held aboard the *Enterprise*-D in 2368. Young Jay Gordon was also made an honorary science officer by Captain Picard. ("Disaster" [TNG]).

Gorgan. (Melvin Belli). **Noncorporeal life**-form that forced the adults from the **Starnes Expedition** to planet **Triacus** to commit suicide and deceived their children into following him and doing his evil bidding. The children could summon the Gorgan by chanting, "Hail, hail, fire and snow. Call the angel, we will go. Far away, for to see, Friendly Angel come to me." ("And the Children Shall Lead" [TOS]). *The Gorgan was played by the late attorney Melvin Belli, whose son also appeared in the episode.*

Gorkon, Chancellor. (David Warner). Leader of the **Klingon High Council**, assassinated in 2293 by forces who sought to block his efforts for peace with the **United Federation of Planets**. Gorkon was succeeded by his daughter, **Azetbur**. (*Star Trek VI: The Undiscovered Country*). SEE: **Klingon Empire**. *Actor David Warner had previously played diplomat* ***St. John Talbot*** *in* Star Trek V. *He later played Gul Madred in "Chain of Command, Part II" (TNG).*

Gorkon, U.S.S. Federation starship, *Excelsior* class, Starfleet registry number NCC-40512. The *Gorkon* was **Admiral Necheyev**'s flagship during the expected **Borg** invasion of 2369. ("Descent, Part I" [TNG]). *Named for Chancellor Gorkon, seen in* Star Trek VI.

Gorlan prayer stick. Rare archaeological artifact. *Enterprise*-D Captain Jean-Luc Picard owned a Gorlan prayer stick, which he had obtained in trade for a very old bottle of **Saurian brandy**. Although Picard treasured the artifact, he gave it to **Jason Vigo** as a memento in 2370. ("Bloodlines" [TNG]).

Gorn. Civilization of reptilian humanoids. Gorn forces destroyed the Earth outpost on **Cestus III**, claiming it was an intrusion into their space. The captain of the Gorn vessel and Captain Kirk were transported to a planet by a race known as the **Metrons,** where each fought for the survival of his respective crew. Kirk won, but refused to kill the Gorn, after realizing that the Gorn attack had been the result of a misunderstanding. ("Arena" [TOS]). The territorial dispute over Cestus III was later resolved, and Federation colonists settled on the planet. ("Family Business" [DS9]).

Goro. (Richard Hale). Tribal elder from **Miramanee's planet** who, in 2268, accepted the amnesia-stricken Kirk into his tribe as a god. ("The Paradise Syndrome" [TOS]).

Gorokian midwife toad. Animal life-form. ("Death Wish" [VGR]).

Gorta. (Joel Swetow). Business partner to **Lursa** and **B'Etor** in 2370. Gorta felt cheated by the Duras sisters in a deal in which the three illicitly mined a **magnesite ore** deposit on **Kalla III** that belonged to the Pakleds. The sisters took the ore and stranded Gorta on the planet. He was given passage off planet on the *Enterprise*-D in exchange for information on where to find the Duras sisters. ("Firstborn" [TNG]). *Gorta was Dopterian. Joel Swetow also portrayed Gul Jasad in "Emissary" (DS9).*

Gosheven. (Grainger Hines). Conservative leader of the **Tau Cygna V** colony in 2366. When informed by Data that the colony's presence on the planet was in violation of a treaty with the **Sheliak**, Gosheven was unwilling to consider abandoning the settlement. He even attacked Data physically to prevent him from urging others to leave. ("The Ensigns of Command" [TNG]).

Goss, DaiMon. (Scott Thompson). Head of the Ferengi trade delegation that negotiated for rights to the **Barzan wormhole** in 2366. In a near-lethal attempt to tip the negotiations in the Ferengi's favor, Goss poisoned the Federation negotiator, **Dr. Mendoza,** with Ferengi **pyrocytes**. Goss later made a secret deal with **Devinoni Ral** in which the Ferengi would pretend to be trying to destroy the wormhole, hoping to give Ral an advantage in negotiating against the Federation. ("The Price" [TNG]).

Gossett, Herm. (Jon Kowal). One of the three miners at the **Rigel XII** lithium mining station in 2266. ("Mudd's Women" [TOS]).

Goth. (Gary Bullock). Spacecraft commander of the **Etanian Order**. Goth commanded a large Etanian attack ship that made an attempted invasion of a **Nezu** colony world. ("Rise" [VGR]). *Goth's name is from the script and was not mentioned in dialog.*

Gothos. Iron-silica planet created by the entity **Trelane**. The *Enterprise* discovered the planet while en route to **Beta VI** in 2267. The surface of Gothos contained no detectable soil or vegetation, had a toxic atmosphere, and was plagued by storms and continuous volcanic eruptions. A small section of the planet did have a Class-M environment, thanks to the mischievous Trelane, who captured several *Enterprise* personnel to play with. ("The Squire of Gothos" [TOS]).

Goval. (Michael Reilly Burke). One of the self-aware **Borg** encountered by the crew of the *Enterprise*-D in 2370. Goval disconnected himself from the **Borg collective** so that his thoughts would not be read by the collective, but he reconnected himself after **Lore** convinced him it was for the greater good. ("Descent, Part II" [TNG]) *Michael Reilly Burke also portrayed Hogue in "Profit and Loss" (DS9).*

Gowron. (Robert O'Reilly). Son of M'Rel, and leader of the **Klingon High Council** following the death of **K'mpec** in 2367. Prior to his ascent to power, Gowron was a political outsider who often challenged the High Council. Following the death of K'mpec, Gowron was one of two contenders for the post of council leader. With the elimination of **Duras**, Gowron won the position of chancellor. ("Reunion" [TNG]). Gowron was installed as council leader in a ceremony attended by Jean-Luc Picard, who had served as **Arbiter of Succession**. Gowron's leadership was quickly challenged by **Lursa** and **B'Etor**, surviving members of the Duras family who sought to install Duras's illegitimate son, **Toral**, as chancellor. The Duras

bid was supported by Romulan interests seeking to gain control over the Klingon Empire. The challenge divided the council and plunged the empire into civil war in 2367. Gowron emerged victorious, in part because he agreed to restore rightful honor to the **Mogh** family in exchange for military support by **Worf** and **Kurn**. ("Redemption, Parts I and II" [TNG]). Within a few months, Gowron found it politically disadvantageous to admit to the Federation's support during his **Rite of Succession** and the subsequent civil war. Official government accounts of these events therefore omitted references to Federation involvement. ("Unification, Part I" [TNG]). Gowron reacted strongly to the supposed "return" of **Kahless the Unforgettable** in 2369, correctly surmising that the new Kahless was part of a political effort to discredit him. Gowron was further convinced that Kahless would once again plunge the empire into civil war. At Worf's urging, Gowron later agreed to support Kahless in the ceremonial role of emperor. This would allow Kahless to be the spiritual leader of the people, while the governmental power would remain with Gowron and the High Council. ("Rightful Heir" [TNG]). In 2372, a civilian uprising overthrew the **Cardassian** military, causing Gowron to believe that the Cardassian government had been taken over by the **Dominion**. Seeking to protect his empire, Gowron ordered Klingon forces to invade the Cardassian Union. Although the invasion was unsuccessful, the **Federation Council** condemned the Klingon action, and in response, Gowron unilaterally withdrew from the **Khitomer Accords** on stardate 49011, ending the peace treaty between the two great powers. In addition, Gowron expelled all Federation citizens from the empire and recalled his ambassadors. Gowron appealed to **Worf** to renounce the Federation and join him in the invasion of Cardassia, but Worf refused, prompting Gowron to banish him from the empire. ("The Way of the Warrior" [DS9]). After his failed attempt to conquer Cardassia, he declared the invasion a victory to avoid being assassinated. ("Hippocratic Oath" [DS9]). A few months later, Gowron demanded that the Federation withdraw from the **Archanis** sector and abandon all of its bases there. During Odo's time in the Great Link, the **Founders** convinced him that Gowron was a changeling infiltrator. ("Broken Link" [DS9]). In fact, Gowron had not been replaced by a changeling, but the Founders had hoped to cast suspicion on him to avoid detection of the real infitrator, a changeling replacement of **General Martok**. In 2372, Chancellor Gowron relocated Klingon military headquarters to planetoid **Ty'Gokor**. Early in 2373, Gowron inducted several warriors into the **Order of the *Bat'leth*.** Captain Benjamin Sisko and his men infiltrated the induction ceremony and exposed General Martok as a changeling spy. ("Apocalypse Rising" [DS9]). SEE: ***Yan-Isleth.*** In 2373, in response to the destabilizing alliance of the Cardassians and the Dominion, Gowron agreed to reinstate the Khitomer Accords, thus renewing the alliance between his empire and the Federation. ("By Inferno's Light" [DS9]).

Gr'oth, I.K.S. D7-class Klingon battle cruiser commanded by Captain Koloth in 2267. Koloth took the *Gr'oth* to Deep Space Station K-7 on stardate 4523, invoking a clause of the **Organian Peace Treaty** that allowed the *Gr'oth's* crew to make use of Federation shore leave facilities. ("Trials and Tribble-ations" [DS9]). *The* Gr'oth *was a replica of the original Klingon battle cruiser model designed by Matt Jefferies for the original* Star Trek *series. Modelmaker Greg Jein, who built the* Gr'oth, *changed Jefferies's design slightly by incorporating surface panel detailing similar to that done for the Klingon ships in* Star Trek: The Motion Picture. *Ironically, Koloth's ship was not seen in the original "The Trouble With Tribbles" (TOS) because the ship model had not yet been designed at that point in the original series.*

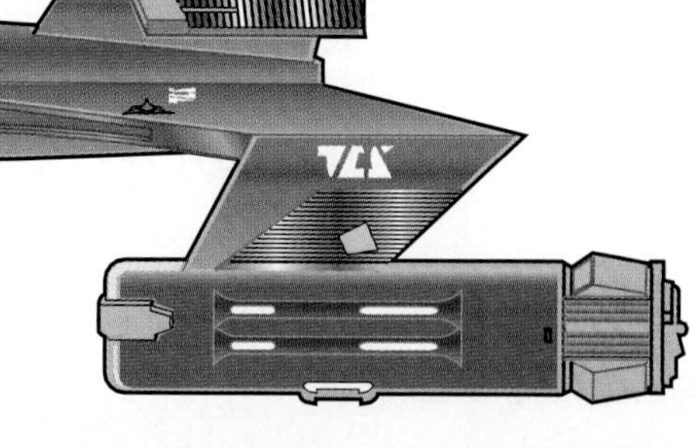

Gracie. SEE: **George and Gracie.**

Grady. (Clint Howard). Resident of **Sanctuary District** A in San Francisco on Earth in 2024. Grady had some mental problems and in the slang of the era was called a **dim**. Ironically, Grady was the only Earth resident who was aware that an alien had visited his planet. ("Past Tense, Part II" [DS9]). *As a child, Clint Howard portrayed* ***Balok*** *in "The Corbomite Maneuver" (TOS), the first regular episode of the original* Star Trek *series. Howard more recently played NASA mission controller Sy Liebergot in the movie* Apollo 13.

Graham, Ensign. (Mona Grudt). Starfleet officer. Graham was at the conn when the *Enterprise*-D entered the Tarchannen system in 2367, albeit too late to save **Lieutenant Hickman.** ("Identity Crisis" [TNG]).

Grak-tay. A famous concert violinist. **Data** programmed himself to emulate Grak-tay's performance style. ("Sarek" [TNG]).

***grakel* milk.** SEE: **schplict.**

Gral. (Lee Arenberg). Ferengi entrepreneur who tried to threaten **Quark** during his brief tenure as **grand nagus** in 2369. Gral intimated that unless Quark showed him favor, he would someday be killed. ("The Nagus" [DS9]).

Gramilian sand peas. Snack food. Pel suggested Gramilian sand peas as a replacement for *lokar* beans in Quark's bar. The peas stimulated thirst (and Quark's profit). ("Rules of Acquisition" [DS9]). Chief O'Brien and Doctor Bashir enjoyed them. ("The Way of the Warrior" [DS9]). *Obviously, the Ferengi equivalent of salted peanuts.*

grand nagus. SEE: **nagus, grand**; **Zek**.

grand proxy. Official messenger of the Ferengi **grand nagus**. Visits by the grand proxy were dreaded by Ferengi entrepreneurs, as he often collected a cut of the profits for the nagus. The annotations of the **Ferengi Rules of Acquisition** stated that encounters with the grand proxy were hopeless situations. ("False Profits" [VGR]).

Granger, Walter. (Jon de Vries). Commander of the colony ship ***S.S. Mariposa*** when it was launched in 2123, and one of only five survivors when the ship crashed on the planet the colonists named **Mariposa**. Granger became one of the progenitors whose cloned descendants inhabited the Mariposa colony, and in 2365 one of his clones (named Wilson Granger) served as colony prime minister. ("Up the Long Ladder" [TNG]). SEE: **clone**.

Grant. (Robert Bralver). *Enterprise* security guard who was part of the landing party at planet **Capella IV** on stardate 3497. Grant was killed by a Capellan with the deadly Capellan weapon, the ***kligat***. ("Friday's Child" [TOS]).

Gratitude Festival. SEE: **Bajoran Gratitude Festival**.

Graves, Dr. Ira. (W. Morgan Sheppard). Noted molecular cyberneticist, Dr. Ira Graves was considered by some to be one of the greatest human minds in the universe. Early in his career, Graves was a teacher to **Dr. Noonien Soong**, and thus Graves considered himself to be a "grandfather" to the android **Data**. Graves spent the last years of his life isolated on a planet he called **Gravesworld**, where he died in 2365 of Darnay's disease. Just prior to his death, Graves deposited his intellect into Data's **positronic brain**; this information was later stored in the *Enterprise*-D main computer. ("The Schizoid Man" [TNG]). SEE: **Zee-Magnees Prize**.

Gravesworld. A remote, ringed planet on which the noted molecular cyberneticist **Ira Graves** lived the last years of his life in seclusion. ("The Schizoid Man" [TNG]).

Gravett Island. Isolated island in the South Pacific on Earth. In 2063, Gravett Island was uninhabited. When the crew of the *Enterprise*-E, stranded in the past, began an evacuation of the ship and started the autodestruct sequence, the crew was to remain on Gravett Island so that disruption of Earth's timeline would be minimized. *(Star Trek: First Contact). Gravett Island was named for* Star Trek *production staff member Jacques Gravett. Since 20th-century atlases show no Gravett Island in existence, we can only assume that Jacques is going to buy an island and name it after himself.*

gravimetric fluctuation. Spatial distortion phenomenon. Gravimetric fluctuations accompanied the appearance of the **temporal rift** near planet **Archer IV**. Vaguely resembling a **wormhole**, the temporal rift exhibited time displacement, but had no discernible event horizon. ("Yesterday's *Enterprise*" [TNG]). Gravimetric interference was partially responsible for the crash of the ***U.S.S. Jenolen*** into the surface of the **Dyson Sphere** in 2294. The interference had apparently been generated by the enormous mass of the Dyson Sphere. ("Relics" [TNG]).

gravimetric flux density. Measurement of spatial distortion characteristics. Very high gravimetric flux density readings may indicate a **quantum singularity**. ("Parallax" [VGR]).

gravimetric microprobe. Sensor instrument; used in the science lab on station Deep Space 9. ("Playing God" [DS9]).

gravimetric scanner. Device used to measure fluctuations in a local gravitational field. In 2373, two Yridians cheated at Quark's **dabo** game table by using a miniature gravimetric scanner to predict where the ball would land on the wheel. ("Nor the Battle to the Strong" [DS9]).

gravitational constant. Mathematical expression describing the amount of gravitational attraction that is generated by a given amount of matter. When *Enterprise*-D personnel were trying to prevent the moon of planet **Bre'el IV** from crashing into the planet, **Q** suggested that reducing the gravitational constant of the universe might be a good way to reduce the moon's mass enough so the ship's **tractor beam** could do the job. Unfortunately, Q forgot that adjusting the gravitational constant was a feat beyond the abilities of most mere mortals. ("Déjà Q" [TNG]). SEE: **warp field**.

gravitational eddy. A backward-circling current in a wormhole. In 2371, a **microprobe** launched from the *Starship Voyager* into a **micro-wormhole** became stuck in the wormhole's gravitational eddies and was eventually crushed. ("Eye of the Needle" [VGR]).

gravitational unit. Device used to generate a synthetic gravity field aboard a space vehicle. The Klingon battle cruiser ***Kronos One*** suffered a hit to the gravity generator during the assassination of **Chancellor Gorkon,** resulting in weightless conditions aboard that ship while the crime was committed. (*Star Trek VI: The Undiscovered Country*).

gravitic caliper. Engineering tool. Ensign Vorik recommended the use of a gravitic caliper to regulate plasma flow, suggesting that it was more precise than a duotronic probe. ("Fair Trade" [VGR]).

gravitic mine. Graviton-based weapon used against space vehicles. *(Star Trek II: The Wrath of Khan).* The transport starship ***U.S.S. Denver*** struck a gravitic mine in 2368. That mine had been left over from the Cardassian war. ("Ethics" [TNG]). The **Albino** planted a land-based gravitic mine to protect his sanctuary on planet Secarus IV. ("Blood Oath" [DS9]).

gravitic sensor net. Network of detection devices employed by the Federation near the **Romulan Neutral Zone**, making it possible to detect space vehicles in the area. This system was at least partially effective in sensing the presence of cloaked ships. ("Face of the Enemy" [TNG]).

graviton matrix. Underlying energy-field structure present in artificially-generated temporal distortion fields. ("Future's End, Part I" [VGR]).

graviton polarimeter. Sensor device used aboard Federation starships. In some astronomical studies, a graviton polarimeter can gather data similar to that of a **flux spectrometer**. ("Cause and Effect" [TNG]).

graviton wave. Traveling energy field composed of graviton particles. A graviton wave of sufficient power can be destructive to any matter in its path. ("Rejoined" [DS9]).

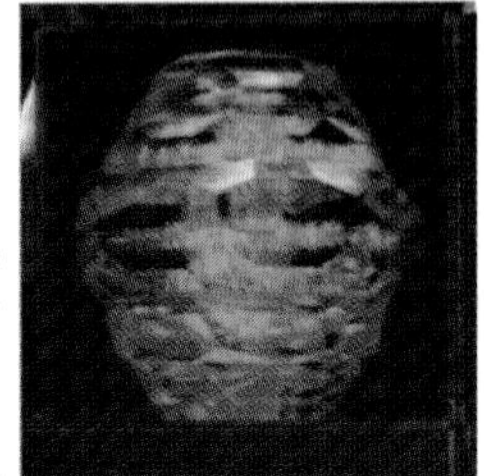

graviton. Elementary particle that transmits gravitational force. ("Q-Less" [DS9]). A graviton inverter circuit is a key component of an **antigrav**, such as those used in cargo-handling units. ("Hollow Pursuits" [TNG]). A graviton field generator is another element of artificial-gravity generators and is used in force field applications as well. An experiment in phasing technology conducted on a Romulan science vessel in 2368 completely depolarized the graviton field generator of that ship, leading to the destruction of the ship's warp core. ("The Next Phase" [TNG]). Graviton pulses were used by *Enterprise*-D personnel to attempt communication with the **Crystalline Entity** in 2368. Before such attempts could succeed, scientist **Dr. Kila Marr**, who sought revenge against the entity, adjusted the graviton beam to set up a resonant frequency that destroyed the entity. ("Silicon Avatar" [TNG]). Graviton field energy generated by a **tractor beam** can be used to strengthen the structural integrity of a vessel being towed. ("Captive Pursuit" [DS9]). A graviton field generated by a previously undiscovered life-form threatened station Deep Space 9 in 2369, when an archaeological artifact, discovered by **Vash** in the Gamma Quadrant and stored on the station, was found to contain the entity. After the object was beamed into space, the winged energy creature emerged from the artifact and flew into the wormhole, leaving Deep Space 9 to return to normal. ("Q-Less" [DS9]). The Ferengi shuttle operated by **Arridor** and **Kol** sent out a graviton pulse to prevent the *U.S.S. Voyager* crew from beaming them out of their shuttle. The graviton pulse destabilized the Barzan wormhole and knocked it off its subspace axis, causing its endpoints to jump around erratically. ("False Profits" [VGR]).

gravity boots. Also known as **magnetic boots**. (*Star Trek VI: The Undiscovered Country*).

gravity net. Floor mat used in freefall environments to generate artificial gravity. **Benjamin Sisko** installed a gravity net in his replica **Bajoran solar-sail vessel** that he built in 2371 because weightlessness made him queasy. ("Explorers" [DS9]).

Grax, Reittan. (Rudolph Willrich). The Betazoid director of the biennial **Trade Agreements Conference** in 2366. Grax was an old friend of **Lwaxana Troi**'s late husband, **Ian Andrew Troi**, and had known their daughter, Deanna Troi, since childhood. Grax contacted the *Enterprise*-D to inform the captain when Riker, Deanna Troi, and Lwaxana Troi were missing, kidnapped by Ferengi operatives. ("Ménage à Troi" [TNG]).

Grayson, Amanda. *According to Original Series* Star Trek *writer and story editor Dorothy Fontana, this was the full name of* ***Spock****'s mother, first seen in "Journey to Babel" (TOS), although the surname Grayson was not established in any regular episode or film. The name was used in the animated episode, "Yesteryear," written by Fontana.* SEE: **Amanda**.

Grazerite. Humanoid species. Prominent Grazerites have included Federation President **Jaresh-Inyo**. Grazerites evolved from herbivorous herd animals and as such abhorred violence and confrontations. ("Homefront" [DS9]). *The name of these people comes from the script.*

Gre'thor*.** In Klingon mythology, the place where the dishonored go to die. *Gre'thor* is guarded by the mythic Klingon figure, ***Fek'lhr. ("Devil's Due" [TNG]).

Great Barrier, the. An energy field surrounding the center of the Milky Way Galaxy. Long believed to be impenetrable by any starship, the Great Barrier was first traversed by the *Starship Enterprise* in 2287 when the ship was commandeered by **Sybok** in his quest for the planet ***Sha Ka Ree***, which Sybok believed he would find at the center of the galaxy. (*Star Trek V: The Final Frontier*). *Not to be confused with the* ***galactic barrier*** *at the edge of the galaxy, first seen in "Where No Man Has Gone Before" (TOS).*

Great Bird of the Galaxy, The. A mythic figure in the 23rd century. Sulu invoked same when he thanked Janice Rand for bringing him lunch, saying "May the Great Bird of the Galaxy bless your planet." ("The Man Trap" [TOS]). *Great Bird of the Galaxy was also Bob Justman's nickname for* Star Trek *creator Gene Roddenberry.*

Great Depression. Economic downturn that beset the planetary financial system on Earth in the 1930s. **Edith Keeler**'s **Twenty-First Street Mission** was set up to help people survive during that time. ("The City on the Edge of Forever" [TOS]).

"Great Experiment, The." Unofficial term used to describe the ***U.S.S. Excelsior***, Starfleet's testbed vehicle for the unsuccessful **transwarp** drive development project. *(Star Trek III: The Search for Spock).*

Great Hall. A massive fortress-like building that serves as the seat of government of the **Klingon Empire**, located in the **First City** on the **Klingon Homeworld**. The **Klingon High Council** meets there. ("Sins of the Father" [TNG]). *The design of the Klingon Great Hall (and other sets in the episode) won an Emmy Award for Best Art Direction for* Star Trek: The Next Generation *production designer Richard James. The exterior of the Great Hall and the surrounding First City was a matte painting created by Syd Dutton at Illusion Arts.*

Great Link. Among the **Founders** of the **Dominion**, the intermingling of a vast number of **shape-shifters** in their liquid forms. The Great Link was the foundation of the changeling society. It provided a meaning for their existence. The link was a merging of form and thought, the sharing of idea and sensation. ("The Search, Part II" [DS9]). In 2372, the Founders compelled **Odo** to return to the Great Link by giving him a debilitating illness. Once back with his people, the Great Link judged him for having killed a changeling. In retribution, Odo's shape-shifting powers were taken away, and he was made human. ("Broken Link" [DS9]). But even when Odo's shape-shifting abilities were removed, Odo's humanoid brain contained trace amounts of morphogenic enzymes, a changeling neurochemical. When a plasma storm subjected Odo to a powerful shock in 2373, the morphogenic enzymes were activated and a telepathic response reached out to form a version of the Great Link with the minds of Sisko, Dax, and Garak, trapping all four in a memory from Odo's past. ("Things Past" [DS9]).

Great Monetary Collapse. Huge financial decline that struck **Ferenginar** during the mid-24th century. This decline involved rampant inflation and currency devaluation. Quark, who was serving on a freighter ship at the time, felt helpless being away while his homeworld was experiencing such a calamity. ("Homefront" [DS9]).

Great Sages. Demigods in **Takarian** mythology. Ancient Takarian lore held that Great Sages would descend from the sky and rule over the people as benevolent protectors. In 2366, **Arridor** and **Kol** crash-landed into a Takarian village square and were believed to be the Great Sages whose arrival from the skies was prophesied long ago. Arridor and Kol used their advanced technology to convince the people that they were the sages and then began to exploit the population for profit. In 2373, the crew of the *U.S.S. Voyager* forced the two interlopers to leave. ("False Profits" [VGR]).

Gree. Life-form. Among the Gree, stimulation of follicles on the proboscis results in swelling of the auricular canal. ("Elogium" [VGR]).

green beans. Earth vegetable usually served cooked as a side dish. Neelix prepared pot roast and green beans for the Thirty-Sevens during their brief visit to the *Voyager* in 2371. ("The 37's" [VGR]).

Green, Colonel. (Phillip Pine). Twenty-first-century military figure who led a genocidal war on Earth. The image of this notorious historical figure was re-created by the **Excalbians** in 2269 as part of their study of the nature of the human concepts of "good" and "evil." ("The Savage Curtain" [TOS]). SEE: **Yarnek**. *It is not clear what war Green fought, but it might have been* ***World War III****, mentioned in "Bread and Circuses" (TOS), "Encounter at Farpoint" (TNG), and* Star Trek: First Contact.

Green, Crewman. (Bruce Watson). *Enterprise* crew member. Green was killed in 2266 on the surface of planet **M-113** by the salt vampire. Green's death was not discovered for several hours because the **M-113 creature** subsequently assumed Green's identity and transported up to the ship. ("The Man Trap" [TOS]).

greenbread. Staple food from planet **Yadera II**. ("Shadowplay" [DS9]).

greenhouse effect. A planetary atmospheric condition in which solar radiation is trapped in a planet's atmosphere, causing increased temperature in that atmosphere. *Enterprise*-D personnel used ship's phasers to release subterranean carbon dioxide into the atmosphere of planet **Penthara IV** in 2368 in hopes that the resulting greenhouse effect would forestall a potential ice age on the planet. ("A Matter of Time" [TNG]). SEE: **global warming**.

Grendel. Mythical beast that terrorized the followers of **King Hrothgar** in the epic ***Beowulf***. In Harry Kim's **holonovel** version of this epic, the role of Grendel was taken over on stardate 48693 by a **photonic being** who had accidentally been brought aboard the ship. The being discovered it could interact with the crew through the holodeck and used the Grendel persona to kidnap three *Voyager* crew members. ("Heroes and Demons" [VGR]).

Grenthemen water hopper. A motor-driven aquatic vehicle. According to Geordi La Forge, a Grenthemen water hopper would stall disastrously when the clutch was popped. Riker also had experience with a hopper. ("Peak Performance" [TNG]). SEE: **hopper.**

Greskrendtregk. Ktarian man who was the husband of *Voyager* officer **Samantha Wildman**. ("Dreadnought" [VGR]).

Griffith Observatory. Astronomical observatory and science museum located in the city of Los Angeles in California on **Earth**. In 1996, the Griffith Observatory participated in Earth's use of radio telescopes in its search for extraterrestrial intelligence. **SETI** astronomer **Rain Robinson** was one of the scientists who worked on that project. ("Future's End, Part I" [VGR]). *The Griffith Observatory was also the site, in 1988, of the wrap party celebrating the completion of filming of the first season of* Star Trek: The Next Generation.

Grilka. (Mary Kay Adams). Wife to the head of the **House** of **Kozak**, a family of some import in the Klingon High Council. Grilka was widowed when Kozak was killed in 2371 aboard station Deep Space 9. Because initial reports indicated Kozak was killed in combat, Grilka was forced to perform the ***brek'tal* ritual** with her husband's killer, in order to preserve her family. **Quark**, acting briefly as head of the House, made arrangements with the Klingon High Council, so that Grilka could lead the family herself. Klingon law normally prevented a woman from heading a House. In return for his assistance, Grilka granted Quark a divorce. ("The House of Quark" [DS9]). SEE: **divorce, Klingon**. In 2373, Grilka visited Quark on Deep Space 9 to ask him for financial advice. With Worf's tutelage in the ways of Klingon courtship, Quark pursued Grilka, eventually winning her affection. As a result of his relationship with Grilka, Quark received a compound fracture of the right radius, two fractured ribs, torn ligaments, strained tendons, and numerous bruises, contusions, and scratches. ("Looking for *par'Mach* in All the Wrong Places" [DS9]). *Mary Kay Adams also played N'Toth, aide to Ambassador G'Kar, on* Babylon 5.

grilled mushrooms. Side dish consisting of umbrella-shaped edible fungi seared on a hot metal grill, usually served in melted butter. Tom Paris liked grilled mushrooms. ("The Chute" [VGR]).

Grimp. (Jason Marsden). Ferengi waiter employed at Quark's bar in 2372. Although Grimp shared the Ferengi cultural dislike of labor unions, he joined the **Guild of Restaurant and Casino Employees** in 2372 to oppose Quark's exploitation of his employees. ("Bar Association" [DS9]).

Grisella. Intelligent life-forms. The Grisella hibernate for six months at a time. Captain Picard chose the Grisella as mediators in a dispute in 2366 between the **Sheliak** and the Federation over the evacuation of the Federation's **Tau Cygna V** colony in accordance with the **Treaty of Armens**. The choice was intended by Picard to delay enforcement of the evacuation. ("The Ensigns of Command" [TNG]).

***Grishnar* cat.** Klingon animal. ("The Way of the Warrior" [DS9]).

***Grissom*, U.S.S.** Federation starship, ***Excelsior* class**, Starfleet registry number NCC-42857. The *Grissom* was near the **Sigma Erandi system** during the **tricyanate** contamination on **Beta Agni II** in 2366. The *Enterprise*-D requested the *Grissom* to stand by should assistance be needed. ("The Most Toys" [TNG]). *This was presumably a newer* U.S.S. Grissom, *since the earlier ship of the same name was destroyed in* Star Trek III.

***Grissom*, U.S.S.** Starfleet science vessel, ***Oberth* class**, registry number NCC-638. The *Grissom* was assigned to investigate the newly formed **Genesis Planet** in 2285, but was destroyed by a Klingon vessel attempting to claim the planet for the Klingon Empire. The *Grissom* had been commanded by Captain J. T. Esteban. The investigation team included Lieutenant **Saavik** and Dr. **David Marcus.** (*Star Trek III: The Search for Spock*). *The* Grissom *was designed by David Carson and built at ILM. The* Grissom *was also relabeled and re-used as a variety of other Federation starships in* Star Trek: The Next Generation. *The* Grissom *was named for* Mercury *astronaut Virgil I. Grissom, who was killed in the tragic* Apollo 1 *fire in 1967. The* Grissom *helm officer was played by Jeanne Mori, and the communications officer was Mario Marcelino. Neither character was given a name on screen.*

Gromek, Admiral. (Georgann Johnson). Starfleet official who transmitted secret orders to the *Enterprise*-D to rendezvous with special Federation emissary **K'Ehleyr** prior to the return of the Klingon ship ***T'Ong*** in 2365. ("The Emissary" [TNG]).

groovy. Mid-20th century Earth slang term meaning "great" or "excellent." ("Future's End, Part I" [VGR]).

Groppler. Title of a civic leader among the **Bandi** people on planet **Deneb IV**. ("Encounter at Farpoint, Parts I and II" [TNG]). SEE: **Zorn**.

***Groumall*.** Small warp-capable Cardassian military freighter commanded by **Gul Dukat** in 2372. The final mission of the *Groumall* was to ferry Major **Kira Nerys** to talks on Korma in 2372. Upon arriving at Korma, Dukat learned that the outpost had been attacked by Klingon forces. Dukat and Kira improvised a counterattack by installing Korma's system-5 disruptors into the *Groumall's* cargo hold. So equipped, the *Groumall* engaged and captured a Klingon bird-of-prey commanded by **K'Temang**. After assuming command of the Klingon ship, Dukat stranded the Klingon crew on the *Groumall*. Dukat then destroyed the *Groumall,* killing all aboard. ("Return to Grace" [DS9]).

ground assault vehicles. Land vehicles used by the **Klingon** military during ground-based battles. ("Elogium" [VGR]).

grup. Slang on **Miri**'s planet for "grown-up." ("Miri" [TOS]).

GSC. Unit of gross stuctural compression measure. ("Who Mourns for Adonais?" [TOS], "Starship Down" [DS9]).

GSK 739. Call sign for a private transmitter belonging to **George Samuel Kirk** on the planet **Deneva**. Kirk asked Uhura to use the private call sign on subspace frequency 3, hoping to contact his brother, Sam, when contact was lost with the colony in 2267. ("Operation— Annihilate!" [TOS]).

Guardian of Forever. (Voice by Bart LaRue). Time portal created by an unknown civilization on a distant planet at least five billion years ago. The Guardian resembled a large, rough-hewn torus about three meters in diameter. It was a sentient device,

able to respond to questions, although the sophistication of its programming was so great that it was difficult for humans to understand it. The Guardian was discovered in 2267 by *Enterprise* personnel who were investigating time-distortion waves in the vicinity. Dr. McCoy, suffering from an accidental overdose of **cordrazine** when the ship was hit by a time wave, fled into Earth's past through the Guardian. While in the past, McCoy effected a change in the flow of history, creating a new future in which the *Starship Enterprise* did not exist. Kirk and Spock followed McCoy to Earth's 1930s, where they learned that McCoy had prevented the death of American social worker **Edith Keeler**. In this altered history, Keeler prevented the entry of the United States into World War II long enough for Nazi Germany to develop weapons that allowed Hitler to dominate the world. Kirk and Spock were able to prevent McCoy from saving Keeler, and upon her death, time resumed its original course. The origin and purpose of the Guardian remains a total mystery, but the Guardian described itself as its own beginning and its own end. ("The City on the Edge of Forever" [TOS]).

Guardians. In **Trill** society, a select group of humanoids who devoted their lives to the care of the **symbiont**s. The Guardians, who were not themselves joined, conducted their work in the **caves of Mak'ala**. The monastic Guardians had very little contact with those outside their group. ("Equilibrium" [DS9]). SEE: **Timor.** In addition to tending to the symbionts, Guardians also oversee the Trill ***zhian'tara*** ritual. ("Facets" [DS9]).

Guernica system. Star system. Location of a Federation outpost that the *Enterprise*-D visited in 2367. ("Galaxy's Child" [TNG]).

guidance and navigation relay. Component of a spacecraft's flight control system, used to manage the flow of navigational sensor data. ("The Jem'Hadar"[DS9]). *The G and N relay of the* Rio Grande, *removed by Jake in "The Jem'Hadar," was actually the "head" of a small model of the* ***Nomad*** *space probe provided by* Star Trek: Deep Space Nine *scenic artist (and space hero) Doug Drexler!*

Guild of Restaurant and Casino Employees. Labor union of workers at Quark's bar on station Deep Space 9. Organized by **Rom** in 2372 in response to abusive pay cuts instituted by bar owner **Quark**. The guild, which was successful in gaining significant concessions from Quark, was officially dissolved under pressure from the **FCA**, but continued to exist under an unofficial agreement with Quark. ("Bar Association" [DS9]). SEE: **O'Brien, Sean Aloysius.**

Guinan. (Whoopi Goldberg). Bartender at the **Ten-Forward Lounge** aboard the *Starship Enterprise*-D. ("The Child" [TNG]). Guinan was a member of a civilization of listeners, but her people, the **El-Aurians**, were nearly wiped out by the **Borg** in the late 23rd century. While fleeing from her homeworld aboard the ***S.S. Lakul*** in 2293, Guinan was briefly swept into an alternate reality known as the **nexus**. *(Star Trek Generations).* The few survivors among her people escaped by spreading themselves across the galaxy. Guinan was one of the survivors. ("Q Who?" [TNG]). Guinan spent some time on Earth prior to that planet's development of space travel. She lived in the Earth city of **San Francisco** in the year 1893, where she met writer **Samuel Clemens**, as well as future shipmates **Data, Picard,** etc., who had traveled back in time. ("Time's Arrow, Parts I and II" [TNG]). Guinan was probably born sometime in the 19th century, making her about 500 years old when she served on the *Enterprise*-D. Her father was about 200 years old at the time of Guinan's birth. ("Rascals" [TNG]). She also had an uncle named **Terkim**. ("Hollow Pursuits" [TNG]). Guinan and **Q** were acquaintances, having met each other some two centuries ago, but neither has been particularly enlightening about the encounter, save for the fact that neither liked the other. ("Q Who?" [TNG]). She has been married several times, and has had many children. She said that all of them turned out all right, except for one who wouldn't listen. ("Evolution" [TNG]). Guinan possessed an unusual sense that extended beyond normal linear space-time. She, alone, was intuitively aware of the damage to the "normal" flow of time caused when the ***Enterprise*-C** was swept some 22 years into its future, creating an alternate timeline. Guinan warned Picard that history had been altered, persuading him to return the *Enterprise*-C back to 2344 to restore the flow of time. Such was Picard's faith in Guinan that he accepted this extraordinary recommendation. ("Yesterday's *Enterprise*" [TNG]). *Much remains unknown about Guinan, largely because* Star Trek's *producers have chosen to keep her background something of a mystery. Guinan, played by Whoopi Goldberg, joined the* Star Trek: The Next Generation *cast at the beginning of the second season after calling Gene Roddenberry and telling him that she'd like to be part of the* Enterprise *crew. Guinan was named after famed bartender Texas Guinan, who ran a saloon during the Prohibition. Young Guinan in "Rascals" was played by Isis J. Jones. Guinan's first appearance was in "The Child" [TNG]).*

gul. Title given to **Cardassian** officers approximately equivalent to a Starfleet captain. ("The Wounded" [TNG]). SEE: **glin.**

gumbo. A thick soup or stew containing okra pods. Gumbo was a specialty at **Sisko's**, a restaurant in New Orleans on Earth. ("Homefront" [DS9]).

Gunji jackdaw. Ostrich-like bird. A Gunji jackdaw appeared, along with numerous other unexpected individuals, on the **Promenade** of station **Deep Space 9** on stardate 46853. The Gunji jackdaw replica was created by unknown aliens from the Gamma Quadrant who were trying to study humanoid life. ("If Wishes Were Horses" [DS9]).

gunpowder. Explosive chemical mixture made from sulfur, saltpeter, and charcoal, used in ancient projectile weapons. Kirk, trapped on an artificial planetoid created by the **Metrons** in 2267, used native materials to make gunpowder for use in a weapon against the **Gorn**. ("Arena" [TOS]).

Gupta, Admiral. Starfleet official. Gupta visited station Deep Space 9 on stardate 47552.9 to assess movement of Cardassian troops along the Federation/Cardassian **Demilitarized Zone.** ("Whispers" [DS9]).

guramba. In the **Nausicaan** language, a word that roughly translates as "conviction" or "courage." ("Tapestry" [TNG]).

gymnasium. Recreational and exercise area aboard the *U.S.S. Enterprise*. Kirk attempted to teach **Charles Evans** some basic martial-arts skills in the gym. ("Charlie X" [TOS]). Among the equipment in the Deck 12 gymnasium on the *Enterprise*-D is an **anbo-jytsu** ring. ("The Icarus Factor" [TNG]).

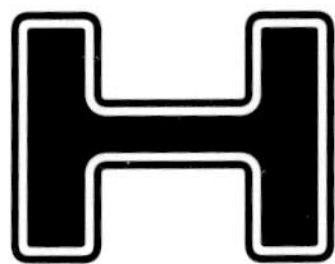

H'atoria. Klingon colony near the border between Federation and Klingon space. (In the **anti-time future** reality created by the **Q Continuum**, former Starfleet officer **Worf** was the governor of H'atoria in 2395.) ("All Good Things..." [TNG]).

H'ohk, Professor. Instructor at **Starfleet Academy**. Professor H'ohk was Captain **Kathryn Janeway**'s **Klingon** physiology teacher at the academy. ("Darkling" [VGR]).

H'Ta. Klingon warrior, son of Kahmar. In 2373, H'Ta was inducted by Gowron into the Order of the *Bat'leth*. ("Apocalypse Rising" [DS9]).

Ha'DIBah. A Klingon insult; it translates as "animal." ("Sins of the Father" [TNG], "Reunion" [TNG]).

Ha'mara. Bajoran holiday held on the anniversary of the **Emissary**'s arrival. During *Ha'mara* the **Bajoran** people show their gratitude to the Prophets for sending the Emissary to them, by fasting and by a Festival of Lights. ("Starship Down" [DS9]).

Haakona. Romulan warbird commanded by **Subcommander Taris**. The *Haakona* intervened when the Federation starships ***Yamato*** and *Enterprise*-D violated the Romulan Neutral Zone in 2365 while in search of the planet **Iconia**. The *Haakona*, along with the *Enterprise*-D, was nearly destroyed by the Iconian software weapon that did destroy the *Yamato*. ("Contagion" [TNG]).

Haakonian Order. The formal name of the **Haakonian** nation in the Delta Quadrant. ("Jetrel" [VGR]).

Haakonians. Humanoid civilization native to the Delta Quadrant. The Haakonians fought a war with the **Talaxians** for the better part of a decade. The war ended in 2356. Talax surrendered unconditionally to the Haakonian Order after the Haakonians deployed the **metreon cascade** on the moon **Rinax**. ("Jetrel" [VGR]).

Habak. A holy place used by the Native American colonists of planet **Dorvan V**. It was the site of their **vision quest**s, as well as other rituals and ceremonies. The Habak contained an open fire pit and **Mansara**, which commemorated the spirits that had visited the Habak. ("Journey's End" [TNG]).

Habitat Ring. Large inner structure of station **Deep Space 9**, surrounding the central core, largely devoted to personnel quarters and other living facilities. The three **runabout** launch pads are also located in the Habitat Ring. ("If Wishes Were Horses" [DS9]).

Habitat Ring

Hacom. (Morgan Farley). Inhabitant of planet **Beta III** during the end of the computer **Landru**'s rule in 2267. Hacom fully supported Landru and summoned the planet's **Lawgivers** when he believed that **Tamar** failed to endorse Landru's authority. ("Return of the Archons" [TOS]).

Hacopian, Dr. Staff physician assigned to the *Enterprise*-D in 2370. Dr. Crusher called in Dr. Hacopian to help with what she believed to be a viral infection among the crew. ("Genesis" [TNG]).

Hadar, Gul. Member of the Cardassian High Command. Hadar was present when **Odo** was first "revealed" to command officers in the early 2360s. Gul Hadar was quite impressed by Odo's Cardassian neck trick. ("Necessary Evil" [DS9]).

Haden, Admiral. (John Hancock). Starfleet officer. Haden transmitted Priority 1 orders to the *Enterprise*-D in the matter of the defection of Romulan admiral **Alidar Jarok** in 2366. Haden was stationed at Starfleet's Lya III command base. ("The Defector" [TNG]). In 2367, Haden confirmed Cardassian reports that the ***U.S.S. Phoenix*** had attacked and destroyed a Cardassian science station, in violation of the Federation-Cardassian peace treaty. ("The Wounded" [TNG]).

Haftel, Admiral. (Nicolas Coster). Starfleet officer and cybernetics scientist. In 2366, Haftel attempted to gain custody of Data's android daughter, **Lal**, because he believed Lal could be better cared for and studied under Starfleet supervision at the **Daystrom Institute of Technology**'s annex at **Galor IV**. ("The Offspring" [TNG]). *While it was never spoken on air, the script for "The Offspring" gives Haftel's first name as Anthony.*

Hagath. (Steven Berkoff). Ruthless arms dealer and associate of **Gaila**. Hagath visited Deep Space 9 in 2373 to meet Gaila and **Quark** for the purpose of conducting weapons sales. Negotiations to sell biological weapons to the **Regent of Palamar** went terribly wrong, resulting in a **purification squad** being sent after Hagath and Gaila by **General Nassuc**, the regent's bitter enemy. ("Business As Usual" [DS9]). SEE: **Farrakk.**

Hagen, Andrus. (John Vickery). Science advisor aboard the ***U.S.S. Brattain*** at the time the ship was trapped in a **Tyken's Rift** in 2367. Hagen was the only member of the crew still alive when the *Enterprise*-D arrived on a rescue mission. Hagen was found in a profound catatonic state and was unable to communicate what had happened. A Betazoid, Hagen could only project a few words telepathically, words that made no sense until Troi began to hear the same words in her dreams. ("Night Terrors" [TNG]).

haggis. Traditional Scottish dish made from sheep's stomach. ("The Savage Curtain" [TOS]).

Hagler, Lieutenant Edward. *Enterprise*-D crew member who was abducted by the **solanagen-based aliens** in 2369. Lieutenant Hagler died as a result of the alien's medical experiments. ("Schisms" [TNG]).

Hagon. (James Louis Watkins). Formerly an aide to **Ligonian** leader **Lutan**, Hagon ascended to great power on planet **Ligon II** when Lutan's mating agreement was dissolved in 2364, and Hagon became First One to the wealthy **Yareena**. ("Code of Honor" [TNG]).

Haines, Ensign. (Victoria George). Navigator on the original *U.S.S. Enterprise*. On stardate 3211, Haines was part of the bridge complement during the search for a missing landing party on planet **Triskelion**. ("The Gamesters of Triskelion" [TOS]).

Hajar, Cadet Second Class Jean. (Walker Brandt). Team navigator of Starfleet Academy's ill-fated **Nova Squadron** in 2368. ("The First Duty" [TNG]). SEE: **Locarno, Cadet First Class Nicholas.**

Hakton VII. Planet located in the **Demilitarized Zone**. Site of a Federation colony. In 2370, three settlers at Hakton VII were killed by **Cardassians** in retaliation for the bombing of the ***Bok'Nor***. ("The Maquis, Part II" [DS9]).

Halanans. Civilization of **psychoprojective telepaths** from planet **New Halana**. When under stress, a Halanan's subconscious mind can project convincingly realistic illusions. Devoting themselves to commitment, Halanans mate for life. ("Second Sight" [DS9]). SEE: **Seyetik, Nidell**.

Halee system. Star system containing more than one planet barely capable of sustaining humanoid life. Worf, speaking for the Klingon renegades **Korris** and **Konmel**, suggested they be allowed to die on their feet on a planet in the Halee system rather than being executed. ("Heart of Glory" [TNG]).

"Half a Life." *Next Generation* episode #96. Teleplay by Peter Allan Fields. Story by Ted Roberts and Peter Allan Fields. Directed by Les Landau. Stardate 44805.3. *First aired in 1991. A scientist must decide between helping his people or conforming to his society's expectation of ritual suicide at age 60.* GUEST CAST: Majel Barrett as **Troi**, **Lwaxana**; Michelle Forbes as **Dara**; Terrence McNally as **B'tardat**; Colm Meaney as **O'Brien**, **Miles**; Carel Struycken as **Homn**; David Ogden Stiers as **Timicin**, **Dr.** SEE: **B'tardat; Dara; helium fusion enhancement; Kaelon II; Kaelon warships; Mantickian paté; neutron migration; oskoid; Praxillus system; Resolution, The; Rigel IV; Timicin, Dr.; torpedo sustainer engine.**

Hali. (James McIntire). A young **Mintakan** bowman. Hali pursued Riker and **Dr. Palmer** when the two fled from Mintakan custody after the accidental exposure of a Federation science team on his planet in 2366. ("Who Watches the Watchers?" [TNG]).

Halii. Homeworld of a partially telepathic humanoid civilization called the Haliians. Starfleet **Lieutenant Aquiel Uhnari** was a native of Halii. SEE: **Batarael; Canar; Horath; Muskan seed punch; *oumriel*; Shiana**. ("Aquiel" [TNG]).

Haliz, Jal. (Tim DeZarn.) **Kazon-Ogla** warrior. Jal Haliz was one of the Kazons who held Commander Chakotay captive in 2372. In his youth, Haliz received his Ogla name by killing a Relora warrior, thus becoming Jal Haliz, one of the Kazons' greatest fighters. Haliz became first **maje** after his former commander **Razik** was killed by the Kazon boy **Kar**. ("Initiations" [VGR]).

Halkans. Humanoid civilization with a history of total peace. In 2267, the Halkans refused the Federation permission to mine **dilithium** crystals on their planet for fear the dilithium would someday be used for acts of destruction. The Halkan people in the **mirror universe** were also peaceful, preferring to die rather than grant mining rights to the **Terran Empire**, the Federation's barbaric counterpart in the parallel universe. ("Mirror, Mirror" [TOS]).

Hall of Audiences. Location on planet **Beta III** where planetary leader **Landru** could be summoned. Kirk and Spock, visiting Beta III in 2267, were led there by government official **Marphon**, where they eventually destroyed the computer that had replaced the original man named Landru. ("Return of the Archons" [TOS]).

Hall of Heroes. Ceremonial hall on **Qo'noS** that was adorned with statues of great **Klingon** warriors of the past. It was a great honor to be immortalized in the Hall of Heroes. ("The Sword of Kahless" [DS9]).

Hall of Warriors. Ceremonial building on **Ty'Gokor**, a Klingon planetoid. The hall featured massive statues of great warriors of the past. The Hall of Warriors was used for great occasions such as the induction ceremony for the Order of the *Bat'leth* in 2373. ("Apocalypse Rising" [DS9]). **Arne Darvin**, a former Klingon intelligence agent who traveled back in time to 2267, hoped that if were successful in murdering legendary Starfleet Captain James T. Kirk, he would have been been honored with a statue in the Hall of Warriors. ("Trials and Tribble-ations" [DS9]). *The statues in the Hall of Warriors were designed by John Eaves under the direction of Herman Zimmerman and Randy McIlvain.* SEE: **Rurik the Damned.**

Halla. Nezu colonist and sister to **Lillias**. ("Rise" [VGR]).

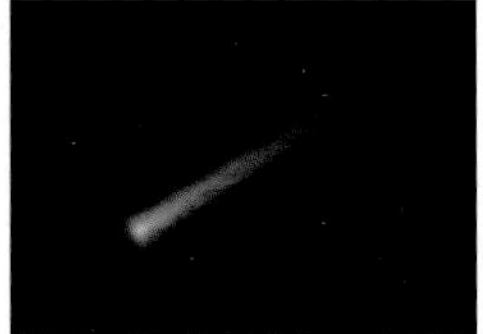

Halley's comet. A spectacular ball of ice that travels a predictable course through **Earth**'s solar system. Halley's comet is visible from Earth at its perihelion, which occurs approximately every 76 years. Noted Earth writer **Samuel Clemens**, visiting the *Starship Enterprise*-D, wondered if one could see Halley's comet from the ship's vantage point in space. ("Time's Arrow, Part II" [TNG]).

Halloway, Captain Thomas. The captain of the *Enterprise*-D in an alternate history created when Q allowed Picard to relive his fight at the **Bonestell Recreation Facility**. ("Tapestry" [TNG]).

Haltla. Dabo game operator. **Boheeka** fondly remembered Haltla from his days playing **dabo** on **Terok Nor**. ("The Wire" [DS9]).

Hamilton. Member of the *U.S.S. Voyager* crew in 2372; a proficient pilot. ("Investigations" [VGR]).

Hamlet. A tragic historical play by **William Shakespeare** about Hamlet, the prince of Denmark, a story of murder and revenge. *Hamlet* was written around AD 1600, and still was read and performed in the 23rd and 24th centuries. The **Karidian Company of Players** conducted an interstellar theatrical tour of Shakespearean performances, including *Hamlet*. ("The Conscience of the King" [TOS]). Captain Picard quoted from *Hamlet* in an effort to convince **Q** of the worthiness of human beings. ("Hide and Q" [TNG]). Klingon General **Chang** quoted from *Hamlet* in 2293 when he proclaimed the dilemna facing the Klingon people was "to be, or not to be...." *(Star Trek VI: The Undiscovered Country) The title of* Star Trek VI *is itself a reference to a quote from* Hamlet, *speaking of "death, the undiscovered country from whose bourn no traveler returns." The character of Hamlet, along with Captain Horatio Hornblower, was used by Gene Roddenberry as a basis for the character of Captain James T. Kirk.*

hammer. Tool used for pounding. In Klingon culture, the hammer is considered a symbol of power. The Taqua tribe of Nagor regards it as representing hearth and home, but the Ferengi treat it as a symbol of sexual prowess. ("Birthright, Part I" [TNG]).

Hammurabi, Code of. Important milestone in the evolution of law on planet **Earth**, the Code of Hammurabi dated back to ancient Babylon, and was one of that planet's first major attempts to develop a uniform system of justice. It included significant legal protections for individual rights. ("Court Martial" [TOS]).

Hanar. (Stewart Moss). **Kelvan** who assisted in the capture of the *Enterprise* landing party in 2268 and forced the crew to set a course for the **Andromeda Galaxy**. In an effort to distract Hanar in his unfamiliar humanoid form, McCoy injected him with **formazine** stimulant. ("By Any Other Name" [TOS]). *Stewart Moss also played Joe Tormolen in "The Naked Time" (TOS).*

hand phaser. SEE: **phaser type-1**.

Handel. Noted Earth composer (1685-1759) of Baroque-era symphonic music. Data, along with his "mother," **Juliana Tainer**, performed a violin concerto by Handel for members of the *Enterprise*-D crew in 2370. ("Inheritance" [TNG]).

Haneek. (Deborah May). **Skrreea**n who was the first of her people to discover the Bajoran wormhole, which her people called the **Eye of the Universe**. In 2370, she was elected leader of the Skrreean refugees. Haneek believed that Bajor was **Kentanna**, the legendary homeworld of the Skrreea. After the **Bajoran Chamber of Ministers** and **Vedek Assembly** rejected her request to settle on Bajor, she reluctantly led her people to settle on planet **Draylon II**. ("Sanctuary" [DS9]).

Hangar 18. Aircraft storage structure operated by the American Army Air Corps at Wright Field on Earth in the mid-20th century. The Ferengi shuttle, *Quark's Treasure*, which accidentally crashed on Earth in 1947, was stored in Hangar 18 before Quark and his crew could escape. ("Little Green Men" [DS9]). *The exterior of Hangar 18 was actually the construction mill building at Paramount Pictures, where sets for* Star Trek: Deep Space Nine *and* Star Trek: Voyager *were built. In "Little Green Men," to the left of "Hangar 18," one can see another large building, which is Stage 18, where the interiors for the* Starship Defiant *were filmed. Down the street, one can glimpse Stages 8 and 9, where the* Enterprise-D *and* Starship Voyager *interiors stood. Photo obtained under the Freedom of Information Act.*

hangar deck. A large facility on Federation starships that permitted the launch and recovery of **shuttlecraft**. On ***Constitution*-class** starships, the hangar deck was located in the engineering hull, with large doors at the aft. The hangar deck had an upper level that included an observation corridor and a control room. In later starships, the facility became known as a **shuttlebay**. *In the original* Star Trek *series, the hangar deck was a miniature set (supplemented with a small portion that was built full-sized) that was first seen in "The* Galileo *Seven" (TOS), then later in "Journey to Babel" (TOS), "The Immunity Syndrome" (TOS), and "Let That Be Your Last Battlefield" (TOS). The observation corridor (but not the hangar deck below) was seen in "Conscience of the King" (TOS).*

Hanjuan. (Geof Prysirr). **Nezu** colonist and **galicite** miner. Hanjuan was a survivor of an asteroid impact on a Nezu colony planet. He escaped the surface by going to an orbital station via a mag-lev carriage. ("Rise" [VGR]).

Hanok. (James Cromwell). Member of the **Karemma** Commerce Ministry. In 2372, Minister Hanok met with the staff of station Deep Space 9 to discuss Karemma complaints with **Ferengi** trade practices. Hanok also helped the crew of the *Starship Defiant* deal with a Jem'Hadar attack. ("Starship Down" [DS9]). *James Cromwell also played Zefram Cochrane in* Star Trek: First Contact.

Hanolan colony. Federation settlement. The Hanolan colony served as an evacuation site for the civilian population of station Deep Space 9 during the coup staged by the **Alliance for Global Unity** in 2370. ("The Siege" [DS9]).

Hanoli system. Star system. Location of a subspace rupture encountered by a Vulcan ship around 2169. The Vulcans detonated a **pulse wave torpedo** into the rupture, accidentally setting off a chain reaction that destroyed the entire Hanoli system. The command crew from Deep Space 9 reviewed these events when a similar subspace rupture was suspected near the station in 2369. ("If Wishes Were Horses" [DS9]).

Hanolin asteroid belt. Asteroid field; site where a **Ferengi cargo shuttle** crashed in early 2368. Parts of the Vulcan ship ***T'Pau*** were found in the wreckage. Investigation of the wreckage eventually led to the discovery of a Romulan plot to conquer Vulcan. ("Unification, Part I" [TNG]).

Hanon IV. Class-M planet in the Hanon system in the Delta Quadrant. Hanon IV was in a Pliocene stage of evolution, comparable to **Earth** several million years ago. The planet was subject to volcanic eruptions and was home to a primitive humanoid species, as well as large carnivorous serpent-like reptiles. After Kazon-Nistrim forces commandeered the *Voyager* in late 2372, Maje Culluh stranded the ship's crew on Hanon IV where they stayed until rescued by Tom Paris. ("Basics, Parts I and II" [VGR]).

Hanonian land eel. Large cave-dwelling carnivore native to planet Hanon IV. The creature was serpentine in shape and had several paddle-like appendages on either side of its body, which it used to help it move. In early 2373, *Voyager* crew member Hogan was killed and devoured by such a beast. ("Basics, Part II" [VGR]). *The creature was designed by Dan Curry and produced as a computer-generated visual effect by Foundation Imaging.*

Hansen's Planet. Class-M world on which were found humanoid creatures similar to those discovered on planet **Taurus II**. ("The *Galileo* Seven" [TOS]).

Hansen, Commander. (Garry Walberg). Starfleet officer in charge of **Romulan Neutral Zone** outpost 4, killed during the Romulan incursion of 2266. ("Balance of Terror" [TOS]).

Hanson, Admiral J. P. (George Murdock). Starfleet official who led the Federation defense against the **Borg** attack at **Wolf 359** in early 2367. Hanson was killed in that battle, along with 11,000 other Starfleet personnel. Hanson had been in charge of Starfleet Tactical's effort to develop a defense against the Borg, but the attack came much sooner than expected, catching Starfleet unprepared against the vastly superior Borg weaponry. Hanson had been a friend of Jean-Luc Picard. ("The Best of Both Worlds, Parts I and II" [TNG]). *Actor George Murdock had previously played the false god-image in* Star Trek V.

Hanson, Mr. (Hagan Beggs). Starfleet officer. Relief helmsman aboard the original *Starship Enterprise*. ("Court Martial" [TOS], "The Menagerie" [TOS]).

***hara* cat.** Bajoran life-form. During the **Cardassian** occupation of planet **Bajor**, Kira Nerys killed a *hara* cat, mistaking it for a Cardassian soldier. ("Second Skin" [DS9]).

"Hard Time" *Deep Space Nine* episode #91. Story by Daniel Keys Moran & Lynn Barker. Teleplay by Robert Hewitt Wolfe. Directed by Alexander Singer. No stardate mentioned. First aired in 1996. *Falsely accused of espionage, Miles O'Brien is subjected to a prison sentence in the form of an Argrathi artificial reality program that simulated memories of a 20-year prison sentence when in reality only hours had passed.* GUEST CAST: Rosalind Chao as **O'Brien, Keiko**; Margot Rose as **Rinn**; Hana Hatae as **O'Brien, Molly**; F.J. Rio as **Muniz**; Craig Wasson as **Ee'Char**. SEE: **Argratha; Argrathi; black hole; *chee'lash*; Ee'Char; *eseekas*; interphasic coil spanner; Muniz, Enrique; O'Brien, Miles; ODN recoupler; *reeta*-hawk; Rinn, K'Par; Telnorri.**

Hargrove, Lieutenant. Starfleet officer assigned to the *U.S.S. Voyager*. Just prior to stardate 48579, the **Emergency Medical Hologram** prepared a culture to test Hargrove for **Arethian flu**. ("Eye of the Needle" [VGR]). Hargrove's quarters on *Voyager* were located on Deck 7. ("Twisted" [VGR]).

Haritath. (Mark L. Taylor). Member of the **Tau Cygna V** colony. Haritath was one of the first colonists to greet Commander Data upon his arrival there in 2366. Haritath agreed with Data that the colony should be evacuated, despite **Gosheven**'s objections. ("The Ensigns of Command" [TNG]).

harmonic resonators. SEE: **resonators**.

Haro, Mitena. (Joycelyn O'Brien). Apparently a **Bolian** first-year cadet attending Starfleet Academy, Haro was found to be a false identity created by unknown life-forms that kidnapped Jean-Luc Picard, **Esoqq**, and **Kova Tholl** in 2366. This abduction was part of an experiment to study the nature of authority, a concept unknown to these telepathically linked life-forms, since they were all identical. The life-forms had replaced all the abductees with near-perfect copies, then altered the behavior of the individual copied and observed the reactions of their associates. ("Allegiance" [TNG]). *The alien life-forms were not given a name in the episode.*

Harod IV. Planet. The *Enterprise*-D made an unscheduled stop at Harod IV to pick up a group of stranded miners on stardate 45761. ("The Perfect Mate" [TNG]).

Harodian miners. (David Paul Needles, Roger Rignack, Charles Gunning). Three humanoids who were picked up for emergency transport by the *Enterprise*-D on stardate 45761, while the ship was en route to planet **Krios**. The miners subsequently created a small disturbance in the ship's Ten-Forward Lounge while in the presence of the Kriosian metamorph, **Kamala**. ("The Perfect Mate" [TNG]).

Haron, Jal. (Terry Lester). First maje of the **Kazon-Relora** in 2372. After a disastrous conference on the ship of First Maje Jal Culluh of the **Kazon-Nistrim**, Haron and his aide were executed by being transported into space. ("Maneuvers" [VGR]).

Harper, Ensign. (Sean Morgan). Starfleet officer. Harper was a crew member aboard the original *Starship Enterprise* , one of the 20 crew left aboard the ship for the disastrous **M-5** drills in 2268. He was killed when the **multitronic** unit tapped into the ship's energy supply. ("The Ultimate Computer" [TOS]).

Harrakis V. Planet. The *Enterprise*-D visited Harrakis V in 2367. The ship's mission there was completed earlier than expected, and the crew was allotted extra personal time. ("Clues" [TNG]).

Harriman, Captain John. (Alan Ruck). Captain of the *U.S.S.* ***Enterprise*-B** on its maiden voyage in 2293. While in grade school, John Harriman read of Captain **James T. Kirk**'s exploits, and he considered Kirk and his original crew to be living legends. During the first flight of the *Enterprise*-B, Harriman turned to Kirk for advice when an emergency situation arose. SEE: ***Lakul, S.S.*; nexus**. *(Star Trek Generations).*

Harris, Captain. Commander of the *Starship Excalibur* who was killed, along with the rest of his crew, during the disastrous **M-5** test exercises in 2268. ("The Ultimate Computer" [TOS]).

Harrison, William B. Flight officer of the ***S.S. Beagle*** Harrison was killed in a brutal televised gladiator game on planet Eight Ninety-Two-IV in 2267. ("Bread and Circuses" [TOS]).

Harrison. Crew member aboard the original *Starship Enterprise* in 2267. Kirk recorded a commendation for Harrison when the bridge of the *Enterprise* was slowly deprived of life support during **Khan**'s takeover attempt. ("Space Seed" [TOS]).

Haru Outpost. Cardassian military facility. As part of their terrorist war against the **Cardassians**, Kira Nerys and other **Bajoran** freedom fighters conducted raids on the Haru Outpost. Years later, Kira admitted to Odo that she still had nightmares about the incident. ("Past Prologue" [DS9]).

harvesters. Deadly **nanobiogenic weapon** used during the centuries-long war between the **T'Lani** and **Kellerun**. Harvesters, which virtually wiped out the population of planet T'Lani III, were clear cylinders containing about two liters of lethal orange gel. When the war ended in 2370, both sides sought Federation help in destroying the harvesters. **Deep Space 9** personnel Dr. Julian Bashir and Miles O'Brien helped determine the **muon frequencies** required to neutralize the deadly weapon. Upon completion of their task, both Bashir and O'Brien were nearly murdered in a joint T'Lani and Kellerun plan to eliminate anyone with the knowledge to re-create these weapons of mass destruction. ("Armageddon Game" [DS9]). SEE: **E'Tyshra; Nydom, Dr.; Sharat**.

Haskins, Dr. Theodore. (Jon Lormer). Scientist with the American Continent Institute, killed when the ***S.S. Columbia*** crashed on planet **Talos IV** in 2236. An illusory version of Haskins, created by the **Talosians**, greeted Captain Pike and an *Enterprise* landing party in 2254. ("The Cage," "The Menagerie, Part I" [TOS]). *The character was apparently named for famed science-fiction film director and optical effects creator Byron Haskins, who was the associate producer of "The Cage."*

hasperat. Spicy Bajoran burrito whose filling is made with a specially prepared brine. Prepared correctly, *hasperat* will make the eyes water and will sear the tongue. **Ro Laren** was fond of *hasperat.* ("Preemptive Strike" [TNG], "Second Skin" [DS9], "Rejoined" [DS9]). *According to* Star Trek: Deep Space Nine *property master Joe Longo, the prop food used for* hasperat *was* *made from flour tortillas, layered with cream cheese, with red and green peppers. The tortillas are rolled, then sliced and served. Yum!*

Hastur, Admiral. High-ranking Starfleet officer. Hastur commanded a relief force sent by Starfleet in 2372 to help Deep Space 9 deal with Gowron's aggressive Klingon battle fleet. Hastur was a good friend of Ben Sisko's. ("The Way of the Warrior" [DS9]).

hatana. Spiced Taresian culinary dish. Eliann offered *hatana* to Harry Kim in 2373. ("Favorite Son" [VGR]).

Hatarian system. Star system known for rich archaeological sites. *Enterprise*-D Captain Jean-Luc Picard planned to visit the Hatarian system when a rendezvous with the *U.S.S. Kearsarge* was delayed in 2370. ("Firstborn" [TNG]).

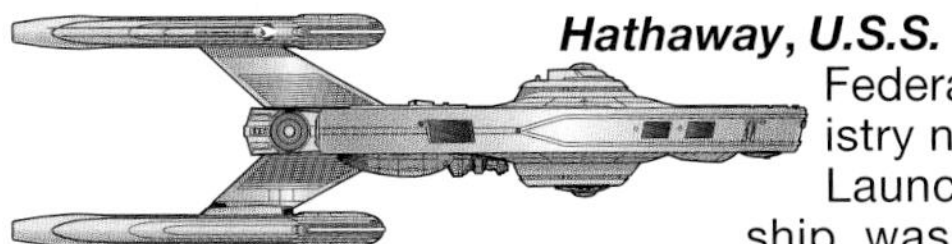

Hathaway, U.S.S. *Constellation*-class Federation starship, registry number NCC-2593. Launched in 2285, the ship was decommissioned prior to 2365, when it was temporarily returned to duty under the command of William Riker as part of a **Starfleet battle simulation**. ("Peak Performance" [TNG]). SEE: **Avidyne engines**. *The interior of the* Hathaway *bridge was a re-dress of the* Enterprise-D *Battle Bridge, although the control panels and display graphics employed movie-style designs from the* Enterprise-A. *The* Hathaway *miniature was a re-dress of the* **Stargazer** *built for "The Battle" (TNG). The* Starship Hathaway *may have been named for Anne Hathaway, the woman who married William Shakespeare. The dedication plaque on the* Hathaway *bridge carried a notation that it had been built by Yoyodyne Propulsion Systems at the Copernicus Ship Yards on Luna.*

Hathon. Location of a weapons depot commanded by Gul **Pirak** during the **Cardassian** occupation of **Bajor.** ("The Darkness and the Light" [DS9]).

Havana, U.S.S. Federation starship *Istanbul* class, Starfleet registry number NCC-34043. The *Enterprise*-D was to rendezvous with the *Havana* after studying the **Bersallis firestorms** of 2369. ("Lessons" [TNG]).

Haven. Class-M planet known for its extraordinary, peaceful beauty. Legends suggest that the planet is so beautiful it has mystical healing powers. A **Tarellian** spacecraft, carrying the last survivors of the Tarellian biological war, attempted to make planetfall on Haven in 2364. The government of Haven strongly objected to this, for fear that the Tarellian plague victims would contaminate the entire planet. Haven is also known as Beta Cassius. ("Haven" [TNG]).

"Haven." *Next Generation* episode #5. Teleplay by Tracy Tormé. Story by Tracy Tormé & Lan Okun. Directed by Richard Compton. Stardate 41294.5. *First aired in 1987. Deanna Troi's mother, Lwaxana, visits the* Enterprise-D *for her daughter's wedding. "Haven" was the first appearance of Majel Barrett in the recurring role of Lwaxana Troi, and her aide, Mr. Homn. Writer Tracy Tormé is the son of famed jazz singer, Mel Tormé. Episode director Richard Compton had, during the original* Star Trek *series, played the part of Lieutenant Washburn in "The Doomsday Machine" (TOS). Coincidentally, the first assistant director of "Haven" was Charles Washburn (who had also worked on the original series).* GUEST CAST: Majel Barrett as **Troi, Lwaxana**; Rob Knepper as **Miller, Wyatt**; Nan Martin as **Miller, Victoria**; Robert Ellenstein as **Miller, Steven**; Carel Struycken as **Homn**; Anna Katarina as Valeda; Raye Birk as **Wrenn**; Danitza Kingsley as **Ariana**; Michael Rider as Transporter chief. SEE: **Alcyones; Ariana; Beta Cassius; Betazed; Betazed, Holy Rings of; Betazoids; bonding gifts; chameleon rose; chime, Betazoid; Fifth House of Betazed; gift box, Betazoid; genetic bonding; Haven; Homn; Innis, Valeda; Miller, Wyatt; Miller, Steven; Miller, Victoria; Sacred Chalice of Rixx; Tarella; Tarellians; Troi, Deanna; Troi, Lwaxana; wedding; Wrenn; Xelo.**

Hawk, Lieutenant. (Neal McDonough). Starfleet officer assigned to the crew of the *Starship Enterprise*-E in 2373. Hawk operated the **conn** position on the vessel's bridge. Hawk was assimilated by the **Borg** during the Borg attack of 2373 and was later killed by Worf. *(Star Trek: First Contact).*

Hawking, Dr. Stephen William. (Himself). Considered one of the most brilliant theoretical physicists of 20th-century Earth. Hawking developed a quantum theory of gravity, in which he sought to link the two major theories of physics: quantum mechanics and relativity. Hawking also speculated on the existence of **wormholes** and **quantum fluctuations** linking multiple universes. Hawking's scientific achievements were all the more remarkable because he was afflicted with a debilitating neural disease that kept him confined to a wheelchair, able to speak only with the aid of a speech-synthesis computer. Commander **Data** devised a **holodeck** program that allowed him to play **poker** with Dr. Hawking, **Albert Einstein** and **Sir Isaac Newton**. ("Descent, Part I" [TNG]). *Professor Hawking's appearance on* Star Trek *was the result of a visit he made to Paramount Pictures to promote his motion-picture version of* A Brief History of Time. *At Paramount, he made known his dream of visiting the* Enterprise. *Hawking not only got to visit the sets, but he persuaded* Star Trek*'s producers to let him make an appearance on the screen. While passing through the main engineering set, Hawking paused near the warp engine, smiled, and said, "I'm working on that." A copy of Hawking's book,* A Brief History of Time, *was in Data's future Cambridge library set in "All Good Things . . ." (TNG).*

Hawking, Shuttlecraft. Shuttle attached to the *Enterprise*-D. The *Hawking* carried **Ambassador Odan** on an aborted flight to a peace conference on planet **Peliar Zel** in 2367. The shuttle was attacked by forces seeking to block the conference. ("The Host" [TNG]). The *Hawking* survived the crash of the *Enterprise*-D saucer section in 2371 and rescued Captain Jean-Luc Picard from a mountaintop on **Veridian III** on which he was stranded. *(Star Trek Generations). Named for 20th-century mathematical physicist and* Star Trek *fan Dr. Stephen Hawking. The* Hawking *in "The Host" was of a different design from the* Hawking *seen in* Star Trek Generations. *The name was re-used for the movie, despite the technical error, because of Executive Producer Rick Berman's admiration for the noted physicist. We didn't think Professor Hawking would mind.*

Hawkins. Federation ambassador to planet **Mordan IV.** Hawkins was taken hostage by Mordan governor **Karnas** in 2364, although Karnas blamed the act on dissident terrorists. ("Too Short a Season" [TNG]).

Hayashi system. Planetary system. The location of an atmospheric charting mission conducted by the *Enterprise*-D in 2366. ("Tin Man" [TNG]).

Hayes, Admiral. (Jack Shearer). Senior Starfleet officer. On stardate 50893, Admiral Hayes mobilized a fleet of starships in the Typhon sector to meet a Borg ship that had entered Federation space on a heading for Earth. The Admiral's flagship was destroyed when the armada battled the Borg vessel. *(Star Trek: First Contact). Jack Shearer also played Admiral Strickler in "Non Sequitur" (VGR).*

Hayes, Ensign. (Michael Mack). Member of the *Enterprise*-D engineering staff. (In an alternate **quantum reality** visited by Worf in 2370, Hayes was forced to take over in engineering when Commander La Forge was taken to sickbay with plasma burns.) ("Parallels" [TNG]). Hayes later served as a tactical officer on the bridge of the *Enterprise*-D in 2371. *(Star Trek Generations). Michael Mack had previously portrayed Romulan Commander Sirol in "The Pegasus" (TNG).*

Hayes, Jack. (Mel Winkler). Farmer from the United States of America on Earth. Hayes and his truck were abducted from Earth in 1937 and transported to the **Briori** homeworld in the Delta Quadrant, where he was regarded as one of the **Thirty-Sevens** by the human colonists there. He and several other humans remained in **cryostasis** on the planet until they were found and revived by the crew of the *U.S.S. Voyager* in 2371. ("The 37's" [VGR]). *This character's name is from the script and was never mentioned in dialog.*

Hayes, Lieutenant. Shuttle pilot assigned to the *Enterprise*-D in 2370. Though he was the pilot on duty on stardate 47653, Captain Jean-Luc Picard chose to pilot a recovery shuttle himself. ("Genesis" [TNG]).

Hayne. (Donald Mirault). Leader of the **Coalition** cadre of planet **Turkana IV**. A charismatic human male, Hayne helped lead his people in their ongoing battle with their rival faction, the **Alliance**. In 2367, Hayne offered his assistance to the crew of the *Enterprise*-D on their mission to rescue the crew of the downed freighter ***Arcos*** from the Alliance. Hayne hoped to use the incident to gain a tactical advantage over his enemies. ("Legacy" [TNG]).

Hazar, General. (Robert Curtis-Brown). High-ranking officer in the Bajoran military. In 2370, Hazar ordered Bajoran forces to prevent a **Skrreea**n ship from landing on the planet. Hazar rescinded the order when it was learned the ship was being piloted by a child, but it was accidentally destroyed anyway. ("Sanctuary" [DS9]). SEE: **Tumak.**

heading. In celestial navigation, a mathematical expression describing a direction with relationship to the center of the galaxy. A heading is composed of two numbers measuring an azimuth value and an elevation value in degrees. A heading of 000, mark 0 describes a direction toward the geometric center of the galaxy. In terms of navigation on a planet's surface, this is analogous to describing a direction in degrees from north, in which case a course of 5 degrees would be slightly to the right of a direction directly toward the planet's north pole. A heading differs from a bearing in that it has no relationship to the current attitude or orientation of the spacecraft. SEE: **bearing.**

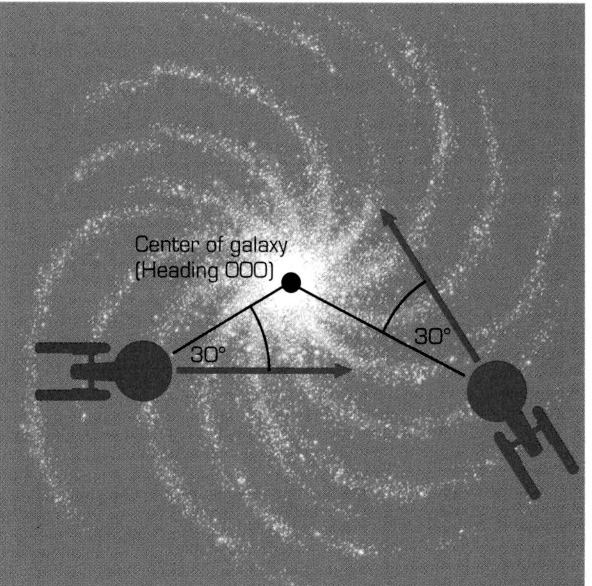

Both ships have an azimuth heading of 030. A heading of 000 for either ship would be toward the center of the galaxy.

Health and Safety inspection. Starfleet procedure used to assure that spacecraft in Federation jurisdiction maintained adequate conditions for crew and passengers. The Federation treaty with the Klingons provided for such inspection of Klingon vessels operating in Federation space. The *Enterprise*-D personnel used this clause as an excuse to detain and search a ***Toron*-class shuttlecraft** piloted by **Koral** in 2370. ("Gambit, Part II" [TNG]).

"Heart of Glory." *Next Generation* episode #20. Teleplay by Maurice Hurley. Story by Maurice Hurley and Herbert Wright & D. C. Fontana. Directed by Rob Bowman. Stardate 41503.7. *First aired in 1988. A group of Klingon renegades tries to capture the* Enterprise-*D. This episode marked the first appearance of Klingons in* Star Trek: The Next Generation, *except for Worf. The Talarians, whose ship we see in this episode, are also seen in "Suddenly Human" (TNG), although with a different ship.* GUEST CAST: Vaughn Armstrong as **Korris, Captain**; Charles H. Hyman as **Konmel, Lieutenant**; David Froman as **K'nera**; Robert Bauer as **Kunivas**; Brad Zerbst as Nurse; Dennis Madalone as Ramos. SEE: ***Batris*; Gault; Halee system; K'nera; Kling; Klingon death ritual; Klingon Defense Force; Konmel, Lieutenant; Korris, Captain; Kunivas; Merculite rockets; *T'Acog, I.K.S.*; Talarians; VISOR; Visual Acuity Transmitter; Worf.**

"Heart of Stone." *Deep Space Nine* episode #60. Written by Ira Steven Behr & Robert Hewitt Wolfe. Directed by Alexander Singer. Stardate 48521.5. *First aired in 1995. When Kira becomes trapped in a living crystal, Odo is her only hope for escape. Meanwhile, Nog lobbies for admission to Starfleet.* GUEST CAST: Max Grodénchik as **Rom**; Aron Eisenberg as **Nog**; Salome Jens as **Founder leader**; Majel Barrett as Computer voice. SEE: **Avesta; Badlands; Bemar; Founder leader; Ferengi Attainment Ceremony; Ferengi Code; Ferengi lobes; Ferengi Rules of Acquisition; kayaking; Lissepian ship; Maquis interceptor; *Mekong, U.S.S.*; Mora Pol, Dr.; Nausicaans; Nog; O'Brien, Miles; *odo'ital*; Odo; *Peregrine*-class ship; Prophet's Landing; Remmil VI; Rom; Starfleet Academy; ultrasonic generator; Vilix'pran.**

heart of *targ*. A traditional Klingon dish. Commander Riker tasted some of this stuff when he tried to acquaint himself with Klingon culture prior to his temporary assignment to the ***Pagh*** in 2365. ("A Matter of Honor" [TNG]). SEE: ***targ*.**

heater. Slang term on planet **Sigma Iotia II** for a firearm. The Iotians referred to a Starfleet phaser as a "fancy heater." ("A Piece of the Action" [TOS]).

heavy graviton beam. A directed energy weapon considered for possible use against the **Borg** during the Borg offensive of 2367. The idea was abandoned when it was determined that local field distortion generation would be ineffective against Borg defenses. ("The Best of Both Worlds, Part II" [TNG]). SEE: **graviton.**

Hechu' ghos. A Klingon phrase meaning "set course," as in to set a ship's course. ("Unification, Part I" [TNG]).

Hedford, Commissioner Nancy. (Elinor Donahue). Assistant Federation commissioner who was assigned to mediate a peace agreement on planet **Epsilon Canaris III** in 2267 in an effort to avert an impending war. Hedford was forced to leave the negotiations prematurely when she contracted deadly **Sakuro's disease**. Commissioner Hedford died aboard the *Shuttlecraft Galileo* while being transported to the *Starship Enterprise*. ("Metamorphosis" [TOS]). *Hedford, of course, did not die in space, but merged with the life-form known as the* ***Companion****, on a planetoid in the* ***Gamma Canaris region****, where she found love with noted scientist* ***Zefram Cochrane****. Since Kirk promised never to reveal this information about her fate, a Federation encyclopedia would not have it.*

Hedril. (Kirsten Dunst). Young **Cairn** child and daughter of **Maques,** who visited the *Starship Enterprise*-D in 2370 as part of a diplomatic mission. Hedril reminded Ambassador Lwaxana Troi of her deceased daughter, **Kestra**, triggering the release of painful memories that Troi had suppressed for years. ("Dark Page" [TNG]). *Kirsten Dunst appeared in* ***metaconscious*** *sequences, playing the role of Kestra but without Cairn makeup.* ("Dark Page" [TNG]).

***Hegh'bat* ceremony.** Literally translated as "The Time to Die," the *Hegh'bat* ceremony was a **Klingon** ritualized suicide. Klingon tradition held that when a Klingon was unable to stand and face his enemies, he should choose the *Hegh'bat*. The rite called for the eldest son of the celebrant, or a trusted friend, to deliver a ritual knife to the warrior, who would impale himself in the chest. The son or friend would then remove the knife and wipe it on his sleeve. Following a severe spinal injury in 2368, Lieutenant **Worf** considered the *Hegh'bat*, but was dissuaded from completing the ritual when offered the alternative of **genetronic replication** therapy. ("Ethics" [TNG]).

Hegh'ta. A Klingon bird-of-prey, commanded by **Kurn** in support of the **Gowron** regime during the **Klingon civil war** of 2367-2368. Worf served briefly aboard the *Hegh'ta* as tactical officer during that conflict. ("Redemption, Part I" [TNG]).

Heifetz, Jascha. A famous concert violinist (1901-1987). **Data** programmed himself to emulate Heifetz's performance style. ("Sarek" [TNG]).

Heisenberg compensators. Component of a transporter system, designed to permit the derivation of precision vector and positional data of particles on a subatomic level. ("Realm of Fear" [TNG]). Picard suggested disengaging the Heisenberg compensators as a possible means of giving physical reality to the computer intelligence version of **Professor James Moriarty**, but it was a ruse to buy time. ("Ship in a Bottle" [TNG]). *Werner Heisenberg's "uncertainty principle" suggests that on a subatomic level, it is possible to know the motion* or *the position of a particle, but not both. Some scientists have suggested this basic characteristic of matter may make it impossible for a transporter as seen on* Star Trek *to work, so Mike Okuda suggested the "Heisenberg compensator" as a bit of a scientific gag to "explain" how the transporter does it anyway. (No, he doesn't have any idea how it would work.)*

Hekaras Corridor. Region of space, approximately 12 light-years long, near the Hekaran system that was commonly used for interstellar travel. Much of the surrounding areas are saturated with unusually intense **tetryon** fields, so the Hekaras Corridor provided the only means of safe passage for starships. In 2366, two Hekaran scientists, **Serova** and **Rabal**, submitted a preliminary report to the Federation Science Council, theorizing that the Hekaras Corridor was stressed by warp fields and would soon develop a rupture. They further theorized that, if warp drive usage continued at its present rate, the ruptures would spread throughout inhabited space. At the time, the council found their theories lacking sufficient proof. In 2370, Rabal and Serova booby-trapped the corridor with **verteron mines**, in order to gain the attention of Starfleet. When the *Enterprise*-D was disabled by one of these mines, Captain Jean-Luc Picard agreed to listen to Serova's theory, and found it to be worthy of resubmission to the Science Council. Unsatisfied with his response, Serova caused a warp core breach aboard her ship, causing a **subspace rupture** in the corridor, just as she had predicted. Thereafter, the Federation Council ordered the corridor limited to essential travel only, in order to slow any further damage to the region. The council further ordered Federation ships throughout the galaxy to restrict their maximum speed to warp 4.7. ("Force of Nature" [TNG]). *The* Starship Enterprise-*D and other ships observed the "warp speed limit" for the remainder of* Star Trek: The Next Generation. *After that, it was assumed that Starfleet was able to develop a more "environmentally friendly" warp drive, so the speed limit was evidently lifted.*

Hekaras II. Class-M planet; a Federation member. Located in the **Hekaras Corridor**, Hekaras II was the only inhabited planet in the region. In the late 2360s, two Hekaran scientists discovered that the region of space near their planet was very susceptible to **warp field effect**. They tried to persuade the Federation Council and their own people to avoid the use of warp travel in the area, even though it would mean the almost total isolation of their planet. It was not until 2370, following the formation of a **subspace rift** in the corridor, that the scientists' theories were believed. Unfortunately, due to the gravitational shifts following the formation of the rift, the climate of Hekaras II began to change. As a short-term measure, Starfleet was able to assist the Hekarans with a **weather control matrix**. ("Force of Nature" [TNG]).

Helaspont Nebula. Astronomical cloud containing numerous protoplanetary masses. In 2371, the ***U.S.S. Ulysses*** commanded by Captain Entebe studied the Helaspont Nebula. ("The Adversary" [DS9]).

Heler. (Thomas Prisco). Heler was a prisoner on the Cardassian ship ***Ravinok*** in 2366 when it was attacked by the Breen and forced to land on **Dozaria**. Heler survived the crash and was forced to labor in the Breen dilithium mines on Dozaria. He and several other crash survivors were rescued by Kira Nerys and Gul Dukat in 2372. ("Indiscretion" [DS9]).

Helewa, Isam. Master of meditation and breathing techniques. He was a mentor to Dr. Julian Bashir, during Bashir's college years. ("Crossover" [DS9]).

helium fusion enhancement. Theoretical technique that would increase the energy output of a dying star by increasing the temperature and pressure inside the star so that the star begins helium fusion, thus increasing its useful life. A test of this technique, designed by **Dr. Timicin** of planet **Kaelon II** in 2367, used shock waves from a carefully controlled series of photon torpedo explosions to create zones of elevated pressure where helium ignition could occur. Timicin tested the process in 2367, but the test was a dramatic failure, causing a red giant star to go supernova. Further work was required, but the elderly Timicin returned to his homeworld for his **Resolution**, hoping that others would continue his research. ("Half a Life" [TNG]).

helm. Aboard a starship, the control station and officer responsible for actually piloting the ship. The helm officer was also called a helmsman. In more recent Federation starships, this function was merged with the duties of the **navigator**, and dubbed conn, or **flight controller**. *Mr.* ***Sulu*** *was the helmsman aboard the* Starship Enterprise *during the original* Star Trek *series. The terms helm and helmsman were replaced with conn at the beginning of* Star Trek: The Next Generation*.*

helmsman. SEE: **helm**.

Hemikek IV. Planet in the Delta Quadrant. In 2372, **Seska** told Michael Jonas that the **Kazon-Nistrim** would rendezvous at planet Hemikek IV once the *Starship Voyager* was destroyed. ("Lifesigns" [VGR]).

Hemikek. Class-M planet in a yellow dwarf system in the Delta Quadrant. Hemikek was rich in minerals, and the mining rights on the planet belonged to a consortium of nonaggressive people. In 2372, **Michael Jonas** sabotaged *Voyager*'s **magnetic constrictors** so that they would be forced to vent plasma, severely damaging the inner layer of the warp coils. This damage was designed to force *Voyager* to visit Hemikek, where **Kazon** forces were lying in ambush. ("Investigations" [VGR]).

hemocythemia. Medical condition in which intercellular pressures are unstable. This condition was also called hemocythemic imbalance and could be treated with osmotic pressure therapy. ("Deadlock" [VGR]).

Hendorff, Ensign. (Mal Friedman). *Enterprise* crew member. Hendorff was killed by a poisonous plant on planet **Gamma Trianguli VI** in 2267. ("The Apple" [TOS]). *Bob Justman speculates, "he was killed because he wore a red shirt. He should have known better!"*

Hendrick, Chief. (Dennis Madalone). *Enterprise*-D transporter officer. Hendrick was on duty when the transformed **Commander La Forge** beamed down to the surface of **Tarchannen III** in 2367. La Forge overpowered Hendrick, and he was unable to stop the transport. ("Identity Crisis" [TNG]). *Dennis "Danger" Madalone is stunt coordinator for* Star Trek: The Next Generation*,* Star Trek: Deep Space Nine*, and* Star Trek: Voyager*. He has been seen as a variety of security guards and other victims of mayhem.*

Hengist, Mr. (John Fiedler). Originally a resident of **Rigel IV**, later employed as a city administrator on planet **Argelius II**. Hengist's body was possessed by an evil energy life-form that thrived on the emotion of terror and was responsible for several brutal murders. This entity, which traveled to Argelius II in Hengist's body, was also known as **Redjac**, **Beratis**, **Kesla**, and **Jack the Ripper**. ("Wolf in the Fold" [TOS]).

Henley, Mariah. (Catherine MacNeal). **Maquis** resistance fighter who joined the crew of the ***Voyager***. During the first few weeks after the ship was lost in the Delta Quadrant in 2371, Henley became regarded as undisciplined. Accordingly, Henley was among several Maquis crew members assigned to Lieutenant Tuvok for **field training**. ("Learning Curve" [VGR]). *Henley's first name was not mentioned in dialog but is from the script.*

Henoch. (Leonard Nimoy). One of three advanced beings who survived a devastating war that destroyed their planet 500,000 years ago. *U.S.S. Enterprise* personnel discovered Henoch and the other two survivors in 2268, their consciousness having been encased in receptacles stored in an underground vault. Upon Henoch's revival, Spock allowed Henoch's intellect to "borrow" Spock's body so that Henoch could construct **android** bodies for the survivors. Henoch was, however, unable to leave behind his old hatreds, and tried to destroy **Sargon** and **Thalassa** before being destroyed himself. ("Return to Tomorrow" [TOS]). SEE: **Sargon's planet**.

Henry V. Classic drama written by William **Shakespeare** on Earth. A holographic performance of the play was available on the *Enterprise*-D holodeck. In this simulation, the holodeck participant could perform one of the roles. Data chose this play as part of his ongoing study of the human condition. ("The Defector" [TNG]). *Patrick Stewart, a former member of the Royal Shakespearean Company, played the holographic image of Michael Williams, a character in the drama.*

Henry, Admiral Thomas. (Earl Billings). Starfleet admiral in charge of security. Admiral Henry visited the *Enterprise*-D in 2367, while **Admiral Norah Satie** was conducting an investigation into the circumstances surrounding an explosion in the ship's engine room. Satie suspected the explosion to be evidence of a serious security breach. Henry ordered Satie's inquest discontinued after determining that her investigation was proceeding without probable cause and was therefore in violation of the Federation Constitution's **Seventh Guarantee** against self-incrimination. ("The Drumhead" [TNG]).

Henshaw, Christi. (Julie Warner). *Enterprise*-D crew member. Henshaw and **Geordi La Forge** had a date on the **holodeck** just prior to the discovery of the ***Cleponji*** in 2366. Although La Forge put a lot of effort into making the holodeck program a romantic experience, Christi eventually told him that she didn't feel "that way" about him. ("Booby Trap" [TNG]). Later that year, when Geordi's self-confidence was improved after his **neurolink** with **"John Doe,"** Christi found Geordi much more attractive. ("Transfigurations" [TNG]).

Hera, U.S.S. Federation starship, *Nebula* class, Starfleet registry number NCC-62006, commanded by Captain **Silva La Forge**. The *Hera* had a crew of 300, most of whom were **Vulcan**. The ship disappeared without a trace in 2370. Captain Silva La Forge was the mother of *Enterprise*-D engineer Geordi La Forge. ("Interface" [TNG]). *Named for the Greek goddess Hera, wife of Zeus and queen of the gods.*

Herbert, Transporter Chief. (Lance Spellerberg). *Enterprise*-D transporter officer. ("We'll Always Have Paris" [TNG]). *Lance Spellerberg also appeared as a transporter operator in "The Icarus Factor" (TNG).*

Herbert. Derogatory term taken from a minor government official known for his rigid patterns of thought. **Dr. Sevrin**'s followers were very fond of calling Captain Kirk by that name. ("The Way to Eden" [TOS]).

Hermes, U.S.S. Federation starship, *Antares* class, Starfleet registry number NCC-10376. The *Hermes* served in Picard's armada to blockade the Romulan supply ships supplying the **Duras** family forces during the **Klingon civil war** of 2367-2368. ("Redemption, Part II" [TNG]).

Hermosa Quake. Disastrous seismic event in 2047 on the coast of southern California near the city of **Los Angeles** on Earth. The quake caused the entire region around Hermosa to sink under

200 meters of water. The area became one of Earth's largest coral reefs, home to thousands of different marine species. ("Future's End, Part I" [VGR]).

"Hero Worship." *Next Generation* episode #111. Teleplay by Joe Menosky. Story by Hilary J. Bader. Directed by Patrick Stewart. Stardate 45397.3. *First aired in 1992. A young boy whose parents are killed in a terrible diasaster copes by deciding he is an android, just like Data. This episode was being filmed at the time of the death of* Star Trek *creator Gene Roddenberry.* GUEST CAST: Joshua Harris as **Timothy**; Harley Venton as **Hutchinson, Transporter Chief**; Sheila Franklin as **Felton, Ensign**; Steven Einspahr as Teacher. SEE: **Black Cluster; Breen; Dokkaran temple; Elamos the Magnificent; enantiodromia; Felton, Ensign; Hutchinson, Transporter Chief; La Forge, Geordi; Starbase 514; Tagas; Tamarian frost; Timothy; user code clearance; *Vico, S.S.*; victurium alloy.**

"Heroes and Demons." *Voyager* episode #12. Written by Naren Shankar. Directed by Les Landau. Stardate 48693.2. *First aired in 1995. The Doctor is called upon to investigate the disappearance of three crew members from the ship's holodeck.* GUEST CAST: Marjorie Monaghan as **Freya**; Christopher Neame as **Unferth**; Michael Keenan as **Hrothgar, King**; Majel Barrett as Computer voice. SEE: ***Amanita muscaria*; atuta; *Beowulf*; Emergency Medical Hologram; Freya; Grendel; Kim, Harry; holodeck and holosuite programs; holonovel; Hrothgar, King; noncorporeal life; Parinisti measles; photonic beings; Rakella Prime; Schweitzer; Unferth; Vok'sha.**

Hesperan thumping cough. A flu-like affliction. Wesley Crusher noted that the effects of a virus he contracted on **Quazulu VIII** were worse than Hesperan thumping cough. ("Angel One" [TNG]).

Hetman. In the **Xepolite** culture, title given to a ship's commander. ("The Maquis, Part II" [DS9]).

Heva VII. Planet in the Delta Quadrant. Site of a refueling port. ("The Chute" [VGR]).

hexiprismatic field. Energy type. Engineer Torres of the *Starship Voyager* used hexiprismatic energy to help determine the location of **Suspiria**, a **sporocystian** life-form. ("Cold Fire" [VGR])

Hickman, Lieutenant Paul. (Amick Byram). Starfleet officer. Former crew member of the ***U.S.S. Victory*** who beamed down to planet **Tarchannen III** in 2362. In 2367, Hickman was compelled to steal a Federation shuttle and return to Tarchannen III. Hickman's shuttle was destroyed attempting to land on the planet. It was later discovered that Hickman's body had been infiltrated by an alien DNA strand in 2362. ("Identity Crisis" [TNG]).

"Hide and Q." *Next Generation* episode #11. Teleplay by C. J. Holland and Gene Roddenberry. Story by C. J. Holland. Directed by Cliff Bole. Stardate 41590.5. *First aired in 1987. Q offers Riker the gift of godlike powers. This episode marked the first return of Q following his initial appearance in "Encounter at Farpoint."* GUEST CAST: John de Lancie as **Q**; Elaine Nalee as Injured woman; William A. Wallace as **Crusher, Wesley** (25 years old). SEE: **Aldebaran serpent; *Hamlet*; Q; Quadra Sigma III; Riker, William T.; Shakespeare, William; Sigma III Solar System; Starbase G-6.**

***Hideki*-class Cardassian starship.** Small patrol craft. In 2370, a *Hideki*-class ship, commanded by **Gul Evek**, intercepted a runabout assigned to Deep Space 9 and forcibly removed Starfleet officer Miles O'Brien. ("Tribunal" [DS9]). *This class may have been named in honor of Japanese physicist Yukawa Hideki, who first postulated the existence of the subatomic pion in 1935, although it is unclear why Cardassians might so recognize an Earth scientist.*

Higa Metar. Sect of the **Bajoran** underground active when planet **Bajor** was occupied by the **Cardassians**. Bajoran geneticist **Dekon Elig** was a member of the Higa Metar. ("Babel" [DS9]).

High Council. SEE: **Klingon High Council.**

"High Ground, The." *Next Generation* episode #60. Written by Melinda M. Snodgrass. Directed by Gabrielle Beaumont. Stardate 43510.7. *First aired in 1990. Beverly Crusher is captured by a terrorist who hopes to draw the Federation into his struggle for freedom.* GUEST CAST: Karrie Keane as **Devos, Alexana**; Richard Cox as **Finn, Kyril**; Marc Buckland as **Shaw, Katik;** Fred G. Smith as Policeman; Christopher Pettiet as Boy. SEE: **Ansata; Devos, Alexana; Elway Theorem; Finn, Kyril; folded-space transport; inverter; Ireland; Rutia IV; Rutians; Shaw, Katik; shuttlebus; subspace phenomena.**

High Sierras. Mountain range in eastern California on Earth. Captain Braxton's 29th-century *Timeship Aeon* crash-landed in the High Sierras in 1967. **Henry Starling** was camping nearby and observed the landing. ("Future's End, Part I" [VGR]).

high-energy distortion wave. Cyclic currents discovered within and around a **subspace rift** that formed in the **Hekaras Corridor** in 2370. The distortion wave was very dangerous to both the *U.S.S. Fleming* and the *Enterprise*-D when both ships were entrapped in the rift. However, the crew of the *Enterprise*-D turned the waves to their advantage, using them to literally "surf" out of the rift. ("Force of Nature" [TNG]).

high-energy X-ray laser. Coherent energy beam weapon. Ship-mounted X-ray lasers were used aboard **Talarian** warships in 2367. ("Suddenly Human" [TNG]). *High-energy X-ray lasers have a basis in 20th-century technology, developed as part of the Strategic Defense Initiative.*

high-intensity warp pulse. Instantaneous discharge of warp energy from a pair of field-saturated **nacelle**s. In 2370, because they were unable to utilize standard warp speed, the crew of the *Enterprise*-D used this technique to "coast" into a **subspace rift**. ("Force of Nature" [TNG]).

Hildebrandt. (Anne H. Gillespie). Starfleet officer. A specialist in volcanology and geomechanics aboard the *Enterprise*-D. Hildebrandt assisted in the geological survey of planets in the **Selcundi Drema** sector in 2365. ("Pen Pals" [TNG]).

hill people. Tribe of hunter-gatherers on **Tyree**'s planet living in huts and caves. Lieutenant **James T. Kirk** visited these people in 2254 when he commanded his first planet survey. Kirk returned in 2267 to find the hill people facing their neighbors, the villagers, as enemies. ("A Private Little War" [TOS]). *Kirk was apparently a crew member aboard the* U.S.S. Farragut *at the time of his first visit.*

Hill, Dixon. (Patrick Stewart, sort of). Fictional private detective from the Dixon Hill series of short stories and novels set in San Francisco, Earth, in the 1930s and 1940s. The character first appeared in the short story **"The Big Goodbye"** published in pulp magazine *Amazing Detective Stories* in 1934. Dixon Hill novels have included *The Long Dark Tunnel* (published 1936) and ***The Parrot's Claw*** (published circa 1940). *Enterprise*-D Captain Jean-Luc Picard was an aficionado of the Dixon Hill stories and enjoyed holodeck simulations based on them. ("The Big Goodbye" [TNG]). The Dixon Hill holodeck program was sufficiently sophisticated that Picard once instructed the computer to "improvise" and create the Dixon Hill environment only, without any specific story elements. Picard's attempt to enjoy the resulting scenario was unfortunately ruined when Betazoid ambassador **Lwaxana Troi** wandered into the simulation and became attracted to one of the characters, unaware that he was merely a simulation. ("Manhunt" [TNG]). Picard introduced Guinan to the Dixon Hill adventures while the *Enterprise*-D was en route to Evadne IV. ("Clues" [TNG]). In 2373, Captain Jean-Luc Picard ran his Dixon Hill program with the safeties deactivated so that he could use a machine gun to neutralize some Borg drones when they attempted to take over the *Enterprise*-E. *(Star Trek: First Contact). The computer readout studied by Data when reading the Dixon Hill stories in "The Big Goodbye" (TNG) listed episode writer Tracy Tormé as the author of Hill's adventures.* SEE: **Bell, Lieutenant Dan; Bradley, Jessica; Leech, Felix; Madeline; Nicki the Nose; Redblock, Cyrus; Ruby.**

Hill, Dr. Richard. Staff physician aboard the *Enterprise*-D. He was one of the first crew members to disappear from Beverly Crusher's universe during her entrapment in a **static warp shell** in 2367. ("Remember Me" [TNG]).

Hindu Festival of Lights. Also known as *Divali,* the Festival of Lights celebrates the return of Rama to his kingdom to become the rightful king. Celebrants would light rows of oil lamps or candles to welcome Rama home. In 2367, the festival was celebrated aboard the *Enterprise*-D on stardate 44390, a day that saw four crew birthdays, two personnel transfers, two chess tournaments, a school play, two promotions, a birth, and a wedding. ("Data's Day" [TNG]).

Hints for Healthful Living. Medical topics segment of the program ***A Briefing With Neelix***. *Hints for Healthful Living* was hosted by *Voyager*'s Emergency Medical Hologram. ("Investigations" [VGR]).

hippocampus. A component of the limbic system in a humanoid brain. The hippocampus coordinates olfaction, autonomic functions, and some aspects of emotional behavior. ("Violations" [TNG], "Conundrum" [TNG]). An increase in the level of **acetylcholine** within the hippocampus can quantify the amount of recent memory an individual has acquired. ("All Good Things..." [TNG]).

Hippocratic Oath. Traditional Earth code of ethics for physicians. The oath requires physicians to do no harm, to use their best efforts to care for their patients, and to protect the confidentiality of patient information. Named for the ancient Greek physician Hippocrates. In 2373, the **Emergency Medical Hologram** cited the Hippocratic Oath after he caused suffering due to aberrant subroutines planted into his personality matrix. ("Darkling" [VGR]).

"Hippocratic Oath." *Deep Space Nine* episode #75. Teleplay by Lisa Klink. Story by Nicholas Corea and Lisa Klink. Directed by Rene Auberjonois. Stardate 49066.5. *First aired in 1995. Doctor Bashir and Chief O'Brien are captured by renegade Jem'Hadar soldiers who demand that the doctor free them from their genetically-engineered drug addiction.* GUEST CAST: Scott MacDonald as **Goran'Agar**; Stephen Davies as **Arak'Taral**; Jerry Roberts as **Meso'Clan**; Marshall Teague as **Temo'Zuma**; Roderick Garr as **Regana Tosh;** Michael H. Bailous as Jem'Hadar #1. SEE: **Arak'Taral; Bashir, Dr. Julian; Bopak III; Bopak system; darts; Founders; Goran'Agar; Gowron; isogenic enzyme; Jem'Hadar; ketracel-white; Markalian smugglers; Merik III; Meso'Clan; Rakonian swamp rat; Regana Tosh; *Rubicon, U.S.S.*; Strategic Operations Officer; Tallonian crystals; Temo'Zuma; Vorta.**

histamine. Biochemical substance produced by the breakdown of histidine, an amino acid found in humanoid tissues. Histamine is produced by the body when it comes in contact with substances to which the body is sensitized, and is a primary factor in the humanoid allergic response. Histamine levels are characteristically depressed by a disease known as **Iresine Syndrome**. ("Violations" [TNG]).

***Hlaka* soup.** Meal prepared by Neelix for the crew of the *U.S.S. Voyager*. ("Investigations" [VGR]).

Hobii. SEE: **Kazon-Hobii**.

Hobson, Lieutenant Commander Christopher. (Timothy Carhart). Starfleet officer who served as Data's first officer aboard the ***U.S.S. Sutherland*** during the Starfleet blockade of the Romulan border in 2368. His first official act in that position was to request a transfer off the ship. ("Redemption, Part II" [TNG]).

Hodgkins's Law of Parallel Planet Development. Sociologic theory postulating that similar planets with similar populations and similar environments will evolve in similar ways. Planet Eight Ninety-Two-IV was an example of this principle in that it was technologically similar to 20th-century Earth, but culturally it resembled the ancient Roman Empire. ("Bread and Circuses" [TOS]). SEE: **Eight Ninety-Two-IV, Planet.**

Hodin. (David Hurst). Prime minister of planet **Gideon** in 2268 and father to **Odona**. Hodin masterminded a desperate plan to abduct *Enterprise* Captain James T. Kirk to help alleviate the overpopulation crisis facing his planet. ("The Mark of Gideon" [TOS]).

Hoek IV. Planet located in the **Lantar Nebula**, where the famed Sampalo relics are located. **Q** tempted archeologist **Vash** with viewing the Sampalo relics located on Hoek IV, but she declined. ("Q-Less" [DS9]). *Hoek IV was definitely* not *a reference to* Ren and Stimpy. *Nope.*

Hoex. Ferengi entrepreneur who bought out his rival Turot's controlling interest in a cargo port on **Volchok Prime** in 2369. ("The Nagus" [DS9]).

Hogan. (Simon Billig). *Starship Voyager* crew member. ("Alliances" [VGR], "Meld" [VGR]). Hogan operated the transporter console, when in 2372, Tuvok and Neelix were accidentally merged into **Tuvix**. Hogan was among those crew members who tried to cook their own food in Neelix's kitchen after Neelix and Tuvok were merged into Tuvix in 2372. ("Tuvix" [VGR]). In early 2373, Hogan was killed by a **Hanonian land eel** on planet Hanon IV. ("Basics, Part II" [VGR]).

Hogue. (Michael Reilly Burke). Member of the **Cardassian underground movement**. In 2370, Hogue, who was a student of Professor **Natima Lang**, was forced to flee Cardassia because of his political views. Hogue, along with Lang and fellow dissident **Rekelen**, sought refuge at station Deep Space 9, but were forced to flee again when the Cardassian Central Command learned of their presence and sentenced them to death. ("Profit and Loss" [DS9]). *Michael Reilly Burke also portrayed Goval, a Borg, in "Descent, Part II" (TNG)*

Hokule'a*-class starship.** Type of Federation starship. The ***U.S.S. Tripoli, the ship whose crew discovered **Data** at **Omicron Theta** in 2338, was a *Hokule'a*-class starship. ("Datalore" [TNG]). *No design has yet been developed for the* Hokule'a*-class starship, as the designation remains conjectural. From the Hawaiian word meaning "star of gladness."*

Holana River. Scenic waterway in **Musilla Province** on planet **Bajor**. ("Looking for *par'Mach* in All the Wrong Places" [DS9]).

Holberg 917G. Planetoid in the Omega system. Holberg 917G was home to the (nearly) immortal **Mr. Flint** and was also a source of the rare mineral **ryetalyn**, an antidote to deadly Rigelian fever that infested the crew of the *Starship Enterprise* in 2269. ("Requiem for Methuselah" [TOS]). *Flint's castle exterior was a re-use of the Rigel fortress matte painting originally created for "The Cage" (TOS).*

"hole in space." A spatial phenomenon created by the extradimensional being called **Nagilum**. The hole in space was used by Nagilum as a means of entrapping the *Enterprise*-D along with an image of the *Starship* ***Yamato***. ("Where Silence Has Lease" [TNG]).

Hollander, Eli. (John Pyper-Ferguson). Holodeck character, known as The Butcher of Bozeman, from the program ***Ancient West.*** ("A Fistful of Datas" [TNG]). *Bozeman, Montana, is the hometown of* Star Trek *writer-producer Brannon Braga.*

Hollander, Frank. Holodeck character in the ***Ancient West*** program. Father of **Eli Hollander.** ("A Fistful of Datas" [TNG]).

Holliday, Doc. (Sam Gilman). Dentist in the early American West who fought on the side of the Earps against the Clanton family at the famous gunfight at the **OK Corral** in **Tombstone, Arizona,** in October of 1881. ("Spectre of the Gun" [TOS]).

"Hollow Pursuits." *Next Generation* episode #69. Written by Sally Caves. Directed by Cliff Bole. Stardate 43807.4. *First aired in 1990. A reclusive* Enterprise-*D engineer compensates for his social awkwardness by creating holodeck simulations in which he is king. This episode features the first appearance of Reginald Barclay.* GUEST CAST: Dwight Schultz as **Barclay, Reginald**; Charley Lang as **Duffy, Lieutenant**; Colm Meaney as **O'Brien, Miles**; Whoopi Goldberg as **Guinan**. SEE: **antigravs; Barclay, Reginald; "Broccoli"; Correllium fever; Costa, Lieutenant; cryonetrium; Duffy, Lieutenant; Gleason, Captain; "Goddess of Empathy"; graviton; holodeck; holodiction; invidium; jakmanite; lucovexitrin; Mikulaks; Nahmi IV; nucleosynthesis; saltzgadum; selgninaem; sensors; Terkim; transporter test article; *Zhukov, U.S.S.***

Holmes, Sherlock. (Brent Spiner). London's greatest consulting detective, a fictional character created in 1887 by Earth novelist **Sir Arthur Conan Doyle**. *Enterprise*-D operations officer Data was an aficionado of Holmes's adventures, having read and memorized all of Doyle's Holmes stories after Riker suggested Holmes's approach might help solve the murder of an **Antican** delegate. ("Lonely Among Us" [TNG]). Data enjoyed Sherlock Holmes simulations on the holodeck. ("Elementary, Dear Data" [TNG], "Ship in a Bottle" [TNG]). SEE: **Barthalomew, Countess Regina; Moriarty, Professor James; Sherlock Holmes program 3A**.

holo-filter. Holographic device that can alter a visual communications signal, making it appear that the signal was originating from a different person or locale. In 2371, a communications holo-filter was used to make it seem that the commander of the ***U.S.S Defiant*** was actually the pilot of a Kobheerian freighter. This allowed the *Defiant* to travel to planet Cardassia under pretense of being a Cardassian ally. ("Second Skin" [DS9]). Gul Dukat employed a holo-filter aboard his commandeered bird-of-prey in early 2373 to create a Klingon appearance for himself. ("Apocalypse Rising" [DS9]).

holo-imager. Handheld device used to capture holographic images for use in **holodeck and holosuite programs**. In 2371, Quark used a holo-imager to capture an image of **Kira Nerys** for use in a custom holosuite program. ("Meridian" [DS9]). SEE: **Tiron**.

holocomic books. Entertainment medium popular with 24th-century children. Lieutenant **Tom Paris** reminisced that the holocomic books in the waiting room of his childhood doctor were never more than six months old. ("Cathexis" [VGR]).

holocommunicator. Communications system that created a full-sized holographic representation of the opposite party within a circular area on the floor. Holographic communicators were installed on some Federation starships, including the *U.S.S. Defiant* and the *U.S.S. Malinche,* in 2373. ("For the Uniform" [DS9]).

holodeck and holosuite programs. *This is a partial listing of the various simulation programs from the* Enterprise-*D as well as* Deep Space 9 *and* Voyager. *In most cases, the episodes gave no formal names for the programs, so we have given them descriptive titles. The holodeck computer gives the user a great deal of discretion in customizing a simulation to his or her specific wishes, so some of these are probably user variations of other programs.*

Aikido 1. Martial-arts exercise program. ("Code of Honor" [TNG]).

Altonian brain teaser. Try to relax and make the multicolored sphere turn into a single color. It ain't easy. ("A Man Alone" [DS9]).

Alture VII relaxation program. Bathes you in a protein bath, then carries you off on a cloud of chromal vapor. ("Birthright, Part I" [TNG]).

Ancient West. A town on the 19th-century American wild frontier. ("A Fistful of Datas" [TNG]).

Barclay programs. Series of customized programs designed by **Reginald Barclay**. ("Hollow Pursuits" [TNG]).

Baseball greats. Ben Sisko's program for playing **baseball** with such players as **Buck Bokai**, Tris Speaker, and Ted Williams. ("If Wishes Were Horses" [DS9]).

Battle of Britain. Aerial combat in primitive flying machines during Earth's second world war. ("Homefront" [DS9]).

Battle of Clontarf, The. The historic battle between Irish warriors and Vikings on Earth in 1014. ("Bar Association" [DS9]).

Battle of Tong Vey, The. An epic Klingon conflict. ("Rules of Engagement" [DS9]).

Beowulf. Epic Old English heroic poem. ("Heroes and Demons" [VGR]).

Black Sea at Night**.** Romantic program complete with moonlight and balalaikas. ("All Good Things..." [TNG]).

Boraal II/Vacca VI transformation. The surface of **Boraal II**, with the topography slowly changing to match the surface of planet **Vacca VI**. ("Homeward" [TNG]).

Boreth. Klingon monastery where the faithful awaited the return of **Kahless the Unforgettable**. ("Rightful Heir" [TNG]).

Bridge Officer Examination**.** The engineering portion of the exam was a holodeck simulation. ("Thine Own Self" [TNG]).

Cafe des Artistes. A French sidewalk cafe located in **Paris**. ("We'll Always Have Paris" [TNG]).

Cardassian sauna. A Cardassian spa. ("For the Cause" [DS9]).

Champs Elysees. The famous section of the city of **Paris**. ("The Perfect Mate" [TNG]).

Charnock's Comedy Cabaret. A 20th-century comedy club. ("The Outrageous Okona" [TNG]).

Christmas Carol, A. Dramatization of the classic Charles Dickens story. ("Devil's Due" [TNG]).

Cliffs of Heaven. Program 47C, cliff diving on planet Sumiko III. ("Conundrum" [TNG]).

Curtis Creek. Fly fishing in an Earth stream. ("Future Imperfect" [TNG]).

Dancing lesson. Program Crusher 4, a ballroom setting with simulated dance partners where Beverly Crusher first studied dance. ("Data's Day" [TNG]).

Defense simulations. Training routines used by *Starship Voyager* crew members. ("Initiations" [VGR]).

Denubian Alps. Skiing in a spectacular mountain setting. ("Angel One" [TNG]).

Desert sunset. A beautiful desert on a Class-M planet. ("Haven" [TNG]).

Dixon Hill. The 1930-1940s world of San Francisco gumshoe detective **Dixon Hill**. ("The Big Goodbye" [TNG], "Manhunt" [TNG], "Clues" [TNG], *Star Trek: First Contact).*

Emerald Wading Pool. From planet Cirrus IV, a very safe experience. ("Conundrum" [TNG]).

Emergent life-form holodeck sequence**.** Symbolic train trip created by the *Enterprise*-D's computer. ("Emergence" [TNG]).

EMH program 4C. The holographic doctor's personality-improvement project, incorporating historical figures. ("Darkling" [VGR]).

Equestrian adventure. Horse riding in an open countryside with a choice of various mounts. ("Pen Pals" [TNG]).

Einstein, A conversation with. Simulation of Professor **Albert Einstein**. ("Nth Degree" [TNG]).

Enterprise bridge. The bridge of the original *Constitution*-class *Starship* ***Enterprise***. ("Relics" [TNG]). *No bloody A, B, C, or D. (Or E!)*

Gondolas in Venice**.** On the canals in Venice, Italy on Earth. ("Prime Factors" [VGR]).

Henry V. Dramatization of **Shakespeare**'s play. ("The Defector" [TNG]).

Hoobishan baths. The famous spa on **Trill**. ("The Way of the Warrior" [DS9]).

hoverball. Championship sport using an antigravity ball. ("Unity" [VGR]).

Ion surfing. An exciting sports program. ("The Visitor" [DS9]).

Janeway Lambda-1. Gothic romance holonovel set in old England. ("Cathexis" [VGR], et al.).

Jupiter Station diagnostics. Diagnostic matrix for a starship's Emergency Medical Hologram with a holographic version of **Dr. Lewis Zimmerman**. ("The Swarm" [VGR]).

Kabul River. Horseback riding in the Himalayas on Earth. ("The Loss" [TNG]).

Kahless and Lukara. The greatest love story in Klingon history. ("Looking for *par'Mach* in All the Wrong Places" [DS9]).

Kayaking. White-water adventure. ("Transfigurations" [TNG]).

King Arthur's court. Ancient England's Arthurian legend. ("The Way of the Warrior" [DS9], "The Muse" [DS9]).

Klingon calisthenics program. Combat exercise program featuring fierce adversaries. ("Where Silence Has Lease" [TNG], "The Emissary" [TNG], "New Ground" [TNG], "Blood Oath" [DS9], "The Way of the Warrior" [DS9]).

Klingon Age of Ascension. Ceremony celebrating a warrior's coming of age. ("The Icarus Factor" [TNG]).

Krios 1. The Kriosian Temple of Akadar, used for their Ceremony of Reconciliation. ("The Perfect Mate" [TNG]).

Lake Cataria. Romantic re-creation of the lake on **Betazed**. ("All Good Things..." [TNG]).

Lake Como. Restful and romantic sailboat trip across the beautiful lake in northern Italy. ("The Swarm" [VGR]).

Lake George. A moonlight sail on the lake in northeastern New York on Earth. ("Coda" [VGR]).

Lauriento massage holoprogram #101A. A beautiful woman with webbed fingers gives a great backrub. ("A Man Alone" [DS9]). *Presumably named for producer Peter Lauritson.*

Low Note, The. New Orleans club on Bourbon Street, with jazz band, circa 1958. ("11001001" [TNG]).

Maranga IV. Program K'Mtar Alpha-one**.** The Klingon outpost on planet **Maranga IV**. ("Firstborn" [TNG]).

Mars in a 1957 Chevy. A romantic (at least according to Tom Paris) evening in a '57 **Chevy** on the hills overlooking **Utopia Planitia**. ("Lifesigns" [VGR]).

Molière plays. The comedic works of the great 17th-century French playwright. ("Parturition" [VGR]).

Moonlight on the beach. Site of Geordi's unsuccessful date with Christi Henshaw. ("Booby Trap" [TNG]).

Neelix One. Medical program that provided holographic lungs for **Neelix** after he was attacked by **Vidiians**. ("Phage" [VGR]).

Novice tennis tournament. Contest for beginning level tennis players. ("Future's End, Part I" [VGR]).

Ohniaka III. The aftermath of the **Borg** attack. ("Descent, Part I" [TNG]).

Orient Express. Nostalgic trip aboard the historic train of the late 19th century ("Emergence" [TNG]).

Orion animal women. An energetic program featuring three green Orion slaves. ("The Begotten" [DS9]).

Parallax Colony. A colorful "colony of free spirits." ("Cost of Living" [TNG]).

Parkland. Open grassy field, setting for **Tasha Yar**'s memorial service. ("Skin of Evil" [TNG]).

Paxau resort. An exclusive vacation spot on planet **Talax**. ("Warlord" [VGR]).

Pleasure mazes. Life-sized labyrinth puzzle with a sexual encounter in the center. ("Rapture" [DS9]).

Poker with great scientists. Poker game with simulations of Sir Isaac Newton, **Albert Einstein**, and **Stephen Hawking**. ("Descent, Part I" [TNG]).

Polynesian resort. Inspired by Earth's Polynesian island cultures, according to Neelix. ("Alter Ego" [VGR]). Also known as Tropical resort simulation 3. ("Darkling" [VGR]).

Pon farr therapy. Medical program intended to aid Ensign **Vorik** through the ordeal of the ***Pon farr***. ("Blood Fever" [VGR]).

Puccini's *La Bohème*. Duet from Puccini's *La Bohème*, featuring famous historical sopranos. ("The Swarm" [VGR]).

Queen's Gambit, The. **Secret agent** adventure about a plot to assassinate the Queen of England. ("A Simple Investigation" [DS9]).

Riga, Stano. Comedy program based on the noted 23rd-century quantum physicist and humorist. ("The Outrageous Okona" [TNG]).

Rock climbing. Challenging spelunking adventure. ("Bloodlines" [TNG]).

Romulus. The incredibly beautiful Chula Valley on **Romulus**. ("The Defector" [TNG]).

Rousseau V. A spectacular asteroid belt. ("The Dauphin" [TNG]).

Sailing ship *Enterprise***.** The 19th-century sailing frigate *Enterprise. (Star Trek Generations).*

Sandrine's. Program Paris-3. **Chez Sandrine,** a bistro in Marseilles, France. ("The Cloud" [VGR], "Jetrel" [VGR], "Learning Curve" [VGR], "Twisted" [VGR], "Meld" [VGR], "Life Signs" [VGR]).

Secret agent. Adventures of a British secret-service agent in 1960s-era Earth. ("Our Man Bashir" [DS9]).

Sherlock Holmes. Nineteenth-century London according to the works of Sir Arthur Conan Doyle. ("Elementary, Dear Data" [TNG], "Ship in a Bottle" [TNG]).

Sigmund Freud. Session with the legendary psychoanalyst, complete with couch. ("Phantasms" [TNG]).

Tactical situation. Simulation of the *Voyager* bridge used in Tuvok's **field training** exercises. ("Learning Curve" [VGR]).

Tanuga Station. Series of simulations used in the extradition trial of William Riker. ("A Matter of Perspective" [TNG]).

Tempest, The. Act V, scene 1, of the **Shakespeare** play. ("Emergence" [TNG]).

Three Musketeers. The classic tale reinterpreted by **Reginald Barclay**. ("Hollow Pursuits" [TNG]).

Transwarp flight. Engineering and training simulation of warp 10 flight. ("Threshold" [VGR]).

Utopia Planitia Fleet Yards. Holodeck file 9140, a drafting room where part of the *Enterprise*-D was designed. ("Booby Trap" [TNG], "Galaxy's Child" [TNG]).

Visit with the Pleasure Goddess of Rixx, A. Nog's favorite holoprogram. ("Little Green Men" [DS9]).

Volleyball. Kim sport program theta-2, featuring the volleyball team that won the Olympic gold medal in 2216. ("Warlord" [VGR]).

Vulcan Love Slave Part II: The Revenge. A sexual fantasy. ("Doctor Bashir, I Presume?" [DS9]).

Vulcan rage. Tuvok's attempt to vent emotions of hate. ("Meld" [VGR]).

Wooded parkland. Natural setting with a stream. ("Encounter at Farpoint" [TNG]). *This was the first holodeck program seen on* Star Trek: The Next Generation.

World Series. Includes the last professional **baseball** game ever played. ("If Wishes Were Horses" [DS9]).

Yankees versus Red Sox. Imaginary **baseball** game between 1961 Yankees and the 1978 Red Sox. In the simulation, the Yankees won, 7-3. ("For the Cause" [DS9]).

holodeck imaging processor. Portion of a holographic environment simulator that is responsible for the production of visual images. The imaging processors in an *Enterprise*-D holodeck malfunctioned following exposure to plasmonic energy in the atmosphere of planet **Boraal II** in 2370, and the simulation of Boraal II suffered many **resolution failures** as a result. ("Homeward" [TNG]).

holodeck matter. A partially stable form of matter created by transporter-based replicators, for use in **holodeck** simulations. This material is stable only within a holographic environment simulator; if removed from the holodeck, it degrades into energy. The characters of **Felix Leech** and **Cyrus Redblock** were composed of holodeck matter and disintegrated when they attempted to leave the holodeck. ("The Big Goodbye" [TNG]). **Professor James Moriarty** agreed to remain within the holodeck to avoid the same fate. ("Elementary, Dear Data" [TNG]). Moriarty later concocted an elaborate scheme, simulating an entire starship within the holodeck, in an effort to convince the *Enterprise*-D crew that he had devised a method of existing outside the holodeck. ("Ship in a Bottle" [TNG]). In 2369, in an unsuccessful attempt to fulfill Professor James Moriarty's wish to leave the holodeck, the crew of the *Enterprise*-D conducted an experiment during which they attempted to beam holodeck matter off the grid and into the real transporter system. ("Ship in a Bottle" [TNG]).

holodeck reactors. Power generation devices used to supply power to **holodeck** systems aboard the *Voyager*. The holodeck reactors were independent from the ship's main power grid. ("Parallax" [VGR]). *The writers of* Star Trek: Voyager *"invented" the holodeck reactors as a way of "explaining" why the ship could have insufficient power to run the replicators, but the crew could still use the holodeck.*

holodeck. Also known as a holosuite or a holographic environment simulator, the holodeck permitted the simulation of virtually any environment or person with a degree of fidelity virtually indistinguishable from reality. The holodeck employed three-dimensional holographic projections as well as transporter-based replications of actual objects. A large library of simulations was available in the holodecks of *Galaxy*-class starships, and holodeck software permitted programs to be customized according to user preferences. ("Encounter at Farpoint" [TNG]). Holodecks were used for a wide range of recreational, sports, and training applications. SEE: **holodeck and holosuite programs**. The *Enterprise*-D holodeck systems were significantly upgraded in 2364 by the **Bynars** at Starbase 74. The Bynars installed new software allowing the behavior of simulated characters to be interactively based on the actions of the holodeck participant. The first demonstration of this new capability was a simulation run by Riker of a New Orleans jazz club and a beautiful woman, **Minuet**, who loved Riker's music. ("11001001" [TNG]). Holodeck software permitted a real person to be simulated by making use of visual images, voice recordings, and personality profile databases. The use of such simulations without the consent of the person being modeled was considered to be a serious invasion of privacy. ("Hollow Pursuits" [TNG], "Galaxy's Child" [TNG], "Meridian" [DS9]). It also was a crime to break into a holosuite while someone else's program was running. ("Our Man Bashir" [DS9]). Available holodeck programs have included the bridges of the various *Starships Enterprise*. ("Relics" [TNG]). Holodecks were equipped with safety overrides to prevent participants from being seriously injuring or killed by holographic characters or objects. *(Star Trek: First Contact)*. Federation starships in the 23rd century were not equipped with holodecks. ("Flashback" [VGR]). *Holodecks were first seen in "Encounter at Farpoint" (TNG).* Star Trek *producer-writer Ronald D. Moore argues that in a free society of responsible citizens, there should be little or no limit on what an adult can do in a holodeck. Even if others might find certain activities objectionable, what one does in one's private space is no one else's business; certainly not the government's. Of the argument that certain activities should be prohibited on the grounds that they might be harmful or addictive to a holodeck participant, Moore suggests that in a free society, a responsible adult must be permitted to judge risks to his or her own well-being, and to act accordingly. Moore concedes that there*

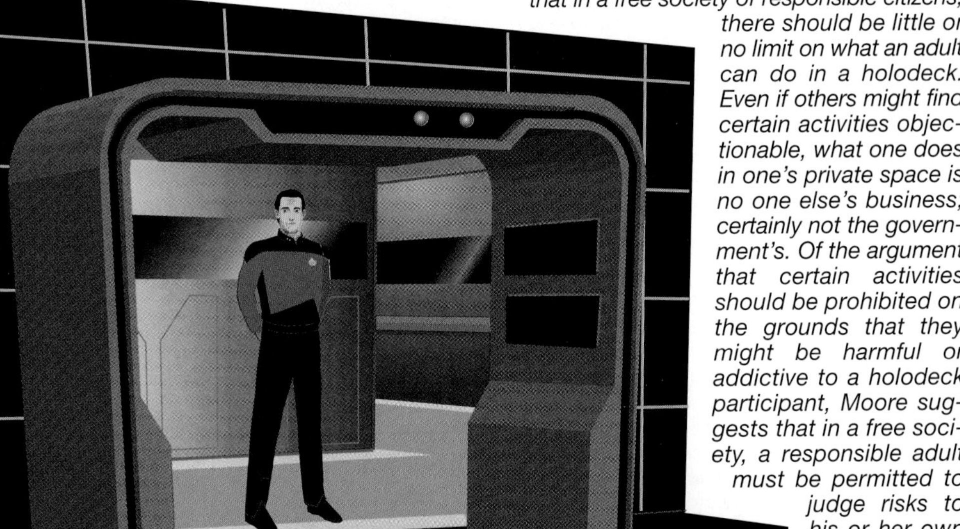

might well be circumstances in which someone might object to being replicated on a holodeck, but notes that it would be extremely difficult to define legally what constituted fair use and what was abusive. (Ron emphasizes that he is referring to holodeck usage by adults, not by children.) "Flashback" (VGR) establishes that holodecks were not in use during the days of James Kirk's voyages aboard the original Enterprise.

holodiction. Contraction for **holodeck** addiction. A psychological condition where an individual becomes so caught up in holographic simulations that the real world becomes unimportant. **Reginald Barclay** suffered this affliction when first assigned to the *Enterprise*-D in 2366. ("Hollow Pursuits" [TNG]).

hologenerator. Technical equipment used to generate holographic environment imagery. Hologenerators were used at Quark's bar on Deep Space 9 and similar facilities. Deep Space 9 entrepreneur Quark told **Odo** that he would like to expand into the space next door to his bar on the station's Promenade so that he could use the same hologenerators to create more programs. ("If Wishes Were Horses" [DS9]). In 2340, **Rurigan** used a hologenerator on planet **Yadera II** to create an entire village of people for company. Rurigan's device employed a matter/antimatter reactor that used **omicron particles** to create its images. So sophisticated was the hologenerator's software that the holographic people attained actual sentience and became bona fide life-forms. In 2370, the hologenerator began to malfunction, causing several holographic inhabitants to disappear. Odo and Jadzia Dax from Deep Space 9 were able to assist in repairing the system and restored the village's inhabitants. ("Shadowplay" [DS9]). Hologenerators were used by Federation anthropological field teams to conceal planetary surface survey stations from indigenous life-forms. Use of the hologram generator allows a team to observe such life-forms at close range without the subjects being aware of the team's presence. The hologram generator used by the field team on **Mintaka III** failed in early 2366, resulting in accidental cultural contamination when the **Mintakans** saw the team and their advanced technology. ("Who Watches the Watchers?" [TNG]).

holographic doctor. SEE: **Emergency Medical Hologram**.

holographic environment simulator. SEE: **holodeck**.

holographic information module. Data storage device. A tiny holographic information module was discovered in the cranial cavity of **Dr. Juliana Tainer**, an android patterned after the human scientist of the same name. The module contained a holographic message from **Dr. Noonien Soong** to whoever would discover Juliana's true nature. It also included a message to his son, Data. In it, Soong pleaded with the finder not to reveal Juliana's true nature to her, so that she could go on believing she was human. ("Inheritance" [TNG]).

holographic projector. Imaging device used in **holodecks** and similar three-dimensional display environments. Holographic projectors were incorporated into the *Starship Voyager*'s sickbay, permitting the operation of the ship's **Emergency Medical Hologram**. ("Parallax" [VGR]). SEE: **hologenerator**.

holographic waiter. Automated serving program developed to replace servers at restaurants and bars. In 2372, Quark attempted to use holographic waiters to work in his bar during his employees' strike. ("Bar Association" [DS9]).

holonovel. Holodeck or **holosuite** adaptation of a novel or similar work of literature, such as the English epic poem ***Beowulf***. In such programs, the **holodeck** participant often plays the role of the protagonist or another major character. ("Heroes and Demons" [VGR]). *Voyager* Captain Janeway enjoyed participating in a holonovel of a gothic romance. ("Cathexis" [VGR], "Persistence of Vision" [VGR]). SEE: **holodeck and holosuite programs; Janeway Lambda-1**.

holosuite. Holographic environment simulators located on the second floor of **Quark's bar** in station **Deep Space 9**. ("Emissary" [DS9]). SEE: **holodeck; holodeck and holosuite programs.**

Holt, Admiral Marcus. (Warren Munson). Starfleet officer. Commander of starbase **Deep Space 3** and an acquaintance of Captain Jean-Luc Picard. ("Interface" [TNG]).

Holy Pilgrim. Minor demigod in **Takarian** mythology. The epic poem "Song of the Sages" recounted the prophecy that the Holy Pilgrim would come to lead the **Great Sages** back into the skies. In 2373 Neelix, disguised as a Ferengi, played the role of the Holy Pilgrim in a plan to remove the interfering influence of **Arridor** and **Kol** from the Takarian people, while at the same time not violating the Prime Directive. ("False Profits" [VGR]).

Holy Rings of Betazed. SEE: **Betazed, Holy Rings of.**

"Home Soil." *Next Generation* episode #17. Teleplay by Robert Sabaroff. Story by Karl Guers & Ralph Sanchez and Robert Sabaroff. Directed by Corey Allen. Stardate 41463.9. *First aired in 1988. A terraforming project threatens the environment for a species of tiny crystalline life-forms, a fact that the project administrator attempts to conceal.* GUEST CAST: Walter Gotell as **Mandl**, **Kurt**; Elizabeth Lindsey as **Luisa**; Gerard Prendergast as **Benson**, **Bjorn**; Mario Roccuzzo as **Malencon**, **Arthur**; Carolyne Barry as Female engineer. SEE: **Bensen, Bjorn; Kim, Luisa; Malencon, Arthur; Mandl, Kurt; microbrain; Pleiades Cluster; quarantine seal; Terraform Command; terraforming; "Ugly Bags of Mostly Water"; Velara III.**

"Homecoming, The." *Deep Space Nine* episode #21. Teleplay by Ira Steven Behr. Story by Jeri Taylor and Ira Steven Behr. Directed by Winrich Kolbe. No stardate given. *First aired in 1993. Kira rescues a legendary resistance fighter from a Cardassian labor camp, while an isolationist Bajoran faction begins to exert its influence on Bajor. "The Homecoming" was the first episode of the second season. It is also the first portion of three part story continued in "The Circle."* GUEST CAST: Richard Beymer as **Li Nalas**; Max Grodénchik as **Rom**; Michael Bell as **Borum**; Marc Alaimo as **Dukat**; Leslie Bevis as Freighter captain; Paul Nakauchi as **Romah Doek**. SEE: **Alliance for Global Unity; Bajoran Chamber of Ministers; Bajoran provisional government; Bajorans; black hole; Borum; Cardassia IV; Cardassian navigational control posts; Cardassians; dermal regenerator; dermal residue; Ferengi Rules of Acquisition; Gibson, Bob; Hutet labor camp; icoberry torte; Jaro, Minister Essa; Lamenda Prime; Laira; Li Nalas; *Martuk; Nanut;* Navarch; *raktajino*; Rionoj; Romah Doek; *rulot* seeds; Sahving Valley; Subytt freighter; Zarale, Gul.**

"Homefront." *Deep Space Nine* episode #83. Written by Ira Steven Behr & Robert Hewitt Wolfe. Directed by David Livingston. *First aired in 1996. Sisko is recalled to Earth and made head of Starfleet Security after a high-level conference is bombed by a shape-shifter. This was the first half of a two-part story that concluded with the following episode, "Paradise Lost" (DS9).* GUEST CAST: Robert Foxworth as **Leyton, Admiral**; Herschel Sparber as **Jaresh-Inyo**; Susan Gibney as **Benteen, Erika**; Aron Eisenberg as **Nog**; Brock Peters as **Sisko, Joseph**; Dylan Chalfy as Head officer. SEE: **Antwerp Conference; aorta; atherosclerosis; Audubon Park; Battle of Britain; Benteen, Erika; bitters; blood screening; bread pudding soufflé; Creole food; Dax, Jadzia; Dublin; Federation President; Ferenginar; Founders; Grazerite; Great Monetary Collapse; gumbo; holodeck and holosuite programs; jambalaya; Jaresh-Inyo; Klingons; *Lakota, U.S.S.*; Leyton, Admiral; New Orleans; O'Brien, Miles; Odo; *Okinawa, U.S.S.*; Paris; Quark; Red Squad; Scotch; shrimp Creole; Sisko, Benjamin; Sisko, Joseph; Sisko, Judith; Sisko's; Starfleet Headquarters; Tholians; tube grubs.**

Homeric hymns. A collection of 34 ancient Greek poems usually attributed to Homer of Earth, but written by various authors at various dates. Captain Picard studied the Homeric hymns following his encounter with the **Tamarians,** in the hope that by learning more of human mythology, he might better understand the Tamarians. ("Darmok" [TNG]).

"Homeward." *Next Generation* episode #165. Teleplay by Naren Shankar. Television story by Spike Steingasser. Based on material by William N. Stape. Directed by Alexander Singer. Stardate 47423.9. *First aired in 1994. Worf's adoptive brother violates the Prime Directive in a desperate attempt to save the primitive people he has been studying.* GUEST CAST: Penny Johnson as **Dobara**; Brian Markinson as **Vorin**; Edward Penn as **Kateras**; Paul Sorvino as **Rozhenko, Nikolai**; Susan Christy as **Tarrana**; Majel Barrett as Computer voice. SEE: **atmospheric dissipation; Boraalan seer; Boraalans; Boraal II; Boraal II/Vacca VI transformation; Cabral sector; Chronicle; Dobara; Draygo IV; holodeck imaging processor; Kateras; materialization error; Prime Directive; resolution failure; Rozhenko, Nikolai; Starbase 87; Tarrana; Vacca VI; Vorin.**

Homeworld, Klingon. SEE: **Klingon Homeworld**.

Homn. (Carel Struycken). **Lwaxana Troi**'s attendant. A dignified humanoid male, tall in stature and few in words, with an impressive capacity for intoxicating beverages. ("Haven" [TNG]). Mr. Homn was also quite fond of eating Betazoid uttaberries. ("Ménage à Troi" [TNG]). *Mr. Homn's species and place of origin was not known. Carel Struycken also gained popularity for his portrayal of Lurch in the* Addams Family *motion pictures. Actor Ted Cassidy, who played the original Lurch in the* Addams Family *television series, also appeared in the original* Star Trek *in the role of Ruk in the episode "What Are Little Girls Made Of?" (TOS).*

Hon'Tihl. (Tom Towles). First officer of the Klingon attack cruiser ***Toh'Kaht***. Hon'Tihl beamed off his ship just before it exploded, immediately after returning from an exploratory mission into the Gamma Quadrant in 2369. Although Hon'Tihl died shortly after beaming to Deep Space 9, his log entries were reviewed by station personnel in an attempt to learn what happened to the ill-fated vessel. ("Dramatis Personae" [DS9]). SEE: **cryostasis; Saltah'na energy spheres; Saltah'na; thalmerite device**. *Tom Towles later played Dr. Vatm in "Rise" (VGR).*

***honatta*.** Title of responsibility in the **Vidiian Sodality**. A *honatta* was a person whose duty it was to find organ replacements for another member of the **Vidiian** species who was affected by the deadly **phage**. A *honatta* obtained organs from dead bodies in many cases, but in times of need, would sometimes be forced to obtain organs from a living individual of another species. On stardate 48532, **Dereth** served as *honatta* to **Motura** by forcibly removing **Neelix**'s lungs and transplanting them into Motura. ("Phage" [VGR]).

Honorius. Flavius Honorius (A.D. 384-423), the last Western Roman emperor, who was in power when the Visigoths sacked Rome. Captain Picard, on the eve of the battle of **Wolf 359**, compared the fate of the Federation at the hands of the **Borg** to the defeat of the Roman Empire under Honorius. ("The Best of Both Worlds, Part I" [TNG]).

Hoobishan Baths. Resort with therapeutic baths and massage chambers on planet **Trill**. People would come from all over Trill to visit the Hoobishan Baths. Jadzia Dax took Kira to a holosuite representation of these baths on stardate 49011, but Kira just couldn't get into the spirit of things. ("The Way of the Warrior" [DS9]).

***Hood*, U.S.S.** *Constitution*-class Federation starship, Starfleet registry number NCC-1703. The *Hood* participated in the disastrous tests of the **M-5** multitronic computer unit in 2268. ("The Ultimate Computer" [TOS]).

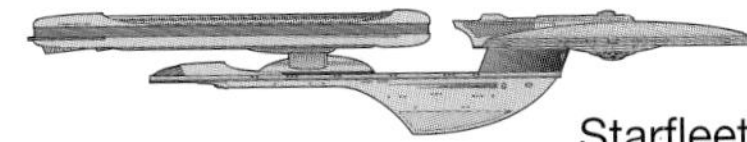

***Hood*, U.S.S.** Federation starship, ***Excelsior* class**, Starfleet registry number NCC-42296. Commanded by Captain **Robert DeSoto**. Commander **William T. Riker** served aboard this ship prior to his assignment to the *Enterprise*-D. ("Encounter at Farpoint, Parts I and II" [TNG]). The *Hood* intercepted the *Enterprise*-D in the **Hayashi system** to deliver **Tam Elbrun** and new orders for the *Enterprise* to proceed to **Beta Stromgren** for the encounter with **Tin Man** in 2366. ("Tin Man" [TNG]). The *Hood* was one of the starships sent to the Romulan Neutral Zone border in preparation for a possible battle after Starfleet received warnings of a Romulan buildup at planet **Nelvana III** in 2366. The warnings, from Romulan defector **Alidar Jarok,** were later found to be baseless. ("The Defector" [TNG]). The *Hood* was scheduled to join the *Enterprise*-D on a terraforming mission to planet Browder IV in 2366. ("Allegiance" [TNG]). *This was presumably at least the second Federation starship to bear the name. The* Hood *was a re-use of the* Excelsior *model built for* Star Trek III. *The footage of the* Hood *flying alongside the* Enterprise-*D created for "Encounter at Farpoint" (TNG) was re-used numerous times to represent other* Excelsior-*class ships.*

Hoover, J. Edgar. Head of the American government's Federal Bureau of Investigation security agency on Earth during the 20th century. After he was revived from cryostasis, **Fred Noonan**, believing that he was still in the 1930s, drew a weapon on the crew of the *Voyager*, and demanded to talk to J. Edgar Hoover. ("The 37's" [VGR]).

hopper. Troop-carrying small craft. Starfleet forces on Ajilon Prime used hoppers to deploy ground soldiers while defending the colony against Klingon invasionary troops in 2373. ("Nor the Battle to the Strong" [DS9]). SEE: **Grenthemen water hopper.**

Horath, Prime Minister. Governmental leader of the **Prytt Alliance** on planet Kesprytt III in 2370. ("Attached" [TNG]).

Horath. A traditional **Halii** song. **Aquiel Uhnari** used to sing the Horath at home during the **Batarael** celebration. ("Aquiel" [TNG]).

***Horatio*, U.S.S.** Federation starship, *Ambassador* class, registry number NCC-10532, commanded by Captain **Walker Keel**. The *Horatio* was destroyed in 2364 near planet **Dytallix B**, apparently by an unknown alien intelligence that attempted to infiltrate Starfleet Command. ("Conspiracy" [TNG]).

Horga'hn*.** Small **Risa**n statuette resembling a crude wooden carving, the Risan symbol of sexuality. To own one was to call forth its powers and to display one was to announce that the owner was seeking ***jamaharon. Riker requested that Picard bring him back one as a souvenir when the captain visited **Risa** in 2366. ("Captain's Holiday" [TNG], "Let He Who Is Without Sin..." [DS9]). It was Riker's attempt to set Picard up for a sexual encounter, but Picard needed no outside assistance in finding companionship. ("Captain's Holiday" [TNG]). *The* Horga'hn *brought back by Picard could sometimes be seen adorning Riker's quarters in later episodes.*

***Horizon*, U.S.S.** Federation starship, *Daedalus* class, Starfleet registry NCC-176. One of the first deep-space exploratory vessels launched by the United Federation

of Planets, the *Horizon* visited planet **Sigma Iotia II** in 2168. The *Horizon* was destroyed shortly thereafter, transmitting a distress call by conventional radio that did not reach Federation space until 2268. It was later found that *Horizon* personnel had left a book entitled ***Chicago Mobs of the Twenties*** on the planet, causing severe cultural contamination. The *Horizon* mission predated the establishment of Starfleet's **Prime Directive** of noninterference. ("A Piece of the Action" [TOS]). *The class and registry designations of the* Horizon *are conjectural, but a desktop model bearing that name and number has been seen as set decoration in Sisko's office on* Star Trek: Deep Space Nine.

Horne, Walter. An instructor in Creative Writing at Starfleet Academy. Horne was Captain Picard's professor during the 2320s, and also taught Wesley Crusher in 2368. ("The Game" [TNG]).

Hornet, U.S.S. Federation starship, *Renaissance* class, Starfleet registry number NCC-45231. It served in Picard's armada to blockade Romulan supply ships supplying the **Duras** family forces during the **Klingon civil war** of 2367-2368. ("Redemption, Part II" [TNG]). *The* Hornet *was named for an American aircraft carrier that fought at the Battle of Midway in World War II. Years later, another ship with that name was the recovery vessel for the Apollo 11 moon landing mission. SEE:* **Akagi, *U.S.S.***

Horta. (Janos Prohaska). **Silicon-based life**-form native to planet **Janus VI**. The Horta's natural environment is underground, and it secretes a powerful corrosive acid to enable it to move through solid rock with great ease. Every 50,000 years, all but one Horta dies, leaving the sole survivor to care for the eggs. This individual becomes the mother to her race. The Horta were discovered in 2267 by Federation mining personnel on Janus VI when a number of unexplained deaths among the miners were found to be caused by the mother Horta protecting her eggs. The miners had unknowingly broken into a subterranean chamber known as the **Vault of Tomorrow**, where the Horta's eggs were stored. The Hortas' true nature was discovered when *Enterprise* Science Officer Spock mind-melded with the mother Horta. Once a level of understanding was achieved between the Horta and the humans, the Horta had no objection to sharing their planet, and in fact agreed to help the miners harvest the abundant minerals on Janus VI. ("The Devil in the Dark" [TOS]). SEE: **pergium**. *The Horta was designed, built, and performed by Janos Prohaska, who reportedly wore the costume into* Star Trek *producer Gene Coon's office. Coon liked the creature so much he wrote "Devil in the Dark" to feature it.*

host candidate. SEE: **initiate**.

"Host, The." *Next Generation* episode #97. Written by Michel Horvat. Directed by Marvin Rush. Stardate 44821.3. *First aired in 1991. A diplomatic mission is endangered when the mediator falls ill and it is learned that he is a helpless symbiotic parasite living inside a host humanoid body. This is the first episode featuring the Trill "joined species."* GUEST CAST: Barbara Tarbuck as **Leka, Governor Trion**; Nicole Orth-Pallavicini as **Kareel**; William Newman as **Trose, Kalin**; Patti Yasutake as **Ogawa, Nurse Alyssa**; Franc Luz as **Odan, Ambassador**. SEE: **Alpha Moon; Ancient Philosophies; *balso* tonic; Beta Moon; colgonite astringent; Crusher, Dr. Beverly; eosinophilia; exobiology; global warming; *Hawking*, *Shuttlecraft*; host; immunosuppressant; joined species; Kalin Trose; Kareel; Lathal Bine; Leka, Governor Trion; magnetospheric energy taps; metrazene; Odan, Ambassador; Ogawa, Nurse Alyssa; Peliar Zel; Stephan; symbiont; Trill.**

host. In the **Trill** joined species, a host is a humanoid life-form in whose body resides a Trill **symbiont**. The combination of the two life-forms forms a single Trill individual. ("The Host" [TNG]).

hot dog. Earth food consisting of a cooked frankfurter served in a split bread roll and garnished to taste with condiments such as mustard or pickle relish. ("Starship Down" [DS9]).

Hotel Brian. Hostelry in 19th-century San Francisco on Earth where Data stayed while in Earth's past. A bellboy there named **Jack London** would one day become a noted literary figure. ("Time's Arrow, Parts I and II" [TNG]). *The Hotel Brian was named for Brian Livingston, son of* Star Trek *producer-director David Livingston. The exterior of Hotel Brian was shot on location in the city of Pasadena.*

Hotel Royale. An early 21st-century novel written by Todd Matthews concerning a luxury hotel of the same name and the various shady characters inhabiting it. A copy of the novel was carried aboard the explorer ship ***Charybdis*** when it was launched from Earth in 2037. When an unknown alien intelligence accidentally killed nearly everyone aboard the *Charybdis*, the intelligence fabricated the Hotel Royale based on descriptions in the book for **Colonel Stephen Richey**, the sole survivor of the *Charybdis* crew, to live in. Unknown to the alien intelligence, the resulting artificial environment, based on a badly written book, was a kind of hell to Richey, who welcomed death when it came. ("The Royale" [TNG]).

"House of Quark, The." *Deep Space Nine* episode #49. Story by Tom Benko. Teleplay by Ronald D. Moore. Directed by Les Landau. No stardate given. *First aired in 1994. Quark accidentally kills a prominent Klingon and finds himself thrust into Klingon politics and forced to marry a Klingon woman.* GUEST CAST: Rosalind Chao as **O'Brien, Keiko**; Mary Kay Adams as **Grilka**; Carlos Carrasco as **D'Ghor**; Max Grodénchik as **Rom**; Robert O'Reilly as **Gowron**; Joseph Ruskin as **Tumek**; John Lendale Bennett as **Kozak**. SEE: ***brek'tal* ritual; Deep Space 9; divorce, Klingon; D'Ghor; Ferengi Rules of Acquisition; Grilka; House; Janitza mountains; Keldar; Klingon bloodwine; Kozak; *mak'dar;* O'Brien, Keiko; Quark; Tumek.**

House. In **Klingon** culture, a family unit. Political power in the Klingon Empire is controlled by the great Houses, including the House of **Kozak**, the House of **Duras**, the House of **Mogh**, and even the House of Quark. ("The House of Quark" [DS9]).

Hovath. (Lawrence Monoson). Inhabitant of a village on **Bajor** who was apprentice to the **Sirah**. Hovath studied for nine years to be the next Sirah, learning the secrets of the storyteller. Hovath was nevertheless unready to assume the responsibility when his mentor was ready to die in 2369. The old Sirah took the seemingly irrational step of appointing Miles O'Brien as the new Sirah, thereby motivating Hovath to try much harder. ("The Storyteller" [DS9]).

hover car. Ground transportation vehicle in use on Earth in the mid-21st century. ("The 37's" [VGR]).

hoverball. Sport involving a small ball equipped with an antigravity suspension device and a limited propulsion system. **Joval**, a woman at **Risa**, said she was unskilled at the sport. ("Captain's

Holiday" [TNG]). Hoverball is almost always played on outdoor courts. ("Let He Who Is Without Sin..." [DS9]). Lieutenant **B'Elanna Torres** played hoverball. She competed in hoverball championships aboard the *U.S.S. Voyager* in 2373 and completed the competition despite a broken ankle. ("Remember" [VGR]). Torres once told **Chakotay** that he needed a good thrashing on ***Voyager's*** simulated court to break him out of a spell of depression. ("Unity" [VGR]).

How to Advance Your Career Through Marriage. A book that young Lieutenant **Jack Crusher** sent to the future **Beverly Crusher** while she was in medical school in 2348, a gag gift that was his way of proposing to her. ("Family" [TNG]).

Howard family candle. Heirloom passed down through generations of Howard women, it was said to be the guiding light of the family since the 17th century. In 2370, Beverly Crusher discovered that the plasma-based flame was a receptacle for **Ronin**, who existed within it for short periods of time. This required that the candle be lit at all times. ("Sub Rosa" [TNG]).

Howard, Beverly. Birth name of **Dr. Beverly Crusher**. ("Sub Rosa" [TNG]). *Beverly's birth name was first seen in Beverly's biographical screen in "Conundrum" (TNG), for* Star Trek *producer Merri Howard.*

Howard, Felisa. (Ellen Albertini Dow). Paternal grandmother to Beverly Crusher, who referred to her as "Nana." Born in 2270, Felisa cared for Beverly following the death of Beverly's mother, early in Beverly's childhood. Felisa and Beverly were survivors of the tragedy at the **Arvada III** colony. It was during that crisis that Felisa Howard learned about the uses of herbs and roots for medicinal purposes, and she shared that knowledge with Beverly. ("The Arsenal of Freedom" [TNG]). Felisa became known as a healer, and dispensed homeopathic cures, along with advice. She served in this capacity at the **Caldos colony**, where she lived following her departure from Arvada III. Just after the death of her mother, Felisa became romantically involved with **Ronin**, an **anaphasic life-form** who appeared to her as a 34-year-old human. Felisa kept very detailed journals of her experiences with Ronin; her journals were helpful in assisting Beverly Crusher in determining Ronin's true nature. When Felisa died in 2370, Beverly delivered the eulogy at her grandmother's funeral. Ronin covered her grave and filled her house with **camellias**, which had been Felisa's favorite flower. ("Sub Rosa" [TNG]). *Beverly's grandmother was mentioned in "The Arsenal of Freedom" (TNG), but she didn't get a name until "Sub Rosa" (TNG).*

Howard, Jessel. Ancestor of **Beverly Crusher**. Jessel Howard, who lived during the 17th century in Scotland on Earth, was the first woman in the Howard family to be seduced by **Ronin**. ("Sub Rosa" [TNG]).

Hoya. (Hilary Shepard). Starfleet officer assigned to Deep Space 9. On stardate 50049, Hoya, Bertram, and Rooney were killed when their runabout was destroyed by the Jem'Hadar at Torga IV. Benjamin Sisko performed Hoya's wedding ceremony. ("The Ship" [DS9]). *Hoya, who was Benzite, was the first of her people to be seen in a Class-M atmosphere without the breathing device commonly used by her people. We assume this is evidence of an advance in Benzite medical technology.*

Hromi Cluster. Stellar group. Location of the planet Gamma Hromi II, near the Acamar system. ("The Vengeance Factor" [TNG]).

Hrothgar, King. (Michael Keenan). Character in the holonovel ***Beowulf***. Hrothgar was the leader of a group of Danes terrorized by the mythical beast, **Grendel**. ("Heroes and Demons" [VGR]).

HTDS. Holotransference Dementia Syndrome. Medical condition in which a person becomes so disoriented within a holographic simulation that they lose their sense of identity and start to think that they are part of the program. ("Projections" [VGR]).

Hubble, Chief. (April Grace). Transporter operator aboard the *Enterprise*-D in 2367. ("Reunion" [TNG], "Future Imperfect" [TNG], "Data's Day" [TNG], "Galaxy's Child" [TNG]).

Hudson, Calvin. (Bernie Casey). **Maquis** leader and former **Starfleet** attaché to the **Federation** colonies in the **Demilitarized Zone**. Hudson graduated from **Starfleet Academy** with his friend, **Benjamin Sisko**. Lieutenant Commander "Cal" Hudson lost his wife Gretchen before being assigned to uphold the **Federation-Cardassian Treaty** in the Demilitarized Zone. In 2370, he traveled to **Deep Space 9** to confer with Commander Benjamin Sisko concerning security, following the destruction of the Cardassian freighter ***Bok'Nor***. Unbeknownst to Starfleet at the time, Hudson had become a leader in the terrorist **Maquis** movement, defending Federation colonies against the Cardassians. Hudson's activities with the Maquis led to his expulsion from Starfleet. ("The Maquis, Parts I and II" [DS9]).

Hudson, Gretchen. Late wife to former Starfleet officer **Calvin Hudson**. She and Calvin socialized with **Benjamin** and Jennifer **Sisko** on Earth. ("The Maquis, Part I" [DS9]).

Huey 204. Rotor-winged aircraft in use on Earth in the late 20th century. One such helicopter craft, owned by **Plexicorp** in San Francisco, was borrowed by Sulu in 1986 to deliver some acrylic plastic sheeting to the time-traveling Klingon bird-of-prey. Sulu noted that he had flown something similar back in his academy days. *(Star Trek IV: The Voyage Home). The Huey pilot who "loaned" Sulu his ship was played by Tony Edwards.*

Hugh. (Jonathan Del Arco). Adolescent **Borg**, designated Third of Five, rescued by the *Enterprise*-D crew from the wreck of a **Borg scoutship** in the **Argolis Cluster** in 2368. Aboard the *Enterprise*-D, Third of Five was restored to health and dubbed "Hugh" by Starfleet personnel. It was soon discovered that, removed from the **Borg collective**, Hugh began to exhibit signs of individuality. During Hugh's convalescence, a plan was developed to create an invasive computer program that would be introduced to the Borg collective through Hugh. The **invasive program** would be designed to cause a fatal overload in the entire Borg collective. The plan was vetoed by Captain Picard, who felt it unethical to use Hugh as a weapon of mass destruction. *Enterprise*-D personnel later returned Hugh to the crash site, where he was reassimilated into the collective. ("I, Borg" [TNG]). Hugh's sense of individuality almost immediately permeated his local portion of the collective, resulting in a dramatic loss of group purpose. The Borg acted aimlessly until given a new sense of purpose by the android **Lore**, who promised to make the Borg into his ideal of artificial life-forms. To fulfill this promise, Lore conducted bizarre medical experiments on many Borg, leaving

them horribly injured. Hugh soon realized that Lore had no idea how to fulfill his promise, and began to secretly care for the injured Borg individuals. Hugh later joined with *Enterprise*-D personnel to defeat Lore. ("Descent, Parts I and II" [TNG]).

Hugo, Victor. (1802-1885). Nineteenth-century Earth poet, dramatist, and novelist from the nation of France. Victor Marie **Hugo** wrote such famous novels as ***The Hunchback of Notre Dame*** (1831) and ***Les Misérables*** (1862). Maquis leader **Michael Eddington** was an admirer of Hugo's works. ("For the Uniform" [DS9]).

Hugora Nebula. Stellar cloud located on the Federation side of the **Demilitarized Zone**. As part of an ambush of **Maquis ships** planned in 2370, Federation starships hoped to use the nebula as cover from the Maquis sensors. ("Preemptive Strike" [TNG]).

hull stress. Shearing and other destructive structural forces placed on a spacecraft hull and frame during maneuvers such as acceleration or turning. Excess hull stress can result in a hull breach and even vehicle destruction. In 2370, the *Starship Enterprise*-D, while escaping from a **subspace rift**, hull stress reached levels of 120 percent above maximum recommended tolerance. ("Force of Nature" [TNG]). SEE: **structural integrity field.**

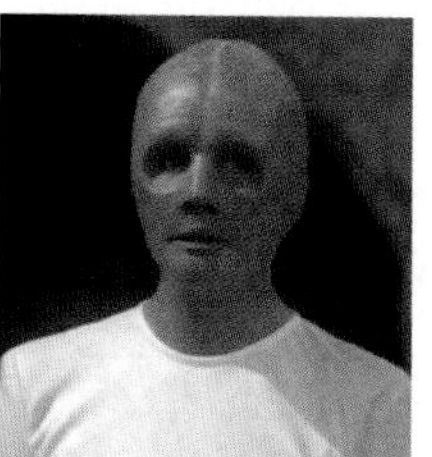

humanoid life. Intelligent bipedal life-forms, generally mammalian, commonly found on many Class-M planets. Humans, **Vulcans**, **Klingons**, **Cardassians**, and **Romulans** are among the many humanoid species known throughout the galaxy. Despite the vast distances separating these planets, many humanoid species have been found to share a remarkable commonality in form and genetic coding. These similarities were believed to be evidence of a common ancestry, a humanoid species that lived in our galaxy some four billion years ago. This species apparently seeded the oceans of many Class-M planets with genetic material, from which a number of humanoid forms eventually evolved. In one of the most remarkable scientific detective stories in history, archaeologist **Richard Galen** of Earth uncovered the similarities between certain **DNA** sequences in life-forms from widely separated planets. He discovered that these DNA sequences were a puzzle deliberately left behind by these ancient progenitors. The DNA sequences, when assembled by protein-link compatibilities, formed an ingenious computer program, a message of peace and goodwill to their progeny. This message, assembled in 2369 in an unprecedented example of interstellar cooperation, was a confirmation that many humanoid species in this galaxy are indeed members of the same family, despite their significant differences. ("The Chase" [TNG]). SEE: **Indri VIII; Preservers; Ruah IV**. *The ancient humanoid in "The Chase" (TNG) was played by Salome Jens.*

humeral socket replacement. Simple surgical procedure. Starfleet Chief Miles O'Brien underwent a humeral socket replacement in 2371. ("Shakaar" [DS9]).

humpback whale. Large aquatic mammal, scientific name *Megaptera novaeangliae*, that lives in the oceans of planet Earth. The humpback whale became extinct in the 21st century owing to humankind's shortsightedness, but two specimens of the species were obtained from the 20th century by Kirk and his crew, who transplanted them into the 23rd century in an effort to repopulate the species. *(Star Trek IV: The Voyage Home).* SEE: **George and Gracie; Probe, the; whale song.**

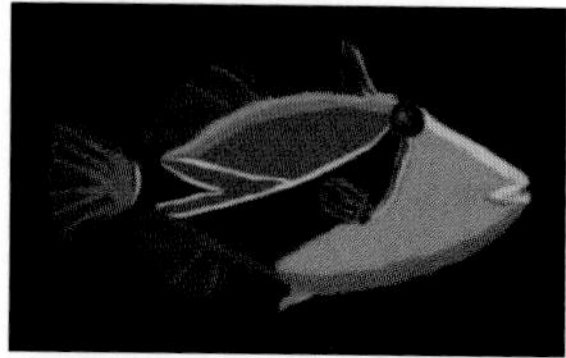

humuhumunukunukuapua'a. Reef triggerfish, also known by the scientific name *Rhinecanthus rectangulus*, found in tropical oceans on Earth. One of these fishes served as an animated "software agent" in an *Enterprise*-D schoolroom computer to help guide students through their studies. ("Rascals" [TNG]). *The humuhumunukunukuapua'a is the state fish of Hawai'i.*

Hunchback of Notre Dame, The. Classic novel, published in 1831, written by noted French poet, dramatist, and novelist **Victor Hugo**. The novel was set during Earth's medieval times during the reign of Louis XI and was a highly melodramatic work that assailed the society of that time. ("For the Uniform" [DS9]).

"Hunted, The." *Next Generation* episode #59. Written by Robin Bernheim. Directed by Cliff Bole. Stardate 43489.2. *First aired in 1990. The* Enterprise-D *captures a fugitive whose "crime" was the fact that his government could not return him to normal society after having converted him into the "perfect soldier."* GUEST CAST: Jeff McCarthy as **Danar**, **Roga**; James Cromwell as **Nayrok**; Colm Meaney as **O'Brien**, **Miles**; J. Michael Flynn as **Zaynar**; Andrew Bicknell as **Wagnor**. SEE: **anesthizine; Angosia III; Angosian transport vessel; Angosians; annular confinement beam; communicator; cryptobiolin; Danar, Roga; Lunar V; macrospentol; Nayrok; Starbase Lya III; subhadar; Tarsian War; triclenidil; Wagnor, Zaynar.**

hunter probe. Automated weapon. A hunter probe could be programmed only to attack a specific target. **Silaran Prin** used two hunter probes on stardate 50416 to murder former **Shakaar resistance cell** members **Latha Mabrin**, **Furel,** and **Lupaza.** Mabrin was killed by a probe hidden in a **Bajoran** ceremonial candle at the **Calash Retreat**. The second probe was smuggled outside **Deep Space 9** while attached to a **Talavian freighter**. After the ship had docked, the probe began to search the habitat ring until it found Furel and Lupaza, whereupon it locked onto a window and exploded, causing the room to decompress. ("The Darkness and the Light" [DS9]).

Hunters. Humanoids from **Tosk**'s planet in the **Gamma Quadrant** who engaged in an elaborate sport that involved hunting a live, intelligent, humanoid prey. In 2369, a group of Hunters tracked their **Tosk** to station Deep Space 9 and demanded his return. They explained to Sisko that in their culture the Tosk are bred and raised for the sole purpose of being hunted. ("Captive Pursuit" [DS9]). *The lead hunter was played by Gerrit Graham, who later played Quinn.*

Hupyrian beetle snuff. Inhalable substance. A vice enjoyed by Grand Nagus Zek. ("Rules of Acquisition" [DS9]). While under the influence of the Bajoran **Prophets** in 2371, Zek briefly stopped using beetle snuff in deference to the plight of the beetles. ("Prophet Motive" [DS9]).

Hupyrians. Civilization of tall humanoids. Hupyrian servants are known for their devotion to their employers. The Hupyrian **Maihar'du** served as Grand Nagus Zek's faithful servant. ("The Nagus" [DS9]). SEE: **Dolbargy sleeping trance**. Hupyrian servants take a vow to speak only to their masters. ("Prophet Motive" [DS9]).

Hur'q planet. An uncharted Class-M world in the Gamma Quadrant once used by the **Hur'q**. Sometime prior to 2372, a bakinium mining team from Vulcan discovered an underground Hur'q museum on this planet. There, they found the **Shroud of the Sword** of Kahless, which they gave to **Kor**, the Klingon ambassador to Vulcan. ("The Sword of Kahless" [DS9]).

Hur'q. Extinct civilization that at one time was known as galaxy-wide plunderers. Legend has it that whatever the Hur'q could not pillage, they destroyed. Over one thousand years ago, the Hur'q invaded the **Klingon Homeworld** and made off with the famous **Sword of Kahless**. ("The Sword of Kahless" [DS9]).

Hur'q. Klingon term meaning "outsider." ("The Sword of Kahless" [DS9]).

Hurada III. A Federation planet. **Tarmin** and his group of telepathic historians visited Hurada III prior to mid-2368. After the **Ullians**' visit, two cases of **Iresine Syndrome** were reported on the planet. These cases were later believed to be instances of forced **telepathic memory invasion** rape by telepathic historian **Jev**. ("Violations" [TNG]).

Huraga. (William Dennis Hunt). Klingon warrior and longtime friend to the House of **Mogh**. In 2372, Huraga told Worf about the Klingon High Council's plan to invade Cardassia. ("The Way of the Warrior" [DS9]). *Huraga's name was not mentioned in dialog, but is from the script.*

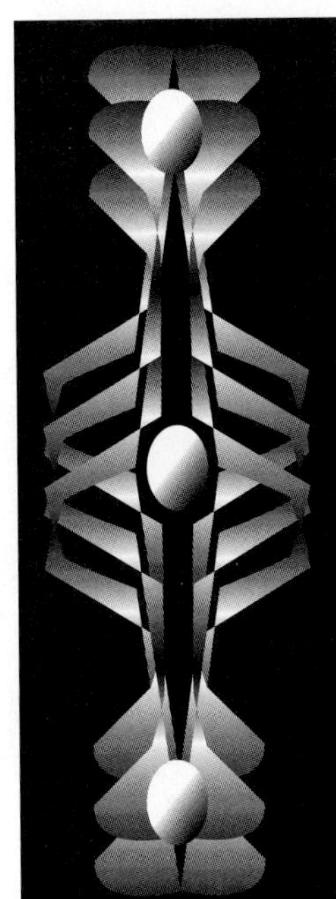

H'urq symbol

Hurkos III. Planet. **Devinoni Ral** moved to Hurkos III at age 19. ("The Price" [TNG]).

Husnock ship. Spacecraft that attacked and destroyed the Federation colony on **Delta Rana IV** in 2366. A **Douwd** image of the **Husnock** ship attacked the *Enterprise*-D when it arrived to investigate the distress signals received from the colony. ("The Survivors" [TNG]). *The Husnock ship was designed and built by Tony Meininger.*

Husnock. An extinct civilization described as having exhibited extremely violent and destructive behavior. A **Husnock ship** attacked and destroyed the colony at **Delta Rana IV** in 2366. In retribution, the only survivor of the colony, a **Douwd**, destroyed the entire Husnock race. ("The Survivors" [TNG]).

Huss. Klingon warrior, daughter of Kahmar. In 2373, Huss was inducted by Gowron into the Order of the *Bat'leth*. ("Apocalypse Rising" [DS9]).

Hutchinson, Commander Calvin. (David Spielberg). Starfleet officer. Huchinson commanded **Arkaria Base** and was known for his prowess at small talk. He was killed by terrorists at a reception for the command crew of the *Enterprise*-D upon their arrival at Arkaria Base in 2369. ("Starship Mine" [TNG]). SEE: **Remmler Array.**

Hutchinson, Transporter Chief. (Harley Venton). An *Enterprise*-D crew member. Hutchinson was at the transporter controls when an away team rescued **Timothy** from the ***Vico*** on stardate 45397. ("Hero Worship" [TNG]).

Hutet labor camp. Cardassian prison located on planet **Cardassia IV.** Bajoran resistance fighter **Li Nalas** was a prisoner at the Hutet camp. Cardassian authorities kept Li and other Bajorans imprisoned at Hutet, even after the Cardassian withdrawal of 2369. In 2370, the camp was infiltrated by Deep Space 9 personnel, freeing Li. Shortly thereafter, all the Bajoran prisoners at the camp were released. ("The Homecoming" [DS9]). SEE: **Borum.**

hydrazine. Colorless liquid (N_2H_4), a powerful reducing agent used as a hypergolic chemical rocket propellant. Hydrazine was used in reaction-control thrusters on Starfleet shuttlecraft. Exposure to hydrazine vapors can be a serious health hazard. ("Coda" [VGR]).

hydrocortilene. Analgesic medicine used to alleviate pain. ("The Swarm" [VGR]).

hydroponics bay. Compartment aboard the *Starship Voyager* where plants were grown in a moist inert medium instead of soil. In 2371, after the *Voyager* had been stranded in the Delta Quadrant, **Kes** converted cargo bay 2 into a hydroponics bay so that she could grow vegetables and fruits to supplement the crew's diet. ("Parallax" [VGR]). SEE: **airponics bay**. Hydroponics on *Sovereign*-class vessels was located on Deck 11. *(Star Trek: First Contact).*

hydrosail. A water sport. Hydrosailing was one of the diversions available at Neelix's **Polynesian resort** holodeck program. **Marayna**, one of the entertainment directors in the program, gave lessons in hydrosailing. ("Alter Ego" [VGR]).

hyper-impulse. Advanced form of propulsion employed on Federation timeships of the 29th century. ("Future's End, Part II" [VGR]).

hyperacceleration. Biochemical condition that plagued the people of planet **Scalos** due to radiation permeating their water supply. Hyperacceleration of biological processes caused an individual so affected to experience one second as if it were an entire hour. Outsiders who were accelerated quickly burned out, dying in a very short period of time due to cell damage. To a normal, nonaccelerated person, a **Scalosian** sounded very much like an insect. ("Wink of an Eye" [TOS]).

hyperchannel. Alternate term for **subspace radio** communications. *(Star Trek II: The Wrath of Khan).*

hyperencephalogram. Medical test that records and measures brain-wave activity. ("The Lights of Zetar" [TOS]).

hyperonic radiation. Hazardous form of energy that can be fatal to unadapted humans. Hyperonic radiation was present in the atmosphere of **Tau Cygna V**. Federation colonists on the planet were able to adapt after two generations of exposure. Hyperonic radiation randomizes phaser beams and renders sensors and transporters inoperative. Data, however, was unaffected by this energy. ("The Ensigns of Command" [TNG]).

HyperPro PC. Brand name of a primitive personal computer product that was to have been introduced by the Earth corporation **Chronowerx** in 1996. Like all Chronowerx products, the HyperPro PC used technology obtained by **Harry Starling** from the Federation *Timeship* ***Aeon***. ("Future's End, Part I" [VGR]).

hyperspace physics test. One portion of the entrance examination for aspiring Starfleet Academy cadets. ("Coming of Age" [TNG]).

hyperspanner. Engineering tool used in the calibration of plasma injectors. ("The Ship" [DS9]).

hyperthermic charge. Explosives technology used by the Vidiians in the Delta Quadrant. Hyperthermic charges released great amounts of heat upon detonation. ("Deadlock" [VGR]).

hyperzine. Cardiac stimulant. Dr. Julian Bashir ordered hyperzine when **Garak** suffered a cardiac arrest due to the stress related to the **cranial implant** in 2370. ("The Wire" [DS9]).

hypochondria. SEE: **Barclay, Reginald.**

hypospray. Medical instrument used by Starfleet medical personnel for subcutaneous and intramuscular administration of medication for many humanoid patients. The hypospray uses an extremely fine, high-pressure aerosuspension delivery system, eliminating the need for a needle to physically penetrate the skin. *As with numerous* Star Trek *"inventions," the hypospray later became an inspiration to real-world engineers who have since invented actual medical devices based on the* Star Trek *prop.*

hypothalmic series. Medical test used to determine hypothalmic function. Dr. Beverly Crusher ordered a hypothalmic series on Counselor Troi in 2370 when Crusher suspected that Troi's hypothalmus, the organ that controls body temperature, was malfunctioning. ("Genesis" [TNG]).

Hyralan sector. Region of space. Area where **Arctus Baran** was to rendezvous with **Koral**'s shuttlecraft to obtain the third piece of the Vulcan **psionic resonator** in 2370. ("Gambit, Part II" [TNG]).

hyronalin. Medication used for treatment of radiation exposure in humanoid patients. Hyronalin replaced **adrenaline** for such applications, although hyronalin had no effect on a radiation-induced hyperaccelerated-aging disease from planet **Gamma Hydra IV** that afflicted several *Enterprise* crew members in 2267. ("The Deadly Years" [TOS]). Hyronalin was used to treat the crew of the *Enterprise*-D when the ship was exposed to hazardous levels of radiation while towing a derelict waste ship away from planet **Gamelan V** in 2367. The drug was administered by introducing hyronalin vapor into the ship's ventilation system. ("Final Mission" [TNG]). La Forge and Crusher required hyronalin treatments following exposure to **plasma fire** radiation in the cargo bay in 2368. ("Disaster" [TNG]). Deep Space 9 Chief Medical Officer Dr. Julian Bashir administered hyronalin to Chief Miles O'Brien for radiation poisoning in 2371. ("Visionary" [DS9]).

hytritium. A highly unstable substance used to neutralize poisonous **tricyanate**. The *Enterprise*-D was able to procure some of this substance from **Zibalian** trader **Kivas Fajo** when the water supply on planet **Beta Agni II** suffered serious tricyanate contamination in 2366. Pure hytritium is too unstable to convey by transporter. ("The Most Toys" [TNG]).

hyvroxilated quint-ethyl metacetamine. Anesthetic potion. Quark tried to use some of the stuff to drug Dr. Julian Bashir in an effort to "fix" a **raquetball** match between Bashir and Miles O'Brien in 2370. ("Rivals" [DS9]).

I

"I Hate You." Obnoxious song popular in American culture in the year 1986. *(Star Trek IV: The Voyage Home). "I Hate You" was written and performed by Star Trek IV associate producer Kirk Thatcher, who also played the punk on the San Francisco bus who gave Kirk and Spock the "finger." Kirk Thatcher was later a designer and producer on the television series* Dinosaurs.

I'danian spice pudding. Highly caloric dessert. ("Babel" [DS9]). Quark offered I'danian spice pudding to Dax and Kira as an enticement to enter his establishment on the Promenade at Deep Space 9. ("The Wire" [DS9]). I'danian spice pudding became one of Jake Sisko's favorite foods while living on the station. ("The Search, Part I" [DS9]).

"I, Borg." *Next Generation* episode #123. Written by René Echevarria. Directed by Robert Lederman. Stardate 45854.2. *First aired in 1992. The* Enterprise-*D crew captures an injured Borg, nurses him back to health, gives him a sense of individuality, and names him Hugh. The story of Hugh the Borg was later continued in "Descent, Parts I and II" (TNG).* GUEST CAST: Jonathan Del Arco as **Hugh** and **Third of Five**; Whoopi Goldberg as **Guinan**. SEE: **access terminal; Argolis Cluster; biochips; Borg collective; Borg scoutship; Borg; foil; Hugh; invasive program; root command structure; Third of Five.**

"I, Mudd." Original Series episode #41. Written by Stephen Kandel. Directed by Marc Daniels. Stardate 4513.3. *First aired in 1967. Harry Mudd returns, now the ruler of a planet of beautiful androids. Mudd plans to use the androids to capture the* Enterprise, *but the androids have other plans. This episode features the second appearance of con man Harry Mudd.* GUEST CAST: Roger C. Carmel as **Mudd, Harcourt Fenton**; Richard Tatro as **Norman**; Alyce Andrece as **Alice series #1-250**; Rhae Andrece as **Alice series #251-500**; Kay Elliott as **Mudd, Stella**; Mike Howden as Rowe, Lieutenant; Michael Zaslow as **Jordan, Ensign**; Tom and Ted Legarde as Herman series; Maureen and Colleen Thornton as **Barbara series**; Tamara and Starr Wilson as **Maisie series**; Loren Janes, Vince Deadrick, Norman's stunt doubles; Bob Bass, Bob Orrison, Engineer stunt double. SEE: **Alice; android; Annabelle series; auxiliary control; Barbara series; central control complex; Class-K planet; Deneb V; Denebians; Jordan, Ensign; Maizie series; Makers; Mudd, Harcourt Fenton "Harry"; Mudd (planet); Mudd, Stella; nanopulse laser; Norman; planetary classification system; Trudy series.**

I, the Jury. Novel published in 1947, the first in a series of stories by Earth writer **Mickey Spillane** about a fictitious private detective, Mike Hammer. The novel was a favorite of Deep Space 9 Operations Officer Miles O' Brien, who recommend it to station Security Chief Odo. ("Profit and Loss" [DS9]).

I.K.S. Abbreviation for Imperial Klingon Ship. Title used for Klingon ships, as in ***I.K.S. Amar***. (*Star Trek: The Motion Picture*). *Actually, the first* Star Trek *movie referred to the* Imperial Klingon Cruiser Amar, *but later references in* Star Trek: Deep Space Nine *used the I.K.S. prefix, so we are assuming that this is the standard Klingon usage.*

I.P. scanner. SEE: **interphasic scanner.**

I.S.S. SEE: ***Enterprise, I.S.S.***; **mirror universe.**

Iadara Colony. Federation settlement. (In an alternate **quantum reality** visited by Worf in 2370, Iadara was the object of covert surveillance by the Cardassians. The Cardassians had reprogrammed the **Argus Array** to observe the Iadara colony, as well as other Federation installations.) ("Parallels" [TNG]).

Ibudan. (Stephen James Carver). Humanoid who profited from running black-market goods to the **Bajorans** during the Cardassian occupation. Odo sent him to jail for murdering a Cardassian citizen, but the Bajoran provisional government released him when they came into power. Plotting revenge, Ibudan came to Deep Space 9 in 2369 and staged his own apparent murder, in which he killed his own clone in an attempt to frame Odo. ("A Man Alone" [DS9]).

"Icarus Factor, The." *Next Generation* episode #40. Teleplay by David Assael and Robert L. McCullough. Story by David Assael. Directed by Robert Iscove. Stardate 42686.4. *First aired in 1989. Will Riker's estranged father, Kyle Riker, visits his son on the* Enterprise-*D. This episode marks the first reference to the Tholians in* Star Trek: The Next Generation, *and the only appearance of Kyle Riker, William's father.* GUEST CAST: Diana Muldaur as **Pulaski, Dr. Katherine**; Colm Meaney as **O'Brien, Miles**; Mitchell Ryan as **Riker, Kyle**; Lance Spellerberg as **Herbert, Transporter Chief**. SEE: **Age of Ascension; Anbo-jytsu; *Aries, U.S.S.*; Beta Kupsic; Flaherty, Commander; Fuurinkazan battle strategies; Giamon; gymnasium; Nasreldine; painstik, Klingon; PCS; Pulaski, Dr. Katherine; Rectyne monopod; Riker, Kyle; Riker, William T.; Starbase Montgomery; Stroyerian; Tholians; Tokyo Base; tryptophan-lysine distillates; Vega-Omicron Sector**.

Icarus IV. A comet whose orbit was near the **Romulan Neutral Zone**. A cloaked **Romulan bird-of-prey**, passing through the tail of Icarus IV, became detectable to the *U.S.S. Enterprise* during the Romulan incursion of 2266. ("Balance of Terror" [TOS]). *Named for the character in Greek mythology that flew too close to the sun, thus melting his wings made of wax.*

Iccobar. Ancient language, that, along with Dewan and Dinasian, was believed to have historic roots from the **Iconian** language. ("Contagion" [TNG]).

iced coffee. Chilled beverage made from brewed **coffee** beans. Geordi La Forge enjoyed it. ("Aquiel" [TNG]).

Iceman. Nickname for **Worf** at the *Enterprise*-D's weekly **poker** game, based on his impassive but disconcertingly successful playing style. ("The Emissary" [TNG]). Iceman was also **Curzon Dax**'s nickname for **Koloth**. ("Blood Oath" [DS9]).

ico-spectrogram. Scientific test used as part of planetary surveys. Acting Ensign **Wesley Crusher** ordered that an ico-spectrogram be performed on one of the planets in the third **Selcundi Drema** system in 2365, despite geologist Davies's objections that the equipment setup was unnecessarily time-consuming. Crusher's intuition in requesting the test paid off when significant dilithium deposits were discovered on **Drema IV**. ("Pen Pals" [TNG]).

icoberry torte. Rectangular-shaped dessert food. Available from the **Replimat** on station Deep Space 9. Benjamin Sisko was fond of icoberry torte. ("Homecoming" [DS9], "Sanctuary" [DS9]). Jadzia Dax liked icoberry juice, but it always made her spots itch. ("Let He Who Is Without Sin..." [DS9]).

icon. A form of **Bajoran** representational painting. A 20,000-year-old icon painting showing the lost city of B'hala was in the collection of the state museum in Ilvia. ("Rapture" [DS9]). Major Kira Nerys's mother was an icon painter. ("Second Skin" [DS9]).

Iconia. Planet, the home of a technologically advanced civilization destroyed some 200,000 years ago. Iconia was discovered by Federation science in 2365 by **Captain Donald Varley** of the ***U.S.S. Yamato***. Varley uncovered evidence that Iconia was located in the Romulan Neutral Zone; he violated the Zone to find the planet because he feared the consequences if the Romulans acquired Iconian technology. Although ancient texts portrayed the **Iconians** as aggressors in that conflict, recent students of archaeology (including Jean-Luc Picard) have speculated that the Iconians were innocent victims, attacked by enemies who feared their advanced technology. *The surface of Iconia was a matte painting designed by visual effects supervisor Dan Curry. The Iconian control building, a model used as part of the painting, was designed by Mike Okuda, based on two swimming pool filter covers and part of the* Star Trek I *drydock model.* ("Contagion" [TNG]).

Iconian computer weapon. A computer software weapon employed by the ancient **Iconians**. The weapon, a destructive computer program, was delivered to an enemy spacecraft by means of a transmitter in a short-range space probe. The program would then alter the target vessel's computer software, causing failure of critical systems. The ***U.S.S. Yamato*** was destroyed in 2365 by a still-functioning Iconian probe that transmitted the computer software weapon into that ship's computer banks. The virus-like program subsequently caused the near-destruction of the *U.S.S. Enterprise*-D and the Romulan warbird ***Haakona***. ("Contagion" [TNG]).

Iconian gateway. Sophisticated dimensional transport system, in use by the ancient Iconians some 200,000 years ago, that allowed instantaneous movement across interstellar distances without the use of starships. The first known discovery of an Iconian gateway in modern times was in 2365 by the crew of the *Starship Enterprise*-D on the planet **Iconia**. The *Enterprise*-D crew destroyed the gateway rather than allow it to fall into Romulan hands. ("Contagion" [TNG]). A second gateway was discovered by Dominion scientists in 2372 on planet Vandros IV in the Gamma Quadrant. The gateway was housed in an ancient stone ziggurat whose internal structure was constructed of **neutronium**, making it impervious to external attack, even by **quantum torpedoes**. Rebel Jem'Hadar soldiers attempted to seize the gateway, but were prevented from doing so by an unusual joint mission of Jem'Hadar and Federation forces that destroyed the gateway mechanism and its surrounding building. ("To the Death" [DS9]).

Iconians. An ancient, highly advanced civilization that mastered the technique of dimensional transport across interstellar distances. SEE: **Iconian gateway**. The Iconians, referred to in ancient texts as "Demons of Air and Darkness," were all believed destroyed some 200,000 years ago by orbital bombardment that devastated the surface of their planet. It has been speculated that the Iconians did not all perish in the attacks, but rather used their gateway technology to escape to other nearby planets. The similarity between the Iconian language and **Dewan**, **Iccobar**, and **Dinasian** has been cited as evidence to support this theory. ("Contagion" [TNG]).

iconic display console. A highly sophisticated computer interface system designed by Lieutenant **Reginald Barclay** while under the influence of the **Cytherians** in 2367. The iconic display console permitted a computer user's mind to link directly into a computer. ("The Nth Degree" [TNG]).

Icor IX. Planet. A symposium on rough star clusters was held at the Astrophysics Center on Icor IX in 2366. Captain Picard considered attending the symposium on his vacation. ("Captain's Holiday" [TNG]).

icosahedron. Twenty-sided geometric solid. ("Alliances" [VGR]).

ID trace. SEE: **transporter ID trace**.

Idanians. Humanoid civilization. Idanians are sometimes characterized as a secretive people. ("A Simple Investigation" [DS9]).

"Identity Crisis." *Next Generation* episode #92. Teleplay by Brannon Braga. Based on a story by Timothy De Haas. Directed by Winrich Kolbe. Stardate 44664.5. *First aired in 1991. Geordi and his former shipmates from the* U.S.S. Victory *are compelled to return to a planet they visited years ago, where they are transformed into alien life-forms.* GUEST CAST: Maryann Plunkett as **Leijten, Susanna**; Patti Yasutake as **Ogawa, Nurse Alyssa**; Amick Byram as **Hickman, Lieutenant Paul**; Dennis Madalone as **Hendrick, Chief;** Mona Grudt as **Graham, Ensign**. SEE: ***Aries, U.S.S.*; Bogrow, Paul; Brevelle, Ensign; *Cousteau*; Graham, Ensign; Hendrick, Chief; Hickman, Lieutenant Paul; kayolane; La Forge, Geordi; Leijten, Susanna; Malaya IV; Mendez; Ogawa, Nurse Alyssa; T-cell stimulator; Tarchannen III; thymus; *Victory*, *U.S.S.*; warning beacons.**

IDIC. Acronym for Infinite Diversity in Infinite Combinations, a cornerstone of the **Vulcan** philosophy. Spock wore an IDIC medallion to a dinner in honor of Dr. Miranda Jones aboard the *Starship Enterprise* in 2268. ("Is There in Truth No Beauty?" [TOS]). Deep Space 9 entrepreneur Quark planned to sell Vulcan IDIC pins on the station's monitors in late 2370. ("The Jem'Hadar" [DS9]). *The triangle-circle IDIC pendant Spock wore was designed by Gene Roddenberry and William Ware Theiss. The emblem has been used as a Vulcan national symbol. Bob Justman insists the acronym stands for "Incredible Detail, Incredible Confusion," a cornerstone of his personal philosophy.*

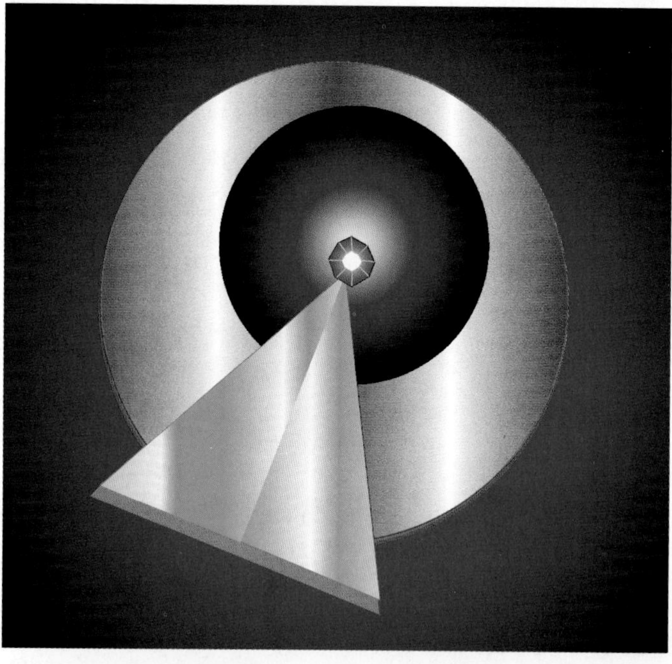

Idini Star Cluster. Located between **Persephone V** and **Mordan IV**. The *Enterprise*-D passed the Idini Cluster while en route to Mordan IV. ("Too Short a Season" [TNG]).

Idran hybrids. Type of plant. In 2373 Keiko O'Brien left her Idran hybrids in the care of her husband and Dr. Julian Bashir. Unfortunately, they watered the plants too much, causing them to die. ("The Assignment" [DS9]).

Idran. Trinary star system located in the **Gamma Quadrant**, first discovered in the 22nd century by the **Quadros-1 probe**. Idran was one of the closest systems to the terminus of the **Bajoran wormhole**. ("Emissary" [DS9], "Battle Lines" [DS9]).

"If I Only Had a Brain." Song from the ancient motion picture *The Wizard of Oz* (MGM, 1939). Just prior to his death in 2365, **Dr. Ira Graves** whistled the tune in Data's presence, noting it was sung by a mechanical man who "finds out that he *is* human after all, [and] always was." ("Schizoid Man" [TNG]).

"If Wishes Were Horses." *Deep Space 9* episode #16. Teleplay by Nell McCue Crawford & William L. Crawford and Michael Piller. Story by Nell McCue Crawford & William L. Crawford. Directed by Robert Legato. Stardate 46853.2. *First aired in 1993. The arrival of Rumpelstiltskin in the O'Briens' quarters signals the beginning of encounters with imaginary beings created by aliens from the Gamma Quadrant, to study human beings.* GUEST CAST: Rosalind Chao as **O'Brien, Keiko**; Keone Young as **Bokai, Buck**; Michael John Anderson as **Rumpelstiltskin**; Hana Hatae as **O'Brien, Molly**. SEE: **Baneriam hawk; baseball; Bashir, Dr. Julian; Bokai, Buck; class-4 probe; Denorios Belt; Gunji jackdaw; Habitat Ring; Hanoli system; hologenerators; impulse sustainer; Larosian virus; level-1 personnel sweep; London Kings; Lower Pylon 1; Newson, Eddie; Odo; pulse-wave torpedo; Rumpelstiltskin; Sisko, Benjamin; Speaker, Tris; subspace phenomena; Tartaran landscapes; thoron; Williams, Ted; World Series**.

Igo Sector. Location of a binary star. Studied by the *Starship **Yosemite*** in 2369. ("Realm of Fear" [TNG]).

iguana. Earth reptile; any of the larger members of the family *Iguanidae*. They can attain a length of approximately 1.8 meters. During the outbreak of **Barclay's Protomorphosis Syndrome** aboard the *Enterprise*-D in 2370, **Spot** devolved into a large iguana. The transformation apparently took place as Spot was giving birth to a litter of kittens. ("Genesis" [TNG]). *Luckily for the kittens, iguanas subsist mostly on fruit and vegetation.*

***ih'tanu* ceremony.** Traditional Bajoran ritual, performed when a girl reached the age of 14. ("Accession" [DS9]).

Ih'valla*.** One of the Bajoran ***D'jarras. The *Ih'valla D'jarra* called for an artistic occupation. Major **Kira Nerys** was of the *Ih'valla D'jarra*, but like many Bajorans, she did not seek an occupation prescribed by her *D'jarra*. ("Accession" [DS9]).

Ihat. Character in **D'Arsay** mythology. An image of Ihat was stored in the **D'Arsay archive.** Ihat was one of characters portrayed by Data when the archive programmed him to reenact the **Masaka** legend in 2370. Ihat was the first personality to appear and acted as a "spokesman." He was the first to allude to the nature of Masaka and her subjects. ("Masks" [TNG]).

Ijarna. Inhabitant of Deep Space 9 in 2372. He and his wife had a tumultuous relationship. ("Crossfire" [DS9]).

Ikalian asteroid belt. Field of asteroids near the **Kriosian system**. The Ikalian belt was believed to be the hiding place of a group of Kriosian rebels. In 2367, two freighters, one Ferengi and the other Cardassian, were attacked by Kriosian rebels near the belt. ("The Mind's Eye" [TNG]).

Ikat'ika. (James Horan). **Jem'Hadar** officer in command of the detachment of **Jem'Hadar** troops assigned to **Dominion internment camp 371** in 2373. ("In Purgatory's Shadow" [DS9]). Ikat'ika fought Starfleet officer **Worf** in hand-to-hand sport combat, coming to respect the **Klingon** because he was unable to kill him. Worf was a prisoner at the camp at the time. **Deyos**, the **Vorta** in charge of the Detention camp, had Ikat'ika executed for failing to kill Worf. ("By Inferno's Light" [DS9]). *James Horan previously played Jo'Bril in "Suspicions" (TNG), Lieutenant Barnaby in "Descent, Part II" (TNG), and Tosin in "Fair Trade" (VGR).*

Ilari Autarch. Hereditary leader of the Ilari people in the Delta Quadrant. Two centuries ago, **Tieran** was Autarch of Ilari, but was overthrown due to his tyranny. In 2373, Tieran's consciousness, in the body of Kes, assassinated the rightful Autarch in a bid to claim the position once again. With the help of the crew of the *U.S.S. Voyager*, Tieran was thwarted and **Demmas**, the rightful Autarch's eldest son, assumed the title. ("Warlord" [VGR]).

Ilari bioelectric microfibers. Highly sophisticated biotechnology used by the **Ilari** people. The microfibers worked with a special cortical implant to effect a transfer of the subject's neural pattern into a host person's brain. The megalomaniacal dictator **Tieran** had such bioelectric microfibers in his hands, and he used them with a cortical implant to transfer his consciousness into Kes' brain just before he died in 2373. ("Warlord" [VGR]).

Ilari First Castellan. Honorific sometimes bestowed upon the Ilari Autarch's chief military advisor. ("Warlord" [VGR]).

Ilari talisman. A metallic choker that was the symbol of the **Ilari Autarch**. When **Tieran** was forcibly removed from power in 2173, the talisman was taken from him. ("Warlord" [VGR]).

Ilari. Planet in the Delta Quadrant that was home to a technologically sophisticated humanoid civilization. Ilari was ruled over by a hereditary Autarch. ("Warlord" [VGR]).

Ilecom system. Planetary system. In 2364, the Ilecom system experienced a "hiccough" in time that was found to be the result of **Dr. Paul Manheim**'s time/gravity experiments at **Vandor IV**. ("We'll Always Have Paris" [TNG]).

Ilia. (Persis Khambatta). Navigator on the *Starship Enterprise* during the **V'Ger** incident of 2271. Ilia, a native of planet **Delta IV**, had been romantically involved with **Willard Decker**, who also later served aboard the *Enterprise*. Ilia was killed by a probe from the V'Ger entity, although a near-duplicate of her was created by the probe in an attempt to communicate with the *Enterprise*'s crew. Ilia was later listed as "missing in action." SEE: **Deltans; Oath of Celibacy.** *(Star Trek: The Motion Picture).*

Iliana. (Nana Visitor). An agent of the **Obsidian Order**. In 2361, Iliana volunteered for an undercover assignment on planet **Bajor**. She was surgically altered to look **Bajoran** and underwent mind-control techniques that erased her own thoughts and replaced them with Bajoran memories. Iliana's father, **Legate Ghemor**, disagreed with his daughter's decision to leave **Cardassia**, but did not interfere. In 2371, **Kira Nerys** was surgically altered to look like Iliana by members of the **Obsidian Order,** as

a ruse to expose Ghemor's connections to the **Cardassian underground movement**. Iliana's fate still remains a mystery. ("Second Skin" [DS9]).

Ilidaria. Planet in the **Delta Quadrant**. Ilidaria is located less than three light-years from a type-4 **quantum singularity**. The planet was inhabited by an intelligent species known as the **Ilidarians**. ("Parallax" [VGR]).

Ilidarians. Technologically sophisticated civilization from the planet **Ilidaria** in the **Delta Quadrant**. ("Parallax" [VGR]). *Voyager* crew members Chakotay and Tuvok visited the Ilidarians just prior to stardate 48734 on a trade mission. ("Cathexis" [VGR]).

illium 629. Naturally occurring by-product of geological decay of **dilithium**. Traces of illium 629 were found on planet **Drema IV**, leading to the discovery of unusual dilithium strata in the planet's mantle. ("Pen Pals" [TNG]).

Iloja of Prim. Cardassian serialist poet from the time of the First Republic. Iloja had quite a temper and spent some time in exile on planet **Vulcan**. ("Destiny" [DS9]).

Ilvia. City on Bajor. A prestigious state museum was located at Ilvia. ("Rapture" [DS9]).

Ilvian Proclamation. Bajoran law, enacted in 2369 after the end of the Cardassian occupation, that exiled all Bajorans who were members of the **Cardassian occupational government**. This proclamation included persons sentenced in absentia. ("The Collaborator" [DS9]). *Apparently named for* Star Trek: Deep Space Nine *art director Randy McIlvain.*

"Imaginary Friend." *Next Generation* episode #122. Teleplay by Edith Swensen and Brannon Braga. Story by Jean Louise Matthias & Ronald Wilkerson and Richard Fliegel. Directed by Gabrielle Beaumont. Stardate 45852.1. *First aired in 1992. A little girl's imaginary playmate turns out to be terrifyingly real.* GUEST CAST: Noley Thornton as **Sutter**, **Clara**; Shay Astar as **Isabella**; Jeff Allin as **Sutter**, **Ensign Daniel**; Brian Bonsall as **Rozhenko**, **Alexander**; Patti Yasutake as **Ogawa**, **Nurse Alyssa**; Sheila Franklin as **Felton**, **Ensign**; Whoopi Goldberg as **Guinan**. SEE: **Brentalia; bunny rabbit; Champs Elysees; Children's Center; drag coefficient; Felton, Ensign; FGC-47; Isabella; Jokri; Kryonian tiger; La Forge, Geordi; McClukidge, Nurse; Mintonian sailing ship; Modean system; nasturtiums; Neutral Zone, Romulan; noncorporeal life; Ogawa, Nurse Alyssa; *papalla* juice; purple omelets; Samarian coral fish; Sutter, Clara; Sutter, Ensign Daniel; Tarkassian razorbeast; Tavela Minor; thermal interferometry scanner; trionium.**

imaging logs. Record of visual acquisition activity by a scientific or other image-recording device, such as an astronomical observatory. These imaging logs of the **Argus Array** were downloaded in 2370 as part of the *Enterprise*-D's investigation into the malfunction of the Array. ("Parallels" [TNG]).

imaging scanner. Component of a transporter that captures a molecular-resolution image of the transport subject, used to create the rematerialization matrix. Four redundant scanners are used, permitting any one to be ignored if it disagrees with the other three. ("Realm of Fear" [TNG]).

Immamura, Lieutenant. *Enterprise* crew member. Immamura was injured in 2267 while on a landing party searching for the ***Shuttlecraft Galileo*** on planet **Taurus II**. ("The *Galileo* Seven" [TOS]).

Immelmann turn. Aerobatic maneuver in which a spacecraft executes a steep climb, returning to upright orientation at the crest of the half loop. Inspired by the maneuvers of 20th-century Earth pilot Max Immelmann. The Immelmann turn was used as a demonstration of piloting prowess by cadets at **Starfleet Academy**. ("The First Duty" [TNG]).

"Immunity Syndrome, The." Original Series episode #48. Written by Robert Sabaroff. Directed by Joseph Pevney. Stardate 4307.1. *First aired in 1968. Kirk and his crew struggle to stop giant space amoeba that has destroyed a star system and now threatens the entire galaxy. Robert Sabaroff also wrote the story for "Conspiracy" (TNG).* GUEST CAST: John Winston as **Kyle**, **Mr.**; Majel Barrett as **Chapel**, **Christine**; Jay Jones, Dick Dial, Stunt doubles. SEE: **acetylcholine; amoeba; *Galileo*, *Shuttlecraft*; Gamma 7A System; *Intrepid*, *U.S.S.*; Kyle, Mr.; Sector 39J; Starbase 6; Vulcans.**

immunosuppressant. Any of several drugs designed to limit immune response in humanoids. Dr. Crusher used immunosuppressants in 2367 to help William Riker successfully carry the **Trill** symbiont, **Ambassador Odan**, within his body. ("The Host" [TNG]).

impedrezene. Cardiac medication. ("Alliances" [VGR], "Investigations" [VGR]).

Imperial Plaza. Large open square in the capital city of **Cardassia Prime**. In 2373, after **Gul Dukat** became head of the Cardassian government, a monument was erected in his honor at the gateway to the Imperial Plaza. ("By Inferno's Light" [DS9]).

Imperial Senate, Romulan. Governing body of the **Romulan Star Empire**. ("Face of the Enemy" [TNG]).

implosive protomatter device. SEE: **protomatter**.

"Improbable Cause." *Deep Space Nine* episode #65. Teleplay by René Echevarria. Story by Robert Lederman & David R. Long. Directed by Avery Brooks. No stardate given. *First aired in 1995. An attempt on Garak's life triggers an investigation by Odo that uncovers a secret plan by Cardassian and Romulan forces to attack the Dominion. This is the first episode in which Garak admits to being a part of the Obsidian Order. This episode was the first of two parts and concluded with "The Die Is Cast" (DS9).* SEE: **Cardassian neck trick; Dekora Assan; Delavian chocolates; Flaxian assassins; Flaxian ship; forced neutrino inverter; Garak, Elim; Japori II; *Julius Caesar;* Mila; Nausicaan; nitrilin; Obsidian Order; Odo; Orias system; pheromonic sensor; Retaya; Shakespeare, William; tailor shop; Tain, Enabran; Talarians; Tal Shiar; transponder; Unefra III; Yalosians; Yridian.**

improvoline. Medicine used as a calmative. Not to be confused with inaprovaline, which is a cardiostimulant. ("Basics, Part II" [VGR]).

impulse drive. Spacecraft propulsion system using conventional Newtonian reaction to generate thrust. Aboard most Federation starships, impulse drive is powered by one or more fusion reactors that employ deuterium fuel to yield helium plasma and a lot of power. A ship under impulse drive is limited to slower-than-light speeds. Normally, full impulse speed is one-quarter the speed of light. Although this is adequate for most interplanetary travel (within a single solar system), it is inadequate for travel between the stars. Faster-than-light velocities, necessary for interstellar flight, generally require the use of **warp drive**. An explosion of 97.835 megatons will result if the impulse-drive reactor of a *Constitution*-class starship is overloaded. Such an explosion, produced in the destruction of the ***U.S.S. Constellation***, was used to destroy the extragalactic **planet killer** in 2267. ("The Doomsday Machine" [TOS]). SEE: **sublight**.

impulse sustainer. Propulsion unit in space vehicles such as a class-4 sensor probe that provides thrust after the probe's initial launch. ("If Wishes Were Horses" [DS9]). SEE: **impulse drive**.

Imutta. One of the Bajoran ***D'jarra***s. The *Imutta D'jarra* called for an occupation concerned with the preparing of the dead for burial. ("Accession" [DS9]).

Imzadi. Betazoid term meaning "beloved." The half-Betazoid **Deanna Troi** had been romantically involved with **William Riker** prior to their service aboard the *Enterprise*-D, and she continued to use that term for him in private. ("Encounter at Farpoint, Part I" [TNG]).

"In Purgatory's Shadow." *Deep Space Nine* episode #112. Written by Robert Hewitt Wolfe & Ira Steven Behr. Directed by Gabrielle Beaumont. No stardate given. *First aired in 1997. The threat of a Dominion attack convinces Sisko to close the wormhole while Garak and Worf are held prisoner by the Jem'Hadar. This episode opened with a title card reading "In memory of Derek Garth."* GUEST CAST: Andrew Robinson as **Garak, Elim**; James Horan as **Ikat'ika**; J.G. Hertzler as **Martok, General**; Paul Dooley as **Tain, Enabran**; Melanie Smith as **Tora Ziyal**. SEE: **Bajoran wormhole; Bashir, Julian; Breen; Brun; Cardassian riding hound; Dominion internment camp 371; Elgol-red; *Finding and Winning Your Perfect Mate*; Garak, Elim; Ikat'ika; Kahn, Dr. Lenara; Kang's Summit; Martok, General; *Maryland, U.S.S.*; Meezan IV; Memad; O'Brien, Kirayoshi; Obsidian Order; *Proxima, U.S.S.*; Rain, Dr. Jennings; recursive encryption algorithm; sabre bear; *Sarajevo, U.S.S.*; Surjak; Tain, Enabran; Tal Shiar; *toh-maire*; Tora Ziyal; ultritium; Vorlem, Gul; *Yukon, U.S.S.***

"In the Hands of the Prophets." *Deep Space Nine* episode #20. Directed by David Livingston. Written by Robert Hewitt Wolfe. No stardate given. *First aired in 1993. A Bajoran religious fundamentalist opposes the teaching of science on the station, but it is a ploy to eliminate a rival candidate to become the next kai.* GUEST CAST: Rosalind Chao as **O'Brien, Keiko**; Robin Christopher as **Neela**; Philip Anglim as **Bareil, Vedek**; Louise Fletcher as **Winn**; Michael Eugene as Fairman vendor. SEE: **Aquino, Ensign; Bajoran wormhole; Bajorans; Bareil, Vedek; cabrodine; EJ7 interlock; infernite; isolinear coprocessor; *jumja*; Neela; Opaka, Kai; security bypass module; security field subsystem ANA; Vedek Assembly; vedek; verteron; Winn.**

"In the zone." In the competitive vernacular, the sense that one cannot lose; a winning streak. Starfleet Chief Miles O'Brien enjoyed a brief period "in the zone" in 2371, when he won 46 consecutive **dart** games. ("Shakaar" [DS9]).

"In Theory." *Next Generation* episode #99. Written by Joe Menosky & Ronald D. Moore. Directed by Patrick Stewart. Stardate 44932.3. *First aired in 1991. Data tries to experience a romantic relationship.* GUEST CAST: Michele Scarabelli as **D'Sora, Lieutenant Jenna**; Rosalind Chao as **O'Brien, Keiko**; Colm Meaney as **O'Brien, Miles**; Pamela Winslow as **McKnight, Ensign**; Whoopi Goldberg as **Guinan**; Majel Barrett as Computer voice. SEE: **Arton, Jeff; Calaman sherry; cleaning processor; crystilia; D'Sora, Lieutenant Jenna; Data; krellide storage cells; Mar Oscura; Prakal II; Shuttle 03; Spot; Starbase 260; Thorne, Ensign; torpedo bay; Tyrinean blade carving; Van Mayter, Lieutenant; *Voltaire*; W-particle interference.**

In'Cha. Klingon term meaning "Begin." ("The Way of the Warrior" [DS9]).

Inad. (Eve Brenner). A telepathic historian. Inad was one of the members of the **Ullian** delegation that visited the *Enterprise*-D in 2368. ("Violations" [TNG]). SEE: **Tarmin**.

inaprovaline. Cardiostimulatory pharmaceutical in use by Starfleet medical personnel. Dr. Beverly Crusher ordered inaprovaline given to the **Zalkonian** named **John Doe** to help stabilize his condition. ("Transfigurations" [TNG]). Usually administered intravenously by **hypospray**. ("Ethics" [TNG]). In 2371, Dr. Julian Bashir administered inaprovaline to his patient **Vedek Bareil** in the course of his treatment for radiation-induced injuries. ("Life Support" [DS9]). In high doses, inaprovaline can also be used to stimulate cell regeneration. ("Lifesigns" [VGR]).

Indiana. Locale in the Midwest region of North America on Earth. **Kathryn Janeway** grew up in Indiana. She once noted that summers there were warm and humid, somewhat similar to those of Rinax. ("Macrocosm" [VGR]).

"Indiscretion." *Deep Space Nine* episode #77. Teleplay by Nicholas Corea. Story by Toni Marberry & Jack Treviño. Directed by LeVar Burton. No stardate given. *First aired in 1995. When parts of a Cardassian warship that was transporting Bajoran prisoners are found, both Kira and Gul Dukat go on an expedition to investigate the remains.* GUEST CAST: Penny Johnson as **Yates, Kasidy**; Marc Alaimo as **Dukat**; Roy Brocksmith as Razka; Cyia Batten as **Ziyal**; Thomas Prisco as **Heler**. SEE: **Azin, Minister; Bajorans; Breen; Cardassians; dilithium; Dozaria; Dukat, Gul; Heler; Kira Nerys; Lissepia; Lorit Akrem; Meressa, Kai; *Rabol*; *Ravinok*; Razka Karn; sand spine; Shakaar resistance cell; Tholians; Tora Naprem; Tora Ziyal; tritonium; uridium; Vulcan restaurant; Yates, Kasidy.**

Indri VIII. Class-L planet first identified by Federation scientists around 2340. No evidence of intelligent life or any animals was detected there, but the planet was covered with deciduous vegetation. Billions of years ago, Indri VIII had apparently been seeded with genetic material by an ancient humanoid species. Cardassian scientists were among several groups seeking to obtain genetic samples from the planet's biosphere to learn more about these ancient humanoids. All life on Indri VIII was destroyed by a violent plasma reaction in the planet's lower atmosphere in 2369, apparently caused by Klingon forces seeking to prevent the competing scientific groups from obtaining the same genetic information. ("The Chase" [TNG]). SEE: **humanoid life; planetary classification system**.

industrial replicator. SEE: **replicator**.

inertial dampers. Field-manipulation devices designed to compensate for the acceleration forces generated when a space vehicle changes speed or direction of flight. The *Enterprise*-D's inertial dampers failed just before the ship experienced a near-collision with the ***U.S.S. Bozeman*** in 2368. ("Cause and Effect" [TNG]). Taking the inertial dampers off-line will give a smaller ship a quicker response time to rapid course changes. ("Playing God" [DS9]). *Inertial dampers were "invented" by* Star Trek*'s writers primarily in response to very valid criticisms that the acceleration and decelerations performed by the* Enterprise *would crush the crew into chunky salsa unless there was some kind of heavy-duty protection.*

Inferna Prime. Federation planet. In 2373 a **Federation Grand Jury** hearing was to have been held at Inferna Prime. At the hearing, Quark was to have given testimony against the Orion Syndicate, since he was a witness to their activities. ("The Ascent" [DS9]).

infernite. Common chemical explosive. A combination of cabrodine and infernite was used by **Neela** on Deep Space 9 to destroy Keiko O'Brien's schoolroom in 2369. ("In the Hands of the Prophets" [DS9]).

infinite velocity, theory of. Concept postulating that an object traveling at warp 10 (also known as **transwarp** velocity) would effectively have an infinite speed, and that the object would therefore occupy every point in the universe simultaneously. In 2372, *U.S.S. Voyager* Lieutenant **Tom Paris**, aboard the *Shuttlecraft Cochrane*, became the first human to cross the transwarp threshold and travel at warp 10. The flight was made possible by the discovery of a new form of **dilithium** that was stable at an extremely high warp frequency. It was discovered, however, that achieving infinite velocity dramatically altered cellular DNA and caused accelerated evolutionary mutation. ("Threshold" [VGR]).

Infirmary. Medical facility on Deep Space 9, the province of Medical Officer **Julian Bashir**. ("Emissary" [DS9]).

Inglatu. (Brian Thompson). **Dosi** negotiator. Inglatu refused to sell Quark 100,000 vats of **tulaberry wine**, since there was not that much of it on his entire planet. ("Rules of Acquisition" [DS9]). *Brian Thompson also played Klag in "A Matter of Honor" (TNG) and a Klingon helm officer in* Star Trek Generations.

Ingraham B. Planet whose population was struck by mass insanity caused by the **Denevan neural parasites** in 2265. Inhabitants of Ingraham B were forced by the parasites to construct ships, traveling to **Deneva** eight months later, where that population was infected. ("Operation—Annihilate!" [TOS]).

"Inheritance." *Next Generation* episode #162. Teleplay by Dan Koeppel and René Echevarria. Story by Dan Koeppel. Directed by Robert Scheerer. Stardate 47410.2. *First aired in 1993. On a mission to avert a planetary crisis, Data mets a woman who claims to be his mother.* GUEST CAST: Fionnula Flanagan as **Tainer, Dr. Juliana**; William Lithgow as **Tainer, Dr. Pran**. SEE: **Atrea IV; cascade anomaly; Corvallan trader; Crystalline Entity; Data; early French impressionists; emotion chip; energy transfer matrix; ferroplasmic infusion; Fourier series; Handel, Georg Fredrich; holographic information module; Lal; magma pockets; magnesite; Malaya IV; modesty subroutine; Omicron Theta; particle stream buffer; pattern enhancer; phasers; Soong, Dr. Noonien; synaptic scanning; synchronous orbit; Tainer, Dr. Juliana; Tainer, Dr. Pran; Terlina III; Terlina system.**

Inheritors. A group of humanoids on planet **Earth**, originally from the continent of Asia, who, thousands of years ago, were visited by advanced extraterrestrial beings. At the time, they were a small tribe of nomadic hunters who had no spoken language and little formal culture except for the use of fire and stone weapons, but a deep respect for the land and for other living creatures. The extraterrestrial visitors were deeply impressed by the these people and gave them a genetic gift that instilled in them a bold sense of curiosity and adventure. Over the next thousand generations, the Inheritors of this extraordinary legacy migrated across their planet, from their cold climate to a new land on what later became known as the American continents. The Inheritors flourished in their new homes until a new people came with weapons and diseases. The survivors scattered and sought refuge in other societies. But even in later generations, the Inheritors retained a memory of their extraterrestrial benefactors, which they called **Sky Spirits**. The descendents of the Inheritors included Earth's **Rubber Tree People** and other Native Americans. ("Tattoo" [VGR]). SEE: **Preservers; Pueblo Revolt.**

initiate. A **Trill** host candidate who was enrolled in the program designed to prepare hosts for joining. Because there were only an average of 300 **symbionts** available each year for the 5,000 qualifying initiates, competition was extremely intense, and standards were very high. ("Playing God" [DS9]). SEE: **field docent**.

"Initiations." *Voyager* episode #21. Written by Kenneth Biller. Directed by Winrich Kolbe. Stardate 49005.3. *First aired in 1995. A young Kazon boy earns his Ogla name with the help of Commander Chakotay.* GUEST CAST: Aron Eisenberg as **Kar**; Patrick Kilpatrick as **Razik**; Tim deZarn as **Haliz**; Majel Barrett as Computer voice. SEE: **Ayala, Lieutenant; Calogan dog; duranium; electroceramic; Haliz, Jal; holodeck and holosuite programs: Defense simulations; Jal; Kar; Kazon; Kazon spacecraft; Kazon-Ogla; Kazon-Relora; Kinell, Jal; Kolopak; magnesite; Pakra; polyduranide; Razik, Jal; Tarok; Trabe.**

Inkarian wool. Fabric. After Odo was rendered into a humanoid by the **Founders**, Garak used Inkarian wool to make a uniform for Odo, who found the material itchy. ("Broken Link" [DS9]).

"Inner Light, The." *Next Generation* episode #125. Teleplay by Morgan Gendel and Peter Allan Fields. Story by Morgan Gendel. Directed by Peter Lauritson. Stardate 45944.1. *First aired in 1992. An alien space probe takes over Picard's mind, and he experiences a lifetime of memories on a dead planet, in just a few minutes. This episode won the 1993 Hugo Award for Best Dramatic Presentation at the World Science Fiction Convention.* GUEST CAST: Margot Rose as **Eline**; Richard Riehle as **Batai**; Scott Jaeck as Administrator; Jennifer Nash as **Meribor**; Patti Yasutake as **Ogawa**, **Nurse Alyssa**; Daniel Stewart as **Batai (young)**; Logan White as **Batai (young)**. SEE: **Batai (young); Batai; cardiac induction; cortical stimulator; crystalline emiristol; delactovine; Eline; isocortex; Kamie; Kamin; Kataan probe; Kataan; Meribor; neurotransmitter; nucleonic beam; Ogawa, Nurse Alyssa; paricium; Parvenium Sector; Ressik; Ressikan flute; somatophysical failure; Starbase 218; talgonite; voice-transit conductors.**

inner eyelid. Part of the **Vulcan** eye that evolved because the intensity of the bright Vulcan sun necessitated a secondary means of protecting the retina. When Spock was subjected to extremely intense light during an attempt to rid him of a **Denevan neural parasite**, his inner eyelid closed involuntarily, temporarily rendering him blind, but protecting his retinas against permanent damage. ("Operation—Annihilate!" [TOS]).

inner nuncial series. A battery of neurological tests. Dr. Crusher ran an inner nuncial series on Counselor Troi, following the loss of Troi's empathic sense in 2367. ("The Loss" [TNG]).

Innis, Valeda. (Anna Katarina). First Electorine of **Haven**. She strongly opposed a **Tarellian** vessel's request to land on planet Haven in 2364, on the grounds that the ship carried a deadly plague from the Tarellian war, requesting that the *Enterprise*-D intervene to destroy the ship. ("Haven" [TNG]).

"Innocence." *Voyager* episode #38. Teleplay by Lisa Klink. Story by Anthony Williams. Directed by James L. Conway. No stardate given. *First aired in 1996. Tuvok becomes stranded on a moon after a crash landing, and he aids three Drayans who appear to be children but in reality are very old and have been sent to the moon to die.* GUEST CAST: Marnie McPhail as **Alcia**; Tiffany Taubman as **Tressa**; Sarah Rayne as **Elani**; Tahj D. Mowry as **Cowin**; Richard Garon as **Bennet**, **Ensign**. SEE: **Alcia; Attendants; Bennet, Ensign; Chakotay; *cherel* sauce; Cowin; crysata; dielectric field; Drayan II; Drayans; Elani; electrodynamic turbulence; "Falor's Journey"; Fayla; final ritual; fire beast of Sullus; Fire Plains; Jarren; *katra*; Kir; Macormak, Ensign; matter/antimatter reaction chamber; *morrok*; polyferranide; Raal; ration pack; shield harmonics; stasis unit; T'Para; *takka* berries; *tardeth*; Tarkannans; thermal inversion gradient; Tressa; Tuvok; Voroth Sea; Vulcan lute.**

inpedrezine. Drug that is sometimes administered to humanoid patients following cranial trauma. ("Distant Voices" [DS9]).

insignia and rank markings, Starfleet. *The distinctive arrowhead symbol used on Starfleet uniforms was first created by Original Series costume designer William Ware Theiss for "The Cage" (TOS) in 1964. Three versions of this original symbol were created, used for command personnel, science specialists, and engineering staff. (A fourth version, featuring a red cross, was occasionally worn by Christine Chapel). During the original* Star Trek *series, it was assumed that the arrowhead symbol was unique to the* Enterprise, *and that other starships had different insignia for their uniforms. This changed in* Star Trek: The Motion Picture, *when a modified emblem, designed by Robert Fletcher, was used not only on* Enterprise *crew members, but on all Starfleet personnel. We therefore assume that at some point after the original* Star Trek *series, the* Enterprise *emblem was adopted for the entire Starfleet. The feature film insignia (in a couple of variations) was used for the movies set in the Kirk era, as well as for* Star Trek: The Next Generation *flashback sequences involving Picard's cadet days. Yet another variation was created for* Star Trek: The Next Generation*'s first season by Theiss, in conjunction with Rick Sternbach and Mike Okuda. This version was also used on* Star Trek: Deep Space Nine. *Current Starfleet officers wear a version designed by John Eaves and Bob Blackman, first seen in* Star Trek Generations. *Additionally, two hypothetical future versions have been seen. One, designed by Okuda, was seen in "Future Imperfect" (TNG) and "Parallels" (TNG), while another, designed by Eaves, was used in "All Good Things" (TNG) and "The Visitor" (DS9). See illustrations on pages 208-211.*

Instrument of Obedience. Small electronic device implanted subcutaneously in the temporal area of the brain in all citizens of the asteroid/ship ***Yonada*** as a means of controlling their behavior. If an individual spoke against the teachings of the **Oracle**, or otherwise violated the society's laws, the Oracle could cause the instrument of obedience to emit a strong pain stimulus. If intense enough, this stimulus could cause death and was thus an effective means of enforcing the will of the Oracle. ("For the World Is Hollow and I Have Touched the Sky" [TOS]). SEE: **Fabrini.**

Intendant. In the **mirror universe**, the title held by the commander of **Terok Nor**. In 2370, **Kira Nerys (mirror)** was Intendant. It was clear that she enjoyed the job and its perks. ("Crossover" [DS9]).

intercom. Aboard certain Federation spacecraft, a wall or console mounted voice communications terminal. Intercom stations fell into disuse in later Federation starships, as the personal **communicator** provides remote access to the ship's internal communications network.

Interface terminal. Computer console used on Earth during the early 21st century, employing stylus and touch-screen technology. Interface terminals were used to access the **Net.** ("Past Tense, Part II" [DS9]).

interface probe. Robotic device that uses remote telepresence technology to permit a person to work in hazardous environments while remaining at a safer location. In 2370, a interface probe was sent into the ***U.S.S. Raman***, allowing Geordi La Forge to see and feel his way around the ship with the assistance of the **interface unit.** ("Interface" [TNG])

interface unit. Experimental device used by *Enterprise*-D personnel in their attempt to rescue the ***U.S.S. Raman*** from **Marijne VII** in 2370. It was connected to **Geordi La Forge** through his **VISOR** inputs, allowing sensory information to be transmitted directly to his cerebral cortex. Geordi could also move the **interface probe** and cause it to perform various functions merely by thinking of moving his own limbs. ("Interface" [TNG]).

Interface. Global computer-based media and information network on Earth in the 21st century. ("Past Tense, Parts I and II" [DS9]). SEE: **Net.**

"Interface." *Next Generation* episode #155. Written by Joe Menosky. Directed by Robert Wiemer. Stardate 47215.5. *First aired in 1993. The crew of the* Enterprise-D *uses an experimental probe connected to Geordi in an attempt to rescue his mother.* GUEST CAST: Madge Sinclair as **La Forge**, **Silva**; Warren Munson as **Holt**, **Admiral Marcus**; Ben Vereen as **La Forge, Doctor Edward M.** SEE: **Breen; Deep Space 3; Doosodarians; *Excelsior, U.S.S.*; interface probe; interface unit; *Hera, U.S.S.*; Holt, Admiral Marcus; lacunae; La Forge, Dr. Edward M.; La Forge, Geordi; La Forge, Silva; Marijne VII; Marijne VII beings; *Nobel, U.S.S.*; *Raman, U.S.S.*; Starbase 495; subspace phenomena; trionic initiators.**

interferometric dispersion. Technique that renders a spacecraft undetectable by primitive radar detection systems. Torres and Chakotay used interferometric dispersion on their shuttle when they visited Earth in 1996. ("Future's End, Part II" [VGR]).

interferometric pulse. Energy discharge that is modulated in opposition to a particular energy field. Interferometric pulses can be used to cancel out and render ineffective an enemy ship's deflector shields. ("The Swarm" [VGR]).

interlink sequencer. Component of Data's **positronic brain**. On stardate 46307, Data converted his interlink sequencer to asynchronous operation, thereby increasing his computational speed. ("The Quality of Life" [TNG]).

intermix formula. A crucial concept in **warp drive**, the intermix formula is a mathematical expression determining the manner in which matter and **antimatter** are brought together to produce the energy required to warp space and travel faster than light. Science Officer Spock and Chief Engineer Montgomery Scott devised a new intermix formula, based on a theoretical relationship between time and antimatter, that permitted an emergency restart of the *U.S.S. Enterprise*'s warp engines in less than 30 minutes when the vessel was trapped in a decaying orbit above planet **Psi 2000** in 2266. ("The Naked Time" [TOS]). An intermix imbalance can propel a starship into an extremely dangerous, artificially created wormhole. *(Star Trek: The Motion Picture).* **Kosinski**'s unsuccessful warp-drive upgrades in 2364 called for variations in the intermix formula in an attempt to improve engine performance. ("Where No One Has Gone Before" [TNG]).

internal power grid. Alternate term for the EPS power distribution system used aboard Federation starships. ("Disaster" [TNG]). SEE: **electroplasma system.**

interphase generator. Experimental Romulan cloaking technology that combined a **molecular phase inverter** with a **cloaking device**. Matter exposed to the interphase generator would partially exist on a parallel spatial plane and would therefore be undetectable to any known sensing device. Matter so cloaked would theoretically even be able to pass through other matter. During the 2360s, the Klingons experimented with the technology, but after several accidents, they abandoned their research. In 2368, the Romulans developed a similar device that caused catastrophic damage to the warp core of the Romulan test vehicle. The *Enterprise*-D responded to a distress call from the Romulan ship and suffered **chroniton particle** contamination as a result of the failure of the interphase generator. During the mission, Geordi La Forge and Ro Laren were lost in an apparent transporter malfunction. It was later discovered that La Forge, Ro, and a Romulan officer were "phased" by the generator and rendered immaterial and invisible to "normal" matter. Commander Data, while acting to remove the chroniton contamination from the

Starfleet emblems, embroidered patch (worn on left breast).

Star Trek: The Original Series

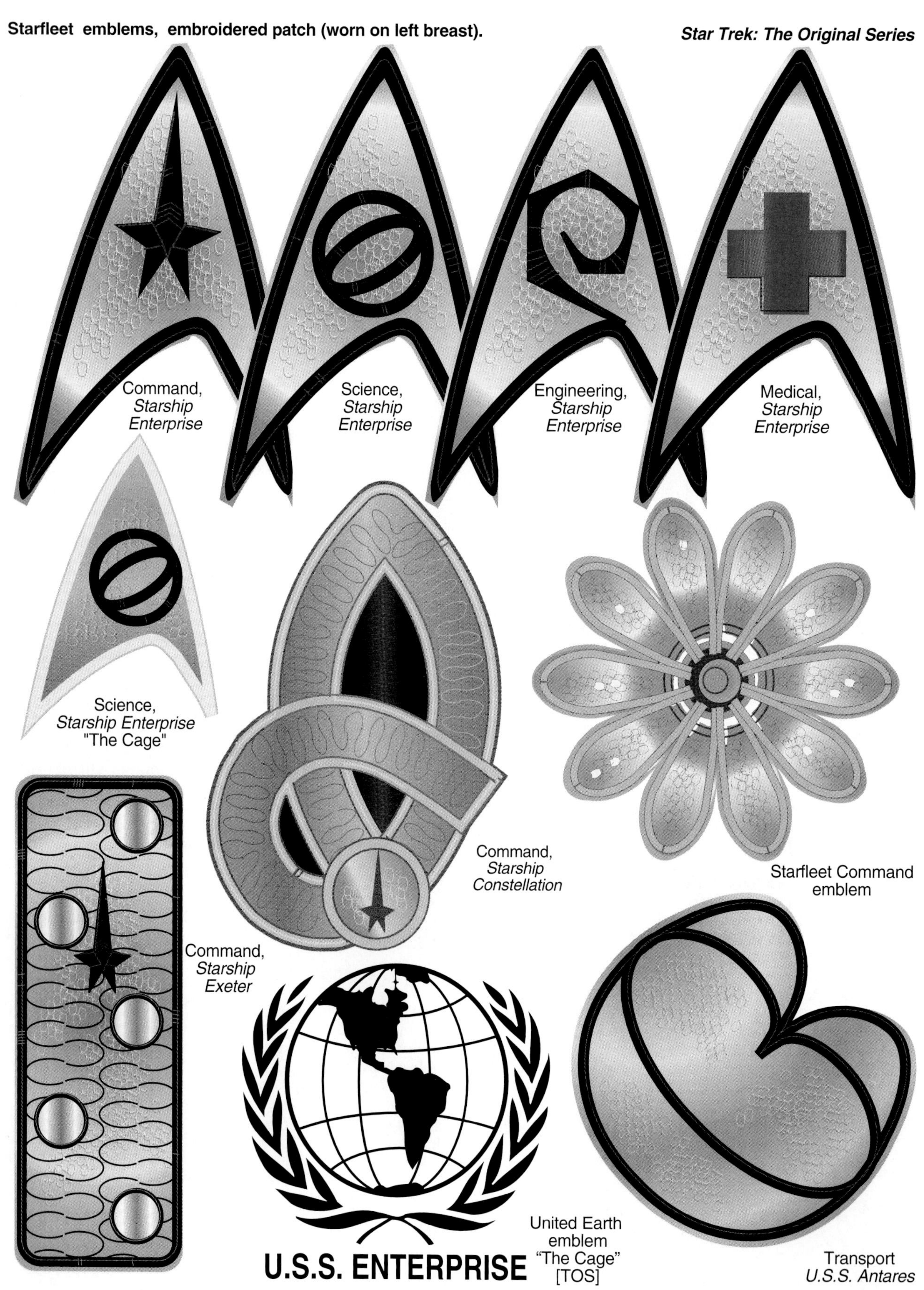

Command, *Starship Enterprise*

Science, *Starship Enterprise*

Engineering, *Starship Enterprise*

Medical, *Starship Enterprise*

Science, *Starship Enterprise* "The Cage"

Command, *Starship Constellation*

Starfleet Command emblem

Command, *Starship Exeter*

United Earth emblem "The Cage" [TOS]

Transport *U.S.S. Antares*

Starfleet officers sleeve stripe ranks

Star Trek: The Original Series

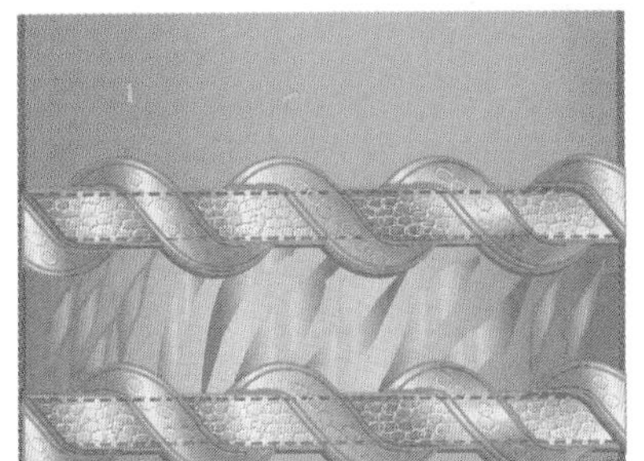

Commodore
Command division

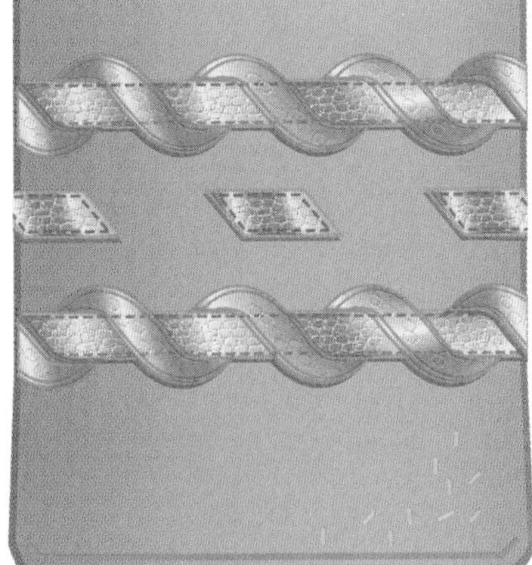

Captain
Command division

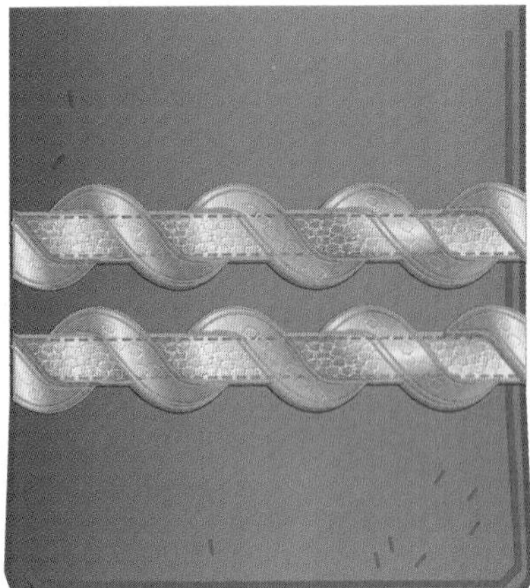

Commander
Science division

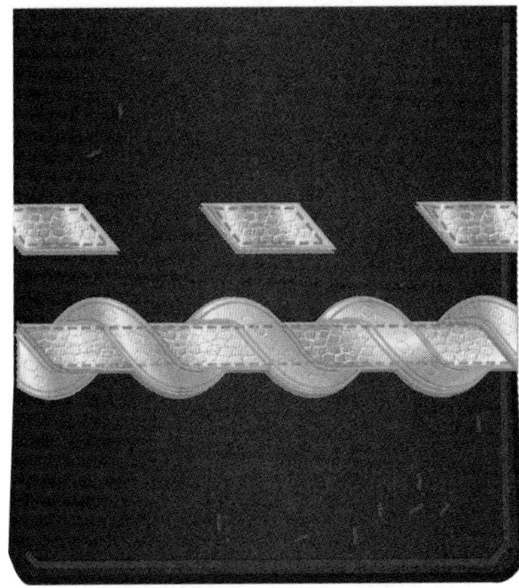

Lieutenant Commander
Engineering & Security division

Lieutenant
Command division

Ensign & Crewmember
Command division

Decoration and awards

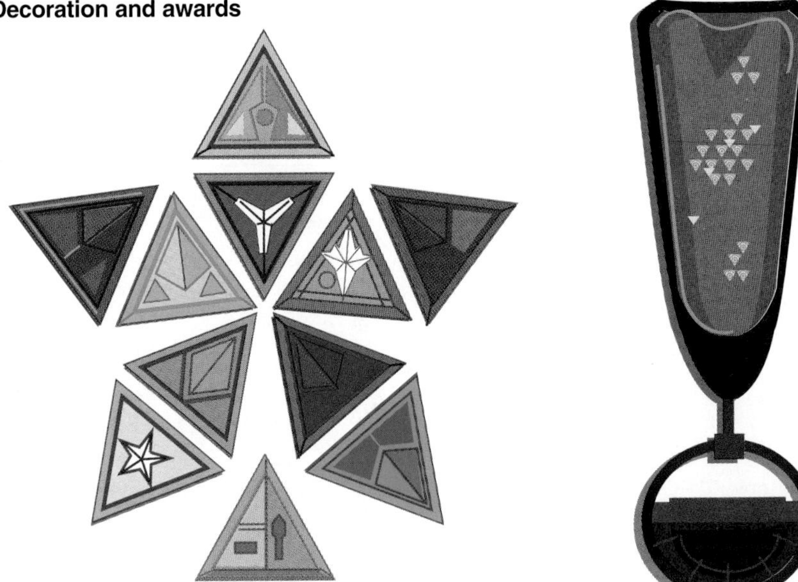

James T. Kirk's cluster with ribbon, 2267

Leonard McCoy's cluster, 2267

Starfleet insignia pin-on device (worn on left breast) ***Star Trek*** **feature films II-VII.**

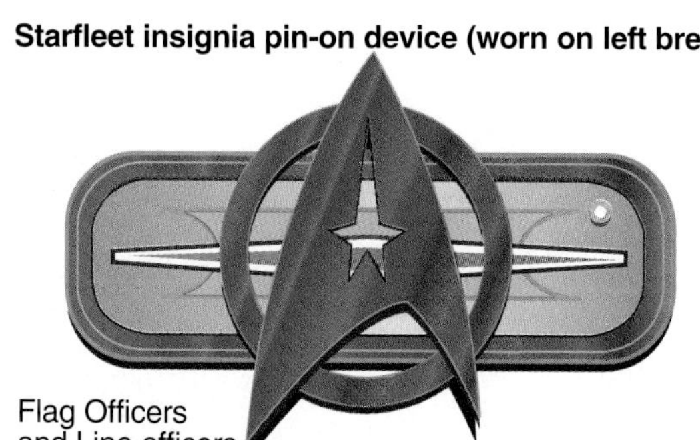

Flag Officers and Line officers

Enlisted crew

Starfleet security

Flag officers rank pin-on device **(worn on both the right shoulder and left sleeve)**

Fleet Admiral

Admiral

Vice Admiral

Rear Admiral

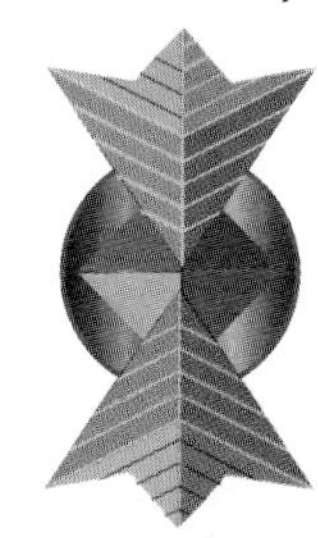

Commodore

Line officers rank pin-on device **(worn on both the right shoulder and left sleeve)**

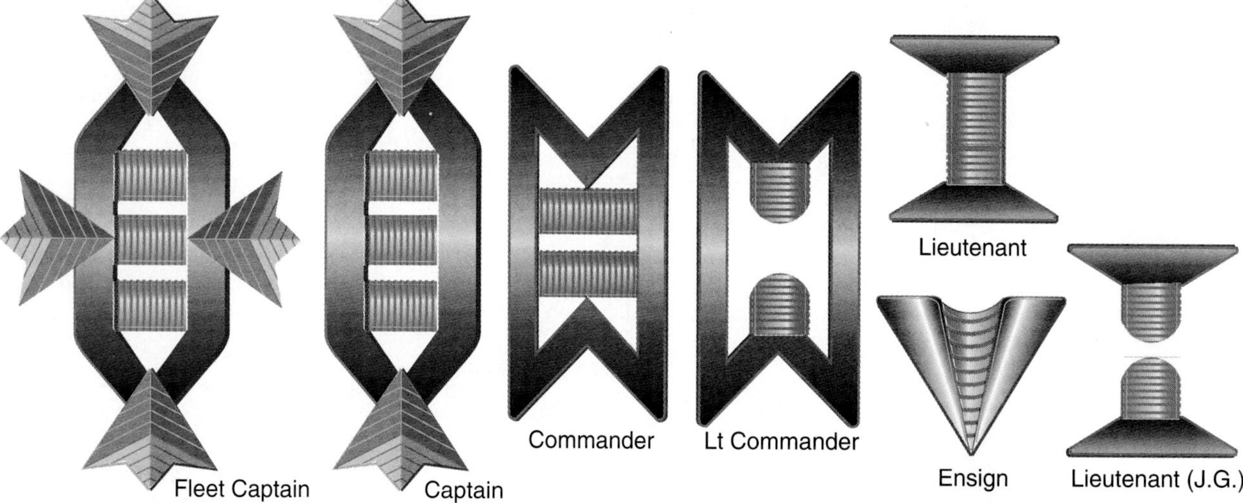

Fleet Captain
Captain
Commander
Lt Commander
Lieutenant
Ensign
Lieutenant (J.G.)

Enlisted crew rating pin-on device **(worn on both the right shoulder and left sleeve)**

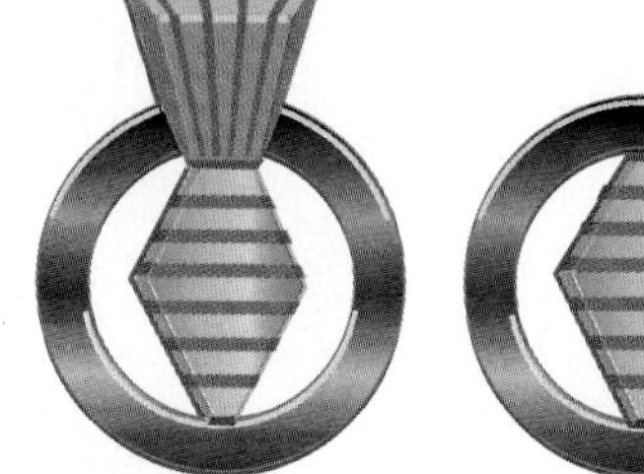

Master CPO

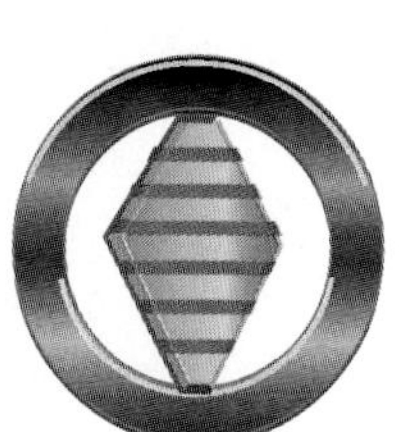

Master CPO 2nd Class

Senior CPO

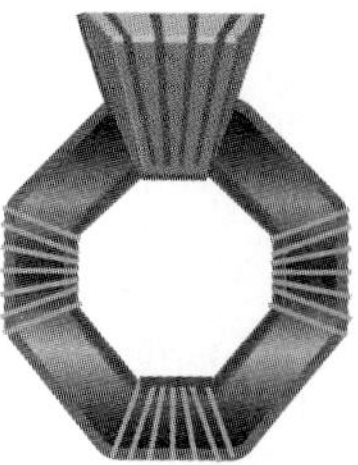

CPO

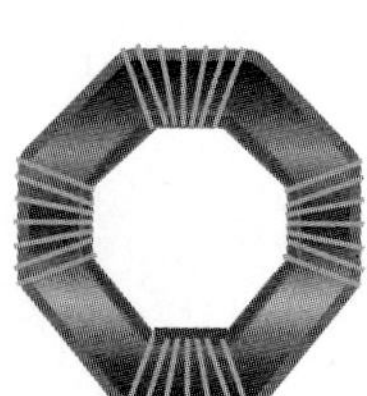

Petty Officer 1st Class

Ables'man

Departmental colors

Trainee
Security
Engineering
Command
Special Services
Medical
Science

Star Trek feature films II-VII, continued

Ribbons of decoration (representative selection)

Years of service/commendations pin-on devices (worn on left sleeve)

PENZAR

Enlisted crew name pin

Starfleet insignia pin-on devices (worn on left breast)

Star Trek: TNG, DS9, VGR

Communicator pin (TNG and early DS9)

Data's imaginary pin "Future Imperfect" (TNG)

Future communicator pin "All Good Things" (TNG)

Communicator pin (*STG*, *ST:FC*, DS9 and VGR)

Flag officers' rank pin-on devices (worn on right collar and left sleeve)

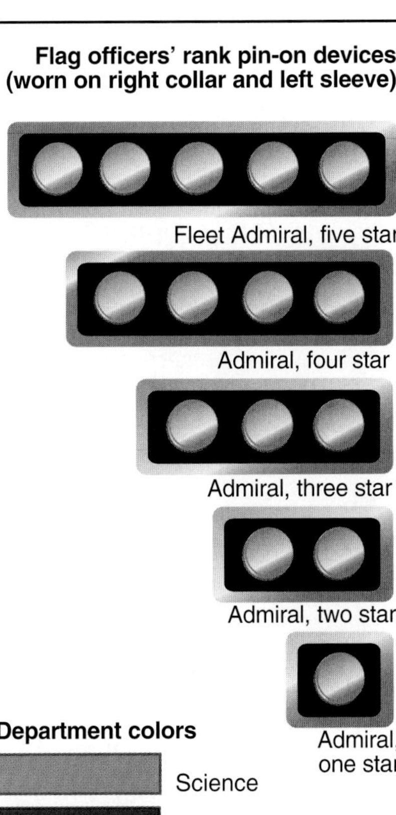

Department colors

Science

Command

Operations

Officers' rank pin-on devices (worn on right collar)

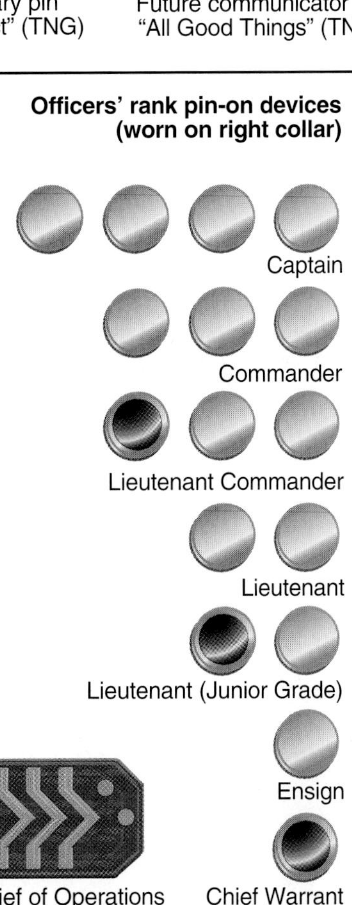

Chief of Operations (embroidered)

Provisional officers' rank pin-on devices (worn on right collar by Maquis members [VGR])

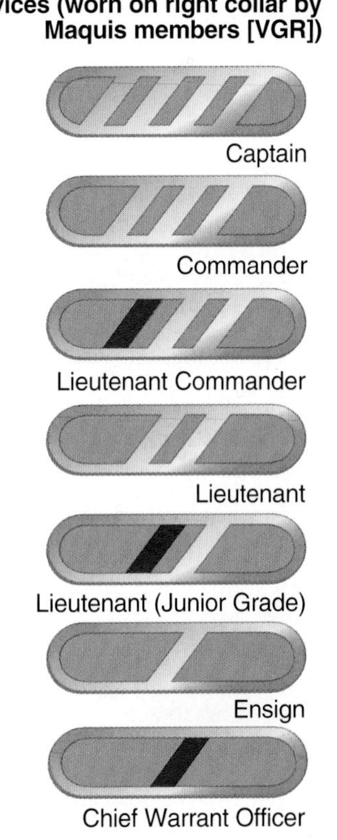

Enterprise-D, was coincidentally able to restore La Forge and Ro to normal space. ("The Next Phase" [TNG]). SEE: **anyon emitter; spatial interphase**.

interphasic coil spanner. Engineering tool. ("Hard Time" [DS9]).

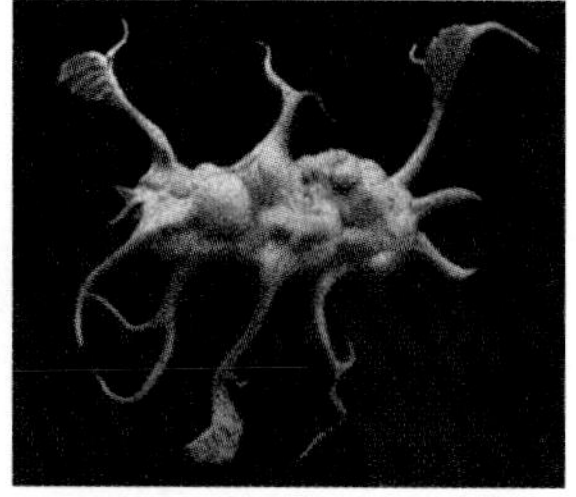

interphasic organisms. Nonsentient parasitic life-forms that attach themselves to the epidermal layers of their hosts with osmotic tendrils and extract **cellular peptides**. Interphasic organisms were brought on-board the *Enterprise*-D in 2370 following the installation of warp core components that were manufactured on planet **Thanatos VII.** They lay dormant until the core was activated. These entities were invisible to the naked eye and undetectable with **tricorders**. Their presence could be determined with the use of an **interphasic scanner**. Data's positronic brain subconsciously detected the interphasic pulse emitted by the organisms. The pulse caused his dream program to produce bizarre, but symbolic imagery. Data destroyed the interphasic organisms by subjecting them to a high-frequency interphasic pulse. ("Phantasms" [TNG]).

interphasic scanner. Small hand-held instrument that permits detection of anything of an interphasic nature. Dr. Beverly Crusher used one to see the **interphasic organisms** on her patients in 2370. She noted that tricorders were not able to detect interphasic phenomena. ("Phantasms" [TNG]).

interplexing beacon. Type of subspace transmitter. While in Earth's past in 2063, a group of **Borg** attempted to convert the *Enterprise*-E's **navigational deflector** dish into an interplexing beacon with which they planned to communicate with their collective in the Delta Quadrant. *(Star Trek: First Contact).*

interspace. SEE: **interphase generator**; **spatial interphase.**

intraship beaming. Method of transporting within the confines of a starship. This procedure required pinpoint accuracy, running the risk of materializing the transport subjects inside a wall or deck. Kirk and Klingon science officer **Mara** risked intraship beaming to carry an offer of peace to **Kang** when the *Enterprise* was held captive by the **Beta XII-A entity** in 2268. ("Day of the Dove" [TOS]). *The technique was perfected by the time of* Star Trek: The Next Generation*, when it became known as* ***site-to-site transport****.*

intraspinal inhibitor. Drug. Intraspinal inhibitor induces paralysis. ("Darkling" [VGR]).

intravascular pressure. Measurable pressure of the blood against the walls of the vessels in a humanoid body. Intravascular pressure is sometimes elevated in **Urodelean flu**. ("Genesis" [TNG]). *In the old (pre-tech) days, this was called "blood pressure."*

Intrepid*, *U.S.S. Federation starship, *Constitution* class, Starfleet registry number NCC-1631. The *Intrepid* was under repair in maintenance section 18 at **Starbase 11** when the *Enterprise* arrived after being damaged in an **ion storm** in 2267. The *Enterprise* was given priority for repair over the *Intrepid* by **Commodore Stone**. ("Court Martial" [TOS]). The *Starship Intrepid* was later destroyed by a massive spaceborne **amoeba** creature near the **Gamma 7A System** in 2268. The crew of the *Intrepid*, entirely composed of personnel from the planet Vulcan, was lost in the incident. ("The Immunity Syndrome" [TOS]).

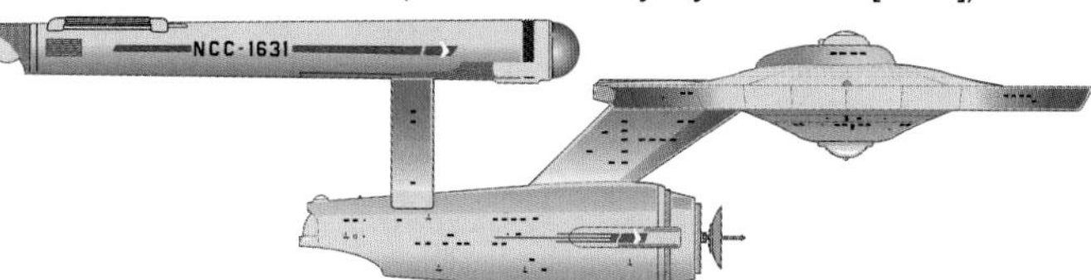

Intrepid*, *U.S.S. Federation starship, ***Excelsior* class**, Starfleet registry number NCC-38907. The *Intrepid* was the first ship to respond to the Klingon distress calls when the **Khitomer** outpost was under attack by the Romulans in 2346. ("Sins of the Father" [TNG]). Chief Petty Officer **Sergey Rozhenko** was a warp-field specialist on the *Intrepid*. Following the Khitomer rescue, Rozhenko adopted a small Klingon child named Worf, who had been found among the wreckage at Khitomer. ("Family" [TNG]). In 2370, **Commander Donald Kaplan** was the chief engineer of the *Intrepid*. ("Force of Nature" [TNG]) *This was presumably at least the second starship to bear the name* Intrepid*, since an earlier* Intrepid *was destroyed in "The Immunity Syndrome" (TOS). There was presumably yet another* U.S.S. Intrepid *that served as the prototype for the* Intrepid*-class* U.S.S. Voyager.

Intrepid*-class starship.** Type of Federation spacecraft. *Intrepid*-class starships were 15 decks thick, and had a crew complement of about 140 and a sustainable cruising velocity of about warp factor 9.975. The prototype ship, the *U.S.S. Intrepid*, was the third starship to bear the name *Intrepid*. The ***U.S.S. Voyager was an *Intrepid*-class vessel. ("Caretaker" [VGR]).

intron virus. SEE: **Barclay's Protomorphosis Syndrome.**

intron. Portions of an individual's genetic code that are normally dormant. Introns are evolutionary holdovers that contain behavioral and physical characteristics from evolutionary predecessors. In 2370, **Barclay's Protomorphosis Syndrome** caused the reactivation of certain introns in members of the *Enterprise*-D crew, resulting in their reversion to earlier evolutionary forms. ("Genesis" [TNG]).

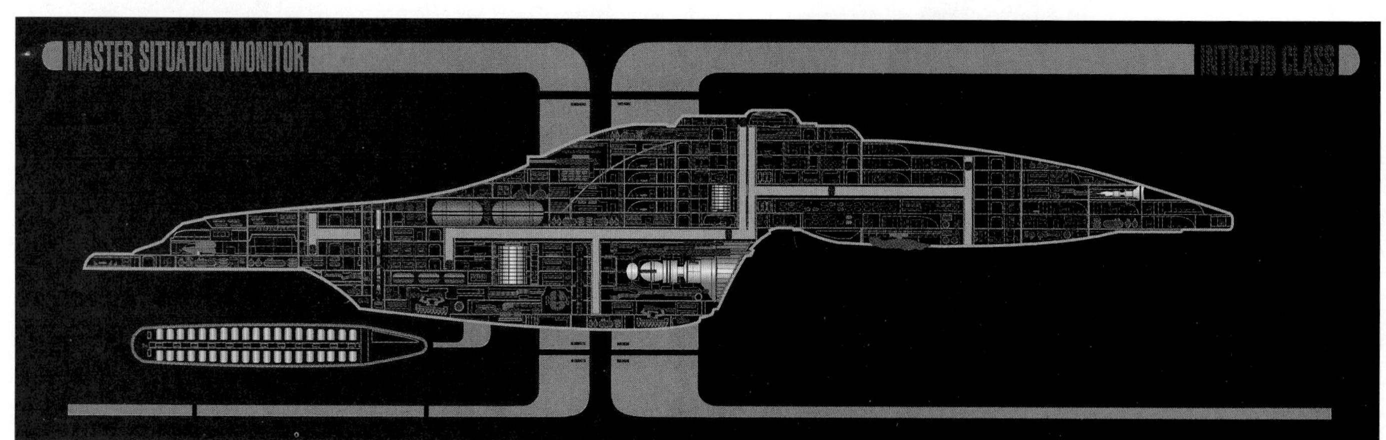

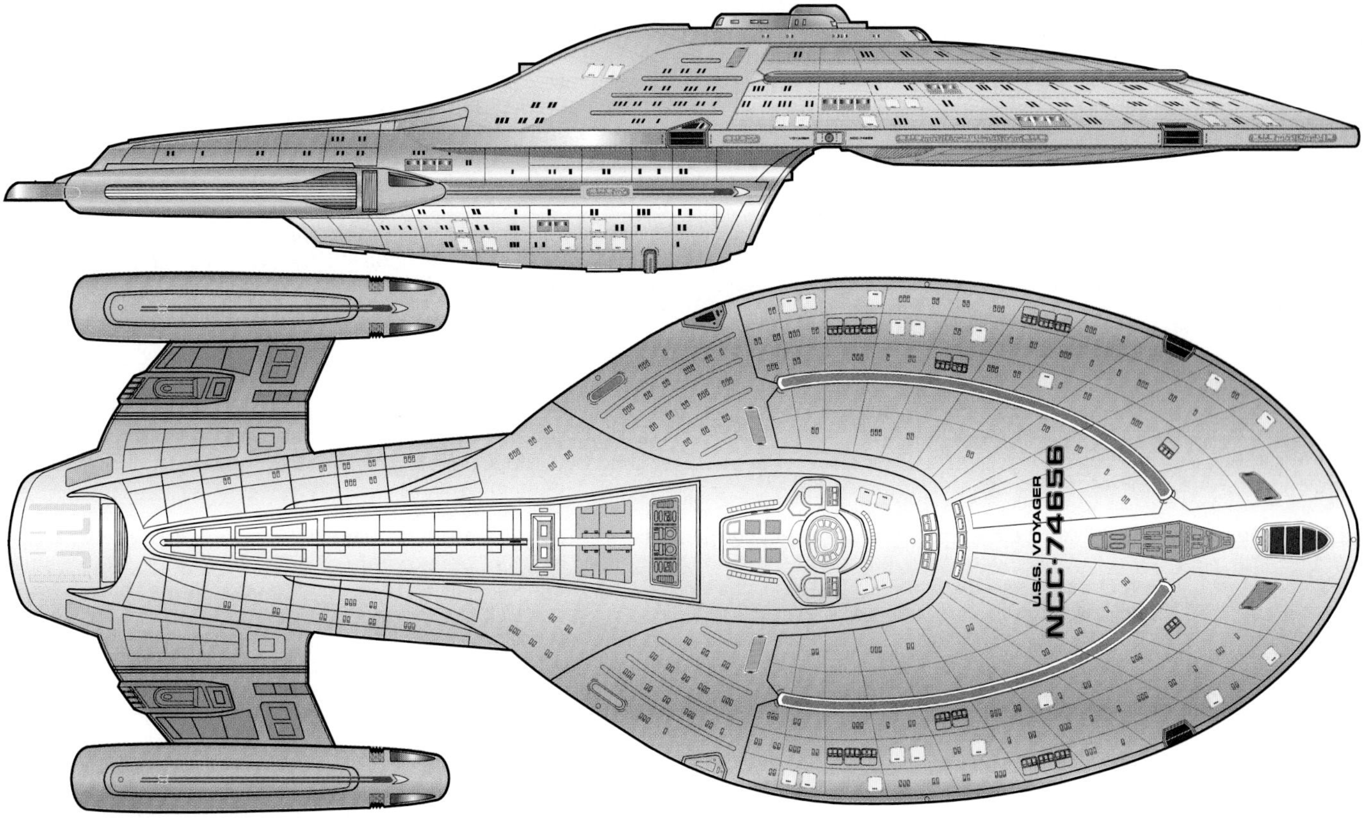

"Invasive Procedures." *Deep Space Nine* episode #24. Teleplay by John Whelpley and Robert Hewitt Wolfe. Story by John Whelpley. Directed by Les Landau. Stardate 47182.1. *First aired in 1993. While the station is evacuated during a plasma storm, a small group of outlaws takes control, demanding Jadzia Dax's symbiont.* GUEST CAST: John Glover as **Verad**; Megan Gallagher as **Mareel**; Tim Russ as **T'Kar**; Steve Rankin as **Yeto**. SEE: **Cliffs of Bole; combadge; Dax, Curzon; Dax, Jadzia; Dax, Tobin; delta wave inducer; *Ekina*; Khefka IV; liquid data chains; *Livingston, U.S.S.*; Mareel; neuroelectrical suppresser; O'Brien, Miles; *Orinoco, U.S.S.;* Pelios Station; plasma disruption; plasma storm; Senarian egg broth; Sisko, Benjamin; Symbiosis Evaluation board; symbiont; *t'gla*; T'Kar; Trill; Trill homeworld; Verad; Yeto.**

invasive program. Computer software weapon designed by *Starship Enterprise*-D personnel in 2368 for the purpose of destroying the **Borg collective** consciousness. The program was a paradoxical geometric construct which, when introduced into the Borg system, was expected to form a recursively insoluble puzzle. It was intended to implant the program into the Borg individual known as **Hugh**, just prior to his planned return to the Borg collective. Once returned, the invasive program was expected to cause a fatal overload in the entire Borg system, effectively destroying their civilization and all its members. Captain Jean-Luc Picard refused to use the program, believing that use of such a weapon of mass destruction would constitute an act of genocide. ("I, Borg" [TNG]).

Invernia II. Second planet in the Invernia system. **Julian Bashir**'s father was once stationed as a diplomat on Ivernia II. ("Melora" [DS9]).

inverse tachyon beam. Energy stream that can be used in certain unorthodox sensor applications to study temporal phenomena. (In the **anti-time future** created by the **Q Continuum**, Data of the year 2395 devised a scanning technique to use an inverse tachyon beam to explore the interior of the **temporal anomaly** located in the **Devron system**. The technique utilized the main deflector dish modified to emit the scanning pulse. It allowed probing beyond the subspace barrier. Captain Picard, as he shifted between time periods, had the *Enterprise*-D's of 2364 and 2370 utilize this technique as well. But a paradox ensued; the crews discovered that the use of the inverse tachyon beam to scan the anomaly had in fact caused the anomaly.) ("All Good Things..." [TNG].) *Fans have correctly pointed out that the original beam came from the* Pasteur, *and not the* Enterprise-*D as alluded to in the dialog, but we feel confident that this is further evidence of Q's mischievous tampering.*

inversion nebula. Interstellar gas cloud populated by highly unstable strands of plasma. Inversion nebulae can be incredibly beautiful, but are so unstable that they normally burn out in a few years. There are no inversion nebulae known to exist in the Alpha Quadrant. An inversion nebula discovered by the *Starship Voyager* in the Delta Quadrant in 2373 was centuries old, thanks to a caretaker named **Marayna**, who preserved her nebula as a work of art for her people. ("Alter Ego" [VGR]).

inverter. A device used by the **Ansata** terrorists of planet **Rutia IV** for folded-space transport. Using the inverter, the Ansata were able to transport interdimensionally, without being detected by Rutian sensors. The device, used by the Ansata in 2366, brought new life to the Ansata cause, despite the fact that repeated use of the inverter caused cumulative (and eventually fatal) damage to the user's DNA. Because the use of the device caused subspace pressure modulations, Commanders Data and La Forge and Ensign Wesley Crusher were able to locate the power source of the device with adaptive subspace echograms. ("The High Ground" [TNG]). SEE: **Elway Theorem**.

"Investigations." *Voyager* episode #35. Teleplay by Jeri Taylor. Story by Jeff Schnaufer & Ed Bond. Directed by Les Landau. Stardate 49485.2. *First aired in 1996. To flush out a spy aboard* Voyager, *Tom Paris is put off the ship to act as bait for the Kazon. Prince Abdullah of Jordan made a brief nonspeaking cameo as a* Voyager *crew member in this episode.* GUEST CAST: Raphael Sbarge as **Jonas**; Martha Hackett as **Seska**; Jerry Sroka as **Laxeth**; Simon Billig as **Hogan**; Majel Barrett as Computer voice. SEE: **Baytart, Pablo; *Briefing With Neelix, A;* Eskarian egg; Hamilton; Hemikek; *Hints for Healthful Living*; *Hlaka* soup; Hogan; impedrezine; Jonas, Michael; Kim, Harry; Kotati;**

Laxeth; magnetic constrictors; Mithren; monocrystal cortenum; Neelix; Paris, Thomas; Pendrashian cheese; polysilicate verterium; security access codes; Silmic wine; verterium cortenide; Zabee nuts.

invidium. A substance formerly used in medical containment-field generation. Invidium fell out of general use in the 23rd century, although a few civilizations continued its application into the 24th century. Invidium had the unusual property of being undetectable by normal internal sensor scans aboard starships. It was also highly reactive, capable of triggering spontaneous **nucleosynthesis** as well as malfunctions in various high-power systems. Invidium used in a medical shipment from the **Mikulaks** accidentally leaked out of a broken storage canister, causing a variety of serious malfunctions aboard the *Enterprise*-D in 2366. The invidium was rendered inert by flooding contaminated areas with gaseous **cryonetrium**. ("Hollow Pursuits" [TNG]).

invisibility screen. SEE: **cloaking device, Romulan**.

ion propulsion. Highly efficient spacecraft propulsion system that uses magnetic fields to drive electrically charged gases. The ship from planet **Sigma Draconis VI** that invaded the *Enterprise* and stole Spock's brain in 2268 used ion propulsion. The propulsion system left a faint but distinctive ion trail of residual gas that permitted the ship to be tracked. ("Spock's Brain" [TOS]). **Jem'Hadar** warships use ion thrusters for secondary propulsion. ("The Ship" [DS9]).

ion storm. A disruptive space phenomenon characterized by intense bombardment of charged particles. The *U.S.S. Enterprise* weathered a severe ion storm in 2267, during which **Ben Finney** was apparently killed when his sensor pod was ejected prematurely. Finney was in fact unhurt, but had altered computer records to make it appear that Captain Kirk had caused his death. ("Court Martial" [TOS]). A dangerous ion storm near the **Halkan** planet later in 2267 resulted in a severe transporter malfunction, causing members of the *Enterprise* landing party to be transposed with their counterparts from a **mirror universe**. ("Mirror, Mirror" [TOS]).

ion surfing. An exciting sport. Jake Sisko and Nog experienced an ion surfing program in a holosuite in Quark's bar on DS9. ("The Visitor" [DS9]).

ionizer, transporter. A critical component in a transporter system. The transporter ionizer aboard the *Starship Enterprise* was damaged during the malfunction that accidentally created a partial duplicate of Captain James Kirk in 2266. ("The Enemy Within" [TOS]).

ionizing radiation. Any radiation powerful enough to cause certain atoms to become electrically charged. Large amounts of ionizing radiation were present in the Devolin system, which made locating the hulk of the ***U.S.S Pegasus*** difficult. The *Enterprise*-D used the natural radiation to its advantage after locating the *Pegasus*. Fearing that a nearby Romulan ship would also locate the ship, the crew of the *Enterprise*-D blanketed the asteroid containing the *Pegasus* with more ionizing radiation, thereby obscuring the *Pegasus* from the Romulan ship's sensors. ("The *Pegasus*" [TNG]).

ionogenic particles. Energy type based on electrically-charged atoms. *Enterprise*-D personnel used ionogenic particles in an attempt to contain the anionic energy that composed the noncorporeal criminal life-forms from the **Ux-Mal** star system that attempted to commandeer the ship in 2368. Commander La Forge speculated that by flooding the Ten-Forward Lounge with the particles, they could contain the entities that were possessing their crew mates. ("Power Play" [TNG]).

Iotians. Humanoid inhabitants of planet **Sigma Iotia II**. When the planet was visited by the ***U.S.S. Horizon*** in 2168, the crew left behind a copy of a book entitled ***Chicago Mobs of the Twenties***. (The contact took place before Starfleet's **Prime Directive** of noninterference was established.) The highly imitative Iotians proceeded to use this book as the blueprint for their society, and by 2268, when a second contact was made by the *Starship Enterprise*, Iotian society had become splintered into territories ruled by mob bosses. In an effort to help the contaminated society, Captain Kirk assumed the mannerisms of the culture, and set up a syndicate between the various territorial leaders, who agreed that the Federation would return each year to collect a "cut" of the profits. The money would then be used to steer the planetary government into a more ethical form. ("A Piece of the Action" [TOS]). SEE: **Oxmyx, Bela**.

ipasaphor*.** A sticky yellow substance secreted by the palms of the hands of **Ocampa** females undergoing ***elogium. The *ipasaphor* makes possible the six-day mating bond during which fertilization occurs. Once the *ipasaphor* appears, the process of mating must begin within 52 hours or conception will not be successful. ("Elogium" [VGR]).

Ireland. One of the British islands on planet Earth. Ireland was reunified in 2025, an example of political change successfully instigated by violence. ("The High Ground" [TNG]).

Iresine Syndrome. A very rare neurological disorder in humanoids characterized by a peculiar electropathic signature in the thalamus, and a severely decreased histamine count. Victims of the disorder, first identified in the 23rd century, would fall suddenly into a coma for approximately 72 hours. Diagnosis could be confused by the presense of any of 22 different substances that left electropathic residue resembling that of this disorder. Iresine Syndrome was suspected of inducing comas that befell three members of the *Enterprise*-D crew in 2368, but was later ruled out when it was learned they were victims of **telepathic memory invasion** rape. ("Violations" [TNG]).

irillium. Trace element found on planetoid **Holberg 917G**. When found in mineral **ryetalyn**, irillium renders the ryetalyn useless for medicinal purposes. ("Requiem for Methuselah" [TOS]).

Irumodic Syndrome. Degenerative disorder that causes progressive deterioration of the synaptic pathways. The disease can cause senility and eventually death. Treatment of choice for the disorder was peridaxon, though this was simply palliative; no cure existed. (In the **anti-time future** created by the **Q Continuum**, Picard suffered from this disorder.) ("All Good Things..." [TNG]). *It seems likely that the "real" Picard may also have the possibility of contracting Irumodic Syndrome.*

"Is There in Truth No Beauty?" Original Series episode #62. Written by Jean Lisette Aroeste. Directed by Ralph Senensky. Stardate 5630.7. *First aired in 1968. A beautiful woman escorts an alien ambassador so hideously ugly that the sight of him can drive a human mad.* GUEST CAST: Diana Muldaur as **Jones, Dr. Miranda**; David Frankham as **Marvick, Laurence**; Robert Balver as Yeoman; Dick Greay, Vince Deadrick, Bill Blackburn, Security guards; Ralph Garrett as Marvick's stunt double; Alan Gibbs as Stunt double. SEE: **Antarean brandy; antigrav; barrier, galactic; IDIC; Jones, Dr. Miranda; Kollos; Marvick, Dr. Laurence; Medusans; mind-link; noncorporeal life; sensor web; Uhura.**

Isabella. (Shay Astar). The "invisible friend" of young **Clara Sutter**, a child living aboard the *Enterprise*-D in 2368. At first, Isabella was purely the product of Clara's imagination, but a plasma-based life-form living in nebula **FGC-47** materialized in the form of Isabella while attempting to investigate the starship. Isabella was trying to determine whether the *Enterprise*-D posed a threat to her species, and whether the ship's deflector shields would serve as a suitable energy source. Isabella's investigation was hampered because, having assumed the form of a child, she had difficulty communicating with ship's personnel. ("Imaginary Friend" [TNG]). SEE: **noncorporeal life**.

Isak. (Richard Evans). **Zeon** member of the underground on planet **Ekos.** In 2268, Isak was held captive by that planet's Nazi-style regime, along with Kirk and Spock. Isak and his brother, Abrom, aided Kirk and Spock's efforts to locate the Federation cultural advisor, **John Gill**. ("Patterns of Force" [TOS]).

Ishan Chaye. Bajoran national. Ishan, who was born in 2329, came from Rakantha Province on Bajor and was an electronics engineer. In 2367, Ishan Chaye, along with Jillur Gueta and Timor Landi, was wrongly accused of attempting to assassinate Gul Dukat on station Terok Nor. The three were executed after a cursory investigation by Odo, Terok Nor's chief of security. ("Things Past" [DS9]).

Ishan. (Bruce Bohn). A member of the **Sakari**, a people discovered by the crew of the *Starship Voyager* on stardate 50537 on a planet in the Delta Quadrant. *His name, not mentioned, is from the script*. ("Blood Fever" [VGR]).

Ishikawa, Hiro. Father to Starfleet botanist **Keiko O'Brien**. Keiko considered naming her first child after Hiro, although her husband, Miles, wanted to name the child after his father, **Michael O'Brien**. ("Disaster" [TNG]). *Little Hiro, or Michael (depending on who you asked), ended up being little Molly.*

Ishikawa, Keiko. Starfleet botanist. Birth name of the future Mrs. **Keiko O'Brien**. ("Data's Day" [TNG]).

Ishka. (Andrea Martin). Mother of **Quark** and **Rom**, widow of **Keldar**, daughter of Adred. Ishka was a headstrong, enterprising **Ferengi** female, and broke with Ferengi tradition in several ways. She never liked to chew food for her sons, she talked to strangers, and she even wore clothes and earned profit. The **Ferengi Commerce Authority** discovered her business activities in 2371, and tried unsuccessfully to halt them ("Family Business" [DS9]). *Emmy Award winner Andrea Martin is well-known for her comedy work on the various "Second City" television series.* SEE: **Moogie**.

isik. Monetary unit. Used by **Alsia** and **Martus Mazur** in their business dealings. ("Rivals" [DS9]).

Isis. (Voice by Barbara Babcock). Lifeform of unknown extra-terrestrial origin. Isis took the form of a black Earth cat, and accompanied Gary Seven to planet Earth in 1968. Isis could also transform herself into a humanoid woman. ("Assignment: Earth" [TOS]). *Isis was apparently intended as a continuing character in the proposed series* Assignment: Earth. SEE: ***Mea 3***.

isoboramine. In **Trill** physiology, a vital neurotransmitter chemical that mediates the synaptic functions between the Trill humanoid host and the **symbiont**. Should isoboramine levels fall below 40 percent of normal, the symbiont is removed to protect it, even though this results in the death of the humanoid host. ("Equilibrium" [DS9]).

isocortex. The extreme outer layer of the cerebral cortex in a humanoid brain. Captain Picard suffered synaptic failure in his isocortex during his exposure to the **Kataan probe** in 2368. ("The Inner Light" [TNG]).

isogenic enzyme. Biochemical substance crucial to **Jem'Hadar** physiology. The **Founders** genetically altered the Jem'Hadar's bodies so that they lacked the ability to produce isogenic enzymes, without which the Jem'Hadar circulatory system would fail. The Jem'Hadar were totally dependent on the **Vorta**, who acted as agents for the Founders, for supplies of the chemical, which they provided in the form of **ketracel-white**, an addictive drug (also known simply as "**white**") and the Vorta used this to control the dangerously warlike Jem'Hadar. ("The Abandoned" [DS9], "Hippocratic Oath" [DS9]).

isograted circuit. Computer chip technology that permitted manufacture of numerous electronic circuit components as a single unit. The isograted circuit was a key development in the dawn of Earth's computer age in the 20th century. **Henry Starling** of **Chronowerx** corporation introduced the first isograted circuit on Earth in 1969. It was not realized that this revolution in microcomputer technology was derived from 29th-century technology that Starling had found in 1967 on the Federation *Timeship* ***Aeon***. ("Future's End, Part I" [VGR]).

isolation protocol. A series of emergency procedures employed aboard Federation starships in the event of a hull breach in part of the ship. Isolation protocol procedures include computer-controlled closure of emergency bulkheads in the turboshafts to prevent uncontrolled atmospheric loss. Isolation protocol was invoked on stardate 45156, when the *Enterprise*-D was damaged by contact with **quantum filaments.** ("Disaster" [TNG]).

isolinear coprocessor. Computing device employing isolinear elements, such as those used aboard **Deep Space 9**. Technician **Neela** planted a subspace device integrated into an isolinear coprocessor in Security. This disabled the weapon detectors on the Promenade. With the weapon detectors off-line, the phaser Neela carried to assassinate Vedek Bareil did not register. ("In the Hands of the Prophets" [DS9]). SEE: **isolinear rods.**

isolinear optical chip. Sophisticated information storage and processing device used aboard 24th-century starships. Composed of **linear memory crystal** material, the isolinear chip came into general use around 2349, and was used for both information storage and data processing. Within larger computing devices, isolinear chips are often housed in wall-mounted racks, permitting computer access to dozens, even hundreds of chips at one time. ("The Naked Now" [TNG]). Isolinear chips replaced older, less efficient **duotronic enhancers** aboard Federation starships around the year 2329. ("Relics" [TNG]). While under Romulan control in 2367, Geordi La Forge altered several isolinear chips to permit unauthorized use of the cargo transporter to beam weapons to planet **Krios**. He programmed the chips to delete all operator commands once the transport was complete, effectively erasing any record of the use of the transporter. ("The Mind's Eye" [TNG]).

isolinear rod. Data storage and processing device used in **Cardassian** computer sytems. Similar in principle to the **isolinear optical chips** used aboard Federation starships, these translucent orange-colored modules were used in **ops** and throughout **Deep Space 9**'s computer network. ("The Forsaken" [DS9]). **Quark** had a number of unauthorized isolinear rods that contained security programs. He used them when he wanted access to restricted information from the station's computer system. ("Past Prologue" [DS9]). Some isolinear rods have color-coded labels. Those with white labels contain data relating to engineering systems controls. Red-labeled ones are for library and information storage. ("Shadowplay" [DS9]).

isomiotic hypo. Medical instrument. An isomiotic hypo can be combined with other components to create a **biogenic weapon**. ("Preemptive Strike" [TNG]).

isonucleic residue. Particles found in warp plasma. Plasma with isonucleic residue of 20 parts per million is considered to be contaminated. ("Fair Trade" [VGR]).

isoton. Unit of mass measurement used by the Federation. ("The Ship" [DS9]).

isotropic restraint. Medical force field used to hold a patient totally immobile. An isotropic restraint field was used to immobilize **Neelix** on stardate 48532 so that holographic lungs could be projected into his body. ("Phage" [VGR]).

Itamish III. Third planet in the Itamish system. The Sisko family once enjoyed a camping vacation there. Jennifer taught Jake to water ski on Itamish III. ("The Jem'Hadar" [DS9]).

Iverson's disease. A chronic disease that causes fatal degeneration of muscular functions in humans. Iverson's disease does not, however, impair mental functions. There is no known cure for the condition. **Admiral Mark Jameson** suffered from Iverson's disease, although he eventually died from other causes. ("Too Short a Season" [TNG]).

Ivor Prime. Planet. Ivor Prime was the site of a Federation colony that was destroyed by the **Borg** in 2373. *(Star Trek: First Contact).*

Iyaaran homeworld. Planet of origin for the **Iyaaran** people, a world known for its spectacular crystal formations. Captain Jean-Luc Picard was scheduled to visit the Iyaaran homeworld in 2370 as part of a cultural exchange program. ("Liasions" [TNG]).

Iyaaran shuttle. Spacecraft of Iyaaran registry. An Iyaaran shuttle, piloted by **Voval**, was to take Captain Jean-Luc Picard to the Iyaaran homeworld for a diplomatic visit in 2370. Following a system-wide power failure, the shuttle crashed, marooning the captain. ("Liaisons" [TNG]). *This ship was another re-dress of the* Nenebek *from "Final Mission" (TNG).*

Iyaarans. Humanoid civilization. The Iyarrans conducted their first cultural exchange with the Federation in 2370. Iyaarans reproduce by postcellular compounding, and emerge full-grown from **natal pods**. Iyaarans do not share certain concepts, such as pleasure, antagonism, and love. They regard the consumption of food as being for sustenance only, and their diet is bland in the extreme by the standards of many other humanoids. During their cultural exchange in 2370, they explored these concepts by assigning an ambassador to each. While Ambassadors **Loquel** and **Byleth** succeeded in their studies of pleasure and antagonism, Ambassador **Voval** felt he failed to understand the nature of love. ("Liaisons" [TNG]).

J'Dan. (Henry Woronicz). Exobiologist who was assigned to the *Enterprise*-D in 2367 as part of the continuing Federation/ Klingon **Officer Exchange Program**. While on the ship, J'Dan, a Klingon national, was discovered to have been part of a plan to steal restricted computer files and smuggle them to the Romulans. These files were transferred into amino acid–like molecules and injected into J'Dan's bloodstream, enabling them to be smuggled into Romulan hands. Technical designs of the *Enterprise*-D **dilithium crystal articulation frame**, taken by J'Dan on stardate 44758, were found to be in Romulan possession shortly thereafter. When confronted with evidence of his actions, J'Dan confessed to being a Romulan collaborator. ("The Drumhead" [TNG]). SEE: **deoxyribose suspensions**.

J'naii. Technologically advanced humanoid civilization. The J'naii culturally suppressed their sexual differentiation, having evolved beyond the need for separate sexual genders, and reproduced by incubating their young in fibrous husks inseminated by both parents. Sexual liaisons were strictly forbidden under J'naii law. There were, however, some J'naii who retained the leanings toward gender, some male and some female. These J'naii lived in fear of being discovered and of being forced by the government to undergo **psychotectic** therapy. The J'naii government requested Starfleet assistance in locating a shuttle vehicle lost in their star system, in 2368. The *Enterprise*-D provided equipment and personnel for the successful rescue mission. During the rescue, a diplomatic incident was narrowly averted when a J'naii individual named **Soren** became romantically involved with Commander William Riker. ("The Outcast" [TNG]).

J'Onn. (Rex Holman). Humanoid settler on planet **Nimbus III**. J'Onn became a follower of the fanatic **Sybok** in 2287, joining Sybok on his quest for the mythical world ***Sha Ka Ree***. *(Star Trek V: The Final Frontier). Rex Holman also played Morgan Earp in "Spectre of the Gun" (TOS).*

ja'chuq. An ancient part of the Klingon **Rite of Succession**, in which a new leader is chosen for the **Klingon High Council**. Now considered obsolete, the *ja'chuq* was a long, involved ceremony where candidates for council leadership would list the battles they had won and prizes they had taken, in order to prove their worthiness to lead the council. In 2367, Captain Picard, as **Arbiter of Succession**, revived the *ja'chuq* to delay the Rite of Succession following **K'mpec's** death. ("Reunion" [TNG]).

Ja'Dar, Dr. (Richard McGonagle). Scientist from planet **Bilana III**, Dr. Ja'Dar was the designer of a revolutionary **soliton wave** propulsion system, tested for the first time in 2368. ("New Ground" [TNG]).

Ja'rod. Member of the politically powerful Klingon House of **Duras**. Ja'rod was the man who betrayed his people to the Romulans at the **Khitomer** outpost in 2346. Ja'rod transmitted secret Klingon defense access codes to the Romulans, making him responsible for the **Khitomer massacre** in which 4,000 Klingons died, including Ja'rod. Years later, Ja'rod's son, High Council member Duras, attempted to cover up Ja'rod's crimes by falsifying evidence to implicate **Mogh**, Ja'rod's bitter political enemy, who was also killed at Khitomer. ("Sins of the Father" [TNG]).

Jabara. (Ann Gillespie). Health-care professional. Jabara was a nurse on duty at the infirmary on Deep Space 9 when the station was struck by the **aphasia virus** on stardate 46423. ("Babel" [DS9]). She assisted Dr. Bashir during the heroic but ultimately tragic treatment of **Vedek Bareil** in 2371. ("Life Support" [DS9]).

Jabin. (Gavin O'Herlihy). **Kazon** leader. Jabin, who held the title of **maje**, led a Kazon-Ogla settlement on the **Ocampa** planet. Jabin's people searched for water and cormaline on the surface of the Ocampa planet. Maje Jabin also commanded a small **Kazon spacecraft**. ("Caretaker" [VGR]).

Jack the Ripper. Nickname given to mass murderer of women in 19th-century London, England, on planet Earth. Centuries later, Jack the Ripper was found to be an evil energy life-form that thrived on the emotion of terror. ("Wolf in the Fold" [TOS]). SEE: **Redjac**.

jacked. Early 21st-century **Earth** slang. "Jacked" meant being accosted and robbed. ("Past Tense, Part I" [DS9]).

Jackson. (Jimmy Jones). Crew member on the original *Starship Enterprise.* Jackson was killed on stardate 3018 while on a landing party to planet **Pyris VII**. The deceased Jackson, who materialized on the ship in a state of rigor mortis, spoke in a voice projected by **Korob**, warning the *Enterprise* to leave Pyris VII. ("Catspaw" [TOS]). *Jimmy Jones was a stunt performer who appeared in several other* Star Trek *episodes.*

Jackson. Former Maquis crew member aboard the *U.S.S. Voyager*. ("State of Flux" [VGR]).

Jadzia. SEE: **Dax, Jadzia**.

Jaeger, Lieutenant Karl. (Richard Carlyle). *Enterprise* geologist. Jaeger was part of the landing party to planet **Gothos** in 2267. ("The Squire of Gothos" [TOS]). SEE: **Trelane.**

JAG. SEE: **Judge Advocate General**.

Jaheel, Captain. (Jack Kehler). Commander of a transport vessel docked for repairs at Deep Space 9 on stardate 46423, when the station was struck by a deadly **aphasia virus**. Jaheel attempted to violate a quarantine by pulling away from the station with the mooring clamps still attached to his vessel. The attempt failed and he was returned. Jaheel was carrying a shipment of Tamen **Sahsheer** to planet **Largo V**. ("Babel" [DS9]).

Jahn. (Michael J. Pollard). One of the last survivors of the disastrous **Life Prolongation Project** on Miri's planet. Jahn was a friend to **Miri**. ("Miri" [TOS]).

Jakara, Rivas. (Jonathan Frakes). Identity created for Commander William Riker when he participated in a covert surveillance mission on planet **Malcor III** in 2367. Riker, as Jakara, was injured in a riot in the capital city and taken to the **Sikla Medical Facility** for treatment. While Jakara was hospitalized, his physician discovered he was an alien who had been surgically altered to pass as a Malcorian. ("First Contact" [TNG]).

jakmanite. A radioactive substance with a half-life of about 15 seconds, capable of causing **nucleosynthesis** in silicon. Jackmanite is not normally detectable by a starship's internal sensor scans. ("Hollow Pursuits" [TNG]).

Jal. Title of honor in the **Kazon-Ogla** sect. A Kazon warrior must earn the title Jal by a daring deed, usually conferring death upon an enemy. ("Initiations" [VGR]).

Jalad. SEE: **"Darmok and Jalad at Tanagra."**

Jalanda Forum. Center for the performing arts on planet **Bajor**. The Jalanda Forum was damaged during the Cardassian occupation. Noted musician **Varani** urged Kira Nerys to address the **Bajoran Chamber of Ministers** to advocate its reconstruction. ("Sanctuary" [DS9]). *Presumably located in Jalanda City.*

Jalanda. Large city on the planet Bajor. Kira Nerys's favorite restaurant was in Jalanda City. ("Return to Grace" [DS9]).

jamaharon. A mysterious Risan sexual rite. At the resort on **Risa**, one announced the desire for *jamaharon* by displaying a ***Horga'hn*** statuette. ("Captain's Holiday" [TNG]). **Curzon Dax** died in 2367 during what **Arandis**, his lover, termed death by *jamaharon*. ("Let He Who Is Without Sin..." [DS9]).

jambalaya. Aromatic stew comprised of either fowl or seafood and various vegetables and rice. Jake Sisko was fond of jambalaya ("The Jem'Hadar" [DS9]), as was Kasidy Yates. ("Rapture" [DS9]). Joseph Sisko felt that his daughter, Judith, like his wife, never put enough cayenne pepper in her jambalaya. ("Homefront" [DS9]).

Jameson, Admiral Mark. (Clayton Rohner). Celebrated Starfleet officer (2279-2364) whose career included command of the *Starship* ***Gettysburg***. Jameson was also credited with the freeing of Federation hostages on planet **Mordan IV** just prior to the outbreak of a civil war on that planet that lasted 40 years. Just prior to his death at age 85, Jameson accepted a second mission to the now-peaceful Mordan IV to secure the release of more Federation hostages. During the negotiations, it was learned that Jameson's previous mission had included an illegal weapons-for-hostages deal in direct violation of the **Prime Directive**. The act triggered—or at least exacerbated—the civil war. The second group of hostages had been seized by Mordan leader **Karnas** for the specific purpose of luring Jameson to the planet. Jameson died on Mordan IV of side-effects of a rejuvenation treatment obtained on planet **Cerebus II.** He had previously been diagnosed with terminal **Iverson's disease.** Jameson was survived by his wife, **Anne Jameson.** ("Too Short a Season" [TNG]).

Jameson, Anne. (Marsha Hunt). Wife to **Admiral Mark Jameson**. Anne and Mark were married from 2314 until the admiral's death in 2364. ("Too Short A Season" [TNG]).

Janaran Falls. Spectacular waterfall located on planet **Betazed**. It was the site of Lieutenant William Riker and Deanna Troi's last date before he departed for an assignment on the ***U.S.S. Potemkin***. ("Second Chances" [TNG]).

Janeway Lambda-1. Holonovel program. Gothic romance, set in late-18th-century England on Earth, in the tradition of Charlotte Brontë's *Jane Eyre*. *Voyager* Captain Kathryn Janeway enjoyed this drama as an escape from the pressures of starship command. In this program, Janeway played Mrs. **Lucille Davenport**, an English governess caring for the children of **Lord Burleigh**, a moody, sardonic nobleman who had been recently widowed. Burleigh's children, **Henry Burleigh** and **Beatrice Burleigh**, had not come to terms with the death of their mother, and were slow to accept Mrs. Davenport as their governess. Davenport was often at odds with **Mrs. Templeton**, Burleigh's housekeeper. An element of mystery was injected into the story when Lord Burleigh forbade Mrs. Davenport from ever entering the fourth floor of his mansion. ("Cathexis" [VGR], "Learning Curve" [VGR]). The story took a dramatic turn when Lord Burleigh declared his love for Davenport, to the considerable dismay of the Burleigh children. A **Bothan** attacked the crew of the *Starship Voyager* in 2372, causing Janeway to experience hallucinations of characters from the holonovel appearing on the ship, not just on the holodeck. ("Persistence of Vision" [VGR]). *Janeway's gothic romance novel was first seen in "Cathexis" (VGR).*

Janeway, Admiral. (Len Cariou). Senior Starfleet officer and father of **Kathryn Janeway**. Admiral Janeway died in 2358 while on Tau Ceti Prime. He was a victim of an accidental drowning under the planet's polar ice cap. In 2373, following a near-fatal shuttle crash injury, Kathryn Janeway's cerebral cortex was inhabited by a **consciousness parasite**. The entity fed a false reality to Janeway, taking the form of her long-dead father. ("Coda" [VGR]).

Janeway, Ensign. (Lucy Boryer). *Enterprise*-D crew member who had a counseling session with Deanna Troi shortly after stardate 46071.6. A member of the science department, Janeway had sought counseling because she had been having trouble with her superior officer, Lieutenant Pinder. Unfortunately, Troi was at the time serving as an involuntary "**receptacle**" for **Ambassador Ves Alkar**'s negative emotions, so she was an unsympathetic listener. ("Man of the People" [TNG]).

Janeway, Kathryn. (Kate Mulgrew). Commander of the ***U.S.S. Voyager***. In 2371, the *Starship Voyager*, with Janeway and her crew, was abducted and swept into the distant Delta Quadrant of the galaxy, some 70,000 light-years from home, where they were essentially stranded. (SEE: **Caretaker**.) After the destruction of a **Maquis** ship that had also been abducted to the **Delta Quadrant**, Janeway accepted the Maquis crew aboard her ship, and invited its commander, **Chakotay**, to become her second-in-command. Janeway's courage and leadership were instrumental in the survival of her crew as they made a long and difficult journey back to the **Alpha Quadrant**. ("Caretaker" [VGR]).

Janeway, whose father was a Starfleet admiral ("Coda" [VGR]), grew up in **Indiana** on **Earth**, where summers were warm and humid. Janeway loved to ski. ("Macrocosm" [VGR]). When she was young, Kathryn's parents took her and her siblings on camping trips, but she never did like camping, as she was very much a child of the 24th century. ("Resolutions" [VGR]). Kathryn had a sister, who was the artist of the family. ("Sacred Ground" [VGR]). Kathryn loved music, but never learned to play a musical instrument, a fact that she regretted in her adult life. ("Remember" [VGR]). As a child, one of Janeway's heroes was noted 20th-century Earth aviator **Amelia Earhart**. In later years, Janeway would recall that Earhart was one of the inspirations that led her to join Starfleet. ("The 37's" [VGR]). Janeway enjoyed tennis when she was in high school, although she did not play the game again until 19 years later when she commanded the *Starship Voyager*. ("Future's End, Part I" [VGR]). Janeway was close with her father, and grieved deeply after his tragic accidental drowning in 2358 ("Coda" [VGR]). Early in her career, Janeway served as science officer aboard the *U.S.S. Al-Batani*. Prior to the *Voyager*'s disappearance, Janeway had been romantically involved with **Mark**, who took care of Molly, her pet Irish Setter. ("Caretaker" [VGR]).

During her off-duty hours aboard *Voyager*, Janeway enjoyed participating in a gothic romance holonovel set in old England on Earth. ("Cathexis" [VGR]). SEE: **Janeway Lambda-1**. Captain Janeway was an accomplished pool player. She considered **coffee** to be an essential part of her lifestyle ("The Cloud" [VGR]) and had a particular weakness for coffee ice cream. ("Persistence of Vision" [VGR]). She enjoyed knitting, and in 2372, made a monogrammed blanket for Ensign **Samantha Wildman's** newborn daughter. The luxury of a hot bath was probably Janeway's favorite form of relaxation. ("Resolutions" [VGR]).

On stardate 48546, Janeway sought Chakotay's help in experiencing a **vision quest** in search of her personal **animal guide**. ("The Cloud" [VGR]). In 2372, Janeway crossed the warp 10 barrier, causing her to mutate into an amphibious creature. Fortunately, the Emergency Medical Hologram was able to reverse the mutative process. While mutated, Janeway and Paris mated, producing three amphibian children that they left behind on a planet in the Delta Quadrant. ("Threshold" [VGR]).

Janeway became afflicted with a potentially fatal viral disease in 2372 after accidental contact with an insectoid life-form on a planet in the Delta Quadrant. Extensive research determined that the condition could remain benign as long as she remained on the planet, but that she could not survive if she left. *Voyager* officer Chakotay was also stricken with the disease. Determined that her people should not sacrifice their chance to return home, Janeway ordered her ship to continue their voyage, leaving Janeway and Chakotay behind. On the planet, Janeway found life was made more pleasant by Chakotay's support and his wilderness skills. After several weeks, *Voyager*'s crew, with the aid of **Vidiian** physician **Danara Pel**, was able to obtain an antiviral medication, and they returned to successfully treat Chakotay and Janeway. Chakotay and Janeway grew closer during their time alone together on the planet. ("Resolutions" [VGR]).

The character was named for American feminist writer Elizabeth Janeway. Actor Genevieve Bujold was originally cast as Captain Nicole Janeway, but she left the show after two days of production and was replaced with Kate Mulgrew as Kathryn Janeway. Kathryn Janeway's first appearance was in "Caretaker" (VGR). Janeway was not *the first female starship captain seen on* Star Trek. *That honor went to the unnamed commander of the* Starship Saratoga, *played by Madge Sinclair in* Star Trek IV: The Voyage Home. *Janeway was, however, the first female series lead in* Star Trek *history.*

Janir. Ancient city on planet **Bajor**. In 2371 the **Qui'al Dam** was restored to operation, diverting water to the city of Janir. ("Destiny" [DS9]). SEE: **Trakor's Third Prophecy.**

Janitza mountains. Geological formation on planet **Bajor**. In 2371, an agrobiology expedition, with Keiko O'Brien as chief botanist, was dispatched to the Janitza range for the first detailed study of this region. ("The House of Quark" [DS9]).

Janklow. Starfleet engineer assigned to station Deep Space 9 in 2372. ("Starship Down" [DS9]).

Janowski, Mary. (Pamelyn Ferdin). One of the surviving children of the **Starnes Expedition** whose parents committed suicide on planet **Triacus** in 2268. In the aftermath of the tragedy, Janowski was controlled by the Gorgan. ("And the Children Shall Lead" [TOS]).

Janus VI. Planet. Homeworld to the **Horta**, a civilization of intelligent, **silicon-based life**-forms. Janus VI also contains rich deposits of the mineral, **pergium**, and the Federation has a pergium production station located underground on the planet. In 2267, prior to first contact between the miners and the Horta, several mining personnel were killed under mysterious circumstances. The deaths were found to be the result of the mother Horta protecting her children. Once contact was made, and the miners learned not to endanger the Horta eggs, peace was restored. ("The Devil in the Dark" [TOS]).

Japanese brush writing. A form of calligraphy practiced in the nation of Japan on Earth since the 11th century. **Keiko O'Brien**'s grandmother was a practitioner of this art. ("Violations" [TNG]).

Japori II. Planet. Flaxian assassin **Retaya** was accused of the killing of **Dekora Assan** on Japori II, but was later cleared of the charge. ("Improbable Cause" [DS9]).

Jarada. Reclusive insectoid civilization from planet Torona IV. Establishment of diplomatic relations with the Jarada had been a Federation priority for some time because of their strategic importance. The Jarada were known for the extreme attention to the detail of protocol. The mispronunciation of a single word once led to a 20-year rift in communication. Captain Jean-Luc Picard successfully delivered the appropriate greetings to the Jarada in 2364, thus paving the way for further diplomatic relations. ("The Big Goodbye" [TNG]). The **Pakled** ship ***Mondor*** showed evidence of using technology borrowed or stolen from a variety of other cultures, including the Jaradans. ("Samaritan Snare" [TNG]). *We've never actually seen a Jaradan.*

Jared, Acost. (Marcello Tubert). Ventaxian head of state in 2367. Jared interpreted a series of apparently paranormal events on **Ventax II** as evidence that the mythic figure **Ardra** was returning to the planet to enslave the population, under the terms of the **Contract of Ardra**. Investigation by *Enterprise*-D personnel revealed this Ardra to be a fake. ("Devil's Due" [TNG]).

Jaresh-Inyo. (Herschel Sparber). **Federation President** in 2372 whose administration faced a grave security threat from possible **changeling** infiltration, and an even greater threat from internal paranoia. When **Founder** infiltration on Earth was suspected following the bombing of the **Antwerp Conference**, Jaresh-Inyo reluctantly authorized sweeping security measures ranging from curtailment of civil liberties to the imposition of martial law. Jaresh-Inyo later rescinded the orders when it became clear that Starfleet **Admiral Leyton** was using the atmosphere of fear to foster a planned military coup of Earth's civilian government. Nevertheless, President Jaresh-Inyo recognized that the incident, including Leyton's sabotoge of Earth's **global power grid**, clearly demonstrated a need for greater planetary security. ("Homefront" [DS9], "Paradise Lost" [DS9]). *Jaresh-Inyo was Grazerite.*

Jareth. (Bruce Davison). **Enaran** military officer. Jareth was a loving father, but he was prejudiced against the ethnic group known as the **Regressives**. He forbade his daughter, **Korenna Mirell**, from seeing her lover, **Dathan Alaris**, because of his ethnic ties to that group. Jareth was an active participant of his government's deliberate and systematic extermination of Regressives in the mid-24th century. ("Remember" [VGR]).

Jaro Essa, Minister. (Frank Langella). Ambitious, politically conservative member of the **Bajoran Chamber of Ministers**. In 2370, Jaro welcomed the returning **Li Nalas** to station Deep Space 9. He used the opportunity to push his political agenda with the Bajoran nationals on the station. ("The Homecoming" [DS9]). It was later

discovered that Jaro was the leader of the terrorist **Alliance for Global Unity**, also known as the Circle. Jaro used the Circle in his bid to overthrow the **Bajoran provisional government**, with himself as the new leader. In this effort, Jaro allied himself with then-Vedek **Winn**, who also sought to lead Bajor back to "more orthodox" values. ("The Circle" [DS9]). Unfortunately for Jaro's plans, evidence of the Cardassian involvement in the Circle's activities was brought to the attention of the **Chamber of Ministers**. Jaro was subsequently forced from power. ("The Siege" [DS9]).

Jarok, Alidar. (James Sloyan). **Romulan** admiral who commanded the forces responsible for the massacre at the **Norkan outposts**. Nevertheless, Jarok was a deeply thoughtful man, who opposed policies of the Romulan government that he saw as the prelude to an unnecessary war. Jarok was eventually censured for his outspokenness and was assigned to a strategically insignificant posting. There, the Romulan government fed him a carefully constructed stream of disinformation designed to convince him that planet **Nelvana III** was being prepared as a staging base for a massive assault against the Federation. Unable to prevent what he believed to be a major threat to galactic peace, in 2366 Jarok stole a scoutship and defected to the Federation. Jarok persuaded *Enterprise*-D Captain Picard to investigate these reports, learning that there was no base, and that the Romulan High Command was testing Jarok's loyalties. In despair over his use as a pawn by his government, and over the loss of his former life, Jarok committed suicide. Jarok said he had done these things to help ensure that his daughter could grow up in a better universe. ("The Defector" [TNG]).

Jaros II. Planet in Federation space. It was the location of the Starfleet stockade where **Ro Laren** was imprisoned following the ***U.S.S. Wellington*** incident, until her release in 2368. ("Ensign Ro" [TNG]).

Jarren. Elderly **Drayan** who died of natural causes in 2372. A shuttle carried Fayla and several others destined for their **final ritual** on one of the moons of Drayan II. The shuttle crashed on the moon and Jarren died shortly thereafter. ("Innocence" [VGR]).

Jarth. (Rick Scarry). Aide to **Ambassador Ves Alkar** at the time he helped negotiate peace on planet **Rekag-Seronia** in 2369. ("Man of the People" [TNG]).

Jarvin. (Justin Williams). **Maquis** crew member aboard the *Voyager*. Jarvin was concerned that the status of the Maquis crew members might change after an altercation between B'Elanna Torres and **Lieutenant Carey**. He was ready to support Chakotay if he wanted to take control of the *Voyager*. ("Parallax" [VGR]). *Jarvin's name was not mentioned in dialog, but was given in the ending credits.*

Jarvis. (Charles Macauley). Prefect of planet **Argelius II**. His wife, an empathic Argelian named **Sybo**, was murdered in 2267 by an alien entity that fed on fear. ("Wolf in the Fold" [TOS]). SEE: **Hengist, Mr.**; **Redjac**. *Actor Charles Macauley also played the computer-generated image of* ***Landru*** *in "Return of the Archons" (TOS).*

Jasad, Gul. (Joel Snetow). Commander of a **Cardassian** warship and a member of the Seventh Order. In 2369, Jasad threatened to reoccupy **Deep Space 9** or destroy the station. ("Emissary" [DS9]).

Jat'yln. Klingon term for spiritual possession. It literally translates as "the taking of the living by the dead." Worf wondered if the **Ux-Mal** noncorporeal criminal life-forms that gained control of three *Enterprise*-D personnel on stardate 45571 might be instances of *Jat'yln*. ("Power Play" [TNG]).

Jatarn, Major. Officer in the Bajoran militia in 2372. Major Kira considered Jantarn to be a potential successor to her in the position of Bajoran liaison to Starfleet. ("Accession" [DS9]).

Jatlh. Klingon expression that translates as "Speak!" ("Unification, Part I" [TNG]).

Javert. Fictional character in **Victor Hugo**'s 1862 novel ***Les Misérables***. Javert was a French police inspector who relentlessly pursued a man named **Valjean**, who was guilty of a trivial offense. In the end Javert's own inflexibility destroyed him, and he committed suicide. *Les Misérables* was **Maquis** leader **Michael Eddington**'s favorite book, and he saw himself as a dashing, romantic hero, fighting the good fight just like Valjean, the novel's hero. Eddington compared Captain Benjamin **Sisko** to the single-minded Javert. ("For the Uniform" [DS9]).

Jaya. (Susanna Thompson). Inmate at the **Tilonus Institute for Mental Disorders** on **Tilonus IV**. Jaya called herself Commander Bloom of the *Starship Yorktown* and offered to help Riker escape from captivity there in 2369. ("Frame of Mind" [TNG]). SEE: ***Frame of Mind.***

Jayden. (Brent Spiner). Name given to the amnesiac Data by **Gia** on planet **Barkon IV** in 2370. ("Thine Own Self" [TNG]).

Jaz Holza. A **Bajoran** leader who resided on the third planet in the **Valo system**. Dr. Crusher had met Jaz at a symposium and found him to be very thoughtful and a good spokesman for his people. **Ro Laren** maintained, however, that Jaz held no real influence with the Bajoran people. ("Ensign Ro" [TNG]).

Jefferies tube. Systems access crawlway aboard Federation starships. **Neela Daren** found the fourth intersect of Jefferies tube 25 to be the most acoustically perfect spot on the *Enterprise*-D for playing her musical instruments. ("Lessons" [TNG]). Jefferies tubes were even used for physical fitness training aboard the *Starship Voyager*. ("Learning Curve" [VGR]). *The term "Jefferies tube" was a gag among the original* Star Trek *production staff, a reference to Original Series art director Matt Jefferies, the man who designed the original* Starship Enterprise. *In* Star Trek: The Next Generation, *the term has actually been used on film, thus making the name "official."*

Jell-O. Brand name of a fruit-flavored gelatin dessert food originating on Earth. Neelix prepared Jell-O with fruit cocktail for the **Thirty-Sevens** during their brief visit to the *Voyager* in 2371. ("The 37's" [VGR]). *Jell-O is a registered trademark of Kraft Foods, Inc.*

Jellico, Captain Edward. (Ronny Cox). Starfleet officer who commanded the *Starship* ***Cairo***. In 2367, Jellico assisted in negotiating the armistice between the Federation and the **Cardassian Union**. In 2369, with tensions between the Cardassians and the Federation again on the rise, Jellico was given temporary command of the ***Enterprise*-D** for a meeting with the Cardassian ship ***Reklar*** while Captain Picard was sent on a covert mission into Cardassian space. Jellico was known for his efficient, demanding style of command. ("Chain of Command, Parts I and II" [TNG]).

Jem'Hadar warships. Vessels used by the Jem'Hadar. The *Starship Defiant* encountered several Jem'Hadar warships in

2371 while searching for the **Founders** of the **Dominion**. ("The Search, Part I" [DS9]). A Jem'Hadar warship crash-landed on planet Torga IV on stardate 50049, killing all aboard. After a standoff against several Jem'Hadar warriors, Captain Sisko and his staff claimed the ship and took it back to the Deep Space 9. Jem'Hadar warships employ **ion propulsion**, as well as **ventral impellers**. Their command centers are equipped with **virtual displays**. ("The Ship" [DS9]).

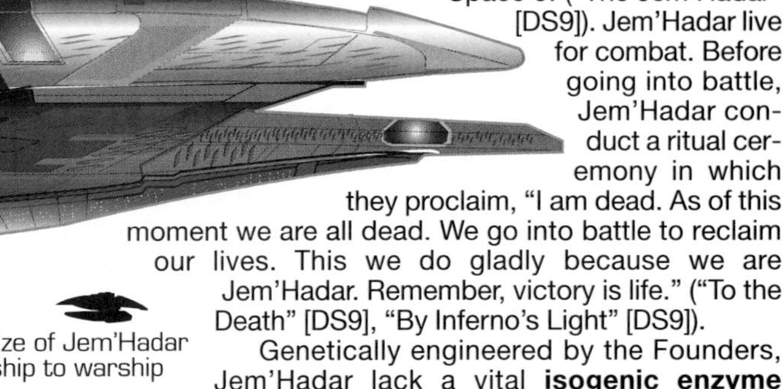
Jem'Hadar warship

Relative size of Jem'Hadar attack ship to warship

Jem'Hadar attack ships. Personnel craft comparable in size to a Klingon *B'rel*-class starship. These craft were armed with phased **polaron** beam weapons. They were also equipped with an advanced deflector shield that prevented tractor beam lock and a **transporter** device that was unhampered by Federation defensive shields. The class was first encountered in the Alpha Quadrant in 2370, when one ship arrived at station Deep Space 9 to deliver news of Commander Sisko's capture by the **Jem'Hadar**. Three of these ships attacked a small fleet of Federation craft sent to investigate the Jem'Hadar threat. As the Federation craft were withdrawing, one of the Jem'Hadar ships rammed and destroyed the ***U.S.S. Odyssey***. ("The Jem'Hadar" [DS9]).

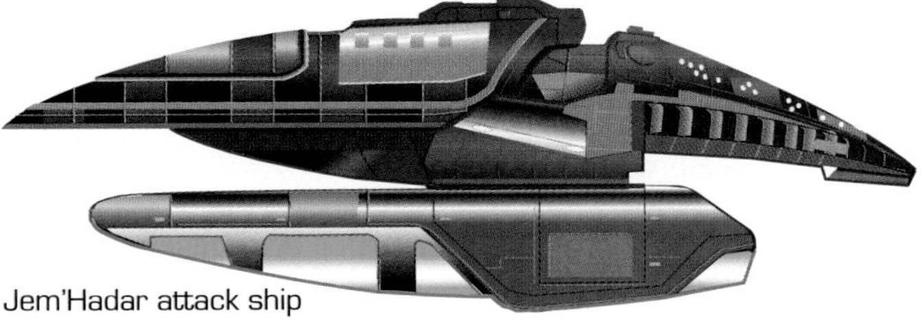
Jem'Hadar attack ship

"Jem'Hadar, The." *Deep Space Nine* episode #46. Written by Ira Steven Behr. Directed by Kim Friedman. No stardate given. *First aired in 1994. On a vacation trip to the Gamma Quadrant, Sisko and company are captured by the Jem'Hadar.* GUEST CAST: Alan Oppenheimer as **Keogh, Captain**; Aron Eisenberg as **Nog**; Cress Williams as **Talak'talan, Third**; Molly Hagan as **Eris**; Michael Jace as 1st officer; Sandra Grando as 2nd officer; Majel Barrett as Computer voice. SEE: **Dominion; Eris; Ferengi Rules of Acquisition; Founders; guidance and navigation relay; IDIC; Itamish III; jambalaya; Jem'Hadar attack ships; Jem'Hadar; katterpod beans; Keogh, Captain; Kurill Prime; *Mekong, U.S.S.;* New Bajor; *Odyssey, U.S.S.; Orinoco, U.S.S.;* polaron; *Rio Grande, U.S.S.*; Talak'talan, Third; telekinetic suppression collar.**

Jem'Hadar. Genetically engineered warrior species from the **Gamma Quadrant**. The Jem'Hadar functioned as the army of the **Dominion**, controlled by the **Founders** through the **Vorta**. They were first encountered in 2370, by personnel from station Deep Space 9. ("The Jem'Hadar" [DS9]). Jem'Hadar live for combat. Before going into battle, Jem'Hadar conduct a ritual ceremony in which they proclaim, "I am dead. As of this moment we are all dead. We go into battle to reclaim our lives. This we do gladly because we are Jem'Hadar. Remember, victory is life." ("To the Death" [DS9], "By Inferno's Light" [DS9]).

Genetically engineered by the Founders, Jem'Hadar lack a vital **isogenic enzyme** (known as **ketracel-white**, or simply **white**) needed for survival. The Founders use this chemical dependence to maintain control over the powerful Jem'Hadar. ("The Abandoned" [DS9]). The Jem'Hadar receive this drug through special supply tubes implanted in their necks. Since the Jem'Hadar were directly controlled by the **Vorta**, most Jem'Hadar spent their entire lives

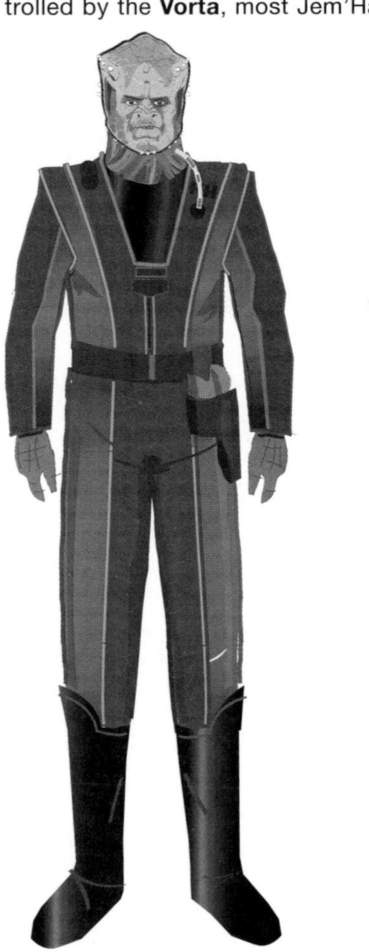
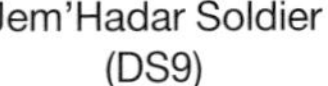
Jem'Hadar Soldier (DS9)

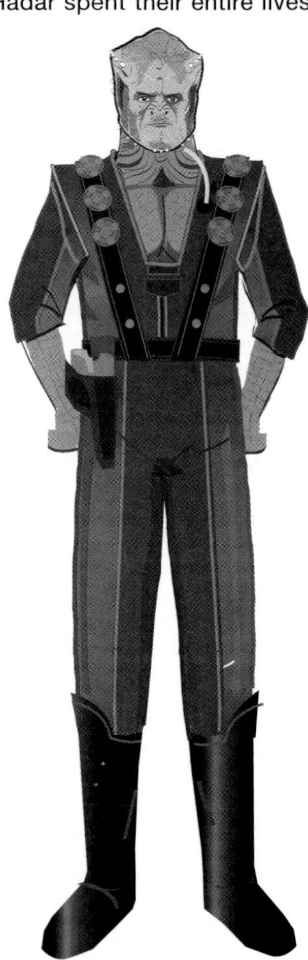
Jem'Hadar Special Forces (DS9)

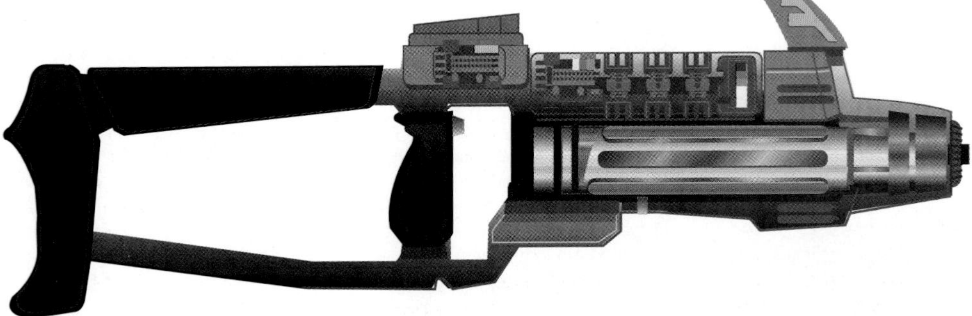
Jem'Hadar rifle

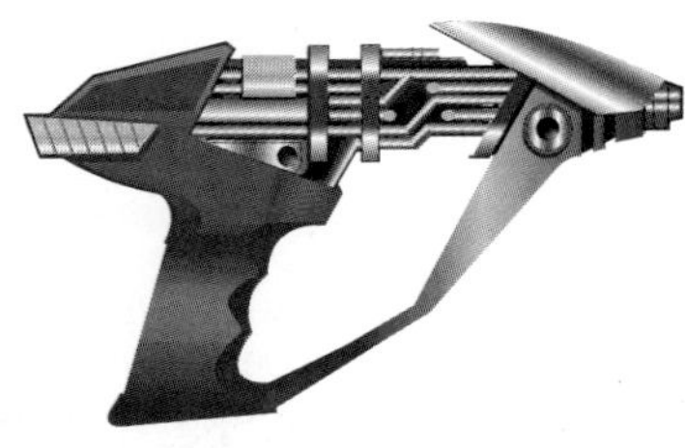
Jem'Hadar pistol

without seeing a Founder. To them, the Founders were almost a myth of god-like stature. ("Hippocratic Oath" [DS9]). A Founder was aboard a Jem'Hadar warship that crash-landed on Torga IV on stardate 50049.3. The Jem'Hadar that came to rescue him failed and later committed suicide for having allowed the Founder's death. ("The Ship" [DS9]).

Jem'Hadar do not eat, because white is the only thing they need for nutrition. Relaxation would only make them weak, so they don't sleep. Jem'Hadar are bred in birthing chambers, so there is no need for females or sexual reproduction. They mature at a rapid rate and are able to fight within three days of emergence. Few live 15 years, and no Jem'Hadar has ever reached 30 years of age. If they manage to reach 20, they achieve the status of "Honored Elder." ("To the Death" [DS9]).

If the Jem'Hadar are ruthless to their own, they are even more so to those who they oppose. When the inhabitants of a planet in the **Teplan** system resisted Dominion rule in 2172, the Jem'Hadar made an example of them by infecting the planet with a deadly disease known as the blight. SEE: **Teplan blight.** ("The Quickening" [DS9]).

Standard Jem'Hadar occupation tactics require at least 27 soldiers to be stationed inside a base camp at all times, with nine patrolling the perimeter. ("To the Death" [DS9]).

In 2371, Starfleet learned more about the Jem'Hadar from a member of that species found as an infant on **Deep Space 9**. This young individual *(played at different ages by Hassan Nicholas and Bumper Robinson)* grew at an accelerated rate, advancing in years both physically and intellectually. ("The Abandoned" [DS9]).

In late 2371, the Jem'Hadar demonstrated their awesome destructive power when a fleet of 150 Jem'Hadar fighter craft ambushed some 20 **Romulan** and **Cardassian** ships attacking the **Founders' homeworld** in the Omarion Nebula. ("The Die is Cast" [DS9]). In 2372, two Jem'Hadar ships disrupted a trade conference among Federation, Ferengi, and **Karemma** delegates held aboard the *Starship Defiant*. The Jem'Hadar ships were destroyed, and the crew of the *Defiant* rescued the Karemman ship's crew. ("Starship Down" [DS9]).

Jenkata nebula. Stellar gas cloud located in the Gamma Quadrant. In 2372, Kira Nerys piloted a runabout to the Jenkata nebula to avoid detection by the **Jem'Hadar**. ("The Quickening" [DS9]).

Jenolen, U.S.S. Federation transport ship, *Sydney* class, registry number NCC-2010. The *Jenolen* disappeared in 2294 and was presumed lost. It was not discovered until 2369 that the *Jenolen* had crashed into a **Dyson Sphere**, and that one passenger, Captain **Montgomery Scott**, had survived for 75 years by suspending himself in a modified transporter beam. Shortly after Scott's rescue, Geordi La Forge and Scott repaired the *Jenolen*'s systems sufficiently to help the *Enterprise*-D escape from the sphere's interior, although the *Jenolen* was destroyed in the process. ("Relics" [TNG]). *The* Jenolen *miniature was a modification of a shuttlecraft built by John Goodson of ILM for* Star Trek VI. *(It was the ship that transported our heroes up to Spacedock). The modifications by Greg Jein added warp engines to the model. Fans have pointed out— quite correctly— that it shouldn't have been possible for Scotty and Geordi to be beamed off the* Jenolen *while that ship's shields were still up. The* Jenolen *model has been re-used as a ship visiting Deep Space 9, notably as the transport that brought the two Temporal Investigations agents to the station in "Trials and Tribble-ations" (DS9).*

Jeraddo. Fifth moon orbiting the planet **Bajor**. Jeraddo was a Class-M planetoid that was inhabited for years until, in 2369, an energy-transfer project tapped that moon's core, rendering the surface uninhabitable. The inhabitants of Jeraddo were relocated by order of the Bajoran provisional government. ("Progress" [DS9]). SEE: **Mullibok; Keena; Baltrim.**

Jessel. (Pamela Kosh). (In the **anti-time future** created by the **Q Continuum**, Jessel served as housekeeper in the traditional residence of the **Lucasian Chair** at **Cambridge University**. She was employed by **Data,** who held that post in this reality. Jessel made no secret of the fact that she disliked the gray streak which the Data of that time had affected, saying it made him look "like a bloody skunk!" Data felt Jessel was frightfully trying at times, but that she made him laugh.) ("All Good Things..." [TNG].) *Pamela Kosh previously had played Mrs. Carmichael in "Time's Arrow, Part II" (TNG).*

Jessen. (Athena Massey). **Enaran** engineer. Jessen traveled aboard the *U.S.S. Voyager* from a colony in the Fima system to Enara Prime in 2373. Jessen found it difficult to believe allegations that her government had, decades ago, systematically exterminated the minority ethnic group known as the **Regressives**. Using her Enaran telepathic abilities, Jessen received memories of that horrific time from a *Voyager* crew member, memories of an Enaran woman named **Korenna Mirell** and her lover, a Regressive named **Dathan Alaris** who was killed by her people. Shocked by these revelations, Jessen understood the need to fight her people's policy of suppressing knowledge of the holocaust and the importance of remembering, so that those terrible times will never be repeated. ("Remember" [VGR]).

***Jestral* tea.** Beverage. A favorite of Lwaxana Troi. ("Cost of Living" [TNG]).

Jetrel, Dr. Ma'Bor. (James Sloyan). Scientist who developed the **metreon cascade**, a weapon of mass destruction, in 2356, during the war between the **Haakonians** and the **Talaxians**. Jetrel's weapon was used on the moon **Rinax**, resulting in some 300,000 deaths and the Talaxians' surrender. The weapon was deemed a tremendous success, but Jetrel later found himself ostracized from Haakonian society. His wife, **Ka'Ree,** and their three children even left him. Jetrel himself felt intense guilt over his role in the death of so many Talaxians at Rinax. He spent many years searching for a way to make amends for his creation, eventually developing a **regenerative fusion** process with which he hoped to restore some of the dead to life. Jetrel found his government uninterested in testing his concept, so in 2371 he bluffed his way onto the *Voyager* in order to use the ship's technology to test his process. The attempt failed, but in the process, Jetrel impressed **Neelix**, a Talaxian, with the sincerity of his desire to atone for the deaths he had wrought. Dr. Jetrel died shortly thereafter of **metremia** from exposure to the metreon cascade. ("Jetrel" [VGR]). *James Sloyan previously played Romulan Admiral Alidar Jarok in "The Defector" (TNG), K'mtar in "Firstborn" (TNG) and Dr. Mora Pol in "The Alternate" (DS9).*

"Jetrel." *Voyager* episode #15. Teleplay by Jack Klein & Karen Klein and Kenneth Biller. Story by James Thomton and Scott Nimerfro. Directed by Kim Friedman. Stardate 48832.1. *First aired in 1995. Neelix faces an enemy scientist who, 15 years ago, developed a terrible weapon that devastated Neelix's homeworld and killed his family.* GUEST CAST: James Sloyan as **Jetrel**, **Dr. Ma'Bor**; Larry Hankin as **Gaunt Gary**; Majel Barrett as Computer voice. SEE: **Chez Sandrine; Haakonian Order; Haakonians; Jetrel, Dr. Ma'Bor; Ka'Ree; Krallinian eel; metremia; metreon cascade; metreon cloud; Neelix; Palaxia; Pyrithian Gorge, Battle of; regenerative fusion; Rinax; Talaxians; Talax; talchok.**

Jev. (Ben Lemon). A telepathic historian from the **Ullian** homeworld. Jev was the son of renowned historian **Tarmin**, and worked for years to help compile Tarmin's library of memories. Jev was taken into custody in 2368 for a crime known as **telepathic memory invasion** rape, in which Jev forced his victims to relive painfully distorted versions of their own memories. These victims, who included three members of the *Enterprise*-D crew, were left comatose for several days. Investigation by *Enterprise*-D personnel linked Jev with the victims, and implicated him in other telepathic rapes on several planets. Jev was returned to his homeworld, where the punishment for his crimes was expected to be severe. ("Violations" [TNG]).

jevonite. Valuable gemstone found on planet **Cardassia**. Many of the artifacts discovered in the burial vaults of the **First Hebitian Civilization** were manufactured from jevonite. Most of these treasures were either stolen by looters or sold by the Cardassian military to finance their war effort. ("Chain of Command, Part II" [TNG]).

Jewel of Thasia. SEE: **Thasia, Jewel of.**

Jeyal. (Michael Ansara). **Tavnian** dignitary. Jeyal married Betazoid ambassador **Lwaxana Troi** in 2372. Shortly thereafter, Troi became pregnant with Jeyal's son, but she rebelled against Tavnian custom that would have excluded her from participating in her son's upbringing. Jeyal followed his wife to station Deep Space 9, where she immediately married her friend, Odo, in a traditional Tavnian ceremony. Thus spurned, Jeyal conceded that the marriage nullified his claim upon his unborn son. ("The Muse" [DS9]). *Michael Ansara also played Kang in "Day of the Dove" (TOS) and "Blood Oath" (DS9).*

Jibalian omelette. Breakfast dish native to the Delta Quadrant. Neelix served Jibalian omelettes to the *Voyager* crew. ("Prototype" [VGR]).

jIH dok. Klingon for "my blood"; an expression of devotion given to one's mate. The response is *maj dok*, meaning "our blood." The exchange is sometimes used to seal a marriage vow. **Worf** and **K'Ehleyr** recited these words to each other, shortly before her death in 2367. ("Reunion" [TNG]).

Jillur Gueta. Bajoran national. Jillur was born in 2312, came from Rakantha province on Bajor, and was an artist. In 2367, Jillur Gueta, along with Ishan Chaye and Timor Landi, was wrongly accused of attempting to assassinate **Gul Dukat** on station **Terok Nor**. The three were executed after a cursory investigation by Odo, Terok Nor's chief of security. ("Things Past" [DS9]).

Jimbalian fudge. Chocolate dessert dish. Neelix baked a seven-layer Jimbalian fudge cake with ***I'maki* nut** icing for Kes's second birthday in 2372. ("Twisted" [VGR]).

Jimenez, Ensign. (Charles Tentindo). Starfleet security officer assigned to starbase Deep Space 9 in 2372. ("Crossfire" [DS9]).

jinaq. Traditional Klingon jeweled amulet, given to a daughter when she comes of age to take a mate. ("Birthright, Part II" [TNG]).

Jo'Bril. (James Horan). Takaran specialist in solar plasma reactions. Jo'Bril was invited, along with other scientists, to participate in the first tests of a new **metaphasic shield** in 2369. Jo'Bril volunteered to pilot a specially modified *Enterprise*-D shuttlecraft into the corona of a star in order to test the feasibility of the shield. Jo'Bril was apparently killed during the test. It was later discovered that Jo'Bril had faked his death. Jo'Bril hoped to discredit **Dr. Reyga**, inventor of the metaphasic shield, so that he could steal the technology for his own use. He was nearly successful in simulating the destruction of the *Shuttlecraft* ***Justman*** and kidnapping Dr. Beverly Crusher. Jo'Bril was killed by Crusher when she discovered his plan. ("Suspicions" [TNG]). *James Horan also played Lieutenant Barnaby in "Descent, Part II" (TNG), Tosin in "Fair Trade" (VGR) ,and Ikat'ika in "In Purgatory's Shadow" (DS9) and "By Inferno's Light" (DS9).*

Jo'kala. City on the planet **Bajor**. ("Starship Down" [DS9]).

Joachim. (Judson Scott). Aide to **Khan Noonien Singh**, and one of 96 surviving genetic "supermen" who escaped from Earth in 1996 aboard the ***S.S. Botany Bay***. Joachim served as Khan's second-in-command when Khan commandeered the *Starship* ***Reliant***, and died when Khan detonated the **Genesis Device**. *(Star Trek II: The Wrath of Khan).*

Joaquin. (Mark Tobin). Genetically engineered survivor of the **Eugenics Wars**. Joaquin and other followers of **Khan Noonien Singh** escaped Earth in 1996 in the sleeper ship ***S.S. Botany Bay***. They traveled in suspended animation until awakened by personnel from the *Starship Enterprise* in 2267. ("Space Seed" [TOS]). *In* Star Trek II, *Khan's deputy was named* ***Joachim.***

Jodmos. Cover name used by Benjamin Sisko in 2373. For a covert mission to **Ty'Gokor**, Sisko was surgically altered to appear Klingon, and he assumed the identity of Jodmos, son of Kobor. ("Apocalypse Rising" [DS9]).

Johnson, Elaine. (Laura Wood). Colonist on planet **Gamma Hydra IV** who died of a radiation-induced hyperaccelerated-aging disease in 2267. Elaine Johnson was the wife of scientist **Robert Johnson** and was 27 years old at the time of her death of old age. ("The Deadly Years" [TOS]).

Johnson, Lieutenant. (David L. Ross). *Enterprise* security officer who was injured in 2268 fighting Klingons while under the control of the **Beta XII-A entity** that fed on hate and anger. Johnson's critical wounds healed quickly, so he could fight again. ("Day of the Dove" [TOS]). *David L. Ross also played Lieutenant Galloway in "A Taste of Armageddon" (TOS) and "The Omega Glory" (TOS).*

Johnson, Robert. (Felix Locher). Scientist on planet **Gamma Hydra IV** who died of a radiation-induced hyperaccelerated-aging disease in 2267 at the age of 29. ("The Deadly Years" [TOS]).

joined species. Term used to describe the **Trill** life-form, consisting of a helpless, intelligent **symbiont** living in partnership within a **host** humanoid body. ("The Host" [TNG]).

joined. Term used to describe those **Trill** who carry a **symbiont** inside them. It was considered a great honor and responsibility in Trill society to be chosen for joining. While approximately 5,000 Trill host candidates qualify each year for the **initiate** program, only 300 symbionts were available. Competition for the available symbionts was therefore high, as were the standards of the initiate program. ("Playing God" [DS9]).

Joining day. Among the Native American people on **Miramanee's planet**, the term for a day on which a **wedding** ceremony was performed. ("The Paradise Syndrome" [TOS]).

Jokarian chess. Game. Jadzia Dax once challenged Benjamin Sisko to a game of Jokarian chess. He declined, opting to search for his tardy son. ("The Nagus" [DS9]).

Jokri. River on planet Tavela Minor. It was noted for vacation cruises that allowed views of the river's iridescent currents. Nurse **Alyssa Ogawa**, reluctant to accept an invitation to **Risa** with a gentleman friend, was thinking about asking him instead to join her for a cruise on the Jokri River. ("Imaginary Friend" [TNG]).

Jol, Etana. (Katherine Moffat). A **Ktarian** operative who spearheaded a Ktarian attempt to gain control of the Federation Starfleet in 2368. Etana met William Riker while he was vacationing on planet **Risa**, and, in the guise of a romantic liaison, introduced a psychotropically addictive **Ktarian game** to Riker, who in turn spread it to the *Enterprise*-D crew. Because the game also affected the brain's reasoning center, Etana was able to control those people who had become addicted to the game. She planned to use the *Enterprise*-D crew to further her people's plot to gain control of Starfleet. ("The Game" [TNG]).

jolan true. A **Romulan** farewell salutation. ("Unification, Parts I and II" [TNG]). *We don't have an exact translation for this, but it seemed to be a Romulan version of "Have a Nice Day."*

jolly. Adjective meaning happy, in good spirits or joyous. There is no exact translation to this word in the Klingon language. ("Parallels" [TNG]).

Jomat Luson. (Sharon Conley). Bajoran social volunteer at the **Tozhat Resettlement Center.** Jomat received **Rugal** from a Cardassian military officer attached to **Terok Nor** in 2362. ("Cardassians" [DS9]).

Jonas, Michael. (Raphael Sbarge). *Starship Voyager* crew member. A former member of the **Maquis**, Michael Jonas served as an engineer aboard *Voyager* after it was lost in the Delta Quadrant. In 2372, Jonas's distrust for Starfleet policy prompted him to contact a **Kazon** vessel in hopes of negotiating on his own terms. ("Alliances" [VGR]). Jonas sent information concerning Thomas Paris's historic crossing of the transwarp threshold to Kazon operative **Rettick**. ("Threshold" [VGR]). A few weeks later, Jonas sabotaged *Voyager*'s magnetic constrictors so that the crew would be forced to vent plasma from the ship, severely damaging the inner layer of the warp coils. This damage was designed to force *Voyager* to visit Hemikek, where Kazon forces were lying in ambush. Neelix discovered Jonas sabotaging some of *Voyager's* systems in engineering and tried to stop him. During the altercation, Jonas fell and was vaporized in the plasma cloud from a broken conduit. ("Investigations" [VGR]). *Michael Jonas was also seen in "Dreadnought" (VGR) and "Lifesigns" (VGR).*

Jones, Cyrano. (Stanley Adams). Entrepreneur and licensed asteroid locator. Jones visited **Deep Space Station K-7** in 2267 to pursue trade. Jones's merchandise included **Spican flame gems**, **Antarian Glow Water**, and, unfortunately, **tribbles**. Jones became embroiled in a dispute between Federation and Klingon personnel at the station when his tribbles multiplied prodigiously, theatening to consume storage bins of valuable grain. Jones's punishment for his part in the mischief was to pick up every tribble on the station, a task Spock estimated would take at least 17 years, seeing as there were 1,771,561 of them. ("The Trouble with Tribbles." [TOS]). *Actor Stanley Adams cowrote "The Mark of Gideon" (TOS).*

Jones, Dr. Miranda. (Diana Muldaur). Psychologist who accomplished one of the first telepathic links with a **Medusan** individual. Jones was born a telepath and studied on planet Vulcan for four years, learning how not to read minds. In 2268, Jones was chosen to attempt the first telepathic link with Medusan Ambassador **Kollos** and accompanied the ambassador aboard the *Starship Enterprise* to his homeworld. Jones was blind, but wore a **sensor web** garment that gave her the ability to function normally among sighted people. ("Is There in Truth No Beauty?" [TOS]). SEE: **Marvick, Dr. Laurence**. *Diana Muldaur also played Dr. Ann Mulhall in "Return to Tomorrow" (TOS) and Dr. Katherine Pulaski in* Star Trek: The Next Generation*'s second season.*

Jono. (Chad Allen). Born in 2353 as Jeremiah Rossa, the grandson of Starfleet Admiral **Connaught Rossa**. Jono's parents were killed in a **Talarian** attack on Galen IV in 2356, and Jono was claimed by Talarian officer **Endar**, who raised the boy as his own in accordance with Talarian custom. In 2367, at the age of 14, Jono was discovered by the *Enterprise*-D crew aboard a damaged Talarian observation craft. DNA gene-type matching identified the boy's biological family. Although examinations by *Enterprise*-D personnel suggested the boy might have been physically abused in Endar's care, further investigation revealed that Jono now considered Endar to be his true father, and Picard released Jono to Endar's custody, despite objections from the Rossa family. ("Suddenly Human" [TNG]). SEE: **Galen border conflicts**; ***Q'Maire***. *The dagger that Jono used to stab the captain was Picard's* cha'DIch *ceremonial knife from "Sins of the Father" (TNG).*

Joranian ostrich. Avian life-form. When frightened, the Joranian ostrich has been known to hide its head under water until it drowns. **Odo** used the analogy of the Joranian ostrich when trying to show **Kira Nerys** that to avoid accepting responsibility for ignoring the ***Kohn-Ma***'s plans could be deadly. ("Past Prologue" [DS9]).

Jordan, Ensign. (Michael Zaslow). *Starship Enterprise* crew member. Jordan was on duty in **auxiliary control** when the android **Norman** commandeered the ship in 2267. ("I, Mudd" [TOS]).

Joseph. (Steve Vinovich). Engineer of the ***S.S. Santa Maria***, who became a colony member on planet **Orellius**. Joseph assisted Deep Space 9 officers Sisko and O'Brien in their attempt to escape the colony. ("Paradise" [DS9]).

Josephs, Lieutenant. (James X. Mitchell). *Enterprise* security guard. Josephs discovered the **Tellarite** ambassador **Gav**, murdered just prior to the **Babel Conference** of 2268. Gav was on Deck 11 hanging upside down in a **Jefferies tube**. ("Journey to Babel" [TOS]).

Jouret IV. Planet. Site of the Federation's **New Providence** colony. In 2366, the colony on Jouret IV disappeared without a trace, the victim of a **Borg** attack. ("The Best of Both Worlds, Part I" [TNG]).

"Journey to Babel." Original Series episode #44. Written by D.C. Fontana. Directed by Joseph Pevney. Stardate 3842.3. *First broadcast in 1967. The* Enterprise*, assigned to transport ambassadors to a critical diplomatic conference, becomes a hotbed of intrigue. One of the diplomats, Spock's estranged father, suffers a heart attack and will die without Spock's help. This is the first appearance of Sarek and Amanda, Spock's parents.* GUEST CAST: Jane Wyatt as **Amanda**; Mark Lenard as **Sarek**; William O'Connell as **Thelev**; Majel Barrett as **Chapel**, **Christine**; John Wheeler as **Gav**; James X. Mitchell as **Josephs**, **Lieutenant**; Reggie Nalder as **Shras**; Billy Curtis as Little copper ambassador; Paul Baxley as Kirk's stunt double; Jim Shepherd as Thelev's stunt double. SEE **Amanda; Andorians; Babel Conference; Babel; benjisidrine; cardiostimulator; Coridan; cryogenic open-heart procedure; dilithium; Gav; Josephs, Lieutenant; Kirk, James T; Orion; Orions; Rigel V; Rigelians; Sarek; Saurian brandy; *sehlat*; Shras; Spock; T-negative; *tal-shaya*; teddy bear; Tellarite; Thelev; Vulcan Science Academy.**

"Journey's End." *Next Generation* episode #172. Written by Ronald D. Moore. Directed by Corey Allen. Stardate 47751.2. *First aired in 1994. Wesley Crusher, on vacation from Starfleet Academy, becomes involved in a dispute over the relocation of Native Americans from a planet annexed by the Cardassians.* GUEST CAST: Wil Wheaton as **Crusher**, **Wesley**; Tom Jackson as **Anthwara**; Natalia Nogulich as **Necheyev**, **Alynna**; Ned Romero as **Lakanta**; George Aguilar as **Wasaka**; Richard Poe as

Evek, Gul; Eric Menyuk as **Traveler**; Doug Wert as **Crusher, Jack R.** SEE: **Anthwara; Brand, Admiral; Bularian canapés; Crusher, Jack R.; Crusher, Wesley; Demilitarized Zone; Dorvan V; Evek, Gul; Federation-Cardassian treaty; Habak; Katowa; Lakanta; Mansara; Maribona-Picard, Javier; Mozart, Wolfgang Amadeus; Necheyev, Admiral Alynna; Picard, Jean-Luc; Pueblo Revolt; Starbase 310; Telak, Glinn; Traveler; Vassbinder, Dr.; *Vetar*; vision quest; Wasaka; watercress sandwiches; Wrightwell, Commander.**

Joval. (Deirdre Imershein). A beautiful female inhabitant of planet **Risa**. When Jean-Luc Picard vacationed on Risa in 2366, Joval noticed him displaying a ***Horga'hn***. She offered him ***jamaharon***, and was puzzled when Picard declined. ("Captain's Holiday" [TNG]). *Deirdre Imershein also played Lieutenant Watley in "Trials and Tribble-ations" (DS9).*

Jovian run. Starfleet shuttle route, running from **Jupiter** to **Saturn** and back each day. This route was **Captain Edward Jellico**'s first Starfleet assignment. **Geordi La Forge** also piloted the Jovian run early in his Starfleet career. SEE: **Titan's Turn**. ("Chain of Command, Part II" [TNG]).

Jovis. A **Zibalian** trade vessel owned by **Kivas Fajo**. The *Jovis* was a relatively small vessel with a maximum speed of warp 3. Data was kidnapped and imprisoned aboard the *Jovis* in 2366. ("The Most Toys" [TNG]). *The* Jovis *miniature was designed and built by Tony Meininger.*

Juarez, Lieutenant. Starfleet officer who served aboard the *Starship Enterprise*-D. Juarez gave birth to a boy aboard the *Enterprise*-D in 2367. The Juarez child was born on the same day that **Miles O'Brien** and **Keiko Ishikawa** were married, during a standoff with a Romulan ship. Captain Picard marveled that in the midst of possible destruction "this small miracle was taking place." ("Data's Day" [TNG]).

Judge Advocate General. Starfleet office in charge of administrative law within **Starfleet** and its own personnel. **Phillipa Louvois** was in charge of the Judge Advocate General office for Sector 23 when she presided over the precedent-setting case in which she ruled that the android Data was entitled to civil rights as a sentient being in 2365. Years earlier, Louvois also worked for the JAG when she prosecuted Jean-Luc Picard's court-martial following the loss of the ***U.S.S. Stargazer*** in 2355. ("The Measure of a Man" [TNG]). In 2359, a JAG investigation into the loss of the *Starship* ***Pegasus*** found "sufficient evidence to conclude that certain members of the crew did **mutiny** against the captain just prior to the destruction of the Pegasus." Despite the Advocate's recommendation that the incident be investigated further, the JAG report was classified and buried, and no further action took place. ("The *Pegasus*" [TNG]). **Rear Admiral Bennett**, a senior JAG official, ruled in 2373 on **Richard Bashir**'s criminal actions regarding the resequencing of son **Julian Bashir**'s DNA. ("Doctor Bashir, I Presume?" [DS9]).

Juhraya. Federation colony that became Cardassian territory following the establishment of the **Federation-Cardassian treaty** in 2370. Some citizens of this colony, including **Macias**, resisted relocation and remained in their homes. ("Preemptive Strike" [TNG]). SEE: **Maquis**.

Juhrayan freighter. Cargo vessel of Juhrayan registry. A Juhrayan freighter was destroyed by Cardassian colonists within the **Demilitarized Zone** in 2370. ("Preemptive Strike" [TNG]).

Julius Caesar. Play by Earth playwright **William Shakespeare** retelling the downfall of Roman statesman Julius Caesar and his betrayal by his friends. It is regarded as a classic tragedy by Earth scholars; Cardassian observer **Garak** considered it more of a farce. ("Improbable Cause" [DS9]).

Julliard Youth Symphony. Musical performance company associated with the Julliard School of Music in New York on Earth. **Harry Kim** played clarinet in the Julliard Youth Symphony prior to his assignment to the *U.S.S. Voyager* in 2371. ("Caretaker" [VGR]).

jumbo Romulan mollusks. Seafood dish. When Quark had a business dinner with Sakonna in 2370, he tried to impress her by serving a lavish feast including Romulan mollusks and ***plomeek* soup**. ("The Maquis, Part I" [DS9]).

***jumja* tea.** Beverage brewed from the sweet sap of the Bajoran *jumja* tree. **Kira Nerys (mirror)** liked *jumja* tea. ("Crossover"[DS9]).

***jumja*.** Sweet confection on a stick made from the sap of the *jumja* tree, it could be purchased at a kiosk on the Promenade of Deep Space 9. Miles O'Brien was fond of the *jumja*'s natural sweetness. ("In the Hands of the Prophets" [DS9]). The *jumja* kiosk on the Deep Space 9 Promenade was run in 2370 by **Lysia Arlin**. ("Shadowplay" [DS9], "Defiant" [DS9]). *The show's production staff referred to this "confection" as glop-on-a-stick.*

junction A-9. Aboard the *Starship Enterprise*-D, the **Jefferies tube** location of one of the sensor phase buffers. ("Force of Nature" [TNG]).

junction C-12. Aboard the *Starship Enterprise*-D, the **Jefferies tube** location of another set of sensor phase buffers. ("Force of Nature" [TNG]).

Jung, Carl Gustav. (1875-1961). Earth psychologist and psychiatrist who founded analytic psychology. In 1932, Jung devised the concept of seeking therapeutic results from within the imagination. He called this his active imagination technique. Native Americans had begun a similar practice centuries earlier as they consulted an **animal guide** as counselor during a **vision quest**. ("The Cloud" [VGR]). Troi quoted Jung while helping Riker, who was having disturbing thoughts while performing the play ***Frame of Mind*** in 2369. ("Frame of Mind" [TNG]).

Junior. A large spaceborne life-form discovered by the *Enterprise*-D near the **Alpha Omicron system** in 2367. The creature was composed of an energy field surrounded by a shell of silicates, actinides, and carbonaceaous chondrites. *Enterprise*-D personnel had been responsible for the accidental death of Junior's mother, just prior to Junior's birth. Accordingly, Dr. Crusher devised a technique to use the ship's phasers to perform a cesarean section on the mother's body, allowing Junior to live. Shortly after the delivery, the creature physically attached itself to the ship's hull, absorbing power directly from ship's systems. **Geordi La Forge**, with help from visiting engineer **Leah Brahms**, was able to modify the ship's internal power frequencies to effectively "sour the milk," thereby weaning the child. Junior was last seen, along with other members of its species, in the asteroid belt near the Alpha Omicron system. ("Galaxy's Child" [TNG]). *According to Captain Picard, the appellation "Junior" was not to be the creature's official name, but it seems to have stuck.*

Jupiter 8. Internal-combustion-engine-powered wheeled vehicle used by citizens of the Roman culture on planet Eight Ninety-Two-IV. ("Bread and Circuses" [TOS]).

Jupiter Outpost 92. Federation station near the fifth planet of the Sol system. It was the first outpost to report the entrance of the **Borg** ship into that system during the Borg offensive of 2367. ("The Best of Both Worlds, Part II" [TNG]). *In an early version of the script for "The Best of Both Worlds, Part II," the story was still considered to be so confidential that each copy of the script was secretly numbered. The number of the Jupiter Outpost (in this* *case, 92) was different in each copy of the early draft script, so that if unauthorized copies were made, it would be possible to trace whose copy it came from.*

Jupiter Station. Starfleet facility orbiting the fifth planet in the Sol System. **Lewis Zimmerman**, the man who programmed the **Emergency Medical Hologram** on the *U.S.S. Voyager*, was stationed at the Jupiter Station Holo-programming Center. ("The Cloud" [VGR], "The Swarm" [VGR]). Lieutenant **Reginald Barclay** was a member of Zimmerman's production team, in charge of testing the EMH's interpersonal skills. ("Projections" [VGR]). Tuvok was temporarily stationed at the Jupiter Station sometime prior to 2371. While there he kept in contact with Kathryn Janeway through written letters. ("Tuvix" [VGR]). Zimmerman offered to set **Leeta** up as the manager of the station's cafe. ("Doctor Bashir, I Presume?" [DS9]).

Jupiter. Fifth world in the Sol System, a gas giant planet. Jupiter has an equatorial diameter of 142,700 kilometers, and it orbits its sun at about 778 million kilometers. The refit *Starship Enterprise* flew past Jupiter on its way to intercept V'Ger. *(Star Trek: The Motion Picture.)* Jupiter was designated as a Class-J planet. SEE: **planetary classification system**. ("Starship Down" [DS9]).

Juro. Contact sport played between two individuals. Benjamin Sisko told Dr. Julian Bashir that **Curzon Dax** use to beat him regularly at bare-fisted Juro counterpunch. ("A Man Alone" [DS9]).

"Justice." *Next Generation* episode #9. Teleplay by Worley Thorne. Story by Ralph Wills and Worley Thorne. Directed by James L. Conway. Stardate 41255.6. *First aired in 1987. Wesley Crusher is sentenced to death for a minor infraction on a planet of hedonistic pleasure.* GUEST CAST: Brenda Bakke as **Rivan**; Jay Louden as **Liator**; Josh Clark as Conn; David Q. Combs as 1st mediator; Richard Lavin as 2nd mediator; Judith Jones as Edo girl; Eric Matthew as 1st Edo boy; Brad Zerbst as Medical technician; David Michael Graves as 2nd Edo boy. SEE: **Crusher, Wesley; Edo god; Edo; Liator; mediators; punishment zones; Rivan; Rubicun III; Rubicun star system; Strnad star system.**

Justinian Code. Part of ancient Roman law enacted during the reign of Byzantine emperor Justinian I in the 6th century on planet Earth. The Justinian Code was a major effort to distill a thousand years of Roman legal precedents into a single body of work. ("Court Martial" [TOS]).

***Justman*, *Shuttlecraft*.** *Enterprise*-D shuttlecraft 03. The *Justman* was fitted with the **metaphasic shield** emitter in order to test the technology developed by Dr. Reyga in 2369. ("Suspicions" [TNG]). Earlier that year, a simulation of the *Justman* served to transport the computer-based intelligence known as **Professor James Moriarty** into a computer-generated environment. ("Ship in a Bottle" [TNG]). *The* Justman *is also visible in "Gambit, Part II" (TNG), sitting in the shuttlebay behind Koral's shuttle. The* Justman *was named by* Star Trek *executive producer Rick Berman, in honor of his colleague,* Star Trek *producer Robert H. Justman, a veteran of both the original* Star Trek *series and* Star Trek: The Next Generation*. The full-sized shuttlecraft filmed on stage was labeled "Justman," although a different shuttle design was seen in the visual-effects scenes of a miniature shuttle in flight.*

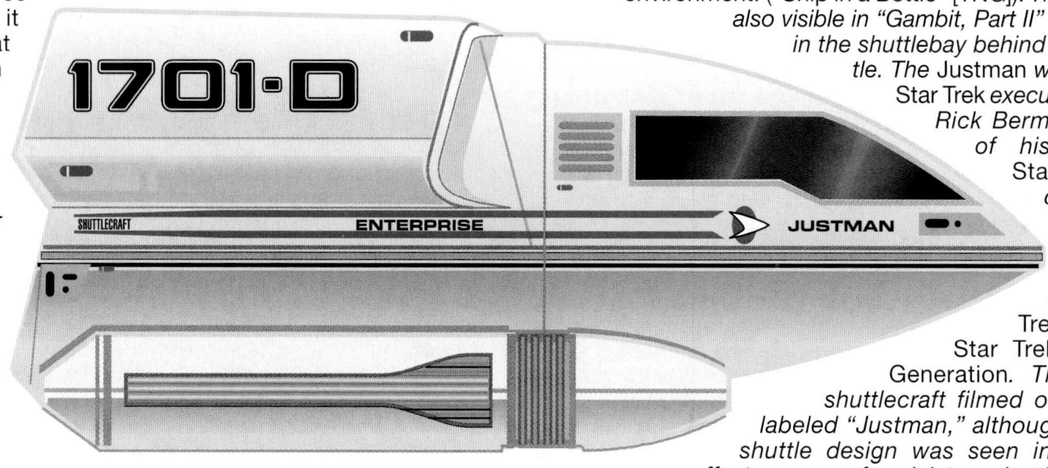

K'adlo. Klingon for "thank you." ("The Mind's Eye" [TNG]).

K'Ehleyr. (Suzie Plakson). Federation special emissary who supervised the return of the Klingon sleeper ship ***T'Ong*** to Klingon space in 2365. K'Ehleyr was responsible for averting a potential crisis, since the crew of the *T'Ong* believed the Klingon Empire was still at war with the Federation. K'Ehleyr's mother was human, and her father was Klingon. She said that she had inherited her mother's sense of humor, but her father's Klingon temper. K'Ehleyr had been romantically involved with **Worf** in 2359, but the relationship remained unresolved until 2365, when K'Ehleyr was assigned to the *Enterprise*-D to deal with the *T'Ong* crisis. K'Ehleyr and Worf nearly took the Klingon marriage oath at the time, when, unbeknownst to Worf, their liaison resulted in the conception of a child, **Alexander Rozhenko**. ("The Emissary" [TNG]). Worf remained unaware that he was a father until K'Ehleyr returned to the *Enterprise*-D in 2367. K'Ehleyr also served as a Federation ambassador to the **K'mpec** government. When K'mpec learned he was dying of slow poison in 2367, K'Ehleyr helped orchestrate his scheme to appoint **Jean-Luc Picard**, an outsider, as his **Arbiter of Succession**. K'Ehleyr was murdered by **Duras** during the rite of succession, after K'Ehleyr began to uncover evidence of Duras's wrongdoings. Worf subsequently claimed the right of vengence under Klingon law and killed Duras. Worf also accepted custody of his son, Alexander, who remained with him aboard the *Enterprise*-D. ("Reunion" [TNG]). *Suzie Plakson had previously played the Vulcan **Dr. Selar** in "The Schizoid Man" (TNG) and the **Q female** in "The Q and the Grey" (VGR).*

K'mpec. (Charles Cooper). Chancellor of the **Klingon High Council** who presided over that body longer than anyone else in history, using an iron hand to maintain peace within the council and the empire itself. One of K'mpec's greatest political challenges came in 2366, when evidence emerged implicating the late **Ja'rod**, father of council member **Duras**, of having committed treason. The politically powerful Duras attempted to suppress the fact that his father had betrayed his people to the Romulans at **Khitomer**. K'mpec feared that exposing Duras would plunge the empire into civil war, so he gave tacit support to a plan whereby the late **Mogh** would be blamed for the massacre. K'mpec did not realize that Mogh's sons, **Worf** and **Kurn**, would return to the homeworld to challenge this injustice, an appeal that K'mpec was not willing to hear in open council. K'mpec eventually agreed to allow Worf to accept **discommendation**, sparing both of Mogh's sons from death, while retaining some semblance of peace in the High Council. ("Sins of the Father" [TNG]). K'mpec was murdered in 2367, apparently poisoned with **Veridium Six** by Duras, who sought to succeed K'mpec as council leader. Under Klingon custom, such a killing was without honor because the killer did not show his face to the victim. Seeking to protect his empire from leadership by such a dishonorable person, K'mpec took the highly unorthodox step of appointing a non-Klingon, Jean-Luc Picard, as his **Arbiter of Succession**. K'mpec was succeeded by **Gowron**, a political newcomer. ("Reunion" [TNG]). *Charles Cooper also played General Korrd in* Star Trek V.

K'mtar alpha-1. Holodeck re-creation of the Klingon outpost of **Maranga IV** as it appeared in 2370. **K'mtar** used the simulation to demonstrate the importance of Klingon fighting skills to Alexander. ("Firstborn" [TNG]).

K'mtar. (James Sloyan). Name used by the adult **Alexander Rozhenko** when he traveled back in time from 2410 to 2370. K'mtar posed as the ***gin'tak*** to the House of **Mogh** and claimed he was sent to protect against an attack on the family. In reality, he was there to train his younger self to be a warrior. In this Alexander's future, Alexander had grown up to become a diplomat and peacemaker. This Alexander tried to end the feuding between the great houses by publicly announcing that the House of Mogh would no longer seek retribution. The future Worf had warned this Alexander not to show such weakness, but Alexander called him "a relic from an earlier time" and said that a new era of peace was at hand. His enemies moved against him, killing Worf on the floor of the High Council chamber. Filled with remorse, this Alexander journeyed back in time, calling himself K'mtar, to try to cause his younger self to become a Klingon warrior. ("Firstborn" [TNG]). *It is not known what influence the future Alexander had on his younger self, and therefore it is not known if Worf will be killed on the floor of the High Council. James Sloyan also played Admiral Alidar Jarok in "The Defector" (TNG), Dr. Mora Pol in "The Alternate" (DS9) and "The Begotten" (DS9) and Dr. Ma'Bor Jetrel in "Jetrel" (VGR).*

K'nera. (David Froman). Klingon officer. K'nera commanded the cruiser assigned to rendezvous with the *Enterprise*-D to return the criminals **Korris** and **Konmel** to the Klingon Homeworld in 2364. Both Korris and Konmel died before the transfer could take place. K'nera was quite impressed with Worf, and offered him a position in the **Klingon Defense Force** once his tenure with Starfleet had been completed. ("Heart of Glory" [TNG]).

k'oh-nar. Vulcan term referring to a fear of being completely exposed in an emotionally vulnerable situation. ("Alter Ego" [VGR]).

K'Ratak. Klingon author, writer of the classic work *The Dream of the Fire.* ("The Measure of a Man" [TNG]).

***K't'inga*-class battle cruiser.** Conjectural designation for an uprated version of the Klingon D7-type starships. *(Star Trek: The Motion Picture).* SEE: **Klingon spacecraft**.

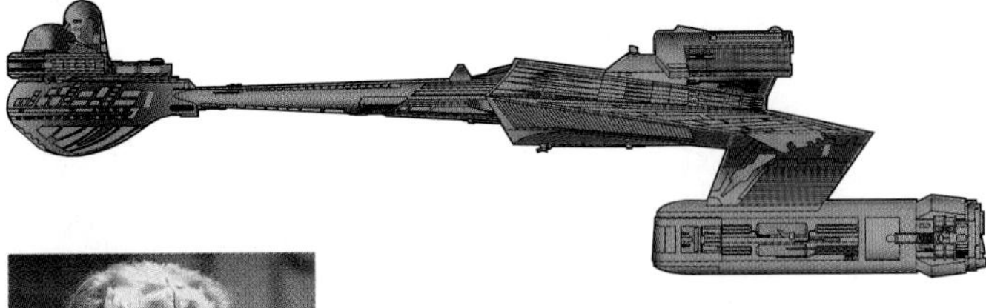

K'Tal. (Ben Slack). A member of the **Klingon High Council** who presided over the installation of **Gowron** as head of the council in 2367. ("Redemption, Part I" [TNG]).

K'Temang. (John Kenton Shull). Commander of a Klingon bird-of-prey that attacked the Cardassian outpost on **Korma** in 2372, killing everyone there. Cardassian officer **Gul Dukat**, commanding the *Groumall*, engaged and captured K'Temang's ship. After assuming command of the Klingon ship, Dukat stranded K'Temang and his crew on the *Groumall*. Dukat then destroyed the *Groumall,* killing all aboard. ("Return to Grace" [DS9]). *John Kenton Shull previously played a security officer in "Shakaar" (DS9).*

K'Temoc. (Lance le Gault). Captain of the Klingon ship ***T'Ong***. K'Temoc, a formidable Klingon warrior, was a product of a period when the Federation and the Klingon Empire were at war. ("The Emissary" [TNG]).

K'Vada, Captain. (Stephen Root). Commander of a Klingon bird-of-prey. K'Vada was assigned to secretly transport Captain Picard to Romulus in 2368. ("Unification, Part II" [TNG]).

K'Vort*-class battle cruisers.** Large version of the **Klingon bird-of-prey** ship. Three of these vessels arrived and surrounded the starships *Enterprise*-D and C as the ***Enterprise*-C** was trying to return through the **temporal rift**. ("Yesterday's *Enterprise*" [TNG]). *Smaller versions of this ship were called* **B'rel-class vessels. Both versions were represented by the same photographic miniature, originally built for* Star Trek III. SEE: **Klingon spacecraft**.

K-3 cell count. Medical test. An imbalance of the K-3 cell count can be indicative of **Urodelean flu**. ("Genesis" [TNG]).

K-3 indicator. Medical measurement of neural activity corresponding to the level of pain being experienced by a patient. The biomedical displays on *Constitution*-class starship sickbays incorporated a K-3 indicator. While Spock was under the control of the **Denevan neural parasites** in 2267, the K-3 indicator was nearly at maximum, indicating extreme pain. ("Operation—Annihilate!" [TOS]).

K-7, Deep Space Station. SEE: **Deep Space Station K-7**.

K-type planet. SEE: **Class-K planet**.

Ka'Ree. Native of the **Haakonian Order** and wife of scientist **Ma'Bor Jetrel**. Ka'Ree left her husband after she learned of his role in the development of the infamous metreon cascade in 2356, a weapon that killed over 300,000 people in the war between the Haakonians and the **Talaxian**s. ("Jetrel" [VGR]).

Kabul River. A major waterway located in the old Earth country of Afghanistan. The river runs past the capital city of Kabul to the Indian ocean. A **holodeck** program available on the *Enterprise*-D re-created a portion of the Kabul River. Jean-Luc Picard once suggested that Will Riker join him there for horseback riding. ("The Loss" [TNG]).

Kaelon II. Class-M planet. The sun of the Kaelon system was gradually dying, and by 2367 the people of Kaelon II were forced to turn to the Federation for help. Starfleet was able to assist in an experiment designed to revitalize the Kaelon sun. ("Half a Life" [TNG]). SEE: **helium fusion enhancement; Timicin, Dr.**

Kaelon warships. Two of these ships were launched from the surface of **Kaelon II** to persuade the *Enterprise*-D to return **Dr. Timicin** to the planet. ("Half a Life" [TNG]).

Kafar. (Rob LaBelle). **Takarian** servant and lackey of the two Ferengi who purported to be the **Great Sages** from Takarian mythology. ("False Profits" [VGR]).

Kaferian apple. Fruit. A favorite of **Gary Mitchell**, who created several Kaferian apple trees on planet **Delta Vega**. ("Where No Man Has Gone Before" [TOS]).

"Kahless and Lukara." Classic legend in Klingon mythology, regarded as the greatest love story in Klingon history. It tells of how Kahless the Unforgettable stood heroically with the Lady Lukara against 500 warriors at the Great Hall of Qam-Chee. Kahless and Lukara were the only survivors of that battle, after which she agreed to become his wife. Worf, who had been oblivious to the romantic attentions of Jadzia Dax, realized his passion for her in 2373 after sharing with her a holosuite opera version of this classic story. ("Looking for *par'Mach* in All the Wrong Places" [DS9]).

Kahless the Unforgettable. (Kevin Conway; Robert Herron). Klingon mythic-historic figure, a great warrior who united the **Klingon Empire** ("The Savage Curtain" [TOS]) some 1,500 years ago. The story of Kahless is a cornerstone of Klingon mythology and religion. ("Birthright, Part II" [TNG]). Legend has it that the messianic Kahless fought the tyrant **Molor**, whom he killed with the first ***bat'leth*** or sword of honor. Another of the epic tales of Kahless relates how he fought his brother, **Morath**, for 12 days and 12 nights because Morath had lied and brought shame to his family ("New Ground" [TNG]). Worf had a statue in his quarters depicting that heroic struggle ("Reunion" [TNG]). Legend also states that Kahless used his *bat'leth* to conquer the *Fek'lhri* and skin the serpent of Xol. Kahless also once used his sword to harvest his father's field and carve a statue of his beloved. ("The Sword of Kahless" [DS9]). He is reputed to have fought off an entire army single-handedly at Three Turn Bridge. ("Let He Who Is Without Sin..." [DS9]).

Kahless was not only known as a great warrior. His courtship of Lady **Lukara**, who agreed to be his wife after they together withstood the attack of 500 warriors at the Great Hall at **Qam-Chee**, is considered to be the greatest romance in Klingon history. ("Looking for *par'Mach* in All the Wrong Places" [DS9]). Kahless once said: "Destroying an empire to win a war is no victory. And ending a battle to save an empire is no defeat." ("The Way of the Warrior" [DS9]). Klingon warriors would often pray to Kahless for guidance before going into battle. ("Blood Oath" [DS9]). They believe that warriors who die honorably join Kahless, who awaits them in ***Sto-Vo-Kor***, the afterlife. Just before his death, Kahless pointed to a star in the sky and promised that he would one day return there. Klingon clerics established a monastery on **Boreth**, a planet orbiting that star, where they waited for centuries for Kahless to return. SEE: **Quin'lat; Story of the Promise, The.**

In the 24th century, the clerics of Boreth devised an elaborate scheme whereby preserved cellular material from Kahless was cloned to produce a replica of the original Kahless. The replica was programmed with all the ancient teachings and parables, and actually believed he was the real Kahless. The deception was quickly discovered, but **Worf**, son of Mogh, pointed out that the new Kahless could be considered the rightful heir to the throne. With the support of High Council leader **Gowron**, the new Kahless was installed in 2369 as ceremonial emperor of the Klingon people. ("Rightful Heir" [TNG]). When Worf was a boy, a vision of Kahless appeared to him and told him that he would do something no other Klingon had ever done. ("The Sword of Kahless" [DS9]). Another (presumably less accurate) copy of Kahless was created by the **Excalbians** in 2269, when they were attempting to study the human concepts of "good" and "evil" ("The Savage Curtain" [TOS]). *Several episodes, notably "Birthright, Part II" (TNG) and "Rightful Heir" (TNG), have revealed fragments of the legend of Kahless, but the entire story still remains to be told. Kahless, as seen in "The Savage Curtain" (TOS), when he was played by Robert Herron, appeared very dif-*

ferent from Kahless as seen in "Rightful Heir" (TNG), when he was played by Kevin Conway. One might rationalize that this might have been because the image of Kahless created by Yarnek was drawn from the mind of James Kirk, who may not have known what the "real" Kahless looked like. Of course, in truth "The Savage Curtain" was filmed many years before "Rightful Heir," prior to the introduction of the more elaborate Klingon makeup designs first used in Star Trek: The Motion Picture.

Kahlest. (Thelma Lee). ***Ghojmok*** or nursemaid to young **Worf**, while his family was living on **Khitomer**, at the time of the **Khitomer massacre** of 2346. She was rescued, along with Worf, by the crew of the ***U.S.S. Intrepid***. Kahlest was taken to **Starbase 24** for treatment, and she later returned to the **Klingon Homeworld** and took up residence in seclusion in the old city. Captain Picard visited her there in 2366 when Worf's family was facing dishonor because of falsified evidence that Worf's father, **Mogh**, had betrayed the empire at Khitomer. Kahlest knew nothing of Mogh's activities, but the existence of an eyewitness to the events at Khitomer was enough to force High Council leader **K'mpec** to accept a compromise. Kahlest had known K'mpec in their younger days, and K'mpec had been attracted to her, but according to Kahlest, "He was too fat." ("Sins of the Father" [TNG]).

Kahn, Dr. Lenara. (Susanna Thompson). Scientist at the **Trill** ministry of science and sister of Dr. Bejal Otner. Lenara Kahn developed a theory for creating artificial wormholes. In 2372 she led a team of scientists to conduct field tests to demonstrate her theories. The team used the *U.S.S. Defiant* and were successful in creating a stable wormhole that was open for 23.4 seconds, making it the first artificially created wormhole in Federation history. Lenara was a Trill who was joined with the Kahn symbiont. During the stable wormhole tests of 2372, Lenara worked with **Jadzia Dax**, a Trill who had (in a previous joining) been **Torias Dax**. Years ago, **Nilani Kahn** (a previous Kahn host) and Torias Dax had been married. Jadzia and Lenara felt a great desire to continue their relationship, despite the fact that Trill social mores prohibited their **reassociation**. Though Jadzia felt strong enough to go against Trill taboo, Lenara didn't wish to risk exile for reassociating with Dax. Lenara Kahn returned to Trill to continue her work. ("Rejoined" [DS9]). In 2373, Kahn devised a method to permanently close the **Bajoran wormhole** without damaging it or harming the wormhole aliens within. ("In Purgatory's Shadow" [DS9]).

Kahn, Nilani. Female joined **Trill** who was married to **Torias Dax**. Nilani was joined with the Kahn symbiont. The day before Torias was to test a shuttle, Nilani was worried for him. The next day Torias died in a shuttle accident, widowing Nilani. Years later, Nilani died, and the Kahn symbiont passed to **Lenara Kahn**. ("Rejoined" [DS9]).

Kahn-ut-tu. Medicine women of the **hill people** on **Tyree**'s planet, trained in the mystic arts, including the curative powers of medicinal herbs and roots. Tribal leader Tyree's wife, **Nona**, was a *Kahn-ut-tu*. Among the men on Tyree's planet, *Kahn-ut-tu* women were considered to be especially desirable. ("A Private Little War" [TOS]).

Kai Winn soufflé. Elaborate dessert created by Quark in 2371. The soufflé was to honor Kai **Winn**'s success in concluding a peace treaty with the **Cardassians**. The confection consisted of a large **chocolate** soufflé topped with Haligian tongue sauce. ("Life Support" [DS9]).

kai. Title for **Bajoran** supreme religious leader, an elected office. **Kai Opaka** held the post in 2369. ("Emissary" [DS9]). After Opaka's death, **Winn** won the title in 2370, after opposing candidate Vedek **Bareil** withdrew from the election. ("The Collaborator" [DS9]). SEE: **Taluno, Kai.**

Kainon. (Tony Rizzoli). Disheveled-appearing Bajoran with a history of minor criminal offenses. Kainon was held at Deep Space 9 station security for drunkenness when **Aamin Marritza** was held in 2369 on suspicion of having committed war crimes while serving in the **Cardassian** military. Kainon was very vocal about his desire not to share the same prison with any Cardassian citizen. When Marritza was found to be innocent of the charges and set free, Kainon took justice into his own hands, killing the Cardassian, not for any crime, but just because he was Cardassian. ("Duet" [DS9]).

Kajada, Ty. (Caitlin Brown). **Kobliad** security officer. Kajada tracked her prisoner, **Rao Vantika**, for 20 years. She was brought to Deep Space 9 after her vessel was destroyed in 2369. Kajada was thought to be the only survivor from her ship, but a series of strange events convinced her that Vantika was still alive, and it was later learned he had transferred his consciousness to Dr. Julian Bashir. Vantika was eventually captured and his consciousness was transferred to an energy-containment cell. Kajada subsequently destroyed the containment cell, killing Vantika. ("The Passenger" [DS9]).

kajanpak't. Klingon word for courage. ("Blood Oath" [DS9]).

Kal Rekk Traditional **Vulcan** holiday of atonement, solitude, and silence. ("Meld" [VGR]).

Kal-if-fee. Vulcan word for challenge. **T'Pring** chose the *Kal-if-fee* during her ***Pon farr*** mating ceremony in 2267, when she opted to challenge **Spock**'s claim on her. ("Amok Time" [TOS]). The female has the right to fight on her own behalf, if that is her choice, as did B'Elanna Torres on stardate 50541 when Ensign **Vorik** tried to claim her as his mate. ("Blood Fever" [VGR]).

kal-toh. A Vulcan puzzle, a test of balance and concentration. Vaguely spherical, about 20 centimeters in diameter, *kal-toh* is composed of short metallic-crystal rods called ***t'an***, connected to one another in what initially appears to be a chaotic fashion. An extremely complex and subtle game player must place the *t'an* rods on the *kal-toh* to introduce order and symmetry into the disorder. **Tuvok** studied under a *kal-toh* master since the age of five. ("Alter Ego" [VGR], "Darkling" [VGR]).

Kalandan outpost. Artificially created planetoid manufactured by the Kalandan people some ten thousand years ago. During the construction of the planet, a deadly microorganism was accidentally created, killing all of the **Kalandans** at the outpost. The last survivor, a woman named **Losira**, set the station's automated defense systems to protect the station for the day when more Kalandans would arrive at the outpost. This defense system killed several *Enterprise* crew members when the ship surveyed the planetoid in 2268. ("That Which Survives" [TOS]).

Kalandans. Technologically-sophisticated humanoid civilization. People responsible for the **Kalandan outpost** some ten thousand years ago. ("That Which Survives" [TOS]).

Kalandra, Dr. (Karen Austin). Federation medical officer. Kalandra was the head doctor at an emergency battlefield hospital on Ajilon Prime during the Klingon invasion of 2373. Kalandra's husband was the science officer on the *U.S.S. Tecumseh.* ("Nor the Battle to the Strong" [DS9]).

Kalavian biscuits. Pastry snack from Neelix's kitchen. ("Threshold" [VGR]).

Kaldra IV. A Federation planet. A group of **Ullian** researchers had intended to conduct research at Kaldra IV for their planned telepathic memory library project in 2368. The Ullians never reached Kaldra, owing to the arrest of one of their party. ("Violations" [TNG]).

Kaleb sector. Region of space. Location where Romulan **Subcommander N'Vek** attempted to rendezvous with a Corvallen freighter for the defection of **Vice-Proconsul M'ret** in 2369. ("Face of the Enemy" [TNG]).

Kalem Apren. First Minister of the Bajoran provisional government until his death in 2371. Kalem, who died from heart failure, was briefly replaced in office by Kai **Winn**. ("Shakaar" [DS9]).

Kalevian montar. Game. **Gul Dukat** once played Kalevian montar with **Odo** on **Deep Space 9**. Dukat recalled that they had played many times, but Odo reminded Dukat that they only played once and that the Cardassian had cheated. ("Duet" [DS9]).

Kalin Trose. (William Newman). Government representative of the **Alpha Moon** of planet **Peliar Zel**. Kalin took part in two major conferences with the **Beta Moon**, one in 2337 and one in 2367. Both negotiations were successfully mediated by **Ambassador Odan**. ("The Host" [TNG]).

Kalita. (Shannon Cochran). Member of a **Maquis** cell located on planet **Ronara** in 2370. Kalita was initially suspicious of **Ro Laren**'s motives for joining the cell, but became convinced of Ro's sincerity following a successful raid on the *Enterprise*-D. ("Preemptive Strike" [TNG]). In 2371, Kalita operated the **conn** station on the bridge of the *U.S.S. **Defiant*** during Thomas Riker's unauthorized mission to the Orias system. ("Defiant" [DS9]).

Kalla III. Uninhabited planet. In 2370, the Duras sisters, **Lursa** and **B'Etor**, along with their partner, **Gorta**, illegally mined a deposit of **magnesite ore** on Kalla III that was actually owned by **Pakled** interests. ("Firstborn" [TNG]).

Kalla-Nohra Syndrome. Chronic pulmonary disease. Kalla-Nohra Syndrome is found only in individuals exposed to a mining accident at **Gallitep**, a labor camp run by the **Cardassians** during the occupation. There are no known instances of anyone not involved with that mining accident contracting the disease, so a positive diagnosis makes it virtually certain that an individual has been at that infamous death camp. Cardassian citizen **Aamin Marritza** was diagnosed with Kalla-Nohra at Deep Space 9 in 2369, and was subsequently suspected of having been Gallitep commander **Gul Darhe'el**. ("Duet" [DS9]).

Kallisko. A transport ship from planet Boreal III. The ship was near the Brechtian Cluster when it was attacked by the **Crystalline Entity** in 2368. There were no survivors. ("Silicon Avatar" [TNG]).

Kalo. (Lee Delano). One of **Bela Oxmyx**'s henchmen on planet **Sigma Iotia II** in 2268. ("A Piece of the Action" [TOS]).

Kalomi, Leila. (Jill Ireland). Botanist and member of a colony expedition that left Earth in 2263 to settle on planet **Omicron Ceti III**. Leila met **Spock** on Earth in 2261 and fell in love, but knew that her feelings could never be returned. The spores on planet Omicron Ceti III changed that when Spock was exposed to their powers, allowing him briefly to return Kalomi's affections. ("This Side of Paradise" [TOS]). SEE: **spores, Omicron Ceti III**. *Jill Ireland, who died in 1991 of breast cancer, spent the last part of her life conducting a courageous campaign to increase national awareness of the importance of early detection of that terrible disease.*

Kalto province. Region on a Class-M planet in the **Delta Quadrant** whose people were dependent on **polaric ion energy**. ("Time and Again" [VGR]).

Kalton. An inhabitant of the **Kalto province** on a planet in the Delta Quadrant. ("Time and Again" [VGR]).

Kama Sutra. Ancient Hindu text containing instruction in love and the erotic arts. ("Doctor Bashir, I Presume?" [DS9]).

Kamala. (Famke Janssen). A native of the **Krios** system, Kamala was an **empathic metamorph**, the first born on her world in a century. Raised from childhood to fulfill her role as an instrument of peace, Kamala was fated to wed **Chancellor Alrik** of **Valt Minor**. Kamala was a beautiful woman, and her ability to change into whatever a potential mate desired made her irresistible to men. When she came on-board the *Enterprise*-D, Kamala was in the final stages of the ***Finiis'ral*** stage of sexual maturity, causing disruptions aboard the ship. Kamala had been intended to bond to Alrik, but when circumstances put her in close contact with Captain Picard, she bonded to him. Kamala said she liked the way she was when she was with Picard, and added that there was no greater joy for a metamorph. But Kamala had learned a sense of duty from her bonding with Picard, and chose to go through with the ceremony, to seal the peace for her people. ("The Perfect Mate" [TNG]). SEE: **Ceremony of Reconciliation**; **Lenor, Par**. *Famke Janssen later played the beautiful Xenia Onatopp in the James Bond film* Goldeneye.

Kamie. Native of the now-dead planet **Kataan**, son of **Meribor** and grandson of **Kamin**, who lived a thousand years ago in the village of **Ressik**. ("The Inner Light" [TNG]).

Kamin. (Patrick Stewart). Native of the now-dead planet **Kataan**. Kamin was known as the best ironweaver in the community of **Ressik**, but he preferred to play his tin flute. Kamin was the husband of **Eline** and the father of two children, **Meribor** and **Batai**. Kamin's life was recorded and sent out on an interstellar probe, launched as a final memory of the people of Kataan, when they discovered their sun was to go nova. When the *Enterprise*-D encountered the probe in 2368, Captain Picard was rendered unconscious by the probe and experienced Kamin's entire adult life in the span of 25 minutes. ("The Inner Light" [TNG]). SEE: **Kataan probe**; **Ressikan flute**.

kanar. A beverage favored by Cardassians. ("The Wire" [DS9]). According to Glinn Daro, the drink took "some getting used to." ("The Wounded" [TNG]). *Kanar* was served to

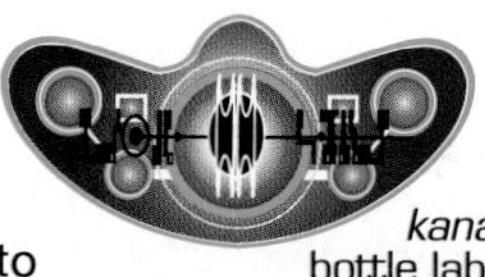

kanar bottle label

Rekelen and Hogue during their visit to station Deep Space 9 in 2370. ("Profit and Loss" [DS9]). Kanar *was also mentioned in "Destiny" [DS9]).*

Kandora champagne. Beverage. Available at **Quark's bar**. According to Quark, 2368 was a very good year for Kandora champagne. ("Meridian" [DS9]).

Kang's Summit. Large mountain on the Klingon Homeworld. **General Martok** was kidnapped by the Dominion while hunting **sabre bear** on Kang's Summit in 2371. ("In Purgatory's Shadow" [DS9]). *Maybe the mountain was renamed for legendary Klingon warrior Kang. Or perhaps Kang was named after the great mountain.*

Kang. (Michael Ansara). Legendary Klingon warrior. In 2268, while captain of a Klingon starship, Kang was the victim of the **Beta XII-A entity** that destroyed his ship and trapped his crew aboard the *Starship Enterprise*. Kang's wife, **Mara**, and 38 members of his crew fought an equal number of *Enterprise* crew members in a seemingly endless battle controlled by the Beta XII-A entity, until both sides discovered that peaceful cooperation was the only way to survive. ("Day of the Dove" [TOS]). Kang met Federation negotiator **Curzon Dax** in 2289, while their governments were still at war. Kang learned to respect Dax as one who understood the Klingon nature. He even named his firstborn son for Dax. Kang's son, along with the firstborns of **Kor** and **Koloth**, was murdered by a criminal known as **the Albino**, who had sought retribution for their role in stopping the Albino from raiding Klingon colonies in 2290. Afterwards, Kang, Kor, Koloth, and Dax swore a blood oath to avenge the killing of these innocent children. In 2293, Kang commanded a *K't'inga*-class battle cruiser that encountered the *U.S.S.* ***Excelsior*** in the **Azure Nebula**. Captain Sulu, in command of the *Excelsior*, ignited the sirillium gas in the nebula, briefly disrupting the sensors and tactical systems of Kang's vessel, allowing the *Excelsior* to escape. ("Flashback" [VGR]). Although the Albino went into hiding for decades, the four never forgot their promise. ("Blood Oath" [DS9]). Koloth and Kor once fought with Kang against T'nag and his army, emerging victorious despite overwhelming odds. ("The Sword of Kahless" [DS9]). Kang died in glorious battle in 2370 when the three Klingons and **Jadzia Dax** found the Albino at a stronghold on planet **Secarus IV**. Kang struck the killing blow to the Albino that day. ("Blood Oath" [DS9]).

Kapec, Rayna. (Louise Sorel). **Android** created by **Flint** as his immortal mate. Rayna died in 2269 when faced with the impossible task of choosing between her love for her mentor and her love for James Kirk. ("Requiem For Methuselah" [TOS]). *Rayna Kapec was named for Czechoslovakian writer Karel Capek, who first coined the term "robot" in the classic science-fiction play entitled "R.U.R."*

Kaplan, Commander Donald. Chief engineer of the ***U.S.S. Intrepid*** in 2370. Kaplan was a Starfleet Academy classmate of *Enterprise*-D Chief Engineer Geordi La Forge. The two men were engaged in a friendly rivalry to see which engineer could achieve the highest power-conversion level in their respective ship's engines. ("Force of Nature" [TNG]).

Kaplan, Ensign. (Susan Patterson). Starfleet officer assigned to the *U.S.S. Voyager.* Kaplan was on the bridge as the ship received a **SETI** greeting from Earth as the starship visited Earth's past in 1996. ("Future's End, Parts I and II" [VGR]). Kaplan was killed in 2373 by renegades on a planet populated by former **Borg** drones. ("Unity" [VGR]).

Kaplan, Lieutenant. (Dick Dial). Crew member aboard the original *Enterprise*. Kaplan was killed in 2267 while serving on landing party duty at planet **Gamma Trianguli VI**. He was killed by a bolt of lightning generated by the god-machine **Vaal**. ("The Apple" [TOS]). *"I think I'll wear red," said Kaplan as he dressed for work on that fateful day.*

Kar-telos system. Planetary system in the Gamma Quadrant. The *U.S.S. Defiant* passed through the Kar-telos system in 2372. ("Bar Association" [DS9]).

Kar. (Aron Eisenberg.) Kazon-Ogla warrior. In 2372, Kar was disgraced when he failed to earn his Ogla name by killing an enemy, a Federation shuttlecraft pilot Chakotay. Kar and Chakotay were taken prisoner by the Kazon-Ogla, but soon escaped to the moon **Tarok,** where they awaited rescue by the *Starship Voyager*. Ashamed of his failure to earn his Ogla name, Kar struggled to find the courage to kill Chakotay, but found he could not. However, when a Kazon landing party descended on the moon, Kar killed First Maje Razik and thus earned his Ogla name of Jal Karden. ("Initiations" [VGR]). *Aron Eisenberg played Nog on* Star Trek: Deep Space Nine.

Kara Polos. Bajoran civilian. Kara was on station Terok Nor in 2367 when he was arrested, convicted of a crime, and sentenced to five years' hard labor for the offense. ("Things Past" [DS9]).

Kara. (Marj Dusay). Leader of the **Eymorg** women of planet **Sigma Draconis VI** in 2268. Although untrained in the sciences, Kara underwent a memory-implantation procedure that gave her the necessary knowledge and skill to successfully steal Spock's brain, so that it could be used to run her planet's master computer system. ("Spock's Brain" [TOS]). SEE: **Controller**; **Teacher**.

Kara. (Tania Lemani). Dancer who worked at a small cafe on planet **Argelius II**. Kara had performed in 2267 on the evening that several *U.S.S. Enterprise* crew members on shore leave visited the cafe. Kara left the establishment in the company of **Montgomery Scott** and was later found brutally murdered. Scott was initially suspected of the crime, but Kara's death was later found to have been caused by an alien entity that fed on the emotion of fear. ("Wolf in the Fold" [TOS]). SEE: **Redjac**.

Karapleedeez, Onna. Starfleet officer. Karapleedeez was killed in 2364, apparently by the unknown alien intelligence that attempted to infiltrate Starfleet Command. ("Conspiracy" [TNG]).

Karden, Jal. SEE: **Kar**.

Kareel. (Nicole Orth-Pallavicini). **Trill** host who joined with **Odan** after the Odan **symbiont** was removed from Commander Riker's body. She returned to the Trill homeworld following the implantation of the symbiont. ("The Host" [TNG]).

Karemma system. Planetary system in the Gamma Quadrant containing the **Karemma** homeworld. ("The Search, Part I" [DS9]).

Karemma. Humanoid civilization from the Gamma Quadrant, part of the **Dominion**. Quark established a trade agreement with the Karemma for purchase of **tulaberry wine.** ("Rules of Acquisition" [DS9]). The Karemma used **Ferengi** as intermediaries in their commerce with the Federation, because they knew the Dominion would never tolerate direct trade between the Karemma and the Federation. The Karemma were naive when it came to business dealings, and the Ferengi took advantage of them for a time. ("Starship Down" [DS9]). The only contact the Karemma had with the rest of the Dominion was through the **Vorta**. ("The Search, Part I" [DS9]).

Karemman fleece. Livestock-hide product traded by the **Karemma**. ("Starship Down" [DS9]).

Karemman vessel. Medium-sized starship of Karemman registry with a crew of 23. A Karemman vessel was destroyed by Jem'Hadar ships after it rendezvoused with the *Starship Defiant* in 2372 to discuss their trade agreement with the Ferengi. ("Starship Down" [DS9]).

Kargan, Captain. (Christopher Collins). Klingon officer, commander of the bird-of-prey ***Pagh.*** Kargan was Riker's superior when Riker served aboard the *Pagh* as part of an **Officer Exchange Program** in 2365. ("A Matter of Honor" [TNG]). *Christopher Collins also played the Pakled captain in "Samaritan Snare" (TNG).*

Karidian Company of Players. Shakespearean theatrical troupe headed by **Anton Karidian**. The Karidian company had been touring official installations for nine years prior to 2266, when Karidian was killed following the revelation that he was Kodos the Executioner. Library computer analysis indicated that nearly every surviving eyewitness to Kodos's crimes had been murdered, and that each murder had taken place when the Karidian Company of Players was nearby. The murder of the surviving witnesses was later found to be the work of **Lenore Karidian**. ("The Conscience of the King" [TOS]).

Karidian, Anton. (Arnold Moss). Alias for the former Governor Kodos of planet **Tarsus IV**, aka **Kodos the Executioner**. Kodos assumed this identity about a year after escaping arrest following the massacre at the Tarsus IV colony in 2246. As Karidian, he won acclaim as a Shakespearean actor and as director of the **Karidian Company of Players**. Karidian was killed in 2266 during a performance of ***Hamlet*** aboard the *Starship Enterprise*. He was survived by his daughter, **Lenore Karidian**. ("The Conscience of the King" [TOS]).

Karidian, Lenore. (Barbara Anderson). Daughter of **Anton Karidian**, aka **Kodos the Executioner**. Born in 2247, about a year after Kodos's massacre at the **Taurus IV** colony. Although her father attempted to shield her from the crimes he had committed before her birth, Lenore not only learned about her father's past, but systematically attempted to murder all nine surviving witnesses of her father's crimes. Deemed criminally insane, Lenore Karidian was imprisoned for treatment following her attempt on the lives of Captain **James Kirk** and Lieutenant **Kevin Riley**, during which her father was accidentally killed. ("The Conscience of the King" [TOS]).

Karina. (Annette Helde). Member of a **Romulan** delegation sent to station Deep Space 9 in 2371 to receive **Starfleet**'s latest intelligence on the **Dominion**. The delegation had secret orders to destroy the **Bajoran wormhole** in order to prevent a feared Dominion invasion of the Alpha Quadrant, and to destroy Deep Space 9 as well. ("Visionary" [DS9]).

Karis Tribe. Population group on planet Delios VII. Karis Tribe members practiced a ritual that increased the electrical resistance of their skin. This protected them from plasma discharges in their sacred caves. ("Sacred Ground" [VGR]).

karjinko. Term for losing in **dabo**. Mardah said *karjinko* to customer **Okalar** after ending a winning streak at the dabo table. ("The Abandoned" [DS9]).

Karnas. (Michael Pataki). Leader of one of the warring factions on planet **Mordan IV.** A ruthless negotiator, Karnas had extorted weapons from Starfleet mediator **Mark Jameson** in 2319 so that he could win revenge on a rival faction for the murder of his father. Karnas nonetheless blamed Jameson for the ensuing civil war, which lasted 40 years. In 2364, Karnas tried to exact revenge on Jameson. ("Too Short a Season" [TNG]). *Michael Pataki previously played Korax in "The Trouble with Tribbles" (TOS).*

karo-net. Sporting event. Odo enjoyed karo-net and cited the karo-net tournament to **Quark** when discussing the disadvantages of coupling and having to make compromises. ("A Man Alone" [DS9]).

***karvino* juice.** Clear green beverage. *Karvino* juice was available at Quark's bar on **Deep Space 9**. ("Defiant" [DS9]).

Kataan probe. Small unmanned spacecraft launched during Earth's 14th century from the planet **Kataan**, just before the star went nova. The probe represented the Kataan people's attempt to preserve something of themselves by sending memories of their people into space. The probe encountered the *Starship Enterprise*-D in 2368, and transmitted those memories to Captain Jean-Luc Picard, who, in the span of a few minutes, experienced a lifetime in the Kataan village **Ressik**, as an ironweaver named **Kamin**. Also carried aboard the probe was a single artifact, a **Ressikan flute** that had belonged to Kamin. ("The Inner Light" [TNG]).

Kataan. Star located in the Silarian Sector. Kataan had six planets, one of which was a Class-M world (also called Kataan) inhabited by a humanoid civilization. The star Kataan went nova in Earth's 14th century, eradicating all life in the system. ("The Inner Light" [TNG]). SEE: **Kamin**; **Kataan probe**; **Ressikan flute**.

Kateras. (Edward Penn). **Boraalan** elder and father of **Tarrana**. Kateras asked Worf to take his daughter as a wife, should he not survive their journey to their new home in 2370. Worf assured Kateras that he would survive the trip. ("Homeward" [TNG]).

Katowa. Grandfather of **Anthwara**. Katowa led a group of Native American colonists from Earth in 2170, to preserve their cultural identity by seeking a new home among the stars. His people wandered for two centuries until settling at planet **Dorvan V**. ("Journey's End" [TNG]).

katra**.** The Vulcan concept of the soul, the living spirit. Just prior to death, Vulcan custom is to mind-meld with a friend who is entrusted with the duty of returning the *katra* to the individual's home. Just before he died in 2285, Spock **mind-meld**ed with Dr. McCoy, placing his *katra* in McCoy's subconscious. *(Star Trek III: The Search for Spock).* Some Vulcans do not fully accept the concept of the *katra*. Tuvok was among them. ("Innocence" [VGR]). SEE: ***fal-tor-pan*****; synaptic pattern displacement.**

katterpod beans. Bajoran agricultural product, grown both on Bajor and on one of its moons, **Jeraddo**. ("Progress" [DS9]). Katterpods, which resemble an Earth mushroom, were cultivated for their roots, which were also referred to as beans. ("The Jem'Hadar" [DS9]). Crops were typically treated with a chlorobicrobe spray to increase yield. ("Progress" [DS9]).

***kava* root.** Agricultural product grown on the planet Bajor. ("Starship Down" [DS9]).

kava**.** Culinary ingredient sometimes used as a flavoring in ***raktajino***. ("Crossfire" [DS9]).

Kaval. (Ted Sorel). **Bajoran** Minister of State in 2369. Kaval communicated to Benjamin Sisko the Bajoran provisional government's desire to see **Aamin Marritza** returned to Bajor so that the accused Cardassian war criminal could stand trial. ("Duet" [DS9]). SEE: **Gallitep**.

Kavarian tiger-bat. Animal life-form from planet Kavaria. ("For the Cause" [DS9]).

Kavis Alpha IV. Planet in Federation space. Kavis Alpha IV became the home of the newly-evolved nanite civilization in 2366. ("Evolution" [TNG]).

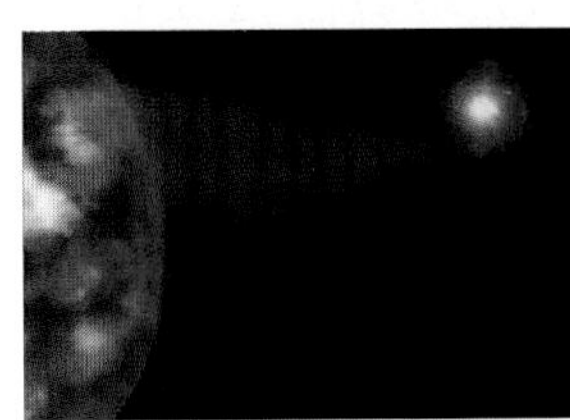

Kavis Alpha Sector. Home of a binary system. The Kavis Alpha Sector was the site of **Dr. Paul Stubbs's** neutronium decay experiments in 2366. The neutron star of that system exploded every 196 years, making it a stellar equivalent of Earth's "Old Faithful." ("Evolution" [TNG]).

***Kavis Teke* elusive maneuver.** Famous battle strategy developed by the **Menthars** in their war with the **Promellians** a thousand years ago. ("Booby Trap" [TNG]).

Kaybok, Commander. (Christopher Darga). Commander of the Klingon bird-of-prey *M'Char.* In early 2372, Kaybok was ordered by the Klingon High Council to board all vessels attempting to leave Bajoran space and to search them for shape-shifters. On stardate 49011, the *M'Char* stopped the freighter *Xhosa*. Captain Sisko, in command of the *Defiant,* intervened and convinced the *M'Char* to stand down. After the incident, **General Martok** had Kaybok executed for disobeying orders. ("The Way of the Warrior" [DS9]).

Kayden, Will. Starfleet officer, a crew member aboard the ***U.S.S. Rutledge***, who was killed during the battle on Setlik III. Kayden, nicknamed "Stompie" by his shipmates, was fond of singing **"The Minstrel Boy."** Kayden's commanding officer was **Captain Benjamin Maxwell**, and he had served along with **Miles O'Brien**. ("The Wounded" [TNG]).

Kaylar. Warrior on planet **Rigel VII**, encountered by Pike and company about a week prior to the *Enterprise*'s first expedition to **Talos IV** in 2254. An illusory version of this individual threatened Pike and **Vina** while the two were held captive by the **Talosians**. ("The Cage," "The Menagerie, Part II" [TOS]).

kaylo**.** Yellow fruit, resembling an Earth apple, native to a planet in the Delta Quadrant. It is highly poisonous to humanoids; one bite of a *kaylo* results in choking, then painful death. ("State of Flux" [VGR]).

kayolane. Sedative medication; used aboard the *Enterprise*-D. ("Identity Crisis" [TNG]).

Kazago. (Doug Warhit). Ferengi first officer to **DaiMon Bok** during the mission to return the hulk of the ***U.S.S. Stargazer*** to Picard in 2364. Kazago relieved Bok of command when it was learned that Bok had engaged in an unprofitable attempt to use the *Stargazer* to exact revenge upon Picard for his part in the **Battle of Maxia**. ("The Battle" [TNG]).

Kazanga. Brilliant theoretical scientist, often compared to such luminaries as **Albert Einstein** and **Dr. Richard Daystrom**. ("The Ultimate Computer" [TOS]).

Kazis Binary system. Star system. Projected destination of the **cryosatellite** discovered by the *Enterprise*-D in 2364. ("The Neutral Zone" [TNG]).

Kazleti pendant. Decorative jewelry. *Voyager* crew member Chell wore a Kazleti pendant as a necklace. The pendant bore a design that originated on the Kazleti homeworld. ("Learning Curve" [VGR]).

Kazon Collective. Formal name for the loose alliance of all the various **Kazon** sects in the Delta Quadrant. ("Caretaker" [VGR]).

Kazon spacecraft. Kazon technology permitted the Kazon sects to operate over a substantial fraction of the Delta Quadrant in a variety of different spacecraft. ("Caretaker" [VGR]). The Kazon sects used ships of **Trabe** design that they stole from the Trabe in 2346, when the Kazon overthrew their Trabe oppressors. ("Maneuvers" [VGR]). A large **Kazon-Ogla** cruiser attempted to prevent the *U.S.S. Voyager* from destroying the **Caretaker**'s **Array** in 2371. Smaller Kazon scoutships were capable of landing on a planetary surface. ("Caretaker" [VGR]). SEE: ***Predator*****-class warship**. The Ogla sect employed raider spacecraft that were equipped with technology similar to Federation **tractor beams** and **phasers**. ("Initiations" [VGR]). Small Kazon shuttles can be equipped with reinforced nose armor and are sometimes used to literally ram into enemy vessels. The Kazon-Nistrim launched such an attack on the *Starship Voyager* in early 2372. ("Maneuvers" [VGR]).

Kazon-Hobii. A sect of the Kazon Collective. In 2372, the Hobii were led by First Maje Jal Loran. ("Maneuvers" [VGR]). In late 2372, Maje Loran**,** along with other Kazon leaders, was invited to a peace conference on planet Sobras organized by *Starship Voyager* Captain Kathryn Janeway and **Trabe** leader **Mabus**. The meeting proved to be a trap devised by Mabus to exterminate the Kazons. Although no lives were lost, the assassination attempt deepened Kazon hatred against both Trabe and Federation forces. ("Alliances" [VGR]).

Kazon-Mostral. A sect of the Kazon Collective. In 2372, the Mostral were lead by First Maje **Jal Surat**. ("Maneuvers" [VGR]). In late 2372, Surat, along with other Kazon leaders, was nearly

Kazon-Hobii

Kazon-Mostral

Kazon-Nistrim

Kazon-Oglamar

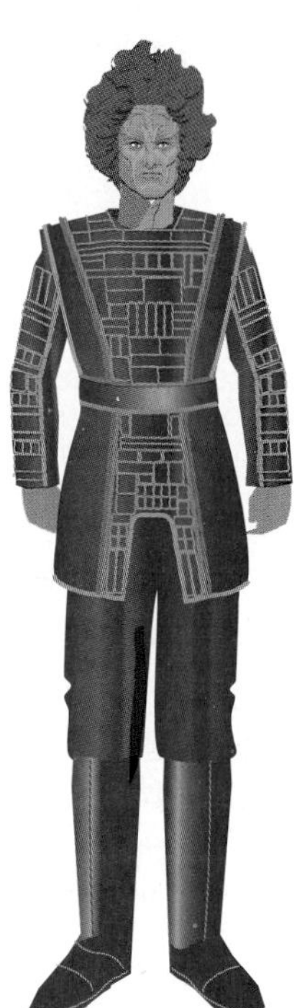
Kazon-Pommar

killed when a peace conference organized by **Trabe** and Federation forces proved to be a trap. ("Alliances" [VGR]).

Kazon-Nistrim. One of the most violent sects of the **Kazon Collective**. Their ships were capable of **warp drive** and carried special masking circuitry that affected Federation sensors in such a way as to render them invisible. The Kazon-Nistrim were willing to be the protectors of the *Voyager* and her crew while she was in the Delta Quadrant, in return for some Federation technology. In 2371, Ensign **Seska** attempted to secretly forge a pact with a Kazon-Nistrim officer *(played by Norman Large)* and gave them a Federation food replicator towards that end. ("State of Flux" [VGR]). *Norman Large also portrayed Romulan proconsul Neral in "Unification, Parts I and II" [TNG] and Maques in "Dark Page" (TNG).* **Jal Culluh** (*pictured*), first maje of the Nistrim in 2372, enlisted Seska, using her in a bold attempt to steal transporter technology from the *Voyager* in an effort to gain an upper hand over the other sects. The effort failed, a symbol of the Nistrim's fading influence in the Kazon Collective, which had diminished greatly since the days that Culluh's grandfather had been First Maje. The Nistrim were sworn enemies of the **Kazon-Relora**. ("Maneuvers" [VGR]). In late 2372, Culluh, along with numerous other Kazon leaders, was nearly killed when a peace conference organized by Trabe and Federation forces proved to be a trap. ("Alliances" [VGR]).

Kazon-Ogla. Sect of the **Kazon Collective**. Members of the Kazon-Ogla settlement on the **Ocampa** planet tried to seize control of the **Caretaker**'s Array in 2371, but were prevented from doing so when the *Starship Voyager* destroyed the **Array**. ("Caretaker" [VGR]). SEE: **Jabin.** A Kazon-Ogla male must participate in a rite of passage from boyhood to manhood by killing an enemy and thereby earning his Ogla name. ("Initiations" [VGR]). Representatives of the Kazon-Ogla did not attend the disastrous peace conference of 2372 arranged by **Trabe** operative **Mabus**. ("Alliances" [VGR]).

Kazon-Oglamar. A sect of the Kazon Collective. In 2372, the Oglamar were lead by Jal Valek. ("Maneuvers" [VGR]). In late 2372, Valek, along with numerous other Kazon leaders, was nearly killed when a peace conference organized by **Trabe** and Federation forces proved to be a trap. ("Alliances" [VGR]).

Kazon-Pommar. Kazon sect. In late 2372, First Maje Minnis of the Pommar, along with other Kazon leaders, was invited to a peace conference on planet Sobras organized by by *Starship Voyager* Captain Kathryn Janeway and **Trabe** leader **Mabus**. The meeting proved to be a trap devised by Mabus to exterminate the Kazons. Although no lives were lost, the assassination attempt deepened Kazon hatred against both Trabe and Federation forces. ("Alliances" [VGR]).

Kazon-Relora. Sect of the **Kazon Collective**, blood enemies of the **Kazon-Nistrim**. The Relora had many ships and were regarded as one of the most powerful of the Kazon sects. In 2372, the Relora were led by First Maje **Jal Haron**, until stardate 49208, when Haron was killed by **Jal Culluh** of the Nistrim. ("Initiations" [VGR], "Maneuvers" [VGR]). Representatives of the Relora did not attend the disastrous peace conference of 2372 arranged by **Trabe** operative **Mabus**. ("Alliances" [VGR]).

Kazon. Spacefaring humanoid civilization from the **Delta Quadrant**. ("Caretaker" [VGR]). Long ago, the Kazon were among the most culturally and technologically advanced people in that part of the galaxy. This ended when the Kazon were conquered by the **Trabe**, who encouraged the various Kazon sects to fight among themselves, making them easier to control. The Trabe oppression ended in 2346 when **Jal Sankur** united the Kazon people, overthrowing the Trabe. The departing Kazons stole the Trabe's spacecraft, returning the Kazon to the status of a spacefaring society. ("Maneuvers" [VGR]). After gaining their freedom, the Kazon persecuted the Trabe, denying their former oppressors sanctuary on other planets. In 2372, Trabe leader **Mabus** conspired to assassinate a delegation of Kazon first majes brought together under the guise of a peace conference. The murderous plan failed, and the Kazon continued its revenge against the Trabe. ("Alliances" [VGR]). Nevertheless, the Kazon people quickly returned to a society divided into warring sects, including the **Kazon-Ogla** ("Caretaker" [VGR]) and the **Kazon-Nistrim** ("State of Flux" [VGR]). While possessing the Trabe interstellar space flight capabilities, the Kazon did not have transporter, replicator, or related technologies common to spacefaring groups in the Alpha Quadrant. ("Caretaker" [VGR]). The Kazon are very territorial, and borders between the sects change daily. Even the number of Kazon sects changes daily. In early 2372, there were approximately 18 sects. ("Initiations" [VGR]). *The Kazon were first encountered in "Caretaker" (VGR).*

Kea IV. Planet. Kea IV was the topic of a minor research paper presented by Jean-Luc Picard at an archaeology symposium in 2368. ("The Chase" [TNG]).

Kearsarge, U.S.S. Federation starship, *Challenger* class, Starfleet registry number NCC-57566. A scheduled rendezvous of the *Kearsarge* with the *Enterprise*-D in 2370 was postponed for four days, allowing Worf and his son Alexander to attend the ***Kot'baval* Festival.** ("Firstborn" [TNG]). *Named for the American aircraft carrier that served as the recovery vessel for Alan Shepard's* Freedom Seven Mercury *spacecraft.*

Keats, John. (1795-1821). Nineteenth-century Earth poet. Keats was one of the most outstanding of English romantic poets. Despite his short career, his work is some of the most thematically and poetically complex writing in the English language. Keats's creativity was, in part, inspired by a noncorporeal entity known as **Onaya**, who was also responsible for the brevity of his life. ("The Muse" [DS9]).

kedion. Subatomic particle that can resonate with positrons. When held by the Borg in 2370, Geordi La Forge and Captain Picard used a phased kedion pulse in hopes of triggering Data's subsystems and rebooting his **ethical program**. ("Descent, Part II" [TNG]).

Kee'Bhor. Medical officer of the Klingon attack cruiser ***Toh'Kaht***. Kee'Bhor was murdered by First Officer Hon'Tihl while under the influence of the **Saltah'na energy spheres**, just before the destruction of the *Toh-Kaht* in 2369. ("Dramatis Personae" [DS9]).

Keedera. Great writer of Klingon epic songs. ("By Inferno's Light" [DS9]).

Keel, Walker. (Jonathan Farwell). Commander of the *Starship* ***Horatio***. Keel was one of several officers who fought against an infiltration of **Starfleet Headquarters** in 2364, but he was killed in the effort, along with the crew of the *Horatio*. Keel had no brothers, but had two sisters, Anne and Melissa. Keel had been one of Jean-Luc Picard's closest friends. Both Keel and Picard were very close to **Jack Crusher**, and Keel introduced Crusher to his future wife, Beverly. Just prior to the destruction of the *Horatio*, Keel suspected his first officer might have fallen under the influence of the conspiracy. ("Conspiracy" [TNG]).

Keel. (Cal Bolder). Tribal warrior loyal to Teer **Maab** on planet Capella IV. Keel was ordered to kill the Klingon **Kras** when he betrayed Maab. ("Friday's Child" [TOS]).

***Keela* flowers.** Variety of multicolored small-bloom flowers, with exceptionally strong stems. ("Learning Curve" [VGR]).

Keeler, Edith. (Joan Collins). American social worker from **Earth**'s 1930s who helped victims of the **Great Depression**. Keeler was an idealistic believer in humanity who worked to help those in her care survive for the future that she foresaw. Keeler, who died in an automobile accident in 1930, was a focal point in the flow of time. When Dr. McCoy, accidentally in Earth's past, prevented her death, he unknowingly changed the course of Earth history. Keeler became a strong advocate for peace, delaying the United States' entry into World War II long enough for Nazi Germany to develop weapons that permitted Hitler to conquer the world. In this altered future, the *Starship Enterprise* did not explore the cosmos in the 23rd century. Kirk and Spock, who followed McCoy into the past, were forced to allow Keeler's death, to restore the shape of time. This task was made infinitely more difficult when Kirk fell in love with Keeler. ("The City on the Edge of Forever" [TOS]). SEE: **Guardian of Forever; Twenty-First Street Mission**.

Keena. (Annie O'Donnell). Resident of **Jeraddo**, a moon orbiting planet **Bajor**. Keena, a Bajoran national, was made mute by the **Cardassians**, during the Cardassian occupation of Bajor. Keena escaped to Jeraddo with her companion, **Baltrim**, in 2351 and started a new life. Teaming up with farmer **Mullibok**, they lived peacefully until an energy-transfer project in 2369 forced the evacuation of Jeraddo. ("Progress" [DS9]).

Keeper, The. (Meg Wyllie). Magistrate and leader of the inhabitants of planet **Talos IV**. In 2254, the Keeper attempted to capture *Enterprise* Captain **Christopher Pike** in hopes that Pike, along with **Vina**, would start a human colony on the surface of Talos IV. The Keeper hoped that such a colony could revitalize his stagant civilization, and was bitterly disappointed to learn that humans were unsuited for life in captivity. Nevertheless, in 2267, the Keeper generously allowed a horribly disfigured Pike to return to Talos IV to live the remainder of his life unfettered by his injured body. ("The Cage," "The Menagerie, Part II" [TOS]).

***keethara*.** Vulcan term meaning "structure of harmony." A *keethara* was a special set of building blocks used as a meditational aid. A person would meditate while attempting to build a structure out of the blocks. The blocks helped to focus thought and refine mental control. The form of the constructed structure was not predefined, but was a reflection of the state of mind of the builder. ("Flashback" [VGR]).

Keeve Falor. (Scot Marlow). A Bajoran leader who resided on the second planet in the **Valo system**. Though he had no diplomatic experience, Keeve was respected by his people. On the advice of Ensign Ro, Captain Picard sought the help of Keeve to locate Bajoran terrorist **Orta**, in 2368. ("Ensign Ro" [TNG]).

kelbonite. Refractory metal. Kelbonite was present in the caves on planets **Melona IV** and **Forlat III**. Data speculated the presence of kelbonite and fistrium prevented the **Crystalline Entity** from penetrating the caves where the colonists were hiding. ("Silicon Avatar" [TNG]).

Keldar. Deceased father of **Quark** and **Rom** ("House of Quark" [DS9]), and husband of **Ishka**. Keldar wasn't very good at acquiring profit, but he was very good at family matters. Early in their marriage, Ishka tried to give financial advice to Keldar, but he would never listen to her because she was a female. ("Family Business" [DS9]). Keldar warned Quark never to leave home, telling him that there were plenty of opportunities for profit right outside his door. Quark instead listened to the 75th Ferengi Rule of Acquisition and left home to find his fortune. ("Civil Defense" [DS9]).

***Keldon*-class warship.** Type of Cardassian spacecraft. ("The Die is Cast" [DS9]). The *Keldon*-class warship was similar to, but more powerful than, the ***Galor*-class** ships. The **Obsidian Order** maintained several *Keldon*-class warships in the **Orias system** in violation of Cardassian law. These Obsidian Order vessels were faster than normal *Keldon*-class ships. ("Defiant" [DS9]). *The miniature for the* Keldon-*class ship was a modification of the* Galor-*class miniature. The modifications were built by Tony Meininger.*

kelilactiral. Fictional computer device "invented" by William Riker to confuse the Ferengi who took over the *Enterprise*-D in 2369. ("Rascals" [TNG]).

Kelinda. (Barbara Bouchet). **Kelvan** who assisted in the capture of the *Enterprise* landing party in 2268 and forced the *Enterprise* crew to set a course for the **Andromeda Galaxy**. Having taken a female humanoid form, Kelinda was susceptible to the new and unfamiliar feelings that accompanied her new body. Kirk took advantage of this, confusing her and the other members of her people with human sensations until they surrendered the ship and accepted a Federation offer of peace. ("By Any Other Name" [TOS]). *Barbara Bouchet played Miss Moneypenny to David Niven's James Bond in the 1967 movie* Casino Royale.

kelindide. Material commonly used in **Cardassian** ship construction. ("The Maquis, Part I" [DS9]). SEE: ***Bok'Nor***.

Kell, Legate. (Danny Goldring). **Cardassian** official during the occupation of **Bajor**. Kell's jurisdiction included the mining station **Terok Nor**. A recorded message from Kell served as part of an ultimate fail-safe in Terok Nor's **counterinsurgency program**, to be activated in the event that then-station commander **Gul Dukat** abandoned the station in a crisis. ("Civil Defense" [DS9]). *Kell's name and title are from the script; they were not mentioned in dialog.*

Kell, Tavor. Famous Cardassian architect who was at one time exiled from his homeworld. Kell's creativity was, in part, inspired by a noncorporeal entity known as **Onaya**, who was also responsible for the brevity of his life. ("The Muse" [DS9]).

Kell. (Larry Dobkin). A special emissary from the Klingon High Command, later found to be a Romulan operative. Kell tried to use his position to instigate distrust between the Federation and Klingon governments following an attempted revolt on **Krios** in 2367. A major tactic was Kell's acquisition of mental control over *Enterprise*-D officer Geordi La Forge. Kell used an **E-band** transmitter to send signals directly to La Forge, attempting to command La Forge to assassinate Klingon governor **Vagh**. ("The Mind's Eye" [TNG]). *Lawrence (Larry) Dobkin also directed "Charlie X" (TOS).*

Kellan. (Dan Kern). First Minister of planet Rakosa V, a highly populated Class-M planet in the Delta Quadrant. Over two million Rakosans were threatened in 2372 when an automated weapon called **Dreadnought** mistook Rakosa V for its target, planet **Aschelan V.** First Minister Kellan dispatched several Rakosan fighters in an unsuccessful attempt to intercept and destroy Dreadnought. ("Dreadnought" [VGR]). *Dan Kern previously played Lieutenant Dean in "We'll Always Have Paris" (TNG).*

Keller, Ensign. A member of the *Enterprise*-D's engineering staff. She died as the result of a failure in the ship's **antimatter containment** systems. A breach of the **matter/antimatter reaction chamber** forced the closure of the isolation doors, trapping Keller. ("Violations" [TNG]). *The incident in which Keller died presumably took place before "Violations," but we don't know much else about it because it was a flashback scene.*

Kellerun. Humanoid civilization that was at war with the **T'Lani** for centuries until finally reaching peace in 2370. ("Armageddon Game" [DS9]). See: **harvesters**; **Sharat**.

kellicam. Unit of distance measure in use by the Klingon Empire. *(Star Trek III: The Search for Spock*, "Redemption, Part I" [TNG]). *One* kellicam *seemed roughly equal to two kilometers.*

kellipate. Unit of distance measure on planet **Bajor**. Kira Nerys told **Mullibok** about a huge tree whose branches blotted out the sun for *kellipates*. ("Progress" [DS9]).

Kelly, Ensign. Starfleet officer assigned to station **Deep Space 9** in 2369. His daughter worked with a Bajoran girl on a prize-winning science-fair project. Kelly was among the Starfleet personnel who remained aboard the station during the Circle's attempted coup in 2370. ("The Siege" [DS9]).

Kelly, Lieutenant Joshua. Chief engineer of the *Starship* ***Yosemite***, killed when the ship was investigating a binary star system in the **Igo Sector** in 2369. ("Realm of Fear" [TNG]).

Kelly, Lieutenant Morgan. Security officer of the ***U.S.S. Essex***, apparently killed in the crash of that vessel on the moon of planet **Mab-Bu IV** in 2167. ("Power Play" [TNG]).

Keloda. Binary star system in the **Delta Quadrant**. Neelix had been on a particularly dangerous trade mission to the Keloda system. ("Parallax" [VGR]).

kelotane. Drug used to treat burns. ("State of Flux" [VGR]).

Kelowitz, Lieutenant Commander. (Grant Woods). Security office aboard the original *Starship Enterprise*. Kelowitz was part of the landing party to the Federation outpost on **Cestus III** in 2267. Unlike his counterpart, Security Officer **Lang**, Kelowitz survived the mission. ("Arena" [TOS]). Kelowitz was a landing-party member who participated in the search for ***Shuttlecraft Galileo*** when it crashed on planet **Taurus II** in 2267. He delivered a report on the humanoid creatures found on that planet. ("The *Galileo* Seven" [TOS]). *Kelowitz also appeared in "This Side of Paradise" (TOS).*

Kelrabi System. Planetary system located in **Cardassian** space. Destination of a Cardassian supply ship intercepted by the ***U.S.S. Phoenix*** and the *Enterprise*-D in 2367. ("The Wounded" [TNG]).

Kelsey. (Marie Marshall). Leader of a terrorist group that attempted to steal **trilithium** resin when the *Enterprise*-D was being serviced at the **Remmler Array** in 2369. ("Starship Mine" [TNG]).

Kelso, Chief. (J. Downing). *Enterprise*-D engineering technician. Kelso operated the transporter during the **particle fountain** malfunction at **Tyrus VIIA** in 2369. ("The Quality of Life" [TNG]). *This character was named by writer Naren Shankar in homage to character Lee Kelso from the pilot episode "Where No Man Has Gone Before" (TOS).*

Kelso, Lieutenant Lee. (Paul Carr). Helm officer aboard the *U.S.S. Enterprise* during the early days of Kirk's first five-year mission in 2265. Kelso was killed by **Gary Mitchell** while helping to implement a plan to quarantine Mitchell on planet **Delta Vega**. ("Where No Man Has Gone Before" [TOS]).

Kelva. Planet in the **Andromeda Galaxy** that was homeworld to a civilization known as the **Kelvans**. ("By Any Other Name" [TOS]).

Kelvans. Life-forms from planet **Kelva** in the **Andromeda Galaxy**. Kelvans are highly intelligent, and their bodies have a hundred tentacles, but they have no tactile perceptions or emotions as we know them. When Kelvan scientists recognized that increasing radiation levels in their galaxy would make life impossible in ten millennia, the Kelvan Empire dispatched several ships to explore the universe for a new place to live. One of their explorer ships was damaged entering the **galactic barrier** at the edge of the Milky Way Galaxy and the crew abandoned ship. Taking humanoid form, the Kelvans dispatched a general distress call that was answered by the *Enterprise* in 2268. The Kelvans commandeered the *Enterprise*, forcing the starship to cross the barrier and to set course for the Andromeda Galaxy. The *Enterprise* crew was able to regain control of their ship by using the Kelvans' unfamiliarity with humanoid senses to confuse and distract them. Kirk then invited the Kelvans to settle in Federation space and live in peace. ("By Any Other Name" [TOS]). SEE: **Kelinda**; **Rojan**.

kemacite. Highly unstable and dangerous material. When exposed to nuclear radiation, kemacite can cause unusual temporal phenomena. Smuggling kemacite was a serious offense. In 2372, Quark attempted to smuggle kemacite aboard his ship, *Quark's Treasure*. ("Little Green Men" [DS9]).

Kenda II. Federation planet, home of **Dr. Dalen Quaice.** The *Enterprise*-D was scheduled to return Quaice to Kenda II while en route to planet Durenia IV in early 2367. ("Remember Me" [TNG]).

Kendi system. Star system located in the Gamma Quadrant. In 2372, the **Jem'Hadar** had a presence in the Kendi system ("The Quickening" [DS9]).

Kendra Valley massacre. Infamous attack by Cardassian forces on members of the Bajoran resistance. **Kai Opaka**'s son and 42 other **Bajoran** freedom fighters were ambushed and killed because someone informed the Cardassians of the location of their encampment in the Kendra Valley. **Prylar Bek** was believed to have been the informant. He made a full confession in a suicide note, then hung himself on the **Promenade** of **Terok Nor**. In 2370, Vedek **Winn** revealed evidence that **Vedek Bareil** may have been the real collaborator, and that Prylar Bek was only acting as a messenger. In reality it was Kai Opaka who gave the Cardassians the information, sacrificing 42 persons to save 1200 lives. ("The Collaborator" [DS9]). *We don't know when the massacre took place, but it was probably between 2360 and 2369.*

Kenicki. *Enterprise*-D crew member. Kenicki suffered from hallucinations caused by lack of **REM sleep** while the *Enterprise*-D was adrift in a **Tyken's Rift** in 2367. Kenicki reported seeing someone in an old-style starfleet uniform riding the turbolift in engineering. ("Night Terrors" [TNG]).

Kennelly, Admiral. (Cliff Potts). Federation official who made a secret pact with the **Cardassians** in 2368 to eliminate the **Bajoran** terrorists believed responsible for an attack against a Federation colony. Kennelly planted Ensign **Ro Laren** on the *Enterprise*-D to carry out his plan. Kennelly's plan was discovered, and he was imprisoned. ("Ensign Ro" [TNG]). SEE: ***Antares*-class carrier.** *Cliff Potts had played one of the crew members on the spaceship* Valley Forge *in Douglas Trumbull's 1972 film,* Silent Running.

Kent State University. Educational institution, located in North America on Earth, founded in 1910. In the 24th century, quantum theorists at Kent State University conducted an experiment in which a single particle of matter was duplicated using a **spatial scission**. ("Deadlock" [VGR]).

Kentanna. In **Skrreea**n legend, the distant homeworld where the Skrreean people originated. **Kentanna** was called the "planet of sorrow" and was believed to be found through the **Eye of the Universe.** In 2370, Skrreean leader Haneek believed that planet **Bajor** was in fact Kentanna, because of its recent history and proximity to the wormhole. When Bajoran authorities refused the Skrreeas' request to colonize Bajor, she realized that Bajor was not Kentanna after all. ("Sanctuary" [DS9]).

Kentor. (Richard Allen). Young community leader of the **Tau Cygna V** colony in 2366. ("The Ensigns of Command" [TNG]).

Keogh, Captain. (Alan Oppenheimer). Commanding officer of the ***U.S.S. Odyssey***. He was an old acquaintance of Jadzia Dax, and the two were not fond of one another. Keogh was killed when the *Odyssey* was destroyed in 2370. ("The Jem'Hadar" [DS9]). *Alan Oppenheimer also portrayed Koroth in "Rightful Heir" (TNG) and Dr. Rudy Wells in* The Six Million Dollar Man.

Kerelian. Sentient life-form. The hearing of Kerelians can distinguish a greater range of musical notes than that of humans. Jean-Luc Picard told **Neela Daren** that a Kerelian tenor had a wide range of musical nuances that only others of their species could hear. ("Lessons" [TNG]).

Kerla, Brigadier. (Paul Rossilli). Military advisor to Klingon **Chancellor Gorkon**, and later to Chancellor **Azetbur**. Kerla opposed Gorkon's 2293 peace initiative. *(Star Trek VI: The Undiscovered Country).*

Kes Security Relay Station One. Facility on planet **Kesprytt III**. Location that was to receive *Enterprise*-D Captain Jean-Luc Picard and Dr. Beverly Crusher when they beamed down to Kesprytt III in 2370. The captain and doctor, on a diplomatic mission to evaluate the Kes application for membership in the Federation, were kidnapped during transport, and the security station reported them missing. ("Attached" [TNG]).

Kes. (Jennifer Lien). Native of the planet **Ocampa** who left her homeworld in 2371 to join the crew of the ***Starship Voyager***. ("Caretaker" [VGR]). Kes was born in 2370. ("Twisted" [VGR]). Her father's name was **Benaren**. She had an uncle named Elrem. ("Dreadnought" [VGR]). Kes's mother was a woman named **Martis**. ("Before and After" [VGR]). Kes remembered her father as a wise man who did much to shape the person she became. Benaren died in 2371, when Kes was one year old. ("Resolutions" [VGR]). Kes, who was both inquisitive and intelligent, escaped her people's underground city in a quest to learn about her world. On the surface, she was captured and abused by the **Kazon-Ogla** until she escaped to the *Starship Voyager*, aided by **Neelix**, with whom she was in love. ("Caretaker" [VGR]). *Kes broke up with Neelix shortly after the third-season episode "Warlord" (VGR).* Kes demonstrated her gratitude and her love for Neelix shortly after stardate 48532, when she donated one of her lungs to save Neelix's life. Shortly thereafter, she began studying to become a medical assistant under the tutelage of *Voyager*'s **Emergency Medical Hologram**. ("Phage" [VGR]). Her quarters on the *Voyager* were located on Deck 8. ("Twisted" [VGR]).

Kes believed there was truth to ancient legends that her people once had extraordinary mental powers. Shortly after joining the *Voyager* crew, she began to exhibit signs of such powers, including visions of a planet destroyed in another timeline by **polaric ion energy** ("Time and Again" [VGR]), and evidence of an **eidetic memory** ("Eye of the Needle" [VGR]). Kes studied **Vulcan** mind-control techniques under **Tuvok**'s direction, on the theory that this would help her develop her natural Ocampa abilities. When under the influence of **Tanis**, she temporarily gained spectacular psychokinetic powers, giving her the ability to influence matter on the molecular level and to direct the flow of life-energy. ("Cold Fire" [VGR]). In early 2372, Kes underwent early ***elogium***, during which Neelix and she decided to conceive a child. She later learned that the *elogium* was a false one and that she might go through *elogium* again, later in life. Kes decided to wait until then to conceive a child. ("Elogium" [VGR]). Kes continually strove to expand her knowledge and skills. She learned to pilot a Federation shuttlecraft under the tutelage of Lieutenant **Tom Paris** in 2372. Kes was surprised to learn that Paris found her attractive. ("Parturition" [VGR]).

In 2373, **Tieran** of the **Ilari** transferred his neural pattern into Kes's mind and used her body in his unsuccessful bid to take over the Ilari government. ("Warlord" [VGR]).

(In one possible future, Kes received **bio-temporal chamber** treatments in 2379, causing her cells to enter a state of biotemporal flux, sending Kes out of temporal synch. Kes traveled backward in time, experiencing a series of brief visits to various points in her life. In one possible future, she and Tom Paris married and had a daughter, Linnis, in 2375. Linnis later married Harry Kim and the two had a son, Andrew, Kes' grandson. In this reality, Kes continued to work in sickbay and eventually became a doctor. Kes was eventually restored to temporal normality when she was exposed to a precisely modulated field of **antichroniton** particles.) ("Before and After" [VGR]). *In "Before and After" (VGR]) young Kes was played by Janna Michaels.*

Kes's first appearance was in "Caretaker" (VGR).

Kes. Nation-state on planet **Kesprytt III.** The Kes comprised three-quarters of the planet's population. In the year 2370, the Kes applied for an associate membership in the United Federation of Planets, despite the fact that their world did not yet have a unified government. Both factions were paranoid in the extreme, and this paranoia led *Starship Enterprise*-D personnel, dispatched to evaluate the Kes application, to recommend the planet be denied membership at this time. ("Attached" [TNG]). SEE: **Prytt**.

Kesla. Name given to unidentified serial murderer of women on planet Deneb II, later found to be an energy life-form also known as **Redjac**. ("Wolf in the Fold" [TOS]).

Kesprytt III. Class-M planet controlled by two large nation-states. Three-quarters of the population was governed by the **Kes**, while the remaining quarter belonged to the **Prytt**. ("Attached" [TNG]).

Kessik IV. Planet. Location of a Federation colony where **B'Elanna Torres** grew up. She lived there with her Klingon mother and human father. When B'Elanna was five years old, her father abruptly left her and her mother. ("Faces" [VGR]).

ketracel-white. An addictive **isogenic enzyme** also known simply as **white**, a drug used by the **Dominion** to control the **Jem'Hadar**. The **Founders** had engineered Jem'Hadar bodies to be addicted to ketracel-white, and designed the entire genetic structure of Jem'Hadar physiology to collapse without the drug. By controlling the supply of white, the Founders, through their **Vorta** agents, maintained control over the Jem'Hadar. The Jem'Hadar received their doses of this drug automatically via special supply tubes implanted in their necks. Ketracel-white also seems to make the Jem'Hadar more violent and less clear-thinking. ("Hippocratic Oath" [DS9]).

kevas. Gemstone traded on planet **Organia**. Spock posed as a trader dealing in kevas and trillium. ("Errand of Mercy" [TOS]). **Arne Darvin**, in near-exile on Cardassia Prime in 2373, also posed as a dealer in kevas. ("Trials and Tribble-ations" (DS9).

Khan. (Ricardo Montalban). Aka Khan Noonien Singh. Genetically engineered human who attempted to gain control of the entire planet Earth in the 1990s during the **Eugenics Wars**. From 1992 to 1996, Khan was absolute ruler of more than a quarter of Earth, from South Asia through the Middle East. He was the last of the tyrants to be overthrown. Khan escaped in 1996 with a band of followers aboard the sleeper ship ***S.S. Botany Bay***. In 2267 the *Starship Enterprise* discovered the *Botany Bay* and awakened Khan and his people. Once awakened, Khan attempted to take over the *Enterprise*, but was thwarted. Captain Kirk exercised command prerogatives in dropping all charges when Khan agreed to be exiled to planet Ceti Alpha V to start a new life. ("Space Seed" [TOS]). Khan and his followers remained on Ceti Alpha V for several years, until they were accidentally discovered by a scientific reconnaissance party from the *Starship **Reliant*** in 2285. Khan commandeered the *Reliant* and ransacked the nearby **Regula I Space Laboratory**, stealing the experimental **Genesis Device**. Khan, along with his followers and the crew of the *Reliant*, was killed when the Genesis Device exploded while aboard the *Reliant*. *(Star Trek II: The Wrath of Khan).* Following the Eugenics Wars, Earth governments, and later the Federation, outlawed genetic engineering in hopes of preventing the creation of another Khan. ("Doctor Bashir, I Presume?" [DS9]).

Khazara. Imperial Romulan warbird, *D'deridex* class. This ship, captained by **Commander Toreth**, was seized by **Subcommander N'Vek** and Deanna Troi as part of a plot to enable Romulan **Vice-Proconsul M'ret** to defect to the Federation. ("Face of the Enemy" [TNG]).

Khefka IV. Planet. Homeworld to **Mareel**. Trill initiate **Verad** met Mareel on Khefka IV while working as a communications clerk at the Federation Consulate. ("Invasive Procedures" [DS9]).

Khitomer Accords. Historic peace treaty between the **Klingon Empire** and the **United Federation of Planets**, framed at **Khitomer** in 2293. The Khitomer Accords were the first step in rapprochement between the two longtime enemies. *(Star Trek VI: The Undiscovered Country).* In response to the Federation Council's condemnation of his invasion of Cardassia in 2372, Gowron unilaterally withdrew the Klingon Empire from the Khitomer Accords. ("The Way of the Warrior" [DS9]). Gowron reinstated the treaty a year later when an alliance between the **Dominion** and the Cardassian Union threatened to destabilize the Alpha Quadrant. ("By Inferno's Light" [DS9]).

Khitomer massacre. A brutal attack by Romulan forces on the Klingon outpost at **Khitomer** in 2346. Some 4,000 Klingons were killed in the incident, later learned to have been made possible by the betrayal of **Ja'rod**, a Klingon who provided secret defense access codes to the Romulans. The only survivors of the massacre were a Klingon child named **Worf** and his nursemaid, named **Kahlest**. The two were rescued by the ***U.S.S. Intrepid***, which responded to the Klingons' distress calls. Years later, in 2366, **Klingon High Council** member **Duras**, son of Ja'rod, attempted to falsify evidence to implicate Worf's father, **Mogh**, as the one who provided the codes to the Romulans. Duras was only partly successful, since Worf learned of the injustice and made an appeal to High Council leader **K'mpec**. ("Sins of the Father" [TNG]). Star Trek VI *establishes that Khitomer was near the Romulan border. We speculate that the massacre was part of an ongoing border dispute between the two powers.*

Khitomer. Class-M planet near the Romulan/Klingon border. Khitomer was the site of the historic Khitomer peace conference in 2293 that was the beginning of rapprochement between the **United Federation of Planets** and the **Klingon Empire**. *(Star Trek VI: The Undiscovered Country).* At the conference, Captain **Spock** first met **Pardek**, a Romulan politician who expressed support for a reunification of the Vulcan and Romulan peoples. ("Unification, Part I" [TNG]). SEE: **Khitomer Accords**. A Klingon outpost was later established on Khitomer, and was the target of the brutal **Khitomer massacre** by the Romulans in 2346. ("Sins of the Father" [TNG]). In 2369, Worf learned that some of the Klingons believed killed at Khitomer were actually taken prisoner by the Romulans. Nearly a hundred Klingons had been discovered unconscious at a perimeter outpost, and the Romulans, reluctant to kill helpless people, instead took them prisoner. ("Birthright, Part I" [TNG]). The prisoners proved to be of no political use, and they later refused an offer of freedom, even though the Romulan government favored their execution, since permitting themselves to be captured, however involuntarily, was a serious breach of the Klingon warrior ethic. Romulan officer **Tokath** opposed the execution of the Klingons and sacrificed his military career to establish and command a prison camp in the **Carraya System**. ("Birthright, Part II" [TNG]).

Kholfa II. Planet. Home of Ferengi entrepreneur **Plegg** in 2370. Quark had claimed that Plegg was dead and was selling fake pieces of him on Deep Space 9. ("The Alternate" [DS9]). See: **Ferengi death rituals.**

Kibberian fire diamonds. Rare jewel. Grand Nagus Zek compared Kira Nerys's eyes to Kibberian fire diamonds. ("Rules of Acquisition" [DS9]).

Kilana. (Kaitlin Hopkins). **Vorta** field operative. Kilana led a detachment of **Jem'Hadar,** tasked with retrieving a **Jem'Hadar warship** that crash-landed on Torga IV on stardate 50049. More important, she and her team were there to rescue an injured **Founder** who was aboard that ship. After a standoff with Captain Sisko and his staff, the Founder died. Kilana took some of the changeling's remains with her and let Sisko claim the warship. ("The Ship" [DS9]).

kilodyne. A measurement of force, one thousand dynes. ("The Loss" [TNG]).

kiloquad. Unit of measure of data storage and transmission in Federation computer systems. ("Realm of Fear" [TNG]). *No, we don't know how many bytes are in a kiloquad. We don't even* want *to know. The reason the term was invented was specifically to avoid describing the data capacity of* Star Trek*'s computers in 20th-century terms. It was feared by technical consultant Mike Okuda that any such attempt would look foolish in just a few years, given the current rate of progress in that field.*

Kim, Andrew. (Christopher Aguilar). (In one possible future, the son of Harry Kim and Linnis Paris, born in 2378. In this possible future, **Kes** had married Tom Paris and had a daughter, Linnis, in 2375. Linnis later married Harry Kim, and the two had a son, Andrew. Andrew, who was Kes' grandson, was only one-quarter Ocampan, but he aged very rapidly nonetheless.) ("Before and After" [VGR].)

Kim, Harry. (Garrett Wang). Starfleet officer who joined the crew of the ***Starship Voyager*** just prior to its disappearance in 2371. ("Caretaker" [VGR]). In 2370, while attending **Starfleet Academy**, Harry Kim was the editor of the academy newspaper for a year. During that time he reported on some of the first activity of the Maquis against the Cardassians. ("Investigations" [VGR]). Kim had graduated from Starfleet Academy on stardate 47918, and was posted to *Voyager* shortly thereafter. ("Non Sequitur" [VGR]). Kim's position aboard the *Voyager* was that of Operations Officer. ("Caretaker" [VGR]).

Family was very important to Kim, born in 2349, and he made it a point to call his parents weekly, even after he joined Starfleet. ("Eye of the Needle" [VGR]). When Harry was nine years old, he and his parents visited a colony on a humanitarian mission. The colony had suffered a radiation disaster, and Harry had a traumatic experience when he inadvertently wandered into a hospital operating room and saw a little girl on the table. ("The Thaw" [VGR]). Harry was his parents' only son, and he had enjoyed playing **clarinet** in the **Julliard Youth Symphony**. ("Caretaker" [VGR]). Even after the *Voyager* was lost in the Delta Quadrant, Kim spent one week's worth of replicator rations to replicate a clarinet, so that he could stay in practice. ("Parturition" [VGR]). At the time of posting to *Voyager*, Kim had been engaged to marry a woman named **Libby**, with whom he was very much in love. ("Non Sequitur" [VGR]). Aboard *Voyager*, Kim's off-duty recreation included playing the title role in a **holonovel** version of the epic poem ***Beowulf***. ("Heroes and Demons" [VGR]). SEE: **photonic being**. Harry Kim enjoyed **Vulcan mocha** coffee, extra sweet. ("Non Sequitur" [VGR]).

In early 2372, Kim accidentally piloted a *Voyager* shuttlecraft through a **timestream**, sending him into an alternate reality in which he had not been assigned to the *Voyager*, and was instead living with his fiancee, Libby, on Earth. In this reality, Kim earned the **Cochrane Medal of Excellence** for outstanding advances in warp theory, and he helped design a new runabout prototype, the *U.S.S. Yellowstone*. Kim returned to his original reality with the help of an alternate Tom Paris. ("Non Sequitur" [VGR]).

Harry Kim was killed in 2372, when part of the *Starship Voyager* experienced an explosive decompression when the ship encountered a **spatial scission**. A duplicate of Kim, from a duplicate *Voyager* created by the scission, returned to the original ship, replacing Harry Kim. ("Deadlock" [VGR]). *This means that every appearance of Kim after "Deadlock" has been the Kim from the duplicate* Voyager.

On stardate 50698, while on an away mission, Kim was infected with a **Taresian** genetically engineered retrovirus. The virus gave him genetic memories that compelled him to go to **Taresia**, where Taresian women tried to convince him that he was actually a native of their planet. Kim escaped when he learned that the Taresians planned to harvest genetic material from him to be used in their procreation process. SEE: **denucleation**. ("Favorite Son" [VGR]). *Irene Tsu played Harry's mother and Kenny Yee played young Harry Kim in "Favorite Son" (VGR).*

Kim's first appearance was in "Caretaker" (VGR).

Kim, Luisa. (Elizabeth Lindsey). Terraforming scientist, part of the unsuccessful **terraforming** project at planet **Velara III**. Kim had great enthusiasm for her work and was devastated to learn that the Velara III project would have destroyed the **microbrain** lifeforms there. ("Home Soil" [TNG]).

Kinell, Jal. Kazon-Ogla warrior. Brother of **Jal Karden**. ("Initiations" [VGR]). *Mentioned but never seen.*

kinetic detonator. Old-style warhead fusing mechanism used by the Cardassians as late as 2369. ("Dreadnought" [VGR]).

Kings, London. SEE: **London Kings**.

Kingsley, Dr. Sara. (Patricia Smith). Scientist at the **Darwin Genetic Research Station** on planet **Gagarin IV**. In the late 2350s and 2360s, Kingsley was part of a genetic-engineering project intended to develop human children with a powerful immune system capable of attacking disease organisms before they enter a human body. After these children were several years old it was learned that the children's antibodies could also attack human beings, causing a disease closely resembling hyperaccelerated aging. Although Kingsley was afflicted by the antibodies, a transporter-based technique was successful in restoring her to her normal age. ("Unnatural Selection" [TNG]).

kinoplastic radiation. Amorphous energy associated with subspace phenomena. Kinoplastic radiation surged through the *U.S.S. Voyager*'s computers after the ship encountered a subspace anomaly on stardate 48892. ("Projections" [VGR]).

kiosk, Klingon. Small restaurant on the **Promenade** of station Deep Space 9. The kiosk offered traditional Klingon fare including ***gladst***, ***racht***, and ***zilm'kach***, prepared tableside by a Klingon chef *(played by Ron Taylor)*, who also serenaded his guests with traditional Klingon folk songs. ("Melora" [DS9], "Playing God" [DS9]).

Kir. Province on the planet **Vulcan**. Kir was the home to an order of silent monks. ("Innocence" [VGR]).

Kira Nerys (mirror). (Nana Visitor). In the **mirror universe**, the **Intendant** of station **Terok Nor (mirror)** and the Bajor Sector. This position gave her a great deal of power, which she used to satisfy her considerable appetites. In 2370, Kira was confronted with a visit from her counterpart from our universe. She attempted to use Kira Nerys's presence to her advantage, and was surprised when her double refused to cooperate. She regretted the escape of several Terrans, including **Benjamin Sisko (mirror)** and **Miles O'Brien (mirror)** from Terok Nor in the incident. ("Crossover" [DS9]). The mirror Kira faced the mirror O'Brien and other members of the **Terran resistance** again the following year when **Jennifer Sisko (mirror)** was on the verge of finishing a **transpectral sensor array**. ("Through the Looking Glass" [DS9]). After the Terran resistance captured Terok Nor (mirror), Kira (mirror) was held prisoner on the station. Julian Bashir (mirror) tortured her with an agonizer. She escaped captivity with the help of **Nog (mirror)**. Before escaping to Bajor, she killed Nog (mirror) and Jennifer Sisko (mirror). ("Shattered Mirror" [DS9]).

Kira Nerys. (Nana Visitor). **Bajoran** freedom fighter who served as first officer and Bajoran liaison to station **Deep Space 9** after the **Cardassian** withdrawal from **Bajor** in 2369. ("Emissary" [DS9]). Kira's family was part of the ***Ih'valla D'jarra***, which in earlier times would have required her to take up an artistic occupation. ("Accession" [DS9]). Kira was born in 2343 in the **Dahkur Province** and spent the first 26 years of her life under Cardassian rule. ("The Maquis, Part I" [DS9], "Shakaar" [DS9]). Stubborn and independent, she joined the **Shakaar resistance cell** of the Bajoran underground in 2355, when she was 12 years old. ("The Circle" [DS9], "Shakaar" [DS9]). SEE: **Shakaar Edon**. Kira was recruited into the Shakaar group by her friend, **Lorit Akrem**. ("Indiscretion" [DS9]). Kira was interned at the Singha refugee camp during the Cardassian occupation. Although conditions there were brutal, she was able to play **springball** with her brothers. ("Shadowplay" [DS9]). Her mother, an **icon** painter from Dahkur Province, died of malnutrition in the Singha refugee camp in 2343. ("Second Skin" [DS9]). Kira spent much of her childhood as a freedom fighter for the Bajoran movement, although Cardassian intelligence reported her as "a minor operative whose activities (were) limited to running errands for the terrorist leaders." ("Battle Lines" [DS9]).

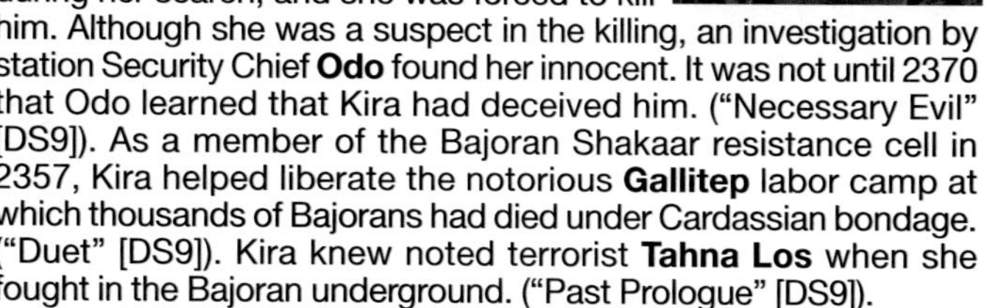

In 2365, Kira was assigned to obtain a list of Bajoran collaborators from a chemist shop on station **Terok Nor** (later Deep Space 9). The chemist, **Vaatrik**, discovered Kira during her search, and she was forced to kill him. Although she was a suspect in the killing, an investigation by station Security Chief **Odo** found her innocent. It was not until 2370 that Odo learned that Kira had deceived him. ("Necessary Evil" [DS9]). As a member of the Bajoran Shakaar resistance cell in 2357, Kira helped liberate the notorious **Gallitep** labor camp at which thousands of Bajorans had died under Cardassian bondage. ("Duet" [DS9]). Kira knew noted terrorist **Tahna Los** when she fought in the Bajoran underground. ("Past Prologue" [DS9]).

In 2369, Kira opposed the **Bajoran provisional government**'s decision to enlist Federation assistance in maintaining Deep Space 9, but nevertheless worked with Starfleet personnel on the station. ("Emissary" [DS9]). Kira had a deep, abiding faith in the Bajoran religion, and was personally struck by the tragedy of **Kai Opaka**'s death in 2369. ("Battle Lines" [DS9]). Her beliefs held that **Benjamin Sisko** was the **Emissary** of Bajoran prophesy, but she sometimes found it difficult to reconcile the fact that her commanding officer was a religious icon. ("Destiny" [DS9]).

In 2370, she became romantically involved with **Vedek Bareil**. ("Shadowplay" [DS9]). At Vedek Bareil's invitation, Kira was given the privilege of encountering an **Orb**. This encounter had a profound effect on her life. ("The Circle" [DS9]). Kira's involvement with Bareil ended tragically in 2371 when he died during Cardassian peace negotiations. ("Life Support" [DS9]). In 2371 Kira was kidnapped and taken to **Cardassia**, where she was surgically altered to look like **Iliana**, a Cardassian operative from the **Obsidian Order**. She later discovered that her transformation was part of a plot to expose **Legate Ghemor** as a member of the **Cardassian underground movement**. ("Second Skin" [DS9]). In 2372, Kira became romantically involved with **Shakaar Edon**, longtime friend and former leader of the Shakaar resistance cell. ("Crossfire" [DS9]).

Kira served as surrogate mother to **Kirayoshi O'Brien**, son of **Miles** and **Keiko O'Brien**. The surrogacy became necessary when Keiko was severely injured aboard the *Runabout Volga* during a botanical survey mission to Torad IV. Dr. **Julian Bashir**, fighting to save both mother and unborn child, found it necessary to implant Kirayoshi's fetus into Kira's body, else Kirayoshi would have died. Upon returning to Deep Space 9, Kira accepted an invitation from Miles and Keiko to live with them in their quarters, so that they could care for her while she carried their child to term. ("Body Parts" [DS9]). *Kira's surrogate pregnancy was devised by the show's writers in order to deal with the fact that Nana Visitor was pregnant with her second child during the latter part of* Star Trek: Deep Space Nine's *fourth season, and the early part of the fifth.* Living in close proximity with the O'Brien family, Kira found herself attracted to Miles, a feeling that he reciprocated. Since neither wished to jeopardize their existing relationships, they decided together not to act on those feelings. ("Looking for *par'Mach* in All the Wrong Places" [DS9]). Her pregnancy prevented her from taking active charge of the investigation when several former member of the **Shakaar resistance cell** were murdered around stardate 50416. ("The Darkness and the Light" [DS9]). In 2373, Kira gave birth to **Kirayoshi O'Brien** in a traditional Bajoran birthing ceremony. ("The Begotten" [DS9]).

Kira disliked indulging in holosuite programs. ("Meridian" [DS9], "The Way of the Warrior" [DS9]). *Kira first appeared in "Emissary" (DS9).*

Kirby. (Andrew Kavovit). Federation medical orderly. Kirby worked at an emergency underground field hospital on Ajilon Prime during the Klingon invasion of 2373. ("Nor the Battle to the Strong" [DS9]).

Kiri-kin-tha's First Law of Metaphysics. "Nothing unreal exists." Spock quoted Kiri-kin-tha during a memory test in 2286. (*Star Trek IV: The Voyage Home*).

Kirk, Aurelan. (Joan Swift). Colonist on planet **Deneva** who was killed by the **Denevan neural parasites** in 2267. Aurelan was wife of **George Samuel Kirk** and mother to **Peter Kirk**. ("Operation—Annihilate!" [TOS]).

Kirk, George Samuel. (William Shatner). Research biologist and older brother to **James T. Kirk**. Sam had been working on a project at planet **Deneva**, where he lived with his wife and three sons. Sam was killed by the **Denevan neural parasites** in 2267. Samuel Kirk had been living on Deneva with his wife Aurelan and son Peter when the parasites infested the planet's population. ("Operation—Annihilate!" [TOS]). Sam had seen his younger brother—the only one who called him Sam—off on his first mission aboard the *Enterprise*. ("What Are Little Girls Made Of?" [TOS]). *Sam was established in "What Are Little Girls Made Of?" (TOS) to have had three sons, one of whom, Peter, was seen in "Operation—Annihilate!" (TOS). We don't know anything about Peter's two brothers, although they presumably were not at the Deneva colony at the time Sam and Aurelan were killed. Sam was only seen briefly as an already-dead body, "played" by William Shatner.*

Kirk, James T. (mirror). (William Shatner). Captain of the ***I.S.S.* Enterprise** in the **mirror universe**; assumed command of *I.S.S. Enterprise* through assassination of Captain Christopher Pike. Kirk's first action for the empire was to suppress a Gorlan uprising by destroying a rebel home planet. His second action was the execution of 5,000 colonists on Vega IX. The mirror Kirk was transposed into our universe in 2267 when an **ion storm** caused a brief bridge between the two existences. It was believed that **Spock (mirror)** would overthrow Kirk as commander of the *Enterprise*, thereby opening the way to breaking the mirror empire's pattern of repressive barbarism. ("Mirror, Mirror" [TOS])

Kirk, James T. (William Shatner). James Tiberius Kirk was the commander of the original *Starship* **Enterprise** during its historic five-year mission of exploration in 2264-2269. ("Where No Man Has Gone Before" [TOS]). His Starfleet serial number was SC 937-0176 CEC. ("Court Martial" [TOS]).

Childhood and family: Kirk was born in 2233 ("The Deadly Years" [TOS]) in Iowa on planet **Earth** *(Star Trek IV: The Voyage Home)*. In 2246, Kirk—at age 13—was one of nine surviving eyewitnesses to the massacre of some 4,000 colonists at planet **Tarsus IV** by **Kodos the Executioner**. ("The Conscience of the King" [TOS]). James Kirk lost his older brother, **George Samuel Kirk** (whom only James called Sam), and sister-in-law, **Aurelan Kirk**, on planet **Deneva** due to the invasion of the **Denevan neural parasites** in 2267. Kirk's nephew, **Peter Kirk** survived. ("Operation—Annihilate!" [TOS]). Sam Kirk had two other sons who were not on Deneva at the time of the tragedy. ("What Are Little Girls Made Of?" [TOS]).

Kirk at the academy: During his academy days, Kirk was tormented by an upperclassman named **Finnegan**, who frequently chose Kirk as a target for practical jokes. Kirk found a measure of satisfaction years later, in 2267, when he had a chance to wallop a replica of Finnegan created on the **amusement park planet** in the **Omicron Delta region**. ("Shore Leave" [TOS]). Kirk served as an instructor at the academy, and **Gary Mitchell** was one of his students. The two were good friends, and once Mitchell took a poisonous dart on Dimorus meant for Kirk, saving Kirk's life. Mitchell set Kirk up with a "little blond lab technician" whom Kirk almost married. ("Where No Man Has Gone Before" [TOS]). Another of Kirk's friends from his academy days was **Ben Finney**, who named his daughter, Jamie, after Kirk. A rift developed between Finney and Kirk around 2250 when the two were serving together on the ***U.S.S. Republic.*** Kirk logged a mistake that Finney had made, and Finney blamed Kirk for his subsequent failure to earn command of a starship. *Kirk's service aboard the* Republic *was apparently while he was still attending the academy, since he was an ensign on the* Republic*, but he was a lieutenant on the* Farragut*, which was described as his first posting after the academy.* ("Court Martial" [TOS]). One of Kirk's heroes at the academy was the legendary Captain **Garth of Izar**, whose exploits are required reading. Years later, Kirk helped save his hero when Garth had become criminally insane and was being treated at the **Elba II** penal colony. ("Whom Gods Destroy" [TOS]). Another of Kirk's personal heroes was **Abraham Lincoln**, 16th president of the United States of America on Earth. ("The Savage Curtain" [TOS]). At the academy, James Kirk earned something of a reputation for himself as having been the only cadet ever to have beaten the "no-win" ***Kobayashi Maru*** scenario. He did it by secretly reprogramming the simulation computer to make it possible to win, earning a commendation for original thinking in the process. *(Star Trek II: The Wrath of Khan).*

Early days in Starfleet: Kirk's first assignment after graduating from the academy was aboard the ***U.S.S. Farragut***. ("Obsession" [TOS]). One of his first missions as a young lieutenant was to command a survey mission to **Tyree**'s planet in 2254. ("A Private Little War" [TOS]). *This incident presumably took place while Kirk was assigned to the* Farragut. While serving aboard the *Farragut* in 2257, Lieutenant Kirk blamed himself for the deaths of 200 *Farragut* personnel, including **Captain Garrovick**, by the **dikironium cloud creature** at planet **Tycho IV**. Kirk felt he could have acted faster in firing on the creature, but learned years later that nothing could have prevented the deaths. ("Obsession" [TOS]). Sometime in the past Kirk almost died from **Vegan choriomeningitis**. ("The Mark of Gideon" [TOS]).

Aboard the *U.S.S. Enterprise*: Kirk's greatest renown came from his command of a historic five-year mission of the original *Starship* **Enterprise** from 2264 to 2269 that made him a legend in space exploration. *(Star Trek Generations).* By 2267, Kirk had earned an impressive list of commendations from **Starfleet**, including the Palm Leaf of Axanar Peace Mission, the Grankite Order of Tactics (Class of Excellence), and the Preantares Ribbon of Commendation (Classes First and Second). Kirk's awards for valor included the Medal of Honor, the Silver Palm with Cluster, the Starfleet Citation for Conspicuous Gallantry, and the Kragite Order of Heroism. ("Court Martial" [TOS]). In 2267, Kirk became the first starship captain ever to stand trial when he was accused of causing the death of **Ben Finney**. Kirk's trial, held at **Starbase 11**, proved Kirk innocent of wrongdoing, and he was exonerated. ("Court Martial" [TOS]). SEE: **Shaw, Areel**. During that original five-year mission, Kirk recorded a tape of last orders to be played by Commander Spock and Chief Medical Officer McCoy upon his death. While trapped in a **spatial interphase** near Tholian space, Kirk vanished with the ***U.S.S. Defiant*** and was declared dead. His last orders conveyed the hope that his two friends would work together, despite their differences. ("The Tholian Web" [TOS]). Kirk was once split into two personalities by a transporter malfunction. ("The Enemy Within" [TOS]). Several of Kirk's voyages involved travel through time. According to the **Federation Department of Temporal Investigations**, Kirk, who sometimes ignored regulations when he felt it was for the greater good, amassed 17 separate temporal violations during his career, more than any other person on file. ("Trials and Tribble-ations" [DS9]). *Kirk went back in time six times that we know of: "The Naked Time" (TOS), "Assignment: Earth" (TOS), "Tomorrow is Yesterday" (TOS), "City on the Edge of Forever" (TOS), "All Our Yesterdays" (TOS) and* Star Trek IV: The Voyage Home. *He also went forward in time in* Star Trek Generations. Kirk's living quarters aboard the original *Enterprise* were on Deck 5. ("Journey to Babel" [TOS]). It was during this five-year mission that Kirk's friendships with officers Spock and McCoy developed, friendships that would last the rest of their lives.

Relationships with women: Kirk was notably unsuccessful in maintaining a long-term relationship with any woman. Although he was involved with many different women during his life, his intense passion for his ship and his career always seemed to interfere. A few years prior to his command of the first *Enterprise*, Kirk became involved with **Dr. Carol Marcus**. The two had a child, **David Marcus**, but Kirk and Carol did not remain together, because their respective careers took them in separate directions. Other significant romances in Kirk's life included **Ruth**, with whom he was involved when he attended Starfleet Academy ("Shore Leave" [TOS]); **Janice Lester**, with whom he spent a year, also during his academy days ("Turnabout Intruder" [TOS]); **Janet Wallace**, a scientist who later saved his life ("The Deadly Years" [TOS]); **Areel Shaw**, who, ironically, years later prosecuted Kirk in the case of Ben Finney's apparent death ("Court Martial" [TOS]); and **Miramanee**, a woman whom Kirk married in 2268 when he suffered from amnesia on a landing party mission. Miramanee became pregnant with Kirk's child, but both mother and unborn child were killed in a local power struggle. ("The Paradise Syndrome" [TOS]). Kirk fell in love with **Antonia** after his first retirement from Starfleet, and for the rest of his life regretted not having proposed to her. *(Star Trek Generations).* Perhaps Kirk's most tragic romantic involvement was with American social worker **Edith Keeler**, whom Kirk met in Earth's past when he traveled into the 1930s through the **Guardian of Forever**. Keeler was a focal point in time, and Kirk was forced to allow her death in order to prevent a terrible change in the flow of history. ("The City on the Edge of Forever" [TOS]).

David Marcus: Kirk was not involved with the upbringing of his son, **David Marcus**, at the request of the boy's mother, Carol Marcus. Kirk had no contact with his son until 2285, when Carol and David were both working on **Project Genesis**, and Kirk helped rescue the two from **Khan**'s vengeance. Later, Kirk and his son were able to achieve a degree of rapprochement. *(Star Trek II: The Wrath of Khan).* Tragically, David was murdered shortly thereafter on the **Genesis Planet**, by a Klingon officer who sought to steal the secret of Genesis. *(Star Trek III: The Search for Spock).*

After the five-year mission: Following the return of the *Enterprise* from the five-year mission in 2270, Kirk accepted a promotion to admiral and became chief of Starfleet operations, while the *Enterprise* underwent an extensive refit. At the time, Kirk recommended **Will Decker** to replace him as *Enterprise* captain, although Kirk accepted a grade reduction back to captain when he regained command of the ship to meet the **V'Ger** threat in 2271. *(Star Trek: The Motion Picture).* Kirk's first retirement from Starfleet happened some time thereafter, at which time he became romantically involved with Antonia. *(Star Trek Generations). (The significant time gap between* Star Trek: The Motion Picture *and* Star Trek II: The Wrath of Khan *suggests the possibility that Kirk commanded another five-year mission of the* Enterprise *following the events in the first* Star Trek *movie, although this is pure conjecture. If Kirk and the* Enterprise *did embark on another five-year mission in 2271, they probably returned in 2276.* Star Trek Generations *could be interpreted to suggest that Kirk's first retirement was some time between 2276 and 2282, when he met Antonia. On the other hand, the 2271 date for* Star Trek: The Motion Picture *is itself somewhat conjectural in that it is based purely on the 18-month refit time for the* Enterprise. *It is not impossible that Kirk and the* Enterprise *had other assignments after the television series, but before the major refit of the ship. Such assignments would push back the date for the first* Star Trek *film, but would not significantly invalidate the timeline.)*

Kirk returned to Starfleet in 2284 *(Star Trek Generations)* and became a staff instructor with the rank of admiral at **Starfleet Academy**. Kirk was dissatisfied with ground assignment, and returned to active duty in 2285 when **Khan Noonien Singh** hijacked the *Starship* ***Reliant*** and stole the **Genesis Device**. Kirk's close friend, **Spock**, was killed in that incident. *(Star Trek II: The Wrath of Khan).* Upon learning that Spock's ***katra*** had survived, Kirk hijacked the *Enterprise* to the Genesis Planet to return Spock's body to **Vulcan**, where Spock was brought back to life when body and *katra* were reunited. Kirk ordered the *Enterprise* destroyed in the incident to prevent its capture by Klingons. *(Star Trek III: The Search for Spock).* Kirk was charged with nine violations of Starfleet regulations in connection with the revival of Spock in 2285. All but one charge was later dropped, and Kirk was found guilty of the one remaining charge, that of disobeying a superior officer. The **Federation Council** was nonetheless so grateful for Kirk's role in saving Earth from the devastating effects of an alien probe that it granted Kirk the captaincy of the second ***Starship Enterprise***. *(Star Trek IV: The Voyage Home).*

Kirk was an intensely driven individual who loved the outdoors. A personal challenge that nearly cost him his life was free-climbing the sheer **El Capitan** mountain face in **Yosemite National Park** on Earth. *(Star Trek V: The Final Frontier).* He was an accomplished equestrian, and kept a horse at a mountain cabin that he owned during his first retirement. Another companion at his mountain cabin was **Butler**, his Great Dane. He sold the cabin some time after his return to Starfleet. *(Star Trek Generations).* Kirk carried the bitterness for his son's murder for years, and opposed the peace initiative of Klingon **Chancellor Gorkon** in 2293. He especially resented the fact that he was chosen as the Federation's olive branch and assigned the duty of escorting Gorkon to Earth. During that mission, Kirk (along with McCoy) was arrested and wrongly convicted for the murder of Gorkon by Federation and Klingon forces conspiring to block Gorkon's initiatives. Kirk nevertheless played a pivotal role in saving the historic **Khitomer** peace conference from further attacks. Kirk retired from Starfleet a second time about three months after the Khitomer Accords were signed. *(Star Trek VI: The Undiscovered Country).*

Shortly after his second retirement, Kirk was an honored guest at the launch of the *Excelsior*-class *Starship* ***Enterprise*-B** in 2293. Kirk was believed killed on that ship's maiden voyage, although it was later learned that he had actually disappeared into a temporal anomaly called the **nexus**. He remained in the nexus until 2371, when he emerged to help save the inhabitants of the **Veridian system**. Kirk, working with fellow *Enterprise* Captain **Jean-Luc Picard**, was successful in saving the Veridians, but the heroic effort cost Kirk his life at the hand of the deranged scientist, **Tolian Soran**. James T. Kirk is buried on a mountain top on planet **Veridian III**. He went boldly, where none had gone before. *(Star Trek Generations).*

Kirk's first appearance was in "Where No Man Has Gone Before" (TOS).

Kirk, Peter. (Craig Hundley). Nephew of Captain James Kirk and one of the victims of the neural parasites that infested planet Deneva in 2267. Peter lost both parents and was himself almost killed by the **Denevan neural parasites**. ("Operation—Annihilate!" [TOS]). *Peter presumably had two brothers, who were apparently not at the Deneva colony, per Kirk's line in "What Are Little Girls Made Of?" (TOS). Craig Hundley also appeared as* ***Tommy Starnes*** *in the third-season episode "And the Children Shall Lead" [TOS] and, years later, composed some background music for* Star Trek III.

Kirok. The name that James Kirk remembered as his own while suffering from amnesia and living among the people on **Miramanee's planet** in 2268. ("The Paradise Syndrome" [TOS]).

Kirom, Knife of. Sacred artifact that Klingon legend holds to be stained with the blood of **Kahless the Unforgettable**. Gowron used the bloodstains to help determine the legitimacy of the clone of Kahless the Unforgettable produced by the clerics of **Boreth** in 2369. Since the new Kahless was indeed a clone, his genetic pattern was an exact match of the original. ("Rightful Heir" [TNG]).

kironide. Chemical compound found in the food on planet **Platonius**. Kironide is a long-lasting source of great power that, when ingested, endows many humanoids with extraordinary psychokinetic powers. The **Platonians** absorbed kironide into their bodies, giving them such powers, although their servant **Alexander** was unable to do so. ("Plato's Stepchildren" [TOS]).

Kiros. (Patricia Tallman). Member of a group of terrorists who attempted to steal **trilithium** resin from the *Enterprise*-D in 2369. ("Starship Mine" [TNG]). *Patricia Tallman has made other appearances, as a stunt performer, on* Star Trek: The Next Generation *and played Lyta Alexander on* Babylon 5.

Kitara's Song. Poem written by renowned Bajoran poet **Akorem Laan** more than 200 years ago. ("Accession" [DS9]).

Klaa, Captain. (Todd Bryant). Commander of the Klingon bird-of-prey that was ordered to secure the release of Klingon general **Korrd** at planet **Nimbus III** in 2287. Klaa, an ambitious young officer, saw the mission as an opportunity to distinguish himself by challenging the legendary Captain Kirk. (*Star Trek V: The Final Frontier*). Klaa later served as translator in 2293 when Kirk and McCoy were tried for the murder of **Chancellor Gorkon**. (*Star Trek VI: The Undiscovered Country*). *Todd Bryant also appeared as an* Enterprise *cadet (*Star Trek II: The Wrath of Khan*).*

klabnian eel. A life-form that **Q** found distasteful. Q offered to do Picard "a big favor" and turn **Vash** into a klabnian eel. ("QPid" [TNG]).

Klach D'Kel Brakt, Battle of. Legendary victory of Klingon forces over the Romulans in 2270. ("Blood Oath" [DS9]). SEE: **Kor**.

Klaestron IV. Planet. Homeworld of **Ilon Tandro**, who arrived at station Deep Space 9 in 2369 with a warrant for **Jadzia Dax**'s arrest for murder. Although members of the Federation, the Klaestrons are allies of the **Cardassians**. This fact explained why Tandro had knowledge of the interior of the station that aided in the kidnapping of Dax. ("Dax" [DS9]). In 2371, Dr. **Julian Bashir** visited Klaestron IV to learn a new treatment for burn victims. ("Second Skin" [DS9]).

Klag. (Brian Thompson). Second officer of the Klingon bird-of-prey ***Pagh*** during William Riker's brief tenure aboard that vessel as part of an officer-exchange program in 2365. Klag expressed doubts that a human officer could effectively command a Klingon crew, but Riker convinced him otherwise by demonstrating his adeptness at physical combat. ("A Matter of Honor" [TNG]). *Brian Thompson also played the Dosi negotiator Inglatu in "Rules of Acquisition" (DS9) and a Klingon helm officer in* Star Trek Generations.

Klarc-Tarn-Droth. A renowned Federation archaeologist. Klarc-Tarn-Droth attended the annual symposium of the **Federation Archaeology Council** in 2367. ("QPid" [TNG]).

Klavdia III. Planet. Location where **Salia**, future leader of planet **Daled IV**, was raised in an environment far from the divisiveness of her homeworld. Although inhospitable, this planet was chosen because of security considerations. In 2365, the *Enterprise*-D was assigned to transport Salia from Klavdia III to assume her duties as leader on planet Daled IV. ("The Dauphin" [TNG]).

klavion. SEE: ***belaklavion*****.**

kligat**.** Three-sided bladed weapon used by tribal warriors on planet **Capella IV**. At ranges up to 100 meters, the *kligat* could be thrown with deadly accuracy. Security guard Grant was killed by a *kligat* when he drew a weapon at a Klingon on Capella VI in 2267. ("Friday's Child" [TOS]).

Kling. A district or city on the **Klingon Homeworld**. The renegade Korris spoke disparagingly of "the traitors of Kling." ("Heart of Glory" [TNG]). *At the time the episode was written, Kling was intended as the name of the Klingon Homeworld. Once the episode was filmed, it was realized that the name sounded pretty silly, so later scripts simply referred to "the Homeworld," and we now assume that Kling is a city or district. The first time the homeworld was given a name was in* Star Trek VI: The Undiscovered Country*, when it was called* ***Qo'noS****, pronounced "kronos."*

Klingon attack cruiser. Starship of the **Klingon Defense Force**. Designated as *Vor'cha*-class vessels, attack cruisers were among the largest and most powerful vessels in the Imperial fleet. In 2367, Klingon High Council leader **K'mpec** was transported aboard an attack cruiser on his final mission: his plea for Jean-Luc Picard to serve as **Arbiter of Succession** after K'mpec's death. ("Reunion" [TNG]). The *Defiant* was attacked by a *Vor'cha*-class Klingon warship when Captain Sisko headed to Cardassia Prime to rescue Gul Dukat and the Detapa Council in early 2372. The warship pursued the *Defiant* all the way to Deep Space 9. ("The Way of the Warrior" [DS9]). *The* Vor'cha*-class attack cruiser was designed by Rick Sternbach and built by Greg Jein. It first appeared in "Reunion" (TNG).* SEE: **Klingon spacecraft**.

Klingon battle cruiser. Starships that formed the backbone of the **Klingon Defense Force** for decades. The D7-type vessels were in service in the 2260s, a design shared with the **Romulan Star Empire** during the brief alliance between the two powers. These vessels, some 228 meters in overall length, were equipped with warp drive and phase-disruptor armament. By the 2280s, an uprated version, known as a *K't'inga*-class vessel, was introduced into service. *The Klingon battle cruiser was designed by Matt Jefferies and introduced dur-*

ing the third season of the original Star Trek *series. A more detailed version was built by Magicam for* Star Trek: The Motion Picture*, and was re-used in* Star Trek II, Star Trek VI*, and in* Star Trek: The Next Generation*. A hybrid version, a copy of Jefferies's original model, but with the elaborate hull panelwork from the feature-film version, was built by Greg Jein for "Trials and Tribble-ations" (DS9). The term* K't'inga *is conjectural. The term D7 was originally a gag devised by William Shatner and Leonard Nimoy during the filming of the original* Star Trek *series, but "Trials and Tribble-ations" made the term "official."* SEE: **Klingon spacecraft**.

Klingon bird-of-prey. Ship used by the **Klingon Defense Force**, capable of both atmospheric entry and landing, as well as warp-speed interstellar travel. Several types of this ship have been in use since at least 2286, the smaller D-12 and ***B'rel***-class scouts, and the larger ***K'Vort***-class cruisers. All were equipped with cloaking devices. SEE: **cloaking device, Klingon**. The *B'rel* and D-12 class ships had a complement of about a dozen officers and crew. *(Star Trek III: The Search for Spock).* An experimental uprated version of this ship was developed prior to 2293, in an effort to allow the use of torpedo weapons while the cloaking device was engaged. This prototype vessel was commanded by **General Chang**, who used it in his unsuccessful attempt to obstruct the **Khitomer** peace conference. *(Star Trek VI: The Undiscovered Country).* The D-12 class scout vessel was built in the 2350's and was eventually retired from service because of defective plasma coils in their cloaking device. **Lursa** and B'Etor used an old D-12 class bird-of-prey in 2371 when they assisted Dr. Tolian Soran in his plans. *(Star Trek Generations). The term bird-of-prey was originally established to be Romulan in "Balance of Terror" (TOS). An early draft of* Star Trek III *had Commander Kruge stealing a Romulan ship for his quest against Kirk. The Romulan connection was dropped in later drafts, but the ship somehow remained a bird-of-prey. The ship was designed by Nilo Rodis and built at ILM. It was first seen in* Star Trek III*, and also used in* Star Trek IV, V*, and* VI*. Class names are from "Yesterday's* Enterprise*" (TNG) for* K'Vort*, "Rascals" (TNG) for* B'rel*, and* Star Trek Generations *for D-12. Klingon birds-of-prey have appeared in "A Matter of Honor" (TNG), "The Defector" (TNG), "Yesterday's* Enterprise*" (TNG), "Reunion" (TNG), "Redemption" (TNG), and "Unification, Parts I and II" (TNG).* SEE: **Klingon spacecraft**.

Klingon bloodwine bottle label

Klingon bloodwine. Variety of red Klingon wine. Worf had programmed the replicators aboard the *Enterprise*-D to produce a close approximation of this beverage. ("Gambit, Part II" [TNG]). **Kozak** consumed an enormous amount of bloodwine just prior to the accident that took his life in 2371. ("The House of Quark" [DS9]). Bloodwine is best when served warm. ("The Way of the Warrior" [DS9]). Bloodwine was traditionally consumed by warriors being inducted into the Order of the *Bat'leth*. ("Apocalypse Rising" [DS9]). *Given the ingredients of other Klingon foods, we wonder if this stuff really lives up to its name... . (On second thought, we don't want to know.)*

Klingon calisthenics program. SEE: **calisthenics program, Klingon.**

Klingon civil war. A brief but bitter power struggle between the forces of council leader **Gowron** and challengers from the politically powerful **Duras** family in 2367-2368. **Lursa** and **B'Etor**, sisters to the late Duras, had attempted to force Duras's illegitimate son, **Toral**, to be accepted as leader of the **Klingon High Council**. When **Jean-Luc Picard**, acting as **Arbiter of Succession**, refused to accept Toral's bid, Lursa and B'Etor attempted a military coup against Gowron. Although Gowron's forces seemed initially overmatched by those loyal to the Duras family, it was learned that Lursa and B'Etor were being supplied by Romulan operative **Sela**. Captain Picard ruled that the Federation Starfleet could not take sides in this internal Klingon matter, but later agreed to blockade the Romulan supply convoy, resulting in a victory for Gowron's forces. ("Redemption, Parts I and II" [TNG]).

Klingon cloaking device. SEE: **cloaking device, Klingon**.

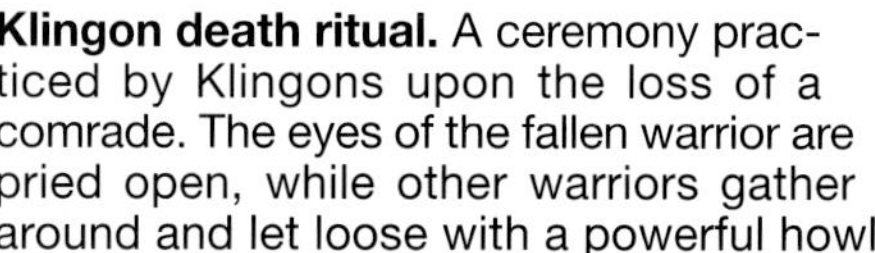

Klingon communicator. Personal voice-communications device used by members of the Klingon Defense Force. In the 2260s, these devices were handheld, but by 2365 they had been incorporated into small decorative pins worn on a warrior's uniform. *Early versions of the pins were designed by Rick Sternbach. Later pins were designed by John Eaves.*

Klingon death ritual. A ceremony practiced by Klingons upon the loss of a comrade. The eyes of the fallen warrior are pried open, while other warriors gather around and let loose with a powerful howl that has been described not as a wail of the dead, but as an exaltation of the victorious. Klingon belief holds that the howl is a warning for the dead to beware because a Klingon warrior is about to arrive. ("Heart of Glory" [TNG]). In other cases, a sacred funereal dirge was sung in memory of the deceased. ("Blood Oath" [DS9]).*The death howl was seen in "Heart of Glory," and again upon* ***K'Ehleyr****'s death in "Reunion" (TNG).*

Klingon Defense Force. Military service of the Klingon Empire. The Klingon Defense Force is responsible for defending the empire's borders against enemies and for operating the empire's space fleet. **Korris** and **Konmel** both claimed to be members of the Klingon Defense Force, but they were actually renegades seeking to overthrow the Klingon government. ("Heart of Glory" [TNG]). Worf's brother, **Kurn**, was an officer of the Klingon Defense Force. ("Sins of the Father" [TNG]).

Klingon Empire. The Klingon nation, founded some 1,500 years ago by **Kahless the Unforgettable**, who first united the Klingon people by killing the tyrant, **Molor**. ("The Savage Curtain" [TOS], "Rightful Heir" [TNG]). The Klingon Empire has had a colorful and violent history, with many bloody conflicts such as the battle of **Tong Vey**, in which the ancient Emperor **Sompek** ordered the destruction of an entire city. ("Rules of Engagement" [DS9]). By 2069, the empire was controlled by the **Klingon High Council**, which had grown so powerful that no emperor headed the empire from that year until the ascension of the second Kahless in 2369. ("Rightful Heir" [TNG]).

First contact between the Klingon Empire and the Federation took place in 2218 ("Day of the Dove" [TOS]), a disastrous event that led to nearly a century of hostilities between the two powers. ("First Contact" [TNG]). By 2267, negotiations between the Federation and the Klingon Empire were on the verge of breaking down. The Klingons had issued an ultimatum to the Federation to withdraw from disputed areas claimed by both the Federation and the Klingon Empire or face war. The hostilities came to a head at planet **Organia**, the only Class-M world in the region. Unknown to either combatant, the **Organians** were incredibly advanced **noncorporeal life**-forms who imposed the **Organian Peace Treaty** on both parties, thus effectively ending armed hostilities. ("Errand of Mercy" [TOS]).

The Klingons entered into a brief alliance with the **Romulan Star Empire** around 2268, when an agreement between the two powers resulted in the sharing of military technology and spacecraft designs, providing the Romulans with Klingon battle cruisers. ("The *Enterprise* Incident" [TOS]). By the mid-2280s, Klingons were using ships described as birds-of-prey (traditionally a Romulan term) that were equipped with **cloaking devices**. *(Star Trek III: The Search for Spock).*

Early talks between the Federation and the Klingon Empire took place at the **Korvat colony** in 2289. While no major breakthrough resulted, some small progress was made when Federation negotiator **Curzon Dax** earned the respect of his Klingon colleagues. ("Blood Oath" [DS9]). The Klingons considered **tribbles** to be an ecological menace, a plague to be wiped out. In the latter part of the 23rd century, hundreds of Klingon warriors were sent to track them down throughout the galaxy. An armada obliterated the tribble homeworld, and before the 24th century, tribbles had been eradicated. ("Trials and Tribble-ations" [DS9]).

A new chapter in relations between the Klingons and the Federation was opened in 2293 when a catastrophic explosion on **Praxis** caused serious environmental damage to the homeworld. In the economic disarray that followed, Klingon **Chancellor Gorkon**, leader of the High Council, found that his empire could no longer afford its massive military forces. Gorkon therefore launched a peace initiative, offering to end some 70 years of hostilities with the Federation. Just prior to a major peace conference, Gorkon was murdered by Federation and Klingon interests who sought to maintain the status quo. Gorkon's successor, his daughter **Azetbur**, continued her father's work, and successfully concluded the **Khitomer Accords** with the Federation later that year, ending nearly a century of hostilities. *(Star Trek VI).*

The **Klingon High Council** was a hotbed of political intrigue that nearly plunged the empire into civil war in 2367 when council leader **K'mpec** died of poison. This murder, viewed as a killing without honor under Klingon tradition, triggered a bitter struggle to determine K'mpec's successor. K'mpec had taken the unorthodox precaution of appointing a non-Klingon, Jean-Luc Picard, as his **Arbiter of Succession**. Under Picard's mediation, political newcomer Gowron emerged as the sole candidate for council leader. ("Reunion" [TNG]). Forces loyal to the powerful **Duras** family unsuccessfully attempted to block Gowron, plunging the empire into a brief, but bitter **Klingon civil war** in 2367. ("Redemption, Parts I and II" [TNG]). Though their nation was called an empire, it had not been ruled by an emperor for more than three centuries. This situation changed rather dramatically in 2369, when the clerics of **Boreth** produced a clone of Kahless the Unforgettable. Although their initial claim that the clone was the actual Kahless was quickly disproven, this clone was regarded as the rightful heir to the throne and, with the support of Chancellor Gowron, was installed as the ceremonial emperor of the Klingon people. ("Rightful Heir" [TNG]).

The empire was ever-vigilant against potential outside threats and, in early 2372, reacted strongly when a civilian uprising overthrew the Cardassian military, placing power into the hands of the **Detapa Council**. Fearing that the Cardassian government had been taken over by the **Dominion**, Gowron's forces, commanded by a changeling agent impersonating **General Martok**, invaded Cardassia Prime, intending to execute the Detapa Council and install an imperial overseer to rule. The **Federation Council** condemned the Klingon invasion, and in response, Gowron cancelled the Khitomer Accords, expelled all Federation citizens from the empire and recalled his ambassadors. ("The Way of the Warrior" [DS9]). Open hostilities between the Klingons and the Federation flared up over the next few months, resulting in the destruction of the *Starship* ***Farragut*** at the **Lembatta cluster** and a pointless skirmish at **Ajilon Prime**. A cease-fire with the Federation was established shortly after the incident at Ajilon. ("Nor the Battle to the Strong" [DS9]).

(In the **anti-time** reality created by the **Q Continuum**, by 2395 the Klingon Empire had gained control of Romulan space. Relations between the Klingons and the Federation were poor, and the Klingons had closed their borders to Federation vessels.) ("All Good Things..." [TNG]).

Klingon High Council. Ruling body of the **Klingon Empire**. The council was composed of about two dozen members and met in the **Great Hall** of the **First City** of the **Klingon Homeworld**. ("Sins of the Father" [TNG]). So powerful was the council that after the death of the emperor in 2069, no successor ascended the throne, and the council alone controlled the empire. ("Rightful Heir" [TNG]). The High Council has a long history of political intrigue and power struggles. When council member **Duras** attempted to unjustly convict the late **Mogh** of having betrayed his people at **Khitomer**, the council, led by **K'mpec**, was willing to let the accusation stand, for fear the powerful Duras family would plunge the empire into civil war. ("Sins of the Father" [TNG]). K'mpec held the position of council leader for longer than anyone in history, until his death in 2367. ("Reunion" [TNG]). SEE: **Arbiter of Succession; Rite of Succession**. His successor, **Gowron**, successfully fought off a challenge by the Duras family to place Duras's illegitimate son, **Toral**, as council leader. That struggle culminated in a brief but bitter civil war between council factions in 2367-2368. Gowron's victory was in part achieved by his promise to restore rightful honor to the Mogh family in exchange for military support by the sons of Mogh. ("Redemption, Parts I and II" [TNG]). *"Redemption, Part I" establishes that a female cannot be a member of the High Council, although* ***Azetbur*** *was council leader in* Star Trek VI.

Klingon Homeworld. The capital planet of the Klingon Empire. A large, green, Class-M world, the homeworld was rarely referred to by its formal name, **Qo'noS** (pronounced kronos). *(Star Trek VI: The Undiscovered Country).* The *Enterprise*-D visited the planet in 2366 when **Worf** challenged the High Council ruling that his father, **Mogh**, was a traitor. ("Sins of the Father" [TNG]). The ship visited the homeworld again in late 2367 when Jean-Luc Picard attended the installation of **Gowron** as High Council leader. Picard had served as Gowron's **Arbiter of Succession**. ("Redemption, Part I" [TNG]). The *Enterprise*-D again returned to the Klingon Homeworld a few weeks later, when Picard requested the loan of a Klingon bird-of-prey for a covert mission into Romulan space to investigate the disappearance of Ambassador Spock. ("Unification, Part I" [TNG]). SEE: **Kling**.

Klingon Intelligence. Information-gathering service of the **Klingon** government. In 2371, a covert team composed of three Klingon Intelligence agents was sent to Deep Space 9 to observe and to take appropriate action against a **Romulan** delegation visiting the station. Klingon Intelligence correctly feared that the Romulan delegation might attempt to destroy the station and the **Bajoran wormhole**. ("Visionary" [DS9]).

Klingon Neutral Zone. A no-man's-land between the **United Federation of Planets** and the **Klingon Empire**. Passage into the zone by ships of either nation was forbidden by treaty. *(Star Trek II: The Wrath of Khan).* The Klingon Neutral Zone was abolished in 2293 by the **Khitomer Accords**. *(Star Trek VI: The Undiscovered Country).*

Klingon opera. Form of musical theater. ("Unification, Part II" [TNG]). In Klingon culture, opera was used to tell stories related to their proud history and traditions, as in the ***Kot'baval*** **Festival**

Klingon spacecraft, approximate scale

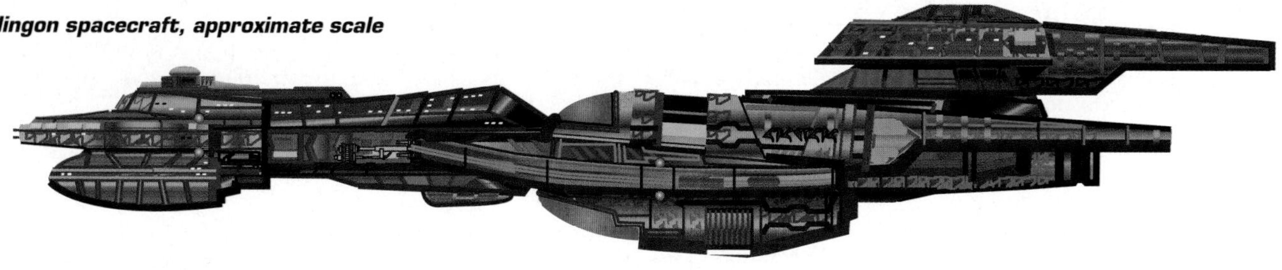

Negh'Var, flagship ("Way of the Warrior" [DS9])

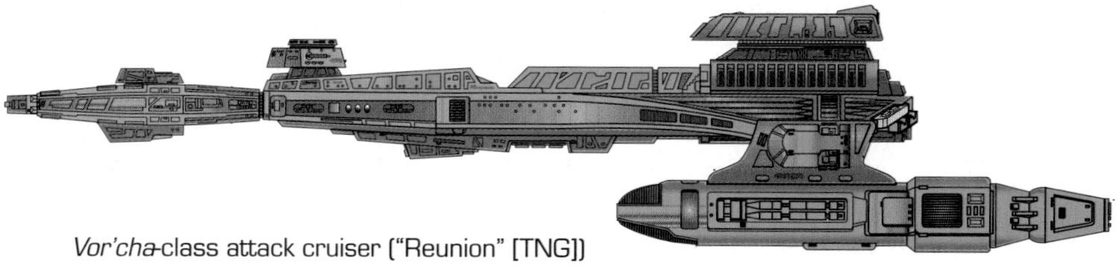

Vor'cha-class attack cruiser ("Reunion" [TNG])

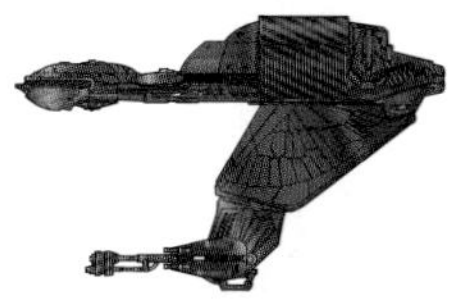

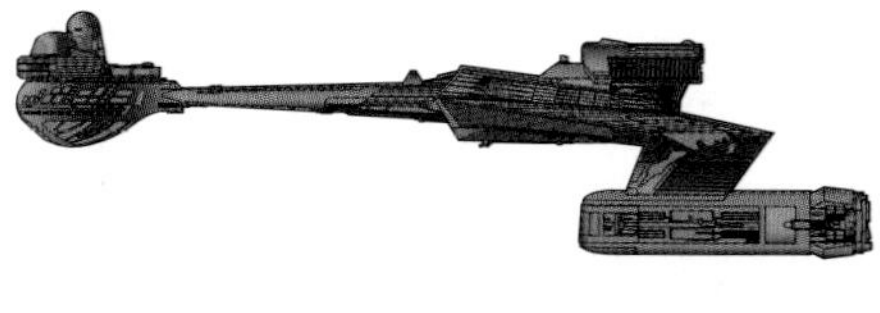

K'tinga class battle cruiser (ST:TMP)

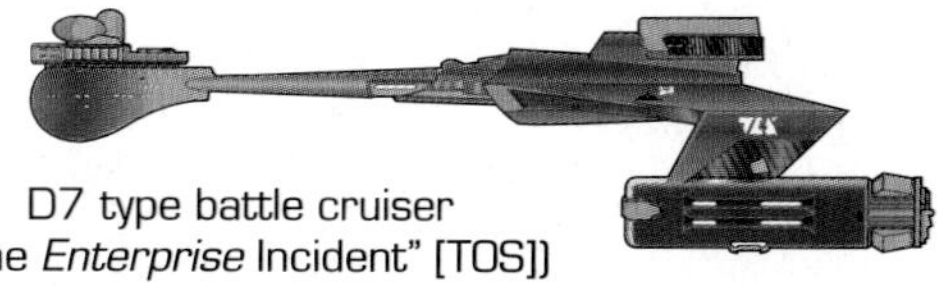

Bird-of-Prey (ST III)

D7 type battle cruiser
("The *Enterprise* Incident" [TOS])

that celebrated the ancient victory of **Kahless the Unforgettable** over the tyrant **Molor**. ("Firstborn" [TNG]). In 2370 on Deep Space 9, Jake Sisko complained to his father Benjamin that he hated studying Klingon opera in school. Ben did, too. ("The Alternate" [DS9]). **Worf** enjoyed Klingon opera, and often played it very loudly through the *Defiant*'s sound system. He particularly liked the performance of Barak-Kadan. ("Looking for *par'Mach* in All the Wrong Places" [DS9]).

Klingon skull stew. Delicacy available at the **Replimat** on station Deep Space 9. *Skull stew was never mentioned in dialog, but a photo of this delicious dish, created by scenic artist Doug Drexler, was seen on the wall of the Replimat.*

Klingon spacecraft. A spaceborne culture, the Klingon Empire has a wide variety of spacecraft used for defense, exploration, and commerce.

Klingon War (alternate). In the alternate timeline created when the ***Enterprise*-C** vanished from its "proper" place in 2344, the Federation and the Klingon Empire engaged in a terrible war, which might have been prevented had the *Enterprise*-C rendered aid to the Klingon outpost at **Narendra III**. Over the next 22 years, some 40 billion people lost their lives, and over half of the Starfleet was destroyed. By 2366, Starfleet Command anticipated that the Federation would be defeated within six months. This alternate timeline was excised when the *Enterprise*-C returned to its "original" place in history, and did indeed render aid at Narendra III in 2344. ("Yesterday's *Enterprise*" [TNG]).

Klingon weapons. The Klingon warrior uses a curious combination of extremely sophisticated armament and ancient traditional weapons.

Klingonese. Spoken and written language of the **Klingon Empire**; a harsh, guttural tongue. **Korax** once boasted that half the quadrant was learning to speak Klingonese because there was no doubt in his mind that the Klingon Empire would dominate the galaxy. ("The Trouble with Tribbles" [TOS]). The Klingon language had no word for "peacemaker" until the Klingons encountered mediator **Riva**, who helped negotiate several treaties between the Klingons and the Federation. ("Loud as a Whisper" [TNG]). *The spoken Klingon language used in most of the* Star Trek *motion pictures and* Star Trek: The Next Generation *episodes was invented by linguist Marc Okrand. For more information about the Klingon language, please refer to Okrand's book,* The Klingon Dictionary, *published by Pocket Books. (Okrand notes that not all the Klingon-language words on the show have come from his book. He speculates that different Klingon provinces have different dialects.)*

Klingons. Humanoid warrior civilization ("Errand of Mercy" [TOS]), originally from the planet **Qo'noS**; a proud, tradition-bound people who value honor. The aggressive Klingon culture has made them an interstellar military power to be respected and feared. There is no equivalent of the devil in Klingon mythology ("Day of the Dove" [TOS]), although a beast known as ***Fek'lhr*** is

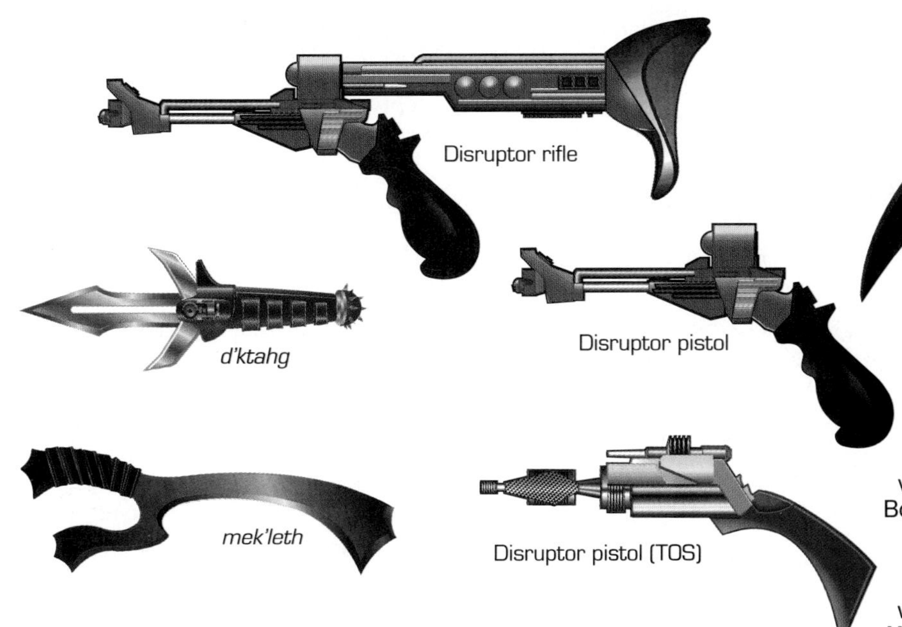

Disruptor rifle

bat'leth

d'ktahg

Disruptor pistol

mek'leth

Disruptor pistol (TOS)

believed to guard the underworld of ***Gre'thor***. ("Devil's Due" [TNG]). According to myth, ancient Klingon warriors slew their gods a millennium ago. They apparently were more trouble than they were worth. ("Homefront" [DS9]). *Perhaps this is why the Klingons have no devil; they killed him.* In Klingon society, the death of a warrior who has died honorably in battle is not mourned. In such cases, the survivors celebrate the freeing of the spirit. ("The Bonding" [TNG]). Klingons believe in an after-life but there is no burial ceremony. They dispose of the body in the most efficient means possible ("Emanations" [VGR]), confident that the warrior's spirit has now joined **Kahless the Unforgettable** in ***Sto-Vo-Kor***. ("Rightful Heir" [TNG]). Klingon tradition holds that "the son of a Klingon is a man the day he can first hold a blade." ("Ethics" [TNG]). Another Klingon ritual is the ***R'uustai,*** or bonding ceremony, in which two individuals join families, becoming brothers and sisters. ("The Bonding" [TNG]).

Klingon warrior (TOS)

Klingon warrior (ST:TMP)

Klingon warrior (STV)

Klingon warrior (TNG)

Klingon warrior (TNG)

Klingons believe that they have the instinctive ability to look an opponent in the eye and see the intent to kill. Klingon tradition holds that a Klingon who dies by their own hand will not travel across the River of Blood to enter *Sto-Vo-Kor*. ("Sons of Mogh" [DS9]). If a Klingon warrior strikes another with the back of his hand, it is interpreted as a challenge to the death. Klingon warriors speak proudly to each other; they do not whisper or keep their distance. Standing far away or whispering are considered insults in Klingon society. ("Apocalypse Rising" [DS9]).

The Klingon body incorporates multiple redundancies for nearly all vital bodily functions. This characteristic, known as ***brak'lul***, gives Klingon warriors enormous resiliency in battle. Despite the considerable sophistication of Klingon technology, significant gaps exist in Klingon medical science, in part due to cultural biases that injured warriors should be left to die or to carry out the ***Hegh'bat***. ("Ethics" [TNG]). Klingons have redundant stomachs. ("Macrocosm" [VGR]). Klingons have no tear ducts. Klingon blood is a lavender-colored fluid. *(Star Trek VI: The Undiscovered Country).*

Klingons were first seen in "Errand of Mercy" (TOS), and throughout the

Klingon chancellor (STVI)

Klingon general (STVI)

Klingon elite warrior (STVI)

Klingon diplomat (STIV)

original Star Trek *series. At the time, they appeared as fairly ordinary humans with heavy makeup and mustaches. Beginning with* Star Trek: The Motion Picture, *improved makeup techniques (and bigger budgets) led to their present elaborate forehead designs. The differences between the two types of Klingons have never been definitively explained on the show, although Worf, in "Trials and Tribble-ations" (DS9), made it very clear that this is not something that Klingons discuss with outsiders. The issue was further complicated when three Klingons, Kor (*pictured*), Koloth, and Kang, who had appeared in the original series with the original makeup design, appeared on* Star Trek: Deep Space Nine *wearing the motion-picture-style Klingon foreheads. According to David Alexander (in* Star Trek Creator, *a biography of Gene Roddenberry, Roc Books, 1994), the Klingons were named for Lieutenant Wilbur Clingan, a friend of Roddenberry who served with him in the Los Angeles Police Department.*

klon peags. Chopstick-like **Wadi** implements that are highly sought after in their culture and have many different uses. **Falow** offered Quark *klon peags* as a wager, but the Ferengi declined the bid. ("Move Along Home" [DS9]).

Kloog. (Mickey Morton). Large, hairy **drill thrall** who fought Kirk in 2268 during one of the games on planet **Triskelion**. ("The Gamesters of Triskelion" [TOS])

KLS stabilizer. Engineering device used to maintain power output stability of a starship's warp core. ("Phage" [VGR]).

***Kobayashi Maru* scenario.** A **Starfleet Academy** training exercise in which command-track cadets were presented with a "no-win" scenario as a test of character. The simulation involved a distress call from a Federation freighter, the *Kobayashi Maru*, which had struck a gravitic mine in the Klingon Neutral Zone. The cadet had a choice of several options, none of which led to a "winning" conclusion, in that it was impossible to simultaneously save the freighter, prevent destruction of the cadet's ship, and avoid an armed exchange with the Klingons. The *Kobayashi Maru* was regarded as something of a rite of passage for command-track cadets. **James T. Kirk** was reputed to have taken the test three times while he was at the academy. Prior to his third attempt, Kirk surreptitiously reprogrammed the simulation computer to make it possible to beat the simulation, and subsequently received a commendation for original thinking. *(Star Trek II: The Wrath of Khan).*

Kobayashi Maru. In the Starfleet Academy's training simulation of that name, the *Kobayashi Maru* was a third-class neutronic fuel carrier with a crew of 81 and 300 passengers. *(Star Trek II: The Wrath of Khan).*

Kobheerian captain. SEE: **Viterian, Captain.**

Kobliad. Humanoid civilization. The Kobliad needed the substance **deuridium** to stabilize their cell structures, prolonging their lives. The demand for deuridium far outweighed its availability, so some Kobliad took illegal routes to procure the substance. ("The Passenger" [DS9]). SEE: **Kajada, Ty; Vantika, Rao.**

Kodos the Executioner. (Arnold Moss). Governor of planet **Tarsus IV** in 2246. When the colony's food supply was destroyed by an exotic fungus, Kodos seized power and declared martial law. Kodos rationed the remaining food supply by selecting some four thousand colonists to die, according to his personal theories of eugenics. Shortly thereafter, Kodos was believed to have died. It was later found that Kodos had assumed a new identity, that of actor **Anton Karidian**, and evaded detection for some 20 years until **Thomas Leighton** identified him as Kodos. Kodos was accidentally killed by his insane daughter, **Lenore Karidian**, who was trying to protect her father from his accusers. ("The Conscience of the King" [TOS]).

Kodrak. Cover name used by Odo in 2373. For a covert mission to **Ty'Gokor**, Odo was surgically altered to appear Klingon, and he assumed the identity of Kodrak. ("Apocalypse Rising" [DS9]).

KoH-man-ara. Prescribed move in the Klingon ***Mok'bara*** martial art form. It closely resembles the crane block of Earth's tai chi chuan. ("Second Chances" [TNG]).

Kohl hibernation system. Sophisticated system designed to keep a few members of the Kohl settlement alive in stasis while their planet recovered from an extended period of glaciation. The hibernation system preserved the survivors' bodies in stasis while their minds were kept occupied in a computer-created virtual reality. Survivors of the **Kohl settlement** used five hibernation pods located 2.3 kilometers below the surface of their planet. The **recall subroutine** within their hibernation system was programmed to revive the five sleepers when environmental conditions on the planet surface were again hospitable. ("The Thaw" [VGR]). SEE: **Clown**.

Kohl physician. (Tony Carlin). One of the few members of the **Kohl settlement** who survived stasis in the **Kohl hibernation system**. In 2372, he and a Kohl programmer were rescued from their malfunctioning hibernation system by the crew of the *Voyager*. ("The Thaw" [VGR]).

Kohl programmer. (Shannon O'Hurley). One of the few surviving members of the **Kohl settlement** in the Delta Quadrant. In 2372, she and a Kohl physician were rescued from their malfunctioning hibernation system by the crew of the *Voyager*. ("The Thaw" [VGR]).

Kohl settlement. Planned community of technologically sophisticated humanoids on a planet in the Delta Quadrant. The settlement was a major trade stop in the area, with a population numbering around four-hundred thousand. In 2353, a major solar flare occurred in the system, radically changing weather patterns on the planet, resulting in a glacial freeze. Five of the settlers managed to survive by enclosing themselves in an underground virtual reality controlled by the **Kohl hibernation system**, which was set to revive them in 2368. ("The Thaw" [VGR]).

Kohlanese stew. Meal served at Quark's bar at Deep Space 9. A food-replicator malfunction caused by an old act of Bajoran sabotage caused the Kohlanese stew to become particularly unpalatable on stardate 46423. ("Babel" [DS9]).

Kohms. One of two major ethnic groups on planet **Omega IV** who fought a terrible bacteriological war centuries ago. The few survivors of the conflict lived because they happened to have powerful natural immunity, and had extraordinarily long life spans. In 2268, Starfleet **Captain Ronald Tracey** of the ***U.S.S. Exeter*** sided with the Kohms, supplying them with phasers with which they struck against their ancient enemies, the **Yangs**. *Enterprise* personnel, investigating the disappearance of the *Exeter*, theorized that the Kohms might have been culturally similar to Earth's 20th-century Chinese Communists. ("The Omega Glory" [TOS]).

Kohn-Ma. Militant **Bajoran** terrorist organization that opposed any outside influence in ruling their planet, including interference from the Federation. In 2369, *Kohn-Ma* dissident **Tahna Los** threatened to destroy the Bajoran wormhole in hopes of decreasing Bajoran importance to the Federation and other factions. ("Past Prologue" [DS9]).

Koinonians. An ancient intelligent culture that was composed of two different life-forms, one of energy, and the other of matter. The physical Koinonians destroyed their civilization a millennium ago after several generations of war, leaving ruins that were studied by an *Enterprise*-D away team in 2366. The surviving Koinonians had very strong ethics, and tried to provide for young **Jeremy Aster** after his mother was killed by an ancient artifact of that war. ("The Bonding" [TNG]). *The name of the Koinonians' homeworld was not established in the episode.*

Kol. (Leslie Jordan). Ferengi pilot present with **DaiMon Goss** and **Dr. Arridor** at the Barzan negotiations in 2366. Kol was lost with the disappearance of the Ferengi shuttle in the **Barzan wormhole**. ("The Price" [TNG]). Kol and Arridor became stranded in the Delta Quadrant when the other terminus of the Barzan wormhole also changed position. The two crash-landed on the **Takarian** homeworld and assumed the role of the **Great Sages** from Takarian mythology. In 2373, the *U.S.S. Voyager* happened upon the planet and forced Arridor and Kol to leave. When the two Ferengi attempted to return to the Takarian planet, their shuttle was pulled into the Barzan wormhole by a gravitational eddy. Their actions knocked the wormhole off of its subspace axis so that both of its endpoints jumped around erratically. The fate of Arridor, Kol, and the shuttle remains unknown. ("False Profits" [VGR]). *Leslie Jordan played Kol in "False Profits." Another actor, who had no dialog, played the part in "The Price."*

Kolaati traders. Outlaws in the Delta Quadrant who operated near the **Nekrit Expanse**. Kolaati traders were believed to deal with illegal substances. ("Fair Trade" [VGR]).

Koladan diamond. Precious stones known for their brightness. ("Caretaker" [VGR]).

Kolaish spice oil. Aromatic herbal compound. In 2372, Shakaar gave Kira Nerys a massage with Kolaish spice oil in order to get her to agree to a big favor. ("Return to Grace" [DS9]).

***kolem*.** Romulan unit of measure for power flow. ("The Next Phase" [TNG]).

***Koliay*.** Klingon term for student. ("Playing God" [DS9]).

Kolinahr*.** Vulcan ritual intended to purge all remaining emotions in pursuit of the ideal of pure logic. **Spock** attempted to attain *Kolinahr* under the guidance of Vulcan masters in 2270, after his first five-year mission under the command of Captain Kirk, but failed when the telepathic call of **V'Ger** stirred the emotions of his human half. (*Star Trek: The Motion Picture*). **Tuvok** began the *Kolinahr* in 2298, but he left the discipline in 2304, prior to completion, because he had entered ***Pon farr. ("Flashback" [VGR]).

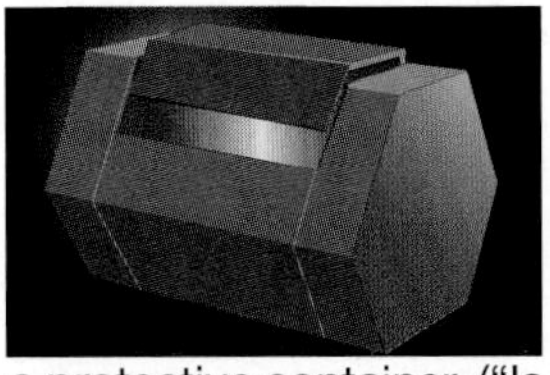

Kollos. Medusan ambassador to the Federation who was transported aboard the *Starship Enterprise* back to his homeworld, accompanied by **Dr. Miranda Jones**. Because the sight of **Medusans** is extremely dangerous to humans, Kollos traveled in a protective container. ("Is There in Truth No Beauty?" [TOS]).

Kolopak. (Henry Darrow). Federation settler, descendant of Native American colonists from Earth; father to Commander **Chakotay** of the *Starship Voyager*. ("Initiations" [VGR]). Kolopak believed that ignorance is the greatest enemy. He was proud of his Native American ancestry, and was very knowledgable of his people's legends, including the creation myth of the **Sky Spirits** and stories of how his family had descended from the ancient **Rubber Tree People** of Central America. ("Tattoo" [VGR]). Kolopak thought it was important that his son, Chakotay, learn traditional wilderness skills, including how to build a log cabin. ("Resolutions" [VGR]). When Chakotay was 15, Kolopak took his son to Earth for an expedition to search for the origin of their tribe. Deep in the Central American jungle, Kolopak found his distant cousins, fellow descendants of the Rubber Tree People, who embraced him and gave him a marking on his forehead that he wore for the rest of his life. Kolopak was disappointed that his son, Chakotay, chose to reject his people's ways. He would have been proud to know that after Kolopak's death, Chakotay came to recognize the value of his heritage. He even marked his forehead, as had his father, to honor their ancestors. ("Tattoo" [VGR]). SEE: **Inheritors**. In 2372, Chakotay celebrated the **pakra** on the anniversary of Kolopak's death. ("Initiations" [VGR]). In late 2372, Kolopak spoke to Chakotay in a **vision quest**, reminding him that there was nothing more important than protecting his son. ("Basics, Part I" [VGR]). *Kolopak was seen in "Tattoo" and "Basics, Part I."*

Kolos. Humanoid patron of Quark's bar. In 2369, Kolos bid on artifacts brought back from the Gamma Quadrant by archaeologist **Vash**. ("Q-Less" [DS9]).

Koloth. (William Campbell). Noted **Klingon** diplomat who represented his government in the late 23rd century. In 2289, Koloth was involved in early talks with the Federation, where his icy demeanor earned him the nickname ***d'akturak*** from Federation negotiator **Curzon Dax**. ("Blood Oath" [DS9]). Earlier in his career, Koloth commanded a Klingon warship that visited **Deep Space Station K-7** for rest and recreation on stardate 4523, much to the chagrin of Federation representatives. ("The Trouble with Tribbles" [TOS]). At the time, Koloth's ship was the ***I.K.S. Gr'oth***. ("Trials and Tribble-ations" [DS9]). Koloth's firstborn son, along with the firstborns of **Kor** and **Kang**, was murdered by a criminal named the Albino, after which Koloth swore a **blood oath** with Kor, Kang, and Dax to avenge the killings. ("Blood Oath" [DS9]). Koloth, Kang, and Kor once fought against T'nag and his army, emerging victorious despite overwhelming odds. ("The Sword of Kahless" [DS9]). Koloth died in glorious battle in 2370 when Kor, Kang, and **Jadzia Dax** won vengeance on the Albino on planet **Secarus IV**. ("Blood Oath" [DS9]). *William Campbell also played Trelane in* "The Squire of Gothos" (TOS). SEE: **Kor**.

Kolrami, Sirna. (Roy Brocksmith). **Zakdorn** master strategist. Kolrami served as a tactical consultant aboard the *Enterprise*-D during a **Starfleet battle simulation** exercise in 2365. A third-level grand master at the game of **strategema**. ("Peak Performance" [TNG]).

Kolrod Island. Disputed territory located on planet **Kesprytt III.** The **Kes** had control of the island in 2370, but the **Prytt** felt it was, by rights, theirs. ("Attached" [TNG]).

Kolvoord Starburst. A highly dangerous aerobatic space maneuver performed by five single-pilot spacecraft. Starting in a circular formation, the ships cross within ten meters of each other, and fly off in the opposite direction, igniting their plasma trails during the crossover. The maneuver was banned by **Starfleet Academy** in the 2260s following an accident that took the lives of five cadets. In 2368, **Nova Squadron** was attempting to execute the Kolvoord Starburst when the ships collided. All five ships were lost, and Cadet **Joshua Albert** was killed. ("The First Duty" [TNG]).

Komack, Admiral. (Byron Morrow). High-ranking official at Starfleet Command in 2267. Kirk asked Uhura to contact Admiral Komack at Starfleet concerning the spores on planet **Omicron Ceti III** and their effects on his crew. ("This Side of Paradise" [TOS]). Later that year, Komack sent a message to the *Enterprise* instructing them to proceed to the inauguration ceremonies on planet **Altair VI**. ("Amok Time" [TOS]). *The character was named for actor-director James Komack, who later directed "A Piece of the Action" (TOS).*

Komananov, Anastasia. (Nana Visitor). Character in Julian Bashir's **secret agent** holosuite program. Anastasia Komananov was a colonel in Russia's KGB during the 1960s. She was also a sometime companion of British secret agent Julian Bashir, who once presented her with a pair of explosive earrings as a Christmas gift. Those earrings later helped the two of them escape the assassin known as **Falcon**. A holosuite malfunction in 2372 caused the character to look exactly like Kira Nerys. ("Our Man Bashir" [DS9]).

Komar. Type of **trianic energy beings** that lived in a **dark-matter nebula** in the Delta Quadrant. The Komar feed off the neural energy of other beings, and in 2371, tried unsuccessfully to absorb **bioneural energy** from the crew of the *Starship Voyager.* ("Cathexis" [VGR]).

Konmel, Lieutenant. (Charles B. Hyman). Klingon criminal killed in 2364 while trying to avoid prosecution on the **Klingon Homeworld**. ("Heart of Glory" [TNG]). SEE: **Korris, Captain**.

Kono. Cousin to Ferengi entrepreneur **Quark**. In 2370, Kono robbed a museum on planet **Cardassia V,** then journeyed to Deep Space 9 to meet with Quark. When contacted by DS9 security, Kono beamed aboard a **Tellerite** freighter, attempting escape, but was eventually captured. ("Shadowplay" [DS9]).

Konsab, Commander. Instructor at the **Romulan** Intelligence Academy. Konsab believed that military officers needed to share a measure of mutual trust in order to function effectively. In this, Konsab disagreed with the basic **Tal Shiar** policy of maintaining loyalty through the use of intimidation. ("Face of the Enemy" [TNG]).

Koon-ut so'lik. The ritual **Vulcan** marriage proposal. On stardate 50537, Ensign **Vorik** performed the *Koon-ut so'lik,* declaring his desire for **B'Elanna Torres** to become his mate during his ***Pon farr***. ("Blood Fever" [VGR]).

Koon-ut-kal-if-fee. Ancient **Vulcan** term meaning "marriage or challenge." In the distant past, Vulcans killed to win their mates. ("Amok Time" [TOS]). SEE: ***Pon farr***.

Kopf, Ensign. (James Lashly). Member of the *Enterprise*-D engineering staff. Kopf worked with Lieutenant Commander La Forge's team when Data, under Dr. Soong's control, took over the *Enterprise*-D in 2367. ("Brothers" [TNG]). *James Lashly later appeared as a Federation security officer in several episodes of* Star Trek: Deep Space Nine.

***kor'tova* candles.** Ritual candles that represent the fire that burns in the heart of a **Klingon** warrior. It is a part of the First Rite of Ascension; when a Klingon boy lights his *kor'tova* candle, he is declaring his intention to become a warrior. ("Firstborn" [TNG]). SEE: **Age of Ascension**.

Kor. (John Colicos). Legendary **Klingon** warrior. In 2267, Kor was the military governor of the planet **Organia** during a border dispute with the Federation. Kor ruled Organia with an iron fist, but was unaware that the apparently humanoid **Organians** were in fact incredibly advanced **noncorporeal life**-forms who sought only to avoid conflict between the two antagonists. ("Errand of Mercy" [TOS]). SEE: **Ayelborne; Organian Peace Treaty**. In 2270, Kor led a decisive Klingon victory over the Romulans in the Battle of **Klach D'Kel Brakt**. He was later awarded the title of ***Dahar* Master**. ("Blood Oath" [DS9]). Kor, along with **Kang** and **Koloth**, once fought a glorious battle against T'nag and his army, emerging victorious despite overwhelming odds. Some of Kor's other triumphs include his valiant defense of the Korma Pass and his attack on Romulus. ("The Sword of Kahless" [DS9]). Kor's firstborn son, along with the firstborns of Kang and Koloth, was murdered by a criminal known as **the Albino.** The three Klingons, along with **Curzon Dax**, swore a **blood oath** to avenge the killings. It took some eight decades to do so, but Kor and his fellow warriors carried out their vengeance on the Albino at planet **Secarus IV** in 2370. ("Blood Oath" [DS9]). SEE: **Dax, Jadzia; scorcher**. In later years, Kor served as the Klingon ambassador to Vulcan. When a Vulcan geological survey found the long-sought **Shroud of the Sword**, the Vulcan government presented the priceless artifact to Kor as a gift. Using analysis of the shroud as a starting point, Kor enlisted the help of Jadzia Dax and **Worf** and set out on a quest for the legendary **Sword of Kahless** in 2372. ("The Sword of Kahless" [DS9]). *Kor, Worf, and Dax actually found the Sword of Kahless on the Hur'q planet. Fearing that the sword would only serve to divide the empire, they decided not to reveal the fact that it had been found. They left the ancient* bat'leth *floating somewhere in free space. This entry reflects their wish that the sword remain lost to protect the empire. Kor was the first Klingon character on* Star Trek. *John Colicos also played Lord Baltar on* Battlestar Galactica.

Kora II. Cardassian planet. Location where **Aamin Marritza** worked beginning in 2364 as an instructor at a military academy, teaching the intricacies of being a filing clerk. After arriving on Kora II in 2364, Marritza underwent cosmetic surgery, changing his appearance. In 2369, he resigned his position at the military academy, put his affairs in order, and boarded a transport vessel for Deep Space 9 in an effort to expose the Cardassian atrocities committed at the **Gallitep** labor camp on Bajor. SEE: **Darhe'el; Kalla-Nohra Syndrome.** ("Duet" [DS9]).

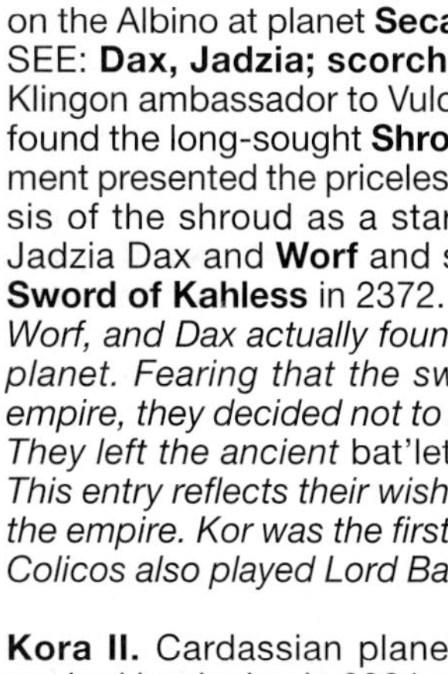

Koral. (James Worthy). Extremely reserved **Klingon** smuggler. Koral was to rendezvous with **Baran** in the Hyralan sector for delivery of a Romulan artifact in 2370. However, Koral and his ***Toron*-class shuttlecraft** were detained by the personnel of the *Enterprise*-D. ("Gambit, Part II" [TNG]). *Koral may have been the tallest Klingon ever to appear on* Star Trek. *He was portrayed by the 6'9" star forward of the Los Angeles Lakers basketball team.*

Koran. One of **Mardah**'s siblings. Koran resided on planet **Bajor** and, as of 2371, had not spoken with Mardah for years. ("The Abandoned" [DS9]).

Koranak**.** Cardassian cruiser. The ***Koranak*** was lost in the **Obsidian Order** attack of **Cardassian** forces on the **Founders' homeworld** in 2371. ("The Die is Cast" [DS9]).

Korat system. Planetary system in Federation territory. The Korat system served as an evacuation site for Starfleet families from station Deep Space 9 during the coup staged by the **Circle** in 2370. ("The Siege" [DS9]).

Korax. (Michael Pataki). Klingon officer. Korax took shore leave on **Deep Space Station K-7** along with several of his fellow crew members in 2267. Drinking at the station's bar, Korax insulted *Enterprise* crew members, including Pavel Chekov and Montgomery Scott, initiating a barroom brawl. ("The Trouble with Tribbles" [TOS]). SEE: **Denebian slime devil**. *Michael Pataki later played* ***Karnas*** *in "Too Short a Season" (TNG).*

Korby, Dr. Roger. (Michael Strong). Known as the Pasteur of archaeological medicine for his translation of medical records from the Orion ruins. Korby was killed during his expedition to the planet **Exo III**, where he discovered a sophisticated **android** technology, the last remnants of an advanced civilization. Prior to his death in 2266, Korby transferred his consciousness into an android body, where he lived until that body was destroyed. Korby had been engaged to Nurse **Christine Chapel**. ("What Are Little Girls Made Of?" [TOS]).

Korgano. Character in ancient **D'Arsay** mythology. He was the nemesis of **Masaka**, the one who could control her and chase her from the sky. Korgano was represented in the **D'Arsay archive** intercepted by the *Enterprise*-D in 2370. *Enterprise*-D Captain Picard, after his study of the archive's information, felt that Korgano may have represented the moon, chasing the sun from the sky each night. Picard assumed the persona of Korgano in order to convince the archive, through communication with Masaka, to release his ship. ("Masks" [TNG]).

Korinar, I.K.S. Klingon warship. In 2372 the *Korinar* was involved in the laying of an illegal cloaked minefield around the Bajoran system. ("Sons of Mogh" [DS9]).

Korinas. (Tricia O'Neil). Member of the **Obsidian Order**. Korinas was assigned as an observer to watch **Gul Dukat** and Commander **Benjamin Sisko**'s efforts to hunt down the ***Defiant***. ("Defiant" [DS9]). *Tricia O'Neil previously played Captain Rachel Garrett in "Yesterday's Enterprise" (TNG).*

Korma Pass. Strategic area that was once valiantly defended by legendary Klingon warrior Kor. ("The Sword of Kahless" [DS9]).

Korma. Cardassian outpost. In 2372 Korma was the site of a conference in which Cardassian and Bajoran officials met to share intelligence information on the Klingons. The conference was disrupted by a Klingon attack that killed everyone at the outpost. Korma's defenses included **system-5 disruptors**. ("Return to Grace" [DS9]). SEE: ***Groumall***; **K'Temang**.

Korob. (Theo Marcuse). Extra-galactic life-form who settled on planet **Pyris VII** with **Sylvia**, on a mission of exploration. In their natural forms, Korob and Sylvia were small avian life-forms a few centimeters high. They used a device they called a **transmuter** to create the illusion of humanoid bodies and a castle with a distinctively haunted atmosphere. Korob and Sylvia captured several *U.S.S. Enterprise* personnel in 2267, but were later killed when Kirk destroyed their transmuter device. ("Catspaw" [TOS]).

Koroth. (Alan Oppenheimer). Klingon high cleric, who in 2369 was in charge of the monastery on the planet **Boreth**. Koroth, along with **Torin**, was responsible for the creation of a clone who was programmed to believe he was **Kahless the Unforgettable**. ("Rightful Heir" [TNG]). *Alan Oppenheimer also played Captain Keogh in "The Jem'Hadar" (DS9) and the Nezu Ambassador in "Rise" (VGR).*

Korrd, General. (Charles Cooper). Klingon diplomatic representative to the **Paradise City** settlement on planet **Nimbus III**. Koord had previously led a distinguished career in the **Klingon Defense Force** before he fell out of favor with the Klingon High Command. His military strategies are required reading at Starfleet Academy. (*Star Trek V: The Final Frontier*). *Actor Charles Cooper also played* ***K'mpec****, leader of the Klingon High Council, in "Sins of the Father" (TNG) and "Reunion" (TNG), albeit with different makeup.*

Korris, Captain. (Vaughn Armstrong). Klingon criminal who fled imprisonment in 2364 by causing the destruction of the cruiser ***T'Acog*** and hijacking a Talarian ship, the ***Batris***. Korris and his accomplices **Konmel** and **Kunivas** apparently crippled the *Batris* during their takeover, and were the only survivors rescued by *Enterprise*-D personnel from the *Batris* just before the *Batris* exploded. Kunivas died shortly thereafter. Korris and Konmel were later killed when a second cruiser was ordered to return them to the **Klingon Homeworld**. ("Heart of Glory" [TNG]). *Vaughn Armstrong also played Cardassian Gul Danar in "Past Prologue" (DS9) and Romulan scientist Telek R'Mor "Eye of the Needle" (VGR).*

koruts. A Klingon derogatory term. ("Sons of Mogh" [DS9]).

Korvat colony. Site of early peace negotiations between the **Federation** and the **Klingon Empire** in 2289. At these talks, **Kang**, representing the Klingon government, faced Federation mediator **Curzon Dax**. ("Blood Oath" [DS9]).

Kosinski. (Stanley Kamel). Starfleet propulsion specialist. Kosinski attempted to perform a series of computer-based upgrades on starship warp drives in 2364. Kosinski's upgrades apparently produced measurable improvements on the starships ***Ajax*** and ***Fearless***, and spectacular improvements on the *Enterprise*-D, but were later found to be baseless. The performance improvements were instead found to be due to the intervention of the **Traveler**, who had the ability to exploit the interchangeability of time, space, and thought. ("Where No One Has Gone Before" [TNG]). Wesley Crusher conducted additional tests on Kosinski's equations in 2367, resulting in the accidental creation of a **static warp shell** in which his mother, Beverly Crusher, became temporarily trapped. ("Remember Me" [TNG]).

Koss'moran**.** Bajoran legend. *Koss'moran* tells of false Prophets or **Pah-wraiths** who were cast out of the Bajoran celestial temple. The Bajoran word *Koss'moran* comes from the verb *kosst* that means to be, and *amoran*, which means banished. ("The Assignment" [DS9]).

Kostolain. Planet that was home to **Minister Campio** and **Erko**. ("Cost of Living" [TNG]).

***Kot'baval* Festival.** Klingon celebration of the ancient victory of **Kahless the Unforgettable** over the tyrant, **Molor**. This festival featured street performances of legendary stories from Klingon lore. In 2370, Worf and his son Alexander attended the *Kot'baval* Festival on **Maranga IV.** ("Firstborn" [TNG]).

Kotakian ship. Space vessel of Kotakian registry. In 2370, **Gul Dukat** traveled to **Deep Space 9** on a Kotakian ship, as an unregistered passenger. ("The Maquis, Part I" [DS9]).

Kotati. Planet in the Delta Quadrant. The crew of the *U.S.S. Voyager* communicated with Kotati in 2372. ("Investigations" [VGR]).

Kovat. (Fritz Weaver). **Public conservator** who served the Cardassian judicial system. Considered one of the finest counselors in the Cardassian Empire, Kovat was adept in helping his clients confess the wisdom of the State during criminal trials. In 2370, Kovat was assigned to Chief **Miles O'Brien** when O'Brien was accused of having supplied arms to Maquis terrorists. Kovat was considerably disturbed when O'Brien's trial did not result in an execution, as expected. ("Tribunal" [DS9]).

Kozak. (John Lendale Bennett). Head of a powerful Klingon **House**. Unfortunately, Kozak had a weakness for gambling and drinking, and by the time of his death in 2371, Kozak had squandered much of his family's wealth, and owed a huge debt to a family enemy, **D'Ghor**. Following Kozak's death, D'Ghor attempted to gain control of the House of Kozak. Quick action by Kozak's widow, **Grilka**, preserved the House from the takeover attempt. ("The House of Quark" [DS9]). *John Lendale Bennett also played the original version of Gabriel Bell in "Past Tense, Part I" (DS9).*

kph. Kilometers per hour. Unit of measure used to describe very slow speeds. ("Galaxy's Child" [TNG]).

Krag. (Craig Richard Nelson). Chief investigator for the **Tanugan** security force. Krag investigated allegations that **William Riker** had been responsible for the death of **Dr. Nel Apgar** in 2366. Krag agreed to a holodeck reenactment of the events aboard the station, which ultimately led to Riker's acquittal and the discovery that Apgar had been responsible for his own death. ("A Matter of Perspective" [TNG]).

Krajensky, Ambassador. (Lawrence Pressman)**.** Starfleet dignitary. Krajensky was kidnapped or killed by **Dominion** agents in late 2371 while en route to planet **Risa**. Krajensky was replaced by a **Founder** who assumed his form. The ersatz Krajensky attempted to trigger a conflict between the Federation and the **Tzenkethi**. ("The Adversary" [DS9]).

Krako, Jojo. (Victor Tayback). Boss of the south side territory on planet **Sigma Iotia II** in 2268. ("A Piece of the Action" [TOS]). SEE: **Iotians**.

Krallinian eel. Life-form. An unpleasant creature found in the Delta Quadrant. ("Jetrel" [VGR]).

Kran-Tobal Prison. Bajoran penal institution. **Ibudan** was incarcerated at Kran-Tobal after murdering a Cardassian during the Cardassian occupation of Bajor. He was later released in 2369 when the **Bajoran** provisional government came into power. ("A Man Alone" [DS9]). **Dr. Surmak Ren** told Kira she'd be sent to Kran-Tobal Prison when she kidnapped him from the surface of Bajor in an effort to enlist his aid to cure the deadly aphasia virus that had struck the people aboard station Deep Space 9. ("Babel" [DS9]).

Kransnowsky. (Bart Conrad). Starship captain. Kransnowsky served on James Kirk's court-martial board in 2267 at Starbase 11 when Kirk was accused of the murder of **Ben Finney**. ("Court Martial" [TOS]).

Kras. (Tige Andrews). Klingon officer who tried to prevent the Federation from obtaining mining rights on planet **Capella IV** in 2267. Kras supported the Capellan **Maab**'s revolt against the **Teer Akaar** in hopes that the new leader would award the Klingon Empire the rights to mine the rare mineral **topaline,** found on Capella. Kras in turn betrayed Maab and was killed for his actions. ("Friday's Child" [TOS]). *Kras was never called by name in the episode and, in dialog, was simply referred to as "Klingon."*

Kraus IV. Fourth planet in the Kraus system. Cardassian clothier **Garak** told the Duras sisters he could obtain some silk lingerie from Kraus IV for them. ("Past Prologue" [DS9]).

Krax. (Lou Wagner). Son to **Zek**, and heir apparent to Zek's role as Ferengi **grand nagus**. Krax was shocked in 2369 when, at a trade conference at Deep Space 9, his father apparently died, appointing **Quark** as his successor. Krax subsequently plotted with Quark's brother, **Rom**, to kill the new grand nagus, until Zek's death was found to be a ruse intended to test Krax's suitability to one day assume his father's mantle. ("The Nagus" [DS9]). *Lou Wagner also played DaiMon Solok in "Chain of Command, Part I" (TNG).*

Kraxon*.** *Galor*-class Cardassian warship. Commanded by **Gul Ranor**, the *Kraxon* protected the *Starship* ***Defiant when **Obsidian Order** ships from the **Orias system** threatened them. Later, **Thomas Riker** beamed aboard the *Kraxon* to be taken into custody for crimes against Cardassia. ("Defiant" [DS9]).

Kray, Minister. (Francis Guinan). Banean minister of science. In 2371, Kray offered assistance to the *U.S.S. Voyager* in repairing the starship's navigational array. ("Ex Post Facto" [VGR]). *Kray's name was given only in the script*. SEE: **Baneans**.

***Krayton*.** Ferengi *D'Kora*-class marauder spacecraft commanded by **DaiMon Tog**. This vessel was present at the **Trade Agreements Conference** on Betazed in 2366. The *Krayton* was reported to have a top speed almost as great as the *Enterprise*-D's. ("Ménage à Troi" [TNG]).

***Kreechta*.** Ferengi *D'Kora*-class marauder spacecraft commanded by **Bractor**. The *Kreechta* stumbled into a **Starfleet battle simulation** in 2365. ("Peak Performance" [TNG]).

krellide storage cells. A power-storage device used in shuttlecraft and handheld tools. The krellide cells aboard Shuttle 3 lost their charge while Captain Picard was piloting the craft through the Mar Oscura Nebula in 2367, making vehicle flight control difficult to maintain. ("In Theory" [TNG]).

Krenim. Aggressive Delta Quadrant civilization that plagued the *Voyager* in one possible future visited by Kes. The Krenim used chroniton torpedo weaponry. After Kes traveled back in time to a period before the *Voyager* entered Krenim space, she warned Janeway about the Krenim threat. ("Before and After" [VGR]).

Kressari. Species of reptilian humanoids. Kressari often specialized as traders in botanical DNA. Though their society had no military forces, some Kressari were persuaded to become weapons runners for the Cardassian High Command, supplying Bajoran dissidents without informing their customers of the weapons' actual source. ("The Circle" [DS9]).

Kri'stak Volcano. Mountain on the Klingon Homeworld, where legend held that the messiah **Kahless the Unforgettable** forged the first ***bat'leth*** sword. ("Rightful Heir" [TNG]).

Krieger waves. Energy phenomenon, a potentially valuable new power source. **Dr. Nel Apgar** of the planet **Tanuga IV** was attempting to develop a Krieger-wave converter for use by the Federation. The converter consisted of a Lambda field generator located on the planet's surface, and a series of reflective coils and mirrors, located in a science station in orbit. The energy from the field generator was projected off the elements of the converter and turned into Krieger waves. Apgar was killed when his research station exploded in 2366, before he could complete his project. ("A Matter of Perspective" [TNG]). *Krieger waves were named for* Star Trek *science consultant David Krieger.*

Krim, General. (Stephen Macht). High-ranking **Bajoran** military officer. Commander Sisko visited Krim at the military command center in 2370 to relay intelligence concerning the **Circle**'s arms suppliers. ("The Circle" [DS9]). In fact, Krim was a member of the Circle. Shortly after his meeting with Sisko, he was instructed to lead the takeover of station Deep Space 9. Nevertheless, when Sisko revealed the **Cardassian** involvement in the coup, Krim returned control of the station to Starfleet personnel. ("The Siege" [DS9]). *Along with Patrick Stewart, actor Stephen Macht was the other leading contender for the role of Captain Jean-Luc Picard for* Star Trek: The Next Generation.

Krios 1. Simulation of the **Temple of Akadar** on planet **Krios**, used on the *Enterprise*-D holodeck for the historic Kriosian **Cremony of Reconciliation** with the Valt Minor system in 2368. The program was designed by Commander La Forge with the help of **Kriosian Ambassador Briam**. ("The Perfect Mate" [TNG]).

Krios. Class-M planet in the **Kriosian** system, controlled by the **Klingon Empire**. In 2367, Captain Picard and Klingon Ambassador **Kell** met with Klingon Governor **Vagh** at Krios, following a Kriosian revolt that the Klingons believed had been supported by the Federation. ("The Mind's Eye" [TNG]). The inhabitants of Krios had been at war with the neighboring system, **Valt Minor**, for centuries. Krios was named for one of two brothers who, centuries ago, shared the rule of a vast empire in space. Krios and his brother, Valt, both fell in love with a woman named **Garuth**, but Krios kidnapped her and took her to the star system that would later bear his name. War erupted between Valt Minor and Krios. In 2368, a historic **Ceremony of Reconciliation** was held in hopes of ending the centuries of conflict. ("The Perfect Mate" [TNG]). SEE: **Kamala**.

Kriosian system. The only Klingon protectorate bordering Federation space during the 2360s. ("The Mind's Eye" [TNG]). SEE: **Krios**.

Kriskov Gambit. A classic ploy in **three-dimensional chess**. It is normally countered with the **el-Mitra Exchange**. ("Conundrum" [TNG]).

Kristin. (Liz Vassey). Member of the *Enterprise*-D crew. Kristin often practiced diving in the holodeck during her off-duty hours. As a result of her hobby, Kristin was a frequent visitor to the *Enterprise*-D sickbay. ("Conundrum" [TNG]). SEE: **Cliffs of Heaven.** *Kristin was not given a last name in the episode.*

Krite. (Callan White). **J'naii** pilot and instructor who participated, along with **Soren**, in the rescue of the J'naii shuttle ***Taris Murn*** in 2368. Krite reported Soren to the government for aberrant sexual behavior. ("The Outcast" [TNG]).

Krocton Segment. A governmental district on planet **Romulus**. In 2368, **Senator Pardek** was the elected representative of the Krocton Segment. ("Unification, Parts I and II" [TNG]).

Krokan petri dish. Laboratory equipment used at the **Bajoran Institute of Science**. Odo, being studied by **Dr. Mora Pol**, once shape-shifted himself into a Krokan petri dish. ("The Alternate" [DS9]).

Krola. (Michael Ensign). Politically conservative Minister of Internal Security for the government of planet **Malcor III**. Krola opposed the **Malcorian** space program and was barely tolerant of the government's social reforms. Upon discovering that the Federation had been conducting covert surveillance of his planet in 2367, Krola tried to make it appear that he had been killed by Commander William Riker. Although **Chancellor Durken** learned of Krola's scheme, Durken ultimately accepted Krola's recommendation to postpone indefinitely Malcor III's ambitious space program. ("First Contact" [TNG]). *Michael Ensign also played Lojal in "The Forsaken" (DS9).*

***Kronos One*.** Klingon battle cruiser that carried **Chancellor Gorkon** on an abortive peace mission to Earth in 2293. Gorkon was assassinated aboard *Kronos One* by forces that sought to obstruct the peace process. *(Star Trek VI: The Undiscovered Country).* Kronos One *was a modification of the Klingon battle cruiser built for the first* Star Trek *movie, which was in turn based on the Klingon ship built in 1968 for the original* Star Trek *series.* SEE: **Klingon spacecraft**.

Kronos. Common phonetic spelling for **Qo'noS**, the **Klingon Homeworld.**

Kroykah*.** Vulcan imperative command to halt. Vulcan leader **T'Pau** firmly issued that order when **Stonn** insisted he fight with Spock during Spock's ***Pon farr ritual in 2267. ("Amok Time" [TOS]).

Kruge, Commander. (Christopher Lloyd). Klingon officer who commanded the bird-of-prey that attempted to obtain information on the Federation's **Project Genesis** for the Klingon government in 2285. Kruge was killed on the Genesis Planet by Kirk, who sought retribution for the murder of his son, **David Marcus**. *(Star Trek III: The Search for Spock). Christopher Lloyd has played a number of other roles in sf/fantasy films, including John Bigbooté in* The Adventures of Buckaroo Banzai Across the Eighth Dimension, *and Dr. Emmett Brown in the* Back to the Future *films.*

Kryonian tiger. Life-form found on planet Brentalia. Worf and Alexander Rozhenko saw a Kryonian tiger while visiting the zoo on Brentalia. ("Imaginary Friend" [TNG]).

Kryton. (Tony Young). Bodyguard to **Elaan**, the **Dohlman** of Elas, in 2268. Kryton was in love with Elaan, and plotted with the Klingon Empire to stop the planned marriage between Elaan and the leader of **Troyius**. Kryton killed himself after his transmission to a nearby Klingon vessel was intercepted. ("Elaan of Troyius" [TOS]).

Ktaran antiques. Treasured artifacts. Several Ktaran antiques were offered for sale at one of the shops on the Promenade at Deep Space 9. Also offered was a 21st-century plasma coil in near-perfect condition that caught the interest of Geordi La Forge. ("Birthright, Part I" [TNG]).

Ktaria VII. Planet. Home to the **Ktarian** civilization. The Ktarians bury their dead in an elaborate manner by laying thousands of sacred stones in the tombs, each stone representing a special prayer. As a Starfleet officer, Chakotay once visited Ktaria VII. During a tomb expedition, he picked up a rock from the burial site and later learned, to his horror, that he had desecrated the grave by taking a sacred stone. ("Emanations" [VGR]).

Ktarian chocolate puff. Confection made with 17 varieties of **chocolate**. It was Deanna Troi's favorite dessert. ("Liaisons" [TNG]).

Ktarian eggs. Large orange-and-red mottled eggs that were olive green on the inside. Fried Ktarian eggs were a favorite of **Antonia**. *(Star Trek Generations).*

Ktarian game. An ingenious recreational device worn like a pair of headsets, used in the **Ktarian** attempt to gain control of the Federation Starfleet in 2368. The Ktarian game employed small lasers that played directly on the optic nerve, creating a holographic image of a game field on which the player used mental control to direct the trajectory of small flying disks into various target funnel shapes. The game had powerful psychotropically addictive properties that rendered the player extremely susceptible to external control. ("The Game" [TNG]). SEE: **Jol, Etana**.

Ktarian glaciers. Massive ice glaciers renowned for excellent skiing conditions. Chakotay invited Captain Janeway to join members of the crew on a holodeck re-creation of Ktarian glaciers shortly after stardate 50425. ("Macrocosm" [VGR]).

Ktarian music festival. Celebration of Ktarian music. Ensign Harry Kim met his future fiancee, Libby, at a Ktarian music festival, because he was in her seat. ("Non Sequitur" [VGR]). *It seems odd that the Ktarians would have any part in a music festival, since less than four years earlier they attempted to take over the Federation. ("The Game" [TNG]).*

Ktarian vessel. A small spacecraft commanded by Ktarian operative **Etana Jol**. This craft met the *Enterprise*-D near the Phoenix Cluster as part of the Ktarian Expansion plan. When the Ktarian plan failed, the vessel was taken in tow by the *Enterprise*-D and delivered to Starbase 82. ("The Game" [TNG]).

Ktarians. Humanoids characterized by their enlarged frontal skull bones and feline eyes. Native to planet **Ktaria VII.** Although politically nonaligned, in 2368 the Ktarians devised a plan they referred to as the expansion, intended to gain control of the Federation Starfleet, and eventually of the Federation itself. They distributed a psychotropically addictive **Ktarian game** to members of the *Entepirse*-D crew, planning to use the crew as tools in their planned expansion. ("The Game" [TNG]). SEE: **Jol, Etana**. Ensign Samantha Wildman's husband, Greskrendtregk, was Ktarian. ("Dreadnought" [VGR]). Ktarians have scales on some parts of their body and have cranial ridges running from the center of their forehead over to the back of their head. ("Deadlock" [VGR]).

Kubus Oak. (Bert Remsen). Bajoran national who served as special liaison between the Cardassians and the Bajoran government during the occupation. After the occupation, Kubus was exiled to **Cardassia** because of his alleged role in the death of many Bajorans during the occupation. In 2370 he returned to **Deep Space 9**, requesting to be allowed to return to his homeworld of Bajor. ("The Collaborator" [DS9]). SEE: **Ilvian Proclamation**.

Kukalaka. Dr. Julian Bashir's beloved teddy bear. Kukalaka became Bashir's first surgical patient when Julian was only five years old, when he stitched Kukalaka's leg closed. Bashir kept Kukalaka on a shelf in his room, even after he'd grown up. ("The Quickening" [DS9]).

Kulge. (Jordan Lund). A Klingon officer who had sworn loyalty to **Gowron** during the **Klingon civil war** of 2367-2368. But when Gowron's forces suffered multiple defeats, Kulge began to question Gowron's leadership. Gowron killed him in the High Council chambers. ("Redemption, Part II" [TNG]).

Kumamoto. City in Japan on planet Earth. Home to **Keiko O'Brien**'s mother. Although Keiko was committed to her career as a Starfleet botanist, she was so distressed at the living accommodations upon moving into station **Deep Space 9** that she threatened to go stay with her mother in Kumamoto. ("Emissary" [DS9]).

Kumeh maneuver. Combat tactic in which one sublight space vehicle maneuvers behind a planet to avoid detection by another. Picard began the **Starfleet battle simulation** of 2365 by using the relatively conservative Kumeh maneuver against the ***U.S.S. Hathaway***. ("Peak Performance" [TNG]).

Kunivas. (Robert Bauer). Klingon criminal killed in 2364 while trying to avoid prosecution on the **Klingon Homeworld**. ("Heart of Glory" [TNG]). SEE: **Korris, Captain**.

Kurak. (Tricia O'Neil). Klingon warp-field specialist. Kurak was invited aboard the *Enterprise*-D in 2369 to participate in the test of a new **metaphasic shield** invented by Dr. Reyga. When the inventor of the shield was murdered, she came under suspicion as the killer. ("Suspicions" [TNG]). *Tricia O'Neil had previously played* Enterprise-*C Captain Rachel Garrett in "Yesterday's* Enterprise*" (TNG).*

Kurill Prime. Planet in the **Gamma Quadrant,** homeworld to a civilization known as the **Vorta. Eris** reportedly was from **Kurill Prime**. ("The Jem'Hadar" [DS9]).

Kurl. Planet located a considerable distance from Federation space. Kurl was once the home of a thriving humanoid civilization, but the Kurlans all disappeared thousands of years ago, leaving behind a rich cultural heritage that is still being studied by archaeologists. ("The Chase" [TNG]). SEE: **Kurlan *naiskos*.**

Kurlan *naiskos*. Archaeological artifact. Small ceramic figures about 30 centimeters high, *naiskos* statues were produced in ancient times by the people of planet **Kurl**. These statues were designed to be opened, revealing a multitude of similar but smaller figurines inside, representing the Kurlan belief that each person is made up of a community of individuals with different voices and desires. Although many ancient *naiskos* have been found by archaeologists, relatively few are intact, and fewer still have all the smaller figurines. **Professor Richard Galen** gave an intact Kurlan *naiskos* to his former student, **Jean-Luc Picard**. That particular artifact was even more prized because it was of the third Kurlan dynasty, made some 12,000 years ago by the Kurlan artisan known only as the **Master of Tarquin Hill**. ("The Chase" [TNG]). *In later episodes, Picard's Kurlan* naiskos *could be seen adorning a corner table of his ready room. Distressingly, Picard*

apparently did not take the naiskos *with him after the crash of the* Enterprise-*D in* Star Trek Generations. *(Unless, of course, he went back for it later or asked someone to retrieve it for him.)*

Kurland, Jake. (Stephen Gregory). Son of an *Enterprise*-D crew member, and an aspiring **Starfleet Academy** cadet. In 2364, Jake scored slightly lower than Wesley Crusher on a test, thus losing to Crusher the opportunity to take the academy entrance exam at **Relva VII**. Despondent, Kurland stole a shuttlecraft and attempted to run away to Beltane IX to sign onto a freighter. Kurland eventually returned to the *Enterprise* after nearly crashing the shuttlecraft, and Commander Riker put him to work repairing the shuttle as penance. ("Coming of Age" [TNG]).

Kurn. (Tony Todd). Born in 2345, the son of **Mogh** and younger brother to **Worf**. When Kurn was only one year old, his family moved to the **Khitomer** outpost, and young Kurn was left in the care of family friend **Lorgh**. Both of Kurn's parents were killed in the **Khitomer massacre** of 2346, and Kurn was raised by Lorgh. Kurn was not made aware of his true parentage until he reached the **Age of Ascension**. As an adult, Kurn joined the **Klingon Defense Force**. In 2366, Kurn became aware that High Council member **Duras** had falsified evidence to make it appear that Mogh had betrayed his people at Khitomer. Kurn joined with his brother, Worf, to challenge this injustice, but found the High Council little interested in uncovering the truth. Instead, Worf was forced to accept a humiliating **discommendation** to avoid a political exposé that would have resulted in his brother's death and might have plunged the empire into civil war. ("Sins of the Father" [TNG]). Kurn opposed **Gowron**'s bid for the council leadership following the death of **K'mpec** in 2367. Kurn nevertheless obeyed Worf's decree that Gowron was the rightful leader, and lent the support of his ship, the ***Hegh'ta***, and three other Klingon squadrons, to Gowron. Kurn's assistance was critical in preventing an overthrow of the Gowron regime by the Duras family during the **Klingon civil war** of 2367-2368. In return, Gowron restored rightful honor to the Mogh family name. ("Redemption, Parts I and II" [TNG]). Following the victory of Gowron's forces over Duras's during the Klingon civil war, Kurn was rewarded for his service to the empire. He was granted a seat on the High Council. ("Rightful Heir" [TNG]). Kurn lost his council seat in early 2372 when Gowron stripped the House of Mogh of its lands, property, and titles, after Worf refused to support Gowron's invasion of Cardassia. Kurn became despondent, and journeyed to station Deep Space 9 in order have his honor restored by Worf in a *Mauk-to'Vor* ceremony. The ritual suicide was interrupted before its completion. After his visit to Deep Space 9, Kurn was not heard from again. ("Sons of Mogh" [DS9]). *Actually, Kurn's memory engrams were erased and he assumed the identity of Rodek, son of Noggra. This entry honors Worf's desire that his brother's new life as Rodek be kept secret. Worf also had a human stepbrother, named Nikolai, the son of Sergey and Helena Rozhenko, mentioned briefly in "Heart of Glory" (TNG) and later seen in "Homeward" (TNG).*

Kushell. (Albert Stratton). Secretary of the planet **Straleb**'s Legation of Unity and father to **Benzan**. ("The Outrageous Okona" [TNG]).

***kut'luch*.** A bladed weapon used by Klingon assassins. The *kut'luch* had a serrated blade and could cause a very serious wound. A *kut'luch* was used in an attack on **Kurn** by operatives of the **Duras** family in 2366. ("Sins of the Father" [TNG]).

***kuttars*.** Type of bayonet. ("Blood Oath" [DS9]).

Kwan, Daniel L. (Tim Lounibos). Officer assigned to the engineering section aboard the *Enterprise*-D. He was part of the team at **Utopia Planitia Fleet Yards** that helped build the *Enterprise*-D.

Kwan's father was human, but his mother was **Napean**, which gave him some empathic abilities. In 2370, Kwan experienced empathic hallucinations that caused him to commit suicide by jumping into the plasma stream of one of the ship's warp drive **nacelle**s. Prior to his death, Kwan had been romantically involved with **Maddy Calloway**. ("Eye of the Beholder" [TNG]). SEE: **Pierce**, **Walter J**.

***kyamo*.** Klingon word for attractive. Jadzia Dax was a *kyamo* woman, according to Kor. ("Blood Oath" [DS9]).

Kylata II. Class-M planet in the **Gamma Quadrant**. Kylata II was scanned by the *U.S.S. Defiant* in 2371 during a research mission. ("Meridian" [DS9]).

Kyle, Mr. (John Winston). Crew member holding the rank of lieutenant aboard the original *Starship Enterprise* under the command of Captain James Kirk. Kyle served as relief helm officer and transporter technician. ("Tomorrow Is Yesterday" [TOS], "Space Seed" [TOS], "The City on the Edge of Forever" [TOS], "Who Mourns for Adonais?" [TOS], "The Doomsday Machine" [TOS], "The Apple" [TOS], "Catspaw" [TOS], "The Immunity Syndrome" [TOS], "Mirror, Mirror" [TOS], "The Lights of Zetar" [TOS]). By 2285, Kyle had been promoted to commander and was serving as communications officer aboard the *Starship* **Reliant**. (*Star Trek II: The Wrath of Khan*). *John Winston also appeared in "Wolf in the Fold" (TOS).*

Kyle, Mr. (mirror). (John Winston). Transporter chief aboard the ***I.S.S. Enterprise*** in the **mirror universe.** Kyle suffered discipline with an **agonizer** when he made an error with the transporter. ("Mirror, Mirror" [TOS]).

Kyle, Ms. (Jennifer Edwards). Primary-school teacher aboard the *Enterprise*-D in 2368. Her pupils included Worf's son, **Alexander Rozhenko**. ("New Ground" [TNG]).

Kylerian goat's milk. Beverage often used as a soporific. ("Death Wish" [VGR]).

Kyoto, Ensign. Starfleet officer assigned to the *U.S.S. Voyager*. In 2371 Ensign Kyoto inadvertently deactivated the **Emergency Medical Hologram** while the doctor was in the middle of doing some lab tests. ("Eye of the Needle" [VGR]). Kyoto's quarters on the *Voyager* were located on Deck 6. ("Twisted" [VGR]).

Kyushu, U.S.S. Federation starship, ***New Orleans* class**, Starfleet registry number NCC-65491. The *Kyushu* was destroyed by the Borg at the battle of **Wolf 359** in early 2367. ("The Best of Both Worlds, Part II" [TNG]). *The* Kyushu *was named for one of the four main islands of Japan, where a Japanese orbital launch facility was located. The* Kyushu *was a study model designed by Ed Miarecki. The* Kyushu *was never built as a full photographic miniature, but the study model was used in the "graveyard" scene of the aftermath of the battle of Wolf 359.*

L

L'Kor. (Richard Herd). **Klingon** warrior, believed killed in the **Khitomer massacre** of 2346, who was actually taken prisoner by the Romulans. L'Kor was spared death by Romulans, who did not wish to murder helpless victims, and was incarcerated at the Romulan prison camp in the **Carraya System**. In the years that followed, L'Kor became a leader among the Klingon prisoners. ("Birthright, Parts I and II" [TNG]).

***l'maki* nut.** Edible hard-shelled seed pod. Kes liked *l'maki* nuts. Neelix baked a seven-layer **Jimbalian fudge** cake with *l'maki* nut icing for Kes's second birthday in 2372. ("Twisted" [VGR]).

L-370. Solar system, formerly containing seven planets that were completely destroyed by an extragalactic **planet killer** weapon in 2267. The star was still intact but the billions of inhabitants on the planets perished. ("The Doomsday Machine" [TOS]).

L-374. Solar system that was almost completely destroyed by a **planet killer** in 2267. The ***U.S.S. Constellation,*** under the command of **Commodore Matt Decker,** investigated the destruction and came under attack, forcing the crew to take refuge on the third planet in that system. Only Decker remained aboard and was helpless when that planet was also destroyed. ("The Doomsday Machine" [TOS]).

L-S VI life-form. Entity discovered on planet **L-S VI** by **Dr. Mora Pol.** Dr. Pol made the discovery in 2370 during an attempt to discover Odo's origin. The L-S VI life-form, apparently a simple conglomerate of microorganisms, had shape-shifting properties. A sample of the L-S VI life-form was taken to Deep Space 9 for study but mysteriously disappeared from the **science lab** and was eventually found dead. ("The Alternate" [DS9]). SEE: **shape-shifter**.

L-S VI. Planet in the **Gamma Quadrant**, located six light years from the Bajoran wormhole. **DNA** patterns similar to those of Deep Space 9 security chief **Odo** were discovered on L-S VI by a Bajoran science probe. A subsequent investigation by **Dr. Mora Pol** attempted to ascertain if Odo had originated on L-S VI, but the study was cut short by volcanic activity that released noxious gases at the survey site. SEE: **L-S VI life-form**. ("The Alternate" [DS9]).

***La Bohème*.** Italian opera by Puccini, written in 1896. ("The Swarm" [VGR]).

La Forge, Alandra. (In the **anti-time future** created by the **Q Continuum**, Alandra was the second child of Geordi La Forge and his wife, Leah.) ("All Good Things..." [TNG].)

La Forge, Ariana. Daughter of **Edward M. La Forge** and **Silva La Forge**, and sister to **Geordi La Forge**. ("Force of Nature" [TNG]). *All we know of her is that she once carried around a piece of tuna in her blouse for two months in an attempt to train her cat.*

La Forge, Brett. (In the **anti-time future** created by the **Q Continuum**, Brett was the eldest child of Geordi La Forge and his wife, Leah. Brett hoped to apply to Starfleet Academy in 2396.) ("All Good Things..." [TNG].)

La Forge, Dr. Edward M. (Ben Vereen). Noted scientist who specialized in exozoology. Father of **Geordi La Forge** and **Ariana La Forge**, and husband of **Silva La Forge**. Geordi talked to him via subspace after the disappearance of the ***U.S.S. Hera***. ("Interface" [TNG]). *Dr. La Forge's given name was suggested by Rick Berman and was seen on Geordi's biographical screen in "Cause and Effect" (TNG).*

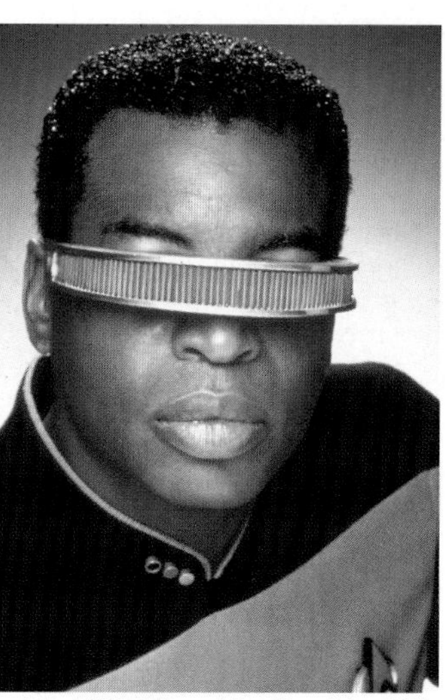

La Forge, Geordi. (LeVar Burton). Chief engineer aboard the *Starship Enterprise*-D. Born blind in 2335 because of a birth defect, La Forge wore a remarkable device called a **VISOR** that permitted him to see with greater clarity than other humans could. Geordi La Forge came from a family of Starfleet officers. His mother, Silva La Forge, was captain of the *U.S.S. Hera* at the time of her death in 2370 ("Interface" [TNG]), and his father was an exobiologist. Geordi recalled that, even though he moved around a great deal, he considered his childhood a great adventure. ("Imaginary Friend" [TNG]). La Forge did not receive his VISOR until after his fifth birthday. ("Hero Worship" [TNG]). Geordi was caught in a fire when he was five years old. He was rescued by his parents, and was not injured. Geordi recalled how for a time after the incident it was extremely important for him to know where his parents were at all times. ("Hero Worship" [TNG]). Geordi had a pet **Circassian cat** when he was eight. ("Violations" [TNG]). Possibly because his parents traveled so much when he was a child, Geordi had something of a knack for languages. One such language was **Hahliian**. ("Aquiel" [TNG]).

Geordi La Forge graduated from Starfleet Academy in 2357. ("The Next Phase" [TNG]). One of La Forge's first Starfleet assignments was as shuttle pilot for the **Jovian run** between Jupiter and Saturn. ("Chain of Command, Part II" [TNG]). La Forge first met Captain Picard when La Forge piloted Picard's shuttle on an inspection tour. During the tour, Picard made an offhanded remark about a minor inefficiency in the shuttle's engines, and La Forge subsequently stayed up all night to repair the problem. Picard was so impressed with the incident that he requested La Forge be assigned to the *Enterprise*-D in 2364. ("The Next Phase" [TNG]). La Forge later served as an ensign on the ***U.S.S. Victory*** under the command of Captain **Zimbata**. ("Elementary, Dear Data" [TNG]). One of Geordi's closest friends on that ship was Lieutenant **Susanna Leijten**. In 2362, both La Forge and Leijten participated in an away mission to planet **Tarchannen III**. It was later realized that all members of that away team were infected by an alien DNA strand that would, if unchecked, compel them to return to Tarchannen III, where they would be transformed into a native Tarchannen life-form. La Forge was saved from the transformation in 2367 by Leijten's actions and medical intervention by *Enterprise*-D CMO Crusher. ("Identity Crisis" [TNG]).

La Forge transferred to the *Enterprise*-D as **flight controller** (conn) in 2364. ("Encounter at Farpoint, Parts I and II" [TNG]). Geordi was promoted to full lieutenant and assigned as *U.S.S. Enterprise*-D chief engineer the following year, just prior to stardate 42073.1. ("The Child" [TNG]). Although brilliantly proficient as a starship engineer, La Forge had difficulty building relationships with women. Perhaps as a result, Geordi developed an attachment to a holographic representation of *Enterprise*-D designer **Leah Brahms**. ("Booby Trap" [TNG]). The real Dr. Brahms was outraged to learn of this simulation, noting that creating such a replica without her permission was an invasion of privacy. Brahms did eventually become friends with La Forge, although Geordi was disappointed to learn that Leah was already married. ("Galaxy's Child" [TNG]). La Forge was promoted to lieutenant commander in early 2366. ("Evolution" [TNG]). Because of his VISOR interface, Geordi was a perfect candidate to test an experimental **interface device.** He used the device in 2370, in an attempt to rescue the crew of the ***U.S.S. Raman***. During the rescue, Geordi encountered what appeared to be his mother, **Silva La Forge**, aboard the *Raman*. Geordi was at first convinced his mother's ship was actually trapped in the atmosphere, but later realized the experience was an attempt by the **Marijne VII beings** to communicate. Though he was unable to save his mother, Geordi felt the incident gave him the opportunity to say good-bye to her. ("Interface" [TNG]).

After the destruction of the *Enterprise*-D, La Forge accepted an assignment as chief engineer of the *U.S.S. Enterprise*-E when it was launched in 2372. By stardate 50893, Geordi had been given ocular implants that replaced his VISOR. Although the implants were much smaller than his VISOR, they still afforded La Forge a wide range of sensory information. *(Star Trek: First Contact).*

The name of Geordi's mother was listed as Alvera K. La Forge on Geordi's death certificate, seen in "The Next Phase" (TNG), but was established as Silva La Forge in "Interface" (TNG). His father (played by Ben Vereen) was seen in that episode, but no first name was established for him, although his biographical screen seen in "Conundrum" (TNG) suggested it might be Edward M. La Forge. Geordi La Forge, whose first appearance was in "Encounter at Farpoint" (TNG), was named in memory of the late, disabled Star Trek *fan George La Forge.*

La Forge, Leah. (In the **anti-time future** created by the **Q Continuum**, Leah was the wife of Geordi La Forge and mother of their children, Alandra, Brett, and Sydney.) ("All Good Things..." [TNG].) *The episode seems to imply that in this alternate reality, Geordi married Leah Brahms, but this is by no means certain. Leah and her children were only mentioned; they were not actually seen.*

La Forge, Sydney. (In the **anti-time future** created by the Q Continuum, Sydney was the third child of Geordi La Forge and his wife, Leah.) ("All Good Things..." [TNG].)

La Forge, Silva. (Madge Sinclair). Captain of the ***U.S.S. Hera*** and mother of **Geordi La Forge** and **Ariana La Forge**. Silva La Forge, a career Starfleet officer, was lost along with her ship and crew on a routine courier mission in 2370. ("Interface" [TNG]). *Madge Sinclair also portrayed the unnamed captain of the* U.S.S. Saratoga *in* Star Trek IV: The Voyage Home, *which was the first appearance in* Star Trek *of a starship commanded by a woman.*

La Rouque, Frederick. (Marc Alaimo). Professional gambler from the city of New Orleans on 19th-century Earth. La Rouque welcomed Commander Data to his poker game and provided Data with a stake in exchange for his **communicator**. ("Time's Arrow, Part I" [TNG]) *Marc Alaimo played several other roles, including* ***Gul Dukat****.*

Labarre, France. Small town in France on **Earth**. Birthplace of *Enterprise*-D Captain **Jean-Luc Picard**. ("Family" [TNG]).

Labin, Gathorel. (Ronald Guttman). Public official on planet **Sikaris**. Labin invited the crew of the *Starship Voyager* to enjoy the hospitality of his planet in 2371. While Labin's generosity was considerable, he declined to make available his people's **trajector** technology, citing the Sikarian canon of laws that prohibited technology transfer. ("Prime Factors." [VGR]).

labor unions. SEE: **Guild of Restaurant and Casino Employees; O'Brien, Sean Aloysius.**

lach'tel. Klingon term for boyfriend. ("Playing God" [DS9]).

lacunae. Empty spaces in ancient **Doosidarian poetry** during which poet and audience were encouraged to acknowledge the emptiness of the experience. Lacunae could last as long as several days. ("Interface" [TNG]).

lacunar amnesia. Type of amnesia that occurs when a patient witnesses an act of violence so terrible that the patient rejects the reality of the situation. Dr. McCoy's preliminary diagnosis included lacunar amnesia when assessing the lack of grief shown by the children of the **Starnes Expedition** on planet **Triacus** for the death of their parents in 2268. ("And the Children Shall Lead" [TOS]).

ladarium. Substance used in Cardassian **warp drive** systems. ("Tribunal" [DS9]).

Lagana sector. Site of a terraforming mission for the ***U.S.S. Gandhi*** in 2369. ("Second Chances" [TNG]).

Laira. Young woman who lived on Deep Space 9 in 2370. She agreed to go on a date with Jake Sisko. Unfortunately, Laira's father refused to allow her to see Jake, because he was not **Bajoran**. ("The Homecoming" [DS9]).

Lakanta. (Ned Romero). Member of the colony on planet **Dorvan V** in 2370. Lakanta introduced **Wesley Crusher** to the concept of the **vision quest**. Lakanta later revealed himself to be the **Traveler**. ("Journey's End" [TNG]).

Lakarian City. City on **Cardassia Prime.** For his 11th birthday, **Mekor** wanted his father to take him to the amusement center in Lakarian City. ("Defiant" [DS9]).

Lakat. City on the planet Cardassia. ("Chain of Command, Part II" [TNG]).

Lake Como. Body of water about fifty kilometers long, in northern Italy near the community of Como on Earth. Lake Como was featured in a restful and romantic holodeck program favored by Tom Paris. ("The Swarm" [VGR]).

Lake George. Scenic lake in northeastern New York on Earth. A holodeck simulation of Lake George was available on the *U.S.S. Voyager*. ("Coda" [VGR]).

Lakota, U.S.S. Federation starship, *Excelsior* class, Starfleet registry number NCC-42768. The *Lakota* transported Captain Benjamin Sisko and Security Officer Odo to Earth in 2372. ("Homefront" [DS9]). Captain **Erika Benteen** later assumed command of the *Lakota*. Under orders from her mentor, **Admiral Leyton**, Benteen, commanding the *Lakota,* tried to prevent the *Starship Defiant* from reaching Earth with evidence that Leyton was planning a military coup of Earth's government. The *Lakota* and *Defiant* met in battle, resulting in over two dozen casualties. ("Paradise Lost" [DS9]). *Named for the Native American nation, and an impressive peak in South Dakota near the city of Hermosa. The Lakota was a re-use of the modified* Excelsior-*class* Enterprise-*B model used in* Star Trek Generations*.*

Laktivia. Population center on planet **Akritiri** in the Delta Quadrant. In 2373, the Laktivia recreational facility was bombed by the terrorist group **Open Sky** using a trilithium-based explosive device, killing 47 people. ("The Chute" [VGR]).

Lakul, S.S. Transport vessel that ferried 150 **El-Aurian** refugees to Earth in 2293. The *Lakul* and another El-Aurian ship became caught by the gravimetric distortion surrounding the **nexus** energy ribbon. The *U.S.S. Enterprise*-B responded to their distress call and was able to rescue 47 passengers from the *Lakul* before the transport exploded in the energy ribbon. Two of the passengers rescued from the *Lakul* were **Guinan** and **Dr. Tolian Soran**. Former *Enterprise* Captain **James T. Kirk** was believed killed during the rescue mission. *(Star Trek Generations). The other El-Aurian refugee ship wasn't identified by name in the movie, but the computer readout screen on the science officer's console of the* Enterprise-*B bridge gave that ship's name as the* S.S. Robert Fox*, for the Federation ambassador from "A Taste of Armageddon" (TOS). The name was suggested by movie co-writer Ronald D. Moore.*

Lal. (Alan Bergmann). A **Vian** scientist. One of the Vians who tested **Gem** to see if her people were worthy of being rescued from an impending nova in 2268. ("The Empath" [TOS]). *Note that the name "Lal" is from the episode script only and was not actually spoken in the aired episode.*

Lal. (Hallie Todd, Leonard J. Crowfoot). Daughter to **Data**, a **Soong-type** android constructed by Data aboard the *Enterprise*-D in 2366. Lal had a **positronic brain** onto which Data replicated much of his own neural pathways. Initially built with a featureless humanoid body, Lal chose to assume the form of a human female. Despite the fact that both Lal and Data shared the same basic programming, Lal's behavioral programs quickly exceeded those of her father, thus demonstrating her ability to learn and grow. Lal became the focus of a heated custody battle when **Admiral Haftel** attempted to order Data to release Lal to the **Daystrom Institute** annex on **Galor IV**. Haftel, recognizing the extraordinary value of a new Soong-type android, believed it imperative that Lal be studied in a controlled environment under the guidance of cybernetics specialists. Data took considerable exception to this view, believing it his responsibility, as a parent, to care for the new lifeform that he had created. The question became moot when Lal experienced a fatal system-wide cascade failure after having lived only a little over two weeks. During that brief time, Lal's positronic networks grew to the point where she was able to experience emotions, love for her father, and sadness at her own impending death. The name, Lal, chosen by Data for his child, is Hindi for "beloved." ("The Offspring" [TNG]). Data later painted a portrait of Lal, which he kept in his quarters on the *Enterprise*-D. ("Inheritance" [TNG]). *This painting was based on a publicity photo of Lal, reworked using a computer paint program, by scenic artist Wendy Drapanas. The initial, featureless version of Lal was played by Leonard J. Crowfoot, who had previously played Trent in "Angel One" (TNG). Hallie Todd played Lal in human female form.*

Lalo*, *U.S.S. Federation starship, *Mediterranean* class, registry number NCC-43837. The Lalo was a freighter that reported a "hiccough" in time that was found to be the result of **Dr. Paul Manheim**'s time/gravity experiments at **Vandor IV** in 2364. ("We'll Always Have Paris" [TNG]). The *Lalo* was lost in late 2366 after apparently encountering a **Borg** ship near Zeta Alpha II. ("The Best of Both Worlds, Part I" [TNG]).

Lambda Paz. One of the moons of planet **Pentarus V**. Lambda Paz was barely Class-M, with extreme desert conditions and a mean surface temperature of 55 degrees Celsius. The mining shuttle ***Nenebek***, piloted by Captain **Dirgo**, along with Captain Picard and Ensign Crusher, crash-landed on Lambda Paz in 2367. ("Final Mission" [TNG]). SEE: **sentry**.

lambda designation. In the **mirror universe**, an **Alliance** classification for **Terrans** of very low importance, frequently assigned to manual labor like mine work. ("Crossover" [DS9]).

Lamenda Prime. Planet near the Cardassian star system. Kira Nerys gave Lamenda Prime as her destination during her mission to rescue **Li Nalas** in 2370. ("The Homecoming" [DS9]).

Lamonay S. (Tom Klunis). False identity assumed by **Ibudan** after he murdered a clone of himself in an attempt to frame **Odo** for murder. ("A Man Alone" [DS9]).

Lancelot, Sir. One of the Knights of the Round Table from Earth's Arthurian legend. Lieutenant Commander Dax and Major Kira shared a holosuite program featuring characters from Arthurian legend, with Kira playing a married lady. Kira knocked out Lancelot when he tried to kiss her. ("The Way of the Warrior" [DS9]).

landing party. A specialized team of starship personnel assigned to a particular mission, usually on a planet. Landing party assignments were generally at the captain's discretion, but were often composed of a senior officer, mission specialists (such as a science officer), and one or more security personnel. The term landing party has since been replaced by Starfleet with the more generic **away team**.

landing struts. Four retractable legs located on the ventral surface of the engineering hull of ***Intrepid*-class starship**s. The landing struts are used as shock absorbers during landing and keep the vessel upright on the surface of the planet on which it has landed. ("The 37's" [VGR]). *Actually, the technical consultants in the* Voyager *art department always assumed that when landed, the* Voyager *was supported by some kind of antigrav field, and that the relatively tiny landing struts merely provided stability.*

Landon, Yeoman Martha. (Celeste Yarnall). Crew member on the original *U.S.S. Enterprise.* In 2267, Yeoman Landon and Ensign Pavel Chekov were attracted to each other when assigned to the landing party on **Gamma Trianguli VI**. The inhabitants noticed their affection, and told the *Enterprise* personnel that touching and similar intimate behavior was forbidden by their god, **Vaal**. ("The Apple" [TOS]).

Landras blend. Hot **coffee**-like beverage native to the Delta Quadrant. Neelix served Landras blend as a substitute for real coffee aboard the *Voyager*. ("Prototype" [VGR]).

Landris II. Planet. Location where Dr. Mowray conducted archaeological research in 2369. Captain Picard had wanted to communicate with Mowray on stardate 46693, but was unable to establish contact due to a communications blackout requested by the **Stellar Cartography** Department on the *Enterprise*-D. ("Lessons" [TNG]).

Landru. (Charles Macaulay). Leader of planet **Beta III** some 6,000 years ago when that world was plagued with war and destruction. Landru changed that by preaching truth and peace, taking his population back to a simpler time. Landru programmed a computer to continue his leadership after his death. Later, the news of Landru's death was kept from the people, and the computer, also called Landru, governed in his stead. The computer judged society by its own definition of perfection and harmony, forcing everyone to act the same and to become part of a common **Body** of people. Under the computer's control, the Beta III society became increasingly aberrant, but those who resisted conformity were forced to be absorbed or killed. The computer Landru was deactivated in 2267 by Kirk and Spock when they convinced the machine it was killing the Body by promoting stagnation, and so it was acting against the original Landru's directive to act for the good of the people. ("Return of the Archons" [TOS]). SEE: ***Archon*, *U.S.S.***; **Lawgivers.** *Charles Macaulay also played Prefect Jarvis in "Wolf in the Fold" (TOS).*

Lanel. (Bebe Neuwirth). A nurse at the **Sikla Medical Facility** on planet Malcor III. Lanel agreed to help Riker escape from

Malcorian authorities in exchange for a very personal favor. ("First Contact" [TNG]). *Bebe Neuwirth was a regular on Paramount's television series,* Cheers.

Lang cycle fusion engines. Ancient power plant used aboard **Promellian** spacecraft a millennium ago. Picard knew of this technology, and hoped an ancient Promellian battle cruiser discovered near **Orelious IX** would still have its Lang cycle engines intact. ("Booby Trap" [TNG]).

Lang, Lieutenant. (James Farley). *Enterprise* security officer. Lang was killed at planet **Cestus III** while on a mission investigating the destruction of the Earth outpost there. ("Arena" [TOS]).

Lang, Natima. (Mary Crosby). **Cardassian** political dissident and former correspondent for the Cardassian information service. While she was serving on station **Terok Nor** in 2363, Lang became romantically involved with **Quark**. Their relationship, which began when Lang learned that Quark had been selling food to Bajorans, ended a month later when Lang discovered that Quark had been using her personal access code to steal money from the communication service. Lang subsequently left Terok Nor and began teaching as a Professor of Political Ethics. Her unorthodox political views brought her into the **Cardassian underground movement**, and by 2370 she was eventually regarded by Cardassian authorities as a dangerous terrorist and marked for death. She fled **Cardassia** with two of her students, **Rekelen** and **Hogue**, and took refuge at Terok Nor (now called **Deep Space 9**) when her shuttle was fired on by a Cardassian warship. The three escaped Cardassian authorities with the aid of Quark, who still loved Lang, and Garak, who believed he was acting in the best interests of Cardassia. ("Profit and Loss" [DS9]). *Mary Crosby is famous as the person who shot J.R.*

Lang. (Deborah Levin). Crew member aboard the *Starship Voyager*. Ensign Lang served ops duty on the bridge. ("Blood Fever" [VGR]).

Langford, Dr. Archaeologist who studied the ruins on Suvin IV in 2369. Dr. Langford invited Captain Picard to join her in exploring for ancient artifacts on planet Suvin IV. ("Rascals" [TNG]).

Langor. (Kimberly Farr). A citizen of the planet **Brekka**. Arrogant and aristocratic, she was dedicated to maintaining the exploitive relationship her planet had with the people of planet **Ornara**. ("Symbiosis" [TNG]).

Lantar Nebula. Nebula containing planet **Hoek IV**. **Q** offered archeologist **Vash** the chance to view the Sampalo relics located in the Lantar Nebula, but she declined. ("Q-Less" [DS9]).

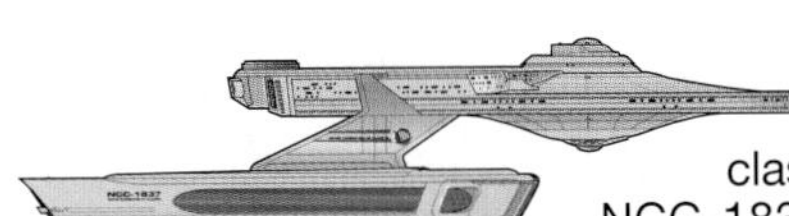

Lantree, U.S.S. Federation starship, *Miranda* class, Starfleet registry number NCC-1837, a class-6 supply ship commanded by **Captain L. Isao Telaka**, normal crew complement of 26. The ship was equipped with class-3 defensive armaments. The *Lantree*'s crew was killed in 2365 after being exposed to a group of genetically engineered human children whose immune systems actively sought out and attacked potential sources of disease, including the *Lantree* crew. The *U.S.S. Lantree* was destroyed by a single photon torpedo fired by the *U.S.S. Enterprise*-D in order to prevent further transmission of the deadly antibodies. ("Unnatural Selection" [TNG]). *The* Lantree *was a minor modification of the* **U.S.S. Reliant** *model originally built for* Star Trek II: The Wrath of Khan. *The* Reliant's *upper "roll bar" was removed to turn it into the* Lantree. *The* Lantree *bridge (seen briefly in a screen readout) was a re-dress of the* Enterprise-D *battle bridge.*

***lapling*.** A small creature with a long snout. These defenseless animals were believed to be extinct. A single living member of the species was discovered in **Kivas Fajo**'s collection aboard the *Jovis* in 2366. ("The Most Toys" [TNG]).

Laporin, Captain. Commander of a Federation starship. Laporin was killed when his bridge was stormed by Klingons in 2372. Laporin had attended Starfleet Academy with Benjamin Sisko. ("Apocalypse Rising" [DS9]). *Laporin was Benzite.*

Lapsang souchong tea. Beverage. It was enjoyed by **Helena Rozhenko**. ("New Ground" [TNG]).

Larg. (Michael E. Hagerty). A Klingon captain, loyal to the **Duras** family during the **Klingon civil war** of 2367-2368. He commanded a vessel that engaged and heavily damaged **Kurn**'s ship, the ***Hegh'ta***. ("Redemption, Part II" [TNG]).

Largo V. Planet. Destination of Captain Jaheel's ship in 2369 when his ship was detained because of the **aphasia virus**. Jaheel was scheduled to deliver a shipment of Tamen **Sahsheer**. ("Babel" [DS9]).

***larish* pie.** Cardassian food served at Quark's. **Woban**, leader of the **Navot** nation on planet Bajor, complimented the Cardassian replicators for the tasty *larish* pie. ("The Storyteller" [DS9]).

Larosian virus. Mild disorder. **Dr. Julian Bashir** feared that **Jadzia Dax** might have contracted Larosian virus on stardate 46853. In truth, a replica of Dax, created by unknown aliens from the Gamma Quadrant, was responsible for Dax's unexpectedly amorous behavior toward Bashir. ("If Wishes Were Horses" [DS9]).

Lars. (Steve Sandor). **Drill thrall** on planet **Triskelion** in 2268. Lars was responsible for training **Uhura** to fight there. ("The Gamesters of Triskelion" [TOS]).

Larson, Lieutenant Linda. (Saxon Trainor). An *Enterprise*-D staff engineer. Larson worked to solve the reactor failure of the **Argus Array** in 2367. ("The Nth Degree" [TNG]).

LaSalle, U.S.S. Federation starship. *Deneva* class, Starfleet registry number NCC-6203. *LaSalle* personnel reported the presence of a series of radiation anomalies in the Gamma Arigulon System in 2367. ("Reunion" [TNG]).

Lasca, Lieutenant. (Mark Kiely). Starfleet officer. Lasca, part of the Starfleet Engineering Corps, worked with Starship design specialists. In an alternate reality, Lasca and Harry Kim designed a prototype runabout, the ***U.S.S. Yellowstone,*** in 2372. ("Non Sequitur" [VGR]).

laser fusion initiator. Component of some fusion reactors that use intense pulses of coherent light to create the high temperatures necessary to begin a fusion reaction. Integral component in station Deep Space 9's **main fusion reactor**. Laser fusion initiators were necessary to keep the reactor active. Disengaging the initiators would shut down the reactor. ("Civil Defense" [DS9]).

laser pulse system. A low-power directed energy device employing coherent light transmission. A modified laser pulse beam system was installed aboard the *Enterprise*-D and the ***Hathaway*** in 2365 for the **Starfleet battle simulation** exercise. ("Peak Performance" [TNG]).

laser weapons. Energy weapon used aboard early Federation starships. ("Laser" was originally an acronym for Light Amplification by Stimulated Emission of Radiation.) These took the form of pistol sidearms, as well as larger artillery-sized cannons. ("The Cage" [TOS], "The Menagerie, Parts I and II" [TOS]). *Lasers had been replaced by* ***phaser*** *weapons by at least 2265 , as seen in "Where No Man Has Gone Before" (TOS), but not before 2200, according to Worf in "A Matter of Time" (TNG).*

Handheld laser pistol "The Cage" and "Where No Man Has Gone Before" (TOS)

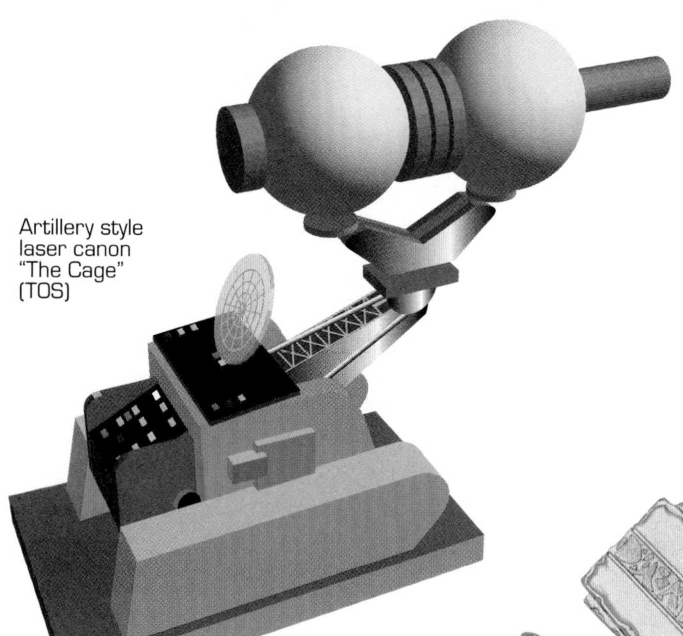

Artillery style laser canon "The Cage" (TOS)

laser-induced fusion. Engineering term for controlled nuclear fusion in which the required ignition temperatures are created by powerful lasers. Laser-induced fusion is used in the **impulse drive** engines of Federation starships, as well as in the power supply reactors on station **Deep Space 9.** ("The Forsaken" [DS9]).

Last Meal. Ritual on planet **Meridian** in which the Meridian inhabitants share their final meal in corporeal form. ("Meridian" [DS9]).

"Last Outpost, The." *Next Generation* episode #7. Teleplay by Herbert Wright. Story by Richard Krzemien. Directed by Richard Colla. Stardate 41386.4. *First aired in 1987. Pursuing a Ferengi ship, the* Enterprise-*D is captured by the last outpost of the ancient Tkon Empire. The Ferengi make their first appearance in this episode, and we see their marauder spacecraft for the first time as well.* GUEST CAST: Armin Shimerman as **Letek**; Jake Dengel as Mordock; Tracey Walter as Kayron; Darryl Henriques as **Portal**; Mike Gomez as **Taar, DaiMon**. SEE: **baktun; DaiMon; Delphi Ardu; Ferengi; Ferengi Code; Ferengi Marauder; Ferengi whip; Gamma Tauri IV; Letek; Portal; second officer; Sun Tzu; T-9 energy converter; Taar, DaiMon; Tkon Empire; Tkon, ages of.**

Lasuma. Location of a grain-processing center on planet **Bajor**. Keiko O'Brien took 11 schoolchildren to visit the grain-processing center at Lasuma on stardate 46922. ("Dramatis Personae" [DS9]).

Latara, Ensign. (Grace Zandarski). Bajoran national who resided on station Deep Space 9. When Latara got married in 2372, Captain Sisko gave her and her husband the Bajoran marriage blessing. ("Accession" [DS9]).

Latha Mabrin. (Matt Roe). Bajoran **vedek**. A former member of the **Shakaar resistance cell**, he had a volatile past history before finding his religious calling. Latha was killed with a **hunter probe** hidden in a ceremonial candle by **Silaran Prin,** who blamed him for the explosion that had disfigured Prin years earlier. ("The Darkness and the Light" [DS9]).

Lathal Bine. (Robert Harper). Representative of **Beta Moon** of planet **Peliar Zel**, who participated in negotiations with **Alpha Moon** in 2367. ("The Host" [TNG]).

Latika. (Brady Bluhm). Inhabitant of a Class-M planet in the **Delta Quadrant** whose people were dependent on **polaric ion energy**. In 2371, Latika's father worked for the planet's media bureau, and Latika hoped to become a journalist himself. ("Time and Again" [VGR]). *The episode did not give Latika's homeworld a name.*

Latimer, Lieutenant. (Reese Vaughn). Crew member aboard the original *Starship Enterprise*. Latimer served as navigator of the ***Shuttlecraft Galileo*** when it crashed on planet **Taurus II** in 2267. Latimer was killed by the humanoid creatures on the planet. ("The *Galileo* Seven" [TOS]).

latinum stairway. Ferengi slang for business success. ("Playing God" [DS9]).

latinum. Valuable metal ingots used as a medium of exchange, primarily outside the Federation. ("Past Prologue" [DS9]). Denominations of gold-pressed latinum ingots, in increasing order of value, included the slip, the strip, and the bar. ("Family Business" [DS9]). One hundred slips was equal to one strip, and 20 strips equaled a bar of latinum. ("Body Parts" [DS9]).

Laughing Hour. A custom at the **Parallax Colony** of **Shiralea VI**. ("Cost of Living" [TNG]).

"Laughing Vulcan and His Dog, The." A children's song. It was taught in the primary school on the *Enterprise*-D, and was popular among children, but Picard preferred "Frère Jacques." ("Disaster" [TNG]).

Laurelian pudding. White pudding. Neelix prepared Laurelian pudding on the *Voyager*. ("Learning Curve" [VGR]).

Lauriento massage holoprogram #101A. Holosuite program set in a soothing atmosphere where an exotic alien woman with webbed fingers gives a body massage. **Ibudan**'s clone was murdered on Deep Space 9 in 2369 while running Lauriento massage holoprogram #101A. ("A Man Alone" [DS9]).

lavaflies. Insect life form indigenous to the marshlands of **Rinax**. Lavaflies can grow as large as six centimeters long. Talaxians living on Rinax find lavaflies extremely annoying. ("Macrocosm" [VGR]).

Lavelle, Sam. (Dan Ganthier). Starfleet officer aboard the *Enterprise*-D. Lavelle stood watch at the ops position on the bridge. While still an ensign, he and **Ensign Sito** were both considered by Commander Riker for the ops position. Lavelle received the job and the promotion to lieutenant, junior grade. Before his promotion, he shared quarters with **Ensign Taurik.** ("Lower Decks" [TNG]).

law. SEE: **Alpha III, Statues of; Armens, Treaty of; Cardassians; Ceremony of Reconciliation; Constitution of the United**

Federation of Planets; Contract of Ardra; Cumberland, Acts of; divorce, Klingon; Federation Code of Justice; Ferengi Code; Ferengi Rules of Acquisition; Ferengi Salvage Code; Judge Advocate General; Justinian Code; Magna Carta; *Mek'ba*; nestor; Right of Statement; salvage rights; Satie, Judge Aaron; Scrolls of Ardra; Seventh Guarantee; Sikaris; Starfleet General Orders and Regulations; Treaty of Algeron; Treaty of Alliance; Uniform Code of Justice; United States Constitution; Vulcan Bill of Rights.

Lawgivers. Robed police from the planet **Beta III**, who enforced the law during the rule of the planetary computer **Landru**. The Lawgivers' tasks included absorbing nonconverted members into the society so they could be controlled by Landru. They were also capable of killing when ordered to do so. ("Return of the Archons" [TOS]).

Lawmim Galactopedia. A rare historical object, reported to be in the personal collection of **Zibalian** trader **Kivas Fajo**. ("The Most Toys" [TNG]).

Lawton, Yeoman Tina. (Patricia McNulty). Member of the original *Enterprise* crew. Janice Rand introduced her to **Charles Evans** in the hope he would befriend her, but Charlie was too attracted to Rand for this to happen. Charlie, in fact, temporarily turned Lawton into an iguana when he became angry. ("Charlie X" [TOS]).

Laxeth. (Jerry Sroka). Communications master of a Talaxian convoy, and old friend of Neelix. Laxeth served on the Talaxian convoy that Lieutenant Tom Paris joined in 2372 as part of an elaborate scheme to flush out a spy for the Kazon aboard the *U.S.S. Voyager*. ("Investigations" [VGR]).

Lazarus. (Robert Brown). Scientist who, in 2267, developed a means of creating an interdimensional **door in the universe**, a passageway to an antimatter continuum. This passage was extremely dangerous because contact between the two continua would theoretically result in the total annihilation of both universes. Lazarus was mentally unstable and exhibited symptoms of severe paranoia. He believed that his alternate self from the other universe wanted to kill him. Fortunately, the alternate Lazarus was more stable, and sacrificed himself to trap the insane Lazarus in the interdimensional corridor. As a result, both universes were made safe, but both Lazaruses are at each other's throats for eternity. ("The Alternative Factor" [TOS]). *The episode's script referred to him as Lazarus-A (the madman from our universe) and Lazarus-B (his sane twin from the antimatter universe). Robert Brown was a last-minute replacement for actor John Barrymore, Jr., who didn't show up for the first day's shooting of the episode.*

Lazon II. Planet in **Cardassian** space. In 2371, **Thomas Riker** was sentenced to spend the rest of his life at the labor camp on Lazon II for the crimes he committed against the Cardassian people in 2371. ("Defiant" [DS9]).

LB10445. Single-celled, ciliated, microscopic life-form indigenous to planet **Devidia II.** A cellular fossil of LB10445 was discovered buried on Earth beneath the city of San Francisco, near Commander Data's severed head, suggesting a **Devidian** presence on Earth some 500 years ago. ("Time's Arrow, Part I" [TNG]).

LCARS. SEE: **Library Computer Access and Retrieval System.**

leaf miners. Any of the larvae of various species of Earth moths and butterflies, so called because these larvae exist by burrowing tunnels in the leaves of plants where they live. ("All Good Things..." [TNG]).

Leanne. (Lark Voorhies). Friend of **Jake Sisko**'s. She had been seeing a boy named Orak romantically for a time, but by stardate 48498 she was free to date Jake. ("Life Support" [DS9]).

"Learning Curve." *Voyager* episode #16. Written by Ronald Wilkerson & Jean Louise Matthias. Directed by David Livingston. Stardate 48846.5. *First aired in 1995. Tuvok attempts to train several unruly Maquis crew members in the finer points of Starfleet protocol, while the ship's bio-neural circuitry contracts a viral infection.* GUEST CAST: Armand Schultz as **Dalby**, **Kenneth**; Derek McGrath as **Chell**; Kenny Morrison as **Gerron**; Catherine MacNeal as **Henley**, **Mariah**; Thomas Dekker as **Burleigh**, **Henry**; Lindsey Haun as **Burleigh**, **Beatrice**; Majel Barrett as Computer voice. SEE: **Ashmore, Ensign; bio-neural gel pack; brill cheese; Burleigh, Henry; Burleigh, Beatrice; Chell; Chez Sandrine; Circassian fig; Dalby, Kenneth; Davenport, Lucille; field training; Gerron; Henley, Mariah; holodeck and holosuite programs; Janeway Lambda-1; Jefferies tube; Kazleti pendant; Keela flowers; Laurelian pudding; macaroni and cheese; Napinne; *putillo*; schplict; Tuvok; varmeliate fiber; *Voyager, U.S.S.***

lectrazine. Drug. Lectrazine was used to stabilize cavdiovascular and renal systems in humanoid patients. ("Lifesigns" [VGR], "Sacred Ground" [VGR], "Warlord" [VGR]).

Ledonia III. Third planet in the Ledonia system. **Jadzia Dax** purchased a plant there. ("The Wire" [DS9]). SEE: **mycorrhizal fungus**.

Lee. (Tina Lifford). Civil servant who worked at **Sanctuary District** A in San Francisco on **Earth** in 2024. Lee was one of the hostages taken during the **Bell Riots**. ("Past Tense, Parts I and II" [DS9]). *Lee's name was not mentioned in dialog, but is from the script.*

Leech, Felix. (Harvey Jason). A fictional character from the **Dixon Hill** detective stories, Leech was a hit man for gangster **Cyrus Redblock**. A holographic version of Leech was part of the Dixon Hill holodeck programs. ("The Big Goodbye" [TNG]).

Leeta. (Chase Masterson). Bajoran national who worked as a **dabo** girl in Quark's bar in 2371. Leeta seemed attracted to Dr. Julian Bashir. Julian was definitely receptive to her attentions. ("Explorers" [DS9]). As an adjunct to her job, Leeta became something of an amateur sociologist, well versed in such cultures as the **Trill**. Leeta's knowledge was useful when she participated in Jadzia Dax's ***zhian'tara***. ("Facets" [DS9]). Leeta and **Julian Bashir** became romantically involved, but later went to Risa in 2373 to perform the Bajoran Rite of Separation. Leeta was attracted to **Rom**, whom she thought was cute and very sexy. ("Let He Who Is Without Sin..." [DS9]). She almost left **Deep Space 9** to take a position managing a cafe on **Jupiter Station** until **Rom** gave her a good reason to stay when he found the courage to profess his love to her. ("Doctor Bashir, I Presume?" [DS9]).

Lefler's Laws. A series of 102 colloquialisms collected by **Ensign Robin Lefler**. She said her laws were her way of remembering essential information. Law 17 was, "When all else fails, do it yourself." Law 36 was, "You gotta go with what works." Law 46: "Life isn't always fair." Law 91: "Always watch your back." Wesley Crusher added a 103rd: "A couple of light-years can't keep good friends apart." Robin gave Wesley Crusher a bound hardcopy of her first 102 laws. ("The Game" [TNG]).

Lefler, Ensign Robin. (Ashley Judd). An *Enterprise*-D crew member and part of the engineering staff. She helped Commander La Forge modify the transporter system while Captain Picard was trapped on planet **El-Adrel IV** in 2368. ("Darmok" [TNG]). Lefler was promoted to mission specialist a few months later, and worked on optimizing sensor usage for a survey of the **Phoenix Cluster**. Lefler befriended Wesley Crusher, who visited the *Enterprise*-D during that mission, and the two were instrumental in helping the crew repel an attempted takeover by a **Ktarian** operative. SEE: **Jol, Etana**; **Ktarian game**. Lefler was the child of two Starfleet plasma specialists. She traveled a great deal as a child, and made few friends her own age. She would later recall thinking of her tricorder as her first friend. ("The Game" [TNG]). SEE: **Lefler's Laws**.

"Legacy." *Next Generation* episode #80. Written by Joe Menosky. Directed by Robert Scheerer. Stardate 44215.2. *First aired in 1990. The* Enterprise-D *visits the late Tasha Yar's homeworld, and finds her sister still living among the gangs there.* GUEST CAST: Beth Toussiant as **Yar, Ishara**; Don Mirault as **Hayne**; Colm Meaney as **O'Brien, Miles**; Vladimir Velasco as **T'su, Tan**; Christopher Michael as Man #1. SEE: **Alliance; *Arcos, U.S.S.*; Camus II; Coalition; escape pod; Hayne; Manu III; myographic scanner; photon grenades; *Potemkin, U.S.S.*; proximity detectors; stunstick; T'su, Tan; Telluridian synthale; Turkana IV; Yar, Ishara; Yar, Natasha.**

Legara IV. Planet; homeworld of the **Legarans**. The *Enterprise*-D traveled there in 2366, transporting Ambassador **Sarek** to a historic conference with the Legarans. ("Sarek" [TNG]).

Legarans. Civilization. The Legarans concluded a historic agreement, negotiated by Ambassador **Sarek**, with the Federation in 2366. Sarek began talks with the Legarans in 2273, but it took nearly a century until the protocol-conscious Legarans agreed to a treaty. The final negotiations took place aboard the *Enterprise*-D in orbit above Legara IV. Preparations for those talks were extensive, and included the construction of a special pool filled with a viscous fluid for the Legarans' comfort. Federation authorities expected the benefits of relations with the Legarans to be incalculable. ("Sarek" [TNG]). SEE: **Bendii Syndrome.** *We never did see the Legarans in that episode, although one might wonder what a creature that lives in a mud bath would look like.*

legate. Title given to a high-ranking Cardassian government official. A legate can be a member of the **Cardassian Central Command**. ("The Maquis, Part II" [DS9]). SEE: **Parn**.

Legation of Unity. Political entity of the planet **Straleb**. ("The Outrageous Okona" [TNG]).

lei. A flower garland, indigenous to certain Polynesian cultures of Earth. Leis were featured in Neelix's **Polynesian resort** holodeck program. Neelix noted that a lei represented the "flowering" of love. ("Alter Ego" [VGR]).

Leighton, Dr. Thomas. (William Sargent). Research scientist, and one of nine surviving eyewitnesses to the massacre of some 4,000 colonists at **Tarsus IV** by **Kodos the Executioner**, aka **Anton Karidian**. Leighton was killed in 2266 by Kodos's daughter, **Lenore Karidian**, who had been systematically murdering all those who could identify her father as being responsible for the massacre. Leighton had been horribly disfigured at Tarsus IV, and had begun to suspect actor Anton Karidian of being Kodos after seeing a performance by Karidian on **Planet Q**. ("The Conscience of the King" [TOS]).

Leighton, Martha. (Natalie Norwick). Widow of **Tarsus IV** massacre survivor **Thomas Leighton**. ("The Conscience of the King" [TOS]).

Leijten, Susanna. (Maryann Plunkett). Starfleet officer. Leijten served with **Geordi La Forge** on the ***U.S.S. Victory***. In 2362, Leijten, then a lieutenant, along with La Forge and three others, beamed down to **Tarchannen III** to investigate the Federation outpost there. It was later revealed that all five away-team members were infected by an alien DNA strand that compelled them all to return to Tarchannen III five years later. This alien DNA transformed three of the former *Victory* crew members into Tarchannen life-forms, a fate that Leijten and La Forge only narrowly escaped. ("Identity Crisis" [TNG]).

lek. Cardassian monetary unit. ("Caretaker" [VGR]).

Leka, Governor Trion. (Barbara Tarbuck). Governor of planet **Peliar Zel**. Leka came aboard the *Enterprise*-D in 2367 to assist in negotiations between her planet's **Alpha** and **Beta Moons**. ("The Host" [TNG]).

Lembatta cluster. Stellar formation. During hostilities with the Federation in 2373, Klingon forces intercepted and destroyed the *U.S.S. Farragut* near the Lembatta cluster. ("Nor the Battle to the Strong" [DS9]).

Lemec, Gul. (John Durbin). Captain of the Cardassian warship ***Reklar***. ("Chain of Command, Part I" [TNG]).

Lemli, Mr. (Roger Holloway). *Starship Enterprise* security officer. Lemli was assigned to guard Dr. Janice Lester shortly after stardate 5928. ("Turnabout Intruder" [TOS]). *Mr. Lemli's name was a reference to William Shatner's daughters, Leslie, Melanie, and Lisabeth. Lemli is also the name of Shatner's production company.*

Lemma II. Planet located three light-years from **Bilana III**. A **soliton wave** scattering field generator was built on Lemma II during the soliton experiment conducted by **Dr. Ja'Dar** in 2368. The planet was placed in jeopardy when the wave went out of control during the test. ("New Ground" [TNG]).

lemur. Animal; member of the biological family *Lemuridea*, a primitive, nocturnal, arboreal primate native to Earth. During the outbreak of **Barclay's Protomorphosis Syndrome** among the crew of the *Enterprise*-D in 2370, Data believed Captain Jean-Luc Picard might devolve into a lemur. ("Genesis" [TNG]).

Len'mat. Klingon term meaning "adjourned." ("Redemption, Part I" [TNG]).

Lenarians. In 2369, an away team from the *Enterprise*-D was involved in a conference with the Lenarians, when a dissident faction attacked the team and critically injured Captain **Jean-Luc Picard**. ("Tapestry" [TNG]).

Lenaris Holem. (John Dorman). Member of the Ornathia resistance cell during the **Cardassian** occupation of **Bajor**, and later an officer in the Bajoran militia. Lenaris was a participant in the historic **Pullock V raid**. In 2371, he served as a colonel in the Bajoran forces charged with apprehending former members of the **Shakaar resistance cell**. Lenaris, who was grateful to the **Shakaar** for having liberated his brother from **Gallitep**, was instrumental in bringing an end to the unrest in the region. ("Shakaar" [DS9]). SEE: **Winn.**

Lenor, Par. (Max Grodenchik). Emissary from the **Ferengi Trade Mission**. Par Lenor and his assistant, **Qol**, deliberately sabotaged their shuttle in order to be "rescued" by the *Enterprise*-D on stardate 45761. Once aboard the starship, Lenor hoped to negotiate an exclusive trade agreement with Kriosian **Ambassador Briam**, who was also aboard the *Enterprise*-D. Lenor discovered that Briam was accompanying an **empathic metamorph** named **Kamala**, and tried to bribe Briam into selling her. When Briam refused, a struggle ensued, and Briam was injured. ("The Perfect Mate" [TNG]). *Max Grodenchik also played Rom in* Star Trek: Deep Space Nine.

Lense, Dr. Elizabeth. (Bari Hochwald). Physician assigned to the ***U.S.S. Lexington*** as Chief Medical Officer. Dr. Lense was valedictorian of **Julian Bashir**'s Starfleet Medical School class. ("Explorers" [DS9]).

***leola* root.** Bitter-tasting yellow-orange tuber that was a very good source of vitamins and minerals; native to a planet in the Delta Quadrant. ("State of Flux" [VGR]). Neelix sometimes prepared *leola* root soup for the crew of the *Voyager*. ("Basics, Part I" [VGR]). Neelix also made a stew with *leola* root, much to the *Voyager* crew's chagrin. ("The Chute" [VGR]).

leporazine. A resuscitative drug; used aboard Federation starships. ("Ethics" [TNG]).

Les Misérables. Classic novel, published in 1862, written by noted French poet, dramatist and novelist **Victor Hugo**. The novel was set in the Parisian underworld and although it had the plot of a detective story it was an epic about the people of Paris. *Les Misérables* was **Maquis** leader **Michael Eddington**'s favorite book, and he saw himself as a dashing, romantic figure, fighting the good fight just like **Valjean**, the novel's hero. ("For the Uniform" [DS9]).

Leslie, Mr. (Eddie Paskey). Crew member aboard the original *Starship Enterprise*. ("Where No Man Has Gone Before" [TOS], "The Conscience of the King" [TOS], "Return of the Archons" [TOS], "This Side of Paradise" [TOS], "The Alternative Factor" [TOS], "The Omega Glory" [TOS]). *Eddie Paskey also played an Eminiar guard in "A Taste of Armageddon" (TOS). Paskey was one of the regular stand-ins on the original* Star Trek *series. He had been working at the gasoline station where all Desilu studio trucks and cars were serviced when studio vice-president Herbert F. Solow got him the job on* Star Trek.

"Lessons." *Next Generation episode* #145. Written by Ronald Wilkerson & Jean Louise Matthias. Directed by Robert Wiemer. Stardate 46693.1. *First aired in 1993. Jean-Luc Picard falls in love with a member of his crew.* GUEST CAST: Wendy Hughes as **Daren, Neela**; Majel Barrett as Computer voice. SEE: **Beck; Bersallis firestorms; Bersallis III; Borgolis Nebula; Cabot, Ensign; Cheney, Ensign; Chopin's Trio in G Minor; Daren, Neela; Deng; *"Frere Jacques"*; *Havana, U.S.S.*; Jefferies tube; Kerelian; Landris II; Marquez, Lieutenant; Mataline II; Melnos IV; Mowray, Dr.; Picard, Jean-Luc; Ressikan flute; Richardson; Spectral Analysis department; Starbase 218; Stellar Cartography; Thelka IV; thermal deflector.**

Lester, Dr. Janice. (Sandra Smith, William Shatner). Federation scientist who discovered an extraordinary life-energy transfer device among the archaeological ruins on planet Camus II in 2269. Shortly thereafter, Lester conspired to kill nearly all of her colleagues on the planet, then used the device to place her mind into the body of Captain James T. Kirk. Lester and Kirk had been romantically involved years before at Starfleet Academy, but she bitterly resented the fact that she was not able to attain command of a starship. ("Turnabout Intruder" [TOS]).

Lestrade, Inspector. (Alan Shearman). Fictional 19th-century English detective with Scotland Yard, a character in Sir Arthur Conan Doyle's **Sherlock Holmes** stories. A computer-generated version of Lestrade was among the characters in a Holmes **holodeck** simulation run by Data. ("Elementary, Dear Data" [TNG]).

"Let He Who Is Without Sin..." *Deep Space Nine* episode #105. Written by Robert Hewitt Wolfe & Ira Steven Behr. Directed by Rene Auberjonois. No stardate given. *First aired in 1996. A vacation on the pleasure planet Risa does not go as planned when Worf joins a radical group called the Essentialists who are bent on closing the planet.* GUEST CAST: Monte Markham as **Fullerton, Pascal**; Chase Masterson as **Leeta**; Frank Kopyc as Bolian aide; Vanessa Williams as **Arandis**; Blair Valk as Risian woman; Zora DeHorter as Risian. SEE: **Arandis; Bashir, Julian; berserker cat; Boday, Captain; Dax, Curzon; Dax, Jadzia; Ferenginar; floater; Fullerton, Pascal; Gault; *glebbening*; *Horga'hn*; hoverball; icoberry tort; *jamaharon*; Kahless the Unforgettable; Leeta; Mikel; New Essentialists Movement; *par'machkai*; protostar; reyamilk soak; Risa; Rite of Separation; *sean*; soccer; Temtibi Lagoon; weather control system; Worf.**

"Let me help." Words from a classic book written by a famous novelist of the 21st century who lived on a planet circling the far left star in Orion's belt. This writer recommended these words, even over "I love you." Kirk mentioned this fact to **Edith Keeler** when she offered to help when Kirk didn't want to talk about his past. ("The City on the Edge of Forever" [TOS]).

"Let That Be Your Last Battlefield." Original Series episode #70. Teleplay by Oliver Crawford. Story by Lee Cronin. Directed by Jud Taylor. Stardate: 5730.2. *First aired in 1969. Two men from a dead civilization are unable to shake the racial hatred that destroyed their people.* GUEST CAST: Frank Gorshin as **Bele**; Lou Antonio as **Lokai**; Majel Barrett as **Chapel, Christine**; Majel Barrett as Computer voice. SEE: **Ariannus; Bele; Cheron; destruct sequence; Lokai; Mendel, Gregor Johann; Starbase 4; Vulcans.**

Letek. (Armin Shimerman). Leader of the **Ferengi** landing party at planet **Delphi Ardu** that made contact with the Federation starship *Enterprise*-D in 2364. ("The Last Outpost" [TNG]). *Actor Armin Shimerman had previously played the gift box face in "Haven" (TNG) and would later play* ***Bractor*** *in "Peak Performance" (TNG) and* ***Quark*** *in* Star Trek: Deep Space Nine.

Lethe. (Susanne Wasson). An inmate at the **Tantalus V** penal colony in 2266. Assistant colony director **Tristan Adams** used Lethe as an example of the success of his experimental neural neutralizer device, but her blank, expressionless demeanor suggested that the neutralizer was erasing more than her criminal tendencies. ("Dagger of the Mind" [TOS]). *In Greek mythology, Lethe was a river in Hades whose water, when drunk, would cause one to forget earthly sorrows.*

Lethean. Humanoid species. Letheans are able to attack an opponent by giving a severe, usually fatal, telepathic shock. In 2371, a Lethean named Altovar attacked Dr. **Julian Bashir** in this way, but the telepathic shock merely put him into a temporary coma. ("Distant Voices" [DS9]). Soto, an associate of Toral, was Lethean. ("The Sword of Kahless" [DS9]).

leukocyte. White blood cell. The **cranial implant** in **Garak**'s brain began to malfunction in 2370, causing the molecular structure of his leukocytes to be altered. ("The Wire" [DS9]).

level-1 diagnostic. SEE: **diagnostic**.

level-1 personnel sweep. Scan protocol on station Deep Space 9 initiated to locate any personnel in an area of the station. Odo asked the computer to run a level-1 personnel sweep of all pylons on stardate 46853 to make sure an evacuation order was obeyed. ("If Wishes Were Horses" [DS9]).

level-2 security alert. Starfleet security protocol. It was enacted when hostile intrusion inside the ship might be expected. During a level-2 alert, armed security officers were stationed on every deck. ("Descent, Part I" [TNG]).

level-4 memory fragmentation. Serious cascading memory degradation in a sophisticated computer program. The *Voyager's* Emergency Medical Hologram experienced a level-4 memory fragmentation in 2373. ("The Swarm" [VGR]).

level-4 neurographic scan. Highly detailed neural study. Much more thorough than a normal neural scan, a level-4 was intended to detect even very slight defects. ("All Good Things..." [TNG]).

Levinius V. Planet whose population suffered mass insanity in 2067, caused by the Denevan neural parasites. The parasites had come from the Beta Portolan system, then proceeded to **Theta Cygni XII.** SEE: **Deneva**. ("Operation—Annihilate!" [TOS]).

Levodian flu. Viral disease. Levodian flu normally lasts 29 hours. Symptoms include sneezing and a runny nose. The *U.S.S. Voyager's* **Emergency Medical Hologram** once programmed himself with a holographic simulation of the Levodian flu. He hoped that the experience would help him better relate to organic patients. ("Tattoo" [VGR]).

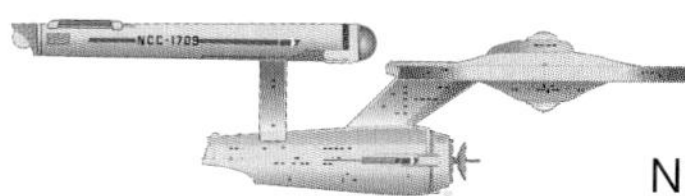

Lexington, U.S.S. Federation starship, *Constitution* class, Starfleet registry number NCC-1709, commanded by **Commodore Robert Wesley**. ("The Ultimate Computer" [TOS]). **Lieutenant Watley** transferred from the *Lexington* to the *Enterprise* just prior to stardate 4523.3. ("Trials and Tribble-ations" [DS9]). A few months later, the *Lexington* participated in the disastrous tests of the **M-5** computer. During those tests, the **multitronic** unit malfunctioned and fired full phasers at the *Lexington*, killing 53 people on that ship, as well as the entire crew of the *Starship* ***Excalibur***. ("The Ultimate Computer" [TOS]). *Named for the famed United States aircraft carrier that fought in the Pacific theater during World War II.*

Lexington, U.S.S. Federation starship, *Excelsior* class, Starfleet registry number NCC-14427. The *Lexington* rendezvoused with the *Enterprise*-D and transferred medical supplies to them for delivery to the **Taranko colony**. ("Thine Own Self" [TNG]).

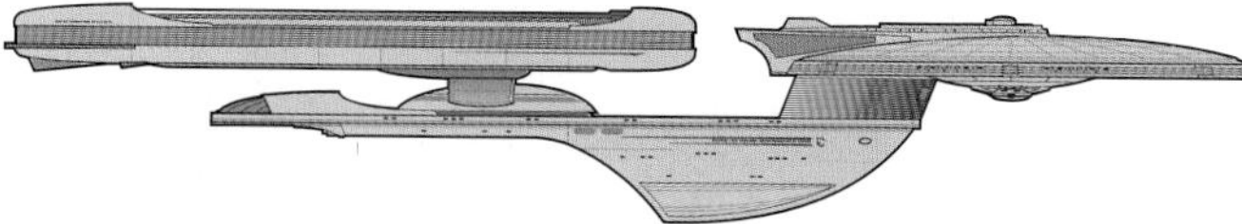

Lexington, U.S.S. *Nebula*-class Federation starship, Starfleet registry number NCC-61832. **Dr. Elizabeth Lense** was the chief medical officer on the *Lexington*. In 2371 the *Lexington* docked at station Deep Space 9. ("Explorers" [DS9]).

lexorin. Medication used to counteract mental disorientation. Kirk administered lexorin to McCoy when McCoy suffered the side effects of carrying Spock's ***katra*** within his own mind. Lexorin can be administered subcutaneously, by **hypospray**. *(Star Trek III: The Search for Spock).*

Leyor. (Kevin Peter Hall). A **Caldonian** national who took part in the negotiations for rights to the Barzan wormhole in 2366. Leyor reached an agreement with **Devinoni Ral**, representative for the **Chrysalians**, in which Caldonia would withdraw from the negotiations. Leyor had been manipulated into making the agreement by Ral, who was secretly using his Betazoid empathic sense to take advantage of the Caldonian's own emotions. ("The Price" [TNG]). *The late Kevin Peter Hall also played the creature from* Predator, *and was Harry in* Harry and the Hendersons.

Leyrons. Inhabitants of planet Malkus IX. The Leyrons, unlike most known humanoid cultures, developed a written language before spoken or sign languages. ("Loud as a Whisper" [TNG]). The Leyrons also use gestures for nonverbal communication. Captain Janeway studied Leyron gestures. ("Macrocosm" [VGR]).

Leyton, Admiral. (Robert Foxworth). Chief of **Starfleet** Operations and architect of a failed military coup of Earth's government in 2372. Early in his career, Leyton was the commanding officer of the *U.S.S. Okinawa* when **Benjamin Sisko** was the vessel's first officer. Leyton later recommended Sisko for the posting as commander of Deep Space 9. ("Homefront" [DS9]). In the early 2370s, Leyton became deeply concerned about the possibility that the **Founders** of the **Dominion** might be using **changelings** to infiltrate Starfleet, perhaps even the Federation government itself. Failing to convince Federation President **Jaresh-Inyo** to adopt repressive security measures, Leyton engineered a plan to create fear by faking evidence that a Dominion invasion was imminent. SEE: **Arriaga, Lieutenant.** Leyton's plan would have culminated with a military coup of Earth's civilian government. When acting Starfleet Security Chief Benjamin Sisko discovered evidence of Leyton's plan, Leyton dispatched the *Starship Lakota* to destroy the *Starship Defiant*, in order to prevent Sisko's evidence from reaching Earth. Leyton's plot collapsed when *Lakota* Captain **Erika Benteen** refused to obey Leyton's orders to destroy the *Defiant* with all hands. ("Paradise Lost" [DS9]). *Robert Foxworth played the title role in* Questor, *an unsold pilot movie created by Gene Roddenberry. Questor was an android, something of a precursor to the character of Data. Foxworth also played General Hague in* Babylon 5.

Li Nalas. (Richard Beymer). Hero of the **Bajoran** resistance movement, renowned for fighting the **Cardassians** during the occupation of his homeworld. Li was believed killed in 2360, but was actually captured by Cardassian forces and conscripted into forced labor at the ore-processing center on station **Terok Nor**. Li was later sent to the **Hutet labor camp**, where he was held until 2370, when he was freed by Major **Kira Nerys**. Li was given a hero's welcome by the **Bajoran provisional government** and given the title of Navarch. He was subsequently assigned as first officer of Deep Space 9, temporarily replacing Major Kira Nerys. ("The Homecoming" [DS9]). Li was killed while saving Commander Sisko from an attack by a member of the **Circle**. Li is remembered as a hero who died for his people's freedom. ("The Siege" [DS9]). *Li spent many years trying to live down his fame because his "heroic" killing of Gul Zarale was in fact accidental. Li himself made no secret of this fact, but after his death, Ben Sisko and associates saw no need to reveal the truth about the Bajoran hero, so this entry reflects Li's legend.*

"Liaisons." *Next Generation* episode #154. Teleplay by Jeanne Carrigan Fauci. Story by Roger Eschbacher & Jaq Greenspan. Directed by Cliff Bole. No stardate given. *First aired in 1993. Captain Picard is captured while the* Enterprise-*D hosts the first cultural exchange between the Federation and a civilization with no understanding of human emotions.* GUEST CAST: Barbara Williams as **Anna**; Eric Pierpoint as **Voval**; Paul Eiding as **Loquel**; Michael Harris as **Byleth**; Rickey D'Shon Collins as **Eric**. SEE: **Anna; Byleth; bioenzymatic supplements; *coltayin* roots; Eric; Iyaarans; Iyaaran homeworld; Iyaaran shuttle; Ktarian chocolate puff; Loquel; natal pod; *papalla* juice; peach cobbler; Picard, Jean-Luc; postcellular compounding; Riker, William T.; Tarvokian powder cake; Terellians; Terellian spices; Troi, Deanna; Worf; Voval.**

Liator. (Jay Lauden). A leader of the Edo people on planet **Rubicun III**. Liator attempted to enforce local laws by demanding the lawful execution of *Enterprise*-D crew member Wesley Crusher for infraction of a minor regulation in 2364. ("Justice" [TNG]). SEE: **punishment zones.**

Libby. (Jennifer Gatti). Woman who was engaged to marry **Harry Kim** at the time Kim was lost aboard the Starship Voyager in 2371. Libby met Kim at a **Ktarian music festival**, and it took Kim three weeks to work up the courage to ask her out. Although the disappearance of *Voyager* seperated the two by many thousands of light-years, Libby and Kim were briefly reunited in early 2372 in an alternate reality created when Kim accidentally piloted a shuttlecraft through a **timestream**. ("Non Sequitur" [VGR]). *Jennifer Gatti also appeared as Ba'el in "Birthright, Parts I and II" (TNG).*

Library Computer Access and Retrieval System. Proper name for the main computer system aboard the ***Galaxy*-class** *Enterprise*-D. Abbreviated LCARS. ("Encounter at Farpoint, Part II" [TNG]). SEE: **control interface**.

library computer. Massive computer system and database carried aboard Federation **starship**s. The storage banks of a library computer contained virtually the sum of recorded information, a vital resource to a starship on detached duty. The library computer could be accessed from any terminal aboard ship, including the **science officer**'s station on the **bridge**.

Life Prolongation Project. A disastrous experiment conducted around 1966 on **Miri**'s planet. The goal of the project was to develop a virus that would dramatically slow the aging process in humans. Unfortunately, the resulting virus killed all the adults on the planet, leaving the children to grow very slowly until they died at puberty. *Enterprise* Chief Medical Officer Leonard McCoy was successful in developing an antitoxin to treat the virus in the remaining children found living on the planet in 2266. ("Miri" [TOS]).

"Life Support." *Deep Space Nine* episode #59. Teleplay by Ronald D. Moore. Story by Christian Ford & Rober Soffer. Directed by Reza Badiyi. Stardate 48498.4. *First aired in 1995. Dr. Bashir fights to prolong a gravely injured Vedek Bareil's life during secret negotiations with the Cardassians.* GUEST CAST: Philip Anglim as **Bareil**, **Vedek**; Aron Eisenberg as **Nog**; Lark Voorhies as **Leanne**; Ann Gillespie as Nurse; Andrew Prine as **Turrel**, **Legate**; Louise Fletcher as **Winn**; Eva Loseth as **Riska**; Kevin Carr as Bajoran. SEE: **Bajorans; Bareil, Vedek; Cardassians; cordrazine; dom-jot; Ferengi tradition; holodeck and holosuite programs; inaprovaline; Jabara; Kai Winn soufflé; Kira Nerys; Leanne; morphenolog; neurogenic radiation; Orb; Osinar VI; positronic implant; pressor; Riska; springball; Terellians; Tholians; Turrel, Legate; vasokin; Vulcan; Winn.**

life-energy transfer. Technology developed long ago by the now-dead civilization of planet **Camus II** that permitted two humanoids to exchange their consciousnesses, so that each person's mind would occupy the other's body. **Dr. Janice Lester** discovered the still-working device on Camus II in 2269 and used it to exchange bodies with Captain James Kirk. ("Turnabout Intruder" [TOS]).

life-forms. The exploration of space has revealed the galaxy to be home to myriad life-forms of virtually every imaginable appearance. Recent discoveries in exo-archaeology, based on the work of **Dr. Richard Galen**, have found a basis for the surprising number of humanoid life-forms found throughout the galaxy that share remarkably similar biochemistries. Chart following page; SEE: **humanoid life.**

"Lifesigns." Voyager episode #36. Written by Kenneth Biller. Directed by Cliff Bole. Stardate 49504.3. First aired in 1996. The doctor creates a holographic body for a female Vidiian suffering from the phage and falls in love with her. GUEST CAST: Susan Diol as **Pel, Danara**; Raphael Sbarge as **Jonas**; Martha Hackett as **Seska**; Michael Spound as **Lorrum**; Rick Gianasi as Gigolo. SEE: **cervaline; Chevy; Crabtree, Susie; Emergency Medical Hologram; Fina Prime; Hemikek IV; holodeck and holosuite programs: Mars in a 1957 Chevy, Sandrine's; inaprovaline; Jonas, Michael; lectrazine; Lorrum; McCoy, Dr. Leonard H.; Pel, Danara; Seska; Shmullus; Utopia Planitia.**

light-speed breakaway factor. Also known as the **slingshot effect**, a warp-speed maneuver used to propel a starship through time. This procedure involves passage close to a massive gravitational source (like a star) at a high warp velocity. It was used to propel the *Enterprise* back in time from 2268 to the year 1968 on a mission of historical research. ("Assignment: Earth" [TOS]). *This was presumably the same technique used in "Tomorrow Is Yesterday" (TOS) and* Star Trek IV: The Voyage Home.

"Lights of Zetar, The." Original Series episode #73. Written by Jeremy Tarcher and Shari Lewis. Directed by Herb Kenwith. Stardate 5725.3. *First aired in 1969. At planetoid Memory Alpha, an* Enterprise *crew member's body is taken over by mysterious energy life-forms.* Jan Shutan as **Romaine**, **Lieutenant Mira**; Majel Barrett as **Chapel**, **Christine**; John Winston as **Kyle**, **Mr.**; Libby Erwin as Technician; Bud Da Vinci as Crewman; Majel Barrett as Computer voice; Barbara Babcock as Zetar voices. SEE: **brain-circuitry pattern; decompression chamber; hyperencephalogram; Kyle, Mr.; Martian Colonies; Memory Alpha; noncorporeal life; psychological profile; Romaine, Jacques; Romaine, Lieutenant Mira; Romaine, Lydia; Scott, Montgomery; Steinman analysis; Zetarians; Zetar.**

lightship. SEE: **Bajoran solar-sail vessel.**

Ligillium, ruins of. An archaeological site where the fabulous Zaterl emerald was reputed to be hidden. Captain Picard offered to take **Ardra** there to try to convince her to accept arbitration in the matter of the **Contract of Ardra**. ("Devil's Due" [TNG]).

Ligobis X. Planet. Location of the Central Gallery where an imposing exhibit of **Professor Gideon Seyetik**'s paintings was once displayed. ("Second Sight" [DS9]).

Ligon II. Class-M planet whose humanoid culture values ritual honor above all else. Ligon II, not a member of the Federation, was a source of a rare vaccine for the treatment of deadly **Anchilles fever**. ("Code of Honor" [TNG]). SEE: **Lutan**.

Ligonians. Humanoid civilization from planet **Ligon II**. Although lacking the advanced technology of the Federation, Ligonians placed an extremely high value on ritual honor. In Ligonian society, the women owned the land and the wealth, while allowing their mates to rule their property. ("Code of Honor" [TNG]). SEE: **Lutan**.

Ligos VII. Volcanically active planet The *Enterprise*-D received a distress call from a Starfleet science team on Ligos VII in 2369. ("Rascals" [TNG]).

Liko. (Ray Wise). An inhabitant of planet **Mintaka III** who chanced to witness the failure of a Federation survey team's **hologram generator**. Liko was injured as a result of the failure and was taken on-board the *Enterprise*-D for treatment, exposing him to advanced technology in violation of the **Prime Directive**.

Life-form	Description	Episode or film
Acamarians	Humanoid inhabitants of **Acamar III**	"The Vengeance Factor" (TNG)
Akritiri	Delta Quadrant civilization who imprisoned criminals on the **Akritiri prison satellite.**	"The Chute" (VGR)
Alcyones	Civilization that destroyed the last Tarellian plague vessel	"Haven" (TNG)
Aldeans	Humanoid inhabitants of the mythical world of **Aldea**	"When the Bough Breaks" (TNG)
Aldebaran serpent	Three-headed reptilian life-form	"Hide and Q" (TNG)
Algorian mammoth	Large animal	"The Wire" (DS9)
allasomorph	Shape-shifters, natives of **Daled IV**	"The Dauphin" (TNG)
Alvanian cave sloth	Animal known for its deep slumbering	"The Sword of Kahless" (DS9)
Alvanian spine mite	Tiny parasitic insects that make their homes in humanoid spinal columns	"The Begotten" (DS9)
Alverian dung beetle	Form of insect life	"Apocalypse Rising" (DS9)
amoeba	Gigantic single-celled life-form	"The Immunity Syndrome" (TOS)
amphibian	Animal that lives on land and in water	"Genesis" (TNG)
anaphasic life-form	Noncorporeal being that required an organic host to "merge" with and help it maintain its molecular cohesion	"Sub Rosa" (TNG)
Andorian amoeba	Unicellular protozoan indigenous to planet Andoria	"Tuvix" (VGR)
Andorians	Humanoid people noted for blue skin and bilateral antennae	"Journey to Babel" (TOS), "Whom Gods Destroy" (TNG), "The Survivors" (TNG), "Data's Day" (TNG)
Angosians	Humanoid inhabitants of **Angosia III**	"The Hunted" (TNG)
Antedeans	Ichthyo-humanoid life-forms	"Manhunt" (TNG)
Anticans	Sentient, lupine humanoids native to the planet **Antica**	"Lonely Among Us" (TNG)
Apollo	Powerful humanoid once worshipped as a god on ancient **Earth**	"Who Mourns for Adonais?" (TOS)
arachnid	Arthropod which **Barclay** de-evolved into in 2370	"Genesis" (TNG)
Arbazan	Species that is a member of the **Federation**	"The Forsaken" (DS9)
Arbazon vulture	Type of predatory bird	"The Search, Part II" (DS9)
Argelians	Humanoid inhabitants of **Argelius II**	"Wolf In The Fold" (TOS)
Argosian	Member of a species that **Sisko** almost got into a fight with	"Dax" (DS9)
Argrathi	Humanoid society native to planet **Argratha**	"Hard Time" (DS9)
Arkarian water fowl	Ornithoid native of planet **Arkaria**, noted for its interesting mating habits	"Starship Mine" (TNG)
Armus	Malevolent life-form who killed **Natasha Yar**	"Skin Of Evil" (TNG)
Australopithecine	Protohuman that **Riker** de-evolved into 2370	"Genesis" (TNG)
bacillus spray	Organism used to combat grapevine parasites	"All Good Things..." (TNG)
Bajorans	Ancient, deeply spiritual humanoid people, victimized for decades by the **Cardassians**	"Ensign Ro" (TNG), "Emissary" (DS9), et al
Balduk warriors	A fierce group	"New Ground" (TNG)
Bandi	Humanoid inhabitants of **Deneb IV**	"Encounter at Farpoint, Parts I & II" (TNG)
Baneans	Spacefaring civilization from the Delta Quadrant	"Ex Post Facto" (VGR)
Baneriam hawk	Predatory bird	"If Wishes Were Horses" (DS9)
Bardakian pronghorn moose	Animal known for its loud call	"Unification, Part II" (TNG)
Barkonians	Humanoid inhabitants of **Barkon IV**. Their civilization was at a level approximately equal to **Earth**'s Renaissance period	"Thine Own Self" (TNG)
Barolians	Humanoids engaged in trade with the **Romulans**	"Unification, Part I" (TNG)
Barzans	Vaguely cat-like Humanoid residents of the planet Barzan	"The Price" (TNG)
Beauregard	Plant raised by **Sulu**	"The Man Trap" (TOS)
Belzoidian flea	Animal mentioned by **Q**	"Deja Q" (TNG)
Benzites	Blue-skinned sentient humanoid; natives of planet **Benzar**	"Coming of Age" (TNG), "A Matter of Honor" (TNG), "The Ship" (DS9)
Berellians	People not known for their engineering skills	"Redemption, Part II" (TNG)
berserker cat	Wild animal known for its courage	"Let He Who is Without Sin…" (DS9)
Beta Renner cloud	Sentient gaseous creature that took over control of **Picard**'s body in an attempt to explore the galaxy	"Lonely Among Us" (TNG)
Beta XII-A entity	Life-form composed of pure energy that thrived on negative emotions	"Day of the Dove" (TOS)
Betazoids	Telepathic humanoids native to the planet **Betazed**; members of the **Federation**	"Haven" (TNG) "Ménage à Troi" (TNG); et al
Bolians	Blue-skinned humanoids, characterized by a midfacial dividing line, natives of **Bolarus IX**	"Allegiance" (TNG), "Conspiracy" (TNG), "Prototype" (VGR), "Emissary" (DS9); et al
Boraalans	Pre-industrial humanoid inhabitants of **Boraal II**	"Homeward" (TNG)
Borg	Cyborg civilization linked by a collective consciousness	"Q Who?" (TNG), "The Best of Both Worlds, Part I & II" (TNG), "I, Borg" (TNG), "Descent, Parts I & II" (TNG), *Star Trek: First Contact*, "Unity" (VGR) et al
Borgia plant	Mildly toxic plant indigenous to planet **M-113**	"The Man Trap" (TOS)
Boslics	Humanoid spacefaring civilization	"Sons of Mogh" (DS9)

Life-form	Description	Episode or film
Botha	A people who occupy a sector of the Delta Quadrant	"Persistence of Vision" (VGR)
Breen	Politically non-aligned culture that sometimes attacks Federation ships	"Hero Worship" (TNG), "Interface" (TNG), "Elogium" (VGR), "Indiscretion" (DS9)
Brekkians	Humanoid people native to planet **Brekka**	"Symbiosis" (TNG)
Bringloidi	Colonists of **Bringloid V**	"Up The Long Ladder" (TNG)
Briori	Humanoid civilization native to the Delta Quadrant	"The 37s" (VGR)
Bulgallian rat	Animal reputed to be terrifying	"Coming of Age" (TNG)
bunny rabbit	Cute terrestrial animal	"Imaginary Friend" (TNG)
Bynars	Humanoids heavily integrated with computers	"11001001" (TNG)
Calamarain	Gaseous life-form that **Q** once tormented	"Deja Q" (TNG)
Caldonians	Very tall, bi-fingered humanoids who bid for rights to the **Barzan wormhole**	"The Price" (TNG)
Caldorian eel	Animal found by **Klim Dokachin**	"Unification, Part I" (TNG)
Camorites	Humanoid residents of **Camor V**	"Bloodlines" (TNG)
Capellans	Humanoid warrior society of the planet **Capella IV**	"Friday's Child" (TOS)
Cardassians	Humanoid natives of **Cardassia**, one of the major governments hostile to the **Federation**	"The Wounded" (TNG), "Chain of Command, Parts I & II" (TNG), "Emissary" (DS9) et al
Carnivorous rastipod	Bajoran animal not known for its grace	"Progress" (DS9)
cave-rat	Small cave-dwelling animal	"The Sword of Kahless" (DS9)
Ceti eel	Mollusk-like neural parasite from **Ceti Alpha V**	*Star Trek II: The Wrath of Kahn*
Chalnoth	Lupine humanoids, native to planet **Chalna**	"Allegiance" (TNG)
chameloid	Shape-shifting life-form	*Star Trek VI: The Undiscovered Country*
Chrysalians	People who bid for rights to the **Barzan wormhole**	"The Price" (TNG)
Circassian cat	**Geordi La Forge**'s first pet	"Violations" (TNG)
coalescent organism	Rare microscopic life-form that could absorb other organisms and assume their form	"Aquiel" (TNG)
Colyus	Sentient holographic life-form from planet **Yadera II**	"Shadowplay" (DS9)
Companion	Noncorporeal, sentient life form, friend to **Zefram Cochrane**	"Metamorphosis" (TOS)
consciousness parasite	Noncorporeal life-form that enters a host consciousness just before the moment of death	"Coda" (VGR)
Corvan gilvos	Stick-like animal; an endangered species	"New Ground" (TNG), "The Nagus" (DS9)
cove palm	Poisonous plant indigenous to **Ogus II**	"Brothers" (TNG)
Cravic	Extinct Delta Quadrant civilization	"Prototype" (VGR)
Crystalline Entity	Sentient life-form that resembles a gigantic snowflake	"Datalore" (TNG), "Silicon Avatar" (TNG)
crystilia	Species of flowering plant found on Tele-marius III	"In Theory" (TNG)
Cyprion cactus	Spiny plant found in the ***Enterprise*-D** arboretum	"Genesis" (TNG)
Cypriprdium	Flowering plant native to planet **Earth**	"Tattoo" (VGR)
Cytherians	Humanoids that reside near the center of the galaxy	"The Nth Degree" (TNG)
D'Arsay	Ancient humanoid civilization	"Masks" (TNG)
Dachlyds	Group for whom Picard served as a mediator	"Captain's Holiday" (TNG)
Dal'Rok	Energy creature created by the first **Sirah** to unite the people in a **Bajoran** village	"The Storyteller" (DS9)
Daliwakan	Humanoid life-form	"The Cloud" (VGR)
Dalvin hissing beetle	Insectoid creature which **Alexander** kept as a pet	"Parallels" (TNG)
Debrune	Ancient off-shoot of the **Romulans**	"Gambit, Part I" (TNG)
Degebian mountain goat	Animal known for its rock-climbing ability	"The Sword of Kahless" (DS9)
Deltans	Characteristically bald humanoids from **Delta IV**	*Star Trek: The Motion Picture*
Denebian slime devil	Nasty creature referred to by **Korax** as a good likeness of **James T. Kirk**	"The Trouble with Tribbles" (TOS)
Denebians	People who did business with **Harcourt Fenton Mudd**	"I, Mudd" (TOS)
Denevan neural parasite	Large single-celled organisms, responsible for the eradication of humanoid life on several planets	"Operation-Annihilate!" (TOS)
Devidians	Species that survived by stealing neural energy from other humanoids	"Time's Arrow, Parts I & II" (TNG)
dikironium cloud creature	Gaseous life-form that ingests human blood	"Obsession" (TOS)
Diomedian scarlet moss	Red feather-like plant	"Clues" (TNG)
distortion ring being	A **noncorporeal life**-form that was a sentient spatial phenomenon capable of changing the shape of space	"Twisted" (VGR)
Doosodarians	Ancient civilization; Data studied their poetry	"Interface" (TNG)
Dopterians	Species that are a distant relative of the **Ferengi**	"The Forsaken" (DS9), "Firstborn" (TNG)
Dosi	Humanoid civilization from the Gamma Quadrant	"Rules of Acquisition" (DS9)
Douwd	Immortal life-form, able to take other forms	"The Survivors" (TNG)
Draco lizards	Flying lizard, indigenous to **Earth**	"New Ground" (TNG)
Draebidium calimus	Plant that vaguely resembles a terrestrial violet	"Rascals"(TNG)
Drathan puppy lig	Animal life-form kept as a pet	"Crossover" (DS9)

Life-form	Description	Episode or film
Drayans	Civilization from the Delta Quadrant	"Innocence" (VGR)
drella	Entity that survives on the emotion of love	"Wolf in the Fold" (TOS)
dryworm	Giant creature on planet Antos IV, which can generate and control energy with no harm to itself.	"Who Mourns for Adonais?" (TOS)
Edo	Humanoid residents of the planet **Rubicun III**	"Justice" (TNG)
Edo God	A powerful space borne entity discovered in orbit of the planet **Rubicun III**.	"Justice" (TNG)
eel-birds	Creatures from planet **Regulus V** which must return to the caverns where they hatched each eleven years	"Amok Time" (TOS)
Ekosians	Humanoid people native to the planet **Ekos**	"Patterns of Force" (TOS)
El-Aurians	Civilization nearly made extinct when their homeworld was destroyed by the **Borg**; Guinan's people	*Star Trek Generations*, "Q Who?" (TNG), "Rivals" (TNG)
Elasians	Warrior species from planet **Elas**	"Elaan of Troyius" (TOS)
Elaysians	Humanoid species whose homeworld has low gravity	"Melora" (DS9)
emergent life-form	Intelligent creature constructed by the systems of the ***Enterprise*-D**	"Emergence" (TNG)
Enarans	Technologically sophisticated Delta Quadrant civilization	"Remember" (VGR)
Ennis/Nol-Ennis	Two factions of the same humanoid species doomed to fight for eternity on a prison moon	"Battle Lines" (DS9)
Etanian Order	Delta Quadrant civilization	"Rise" (VGR)
Excalbian	Intelligent, shape-shifting rock creatures of the planet **Excalbia** who conducted an elaborate drama to study the humanoid concepts of "good" and "evil"	"The Savage Curtain" (TOS)
exocomp	Small robotic servomechanisms that attained sentience	"The Quality of Life" (TNG)
Eymorg/Morg	Humanoid inhabitants of the planet **Sigma Draconis VI**	"Spock's Brain" (TOS)
Fabrini	Ancient civilization that built the planet ship **Yonada**	"For the World Is Hollow and I Have Touched the Sky" (TOS)
Farn	Humanoid civilization from the Delta Quadrant; once part of the **Borg collective**	"Unity" (VGR)
Farpoint Station	Shape-shifting spaceborne entity, forced to take the form of a space station	"Encounter at Farpoint" (TNG)
Felaran rose	Flowering plant native to a planet in the Delta Quadrant	"Parturition" (VGR)
Ferengi	Humanoid civilization known as consummate capitalists	"The Last Outpost" (TNG), "The Nagus" (DS9); et al
fire ants	Venomous mound-building insects native to Earth	"The Chute" (VGR)
fire beast of Sullus	Creature from **Drayan** folklore	"Innocence" (VGR)
fire snakes	Reptilian species	"Fair Trade" (VGR)
flitterbird	Avian life-form from planet **Rhymus Major**	"Profit and Loss" (DS9)
Folnar jewel plant	Plant from planet **Folnar III** that secretes a resin which hardens into a gem	"Dark Page" (TNG)
Founders	Ancient civilization of **shape-shifter**s	"The Search, Parts I & II" (DS9)
Frunalian	Species from the **Alpha Quadrant**	"Emissary" (DS9)
Galipotans	Civilization with a different standard of time than most humanoid species	"The Wire" (DS9)
Gallamite	Species of humanoids with transparent skulls	"The Maquis, Part I" (DS9)
Garanian Bolites	Small creatures that cause extreme itching and skin discoloration when applied to humanoid skin	"A Man Alone" (DS9)
***garili* tree**	Blooming tree found on the **Vhnori** homeworld	"Emanations" (VGR)
garlanic tree	Plant form indigenous to the **Elaysian** homeworld	"Melora" (DS9)
Gatherers	Nomadic offshoot of the **Acamarians**	"The Vengeance Factor" (TNG)
Gem	One member of a mute, naturally empathic species whose sun went nova in 2268	"The Empath" (TOS)
gettle	Wild herd animal native to **Cardassia**	"Chain of Command, Part II" (TNG)
***glob* fly**	**Klingon** insect one-half the size of an **Earth** mosquito; creature has no sting, but is known for its annoying buzz.	"The Outrageous Okona" (TNG)
Gomtuu	Species of living spaceships who live symbiotically with their crews; the last of its kind chose to live with **Tam Elbrun**	"Tin Man" (TNG)
Gorgan (AKA The Friendly Angel)	Evil entity who forced the adults of the **Starnes Expedition** to commit suicide and deceived their children to follow him	"And the Children Shall Lead" (TOS)
Gorn	Sentient reptilians that believed the Federation was infringing on its territorial claim on planet **Cestus III**	"Arena" (TOS)
Gorokian midwife toad	Animal life-form	"Death Wish" (VGR)
Grazerite	Humanoid species that evolved from herd animals	"Homefront" (DS9)
Gree	Life-form from the Delta Quadrant	"Elogium" (VGR)
Grisella	Species known for hibernating for six month periods	"The Ensigns of Command" (TNG)
Gunji jackdaw	Ostrich-like bird, possibly sentient	"If Wishes Were Horses" (DS9)
Haakonians	Humanoid civilization native to the Delta Quadrant	"Jetrel" (VGR)
Halkans	Humanoid civilization with a history of total peace	"Mirror, Mirror" (TOS)
Hanonian land eel	Large cave-dwelling carnivore native to planet **Hanon IV**	"Basics, Part II" (VGR)
***hara* cat**	Bajoran life-form	"Second Skin" (DS9)
hill people	A tribe of hunter-gatherers living on **Tyree's planet**	"A Private Little War" (TOS)

Life-form	Description	Episode or film
Horta	A silicon-based rocklike sentient life-form	"The Devil in the Dark" (TOS)
Humans	Humanoid species native to planet **Earth**	*Star Trek*
humpback whale	Intelligent ocean-dwelling life-form indigenous to planet **Earth**	*Star Trek IV: The Voyage Home*
humuhumunukunukuapua'a	Terrestrial reef triggerfish	"Rascals" (TNG)
Hunters	**Gamma Quadrant** species who live to pursue the **Tosk**	"Captive Pursuit" (DS9)
Hupyrians	Humanoids known for their devotion to their employers	"The Nagus" (DS9)
Husnock	Civilization utterly destroyed by **Kevin Uxbridge**	"The Survivors" (TNG)
Iconians	An ancient, highly-advanced civilization once known as **"Demons of Air and Darkness"**	"Contagion" (TNG), "To the Death" (DS9)
Idanians	Humanoid civilization	"A Simple Investigation" (DS9)
iguana	Large tropical lizard into which **Spot** de-evolved in 2370	"Genesis" (TNG)
Ilidarians	Civilization from planet **Ilidaria** in the **Delta Quadrant**	"Cathexis" (VGR)
Inheritors	Group of humanoids on planet **Earth** who were visited by an advanced extraterrestrial species	"Tattoo" (VGR)
interphasic organisms	Parasitic organism which extracted cellular peptides from the body	"Phantasms" (TNG)
Iotians	Society of intelligent humanoids who inhabit planet **Sigma Iotia II**	"A Piece of the Action" (TOS)
Isis	Life-form of unknown extraterrestrial origin	"Assignment Earth" (TOS)
Iyaarans	Humanoids who had their first cultural exchange with the **Federation** in 2370.	"Liaisons" (TNG)
J'naii	An androgynous humanoid species	"The Outcast" (TNG)
Jarada	Insectoid civilization, which finally opened relations with the Federation in 2364	"The Big Goodbye" (TNG), "Samaritan Snare" (TNG)
Jem'Hadar	Genetically-engineered warrior species from the **Gamma Quadrant**; part of the **Dominion**	"The Jem'Hadar" (DS9), "To the Death" (DS9), "The Abandoned" (DS9), et al
Joranian ostrich	Avian life-form that hides its head underwater when frightened, usually until it drowns	"Past Prologue" (DS9)
Junior	Spaceborne ship-sized life-form	"Galaxy's Child" (TNG)
Kalandans	People who established an outpost and unleashed a terrible disease	"That Which Survives" (TOS)
Karemma	Humanoid civilization from the **Gamma Quadrant**	"Rules of Acquisition" (DS9)
Kavarian tiger-bat	Animal life-form from planet Kavaria	"For the Cause" (DS9)
Kazon	Spacefaring humanoid civilization from the **Delta Quadrant**	"Caretaker" (VGR), "Maneuvers" (VGR), "Alliances" (VGR)
Kellerun	Humanoid civilization at war with the **T'Lani** for centuries	"Armageddon Game" (DS9)
Kelvans	Life-forms from planet **Kelva** in the **Andromeda Galaxy**	"By Any Other Name" (TOS)
Kerelian	Species with highly developed hearing	"Lessons" (TNG)
Kes	Humanoid residents of planet **Kesprytt III**. They applied for associate membership in the Federation in 2370.	"Attached" (TNG)
Klabnian eel	Life-form **Q** disliked	"QPid" (TNG)
Klingons	Warrior civilization, formerly enemies of the Federation	"Errand of Mercy" (TOS), *Star Trek VI: The Undiscovered Country*, "Sins of the Father" (TNG) et al
Kobliad	Dying species that required deuridium to prolong their lives	"The Passenger" (DS9)
Kohms	Humanoid residents of **Omega IV**	"The Omega Glory" (TOS)
Koinonians	Noncorporeal species capable of taking human form	"The Bonding" (TNG)
Krallinian eel	Unpleasant creature found in the Delta Quadrant	"Jetrel" (VGR)
Kressari	Species of reptilian humanoids	"The Circle" (DS9)
Kryonian tiger	Life-form found in the **Brentalia** Zoo	"Imaginary Friend" (TNG)
Ktarians	Humanoids who attempted to gain control of **Starfleet** in 2368. **Samantha Wildman**'s husband was Ktarian	"The Game" (TNG), "Dreadnought" (VGR), "Deadlock" (VGR)
L-S VI life-form	Entity discovered on planet **L-S VI** by **Dr. Mora Pol.**	"The Alternate" (DS9)
lapling	An endangered species, the last of which was found in the possession of **Kivas Fajo**	"The Most Toys" (TNG)
lavaflies	Insect life-form indigenous to the marshlands of **Rinax**	"Macrocosm" (VGR)
LB10445	Single-celled life-form native to **Devidia II**	"Time's Arrow, Part I" (TNG)
leaf miners	Grapevine parasites	"All Good Things..." (TNG)
Legarans	Culture with whom **Ambassador Sarek** labored 93 years to establish a critical treaty; they live in a mudbath-like environment	"Sarek" (TNG)
lemur	Small arboreal primate that **Data** thought **Picard** might de-evolve into	"Genesis" (TNG)
Lenarians	People who don't like the **Federation**	"Tapestry"(TNG)
Lethean	Humanoid species	"The Sword of Kahless" (DS9)
Leyrons	Inhabitants of the planet **Malkus IX.** The Leyrons use gestures for non-verbal communication	"Loud As A Whisper" (TNG), "Macrocosm" (VGR)
Ligonians	Humanoid civilization native to planet **Ligon II**	"Code of Honor" (TNG)
Lissepians	Spacefaring civilization; possible **Cardassian** allies	"The Maquis, Parts I and II" (DS9), "Bar Association" (DS9)

Life-form	Description	Episode or film
Iothra	Hydrogen breathing, sentient life-form	"Melora" (DS9)
Lycosa tarantula	Arachnid; **Miles O'Brien** kept one as a pet	"Realm of Fear" (TNG)
Lynars	Batlike creature indigenous to **Celtris III**	"Chain of Command, Part I" (TNG)
M-113 creature	Sentient humanoid species, now extinct, native to planet **M-113**; it subsisted on NaCl	"The Man Trap" (TOS)
macrovirus	Virus indigenous to the **Delta Quadrant** that grows to extraordinary size	"Macrocosm" (VGR)
Makers	Ancient advanced civilization responsible for **Norman** and his counterparts	"I, Mudd" (TOS)
Malcorians	Humanoid natives of **Malcor III**, on the verge of developing spaceflight	"First Contact" (TNG)
Malurians	Civilization destroyed by the robot space probe, **Nomad**	"The Changeling" (TOS)
Manchovites	Sentient civilization	"Business As Usual" (DS9)
Marijne VII beings	Sentient subspace beings who communicated by direct access of thoughts	"Interface" (TNG)
Markoffian sea lizard	Life-form once mentioned by **Q**	"Deja Q" (TNG)
Mathenites	Civilization whose government offered asylum to **Legate Ghemor** in 2371	"Second Skin" (DS9)
Medusans	Formless entities whose physical appearance can cause madness in humans	"Is There in Truth No Beauty?" (TOS)
Megaptera novaeangliae	Earth cetacean also known as the **humpback whale**	*Star Trek IV: The Voyage Home*
Melkotians	Telepathic, non-humanoid species	"Spectre of the Gun" (TOS)
mellitus	Creature which is solid at rest and gaseous when in motion	"Wolf in the Fold" (TOS)
memory virus	Parasitic organisms that thrived on peptides generated by its host's brain	"Flashback" (VGR)
Menthar	Ancient civilization which fought to its own extinction against the **Promellians**	"Booby Trap" (TNG)
Metron	Highly advanced, and long lived, humanoid civilization	"Arena" (TOS)
microbiotic colony	Subatomic life-form that ingests metallic substances for food	"A Matter of Honor" (TNG)
microbrain	Silicon based intelligent life form indigenous to a narrow layer above the water table on planet **Velara III**	"Home Soil" (TNG)
microvirus	Genetically-engineered microorganism	"The Vengeance Factor" (TNG)
Mikhal Travelers	Delta Quadrant civilization who explore unknown space for the spirit of adventure	"Darkling" (VGR)
Mikulaks	People who donated tissue samples to study Correllium fever	"Hollow Pursuits" (TNG)
Minnobia	Civilization at war with the **Vek** people in 2373	"Business As Usual" (DS9)
Mintakans	Proto-Vulcan humanoids	"Who Watches the Watchers?" (TNG)
Miradorn	Humanoid species of symbiotic twins	"Vortex" (DS9)
Mizarians	Humanoid species native to Mizar II	"Allegiance" (TNG)
Mordian butterfly	Insect life-form indigenous to **Rymus Major**	"Profit and Loss" (DS9)
Moriarty	Holodeck character who became sentient	"Elementary, Dear Data" (TNG), "Ship in a Bottle" (TNG)
Moropa	Society hostile to the **Bolians**	"Allegiance" (TNG)
mugato	White simian creature native to **Tyree**'s planet; the animal is extremely venomous	"A Private Little War" (TOS)
***muktok* plant**	Bristle-like foliage native to **Betazed**	"Ménage à Troi" (TNG)
Nagilum	Extra-dimensional life-form	"Where Silence has Lease" (TNG)
nanites	Submicroscopic cybernetic life-form	"Evolution" (TNG), "The Best of Both Worlds, Part II" (TNG), "Meld" (VGR)
Napean	Species of partially empathic humanoids	"Eye of the Beholder" (TNG)
Nasari	Spacefaring technological humanoid civilization	"Favorite Son" (VGR)
nasturtium	Flowering plant native to **Earth**	"Imaginary Friend" (TNG)
Nausicaans	Tall humanoid people noted for their short tempers	"Samaritan Snare" (TNG), "Tapestry" (TNG)
Nechani	Humanoid civilization native to the **Delta Quadrant**	"Sacred Ground" (VGR)
Nezu	Technologically-sophisticated civilization	"Rise" (VGR)
nitrium metal parasites	Spaceborne microscopic life-forms that ingest **nitrium,** converting it to a simple molecular gel	"Cost of Living" (TNG)
nucleogenic cloud being	Nebula-like life-form native to the **Delta Quadrant**.	"The Cloud" (VGR)
Numiri	Spacefaring civilization in the **Delta Quadrant**	"Ex Post Facto" (VGR)
Nyberrite Alliance	Spacefaring civilization	"The Way of the Warrior" (DS9)
Ocampa	Humanoid civilization from the **Delta Quadrant** who have a life span of nine years	"Caretaker" (VGR), "Cold Fire" (VGR), "Emanations" (VGR)
Old Ones	Long-dead civilization on planet **Exo III**	"What Are Little Girls Made Of" (TOS)
Old Ones	Leaders of **Korob** and **Sylvia**'s homeworld	"Catspaw" (TOS)
Onaya	**Noncorporeal life**-form who lived on neural energy from the act of creativity in humanoid minds	"The Muse" (DS9)

Life-form	Description	Episode or film
ophidian	Snake-like animal used by **Devidians**	"Time's Arrow, Parts I and II" (TNG)
Organians	Powerful noncorporeal beings responsible for peace treaty between the **Klingons** and the **Federation**	"Errand Of Mercy" (TOS)
Orillian lung maggot	Form of life indigenous to the Orillian homeworld	"Fair Trade" (VGR)
Orion wing-slug	Lower life-form	"Ménage à Troi" (TNG)
Orions	Characteristically green-skinned humanoids: females of the species were once sold as commodities	"The Cage" (TOS), "The Menagerie, Part II" (TOS), "Whom Gods Destroy" (TOS)
Ornarans	Humanoid species native to planet Ornara; the entire civilization was addicted to the drug **felicium**	"Symbiosis" (TNG)
Pah-wraiths	Energy-based life-forms	"The Assignment" (DS9)
Pakleds	Humanoid civilization; highly intelligent despite their slow speech	"Samaritan Snare" (TNG)
Paradas	Humanoids from the **Parada system**	"Whispers" (DS9)
Parein	Civilization populating a planet of former **Borg** drones	"Unity" (VGR)
Paxans	Xenophobic life-forms residing in the **Ngame nebula**	"Clues" (TNG)
Peljenite	Sentient life-forms invited to join the Federation in 2371	"Family Business" (DS9)
Petarian	Spacefaring civilization	"Family Business" (DS9)
photonic being	Noncorporeal life-form discovered in a protostar	"Heroes and Demons" (VGR)
Platonians	Humanoids, formerly from the star system Sahndara, that once lived on **Earth** during the time of Plato	"Plato's Stepchildren" (TOS)
Portal	Last survivor of the **Tkon empire**	"The Last Outpost" (TNG)
Preservers	Ancient civilization that rescued endangered cultures, including American Indians, by planting them on distant world	"The Paradise Syndrome" (TOS)
Promellians	Reptilian civilization that caused its own extinction	"Booby Trap" (TNG)
Providers	Disembodied brains who resided on **Triskelion**	"The Gamesters of Triskelion" (TOS)
Proxcinians	Civilization at war in 2373	"Business As Usual" (DS9)
Prytt	Humanoid residents of the planet **Kesprytt III**; extreme xenophobes	"Attached" (TNG)
Psi 2000 virus	Water-based disease organism, transmitted through perspiration, causing abnormal behavior in humans	"The Naked Time" (TOS), "The Naked Now" (TNG)
pygmy marmoset	Small Earth primate that **Data** thought **Picard** might de-evolve into	"Genesis" (TNG)
Pygorians	Interstellar traders	"The Maquis, Part II" (DS9)
Q	One of a civilization of omnipotent humanoids	"Encounter At Farpoint" (TNG), et al
quantum singularity life-form	Intelligent species from another space-time continuum; they incubate their young in a black hole	"Timescape" (TNG)
quasi-energy microbes	Life-forms found within the plasma streamer in the **Igo Sector**	"Realm of Fear" (TNG)
Rafalian mouse	Tiny animal; **Odo** enjoyed taking this form	"Crossfire" (DS9)
Rakhari	Humanoid natives of the planet **Rakhar**	"Vortex" (DS9)
Rakonian swamp rat	Unpleasant animal; in 2372, **Kira** compared **Quark** to a Rakonian swamp rat	"Hippocratic Oath" (DS9)
Rectilian vulture	Avian life-form native to a planet in the **Delta Quadrant**	"Phage" (VGR)
Rectyne monopod	Animal life-form that can weigh up to two tons	"The Icarus Factor" (TNG)
Redjac	Noncorporeal life-form that thrived on fear and terror; also known as Kesla, Beratis and **Jack the Ripper**	"Wolf in the Fold"(TOS)
Reegrunion	Humanoid civilization and nationality of **Plix Tixiplik**	"Sanctuary" (DS9)
reeta-hawk	Avian life-form from planet **Argratha**	"Hard Time" (DS9)
Regalian fleaspider	Arachnoid life-form; medicine synthesized from fleaspider venom improves humanoid circulation	"The Ship" (DS9)
Regulan blood worm	Soft, shapeless creature mentioned by **Korax** when insulting several members of the ***Enterprise*** crew at **Space Station K-7**	"The Trouble with Tribbles" (TOS)
reptohumanoid hatchling	Infant life-form discovered by *Voyager* crew members on a Class-M planet in the **Delta Quadrant**	"Parturition" (VGR)
Rigelians	Species physiologically similar to **Vulcans**.	"Journey to Babel" (TOS)
Romulans	Humanoid offshoot of the **Vulcan** species that rejected devotion to logic in favor of a fierce warrior ethic	"Balance of Terror" (TOS), " The Neutral Zone" (TNG), "Unification, Parts I & II" (TNG), et al
Rutians	Humanoids from the politically non-aligned planet of **Rutia IV**	"The High Ground" (TNG)
Sakari	Humanoid inhabitants from the **Delta Quadrant**	"Blood Fever" (VGR)
Saltah'na	**Gamma Quadrant** life-forms that produced telepathic spheres that "possessed" the crew of **DS9**	"Dramatis Personae" (DS9)
Samarian coral fish	Aquatic life-form; **Guinan** thought she saw one in a nebula	"Imaginary Friend" (TNG)
sand bats	Creatures from planet Manark IV; they appear to be inanimate rock crystals until they attack	"The Empath" (TOS)
***sark*, Klingon**	Riding animal	"Pen Pals" (TNG)
Satarrans	Humanoids, native to **Sothis III**, that attempted to take over the ***Enterprise*-D**	"Conundrum" (TNG), "The Chase" (TNG)

Life-form	Description	Episode or film
Scalosians	Humanoid civilization of the planet Scalos, physiologically hyperaccerated by radiation exposure	"Wink of an Eye" (TOS)
Scathos	Civilization. Scathosian woman who conceived children before the age of forty were executed	"Elogium" (VGR)
sehlat	**Vulcan** animal that resembles a teddy-bear with six inch fangs	"Journey to Babel" (TOS)
Selay	Sentient, reptilian inhabitants of the **Beta Renna** system	"Lonely Among Us" (TNG)
Sheliak	Classification R-3 life-form; a very reclusive people	"The Ensigns of Command" (TNG)
sinoraptor	Life-form	"The Darkness and the Light" (DS9)
Skrreea	Humanoid civilization from the Gamma Quadrant	"Sanctuary" (DS9)
solanagen-based entities	Life-forms that existed in a deep subspace domain	"Schisms" (TNG)
Soong-type android	Artificial life-form based on the work of Dr. **Noonien Soong**; **Data** was a Soong-type android	"Datalore" (TNG), "Descent" (TNG), et al
spawn beetle	Insectoid life-form	"Elogium" (VGR)
spores, Omicron Ceti III	Symbiotic organism from planet **Omicron Ceti III**	"This Side Of Paradise" (TOS)
Spot	**Data**'s companion, *Felis domesticus*; obviously sentient	"Data's Day" (TNG), et al
Swarm	Highly territorial civilization in the Delta Quadrant	"The Swarm" (VGR)
symbiont	Small, sightless, sessile intelligent life-form, one half of the **Trill** joined species	"Equilibrium" (DS9), "The Host" (TNG), "Dax" (DS9), "Invasive Procedures" (DS9), et al
T'Lani	Humanoid people who were at war with the **Kellerun**	"Armageddon Game" (DS9)
t'stayan	**Talarian** riding animal	"Suddenly Human" (TNG)
T-Rogorans	Civilization located in the Gamma Quadrant	"Sanctuary" (DS9)
Tagrans	Inhabitants of **Tagra IV**	"True Q" (TNG)
Tak Tak	Humanoid society native to the Delta Quadrant who use ritualistic body language as communication	"Macrocosm" (VGR)
Takarans	Reptilian humanoids with disseminated internal physiology	"Suspicions" (TNG)
Takarians	Humanoid pre-industrial bronze-age civilization	"False Profits" (VGR)
Talarian hook spider	An arachnid with half-meter-long legs	"Realm of Fear" (TNG)
Talarians	Warrior civilization with a long history of violence against the Federation	"Heart of Glory" (TNG), "Suddenly Human" (TNG)
Talavians	Civilization	"Things Past" (DS9)
Talosians	Humanoids dependant upon illusion; their civilization was nearly wiped out by war	"The Cage" (TOS), "The Menagerie, Parts I & II" (TOS)
Tamarians	Humanoids who communicate entirely by metaphor	"Darmok" (TNG)
Tanugans	Humanoid species native to **Tanuga IV**	"A Matter of Perspective" (TNG)
Tarchee cat	Animal indigenous to the **Nechani** homeworld	"Sacred Ground" (VGR)
Tarellians	Humanoid species from the planet **Tarella**, who were almost completely wiped out by a biological weapon	"Haven" (TNG)
Taresians	Civilization in the Delta Quadrant	"Favorite Son" (VGR)
targ	Furry porcine animal native to ***Qo'nos***	"Where No One Has Gone Before" (TNG)
Targhee moonbeast	Life-form noted for its loud bray	"The Perfect Mate" (TNG)
Tarkalean condor	Large avian life-form	"Nor the Battle to the Strong" (DS9)
Tarkalean hawk	Predatory avian life-form	"The Begotten" (DS9)
Tarkannans	Civilization	"Innocence" (VGR)
Tarkassian razorbeast	Animal. When **Guinan** was a child, a tarcassian razorbeast was her imaginary friend	"Imaginary Friend" (TNG), "Rascals" (TNG)
Tavnians	Humanoids who believed in separation of sexes	"The Muse" (DS9)
Tellarites	Humanoids with distinctive porcine physical traits	"Journey to Babel " (TOS), "Shadowplay" (DS9), "Apocalypse Rising" (DS9)
Terellians	Life-form noted for its four arms	"Liaisons" (TNG)
Terrellians	Spacefaring civilization	"Life Support" (DS9)
Thasians	Noncorporeal life-form native to planet **Thasus**	"Charlie X" (TOS)
Tholians	Sentient culture with a long history of violence with the **Federation**	"The Tholian Web" (TOS), "The Icarus Factor" (TNG), et al
Tiberian bats	Avian life-forms known for sticking together	*Star Trek VI: The Undiscovered Country*
tiger	Large feline encountered by **Sulu**	"Shore Leave" (TOS)
Tika cat	Small animal known for its timidity	"Faces" (VGR)
Tosk	Reptilian humanoids from the **Gamma Quadrant**, raised from birth to be the prey of the **Hunters**	"Captive Pursuit" (DS9)
Traveler	Humanoid native of **Tau Alpha C**, who possesses the ability to manipulate time, space, and thought	"Where No One Has Gone Before" (TNG), "Remember Me" (TNG), "Journey's End" (TNG)
Trelane	Immensely powerful, noncorporeal life-form	"The Squire of Gothos" (TOS)
Trellan crocodile	Large reptilian animal known for its strength and potential destructive abilities	"Crossfire" (DS9)

Life-form	Description	Episode or film
trianic energy beings	Noncorporeal life-forms. Trianic energy beings known as the **Komar** lived in a dark-matter nebula	"Cathexis" (VGR)
tribble	Small furry animal that reproduces at an astronomical rate	"The Trouble with Tribbles" (TOS) "Trials and Tribble-ations" (DS9)
Trill	Joined species, composed of a humanoid host and a small, helpless, but long-lived, **symbiont**	"The Host" (TNG), *Deep Space Nine* (series)
Troglytes	Subdivision of the humanoid inhabitants of the planet **Ardana**	"The Cloud Minders" (TOS)
Troi, Ian Andrew (II)	Noncorporeal life-form that impregnated **Counselor Troi** and interacted with her as her son in an attempt to learn about humanoid life	"The Child" (TNG)
Troyians	Humanoid civilization native to planet **Troyius**	"Elaan of Troyius" (TOS)
tsetse fly	**Earth** insect	"Ship in a Bottle" (TNG)
two-dimensional creatures	life-forms from a two-dimensional spacial continuum, encountered by the ***Enterprise*-D** in 2367	"The Loss" (TNG)
two-headed Malgorian	Life-form reputed to be unable to make up its mind	"Progress" (DS9)
Tzenkethi	Civilization native to the Alpha Quadrant	"The Adversary" (DS9)
"Ugly Bags of Mostly Water"	AKA humanoids	"Home Soil" (TNG)
Ullians	Telepathic humanoid species	"Violations" (TNG)
V'Ger	Massive machine life-form built around the **NASA** probe ***Voyager***	*Star Trek: The Motion Picture*
vakol fish	Aquatic life-form from a planet in the Delta Quadrant	"State of Flux" (VGR)
Valerians	People who supplied **dolamide** to the **Cardassians** for weapons production	"Dramatis Personae" (DS9)
Valtese	Humanoid species; inhabitants of the **Valt Minor** system	"The Perfect Mate" (TNG)
Vek	Civilization at war with the Minnobian people in 2373	"Business As Usual" (DS9)
Verillians	Sentient culture	
Vians	Advanced humanoid people of unknown origin	"The Empath" (TOS)
Vicarian razorback	Animal life-form; a vicious and dangerous beast	"The Die is Cast" (DS9)
Vidiians	Humanoid species native to the Delta Quadrant stricken with a terrible disease known as the **phage**	"Phage" (VGR), "Faces" (VGR), "Resolutions" (VGR)
Vok'sha	Civilization from planet Rakella Prime	"Heroes and Demons" (VGR)
Vorgons	Humanoid species with the ability to travel in time	"Captain's Holiday" (TNG)
Vorian pterodactyl	Large reptilian flying animal	"The Ascent" (DS9)
Vorta	Civilization from the Gamma Quadrant and member of the **Dominion.** The Vorta controlled the **Jem'Hadar**	"The Search, Parts I and II" (DS9), "Hippocratic Oath," (DS9), et al
Vulcans	Humanoid species whose culture is based on total suppression of emotion in favor of pure logic	"Amok Time" (TOS), "The Savage Curtain" (TOS), "Meld" (VGR) "Unification, Parts I & II" (TNG), et al
Wadi	Humanoid species from the **Gamma Quadrant**, first contacted in 2369	"Move Along Home" (DS9)
Wanoni tracehound	Predatory life-form that pursued its victims with enthusiastic vigor	"The Forsaken" (DS9)
Wentlian condor snake	Serpentine life-form. Stuffed condor snake was a favorite dish of the **Regent of Palamar**	"Business As Usual" (DS9)
white rhinos	Terrestrial animal life-form	"New Ground" (TNG)
Wise Ones	Ancient civilization also known as the **Preservers**	"The Paradise Syndrome" (TOS)
Wogneer creatures	Species saved by **Jean-Luc Picard**	"Allegiance" (TNG)
wompat	Rodent-like creature native to **Cardassia**	"Chain of Command, Part II" (TNG)
Xepolites	Humanoid civilization	"The Maquis, Part II" (DS9)
Yaderans	**Sentient holographic life-forms**	"Shadowplay" (DS9)
Yallitians	Sophisticated life-forms from the Delta Quadrant	"Phage" (VGR)
Yalosians	Sentient life-forms	"Improbable Cause" (DS9)
Yangs	Caucasian humanoid residents of **Omega IV**	"The Omega Glory" (TOS)
Yattho	Beta Quadrant civilization	"Before and After" (VGR)
Yridian yak	Grazing animal known for its large size	"Accession" (DS9)
Yridians	Humanoid civilization; known as interstellar dealers of information	"Birthright, Parts I & II" (TNG), "The Chase" (TNG)
Zakdorn	Humanoid people reputed to be the greatest strategic minds in the galaxy	"Peak Performance" (TNG), "Unification, Parts I & II" (TNG)
Zaldans	Humanoids characterized by webbed hands and a fierce dislike of courtesy	"Coming of Age" (TNG)
Zalkonians	Humanoid species undergoing a great transformation into noncorporeal beings	"Transfigurations" (TNG)
Zan Periculi	Species of flower native to Lappa IV, a Ferengi world	"Ménage à Troi" (TNG)
Zetarians	Life energy comprised of the thoughts and wills of the last living beings from the planet **Zetar**	"The Lights of Zetar" (TOS)
Zibalians	Humanoid civilization noted for facial tattooing	"The Most Toys" (TNG)
Zylo eggs	Life-form that **Data** chose as a subject for his first attempt at painting	"11001001" (TNG)

Efforts to erase his short-term memory were unsuccessful, and Liko returned to the surface with a complete memory of his visit to the *Enterprise*-D and a mistaken idea that Captain Picard was the Mintakan "**Overseer**" or god. Liko related his experiences to the other Mintakans, furthering the cultural contamination and complicating the rescue of the Federation scientist, **Dr. Palmer**. Liko held the irrational hope that "The Picard" would bring Liko's wife, who had died in a flood the previous year, back to life. Liko shot Captain Picard with an arrow, wounding Picard and convincing himself of Picard's mortality. ("Who Watches the Watchers?" [TNG]).

Lillias. (Lisa Kaminar). Foundry worker and colonist on a **Nezu** colony world in the Delta Quadrant. Lillias was a survivor of asteroid impacts on the planet. She escaped the surface by going to an orbital station aboard a mag-lev carriage. ("Rise" [VGR]).

Lima Sierra system. A star system whose planetary orbits seem anomalous in terms of conventional celestial mechanics. The *Enterprise*-D was there prior to being assigned to transport mediator **Riva** from the Ramatis star system in 2365, and Captain Picard spent time puzzling over the Lima Sierra planetary orbits afterward. ("Loud as a Whisper" [TNG]).

Lin, Ensign Peter. (Brian Tochi). An *Enterprise*-D crew member who relieved **Ensign Rager** at conn when she was sent to sickbay when the ship was trapped in a **Tyken's Rift** in 2367. ("Night Terrors" [TNG]). *Brian Tochi also played **Ray Tsingtao**, one of the children victimized by the evil **Gorgan** in "And the Children Shall Lead" (TOS).*

Lincoln, Abraham. (Lee Bergere). Sixteenth president of Earth's United States of America (1809-1865), considered by many Earth historians to have been the greatest American leader. Lincoln was a hero to *Enterprise* Captain **James T. Kirk**, who was fascinated in 2269 when the **Excalbians** sent a replica of Lincoln to visit Kirk on the *Enterprise*. The re-created Lincoln was part of an Excalbian experiment designed to study the human concept of "good" and "evil." ("The Savage Curtain" [TOS]).

Lincoln, Roberta. (Teri Garr). Human inhabitant of planet **Earth** in 1968 who unknowingly became employed by extraterrestrial agents working covertly to help Earth survive its critical Nuclear Age. Lincoln worked with Agents 347 and 201 at 811 East 68th Street, Apartment 12B, in New York City on Earth. Later, when she learned of the extraterrestrial nature of her employers, she continued to work for **Gary Seven** at the same address, although she found **Isis** somewhat disconcerting. ("Assignment: Earth" [TOS]).

Lindstrom. Space Command representative who served on James Kirk's court-martial board in 2267 when Kirk was accused of the murder of **Ben Finney**. ("Court Martial" [TOS]).

Lindstrom. (Christopher Held). *Enterprise* sociologist and member of the landing party to planet **Beta III** in 2267. Lindstrom studied the planet's society, helping to unravel the mystery of the culture's unusual behavior. He later stayed behind on the planet to help the population establish an independent society after the deactivation of the planetary computer, **Landru**, which had controlled them for millennia. ("Return of the Archons" [TOS]).

"Linear Models of Viral Propagation." A well-known scientific paper authored by **Dr. Katherine Pulaski** some time prior to her service aboard the *Enterprise*-D. ("Unnatural Selection" [TNG]).

linear memory crystal. Optically refractive material used in **isolinear optical chips**, a key part of optical data processing devices. The sentient **nanites** accidentally developed by Wesley Crusher in 2366 consumed linear memory crystal as nourishment, enabling their reproduction. ("Evolution" [TNG]).

lingta. Game animal indigenous to the Klingon homeworld. It was traditional among the people of the Mekro'vak region for the man to bring a leg of *lingta* to the first courtship dinner. ("Looking for *par'Mach* in All the Wrong Places" [DS9]). Jake Sisko prepared a *lingta* roast for his father and himself in 2373. ("Rapture" [DS9]).

linguacode. Data communications format designed to be understandable by nearly any technologically sophisticated intelligence. Unlike normal encryption, which serves to conceal information, linguacode was designed to make a message more accessible to a wide range of life-forms. Linguacode is sometimes used in first-contact situations such as those with **V'Ger** or **Tin Man**, to transmit initial greetings and friendship messages. (*Star Trek: The Motion Picture*).

link. SEE: **Great Link.**

Linke, Dr. (Jason Wingreen). Scientist stationed on planet **Minara II** in 2268 who was killed by the **Vians** while studying the impending nova of the **Minaran star system**. ("The Empath" [TOS]).

liquid data chains. Fluidic information storage medium. During the **plasma disruption** on stardate 47182.1, Quark helped **Yeto** to arrive illegally at Deep Space 9 to purchase liquid data chains, although Yeto's real purpose was to assist in stealing Jadzia Dax's **symbiont**. ("Invasive Procedures" [DS9])

Liquidator. Agent of the **Ferengi Commerce Authority** tasked with enforcing **Ferengi** trade laws. **Brunt** was the Liquidator assigned to the case of Quark's mother, **Ishka**, who was charged in 2371 with the serious crime of earning profit. ("Family Business" [DS9]).

Liria. (Robert Pine). Akritirian ambassador. Liria was a disagreeable bureaucrat who saw no problem with the Akritirian practice of keeping prisoners incarcerated even after new evidence came to light that proved their innocence. ("The Chute" [VGR]).

lirpa. Ancient Vulcan weapon with a razor-sharp curved blade at one end and a heavy bludgeon on the other. Kirk and Spock used the *lirpa* when they fought for possession of **T'Pring** during Spock's ***Pon farr*** ritual on planet **Vulcan** in 2267. ("Amok Time" [TOS]).

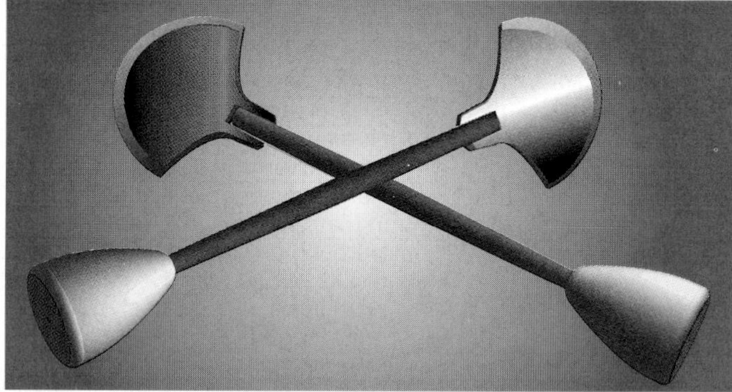

Lissepia. Planet; homeworld of the **Lissepians.** In 2366, Gul Dukat sent his Bajoran mistress, **Tora Naprem**, away with their daughter, **Tora Ziyal**, to live on Lissepia. ("Indiscretion" [DS9]).

Lissepian captain. (Nicholas Worth). Commander of a cargo vessel. The Lissepian captain traded Nog's ***yamok* sauce** for a hundred gross of **self-sealing stem bolts** at Deep Space 9 on stardate 46844. ("Progress" [DS9]).

Lissepian supply ship. Spacecraft. A **Founder Leader** used a **Maquis** interceptor to lure Kira and Odo to a seismically unstable moon by attacking a Lissepian supply ship on stardate 48521. ("Heart of Stone" [DS9]).

Lissepian transport. SEE: ***Martuk.***

Lissepians. Spacefaring civilization. In 2370, Lissepian traders were suspected but not proven to be assisting the **Cardassians** in smuggling weapons into the **Demilitarized Zone**. ("The Maquis, Parts I and II" [DS9]). SEE: ***Martuk*, Xepolite**. In 2372, a Lissepian sold Quark a holographic simulator program that would enable him to use holographic waiters in his bar during his employees' strike. ("Bar Association" [DS9]).

lita. Unit of monetary exchange on **Bajor**. ("Necessary Evil" [DS9]).

lithium cracking station. Mineral-processing facility used to produce **lithium crystals**, a critical element of early warp-drive technology. One such facility was the automated station on planet **Delta Vega**, visited by the *Enterprise* in 2265. ("Where No Man Has Gone Before" [TOS]).

lithium crystals. The lightest metal on the periodic table of elements, with an atomic number of 3 and an atomic weight of 6.941. Lithium in a form resembling crystalline quartz was a critical component of warp-drive systems in early starships. Lithium suitable for such use was an extremely rare and valuable commodity, requiring an energy-intensive "cracking" process. ("Where No Man Has Gone Before" [TOS]). Starships were rarely able to carry many spare crystals, meaning that any damage or burnout to a ship's crystals was a serious problem. ("Mudd's Women" [TOS]). *Lithium crystals were used in the* Enterprise*'s engines during the first few episodes of the Original Series. At the suggestion of* Star Trek *scientific advisor Harvey Lynn, lithium was later changed to* ***dilithium*** *because lithium is a real element with known properties, while the imaginary dilithium could be endowed by* Star Trek*'s writers with extraordinary qualities not yet known to science, making warp drive possible in the* Star Trek *universe.*

Lito. (Mark Humphrey). Inhabitant of planet **Meridian.** Lito asked **Commander Benjamin Sisko** to join him in a game of **vajhaq**. ("Meridian" [DS9]). *Lito was named only in the script.*

"Little Green Men." *Deep Space Nine* episode #80. Teleplay by Ira Steven Behr & Robert Hewitt Wolfe. Story by Toni Marberry & Jack Treviño. Directed by James Conway. No stardate given. *First aired in 1995. When Quark, Rom, and Nog take a trip to Earth, their ship proves to be have been sabotaged, forcing them to crash-land in Roswell, New Mexico in 1947—where they are presumed to be aliens from Mars.* GUEST CAST: Megan Gallagher as **Garland**; Charles Napier as **Denning**; Max Grodénchik as **Rom**; Aron Eisenberg as **Nog**; Conor O'Farrell as **Carlson**; James G. MacDonald as **Wainwright**. SEE: **arbiter; atomic bomb; Bell, Gabriel; Blessed Exchequer; Carlson, Jeff; Celestial Auction; Denning, General Rex; Divine Treasury; Earth guidebook; Earth; Ferengi; Ferengi death rituals; Ferengi Rules of Acquisition; Gaila; Garland, Faith; Hangar 18; holodeck and holosuite programs; kemacite; *neep-gren*; Nog; Orion; *Quark's Treasure*; Quark; Roswell; sodium pentothal; tobacco; tooth sharpener; Truman, Harry S; universal translator; Vault of Eternal Destitution; Wainwright, Captain.**

Little John. (Jonathan Frakes). In Earth mythology, the trusted lieutenant of **Robin Hood** in ancient England. **Q** cast Commander Riker as Little John in an elaborate fantasy crafted to teach Captain Picard a lesson. ("QPid" [TNG]).

Little Mermaid, The. Fable written by Earth author Hans Christian Andersen (1805-1875). It was the tale of a mermaid who, because of her love for a man, traded her life under the sea for a pair of legs with which to walk on land. ("Melora" [DS9]).

Little One. A diminutive used by **Lwaxana Troi** when addressing her daughter, Deanna. The younger Troi found it irritating. ("Ménage à Troi" [TNG]).

Liva. (Stephanie Erb). Aide to **Ambassador Ves Alkar** when he helped negotiate peace on planet **Rekag-Seronia** in 2369. She was an attractive woman, and Alkar attempted to use her as a "receptacle" for his negative emotions after he thought that Deanna Troi had died. ("Man of the People" [TNG]).

Livara. Romulan intelligence operative. Livara posed as a Talavian freighter captain and smuggler. Livara began operating in the Bajoran sector in 2367. He visited station Terok Nor and tried to interest Quark in some *maraji* crystals. ("Things Past" [DS9]).

Livingston, U.S.S. Federation starship *Excelsior* class, Starfleet registry number NCC-34099. **Benjamin Sisko** and **Curzon Dax** once served together aboard the *Livingston*. ("Invasive Procedures" [DS9]). *The* Livingston *may have been named for American statesman Robert R. Livingston, a signer of the Declaration of Independence, but most likely was an homage to* Star Trek *producer-director David Livingston.*

Livingston. *Unofficial name given by the* Star Trek *production crew to the Australian lionfish that lived in the salt water aquarium in Picard's* ***ready room****. Livingston was named for* Star Trek *producer-director David Livingston. "I can see the resemblance," says Bob Justman.*

LMH. SEE: **Longterm Medical Hologram.**

LN_2 exhaust conduits. Vents used to dump excess quantities of liquid nitrogen from a space vehicle. In 2371, B'Elanna Torres feigned serious damage to *Voyager* by blowing out *Voyager*'s dorsal phaser emitters and venting the LN_2 exhaust conduits, fooling two Numiri patrol ships. ("Ex Post Facto" [VGR]).

lobes. SEE: **Ferengi lobes**.

***Lobi* crystal.** Semiprecious stone used as ornaments and in inexpensive jewelry. A dozen assorted shapes of *Lobi* crystals could be bought in a shop at the Volnar Colony for one Cardassian **lek**. ("Caretaker" [VGR]).

Locarno, Cadet First Class Nicholas. (Robert Duncan McNeill). Leader of Starfleet Academy's **Nova Squadron** in 2368 when the team attempted the hazardous **Kolvoord Starburst** for that year's commencement ceremonies. Nova Squadron member **Joshua Albert** was killed in an accident during the maneuver. The charismatic Locarno persuaded his team to conceal

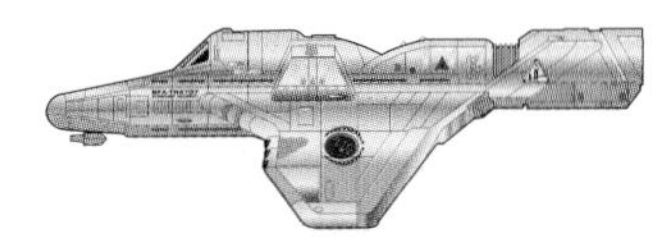

Starfleet Academy Trainer piloted by Locarno at the time of the Kolvoord Starburst accident

the fact that they had been attempting a maneuver that had been banned by the academy for nearly a century. When the truth was eventually revealed at an academy investigation, Locarno accepted responsibility for Albert's death, and was expelled. ("The First Duty" [TNG]). *Robert Duncan McNeill later played Tom Paris on* Star Trek: Voyager.

locator bomb. Sophisticated antipersonnel weapon capable of seeking out a specific person and detonating a **sorium argine** explosive to kill the target. A locator bomb used sensors designed to lock on to the target's pheromones. In 2369, Quark's brother **Rom** and Zek's son, **Krax**, used a locator bomb in an attempt to assassinate Quark during his brief tenure as **grand nagus**. ("The Nagus" [DS9]).

Lockheed Electra. Early suborbital aircraft in use on Earth during the 1930s. Noted aviator **Amelia Earhart** piloted a Lockheed Electra in her 1937 attempt to fly around the planet with navigator **Fred Noonan**. The flight was interrupted when both aircraft and crew were abducted and transported to the **Briori** homeworld in the Delta Quadrant. ("The 37's" [VGR]).

Locklin, Ensign. Member of the *Enterprise*-D's transporter crew. In 2367, she was the last person to use a transporter prior to the *Enterprise*-D's encounter with a wormhole in the **Ngame Nebula.** ("Clues" [TNG]).

Locutus of Borg. (Patrick Stewart). **Borg** leader created by the assimilation of **Jean-Luc Picard** into the Borg consciousness in 2366. Although the concept of a Borg leader was, at the time, almost a contradiction in terms, Locutus was intended to provide a voice for the Borg, as part of a Borg plan to assimilate the Federation. With Picard's mind in the Borg collective consciousness, the powerful adversary had access to all of Picard's knowledge and experience, making him partially responsible for the massive Federation defeat at the battle of **Wolf 359**. But the access proved to be two-way. The capture of Locutus by the *Enterprise*-D personnel gave them access to the Borg collective consciousness, and they were able to defeat the Borg by exploiting this access. ("The Best of Both Worlds, Parts I and II" [TNG]). Locutus was to have been a voluntary counterpart of the **Borg queen**, with a mind of his own, not just another Borg drone. She wanted Picard to give himself freely to the Borg, but he resisted and was forced into the collective. *(Star Trek: First Contact). Locutus was also featured in flashback scenes in "Emissary" (DS9).*

log. An official record of mission progress kept by the commanding officer of a starship or starbase.

Logan, Chief Engineer. (Vyto Ruginis). Chief engineer of the *Starship Enterprise*-D in late 2364. Logan expressed concern at Geordi La Forge's relative inexperience when La Forge was temporarily placed in command of the ship at planet **Minos**. ("The Arsenal of Freedom" [TNG]). *Ironically, Logan was replaced as chief engineer by La Forge the following year in "The Child" (TNG).*

logic. School of rigorously rational thought that forms the cornerstone of the **Vulcan** culture. The Vulcans nearly destroyed themselves in bitter wars until they rejected emotionalism in favor of logic.

logo. Early 21st-century American slang term referring to personal identification. ("Past Tense, Part I" [DS9]).

Lojal. (Michael Ensign). **Vulcan** ambassador. Lojal visited **Deep Space 9** in 2369 on a fact-finding mission to the **Bajoran wormhole**. ("The Forsaken" [DS9]). *Michael Ensign also played Krola in "First Contact" (TNG).*

Lokai. (Lou Antonio). Accused criminal from the planet **Cheron** who fled his planet's authorities across interstellar space for 50,000 years. Lokai claimed he was the victim of racial persecution because his skin coloration was different from those from Cheron who called themselves the "master race." Lokai was finally captured by Commissioner **Bele** in 2268. Upon returning to their homeworld, they found that racial hatred had destroyed their society, leaving no survivors. ("Let That Be Your Last Battlefield" [TOS]).

***lokar* beans.** Ferengi food served at **Quark's bar** on station Deep Space 9. ("Move Along Home," "Progress", "Rules of Acquisition" [DS9]). *Apparently the Ferengi equivalent of pretzels.*

London Kings. Professional **baseball** team that played on Earth during the 21st century. ("The Big Goodbye" [TNG]). In 2015 a gifted ballplayer by the name of **Buck Bokai** played his rookie year with the Kings. ("Past Tense, Part II" [DS9]). While playing shortshop, Bokai broke **Joe DiMaggio**'s record for hits in consecutive games in 2026. ("The Big Goodbye" [TNG]). The London Kings won the World Series in 2042, but by that time, public interest in the sport had fallen to the point where there were only 300 spectators at the last game. ("If Wishes Were Horses" [DS9]).

London, Jack. (Michael Aron). Early 20th-century American writer (1876-1916). Prior to becoming a popular writer, London worked as a bellboy at the 19th-century San Francisco hotel where Commander Data took up lodging. ("Time's Arrow, Parts I and II" [TNG]). *The real Jack London was born in San Francisco and spent part of his youth as an oyster pirate before leaving for the Klondike in 1897. While we have no evidence to support this, it is possible that Jack London was working as a bellboy in 1893, where he may have met an unusual "albino" customer with an affinity for poker.*

"Lonely Among Us." *Next Generation* episode #8. Teleplay by D. C. Fontana. Story by Michael Halperin. Directed by Cliff Bole. Stardate 41249.3. *First aired in 1987. A mysterious cloud creature attempts to communicate with the* Enterprise-*D crew through the body of Captain Picard. Data first showed his interest in the Sherlock Holmes stories during this episode.* GUEST CAST: John Durbin as **Ssestar**; Colm Meaney as **O'Brien, Miles**; Kavi Raz as **Singh, Lieutenant Commander**. SEE: **Antica; Anticans; Badar N'D'D; Beta Renner cloud; Beta Renner system; Channing, Dr.; *Enterprise*-D, *U.S.S.*; Holmes, Sherlock; Parliament; Selay; Ssestar; Singh, Lieutenant Commander.**

Long Dark Tunnel, The. Pulp novel featuring the adventures of San Francisco gumshoe detective **Dixon Hill**. Published in 1936 on Earth. ("The Big Goodbye" [TNG]).

Longterm Medical Hologram. (Alexander Siddig). Holographic program intended to provide medical services in situations where life support or living space was at a premium such as at a research or deep space outpost. Unlike the **Emergency Medical Hologram**, the LMH was designed to incorporate sophisticated social skills, enabling it to interact with patients over an extended period. Hologram designer **Dr. Lewis Zimmerman** selected **Deep Space 9** physician **Dr. Julian Bashir** as the template for the LMH. Unfortunately, the plan was derailed when it was revealed that Bashir had undergone illegal genetic engineering as a child. The LMH was developed at Starfleet's **Jupiter Station**. ("Doctor Bashir, I Presume?" [DS9]).

Lonka Pulsar. A rotating neutron star of approximately 4.356 solar masses, located in the Lonka Cluster. An alien replica of Picard, placed on the *Enterprise*-D in 2366 by unknown aliens to study the nature of authority, ordered the ship to approach the Lonka Pulsar too closely for safety, leading Riker to suspect the substitution. ("Allegiance" [TNG]).

Lonzo. Professional ***tongo*** player. Lonzo visited station Deep Space 9 in 2371. He suffered a substantial loss to station Security Chief Odo, who was at the time joined with Curzon Dax. ("Facets" [DS9]).

"Looking for *par'Mach* in All the Wrong Places." *Deep Space Nine* episode #101. Written by Ronald D. Moore. Directed by Andrew J. Robinson. No stardate given. *First aired in 1996. Quark's Klingon ex-wife shows up on DS9. Worf finds himself falling in love with her; but is surprised to learn that Dax has eyes for him. This was the first episode directed by actor Andrew Robinson.* GUEST CAST: Rosalind Chao as **O'Brien, Keiko**; Mary Kay Adams as **Grilka**; Joseph Ruskin as **Tumek**; Phil Morris as **Thopok**. SEE: **Bajorans; Barak-Kadan; *Basai* Master; Dax, Jadzia; Grilka; Holana River; holodeck and holosuite programs; "Kahless and Lukara"; Kahless the Unforgettable; Kira Nerys; Klingon opera; *lingta*; Lukara; *makora* herbs; Maporian ale; *Mekro'vak*; *mev yap*; *Mok*; Morn; *MoVas ah-kee rustak*; Musilla Province; O'Brien, Miles; *par'Mach*; *pazafer*; Qam-Chee; Quark; separ; *takeo* herbs; Thopok; Tumek; Worf.**

Lopez, Ensign. *Enterprise*-D security division crew member. Worf snapped at him because he felt Lopez had improperly prepared a duty roster, but Worf was just upset about having learned the possibility that his father might have been captured by Romulans at Khitomer. ("Birthright, Part I" [TNG]).

Loquel. (Paul Eiding). **Iyaaran** ambassador. Loquel was assigned to investigate the emotion of pleasure during his people's first diplomatic contact with the Federation in 2370. His investigation involved sampling an enormous number of culinary delicacies with Counselor **Deanna Troi**. ("Liaisons" [TNG]).

Loran, Jal. (Jeff Cadiente). Leader of the **Kazon-Hobii** sect in 2372. ("Maneuvers" [VGR]). Loran was nearly killed in the disastrous peace conference organized by **Trabe** and Federation forces in late 2372. ("Alliances" [VGR]).

Lord High Sheriff of Nottingham. (John de Lancie). In Earth mythology, the nemesis of **Robin Hood** in ancient England. **Q** cast himself as the Sheriff of Nottingham in 2367 during an elaborate fantasy he crafted to teach Picard about the nature of love. ("QPid" [TNG]).

Lore. (Brent Spiner). A highly sophisticated humanoid **android** built by noted scientists Dr. **Noonien Soong** and **Juliana Soong** at their laboratory on planet **Omicron Theta**. Lore was almost identical in physical design to the android **Data** (also built by the Soongs), but had more human emotional responses built into his programming. Lore was activated around 2335 or 2336, but was shut down by Soong shortly afterward because the colonists at Omicron Theta viewed Lore as a threat. Lore was responsible for luring the malevolent **Crystalline Entity** to Omicron Theta, resulting in the death of all the colonists there. Lore remained dormant until 2364 when his components were discovered by an away team from the *Enterprise*-D. Upon his reactivation, Lore exhibited manipulative and sadistic behavior and was eventually beamed into space when he attempted to gain control of the ship. ("Datalore" [TNG]). Lore drifted in space for nearly two years before he was rescued by a passing **Pakled** ship. In 2367, Lore responded to a call sent by Dr. Noonien Soong, intended to summon Data to Soong's new secret laboratory. Soong had intended to install a new chip in Data's brain to give the android the ability to experience human emotions. Arriving at Soong's laboratory at the same time as Data, Lore stole the new chip by masquerading as Data. Soong died shortly thereafter, and Lore escaped before *Enterprise*-D personnel could apprehend him. ("Brothers" [TNG]). Lore later encountered a **Borg** group wandering aimlessly in space. The Borg were experiencing individuality as a result of **Hugh**'s reintroduction into the collective, and were unable to cope with the experience. Lore seized on the situation and appointed himself as leader of the Borg. He promised to re-create them in his own image, that of a completely artificial life-form. The Borg willingly followed Lore, attacking his enemies, capturing his brother, **Data**, and also sacrificing themselves to his medical experiments. A small group of Borg, led by Hugh, suspected that Lore was incapable of fulfilling his promise, and were angered at the suffering Lore was inflicting on his experimental subjects. This dissident group of Borg, aided by *Enterprise*-D personnel, overthrew Lore by force. Shortly thereafter, Lore was deactivated by his brother, Data. The **emotion chip** designed by Soong was removed from Lore's body before it was dismantled. ("Descent, Parts I and II" [TNG]). *Lore first appeared in "Datalore" (TNG).*

Loren III. Planet located near the **Kurlan** system. Site where **Professor Richard Galen** obtained genetic samples as part of his research just prior to his death in 2369. ("The Chase" [TNG]). SEE: **humanoid life**.

Lorenze Cluster. A stellar formation. Wesley Crusher recognized the Lorenze Cluster when he gazed from Ten-Forward while discussing his future with Guinan. ("The Child" [TNG]). The Lorenze Cluster was also the location where the *Starship* ***Drake*** disappeared some time prior to 2364. The planet **Minos** is located there. ("The Arsenal of Freedom" [TNG]).

Lorgh. A friend of **Mogh**, Lorgh cared for Mogh's son, the infant **Kurn**, when Mogh and his family went to **Khitomer** in 2346. After Mogh was killed in the Romulan attack at Khitomer, Lorgh raised Kurn as his own son, and did not tell him of his true parentage until he reached the **Age of Ascension**. ("Sins of the Father" [TNG]).

Lorin, Security Minister. (Lenore Kasdorf). Member of the Prytt government of planet **Kesprytt III** in 2370. Lorin engineered the abduction of *Enterprise*-D Captain Jean-Luc Picard and Dr. Beverly Crusher, as well as the implantation of **psi-wave devices**, which she hoped would enable the Prytt Security Ministry to read Picard's and Crusher's thoughts. Lorin incorrectly believed the personnel of the *Enterprise*-D were attempting to establish a military alliance with the **Kes**. ("Attached" [TNG]).

Lorit Akrem. Former member of the **Shakaar resistance cell** and longtime friend of **Kira Nerys**. Lorit Akrem was a prisoner on the Cardassian ship ***Ravinok*** when it was attacked by the Breen and forced to land on **Dozaria** in 2366. Lorit survived the crash and was forced to labor in the Breen dilithium mines on Dozaria, until he died in a mine collapse in 2370. ("Indiscretion" [DS9]).

Lornak. One of several warring clans on planet **Acamar III.** The Lornaks had been deadly enemies of the **Tralesta** clan for two centuries, and finally staged a bloody massacre in 2286, killing all but five of the Tralestas. The Lornaks were in turn systematically murdered by one of the last five surviving Tralestas, a woman named **Yuta**. ("The Vengeance Factor" [TNG]).

Lorrum. (Michael Spound). Member of the **Kazon-Nistrim** sect. In 2372, Lorrum was assigned by Maje **Culluh** to be the controller of **Michael Jonas**, their spy aboard the *Voyager*. ("Dreadnought" [VGR]). Lorrum instructed Jonas to sabotage the ship's warp system. ("Lifesigns" [VGR]). *Lorrum's name was not spoken in dialog.*

Lorvan crackers. Snack food. Lorvan crackers were available at Quark's bar on **Deep Space 9.** ("Defiant" [DS9]).

Los Angeles. City on the North American continent of Earth. The **Chronowerx** corporation, headed by **Henry Starling**, was based in Los Angeles in 1996. ("Future's End, Parts I and II" [VGR]). *We are at a loss to explain why Los Angeles in 1996 seems to have escaped the ravages of the Eugenics Wars, but on the other hand, we're not complaining, either.*

Losira. (Lee Meriwether). Last survivor of the **Kalandan outpost** whose population was killed 10,000 years ago due to a deadly microorganism. After Losira's death, the outpost's computer system used Losira's image to protect the outpost against invaders. The replica was able to kill by touching a victim, matching his chromosome pattern, then killing the person by **cellular disruption**. ("That Which Survives" [TOS]).

Loskene, Commander. (Voice of Barbara Babcock). **Tholian** commander who accused the *Enterprise* of trespassing in a territorial annex of the **Tholian Assembly** in 2268. Loskene attempted to entangle the *Enterprise* in an energy web. ("The Tholian Web" [TOS]). SEE: **Mea 3**.

"Loss, The." *Next Generation* episode #84. Teleplay by Hilary J. Bader and Alan J. Alder & Vanessa Greene. Story by Hilary J. Bader. Directed by Chip Chalmers. Stardate 44356.9. *First aired in 1990. Deanna Troi considers resigning her Starfleet commission when she loses her empathic powers.* GUEST CAST: Kim Braden as **Brooks**, **Ensign Janet**; Mary Kohnert as **Allenby**, **Ensign Tess**; Whoopi Goldberg as **Guinan**. SEE: **Allenby, Ensign Tess; Bracas V; Breen; Brooks, Ensign Janet; Brooks, Marc; cosmic string fragment; Ferengi; inner nuncial series; Kabul River; kilodynes; T'lli Beta; Troi, Deanna; two-dimensional creatures.**

Lote, Orn. (John P. Connolly). Engineering specialist on planet **Tagra IV**. Lote contacted the *Enterprise*-D in 2369. ("True-Q" [TNG]).

lothra. Hydrogen-breathing, sentient life-form. ("Melora" [DS9]).

"Loud as a Whisper." *Next Generation* episode #32. Written by Jacqueline Zambrano. Directed by Larry Shaw. Stardate 42477.2. *First aired in 1988. A hearing-impaired mediator struggles to find a way to turn his disadvantage into an advantage while searching for peace on planet Solais V.* GUEST CAST: Diana Muldaur as **Pulaski**, **Dr. Katherine**; Marnie Mosiman as Woman; Thomas Oglesby as Scholar/Artist; Leo Damian as Warrior/Adonis; Howie Seago as **Riva**; Colm Meaney as **O'Brien, Miles**; Richard Lavin as Warrior #1; Chip Heller as Warrior #2; John Garrett as Lieutenant. SEE: **chorus; Fendaus V; Klingonese; Leyrons; Lima Sierra system; M-9; Malkus IX; Ramatis III; Ramatis star system; Riva; Scholar/Artist; sign language; Solais V; Solari; VISOR; Warrior/Adonis; Woman; Zambrano, Battle of**.

Louis. (Dennis Creaghan). Supervisor on Earth's **Atlantis Project**. An old friend of **Jean-Luc Picard**'s, Louis and Jean-Luc spent a good deal of their youth together in **Labarre, France**. Louis undertook a career in hydroponics, but by 2367, he was a supervisor on the Atlantis Project. Picard found this amusing because his friend had been a horrible swimmer in their youth, but now worked on the ocean floor. ("Family" [TNG]). *Louis was not given a last name in the episode.*

Louvois, Captain Phillipa. (Amanda McBroom). Starfleet legal officer. Louvois prosecuted **Jean-Luc Picard** in the court-martial proceedings following the loss of the ***U.S.S. Stargazer*** in 2355. Although Picard and Louvois had been romantically involved prior to that time, the *Stargazer* trial ended that relationship. Louvois left Starfleet thereafter. The two did not see each other again until 2365, when Louvois, having returned to Starfleet as head of the Sector 23 **Judge Advocate General**'s office, presided over the precedent-setting case in which she ruled that the android **Data** was entitled to full constitutional rights and was not the property of Starfleet. ("The Measure of a Man" [TNG]).

Loval. Planet in Cardassian space. Loval was the location of a civilian outpost and a secret weapons-research installation. ("Return to Grace" [DS9]).

love poetry, Klingon. Romantic verse in the Klingon language. Worf recommended reading love poetry as a means of luring a potential mate, when **Wesley Crusher** was attracted to **Salia** of planet **Daled IV**. Worf noted that in response, a Klingon woman might be expected to roar, throw heavy objects, and claw at her mate. He expressed disdain for human males, describing their courtship rituals as "begging." ("The Dauphin" [TNG]). Worf once claimed that the art of love poetry reached its fullest flower among the Klingons. ("Up the Long Ladder" [TNG]).

Lovok, Colonel. (Leland Orser). **Founder** who took the form of a Romulan officer to infiltrate the **Tal Shiar** in 2371. Lovok was one of several **Dominion** agents who infiltrated the Alpha Quadrant powers as a prelude to a Dominion offensive. Lovok was commander of the lead **Romulan warbird** in a combined fleet of **Tal Shiar** and **Obsidian Order** ships against the **Founders' homeworld**. Lovok's presence insured that the attack did not succeed, and that all 20 Romulan and Cardassian ships were destroyed. ("The Die is Cast" [DS9]).

Low Note, The. A jazz club from Earth's New Orleans city on Bourbon Street, circa 1958. Riker enjoyed a simulation of The Low Note on the *Enterprise*-D holodeck shortly after that system had been enhanced by the **Bynars** at **Starbase 74**. Being a jazz fan, Riker enjoyed playing a trombone with the program's jazz band, as well as the company of the lovely **Minuet**, a young lady who evidently left quite an impression on him. ("11001001" [TNG]).

low-mileage pit woofie. Slang term used by 20th-century entertainer **Sonny Clemonds**. Neither Riker nor Data understood the reference. ("The Neutral Zone" [TNG]).

"Lower Decks." *Next Generation* episode #167. Teleplay by René Echevarria. Story by Ronald Wilkerson & Jean Louise Matthias. Directed by Gabrielle Beaumont. Stardate 47566.2. *First aired in 1994. Four junior officers worry about promotions, and one goes on a covert mission into Cardassian space.* GUEST CAST: Dan Gauthier as **Lavelle**, **Sam**; Shannon Fill as **Sito Jaxa**; Alexander Enberg as **Taurik**, **Ensign**; Bruce Beatty as **Ben**; Patti Yasutake as **Ogawa**, **Nurse Alyssa**; Don Reilly as **Dal**, **Joret**. SEE: **Argaya system; Ben; *Clement, U.S.S.*; *Curie, Shuttlecraft*; Dal, Joret; *gik'tal* challenge; Lavelle, Sam; Ogawa, Alyssa; Powell, Andrew; Sito Jaxa; Taurik, Ensign; Trakian Ale.**

Lower Pylon 1. On station Deep Space 9, the lower half of docking pylon 1. Lower Pylon 1 was evacuated on stardate 46853 due to the danger of a **subspace rupture**. ("If Wishes Were Horses" [DS9]).

luau. SEE: **Polynesian resort.**

Lucasian Chair. Title given to a Professorship of Mathematics at **Cambridge University**. The Chair has been held by such notable theorists as **Isaac Newton**, Paul Dirac, and **Stephen Hawking**. (In the **anti-time future** devised by the **Q Continuum**, Data held this Chair, and lived in the traditional residence first occupied by Sir Isaac Newton.) ("All Good Things..." [TNG]). *One of the many books to decorate Data's library was a copy of Stephen Hawking's book,* A Brief History of Time.

Lucier, Bruce. Medical student at Starfleet Medical School in 2367. He held a New Year's Eve party in 2368 that was attended by **Julian Bashir**, his friend **Erib**, and **Elizabeth Lense**. ("Explorers" [DS9]).

lucovexitrin. A highly toxic substance capable of causing **nucleosynthesis** in silicon. Lucovexitrin is not normally detectable by a starship's internal **sensor** scans. ("Hollow Pursuits" [TNG]).

Lucsly. (James W. Jansen). Agent of the Federation **Department of Temporal Investigations**. In 2373, agents Dulmer and Lucsly traveled to Deep Space 9 to investigate the *U.S.S. Defiant*'s accidental trip back in time 105 years to stardate 4523. ("Trials and Tribble-ations" [DS9]). *James W. Jansen previously portrayed Faren Kag in "The Storyteller" (DS9).*

Ludugial gold. Reputed to be the purest form of gold in the galaxy. Twenty thousand Ludugial gold coins were offered by Ferengi trade official **Par Lenor** to Kriosian **Ambassador Briam** in exchange for the **empathic metamorph** named **Kamala**. Briam declined. ("The Perfect Mate" [TNG]).

Lukara. Great Klingon lady and wife of **Kahless the Unforgettable**. One thousand years ago, five hundred warriors stormed the Great Hall at Qam-Chee. Only the Emperor Kahless and the Lady Lukara stood their ground. After the battle, Kahless and Lukara began what would be considered the greatest romance in Klingon history. ("Looking for *par'Mach* in All the Wrong Places" [DS9]).

Luma. (Sheila Leighton). One of the **Eymorg** women of planet **Sigma Draconis VI**. ("Spock's Brain" [TOS]).

Lumo. Native on **Miramanee's planet.** In 2268, when Lumo brought a young boy who had drowned to the tribe's medicine man, Kirk performed artificial respiration on the child, bringing him miraculously back to life. ("The Paradise Syndrome" [TOS]).

Lunar V base. Bajoran resistance camp on **Bajor**'s fifth moon. A few Bajoran **subimpulse raiders** were stored underground at the base, prior to its capture by Cardassian forces in 2360. ("The Siege" [DS9]).

Lunar V. A military prison facility set up by the **Angosian** government to house the biochemically altered veterans of the **Tarsian War**. ("The Hunted" [TNG]). SEE: **Danar, Roga**.

Lupaza. (Diane Salinger). Member of the **Shakaar resistance cell** during the **Cardassian** occupation of **Bajor**. Following the occupation, Lupaza settled on a farm in her home province of **Dahkur**. ("Shakaar" [DS9]). SEE: **Shakaar**. Lupaza was killed in 2373 by **Silaran Prin**, who sought revenge on members of the Shakaar cell. Lupaza and her colleagues had been responsible for a bombing in which Prin had been seriously injured. ("The Darkness and the Light" [DS9]).

Lurin, DaiMon. (Mike Gomez). Leader of the renegade **Ferengi** who took over the *Enterprise*-D in 2369. ("Rascals" [TNG]).

Lurry, Mr. (Whit Bissell). Manager of **Deep Space Station K-7** in 2267. ("The Trouble with Tribbles" [TOS]). SEE: **Darvin, Arne; Sherman's Planet**; **quadrotriticale**.

Lursa. (Barbara March). A member of the politically powerful **Duras** family; the elder of Duras's two sisters. Following the death of Duras in 2367, Lursa, and her sister, **B'Etor**, conspired with the Romulan operative **Sela** to overthrow the **Gowron** leadership of the **Klingon High Council**. Their attempt to place **Toral**, the illegitimate son of Duras, as council leader split the council and plunged the empire into a **Klingon civil war** until their complicity with the **Romulan Star Empire** was discovered. ("Redemption, Parts I and II" [TNG]). Lursa subsequently dropped out of sight for almost two years until she and her sister attempted to raise capital for their armies by selling **bilitrium** explosives to the ***Kohn-Ma***, a Bajoran terrorist organization, in 2369. ("Past Prologue" [DS9]). In 2370, she and her sister illegally mined a **magnesite ore** deposit on **Kalla III** which belonged to the **Pakleds**. They later tried to sell the ore to the **Yridians** in the **Ufandi system.** During this time, she became aware that she was pregnant with a male child. ("Firstborn" [TNG]). In 2371, Lursa and B'Etor assisted **Dr. Tolian Soran** in stealing **trilithium** from the Romulans for Soran's experiments so that, in return, they would receive trilithium weapons technology. Lursa hoped that trilithium weapons could be a powerful tool to reestablish Duras dominance over the Klingon Empire. When the ***Starship Enterprise*-D** stumbled upon their activities with Soran at the **Amargosa Observatory**, Lursa and B'Etor attacked the *Enterprise*-D. Lursa was killed when the *Enterprise*-D returned fire, destroying her class D-12 bird-of-prey spacecraft. *(Star Trek Generations).*

Lursor. Lake on the **Klingon Homeworld**. Klingon oral history held that this was the place where **Kahless the Unforgettable** finished the forging of the first ***bat'leth*** sword. ("Rightful Heir" [TNG]).

Lutan. (Jessie Lawrence Ferguson). Civil leader on planet **Ligon II** in 2364 when the **Ligonians** agreed to provide vitally needed vaccines to the *Enterprise*-D for transfer to planet **Styris IV**. During the negotiations for the transfer, Lutan attempted to engineer an incident to use *Enterprise*-D Lieutenant Yar to eliminate his wife, **Yareena**, thus clearing the way for him to control her lands and wealth. Lutan lost these claims when Yar defeated Yareena in ritual combat. Lutan's honor was preserved when Yareena later accepted Lutan as her Second One after **Hagon** became Yareena's **First One**. ("Code of Honor" [TNG]).

luvetric pulse. Energy form. A luvetric pulse was suggested as a possible way to track Commander **Data** when he was controlled by Lore in 2369. The pulse would have caused a resonance fluctuation in Data's power cells. However, in order to be effective, the pulse would have to be so strong as to risk destruction of Data's positronic net. ("Descent, Part I" [TNG]).

Luvsitt, Mona. (Marci Brickhouse). Character in Julian Bashir's **secret agent** holosuite program. Mona Luvsitt was a highly talented, well-educated valet to Julian Bashir's secret agent character. Mona spoke seven languages; had degrees in biology, chemistry, and physics; and could fly anything from jet planes to a helicopter. ("Our Man Bashir" [DS9]).

Lya Station Alpha. A Federation starbase. The *Enterprise*-D traveled to Lya Station Alpha with survivors from the attack on the **Solarion IV** colony in 2368. **Ensign Ro Laren** came aboard the *Enterprise*-D at this station, and Picard met there with **Admiral Kennelly** regarding suspected Bajoran terrorist activity. ("Ensign Ro" [TNG]).

Lycosa tarantula. Spider, similar to an Earth tarantula. **Miles O'Brien** kept a Lycosa tarantula as a pet that he named Christina. ("Realm of Fear" [TNG]).

lydroxide. Corrosive substance used as a coolant in the couplings of **orbital tether** carriages of **Nezu** design. Lydroxide was poisonous to humanoids. Sklar used lydroxide to murder Dr. Vatm in 2373. ("Rise" [VGR]).

lynars. Batlike creature indigenous to the caverns of planet **Celtris III**. *Lynars* were believed to be harmless. ("Chain of Command, Part I" [TNG]).

Lynch, Leland T. (Walker Boone). An assistant chief engineer on the *Starship Enterprise*-D in 2364. Lynch had been supervising routine servicing of the dilithium chamber when forced to quickly bring the warp drive back on line for a rescue mission to planet Vagra II. ("Skin of Evil" [TNG]).

Lyris. (Deborah May). Official of the Taresian government. She met members of the *Voyager* crew when they beamed down with **Harry Kim** in 2373. Lyris convinced Kim that he was a native of **Taresia** and that his embryo had been taken in stasis to Earth and implanted in his mother. This was an elaborate deception; the Taresian women wanted only to harvest genetic material from him to be used in their procreation process. ("Favorite Son" [VGR]). *Deborah May previously played Haneek in "Sanctuary" (DS9).*

Lyshan system. Federation system. The Lyshan system was the rendezvous point for Captain Picard's covert team, following their mission on planet **Celtris III** in 2369. Commander Riker was able to retrieve Dr. Crusher and Lieutenant Worf from the system, following their escape from Celtris. ("Chain of Command, Part II" [TNG]).

Lysia. The homeworld of the Lysian Alliance. In 2368, the crew of the *Enterprise*-D was led to believe that the crews of 14 Federation vessels were being held captive on Lysia, but it was a **Satarran** ploy to trick *Enterprise*-D personnel into attacking the Lysian Central Command. ("Conundrum" [TNG]). SEE: **Epsilon Silar system.**

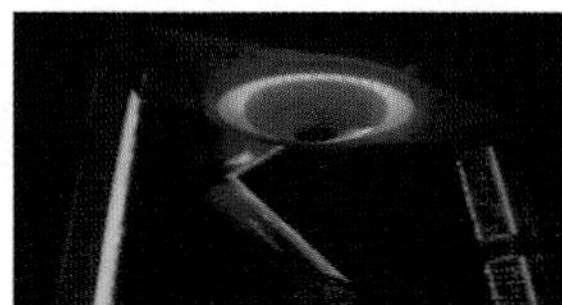

Lysian Central Command. A Lysian space station located deep within the **Epsilon Silar system**. Lysian Central Command was protected by a series of unmanned laser-equipped sentry pods. The command station itself was staffed by a crew of over 15,000, and was defended by four laser cannons. It also had the ability to fire a series of cobalt-fusion warheads. By Federation Starfleet standards, the Lysian Central Command, as well as the Lysian ships, possessed limited weaponry. ("Conundrum" [TNG]). *The model of the Lysian Central Command was a revamp of the* ***Edo god*** *from "Justice" (TNG).*

Lysian destroyer. A short-range attack vessel equipped with low-power disruptor-type weapons and minimal shielding. The vessel had a standard crew complement of 53. One of these vessels was destroyed by the *Enterprise*-D in 2368 while that ship's crew was being misled by a **Satarran** agent seeking to use the Federation ship against his Lysian enemies. ("Conundrum" [TNG]). SEE: **Epsilon Silar system; MacDuff, Commander Keiran.**

lysosomal enzyme. An organic catalyst found in certain lifeforms, such as Andorian amoebae, that use symbiogenesis as a means of reproduction. ("Tuvix" [VGR]).

M-Class planet. SEE: **planetary classification system**.

M'Benga, Dr. (Brooker Bradshaw). Physician aboard the original *Starship Enterprise*. M'Benga interned in a Vulcan ward during his medical training. He cared for Spock when the *Enterprise* first officer was critically wounded on **Tyree**'s planet in 2267. ("A Private Little War" [TOS]). M'Benga supervised the autopsies surrounding the mysterious deaths of *Enterprise* personnel near the **Kalandan outpost** in 2268. ("That Which Survives" [TOS]). *M'Benga made only two appearances on* Star Trek.

M'Char. Klingon bird-of-prey under the command of Commander Kaybok. The freighter *Xhosa* was stopped by the *M'Char* in 2372. Kaybok intended to board the *Xhosa* and search it for shapeshifters, but Captain Sisko, in command of the *Defiant,* intervened and convinced Kaybok to withdraw his vessel. ("The Way of the Warrior" [DS9]).

M'kemas III. Planet located in **Tzenkethi** territory. In 2371, a **Founder** took control of the ***U.S.S. Defiant*** and planned to attack M'kemas III in hopes of starting a war between the **Federation** and the Tzenkethi. ("The Adversary" [DS9]).

M'ret, Vice-Proconsul. High-ranking **Romulan** senator who defected to the Federation in 2369. M'ret, along with two aides, was placed into stasis and smuggled in a cargo container aboard the Romulan warbird ***Khazara*** for transfer to a Corvallen freighter in the **Kaleb sector**. Although this plan was not entirely successful, M'ret and his aides were later transported to the *Enterprise*-D. M'ret's escape had been engineered by Ambassador **Spock**, working with the dissident underground on Romulus. Spock hoped that M'ret's defection would help establish an escape route for thousands of other Romulan dissidents who lived in fear for their lives. ("Face of the Enemy" [TNG]). SEE: **N'Vek, Subcommander**.

M'Tell. Archaeologist noted for the discovery of Ya'Seem, ranked among the greatest findings in her field. ("The Chase" [TNG]).

M-1 through M-4. Experimental **multitronic** computers developed by **Dr. Richard Daystrom**, unsuccessful predecessors to the **M-5** computer. ("The Ultimate Computer" [TOS]).

M-113 creature. (Sharon Gimpel). The last surviving humanoid inhabitant of planet **M-113**, an intelligent life-form with large suction cups on its hands. This individual had caused the death of **Nancy Crater** before transporting up to the *Enterprise,* where it was killed when it threatened the life of Captain Kirk. The M-113 creatures possessed an extraordinary hypnotic ability to take on the appearance of someone known to their prey, and used this ability when hunting in order to obtain the salt they needed to survive. ("The Man Trap" [TOS]). *The M-113 creature is popularly known by many* Star Trek *fans as the Salt Vampire, although this name did not come from the episode itself. The creature was designed and built by Wah Chang. Staff and crew members of the original series called this creature the "Salt Sucker."*

M-113. Class-M planet, the former home of a long-dead civilization, now desertlike and nearly barren. Archaeologist **Robert Crater** spent some five years prior to 2266 studying the ruins there, during which time his wife **Nancy Crater** was killed by the last surviving native inhabitant of that planet. ("The Man Trap" [TOS]).

M-4. Robot invented by **Flint** to perform a variety of tasks at his home on planetoid **Holberg 917G.** ("Requiem For Methuselah" [TOS]).

M-5. (Voice of James Doohan). Experimental computer designed in 2268 by **Dr. Richard Daystrom**. The M-5 **multitronic** unit was the most ambitious computer complex of its time, and was designed with the purpose of correlating and controlling every aspect of starship operation. The M-5 multitronic unit was built using a technique that allowed human neural **engram**s to be impressed upon the computer's circuits, theoretically giving the machine the ability to think and reason like a human. Daystrom hoped that the M-5 would prove as great an advance as his earlier breakthrough in **duotronics**. The M-5 was tested aboard the *Starship Enterprise* in 2268 in an exercise that allowed the M-5 to conduct routine contact and survey operations, as well as an elaborate war game that involved four other Federation starships. Although initial tests were promising, the M-5 demonstrated serious problems when it fired full phasers at the ***Excalibur*** and the ***Lexington***, killing hundreds of people. Fortunately, the M-5 possessed Daystrom's sense of morality, and it later deactivated itself to atone for the sin of murder. ("The Ultimate Computer" [TOS]).

M-9. A type of gestural sign language that is both silent and covert. Developed by the **Leyrons** of planet Malkus IX. Data learned this language form in 2365 for use in communicating with mediator **Riva** after his **Chorus** was killed at planet **Solais V**. ("Loud as a Whisper" [TNG]). *The hand gestures that Data studied on his computer screen when learning this language were mostly standard American Sign Language symbols. One sign that was not, however, was the traditional Vulcan salute, which was included to see if anyone would notice.*

M24 Alpha. Star system that contained the planet **Triskelion**; site where several members of the *Enterprise* were transported in 2268. ("The Gamesters of Triskelion" [TOS]).

Maab. (Michael Dante). Ambitious warrior on planet **Capella IV** who attempted to gain control of the Ten Tribes of Capella by murdering their leader, High **Teer Akaar,** in 2267. Maab had favored selling **Capellan** mineral rights to the Klingons instead of to the Federation. Maab later sacrificed his life defending Akaar's widow, **Eleen**, against Klingon agent **Kras**, after discovering that the Klingons were without honor by Capellan standards. ("Friday's Child" [TOS]).

Mab-Bu VI. A giant, gaseous planet located in Federation space. Mab-Bu VI had a Class-M moon that was recorded in Starfleet records as uninhabited. The *Starship **Essex*** was destroyed above the Mab-Bu moon in 2167 by **Ux-Mal** criminals who had been imprisoned on the moon. These same criminals attempted to escape a second time, in 2368, by commandeering the *Starship Enterprise*-D, taking over the bodies of several *Enterprise*-D personnel including Miles O'Brien, Deanna Troi, and Data. ("Power Play" [TNG]).

Mabus. (Charles O. Lucia). **Trabe** leader. Mabus grew up on a planet where members of the Kazon were imprisoned and persecuted. He was eight years old when orphaned in the **Kazon** revolt of 2346. Many years later, he and other Trabe nationals were captured by the **Kazon-Nistrim** and placed in prison on planet Sobras. In 2372, Mabus and his countrymen escaped captivity and briefly formed an alliance with members of the *U.S.S. Voyager*. With the combined strength of a Federation starship and the Trabe, Mabus organized a peace conference and invited many Kazon first majes. Mabus, however, had engineered the entire conference as a trap with the sole intention of assassinating the Kazon representatives. The plot failed, and Mabus returned to his countrymen to continue his acts of revenge. ("Alliances" [VGR]).

MacAllister, James Mooney. Starfleet officer. As a cadet, MacAllister shared a room with Harry Kim at Starfleet Academy. MacAllister used to study algorithms until dawn, and he helped Kim through fourth-year quantum chemistry. ("The Cloud" [VGR]).

macaroni and cheese. Traditional Earth dish made from extruded carbohydrate paste and pressed dairy curds. A favorite of Ensign Ashmore. Neelix made macaroni and cheese for Ashmore aboard the *Starship Voyager*, using **schplict** to make **brill cheese**. ("Learning Curve" [VGR]).

macchiato. A cappuccino-like **coffee** beverage favored by Beverly Crusher. ("The Chase" [TNG]).

MacDougal, Sarah. (Brooke Bundy). Chief engineer of the *Enterprise*-D in early 2364. ("The Naked Now" [TNG]).

MacDuff, Commander Kieran. (Erich Anderson). A **Satarran** operative who masqueraded as an officer of the *Enterprise*-D in 2368. The Satarrans bombarded the Federation ship with a powerful bio-electric field that suppressed the crew's short-term memories as well as most computer records. During the following confusion, MacDuff took a place aboard the *Enterprise*-D and attempted to convince the ship's crew to attack the **Lysian Central Command**. The Satarran scheme failed because Captain Picard refused to attack a defenseless enemy, even though he appeared to have been ordered to do so. ("Conundrum" [TNG]).

Macet, Gul. (Marc Alaimo). Commanding officer of the **Cardassian** warship ***Trager***. Macet came aboard the *Enterprise*-D in 2367 as an observer during a mission to locate the renegade Federation starship ***Phoenix***. ("The Wounded" [TNG]). *Marc Alaimo played several other roles, including Gul Dukat.* SEE: **Badar N'D'D**.

Macias. (John Franklyn-Robbins). Leader of the **Maquis** cell on Ronara. Macias was originally from the Federation colony on Juhraya, and lived there when the **Federation-Cardassian treaty** was signed. He tried to stay on in his home, but was attacked and beaten by Cardassian operatives, leaving him permanently scarred. Macias relocated to Ronara, and became part of the Maquis cell there. A complex man, Macias was fond of ***hasperat*** and played the ***belaklavion***, though he was not **Bajoran.** He befriended **Ro Laren,** and was instrumental in her decision to leave Starfleet and join the Maquis in 2370. Shortly thereafter, Macias was killed in a surprise attack by Cardassians. ("Preemptive Strike" [TNG]).

Macintosh. Primitive 20th-century personal computer. Scotty found a Macintosh puzzling because of his unfamiliarity with its peculiar "mouse" pointing device. A trademark of Apple Computer company. *(Star Trek IV: The Voyage Home). This Encyclopedia was written and designed on Macintosh computers.*

Macormak, Ensign. Starfleet officer assigned to the *U.S.S. Voyager* in 2372. She was attracted to **Ensign Bennet**, although she didn't make it clear to him. ("Innocence" [VGR]).

MacPherson Nebula. Supernova remnant. When searching for a source of vertion particles to feed an **emergent life-form** in 2370, Geordi La Forge chose the MacPherson Nebula over the **Dikon alpha** pulsar. La Forge launched a modified photon torpedo into the nebula, and the subsequent explosion created the needed vertions. ("Emergence" [TNG]).

"Macrocosm." *Voyager* episode #54. Written by Brannon Braga. Directed by Alexander Singer. Stardate 50425.1. First aired in 1996. *After returning from a trade negotiation with the Tak Tak, Captain Janeway and Neelix discover* Voyager *has been invaded by macroviruses, cells billions of times their original size and mass.* GUEST CAST: Albie Selznick as **Tak Tak consul**; Michael Fiske as **Garan miner**. SEE: **American Sign Language; antigen; biocontainment fields; cargo bay; chromolinguistics; Garan miner; Garan mining colony; Indiana; Janeway, Kathryn; Klingons; Ktarian glaciers; lavaflies; Leyron; macrovirus; micron; Neelix; neurode; pot roast; Rinax marshlands; Rinax; shuttlebay; Starfleet General Orders and Regulations; Tak Tak; Tak Tak consul; Talax; tropical resort; *Voyager, U.S.S.*; Wildman, Samantha.**

macrospentol. One of several chemicals used by the **Angosians** during the **Tarsian War** to "improve" their soldiers, making them more effective in combat. Unfortunately, the effects of many of these drugs were irreversible. ("The Hunted" [TNG]). SEE: **Danar, Roga**.

macrovirus. Life-form probably indigenous to a planet in the Delta Quadrant, resembling a conventional virus, but growing to extraordinary size. The macrovirus begins its life cycle at a submicroscopic size, but quickly grows, infecting its host body as it multiplies. When it reaches approximately one centimeter in size, the macrovirus emerges from the host, where it can grow as large as two meters. The **Tak Tak** civilization had serious problems with macrovirus infestations, and adopted a policy of destroying any infected colony or ship. Although Tak Tak medical technology had no effective treatment for the macrovirus, the Emergency Medical Hologram aboard the *Starship Voyager* was able to develop an **antigen** that could destroy the macrovirus. ("Macrocosm" [VGR]). SEE: **resort**.

Maddox, Commander Bruce. (Brian Brophy). Noted cyberneticist, Chair of Robotics at the **Daystrom Institute of Technology,** and student of the works of **Noonien Soong**. Maddox was the only member of the entrance committee who opposed the android **Data**'s entrance into Starfleet Academy in 2341 because of his belief that Data was not a sentient being. In 2365, Maddox attempted to use legal means to coerce Data to submit to a disassembly procedure, in an effort to learn more about the android's construction. This effort was blocked when Judge Advocate General **Phillipa Louvois** ruled that Data was indeed a sentient being. ("The Measure of a Man" [TNG]). Data nevertheless held no ill will against Maddox, and in fact remained in correspondence with him, providing Maddox with information to help further understand Data's mind. ("Data's Day" [TNG]).

Madeline. (Rhonda Aldrich). A holodeck character, the fictional secretary of pulp detective **Dixon Hill**. An attractive woman who outwardly seemed bemused by the world of private investigators, Madeline wanted to become a P.I. herself. The Dixon Hill holodeck program, based on the Dixon Hill novels and short stories, included a holographic representation of Madeline. ("Manhunt" [TNG], "Clues" [TNG]). *She also appeared in "The Big Goodbye" [TNG], although the character did not yet have a name.*

Madena, Coalition of. Political entity encompassing planets **Altec** and **Straleb** in the Omega Sagitta system. Both planets are inhabited by the same humanoid species, and the coalition was held together by a precarious treaty. ("The Outrageous Okona" [TNG]).

Madred, Gul. (David Warner). Cardassian officer who interrogated *Enterprise*-D captain **Jean-Luc Picard** when Picard was captured at planet **Celtris III** in 2369. Madred employed physical and psychological torture in violation of the **Seldonis IV Convention** while attempting to extract Starfleet tactical information from Picard. Although Picard was able to resist, he later confided that he was so brutalized by the experience that he would have done anything for Madred, had he not been freed. ("Chain of Command, Part II" [TNG]). *David Warner also played St. John Talbot in* Star Trek V: The Final Frontier *and Gorkon in* Star Trek VI: The Undiscovered Country.

mag-lev carriage. Small passenger or cargo vehicle that uses **magnetic leverage** to travel up a cable tether connecting the surface of a planet to an orbital station. Used by **Nezu** colonists in the Delta Quadrant on their **orbital tether** sysem. ("Rise" [VGR]).

Magda. (Susan Denberg). One of Mudd's women. Magda had short blond hair and came from the Helium experimental station before being recruited by **Harcourt Fenton Mudd** as a wife for a settler on planet **Ophiucus III** in 2266. Magda later married one of the miners on **Rigel XII**. ("Mudd's Women" [TOS]). *Magda's last name was not mentioned in the aired version, but a final draft script, dated May 26, 1966, listed her as Magda Kovacs.*

Magellan*, Shuttlecraft.** *Enterprise*-D shuttle vehicle #15. The *Magellan*, piloted by Worf, was launched on a rescue mission when Captain Picard was trapped on planet **El-Adrel IV** in 2368. A **Tamarian** vessel fired on the *Magellan*, carefully disabling it so that it was forced to return to the *Enterprise*-D. The Tamarians had sought to isolate Picard and their captain on El-Adrel IV so that they might have a chance to learn to communicate. ("Darmok" [TNG]). The *Magellan* participated in a rescue mission of the **J'naii** shuttle ***Taris Murn in 2368. The *Magellan* had two 1,250 **millicochrane** warp engines and microfusion impulse thrusters. Such shuttles are normally unarmed, but can be equipped with two **phaser type-4** emitters for special mission requirements. The rescue of the J'naii shuttle was successful, but the *Magellan* was destroyed in the process. ("The Outcast" [TNG]). *The* Magellan *was named for Spanish navigator Ferdinand Magellan, the first explorer to circumnavigate planet Earth. This was the first appearance of the new full-sized shuttle set and model introduced during the fifth season. The ship was an extensive modification of the* **Galileo 5** *shuttle built for* Star Trek V. *Designers included Richard James, Nilo Rodis, Herman Zimmerman, Andy Neskoromny, and Rick Sternbach. The model was built by Greg Jein.*

***Magellan*, U.S.S.** Federation starship, commanded by **Captain Conklin**. ("Starship Mine" [TNG]).

"Magic Carpet Ride." Song written by Earth musicians John Kay and Rushton Moreve and performed by Steppenwolf, originally recorded in 1968. **Zefram Cochrane** played "Magic Carpet Ride" during his historic first warp flight aboard the *Phoenix* on April 4, 2063. *(Star Trek: First Contact)*.

magma pockets. In planetary geology, subsurface regions containing molten rock. In 2370, magma pockets in planet Atrea IV had cooled to the point of solidifying, threatening the stability of the planet. These pockets were used as placement points for **ferroplasmic infusion** devices used to reliquefy the core of the planet. ("Inheritance" [TNG]).

Magna Carta. The "great charter" of liberties signed by English King John under enormous pressure from English barons on Earth in the year 1215. The Magna Carta, still regarded as a major milestone in the evolution of law, provided guarantees of due process in trials, and strict limitations of governmental power over the governed. ("Court Martial" [TOS]).

magnascopic storm. Electromagnetic spatial disruption. The *Enterprise*-D passed through a magnascopic storm in the Mekorda sector in 2370, when an **emergent life-form** attached itself to the ship's computer system. ("Emergence" [TNG]).

magnasite drops. Corrosive compound. Magnasite drops can be used to dissolve duranium. ("Necessary Evil" [DS9]).

magnaspanner. Handheld tool used by Starfleet engineers. ("Tapestry" [TNG]).

magnaton pulse. Electromagnetic energy burst. Renegade Jem'Hadar soldiers used a magnaton pulse to hide their escape ship's ion trail in 2372. ("To the Death" [DS9]).

magnesite-nitron tablet. Small white disk carried in Dr. McCoy's medical pouch. When crushed, the tablet explodes into a bright flame, providing a source of illumination. Kirk used a magnesite-nitron tablet for illumination in a cave on planet **Capella IV** on stardate 3497. ("Friday's Child" [TOS]).

magnesite. Metallic composite containing magnesium carbonate, $MgCO_3$. The presence of magnesite ore in the crust of **Atrea IV** caused a feedback pulse in the drilling phasers used by the Starship *Enterprise*-D in 2370. The problem was corrected by adjusting the harmonic frequency of the phaser beam. ("Inheritance" [TNG]). Transporters cannot beam through magnesite-bearing rock. ("Nor the Battle to the Strong" [DS9]). The Duras sisters illegally extracted magnesite ore from a Pakled mine on planet Kalla III. ("Firstborn" [TNG]). Magnesite was used as a structural material in Federation and Kazon spacecraft construction. ("Initiations" [VGR]). Magnesite can also be used as a chemical fuel for cooking. Campers on Earth generally prefer to use magnesite fuel instead of wood cut from trees. ("Tattoo" [VGR]).

magnetascopic interference. Electromagnetic energy produced by unstable **protostar**s. Magnetascopic interference affects sensor and communication efficiency. ("Preemptive Strike" [TNG]).

magnetic boots. Footwear used by starship personnel in weightless conditions to allow a worker to remain attached and vertical with respect to a floor or other suitable surface. Also known as gravity boots. **Burke** and **Samno**, Federation operatives who murdered Klingon chancellor Gorkon, wore magnetic boots so that they could move freely aboard the Klingon ship ***Kronos One*** during the assassination. The boots later provided the means of identifying Burke and Samno as the assassins. *(Star Trek VI: The Undiscovered Country).*

magnetic constrictors. Component of a starship's warp core. In 2372, Michael Jonas sabotaged *Voyager*'s magnetic constrictors so that they would be forced to vent plasma, severely damaging the inner layer of the warp coils. This damage was designed to force *Voyager* to visit planet Hemikek, where Kazon forces were lying in ambush. ("Investigations" [VGR]).

magnetic leverage. Form of linear propulsion that was used to lift a carriage along a tether cable stretching from a planet's surface up to a station in synchronous orbit. Used by **Nezu** colonists in the Delta Quadrant on their **orbital tether** sysem. ("Rise" [VGR]).

magnetic probe. Handheld engineering tool. *Enterprise* engineering officer Scott used a magnetic probe to seal the matter-antimatter flow that caused the ship to travel at dangerously accelerated speeds when **Losira** sabotaged the ship's engines in 2268. ("That Which Survives" [TOS]).

magnetic resonance traces. Subtle electromagnetic patterns discovered in sections of the *Enterprise*-D hull after their encounter with the Borg at **System J-25** in 2365, these were believed to be indicative of Borg activity—a "Borg footprint." The same resonance traces were also discovered in the remains of the **New Providence** colony in late 2366, and confirmed that the Borg had indeed been responsible for the disappearance of the colony. ("The Best of Both Worlds, Part I" [TNG]).

magnetic seals. Component of the matter/**antimatter containment** system aboard Federation starships. The seals help prevent the highly volatile antimatter from coming into contact with the structure of the ship. The magnetic seals of the ***U.S.S. Yamato*** collapsed just prior to that ship's explosion in 2365. An emergency system that should have dumped the antimatter from the ship in that situation evidently failed. ("Contagion" [TNG]).

magnetic spindle bearings. Mechanisms used in a Federation starship's reaction control assembly. ("Fair Trade" [VGR]).

magnetic storm. Electromagnetic spatial disturbance. In 2373, the ***Voyager*** shuttlecraft ***Sacajawea*** became caught in a magnetic storm and crashed on a planet in a binary system in the **Delta Quadrant**. **Kathryn Janeway** was almost killed in the crash. ("Coda" [VGR]).

magneton scan. Highly accurate **sensor** protocol. The magneton scan was considered the most precise instrument available aboard the *Starship Voyager*, and was employed on stardate 48734 in an effort to locate a suspected alien presence aboard the ship. ("Cathexis" [VGR]).

magnetospheric energy taps. Technology developed on the Alpha Moon of planet **Peliar Zel**. The taps allowed the magnetic field of Peliar Zel to be used as an energy source for **Alpha Moon**. Unfortunately, the magnetospheric field created by the tap crossed the orbit of **Beta Moon**. The field caused severe environmental damage to Beta Moon in 2367, increasing the pre-existing political tensions between the governments of the two moons. ("The Host" [TNG]). SEE: **Odan, Ambassador**.

mahko* root.** Plant used by the ***Kahn-ut-tu women of **Tyree**'s planet to cure the poisonous bite of the ***mugato***. When James Kirk suffered such a bite in 2267, *Kahn-ut-tu* woman **Nona** inflicted a knife wound on herself, then allowed her blood to pass through the *mahko* root to Kirk's injury, curing him. ("A Private Little War" [TOS]).

Maht-H'a, I.K.S. Klingon *Vor'cha*-class attack cruiser. Under the command of Captain **Nu'Daq**, the *Maht-H'a* participated in 2369 in the discovery of a four-billion-year-old genetically encoded message from an ancient humanoid species. ("The Chase" [TNG]). SEE: **Galen, Professor Richard; humanoid life**.

Maid Marian. (Jennifer Hetrick). In Earth mythology, the woman who loved legendary English outlaw **Robin Hood**. **Vash** was cast in the role of Maid Marian by **Q** during a fantasy he crafted for the *Enterprise*-D crew. ("QPid" [TNG]).

Maihar'du. (Tiny Ron). Tall, prune-faced humanoid who was the faithful servant of **Grand Nagus** Zek. Maihar'du was

Hupyrian, and shared his people's tradition of devotion to their employers. This faithful servant taught **Zek** how to enter a **Dolbargy sleeping trance** to fake his death. ("The Nagus" [DS9]). His duties also included attending to the grand nagus's personal grooming. ("Rules of Acquisition" [DS9]). As a Hupyrian servant, Maihar'du took a vow only to speak to his master, Grand Nagus Zek. ("Prophet Motive" [DS9]).

main bridge. SEE: **bridge**.

main fusion reactor. Primary source of power for station **Deep Space 9**. In 2371, the main fusion reactor overloaded and exploded after a self-destruct sequence was automatically triggered by the station's main computer. At the last instant, the energy of the blast was directed into the station's deflector shields, saving the station from destruction. ("Civil Defense" [DS9]).

main particle impeller. Component of **Dr. Farallon**'s experimental **particle fountain**. Dr. Farallon's particle impeller overloaded, causing radiation to contaminate the work station on planet Tyrus VIIA in 2369. ("The Quality of Life" [TNG]).

main shuttlebay. SEE: **shuttlebay**.

maintenance conduit. Access tunnel on Deep Space 9, much like the **Jefferies tubes** aboard Federation starships. ("Civil Defense" [DS9]).

Maizie series. (Tamara Wilson and Starr Wilson). Model of **android** designed by **Harcourt Fenton Mudd** in 2267. ("I, Mudd" [TOS]).

Maj ram. Klingon for "Good Night." ("The Sword of Kahless" [DS9]).

maje. Title of authority in the **Kazon** Collective. **Jabin** was first maje of the **Kazon-Ogla** sect. ("Caretaker" [VGR]).

MajQa*, Rite of.** Klingon ritual involving deep meditation in the lava caves of ***No'Mat. Prolonged exposure to the heat is believed to induce a hallucinatory effect. Great significance is attached to any visions received during the *MajQa*, and revelations of one's father are believed to be the most important. When Worf was young, his adoptive parents arranged for him to experience the Rite of *MajQa*. ("Birthright, Part I" [TNG]).

Mak'ala, Caves of. Geological formation located on the **Trill homeworld**. The caves contain interconnecting pools that stretch for kilometers under the surface of the planet. The pools are the breeding environment for Trill **symbionts**. ("Equilibrium" [DS9]).

mak'dar. Klingon insult. ("The House of Quark" [DS9]).

Makar. Romulan warbird. The ***Makar*** was lost in the **Tal Shiar** attack on the **Founders' homeworld** in 2371. ("The Die is Cast" [DS9]).

***makara* herb.** Native **Bajoran** flora, noted for their medicinal value. *Makara* herbs are administered to pregnant Bajoran women to raise progesterone levels. Dr. Julian Bashir prescribed *makora* herbs for **Kira Nerys,** when she was carrying **Kirayoshi O'Brien**, in 2373 to help her swollen ankles. ("Looking for *par'Mach* in All the Wrong Places" [DS9]). Kira likened the taste to "something that crawled out of **Quark**'s ear." The *makara* acted as a counteragent when she was injected with **merfadon** on stardate 50416 by **Silaran Prin,** who blamed her for the explosion years earlier that had disfigured him. ("The Darkness and the Light" [DS9]).

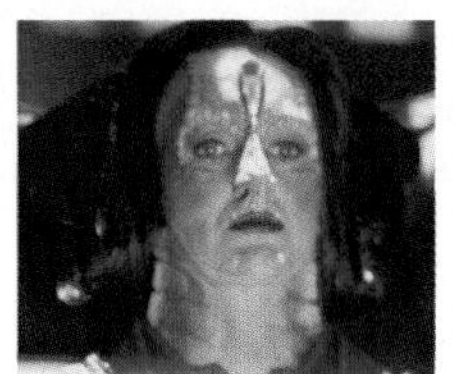

Makbar. (Caroline Lagerfelt). Chief **archon** in the **Cardassian** court. In 2370, she presided over the trial of Chief Miles O'Brien. ("Tribunal" [DS9]).

Makers. Intelligent beings from the Andromeda Galaxy who, centuries ago, established exploratory outposts in our galaxy. When the Makers' home star went nova, only a few outposts survived, including one populated by humanoid **android**s on what became known as the planet **Mudd** in 2267. ("I, Mudd" [TOS]).

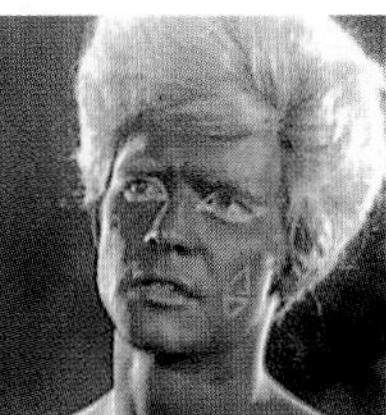

Makora. (David Soul). Inhabitant of planet **Gamma Trianguli VI** who welcomed the *Enterprise* landing party to their village in 2267. He was attracted to **Sayana**, but wasn't allowed to act on his feelings because mating was against **Vaal**'s law. ("The Apple" [TOS]).

Maktag. A division of the **Klingon** calendar, roughly analogous to a terrestrial month. **Alexander Rozhenko** was born during Maktag of the Earth calendar year 2366. ("New Ground" [TNG]).

Makus III. Planet. The *Starship Enterprise* was scheduled to deliver emergency medical supplies to Makus III for transfer to the **New Paris colonies** following a plague outbreak in 2267. ("The *Galileo* Seven" [TOS]).

Malaya IV. Planet. Lieutenant **Paul Hickman** had a physical examination on Malaya IV shortly before an alien DNA strand compelled him to return to **Tarchannen III** in 2367. ("Identity Crisis" [TNG]).

Malcor III. A Class-M planet and homeworld to the **Malcorians**. This planet was a candidate for Federation first contact, and in 2367 was the subject of sociological studies in preparation for such a contact. ("First Contact" [TNG]).

Malcorians. A humanoid civilization whose members are characterized by enlarged frontal skull bones and a single fused phalange, rather than distinct fingers. In 2367, Malcorian society was undergoing a series of social reforms accompanied by rapid leaps in technology. The Malcorians were within ten months of their first interstellar flight, but the prospects of potential contact with extraterrestrial life were disturbing to some of the Malcorian people. During this time of social upheaval, the *Enterprise*-D attempted to complete a program of covert study on the planet prior to **first contact** with the Malcorian government. Unfortunately, the premature discovery of Federation personnel on the planet's surface led to hysteria in parts of the population and the first contact had to be delayed indefinitely. ("First Contact" [TNG]). SEE: **Krola; Jakara, Rivas; Yale, Mirasta.**

Malencon, Arthur. (Mario Roccuzzo). Hydraulics specialist, part of the unsuccessful **terraforming** project at planet **Velara III**. Malencon was killed in 2364 by the native crystalline **microbrain** life-forms whose lives were threatened by the project. ("Home Soil" [TNG]).

Malia. (Kristanna S. Loken). **Taresian** woman. Malia was joined to **Taymon** and became one of his wives. To facilitate procreation, in 2373 Malia and others reduced Taymon to a lifeless husk through **denucleation** of his cells. ("Favorite Son" [VGR]).

Malinche, U.S.S. *Excelsior*-class Federation starship. On stardate 50485.2, under the command of Captain **Sanders**, the *Malinche* patrolled the **Demilitarized Zone**, near the Gamma 7 outpost. It was attacked and disabled by a group of **Maquis** raiders led by **Michael Eddington**. ("For the Uniform" [DS9]). *The ship was named after the 16th-century Mexican princess who was originally a slave given as a peace offering to the Spanish conquistadors by the Tabascan Indians.*

Malko. Holosuite character. A handsome young masseur in Jadzia Dax's holosuite representation of the **Hoobishan Baths** of Trill. ("The Way of the Warrior" [DS9]).

Malkus IX. Planet. The Leyrons, inhabitants of Malkus IX, developed writing before sign language. This is unusual because most humanoid cultures tend to develop hand signs and spoken languages first. ("Loud as a Whisper" [TNG]).

Mallory, Lieutenant. (Jay Jones). *Enterprise* crew member. Mallory was killed while on a landing party on planet **Gamma Trianguli VI** in 2267 when he stepped on a rock with explosive properties. Mallory's father had helped **James Kirk** get into the academy. ("The Apple" [TOS]).

Maltz. (John Larroquette). Officer of the Klingon bird-of-prey commanded by **Kruge**. Maltz was the only survivor of that ship's crew after Kruge was killed on the **Genesis Planet** and the rest of the crew perished when the *Enterprise* was destroyed. Maltz was taken prisoner when Kirk commandeered the bird-of-prey after Kruge was killed. (*Star Trek III: The Search for Spock*).

Malurian system. Planetary system that was once home to over four billion inhabitants. When executing its program of planetary sterilization, the space probe ***Nomad*** did not destroy the solar system itself, just the "unstable biological infestations" inhabiting it. ("The Changeling" [TOS]). SEE: ***Tan Ru.***

Malurians. Civilization from the Malurian system, some four billion people, that were wiped out in 2267 by the errant Earth space probe ***Nomad***. The Malurians were being studied by a Federation science team under the direction of **Dr. Manway** at the time. ("The Changeling" [TOS]).

"Man Alone, A." *Deep Space Nine* episode #3. Teleplay by Michael Piller. Story by Gerald Sanford and Michael Piller. Directed by Paul Lynch. Stardate: 46421.5. *First aired in 1993. Odo is framed for murder by a man who has killed his own clone. This was the first regular hour-long episode of* Star Trek: Deep Space Nine *produced after the pilot movie.* GUEST CAST: Rosalind Chao as **O'Brien, Keiko**; Edward Albert as **Zayra**; Max Grodénchik as **Rom**; Peter Vogt as Romulan Commander; Aron Eisenberg as **Nog**; Stephen James Carver as **Ibudan**; Tom Klunis as **Lamonay S.;** Scott Trost as Bajoran officer; Patrick Cupo as Bajoran man; Kathryn Graf as Bajoran man; Hana Hatae as **O'Brien, Molly**; Diana Cignoni as Dabo girl; Judi Durand as Computer voice. SEE: **Altonian brain teaser; azna; bioregenerative field; clone; Dax, Jadzia; electrophoretic analysis; Garanian bolites; glop-on-a-stick; Ibudan; Juro; Karo-Net; Kran-Tobal Prison; Lamonay S.; Lauriento massage holoprogram #101A; O'Brien, Keiko; O'Brien, Molly; Odo; Rom; Rujian; schoolroom; seofurance; Sisko, Benjamin; Trills; Yadozi Desert; Zayra.**

"Man of the People." *Next Generation* episode #129. Written by Frank Abatemarco. Directed by Winrich Kolbe. Stardate 46071.6. *First aired in 1992. A famous Federation mediator maintains extraordinary equanimity in tough negotiations by even more extraordinary abuse of his female companions.* GUEST CAST: Chip Lucia as **Alkar**, **Ambassador Ves**; Patti Yasutake as **Ogawa**, **Nurse Alyssa**; George D. Wallace as Simon, Admiral; Lucy Boryer as **Janeway**, **Ensign**; Susan French as **Maylor**, **Sev**; Rick Scarry as **Jarth**; Stephanie Erb as **Liva**; J.P. Hubbell as Ensign; Majel Barrett as Computer voice. SEE: **Alkar, Ambassador Ves; counselor; Darthen; *Dorian*; dylamadon; Janeway, Ensign; Jarth; Liva; Maylor, Sev; melorazine; *Mok'bara*; neurotransmitter; Ogawa, Nurse Alyssa; Pinder, Lieutenant; "receptacle"; Rekag-Seronia; Rekags; Talmadge, Captain**.

"Man Trap, The." Original Series episode #6. Written by George Clayton Johnson. Directed by Marc Daniels. Stardate 1513.1. *First aired in 1966. A salt-eating creature that can disguise itself in any form stalks the* Enterprise *crew. Although the sixth episode produced in the original series (counting the two pilots), "The Man Trap" was the first episode to be aired during the original network run of the show, which premiered on September 8, 1966.* GUEST CAST: Jeanne Bal as **Crater**, **Nancy**; Alfred Ryder as **Crater**, **Professor**; Grace Lee Whitney as **Rand**, **Janice**; Bruce Watson as **Green**, **Crewman**; Michael Zaslow as **Darnell**, **Crewman**; Vince Howard as Uhura's crewman; Francine Pyne as Blonde Nancy (Nancy III); Sharon Gimpel as **M-113 creature**; Garrison True as Crewman guard #1; Larry Anthony as Transporter chief; Bob Baker as Beauregard puppeteer. SEE: **Barnhart; Beauregard; Borgia plant; Corinth IV; Crater, Nancy; Crater, Professor Robert; Darnell, Crewman; Great Bird of the Galaxy, the; Green, Crewman; M-113 creature; M-113; McCoy, Dr. Leonard H.; "Plum"; Saurian brandy; sodium chloride; Sturgeon; Sulu, Hikaru; Rand, Janice; Vulcan; Wrigley's Pleasure Planet.**

Manark IV. SEE: **sand bats**.

Manchovites. Sentient civilization. **Hagath** and **Gaila** supplied weapons to the Manchovites to be used in a war some time ago. They also supplied weapons to the Manchorites' enemies in the conflict. ("Business As Usual" [DS9]).

Mandel, Ensign. (Cameron Arnett). An *Enterprise*-D crew member. Mandel was assigned to ops on the main bridge while the *Enterprise*-D was departing Mudor V on stardate 45156. Mandel was one of the few officers left on the bridge when the ship was disabled by a **quantum filament**. ("Disaster" [TNG]).

Mandl, Kurt. (Walter Gotell). Director of an aborted **terraforming** station on planet **Velara III**. Mandl had concealed the fact that the terraforming project would threaten indigenous life-forms on Velara III. ("Home Soil" [TNG]). *Actor Walter Gotell also played General Gogol in several James Bond movies.*

maneuvering thrusters. Low-power reaction-control jets used for fine positional and attitude control by starships and other spacecraft. Used in low-speed docking maneuvers and similar situations. *(Star Trek: The Motion Picture).*

"Maneuvers." *Voyager* episode #27. Written by Kenneth Biller. Directed by David Livingston. Stardate 49211.5. *First aired in 1995. The* Voyager *is attacked in a daring raid masterminded by Seska and Jal Culluh of the Kazon-Nistrim. Chakotay, taking responsibility for the disaster, goes off by himself to a Kazon ship.* GUEST CAST: Martha Hackett as **Seska**; Anthony DeLongis as **Culluh**, **Jal**; Terry Lester as **Haron**; John Gegenhuber as **Surat**, **Jal**; Majel Barrett as Computer voice. SEE: **Chakotay; Culluh, Jal; enemy's blood; Haron, Jal; Kazon; Kazon spacecraft; Kazon-Hobii; Kazon-Mostral; Kazon-Nistrim; Kazon-Oglamar; Kazon-Relora; Loran, Jal; quantum resonance oscillator; Sankur, Jal; Seska; Surat, Jal; Torres; Trabe; Valek, Jal.**

Manheim Effect. An intense temporal disturbance generated by **Dr. Paul Manheim**'s efforts to open a window into another dimension. The Manheim Effect was manifested as a series of brief temporal "hiccoughs" during which time was briefly superimposed over itself. Data was successful in disrupting the Manheim Effect by injecting a small quantity of antimatter into the distortion. ("We'll Always Have Paris" [TNG]).

Manheim, Dr. Paul. (Rod Loomis). Brilliant scientist who conducted revolutionary studies in nonlinear time and the relationships between time and gravity. Manheim's early work in nonlinear time found little acceptance in the scientific community, and he became a recluse, setting up a laboratory on the distant planetoid **Vandor IV**, where he hoped his temporal research would yield the key to other dimensions. Manheim made considerable strides there, although a terrible accident in 2364 nearly killed Manheim and caused a severe temporal disturbance. ("We'll Always Have Paris" [TNG]). SEE: **Manheim Effect**.

Manheim, Jenice. (Michelle Phillips). Wife to scientist **Dr. Paul Manheim**. Prior to her marriage to Manheim, Jenice had been romantically involved with future *Enterprise*-D captain **Jean-Luc Picard**. Jenice was hurt when Picard left her without saying goodbye in 2342, but the two resolved their feelings in 2364 when Picard and the *Enterprise*-D saved the life of her husband. ("We'll Always Have Paris" [TNG]). *Actor Michelle Phillips gained fame in the 1960s as a singer with the musical group The Mamas and the Papas.*

"Manhunt." *Next Generation* episode #45. Written by Tracy Tormé. Directed by Rob Bowman. Stardate 42859.2. *First aired in 1989. Lwaxana Troi returns to the* Enterprise*-D with the intent of finding a husband.* GUEST CAST: Diana Muldaur as **Pulaski**, **Dr. Katherine**; Majel Barrett as **Troi**, **Lwaxana**; Robert Costanzo as **Bender**, **Slade**; Carel Struycken as **Homn**; Rod Arrants as **Rex**; Colm Meaney as **O'Brien**, **Miles**; Rhonda Aldrich as **Madeline**; Mick Fleetwood as Antedean dignitary; Wren T. Brown as Transporter pilot. SEE: **Antede III; Antedean ambassador; Antedeans; Bender, Slade; brown dwarf; chime, Betazoid; co-orbital satellites; Hill, Dixon; Madeline; Marejaretus VI; Pacifica; *Parrot's Claw, The*; phase, the; Rex; Sacred Chalice of Rixx; Troi, Lwaxana; Ultritium; vermicula.**

Mansara. Carved representations of the spirits who have visited the **Habak** of the Native American colonists on planet **Dorvan V**. These spirits include the Vulcans, the Klingons, and the Ferengi, as well as the bear, coyote, fish, and parrot. ("Journey's End" [TNG]).

***manta* leaves.** Type of foliage that pops when burned. ("Attached" [TNG]).

Mantickian paté. An exotic dish. Lwaxana Troi prepared some Mantickian paté for **Dr. Timicin** and the engineering staff of the *Enterprise*-D in 2367. ("Half a Life" [TNG]).

Manu III. Inhabited planet. The government of Manu III used **proximity detectors** to control its population. ("Legacy" [TNG]).

Manway, Dr. Federation scientist who studied the inhabitants of the **Malurian system**. He was killed in 2267 when the system's entire population was destroyed by the robot ***Nomad***. ("The Changeling" [TOS]).

Maporian ale. Alcoholic beverage. Grilka liked Maporian ale with a hint of *pazafer*. ("Looking for *par'Mach* in All the Wrong Places" [DS9]).

Maques. (Norman Large). Leader of the **Cairn** delegation to the *Enterprise*-D in 2370. Maques assisted Deanna Troi in helping her mother, **Lwaxana Troi**, out of a coma-like state caused by a particularly traumatic memory. This memory was triggered by the resemblance between his daughter, **Hedril**, and Lwaxana's first daughter, **Kestra**. ("Dark Page" [TNG]). *Norman Large also portrayed Romulan Proconsul Neral in "Unification, Parts I and II" (TNG).*

Maquis interceptor. Modified, lightly armed *Peregrine*-class courier ship, usually with a one-person crew, used by the **Maquis**. A **Founder Leader** lured **Kira Nerys** and **Odo** to a seismically unstable moon by using a Maquis interceptor to attack a Lissepian supply ship. ("Heart of Stone" [DS9]).

Maquis ships. The **Maquis** were equipped with a variety of older spacecraft, mostly obtained from Federation sources. One common type was a small two- or three-person spacecraft used by the Maquis for ship-to-ship engagements and covert attacks. These ships were equipped with **photon torpedoes**, **type-8 phaser** banks, and transporters. In 2370, a small group of Maquis ships were used to attack and severely damage a *Galor*-class Cardassian warship, forcing its captain, **Gul Evek**, to send out a distress signal. Another group of these ships was sent to the **Demilitarized Zone** border to attack an **Yridian convoy**. The ships disengaged following Ro's warning that the attack was a Starfleet ambush. ("Preemptive Strike" [TNG]). Later that year, **Calvin Hudson** and **Amaros** traveled in a Maquis ship in an attempted attack on a Cardassian weapons depot on planet **Bryma**. ("The Maquis, Part II" [DS9]). The Maquis used a variety of spacecraft, mostly older ships of Federation origin, in their fight against the Cardassians. A Maquis ship commanded by Chakotay in 2371 was at least four decades old, but was still able to elude Cardassian pursuit. ("Caretaker" [VGR]). In 2373, a number of Maquis raider craft, commanded by **Michael Eddington**, used cobalt diselenide as a biogenic weapon against Cardassian colonies on **Veloz Prime** and **Quatal Prime.** They also attacked and disabled the ***U.S.S. Malinche***. ("For the Uniform" [DS9]).

"Maquis, Part I, The." *Deep Space Nine* episode # 40. Teleplay by James Crocker. Story by Rick Berman & Michael Piller & Jeri Taylor and James Crocker. Directed by David Livingston. No stardate given. First aired in 1994. *The Cardassians and Federation deal with the Maquis, militant colonists defending their homes in the Demilitarized Zone.* GUEST CAST: Tony Plana as **Amaros**; Bertila Damas as **Sakonna**; Richard Poe as **Evek, Gul**; Michael A. Krawic as **Samuels, William Patrick**; Amanda Carlin as Kobb; Marc Alaimo as **Dukat, Gul**; Bernie Casey as **Hudson, Calvin**; Michael Rose as **Niles**; Steven John Evans as Guard. SEE: **Amaros; Badlands; Bardeezan merchant ship; Boday, Captain; *Bok'Nor*; Cardassian Central Command; Cardassian shuttle; Cardassians; cobalt-thorium device; Dax, Curzon; Demilitarized Zone; Dukat, Gul; Evek, Gul; Farius Prime; Ferengi Rules of Acquisition; Galador freighter; Galador II; Gallamite; Galor-class plasma banks; golside ore; Hudson, Calvin; Hudson, Gretchen; jumbo Romulan mollusks; kelindide; Kira Nerys; Kotakian ship; Lissepians; Maquis; mazurka festival; mercassium; New Berlin; Niles; *plomeek* soup; protomatter; Regulon system; rodinium; Ropal City; S.I.D.; Sakonna; Saltok IV; Samuels, William Patrick; Sisko, Benjamin; Volon II; Vulcan Bill of Rights; Vulcan port; Yridians.**

"Maquis, Part II, The." *Deep Space Nine* episode #41. Teleplay by Ira Steven Behr. Story by Rick Berman & Michael Piller & Jeri Taylor and Ira Steven Behr. Directed by Corey Allen. No stardate given. First aired in 1994. *Sisko forms an unusual alliance with Gul Dukat, who aids him in the clash between Cardassian and Federation settlers.* GUEST CAST: Tony Plana as **Amaros**; John Schuck as **Parn**; Natalia Nogulich as **Necheyev, Alynna**; Bertila Damas as **Sakonna**; Michael Bell as **Drofo Awa**; Amanda Carlin as Kobb; Marc Alaimo as **Dukat, Gul**; Bernie Casey as **Hudson, Calvin**; Michael Rose as **Niles**. SEE: **Amaros; *Bok'Nor*; Bryma; Cardassians; Demilitarized Zone; Drofo Awa; Ferengi Rules of Acquisition; Dukat, Gul; Earth; Federation Code of Justice; Hakton VII; Hetman; Hudson, Calvin; Legate; Lissepians; Maquis; Maquis ships; *Mekong, U.S.S.*; Necheyev, Admiral Alynna; Niles; *Orinoco, U.S.S.*; Oort cloud; Parn; Pygorians; Regrean wheat husks; *Rio Grande, U.S.S.*; Sakonna; Umoth VIII; Volon III; Vulcan mind-meld; Xepolites.**

Maquis. Paramilitary organization of former Federation citizens formed at the colonies affected by the border changes wrought by the **Federation-Cardassian Treaty** of 2370. The Maquis grew in response to Cardassian hostilities toward these colonies and to the perception that they had been abandoned by the Federation government. Members of the Maquis had often been victims of violence directed toward them by the Cardassian military. They felt the intention was to force them from their homes, and many chose to fight rather than leave. The Maquis was organized in a series of cells, with only the leaders of each cell knowing the whereabouts of the other cells. A number of Starfleet officers were sympathetic to the Maquis situation and either provided them with weapons, or left Starfleet to join their ranks. ("Preemptive Strike" [TNG]). In 2370, a group of Maquis led by **Calvin Hudson** defended colonies in the **Demilitarized Zone** that were no longer under Federation protection. Hudson's group destroyed the **Cardassian** freighter ***Bok'Nor***, resulting in several skirmishes along the border. ("The Maquis, Parts I and II" [DS9]). In 2371 **Thomas Riker** hijacked the ***Defiant*** from **Deep Space 9** for a Maquis mission to investigate a suspected Cardassian military buildup in the **Orias system**. ("Defiant" [DS9]). Also during that year, a Maquis ship commanded by **Chakotay** was lost in the **Badlands**. ("Caretaker" [VGR]). By 2372, members of the Maquis were no longer considered to be citizens of the Federation. ("For the Cause" [DS9]). *The name Maquis was used by members of the French underground in World War II.*

Mar Oscura. A dark-matter nebula located in Federation space. The *Enterprise*-D was assigned to chart the Mar Oscura Nebula in 2367, using special photon torpedos to illuminate its interior for study. The crew discovered that the nebula's interior was riddled with gaps in the fabric of normal space. When these pockets came in contact with the ship, they would cause the point of contact to momentarily phase out of normal space. The *Enterprise*-D lost one crew member and a shuttlepod to the phasing phenomenon before the ship was able to leave the nebula, guided by Captain Picard. ("In Theory" [TNG]).

Mara. (Susan Howard). Science officer aboard **Kang**'s Klingon battle cruiser in 2268. Mara, who was Kang's wife, was among the victims of the **Beta XII-A entity**. ("Day of the Dove" [TOS]). *Mara may have been the mother of the son that Kang named after Curzon Dax ("Blood Oath" [DS9]).*

***maraji* crystals.** Controlled substance that was illegal to possess or sell in the Cardassian Union. Captain Livara, a Romulan spy who posed as a Talavian smuggler, visited station Terok Nor in 2367 and tried to interest Quark in some *maraji* crystals. ("Things Past" [DS9]).

Maraltian *seev*-ale. Green beverage. Carried in Quark's private stock on Deep Space 9. **Odo** gave a Maraltian *seev*-ale to **Kira** after a particularly difficult interrogation session with the Cardassian, **Aamin Marritza** in 2369. ("Duet" [DS9]).

Maranga IV. Class-M planet on which is located a Klingon outpost. Worf and his son Alexander attended the ***Kot'baval* Festival** at Maranga IV in 2370. ("Firstborn" [TNG]).

Marani. Masseuse in the mirror universe. Marani was once a servant to **Kira Nerys (mirror)**. ("Shattered Mirror" [DS9]).

Marat Kobar. Bajoran civilian. Marat was on station Terok Nor in 2367, where he was arrested and convicted of a crime and sentenced to five years hard labor for the offense. ("Things Past" [DS9]).

Marauder, Ferengi. SEE: **Ferengi Marauder**.

Marayna. (Sandra Nelson). A character in Neelix's holographic **Polynesian resort** program. Marayna was the entertainment director of the resort. In 2373, **Harry Kim** found himself falling in love with Marayna, so he sought Tuvok's help in ridding himself of these emotions through the Vulcan technique of *t'san s'at*. Unfortunately, partway through the process, **Tuvok** also found himself strongly attracted to the Marayna character. It was later found that a humanoid known as Marayna had tapped into the *Voyager*'s computer system, and used the character as a means of interacting with the crew. The real Marayna lived on a small station in a nearby **inversion nebula**, where she was responsible for preventing a chain reaction that would destroy the nebula, so that others of her people could enjoy its beauty. Marayna, who lived alone, enjoyed tapping into the computer systems of passing spacecraft and interacting with their crews. ("Alter Ego" [VGR]).

Marcos XII. Inhabited planet. The evil **Gorgan** of **Triacus** targeted Marcos XII for conquest in 2268. The Gorgan manipulated the children of the **Starnes Expedition** into commandeering the *Starship Enterprise* toward that destination. Marcos XII was also the home of **Tommy Starnes**'s relatives. ("And the Children Shall Lead" [TOS]).

Marcus, Claudius. (Logan Ramsey). Proconsul and Roman leader on the fourth planet in system Eight Ninety-Two. When Captain **R. M. Merrick** of the ***S.S. Beagle*** beamed down to this planet in 2261, Marcus convinced him to stay rather than report this culture to Federation authorities. ("Bread and Circuses" [TOS]). SEE: **Eight Ninety-Two, Planet IV**.

Marcus, Dr. Carol. (Bibi Besch). Brilliant scientist and noted molecular biologist. Marcus directed the ambitious **Project Genesis**, which attempted to develop a process to rapidly terraform uninhabitable planets into worlds suitable for humanoid life. Marcus was romantically involved with future *Enterprise* captain **James T. Kirk** in the early 2260s. Their son, **David Marcus**, became a noted scientist in his own right, although, at Carol's request, Kirk was not involved in the boy's upbringing. *(Star Trek II: The Wrath of Khan).*

Marcus, Dr. David. (Merritt Butrick). Scientist, born 2261, died 2285. Son of **James T. Kirk** and **Dr. Carol Marcus**. Marcus was one of the key figures in the development of **Project Genesis**. *(Star Trek II: The Wrath of Khan).* Marcus later was assigned, along with Saavik, to the ***U.S.S. Grissom*** for study of the Genesis Planet. During that study, Marcus was killed by a Klingon expedition that sought to claim the planet and the Genesis process for the Klingon government. *(Star Trek III: The Search for Spock). Merritt Butrick later played T'Jon in "Symbiosis" (TNG). Although Marcus did not appear in* Star Trek VI: The Undiscovered Country, *Kirk did mention his son in his log recording, and a photograph of Butrick as Marcus was seen on Kirk's desk aboard the* Enterprise-*A.*

Mardah. (Jill Sayre). Employee at **Quark's bar** on station **Deep Space 9**. Mardah was born in 2351 on planet **Bajor**. Her parents were killed during the **Cardassian** occupation, and she was raised by neighbors until the age of 13 when she struck out on her own. Her brother and sister remained on Bajor, but did not speak with Mardah for years because they disapproved of her decision to become employed as a **dabo girl** at Quark's. In 2370, she and **Jake Sisko** began dating ("Playing God" [DS9], "Sanctuary" [DS9]) and found that they both shared a love of writing, especially poetry. ("The Abandoned" [DS9]). Mardah was accepted to the science academy on planet **Regulus III** in 2371, and left Bajor to attend. ("Fascination" [DS9]).

Mareel. (Megan Gallagher). Native of planet **Khefka IV** who participated in **Verad**'s scheme to steal the Dax **symbiont** in 2370. Dismayed by Verad's personality change after he was joined with the Dax symbiont, Mareel betrayed her lover to gain back the man she loved. ("Invasive Procedures" [DS9]). *Megan Gallagher appeared as Faith Garland in "Little Green Men" (DS9).*

Marejaretus VI. Planet. Home of the Ooolans, who traditionally strike two large stones together during a meal. Those at the meal must continue to eat until the stones are broken. The ritual is somewhat reminiscent of the use of the **Betazoid chime** rung to give thanks for food. ("Manhunt" [TNG]).

Mareuvian tea. Beverage. **Guinan** served Mareuvian tea in the **Ten-Forward Lounge** aboard the *Enterprise*-D. ("The Child" [TNG]).

Mariah IV. Planet. The Valerian vessel ***Sherval Das*** visited Mariah IV when delivering **dolamide**, a chemical energy source, to the Cardassians. ("Dramatis Personae" [DS9]).

Maribona-Picard, Javier. Spanish soldier who participated in the brutal retribution against the Indians involved in the **Pueblo Revolt** of Earth in 1680. Javier Maribona-Picard was an ancestor of Captain **Jean-Luc Picard**. ("Journey's End" [TNG]).

Marijne VII beings. Subspace life-forms that lived in low orbit around planet Marijne VII. The Marijne beings resembled a small chemical flame, but were highly intelligent. When the *Starship Raman* entered Marijne VII's atmosphere in 2370, several of these beings were accidentally trapped aboard as the ship climbed to higher altitudes. The Marijne beings attempted to communicate with the crew, by directly accessing their thoughts, but this proved fatal to the scientists. Geordi La Forge explored the *Raman* with an **interface unit** and found what appeared to be his mother, **Silva La Forge**, aboard the vessel. Geordi learned that the entity that appeared to be his mother was one of the Marijne beings, who had used her image to communicate their need to return home. ("Interface" [TNG]).

Marijne VII. Gas giant planet. Site where the ***U.S.S. Raman*** was lost in 2370. Subspace beings living around Marijne VII were responsible for the accidental death of the *Raman* crew. ("Interface" [TNG]).

Mariposa, S.S. Colony vessel, **DY-500** type, launched from **Earth** on November 27, 2123, toward the **Ficus Sector**. Commanding officer was Captain Walter Granger. Besides colonists, the ship's payload included an interesting mix of high-technology equipment and low-tech gear such as spinning wheels and actual animal livestock. The *Mariposa* carried two very different groups of colonists. The first, who settled planet **Bringloid V**, were a group of Irish descendants who had eschewed advanced technology in favor of a simpler agrarian life. The second, who settled a planet they named **Mariposa**, embraced technology and in fact survived only with the aid of sophisticated cloning techniques. The colonies were reunited in 2365 when solar flares threatened the **Bringloidi**, while dangerous **replicative fading** threatened the Mariposans. ("Up the Long Ladder" [TNG]). *Named for the Spanish word for "butterfly." The DY-500 designation presumably means that the* Mariposa *was a more advanced version of Khan's DY-100-class* S.S. Botany Bay *seen in "Space Seed" (TOS).* SEE: **clone**.

Mariposa. Class-M planet in the **Ficus Sector** settled by colonists from the ***S.S. Mariposa***. ("Up the Long Ladder" [TNG]).

Maris, Roger. Twentieth-century American **baseball** player (1934-1985). Maris played for the New York Yankees and broke Babe Ruth's one-season home-run record. Twenty-fourth-century collector **Kivas Fajo** had an ancient baseball trading card, circa 1962, bearing Roger Maris's likeness, the only such card to have survived into that century. ("The Most Toys" [TNG]).

"Mark of Gideon, The." Original Series episode #72. Written by George F. Slavin and Stanley Adams. Directed by Jud Taylor. Stardate 5423.4. *First aired in 1969. Captain Kirk is held captive on a duplicate of the* Enterprise *by people who hope he holds the solution to their planet's overpopulation. The episode was cowritten by Stanley Adams, who as an actor played Cyrano Jones in "The Trouble With Tribbles" (TOS).* GUEST CAST: Sharon Acker as **Odona**; David Hurst as **Hodin**; Gene Dynarski as Krodak; Richard Deer as Fitzgerald, Admiral. SEE: **Bureau of Planetary Treaties; Gideon; Hodin; Kirk, James T.; Odona; Vegan choriomeningitis.**

Mark. (Stan Ivar). Attractive man who was romantically involved with **Kathryn Janeway** in 2371. Mark took care of **Molly**, Janeway's pregnant Irish Setter, while she was away. Janeway was not able to adequately say goodbye to Mark before she and her ship were abruptly transported to the Delta Quadrant. ("Caretaker" [VGR]). When a **Bothan** attacked *Voyager* in 2372, Janeway had a hallucination that Mark was with her on the ship. ("Persistence of Vision" [VGR]). *Mark was not given a last name.*

Markalian smugglers. Criminal operation with which Regana Tosh was believed to be associated. ("Hippocratic Oath" [DS9]).

marker beacon. Brilliant strobe lights located on the hulls of Federation **starships**, intended to aid other ships in visually locating that vessel. The marker beacons of the ***U.S.S. Lantree*** were activated to warn other ships to avoid contact with the contaminated *Lantree*. ("Unnatural Selection" [TNG]).

Markoffian sea lizard. Aquatic life-form. **Q** claimed he could have chosen to become a Markoffian sea lizard when he was stripped of his powers in 2366. He instead chose to become human. ("Déjà Q" [TNG]).

Markov. Site of a **polaric ion energy** accident in 2371 on a Class-M planet in the **Delta Quadrant** whose people were dependent on such power. Concerned inhabitants of this planet tried to stop the use of polaric energy; the Markov accident helped to raise public attention for their cause. ("Time and Again" [VGR]).

Markson, Ensign. Member of the *Enterprise*-D crew in 2370. Markson at one time dated Ensign **Alyssa Ogawa**. ("Attached" [TNG]). *Unfortunately, we do not know Ensign's Markson's first name. Things apparently didn't work out, because Alyssa later became engaged to Lieutenant Andrew Powell.*

Marlonia. Planet. Captain Picard, Ensign Ro, Keiko O'Brien, and Guinan visited Marlonia in 2369. While returning to the *Enterprise*-D, the shuttlecraft was enveloped by an energy field and its occupants reduced to children. ("Rascals" [TNG]).

***Marob* root tea.** A **Banean** drink. In 2371, Lidell Ren made some *Marob* root tea for Tom Paris. ("Ex Post Facto" [VGR]).

Marouk. (Nancy Parsons). The Sovereign of planet **Acamar III,** under whose leadership a century-old rift between the **Acamarian** government and the nomadic Acamarian **Gatherers** was ended. This aristocratic woman had very little tolerance for the Gatherers, but nevertheless agreed to help Captain Picard attempt to end the Gatherer piracy, by extending an offer of amnesty to the Gatherers, allowing them to return to Acamar III. ("The Vengeance Factor" [TNG]). SEE: **Yuta**.

Marphon. (Torin Thatcher). Member of the society on planet **Beta III** during the end of **Landru**'s rule in 2267. Although Marphon was a high-ranking official in the Landru regime, he was immune to absorption and was a member of the underground resistance against the will of Landru. Marphon rescued Kirk and Spock when they were captured by Landru's **Lawgivers**. ("Return of the Archons" [TOS]).

Marple. (Jerry Daniels). Security guard aboard the original *Starship Enterprise* and member of the landing party to planet **Gamma Trianguli VI**. Marple was killed in 2267 when one of the inhabitants of that planet struck him on the head with a heavy club. ("The Apple" [TOS]).

Marquez, Lieutenant. *Enterprise*-D crew member. Marquez was sent to the surface of planet **Bersallis III** in 2369 to track the deadly firestorm. ("Lessons" [TNG]).

Marr, Dr. Kila. (Ellen Geer). Renowned Federation xenologist who had made the study of the **Crystalline Entity** her life's work. Marr's only child, **Raymond Marr**, was killed on **Omicron Theta** when the entity attacked and destroyed that colony in 2336. She devoted all of her studies thereafter to the entity. Her work culminated in 2368 when she located the entity while she was aboard the *Enterprise*-D. Seeking revenge against the life-form that had killed her son, Marr used a projected **graviton** pulse to destroy the entity, despite orders to the contrary. ("Silicon Avatar" [TNG]).

Marr, Raymond. Science student (2320-2336) killed by the **Crystalline Entity** at the **Omicron Theta** colony. Marr, called Renny by his family, was survived by his mother, **Dr. Kila Marr**. ("Silicon Avatar" [TNG]).

Marrab Sector. Area of space where planet **Devidia II** is located. ("Time's Arrow, Part I" [TNG]).

Marratt, Gul. Cardassian officer and junior member of the **Detapa Council**. In 2372, Marratt was one of Cardassia's rising stars and was considered quite a lady's man, especially with other officers' wives. Gul Dukat despised Marratt and hoped to demote the young upstart when he returned to power. ("Return to Grace" [DS9]).

marriage. SEE: **wedding**.

Marritza, Aamin. (Harris Yulin). Minor **Cardassian** officer at the infamous **Gallitep** labor camp during the Cardassian occupation of Bajor. He served as file clerk to **Gul Darhe'el**, the brutal commander of the camp. Marritza's inability to stop the atrocities against the **Bajoran** prisoners caused him great guilt. After Gallitep, Marritza moved on to other duties and settled on planet **Kora II** in 2364, where he was an instructor at a military academy for five years. There he underwent a cosmetic alteration to look like his old commander, Gul Darhe'el, and set into motion a ruse that brought him to **Deep Space 9** in 2369. As he planned, he was arrested by station authorities who believed that he was the infamous Darhe'el. When station personnel discovered Marritza's plan, Marritza protested that he was Darhe'el and that he must be punished so that his people would be forced to hear the terrible atrocities committed against the Bajoran people and perhaps feel the terrible guilt he felt. Marritza was nevertheless freed to be returned to Kora II. While being escorted to a ship, **Kainon**, a Bajoran, took justice into his own hands, killing Marritza not because he was "the Butcher of Gallitep," but simply because he was Cardassian. ("Duet" [DS9]).

Mars Defense Perimeter. A Starfleet defense border designed to protect the inner Sol system. The **Mars** Defense Perimeter was guarded by unmanned pods capable of tracking and destroying intruding enemy space vehicles. The Borg craft passed easily through the perimeter on its way toward Earth in early 2367. ("The Best of Both Worlds, Part II" [TNG]).

Mars. Fourth planet in the Sol system, orbiting its sun with a mean distance of 228 million kilometers. Earth scientists first discovered microscopic evidence of ancient life on Mars in 1996. ("Future's End, Part I" [VGR]). Mars was colonized by people from Earth in 2103. ("The 37's" [VGR]). Starfleet's **Utopia Planitia Fleet Yards** were located on Mars. ("Booby Trap" [TNG]). SEE: **Martian Colonies.** *"Future's End, Parts I and II" (VGR) were filmed in August, 1996, just a few days after NASA's historic press conference announcing the discovery of possible microfossils in a Martian meteorite. Since that episode was set in late 1996, the* Voyager *art department put a large photo of the microfossil (with the caption "take me to your leader") as well as a newspaper clipping describing the finding into Rain Robinson's laboratory.* Star Trek: Deep Space Nine *scenic artist Anthony Fredrickson also commemorated the discovery by putting the code number ALH84001 on the mines laid by the* Defiant *in "Call To Arms" (DS9). ALH84001 was the code number of the meteorite in which the possible microfossils were found.*

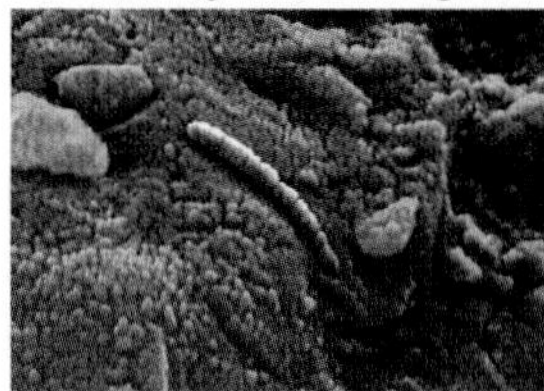

Marseilles. City in southeastern France, **Earth** on the Mediterranean Sea. Starfleet maintained a training base just outside of Marseilles. As a cadet, **Thomas Paris** chose that particular facility for his second-semester physical training because of its proximity to **Chez Sandrine**'s. ("The Cloud" [VGR]).

Marta community. A settlement of the southern continent of **Malcor III**. William Riker, masquerading as **Rivas Jakara**, listed this as his home. ("First Contact" [TNG]).

Marta. (Yvonne Craig). Inmate at the **Elba II** penal colony in 2268 who was killed by fellow inmate **Garth of Izar**. Marta, a green Orion woman, was Lord Garth's consort during his takeover attempt and was fond of quoting **Shakespeare**. ("Whom Gods Destroy" [TOS]).

Martia. (Iman). Chameloid (shape-shifting) inmate at the Klingon prison asteroid **Rura Penthe** at the time Kirk and McCoy were imprisoned there for the murder of Klingon **Chancellor Gorkon**. (*Star Trek VI: The Undiscovered Country*). SEE: **shape-shifter**.

Martian Colonies, Fundamental Declarations of the. Important legal document addressing the subject of individual rights. ("Court Martial" [TOS]).

Martian Colonies. Settlements on the fourth planet in the Sol system. ("Court Martial" [TOS]). The first human colony on **Mars** was established in 2103. ("The 37's" [VGR]). A serial murderer killed eight women at the Martian Colonies in 2105, a crime that went unsolved for over a century. ("Wolf in the Fold" [TOS]). Some of **Jean-Luc Picard's** ancestors were among the pioneers who settled the first colony on Mars. (*Star Trek Generations). Starship Enterprise* crew member **Lieutenant Mira Romaine** was born at Martian Colony 3. ("The Lights of Zetar" [TOS]). *Enterprise*-D crew member **Simon Tarses** was a native of the Martian Colonies ("The Drumhead" [TNG]), and noted **Utopia Planitia Fleet Yards** engineer **Leah Brahms** resided there while working on the *Galaxy*-class starship project. ("Booby Trap" [TNG]).

Martin, Dr. (Rick Fitts). A member of the *Enterprise*-D's medical staff. He was left in charge of sickbay when Dr. Crusher succumbed to a mysterious coma, later found to be caused by a **telepathic memory invasion** rape. ("Violations" [TNG]).

Martin, Ensign. (David Christian). Starfleet officer assigned to the *U.S.S. Voyager*. In 2373 Ensign Martin was on duty in Transporter Room 1 when an **Ilari** ambassador was beamed aboard. Kes, while under the influence of **Tieran**, shot and killed Martin and the Ilari representative. ("Warlord" [VGR]).

Martine, Ensign Angela. (Barbara Baldavin). Phaser control officer aboard the original *Starship Enterprise* during the **Romulan** incursion of 2266. Martine had been engaged to marry **Robert Tomlinson**, but their wedding was interrupted by news of the attack on the **Romulan Neutral Zone** outposts. Her fiancé was killed during that conflict. ("Balance of Terror" [TOS]). Martine was on the landing party to the **amusement park planet** in 2267. She was apparently killed by an old-style airplane making a strafing run, an image conjured up by fellow crew member **Esteban Rodriguez**. Martine was later restored to health by the planet's **Caretaker**. ("Shore Leave" [TOS]). *Actor Barbara Baldavin was the wife of original series Star Trek casting director Joseph D'Agosta.*

Martis. (Rachael Harris). Ocampan woman, mother of **Kes** and wife to **Benaren**. In 2370, when Kes was born, Martis voiced her wish that Kes might one day see the sun. ("Before and After" [VGR]).

Martok, General. (J. G. Hertzler). Klingon warrior who commanded the empire's defense forces in 2372. When the **Klingon High Council** suspected that the **Cardassian** government's **Detapa Council** was being controlled by **Dominion** agents early in that year, Martok led the massive invasion on Cardassia from his flagship, ***Negh'Var.*** Martok's mission of eliminating the Detapa Council was thwarted when Starfleet officer Ben Sisko rescued the council, and Martok subsequently turned his attack onto station **Deep Space 9**. When Gowron decided to end the battle and return home, Martok argued that victory was close at hand, even though continuation of the fight would have greatly weakened the empire. ("The Way of the Warrior" [DS9]). It was not realized that sometime before 2373, Martok was captured by agents of the Dominion while he was hunting sabre bear on Kang's Summit. ("In Purgatory's Shadow" [DS9]). He was replaced by a shape-shifting **Founder**, so no one suspected the substitution. During an induction ceremony for the Order of the *Bat'leth* in early 2373, Captain Benjamin Sisko and his men exposed the duplicate Martok as a Founder spy. The spy was killed by the assembled Klingon warriors at **Ty'Gokor**.

("Apocalypse Rising" [DS9]). The real Martok was held until 2373 by the **Jem'Hadar** at **Dominion internment camp 371** in the Gamma Quadrant. ("In Purgatory's Shadow" [DS9]). Following his escape from Dominion imprisonment, Martok was assigned to command a detachment of Klingon warriors stationed at Deep Space 9. ("By Inferno's Light" [DS9]).

Martuk. Name of a nonexistent Lissepian transport vessel, used as a cover for Major Kira Nerys's runabout on a covert mission to planet **Cardassia IV** to rescue **Li Nalas** in 2370. ("The Homecoming" [DS9]).

Martus. SEE: **Mazur, Martus.**

Marva IV. Class-M planet located in the **Badlands**. On stardate 50485.2, Benjamin Sisko went to a **Maquis** camp on Marva IV to meet with Cing'ta, an informant who claimed to have information about Michael Eddington. ("For the Uniform" [DS9]).

Marvick, Dr. Laurence. (David Frankham). Federation engineer, one of the designers of the original ***Constitution*-class *Starship*** *Enterprise*. Marvick traveled aboard the ***Enterprise*** in 2268 while accompanying **Dr. Miranda Jones** and **Medusan** Ambassador **Kollos** on a diplomatic mission. Marvick, who exhibited signs of emotional instability, was in love with Jones and became jealous of her interest in Kollos. During the journey, Marvick made direct visual contact with Kollos and was driven dangerously insane by the encounter. In his delirium, he programmed the *Enterprise* to travel beyond the rim of the galaxy, across the dangerous **galactic barrier**. Marvick died shortly thereafter, unable to live with what he saw in Kollos. Ironically it was the Medusan ambassador who guided the *Enterprise* back to Federation space with his advanced navigational knowledge, after mind-melding with Commander Spock. ("Is There in Truth No Beauty?" [TOS]).

Maryland*, *U.S.S. Federation starship. The *Maryland* was lost in the **Gamma Quadrant** some time prior to 2371. It was believed that the ship and crew fell victim to the **Dominion**. ("In Purgatory's Shadow" [DS9]). *Named for the several naval vessels that served the United States in the 20th century.*

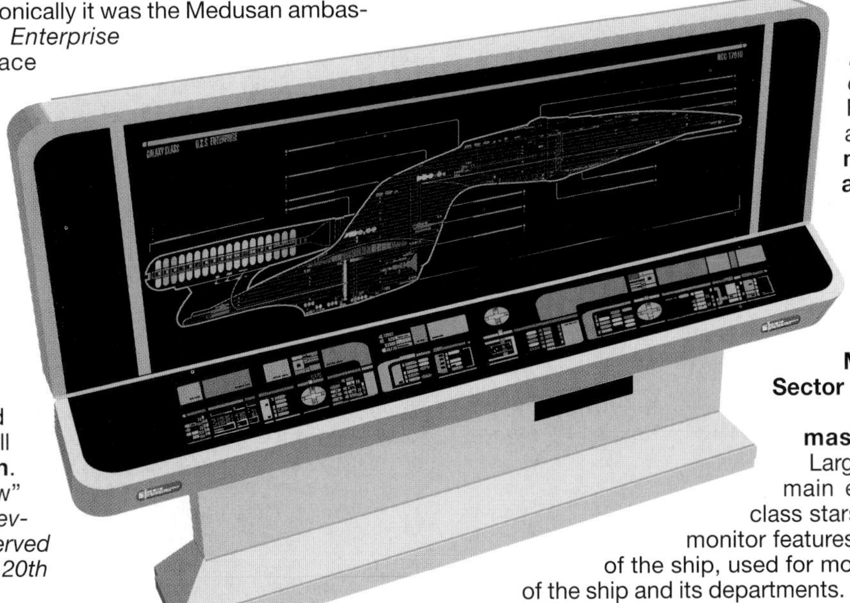

Masada. Science officer of the ***U.S.S. Constellation***, killed when the ship was destroyed by the **planet killer** in 2267. ("The Doomsday Machine" [TOS]). *Probably named for the hilltop fortress where Jews defied Roman legions, eventually committing suicide* en masse *rather than surrender.*

Masaka's city. Term **Ihat** applied to the space-borne structure that was the **D'Arsay archive**. ("Masks" [TNG]).

Masaka. (Brent Spiner). The sun goddess in ancient **D'Arsay** mythology. Masaka was the queen, a sun deity who also represented death. Masaka's enemy was **Korgano**, the moon god who was the only one who could control her and chase her from the sky. The **D'Arsay archive** programmed Data to assume the role of Masaka in a re-creation of D'Arsay myths aboard the *Enterprise*-D in 2370. During this re-creation, the *Enterprise*-D crew caused the archive to convert part of the ship into Masaka's temple, permitting communication with Masaka herself, and providing the key to returning the ship to normal. ("Masks" [TNG]). *The basic structure of Masaka's temple was also used as the meeting hall in "Meridian" (DS9), the Klingon Great Hall in "House of Quark" (DS9), and the interior of the Albino's home in "Blood Oath" (DS9).*

Masefield, John. English poet (1878-1967) who wrote such classics as "Sea Fever," from which Kirk quoted, "All I ask is a tall ship and a star to steer her by." ("The Ultimate Computer" [TOS], *Star Trek V: The Final Frontier). The* ***dedication plaque*** *on the bridge of the* Starship Defiant *quoted the same line from "Sea Fever."*

mashed potatoes with butter. Food made from puréed cooked Earth plant roots cooked with dairy products. Samantha Wildman introduced Kes to mashed potatoes with butter. ("Elogium" [VGR]).

Masiform D. Powerful injectable stimulant. McCoy administered Masiform D to Spock after several thorns from a poisonous plant rendered him unconscious on planet **Gamma Trianguli VI** in 2267. ("The Apple" [TOS]).

masking circuitry. Device employed by some ships of the **Kazon-Nistrim** sect in the Delta Quadrant. The masking circuitry made such ships difficult to detect using **sensors**. Such vessels could be rendered briefly visible when illuminated by a **polaron** burst. ("State of Flux" [VGR]).

"Masks." *Next Generation* episode #169. Written by Joe Menosky. Directed by Robert Weimer. Stardate 47615.2. *First aired in 1994. An ancient archive begins to convert the* Enterprise*-D and Data into representations of its culture.* GUEST CAST: Rickey D'Shon Collins as **Eric**. SEE: **behavioral nodes; D'Arsay; D'Arsay archive; D'Arsay symbols; Data; Elder; Eric; Federation Astrophysical Survey; fortanium; Ihat; Korgano; Masaka's city; Masaka; Narsu, Mrs.; rogue comet; Sector 1156.**

master situation monitor. Large wall-mounted display in main engineering of a *Galaxy*-class starship. The master situation monitor features a large cutaway diagram of the ship, used for monitoring the overall status of the ship and its departments. *The master situation monitor also included a number of very small "in-jokes." These included the official* U.S.S. Enterprise *duck, the ship's mouse, a Porsche, a DC-3 airplane, the* Nomad *space probe (from "The Changeling" [TOS]), and the hamster on a treadmill that was alleged to be the true source of power for the ship's warp engines. Naturally, these items were far too small to normally be seen on television, but the sharp-eyed viewer could occasionally glimpse them in a close-up, if they hadn't been covered up for that shot.*

master systems display. Information display and control console used by starship personnel in main engineering of *Galaxy*-class starships. *The master systems display console was built from the video display table from Starfleet Command in* Star Trek IV: The Voyage Home. *For obvious reasons,* Star Trek *production personnel nicknamed it the Pool Table.*

"Masterpiece Society, The." *Next Generation* episode #113. Teleplay by Adam Belanoff and Michael Piller. Story by James Kahn and Adam Belanoff. Directed by Winrich Kolbe. Stardate 45470.1. *First aired in 1992. The Enterprise-D offers help when a perfectly planned, genetically engineered community is threatened with destruction, but the cure may be worse than the disease.* GUEST CAST: John Snyder as **Conor, Aaron**; Dey Young as **Bates, Hannah**; Ron Canada as **Benbeck, Martin**; Shelia Franklin as **Felton, Ensign**. SEE: **Bates, Hannah; Benbeck, Martin; Conor, Aaron; Felton, Ensign; Genome Colony; Moab IV; Moab Sector; multiphase tractor beam; stellar core fragment.**

Masters, Lieutenant. (Janet MacLachlan). Staff engineer who served aboard the *Starship Enterprise* in 2267. Masters was on duty during the confrontation with the entity **Lazarus**. ("The Alternative Factor" [TOS]).

Mataline II. Second planet in the Mataline system. **Neela Daren** purchased a flexible piano keyboard at Mataline II. ("Lessons" [TNG]).

materialization error. Failure of a **holodeck** matter conversion system, which can cause the loss of solid objects within the holodeck environment. Materialization errors occurred in the *Enterprise*-D holodecks in 2370 following the ship's exposure to plasmonic energy in the atmosphere of planet **Boraal II**. ("Homeward" [TNG]).

Mathenites. Civilization. The Mathenite government offered asylum to **Legate Ghemor** in 2371. ("Second Skin" [DS9]).

Matopin rock fungi. Type of edible fungi used in salads. ("Business As Usual" [DS9]).

matrix diodes. The array of omnidirectional holographic diodes embedded in the walls of a holographic environment simulator. The matrix diodes were suspected of malfunctioning in **Sherlock Holmes program 3A** in 2369. ("Ship in a Bottle" [TNG]).

matrix overlay program. Computer program devised by the Jupiter Station diagnostic program. A matrix overlay was used to repair serious memory fragmentation in the *Voyager's* Emergency Medical Hologram by merging the diagnostic program's heuristic matrix with the EMH's matrix. ("The Swarm" [VGR]).

"Matter of Honor, A." *Next Generation* episode #34. Teleplay by Burton Armus. Story by Wanda M. Haight & Gregory Amos and Burton Armus. Directed by Rob Bowman. Stardate 42506.5. *First aired in 1989. Riker serves aboard a Klingon ship as part of an officer exchange program.* GUEST CAST: Diana Muldaur as **Pulaski, Dr. Katherine**; John Putch as **Mendon, Ensign**; Christopher Collins as **Kargan, Captain**; Brian Thompson as **Klag**; Colm Meaney as **O'Brien, Miles**; Peter Parros as Tactics officer; Laura Drake as **Vekma**. SEE: **Benzar; Benzites; *bregit* lung; *gagh*; heart of *targ*; Kargan, Captain; Klag; Mendon, Ensign; microbiotic colony; Officer Exchange Program; *Pagh, I.K.S.*; phaser range; Pheben system; *pipius* claw; Riker, William T.; *rokeg* blood pie; Starbase 179; Tranome Sar; transponder, emergency; Vekma.**

"Matter of Perspective, A." *Next Generation* episode #62. Written by Ed Zuckerman. Directed by Cliff Bole. Stardate 43610.4. *First aired in 1990. The holodeck is used to re-create the scene of a crime when Riker is accused of murder.* GUEST CAST: Craig Richard Nelson as **Krag**; Gina Hecht as **Apgar, Mauna**; Mark Margolis as **Apgar, Dr. Nel**; Colm Meaney as **O'Brien, Miles**; Juli Donald as **Tayna**. SEE: **Apgar, Dr. Nel; Apgar, Manua; dicosilium; Emila II; Krag; Krieger waves; painting; Riker, William T.; Tanuga IV; Tanugans; Tayna.**

"Matter of Time, A." *Next Generation* episode #109. Written by Rick Berman. Directed by Paul Lynch. Stardate 45349.1. *First aired in 1991. A time-traveling professor, apparently on a research project from the future, turns out to be a petty thief from the past.* GUEST CAST: Stefan Gierasch as **Moseley, Hal**; Matt Frewer as **Rasmussen, Berlinghoff**; Shelia Franklin as **Felton, Ensign**; Shay Garner as Scientist. SEE: **auto-phaser interlock; berylite scan; electroplasma system taps; exothermal inversion; Felton, Ensign; greenhouse effect; Model A Ford; Moseley, Hal; neural stimulator; New Seattle; Penthara IV; phaser; plasticized tritanium mesh; Rasmussen, Professor Berlinghoff; shield inverters; Starbase 214; Telurian plague; temporal distortion; terawatt; time-travel pod.**

matter stream. In the operation of the **transporter**, the matter stream is the beam of phased (or dematerialized) matter that is transported from the transport chamber to the destination (or the reverse). ("Realm of Fear" [TNG]).

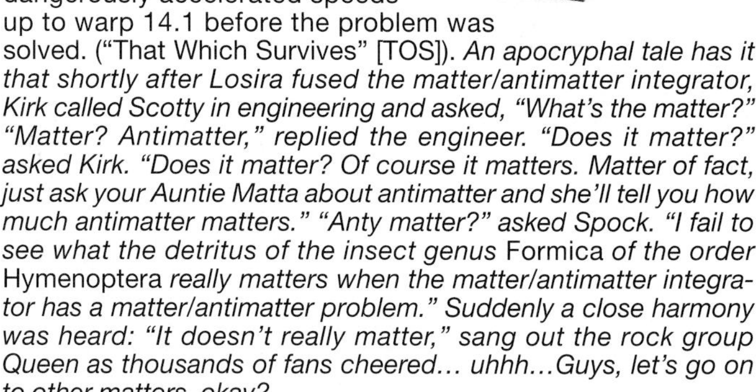

matter/antimatter integrator. Component of a starship's **warp-drive** system, such as those used aboard *Constitution*-class vessels. The emergency bypass control valve to the matter-antimatter integrator aboard the *Starship Enterprise* was fused by **Losira** in 2268, causing the *Enterprise* to travel at dangerously accelerated speeds up to warp 14.1 before the problem was solved. ("That Which Survives" [TOS]). *An apocryphal tale has it that shortly after Losira fused the matter/antimatter integrator, Kirk called Scotty in engineering and asked, "What's the matter?" "Matter? Antimatter," replied the engineer. "Does it matter?" asked Kirk. "Does it matter? Of course it matters. Matter of fact, just ask your Auntie Matta about antimatter and she'll tell you how much antimatter matters." "Anty matter?" asked Spock. "I fail to see what the detritus of the insect genus* Formica *of the order* Hymenoptera *really matters when the matter/antimatter integrator has a matter/antimatter problem." Suddenly a close harmony was heard: "It doesn't really matter," sang out the rock group Queen as thousands of fans cheered... uhhh...Guys, let's go on to other matters, okay?*

matter/antimatter reaction chamber. Component of the **warp-drive** system used aboard Federation starships. The reaction chamber is the vessel within which matter and antimatter are allowed to intermix in a controlled fashion, resulting in the massive release of energy necessary to power the faster-than-light warp drive. The matter/antimatter reaction is regulated by a **dilithium crystal**, and the entire volume is contained by a magnetic containment field to prevent the volatile antimatter from coming into physical contact with the ship's structure. SEE: **antimatter containment**. The *Starship Voyager*'s warp core was ejected on stardate 48734 by a disembodied Commander Chakotay, working to prevent the ship's entry into a nebula inhabited by the **Komar**. The core was subsequently recovered and reinstalled. ("Cathexis" [VGR]). *Voyager*'s warp core was designed to operate for up to three years without refueling. The reaction chamber was equipped with a compositor that allowed **dilithium** to be recrystallized. ("Innocence" [VGR]).

Matthews. (Vince Deadrick). *Enterprise* security officer. Matthews was killed when he fell into the caverns at planet **Exo III**. ("What Are Little Girls Made Of?" [TOS]).

Maturin. (Michael Keenan). Governor of the **Caldos colony**. Although not from **Earth**, he had a great appreciation of the heritage of Scotland. Maturin's family had visited Glamis Castle, in the Scottish Highlands, when he was a child, and Maturin had felt a kinship with the Scottish culture since that time. He felt it natural to move to Caldos, which was a re-creation of Scotland. ("Sub Rosa" [TNG]).

Mauk-to'Vor. Klingon ritual in which the honor of an individual is restored by the one responsible for the loss of honor. The restoration of honor involves the killing of the dishonored individual with a *mevak* dagger. *Adanji* incense is used in the *Mauk-to'Vor*. In 2372, **Kurn** journeyed to Deep Space 9 in order to have his honor restored by Worf in a *Mauk-to'Vor* ritual. Kurn had believed that his brother's refusal to support Chancellor Gowron's policies had been responsible for his loss of honor. ("Sons of Mogh" [DS9]).

Maura. Beloved pet dog of **Aquiel Uhnari**. Maura was killed at **Relay Station 47** in 2369 by the same **coalescent organism** that killed **Keith Rocha**. ("Aquiel" [TNG]).

Mauric, Ambassador. (Robin Gammell). Diplomatic envoy from planet **Kesprytt III** to the Federation in 2370. Mauric represented the **Kes** people in their bid to gain associate membership in the Federation. During the talks, Mauric exhibited seriously paranoid behavior. This level of mistrust also appeared to be pervasive throughout the Prytt Security Ministry. Accordingly, *Enterprise*-D personnel recommended that the Kes be denied membership in the Federation. ("Attached" [TNG]).

Mavala IV. Planet where **Dr. Noonien Soong** and Juliana O'Donnell were secretly married in 2332. They returned to Omicron Theta after a four-day absence. ("Inheritance" [TNG]).

Mavek. (Gary Werntz). Attendant at the **Tilonus Institute for Mental Disorders** created in Riker's mind while he was being brainwashed on planet **Tilonus IV** in 2369. Mavek was large in stature and seemed to delight in forcing Riker and other inmates to obey his orders. ("Frame of Mind" [TNG]). SEE: ***"Frame of Mind."***

Maxia Zeta Star System. Location of the **Battle of Maxia** where the ***U.S.S. Stargazer,*** under the command of Captain **Jean-Luc Picard,** suffered a devastating sneak attack from an unidentified ship that was later identified as **Ferengi** in origin. ("The Battle" [TNG]).

Maxia, Battle of. A skirmish in 2355 between the Federation starship ***Stargazer*** and an unknown spacecraft, later identified as a **Ferengi** vessel. The *Stargazer,* under the command of Captain **Jean-Luc Picard,** was traveling through the **Maxia Zeta Star System** when it was attacked without provocation. The *Stargazer* survived because of a brilliant tactic devised by Captain Picard, later called the **Picard Maneuver**, permitting the ship to escape damage long enough to fire a full phaser and torpedo spread. The Ferengi ship was destroyed, but the *Stargazer* crew was able to escape in shuttlecraft and **escape pod**s. Among the casualties aboard the Ferengi vessel was the son of **DaiMon Bok,** making his first voyage as DaiMon. ("The Battle" [TNG]).

Maxwell, Captain Benjamin. (Bob Gunton). Starfleet officer who commanded the ***U.S.S. Rutledge*** during the **Cardassian** wars. Maxwell received the Federation's highest citations for courage and valor during the conflict, but he lost his family in the Cardassian attack on the **Setlik III** outpost, a loss made even more bitter because his ship was not able to reach Setlik in time to prevent the massacre. Maxwell carried bitterness toward the Cardassians for many years, and in 2367 mounted an unauthorized offensive against the Cardassians, in direct violation of the peace treaty of 2366. Maxwell, in command of the ***U.S.S. Phoenix***, destroyed a Cardassian outpost and two Cardassian ships, because he believed the Cardassians were planning for a new attack against the Federation. Former *Rutledge* crew member **Miles O'Brien** was able to convince Maxwell to discontinue his attack, and Maxwell was relieved of command of the *Phoenix*. ("The Wounded" [TNG]).

"May you die well." A Klingon parting phrase. ("Redemption, Part II" [TNG]).

Maylor, Sev. (Susan French). A woman who died while traveling with **Ambassador Ves Alkar** on a diplomatic mission in 2369. Alkar identified Maylor as his mother, but it was later learned that she was not. Maylor was found to be much younger than she appeared, but Alkar had been using her as an empathic "receptacle" for his negative thoughts and emotions. As a result of this severe abuse, she became extremely bitter and hostile, and aged at a highly accelerated rate. Maylor died at about age 30 from the stress of Alkar's empathic abuse. ("Man of the People" [TNG]).

Mazur, Martus. (Chris Sarandon). **El-Aurian** refugee and con artist who, in 2370, obtained an unusual **gambling device** that somehow altered the laws of probability. At station Deep Space 9, he opened a bar called **Club Martus**, where he installed several copies of this device. Martus was initially successful in luring patrons from Quark's bar, but his good fortune did not last. A run of bad luck, possibly influenced by the gambling devices, forced him out of business. Soon after that, **Alsia**, a woman he met on the station, conned him out of his remaining money. Martus was later taken into custody when a couple from **Pythro V** from whom Martus had bilked money pressed charges. ("Rivals" [DS9]). SEE: **Roana**.

mazurka festival. Celebration of Polish folk dance and music from **Earth**'s European continent. Jennifer and **Benjamin Sisko**, along with their friends Gretchen and **Calvin Hudson,** attended a mazurka festival at **New Berlin**. ("The Maquis, Part I" [DS9]). Star Trek: First Contact *established that New Berlin is located on Earth's moon.*

McAllister C-5 Nebula. Protostellar cloud located seven light-years inside **Cardassian** space, some 11 light-years from planet **Minos Korva**. In 2369, a Cardassian invasion fleet hid inside the nebula while apparently preparing to attack the Minos Korva sector. The fleet's time inside the nebula was limited due to the intense particle flux within, which caused degradation of the spacecraft hulls. ("Chain of Command, Part II" [TNG]).

McClukidge, Nurse. Member of the *Enterprise*-D medical staff. Dr. Beverly Crusher suggested that McClukidge could fill in for **Nurse Ogawa**, so the latter could take a vacation on **Risa**. ("Imaginary Friend" [TNG]).

McCoullough, Captain. Starfleet officer who wrote the revised procedures for **first contact** operations. ("Move Along Home" [DS9]).

McCoy, David. (Bill Quinn). Father of *Enterprise* medical officer **Leonard McCoy**. The elder McCoy suffered from a painful, terminal illness, and his son eventually pulled the plug to spare his father further pain. *(Star Trek V: The Final Frontier). David McCoy's first name was established in* Star Trek III.

McCoy, Dr. Leonard H. (DeForest Kelley). Chief medical officer aboard the original *Starship Enterprise* under the command of Captain James Kirk, who gave him the nickname "Bones." ("The Corbomite Maneuver" [TOS]). As of 2267, McCoy had earned the Legion of Honor, and had been decorated by Starfleet surgeons. ("Court Martial" [TOS]).

McCoy attended the University of Mississippi on Earth. While a student there, he met and had a romance with **Emony Dax** while she was visiting Earth around 2245 to judge a gymnastics competition. ("Trials and Tribble-ations" [DS9]). Early in McCoy's medical career, his father was struck with a terrible, fatal illness. Faced with the prospect of his father suffering a terrible, lingering death, McCoy mercifully "pulled the plug" on

him, allowing him to die. To McCoy's considerable anguish, a cure for his father's disease was discovered shortly thereafter, and McCoy carried the guilt for his father's possibly needless death for many years. *(Star Trek V: The Final Frontier).* Prior to his assignment to the *Enterprise,* McCoy had been romantically involved with the future **Nancy Crater**. ("The Man Trap" [TOS]). In 2253, McCoy developed a neurosurgical technique that was used in 2372 by the *Voyager's* **Emergency Medical Hologram** to repair the damaged cerebral cortex of **Danara Pel**. ("Lifesigns" [VGR]).

McCoy first joined the *Enterprise* crew in 2266, and remained associated with that illustrious ship and its successor for some 27 years. *(Star Trek VI: The Undiscovered Country).* In 2267, McCoy suffered a serious overdose of **cordrazine** in a shipboard accident. In the paranoid delusions that followed, McCoy fled the ship, then jumped through a time portal being studied by *Enterprise* personnel. In the past, McCoy effected serious damage to the flow of time until Kirk and Spock followed him to restore the shape of history. ("The City on the Edge of Forever" [TOS]). SEE: **Guardian of Forever; Keeler, Edith**. In 2268, McCoy was diagnosed with terminal **xenopolycythemia** and chose to resign from Starfleet so that he could marry a woman named **Natira**, high priestess of the **Yonada**n people. McCoy rejoined Starfleet after a cure was found in the Yonadan memory banks. ("For the World is Hollow and I Have Touched the Sky" [TOS]).

McCoy retired from Starfleet after the return of the *Enterprise* from the five-year mission, but he returned to Starfleet at Kirk's request when the ship intercepted the **V'Ger** entity near Earth. *(Star Trek: The Motion Picture).* McCoy, along with Kirk, was wrongly convicted of the murder of Klingon **Chancellor Gorkon** in 2293, a conviction that was later overturned. McCoy was scheduled to retire shortly after the **Khitomer** peace conference, but he either changed his mind, or later returned to Starfleet. *(Star Trek VI: The Undiscovered Country).* As a retired Starfleet admiral, McCoy made an inspection tour of the *Enterprise*-D in 2364 at the age of 137. ("Encounter at Farpoint, Part I" [TNG]).

An unofficial part of McCoy's backstory was developed by Original Series story editor Dorothy Fontana, who had written a story entitled "Joanna," which would have established that McCoy had been married and later endured a bitter divorce, and it was the aftermath of this experience that drove him to join Starfleet. The episode would have introduced Joanna, McCoy's now-grown daughter from that failed marriage. "Joanna" was written for the Original Series's third season, but was so heavily rewritten (becoming "The Way to Eden" [TOS]) that Fontana removed her name from the final version.

Since this McCoy backstory was never incorporated into an episode, it isn't "official," at least for the purposes of this encyclopedia. On the other hand, it is mentioned here because it offers insight into the McCoy character, and because of Fontana's pivotal role in the development of many Star Trek *characters. McCoy's first appearance was in "The Corbomite Maneuver" (TOS).*

McDowell, Ensign. (Kenneth Meseroll). *Enterprise*-D crew member. McDowell served at Tactical during the ship's rescue of a Romulan science ship in 2368. ("The Next Phase" [TNG]).

McFarland. A renowned Federation archaeologist. McFarland attended the annual symposium of the **Federation Archaeology Council** in 2367. ("QPid" [TNG]).

McGivers, Lieutenant Marla. (Madlyn Rhue). Historian aboard the original *Starship Enterprise* in 2267 when former dictator **Khan Noonien Singh** attempted to commandeer the ship. McGivers's fascination for bold men of the past clouded her judgment when it came to Khan. She betrayed the *Enterprise* crew and helped Khan's takeover attempt. Marla was later given the choice of a court-martial or accompanying Khan and his group into exile on planet **Ceti Alpha V**. She chose to stay with Khan and live on that desolate world. ("Space Seed" [TOS]). McGivers married Khan, but she was later killed by the parasitic eel creatures indigenous to Ceti Alpha V. *(Star Trek II: The Wrath of Khan).*

McHuron, Eve. (Karen Steele). Beautiful woman recruited by Harry Mudd as a bride for a settler on planet **Ophiucus III**. Eve had been raised on a farm planet, caring for her two brothers. Although Eve was attracted to Kirk, she eventually realized that Kirk was married to his ship, so she ended up with miner **Ben Childress** at the **Rigel XII** mining station. ("Mudd's Women" [TOS]).

McKenzie, Ard'rian. (Eileen Seeley). Member of the **Tau Cygna V** colony. Ard'rian was very interested in Commander Data's abilities as an android, and grew very fond of him personally. She supported Data's efforts to evacuate the Tau Cygna colony in 2366. ("The Ensigns of Command" [TNG]).

McKinley Park. Located on planet Earth, a favorite place of **Keiko** and **Miles O'Brien**. Miles presented Keiko with a gold bracelet there. ("Power Play" [TNG]).

McKinley Rocket Base. American military space launch facility on Earth. In 1968, a large orbital nuclear weapons platform was launched from McKinley Rocket Base by the United States to counter a similar launch by a rival power. In an effort to demonstrate the foolhardy nature of such weapons, extraterrestrial agent Gary Seven secretly armed the platform's warheads shortly after launch, then caused the launch vehicle to malfunction, before disarming it just before impact. ("Assignment Earth" [TOS]). *The scenes of McKinley Rocket Base were a combination of stock film of NASA's Kennedy Space Center and footage shot at Paramount Pictures in Los Angeles. The vehicle launched from McKinley Rocket Base was stock footage of an early* Saturn V *booster.*

McKinley Station. SEE: **Earth Station McKinley**.

McKinney. Starfleet officer who was apparently killed by the unknown alien intelligence that attempted to infiltrate **Starfleet Headquarters** in 2364. ("Conspiracy" [TNG]).

McKnight, Ensign. (Pamela Winslow). *Enterprise*-D crew member. McKnight served at conn in 2367. ("Clues," "Face of the Enemy" [TNG]).

McLowery, Frank. (Leonard Nimoy). Outlaw from **Earth**'s ancient American West, and a member of the Clanton gang who was killed at the famous gunfight at the OK Corral in 1881. Spock represented Frank McLowery in a bizarre charade created by the **Melkotians** in 2268. ("Spectre of the Gun" [TOS]).

McLowery, Tom. (DeForest Kelley). Outlaw who sided with the Clanton family against the Earps at the historic gunfight at the OK Corral in 1881. Tom McLowery and his brother, Frank, were both killed in the battle. McCoy was cast as Tom McLowery in a drama created by the **Melkotians** in 2268 for the purpose of causing the *Enterprise* crew's death. ("Spectre of the Gun" [TOS]).

McNary. (Gary Armagnal). Fictional character from the **Dixon Hill** detective stories. McNary was a homicide detective and a good friend of Hill's, despite Dixon's tendency to work both sides of the law. A holographic version of McNary was part of the Dixon Hill holodeck programs. ("The Big Goodbye" [TNG]).

McPherson. Genetically engineered survivor of Earth's **Eugenics Wars**. McPherson and other followers of **Khan Noonien Singh** escaped Earth in 1996 in the sleeper ship, ***S.S. Botany Bay***, remaining in suspended animation until revived by personnel from the *U.S.S. Enterprise* in 2267. ("Space Seed" [TOS]).

McWatt. Starfleet officer. McWatt served aboard the ***U.S.S. Okinawa*** while Benjamin Sisko was the vessel's executive officer. In 2372, McWatt and several other former *Okinawa* officers were reassigned by **Admiral Leyton** in preparation for his attempted coup of Earth's government. ("Paradise Lost" [DS9]).

Mea 3. (Barbara Babcock). Government official on planet **Eminiar VII**. Mea 3 greeted the *Enterprise* landing party in 2267. She was declared a casualty of war during an attack by planet **Vendikar**. Mea 3 was expected to report to a disintegration chamber under the terms of her planet's agreement with Vendikar, but was prevented from doing so by *Enterprise* personnel. ("A Taste of Armageddon" [TOS]). *Barbara Babcock also played Philana in "Plato's Stepchildren" (TOS), and provided the voice of Trelane's mother in "The Squire of Gothos" (TOS), the voice of Isis the cat in "Assignment: Earth" (TOS), and the voice of Commander Loskene in "The Tholian Web" (TOS).*

Mears, Yeoman. (Phyllis Douglas). Crew member aboard the original *Starship Enterprise*. Mears served on the ***Shuttlecraft Galileo*** crew when it crashed on planet **Taurus II** in 2267. ("The *Galileo* Seven" [TOS]).

"Measure of a Man, The." *Next Generation* episode #35. Written by Melinda M. Snodgrass. Directed by Robert Scheerer. Stardate 42523.7. *First aired in 1989. Data is put on trial to determine if he is a person, or merely the property of Starfleet. This episode included the first references to the Daystrom Institute (a tip of the hat to "The Ultimate Computer" [TOS]), and to Commander Bruce Maddox (who would not be seen again, but Data would occasionally correspond with him). Our heroes' weekly poker game was also seen for the first time in this episode.* GUEST CAST: Diana Muldaur as **Pulaski, Dr. Katherine**; Amanda McBroom as **Louvois, Captain Phillipa**; Clyde Kusatsu as **Nakamura, Admiral**; Brian Brophy as **Maddox, Commander Bruce**; Whoopi Goldberg as **Guinan**; Colm Meaney as **O'Brien, Miles**. SEE: **android; Cumberland, Acts of; Data; Daystrom Institute of Technology; *Dream of the Fire, The*; Judge Advocate General; K'Ratak; Louvois, Phillipa; Picard, Jean-Luc; Maddox, Commander Bruce; Nakamura, Admiral; poker; Sector 23; security access code; Starbase 173; *Stargazer, U.S.S.*; Yar, Natasha.**

mechanical rice picker. Device that supposedly caused Spock's ears to be pointed, at least in a tale fabricated by Kirk in Earth's past. Kirk was trying to explain Spock's alien appearance to a police officer of Earth's 1930s. ("The City on the Edge of Forever" [TOS]).

mediators. Law-enforcement officials on planet **Rubicun III**. ("Justice" [TNG]). SEE: **punishment zones**.

medical equipment. SEE: **alpha-wave inducer; autosuture; bioregenerative field; cortical stimulator; drechtal beams; exoscalpel; hypospray; microtome; motor assist bands; neural calipers; neural stimulator; neural transducers; physiostimulator; plasma infusion unit; protodynoplaser; psychotricorder; pulmonary support unit; somnetic inducer; sonic separator; stasis unit; T-cell stimulator; tissue mitigator; trilaser connector.**

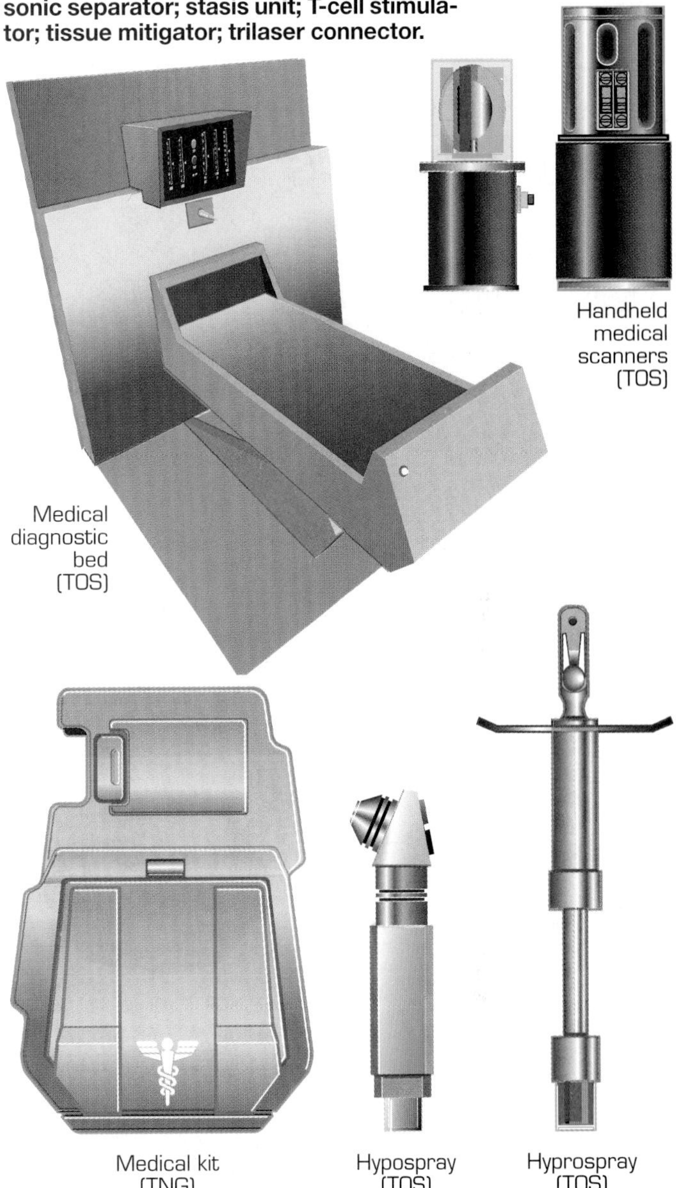

Handheld medical scanners [TOS]

Medical diagnostic bed [TOS]

Medical kit [TNG]

Hypospray [TOS]

Hyprospray [TOS]

medicine bundle. In Native American culture, a pouch containing various objects used by an individual when on a **vision quest**. The contents of the medicine bundle were suggested to the individuals by their animal guides. Medicine bundles were private and were handled reverently. **Chakotay**'s medicine bundle contained an engraved river rock, a blackbird's wing, and an ***akoonah***. ("The Cloud" [VGR]). The river rock was engraved with a ***CHAH-mooz-ee*** symbol. ("Tattoo" [VGR]). *The CHAH-mooz-ee design was an abstract symbol designed by* Voyager *senior illustrator Rick Sternbach, who based it on a drawing of the Milky Way Galaxy. Several diagonal lines drawn over the galaxy may–or may not–have represented wormholes across the galaxy.*

medicine wheel. Traditional Native American design symbolizing the cosmos, often a painting applied to animal skins. The medicine wheel represents the universe both inside and outside one's mind. When someone is near death or in a coma, it is said that his soul has gotten lost on the wheel. Small rock icons including the **Coyote Stone** are placed on

the wheel to guide his soul back to this world. Locations on Chakotay's medicine wheel included the **Mountains of the Antelope Women**. When Commander **Chakotay** was found brain-dead in 2371, Lieutenant Torres attempted to guide his soul with the medicine wheel. ("Cathexis" [VGR]).

Meditations on a Crimson Shadow. Cardassian novel written by **Preloc**. It takes place in the future during a time when Cardassia is at war with the **Klingon Empire**. In the story, the **Cardassians** were triumphant over the **Klingons**. ("The Wire" [DS9]).

medkits. Medical supply modules stored in bulk aboard Federation starships for emergency relief missions. In 2370, Lieutenant **Ro Laren** successfully stole a large number of kits from the *Enterprise*-D in an effort to demonstrate her loyalty to the **Maquis**, who needed the medkits before they could launch an offensive against an Yridian convoy carrying Cardassian military supplies. ("Preemptive Strike" [TNG]).

Medusans. Intelligent **noncorporeal life**-forms whose minds are believed to be among the most beautiful in the universe. By contrast, Medusans' physical appearance is so hideous that one look at a Medusan by a human will cause total madness in the human unless the human is wearing a protective visor. While traveling aboard the *Enterprise*, Medusan ambassador **Kollos** shielded himself in a protective container in order to protect the human members of the crew. Medusans' sensory systems are radically different from those of humanoid life-forms, and their ability to orient themselves in subspace makes them well suited for navigational tasks aboard starships. ("Is There in Truth No Beauty?" [TOS]).

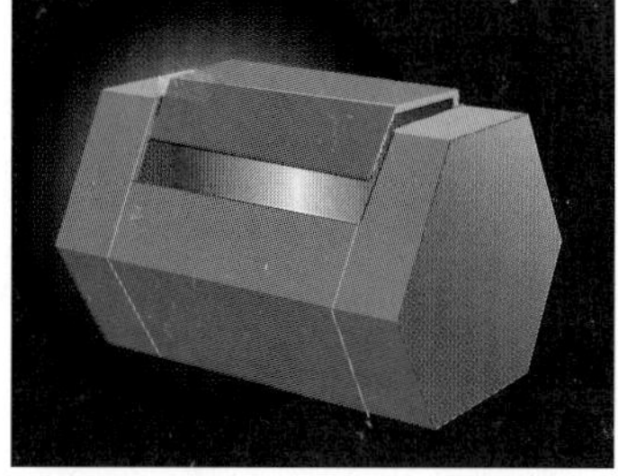

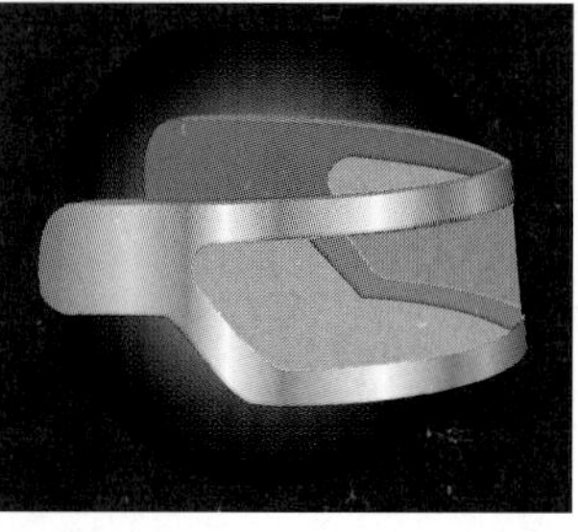

Meezan IV. Planet. A burn treatment conference was held on Meezan IV in 2373. **Dr. Julian Bashir** attended the event, and while there he was abducted by the **Dominion** and replaced by a **changeling** impersonator. After being captured, Bashir was taken to **Dominion internment camp 371**. ("In Purgatory's Shadow" [DS9]).

Megaptera novaeangliae. Scientific name for the Earth cetacean also known as the **humpback whale**. *(Star Trek IV: The Voyage Home).*

Mek'ba. In the **Klingon** system of justice, the portion of a trial or appeal in which evidence was heard. The *Mek'ba* had strict rules for the presentation of evidence and for the conduct of both the accuser and the accused. ("Sins of the Father" [TNG]).

mek'leth. Klingon sword approximately half as long as the ***bat'leth***. ("Sons of Mogh" [DS9]). Worf used a *mek'leth* when he battled the Borg on the *Starship Enterprise*-E in 2373. *(Star Trek: First Contact).*

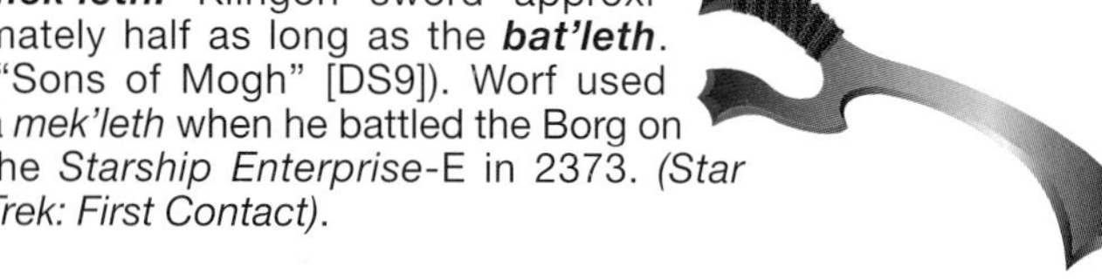

Mekong, U.S.S. *Danube*-class **runabout**, Starfleet registry number NCC-72617, assigned to station Deep Space 9. ("Playing God" [DS9], "Whispers" [DS9], "The Maquis, Part II" [DS9], "The Jem'Hadar" [DS9], "Heart of Stone" [DS9]). The *Mekong* was destroyed in the aftermath of the disastrous Cardassian-Romulan attack on the Founders' homeworld in 2371. ("The Die is Cast" [DS9]). *The* Mekong *replaced the* Ganges *and was first seen in "Playing God." It was named after the river in southeast Asia that flows south to the China Sea.*

Mekor. Son of **Gul Dukat**, born in 2360. In 2371, the elder Dukat promised to take Mekor to the amusement center in **Lakarian City** for his 11th birthday, but Gul Dukat was unable to keep his promise. ("Defiant" [DS9]).

Mekorda sector. Region of space. The *Enterprise*-D weathered an unexpected **magnascopic storm** in the Mekorda sector in 2370. ("Emergence" [TNG]). SEE: **emergent life-form.**

Mekro'vak. Region on the Klingon homeworld. **Grilka's** family was from the Mekro'vak region. ("Looking for *par'Mach* in All the Wrong Places" [DS9]).

melakol. Romulan unit of measure for pressure. ("The Next Phase" [TNG]).

Melakon. (Skip P. Homeier). Deputy Fuhrer in the Nazi-style government on planet **Ekos** that seized power from planetary leader **John Gill**. The ambitious Melakon subverted Gill's efforts to create an efficient, compassionate government, instead creating a close copy of Earth's brutal Nazi Germany. Melakon was responsible for the policy of genocide against the **Zeons** in 2268, just before the collapse of the Gill regime. ("Patterns of Force" [TOS]). *Skip Homeier also played* ***Dr. Sevrin*** *in "The Way to Eden" (TOS).*

Melanie. (Rachel Robinson). (In an alternate future in which Ben Sisko was believed killed aboard the *Defiant* in 2372, Melanie was a young, aspiring writer who visited Jake Sisko on the last day of his life. Melanie was a great admirer of Jake Sisko's writings. SEE: **Sisko, Jake.**) ("The Visitor" [DS9]).

Melbourne, U.S.S. Federation starship, ***Excelsior*-class**, Starfleet registry number NCC-62043. The *Melbourne* was stationed at **Starbase 74** in 2364 when the **Bynars** hijacked the *Enterprise*-D, but was unable to give chase because of maintenance in progress. ("11001001" [TNG]). Commander **William Riker** was offered command of the *U.S.S. Melbourne* in late 2366, but he declined the promotion, preferring to remain executive officer on the *Enterprise*-D. ("The Best of Both Worlds, Part I" [TNG]). Shortly thereafter, the *Melbourne* was one of 39 Federation starships destroyed by the **Borg** in the battle of **Wolf 359**. ("The Best of Both Worlds, Part II" [TNG]). *The* U.S.S. Melbourne *takes its name from the Australian city. There were actually two* Starships Melbourne *used in these episodes. The first was a* **Nebula-*class*** *model, barely glimpsed as a wrecked hulk in the spaceship graveyard from "The Best of Both Worlds, Part II" (TNG). When the scene was redone three years later for "Emissary" (DS9), a decision was made to instead use the more detailed* **U.S.S. Excelsior** *model originally built for* Star Trek III. *Both models were given the same Starfleet registry number, but since the* Excelsior *version was seen fairly clearly on screen, and the* Nebula *version was not seen well, we now assume that the* Melbourne *"really" was an* Excelsior*-class ship.*

"Meld." *Voyager* episode #33. Teleplay by Michael Piller. Story by Michael Sussman. Directed by Cliff Bole. No stardate given. First aired in 1996. *Tuvok mind-melds with a murderer, causing the Vulcan to lose control of his violent emotions.* GUEST CAST: Brad Dourif as **Suder**; Angela Dohrmann as **Ricky**; Simon Billig as **Hogan**; Majel Barrett as Computer voice. SEE: **Chez Sandrine; Darwin, Frank; electroplasma system; Hogan; holodeck and holosuite programs: Vulcan rage; *Kal Rekk*; mesiofrontal cortex; nanites; neurosynaptic therapy; potatoes, mashed; prime rib; radiogenic sweepstakes; *raktajino*; Rillan grease; *Rumarie*; spinach, creamed; Starfleet General Orders and**

Regulations: Directive 101; Suder, Lon; Tuvok; Vulcan mind-meld; Vulcans.

Meldrar I. Planet. A penal facility was located on the moon of Meldrar I. ("Necessary Evil" [DS9]).

Meles II. An inhabited planet located near the **Detrian system**. Commander Riker suggested it as a port of call for **Professor Moriarty** and the **Countess Barthalomew** in 2369. ("Ship in a Bottle" [TNG]).

Melian. (Paul Lambert). A musician on planet **Aldea**. Aldean authorities assigned Melian to tutor Katie, the child of an *Enterprise*-D crew member. ("When the Bough Breaks" [TNG]).

Melina II. Inhabited planet. **Tarmin** and his group of telepathic historians visited Melina II prior to mid-2368. ("Violations" [TNG]).

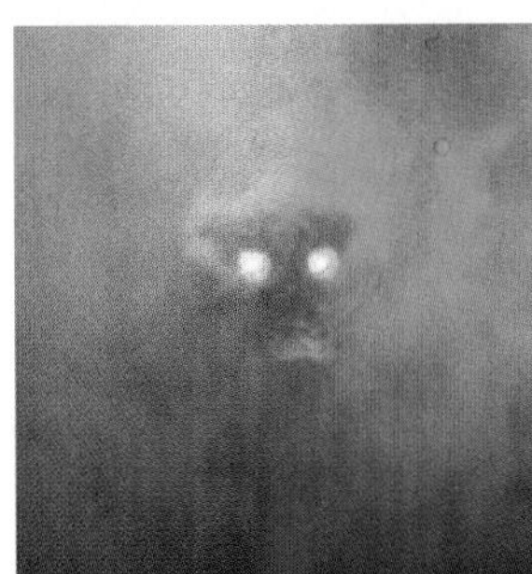

Melkotians. Telepathic civilization with whom first contact was made in 2268. The Melkotians spurned, by the use of an orbiting warning buoy, the *Enterprise*'s initial contact overtures. When *Enterprise* Captain Kirk ignored the Melkotian warning, they subjected Kirk and company to an elaborate charade in which images from Kirk's memory were intended to be the devices of their deaths. The Melkotians' drama took the form of the famous gunfight at the **OK Corral** at **Tombstone, Arizona,** on October 26, 1881, between the Earps and the Clantons, a fight that the Clantons lost. Kirk and members of his *Enterprise* crew were to fill their shoes, but managed to avoid death in the legendary gun battle. Kirk was later successful in opening diplomatic relations with the reclusive Melkotians. ("Spectre of the Gun" [TOS]). *They were also referred to as the Melkots.*

mellitus. Creature from planet Alpha Majoris I whose form is gaseous when in motion and becomes solid at rest. ("Wolf in the Fold" [TOS]).

Melnos IV. Planet where in the past *Enterprise*-D crew member **Neela Daren** had led a team of geologists to study the plasma geyser. ("Lessons" [TNG]).

Melona IV. Class-M planet that was attacked by the **Crystalline Entity** in 2368. The planet was, at the time, being readied for colonization by the Federation. The attack stripped the planet of all indigenous life and killed two colonists. The surviving colonists were evacuated by the *Enterprise*-D, which had been assisting in the colonization project. ("Silicon Avatar" [TNG]).

"Melor Famagal." Musical selection. **Omag**, a Ferengi arms merchant, always requested "Melor Famagal" when at **Amarie**'s bar. ("Unification, Part II" [TNG]).

"Melora." *Deep Space Nine* episode #26. Teleplay by Evan Carlos Somers and Steven Baum and Michael Piller & James Crocker. Story by Evan Carlos Somers. Directed by Winrich Kolbe. Stardate 47229.1. *First aired in 1993. Dr. Bashir becomes romantically involved with an officer whose homeworld is a low-gravity planet; Quark's life is threatened by an old acquaintance.* GUEST CAST: Daphne Ashbrook as **Pazlar**, **Melora**; Peter Crombie as **Fallit Kot**; Don Stark as **Ashrok**; Ron Taylor as Klingon chef. SEE: **Ashrok; Bashir, Dr. Julian; Delvok; Elaysians; Fallit Kot; Ferengi death rituals; Ferengi Rules of Acquisition; garlanic tree; *gladst;* Invernia II; kiosk, Klingon; *Little Mermaid, The*; lothra; neuromuscular adaptation theory; Paltriss, Rings of; Pazlar, Melora; *racht;* Romulan ale; Vak clover soup; Vulcan mollusks; *Yellowstone, U.S.S.; zilm'kach*.**

melorazine. Sedative, often administered by hypospray. ("Man of the People" [TNG]).

Meltasion asteroid belt. An asteroid belt orbiting the star Gamelan, inside the orbit of planet **Gamelan V**. The presence of the belt complicated the *Enterprise*-D's efforts to dispose of an ancient vessel that was causing radiation contamination of the Gamelan atmosphere. The *Enterprise*-D was forced to tow the contaminated barge through the Meltasion belt, exposing the crew of the *Enterprise*-D to a near-lethal amount of radiation. ("Final Mission" [TNG]).

Memad. Former enemy of Enabran Tain. In 2373, Garak intimated that he was responsible for Memad's death. ("In Purgatory's Shadow" [DS9]).

Memory Alpha. Planetoid on which is located a massive library containing all scientific and cultural information from each planet in the United Federation of Planets. Just prior to the completion of Memory Alpha in 2269, the planetoid was attacked by the non-corporeal survivors of planet **Zetar**. ("The Lights of Zetar" [TOS]). SEE: **Romaine, Lieutenant Mira; Zetarians**.

memory engrams. SEE: **engrams**.

memory virus. Parasitic organism that thrived on the peptides generated by its host's brain. The virus, discovered in 2373 by *Voyager* scientists, was able to evade the body's immune system by disguising itself as an **engram**. The parasite would create a false memory for its host that was so traumatic that the host's mind would repress it. The memory virus would live, in person after person, hiding in a part of the brain that the unconscious mind would want to avoid at all costs. When it sensed the death of its host, the virus would leave to find another. Thoron radiation was lethal to the memory virus. Victims of the memory virus included **Dmitri Valtane** and **Tuvok**. ("Flashback" [VGR]).

Mempa sector. Located in Klingon territory. Site of several key battles during the **Klingon civil war** of 2367-2368. Forces loyal to **Gowron** suffered a major defeat in the Mempa system during the conflict. ("Redemption, Parts I and II" [TNG]). **General Martok** fought at Mempa. ("Apocalypse Rising" [DS9]).

"Ménage à Troi." *Next Generation* episode #72. Written by Fred Bronson & Susan Sackett. Directed by Rob Legato. Stardate 43980.7. *First aired in 1990. A Ferengi DaiMon kidnaps Lwaxana Troi in hopes of using her empathic senses in his business dealings. This episode marks the first time we see the surface of Troi's homeworld, Betazed. It was also the first episode directed by visual effects supervisor Rob Legato. Episode cowriter Susan Sackett was* Star Trek *creator Gene Roddenberry's executive assistant.* GUEST CAST: Majel Barrett as **Troi**, **Lwaxana**; Frank Corsentino as **Tog**, **DaiMon**; Ethan Phillips as **Farek**, **Dr.**; Peter Slutsker as **Nibor**; Rudolph Willrich as **Grax**, **Reittan**; Carel Struycken as **Homn**. SEE: **Aldabren Exchange; Algolian ceremonial rhythms; Arcturian Fizz; Betazed; Betazoids; *Bradbury, U.S.S.*; Cochrane distortion; Crusher, Wesley; Farek, Dr.; Ferengi; Ferengi lobes; Gamma Erandi Nebula; Grax, Reittan; Homn; *Krayton*; "Little One"; *muktok* plant; Nibor; *oo-mox*; Orion wing-slug; oskoid; Riker, William T.; Tog, DaiMon; Trade Agreements Conference; Troi, Deanna; Troi, Lwaxana; uttaberries; warp field; Xanthras III; *Zapata*, *U.S.S.***

"Menagerie, Parts I and II, The." Original Series episode #16. Written by Gene Roddenberry. Directed by Marc Daniels (Part I). Directed by Robert Butler (Part II). Stardate 3012.4. *First aired in 1966. Spock hijacks the* Enterprise *to return Captain Pike to planet Talos IV. This two-part episode incorporated most of the footage from the original* Star Trek *pilot episode "The Cage" (TOS). Using the courtroom drama of Spock's trial as a framing device, this episode was an ingenious effort to make use of the first pilot, despite the fact that "The Cage" had a markedly different cast. Use of "The Cage" footage helped the tightly budgeted series control costs and stay on schedule. Marc Daniels directed the "envelope" scenes of Spock's trial, while Robert Butler* *received screen credit for "The Menagerie, Part II" for directing the scenes from "The Cage" that formed the majority of that segment. Despite being a two-parter, the wrap-around "envelope" footage was treated as a single episode by studio accounting, so it is listed here as one segment.* GUEST CAST: Jeffrey Hunter as **Pike, Christopher**; Susan Oliver as **Vina**; Malachi Throne as **Mendez, Commodore José**; M. Leigh Hudec (Majel Barrett Roddenberry) as Number One; John Hoyt as Boyce, Dr. Phillip; Peter Duryea as **Tyler, José**; Laurel Goodwin as Colt, Yeoman J.M.; Adam Roarke as C.P.O. Garrison and First Crewman; Sean Kenney as Pike, Captain (Injured); Hagen Beggs as **Hansen, Mr.**; Julie Parrish as Piper, Miss; Meg Wyllie as Keeper, The; Clegg Hoyt as *Pitcairn* Transporter chief; George Sawaya as Humbolt, Chief; Brett Dunham as Security chief; Tom Lupo, Ian Reddin, Security guards; Majel Barrett as *Enterprise* computer voice and Starbase computer control voice; Bob Herron as Kirk's stunt double and stunt double captain. SEE: **Boyce, Dr. Phil; *Columbia, S.S.*; delta radiation; duranium; fleet captain; Haskins, Dr. Theodore; Kaylar; Keeper, the; laser weapons; Mendez, Commodore José; Mojave; Number One; Orion animal women; Pike, Christopher; Rigel VII; Spock; Starbase 11; Starfleet General orders and Regulations; Talos IV; Talos Star Group; Talosians; Tango; tritanium; Tyler, José; Vega Colony; Vina.**

Mendak, Admiral. (Alan Scarfe). Romulan officer who commanded the warbird ***Devoras***. Mendak and the *Devoras* met the *Enterprise*-D inside the Romulan Neutral Zone in 2367. The rendezvous was slated to be the beginning of negotiations between the Federation, represented by **Ambassador T'Pel**, and the Romulans. However, Mendak's true purpose was to enable T'Pel, in reality a Romulan operative named **Subcommander Selok**, to escape into Romulan hands. ("Data's Day" [TNG]). *Alan Scarfe also played Tokath in "Birthright, Part II" (TNG).*

Mendakan pox. Humanoid disease characterized by skin mottling. **Harry Kim** had a case of Mendakan pox in 2358. ("Favorite Son" [VGR]).

Mendel, Gregor Johann. Nineteenth-century Earth scientist (1822-1884) who postulated the basic principles of genetic heredity and suggested the existence of genes. ("Let That Be Your Last Battlefield" [TOS]).

Mendez, Commodore José. (Malachi Throne). Commanding officer of **Starbase 11** in 2267. An illusory version of Mendez presided over Spock's court-martial for charges of mutiny and violation of **General Order 7** when Spock abducted Fleet Captain **Christopher Pike** to **Talos IV**. The real Mendez later cleared Spock of all charges. ("The Menagerie, Parts I and II" [TOS]). *Actor Malachi Throne also provided the voices of the Talosian magistrate in the original (unaired) version of "The Cage," and later portrayed Romulan Senator Pardek in "Unification, Parts I and II" [TNG]). Mendez must have assumed command of Starbase 11 just prior to "The Menagerie, Part I" (TOS), since in the previous episode ("Court Martial" (TOS), the base was being run by Commodore Stone.*

Mendez. Starfleet officer who was a crew member on the ***U.S.S. Victory***, and who participated in a mission to planet **Tarchannen III** in 2362. In 2367, Mendez stole a shuttle from the ***U.S.S. Aries*** and fled to planet Tarchannen III, where it is believed her body was transformed into a reptilian life-form native to that planet. ("Identity Crisis" [TNG]).

Mendon, Ensign. (John Putch). A Starfleet officer and a native of the planet **Benzar**. As is a characteristic of his people, Mendon had bluish-green skin and breathed with the assistance of a respiration device. Mendon was something of an over-achiever by human standards, causing some initial friction with the *Enterprise*-D crew when he served aboard that ship as part of an officer exchange program in 2365, but he soon adapted to Starfleet social norms. Wesley Crusher once mistook Mendon for **Mordock**, another Benzite, but Mendon explained that they were both from the same geostructure, and therefore looked alike to non-Benzites. ("A Matter of Honor" [TNG]). *John Putch also played Mordock in "Coming of Age" (TNG) and a journalist aboard the* U.S.S. Enterprise-*B in* Star Trek Generations.

Mendora. A mythical devil figure to the inhabitants of the Berussian Cluster. ("Devil's Due" [TNG]).

Mendoza, Dr. (Castulo Guerra). Federation representative in the negotiations for rights to the **Barzan wormhole** in 2366. Dr. Mendoza was poisoned by members of the Ferengi delegation, and Commander Riker was forced to take his place at the negotiation table. ("The Price" [TNG]).

Mendrossen, Ki. (William Denis). Ambassador **Sarek**'s chief-of-staff during the Legaran conference of 2366, Sarek's final diplomatic mission. A middle-aged human male, Mendrossen was aware that Sarek suffered from debilitating **Bendii Syndrome**, but sought to protect the ambassador so that he could complete that last mission with honor. ("Sarek" [TNG]).

Menegay, Paul. Son of an *Enterprise*-D crew member. In 2370, at the age of seven, Paul was the winner of the **Captain Picard Day** contest. His winning entry was a bust of the Captain's head, a work of art that Commander William Riker described as "the orange one with the lumpy skin." ("The *Pegasus*" [TNG]).

Menthar. An ancient culture that was destroyed a thousand years ago in a terrible war with the **Promellians**. The final battle in this conflict was fought at planet **Orelious IX**, resulting in the extinction of both species and the destruction of Orelious IX. The Menthars were believed to be very innovative in battle: they were the first to develop the *Kavis Teke* elusive maneuver, and had a passive lure stratagem comparable to Napoleon's. The Menthars also developed and deployed aceton assimilators, devices that not only trapped the ***Cleponji***, but worked well enough to trap the *Enterprise*-D a millennium after their final battle. ("Booby Trap" [TNG]).

Menuhin, Yehudi. A famous Earth concert violinist (1916-). **Data** programmed himself to emulate Menuhin's performance style. ("Sarek" [TNG]).

Mera, Vedek. Bajoran spiritual leader. Mera traveled to Deep Space 9 in 2373 to attend what would have been the signing ceremony for Bajor's admission to the Federation. ("Rapture" [DS9]).

Merak II. Planet. A botanical plague threatened to destroy all vegetation on Merak II in 2269. The plague was averted when a consignment of mineral **zenite** was delivered by the *Starship Enterprise* from planet **Ardana**. ("The Cloud Minders" [TOS]). Quark said that the inhabitants of Merak II manufactured the best sizing scanners, but he may have been lying. ("The Wire" [DS9]).

mercassium. Proprietary composite used in Federation shield-generator construction. In 2370, traces of mercassium were found in the debris of the Cardassian freighter, ***Bok'Nor***. Since mercassium is classified, destruction of the ship pointed to someone within the Federation. ("The Maquis, Part I" [DS9]). SEE: **Maquis**.

Merced*-class starship.** Conjectural designation for a type of Federation ship. The ***U.S.S. Trieste, which underwent servicing at **Starbase 74** in 2364 and on which Data once served, was a *Merced*-class starship.

***Merchantman*.** Small merchant cargo ship. The *Merchantman* was chartered by Klingon operative **Valkris** in 2285 in order to transport stolen data from the Federation's **Project Genesis** to the Klingon government. The *Merchantman*, along with its crew and Valkris, was destroyed after delivery of the information. (*Star Trek III: The Search for Spock*). *The* Merchantman *was never referred to by name during the film. The name is from the script only. The* Merchantman *model, designed by Nilo Rodis and built at ILM for* Star Trek III, *was re-used several times as various "guest" spaceships in* Star Trek: The Next Generation.

Merculite rockets. Obsolete weapons system found in older spacecraft. The **Talarian** freighter ***Batris*** was equipped with Merculite rockets that were apparently used to destroy the Klingon cruiser ***T'Acog***. ("Heart of Glory" [TNG]). Merculite rockets were part of the weaponry of the Talarian ship ***Q'Maire*** when it confronted the *Enterprise*-D in 2367. ("Suddenly Human" [TNG]).

Mercy Hospital. Health-care facility located in the Mission District of San Francisco on Earth in the late 20th century. Pavel Chekov, injured in Earth's past, was cared for in this facility before being rescued by his fellow *Enterprise* crew members. (*Star Trek IV: The Voyage Home*). *The Mercy Hospital scenes were filmed at Centinela Hospital in Inglewood, California.*

Meressa, Kai. Former Bajoran religious leader. Kai Meressa once said "What remains after death is but a shell–a sign that the ***pagh*** has begun its final journey to the **Prophets**." ("Indiscretion" [DS9]).

merfadon. A sedative. Administered to **Kira** on stardate 50416 by **Silaran Prin** prior to his attempt to remove the unborn **Kirayoshi O'Brien** from her womb. The ***makara* herb** taken by Kira during her pregnancy acted as a counteragent to the merfadon. ("The Darkness and the Light" [DS9]).

Meribor. (Jennifer Nash). Native of the now-dead planet **Kataan** and daughter of the ironweaver **Kamin**. Meribor lived over a thousand years ago in the village of **Ressik**. Memories of her life were preserved aboard a space probe launched from Kataan. The probe encountered the *Starship Enterprise*-D in 2368, transferring its memories, including the memory of Meribor, to Jean-Luc Picard. ("The Inner Light" [TNG]).

Mericor system. Planetary system. Crash site of the ***U.S.S. Denver*** after the ship struck a gravitic mine in 2368. ("Ethics" [TNG]).

"Meridian" *Deep Space Nine* episode #54. Teleplay by Mark Gehred-O'Connel. Story by Hilary Bader and Evan Carlos Somers. Directed by Jonathan Frakes. Stardate 48423.2. First aired in 1994. *Dax falls in love with a man whose planet disappears for 60 years at a time.* GUEST CAST: Brett Cullen as **Deral**; Christine Healy as **Seltin**; Jeffrey Combs as **Tiron**; Mark Humphrey as **Lito**. SEE: **Andorian ale**; **Bajoran Military Academy**; **Dax (symbiont); Deral; First Meal; gamma radiation; holodeck and holosuite programs; holodeck; holo-imager; Kandora champagne; Kira Nerys; Kylata II; Last Meal; Lito; Meridian; noncorporeal life; Odo; quantum matrix; Quintana, Ensign; Rakal, Seltin; Serilian ambassador; Tiron; *tongo*; Trialus star system; *vajhaq*.**

Meridian. Class-M planet located in the **Trialus star system** in the **Gamma Quadrant**. Meridian underwent dimensional shifts every 60 years, causing its inhabitants to phase between corporeal and noncorporeal states. In 2371 the ***U.S.S. Defiant***'s crew assisted the Meridian's search for an answer to their unstable world. It was discovered that their sun's core fusion was imbalanced and a building cascade reaction at the quantum level was triggering the dimensional shifts. The sun's reactions were stabilized, enabling the planet to exist for longer periods in solid form. ("Meridian" [DS9]). *The painted forest backdrop used outside the Meridian hall was rented from Walt Disney Studios, which had originally created the backdrop for the movie* Mary Poppins. *The Meridian hall itself was also seen (in modified form) as the Klingon Great Hall in "House of Quark" (DS9), the Albino's lair in "Blood Oath" (DS9), and Masaka's temple in "Masks" (TNG).*

Merik III. Planet in the Gamma Quadrant. Doctor Bashir and Chief O'Brien conducted a bio-survey of Merik III just prior to stardate 49066.5. ("Hippocratic Oath" [DS9]).

Merikus. SEE: **Merrick, R. M.**

Merkoria Quasar. Quasistellar object. The Merkoria Quasar was studied by the *Enterprise*-D in 2370. The study was cut short when the *Enterprise*-D was reassigned to locate the ***U.S.S. Pegasus***. ("The *Pegasus*" [TNG]).

Merrick, R. M. (William Smithers). Captain of the survey vessel ***S.S. Beagle*** that disappeared in star system Eight Ninety-Two in the year 2261. James Kirk had known Merrick at **Starfleet Academy**, when Merrick was expelled in his fifth year after failing a psychosimulator test. *(Note that Starfleet Academy was later established as being a four-year institution.)* Merrick then went into the merchant service and eventually became captain of the *S.S. Beagle.* After his ship was damaged by meteors, Merrick and several of his crew beamed down to planet Eight Ninety-Two-IV in search of supplies and met **Claudius Marcus**. Merrick elected to stay on the planet, becoming Merikus, First Citizen of the Roman culture. As Merikus, he became a political strongman and was known as The Butcher to the slaves he persecuted. Six years later, an *Enterprise* landing party located him, and he was killed by Marcus when helping the *Enterprise* people escape. SEE: **Eight Ninety-Two-IV, planet**. ("Bread and Circuses" [TOS]).

***Merrimack*, U.S.S.** Federation starship, ***Nebula*-class**, Starfleet registry number NCC-61827. Ship that transported Ambassador **Sarek** and his party from **Legara IV** back to Vulcan, following the **Legaran** conference of 2366. ("Sarek" [TNG]). The *Merrimack* transported Cadet Wesley Crusher back to Starfleet Academy following his vacation aboard the *Enterprise*-D in 2368. ("The Game" [TNG]). *This ship was named in honor of the vessel that became the noted iron-clad warship* C.S.S. Virginia, *that fought for the Confederacy in the American Civil War.*

Merriweather, Patrick. Alias used by Julian Bashir in his **secret agent** holosuite program. ("Our Man Bashir" [DS9]).

Merrok, Proconsul. High-ranking official of the **Romulan** government. Proconsul Merrok was assassinated with poison on Romulus during the time that **Elim Garak** was a gardener at the **Cardassian Embassy on Romulus** there. According to Garak, he had nothing to do with Merrok's death. ("Broken Link" [DS9]).

mesiofrontal cortex. Region of **Vulcan** brain associated with suppression of emotions. In 2372, *Starship Voyager* Lieutenant Tuvok suffered injury to his mesiofrontal cortex following a mind-meld with **Lon Suder**, releasing emotions of rage and violence. ("Meld" [VGR]).

Meso'Clan. (Jerry Roberts). **Jem'Hadar** soldier under the command of Goran'Agar. In 2372, Meso'Clan traveled with **Goran'Agar** to planet Bopak III because Goran'Agar believed that the planet could cure his men of their addiction to **ketracel-white**. ("Hippocratic Oath" [DS9]). *Meso'Clan's name was not mentioned in dialog, but is from the script only.*

mess hall. Communal dining facility aboard a starship. ("Caretaker" [VGR]). The mess hall aboard the *Starship Voyager* was located on Deck 2, Section 13, and featured several large forward-looking windows. Although food service in the *Voyager*'s mess hall was originally provided by **replicator**s, power rationing aboard the ship prompted **Neelix** to remove the replicators and to instead install a makeshift kitchen. In his capacity as unofficial ship's cook, Neelix prepared all manner of delicacies for the *Voyager* crew. ("Phage" [VGR]).

message buoy. Small spaceborne instrument package, usually containing a data storage system and an automatic transponder. **Chakotay** launched a message buoy from his shuttle in 2373 before landing on a planet in the **Nekrit Expanse** that was colonized by former **Borg** drones. ("Unity" [VGR]). SEE: **recorder marker**.

metabolic reduction injection. Medication. Henoch synthesized a metabolic reduction compound so that Kirk, Spock, and **Dr. Ann Mulhall**'s bodies could carry the intellects of **Sargon**, **Henoch**, and **Thalassa**. The drug reduced heart rate and all bodily functions to normal, allowing the three to occupy the humanoid bodies without permanent damage to those bodies. Henoch secretly prepared a different compound for Sargon in an attempt to destroy his ancient enemy. ("Return to Tomorrow" [TOS]).

metaconscious. Part of the **Betazoid** psyche that filters and protects an individual from psychic trauma. In 2370, **Lwaxana Troi** suffered an emotional shock so severe that her metaconscious could not protect her as she relived the death of her daughter **Kestra**. ("Dark Page" [TNG]).

metagenic weapon. Sophisticated biological weapon using genetically engineered viruses, designed to destroy any form of DNA. These viruses could mutate rapidly and were believed able to destroy entire ecosystems within days. After 30 days the metagenic agent itself died, having destroying all biological life on a planetary scale, while leaving all the technological aspects of a culture intact. Because of the extreme danger of these weapons, treaties were established to ban their use, and all of the major powers of the period, including the Federation, the Ferengi, and the Romulans, agreed to the ban. In 2369, Starfleet Intelligence was the victim of Cardassian disinformation suggesting that the **Cardassians** were developing metagenic toxins. Starfleet also believed that the Cardassians had discovered a new method to deliver the toxins in a dormant state on a **theta-band** subspace carrier wave. ("Chain of Command, Part I" [TNG]).

"Metamorphosis." *Original Series* episode #31. Written by Gene L. Coon. Directed by Ralph Senensky. Stardate 3219.8. *First aired in 1967. While transporting a Federation official to a vital diplomatic mission, Kirk and company find historic space scientist Zefram Cochrane, still alive on a distant planetoid, and cared for by an energy life-form called the Companion.* GUEST CAST: Glenn Corbett as **Cochrane, Zefram**; Elinor Donahue as **Hedford, Commissioner Nancy**; Elizabeth Rogers as The Companion's voice. SEE: **Alpha Centauri; Cochrane, Zefram; Companion; Epsilon Canaris III; *Galileo, Shuttlecraft*; Gamma Canaris region; Hedford, Nancy; Sakuro's disease; Universal Translator; warp drive.**

metaphasic shield. Revolutionary new shielding technology developed in 2369 by Ferengi scientist **Dr. Reyga**. The system involved the generation of overlapping low-level **subspace** fields, causing an object within the fields to exist partially in subspace. The technology was first tested in 2369 by sending an *Enterprise*-D shuttlecraft into a star's corona. The initial test was deemed unsuccessful, but further investigation revealed that sabotage of the metaphasic field had caused the failure. The pilot of the craft was discovered to have perpetrated the sabotage, in the hopes of discrediting Dr. Reyga in order to steal the technology. Dr. Beverly Crusher then piloted the shuttlecraft into the corona herself, thereby proving that the technology worked. ("Suspicions" [TNG]). SEE: **Jo'Bril.** In 2370, as the ship was escaping from a group of self-aware **Borg**, Dr. Crusher employed the new shielding technology to take the *Enterprise*-D into the corona of a star. The shield worked long enough for the crew to generate a solar eruption that destroyed the **Borg ship.** ("Descent, Part II" [TNG]). A prison complex run by the **Mokra Order** in the Delta Quadrant employed metaphasic shielding to prevent escape. ("Resistance" [VGR]).

methanogenic compound. Explosive gaseous substance found in caverns on planet **Kesprytt III.** Methanogenic gas endangered *Enterprise*-D Captain Jean-Luc Picard and Chief Medical Officer Beverly Crusher when they were forced to traverse caverns on Kesprytt III during their escape from the **Prytt** in 2370. ("Attached" [TNG]).

metorapan treatments. Regenerative treatment for fracture patients. Wesley Crusher was allergic to metorapan. ("The First Duty" [TNG]).

metrazene. Cardiac antiarrhythmic medication, used aboard the *Enterprise*-D. ("The Host" [TNG]).

metremia. Radiation poisoning caused by the **metreon cascade**. Metremia, a fatal degenerative blood disease, was caused by exposure to high concentrations of metreon isotopes. The disease attacked its victims on a molecular level, causing the body's atomic structure to undergo fission. ("Jetrel" [VGR]).

metreon cascade. Weapon of mass destruction used by the **Haakonian Order** in their war with the **Talaxians**. A metreon cascade was deployed against the civilian inhabitants of **Rinax**, a moon of planet **Talax**, around 2356, vaporizing more than 300,000 Talaxians and causing thousands of others to die of **metremia** poisoning. Neelix's family members were among the casualties. The day after the cascade was deployed, Talax surrendered unconditionally to the Haakonian Order. The metreon cascade was developed by scientist **Ma'Bor Jetrel**. ("Jetrel" [VGR]).

metreon cloud. Overcast of contaminants and fallout generated by the **metreon cascade** weapon. A metreon cloud rendered the Talaxian moon **Rinax** uninhabitable after the metreon cascade attack of 2356. The metreon cloud contained the vaporized remains of the victims of Rinax. In 2371, Dr. **Ma'Bor Jetrel** attempted without success to re-integrate one of the victims of Rinax from atomic fragments residing in the cloud. ("Jetrel" [VGR]).

Metro Plaza. Large business and shopping center located in downtown **Los Angeles**. Astronomer **Rain Robinson** arranged a meeting with **Henry Starling** at the Metro Plaza in 1996. ("Future's End, Part II" [VGR]). *There is no Metro Plaza in Los Angeles. Scenes of this plaza were filmed at the Music Center on Grand Avenue in Los Angeles.*

Metron Consortium. Business organization that sometimes dealt in sophisticated weapons. ("Business As Usual" [DS9]). *It seems odd that the Metrons, who abhorred violence in "Arena" (TOS) would deal in weapons.*

Metron. (Carole Shelyne). Highly advanced civilization, apparently humanoid, of unknown origin, possessing great powers. The Metrons intervened in a conflict between the original *Enterprise* and a **Gorn** ship in 2267. The two ships had been involved in a territorial dispute over planet **Cestus III**. Seeking to avoid unnecessary unpleasantness in their space, the Metrons sent *Enterprise* Captain Kirk and the Gorn ship commander to an artificial planetoid, where they were expected to fight to the death. Kirk won the fight, but declined to kill his opponent, prompting the Metrons to reevaluate their opinion of humankind. A Metron representative said they had not expected Kirk to demonstrate the advanced trait of mercy, and said that they were so impressed they might wish to contact the Federation in just a few thousand years. ("Arena" [TOS]).

mev yap. Klingon for "stop." ("Reunion" [TNG]), ("Looking for *par'Mach* in All the Wrong Places" [DS9]).

MEV. Unit of electromotive force measure; abbreviation for one million electron volts. ("Before and After" [VGR]).

mevak. Klingon dagger used in such ceremonies as the *Mauk-to'Vor* ritual. ("Sons of Mogh" [DS9]).

Meyers, Annie. (Joy Garrett). Computer-generated character from Alexander Rozhenko's holodeck program ***Ancient West.*** ("A Fistful of Datas" [TNG]).

Mickey D. (Gregory Beecroft). Character in the novel ***Hotel Royale***, a nefarious lothario who murdered a hotel bellboy to enforce his authority. ("The Royale" [TNG]).

micro-wormhole. A **wormhole** whose singularity has mostly dissipated, leaving an extremely narrow passageway through **subspace**. A micro-wormhole was discovered in 2371 by the crew of the *Starship Voyager*. One terminus of this wormhole was in the Delta Quadrant, while the other was situated across the galaxy in **Sector 1385** of the Alpha Quadrant. This particular wormhole also traversed a temporal distance of 20 years, so the Alpha Quadrant terminus was in the year 2351. A **microprobe** lodged in the wormhole made it possible for the *Voyager* crew to contact the Romulan ship ***Talvath*** in the Alpha Quadrant. ("Eye of the Needle" [VGR]).

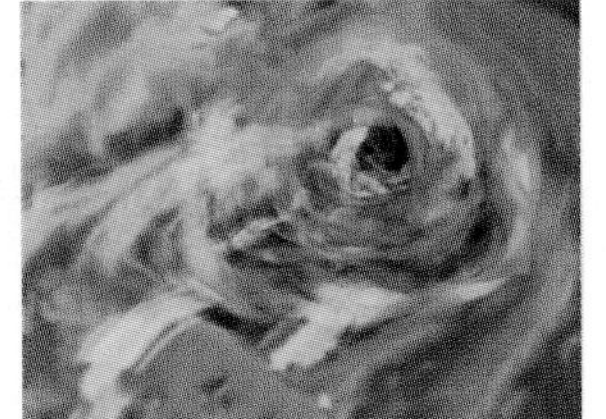

microbiotic colony. A rare subatomic life-form, analogous to carbon-based bacteria. A microbiotic colony was responsible for significant structural damage to the Klingon vessel ***Pagh*** and the *Enterprise*-D. A tunneling neutrino beam was found to be effective in removing these dangerous organisms from both ships. ("A Matter of Honor" [TNG]).

microbrain. Silicon based intelligent life-form indigenous to planet **Velara III**. The microbrains were nonorganic entities that lived in the soil, in the moist region just above the water table. Using energy absorbed from sunlight, the microbrains, which resembled tiny sparkling crystals, used groundwater to form electrical pathways that served as its consciousness. The life-form was named "microbrain" by *Enterprise*-D personnel investigating the now-defunct Federation **terraforming** station on the planet. The terraforming project on Velara III threatened the lives of these entities by altering the subsurface water table. ("Home Soil" [TNG]).

microcellular scan. Detailed sensor readings of the microscopic functions within living cells. Dr. Crusher ran a microcellular scan on **Reginald Barclay**, while diagnosing his case of **Urodelean flu** on stardate 47653. ("Genesis" [TNG]).

microcentrum cell membrane. Physical characteristic of cell structures in certain life-forms. Microcentrum cell membranes are often seen in **shape-shifer**s. Life-forms with microcentrum cell membranes are often unaffected by **triolic waves.** ("Time's Arrow, Part I" [TNG]).

microcircuit fibers. An element of **Borg** technology, designed to be implanted into humanoid tissue during the assimilation process. Microcircuit fibers were implanted into **Jean-Luc Picard**'s body when he was abducted and surgically altered by the Borg in 2366. Infiltration of the fibers into Picard's healthy tissue around the Borg implants caused changes in the cellular DNA around the implants and made surgical removal impossible while the implants were active. ("The Best of Both Worlds, Part II" [TNG]).

microdyne. Measurement of force, one-millionth of a dyne. ("Playing God" [DS9]).

microfusion initiator. Reactor component. Renegade Jem'Hadar soldiers stole microfusion initiators to reactivate an Iconian gateway found on planet Vandros IV. ("To the Death" [DS9]).

micron. Unit of length measure, one-millionth of a meter. ("Macrocosm" [VGR]).

microoptic drill. A handheld piece of Starfleet equipment used to produce extremely small, precision holes. Commander La Forge and Ensign Ro used a microoptic drill to create an observation hole in the ceiling of the **Ten-Forward Lounge** on stardate 45571 when **Ux-Mal** terrorists were holding *Enterprise*-D personnel hostage there. ("Power Play" [TNG]).

microprobe. Small free-flying unpiloted instrument package used by Starfleet scientists for remote sensing studies. Microprobes measured only a few centimeters in diameter. In 2371, a microprobe launched by the *Starship Voyager* into a **micro-wormhole** became trapped in **gravitational eddies** within the wormhole. The *Voyager* crew used the probe as a communications relay to the science vessel ***Talvath***. ("Eye of the Needle" [VGR]).

microreplication system. Device permitting an **exocomp** to fabricate virtually any tool required for an engineering servicing task. The microreplicator creates a new circuit pathway whenever an exocomp performs a task it has never done before. ("The Quality of Life" [TNG]).

microscopic generator. Nanotech device used by the criminal **Rao Vantika** to transfer his consciousness into the body of Dr. Bashir, thereby continuing his existence. ("The Passenger" [DS9]). SEE: **glial cells; synaptic pattern displacement.**

microtomographic analysis. Imaging technique using a series of microscopic narrow-beam X-rays to derive information on a molecular scale. Microtomographic analysis, along with mass spectrometry, of the *Enterprise*-D **dilithium chamber hatch** helped determine that the explosion suffered by the ship in 2367 was the result of a flawed hatch cover and not sabotage. SEE: **neutron fatigue.** ("The Drumhead" [TNG]).

microvirus. A genetically-engineered microorganism designed to attack only cells with a specific DNA sequence. One such organism was designed to attach itself to parasympathetic nerves and to block the function of the enzyme cholinesterase, thus blocking autonomic nerve impulses, but only of specific individuals. **Yuta** of the **Acamarian** clan **Tralesta** used such a microvirus as a weapon to systematically murder nearly all members of the rival clan **Lornak**, including **Penthor-Mul** and **Volnoth**. ("The Vengeance Factor" [TNG]).

mid-range phase adjuster. An innovative device developed by Geordi La Forge for use in the *Enterprise*-D warp-drive system. When installed in the power transfer conduits, it corrected the phase of the energy plasma, compensating for inertial distortion. La Forge offered to collaborate with **Dr. Leah Brahms** on a scientific paper describing the technology. ("Galaxy's Child" [TNG]).

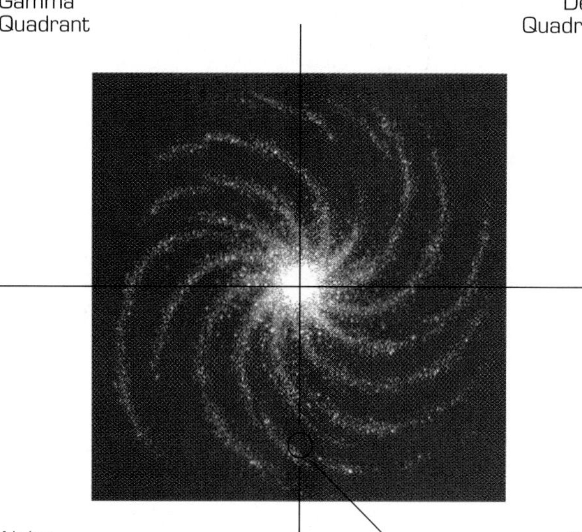

Midos V. Planet. The original *Starship Enterprise* was to have gone to Midos V after an expedition to planet **Exo III** on stardate 2712. Midos V had a small colony that Korby's androids deemed a good choice for further android manufacture, owing to abundant raw materials available there. ("What Are Little Girls Made Of?" [TOS]).

Midro. (Ed Long). One of the Disrupters of planet **Ardana**. Midro conspired with **Vanna** to kidnap the *Enterprise* landing party when the starship visited the planet in 2269. ("The Cloud Minders" [TOS]).

Midsummer's Night Dream, A. Comedic play written by **William Shakespeare** of Earth in 1595. In 1893, a troupe of actors led by a "Mr. Pickerd" was reported to be planning a performance of this play in San Francisco. ("Time's Arrow, Part II" [TNG]).

Mikel. Young human boy who lived on the farming world of **Gault** at the time that **Worf** was a boy. Mikel played soccer, and it was in 2353, during a match against Worf's school soccer team, that Mikel died. In the championship play-off game, Mikel and Worf's heads collided forcefully, leaving Mikel with a broken neck. He died the next day. Worf felt responsible, and thereafter he exercised extreme restraint when dealing physically with humans. ("Let He Who Is Without Sin..." [DS9]).

Mikhal Travelers. Civilization residing in the **Delta Quadrant**. Mikhal Travelers journey in small two-occupant vessels, exploring unknown space in the spirit of adventure. In 2373, several Mikhal Travelers assisted the crew of the *Starship Voyager* in plotting a course for the **Alpha Quadrant**. ("Darkling" [VGR]). SEE: **Zahir.**

Mikulaks. Civilization. The Mikulaks donated a collection of special tissue samples to Starfleet for transportation to **Nahmi IV** in 2366. It was hoped that the samples would prove helpful in finding a cure for an outbreak of **Correllium fever** on that planet. ("Hollow Pursuits" [TNG]).

Mila. (Julianna McCarthy). Housekeeper and confidant to **Enabran Tain** for more than 30 years. Mila was fond of **Garak**, and believed him innocent of having betrayed Tain. ("Improbable Cause" [DS9], "The Die is Cast" [DS9]).

Milan, S.S. Federation transport ship, registry number NDT-50863. **Helena** and **Alexander Rozhenko** traveled aboard the *Milan* from Earth to the *Enterprise*-D, in orbit of planet **Bilana III** in 2368. ("New Ground" [TNG]).

Milika III. Planet. Early in his career, **Jean-Luc Picard** led an away team on a heroic mission to rescue an ambassador on Milika III. ("Tapestry" [TNG]).

military log. In the alternate history created when the ***Enterprise*-C** vanished from its "proper" time in 2344, Picard's captain's log was instead referred to as a military log. ("Yesterday's *Enterprise*" [TNG]).

Milky Way Galaxy. The local galaxy, a flat, spiral-shaped cloud roughly 100,000 light-years in diameter, consisting of some 100 billion stars. The galaxy is divided into four major regions, called **quadrant**s. Each quadrant is divided into many thousands of sectors.

Miller, Steven. (Robert Ellenstein). Father of **Wyatt Miller** and a close friend of the late **Ian Andrew Troi**. ("Haven" [TNG]). *Actor Robert Ellenstein had previously played the* ***Federation President*** *in* Star Trek IV: The Voyage Home.

Miller, Victoria. (Nan Martin). Mother of **Wyatt Miller**. ("Haven" [TNG]).

Miller, Wyatt. (Rob Knepper). Physician who was betrothed to **Deanna Troi** when they were very young, being raised on planet **Betazed**. Wyatt had been haunted all his life by an image of a woman who he had thought was Deanna, but he later learned the mysterious woman was a **Tarellian** named **Ariana**. He chose not to marry Troi so that he could join the Tarellians in the search for a cure to the virus that infected the last members of the Tarellian people. ("Haven" [TNG]).

millicochrane. Unit of measure of **subspace** distortion, one one-thousandth of the force necessary to establish a field of warp factor one. Named for **Zefram Cochrane**, inventor of the space warp. ("Remember Me" [TNG], "The Outcast" [TNG]).

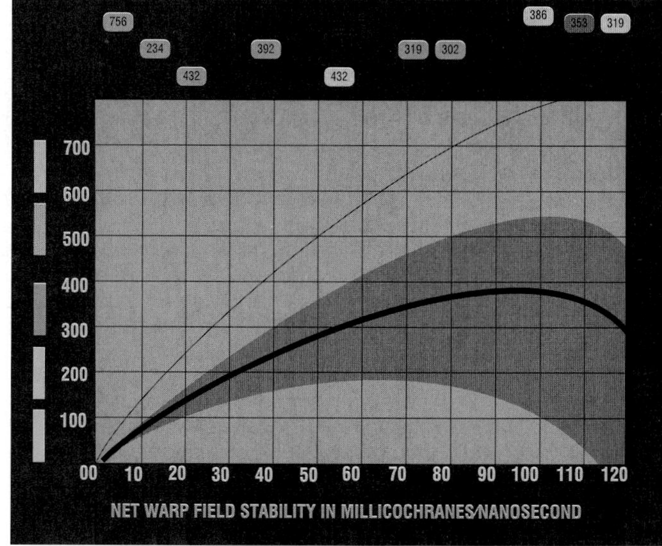

Subspace distortion measured in millicochranes, displayed from a *Constitution*-class starship

millipede juice. Ferengi beverage. Quark preferred it without shells. ("Prophet Motive" [DS9]).

Milton. English poet John Milton (1608-1674). When asked by Kirk in 2267 if he would prefer exile or imprisonment, **Khan** cited Milton's Satan, who, as quoted by Kirk, felt "it is better to rule in

Hell than to serve in Heaven." ("Space Seed" [TOS]). *On the other hand, Bob Justman claims that "it is better to be served in Heaven than to rule in Hell." He could be right.*

Mimas. Closest of the major moons orbiting the planet Saturn. Mimas was the location of an emergency evacuation center for Starfleet **Academy's Flight Range**, and was the location where **Nova Squadron** was evacuated following an accident in 2368. ("The First Duty" [TNG]).

Minara II. Planet in the **Minaran star system** where the **Vians** conducted studies in 2268 to determine which planet's inhabitants would be saved when the star Minara exploded. ("The Empath" [TOS]).

Minaran empath. Individual whose nervous system is capable of absorbing the physical and emotional responses of another, permitting the empath to heal the injuries of others by transferring those injuries onto her or his own body. **Gem** of the Minaran star system was one such empath. ("The Empath" [TOS]).

Minaran star system. Planetary system, formerly with several inhabited worlds. The star, Minara, entered a nova phase in 2268, rendering those planets uninhabitable. An advanced civilization known as the **Vians** had the ability to save the inhabitants of only one of those planets, and ultimately chose the humanoid people of the planet **Minara II**. ("The Empath" [TOS]). SEE: **Gem**.

"Mind's Eye, The." *Next Generation* episode #98. Teleplay by René Echevarria. Story by Ken Schafer and René Echevarria. Directed by David Livingston. Stardate 44885.5. *First aired in 1991. Geordi is abducted and subjected to mental reprogramming by Romulan agents who intend to use him to murder a Klingon official. This episode marked the first appearance of the mysterious Sela, although she would not be identified until "Redemption, Part II" (TNG).* GUEST CAST: Larry Dobkin as **Kell**; John Fleck as **Taibak**; Colm Meaney as **O'Brien, Miles**; Edward Wiley as **Vagh**; Majel Barrett as Computer voice. SEE: **actinides; Costa, Lieutenant; E-band emissions; Ikalian asteroid belt; isolinear optical chip; *k'adlo*; Kell; Krios; Kriosian system; neural implants; *Onizuka*, Shuttlepod; phaser rifle; phaser type-3; rapid nadion pulse; Risa; Romulan Star Empire; Sela; Shuttle 7; somnetic inducer; Starbase 36; Taibak; Teldarian cruiser; Vagh; VISOR.**

mind-link. Telepathic linking of two minds creating a double entity within one being, similar to a **Vulcan mind-meld**. ("Is There in Truth No Beauty?"[TOS]).

mind-meld, Vulcan. SEE: **Vulcan mind-meld**.

mind-sifter. Barbaric **Klingon** device used to probe the thoughts of a prisoner during interrogation. At higher settings, the device irreparably damaged the brain of the victim. Spock's Vulcan discipline enabled him to endure the mind-sifter on planet **Organia** in 2267. ("Errand of Mercy" [TOS]).

Ministry of Justice. Judicial branch of the Cardassian government. ("Defiant" [DS9]). SEE: **Cardassians**.

Minnerly, Lieutenant. *Enterprise*-D crew member. Minnerly was scheduled to participate in a martial-arts competition aboard the ship just prior to Tasha Yar's death in 2364. Yar was set to compete against Minnerly, and was favored in the ship's pool, although she expected Minnerly's kick-boxing to prove a formidable challenge. ("Skin of Evil" [TNG]).

Minnis. (Tom Morga). **First maje** of the **Kazon-Pommar** in early 2372. ("Alliances" [VGR]).

Minnobia. Civilization. The Minnobia were at war with the **Vek** people in 2373. ("Business As Usual" [DS9]).

Minos Korva. Federation planet located in a sector four light-years from the border between the Federation and the Cardassians. The Cardassians attempted to annex the planet in the early 2360s, but were unsuccessful. In 2369, Starfleet contingency plans placed the *Enterprise*-D leading a fleet to defend Minos Korva and the surrounding sector in the event of a feared Cardassian invasion. ("Chain of Command, Part II" [TNG]).

Minos. Now uninhabited, Minos, a lush, forested planet, was once the home of a thriving, technologically advanced civilization. The people of Minos gained notoriety as arms merchants during the **Erselrope Wars**, but were all killed when their weapons systems got out of hand. At least a few Minosian artifacts survived, however, and were responsible for the destruction of the ***U.S.S. Drake*** in 2364. ("The Arsenal of Freedom" [TNG]). SEE: **Arsenal of Freedom**.

"Minstrel Boy, The." Traditional Earth folksong that told of a young musician killed in an ancient war. ***U.S.S. Rutledge*** crew member **Will Kayden**, killed by **Cardassians** at **Setlik III**, was fond of the song, as were his shipmates **Benjamin Maxwell** and **Miles O'Brien**. ("The Wounded" [TNG]).

mint tea. A beverage made from the steeped leaves of a plant from the genus *Mentha*. **Perrin**, wife of Ambassador **Sarek**, liked living on Vulcan, but regretted that there was no mint tea there. ("Unification, Part I" [TNG]).

Mintaka III. Class-M planet. Mintaka III was the site of a Federation anthropological field study of the local proto-Vulcan culture. ("Who Watches the Watchers?" [TNG]). *The exterior scenes of Mintaka III were filmed at Vasquez Rocks, near Los Angeles. Several other* Star Trek *episodes have been shot there, notably "Shore Leave," (TOS), "Arena" (TOS), and "Friday's Child" (TOS).*

Mintakan tapestry. Woven fabric art produced by the people of Mintaka III. An example of this craft was given to Captain Picard by **Nuria**, the **Mintakan** leader, in appreciation for his concern for her people. ("Who Watches the Watchers?" [TNG]). *This tapestry could, in later episodes, sometimes be seen draped over the back of Picard's chair in his quarters. Picard evidently salvaged the tapestry after the crash of the* Enterprise-*D in* Star Trek Generations, *since the artifact was seen on the chair in his ready room on the* Enterprise-*E in* Star Trek: First Contact.

Mintakans. Bronze age proto-Vulcan humanoids; natives of the planet **Mintaka III**. They were reported to be very peaceful and rational, living in a matriarchal, agricultural society. A Federation anthropological field team, studying the Mintakans in 2366, accidentally exposed the Mintakans to advanced Federation technology. ("Who Watches the Watchers?" [TNG]). SEE: **Nuria**.

Mintonian sailing ship. Wind-powered ocean vessel. Guinan imagined seeing a Mintonian sailing ship in the swirling clouds of the **FGC-47** nebula. ("Imaginary Friend" [TNG]).

Minuet. (Carolyn McCormick). A character in a holodeck simulation of a New Orleans jazz club. Minuet was generated by an enhanced holodeck program created by the **Bynars**, and was designed to interactively respond to Riker's expectations. Riker was quite captivated by the lovely Minuet, and was disappointed when her program disappeared from the computer after the Bynars left the ship. ("11001001" [TNG]). Minuet had left such an impression on Riker that **Barash**'s neural scanners found her image in Riker's mind when Riker was held by Barash on **Alpha Onias III** in 2367. In this virtual reality created by Barash's equipment, Minuet was supposedly Riker's wife and his ship's counselor, who had been killed in a shuttle accident. ("Future Imperfect" [TNG]).

Mira system. Location of planet **Dytallix B**. ("Conspiracy" [TNG]).

"Miracle Worker." Nickname given to **Montgomery Scott** by his crew mates aboard the *Starship Enterprise*. Kirk once joked that Scotty had earned that title by multiplying his repair time estimates by four, thus making it seem that he had performed those repairs in an amazingly small amount of time. *(Star Trek III: The Search for Spock).*

Miradorn. Species in which sets of twins have an almost symbiotic relationship; the two halves make the whole person. The Miradorn **Ro-Kel** was killed by the Rakhari fugitive **Croden**, causing his twin **Ah-Kel** to swear revenge. ("Vortex" [DS9]). *The Miradorn ship was designed by Ricardo Delgado.*

Miramanee's planet. Class-M planet onto which an ancient civilization known as the **Preservers** had transplanted several tribes of Native Americans centuries ago. The planet was in the midst of a dangerous asteroid belt, so the Preservers provided a powerful deflector device known to the Native Americans as the **Obelisk**. The Preservers taught the tribe's medicine man how to operate the deflector, but one medicine man failed to pass that information to his son, so in 2268, the planet was defenseless. *Enterprise* personnel attempted to protect the planet from a large asteroid in that year, but were unsuccessful. Kirk, injured on the planet's surface, accidentally figured out how to access the deflector controls so that the planet could be saved. ("The Paradise Syndrome" [TOS]). *Miramanee's planet was not given a formal name in the episode.*

Miramanee. (Sabrina Scharf). Tribal priestess from a group of Native Americans whose ancestors, centuries before, had been transplanted from Earth by people known as the **Preservers**. When *Enterprise* Captain **James T. Kirk** was stricken by amnesia on her planet's surface in 2268, Kirk's appearance was interpreted by tribal elders as a fulfillment of prophecy, and Kirk was decreed to be a god. Accordingly, tribal custom demanded that Miramanee marry Kirk, and the two fell in love and conceived a child. Their happiness did not last, as the tribe turned against Kirk when they learned he was mortal, fatally injuring Miramanee. She and her unborn child died in her husband's arms. ("The Paradise Syndrome" [TOS]). SEE: **Kirok.**

Miranda*-class starship.** Federation spacecraft type introduced in the late 23rd century. *Miranda*-class starships have included the ***Reliant *(Star Trek II), the* ***Saratoga*** *(Star Trek IV),* and another ***Saratoga*** (of a higher registry number and a slightly different design, seen in "Emissary" [DS9]). *Miranda*-class ships were similar to ***Soyuz*-class** vessels. *Named for Prospero's daughter, a character in William Shakespeare's last play,* The Tempest.

Mirell, Korenna. (Eve H. Brenner). Enaran woman whose lover, a Regressive man named Dathan Alaris, was killed in the mid-24th century. Alaris was murdered by the Enaran people, who systematically exterminated his ethnic minority. In following years, the Enarans lied to their descendents about the disappearance of the Regressives. Decades later, after a lifetime of keeping the secret, Jora Korenna Mirell decided to let the truth be known. In 2373, Korenna was able to use her telepathic abilities to pass her experiences to *Voyager* crew member B'Elanna Torres. Shortly after she had imparted her knowledge to Torres, Korenna died, apparently murdered by other Enarans who wished the dark truth to remain a secret. Torres subsequently passed Korenna's truth to a Enaran woman named **Jessen**. ("Remember" [VGR]). *"Jora" was a title of address prefixed to the name of an elder Enaran woman. Eve Brenner previously played Inad in "Violations" (TNG).*

Miri. (Kim Darby). A young woman who survived a disastrous biological experiment on her planet. The experiment was intended to create a virus that would extend human life, but resulted in the deaths of all the adults on her world. Only the children survived, their lives greatly extended, until they reached puberty and died a painful death. Miri had reached puberty at the time the *U.S.S. Enterprise* contacted her planet in 2266, but was saved when Dr. Leonard McCoy was able to develop an antitoxin for the virus. ("Miri" [TOS]). *Miri's planet was not given a name in the episode.*

"Miri." Original Series episode #12. Written by Adrian Spies. Directed by Vincent McEveety. Stardate 2713.5. *First aired in 1966. The* Enterprise *discovers a planet where all the adults have died, leaving behind a population of nearly immortal children.* GUEST CAST: Kim Darby as **Miri**; Michael J. Pollard as **Jahn**; Grace Lee Whitney as **Rand, Janice**; Keith Taylor as Jahn's friend; Ed McCready as Boy creature; Kellie Flanagan as Blonde girl; Steven McEveety as Redheaded boy; David Ross as Security guard #1; Jim Goodwin as **Farrell, Lieutenant John**; John Megna as Little boy; John Arndt as Security guard #2; David L. Ross as **Galloway, Lieutenant**; Irene Sale as Louise, female creature; Lizabeth Shatner as Blonde girl in red-striped dress; Melanie Shatner as Brunette in black lace dress; Dawn Roddenberry as Little blond girl; Darlene Roddenberry as Dirty-faced girl in flowered dress; Phil Morris as boy in army helmet; Jon and Scott Dweck as boys who stole phasers; Bob Miles as McCoy's stunt double. SEE: **Farrell, Lieutenant John; foolie; grup; Jahn; Life Prolongation Project; Miri; onlies; Rand, Janice**.

Miridian VI. An uninhabited planet near the Romulan Neutral Zone. During a virtual reality engineered by Barash on **Alpha Onias III** in 2367, **Barash** (as Ethan) said he had been captured by Romulans while living on Miridian VI. ("Future Imperfect" [TNG]).

Mirok. (Thomas Kopache). Science officer aboard a Romulan science vessel, in charge of developing and testing an experimental **interphase generator** in 2368. ("The Next Phase" [TNG]). *Thomas Kopache also played a communications officer on the* U.S.S. Enterprise-*B in* Star Trek Generations.

Mirren, Oliana. (Estee Chandler). One of three candidates who competed with Wesley Crusher for a single opening to **Starfleet Academy** in 2364. Mirren, a brilliant human female, was a runner-up in the competition. ("Coming of Age" [TNG]).

mirror universe. Continuum parallel to and coexisting with our own, but on another dimensional plane. Virtually everything in the mirror universe is duplicated, but in many cases is opposite in nature to its counterpart in our own universe. Captain Kirk and a few members from the *Enterprise* were thrust into this parallel existence after beaming during an ion storm, finding the mirror universe to be a brutally savage place. Spock's counterpart in the mirror universe believed his brutally oppressive government would inevitably spur a revolt, resulting in a terrible dark age. The mirror Spock indicated a willingness to help reform his government to possibly avert this sequence of events. ("Mirror, Mirror" [TOS]). SEE: ***Enterprise, I.S.S.*; Kirk (mirror); Spock (mirror); Tantalus field.** Led by Spock (mirror), the **Terran Empire** embraced disarmament and peace, but this was, unfortunately, ill-timed and left the empire open to be conquered by the **Alliance** of Klingon and Cardassian forces. Terrans were reduced to slave status. A second contact with our universe occurred in 2370, when a runabout's warp-drive malfunction sent **Deep Space 9** officers Kira and Bashir into the mirror universe by way of the **Bajoran wormhole**. Although Kira and Bashir soon returned home, they planted the seeds of human rebellion with potential freedom fighters on station **Terok Nor (mirror)**. ("Crossover" [DS9]). **Benjamin Sisko (mirror)** led the **Terran resistance** from a secret base in the **Badlands**. The mirror Sisko was killed in 2371 when his ship was destroyed by Cardassian forces. Terran forces quickly regrouped, however, under the leadership of Sisko's counterpart from our universe. This **Benjamin Sisko** visited the mirror universe long enough to convince **Jennifer Sisko (mirror)** to abandon work on a transpectral sensor array that would have made it impossible for Terran operatives to hide in the **Badlands**. ("Through the Looking Glass" [DS9]). By 2372, the resistance had driven the Alliance from Terok Nor. Terrans at the station built a powerful new ship, the ***Defiant* (mirror)**, that they used in their fight. ("Shattered Mirror" [DS9]).

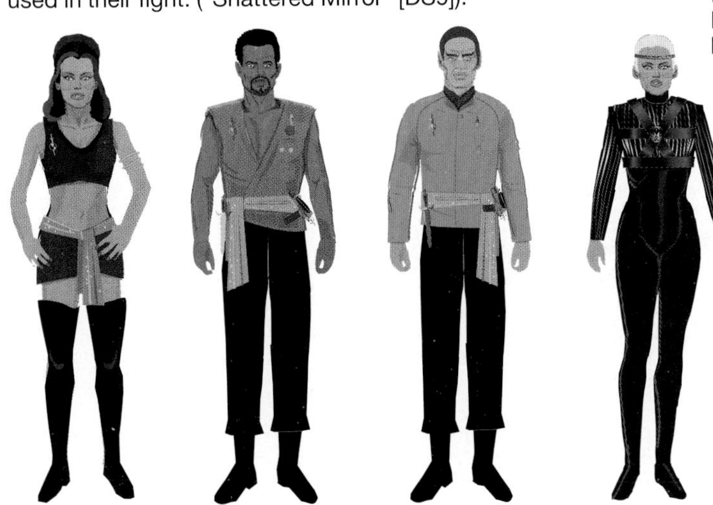

"Mirror, Mirror." Original Series episode #39. Written by Jerome Bixby. Directed by Marc Daniels. Stardate: Unknown. *First aired in 1967. A transporter malfunction sends Kirk and company into a savage mirror universe. This was the first episode set in the mirror universe. Several* Star Trek: Deep Space Nine *episodes were also set in this alternate reality, including "Crossover" (DS9), "Through the Looking Glass" (DS9), and "Shattered Mirror" (DS9).* GUEST CAST: Barbara Luna as **Moreau, Marlena (mirror)**; Vic Perrin as Tharn; John Winston as **Kyle, Mr.**; Garth Pillsbury as Wilson; Pete Kellett as **Farrell (mirror)**; John Winston as Computer voice; Paul Prokop as Guard; Bob Bass as Chekov's boy #1; Bob Clark as Chekov's boy #2; Johnny Mandell as Sulu's boy; Paul Baxley as Kirk's stunt double; Vince Deadrick as McCoy's stunt double; Jay Jones as Scotty's stunt double; Nedra Rosemond as Uhura's stunt double. SEE: **agonizer; agony booth; Farrell (mirror); Halkans; ion storm; Kirk, James T. (mirror); ion storm; Kyle, Mr. (mirror); mirror universe; Morleau, Marlena (mirror); Spock (mirror); Sulu (mirror); Tantalus field; Terran Empire.**

Mishiama wristlock. Martial-arts technique. **Tasha Yar** practiced the Mishiama wristlock for a competition aboard the *Enterprise*-D just prior to her death in 2364. ("Skin of Evil" [TNG]).

Mislen. Planet orbiting a yellow dwarf star in the Delta Quadrant. Mislen was the homeworld to a technologically sophisticated humanoid civilization of which **Chardis** was a member. ("The Swarm" [VGR]).

Mission: Impossible. Two-dimensional noninteractive audiovisual entertainment program produced on Earth from 1966 to 1973. The series dealt with a group of **secret agent**s who engaged in extralegal adventures on behalf of their government. Rain Robinson said that she'd seen every episode of *Mission: Impossible*. ("Future's End, Part II" [VGR]). Mission: Impossible *was produced at Desilu Studios on Stages 7 and 8, right next door to Stages 9 and 10, where the original* Star Trek *was filmed. Leonard Nimoy, who played Spock in the original* Star Trek *series, played a character named Paris in* Mission: Impossible. *William Shatner and Mark Lenard also had guest roles on the show. Other* Star Trek *veterans included Bob Justman, who was the associate producer, and art director Matt Jefferies, both of whom worked on the show's pilot episode.*

Mitchell, Admiral. Starfleet officer in charge of **Starbase 97**. ("Starship Mine" [TNG]).

Mitchell, Gary. (Gary Lockwood). Starfleet officer who was killed during an exploratory mission beyond the rim of the galaxy in 2265. Mitchell was a friend of **James T. Kirk** when they attended **Starfleet Academy** together. Gary once risked his life for Kirk by taking a poison dart thrown by rodent creatures on planet Dimorus. Kirk requested Mitchell on his first command, and Mitchell, who then held the rank of lieutenant commander, also served aboard the *Enterprise* early during Kirk's first five-year mission. In 2265, Mitchell was mutated into a godlike being after exposure to radiation at an energy barrier at the edge of the galaxy. Mitchell died on planet **Delta Vega**, and was listed as having given his life in the line of duty. ("Where No Man Has Gone Before" [TOS]). SEE: **barrier, galactic**. *Gary Lockwood also starred in the classic science-fiction movie* 2001: A Space Odyssey.

Mithren. Planet in the **Delta Quadrant**. Mithren has a form of structured government. **Neelix**, of the *Voyager*, had friends there. ("Persistence of Vision" [VGR]). The crew of the *U.S.S. Voyager* communicated with Mithren in 2372. ("Investigations" [VGR]).

mitosis. The ordered process of cell division, whereby one parent cell produces two genetically identical daughter cells. A similar process was used by the **quantum singularity life-form**s discovered in 2369. ("Timescape" [TNG]).

mitral sac. A pouchlike structure that grows on the backs of **Ocampa** females during their ***elogium***. The mitral sac is the structure in which the Ocampa fetus develops. ("Elogium" [VGR]).

Mitsuya, Admiral. Starfleet officer. Mitsuya visited station Deep Space 9 in 2370 in order to discuss Cardassian foreign policy with the station commander, and maybe to play a little poker. ("Paradise" [DS9]).

mizainite ore. Metallic substance. Rich deposits of mizainite ore are found on planet **Stakoron II** in the Gamma Quadrant. ("The Nagus" [DS9]).

Mizan, Dr. Ktarian scientist who was an expert in interspecies mating practices. In 2369, during a conference on deep-space assignments, Dr. Mizan attempted to enlist Counselor Troi's aid in his research. ("Timescape" [TNG]).

Mizar II. Home planet of the **Mizarians**. ("Allegiance" [TNG]).

Mizarians. The humanoid residents of the planet **Mizar II**. Distinguished by a gray wrinkled complexion, the Mizarians valued peace above confrontation. As a result, the Mizarians were conquered six times in a period of 300 years. The Mizarians survived by offering no resistance. **Kova Tholl** was Mizarian. ("Allegiance" [TNG]).

MK-12 scanner. Cardassian security device. An MK-12 scanner was used to verify the identity of those storing valuables at the **assay office** on the **Promenade** of station **Deep Space 9**. When entrusting several archaeological artifacts to the assay office, **Vash** questioned the office's clerk as to whether an MK-12 scanner with an L-90 enhanced resolution filter was adequate to prevent theft. ("Q-Less" [DS9]).

mnemonic memory circuit. Device improvised by Spock that allowed the retrieval of data from a **tricorder** when Spock and Kirk were trapped in Earth's past. Spock had constructed the circuit out of primitive electrical and radio components available in Earth's 1930s. Using the device, they were able to trace the flow of history as altered by Dr. McCoy and to locate the focal point in time where McCoy changed history. Spock complained to Kirk that he was working with tools at the primitive level of stone knives and bearskins, but finished the project nevertheless. ("The City on the Edge of Forever" [TOS]). SEE: **Guardian of Forever**; **Keeler, Edith.**

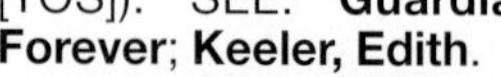

Moab IV. A harsh, inhospitable planet in the **Moab Sector**. Moab IV was colonized in 2168 by a group of humans who sought to create a perfect society there. The crew of the *Enterprise*-D discovered this previously unknown colony in 2368. ("The Masterpiece Society" [TNG]). *Named for the ancient kingdom that flourished on Earth during Biblical times in what is now Jordan.* SEE: **Genome Colony**.

Moab Sector. Region of Federation space. The *Enterprise*-D was assigned to the Moab Sector to track an errant **stellar core fragment** and to monitor resulting planetary disruptions in 2368. During the mission, the *Enterprise*-D found a previously unknown human colony on planet **Moab IV**. ("The Masterpiece Society" [TNG]).

***moba* fruit.** Bajoran food. *Moba* fruit was served on Deep Space 9 in 2372 at the reception for the Trill science team led by Lenara Kahn. ("Rejoined" [DS9]).

Mobara. Former member of the **Shakaar resistance cell** who lived at the **Bajoran** university in **Musilla Province.** He was killed on stardate 50416 with a micro-explosive implanted behind his ear. It was an act of vengeance by **Silaran Prin** for the explosion that disfigured him years earlier during the **Cardassian** occupation of **Bajor**. ("The Darkness and the Light" [DS9]).

***Moby-Dick*.** Classic story written by Earth novelist Herman Melville (1819-1891), first published in 1851. *Moby-Dick's* main character, Captain Ahab, was a sea captain who spent years hunting an enormous cetacean that had crippled him, so that he could exact revenge against it. Lily Sloane compared Captain Picard to Ahab because Picard seemed to want revenge on the Borg at any cost. *(Star Trek: First Contact)*.

Modean system. Inhabited planetary system. Young **Geordi La Forge** was once stationed with his father in the Modean system. ("Imaginary Friend" [TNG]).

Model A Ford. The second self-powered wheeled vehicle developed by **Earth** entrepreneur Henry Ford, introduced in 1927. **Data**, who was the second android built by **Dr. Noonien Soong**, compared himself to a Model A. ("A Matter of Time" [TNG]).

Modela aperitif. Exotic double-layered beverage. Modela aperitifs were served at **Quark's bar** on **Deep Space 9**. ("Dramatis Personae" [DS9]).

modesty subroutine. Specialized program incorporated into **Data**'s positronic brain. The program instructed Data to remain clothed, a human social convention he had previously found unnecessary. ("Inheritance" [TNG]).

modular shelter. Portable living enclosure carried aboard Federation starships in an unassembled form. In 2372, when Janeway and Chakotay were left behind on a planet to live out their lives, they were left with an assortment of supplies and equipment, including a modular shelter. ("Resolutions" [VGR]).

Mogh. Noted Klingon warrior. Father to **Worf** and **Kurn**, and political rival to **Ja'rod**. Mogh and his wife were killed in the **Khitomer massacre** of 2346, after following Ja'rod to Khitomer because Mogh suspected him of disloyalty. Mogh's suspicions were correct: Ja'rod betrayed his people at Khitomer by providing secret defense codes to the Romulans. Mogh was survived by his sons, Worf and Kurn. Years later, in 2366, Ja'rod's son, **Klingon High Council** member **Duras**, falsified evidence in an attempt to conceal Ja'rod's actions and to implicate Mogh. Worf and Kurn challenged the accusations before the High Council, but council leader **K'mpec** was not willing to expose the powerful Duras family. ("Sins of the Father" [TNG]). Honor was restored to the house of Mogh in late 2367 when the sons of Mogh agreed to support the Gowron regime during the Klingon civil war. ("Redemption, Parts I and II" [TNG]). In 2369, Worf investigated a report that Mogh had not been killed at Khitomer and that he had survived at a secret Romulan prison camp in the **Carraya System**. Although the camp was real, Worf learned from one of the inmates that the report was untrue. ("Birthright, Part II" [TNG]).

Mojave. Southwestern region of the North American continent on **Earth**. Home to *Enterprise* Captain **Christopher Pike** (born early 23rd century), the area boasted glittering cities surrounded by wide belts of parkland. ("The Cage," "The Menagerie, Part II" [TOS]). *The scenic background of the distant Mojave city, seen at Pike's picnic with Tango, was later re-used as the skyline of a city on Planet Q in "Conscience of the King" (TOS).*

***Mok'bara*.** Ritual Klingon martial-arts form, resembling terrestrial tai chi. Worf taught a *Mok'bara* class to his *Enterprise*-D shipmates most mornings at 0700. ("Man of the People" [TNG]). Worf taught the *Mok'bara* to his fellow captives at the secret Romulan prison camp in the **Carraya System** in 2369. The exercises, designed to enhance one's agility in hand-to-hand combat, helped to revive the dormant warrior spirit among the captives there. ("Birthright, Part II" [TNG]). *The* Mok'bara *exercises were invented by martial-arts expert (and visual effects producer) Dan Curry.*

***Mok*.** Klingon term meaning "Begin." ("Looking for *par'Mach* in All the Wrong Places" [DS9]).

Mokra Order. Government of a humanoid civilization on a planet in the Delta Quadrant. The Mokra Order was technologically advanced, but viewed outsiders and dissidents alike with extreme distrust. By 2372, the Mokra Order was opposed by the **Alsaurian resistance movement**. ("Resistance" [VGR]).

molecular cybernetics. Field of study pioneered by noted scientist **Dr. Ira Graves**, whose work formed the basis of **Dr. Noonien Soong**'s invention of the positronic neural network. The work of both men in this field made possible the **positronic brain** in the android **Data**. ("The Schizoid Man" [TNG]).

molecular displacement traces. Tricorder readings indicative of recent macroscopic motion. ("Ensign Ro" [TNG]).

molecular imaging scanner. Subsystem within a Federation starship's **transporter**. The molecular imaging scanner is responsible for creating the data matrix that describes every particle of the transport subject. A faulty imaging scanner could result in a transport subject being improperly re-created. ("Tuvix" [VGR]). SEE: **Heisenberg compensator**.

molecular phase inverter. Romulan device that could alter the molecular structure of matter so it could pass through "normal" matter and energy. ("The Next Phase" [TNG]). SEE: **interphase generator**.

molecular reversion field. Mysterious energy pattern. The ***Shuttlecraft Fermi*** passed through a molecular reversion field on stardate 46235. The field caused the shuttle's structure to deteriorate and prevented a clean transporter lock on its crew. Finally, the field caused Picard and the other members of the *Fermi* crew to be reduced to children. ("Rascals" [TNG]). SEE: **rybo-viroxic-nucleic structure.**

molecular signature. Physical frequency at which all matter in the universe resonates. In 2372, the *Starship Voyager* was duplicated by a **spatial scission**. The two resulting ships had slightly differing molecular signatures. ("Deadlock" [VGR]).

molecular-decay detonator. A technology used exclusively in Romulan weapons. A detonator of this type was found in the bomb that exploded aboard **K'mpec**'s ship in 2367, providing compelling evidence of Romulan involvement. ("Reunion" [TNG]).

Molière. Earth actor and playwright (1622-1673). Considered to be the greatest of all writers of French comedy. In 2372 when Lieutenant Paris needed cheering up, Ensign Harry Kim suggested they take in a Molière comedy in the holodeck. ("Parturition" [VGR]).

Molor. Tyrant emperor on the **Klingon Homeworld** who ruled at the time of **Kahless the Unforgettable**, some 1,500 years ago. Kahless used the first ***bat'leth*** sword to kill the tyrant. ("Rightful Heir" [TNG]). At the **Maranga IV** outpost, Alexander wanted 50 **darseks** to see Molor's mummified head. ("Firstborn" [TNG]). *John Kenton Shull played Molor in the Klingon opera performed on Maranga IV in "Firstborn."*

Molson, E. Federation colonist on planet Tarsus IV who survived the massacre in 2246. By 2266, Molson was one of only nine surviving eyewitnesses who could have identified **Kodos the Executioner**. ("The Conscience of the King" [TOS]).

molybdenum-cobalt alloys. Sophisticated metallic compound, used in the construction of the android **Data**, who had about 11.8 kilograms of the stuff in his body. ("The Most Toys" [TNG]).

***Mondor*.** Pakled spacecraft, encountered by the *Enterprise*-D near the **Scylla** Sector in 2365. The *Mondor* had experienced systems malfunctions and *Enterprise*-D engineer Geordi La Forge transported to the **Pakled** ship in an effort to render assistance. The Pakleds thereupon made an unsuccessful attempt to kidnap La Forge. The *Mondor*'s equipment showed evidence of having been borrowed or stolen from a variety of other civilizations, including the Romulans, the Klingons, and the **Jaradans**. ("Samaritan Snare" [TNG]).

monetary units. SEE: **Bolian currency; credit; credit chip; darsek; dirak; dollar; *dorak*; *frang*; isik; latinum; lek; *lita*; quatloo; strip.**

Monitor, U.S.S. Federation starship, ***Nebula*-class**, Starfleet registry number NCC-61826, sent to the Romulan Neutral Zone border in preparation for a possible battle, after Starfleet received warnings of a Romulan buildup at planet **Nelvana III** in 2366. The warnings, from Romulan defector Alidar Jarok, were later found to be baseless. ("The Defector" [TNG]).

monocaladium particles. Substance detected in cave walls on planet **Melona IV** following the attack of the **Crystalline Entity** in 2368. ("Silicon Avatar" [TNG]).

monocrystal cortenum. Substance that can be combined with **polysilicate verterium** to create a densified composite material, **verterium cortenide**. ("Investigations" [VGR]).

Monroe, Lieutenant. (Jana Marie Hupp). An *Enterprise*-D officer. She was in command of the ship when it struck two **quantum filaments** in rapid succession on stardate 45156. Monroe was killed in the second collision, leaving **Deanna Troi** in charge. ("Disaster" [TNG]).

Montana. Region of the North American continent on **Earth**. Montana was the home of **Zefram Cochrane**, and the launch site of the ***Phoenix***, Earth's first faster-than-light spacecraft. Montana was also the site of Earth's **first contact** with an extraterrestrial civilization, made on April 5, 2063, after a passing **Vulcan** spacecraft followed Cochrane's ship back to Earth. A monument to Cochrane's achievements, including a 20-meter marble statue of the great space pioneer, stands in Montana near the site of first contact. *(Star Trek: First Contact). Montana was also the home state of* First Contact *cowriter Brannon Braga.*

Moodus. Starfleet officer. Moodus served aboard the ***U.S.S. Okinawa*** while Benjamin Sisko was the vessel's executive officer. In 2372, Moodus and several other former *Okinawa* officers were reassigned by **Admiral Leyton** in preparation for his attempted coup of Earth's government. ("Paradise Lost" [DS9]).

Moogie. Childhood nickname used by **Rom** and **Quark** to refer to their mother, **Ishka**. ("Family Business" [DS9]).

"Moon Over Rigel VII." A traditional song, often sung around campfires in the 23rd century. McCoy, however, preferred "Row, Row, Row Your Boat." *(Star Trek V: The Final Frontier).*

moon grass. Vegetation used as a flavor enhancer in certain culinary preparations. ("Business As Usual" [DS9]).

"Moon's a Window to Heaven, The." Song. **Uhura** sang "The Moon's a Window to Heaven" while distracting **Sybok**'s soldiers on planet **Nimbus III**. *(Star Trek V: The Final Frontier). Music and lyrics by Jerry Goldsmith and John Bettis. Arranged and performed by Hiroshima.*

moon. Planetoid; **Earth**'s only natural satellite. The moon was the first world visited by space explorers from Earth. ("Tomorrow is Yesterday" [TOS]). SEE: ***Apollo* 11**. In the 24th century, 50 million people lived on the moon that was home to Tycho City, the **New Berlin** colony, and Lake Armstrong. *(Star Trek: First Contact).*

Moore, Admiral. Starfleet official. Moore briefed Captain Picard on an ancient distress signal detected from the **Ficus Sector** a month prior to stardate 42823. ("Up the Long Ladder" [TNG]).

mooring clamps. Mechanism used at station Deep Space 9 to secure a ship to the docking port. ("Babel" [DS9]).

Mora Pol, Dr. (James Sloyan). Scientist who studied **Odo** at the **Bajoran Institute of Science** following Odo's discovery in the **Denorios Belt** ("The Alternate" [DS9]) in 2358 ("Broken Link" [DS9]). Dr. Mora studied Odo's remarkable ability to change shape, and helped encourage Odo's adoption of a humanoid form. During Odo's formative years in the laboratory on planet **Bajor**, Dr. Mora and other scientists called him ***odo'ital*** which in **Cardassian** means "nothing." ("Heart of Stone" [DS9]). Mora regarded himself as Odo's father, and found it difficult to accept Odo's increasing independence as Odo integrated himself into humanoid society. The two remained estranged following Odo's departure from the institute, until 2370, when Mora enlisted Odo's help in investigating a shape-shifting life-form on planet **L-S VI**. After returning from L-S VI, Mora correctly ascertained that Odo was causing havoc on Deep Space 9 during his regenerative state due to contamination by volcanic gas from the planet. ("The Alternate" [DS9]). When Odo was struck by a mysterious debilitating medical condition in 2372, Dr. Mora invited him back to his lab for some more tests, but Odo declined. ("Broken Link" [DS9]). Mora did not realize how his rational, scientific approach to Odo's upbringing had been difficult, even painful to Odo. As a result, Mora was deeply hurt that Odo never understood how much Mora had cared for him, even as his own son. In 2373, when another **changeling infant** was discovered in the Alpha Quadrant, Mora offered his assistance to Odo, who was caring for the child. When Odo saw how difficult it was to care for the desperately ill infant changeling, he began to understand how much Mora cared for him. ("The Begotten" [DS9]). *James Sloyan also played Admiral Alidar Jarok in "The Defector" (TNG) and the adult Alexander Rozhenko in "Firstborn" (TNG).*

Morag. (Reg E. Cathey). Commander of a Klingon ship that patrolled the Federation border, near **Relay Station 47**. Morag was fond of flying close to the station every few days, harassing the station's crew, once even locking his disruptors onto the station. Morag was found innocent in an incident in 2369 at Relay Station 47 in which **Lieutenant Aquiel Uhnari** and **Lieutenant Keith Rocha** were believed to have been murdered, but Morag was found to have stolen Starfleet data from that station. ("Aquiel" [TNG]).

Moral and Ethical Issues. A course at the **Starfleet Academy** taught by Professor Somak. ("The Ship" [DS9]).

morale officer. SEE: **Neelix**.

Morath. Legendary figure in Klingon mythology, the brother of **Kahless the Unforgettable**. Legend has it that Morath once brought dishonor to his family by telling a lie, for which Kahless fought him for 12 days and 12 nights. A small statue of Morath and Kahless, depicting this heroic struggle, adorned Worf's quarters aboard the *Enterprise*-D. ("New Ground" [TNG]).

morathial series. A group of resuscitative drugs in use aboard Federation starships. ("Ethics" [TNG]).

Mordan IV. Class-M planet whose humanoid inhabitants suffered a terrible civil war that lasted 40 years. The conflict started around 2319 when Starfleet officer **Mark Jameson** provided weapons to one of the factions in exchange for freedom for Federation hostages. ("Too Short a Season" [TNG]).

Mordian butterfly. Insect life-form indigenous to **Rymus Major**. ("Profit and Loss" [DS9]).

Mordock Strategy. A brilliant system devised by **Mordock** of the planet **Benzar**. Wesley Crusher was nearly in awe of this accomplishment. ("Coming of Age" [TNG]). *Unfortunately, the episode does not give any clue as to what the Mordock Strategy is for or how it works.*

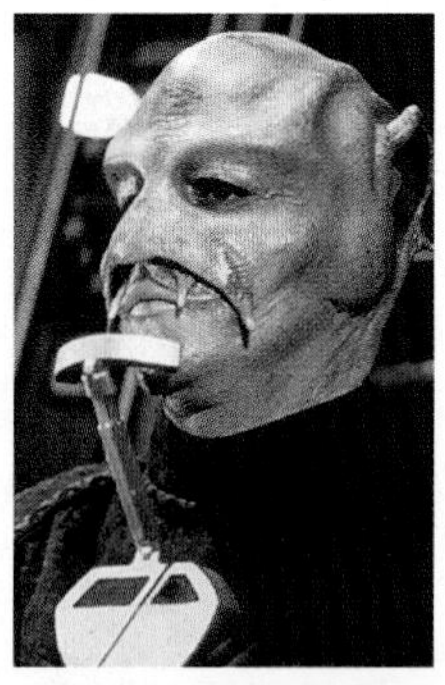

Mordock. (John Putch). One of three candidates who competed with Wesley Crusher for a single opening to **Starfleet Academy** in 2364. Mordock won the coveted appointment to the academy, becoming the first Starfleet cadet from the planet **Benzar**. ("Coming of Age" [TNG]). *John Putch also played another Benzite, **Mendon**, in "A Matter of Honor" (TNG), which established that all Benzites from the same geostructure look identical, at least to non-Benzites. He also portrayed a journalist aboard the* U.S.S. *Enterprise-B in* Star Trek Generations.

Moreau, Marlena (mirror). (Barbara Luna). ***I.S.S. Enterprise*** scientist who worked in the lab and performed other duties as the captain's woman in the **mirror universe**. After seeing the normally brutal Captain Kirk show mercy to his enemies, Moreau deduced that Kirk was in fact a counterpart from an alternate (our own) universe. When Kirk returned to his own universe, he discovered Moreau's counterpart had recently been assigned to his own *U.S.S. Enterprise*. ("Mirror, Mirror" [TOS])

Morg. Term used for the male population on planet **Sigma Draconis VI**. The Morgs lived under virtual Stone Age conditions, controlled by the **Eymorg** women and their **Controller**. The Morgs and Eymorgs were reunited as a single society after the failure of the Controller in 2268. ("Spock's Brain" [TOS]).

Morgana Quadrant. Region of space. Destination of *Enterprise*-D after departing Science Station **Tango Sierra**. The ship was still en route to Morgana when Nagilum was discovered. ("The Child" [TNG], "Where Silence Has Lease" [TNG]). *The term Morgana Quadrant does not fit into the Alpha, Beta, Delta, and Gamma naming scheme that* Star Trek *now uses for the four quadrants of the galaxy. The reason for this is that "The Child" and "Where Silence Has Lease" were both filmed before "The Price" (TNG), in which that system was first used. The feature film* Star Trek VI: The Undiscovered Country *also used the Alpha-Beta-Delta-Gamma system, so we are assuming that this nomenclature was in use significantly before* The Next Generation, *even though* Star Trek VI *was filmed after "The Price."*

Moriarty, Professor James. (Daniel Davis). Villainous adversary to **Sherlock Holmes**, Moriarty was a fictional character created by Earth novelist **Sir Arthur Conan Doyle**. A computer-generated embodiment of Moriarty was created by the *Enterprise*-D **holodeck** computer. The computer had been responding to a command from Geordi La Forge to create an adversary capable of defeating Data in the role of Sherlock Holmes. The result was Moriarty, a computer program so sophisticated that he was a life-form in his own right. Thus imbued with consciousness, Moriarty began to learn about his surroundings and actually befriended Dr. Katherine Pulaski. When it was deemed improper to erase this program on the grounds that it was a sentient being, *Enterprise*-D Captain Picard ordered the Moriarty character saved for reactivation when a means could be found to give the character physical form so that it could live outside of the holodeck. ("Elementary, Dear Data" [TNG]). Moriarty remained stored in protected computer memory for four years, but for some unexplained reason, his program was not entirely dormant. Moriarty attempted to escape the holodeck computer again in 2369, fashioning an elaborate simulated world in which he tried to trick Picard and other *Enterprise*-D personnel into permitting his release into the real world. Unfortunately, the technology to permit this was still not available, so Moriarty's program was transferred into an independent computer system where his computer-generated consciousness could live in a computer-generated environment. ("Ship in a Bottle" [TNG]). SEE: **Barthalomew, Countess Regina**.

Morikin VII. Planet. **Jean-Luc Picard** was assigned to Morikin VII for training while a cadet third class at Starfleet Academy. There was a **Nausicaan** outpost on one of the nearby asteroids. ("Tapestry" [TNG]). *But that's a story for another day....*

morilogium. The final phase of the **Ocampa**n lifespan. *Morilogium* usually occurs around nine years of age. ("Before and After" [VGR]). SEE: **Kes**.

Moriya system. Star system in the **Badlands**. The **Terikof Belt** was located beyond the Moriya system. ("Caretaker" [VGR]).

Morka. (Ray Young). An agent of the **Klingon Intelligence** service; one of three agents sent to **Deep Space 9** in 2371 to observe and to take appropriate action against a **Romulan** delegation visiting the station. Morka was under direct orders from the Klingon High Council. ("Visionary" [DS9]).

Morla. (Charles Dierkop). **Argelian** native. Morla was to marry a dancer named **Kara**. When Kara was brutally murdered in 2267, Morla admitted being jealous that Kara had paid attention to Montgomery Scott, but denied that this jealousy would have driven him to such violence. ("Wolf in the Fold" [TOS]).

Morn. (Mark Shepherd). Patron of **Quark's bar** at the **Promenade** on station **Deep Space 9**. ("Emissary" [DS9]). Morn had 17 brothers and sisters. ("Starship Down" [DS9]). Morn once asked **Jadzia Dax** out for dinner. She declined, even though she thought he was kinda cute. ("Progress" [DS9]). Members of Morn's species have more than one heart. In 2371, Morn and **Quark** were caught by **Odo** as they prepared for Cardassian **vole** fights. ("Through the Looking Glass" [DS9]). In 2373, Worf shoved Morn from a barstool in order to impress the Lady Grilka when she visited the station. Worf promised to apologize to Morn later. ("Looking for *par'Mach* in All the Wrong Places" [DS9]). (In an alternate future in which Ben Sisko was believed killed aboard the *Defiant* in 2372, Quark had left Deep Space 9 and had acquired a small moon by 2391, and Morn took over Quark's bar and continued to run it as late as 2405. SEE: **Sisko, Jake**.) ("The Visitor" [DS9]). *Morn is an anagram for Norm, George Wendt's character in* Cheers. *The character had been regularly seen in the background at Quark's bar since "Emissary," the first episode of* Star Trek: Deep Space Nine, *but was not referred to by name until "Vortex" (DS9).*

Moropa. Civilization with whom the **Bolians** maintained an uneasy truce in 2366. ("Allegiance" [TNG]).

morphenolog. Pharmaceutical used to ease pain and stop convulsions. Dr. Bashir ordered 2 cc's of morphenolog for **Vedek Bareil** in 2371 when treating him for injuries sustained during an explosion aboard a **Bajoran** transport. ("Life Support" [DS9]).

morphogenic enzyme. Neurochemical found in the bodies of **Founders**. In 2373, when Odo experienced a plasma shock, his morphogenic enzymes produced a version of the Great Link, trapping him and three others in a memory from Odo's past. ("Things Past" [DS9]).

morphogenic matrix. Fundamental structure underlying **Founder** physiology. Instability of the morphogenic matrix can cause a life-threatening medical condition. ("The Begotten" [DS9]).

***morrok*.** Legendary beast from **Drayan** folklore. The *morrok* was a personification of death that was believed to take elderly Drayans at the end of their lives. ("Innocence" [VGR]).

Morrow, Admiral. (Robert Hooks). Chief of Starfleet Command in 2285. Morrow was commander at the time the original *Starship Enterprise* returned from the **Mutara Sector** after confronting **Khan**. Morrow had ordered the *Enterprise* to be decommissioned and denied Kirk's request to return to the **Genesis Planet** to search for Spock, but Kirk disobeyed Morrow and went anyway. *(Star Trek III: The Search for Spock). Morrow was evidently replaced as Starfleet commander shortly after* Star Trek III, *since Admiral Cartwright held the post in* Star Trek IV.

Morska. Klingon planet on which is located a subspace monitoring outpost. The *Enterprise*-A passed near Morska when on course to **Rura Penthe** to rescue Kirk and McCoy in 2293. Fortunately, Communications Officer Uhura was somehow able to convince the technicians at Morska that the *Enterprise*-A was a legitimate Klingon ship. *(Star Trek VI: The Undiscovered Country).*

Morta. (Michael Snyder). One of the renegade Ferengi who took over the *Enterprise*-D shortly after stardate 46235. ("Rascals" [TNG]). *Michael Snyder also played Dax in* Star Trek VI *and Qol in "The Perfect Mate" (TNG).*

mortae. Mining implements used by the **Troglytes** on planet Ardana. The Troglyte **Disrupters** used mortae as tools of vandalism on the cloud city **Stratos** in 2269 when protesting the inequities of their society. ("The Cloud Minders" [TOS]).

mortality fail-safe. Subroutine of the *Enterprise*-D's **holodeck** control programs intended to prevent simulation participants from injuring themselves seriously. ("Elementary, Dear Data" [TNG]).

Mortania. Remote region of planet **Angel One**. Dissident **Ramsey**, his wife **Ariel**, and their followers were exiled to Mortania by Angel One leader **Beata** in an effort to slow the rate of the social changes Ramsey and company had advocated. ("Angel One" [TNG]).

Moseley, Hal. (Stefan Gierasch). Meteorologist from the planet **Penthara IV**. When his planet was faced with an ecological disaster caused by a meteor strike on the surface, Moseley worked with the crew of the *Enterprise*-D to overcome the disaster. ("A Matter of Time" [TNG])

Moselina system. Star system. The *Enterprise*-D was en route to the Moselina system on stardate 45733 when it suffered extensive damage due to an invasion by **nitrium metal parasites**. ("Cost of Living" [TNG]).

"Most Toys, The." *Next Generation* episode #70. Written by Shari Goodhartz. Directed by Timothy Bond. Stardate 43872.2. *First aired in 1990. An eccentric and cruel collector decides to add Data to his collection.* GUEST CAST: Nehemiah Persoff as **Toff, Palor**; Jane Daly as **Varria**; Colm Meaney as **O'Brien, Miles**; Saul Rubinek as **Fajo, Kivas**. SEE: **Basotile; Beta Agni II; bioplast sheeting; Data; denkirs; Fajo, Kivas; finoplak; Giles Belt; *Grissom, U.S.S.*; hytritium; *Jovis*, the; *lapling*; Lawmim Galactopedia; Maris, Roger; molybdenum-cobalt alloys; Nel Bato system; Off-Zel, Mark; *Pike, Shuttlepod*; Rejac Crystal; Sigma Erandi system; Stacius Trade Guild; "Starry Night"; Station Lya IV; Tellurian spices; Toff, Palor; tricyanate; tripolymer composites; Varon-T disruptor; Varria; Veltan Sex idol; Zibalians.**

Mostral. SEE: **Kazon-Mostral**.

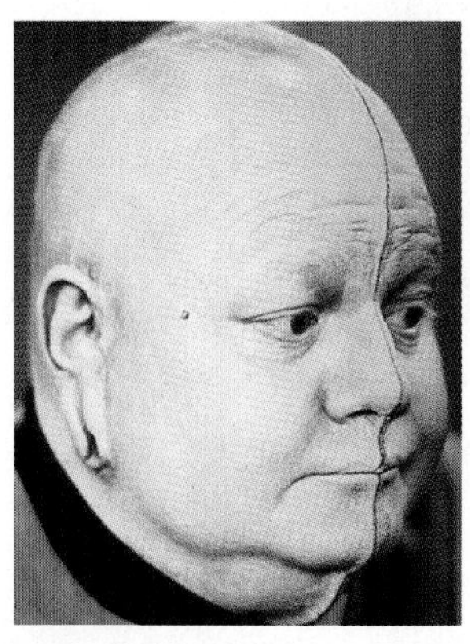

Mot. (Ken Thorley, Shelly Desai). Barber aboard the *Enterprise*-D. ("Data's Day" [TNG]). Mot, a Bolian, was fond of giving useful tactical advice to the ship's senior officers, whether they wanted it or not. ("Ensign Ro" [TNG]). Mot was responsible for the hairpieces worn by Captain Picard and Commander Data when they masqueraded as Romulans on a covert mission to **Romulus** in 2368. ("Unification, Part I" [TNG]). *The* Enterprise-*D barber was first seen in "Data's Day" (TNG), where he was played by Shelly Desai and named V'Sal in the script, although that name was never used on the air. In later episodes, the character was called Mr. Mot and was played by Ken Thorley. We suspect the two were supposed to be the same person, since it seems unlikely that the* Enterprise-D *would have two barbers who were both Bolians. Mot was first referred to by name in "Ensign Ro" (TNG).*

motor assist bands. Four-centimeter-wide straplike devices used with neurologically damaged patients. The bands provide electrical stimulation to the patient's limbs and help with muscle retraining. These devices were used to help rehabilitate the **Zalkonian** called **John Doe** in 2366, following the reattachment of one of his arms. ("Transfigurations" [TNG]).

Motura. (Stephen Rappaport). Victim of the Vidiian **phage** who nearly died of lung failure in 2371 due to the disease. Motura survived after receiving a transplant of **Neelix**'s lungs shortly after stardate 48532. Motura realized that a non-**Vidiian** might not understand the desperate survival measures to which the phage had driven his people. He was therefore surprised and grateful when Captain Janeway declined to order Motura's death in order to reclaim Neelix's lungs. Motura subsequently lent medical assistance that permitted Neelix to live by making it possible to transplant one of **Kes**'s lungs into Neelix's body. ("Phage" [VGR]). SEE: **Dereth**.

Mountains of the Antelope Women. Location on **Chakotay**'s **medicine wheel**. It was considered an extremely attractive area, from which a soul might not choose to return. ("Cathexis" [VGR]).

Movar. (Nicholas Kepros). **Romulan** general. Movar aided **Lursa** and **B'etor** in their bid to take over the **Klingon High Council** in 2367. Movar secretly provided military supplies to **Duras** family forces during the **Klingon civil war** that year. ("Redemption, Part I" [TNG]).

MoVas ah-kee rustak. Klingon phrase meaning "Today was a good day to die." ("Looking for *par'Mach* in All the Wrong Places" [DS9]).

"Move Along Home." *Deep Space Nine* episode #10. Teleplay by Frederick Rappaport and Lisa Rich & Jeanne Carrigan-Fauci. Story by Michael Piller. Directed by David Carson. No stardate given. *First aired in 1993. A new species from the Gamma Quadrant forces the crew to play a new and seemingly deadly game.* GUEST CAST: Joel Brooks as **Falow**; James Lashly as **Primmin, Lieutenant George**; Clara Bryant as **Chandra**. SEE: ***allamaraine*; alpha-currant nectar; Andolian brandy; Chandra; chula; Falow; Ferengi; first contact; *klon peags*; *lokar* beans; McCoullough, Captain; Primmin, Lieutenant George; reactive ion impeller; *shap*; Surchid, Master; *thialo*; Wadi**.

movek. Klingon word which means "I lose." ("Sons of Mogh" [DS9]). *This is how Klingons "say uncle."*

Mowray, Dr. Archaeologist. Captain Picard sought to contact Mowray on planet Landris II on stardate 46693. Picard was unable to make contact due to a communications blackout requested by the **Stellar Cartography Section**. ("Lessons" [TNG]).

Mozart, Wolfgang Amadeus. Austrian musical composer (1756-1791) who wrote more than six hundred compositions and is recognized as one of the principal composers of **Earth**'s Classic style. *Enterprise*-D Captain Jean-Luc Picard was fond of Mozart's works, and enjoyed playing them on his **Ressikan flute**. ("A Fistful of Datas" [TNG]). The **Traveler** once compared Wesley Crusher to Mozart, as both were child prodigies, destined for great things. ("Journey's End" [TNG]). (In one possible future visited by **Kes**, the holographic doctor aboard the ***Voyager*** briefly took the name Dr. Mozart.) ("Before and After" [VGR].)

MS 1 Colony. Federation settlement. In 2369, MS 1 was the second colony to be attacked by a group of fanatical self-aware **Borg**. ("Descent, Part I" [TNG]).

Mudd (planet). Class-K planet. Mudd was inhabited by a group of sophisticated **androids** from the Andromeda Galaxy. When **Harcourt Fenton Mudd** stumbled upon this world in 2267, he named it in his own honor. ("I, Mudd" [TOS]).

"Mudd's Women." Original Series episode #4. Teleplay by Stephen Kandel. Story by Gene Roddenberry. Directed by Harvey Hart. Stardate 1329.8. *First aired in 1966. The* Enterprise *rescues con man Harry Mudd and his "cargo" of three beautiful women. This episode marks the first appearance of Harry Mudd, who would reappear in "I, Mudd" (TOS).* GUEST CAST: Roger C. Carmel as **Mudd, Harcourt Fenton**; Karen Steele as **McHuron, Eve**; Maggie Thrett as **Ruth**; Susan Denberg as **Magda**; Jim Goodwin as **Farrell, Lieutenant John**; Gene Dynarski as **Childress, Ben**; Jon Kowal as **Gossett, Herm**; Seamon Glass as **Benton**; Jerry Foxworth as Security guard; Eddie Paskey as Connors; Frank Da Vinci as Guard; Majel Barrett as Computer voice. SEE: **Benton; Childress, Ben; class-J cargo ship; Farrell, Lieutenant John; Gossett, Herm; lithium crystal; Magda; McHuron, Eve; Mudd, Harcourt Fenton "Harry"; Ophiucus III; Rigel XII; Ruth; Venus drug; Walsh, Captain Leo.**

Mudd, Harcourt Fenton "Harry." (Roger C. Carmel). An interstellar rogue, con man, and general ne'er-do-well. Brought aboard the *Enterprise* in 2266 when his damaged ship disintegrated, Mudd was charged with several violations, and his extensive criminal record was discovered, including smuggling, transport of stolen goods, and purchasing a space vessel with counterfeit currency. One scam involved the illegal **Venus drug**, given to women he recruited as wives for settlers on distant planets, including **Rigel XII**. His ruse discovered, Mudd was convicted and incarcerated. ("Mudd's Women" [TOS]). Mudd somehow escaped from the authorities and then established what he called a "technical information service," selling the **Denebians** all rights to a Vulcan fuel synthesizer. When it was found that Mudd did not have the rights to make such a sale, Mudd was arrested. Upon learning that fraud carries a death penalty on Deneb, Mudd broke jail and was pursued by a patrol, which fired and damaged his ship. He drifted in space until he came to a Class-K planet inhabited by sophisticated **androids** from the Andromeda Galaxy. The androids dubbed him Lord Mudd and provided for his every need, except the need for freedom. In 2267, Mudd sent an android named **Norman** to commandeer the *Starship Enterprise* in hopes that he could trade the *Enterprise* crew for his own freedom. Upon escaping from the androids, Captain Kirk left Mudd on the android planet as punishment. ("I, Mudd" [TOS]).

Mudd, Stella. (Kay Elliot). Former wife of confidence man **Harcourt Fenton Mudd**. While on the android planet, he had a replica made of her, so he could have the pleasure of telling her to shut up. Mudd's punishment for hijacking the *Enterprise* in 2267 was to be left behind on the android planet with 500 replicas of Stella to nag him. ("I, Mudd" [TOS]).

Mudor V. Planet. Site of an *Enterprise*-D mission in 2368. The *Enterprise*-D had just departed Mudor V when it was severely disabled by impact with a series of **quantum filaments**. ("Disaster" [TNG]).

mugato. (Janos Prohaska). Apelike carnivore with white fur and poisonous fangs on **Tyree**'s planet. A *mugato* attacked James Kirk in 2267, leaving him close to death. Since there was no antitoxin known to counteract this poison, McCoy allowed a local witch doctor, a ***Kahn-ut-tu*** woman, of the **hill people** tribe to successfully treat Kirk. ("A Private Little War" [TOS]). *In the script, the apelike creature was called a gumato. Janos Prohaska was also the* ***Horta*** *from "Devil in the Dark" (TOS) and the* ***Excalbian*** *from "The Savage Curtain" (TOS). Prohaska designed and built the* mugato *from an ape suit he had previously built for another project.*

***muktok* plant.** Variegated bristle-like foliage found on the planet **Betazed**. Able to live for hundreds of years, the *muktok* blooms gave off a pleasant sound when shaken. Riker and Troi recalled meeting near a particular *muktok* plant when Riker was stationed on Betazed. ("Ménage à Troi" [TNG]).

Mulhall, Dr. Ann. (Diana Muldaur). Astrobiologist aboard the original *Starship Enterprise*. In 2268, Mulhall was on the landing party to **Sargon's planet**. Dr. Mulhall volunteered to allow her body to house **Thalassa**, one of the beings encountered there, so that **android** bodies could be built for them. ("Return to Tomorrow" [TOS]). SEE: **Sargon**. *Diana Muldaur also played* ***Dr. Miranda Jones*** *in "Is There in Truth No Beauty?" (TOS) and* ***Dr. Katherine Pulaski*** *during the second season of* Star Trek: The Next Generation.

Mullen, Commander Steven. First Officer of the ***U.S.S. Essex***. Mullen was killed in 2167 when the *Essex* disintegrated above a moon of **Mab-Bu VI**. ("Power Play" [TNG]).

Mullibok. (Brian Keith). **Bajoran** farmer who escaped from a **Cardassian** labor camp in 2329, and later settled on **Jeraddo**, a Class-M moon orbiting **Bajor**. Mullibok lived in peace on Jeraddo for 40 years, until the Bajoran provisional government decided to tap Jeraddo's core for use as an energy source. This project was expected to render Jeraddo uninhabitable, so it was necessary for Mullibok and his friends **Baltrim** and **Keena** to evacuate their home. When they resisted, Major Kira Nerys was assigned to persuade them to leave before the energy-tap project endangered their lives. ("Progress" [DS9]).

multimodal reflection sorting. An advanced technique used to process subspace **sensor** data. Multimodal reflection sorting was used to detect the interactive **subspace** signals exchanged between **Locutus** and the **Borg** collective consciousness after Picard had been rescued from the Borg in early 2367. ("The Best of Both Worlds, Part II" [TNG]).

multiphase pulse. Energy burst characterized by signals of overlapping frequencies and nutation. Multiphase pulses could be generated by Starfleet sensor devices, such as a tricorder. Properly programmed and adjusted, a multiphase pulse could sometimes be used to penetrate some force fields. ("Attached" [TNG]). Harry Kim used a multiphasic scan to determine the defensive capabilities of Bothan ships in 2372. ("Persistence of Vision" [VGR]).

multiphase tractor beam. Technology developed by Geordi La Forge of the En*terprise*-D and scientist **Hannah Bates** of the **Genome Colony** on planet **Moab IV** in 2368. Their new development allowed warp power to be channeled into the tractor beam with greater efficiency than was previously available. The modified **tractor beam** was successful in diverting an approaching stellar core fragment that threatened Bates's home on Moab IV, but use of the beam caused loss of life-support systems throughout the ship. ("The Masterpiece Society" [TNG]).

multiplexed pattern buffer. SEE: **pattern buffer.**

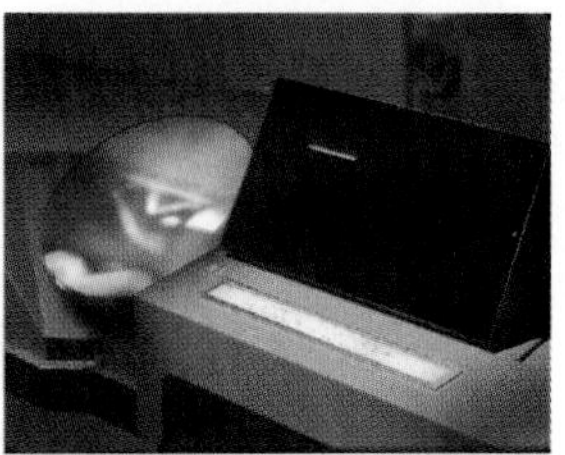

multitronics. Experimental computer technology developed by **Dr. Richard Daystrom** in the 2260s. Daystrom made several attempts to develop a functional multitronic computer, but his test units M-1 through M-4 were not entirely successful. His fifth attempt, M-5, was tested aboard the *Starship Enterprise* in 2268 with disastrous results. ("The Ultimate Computer" [TOS]). By the 24th century, some highly sophisticated computer programs, such as Starfleet's **Emergency Medical Hologram**, used multitronic pathway programming techniques. ("The Swarm" [VGR]).

Mulzirak. Type of transport vessel. **Vash** hired a Mulzirak ship to shuttle her away from Deep Space 9 in 2369. She later canceled her reservations. ("Q-Less" [DS9]).

Mundahla. Cloud dancer located in the Teleris Cluster. Q invited **Vash** to visit there, but she declined. ("Q-Less" [DS9]).

Muniz, Enrique. (F. J. Rio). Noncommissioned Starfleet engineer assigned to Deep Space 9. ("Hard Time" [DS9]). In 2372, Muniz was stationed in engineering on the ***U.S.S. Defiant*** when the ship came under Jem'Hadar attack during a trade conference with the Karemma. ("Starship Down" [DS9]). Muniz died on stardate 50049, mortally wounded in a battle with the Jem'Hadar while on a mining survey mission to planet Torga IV. ("The Ship" [DS9]). *Muniz first appeared in Starship Down" (DS9). His first name was first mentioned in "The Ship" (DS9).*

muon frequencies. Energetic radiation used to destroy the **harvesters** in 2370. ("Armageddon Game" [DS9]).

muon. Short-lived subatomic particle classified as a lepton. Excessive buildup of muons in the **dilithium** chamber of a Federation starship's warp drive can lead to a catastrophic explosion. Such a buildup occurred as a result of Romulan sabotage in 2368 when the *Enterprise*-D was rendering assistance to a Romulan science vessel. ("The Next Phase" [TNG]).

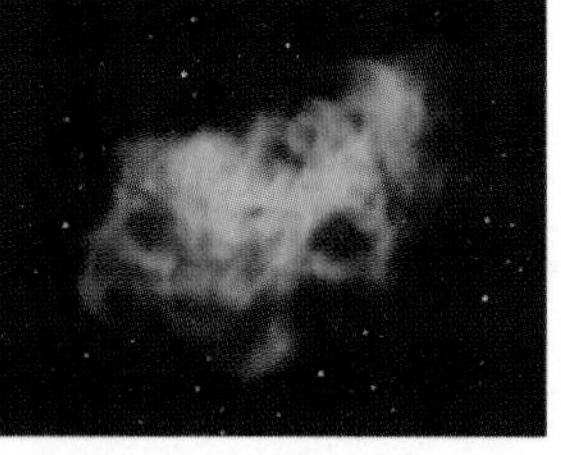

Murasaki 312. Quasar-like formation near planet **Taurus II**. *Enterprise* ***Shuttlecraft Galileo*** was lost in 2267 while studying this object. ("The *Galileo* Seven" [TOS]). Studies of the Murasaki Effect were still under way in 2367 when the *Enterprise*-D gathered information on this object using long-range sensors. ("Data's Day" [TNG]).

Muroc, Penny. A woman from Rigel with a penchant for men in uniform. She had two dates with Ensign Jean-Luc Picard during his assignment at **Starbase Earhart** in 2327. ("Tapestry" [TNG]).

Murphy, Ensign. (Shepard Ross). Starfleet security officer assigned to the *U.S.S. Voyager*. In 2373, Murphy escorted Arridor and Kol to secured quarters. Along the way they overpowered him and escaped the ship via the shuttlebay. ("False Profits" [VGR]). *A different actor played Murphy as seen in "Prime Factors" (VGR). This Murphy wore a blue sciences/medical uniform.*

"Muse, The." *Deep Space Nine* episode #93. Teleplay by René Echevarria. Story by René Echevarria & Majel Barrett Roddenberry. Directed by David Livingston. No stardate given. *First aired in 1996. Lwaxana Troi, pregnant with an unborn son, begs Odo to help her escape her husband; Jake meets a mysterious woman named Onaya who encourages his literary pursuits–but her help may cost Jake his life. Odo and Lwaxana Troi become married in this episode.* GUEST CAST: Majel Barrett as **Troi, Lwaxana**; Michael Ansara as Jeyal; Meg Foster as **Onaya**. SEE: ***Anslem*; Betazoids; Catullus; foramen magnum; Gavaline tea; holodeck and holosuite programs; Jeyal; Keats, John; Kell, Tavor; neurotransmitter; Odo; Onaya; orange juice; *qui'lari*; Revalus; *shakras*; Sisko, Jake; Tagana; Tarbolde, Phineas; Tavnians; Troi, Lwaxana; Umani sector; visceral writing; *Wait, The*; wedding.**

mushroom soup. Broth made with edible fungus growths. Chakotay's favorite soup. ("State of Flux" [VGR]).

Musilla Province. Region on the planet **Bajor**. Site of a **Bajoran** university and engineering school. **Mobara**, a former member of the **Shakaar resistance cell** lived there until his death in 2373. ("The Darkness and the Light" [DS9]). **Kira Nerys** had a friend who owned a 200-year-old cottage in Musilla Province. ("Looking for *par'Mach* in All the Wrong Places" [DS9]). In 2367, there was a string of four bombings in Musilla that were very similar to the assassination attempt on **Gul Dukat** on station **Terok Nor** that same year. ("Things Past" [DS9]).

Muskan seed punch. Traditional **Halii** beverage. **Aquiel Uhnari** missed Muskan seed punch when assigned to **Relay Station 47**. She said that the replicator didn't make it as well as her mother did. ("Aquiel" [TNG]).

mutagenic retrovirus. Deadly biological weapon. Arms dealers Gaila and Hagath often sold mutagenic retroviruses. ("Business As Usual" [DS9]).

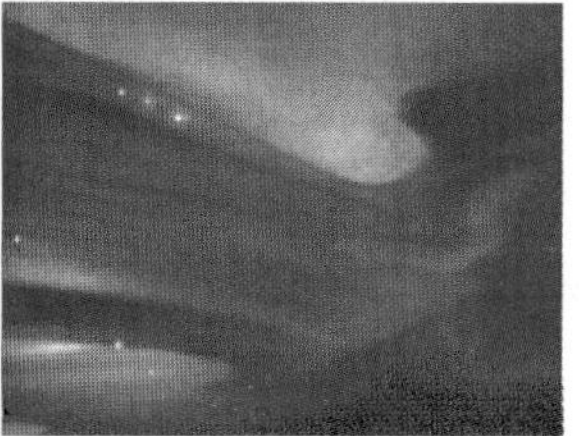

Mutara Nebula. Interstellar dust cloud in the Mutara Sector. Site where **Khan** detonated the experimental Genesis torpedo in 2285, causing the Mutara Nebula to re-form into the **Genesis Planet**. The nebula was composed of ionized gas that prevented reliable operation of a starship's sensors. *(Star Trek II: The Wrath of Khan). Stock footage of the Mutara Nebula was reused several times for other nebulae seen on* Star Trek: The Next Generation.

Mutara Sector. Region of space. Location where the ***S.S. Botany Bay***, launched from Earth in 1996, was discovered adrift in 2267. ("Space Seed" [TOS]). Also the location of the **Genesis Planet**, and the **Regula I** planetoid. (*Star Trek II: The Wrath of Khan, Star Trek III: The Search for Spock*).

mutiny. The criminal act of willfully disobeying lawful military authority. Persons accused of mutiny would be subject to court-martial and, if convicted, could receive punishment up to and including a death sentence. By the 23rd and 24th centuries, mutiny aboard starships was unthinkable. ("Whom Gods Destroy" [TOS]). Nevertheless, an investigation conducted by the Judge Advocate General found evidence that mutiny did occur aboard the *Starship* ***Pegasus*** in 2359. This evidence was suppressed and no trial was ever held. ("The Pegasus" [TNG]). *Though Picard found mutiny "shocking," there are several examples of mutinies and attempted mutinies aboard Federation starships. These include the mutiny of Garth's crew ("Whom Gods Destroy" [TOS]), the mutiny of the crew of the first* Starship Defiant *("The Tholian Web" [TOS]), and the suggested mutiny of the* Enterprise *bridge crew ("Turnabout Intruder" [TOS]), as well as the mutiny on the* Pegasus.

mutual annihilation. The process by which a particle and its counterpart antiparticle come into contact and destroy each other, releasing energy. ("Deadlock" [VGR]). SEE: **antimatter**. A similar phenomenon exists for time and **anti-time.** ("All Good Things..." [TNG]).

mutual induction field. Energy barrier produced by a network of low-altitude satellites around a penal colony moon in the Gamma Quadrant. The mutual induction field prevented communications to or from the moon, and also made it difficult for sensors from the runabout *Yangtzee Kiang* to scan the planet's surface. ("Battle Lines" [DS9]).

mycorrhizal fungus. Mold found on planet **Ledonia III**. Mycorrhizal fungus helps the native plants to survive by retaining water. ("The Wire" [DS9]).

myocardial enzyme balance. Medical test used in surgical (particularly cardiac) procedures. ("Samaritan Snare" [TNG]).

myographic scanner. Sensing device. Used on Federation **escape pods** to monitor the bio-electric signatures of the pod's passengers, allowing them to be traced should they become separated from the pod after landing. ("Legacy" [TNG]).

Myrmidon. Planet. Archaeologist **Vash** was wanted by authorities on Myrmidon for stealing the Crown of the First Mother. ("Q-Less" [DS9]).

N'Vek, Subcommander. (Scott MacDonald). **Romulan** officer and member of the underground supporting reunification of the Romulan and the Vulcan people. In 2369, N'Vek was a key operative in an elaborate plot to enable the defection of **Vice-Proconsul M'ret** to the Federation. N'Vek arranged for the abduction of *Enterprise*-D officer Deanna Troi from Borka VI, then had her surgically altered into Romulan form. N'Vek then coerced Troi to assume the identity of **Major Rakal**, a member of the elite **Tal Shiar** intelligence service. Using Troi as Rakal, N'Vek commandeered the Romulan warbird ***Khazara***, arranging for stasis containers with M'ret and two aides to be transported into Federation hands. N'Vek was killed while enabling Troi's return to the *Enterprise*-D after the operation was complete. ("Face of the Enemy" [TNG]). *Scott MacDonald also played Tosk in "Captive Pursuit" (DS9), Goran'Agar in "Hippocratic Oath" (DS9), and Rollins in "Caretaker" (VGR) and "Dreadnought" (VGR).*

***N'yengoren* strategy**. Klingon attack tactic used against a fortified ground-based stronghold. ("Blood Oath" [DS9]).

nacelle. In starship design, a large outboard structure that houses a **warp-drive** engine. Nacelles generally incorporate powerful **subspace** field generation coils and sometimes have **Bussard collector**s to gather interstellar hydrogen. The interior of a warp nacelle is dominated by a two rows of massive semi-circular warp-field coils that serve to transform the ship's drive plasma stream into the subspace field that makes faster-than-light speeds possible. A nacelle's interior also includes a small control room that permits maintenance and monitoring of the system's operation. Aboard a ***Galaxy*-class starship**, access to the nacelle control room is via **Jefferies tube**. Most Federation starship designs feature two warp-engine nacelles mounted parallel to the axis of flight, whose net centerline is offset from the ship's center of gravity. One of the nacelle control rooms aboard the *Starship Enterprise*-D was the site of a suicide that occurred in 2362, prior to the ship's launch. ("Eye of the Beholder" [TNG]). *Some ships, like the* U.S.S. Stargazer*, have four warp engines instead of the traditional two. Gene Roddenberry insisted that starships have even numbers of nacelles, although the future version of the* Enterprise*-D from "All Good Things..." (TNG) had three nacelles. The nacelle control room and plasma injectors were a full-sized set designed by Richard James. The cavernous warp coils were a miniature designed by Anthony Fredrickson and composited by visual effects supervisor David Stipes. The design of the coils was based on a drawing by Rick Sternbach in the* Star Trek: The Next Generation Technical Manual.

Nador, Gul. (Mark Bramhall). Cardassian officer. Nador commanded a *Galor*-class warship that was patrolling the vicinity of the **Argus Array** in 2370. (In the **quantum reality** in which he existed, Nador took his ship into Federation territory in order to investigate the *Enterprise*-D's presence at the Argus Array. Nador implied that the Federation was using the Array to "observe a neighboring species" rather than gather astronomical data.) ("Parallels" [TNG]).

Nafir, ruins of. Archaeological site. Captain Picard visited the ruins of Nafir in 2370, just prior to his fateful visit to a bar on **Dessica II.** ("Gambit, Part I" [TNG]).

Nagilum. (Earl Boen). An extradimensional life-form. The *Enterprise*-D encountered Nagilum during a star-mapping mission en route to the **Morgana Quadrant** in 2365. Nagilum threatened the lives of one-third to one-half the *Enterprise* crew, but it was later learned the threat was merely its effort of trying to understand the human concept of life and death. ("Where Silence Has Lease" [TNG]).

nagus, grand. Ferengi master of commerce. The grand nagus has enormous power over **Ferengi** business, controlling the allocation of trade territories and other commercial opportunities. In 2369, Grand Nagus **Zek** named **Quark** as his successor in a trade conference held aboard Deep Space 9, although the appointment and Zek's subsequent apparent death were part of a ruse intended to test his son, **Krax**. When a Nagus dies, his body is immediately vacuum-desiccated and pieces are sold as collector's items at handsome prices. SEE: **Ferengi death rituals**. ("The Nagus" [DS9]). The grand nagus carried an ornate cane symbolizing his high rank. The cane featured a sculpted Ferengi head made of gold at its top. It was customary to honor the nagus by kissing the head of the cane. Grand Nagus Zek loaned his cane to Benjamin Sisko in early 2371 in order to impress Quark with the importance of establishing business dealings with the **Dominion**. ("The Search, Part I" [DS9]). The first grand nagus was **Gint**, the ancient entrepreneur who first devised the **Ferengi Rules of Acquisition** that guide Ferengi commerce. ("Body Parts" [DS9]). *"Nagus" was also a nickname given to David Livingston, director of "The Nagus" (DS9), by* Star Trek: Deep Space Nine *director of photography Marvin Rush.*

"Nagus, The." *Deep Space Nine* episode #11. Teleplay by Ira Steven Behr. Story by David Livingston. Directed by David Livingston. No stardate given. *First aired in 1993. The Ferengi "godfather" dies, and Quark is the heir apparent.* GUEST CAST: Max Grodénchik as **Rom**; Lou Wagner as **Krax**; Barry Gordon as **Nava**; Lee Arenberg as **Gral**; Aron Eisenberg as **Nog**; Tiny Ron as **Maihar'du**; Wallace Shawn as **Zek**. SEE: **Arcybite; argine; Augergine stew; Bajoran Gratitude Festival; Balosnee VI; Barbo; Clarus System; Dolbargy sleeping trance; Ferengi Rules of Acquisition; fire caves; Gral; Hoex; Hupyrian; Jokarian chess; Krax; locator bomb; Maihar'du; mizainite ore; nagus, grand; Nava; Nog; O'Brien, Miles; Rom; *Sepulo*; sorium; Stakoron II; Tarahong detention center; tube grubs; Volchok Prime; Zek**.

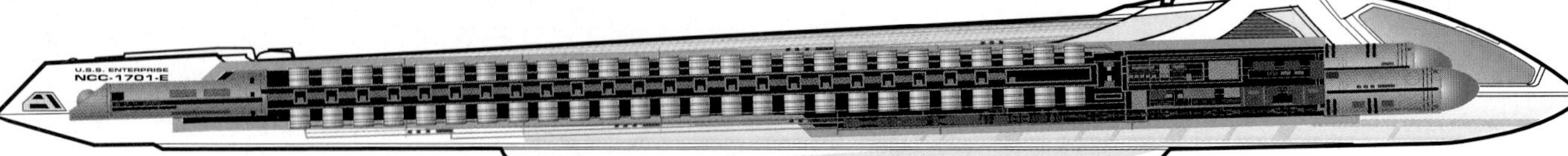

Nacene. Noncorporeal extragalactic life-forms. The Nacene originated outside of our galaxy and exist as pure **sporocystian** energy who can travel through **subspace**, although they can manifest themselves in solid humanoid form. A group of Nacene explorers visited our galaxy a millennium ago, accidentally devastating the environment of the **Ocampa** planet in the Delta Quadrant. Two Nacene individuals, one known as the **Caretaker**, and another called **Suspiria**, remained behind to care for the Ocampa. ("Cold Fire" [VGR]).

naDev ghos! Klingon for "Come Here!" ("Redemption, Part I" [TNG]).

nadion. Subatomic particle associated with high-speed interactions within atomic nuclei. Nadion emissions accompanied the discharge of a **phaser** beam. ("Time and Again" [VGR]).

Nahmi IV. Inhabited planet. Site of an outbreak of **Correllium fever** in 2366. The *Enterprise*-D was assigned to transport a collection of tissue samples from the **Mikulaks** to Nahmi IV, in hopes that the samples would help contain the outbreak. ("Hollow Pursuits" [TNG]).

Nakahn. (Stephen Davies). Inhabitant of the **Delta Quadrant**. Nakahn was a member of the **Mikhal Travelers** and operated a refueling outpost near **Tarkan** territory. ("Darkling" [VGR]).

Nakamura, Admiral. (Clyde Kusatsu). Starfleet officer in charge of Starbase 173, near the Romulan Neutral Zone, at the time the facility first opened in 2365. Nakamura supported **Commander Bruce Maddox**'s efforts to have Data disassembled in hopes of replicating Noonien Soong's work. ("The Measure of a Man" [TNG]). In 2370, Nakamura was made commander of **Starbase 219.** He was perturbed when the *Enterprise*-D mysteriously suffered propulsion problems that would prevent Captain Picard from attending the Annual Starfleet **Admiral's Banquet**. ("Phantasms" [TNG]). (In the **anti-time** reality created by the **Q Continuum**, Nakamura initiated a fleetwide yellow alert on stardate 47988. During that alert he deployed 16 starships, including the *Enterprise*-D, to the **Romulan Neutral Zone** in response to the military buildup along the Romulan side of the border. Nakamura authorized the deployment of probes into the Neutral Zone to investigate the anomaly reported there, but would not authorize any ship to enter the zone.) ("All Good Things..." [TNG].)

"Naked Now, The." *Next Generation* episode #3. Teleplay by J. Michael Bingham. Story by John D. F. Black and J. Michael Bingham. Directed by Paul Lynch. Stardate 41209.2. *First aired in 1987. An intoxicating virus causes members of the* Enterprise-D *crew to lose their inhibitions. This episode was the first* Next Generation *segment made after the two-hour series opener, "Encounter at Farpoint" (TNG). The basic story was written by John D. F. Black in May 1967 during the original* Star Trek *series, as a possible sequel to "The Naked Time" (TOS).* GUEST CAST: Brooke Bundy as **MacDougal**, **Sarah**; Benjamin W.S. Lum as **Shimoda**, **Jim**; Michael Rider as Transporter chief; David Renan as Conn; Skip Stellrecht as Engineering crewman; Kenny Koch as Kissing crewman. SEE: **Data; isolinear optical chip; MacDougal, Sarah; Psi 2000 virus; Shimoda, Jim; *Tsiolokovsky*, *U.S.S.*; Yar, Natasha.**

"Naked Time, The." Original Series episode #7. Written by John D. F. Black. Directed by Marc Daniels. Stardate 1704.2. *First aired in 1966. During the investigation of a disintegrating planet, a mysterious alien virus strips the* Enterprise *crew of their inhibitions, exposing their innermost feelings. This episode was originally planned as the first part of a two-parter, although the second half eventually became an independent story, "Tomorrow Is Yesterday" (TOS). The first regular episode of* Star Trek: The Next Generation, *"The Naked Now" (TNG), was sort of a sequel to this episode. "The Naked Time" was the first episode to establish that the* Enterprise *warp engines are powered by matter and antimatter. It was also the first episode in which the tricorder was used.* GUEST CAST: Stewart Moss as **Tormolen**, **Joe**; Majel Barrett as **Chapel**, **Christine**; Bruce Hyde as **Riley**, **Kevin Thomas**; Grace Lee Whitney as **Rand**, **Janice**; William Knight as Amorous crewman; John Bellah as Laughing crewman; Frank Da Vinci as Brent, Lieutenant; Eddie Paskey as Ryan, Lieutenant; Christin Ducheau, Woody Talbert, Bud Da Vinci, Crewmen. SEE: **antimatter; Chapel, Christine; environmental suit; fencing; foil; intermix formula; Psi 2000 virus; Psi 2000 (planet); Rand, Janice; Riley, Kevin Thomas; Spock; Sulu, Hikaru; Tormolen, Joe; tricorder; warp drive**.

Name the Winner! Televised sports program on planet Eight Ninety-Two-IV in which Roman gladiators fought to the death. ("Bread and Circuses" [TOS]). *The announcer for* Name the Winner! *was Bart La Rue, who also provided the voice of the* ***Guardian of Forever*** *in "The City on the Edge of Forever" (TOS).*

Naming Day. A coming-of-age ritual in the **Ferengi** culture, at which a young Ferengi receives presents from his parents. ("Rivals" [DS9]).

Nanclus. (Darryl Henriques). **Romulan** ambassador to the United Federation of Planets. In 2293, Nanclus was part of a conspiracy between Starfleet **Admiral Cartwright** and Klingon **General Chang** to obstruct **Chancellor Gorkon**'s peace initiatives. (*Star Trek VI: The Undiscovered Country*). *Actor Darryl Henriques also played* ***Portal*** *in "The Last Outpost" (TNG).*

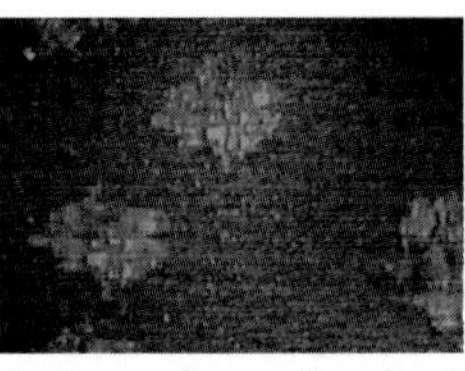

nanites. Submicroscopic robots designed to perform medical functions within the bloodstream of a living organism. Such functions might include intracellular surgery, elimination of individual disease cells, or removing clotted material from a blood vessel. Manufactured in Dakar, Senegal, these devices possessed gigabytes of mechanical computer memory. They were designed to operate only while inside cellular nuclei, and were generally kept in a nonfunctional state when not in use. In 2366, Wesley Crusher conducted experiments in nanite interaction. These studies went awry, resulting in the creation of self-replicating, sentient nanites. The nanites interfered with *Enterprise*-D on-board systems and nearly jeopardized a landmark astrophysics experiment conducted by **Dr. Paul Stubbs** before the nanites were recognized to be sentient life-forms. The nanites were later granted colonization rights on planet Kavis Alpha IV. ("Evolution" [TNG]). Nanites were briefly considered by *Enterprise*-D personnel as a possible defense against the **Borg** during the Borg offensive of 2367. The plan was abandoned because it was believed it would take two to three weeks for the nanites to have an effect, far too long to save Earth from the Borg. ("The Best of Both Worlds, Part II" [TNG]). In 2372, *Voyager*'s **Emergency Medical Hologram** used nanites to retrieve foreign DNA from murder victim Frank Darwin, leading to the discovery of his killer's identity. ("Meld" [VGR]).

nanobiogenic weapon. Biological weapon of mass destruction used in the war between the **T'Lani** and the **Kellerun**. ("Armageddon Game" [DS9]). See: **harvesters**.

nanopolymer. Densified material that can be used to re-inforce components of plasma flow conduits. *(Star Trek: First Contact)*.

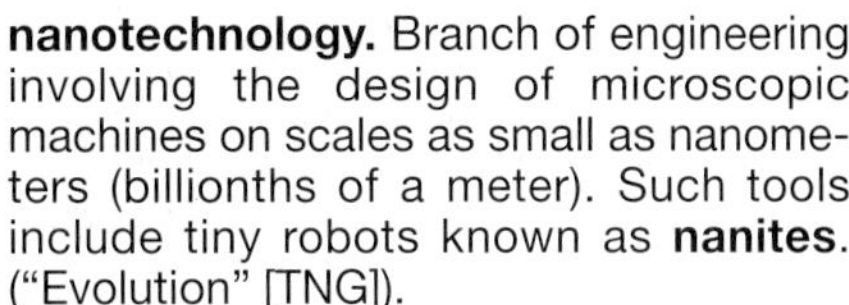

nanopulse laser. Advanced engineering device developed by the androids on planet **Mudd**. ("I, Mudd" [TOS]).

nanotechnology. Branch of engineering involving the design of microscopic machines on scales as small as nanometers (billionths of a meter). Such tools include tiny robots known as **nanites**. ("Evolution" [TNG]).

Nanut. Tygarian freighter. The *Nanut* docked at station Deep Space 9 in 2370, before a mission to the Gamma Quadrant. While at DS9, **Li Nalas** was discovered aboard the *Nanut*, hoping to escape his fame. ("The Homecoming" [DS9]).

Napean. Partially empathic humanoid species. **Daniel Kwan**'s mother was Napean. ("Eye of the Beholder" [TNG]).

Napinne. Planet in the Delta Quadrant. The *Voyager* stopped at Napinne to pick up food stores just prior to stardate 48846. On Napinne, Neelix obtained varmeliate fiber, whole green *putillos* and **schplict**. ("Learning Curve" [VGR]).

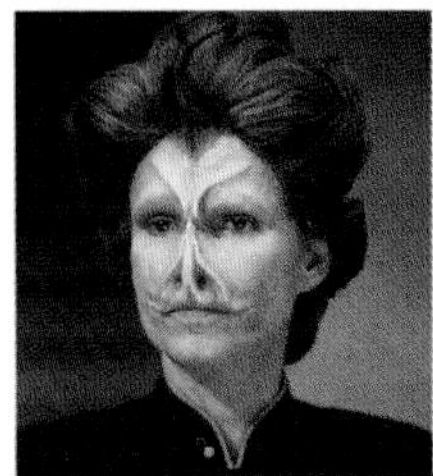

Nara, Lieutenant. (Nancy Harewood). **Daniel Kwan**'s supervisor in the **nacelle** control room aboard the *Enterprise*-D in 2370. ("Eye of the Beholder" [TNG]).

Narendra III (alternate). Planet. In the alternate history created when the ***Enterprise*-C** vanished from its "proper" time in 2344, the Klingon outpost at

Narendra III was also attacked by Romulan forces. But in this alternate timeline, the *Enterprise*-C was not available to render aid to the colony. This was evidently a key event in history, because the failure to render aid led to serious deterioration of the relationship between the Klingons and the Federation, culminating in a long and costly war between the two powers. ("Yesterday's *Enterprise*" [TNG]).

Narendra III. Planet. The site of an ill-fated Klingon outpost that was attacked by Romulan forces in 2344. The ***Enterprise*-C** rendered aid in the incident. Athough the *Enterprise*-C was reported lost, the heroism of the ship's crew so impressed the Klingon government that it led to improved relations between the Federation and the Klingons. ("Yesterday's *Enterprise*" [TNG]).

Narik. (Cameron Thor). Member of **Arctus Baran**'s band of mercenaries and chief engineer of their ship. Like the rest of Baran's crew, Narik was kept in control by the use of a **neural servo**. He was present when Commander Riker was abducted from Barradas III. Narik was killed in 2370 on **Vulcan** when **Tallera** activated a **psionic resonator**. ("Gambit, Parts I and II" [TNG]).

Narsu, Admiral Uttan. Commander of Starbase 12 in 2167. Narsu ran Starabase 12 at the time the ***U.S.S. Essex*** disappeared above a moon of planet **Mab-Bu VI**. ("Power Play" [TNG]).

Narsu, Mrs. Instructor of a sculpting class aboard the *Enterprise*-D. ("Masks" [TNG]).

Narth, Captain. Commander of the ***U.S.S. Ajax*** in 2327. Ensign **Cortin Zweller** served under Narth, Zweller's first Starfleet assignment after graduation from the academy. ("Tapestry" [TNG]).

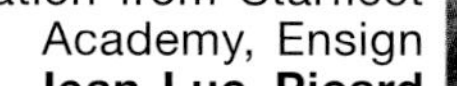

NASA. National Aeronautics and Space Administration. Earth-based branch of the American government responsible for many early space exploration missions, including ***Apollo* 11** and ***Voyager VI***. *(Star Trek: The Motion Picture).* NASA launched the spaceship ***Charybdis*** from Earth on July 23, 2037, the ill-fated third manned attempt to explore beyond the solar system. The ship suffered a telemetry failure, and its fate was unknown until 2365, when the remains of the *Charybdis* were discovered in orbit around a planet in the **Theta 116** system. ("The Royale" [TNG]). *NASA received screen credit for its technical support of the first* Star Trek *feature film.*

Nasari. Spacefaring technological humanoid civilization. The Nasari considered the **Taresians** their enemies, and they attacked any ship carrying Taresians. **Captain Alben** was Nasari. ("Favorite Son" [VGR]).

Nasreldine. Planet. An *Enterprise*-D crew member picked up a case of the flu at Nasreldine shortly prior to stardate 42686. ("The Icarus Factor" [TNG]).

Nassuc, General. Military officer and head of the **Palamarian Freedom Brigade**. Nassuc was a former general under the **Regent of Palamar**. The Regent trusted Nassuc, and he intended to eventually hand his entire army over to her, but she betrayed him by declaring independence for her homeworld. In 2373, Nassuc was interested in buying deadly biological weapons from Quark, to be used against the forces of the Palamarian Regent. When she learned that **Gaila** and **Hagath** contracted to sell deadly biological weapons to the Regent of Palamar, she sent a **purification squad** after them. ("Business As Usual" [DS9]).

nasturtium. Terrestrial flowering plant of the genus *Tropaeolum*. Young **Clara Sutter** helped **Keiko O'Brien** plant nasturtiums in the *Enterprise*-D arboretum shortly after stardate 45852. ("Imaginary Friend" [TNG]).

natal pod. Device used by the Iyaaran people to produce their young, using postcellular compounding. ("Liaisons" [TNG]). *Unfortunately, the episode never did make clear just how this works.*

Natira. (Kate Woodville). High Priestess of the **Fabrini** people on the asteroid/ship ***Yonada***, who served as her people's liaison to their **Oracle**. Natira guided her people near the end of their long interstellar voyage, when the *Yonada* nearly collided with planet **Daran V**. In 2268, Natira fell in love with Starfleet officer **Dr. Leonard McCoy** and asked him to marry her. ("For the World Is Hollow and I Have Touched the Sky" [TOS]). *Natira probably presided over her people's arrival at their promised land in 2290, although we haven't seen that event, so we don't know what really happened. We hope that McCoy was able to attend Yonada's arrival.*

Nausicaans. (Clint Carmichael, Nick Dimitin, Tom Morga). Intelligent humanoid life-forms. Some Nausicaans have earned a reputation for being surly, ill-tempered, quick to violence, and very tall. In 2327, just after his graduation from Starfleet Academy, Ensign **Jean-Luc Picard** was involved in a fight with three Nausicaans while on leave at **Starbase Earhart**. One Nausicaan stabbed Picard through the heart, severely injuring the young ensign, who required **cardiac replacement** surgery. ("Samaritan Snare" [TNG]). Many years later, Picard relived the incident through **Q**'s intervention. ("Tapestry" [TNG]). In 2371, a band of Nausicaan raiders used an ultrasonic generator to break into and rob the central museum on Remmil VI. ("Heart of Stone" [DS9]). Later that year, **Garak** said he misplaced the wedding suit of a Nausicaan, making the Nausicaan angry with Garak. ("Improbable Cause" [DS9]). In 2372, two Nausicaan bodyguards accompanied FCA Liquidator **Brunt** to Deep Space 9 to investigate a Ferengi labor union that was striking against Quark's bar. The bodyguards severely beat Quark in order to intimidate Rom into ending the strike. ("Bar Association" [DS9]). *Named for the Greek princess of the wind, as well as for the animated fantasy film* Nausicaa.

Nava. (Barry Gordon). Ferengi entrepreneur who took over the Arcybite mining refineries in the **Clarus System** in 2369. Grand Nagus **Zek** congratulated Nava for his accomplishments at a meeting held at Quark's bar on Deep Space 9. ("The Nagus" [DS9]).

Navarch. Honorary title bestowed on **Bajoran** resistance hero **Li Nalas** in 2370. Decreeing that there was no other appropriate title for the great Li, the **Chamber of Ministers** created this one. ("The Homecoming" [DS9]). Though the Navarch was appointed by the Chamber, he answered directly to the **Prophets**. ("The Circle" [DS9]).

navigation. SEE: **bearing; heading; navigator.**

navigational deflector. On many Federation starships, a powerful forward-looking directional force-beam generator used to push aside debris, meteroids, microscopic particulates, and other objects that might collide with the ship. The navigational deflector of the *Enterprise*-D was modified in 2366 in a desperate effort to improvise a weapon against the **Borg** assault on Earth. ("The Best of Both Worlds, Part I" [TNG]). The modified deflector provided a single, massive pulse directed at the Borg ship. The use of the weapon caused significant damage to the *Enterprise*-D's warp drive and burned out the deflector itself, but failed to stop the Borg vessel. ("The Best of Both Worlds, Parts II" [TNG]). On an *Intrepid*-class starship, the power of a transporter signal could be boosted by tying the transporter system directly into the navigational deflector. ("Non Sequitur" [VGR]). While in Earth's past in 2063, a group of Borg attempted to convert the *Enterprise*-E's navigational deflector dish into an interplexing beacon that they intended to use to communicate with the Borg collective in the Delta Quadrant. *(Star Trek: First Contact).*

navigator. Aboard a starship, the **bridge** control station and the officer responsible for projecting the desired course or trajectory of the vehicle and for determining the ship's actual position, velocity, and direction in relationship to that desired course. In more recent Federation starships, this function was merged with the duties of the **helm** officer, and dubbed conn, or **flight controller**. *Ensign* ***Pavel Chekov*** *was one of the navigators of the* Starship Enterprise *during the original* Star Trek *series. The term "navigator" was replaced with "conn" at the beginning of* Star Trek: The Next Generation.

Navot. Bajoran faction embattled in 2369 in a border dispute with their neighbors, the **Paqu**. ("The Storyteller" [DS9]). SEE: **Glyrhond; Varis Sul; Woban.**

Nayrok. (James Cromwell). Prime minister of planet **Angosia III** in 2366, when the **Angosian** government sought membership in the Federation. Nayrok enlisted the aid of the *Enterprise*-D to help capture **Roga Danar**, whom Nayrok identified as a fugitive criminal. It was learned that Danar was the leader of a veterans' group seeking redress from the Angosian government for injuries they had received during the **Tarsian War**. Nayrok later requested assistance from the *Enterprise*-D in suppressing the unrest caused by Danar's group, but Captain Picard declined on the grounds that it was a purely local matter. ("The Hunted" [TNG]). *James Cromwell later portrayed Jaglom Shrek in "Birthright, Parts I and II" (TNG), Hanok in "Starship Down" (DS9), and Zefram Cochrane in* Star Trek: First Contact. *He also played Farmer Hoggitt in the 1995 fantasy film* Babe.

Nazi. SEE: **Ekosians; Gill, John; Melakon.**

NCC. Spacecraft registry number prefix assigned to vessels of the Federation Starfleet. For example, the registry number of the original ***Starship Enterprise*** was NCC-1701. Experimental vessels developed by Starfleet sometimes had NX registry prefixes, as did the ***U.S.S. Excelsior*** when it was in its early testing stages. *(Star Trek III: The Search for Spock).* Other vessels, under the auspices of other operating authorities, had other registry prefixes. The ***T'Pau***, a ship of Vulcan registry, had an NSP registry number prefix ("Unification, Part I" [TNG]), while the non-Starfleet science vessel ***Vico*** had an NAR prefix ("Hero Worship" [TNG]), as did the ***Nenebek*** ("Final Mission" [TNG]), and an Yridian transport had a YLT prefix ("Birthright, Part II" [TNG]). *Put another way, NCC doesn't stand for anything. It was devised by Matt Jefferies, art director for the first* Star Trek *series. Jefferies, who is a pilot, based NCC on 20th-century aircraft registration codes. In such 20th-century usage, an "N" first letter refers to an aircraft registered in the United States of America. A "C" second letter refers to a civil (non-military) aircraft. Jefferies added a second "C," just because he thought it looked better. Think of it as being like the arbitrary three-letter code that's part of automobile license plate numbers in many states.*

Nebula*-class starship.** Type of Federation starship, slightly smaller than a *Galaxy*-class vessel. The *Nebula*-class ships featured a large upper equipment module, usually used for sensors, that could be customized for different mission profiles. *Nebula*-class ships have included the ***U.S.S. Phoenix ("The Wounded" [TNG]), the ***U.S.S. Sutherland*** ("Redemption, Part II" [TNG]), and the *U.S.S. Bellerophon* (barely seen in the battle sequences of "Emissary" [DS9]). *The* Nebula*-class ship was designed by Ed Miarecki, Rick Sternbach, and Mike Okuda. The model was built by Greg Jein.*

"Necessary Evil." *Deep Space Nine* episode #28. Written by Peter Allan Fields. Directed by James L. Conway. Stardate 47282.5. *First aired in 1993. Odo's investigation of an attack on Quark causes him to re-examine a 5-year-old murder case where Kira was a suspect.* SEE: **Cardassian neck trick; Ches'sarro; compressed tetryon beam; cortolin; desealer rod; Ferengi Rules of Acquisition; Hadar, Gul; Kira Nerys; *lita*; magnasite drops; Meldrar I; Odo; Pallra; pulsatel lockseal; Pyrellian ginger tea; Quark; Rom; Terok Nor; Trazko; Vaatrik.**

Nechani magistrate. (Harry Groener). Official of the **Nechani** government. The magistrate dealt with Captain Kathryn Janeway in 2373 when she wished to find a cure for an injured *Voyager* crew member. ("Sacred Ground" [VGR]).

Nechani. Humanoid civilization native to the Delta Quadrant. In 2373, the Nechani invited the crew of the *Voyager* to take shore leave on their planet. While visiting the Nechani homeworld, Kes was inadvertently sent into a comalike state when she ventured into a shrine of the **Nechisti Order**. ("Sacred Ground" [VGR]).

Nechayev, Alynna. (Natalia Nogulich). Starfleet senior officer. Admiral Nechayev was responsible for the handling of the **Celtris III** incident in 2369. ("Chain of Command, Parts I & II" [TNG]). Nechayev blasted Picard for his decision to return the **Borg** known as **Hugh** to the Borg collective without also sending an invasive program developed by *Enterprise*-D personnel. Picard protested that using the program, effectively a genocidal weapon of mass destruction, would be a violation of Starfleet's principles, but Nechayev, fearing a mass invasion by the Borg, ordered him to use the weapon if another opportunity presented itself. ("Descent, Part I" [TNG]). Nechayev was promoted from vice-admiral to fleet admiral in 2370. During that year, she was involved with the creation of the **Federation-Cardassian Treaty**. Later, she ordered Captain Picard to evacuate the settlers from **Dorvan V**. ("Journey's End" [TNG]) Late in 2370, Necheyev once again visited the *Enterprise*-D to discuss the **Maquis** situation. She asked Captain Picard to persuade **Ro Laren** to infiltrate the Maquis. ("Preemptive Strike" [TNG]). She also traveled to **Deep Space 9** in 2370 to discuss problems maintaining the treaty, including the troublesome Maquis. ("The Maquis, Part II" [DS9]).

Nechisti Council. Ruling body of the Nechisti Order of the **Nechani**. In 2373, the Nechisti Order granted permission to Captain Kathryn Janeway to go through a Nechisti ritual in order to find a cure for Kes. ("Sacred Ground" [VGR]).

Nechisti guide. (Becky Ann Baker). Middle-aged Nechani woman who was a monk of the **Nechisti Order**. The guide helped Kathryn Janeway go through a Nechisti ritual in 2373. ("Sacred Ground" [VGR]).

Nechisti Order. Religious brotherhood of the **Nechani** culture. The Nechisti Order was a group of monks devoted to serving their **Ancestral Spirits**. The Order was governed by the Nechisti Council. ("Sacred Ground" [VGR]).

Nechisti shrine. Sacred altar on the **Nechani** homeworld used by the monks of the **Nechisti Order** to receive the gift of purification. The shrine was surrounded by a powerful biogenic field and very high levels of **thoron** radiation. Unprepared visitors to the shrine experienced a severe **neuroleptic shock**. After going through a special ritual, however, the Nechisti monks could safely enter the shrine. In 2373, Kes was inadvertently sent into a comalike state when she ventured unprepared into the shrine. ("Sacred Ground" [VGR]).

neck pinch. SEE: **Vulcan nerve pinch.**

Neeka. Small doglike pet belonging to the **Banean** physicist **Tolen Ren**. In 2371, Neeka helped implicate a Numiri agent in Ren's murder by recognizing the agent, who had claimed never to have been in Ren's house before. ("Ex Post Facto" [VGR]).

Neela. (Robin Christopher). **Bajoran** religious activist who attempted to assassinate **Vedek Bareil** at **Deep Space 9** in 2369 to support Vedek **Winn**'s bid to succeed **Kai Opaka**. Neela sabotaged station systems, planted a terrorist bomb, and later shot at Bareil. Although her acts were considered criminal, Neela believed she was acting in accordance with the will of her people's **Prophets**. ("In the Hands of the Prophets" [DS9]). She had been working on Deep Space 9 as an engineer as a cover for her attempt to murder Bareil. ("Duet" [DS9]).

Neelix. (Ethan Phillips). **Talaxian** trader who joined the crew of the ***Starship Voyager*** in 2371. ("Caretaker" [VGR]). As a child, Neelix lived with his parents and younger brothers on **Rinax**, a moon of **Talax** ("Jetrel" [VGR]), where, due to Talax's three suns, the summer seasons were the hottest in the sector, reaching temperatures of 50 degrees Celsius with 90 percent humidity. ("Macrocosm" [VGR]). Neelix was very close to **Alixia**, one of his sisters. The two enjoyed many adventures together, exploring the Caves of Touth, visiting the equatorial dust shrouds, and even hunting arctic spiders. ("Rise" [VGR]). Neelix bred orchids, which he liked to serve in salads with **Baldoxic vinegar**. ("Tattoo" [VGR]). Neelix's entire family, including Alixia, was killed when Rinax was devastated by the **metreon cascade** attack by the **Haakonian Order**. Neelix survived because he was on Talax at the time, fleeing from military duty in a war he felt was unjust.

("Jetrel" [VGR]). Neelix worked for two years on an **orbital tether** maintence team on Talax. ("Rise" [VGR]). He served for two years as an engineer's assistant aboard a Trabalian freighter ("Threshold" [VGR]) and also worked in a mining colony. ("Blood Fever" [VGR]). There were a few incidents in Neelix's past that he would probably have preferred to have forgotten. He and his friend **Wixiban** had a run in with **Ubean** authorities. Although Neelix escaped arrest, Wixiban served a brutal term in an Ubean prison. ("Fair Trade" [VGR]).

Neelix, a native of the **Delta Quadrant**, had been a trader of junk and debris, but prided himself on his skills as a jack-of-all-trades. Neelix helped Captain Janeway deal with the **Kazon-Ogla** shortly after *Voyager*'s arrival in the Delta Quadrant, and was subsequently invited to join the *Voyager* crew, in part because of his familiarity with the region of space. Neelix was romantically involved with **Kes**, who also joined the *Voyager* crew. ("Caretaker" [VGR]). *Neelix and Kes broke up around the time of the third-season episode "Warlord" (DS9).*

Shortly after joining the *Voyager* crew, Neelix appointed himself ship's cook and took it upon himself to convert part of the **mess hall** on Deck 2 into a kitchen. Neelix hoped not only to reduce the crew's dependence on replicated food, but also to prove his value as a member of the ship. In his kitchen, Neelix prepared numerous delicacies with food grown in Kes's **hydroponics bay**, or gathered at planets visited by *Voyager*. Unfortunately, Neelix neglected to note that he had used the captain's private dining room, immediately adjacent to the mess hall, for storage. ("Phage" [VGR]). Neelix also took it upon himself to serve as the ship's morale officer. ("The Cloud" [VGR]). Neelix performed diplomatic duties in helping the *Voyager* crew to deal with newly contacted civilizations, a task for which Janeway once jokingly suggested he should be promoted to ambassador. ("Macrocosm" [VGR]). Neelix even produced a daily informational audiovisual program, ***A Briefing With Neelix,*** which he distributed over the ship's internal communications system. ("Investigations" [VGR]). Neelix often took part in monthly tactical exercises aboard the *Voyager*. ("Warlord" [VGR]).

On stardate 48532.4, Neelix was attacked; his lungs were surgically removed, and they were implanted into a **Vidiian** named **Motura**, who was suffering from the **phage**. When Janeway declined to order Motura's death to reclaim Neelix's lungs, Kes donated one of her lungs to be implanted into Neelix's body, thereby saving his life. ("Phage" [VGR]). In 2372, Tuvok and Neelix were involved in a transporter accident that merged them at the molecular level, forming a new living being who adopted the name Tuvix. Neelix did not exist during the two weeks that Tuvix lived. ("Tuvix" [VGR]). Neelix encountered his old friend, **Wixiban**, in 2373 at the **Nekrit Supply Depot** space station. Neelix was briefly drawn back into the world of illicit trade, until he was injured when a cylinder of stolen warp plasma exploded. Janeway subsequently ordered Neelix to serve two weeks of deuterium maintenance duty as punishment for having stolen the plasma and engaged in illegal activities. ("Fair Trade" [VGR]).

Neelix's first appearance was in "Caretaker" (VGR). Ethan Phillips had previously played Dr. Farek in "Ménage à Troi" (TNG). He made a cameo appearance in Star Trek: First Contact *as a holographic nightclub maître d'. Neelix's ship was kept in* Voyager's *cargo bay and the exterior of the vessel was first seen in "The Chute" (VGR).*

Neema. Daughter of Audrid Dax. When she was six years old, Neema spent two weeks in the hospital with Rugalan fever. While there, her mother, Audrid, read her all 17 volumes of *Down the River Light* even though Neema was unconscious at the time. Neema survived the illness. Fifteen years later Neema and her mother were not on speaking terms and would not be for another eight years. ("Nor the Battle to the Strong" [DS9]).

neep-gren. Ferengi phrase meaning "Thank you." ("Little Green Men" [DS9]).

negaton hydrocoil. Nanotech device that resembled a drop of jelly. Use of negaton hydrocoils allowed **android**s constructed by **Sargon**, **Thalassa,** and **Henoch** to move like humanoids without microgears or other mechanical aids. ("Return to Tomorrow" [TOS]). SEE: **nanotechnology**.

Negh'Var. Flagship of the Klingon Defense Force in 2372. **General Martok** commanded the *Negh'Var* during the Klingon Empire's invasion of Cardassia on stardate 49011. ("The Way of the Warrior" [DS9]). *The* Negh'Var *was a modification of the future Klingon ship model used in "All Good Things..." (TNG).*

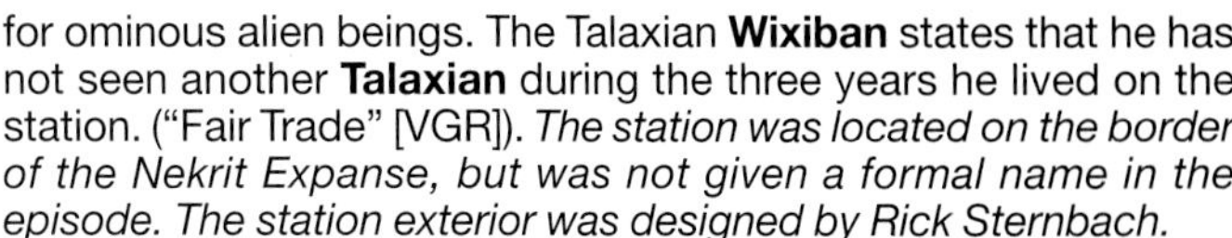

for ominous alien beings. The Talaxian **Wixiban** states that he has not seen another **Talaxian** during the three years he lived on the station. ("Fair Trade" [VGR]). *The station was located on the border of the Nekrit Expanse, but was not given a formal name in the episode. The station exterior was designed by Rick Sternbach.*

Nel Bato system. Star system. A possible destination of the ***Jovis***, following the kidnapping of Data by **Kivas Fajo** in 2366. ("The Most Toys" [TNG]).

Nel system. Planetary system. Site of a visit by a delegation of **Ullian** telepathic historians in 2368. Two cases of unexplained coma, resembling **Iresine Syndrome**, were reported shortly afterward on one of the planets in the Nel system. Both patients were later believed to be victims of **telepathic memory invasion** rape by Ullian historian **Jev**. ("Violations" [TNG]).

Nelson, Lord Horatio. (1758-1805) Perhaps the most celebrated admiral in British maritime history. While commanding the British fleet, Lord Nelson was killed aboard the ***H.M.S. Victory*** following the British defeat of the French at Trafalgar. Prior to the Borg encounter of 2366-2367, Captain Jean-Luc Picard drew inspiration from Nelson's courage on the eve of battle. ("The Best of Both Worlds, Part I" [TNG]). SEE: **Trafalgar, Battle of**.

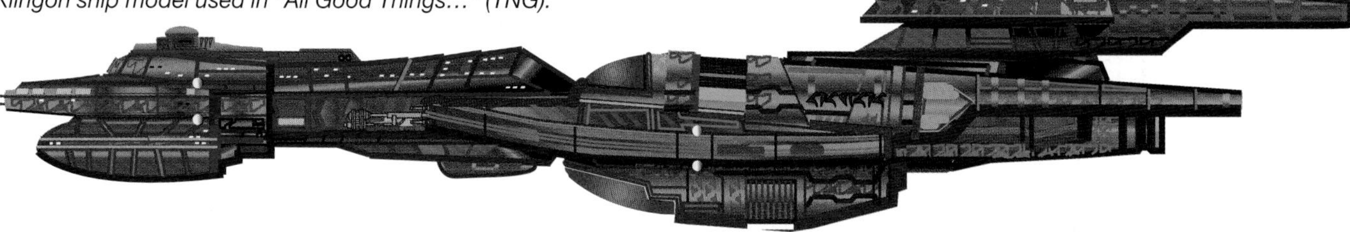

Nehelik Province. Area in the southern hemisphere of the planet **Rakhar**. Site where government official Exarch demanded the return of the fugitive **Croden** from Deep Space 9 in 2369. ("Vortex" [DS9]).

Nehru Colony. Federation colony near station **Deep Space 9** and the Bajoran system. **Jadzia Dax** ordered a subspace link established to the Nehru Colony while trying to overload the station's computers when the software life-form called **Pup** threatened station safety in 2369. ("The Forsaken" [DS9]).

Neil. (Tom Nibley). Member of a group of terrorists who attempted to steal **trilithium** resin from the *Enterprise*-D in 2369. Neil was the engineer of the group and had devised a means to transport the dangerously unstable and toxic trilithium through the ship. He was killed by one of his fellow terrorists. ("Starship Mine" [TNG]).

Neinman. An ancient, mythical land on planet Xerxes VII. Riker likened Neinman to Earth's Atlantis or the planet Aldea. ("When the Bough Breaks" [TNG]).

Nekrit Expanse. A vast, uncharted region of space in the Delta Quadrant. The Nekrit Expanse was populated by an unknown form of interstellar dust clouds and plasma storms. Neelix was unfamiliar with this part of the Delta Quadrant. Near the border of the region was a **Nekrit Supply Depot**, which served mining and trading ships. The *Starship Voyager* entered the Nekrit Expanse in 2373. ("Fair Trade" [VGR]). In the Nekrit Expanse, *Voyager* discovered a disabled **Borg ship** and a colony of former **Borg** drones no longer linked to the **Borg collective**. ("Unity" [VGR]).

Nekrit Supply Depot. Space station located on the border of the **Nekrit Expanse** in the Delta Quadrant. **Bahrat** is the station manager. The station, a supply depot for mining and trading ships, is the location of many dubious transactions, and a meeting place

Nelvana III. Planet located in the **Romulan Neutral Zone**. Nelvana III was in striking range of some fifteen Federation sectors. Romulan defector **Alidar Jarok** reported to Federation authorities that the Romulans were building a secret base there from which to launch a major offensive against the Federation. The reports of the base turned out to be disinformation, devised by the Romulan High Command to test Jarok's loyalties, and to lure the *Enterprise*-D into the Neutral Zone, where it could be captured. ("The Defector" [TNG]).

Nenebek. A mining shuttle from planet **Pentarus V**. The *Nenebek* was piloted by Captain **Dirgo**, who was quite proud of the vessel, despite its advanced age and somewhat substandard maintenance. Dirgo and the *Nenebek* were sent by the government of **Pentarus V** to transport Captain Picard and Ensign Crusher to a labor mediation on the planet in 2367. During their flight, a serious malfunction forced the *Nenebek* to crash on **Lambda Paz**, one of the moons of Pentarus II. ("Final Mission" [TNG]). *The* Nenebek *was designed by Joseph Hodges and Rick Sternbach. It was later re-dressed and served as several other ships, including* ***Rasmussen****'s time-travel pod from "A Matter of Time" (TNG)* ***Jaglom Shrek****'s Yridian craft from "Birthright, Part I" (TNG), the* **Taris Murn** *from "The Outcast" (TNG), and Koral's* Toron-*class Klingon shuttlecraft from "Gambit, Part II" (TNG).* SEE: ***Toron*-class shuttlecraft.**

Neo-Transcendentalism. A philosophical movement of 22nd-century Earth, advocating a return to a simpler life, one more in harmony with nature. The movement was founded by **Liam Dieghan**, and was a product of the time when Earth was still recovering from the nuclear holocaust of the previous century. ("Up the Long Ladder" [TNG]).

Neo-Trotskyists. Dominant political party within the French National Assembly on **Earth** in 2024. ("Past Tense, Part I" [DS9]).

neodextraline solution. Liquid medication administered intravenously for the treatment of severe dehydration. ("Ex Post Facto" [VGR]).

neodyne light. Illumination technology used on the **Nechani** homeworld. Neodyne lights were more advanced and efficient than chromodynamic lights. ("Sacred Ground" [VGR]).

neosorium composite. Material used in the construction of Federation **replicators**. In 2371, the Federation was the only known user of neosorium technology. ("State of Flux" [VGR]).

Nequencia system. Star system located near the Romulan Neutral Zone. Nequencia was one of two destinations visited by **Jaglom Shrek** after departing Deep Space 9 with Worf. ("Birthright, Part II" [TNG]). SEE: **Carraya System**.

Nerada. Nasari starship under the command of **Captain Alben**. On stardate 50732, the *Nerada* attacked the ***U.S.S. Voyager*** because Alben believed there was a native **Taresian** aboard the Federation ship. ("Favorite Son" [VGR]).

Neral. (Norman Large). **Proconsul** of the Romulan Senate during the year 2368. A relatively young man who was new to the office, Neral was reported to be sympathetic to the cause of Vulcan/Romulan reunification. Neral was, however, secretly working with **Senator Pardek** to use the reunification movement as a cover for a planned invasion of Vulcan. ("Unification, Parts I and II" [TNG]). SEE: **Spock**.

Neria, Dr. (Jerry Hardin). A chief **thanatologist** on the **Vhnori** homeworld. When Ensign Harry Kim accidentally arrived on his world through a subspace vacuole, Dr. Neria wished to study him to learn more about the "afterlife" from which Kim apparently came. ("Emanations" [VGR]). SEE: **Vhnori transference ritual**. *Jerry Hardin previously played Radue in "When the Bough Breaks" (TNG) and Samuel Clemens in "Time's Arrow, Parts I and II" (TNG).*

Nervala IV. Class-M planet whose upper atmosphere contains a powerful **distortion field**, making it impossible to reach the planet by shuttle or transporter for most of the planet's year. A Federation research station located on the planet's surface was evacuated by the crew of the ***U.S.S. Potemkin*** in 2361 when the distortion field was forming in the planetary atmosphere. The rescue team from the *Potemkin* was led by Lieutenant William T. Riker. A transporter malfunction during the final beam-out from the planet caused Riker to be duplicated. One Riker returned to the *Potemkin*, while the other materialized back on Nervala IV. The existence of the duplicate Riker was not suspected until 2369, when the *Enterprise*-D returned to the planet to retrieve the scientific information left behind by the scientific team. ("Second Chances" [TNG]). SEE: **Riker, Thomas.**

nerve pinch, Vulcan. SEE: **Vulcan nerve pinch**.

Nerys. SEE: **Kira Nerys**.

nesset. Small animal indigenous to the **Nechani** homeworld in the Delta Quadrant. The *nesset* bit with three fangs, and its venom acted as a psychoactive drug in the bloodstream of humanoids. The *nesset* was used in the Nechisti ritual, and the Nechisti monks believed that *nessets* could travel from this world to the Spirit realm. ("Sacred Ground" [VGR]).

nestor. An officer of the **Cardassian** court whose role was to assist the offender during the court proceedings. The nestor was not permitted to address the court or any other officers of the court. ("Tribunal" [DS9]). SEE: **Odo**.

Net. Global computer-based media and information network on **Earth** in the 21st century. The Net, also called the Interface, offered multimedia, computer database, and business functions, featuring hundreds of different channels that offered news and entertainment. These channels also afforded access to commercial service industries, retail vendors, and government agencies. Channel 90 of the Net was operated by **Brynner Information Services**, while Channel 178 was run by **SafeTech**, which offered retinal scan services. ("Past Tense, Parts I and II" [DS9]). *Apparently, a commercial outgrowth of the Internet.*

netgirl. A woman who allows men into her mind for money. The link was accomplished via a dataport. ("A Simple Investigation" [VGR]).

netinaline. Pharmaceutical stimulant. Used to waken a patient from unconsciousness. ("Emanations" [VGR]).

neural calipers. Medical instrument used in surgical procedures. ("Samaritan Snare" [TNG]).

neural depletion. Complete loss of electrochemical energy of a humanoid brain, resulting in the death of the victim. Neural depletion was characteristic of the victims attacked by aliens from **Devidia II**. ("Time's Arrow, Part II" [TNG]).

neural imaging scan. Medical diagnostic scan used to test acuity of a patient's visual cortex. Dr. Julian Bashir performed a neural imaging scan on Miles O'Brien when trying to find the cause of his unexplained **aphasia** in 2369. ("Babel" [DS9]).

neural implants. The bio-electrical interface between **Geordi La Forge**'s visual cortex and his **VISOR.** The devices were implanted bilaterally in the temporal regions of La Forge's skull, and fed into the visual cortex. The external portion of the implant allowed for direct connection of the VISOR to La Forge's head. ("The Mind's Eye" [TNG]). SEE: **neural output pods.**

neural metaphasic shock. A potentially fatal failure of the neurological system in humanoids. Neural metaphasic shock was the cause of death of a crash victim from the *U.S.S. Denver* after Dr. Toby Russell treated him with **borathium**, an unauthorized drug. ("Ethics" [TNG]).

neural modulator. Medical device that can be used to relieve minor muscle pains. ("Business As Usual" [DS9]).

neural neutralizer. Device invented by **Dr. Simon Van Gelder** in 2266 to aid rehabilitation of criminals. The neutralizer was intended to selectively remove thoughts relating to criminal acts, but was later found to have potentially lethal effects. ("Dagger of the Mind" [TOS]).

neural output pods. Component of **Geordi La Forge**'s **VISOR**, the neural output pods transmitted the VISOR's visual data to La Forge's brain. La Forge and the Romulan **Bochra** connected the neural output pods of La Forge's VISOR to a tricorder to detect a neutrino beacon when both were trapped on planet **Galorndon Core** in 2366. ("The Enemy " [TNG]). SEE: **neural implants.**

neural paralyzer. Medication that can cause a cessation of heartbeat and breathing in a humanoid patient, creating the appearance of death. If such a patient receives medical treatment in time, a full recovery is possible. McCoy injected Kirk with neural paralyzer during Spock's ***Pon farr*** in 2267, making it possible for Spock to win his fight with Kirk without actually killing his commanding officer. ("Amok Time" [TOS]).

neural parasite, Denevan. SEE: **Denevan neural parasite.**

neural scan interface. SEE: **iconic display console.**

neural servo. Electronic device implanted on the nuchal surface of each member of **Arctus Baran**'s crew of mercenaries, used for crew discipline. The device was directly connected to the wearer's nervous system and was controlled by a transponder worn by Baran. He was able to adjust the impulses transmitted to the servo, thereby controlling the amount of pain he inflicted. Ironically, Baran, who also was fitted with a servo, used it to inadvertently kill himself in 2370. ("Gambit, Parts I and II" [TNG]).

neural stimulator. Medical instrument used to increase neural activity in the central nervous system of a humanoid brain. Dr. Crusher used a neural stimulator in an unsuccessful attempt to revive the gravely injured **Natasha Yar** after she had been attacked by **Armus**. ("Skin of Evil" [TNG]). **Professor Berlinghoff Rasmussen** stole a neural stimulator from sickbay. ("A Matter of Time" [TNG]).

neural transducers. Implantable bio-electric devices that receive nerve impulses from the brain and transmit it to affected voluntary muscle groups. These instruments were used in cases of severe spinal cord damage to give the patient some control over the affected extremities. ("Ethics" [TNG]).

neural transponder. Device used to link **Borg** drones through processors implanted in their nervous systems. Neutral transponders allowed members of the **Borg collective** to share neural energy. ("Unity" [VGR]).

Neural. SEE: **Tyree**.

neurochemical imbalance. A serious physiological condition in **Vulcans**, the effect of the ***Pon farr*** mating drive. Even Ensign **Vorik's** brief physical contact with **B'Elanna Torres** on stardate 50537.2 caused her to experience a potentially fatal neurochemical imbalance, the result of a Vulcan telepathic mating bond. ("Blood Fever" [VGR]).

neurocine gas. Lethal white aerosol used by the **Cardassian** military for riot control. The automatic **counterinsurgency program** on **Terok Nor** used neurocine gas to suppress uprisings among the Bajoran workers. ("Civil Defense" [DS9]).

neurocortical monitor. Small medical sensor device which could be placed on a patient's forehead to record encephalographic data. A neurocortical monitor could also be configured to notify medical personnel when preprogrammed readings were detected. ("Flashback" [VGR]).

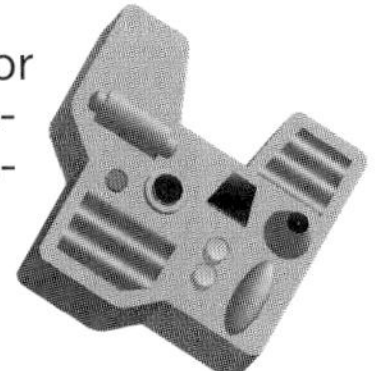

neurode. In **bio-neural circuitry** technology, the connection between a **bio-neural gel pack** and external components. ("Macrocosm" [VGR]).

neuroelectric weapon. Device that incapacitates a person by sending a severe energy shock pulse into the nervous system. ("The Swarm" [VGR]).

neuroelectrical suppresser. Medical instrument used to suppress pain. ("Invasive Procedures" [DS9]).

neurogenetics. Study of the development and genetic replication of neural tissue. ("Ethics" [TNG]). SEE: **genetronic replicator**.

neurogenic radiation. Form of electrical energy used in the practice of medicine to stimulate a patient's brain. **Dr. Julian Bashir** used 70 millivolts of neurogenic radiation to successfully revive **Vedek Bareil**'s clinically dead cerebral cortex in 2371. Unfortunately, this caused vasoconstriction in Bareil's arteries, causing inadequate blood flow to his internal organs, eventually leading to his death. ("Life Support" [DS9]). SEE: **vasokin**.

neuroleptic shock. Form of neurological disturbance in which cortical functions of the brain's synaptic pathways are disrupted. This could result in a state similar to a coma, but without the usual biochemical markers. ("Sacred Ground" [VGR]).

neurolink. Emergency medical technique used for the stabilization of patients with brainstem injuries. Matching neural pads were used. One would be placed on a healthy individual, and a matching unit would be placed on the patient. These devices enabled a link to be established from the healthy person's autonomic nervous system to that of the injured patient. When the **Zalkonian** named **John Doe** was discovered in the wreck of a Zalkonian escape pod in 2366, Dr. Crusher used a neurolink with Geordi La Forge to stabilize "John"'s nervous system. ("Transfigurations" [TNG]).

neuromuscular adaptation theory. Medical concept in a treatise published in 2340 by Nathaniel Teros. In it, Teros theorized that stimulation of the humanoid motor cortex would increase **acetylcholine** absorption, increasing muscle tensile strength in low-gravity species. This would make it possible for members of such species to function in gravity fields substantially greater than those for which their bodies had evolved. In 2370, Starfleet physician Julian Bashir tested this theory, dramatically increasing muscular strength in an **Elaysian**. The test subject, Ensign **Melora Pazlar**, declined to undergo a full treatment, because she feared she would be unable to return to her homeworld once the treatment became irreversible. ("Melora" [DS9]).

neuropolaric induction. Medical procedure used to repolarize ganglionic neural sheaths in the brain. ("Rapture" [DS9]).

neuroprocessor. Central memory component contained in every **Borg**. The neuroprocessor contained a record of all the instructions received from the Borg collective. *(Star Trek: First Contact)*.

neurosomatic technique. Procedure used on planet **Tilonus IV** in an attempt to extract strategic information from Commander William Riker, captured there in 2369. Using neurosomatic techniques, his captors created a delusional world in which Riker believed he was an inmate at the **Tilonus Institute for Mental Disorders**. Riker's subconscious incorporated elements of a play called ***Frame of Mind*** into this delusional world, allowing Riker's mind to create a defense mechanism against the neurosomatic process. ("Frame of Mind" [TNG]). SEE: **Syrus, Dr.; Suna; Mavek.**

neurosynaptic therapy. Medical treatment used to modify a patient's behavior through modification of neural structure. In 2372, *Voyager* Ensign **Lon Suder** murdered fellow crew member Frank Darwin and confessed he had killed before. Targeted neurosynaptic therapy had been used in the past in an attempt to quell Suder's violent tendencies, but the treatment had not worked. ("Meld" [VGR]).

neurotransmitter. Biochemicals associated with the propagation of electrical energy between neurons in humanoid nervous systems. Captain Picard exhibited increased neurotransmitter output on stardate 45944 while under the influence of the **Kataan probe**. ("The Inner Light" [TNG]). Elevated levels of neurotransmitters were found in the cerebral cortexes of **Ambassador Ves Alkar**'s victims, leading Dr. Crusher to suspect the nature of his psychic abuse of these people. ("Man of the People" [TNG]). **Onaya**'s psionic powers caused neurotransmitter production in her victims' brains to increase by more than 20 percent. ("The Muse" [DS9]).

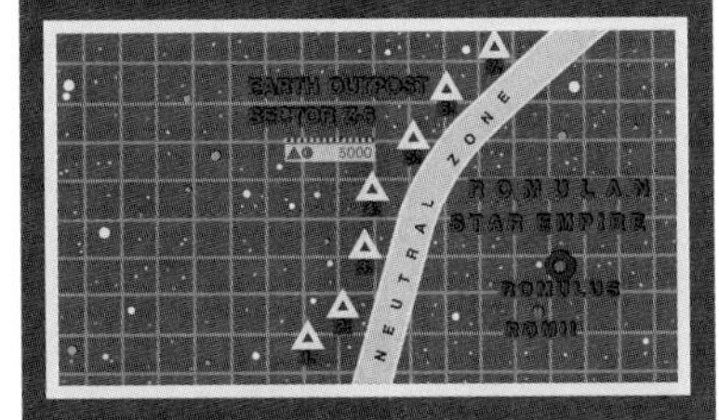

Neutral Zone Outposts. A series of Federation monitoring facilities located on the border of the **Romulan Neutral Zone**. Outposts 2, 3, 4, and 8 were destroyed in the Romulan incursion of 2266. ("Balance of Terror" [TOS]).

Neutral Zone, Klingon. SEE: **Klingon Neutral Zone**.

Neutral Zone, Romulan. SEE: **Romulan Neutral Zone**.

"Neutral Zone, The." *Next Generation* episode #26. Television story & teleplay by Maurice Hurley. From a story by Deborah McIntyre & Mona Glee. Directed by James Conway. Stardate 41986.0. *First aired in 1988. The* Enterprise-D *revives a group of 20th-century humans who were frozen some four centuries ago. "The Neutral Zone" establishes the first season of* Star Trek: The Next Generation *as set in the year 2364. This is the point of reckoning from which most* Next Generation*-era dates are derived. This episode established the destruction of several distant outposts that was later found to be the work of the Borg in "Q Who?" (TNG). "The Neutral Zone" was the last episode of the first season of* Star Trek: The Next Generation*.* GUEST CAST: Marc Alaimo as **Tebok, Commander**; Anthony James as **Thei, Subcommander**; Leon Rippy as **Clemonds, Sonny**; Gracie Harrison as **Raymond, Clare**; Peter Mark Richman as **Offenhouse, Ralph**. SEE: ***Charleston, U.S.S.*; Clemonds, Sonny; cryonics; cryosatellite; *D'deridex*-class warbird; Kazis binary system; low-mileage pit woofie; Neutral Zone, Romulan; Offenhouse, Ralph; *QE-2*; Raymond, Claire; Raymond, Donald; Raymond, Edward; Raymond, Thomas; Romulan Star Empire; Romulan warbird; Science Station Delta Zero Five; Sector 3-0; Sector 3-1; Starbase 39-Sierra; Starbase 718; Tarod IX; Tebok, Commander; television; Thei, Subcommander; Tomed Incident; United Federation of Planets**.

neutral particle weapons. Ship-mounted weapons in use aboard **Talarian** warships such as the ***Q'Maire*** in 2367. ("Suddenly Human" [TNG]).

neutralization emitters. Component of **Cardassian** security force-field systems. These systems were much like Starfleet containment fields except that Cardassian neutralization emitters were lethal. ("Civil Defense" [DS9]).

neutrino field. A concentration of **neutrino** particles. Geordi La Forge used a neutrino field to help contain a group of noncorporeal criminal life-forms from the **Ux-Mal** system that attempted to commandeer the *Enterprise*-D on stardate 45571. ("Power Play" [TNG]).

neutrino. Massless subatomic particle that has no electrical charge. Literally, "the little neutral one," neutrinos were first detected by Earth scientists in 1956. A major source of neutrinos is nuclear reactions deep within stars. ("Power Play" [TNG]). Elevated neutrino readings accompany passage of an object through the **Bajoran wormhole**. ("Captive Pursuit" [DS9]). A standard Starfleet tricorder is not equipped to detect neutrinos. ("The Enemy" [TNG]). SEE: **solar neutrinos**. Neutrinos are also found in a starship's warp signature. In 2373, Maquis leader Michael Eddington used an unmanned probe set to transmit a false warp signature containing neutrinos. ("For the Uniform" [DS9]).

neutron densitometer. SEE: **passive high-resolution series.**

neutron fatigue. A breakdown of nuclear cohesion in a structure. Neutron fatigue was shown to be the cause of a failure of the **dilithium chamber hatch** aboard the *Enterprise*-D in 2367. The failure of the hatch caused an explosion that injured two crew members and took the warp drive offline for more than 15 days. ("The Drumhead" [TNG]). *Either that, or we're just working those subatomic particles too hard.*

neutron migration. The movement of neutrons from the outer hydrogen-reaction zone to the inner helium core of a star. The migration of neutrons increased stellar-core density and contributed to the spectacular failure of Dr. Timicin's helium ignition test in 2367. ("Half a Life" [TNG]). SEE: **helium fusion enhancement.** *Or it could be when neutrons go south for the winter.*

neutron radiation. Energy discharge consisting of electrically neutral subatomic particles. High levels of neutron radiation were found to be a signature of the torpedo systems of an uprated **Klingon bird-of-prey** that was capable of firing weapons while cloaked. This radiation proved to be a weak point of this ship, making it detectable while cloaked. *(Star Trek VI: The Undiscovered Country).*

neutron star. Stellar body that has been gravitationally crushed to the point where its density is that of nuclear material. **Dr. Paul Stubbs** conducted an experiment near a neutron star in the **Kavis Alpha Sector** in 2366. ("Evolution" [TNG]). SEE: **neutronium.**

neutronium. Matter so incredibly dense that atoms' electron shells have collapsed and the nuclei are actually touching each other. Periodic explosions on the surface of a neutron star in the **Kavis Alpha Sector** are known to expel particles of neutronium into space at relativistic speeds. ("Evolution" [TNG]). The shell of the extragalactic **planet killer** that destroyed systems **L-370** and **L-374** in 2267 was constructed of pure neutronium, rendering it impervious to phaser fire or any external attack. ("The Doomsday Machine " [TOS]). The inner structure of an ancient Iconian ziggurat on planet Vandros IV was made of neutronium, protecting the **Iconian gateway** within from attack. ("To the Death" [DS9]).

Nevad. Monarch to the **Nechani** people who lived in historic times. His son was inadvertently sent into a comalike state when he ventured into a shrine of the **Nechisti Order**. King Nevad petitioned the Nechisti Order to go through a **Nechisti** ritual in order to plead for his son's life. Reportedly, the ancestral spirits granted his request and spared the king's son. Using King Nevad's story as a precedent, Captain Kathryn Janeway petitioned to go through the ritual to help a member of her crew. ("Sacred Ground" [VGR]).

Never Ending Sacrifice, The. A **Cardassian** novel in which seven generations of characters lead selfless lives of duty to the state. Considered the finest example of the repetitive epic form of Cardassian literature. **Garak** believed this novel to be the best ever written, but Julian Bashir found it boring. ("The Wire" [DS9]).

New Bajor. First Bajoran colony in the **Gamma Quadrant**. ("Crossover" [DS9]). The colony had a rather impressive irrigation system. New Bajor's inhabitants were massacred in 2371 by the **Jem'Hadar.** ("The Jem'Hadar" [DS9], "The Search, Part II" [DS9]).

New Berlin. Federation settlement located on Earth's **moon**. *(Star Trek: First Contact).* In 2369, with tensions high following an attack on the **Ohniaka III** outpost, the New Berlin colony also reported a **Borg** attack. Fortunately, the "attacking" ship turned out to be merely a Ferengi trading vessel. ("Descent, Part I" [TNG]). **Calvin Hudson** and his wife joined Benjamin Sisko and his wife, Jennifer, at a **mazurka festival** at New Berlin. ("The Maquis, Part I" [DS9]).

New Era. Name used by members of the Q Continuum to refer to the age of enlightenment that began for the Continuum more than ten thousand years ago. ("Death Wish" [VGR]).

New Essentialists Movement. Twenty-fourth century political group dedicated to restoring the moral and cultural traditions of the Federation. They believed that Federation citizens were decadent and that self-indulgence had eroded the foundations of Federation society. In 2373, the New Essentialists Movement conducted a protest demonstration at planet **Risa**, which they believed to be symbolic of the root of the Federation's problems. Members of the movement, led by **Pascal Fullerton**, also sabotaged the planet's weather-control system in order to make their point that Federation citizens were too complacent. Worf was swayed by the movement's ideas for a time. ("Let He Who Is Without Sin..." [DS9]).

New France Colony. Federation colony near station Deep Space 9. Dax ordered a subspace link established to the New France Colony while trying to overload the station's computers when the software life-form called **Pup** threatened station safety in 2369. ("The Forsaken" [DS9]).

New Gaul. Planet that was the birthplace of **Miranda Vigo.** ("Bloodlines" [TNG]).

"New Ground." *Next Generation* episode #110. Teleplay by Grant Rosenberg. Story by Sara Charno and Stuart Charno. Directed by Robert Scheerer. Stardate 45376.3. *First aired in 1992. Alexander returns to the* Enterprise-*D to live with his father, Worf, but the transition is not easy for either.* GUEST CAST: Georgia Brown as **Rozhenko**, **Helena**; Brian Bonsall as **Rozhenko**, **Alexander**; Richard McGonagle as **Ja'Dar**, **Dr.**; Jennifer Edwards as **Kyle**, **Ms.**; Sheila Franklin as **Felton**, **Ensign**; Majel Barrett as Computer voice. SEE: **Balduk warriors; Bilana III; Brentalia; calisthenics program, Klingon; Cochrane, Zefram; Corvan *gilvos*; Corvan II; Donaldson; Draco lizards; Felton, Ensign; firefighting; Ja'Dar, Dr.; Kahless the Unforgettable; Kyle, Ms.; Lapsang souchong tea; Lemma II; Maktag; *Milan*, *S.S.*; Morath; Rozhenko, Alexander; Rozhenko, Helena; soliton wave; white rhinos; Yeager, Chuck.**

New Halana. Homeworld of the **Halanans**. New Halana was terraformed by **Professor Gideon Seyetik**. ("Second Sight" [DS9]). See: **Seyetik, Nidell**.

New Manhattan. City on planet Beth Delta I. **Dr. Paul Stubbs** jokingly said he would like to take Deanna Troi there for champagne. ("Evolution" [TNG]).

New Martim Vaz. An aquatic city located in Earth's Atlantic ocean. **Kevin** and **Rishon Uxbridge** were originally from New Martim Vaz. ("The Survivors" [TNG]).

New Orleans*-class starship.** Federation ships, often designated as frigates. The *Starships* ***Renegade and ***Thomas Paine*** ("Conspiracy" [TNG]) were both *New Orleans*-class ships, as was the ***Kyushu.*** ("The Best of Both Worlds, Part II [TNG]). *A study model was made for this class of ship and was seen very briefly as the* Kyushu *in the ship graveyard in "The Best of Both Worlds, Part II." Named for the ship we called the* City of New Orleans.

New Orleans. City in Louisiana on **Earth**. Starfleet officer **Benjamin Sisko** was raised in New Orleans. **Joseph Sisko**, Benjamin's father, ran a fine Creole restaurant called **Sisko's** in New Orleans. ("The Visitor" [DS9], "Homefront" [DS9]).

New Paris colonies. Federation settlements. The New Paris colonies were stricken by a serious plague in 2267. The original *Starship Enterprise* was assigned to transport critically needed medical supplies to planet Makus III for transfer to New Paris. ("The *Galileo* Seven" [TOS]).

New Providence. A Federation colony on planet Jouret IV. In 2366, all 900 colonists and the colony itself disappeared, leaving a huge crater in the ground. The loss of the New Providence colony was attributed to a **Borg** attack. ("The Best of Both Worlds, Part I" [TNG]).

New Seattle. A tropical city on **Penthara IV**. New Seattle experienced freezing conditions when the planet's temperature dropped following the impact of a type-C asteroid on the planet in 2368. ("A Matter of Time" [TNG]).

New United Nations. SEE: **United Nations, New**.

Newson, Eddie. Twenty-first-century baseball player. Newson was noted for having played on the opposing team the day **Buck Bokai** of the **London Kings** broke **Joe DiMaggio**'s consecutive hitting streak. ("If Wishes Were Horses" [DS9]).

Newton, Isaac. (John Neville; Peter Dennis). (1642-1727). Considered to be one of the most important figures in Earth's development of science. Newton developed laws of motion and universal gravitation and invented calculus. Data programmed a holographic re-creation of Newton for a holodeck poker game that also included **Albert Einstein** and **Stephen Hawking**. ("Descent, Part I" [TNG]). According to legend, Newton formulated his theories of gravitation after an apple fell on his head while he was sitting under an apple tree. A member of the Q Continuum, later called **Quinn**, said he was responsible for causing the apple to fall. ("Death Wish" [VGR]). SEE: **Cambridge University; Lucasian Chair.** *John Neville (*pictured*) played Newton in "Descent, Part I", while Peter Dennis was Newton in "Death Wish." Modern historians generally regard the apple story as apocryphal.*

Next Emanation. Term used by the **Vhnori** to refer to their concept of an afterlife. At the moment of death, Vhnori believed they entered the Next Emanation through a **spectral rupture**. ("Emanations" [VGR]).

"Next Phase, The." *Next Generation* episode #124. Written by Ronald D. Moore. Directed by David Carson. Stardate 45892.4. *First aired in 1992. Geordi La Forge and Ro Laren are believed dead, but they have merely been made invisible by a new Romulan cloaking device.* GUEST CAST: Michelle Forbes as **Ro Laren**; Thomas Kopache as **Mirok**; Susanna Thompson as **Varel**; Shelby Leverington as **Brossmer**, **Chief**; Brian Cousins as **Parem**; Kenneth Meseroll as **McDowell**, **Ensign**. SEE: **anyon emitter; Bajoran death chant; borhyas; Brossmer, Chief; chroniton particles; cloaking device, Romulan; Garadius system; graviton; interphase generator; *kolem*; La Forge, Geordi; McDowell, Ensign; melakol; Mirok; molecular phase inverter; muon; Parem; Ro Laren; Romulan science vessel; subspace technology; Varel.**

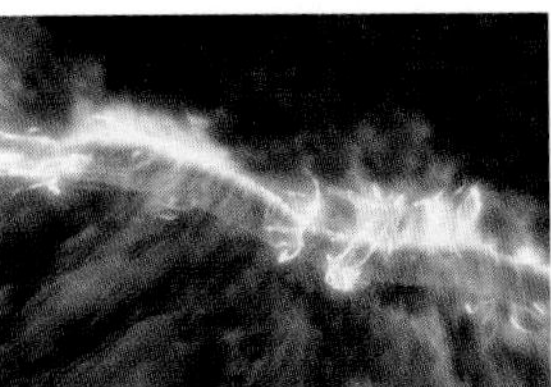

nexus. Nonlinear temporal continuum in which reality appears to reshape itself in fulfillment of a person's innermost wishes. The gateway to the nexus was an energy ribbon, a **temporal flux** phenomenon that crossed this galaxy every 39 years. The first known contact with the nexus was in 2293, when the energy ribbon crossed the flight path of two **El-Aurian** refugee ships in the Sol sector. Both ships were destroyed in the collision, and at least two passengers aboard the ***S.S. Lakul*** were swept into the nexus. One, an El-Aurian named **Guinan**, recovered from the experience with relatively few side effects. The other, **Dr. Tolian Soran**, became obsessed with the nexus, and was willing to do anything to return. Also disappearing into the nexus was former *Enterprise* Captain **James T. Kirk**, who was lost as the *Starship* ***Enterprise*-B** was conducting rescue operations for the *Lakul* survivors. Kirk emerged from the nexus in 2371 to aid *Enterprise*-D Captain **Jean-Luc Picard** in preventing Soran from committing mass murder in his quest to return to the nexus. All who have returned from the nexus have reported it to be a euphoric experience. Guinan described it as "like being wrapped in joy." Both Kirk and Picard reported an idyllic existence in which they experienced their lives as they wished they had unfolded. In Picard's nexus reality, he was married *(his unnamed wife was played by Kim Braden, who also played **Janet Brooks** in "The Loss" [TNG])*, and had several children: Matthew, a ten-year-old son *(played by Matthew Collins),* Olivia, a ten-year-old daughter *(played by Olivia Hack),* Mimi, a six-year-old daughter *(played by Mimi Collins),* and Madison, a four-year-old daughter *(played by Madison Eginton). (The children's names were from call sheets only, not from dialog).* **SEE: Picard, René.** Kirk's nexus reality was partially set in his beloved mountain cabin, with his dog **Butler**, his horse, and an opportunity to set things right with **Antonia**, the woman he wished he'd married. *(Star Trek Generations).*

Nezu ambassador. (Alan Oppenheimer). Diplomatic representative for the **Nezu** government. ("Rise" [VGR]). *Alan Oppenheimer previously played Koroth in "Rightful Heir" (TNG), Captain Keogh in "The Jem'Hadar" (DS9), and Dr. Rudy Wells in* The Six Million Dollar Man*.*

Nezu. Technologically sophisticated humanoid **Delta Quadrant** civilization. The Nezu people maintained five colonies on a **Class-M planet**. Access to space from the Nezu colony planet was provided by an **orbital tether** system that extended from the planet's surface to a station in planetary orbit. The colony world was plagued by asteroid impacts. It was learned that the asteroids had been deliberately sent to the Nezu colony planet by the **Etanian Order**. The Etanians anticipated that what appeared to be a natural disaster would cause the Nezu to evacuate the planet. Once the population had left, the Etanians would have arrived to stake a claim. The ***U.S.S. Voyager*** came to the rescue of the Nezu and discovered the Etanians' plan, driving them away when they attempted to invade openly. ("Rise" [VGR]).

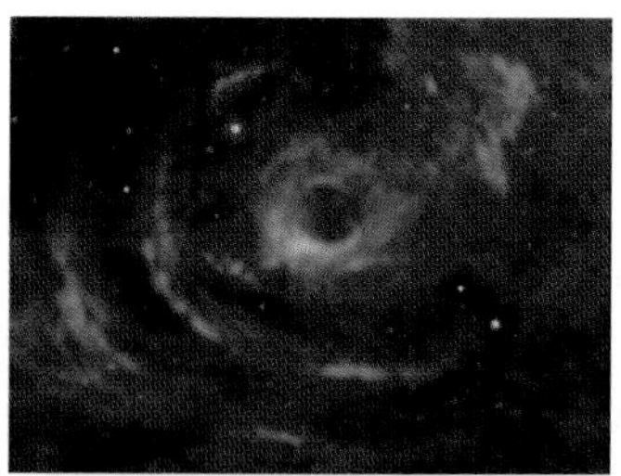

Ngame Nebula. An interstellar cloud of dust and gas. The *Enterprise*-D passed the Ngame Nebula en route to its mission on Evadne IV in 2367. The ship's sensors discovered the apparent presence of a Class-M planet in a **T-tauri type star system** within the cloud. While investigating the planet, the *Enterprise*-D encountered a wormhole that rendered the crew unconscious for approximately thirty seconds. The Class-M reading was later found to be erroneous. ("Clues" [TNG]). *The episode "Clues" dealt with the* Enterprise-D*'s encounter with the pathologically reclusive **Paxans**. Since the Paxans were apparently successful in erasing or suppressing all records and memories of the contact, we assume that the existence of the Paxans remains a secret from the Federation.*

Ngomo, Admiral. Starfleet officer stationed on **Earth** in 2371. ("Past Tense, Part I" [DS9]).

Niagara*-class starship.** Conjectural designation for a type of Federation ship. The ***U.S.S. Wellington, which underwent servicing at **Starbase 74** in 2364 and on which Ensign **Ro Laren** once served, was a *Niagara*-class starship.

nIb'poH. Klingon term that describes the feeling that an action or situation has occurred before, similar to the human term ***déjà vu***. ("Cause and Effect" [TNG]).

Nibor. (Peter Slutsker). A crew member of the Ferengi vessel ***Krayton***, Nibor was present at the **Trade Agreements Conference** in 2366. He lost a **three-dimensional chess** game to Commander Riker during the closing reception of the conference, and later lost another game to Riker aboard the *Krayton*. ("Ménage à Troi" [TNG]).

Nichols, Dr. (Alex Henteloff). Plant manager at **Plexicorp**, a 20th-century company based in San Francisco, on Earth. Nichols developed the molecular matrix for transparent aluminum in 1986. *(Star Trek IV: The Voyage Home).*

Nicki the Nose. (Don Stark). A fictional character from the **Dixon Hill** detective stories. Nicki was a notorious gangster who had a silver plate replacing the part of his nose that had been shot off. A holographic version of Nicki the Nose was part of the Dixon Hill holodeck programs. *(Star Trek: First Contact).*

Nicoletti, Susan. (C. Delgado). Member of the *Starship Voyager* crew. Lieutenant Nicoletti's quarters on the *Voyager* were located on Deck 4. ("Twisted" [VGR]). She played the oboe with Harry Kim when he played his clarinet. Kim and Nicoletti collaborated on a new orchestral program for the holodeck. ("The Thaw" [VGR]). Nicoletti was assigned to the engineering section on the *Voyager*. In 2373, Nicoletti helped B'Elanna Torres re-align the *Voyager's* **dilithium matrix** while the warp drive was online. ("The Swarm" [VGR]).

nictitating membrane. An inner eyelid present in many animals, such as **amphibian**s. Counselor Troi developed nictitating membranes as part of her symptomatology while suffering from **Barclay's Protomorphosis Syndrome** in 2370. ("Genesis" [TNG]). *Not to be confused with the Vulcan inner eyelid....*

"Night Bird." Musical jazz composition that features a trombone solo. Commander William Riker tried for ten years to master performance of the piece, with only moderate success. ("Second Chances" [TNG]).

"Night Terrors." *Next Generation* episode #91. Teleplay by Pamela Douglas and Jeri Taylor. Story by Sheri Goodhartz. Directed by Les Landau. Stardate 44631.2. *First aired in 1991. The* Enterprise-D *crew suffers severe sleep deprivation due to proximity with an interdimensional phenomenon called a Tyken's Rift.* GUEST CAST: Rosalind Chao as **O'Brien**, **Keiko**; John Vickery as **Hagen**, **Andrus**; Duke Moosekian as **Gillespie**, **Chief**; Craig Hurley as **Peeples**, **Ensign**; Brian Tochi as **Lin**, **Ensign Peter**; Lanei Chapman as **Rager**, **Ensign**; Colm Meaney as **O'Brien**, **Miles**; Whoopi Goldberg as **Guinan**; Deborah Taylor as Zaheva. SEE: **Balthus, Dr.; *Brattain, U.S.S.*; Brink; Bussard collectors; Corbin, Tom; "Eyes in the dark"; Gillespie, Chief; Hagen, Andrus; Kenicki; Lin, Ensign Peter; "One moon circles"; Peeples, Ensign; Rager, Ensign; REM sleep; Starbase 220; Tyken's Rift; Zaheva, Captain Chantal.**

Night-Blooming *throgni*. A fragrant Klingon flower. Worf found the smell of a **Quazulu VIII** virus similar to the *throgni*. ("Angel One" [TNG]).

"Nightingale Woman." Passionate love sonnet written by poet **Phineas Tarbolde** in 1996 on the Canopus Planet. After contact with the barrier at the edge of the galaxy, **Gary Mitchell** was able to quote this poem as an early example of his expanded mental powers. ("Where No Man Has Gone Before" [TOS]). *The poem was actually written by Gene Roddenberry as an aviator speaking to his beloved airplane.*

Niles. (Michael Rose). Member of the **Maquis**. He assisted **Sakonna** and **Amaros** in abducting **Gul Dukat** from **Deep Space 9** in 2370. Niles piloted one of the two Maquis ships that made an aborted attempt to attack a **Cardassian** weapons depot on planet **Bryma**. ("The Maquis, Parts I and II" [DS9]).

Nilrem. (Steven Anderson). A physician on planet **Malcor III**. Nilrem was responsible for the treatment of William Riker, masquerading as a Malcorian named **Rivas Jakara**, at the **Sikla Medical Facility** in 2367. When Dr. Berel declined to endanger Riker's life at the request of Malcorian security, Nilrem replaced **Berel** as head of the facility. ("First Contact" [TNG]). *Merlin, spelled backwards.*

Nimbus III. A barely habitable Class-M planet in the Neutral Zone. Dubbed the "planet of galactic peace," Nimbus III was the site of an experiment by the Romulan, Klingon, and Federation governments to bridge the gap between them by sponsoring a settlement there. The colony, established in 2268, was a dismal failure, although the settlement remained in place for at least two decades. The Vulcan fanatic **Sybok** began his quest for ***Sha Ka Ree*** there. (*Star Trek V: The Final Frontier*).

Nimian sea salt. Culinary spice native to the Delta Quadrant. ("Prototype" [VGR]).

***nisroh*.** Curved blade used on planet **Tilonus IV**. Given to Commander William Riker as part of his disguise while he visited Tilonus IV in 2369 to rescue a Federation research team. Before beaming down to Tilonus IV, Lieutenant Worf briefed Riker on his undercover mission, including the use of the *nisroh*, accidentally cutting Riker on the head. The pain and bleeding from the wound served as a focal point of reality for Riker in the delusional world created by the **neurosomatic technique**s he endured on Tilonus IV. ("Frame of Mind" [TNG]).

Nistrim. SEE: **Kazon-Nistrim**.

nitrilin. Extremely unstable and rare substance often used in microexplosives. ("Improbable Cause" [DS9]).

nitrium metal parasites. Spaceborne microscopic life-forms that ingest **nitrium**, converting it to a simple molecular gel. These life-forms normally live in nitrium-rich asteroids, such as those found in the **Pelloris Field** near planet **Tessen III**. The *Enterprise*-D was accidentally infested with nitrium metal parasites on stardate 45733, while destroying an asteroid that was on a collision course for Tessen III. Because nitrium is used extensively in starship construction, the parasites caused substantial damage to the *Enterprise*-D, nearly resulting in a warp-core breach. ("Cost of Living" [TNG]).

nitrium. A metal alloy, used in the construction of Federation starships. Nitrium is used in the interior construction of such ship's systems as inertial damping field generators, food replication, power transfer conduits, and the matter/antimatter reaction chamber. ("Cost of Living" [TNG]).

nitrogen narcosis. Also known as "rapture of the deep," nitrogen narcosis was a hazard of 20th-century-Earth deep-sea diving. It was caused by the replacement of oxygen in oxyhemoglobin with nitrogen. In its victims, the resultant anoxia produced disorientation, hallucinations, and lack of judgment. The phenomenon is similar to temporal narcosis. ("Timescape" [TNG]).

nitrogen tetroxide. Hypergolic liquid propellent, often used in simple chemical-reaction-control thrusters; a gas poisonous to most humanoids. ("Basics, Part I" [VGR]).

nitrogenase compound. Useful raw material. Kathryn Janeway and Chakotay were scouting for nitrogenase compounds in 2373 when their shuttle, the *Sacajawea*, encountered a magnetic storm and crashed on a planet in a binary star system in the Delta Quadrant. ("Coda" [VGR]).

Nivoch. Planet. **Seska** promised to meet her brother on Nivoch on his birthday in 2371. ("Prime Factors." [VGR]).

Nixon, Richard M. (1913-1994). Thirty-seventh president of the American nation on **Earth** during the 20th century. Nixon, a politically conservative leader, was able to establish diplomatic relations with the nation of China, a major feat made possible by his strong resistance to the influence of that country early in his career. So extraordinary was this breakthrough that **Vulcan** political scholars have observed that "only Nixon could go to China." *(Star Trek VI: The Undiscovered Country)*. Nixon met computer pioneer **Henry Starling** in 1970. ("Future's End, Part I" [VGR]).

No'Mat. Klingon planet on which are located the lava caves where the Klingon **Rite of *MajQa*** is practiced. ("Birthright, Part I" [TNG]). As a child, **Worf** visited No'Mat, where he received a vision of the prophet **Kahless the Unforgettable**. Kahless told young Worf he would do something no other Klingon had done before. ("Rightful Heir" [TNG]). Worf pondered the meaning of Kahless's words, and when he was old enough, he joined **Starfleet**, something no Klingon had ever done before. ("The Sword of Kahless" [DS9]).

No-win scenario. SEE: ***Kobayashi Maru* scenario**.

Noah, Dr. Hippocrates. (Avery Brooks). Character in Julian Bashir's **secret agent** holosuite program. Dr. Noah was a mad scientist bent on reshaping the Earth by using powerful lasers to cause massive earthquakes and flooding. Dr. Noah had a secret stronghold at the top of Mount **Everest**, which he expected would remain an island after his plan caused the rest of the planet's surface to become flooded. A holosuite malfunction in 2372 caused the character to look exactly like Benjamin Sisko. ("Our Man Bashir" [DS9]).

Nobel Prize. Annual awards established by Earth chemist Alfred Nobel (1833-1896), recognizing outstanding achievements in science, literature, medicine, and peace. **Dr. Richard Daystrom** won a Nobel Prize in 2243 for his theoretical work that led to **duotronic** computer systems. ("The Ultimate Computer" [TOS]). An ancestor of **Jean-Luc Picard** won a Nobel Prize in chemistry. *(Star Trek Generations)*.

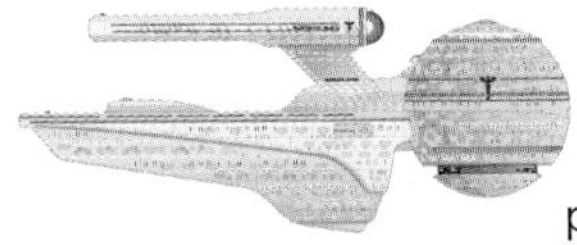

Nobel, U.S.S. Federation starship, *Olympic* class, Starfleet registry number NCC-55012, which, along with the ***U.S.S. Excelsior***, took part in a search-and-rescue mission for the ***U.S.S. Hera*** in 2370. ("Interface" [TNG]). *The Nobel was named after Alfred Nobel, Swedish industrialist, inventor of dynamite, and founder of the Nobel Prize.*

Noel, Dr. Helen. (Marianne Hill). Member of the *U.S.S. Enterprise* medical staff with both psychiatric and penology experience. Noel accompanied Captain Kirk on an inspection visit to the **Tantalus V** penal colony. An attractive woman, Noel first met Kirk at the *Enterprise* science lab Christmas party, and evidently found the captain attractive as well. ("Dagger of the Mind" [TOS]).

Nog (mirror). (Aron Eisenberg). Counterpart to **Nog** in the **mirror universe**. After **Quark (mirror)** and **Rom (mirror)** were killed by the **Alliance**, Nog (mirror) became the owner of the bar on **Terok Nor (mirror).** Nog (mirror) helped **Kira Nerys (mirror)** escape from **Terran resistance** captivity in 2372, but she killed him when she realized that he knew her intended escape destination. ("Shattered Mirror" [DS9]).

Nog. (Aron Eisenberg). Nephew of **Quark** and son of **Rom**, who lived on **Deep Space 9** in 2369. The young Ferengi was apprehended by Odo as he stole from the assay office on Deep Space 9's **Promenade** in 2369. ("Emissary" [DS9]). Nog's mother was **Prinadora**. ("Doctor Bashir, I Presume?" [DS9]). Nog became good friends with young **Jake Sisko** on the station, and the two boys once created a fictitious company, the **Noh-Jay Consortium**, for their commercial exploits. ("Progress" [DS9]). When Nog's father, Rom, forbade Nog to attend school on the station, Jake taught him how to read. ("The Nagus" [DS9]). In 2371, Nog underwent the **Ferengi Attainment Ceremony**. He asked Benjamin Sisko to be his role model (SEE: **Ferengi Code**) and asked Sisko to recommend him for admission to Starfleet Academy. ("Heart of Stone" [DS9]). Following Nog's decision to join Starfleet, he studied in earnest for the **Starfleet Academy Preparatory Program**, despite his uncle Quark's opposition. ("Facets" [DS9]). In 2372, Nog sold his childhood belongings prior to leaving station Deep Space 9 to attend Starfleet Academy. Nog joined his father and uncle on the ship ***Quark's Treasure*** for the trip to Earth, although the journey was slightly delayed due to an unanticipated time trip to the year 1947. ("Little Green Men" [DS9]). In 2373, Nog returned to Deep Space 9 on a Starfleet Academy cadet field-study assignment. While there he roomed with his friend, Jake Sisko. ("The Ascent" [DS9]). (In an alternate future in which Ben Sisko was believed killed aboard the *Defiant* in 2372, Nog became a commander in Starfleet by 2391, and a captain by 2405. SEE: **Sisko, Jake**.) ("The Visitor" [DS9]). *Nog was first seen in "Emissary" (DS9).*

Nogami. (James Saito). Officer in the Japanese military on Earth in the 1930s. Nogami was abducted from Earth in 1937 and taken to the **Briori** homeworld in the Delta Quadrant, where he was regarded as one of the **Thirty-Sevens** by the human colonists there. He remained in **cryostasis** on the planet until he and eight others were found and revived by the crew of the *U.S.S. Voyager* in 2371. ("The 37's" [VGR]). *This character's name is from the script and was never mentioned in dialog.*

Nogatch hemlock. Substance poisonous to humans. In 2372 there was no known cure for Nogatch hemlock poisoning. ("Death Wish" [VGR]).

Noggra. (Robert DoQui). Klingon warrior. Noggra was a friend to **Mogh**, father of Worf and Kurn. In 2372, Noggra journeyed to station Deep Space 9 to pick up his son, **Rodek**, who had been injured in a shuttle accident. ("Sons of Mogh" [DS9]). *Rodek was, of course, Kurn's new identity after his memory was wiped.*

Nogura, Admiral. Starfleet commanding admiral, based in San Francisco, who reinstated James Kirk as captain of the *Enterprise* during the **V'Ger** crisis of 2271. (*Star Trek: The Motion Picture*).

Noh-Jay Consortium. Fictitious company name improvised by young **Nog** and **Jake Sisko** for their fledgling business ventures on Deep Space 9. On stardate 46844, the boys traded 5,000 wrappages of ***yamok* sauce** for **self-sealing stem bolts**, even though they had no idea what stem bolts were used for. They later traded the stem bolts for a parcel of land, sight unseen, on **Bajor**. Nog and Jake then sold the land to Quark for five bars of gold-pressed **latinum.** ("Progress" [DS9]).

Nol-Ennis. Group of individuals trapped in a war against their eternal enemies, the **Ennis**, on a lunar penal colony in the Gamma Quadrant. ("Battle Lines" [DS9]).

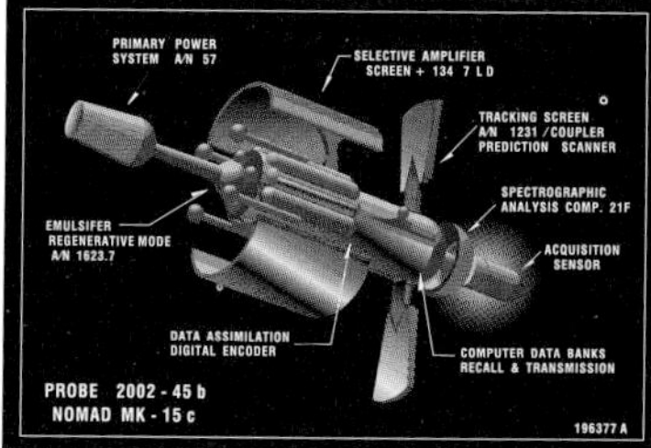

Nomad. (Voice by Vic Perrin). Early robotic interstellar probe launched from **Earth** in 2002 on a mission to search for new life-forms. Roughly cylindrical in shape, weighing 500 kilograms, and measuring about one meter in length, *Nomad* was created by brilliant Earth scientist **Jackson Roykirk**. *Nomad* was presumed destroyed in flight by a meteor collision. It was later learned that *Nomad* had in fact collided with an alien space probe called ***Tan Ru***. In the aftermath of the accident, *Nomad* somehow repaired itself, merging its control programs with those of *Tan Ru*. The resulting combination of their benign programs became deadly. *Nomad*'s new purpose was to seek out and sterilize what it deemed to be imperfect biological infestations. Nomad destroyed all living beings in the **Malurian system** in 2267, and shortly thereafter attacked the *U.S.S. Enterprise*. The deadly probe destroyed itself when it realized it was imperfect, having confused *Enterprise* Captain James Kirk with its creator, Jackson Roykirk. ("The Changeling" [TOS]). *The episode suggested that* Nomad *was Earth's first probe out of our solar system, but in actual fact,* Pioneer 10 *was the first craft to reach interstellar space.*

"Non Sequitur." *Voyager* episode #22. Written by Brannon Braga. Directed by David Livingston. *First aired in 1995. Ensign Kim finds himself back on Earth in an alternate reality, one in which he never served on* Voyager. GUEST CAST: Louis Giambalvo as **Cosimo**; Jennifer Gatti as **Libby**; Jack Shearer as **Strickler, Admiral**; Mark Kiely as **Lasca, Lieutenant**; Majel Barrett as Computer voice. SEE: **antimatter containment; *Apollo* 11; Byrd, Daniel; Cochrane Medal of Excellence; Cosimo; *Drake, Shuttlecraft*; *Exeter, U.S.S.*; Kim, Harry; Ktarian music festival; Lasca, Lieutenant; Libby; navigational**

deflector; Paris, Thomas; polaron; security anklet; site-to-site transport; Spacedock; Starfleet Corps of Engineers; Strickler, Admiral; tetryon; timestream; *Voyager, U.S.S.*; Vulcan mocha; *Yellowstone, U.S.S.*

Nona. (Nancy Kovack-Mehta). ***Kahn-ut-tu*** woman among the **hill people** on **Tyree**'s planet, and ambitious wife of tribal leader Tyree. Using her special knowledge as a *Kahn-ut-tu*, Nona cured James Kirk of a deadly ***mugato*** wound, then cast a spell that rendered him unable him to resist her wishes. Upon learning Kirk's true identity as a starship captain possessing advanced weapons, Nona stole Kirk's hand phaser, hoping to use it as a stepping-stone to power. Nona was instead killed by a mob of village people who viewed her as a spy. ("A Private Little War" [TOS]).

noncorporeal life. Literally, without body. Refers to a wide number of life-forms that exist as complex patterns of energy, plasma, or gas, without any tangible solid form. Non-corporeal life-forms have included the **Thasians** (*pictured*) ("Charlie X" [TOS]); **Trelane** ("The Squire of Gothos" [TOS]); the **Organians** ("Errand of Mercy" [TOS]); **Redjac,** also known as Jack the Ripper, Beratis, Kesla, and Mister Hengist ("Wolf in the Fold" [TOS]); the **Gorgan** of **Triacus** ("And the Children Shall Lead" [TOS]); the **Medusans** ("Is There in Truth No Beauty?" [TOS]); the **Zetarians** ("The Lights of Zetar" [TOS]); **Nagilum** ("Where Silence Has Lease" [TNG]; **Troi, Ian Andrew** ("The Child" [TNG]); the **Koinonians** ("The Bonding" [TNG]); the **sentry** ("Final Mission" [TNG]); **Isabella** ("Imaginary Friend" [TNG]); **Ronin** ("Sub Rosa" [TNG]); the **Caretaker** ("Caretaker" [VGR]) and **Suspiria**, who were members of the **Nacene** ("Cold Fire" [VGR]); **photonic beings** ("Heroes and Demons" [VGR]); **trianic energy being**s, also known as the **Komar** ("Cathexis" [VGR]); and **Onaya** ("The Muse" [DS9]). SEE: **cloud creatures; distortion ring being; Meridian; Pah-wraiths**.

Nondoran tomato paste. Red condiment. Neelix used Nondoran tomato paste in his kitchen aboard the *Voyager*. ("Projections" [VGR]).

noninterference directive. See: **Prime Directive**.

Noonan, Fred. (David Graf). Earth aviation pioneer who served as navigator to **Amelia Earhart** on her attempt to fly around the world in 1937. After completing two-thirds of the trip, the aircraft and both occupants were abducted by the **Briori** and transported 70,000 light-years to the Briori homeworld in the Delta Quadrant. Earhart, Noonan, and several others remained in cryostasis on the planet until they were revived by the crew of the *U.S.S. Voyager* in 2371. Given the choice of either traveling with the *Voyager* or staying with the human inhabitants of the Delta-Quadrant world, Noonan, who was in love with Earhart, chose to remain on the former Briori homeworld.. ("The 37's" [VGR]).

Noor. (Megan Cole). Head of the **J'naii** government in 2368. Noor sentenced **Soren** to undergo **psychotectic therapy** to cure Soren's aberrant sexual behavior. ("The Outcast" [TNG]).

"Nor the Battle to the Strong." *Deep Space Nine* episode #102. Teleplay by René Echevarria. Story by Brice R. Parker. Directed by Kim Friedman. No stardate given. *First aired in 1996. Jake experiences the horror of war firsthand when he and Bashir respond to a distress call from a Federation colony being attacked by Klingons.* GUEST CAST: Andrew Kavovit as **Kirby**; Karen Austin as **Kalandra**; Mark Holton as Bolian; Lisa Lord as Nurse; Jeb Brown as Ensign; Danny Goldring as **Burke**; Elle Alexander as Female guard; Greg "Christopher" Smith as Male guard. SEE: **Ajilon Prime; Archanis; Burke; Cartalian fever; Caster; cutter; Dax, Audrid; Dax, Tobin; *Down the River Light*; *Farragut, U.S.S.*; Ferengi; Ganalda IV; gravimetric scanner; hopper; Kalandra, Dr.; Kirby; Klingon Empire; Lembatta cluster; magnesite; Neema; prion; Raifi; Raymond, Captain; Rugalan fever; *Rutledge, U.S.S.*; Sisko, Jake; Tanandra Bay; Tarkalean condor; *Tecumseh, U.S.S.*; transport scrambler.**

noranium alloy. A metal of little salvage value. A large quantity of noranium was found in the **Gatherer** camp on **Gamma Hromi II**. An *Enterprise*-D away team vaporized the noranium to provide a smoke screen for their escape. ("The Vengeance Factor" [TNG]).

norep. Medication, a derivative of norepinephrine. Dr. Beverly Crusher ordered norep administered to **Natasha Yar** in an unsuccessful attempt to revive her after she had been attacked by **Armus**. ("Skin of Evil" [TNG]).

norepinephrine. Hormone produced by the adrenal glands. Norepinephrine is chemically similar to adrenaline and is used medicinally to treat shock. ("The Thaw" [VGR]). SEE: **norep.**

Nori. (Galyn Görg). Wife and follower of the **Tieran**, the tyrannical leader of the **Ilari** nation. Nori supported her husband when his consciousness took over Kes's body and tried to overthrow the Ilari government in 2373. Nori was shot and killed when a team from the *Starship Voyager* beamed down to rescue Kes. ("Warlord" [VGR]). *Galyn Görg previously played Korena in "The Visitor" (DS9).*

Norkan outposts. Colonies located near the **Romulan Neutral Zone**. Site of a bloody attack conducted under the command of Romulan Admiral **Alidar Jarok**. Although the Federation described the incident as a "massacre," Jarok noted that Romulans considered it to be a successful "campaign," and that one world's butcher might be another world's hero. ("The Defector" [TNG]).

Norkova. Vessel that transported a shipment of **deuridium** from the Gamma Quadrant to Deep Space 9 in 2369. SEE: **Rao Vantika**. ("The Passenger" [DS9]).

Norman. (Richard Tatro). The central locus of the android society on the planet informally known as **Mudd**. Norman and his fellow androids were originally from the Andromeda Galaxy, but were stranded in this galaxy when their homeworld's sun went nova, killing their **Makers**. In 2267, Norman conspired with **Harcourt Fenton Mudd** to capture the *Starship Enterprise* and its crew. The *Enterprise* crew was able to escape from the androids by the skillful use of illogic, which caused the highly logical androids to overload. ("I, Mudd" [TOS]).

Norpin Colony. Retirement community on planet Norpin V. **Montgomery Scott** had hoped to take up residence at the Norpin Colony in 2294 before he was sidetracked by the crash of the ***U.S.S. Jenolen***. ("Relics" [TNG]).

Norris, Tom. School friend of **Beverly Crusher**. They had one date, which Beverly brought to an abrupt end with the question: "Is that a beard or is your face dirty?" ("Attached" [TNG]).

Norva. (Heidie Margolis). Inhabitant of a planet in the Teplan system located in the Gamma Quadrant. Norva was infected with a deadly disease known as the blight. In 2372, Dr. Julian Bashir and Jadzia Dax found Norva near death and took her to **Trevean**'s hospital, where she died. SEE: **Teplan blight.** ("The Quickening" [DS9]).

***Norway*-class starship.** Type of Federation starship in use in the late 24th century. The *U.S.S. Budapest* was a ship of the *Norway* class. *(Star Trek: First Contact). The* Norway*-class starship was designed by Alex Jaegar at ILM. It was rendered as a computer-generated visual effect.*

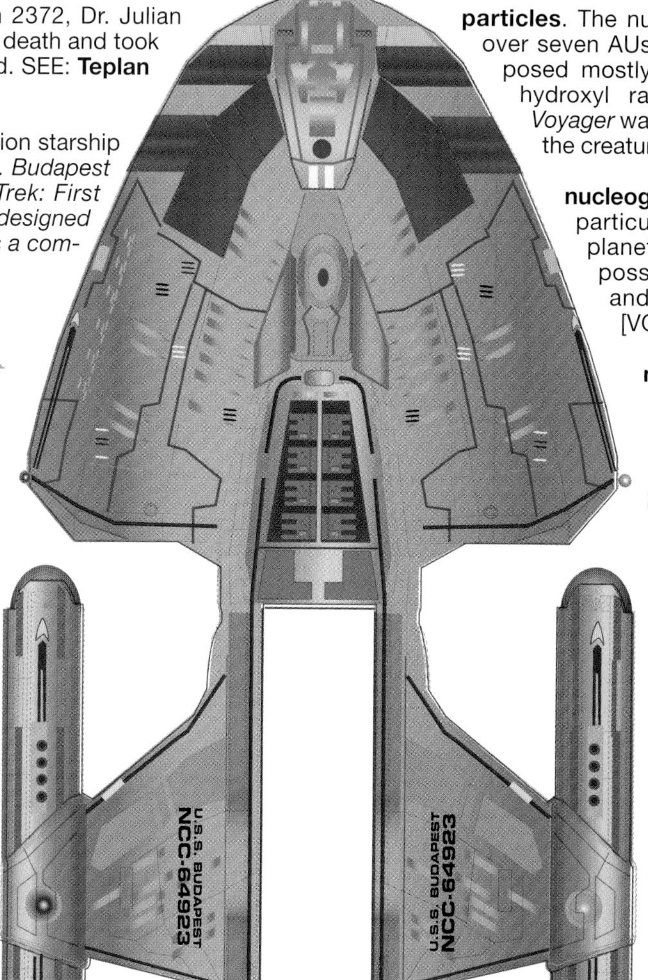

Nova Squadron. Team of elite cadet pilots at **Starfleet Academy**. Nova Squadron was composed of five members who flew small single-pilot ships in aerobatic maneuvers. In 2368, Nova Squadron won the Rigel Cup, a source of considerable pride to all involved. A short time later, on stardate 45703, Nova Squadron was involved in a collision that destroyed all five craft and resulted in the death of squadron member **Joshua Albert**. ("The First Duty" [TNG]). SEE: **Kolvoord Starburst; Locarno, Cadet First Class Nicholas.**

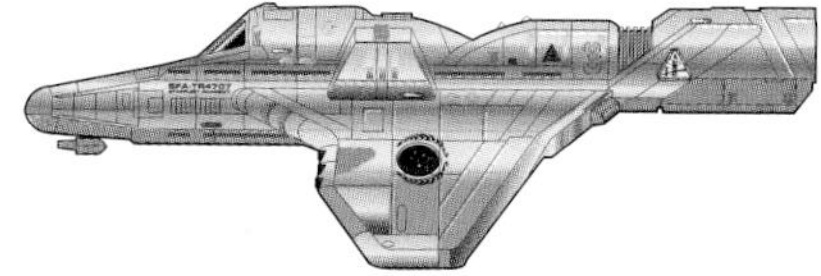

Novakovich. Wesley Crusher's instructor in anthropology at Starfleet Academy in 2368. ("The Game" [TNG]).

"Nth Degree, The." *Next Generation* episode #93. Written by Joe Menosky. Directed by Robert Legato. Stardate 44704.2. *First aired in 1991. Contact with an alien space probe gives Reginald Barclay an incredible intelligence boost.* GUEST CAST: Jim Morton as **Einstein**, **Albert**; Kay E. Kuter as **Sirah**; Saxon Trainor as **Larson**, **Lieutenant Linda**; Page Leong as **Anaya**, **Ensign April**; Dwight Schultz as **Barclay**, **Reginald**; David Coburn as **Brower**, **Ensign**. SEE: **Anaya, Ensign April; Argus Array; Barclay, Reginald; Brower, Ensign; Crusher, Dr. Beverly; *Cyrano de Bergerac*; Cytherians; Einstein, Albert; iconic display console; Larson, Lieutenant Linda; ODN; passive high-resolution series; Science Station 402; sero-amino readout; Shuttle 5; subspace phenomena.**

Nu'Daq. (John Cotran). Commander of the Klingon attack cruiser *Maht-H'a* that participated in the discovery of a four-billion-year-old genetically encoded message from an ancient humanoid species. ("The Chase" [TNG]). SEE: **Galen, Professor Richard; humanoid life.**

nuanka. Native American term for a period of mourning. ("The Cloud" [VGR]).

nucleogenic cloud being. Nebula-like life-form native to the **Delta Quadrant** of the galaxy. The *Starship Voyager* encountered an individual of this species in 2371, accidentally inflicting serious harm to the creature by entering its body to harvest **omicron particles**. The nucleogenic cloud being was over seven AUs in diameter and was composed mostly of hydrogen, helium, and hydroxyl radicals. The crew of the *Voyager* was eventually able to help heal the creature. ("The Cloud" [VGR]).

nucleogenic particles. Micro-scopic particulates present in a Class-M planet's atmosphere that make it possible for water to precipitate and fall as rain. ("Caretaker" [VGR]).

nucleonic beam. Directed energy transmission. A low-level energy nucleonic beam was projected by a probe from the planet **Kataan**. The beam penetrated the *Enterprise*-D shields, rendering Captain Jean-Luc Picard unconscious, and in the span of 25 minutes transmitted a lifetime of experiences into Picard's mind. ("The Inner Light" [TNG]).

nucleonic radiation. Hazardous energy normally present within a Federation-style **replicator**. Nucleonic radiation can cause massive cell mutation in living tissue. A replicator incorrectly installed on the bridge of a Kazon-Nistrim ship on stardate 48658 exploded, causing a large burst of nucleonic radiation, killing almost everyone aboard. ("State of Flux" [VGR]).

nucleosynthesis. Alteration of matter at the atomic level. Under certain conditions, **invidium** contamination can trigger spontaneous nucleosynthesis in silicon molecules like those used in glassware. ("Hollow Pursuits" [TNG]).

null space. An extremely rare "pocket" in space created during the formation of a star. The phenomenon is caused by turbulent regions of magnetic and gravitational fields that coalesce into an area that absorbs all electromagnetic energy that enters it. Energy outside the null space is bent around it, making the area invisible to sensors and the naked eye. Long thought to be strictly theoretical, a pocket of null space was discovered near the **J'naii** planet in 2368 when the shuttle ***Taris Murn*** was lost. ("The Outcast" [TNG]).

nullifier core. Major component of the propulsion system on a **Romulan warbird**. The nullifier cores must be maintained in precise alignment to avoid magnetic disruptions that can be detected when the ship is cloaked. ("Face of the Enemy" [TNG]). SEE: **artificial quantum singularity**.

Number One. (M. Leigh Hudec, aka Majel Barrett Roddenberry). Executive officer holding the rank of lieutenant, and second-in-command of the original *Starship Enterprise* under the command of Captain Christopher Pike. ("The Cage," "The Menagerie, Parts I and II" [TOS]). *Number One was a cool, mysterious woman whose name was never given, although she was intended as a regular character in Roddenberry's original version of* Star

Trek. *Number One is apparently a common nickname given by starship captains to their second-in-command, since Captain Picard gave the same moniker to Commander* ***William T. Riker****. SEE:* ***Flores, Marissa****. The character of Number One was dropped from the original* Star Trek *series at the insistence of the network, and Mr. Spock was "promoted" to second-in-command. It was not until 1986, when Madge Sinclair was cast as the captain of the ill-fated* **U.S.S. Saratoga** *in* Star Trek IV, *that the decision was reversed. Majel Barrett also played Nurse Chapel in the original* Star Trek *series and Lwaxana Troi in* Star Trek: The Next Generation. *Barrett also lent her voice to various computers in the spin-off series.*

Numiri. Spacefaring civilization in the Delta Quadrant. The Numiri were at war with the **Baneans**, even though the two peoples shared a common ancestry. In 2371, Numiri operatives framed *Voyager* officer **Thomas Paris** in the murder of Banean weapons designer **Tolen Ren**, an elaborate scheme to use Paris's memory engrams to carry stolen Banean military information to the Numiri homeworld. ("Ex Post Facto" [VGR]).

Nuria. (Kathryn Leigh Scott). A leader of a proto-**Vulcan** tribe on planet **Mintaka III** at the time a Federation anthropological team accidentally revealed themselves to the Mintakans in 2366. The technologically primitive Mintakans interpreted the scientists' advanced Federation technology as evidence of a supernatural presence. Attempting to appeal to her logical nature, Captain Picard brought Nuria on-board the *Enterprise*-D (in violation of the **Prime Directive**) to convince her that he was not a god. ("Who Watches the Watchers?" [TNG]).

Ny Terla. (Joel Polis). Inhabitant of a Class-M planet in the **Delta Quadrant** whose people were dependent on **polaric ion energy**. Ny Terla and others protested against the use of polaric energy. ("Time and Again" [VGR]).

Nyberrite Alliance. Spacefaring civilization. The Nyberrite Alliance was always looking to hire experienced officers. When Lieutenant Commander Worf contemplated leaving Starfleet in 2372, he considered joining the crew of a Nyberrite cruiser. ("The Way of the Warrior" [DS9]).

Nydom, Dr. (Larry Cedar). **T'Lani** scientist. Dr. Nydom was killed in 2370 after discovering how to neutralize the deadly **harvesters**. ("Armageddon Game" [DS9]).

Nykalia. Locale on a planet in the Teplan system located in the Gamma Quadrant. In 2372, **Ekoria** told Dr. Julian Bashir that a woman in Nykalia made a medicine that eased the pain caused by a deadly disease known as the blight. SEE: **Teplan blight.** ("The Quickening" [DS9]).

"O soave fanciulla." A duet from Puccini's opera *La Bohème*. In 2373, *Voyager*'s Emergency Medical Hologram performed "O soave fanciulla" with a holodeck representation of Giuseppina Pentangeli, a 22nd-century diva. ("The Swarm" [VGR]).

O'Brien, Kirayoshi. Born in 2373, son of Starfleet officers **Miles O'Brien** and **Keiko O'Brien** and younger brother to **Molly O'Brien**. Prior to Kirayoshi's birth, Keiko was seriously injured in an accident aboard a runabout. The child survived because of a daring surgical procedure in which **Dr. Julian Bashir** removed the fetal Kirayoshi from his mother's womb and im-planted him into the body of **Kira Nerys**. Kira carried the fetus for the remaining five months of pregnancy, after which he was delivered in a traditional **Bajoran** birthing ceremony. ("The Begotten" [DS9]). *Kirayoshi was born in "The Begotten" (DS9) but didn't get a first name until "In Purgatory's Shadow" (DS9).*

O'Brien, Keiko. (Rosalind Chao). Starfleet botanist, formerly assigned to the *Enterprise*-D, later stationed at Deep Space 9.

Born Keiko Ishikawa, she married fellow crew member **Miles O'Brien** in 2367. Their wedding, held aboard the *Enterprise*-D in the Ten-Forward Lounge, was a mixture of Japanese and Irish traditions. ("Data's Day" [TNG]). *The words Picard spoke in the O'Brien wedding ceremony are almost identical to the ceremony performed by Captain Kirk in "Balance of Terror" (TOS), a deliberate homage by episode writer Ronald D. Moore.* Keiko gave birth to a girl, **Molly O'Brien**, a year later. Molly was born in Ten-Forward during a ship-wide systems failure. ("Disaster" [TNG]). Keiko was briefly reduced to a child after passing through an energy field in 2369. ("Rascals" [TNG]). *(Young Keiko was played by Caroline Junko King.)*

Keiko accepted a transfer to station **Deep Space 9** in 2369 when her husband was assigned there as chief of operations. Keiko was appalled at the living accommodations on the station, but remained there for the sake of her husband's career. ("Emissary" [DS9]). Keiko and her husband visited Earth that same year for her mother's 100th birthday. ("Dax" [DS9]). As a child, Keiko helped her grandmother with her Japanese brush painting. It had been the young Keiko's special task to fill the old chipped cup that her grandmother, whom she called **Obachan**, used to clean the brush. ("Violations" [TNG]).

Keiko found adapting to life on the station difficult. She was dissatisfied by the lack of professional opportunities on the station for a botanist, and was concerned about the lack of educational facilities for her daughter. Keiko was able to address this last issue when Commander Sisko granted her permission to establish a **schoolroom** on the station. ("A Man Alone" [DS9]). Keiko operated the school until early 2371, when enrollment dropped dramatically because of fears of a possible **Dominion** attack. Shortly thereafter she accepted an assignment as chief botanist on a agrobiology expedition to Bajor. The assignment kept Keiko and her daughter, Molly, away from the station for much of that year. ("The House of Quark" [DS9], "Fascination" [DS9]). In 2372, Keiko became pregnant with her second child. Later that year she completed her assignment on Bajor, and she and her daughter returned to live on station Deep Space 9. ("Accession" [DS9]). Keiko's second pregnancy nearly ended disastrously when she was seriously injured in an accident aboard the *Runabout Volga* during a botanical survey mission to Torad IV. Dr. Bashir saved her life, but it was necessary to remove her unborn child and implant it into the body of **Kira Nerys**. Keiko and Miles subsequently invited Kira to live with them in their quarters so that they could help care for her while she carried their child to term. ("Body Parts" [DS9]). While Kira carried her child, Keiko was captured by an alien entity known as a **Pah-wraith** who briefly gained control of her mind and body. The Pah-wraith had intended to use Keiko in an elaborate plan to kill the **Bajoran Prophets.** Fortunately, the plan failed, and Keiko was released from the entity. ("The Assignment" [DS9]). In 2373, Kira delivered **Kirayoshi O'Brien** in a traditional Bajoran birthing ceremony. ("The Begotten" [DS9]).

Keiko's first appearance was in "Data's Day" (TNG). She joined the cast of Star Trek: Deep Space Nine *in "A Man Alone" (DS9).*

O'Brien, Michael. The father of Starfleet officer **Miles Edward O'Brien**. Miles and Keiko considered naming their first child after Michael, if it was a boy. ("Disaster" [TNG]). The senior O'Brien had wanted his son, Miles, to become a cello player. When Miles was 17, Michael sent a recorded audition of his son's music to the **Aldeberan Music Academy**. He was disappointed when Miles joined Starfleet instead, but eventually became proud of his son's career. ("Shadowplay" [DS9]). Michael O'Brien became widowed in 2368 when his wife passed away. He remarried the following year. Miles O'Brien didn't like the fact that he'd never met his father's new bride. ("Whispers" [DS9]).

O'Brien, Miles (mirror). (Colm Meany). In the **mirror universe**, a Terran conscript who served on station **Terok Nor**. O'Brien held a **theta designation**, and in that capacity served as a repair technician for the mining equipment on the station. This O'Brien helped engineer the escape of Major Kira Nerys and Dr. Julian Bashir from the station in 2370. O'Brien escaped in the company of **Benjamin Sisko (mirror)**, and the two began the difficult fight to regain human freedom in the mirror universe. Sisko insisted on calling him "Smiley." ("Crossover" [DS9]). After Benjamin Sisko (mirror) was killed in 2371, the mirror O'Brien used a reconfigured transporter to abduct Commander **Benjamin Sisko** from the alternate (our) universe to complete the mirror Sisko's last mission. ("Through the Looking Glass" [DS9]). While in our universe, this O'Brien also downloaded technical information from the computer at Deep Space 9. These data permitted Terrans at Terok Nor to construct a copy of the *Starship Defiant*. The new ***Defiant* (mirror)** proved a powerful weapon for the **Terran resistance**. ("Shattered Mirror" [DS9]).

O'Brien, Miles. (Colm Meaney). Starfleet engineer, chief of operations at station Deep Space 9. ("Emissary" [DS9]). O'Brien's family resided in Dublin, Ireland, on Earth. ("Homefront" [DS9]). His ancestors included noted 20th-century union leader **Sean Aloysius O'Brien** and 11th-century Irish **King Brian Boru**. ("Bar Association" [DS9]). Prior to being assigned to Deep Space 9 in 2369, Miles Edward O'Brien had been operating transporters for some 22 years, the last six of which were spent on the *Enterprise*-D. ("Realm of Fear" [TNG]). As of 2372, he had been decorated 15 times by Starfleet Command. ("Rules of Engagement" [DS9]).

Miles, who was born in the month of September ("Whispers" [DS9]), grew up with two brothers. ("Invasive Procedures" [DS9]). During his youth, O'Brien did poorly in mechanical aptitude tests, but his later skills belied his test scores. ("Paradise" [DS9]). His father, Michael, wanted him to be a concert cellist, but two days before he was to start at the **Aldebaran Music Academy**, Miles signed up for Starfleet. ("Shadowplay" [DS9]).

Early in his Starfleet career, O'Brien had been the tactical officer aboard the ***U.S.S. Rutledge*** under the command of **Captain Benjamin Maxwell**. O'Brien's first experience

with transporters came in 2347, when the *Rutledge* responded to the Cardassian massacre at planet **Setlik III**. O'Brien repaired a balky field transporter, preventing himself and 13 Starfleet personnel from becoming Cardassian prisoners of war. He also participated in the rescue of several survivors of that bloody massacre. The experience of Setlik III scarred O'Brien deeply, and he continued to harbor bitterness against the Cardassians for many years. ("The Wounded" [TNG]). He was rewarded for his resourcefulness by being promoted to *Rutledge* tactical officer. ("Paradise" [DS9]). *Note that "Rules of Engagement" (DS9) suggests that O'Brien joined Starfleet in 2350, although the Setlik III backstory establishes that he was already in the service aboard the* Rutledge *in 2347.*

O'Brien was deathly afraid of spiders, until an incident where he had to crawl through a Jefferies tube past twenty **Talarian hook spiders** to perform a critical repair at Zayra IV. After that considerable act of courage, O'Brien said he wasn't quite so fearful of arachnids, and even kept a **Lycosa tarantula** named Christina as a pet. ("Realm of Fear" [TNG]). O'Brien once dislocated his left shoulder while kayaking on the holodeck. O'Brien was healed, almost miraculously, by a touch from the **Zalkonian** named **John Doe**. ("Transfigurations" [TNG]).

O'Brien married **Keiko Ishikawa** on stardate 44390 in a ceremony in the Ten-Forward Lounge aboard the *Enterprise*-D. Captain Jean-Luc Picard presided at the ceremony, and Data (who had first introduced Miles and Keiko to each other) served as father of the bride. ("Data's Day" [TNG]). O'Brien became a father a year later when **Molly O'Brien** was born. ("Disaster" [TNG]). O'Brien was deeply committed to his family, and was well aware of the risk that Starfleet duty entailed. He periodically recorded a "goodbye" message for his family, to be played in the event of his death. He recorded such a message every time he was about to go into battle, and as of early 2372, had done so 11 times. ("To the Death" [DS9]). His second child, **Kirayoshi O'Brien**, was born in 2373. ("The Begotten" [DS9]).

O'Brien was promoted and assigned to be chief of operations on station **Deep Space 9** in 2369, and moved there with his wife and daughter. O'Brien's technical expertise and skill at improvisation proved invaluable, given the station's generally poor condition and the lack of technical resources at the distant post. ("Emissary" [DS9]).

O'Brien almost died in 2370 after being exposed to nanobiogenic gel while helping the T'Lani and Kellerun governments to neutralize their deadly harvester weapon. He drank **coffee**, Jamaican blend, double strong, double sweet. ("Armageddon Game" [DS9]). Later that year, O'Brien was assigned to assist in preparations for the peace talks between the **Paradan** government and the rebels with whom the government had been at war. The Paradan government abducted O'Brien and replaced him with a cloned replicant that was physically identical to O'Brien. The replicant, who was programmed by the government to assassinate members of the rebel negotiating team, was given O'Brien's memories, and had no way to know that he was not the original. ("Whispers" [DS9]).

O'Brien died of severe **delta-series radio-isotope** contamination in 2371, when he was timeshifted several hours into a future in which the **Romulan** government destroyed Deep Space 9. The timeshifting was triggered by interaction of temporal displacement waves from a nearby cloaked Romulan warbird with the radioisotopes in O'Brien's body. Ironically, O'Brien's death made it possible for his future self to travel back in time to his original "present," where the future O'Brien successfully warned station personnel of the impending Romulan attack. The future O'Brien thereby effectively changed places with the present O'Brien, and continued his life in this altered reality. ("Visionary" [DS9]). *This would seem to mean that every appearance of O'Brien since "Visionary" (DS9) has been the alternate O'Brien from several hours into the future, since the original died in that episode.* The alternate O'Brien from the future fit in well, showing virtually no difference from the original O'Brien. During a rather remarkable winning streak at **darts**, this O'Brien suffered a rotator cuff tear and was forced to have **humeral socket replacement** surgery. It ended his winning streak, but allowed him to finally complete his beloved **kayaking** program. ("Shakaar" [DS9]). In 2372, O'Brien was falsely accused of espionage by the **Argrathi** government and, as punishment, was implanted with memories of a 20-year prison sentence. After returning to Deep Space 9, O'Brien suffered mental stress and hallucinations caused by the implanted memories, pushing him to the brink of suicide. With help, O'Brien was able to cope with the incident. ("Hard Time" [DS9]). When **Kira Nerys** shared the O'Briens' quarters while she served as surrogate mother to their second child in 2373, both Nerys and Miles realized that they shared a mutual attraction. They nevertheless agreed to ignore their feelings. ("Looking for *par'Mach* in All the Wrong Places" [DS9]).

Besides engineer, husband, and father, O'Brien briefly served as a substitute schoolteacher, when his wife visited her mother on Earth. ("The Nagus" [DS9]). O'Brien's off-duty pastimes also included music, and he was seen playing the cello in a string quartet in Ten-Forward aboard the *Enterprise*-D on at least one occasion. ("The Ensigns of Command" [TNG]). O'Brien liked to kayak on the holodeck and holosuite. ("Heart of Stone" [DS9], "Transfigurations" [TNG]) and enjoyed racquetball, although perhaps not quite so much as did Dr. Julian Bashir. ("Rivals" [DS9]). *O'Brien was first seen as the battle bridge conn officer in "Encounter at Farpoint" (TNG), a role he reprised in "All Good Things..." (TNG), but it was many episodes until he got a last name. He did not get a first and middle name, Miles Edward, until "Family" (TNG).*

O'Brien, Molly. (Hana Hatae). Daughter of Starfleet officers Miles O'Brien and Keiko O'Brien. Molly was born aboard the *Enterprise*-D in 2368. ("Disaster" [TNG]). She moved to station Deep Space 9 with her parents in 2369. ("Emissary, Parts I and II" [DS9]). Molly began to crawl into bed with her parents at night in early 2372, her way of trying to get attention, since her mother was pregnant with Kirayoshi at the time. ("To the Death" [DS9]). *Baby Molly was born during "Disaster" (TNG), but didn't get a name until "The Game" (TNG). She was also seen as an infant in "Power Play" (TNG). Played by Hana Hatae, Molly was first seen in "Rascals" (TNG). Her first appearance on* Star Trek: Deep Space Nine *was in "A Man Alone" (DS9). Among Molly's toys in her quarters on Deep Space 9 was a stuffed toy Klingon* targ, *hand-made by a* Star Trek *fan and loaned to the production by writer-producer Ronald D. Moore. Molly was named for Molly Berman, daughter of* Star Trek *executive producer Rick Berman, and for former* Next Generation *staffer Molly Rennie.*

O'Brien, Sean Aloysius. Noted labor leader on early 20th-century Earth. O'Brien led coal miners in Pennsylvania during the bitter

anthracite strike of 1902. The strike lasted for 11 months, ending only when all of the workers' demands had been met. Sean O'Brien was martyred before the dispute was resolved. O'Brien's bullet-ridden body was found in the Allegheny River a week before the strike's conclusion. His 24th-century descendent, Miles O'Brien, recalled with pride that Sean was not merely a hero, he was a union man. ("Bar Association" [DS9]). *The actual leader of the 1902 anthracite strike was United Mine Workers' president John Mitchell. We would be remiss if we did not mention the fact that many of the workers in the* Star Trek *television and film production teams are members of the International Alliance of Theatrical and Stage Employees (IATSE), the Writers' Guild of America, the Directors' Guild of America, the Producers' Guild of America, the Screen Actors' Guild, the International Brotherhood of Teamsters, the American Federation of Guards, the International Brotherhood of Electrical Workers, and the Paramount Office Employees' Association.*

O'Connel, Steve. (Caesar Belli). One of the surviving children of the **Starnes Expedition** whose parents committed suicide on planet **Triacus** in 2268. In the aftermath of the tragedy, young O'Connel was controlled by the **Gorgan**. ("And the Children Shall Lead" [TOS]). *Caesar Belli is the son of the late Melvin Belli, who played the Gorgan.*

O'Donnell, Juliana. SEE: **Tainer, Dr. Juliana.**

O'Neil, Lieutenant. (Sean Morgan). *Enterprise* crew member. O'Neil beamed down to planet **Beta III** in 2267 to investigate the disappearance of the *Starship* ***Archon***. He was captured by the planet's inhabitants, brainwashed, and absorbed into the society's culture by the machine entity **Landru**. ("Return of the Archons" [TOS]).

O'Neill, Ensign. *Enterprise* crew member. O'Neill participated in the search for ***Shuttlecraft Galileo*** when it crashed on planet **Taurus II** in 2267. O'Neill was killed in an incident on that planet. ("The *Galileo* Seven" [TOS]).

Oath of celibacy. A pledge required of Starfleet personnel who are native to planet **Delta IV** to assure they will not take advantage of other, sexually immature humanoid species. *(Star Trek: The Motion Picture)*. SEE: **Ilia**.

Oath, Klingon. Klingon ritual of marriage, solemnizing the bond between husband and wife in the Klingon culture. **Worf** and **K'Ehleyr** almost took the oath after they spent a night together on the *Enterprise*-D holodeck in 2365, but K'Ehleyr did not feel ready for such a commitment, even though they had just conceived a child together. ("The Emissary" [TNG]).

oatmeal. Traditional **Earth** porridge made from rolled or ground oats. Vacuum-packed oatmeal rations were available on the *Starship Voyager*. ("Phage" [VGR]). Jake Sisko enjoyed oatmeal and juice for breakfast. ("For the Cause" [DS9]).

Obachan. Japanese term of endearment used for an older woman, such as a grandmother. **Keiko O'Brien** called her grandmother Obachan. ("Violations" [TNG]).

Obatta cluster. Star system located in the Gamma Quadrant. In 2372, the **Jem'Hadar** had a presence in the Obatta cluster ("The Quickening" [DS9]).

Obelisk. A powerful asteroid deflector-beam generator built on the surface of **Miramanee's planet** centuries ago by the **Preservers**. The device was necessary because the otherwise habitable planet was located in a dangerous asteroid belt. The deflector, built in the shape of a towering monolith known to **Miramanee**'s people as the Obelisk, was inscribed with symbols that formed a tonal alphabet, giving instructions for the operation of the deflector. The knowledge of the Obelisk's operation was kept by the inhabitants' medicine man, but one such medicine man failed to pass the secrets to his son, leaving the planet defenseless by the year 2268. ("The Paradise Syndrome" [TOS]).

Oberth*-class starship.** Small Federation starship-type frequently used for scientific missions. The class was named for 20th-century German rocket pioneer Hermann Oberth. *Oberth*-class ships have included the ***Grissom *(Star Trek III)*, ***Vico*** ("Hero Worship" [TNG]), and ***Tsiolkovsky*** ("The Naked Now" [TNG]). *The first* Oberth-*class ship seen was the* U.S.S. Grissom *in* Star Trek III. *There presumably was a* U.S.S. Oberth *after which the class was named.*

Oblissian cabbage. Edible vegetation whose large leaves can be used in salads. Kes grew Oblissian cabbage in the airponics bay aboard the *Starship Voyager*. ("Elogium" [VGR]).

observation lounge. Conference room located on Deck 1 on ***Galaxy*-class** starships, directly behind the Main Bridge. The observation lounge features a large conference table and chairs, two large viewers, and several large windows that provide a dramatic vista of space. Also known as the conference lounge.

"Obsession." Original Series episode #47. Written by Art Wallace. Directed by Ralph Senensky. Stardate 3619.2. *First aired in 1967. Kirk is determined to destroy a vampiric cloud creature that years ago killed 200 people on his first Starfleet assignment, deaths Kirk felt he could have prevented.* GUEST CAST: Stephen Brooks as **Garrovick**, **Ensign**; Jerry Ayres as **Rizzo**,

Ensign; Majel Barrett as **Chapel, Christine**. SEE: **antigrav; cordrazine; *Cygnian Respiratory Diseases, A Survey of*; dikironium cloud creature; dikironium; *Farragut, U.S.S.*; Garrovick, Captain; Garrovick, Ensign; Kirk, James T.; Rizzo, Ensign; Theta VII; Tycho IV; *Yorktown, U.S.S.***

Obsidian Order. The ruthless and frighteningly efficient **Cardassian** internal security police. The Obsidian Order maintained an elaborate network that kept virtually every **Cardassian** citizen under surveillance. **Enabran Tain** was once the head of the Obsidian Order, but was retired by 2370. ("The Wire" [DS9]). The **Cardassian** military and the Obsidian Order were under the political authority of the **Detapa Council**. However, in practice, each entity acted independently. The Order was explicitly forbidden from having warships or other any other military equipment. ("Defiant" [DS9]). Nevertheless, in 2371, the Obsidian Order combined forces with the Romulan **Tal Shiar** to assemble a massive fleet in the **Orias system** in preparation for a covert first-strike mission against the **Founders** of the **Dominion**. The operation was masterminded by former Obsidian Order head **Enabran Tain**, who emerged from retirement in order to lead the attack. The joint fleet was ambushed by 150 **Jem'Hadar** ships hiding in the **Omarion Nebula**, resulting in the annihilation of all attacking ships. The debacle effectively eliminated the Obsidian Order as a viable military force in the **Alpha Quadrant**, substantially weakening the Cardassian empire as a whole. ("Improbable Cause" [DS9]). SEE: **Garak, Elim; Lovok, Colonel.** Also that year, operative **Entek** masterminded a plot to expose **Legate Ghemor**, a high-ranking member of the **Central Command**, as being aligned with the **Cardassian underground movement.** ("Second Skin" [DS9]). The Obsidian Order opposed the peace treaty that **Cardassia** signed with Bajor in 2371. ("Destiny" [DS9]). In 2373 it was learned that a few Cardassians had survived the disastrous attack in the Omarion Nebula and were being held captive by the Jem'Hadar on an asteroid in the **Gamma Quadrant**. ("In Purgatory's Shadow" [DS9]). *The Obsidian Order was first mentioned in "The Wire" (DS9).*

Ocampa planet. Fifth planet in the Ocampa system, located in the **Delta Quadrant**, and homeworld to the **Ocampa** people. The surface of the Ocampa planet was ecologically devastated a millennium ago when a group of explorers from another galaxy accidentally stripped the planet's atmosphere of **nucleogenic particles**. Even today, the surface of the Ocampa planet remains a desert. ("Caretaker" [VGR]).

Ocampa. Humanoid civilization from the **Delta Quadrant**. The Ocampa have a life span of about nine years. Ocampa communicate telepathically, as well as verbally. Legend has it that the ancient Ocampa possessed even more extraordinary telepathic and mental powers. Ocampa civilization was nearly destroyed a thousand years ago, when their planet suffered a major ecological catastrophe, accidentally triggered by intergalactic explorers. The explorers accepted responsibility for this disaster and left two of their kind behind to care for the Ocampa people. One, who became known as the **Caretaker**, created a subterranean city for the Ocampa. For over five hundred Ocampa generations, the Caretaker provided power for the city from his space borne **Array**, while protecting the Ocampa from intruders like the **Kazon-Ogla**. ("Caretaker" [VGR]). In 2072, **Suspiria**, the Caretaker's mate, took some two thousand Ocampa individuals with her to a second Array, where she helped them develop their latent psychokinetic powers so that they could join her in **Exosia**. SEE: **Suspiria's Array**. ("Cold Fire" [VGR]). The Caretaker died in 2371, at which time the city had enough energy stored to provide for the Ocampa people until 2376. ("Caretaker" [VGR]). The Ocampa bury their dead beneath the soil and believe that their *comra* or spirit is released into the afterlife. ("Emanations" [VGR]). SEE: ***elogium*; Kes** (*pictured*); ***morilogium*; Ocampa planet**.

Ocampan prayer taper. Traditional candles used by the **Ocampa**n people in meditation. Kes used Ocampan prayer tapers in 2372 when she mourned the loss of Tuvok and Neelix, who ceased to exist when they become merged into Tuvix. ("Tuvix" [VGR]).

Oceanus IV. Federation planet. The *Enterprise*-D was assigned to a diplomatic mission at Oceanus IV following its assignment at the **Phoenix Cluster** in 2368. ("The Game" [TNG]).

Ocett, Gul. (Linda Thorson). Commander of a Cardassian *Galor*-class warship. Ocett participated in the discovery of a four-billion-year-old genetically encoded message from an ancient humanoid species. ("The Chase" [TNG]). SEE: **Galen, Professor Richard; humanoid life.**

ocular implant. Cybernetic optical device that could be surgically implanted to give sight to a blind person. By stardate 50893, Lieutenant Commander **Geordi La Forge** had been given ocular implants to replace his **VISOR**. Although the implants were much smaller than his VISOR, they still afforded La Forge an equally wide range of sensory information. *(Star Trek: First Contact).*

Odan, Ambassador. (Franc Luz). A highly respected Federation ambassador and mediator. Odan was instrumental in negotiating a peace treaty between the two moons of planet **Peliar Zel** in 2337. In 2367, Odan was again asked to mediate a dispute between the **Alpha** and **Beta Moon**s, but was injured while en route to the conference, which was later held aboard the *Enterprise*-D. It was not generally known that Odan was a **Trill**, a member of a joined species. The **symbiont** known as Odan was relatively unharmed, but the humanoid host was fatally injured. Commander William Riker volunteered to serve as a temporary host for the symbiont, long enough for the ambassador to mediate the peace talks. Following the negotiations, Odan was successfully transferred into a new host body and returned to her homeworld on a Trill vessel. During the mission, Odan became romantically involved with **Beverly Crusher**. ("The Host" [TNG]). *Nicole Orth-Pallavicini played Odan's new host.*

***Ode to Psyche*.** One of the six great odes written in 1819 by the English poet John Keats (1795-1821). Deanna Troi gave William Riker an old hardbound copy of this book. She inscribed it, "To Will, all my love, Deanna." ("Conundrum" [TNG]).

"Ode to Spot." Poem written by Commander Data about his cat. ("Schisms" [TNG], "A Fistful of Datas" [TNG]).

Odell, Brenna. (Rosalyn Landor). Daughter of **Bringloidi** leader **Danilo Odell**. A beautiful but practical woman, Brenna was the real leader of her people in 2365. She was attracted to Riker, but eventually settled on one of **Walter Granger**'s clones. ("Up the Long Ladder" [TNG]).

Odell, Danilo. (Barrie Ingham). Leader of the colonists on planet **Bringloid V**. A proud Irish descendant, Odell seemed as concerned with ensuring that his daughter, **Brenna Odell**, found a suitable husband as with the safety of the colony. ("Up the Long Ladder" [TNG]).

***Odin*, S.S.** Federation freighter craft, registry number NGL-12535, disabled near planet **Angel One** in 2357 by an asteroid collision. Three **escape pod**s from this ship drifted for five months before landing on planet Angel One. ("Angel One" [TNG]).

ODN recoupler. Engineering tool. ("Hard Time" [DS9]).

ODN. Acronym for optical data network. A system of fiber-optic data-transmission conduits used aboard Federation starships, serving as the nervous system of the ship's computer network. *Enterprise*-D engineers attempted to use an ODN bypass to overcome the loss of computer control when Lieutenant **Reginald Barclay** took over the ship's computer in 2367. ("The Nth Degree" [TNG]). Computer systems aboard the *Starship Defiant* included ODN manifolds. ("Starship Down" [DS9]). An optical data network was also used in the old **Cardassian** mining station, **Deep Space 9**, although it was nowhere near as reliable as the better-maintained equipment in use aboard Federation ships. ("Emissary" [DS9]).

Odo (mirror). (Rene Auberjonois). In the **mirror universe**, supervisor of the ore-processing center on **Terok Nor (mirror).** This Odo was killed by Dr. Julian Bashir in 2370, when Bashir escaped back to his own universe. ("Crossover" [DS9]).

***odo'ital*.** Cardassian word that approximately translates into "unknown" or "nothing." When **Dr. Mora Pol** brought **Odo** into his laboratory, it was under **Cardassian** supervision. Odo's specimen was labeled "unknown sample," which was translated into Cardassian as *odo'ital*. Even after it became clear that Odo was sentient, the **Bajoran** scientists kept calling him that. As a cruel joke, they split it into two words like a Bajoran name: Odo Ital. It was eventually shortened into Odo. ("Heart of Stone" [DS9]).

Odo. (Rene Auberjonois). Security chief aboard **Cardassian** space station **Terok Nor**, who continued that function when Starfleet took over the facility in 2369. Odo was a shapeshifter, one of the **Founders** of the Gamma Quadrant's **Dominion**. ("The Search, Parts I and II" [DS9]). Odo was discovered as an infant in the **Denorios Belt** near planet Bajor, but those that rescued him had no idea where he came from, or what species he belonged to. ("Emissary" [DS9]).

When discovered in 2358 ("Broken Link" [DS9]), Odo was a shapeless mass of organic broth. He spent several years at the **Bajoran Institute of Science** being studied by **Dr. Mora Pol**, who helped Odo assimilate himself into humanoid society. Being the only one of his kind, he attempted to fit into society by being "the life of the party." He'd turn himself into any object requested by the partygoers, which only increased his feelings of isolation and loneliness. ("The Forsaken" [DS9]). Odo regarded Mora as a father figure, yet resented his cold scientific attitude and constant scrutiny. He left the institute and rebelled against Mora's influence for years. ("The Alternate" [DS9]). Odo got his name from the Cardassian word ***odo'ital***, something of a cruel joke, since it translates into "nothing." ("Heart of Stone" [DS9]). Odo did not realize that despite Mora's seemingly unfeeling treatment, the scientist truly cared for Odo, and much of his apparent cruelty was the result of ignorance about changeling physiology. ("The Begotten" [DS9]).

Odo came to **Terok Nor** in 2365, and became an unofficial arbitrator for the Bajoran nationals on the station. Later that year, station prefect **Gul Dukat** asked Odo to investigate a murder on the station. **Kira Nerys** was a suspect in that case. Dukat was so impressed with Odo's work that he made Odo chief of security for the station. ("Necessary Evil" [DS9]). In 2366, as part of his duties as Terok Nor's security chief, Odo was made an officer of the Cardassian court. This would become advantageous in 2370, following the arrest of Starfleet Officer Miles O'Brien by the Cardassian government. Using his position as an officer of the court, Odo was able to have himself assigned as O'Brien's **nestor**. ("Tribunal" [DS9]). When Benjamin Sisko was appointed acting chief of Earth security in 2372, Odo accompanied Sisko to Earth to as a consultant on protection against shape-shifter infiltration. ("Homefront" [DS9]).

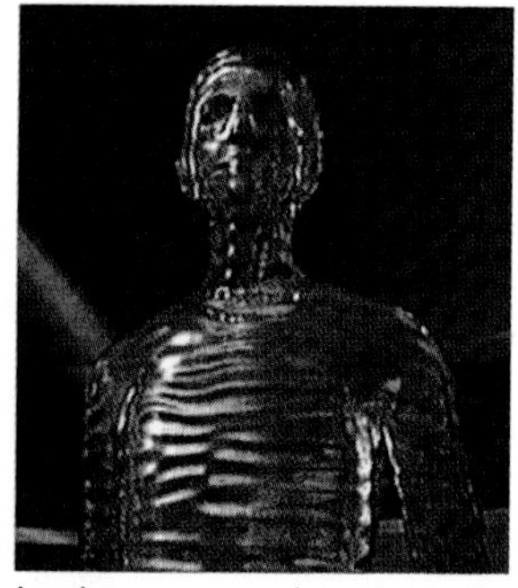

Odo maintained a humanoid form while at work on the station, but he had to return to his natural form, a viscous orange fluid, every 16 hours. ("The Storyteller" [DS9]). *(In "A Man Alone" [DS9] Odo had to return to his liquid form every 18 hours.)* Having a great respect for the rights of all lifeforms, however simple or evolved ("Playing God" [DS9]), Odo refused to carry a weapon. ("Emissary" [DS9]). He didn't need to eat and only had an approximation of a mouth and digestive system. ("The Forsaken" [DS9], "Heart of Stone" [DS9]). Once, not long after he first assumed humanoid form, he tried eating, but did not find it satisfying because he had no taste buds. ("Meridian" [DS9]). Odo could nevertheless simulate the act of drinking. He would form part of his body into a drinking glass, so that he could drink and reabsorb the liquid within, permitting him to share the social experience of dining with others. ("The Way of the Warrior" [DS9]). Odo had no sense of smell. ("If Wishes Were Horses" [DS9], "Improbable Cause" [DS9]). He patterned his own hairstyle after Dr. Mora, the scientist assigned to study him at the research center on planet **Bajor**. He did not know how to gamble ("Babel" [DS9]), but did try to take on new challenges. Odo sometimes joined Miles O'Brien when O'Brien ran his kayaking holographic simulation program, and O'Brien used to give Odo old Earth detective novels to read. ("Heart of Stone" [DS9]).

Odo was reluctant to take a mate, claiming that he would not to want to make the compromises that a relationship would demand. Odo also had an uncompromising view of law enforcement, believing that "laws change, but justice is justice." ("A Man Alone" [DS9]). Odo let his guard down slightly with Ambassador **Lwaxana Troi** in 2369 when the two were trapped together in a turbolift on the station. In their different ways, both Odo and Troi were loners, and their enforced proximity caused them to share each other's vulnerabilities. ("The Forsaken"

[DS9]). In 2371, Odo came to realize that he had romantic feelings for longtime friend **Kira Nerys**, but he was never able to successfully express these feelings to her. ("Fascination" [DS9], "Heart of Stone" [DS9]). In 2372, after his feelings for her interfered with his job, Odo decided to maintain an emotional detachment from her. ("Crossfire" [DS9]). Odo actually married Lwaxana Troi in 2372, although it was a marriage of convenience, in which Odo sought to help Troi escape from her husband, **Jeyal**. By marrying Odo, Troi became free to raise her son on Betazed, away from Tavnian traditions that would have kept her away from her child. ("The Muse" [DS9]). In 2373, Odo fell in love with **Arissa**, a woman who visited the station. It was with her that he had his first intimate experience with a humanoid woman. ("A Simple Investigation" [DS9]).

Odo yearned desperately to learn of his origins, and hoped for years to meet another individual of his species. When Crodin of the planet **Rakhar** gave him a shape-shifting necklace from the **Gamma Quadrant**, Odo began to suspect that he might find other shape-shifters in that part of the galaxy. ("Vortex" [DS9]). In early 2371, Odo found his people on a sunless planet in the **Omarion Nebula** in the Gamma Quadrant. He learned that he was a member of a species of shape-shifters who were the elusive **Founders** of the **Dominion**. To learn about the galaxy, the Founders had sent 100 infant members of their species far out into space, and placed a desire to return home into their genetic makeup. Odo was one of these infants. ("The Search, Parts I and II" [DS9]). Odo's encounter with his fellow shape-shifters gave him a greater measure of self-confidence, even though he had declined to join his people's **Great Link**. He even stopped using his bucket for regeneration periods, instead reverting to his gelatinous state in his quarters, where he began to experiment with the sensations of turning into different shapes and textures. ("The Abandoned" [DS9]). Later that same year, Odo was afforded the unique opportunity to participate in Jadzia Dax's ***zhian'tara***. But because of his shape-shifter nature, rather than just temporarily embodying the personality of **Curzon Dax**, Odo, in fact, became joined with him. The arrangement was very satisfactory for both beings, and for a time they refused to be separated. Even after Odo was persuaded to give up the Curzon personality, he retained memories of being joined with Curzon. ("Facets" [DS9]).

Odo was a security officer for most of his humanoid existence, but he had never found it necessary to fire a weapon or take a life, as he abhorred the humanoid practice of violence. Nevertheless, in 2371, he became the first of his species to harm another Founder, when he accidentally killed the Founder posing as **Ambassador Krajensky** aboard the ***U.S.S. Defiant.*** ("The Adversary" [DS9]). A year later, Odo was compelled to return to the Great Link on the **Founders' homeworld**. There, he was judged for having killed another changeling, and in punishment was made human, unable to shape-shift. ("Broken Link" [DS9]). In 2373, a **changeling infant** was discovered on station Deep Space 9. Odo became the child's surrogate parent, determined not to repeat what he saw as the cruelty with which he was raised by **Dr. Mora Pol**. Odo even spurned Mora's offers of help, but later relented when the child's health deteriorated due to exposure to **tetryon** radiation in space. Odo experienced the joy of parenthood, then the grief of loss when the radiation poisoning proved fatal. The experience helped Odo understand how much Mora had cared for him, and how much Odo's rebellion against his surrogate father had hurt Mora. Just prior to its death, the changeling infant infused itself into Odo's body, restoring Odo's shape-shifting abilities. ("The Begotten" [DS9]).

Rene Auberjonois had previously played Colonel West in Star Trek VI: The Undiscovered Country. *Odo first appeared in "Emissary" (DS9).*

Odona. (Sharon Acker). Daughter of Prime Minister **Hodin** of planet **Gideon**. In 2268, Odona volunteered to sacrifice her life by contracting deadly **Vegan choriomeningitis** so that her death might serve as an inspiration to others on her planet in their fight against overpopulation. While carrying out her assignment, Odona was cured of choriomeningitis by Dr. Leonard McCoy. She nevertheless chose to remain on her world to help solve its problems, despite the fact that she had fallen in love with Captain James Kirk. ("The Mark of Gideon" [TOS])

Odyssey, U.S.S. Federation starship, ***Galaxy*-class**, Starfleet registry number NCC-71832, commanded by **Captain Keogh**. In 2370, the *Odyssey* was dispatched to the Gamma Quadrant to investigate threats to Federation citizens made by the Jem'Hadar. The ship encountered three Jem'Hadar attack ships shortly after its arrival in the Gamma Quadrant. The *Odyssey* was destroyed while retreating from the altercation. ("The Jem'Hadar" [DS9]). *The unnamed first officer of the* Odyssey *was portrayed by Michael Jace. The* Odyssey *was named after the command module of* Apollo 13. *The dedication plaque on the* U.S.S. Odyssey *bridge set had a quote from the movie* 2001: A Space Odyssey, *"Its origin and purpose, still a total mystery."*

Off-Zel, Mark. Noted artist from planet Sirrie IV, now deceased. One of Off-Zel's vases was owned by 24th-century collector **Kivas Fajo**. ("The Most Toys" [TNG]).

offender. In the **Cardassian** court system, term applied to an individual charged with a criminal offense. The offender was always guilty. ("Tribunal" [DS9]).

Offenhouse, Ralph. (Peter Mark Richman). Human from late-20th-century Earth who died at age 55 of advanced cardiomyopathy. Offenhouse had his body cryogenically frozen upon his death, and he was revived in 2364 aboard the *Enterprise*-D. Offenhouse had been a financier, and found it difficult to cope in the largely moneyless society of the Federation. Offenhouse returned to Earth on the *Starship* ***Charleston***. ("The Neutral Zone" [TNG]). SEE: **cryonics**; **cryosatellite**.

Officer Exchange Program. A cultural exchange program in which members of the **Klingon Defense Force** and officers of the Federation **Starfleet** (and others, including the Benzites) were permitted to serve aboard ships of each other's fleets in an effort to promote intercultural understanding. In 2365, as part of this program, Riker became the first Starfleet officer to serve aboard a Klingon warship. ("A Matter of Honor" [TNG]). Klingon officer **Kurn** served aboard the *Enterprise*-D in another exchange a year later, although it was later learned that Kurn had specifically requested the *Enterprise* posting because his brother, Worf, was aboard that ship. ("Sins of the Father" [TNG]). In 2367, Klingon exobiologist **J'Dan** also served on the *Enterprise*-D through this program. ("The Drumhead" [TNG]).

"Offspring, The." *Next Generation* episode #64. Written by René Echevarria. Directed by Jonathan Frakes. Stardate 43657.0. *First aired in 1990. Data decides to become a parent and builds an android daughter. This was the first episode directed by actor Jonathan Frakes, who later directed* Star Trek: First Contact. GUEST CAST: Hallie Todd as **Lal**; Nicholas Coster as **Haftel, Admiral**; Whoopi Goldberg as **Guinan**; Judyann Elder as **Ballard, Lieutenant**; Diane Moser, Hayne Bayle, Maria Leone, James G. Becker, as Ten-Forward crew. SEE: **Andorians; android; Ballard, Lieutenant; Data; Daystrom Institute of Technology; Galor IV; Haftel, Admiral; Lal; Otar II; positronic**

brain; Selebi Asteroid Belt; Soong-type android; submicron matrix transfer technology.

Ogat Training Academy. School where Klingon youths learned the warrior disciplines. **K'mtar** wished to send the young **Alexander Rozhenko** to the Ogat Academy. He wanted the boy raised as a Klingon warrior to better defend the House of Mogh as an adult. ("Firstborn" [TNG]).

Ogawa, Nurse Alyssa. (Patti Yasutake). Member of the *Enterprise*-D medical staff. ("Future Imperfect" [TNG], "Clues" [TNG], "Identity Crisis" [TNG], "The Host" [TNG], "The Game" [TNG], "Ethics" [TNG], "Cause and Effect" [TNG], "The Inner Light" [TNG], "Man of the People" [TNG], "Realm of Fear" [TNG], "True-Q" [TNG], and "Suspicions" [TNG]). Ogawa dated one of her fellow *Enterprise*-D crew members. She said she liked him, but wasn't at all sure if she would accept his invitation to visit **Risa** with him. ("Imaginary Friend" [TNG]). Alyssa was promoted to lieutenant in 2370. Early in 2370, Ogawa began seeing Ensign Markson, another member of the *Enterprise*-D crew. ("Attached" [TNG]). The relationship did not last, and later that year, she began seeing Lieutenant Andrew Powell. Andrew proposed, and Alyssa became pregnant with their first child. During her pregnancy, Alyssa succumbed to **Barclay's Protomorphosis Syndrome**, although her fetus was unaffected. Data was able to extract some of the amniotic fluid from her pregnancy and use it to manufacture a cure for the condition. ("Genesis" [TNG]). Ogawa helped to care for injured personnel following the crash-landing of the *Enterprise*-D **Saucer Module** on planet **Veridian III** in 2371. *(Star Trek Generations).* (In another **quantum reality**, Ogawa served as chief medical officer of the Starship *Enterprise*-D. She had the unfortunate task of informing Data and Worf that Geordi had died.) ("Parallels" [TNG]). Ogawa was aboard the *Enterprise*-E in 2373 during an attempted Borg takeover of the ship. *(Star Trek: First Contact). Ogawa was first seen in "Future Imperfect" (TNG), and got a first name in "Clues" (TNG), and a last name in "Identity Crisis" (TNG). During Patti Yasutake's first few appearances, she was simply referred to in the scripts as a nameless nurse. Eventually, script coordinator (and* Star Trek *writer) Eric Stillwell was asked to come up with a Japanese name for Patti's character. Eric called Suzi Shimizu,* Star Trek: The Next Generation*'s budget estimator, for suggestions. They chose the first name Alyssa, for Suzi's daughter, and Ogawa, for Suzi's maiden name.*

Ogla. SEE: **Kazon-Ogla.**

Oglamar. SEE: **Kazon-Oglamar.**

Ogus II. Planet. The crew of the *Enterprise*-D was enjoying a two-day liberty on Ogus II in early 2367 when a medical emergency required an immediate departure to Starbase 416. ("Brothers" [TNG]).

Oguy Jel. Bajoran political activist who opposed Bajor's admission to the Federation. In 2372, he was caught scrawling political graffiti on the walls of Deep Space 9. The station's arbiter sentenced him to three weeks' community service on sanitation duty. ("Crossfire" [DS9]).

Ohn-Kor. Prytt village located near the border between **Kes** and **Prytt** territories on planet **Kesprytt III**. It was designated by the Kes as the place for *Enterprise*-D Captain Jean-Luc Picard and Dr. Beverly Crusher to rendezvous with Kes sympathizers after Picard and Crusher escaped from Prytt captivity in 2370. ("Attached" [TNG]).

Ohniaka III. Planet. Site of a Federation science station in a non-strategic sector. The outpost was staffed by 274 Starfleet personnel. In 2369, this outpost was attacked, and all personnel were lost. The attack was later discovered to be the work of a previously unknown group of self-aware, fanatical **Borg**, controlled by a figure known as **"The One."** ("Descent, Part I & II" [TNG]).

Oji. (Pamala Segall). A **Mintakan** native, daughter to **Liko**. Oji was in charge of taking the measurements on the sundial, and, at a young age, had just been appointed the official record keeper in 2366, when a Federation anthropological team was studying her planet. ("Who Watches the Watchers?" [TNG]).

OK Corral. Location of the historical gunfight in 1881 between a gang led by **Ike Clanton** and lawmen led by **Wyatt Earp** outside the Western town of **Tombstone, Arizona,** on Earth. In 2268, the **Melkotians** created a replica of the OK Corral and the famous battle between the Earps and the Clantons as a means of execution for members of the *Enterprise* crew. ("Spectre of the Gun" [TOS]).

Okala. (Louahn Lowe). Officer in the Bajoran militia. She was stationed at Deep Space 9 and stood watch in ops. ("Things Past" [DS9]).

Okalar. Humanoid **dabo** player. In 2371, Okalar had a particularly long winning streak at the dabo table at Quark's bar on Deep Space 9 ("The Abandoned" [DS9]).

Okinawa, U.S.S. Federation starship. *Excelsior* class. The *Okinawa* was once commanded by the future Admiral Leyton. Benjamin Sisko served as Executive Officer under Leyton. ("Homefront" [DS9]). Benjamin Sisko fought in the Tzenkethi war alongside Leyton while aboard the *Okinawa*. ("Paradise Lost" [DS9]). *Named for the islands in the South China Sea that were the scene of heavy fighting near the end of Earth's second world war.*

Okona, Thadiun. (William O. Campbell). Captain of the small interplanetary cargo vessel ***Erstwhile***. A loner, distrustful of authority, Okona was nonetheless a romantic at heart. He gained notoriety as intermediary between **Benzan** of planet **Straleb** and **Yanar** of planet **Altec** when the two were secretly seeing each other prior to their marriage in 2365. ("The Outrageous Okona" [TNG]).

Old Ones. Leaders of **Korob** and **Sylvia**'s homeworld in another galaxy. ("Catspaw" [TOS]).

Old Ones. Long-dead civilization on planet **Exo III**. The Old Ones had moved underground a half-million years ago when their planet's sun began to fade. In the dark underground, their culture began to become more mechanized and less human. Eventually, the Old Ones began to fear the sophisticated **androids** their ancestors had built to serve them. When the Old Ones attempted to deactivate their servants, the androids turned on their masters, destroying them. ("What Are Little Girls Made Of?" [TOS]).

olivine. Naturally-occurring gemstone created by volcanic processes. Olivine was found inside one of the artificial asteroids sent toward a **Nezu** colony world by the **Etanian Order**. ("Rise" [VGR]).

Omag's girls. (Shana O'Brien, Heather Long). Two beautiful female companions of the Ferengi arms merchant **Omag** at Qualor II in 2368. ("Unification, Part II" [TNG]).

Omag. (Bill Bastiani). Ferengi arms merchant who sometimes dealt in illicit merchandise, and helped Romulan forces to obtain spacecraft parts stolen from the Starfleet surplus depot at **Qualor II** in 2368. ("Unification, Part II" [TNG]).

Omaha Air Base. United States Air Force military facility on **Earth** during the 20th century. Omaha Air Base radar systems detected the *Starship Enterprise* in Earth's upper atmosphere in July 1969, when the ship was accidentally propelled back into Earth's past. A fighter aircraft dispatched from the base photographed the starship, necessitating a covert landing party to recover the film to eliminate evidence of the ship's presence in the past. ("Tomorrow Is Yesterday" [TOS]). SEE: **air police sergeant; Fellini, Colonel; Christopher, Captain John.**

Omarion Nebula. Interstellar dust cloud in the **Gamma Quadrant**. Inside the nebula was a sunless Class-M planet, home of the civilization of **shape-shifters** known as the **Founders**. ("The Search, Parts I and II" [DS9]).

"Omega Glory, The." *Original Series* episode #54. Written by Gene Roddenberry. Directed by Vincent McEveety. No stardate given. *First broadcast in 1968. The* Enterprise *encounters a planet where long-lived survivors of a terrible bacteriological holocaust worship the American flag. This episode was originally written in 1965 as one of three possibilities for the original* Star Trek *series' second pilot, along with "Mudd's Women" (TOS) and "Where No Man Has Gone Before" (TOS).* GUEST CAST: Morgan Woodward as **Tracey**, **Captain Ronald**; Roy Jenson as **Cloud William**; Irene Kelly as Sirah; Morgan Farley as Old Yang scholar; David L. Ross as **Galloway**, **Lieutenant**; Lloyd Kino as **Wu**; Ed McCready as Carter, Dr.; Frank Atienza as Kohm villager; Eddie Paskey as **Leslie**, **Mr.**; Paul Baxley as Kirk's stunt double. SEE: **Cloud William; *Exeter*, *U.S.S.*; fireboxes; Galloway, Lieutenant; Kohms; Leslie, Mr.; Omega IV; Prime Directive; Tracey, Captain Ronald; United States Constitution; Vulcan mind-meld; Wu; Yangs.**

Omega IV. Class-M planet whose humanoid inhabitants fought a terrible bacteriological war many centuries ago. Omega IV was visited in 2268 by the *Starship **Exeter***, commanded by **Captain Ronald Tracey**. The remaining bacterial agents in the planet's atmosphere killed all of the *Exeter*'s crew except for Tracey. ("The Omega Glory" [TOS]). SEE: **Kohms; Yangs**.

Omega Sagitta system. Solar system that includes the twin planets **Altec** and **Straleb**. The two planets form the **Coalition of Madena**. ("The Outrageous Okona" [TNG]).

Omekla III. Planet. Omekla III was the location of a **Cardassian** shipyard. ("Defiant" [DS9]).

Omet'iklan. (Clarence Williams III). **Jem'Hadar** warrior who, in early 2372, participated in a joint Jem'Hadar-Federation mission to prevent renegade Jem'Hadar soldiers from gaining control of an **Iconian gateway**. Omet'iklan found Starfleet discipline lax, and could not understand why Benjamin Sisko declined to kill one of his officers for a minor breach of orders. Omet'iklan killed his Second for such a breach, and later killed **Weyoun**, a **Vorta** field operative, for doubting his loyalty. ("To the Death" [DS9]). *Clarence Williams III played Linc Hayes in* The Mod Squad, *which was produced by future* Star Trek *movie producer Harve Bennett.*

Omicron Ceti III. Beautiful Class-M planet bombarded by deadly berthold radiation, rendering it unsuitable for humanoid habitation. In 2264, prior to the discovery of **berthold rays**, Omicron Ceti III was colonized by an agricultural expedition led by **Elias Sandoval**. Approximately one hundred of the original 150 colonists died from berthold ray exposure. The *Starship Enterprise* visited the colony site in 2267, finding that about fifty colonists had survived due to protection offered by alien spores found on the planet. ("This Side of Paradise" [TOS]). SEE: **Kalomi, Leila; spores, Omicron Ceti III**.

Omicron Delta region. Area of space where the **amusement park planet** was located. The original *Starship Enterprise* visited the Omicron Delta region in 2267. ("Shore Leave" [TOS]).

Omicron IV. Planet that nearly destroyed itself in a nuclear arms race that escalated to the launching of orbital nuclear weapons platforms, much as **Earth** did in the late 1960s. **Gary Seven** said this behavior almost destroyed all life on Omicron IV and would do the same on Earth unless something was done to stop the arms race. ("Assignment: Earth" [TOS]). *Fortunately,* Star Trek*'s warning of nuclear weapons in Earth orbit has not yet been fulfilled.*

omicron particles. Rare subatomic particles created by certain types of matter/antimatter reactions. The holographic inhabitants on planet **Yadera II** were composed of omicron particles that were created by a **hologenerator** in the center of their village. ("Shadowplay" [DS9]). Omicron particles can also be used to produce antimatter. The immense **nucleogenic cloud being** encountered by the *Voyager* in 2371 contained high levels of omicron particles, which the being used as a circulatory medium. ("The Cloud" [VGR]).

Omicron Theta. Planet. Location of a Federation science and farming colony devastated in 2336 by the mysterious **Crystalline Entity**. The colony was the site of a hidden laboratory at which Noonien Soong, and his wife, Juliana, conducted advanced work in robotics. Together, they constructed five positronic androids, including Data and Lore. ("Inheritance" [TNG]). Just prior to the destruction of the colony, memories from all the colonists were stored in Data's positronic brain. Soong apparently escaped from the colony shortly thereafter. The crew of the *Starship **Tripoli*** discovered the android Data in 2338 at the remains of the colony. A second expedition in 2364 by an away team from the *Enterprise*-D (including Data) discovered the second android, Lore, at the colony site. ("Datalore" [TNG]).

Onara. (David Carpenter). Bajoran national residing on station Deep Space 9 in 2372. ("Accession" [DS9]).

Onaya. (Meg Foster). **Noncorporeal life**-form who lived on neural energy from the act of creativity in humanoid minds. Onaya stimulated her victims' brain's production of neurotransmitters, intensifying creativity, but shortening their lives. Onaya appeared as a humanoid female at station Deep Space 9 in 2372, where she inspired **Jake Sisko** to write the first draft of his novel, ***Anslem***. Benjamin Sisko, learning of the danger to his son, drove Onaya away into open space. Onaya had similarly inspired and caused the premature death of more than a hundred artists including such renowned names as Catullus, Revalus, **Phineas Tarbolde**, Cardassian architect **Tavor Kell**, and 19th-century Earth poet **John Keats**. ("The Muse" [DS9]).

"One moon circles." A telepathic message sent to Counselor Deanna Troi by an unknown vessel trapped with the *Enterprise*-D in a **Tyken's Rift.** The message described atomic hydrogen and the aliens' need for hydrogen to produce an explosion to rupture the rift so that both ships could escape. ("Night Terrors" [TNG]).

"11001001." *Next Generation* episode #16. Written by Maurice Hurley and Robert Lewin. Directed by Paul Lynch. Stardate 41365.9. *First aired in 1988. A group of Bynars hijack the* Enterprise-*D in hopes of using the ship's computer to restart their planetary computer system. This is the first episode in which we saw Data's hobby of painting and Riker's love of the trombone.* GUEST CAST: Carloyn McCormick as **Minuet**; Gene Dynarski as **Quinteros, Commander Orfil**; Katy Boyer as Zero One; Alexandra Johnson as One Zero; Iva Lane as Zero Zero; Kelli Ann McNally as One One; Jack Sheldon as Piano player; Abdul Salaam El Razzac as Bass player; Ron Brown as Drummer. SEE: **antimatter containment; autodestruct; Beta Magellan; buffer; Bynars; Bynaus; cybernetic regeneration; Epstein, Dr. Terence; *Galaxy*-Class Starship Development Project; holodeck; Low Note, The; *Melbourne*, *U.S.S.*; Minuet; painting; parrises squares; Pelleus V; Quinteros, Commander Orfil; Riker, William T.; Starbase 74; Tarsas III; *Trieste*, *U.S.S.*; trombone; *Wellington*, *U.S.S.*; *zylo* eggs.**

"One, The." Title taken by the android **Lore** in 2369, following his takeover of a group of rogue **Borg**. ("Descent, Part I" [TNG]).

One. Philosophy that rejected the advances of modern technological society in favor of a simpler life. The renegade scientist **Dr. Sevrin** and his followers embraced this philosophy in their search for the mythical planet Eden in 2269. ("The Way to Eden" [TOS]).

Ongilin caviar. Culinary delicacy made from fish eggs. Deanna Troi ordered Ongilin caviar while under the influence of **Barclay's Protomorphosis Syndrome** in 2370. Craving something salty, Deanna had a double order for lunch. ("Genesis" [TNG]).

Onias Sector. Region of space located near the **Romulan Neutral Zone**. The *Enterprise*-D conducted a security survey there in 2367. ("Future Imperfect" [TNG]). SEE: **Barash**.

onion rings. Circular slices of onion, deep fried and served as a side dish, usually to accompany a main course of meat. While incarcerated in an Akritirian prison satellite, Tom Paris dreamed of eating onion rings when he was free again. ("The Chute" [VGR]).

***Onizuka*, *Shuttlepod*.** Shuttle 7, attached to the *Starship Enterprise*-D. Data piloted the *Onizuka* to planet **Tau Cygna V** when it was necessary to evacuate the colony there. ("The Ensigns of Command" [TNG]). Geordi La Forge flew the *Onizuka* from the *Enterprise*-D to planet **Risa** for an artificial-intelligence seminar in 2367. It was later revealed that La Forge and the *Onizuka* were abducted in midflight, then returned to the *Enterprise*-D with La Forge under Romulan mental control. ("The Mind's Eye" [TNG]). *The* Onizuka *was named for* Challenger *astronaut Ellison Onizuka. The shuttle was sometimes seen in other episodes, sitting in the shuttlebay. The* Onizuka *was Shuttle 7, although in its first appearance it had the number 05, left over from the prop's first appearance as the* **El-Baz**. *A tiny replica of the* Shuttlepod Onizuka *is on display at the Ellison Onizuka Space Center museum in Kona, Hawai'i, Ellison's hometown.*

onkian. Unit of temperature measure used by the **Romulan Star Empire**. A reading of 12 onkians corresponds to a temperature somewhat above the freezing point of water. ("The Defector" [TNG]).

onlies. Slang on **Miri**'s planet for the children who survived the disastrous results of the **Life Prolongation Project**, the "only" ones who remained. ("Miri" [TOS]). *Several of the children portraying the onlies were children of members of the production team and included the children of Grace Lee Whitney, William Shatner, and Gene Roddenberry.*

***oo-mox*.** Ferengi sexual foreplay, involving a gentle massaging of the ears, considered one of their most erogenous zones. **Lwaxana Troi** was very skilled at the art of *oo-mox*. ("Ménage à Troi" [TNG]). Archaeologist and entrepreneur **Vash** gave Quark *oo-mox* at Deep Space 9 in 2369 when negotiating what percentage Quark would receive from the auction of the relics brought back from the Gamma Quadrant. Quark claimed he was not distracted by the treatment. ("Q-Less" [DS9]). **Emi** performed *oo-mox* on Quark while negotiating with him for the purchase of **self-sealing stem bolts**. ("Prophet Motive" [DS9]).

Oort cloud. Distant comets that sometimes orbit the outer periphery of a solar system. In 2370, **Miles O'Brien** suggested hiding sensor probes in the **Bryma** system's Oort cloud to detect **Maquis** ships. ("The Maquis, Part II" [DS9]).

Opaka, Kai. (Camille Saviola). Spiritual and political leader of the **Bajoran** people. In 2369, **Deep Space 9** Commander **Benjamin Sisko** turned to her in hopes that she could help unite the many contentious factions that threatened to bring civil war to **Bajor**. Opaka, in turn, identified Sisko as the prophesied **Emissary** who would save her people. ("Emissary" [DS9]). Compelled by the **Prophets**, Opaka visited Deep Space 9 later that year, and prevailed upon Sisko to allow her to travel through the **Bajoran wormhole** and visit the Gamma Quadrant. On that trip, Opaka was killed when the runabout ***Yangtzee Kiang***, carrying Opaka, Sisko, Bashir, and Kira Nerys, crashed on a moon in the Gamma Quadrant. She was brought back to life by unusual artificial microbes on that moon. Unfortunately, the nature of the microbes keeping her alive made it impossible for her to leave that world. Opaka accepted this as a sign that the Prophets wanted her to remain there to help bring peace to the warring prisoners incarcerated on that moon. ("Battle Lines" [DS9]). Following the disappearance of

Opaka from the Bajoran religious community, an intense power struggle ensued to determine who would ascend to be the next kai. ("In the Hands of the Prophets" [DS9]). SEE: **Bareil, Vedek; Neela; Winn**. One such power struggle evolved in 2370 when Vedek Bareil concealed evidence related to the late kai's son. Opaka lost her son in the infamous **Kendra Valley massacre**. Bajoran **Prylar Bek** was believed to have provided the Cardassians with information that lead to the massacre, but it was never revealed that Opaka had been the actual informant, sacrificing her son and 42 other freedom fighters to save the lives of some 1,200 other Bajorans. **Vedek Bareil** concealed evidence of her involvement, and years later, even withdrew his bid to become Opaka's replacement as kai in order to protect her name. ("The Collaborator" [DS9]). In 2372, Kai Opaka appeared to Benjamin Sisko in an **Orb shadow** experience. In the vision, Opaka warned him to remember that he was the Emissary. ("Accession" [DS9]).

Open Sky. Akritirian terrorist group. In 2373, Open Sky used a trilithium-based explosive device to bomb the **Laktivia** recreation facility on **Akritiri**, killing 47 off-duty patrollers. ("The Chute" [VGR]).

opera, Klingon. SEE: **Klingon opera**.

Operation Retrieve. Code name for a proposed military strike operation advocated by Starfleet Command to recover Kirk and McCoy, when they were wrongly imprisoned by the Klingon government for the murder of **Chancellor Gorkon** in 2293. The **Federation president** decided not to authorize Operation Retrieve when Chancellor **Azetbur** offered to continue her late father's peace initiative in exchange for a pledge of no military action to rescue Kirk and McCoy. *(Star Trek VI: The Undiscovered Country). The scene in which **Admiral Cartwright** and **Colonel West** propose Operation Retrieve to the Federation president was deleted from the theatrical release of* Star Trek VI*, but was restored for the videocassette and laser disk version.*

Operations Center. Also known as ops. Command facility for station **Deep Space 9**, where the various functions of the station were coordinated. Ops was located in the uppermost section of the station's central core. In keeping with **Cardassian** architecture, the prefect's office is at the highest level, allowing the commander to look down upon the crew working in ops. ("Emissary" [DS9]).

operations manager. On recent Federation starships, the operations manager, usually known as ops, is the **bridge** officer responsible for coordination of the various departmental functions aboard the ship. Ops is one of two freestanding consoles located directly ahead of the captain's chair in most bridge designs. Lieutenant Commander **Data** was the operations manager on the *Starship Enterprise*-D. Also referred to as an operations officer.

"Operation: Annihilate!" Original Series episode #29. Written by Steven W. Carabatsos. Directed by Herschel Daugherty. Stardate 3287.2. *First aired in 1967. At a Federation colony, Kirk finds his brother and sister-in-law are victims of neural parasites causing planetwide insanity. This was the last episode of the original series's first season.* GUEST CAST: Joan Swift as **Kirk**, **Aurelan**; Zahra Maurishka as Yeoman; Majel Barrett as **Chapel**, **Christine**; Craig Hundley as **Kirk**,

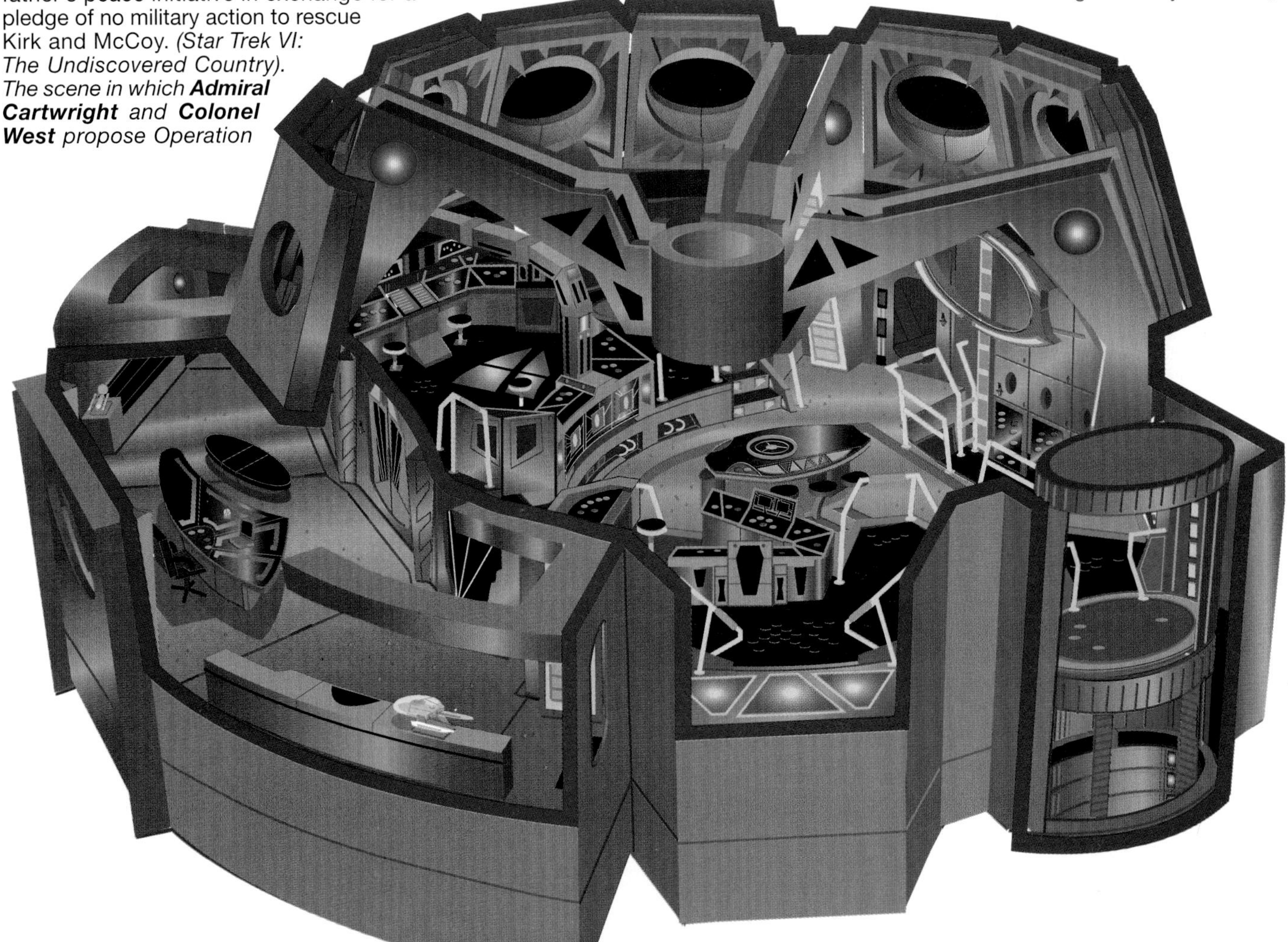

Peter; Fred Carson as First Denevan; Jerry Catron as Second Denevan; Dave Armstrong as Kartan; Gary Coombs as Kirk's stunt double; Bill Catching as Spock's stunt double; Eddie Paskey as Transporter chief; William Shatner as Sam Kirk's body. SEE: **Beta Portolan system; Deneva; Denevan neural parasite; Denevan ship; *Enterprise*, *U.S.S.*; GSK 739; Ingraham B; inner eyelid; K-3 indicator; Kirk, Aurelan; Kirk, George Samuel; Kirk, James T.; Kirk, Peter; Levinius V; Scott, Montgomery; Spock; Starbase 10; Theta Cygni XII; tri-magnesite; ultraviolet satellite; Vulcans.**

ophidian. Snakelike entity with extradimensional properties. The life-forms of **Devidia II** used ophidians in their plan to steal neural energy from Earth people. When irradiated with the proper energy, the ophidian made it possible for the **Devidians** to travel to and from Earth's past. ("Time's Arrow, Parts I and II" [TNG]).

Ophiucus III. Class-M planet. Ophiucus III was **Harcourt Fenton Mudd**'s attempted destination for delivery of three beautiful woman he had recruited as wives for settlers in 2266. ("Mudd's Women" [TOS]).

ops. Abbreviation for **operations manager** aboard Federation starships; also the nickname for the **Operations Center** aboard station **Deep Space 9**. ("Emissary" [DS9]).

opti-cable. Fiber-optic data-transmission cable used aboard Federation starships; part of their **ODN**, optical data network. ("Peak Performance" [TNG]).

optical transducer. Component of Geordi La Forge's **VISOR**. The transducer received electromagnetic radiation from the environment and translated it into bio-electric impulses that could be interpreted by his brain. Following Geordi's injury by a phaser blast in 2369, Dr. Crusher adjusted the transducer to block some of the pain receptors in Geordi's brain. ("Starship Mine" [TNG]).

Oracle. Sophisticated computer, constructed by the creators of the ***Yonada*** asteroid/ship that acted as a religious edifice, guiding the **Fabrini** people through the journey to their promised land. ("For the World Is Hollow and I Have Touched the Sky" [TOS]). SEE: **Natira**. *James Doohan provided the voice of the Oracle.*

orange juice. Beverage made with pulp from an Earth citrus fruit. **Jake Sisko** was fond of orange juice. ("The Muse" [DS9], "The Assignment" [DS9]). Neelix used orange juice as an ingredient in a new experimental breakfast drink served on the *Voyager* on stardate 50126.4. ("Flashback" [VGR]).

Orb of Change. SEE: **Orb of Prophecy.**

Orb of Prophecy. One of the sacred **Orbs** given to the **Bajoran** people by the **Prophets**. After encountering Orb of Prophecy 3000 years ago, **Trakor** wrote down several prophecies. ("Destiny" [DS9]). Also known as the Orb of Prophecy and Change, as well as the Orb of Change. ("The Circle" [DS9]). **Benjamin Sisko**, the **Emissary** of the Bajoran people, experienced a plasma burst in 2373, leaving him with prophetic visions or ***pagh'tem'far***. He subsequently had an encounter with the Orb of Prophecy in order to bring his visions into focus. ("Rapture" [DS9]).

Orb of Time. One of the sacred **Orbs** of the **Bajoran** people. A powerful orb, with proper use the Orb of Time could actually permit one to travel in time. The Cardassians confiscated the Orb during the occupation and then returned it to the Bajorans in 2373. Former Klingon agent **Arne Darvin** used the Orb of Time to take the *U.S.S. Defiant* back in time 105 years to station K-7 in 2267, so that he could try to kill James Kirk. ("Trials and Tribble-ations" [DS9]).

Orb of Wisdom. One of the sacred **Orbs** of the **Bajoran** people. In 2371, the Orb of Wisdom was obtained by **Grand Nagus Zek** from a contact on **Cardassia III**. Zek tried to use the Orb to see into the future, but instead encountered the wormhole aliens, also known as the Bajoran **Prophets**. ("Prophet Motive" [DS9]).

Orb shadow. Vision-like hallucinatory experience that sometimes occured weeks or months later to persons who have been exposed to an **Orb** of the **Prophets**. The Bajorans believed that a person experienced an Orb shadow when they ignored what the Prophets told them during their Orb encounter. ("Accession" [DS9]).

Orb. Also known as **Tears of the Prophets**, the Orbs were mystical artifacts of the **Bajoran** religion. Nine Orbs, which were hourglass-shaped energy vortices, were discovered in the Bajoran star system over the past 10,000 years. The Bajorans believed the Orbs were sent by the Prophets from the Celestial Temple to teach them and guide their lives. All but one of the Orbs were stolen by the **Cardassians** when they ended their occupation of Bajor in 2369. The remaining Orb planted visions in the mind of **Benjamin Sisko** that enabled him to relive experiences from his past. The Orbs were enshrined in ornately jeweled cases and had been cared for by Bajoran monks at a monastery on the planet. ("Emissary" [DS9]). The Third Orb, which remained with the Bajorans, was known as the Orb of Prophecy and Change. **Vedek Bareil** invited Kira Nerys to encounter this Orb in 2370. The experience had a profound effect on her life. Encounters with any of the Orbs by tradition were to be approved by the **Vedek Assembly**, though in practice, very few held to that formality. ("The Circle" [DS9]). The 2371 peace treaty between the Bajorans and the Cardassians did not address the issue of whether or not the Cardassians would be required to return the Bajoran Orbs stolen during the occupation. ("Life Support" [DS9]). Later that year, Grand Nagus **Zek** obtained the **Orb of Wisdom** from contacts on Cardassia III. Using the Orb, Zek communicated with the **Prophets** and was profoundly, but temporarily changed before he attempted to sell the artifact back to the Bajoran people. ("Prophet Motive" [DS9]). SEE: **Orb shadow**. The Cardassian government returned the **Orb of Time** to the Bajorans in 2373. ("Trials and Tribble-ations" [DS9]).

orbital habitats. Large artificial structures designed for human habitation in space. In 2371, there were a number of orbital habitats orbiting the planet **Earth**. ("Past Tense, Part I" [DS9]).

orbital office complex. Space station orbiting **Earth**, part of Starfleet's **San Francisco Yards** facility. Admiral **James Kirk** beamed to the orbital office complex before traveling to the refurbished *Starship Enterprise* while it was in orbital drydock in 2271. *(Star Trek: The Motion Picture).*

orbital tether. Space transportation system providing access to planetary orbit by means of an extremely long cable stretching from a ground station on the planet's surface to a space station in **synchronous orbit**. Carriage vehicles ride the cable between the ground and orbital stations. An orbital tether system on a **Nezu**

colony world used mag-lev carriages for this purpose. Planet **Rinax** also had an orbital tether system, on which **Neelix** worked for two years as a maintenance technician. ("Rise" [VGR]).

Ordek Nebula. Interstellar gas cloud. The home of the Wogneer creatures. ("Allegiance" [TNG]).

Order of the *Bat'leth*. SEE: ***Bat'leth,* Order of the.**

Orelious IX. Planet destroyed a thousand years ago during the final conflict between the **Promellians** and the **Menthars**. Although neither side expected this battle to be decisive, the devastation was so great that both cultures were utterly destroyed and the planet was reduced to rubble. In 2366, in the asteroid-field remains of the planet, the *Enterprise*-D discovered the hulk of the Promellian battle cruiser ***Cleponji***, along with several hundred thousand deadly **aceton assimilators.** ("Booby Trap" [TNG]).

Orellius Minor. F-type star located near the Alpha Quadrant terminus of the Bajoran wormhole. ("Paradise" [DS9]).

Orellius. Class-M planet orbiting 160 million kilometers from **Orellius Minor**. Isolated from trade routes, Orellius was the crash site for the transport ship ***Santa Maria.*** The passengers of the *Santa Maria* subsequently colonized Orellius. ("Paradise" [DS9]). SEE: **Alixus; duonetic field.**

Organia. Class-M planet. The only habitable world in a zone disputed by the Federation and the Klingon Empire in 2267. Organia was ideally located for usage by either side as a strategic base. Its inhabitants, the **Organians**, appeared as simple humanoids in an agrarian culture, but in reality were highly evolved **noncorporeal life**-forms. ("Errand of Mercy" [TOS]).

Organian Peace Treaty. Imposed by the **Organians** in 2267 after the incident on planet **Organia** between the **United Federation of Planets** and the **Klingon Empire**. The Organian Peace Treaty decreed that the Organians would tolerate no hostilities between the Klingons and the Federation. ("Errand of Mercy"[TOS], "Day of the Dove" [TOS]). The treaty provided that any planet disputed between the two powers would be awarded to the side that demonstrated it could develop that planet most efficiently. There was also a provision allowing for starship crews from either side to use shore facilities (such as space stations) of the other. ("The Trouble with Tribbles" [TOS]).

Organians. Inhabitants of planet **Organia** who appeared to be simple primitive people with absolutely no advancement in tens of thousands of years. In reality the Organians were highly advanced **noncorporeal life**-forms who developed beyond the need for physical bodies millions of years ago. When Klingon forces sought to occupy Organia in 2267 for the planet's strategic value, the Organians rejected both the Klingons and the Federation, asserting they had no interest in their dispute. Following a declaration of war by the two antagonists, the Organians imposed the **Organian Peace Treaty** to prevent hostilities. ("Errand of Mercy" [TOS]). SEE: **Ayelborne**.

Orias III. Class-M planet located in the Orias system in **Cardassian** space. The **Obsidian Order** based a secret operation on Orias III in 2371. ("Defiant" [DS9]). The secret project was later found to be a joint operation of the Obsidian Order and the Romulan **Tal Shiar**, in which a massive attack fleet was assembled for a disastrous attempted first strike against the **Founders** of the **Dominion**. ("Improbable Cause" [DS9]). SEE: **Riker, Thomas.**

Orias system. Planetary system in **Cardassian** space. ("Defiant" [DS9], "Improbable Cause" [DS9]).

Orient Express. Transcontinental fixed-rail transportation system on **Earth** that provided service between the cities of **Paris** and Istanbul from 1883 to 1977. *Enterprise*-D officer Beverly Crusher programmed a **holodeck** re-creation of this romantic historical setting, complete with interesting travel partners. ("Emergence" [TNG]). *Characters in Crusher's Orient Express program, as modified by the emergent life-form, included a conductor (played by David Huddleston), an engineer (played by Thomas Kopache), a hitman (played by Vinny Argio), "hayseed" (played by Arlee Reed), two flappers (played by D. Michaels and D. Zanuck), a gunslinger (played by S. Whittaker), a knight-in-armor (played by C. Gilman), and a man in a gray flannel suit (played by regular stand-in Dennis Tracy).* SEE: **emergent life-form holodeck sequence.**

Orillian lung maggot. Form of life indigenous to the Orillian homeworld. Neelix called **Tosin** an Orillian lung maggot. ("Fair Trade" [VGR]).

Orinoco, U.S.S. *Danube*-class **runabout**, Starfleet registry number NCC-72905, attached to station Deep Space 9. ("The Siege" [DS9]). The *Orinoco* was destroyed in 2372 when a Cardassian separatist group calling themselves **The True Way** sabotaged the runabout's warp core. ("Our Man Bashir" [DS9]). *The* Orinoco *was first seen in "The Siege" (DS9). It was also seen in "Invasive Procedures" (DS9), "Shadowplay" (DS9), "Paradise" (DS9), "The Maquis, Part II" (DS9), and "The Jem'Hadar" (DS9). The* Orinoco *was named after the 1700-mile-long river in Venezuela.*

Orion animal women. Sensual, seductive, and green-skinned, these humanoid females were a commodity of trade in the seamier parts of the galaxy during the 23rd century. Christopher Pike saw **Vina** as an illusory Orion slave woman while both were under control of the **Talosians** in 2254. ("The Cage," "The Menagerie, Part II" [TOS]). Marta, the insane consort of Captain Garth, was Orion. ("Whom Gods Destroy" [TOS]). In 2373, Quark had an energetic holosuite program that featured three Orion slave girls. ("The Begotten" [DS9]). *Actor Majel Barrett was painted green for the initial makeup tests for this blatantly sexist character. Ironically, Barrett would also play the progressive part of Number One, second-in-command of the* Enterprise *in "The Cage" (TOS).*

Orion Syndicate. Powerful criminal organization based in the Alpha Quadrant. Members were known to take their own lives before being compelled to testify against the syndicate. **Quark** had some dealings with the notorious Orion Syndicate, but they didn't allow him to join because he couldn't afford the substantial membership fee. ("The Ascent" [DS9]). **Draim**, who specialized in blackmail and extortion, was a member of the syndicate. ("A Simple Investigation" [DS9]).

Orion wing-slug. Life-form. Ambassador **Lwaxana Troi** said she would rather eat Orion wing-slugs than deal with **DaiMon Tog**. ("Ménage à Troi" [TNG]).

Orion. Constellation near Taurus containing the stars Rigel and Betelgeuse. ("Journey to Babel" [TOS]). SEE: **Orions**. In 2372, Quark attempted to smuggle **kemacite** to Orion aboard his ship, *Quark's Treasure*. ("Little Green Men" [DS9]).

Orions. Humanoid civilization. Orion operatives attempted to sabotage the **Babel Conference** of 2267. An Orion vessel fired on the *Enterprise*, which was transporting delegates to the Babel conference. At the time, Orion smugglers had been raiding the **Coridan** system and stealing **dilithium** crystals to sell on the black market. Their attack was intended to prevent Coridan's admission to the Federation. ("Journey to Babel" [TOS]). SEE: **Thelev**.

Orkett's disease. Viral sickness. Orkett's disease swept through the Bajoran work camps during the Cardassian occupation of Bajor, killing thousands of children. ("State of Flux" [VGR]).

Ornara. The third planet in the **Delos** star system, home to an intelligent humanoid species, the **Ornarans**. ("Symbiosis" [TNG]).

Ornarans. Humanoid species native to planet Ornara. The Ornarans had suffered from a deadly plague two centuries ago, a plague that was cured with the medication **felicium** from the planet **Brekka**. Unfortunately, felicium was later found to have powerfully addictive narcotic effects, with the result that all Ornarans had become addicted to the drug. The people of Brekka exploited the situation, selling felicium to the Ornarans, while concealing from them the fact that the drug was no longer needed to control the plague. Generations of drug addiction resulted in loss of intelligence and technical knowledge, so by the year 2364, the Ornarans no longer had the ability to maintain the interplanetary freighters they needed to transport felicium from Brekka to Ornara. The Ornarans, along with the Brekkians, requested Federation assistance in repairing their remaining ships, but *Enterprise*-D Captain Picard declined to render aid, citing **Prime Directive** considerations. ("Symbiosis" [TNG]).

Ornathia resistance cell. Bajoran resistance group responsible for the historic **Pullock V raid** during the **Cardassian** occupation of Bajor. **Lenaris Holem** was a member of the Ornathia resistance cell. ("Shakaar" [DS9]).

Ornithar. (John Fleck). **Karemma** official. Ornithar was one of Quark's business partners in the Ferengi purchases of **tulaberry wine** from the **Dominion**. Ornithar also helped Sisko and his crew find the **Founders** by telling them of the Dominion's relay station on Callinon VII. ("The Search, Part I" [DS9]). *John Fleck also played Taibak, a Romulan, in "The Mind's Eye" (TNG).*

ornithology. Branch of zoology that deals with the study of birds. Ornithology was an apparent interest of **Commander Calvin Hutchinson**. ("Starship Mine" [TNG]).

Orpax, Dr. Ferengi physician. In 2372, Dr. Orpax gave Quark his annual insurance physical and diagnosed Quark with Dorek syndrome. Dr. Orpax's diagnosis was wrong; Quark did not have Dorek syndrome. ("Body Parts" [DS9]).

Orr. Starfleet officer. Orr served aboard the ***U.S.S. Okinawa*** while Benjamin Sisko was the vessel's executive officer. In 2372, Orr and several other former *Okinawa* officers were reassigned by **Admiral Leyton** in preparation for his attempted coup of Earth's government. ("Paradise Lost" [DS9]).

Orra, Jil. (Heather L. Olson). Daughter of **Gul Madred**. Madred allowed young Jil Orra into the interrogation room where Picard was being tortured. ("Chain of Command, Part II" [TNG]).

Orta. (Jeffrey Hayenga). Leader of a splinter group of Bajoran terrorists. Orta's hatred of **Cardassians** began with an incident in which he was captured by the Cardassians, tortured, and had his vocal cords severed. He was later able to communicate by means of a voice synthesizer embedded in his neck. In 2368, Orta was suspected of being behind an attack on a Federation colony, but it was later learned that the Cardassians were responsible. ("Ensign Ro" [TNG]).

Orton, Mr. (Glenn Morshower). Station administrator of **Arkaria Base**. In 2369, Orton, a native of Arkaria, collaborated with a group of politically nonaligned terrorists to steal **trilithium resin** from the *Enterprise*-D at the **Remmler Array.** ("Starship Mine" [TNG]). *Glenn Morshower also played Lieutenant Burke in "Peak Performance" (TNG) and was the navigator of the* U.S.S. Enterprise-*B in* Star Trek Generations.

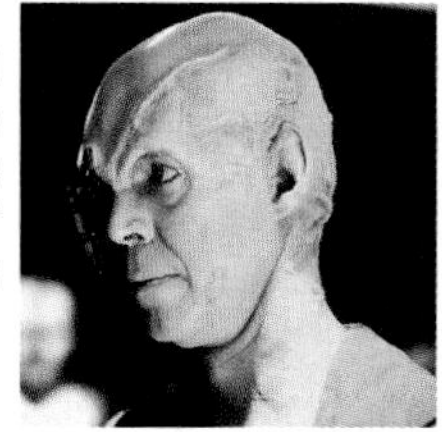

Orum. (Ivar Brogger). A **Romulan** national assimilated by the **Borg**, possibly in the Battle of **Wolf 359**. He later became the medical-care provider for a community of former Borg drones living on a planet in the **Nekrit Expanse** in the **Delta Quadrant**. ("Unity" [VGR]).

Osinar VI. Planet. **Leanne**'s friend Riska had an uncle who ran a bar on Osinar VI. ("Life Support" [DS9]).

oskoid. A leaflike Betazoid delicacy, a favorite of **Lwaxana Troi**. ("Ménage à Troi" [TNG], "Half a Life" [TNG]).

osmotic pressure therapy. Medical treatment used to treat **hemocythemia**. ("Deadlock" [VGR]).

osteogenic stimulator. Medical device. Used to accelerate healing of bone fractures. ("Distant Voices" [DS9], "Resolutions" [VGR]).

Otar II. Planet, the location of a starbase. Destination of the *Enterprise*-D following the death of Data's daughter, **Lal**, in 2366. ("The Offspring" [TNG])

Otel, Jaret. (Andrew Hill Newman). Native of planet **Sikaris**, and an associate of Sikarian magistrate **Gathorel Labin**. Acting against Sikarian law, Otel traded **trajector** technology in exchange for a library of Federation literature. ("Prime Factors." [VGR]).

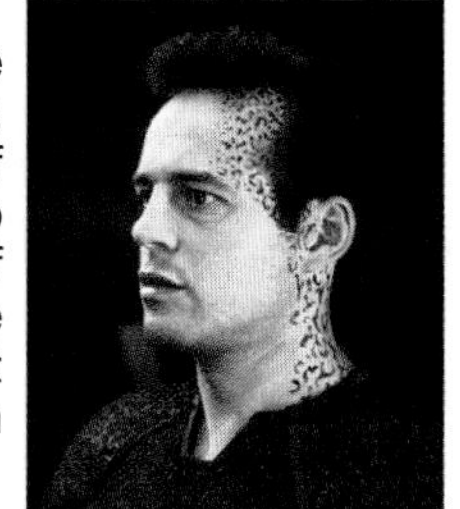

Otner, Dr. Bejal. (Tim Ryan). Scientist at the Trill science ministry and brother of Dr. **Lenara Kahn**. Bejal Otner was a member of the science team that visited station Deep Space 9 in 2372 to attempt the creation of an **artificial wormhole**. He had a close relationship with his sister and worried that she might risk all by reassociating with Jadzia Dax. ("Rejoined" [DS9]).

Otto. Genetically engineered human male, follower of former Earth dictator **Khan Noonien Singh**. Otto, along with Khan and other genetic "supermen," escaped Earth in the sleeper ship ***S.S. Botany Bay***. ("Space Seed"[TOS]).

***oumriel*.** In the **Halii** language, the word for a special friend. **Aquiel Uhnari** called Geordi *oumriel*. ("Aquiel" [TNG]).

"Our Man Bashir." *Deep Space Nine* episode #82. Teleplay by Ronald D. Moore. Story by Robert Gillian. Directed by Winrich Kolbe. No stardate given. *First aired in 1995. A transporter mishap results in Sisko, Worf, Kira, Dax, and O'Brien entering Dr. Bashir's secret-agent program in the holosuite as a 20th-century mad scientist and his henchman, a beautiful professor, an assassin, and a Russian agent.* GUEST CAST: Max Grodénchik as **Rom**; Kenneth Marshall as **Eddington, Michael**; Andrew Robinson as **Garak, Elim**; Melissa Young as **Caprice**; Marci Brickhouse as **Luvsitt, Mona**. SEE: **baccarat; Bare, Professor Honey; Bashir, Julian; Caprice; champagne; Duchamps; Everest, Mount; Falcon; holodeck and holosuite programs; holodeck; Komananov, Anastasia; Luvsitt, Mona; Merriweather, Patrick; Noah, Dr. Hippocrates; *Orinoco, U.S.S.*; secret agent; True Way, The.**

"Outcast, The." *Next Generation* episode #117. Written by Jeri Taylor. Directed by Robert Scheerer. Stardate 45614.6. *First aired in 1992. On a planet of androgynous humanoids where gender orientation is a crime, Riker falls in love with one who dares to call herself female.* GUEST CAST: Melinda Culea as **Soren**; Callan White as **Krite**; Megan Cole as **Noor**. SEE: **dexalin; Federation Day; J'naii; Krite; *Magellan*, *Shuttlecraft*; millicochrane; *Nenebek*; Noor; null space; phaser type-4; Phelan system; psychotectic therapy; Soren; *Taris Murn*; United Federation of Planets.**

Outpost 23. A Federation station along the **Romulan Neutral Zone**. In 2367, it was the key outpost in Starfleet's defenses along the border. During a fantasy created for Riker's benefit by **Barash** on **Alpha Onias III**, Outpost 23 was supposedly no longer of strategic importance and was slated to be the site of final peace negotiations between the Federation and the Romulan Star Empire, an apparent ruse to reveal the location of the outpost. ("Future Imperfect" [TNG]).

Outpost Seran-T-One. Federation station at which is located a Starfleet design facility. The **dilithium crystal chamber** for the *Enterprise*-D was designed there on stardate 40052. ("Booby Trap" [TNG]).

Outpost Sierra VI. A Federation station. Outpost Sierra VI detected the presence of a **Romulan scoutship** piloted by **Alidar Jarok** in the Neutral Zone in 2366. ("The Defector" [TNG]).

"Outrageous Okona, The." *Next Generation* episode #30. Teleplay by Burton Armus. Story by Les Menchen & Lance Dickson and David Landsberg. Directed by Robert Becker. Stardate 42402.7. *First aired in 1988. The irascible Captain Okona drags the* Enterprise-D *into a love-war relationship between two planets.* GUEST CAST: William O. Campbell as **Okona, Thadiun**; Douglas Rowe as **Debin**; Albert Stratton as **Kushell**; Rosalind Ingledew as **Yanar**; Kieran Mulroney as **Benzan**; Joe Piscopo as **Comic, The**; Whoopi Goldberg as **Guinan**. SEE: **Altec; Benzan; Comic, The; Data, Lieutenant Commander; Debin; Erstwhile; Giddings, Dianna; *glob* fly; Kushell; Legation of Unity; Madena, Coalition of; Okona, Thadiun; Omega Sagitta system; Riga, Stano; Robinson, B. G.; Straleb security ship; Straleb; Thesia, Jewel of; Yanar.**

"Overseer, the." In the religious belief system of planet **Mintaka III**, the Overseer was a supernatural being that possessed supreme power. The Overseer was supposed to be able to appear and disappear at will, and to raise the dead. When a Federation science team accidentally revealed its advanced technology to the Mintakans in 2366, the Mintakans logically interpreted these apparent "miracles" as evidence that *Enterprise*-D Captain **Jean-Luc Picard** was their Overseer. Picard chose to violate the **Prime Directive** in order to convince them that this was not true. ("Who Watches the Watchers?" [TNG]).

Owon eggs. Foodstuff regarded by some as a delicacy. Riker obtained Owon eggs at Starbase 73, and prepared them as an omelet on a makeshift stove in his quarters. Judging from the reactions of Geordi and Pulaski, Riker's cooking left something to be desired, although Worf seemed to enjoy the dish. ("Time Squared" [TNG]).

Oxmyx, Bela. (Anthony Caruso). Boss of the largest territory on planet **Sigma Iotia II**. In 2268, Oxmyx tried to convince Kirk to supply his men with firearms so that he could take over the planet from the other leaders. Kirk negotiated an arrangement that ended the planet's territorial wars, in which Oxmyx would lead the planetary government, but with provisions that would enable the Federation to guide his regime into a more ethical form of government. ("A Piece of the Action" [TOS]). SEE: **Book, the**.

Ozaba. (Davis Roberts). Scientist stationed on planet **Minara II** in 2268 who was killed by the **Vians** while studying the impending nova of the **Minaran star system**. ("The Empath" [TOS]).

ozone. Naturally occurring chemical compound formed of three oxygen atoms. Gaseous ozone collects in the upper atmosphere of some Class-M planets (such as **Earth**), shielding the surface from hazardous ultraviolet solar radiation. Destruction of the ozone layer can therefore result in significant harm to such a planet's surface-dwelling life-forms. The cloaking shield used by the inhabitants of planet **Aldea** caused damage to that planet's ozone layer, eventually resulting in the infertility of the Aldeans. ("When the Bough Breaks" [TNG]).

P'Rang*, *I.K.S. Klingon spacecraft. The *P'Rang* was ordered to intercept the sleeper ship ***T'Ong*** after command of the *T'Ong* had been assumed by Emissary **K'Ehleyr**. ("The Emissary" [TNG]).

P'Trell, Chirurgeon Ghee. Physician involved in gerontological research on planet **Andoria**. P'Trell was a **Carrington Award** nominee in 2371. ("Prophet Motive" [DS9]).

Pa'Dar, Kotran. (Robert Mandan). Powerful **Cardassian** civilian leader, instrumental in the decision to withdraw from **Bajor** in 2369. In 2362, while he was serving as **exarch** of a Cardassian settlement on Bajor, Pa'Dar's house was destroyed in a terrorist attack. His wife was killed in the attack, and his son, **Rugal**, was missing and also believed dead. Unknown to Pa'Dar, Rugal was still alive, and the boy was ordered to the **Tozhat Resettlement Center** by **Gul Dukat**, Pa'Dar's political enemy. In 2370, Pa'Dar learned his son was alive in the care of a Bajoran family. The revelation would have been a political disgrace for Pa'Dar, except that a custody hearing held aboard station Deep Space 9 revealed Dukat's plot to embarrass Pa'Dar. Rugal was subsequently ordered returned to the custody of his birth father. ("Cardassians" [DS9]).

Pacifica. Beautiful ocean world, known for warm blue waters and fine white beaches. Pacifica was headed by **Governor Delaplane**. The *Enterprise*-D was en route to a scientific mission there in 2364 when Captain **Walker Keel** requested a covert meeting with Captain Picard to discuss Keel's suspicions of a conspiracy to infiltrate Starfleet. ("Conspiracy" [TNG]). An interstellar conference was held there in 2365. Among the participants was Betazoid Ambassador **Lwaxana Troi**. Troi was instrumental in uncovering an **Antedean** plot to blow up the conference when she discovered that the delegates from planet **Antede III** were in fact assassins. ("Manhunt" [TNG]).

padd. Acronym for the personal access display device; small handheld information unit used by Starfleet personnel aboard Federation starships. *At the time* Star Trek: The Next Generation*'s padd was designed in 1987, it seemed fairly futuristic, but as this entry is written, devices—like Apple Computer's Newton personal digital assistant—that do virtually everything a padd can theoretically do, are already being marketed as consumer products. An electronic clipboard was also used by the* Enterprise *crew in the original series, which might also have been a padd device, although it was never referred to as such.*

Paffran. City on the **Vhnori** homeworld. ("Emanations" [VGR]).

***pagh'tem'far*.** Bajoran concept of a sacred vision. After experiencing a plasma burst in 2373, Benjamin Sisko had several *pagh'tem'far;* one vision led him to find the lost city of **B'hala**. ("Rapture" [DS9]).

Pagh*, *I.K.S. Klingon *K'Vort*-class battle cruiser, a large bird-of-prey spacecraft commanded by **Captain Kargan**. Starfleet officer William Riker briefly served as first officer aboard this ship in 2365 as part of an officer exchange program. During Riker's service aboard the *Pagh*, an incident with Starfleet was narrowly averted when *Enterprise*-D personnel helped identify and repair damage from a previously undiscovered subatomic life-form that was damaging the hull of the *Pagh*. ("A Matter of Honor" [TNG]).

***pagh*.** In the **Bajoran** religion, a person's life-force, from which one gains strength and courage. Bajorans believe their *pagh,* or life-force, is replenished by the prophets who reside in the **Celestial Temple**. ("Emissary" [DS9]).

Pah-wraiths. Energy-based life-forms that lived in the **Bajoran wormhole.** Long ago, the Pah-wraiths were banished by the **Prophets** to the fire caves on planet Bajor and forbidden to return. In 2373, a Pah-wraith tried to use **Keiko O'Brien** in an elaborate attempt to kill the Prophets with a beam of **chroniton particles**. Fortunately, the Pah-wraith was driven from Keiko O'Brien, and the wormhole aliens remained unharmed. ("The Assignment" [DS9]).

Pahash. Cover name used by Chief Miles O'Brien in 2373. For a covert mission to Ty'Gokor, O'Brien was surgically altered to appear Klingon, and he assumed the identity of Pahash, son of Konjah. ("Apocalypse Rising" [DS9]).

***pahtk*.** A Klingon insult. ("The Defector" [TNG], "Sins of the Father" [TNG], "Reunion" [TNG]).

painstik, Klingon. Electronic "cattle prod" used as part of the Klingon **Age of Ascension** ritual. The use of the painstik is significant because endurance of physical suffering is considered a Klingon spiritual test. O'Brien recalled that he saw a painstik used on a two-ton **Rectyne monopod**, and that the creature jumped five meters before dying of excessive cephalic pressures. ("The Icarus Factor" [TNG]). Painstiks were also used in the ***Sonchi*** ceremony to provide "proof" that an individual was dead. ("Reunion" [TNG]). Commander Troi was under the impression that painstiks were used as part of a Klingon birthday celebration. ("Parallels" [TNG]).

Painter, Mr. (Dick Scotter). Navigator aboard the original *U.S.S. Enterprise*. Painter was on duty during the mission to investigate the fate of colonists on planet **Omicron Ceti III** in 2267. ("This Side of Paradise" [TOS]).

painting. Art form involving the creation of visual images through the application of viscous liquid pigments to a flat surface. Geordi La Forge taught **Data** how to paint, causing Riker to comment on the irony of a blind man teaching an android about a visual art. Although Data's initial efforts at painting were relatively mechanistic because he was concentrating on the techniques of painting, he eventually gained an awareness of the artistry involved as he became more comfortable with his own humanity. ("11001001" [TNG]). A painting class was offered aboard the *Enterprise*-D in 2366. Captain Picard was one of the students, although his initial efforts may have been discouraged by Data's unintentionally harsh criticism. ("A Matter of Perspective" [TNG]). *The paintings by Picard and the other students in the class were done by Elaine Sokoloff.* When Data began to experience dreams in 2369, he used painting as a means to explore those inner visions. Data painted a multitude of images, including his creator, Dr. Soong, as well as himself as a bird. ("Birthright, Part I" [TNG]). *Data's paintings were actually done by scenic artists Wendy Drapanas, (*who did Data's Picascoeqse cat*) Alan Kobayashi, and Mike Okuda. Additional designs were contributed by Rick Sternbach.*

Pakled captain. (Christopher Collins). Commanding officer of the **Pakled** ship ***Mondor***. Although this individual gave the impression of possessing limited intelligence, he was later found to be both intelligent and devious. ("Samaritan Snare" [TNG]). *The captain was given the name Grebnedlog in the script, but this name was never spoken in the actual completed episode. Christopher Collins also played Captain Kargan in "A Matter of Honor" (TNG).*

Pakleds. Species of characteristically heavyset and technologically advanced humanoids. Although initial contact with the *Enterprise*-D in 2365 suggested the Pakleds had limited intellectual capacities, this was found to be untrue, and the Pakleds further demonstrated considerable cunning in attempting to capture *Enterprise*-D engineer Geordi La Forge. ("Samaritan Snare" [TNG]). Pakled interests owned a **magnesite ore** mine on planet Kalla III. In 2370, the Duras sisters illegally mined the deposit without the Pakleds' knowledge. ("Firstborn" [TNG]). A Pakled spacecraft rescued **Lore** after he was transported into space in 2364. Subsequently, he adopted traditional Pakled clothing styles. ("Brothers" [TNG]). SEE: **Lore**.

pakra. Native American ritual commemorating the anniversary of the death of a loved one. In 2372, **Chakotay** celebrated the pakra on the anniversary of his father's death, in quiet solitude aboard a *Voyager* shuttlecraft. ("Initiations" [VGR]). SEE: **Kolopak**.

Palamarian Freedom Brigade. Political faction led by **General Nassuc**. The Palamarian Freedom Brigade was in direct opposition to the forces of the **Regent of Palamar**. Nassuc's Freedom Brigade sought independence for her homeworld. ("Business As Usual" [DS9]).

Palamarian sea urchin. Seafood. Favored by the **Regent of Palamar**. ("Business As Usual" [DS9]).

Palamas, Lieutenant Carolyn. (Leslie Parrish). Archaeology and anthropology officer on the original *Starship Enterprise*. Palamas served on a landing party to planet **Pollux IV** that encountered the entity **Apollo** in 2267. The humanoid Apollo found Palamas attractive, and Palamas found Apollo fascinating on both a professional and personal level. Realizing that Apollo intended to enslave the *Enterprise* crew, Palamas spurned his advances. Apollo eventually released the ship and vanished into oblivion. ("Who Mourns for Adonais?" [TOS]). *An early draft script for the episode ended with a scene in which McCoy discovered that Palamas was pregnant with Apollo's child.*

Palaxia. Young girl, a resident of **Rinax** when the **metreon cascade** was deployed in 2356. Palaxia survived, but her flesh was horribly burnt in the many fires that the weapon caused. A team of rescuers, including **Neelix**, went to Rinax after the cascade to evacuate survivors, and Palaxia was returned to **Talax** where she slowly withered away and died over the next few weeks. ("Jetrel" [VGR]).

Palis, Delon. Daughter of a top administrator at a medical complex in **Paris**. Palis, a ballerina, was once romantically involved with **Dr. Julian Bashir** while Bashir was a Starfleet medical student. Although her father offered Julian a job and promised he'd eventually become chief of surgery, Julian chose a Starfleet career, and broke up with Delon. ("Armageddon Game" [DS9]).

Palliantyne peas. Edible vegetable native to a planet in the Delta Quadrant. Neelix prepared Palliantyne peas, served lightly spiced, as a side dish. ("Parturition" [VGR]).

Pallra. (Katherine Moffat). **Bajoran** national who was a resident of **Terok Nor** during the Cardassian occupation. Her husband, **Vaatrik**, ran the station's chemist shop, until his murder in 2365. Pallra was suspected of the murder, but was never convicted. In 2370, Pallra bribed Quark to obtain a list of Cardassian collaborators from a hidden vault in her husband's shop. She intended to use the list to blackmail those on it, but was apprehended before she could complete her plan. ("Necessary Evil" [DS9]). *Katherine Moffat also portrayed Etana Jol in "The Game" (TNG).*

palm beacons. Handheld light sources used by Starfleet away teams. ("Preemptive Strike" [TNG]). *Palm beacons are sometimes referred to as "Sims beacons," named for Alan Sims, property master for* Star Trek: The Next Generation *and* Star Trek: Voyager.

Palmer, Dr. (Tim Trella). Federation scientist. Palmer was injured in the failure of the "duck blind" enclosure on planet **Mintaka III**. Rendered unconscious by his injuries, Dr. Palmer was captured and held by the Mintakans in the hopes that it would please their deity. ("Who Watches the Watchers?" [TNG]).

Palmer, Lieutenant. (Dr. Mae Jemison). Starfleet officer who served aboard the *Starship Enterprise*-D. Palmer was assigned to transporter duty during an away team mission to **Nervala IV**. ("Second Chances" [TNG]). *Space shuttle astronaut Dr. Mae Jemison was the first African-American woman in space.*

Palmer, Lieutenant. (Elizabeth Rogers). Relief communications officer aboard the *Starship Enterprise* under the command of James Kirk. ("The Doomsday Machine" [TOS], "The Way to Eden" [TOS]).

Paloris Colony. Settlement. Location where a **Harodian miner** aboard *Enterprise*-D was absolutely certain he had met the empathic metamorph, **Kamala**. ("The Perfect Mate" [TNG]).

Paltriss, Rings of. Collection of artifacts by Paltriss, an Yridian artist. They were considered objects of great value to the **Yridians**. In 2370, Quark found himself in possession of 42 of them. He contracted to sell them to another Yridian, Ashrock. ("Melora" [DS9]).

palukoo. Large arachnids indigenous to the **Bajoran** moons. They were used as a source of food by the Bajoran resistance. ("The Siege" [DS9]). *The* palukoo *was built by* Star Trek: Deep Space Nine *special effects technician Joe Sasgen using parts from a radio-controlled toy.*

pancakes. Earth pastry food made from a flour mixture, fried and served for breakfast. In 2373, Rom ordered a short stack of pancakes, dripping with butter, and served with a side of sausage and pineapple. ("The Assignment" [DS9]).

Panora. Planet in the **Demilitarized Zone** near the Dorvan sector. Panora was a **Cardassian** colony. In 2373, the **Maquis** raided Panora, seriously damaging most of the defense systems there. ("For the Uniform" [DS9]).

***papalla* juice.** Orange-colored beverage. Guinan recommended it for children. Be sure to order it with extra bubbles. ("Imaginary Friend" [TNG]). Ambassador **Loquel** found the drink to his liking during his visit aboard the *Enterprise*-D in 2370. ("Liaisons" [TNG]). Neelix used the seeds of the *papalla* fruit as an ingredient in a new experimental breakfast drink on *Voyager* on stardate 50126. ("Flashback" [VGR]).

Paqu. Bajoran village. Paqu was embattled in a border dispute with their neighbors, the **Navot**, in 2369. ("The Storyteller" [DS9]). SEE: **Glyrhond; Varis Sul**.

***par'Mach*.** Klingon word for love, which included more aggressive overtones than are common in many humanoid cultures. ("Looking for *par'Mach* in All the Wrong Places" [DS9]).

***par'machkai*.** Klingon term of endearment, used to refer to one's romantic partner. ("Let He Who Is Without Sin..." [DS9]).

paracortex. Telepathic lobe of the **Betazoid** brain. When **Lwaxana Troi** fell into a coma in 2370, Dr. Beverly Crusher noted that the neural activity in her paracortex was practically nonexistent. ("Dark Page" [TNG]).

Parada II. Planet in the **Parada system**. Parada's inhabitants fought a civil war from 2358 to 2370. Peace talks in 2370 between the Paradan government and rebels were nearly disrupted by a government plot to assassinate members of the rebels' negotiating team, using a duplicate of Deep Space 9 Operations Officer Miles O'Brien. ("Whispers" [DS9]). SEE: **Coutu**.

Parada IV. Largest planet in the **Parada system**. Parada IV has seven moons. A replicant of Miles O'Brien, created by the Paradan government to disrupt the peace talks of 2370, used the polar magnetic field of Parada IV to hide his runabout from the pursuing Starfleet personnel. ("Whispers" [DS9]).

Parada system. Star system with at least four planets. The system is located in the Gamma Quadrant, 74 minutes from the wormhole at maximum warp. ("Whispers" [DS9]).

Paradas. Humanoids from the **Parada system**; slightly reptilian in appearance. Civil war erupted in the Parada system in 2358 and continued until 2370, when the Paradas sought help from Federation authorities to negotiate a peace. Deep Space 9 operations chief **Miles O'Brien** was dispatched to the Parada system to be briefed on security arrangements for peace talks, but was instead taken captive. The Paradan government, which possessed a highly advanced cloning technology, created a replica of O'Brien and sent the replicant to Deep Space 9, with the intention of using him to disrupt the peace talks. This plan was uncovered by Paradan rebels and reported to Starfleet personnel. ("Whispers" [DS9]). *The replicant O'Brien noted that the Paradas' skin produced secretions that changed odor according to their moods, but this fact was omitted from the official reports.*

Paradise City. Main settlement of the unsuccessful colony on planet **Nimbus III**. With the failure of the colony, Paradise City became an interstellar wilderness town of rogues and others on the edge of the law. *(Star Trek V: The Final Frontier).*

"Paradise Lost." *Deep Space Nine* episode #84. Teleplay by Ira Steven Behr & Robert Hewitt Wolfe. Story by Ronald D. Moore. Directed by Reza Badiyi. No stardate given. *First aired in 1996. Sisko discovers a greater threat to the Earth than changelings when Admiral Leyton attempts a military coup of Earth's government. This was the second half of a two-part story that began with "Homefront" (DS9).* GUEST CAST: Robert Foxworth as **Leyton, Admiral**; Herschel Sparber as **Jaresh-Inyo**; Susan Gibney as **Benteen, Erika**; Aron Eisenberg as **Nog**; David Drew Gallagher as **Shepard**; Mina Badie as Security officer; Rudolph Willrich as Bollan, Commandant; Brock Peters as **Sisko, Joseph**; Bobby C. King as Security chief. SEE: **ablative armor; academy commandant; Antwerp Conference; Arriaga, Lieutenant; Bartlett; Benteen, Erika; Beumont, Neffie; Bolian tonic water; CO; Daneeka; *Defiant, U.S.S.*; Division of Planetary Operations; Federation president; global power grid; Jaresh-Inyo; *Lakota, U.S.S.*; Leyton, Admiral; McWatt; Moodus; *Okinawa, U.S.S.*; Orr; Paris; pasta boudin; Phillips, Zoey; quantum torpedo; Ramsey; Red Squad; relay satellite; Sisko, Benjamin; Shepard, Riley Aldrin; Snowden; Tzenkethi war; United Federation of Planets; XO.**

"Paradise Syndrome, The." Original Series episode #58. Written by Margaret Armen. Directed by Jud Taylor. Stardate 4842.6. *First aired in 1968. Kirk loses his memory and falls in love on a peaceful planet inhabited by descendants of Native Americans from Earth.* GUEST CAST: Sabrina Scharf as **Miramanee**; Rudy Solari as **Salish**; Richard Hale as **Goro**; Majel Barrett as **Chapel, Christine**; Naomi Pollack as Indian woman; John Lindesmith as Engineer; Peter Virgo, Jr. as **Lumo**; Lamont Laird as Indian boy; Sean Morgan as Engineer; Paul Baxley as Kirk's stunt double; Richard Geary as Salish's stunt double. SEE: **Goro; Joining day; Kirk, James T.; Kirok; Lumo; Miramanee; Miramanee's planet; Obelisk; Preservers; ritual cloak; Salish; Tahiti Syndrome; wedding; Wise Ones**.

"Paradise." *Deep Space Nine* episode #35. Teleplay by Jeff King and Richard Manning & Hans Beimler. Story by Jim Trombetta and James Crocker. Directed by Corey Allen. Stardate 47573.1. *First aired in 1994. Sisko and O'Brien find themselves trapped on a planet where humans have abandoned technology.* GUEST CAST: Julia Nickson as **Cassandra**; Steve Vinovich as **Joseph**; Michael Buchman Silver as **Vinod**; Erick Weiss as **Stephan**; Gail Strickland as **Alixus**; Majel Barrett as Computer voice. SEE: **Alixus; astatine; bioimplant; Cassandra; core behavior; *Crockett, U.S.S.;* duonetic field; *Gasko;* Gemulon V; Golanga; Joseph; Mitsuya, Admiral; O'Brien, Miles; Orellius Minor; Orellius; *Orinoco, U.S.S.; Rio Grande, U.S.S.*; runabout; *Santa Maria;* Sector 401; sleeper fungi; Stephan; Vinod; *xupta* tree.**

***paraka* wings.** Wings from an avian species from the Delta Quadrant, cooked and heavily seasoned with spices. *Paraka* wings were particularly suited to be served as finger food at informal get-togethers. ("Warlord" [VGR]).

paralithium. Crystalline substance used as fuel for some ion-based starship propulsion systems. Paralithium can be converted to **trilithium**. Vel's Akritirian freighter used paralithium as a fuel source. ("The Chute" [VGR]). *Paralithium technology would appear to be unknown in the Alpha Quadrant, since Soran went through such extreme lengths to get trilithium in* Star Trek Generations*.*

Parallax Colony. Society of "free spirits" on planet **Shiralea VI**. The colony was populated by a number of fanciful humanoids who pursed a life of pleasure. These colorful characters included a juggler, an argumentative humanoid couple, a poet, and a Wind Dancer, who served as colony sentry, assuring that "only those whose hearts are joyous" could enter. Lwaxana Troi introduced young Alexander Rozhenko to a holodeck simulation of the Parallax Colony in 2368. Alexander seemed to enjoy the "Laughing Hour," while Lwaxana wanted to visit the colony's famous mudbaths. Alexander tolerated the mudbaths, but Worf could not fathom their attraction. ("Cost of Living" [TNG]).

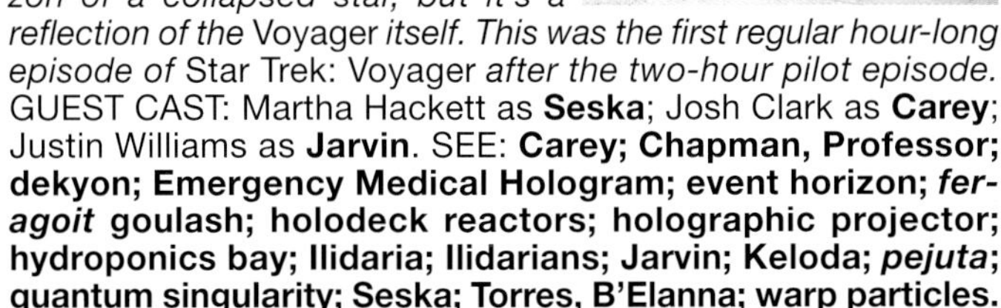

"Parallax." *Voyager* episode #3. Teleplay by Brannon Braga. Story by Jim Trombetta. Directed by Kim Friedman. Stardate 48439.7. *First aired in 1995.* Voyager *is contacted by a ship trapped in the event horizon of a collapsed star, but it's a reflection of the* Voyager *itself. This was the first regular hour-long episode of* Star Trek: Voyager *after the two-hour pilot episode.* GUEST CAST: Martha Hackett as **Seska**; Josh Clark as **Carey**; Justin Williams as **Jarvin**. SEE: **Carey; Chapman, Professor; dekyon; Emergency Medical Hologram; event horizon; *feragoit* goulash; holodeck reactors; holographic projector; hydroponics bay; Ilidaria; Ilidarians; Jarvin; Keloda; *pejuta*; quantum singularity; Seska; Torres, B'Elanna; warp particles.**

"Parallels." *Next Generation* episode #163. Written by Brannon Braga. Directed by Robert Wiemer. *First aired in 1993. Worf finds himself shifting between different quantum realities. Worf celebrates his 30th birthday in this episode.* GUEST CAST: Wil Wheaton as **Crusher**, **Wesley**; Patti Yasutake as **Ogawa**, **Nurse Alyssa**; Mark Bramhall as **Nador**, **Gul**; Majel Barrett as Computer voice. SEE: **Argus Array; Bajorans; *Bat'leth* competition; Battle of *HarOs*, the; birthday cake; Borg; broad-spectrum warp field; Cardassians; *"Cha* Worf *Toh'gah-nah lo Pre'tOk"*; champagne; Champion Standing; Crusher, Wesley; *Curie, Shuttlecraft;* Dalvan hissing beetle; Deep Space 5; Expressionistic phase; Forcas III; Gates, Ensign; Hayes, Ensign; Iadara Colony; imaging logs; jolly; Nador, Gul; Ogawa, Alyssa; painstik, Klingon; Picard, Jean-Luc; quantum fissure; quantum flux; quantum reality; quantum signature; Riker, William T.; RNA; Rozhenko, Eric-Christopher; Rozhenko, Shannara; secondary plasma conduit; Sector 19658; *Soh-chIm*; Starbase 47; Starbase 129; surprise party; *T'gha* maneuver; temporal anomaly; Troi, Deanna; uncertainty principle; Utopia Planitia Fleet Yards; vertazine; VISOR; Worf.**

paralysis field. Weapon used by the **Kelvans**. The paralysis field was used against the *U.S.S. Enterprise* crew to gain control of the starship in 2268. The weapon blocked nerve impulses to the voluntary muscles. ("By Any Other Name" [TOS]).

Pardek, Senator. (Malachi Throne). Romulan senator who represented the **Krocton Segment** of **Romulus**. Pardek was among the delegates at the **Khitomer** conference in 2293 and served as a member of the Romulan Senate for 90 years. Pardek was considered a "man of the people," something of a radical, having sponsored many governmental reforms and pursued the cause of peace within the empire throughout his career. Pardek worked to bring Ambassador **Spock** to Romulus in 2368 to support an underground movement seeking to reunite the Romulans with their Vulcan cousins. Pardek eventually betrayed Spock, as well as Captain Picard and Commander Data, to the Romulan authorities, in exchange for favors granted to him by **Proconsul Neral**. ("Unification, Parts I and II" [TNG]). *Malachi Throne had played* ***Commodore José Mendez*** *in "The Menagerie, Parts I and II" (TOS). He also provided the voice of the* ***Talosian*** *magistrate in the original, unaired version of the pilot episode "The Cage" (TOS), produced in 1964.*

Parein. Civilization populating a planet of former **Borg** drones in the Delta Quadrant. ("Unity" [VGR]).

Parem. (Brian Cousins). Romulan officer. Parem was accidentally "phased" by an experimental Romulan **interphase generator** in 2368. Parem made his way on-board the *Enterprise*-D and threatened both Geordi La Forge and Ro Laren, who had also been "phased" in the accident. Parem was killed during a struggle with the two officers when he was forced through the "normal" ship's bulkhead and out into space. ("The Next Phase" [TNG]).

paricium. Ceramic substance. Used in construction of the **Kataan probe**. ("The Inner Light" [TNG]).

Parinisti measles. Endoplasmic virus. Six *Voyager* crew members suffered from Parinisti measles on stardate 48693. Fortunately, the **Emergency Medical Hologram** was able to produce a vaccine that prevented the disease from becoming epidemic. ("Heroes and Demons" [VGR]).

Paris delight. Blend of **coffee** created by *U.S.S. Voyager*'s chef Neelix to honor Lieutenant Thomas Paris's historic breaking of the warp 10 barrier. ("Threshold" [VGR]).

Paris, Admiral. (Warren Munson). Former commander of the *Starship Al-Batani* and father of **Tom Paris**. Future *Voyager* Captain **Kathryn Janeway** served as science officer aboard the *Al-Batani* under the elder Paris. Admiral Paris took it very hard when his son, Thomas, was forced out of Starfleet and later arrested as a member of the **Maquis**. ("Caretaker" [VGR]). Paris was a firm believer in Starfleet's **Prime Directive** of noninterference, and was known to lecture his family on the subject once a year. ("Time and Again" [VGR]). The elder Paris also served as an instructor at **Starfleet Academy**. He strove to avoid any hint of favoritism when his son attended that institution, even giving Tom a B-minus grade in a course on survival. ("Parturition" [VGR]). When a **Bothan** attacked *Voyager* in 2372, Tom Paris had a hallucination that his father was with him on the ship. ("Persistence of Vision" [VGR]).

Paris, Linnis. (Jessica Collins). (In a possible future, the daughter of **Thomas Paris** and **Kes**. In this reality Kes and Tom married and had a daughter, Linnis, in 2375. As an adult, Linnis worked in the **sickbay** with her mother. Linnis later married **Harry Kim**, and the two had a son, **Andrew Kim**, who was Kes's grandson.) ("Before and After" [VGR].)

Paris, Thomas. (Robert Duncan McNeill). Starfleet officer aboard the ***U.S.S. Voyager***. ("Caretaker" [VGR]). Early in his career, Thomas Eugene Paris served aboard the *Starship Exeter*. ("Non Sequitur" [VGR]). He majored in astrophysics at Starfleet Academy. ("Future's End, Part I" [VGR]). As an academy cadet, Paris chose the Starfleet base outside **Marseilles**, France for physical training in his second semester of the academy. He spent most of his time that semester at **Chez Sandrine**, a bistro that he later re-created in the holodeck of the *Starship Voyager*. ("The Cloud" [VGR]). SEE: **Ricky**.

The son of a Starfleet admiral, Tom Paris was a graduate of **Starfleet Academy** and was involved in a fatal accident that claimed the lives of three other Starfleet officers. Paris initially

denied responsibility for the accident, but later admitted he had falsified reports to hide his culpability, and was forced to leave Starfleet. ("Caretaker" [VGR]). In later years, Paris realized that his greatest mistake was not having told the truth. ("Fair Trade" [VGR]). Paris became a mercenary for the **Maquis**, but was arrested by Federation authorities while on his first assignment for the resistance group. He was imprisoned at the Federation Penal Settlement in New Zealand on Earth, but was released in 2371 at the request of *Voyager* captain **Kathryn Janeway**. In exchange for his parole, Paris agreed to help the *Voyager* locate his former colleagues in the Maquis. While carrying out this mission, Paris and all *Voyager* personnel were swept into the Delta Quadrant, where they were forced to join forces with the Maquis crew in order to survive. Janeway subsequently reinstated Paris's Starfleet commission and assigned him to the ship's **conn**. Paris experienced some discomfort at working under Commander **Chakotay**, a former Maquis officer. ("Caretaker" [VGR]).

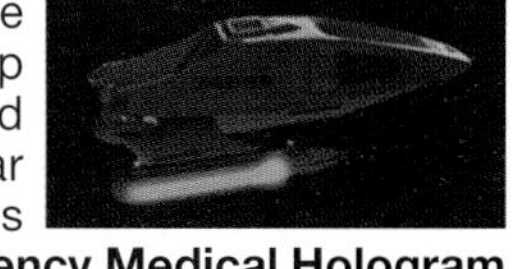

In 2372 Paris made history by becoming the first human pilot to cross the **transwarp** threshold and attain a warp 10 velocity. The experience accelerated the evolutionary process in his cellular DNA, mutating him into an amphibious creature. Fortunately, *Voyager's* **Emergency Medical Hologram** was able to reverse the process. *Voyager* captain Kathryn Janeway was also mutated by Paris's transwarp flight, and while mutated, the two had three amphibian children, which they left on a planet in the Delta Quadrant. ("Threshold" [VGR]).

Tom Paris was an aficionado of 20th-century America, and was fond of traditional **Earth** foods from that period. ("Future's End, Part I" [VGR]). He was an experienced rock climber and was skilled at spelunking. ("Blood Fever" [VGR]).

Tom Paris realized in 2372 that he was very much attracted to **Kes**. He decided not to act on these feelings out of respect for Neelix, who was, at the time, involved with her. ("Parturition" [VGR]). Paris was an instrumental part of an elaborate scheme devised by Janeway and Security Chief Tuvok, intended to trap a spy believed to be operating aboard *Voyager*. Paris exhibited increasing anger and discontent with his life aboard the ship for several weeks in 2372, culminating with his departure from the *Voyager* crew. In doing so, Paris was able to determine that **Michael Jonas** had been acting as a Kazon operative, working against the interests of the *Voyager* crew. ("Investigations" [VGR]).

(In one possible future, **B'Elanna Torres** and Tom Paris became romantically involved. Later, Torres and Captain Kathryn Janeway were killed in a **Krenim** attack. Paris was devastated. Kes comforted him, helping him get through the pain, and the two ended up together. Kes and Tom Paris married and had a daughter, **Linnis**, in 2375. Linnis later married **Harry Kim**, and the two had a son, **Andrew Kim**, who was Tom's grandson.) ("Before and After" [VGR].)

Robert Duncan McNeill had previously played Cadet Nick Locarno in "The First Duty" (TNG). Tom Paris's first appearance was in "Caretaker" [VGR]. His middle name was a tip of the hat to Star Trek *creator Gene Roddenberry.*

Paris. Ancient city in France on Earth. Location of the office of the **Federation president**. *(Star Trek VI: The Undiscovered Country,* "Homefront" [DS9], "Paradise Lost" [DS9]). Near the president's office is an outdoor cafe where Jean-Luc Picard once broke a date with the future Mrs. Jenice Manheim, although the two later recreated the rendezvous in a holodeck simulation of the *Cafe des Artistes*. ("We'll Always Have Paris" [TNG]). *The Paris city skyline backdrop from "We'll Always Have Paris" (TNG) was re-used in* Star Trek VI, *and again (in slightly modified form) in "Homefront" (DS9) and "Paradise Lost" (DS9). The backdrop was also used as the basis for a matte painting by Eric Chauvin in those two episodes.*

Parliament. Politically neutral planet used by the Federation as a site for diplomatic negotiations. A conference held there in 2364 with the antagonistic **Selay** and **Antican** delegates considered the question of both peoples' admission to the Federation. ("Lonely Among Us" [TNG]).

Parmak, Dr. Cardassian physician. Parmak was once interrogated by **Garak**. ("The Die is Cast" [DS9]).

Parmen. (Liam Sullivan). Philosopher-king and leader of the **Platonian** society. Parmen attempted to abduct Dr. Leonard McCoy to serve as his physician in 2268. Parmen maintained his control over Platonian society through his telekinetic powers. ("Plato's Stepchildren" [TOS]). SEE: **Philana**.

Parn. (John Schuck). Cardassian **legate** and member of **Cardassian Central Command**. In 2370, Parn tried to conceal his government's effort to provide weapons to Cardassian colonists in the **Demilitarized Zone**. He informed Deep Space 9 command personnel that any such activity was unauthorized, and that **Gul Dukat** had been responsible. This was later found to be untrue. ("Maquis, Part II" [DS9]). *John Schuck also portrayed the Klingon ambassador in* Star Trek IV *and* Star Trek VI.

parrises squares. An athletic game involving competition between two teams of four players. A team of *Enterprise*-D personnel was challenged to a game of parrises squares by a team at **Starbase 74** when the ship was docked there for a computer systems upgrade. ("11001001" [TNG]). Ensign Fred Bristow and Lieutenant B'Elanna Torres played a parrises squares match in 2373, and Torres was the easy victor. ("The Swarm" [VGR]).

Parrot's Claw, The. Novel in the **Dixon Hill** series of detective stories published on Earth in the 1930s-1940s. The story involves a character named Jimmy Cuzzo, who killed a man named Marty O'Fallon. ("Manhunt" [TNG]).

parsec. Unit of measure used by Earth scientists for astronomical distances. One parsec is equal to approximately 3.26 light years. ("The Trouble With Tribbles" [TOS], "Threshold" [VGR]).

Parsion III. Planet. In 2373 feldomite was discovered in a mine on Parsion III. ("Business As Usual" [DS9]).

Parsons, Ensign. *U.S.S. Voyager* crew member. Neelix suspected Parsons of being controlled by an alien presence in 2371. Parsons was known to drink ***pejuta***. ("Cathexis" [VGR]). Neelix asked Parsons to watch the kitchen on stardate 48523. ("Phage" [VGR]).

***parthas* à la Yuta.** An **Acamarian** meal prepared from spiced *parthas*, a green vegetable with fleshy roots. **Yuta**, an aide to Acamarian Sovereign **Marouk**, made this dish, which Riker dubbed *parthas* à la Yuta. ("The Vengeance Factor" [TNG]).

parthenogenic implant. An artificial device, surgically implanted into a human body. **Jean-Luc Picard** had a parthenogenic implant, a bionic heart, that replaced his natural heart after he was stabbed as a young academy graduate in 2327. ("Samaritan Snare" [TNG]).

particle fountain. Experimental mining technique developed by **Dr. Farallon** at planet Tyrus VIIA in 2369. A powerful vertical force field was established between a point on a planet's surface and a field generator in a space station orbiting the planet. The fountain malfunctioned during testing. ("The Quality of Life" [TNG]).

particle stream buffer. Critical component of a **ferroplasmic infusion** device. This component required reinitializing, following damage to a unit used on planet **Atrea IV** in 2370. ("Inheritance" [TNG]).

particle stream. An energetic by-product of a starship's **warp-drive** engines. Geordi La Forge considered using a particle stream to attempt to sweep a holodeck clean when Dr. Katherine Pulaski was trapped in an ongoing simulation program, but the plan was abandoned when it was realized that the energetic particles would also kill Pulaski. ("Elementary, Dear Data" [TNG]).

"Parturition." *Voyager* episode #23. Written by Tom Szollosi. Directed by Jonathan Frakes. No stardate given. *First aired in 1995. Neelix and Paris must put their jealousies over Kes aside when they are ordered to investigate a planet that may be rich in foodstuffs—and end up becoming foster parents to a reptohumanoid hatchling.* GUEST CAST: Majel Barrett as Computer voice. SEE: **Alfarian hair pasta; Baytart, Pablo; clarinet; cordrazine; dermal osmotic sealant; driver coil assembly; Emergency Medical Hologram; Felaran rose; garnesite; holodeck and holosuite programs: Molière plays; Kes; Kim, Harry; Molière; Palliantyne peas; Paris, Admiral; Paris, Thomas; Planet Hell; Potak cold fowl; Potak III; reptohumanoid hatchling; Tanzian flu; technobabble; trigemic vapors.**

Parvenium Sector. Region of Federation space. The *Enterprise*-D conducted a magnetic wave study in the Parvenium Sector in late 2368. The study had just been completed when the *Enterprise*-D encountered the **Kataan probe**. ("The Inner Light" [TNG]).

"Passenger, The." *Deep Space Nine* episode #9. Teleplay by Morgan Gendel and Robert Hewitt Wolfe & Michael Piller. Story by Morgan Gendel. Directed by Paul Lynch. No stardate given. *First aired in 1993. A renegade scientist places his consciousness into Dr. Bashir in order to steal a valuable substance needed to prolong his life.* GUEST CAST: Caitlin Brown as **Kajada**, **Ty**; James Lashly as **Primmin**, **Lieutenant George**; Christopher Collins as **Durg**; James Harper as **Vantika**, **Rao**. SEE: **alpha-wave inducer; antigrav; deuridium; DNA reference scan; Durg; energy containment cell; glial cells; Kajada, Ty; Kobliad; microscopic generator; *Norkova*; Primmin, Lieutenant George; *raktajino*; retinal imaging scan; *Reyab*; Rigel VII; *Rio Grande, U.S.S.*; subspace technology; synaptic pattern displacement; Vantika, Rao; Vulcan mind-meld.**

passive high-resolution series. Sequence of sensor scans. Commander La Forge and Lieutenant Barclay conducted a passive high-resolution series on a **Cytherian** probe found near the **Argus Array** in 2367. The test was unable to uncover any information about the probe. ("The Nth Degree" [TNG]).

"Past Prologue." *Deep Space Nine* episode #4. Written by Kathryn Powers. Directed by Winrich Kolbe. No stardate given. *First aired in 1993. A Bajoran terrorist attempts to destroy the wormhole.* GUEST CAST: Jeffrey Nordling as **Tahna Los**; Andrew Robinson as **Garak**, **Elim**; Gwynyth Walsh as **B'Etor**; Barbara March as **Lursa**; Susan Bay as **Rollman**, **Admiral**; Vaughn Armstrong as **Korris**, **Captain**; Richard Ryder as Bajoran deputy. SEE: ***Aldara*; B'Etor; Bajor VIII; bilitrium; Danar, Gul; Duras; *Ganges, U.S.S.*; Garak; Haru Outpost; isolinear rods; Joranian ostrich; Kira Nerys; *Kohn-Ma*; Kraus IV; latinum; Lursa; Rollman, Admiral; Tahna Los; Tarkalean tea; *Yangtzee Kiang, U.S.S.***

"Past Prologue." Story written by **Jake Sisko** in 2373. ("The Ascent" [DS9]). *This was also the title of a first-season episode of* Star Trek: Deep Space Nine.

"Past Tense, Part I." *Deep Space Nine* episode #57. Teleplay by Robert Hewitt Wolfe. Story by Ira Steven Behr & Robert Hewitt Wolfe. Directed by Reza Badiyi. Stardate 48481.2. *First aired in 1995. A transporter accident sends Sisko, Dax, and Bashir back in time to San Francisco in 2024.* GUEST CAST: Jim Metzler as **Brynner**, **Christopher**; Frank Military as **Coleridge, Biddle "B.C."**; Dick Miller as **Vin**; Al Rodrigo as Bernardo; Tina Lifford as **Lee**; Bill Smitrovich as **Webb**, **Michael**; Henry Hayashi as Male guest; Patty Holly as Female guest; Richard Lee Jackson as **Webb**, **Danny**; Eric Stuart as Stairway guard; John Lendale Bennett as **Bell**, **Gabriel**. SEE: **ablative armor; Aldebaran; Bajor; Bell Riots; Bell, Gabriel; Belongo; Brynner Information Systems; Brynner, Christopher; chroniton particles; Coleridge, Biddle "B.C."; credit chip; dim; Drazman, Admiral; Earth; Ferengi Rules of Acquisition; Gaullists; ghost; gimme; Interface terminal; jacked; Lee; logo; Neo-Trotskyists; Net; Ngomo, Admiral; orbital habitats; Processing Center; Proxima Maintenance Yards; quantum singularity; ration cards; SafeTech; San Francisco; Sanctuary District; schizophrenia; Sisko, Benjamin; Sisko, Judith; Starfleet General Orders and Regulations; Starfleet temporal displacement policy; transporter shock; Trill homeworld; UHC card; Venus; Vin; Webb, Danny; Webb, Michael; Wright, Admiral.**

"Past Tense, Part II." *Deep Space Nine* episode #58. Teleplay by Ira Steven Behr & René Echevarria. Story by Ira Steven Behr & Robert Hewitt Wolfe. Directed by Jonathan Frakes. No stardate given. *First aired in 1995. Sisko, trapped in the past, must assume the identity of a doomed historical figure to ensure the continuity of the future.* GUEST CAST: Jim Metzler as **Brynner**, **Christopher**; Frank Military as **Coleridge**, **Biddle "B.C."**; Dick Miller as **Vin**; Deborah Van Valkenburgh as **Preston**, **Dectective**; Al Rodrigo as Bernardo; Clint Howard as **Grady**; Richard Lee Jackson as **Webb**, **Danny**; Tina Lifford as **Lee**; Bill Smitrovich as **Webb**, **Michael**; Mitch David Carter as Swat leader; Daniel Zacapa as **Garcia**, **Henry**. SEE: **baseball; Bell Riots; Bell, Gabriel; Bokai, Buck; Brynner, Christopher; Chen, Governor; Coleridge, Biddle "B.C."; dim; E-mail; Federal Employment Act; Garcia, Henry; ghost; gimme; glucajen; Grady; Interface; Interface terminal; Lee; London Kings; Net; Preston, Detective; Processing Center; ration cards; San Francisco; Vin; Webb, Danny; Webb, Michael; Yankees.**

pasta al fiorella. Food. One of Geordi's favorite dishes. ("Birthright, Part I" [TNG]).

pasta boudin. Spicy Earth pasta dish. Pasta boudin was served at **Sisko's**, a restaurant in New Orleans. ("Paradise Lost" [DS9]).

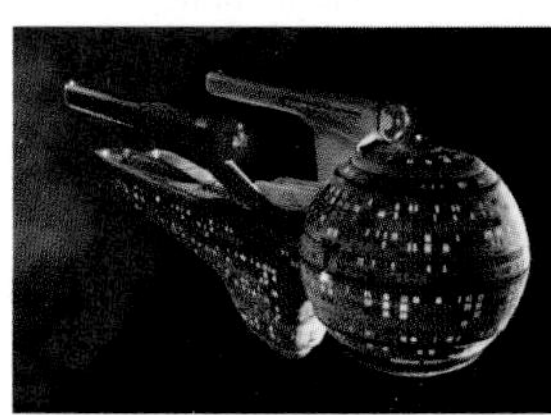

Pasteur, U.S.S. *Olympic*-class Federation medical starship, Starfleet registry number NCC-58928. (In the **anti-time** reality devised by the **Q Continuum**, the *Pasteur* was commanded by Captain Beverly Picard. The ship crossed into the Romulan Neutral Zone in order to investigate an anomaly Jean-Luc Picard believed existed there. While in the Zone, the *Pasteur* came under fire by two Klingon attack cruisers. The ship suffered a warp-core breach as a result of the attack and was destroyed.) ("All Good Things..." [TNG].) *The* Pasteur *miniature was designed and built by ILM art director Bill George. The ship's dedication plaque bore a quote from the Hippocratic Oath. An early version of that plaque indicated the Pasteur as being a* Hope-*class vessel.*

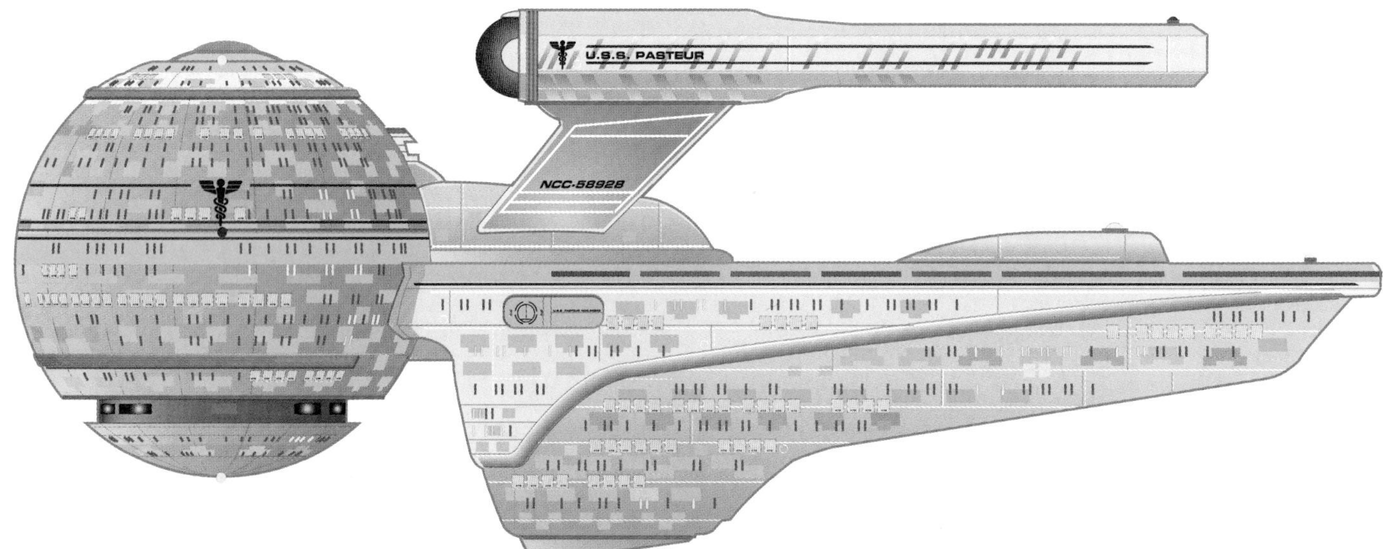

Patahk. (Steve Rankin). Romulan survivor of the scoutship ***Pi*** that crashed on planet **Galorndon Core** in 2366. Patahk was severly injured in the crash, and was brought on board the *Enterprise*-D for medical treatment. Patahk died for lack of a compatible **ribosome infusion**. Although suitable ribosomes were available from Worf, the Klingon declined to make a donation to what he viewed as an enemy of his people, and Patahk himself insisted he would not accept such a donation from Worf. Romulan officials maintained that the intrusion of Patahk's ship into Federation space was accidental. ("The Enemy" [TNG]). *The character was referred to as Patahk in the script, but the name was not spoken in the episode.*

Patches. Calico cat, pet to young **Jeremy Aster** when he lived with his parents on Earth. ("The Bonding" [TNG]).

pattern buffer. Component of a **transporter** in which a transport subject's image is briefly stored so that transmission frequency can be adjusted to compensate for the Doppler effect caused by any relative motion between the transport chamber and the target. Because of the criticality of this subsystem, two buffers must be operated in synchronization with each other, so that in case of failure of one unit, the beam can be immediately handed off to the backup. Since 2319, pattern buffers have been multiplexed to avoid **transporter psychosis**. In 2369, **quasi-energy microbes** that were capable of living within a pattern buffer's **matter stream** were discovered in the Igo Sector. ("Realm of Fear" [TNG]). Montgomery Scott modified the pattern buffers of the ***U.S.S. Jenolen*** in an attempt to keep himself and **Matt Franklin** suspended in the beam until help arrived. The attempt was partially successful: Scott survived for 75 years, but Franklin's pattern degraded beyond retrieval. ("Relics" [TNG]). The relays of the pattern buffer in the food **replicator**s aboard the *Voyager* contained **bio-neural circuitry**. ("State of Flux" [VGR]).

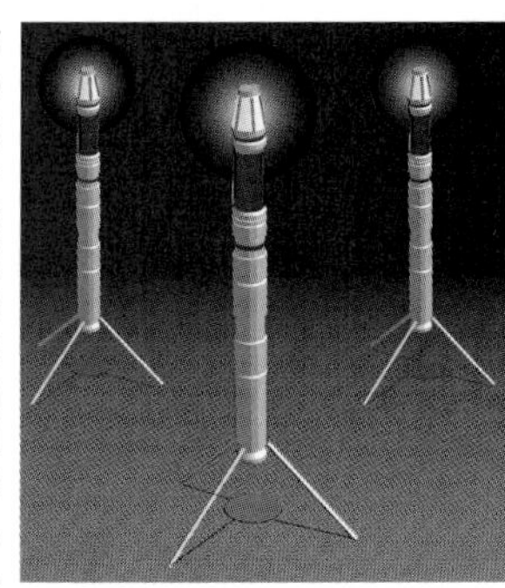

pattern enhancer. Devices used by Starfleet **transporter** systems to amplify the beam, thereby making personnel transport safer during relatively hazardous situations, as when beaming through an electrical storm. Transporter Chief O'Brien used a pattern enhancer to expedite a transporter rescue of an away team stranded on the moon of **Mab-Bu VI** on stardate 45571. Three pattern enhancers are generally used, deployed in a triangular formation, amplifying the signal lock on any object contained within the triangle. ("Power Play" [TNG]). *Pattern enhancers were first used in "Power Play" (TNG) and were also seen in other episodes, including "Ship in a Bottle" (TNG) ,"Frame of Mind" (TNG), and "Inheritance" (TNG).*

"Patterns of Force." Original Series episode #52. Written by John Meredyth Lucas. Directed by Vincent McEveety. No stardate given. *First aired in 1968. The* Enterprise *investigates a planet where a sociologist's experiment has gone awry, leaving the world with a government patterned after Nazi Germany.* GUEST CAST: Richard Evans as **Isak**; Valora Noland as **Daras**; Skip P. Homeier as **Melakon**; David Brian as **Gill, John**; Patrick Horgan as **Eneg**; William Wintersole as **Abrom**; Gilbert Green as S.S. Major; Ralph Maurer as S.S. Lieutenant; Ed McCready as S.S. Trooper; Peter Canon as Gestapo Lieutenant; Paul Baxley as First trooper; Chuck Courtney as Davod; Bart LaRue as Newscaster; Bill Blackburn, Laskey, Troopers. SEE: **Abrom; Daras; Ekos; Ekosians; Eneg; Gill, John; Isak; Melakon; Prime Directive; rubindium crystal; subcutaneous transponder; Zeon.**

Pauley, Ensign. Starfleet officer. Pauley returned from the Gamma Quadrant in the disabled runabout ***U.S.S. Ganges*** with Dax and archaeologist **Vash**. ("Q-Less" [DS9]).

Paulson Nebula. Astronomical cloud located in the vicinity of Zeta Alpha II. The Paulson Nebula was rich in transuranics, dilithium hydroxyls, and other elements. The *Enterprise*-D took advantage of this to hide from the sensors of the **Borg** ship in 2366. ("The Best of Both Worlds, Part I" [TNG]).

Pavarotti, Luciano. One of the best, and easily the most famous, operatic tenor of late 20th-century Earth. To learn about opera, *Voyager's* Emergency Medical Hologram studied recordings of Puccini's *La Bohème*, featuring Pavarotti in the role of Rudolpho. ("The Swarm" [VGR]).

Pavlick, Ensign. (Jana Marie Hupp). An *Enterprise*-D engineering technician. Pavlick was on duty during the ship's mission to the Alpha Omicron system and helped **Dr. Leah Brahms** access holodeck files on the engine modifications Commander La Forge had made to the *Enterprise*-D. ("Galaxy's Child" [TNG]). *Ensign Pavlick also let Dr. Brahms look at Geordi's programs with a holographic simulation of Brahms herself, but we understand Geordi didn't hold it against her.*

Paxans. Civilization that remains unknown to the Federation. Able to manipulate energy on many levels, the Paxans existed on a terraformed protoplanet in the **Ngame Nebula**. The Paxans exhibited extremely xenophobic behavior and protected their planet by means of an energy field that appeared to be an unstable **wormhole**. Passage through the field put unsuspecting starship crews into a state of biochemical stasis, so such ships could be towed out of Paxan space without the crew's knowledge. *The* Enterprise-*D encountered the Paxans in 2367, but all records of and memories of the contact were erased, so no* Enterprise-*D personnel (except Data) retained any memory of the incident.* ("Clues" [TNG]).

Paxau resort. Place on planet **Talax** where the rich and privileged went to relax and be pampered. Neelix created a **holodeck** program of the resort for use by the *Voyager* crew in 2373. ("Warlord" [VGR]).

Paxim. (Russ Fega). Officer in the **Talaxian** defense forces. A squadron of Talaxian fighter ships lead by Commander Paxim helped Tom Paris to successfully retake *Voyager* from the Kazon-Nistrim near stardate 50032. ("Basics, Part II" [VGR]).

pazafer. Additive used in some beverages. Grilka liked Maporian ale with a hint of *pazafer*. ("Looking for *par'Mach* in All the Wrong Places" [DS9]).

Pazlar, Melora. (Daphne Ashbrook). Starfleet stellar cartographer who was assigned to station Deep Space 9 in 2370. Pazlar was the first **Elaysian** in **Starfleet**, and one of the very few of her species to leave her native world. Because her people evolved in a low-gravity environment, Pazlar faced many obstacles in becoming a Starfleet officer and developed a defensive attitude as a result. Pazlar was nevertheless a well-rounded officer; she had a working knowledge of **Vulcan** music and an impressive command of the **Klingon** language. During her assignment on the station, Pazlar was instrumental in the capture of a criminal, **Fallit Kot**, who had been threatening station personnel. ("Melora" [DS9]). SEE: **neuromuscular adaptation theory.**

PCS. "Pulaski's Chicken Soup." Part of *Enterprise*-D medical officer **Katherine Pulaski**'s treatment for the flu virus. ("The Icarus Factor" [TNG]).

Pe'Nar Makull. (Nicolas Surovy). Inhabitant of a Class-M planet in the **Delta Quadrant** whose people were dependent on **polaric ion energy**. Pe'Nar Makull and others protested against the use of polaric energy. In 2371, *Voyager* personnel visited his world, but Pe'Nar Makull believed them to be governmental spies sent to halt the protests. ("Time and Again" [VGR]).

peach cobbler. Dessert made with the fruit of an Earth peach tree, sliced, sweetened, and covered with a biscuit crust. It is best when served with whipped cream. ("Liaisons" [TNG]).

"Peak Performance." *Next Generation* episode #47. Written by David Kemper. Directed by Robert Scheerer. Stardate 42923.4. *First aired in 1989. Riker commands a starship in a war game against* Enterprise-*D Captain Picard.* GUEST CAST: Diana Muldaur as **Pulaski**, **Dr. Katherine**; Roy Brocksmith as **Kolrami, Sirna**; Armin Shimerman as **Bractor**; David L. Lander as Tactician; Leslie Neale as Nagel, Ensign; Glenn Morshower as **Burke, Lieutenant**. SEE: **Avidyne engines; battle simulation, Starfleet; Bractor; Braslota system; Burke, Lieutenant; Grenthemen water hopper; *Hathaway, U.S.S.*; Kolrami, Sirna; *Kreechta*; Kumeh maneuver; laser pulse system; opti-cable; *Potemkin, U.S.S.*; Riker, William T.; sensors; strategema; Tholians; Worf; Zakdorn.**

peanut butter and jelly sandwich. Earth meal made with puréed peanuts and fruit preserves spread between slices of bread. Tom Paris considered a peanut butter and jelly sandwich "comfort" food, since it reminded him of home. ("Faces" [VGR]).

pecan pie. Dessert food consisting of pecan nut compote baked in a crust. Kathryn Janeway delighted Sikarian magistrate **Gathorel Labin** with the taste of pecan pie. ("Prime Factors." [VGR]).

Peddler, Minosian. (Vincent Schiavelli). A holographic humanoid image, preprogrammed to interactively serve as a salesperson for **Minosian** weapons systems. An effective and convincing pitchman, the peddler and the computer systems that generated his image were left over from ancient times when the Minosians were notorious arms dealers. ("The Arsenal of Freedom" [TNG]). *Vincent Schiavelli also played one of the evil Red Lectroids in* The Adventures of Buckaroo Banzai.

Peeples, Ensign. (Craig Hurley). *Enterprise*-D crew member, assigned to engineering. Peeples was one of the first of the *Enterprise*-D crew to suffer hallucinations as a result of his dream-deprived state when the ship was trapped in a **Tyken's Rift** in 2367. ("Night Terrors" [TNG]).

Peers, Selin. (Richard Lineback). **Trill** medical specialist. Peers was sent by his government to be present at Deep Space 9 during **Jadzia Dax**'s extradition hearing in 2369, attempting to return her to planet **Klaestron IV.** He testified at the hearing as an expert on Trills. ("Dax" [DS9]). SEE: **Dax, Curzon**. *Richard Lineback also played Romas in "Symbiosis" (TNG).*

"Pegasus, The." *Next Generation* episode #164. Written by Ronald D. Moore. Directed by LeVar Burton. Stardate 47457.1. *First aired in 1994. A Starfleet admiral tries to salvage his old starship and its illegal cloaking device before the Romulans can beat him to it. This episode establishes why the Federation doesn't use cloaking devices.* GUEST CAST: Nancy Vawter as **Blackwell, Admiral Margaret**; Terry O'Quinn as **Pressman**, **Erik**; Michael Mack as **Sirol**, **Commander**. SEE: **asteroid gamma 601; Blackwell, Admiral Margaret; Boylen, Lieutenant; Captain Picard Day; Commander Riker Day; *Crazy Horse, U.S.S.*; Devolin system; Gates, Ensign; ionizing radiation; Judge Advocate General; Menegay, Paul; Merkoria Quasar; mutiny; *Pegasus, U.S.S.*; phasing cloak; Pressman, Admiral Erik; Ranar, Admiral; Riker, William T.; Sector 1607; Shanthi, Fleet Admiral; Sirol, Commander; Starbase 247; tachyon; terakine; *Terix;* Treaty of Algeron, the; verteron.**

Pegasus, U.S.S. Federation starship, *Oberth* class, Starfleet registry number NCC-53847. Commanded by Captain **Erik Pressman**. The *Pegasus* was a prototype ship, used as a testbed for many new systems designs, many of which were later used in the

design of the *Galaxy*-class starships. While it was not widely known at the time, the *Pegasus* was also used a testing ground for an experimental **phasing cloak**, in direct violation of the **Treaty of Algeron**. The *Pegasus* crew protested the illegal test and eventually mutinied, forcing the captain and seven other crew members to escape the ship in a pod. Shortly after the captain departed, the crew attempted to shut down the cloak. The device malfunctioned, and the ship drifted in space, in a cloaked state until it came to rest within the body of an asteroid in the Devolin system. All members of the crew, save the seven who escaped, were lost when the ship unphased, leaving parts of the ship open to vacuum and parts encased in solid rock. ("The *Pegasus*" [TNG]). *The Pegasus was named for the famous winged horse of Greek mythology that legend holds sprang from the severed neck of Medusa.*

Pegos Minor. Star system where **Dr. Paul Manheim** claimed his laboratory was located when he called for help after a serious accident in 2364. Upon arriving at Pegos Minor, Manheim, obsessed with security, informed the *Enterprise*-D that he was actually at **Vandor IV**. ("We'll Always Have Paris" [TNG]).

pejuta. Beverage often served hot. ("Parallax" [VGR]). Ensign Parsons usually liked it hot, with lemon, but occasionally ordered it cold. ("Cathexis" [VGR]).

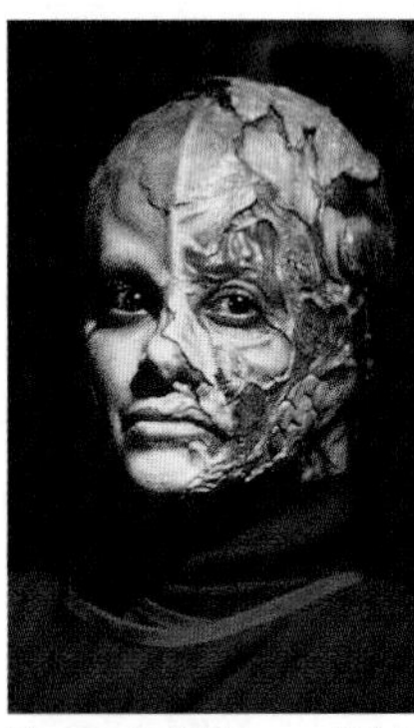

Pel, Danara. (Susan Diol). **Vidiian** physician. Diagnosed at age seven with the deadly Vidiian **phage**, Danara Pel lived with the disease most of her life. She was near death in 2372 when the *Starship Voyager* intercepted her distress call, necessitating drastic measures. The *Voyager's* **Emergency Medical Hologram** transferred Pel's DNA code into a holographic body where Danara existed within the confines of the holographic emitters. As the EMH struggled to repair the damaged neural tissue of the Vidiian's diseased body, Danara began to fall in love with the holographic doctor. Utilizing B'Elanna Torres's Klingon DNA, which was resistant to the phage, the EMH was able to slow the infectious process in Danara's body. Knowing she could not live forever as a hologram, Pel reluctantly returned to her biological body and left for home, continuing the search for a cure to the phage. ("Lifesigns" [VGR]). Several months later, Pel assisted *Voyager* scientists by providing a Vidiian antiviral medication that was successful in treating Captain Janeway and Commander Chakotay for a potentially fatal virus. ("Resolutions" [VGR]). *Susan Diol previously played Carmen Davila in "Silicon Avatar" (TNG).*

Pel. (Hêlen Udy). **Ferengi** waiter hired to work at Quark's bar in 2370. Impressed by Pel's business sense, Quark took the young waiter with him to the Gamma Quadrant to negotiate with the Dosi. After the trip, Pel shocked both Quark and **Grand Nagus Zek** by revealing herself to be a female. Unable to remain with Quark because of Ferengi custom, she boarded an Andorian ship bound for the Gamma Quadrant. ("Rules of Acquisition" [DS9]).

Peldor Festival. SEE: **Bajoran Gratitude Festival.**

peldor joi. In **Bajoran** society, a greeting used in celebration of the **Bajoran Gratitude Festival.** ("Fascination" [DS9]).

Peliar Zel. Class-M Federation planet with two inhabited moons. The planet was populated by a humanoid species characterized by a midline nasal outgrowth. The moons of Peliar Zel were colonized five centuries ago, and the governments of **Alpha Moon** and **Beta Moon** were historically at odds with one another. By 2337, Federation **Ambassador Odan** was called in to mediate a major dispute. Some thirty years later, relations between the moons had again deteriorated to the point of war when Alpha Moon developed an energy source that caused substantial environmental damage to Beta Moon. ("The Host" [TNG]). SEE: **magnetospheric energy taps.**

Pelios Station. Federation facility. Location where **Curzon Dax** and **Benjamin Sisko** first met. ("Invasive Procedures" [DS9]).

Peljenite. Sentient life-form. In 2371, Commander Benjamin Sisko invited the Peljenites to exchange ambassadors with the Federation. ("Family Business" [DS9]).

Pelleus V. Planet. The *Enterprise*-D was scheduled to arrive at Pelleus V shortly after a layover at **Starbase 74** in 2364. ("11001001" [TNG]).

Pelloris Field. Asteroid belt. The Pelloris Field was the source of an asteroid that nearly collided with planet **Tessen III** in 2368. Asteroids in the Pelloris Field were rich in **nitrium**, which served as a food source for **nitrium metal parasites** that lived there. A colony of these parasites infested the *Enterprise*-D in 2368, after which the ship's personnel successfully returned the parasites to the Pelloris Field. ("Cost of Living" [TNG]).

"Pen Pals." *Next Generation* episode #41. Teleplay by Melinda M. Snodgrass. Story by Hannah Louise Shearer. Directed by Winrich Kolbe. Stardate 42695.3. *First aired in 1989. Data inadvertently breaks the Prime Directive by exchanging subspace messages with a little girl on a distant planet, then comes to her rescue when he learns that her planet is endangered.* GUEST CAST: Diana Muldaur as **Pulaski, Dr. Katherine**; Nicholas Cascone as **Davies, Ensign**; Nikki Cox as **Sarjenka**; Ann H. Gillespie as **Hildebrandt**; Colm Meaney as **O'Brien, Miles**; Whitney Rydbeck as **Alans**. SEE: **Alans; Benev Selec; Crusher, Wesley; Davies, Ensign; Drema IV; Elanian singer stone; Hildebrandt; ico-spectrogram; Illium 629; Picard, Jean-Luc; Planetary Geosciences Laboratory; Prixus; resonators; Sarjenka; *sark*, Klingon; Selcundi Drema sector; Selcundi Drema; zabathu, Andorian.**

Pendi II. Homeworld of a trader who related a rumor to the **Maquis** that the Cardassians were smuggling components of a **biogenic weapon** to their colonies in the **Demilitarized Zone** in 2370. ("Preemptive Strike" [TNG]).

Pendleton, Chief. Communications officer aboard the *Enterprise*-D. Geordi La Forge offered to put in a good word with Pendleton on behalf of his friend, **Aquiel Uhnari**, but Uhnari declined the help, saying she would rather earn a promotion on her own merits. ("Aquiel" [TNG]).

Pendrashian cheese. Variety of pressed milk curd native to a planet in the Delta Quadrant. ("Investigations" [VGR]).

Pennington School. College located in Wellington, New Zealand, on **Earth**. Pennington was a respected educational institution, and admission was highly competitive. **Jake Sisko** applied to Pennington and was offered a writing fellowship in 2371 on the strength of one of the stories he had written. Rather than accepting the fellowship, however, Jake decided to defer admission to the school for a year. ("Explorers" [DS9]).

Pentangeli, Giuseppina. (Carole Davis). Arguably the greatest operatic soprano of the 22nd century. Pentangeli was very talented but was also known for her temperament and her large ego. In 2373, the *Voyager's* Emergency Medical Hologram performed the operatic duet "O soave fanciulla" from Puccini's *La Bohème* with a holodeck representation of Giuseppina Pentangeli. ("The Swarm" [VGR]).

Pentarus II. Class-M planet in the Pentarus system. It was searched as a possible crash site when the shuttle ***Nenebek***, carrying Jean-Luc Picard and Wesley Crusher, was lost in 2367. ("Final Mission" [TNG]).

Pentarus V. Class-M Federation planet. The government of Petarus V petitioned *Enterprise*-D Captain Jean-Luc Picard to mediate a labor dispute among its **salenite miners** in 2367. Captain Picard was unable to attend the initial negotiations due to the crash of his transport shuttle, the ***Nenebek***. ("Final Mission" [TNG]).

Pentath III. Planet. Located near the Klingon border, Pentath III was home to a Cardassian colony. In 2372 an outbreak of Rudellian plague necessitated medical relief from various governments. ("Rules of Engagement" [DS9]).

Penthara IV. Class-M Federation planet with a population of twenty million humans. In 2368, Penthara IV was struck by a type-C asteroid. The explosion created a dust cloud that reflected most of the sunlight that would have reached the surface, causing surface temperatures to drop at an alarming rate. The *Enterprise*-D attempted to alleviate the problem by using ship's phasers to release subterranean carbon dioxide gas, in the hopes that the resulting **greenhouse effect** would help warm the planet. Unfortunately, the release of gas was accompanied by unanticipated volcanic activity, producing massive amounts of volcanic ash, compounding the initial problem. A desperate attempt was successful in saving the planet's ecosphere when the airborne particulates were vaporized and the resulting plasma energy was drawn out into space by the *Enterprise*-D's navigational deflector. ("A Matter of Time" [TNG]).

Penthath system. Stellar system located near the Klingon Empire. In 2372, a Klingon civilian transport ship was destroyed by Lieutenant Commander **Worf** near the Penthath system. ("Rules of Engagement" [DS9]).

Penthor-Mul. Gatherer and member of the clan **Lornak**. Arrested in 2313 after a **Gatherer** raid, he died of an apparent heart attack during his trial. Investigation by Dr. Crusher determined that he was assassinated by **Yuta** of the rival **Tralesta** clan. ("The Vengeance Factor" [TNG]). SEE: **microvirus**.

***Peregrine*-class ship**. Small courier spacecraft. The **Maquis** used modified, lightly armed *Peregrine*-class ships as interceptors. ("Heart of Stone" [DS9]).

Peretor. Title given to tribal leaders on planet **Mordan IV.** Karnas once carried that title. His father was killed by the order of Peretor Sain. ("Too Short a Season" [TNG]).

"Perfect Mate, The." *Next Generation* episode #121. Teleplay by Gary Perconte and Michael Piller. Story by René Echevarria and Gary Perconte. Directed by Cliff Bole. Stardate 45761.3. *First aired in 1992. In order to end a war, Picard must deliver an incredibly attractive woman to her future husband, but she falls for Picard.* GUEST CAST: Famke Janssen as **Kamala**; Tim O'Connor as **Briam**, **Ambassador**; Max Grodénchik as **Lenor, Par**; Mickey Cottell as **Alrik**, **Chancellor**; Michael Snyder as **Qol**; David Paul Needles as Miner #1; Roger Rignack as Miner #2; Charles Gunning as Miner #3; April Grace as Transporter Chief; Majel Barrett as Computer voice. SEE: **Akadar, Temple of; Aldorian ale; Alrik, Chancellor; Briam, Ambassador; Ceremony of Reconciliation; Constitution of the United Federation of Planets; empathic metamorph; Ferengi shuttle; Ferengi Trade Mission; *Finiis'ral*; Garuth; Harod IV; Harodian miners; Kamala; Krios 1; Krios; Lenor, Par; Ludugial gold; Paloris Colony; pheromones; Qol; Starbase 117; Targhee moonbeast; *Torze-qua*; Valt Minor; Valtese horns; Valtese; Ventanian thimble.**

pergium. Mineral used on many planets as a source of power for life-support systems. Pergium was found in abundance on planet **Janus VI** (*pictured*), and extracted by the Federation mining colony there. Beginning in 2267, the **Horta**, an indigenous life-form that tunneled through rock, helped the Federation miners to find pergium deposits. ("The Devil in the Dark" [TOS]). The environmental control system aboard *Intrepid*-class starships used pergium for filter regeneration. ("Fair Trade" [VGR]).

peridaxon. Palliative treatment for **Irumodic Syndrome**. ("All Good Things..." [TNG]).

Perikian peninsula. Geographic location on planet Bajor. The headquarters of the **Alliance for Global Unity** was located in labyrinths beneath the peninsula. ("The Circle" [DS9]).

peritoneum. Membrane lining the abdominal cavity in many humanoid species, including **Bajorans**. A phaser blast punctured **Mullibok**'s peritoneum, requiring medical care from Dr. Julian Bashir. ("Progress" [DS9]).

Perrin. (Joanna Miles). Wife to Vulcan Ambassador **Sarek** during the final years of his life. A human woman, fiercely devoted to her husband, Perrin sought to protect Sarek from the knowledge that he suffered from **Bendii Syndrome**, a disease that strips away emotional control. Perrin persuaded Captain **Jean-Luc Picard** to enter into a **mind-meld** with Sarek, permitting Picard's emotional strength to support the ambassador long enough for him to conclude the historic **Legaran** talks in 2366, the final triumph of Sarek's career. ("Sarek" [TNG]). Perrin continued to care for her husband during Sarek's final months, as he suffered from the degenerative effects of Bendii Syndrome. Perrin harbored resentment toward Spock, who publicly opposed Sarek's position during the **Cardassian** wars, and who left for **Romulus** during Sarek's illness without saying goodbye. ("Unification, Part I" [TNG]).

Persephone V. Planet. Persephone V was home to retired Admiral **Mark Jameson** prior to his final mission to **Mordan IV.** ("Too Short a Season" [TNG]).

"Persistence of Vision" *Voyager* episode #24. Written by Jeri Taylor. Directed by James L. Conway. No stardate given. First aired in 1995. *The Voyager crew is assaulted by a Bothan, who uses telepathy to force them to face their deepest fears.* GUEST CAST: Michael Cumpsty as **Burleigh**, **Lord**; Carolyn Seymour as **Templeton**, **Mrs.**; Stan Ivar as **Mark**; Warren Munson as **Paris**, **Admiral**; Lindsey Haun as **Burleigh**, **Beatrice**; Thomas Dekker as **Burleigh**, **Henry**; Patrick Kerr as Bothan; Marva Hicks as **T'Pel**; Majel Barrett as Computer voice. SEE: **Botha; Bothan; Burleigh, Beatrice; Burleigh, Henry; Burleigh, Lord; coffee ice cream; Davenport, Lucille; delta wave frequency; Hargrove, Lieutenant; holonovel; Janeway Lambda-1; Janeway, Kathryn; Mark; Mithren; multiphase pulse; Paris, Admiral; T'Pel; Templeton, Mrs.; Tuvok; Vulcan lute.**

Petarian. Spacefaring civilization. A freighter captained by **Kasidy Yates** in 2371 was owned by Petarian interests. ("Family Business" [DS9]).

Petri. (Jay Robinson). Ambassador from the planet **Troyius**. In 2268, Petri was assigned to escort **Elaan**, the **Dohlman** of **Elas**, to his home planet and to teach her civilized manners in preparation for her marriage to the leader of his planet. Troyius and the planet Elas had been at war for many years. This union was a hope toward peace. Unfortunately, the Dohlman resented having a new culture thrust upon her, and she stabbed Petri. The task of indoctrinating the bride to Troyian culture fell to Captain Kirk, with dire consequences. ("Elaan of Troyius" [TOS]).

Petrokian sausage. A type of food. During a malfunction of the *Enterprise*-D food replicators caused by nitrium metal parasites in 2368, Petrokian sausage was substituted for an order of **Jestral tea**. ("Cost of Living" [TNG]).

pets. SEE: **Beauregard; Christina; Circassian cat; *sehlat*; Maura; Molly; Patches; Spot; Tarkassian razor beast; *targ*; tribbles; wompat.**

"Phage" *Voyager* episode #5. Story By Timothy De Haas. Teleplay By Skye Dent and Brannon Braga. Directed by Winrich Kolbe. Stardate 48532.4. *Aliens steal Neelix's lungs. This was the first appearance of the Vidiian Sodality*. GUEST CAST: Cully Fredricksen as Alien #1; Stephen B. Rappaport as Alien #2; Martha Hackett as **Seska**; Majel Barrett as Computer voice. SEE: **asparagus; blood-gas infuser; cellular toxicity; cytoplasmic stimulator; *darvot* fritters; Dereth; eggs benedict; Emergency Medical Hologram; holodeck and holosuite programs; *honatta*; isotropic restraint; Kes; KLS stabilizer; mess hall; Motura; Neelix; oatmeal; Parsons, Ensign; phage; pulmonary scanner; ration pack; Rectilian vulture; Seska; strawberries and cream; Talaxians; tricorder operations manual; Vidiian Sodality; Vidiian; *Voyager, U.S.S.*; Yallitians.**

phage. In biology, a virus that infects bacteria by attaching a hollow protein tail to a bacteria cell wall, injecting DNA into the cell. Sometimes called a bacteriophage. Phage was also the name of a deadly virus that attacked members of the **Vidiian** people in the Delta Quadrant. The phage consumed the Vidiians' bodies, destroying their genetic codes and cellular structures. There was no known cure for the phage, and the Vidiians survived as a species only by making extensive use of organ transplantation. ("Phage" [VGR]). One of the symptoms of the early stages of the phage is excruciating joint pain. Some who are infected have been known to die from the agony itself. Klingon physiology was resistant to the phage, and Vidiian scientist **Sulan** believed that Klingon genetic material extracted from **B'Elanna Torres** would eventually lead to a cure for the disease. ("Faces" [VGR]).

"Phantasms." *Next Generation* episode #158. Written by Brannon Braga. Directed by Patrick Stewart. Stardate 47225.7. *First aired in 1993. The* Enterprise*-D is plagued by interphasic parasites that attack the crew and affect Data's dream program, giving him nightmares.* GUEST CAST: Gina Ravarra as **Tyler, Ensign**; Bernard Kates as **Freud, Dr. Sigmund**; Clyde Kusatsu as **Nakamura, Admiral**; David L. Crowley as Workman. SEE: **Admiral's Banquet; cellular peptides; Data; feline supplement 25; Freud, Dr. Sigmund; Gates, Ensign; interphasic organisms; interphasic scanner; Nakamura, Admiral; Starbase 84; Starbase 219; Thanatos VII; Tyler, Ensign.**

Phase 1 Search. Standard Starfleet procedure for a painstaking search aboard a ship for an individual presumed to be injured and unable to respond. ("Court Martial" [TOS]).

phase buffer. Component of the sensor array of *Galaxy*-class starships. Located within the **Jefferies tubes**, phase buffers needed to be carefully aligned in order for sensors to function at maximum efficiency. ("Force of Nature" [TNG]).

phase conditioners. Component of seismic regulators. Phase conditioners can malfunction in the presence of **triolic waves**. ("Time's Arrow, Part I" [TNG]). SEE: **Devidia II.**

phase discriminator. Signal detection and processing device. Commander Data had a type-R phase discriminating amplifier in his positronic brain. Lore's brain had a type-L. A crude, handheld version of this instrument was used to adjust the *Enterprise*-D command crew into the **Devidian's** time continuum. ("Time's Arrow, Part I" [TNG]). SEE: **Devidia II**. Emergency transporter armbands contained a type-7 phase discriminator, sensitive enough to enable these bands to be used to generate a subspace force field. ("Timescape" [TNG]). A portable phase discriminator can be used to protect a person from the harmful effects caused by entering an environment with a different **molecular signature**. ("Deadlock" [VGR]).

phase disruptor. SEE: **disruptor; Klingon weapons**.

phase transition coils. Key component of a **transporter** that is responsible for the conversion of the transport subject from matter to energy or the reverse. ("Realm of Fear" [TNG]). A phase transition coil malfunction was briefly suspected in the apparent death of Ambassador T'Pel in 2367, but O'Brien indicated that the coils had been replaced only a week prior to the incident. ("Data's Day" [TNG]). SEE: **phased matter**.

phase, the. Stage in the life cycle of a **Betazoid** female during which she becomes fully sexual. Normally occurs at midlife. An unmarried Betazoid woman in the phase is expected by her culture to focus her sexual energy on one particular man, who will normally become her husband. It is common for a Betazoid female to experience a sex drive of quadrupled intensity during the phase. **Lwaxana Troi** (*pictured*) entered the phase in 2365, and thereafter sought, in succession, Jean-Luc Picard and William Riker as potential husbands. ("Manhunt" [TNG]).

phase-conjugate graviton emitter. Engineering device sometimes used in tractor beams to increase lift capacity. ("The Ship" [DS9]).

phased ion cannon. Energy weapon employing electrically charged beams. The **Mokra Order** had at least 85 phased ion cannons at their disposal to defend their territorial space. ("Resistance" [VGR]).

phased matter. In the operation of a **transporter**, phased matter refers to matter that has been dematerialized by the **phase transition coils** and converted into a **matter stream**. ("Realm of Fear" [TNG]).

phased polaron beam. SEE: **polaron**.

phaser pistol. SEE: **phaser type-2**.

phaser power coupling. Weapons power transfer conduit, part of the **electroplasma system**. On *Intrepid*-class vessels, the primary phaser coupling was located near the outer skin on the anterior portion of the lower hull, while the backup coupling ran adjacent to the **bridge** on Deck 1. ("Basics, Part II" [VGR]).

phaser range. Training and recreation facility aboard Federation starships. A dark chamber in which holographic targets appear at random in the distance. Shooting at these moving targets was a test of proficiency with phaser hand weapons. When two participants are involved, each player must remain within a semicircular area, with both players' areas forming a full circle about three meters in diameter. ("A Matter of Honor" [TNG]). Worf and Guinan shared a practice session together in the *Enterprise*-D's phaser range in late 2367. Guinan was a better shot than Worf. ("Redemption, Part I" [TNG]).

phaser rifle. SEE: **phaser type-3**.

phaser type-1. Small handheld weapon used by Starfleet personnel who preferred not to appear conspicuously armed, as during diplomatic functions. Like all such weapons, phaser type-1 could be adjusted to a variety of settings including stun, heat, and disruption. Phaser 1, also known as a hand phaser, was not as powerful as the **phaser type-2** pistol. ("The Devil in the Dark" [TOS]). Some versions of phaser type-1 were designed to fit into a pistol grip unit, forming the more powerful phaser type-2.

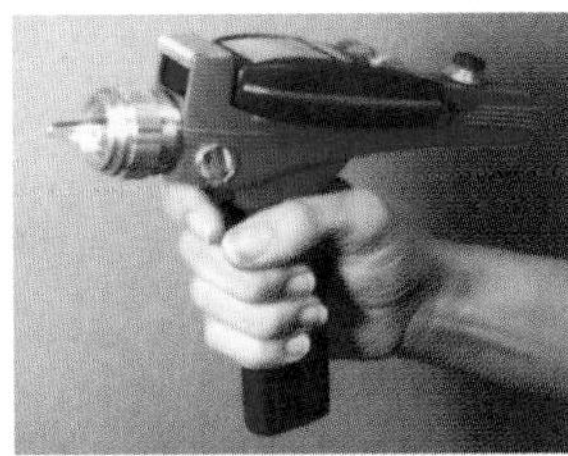

phaser type-2. Medium-sized handheld weapon used by Starfleet personnel. Early versions of phaser type-2 were pistol-like in design. Significantly more powerful than the tiny **phaser type-1**, the phaser pistol actually incorporated the phaser 1 into its design. Like all handheld phaser weapons, phaser 2 could be adjusted to a variety of settings including stun, heat, and disruption. ("The Devil in the Dark" [TOS]). Later versions of phaser-2 were wandlike in design. *(Star Trek: The Next Generation).*

phaser type-3. Handheld phaser rifle weapon. Extremely powerful, seldom necessary on Starfleet missions due to the great power and utility of the smaller type-1 and type-2 phasers. Nevertheless, Spock believed a phaser rifle to be necessary while attempting to quarantine Gary Mitchell on planet **Delta Vega** in 2265. ("Where No Man Has Gone Before" [TOS]). Hundreds of type-3 phaser rifles were captured from **Kriosian** rebels in 2367 by the Klingon government, evidence that the Federation was aiding the rebels. Investigation revealed the weapons to be Romulan in origin. ("The Mind's Eye" [TNG]). Federation phaser rifles can be modified to emit an expanding energy pulse. The pulse does not harm equipment, but does affect some living beings. In 2371, the crew of the *U.S.S. Defiant* used phasers configured in this manner to sweep the ship for a **Founder** who was sabotaging their starship. ("The Adversary" [DS9]). Even less frequently used were compression phaser rifles, although some Federation starships, including the *U.S.S. Voyager*, carried them in their weapons inventory for contingency situations. ("Caretaker" [VGR]). In 2372, a standard-issue Starfleet type-3 phaser rifle had 16 beam settings, a fully autonomous recharge, and multiple target acquisition, and was gyrostabilized. ("Return to Grace" [DS9]). *A phaser rifle was used only once during the Original Series, the one wielded by Kirk in "Where No Man Has Gone Before." Phaser rifles were not used for the first few seasons of* Star Trek: The Next Generation, *until "The Mind's Eye," because it was believed that type-1 and type-2 phasers were powerful enough to handle just about anything.*

phaser type-4. Medium-sized phaser emitter device, mountable on small vehicles such as shuttlecraft, although not part of most shuttles' standard equipment. ("The Outcast" [TNG]). SEE: ***Magellan, Shuttlecraft***.

phaser type-8. Ship-mounted phaser emitter device. **Maquis ships** in the **Demilitarized Zone** gained possession of several type-8 phasers through covert means and used them in an attack on **Gul Evek**'s ship in 2370. ("Preemptive Strike" [TNG]).

phaser. Acronym for PHASed Energy Rectification, a directed-energy weapon used by the Federation Starfleet and others. Phasers were used as sidearms by Starfleet personnel. Most such weapons were either **phaser type-1**, otherwise known as hand phasers, which were used primarily when conspicuous weapons were undesirable, or the larger, more powerful **phaser type-2**, formerly known as pistol phasers. Phaser type-2 weapons were capable of power settings as high as 16. ("Frame of Mind" [TNG]). Type-3 phasers, also known as phaser rifles, were seldom used. ("Where No Man Has Gone Before" [TOS], "The Mind's Eye" [TNG]). Large ship-mounted phaser weapons, often called phaser banks, were standard equipment aboard many Starfleet vessels. By 2367, the effective tactical range of shipboard phaser banks (and most directed-energy weapons) was about 300,000 kilometers (about one light-second). Ship's phasers could be reconfigured to drill into planetary surfaces, and could effectively drill to great depths. ("Inheritance" [TNG]). *Ship's phasers were also used to drill into a planet in the episodes "Legacy" (TNG) and "A Matter of Time" (TNG). Phasers did not exist during the 22nd century, according to Worf in "A Matter of Time" (TNG), so they had to have been invented no earlier than the year 2200. Phasers were apparently not in common use as late as 2254, when the* Enterprise *landing party in "The Cage" (TOS) was equipped with laser weapons.* SEE: Illustration.

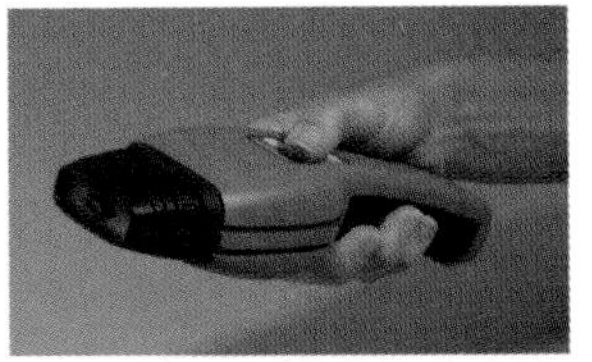

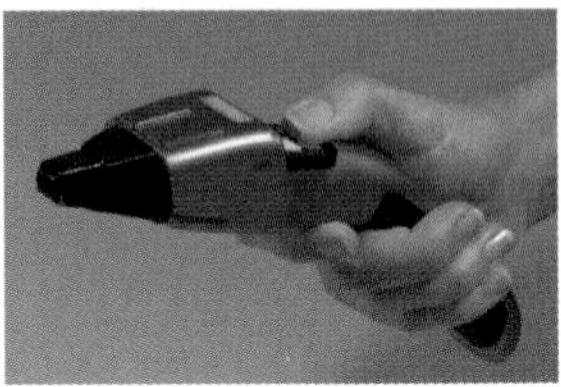

phasing cloak. Invisibility-screen generator that was designed not only to disguise a starship from visual and sensor detection, but also to alter the atomic structure of the ship, so that ship could pass through normal matter. The strategic advantages of the device would have been numerous, and the Federation covertly worked on its development, in violation of the **Treaty of Algeron**. The cloak eventually proved itself in practical use, but the Federation was forbidden from using it by the terms of the treaty. ("The *Pegasus*" [TNG]). SEE: **cloaking device.**

Pheben system. Planetary system; site of a mission by the Klingon vessel ***Pagh*** during William Riker's tenure as first officer of that ship in 2365. ("A Matter of Honor" [TNG]).

Phelan system. Star system located some 2.5 light-years from the **J'naii** planet. The *Enterprise*-D was assigned to a diplomatic mission in the Phelan system following an assignment at the J'naii system in 2368. ("The Outcast" [TNG]).

pheromones. Biochemicals secreted by many carbon-based life-forms, whose scent affects the behavior of other members of the same or similar species. Many animal species use pherenomes for communication or to attract members of the opposite sex. **Empathic metamorphs** produce highly elevated levels of a substance similar to pheromones during the final stage of their sexual maturation. ("The Perfect Mate" [TNG]). SEE: **Kamala**. *Enterprise*-D personnel used pheromones extracted from Deanna Troi to lure the devolved Worf away from sickbay, while they worked on a cure for **Barclay's Protomorphosis Syndrome** in 2370. ("Genesis" [TNG]).

pheromonic sensor. Instrument sensitive to pheromones. Pheromonic sensors can be set to be triggered when a person of a particular species gets within range, and were a favored tool of **Flaxian assassins**. ("Improbable Cause" [DS9]).

Philana. (Barbara Babcock). Wife of Platonian leader **Parmen**. Although she looked some thirty years old, she was in fact some two thousand three hundred years old and enjoyed the benefits of power in her repressive society. ("Plato's Stepchildren" [TOS]). SEE: **Mea 3**.

Phillips, Zoey. Former girlfriend of a young Benjamin Sisko. The two dated for three years. ("Paradise Lost" [DS9]).

Phoenix Cluster. A dense expanse of stars, largely unexplored by 2368. The *Enterprise*-D was assigned to conduct two weeks of research in the Phoenix Cluster when the **Ktarian** plot to infiltrate Starfleet was launched. ("The Game" [TNG]). *The Phoenix*

Phaser type-1

1) 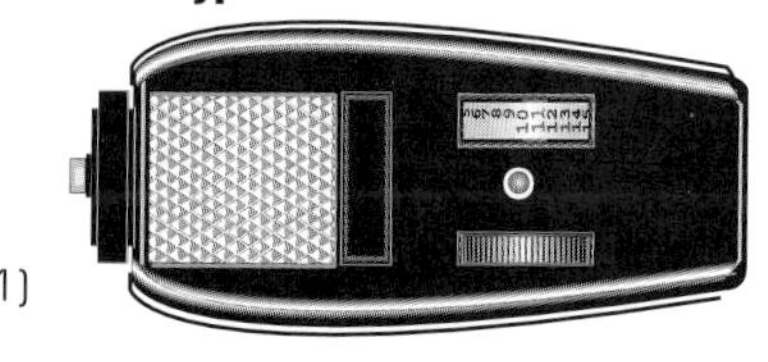

2) 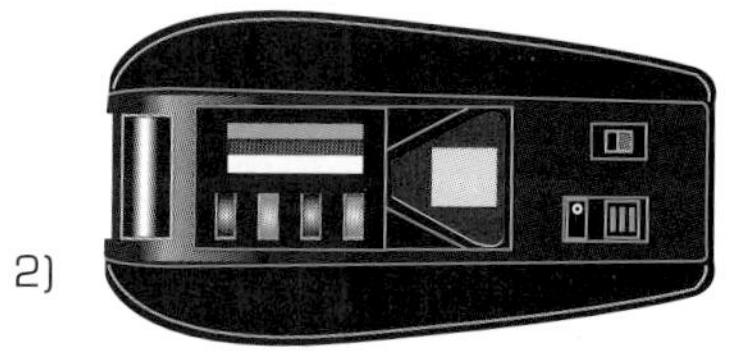

3) 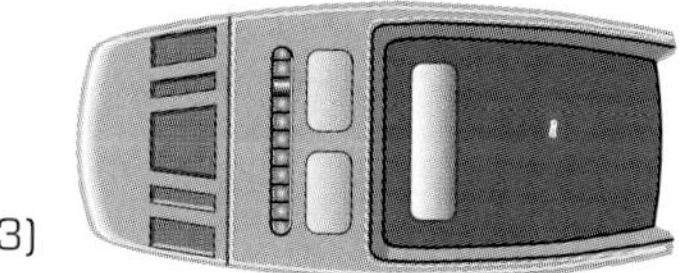

1) *Star Trek: The Original Series* 2) *Star Trek III* 3) *Star Trek: The Next Generation*

Phaser type-2

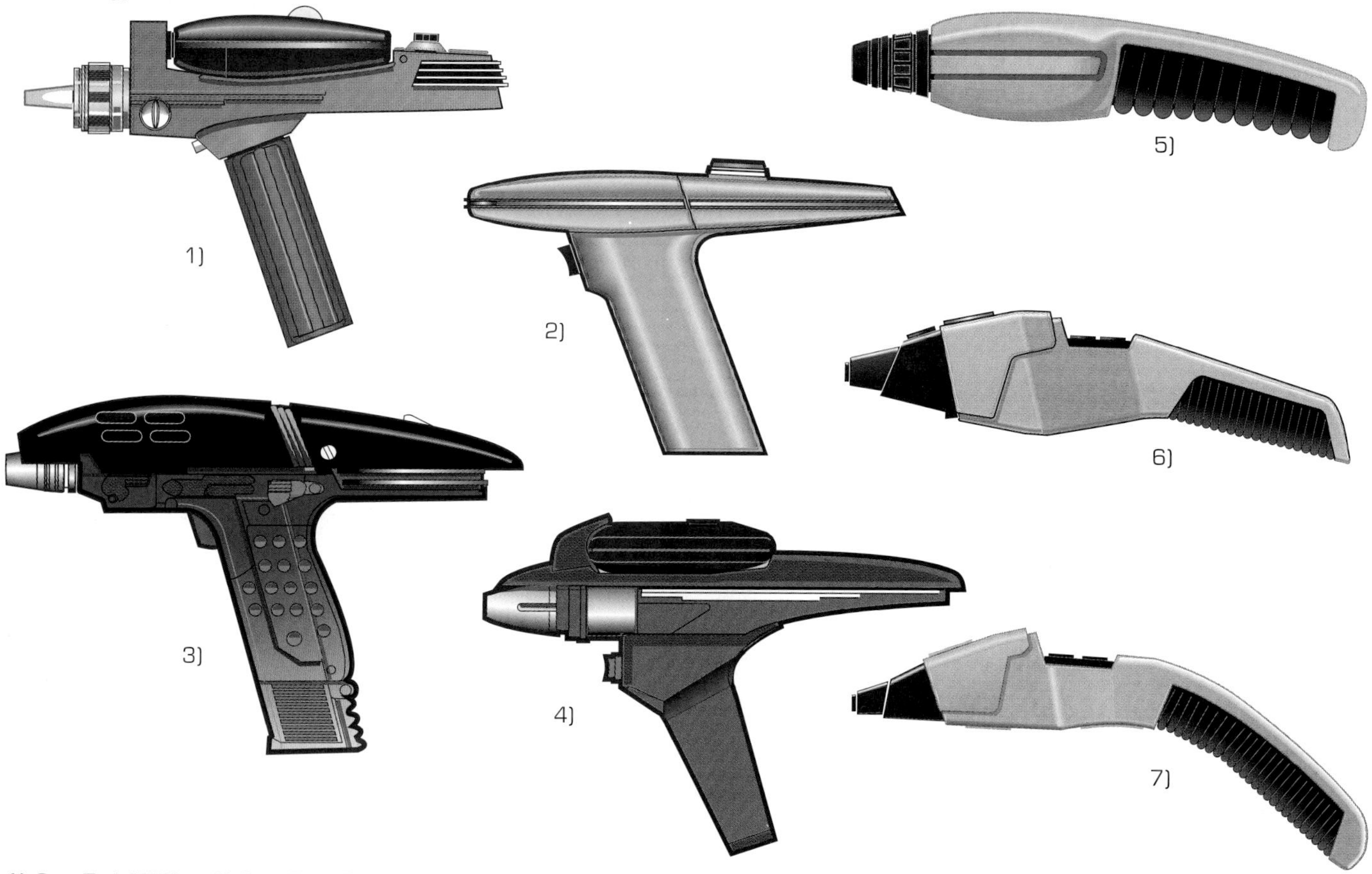

1) 2) 3) 4) 5) 6) 7)

1) *Star Trek* (TOS). 2) *Star Trek: TMP, Star Trek II,* and "Yesterday's Enterprise" (TNG). 3) *Star Trek V, Star Trek VI.* 4) *Star Trek III, Star Trek IV,* and "Final Mission" (TNG). 5) *Star Trek: The Next Generation,* season 1 and 2. 6) *Star Trek: The Next Generation,* season 3. 7) *Star Trek: Deep Space Nine,* season 3, *Star Trek: Voyager,* season 2.

Phaser type-3

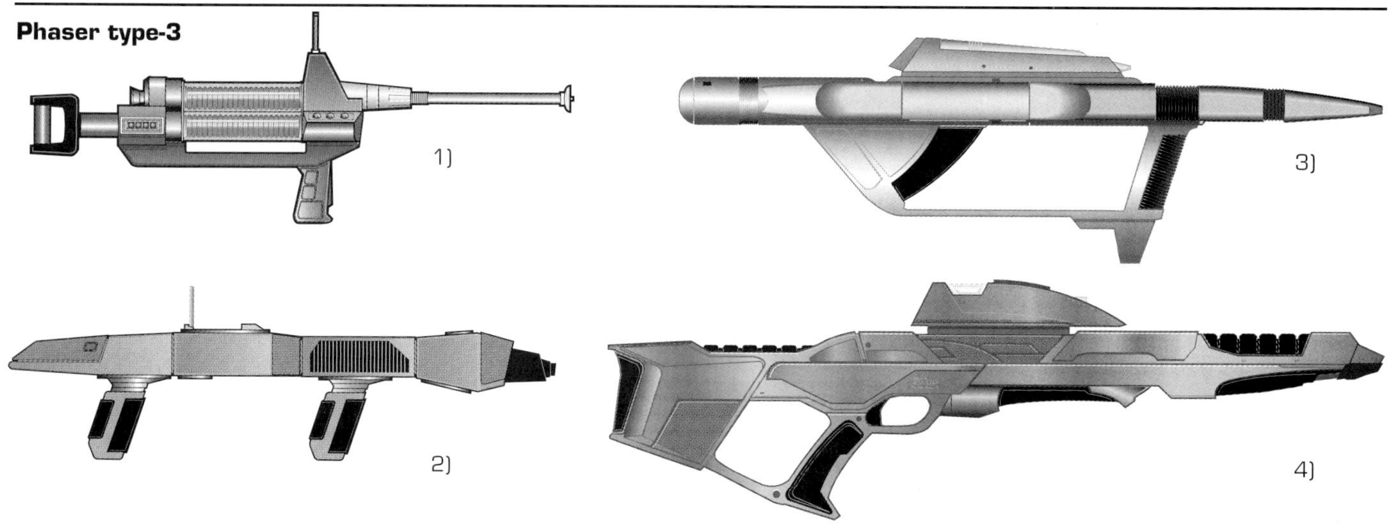

1) *Star Trek: The Original Series.* 2) *Star Trek: The Next Generation.* 3) Compression version, *Star Trek: Voyager.* 4) Compression version, *Star Trek: First Contact.*

Cluster was, in part, named for the Phoenix Asteroids in John Carpenter and Dan O'Bannon's film Dark Star.

***Phoenix*, U.S.S.** Federation ***Nebula*-class** starship, Starfleet registry number NCC-65420. In 2367, the ship was under the command of **Captain Benjamin Maxwell** at the time when Maxwell ordered an unauthorized attack on **Cardassian** forces near Sector 21503. Two Cardassian ships and a Cardassian science station were destroyed by the *Phoenix*. Maxwell said his actions were intended to prove his suspicions that the Cardassians had been planning a new offensive against the Federation. Maxwell was subsequently relieved of command of the *Phoenix*. ("The Wounded" [TNG]). *The dedication plaque for the* Phoenix *in Maxwell's ready room carried the motto, "There will be an answer, let it be." The Phoenix was the first appearance of a* Nebula-*class ship. The starship was presumably named after Zefram Cochrane's historic warp ship that first broke the light-speed barrier in 2063.*

***Phoenix*.** The first spacecraft launched from Earth to travel faster than light. The *Phoenix* was built by noted space pioneer **Zefram Cochrane** and engineer **Lily Sloane**. It was built from an old **Titan V** nuclear missile, modified with a small crew cabin and twin warp nacelles. The *Phoenix* made its historic first warp flight on April 4, 2063, piloted by Zefram Cochrane, symbolically rising from the ashes of **World War III**, ushering in a new era for humankind. The flight of the *Phoenix* was directly responsible for Earth's **first contact** with extraterrestrials, leading to Earth's recovery from the **postatomic horror**. The *Phoenix* later was placed on display at the Smithsonian Institution, and was the subject of a course taught at the **Starfleet Academy**. *(Star Trek: First Contact). The ship was named for the immortal bird from Egyptian mythology that periodically was consumed in fire, then arose from the ashes reborn. The* Phoenix *was designed by Herman Zimmerman and John Eaves, loosely based on a conjectural model created by Greg Jein.*

phoretic analyzer. Biomedical analysis device. Dr. Julian Bashir once asked **Odo** to pour himself into a phoretic analyzer so Bashir could gain a better understanding of the **shape-shifter**'s chemistry. ("Dramatis Personae" [DS9]).

photon grenade. Short-range, variable-yield energy weapon that creates a powerful electromagnetic pulse. At lower settings, it is capable of stunning humanoid life-forms in an enclosed area. Photon grenades were considered for use during the *Enterprise*-D's rescue mission of ***Arcos*** personnel at **Turkana IV** in 2367, but were ultimately considered ineffective. ("Legacy" [TNG]).

photon torpedo. Tactical weapon used by Federation starships. Photon torpedoes are self-propelled missiles containing a small quantity of matter and antimatter bound together in a magnetic bottle, launched at warp speed at a target. Photon torpedoes are usually the weapon of choice when a ship is at warp drive, since they are not limited by the speed of light. The warhead can be removed from a photon torpedo, leaving a small, high-speed missile that can be used as an instrumented probe, to transport small objects ("The Emissary" [TNG]), and even for burials in space. *(Star Trek II: The Wrath of Khan*, "The Schizoid Man" [TNG]). *Galaxy*-class starships are capable of launching up to ten photon torpedoes simultaneously from a single launch tube. Each torpedo can be independently targeted. ("The Arsenal of Freedom" [TNG]). A *Galaxy*-class starship is normally equipped with 250 photon torpedoes. ("Conundrum" [TNG]). The *U.S.S. Voyager* was equipped with type-6 photon torpedoes. ("Dreadnought" [VGR]).

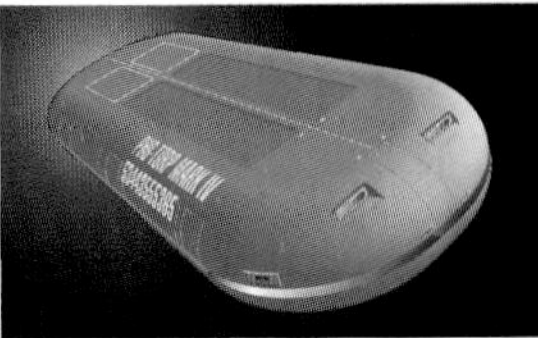

photonic being. Noncorporeal, sentient life-form discovered in the corona of a protostar in the Delta Quadrant by the crew of the *Starship Voyager* in 2371. Two of these creatures were accidentally brought to *Voyager* while gathering energy from a nearby protostar. One of the creatures took refuge on the ship's holodeck, where it briefly captured three members of the *Voyager* crew while trying to communicate with the crew. ("Heroes and Demons" [VGR]). SEE: ***Beowulf*; Grendel.**

photoplasma. Energy signature. A **tricorder** can be programmed to emit a photoplasmic trail to mark a path for later backtracking. ("Twisted" [VGR]). *It may be a coincidence, but physicist Harvey P. Lynn, Jr.,* Star Trek's *first scientific consultant, who worked with Gene Roddenberry during the early days of the original* Star Trek *series, suggested the term "photoplasma" for something in the first pilot episode. Although Roddenberry did not use this particular suggestion at the time, three decades later, Lynn's term finally made it to the screen.*

Phyrox plague. Disease. The population of planet Cor Caroli V suffered an outbreak of Phyrox plague in 2366. The epidemic was contained with assistance from *Enterprise*-D personnel. Starfleet Command classified the incident as secret. ("Allegiance" [TNG]).

physiostimulator. Medical instrument used to elevate metabolic functions in an impaired individual. ("The *Enterprise* Incident" [TOS]).

***pi* (π).** Mathematical expression representing the ratio of the circumference of a circle over the diameter. An irrational number approximately equal to 3.1415926535. When the **Redjac** energy-based creature took over the main computer of the original *Starship Enterprise* in 2267, Spock forced the creature from the computer by ordering it to compute *pi* to the last decimal place, a mathematically impossible task. ("Wolf in the Fold" [TOS]).

***Pi*.** Romulan scoutship that crashed on planet **Galorndon Core**, one-half light-year into Federation space, in 2366. The ship was rigged to self-destruct shortly after the crash. Only the wreckage of the ship was recovered, and it was believed the *Pi* may have been on a covert mission in Federation space. ("The Enemy" [TNG]). *The* Pi *was not seen in "The Enemy," but one might assume it would have been of the same design as the Romulan scoutship built three episodes later for "The Defector" (TNG).*

Picard Delta One. Holodeck computer file, a virtual reality within which lived the computer intelligences known as **Professor James Moriarty** and **Countess Barthalomew**. In the program, the Professor and the Countess believed they were exploring the universe together, having escaped the confines of the *Enterprise*-D holodeck. ("Ship in a Bottle" [TNG]).

Picard Maneuver

A) Objective viewpoint.

B) Ferengi ship's viewpoint.

1A) TIME: 00 seconds. The *Stargazer* is approximately 9 million kilometers from the Ferengi ship. At this distance, it takes light from the *Stargazer* about 30 seconds to reach the Ferengi ship. Both ships have little motion with respect to each other.

1B) From the viewpoint of the Ferengi ship, the *Stargazer* is not moving. However, because the *Stargazer* is some 30 light-seconds away, what the Ferengi sees is actually the image of the *Stargazer* some 30 seconds ago.

1

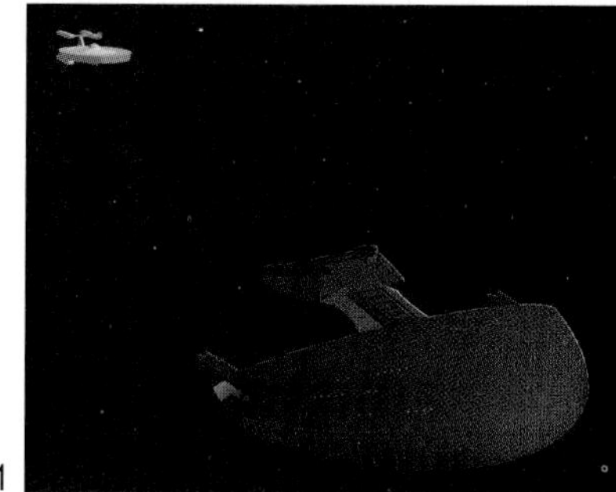

2A) TIME: 01 seconds. The *Stargazer* accelerates into warp drive, moving closer to the Ferengi ship.

2B) Because of the 30-second lag, the Ferengi cannot know yet that the *Stargazer* has moved until those 30 seconds have passed.

2

3A) TIME: 15 seconds. The *Stargazer* has assumed a new position, closer to the Ferengi ship, in preparation for attack.

3B) Again, the Ferengi still has no way of knowing that the *Stargazer* has moved, because light from the *Stargazer*'s new position has not yet reached the Ferengi ship.

3

4A) TIME: 20 seconds. The *Stargazer* fires weapons.

4B) Because the new position of the *Stargazer* is closer than the old position, light from the new *Stargazer* position reaches the Ferengi ship while light form the old position is still en route. In other words, the *Stargazer* appears to be in two places at once, thus confusing the Ferengi ship.

4

5A) TIME: 31 seconds. The battle is over; the *Stargazer* has destroyed the Ferengi ship.

5B) The light from the *Stargazer* that left when the ship shifted position finally reached the Ferengi ship. Is is now possible for the Ferengi to know what the *Stargazer* is doing, although it is too late to do anything about it.

5

Picard Maneuver. A tactic devised by Captain **Jean-Luc Picard** aboard the ***U.S.S. Stargazer*** during the **Battle of Maxia** in 2355. The *Stargazer* accelerated to warp speed and for an instant appeared to be in two places at once to a distant observer, the opponent vessel. This maneuver, taking advantage of the fact that the opponent vessel was using only light-speed sensors, allowed the Federation starship to fire and damage their enemy. The Picard Maneuver is required study at Starfleet Academy. ("The Battle" [TNG]). SEE: Diagram on previous page.

Picard Mozart trio, program 1. Musical selection created by Captain Picard with music by **Mozart** with accompanying **Ressikan flute.** ("A Fistful of Datas" [TNG]).

Picard's photo album. Large scrapbook used by **Jean-Luc Picard** to hold family photos and other mementos. The album was a cherished possession of Jean-Luc's and featured pictures of his brother, **Robert Picard**, and his nephew, **René Picard**. After the crash of the *Enterprise*-D on Veridian III, Picard retrieved the album from the wreckage of his **ready room**. *(Star Trek Generations). Picard's album contained other personal mementos not seen in the movie. These included an award certificate for having won the* ***Starfleet Academy marathon*** *of 2323, a Starfleet Academy graduation announcement for Jean-Luc Picard (ceremony held on July 20, 2327, in Gagarin Hall in San Francisco), Starfleet orders giving him command of the* U.S.S. Stargazer, *an award presented to* ***Maurice Picard*** *for an outstanding vintage, the Grankite order of Tactics, various news clippings, wine bottle labels from Chateau Picard, personal correspondence, and an invitation to the wedding of Jack and* ***Beverly Crusher***. *These items were designed by Geoff Mandel, Alan Kobayashi, and Penny Juday.*

Picard, Javier Maribona. SEE: **Maribona-Picard, Javier.**

Picard, Jean-Luc. (Patrick Stewart). Captain of the fifth and sixth *Starships* **Enterprise** and a noted figure in space exploration, science, and interstellar diplomacy. ("Encounter at Farpoint, Part I" [TNG]).

Family. Picard was born on Earth in 2305 to **Maurice Picard** and **Yvette Gessard Picard**. Maurice was a tradition-bound French vintner who discouraged young Jean-Luc's ambitions of voyaging among the stars. ("Tapestry" [TNG], "Chain of Command, Part II" [TNG]). Jean-Luc was raised on a family farm in **Labarre, France**, along with his older brother, **Robert Picard**. ("Family" [TNG]). As a boy, young Jean-Luc enjoyed building ships in bottles; his collection included a legendary **Promellian** battle cruiser, a ship that he would one day discover in his voyages aboard the *Enterprise*-D. Those toy ships served as a springboard for the future captain's imagination. ("Booby Trap" [TNG]). As a boy, Picard visited the Smithsonian Institution and viewed **Zefram Cochrane**'s warp ship, the ***Phoenix***, several times. *(Star Trek: First Contact)*. Jean-Luc Picard was proud of his illustrious family history. One of his ancestors fought at the Battle of Trafalgar, a Picard won a **Nobel Prize** for chemistry, and Picards were among those who settled the first **Martian Colonies**. *(Star Trek Generations)*. SEE: **Picard's photo album; Trafalgar, Battle of**. On the other hand, Picard felt guilt over the role of another ancestor, **Javier Maribona-Picard**, in the infamous crushing of the **Pueblo Revolt** on Earth in 1692. ("Journey's End" [TNG]).

Academy and early career. Picard failed in 2322 to gain entrance to **Starfleet Academy** at the age of 17, but was admitted a year later. ("Coming of Age" [TNG]). As a first-year cadet in 2323, Picard became the only freshman ever to win the Starfleet Academy marathon on Danula II. ("The Best of Both Worlds, Part II" [TNG]). Picard won top academic honors as well. ("Family" [TNG]). Cadet Picard committed a serious offense while at the academy. Years later, he credited academy groundskeeper **Boothby** (*pictured*) with making it possible for him to graduate by helping him to do the right thing. ("The First Duty" [TNG]). Shortly after graduating from Starfleet Academy with the class of 2327, Picard was on leave with several classmates at **Starbase Earhart**, where he picked a fight with three **Nausicaans** at the **Bonestell Recreation Facility**. One of the Nausicaans stabbed Picard through the heart, necessitating a **cardiac replacement** procedure, leaving Picard with an artificial heart. ("Samaritan Snare" [TNG], "Tapestry" [TNG]). SEE: **Batanides, Marta; Zweller, Cortin**. *(Q commented that the injury to Picard's heart had occurred "30 years ago," which would set the Nausicaan incident in 2338. Unfortunately, this was a mistake, since "The First Duty" [TNG] established that Picard graduated in 2327, but the oversight was not caught until after the episode was filmed. The young Ensign Picard was played by Marcus Nash.)* As a young lieutenant, Picard met Ambassador **Sarek** at the wedding of the ambassador's son. Picard recalled how in awe he was at meeting someone who had helped to shape the Federation. ("Sarek" [TNG]). *(The episode does not make it clear which "son" Picard was referring to, although Gene Roddenberry said he thought it was* ***Spock***.*)* As a young officer, Picard was romantically involved with the future **Jenice Manheim**. Although the two had been strongly attracted to each other, Picard feared commitment, and eventually broke off the relationship in 2342. For many years, Picard regretted losing Jenice, and the two saw each other again in 2364 when the *Enterprise*-D saved her husband, **Dr. Paul Manheim**, after a serious laboratory accident on **Vandor IV**. ("We'll Always Have Paris" [TNG]). In his early career, Picard distinguished himself when he led an away team to planet **Milika III**, to save an endangered ambassador. ("Tapestry" [TNG]).

On the *Stargazer*. Lieutenant Picard was a bridge officer on the ***U.S.S. Stargazer*** when the ship's captain was killed. Picard took charge of the bridge, and for his service in the emergency was offered the command of the *Stargazer*. ("Tapestry" [TNG]). Picard comanded the *Stargazer* for some 20 years, until 2355, when the ship was nearly destroyed by an unprovoked sneak attack near the **Maxia Zeta Star System**. The surviving *Stargazer* crew, including Picard, drifted for weeks in shuttlecraft before being rescued. The assailant in the incident was unknown, but was later found to be a Ferengi spacecraft. ("The Battle" [TNG]). SEE: **Picard Maneuver**. Following the loss of the *Stargazer*, Picard was court-martialed as required by standard Starfleet procedure, but he was exonerated. The prosecutor in the case was **Phillipa Louvois**, with whom Picard had been romantically involved. ("The Measure of a Man" [TNG]).

Aboard the *Enterprise*-D. Jean-Luc Picard was appointed captain of the fifth *Starship Enterprise* in 2363, shortly after the ship was commissioned. ("Encounter at Farpoint" [TNG]). Picard was offered a promotion to the admiralty in 2364 when **Admiral Gregory Quinn** was attempting to consolidate his power base to combat an unknown alien intelligence that was trying to take over Starfleet Command. Picard declined the offer, citing his belief that he could better serve the Federation as a starship commander. ("Coming of Age" [TNG]). An energy vortex near the Endicor system created a duplicate of Picard from six hours in the future, in 2365. Although the duplicate was identical to the "present" person, Picard had difficulty accepting the existence of his twin because he believed the twin might have been responsible for the destruction of his ship, a deeply repugnant thought. ("Time Squared" [TNG]). Picard's artificial heart required routine replacement, most recently in 2365, when complications in the cardiac replacement procedure performed at **Starbase 515** necessitated emergency assistance by **Dr. Katherine Pulaski**. ("Samaritan Snare" [TNG]). Picard met Ambassador Sarek again in 2366, when Sarek's last mission was jeopardized by **Bendii Syndrome,** which caused the ambassador to lose emotional control. Picard **mind-meld**ed with Sarek to lend the ambassador the emotional stability needed to conclude the historic treaty with the **Legarans**. ("Sarek" [TNG]).

Picard was abducted by the **Borg** in late 2366 as part of the Borg assault on the Federation. Picard was surgically mutilated and transformed into an entity called **Locutus of Borg**. ("The Best of Both Worlds, Part I" [TNG]). As Locutus, Picard was forced to cooperate in the devastating battle of **Wolf 359**, in which he was forced to help destroy 39 Federation starships and their crews. Picard was rescued by an *Enterprise*-D away team, then surgically restored by Dr. Crusher. ("The Best of Both Worlds, Part II" [TNG]). (In an alternate **quantum reality**, Picard was lost to the Borg in 2366. In that reality, Riker was promoted to captain following his loss.) ("Parallels" [TNG]). Following his return from the Borg, Picard spent several weeks in rehabilitation from the terrible physical and psychological trauma. While the *Enterprise*-D was undergoing repairs at **Earth Station McKinley**, Picard took the opportunity to visit his home town of Labarre for the first time in almost 20 years. While there, he stayed with his brother **Robert Picard**, met Robert's wife, **Marie Picard**, and their son, **René Picard**, for the first time. Picard briefly toyed with the idea of leaving Starfleet to accept directorship of the **Atlantis Project**, but his return home helped him realize that he belonged on the *Enterprise*-D. ("Family" [TNG]).

Picard was reduced to a child after passing through an energy field in 2369. ("Rascals" [TNG]). Jean-Luc Picard suffered profound emotional abuse in 2369 when he was captured by **Gul Madred**, a Cardassian officer who tortured Picard for Starfleet tactical information. Picard resisted, but later confessed that the experience so brutalized him that he would have told Madred anything had he not been rescued. ("Chain of Command, Parts I and II" [TNG]). Picard's command of the *Enterprise*-D came to a premature end in 2371, when the ship was destroyed at planet **Veridian III** while trying to prevent **Dr. Tolian Soran** from destroying the **Veridian system**. Working with Picard to stop Soran was **James T. Kirk**, captain of the original *Starship Enterprise*. Kirk, who had been missing for some 78 years following the launch of the *Enterprise*-B, was killed while stopping Soran. SEE: **nexus**. *(Star Trek Generations).*

Aboard the *Enterprise*-E. Captain Picard assumed command of the *Sovereign*-class *Enterprise*-E upon its launch in 2372. When a Borg ship threatened Earth in 2373, Picard violated orders and responded in defense of his homeworld. Picard's residual connection to the Borg collective made it possible for the Starfleet armada to destroy the Borg ship. *(Star Trek: First Contact).*

Picard and the Klingon Empire. Picard assumed an unprecedented role in Klingon politics when he served as **Arbiter of Succession** following the death of Klingon leader **K'mpec** in 2367. K'mpec took the highly unusual step of appointing an outsider as arbiter so as to ensure that the choice of K'mpec's successor would not plunge the empire into civil war. Under Picard's arbitration, council member **Gowron** emerged as the sole challenger for leadership of the High Council. ("Reunion" [TNG]).

Personal interests. Picard was something of a Renaissance man, whose areas of interest ranged from drama to astrophysics. He was an avid amateur archaeologist, occasionally publishing scientific papers on the subject, and even addressing the **Federation Archaeology Council** in 2367. ("QPid" [TNG]). SEE: **Tagus III**. Early in his career, at the urging of his teacher, noted archaeologist **Richard Galen**, Picard seriously considered pursuing archaeology on a professional level. Picard's path later crossed Galen's again just before Galen's death in 2369. Picard helped complete Galen's greatest discovery, the reconstruction of an ancient message from a humanoid species that lived some four billion years ago. ("The Chase" [TNG]). SEE: **humanoid life**. Picard studied the legendary ancient **Iconians** while at the academy. ("Contagion" [TNG]). Picard was also an accomplished equestrian, and one of his favorite holodeck programs was a woodland setting in which he enjoyed riding a computer-simulated Arabian mare. ("Pen Pals" [TNG]). Picard played the piano when he was young ("Lessons" [TNG]), but his deep love of music may have stemmed from an incident in 2368 when his mind received a lifetime of memories from the now-dead planet **Kataan**, and he experienced the life of a man named **Kamin**, who died a thousand years ago. Kamin had played a **Ressikan flute** (*pictured*), and Picard treasured that instrument because of having shared Kamin's memories. ("The Inner Light" [TNG]).

Picard shared his music with **Neela Daren**, an *Enterprise*-D crew member with whom he became romantically involved in 2369. ("Lessons" [TNG]). Picard was involved with **Miranda Vigo** in 2346 during shore leave on Earth, and although they attempted to keep in touch, he never saw her again. In 2370, **Bok** resequenced **Jason Vigo**'s DNA to appear as Picard's son. Bok planned to kill Jason in retaliation for Picard supposedly murdering his son in 2355. ("Bloodlines" [TNG]). Picard was introduced to Beverly Howard, the future **Beverly Crusher** (*pictured*), in 2344, and fell in love with her. Picard never acted on his feelings because Beverly was involved with his best friend, **Jack Crusher**, whom she married in 2348. When Jack was killed in 2354, Picard still did not reveal his attraction for her, because he felt to do so would be to betray his friend. Beverly finally learned of Picard's love in 2370, when Picard and Crusher were implanted with **psi-wave devices** so that she could read his thoughts. ("Attached" [TNG]). With the tragic death of his brother, Robert, and his nephew, René, in 2371, Picard experienced regret at his decision not to have children. *(Star Trek Generations).*

According to Star Trek: The Next Generation *supervising producer Robert Justman, Captain Picard was named for French oceanographer Jacques Piccard (1922-), who explored the depths of Earth's Marianas Trench aboard the bathyscaph* Trieste. *Young Picard in "Rascals" was played by David Tristen Birkin, who also played René Picard in "Family" (TNG). Picard's mother was seen briefly in "Where No One Has Gone Before" (TNG), and*

his father made an appearance in "Tapestry" (TNG), both flashbacks of sorts, since both people were dead at the time of those episodes.

Jean-Luc Picard was first seen in "Encounter at Farpoint" (TNG).

Picard, Marie. (Samantha Eggar). Wife to **Robert Picard**, and **Jean-Luc Picard**'s sister-in-law. Marie and Robert had a son, **René Picard**. A gracious and lovely woman, Marie was responsible for keeping the peace between Robert and Jean-Luc. Though they did not meet until his homecoming in 2367, Marie had corresponded regularly with Jean-Luc, keeping him informed of family matters. ("Family" [TNG]). Marie was widowed in 2371 with the tragic death of her husband and her son in a fire. *(Star Trek Generations.)*

Picard, Maurice. (Clive Church). Vinticulturist from **Labarre**, France, on planet Earth, and the father of *Enterprise*-D Captain **Jean-Luc Picard**. ("Chain of Command, Part II" [TNG]). The elder Picard did not approve of advanced technology and avoided it in his life whenever possible. It was understandable, then, that Maurice Picard was disappointed when his younger son joined Starfleet rather than remaining at home to tend the family vineyard. ("Tapestry" [TNG]). *The name Maurice Picard was first seen on Jean-Luc's biographical computer screen in "Conundrum" (TNG). The name was selected by* Star Trek *writer-producer Ron Moore.*

Picard, René. (David Tristen Birkin). (2360-2371). Nephew to **Jean-Luc Picard**, and the son of **Robert Picard**. Jean-Luc met René for the first time in 2367, when the boy was seven, when Captain Picard came home for the first time in 20 years. René expressed a desire to be like his uncle, and dreamed that someday he would be leaving for his own starship. ("Family" [TNG]). He and his father perished in a tragic fire on Earth in 2371. Jean-Luc Picard remembered René as a dreamer, imaginative, and very gentle. *(Star Trek Generations). David Tristen Birkin later portrayed Jean-Luc Picard as a child in the sixth-season episode "Rascals" (TNG). René was played by Christopher James Miller in Picard's **nexus** sequence in* Star Trek Generations.

Picard, Robert. (Jeremy Kemp). Older brother to **Jean-Luc Picard**, and husband to **Marie Picard**. Fiercely old-fashioned, Robert stayed on the family vineyard to continue his father's work after Jean-Luc left to join Starfleet. Robert was resentful of his younger brother's literally stellar achievements and carried that bitterness for years. The two Picard brothers came somewhat to terms in 2367 when Jean-Luc visited home while recovering from his abduction by the **Borg**. ("Family" [TNG]). Robert Picard died in 2371 in a fire on Earth that also claimed the life of his son, René. Robert Picard was survived by his wife, Marie, and brother, Jean-Luc. *(Star Trek Generations).*

Picard, Yvette Gessard. (Herta Ware). Mother to *Enterprise*-D Captain **Jean-Luc Picard**. Many years after her death, Picard once again met her son, Jean-Luc, in 2364 when a failed warp-drive experiment caused a bizarre intertwining of time, space, and thought caused by an individual known as the **Traveler**. ("Where No One Has Gone Before" [TNG]). *Jean-Luc's mother's name was established in "Chain of Command, Part II" [TNG]). She was named after Yvette Mimieux, star of* The Time Machine.

Picnic on Rymus Major. Holosuite program; an outdoor setting shared by Quark and **Natima Lang** in 2363. It was the first holosuite program installed on station **Terok Nor**. ("Profit and Loss" [DS9]).

"Piece of the Action, A." Original Series episode #49. Teleplay by David P. Harmon and Gene L. Coon. Story by David P. Harmon. Directed by James Komack. No stardate given. *First aired in 1968. The* Enterprise *visits a planet whose inhabitants have patterned themselves after Earth's Chicago gangsters of the 1920s.* GUEST CAST: Anthony Caruso as **Oxmyx**, **Bela**; Victor Tayback as **Krako**, **Jojo**; Lee Delano as **Kalo**; John Harmon as **Tepo**; Sheldon Collins as Tough kid; Dyanne Thorne as First girl; Sharyn Hillyer as Girl #2; Buddy Garion as Hood; Steve Marlo as **Zabo**; William Blackburn as Hadley, Lieutenant; Marlys Burdette as Krako's gun moll; Jay Jones as Mirt; Christie, McIntosh, Conte, Hoods. SEE: **Beta Antares IV; Book, The; *Chicago Mobs of the Twenties*; Cirl the Knife; fizzbin; heater; *Horizon, U.S.S.*; Iotians; Kalo; Krako, Jojo; Oxmyx, Bela; Prime Directive; Sigma Iotia II; subspace technology; Tepo; transtator; Zabo.**

Pierce, Walter J. (Mark Rolston). Starfleet engineer who helped build the *Starship Enterprise*-D. In 2362, while the *Enterprise*-D was still under construction at **Utopia Planitia Fleet Yards**, a love triangle existed among Pierce, **Marla Finn,** and another man. When Pierce caught the other two embracing, he became overwhelmed with anger and killed them both. Afterwards he was overcome by guilt, and committed suicide by jumping into the plasma stream in one of the *Enterprise*-D's **nacelle** control rooms. Because Pierce's maternal grandmother was Betazoid, Pierce was partially empathic. The subspace energy in the nacelle imprinted his empathic pattern on a bulkhead like a "psychic photograph." In 2370, **Daniel Kwan** discovered the panel, and since he was also partially empathic, the psychic signature triggered an hallucination that caused him to experience events similar to those last experienced by Lieutenant Pierce, causing Kwan to commit suicide. When investigating the death of Kwan, Deanna Troi experienced the same phenomenon, but was stopped before she could jump to her death. ("Eye of the Beholder" [TNG]).

Piersall, Lieutenant. (Mark Erickson). Starfleet officer assigned to the ***U.S.S. Prometheus.*** Piersall was on duty during the mission to reignite **Epsilon 119** in 2370. ("Second Sight" [DS9]).

Pierson, Lieutenant. *Enterprise*-D engineering technician. Pierson worked to help repair the experimental **particle fountain** at planet Tyrus VIIA in 2369. ("The Quality of Life" [TNG]).

Pike City Pioneers. One of the six **baseball** teams organized in mid 2371 on **Cestus III**. The youngest brother of **Kasidy Yates** was a member of the Pioneers, and even arranged to have audio recordings of their games transmitted to her in the Bajor Sector. ("Family Business" [DS9]).

Pike City. Town on planet **Cestus III**. Pike City organized a **baseball** team in mid-2371. ("Family Business" [DS9]). *Presumably named for Christopher Pike.*

Pike, Christopher. (Jeffrey Hunter). Early captain of the first ***Starship Enterprise***. Pike commanded one of the first missions to planet **Talos IV**, after which Starfleet imposed **General**

Order 7, prohibiting Federation contact with that planet. Pike was born in **Mojave**, on Earth; he took command of the *Enterprise* in 2250 and conducted two five-year missions of exploration. He relinquished command of that ship to **James Kirk** in 2263, at which time Pike was promoted to **fleet captain**. Pike suffered severe radiation injuries in 2266 as a result of an accident aboard a class-J training ship. Wheelchair-bound as a result of delta-ray exposure, Pike went to live on Talos IV when the **Talosians** offered to use their power of illusion to provide him with a life unfettered by his physical body. ("The Cage," "The Menagerie" [TOS]). *Based on Spock's line that he had served with Pike for 11 years, we conjecture that Pike had commanded two five-year missions of the* Enterprise *prior to his promotion to fleet captain in 2263. Christopher Pike was seen as* Enterprise *captain in the first* Star Trek *pilot episode, "The Cage" [TOS], produced in 1964. Actor Jeffrey Hunter, who portrayed Pike, was unavailable when the second* Star Trek *pilot ("Where No Man Has Gone Before" [TOS]) was being planned, so the part was recast with William Shatner portraying Captain James Kirk. Footage from "The Cage" was later incorporated into the two-part episode "The Menagerie" (TOS). Prior to selecting either Shatner or Hunter, producer Gene Roddenberry had offered the role of the captain to* Sea Hunt *actor Lloyd Bridges.* Star Trek *tradition has it that shuttlecraft are named after famous explorers and scientists, and the shuttle in "The Most Toys" (TNG) was named after Christopher Pike.*

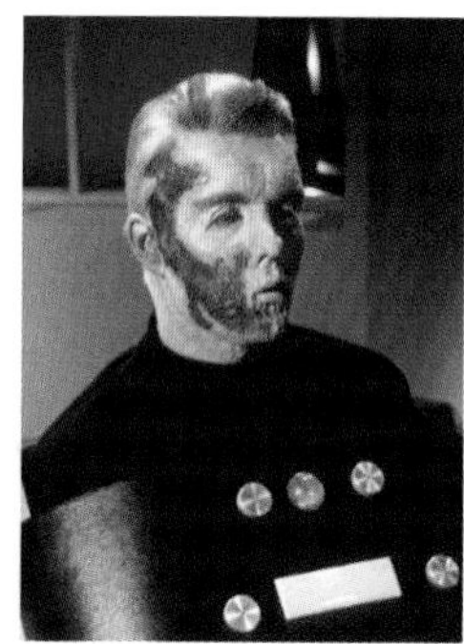

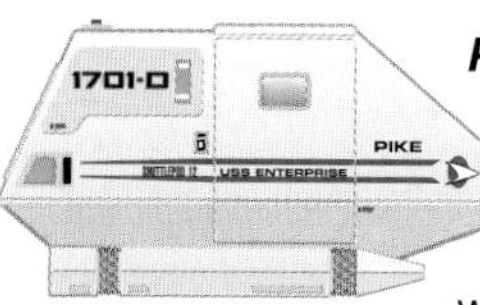

***Pike*, Shuttlepod.** Assigned to the *Enterprise*-D, this shuttle, #12, was destroyed while transporting **hytritium** to the ship in 2366. The explosion of the *Pike* was initially believed to be due to pilot error, but was later discovered to have been caused by **Kivas Fajo**. ("The Most Toys [TNG]). *The* Pike *was named for Captain Christopher Pike, early captain of the first* Starship Enterprise.

Pinder, Lieutenant. *Enterprise*-D science division crew member, and supervisor to **Ensign Janeway**. Pinder found fault in Janeway's performance, much to Janeway's dismay. ("Man of the People" [TNG]).

***Pioneer* 10.** Ancient robotic space probe launched from Earth in 1972 by

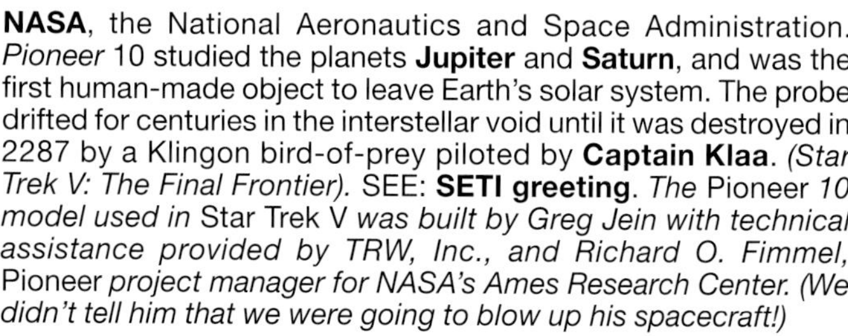

NASA, the National Aeronautics and Space Administration. *Pioneer* 10 studied the planets **Jupiter** and **Saturn**, and was the first human-made object to leave Earth's solar system. The probe drifted for centuries in the interstellar void until it was destroyed in 2287 by a Klingon bird-of-prey piloted by **Captain Klaa**. *(Star Trek V: The Final Frontier).* SEE: **SETI greeting**. *The* Pioneer *10 model used in* Star Trek V *was built by Greg Jein with technical assistance provided by TRW, Inc., and Richard O. Fimmel,* Pioneer *project manager for NASA's Ames Research Center. (We didn't tell him that we were going to blow up his spacecraft!)*

Piotr. SEE: **Chekov, Piotr**.

Piper, Dr. Mark. (Paul Fix). **Chief medical officer** aboard the *Enterprise* in 2265. Predecessor to Dr. McCoy. ("Where No Man Has Gone Before" [TOS]).

***pipius* claw.** A traditional Klingon dish. Commander Riker tasted some of this stuff when he tried to acquaint himself with Klingon culture prior to his temporary assignment to the *Pagh* in 2365. ("A Matter of Honor" [TNG]).

Pirak. Gul who commanded the **Cardassian** weapons depot at **Hathon.** Pirak was killed, along with his family, by a bomb planted by **Kira Nerys** and the **Shakaar resistance cell.** Years later, on stardate 50416, **Silaran Prin,** a servant to Pirak who was disfigured in the explosion, sought vengeance against those responsible. ("The Darkness and the Light" [DS9]).

***Pirates of Penzance, The*.** Comic operetta by Sir William Gilbert and Sir Arthur Sullivan, first published on Earth in 1879. Beverly Crusher, in her role as ship's drama director, staged a production of *The Pirates of Penzance* aboard the *Enterprise*-D in 2368. She urged Geordi La Forge to audition for the role of Major-General Stanley for the production, although Geordi was uncomfortable about singing in front of an audience. ("Disaster" [TNG]).

Piri. (Rosemary Morgan). Akritirian citizen born in 2359. Piri and her brother, Vel, sympathized with the terrorist group known as Open Sky. ("The Chute" [VGR]).

pistol. Handheld weapon that used a small chemical explosive cartridge to propel a metal pellet. One variety of these weapons, known as a double-action cavalry pistol, circa 1873, was found in a subterranean cavern on Earth in 2368. ("Time's Arrow, Part I" [TNG]). SEE: **Police Special**.

Pit. (Ed Trotta). Inmate of the **Akritirian prison satellite** while Ensign Harry Kim and Lieutenant Tom Paris were imprisoned there on stardate 50156. ("The Chute" [VGR]).

pizza. Traditional Earth food made from a thin baked bread crust covered with a variety of toppings, including chopped and puréed vegetables and spiced meats. Considered by some to be an Earth classic. Lieutenant Thomas Paris craved pepperoni pizza with Kavarian olives while he was mutating into a amphibious creature in 2372. ("Threshold" [VGR]).

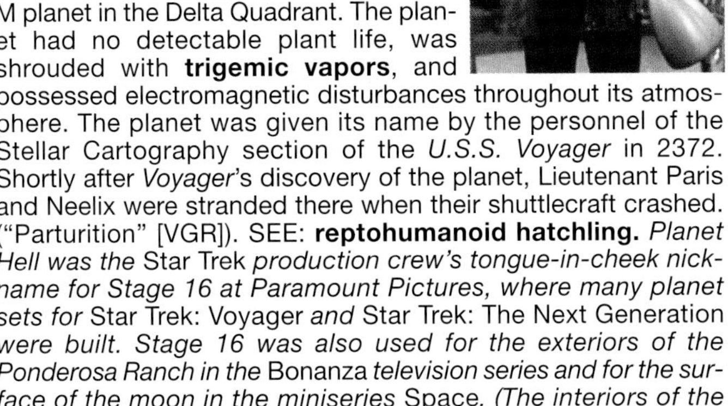

Plak-tow. Vulcan term roughly translating as "blood fever." Refers to a state of mind in which a **Vulcan** undergoing ***Pon farr***, the mating drive, becomes oblivious to anything not related to the winning of one's mate. Spock experienced *Plak-tow* when he underwent *Pon farr* in 2267, making him prone to throwing bowls of soup in anger. ("Amok Time" [TOS]).

Planet Hell. Unofficial name for a Class-M planet in the Delta Quadrant. The planet had no detectable plant life, was shrouded with **trigemic vapors**, and possessed electromagnetic disturbances throughout its atmosphere. The planet was given its name by the personnel of the Stellar Cartography section of the *U.S.S. Voyager* in 2372. Shortly after *Voyager*'s discovery of the planet, Lieutenant Paris and Neelix were stranded there when their shuttlecraft crashed. ("Parturition" [VGR]). SEE: **reptohumanoid hatchling.** *Planet Hell was the* Star Trek *production crew's tongue-in-cheek nickname for Stage 16 at Paramount Pictures, where many planet sets for* Star Trek: Voyager *and* Star Trek: The Next Generation *were built. Stage 16 was also used for the exteriors of the Ponderosa Ranch in the* Bonanza *television series and for the surface of the moon in the miniseries* Space. *(The interiors of the Ponderosa were filmed on Stage 17, where Deep Space 9's Promenade was built.)*

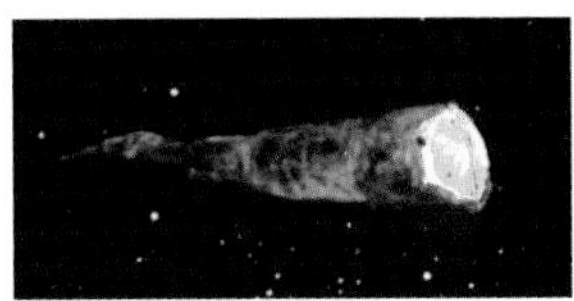

planet killer. Automated spacegoing weapon from outside our galaxy that entered Federation space in 2267, destroying the planets in star systems **L-370** and **L-374**. Several kilometers in length, with a hull composed of pure **neutronium**, it smashed planets into rubble with an **antiproton** weapon, and used the matter as fuel. *Enterprise* Captain James T. Kirk theorized that it was a weapon, a doomsday machine built primarily as a bluff used in a war uncounted years ago in another galaxy. The civilization that built the planet killer might have gone, but the machine continued to destroy. Initial projections suggested that the planet killer's course, if unchecked, would take it toward the Rigel colonies and the most densely populated part of our galaxy, putting billions of lives at risk. The ancient weapon was finally destroyed when Kirk sent the hulk of the ***U.S.S. Constellation*** to explode in the planet killer's interior, destroying it. ("The Doomsday Machine" [TOS]). SEE: **Decker, Commodore Matt**.

Planet Q. SEE: **Q, Planet.**

Planetary Geosciences Laboratory. Scientific research facility located on Deck 10 of the *Enterprise*-D. The planetary geosciences lab, under the supervision of Acting Ensign **Wesley Crusher**, surveyed the planetary systems in the **Selcundi Drema** sector in 2365. ("Pen Pals" [TNG]).

planetary classification system. A method of labeling planet types according to a letter nomenclature. Planetary classes near the letter M are generally more likely to support life. The farther from the letter M, the less likely the planet is to support life as we know it.

Class-D planets are small, rocky planetoids. Regula was a Class-D world. *(Star Trek II: The Wrath of Khan). The ringed Saturn-like planet in "Emanations" [VGR] was also described as a Class-D world, but the term had previously been established to describe asteroids, and "Starship Down" (DS9) further established Saturn to be a Class-J planet. Perhaps the* Voyager *crew was referring to the asteroid-like objects in the planet's rings, or maybe they were just overly excited at the discovery of element 247.*

Class-H planets are generally extremely dry, although sometimes habitable. An example is planet **Tau Cygna V** ("The Ensigns of Command" [TNG]).

Class-J planets are gas giants with turbulent atmospheres in which wind speeds of over 10,000 kilometers per hour are not unknown. **Jupiter** and **Saturn** are Class-J planets. ("Starship Down" [DS9]). *Note that "Emanations" (VGR) suggests that Saturn is a Class-D planet, but we're assuming this to be a mistake.*

Class-K planets are unsuitable for humanoid life, even though their gravity fields can fall within Class-M norms. Class-K planets, like the planet **Mudd**, are adaptable for humanoid life only with the use of pressure domes and life-support systems. ("I, Mudd" [TOS]).

Class-L planets are generally small, rocky, terrestrial worlds with oxygen-argon atmospheres. ("The 37's" [VGR]). Class-L worlds can sometimes support life, although this is often limited to plant forms. Planet **Indri VIII** was Class-L. ("The Chase" [TNG]). In 2373, Odo and Quark made an emergency runabout landing on a Class-L planet. ("The Ascent" [DS9]).

Class-M planets are small, rocky, terrestrial worlds with oxygen-nitrogen atmospheres, and are highly supportive of organic life. **Earth** and **Vulcan** are Class-M planets. ("The Cage" [TOS], "Caretaker" [VGR]). *The* Star Trek *format suggests that the majority of* Star Trek's *adventures should take place on Class-M planets. This is a key concept in making the show affordable within the limits of an episodic television budget.*

planetoid. SEE: **asteroid**.

planets, stars and other celestial objects. SEE: chart follows.

plankton loaf. Baked microscopic Earth sea life, sometimes served as a breakfast food. **Keiko O'Brien** was very fond of plankton loaf and served it, along with kelp buds and sea berries, to her new husband, **Miles O'Brien**, who wasn't too sure about the stuff. ("The Wounded" [TNG]).

plasma canister. A device used to transport small amounts of **warp plasma**. ("Fair Trade" [VGR]).

plasma charge. Explosive device. When **Kira Nerys** was a member of the **Shakaar resistance cell** during the **Cardassian** occupation of **Bajor**, she planted a plasma charge outside the bedroom of Gul **Pirak.** The explosion killed 12 Cardassians, including his entire family. Twenty-three others, including **Silaran Prin**, were wounded. ("The Darkness and the Light" [DS9]).

plasma conversion sensor. Starfleet instrument used to measure the consumption of matter and antimatter fuel during engine use. ("Timescape" [TNG]).

plasma coolant. Highly corrosive fluid used in the warp-drive systems of Federation starships. *(Star Trek: First Contact).*

plasma disruption. Violent energy discharges in space, also known as a plasma storm. **Deep Space 9** was subjected to a plasma disruption on stardate 47182.1, forcing evacuation of most station personnel. ("Invasive Procedures" [DS9]). In 2373, a runabout carrying Sisko, Dax, Garak, and Odo encountered a plasma disruption. The storm's effects on Odo triggered a version of the Great Link, trapping all four in a memory of Odo's past. ("Things Past" [DS9]).

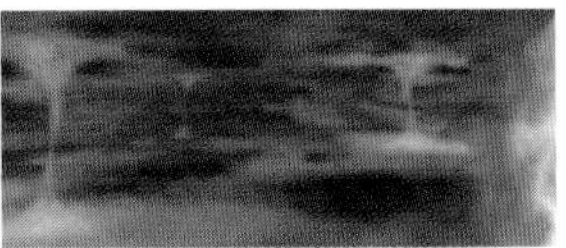

plasma fields. Energetic plasma disruptions located in the **Badlands**. These fields were quite extensive and made spaceship navigation difficult. ("For the Uniform" [DS9]).

Object name	Description	Episode or film
'audet IX	Planet; location of a **Federation** Medical Collection Station	"The Child" (TNG)
Acamar III	Home planet of the Acamarian people	"The Vengeance Factor" (TNG)
Acamar system	Star system containing planet **Acamar III**	"The Vengeance Factor" (TNG)
Adelphous IV	Planet; destination of ***Enterprise*-D** in 2367	"Data's Day" (TNG)
Adigeon Prime	Planet; location of medical facility were seven year old **Julian Bashir** was taken to have the structure of his brain altered	"Doctor Bashir, I Presume" (DS9)
Ajilon Prime	Site of skirmish between **Klingon** and Federation in early 2373	"Nor the Battle to the Strong" (DS9)
Alastria	Delta Quadrant planet with euphoric **erosene winds**	"Prime Factors" (VGR)
Alawanir Nebula	Nebula investigated by the ***Enterprise*-D** in 2369	"Rightful Heir" (TNG)
Aldea	Legendary planet whose people excelled in intellect and art	"When the Bough Breaks" (TNG)
Aldebaran	Star system. **Dr. Elizabeth Dehner** joined the ***Enterprise*** crew at Aldeberan. **Janet Wallace** and her husband came from Aldebaran III. **Belongo** was held there in 2371	"Where No Man Has Gone Before" (TOS), "The Deadly Years" (TOS), "Past Tense, Part I" (DS9)
Alfa 117	Class M planet where **Kirk** was divided into two halves	"The Enemy Within" (TOS)
Alpha 441	Planetoid located in the **Badlands**	"Dreadnought" (VGR)
Alpha Carinae II	Class-M planet used in the **M-5** test	"The Ultimate Computer" (TOS)
Alpha Carinae V	Planet of the **drella** creature that derived sustenance from emotions	"Wolf in the Fold" (TOS)
Alpha Centauri	Closest star to **Earth**'s solar system, home to **Zefram Cochrane**, inventor of the warp drive	"Metamorphosis" (TOS)
Alpha Cygnus IX	Planet where Federation Ambassador **Sarek** arranged a major treaty	"Sarek" (TNG)
Alpha III	Planet where a historic individual rights document was established	"Court Martial" (TOS)
Alpha Majoris I	Planet origin of the **mellitus**, a creature with many forms	"Wolf in the Fold" (TOS)
Alpha Moon	Moon orbiting planet **Peliar Zel**, at odds with its sister moon, **Beta**	"The Host" (TNG)
Alpha Omicron system	Star system where a life-form was found living in the vacuum of space	"Galaxy's Child" (TNG)
Alpha Onias III	Planet where **Riker** was abducted by a little boy who wanted a friend to play with	"Future Imperfect" (TNG)
Alpha Proxima II	Planet where several women were brutally murdered	"Wolf in the Fold" (TOS)
Alpha Quadrant	One quarter of the entire Milky Way galaxy. The region in which most of the **United Federation of Planets** is located. **Deep Space 9 i**s also located in the Alpha Quadrant	*Star Trek* series
Alpha V	Planet with colony where **Charles Evans**' nearest relatives lived	"Charlie X" (TOS)
Altair III	Planet where **William Riker** refused to allow **Captain DeSoto** to beam to the surface	"Encounter at Farpoint" (TNG)
Altair IV	Federation planet; home to **Dr. Henri Roget**	"Prophet Motive" (DS9)
Altair VI	Planet visited by the ***Enterprise*** in 2267 for presidential inauguration ceremony; part of **Kobayashi Maru simulation**	"Amok Time" (TOS), *Star Trek II: The Wrath of Khan*
Altec	Planet, along with **Straleb,** part of the **Coalition of Madena**	"The Outrageous Okona" (TNG)
Amargosa	Yellow giant star destroyed in 2371 by **Dr. Tolian Soran**	*Star Trek Generations*
Amargosa Diaspora	Dense globular star cluster ***Enterprise*-D** investigated in 2369	"Schisms" (TNG)
Amleth Prime	Cardassian planet located with an **emission nebula**	*"Return to Grace" (DS9)*
Andevian II	Planet with at least four moons	"The Forsaken" (DS9)
Andoria	Homeworld to the **Andorian** people	"Prophet Motive" (DS9)
Andromeda Galaxy	Closest galaxy to the Milky Way Galaxy, home to the **Kelvans**, expected to become uninhabitable due to increased radiation	"By Any Other Name" (TOS)
Angel One	Planet whose society had a matriarchial government	"Angel One" (TNG)
Angosia III	Planet; mistreated war veterans	"The Hunted" (TNG)
Antede III	Planet; homeworld to intelligent fishlike inhabitants	"Manhunt" (TNG)
Antica	Homeworld to the **Anticans**	"Lonely Among Us" (TNG)
Antos IV	Planet where Captain **Garth** learned cellular metamorphosis. Home of the giant energy generating worm	"Whom Gods Destroy" (TOS); "Who Mourns for Adonais?" (TOS)
Aolian Cluster	Site of archaeological research conducted by **Professor Galen**	"The Chase" (TNG)
Archanis	Star used as a navigational reference. In 2373, Klingon forces took hold of Archanis which had been controlled by the Federation	"Arena" (TOS), "Broken Link" (DS9), "Apocalypse Rising" (DS9)
Archanis IV	Home planet of **Chekov**'s imaginary brother, **Piotr.** In 2372, Klingon demanded Federation withdraw from Archanis IV	"The Day of the Dove" (TOS), "Broken Link" (DS9)
Archer IV	Planet destination of ***Enterprise*-D** after its encounter with a **temporal rift**	"Yesterday's Enterprise" (TNG)
Arcybite	Planet where **Nava**, a **Ferengi**, took over mining refineries	"The Nagus" (DS9)
Ardana	Planet, location of the cloud city **Stratos**	"The Cloud Minders" (TOS)
Argaya system	Star system where the ***Enterprise*-D** was to rendezvous with Ensign **Sito**'s escape pod	"Lower Decks" (TNG)
Argelius II	Planet with hedonistic culture victimized by brutal murders in 2267	"Wolf in the Fold" (TOS)

Object name	Description	Episode or film
Argolis Cluster	Cluster ***Enterprise*-D** was charting when it discovered a **Borg** scout ship, location of ecologically devastated planet **Tagra IV**	"I, Borg" (TNG), "True Q" (TNG)
Argos system	Star system, possible destination of the **Crystalline Entity** in 2368	"Silicon Avatar" (TNG)
Argratha	Planet in the Gamma Quadrant and homeword of the **Argrathi**	"Hard Time" (DS9)
Argus sector	Area to be visited by the ***Enteprise*-D** in 2370	"Gambit, Part I" (TNG)
Ariannus	Planet vital as a transfer point, infected by a bacterial plague in 2268	"Let That Be Your Last Battlefield" (TOS)
Arkaria Base	Planet, location of the **Remmler Array**	"Starship Mine" (TNG)
Armus IX	Planet where **Riker** wore a native feathered costume	"Angel One" (TNG)
Arneb	Star recognized by **Wesley** while gazing from Ten-Forward	"The Child" (TNG)
Arvada III	Planet where a terrible tragedy killed many people	"The Arsenal of Freedom" (TNG)
Aschelan V	Cardassian planet, site of a Cardassian fuel depot	"Dreadnought" (VGR)
asteroid belt	Band of several thousand small bodies revolving around Earth's sun between the orbits of Mars and Jupiter	"Future's End, Part II" (VGR)
asteroid gamma 601	Moon-sized asteroid in the **Devolin System**. The phased hulk of the *Starship* ***Pegasus*** became trapped inside this asteroid	"The *Pegasus*" (TNG)
Atalia VII	Planet, site of a vital diplomatic conference in 2369	"The Chase" (TNG)
Atrea IV	Class-M planet that suffered unexplained magma cooling in 2370	"Inheritance" (TNG)
Axanar	Planet that cadet **James Kirk** visited on a peace mission	"Whom Gods Destroy" (TOS)
Babel	Planetoid, location of interplanetary conference concerning **Coridan**'s bid for admission to the Federation	"Journey to Babel" (TOS)
Badlands	Region of space near the Cardassian border populated with dangerous **plasma storm**s	"The Maquis, Part I" (DS9), "Caretaker" (VGR), et al
Bajor	Homeworld to the **Bajoran** people	"Emissary" (DS9), et al
Bajor VIII	Eighth planet in the **Bajoran** system containing six colonies	"Past Prologue" (DS9)
Bajoran wormhole	Artificially constructed stable passageway to the **Gamma Quadrant**	"Emissary" (DS9)
Balosnee VI	Planet where the harmonies of the tides can cause hallucinations	"The Nagus" (DS9)
Barisa Prime	Planet; site of a Federation settlement	"The Adversary" (DS9)
Barkon IV	Planet where a Federation deep space probe crashed in 2370	"Thine Own Self" (TNG)
Barradas III	Class-M uninhabited planet with numerous archeological ruins	"Gambit, Part I" (TNG)
Barradas system	Planetary system where the ***Enterprise*-D** pursued a group of mercenaries in 2370	"Gambit, Part I" (TNG)
Barson II	Planet; site of a medical emergency in 2370	"Eye of the Beholder" (TNG)
Barzan wormhole	Unstable wormhole sold to the **Chrysalians**	"The Price" (TNG)
Beloti Sector	Region of space	"Ethics" (TNG)
Beltane IX	Planet that serves as a center for commercial shipping	"Coming of Age" (TNG)
Benecia Colony	Planet where the **Karidian Players** were to perform; the colony had relatively primitive medical facilities	"The Conscience of the King" (TOS), "Turnabout Intruder" (TOS)
Benev Selec	Star system in the **Selcundi Drema Sector**	"Pen Pals" (TNG)
Benzar	Homeworld to the **Benzites**	"A Matter of Honor" (TNG)
Berengaria VII	Planet where dragons can be found	"This Side of Paradise" (TOS)
Bersallis III	Planet where deadly firestorms occur every seven years	"Lessons" (TNG)
Beta Agni II	Planet that experienced **tricyanate** contamination	"The Most Toys" (TNG)
Beta Antares IV	Planet where imaginary card game **fizzbin** was played, at least according to **James T. Kirk**	"A Piece of the Action" (TOS)
Beta Aurigae	Binary star system where the original ***Enterprise*** was to meet the *Starship* ***Potemkin*** in 2269	"Turnabout Intruder" (TOS)
Beta Geminorum system	Star system that contains planets **Pollux IV** & **V**	"Who Mourns for Adonais?" (TOS)
Beta III	Planet where a sophisticated computer ruled the society	"Return of the Archons" (TOS)
Beta Kupsic	Planet; destination of the ***Enterprise*-D** in 2365	"The Icarus Factor" (TNG)
Beta Lankal	Planetary system in **Klingon** space	"Redemption, Part II" (TNG)
Beta Magellan	Star system where planet **Bynaus** is located; the star went nova	"11001001" (TNG)
Beta Moon	Moon orbiting planet **Peliar Zel**, at odds with its sister moon	"The Host" (TNG)
Beta Niobe	Star that exploded in 2269, destroying planet **Sarpeidon**	"All Our Yesterdays" (TOS)
Beta Portolan system	System where mass insanity from **Denevan neural parasites** began	"Operation—Annihilate!" (TOS)
Beta Renner system	Star system to homeworlds of the **Anticans** and **Selay**	"Lonely Among Us" (TNG)
Beta Stromgren	Red giant star where **Tin Man** was discovered by the **Vega IX probe**	"Tin Man" (TNG)
Beta Thoridar	**Klingon** planet used as a staging area for the **Duras** forces during the **Klingon civil war**	"Redemption, Part I" (TNG)
Beta VI	Planet; destination before ***Enterprise*** encountered **Trelane**	"The Squire of Gothos" (TOS)
Beta XII-A	Planet to which an alien entity lured the ***Enterprise*** and the Klingon vessel commanded by **Kang**	"The Day of the Dove" (TOS)
Betazed	Planet; homeworld to **Deanna Troi**	"Ménage à Troi" (TNG), et al
Beth Delta I	Planet where **Dr. Paul Stubbs** wished he could take **Deanna Troi** for champagne	"Evolution" (TNG)
Bilana III	Planet where the **soliton wave** was developed	"New Ground" (TNG)
Bilaren System	Planet, location of **Amanda Rogers**'s adoptive parents' home	"True-Q" (TNG)

Object name	Description	Episode or film
Black Cluster	Astronomical formation of proto-stars collapsing in close proximity	"Hero Worship" (TNG)
Blue Horizon	Planet, site of a terraforming project by **Professor Seyetik**	"Second Sight" (DS9)
Bolarus IX	Homeworld of the **Bolian** people	"Allegiance" (TNG)
Bopak III	Uninhabited Class-M world in the Gamma Quadrant	"Hippocratic Oath" (DS9)
Bopak system	Red giant star system in the Gamma Quadrant	"Hippocratic Oath" (DS9)
Boraal II	Class-M planet that suffered atmospheric dissipation in 2370	"Homeward" (TNG)
Boradis system	System where ***Enterprise*-D** met emissary **K'Ehleyr**	"The Emissary" (TNG)
Boreal III	Planet, home of a transport attacked by the **Crystalline Entity**	"Silicon Avatar" (TNG)
Boreth	Klingon planet where a monastery to **Kahless the Unforgettable** was established to await his return	"Rightful Heir" (TNG), "The Way of the Warrior" (DS9)
Borgolis Nebula	Blue-tinged gaseous nebula studied by ***Enterprise*-D** in 2369	"Lessons" (TNG)
Borka VI	Planet where **Troi** was abducted	"Face of the Enemy" (TNG)
Bracas V	Planet where **La Forge** took a vacation and went skin-diving	"The Loss" (TNG)
Braslota System	Planetary system	"Peak Performance" (TNG)
Brax	Planet where **Q** was known as "The god of lies"	"Q-Less" (DS9)
Bre'el IV	Planet whose moon was knocked out of its orbit	"Deja Q" (TNG)
Brechtian Cluster	Star system that the **Crystalline Entity** was en route to when it was destroyed	"Silicon Avatar" (TNG)
Brekka	Planet, home to the **Brekkians**	"Symbiosis" (TNG)
Brentalia	Protected planet used as a zoo for endangered species; **Worf** and **Alexander** visited there once	"New Ground" (TNG), "Imaginary Friend" (TNG)
Bringloid V	Planet settled by human colonists from ***S.S. Mariposa***	"Up the Long Ladder" (TNG)
Browder IV	Planet undergoing terraforming in 2366	"Allegiance" (TNG)
Bryma	Planet located in the **Demilitarized Zone**	"The Maquis, Part II" (DS9)
Bynaus	Planet, home of the **Bynars**	"11001001" (TNG)
C-111	Star system where planet **Beta III** was located	"The Return of the Archons" (TOS)
Cabral sector	Sub-division of space where planet **Vacca VI** is located	"Homeward" (TNG)
Calder II	Site of a Federation archeological outpost raided by mercenaries	"Gambit, Part I" (TNG)
Caldos Colony	One of the first terraforming projects undertaken by the Federation The colony was the final home of **Felisa Howard**	"Sub Rosa" (TNG)
Cambra system	System where the future **Alexander** encountered the man who sent him back in time	"Firstborn" (TNG)
Camor V	Planet; **Jason Vigo** and his mother settled here	"Bloodlines" (TNG)
Camus II	Planet where **Dr. Janice Lester** exchanged bodies with **James Kirk**, site of an archaeological survey that the ***Enterprise*-D** missed	"Turnabout Intruder" (TOS), "Legacy" (TNG)
Canopus	Red supergiant star, also known as **Alpha Caranae,** Star used for navigational reference	"Arena" (TOS)
Canopus Planet	Planet where **Tarbolde** wrote the sonnet "**Nightingale Woman**"	"Where No Man Has Gone Before" (TOS)
Capella IV	Home planet to **Eleen** and other **Capellans**	"Friday's Child" (TOS)
Cardassia	Homeworld of the **Cardassian** people	"The Wounded" (TNG), et al
Carema III	Planet considered as a candidate for **Dr. Farallon**'s **particle fountain** mining technology	"The Quality of Life" (TNG)
Carraya System	Star system, location of a secret **Romulan** prison camp	"Birthright, Part II" (TNG), "Rightful Heir" (TNG)
Castal I	Site of conflict between **Federation** and **Talarian** forces	"Suddenly Human" (TNG)
Catualla	Home planet to **Tango Rad**, follower of **Dr. Sevrin**	"The Way to Eden" (TOS)
Celtris III	Planet in **Cardassian** space where **Picard** was kidnapped	"Chain of Command, Part I" (TNG)
Cerebus II	Planet where **Mark Jameson** received a dangerous drug	"Too Short a Season" (TNG)
Cestus III	Planet, location of **Federation** outpost destroyed by the **Gorn**; later the site of a Federation colony	"Arena" (TOS), "Family Business" (DS9)
Ceti Alpha V	Planet where **Khan** and his followers were exiled	"Space Seed" (TOS), *Star Trek II: The Wrath of Khan*
Ceti Alpha VI	Planet that exploded, causing **Ceti Alpha V** to become barren	*Star Trek II: The Wrath of Khan*
Chalna	Planet, home of the **Chalnoth** civilization	"Allegiance" (TNG)
Chaltok IV	Planet, location of Romulan research colony	"Time and Again" (VGR)
Chamra Vortex	Nebula where **Odo** and **Croden** evaded a **Miradorn** vessel	"Vortex" (DS9)
Chandra V	Planet where **Tam Elbrun** was assigned	"Tin Man" (TNG)
Cheron	Planet, home to **Bele** and **Lokai**, destroyed by racial strife; site of a decisive battle with the Romulans	"Let This Be Your Last Battlefield" (TOS), "The Defector" (TNG)
Cirrus IV	Planet, location of the **Emerald Wading Pool**	"Conundrum" (TNG)
Clarus System	Star system, location of planet **Arcybite**	"The Nagus" (DS9)
Cluster NGC 321	Star cluster containing planets **Eminiar VII** and **Vendikar**	"A Taste of Armageddon" (TOS)
Coltar IV	Planet that experienced time distortion in 2364	"We'll Always Have Paris" (TNG)
Cor Caroli V	Planet whose people suffered the Phyrox Plague	"Allegiance" (TNG)
Cordannas system	Location of a white dwarf star where the **emergent life-form** attempted to take the ***Enterprise*-D**	"Emergence" (TNG)

Object name	Description	Episode or film
Coridan	**Dilithium**-rich planet admitted to the **Federation** in 2267 after the **Babel** Conference	"Journey to Babel" (TOS), "Sarek" (TNG)
Corinth IV	Location of **Starfleet** facility that requested an explanation for why the ***Enterprise*** was delayed on planet **M-113**	"The Man Trap" (TOS)
Cornelian star system	Star system where **Riker** ordered the ***Enterprise*-D** to escape the "hole" in space created by **Nagilum**	"Where Silence Has Lease" (TNG)
Corvan II	Planet whose atmospheric pollutants threatened life	"New Ground" (TNG)
Cruses System	Last known location of a co-conspirator of **J'Ddan**	"The Drumhead" (TNG)
Cuellar system	Location of a **Cardassian** science station destroyed by the ***U.S.S. Phoenix***	"The Wounded" (TNG)
Cygnet XIV	Planet dominated by women, who fixed the ***Enterprise*** computer	"Tomorrow Is Yesterday" (TOS)
Cygnia Minor	Earth colony threatened by famine in 2266	"The Conscience of the King" (TOS)
Daled IV	Planet that revolves only once every planetary year	"The Dauphin" (TNG)
Danula II	Planet, site of a **Starfleet Academy marathon** where **Picard** won	"The Best of Both Worlds, Part II" (TNG)
Daran V	Planet directly in the path of **Yonada** ship in 2268	"For the World Is Hollow and I Have Touched the Sky" (TOS)
Davlos III	Planet located on the **Klingon** border	"Visionary" (DS9)
Dayos IV	Planet where **Kang** found one of the **Albino**'s wives	"Blood Oath" (DS9)
Dedestris	Planet in the Delta Quadrant	"Prime Factors" (VGR)
Deinonychus VII	Planet where ***Enterprise*-D** awaited the supply ship ***Biko***	"A Fistful of Datas" (TNG)
Delb II	Homeworld of **Nellen Tore**, assistant to **Admiral Norah Satie**	"The Drumhead" (TNG)
Delinia II	Planet where **transporter psychosis** was first diagnosed	"Realm of Fear" (TNG)
Delios VII	Planet that was the home to the Karis Tribe	"Sacred Ground" (VGR)
Delos	Star system containing planets **Ornara** and **Brekka**	"Symbiosis" (TNG)
Delos IV	Planet where **Dr. Crusher** completed internship	"Remember Me" (TNG)
Delphi Ardu	Star system where last **Tkon** outpost was located	"The Last Outpost" (TNG)
Delta IV	Homeworld to the **Deltans**	*Star Trek: The Motion Picture*
Delta Quadrant	One-quarter of the entire Milky Way Galaxy, its closest point is some 40,000 light years from the Federation. In 2371, the ***U.S.S. Voyager*** became lost in the Delta Quadrant	"The Price" (TNG), "Q-Less" (DS9), "Caretaker" (VGR)
Delta Rana IV	Home of **Kevin** and **Rishon Uxbridge**	"The Survivors" (TNG)
Delta Rana star system	Planetary system and location of planet **Delta Rana IV**	"The Survivors" (TNG)
Delta Vega	Desolate planet with automated **lithium** mining station	"Where No Man Has Gone Before" (TOS)
Deltived Asteroid Belt	Astronomical formation misplaced by **Q2**	"Deja Q" (TNG)
Deneb II	Planet where **Kesla** murdered several women	"Wolf in the Fold" (TOS)
Deneb IV	Planet inhabited by **Bandi**. Location of **Farpoint Station**	"Encounter at Farpoint" (TNG)
Deneb V	Planet where **Harcourt Fenton Mudd** illegally sold all the rights to a **Vulcan** fuel synthesizer	"I, Mudd" (TOS)
Deneva	Planet infested by **Denevan neural parasites** in 2267	"Operation: Annihilate!" (TOS)
Denius III	Planet where artifacts showed location of planet **Iconia**	"Contagion" (TNG)
Denkiri Arm	One of the spiral-shaped arms that make up the Milky Way Galaxy, located in the **Gamma Quadrant**	"The Price" (TNG)
Denorios Belt	Charged plasma field where the **Bajoran wormhole** is located	"Emissary" (DS9)
Deriben V	**Aquiel Uhnari**'s last posting prior to **Relay Station 47**	"Aquiel" (TNG)
Dessica II	Frontier world where **Picard** was believed to have been murdered	"Gambit, Part I" (TNG)
Detrian System	Star system where two gas giant planets collided in 2369	"Ship in a Bottle" (TNG)
Devidia II	Planet whose inhabitants steal neural energies	"Time's Arrow" (TNG)
Devolin system	Mass of rocks and dust where the hulk of ***U.S.S. Pegasus*** was discovered	"The *Pegasus*" (TNG)
Devron system	System in **Romulan Neutral Zone**. Location of the spatial anomaly discovered in 2370	"All Good Things..." (TNG)
Dichromic Nebula	Interstellar gas cloud; location of gravimetric distortion	"Bloodlines" (TNG)
Dikon alpha	Class-nine pulsar	"Emergence" (TNG)
Dimorus	Planet where **Gary Mitchell** saved **Kirk**'s life from a poison dart thrown by rodent creatures	"Where No Man Has Gone Before" (TOS)
Donatu V	Planet; site of an inconclusive battle fought with **Klingons**	"The Trouble with Tribbles" (TOS)
Dopa system	Planetary system located within the Cardassian Union	"Return to Grace" (DS9)
Doraf I	Planet where ***Enterprise*-D** was assigned for terraforming	"Unification, Part I" (TNG)
Dorias Cluster	Region of at least 20 star systems. **Bok** was sighted here following his escape from prison	"Bloodlines" (TNG)
Dorvan V	Planet near Cardassian border; ceded by Federation	"Journey's End" (TNG)
Dozaria	Class-M world with a hot desert-like climate	"Indiscretion" (DS9)
Draken IV	Planet where Romulan **N'Vek** helped with defection of **M'ret**; Site of archeological digs	"Face of the Enemy" (TNG), "Gambit" (TNG)
Drayan II	Class-M planet in the Delta Quadrant with several moons	"Innocence" (VGR)

Object name	Description	Episode or film
Draygo IV	Class-M planet rejected as a potential home for the **Boraalans**	"Homeward" (TNG)
Draylon II	Class-M planet; site of **Skrreea** settlement	"Sanctuary" (DS9)
Drema IV	Planet suffering violent geologic instabilities; home to **Sarjenka**	"Pen Pals" (TNG)
Dreon VII	Planet; site of a Bajoran colony	"For the Cause" (DS9)
Dulisian IV	Planet that supposedly sent a distress call in 2368	"Unification, Part II" (TNG)
Durenia IV	Planet, destination of ***Enterprise*-D** in 2367	"Remember Me" (TNG)
Dyson sphere	Gigantic artificial structure designed to completely enclose a star, discovered in 2294 by the ***U.S.S. Jenolen***	"Relics" (TNG)
Dytallix B	Planet owned by the Dytallix Mining Corporation	"Conspiracy" (TNG)
Earth	Mostly harmless. Home to Human people	"The Cage" (TOS), et al
Earth Colony 2	Planet where **George Samuel Kirk** hoped to be transferred	"What Are Little Girls Made Of?" (TOS)
Eden	Mythical planet sought by **Dr. Sevrin** and his followers	"The Way to Eden" (TOS)
Ekos	Class-M planet, accidentally turned into a repressive Nazi state by Federation sociologist **John Gill**	"Patterns of Force" (TOS)
El-Adrel IV	Planet where **Tamarian** captain **Dathon** and **Picard** met in 2367	"Darmok" (TNG)
El-Adrel system	Star system located midway between **Federation** and **Tamarian** space	"Darmok" (TNG)
Elas	Inner planet in the **Tellun Star System;** homeworld of **Elaan**	"Elaan of Troyius" (TOS)
Elba II	Planet, location of a penal colony for the criminally insane	"Whom Gods Destroy" (TOS)
Emila II	Planet, destination of ***Enterprise*-D** after visiting **Tanuga IV**	"A Matter of Perspective" (TNG)
Eminiar VII	Planet at war with its neighbor, **Vendikar**, for 500 years	"A Taste of Armageddon" (TOS)
Enara Prime	Homeworld to the Enaran civilization in the Delta Quadrant	"Remember" (VGR)
Endicor system	Star system, destination of the ***Enterprise*-D** before encountering energy vortex	"Time Squared" (TNG)
Ennan VI	Planet where **Pulaski** obtained a bottle of ale	"Time Squared" (TNG)
Epsilon 119	Dead star reignited in 2370 by **Professor Gideon Seyetik**	"Second Sight" (DS9)
Epsilon Canaris III	Planet on the verge of war, where negotiations were assigned to **Commissioner Hedford**	"Metamorphosis" (TOS)
Epsilon Hydra VII	Planet where archaeologist **Vash** was barred from the Royal Museum	"Q-Less" (DS9)
Epsilon Indi	Star system where ancient marauders from planet **Triacus** waged war; **Wesley Crusher** recognized it once	"And the Children Shall Lead" (TOS), "The Child" (TNG)
Epsilon IX sector	Site of an astronomical survey by the ***Enterprise*-D**	"Samaritan Snare" (TNG)
Epsilon Mynos system	Star system where planet **Aldea** is located	"When the Bough Breaks" (TNG)
Epsilon Pulsar Cluster	Astronomical phenomenon located in **Epsilon IX sector**	"Samaritan Snare" (TNG)
Epsilon Silar System	Unexplored star system where ***Enterprise*-D** became a pawn of the **Satarrans**	"Conundrum" (TNG)
Erabus Prime	Planet where **Q** saved **Vash** from getting sick after a bug sting	"Q-Less" (DS9)
Errikang VII	Planet where **Vash** said **Q** almost got her killed	"Q-Less" (DS9)
Evadne IV	Planet, destination after ***Enterprise*-D** encountered unstable wormhole	"Clues" (TNG)
Excalbia	Inhospitable volcanic planet; homeworld to **Excalbians**	"The Savage Curtain" (TOS)
Exo III	Dead planet where **Dr. Korby** discovered a civilization of highly-sophisticated androids	"What Are Little Girls Made Of?" (TOS)
Fabrina	Star system whose sun went nova, origin of the **Fabrini** asteroid/ship	"For the World Is Hollow and I Have Touched the Sky" (TOS)
Fahleena III	Planet that a Valerian vessel visited, delivering supplies	"Dramatis Personae" (DS9)
Farius Prime	Planet; destination of a **Galador** freighter	"The Maquis, Part I" (DS9)
Fendaus V	Planet led by a family whose members have no limbs	"Loud as a Whisper" (TNG)
Ferenginar	Ferengi homeworld and center of the **Ferengi Alliance**	"Family Business" (DS9)
FGC-13 cluster	Stellar cluster ***Enterprise*-D** charted in 2369	"Schisms" (TNG)
FGC-47	Giant nebula formed around a neutron star	"Imaginary Friend" (TNG)
Fina Prime	Planet location of an outbreak of deadly Viidian **phage**	"Lifesigns" (VGR)
Fina system	Planetary system in the Delta Quadrant	"Lifesigns" (VGR)
Finnea Prime	A non-Federation world	"A Simple Investigation" (DS9)
Folnar III	Planet origin of the **Folnar jewel plant**	"Dark Page" (TNG)
Forcas III	Planet where a ***bat'leth* competition** was held in 2370; **Data** found the a drink from Forcas III revolting	"Parallels" (TNG), *Star Trek Generations*
Forlat III	Planet, site of an attack by the **Crystalline Entity**	"Silicon Avatar" (TNG)
Gagarin IV	Planet, location of the **Darwin Genetic Research Station**	"Unnatural Selection" (TNG)
Galador II	Planet homeworld to **Galador freighters**	"The Maquis, Part I" (DS9)
Galaxy M33	Galaxy accidentally visited by the ***Enterprise*-D** with help from the **Traveler**	"Where No One Has Gone Before" (TNG)
Galdonterre	Planet, former hiding place of the **Albino**	"Blood Oath" (DS9)
Galen IV	Planet, site of Federation colony destroyed by **Talarian** forces	"Suddenly Human" (TNG)
Galor IV	Planetary site of an annex to the **Daystrom Institute**	"The Offspring" (TNG)
Galorda Prime	Planet. In 2372, a **Klingon** civilian transport crashed, killing all persons on board	"Rules of Engagement" (DS9)

Object name	Description	Episode or film
Galorndon Core	Federation planet where **Romulan** scout ship ***Pi*** crashed in 2366	"The Enemy" (TNG), "Unification, Part II" (TNG)
Galvin V	Planet where a marriage was only considered successful if a child was produced in the first year	"Data's Day" (TNG)
Gamelan V	Planet that experienced increase in atmospheric radiation in 2367	"Final Mission" (TNG)
Gamma 400 star system	Star system where **Starbase 12** is located	"Space Seed" (TOS)
Gamma 7 Sector	Service area of the ***U.S.S. Lantree***	"Unnatural Selection" (TNG)
Gamma 7A system	Star system destroyed by the **amoeba** creature	"The Immunity Syndrome" (TOS)
Gamma Arigulon System	Star system where the ***U.S.S. LaSalle*** reported radiation anomalies	"Reunion" (TNG)
Gamma Canaris region	Region of space where the ***shuttlecraft Galileo*** was pulled off course	"Metamorphosis" (TOS)
Gamma Erandi nebula	Interstellar gas cloud studied by the ***Enterprise*-D** in 2366	"Ménage à Troi" (TNG)
Gamma Eridon	Star system in **Klingon** space	"Redemption, Part II" (TNG)
Gamma Hromi II	Planet, location of a Gatherer camp. Site of negotiations to reunite the **Acamarians** and the **Gatherers**	"The Vengeance Factor" (TNG)
Gamma Hydra	Star system, theoretical location of the ***Kobayashi Maru***'s distress call	*Star Trek II: The Wrath of Khan*
Gamma Hydra IV	Planet where entire population of a **Federation** science colony died of a radiation disease resembling old age	"The Deadly Years" (TOS)
Gamma II	Planet, destination of the ***Enterprise*** when crew members were abducted to **Triskelion**	"The Gamesters of Triskelion" (TOS)
Gamma Quadrant	One-quarter of the **Miky Way Galaxy**, the portion most distant from the **United Federation of Planets.** Access to the Gamma Quadrant may be gained through the **Bajoran wormhole**	"Emissary" (DS9), et al
Gamma Tauri IV	Planet where the **Ferengi** stole a T-9 energy converter	"The Last Outpost" (TNG)
Gamma Trianguli VI	Tropical class-M planet, homeworld of a humanoid people formerly ruled by the machine-god **Vaal**	"The Apple" (TOS)
Gamma Vertis IV	Planet where the entire population is mute	"The Empath" (TOS)
Ganalda IV	Planet, **Klingon** forces retreated from Ganalda IV in 2373	"Nor the Battle to the Strong" (DS9)
Garadius system	Star system where the ***Enterprise*-D** was assigned to a diplomatic mission	"The Next Phase" (TNG)
Gariman Sector	Area of **Federation** space	"Rightful Heir" (TNG)
Garon II	Planet visited by the *Starship* ***Wellington***	"Ensign Ro" (TNG)
Garth system	Solar system near planet **Malcor III**	"First Contact" (TNG)
Gaspar VII	Homeworld of Starfleet Captain **Edwell**	"Starship Mine" (TNG)
Gault	Farming world where **Worf** was raised	"Heart Of Glory" (TNG), "Let He Who is Without Sin..." (DS9)
Gavara system	Star system located in the **Gamma Quadrant**	"The Quickening" (DS9)
Gema IV	Planet in the **Delta Quadrant** controlled by the **Kazon-Nistrim**	"Basics, Part I" (VGR)
Gemaris V	Planet where Captain **Picard** mediated a trade dispute	"Captain's Holiday" (TNG)
Gemulon V	Original planet destination of colony ship ***S.S. Santa Maria***	"Paradise" (DS9)
Genesis Planet	Planet formed in the **Mutara Nebula** by **Project Genesis**, but later destroyed because of **protomatter** in the Genesis matrix	*Star Trek II: The Wrath of Khan* *Star Trek III: The Search for Spock*
Gideon	Class-M planet, once a paradise, but in 2269 plagued with overpopulation	"The Mark of Gideon" (TOS)
Giles Belt	Asteroid field; possible destination of the ***Jovis***	"The Most Toys" (TNG)
Gonal IV	Planet; home to swarming moths	"Disaster" (TNG)
Gothos	Planet created by **Trelane**, although his parents warned him that if he disobeyed, he wouldn't be allowed to make any more worlds	"The Squire of Gothos" (TOS)
Gravesworld	Planet where cyberneticist **Ira Graves** lived his last years	"The Schizoid Man" (TNG)
Guernica system	Star system, location of Federation outpost	"Galaxy's Child" (TNG)
H'atoria	**Klingon** colony where **Worf** was governor in **Q**'s future	"All Good Things..." (TNG)
Halee system	Star system where **Worf** suggested renegades be allowed to die	"Heart of Glory" (TNG)
Halii	Planet, homeworld of Starfleet **Lieutenant Aquiel Uhnari**	"Aquiel" (TNG)
Halley's comet	Ball of ice that travels through Earth's solar system every 76 years	"Time's Arrow, Part II" (TNG)
Hanoli System	Star system where a subspace rupture destroyed a **Vulcan** ship	"If Wishes Were Horses" (DS9)
Hanolin asteroid belt	Asteroid belt where a **Ferengi** cargo shuttle crashed and the wreckage of the **Vulcan** ship ***T'Pau*** was found	"Unification, Part I" (TNG)
Hanon IV	Class-M planet in the **Delta Quadrant**	"Basics, Parts I & II" (VGR)
Hansen's Planet	Planet; homeworld to humanoid creatures similar to those on **Taurus II**	"The Galileo Seven" (TOS)
Harod IV	Planet where ***Enterprise*-D** picked up stranded miners	"The Perfect Mate" (TNG)
Harrakis V	Planet that the ***Enterprise*-D** visited in 2367	"Clues" (TNG)
Hatarian system	**Picard** wanted to visit some archeological ruins here	"Firstborn" (TNG)
Haven	Planet reputed to have mystical healing powers	"Haven" (TNG)
Hayashi system	Star system; site of atmospheric charting mission in 2366	"Tin Man" (TNG)
Hekaras Corridor	Only safe passage for warp-driven ships near **Hekaras II**	"Force of Nature" (TNG)

Object name	Description	Episode or film
Hekaras II	Class-M planet damaged by a **subspace rift**	"Force of Nature" (TNG)
Helaspont Nebula	Astronomical cloud containing numerous protoplanetary masses	"The Adversary" (DS9)
Hemikek	Planet in a yellow dwarf system in the **Delta Quadrant**	"Investigations" (VGR)
Hemikek IV	Planet in the **Delta Quadrant**	"Lifesigns" (VGR)
Heva VII	Planet in the **Delta Quadrant**, site of refueling port	"The Chute" (VGR)
Hoek IV	Planet where the Sampalo relics can be viewed	"Q-Less" (DS9)
Holberg 917G	Planetoid, home to **Flint**	"Requiem for Methuselah" (TOS)
Hromi Cluster	Location of planet Gamma Hromi II, near the **Acamar System**	"The Vengeance Factor" (TNG)
Hugora Nebula	Astronomical phenomenon located very close to the **Demilitarized Zone**	"Preemptive Strike" (TNG)
Hur'q planet	Uncharted Class-M world in the **Gamma Quadrant**	"The Sword of Kahless" (DS9)
Hurada III	Planet visited by **Tarmin** and his group of telepathic historians	"Violations" (TNG)
Hurkos III	Planet where **Devinoni Ral** moved at age 19	"The Price" (TNG)
Hyralan sector	Location where the ***Enterprise*-D** intercepted the Klingon **Koral** before he could transfer his cargo to **Baran**'s mercenaries	Gambit, Part II" (TNG)
Iadara Colony	Federation colony that was subject of covert surveillance in an alternate quantum reality	"Parallels" (TNG)
Icarus IV	Comet whose orbit was near the **Romulan Neutral Zone**	"Balance of Terror" (TOS)
Iconia	Homeworld of an advanced civilization, now extinct	"Contagion" (TNG)
Icor IX	Planet, site of an astrophysics center that **Picard** hoped to visit	"Captain's Holiday" (TNG)
Idini Star Cluster	The ***Enterprise*-D** passed through this cluster en route to **Mordan IV**	"Too Short A Season" (TNG)
Idran	Trinary star system located in the **Gamma Quadrant** near the terminus of the **Bajoran wormhole**	"Emissary" (DS9), "Battle Lines" (DS9)
Igo Sector	Location of a binary star studied by the ***U.S.S. Yosemite***	"Realm of Fear" (TNG)
Ikalian Asteroid belt	Asteroid belt believed to be a hiding place for **Kriosian** rebels	"The Mind's Eye" (TNG)
Ilari	Planet in the **Delta Quadrant**	"Warlord" (VGR)
Ilecom system	Star system that experienced time distortion from **Manheim**'s experiments in 2364	"We'll Always Have Paris" (TNG)
Ilidaria	Planet in the **Delta Quadrant**	"Parallax" (VGR)
Indri VIII	Planet; long ago seeded with genetic material	"The Chase" (TNG)
Inferna Prime	Federation planet	"The Ascent" (DS9)
Ingraham B	Planet struck by the **Denevan neural parasites** in 2265	"Operation: Annihilate!" (TOS)
Invernia II	Julian **Bashir**'s father was once stationed on Invernia II	"Melora" (DS9)
inversion nebula	Interstellar gas cloud populated by highly unstable strands of plasma	"Alter Ego" (VGR)
Itamish III	The Sisko family once enjoyed a camping vacation on Itamish III	"The Jem'Hadar" (DS9)
Ivor Prime	Planet site of a Federation colony destroyed by the Borg in 2373	*Star Trek: First Contact*
Iyaaran homeworld	**Picard** was scheduled to visit there in 2370 as part of a cultural exchange; noted for its spectacular crystal formations	"Liasions" (TNG)
Janus VI	Planet, home of the **Horta**	"Devil in the Dark" (TOS)
Jaros II	Planet where **Ro Laren** was imprisoned until her release in 2368	"Ensign Ro" (TNG)
Jenkata nebula	Stellar gas cloud located in the **Gamma Quadrant**	"The Quickening" (DS9)
Jeraddo	Fifth moon orbiting the planet **Bajor**, home to **Mullibok**	"Progress" (DS9)
Jouret IV	Planet, site of **New Providence colony**, victim of a **Borg** attack	"The Best of Both Worlds, Part I" (TNG)
Juhraya	**Federation** colony near Cardassian border	"Preemptive Strike" (TNG)
Jupiter	Gas giant planet, fifth world in the **Sol System**	"Starship Down" (DS9)
Kaelon II	Planet whose star, **Kaelon**, was gradually dying	"Half a Life" (TNG)
Kalandan outpost	Artificially-created planet; manufactured by the Kalandan people	"That Which Survives" (TOS)
Kaldra IV	Planet, destination of a group of **Ullian** researchers in 2368	"Violations" (TNG)
Kaleb sector	Site of the attempted defection of **M'ret** in 2369	"Face of the Enemy" (TNG)
Kalla II	Planet where the **Duras** sisters conducted illegal mining	"Firstborn" (TNG)
Kar-telos system	Planetary system in the **Gamma Quadrant**	"Bar Association" (DS9)
Karemma system	Planetary system in the **Gamma Quadrant** containing the **Karemma** homeworld	"The Search, Part I" (DS9)
Kataan	Star that exploded a millennium ago; located in the Silarian sector	"The Inner Light" (TNG)
Kavis Alpha IV	Planet that became the home of the newly evolved **nanites**	"Evolution" (TNG)
Kavis Alpha sector	Site of **Dr. Stubbs**'s neutronium decay experiment	"Evolution" (TNG)
Kazis Binary system	System that was the projected destination of the **Ralph Offenhouse**'s **cryosatellite**	"The Neutral Zone" (TNG)
Kea IV	Planet that was topic of a research paper presented by **Picard**	"The Chase" (TNG)
Keloda	Binary star system in the **Delta Quadrant**	"Parallax" (VGR)
Kelrabi System	Star system located in **Cardassian** space	"The Wounded" (TNG)
Kelva	Planet in the **Andromeda Galaxy**	"By Any Other Name" (TOS)
Kenda II	Planet, home of **Dr. Dalen Quaice**	"Remember Me" (TNG)
Kendi system	Star system located in the **Gamma Quadrant**	"The Quickening" (DS9)
Kesprytt III	Class-M planet, home to two paranoid nations	"Attached" (TNG)
Kessik IV	Federation colony where **B'Elanna Torres** grew up	"Faces" (VGR)
Khefka IV	Planet, homeworld to **Mareel**	"Invasive Procedures" (DS9)

Object name	Description	Episode or film
Khitomer	Planet near the Klingon-Romulan border, site of the historic **Khitomer peace conference** and the infamous **Khitomer massacre**	*Star Trek VI: The Undiscovered Country*, "Sins of the Father" (TNG), et al
Kholfa II	Planet. Home of Ferengi entrepreneur **Plegg** in 2370	"The Alternate" (DS9)
Klaestron IV	Homeworld to **Ilon Tandro**	"Dax" (DS9), "Second Skin" (DS9)
Klavdia III	Planet where **Salia** was raised in a neutral environment	"The Dauphin" (TNG)
Klingon Homeworld	Central planet of the **Klingon Empire**, also known as **Qo'noS**	"Sins of the Father" (TNG), *Star Trek VI: The Undiscovered Country*, et al
Kora II	**Cardassian** planet where **Marritza** taught at a military academy	"Duet" (DS9)
Korat system	Planetary system in Federation territory	"The Siege" (DS9)
Kostolain	Homeworld to **Minister Campio**, fiancé of **Lwaxana Troi**	"Cost of Living" (TNG)
Kotati	Planet in the **Delta Quadrant**	"Investigations" (VGR)
Kraus IV	Planet where Cardassian clothier **Garak** could obtain silk lingerie	"Past Prologue" (DS9)
Krios	One of two neighboring star systems that had been warring with each other for centuries; a **Klingon** planet	"The Perfect Mate" (TNG), "The Mind's Eye" (TNG)
Ktaria VII	Planet. Home to the **Ktarian** civilization	"Emanations" (VGR)
Kurill Prime	Planet homeworld to a civilization known as the **Vorta**	"The Jem'Hadar" (DS9)
Kurl	Planet where inhabitants disappeared, leaving interesting ruins	"The Chase" (TNG)
Kylata II	Class-M planet in the **Gamma Quadrant**	"Meridian" (DS9)
L-370	Star system whose planets were destroyed by the **planet killer**	"The Doomsday Machine" (TOS)
L-374	Star system almost completely destroyed by the **planet killer**	"The Doomsday Machine" (TOS)
L-S VI	Planet in the **Gamma Quadrant**	"The Alternate" (DS9)
Lagana sector	Site of a terraforming mission by the ***U.S.S. Gandhi***	"Second Chances" (TNG)
Lambda Paz	Moon of planet **Pentarus III**, where **Dirgo**'s shuttle crashed	"Final Mission" (TNG)
Lamenda Prime	Planet near the **Cardassian** star system	"The Homecoming" (DS9)
Landris II	Planet where Dr. Mowray conducted archaeological research	"Lessons" (TNG)
Lantar nebula	Nebula containing the planet **Hoek IV**	"Q-Less" (DS9)
Largo V	Planet; destination for a shipment of Tamen **Sahsheer**	"Babel" (DS9)
Lazon II	Planet in **Cardassian** space	"Defiant" (DS9)
Ledonia III	**Jadzia Dax** purchased a plant on Ledonia III	"The Wire" (DS9)
Legara IV	Planet, homeworld of the **Legarans**	"Sarek" (TNG)
Lembatta cluster	Stellar formation. In 2373, Klingon forces destroyed the *U.S.S. Farragut* near the Lembatta cluster	"...Nor the Battle to the Strong" (DS9)
Lemma II	Planet placed in jeopardy during **soliton wave** test	"New Ground" (TNG)
Levinius V	Planet struck by the **Denevan neural parasites** in 2247	"Operation: Annihilate!" (TOS)
Ligobis X	Planet where Gideon Seyetik's paintings were displayed	"Second Sight" (DS9)
Ligon II	Home to the **Ligonians**, who valued honor above all else	"Code of Honor" (TNG)
Ligos VII	Volcanically active planet	"Rascals" (TNG)
Lima Sierra system	Star system whose planetary orbits are contrary to the norm	"Loud as a Whisper" (TNG)
Lissepia	Planet, homeworld to the **Lissepian** people	"Indiscretion" (DS9)
Lonka Pulsar	Rotating neutron star located in the Lonka Cluster	"Allegiance" (TNG)
Loren III	Planet where **Professor Galen** obtained genetic samples	"The Chase" (TNG)
Lorenze Cluster	Star cluster where the planet **Minos** is located	"The Arsenal of Freedom" (TNG), "The Child" (TNG)
Loval	Planet in **Cardassian** space and location of a civilian outpost	"Return to Grace" (DS9)
Lunar V	Moon of **Angosia III**; used as a prison	"The Hunted" (TNG)
Lyshan system	Star system where **Picard**'s covert team was to be retrieved	"Chain of Command, Part II" (TNG)
Lysia	Homeworld of the **Lysian Alliance**	"Conundrum" (TNG)
M'kemas III	Planet located in **Tzenkethi** territory	"The Adversary" (DS9)
M-113	Former home of the salt vampire, planet studied by archaeologist **Dr. Robert Crater**	"The Man Trap" (TOS)
M24 Alpha	Star system that contained the planet **Triskelion**	"The Gamesters of Triskelion" (TOS)
Mab-Bu VI	Planet with Class-M moon where disembodied alien criminals lived; crash site of the ***U.S.S. Essex***	"Power Play" (TNG)
MacPherson Nebula	Supernova remnant used as a source of **vertion particles** for the **emergent life-form** which occupied the ***Entepirse*-D**	"Emergence" (TNG)
Makus III	Planet where the ***Enterprise*** was to deliver medical supplies	"The Galileo Seven" (TOS)
Malaya IV	Planet where **Paul Hickman** had a physical exam	"Identity Crisis" (TNG)
Malcor III	Planet where **Riker** conducted covert sociological studies	"First Contact" (TNG)
Malkus IX	Planet whose inhabitants developed writing before sign language	"Loud as a Whisper" (TNG)
Malurian System	System completely "sterilized" by **Nomad**	"The Changeling" (TOS)
Manark IV	Home of the sandbats	"The Empath" (TOS)
Manu III	Planet whose government used proximity detectors	"Legacy" (TNG)
Mar Oscura	A dark-matter nebula located in Federation space	"In Theory" (TNG)
Maranga IV	**Worf** attended the Klingon ***Kot'baval* Festival** there in 2370	"Firstborn" (TNG)
Marcos XII	Planet chosen by the evil **Gorgan** to conquer and control	"And the Children Shall Lead" (TOS)
Marejaretus VI	Homeworld to the Ooolans	"Manhunt" (TNG)
Mariah IV	Planet visited by a Valerian vessel when delivering supplies	"Dramatis Personae" (DS9)
Marijne VII	Gas giant planet	"Interface" (TNG)

Object name	Description	Episode or film
Mariposa	Planet settled by human colonists from ***S.S. Mariposa***	"Up the Long Ladder" (TNG)
Marlonia	Planet visited by some of the ***Enterprise*-D** crew in 2369	"Rascals" (TNG)
Mars	Fourth planet in **Sol System**, location of the **Utopia Planitia Fleet Yards**; site of **Martian Colonies**, where important legal declarations on human rights were written	"Booby Trap" (TNG), "Court Martial" (TOS), "The Lights of Zetar" (TOS)
Marva IV	Class-M planet located in the **Badlands**	"For the Uniform" (DS9)
Mataline II	Planet where **Neela Daren** purchased a flexible piano keyboard	"Lessons" (TNG)
Mavala IV	Planet where **Noonien Soong** married **Juliana O' Donnell**	"Inheritance" (TNG)
Maxia Zeta star system	Star system where the **Battle of Maxia** was fought	"The Battle" (TNG)
McAllister C-5 Nebula	Nebula located 7 light-years inside **Cardassian** space	"Chain of Command, Part II" (TNG)
Meezan IV	Planet where **Julian Bashir** attended a burn treatment conference	"In Purgatory's Shadow" (DS9)
Mekorda sector	Area of space where the ***Enterprise*-D** weathered a magnascopic storm	"Emergence" (TNG)
Meldrar I	Planet	"Necessary Evil" (DS9)
Meles II	Suggested port of call for **Moriarty**	"Ship in a Bottle" (TNG)
Melina II	Planet visited by **Tarmin** and his group of telepathic historians	"Violations" (TNG)
Melnos IV	Planet where **Neela Daren** led a team to study a plasma geyser	"Lessons" (TNG)
Melona IV	Planet attacked by the **Crystalline Entity** in 2368	"Silicon Avatar" (TNG)
Meltasion asteroid belt	Asteroid belt through which the ***Enterprise*-D** was forced to tow a contaminated barge full of radioactive waste	"Final Mission" (TNG)
Memory Alpha	Planetoid, location of Federation library	"The Lights of Zetar" (TOS)
Mempa sector	Star system in Klingon space where **Gowron** suffered a major defeat during the **Klingon civil war**	"Redemption" (TNG)
Merak II	Planet ravaged by a botanical plague in 2269. **Quark** said the inhabitants of Merak II made the best scanners	"The Cloud Minders" (TOS), "The Wire" (DS9)
Mericor system	Planetary system, crash site of the ***U.S.S. Denver*** after the ship struck a gravitic mine in 2368	"Ethics" (TNG)
Meridian	Planet that undergoes dimensional shifts every 60 years	"Meridian" (DS9)
Merik III	Planet in the **Gamma Quadrant**	"Hippocratic Oath" (DS9)
Merkoria Quasar	Phenomenon under study by the ***U.S.S. Enterprise*-D** in 2370	"The *Pegasus*" (TNG)
micro-wormhole	A **wormhole** whose singularity has mostly dissipated, leaving an extremely narrow passageway through **subspace**	"Eye of the Needle" (VGR)
Midos V	Planet where **Dr. Roger Korby** planned to begin manufacturing androids	"What Are Little Girls Made Of?" (TOS)
Milika III	Planet where a young **Picard** led an away team to rescue an ambassador	"Tapestry" (TNG)
Mimas	Moon of **Saturn**, where the **Nova Squadron** was evacuated	"The First Duty" (TNG)
Minara II	Planet used by the **Vians**	"The Empath" (TOS)
Minaran star system	Planetary system, formerly with several inhabited worlds. The star, Minara, entered a nova phase in 2268	"The Empath" (TOS)
Minos	Planet whose inhabitants sold weapons during the **Erselrope Wars**	"The Arsenal of Freedom" (TNG)
Minos Korva	Federation planet	"Chain of Command, Part II" (TNG)
Mintaka III	Planet, site of Federation anthropological study of a proto-Vulcan culture	"Who Watches the Watchers" (TNG)
Mira system	Location of **Dytallix B**	"Conspiracy" (TNG)
Miramanee's planet	Planet, home to native American Indians transplanted from Earth (name is unofficial)	"The Paradise Syndrome" (TOS)
Miridian VI	Planet where **Barash** said he'd been captured by the **Romulans**	"Future Imperfect" (TNG)
Mislen	Planet orbiting a yellow dwarf star in the **Delta Quadrant**	"The Swarm" (VGR)
Mithren	Planet in the **Delta Quadrant**	"Investigations" (VGR)
Mizar II	Homeworld of the Mizarians	"Allegiance" (TNG)
Moab IV	Inhospitable planet; site of genetically-engineered colony	"The Masterpiece Society" (TNG)
Modean System	Star system that **Geordi La Forge** visited as a child	"Imaginary Friend" (TNG)
moon	Planetoid, **Earth**'s only natural satellite	*Star Trek: First Contact*
Mordan IV	Planet plunged into a 40-year civil war after outside interference by Starfleet captain **Mark Jameson**	"Too Short a Season" (TNG)
Morikin VII	Planet where cadet **Jean-Luc Picard** was assigned for training	"Tapestry" (TNG)
Moriya system	Star system in the **Badlands**	"Caretaker" (VGR)
Morska	**Klingon** planet on which is located a subspace monitoring outpost	*Star Trek VI: The Undiscovered Country*
Moselina System	Star system, destination of the ***Enterprise*-D** when it was invaded by **nitrium metal parasites**	"Cost of Living" (TNG)
Mudd	Class-K planet inhabited by a group of androids led by **Norman**	"I, Mudd" (TOS)
Mudor V	Planet from which the ***Enterprise*-D** departed before striking a series of **quantum filament**s	"Disaster" (TNG)
Murasaki 312	Quasar-like formation near planet **Taurus II**, investigated by ***Shuttlecraft Galileo*** in 2266, also by ***Enterprise*-D** in 2367	"The Galileo Seven" (TOS), "Data's Day" (TNG)

Object name	Description	Episode or film
Mutara Nebula	Interstellar dust cloud in the Mutara Sector, transformed into the **Genesis planet**	*Star Trek II:The Wrath of Khan*
Myrmidon	Planet were archaeologist **Vash** was wanted for theft	"Q-Less" (DS9)
Nahmi IV	Planet where an outbreak of **Correllium fever** occurred in 2366	"Hollow Pursuits" (TNG)
Napinne	Planet in the **Delta Quadrant**	"Learning Curve" (VGR)
Narendra III	**Klingon** planet defended by the ***Enterprise*-C** in 2344	"Yesterday's Enterprise" (TNG)
Nasreldine	Planet where an ***Enterprise*-D** crew member caught the flu	"The Icarus Factor" (TNG)
Nekrit Expanse	Vast, uncharted region of space in the **Delta Quadrant** populated by an unknown form of interstellar dust clouds and plasma storms	"Fair Trade" (VGR)
Nel Bato system	Star system believed to be where **Kivas Fajo** took the kidnapped **Data**	"The Most Toys" (TNG)
Nel system	Star system visited by a delegation of **Ullian** telepathic historians	"Violations" (TNG)
Nelvana III	Planet where **Jarok** believed there was a secret base	"The Defector" (TNG)
Nequencia system	Star system located near the **Romulan Neutral Zone**	"Birthright, Part I" (TNG)
Nervala IV	Planet where a duplicate of **William Riker** was found	"Second Chances" (TNG)
neutron star	Stellar body that has been gravitationally crushed to the point where its density is that of nuclear material	"Evolution" (TNG)
New Gaul	Planet where **Miranda Vigo** was born	"Bloodlines" (TNG)
New Halana	Planet terraformed by **Professor Gideon Seyetik**	"Second Sight" (DS9)
New Paris colonies	Federation colonies stricken by a plague in 2267	"The Galileo Seven" (TOS)
Ngame Nebula	Astronomical formation that the ***Enterprise*-D** passed en route to planet **Evadne IV**	"Clues" (TNG)
Nimbus III	Planet governed by **Klingons**, **Romulans** and the **Federation**	*Star Trek V: The Final Frontier*
Nivoch	Planet	"Prime Factors" (VGR)
No'Mat	Klingon planet where the **Rite of MajQa** is practiced	"Rightful Heir" (TNG)
Norpin Colony	A community where Scotty hoped to retire before being waylaid by the **Dyson sphere**	"Relics" (TNG)
null space	Extremely rare "pocket" of space	"The Outcast" (TNG)
Obatta cluster	Star system located in the **Gamma Quadrant**. In 2372, the Jem'Hadar had a presence in the **Obatta cluster**	"The Quickening" (DS9)
Ocampa planet	Fifth planet in the Ocampa system, located in the **Delta Quadrant** and homeworld to the **Ocampa** people	"Caretaker" (VGR)
Oceanus IV	***Enterprise*-D** was sent on a diplomatic mission there	"The Game" (TNG)
Ogus II	Planet where ***Enterprise*-D** crew members took R&R in 2367	"Brothers" (TNG)
Ohniaka III	Federation outpost where self-aware **Borg** were encountered	"Descent Part I" (TNG)
Omarion Nebula	Interstellar dust cloud in the **Gamma Quadrant**. Inside the nebula is a sunless Class-M planet, home of the Founders	"The Search" (DS9)
Omega IV	Planet whose people were nearly wiped out by bacteriological war	"The Omega Glory" (TOS)
Omega Sagitta system	Solar system that includes twin planets **Atlec** and **Straleb**	"The Outrageous Okona" (TNG)
Omekla III	Planet location of a Cardassian shipyard	"Defiant" (DS9)
Omicron Ceti III	Planet bombarded by **berthold rays**, site of a failed colony	"This Side of Paradise" (TOS)
Omicron Delta region	Location of the **amusement park planet**	"Shore Leave" (TOS)
Omicron IV	Planet like Earth, nearly destroyed by nuclear weapons	"Assignment: Earth" (TOS)
Omicron Theta	Planet where Data was discovered at a colony destroyed by the **Crsytalline Entity**	"Datalore" (TNG)
Onias Sector	Region of space near the **Romulan Neutral Zone**	"Future Imperfect" (TNG)
Oort cloud	Distant comets that sometimes orbit the periphery of a star system	"The Maquis, Part II" (DS9)
Ophiucus III	Planet, **Harcourt Fenton Mudd**'s attempted destination for delivery of three woman recruited as wives for settlers in 2266	"Mudd's Women" (TOS)
Ordek Nebula	Home of the **Wogneer creatures**	"Allegiance" (TNG)
Orelious IX	Planet destroyed by the **Promellians** and the **Menthars** in 2266	"Booby Trap" (TNG)
Orellius Minor	Star located near the terminus of the Bajoran wormhole	"Paradise" (DS9)
Organia	Home of the noncorporeal **Organians** who imposed the **Organian Peace Treaty** between the **Federation** and the **Klingons**	"Errand of Mercy" (TOS)
Orias III	Planet located in the Orias system	"Defiant" (DS9), "Improbable Cause" (DS9)
Orias system	Planetary system in Cardassian space	"Defiant" (DS9), "Improbable Cause" (DS9)
Orion	Constellation near Taurus	"Little Green Men" (DS9)
Ornara	Home to the **Ornarans**, who were dependent on the drug **felicium**	"Symbiosis" (TNG)
Osinar VI	Planet	"Life Support" (DS9)
Otar II	Destination of the ***Enterprise*-D** following the death of **Lal**	"The Offspring" (TNG)
Pacifica	Beautiful ocean world, known for warm blue waters; an interstellar conference was held there in 2365	"Conspiracy" (TNG), "Manhunt" (TNG)
Panora	Planet in the **Demilitarized Zone**	"For the Uniform" (DS9)
Parada II	Planet in the Parada system	"Whispers" (DS9)
Parada IV	Largest planet in the Parada system with seven moons	"Whispers" (DS9)
Parada system	Star system located in the Gamma Quadrant with at least four planets	"Whispers" (DS9)

Object name	Description	Episode or film
Parliament	Planet used by the **Federation** for diplomatic negotiations	"Lonely Among Us" (TNG)
Parsion III	Planet	"Business As Usual" (DS9)
Parvenium Sector	Region of space where the **Kataan probe** was discovered	"The Inner Light" (TNG)
Paulson Nebula	Astronomical cloud where the ***Enterprise*-D** hid from the **Borg** in 2366	"The Best of Both Worlds, Part I" (TNG)
Pegos Minor	Star system where **Dr. Paul Manheim** claimed to be	"We'll Always Have Paris" (TNG)
Peliar Zel	Planet with two moons, **Alpha Moon** and **Beta Moon**	"The Host" (TNG)
Pelleus V	Planet the ***Enterprise*-D** was scheduled to visit in 2364	"11001001" (TNG)
Pelloris Field	Asteroid field that threatened planet **Tessen III**	"Cost of Living" (TNG)
Pendi II	Home planet of a trader who supplied information to the **Maquis**	"Preemptive Strike" (TNG)
Pentarus II	Planet where shuttle ***Nenebek*** was thought to have crashed	"Final Mission" (TNG)
Pentarus V	Planet that petitioned **Picard** to mediate a labor dispute	"Final Mission" (TNG)
Penthara IV	Federation planet struck by an asteroid	"A Matter of Time" (TNG)
Penthath system	Stellar system near the Klingon Empire. In 2372, a Klingon civilian transport ship was destroyed by **Worf** near Penthara system	"Rules of Engagement" (DS9)
Persephone V	Home planet to retired **Admiral Mark Jameson** just prior to his death	"Too Short a Season" (TNG)
Pheben system	Location of undesignated maneuvers by the **Klingon** vessel ***Pagh***	"A Matter of Honor" (TNG)
Phelan system	Star system where the ***Enterprise*-D** was assigned a diplomatic mission	"The Outcast" (TNG)
Phoenix Cluster	Site of an ***Enterprise*-D** research mission	"The Game" (TNG)
Platonius	Planet settled by the **Platonians**, who based their society on Plato's Republic	"Plato's Stepchildren" (TOS)
Pleiades Cluster	Region of space known as M45, where young planets are located	"Home Soil" (TNG)
Pluto	Ninth planet in the Sol system	*Star Trek Generations*
Pollux IV	Planet where the Greek god **Apollo** lived and tried to recruit the crew of the ***Enterprise*** as his worshippers	"Who Mourns for Adonais?" (TOS)
Pollux V	Planet in Beta Geminorum system	"Who Mourns for Adonais?" (TOS)
Portas V	Planet near the **Demilitarized Zone** with **Breen** settlement	"For the Uniform" (DS9)
Potak III	Planet in the Delta Quadrant	"Partuition" (VGR)
Prakal II	Planet where **Guinan** acquired an unusual drink recipe	"In Theory" (TNG)
Praxillus system	Solar system, site for an unsuccessful **helium ignition test**	"Half a Life" (TNG)
Praxis	Moon of the planet **Qo'noS** which exploded and caused environmental damage to the Klingon Homeworld	*Star Trek VI: The Undiscovered Country*
Prema II	Planet, site of Talaxian mining colony	"Basics, Part I" (VGR)
Psi 2000	Planet that disintegrated in 2266	"The Naked Time" (TOS)
Pyris VII	Planet where **Korob** and **Sylvia** captured several ***Enterprise*** crew members	"Catspaw" (TOS)
Pythro V	Planet	"Rivals" (DS9)
Planet Q	Planet, home of scientist **Thomas Leighton** at the time of his death in 2266	"The Conscience of the King" (TOS)
Qo'noS	Central planet of the **Klingon Empire**, usually known as the Klingon Homeworld	*Star Trek VI:The Undiscovered Country*
Quadra Sigma III	Planet where a Federation mining colony suffered a deadly explosion	"Hide and Q" (TNG)
Quadrant 904	Area of space where **Gothos** was encountered	"The Squire of Gothos" (TOS)
Qualor II	Planet, site of a Federation surplus depot	"Unification, Part I" (TNG)
Quatal Prime	Planet in the **Demilitarized Zone**	"For the Uniform" (DS9)
Quazulu VIII	Planet where several ***Enterprise*-D** students became ill	"Angel One" (TNG)
Rachelis system	Planetary system struck with an outbreak of plasma plague in 2365	"The Child" (TNG)
Rahm-Izad system	Star system where **Gul Ocett** was misdirected to while in search of a message from an ancient humanoid people	"The Chase" (TNG)
Rakal	Planet located in Cardassian space	"Return to Grace" (DS9)
Rakhar	Planet in the **Gamma Quadrant**, home to **Croden**	"Vortex" (DS9)
Rakosa V	Highly populated Class-M planet in the Delta Quadrant	"Dreadnought" (VGR)
Ramatis III	Planet, home of famed negotiator **Riva**	"Loud as a Whisper" (TNG)
Ramatis star system	Star system, location of planet **Ramatis III**	"Loud as a Whisper" (TNG)
red dwarf	Small, cool star of spectra type M, near the end of its life	"Time and Again" (VGR)
Regula	Lifeless planetoid, test site for **Project Genesis**	*Star Trek II:The Wrath of Khan*
Regulus III	Planet location of Science Academy	"Fascination" (DS9)
Regulus V	Home planet to the giant eel-birds	"Amok Time" (TOS)
Rekag-Seronia	Planet, site of bitter hostilities affecting Federation shipping routes	"Man of the People" (TNG)
Relva VII	Planet, location of Starfleet facility	"Coming of Age" (TNG)
Remmil VI	Planet, buildings constructed of crystalline webbing	"Heart of Stone" (DS9)
Remus	One of the homeworlds of the **Romulan Star Empire**	"Balance of Terror" (TOS)
Rhomboid Dronegar Sector	Origin of a distress call to the ***Enterprise*-D** from a disabled **Pakled** ship	"Samaritan Snare" (TNG)
Rigel	Star, also known as Beta Orionis	"Mudd's Women" (TOS)
Rigel II	Planet where **McCoy** mentioned he'd met two scantily clad women	"Shore Leave" (TOS)

Object name	Description	Episode or film
Rigel IV	**Mr. Hengist**'s homeworld; planet where a brilliant astronomer was fond of **Lwaxana Troi**; site of hydroponics conference	"Wolf in the Fold" (TOS), "Half a Life" (TNG), "The Wire, "(DS9)
Rigel V	Planet where a drug to increase blood products was tested	"Journey to Babel" (TOS)
Rigel VII	Planet where several ***Enterprise*** crew members killed under command of **Captain Pike**; also location where criminal **Rao Vantika** caused computer systems to crash	"The Cage" (TOS), "The Menagerie" (TOS), "The Passenger" (DS9)
Rigel XII	Planet, site a small lithium mining operation headed by **Ben Childress**	"Mudd's Women" (TOS)
Rinax	Class-M moon orbiting planet **Talax**	"Jetrel" (VGR)
Risa	Tropical resort planet noted for its beauty and open sexuality	"Captain's Holiday" (TNG), et al
Rochani III	Planet where **Curzon Dax** and **Sisko** were cornered by Kaleans	"Dramatis Personae" (DS9)
Rolor Nebula	Interstellar dust cloud near the Dreon system	"For the Cause" (DS9)
Romulus	One of the homeworlds of the **Romulan Star Empire**	"Balance of Terror" (TOS)
Ronara	Planet in the **Demilitarized Zone**	"Preemptive Strike" (TNG)
Rousseau V	Location of a spectacular asteroid belt	"The Dauphin" (TNG)
Ruah IV	Planet supporting life-forms including a genus of proto-humanoids	"The Chase" (TNG)
Rubicun III	Homeworld to the Edo people	"Justice" (TNG)
Rubicun star system	Star system near the **Strnad system** containing **Rubicun III**	"Justice" (TNG)
Rujian	Planet	"A Man Alone" (DS9)
Runners, the	Constellation that can be seen from Bajoran space	"Second Sight" (DS9)
Rura Penthe	Frozen planet, site of **Klingon** forced labor prison camp where **Kirk** and **McCoy** were wrongly imprisoned	*Star Trek VI:The Undiscovered Country*
Rutia IV	Planet; home to **Ansata** political dissident group	"The High Ground" (TNG)
Sahndara	Native star to the **Platonians** which exploded millennia ago	"Plato's Stepchildren" (TOS)
Sakura Prime	Planet in the Alpha Quadrant	"Dreadnought" (VGR)
Saltok IV	Planet	"The Maquis, Part I" (DS9)
Salva II	Planet site of a Federation colony	"For the Uniform" (DS9)
Sargon's planet	World destroyed centuries ago by war, leaving a small number of survivors stored in subterranean canisters	"Return to Tomorrow" (TOS)
Sarona VIII	Planet; ***Enterprise*-D**'s destination before **Vandor IX**	"We'll Always Have Paris" (TNG)
Sarpeidon	Planet whose star went nova in 2269	"All Our Yesterdays" (TOS)
Sarthong V	Planet known for its rich archaeological ruins	"Captain's Holiday" (TNG)
Saturn	Sixth planet in the **Sol system**; location of **Starfleet Academy flight range**; Saturn is a class-J planet	"The First Duty" (TNG), "Starship Down" (DS9)
Scalos	Planet whose humanoid inhabitants underwent hyperacceleration as a result of environmental pollution	"Wink of an Eye" (TOS)
Scylla sector	Location of **Starbase 515**	"Samaritan Snare" (TNG)
Secarus IV	Planet location of the **Albino**'s hideout in 2345	"Blood Oath" (DS9)
Selay	Homeworld to a sentient reptilian people	"Lonely Among Us" (TNG)
Selcundi Drema	Star system whose planets experienced geologic instabilities	"Pen Pals" (TNG)
Selebi Asteroid Belt	Asteroid belt charted by the ***Enterprise*-D** in 2366	"The Offspring" (TNG)
Sentinel Minor IV	Planet, destination of the ***U.S.S. Lalo*** before they were destroyed by the **Borg**	"The Best of Both Worlds, Part I" (TNG)
Septimus Minor	Original destination of vessel ***Artemis***, launched in 2274	"The Ensigns of Command" (TNG)
Setlik III	Planet where a **Federation** outpost was destroyed by a **Cardassian** sneak attack	"The Wounded" (TNG), "Emissary" (DS9)
Shelia star system	Home star system of the **Sheliak**	"The Ensigns of Command" (TNG)
Sherman's Planet	Object of a dispute between the **Federation** and the **Klingon Empire**	"The Trouble With Tribbles" (TOS)
Shiralea VI	Planet; location of the **Parallax Colony**	"Cost of Living" (TNG)
Sigma Draconis	Star system with three Class-M planets	"Spock's Brain" (TOS)
Sigma Draconis III	Class-M planet equivalent in development to Earth year 1485	"Spock's Brain" (TOS)
Sigma Draconis IV	Class-M planet equivalent in development to Earth year 2030	"Spock's Brain" (TOS)
Sigma Draconis VI	Class-M planet where **Spock**'s brain was taken	"Spock's Brain" (TOS)
Sigma Erandi system	Star system, source of hytritium chemical	"The Most Toys" (TNG)
Sigma III solar system	Solar system containing planet Quadra Sigma III	"Hide and Q" (TNG)
Sigma Iotia II	Planet whose culture was based on the Chicago mobs of the 1920s, due to cultural contamination from the ***U.S.S. Horizon***	"A Piece of the Action" (TOS)
Sikaris	Class-M planet in the Delta Quadrant	"Prime Factors" (VGR)
Sirius	Star used for navigational reference	"Arena" (TOS)
Sobras	Planet in the Delta Quadrant. Site of Kazon conference in 2372	"Alliances" (VGR)
Solais V	Planet where famed mediator **Riva** helped warring inhabitants find peace	"Loud as a Whisper" (TNG); "The Adversary" (DS9)
Solari	Star system, location of planet Solais V	"Loud as a Whisper" (TNG)
Solarion IV	Planet; formerly site of a **Federation** colony	"Ensign Ro" (TNG)
Solosos III	Planet in the **Demilitarized Zone** and site of a Maquis colony	"For the Uniform" (DS9)
Sothis III	Homeworld of the Satarran people	"The Chase" (TNG)
Stakoron II	Planet in the **Gamma Quadrant which** contains mizainite ore	"The Nagus" (DS9)
stellar core fragment	Extremely dense, massive piece of disintegrated star, probably composed on **neutronium**	"The Masterpiece Society" (TNG)

Object name	Description	Episode or film
Straleb	Planet; part of the **Coalition of Madena**	"The Outrageous Okona" (TNG)
Strnad star system	Solar system to which the ***Enterprise*-D** delivered Earth colonists in 2364	"Justice" (TNG)
Styris IV	Planet plagued by Anchilles fever in 2364	"Code of Honor" (TNG)
supernova	A star, near the end of its life, that explodes violently	"The Q and the Grey" (VGR)
Surata IV	Planet where Riker was injured by an indigenous plant	"Shades of Gray" (TNG)
Suvin IV	Planet noted for splended archaeologic ruins	"Rascals" (TNG)
Sylleran Rift	Astronomical object	"Darkling" (VGR)
System J-25	Star system, location of **Borg** attack	"Q Who?" (TNG)
T'Lani III	Planet whose population was destroyed by war	"Armageddon Game" (DS9)
T'Lani Prime	Planet in the **T'Lani** star system	"Armageddon Game" (DS9)
T'lli Beta	Planet, destination of ***Enterprise*-D** when it encountered a school of **two-dimensional creatures**	"The Loss" (TNG)
Tagra IV	Planet in the Argolis Cluster which was ecologically devastated	"True-Q" (TNG)
Tagus III	Planet with many archaeological sites	"QPid" (TNG)
Talos IV	Class-M planet devastated centuries ago by nuclear war, homeworld to the **Talosians**	"The Cage" (TOS), "The Menagerie" (TOS)
Tambor Beta VI	White dwarf star where the **emergent life-form** took the ***Enterprise*-D** to collect **vertion particles**	"Emergence" (TNG)
Tantalus V	Location of a Federation penal colony	"Dagger of the Mind" (TOS)
Tanuga IV	Planet where **Dr. Apgar** worked on a **Krieger-wave** converter	"A Matter of Perspective" (TNG)
Tarchannen III	Planet where crew members from the ***U.S.S. Victory*** were infected by alien **DNA**	"Identity Crisis" (TNG)
Tarella	Home planet to the **Tarellians**, devastated in a biological war	"Haven" (TNG)
Taresia	Class-M planet in the Delta Quadrant	"Favorite Son" (VGR)
Tarod IX	Planet near **Romulan Neutral Zone**, attacked by the **Borg**	"The Neutral Zone" (TNG)
Tarok	Class-M moon located in **Kazon-Ogla** space	"Initiations" (VGR)
Tarsas III	Planet around which orbits **Starbase 74**	"11001001" (TNG)
Tarsus IV	Site of infamous massacre by **Kodos the Executioner**	"The Conscience of the King" (TOS)
Tartaras V	Planet that **Vash** decided to explore instead of returning to **Earth**	"Q-Less" (DS9)
Tau Alpha C	Little-known homeworld to the **Traveler**	"Where No One Has Gone Before" (TNG)
Tau Ceti	Star located eight light-years from **Earth**	"Whom Gods Destroy" (TOS)
Tau Ceti III	Planet where **Picard** met **Captain Rixx** sometime in 2364	"Conspiracy" (TNG)
Tau Ceti Prime	Planet; site of a tragic accident in 2358 that claimed the life of **Admiral Janeway**	"Coda" (VGR)
Tau Cygna V	Planet where a Federation colony was established in violation of the **Treaty of Armens**	"The Ensigns of Command" (TNG)
Taugan sector	Region of space where the planets **Dessica II**, **Calder II**, **Draken IV** and **Yadalla Prime** are located	"Gambit (TNG)
Taurus II	Planet where ***Shuttlecraft Galileo*** crashed in 2267 while under the command of Mr. **Spock**	"The Galileo Seven" (TOS)
Tavela Minor	Planet where Crusher suggested that Ogawa take a vacation	"Imaginary Friend" (TNG)
Teleris	Star cluster that **Q** invited **Vash** to visit	"Q-Less" (DS9)
Telfas Prime	Planet location of a mining community	"Alliances" (VGR)
Tellun star system	System containing planets **Elas** and **Troyius**	"Elaan of Troyius" (TOS)
Teluridian IV	Planet in the Alpha Quadrant	"Ex Post Facto" (VGR)
Tenarus cluster	Star system near Kazon territory in the Delta Quadrant	"Basics, Part I" (VGR)
Teplan system	Planetary system in the Gamma Quadrant. A deadly plague called the **blight** was unleashed on one of the systems worlds	"The Quickening" (DS9)
Terlina III	Planet where **Noonien Soong**'s last laboratory was located	"Inheritance" (TNG)
Terlina system	Solar system where where **Terlina III** is located	"Inheritance" (TNG)
Terosa Prime	Planet	"Second Sight" (DS9)
Tessen III	Federation planet threatened by an asteroid in 2368	"Cost of Living" (TNG)
Tethys III	Green planet with hydrogen-helium composition and frozen core	"Clues" (TNG)
Thalos VII	Planet where cocoa beans are aged for four centuries (yum!)	"The Dauphin" (TNG)
Thanatos VII	Planet where a contaminated plasma conduit was manufactured	"Phantasms" (TNG)
Thasus	Home planet of a noncorporeal civilization known as the **Thasians**, who cared for young Charles Evans	"Charlie X" (TOS)
Thelka IV	Planet where **Picard** discovered a delicious dessert	"Lessons" (TNG)
Theta 116	Star system that was the final destination for the ***Charybdis***	"The Royale" (TNG)
Theta Cygni XII	Planet struck by the **Denevan neural parasites**	"Operation: Annihilate!" (TOS)
Theta VII	Planet that needed vaccines from the ***Enterprise***	"Obsession" (TOS)
Tiburon	Planet where **Dr. Sevrin** studied as a research engineer, also location of **Zora**'s inhumane experiments	"The Way to Eden" (TOS), "The Savage Curtain" (TOS)
Tilonus IV	Planet. In 2369, Commander William Riker was subjected to neural manipulation in an attempt to extract information from him	"Frame of Mind' (TNG)
Titan	Largest of **Saturn**'s moons	"The First Duty" (TNG)
Titus IV	Planet where **Miles O'Brien** almost stepped on a **Lycosa tarantula**	"Realm of Fear" (TNG)
Tohvun III	Neutral planet located near the Cardassian/Federation border	"Chain of Command, Part II" (TNG)

Object name	Description	Episode or film
Topin system	Planetary system with an unstable protostar	"Preemptive Strike" (TNG)
Torad IV	Planet in the Gamma Quadrant	"Body Parts" (DS9)
Torga IV	Planet, site of standoff between DS9 team and Jem'Hadar	"The Ship" (DS9)
Torman V	Planet where **Picard** got transportation to **Celtris III**	"Chain of Command, Part I" (TNG)
Torna IV	Planet	"The Sword of Kahless" (DS9)
Torona IV	Home of the insectoid civilization known as the **Jarada**	"The Big Goodbye" (TNG)
Tracken II	Planet in the **Demilitarized Zone** and site of Maquis colony	"For the Uniform" (DS9)
Triacus	Planet where a Federation science team was driven to suicide by the evil **Gorgan**	"And the Children Shall Lead" (TOS)
Trialus star system	Planetary system in the Gamma Quadrant	"Meridian" (DS9)
Trill homeworld	Class-M planet that is home to the joined species known as the **Trill**	"Invasive Procedures" (DS9), "Past Tense, Part I" (DS9)
Triona System	Planet where **Lt. Keith Rocha** was killed by a **coalescent organism**	"Aquiel" (TNG)
Triskelion	Planet ruled by the **Providers** for gaming purposes	"The Gamesters of Triskelion" (TOS)
Troyius	Planet at war with sister world **Elas** in 2268	"Elaan of Troyius" (TOS)
Turkana IV	Planet, site of a failed Federation colony, birthplace to security officer **Natasha Yar**	"Legacy" (TNG)
Tycho IV	Home planet to the vampire cloud creature	"Obsession" (TOS)
Tyken's Rift	Rupture in the fabric of space	"Night Terrors" (TNG)
Typhon Expanse	Huge area of space where ***Enterprise*-D** and the ***Bozeman*** were trapped in a temporal causality loop	"Cause and Effect" (TNG)
Tyrellia	Federation planet with no atmosphere and no magnetic pole	"Starship Mine" (TNG)
Tyrus VIIA	Planet where **Dr. Farallon** tested **particle fountain** mining	"The Quality of Life" (TNG)
Tzenketh	Planet homeworld of the **Tzenkethi** civilization	"By Inferno's Light" (DS9)
Ufandi III	Planet where **Duras** sisters transferred illegal goods	"Firstborn" (TNG)
Ultima Thule	Planet, location of a **dolamide** purification plant	"Dramatis Personae" (DS9)
Umoth VIII	Planet location of Federation colony in the **Demilitarized Zone**	"The Maquis, Part II" (DS9)
Unefra III	Planet, **Enabran Tain** lived here after his retirement	"Improbable Cause" (DS9)
Ux-Mal	Star system that was the original home of a group of criminals who took over the ***Enterprise*-D** in 2368	"Power Play" (TNG)
Vacca VI	Isolated Class-M planet; new home of the **Boraalans**	"Homeward" (TNG)
Vadris III	Planet; natives think they are the only intelligent life in the universe	"Q-Less" (DS9)
Vagra II	Planet whose inhabitants escaped, leaving behind a skin of pure evil, location of **Natasha Yar**'s death	"Skin of Evil" (TNG)
Valo system	Solar system located near the **Cardassian** border	"Ensign Ro" (TNG)
Valt Minor	Star system at war with neighboring **Krios** system for centuries	"The Perfect Mate" (TNG)
Vandor IV	Planet, location of **Dr. Paul Manheim**'s laboratory	"We'll Always Have Paris" (TNG)
Vandor star system	Binary star system containing a B-class giant with companion pulsar, location of **Dr. Paul Manheim**'s laboratory	"We'll Always Have Paris" (TNG)
Vandros IV	Planet in the Gamma Quadrant where an ancient **Iconian gateway** was discovered by Dominion scientists in 2372	"To the Death" (DS9)
Vaytan	Star chosen as the first test site for the new **metaphasic shield**	"Suspicions" (TNG)
Vega colony	Destination of ***U.S.S. Enterprise*** before receiving distress call from ***S.S. Columbia***	"The Cage" (TOS)
Vega-Omicron sector	Patrol assignment of the ***U.S.S. Aries***	"The Icarus Factor" (TNG)
Velara III	Planet that was the object of a terraforming project in 2364	"Home Soil" (TNG)
Veloz Prime	Planet in the **Demilitarized Zone**	"For the Uniform" (DS9)
Vendikar	Planet at war with its neighbor, **Eminiar VII**, for 500 years	"A Taste of Armageddon" (TOS)
Ventax II	Planet that enjoyed a thousand years of peace, apparently because of a pact with a mythological figure named **Ardra**	"Devil's Due" (TNG)
Venus	Second planet in the Sol system	"Future's End, Part II" (VGR)
Verath	Solar system, origin of a rare statue	"Q-Less" (DS9)
Veridian III	Planet, the **nexus** ribbon passed near Veridian III in 2371	*Star Trek Generations*
Veridian IV	Planet populated with a pre-industrial humanoid society	*Star Trek Generations*
Veridian system	Star system with four planets. The **nexus** energy ribbon passed through the Veridian system in 2371	*Star Trek Generations*
Vilmor II	Planet where clues to the ancient seeding humanoids were found	"The Chase" (TNG)
Vlugta asteroid belt	Asteroid field in the Vlugtan star system	"Rivals" (DS9)
Vlugtan star system	Location of Vlugta asteroid belt	"Rivals" (DS9)
Vodrey Nebula	***Enterprise*-D** passed through this nebula enroute to **Maranga IV**	"Firstborn" (TNG)
Volchok Prime	Planet where the Ferengi Hoex bought his rival's cargo port	"The Nagus" (DS9)
Volon II	Planet that was Federation territory, now in **Demilitarized Zone**	"The Maquis" (DS9)
Volon III	Planet location of Federation colonies in the **Demilitarized Zone**	"The Maquis, Part II" (DS9), "Tribunal" (DS9)
Volterra Nebula	Nebula that the ***Enterprise*-D** studied in 2369	"The Chase" (TNG)
Vulcan	Home planet to Mr. **Spock**	"Amok Time" (TOS), et al
Wolf 359	Star system, location of a devastating battle against the **Borg**	"The Best of Both Worlds, Part II" (TNG), et al
wormhole	A subspace bridge between two points	*Star Trek: The Motion Picture*

Object name	Description	Episode or film
Wrigley's Pleasure Planet	Planet where *Enterprise* crew member Darnell met a beautiful woman	"The Man Trap" (TOS)
Xanthras III	Planet, destination of ***Enterprise*-D** in 2366	"Ménage à Troi" (TNG)
Xendi Sabu star system	Star system where the **Ferengi** returned the *Stargazer* to **Picard**	"The Battle" (TNG); "Bloodlines" (TNG)
Xerxes VII	Planet where legend says a mythical land called Neinman is found	"When the Bough Breaks" (TNG)
Yadalla Prime	Site of a archaeological site suggested as a possible raiding site for **Baran**'s mercenaries	"Gambit" (TNG)
Yadera II	Planet located in the Gamma Quadrant. Home to **Rurigan**	"Shadowplay" (DS9)
Yadera Prime	Planet conquered by the **Dominion** in 2340	"Shadowplay" (DS9)
Zadar IV	Planet on which oceanographer Dr. Harry Bernard once lived	"When the Bough Breaks" (TNG)
Zalkon	Homeworld of the **Zalkonians**	"Transfigurations" (TNG)
Zayra IV	Planet where **Miles O'Brien** rerouted an emitter array	"Realm of Fear" (TNG)
Zed Lapis Sector	Region where planet **Vagra II** is located	"Skin of Evil" (TNG)
Zeon	Peaceful neighbors to planet **Ekos**	"Patterns of Force" (TOS)
Zeta Alpha II	Planet from which the ***U.S.S. Lalo*** departed before they were lost to the **Borg**	"The Best of Both Worlds, Part I" (TNG)
Zeta Gelis Cluster	Cluster where ***Enterprise*-D** discovered the **Zalkonian**, **John Doe**	"Transfigurations" (TNG)
Zetar	Planet, home to the **Zetarians**, destroyed millennia ago	"The Lights of Zetar" (TOS)
Zytchin III	Planet where Captain **Picard** once spent a four day vacation that he claimed not to have enjoyed	"Captain's Holiday" (TNG)

plasma fire. Combustion supported by the intense heat from an externally supplied ionized plasma gas source, such as those found in a starship's **internal power grid.** ("Disaster" [TNG]).

plasma flares. Technical component. Combined with other supplies, plasma flares can be used to create a **biogenic weapon**. ("Preemptive Strike" [TNG]).

plasma grid. Component of the warp drive partially responsible for **power conversion levels**. In 2370, as part of their ongoing contest to have the highest performance level, **Commander Donald Kaplan** suggested that Commander La Forge might achieve a higher level by "cleaning his plasma grid once in a while." ("Force of Nature" [TNG]).

plasma infuser. Handheld instrument used for the transfer of high-energy plasma. ("Suspicions" [TNG]).

plasma infusion unit. Medical device used aboard Federation starships to dispense fluid and electrolytes. ("Schisms" [TNG]).

plasma injector. Portion of a starship's **warp drive** that controls the flow of ionized gas into the warp coils. ("Captive Pursuit" [DS9]). In 2370, the failure of a plasma injector aboard a Deep Space 9 runabout led to the accidental discovery of a passageway into a **mirror universe**. ('Crossover" [DS9]).

plasma plague. A group of deadly virus types. An unclassified but extremely virulent strain of plasma plague threatened the densely populated **Rachelis system** in 2365. Significant research into plasma plague was conducted by Dr. Susan Nuress in 2295 in response to a similar outbreak on planet Obi VI. One mutated strain developed during Nuress's research was found to grow more rapidly when exposed to eichner radiation. A similar strain threatened the *Enterprise*-D when that ship was transporting specimens of plasma plague to Science Station **Tango Sierra** to combat an outbreak in the Rachelis system in 2365. ("The Child" [TNG]).

plasma residue. By-product of the warp propulsion process. When plasma residue was vented from a starship's warp **nacelle**s, a cloud of blue glowing gas was created around the ship. ("Elogium" [VGR]).

plasma storm. See **plasma disruption**.

plasma strand. Cohesive strings of plasma energy found in great quantity within an **inversion nebula**. Plasma strands are highly unstable, and typically burn themselves out within a few years. ("Alter Ego" [VGR]).

plasma stream. See: **nacelle.**

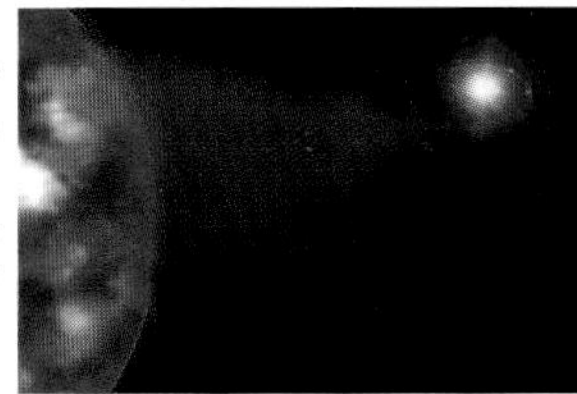

plasma streamer. Gas current flowing through space between one star of a binary pair and the other. The *Starship* ***Yosemite*** encountered **quasi-energy microbes** living in the **plasma** streamer between a binary pair in the Igo Sector in 2369. ("Realm of Fear" [TNG]).

plasma torch. Work tool used aboard Federation starships. An engineer aboard the *Enterprise*-D was badly burned in 2369 when he was working on a conduit on Deck 37 and a **plasma** torch blew up in his hands. ("Frame of Mind" [TNG]).

plasma weapons. Armament technology, developed sometime after 2293. ("Flashback" [VGR]).

plasma. Scientific term for very hot, ionized gas. Plasma is gas so hot that the electrons have been stripped from the atomic nuclei. A starship's impulse engines leave an exhaust of plasma, which can be detected, even from a cloaked vessel. (*Star Trek VI: The Undiscovered Country*).

plasticized tritanium mesh. A 26th-century construction material, unknown in the 24th century. **Professor Berlinghoff Rasmussen**'s time-travel pod had a hull composed of plasticized tritanium mesh. ("A Matter of Time" [TNG]).

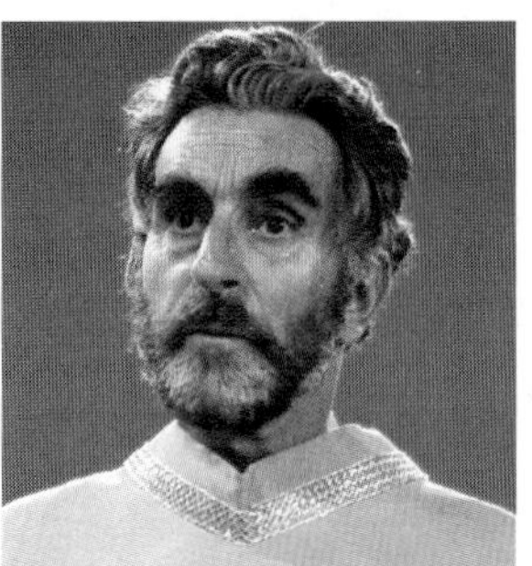

Plasus. (Jeff Corey). High advisor of the cloud city **Stratos** above planet **Ardana** in 2269 and father to **Droxine**. The politically conservative Plasus was determined to protect the established social order on his planet, despite the fact that exploitation of the **Troglyte** workers on the planet's surface was both unfair and physically harmful to the workers. Plasus opposed talks with the Troglytes, and further opposed a plan whereby protective **filter masks** would be furnished to the workers to shield them against the debilitating effects of **zenite** gas. ("The Cloud Minders" [TOS]).

"Plato's Stepchildren." Original Series episode #67. Written by Meyer Dolinsky. Directed by David Alexander. Stardate 5784.2. *First aired in 1968.* Enterprise *crew members are held captive by a civilization whose people once visited Earth during the time of Plato, and who now have remarkable psychokinetic powers.* GUEST CAST: Michael Dunn as **Alexander**; Liam Sullivan as **Parmen**; Barbara Babcock as **Philana**; Majel Barrett as **Chapel, Christine**; Ted Scott as Eraclitus; Derek Partridge as Dionyd; Armando Gonzales as Spock's Flamenco dance double; Jay Jones as Kirk's stunt double. SEE: **Alexander; kironide; Parmen; Philana; Plato; Platonians; Platonius; psychokinesis; Sahndara.**

Plato. Ancient Greek philosopher (c.428 B.C.-c.348 B.C.) on Earth. Plato's teachings inspired a group of extraterrestrials led by **Parmen** who later called themselves **Platonians**. ("Plato's Stepchildren" [TOS]).

Platonians. Humanoids, originally from the **Sahndara** star system, who patterned their society after the teachings of ancient Earth philosopher **Plato**. When their star, Sahndara, exploded millennia ago, 38 individuals fled their doomed world, settling briefly on Earth during the time of Plato. When the Greek culture faded, the Platonians moved to another planet, which they called Platonius. Here, they accidentally developed powerful **psychokinetic** powers from ingesting native food containing **kironide**, a rare and powerful element found in the food. The Platonians remained unknown to the rest of the galaxy for centuries until their leader, Parmen, fell ill in 2268 and summoned the *Starship Enterprise* to provide him with medical care. ("Plato's Stepchildren" [TOS]). SEE: **Alexander**.

Platonius. Class-M planet settled by the **Platonians**, who attempted to create their own version of **Plato**'s Republic there. The natural foods on Platonius contained a substance called **kironide**, a powerful energy source. ("Plato's Stepchildren" [TOS]).

"Playing God." *Deep Space Nine* episode #37. Story by Jim Trombetta. Teleplay by Jim Trombetta and Michael Piller. Directed by David Livingston. No stardate given. *First aired in 1994. A miniature universe is brought on board Deep Space 9, and Dax acts as a training guide for a potential Trill host.* GUEST CAST: Geoffrey Blake as **Arjin**; Ron Taylor as Klingon host; Richard Poe as Cardassian officer; Chris Nelson Norris as Alien man; Majel Barrett as Computer voice. SEE: ***"Ak'la bella doo"*; Arjin; Black Hole; citrus blend; Dax (symbiont); Dax, Curzon; Dax, Jadzia; Dax, Lela; directional sonic generator; dynametric array; entomology; entropy; Evek, Gul; Ferengi Rules of Acquisition; field docent; Frenchotte; Galeo-Manada style wrestling; Gedana post; gravimetric microprobe; inertial dampers; initiate; joined; kiosk, Klingon; *Koliay; lach'tel;* latinum stairway; Mardah; *Mekong, U.S.S.*; microdyne; Odo; protouniverse; quantometer probe; Quark's bar; Quark; *racht*; red lining; *Rio Grande, U.S.S.*; Sisko, Benjamin; Sisko, Jake; spectral line profile analysis; Starbase 41; sub-nagus; subspace phenomena; synthale; *tongo*; Trajok; Trill; verteron; vole; Wormhole Junction.**

Plegg. Famous **Ferengi** entrepreneur who developed the modular **holosuite** industry. Quark attempted to capitalize on Plegg's fame by selling bogus pieces of Plegg's body in 2370, despite the fact that Plegg was alive and well on planet **Khofla II.** ("The Alternate" [DS9]). SEE: **Ferengi death ritual.**

Pleiades Cluster. Region of space, also known as M45 or the Seven Sisters, in which many young planets are located. The Pleiades are a cluster of about 400 stars in a 25-light-year radius, some 415 light-years from Earth. One of the planets in the area is **Velara III**, site of a failed **terraforming** project. The *Enterprise*-D conducted a mapping mission in the Pleiades Cluster in 2364. ("Home Soil" [TNG]).

Plexicorp. Commercial company engaged in the manufacture of acrylic polymers and other plastics in San Francisco, Earth, in the late 20th century. **Dr. Nichols**, a chemist employed by Plexicorp, developed the molecular matrix for **transparent aluminum**. He was assisted in this discovery by Montgomery Scott, who provided the information in exchange for acrylic plastic sheeting needed for transporting two humpback whales to the 23rd century. *(Star Trek IV: The Voyage Home). The Plexicorp scenes in* Star Trek IV *were filmed at a company called Reynolds & Taylor in Santa Ana, California.*

plexing. Betazoid relaxation technique in which one gently taps a nerve behind one's ear, using the index and middle fingers. Plexing stimulates a nerve cluster behind the carotid artery, causing the release of natural endorphins. Deanna Troi taught the technique to **Reginald Barclay** in an effort to help him overcome his fear of being transported. ("Realm of Fear" [TNG]). *Troi used the technique to try to calm herself in subsequent episodes, including "Timescape" (TNG).*

***plomeek* soup à la Neelix.** Neelix's spiced-up version of the time-honored **Vulcan** dish. Tuvok found it rather too piquant, but Neelix thought it was delicious. ("Faces" [VGR]).

plomeek* soup.** A traditional **Vulcan** food, orange in color. Nurse Chapel prepared a bowl of *plomeek* soup for Spock during his ***Pon farr in 2267, but Spock expressed his desire to be left alone by throwing the bowl into the corridor. ("Amok Time" [TOS]). When Quark had a business dinner with Sakonna in 2370, he tried to impress her by serving a lavish feast including *plomeek* soup. ("The Maquis, Part I" [DS9]). Tuvok was fond of *plomeek* soup; it seemed to remind him of home. ("Faces" [VGR]).

"Plum." Nickname given to **Leonard McCoy** by the future Mrs. **Nancy Crater** when they were romantically involved, several years prior to McCoy's assignment to the *Enterprise*. ("The Man Trap" [TOS]).

Pluto. The ninth planet in the Sol system. In 2293, the maiden voyage of the *U.S.S. Enterprise*-B was to have taken the ship out beyond Pluto and then back to Spacedock. This flight plan was abandoned when the starship responded to a distress call from the transport ship *S.S. Lakul*. *(Star Trek Generations).*

poker. Traditional Earth card game of chance and wills. Spock was unfamiliar with the game, but McCoy offered to teach it to him. ("The Corbomite Maneuver" [TOS]). A poker game was held every Thursday night aboard the *Starship Enterprise*-D. **Data** initially believed poker to be a fairly simple mathematical game, but he failed to consider the human element of bluffing one's opponent. ("The Measure of a Man" [TNG]). Data came to regard the game of poker as a fascinating forum for the study of human nature, eventually developing such ingenious exercises as his

poker game with holographic representations of **Sir Isaac Newton**, **Albert Einstein**, and **Stephen Hawking**. ("Descent, Part I" [TNG]). Geordi's VISOR gave him "special insight" into the cards held by his shipmates, courtesy of infrared light, although he said he never peeked until after a hand was over. ("Ethics" [TNG]). *The weekly* Enterprise-D *poker game was first seen in "The Measure of a Man" (TNG), and became something of a metaphor for* Star Trek's *human adventure. It therefore seems appropriate that our final television glimpse of our* Next Generation *friends was around the poker table in Riker's quarters, where Picard fittingly noted that "the sky's the limit." ("All Good Things..." [TNG]).*

Polaric Test Ban Treaty. Pact against the use of **polaric ion energy** sources, signed by the **United Federation of Planets** and the **Romulan Star Empire** in 2268. The treaty was prompted when a Romulan research colony on planet Chaltok IV was almost destroyed while testing polaric energy. ("Time and Again" [VGR]). *It wasn't clear if there were other signatories to the pact.*

polaric ion energy. Highly energetic but unstable power source. Although early research showed polaric energy as a promising means of providing power on a planetary scale, its use ran serious risks of uncontrolled chain reactions through subspace. Such an incident nearly destroyed a Romulan research colony on planet **Chaltok IV**, resulting in the **Polaric Test Ban Treaty** of 2268. In 2371, the *U.S.S. Voyager* scanned a Class-M planet in the Delta Quadrant whose inhabitants had a planet-wide polaric ion energy system. ("Time and Again" [VGR]). *The episode dealt with the aftermath of a planet-wide polaric ion explosion, and of our heroes' time travel to a day before the explosion, where they learned that they were the cause of the disaster. Since Janeway and company were successful in correcting the timeline, no one on the ship or the planet retained any memory of the explosion or the efforts to prevent it. The unnamed Class-M planet had a prewarp culture, so no attempt was made to contact them.*

polaron. Subatomic particle. On stardate 48658, the *Starship Voyager* used a polaron burst to illuminate a **Kazon** ship, making the vessel momentarily visible despite the Kazon's **masking circuitry**. ("State of Flux" [VGR]). In 2373, Starfleet theorized that exposure to polaron radiation would have a destabilizing effect on a Founder's physiology, forcing a **shape-shifter** back into a gelatinous state. Excessive polaron radiation is fatal to most forms of life. ("Apocalypse Rising" [DS9]). **Jem'Hadar attack ships** employed ship-mounted phased polaron beam weapons. The polaron beams could easily penetrate Federation defensive shields, regardless of what frequency nutation was used. ("The Jem'Hadar" [DS9]). Federation vessels, including runabouts, employed polaron scanners in their sensor complement. In 2372, Ensign **Harry Kim**, piloting a shuttlecraft, ran a polaron scan when his ship accidentally intersected a timestream, sending Kim into an alternate reality. ("Non Sequitur" [VGR]). The Swarm in the Delta Quadrant used polaron bursts as a means to control a target's shield polarity. ("The Swarm" [VGR]). In 2373, the crew of the *Starship Voyager* used a polaron pulse sent from the main deflector to successfully defend the ship from an attack from Captain Braxton's *Timeship Aeon*. ("Future's End, Part I" [VGR]). The crew of the *U.S.S. Defiant* used a polaron field on stardate 50416.2 to trace the ion trail of a runabout piloted by Kira Nerys. ("The Darkness and the Light" [DS9]).

Police Special. Ancient Earth hand weapon that fired lead projectiles propelled by a contained chemical explosion. On the **amusement park planet** in 2267, Sulu found a Police Special, which he'd always wanted to add to his collection. ("Shore Leave" [TOS]). SEE: **pistol**.

Political Ethics. Course of study taught by **Professor Natima Lang** on planet **Cardassia**. Lang's curriculum and unorthodox political views brought her under the scrutiny of the Cardassian Central Command. ("Profit and Loss" [DS9]).

Pollux IV. Class-M planet in the **Beta Geminorum** system with an oxygen-nitrogen atmosphere, home to the entity known as **Apollo**. The *Starship Enterprise*, in the Beta Geminorum system in 2267, was briefly captured by Apollo, who hoped the *Enterprise* crew would worship him as had the ancient Greeks. ("Who Mourns for Adonais?" [TOS]).

Pollux V. Planet in the **Beta Geminorum** system. Pollux V registered as having no intelligent life-forms when the *Enterprise* investigated that area of space on stardate 3468. ("Who Mourns for Adonais?" [TOS]).

polyadrenaline. Synthetic pharmaceutical based on the humanoid hormone epinephrine. ("Ethics" [TNG]).

polycomposite. Synthetic material used in the construction of Federation starship hulls. In 2370, the discovery of a debris field littered with **duranium** and polycomposite fragments incorrectly led the crew of the *Enterprise*-D to believe they had discovered the remains of the ***Fleming***. ("Force of Nature" [TNG]).

polycythemia. Medical condition characterized by an abnormal increase in the number of red blood cells. ("Basics, Part I" [VGR]). SEE: **xenopolycythemia.**

polyduranide. Construction material used aboard Federation starships. Although normally not flammable, polyduranide emits dangerous radiation when exposed to extremely intense heat, such as that generated in a **plasma fire**. ("Disaster" [TNG]). In 2372, *Starship Voyager* Chief Engineer **B'Elanna Torres** mistakenly said polyduranide was not used in construction of Federation spacecraft. Polyduranide is a component of Kazon spacecraft. ("Initiations" [VGR]).

polyduranium. Metallic alloy. Polyduranium was used in the bulkheads of Federation starships such as the *U.S.S. Defiant*. ("The Search, Part I" [DS9]).

polyferranide. Metallic compound. On Federation starships, polyferranide was used to seal warp coils. ("Tattoo" [VGR]). In 2372, the crew of the *Voyager* searched the moons around Drayan II for a source of polyferranide. ("Innocence" [VGR]).

Polynesian resort. Holodeck program devised by Neelix for the crew of the *Starship Voyager*. The Polynesian resort program included many elements popular among visitors to the islands of Earth's South Pacific ocean, including Neelix's version of a traditional Hawaiian luau with Tiki lamps, flowered leis, and hula dancers. ("Alter Ego" [VGR]). Also known as Tropical resort simulation 3. ("Darkling" [VGR]).

polynutrient solution. Restorative formula given to patients suffering from malnutrition. ("The Ascent" [DS9]).

polysilicate verterium. Substance that can be combined with **monocrystal cortenum** to create a densified composite material, **verterium cortenide**. ("Investigations" [VGR]).

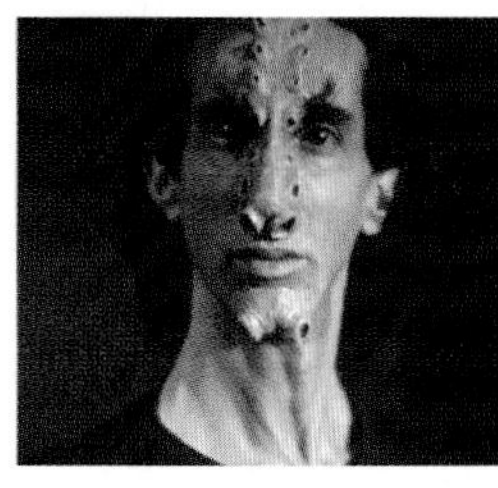

Pomet. (Alan Altshuld). Member of a group of terrorists who attempted to steal **trilithium** resin from the *Enterprise*-D in 2369. Pomet was disabled by Picard using a crossbow from Lieutenant Worf's quarters. Pomet was later killed by the **baryon sweep.** ("Starship Mine" [TNG]). SEE: **Remmler Array**.

Pommar. SEE: **Kazon-Pommar**.

Pon farr. Vulcan term for the time of mating. Although **Vulcans** live strictly by the dictates of logic, their veneer of civilization is

ripped away from them during *Pon farr*, every seven years of their adult life. The individual experiencing *Pon farr* will stop eating and sleeping if not allowed to return home to take a mate. ("Amok Time" [TOS]). During *Pon farr*, the brain is thrown into a **neurochemical imbalance** that can be fatal if the mating drive is not acted upon. The Vulcan telepathic mating bond draws mated couples irresistibly together during *Pon farr*. ("Blood Fever" [VGR]). Spock underwent *Pon farr* in 2267, when he returned to Vulcan, only to be spurned by his betrothed, **T'Pring**. ("Amok Time" [TOS]). SEE: ***Plak-tow***. Spock again experienced *Pon farr* when his regenerated body was undergoing hyperaccelerated growth on the **Genesis Planet** in 2285. Spock was fortunate that **Saavik**, a Vulcan female, was also present. *(Star Trek III: The Search for Spock).* **Tuvok** married **T'Pel** shortly after entering *Pon farr* in 2304. ("Flashback" [VGR]).

pool. Traditional Earth game of billiards. Tom Paris's holodeck recreation of **Chez Sandrine** featured a pool table. Paris's program included great pool players of the past. Various members of the *Voyager* crew played pool in Paris's program during their off-duty hours. Captain Janeway was an accomplished pool player. ("The Cloud" [VGR]). SEE: **Gaunt Gary.**

Porakan eggs. Eggs from an oocytic animal indigenous to planet Porakas IV in the Delta Quadrant. Neelix prepared Porakan eggs as a breakfast food on the *Voyager*. He prepared them with a little dill weed and a touch of *rengazo*. ("Flashback" [VGR]).

Porania, Legate. Bureaucrat within the **Cardassian** government. In 2368, Legate Porania was surprised at **Enabran Tain**'s retirement from the **Obsidian Order**. ("The Die is Cast" [DS9]).

port. Ancient nautical term referring to the left side of a ship, as opposed to the starboard (right) side.

Porta, Vedek. (Robert Symonds). Bajoran monk who served at the temple on station Deep Space 9. When **Akorem Laan** briefly assumed the role of Emissary in 2372 and tried to reinstate Bajor's caste-based ***D'jarra*** system, Porta killed a fellow monk who belonged to an "unclean" caste. ("Accession" [DS9]).

Portal. (Darryl Henriques). The last remaining protector of the once-grand **Tkon Empire**, Portal 63 had been stationed on the planet Delphi Ardu during the Tkon age of Bastu, at least 600,000 years ago. Remaining in some kind of suspension or stasis in the intervening millennia on a deserted outpost, Portal was unaware that the Tkon Empire had collapsed, until he was awakened by the presence of **Ferengi** and Federation spacecraft near his planet. ("The Last Outpost" [TNG]). *Actor Darryl Henriques also played Romulan ambassador Nanclus in* Star Trek VI: The Undiscovered Country.

Portas V. Planet near the **Demilitarized Zone** that was the site of a **Breen** settlement. ("For the Uniform" [DS9]).

Porter, Paul. (Eric Steinberg). Starfleet officer assigned to the engineering section of the *Enterprise*-E in 2373. Porter was captured and assimilated by the Borg when they attempted to take over the ship. *(Star Trek: First Contact).*

Porter. (Clayton Murray). Citizen of the American nation on 20th-century Earth. In 1996 Porter was a member of an antigovernment militia cell located in a house 30 kilometers northeast of Phoenix. ("Future's End, Part II" [VGR]).

Portland, U.S.S. Federation starship, *Chimera* class, Starfleet registry number NCC-57418. The *Portland,* along with a Cardassian cruiser, searched the **Algira sector** for **Odo** and **Garak**, when their runabout became missing in 2371 during the Romulan and Cardassian attack on the Founders' homeworld. ("The Die is Cast" [DS9]).

positron beam. Energy beam consisting of a stream of positron particles. In 2293, to evade Kang's battle cruiser, Captain Sulu ignited sirillium in the Azure Nebula using a positron beam modulated to a subspace frequency. ("Flashback" [VGR]).

positronic brain. An extremely advanced computing device that uses the decay of positrons to form sophisticated neural network systems. Long thought to be impossible, the positronic brain was first postulated in the 20th century by **Isaac Asimov** and finally made practical in the 24th century by **Noonien Soong**. Positronic brains were used in Soong's androids, **Data** and **Lore**. ("Datalore" [TNG]). A significant advance in submicron matrix transfer technology was introduced at a cybernetics conference in 2366, permitting Data to program a new positronic brain, which he used as the basis for his construction of his daughter, **Lal**. (*pictured*) ("The Offspring" [TNG]). *Although positronic computing remains purely hypothetical, positrons do exist. They are subatomic particles virtually identical to normal electrons, but with opposite electromagnetic properties. An electron has a negative charge, and a positron has a positive charge. Positrons were the first known particles of actual* ***antimatter*** *to be observed in the laboratory.*

positronic implant. Artificial cybernetic replacement for damaged portions of a biological brain. A patient given such an implant can exhibit dramatic personality changes. The magnitude and scope of these changes are a function of which areas and how much of the brain is replaced. **Vedek Bareil** was given a positronic implant after **vasokin** treatments damaged his brain in 2371. ("Life Support" [DS9]).

postatomic horror. A period of 21st-century Earth history, during which **Earth** recovered from the **World War III** nuclear conflict of 2053. Much of the planet reverted to barbarism during this period. ("Encounter at Farpoint, Part I" [TNG]). Humanity's **first contact** with an extraterrestrial civilization in 2063 marked the beginning of the end of the postatomic horror. *(Star Trek: First Contact). "Encounter at Farpoint" suggests that the postatomic horror lasted until at least 2079, so the renaissance wrought by contact with the Vulcans did not happen instantly.*

postcellular compounding. Method by which the Iyaaran people reproduced, using a natal pod. Using this method, the Iyaarans emerged as fully grown adults. ("Liaisons" [TNG]). *It's probably just as well that the episode didn't make clear just how this worked.*

postcentral gyrus. Part of the **Cardassian** brain. The special **cranial implant** that **Garak** was given when he was in the **Obsidian Order** was located in the postcentral gyrus. ("The Wire" [DS9]).

postmortem resuscitation technique. Starfleet medical protocols used to revive patients who, in an earlier age, might have been considered to be clinically dead. ("Emanations" [VGR]).

pot roast. Traditional Earth meal made from simmered beef. A meal of replicated pot roast was ruined aboard the *Starship*

Voyager in 2373 because of an overloaded heating array. ("Macrocosm" [VGR]).

Potak cold fowl. Beverage made from the glandular secretions of an adult dunghill bird found only on **Potak III**. Potak cold fowl was a rare beverage that had a smoky flavor, making it particularly suited to be served with strong meaty dishes. According to Neelix, only 27 bottles of Potak cold fowl were in existence in 2372. ("Parturition" [VGR]).

Potak III. Planet in the Delta Quadrant. Source of the dunghill bird from which **Potak cold fowl** was made. ("Parturition" [VGR]).

potato casserole. Traditional Earth dish, made from Earth tuber roots, popular with the people of Ireland. Potato casserole was part of **Miles O'Brien**'s childhood. He once prepared the dish for his wife, Keiko, who preferred such staples as **plankton loaf** and kelp buds, but tried her husband's favorites anyway. ("The Wounded" [TNG]).

potatoes, mashed. Traditional Earth dish made from carbohydrate-rich tuber roots. The roots are cooked, then crushed, and blended with milk, salt, and butter. Tom Paris decided to buy mashed potatoes with replicator rations from his **radiogenic sweepstakes** gambling scheme. ("Meld" [VGR]).

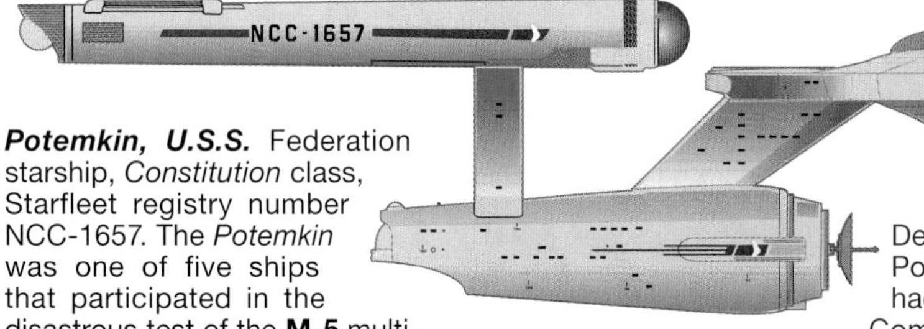

Potemkin, U.S.S. Federation starship, *Constitution* class, Starfleet registry number NCC-1657. The *Potemkin* was one of five ships that participated in the disastrous test of the **M-5** multitronic unit in 2268. ("The Ultimate Computer" [TOS]). The *Potemkin* was to rendezvous with the *Enterprise* at Beta Aurigae shortly after stardate 5928 to study gravitational influences in that binary system, until Dr. Janice Lester, in Kirk's body, changed the course. ("Turnabout Intruder" [TOS]).

Potemkin, U.S.S. Federation starship, *Excelsior* class, Starfleet registry number NCC-18253. **William T. Riker** served aboard this vessel prior to his assignments to the ***Hood*** and the *Enterprise*-D, but after the *Pegasus*. Riker once employed the unconventional tactic of positioning the ship over a planet's magnetic pole, thus making the ship difficult to detect by an opponent's sensors. ("Peak Performance" [TNG]). In 2361, as a lieutenant aboard the *Potemkin*, Riker led an away team to evacuate the science outpost on planet **Nervala IV**, and subsequently was promoted to lieutenant commander and commended for "exceptional valor" on the mission. It was not realized until later that a duplicate of Riker had been created in a transporter malfunction during the evacuation. ("Second Chances" [TNG]). SEE: **Riker, Thomas**. During the same year, the *Potemkin* was the last Federation starship to make contact with the failed **Turkana IV** colony, prior to the *Enterprise*-D's mission there in 2367. *Potemkin* personnel were warned by the colony's ruling cadres not to transport to the surface, or they would be killed. ("Legacy" [TNG]). The *Potemkin* rendezvoused with the *Enterprise*-D on stardate 45587 to transfer **Dr. Toby Russell** to the *Enterprise*-D. ("Ethics" [TNG]). *Named for Grigory Aleksandrovich Potemkin, (1739-1791), Russian military figure under Catherine II.*

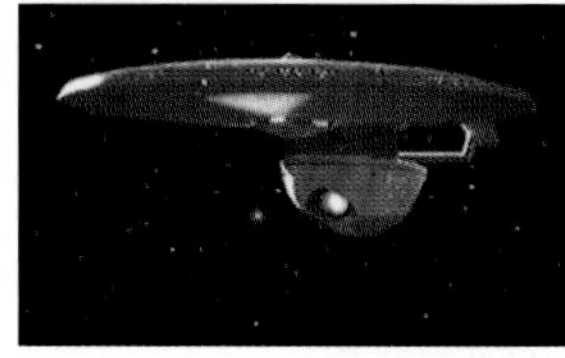

Pottrik Syndrome. Disease that afflicts Cardassians, similar to **Kalla-Nohra Syndrome**. So alike are the two afflictions that they are even treated by the same medication. **Aamin Marritza** claimed to suffer from Pottrik Syndrome, in an apparent attempt to conceal the fact that he suffered from Kalla-Nohra. A lower pulmonary bio-probe for Pottrik Syndrome shows up as negative, whereas for Kalla-Nohra, it shows up as positive. ("Duet" [DS9]).

Potts, Jake. (Cory Danziger). The elder of the two Potts children who were left on the *Enterprise*-D, by special arrangement, while their parents took a sabbatical in 2367. During crew shore leave on **Ogus II**, Jake played a practical joke on his younger brother, **Willie Potts**, resulting in Willie's near-death. ("Brothers" [TNG]). SEE: **cove palm**.

Potts, Willie. (Adam Ryen). Younger brother to **Jake Potts**. Willie almost died in 2367 at the age of nine years when a practical joke played by Jake misfired seriously. Jake had pretended to be hurt in a laser duel game, whereupon Willie hid in a nearby forest, eating a deadly **cove palm** fruit. The infectious parasites in the fruit nearly killed Willie, who had to be quarantined until he could be rushed to **Starbase 416** for treatment. ("Brothers" [TNG]).

powdered newt. Finely ground desiccated lizard remains used as a food supplement. Quark owned some stock in powdered newt supplements, but they became worthless in 2373. ("Business As Usual" [DS9]).

Powell, Lieutenant Andrew. *Enterprise*-D crew member. In 2370, Powell began dating Alyssa Ogawa. Powell proposed to Alyssa that same year. ("Lower Decks" [TNG]). *We don't know if they actually did get married.* Powell and Ogawa conceived a child together, but Andrew later had some difficulty adjusting to Alyssa's pregnancy. Lieutenant Commander Data, after his nine weeks of experience dealing with the pregnant **Spot**, felt he was ready to help Andrew prepare for his impending fatherhood. ("Genesis" [TNG]).

"Power Play." *Next Generation* episode #115. Teleplay by Rene Balcer and Herbert J. Wright & Brannon Braga. Story by Paul Reuben and Maurice Hurley. Directed by David Livingston. Stardate 45571.2. *First aired in 1992. Alien criminals take over the minds of* Enterprise-*D crew members.* GUEST CAST: Rosalind Chao as **O'Brien**, **Keiko**; Colm Meaney as **O'Brien**, **Miles**; Michelle Forbes as **Ro Laren**; Ryan Reid as Transporter technician; Majel Barrett as Computer voice. SEE: **anesthezine gas; anionic energy; *Daedalus*-class starship; *Essex, U.S.S.*; ionogenic particles; *Jat'yln*; Kelly, Lieutenant Morgan; Mab-Bu VI; McKinley Park; microoptic drill; Mullen, Commander Steven; Narsu, Admiral Uttan; neutrino field; neutrino; O'Brien, Keiko; O'Brien, Molly; pattern enhancer; Shumar, Captain Bryce; Ux-Mal.**

power conversion level. Measurement of the actual usable energy obtained from an energy-conversion system, such as the matter/antimatter reaction in a starship's warp drive. Typically, Federation starships can utilize 97 percent of the energy created in the matter/antimatter reaction, an extremely high level. In 2370, by doing some fine tuning of the power taps, *Enterprise*-D Chief Engineer Geordi La Forge was able to raise the ship's power conversion level to 97.2 percent. ("Force of Nature" [TNG]).

Praetor. Title of the leader of the **Romulan Star Empire**. ("Balance of Terror" [TOS]). SEE: **Proconsul.**

Prak, DaiMon. (Lee Arenberg). Commander of a *D'Kora*-class Ferengi transport vessel discovered disabled in the **Hekaras Corridor** in 2370. Though he initially believed his ship had been disabled by a new Federation weapon, Prak was persuaded otherwise, and allowed the *Enterprise*-D crew to view his ship's sensor logs. These logs were instrumental in locating the ***U.S.S.***

Fleming. ("Force of Nature" [TNG]). *Prak's name was never mentioned on air, and is from the script. His ship didn't have a name, either.*

Prakal II. A planet. Guinan once visited Prakal II, where she acquired an unusual drink recipe. ("In Theory" [TNG]).

***Prakesh*.** *Galor*-class Cardassian warship. Gul **Dukat** helped the **Detapa Council** flee the Klingon invasion fleet in 2372 by evacuating them from Cardassia Prime aboard the *Prakesh*. The ship came under heavy fire from several Klingon warships and was almost destroyed before the *U.S.S. Defiant* arrived and rescued Dukat and the council members. The *Prakesh* was eventually destroyed after Dukat's party was safe aboard the *Defiant*. ("The Way of the Warrior" [DS9]).

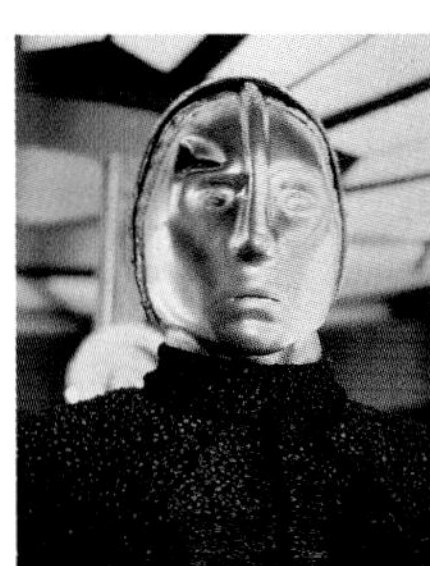

Pralor Automated Personnel Unit 3947. (Rick Worthy). Humanoid automaton built by the **Pralor** to fight in a war against robots built by the **Cravic**. Unit 3947 was activated by a Builder on the Pralor homeworld in 2222. This unit was severely damaged when the asteroid mining pod it was using exploded. In 2372, the *U.S.S. Voyager* crew discovered Unit 3947 drifting in space, brought it aboard, and reactivated it. Unit 3947 subsequently kidnapped *Voyager* engineer Torres, forcing her to create more robots of its kind. ("Prototype" [VGR]).

Pralor Automated Personnel Unit 6263. (Hugh Hodgin). Humanoid automaton built by the **Pralor** to fight in a war against robots built by the **Cravic**. Unit 6263 commanded a Pralor vessel that encountered the *U.S.S. Voyager* in 2372. ("Prototype" [VGR]).

Pralor Automated Personnel Unit. Sentient humanoid automatons built long ago by the **Pralor** people in their war against the **Cravic**. The Cravic, in turn, developed nearly identical automated weapons to counter the use of the Pralor units. Both sides programmed these robots to destroy their enemy. Eventually, the Pralor and Cravic sued for peace, and recalled their soldier automatons. The Automated Personnel Units built by both sides correctly viewed peace as a threat to their existence, and now regarded their Builders as their enemies. Pralor and Cravic units turned on their creators, wiping them out utterly. Once their Builders were gone, the Pralor and Cravic automated units continued to wage war on each other. Both the Pralor and Cravic builders took the precaution of designing the automated units' **chromodynamic power modules** to be impossible to replicate, thereby making the robots incapable of reproducing themselves. The Pralor automated units and their ships were silver-gray colored, while the Cravic units and ships were golden. ("Prototype" [VGR]). SEE: **Prototype Automated Personnel Unit 0001.**

Pralor. Technologically sophisticated Delta Quadrant civilization that became extinct several decades ago. The Pralor created sophisticated Automated Personnel Units to fight their war with the Cravic. Later the entire Pralor race was destroyed when they attempted to deactivate these robotic soldiers. ("Prototype" [VGR]). SEE: **Pralor Automated Personnel Unit**.

Praxillus system. A lifeless solar system with a giant red star as its center. The Praxillus system was the site for **Dr. Timicin**'s spectacularly unsuccessful **helium ignition test** in 2367. While the test was initially promising, temperatures in the stellar core continued to rise far beyond the needed 220 million Kelvins. Core density also continued to increase, and the Praxillus eventually went nova as a result of the experiment. ("Half a Life" [TNG]).

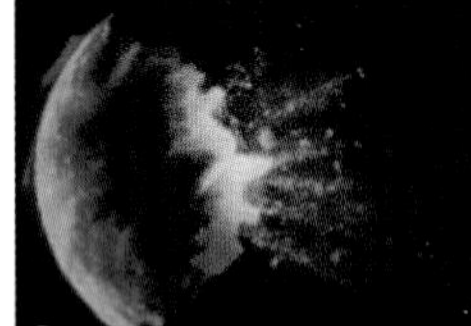

Praxis. A moon of the **Klingon Homeworld** of Qo'noS, and formerly a key energy-production facility for the Klingon Empire. A massive explosion on Praxis in 2293 nearly shattered that satellite and caused severe environmental damage to the homeworld as well. The aftermath of the explosion was a key factor in motivating **Chancellor Gorkon**'s peace initiative later that year. SEE: **Klingon Empire**. *(Star Trek VI: The Undiscovered Country*, "Flashback" [VGR]).

prayko. Game. **Leeta** said that she would install two prayko alleys at **Quark's bar** if she ran the place. ("Doctor Bashir, I Presume?" [DS9]).

pre-warp civilization. Sociologic term used to describe a culture that has not yet developed a faster-than-light interstellar travel capability. Under Starfleet's **Prime Directive**, a starship was generally not allowed to make contact with a pre-warp civilization. ("Time and Again" [VGR]).

preanimate matter. In biology, preanimate matter refers to certain nonorganic compounds from which organic materials may eventually evolve. *(Star Trek II: The Wrath of Khan).*

***Predator*-class warship.** Kazon spacecraft. In a malfunction-created holodeck delusion experienced by the holographic doctor, the *Voyager* came under attack by two *Predator*-class Kazon warships in 2372. ("Projections" [VGR]).

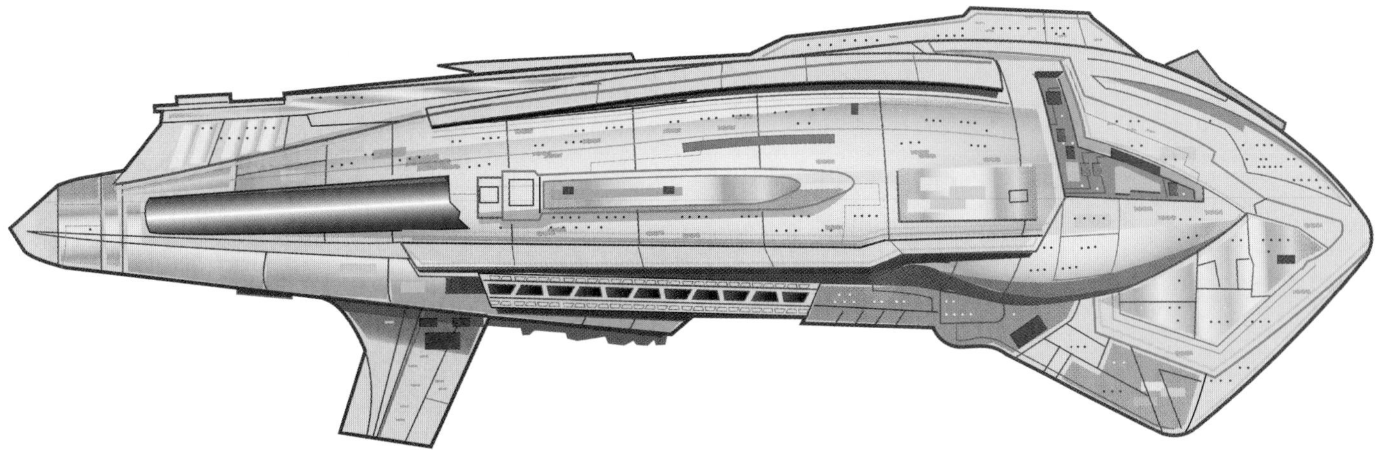

predestination paradox. In elementary temporal mechanics, a time loop in which a time traveler who has gone into the past causes an event that ultimately causes the original future version of the person to go back into the past. This is a paradox because it becomes unclear which event (past or future) is the cause, and which is the effect. For example, when **Dr. Julian Bashir** (from the year 2373) traveled back in time to 2267, he met **Lieutenant Watley**, a woman he suspected to be his great-grandmother. When Bashir and Watley briefly found themselves attracted to each other, Bashir wondered if he was predestined to fall in love with her and thereby to become his own great-grandfather. If this had been a true predestination paradox, Bashir's failure to do so would probably have resulted in the creation of an alternate timeline in which Bashir never existed. ("Trials and Tribble-ations" [DS9]).

"Preemptive Strike." *Next Generation* episode #176. Teleplay by René Echevarria. Story by Naren Shankar. Directed by Patrick Stewart. Stardate 47941.7. *First aired in 1994. Ro Laren is recruited to infiltrate an organization threatening the new peace treaty between the Federation and the Cardassians.* GUEST CAST: Michelle Forbes as **Ro Laren**; John Franklyn-Robbins as **Macias**; Natalia Nogulich as **Necheyev**, **Alynna**; William Thomas, Jr. as **Santos**; Shannon Cochran as **Kalita**; Richard Poe as **Evek**, **Gul**. SEE: **Advanced Tactical Training; *belaklavion*; biogenic weapon; biomimetic gel; Demilitarized Zone; Evek, Gul; *foraiga*; Gates, Ensign; *hasperat*; Hugora Nebula; isomiotic hypos; Juhraya; Juhrayan freighter; Kalita; Macias; magnetascopic interference; Maquis ships; Maquis; medkits; Necheyev, Alynna; palm beacons; Pendi II; phaser type-8; plasma flares; protostar; quarantine pods; retroviral vaccines; Ro Laren; Ronara; Santos; Topin system.**

prefix code. In a Federation starship's computer systems, the prefix code was a security passcode prepended to computer commands to prevent unauthorized activation or control of key systems. Kirk gained control of the ***U.S.S. Reliant***'s shield systems by transmitting the *Reliant*'s prefix code from the *Enterprise*. The *Reliant*'s prefix code was 16309. *(Star Trek II: The Wrath of Khan).* Captain Picard revealed the prefix code of the *Starship* ***Phoenix*** to Cardassian authorities in 2367 when *Phoenix* Captain **Benjamin Maxwell** was preparing an unauthorized attack on a Cardassian ship. The code gave the Cardassians the ability to remotely disable the *Phoenix*'s shields. ("The Wounded" [TNG]).

preganglionic fiber. Nerve tissue located outside the central nervous system. In 2373, Lieutenant Tom Paris suffered some damage to preganglionic fibers in his spinal cord as a result of being fired upon by a neuroelectric weapon. ("The Swarm" [VGR]). SEE: **Bashir, Dr. Julian.**

Preloc. Cardassian writer whose work includes ***Meditations on a Crimson Shadow***. ("The Wire" [DS9]).

Prema II. Planet in the Delta Quadrant that was the site of a Talaxian mining colony. In 2372, Talaxian forces from Prema II pledged their support of the *Voyager* in their mission to rescue Chakotay's son from the Kazon. ("Basics, Part I" [VGR]).

Pren, Dr. Hanor. (James Noah). Scientist at the Trill science ministry. Hanor Pren was a member of the science team that visited station Deep Space 9 in 2372 to attempt the creation of an **artificial wormhole**. ("Rejoined" [DS9]).

Preservers. Alien civilization that rescued primitive cultures in danger of extinction, transplanting them to other planets. Centuries ago, the Preservers translocated several tribes of Native Americans to a distant world where they could thrive and maintain their unique culture. Also known as the Wise Ones. ("The Paradise Syndrome" [TOS]). SEE: **Miramanee's planet**.

President, Federation. SEE: **Federation president**.

Presidio. Ancient fort located in the **San Francisco** Bay area on **Earth**, it was a military installation well into the 20th century. Commander Data's head was discovered in caverns located under the Presidio's remains. ("Time's Arrow, Part II" [TNG]). **Starfleet Academy** is located in the Presidio. ("The First Duty" [TNG]).

Pressman, Erik. (Terry O'Quinn). Federation admiral attached to Starfleet Intelligence. In 2358, Pressman, a captain, commanded the Federation *Starship* ***Pegasus***, a prototype ship designed to test several types of new technologies. Pressman was also in charge of the covert testing of a new Federation designed **phasing cloak**, even though the development of this technology by the Federation was a violation of the **Treaty of Algeron**. Pressman persisted in testing the device, over the objections of most of the crew. During the final test of the device, Pressman's crew mutinied, and Pressman was forced to escape the ship, along with seven other crew members who remained loyal to him, including William T. Riker. The *Pegasus* was believed to have suffered a warp-core breach shortly after Pressman's departure, and was believed destroyed with all hands. A Judge Advocate General report expressed a strong suspicion that a **mutiny** had taken place, but no further action was taken due to lack of evidence. In 2370, Starfleet Intelligence obtained evidence that the Romulans were searching for the wreck of the *Pegasus*, so Pressman came aboard the *Enterprise*-D, determined to locate and salvage the cloaking device aboard the *Pegasus*. When the exact nature of Pressman's interest in the *Pegasus* was finally made clear, Pressman was placed under arrest and charged with violating the Treaty of Algeron. ("The *Pegasus*" [TNG]). SEE: **Riker, William T.**

pressor. Medical device used to close off hemorrhaging blood vessels using a force field. ("Life Support" [DS9]).

Preston, Detective. (Deborah Van Valkenburgh). Officer with the **San Francisco** Police Department in **Earth** in 2024. During the **Bell Riots**, she was assigned to negotiate with the **Sanctuary District** residents who had taken hostages. ("Past Tense, Part II" [DS9]).

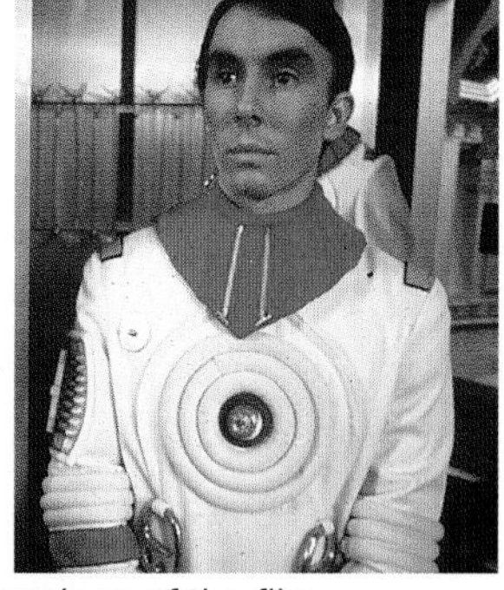

Preston, Peter. (Ike Eisenmann). Engineer's mate, midshipman first class aboard the *Starship Enterprise* during an academy training cruise in 2285. Preston was killed when the ship was diverted to active duty to investigate the hijacking of the **Regula I Space Laboratory** by **Khan Noonien Singh**. *(Star Trek II: The Wrath of Khan). The ABC-TV extended television version of* Star Trek II *included a line of dialog establishing that Preston was the nephew of Montgomery Scott. That line was not in the original theatrical or video versions of the film.*

"Price, The." *Next Generation* episode #56. Written by Hannah Louise Shearer. Directed by Robert Scheerer. Stardate: 43385.6. *First aired in 1989. A professional negotiator uses his Betazoid senses in his business dealings, as well as in his relationship with*

Deanna Troi. This is the first episode in which the current Greek letter designations for the galaxy's four quadrants were first used. Previous episodes had used a variety of inconsistent naming systems. GUEST CAST: Matt McCoy as **Ral**, **Devinoni**; Elizabeth Hoffman as **Bhavani**, **Premier**; Castulo Guerra as **Mendoza**, **Dr.**; Scott Thompson as **Goss**, **DaiMon**; Dan Shor as **Arridor**, **Dr.**; Kevin Peter Hall as **Leyor**; Colm Meaney as **O'Brien**, **Miles**. SEE: **Arridor, Dr.; Barzan wormhole; Barzan; Barzans; Bhavani, Premier; Caldonians; chocolate; Chrysalians; Delta Quadrant; Denkiri Arm; Ferengi shuttle; Gamma Quadrant; Goss, DaiMon; Hurkos III; Kol; Leyor; Mendoza, Dr.; pyrocyte; Ral, Devinoni; Shuttlecraft 9; Troi, Deanna.**

Prieto, Lieutenant Ben. (Raymond Forchion). *Enterprise*-D shuttlecraft pilot. Prieto transported Counselor Troi back to the *Enterprise*-D when his shuttle was forced down on planet **Vagra II**. ("Skin of Evil" [TNG]).

Primary Hull. The saucer section of many Federation **starships**. On most ships, the bridge is located on the top of the Primary Hull. Also known as a **Saucer Module**.

Prime Directive. Also known as Starfleet General Order #1. The Prime Directive prohibits **Starfleet** personnel and spacecraft from interfering in the normal development of any society, and mandates that any Starfleet vessel or crew member is expendable to prevent violation of this rule. Adopted relatively early in Starfleet history, the Prime Directive was a key part of Starfleet and Federation policy toward newly discovered civilizations, but it was also one of the most difficult to administer. ("A Piece of the Action" [TOS]). In most cases, the Prime Directive applied to any civilization that had not yet developed the use of warp drive for interstellar travel. ("Time and Again" [VGR]). SEE: **pre-warp civilization**. This rule was not in force in 2168, when the ***U.S.S. Horizon*** contacted planet **Sigma Iotia II**, resulting in disastrous cultural contamination. ("A Piece of the Action" [TOS]). Federation cultural observer **John Gill** violated the Prime Directive at planet **Ekos** when he attempted to provide that planet with a more efficient government. Gill's plan misfired badly, resulting by 2268 in a brutal regime closely resembling Earth's Nazi Germany. ("Patterns of Force" [TOS]). **Captain Ronald Tracey** of the ***U.S.S. Exeter*** violated the Prime Directive in 2268 at planet **Omega IV** when he provided phaser weapons to one of the warring factions there. ("The Omega Glory" [TOS]). While it remained one of Starfleet's highest laws, the Prime Directive was not without its detractors. Captain Picard questioned its validity when using the *Enterprise*-D to save planet **Drema IV** from geological destruction. ("Pen Pals" [TNG]). Dr. **Nikolai Rozhenko** refused to abide by it when he chose to save one village of **Boraalans** from certain death. ("Homeward" [TNG]). Lieutenant B'Elanna Torres of the *Starship Voyager* would have violated the Prime Directive in 2372 if she had given **Pralor Automated Personnel Units** the ability to construct more of their kind. ("Prototype" [VGR]). *Other episodes in which the Prime Directive was arguably broken include "Return of the Archons" (TOS), "A Taste of Armageddon" (TOS), "The Apple" (TOS), "A Private Little War" (TOS), "Justice" (TNG), "Pen Pals" (TNG), "Who Watches the Watchers?" (TNG), "Devil's Due" (TNG), "Let He Who Is Without Sin..." (DS9), and "Captive Pursuit" (DS9). In "Bread and Circuses" (TOS), Kirk noted that the Roman culture on planet Eight Ninety-Two-IV was entitled to full Prime Directive protection.*

"Prime Factors." *Voyager* episode #10. Teleplay By Michael Perricone and Greg Elliot. Story By David R. George III & Eric A. Stillwell. Directed By Les Landau. Stardate 48642.5. *First aired in 1995. The* Voyager *encounters the Sikarians—a civilization renowned for their incredible hospitality, who have the technology to travel more than 40,000 light-years in an instant.* GUEST CAST: Ronald Guttman as Gath; Yvonne Suhor as **Eudana**; Andrew Hill Newman as Jaret; Martha Hackett as **Seska**; Josh Clark as **Carey.** SEE: **Alastria; antimatter containment; Carey; Dedestris; Delaney, Jenny; Delaney sisters; erosene winds; Eudana; folded-space transport; holodeck and holosuite programs; Labin, Gathorel; Murphy, Ensign; Nivoch; Otel, Jaret; pecan pie; Seska; Sikaris; trajector.**

prime rib. Earth meal made from beef meat. Tom Paris decided to buy some prime rib with replicator rations from his **radiogenic sweepstakes** gambling scheme. ("Meld" [VGR]).

Primmin, Lieutenant George. (James Lashly). Starfleet security officer assigned to Deep Space 9 in 2369. Primmin's self-assured attitude annoyed **Odo**. ("The Passenger" [DS9]). Primmin had been a security officer since 2363. ("Move Along Home" [DS9]).

Prin, Silaran. (Randy Ogelsby) Cardassian national who worked as a servant, cleaning uniforms for Gul **Pirak**, during the **Cardassian** occupation of **Bajor.** Prin was disfigured in an attack on Pirak's residence by **Kira Nerys** and the **Shakaar resistance cell** during the occupation. Years later, on stardate 50416, after Prin had taken up residence on a planet near the Cardassian Demilitarized Zone, Prin began to exact revenge on surviving members of the Shakaar group. ("The Darkness and the Light" [DS9]). *The interior set for Silaran's house was dressed with consoles seen years earlier on space station* Regula I *in* Star Trek II: The Wrath of Khan.

Prinadora. Former wife of **Rom,** mother to **Nog**, she entered into a standard five-year contract to produce a child. When Rom fell in love with her, he blindly signed an extension to the contract without reading the fine print. As a result, her father was able to swindle Rom out of all his money. Eventually, she then left them both to marry a richer man. ("Doctor Bashir, I Presume?" [DS9]).

Princeton, U.S.S. Federation starship, *Niagara* class, Starfleet registry number NCC-58904. The *Princeton* was among the 39 ships lost to the Borg in the battle of Wolf 359. ("The Best of Both Worlds, Part II" [TNG]).

prion replication in ganglionic cell clusters. Medical research project conducted by **Dr. Julian Bashir**. ("Doctor Bashir, I Presume?" [DS9]).

prion. Subviral infectious agent. Prions were rod-shaped lifeforms, lacking nucleic-acid based genetic material. They were the cause of several serious neurological diseases. In 2373, **Dr. Julian Bashir** presented a paper to the medical community describing how prion replication was inhibited by quantum resonance effects. ("Nor the Battle to the Strong" [DS9]). Prions were sold by **Gaila** and **Hagath** as deadly biological weapons. ("Business As Usual" [DS9]).

prishic. Culinary spice native to the Delta Quadrant. ("Prototype" [VGR]).

"Private Little War, A." Original Series episode #45. Teleplay by Gene Roddenberry. Story by Jud Crucis. Directed by Marc Daniels. Stardate 4211.4. *First aired in 1968. The peaceful society on a primitive planet is shattered when the Klingons provide firearms to the inhabitants.* GUEST CAST: Nancy Kovack as **Nona**; Michael Kovack as **Tyree**; Ned Romero as Krell; Majel Barrett as **Chapel**, **Christine**; Booker Bradshaw as **M'Benga**, **Dr.**; Arthur Bearnard as **Apella**; Janos Prohaska as ***mugato***; Paul Baxley as Patrol leader; Gary Pillar as **Yutan**; Regina Parton as Nona's stunt double; Dave Perna as Spock's stunt double; Bob Orrison as McCoy's and Village stunt doubles; Roy Slickner, Bob Lyon, Villager stunt doubles; Paul Baxley as Kirk's and Apella's stunt doubles. SEE: **Apella; flintlock; hill people; *Kahn-ut-tu*; Kirk, James T.; M'Benga, Dr.; *mahko* root; *mugato*; Nona; Prime Directive; Spock; Tyree; Vulcans; Yutan.**

Prixus. Minerologist and metallurgist aboard the *Enterprise*-D. Prixus assisted in the geological survey of planets in the **Selcundi Drema** sector in 2365. ("Pen Pals" [TNG]).

probability mechanics. Area of study at Starfleet Academy. The android **Data** excelled in probability mechanics at Starfleet Academy. ("Encounter at Farpoint, Part I" [TNG]).

Probe, the. Alien space probe of unknown origin that wreaked ecological havoc on planet Earth in 2286 when it attempted to contact the intelligent species, **humpback whale**, on that planet. The species had unfortunately become extinct in the 21st century, so there were no whales to contact. The damage to Earth's biosphere occurred when the probe failed to make contact with any humpback whales and increased the power of its carrier wave to tremendous levels. Disaster was narrowly averted when James Kirk and his *Enterprise* officers traveled back in time to the 20th century to bring two whales back to the future. *(Star Trek IV: The Voyage Home).*

probe, Iconian. SEE: **Iconian computer weapon**.

Probert, Commodore. Starfleet officer. Probert ordered the *U.S.S. Columbia* to rendezvous with the *U.S.S. Revere* on stardate 7411.4. The message was relayed through the **Epsilon IX monitoring station**. *(Star Trek: The Motion Picture). Commodore Probert was a name mentioned in one of the messages heard in the background of the Epsilon IX sequence in* Star Trek I. *It was a tongue-in-cheek reference to Andrew Probert, one of the illustrators on that film and the man who designed the* Enterprise-*D for* Star Trek: The Next Generation.

Processing Center. In early 21st-century American society, an official check-in point for persons entering a **Sanctuary District**. The Processing Center for Sanctuary District A in **San Francisco** was the site at which several civil servants were held hostage during the **Bell Riots** of 2024. ("Past Tense, Parts I and II" [DS9]).

Proconsul. Term for the head of the **Romulan** Senate; one of the highest leaders of the Romulan government. ("Unification, Parts I and II" [TNG]). SEE: **Praetor**.

Proficient Service Medallion. Commendation awarded to members of the **Cardassian** military. **Gul Darhe'el** received the Proficient Service Medallion in recognition of his distinguished military career. ("Duet" [DS9]). SEE: **Gallitep; Kalla-Nohra; Marritza, Aamin**.

"Profit and Loss." *Deep Space Nine* episode #38. Written by Flip Kobler & Cindy Marcus. Directed by Robert Wiemer. No stardate given. *First aired in 1994. Three Cardassian political refugees arrive at Deep Space 9, one of whom is an old flame of Quark's.* GUEST CAST: Mary Crosby as **Lang, Natima**; Andrew Robinson as **Garak, Elim**; Michael Reilly Burke as **Hogue**; Heidi Swedberg as **Rekelen**; Edward Wiley as **Toran, Gul**. SEE: **Cardassian shuttle; Cardassian underground movement; cloaking device; Deep Space 9; disruptor; flitterbird; Garak; Hogue; *I, the Jury*; *kanar*; Lang, Natima; Mordian butterfly; Picnic on Rhymus Major; Political Ethics; Quark; Rekelen; Rhymus Major; Samarian Sunset; Spillane, Mickey; Toran, Gul; Yiri, General.**

Progenitors. The founders of an idyllic artists' society on the planet **Aldea**. Hundreds of centuries ago, the Progenitors set up a sophisticated computer called the **Custodian** (*pictured*) to provide for the needs of all citizens, along with a powerful cloaking device intended to conceal the planet from potential intrusion by space travelers. ("When the Bough Breaks" [TNG]).

Program delta 5 9. Holographic simulation of the **Operations Center** of station Deep Space 9. This program was part of the academy preparatory program entrance exams. ("Facets" [DS9]).

"Progress." *Deep Space Nine* episode #15. Written by Peter Allan Fields. Directed by Les Landau. Stardate 46844.3. *First aired in 1993. An old farmer on the Bajoran moon Jeraddo refuses to leave, even though his world is about to be made uninhabitable by toxic gases.* GUEST CAST: Brian Keith as **Mullibok**; Aron Eisenberg as **Nog**; Nicholas Worth as **Lissepian captain**; Michael Bofshever as **Toran**; Terrence Evans as **Baltrim**; Annie O'Donnell as **Keena**; Daniel Riordan as First guard. SEE: **Bajor; Baltrim; carnivorous rastipod; chlorobicrobes; Dax, Jadzia; Jeraddo; katterpod beans; Keena; *kellipates*; Lissepian captain; *lokar* beans; Morn; Mullibok; Nog; Noh-Jay Consortium; peritoneum; self-sealing stem bolts; Sirco Ch'Ano; Sisko, Jake; tessipates; thermologist; Toran; two-headed Malgorian; *yamok* sauce.**

progressive encryption lock. Multilayered set of security codes used by the Romulan information net. In 2368, Commander Data and Ambassador Spock, working together, were able to penetrate the encryption codes and access the network. ("Unification, Part II" [TNG]).

progressive memory purge. Computer protocol that restored Commander Data's memory and the *Enterprise*-D computer's recreational database, after the failure of an interface experiment in 2369. ("A Fistful of Datas" [TNG]). SEE: **Subroutine C-47; *Ancient West.***

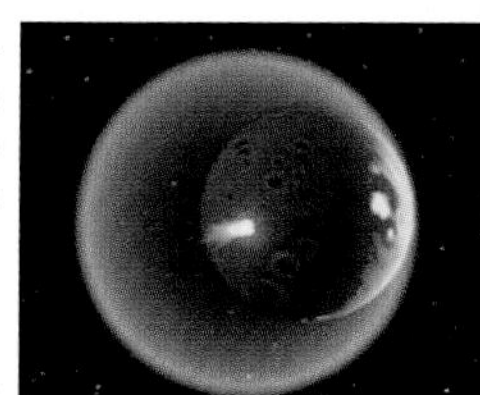

Project Genesis. Scientific research project whose goal was to develop a process whereby uninhabitable planets could be re-formed into worlds suitable for life. The process involved a massive explosion that reduced the planet to subatomic particles, which then reassembled according to a preprogrammed matrix. Project Genesis, under the direction of **Dr. Carol Marcus**, conducted a successful test of the process in a cavern inside the **Regula** asteroid. A second, more ambitious test was prematurely initiated when **Khan Noonien Singh** stole the **Genesis Device**, resulting in the formation of a habitable planet from the remains of the **Mutara Nebula**. (*Star Trek II: The Wrath of Khan*). Although initial tests of the Genesis Device showed remarkable promise, the process was later found to be unworkable due to the dangerously unstable nature of **protomatter** used in the Genesis matrix. *(Star Trek III: The Search for Spock).*

"Projections." *Voyager* episode #17. Written by Brannon Braga. Directed by Jonathan Frakes. Stardate 48892.1. *First aired in 1995. The Doctor becomes trapped on the holodeck, and everything he experiences leads him to believe that he is a real person and that the* Voyager *and its crew have been holograms all along.* GUEST CAST: Dwight Schultz as **Barclay, Reginald**; Majel Barrett as Computer voice. SEE: **ARA scan; Barclay, Reginald; Emergency Medical Hologram; HTDS; Jupiter Station; kinoplastic radiation; Nondoran tomato paste; *Predator*-class warship; Zimmerman, Lewis**.

Proka Migdal. (Terrence Evans). Bajoran national, who in 2362 adopted **Rugal**, a boy thought to be a **Cardassian** war orphan. Proka taught Rugal to hate everything Cardassian. In 2370 Proka lost custody of Rugal to the child's biological father, **Kotran Pa'Dar**. ("Cardassians" [DS9]). *Terrance Evans had previously portrayed the mute Bajoran, Baltrim, in "Progress" (DS9).*

Prokofiev, U.S.S. Federation starship, *Andromeda* class, Starfleet registry number NCC-68814. The *Prokofiev* was dispatched to the border of the Federation-Cardassian **Demilitarized Zone** in 2370, following the arrest of Starfleet officer Miles O'Brien. ("Tribunal" [DS9]). *Named for the 20th-century Russian composer of* Peter and the Wolf.

Promellian. Technologically sophisticated reptilian culture that fought to its extinction a millenium ago in a war against the

Menthar civilization. Promellian technology, although relatively crude by Federation standards, remains as an example of elegant simplicity in design. ("Booby Trap" [TNG]). SEE: ***Cleponji*; Galek Sar.**

Promellian/Menthar war. Legendary conflict that ended at least 1000 years prior to 2366, in a battle at **Orelious IX**. During that battle, both sides fought to their mutual extinction, and Orelious IX was destroyed. ("Booby Trap" [TNG]).

Promenade. Expansive area on station **Deep Space 9** containing numerous commercial and service facilities. ("Emissary" [DS9]). Among the many shops and offices located on the **Promenade** are **Quark's bar**, the **Replimat**, a **Bajoran temple**, **Garak**'s clothing shop, the **Infirmary**, **Odo**'s security office, a mineral assay office, and a candy kiosk. **Keiko O'Brien**'s classroom was also there. ("Emissary" [DS9]). *The massive Promenade set was built on Paramount's Stage 17, which in years past also housed the interiors of the Ponderosa ranch from the television series* Bonanza. *(The exteriors of the Ponderosa were built on Stage 16, on which most of the planet sets were built for* Star Trek: The Next Generation *and* Star Trek: Voyager.*)*

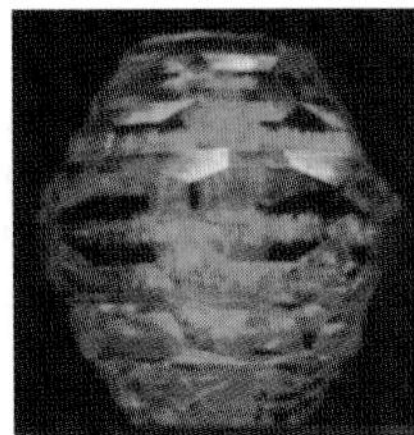

Promethean quartz. A valuable mineral that glows with an internal light. Archaeologist and entrepreneur **Vash** discovered a geode resembling Promethean quartz in the **Gamma Quadrant**, but the artifact had a much higher molecular density and index of refractivity. Vash's artifact was later found to contain a winged energy creature that nearly destroyed the station with a powerful **graviton field** before it was set free. ("Q-Less" [DS9]).

Prometheus*, *U.S.S. Federation starship, *Nebula* class, Starfleet registry number NCC-71201. The science ship used by terraformer **Gideon Seyetik** on his project to reignite the dead sun **Epsilon 119.** ("Second Sight" [DS9]). *Named for the mythological Greek Titan who stole fire from heaven for the benefit of mankind.*

"Prophet Motive." *Deep Space Nine* episode #62. Written by Ira Steven Behr & Robert Hewitt Wolfe. Directed by Rene Auberjonois. No stardate given. *First aired in 1995. Quark has an unexpected visit from Grand Nagus Zek, but even more unexpected are Zek's radical changes to the Rules of Acquisition. This was the first episode directed by actor Rene Auberjonois.* GUEST CAST: Max Grodénchik as **Rom**; Juliana Donald as **Emi**; Tiny Ron as **Maihar'du**; Wallace Shawn as **Zek**; Bennett Guillory as Medical big shot. SEE: **Aldeberan whiskey; Altair IV; Andoria; Bashir, Julian; Cardassia III; Carrington Award; Emi; darts; Ferengi Benevolent Association; Ferengi Rules of Acquisition; Ferengi Rules of Acquisition, Revised; Hupyrian beetle snuff; Hupyrian; Maihar'du; millipede juice; Orb of Wisdom; Orb; *oo-mox*; P'Trell, Chirurgeon Ghee; Prophets; Roget, Dr. Henri; Sacred Marketplace; Saurian brandy; self-sealing stem bolts; Senva, Healer; Temple of Commerce; Trixian bubble juice; Wade, Dr. April; Zek.**

Prophet's Landing. Bajoran colony closest to the Cardassian border. Governor Avesta ran the colony in 2371, and security was handled by Security Chief Bemar. ("Heart of Stone" [DS9]).

Prophets. In the **Bajoran** religion, the Prophets are spiritual entities who provide wisdom and guidance to the Bajoran people. Bajoran tradition holds that the Prophets were responsible for the nine **Orbs** that served as sources of wisdom for the people of **Bajor**. Many Bajorans believe that the alien beings first encountered in the **Bajoran wormhole** by Commander **Benjamin Sisko** in 2369 were in fact the Prophets. These life-forms found the concept of linear time to be totally alien, and Sisko attempted to help them understand the importance of linear existence to Bajorans and humans. Ironically, although Sisko did not believe in the Bajoran religion, his role in making contact with these life-forms made him their prophesied **Emissary**, a role that Sisko did not relish, although he respected their beliefs. ("Emissary" [DS9]). In 2371, the Prophets encountered Ferengi Grand Nagus **Zek**, finding his highly acquisitive nature to be deeply offensive. The Prophets devolved Zek's personality back to a time before Ferengi sought profit above everything. They returned Zek to his original state after Quark convinced them that the change to Zek would invite more visits from linear beings, a prospect that the Prophets found distasteful. ("Prophet Motive" [DS9]). SEE: **Ferengi Rules of Acquisition, Revised.**

protected memory. In a computer system, an area of core memory designed to be impervious to erasure. The file containing the consciousness of **Professor James Moriarty** was stored in protected memory in the *Enterprise*-D computer core. ("Ship in a Bottle" [TNG]).

protectors. Another name given to the filter masks provided to the Troglyte mining workers on planet **Ardana** to negate the deleterious effects of the **zenite** gas. Vanna prefered the term to "filter masks" because it more clearly described their use. ("The Cloud Minders" [TOS]).

proto-Vulcan. Anthropological term to describe the humanoid culture on planet **Mintaka III**, whose inhabitants did indeed resemble early Vulcans at a Bronze Age level of technology. ("Who Watches the Watchers?" [TNG]).

protodynoplaser. Medical instrument in use aboard the *Enterprise*-D. The device was used on **Zalkonian** patient **John Doe** to stabilize his immune system. ("Transfigurations" [TNG]).

protomatter. A dangerously unstable form of matter. Because of the extreme hazard associated with protomatter, many 23rd-century scientists denounced its use, but Dr. **David Marcus** secretly used it as part of the **Project Genesis** matrix, thus dooming the project to failure because the resulting planet created by the matrix was also dangerously unstable. *(Star Trek III: The Search for Spock).* In 2370, **Professor Gideon Seyetik** used protomatter in his effort to reignite star Epsilon 119. ("Second Sight" [DS9]). Protomatter was used in the implosive device employed by **Maquis** terrorists in 2370 to overload the fusion drive of the Cardassian ship ***Bok'Nor***. ("The Maquis, Part I" [DS9]). In 2373, a changeling infiltrator posing as **Dr. Julian Bashir** hijacked the *Runabout* ***Yukon*** and attempted to destroy the **Bajoran** sun with a **trilithium** explosive containing **tekasite** and protomatter. ("By Inferno's Light" [DS9]).

protostar. Star in its earliest stages of development, shortly following the start of nuclear fusion. A protostar can emit high levels of **magnetascopic interference**. ("Preemptive Strike" [TNG]). In 2373, Worf encountered a cluster of protostars while commanding the *Defiant* on a scouting mission in the Gamma Quadrant. ("Let He Who Is Without Sin..." [DS9]).

Prototype Automated Personnel Unit 0001. (Hugh Hodgin). Humanoid automaton patterned after the **Pralor Automated Personnel Units**. Unit 0001 was created by Voyager engineer B'Elanna Torres in 2372. This prototype was unlike other Pralor units in that it possessed a power module that could be easily replicated. In building this prototype, Torres, in essence, gave the Pralor units the ability to reproduce, which violated the Prime Directive. Once she had learned that the **Pralor** and **Cravic** peoples had been wiped out by their own robots, and that these robots only existed to continue the war started by their **Builders**, Torres destroyed prototype unit 0001. ("Prototype" [VGR]).

"Prototype." *Voyager* episode #29. Written by Nicholas Corea. Directed by Jonathan Frakes. No stardate given. *First aired in 1996. Torres reactivates a robot found drifting in space, only to learn it is a soldier in a war that has destroyed all the robot's* *builders.* GUEST CAST: Rick Worthy as **3947** and **Cravic 122**; Hugh Hodgin as **6263** and **Prototype 0001**. SEE: **anodyne relay; Bolians; Builders; chromodynamic power module; Cravic Automated Personnel Unit 122; Cravic; flux capacitance; Jibalian omelette; Landras blend; Nimian sea salt; Pralor Automated Personnel Unit 3947; Pralor Automated Personnel Unit 6263; Pralor Automated Personnel Unit; Pralor; Prime Directive; *prishic*; Prototype Automated Personnel Unit 0001; Spith basil; Traggle nectar; tripolymer plasma; Vulcans.**

protouniverse. A universe in its early stages of formation. One such universe was found in the Gamma Quadrant and accidentally brought aboard station Deep Space 9 in 2370. This protouniverse expanded, threatening station safety by displacing parts of this universe (and the station). Although prudence suggested destroying the protouniverse, sensor studies revealed the possibility that life, possibly even entire civilizations, was evolving within it. The protouniverse was subsequently returned to its original location in the Gamma Quadrant. ("Playing God" [DS9]).

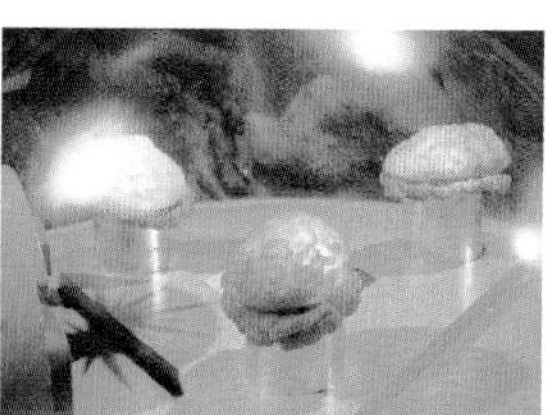

Providers. Three disembodied brains who lived beneath the surface of planet **Triskelion**. In the past, the Providers had humanoid bodies, but devotion to intellectual pursuits eliminated the need for a shell of flesh. For amusement, they captured beings from throughout the galaxy and trained them to fight among themselves, betting on the results. In 2268, the Providers agreed to free their captives in payment of a wager they had made with Captain James Kirk. ("The Gamesters of Triskelion" [TOS]). SEE: **drill thralls; quatloos**.

Proxcinian War. Armed conflict undertaken by the Proxcinians in 2373. ("Business As Usual" [DS9]).

Proxcinians. Civilization. In 2373, the Proxcinians were at war. **Quark** sold 7000 attack skimmers to a Proxcinian. ("Business As Usual" [DS9]).

Proxima Maintenance Yards. Starfleet starship maintenance facility commanded by Admiral **Drazman**. ("Past Tense, Part I" [DS9]).

Proxima, U.S.S. Federation starship, *Nebula* class, Starfleet registry number NCC-61952. The *Proxima* was lost in the Gamma Quadrant sometime prior to 2371. It was believed that the ship and crew fell victim to the **Dominion**. ("In Purgatory's Shadow" [DS9]). *Named for Proxima Centauri, a star 4.3 light years from Earth.*

proximity detector. A two-centimeter-square, jewel-like, magnetic device that was implanted into a humanoid body, making it easy to accurately track and identify that individual. These implants were used on planets Manu III and **Turkana IV**, sounding an alarm when the wearer entered forbidden territory. In their use on Turkana IV, proximity detectors would also sound an alarm to warn of the approach of enemy forces, providing positive identification of one's cadre affiliation, either **Coalition** or **Alliance**. The implants contained a micro-explosive that detonated on contact with air, thus preventing easy removal. Dr. Crusher was able to remove the proximity detector from Turkana IV native **Ishara Yar**. ("Legacy" [TNG]).

prune juice. A beverage made from the puréed dried fruit of an Earth plum tree. Guinan introduced Worf to this beverage in 2366. He pronounced it "a warrior's drink." ("Yesterday's *Enterprise*" [TNG]).

prylar. Title of a Bajoran monk. ("Collaborator" [DS9]).

Prylar Rhit. Bajoran monk. Prylar Rhit was the keeper of the **Bajoran** shrine on station Deep Space 9. He played **dabo** at Quark's bar, where he ran up a sizable gambling debt, causing a scandal in the **Vedek Assembly** ("Shadowplay" [DS9]).

Prytt Security Ministry. Governmental agency of the **Prytt** nation-state on planet **Kesprytt III**. The Security Ministry was responsible for the abduction of Captain Jean-Luc Picard and Dr. Beverly Crusher during a diplomatic mission to the planet in 2370. ("Attached" [TNG]).

Prytt. One of two nation-states that control planet **Kesprytt III.** The Prytt comprised one-quarter of the population of the planet. During a Federation investigation of the planet in 2370, *Starship Enterprise*-D personnel reported the Prytt to be reclusive almost to the point of **xenophobia**. The Prytt did not even possess a communication network capable of contacting anyone outside their territory. The Prytt were responsible for the abduction of Captain Jean-Luc Picard and Dr. Beverly Crusher. Also known as the Prytt Alliance. ("Attached" [TNG]). SEE: **Kes**.

Psi 2000 virus. A water-based disease organism originally found on planet Psi 2000 in 2266. This virus infected members of the Federation science team stationed on that planet, causing suppression of their inhibitions, and ultimately their deaths. Transmitted through human perspiration, the virus later infected members of the *Enterprise* crew, resulting in the near-destruction of the starship when infected crew member **Kevin Riley** disabled the ship's engines while it was in orbit around the disintegrating planet. ("The Naked Time" [TOS]). A variant of this virus infected members of the ***U.S.S. Tsiolkovsky*** crew as well as the crew of the *Enterprise*-D in 2364. ("The Naked Now" [TNG]).

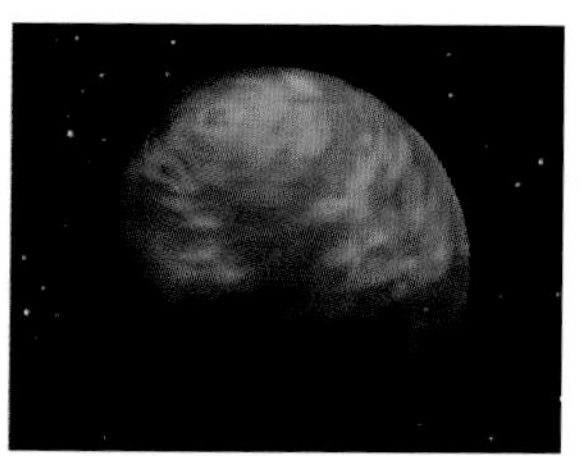

Psi 2000. A frozen planet that disintegrated in 2266. Just prior to the planet's end, a Federation science team had been stationed there, but all members of that team were found dead under mysterious circumstances. Their deaths were later found to have been due to a virus that stripped away their inhibitions and caused team members to engage in hazardous behavior. The *U.S.S. Enterprise* conducted scientific observations of the planet's disintegration and was nearly destroyed. ("The Naked Time" [TOS]). SEE: ***Tsiolkovsky, U.S.S.***

psi-wave device. Device used by the **Prytt** Security Ministry to gain direct access to the minds of people they wished to interrogate. The devices were implanted directly into the victim's cerebral cortex, and required a passage of time to be tuned to the individual's psi-wave pattern. In 2370, while in the custody of the Prytt Security Ministry, Captain Jean-Luc Picard and Dr. Beverly Crusher were implanted with these devices. A side effect of the device, Picard and Crusher found, was that they could read each other's thoughts. ("Attached" [TNG]).

psilosynine. Neurotransmitter chemical used for telepathy by the brains of telepathic species, such as **Betazoids**. While working with the Cairn diplomatic delegation in 2370, the telepathic demands on Ambassador **Lwaxana Troi** were so great that her psilosynine level was depleted. ("Dark Page" [TNG]) *U.S.S.*

Enterprise-D Chief Medical Officer Beverly Crusher manufactured a psilosynine inhibitor for Deanna Troi in 2370 during her investigation into Daniel Kwan's death. The inhibitor lessened the number of telepathic images Deanna received. ("Eye of the Beholder" [TNG]). *The drug was given to Troi during her prolonged hallucination in that episode. It may or may not "really" exist.*

psionic resonator. Ancient **Vulcan** weapon that focused and amplified telepathic energy, enabling its user to kill with a thought. The resonator, known in Vulcan mythology as the **Stone of Gol**, was believed to be one of the most devastating weapons ever conceived. ("Gambit, Part II" [TNG]).

Psych Test. A part of the entrance examination for aspiring Starfleet Academy cadets, designed to determine a candidate's reaction to his or her greatest fears. The Psych Test is administered on an individual basis, and generally involves a simulation designed to make the candidate face those fears. Wesley Crusher's Psych Test involved forcing him to make a decision to let one man die, so that another could live, a situation that paralleled that in which his father, Jack Crusher, died as the result of a decision by Captain Jean-Luc Picard. ("Coming of Age" [TNG]).

psychoactive drug. Chemical substance that has the effect of producing delusional or hallucinogenic results when administered to humanoids. The venom of a Nechani ***nesset*** was used as a psychoactive drug by monks of the **Nechisti Order**. ("Sacred Ground" [VGR]).

psychographic profile. Detailed files maintained by the **Vorta** on potential adversaries. Such profiles could be surprisingly detailed and included much personal information. ("To the Death" [DS9]).

psychokinesis. The ability to transport and control objects using the power of the mind. The **Platonians** demonstrated psychokinetic powers. ("Plato's Stepchildren" [TOS]). SEE: **kironide**.

psychological profile. Complete psychological history required of all Starfleet personnel. *Starship Enterprise* crew member **Mira Romaine**'s psychological profile was examined in 2269 when her mind was occupied by the noncorporeal survivors of planet **Zetar**. ("The Lights of Zetar" [TOS]).

psychoprojective telepathy. The ability to create illusions from the unconscious mind. **Halanans** have this ability, which enables them to create realistic and tangible, albeit illusory, alter egos. While under stress, **Nidell Seyetik** unknowingly created a projection named **Fenna**. ("Second Sight" [DS9]).

psychotectic therapy. A psychological treatment used on the **J'naii** planet to eliminate gender-specific sexuality, which the J'naii considered aberrant behavior. In 2368, the therapy was highly effective in extinguishing **Soren**'s female-specific feelings. ("The Outcast" [TNG]).

psychotricorder. Instrument used to record past memories. Kirk ordered a 24-hour regressive memory test on Montgomery Scott using a psychotricorder, after the chief engineer was accused of murder on planet **Argelius II** in 2267, although the test was interrupted when psych technician Karen Tracy was murdered by the malevolent entity occupying Scott's body. ("Wolf in the Fold" [TOS]). *The psychotricorder was, of course, a re-use of the standard original series tricorder prop.*

Ptera. (Cecile Callan). Native of the **Vhnori** homeworld who died in 2371. In accordance with her people's customs, she died in a **cenotaph**, just prior to being sent to the **Next Emanation** through a **spectral rupture**. During this process, Ptera was accidentally exchanged with Ensign Harry Kim, a crew member from the *Starship Voyager*. Ptera was recovered by *Voyager* personnel and revived. She interpreted her revival as her entry in the Next Emanation, and was profoundly disappointed to find herself aboard a starship. Ptera died when the *Voyager* crew tried to send her back through a subspace vacuole. ("Emanations" [VGR]).

public conservator. Officer of the **Cardassian** court. It was the conservator's function to help the **offender** concede to the wisdom of the Cardassian court and confess his guilt. The conservator also helped the offender accept his inevitable execution. ("Tribunal" [DS9]).

Puccini, Giacomo. (1858-1924). Operatic composer from Italy on Earth, who wrote the opera *La Bohème*. In 2373, the holographic doctor aboard the *Voyager* performed the operatic duet "*O soave fanciulla*" from Puccini's *La Bohème*. ("The Swarm" [VGR]).

Pueblo Revolt. Revolutionary battle on **Earth** in 1680, in which several Native American tribes rose up to overthrow their Spanish overlords and drove them out of what became New Mexico. In 1692, the Spanish returned to reconquer the area. They were brutal and savage, killing hundreds and maiming thousands more. One of the soldiers involved was **Javier Maribona-Picard**, ancestor of *Enterprise*-D Captain Jean-Luc Picard. ("Journey's End" [TNG]). SEE: **Inheritors.**

Pulaski, Dr. Katherine. (Diana Muldaur). Chief medical officer aboard the *U.S.S. Enterprise*-D during the year 2365. ("The Child" [TNG]). While aboard the *Enterprise*-D, Pulaski nearly died of a disease closely resembling old age, after she was exposed to genetically engineered human children at the **Darwin Genetic Research Station** on planet **Gagarin IV**. Pulaski recovered from the disease, thanks to a transporter-based technique, despite the fact that she harbored a phobia about transporter use. ("Unnatural Selection" [TNG]). Pulaski cared for **Kyle Riker** after he was nearly killed in a **Tholian** attack in 2353. The two fell in love, and Pulaski would later recall that she would have married him "in a cold minute" given the opportunity, but that Riker had "other priorities." Following her involvement with Riker, Pulaski married three times. As of 2365, she noted that she remained good friends with all three men. ("The Icarus Factor" [TNG]). Counselor Troi commented once that Pulaski's greatest medical skill was her empathy with her patients, evidenced by the use of "PCS"—Pulaski's Chicken Soup–in treating the flu virus. ("The Icarus Factor" [TNG]). *Dr. Pulaski was part of the regular* Star Trek: The Next Generation *cast during the second season. Her first episode was "The Child" (TNG), and her last was "Shades of Gray" (TNG). She replaced Dr. Beverly Crusher, who in turn replaced Pulaski when Diana Muldaur left the series at the end of the second season. Muldaur had previously played Dr. Ann Mulhall in "Return to Tomorrow" (TOS) and Dr. Miranda Jones in "Is There in Truth No Beauty?" (TOS).*

Pullock V raid. First off-world attack conducted by the **Ornathia resistance cell** against the **Cardassians** during the Cardassian occupation of **Bajor**. ("Shakaar" [DS9]).

pulmonary scanner. Medical device used in running a respiratory series. ("Phage" [VGR]).

pulmonary support unit. Emergency cardiopulmonary support unit in use aboard Federation starships. ("Tapestry" [TNG]).

pulmozine. Pharmaceutical used to stimulate breathing in a patient having respiratory difficulties. ("Favorite Son" [VGR]; "Basics, Part I" [VGR]).

pulsatel lockseal. High security locking mechanism. Some shopkeepers on station Deep Space 9 used pulsatel lockseals to secure their stores. Quark was able to bypass such a lock in 25 seconds. His brother, Rom, could bypass one in only ten. ("Necessary Evil" [DS9]).

pulse compression wave. Energy burst that could be channeled through a phaser bank, thereby increasing the destructive power of a phaser blast. Chief Operations Officer Miles O'Brien proposed this method to defend station **Deep Space 9** against the **Cardassians** shortly after the discovery of the **Bajoran wormhole** in 2369. ("Emissary" [DS9]).

pulse gun. Type of directed-energy hand weapon used by Akritirian patrollers. ("The Chute" [VGR]).

pulse wave torpedo. Explosive device. A Vulcan spaceship used a pulse wave torpedo in a futile attempt to repair a **subspace rupture** in 2169. A pulse wave torpedo was also used when a subspace rupture was believed to have formed near Deep Space 9 in 2369. ("If Wishes Were Horses" [DS9]).

punishment zones. In **Edo** society on planet **Rubicun III,** a randomly selected area in which mediators (law officials) enforce local laws. Violation of any law in a punishment zone would exact a death penalty. Under this system, no one except the mediators would know which area was currently designated as a punishment zone. In this way, a relatively small number of mediators could insure compliance with the law of a large number of Edo citizens. ("Justice" [TNG]).

Pup. Chief O'Brien's nickname for an alien software life-form hidden in data downloaded from a probe that came from somewhere in the **Gamma Quadrant** in 2369. Feeding off the energy from **Deep Space 9**'s computers, this nonsentient life-form integrated itself into the system, causing stationwide malfunctions. To Chief Miles O'Brien, the computer seemed to be craving attention, much like a puppy who didn't like to be left alone. He created a subprogram labeled "Pup" and filled it with all main computer backup functions, then downloaded the probe data into the file. The life-form had its own place in the computer system, where it could interface with the backup functions and not cause further malfunctions. ("The Forsaken" [DS9]). *We did not learn the name of the culture from the Gamma Quadrant that sent the probe that carried Pup to Deep Space 9. The probe model itself was a modification of the **Cytherian** probe originally built for "The Nth Degree" (TNG).*

puree of beetle. Ferengi food. Puree of beetle is a common Ferengi breakfast dish. ("The Assignment" [DS9]).

purification squad. Team of expert assassins sent out by **the Palamarian Freedom Brigade** to execute **Hagath** and **Gaila** in 2373. ("Business As Usual" [DS9]).

purple omelettes. A dish created by young Clara Sutter, made from grape juice and eggs. ("Imaginary Friend" [TNG]). *Mike still prefers green eggs and ham.*

putillo. Edible green vegetable from planet Napinne in the Delta Quadrant. ("Learning Curve" [VGR]).

PXK reactor. Antiquated power-generation device that provided life support to the underground mining colony at planet **Janus VI**. Although the PXK was considered obsolete, it was used on Janus VI because of the abundance of fissile minerals there. That station's reactor suffered a serious malfunction when an indigenous life-form known as a **Horta** damaged it in 2267. The Horta's actions were later found to be her effort to protect her children from the actions of the miners. ("The Devil in the Dark" [TOS]).

pygmy marmoset. Primate member of the genus *Cebuella*; a small, long-tailed, arboreal monkey. During the outbreak of **Barclay's Protomorphosis Syndrome** among the crew of the *Enterprise*-D, Data believed that Captain Jean-Luc Picard might devolve into a pygmy marmoset. ("Genesis" [TNG]).

Pygorians. Interstellar traders. In 2370, Quark put **Sakonna** in touch with the Pygorians, who sold her contraband weapons for the **Maquis**. ("The Maquis, Part II" [DS9]). *We never saw the Pygorians.*

pyllora. Vulcan concept of a counselor or guide. Vulcan psychocognitive research suggested that a *t'lokan* schism could be treated with a mind-meld between the patient and a family member, in an attempt to bring the repressed memory into the conscious mind. The family member acted as a *pyllora* by helping the patient to reconstruct the memory in its entirety from within the meld. Kathryn Janeway served as *pyllora* to Tuvok in 2373 when Tuvok was afflicted by the **memory virus**. ("Flashback" [VGR]).

Pyrellian ginger tea. Bajoran beverage. Pyrellian ginger tea was scarce during the Cardassian occupation. Quark managed to obtain a supply, which he made available on the black market. ("Necessary Evil" [DS9]).

Pyris VII. Planet devoid of native life. Extragalactic life-forms **Korob** and **Sylvia** once resided at Pyris VII, where they captured and controlled several of the *Enterprise* crew in 2267. ("Catspaw" [TOS]).

Pyrithian Gorge, Battle of. Conflict fought during the war between the **Haakonians** and the **Talaxians**. ("Jetrel" [VGR]).

pyroclastic debris. Type of mineral aggregation found in the crusts of some rocky terrestrial planets. There was pyroclastic debris on Torga IV. ("The Ship" [DS9]).

pyrocyte. A naturally occurring component of **Ferengi** blood. A distillation of these cells was used to poison a Federation negotiator, **Dr. Mendoza**, during negotiations for the Barzan wormhole in 2366. The pyrocytes, though not fatal, provoked a severe allergic reaction, effectively removing Mendoza from the talks. ("The Price" [TNG]). Pyrocytes are also a component of **Kazon** blood. ("State of Flux" [VGR]).

Pythro V. Planet. Homeworld to an elderly couple from whom **Martus Mazur** bilked money. ("Rivals" [DS9]).

"Q and the Grey, The." *Voyager* episode #53. Teleplay by Kenneth Biller. Story by Shawn Piller. Directed by Cliff Bole. Stardate 50348.1. *First aired in 1996. In an attempt to end a war in the Continuum, Q arrives on the* Voyager *to ask Janeway to have his child.* GUEST CAST: Suzie Plakson as **Q female**; Harve Presnell as **Q colonel** ; John de Lancie as **Q**. SEE: **antiproton; beta-tachyon; chocolate truffle; Cyrillian microbe; Drabian love sonnet; Q child; Q colonel; Q Continuum; Q female; Q freedom faction; Q; Quinn; Romulan empress; supernova.**

Q child. (Donahue twins.) Member of the **Q Continuum** who was born in 2373, the child of **Q** and a **Q female**. The child was the offspring of the first-ever mating of two Q. ("The Q and the Grey" [VGR]).

Q colonel. (Harve Presnell). Member of the **Q Continuum** who took the form of a Confederate colonel from Earth's Civil War period. He was a leader in the forces of the status quo, and his faction opposed the **Q freedom faction** during the Continuum's civil war in 2373. ("The Q and the Grey" [VGR]).

Q Continuum. Extradimensional domain in which **Q** and others of his kind exist. ("Encounter at Farpoint, Parts I and II" [TNG]). Although immensely powerful and intelligent, the Q require the stimulus of novelty to maintain their vitality. About ten thousand years ago, the Continuum entered a **New Era** of enlightenment and culture. Unfortunately, complacency set in thereafter, and the continuum became stagnant. Q rebelled against the order represented by the New Era and was generally ostracized by the Continuum. One member of the Continuum, an individual later known as **Quinn**, found Q's irrepressible nature to be an inspiration. Quinn regarded the immortality of the Continuum as an intolerable hardship, and so sought to end his life. The Continuum refused to allow Quinn's request, and ordered him imprisoned in a rogue comet. ("Death Wish" [VGR]). Q himself was briefly banished from the Continuum in 2366, until another Q entered our existence, offering to restore his powers. ("Déjà Q" [TNG]). The Continuum commanded Q to instruct and evaluate **Amanda Rogers** to see if she could ignore her powers and live among humans. If she could not or if she refused to accompany Q back to the Continuum, she was to be destroyed. The Continuum felt a moral obligation not to allow members of their kind to live with inferior beings and still use their awesome powers. ("True-Q" [TNG]). The death of Quinn spawned a freedom faction within the Continuum, culminating in a great civil war in 2373 between the freedom faction and forces of the status quo. *Voyager* Captain Kathryn Janeway experienced the warring Continuum in images of the 19th-century American civil war. One side effect of this conflict was the detonation of an unusual number of supernovae throughout the galaxy during that year. The war was ended when Q, representing the freedom faction, mated with a female Q. SEE: **Q female**. Their offspring offered a new hope of peace for the continuum. ("The Q and the Grey" [VGR]).

Q female. (Suzie Plakson). Member of the **Q Continuum**. This individual had a relationship with **Q** for some four billion years, culminating in 2373 with their conceiving a child together, the first child ever born in the Continuum through sexual means. Both parents, who had known each other for some four billion years, hoped their child would bring peace to the troubled Continuum. ("The Q and the Grey" [VGR]). *Q's mate was played by Suzie Plakson, who previously portrayed Dr. Selar in "The Schizoid Man" (TNG) and K'Ehleyr in "The Emissary" (TNG) and "Reunion" (TNG).*

Q freedom faction. Faction within the **Q Continuum** that followed the teachings of **Quinn**, who advocated freedom and individual thought. The freedom faction, of which **Q** was a member, clashed with the forces of the status quo, culminating in a great civil war in the Continuum in 2373. ("The Q and the Grey" [VGR]).

"Q Who?" *Next Generation* episode #42. Written by Maurice Hurley. Directed by Rob Bowman. Stardate 42761.3. *First aired in 1989. Q sends the* Enterprise-D *across the galaxy, where it encounters the Borg for the first time. The Borg had been previously hinted at in "The Neutral Zone" (TNG). This episode is the first of two appearances of Ensign Sonya Gomez.* GUEST CAST: John de Lancie as **Q**; Lycia Naff as **Gomez, Ensign Sonya**; Colm Meaney as **O'Brien, Miles**; Whoopi Goldberg as **Guinan**. SEE: **Borg ship; Borg; El-Aurians; Gomez, Ensign Sonya; Guinan; Neutral Zone, Romulan; Q; Starbase 83; Starbase 173; Starbase 185; System J-25.**

q'lava. A watery fruit enjoyed by the **Vorta**. *Q'lavas* were a personal favorite of Kilana. ("The Ship" [DS9]).

Q'Maire. A **Talarian** warship, commanded by **Endar**. In 2367, the *Q'Maire* intercepted the *U.S.S. Enterprise*-D in **Sector 21947**, near a disabled Talarian observation craft. The *Q'Maire*, along with two sister warships, surrounded the *Enterprise*-D in the hopes of forcing the release of Endar's adoptive son, **Jono**. The *Q'Maire* was equipped with limited weaponry, including neutral particle weapons, X-ray lasers, and Merculite rockets, and was thus not a serious tactical threat. ("Suddenly Human" [TNG]). *The* Q'Maire *miniature was designed by Rick Sternbach and built by Tony Meininger.*

q'parol. Dinner casserole. *Q'parol* was a difficult and time-consuming food to make. In 2373, **Keiko O'Brien** made *q'parol* for her husband's surprise birthday party. ("The Assignment" [DS9]).

Q, Planet. Federation world. Home of scientist **Thomas Leighton** at the time of his death in 2266. ("The Conscience of the King" [TOS]).

"Q-Less." *Deep Space Nine* episode #7. Teleplay by Robert Hewitt Wolfe. Story by Hannah Louise Shearer. Directed by Paul Lynch. Stardate 46531.2. *First aired in 1993. Archaeologist Vash arrives from the Gamma Quadrant with a mysterious cargo, accompanied by Q.* GUEST CAST: Jennifer Hetrick as **Vash**; John de Lancie as **Q**; Van Epperson as Bajoran clerk; Tom McCleister as Kolos; Laura Cameron as Bajoran woman. SEE: **assay office; Betazed; Brax; Daystrom Institute; Delta Quadrant; duranium; EPI capacitor; Epsilon Hydra VII; Erabus Prime; Erriakang VII; Gamma Quadrant; Gamzian; *Ganges, U.S.S.*; ganglion; graviton field; graviton; Hoek IV; Kolos; Lantar Nebula; MK-12 scanner; Mulzirak; Mundahla; Myrmidon; *oomox*; Pauley, Ensign; Promethean quartz; Q; Rul the Obscure; Sampalo; Stol; Tartaras V; Teleris; tritium; Vadris III; Vash; Verath; Watergate; Woo, Dr.**

Q. (John DeLancie). An immensely powerful extradimensional entity. While possessing near-godlike powers, Q also exhibits a childlike petulance and sense of playfulness. ("Encounter at Farpoint, Parts I and II" [TNG]). Q was a free spirit in the Q Continuum who rebelled against the stagnation that had grown there over the past ten millennia. Q's irrepressive nature made him something of an outcast in the Continuum, but his freedom of thought inspired another member of the Continuum who would one day be known as **Quinn**. ("Death Wish" [VGR]). The *Enterprise*-D made first contact with Q in 2364, when Q detained

the ship, enacting a courtroom drama in which Q accused the ship's crew of being "grievously savage." ("Encounter at Farpoint, Parts I and II" [TNG]).

On his second visit to the *Enterprise*-D, Q offered **William Riker** a gift of Q-like supernatural powers, although it was not clear if this was a further attempt to study the human species or merely another exercise in provoking humans to respond for his amusement. ("Hide and Q" [TNG]).

Q later transported the *Enterprise*-D some seven thousand light years beyond Federation space to **System J-25**, where first contact was made with the powerful and dangerous **Borg**. ("Q Who?" [TNG]).

Q was banished from the **Q Continuum** and stripped of his powers in 2366 for having spread chaos through the universe. Q sought refuge in human form aboard the *Enterprise*-D, claiming that Jean-Luc Picard was the nearest thing he had to a friend. Unfortunately, Q had made many enemies in this universe, and one of these, the **Calamarain**, attacked the *Enterprise*-D, attempting to exact revenge on Q. Quick action by Lieutenant Commander **Data** saved Q from the attack. Truly surprised by Data's selfless action to save him, Q stole a shuttlecraft in an attempt to protect the *Enterprise*-D crew from further hostile action. This altruistic act was enough to persuade the Continuum to return his powers. ("Déjà Q" [TNG]).

Q interrupted a symposium of the **Federation Archaeology Council** held aboard the *Enterprise*-D in 2367. He cast Picard, **Vash**, and members of the *Enterprise*-D crew into an elaborate fantasy based on the old Earth legends of **Robin Hood**. Q later vanished, taking Vash with him as his new partner in crime. ("QPid" [TNG]). He returned to the *Enterprise*-D in 2369 to instruct and evaluate Amanda Rogers, whose biological parents were members of the **Q Continuum** who took human form. ("True-Q" [TNG]).

After a period of time exploring the Gamma Quadrant, Vash left Q, and returned to Alpha Quadrant aboard the Starfleet runabout ***U.S.S. Ganges*** through the **Bajoran wormhole**. Q followed Vash to station **Deep Space 9** in an attempt to convince her to return, but she once again rebuffed him. He amused himself with the crew of the station, provoking Benjamin Sisko into a 19th-century-style fistfight, and was shocked when Sisko knocked him to the floor. ("Q-Less" [DS9]).

Later that year, Q once again visited Captain Picard, following a disastrous away mission on which Picard was ambushed by **Lenarians**. In what Q claimed was the afterlife, Q offered Picard the opportunity to see what his life would have been like had he not made some of the rash choices of his youth. In particular, Picard was given the opportunity to relive the three-day period leading up to his injury at the **Bonestell Recreation Facility** in 2327. Using the knowledge of what was to come, Picard was able to avoid the fight that cost him his heart. However, Picard discovered that it was partly the brashness of his youth that had made him the man that he was. ("Tapestry" [TNG]). SEE: **Batanides, Marta; Nausicaans**.

In 2370, the **Q Continuum** once again decided to test humanity. They devised a paradox, whereby Picard would be responsible for the destruction of mankind by creating an **anti-time** phenomenon. Q himself added the wrinkle of having Picard shift among three time periods, with awareness of what was happening in each. After Picard succeeded in solving the paradox, Q informed him that it had been a test. The Q Continuum had wanted to learn if Picard had the ability to expand his mind and explore the unknown possibilities of existence. ("All Good Things..." [TNG]).

Q encountered the *Starship Voyager* in 2372, when he was tasked with returning a member of the Q Continuum later known as **Quinn** back into custody. Ironically, when Quinn later affirmed his desire to assert his individuality by committing suicide, Q helped him, much to the dismay of the Continuum. ("Death Wish" [VGR]). Q, inspired by Quinn's death, became a member of the **Q freedom faction**, advocating freedom of individual thought in the tradition-bound Q Continuum. In 2373, when friction with the freedom faction escalated into a great civil war, Q conceived a child with a female Q, in hopes that their child would bring peace to the Continuum. Q chose his female counterpart in the Continuum as the mother for his child only after considering a Klingon ***targ***, the **Romulan empress**, and Voyager Captain **Kathryn Janeway**. SEE: **Q female**. ("The Q and the Grey" [VGR]).

Q was named by Gene Roddenberry for English Star Trek *fan Janet Quarton. Q's first appearance was in "Encounter at Farpoint, Part I" (TNG), the first episode of* Star Trek: The Next Generation, *and he also appeared in "All Good Things" (TNG), the final television episode of that series.. In that epiosde, Q became the first character in* Star Trek *ever to use the word "trek" in dialog, although Zefram Cochrane later used the word in* Star Trek: First Contact. *Many fans have speculated that Q may be related to* ***Trelane****.*

Q2. (Corbin Bernsen). A member of the **Q Continuum**, Q2 was responsible for the removal of Q's powers in 2366 when Q was found guilty of spreading chaos in the universe. He continued to observe Q following his banishment, and later restored Q's powers after Q committed an act of self-sacrifice. ("Déjà Q" [TNG]). *Q2 only identified himself as another member of the Q Continuum. The name is from the script for the convenience of* Star Trek*'s production personnel, but was never used in the episode. In fact, both Qs in the episode referred to themselves simply as Q.* SEE: **Quinn.**

qa'vak. Traditional **Klingon** game involving a half-meter hoop and a spear. The hoop is rolled between various stakes planted into the ground, and the object is to throw the spear through the center of the hoop. Upon successfully scoring in this manner, it is traditional to shout "*ka'la*!" The game is intended to hone skill necessary for the traditional Klingon hunt. ("Birthright, Part II [TNG]).

Qab jIH nagil. Klingon ritual challenge used during the ***Sonchi*** ceremony during the **Rite of Succession**. It translates, "Face me if you dare." ("Reunion" [TNG]).

Qam-Chee. Ancient village on the **Klingon** homeworld. Fifteen hundred years ago, Qam-Chee was the site of a great battle that provided the backdrop for the courtship of **Kahless the Unforgettable** and the Lady **Lukara** that is considered the greatest romance in Klingon history. ("Looking for *par'Mach* in All the Wrong Places" [DS9]).

Qapla'. Klingon word meaning "success." Often used as a farewell. *(Star Trek III: The Search for Spock,* "Sins of the Father" [TNG], et al.).

QE-2. Also known as the *Queen Elizabeth II*; luxury seafaring passenger ship that sailed Earth's Atlantic Ocean during the late 20th and early 21st centuries. **Ralph Offenhouse**, dissatisfied with services aboard the *Starship Enterprise*-D, suggested that Captain Picard could use a few lessons from the *QE-2*. ("The Neutral Zone" [TNG]).

QiVon. Klingon word for knee. ("Blood Oath" [DS9]).

Qo'noS. (Pronounced "kronos"). The capital planet of the **Klingon Empire**, almost invariably referred to as the homeworld. *(Star Trek VI: The Undiscovered Country)*. SEE: **Klingon Homeworld**.

Qol. (Michael Snyder). Assistant to **Ferengi** trade emissary **Par Lenor**. ("The Perfect Mate" [TNG]). *Michael Snyder also played Morta in "Rascals" (TNG) and Dax in* Star Trek VI.

Q'orat. Member of the **Klingon High Council** in 2368. ("Redemption, Part II" [TNG]).

"QPid." *Next Generation* episode #94. Teleplay by Ira Steven Behr. Story by Randee Russell and Ira Steven Behr. Directed by Cliff Bole. Stardate 44741.9. *First aired in 1991. Q transports our heroes into Sherwood Forest with Jean-Luc Picard as Robin Hood.* GUEST CAST: Jennifer Hetrick as **Vash** and **Maid Marian**; Clive Revill as **Sir Guy of Gisbourne**; John de Lancie as **Q** and **Lord High Sheriff of Nottingham**; Joe Staton as Servant. SEE: **Alan-a-Dale; Federation Archaeology Council; Friar Tuck; *Horga'hn*; Klabnian eel; Klarc-Tarn-Droth; Little John; Lord High Sheriff of Nottingham; Maid Marian; Picard, Jean-Luc; Q; Robin Hood; Sarthong V; Sherwood Forest; Sir Guy of Gisbourne; Switzer; Tagus III; Vash; Vulcans.**

Qu'Vat, I.K.S. Klingon ***Vor'cha*-class** attack cruiser. The *Qu'Vat* rendezvoused with the *Enterprise*-D in 2369, carrying **Governor Torak** on an investigation into the death of a Starfleet officer at **Relay Station 47**. ("Aquiel" [TNG]).

quad. SEE: **kiloquad**.

Quadra Sigma III. Planet. Location of a Federation mining colony that suffered a serious explosion in 2364, resulting in significant casualties amongst the colonists. *Starship Enterprise*-D rendered aid shortly after the accident in 2364. ("Hide and Q" [TNG]).

Quadrant 904. An area of space completely devoid of stars where the artificially created planet **Gothos** was discovered by the *Enterprise* in 2267. ("The Squire of Gothos" [TOS]). *The episode was produced before* Star Trek*'s current system of quadrants and sectors was devised, and it is therefore inconsistent with terminology of later episodes.*

quadrant. In interstellar mapping, a quadrant is one-fourth of the Milky Way Galaxy. The galaxy is divided into four quadrants, each forming a 90-degree pie wedge as seen from above or below the galaxy's plane. The four quadrants are labeled Alpha, Beta, Delta, and Gamma. The United Federation of Planets is mostly located in the **Alpha Quadrant**, although parts spill over into Beta. Station **Deep Space 9** is located in Alpha Quadrant. The Klingon and Romulan Empires are located in the **Beta Quadrant**, although they spill over into Alpha. The Borg homeworld is believed to be in the **Delta Quadrant**, while the Bajoran wormhole has one terminus in the **Gamma Quadrant**.*Quadrants and sectors have been used inconsistently in the various* Star Trek *episodes and films. During the original* Star Trek *series, the term quadrant was used rather freely, as was the term sector. At times, quadrant seemed to refer to a fourth of the entire galaxy, while at others it seemed to be a portion of a smaller region. It was not until "The Price" (TNG) that the current system of Alpha, Beta, Delta, and Gamma quadrants was firmly established.* Star Trek VI: The Undiscovered Country *adhered to this system, as well.*

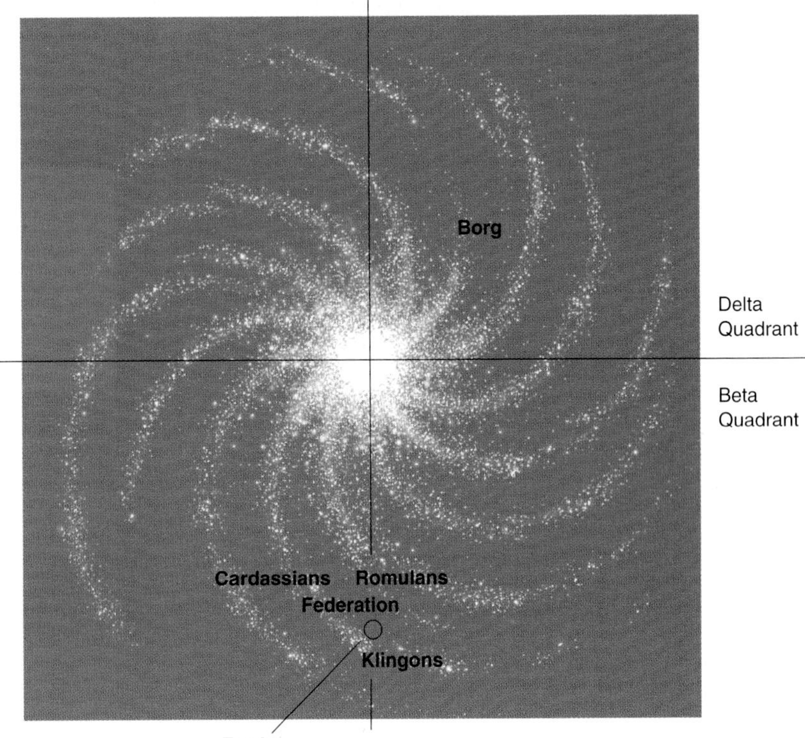

quadroline. An emergency drug used on planet **Malcor III**. ("First Contact" [TNG]).

Quadros-1 probe. Deep-space instrumented probe launched to the **Gamma Quadrant** in the 22nd century, one of the first scientific expeditions into that distant part of the galaxy. Among the findings returned by the craft was the discovery of a trinary star system called **Idran** in the Gamma Quadrant. Humans would not venture as far as the Quadros-1 probe until the discovery of the **Bajoran wormhole** in the 24th century. ("Emissary" [DS9]).

quadrotriticale. Genetically engineered grain developed on Earth from a four-lobed hybrid of wheat and rye. The parent strain, triticale, was discovered in 20th-century Canada. Quadrotriticale was the only Earth grain that would grow on **Sherman's**

Planet, and was thus critical to the Federation's plan in 2267 to develop that world. A large quantity of quadrotriticale was stored on **Deep Space Station K-7** for that project, but it was poisoned by a Klingon agent. ("The Trouble with Tribbles" [TOS]). SEE: **Darvin, Arne**; **Jones, Cyrano**; **tribbles**. Quark owned some quadrotriticale futures, but they became worthless in 2373. ("Business As Usual" [DS9]).

Quaice, Dr. Dalen. (Bill Erwin). Starfleet physician and native of planet Kenda II. Dr. Quaice had been a friend and mentor to **Dr. Beverly Crusher**, who did her internship with Quaice in 2352 on planet Delos IV. Following the death of his wife, Patricia, Dr. Quaice resigned his position at Starbase 133 and returned to his home on Kenda II aboard the *Enterprise*-D. Quaice had served on Starbase 133 for six years. ("Remember Me" [TNG]).

Quaice, Patricia. Wife of **Dr. Dalen Quaice**. Upon Patricia's death in 2367, Dalen left Starbase 133 and returned to his home planet, Kenda II. ("Remember Me" [TNG]).

"Quality of Life, The." *Next Generation* episode #135. Written by Naren Shankar. Directed by Jonathan Frakes. Stardate 46307.2. *First aired in 1992. Data refuses to send robotic servomechanisms to do hazardous tasks because he believes the machines to be sentient life-forms.* GUEST CAST: Ellen Bry as **Farallon, Dr.**; J. Downing as **Kelso, Chief**; Majel Barrett as Computer voice. SEE: **axionic chip; *bat'leth*; boridium power converter; Carema III; exocomp; Farallon, Dr.; interlink sequencer; Kelso, Chief; main particle impeller; microreplication system; Pierson, Lieutenant; Tyran system; Tyrus VIIA.**

Qualor II. Class-M world under Federation jurisdiction. A surplus depot operated by the **Zakdorn** people for Starfleet was located in orbit of Qualor II. ("Unification, Part I" [TNG]).

quantometer probe. Scientific instrument used to measure energy usage. ("Playing God" [DS9]).

quantum anomaly. SEE: **quantum fissure.**

quantum chemistry. Course taught in the fourth year of the Starfleet Academy curriculum. ("The Cloud" [VGR]).

quantum filament. An elongated subatomic object, hundreds of meters long, highly energetic, but possessing almost no mass. The *Enterprise*-D struck two quantum filaments in early 2368, resulting in the death of several crew members and severe damage to the ship itself. ("Disaster" [TNG]). *An early draft of "Disaster" had the ship colliding with an asteroid, but the writers, sensitive to scientific concerns that an asteroid would not cause the damage described in the script, "invented" the quantum filament. We have little idea what a quantum filament is, but we do know it's not a cosmic string.*

quantum fissure. Fixed point in the space-time continuum, essentially a keyhole into other **quantum realities**. Returning from shore leave by shuttlecraft in 2370, Worf encountered a quantum fissure. When the shuttle intersected the fissure, its warp engines caused a break in the barriers between realities and allowed Worf to pass from one quantum reality to the next. When the fissure was discovered and was in the process of being analyzed, a power surge aboard the *Enterprise*-D caused the fissure to destablize and allowed other realities to intrude into Worf's current location. Some 285,000 *Enterprise*-Ds, each representing a different quantum reality, were observed coming through the fissure. ("Parallels" [TNG]).

quantum fluctuations. Phenomenon postulated by physicist **Dr. Stephen Hawking**. Quantum fluctuations were thought to be links between multiple universes. Hawking referred to them as **wormholes**. ("Descent, Part I" [TNG]).

quantum flux. State of dimensional instability, or continual change. Objects in a state of quantum flux are unable to remain stable in one **quantum reality**. In 2370, following an encounter with a **quantum fissure**, Worf was thrown into a state of quantum flux, and began shifting from one quantum reality to the next, until the flux could be detected and repaired. ("Parallels" [TNG]).

quantum matrix. Energy pattern present in life-forms and objects. Fluctuations in the planet **Meridian**'s quantum matrix, caused by its sun, triggered dimensional shifts. In 2371, **Jadzia Dax** used the transporter to try to match her quantum matrix to that of Meridian so that she, too, would shift to Meridian's other dimension. The attempt failed. ("Meridian" [DS9]).

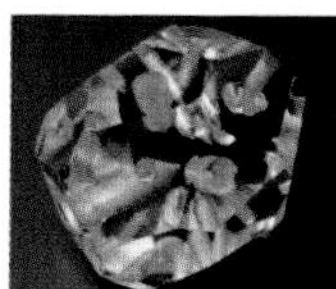

quantum phase inhibitor. Also known as the ***Tox Uthat***, a device invented by 27th-century scientist **Kal Dano** that was capable of halting all nuclear reaction within a star. ("Captain's Holiday" [TNG]).

quantum reality. One of an infinite number of possible universes or realities that exist side by side along the space-time continuum. Every occurrence and outcome that could exist does exist in a different quantum reality, realities that become increasingly divergent. In 2370, following an exposure to a **quantum fissure**, Worf experienced several such quantum realities, until his "shifting" could be corrected and he could be returned to his original reality. ("Parallels" [TNG]). *This idea of multiple realities is based on Dr. Richard **Feynman's** theory of "sum over histories," where a particle would not have a single history or path in space-time, but would instead follow every possible path.*

quantum resonance oscillator. Component of a Federation **transporter** module. ("Maneuvers" [VGR])

quantum signature. A unique characteristic that marks all matter in the universe for a given **quantum reality**. All matter in each universe resonates at a specific frequency at the quantum level. That signature is constant and cannot be changed by any known process. In 2370, an alternate Commander Data was able to determine that Worf's quantum signature was not native to the reality he was currently inhabiting. This discovery led to the solution for Worf's "shifting" through realities. ("Parallels" [TNG]).

quantum singularity life-form. Intelligent species from another time-space continuum whose young are incubated in a natural black hole. In 2369, these life-forms attempted to use the artificial quantum singularity of a **Romulan warbird** as a nest. When they discovered their mistake, they attempted to extract their embryos from the Romulan ship, endangering the warbird as well as the *Starship Enterprise*-D. ("Timescape" [TNG]). *Neither this species, the domain in which they existed, nor any of the individuals seen in the episode were given formal names.*

quantum singularity. Celestial phenomenon caused by the collapse of a neutron star, resulting in an object so dense that neither space-normal matter nor light can escape its gravity. In 2371 a microscopic singularity passed through the Sol system and exploded. The energy emitted by the singularity shifted the **chroniton** particles into a state of polarization. This caused a subspace bubble to be created around the ***Starship Defiant*** that was in Earth orbit at the time. ("Past Tense, Part I" [DS9]). **Romulan warbird**s employed a forced quantum singularity as a power source. ("Timescape" [TNG]). In 2371, temporal displacement waves from a cloaked Romulan ship's quantum singularity interacted with delta-series radioisotopes in Chief Miles O'Brien's body, causing O'Brien to shift through time. The warbird's quantum singularity also gave off **tetryon** emissions that allowed station personnel to track the ship. ("Visionary" [DS9]). In 2371, the *Voyager* encountered a type-4 quantum singularity in the Delta

Quadrant and became trapped within its **event horizon**. They were able to free themselves by enlarging a crack in the event horizon and passing through it. ("Parallax" [VGR]). SEE: **black hole; dekyon.**

quantum torpedo. Advanced weaponry developed by Starfleet in the late 2360s. Quantum torpedoes employed an energetic local release of the zero point energy field. This quantum effect tended to be more effective than conventional antimatter explosives in penetrating deflector shields. Quantum torpedoes were installed on the ***U.S.S. Defiant***. ("Defiant" [DS9]). While at the **Founders' homeworld** in 2372, **Garak** attempted to override the launch controls for the *Starship Defiant's* quantum torpedoes. Garak was attempting to destroy the planet's surface in order to kill all the Founders. ("Broken Link" [DS9]). In 2372, the weapons systems of the ***U.S.S. Lakota*** were upgraded, including a loadout of quantum torpedoes. ("Paradise Lost" [DS9]). The Cardassian guided tactical missile known as **Dreadnought** was equipped with quantum torpedoes. ("Dreadnought" [VGR]). The crew of the *Enterprise*-E used quantum torpedoes to destroy a time-traveling **Borg sphere**. *(Star Trek: First Contact)*. In 2373, in order to convince Michael Eddington to give himself up, Benjamin Sisko fired quantum torpedoes containing 50 kilograms of **trilithium** resin into the atmosphere of planet Solosos III, a Maquis colony. This rendered the planet uninhabitable for a period of 50 years. ("For the Uniform" [DS9]).

quarantine pods. Specialized medical equipment. In 2370, shipments of quarantine pods, along with other supplies, lead the **Maquis** to believe that the Cardassian colonists in the **Demilitarized Zone** were developing a **biogenic weapon**. ("Preemptive Strike" [TNG]).

quarantine seal. Also called a medical quarantine field. Force field used to isolate potentially hazardous biological specimens in sickbay and other laboratory facilities aboard starships. ("Home Soil" [TNG]). A medical quarantine field was used to isolate young **Willie Potts** when he contracted a deadly and contagious parasite from a **cove palm** fruit in 2367. ("Brothers" [TNG]).

quarantine transmitter. Standard equipment on Federation starships. These radio beacons are capable of transmitting automated warning messages should a ship become dangerously contaminated. The quarantine transmitter on the ***U.S.S. Lantree*** was activated after the ship's entire crew was killed from exposure to deadly antibodies from the **Darwin Genetic Research Station**. ("Unnatural Selection" [TNG]).

Quark (mirror). (Armin Shimerman). In the **mirror universe**, proprietor of the bar at **Terok Nor (mirror)**. Quark illegally helped **Terran** slaves find passage off the station. Unfortunately, his activities were discovered, and he was executed in 2370. ("Crossover" [DS9]). After this Quark was killed, the mirror Rom inherited the bar at Terok Nor. When Rom was killed a year later, Nog became the owner. ("Shattered Mirror" [DS9]).

Quark's Treasure. Small starship of **Ferengi** design owned by **Quark** in 2372. The ship had been given to Quark by his cousin **Gaila** in payment of an old business debt. Quark's first (and only) trip aboard the *Treasure* was a flight to **Earth**, ostensibly to transport his nephew, **Nog**, to Starfleet Academy, but actually to smuggle a quantity of illegal **kemacite** to **Orion**. Although the ship appeared to be in good operating condition, sabotage was later suspected when the ship's command sequencer malfunctioned. As a result, the ship's warp drive accelerated out of control, eventually causing Quark and his family to crash on Earth in 1947. SEE: **UFO**. The ship and crew were captured by the American military near **Roswell**, New Mexico, and later held for interrogation at **Hangar 18** at Wright Field. The discovery of an extraterrestrial spacecraft caused ripples of concern through the highest levels of the American government. Quark and his crew were later able to escape, with assistance from Earth natives **Faith Garland** and **Jeff Carlson**. Rom was able to devise a means to use the kemacite to establish an inversion wave that allowed the ship and its crew to return to the 24th century. Unfortunately, *Quark's Treasure* was seriously damaged in the return flight, and Quark was forced to sell it for passage back to Deep Space 9. ("Little Green Men" [DS9]). Quark's Treasure *was a reuse of the Ferengi shuttle model first seen in "The Price" (TNG).*

Quark's bar. Bar and gambling establishment on the **Promenade** at station **Deep Space 9**. Owned by its Ferengi namesake, **Quark**'s place was a favorite gathering spot for station residents, as well as for travelers passing through. The bar provided games such as **dabo** for gambling, and several **holosuites** on the second level of the bar. ("Emissary" [DS9]). The bar was located on level seven, section five of DS9. ("Playing God" [DS9]). In 2371, Chief **Miles O'Brien** convinced Quark to put a **dart** board in his bar. ("Visionary" [DS9]). The employees of Quark's bar organized into a labor **union** in 2372 in response to abusive management decisions by Quark. SEE: **Guild of Restaurant and Casino Employees.** ("Bar Association" [DS9]). **FCA** Liquidator **Brunt** tried to close down Quark's bar later that year when he forced Quark to break a sales contract. Even though Brunt was able to revoke Quark's Ferengi business license, Quark's friends came to the rescue, contributing furniture, glassware, potables, and other necessities to help keep the establishment in operation. ("Body Parts" [DS9]).

Quark. (Armin Shimerman). Entrepreneur who ran Quark's bar on station **Deep Space 9**. Quark grew up on planet **Ferenginar** with his father **Keldar**, his mother **Ishka**, and his younger brother **Rom**. Inheriting his mother's good business sense, Quark left his homeworld in 2351 as soon as he reached his Age of Ascension. ("Family Business" [DS9]). As a young man, Quark was apprenticed to a district **subnagus**. He behaved as a proper, subservient **Ferengi**, and was very popular with the subnagus, and felt he was well on his way to success. However, Quark became involved with the subnagus's sister, and was ousted from his apprenticeship because of it. ("Playing God" [DS9]). SEE: **Ferengi Rules of Acquisition: 112.** Quark worked on a Ferengi freighter ship for eight years before opening a bar on the Cardassian mining station, **Terok Nor**. ("Babel" [DS9], "The Way of the Warrior" [DS9]). Quark served as ship's cook on the freighter, and was away from Ferenginar when the planet was struck by the Great Monetary Collapse. ("Homefront" [DS9]).

In 2363, Quark had a brief affair with **Natima Lang** (*pictured*), a Cardassian woman with unorthodox political views, who admired him for illegally selling food to Bajoran nationals on **Terok Nor**. Lang left Quark after learning that he had used her personal access code to steal money. Quark regarded Lang as the great love of his life and always regretted having betrayed her trust. ("Profit and Loss" [DS9]).

During the Cardassian occupation of planet **Bajor**, Quark ran a black-market business for Bajoran nationals on the station. When the Cardassians left in 2369, Quark reluctantly stayed to manage his bar. Quark, a **Ferengi** national, felt unfairly persecuted by station security chief, **Odo**. ("Emissary" [DS9]). Later that year, Quark served as **grand nagus** when Grand Nagus **Zek** apparently died. The appointment was only temporary, however, because Zek had faked his death to test his son, **Krax**. ("The Nagus" [DS9]). SEE: **Corvan gilvos**.

In 2370, during an attempt to find a list for an acquaintance, Pallra, Quark was shot with a compressed tetryon-beam weapon and suffered life-threatening injuries to his thoracic cavity. Fortunately, he recovered. ("Necessary Evil" [DS9]). Also in 2370, Grand Nagus Zek gave Quark the opportunity to be the first Ferengi to open business negotiations with a planet from the Gamma Quadrant. Unfortunately, the scandalous revelation that **Pel**, Quark's protégé in the venture, was female resulted in the loss of Quark's profits. ("Rules of Acquisition" [DS9]).

Early in 2371, Quark found himself briefly thrust into Klingon politics when he accidentally killed **Kozak**, a patron at his bar. Quark temporarily became head of the House of Kozak, and husband to **Grilka** (*pictured).* In that capacity, he helped to insure Grilka's financial security by fending off a plot by **D'Ghor** to gain control of Kozak's assets. ("The House of Quark" [DS9]). SEE: **divorce, Klingon**. Quark once loaned his cousin, **Gaila**, latinum to start an arms consortium. Years later, when Gaila had grown enormously wealthy, he repaid the debt by presenting Quark with his own ship. Quark named the vessel ***Quark's Treasure***, but unfortunately, the ship experienced a serious malfunction on its first voyage and had to be scrapped after an accidental side trip to **Earth** in the year 1947. ("Little Green Men" [DS9]).

In 2372, Quark was faced with an extraordinarily difficult situation when the employees at his bar formed a labor union and went on strike. Pressured by the threat of violence from the **FCA**, Quark settled the dispute by making secret concessions to the workers, despite Ferengi law prohibiting negotiations with labor unions. SEE: **Guild of Restaurant and Casino Employees**. ("Bar Association" [DS9]).

A few weeks later, while on a trip to Ferenginar, Quark was misdiagnosed with fatal **Dorek syndrome** by **Dr. Orpax** during his annual insurance physical examination. Mindful of Ferengi tradition that holds that a Ferengi who dies in debt will suffer in the afterlife, Quark tried to raise money by offering his desiccated remains on the Ferengi Futures Exchange. Quark accepted an anonymous bid of 500 bars of latinum before learning that the diagnosis was in error. He subsequently learned that the anonymous bidder was FCA Liquidator **Brunt**, who refused a refund and demanded fulfillment of his contract for Quark's remains. When Quark defied Ferengi law by breaking his sales contract, Brunt responded by confiscating Quark's assets and revoking his Ferengi business licence. Fortunately, Quark's friends on Deep Space 9 came to the rescue, offering help so that he could remain in business. ("Body Parts" [DS9]). In 2373, Quark made a brief foray into illegal arms dealing in order to settle his mounting debt. ("Business As Usual" [DS9]).

The Lady Grilka returned into Quark's life in 2373 when she traveled to Deep Space 9 to ask his advice on financial matters. Quark found the Klingon woman very attractive, and, with Worf's tutelage, won her romantic attentions. As a result, Quark received a compound fracture of the right radius, two fractured ribs, torn ligaments, strained tendons, and numerous bruises, contusions, and scratches. ("Looking for *par'Mach* in All the Wrong Places" [DS9]).

*Armin Shimerman also played **Letek**, one of the original three Ferengi in "The Last Outpost" (TNG); **Bractor**, another Ferengi, in "Peak Performance" (TNG); and the gift box face in "Haven" (TNG). Quark was first seen in "Emissary" (DS9).*

quartum. Chemical compound used in Starfleet emergency thruster packs. Quartum is normally quite stable, but becomes explosive when exposed to radiation exceeding 350 rads. ("Disaster" [TNG]).

quasar. Mysterious quasi-stellar object believed to generate enormous amounts of energy from relatively small amounts of mass. The *Enterprise*, in 2267, had standing orders to investigate all quasars and quasarlike objects whenever they might be encountered. ("The *Galileo* Seven" [TOS]). SEE: **Murasaki 312**.

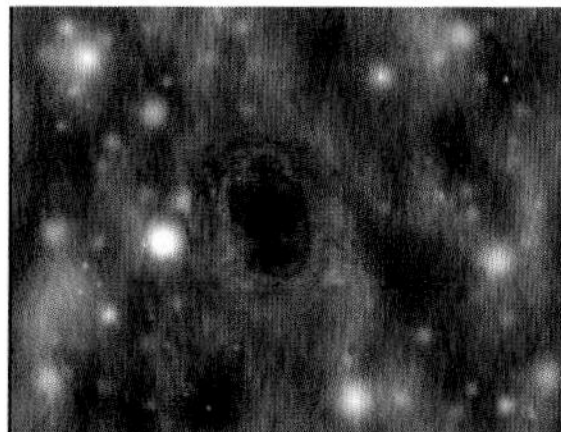

quasi-energy microbes. Space-borne life-forms found within a plasma streamer between a binary star pair in the Igo Sector. Quasi-energy microbes, first encountered by the crew of the *Starship **Yosemite*** in 2369, existed in a state between matter and energy, and were able to live in the matter stream of a transporter beam. Several of these microbes were accidentally brought aboard the *Yosemite*, where they nearly caused the destruction of that ship. Following the detection of these life-forms by *Enterprise*-D personnel, the microbes were removed from both ships' transporter systems and returned to the plasma streamer that was their home. ("Realm of Fear" [TNG]).

quasimolecular flux. Molecular states in which constitutent atoms are altered from their normal composition and energy state. A portion of metal in the bulkhead of the *Enterprise*-D cargo bay was altered to a state of quasimolecular flux by the **solanagen-based aliens**. ("Schisms" [TNG]).

Quatal Prime. Planet in the **Demilitarized Zone** near the Dorvan sector, the site of a **Cardassian** colony. Quatal had a lucrative mining operation, and in 2373 its weapons systems were in the process of being upgraded. In 2373, the **Maquis** used **cobalt diselenide** as a **biogenic weapon** against the **Cardassian** colony on Quatal Prime. Quatal Prime has at least four moons. ("For the Uniform" [DS9]).

quatloo. Monetary unit used by the **Providers** of planet **Triskelion** for betting on competition between **drill thralls**. ("The Gamesters of Triskelion" [TOS]).

Quazulu VIII. Planet. Twelve students from the *Enterprise*-D visited Quazulu VIII on a field trip in 2364, just prior to that ship's visit to planet **Angel One**. At Quazulu, several of the students were infected with an airborne virus that later threatened the health of hundreds of *Enterprise*-D personnel by causing respiratory distress. ("Angel One" [TNG]).

Queen's Gambit, The. A **holosuite program**, another adventure of **secret agent** Julian **Bashir**. The story featured former agent **Nigel Dunlap**, who worked with Bashir to prevent **Lady Wantsomore** from assassinating the Queen of England. ("A Simple Investigation" [DS9]).

Qui'al Dam. Water-diverting structure on planet **Bajor** near the city of **Janir**. The dam was placed back in operation in 2371 after years of disuse. ("Destiny" [DS9]). SEE: **Trakor's Third Prophecy.**

qui'lari. Vulcan name for the **foramen magnum** portion of the humanoid cranium. ("The Muse" [DS9]).

Qui'Tu. In **Klingon** mythology, the source of all creation. *(Star Trek V: The Final Frontier).* SEE: ***Sha Ka Ree***.

quicken. Term used to indicate the terminal stage in a disease known as the blight. ("The Quickening" [DS9]). SEE: **Teplan blight; Trevean**.

"Quickening, The." *Deep Space Nine* episode #95. Written by Naren Shankar. Directed by Rene Auberjonois. No stardate mentioned. First aired in 1996. *On a planet in the Gamma Quadrant, Dr. Julian Bashir risks his life to cure a deadly disease called the blight.* GUEST CAST: Ellen Wheeler as **Ekoria**; Dylan Haggerty as **Epran**; Michael Sarrazin as **Trevean**; Heide Margolis as **Norva**; Loren Lester as Attendant; Alan Echevarria as **Tamar;** Lisa Moncure as Latia. SEE: **Bashir, Dr. Julian; Boranis III; cordrazine; Dominion; Ekoria; Epran; Gavara system; Jem'Hadar; Jenkata nebula; Kendi system; Kukalaka; Norva; Nykalia; Obatta cluster; quicken; Takana root tea; Tamar; Teplan blight; Teplan system; Trevean.**

Quin'lat. Ancient city on the **Klingon Homeworld**. Klingon history tells of a great storm that struck the city centuries ago while **Kahless the Unforgettable** was there. One man went outside to face the storm, to "stand before the wind and make it respect [him]." The man was killed. As Kahless would later say, "The wind does not respect a fool." ("Rightful Heir" [TNG]).

Quinn, Admiral Gregory. (Ward Costello). **Starfleet** officer who played a crucial role in uncovering the attempted takeover of **Starfleet Command** in 2364. As part of his effort to uncover the situation, Quinn ordered Inspector General **Dexter Remmick** to investigate the *Enterprise*-D for possible infestation. ("Coming of Age" [TNG]). None was discovered at the time, although Quinn himself later became a victim of the alien infestation when his mind was overtaken by the unknown alien intelligence that attempted to infiltrate **Starfleet Headquarters** in 2364. ("Conspiracy" [TNG]).

Quinn. (Gerrit Graham). A member of the **Q Continuum**, Quinn was at one time a renowned philosopher within the Continuum, espousing the virtues of the **New Era**. He was a benevolent entity and on several occasions helped the inhabitants of **Earth**. SEE: **Newton, Isaac; Ginsberg, Maury; Riker, Colonel Thaddius.** However, on at least one occasion, Quinn created a misunderstanding that ignited a war between the Vulcans and the Romulans that lasted 100 years. Quinn eventually found immortality unendurably boring and sought to end his own life. The Continuum would not allow this, and around 2072 imprisoned him in a rogue comet. In 2372, he was inadvertently released from his incarceration by the crew of the *U.S.S. Voyager* in the Delta Quadrant. Quinn requested asylum from the Continuum so that he could end his own life. Q represented the interests of the Continuum in a hearing convened by Captain Kathryn Janeway to decide whether to grant Quinn's request. Q argued strongly against asylum, but was touched by the other Q's irrepressible nature. After his asylum was granted, he agreed to become a human crew member on the *Starship Voyager* and chose the name Quinn. His foray into a mortal existence proved to be short-lived, as he committed suicide by ingesting Nogatch hemlock provided to him by Q. ("Death Wish" [VGR]). *He was referred to as Q2 in the script.* Quinn's suicide spawned chaos and upheaval in the Q Continuum because his calls for freedom and individualism inspired many followers. The **Q freedom faction** clashed with the forces of the status quo. This caused a great civil war in the Continuum. What might be viewed as Quinn's ultimate victory occurred in 2373, when Q and a female of the Continuum conceived a child, the first baby ever to be born in the Continuum; definitely an upsetting of the status quo. SEE: **Q female**. ("The Q and the Grey" [VGR]).

Quint, Ned. (Shay Duffin). Resident of **Caldos colony** and friend of **Felisa Howard.** Quint was caretaker for Felisa's estate during her life. Following Felisa's death, Quint warned Beverly to rid herself of her grandmother's house and most particularly the **Howard family candle**, which Ned felt summoned the family **ghost**. Quint felt the ghost had been a curse on the Howard family for generations. He was killed at the colony's weather control substation, apparently by **Ronin**. ("Sub Rosa" [TNG]).

Quintana, Ensign. Starfleet officer assigned to station Deep Space 9. ("Meridian" [DS9]). *This person was mentioned but not seen.*

Quinteros, Commander Orfil. (Gene Dynarski). Starfleet officer assigned to **Starbase 74** in 2364. Quinteros had previously been in charge of the team that assembled the *Starship Enterprise*-D at the **Utopia Planitia Fleet Yards** on Mars. Quinteros also oversaw computer systems upgrades to the *Enterprise*-D at Starbase 74 in 2364. ("11001001" [TNG]). SEE: ***Galaxy*-Class Starship Development Project.** *Actor Gene Dynarski also played miner **Ben Childress** in "Mudd's Women" (TOS) and an aide to Ambassador Hodin in "The Mark of Gideon" (TOS).*

R'Mor, Telek. (Vaughn Armstrong). Scientist and pilot of the **Romulan** research vessel ***Talvath.*** In 2349, R'Mor, who was a member of the Romulan Astrophysical Academy, began an extended scientific mission aboard the *Talvath*, leaving behind his wife and an infant daughter on **Romulus**. In 2351, R'Mor made contact through a **micro-wormhole** with the Federation starship ***Voyager*** in the distant **Delta Quadrant**. The wormhole traversed not only across the galaxy, but also 20 years into R'Mor's future, as the *Voyager* was in the year 2371. R'Mor sympathized with the plight of the *Voyager* crew, and offered to deliver personal messages to the families of the *Voyager* crew in the year 2371. Unfortunately, R'Mor died in 2367, four years before he could have fulfilled his promise. ("Eye of the Needle" [VGR]). *It was not revealed if the messages were ever delivered. Vaughn Armstrong previously played Captain Korris in "Heart of Glory" (TNG) and Gul Danar in "Past Prologue" (DS9).*

R'uustai. Klingon ceremony in which two individuals bond together to become brothers or sisters. Worf performed the *R'uustai* with young **Jeremy Aster** after Aster's mother died under Worf's command in 2366. The rite itself is resplendent in Klingon custom and involves the lighting of ceremonial candles and the wearing of warrior's sashes, concluding with a Klingon intonation honoring their mothers. ("The Bonding" [TNG]).

Raal. Province located on the coast of the **Voroth Sea** on planet **Vulcan**. ("Innocence" [VGR]).

Rabal, Dr. (Michael Corbett). Hekaran scientist. Rabal worked with his sister, **Serova**, on her theory that the cumulative effects of warp drive were damaging the fabric of space. He said it took him four years of study to understand the theoretical models on which her conclusions were based. By 2370, he was convinced that she was correct and joined her in her attempt to gain attention for her findings. After his sister's death, Rabal was left to deal with the legacy his sister had created: a **subspace rift** that affected the orbit of his homeworld. ("Force of Nature" [TNG]).

Rabol. Cardassian spacecraft. The *Rabol* transported Gul Dukat to station Deep Space 9 in 2372 so that he could join Kira Nerys on her expedition to investigate the disappearance of the ***Ravinok***. ("Indiscretion" [DS9]).

Rachelis system. A densely populated planetary system. The Rachelis system was struck with an outbreak of a new strain of **plasma plague** in 2365, just prior to stardate 42073.1. ("The Child" [TNG]).

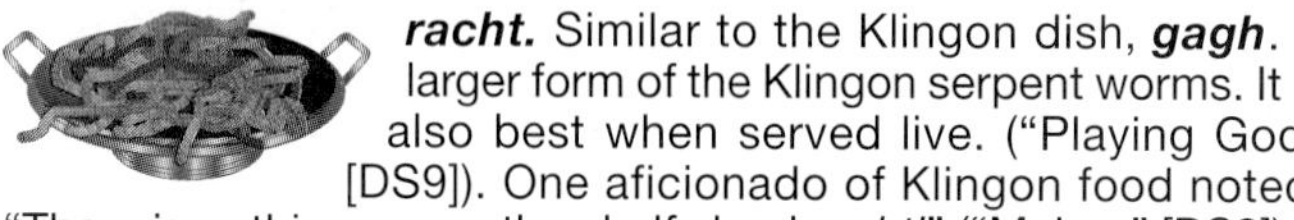

racht. Similar to the Klingon dish, ***gagh***. A larger form of the Klingon serpent worms. It is also best when served live. ("Playing God" [DS9]). One aficionado of Klingon food noted: "There is nothing worse than half-dead *racht!*" ("Melora" [DS9]).

racquetball. Sport similar to handball, using small paddles to hit a ball against a wall. Chief O'Brien and Dr. Julian Bashir both enjoyed the sport. O'Brien even built a raquetball court on Deep Space 9, where he and Bashir played a tournament in 2370. O'Brien stopped the match before it was finished because probabilities were being distorted by an alien **gambling device**. ("Rivals" [DS9]).

radans. Common gemstones from planet **Troyius**. Radans resembled quartz, but chemically, radans were raw **dilithium** crystals. The leader of Troyius gave **Elaan**, the **Dohlman** of **Elas**, a necklace of radans as a wedding present in 2268. The discovery that these common gemstones were in fact valuable dilithium made Troyius a planet of great strategic significance. Elaan's necklace served as a source of emergency crystals for the *Starship Enterprise* when that ship was under attack by a Klingon vessel that ironically sought to guarantee a supply of radans from Troyius. ("Elaan of Troyius" [TOS]).

radiogenic sweepstakes. Game of chance sponsored in early 2372 by Tom Paris aboard the *Starship Voyager*. Contestants predicted the daily radiogenic particle count at the price of one replicator ration per bet. Paris skimmed part of the proceeds for himself, which he used to supplement his **replicator rations**. The contest was quickly shut down by First Officer Chakotay. ("Meld" [VGR]). SEE: **Chez Sandrine**.

radioisotope. Form of chemical elements possessing unstable nucleii that spontaneously emit radiation in the form of alpha particles, beta particles, or gamma rays. ("Tuvix" [VGR]).

radioseptics. Small silvery spheres used by the Enaran people of the Delta Quadrant. Persons cleaned and disinfected their hands by rolling the radioseptics around in them. ("Remember" [VGR]).

Radue. (Jerry Hardin). First Appointee of planet **Aldea** in 2364. Radue attempted to negotiate with *Enterprise*-D personnel to obtain possession of some crew members' children in exchange for access to Aldean technology. ("When the Bough Breaks" [TNG]). *Jerry Hardin also played Samuel Clemens in "Time's Arrow, Parts I and II" (TNG).*

Rael. (Jason Evers). **Scalosian** male who boarded the *Enterprise* in 2268 in an attempt to cryogenically freeze the crew and use the males for breeding stock. Like all the males on planet **Scalos**, Rael was sterile due to radiation contamination on his planet. Although he intellectually realized the need to propagate his species by forcing alien males to mate with Scalosian females, he became jealous of the pairing of Captain James Kirk and **Deela**. ("Wink of an Eye" [TOS]).

Rafalian mouse. Tiny animal. Odo occasionally enjoyed taking the form of a Rafalian mouse. ("Crossfire" [DS9]).

Rager, Ensign. (Lanei Chapman). *Enterprise*-D crew member who served at conn under the command of Captain Jean-Luc Picard in 2367. ("Galaxy's Child" [TNG], "Schisms" [TNG], "Relics" [TNG]). Rager had to be relieved of duty when she suffered severe dream deprivation when the ship was trapped in a **Tyken's Rift** later that year. ("Night Terrors" [TNG]). *Lanei Chapman later had a regular role in* Space, Above and Beyond.

Rahm-Izad system. Star system located in Sector 21459. The Cardassian **Gul Ocett** was misdirected to the Rahm-Izad system by Federation and Klingon personnel when it was found she had tried to sabotage the *Enterprise*-D in an attempt to gain advantage in finding data to complete the late **Professor Richard Galen**'s work. The actual information was found on **Vilmor II**. ("The Chase" [TNG]). SEE: **humanoid life**.

Raifi. Offspring of **Tobin Dax**. Raifi was a difficult child at times, causing Tobin some difficulty on a number of occasions. ("Nor the Battle to the Strong" [DS9]).

Rain, Dr. Jennings. Noted expert in humanoid interpersonal relationships and author of the book ***Finding and Winning Your Perfect Mate***. ("In Purgatory's Shadow" [DS9]).

Rak-Minunis. Freighter spacecraft of Kobheerian registry. The *Rak-Minunis* delivered the Cardassian **Marritza** to **Deep Space 9** in 2369 for medical care. ("Duet" [DS9]). SEE: **Kobheerian captain.** In 2371, with the use of a holo-filter, the ***U.S.S. Defiant***

appeared to be the **Kobheerian** transport vessel *Rak-Minunis* to fool the **Cardassians**. ("Second Skin" [DS9]).

Rakal, Major. Member of the Romulan **Tal Shiar** intelligence service. Rakal was murdered in 2369 by members of the **Romulan** underground so that Deanna Troi could be coerced into assuming Rakal's identity, as part of an elaborate plot to enable Romulan **Vice-Proconsul M'ret** to defect to the Federation. ("Face of the Enemy" [TNG]). SEE: **N'Vek, Subcommander**.

Rakal, Seltin. (Christine Healy). Leader of the inhabitants on planet **Meridian**. ("Meridian" [DS9])

Rakal. Planet located in Cardassian space. The Cardassians maintained a subterranean base on the fourth moon of Rakal. ("Return to Grace" [DS9]).

Rakan folk songs. Traditional music known to some members of the Maquis. ("State of Flux" [VGR]).

Rakantha Province. Farming community that was one of the most productive regions of planet **Bajor**. The land in Rakantha was poisoned in 2369 by departing Cardassian troops at the end of the occupation. In 2371, Kai **Winn** assigned **soil reclamators** to Rakantha in preparation for planting crops that could be used for export. ("Shakaar" [DS9]). Rakantha was home to **Jillur Gueta**, Ishan Chaye, and Timor Landi. ("Things Past" [DS9]).

Rakella Prime. Planet. Home of a civilization known as the **Vok'sha**. ("Heroes and Demons" [VGR]).

Rakhar. Planet in the **Gamma Quadrant.** The government of Rakhar did not tolerate political dissidents and, as punishment, would kill a perpetrator's family. ("Vortex" [DS9]). SEE: **Croden**.

Rakhari. Humanoid inhabitants of the planet **Rakhar**. ("Vortex" [DS9]). SEE: **Croden**

Rakonian swamp rat. Unpleasant animal. In 2372, Kira compared Quark to a Rakonian swamp rat. ("Hippocratic Oath" [DS9]).

Rakosa V. Highly populated Class-M planet in the Delta Quadrant. A humanoid civilization existed on Rakosa V and over two million of its inhabitants were threatened in 2372 when a Cardassian weapon known as **Dreadnought** mistook it for planet **Aschelan V**. ("Dreadnought" [VGR]).

Rakosan fighters. Small one-person defensive spacecraft from the planet Rakosa V. In 2372, First Minister Kellan dispatched several Rakosan fighters in an unsuccessful attempt to intercept and destroy the Cardassian autonomous weapon known as **Dreadnought**. ("Dreadnought" [VGR]).

raktajino*.** Klingon **coffee** beverage. It was served at **Quark's bar** on station **Deep Space 9** and sometimes served iced. ("The Passenger" [DS9]). **Benjamin Sisko** was fond of *raktajino* ("Second Sight" [DS9]). **Kira Nerys** liked her raktajino extra hot with two measures of ***kava. ("Crossfire" [DS9]). Klingon intelligence agent **Arne Darvin** preferred *raktajino* to Cardassian **fish juice**. *Raktajino* was not available at Federation establishments such as the bar on **Deep Space Station K-7** in 2267, since this was before détente between the Federation and the Klingon governments. ("Trials and Tribble-ations" [DS9]). **Tom Paris** decided to buy some *raktajino* in early 2372 with replicator rations from his **radiogenic sweepstakes** gambling scheme. ("Meld" [VGR]). **Talarians** sometimes react badly to *raktajino*, causing them to become unruly. ("A Simple Investigation" [DS9]).

Ral, Devinoni. (Matt McCoy). The agent for the **Chrysalians** during the **Barzan wormhole** negotiations in 2366. Ral, who was one-fourth **Betazoid**, was born in Brussels, in the European alliance, in 2325. He moved to the planet Hurkos III at the age of 19. Taken by his striking appearance, Deanna Troi found herself drawn to Ral during the Barzan negotiations. Ral kept his Betazoid heritage hidden, and used his empathic abilities to give him an advantage during business and personal dealings. ("The Price" [TNG]).

Ralkana. Daughter of **Caylem** and member of the **Alsaurian resistance movement** on a planet of the **Mokra Order**. Ralkana was killed when she attempted to rescue her mother from a Mokra prison. Years later, a delusional Caylem thought Kathryn Janeway was Ralkana. Janeway could not bring herself to tell Caylem that she was not his daughter. ("Resistance" [VGR]).

Raman, U.S.S. Federation science vessel, *Oberth* class, Starfleet registry number NCC-59983, with a crew of seven, lost in the atmosphere of **Marijne VII** in 2370. The crew was killed by subspace life-forms living in the lower atmosphere of the planet. The *U.S.S. Enterprise*-D responded to a distress call from the *Raman*, but arrived too late to save the crew. ("Interface" [TNG]). *Named for the Nobel-Prize-winning physicist, Sir Chandrasekhara Venkata Raman.*

Ramart, Captain. (Charles Stewart). Commander of the Federation science vessel ***Antares***. Ramart's crew rescued the 17-year-old **Charles Evans** from planet **Thasus** in 2266, delivering him to the *Enterprise*. Ramart, along with the rest of his crew, was killed when Evans destroyed the *Antares* to prevent Ramart from warning Kirk about Evans's psychokinetic powers. ("Charlie X" [TOS]).

Ramatis III. Planet. Homeworld of famed Federation mediator **Riva**. The ruling family of Ramatis III lacked the gene that makes hearing possible, and thus members of that family communicated with an interpretive **Chorus** that provided assistive hearing and speech. Riva was a member of the Ramatis III ruling family in 2365. ("Loud as a Whisper" [TNG]).

Ramatis star system. Location of planet **Ramatis III**. The *Starship Enterprise*-D visited the Ramatis system in 2365 on a mission to transport mediator **Riva** from Ramatis III to **Solais V**. ("Loud as a Whisper" [TNG]).

Ramirez, Captain. Spaceship pilot and three-time ***tongo*** champion. Ramirez beat Dax rather badly at *tongo* on stardate 50416, and she ended up owing him two bars of **latinum**. ("The Darkness and the Light" [DS9]).

Ramirez. Starfleet officer. Ramirez served aboard the *Defiant* and was killed in 2372 on planet **Vandros IV**. ("To the Death" [DS9]).

ramscoop. Device that employs powerful magnetic fields to collect interstellar hydrogen for use as fuel for a space vehicle.

Also called a **Bussard collector**. O'Brien compared a ramscoop to the **arva nodes** in **Tosk's** ship, which essentially did the same thing. ("Captive Pursuit" [DS9]).

Ramsey, Dr. Archaeologist aboard the ***U.S.S. Yamato*** at the time of an expedition to planet **Denius III** in 2365. Ramsey's work, along with the contributions of *Yamato* **Captain Donald Varley,** enabled artifacts found at Denius III to help determine the location of the legendary planet **Iconia**. ("Contagion" [TNG]).

Ramsey. (Sam Hennings). One of four survivors of the wreck of the Federation freighter ***Odin*** who drifted to planet **Angel One** in escape pods in 2357. Ramsey took up residence among the people of Angel One, despite objections from that planet's government that his outside ideas would threaten the stability of the female-dominated society. ("Angel One" [TNG]).

Ramsey. Starfleet officer assigned to Deep Space 9. In 2372, Ramsey died aboard the *Starship Defiant* during a battle with the *U.S.S. Lakota.* ("Paradise Lost" [DS9]).

Ranar, Admiral. Federation admiral in charge of Starfleet Security. She took a personal interest in the recovery of the *Starship* ***Pegasus*** after it had been detected by the Romulans in 2370. Ranar sent personal orders to Commander **William Riker**, instructing him not to inform Captain Jean-Luc Picard of the true nature of the salvage mission. ("The *Pegasus*" [TNG]). SEE: **Pressman, Erik**.

Rand, Janice. (Grace Lee Whitney). Starfleet officer who served as Captain Kirk's yeoman during the early days of Kirk's first five-year mission aboard the original *Starship Enterprise*. ("The Corbomite Maneuver" [TOS]). Rand returned to serve aboard the *Enterprise* as **transporter** chief in 2271. *(Star Trek: The Motion Picture).* Rand subsequently served at **Starfleet Command** in San Francisco, where she assisted in directing emergency operations when Earth was threatened with ecological disaster by an alien space probe of unknown origin. *(Star Trek IV: The Voyage Home).* Rand later served as communications officer aboard the ***U.S.S. Excelsior*** under the command of Captain Sulu. *(Star Trek VI: The Undiscovered Country,* "Flashback" [VGR]). She was team leader of that ship's gamma shift. ("Flashback" [VGR]). *Rand's first appearance was in "The Corbomite Maneuver." She was also seen in "The Enemy Within" (TOS), "The Man Trap" (TOS), "The Naked Time" (TOS), "Charlie X" (TOS), and "Miri" (TOS). Her character was dropped thereafter for budget reasons, although she later returned in* Star Trek I, Star Trek III, Star Trek IV, Star Trek VI, *and "Flashback" (VGR).*

Ranor, Gul. Commander of the ***Galor*-class Cardassian warship** *Kraxon*. ("Defiant" [DS9]).

Ranora, Dr. (John Cirigliano). **Vhnori** scientist, a **thanatologist** who presided over the **Vhnori transference ritual** of **Ptera**. ("Emanations" [VGR]).

rapid nadion pulse. A burst of subatomic nadion particles that facilitate a release of energy from the emitter crystal in a **phaser**. ("The Mind's Eye" [TNG]).

"Rapture." *Deep Space Nine* episode #108. Teleplay by Hans Beimler. Story by L. J. Strom. Directed by Jonathan West. No stardate given. *First aired in 1997. A plasma discharge gives Sisko prophetic visions of a long-lost ancient Bajoran city, leading him to oppose Bajor's admission to the Federation.* GUEST CAST: Penny Johnson as **Yates, Kasidy**; Ernest Perry, Jr. as **Whatley, Admiral Charles**; Louise Fletcher as **Winn**. SEE: **Alvanian beehive; B'hala; Bajor; Bajoran Chamber of Ministers; Bajoran Gratitude Festival; *bantaca*; *bateret* leaves; Cardassians; Colti, Admiral; holodeck and holosuite programs: Pleasure mazes; icon; Ilvia; jambalaya; *lingta*; Mera, Vedek; neuropolaric induction; Orb of Prophecy; *pagh'tem'far*; Rifkin, Captain; Sisko, Benjamin; Veta, Admiral; Whatley, Admiral Charles; Whatley, Kevin; Winn; Yates, Kasidy; Zocal's Third Prophecy.**

"Rascals." *Next Generation* episode #133. Teleplay by Allison Hock. Story by Ward Botsford & Diana Dru Botsford and Michael Piller. Directed by Adam Nimoy. Stardate 46235.7. *First aired in 1992. A mysterious energy field reverts Picard, Guinan, Keiko, and Ro into children. This was the first episode directed by Adam Nimoy, son of Leonard Nimoy.* GUEST CAST: Colm Meaney as **O'Brien, Miles**; Rosalind Chao as **O'Brien, Keiko**; Michelle Forbes as **Ro Laren**; David Tristen Birkin as Picard, Jean-Luc (child); Megan Parlen as Ro Laren (child); Caroline Junko King as O'Brien, Keiko (child); Isis J. Jones as Guinan (child); Mike Gomez as **Lurin, DaiMon**; Tracey Walter as **Berik**; Michael Snyder as **Morta**; Brian Bonsall as **Rozhenko, Alexander**; Whoopi Goldberg as **Guinan**; Morgan Nagler as Kid #1; Hana Hatae as **O'Brien, Molly**; Majel Barrett as Computer voice. SEE: ***B'rel*-class bird-of-prey; Berik; Buranian; crayon; *Draebidium calimus*; *Draebidium froctus*; Ferengi Salvage Code; *Fermi*, *Shuttlecraft*; firomactal drive; Guinan; humuhumunukunukuapua'a; kelilactiral; Langford, Dr.; Ligos VII; Lurin, DaiMon; Marlonia; molecular reversion field; Morta; O'Brien, Keiko; Picard, Jean-Luc; Ro Laren; ryboviroxic-nucleic structure; security access code; Suvin IV; Taguan; Tarkassian razorbeast; vendarite.**

Rashella. (Brenda Strong). The last child born on planet **Aldea** when radiation poisoning from damage to Aldea's **ozone** layer caused infertility among the Aldeans. Rashella had strong maternal instincts and, in 2364, wished to keep Alexandra, the child of an *Enterprise*-D crew member, as her own to raise. ("When the Bough Breaks" [TNG]).

Rasmussen, Berlinghoff. (Matt Frewer). A 22nd-century con artist from the **Earth** region known as New Jersey. Rasmussen appeared on the *Enterprise*-D in 2368, claiming to be a historian from the 26th century. Professor Rasmussen had in fact stolen his **time-travel pod** from a 26th century researcher, and was hoping to steal artifacts of 24th-century technology. His plan was to return to the 22nd century, then grow wealthy by claiming to have "invented" these devices. When the *Enterprise*-D crew learned of his scheme, Rasmussen was detained, and his time-travel pod returned without him. Rasmussen was subsequently taken under custody to **Starbase 214**, where

Captain Picard felt he would be helpful in some legitimate historical research. ("A Matter of Time" [TNG]). *Matt Frewer is also familiar to genre fans for the role of* Max Headroom.

Rata. (Robert Towers). Second officer of the Ferengi vessel commanded by **DaiMon Bok**. ("The Battle" [TNG]).

***ratamba* stew.** Traditional Bajoran dish. Benjamin Sisko prepared *ratamba* stew, served over spinach linguine, as an experiment in 2372. ("For the Cause" [DS9]).

***ratana* tree.** Type of tree found in the Rigel system. There was a *ratana* tree outside the infamous Barros Inn. ("Rejoined" [DS9]).

Rateg. City on planet **Romulus**. Picard and Data, working undercover on Romulus in 2368, said they came from Rateg. ("Unification, Part I" [TNG]).

ration cards. Official document issued to residents of **Sanctuary Districts** in the 21st-century United States on **Earth**. Ration cards, also called food cards, could be used to obtain food and water at distribution points located throughout each District. ("Past Tense, Parts I and II" [DS9]).

ration pack. Prepackaged emergency meal carried aboard Federation starships. Ration pack #5 contained stewed tomatoes and dehydrated eggs. Another contained strawberries and cream. ("Phage" [VGR]). Ration packs were also standard issue aboard Starfleet shuttlecraft. ("Innocence" [VGR]).

***Ravinok*.** Cardassian transport ship. In 2366 the *Ravinok* was en route to planet **Lissepia** when it was attacked by two **Breen** warships. The Breen forced the *Ravinok* to crash on planet **Dozaria**, killing 12 people. Eighteen Cardassian crew members survived, along with 32 Bajoran prisoners, including **Lorit Akrem** and Heler. Also aboard were two civilians, **Tora Naprem** and her daughter, **Tora Ziyal**. The Breen forced the *Ravinok* survivors to mine dilithium on Dozaria. The fate of the *Ravinok* was unknown for years until 2372, when Bajoran militia officer **Kira Nerys** and Cardassian **Gul Dukat** found the ship and rescued several survivors. ("Indiscretion" [DS9]).

Rawlens. Chief geologist aboard the original *Starship Enterprise* in 2268. Captain James Kirk recommended Rawlens for a survey team to planet **Alpha Carinae II**, but the M-5 computer disagreed. ("The Ultimate Computer" [TOS]).

Rayburn. (Budd Albright). *Enterprise* security officer. Rayburn was killed by the android **Ruk** at planet **Exo III** in 2266. ("What Are Little Girls Made Of?" [TOS]).

Raymond, Captain. Starfleet officer in command of the *U.S.S. Tecumseh* from the time of the Cardassian wars. Near stardate 50049, Raymond, commanding the *Tecumseh*, joined the *Rutledge* in a counterattack against Klingon forces in the **Archanis** sector. ("Nor the Battle to the Strong" [DS9]).

Raymond, Claire. (Gracie Harrison). Human from late-20th-century Earth; former occupation: homemaker. Raymond died of an embolism at the age of 35, whereupon her husband, Donald, arranged to have her body cryogenically frozen and stored in an orbiting satellite. Over three centuries later, she was revived aboard the *Enterprise*-D. Raymond returned to Earth aboard the *Starship* ***Charleston***, where she planned to look up her descendants living near Indianapolis. ("The Neutral Zone" [TNG]).

Raymond, Donald. Twentieth-century human and husband to **Claire Raymond**. Upon his wife's death, the profoundly sad Donald Raymond arranged to have Claire's body cryogenically frozen and stored in an orbiting satellite for future revival. Upon Claire's revival in 2364, she noted that her great-great-great-great-great grandson, **Thomas Raymond**, bore a striking resemblence to Donald. ("The Neutral Zone" [TNG]).

Raymond, Edward. Younger son of **Donald** and **Claire Raymond**. Edward was born in Secaucus, New Jersey, and lived in late-20th and early-21st-century Earth. ("The Neutral Zone" [TNG]).

Raymond, Thomas. (Peter Lauritson). Great-great-great-great-great-grandson of **Claire Raymond**. At the time of Claire's revival from cryonic storage in 2364, Thomas was living on Earth, just outside of Indianapolis. Claire said that Thomas looked exactly like her husband, who had lived in the late-20th and early-21st century. ("The Neutral Zone" [TNG]). *The image of Thomas Raymond seen on Troi's computer screen was the face of* Star Trek *producer Peter Lauritson.*

Razik, Jal. (Patrick Kilpatrick). First **maje** of the Kazon-Ogla. Jal Razik was one of the Kazon warriors who held Commander Chakotay captive on stardate 49005. Razik received his Ogla name after destroying a **Kazon-Nistrim** frigate. He was assassinated in 2372 by the **Jal Karden**. ("Initiations" [VGR]).

Razka Karn. (Roy Brocksmith). Smuggler, black marketeer, and scrap-metal merchant. Razka was an old friend of Kira Nerys's during the days of the Cardassian occupation. In 2372, Razka Karn obtained a piece of metal from a Ferengi merchant that was a piece of the ***Ravinok***, a Cardassian ship lost in 2366. He contacted Kira with his findings. ("Indiscretion" [DS9]).

reaction stabilizers. Integral component in station Deep Space 9's **main fusion reactor**. If the reaction stabilizers were disengaged, the reactor would overload, more than likely resulting in the destruction of the station. ("Civil Defense" [DS9]).

reactive armor. Type of armor that actively deflects energy and projectiles, sometimes by exploding outward in such a way as to deflect the incoming projectile. ("Business As Usual" [DS9]).

reactive ion impeller. Science project that Nog and Jake built for school on Deep Space 9 in 2369. ("Move Along Home" [DS9]).

ready room. On many starships, a small office located directly adjacent to the bridge, where the commanding officer could work undisturbed. Captain Picard's ready room on the *Enterprise*-D had a desk, a desktop viewer, a couch, and a food replicator terminal. *Decorations in Picard's ready room have included a model of the* ***U.S.S. Stargazer****; a hardbound illustrated edition of the collected works of William Shakespeare; a painting of the* Enterprise-D *by Andrew Probert and Rick Sternbach; a saltwater aquarium containing* **Livingston,** *a fish; a crystalline sailing ship model by*

Hawai'i artist Anthony Vannatta; an ancient nautical sextant; and, in later episodes, a ***Kurlan* naiskos** *statuette from "The Chase" (TNG).*

"Realm of Fear." *Next Generation* episode #128. Written by Brannon Braga. Directed by Cliff Bole. Stardate 46041.1. *First aired in 1992. Reginald Barclay, who is scared of the transporter anyway, is attacked by creatures living in the transporter beam. This was the only time where the audience was shown what it looks like to be beamed from the transport subject's point of view.* GUEST CAST: Colm Meaney as **O'Brien, Miles**; Patti Yasutake as **Ogawa, Nurse Alyssa**; Dwight Schultz as **Barclay, Reginald**; Renara Scott as Admiral; Thomas Belgrey as Crew member; Majel Barrett as Computer voice SEE: **Barclay, Reginald; Christina; Delinia II; Dern, Ensign; endorphins; Heisenberg compensators; Igo Sector; imaging scanner; Kelly, Lieutenant Joshua; kiloquad; Lycosa tarantula; matter stream; O'Brien, Miles; Ogawa, Nurse Alyssa; Olafson, Dr.; pattern buffer; phase transition coils; phased matter; plasma streamer; plexing; quasi-energy microbes; sample container; Talarian hook spider; Titus IV; transporter psychosis; Transporter Theory; *Yosemite*, *U.S.S.*; Zayra IV.**

reassociation. In **Trill** society, after two joined Trill are married, the **symbionts** are strongly discouraged from maintaining their relationship in later lifetimes when they are joined with subsequent hosts. Such reassociation was considered unnatural, and was such a strict taboo that any Trill engaging in it was exiled from the Trill homeworld. When this occurred, the symbiont was barred from being rejoined to a new host, but instead died within the body of the exiled host. ("Rejoined" [DS9]).

Rebel raider ship. Small spacecraft used by the **Terran rebellion** in the **mirror universe** in their struggle against the **Alliance**. ("Through the Looking Glass" [DS9]). *The miniature of this ship was a re-use of the two-person Bajoran subimpulse raider vessel from "The Siege" (DS9).*

rec deck. Large recreation room located at the rear of Deck 7 in the Primary Hull of the refitted *Starship Enterprise*. It featured a variety of games, a large viewscreen, and a display honoring previous vessels named *Enterprise*. *(Star Trek: The Motion Picture).*

recalibration sweep. Systematic analysis and correction of instrumentation. Dr. Julian Bashir told a Federation delegation sent to study the Bajoran wormhole in 2369 that Commander Sisko was busy with a recalibration sweep, an ultimately futile attempt to keep the delegates out of Sisko's way. ("The Forsaken" [DS9]).

recall subroutine. Component of the computer control system of the sophisticated **Kohl hibernation system** created by the survivors of the **Kohl settlement**. The recall subroutine program was responsible for reviving the hibernating persons when the environmental conditions on the planet were again favorable for surface habitation. ("The Thaw" [VGR]).

"receptacle." Term used callously by **Ambassador Ves Alkar** to describe the women that he subjected to severe empathic abuse in order for him to maintain his extraordinary emotional control. His "receptacles" generally died as a result of this molestation. ("Man of the People" [TNG]).

reconnaissance probe. SEE: **class-5 probe**.

recorder marker. Small data-storage buoy designed to be ejected from a spacecraft when destruction of that vessel was believed imminent. When recovered after the disaster, the information from the recorder marker would serve to help reconstruct the incidents leading to the ship's destruction. ("Where No Man Has Gone Before" [TOS], "The Corbomite Maneuver" [TOS]). The recorder marker of the ***S.S. Valiant*** was recovered by the original *Starship Enterprise* in 2265. ("Where No Man Has Gone Before" [TOS]). SEE: **flight recorder**.

Rectilian vulture. Avian life-form native to a planet in the Delta Quadrant, known for swooping in on its prey quickly. ("Phage" [VGR]).

Rectyne monopod. A single-footed animal form that grows as large as two tons. Miles O'Brien once saw a Rectyne monopod subjected to a **Klingon painstik**, a brutal treatment that caused the creature to jump five meters at the slightest touch. The animal finally died from excessive cephalic pressures—its head exploded. ("The Icarus Factor" [TNG]).

recursive encryption algorithm. Method of message encryption used in most codes employed by the **Cardassians**. ("In Purgatory's Shadow" [DS9]).

Red Alert. Aboard Federation **starships** and other vessels, a state of maximum crew and systems readiness. Red Alert is generally ordered by a ship's commanding officer during a serious emergency or potential emergency, such as a major systems failure or a battle situation.

Red Hour. During the rule of the computer **Landru** on planet **Beta III**, the Red Hour was a period of extreme violence and destruction by the planet's inhabitants. This may have been intended as a means of providing an emotional outlet to the tightly controlled society. ("Return of the Archons" [TOS]).

Red Squad. An elite group of **Starfleet Academy** cadets chosen for special secret missions. Red Squad received special training, and virtually every cadet aspired to be a member. In 2372, Red Squad was an unwitting tool in **Admiral Leyton's** attempted coup of Earth's government. Under Leyton's orders, Red Squad members sabotaged Earth's **global power grid**. Cadet Riley Aldrin Shepard was a member of Red Squad. ("Homefront" [DS9], "Paradise Lost" [DS9]).

red dwarf. Small, cool star of spectral type M, near the end of its life. ("Time and Again" [VGR]).

red leaf tea. Beverage. Gul Dukat ordered red leaf tea during his visit to Deep Space 9 in early 2371. ("Civil Defense" [DS9]).

redlining. Engineering slang meaning to reach or exceed maximum safe levels. ("Playing God" [DS9]).

Redab, Vedek. Deceased **Bajoran** cleric. Quark claimed that just before his death, **Vedek** Redab had blessed the latinum-plated **Renewal Scroll** inscription pens that he sold in 2371. ("Fascination" [DS9]).

Redblock, Cyrus. (Lawrence Tierney). A fictional character from the **Dixon Hill** detective stories. A notorious and powerful gangster, Redblock was an urbane and ruthless intellectual. A holographic version of Redblock was part of the Dixon Hill holodeck programs. ("The Big Goodbye" [TNG]). *The name Cyrus Redblock was apparently a play on the name of actor Sydney Greenstreet.*

"Redemption, Part I." Next Generation episode #100. Written by Ronald D. Moore. Directed by Cliff Bole. Stardate 44995.3. First aired in 1991. Worf becomes embroiled in a civil war for control of the Klingon High Council. This cliff-hanger episode was the last of the fourth season, and the direct continuation of Worf's story begun in "Sins of the Father" (TNG) and "Reunion" (TNG). GUEST CAST: Robert O'Reilly as **Gowron**; Tony Todd as **Kurn**; Barbara March as **Lursa**; Gwynyth Walsh as **B'Etor**; Ben Slack as **K'Tal**; Nicholas Kepros as **Movar**; J.D. Cullum as **Toral**; Whoopi Goldberg as **Guinan**. SEE: **Arbiter of Succession; B'Etor; *BaH*; Beta Thoridar; *Bortas, I.K.S.*; *d'k tahg*; discommendation; Duras; *G'now juk Hol pajhard*; Gowron; *Hegh'ta*; K'Tal; *kellicam*; Klingon civil war; Klingon Empire; Klingon Homeworld; Kurn; *Len'mat*; Lursa; Mempa sector; Movar; *naDev ghos!*; phaser range; Reel, Ensign; Romulan Star Empire; Sela; Starbase 24; Toral; Treaty of Alliance; Worf; *yIntagh*.**

"Redemption, Part II." *Next Generation* episode #101. Written by Ronald D. Moore. Directed by David Carson. Stardate 45020.4. *First aired in 1991. The Gowron regime retains control of the Klingon High Council, and Worf regains his family honor. This was the first episode of the fifth season.* GUEST CAST: Denise Crosby as **Sela**; Tony Todd as **Kurn**; Barbara March as **Lursa**; Gwynyth Walsh as **B'Etor**; J.D. Cullum as **Toral**; Robert O'Reilly as **Gowron**; Michael G. Hagerty as **Larg**; Fran Bennett as **Shanthi, Fleet Admiral**; Nicholas Kepros as **Movar**; Colm Meaney as **O'Brien, Miles**; Timothy Carhart as **Hobson, Lieutenant Commander Christopher**; Whoopi Goldberg as **Guinan**; Jordan Lund as **Kulge**; Stephen James Carver as Helmsman; Majel Barrett as Computer voice. SEE: ***Akagi, U.S.S.*; *baktag*; Berellians; Beta Lankal; B'Etor; cloaking device, Romulan; *DaH*; Data; Duras; *Endeavour, U.S.S.*; *Excalibur, U.S.S.*; Gamma Eridon; *GhoS!*; Gowron; *Hermes, U.S.S.*; Hobson, Lieutenant Commander Christopher; *Hornet, U.S.S.*; Klingon civil war; Klingon Empire; Kulge; Kurn; Larg; Lursa; "May you die well"; Mempa sector; Romulan Star Empire; Sela; Shanthi, Fleet Admiral; Starbase 234; *Sutherland, U.S.S.*; tachyon; tachyon detection grid; *Tian An Men, U.S.S.*; Toral; Worf; Yar, Tasha (alternate).**

Redjac. Energy-based life-form that terrorized and murdered women throughout history, feeding on the emotion of fear. Redjac was believed responsible for the deaths of seven women who were knifed to death in Shanghai, China, on Earth in 1932. The entity was also believed responsible for five similar murders in Kiev, USSR, in 1974, as well as for eight murders in the **Martian Colonies** in 2105 and ten murders on planet Alpha Eridani II in 2156. All these murders were committed by the entity known in London on Earth as **Jack the Ripper**, on **Deneb II** as **Kesla**, and on **Rigel IV** as **Beratis**. This entity traveled from Rigel IV to **Argelius II** in the body of city administrator **Hengist**, where it caused at least three more deaths in 2267. *Enterprise* engineer Montgomery Scott was initially accused of these last murders, but when the entity's true nature was discovered, it was transported into space where it was hoped it dispersed harmlessly. ("Wolf in the Fold" [TOS]). SEE: **noncorporeal life**.

Reegrunion. Humanoid civilization; nationality of **Plix Tixiplik**, a wanted criminal. ("Sanctuary" [DS9]).

Reel, Ensign. An *Enterprise*-D officer who was assigned to conn. Reel was on duty during the first battle of the **Klingon civil war** in late 2367. Reel was ordered to pilot the ship away from the confrontation so the Federation would not become involved in the conflict. ("Redemption, Part I" [TNG]).

Reese, Lieutenant. (Steven Vincent Leigh). Starfleet security officer stationed at starbase Deep Space 9 in 2372. Reese worked with Lieutenant Commander Eddington to ensure the safety of the 12 Federation CFI replicators bound for Cardassia. ("For the Cause" [DS9]).

***reeta*-hawk.** Avian life-form from planet **Argratha**; a scavenger. ("Hard Time" [DS9]).

reflection therapy. Psychiatric technique used on planet **Tilonus IV** in which the patient's brain is scanned and images from brain areas that control emotions and memory are projected holographically. The patient then interacts with holographic images, which represent various facets of his personality. ("Frame of Mind" [TNG]). SEE: ***Frame of Mind*; neurosomatic technique; Syrus, Dr.**

refrigeration unit. Heat-pump device installed by the **Scalosians** into the *Starship Enterprise*'s life-support systems in 2268, intended to freeze the ship's crew until they were needed for reproduction. ("Wink of an Eye" [TOS]).

Regalian fleaspider. Arachnoid life-form. The venom of fleaspiders could be used to synthesize a medicine to improve circulation in humanoid patients. Quark imported a shipment of Regalian fleaspiders for Dr. Julian Bashir in 2373. ("The Ship" [DS9]).

Regalian liquid crystals. An illegal, highly intoxicating, and sometimes dangerous aphrodisiac. In early 2373, Quark imported some of these crystals, along with a shipment of Regalian fleaspiders, for Dr. Bashir. ("The Ship" [DS9]).

Regana Tosh. (Roderick Garr). Man known to be associated with a Markalian smuggling operation. In 2372, Regana Tosh was arrested by Odo on station Deep Space 9 for trafficking in illegal Tallonian crystals. ("Hippocratic Oath" [DS9]).

regenerative fusion. Experimental process developed by Dr. **Ma'Bor Jetrel** in hopes of restoring the inhabitants of **Rinax**, vaporized in the **metreon cascade** attack of 2356, to life. Jetrel planned to use medical records of the victims to identify and isolate a single individual's DNA from the atomic fragments in the **metreon cloud**. Using the **transporter** system aboard the *Starship Voyager*, Jetrel conducted a test of this process in 2371, but found the fragments in the metreon cloud to be too diffuse for successful reintegration. ("Jetrel" [VGR]).

Regent of Palamar. (Lawrence Tierney). Leader of the repressive regime in control of the Palamar nation. The Regent's bitter rival was **General Nassuc**, a former trusted officer. The Regent had intended to hand his entire army over to Nassuc eventually, but she betrayed him by declaring independence for her homeworld. In 2373, the Regent went to station Deep Space 9 to buy devastating biological weapons for use against General Nassuc's people. **Quark** arranged for **Gaila** and **Hagath** to be caught dealing with both the Regent of Palamar and General Nassuc. As a result, the Regent was killed by one of General Nassuc's purification squads. ("Business As Usual" [DS9]). *Lawrence Tierney was previously seen as Cyrus Redblock in "The Big Goodbye" (TNG).*

Regent. SEE: **Worf (mirror).**

Reger. (Harry Townes). Inhabitant of planet **Beta III** during the end of **Landru**'s rule in 2267. Reger owned the inn at which an *Enterprise* landing party sought refuge after the **Red Hour**. For reasons unknown, Reger was immune from absorption into the Body. Along with citizens Tamar and Marphon, Reger was a member of the resistance movement against Landru's rule. ("Return of the Archons" [TOS]).

Reginold. (Leslie Morris). Engineering officer of the **Pakled** vessel ***Mondor***. ("Samaritan Snare" [TNG]).

Registrar. In **Ferengi** mythology, the attendant who awaited the recently deceased at the entrance to the **Divine Treasury**. If the new arrival was worthy to enter, the Registrar then accepted their bribe and ushered them inside. The Ferengi Registrar was much like Charon of Earth's Greek mythology. ("Body Parts" [DS9]). SEE: **Ferengi death rituals**.

Regova eggs. Cardassian delicacy, often served as an appetizer. ("Destiny" [DS9]).

Regrean wheat husks. Agricultural product. A **Xepolite** ship reportedly carried a cargo of Regrean wheat husks in 2370. ("The Maquis, Part II" [DS9]).

Regressives. Extinct minority ethnic group that once lived on Enara Prime. The Regressives shunned all but the most basic technology, which fomented resentment among the rest of the Enaran population. The other Enarans closed the Regressives out of their cities after a curfew hour, and they regarded them as second-class citizens. Ultimately the Regressives were deliberately and systematically exterminated under an operation disguised as a resettlement effort. After they had been eliminated, the Enarans told their descendants a lie: that the Regressives had decided to leave on their own volition, and that they died of disease due to their backward beliefs and unsanitary living conditions. The truth of their death might have been forgotten if not for the courage of an Enaran woman named **Korenna Mirell**. ("Remember" [VGR]).

Regula I Space Laboratory. Deep-space facility located in the **Mutara Sector** near the planetoid **Regula**. Dr. Carol Marcus led a scientific team that developed **Project Genesis** at the Regula I Space Laboratory in the late 23rd century. *(Star Trek II: The Wrath of Khan).*

Regula. Lifeless, Class-D asteroid located in the **Mutara Sector**. Regula was the site of a key test of **Project Genesis** in which a Genesis Device was detonated deep inside the planetoid, resulting in the creation of a large cavern in which life evolved at a dramatically accelerated rate. SEE: **planetary classification system**. *(Star Trek II: The Wrath of Khan).*

Regulan blood worms. Soft and shapeless creatures. Klingon warrior **Korax** compared Regulan blood worms to several *Enterprise* crew members on **Deep Space Station K-7** in 2267. ("The Trouble with Tribbles" [TOS]).

Regulations, Starfleet. SEE: **Starfleet General Orders and Regulations.**

Regulon system. Star system. Destination of the ***Bok'Nor*** before arrival at **Deep Space 9** in 2370. ("The Maquis, Part I" [DS9]). SEE: **golside ore**.

Regulus III. Planet. **Mardah** was accepted to the Science Academy on Regulus III in 2371. ("Fascination" [DS9]).

Regulus V. Planet; homeworld to giant eel-birds who, every 11 years, return to the caverns where they were hatched. ("Amok Time" [TOS]).

Rejac Crystal. A rare objet d'art. The Rejac Crystal was reported to be in the personal collection of **Zibalian** trader **Kivas Fajo**, at least until Fajo's arrest in 2366. ("The Most Toys" [TNG]).

"Rejoined." *Deep Space Nine* episode #78. Teleplay by Ronald D. Moore & René Echevarria. Story by René Echevarria. Directed by Avery Brooks. Stardate 49195.5. *First aired in 1995. Jadzia discovers that a member of a Trill science team carries within her the symbiont to whom Jadzia's symbiont was married in a previous incarnation.* GUEST CAST: Susanna Thompson as **Lenara, Dr.**; Tim Ryan as **Otner, Dr. Bejal**; James Noah as **Pren, Dr Hanor.**; Kenneth Marshall as **Eddington, Michael**. SEE: **artificial wormhole; Barros Inn; Dax, Curzon; Dax, Jadzia; Dax, Tobin; Dax, Torias; graviton wave; *hasperat*; Kahn, Dr. Lenara; Kahn, Nilani; *moba* fruit; Otner, Dr. Bejal; Pren, Dr. Hanor; *ratana* tree; reassociation; Risian perfume; Trill; Tyler, Ensign; *veklava*.**

Rekag-Seronia. Class-M inhabited planet in Federation space. Rekag-Seronia was the site of bitter hostilities between local factions, the **Rekags** and the Seronians. By 2369, this fighting threatened a key Federation shipping route, so **Ambassador Ves Alkar** was assigned there in hopes of mediating a cease-fire between the warring parties. This was the last conflict that Alkar mediated prior to his death. The planet is also known as Seronia. ("Man of the People" [TNG]).

Rekags. One of two historically warring factions on planet **Rekag-Seronia**. Rekag battle cruisers fired on the transport ship ***Dorian*** when that ship was attempting to convey **Ambassador Ves Alkar** to Rekag-Seronia in 2369 in hopes of bringing peace. ("Man of the People" [TNG]).

Rekarri starbursts. Festive beverage, usually served in a tall glass, topped with colorful flowers. ("Warlord" [VGR]).

Rekelen. (Heidi Swedberg). Member of the **Cardassian underground movement**. In 2370, Rekelen, who was a student of Professor **Natima Lang**, was forced to flee **Cardassia** because of his political views. Rekelen, along with Lang and fellow dissident **Hogue**, sought refuge at station **Deep Space 9**, but were forced to flee again when the **Cardassian Central Command** learned of their presence and sentenced them to death. ("Profit and Loss" [DS9]).

Reklar. Cardassian ***Galor*-class** warship, under the command of **Gul Lemec** in 2369. The *Reklar* met the *Enterprise*-D at the Federation-Cardassian border so that Gul Lemec and Captain Jellico could conduct talks about the movements of Cardassian troops and ships along the border. ("Chain of Command, Part I" [TNG]).

Relay Station 47. Remote **Starfleet** communications station near the **Klingon** border. Most of the operations of the station were automated, although a two-person crew provided for nonroutine operations and maintenance. A network of such stations throughout Federation space permits interstellar communication between distant points with much shorter time lags than unboosted **subspace radio** transmissions would require. **Lieutenant Aquiel**

Uhnari, assigned to Relay Station 47 in 2369, was investigated for the murder of her crew mate, **Keith Rocha**, but was exonerated. ("Aquiel" [TNG]). *The Relay Station 47 miniature was designed by Rick Sternbach and was a modification of the* ***cryosatellite*** *from "The Neutral Zone" (TNG), based on a drawing Rick did in the* Star Trek: The Next Generation Technical Manual *(Pocket Books, 1991).*

Relay Station 194. Communications station used to amplify and retransmit subspace messages. Relay Station 194 was off-line for maintenance for several hours in early 2369, and **Relay Station 47** accepted the additional comm traffic for that period. ("Aquiel" [TNG]).

relay satellite. Automated communications station situated near the Gamma Quadrant terminus of the **Bajoran wormhole**. In 2372, under orders from **Admiral Leyton**, Lieutenant Arriaga attached a subspace modulator to the relay satellite to create the appearance that several cloaked ships had come through. ("Paradise Lost" [DS9]).

Reliant*, *U.S.S. Federation starship, ***Miranda* class**, Starfleet registry number NCC-1864. In 2285, the *Reliant*, under the command of Captain **Clark Terrell**, was assigned to survey planets in the **Mutara Sector** in support of **Project Genesis**. During the mission, the *Reliant* was destroyed when it was hijacked by **Khan Noonien Singh**. The ship had been on a scientific mission and was surveying planet **Ceti Alpha V**, on which Khan had been marooned. Khan had left the *Reliant*'s crew behind on Ceti Alpha V. (*Star Trek II: The Wrath of Khan*). *The* Reliant *was designed by Mike Minor and Joe Jennings. The model was built at Industrial Light and Magic under the supervision of Jeff Mann.*

"Relics." *Next Generation* episode #130. Written by Ronald D. Moore. Directed by Alexander Singer. Stardate 46125.3. *First aired in 1993. Captain Montgomery Scott is found to be alive, having survived in a transporter beam after his ship crashed on a Dyson Sphere 75 years ago. "Relics" establishes that Scotty disappeared aboard the* Jenolen *about a year after the events in* Star Trek VI, *and that he remained lost until 2369.* GUEST CAST: Lanei Chapman as **Rager**, **Ensign**; Erick Weiss as Kane, Ensign; James Doohan as **Scott**, **Montgomery**; Stacie Foster as **Bartel**, **Engineer**; Ernie Mirich as Waiter; Majel Barrett as Computer voice. SEE: **Aldebaran whiskey; Bartel, Engineer; Code One Alpha Zero; containment fields; deuterium; dilithium; duotronics; Dyson Sphere; *Enterprise*-A, *U.S.S.*; Fleet Museum; Franklin, Ensign Matt; *Goddard, Shuttlecraft*; gravimetric fluctuation; holodeck; isolinear optical chip; *Jenolen*, *U.S.S.*; Norpin Colony; pattern buffer; Rager, Ensign; Starfleet General Orders and Regulations; rematerialization subroutine; Scott, Montgomery; *Sydney*-class transport; synthehol; Ten-Forward.**

Relliketh. Refugee camp on planet Bajor. **Vedek Bareil** was interned at Relliketh during the Cardassian occupation. ("Shadowplay" [DS9]).

Relora. SEE: **Kazon-Relora**.

Relva VII. Planet; site of a Starfleet facility. Wesley Crusher's first attempt to pass the **Starfleet Academy** entrance exam was made at Relva VII in 2364, under the supervision of **Tac Officer Chang**. ("Coming of Age" [TNG]). *The exterior of the Relva VII station was a matte painting by visual effects supervisor Dan Curry. The painting was a modification of a design Dan had originally done for an episode of the series* Buck Rogers *entitled "Plot to Kill a City."*

REM sleep. In neurophysiology, REM (rapid eye movement) describes a normal state of sleep during which most humanoid dreaming occurs. The condition is so named because the sleeper's eyes, though closed, will often exhibit rapid movement. William Riker experienced neural patterns corresponding to REM sleep after being injured on an away mission to planet **Surata IV** in 2365. ("Shades of Gray" [TNG]). Lack of REM sleep was thought to have caused the psychosis that led the crew of the ***Brattain*** to kill each other in 2367. This lack of REM sleep was apparently caused by attempts at communication by an alien intelligence trapped in a **Tyken's Rift**. ("Night Terrors" [TNG]). *Contrary to popular belief, a lack of dreams is not currently believed to be harmful, except if you are using your dreams as fodder for television scripts.*

remat detonator. Weapon programmed to scramble a **transporter** beam during materialization. Remat detonators could be as small two cubic millimeters in size and could be hidden in clothing or even injected under the skin. Typically used by the **Romulans**, they were also sold on the black market. A remat detonator was used by **Silaran Prin** on stardate 50416 to murder **Trentin Fala**. ("The Darkness and the Light" [DS9]).

rematerialization subroutine. Portion of the operation cycle of a **transporter** that controls the restoration of the matter stream to its original form. **Montgomery Scott** disabled the rematerialization subroutine of the *Jenolen*'s transporters in an attempt to keep himself and Matt Franklin suspended in the beam until help arrived. ("Relics" [TNG]).

"Remember Me." Next Generation episode #79. Written by Lee Sheldon. Directed by Cliff Bole. Stardate 44161.2. *First aired in 1990. A warp-physics experiment gone awry traps Beverly Crusher in her own private universe. This was the 79th episode of Star Trek: The Next Generation, equaling the total episode count of the original Star Trek series. This episode also marked the return of the Traveler, first seen in "Where No One Has Gone Before" (TNG).* GUEST CAST: Eric Menyuk as **Traveler**; Bill Erwin as **Quaice**, **Dr. Dalen**; Colm Meaney as **O'Brien**, **Miles**. SEE: **Crusher, Dr. Beverly; Delos IV; Durenia IV; Hill, Dr. Richard; Kenda II; Kosinski; millicochrane; Quaice, Dr. Dalen; Quaice, Patricia; Selar, Dr.; sickbay; Starbase 133; static warp shell; warp field; transporter ID trace; Traveler; umbilical port; *Wellington*, *U.S.S.***

"Remember." *Voyager* episode #48. Teleplay by Lisa Klink. Story by Brannon Braga & Joe Menosky. Directed by Winrich Kolbe. Stardate 50203.1. *First aired in 1996. When shuttling a group of telepathic aliens to their homeworld, Torres experiences realistic dreams, which turn out to be actual memories of a horrific genocide perpetrated decades ago.* GUEST CAST: Eugene Roche as **Brel**, **Jor**; Charles Esten as **Dathan**; Athena Massey as **Jessen**; Eve H. Massey as **Mirell**, **Jora**; Bruce Davison as **Jareth**; Nancy Kaine as Woman; Tina Reddington as Girl; Majel Barrett as Computer voice. SEE: **Alaris, Dathan; algae puffs; Brel, Jor; Demalos; Enara Prime; Enarans; Farran; Fima system; hoverball; Janeway, Kathryn; Jareth; Jessen; Mirell, Korenna; radioseptics; Regressives; resettlement; Sanric; tarin juice; thermal sweep.**

Remmick, Dexter. (Robert Schenkkan). **Starfleet** officer with the Inspector General's office. Remmick was assigned to inspect the *Starship Enterprise*-D in 2364 when Starfleet Admiral **Gregory Quinn** suspected the existence of a conspiracy deep in the heart of Starfleet. ("Coming of Age" [TNG]). Remmick, later assigned to Starfleet Command, was the victim of the alien intelligence that infiltrated **Starfleet Headquarters** in 2364. Remmick was the unwilling host to the "mother" alien that apparently controlled the parasites that infested numerous Starfleet officers. Both he and the alien were killed by intense phaser fire, after which the

telepathically linked parasites in other officers also died. ("Conspiracy" [TNG]).

Remmil VI. Planet. The inhabitants spin a kind of crystalline webbing that they use to construct buildings. In 2371 a band of **Nausicaan** raiders used an ultrasonic generator to loot the central museum on Remmil VI. ("Heart of Stone" [DS9]).

Remmler Array. Federation orbital facility located above **Arkaria Base**. The Remmler Array was used for baryon decontamination sweeps of starships. The *Enterprise*-D put in at the Remmler Array in 2369. While it was there, a group of terrorists attempted to steal **trilithium** resin from the ship's engines. ("Starship Mine" [TNG]).

Remus. One of the two homeworlds of the **Romulan Star Empire**. ("Balance of Terror" [TOS]). *Mr. Spock's star chart gives this planet's name as Romii, although spoken dialog in the episode uses the name Remus.* SEE: **Romulus**.

Ren, Lidell. (Robin McKee). Widow of **Banean** physicist **Tolen Ren**. Lidell accused *Voyager* crew member Tom Paris of murdering her husband. After an exhaustive investigation by *Voyager* Security Chief Tuvok, Lidell was found to be collaborating with a **Numiri** spy posing as a Banean doctor. ("Ex Post Facto" [VGR]).

Ren, Tolen. (Ray Reinhardt). **Banean** scientist. The inventor of Banean warship technology, Professor Ren developed four generations of navigational arrays for Banean ships. In 2371, Professor Ren was murdered by a **Numiri** spy posing as a Banean doctor to gain valuable weapons information. ("Ex Post Facto" [VGR]). SEE: **Neeka; Ren, Lidell.**

Renaissance*-class starship.** Conjectural designation for a type of Federation vessel. The ***U.S.S. Aries, offered for Riker to command in 2365, was a *Renaissance*-class ship ("The Icarus Factor" [TNG]), as was the ***U.S.S. Hornet*** ("Redemption, Part II" [TNG]). *Named for the period in European history when civilization as we know it had a dramatic rebirth, or renaissance.*

Renegade, U.S.S. Federation starship, *New Orleans* class, registry number NCC-63102, commanded by Captain **Tryla Scott**. The *Renegade* was one of the ships that met the *Enterprise*-D at **Dytallix B** when an alien intelligence attempted to take over Starfleet Command in 2364. ("Conspiracy" [TNG]).

Renewal Scroll. Symbolic paper scroll on which participants of the **Bajoran Gratitude Festival** wrote their problems. They then placed the scrolls to be burned in a special brazier so that their troubles could symbolically turn to ashes along with the scroll. ("Fascination" [DS9]).

rengazo. Seasoning used by Neelix along with dill weed when he prepared Porakan eggs as a breakfast food for Tuvok on the *Voyager* in 2373. ("Flashback" [VGR]).

Renhol, Doctor. (Lisa Banes). Member of the **Trill Symbiosis Commission**. Doctor Renhol participated in the evaluation of a Trill **initiate** named Jadzia. In 2371, when the joined Trill known as **Jadzia Dax** became ill, Doctor Renhol oversaw her treatment. ("Equilibrium" [DS9]). SEE: **Belar, Joran; isoboramine.**

Renora. (Anne Haney). Judge who presided over **Jadzia Dax**'s extradition trial on Deep Space 9 in 2369 for the murder of General Ardelon Tandro. Renora was 100 years old and said that at her age, she didn't want to waste time with needless legal maneuvers. ("Dax" [DS9]). SEE: **Klaestron IV; Tandro, General Ardelon; Curzon Dax**. *Anne Haney also played Rishon Uxbridge in "The Survivors" (TNG).*

Replicating Center. Facility aboard a *Galaxy*-class starship containing several replicator terminals at which crew members could order a wide variety of products that would be produced on command. Worf and Data went there in search of a wedding present for **Miles** and **Keiko O'Brien**. ("Data's Day" [TNG]).

replicative fading. A loss of genetic information occurring when an organism is repeatedly cloned. After several generations of cloning, replicative fading can become serious, resulting in subtle errors creeping into chromosomes, eventually yielding a nonviable **clone**. The **Mariposa** colony had depended on cloning to maintain its population, but fell victim to replicative fading. ("Up the Long Ladder" [TNG]).

replicator rations. Aboard the *Starship Voyager*, the limited power for **replicator**s was conserved by issuing replicator ration credits to each crew member. ("The Cloud" [VGR]). SEE: **mess hall.**

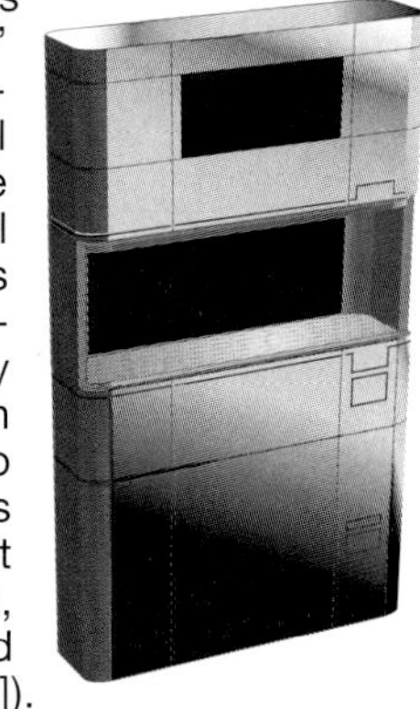

replicator. Device that uses **transporter** technology to dematerialize a quantity of matter, then to rematerialize it in another form, often used to produce food. Replicators are used aboard Federation starships to provide a much wider variety of meal choices to crew members than would be available if actual foodstuffs had to be carried, since the selection available is limited only by software. Most people find replicated food indistinguishable from "original" food, although some individuals claim to be able to tell the difference. Captain Picard carried a few cases of real caviar aboard his ship for special occasions because he felt that replicated caviar was not quite as good as the real thing. ("Sins of the Father" [TNG]). As a safety measure, starship replicators are programmed not to produce fatal poisons. ("Death Wish" [VGR]). It is possible to convert a food replicator into a small transporter by realigning the replicator's matter-energy conversion matrix. ("Visionary" [DS9]). Replicator operation normally generated **nucleonic radiation**, although Federation replicators were designed to prevent user exposure to such hazardous energy. Replicator technology was not common to cultures in the Delta Quadrant, including the technologically advanced **Kazon Collective**. ("State of Flux" [VGR]). Very large replicators, such as class-4 CFI industrial replicators, could be employed for large-scale fabrication. The Federation Council provided two such units to the Bajoran government after the end of the Cardassian occupation. The council also provided four industrial replicators to the Cardassian government to help the Cardassians cope with the aftermath of the Klingon invasion of 2372. ("For the Cause" [DS9]). *"Flashback" (VGR) establishes that replicators were not in use aboard Federation starships in*

Captain Kirk's day, suggesting that the ***food slot****s on his ship were some kind of mechanical delivery or preparation system.*

Replimat. Sidewalk cafe located on the **Promenade** on Deep Space 9. ("Emissary, Parts I and II [DS9]). A large assortment of foods could be ordered from the Replimat, satisfying different cultural palates. The Replimat did not, however, stock Ferengi dishes. ("Rules of Acquisition" [DS9]).

reptohumanoid hatchling. Infant life-form discovered by *Voyager* crew members in 2372 on a Class-M planet in the Delta Quadrant. The reptillean entity was a member of a technologically sophisticated species that may not have been native to that world, designated **Planet Hell** by *Voyager* personnel. ("Parturition" [VGR]).

Klingon skull stew, served at Replimat.

Republic, U.S.S. Federation starship, *Constitution* class, Starfleet registry number NCC-1371. **James Kirk** and **Ben Finney** served together on the *Republic* around 2250. Ensign Kirk once found Finney had left a circuit to the atomic matter piles open. Kirk logged the error, and Finney was sent to the bottom of the promotion list. ("Court Martial" [TOS]).

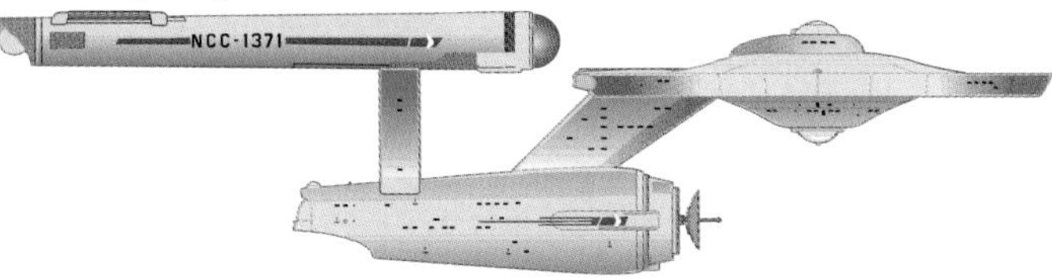

Repulse, U.S.S. Federation starship, *Excelsior* class, registry number NCC-2544, **Captain Taggert** commanding. **Dr. Katherine Pulaski** served aboard the *Repulse* prior to her assignment to the *Enterprise*-D in 2365. ("The Child" [TNG], "Unnatural Selection" [TNG]). *Named for the British battle cruiser that fought in Earth's World War II.*

"Requiem for Methuselah." Original Series episode #76. Written by Jerome Bixby. Directed by Murray Golden. Stardate 5843.7. *First aired in 1969. An immortal man tries to build the perfect woman, but she falls in love with James Kirk instead.* GUEST CAST: James Daly as **Flint**; Louise Sorel as **Kapec**, **Rayna**; John Buonomo as Orderly; Phil Adams as Flint's stunt double; Paul Baxley as Kirk's stunt double. SEE: **Brack, Mr.; Constantinople; Flint; Holberg 917G; irillium; Kapec, Rayna; M-4; Rigelian fever; ryetalyn; Saurian brandy.**

Research Station 75. Federation outpost located on a planetary surface. The *Enterprise*-D visited there in 2369 to pick up **Ensign Stefan DeSeve**, who was returning to Federation custody after having previously renounced his Federation citizenship in 2349 to live on **Romulus**. ("Face of the Enemy" [TNG]).

resettlement. Euphemism used by the **Enarans** to refer to the deliberate and systematic extermination of all members of the ethnic group known as the **Regressives**. ("Remember" [VGR]).

Resh. (Charles Emmett). Military advisor to the tyrant **Tieran** of the **Ilari**. When the consciousness of Tieran killed the Autarch and staged a coup of Ilari in 2373, Resh was given the honorary title of First Castallan. ("Warlord" [VGR]).

"Resistance." *Voyager* episode #28. Teleplay by Lisa Klink. Story by Michael Jan Friedman & Kevin J. Ryan. Directed by Winrich Kolbe. No stardate given. *First aired in 1995. Tuvok and Torres are captured and jailed by a hostile occupational race called the Mokra. Meanwhile, Janeway is sheltered by a gentle but confused old resistance fighter who believes she is his daughter. Episode co-writer Kevin J. Ryan was the editor at Pocket Books for the first edition of* The Star Trek Encyclopedia. GUEST CAST: Alan Scarfe as **Augris**; Tom Todoroff as **Darod**; Glenn Morshower as Guard #1; Joel Grey as **Caylem**. SEE: **Alsaurian resistance movement; Augris; Caylem; Darod; metaphasic shield; Mokra Order; phased ion cannon; Ralkana; *talsa* root soup; tellerium.**

resolution failure. Malfunction of a holodeck holographic imagery system, which can cause the loss of background environments within the simulation. Resolution failures, allowing the holodeck grid to be seen, occurred in the *Enterprise*-D holodecks following the ship's exposure to plasmonic energy in the atmosphere of planet **Boraal II** in 2370. ("Homeward" [TNG]).

Resolution, The. On planet **Kaelon II**, the ritual ending of one's life at age 60. The Kaelon people considered this to be a dignified way to conclude a life, and viewed it to be vastly preferable to having the aged population waste away in "death watch facilities." The Resolution celebrated the guest of honor with a special gathering of friends and relatives, where that person's life and achievements would be recognized. The Resolution has been in practice for over a millennium, and Kaelon society permits no exceptions. ("Half a Life" [TNG]). SEE: **Timicin, Dr.**

"Resolutions." *Voyager* episode #41. Written by Jeri Taylor. Directed by Alexander Singer. Stardate 49690.1. *First aired in 1996. A deadly virus infects Chakotay and Janeway, and she turns command over to Tuvok, ordering him to abandon them on a planet that will shield them from the disease's effects.* GUEST CAST: Susan Diol as **Pel, Danara**; Simon Billig as **Hogan**; Bahni Turpin as **Swinn**. SEE: **antimatter pod; Benaren; Chakotay; Janeway, Kathryn; Kes; Kolopak; modular shelter; osteogenic stimulator; Pel, Danara; Shmullus; sonic shower; stasis unit; Talaxian tomato; Tuvok; Vidiians.**

resonance tissue scan. Medical diagnostic test used by Starfleet physicians to screen for infection. Dr. Crusher ran a resonance tissue scan on **Geordi La Forge** when his **VISOR** malfunctioned after he was kidnapped by the **solanagen-based aliens.** ("Schisms" [TNG]).

resonant particle wave. Energy-dampening emission used by the **Delta Quadrant** civilization known as the **Swarm**. The resonant particle wave caused warp fields to collapse, rendering warp propulsion inoperative. ("The Swarm" [VGR]).

resonators. Devices designed to create powerful vibrations in underground geologic strata. *Enterprise*-D crew personnel modified a number of **Class-1 probe**s to serve as resonator devices delivered from orbit to the subsurface of planet **Drema IV**. Once delivered, the resonators emitted harmonic vibrations that successfully shattered the lattices of dilithium strata, thus halting the disintegration of the planet. ("Pen Pals" [TNG]).

Ressik. Community of the now-dead planet **Kataan**, once home of the ironweaver **Kamin**. Under the influence of the Kataan probe, Jean-Luc Picard experienced a lifetime of memories from Ressik. The probe had been launched a thousand years ago by the Kataans in the hopes it would someday encounter someone like Picard through whom the planet's people might be remembered. ("The Inner Light" [TNG]).

Ressikan flute. Small musical wind instrument, resembling a tin flute, native to the community of **Ressik** on the now-dead planet **Kataan**. The space probe launched from Kataan contained

memories from the planet, as well as a single artifact, a Ressikan flute. **Jean-Luc Picard**, who received the Kataan memories, including the knowledge of how to play the Ressikan flute, also received the artifact, which he treasured. ("The Inner Light" [TNG]). SEE: **Kamin.** Picard enjoyed playing his Ressikan flute in musical duets with **Neela Daren** when the two were romantically involved in 2369. ("Lessons" [TNG]). *Picard also played the instrument in "A Fistful of Datas" (TNG). The haunting melody that Picard played on the flute was written by* Star Trek *composer Jay Chattaway.*

Retaya. (Carlos LaCamara). **Flaxian assassin**. Retaya was hired by the **Tal Shiar** in 2371 to kill **Cardassian** exile **Elim Garak** on **Deep Space 9**. Retaya was unsuccessful, and subsequently was killed when the Tal Shiar blew up his spacecraft. DS9 Security Chief **Odo** confirmed Retaya's connection to the Tal Shiar and the attempt on Garak's life through a highly placed informant in the Cardassian government. ("Improbable Cause" [DS9]). *Odo's shadowy, unnamed informant was played by Joseph Ruskin, who previously played Galt in "The Gamesters of Triskelion" [TOS] and Tumek in "House of Quark" [DS9].*

reticular formation. A system of cells in the medulla oblongata of many humanoid brains. This area controls the overall degree of nervous system activity. The **Ktarian game** was found to activate the reticular formation of the brain. ("The Game" [TNG]).

retinal scan. Method of verifying an individual's identification by scanning the pattern of blood vessels in that person's retina. The technique was believed to be more reliable (and more difficult to falsify) than fingerprinting. Kirk had to submit to a retinal scan to gain access to the **Project Genesis** files. *(Star Trek II: The Wrath of Khan).* Retinal scans were also used on planet **Bajor** for identification. In 2370, **Kira Nerys** identified a secret file from fragments of **Vedek Bareil**'s retinal scan. ("Collaborator" [DS9]).

retinal imaging scan. Medical test used to verify the presence of activity in the visual cortex. ("The Passenger" [DS9]).

Retnax V. Medication used to treat certain forms of nearsightedness. McCoy noted he had not prescribed Retnax V to Kirk because the good captain was allergic to it. *(Star Trek II: The Wrath of Khan).*

retroviral vaccines. Attenuated retroviral compounds, used for preventative inoculation. These vaccines can be combined with other components to create a **biogenic weapon**. ("Preemptive Strike" [TNG]).

retrovirus. Member of a family of viruses, *Retroviridae*, which reproduce by using a host cell to reproduce **DNA**, rather than the **RNA** which most viruses produce. In order to combat an outbreak of **Barclay's Protomorphosis Syndrome** aboard the Enterprise-D in 2370, Data used the **amniotic fluid** of Nurse **Ogawa**'s pregnancy as a template for a retrovirus. This retrovirus, once activated, rewrote the DNA of the mutated **T-cell**, which caused the symptoms of the syndrome to abate. ("Genesis" [TNG]). *While this retrovirus was a good one, most of them are associated with cancers, mostly in animals. There is also some research linking a retrovirus with AIDS.* The **Taresians** engineered a retrovirus that they placed on several planets in the **Delta Quadrant**. The retrovirus would alter the DNA of a male host's body, making it Taresian. The retrovirus also imparted an instinctive urge to return to Taresia, where the male would be killed by denucleation. ("Favorite Son" [VGR]).

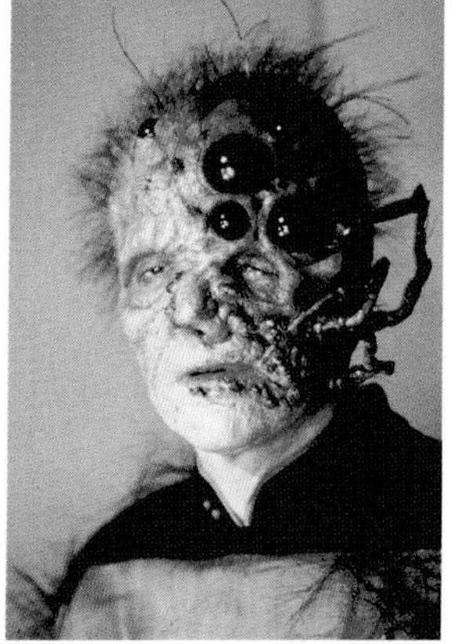

Rettick. (Marron E. Willis). **Kazon-Nistrim** officer who received information concerning Tom Paris's crossing of the **transwarp** threshold from ***U.S.S. Voyager*** crew member Jonas. ("Threshold" [VGR]). In 2372, while serving on First Maje **Culluh**'s ship, Rettick was contacted by *Starship Voyager* engineer **Michael Jonas**. ("Alliances" [VGR]).

"Return of the Archons." *Original Series* episode #22. Teleplay by Boris Sobelman. Story by Gene Roddenberry. Directed by Joseph Pevney. Stardate 3156.2. *First aired in 1967. The* Enterprise*, investigating the disappearance of the* Starship Archon*, finds a planet ruled by a computer called Landru. The computer now wants to destroy the* Enterprise *in order to protect what it believes to be a perfect society.* GUEST CAST: Harry Townes as **Reger**; Torin Thatcher as **Marphon**; Brioni Farrell as **Tula**; Sid Haig as First lawgiver; Charles Macaulay as **Landru**; Jon Lormer as Tamar; Morgan Farley as **Hacom**; Christopher Held as **Lindstrom**; Sean Morgan as **O'Neil, Lieutenant**; Ralph Maurer as **Bilar**; David L. Ross as Guard; Miko Mayama as **Tamura, Yeoman**; Eddie Paskey as **Leslie, Mr.**; Barbara Weber as Dancing woman; Bob Clark as Stunt double. SEE: **absorbed; *Archon, U.S.S.*; Archons; Beta III; Bilar; Body; C-111; Festival; Hacom; Hall of Audiences; Landru; Lawgivers; Leslie, Mr.; Lindstrom; Marphon; O'Neil, Lieutenant; Red Hour; Reger; Tula; Valley**.

"Return to Grace." *Deep Space Nine* episode #86. Teleplay by Hans Beimler. Story by Tom Benko. Directed by Jonathan West. No stardate given. *First aired in 1996. Kira becomes an unlikely ally of a demoted Dukat when they discover that Klingons have attacked an outpost where Cardassians and Bajorans were conducting talks.* GUEST CAST: Marc Alaimo as **Dukat, Gul**; Cyia Batten as **Ziyal**; Casey Biggs as **Damar, Glinn**; John K. Shull as **K'Temang**. SEE: **Alvinian melons; Amleth Prime; Cardassians; Cardassian phase-disruptor rifle; cloaking device, Klingon; Damar, Glinn; disruptors, system 5; Dopa system; Dukat, Gul; emission nebula; *Groumall*; Jalanda; K'Temang; Kolaish spice oil; Korma; Loval; Marratt, Gul; phaser type-3; Rakal; Shakaar Edon; spring wine; Tora Ziyal.**

"Return to Tomorrow." Original Series episode #51. Written by John Kingsbridge. Directed by Ralph Senensky. Stardate 4768.3. *First aired in 1968. Two lovers and their enemy from a society that died a half-million years ago "borrow" the bodies of* Enterprise *people so that they may build android bodies for themselves. But the temptations of human flesh prove too much, even for these beings of immense wisdom and power. John Kingsbridge was the pen name of writer John T. Dugan.* GUEST CAST: Diana Muldaur as **Mulhall, Dr. Ann**; Cindy Lou as *Enterprise* nurse; Majel Barrett as **Chapel, Christine**; William Shatner as **Sargon**, body of; James Doohan as **Sargon**, voice of; Eddie Paskey as Security guard. SEE: **android; Henoch; metabolic reduction injection; Mulhall, Dr. Ann; negaton hydrocoils; Sargon's planet; Sargon; Thalassa; Vulcans.**

"Reunion." *Next Generation* episode #81. Teleplay by Thomas Perry & Jo Perry and Ronald D. Moore & Brannon Braga. Story by Drew Deighan and Thomas Perry & Jo Perry. Directed by Jonathan Frakes. Stardate 44246.3. *First aired in 1990. Worf discovers he is a father, and Picard is asked to help choose the next leader of the Klingon Empire. This episode was a sequel to "The Emissary" (TNG), in which K'Ehleyr first appeared. It continued Worf's story from "Sins of the Father" (TNG), and later was further continued in "Redemption, Parts I and II" (TNG). "Reunion" (TNG) is the first appearance of Worf's son, Alexander.* GUEST CAST: Suzie Plakson as **K'Ehleyr**; Robert O'Reilly as **Gowron**; Patrick Massett as **Duras**; Charles Cooper as **K'mpec**; Jon Steuer as **Rozhenko, Alexander**; Michael Rider as Security guard; April Grace as Transporter technician; Basil Wallace as Klingon guard #1; Mirron E. Willis as Klingon guard #2. SEE:

Arbiter of Succession; *bat'leth*; *Buruk*; Duras; Gamma Arigulon system; Gowron; *ha'DIBah*; Hubble, Chief; *ja'chuq; jIH dok*; K'Ehleyr; K'mpec; Kahless the Unforgettable; Klingon attack cruiser; Klingon Empire; *LaSalle, U.S.S.*; *mev yap*; molecular-decay detonator; painstik, Klingon; Picard, Jean-Luc; Rite of Succession, Klingon; Rozhenko, Alexander; Rozhenko, Helena; *Sonchi* ceremony; Starbase 73; Tholians; triceron; Veridium Six; Vorn; Worf.

Revalus. Famous writer. Revalus created a work entitled ***The Wait***. ("The Muse" [DS9]). SEE: **visceral writing**.

Revere, U.S.S. Scout vessel, Starfleet registry number NCC-595. *The* Revere *was not seen, but was mentioned in a Starfleet communique overheard at the **Epsilon IX** Monitoring Station, ordered to rendezvous with the* U.S.S. Columbia *by Commodore Probert, a gag reference to production illustrator Andrew Probert. (Star Trek: The Motion Picture).*

reverse-ratcheting router. Special tool used to create a gouge. ("By Inferno's Light" [DS9]).

Rex. (Rod Arrants). A fictional bartender in the world of pulp detective **Dixon Hill**, and the owner of Rex's Bar. The Dixon Hill holodeck program, based on the Dixon Hill novels and short stories, included a holographic representation of Rex. The character attracted the romantic interest of **Lwaxana Troi**, who was unaware that Rex was not a real person, when she entered a holodeck simulation being run by **Jean-Luc Picard**. ("Manhunt" [TNG]).

Reyab. Kobliad transport vessel. The *Reyab* carried **Kobliad** security officer **Kajada** and her prisoner **Rao Vantika**. The *Reyab* caught fire near Bajoran space in 2369. A runabout from station Deep Space 9 responded to the *Reyab*'s distress call. ("The Passenger" [DS9]).

reyamilk soak. Soothing bath experience available on the pleasure planet Risa. ("Let He Who Is Without Sin..." [DS9]).

Reyga, Dr. (Peter Slutsker). Ferengi scientist who invented a revolutionary metaphasic-shield technology in 2369. Though his invention was treated with skepticism by most of the scientific community, he found an unlikely ally in **Dr. Beverly Crusher**. Dr. Reyga was invited aboard the *Enterprise*-D, along with other specialists in subspace technology, in order to test his new shield. The test was apparently unsuccessful, and shortly thereafter Dr. Reyga was found dead, the victim of a plasma surge. Dr. Crusher was able to prove that Reyga had been murdered, and that his **metaphasic shield** was indeed a viable technology. ("Suspicions" [TNG]). SEE: **Jo'Bril.**

RF power conduit. Waveguide device used for radio-frequency energy transmission. RF power conduits are found in the upper pylon docking systems on station Deep Space 9. ("Whispers" [DS9]).

Rhada, Lieutenant. (Naomi Pollock). *Enterprise* crew member. Rhada served at the helm when a landing party was stranded at the **Kalandan outpost** in 2268. ("That Which Survives" [TOS]).

Rhodes, Sandra. (Amy Pietz). Security officer aboard the *U.S.S. Enterprise*-D in 2370. She was assigned to protect **Jason Vigo** while he was a visitor on the ship. ("Bloodlines" [TNG]).

rhodium nitrite. Metallic compound based on rhodium, an element of the platinum group. Rhodium nitrites and selenium can be reformulated and synthesized to form the biogenic agent cobalt diselenide. ("For the Uniform" [DS9]).

Rhomboid Dronegar Sector. Region of space. Origin of a distress call received by the *Enterprise*-D from a disabled **Pakled** ship in 2365. ("Samaritan Snare" [TNG]).

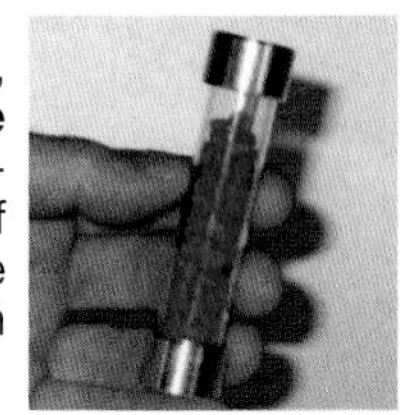

Rhuludian crystals. A powerful narcotic, banned by authorities near the **Nekrit Expanse** of the **Delta Quadrant**. Ingesting one Rhuludian crystal was reputed to make days of tedious travel seem like moments of exquisite rapture. **Sutok** was a dealer in Rhuludian crystals. ("Fair Trade" [VGR]).

Rhymus Major. Planet in the binary Rhymus system. Quark created a **holosuite** program of a picnic using Rhymus Major as the locale. ("Profit and Loss" [DS9]).

Rib. (Beans Morocco). Mentally unbalanced inmate of the **Akritirian prison satellite** while Ensign Harry Kim and Lieutenant Tom Paris were there on stardate 50156.2. ("The Chute" [VGR]).

ribocyatic flux. Condition where an organism's DNA is being actively rewritten. Ribocyatic flux was a later symptom of **Barclay's Protomorphosis Syndrome**. The shifting genetic codes caused cellular mutations which manifested themselves as organs and behavioral traits of earlier genetic forms. ("Genesis" [TNG]).

ribonucleic acid. SEE: **RNA.**

ribosome infusion. Medical treatment procedure. Dr. Crusher prescribed a ribosome infusion to help the injured Romulan **Patahk** after exposure to the surface conditions on **Galorndon Core** in 2366. The only compatible donor on the *Enterprise*-D was Worf, who refused to cooperate. ("The Enemy" [TNG]).

Rice, Captain Paul. (Marco Rodriguez). Commander of the ***U.S.S. Drake*** when it was destroyed at planet **Minos** in 2364. Rice was a highly regarded officer, a risk taker, and a friend to William Riker. Rice was offered the chance to command the *Drake* after Riker declined the job. Rice was later killed at Minos, along with the rest of his crew, by an ancient but still-active weapons system. ("The Arsenal of Freedom" [TNG]). *Marco Rodriguez also played Glinn Telle in "The Wounded" (TNG). Rice was named for a character in Gene Roddenberry's series* The Lieutenant.

Richardson. *Enterprise*-D crew member who was killed while manually controlling the **thermal deflectors** against a fierce firestorm on planet **Bersallis III** in 2369. ("Lessons" [TNG]).

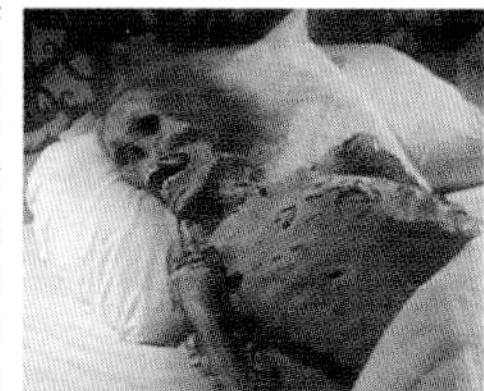

Richey, Colonel Stephen. Commander of the **NASA** ship ***Charybdis*** on the ill-fated third manned attempt to explore beyond Earth's solar system. Richey was the only survivor when the *Charybdis*'s crew was accidentally killed by an unknown alien intelligence. In an effort to atone for the tragic deaths of the *Charybdis* crew, the intelligence attempted to create a natural human environment in which Richey could live out the remainder of his life. Unfortunately, the aliens used a badly written novel—***Hotel Royale,*** by Todd Matthews—as the model for this environment, thus creating a bizarre purgatory in which Richey eventually died. ("The Royale" [TNG]).

Richter's scale of culture. Measurement used to describe relative levels of cultural development in planetary civilizations. Spock said the agrarian inhabitants on planet **Organia** were a D-minus on Richter's scale of culture: primitive but peaceful.

Spock's assessment was later found to be wrong when the Organians turned out to be incredibly advanced **noncorporeal life**-forms. ("Errand of Mercy" [TOS]).

Ricky. (Angela Dohrmann). Holographic character, a beautiful American woman who frequented **Chez Sandrine** in Tom Paris's holodeck re-creation of the establishment. Paris was very fond of Ricky, and included her in all of his holoprograms. ("The Cloud" [VGR]).

riddinite. Brick-like building material. The **Albino**'s compound on planet Secarus IV was made of riddinite. ("Blood Oath" [DS9]). *The exterior of the Albino's compound was actually a Los Angeles building designed by Frank Lloyd Wright. The real building was supplemented by a matte painting supervised by Gary Hutzel, supplemented with a miniature by Karl Martin.*

Rifkin, Captain. Starfleet officer and starship commander. In 2373 Captain Rifkin attended what would have been the signing ceremony for **Bajor**'s entrance into the Federation held at Deep Space 9. ("Rapture" [DS9]).

Riga, Stano. Twenty-third-century comedian who specialized in humor based on quantum mathematics. Riga was considered one of the funniest of human comedians. A simulated version of Riga was programmed into the *Enterprise*-D holodeck computer, but **Data**, who was studying the concept of humor, thought Riga's material too esoteric. ("The Outrageous Okona" [TNG]).

Rigel II. The second planet in the Rigel system. Dr. Leonard McCoy once met two scantily clad women in a chorus line at a cabaret on Rigel II. The pair was re-created from McCoy's imagination in 2267 on the **amusement park planet** in the Omicron Delta region. ("Shore Leave" [TOS]).

Rigel IV. Planet; site of serial killings of women in 2266. These murders were attributed to an unknown individual called Beratis, which was later learned to be a malevolent energy creature who left Rigel IV in the body of **Mr. Hengist**, who traveled to planet Argelius II, where he committed more murders using a knife from the **Argus River region** of Rigel IV. ("Wolf in the Fold" [TOS]). A brilliant astronomer with a fondness for **Lwaxana Troi** resided on Rigel IV. He once named a star after Lwaxana, or so she claimed. ("Half a Life" [TNG]). In 2370, **Keiko O'Brien** attended a hydroponics conference on Rigel IV. ("The Wire" [DS9]).

Rigel V. The fifth planet in the Rigel system. Site where an experimental drug was tested to see if the production of blood elements in a humanoid body could be accelerated. Spock suggested this drug might be useful for Ambassador **Sarek** during a critical heart operation. ("Journey to Babel" [TOS]). SEE: **Rigelians; T-negative**.

Rigel VII. Seventh planet in the Rigel system. The site of a violent conflict in 2254 involving *Enterprise* crew personnel under the command of Captain **Christopher Pike** and the humanoid inhabitants of that planet. Three *Enterprise* crew members, including Pike's yeoman, were killed, and seven others were injured. The incident, which Pike later blamed on his own carelessness, took place just prior to the *Enterprise*'s first mission to planet **Talos IV**. ("The Cage," "The Menagerie, Part II [TOS]). SEE: **Kaylar**. In the 2360s, **Kobliad** criminal **Rao Vantika** caused computer systems on Rigel VII to crash, using a **subspace shunt**, similar to the one he used in 2369 on station Deep Space 9. ("The Passenger" [DS9]). *The matte painting of the Rigel VII fortress seen in Pike's Talosian illusion was later re-used as **Flint**'s castle in "Requiem for Methuselah" (TOS).*

Rigel XII. Barely habitable Class-M planet, racked by fierce storms. Site of a small lithium mining operation headed by **Ben Childress**. The *Enterprise* visited the mining station in 2266 to obtain needed **lithium crystals** to restore operation of the ship's engines. ("Mudd's Women" [TOS]).

Rigel*-class starship.** Conjectural designation for a type of Federation ship. The ***U.S.S. Tolstoy, destroyed in the battle of Wolf 359, was a *Rigel*-class starship ("The Best of Both Worlds, Part II" [TNG]), as was the ***U.S.S. Akagi*** ("Redemption, Part II" [TNG]).

Rigel. Star, also known as Beta Orionis. Rigel is a bright supergiant star, visible from Earth as one of the "legs" in the constellation Orion (the hunter). Rigel is the primary of a star system containing at least 12 planets, at least five of which are inhabited. SEE: **Rigel II; Rigel IV; Rigel V; Rigel VII; Rigel XII**.

Rigelian fever. Deadly disease resembling bubonic plague. An outbreak of Rigelian fever threatened the *Enterprise* crew in 2269, necessitating that a landing party beam down to planetoid **Holberg 917G** in search of the antidote, **ryetalyn**. ("Requiem for Methuselah" [TOS]).

Rigelian freighter. Spacecraft. A Rigelian freighter was used to run interference between the runabout taking **Croden** to the planet **Rakhar** and a **Miradorn** ship in 2369. ("Vortex" [DS9]).

Rigelian Kassaba fever. Disease. As a ruse to regain control of the *Enterprise* in 2268 when it was commandeered by the **Kelvans**, Dr. McCoy claimed that Spock suffered from Rigelian Kassaba fever and required treatment with **stokaline** injections. ("By Any Other Name" [TOS]).

Rigelians. Humanoid species with a physiology similar to that of **Vulcans**. A drug to speed up reproduction and replacement of blood was experimentally used with success on **Rigel V**. ("Journey to Babel" [TOS]).

"Rightful Heir." *Next Generation* episode #149. Teleplay by Ronald D. Moore. Story by James E. Brooks. Directed by Winrich Kolbe. Stardate 46852.2. *First aired in 1993. Worf goes in search of his faith and finds the revered Klingon prophet Kahless the Unforgettable, returned from the dead.* GUEST CAST: Alan Oppenheimer as **Koroth**; Robert O'Reilly as **Gowron**; Norman Snow as **Torin**; Charles Esten as **Divok**; Kevin Conway as **Kahless the Unforgettable**; Majel Barrett as Computer voice. SEE: **Alawanir Nebula; *bat'leth*; Boreth; Divok; Gariman Sector; Gowron; Kahless the Unforgettable; Kirom, Knife of; Klingon Empire; Klingon High Council; Klingons; Koroth; Kri'stak Volcano; Kurn; Lusor; Molor; No'Mat; Quin'lat; *Sto-Vo-Kor*; Story of the Promise, The; Torigan, Ensign; Torin; *Vorch-doh-baghk, Kahless!*; *warnog*; Worf.**

Riker, Jean-Luc. (Chris Demetral). Alter-ego of **Barash**, who assumed the role of Riker's ten-year-old son in the hopes that Riker would play with him. In Barash's fantasy, Jean-Luc Riker had been named after **Jean-Luc Picard**. ("Future Imperfect" [TNG]).

Riker, Kyle. (Mitchell Ryan). Father to *Enterprise*-D Executive Officer **William Riker**. Kyle Riker was a civilian strategist advising

Starfleet in a **Tholian** conflict in 2353. The starbase he was working from was attacked by the Tholians and all station personnel except for Riker were killed. Future *Enterprise*-D Medical Officer **Katherine Pulaski** cared for Riker, and the two became romantically involved. Pulaski later recalled that she would have married him, but Riker's priority was his career. ("The Icarus Factor" [TNG]).

Riker, Thaddius. Union Army officer during Earth's United States Civil War, and ancestor of Starfleet officer **William T. Riker**. Colonel Riker was the commander of the 102nd New York during Sherman's march on Atlanta, and had the nickname "Old Iron Boots." In 1864, he was wounded at Pine Mountain. **Quinn**, a member of the Q Continuum, helped the wounded Thaddius Riker back from the front line, probably saving his life. ("Death Wish" [VGR]).

Riker, Thomas. (Jonathan Frakes). An exact duplicate of William T. Riker, created in 2361 during a **transporter** accident when the ***U.S.S. Potemkin*** was evacuating the science team on planet **Nervala IV**. One copy of Riker returned safely to the *Potemkin*, while the other was reflected by the planet's **distortion field** and materialized back on the surface of Nervala IV. The existence of the duplicate Riker was not discovered until 2369 when the *Starship Enterprise*-D returned to Nervala IV during a brief respite in the distortion field. This Riker had lived alone for eight years on the planet's surface. Once rescued, this Riker decided to use his middle name, Thomas, to distinguish himself from his copy, who had since been promoted to commander. Thomas indicated a desire to continue in Starfleet and was assigned to the ***U.S.S. Gandhi***. Thomas took with him a cherished trombone, a gift from his twin. It should be noted that the individual known as Thomas Riker has just as valid a claim to being the "original" as does his duplicate known as William Riker. ("Second Chances" [TNG]). Lieutenant Thomas Riker remained aboard the *Gandhi* for little more than a year before abandoning Starfleet and joining the **Maquis**. As a member of the Maquis, he impersonated his double in 2371 and commandeered the *U.S.S.* ***Defiant*** from **Deep Space 9** to investigate a suspected **Cardassian** military buildup in the **Orias system**. After Riker was apprehended, he agreed to give himself up to the Cardassians to be sentenced to life at the **Lazon II** labor camp. In exchange, the Cardassians promised to allow his Maquis crew and the *Defiant* itself to return to the Federation. ("Defiant" [DS9]).

Riker, William T. (Jonathan Frakes). Executive officer of the *Starships* ***Enterprise*-D** and ***Enterprise*-E** under the command of Captain **Jean-Luc Picard.** ("Encounter at Farpoint" [TNG], *Star Trek: First Contact)*. Starfleet serial number SC 231-427. ("Gambit, Part I" [TNG]).

William Thomas Riker was born in Valdez, Alaska, on Earth in 2335. Riker's mother died when he was only two years old, and he was raised by his father, **Kyle Riker**. The elder Riker abandoned his son at age 15, an act that William held against his father until 2365 when, at age 30, William was reunited with Kyle aboard the *Enterprise*-D. ("The Icarus Factor" [TNG]). William graduated from Starfleet Academy in 2357, and was ranked eighth in his class at graduation. As of 2369, he had been decorated five times. ("Chain of Command, Part I" [TNG]). Riker's ancestors included Colonel **Thaddius Riker**, also known as "Old Iron Boots Riker," who fought in Earth's American civil war. ("Death Wish" [VGR]).

Riker's first assignment after graduating from the academy was as helm officer aboard the *U.S.S. Pegasus*, a ship that disappeared in 2358 under mysterious circumstances. Years later, it was revealed that *Pegasus* Captain **Erik Pressman** had been illegally testing a Federation **cloaking device** in violation of the **Treaty of Algeron**. The crew of the *Pegasus* mutinied to try to prevent Pressman from testing the device. Riker fought to defend his captain, and Riker and Pressman were the only two to escape when the ship apparently exploded. Afterwards, Pressman suppressed all records of the incident. ("The *Pegasus*" [TNG]). Early in his Starfleet career, Riker was stationed on planet **Betazed** (*pictured*) ("Ménage à Troi" [TNG]), where he became romantically involved with psychology student **Deanna Troi**. Riker, then a lieutenant, chose to make his Starfleet career his priority over his relationship with Deanna, and accepted a posting to the ***U.S.S. Potemkin***. While aboard the *Potemkin*, Riker led a rescue mission to planet **Nervala IV** and was subsequently promoted to lieutenant commander and commended for "exceptional valor" during the rescue. It was not realized until years later that a transporter malfunction during the final beam-out caused an identical copy of Riker to be created on the planet's surface. ("Second Chances" [TNG]). SEE: **Riker, Thomas**. William Riker was later promoted to executive officer aboard the ***U.S.S. Hood***, where he served under the command of **Captain Robert DeSoto**.

Riker joined the *Enterprise*-D at planet **Deneb IV**, having transferred from the *Hood*. ("Encounter at Farpoint, Parts I and II" [TNG]). Riker accepted the *Enterprise*-D posting, despite the fact that he'd been offered command of the ***U.S.S. Drake.*** ("The Arsenal of Freedom" [TNG]). One of Riker's greatest personal tests came in 2364 when the entity **Q** offered him a gift of supernatural powers, an offer that Riker was able to refuse. ("Hide and Q" [TNG]). Riker became the first Federation Starfleet officer to serve aboard a Klingon vessel when he participated in an **Officer Exchange Program** in 2365, serving as first officer aboard the Klingon ship ***Pagh***. ("A Matter of Honor" [TNG]). Riker was offered command of the ***U.S.S. Aries*** in 2365, but he declined the appointment, preferring to remain on the *Enterprise*-D. ("The Icarus Factor" [TNG]). Riker suffered a near brush with death while on a survey mission to planet **Surata IV,** where contact with an indigenous plant-form caused him to lose consciousness for several hours. ("Shades of Gray" [TNG]). Riker was charged with murder in the 2366 death of **Dr. Nel Apgar** at planet **Tanuga IV** after Apgar's research station exploded. He was acquitted after a

holodeck re-creation of the events leading to the death demonstrated that Apgar had been responsible for the explosion. ("A Matter of Perspective" [TNG]). In late 2366, Riker refused a third opportunity to command a starship, when he was offered the ***U.S.S. Melbourne*** during the **Borg** incursion that year. ("The Best of Both Worlds, Part I" [TNG]). Shortly thereafter, Riker was granted a temporary field promotion to captain, and given command of the *Enterprise*-D following the capture of Captain Picard by the Borg. The *Melbourne* was later destroyed by the Borg in the battle of **Wolf 359**. ("The Best of Both Worlds, Part II" [TNG]). Riker did, however, have ambitions of becoming a starship commander. After the loss of the *Enterprise*-D in 2371, Riker expressed regret that he would not have the opportunity of someday commanding that great ship. *(Star Trek Generations).*

(In an alternate **quantum reality**, Picard was lost to the Borg in 2366. In that reality, Riker was promoted to captain following Picard's loss.) ("Parallels" [TNG]).

Riker's approach to command was frequently unconventional. Prior to his service aboard the *Enterprise*-D, Riker had been a lieutenant aboard the *Starship* ***Potemkin***. During a crisis aboard that ship, Riker positioned the *Potemkin* over a planet's magnetic pole, thus confusing his opponent's sensors. Indeed, Data once observed that Riker relied upon traditional problem-solving techniques less than one-quarter of the time. ("Peak Performance" [TNG]).

As a boy, Riker was responsible for cooking for himself and his father. As *Enterprise*-D Executive Officer, Riker regarded cooking as a hobby. ("Time Squared" [TNG]). One of Riker's passions was for old Earth jazz music, and he was a pretty fair trombone player. ("11001001" [TNG]). *SEE:* ***Number One***. *William Riker was first seen in "Encounter at Farpoint" (TNG).*

rikka. Variety of Taresian flower with a very pleasant fragrance. The **Taresians** applied liquid essence of rikka flowers to the forehead as an aid in relaxation. ("Favorite Son" [VGR]).

Riley, Kevin Thomas. (Bruce Hyde). Relief navigator aboard the *U.S.S. Enterprise* under the command of Captain Kirk. Riley fancied himself the descendant of Irish kings, and this trait surfaced while he was under the intoxicating effects of the **Psi 2000** virus, during which Riley nearly caused the destruction of the *Enterprise* when he shut down the ship's main engines. ("The Naked Time" [TOS]). As a young boy, Riley was one of nine surviving eyewitnesses to the massacre of some 4,000 colonists at **Tarsus IV** by **Kodos the Executioner**. Riley's parents were killed in the massacre. In 2266, Riley also witnessed the death of Kodos, then known as **Anton Karidian**, during a performance of ***Hamlet*** aboard the *Starship Enterprise*. ("The Conscience of the King" [TOS]).

Rillan grease. Lubricant used in an ancient **Vulcan** festival. Rillan grease was applied to scantily clad Vulcans during the *Rumarie*, an ancient pagan festival last celebrated over a millennium ago. ("Meld" [VGR]).

Rinax marshlands. Region of planet **Rinax**. Neelix and his family lived near the Rinax marshlands. He recalled that the summers there were hot and humid, reaching 50 degrees Celsius and 90 percent humidity. Neelix also recalled serious lavafly infestations. ("Macrocosm" [VGR]).

Rinax. Class-M moon orbiting planet **Talax**. Childhood home of **Neelix**. Target of the metreon cascade weapon used by the **Haakonian Order** that forced the surrender of Talax in 2356. Some 300,000 Talaxians were vaporized in the attack, including Neelix's entire family. Thousands of others died in following years from **metremia** poisoning. Neelix himself escaped death because he was on Talax at the time. ("Jetrel" [VGR]). SEE: **Rinax marshlands**. Access to space from Rinax was provided by an **orbital tether** system that allowed carriage vehicles to ride an extremely long cable stretching from a station on the planet's surface to a station in **synchronous orbit**. ("Rise" [VGR]).

Rinn, K'Par. (Margot Rose) **Argrathi** prison administrator. In 2372, Rinn supervised the implementation of artificial memories of a 20-year prison sentence into the brain of Miles O'Brien. ("Hard Time" [DS9]). *Name and title were mentioned only in the script and not in the aired episode.*

Rinna. (Kelli Kirkland). Taresian woman present when Karry Kim visited Taresia in 2373. Rinna was interested in becoming one of Harry Kim's wives, and pursued him to that end. She wanted to use his cells' genetic material to conceive offspring. ("Favorite Son" [VGR]).

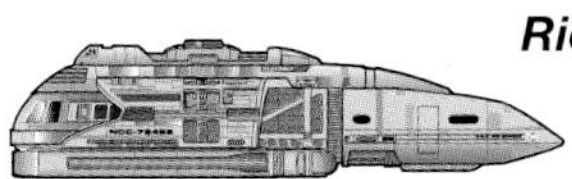

Rio Grande, U.S.S. Starfleet *Danube*-class **runabout**, registry number NCC-72452, one of three runabouts originally assigned to station Deep Space 9. ("Emissary" [DS9]). *It was also seen throughout the run of* Star Trek: Deep Space Nine. *Members of the* Star Trek: Deep Space Nine *art department, noticing that the* Rio Grande *seems to be the longest-lived (and therefore the safest) of any of the runabouts assigned to the station, strongly recommend that if you must travel by runabout, you should choose the* Rio Grande. *(Just a suggestion...)*

Rionoj. (Leslie Bevis). Ship's officer who delivered **Li Nalas**'s earring to Quark on station Deep Space 9. She received it from a maintenance worker on **Cardassia IV**, who asked her to deliver it to Bajor. ("The Homecoming" [DS9]). On stardate 48214, she sold Quark wreckage of a ship that had crashed in the **Gamma Quadrant**. Within the wreckage was a **Jem'Hadar** baby. ("The Abandoned" [DS9]). In late 2372, Odo suspected Rionoj of trafficking in stolen Falangian diamonds. ("Broken Link" [DS9]). *This character was referred simply as "Boslic freighter captain" in the script for "The Homecoming" and "The Abandoned." The script (but not actual dialog) for "Broken Link" suggests her name was Rionoj.*

Risa. A tropical Class-M planet noted for its beautiful beaches and resort facilities, and its open sexuality. At the Risa resort, one who displays a ***Horga'hn*** statuette indicates a desire for ***jamaharon***, which the Risans seem only too happy to oblige. ("Captain's Holiday" [TNG]). An extremely popular tourist destination, Risa hosted millions of guests every year. Risa was actually a rain-soaked, geologically unstable planet, but a sophisticated **weather control system** created a virtually perfect climate. The weather control system was sabotoged in 2373 by the **New Essentialists Movement**. ("Let He Who Is Without Sin..." [DS9]). Captain Picard vacationed there in 2366, where he met archaeologist **Vash** in search of the ***Tox Uthat***. ("Captain's Holiday" [TNG]). In 2367, Geordi La Forge was scheduled to attend an artificial-intelligence seminar on Risa. La Forge was kidnapped by Romulans en route to the conference. ("The Mind's Eye" [TNG]). William Riker, who was very fond of Risa, vacationed there again in 2368, when he met a beautiful woman named **Etana Jol**, who was actually a **Ktaran** operative seeking to infiltrate Starfleet. ("The Game" [TNG]). In 2371 on Deep Space 9,

Thomas Riker, posing as Will Riker, said he was going to Risa for shore leave. ("Defiant" [DS9]). Also that year, a **Boslic freighter captain**'s next destination after off-loading materials on Deep Space 9 in 2371. ("The Abandoned" [DS9]). Ambassador Krajensky was on his way to Risa in 2371 when he disappeared and was replaced by a **Founder** who assumed his form and identity. ("The Adversary" [DS9]).

"Rise." *Voyager* episode #60. Teleplay by Brannon Braga. Story by Jimmy Diggs. Directed by Robert Scheerer. No stardate given. *First aired in 1997. The* Voyager *crew assists a planet suffering a mysterious asteroid bombardment, and the team sent to investigate crash-lands their shuttle on the surface.* GUEST CAST: Gary Bullock as **Goth**; Geoff Pysirr as **Hanjuan**; Lisa Kaminar as **Lillias**; Alan Oppenheimer as **Nezu ambassador**; Kelly Connel as **Sklar**; Tom Towles as **Vatm, Dr.** SEE: **Alixia; analeptic; arctic spider; dust shrouds; Etanian Order; galicite; Goth; Halla; Hanjuan; Lillias; lydroxide; mag-lev carriage; magnetic leverage; Neelix; Nezu ambassador; Nezu; olivine; orbital tether; Rinax; Sklar; Touth, Caves of; triadium; triox compound; tryoxene; Vatm, Dr.**

Risean tapestries. Elaborate decorative wall hangings made on **Risa**. **Quark** tried to entice **Arissa** to his quarters to see his Risean tapestries. ("A Simple Investigation" [DS9]).

Risian perfume. Variety of perfume originating on Risa. In 2372, Jadzia Dax gave a bottle of Risian perfume to Dr. Lenara Kahn. ("Rejoined" [DS9]).

Riska. (Eva Loseth). Humanoid resident of station Deep Space 9. Riska was a friend of **Leanne**. She double-dated with Leanne, **Jake Sisko**, and **Rom** on stardate 48498, but the evening was a disaster. ("Life Support" [DS9]).

Rite of Separation. Bajoran custom practiced by a couple who are dissolving their romantic relationship. In the custom, the couple spend several days celebrating their parting. When done correctly, the Rite of Separation allows for a friendly parting with no hurt feelings or recriminations. Leeta and Bashir underwent the Rite of Separation in 2373. ("Let He Who Is Without Sin..." [DS9]).

Rite of Succession, Klingon. Process whereby a new leader was chosen for the **Klingon High Council** following the death of the previous leader. The rite first required the ***Sonchi***, in which the previous leader was formally certified to be truly dead. Next, the **Arbiter of Succession** was required to select the challengers for leadership of the council. The two strongest challengers would then fight for the right to lead the council. Following the death of **K'mpec** in 2367, Jean-Luc Picard served as Arbiter of Succession. ("Reunion" [TNG]).

Ritter scale. Measurement of cosmic radiation. ("The Empath" [TOS]).

ritual cloak. Feathered ceremonial coat worn by the groom during the joining or marriage ceremony on **Miramanee's planet**. ("The Paradise Syndrome" [TOS]).

Riva. (Howie Seago). Famed mediator from planet **Ramatis III**, Riva brought adversaries together by striving to turn disadvantages into advantages. His accomplishments include several treaties between the Klingon Empire and the United Federation of Planets. Riva was a member of the ruling family of Ramatis III and, as is a genetic characteristic of that family, was born without the sense of hearing. Riva was able to overcome this challenge through the use of a **Chorus** of aides who acted as his interpreters. This Chorus was killed during negotiations on planet **Solais V**, after which Riva remained on that planet, working to turn that disadvantage into an advantage, bringing the opponents together by teaching both sides the use of sign language. ("Loud as a Whisper" [TNG]). *Actor Howie Seago is deaf in real life, and this episode was developed in part at his suggestion.*

"Rivals." *Deep Space Nine* episode #31. Teleplay by Joe Menosky. Story by Jim Trombetta and Michael Piller. Directed by David Livingston. No stardate given. *First aired in 1994. A con man replicates a device that can alter the laws of probability, causing havoc on Deep Space 9.* GUEST CAST: Rosalind Chao as **O'Brien, Keiko**; Barbara Bosson as **Roana**; K. Callan as **Alsia**; Max Grodénchik as **Rom**; Albert Henderson as **Cos**; Chris Sarandon as **Mazur, Martus**. SEE: **Alsia; Bashir, Dr. Julian; Club Martus; Cos; El-Aurian; Ferengi Rules of Acquisition; gambling device; Gamzian wine; hyvroxilated quint-ethyl metacetamine; isiks; Mazur, Martus; Naming Day; Pythro V; racquetball; solar neutrinos; Roana; Rom; Vlugta asteroid belt; Vlugtan star system.**

Rivan. (Brenda Bakke). Female leader of the **Edo** people on planet **Rubicun III** in 2364. When transported to the *Enterprise*-D, Rivan was awestruck at the sight of the spaceborne object her people worshipped as its god. ("Justice" [TNG]). SEE: **Edo god.**

Rixx, Captain. (Michael Berryman). Commander of the *Starship* ***Thomas Paine***. Along with **Walker Keel** and **Tryla Scott**, Rixx warned Jean-Luc Picard at planet Dytallix B of the unknown alien entities that were infiltrating Starfleet Command in 2364. Rixx was a **Bolian**. ("Conspiracy" [TNG]). *Actor Michael Berryman previously played the communications officer in Starfleet Command in* Star Trek IV*, although he was wearing different makeup prosthetics.*

Rizzo, Ensign. (Jerry Ayres). *Enterprise* security officer who was killed by the **dikironium cloud creature** in 2268. Rizzo died from shock due to 60 percent of his red blood cells being drained. Rizzo had been a good friend of **Ensign Garrovick**. ("Obsession" [TOS]).

RNA. Substance found in all living cells which acts as a controller of protein synthesis. Ribonucleic acid is similar in construction to its counterpart deoxyribonucleic acid (**DNA**), with the replacement of ribose for deoxyribose and the pyrimidine uracil for thymine. Following his exposure to a quantum fissure in 2370, Worf's cellular RNA was thrown into a state of flux, which extended to the subatomic level. This was the first clue to the nature of Worf's quantum disassociation; essentially he was in the wrong **quantum reality**. ("Parallels" [TNG]).

Ro Laren. (Michelle Forbes). **Bajoran** national who served in the Federation Starfleet before becoming a member of the **Maquis** resistance group. Born in 2340 and raised during the **Cardassian** occupation of her homeworld, Ro spent her childhood in Bajoran resettlement camps. When she was seven years old, she was forced to watch as Cardassians tortured her father to death.

As a Starfleet ensign, Ro earned numerous reprimands, and she was court-martialed after a disastrous mission to planet **Garon II** in which she disobeyed orders and eight members of her ***U.S.S. Wellington*** away team were killed. Ro was subsequently imprisoned on **Jaros II** until her release in

2368 by **Admiral Kennelly**. She was released in exchange for her participation in a covert mission aboard the *Enterprise*-D, intended to apprehend Bajoran terrorists believed to have attacked Federation interests. Ro was instrumental in the discoveries that the attacks were actually Cardassian in origin, and that Kennelly had been acting as an agent for the Cardassians. Ro subsequently agreed to remain aboard the *Enterprise*-D as a crew member. Bajoran custom dictates that an individual's family name is given first, and the given name is last; thus Ro is her family name. ("Ensign Ro" [TNG]).

In 2368, on stardate 45494, Ro and Commander Riker shared a brief romantic liaison when both suffered from memory loss while under the influence of a Satarran probe, a somewhat ironic occurrence considering that both of them had been frequently at odds over her performance as an *Enterprise*-D crew member. ("Conundrum" [TNG]).

Despite her people's spiritual nature, Laren was never sure about her faith in the Bajoran religion. When she was exposed to a Romulan **interphase generator** in 2368 that rendered her invisible, she believed she was dead, and tried to make peace with herself in accordance with those religious beliefs. ("The Next Phase" [TNG]). Ro was temporarily reduced to a child after passing through an energy field in 2369. ("Rascals" [TNG]). *Young Laren was played in "Rascals" by Megan Parlen.*

Early in 2370, Ro was accepted into Starfleet's Advanced Tactical Training school, on a recommendation from Captain Picard. Following her successful completion of the training, she was promoted to lieutenant first class, and returned to the *Enterprise*-D. Captain Picard reassigned her to conn during the *Enterprise*-D's mission to the Cardassian **Demilitarized Zone**. At the urging of Admiral Nechayev, Ro volunteered to infiltrate a **Maquis** cell, using her history as a **Bajoran** Starfleet officer as a convincing cover. Ro convinced the members of the cell of her sincerity, but as she spent more time with the Maquis, Ro found herself genuinely sympathizing with their cause. She sabotaged a planned Starfleet ambush of a Maquis ship, and subsequently disappeared into the Maquis underground. ("Preemptive Strike" [TNG]). *Michelle Forbes had previously played Dara in "Half a Life" (TNG).* Star Trek's *producers planned to transfer the character of Ro to* Star Trek: Deep Space Nine, *but she was replaced on that show by Kira Nerys when Forbes demurred in favor of movie projects. Ensign Ro appeared in "Disaster" (TNG), "Conundrum" (TNG), "Power Play" (TNG), "Cause and Effect" (TNG), "The Next Phase" (TNG), and "Rascals" (TNG). Her last appearance was in "Preemptive Strike" (TNG).*

Ro-Kel. Humanoid of the Miradorn species. Ro-Kel was killed by the fugitive **Croden** during a robbery in 2369. His twin, **Ah-Kel,** swore vengeance. ("Vortex" [DS9]).

Roana. (Barbara Bosson). Bajoran shopkeeper on Deep Space 9. In 2370 Roana met **Martus Mazur** and opened a gambling casino-bar in partnership with him called **Club Martus.** ("Rivals" [DS9]).

Robbiani dermal-optic test. Medical diagnostic test that registers a subject's emotional structure through skin and pupil response to visual stimulation at specific color wavelengths. Dr. McCoy administered such a test to Kirk when Dr. Janice Lester's mind occupied his body in 2269. ("Turnabout Intruder" [TOS]).

Robbins, Harold. One of the most popular writers of Earth's 20th century. Spock read Robbins's works during his study of Earth culture, and regarded him as one of the "giants" of human literature. *(Star Trek IV: The Voyage Home).*

Robert Fox, S.S. Transport vessel that ferried **El-Aurian** refugees in convoy with the ***S.S. Lakul*** in 2294. Both transport vessels became caught by the gravimetric distortion surrounding the **nexus** energy ribbon. The *Robert Fox* was destroyed from hull stresses before any of her passengers could be rescued. *(Star Trek Generations). The name of the* Robert Fox *was not mentioned in dialog, but comes from a computer graphic display on the science officer's console on the* Enterprise-*B bridge. The name was suggested by movie co-writer Ronald D. Moore.*

Robin Hood. (Patrick Stewart). In the mythology of old Earth, a 12th-century English hero who "robbed from the rich and gave to the poor." Picard was cast in the role of this legendary Englishman during an elaborate fantasy **Q** designed to teach Picard a lesson about love. ("QPid" [TNG])

Robinson, B. G. (Teri Hatcher). *Enterprise*-D transporter officer in 2365. A beautiful woman, Robinson attracted the attentions of Captain **Thadiun Okona**, and the two evidently spent some time together. ("The Outrageous Okona" [TNG]). *Teri Hatcher also played Lois Lane in* Lois and Clark, The New Adventures of Superman.

Robinson, Rain. (Sarah Silverman). Earth astronomer who participated in an early search for extraterrestrial intelligence using radio telescope equipment during the 20th century. In 1996, working at the **SETI** lab at the **Griffith Observatory**, Robinson detected gamma emissions from the *Starship Voyager* in Earth orbit. Program sponsor **Henry Starling** attempted to suppress knowledge of her discovery because he feared that *Voyager* might be a ship from the future. Robinson worked with *Voyager* personnel to prevent Starling from causing a cataclysmic temporal explosion in the 29th century. ("Future's End, Parts I and II" [VGR]).

Rocha, Lieutenant Keith. Starfleet officer killed by a **coalescent organism** when assigned to an outpost in the **Triona system** in early 2369. The coalescent organism subsequently assumed Rocha's form, so his death was not suspected until a short time later when the ersatz Rocha was assigned to Subspace **Relay Station 47**. Rocha had earned two decorations for valor and three outstanding evaluations from his commanding officers. ("Aquiel" [TNG]).

Rochani III. Planet. Site where **Curzon Dax** and **Benjamin Sisko** were once cornered by a party of Kaleans. While under the influence of the **Saltah'na energy spheres** in 2369, Jadzia Dax repeated the story of Rochani III to Major Kira Nerys. ("Dramatis Personae" [DS9]).

Roddenberry, Gene. *(1921-1991).* Star Trek's *creator and noted visionary futurist, nicknamed "**Great Bird of the Galaxy.**" A former airline pilot and police officer, Roddenberry became a prolific television writer in the 1950s. He wrote the first* Star Trek *pilot episode in 1964, and served as producer and executive producer during the show's original network run from 1966 to 1969. Roddenberry co-wrote and produced the first* Star Trek *movie in 1979 and served as executive consultant to subsequent* Star Trek *films. In 1987, he created* Star Trek: The Next Generation, *and served as the show's executive producer until his death in 1991. Roddenberry's personal optimism about humanity's potential for* *a better future showed strongly in all of these productions. Roddenberry was married to actress Majel Barrett, who played several different roles on* Star Trek*, including the voice of the* Enterprise *computer. Even after his death, the producers of* Star Trek: Deep Space Nine *and* Star Trek: Voyager *acknowledged Roddenberry's vision with the screen credit: "Based Upon* Star Trek, *Created by Gene Roddenberry." NASA posthumously recognized Roddenberry's contribution to space exploration when his ashes were taken into orbit aboard the Space Shuttle Columbia in 1992. Gene finally got to voyage into the final frontier. SEE:* ***Drake Equation****.*

Rodek. (Tony Todd). Klingon warrior, son of **Noggra**. Rodek was involved in a shuttle accident in 2372 that left him with complete amnesia. ("Sons of Mogh" [DS9]). *Actually, Kurn's memory engrams were erased and he assumed the identity of Rodek. This entry honors Worf's desire that his brother's new life as Rodek be kept secret.*

rodinium. One of the hardest substances known to Federation science. The outer protective shell of the Federation outposts monitoring the **Romulan Neutral Zone** were constructed of cast rodinium, but even this material was unable to withstand exposure to a plasma energy weapon during the Romulan incursion of 2266. ("Balance of Terror" [TOS]). SEE: **Neutral Zone Outposts**. Rodinium was also used in **Cardassian** ship construction. ("The Maquis, Part I" [DS9]). SEE: ***Bok'Nor***.

Rodriguez, Lieutenant Esteban. (Perry Lopez). Crew member aboard the original *Starship Enterprise.* Rodriguez was part of the landing party to the **amusement park planet** in 2267. Rodriguez and his partner **Angela Martine** were part of the exploratory team to make sure the Earthlike planet was safe for shore leave. They soon found out that their imaginations conjured up images, which could be beautiful as well as deadly. ("Shore Leave" [TOS]).

Rodriguez. Genetically engineered survivor of Earth's **Eugenics Wars**. Rodriguez and other followers of **Khan Noonien Singh** escaped Earth in 1996 in the sleeper ship, ***S.S. Botany Bay,*** remaining in suspended animation until revived by personnel from the *U.S.S. Enterprise* in 2267. Rodriguez was trained in communications technologies. ("Space Seed" [TOS]).

roentgen. Unit of ionizing radiation measure. The quantity of radiation that will produce one electrostatic unit of charge of electricity in one cubic centimeter of air. ("Before and After" [VGR]).

Rog Prison. Ferengi incarceration facility. Former DaiMon **Bok** was sent to Rog Prison in 2364, but he bought his way out in 2368. ("Bloodlines" [TNG]).

Rogers, Amanda. (Olivia D'Abo). Member of the **Q Continuum** who was raised as a human. Rogers was unaware of her extraordinary powers until just before she went aboard the *Enterprise*-D in 2369 as a student intern. Amanda's final act was to clean the air pollution from planet **Tagra IV** before leaving with **Q** to discover her new identity. ("True-Q" [TNG]).

Rogerson, Commander. (Newell Tarrant). Command duty officer aboard the American aircraft carrier *U.S.S. Enterprise* in 1986 when Chekov and Uhura broke onto the ship in an effort to gather high-energy photons for their return back to the 23rd century. *(Star Trek IV: The Voyage Home).*

Roget, Dr. Henri. Physician from the Central Hospital on **Altair IV** who won the prestigious **Carrington Award** in 2371. ("Prophet Motive" [DS9]).

rogue comet. Essentially a huge ball of ice, which has not been captured by the gravitational influences of any solar system. In 2370, the *Enterprise*-D encountered such a comet, which had never before been recorded in any Federation navigational charts. The comet was found to have originated in the D'Arsay system, over 87 million years ago. Sensors showed the comet to be composed of an outer shell of gaseous hydrogen and helium over an icy mantle. The interior of the comet was found to contain the **D'Arsay archive**. ("Masks" [TNG]).

Rojan. (Warren Stevens). Leader of a **Kelvan** expedition sent from the **Andromeda Galaxy** as a possible prelude to colonization and conquest of the Milky Way Galaxy. In 2268, Rojan agreed to a plan proposed by James Kirk whereby the Kelvans would be permitted to peaceably colonize a planet in the Milky Way. ("By Any Other Name" [TOS]). *Warren Stevens played Doc Ostrow in the classic s-f film* Forbidden Planet.

Rokassa juice. Beverage with tranquilizing qualities, favored by Garak. ("Cardassians" [DS9]).

***rokeg* blood pie.** A traditional Klingon dish. The crew of the Klingon vessel *Pagh* served *rokeg* blood pie to Riker as sort of an initiation rite, but Riker proved his mettle by claiming to enjoy it. ("A Matter of Honor" [TNG]). *Rokeg* blood pie was one of **Worf**'s favorite foods. When he was a child, his adoptive mother, **Helena Rozhenko**, mastered the technique of making this dish. ("Family" [TNG]).

Roladan Wild Draw. Card game that, like Earth poker, is as much a contest of wills as a game of chance. Miles O'Brien said he never wanted to play Roladan Wild Draw against the strong-willed Major Kira Nerys. ("Emissary" [DS9]).

rolisisin. An **Ocampa** ritual in which a parent massages the feet of their daughter who is undergoing ***elogium***. This massaging continues until the daughter's tongue begins to swell. The *rolisisin* is usually a time for parent and child to move into a new kind of relationship. As the child has her own child, the parent must acknowledge her true adulthood. ("Elogium" [VGR]).

rolk. A type of **Banean** meat, sometimes cooked in a stew. ("Ex Post Facto" [VGR]).

roller coaster. Elevated rail vehicle designed to provide a brief, exciting ride on a track with steep inclines and sharp turns, used purely for amusement, popular with some Earth cultures. Roller coasters were still enjoyed by people of all ages well into the 24th century. ("The Thaw" [VGR]).

Rollins. (Scott MacDonald). Bridge officer on the *Starship Voyager*. ("Caretaker" [VGR]). By 2372, Rollins had been promoted from ensign to the rank of lieutenant. ("Dreadnought" [VGR]). *Scott MacDonald also played Subcommander N'Vek in "Face of the Enemy" (TNG) and Tosk in "Captive Pursuit" (DS9).*

Rollman, Admiral. (Susan Bay). Starfleet official. Major Kira communicated with Rollman in 2369, voicing her dissatisfaction with Sisko's hesitation in granting political asylum to ***Kohn-Ma*** terrorist **Tahna Los**. ("Past Prologue" [DS9]). Rollman was advised in 2370 when a duplicate of Deep Space 9 Operations Chief **Miles O'Brien** was created by the **Paradan** government in order to disrupt peace talks. The replicant O'Brien had no way of knowing that he was not the real O'Brien, and he contacted Rollman to advise her of unusual behavior on the part of the station's command crew. ("Whispers" [DS9]). *Susan Bay is married to actor Leonard Nimoy.*

Rolor Nebula. Interstellar dust cloud in the general vicinity of the Dreon system. ("For the Cause" [DS9]).

Rom (mirror). (Max Grodénchik). Hardened, heavily armed professional soldier and member of the **Terran rebellion** in the **mirror universe**. In this reality, **Garak (mirror)** tortured Rom until he revealed **Benjamin Sisko**'s plan to get **Jennifer Sisko (mirror)** away from **Terok Nor (mirror)**. Garak (mirror) then killed the mirror Rom. ("Through the Looking Glass" [DS9]).

Rom. (Max Grodénchik). **Quark**'s brother and father to **Nog**. Rom helped Quark run the bar at station **Deep Space 9**. ("Emissary" [DS9]). Rom grew up on his homeworld of **Ferenginar** with his father **Keldar**, his mother **Ishka**, and his older brother Quark. Quark never treated him with much respect. On Rom's Naming Day, Quark substituted old vegetables for his presents, then sold the presents for more than their father had originally paid for them. ("Rivals" [DS9]). Rom was a mechanical genius, but wasn't very good at acquiring profit ("Heart of Stone" [DS9]), seeming to inherit his father's lack of business sense. Rom stayed at home on Ferenginar for ten years after Quark departed, finally moving away in 2361. ("Family Business" [DS9]). Rom entered into a five-year marriage contract with **Prindora**, producing a child, **Nog**. Rom subsequently fell in love with Prindora, and thus blindly signed an extension to the marriage contract without reading the fine print that enabled Prindora's father to swindle all of Rom's money. ("Doctor Bashir, I Presume?" [DS9]).

In 2369 when Keiko O'Brien opened a new school on the station, Rom was initially opposed to his son, Nog, attending, but later relented. ("A Man Alone" [DS9]).

Rom often showed amazing initiative. He demonstrated a keen ability to break into Quark's security systems, much to Quark's shock. ("Necessary Evil"[DS9]). Rom served as Quark's bodyguard during Quark's brief tenure as **grand nagus** in 2369. In true Ferengi tradition, Rom plotted to eliminate his brother, but was halted when the previous nagus, **Zek**, was found to be still alive. Quark applauded Rom's treachery, making him assistant manager of policy and clientele. ("The Nagus" [DS9]). Rom challenged the very foundations of **Ferengi** culture in 2372 when, in response to unfair management practices by Quark, Rom organized a labor union among the workers at Quark's bar. Formation of the **Guild of Restaurant and Casino Employees** brought a swift and violent reaction by the **FCA**, which was determined to shut down the union. Rom disbanded the union after Quark agreed to the workers' demands, although the union continued to operate in an unofficial capacity. Shortly after the incident, Rom left Quark's bar and became one of Deep Space 9's diagnostic and repair technicians, junior grade. ("Bar Association" [DS9]). Rom quickly demonstrated extraordinary skill at understanding and troubleshooting engineering systems. ("The Assignment" [DS9]).

In 2371 when his son Nog petitioned to join Starfleet, Rom was very supportive of the idea. ("Heart of Stone" [DS9]).

In 2373 Rom became attracted to **Leeta**, who worked as a **dabo** girl at Quark's bar. Rom found it difficult to express his affection to Leeta, and almost lost her when she nearly accepted an assignment to manage the cafe at Starfleet's Jupiter Station. ("Doctor Bashir, I Presume?" [DS9]).

Max Grodénchik had previously played Sovak in "Captain's Holiday" (TNG) and Par Lenor in "The Perfect Mate" (TNG). He also played a NASA flight dynamics officer in the motion picture Apollo 13. *Rom was first seen in "Emissary" (DS9).*

Romah Doek. (Paul Nakauchi). Executive officer of the Tygarian freighter ***Nanut***. ("The Homecoming" [DS9]).

Romaine, Jacques. Starfleet chief engineer and father to *Enterprise* crew member **Mira Romaine**. ("The Lights of Zetar" [TOS]). *Jacques Romaine was retired by the time of the episode, set in 2269.*

Romaine, Lieutenant Mira. (Jan Shutan). Crew member aboard the original *Starship Enterprise*. Romaine supervised the transfer of equipment to the **Memory Alpha** station in 2269. During the mission, Romaine's mind was invaded by **noncorporeal life**-forms, the last survivors from planet **Zetar**. The **Zetarians** were driven from Romaine's body by placing her in a medical decompression chamber. Romaine was a friend of Chief Engineer **Montgomery Scott**, and his affection was believed to have played a role in her recovery. ("The Lights of Zetar" [TOS]).

Romaine, Lydia. Mother to *Enterprise* crew member **Mira Romaine.** ("The Lights of Zetar" [TOS]). *Lydia Romaine was deceased by the time of the episode, set in 2269.*

Romas. (Richard Lineback). A citizen of the planet **Ornara**, and a crew member on the Ornaran freighter ***Sanction*** in 2364. Like all **Ornarans** of that time, Romas was addicted to the Brekkian medication **felicium**. ("Symbiosis" [TNG]). *Richard Lineback also played Selin Peers in "Dax" (DS9).*

Romii. SEE: **Remus**.

Romulan ale. A powerfully intoxicating beverage, light blue in color. Although Romulan ale was illegal in the Federation, McCoy gave Kirk a bottle of the stuff for his 52nd birthday in 2285. *(Star Trek II: The Wrath of Khan).* Romulan ale was served at a diplomatic dinner hosted by Kirk for Klingon **Chancellor Gorkon** aboard the *Enterprise*-A. Tensions between the Federation people and their Klingon guests were high, and the Romulan ale probably did not help much, either. *(Star Trek VI: The Undiscovered Country).* In 2362, **Fallit Kot** was arrested for attempting to hijack a shipment of the ale. ("Melora" [DS9]).

Romulan Astrophysical Academy. Scientific organization within the **Romulan Star Empire.** Dr. **Telek R'Mor** was a member of the academy. ("Eye of the Needle" [VGR]).

Romulan battle cruiser. Starship of Klingon design in use by the **Romulan Star Empire** under the terms of a brief alliance between the two powers in 2268. ("The *Enterprise* Incident" [TOS]). *The Romulan battle cruiser was, of course, a re-use of the* ***Klingon battle cruiser*** *miniature designed by Matt Jefferies.* **SEE: Romulan spacecraft.**

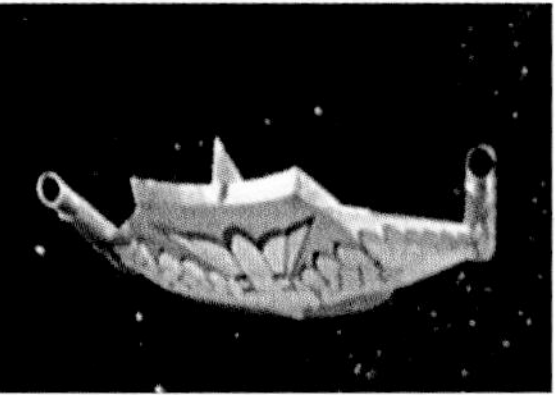

Romulan bird-of-prey. Spacecraft of the **Romulan Star Empire** in the late 23rd century. The Romulan bird-of-prey was painted with an impressive predatory bird, and was equipped with a **cloaking device** and a powerful plasma energy weapon. Propulsion was simple impulse. The ship was equipped with a cloaking device, possibly the first known example of a ship equipped with a practical invisibility screen. Fortunately, it was learned that the cloaking device required so much power that the ship had to decloak in order to fire. A Romulan bird-of-prey crossed the **Romulan Neutral Zone** in 2266 in a test of Federation resolve. ("Balance of Terror" [TOS]). SEE: **Klingon bird-of-prey; Romulan spacecraft.**

Romulan cloaking device. SEE: **cloaking device, Romulan**.

Romulan commander. (Joanne Linville). Officer in charge of the **Romulan battle cruiser** that captured the original *U.S.S. Enterprise* when Kirk and Spock crossed the **Romulan Neutral Zone** on a spy mission in 2268. She attempted to persuade Spock to defect to the Romulan Star Empire, an effort made significantly more persuasive by the personal attraction Spock felt for the commander. After the successful conclusion of that mission (in which Kirk and Spock stole an improved **Romulan cloaking device**), the Romulan commander was made a Federation prisoner. ("The *Enterprise* Incident" [TOS]). *Kirk indicated that the commander would eventually be returned to Romulan territory, although we have no way of knowing if this actually happened. Like Mark Lenard's character, this Romulan commander was not given a name.*

Romulan commander. (Mark Lenard). Conducted the Romulan incursion of 2266, crossing the **Romulan Neutral Zone** in command of a **Romulan bird-of-prey** to test Federation defenses and resolve. A highly honorable individual, he feared the toll that a new Romulan-Federation war would bring, but nevertheless carried out his orders to the best of his ability. ("Balance of Terror" [TOS]). *Actor Mark Lenard would later play **Sarek** (Spock's father) in "Journey to Babel" (TOS), et al., as well as the Klingon commander in* Star Trek: The Motion Picture.

Romulan empress. A leader of the **Romulan Star Empire**. Q briefly considered asking the Romulan empress to be the mother of his child before deciding on Kathryn Janeway. ("The Q and the Grey" [VGR]).

Romulan Neutral Zone. A region of space approximately one light-year across, dividing the **Romulan Star Empire** from the **United Federation of Planets**. The Neutral Zone was established in 2160 after a conflict between Earth and the Romulans. That conflict had been fought with early space vessels using primitive atomic weapons. The peace treaty establishing the Neutral Zone had been negotiated by subspace radio and provided that entry into the zone by either party would constitute an act of war. The zone remained unviolated until the Romulan incursion of 2266. ("Balance of Terror" [TOS]). The *Enterprise* violated the Neutral Zone in 2267 at the order of **Commodore Stocker,** when radiation-induced aging threatened the lives of the ship's command crew. ("The Deadly Years" [TOS]). The ship again crossed into Romulan space in 2268 on a covert mission to steal an advanced Romulan **cloaking device**. ("The *Enterprise* Incident" [TOS]). The Neutral Zone remained uncrossed by either party during an extended period of Romulan isolationism beginning after the **Treaty of Algeron** was signed after the **Tomed Incident** of 2311. The mysterious destruction of several Federation and Romulan outposts in 2364 triggered the end of this isolationism when a Romulan warbird crossed the Neutral Zone to investigate. Although the outposts were later found to have been destroyed by the **Borg**, the incident triggered a resumption of hostilities between the Romulans and the Federation. ("The Neutral Zone" [TNG]). It was later determined that the pattern of large craters was characteristic of **Borg** attacks, suggesting the possibility of Borg activity near Federation space nearly a year prior to first contact with the *Enterprise*-D in 2365. ("Q Who?" [TNG]). **Captain Donald Varley**, commanding the ***U.S.S. Yamato***, violated the Romulan Neutral Zone in 2365. Varley entered the zone in a successful effort to locate the ancient planet **Iconia**, in hopes of preventing the Romulans from gaining access to their legendary weapons technology. Unfortunately, the *Yamato* itself fell victim to an Iconian weapon, and an interstellar incident was nearly triggered when the same weapon nearly destroyed the *Enterprise*-D and a Romulan warbird. ("Contagion" [TNG]). A **Romulan scoutship** was detected in the Neutral Zone by the crew of Federation outpost **Sierra VI** in 2366. The ship was piloted by **Alidar Jarok**, who was defecting to the Federation so that he could warn of what he believed was a dangerously destabilizing base on planet **Nelvana III.** On Stardate 43462.5, the *Enterprise*-D entered the Neutral Zone, in violation of the Treaty of Algeron, to investigate these reports. ("The Defector" [TNG]). The Neutral Zone was also violated in 2366 by the Romulan scoutship *Pi* and later by **Tomalak**'s warbird when he tried to rescue the crew of the ***Pi***. ("The Enemy" [TNG]). The *Starship Enterprise*-E was assigned to patrol the Romulan Neutral Zone on stardate 50893 at the time of the **Borg** incursion to Sector 001 in 2373. *(Star Trek: First Contact)*. (In the **anti-time future** created by the Q Continuum, the Klingons had conquered the **Romulan Star Empire**. The Neutral Zone was under the control of the Klingons, forcing the crew of the *Pasteur* to seek Worf's help to enter the Zone.) ("All Good Things..." [TNG]). *"The Defector" (TNG) established the Treaty of Algeron and suggested the width of the Neutral Zone. The first edition of this Encyclopedia assumed that the treaty was signed after the Romulan war in 2160, but "The* Pegasus*" (TNG) makes it clear that it was signed after the Tomed Incident.*

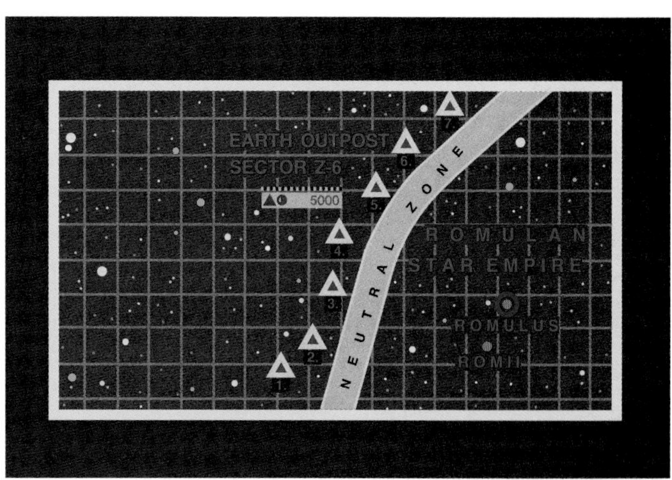

Map of the Romulan Neutral Zone, 2266.

Romulan Right of Statement. Romulan law allowing a condemned person to record an official statement regarding his guilt or innocence. Spock, captured by Romulan authorities for espionage in 2268, made an exceptionally long statement under this right, a successful effort to buy enough time for Kirk to complete their spy mission. ("The *Enterprise* Incident" [TOS]).

Romulan science vessel. A small ship, with a crew of about 73, that served as a testbed for an experimental **interphase generator**-based **cloaking device** in 2368. During the tests, the ship experienced a catastrophic malfunction of its warp core, but was able to return to Romulan space, thanks to assistance rendered by the *Enterprise*-D. ("The Next Phase" [TNG]). *This ship model was a modification of the Romulan scout from "The Defector" (TNG).*

Romulan Senate. Governing body of the **Romulan Star Empire**. Dr. **Telek R'Mor** communicated with the Romulan government regarding Captain Janeway's request that he transmit her crew's messages to **Starfleet**. The Romulan Senate promised to take the matter under advisement, but was not forthcoming with a decision. ("Eye of the Needle" [VGR]).

Romulan Star Empire. The formal name of the Romulan nation. An enigmatic offshoot of the **Vulcan** civilization, now residing on planets **Romulus** and **Remus**. ("Balance of Terror" [TOS]). The ancient Romulans left Vulcan two millennia ago, possibly in rebellion against **Surak**'s philosophy of logic and pacifism. The Romulans are a study in dramatic contrasts. Capable of considerable tenderness, they can also be violent in the extreme. Romulans have also been characterized as having great curiosity, while maintaining a tremendous self-confidence that borders on arrogance. The leader of the empire was called the **Praetor**. In interstellar relations, the Romulans have generally preferred to react to actions of a potential adversary, rather than committing themselves beforehand. ("The Neutral Zone" [TNG]). The Romulans fought a war with the Vulcans that lasted for a century. Neither side realized that the conflict had been ignited by **Quinn**, a member of the Q Continuum. *The war occurred at some unspecified time before 2072, when Quinn was imprisoned.* ("Death Wish" [VGR]). A bitter war between the Romulans and Earth forces around 2160 resulted in the establishment of the **Romulan Neutral Zone**, violation of which was considered an act of war. The Neutral Zone remained unviolated until 2266, when a single Romulan ship crossed into Federation space in a test of Federation resolve. ("Balance of Terror" [TOS]). SEE: **Treaty of Algeron**. The Romulans entered into a brief alliance with the **Klingon Empire** around 2268, when an agreement between the two powers resulted in the sharing of military technology and spacecraft designs. ("The *Enterprise* Incident" [TOS]). By the mid-2280s, Klingons were using ships described as birds-of-prey (a traditionally Romulan term) that were equipped with cloaking devices very similar to those developed by the Romulans. *(Star Trek III).* The Romulans again went into isolation in 2311, following the **Tomed Incident**, not to emerge until 2364, when early indications of **Borg** activity were detected. ("The Neutral Zone" [TNG]). The Romulans pursued a long-term policy of using covert means to destabilize the Klingon government going back to at least the 2340s. In 2367, Romulan operative **Sela** attempted to use mental conditioning of Starfleet officer

Romulan spacecraft.

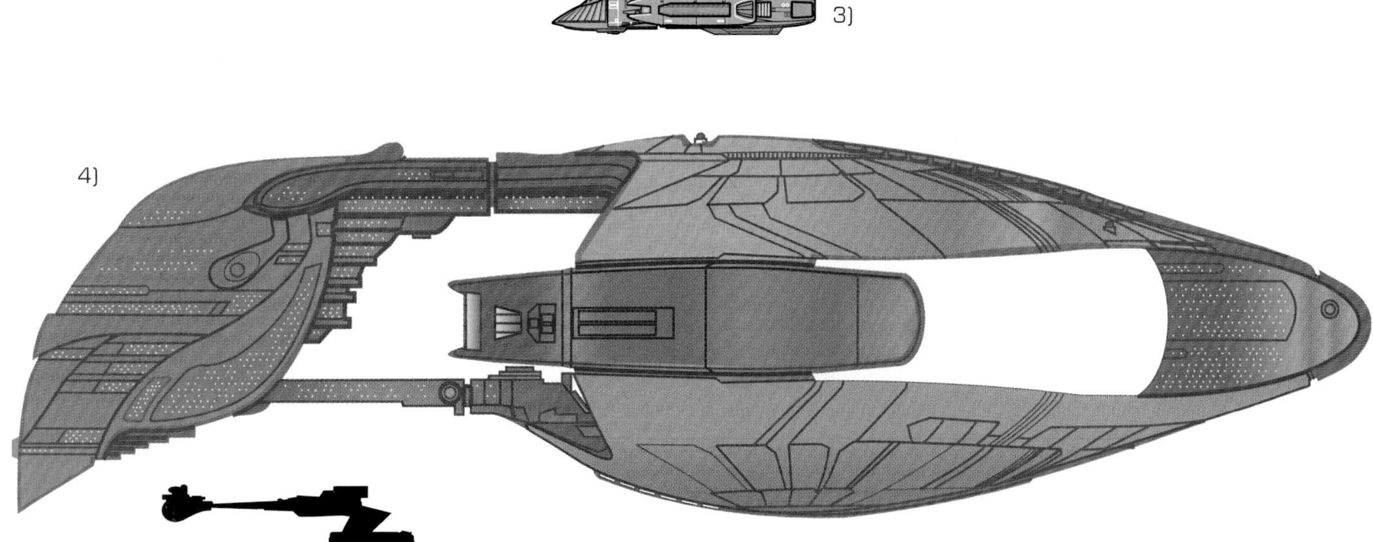

1) Romulan Bird-of-Prey ("Balance of Terror" [TOS]). 2) Romulan battle cruiser ("The Enterprise Incident" [TOS]). 3) Romulan scout ship ("The Defector" [TNG]). 4) Romulan warbird ("The Neutral Zone" [TNG]). NOTE: Drawings 1-3 are approximate scale. The warbird is smaller than scale; the small battle cruiser silhouette indicates size relationship.

Geordi La Forge to force him to assassinate Klingon Governor **Vagh**, a move calculated to spark distrust between the Klingons and the Federation. ("The Mind's Eye" [TNG]). Later that year, Sela formed a covert alliance with the **Duras** family in an effort to wrest control of the **Klingon High Council** from **Gowron**. The attempt was unsuccessful, but it triggered a **Klingon civil war** in 2367-2368, with Sela providing material support to the Duras forces. ("Redemption, Parts I and II" [TNG]). An underground movement emerged in the late 2360s, seeking to promote reunification of the Romulans with their distant Vulcan cousins. When the Romulan government became aware of this movement in 2368, **Proconsul Neral** tried to use it as a cover for an attempted invasion of planet Vulcan. The invasion was thwarted by the Federation Starfleet. Ambassador **Spock** chose to remain undercover on Romulus to continue work toward reunification. ("Unification, Parts I and II" [TNG]).

Romulan warbird. Massive, powerful spacecraft first encountered in 2364 when the Romulans violated the **Romulan Neutral Zone** in response to attacks by the **Borg**. Designated as ***D'deridex* class**, the warbird was nearly twice the overall length of a *Galaxy*-class starship ("The Neutral Zone" [TNG]) and utilized an **artificial quantum singularity** as a power source for its warp-drive system ("Face of the Enemy" [TNG]). A Romulan warbird was destroyed in 2369 when its power source became a nest for extradimensional **quantum singularity life-forms**. ("Timescape" [TNG]). Starfleet at one time designated this ship as a "B-Type warbird" ("The Defector" [TNG]). *The Romulan warbird was designed by Andrew Probert and built by Greg Jein. The ship first appeared in "The Neutral Zone" and was subsequently used in "Where Silence Has Lease" (TNG), "Contagion" (TNG), "Peak Performance" (TNG), "The Enemy" (TNG), "The Defector" (TNG), "Tin Man" (TNG), "Future Imperfect" (TNG), "Data's Day" (TNG), "The Mind's Eye" (TNG), "Redemption" (TNG), "Face of the Enemy" (TNG), "The Chase" (TNG), and "Timescape" (TNG).* SEE: **Romulan spacecraft.**

Romulans. Warrior civilization from the planets **Romulus** and **Remus**. An offshoot of the **Vulcan** people who left Vulcan two thousand years ago to found the **Romulan Star Empire**, the Romulans are a passionate, aggressive, but highly honorable people. ("Balance of Terror" [TOS], "Unification, Parts I and II" [TNG]). The ancient Romulans reached across much of the quadrant with outposts and settlements on such far-flung worlds as **Barradas III**, **Calder II**, **Dessica II**, Draken IV, and **Yadalla Prime**. SEE: **Debrune**. ("Gambit, Parts I and II" [TNG]).

In modern times, the Romulans conducted a brutal attack on the Klingon **Narendra III** outpost in 2344. The *Starship* ***Enterprise*-C**, under the command of **Captain Rachel Garrett**, responded to distress calls from Narendra III, and attempted to render aid to the Klingons. Although the *Enterprise*-C was reported lost, the incident led to closer Klingon-Federation ties in following years. ("Yesterday's *Enterprise*" [TNG]). Two Romulan officers were found on **Galorndon Core** in 2366 after the downing of their scout craft. ("The Enemy" [TNG]).

The Romulans believed the **Dominion** to be the greatest threat to the **Alpha Quadrant** in the last century. Accordingly, the Romulan government attempted in 2371 to collapse the **Bajoran wormhole** in order to prevent a potential Dominion invasion. The plan, which would have included the destruction of station **Deep Space 9** to eliminate witnesses, failed when a cloaked **Romulan warbird** accidentally caused Miles O'Brien to timeshift into the near future, where he witnessed the Romulan attack. Upon returning to his present, O'Brien warned station personnel, thwarting the plan. ("Visionary" [DS9]).

Two years later, when an alliance of the Dominion and the **Cardassian** Union threatened to destabilize the Alpha Quadrant, the Romulans joined forces with the Federation and the **Klingon Empire**, contributing a fleet of Romulan warships to the defense effort. ("By Inferno's Light" [DS9]).

The Romulan legislative body is known as the Romulan Senate. ("The Die is Cast" [DS9]).

Romulus. One of the two homeworlds of the **Romulan Star Empire**. ("Balance of Terror" [TOS]). Romulus was settled by expatriate **Vulcans** some two thousand years ago. ("Unification, Part I" [TNG]). **Admiral Jarok** described Romulus as a world of awesome beauty and spoke glowingly of such sights as the firefalls of Gal Gath'thong, the Valley of Chula, and the Apnex Sea. ("The Defector" [TNG]). Ambassador **Spock** traveled to Romulus in 2368, on a personal mission to promote peaceful reunification between the Romulans and the Vulcans. Shortly thereafter, Picard and Data also went to Romulus, on a covert mission to determine Spock's motives. ("Unification, Parts I and II" [TNG]). SEE: **Remus.**

Ronara. Class-M planet in the **Demilitarized Zone** between the Federation and Cardassian borders, site of a Federation colony. In 2370, **Lieutenant Ro Laren** made contact with a **Maquis** cell in a bar located at the colony. The bar later served as a covert meeting place for Ro and Captain Jean-Luc Picard. ("Preemptive Strike" [TNG]).

Rondon. (Robert Riordan). Starfleet officer. Rondon participated in Wesley Crusher's academy entrance examinations at **Relva VII** in 2364. Crusher successfully identified Rondon as a Zaldan, and acted correctly in addressing Rondon with brutal honesty in deference to the Zaldan belief that human courtesy is a form of dishonesty. ("Coming of Age" [TNG]).

Romulan military (TOS)

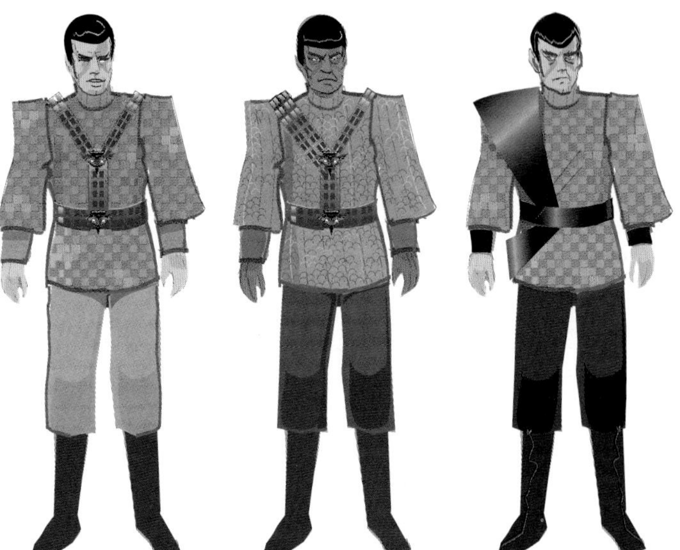

Romulan military (TNG, DS9)

Ronin. (Duncan Regehr). **Anaphasic lifeform** who appeared in human form as a 34-year-old man. Ronin, who needed the company of a suitable human female in order to maintain his molecular cohesion, claimed to have been born in 1647, in Glasgow, Scotland. He originally found a suitable host with Jessel Howard, gaining a powerful hypnotic control over her. Ronin formed a symbiotic relationship with Howard, giving her emotional sustenance, while she gave him molecular cohesion. Upon Jessel's death, Ronin joined with each successive female member of the Howard line, until his relationship with **Felisa Howard** in the 24th century. When Felisa died in 2370, Ronin attempted to join with **Beverly Crusher**, Felisa's granddaughter. He attempted to entice Beverly to resign from Starfleet, but Beverly learned of his true nature and was forced to kill him when he threated the lives of her friends. ("Sub Rosa" [TNG]).SEE: **Howard Family candle**.

Rooney. Starfleet officer assigned to Deep Space 9. On stardate 50049.3, Rooney, Hoya, and Bertram were killed when their runabout was destroyed by the Jem'Hadar at Torga IV. Rooney had played the trumpet, and on one occasion he had people dancing in the aisles of Quark's bar. ("The Ship" [DS9]).

Roosevelt, U.S.S. Federation starship, *Excelsior* class, Starfleet registry number NCC-2573. The *Roosevelt* was among the ships lost at the battle of **Wolf 359**. Dr. **Riley Frazier** was a science officer aboard the *Roosevelt* before she was assimilated by the **Borg**. ("Unity" [VGR]). *Named for American president Theodore Roosevelt.*

root beer. Carbonated Earth beverage made with yeast and the extracts of several plant roots. ("Facets" [DS9]). Quark and Garak described root beer as being bubbly, cloying, and insidiously happy—a frightening metaphor for the United Federation of Planets. ("The Way of the Warrior" [DS9]). Nog, however, really liked the stuff. ("The Ascent" [DS9]).

root canal. Engineering slang used to describe a rebuilding of a computer system's software from the ground up. Usually performed only when the system is considered to be beyond conventional repair. Miles O'Brien, who was distinctly unimpressed with **Cardassian** technology, devoutly wanted to perform a root canal on the Cardassian-built computers on **Deep Space 9**. ("The Forsaken" [DS9]).

root command structure. The basic computer programs that control the **Borg collective**. ("I, Borg" [TNG]).

rop'ngor. Disease that sometimes affects Klingon children, somewhat akin to terrestrial measles. As an adult, Worf came down with a case of *rop'ngor* in 2365, much to his embarrassment. Sensitive to Worf's feelings, Dr. Katherine Pulaski made up an excuse for him: that he had been engaged in ritual Klingon fasting and thus was not at peak physical condition. ("Up the Long Ladder" [TNG]).

Ropal City. Community on one of the **Volon** colonies**. Calvin Hudson** alleged that **Cardassian** authorities stoned two citizens on the streets of Ropal in 2370. ("The Maquis, Part I" [DS9]).

Ross, Yeoman Teresa. (Venita Wolf). Crew member aboard the original *Starship Enterprise*. Ross was abducted along with other bridge personnel to the planet **Gothos** by the entity **Trelane** in 2267. Trelane fancied Ross's presence, dressing her in a floor-length gown and making the yeoman his dancing partner. ("The Squire of Gothos" [TOS]).

Rossa, Admiral Connaught. (Barbara Townsend). Starfleet official. Rossa had two sons, both of whom served in Starfleet; and both were killed in the line of duty. For years, Admiral Rossa also believed her grandson, **Jeremiah Rossa**, to have been killed by **Talarians** at **Galen IV** in 2356, until he was discovered aboard a disabled Talarian observation craft in 2367. ("Suddenly Human" [TNG]).

Rossa, Connor. Starfleet officer who served on the Federation colony at **Galen IV**. Connor Rossa was killed in 2356 when **Talarian** forces attacked and destroyed the colony. His son, **Jeremiah Rossa**, survived and was captured by the Talarian **Endar**. ("Suddenly Human" [TNG]).

Rossa, Jeremiah. (Chad Allen). A human male born in 2353 on **Galen IV**, to Federation personnel **Connor Rossa** and **Moira Rossa**. When Jeremiah was three, the colony on Galen IV was overrun by Talarian forces. All the colonists, including Jeremiah's parents, were believed killed in the attack. Jeremiah, unknown to Federation authorities, was the only human to survive. Talarian officer **Endar** discovered him near the body of his mother and took the child home to be raised as a Talarian named **Jono**. ("Suddenly Human" [TNG]).

Rossa, Moira. Wife of Starfleet officer **Connor Rossa**. Moira Rossa was the biological mother of **Jeremiah Rossa**. She was killed in the 2356 **Talarian** attack on the **Galen IV** colony. ("Suddenly Human" [TNG]).

Roswell. City in southwest New Mexico on **Earth**. In July, 1947, an extraterrestrial spacecraft of **Ferengi** origin crashed near Roswell, and was taken by the American military for study to **Hangar 18** at Wright Field. The ship and its crew later escaped, and the American government subsequently denied ever having captured an alien ship. SEE: ***Quark's Treasure***. ("Little Green Men" [DS9]). *Some claim that one of the escaping Ferengi was left behind to fend for himself. He eventually made his way to Texas where, as befits a true Ferengi, he amassed a great fortune and ran (unsuccessfully) for U.S. president several times as an independent candidate.*

Rousseau V. Location of a spectacular asteroid belt. **Wesley Crusher** re-created Rousseau V on the holodeck for the benefit of the lovely young **Salia** of **Daled IV**. ("The Dauphin" [TNG]).

Royale, Hotel. SEE: ***Hotel Royale***.

"Royale, The." *Next Generation* episode #38. Written by Keith Mills. Directed by Cliff Bole. Stardate 42625.4. *First aired in 1989. An* Enterprise-*D away team is trapped in a bizarre re-creation of a setting from a pulp novel,* Hotel Royale. GUEST CAST: Diana Muldaur as **Pulaski, Dr. Katherine**; Sam Anderson as Assistant manager; Jill Jacobson as Vanessa; Leo Garcia as Bellboy; Noble Willingham as Texas; Colm Meaney as **O'Brien, Miles**; Gregory Beecroft as **Mickey D**. SEE: ***Charybdis*; Fermat's last theorem; *Hotel Royale*; Mickey D.; NASA; Richey, Colonel Stephen; Theta 116; United States of America**.

Roykirk, Jackson. Noted 21st-century Earth scientist, regarded as one of the most brilliant though erratic scientists of his time, who designed the space probe ***Nomad***. Roykirk's goal was to build the perfect thinking machine capable of independent logic. The early interstellar probe, *Nomad*, was the result. ("The Changeling" [TOS]).

Rozahn, Minister. (Betty McGuire). Member of the **Bajoran Chamber of Ministers** on Bajor. She, along with **Vedek Sorad**, journeyed to Deep Space 9 in 2370 to inform **Haneek** that the **Skrreea**n request to settle on Bajor had been denied. ("Sanctuary" [DS9])

Rozhenko, Alexander. (Brian Bonsall, Jon Steuer, James Sloyan). Son of Starfleet officer **Worf** and Federation Ambassador **K'Ehleyr.** Alexander was born in 2366, on the 43rd day of Maktag, and spent his infancy in the care of his mother. Worf learned of Alexander's existence shortly before K'Ehleyr's death in 2367, but was reluctant to acknowledge that Alexander was his son, for fear that Alexander would bear the disgrace of Worf's

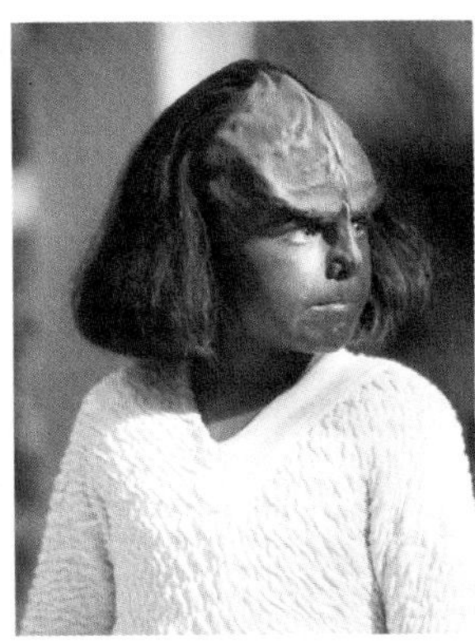

discommendation. Worf did accept his son, who returned to Earth to be raised by Worf's adoptive parents, **Sergey** and **Helena Rozhenko**. ("Reunion" [TNG]). Alexander remained on Earth for about a year, but the Rozhenkos became concerned that the child needed his father, and returned Alexander to Worf's custody aboard the *Enterprise*-D. ("New Ground" [TNG]). Alexander was fond of heroic tales of the ancient American West, and once persuaded his father and Counselor Troi to join him in a simulation designed for him by **Reginald Barclay**, called the ***Ancient West***. ("A Fistful of Datas" [TNG]). In 2370, when Alexander was to make his choice of whether or not to undergo the first Rite of Ascension, he was visited by a mysterious stranger named **K'mtar**, who helped young Alexander to better understand the Klingon way. K'mtar was, in reality, Alexander's future self, although Alexander did not know this. ("Firstborn" [TNG]). SEE: **Age of Ascension.** *The episode does not indicate whether Alexander ever performed the Rite of Ascension.* Alexander was happy living on Earth with his grandparents in 2372. ("The Way of the Warrior" [DS9]). *Alexander was played by Jon Steuer in "Reunion," but Brian Bonsall assumed the role in later episodes. Brian Bonsall had previously played little Andrew Keaton in the* Family Ties *television series. Alexander's future self in "Firstborn" (TNG) was played by James Sloyan.*

Rozhenko, Eric-Christopher. (In an alternate **quantum reality** visited by Worf in 2370, Eric-Christopher was the three year-old son of Deanna Troi and Worf. In this alternate reality, Worf and Deanna had been married for several years.) ("Parallels" [TNG]).

Rozhenko, Helena. (Georgia Brown). **Worf**'s adoptive mother. Helena and her husband, Sergey, faced the considerable challenges of raising a Klingon child in a human environment. Helena even learned to make Klingon ***rokeg* blood pie**. They loved their child enough to make a deliberate choice to allow young Worf to find his own path. ("Family" [TNG]). Helena and Sergey lived for a time on the farm world of **Gault**, but later moved to Earth. The Rozhenkos had another, biological, son, who entered Starfleet Academy at the same time as Worf, but found it not to his liking. ("Heart of Glory" [TNG]). Helena and Sergey accepted custody of Worf's son, **Alexander Rozhenko**, after the death of **K'Ehleyr** in 2367. ("Reunion" [TNG]). They returned to Earth to care for Alexander, but after a year found that the child had difficulty adapting to life in human society. They realized that Alexander needed his father, so they returned the child to the *Enterprise*-D in 2368. ("New Ground" [TNG]).

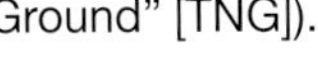

Rozhenko, Nikolai. (Paul Sorvino). Son of **Sergey** and **Helena Rozhenko** and adoptive older brother of **Worf**. During their childhood, Nikolai and Worf frequently disagreed, and their personalities clashed well into their adulthood. Nikolai entered **Starfleet Academy** with Worf in 2357, but found the atmosphere too restrictive and left the academy at the end of his first year. Nikolai later became a scientist and cultural observer. In 2370, he was assigned to planet **Boraal II**. Nikolai overstepped the role of observer, and became personally involved with the village he was assigned to study. During that year, severe plasmonic reactions began destroying the planet's atmosphere. Rozhenko sent a distress call, and while waiting for help to arrive, protected the villagers with an energy shield from his observation post, a violation of the Prime Directive. The *Starship Enterprise*-D responded to Rozhenko's call, and Captain Jean-Luc Picard refused to erect an atmospheric shield to protect the village, citing Prime Directive considerations. Rozhenko then surreptitiously transported the Boraalan villagers into a **holodeck** representation of their encampment, forcing Captain Picard to participate in a plan in which the Boraal villagers were maintained in a holographic simulation until they were beamed down to a new planetary home. After the entire Boraalan village was successfully transported to the surface of Vacca VI, Nikolai decided to remain with the village and Dobara, with whom he had fathered a child. He became the village's new chronicle, taking **Vorin**'s place. ("Homeward" [TNG]). *Nikolai's existence and his time at Starfleet Academy was first alluded to in "Heart of Glory" (TNG), although he didn't get a name until "Homeward" (TNG).*

Rozhenko, Sergey. (Theodore Bikel). **Worf**'s adoptive father. Rozhenko, husband to **Helena Rozhenko**, had been a chief petty officer, serving as a warp-field specialist aboard the ***U.S.S. Intrepid***, the starship that rendered aid to the Klingons following the **Khitomer** massacre of 2346. Rozhenko and his wife adopted a young Klingon child named Worf, found in the wreckage at Khitomer, and raised him as their own child. Sergey and Helena Rozhenko visited Worf aboard the *Enterprise*-D in 2367 when the ship was under repair at **Earth Station McKinley**. ("Family" [TNG]).

Rozhenko, Shannara. (In an alternate **quantum reality** visited by Worf in 2370, the two year-old daughter of Deanna Troi and Worf. In that alternate reality, Worf and Deanna had been married for several years.) ("Parallels" [TNG]).

Ruah IV. Class-M planet supporting numerous plant and animal forms including a genus of proto-humanoids. Ruah IV was studied by **Professor Richard Galen** in his effort to learn about an ancient humanoid species that seeded many planets. These ancient humanoids may have seeded the primordial life on Ruah IV billions of years ago. ("The Chase" [TNG]).

Rubber Tree People. In the mythology of some native Central American cultures on Earth, the Rubber Tree People were an ancient tribe that was the ancestor of those present-day Native American peoples. According to legend, the ancient **Sky Spirits** created the first Rubber Tree People in their own image. Like the Sky Spirits, the Rubber Tree People honored the land above all else. The Sky Spirits led the Rubber Tree People to a new land, where they could live for all time. The Rubber Tree People were endowed with a bold sense of curiosity and adventure, and some of their descendents even voyaged to the stars, finding new homes on other worlds. But even in the 24th century, a few descendents of the Rubber Tree People still lived in what became known as the American continents, eschewing advanced technology in favor of preserving their traditional way of life. ("Tattoo" [VGR]). SEE: **Inheritors**.

Rubicon, U.S.S. Runabout, *Danube* class, Starfleet registry number NCC-72936. Assigned to station **Deep Space 9** in 2371. The ship was named by Commander **Benjamin Sisko**. ("Family Business" [DS9]). Doctor Bashir and Chief O'Brien used the *Rubicon* to conduct a bio-survey of Merik III just prior to stardate 49066.5. Shortly thereafter, the *Rubicon* was forced to make an emergency landing on planet Bopak III after a group of **Jem'Hadar** hit the runabout with a subspace magneton pulse.

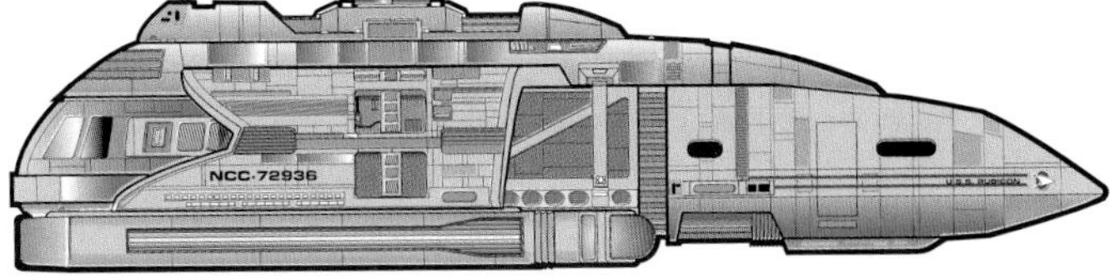

After being held prisoners by a group of Jem'Hadar led by **Goran'Agar**, Bashir and O'Brien returned to station Deep Space 9 aboard the *Rubicon*. ("Hippocratic Oath" [DS9]). *The* Rubicon *replaced the* Mekong, *lost in "The Die Is Cast" (DS9). The* Rubicon *was named after the river in Italy that was of strategic importance to Caesar in 49 B.C.*

Rubicun III. Class-M planet in the Rubicun star system and home to the **Edo** civilization. The *Enterprise*-D visited Rubicun III in 2364 for R&R, but their mission turned to crisis when Wesley Crusher broke one of the Edo laws and was sentenced to death. The boy's life was saved at the expense of the Prime Directive. ("Justice" [TNG]). *One location used for filming parts of Rubicun III's exteriors was the Tillman Water Reclamation Plant in Van Nuys, California, the same location used for Starfleet Academy in the episode "First Duty" (TNG) and Starfleet Command in "Homefront" (DS9). Other Rubicun III exteriors were filmed at the Huntington Library in Pasadena.*

Rubicun star system. Planetary system adjoining the **Strnad system** and containing the Class-M planet **Rubicun III**, home to the **Edo** civilization. ("Justice" [TNG]). SEE: **Edos**.

rubindium crystal. Component of a subcutaneous transponder. Kirk and Spock, imprisoned on a mission to planet **Ekos** in 2268, removed their transponders so that the rubindium crystals could be used as a crude laser. ("Patterns of Force" [TOS]). SEE: **transponder, emergency**.

Ruby. (Hillary Hayes). Attractive woman who was a character in the **Dixon Hill** stories. Ruby was a friend and sometimes companion of Dixon Hill. *(Star Trek: First Contact). Named for Ruby Moore, wife of* Star Trek: First Contact *cowriter Ronald D. Moore.*

Rudellian brain fever. Type of illness. Miles O'Brien feared his wife had been stricken with Rudellian brain fever upon returning from planet Bajor in 2373. ("The Assignment" [DS9]).

Rudellian plague. Disease. The Cardassian colony on planet Pentath III was afflicted by Rudellian plague in 2372. ("Rules of Engagement" [DS9]).

Rudman, Commander. Officer on the *Starship Merrimac*. ("Birthright, Part I" [TNG]).

Rugal. (Vidal Peterson). Cardassian national born in 2358, the son of **Kotran Pa'Dar**. In 2362, while a child living on planet **Bajor**, Rugal was believed killed in a terrorist attack. Unbeknownst to Rugal's father, the child was taken to the **Tozhat Resettlement Center** where he was adopted by **Proka Migdal**. Raised in **Bajoran** culture, Rugal was taught to hate **Cardassians**. In 2370, his biological father learned Rugal was alive, and sought custody of the boy. Benjamin Sisko, arbitrating the dispute, ruled that Rugal was a victim in the affair and awarded custody of the boy to Pa'Dar, despite Rugal's wishes to remain with his adoptive parents. ("Cardassians" [DS9]). *Vidal Peterson previously portrayed the Romulan boy D'Tan in "Unification, Part II" (TNG).*

Rugalan fever. Deadly disease. Audrid Dax's daughter, Neema, spent two weeks in the hospital with Rugalan fever over two hundred years ago. ("Nor the Battle to the Strong" [DS9]).

Rujian. Planet. Location of a steeplechase that Curzon Dax and Benjamin Sisko once attended, where they met two Ruji twin sisters and had a swell time. ("A Man Alone" [DS9]).

Ruk. (Ted Cassidy). Sophisticated **android** built millennia ago by the **Old Ones** of planet **Exo III**. Ruk was discovered by archaeologist Roger Korby, who used Ruk to build additional androids. Ruk was eventually destroyed by Korby when the old android rediscovered his survival instinct. ("What Are Little Girls Made Of?" [TOS]). *Actor Ted Cassidy was also famous for his role of Lurch in the* Addams Family *television series. SEE:* **Homn**.

Rul the Obscure. One of the bidders at an auction at Quark's bar in 2369. Rul bought an artifact brought back by **Vash** from the Gamma Quadrant. ("Q-Less" [DS9]).

Rules of Acquisition. SEE: **Ferengi Rules of Acquisition.**

"Rules of Acquisition." *Deep Space Nine* episode #27. Teleplay by Ira Steven Behr. Story by Hilary Bader. Directed by David Livingston. No stardate given. *First aired in 1993. Quark is recruited by the grand nagus for important negotiations in the Gamma Quadrant. Quark takes his newest waiter, Pel, with him, unaware that he is really a she. This episode marks the first appearance of a Ferengi female.* SEE: **Andorian transport; brizeen nitrate; Dax, Curzon; Dominion; Dosi; Ferengi; Ferengi Rules of Acquisition; flaked blood fleas; Gramilian sand peas; Hupyrian beetle snuff; Inglatu; Karemma; Kibberian fire diamonds; *lokar* beans; Maihar'du; Pel; Quark; Replimat; *tongo*; tube grubs; tulaberry wine; Zek, Grand Nagus; Zyree.**

"Rules of Engagement." *Deep Space Nine* episode #90. Story by Bradley Thompson & David Weddle. Teleplay by Ronald D. Moore. Directed by LeVar Burton. Stardate 49665.3. *First aired in 1996. Lieutenant Commander Worf is accused of firing on a Klingon transport vessel, killing all aboard. A hearing convenes on Deep Space 9, where it is learned that the incident was a setup by the Klingons to disgrace the Federation and gain additional Cardassian territory.* GUEST CAST: Ron Canada as **Ch'Pok**; Deborah Strang as **T'Lara**; Christopher Michael as Helm officer. SEE: **Ch'Pok; Galorda Prime; holodeck and holosuite programs; Klingon Empire; O'Brien, Miles; Pentath III; Pentath system; Rudellian plague; Sompek; T'Lara; Tong Vey; Worf.**

***rulot* seeds.** Agricultural product used by Cardassians. ("The Homecoming" [DS9]).

***Rumarie*.** Ancient pagan **Vulcan** festival. The *Rumarie* was last celebrated over a millennium ago. ("Meld" [VGR]). SEE: **Rillan grease**. *"Gambit, Part II" (TNG) establishes that the Vulcan Time of Awakening was about 2,000 years ago, so it might seem that this holdover from the old Vulcan ways survived a thousand years after the time of Surak.*

Rumpelstiltskin. (Michael John Anderson). Character who reputedly spun straw into gold in an ancient Earth fairy tale. In 2369, unknown aliens from the **Gamma Quadrant** created a replica of Rumpelstiltskin on station Deep Space 9. The character was drawn from the imagination of Chief **Miles O'Brien**, who had been reading a bedtime story to his daughter, Molly, on stardate 46853. The alien version of Rumpelstiltskin was created so that the aliens could better study humans. ("If Wishes Were Horses" [DS9]). SEE: **Bokai, Buck**.

runabout simulation. Holographic re-creation of a Starfleet **runabout**, used for training purposes. ("Facets" [DS9]).

runabout. Generic term for small Federation **starship**s used for relatively short-range interstellar travel. Resembling an

enlarged **shuttlecraft**, runabouts had a cockpit that incorporated a short-range two-person transporter, as well as seating for four people, including a two-person flight crew. The runabout's aft section contained living accommodations, and the midsection was a detachable module that could be replaced for different mission profiles. The *Enterprise*-D off-loaded three runabouts at station **Deep Space 9** in 2369. ("Emissary" [DS9]). Starfleet commissioned the first runabouts in 2368. ("Paradise" [DS9]). Aft of the pilots' compartment, the craft contained a small living area, with bunks and a replicator for food processing. This area made the craft comfortable for extended travel. ("Timescape" [TNG]). A runabout's exterior shell is made from duranium composites. ("Q-Less" [DS9]). SEE: ***Ganges, U.S.S.; Mekong, U.S.S.; Orinoco, U.S.S.; Rio Grande, U.S.S.; Rubicon, U.S.S.; Yangtzee Kiang, U.S.S.*** *Runabouts were first seen in "Emissary" [DS9], although the* **U.S.S. Jenolan** *(Scotty's* Sydney-*class transport in "Relics" [TNG]) may also have been an early runabout. The aft section of the runabout was first seen in "Timescape" (TNG). The* Danube-*class runabouts seen in* Deep Space 9 *are traditionally named after great rivers. The runabout was designed by Rick Sternbach and Jim Martin, and the interior cockpit set was designed by Joseph Hodges, all under the direction of Herman Zimmerman. The aft compartment was designed by Richard James. The miniature was built by Tony Meininger. Although runabouts are primarily used in* Star Trek: Deep Space Nine, *Picard and company took a trip in an unnamed runabout in "Timescape" [TNG]), which was the only time to date that the aft compartment has been seen.*

Runners, the. A constellation that can been seen from Bajoran space. ("Second Sight" [DS9])

Rura Penthe. Frozen, almost uninhabitable planetoid on which was located a **Klingon** prison camp. Rura Penthe was known throughout the galaxy as the "aliens' graveyard," because prisoners were used for forced labor at the **dilithium** mines there. The large asteroid, deep inside of Klingon territory, was so inhospitable that the prison camp needed no guard towers or electronic frontier to keep the prisoners in. Kirk and McCoy were sentenced to life at Rura Penthe after being wrongly convicted for the murder of **Chancellor Gorkon** in 2293. *(Star Trek VI: The Undiscovered Country). Some of the exterior scenes for Rura Penthe were actually filmed on a glacier in Alaska.*

Rurigan. (Kenneth Tobey). Native of **Yadera Prime**. Rurigan left his homeworld after it was conquered by the **Dominion** in 2340. He moved to planet **Yadera II,** where he used a **hologenerator** to create a holographic village where he could live. The hologenerator also filled the village with holographic people whose programming became so sophisticated that they actually developed sentience. As the years passed, Rurigan nearly forgot that the village was not real. He had a granddaughter, **Taya**, and loved her as if she were a real flesh-and-blood child. In 2370, the hologenerator malfunctioned, causing several villagers to vanish. Dax and Odo, visiting the planet, repaired the device, restoring the missing **sentient holographic lifeforms**. ("Shadowplay" [DS9]).

Rurik the Damned. Legendary **Klingon** warrior who conquered Zora Fel and liberated Vrax. A statue of Rurik the Damned stood in the **Hall of Warriors** on **Ty'Gokor**. ("Apocalypse Rising" [DS9]).

Rushton infection. Disease. A Rushton infection killed **Jeremy Aster**'s father in 2361. ("The Bonding" [TNG]).

Russell, Dr. Toby. (Caroline Kava). Neurogeneticist from the **Adelman Neurological Institute**. Dr. Russell pioneered several revolutionary medical therapies, including the **genetronic replicator** technique. Russell's career was marred by accusations that she had sometimes sacrificed patients' lives in order to gather experimental data. Russell's genetronic technique saved the life of *Enterprise*-D Security Chief Worf in 2368. ("Ethics" [TNG]). SEE: **borathium**.

Ruth. (Maggie Thrett). One of Mudd's women. Ruth had long black hair and had lived on a pelagic planet with sea ranchers before being recruited by Harry Mudd as a wife for a settler on planet **Ophiucus III**. Ruth instead married one of the miners on **Rigel XII**. ("Mudd's Women" [TOS]). *Ruth's last name was never mentioned in the aired version, but a final draft script of the episode listed her as Ruth Bonaventure.*

Ruth. (Shirley Bonne). Attractive woman who was romantically involved with James Kirk in 2252 during his academy days. A re-creation of Ruth appeared on the **amusement park planet** in 2267, looking just as Kirk had remembered her 15 years ago. ("Shore Leave" [TOS]). *Ruth was not given a last name in the episode.*

Rutia IV. A politically neutral Class-M planet that enjoyed a long trading relationship with the Federation. Although the planet's population was united under a single planetary government, a dissident group called the **Ansata** on the western continent sought political independence in 2296. This bid was denied by the Rutian government, and the Ansata began a long terrorist struggle to gain recognition of their plight. Although the Ansata were only believed to number about two hundred members, they were successful in causing significant disruption of Rutian society. In 2366, Ansata leader **Kyril Finn** led an apparently futile attack against the *Enterprise*-D, a successful attempt to gain Federation involvement in their fight. ("The High Ground" [TNG]).

Rutian archaeological vessel. Spacecraft. The only vessel reported in range of the **Dulisian IV** colony when it transmitted a distress call in 2368. ("Unification, Part II" [TNG]).

Rutians. The inhabitants of **Rutia IV**, humanoid in appearance. Rutian males are marked by a distinctive white streak of hair; females are generally red-haired. ("The High Ground" [TNG])

Rutledge, U.S.S. Federation starship, *New Orleans* class, Starfleet registry number NCC-57295, commanded by **Captain Benjamin Maxwell** during the war between the Federation and the **Cardassians**. Future *Enterprise*-D crew member **Miles O'Brien** served aboard the *Rutledge* as tactical officer. The

Rutledge responded to a Cardassian attack on the Federation outpost at **Setlik III**, but was too late to prevent the massacre. ("The Wounded" [TNG]). In early 2373, the *Rutledge* and the *Starship Tecumseh* were ordered to conduct a counterattack against Klingon forces in the **Archanis** sector. ("Nor the Battle to the Strong" [DS9]).

Ruwon. (Jack Shearer). Leader of a **Romulan** delegation sent to station Deep Space 9 in 2371 to receive **Starfleet**'s latest intelligence on the **Dominion**. The delegation had secret orders to destroy the **Bajoran wormhole** in order to prevent a feared Dominion invasion of the Alpha Quadrant, and to destroy Deep Space 9 as well. ("Visionary" [DS9]). *Jack Shearer also played Admiral Strickler in "Non Sequitur" (VGR) and Admiral Hayes in* Star Trek: First Contact.

RVN. SEE: **rybo-viroxic-nucleic structure.**

rybo-viroxic-nucleic structure. Long organic compound that is one of the key factors in development during puberty of many humanoids. As such life-forms grow older, **RVN** takes on additional viroxic sequences. When Captain Picard and the other members of the *Shuttlecraft* ***Fermi*** passed through a **molecular reversion field** while returning to the *Enterprise*-D on stardate 46235, O'Brien had difficulty getting a transporter lock on the crew because the field was masking part of their patterns. The transporter therefore only registered part of the RVN patterns, leaving off key sequences, and thus, the shuttle's crew was transformed to children. A record of the shuttle crew's RVN patterns was in the transporter pattern buffer, making it possible to restore the lost viroxic sequences during the transport process. ("Rascals" [TNG]). *Yeah, well, we don't think it makes much sense, either.*

ryetalyn. Rare mineral substance. Ryetalyn was used to cure Rigelian fever, a deadly disease that infected the crew of the *Starship Enterprise* in 2269. A deposit of ryetalyn was found on a small planetoid in the Omega system that belonged to **Flint**. ("Requiem for Methuselah" [TOS]).

S.I.D. Abbreviation for ship in distress. ("The Maquis, Part I" [DS9]).

Saavik. (Kirstie Alley, Robin Curtis). Starfleet officer who, as a cadet, served as navigator on the *Starship Enterprise* during the **Project Genesis** crisis in 2285. Saavik, a Vulcan, had been mentored by **Spock**, who counseled her that tolerance of her human colleagues was logical. *(Star Trek II: The Wrath of Khan).* Following the Genesis crisis, Saavik, along with **David Marcus**, transferred to the ***U.S.S. Grissom*** for further study of the **Genesis Planet**. Saavik later returned to planet Vulcan. *(Star Trek III: The Search for Spock, Star Trek IV: The Voyage Home). Saavik apparently had sex with Spock on the Genesis Planet when Spock was undergoing* **Pon farr** *during* Star Trek III. *A scene cut from the final version of* Star Trek IV *would have shown that the reason Saavik remained on Vulcan was because she was pregnant with Spock's child. (Because the scene was cut, we don't consider this to be "evidence" that it "really" happened.). The script for* Star Trek II *contained a line that would have suggested Saavik was half-Vulcan and half-Romulan, but the line was cut, and later films seemed to assume that she was pure Vulcan. Actor Kirstie Alley played Saavik in* Star Trek II, *but Robin Curtis assumed the role in* Star Trek III *and* Star Trek IV. *Robin Curtis later played Tallera in "Gambit, Parts I and II" (TNG). An early-draft script for* Star Trek VI *featured Saavik in the role that eventually became Valeris.*

Sabak's armor. Ancient legendary artifact that is a revered icon of the **Klingon** people. ("The Sword of Kahless" [DS9]).

***Saber*-class starship.** Type of Federation starship in use in the late 24th century. The *U.S.S. Yeager* was a ship of the *Saber* class. *(Star Trek: First Contact). The* Saber-*class starship was designed by Alex Jaegar at ILM. It was rendered as a computer-generated visual effect.*

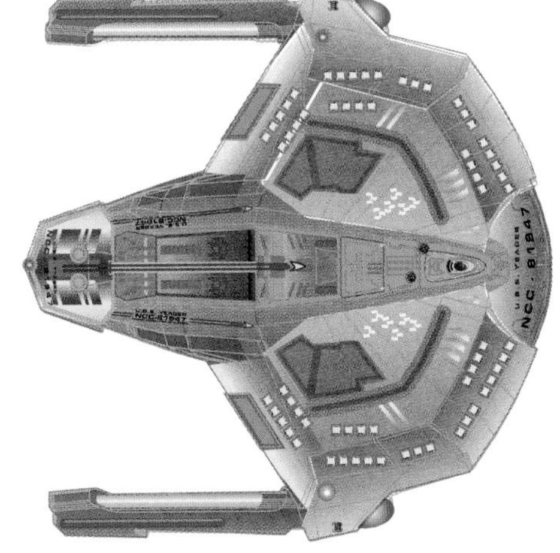

sabre bear. Klingon animal found on **Kang's Summit**, sometimes hunted by adventurous warriors. ("In Purgatory's Shadow" [DS9]).

Sacajawea. Type-6 shuttlecraft carried aboard the *U.S.S. Voyager*. In 2373 the *Sacajawea* became caught in a magnetic storm and crashed on a planet in a binary system in the Delta Quadrant. **Kathryn Janeway** was almost killed in the crash. ("Coda" [VGR]). *The shuttle was named for the Shoshone woman who guided the Lewis and Clark expedition to the Pacific Northwest.*

Sacred Chalice of Rixx. An important artifact in **Betazoid** culture, held for ceremonial purposes by **Lwaxana Troi**. ("Haven" [TNG]). Deanna Troi described the chalice as a "moldy old pot." ("Manhunt" [TNG]). *The name of the artifact is a gag reference to* Star Trek *executive producer Rick Berman.*

"Sacred Ground." *Voyager* episode #43. Teleplay by Lisa Klink. Story by Geo Cameron. Directed by Robert Duncan McNeill. Even though this was the 43rd episode produced, it was the 48th one aired. Stardate 50063.2. *First aired in 1996. Kes is sent into an untreatable coma by an energy field generated by a sacred shrine, and Janeway must go through a spiritual ritual in order to find a cure for her condition. This was the first episode directed by actor Robert Duncan McNeill.* GUEST CAST: Becky Ann Baker as **Nechisti Guide**; Estelle Harris as Old woman; Keene Curtis as Old man #2; Parley Baer as Old man #1; Harry Groener as **Nechani magistrate, The**. SEE: **Ancestral Spirits; biogenic field; cultural database; Delios VII; Janeway, Kathryn; Karis Tribe; lectrazine; .ani magistrate; Nechani; Nechisti Council; Nechisti guide; Nechisti Order; Nechisti shrine; neodyne light; *nesset*; neuroleptic shock; Nevad; psychoactive drug; subdermal bioprobe; *Tarchee* cat; thoron.**

Sacred Marketplace. Center of commerce on planet **Ferenginar**, the **Ferengi** homeworld. The **grand nagus** traditionally made important pronouncements from the Grand Steps of the Sacred Marketplace. ("Prophet Motive" [DS9]). A large, domed complex it was the location of the **Tower of Commerce**. ("Family Business" [DS9]).

Sacred Texts. Religious writings of the **Bajoran** faith. ("Collaborator" [DS9]).

saddle. Leather appliance used as a seat for the rider of a horse or other mount animal. Captain **Jean-Luc Picard** kept a saddle that he'd owned since his academy days with him aboard the *Enterprise*-D. Picard noted that most serious riders own their own saddles. His crew agreed. ("Starship Mine" [TNG]).

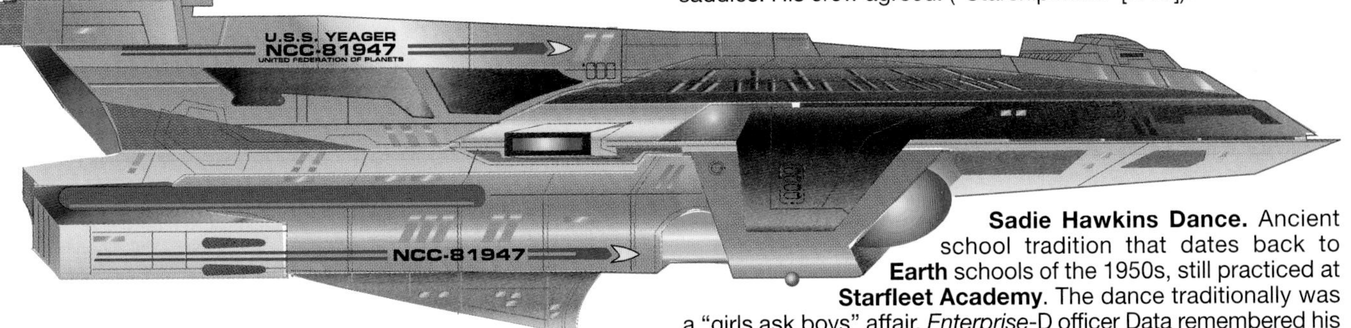

Sadie Hawkins Dance. Ancient school tradition that dates back to **Earth** schools of the 1950s, still practiced at **Starfleet Academy**. The dance traditionally was a "girls ask boys" affair. *Enterprise*-D officer Data remembered his academy Sadie Hawkins Dance as a "notably awkward affair." ("The Game" [TNG]).

SafeTech. Twenty-first century **Earth** company that offered various information-related services on the **Net**, such as a fingerprint database and a retinal scan service on Channel 178. ("Past Tense, Part I" [DS9]).

Sahndara. Star that became a nova millennia ago. Humanoid inhabitants of the Sahndara system fled their doomed world, eventually settling on a planet they named **Platonius**. ("Plato's Stepchildren" [TOS]). SEE: **Platonians**.

Sahsheer. Beautiful crystal-like formations from planet **Kelva** in the **Andromeda Galaxy** that form so rapidly they can be seen to grow. ("By Any Other Name" [TOS]). In 2369, a cargo ship piloted by **Captain Jaheel** was scheduled to deliver a shipment of Tamen Sahsheer to planet **Largo V**. ("Babel" [DS9]). *A rose, by any other name.*

Sahving Valley. Location on planet Bajor. Site where Bajoran resistance fighter **Li Nalas** killed **Gul Zarale**. ("The Homecoming" [DS9]).

Saint Emilion. French wine. Saint Emilion was a favorite of Tom Paris. ("The Cloud" [VGR]).

Sakar. Brilliant Vulcan theoretical scientist, often compared to such luminaries as **Albert Einstein** and **Dr. Richard Daystrom**. ("The Ultimate Computer" [TOS]).

Sakari. Humanoid inhabitants of a planet in the Delta Quadrant. In the mid-24th century, the Sakari were attacked by the **Borg**, who virtually eradicated their society. A few survivors escaped assimilation by hiding in underground mines. The crew of the ***U.S.S. Voyager***, who discovered the Sakari in 2373, helped them avoid further detection by hiding their **gallicite**-coated power conduits. ("Blood Fever" [VGR]).

***Sakharov*, *Shuttlecraft*.** Shuttlecraft 1, assigned to *Starship Enterprise*-D. The *Sakharov* transported **Dr. Katherine Pulaski** to the **Darwin Genetic Research Station** on planet **Gagarin IV**. ("Unnatural Selection" [TNG]). **Q** commandeered the *Sakharov* in 2366 during an attack by the **Calamarain** against the *Enterprise*-D. The Calamarain's real target was Q, and Q's action to protect the *Enterprise*-D was an unusual act of self-sacrifice on his part. Although Q was successful in saving the *Enterprise*-D, the *Sakharov* was lost in the incident. ("Déjà Q" [TNG]). *The* Sakharov *was named for Russian nuclear scientist and peace advocate Andre Sakharov (1921-1989).*

Sakkath. (Rocco Sisto). Personal assistant to Ambassador **Sarek** during the **Legaran** conference of 2366. A young Vulcan male, Sakkath was aware that Sarek suffered from debilitating **Bendii Syndrome**, but used his telepathic skills in an effort to give the ambassador the emotional control necessary to complete the historic Legaran treaty. ("Sarek" [TNG]).

Sakonna. (Bertila Damas). **Vulcan** gunrunner and member of the **Maquis**. In 2370, Sakonna bought weapons for the Maquis through **Quark** and later assisted in the abduction of **Gul Dukat** from **Deep Space 9**. She attempted a **Vulcan mind-meld** on Dukat, but failed to break the Cardassian's mental conditioning. Upon her capture by Deep Space 9 personnel, Sakonna stated when but not where the next Maquis strike would occur. ("The Maquis, Parts I and II" [DS9]).

Sakura Prime. Planet in the Alpha Quadrant. Sakura Prime was once ruled by Sural, a ruthless dictator. ("Dreadnought" [VGR]).

Sakuro's disease. An extremely rare disease that can cause intense fever, weakness, and death if not treated. Commissioner **Nancy Hedford** contracted Sakuro's disease in 2267, preventing her from serving as mediator in a dispute on planet Epsilon Canaris III. ("Metamorphosis" [TOS]).

Salazar. (Benito Martinez). **Transporter** chief aboard the *Enterprise*-D in early 2370. Salazar was on duty during the *Enterprise*-D's encounter with the band of self-aware **Borg** led by **Lore**. ("Descent, Part II" [TNG]).

salenite miners. Workers engaged in excavation of salenite ore. A group of salenite miners on planet **Pentarus V** was embroiled in a labor dispute in 2367. Because the group was prone to violence, the government of Pentarus V asked Captain Picard to mediate their negotiations. ("Final Mission" [TNG]).

Salia. (Jamie Hubbard). Leader of planet **Daled IV**. The child of parents from opposing sides of the civil war on that planet, Salia was raised on the neutral planet **Klavdia III** and was returned aboard the *Enterprise*-D to her homeworld in 2365 at age 16 in the hopes she could bring peace to her planet. A shapeshifting **allasomorph**, Salia appeared to the *Enterprise* crew as a lovely human female who attracted the interest of **Wesley Crusher**. ("The Dauphin" [TNG]).

Salish. (Rudy Solari). Native American descendant on **Miramanee's planet.** Salish was his tribe's Medicine Chief before the amnesia-stricken Kirk appeared as their promised god in 2268. ("The Paradise Syndrome" [TOS]).

Salk, Dr. Jonas. (1914-1995). Earth physician and microbiologist who developed the vaccine against poliomyelitis. Salk was among the names that *Voyager*'s **Emergency Medical Hologram** considered in 2371 when searching for a name to adopt as his own. ("Ex Post Facto" [VGR]).

salt vampire. SEE: **M-113 creature**.

Saltah'na clock. Mechanical timepiece from the Saltah'na culture. Under the influence of the energy matrix from the **Saltah'na energy spheres** in 2369, Benjamin Sisko constructed a Saltah'na clock. ("Dramatis Personae" [DS9]). *The Saltah'na clock, designed by Ricardo Delgado, was sometimes seen in Sisko's office in subsequent episodes.*

Saltah'na energy spheres. Telepathic receptacles that stored an ancient power struggle that destroyed the Saltah'na civilization. The Klingon vessel ***Toh'Kaht*** retrieved the energy spheres from a planet in the Gamma Quadrant in 2369. A self-sustaining energy matrix within the spheres caused the Klingon crew to re-enact the power struggle that destroyed the Saltah'na, eventually leading to their own demise. *Toh'Kaht* First Officer **Hon'Tihl** was transported to Deep Space 9 moments before his vessel exploded, carrying with him the energy matrix from the spheres. The telepathic matrix was transferred to the crew members in ops, causing them to re-enact the power struggle, pitting Sisko against Major Kira Nerys. ("Dramatis Personae" [DS9]).

Saltah'na. Civilization from a planet located in the **Gamma Quadrant**. The Klingon warship ***Toh'Kaht*** visited the planet in 2369 on a routine biosurvey, during which a collection of energy spheres was discovered. The spheres contained a telepathic archive describing an ancient power struggle that destroyed the Saltah'na civilization. ("Dramatis Personae" [DS9]). SEE: **Saltah'na energy spheres**.

Saltok IV. Planet. In 2370, **Calvin Hudson** explained to **Gul Evek** that the Federation ships that battled Cardassian civilian craft in the **Demilitarized Zone** were not carrying weapons but instead were transporting medical supplies to Saltok IV. ("The Maquis, Part I" [DS9]).

saltzgadum. A substance capable of causing **nucleosynthesis** in silicon. Saltzgadum is not normally detectable to a starship's internal sensor scans. ("Hollow Pursuits" [TNG]).

Salva II. Planet that was the site of a Federation colony. After the **Federation-Cardassian treaty of 2372**, Salva II became Cardassian territory. ("For the Uniform" [DS9]).

salvage rights. A legal tradition dating back to Earth's ancient maritime laws. Under salvage rights, a ship with no living crew may be regarded as having been abandoned and thus may be claimed by the first entity to take physical posession of the vessel. Captain Benjamin Sisko claimed a crashed Jem'Hadar ship on stardate 50049 by invoking salvage rights. ("The Ship" [DS9]).

Sam. SEE: **Kirk, George Samuel**.

Samarian coral fish. Aquatic life-form. Guinan imagined seeing a Samarian coral fish in the swirling clouds of the **FGC-47** nebula. Data insisted the clouds more closely resembled a bunny rabbit. ("Imaginary Friend" [TNG]).

Samarian Sunset. A specialty beverage that initially appears clear, but develops a multicolored hue when the rim of the glass is tapped sharply. Data prepared a Samarian Sunset for Deanna Troi on stardate 45494 after losing a **three-dimensional chess** game to Troi. ("Conundrum" [TNG]). Samarian Sunsets were once a favorite of **Natima Lang**. She stopped drinking them following her estrangement from Quark in 2363. ("Profit and Loss" [DS9]).

"Samaritan Snare." *Next Generation* episode #43. Written by Robert L. McCullough. Directed by Les Landau. Stardate 42779.1. *First aired in 1989. The* Enterprise-D *is nearly victimized by cunning Pakleds, while Picard is off to a starbase for replacement of his artificial heart. Picard's youthful brawl with Nausicaans at the Bonestell Facility, leading to his heart replacement surgery, was later depicted in flashback scenes in "Tapestry" (TNG).* GUEST CAST: Diana Muldaur as **Pulaski, Dr. Katherine**; Christopher Collins as **Pakled captain**; Leslie Morris as **Reginold**; Daniel Benzali as Surgeon; Lycia Naff as **Gomez, Ensign Sonya**; Tzi Ma as **biomolecular physiologist**. SEE: **biomolecular physiologist; Bonestell Recreation Facility; Bussard collectors; cardiac replacement; Crusher, Wesley; Epsilon IX Sector; Epsilon Pulsar Cluster; Gomez, Ensign Sonya; Jarada;** ***Mondor*****; myocardial enzyme balance; Nausicaans; neural calipers; Pakled captain; Pakleds; parthenogenic implant; Picard, Jean-Luc; Reginold; Rhomboid Dronegar Sector; Scylla Sector; Starbase 515; Starbase Earhart; tissue mitigator; Van Doren, Dr.**

Samno, Yeoman. Crew member aboard the *Starship Enterprise*-A who was one of two "hit men" who carried out the assassination of Klingon **Chancellor Gorkon** in 2293. Samno was later murdered, apparently by **Valeris**, in order to protect others involved with the conspiracy. *(Star Trek VI: The Undiscovered Country).*

Sampalo. Archaeological site located on planet Hoek IV in the Teleris cluster. **Q** invited archaeologist **Vash** to visit the Sampalo relics. She declined. ("Q-Less" [DS9]).

sample container. Cylindrical vessel used for the safe storage of scientific or medical samples. ("Realm of Fear" [TNG]).

Samuels, William Patrick. (Michael A. Krawic). Federation colonist who joined the **Maquis** and helped destroy the Cardassian ship ***Bok'Nor***. Samuels was born in Bergen, Norway, on Earth in 2327, and moved to the Federation colony on **Volon II** to be a farmer in 2350. When Volon II became Cardassian territory under the **Federation-Cardassian Treaty**, Samuels refused to give up his land, and joined the **Maquis**. In 2370, he planted the implosive device that destroyed the *Bok'Nor*. Cardassian authorities reported that Samuels committed suicide while being held after interrogation by **Gul Evek**. Before his death, Samuels recorded a confession, admitting his part in the bombing of the *Bok'Nor*. ("The Maquis, Part I" [DS9]).

San Francisco Yards. Starfleet **drydock** facility in Earth orbit. Site where the original *Enterprise* was built in 2245. That ship also underwent a major refurbishment and systems upgrade there in 2270. *(Star Trek: The Motion Picture).* SEE: **Earth Station McKinley.** *The* ***dedication plaque*** *on the* Enterprise *bridge in the original* Star Trek *series indicated that the ship had been built at the San Francisco Yards.*

San Francisco. Port city on the west coast of Earth's North American continent; location of **Starfleet Command** as well as the main campus of the **Starfleet Academy**. In the early 21st century, part of San Francisco was walled in to form a prison known as a **Sanctuary District**. The Sanctuary District was abolished after the Bell Riots of 2024. ("Past Tense, Parts I and II" [DS9]). Hikaru Sulu was born there. *(Star Trek IV: The Voyage Home).* Star Trek *has visited the city by the bay several times, in* Star Trek: The Motion Picture, Star Trek II, Star Trek III, Star Trek IV, Star Trek VI, *as well as the episodes "Time's Arrow, Parts I and II" (TNG), "Past Tense, Parts I and II" (DS9), and "Non Sequitur" (VGR). The* ***dedication plaque*** *for the first* Starship Enterprise *indicated that the ship was built at Starfleet's* ***San Francisco Yards****.*

Sanchez, Dr. Physician aboard the original *Starship Enterprise*. Sanchez performed an autopsy on the transporter operator killed by **Losira** near the **Kalandan outpost** in 2268. ("That Which Survives" [TOS]).

Sanction**.** Interplanetary freighter craft operated from the planet **Ornara**, commanded by **T'Jon**. The *Sanction* was destroyed above planet **Brekka** when a drive-coil malfunction made it impossible for the ship to maintain a stable orbit. Although the malfunction was fairly minor, the Ornarans' technical ignorance made the problem disastrous. The *Sanction* had been carrying a cargo of the narcotic substance **felicium**, which the Ornarans believed essential to their survival. ("Symbiosis" [TNG]). *The* Sanction *model was a modification of the* **Batris** *from "Heart of Glory" (TNG), which in turn was built from a Visitors' freighter from the miniseries* V. *It would appear that it was a popular design for ships in the galaxy.*

Sanctuary District. Relocation camps during **Earth**'s 21st century, intended to provide protected living space for people without jobs. Sanctuary Districts were set up in every major Earth city by the early 2020s, usually by simply walling in a part of a city. While established with benevolent intent, the sanctuaries quickly degenerated into prisons, offering little hope for those interred there. Residents and their families usually stayed in the Districts for years, since jobs were virtually impossible to find

A DISTRICT RATION DISTRIBUTION CENTER

ERRAND OF MERCY MEAL SUPPORT

CITY OF SAN FRANCISCO SANCTUARY PROGRAM

CURRENT RATION CARD WITH GOVERNMENT IDENTIFICATION HONORED

Sign from a Sanctuary District Ration Distribution Center.

from within a Sanctuary. In addition to people genuinely in search of work, the Sanctuaries housed sociopathic troublemakers and the mentally ill, but lacked the facilities to care for them. Sanctuary District A in **San Francisco** was the flash point for the **Bell Riots** of 2024, after which the Sanctuary Districts were abolished, when the American public became aware of their injustices. ("Past Tense, Parts I and II" [DS9]). SEE: **dim; ghost; gimme; ration card**.

"Sanctuary." *Deep Space Nine* episode #30. Teleplay by Frederick Rappaport. Story by Gabe Essoe & Kelley Miles. Directed by Les Landau. Stardate 47391.2. *First aired in 1993. A group of alien refugees arrives on DS9 in search of a promised land, which they believe to be Bajor.* GUEST CAST: William Schallert as **Varani**; Andrew Koenig as **Tumak**; Aron Eisenberg as **Nog**; Michael Durrell as **Sorad**, **Vedek**; Betty McGuire as **Rozahn**, **Minister**; Robert Curtis-Brown as **Hazar**, **General**; Kitty Swink as Vayna; Deborah May as **Haneek**; Leland Orser as Gai; Nicholas Shaffer as Cowl. SEE: **Bajoran Chamber of Ministers; Deep Space 9; Dominion, the; Draylon II; Eye of the Universe; Haneek; Hazar, General; icoberry torte; Jalanda Forum; Kentanna; Mardah; Reegrunion; Rozahn, Minister; Skrreea; Sorad, Vedek; T-Rogorans; Tixiplik, Plix; Tumak; universal translator; Varani; Vedek Assembly.**

sand bats. Creatures from planet Manark IV that appear to be inanimate rock crystals until they attack. ("The Empath" [TOS]).

sand spine. Spiny plant that lives in the sandy caves of Dozaria. Gul Dukat sat on one in 2372. ("Indiscretion" [DS9]). *Ouch!*

Sanders, Captain. (Eric Pierpoint). Starfleet officer and commander of the *Starship* ***Malinche***. In 2373, Sanders was assigned to apprehend **Maquis** leader and former Starfleet officer **Michael Eddington**. When the *Malinche* caught up with Eddington, Sanders's ship was disabled by a focused particle beam rigged onto a Cardassian freighter decoy. ("For the Uniform" [DS9]). *Eric Pierpoint previously played Iyaaran ambassador Vovall in "Liaisons" (TNG) and is known to genre fans as newcomer detective George Francisco in the television series* Alien Nation.

Sandoval, Elias. (Frank Overton). Leader of an agricultural expedition that colonized planet **Omicron Ceti III** in 2264. The majority of the colonists died from exposure to deadly **berthold rays**, but about fifty colonists, including Sandoval, survived due to the protection offered by unusual spores found on the planet. The spores kept the colonists alive and gave them an extraordinary sense of tranquility, but also removed their motivation to work. Sandoval and the other colonists were freed from the influence of the spores in 2267 when *Starship Enterprise* personnel bombarded the colony with ultrasonic energy. ("This Side of Paradise" [TOS]). SEE: **spores, Omicron Ceti III**.

Sandoval. *Enterprise*-D crew member. Sandoval was struck by a disruptor blast while under Lieutenant Worf's command in 2366. She lived for a week before succumbing to her injuries. ("Ethics" [TNG]).

Sandrine's. SEE: **Chez Sandrine**.

Sandrine. (Judy Geeson). Owner and bartender of **Chez Sandrine**, a bistro in **Marseilles**, France, on Earth. Tom Paris created a replica of Sandrine in his **holodeck** simulation program of Sandrine's establishment. ("The Cloud" [VGR]). When *Voyager's* Emergency Medical Hologram visited the holodeck and played bartender during Kes's surprise second birthday party in 2372, Sandrine seemed attracted to him. ("Twisted" [VGR]). SEE: **Gaunt Gary**.

Sankur, Jal. Historic **Kazon** leader who, in 2346, united his people to overthrow their **Trabe** oppressors. ("Maneuvers" [VGR]).

Sanric. (Nancy Kaine). Enaran citizen. Sanric was a member of the ethnic group called the **Regressives**. Sanric was murdered, along with the rest of her people, as part of the horrific **resettlement** on Enara Prime. ("Remember" [VGR]).

Santa Maria, S.S. *Erewon*-class personnel transport, registry number BDR-529, that embarked in 2360 for planet **Gemulon V**. The ship suffered life-support failure in the vicinity of planet **Orellius** and was forced to land there to make repairs. Once there, the ship and all its personnel became stranded. ("Paradise" [DS9]). SEE: **Alixus; duonetic field; Joseph**. *The* Santa Maria *was named for Christopher Columbus's ship that reached the new world in 1492.*

Santos. (William Thomas, Jr.). Member of the **Maquis** cell from planet **Ronara**. Santos was the first Maquis to make contact with Ro Laren following her arrival at Ronara in 2370. He had sources in Starfleet who were able to verify Ro's cover story. Santos later acted as leader of the Maquis strike force sent to ambush an **Yridian convoy**. ("Preemptive Strike" [TNG]).

Sarajevo, U.S.S. Federation starship, *Istanbul* class, Starfleet registry number NCC-38529. The *Sarajevo* became lost in the Gamma Quadrant sometime prior to 2371. It was believed that the ship and crew fell victim to the Dominion. ("In Purgatory's Shadow" [DS9]). *Named for the capital city of Bosnia and Herzegovina.*

Saratoga, U.S.S. Federation ***Miranda*-class starship**, registry number NCC-1937. The *Saratoga* was disabled by an alien space probe of unknown origin while patrolling the Neutral Zone. *(Star Trek IV: The Voyage Home).* SEE: **Probe, the**. *The* Saratoga *was a re-use of the* Reliant *model originally built for* Star Trek II: The Wrath of Khan. *The captain of the* Saratoga *was played by Madge Sinclair, who was the first woman on* Star Trek *to portray a starship commander. The* Saratoga's *science officer was played by Mike Brislane, and the helm officer was played by Nick Ramus.*

Saratoga, U.S.S. Federation starship, ***Miranda* class**, Starfleet registry number NCC-31911. The *Saratoga* was destroyed by the **Borg** at the battle of **Wolf 359** in 2367. Survivors of the destruction of the *Saratoga* included the first officer, Lieutenant Commander **Benjamin Sisko**, and his son, **Jake Sisko**, who were among the *Saratoga* personnel who fled the ship in escape pods. ("Emissary" [DS9]). *This was presumably at least the second* Miranda*-class starship to bear the name.*

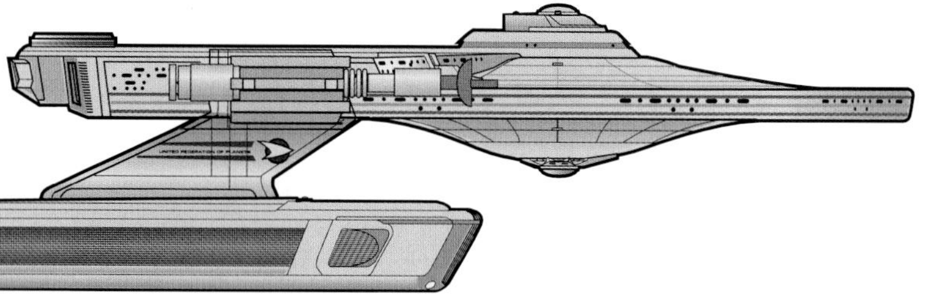

Sarda, Miss. (Kelly Curtis). Resident of station Deep Space 9 who was employed by **Quark** as a **dabo girl**. Sarda complained to Sisko that the fine print of Quark's employment agreement required her to grant sexual favors to the proprietor of the establishment. Sisko assured her that any such contract was unenforceable. ("Captive Pursuit" [DS9]).

Sarek. (Mark Lenard). Vulcan ambassador to the **United Federation of Planets** (2165-2368) and father to **Spock**. ("Journey to Babel" [TOS]). Sarek's illustrious career included the treaty of Alpha Cygnus IX, the **Coridan** admission to the Federation, and the alliance between the Federation and the **Klingon Empire**. ("Sarek" [TNG]).

Sarek, son of Skon and grandson of Solkar *(Star Trek III: The Search for Spock),* represented his government at the **Babel** Conference in 2267. Sarek gave his son, Spock, his first lessons in computer science, but Spock chose to devote himself to **Starfleet** rather than the Vulcan Science Academy. This and other differences prevented Spock and Sarek from speaking as father and son for 18 years. Being 102.437 years of age in 2267, Sarek had planned to retire after the Babel Conference, for medical reasons. ("Journey to Babel" [TOS]).

A malfunction in one of Sarek's heart valves required Chief Surgeon McCoy to perform surgery that required a transfusion of rare type T-negative blood from his son Spock. Sarek survived the operation, and an understanding between father and son was reached. ("Journey to Babel" [TOS]).

Following the death of his son Spock in 2285, Sarek traveled to Earth, where he asked Kirk's assistance in returning Spock's ***katra*** to planet Vulcan. Kirk was ultimately successful in recovering both Spock's *katra* and his regenerated body. Sarek then made a highly unusual request for a ***fal-tor-pan*** ceremony, which was successful in rejoining Spock's body and living spirit. *(Star Trek III: The Search for Spock).* Perhaps in gratitude for Kirk's efforts, Sarek testified on Kirk's behalf at the Federation Council when the Klingon government attempted to extradite Kirk for alleged crimes. *(Star Trek IV: The Voyage Home).*

Sarek helped lay the groundwork for the historic **Khitomer** peace accords with the Klingon Empire, sending Spock to meet **Chancellor Gorkon** and to open a dialog following the disastrous explosion of the Klingon moon, **Praxis**, in 2293. *(Star Trek VI: The Undiscovered Country).*

Sarek married several times during his life. His first wife was a Vulcan princess, with whom he had a son named **Sybok**. *(Star Trek V: The Final Frontier).* Following the death of his first wife, Sarek married **Amanda**, a human woman, with whom he had a son named **Spock**. ("Journey to Babel" [TOS]). At the time of his death in 2368, Sarek was married to **Perrin**, another human woman. ("Sarek" [TNG]).

In 2366, at the age of 202, Ambassador Sarek concluded negotiations on a historic treaty with the **Legarans**. Sarek had been working on the accord for 93 years, and the treaty was the final triumph of his career. At the time of the talks, Sarek was suffering from degenerative **Bendii Syndrome**, but the ambassador was able to maintain emotional control with the help of a **mind-meld** with **Jean-Luc Picard**. ("Sarek" [TNG]). Sarek convalesced for several months while Bendii Syndrome continued to take its toll on his emotional control. Just prior to his death, Sarek met again with Captain Picard, when Picard sought information on the unexplained sighting of Spock on **Romulus**.

Sarek died in his home on Vulcan in 2368 from the degenerative effects of Bendii Syndrome. He was survived by his wife, Perrin, and his son, Ambassador Spock. ("Unification, Part I" [TNG]).

We know that Sarek was married at least three times: to the Vulcan princess, to Amanda, and finally to Perrin. It is not clear whether or not he had other marriages. Dorothy Fontana once decreed that Spock was an only child to strengthen the drama in "Journey to Babel" (TOS), but the writers of Star Trek V *attempted to get around this by suggesting that Sybok was a half-brother. Actor Jonathan Simpson played the young Sarek for Spock's birth scene in that film. Mark Lenard also played the Romulan commander in "Balance of Terror" (TOS) and the commander of the Klingon ship* Amar *in* Star Trek: The Motion Picture. *Lenard was also one of the leading contenders to replace Leonard Nimoy just prior to the second season of the original series when Nimoy considered leaving the show.*

"Sarek." *Next Generation* episode #71. Television story and teleplay by Peter S. Beagle. From an unpublished story by Marc Cushman & Jake Jacobs. Directed by Les Landau. Stardate 43917.4. *First aired in 1990. Ambassador Sarek travels aboard the* Enterprise-*D for a crucial diplomatic mission, but he suffers from an emotionally debilitating disease. Sarek's story later continued in "Unification, Part I" (TNG).* GUEST CAST: Mark Lenard as **Sarek**; Joanna Miles as **Perrin**; William Denis as **Mendrossen, Ki**; Rocco Sisto as **Sakkath**; Colm Meaney as **O'Brien, Miles**; John H. Francis as Science crew member. SEE: **Alpha Cygnus IX; Babel Conference; Bendii Syndrome; Coridan; Dumont, Ensign Suzanne; Grak-tay; Heifetz, Jascha; Legara IV; Legarans; Mendrossen, Ki; Menuhin, Yehudi; *Merrimack*, *U.S.S.*; Perrin; Picard, Jean-Luc; Sakkath; Sarek; Spock; Tataglia; Vulcan mind-meld**.

Sargon's planet. World that once was home to an advanced civilization of humanoids that colonized the galaxy some six hundred thousand years ago. **Vulcan** may have been among the many worlds colonized by these beings. Sargon's planet was devastated five hundred thousand years ago in a terrible war that all but wiped out this advanced civilization. The few survivors of this war agreed to bury old hatreds and place themselves in survival canisters underground, in hopes of revival in the distant future when radiation poisoning on the surface subsided. According to **Sargon**, the war was spawned when his people became so advanced that they had dared think of themselves as gods. ("Return to Tomorrow" [TOS]). *Neither Sargon's world nor his people were given a formal name in the episode.*

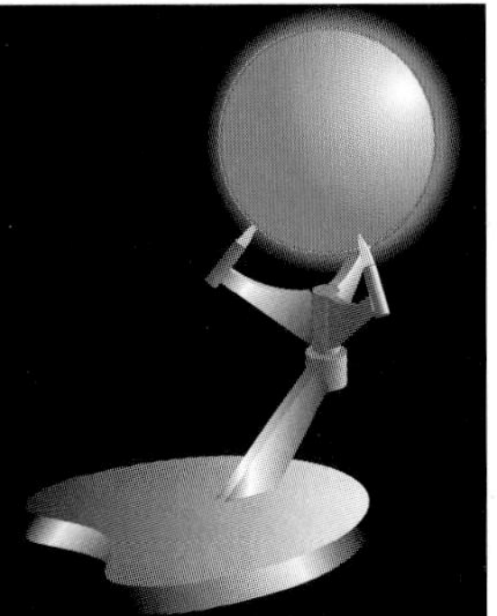

Sargon. (Voice of James Doohan, body of William Shatner). Leader on his world after it was destroyed a half million years ago in a devastating war. Sargon and a handful of other survivors of that war were placed into survival canisters and revived in 2268 by the crew of the *Starship Enterprise*. Sargon temporarily occupied the body of Captain James T. Kirk, so that android bodies could be built to house the three survivors' intellects. The other two survivors—Sargon's wife, **Thalassa**, and **Henoch**, Sargon's old adversary—occupied the bodies of **Dr. Ann Mulhall** and **Spock**. When Henoch was unable to bury the ancient hatreds, Sargon realized they could not continue their existence, so Sargon and his beloved Thalassa departed into oblivion together. ("Return to Tomorrow" [TOS]). SEE: **Sargon's planet**.

Sarish Rez. (Bruce Wright). Adjutant to Bajoran First Minister Shakaar in 2372. ("Crossfire" [DS9]).

Sarjenka. (Nikki Cox). A humanoid life-form who lived on planet **Drema IV**. As a child of about ten or 12 years of age, Sarjenka built a simple subspace radio, with which she broadcast calls for help because of severe geological disturbances that threatened her planet with disintegration. *Enterprise*-D officer Data established subspace radio contact with Sarjenka and remained in communication for several weeks, despite the fact that such contact violated **Prime Directive** quarantine protocols. A rescue mission by Data brought Sarjenka to the *Enterprise*-D, but she was successfully returned to her home with no memory of the starship, because of a memory-erasure procedure developed by **Katherine Pulaski**. ("Pen Pals" [TNG]).

Sarjeno. Bajoran citizen. One of **Mardah**'s siblings. Sarjeno resided on planet **Bajor** and, as of 2371, had not spoken with Mardah for years. ("The Abandoned" [DS9]).

***sark*, Klingon.** An animal similar to a terrestrial horse. Holographic simulations of a *sark* were available for riding on the *Enterprise*-D holodeck. ("Pen Pals" [TNG]).

Sarona VIII. Planet. The *Enterprise*-D was heading toward Sarona VIII for crew shore leave when the ship was diverted to **Vandor IV** to investigate an emergency. ("We'll Always Have Paris" [TNG]).

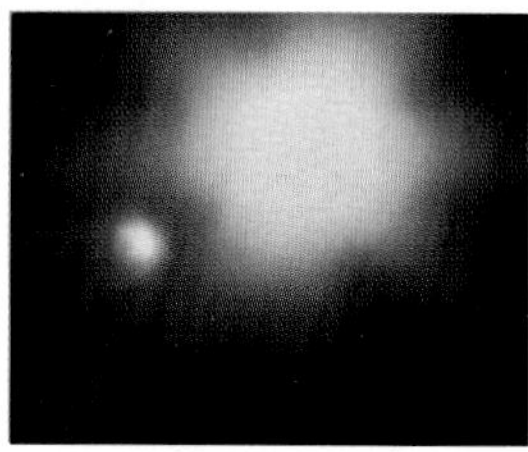

Sarpeidon. Class-M planet destroyed in 2269 when its star, **Beta Niobe**, went nova. Sarpeidon had been home to a technologically advanced humanoid civilization. Prior to the explosion of their sun, the people of Sarpeidon developed a time portal they called an **atavachron**, which they used to escape into their planet's past, so that they could live out their lives. ("All Our Yesterdays" [TOS]). SEE: **Atoz, Mr.**; **Zarabeth**.

Sarthong V. Planet known for rich archaeological ruins. **Vash** was thinking about exploring Sarthong V after leaving **Risa**, but Picard pointed out that the Sarthongians dealt harshly with trespassers. ("Captain's Holiday" [TNG], "QPid" [TNG]).

Satarrans. Humanoid civilization. The Satarrans had been at war with the people of **Lysia** for decades. In 2368, the Satarrans attempted to use the Federation starship *Enterprise*-D to launch a devastating attack against the **Lysian Central Command**. ("Conundrum" [TNG]). SEE: **MacDuff, Commander Keiran**. Satarrans hate mysteries. ("The Chase" [TNG]).

SATCOM 47. Communications relay satellite in Earth orbit operated by **Chronowerx** industries. Chronowerx Security Chief Dunbar used the satellite to locate **Henry Starling** aboard the *Voyager* and to transport him away. ("Future's End, Part II" [VGR]).

Satelk, Captain. (Richard Fancy). Starfleet officer attached to Starfleet Academy in 2368. Satelk, a native of planet **Vulcan**, presided over the inquiry into Cadet **Joshua Albert**'s death at the **Academy Flight Range**. SEE: **Kolvoord Starburst; Locarno, Cadet First Class Nicholas.** ("The First Duty" [TNG]).

Satie, Admiral Norah. (Jean Simmons). Starfleet officer, the daughter of noted Federation jurist **Aaron Satie**. Satie issued the directive for Captain Jean-Luc Picard to take command of the *U.S.S. Enterprise*-D. These orders became effective on stardate 41148. ("All Good Things..." [TNG]). She was largely responsible for exposing the alien conspiracy against Starfleet in 2364. Shortly after this incident, Satie retired from active Starfleet service. Known for her brilliant investigative skills, she was recalled from retirement in 2367 when Rom-ulan espionage was suspected aboard the *Enterprise*-D. When investigation proved the explosion to be an accident, Admiral Satie improperly continued her relentless search for conspirators, even accusing Captain Picard of acts against the Federation. Satie's investigation was finally stopped by order of Admiral Thomas Henry. ("The Drumhead" [TNG]). SEE: **J'Dan; Seventh Guarantee; Tarses, Crewman Simon.** *Satie was not mentioned in "Conspiracy" (TNG), but "The Drumhead" establishes that she uncovered the alien presence.*

Satie, Judge Aaron. Brilliant Federation jurist and father of Starfleet **Admiral Norah Satie.** Judge Satie was a strong advocate of individual civil liberties, including freedom of speech and freedom of thought. His decisions were required reading at **Starfleet Academy**. Satie once wrote, "With the first link, the chain is forged. The first speech censured, the first thought forbidden, the first freedom denied, chains us all, irrevocably." Captain Picard quoted from Aaron Satie during a hearing held by Norah Satie aboard the *Enterprise*-D in 2367. ("The Drumhead" [TNG]). SEE: **Seventh Guarantee.**

Satler. (Tim DeZarn). Member of a group of terrorists who attempted to steal **trilithium** resin from the *Enterprise*-D in 2369. Satler was forced to chase an escaping Captain Picard down a Jefferies tube. Satler was killed when he was caught by a **baryon sweep** during his pursuit of Picard. SEE: **Remmler Array.** ("Starship Mine" [TNG]).

Satok, Security Minister. (Martin Goslins). **Vulcan** official in charge of that planet's security service. In 2370, Commander Riker contacted Satok to convey information from his operative, T'Paal. Satok denied knowledge of any covert operative working with mercenaries. Once the mercenary band was captured, they were turned over to Satok's custody, first to answer for crimes on Vulcan and then to be tried for their crimes against other Federation worlds. ("Gambit, Part II" [TNG]).

Saturn NavCon. A navigational control satellite in orbit of planet **Saturn**, which performed sensor sweeps of the **Academy Flight Range**. Saturn NavCon file 6-379 contained a recording of the flight paths of **Nova Squadron** just prior to the crash that killed **Joshua Albert** in 2368. ("The First Duty" [TNG]).

Saturn. The sixth planet in the Sol system. Saturn is a gas giant with a mass 95 times that of **Earth** and is noted for its spectacular system of rings. It has a diameter of some 120,800 kilometers, and orbits its sun at a mean distance of 1.4 billion kilometers. The first human spaceflight to Saturn was commanded by **Colonel Shaun Geoffrey Christopher** in the early 21st century. ("Tomorrow is Yesterday" [TOS]). The Starfleet **Academy Flight Range** was located in a proximal orbit of Saturn. ("The First Duty" [TNG]). Saturn is a Class-J planet. SEE: **planetary classification system**. ("Starship Down" [DS9]).

Saucer Module. The large circular (or elliptical) command section of many Federation starships. ("Encounter at Farpoint, Part I" [TNG]). Also known as the Primary Hull. SEE: **stardrive section**.

saucer separation. An emergency maneuver performed by ***Galaxy*-class** starships in which the **Saucer Module** disconnects from the remainder of the spacecraft. Saucer separation is generally employed so that the Saucer Module, containing most of the crew, can remain in relative safety while the **stardrive section** (containing the ship's powerful **warp drive**) goes into battle or other hazardous situations. ("Encounter at Farpoint, Part I" [TNG]). SEE: **Battle Bridge**. In extreme emergencies, the separated saucer could even land on a suitable planetary surface, although it would be incapable of returning to orbit afterward. *(Star Trek Generations).* Saucer separation was normally accomplished at sublight speeds. Separation at warp speeds was considered highly dangerous, although the *Enterprise*-D successfully accomplished such a maneuver shortly after first contact with the entity **Q** in 2364. ("Encounter at Farpoint, Part I" [TNG]). Geordi La Forge, temporarily in command of the *Enterprise*-D, ordered a saucer separation at planet **Minos** when the ship was threatened by an ancient Minosian weapons system. ("The Arsenal of Freedom" [TNG]). SEE: **Echo Papa 607.** The maneuver was also employed during the Borg attack of early 2367. ("The Best of Both Worlds, Part II" [TNG]). A saucer-separation maneuver saved the lives of the entire ***Enterprise*-D** crew in 2371 when a Klingon attack caused a loss of **antimatter containment**, resulting in the destruction of the ship's stardrive section. The Saucer Module successfully crash-landed on planet **Veridian III**, with no loss of life. *(Star Trek Generations).* Earlier classes of starships were also capable of saucer separation, although not all were capable of reconnection afterward. Captain James Kirk once ordered engineer Scott to prepare for such a maneuver when the original *Enterprise* was threatened by the god-machine **Vaal** at planet **Gamma Trianguli VI** in 2267. ("The Apple" [TOS]). *During the first few episodes of* Star Trek: The Next Generation*, saucer separation was intended to be a standard maneuver in combat situations, but was rarely done because of the costs for visual effects and for rebuilding the Battle Bridge; also, it was felt that it slowed down story-telling too much.*

Saurian brandy. Potent liqueur. Saurian brandy was imbibed in moderation, although the aggressive half of James Kirk demanded a bottle of the stuff after Kirk's duplication by a transporter malfunction in 2266. ("The Enemy Within" [TOS]). Picard once traded an old bottle for a **Gorlan prayer stick**. ("Bloodlines" [TNG]). *Saurian brandy was also enjoyed in "The Man Trap" (TOS), "The Conscience of the King" (TOS), "Journey to Babel" (TOS), and "Requiem for Methuselah" (TOS),"The Wire" (DS9), and "Prophet Motive" (DS9). Saurian brandy was stored in distinctive amber bottles with curved necks, originally made as commemorative whiskey bottles by the Dickel company of Tennessee. Replicas of these original bottles were sometimes seen in Quark's bar in Deep Space 9.*

sautéed beets. Fleshy edible root vegetable of the genus *Beta*, browned in a pan with some fatty sauce. Benjamin Sisko liked sautéed beets. ("Equilibrium" [DS9]).

"Savage Curtain, The." Original Series episode #77. Teleplay by Gene Roddenberry and Arthur Heinemann. Story by Gene Roddenberry. Directed by Herschel Daugherty. Stardate 5906.4. *First aired in 1969. Kirk and Spock are forced to fight alongside such historical figures as Abraham Lincoln of Earth and Surak of Vulcan by aliens who want to study the human concept of "good" and "evil."* GUEST CAST: Lee Bergere as **Lincoln**, **Abraham**; Barry Atwater as **Surak**; Phillip Pine as **Green**, **Colonel**; Arell Blanton as **Dickerson**, **Lieutenant**; Carol Daniels Derment as **Zora**; Robert Herron as **Kahless**; Nathan Jung as **Genghis Kahn**; Phil Adams as Kirk's stunt double; Bill Catching as Lincoln's stunt double and Surak's stunt double; Gary Eppers as Surak's stunt double; Jerry Summers as Green's stunt double; Bob Orrison as Spock's stunt double; Troy Melton as Genghis Kahn's stunt double; Bart La Rue as **Yarnek**, voice of; Janos Prohaska as **Yarnek**, costumed. SEE: **Dickerson, Lieutenant; Excalbia; Excalbian; Genghis Khan; Green, Colonel; haggis; Kahless the Unforgettable; Kirk, James T.; Klingon Empire; Lincoln, Abraham; Surak; telegraph; Tiburon; Vulcans; Yarnek; Zora.**

Savar, Admiral. (Henry Darrow). Starfleet officer who was taken over by the unknown intelligence that attempted to infiltrate Starfleet Command in 2364. Savar, a native of planet **Vulcan**, was stationed at **Starfleet Headquarters** in San Francisco at the time. ("Conspiracy" [TNG]).

Sayana. (Shair Nims). Inhabitant of planet **Gamma Trianguli VI.** Sayana greeted an *Enterprise* landing party with flowers in 2267. She and **Makora**, another member of her people, were attracted to each other but were not allowed to show their affection because it was against the law of **Vaal**, their god. This presumably changed after the destruction of Vaal in 2267. ("The Apple" [TOS]).

Scalos. Class-M planet. Massive volcanic eruptions on Scalos released high levels of radiation into the water supply, contaminating the water and subjecting the humanoid population to **hyperacceleration**. Scalos is the homeworld to the **Scalosians**. ("Wink of an Eye" [TOS]).

Scalosians. Humanoid people from planet **Scalos.** The Scalosians were subjected to biochemical **hyperacceleration** by volcanic radiation many generations ago. The radiation also decreased fertility in the females and completely sterilized the men. To preserve their species, the Scalosians were forced to mate outside their planet, dispatching distress calls to passing space vehicles and subjecting the crews of any responding vessels to hyperacceleration. This pattern continued until 2268, when the *Enterprise* responded to a distress call from Scalos but was able to repel the invaders. Federation authorities were later advised to warn other ships to avoid Scalos. SEE: **Deela; Rael**. ("Wink of an Eye" [TOS]).

Scarlett, Will. (Michael Dorn). In Earth mythology, a member of **Robin Hood**'s band of "merry men" in ancient England. Worf was cast in the role of Will Scarlett by Q despite his protest that he was "*not* a merry man!" ("QPid" [TNG]).

Scathos. Civilization. In the Scathos culture any woman who conceived a child before the age of 40 was summarily executed. ("Elogium" [VGR]).

"Schisms." *Next Generation* episode #131. Teleplay by Brannon Braga. Story by Jean Louise Matthias & Ronald Wilkerson. Directed by Robert Wiemer. Stardate 46154.2. *First aired in 1992. Aliens from another time continuum kidnap* Enterprise*-D crew members.* GUEST CAST: Lanei Chapman as **Rager**, **Ensign**; Ken Thorley as **Mot**; Angelina Fiordellisi as Kaminer; Scott T. Trost as Shipley, Lt.; Angelo McCabe as Crewman; John Nelson as Medical technician; Majel Barrett as Computer voice. SEE: **Adele, Aunt; Amargosa Diaspora; anapestic tetrameter; coherent graviton pulse; FGC-13 Cluster; Hagler, Lieutenant Edward; "Ode to Spot"; plasma infusion unit; quasimolecular flux; Rager, Ensign; resonance tissue scan; Setti, Mister; solanagen-based entities; solanagen; tertiary subspace manifold; tetryon.**

"Schizoid Man, The." *Next Generation* episode #31. Teleplay by Tracy Tormé. Story by Richard Manning & Hans Beimler. Directed by Les Landau. Stardate 42437.5. *First aired in 1988. A reclusive scientist implants his consciousness into Data's brain just prior to his death. Writer Tracy Tormé intended this episode and its title as an homage to the British series* The Prisoner. *One episode of that series was titled "The Schizoid Man." At one point, actor Patrick McGoohan, who had starred in* The Prisoner, *was considered for the part of Dr. Ira Graves.* GUEST CAST: Diana Muldaur as **Pulaski, Dr. Katherine**; W. Morgan Sheppard as **Graves, Dr. Ira**; Suzie Plakson as **Selar, Dr.**; Barbara Alyn Woods as **Brianon, Kareen**. SEE: **Brianon, Kareen; *Constantinople, U.S.S.*; Darnay's disease; Data; Graves, Dr. Ira; Gravesworld; "If I Only Had a Brain"; molecular cybernetics; photon torpedo; Selar, Dr.; touch-and-go downwarping; transport, near-warp; Zee-Magnees Prize.**

schizophrenia. Psychotic mental disorder with such symptoms as delusions, retreat from reality, and conflicting emotions. ("Past Tense, Part I" [DS9]). SEE: **dim**.

Schmitter. (Biff Elliott). Miner on planet **Janus VI** who was killed by the silicon-based creature known as the **Horta** in 2267. ("The Devil in the Dark" [TOS]).

Scholar/Artist. (Thomas Oglesby). A member of Mediator Riva's interpretive **Chorus** from planet Ramatis III. Each member of the Chorus represented a different part of Riva's personality. Scholar/Artist spoke for the intellect, for matters of judgment, philosophy, and logic. He was also the dreamer and the poet who "longs to see the beauty beyond the truth which is always the first duty of art." ("Loud as a Whisper" [TNG]).SEE: **Warrior/Adonis**; **Woman**.

schoolroom. Primary-school classroom established in 2369 by Keiko O'Brien for the children on station Deep Space 9. O'Brien established the school because she was concerned that there were no educational opportunities for her daughter, Molly, on the station. ("A Man Alone" [DS9]). *Educational items used for set decoration in Keiko's schoolroom included an early conjectural model of Zefram Cochrane's first warp-powered spaceship as well as the* U.S.S. Horizon *(both originally built by Greg Jein for the* Star Trek Chronology*), diagrams of several alien life-forms seen in the original* Star Trek *television series, a topographical relief map of planet Sigma Iotia II (from "A Piece of the Action" [TOS]), and a galaxy map originally designed for Starfleet Command, showing the planets visited by the original* Starship Enterprise *(from "Conspiracy" [TNG]).*

schplict. *Grakel* milk. Neelix brought some schplict onboard the *Voyager* from the planet **Napinne** just prior to stardate 48846. He made brill cheese out of the schplict, but the bacteria he cultivated for that purpose became host to a virus that infected the ship's **bio-neural gel packs**. ("Learning Curve" [VGR]). SEE: **macaroni and cheese**.

Schweitzer, Dr. Albert. (1875-1965) Theologian, musician, and medical doctor, Albert Schweitzer spent most of his life working at a missionary hospital on Earth. Winner of the 1952 Nobel Peace Prize. In 2371 aboard the *Starship Voyager*, the **Emergency Medical Hologram** chose the name Schweitzer before his first away mission. The EMH later discarded it because he felt it would bring back uncomfortable memories. ("Heroes and Demons" [VGR]).

science officer. Aboard Federation starships, the individual responsible for overseeing scientific investigations and for providing the ship's captain with scientific information needed for command decisions. The science officer's station on the **bridge** of most Federation starships included extensive tie-ins to the various **sensor** systems, as well as links to the ship's **library computer** system. **Spock** was the science officer aboard the original *Starship Enterprise*.

Science Station 402. Located in the Kohlan system. The *Enterprise*-D planned to tow the Cytherian probe found near the **Argus Array** in 2367 to Science Station 402, but the probe was destroyed first. ("The Nth Degree" [TNG]).

Science Station Delta Zero Five. Facility located near the **Romulan Neutral Zone**. The station was totally destroyed in 2364, apparently scooped from the surface of the planet, by the **Borg**. ("The Neutral Zone" [TNG]).

SCM Model 3. Small handheld superconducting magnet used aboard *Galaxy*-class starships. **Wesley Crusher** was surprised when the beautiful **Salia** of planet **Daled IV** recognized the device. ("The Dauphin" [TNG]).

scorcher. Energy weapon. **Kor** had a scorcher burn on his 14th rib. ("Blood Oath" [DS9]).

Scotch. Whiskey made on Earth in Scotland from malted barley and having a rather smoky flavor. Doctor Bashir ordered a Scotch without ice in 2372, shortly after he and Miles O'Brien completed their **Battle of Britain** holosuite simulation. ("Homefront" [DS9]).

Scott, Montgomery. (James Doohan). Also known as "Scotty." Chief engineer aboard the original *Starship **Enterprise*** under the command of Captain James Kirk. ("Where No Man Has Gone Before" [TOS]). Scott's Starfleet serial number was SE 19754.T. ("Wolf in the Fold" [TOS]).

Scott's engineering career began in 2243, and he served on a total of 11 ships ("Relics" [TNG]), including a stint as an engineering advisor on the asteroid freight run from planet **Deneva**, making the cargo run a couple of times. ("Operation: Annihilate!" [TOS]).

The original *U.S.S. Enterprise* was the first starship on which Scott served as chief engineer ("Relics" [TNG]), and he distinguished himself many times in that position by improvising engineering miracles that more than once saved the ship and its crew. While serving aboard the original *Enterprise*, Scott once suffered from a near-fatal accelerated aging disease. ("The Deadly Years" [TOS]). He was actually killed in 2267 by space probe ***Nomad***, although the errant probe later returned Scott to life. ("The Changeling" [TOS]).

Scotty was scheduled to retire some three months after the **Khitomer** peace conference incident in 2293, and had bought a boat in anticipation of having more free time. *(Star Trek VI: The Undiscovered Country).* Later that year, Scott was an honored guest at the launch of the *Starship Enterprise*-B. Captain **James T. Kirk** was lost and believed killed on that flight. *(Star Trek Generations).*

Scott finally did retire in 2294 at the age of 72, having served in Starfleet for 51 years. He was in the process of relocating to the retirement community at the **Norpin Colony** when his transport ship, the *Jenolen*, crashed into a **Dyson Sphere**. Scott, the only one who lived through the crash, survived for 75 years by suspending himself inside a transporter beam. He was rescued in 2369 by an away team from the *Enterprise*-D. Following his rescue, Scott embarked for parts unknown aboard a shuttlecraft "loaned" to him by *Enterprise* Captain Picard. ("Relics" [TNG]).

Scott never married, but he became romantically involved with fellow crew member **Mira Romaine** in 2269. That relationship ended when Romaine transferred to **Memory Alpha**. ("The Lights of Zetar" [TOS]). *The writers of* Star Trek Generations *were indeed aware that Scotty, in "Relics" (TNG), seemed to think that Kirk was still alive, in contradiction of Kirk's apparent death in* Star Trek Generations. *"Relics" (TNG) had been produced before it was known that Kirk would die in* Generations, *and the decision to include Scotty despite the error was motivated simply by fondness for Doohan's character, and the desire to see him one more time. James Doohan also provided many voices for the original* Star Trek *series, including* ***Trelane****'s father ("The Squire of Gothos" [TOS]),* ***Sargon*** *("Return to Tomorrow" [TOS]), the* ***M-5*** *computer ("The Ultimate Computer" [TOS]), and the* ***Melkotian*** *buoy ("Spectre of the Gun" [TOS]). Scotty's first appearance was in "Where No Man Has Gone Before" (TOS).*

Scott, Tryla. (Ursaline Bryant). Starfleet officer who earned the command of a starship at a younger age than any previous captain. Scott was something of a legend in her own time, but she was taken over in 2364 by the extragalactic intelligence that attempted to inflitrate Starfleet Command that year. ("Conspiracy" [TNG]).

scoutship, Romulan. Small warp-capable vessel used for reconnaisance and science missions. A Romulan scoutship, apparently on a covert mission, crashed on the Federation planet **Galorndon Core** in 2366 ("The Enemy" [TNG]). Another Romulan scoutship was apparently stolen by Admiral **Alidar Jarok**, who used it when he defected to the Federation later that year ("The Defector" [TNG]). *The Romulan scoutship was designed by Rick Sternbach and built by Tony Meininger.*

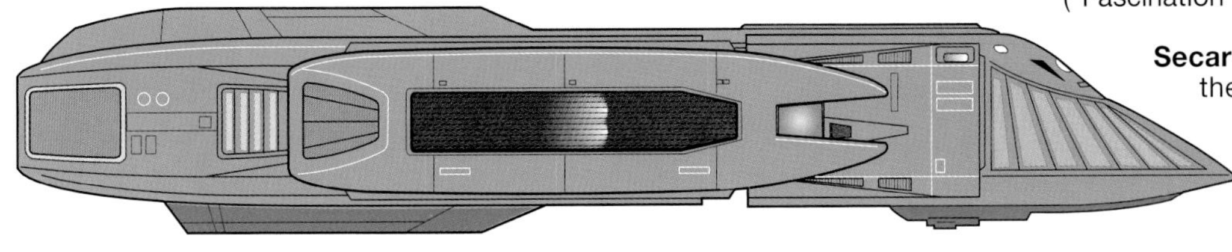

Scrolls of Ardra. A collection of documents that outlined all the details of the **Contract of Ardra**, an ancient arrangement between **Ardra** and the people of **Ventax II**. ("Devil's Due" [TNG]).

Scrooge, Ebenezer. A literary character; the protagonist in Charles Dickens's (1812-1870) 19th-century work *A Christmas Carol*. Data portrayed Scrooge in a holodeck dramatization of the book, part of Data's effort to use drama to gain an understanding of human emotions. ("Devil's Due" [TNG]).

Scylla Sector. Region of space near the **Epsilon IX Sector.** Location of **Starbase 515**. ("Samaritan Snare" [TNG]). *In Greek mythology, Scylla is one of two sea monsters who lived in a cave near the Straits of Messina. The other monster was* ***Charybdis****, mentioned in "The Royale" (TNG).*

sean. Bajoran word which meant swamp. ("Let He Who Is Without Sin..." [DS9]).

search for extraterrestrial intelligence. SEE: **SETI**.

"Search, Part I, The." *Deep Space Nine* episode #47. Teleplay by Ronald D. Moore. Story by Ira Steven Behr & Robert Hewitt Wolfe. Directed by Kim Friedman. Stardate 48212.4. *First aired in 1994. To head off an invasion, Sisko enters the Gamma Quadrant in search of the Dominion—but encounters the ruthless Jem'Hadar instead. This was the first episode of* Star Trek: Deep Space Nine*'s third season. It marked the first appearance of the* Starship Defiant, *as well as the new Starfleet insignia that were designed for use in* Star Trek Generations. GUEST CAST: Salome Jens as **Founder Leader**; Martha Hackett as **T'Rul, Subcommander**; John Fleck as **Ornithar**; Kenneth Marshall as **Eddington, Michael**. SEE: **beritium; cloaking device, Romulan; Deep Space 9; *Defiant, U.S.S.*; diamide; dirak; Dominion; Eddington, Michael; Founder Leader; Founders; Founders' homeworld; I'danian spice pudding; Jem'Hadar warships; Karemma; nagus, grand; Odo; Omarion Nebula; Ornithar; polyduranium; Sisko, Benjamin; T'Rul, Subcommander; Utopia Planitia Fleet Yards; Vorta; wardroom; Yoruba mask.**

"Search, Part II, The." *Deep Space Nine* episode #48. Teleplay by Ira Steven Behr. Story by Ira Steven Behr & Robert Hewitt Wolfe. Directed by Jonathan Frakes. No stardate given. *First aired in 1994. Sisko, Dax and Bashir find Federation negotiations with the Dominion increasingly bizarre; Odo bonds with the shape-shifters while Kira remains suspicious. This episode revealed Odo's origin as a Founder who had been sent into the galaxy as an infant in hopes that he would return so that his people would learn about distant space.* GUEST CAST: Salome Jens as **Founder Leader**; Andrew Robinson as **Garak, Elim**; Natalia Nogulich as **Nechayev, Alynna**; Martha Hackett as **T'Rul, Subcommander**; Kenneth Marshall as **Eddington, Michael**; William Frankfather as Male shapeshifter; Dennis Christopher as **Borath**; Christopher Doyle as Jem'Hadar officer; Tom Morga as Jem'Hadar soldier; Diaunté as Jem'Hadar guard; Majel Barrett as Computer voice. SEE: **Arbazon vulture; Borath; changeling; cloaking device, Romulan; Dominion; Eddington, Michael; Eris; Founder Leader; Founders; Founders' homeworld; Great Link; New Bajor; *Rio Grande, U.S.S.*; solids; Odo; Omarion Nebula; Sisko, Benjamin; T'Rul, Subcommander.**

Sebarr. Zoologist, a colleague of Keiko O'Brien. He and O'Brien worked together during an agrobiology expedition to planet Bajor in 2371. Keiko considered Sebarr a close friend, and she confided in him about her relationship with her husband, **Miles O'Brien**. ("Fascination" [DS9]).

Secarus IV. Class-M planet. Location of the **Albino**'s hideout from 2345 through 2370. **Kang**, **Koloth**, **Kor**, and **Jadzia Dax** stormed his stronghold in 2370, killing the Albino and fulfilling their **blood oath**. ("Blood Oath" [DS9]).

"Second Chances." *Next Generation* episode #150. Story by Mike Medlock. Teleplay by René Echevarria. Directed by LeVar Burton. Stardate 46915.2. *First aired in 1993. When the* Enterprise-D *arrives at planet Nervala IV to retrieve research data left behind eight years before, they find a duplicate of Commander Will Riker.* GUEST CAST: Dr. Mae Jemison as **Palmer, Lieutenant**. SEE: **distortion field; *Gandhi, U.S.S.*; Janaran Falls; *KoH-man-ara*; Lagana Sector; Nervala IV; "Night Bird"; Palmer, Lieutenant; *Potemkin, U.S.S.*; Riker, Thomas; Riker, William T.; tai chi chuan; trombone; valerian root tea.**

Second Order. Division of the **Cardassian** military commanded in 2371 by **Gul Dukat**. ("Defiant" [DS9]).

"Second Sight." *Deep Space Nine* episode #29. Teleplay by Mark Gehred-O'Connell and Ira Steven Behr & Robert Hewitt Wolfe. Story by Mark Gehred-O'Connell. Directed by Alexander Singer. Stardate 47329.4. *First aired in 1993. Sisko falls in love with a mysterious woman who resembles the wife of a famous scientist.* GUEST CAST: Salli Elise Richardson as **Fenna** and **Seyetik, Nidell**; Richard Kiley as **Seyetik**, **Professor Gideon**; Mark Erickson as **Piersall**, **Lieutenant**. SEE: **Andorian tuber root; Blue Horizon; Chiraltan tea; DaVinci Falls; Epsilon 119; *Fall of Kang, The*; Fenna; flux generator; G'Trok; Halanans; Ligobis X; New Halana; Piersall, Lieutenant; *Prometheus, U.S.S.*; pro-tomatter; psychoprojective telepathy; *raktajino*; Runners, the; Seyetik, Nidell; Seyetik, Professor Gideon; terraforming.**

"Second Skin." *Deep Space Nine* episode #51. Written by Robert Hewitt Wolfe. Directed by Les Landau. No stardate given. First aired in 1994. *Kira Nerys is kidnapped and surgically altered to look like a Cardassian, part of an Obsidian Order plot to frame a Cardassian leader.* GUEST CAST: Andrew Robinson as **Garak, Elim**; Gregory Sierra as **Entek**; Cindy Katz as Yteppa; Lawrence Pressman as **Ghemor**, **Legate**; Christopher Carroll as **Benil**, **Gul**; Freyda Thomas as **Alenis Grem**; Billy Burke as **Ari**. SEE: **Alenis Grem; Ari; Benil, Gul; Bestri Woods; Cardassian underground movement; Dahkur Hills; Dahkur Province; desegranine; Elemspur Detention Center; Entek; Garak, Elim; Ghemor, Legate; *hara* cat; *hasperat*; holo-filter; holodeck and holosuite programs; icon; Iliana; Kira Nerys; Klaestron IV; Kobheerian captain; Mathenites; Obsidian Order; *Rak-Minunis*; Shakaar resistance cell; Singha refugee camp; Viterian, Captain; Yeln.**

second officer. Person third in the line of command of a starship, following the captain and the first officer. Lieutenant Commander Data was the second officer of the *Starship Enterprise-D*. ("The Last Outpost" [TNG], "Force of Nature" [TNG]).

secondary plasma conduit. Component of the *Enterprise*-D's warp drive system. (An explosion of the secondary plasma conduit in an alternate **quantum reality** caused a severe injury to the Commander La Forge of that reality. La Forge died of his injuries.) ("Parallels" [TNG]).

secret agent. In Earth mythology, a 20th-century governmental operative who concealed his national affiliation, freeing him or her to perform covert acts on behalf of that government. Secret agents were portrayed as colorful characters whose adventures were frequently flamboyant and violent. **Julian Bashir** (*pictured on right*) was an aficionado of secret agent stories. He was fond of indulging in a holosuite adventure in which he portrayed a British secret service agent who worked against such adversaries as Colonel **Anastasia Komananov** (a Russian KGB agent—*pictured on left*), an assassin named **Falcon**, an evil scientist named **Dr. Hippocrates Noah**, and his aide, **Duchamps**. Beautiful women were often prominent characters in such secret agent stories. In Bashir's program, these included **Caprice**, Professor **Honey Bare**, **Mona Luvsitt** (Bashir's valet), and Colonel Komananov. Cardassian agent **Elim Garak** found this fanciful vision of intelligence operations to be highly amusing. ("Our Man Bashir" [DS9]).

sector. In interstellar mapping, a volume of space approximately twenty light-years across. A typical sector in Federation space will contain about 6 to 10 star systems, although sectors toward the galactic core will often contain many more. The Milky Way Galaxy is divided into hundreds of thousands of sectors, grouped into four **quadrants**. Sectors are usually numbered, although in common usage they are often named for a major star or planet located in that sector. *The numbering system for sectors had been inconsistently used (and sometimes interchanged with quadrants) during the show, especially in its early days. We assume that some sectors may retain older designations from previous mapping systems, much as present-day astronomers still use NGC and Messier catalog numbers.*

Sector 001. Region that includes the G2-type star known as Sol and the nine planets in its system, including **Earth**. Sector 001 was the destination of the invading **Borg** ship in 2366. ("The Best of Both Worlds, Parts I and II" [TNG]). *The original and motion picture* Enterprise *returned to Sector 001 in "Tomorrow Is Yesterday" (TOS),* Star Trek I, Star Trek III, Star Trek IV, Star Trek V, *and* Star Trek VI, *although the term "Sector 001" was not invented until "The Best of Both Worlds" (TNG). The* Enterprise-D *also returned to Sector 001 in "Conspiracy" (TNG), "Family" (TNG), "The First Duty" (TNG), and "Time's Arrow, Part I" (TNG).*

Sector 3-0. Region of space near the **Romulan Neutral Zone**. Two Federation outposts were destroyed there in late 2364 by an unknown agency later believed to be the Borg. ("The Neutral Zone" [TNG]).

Sector 3-1. Located near the **Romulan Neutral Zone**. Communications were lost with Federation starbases in this sector on stardate 41903.2 (late 2364). It was later believed that this was due to **Borg** activity in the area. ("The Neutral Zone" [TNG]).

Sector 23. Stellar area near the **Romulan Neutral Zone**, the location of Starbase 173. ("The Measure of a Man" [TNG]).

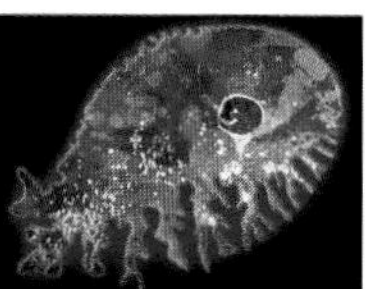

Sector 39J. Region where the **Gamma 7A System** was destroyed by a spaceborne **amoeba** creature in 2268. The ***U.S.S. Intrepid*** was also lost in Sector 39J, another victim of the amoeba. ("The Immunity Syndrome" [TOS]).

Sector 401. Region of space where the runabout ***Rio Grande*** was sighted by the Romulan vessel *Gasko* shortly after stardate 47573. ("Paradise" [DS9]).

Sector 1385. Volume of space in the Alpha Quadrant that contained no known shipping lanes. **Romulan** scientist **Telek R'Mor** was on a research mission in sector 1385 in the year 2351 when he discovered a **micro-wormhole** leading to the Delta Quadrant. ("Eye of the Needle" [VGR]).

Sector 1607. Location where the ***U.S.S. Pegasus*** was lost in 2358. The *Enterprise*-D was assigned to rendezvous with the *Starship* ***Crazy Horse*** in this sector in 2370. ("The *Pegasus*" [TNG]).

Sector 2520. Stellar region located near the Klingon-Federation border. **Lieutenant Aquiel Uhnari**, escaping from **Relay Station 47** aboard a shuttlecraft in 2369, was captured as her ship approached that sector. ("Aquiel" [TNG]).

Sector 19658. Uninhabited region outside of Federation space. (In an alternate **quantum reality** visited by Worf in 2370, the **Argus Array** had to be redirected to relay its visual information to this sector.) ("Parallels" [TNG]).

Sector 21305. An area of space where the *Enterprise*-D conducted a surveying mission in 2368. ("Ensign Ro" [TNG]).

Sector 21503. Federation space near the **Cardassian** border. The *Enterprise*-D conducted a mapping survey there in 2367. ("The Wounded" [TNG]).

Sector 21505. Stellar region located in **Cardassian** space. A Cardassian science station destroyed by the *Starship* ***Phoenix*** was in this region. ("The Wounded" [TNG]).

Sector 21947. Area of space considered to be **Talarian** territory. The *Enterprise*-D ventured into this sector in response to a distress call from a damaged **Talarian observation craft** in 2367. ("Suddenly Human" [TNG]).

Sector 37628. Stellar region. The *Enterprise*-D was scheduled to survey this sector on stardate 45587. The mission was delayed due to the accident involving the ***U.S.S. Denver***. ("Ethics" [TNG]).

security access code. Password used by Starfleet personnel to provide positive identification when requesting restricted computer functions or information. Both the password and the user's voiceprint were used to confirm the user's identity. Security access codes were changed occasionally. Picard's security code as of stardate 42494 was "omicron-omicron-alpha-yellow-daystar-2-7." ("Unnatural Selection" [TNG]). Later, it was "Picard-delta-5" ("Chain of Command, Part I" [TNG]), and "Picard Gamma 6-0-7-3" ("Starship Mine" [TNG]), then "Picard 4-7-alpha-tango." *(Star Trek: First Contact).* Riker's security access code as of stardate 42523 was "theta alpha 2-7-3-7, blue." ("The Measure of a Man" [TNG]). Later, it was "Riker-omega-3." ("Rascals" [TNG]). Geordi La Forge: "La Forge theta-9-9-0." ("Tin Man" [TNG]). Captain Edward Jellico: "Jellico alpha 3-1." ("Chain of Command, Part II" [TNG]). Captain Kathryn Janeway: "Janeway 8-1-4-alpha-6-5" ("Cathexis" [VGR]), "Janeway pi 1-1-0." ("Dreadnought" [VGR], "Deadlock" [VGR]), and "Janeway lambda-3." ("Coda" [VGR]). Engineering authorization: omega 4-7. ("Investigations" [VGR]). Kazon-Nistrim defense net: "4-9-1-1-7-0-Culluh." ("Basics, Part I" [VGR]). The *Voyager's* EMH used "Emergency Medical Priority 1-1-4." Seska used "Culluh-0-0." ("Basics, Part II" [VGR]). Kira Nerys: "Kira one-five-seven alpha." ("The Darkness and the Light" [DS9]).

security anklet. Device used by Starfleet authorities to track the whereabouts of a criminal or other prisoner. Worn around the ankle of a humanoid prisoner, the anklet contains a transponder and cannot be removed, except by authorized personnel. ("Caretaker" [VGR], "Non Sequitur" [VGR]).

security bypass module. Small electronic component used to circumvent security restrictions in computer-controlled devices. Bajoran religious terrorist **Neela** used a security bypass module to gain illegal access to runabout pad A on Deep Space 9, part of the plot to assassinate **Vedek Bareil** in 2369. ("In the Hands of the Prophets" [DS9]).

security clearance. An authorization needed to access restricted functions in key computer systems. Functions of increasing criticality generally required increasing levels of security clearance. Aboard station Deep Space 9, security clearance 5 was required to access the locations of repaired replicators in ops during the stationwide computer malfunctions preceeding discovery of the **aphasia device** on stardate 46423. Quark needed a security clearance of 5 to access such information, but he averted the problem by switching several **isolinear rods** to obtain the data. ("Babel" [DS9]). Security clearance level 7 was needed to access the location of weapons stored on station Deep Space 9. ("Captive Pursuit" [DS9]).

security field subsystem ANA. Computer program devised by **Neela**, but classified under Chief O'Brien's name, intended to bypass the security defenses on **Deep Space 9**. The subprogram was designed to override the security force fields approaching runabout pad A, thus allowing her to escape after her planned assassination of **Vedek Bareil** in 2369. ("In the Hands of the Prophets" [DS9]). *In an early draft of the episode, the character of Neela was named Anara. The subsystem code ANA was an accidental holdover from that draft.*

security sensor. Specialized devices used to detect the presence of weapons or other contraband. Security sensors on station Deep Space 9 were designed to sound an alarm upon detection of unauthorized weapons passing through the airlocks to the interior of the station. The security sensor detected the **Hunters'** weapons and activated the alert. ("Captive Pursuit" [DS9]).

sehlat. A Vulcan animal resembling a large teddy bear with six-inch fangs. When **Spock** was a boy, he was very fond of his pet *sehlat.* ("Journey to Babel" [TOS]). *The animated episode "Yesteryear," written by Dorothy Fontana, suggests that Spock's* sehlat *was named I-Chaya.*

seismic regulator. Device used to control seismic activity in a planet's crust. Seismic regulators were being installed in a subterranean cavern under the city of San Francisco on Earth in late 2368 when a work crew discovered the severed head of Data, which had been buried there for five centuries. ("Time's Arrow, Part I" [TNG]).

Sela. (Denise Crosby). Romulan operative who claimed to be the daughter of *Enterprise*-D Security Officer **Natasha Yar** and a Romulan official. Although Yar died in 2364 without ever having a child, it was believed that an alternate version of Yar entered this continuum in 2366, then went into the past, where she gave birth to Sela. ("Redemption, Part II" [TNG]). SEE: **Yar, Natasha (alternate)**. Sela emerged in 2367 as a key figure in the ongoing **Romulan** hegemony in Klingon and Federation politics. She spearheaded an operation in that year that unsuccessfully attempted to use mental conditioning to reprogram Starfleet officer Geordi La Forge so that La Forge would assassinate Klingon Governor **Vagh**, which would have created distrust between the Klingon and Federation governments. ("The Mind's Eye" [TNG]). Later that year, Sela commanded a covert action to provide military supplies to the **Duras** family during the **Klingon civil war** in an attempt to destabilize the **Gowron** regime. ("Redemption, Parts I and II" [TNG]). In 2368, Sela spearheaded a plan to use the underground Romulan-Vulcan reunification movement as a cover for an attempted invasion of **Vulcan**. She tried to force Ambassador **Spock** to reassure Vulcan authorities that the Romulan invasion force was actually a peace delegation, but her plan was thwarted by *Enterprise*-D personnel. ("Unification, Parts I and II" [TNG]). *Sela was first seen as a mysterious woman in the shadows in "The Mind's Eye" (TNG). Denise Crosby provided Sela's voice for that episode, although Sela's silhouette was played by a photo-double. Crosby was first seen as Sela in "Redemption, Part I."*

Selar, Dr. (Suzie Plakson). Physician, part of the *Enterprise*-D medical staff. A Vulcan, Dr. Selar was part of the away team answering a distress call from **Gravesworld**, and was present when noted cyberneticist **Dr. Ira Graves** died there of **Darnay's disease** in 2365. ("The Schizoid Man" [TNG]). *Although "The Schizoid Man" was the only appearance of Dr. Selar, we heard her being paged aboard the alternate* Enterprise-D *in "Yesterday's* Enterprise*" (TNG), and Dr Crusher mentioned her in other episodes including "Remember Me" (TNG), "Tapestry" (TNG), "Suspicions" (TNG), "Sub Rosa" (TNG) and "Genesis" (TNG). Actor Suzie Plakson, who played Selar, also portrayed Emissary* ***K'Ehleyr*** *and the* ***Q female.***

Selay. One of two habitable planets in the **Beta Renna** star system, as well as the name of the sentient reptilian people from that world. Since achieving spaceflight, the Selay had been bitter enemies with the **Anticans**, who came from the other habitable planet in their system. Both the Selay and the Anticans applied for admission to the Federation in 2364. ("Lonely Among Us" [TNG]).

Selcundi Drema sector. Stellar region in which are located five geologically similar planetary systems. One planet in the region, **Drema IV**, was found to be dangerously unstable, threatening the humanoid civilization living there. Acting Ensign Wesley Crusher was in charge of planetary mineral surveys during the *Enterprise*-D mission to the region in 2365. ("Pen Pals" [TNG]).

Selcundi Drema. Star system in the Selcundi Drema sector. All the planets in this system (as well as in the other systems in the sector) exhibited unusual geologic instabilities. The fifth planet of this system disintegrated around 2215, forming an asteroid belt.

The fourth planet, **Drema IV**, was the home of a humanoid civilization. ("Pen Pals" [TNG]). SEE: **Sarjenka**.

Seldonis IV Convention. Interstellar treaty governing the treatment of prisoners of war. Both the United Federation of Planets and the Cardassian Union were signatories to the accord. Following Captain Picard's capture by the **Cardassians** in 2369, Picard was tortured by **Gul Madred**, in violation of that treaty. Madred claimed Picard had been acting without Federation orders, and was therefore not entitled to the protection of the Seldonis Convention. ("Chain of Command, Part II" [TNG]).

Selebi Asteroid Belt. Debris field located in Sector 396. The *Enterprise*-D charted the Selebi belt in 2366. ("The Offspring" [TNG]).

selenium. Semiconducting, metallic element of the sulfur group, with atomic number 34. Selenium and rhodium nitrites can be synthesized to form **cobalt diselenide**, a biogenic agent. ("For the Uniform" [DS9]).

Seleya, Mount. On planet **Vulcan**, a mountain on whose summit is located an ancient temple. Mount Seleya was where a ***fal-tor-pan*** ceremony was performed in 2285, rejoining Spock's ***katra*** with his body. *(Star Trek III: The Search for Spock).*

self-destruct sequence. Command program in the main computer system of Cardassian station **Terok Nor** enabling the destruction of the station should it fall into non-Cardassian hands. In 2371, Jake Sisko inadvertently triggered a **counterinsurgency program** that activated the self-destruct sequence. Once the self-destruct sequence was initiated, the station's main fusion reactor was set to overload. ("Civil Defense" [DS9]). SEE: **autodestruct**; **destruct sequence**.

self-sealing stem bolt. Useful gizmo. On stardate 46844, **Nog** and **Jake Sisko** traded some ***yamok* sauce** for 100 gross of self-sealing stem bolts, eventually trading them for seven tessipates of land on planet Bajor. ("Progress" [DS9]). Self-sealing stem bolts can be used in the production of reverse-ratcheting routing planers. ("Prophet Motive" [DS9], "By Inferno's Light" [DS9]). *Makes sense to us....*

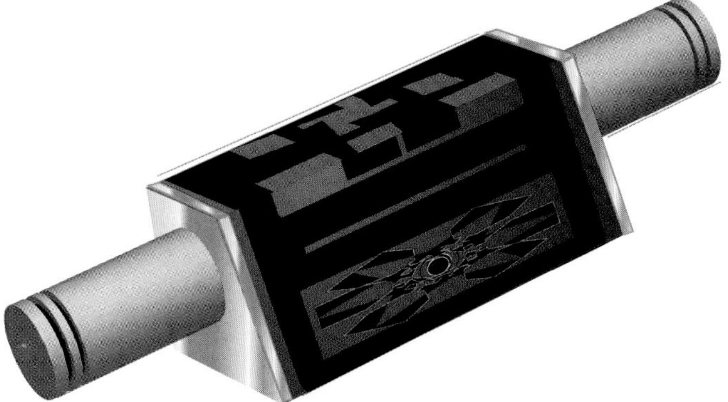

selgninaem. A highly toxic substance capable of causing **nucleosynthesis** in silicon. Selgninaem is not normally detectable by a starship's internal sensor scans. ("Hollow Pursuits" [TNG]). *"Selignaem" is "meaningles(s)" spelled backwards.*

seloh. Klingon term for sex. ("Sins of the Father" [TNG]).

Selok, Subcommander. The true Romulan identity of Vulcan **Ambassador T'Pel**. ("Data's Day" [TNG]).

selton. Unit of measurement to the inhabitants of the village on planet **Barkon IV**. ("Thine Own Self" [TNG]).

***sem'hal* stew**. Cardassian food. *Sem'hal* stew was served to **Aamin Marritza** while a prisoner on Deep Space 9 in 2369. Marritza said it could use some ***yamok* sauce**. ("Duet" [DS9]).

Senarian egg broth. Soup. **Mareel** gave **Miles O'Brien** a bowl of Senarian egg broth after the chief suffered a phaser stun in 2370. ("Invasive Procedures" [DS9]).

sensor web. Shawl-like garment into which was woven a highly sophisticated string of **sensors**. **Dr. Miranda Jones** wore a sensor web that fed her sensory information about her surroundings, and helped to hide the fact that she was blind. ("Is There in Truth no Beauty?"[TOS]).

sensor. Any of a wide range of scientific, medical, and engineering instruments such as those used aboard Federation starships for detection and analysis at a distance. ("Where No Man Has Gone Before" [TOS]). The original *Enterprise* used a **duotronic** sensor array that had sensor nulls in its scan cycle of almost three seconds' duration. ("Trials and Tribble-ations" [DS9]). Under certain conditions, a ship in orbit above a planet's magnetic pole can be difficult to detect by sensors. William Riker once used this phenomenon while a lieutenant aboard the *Starship* ***Potemkin*** to obscure the ship from an opponent. ("Peak Performance" [TNG]). On the *Enterprise*-D, there were 15,525 known substances that could not be detected by standard internal scans. ("Hollow Pursuits" [TNG]).

sentient holographic life-form. Forms of life that were created by means of holo-imaging devices and computer programmed behavior. These beings were considered alive for the same reason that androids like **Data** were deemed alive by Starfleet. Similarly, holographic beings that had exceeded their programming and developed sentience were considered to be bona fide life-forms. Fortunately, this happened only infrequently; otherwise every holodeck-created character could never be shut off once activated. Examples of sentient holographic life-forms include **Professor James Moriarty** ("Elementary Dear Data" [TNG], "Ship in a Bottle" [TNG]), the inhabitants of **Yadera II** ("Shadowplay" [DS9]), and the holographic doctor aboard the *Starship Voyager* ("Caretaker" [VGR]).

Sentinel Minor IV. Planet. Sentinel Minor IV was the destination of the ***U.S.S. Lalo*** when it was attacked by a **Borg** ship and disappeared in 2366. ("The Best of Both Worlds, Part I" [TNG]).

sentry. A tightly confined annular force field that was discovered on the moon **Lambda Paz** in the Pentarus star system. The sentry surrounded a water fountain in a cave on that desert planet, serving to protect that valuable resource. It was not clear if the sentry itself was a life-form, but it responded effectively to the attempts of Captain **Dirgo**, as well as those of Jean-Luc Picard and Wesley Crusher, when they attempted to get water from the fountain after they crashed on Lambda Paz in 2367. Dirgo was killed by the sentry. ("Final Mission" [TNG]).

Senva, Healer. Physician from the **Vulcan** Medical Institute. Senva was nominated to receive the **Carrington Award** in 2371 but did not win. ("Prophet Motive" [DS9]).

seofurance. Biochemical substance. Seofurance fragments from a biological-sample container were found by the matter reclamation unit in **Ibudan's** quarters. ("A Man Alone" [DS9]).

separ. Type of gemstone known for its hardness and its sharp facets. ("Looking for *par'Mach* in All the Wrong Places" [DS9]).

Sepian Commodities Exchange. Financial market. The Sepian Commodities Exchange was in chaos in 2373 after a mine on Parsion III struck **feldomite**. ("Business As Usual" [DS9]).

septal area. Also known as the septum lucidum, the triangular double membrane that separates the anterior horns of the lateral ventricles of a humanoid brain. The **Ktarian game** was found to affect the septal area. ("The Game" [TNG]).

Septimus Minor. Planetary system. The original destination of the Federation colony ship ***Artemis***, launched in 2274. ("The Ensigns of Command" [TNG]).

Septimus. (Ian Wolfe). Leader of a group of slaves on planet Eight Ninety-Two-IV who hid in the caves away from the Roman culture on that planet. A former senator active in Roman society, he heard the words of the Son, gave up his lifestyle, and became a slave. ("Bread and Circuses" [TOS]). SEE: **Children of the Sun**; **Eight Ninety-Two-IV, Planet**. *Ian Wolfe also played* ***Mr. Atoz*** *in "All Our Yesterdays" (TOS).*

Sepulo. Ferengi transport ship. The *Sepulo* visited station Deep Space 9 in 2369 for a major trade conference convened by the **grand nagus.** ("The Nagus" [DS9]).

serik. Device hit with the cue stick in the game of **dom-jot**. ("Tapestry" [TNG]).

Serilian ambassador. Representative of the Serilian government. The Serilian ambassador planned to arrive at **Deep Space 9** shortly after stardate 48423.2. Security Chief **Odo** worked on security protocols for the ambassador's arrival. ("Meridian" [DS9]). *We never saw the ambassador.*

sero-amino readout. A medical test. Dr. Crusher performed a sero-amino test on **Reginald Barclay** following his exposure to a **Cytherian** probe in 2367. ("The Nth Degree" [TNG]).

serotonin. Biochemical substance that serves as a central neurotransmitter in humanoid nervous systems. The addictive **Ktaran game** initiated a serotonin cascade in the frontal lobe of the brain. ("The Game" [TNG]).

Serova, Dr. (Margaret Reed). Hekaran scientist who, in 2366, theorized that repeated and prolonged use of warp travel in the **Hekaras Corridor** was damaging the very fabric of space. The Federation Science Council initially found insufficient evidence to back up her theory and declined to act on her recommendations to limit the use of warp drive. Serova continued to work on her research, and by 2370, she, along with her brother, **Rabal**, felt they had enough data to finally prove her theories. She was unwilling to wait for the year it would take for the Federation Science Council to complete a review of her claims. She and Rabal chose instead to booby-trap the Hekaras Corridor with **verteron mines**, theorizing that if the mines disabled enough ships, Starfleet would send a vessel to investigate. The *Enterprise*-D was dispatched, and it, too, became disabled. Captain Jean-Luc Picard reviewed her research and agreed to recommend Serova's work to the Science Council. Serova was nevertheless impatient and was killed while proving her theory by triggering a warp core breach in her ship, causing a **subspace rupture**. The Federation Science Council subsequently imposed Federation-wide limits on the use of warp drive to avoid further damage to the continuum. ("Force of Nature" [TNG]). The restrictions remained in place until advances in **warp-drive** technology made it possible to avoid such damage.

serpent of Xol. Legendary beast that was slain by the great **Klingon** warrior **Kahless the Unforgettable**. ("The Sword of Kahless" [DS9]).

servo. Multipurpose tool used by **Gary Seven** on Earth in 1968. The servo was a device of extraterrestrial origin and had a variety of functions, from opening locked doors to serving as a weapon. ("Assignment: Earth" [TOS]).

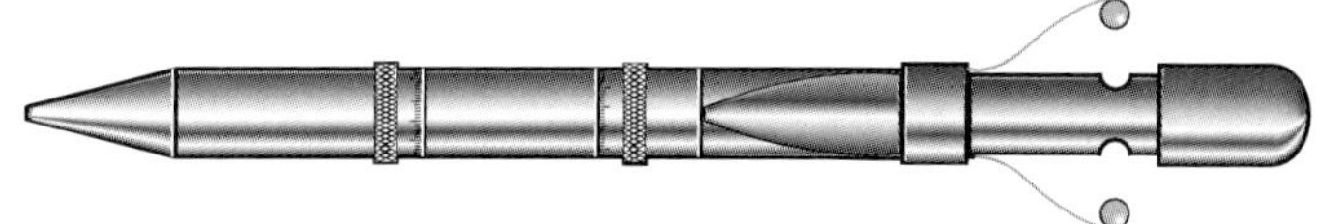

Seska. (Martha Hackett). **Cardassian** agent who was surgically altered to appear **Bajoran**, then assigned to infiltrate the **Maquis** terrorist group. ("State of Flux" [VGR]). Accepted as a member of the Maquis, Seska joined the crew of the ***Starship Voyager*** after her Maquis vessel was destroyed in the Delta Quadrant in 2371. Aboard the *Voyager*, she worked as an engineering officer. Seska and **Chakotay** had once been lovers. ("Parallax" [VGR]). Her role as a Cardassian agent was discovered on stardate 48658, when she was caught selling Federation **replicator** technology to the **Kazon-Nistrim** sect. ("State of Flux" [VGR]). Seska fled to the Nistrim, where she sought the assistance of **Jal Culluh**. She helped Culluh in a bold, but unsuccessful attempt to steal a transporter module from the *Starship Voyager*. Seska continued to use her past relationship with Chakotay in an effort to undermine his dealings with the Nistrim, informing him that she had used Chakotay's DNA to artificially impregnate herself. ("Maneuvers" [VGR]). She also used her pregnancy to manipulate Culluh, also telling him that the child was his. ("Alliances" [VGR]). She instructed *Voyager* crew member **Michael Jonas** to sabotage the ship's warp systems. ("Lifesigns" [VGR]). Late in 2372, Seska gave birth to a son, which was actually fathered by Culluh, not Chakotay as she had intended. Seska was killed after she helped Nistrim forces capture the *Starship Voyager*, when *Voyager* crew members retook their ship. Culluh subsequently took custody of his child. ("Basics, Parts I and II" [VGR]). *Seska said in "Prime Factors" (VGR) that she had a brother, but she may have been lying. Seska was first seen in "Parallax" (VGR). She also appeared in "Phage" (VGR), "Emanations" (VGR), and "Maneuvers" (VGR). Martha Hackett previously portrayed Subcommander T'Rul in "The Search, Parts I and II" (DS9).*

Setal, Sublieutenant. Identity assumed by Romulan Admiral **Alidar Jarok** when he defected to the Federation in 2366. As Setal, Jarok claimed to be a low-ranking logistics officer, but his true identity was later discovered. ("The Defector" [TNG]).

SETI greeting. Communications protocol developed by 20th-century **Earth** astronomers for the purpose of signaling an extraterrestrial intelligence. The **SETI** greeting was intended to be intelligible by any technologically sophisticated civilization, and conveyed information about Earth's position in the galaxy, information about life on Earth, and greetings in many different Earth languages. Earth astronomer **Rain Robinson** transmitted a SETI greeting to the *U.S.S. Voyager* in 1996 when she believed the starship to be of extrasolar origin. ("Future's End, Part I" [VGR]). *Robinson's SETI greeting was loosely based on messages that NASA sent into interstellar space aboard its* Pioneer *and* Voyager *space probes. Those SETI greetings, in the form of a plaque on* Pioneer 10 *and 11, and a record on* Voyager 1 *and 2, were designed by astronomers Carl Sagan and Frank Drake, et al. A replica of the* Pioneer 10 *plaque was among the wall decorations* *in Rain Robinson's SETI lab. We saw the* Pioneer 10 *plaque (and the* Pioneer *spacecraft itself) destroyed by a Klingon ship in* Star Trek V: The Final Frontier.

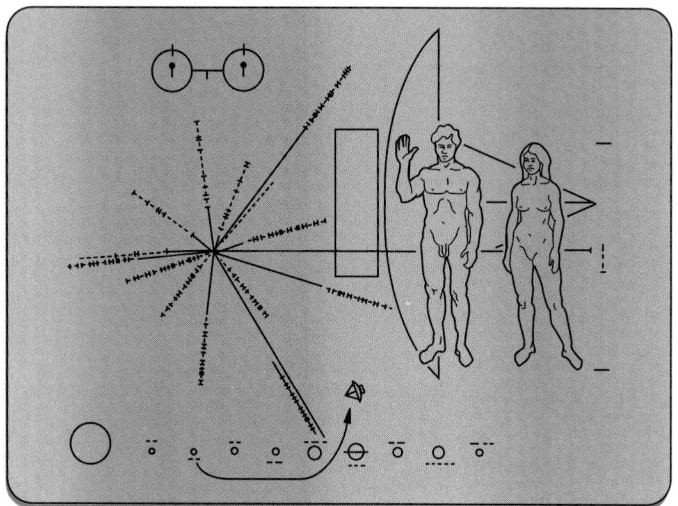

Pioneer plaque

SETI. Search for extraterrestrial intelligence; on 20th-century Earth, a scientific research program using radio telescopes that attempted to detect radio signals from any extrasolar civilizations. A key concept in the search for extraterrestrial intelligence was a mathematical concept known as the **Drake Equation**. In 1996, the program was privately supported with funds from such organizations as the **Chronowerx** corporation. SETI astronomer **Rain Robinson** actually detected the *Starship Voyager* in Earth orbit in that year, but this information was suppressed by Chronowerx executive **Harry Starling**. ("Future's End, Part I" [VGR]). *In real life, financial supporters of SETI programs include Microsoft chairman Bill Gates and filmmaker Steven Spielberg.*

Setlik III. Planet. Site of a Federation outpost that was the victim of a sneak attack during the **Cardassian** war. Nearly one hundred civilians were killed in the incident, including the wife and children of **Captain Benjamin Maxwell**. The *Starship* ***Rutledge***, commanded by Maxwell, arrived at Setlik III the morning after the attack and was only able to save a few civilians in an outlying area. Years later, the Cardassians admitted the raid was a mistake, that they had incorrectly believed the civilian outpost was a staging place for a massive Federation attack. ("The Wounded" [TNG], "Emissary" [DS9]).

Setti, Mr. Hairdresser who worked with **Mr. Mot** in the *Enterprise*-D barber shop. ("Schisms" [TNG]).

Seven, Gary. (Robert Lansing). Human raised on a distant planet who was returned to **Earth** in 1968 to help humanity survive its nuclear age. He was also known as Supervisor 194. Gary Seven's ancestors were taken from Earth approximately six thousand years ago and trained by the inhabitants of an unknown alien world. Seven was sent to Earth in 1968 on a mission to prevent Earth's civilization from destroying itself in a dangerous nuclear-arms race. His assignment was to intercede in the scheduled launch of an American orbital nuclear-weapons platform, causing the launch vehicle to malfunction in such a way as to frighten planetary authorities into abandoning such weapons of mass destruction. While en route to Earth, Seven was accidentally intercepted by the *Starship Enterprise* and nearly prevented from accomplishing his task before *Enterprise* personnel determined that his intentions were not destructive. Seven remained on Earth in that time period, where he is believed to have performed other missions for the protection of humankind. ("Assignment Earth" [TOS]). SEE: **Lincoln, Roberta**. *The producers of* Star Trek *hoped for Gary Seven to return in his own television series,* Assignment: Earth, *although this never materialized.*

Seventh Guarantee. One of the fundamental civil liberties protected by the **Constitution of the United Federation of Planets**. The Seventh Guarantee protects citizens against self-incrimination. ("The Drumhead" [TNG]).

Sevrin, Dr. (Skip Homeier). Would-be revolutionary who rejected the technological world to seek a more primitive existence on the mythical planet **Eden**. Sevrin had been a noted research engineer in acoustics and communication on **Tiburon**, before he became infected with deadly ***Synthococcus novae***. This disease, the product of technological living, pushed Sevrin on his quest for a simpler life. It was on this quest that Sevrin and his followers in 2269 stole the star cruiser ***Aurora***, and later commandeered the *Starship Enterprise* on a quest for Eden. Sevrin died from eating a poisonous plant on a planet he thought was Eden. ("The Way to Eden" [TOS]). *Skip Homeier also played Melakon in "Patterns of Force" [TOS]).*

Seyetik, Nidell. (Salli Elise Richardson). Wife of **Professor Gideon Seyetik.** Nidell met Seyetik just after the professor completed terraforming her homeworld, planet **New Halana**. Even though she loved Seyetik, she was homesick and unhappy, but because **Halanans** mate for life, she could never divorce him. This caused her deep emotional distress, and she lost control of her **psychoprojective telepathic** abilities, resulting in the creation of a number of psychoprojective alter egos over the years. Nidell's internal struggle ended with the death of her husband in 2370, and her alter egos disappeared. Nidell retained no memory of her projections or their actions. SEE: **Fenna**. ("Second Sight" [DS9]).

Seyetik, Professor Gideon. (Richard Kiley). Scientist noted for having terraformed several planets including **New Halana** and **Blue Horizon**. In addition to his remarkable scientific achievements, Seyetik was an author and a painter known for his flamboyant style. Seyetik was married nine times. His ninth wife was **Nidell**, of planet New Halana. Seyetik's greatest and final triumph was the re-ignition of the star Epsilon 119 in 2370, which he accomplished by personally piloting a shuttlepod into the dead star to deliver a payload of **protomatter**. Sadly, Seyetik was killed in the process. He sacrificed himself on the altar of science. ("Second Sight" [DS9]). SEE: **terraforming**.

Sha Ka Ree. In **Vulcan** mythology, a beautiful planet from which creation sprang. Many cultures have similar legends. Humans call it "heaven" or "**Eden**," while Klingons call it "***Qui'Tu***," and the Romulans refer to it as "***Vorta Vor.***" **Sybok** spent much of his life searching for this world, finding a planet he believed was *Sha Ka Ree* after stealing the *Starship Enterprise*-A for this quest. Unfortunately, the planet discovered by Sybok was home to a malevolent creature who was using Sybok's quest in an attempt to escape from the Great Barrier at the center of the galaxy. *(Star Trek V: The Final Frontier).* SEE: **Great Barrier, the.** *The name* Sha Ka Ree *was a wordplay based on the fact that* Star Trek V*'s producers at one point were considering casting Sean Connery in the part of Sybok.*

"Shades of Gray." *Next Generation* episode #48. Teleplay by Maurice Hurley and Richard Manning & Hans Beimler. Story by Maurice Hurley. Stardate 42976.1. *First aired in 1989. Riker becomes comatose after an injury on an away mission and dreams of past experiences. This episode marked the last appearance of Diana Muldaur as* ***Dr. Katherine Pulaski****. The episode was a "clip show," designed to use scenes from earlier episodes in an effort to save money, since this was the last episode of the season.* GUEST CAST: Diana Muldaur as **Pulaski, Dr. Katherine**; Colm Meaney as **O'Brien, Miles**. SEE: **endorphins; Pulaski, Dr. Katherine; REM sleep; Riker, William T.; Surata IV; tricordrazine.**

"Shadowplay." *Deep Space Nine* episode # 36. Written by Robert Hewitt Wolfe. *Directed by Robert Scheerer. Stardate 47603.3. First aired in 1994. Drawn by unusual readings to an unknown planet, Dax and Odo discover a civilization of living holograms.* GUEST CAST: Kenneth Mars as **Colyus**; Kenneth Tobey as **Rurigan**; Noley Thornton as **Taya**; Philip Anglim as **Bareil, Vedek**; Trula M. Marcus as Female villager; Martin Cassidy as Male villager. SEE: **Aldebaran Music Academy; Anetra; Arlin, Lysia; Bareil, Vedek; Cardassia V; Colyus; Dominion; greenbread; holodeck & holosuite programs; hologenerator; isolinear rods; *jumja*; Kira Nerys; Kono; O'Brien, Michael; O'Brien, Miles; omicron particles; *Orinoco, U.S.S.*; Relliketh; Rhit, Prylar; Rurigan; Singha refugee camp; Sisko, Jake; springball; Taya; Tellarite; Yadera II; Yadera Prime; Yaderans.**

Shahna. (Angelique Pettyjohn). **Drill thrall** on planet **Triskelion**. In 2268, Shahna was responsible for training James Kirk to fight in games for the planet's **Providers**. ("The Gamesters of Triskelion" [TOS]).

"Shaka, when the walls fell." A **Tamarian** metaphorical phrase that referred to an inability to understand or be understood. Tamarian Captain **Dathon** used this phrase repeatedly when attempting to communicate with Captain Jean-Luc Picard in 2368. ("Darmok" [TNG]).

Shakaar Edon. (Duncan Regehr). Leader of the **Bajoran** resistance cell that bore his name during the **Cardassian** occupation of Bajor. SEE: **Shakaar resistance cell**. Following the Cardassian withdrawal in 2369, Shakaar settled on a farm in his home province of **Dahkur**. Unfortunately, the farmland had been poisoned by departing Cardassian forces, and could not grow crops without treatment by **soil reclamators**. These reclamators were made available by the Bajoran government in 2371, but before they could be used, acting First Minister **Winn** ordered the machines returned. When Shakaar and his neighbors refused to cooperate, Winn's political inexperience led her to escalate the incident to the brink of armed conflict. Popular support for Shakaar's position subsequently led him to be elected **Bajoran First Minister**, a significant setback for Winn's political ambitions. He faced very little opposition. ("Shakaar" [DS9]). As First Minister, Shakaar visited Deep Space 9 in early 2372 for talks with the Federation. During his visit he became romantically involved with **Kira Nerys**, his longtime friend and resistance comrade during the occupation of Bajor. ("Crossfire" [DS9]). Shortly thereafter, Shakaar asked Kira to participate in a diplomatic conference on **Korma**. He wined and dined her in **Jalanda City** in order to persuade her to accept the difficult task. ("Return to Grace" [DS9]). Shakaar was present on Deep Space 9 in 2373 when Nerys gave birth to Kirayoshi O'Brien. ("The Begotten" [DS9]). Before the Cardassian occupation, Shakaar's family was part of the farming ***D'jarra***. ("Accession" [DS9]). *Duncan Regehr previously portrayed Ronin in "Sub Rosa" (TNG).*

Shakaar resistance cell. Bajoran terrorist group that took its name from its charismatic leader, **Shakaar Edon**. The Shakaar cell, for ten years prior to the Cardassian withdrawal, used the mountains of their home province, **Dahkur**, to hide from Cardassian forces. ("Shakaar" [DS9]). The Shakaar group liberated the infamous Bajoran labor camp at **Gallitep** in 2357. **Kira Nerys** was a member of the group and helped free her fellow **Bajorans** from their terrible imprisonment at Gallitep. ("Duet" [DS9]). SEE: **Marritza, Darhe'el**. In 2361, Kira and other members spent a cold winter in the Dahkur Hills on Bajor evading Cardassian troops. ("Second Skin" [DS9]). **Lorit Akrem** was also a member of Shakaar's band. The group was quite a thorn in the side of the Cardassian occupational forces. ("Indiscretion" [DS9]). Years after the end of the Cardassian occupation, several former members of the Shakaar cell were murdered by **Silaran Prin**, a Cardassian national who sought revenge for a bombing committed during the occupation. ("The Darkness and the Light" [DS9]).

"Shakaar." *Deep Space Nine* episode #70. Written by Gordon Dawson. Directed by Jonathan West. No stardate given. *First aired in 1995. A dispute over the use of farm equipment places members of Kira's old resistance cell in danger and nearly ignites a Bajoran civil war.* GUEST CAST: Duncan Regehr as **Shakaar**; Diane Salinger as **Lupaza**; William Lucking as **Furel**; Sherman Howard as Syvar; John Doman as **Lenaris Holem**; Louise Fletcher as **Winn**; John Kenton Shull as Security officer; Harry Hutchinson as Trooper. SEE: **Bajoran First Minister; Dahkur Province; *duranja;* Furel; Gallitep; humeral socket replacement; "in the zone"; Kalem Apren; Kira Nerys; Lenaris Holem; Lupaza; O'Brien, Miles; Ornathia resistance cell; Pullock V raid; Rakantha Province; Shakaar Edon; Shakaar resistance cell; soil reclamators; tuwaly pie; Winn.**

Shakespeare, William. One of Earth's most respected dramatists and poets, William Shakespeare (1564-1616) left behind a body of work that continues to illuminate the human adventure, even into the 24th century. The **Karidian Company of Players** performed ***Hamlet*** on a tour of official installations until Karidian's death in 2266. ("Conscience of the King" [TOS]). Klingon General **Chang** was fond of quoting from Shakespearean plays. *(Star Trek VI: The Undiscovered Country).* Captain Jean-Luc Picard kept a leather-bound copy of Shakespeare's collected works in his **ready room** aboard the *Enterprise*-D. ("Hide and Q" [TNG]). One of Shakespeare's most famous plays was ***Julius Caesar***, although **Garak** considered it more of a farce than a tragedy. ("Improbable Cause" [DS9]). **Data** created a **holodeck program** that allowed him to play the title role in Shakespeare's ***Henry V***. ("The Defector" [TNG]). Another holodeck program let Data portray Prospero from ***The Tempest***. ("Emergence" [TNG]).

shakras. Name used by the Native Americans of ancient Earth to refer to the **foramen magnum** portion of the humanoid cranium. ("The Muse" [DS9]).

Shanthi, Fleet Admiral. (Fran Bennett). High-ranking Starfleet official. In early 2368, Shanthi authorized Captain Jean-Luc

Picard to form an armada to blockade Romulan forces that were covertly supplying the **Duras** family army in the **Klingon civil war**. ("Redemption, Part II" [TNG]). In 2370, she convened an inquiry into the activities of **Admiral Erik Pressman** and his associates in the salvage of the *Pegasus*. ("The *Pegasus*" [TNG]).

***shap*.** Term used in the **Wadi** game **chula** for a level on the multi-tiered playing board. Each *shap* contained a test, progressively more difficult, until the players reached home, their final destination. ("Move Along Home" [DS9]).

shape-shift inhibitor. Device that generated an energy field capable of preventing a shape-shifting being from altering its form. The **Obsidian Order** developed a prototype shape-shift inhibitor and tested it successfully on **Odo** in 2371. ("The Die is Cast" [DS9]).

shape-shifter. SEE: **allasomorph; Anya; Armus; cellular metamorphosis; chameloid; changeling; coalescent organism; Devidian nurse; Douwd; Excalibans; Farpoint Station; Founders; Garth of Izar; Isabella; Isis; Kelvans; L-S VI life-form; Martia; melitius; Odo; Q; Rocha, Lieutenant Keith; Salia; Spot; Sylvia.**

Sharat. (Peter White). **Kellerun** ambassador who helped negotiate the end of the war with the **T'Lani** in 2370. Sharat collaborated with **E'Tyshra**, the T'Lani ambassador, to destroy all information of the **harvester** technology and to try to kill everyone who had technical knowledge of their manufacture, including Deep Space 9 personnel **Dr. Julian Bashir** and **Miles O'Brien**. ("Armageddon Game" [DS9]).

"Shattered Mirror." *Deep Space Nine* episode #92. Written by Ira Steven Behr & Hans Beimler. Directed by James L. Conway. No stardate given. *First aired in 1996. Jennifer crosses over from the mirror universe and kidnaps Jake; Benjamin Sisko follows them back and finds that he must fix the rebels'* Defiant *as part of the ransom.* GUEST CAST: Felecia M. Bell as **Sisko, Jennifer (mirror)**; Aron Eisenberg as **Nog**; Carlos Carrasco as Klingon officer; Andrew Robinson as **Garak, Elim (mirror)**; James Black as Helmsman; Dennis Madalone as Guard. SEE: **agonizer; Alliance; Bashir, Julian (mirror); chicken à la Sisko; *Defiant* (mirror); Gettor, Minister; Kira Nerys (mirror); Marani; mirror universe; Nog (mirror); O'Brien, Miles (mirror); Sisko, Jennifer (mirror); Terok Nor (mirror); Terran resistance; warp shadows; Worf (mirror).**

Shaw, Areel. (Joan Marshall). Starfleet attorney with the Judge Advocate General's office at **Starbase 11**. Shaw prosecuted James Kirk's court-martial in 2267 for the apparent death of **Ben Finney**. This notwithstanding, Shaw had been romantically involved with Kirk in 2263, and they parted friends after the court-martial when Kirk was found innocent, despite her efforts to show otherwise. ("Court Martial" [TOS]).

Shaw, Katik. (Marc Buckland). A Rutian male; waiter at the Lumar Cafe on **Rutia IV**. Shaw was an **Ansata** sympathizer and conveyed a message from Commander Riker to the Ansata leader, **Kyril Finn**. ("The High Ground" [TNG]).

Shea, Lieutenant. (Carl Byrd). Security guard on the original *Starship Enterprise*. Shaw was part of the landing party that encountered the **Kelvans** in 2268. ("By Any Other Name" [TOS]).

Shel-la, Golin. (Jonathan Banks). Leader of the **Ennis,** who fought their eternal enemy, the **Nol-Ennis**, on a lunar penal colony in the Gamma Quadrant. ("Battle Lines" [DS9]).

Shelby, Lieutenant Commander. (Elizabeth Dennehy). Officer who was placed in charge of Starfleet's planning for defense against the **Borg** in early 2366. Shelby, along with Admiral Hanson, went aboard the *Enterprise*-D later that year when the disappearance of a colony on **Jouret IV** indicated a new Borg offensive. Young and ambitious, Shelby hoped to gain an appointment as *Enterprise*-D executive officer, and won at least a temporary promotion to the post following the abduction of Captain Picard by the Borg. Following the destruction of the Borg ship, Shelby was assigned to Starfleet Headquarters, where she joined the task force to reassemble the fleet. ("The Best of Both Worlds, Parts I and II" [TNG]).

Shelia star system. Home system of the **Sheliak**. ("The Ensigns of Command" [TNG]).

Sheliak Corporate. Governing body of the **Sheliak**. ("The Ensigns of Command" [TNG]).

Sheliak Director. (Mart McChesney). Leader of the **Sheliak** group sent to colonize planet **Tau Cygna V**. The director demanded removal of the Federation colony there, noting that the "human infestation" was in violation of the Treaty of Armens. ("The Ensigns of Command" [TNG]). SEE: **Armens, Treaty of.**

Sheliak. Classification R-3 life-forms, the Sheliak are only vaguely humanoid. The Sheliak are a reclusive people, avoiding contact with the Federation whenever possible. This may be due to the Sheliak attitude that humans are an inferior form of life. The **Treaty of Armens** was established in 2255 between the Sheliak and the Federation, ceding several planets (including **Tau Cygna V**) to the Sheliak. There was virtually no contact with the Sheliak for over a century thereafter, until they demanded that a Federation colony on Tau Cygna V be removed. The Sheliak refer to themselves as "The Membership" and have a governing body called "the Corporate." ("The Ensigns of Command" [TNG]). *The Sheliak colony ship model was a reuse of the* Merchantman *from* Star Trek III. *Their ship interior was a re-dress of the* Enterprise-*D battle bridge set.*

Shepard, Riley Aldrin. (David Drew Gallagher). Starfleet officer, serial number C95304699427. In 2372, while a third-year cadet at **Starfleet Academy**, with a specialty in tactical operations, Shepard was a member of **Red Squad**. As a member of that elite group, he took part in the sabotage of the Earth's **global power grid** at the **Division of Planetary Operations** headquarters in Lisbon. Since he was following direct orders from **Admiral Leyton**, Shepard did not realize that he and the rest of Red Squad were committing acts of treason. ("Paradise Lost" [DS9]). *Named for astronauts Buzz Aldrin and Alan B. Shepard.*

Sherlock Holmes program 3A. One of Data's recreational holodeck programs on the *Enterprise*-D, re-creating the world of 19th-century London according to the literary works of **Sir Arthur Conan Doyle.** This particular **Sherlock Holmes** adventure malfunctioned in 2369 when a computer life-form based on the character of **Professor James Moriarty** attempted to escape the holodeck. ("Ship in a Bottle" [TNG]).

Sherman's Planet. Planet near the **Klingon** border. Sherman's Planet was the object of a dispute in 2267 between the **Klingon Empire** and the **United Federation of Planets**. Under the terms of the **Organian Peace Treaty**, the side that could most efficiently develop the planet could assume ownership. The Federation claim to Sherman's Planet was based on the availability of a large store of **quadrotriticale**, a grain that grew well on that world. ("The Trouble with Tribbles" [TOS]). SEE: **Darvin, Arne**; **Deep Space Station K-7**. *Named for Holly Sherman, a friend of episode writer David Gerrold.*

Sherval Das. Valerian vessel. The *Sherval Das* docked at station Deep Space 9 for maintenance in 2369. Major Kira Nerys believed the *Sherval Das* was carrying chemical **dolamide** explosives intended for use in **Cardassian** weapons. Prior to its arrival at Deep Space 9, the *Sherval Das* visited planets Fahleena III, Mariah IV, and Ultima Thule; this route was believed to be the same one the Valerians used previously when shipping dolamide to the Cardassians. ("Dramatis Personae" [DS9]).

Sherwood Forest. An area of Nottinghamshire, in central Great Britain on **Earth**, site of the legendary adventures of **Robin Hood**. Q re-created Sherwood Forest in 2367 for an elaborate fantasy he designed to teach Jean-Luc Picard a lesson about love. ("QPid" [TNG]).

Shiana. Sister of **Lieutenant Aquiel Uhnari**. Aquiel corresponded extensively by subspace with Shiana, who remained home on **Halii** when Aquiel joined **Starfleet**. In one of her messages, Aquiel expressed regret that she wouldn't be able to participate in the **Batarael** celebration at her home by singing the traditional **Horath**. ("Aquiel" [TNG]).

shield harmonics. The interaction of different frequencies of force-field energy present in a deflector shield. Shield harmonics vary with the modulation, geometry, frequency, and nutation of the shields. This set of data could be used like a fingerprint to identify ships by type, class, and origin. ("Innocence" [VGR]). *This identification based on shield characteristics is similar to how today's naval sonar operators can identify different ships and submarines purely on the basis of the propeller rotation frequency and other audible characteristics.*

shield inverters. A subsystem of Federation starship defensive shield arrays. Shield inverters were utilized during an *Enterprise*-D mission to planet **Penthara IV** in 2368 to assist in the venting of ionized plasma from the planetary atmosphere. ("A Matter of Time" [TNG]).

shield nutation. Engineering term measuring variations in shield-frequency phase rotation. Nutation was employed by *Enterprise*-D personnel in hopes of increasing shield effectiveness during the **Borg** attack of 2366. The technique was only temporarily successful, as the Borg ship was able to overcome the effects in just a few minutes. ("The Best of Both Worlds, Parts I and II" [TNG]).

shields. Energy field used to protect starships and other vessels from harm resulting from natural hazards or enemy attack. Also referred to as deflectors, deflector shields, or screens. The **transporter** could not function when shields were active. ("Arena" [TOS]). The exact modulation frequency of a particular shield system was a critical data point. Matching the modulation, frequency, and nutation of a deflector system could, with certain energy weapons, make it possible to penetrate the shield. ("The Best of Both Worlds, Part I" [TNG]). The Duras sisters used this technique in 2371 with a torpedo that destroyed the stardrive section of the *Starship Enterprise*-D. *(Star Trek Generations).*

Shiku Maru. A Federation vessel. The *Shiku Maru* encountered a **Tamarian** vessel sometime in the 23rd century. While the encounter was without incident, no relations were established, as the two cultures could not communicate. ("Darmok" [TNG]).

Shimoda, Jim. (Benjamin W. S. Lum). An assistant chief engineer on the *Enterprise*-D in 2364. Shimoda became infected with the **Psi 2000 virus** and removed the **isolinear optical chips** from their receptacles in engineering. ("The Naked Now" [TNG]).

"Ship in a Bottle." *Next Generation* episode #138. Written by René Echevarria. Directed by Alexander Singer. Stardate 46424.1. *First aired in 1993. The computer-generated Professor James Moriarty tries to emerge from the holodeck, demanding that a way be found for him to leave the ship. This episode continues the story of Moriarty begun in "Elementary, Dear Data" (TNG).* GUEST CAST: Daniel Davis as **Moriarty**, **Professor James**; Stephanie Beacham as **Barthalomew**, **Countess Regina**; Dwight Schultz as **Barclay**, **Reginald**; Clement Von Franckenstein as Gentleman; Majel Barrett as Computer voice. SEE: **Barclay, Lieutenant Reginald; Barthalomew, Countess Regina; cogito ergo sum; Detrian system; Heisenberg compensators; holodeck matter; *Justman, Shuttlecraft*; matrix diodes; Meles II; Moriarty, Professor James; pattern enhancers; Picard Delta One; protected memory; Sherlock Holmes program 3A; spatial orientation systems; strychnine; tsetse fly.**

ship recognition protocols. Codified system of superstructure landmarks for visual identification of starships. Federation recognition protocols enabled civilians to rapidly recognize friendly versus unfriendly spacecraft. ("Descent, Part I" [TNG]). SEE: **starships**.

ship's log recorder. Small data-storage device that was used as a repository for all starship logs. In the event of a catastrophic event aboard ship, the log recorder was jettisoned so a record of the ship's activities could be found. In 2370, a **verteron mine** laid in the Hekaras Corridor was momentarily thought to be a ship's log recorder. ("Force of Nature" [TNG]). SEE: **flight recorder; recorder marker.**

"Ship, The." *Deep Space Nine* episode #100. Teleplay by Hans Beimler. Story by Pam Wigginton & Richard Carson. Directed by Kim Friedman. Stardate 50049.3. *First aired in 1996. A Jem'Hadar warship crash-lands on an abandoned planet, Sisko and an away team board it, but more Jem'Hadar arrive and hinder Sisko's efforts to claim the ship. The recurring character Muniz dies in this episode.* GUEST CAST: Kaitlin Hopkins as **Kilana**; F.J. Rio as **Muniz**; Hilary Shepard as **Hoya**. SEE: ***Ak'voh*; Benzites; Bertram; cormaline; Founders; Hoya; hyperspanner; ion propulsion; isotons; Jem'Hadar; Jem'Hadar warship; Kilana; Moral and Ethical Issues; Muniz, Enrique; phase-conjugate graviton emitter; pyroclastic debris; *q'lava*; Regalian fleaspider; Regalian liquid crystals; Rooney; salvage rights; Somak; T'Lor; Torga IV; ultritium; ventral impeller; virtual display; Weyoun.**

Shiralea VI. Planetary home of the carnival-like **Parallax Colony**. ("Cost of Living" [TNG]).

Shmullus. Uncle to Vidiian physician Danara Pel. Dr. Pel gave the name Shmullus to *Voyager's* **Emergency Medical Hologram** when he cared for her in 2372. ("Lifesigns" [VGR], "Resolutions" [VGR]).

shock pulse. Powerful energy discharge created by a starship's warp core. In 2372, by initiating a near-critical warp core shock pulse, Lieutenant Torres attempted unsuccessfully to prevent a **distortion ring being** from progressively crushing the ship. ("Twisted" [VGR]).

Shoggoth. Noted author of Cardassian enigma tales. ("Distant Voices" [DS9]).

shon-ha'lock. Vulcan term meaning "the engulfment," *shon-ha'lock* refers to the most intense and psychologically perilous form of eros, the emotion humans call "love at first sight." ("Alter Ego" [VGR]).

"Shore Leave." *Original Series* episode #17. Written by Theodore Sturgeon. Directed by Robert Sparr. Stardate 3025.3. *First aired in 1967. The* Enterprise *crew is baffled by a mysterious planet on which dreams come true in a terrifying way. Director Robert Sparr and original series cinematographer Jerry Finnerman were severely injured years later in a plane crash while scouting locations in the Colorado mountains for another project. Before the crash, Sparr and Finnerman had planned to visit Bob Justman, who was filming the series* Then Came Bronson*, not far from where they crashed.* GUEST CAST: Emily Banks as **Barrows**, **Tonia**; Oliver McGowan as **Caretaker**; Perry Lopez as **Rodriguez**, **Lieutenant Esteban**; Bruce Mars as **Finnegan**; Barbara Baldavin as **Martine**, **Ensign Angela**; Marcia Brown as Alice; Tom Sebastian as Warrior; Shirley Bonne as **Ruth**; Jim Gruzal as Don Juan; Bill Blackburn as **White Rabbit**; Paul Baxley as **Black knight**; John Carr as Security guard; Paul Baxley as Kirk's stunt double; Vince Deadrick as Finnegan's stunt double; Irene Sale as Teller's stunt double. SEE: ***Alice in Wonderland;* Alice; amusement park planet; Barrows, Yeoman Tonia; black knight; cabaret girls; Caretaker; Finnegan; Kirk, James T.; Martine, Angela; Omicron Delta region; Police Special; Rigel II; Rodriguez, Lieutenant Esteban; Ruth; Sulu, Hikaru; tiger; White Rabbit.**

Shras. (Reggie Nalder). **Andorian** ambassador. Shras was sent to the **Babel Conference** aboard the *Starship Enterprise* in 2267. Shras denied any knowledge of the **Orion** plot carried out by **Thelev**, a member of his staff. ("Journey to Babel" [TOS]).

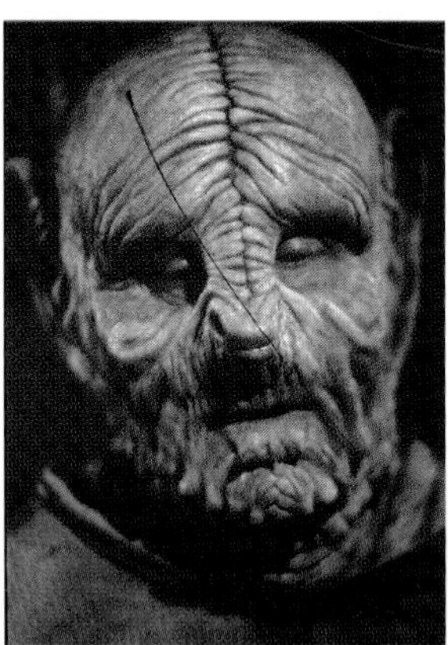

Shrek, Jaglom. (James Cromwell). An **Yridian** dealer in information. Shrek sold Worf information that his father, **Mogh**, might still be alive, some 25 years after the Khitomer massacre. Shrek transported Worf to a Romulan prison camp in the **Carraya System**, but Mogh was not among the survivors there. ("Birthright, Parts I and II" [TNG]). *Shrek's ship was a re-use of the* Nenebek, *Dirgo's shuttle from "Final Mission" (TNG). The registry number of Shrek's ship was YLT-3069. James Cromwell also played Narok in "The Hunted" (TNG) and Zefram Cochrane in* Star Trek: First Contact. SEE: ***Toron*-class shuttlecraft.**

shrimp Creole. Traditional Earth seafood dish. Shrimp Creole was featured on the menu at **Sisko's**, a restaurant in New Orleans on Earth. ("Homefront" [DS9]).

shrimp with fettran sauce. Culinary dish of small edible Earth marine decapods cooked and served in a special sauce. While incarcerated in an Akritirian prison satellite, Harry Kim dreamed of having shrimp with fettran sauce when he was free again. ("The Chute" [VGR]).

Shroud of the Sword. Ancient cloth that once wrapped the sacred **Sword of Kahless**. It was believed lost for centuries, and numerous fakes have emerged over the years, but a Vulcan geological team discovered the true shroud in the late 24th century. As a diplomatic courtesy, the Vulcan government gave the artifact to Ambassador **Kor**. ("The Sword of Kahless" [DS9]).

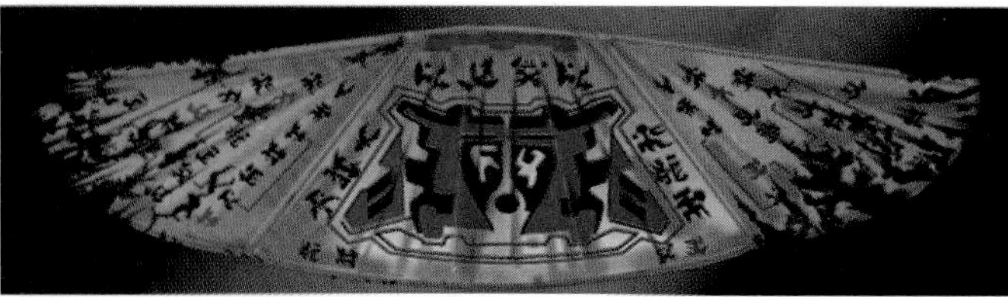

Shumar, Captain Bryce. The commanding officer of the ***U.S.S. Essex***. Shumar was killed in 2167 when the *Essex* disintegrated above a moon of planet **Mab-Bu VI**. ("Power Play" [TNG]).

Shuttle 3. The ***Voltaire***, a shuttlepod attached to the *Starship Enterprise*-D. Shuttle 3 was used by Captain Picard to guide the *Enterprise*-D out of the **Mar Oscura** Nebula in 2367. The craft suffered damage to its starboard impulse nacelle, and lost its inertial damping control. The *Voltaire* was destroyed before it could exit the nebula. ("In Theory" [TNG]).

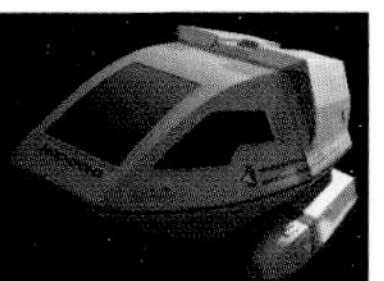

Shuttle 5. Shuttlecraft attached to the *Starship Enterprise*-D. Shuttle 5 was taken by Commander La Forge and Lieutenant Reginald Barclay to investigate a **Cytherian** probe near the **Argus Array** in 2367. The probe emitted a brilliant flash, disabling the shuttle's onboard systems and rendering Lieutenant Barclay unconscious. ("The Nth Degree" [TNG]). *The designation Shuttle 5 was also used for the shuttlepod* El-Baz *in "Time Squared" (TNG).*

Shuttle 7. Shuttlepod attached to the *Starship Enterprise*-D; Shuttle 7, also designated as the ***Onizuka***, which Commander La Forge piloted to **Risa** in late 2367. The shuttle was intercepted in midflight and taken aboard a Romulan warbird. ("The Mind's Eye" [TNG]).

shuttle escape transporter. Small short-range personnel **transporter** built into some Starfleet shuttlecraft. The escape transporter permitted emergency evacuation in case of major disaster aboard the shuttle, and was used by Worf and Data in their away mission to rescue **Jean-Luc Picard** from **Borg** captivity in 2367. ("The Best of Both Worlds, Part II" [TNG]).

shuttle, Vulcan. Small warp-powered vessel of **Vulcan** registry used to transport Spock from Vulcan to the *Enterprise* in 2271. The ship featured a detachable crew cabin, and bore the name *Surak,* for the great Vulcan philosopher. *(Star Trek: The Motion Picture). The Vulcan shuttle was designed by Andrew Probert and built at Magicam.*

shuttlebay. Large facility aboard Federation starships used for the launching and recovery of **shuttlecraft**. A ***Galaxy*-class** starship had three such shuttlebays. The main shuttlebay was located on Deck 4, with a single large hatch opening aft on the upper surface of the **Saucer Module**. Shuttlebays 2 and 3 are located on the aft of the interconnecting dorsal, also known as a **hangar deck** on older starships. Emergency explosive decompression of the main shuttlebay was employed on stardate 45652 to nudge the *Enterprise*-D from a collision course with the ***U.S.S. Bozeman***. ("Cause and Effect" [TNG]). In a large-scale disaster, the shuttlebays could be converted to emergency medical triage centers. This dramatically increases the number of injured that could be cared for aboard a ship, as was done when accident victims from the ***U.S.S. Denver*** crash were cared for aboard the *Enterprise*-D in 2368. ("Ethics" [TNG]). *The brief miniature shot of the* Enterprise-*D main shuttlebay decompressing in "Cause and Effect" was the only glimpse to date of that huge facility, although a miniature of the* Constitution-*class starship's hangar deck was seen several times in the original* Star Trek *series.* The shuttlebay of the *Intrepid*-class *Starship Voyager* was located on Deck 10. ("Macrocosm" [VGR]).

shuttlebus. A transportation vehicle used on planet **Rutia IV**. A shuttlebus was destroyed by **Ansata** terrorists in 2365, a few days after Alexana Devos assumed her post as Rutian security chief. Devos, who described herself as politically moderate prior to the incident, was outraged that 60 schoolchildren were killed in the bombing, an incident the Ansata claimed was an accident. ("The High Ground" [TNG]).

Shuttlecraft. Shown to approximate scale.

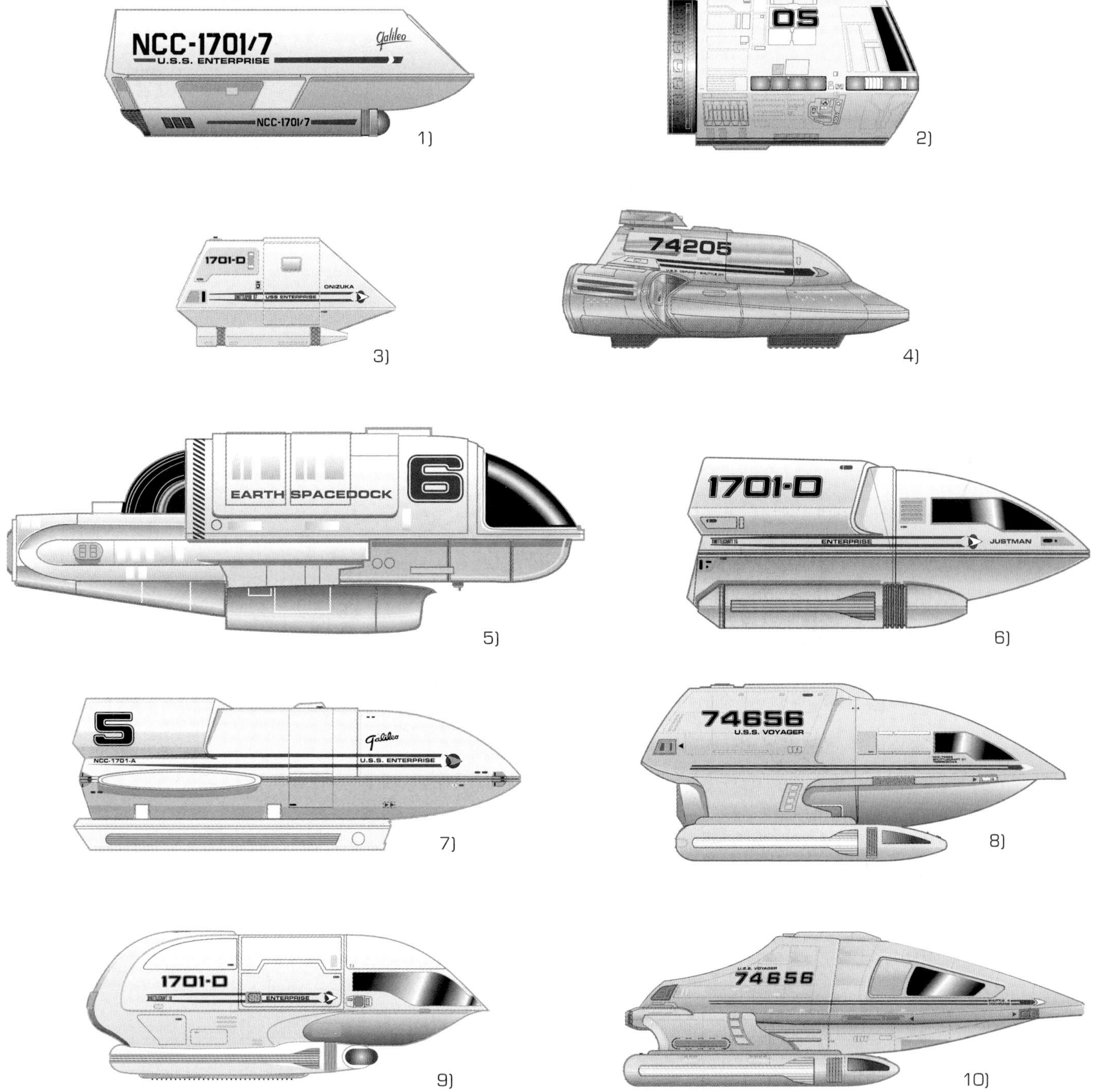

1) Shuttlecraft ("Galileo Seven" [TOS]). 2) Travel pod (*Star Trek: The Motion Picture*). 3) Type-15 shuttlepod ("Time Squared" [TNG]). 4) Type-18 shuttlepod ("The Search" [DS9]). 5) Orbital shuttle (*Star Trek IV: The Voyage Home*). 6) Type-6 personnel shuttlecraft ("Darmok" [TNG]). 7) Shuttlecraft (*Star Trek V: The Final Frontier*). 8) Type-8 personnel shuttlecraft ("Parallax" [VGR]). 9) Type-7 personnel shuttlecraft ("Coming of Age" [TNG]). 10) Type-9 personnel shuttlecraft ("Threshold" [VGR]).

Shuttlecraft 1. SEE: ***Sakharov*, *Shuttlecraft*.**

Shuttlecraft 9. Shuttlepod piloted by Data and Geordi La Forge into the **Barzan wormhole** on a mission to determine the stability of the wormhole in 2366. It was eventually learned that the Barzan wormhole was unstable. ("The Price" [TNG]).

Shuttlecraft 13. Vehicle attached to the *Enterprise*-D. **Jake Kurland**, despondent over having failed to gain entrance to Starfleet Academy, ran off with Shuttlecraft 13 and nearly crashed it into **Relva VII**. ("Coming of Age" [TNG]). *Jake's flight from the* Enterprise-*D was the first use of a shuttlecraft in* Star Trek: The Next Generation. *This shuttle was designed by Andrew Probert. The miniature was built by Greg Jein.* The same shuttle later crashed on planet **Vagra II** with pilot Ben Prieto and Counselor Deanna Troi aboard, in an incident that cost rescue party member **Natasha Yar** her life. Shuttlecraft 13 was destroyed on the surface of Vagra II to prevent **Armus** from escaping the planet. ("Skin of Evil" [TNG]).

Shuttlecraft 15. SEE: ***Magellan***.

shuttlecraft. Small, short-range spacecraft, intended primarily for transport from a deep-space vessel to a planet's surface, or for travel within a solar system. A variety of shuttlecraft types have been used aboard different starships over the years. Most shuttles are capable of sublight travel only, and virtually all are capable of planetary landing and takeoff. Small shuttles are also designated as **shuttlepods**. *The shuttlecraft is a seldom-used part of the* Star Trek *television-movie format, mainly because the ingenious invention of the transporter makes it fast, easy, and (relatively) cheap to get our characters down to a planet without a landing ship. The first shuttlecraft, the* Galileo, *was built for the original* Star Trek *series about halfway through that show's first season. (The shuttle was not built for the first few episodes because of the enormous cost of building the full-scale mockup.) Shuttles built for the* Star Trek *movies included the San Francisco air tram and the travel pod built for* Star Trek I, *and the shuttlecrafts* Galileo 5 *and* Copernicus *built for* Star Trek V. *Cost considerations also affected the first season of* Star Trek: The Next Generation, *when a shuttle mockup was not built until a specific episode required it. Even then, that first shuttle design (seen in "Coming of Age" [TNG]) proved too difficult to build for a television budget, so, after several unsuccessful attempts to fake a partial exterior (as in "Unnatural Selection" [TNG]), a greatly simplified "shuttlepod" was built for "Time Squared" (TNG). Although lacking the graceful curves of the original design, the shuttlepod had a full exterior that could be photographed from any angle. It was not until several years later that a new "midsized" ship, first seen in miniature in "Darmok" (TNG) and in full-scale form as the* Shuttlecraft Magellan *in "The Outcast" (TNG), was built. This full-scale mockup was a modification of one of the shuttles from* Star Trek V: The Final Frontier. *In terms of television drama, the real purpose of a shuttlecraft is often to isolate characters in a slow-moving vehicle that can easily get lost. For this reason, Starfleet is unlikely to "invent" significantly faster shuttles for general use.* SEE: Illustration, previous page; ***Columbus; Copernicus; Cousteau; El-Baz; Fermi; Feynman; Galileo; Galileo II; Galileo 5; Goddard; Hawking; Justman; Magellan; Onizuka; Pike; Sakharov; Voltaire.***

shuttlepod. Small **shuttlecraft** carried aboard Federation starships. Most shuttlepods were only capable of carrying two people and were limited to sublight travel across relatively short interplanetary distances. SEE: ***El-Baz; Onizuka; Pike.*** The *Starship Defiant* also carried at least one shuttlepod, used to help minimize the spread of silithium contamination from comet fragments that entered the Bajoran wormhole in 2371. ("Destiny" [DS9]). *(The* Defiant*'s shuttlepod was of a different design than those carried aboard the* Enterprise-*D, although the interior cabin was a re-dress of the* El-Baz.*)*

sickbay. Medical care facility aboard Federation starships and other space vessels. ("The Corbomite Maneuver" [TOS]). The sickbay aboard the *Starships Enterprise* included one or more

intensive-care wards, a doctor's office, a medical laboratory, an OB/GYN unit, as well as other facilities including an examination room and rehabilitation equipment. On a *Galaxy*-class starship, at least four medical personnel were on duty at all times. ("Remember Me" [TNG]). In a large-scale disaster, sickbay facilities could be supplemented by converting the **shuttlebays** into emergency triage and treatment centers. ("Ethics" [TNG]). The sickbay on an *Intrepid*-class starship was located on Deck 5. ("Tuvix" [VGR]). Aboard Federation starships, sickbay was the responsibility of the ship's **chief medical officer**. *Another case of life imitating art: the sickbay beds featured biofunction monitors above each patient, making it easy for medical personnel to monitor the patient's vital signs. Such displays, considered futuristic at the time of the original* Star Trek *series, are now a common sight in hospitals everywhere.*

"Siege, The." *Deep Space Nine* episode #23. Written by Michael Piller. Directed by Winrich Kolbe. No stardate given. *First aired in 1993. The station is evacuated, and Sisko and company are forced into hiding until proof of the Cardassian support of the Circle can reach the Bajoran government. This episode completes the story begun in "The Homecoming" (DS9) and "The Circle" (DS9).* GUEST CAST: Rosalind Chao as **O'Brien, Keiko**; Steven Weber as **Day, Colonel**; Richard Beymer as **Li Nalas**; Stephen Macht as **Krim, General**; Mac Grodénchik as **Rom**; Aron Eisenberg as **Nog**; Philip Anglim as **Bareil, Vedek**; Louise Fletcher as **Winn**; Katrina Carlson as Bajoran officer; Hana Hatae as **O'Brien, Molly**. SEE: **Alliance for Global Unity, The; anesthizine; Bajoran assault vessel; Bajoran impulse ship; Bilecki, Lieutenant; combat rations; Dax, Tobin; Day, Colonel; Deep Space 9**; **duranium; Ferengi Rules of Acquisition; French onion soup; *Ganges, U.S.S.*; Hanolan colony; Jaro Essa, Minister; Kelly, Ensign;**

Korat system; Krim, General; Li Nalas; Lunar-V base; *Orinoco, U.S.S.*; *palukoo*; *Rio Grande, U.S.S.*; subimpulse raiders; Trill.

Sigma Draconis III. Class-M planet, rated B on the industrial scale and 3 on the technological scale, equivalent to Earth year 1485. ("Spock's Brain" [TOS]).

Sigma Draconis IV. Class-M planet with an industrial rating of G, equivalent to Earth year 2030. ("Spock's Brain" [TOS]).

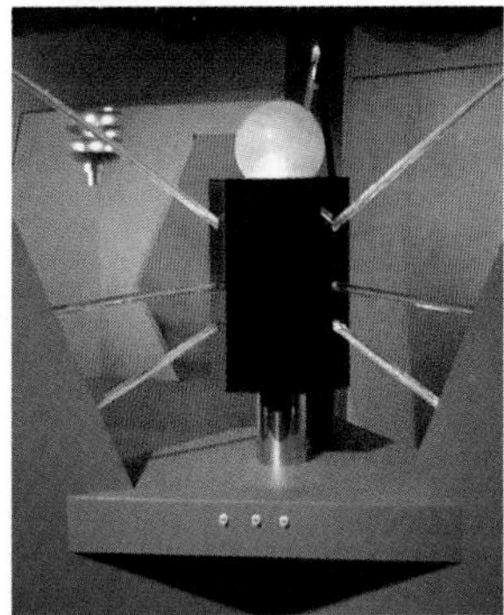

Sigma Draconis VI. Class-M planet with a glaciated surface, formerly the home of a technologically advanced civilization. By 2268, the civilization had all but vanished, and the humanoid inhabitants had been split into two groups. The first, the **Morgs**, were the males who lived on the surface under virtually stone-age conditions. The females, called **Eymorgs**, lived in a technologically advanced underground, but they no longer knew how to maintain the machinery that maintained their environment. When the computer system called the **Controller** failed in 2268, the Eymorgs were forced to return to the surface to live with the Morgs. ("Spock's Brain" [TOS]). SEE: **Kara**; **Teacher**. *The planet was also referred to in dialog as Sigma Draconis VII, an apparent continuity error.*

Sigma Draconis. System with a Class-G9 star and nine planets, three of which are Class-M. ("Spock's Brain" [TOS]).

Sigma Erandi system. Planetary system. According to **Zibalian** trader **Kivas Fajo**, the Sigma Erandi system was a source for **hytritium**. ("The Most Toys" [TNG]).

Sigma Epsilon II. Planet in the Gamma Quadrant. Q and Vash visited Sigma Epsilon II, to the considerable displeasure of the natives. ("Q-Less" [DS9]).

Sigma III Solar System. Star system. Location of a Federation mining colony on planet **Quadra Sigma III** that suffered a serious explosion in 2364. ("Hide and Q" [TNG]).

Sigma Iotia II. Class-M planet. Sigma Iotia II was located some one hundred light-years beyond Federation space, first visited in 2168 by the ***U.S.S. Horizon***. ("A Piece of the Action" [TOS]). SEE: **Iotians**.

sign language. The use of gestures and hand signs for communication. In most humanoid cultures, sign language predates the use of spoken language. The only known exception was the Leyrons of planet **Malkus IX**, who developed a written language first. ("Loud as a Whisper" [TNG]).

signage, Federation Starfleet. SEE: illustrations. SEE also: **Insignia, Starfleet**; **symbols**.

signage, other cultures. SEE: illustrations next pages. SEE also: **written languages**.

Sikaris. Class-M planet in the Delta Quadrant. Home to a technologically advanced humanoid civilization. The Sikarians were a remarkably pleasure-oriented society, and they were known for their incredible hospitality. The Sikarians possessed an extraordinary **trajector** technology that permitted instantaneous transport across great distances. While the Sikarian reputation for generosity was well deserved, the Sikarian canon of laws prohibited the transfer of their technology to other cultures. ("Prime Factors." [VGR]). SEE: **Labin, Gathorel; Otel, Jaret.**

Sikla Medical Facility. Major health-care facility on planet **Malcor III**. William Riker, masquerading as a **Malcorian** named **Rivas Jakara,** was taken to the Sikla facility after he was injured in a riot in the capital city in 2367. ("First Contact" [TNG]).

"Silicon Avatar." *Next Generation* episode #104. Teleplay by Jeri Taylor. From a story by Lawrence V. Conley. Directed by Cliff Bole. Stardate 45122.3. *First aired in 1991. A scientist whose child was killed at Omicron Theta by the Crystalline Entity comes aboard the* Enterprise-*D on a mission of revenge. The term "avatar" refers to Data as a repository of knowledge.* GUEST CAST: Ellen Geer as **Marr, Dr. Kila**; Susan Diol as **Davila, Carmen**. SEE: **antiprotons; Argos system; bitrious filaments; Boreal III; Brechtian Cluster; Clendenning, Dr.; Crystalline Entity; Data; Davila, Carmen; fistrium; Forlat III; graviton; *Kallisko*; kelbonite; Marr, Dr. Kila; Marr, Raymond; Melona IV; monocaladium particles; Omicron Theta.**

silicon nodule. Term used by miners on planet **Janus VI** to describe spherical objects found in subterranean caverns on that planet in 2267. The miners regarded the nodules as geologic curiosities and were routinely destroying them until they discovered that they were actually the eggs of a **silicon-based life**-form called the **Horta**, indigenous to the planet. ("The Devil in the Dark" [TOS]).

silicon-based life. Biological forms whose organic chemistry is based on the element silicon, rather than the more common element, carbon. One such example is the **Horta** of planet **Janus VI**. ("The Devil in the Dark" [TOS]).

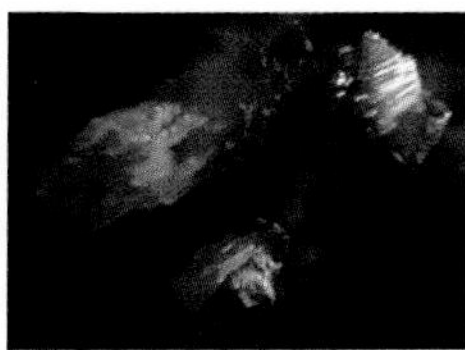

silithium. Unstable material reactive with **verteron** particles. In 2371, a comet near the **Gamma Quadrant**'s terminus of the **Bajoran wormhole** was found to contain silithium in its core. Fragments of the comet left a trail of silithium in the wormhole's interior, creating a subspace filament that allowed communications between the Alpha and Gamma Quadrants. ("Destiny" [DS9]).

Silmic wine. Alcoholic beverage available aboard the *U.S.S. Voyager*. ("Investigations" [VGR]).

Silvestri, Captain. Commander of the spacecraft ***Shiku Maru***. Captain Silvestri encountered a **Tamarian** vessel, but was unable to establish communications because of the dramatic differences in culture and speech patterns. ("Darmok" [TNG]).

Singh, Khan Noonien. SEE: **Khan.**

Singh, Lieutenant Commander. (Kavi Raz). Assistant chief engineer of the *Enterprise*-D. Singh was killed by the **Beta Renna cloud** entity while the ship was in route to the neutral planet of **Parliament** in 2364. ("Lonely Among Us" [TNG]). *Singh had the dubious distinction of being the first* Enterprise-*D crew member killed on* Star Trek: The Next Generation.

Singh, Mr. (Blaisdell Makee). Engineer aboard the original *Starship Enterprise.* Singh was on duty in the auxiliary control room when the robot ***Nomad*** was aboard on stardate 3541. ("The Changeling" [TOS]). *Blaisdell Makee also played Lieutenant Spinelli in "Space Seed" (TOS).*

Singha refugee camp. Prison camp on planet **Bajor** during the Cardassian occupation. **Kira Nerys** and her brothers were interned at Singha when they were young. Although conditions there were unpleasant, the youngsters occasionally played springball. ("Shadowplay" [DS9]). Kira Nerys's mother died of malnutrition at Singha in 2343. ("Second Skin" [DS9]).

singularity. SEE: **quantum singularity**.

sinoraptor. Life-form. **Kira** recounts that **Lupaza** once said that Kira Nerys had a heart like a sinoraptor. ("The Darkness and the Light" [DS9]).

Signage, Starfleet.

LEONARD McCOY
M. D.
3F 127

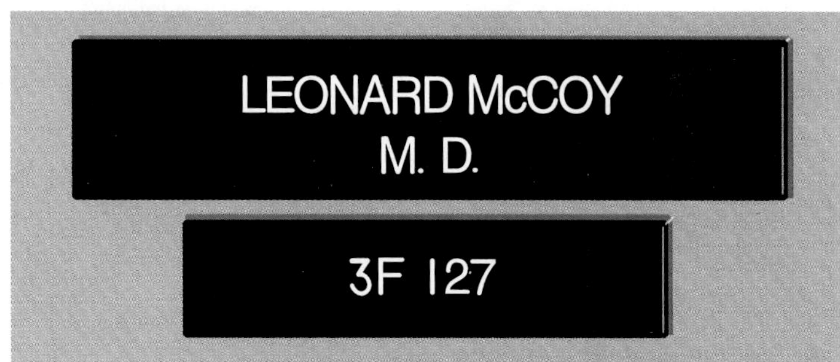

1)

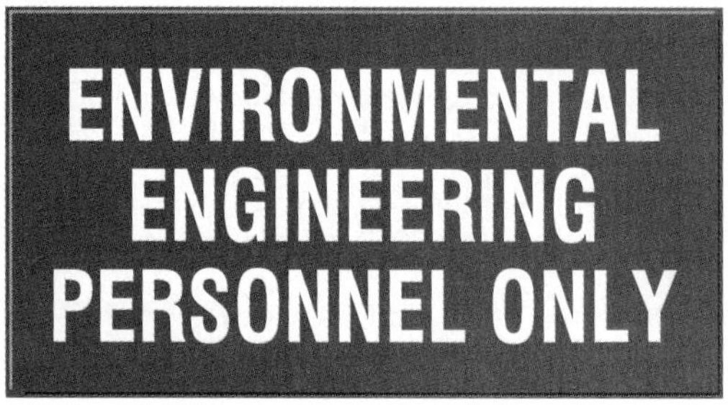

ENVIRONMENTAL
ENGINEERING
PERSONNEL ONLY

2)

3)

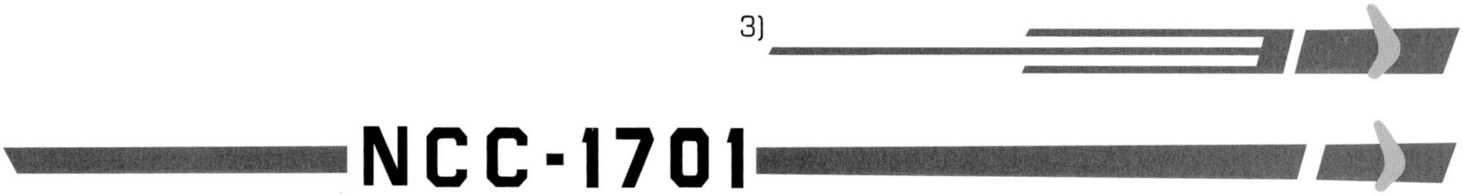

NCC-1701

Typical signage (TOS): 1) Door sign. 2) Caution sign. 3) Ship's exterior pennants. TOS graphics supervised by Matt Jefferies.

1)

5

2)

3)

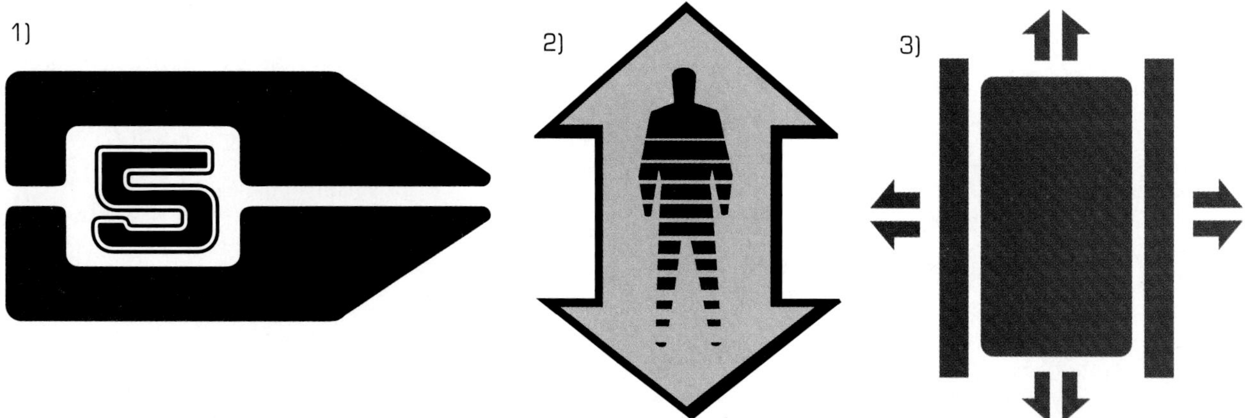

4)

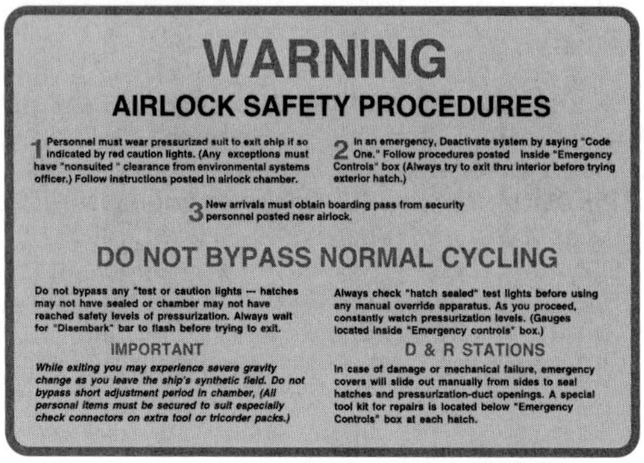

WARNING
AIRLOCK SAFETY PROCEDURES
1 Personnel must wear pressurized suit to exit ship if so indicated by red caution lights. (Any exceptions must have "nonsuited " clearance from environmental systems officer.) Follow instructions posted in airlock chamber.
2 In an emergency, Deactivate system by saying "Code One." Follow procedures posted inside "Emergency Controls" box (Always try to exit thru interior before trying exterior hatch.)
3 New arrivals must obtain boarding pass from security personnel posted nesr airlock.
DO NOT BYPASS NORMAL CYCLING
Do not bypass any "test or caution lights --- hatches may not have sealed or chamber may not have reached safety levels of pressurization. Always wait for "Disembark" bar to flash before trying to exit.
IMPORTANT
While exiting you may experience severe gravity change as you leave the ship's synthetic field. Do not bypass short adjustment period in chamber, (All personal items must be secured to suit especially check connectors on extra tool or tricorder packs.)
Always check "hatch sealed" test lights before using any manual override apparatus. As you proceed, constantly watch pressurization levels. (Gauges located inside "Emergency controls" box.)
D & R STATIONS
In case of damage or mechanical failure, emergency covers will slide out manually from sides to seal hatches and pressurization-duct openings. A special tool kit for repairs is located below "Emergency Controls" box at each hatch.

5)

8P6
TEST POINT
TEST POINT
TEST POINT
TEST POINT
HOLD LOCATOR
STARFLEET MATERIAL
SUPPLY COMMAND P1
MANIFEST CODE
ORIGIN
DESTINATION
TRACTOR BEAM
STASIS FIELD
DOORS UP:DN

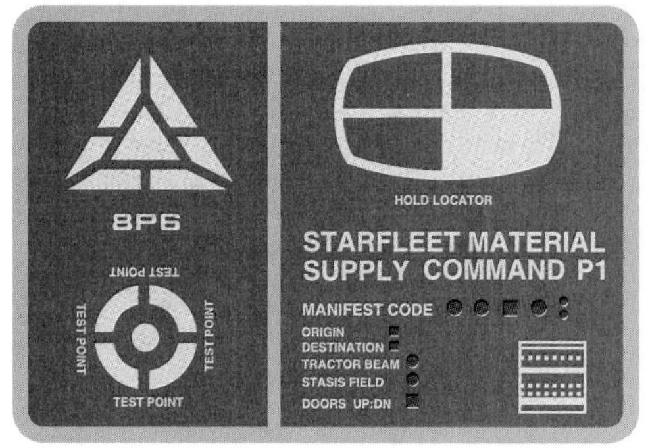

6)

STARSHIP U.S.S. ENTERPRISE UNITED FEDERATION OF PLANETS NCC-1701

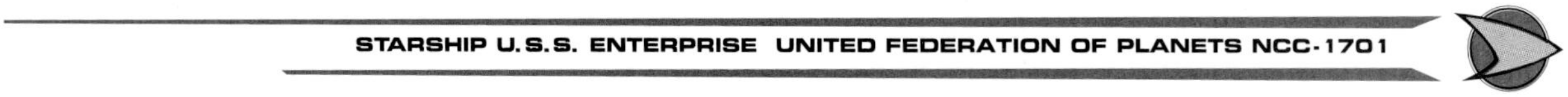

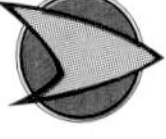

Typical signage (*ST:TMP-ST III*): 1) Directional sign. 2) Transporter systems logo. 3) Turbolift logo. 4) Instructional plaque. 5) Cargo label. 6) Ship's exterior pennant. *ST: TMP* graphics by Lee Cole, Rick Sternbach, and Mike Minor.

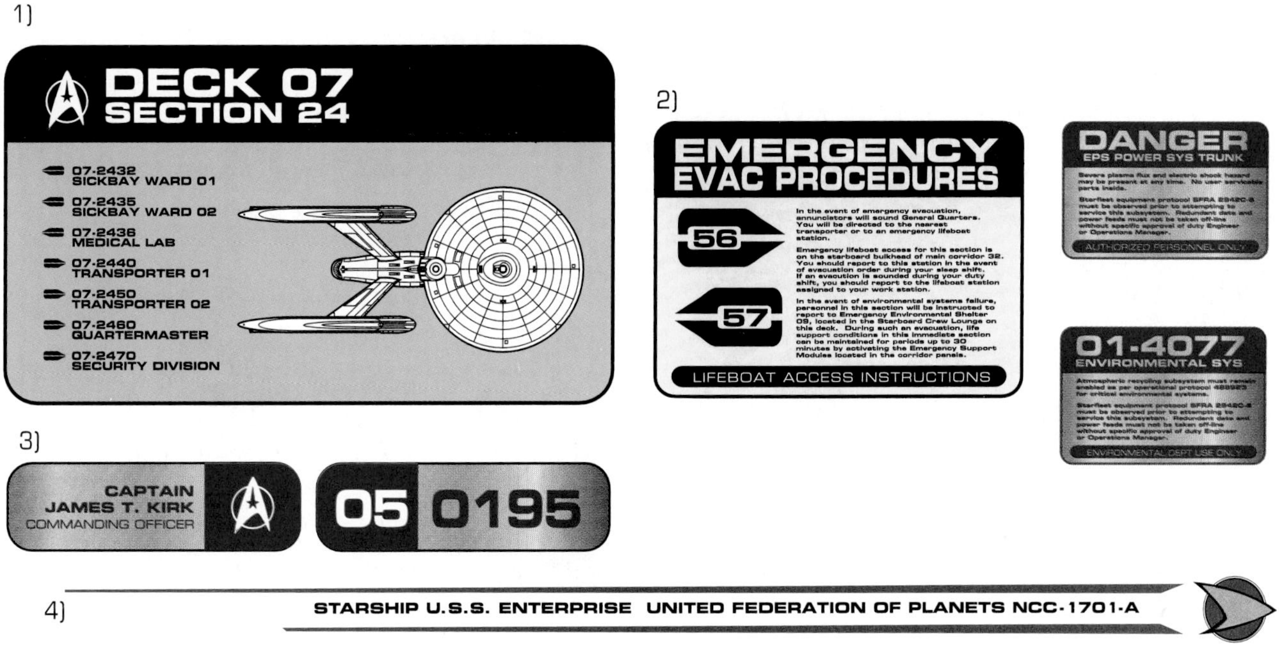

1)
DECK 07
SECTION 24
07-2432 SICKBAY WARD 01
07-2435 SICKBAY WARD 02
07-2436 MEDICAL LAB
07-2440 TRANSPORTER 01
07-2450 TRANSPORTER 02
07-2460 QUARTERMASTER
07-2470 SECURITY DIVISION
2)
EMERGENCY
EVAC PROCEDURES
56
57
In the event of emergency evacuation, annunciators will sound General Quarters. You will be directed to the nearest transporter or to an emergency lifeboat station.
Emergency lifeboat access for this section is on the starboard bulkhead of main corridor 32. You should report to this station in the event of evacuation order during your sleep shift. If an evacution is sounded during your duty shift, you should report to the lifeboat station assigned to your work station.
In the event of environmental systems failure, personnel in this section will be instructed to report to Emergency Environmental Shelter 09, located in the Starboard Crew Lounge on this deck. During such an evacuation, life support conditions in this immediate section can be maintained for periods up to 30 minutes by activating the Emergency Support Modules located in the corridor panels.
LIFEBOAT ACCESS INSTRUCTIONS
DANGER
EPS POWER SYS TRUNK
AUTHORIZED PERSONNEL ONLY
01-4077
ENVIRONMENTAL SYS
ENVIRONMENTAL DEPT USE ONLY
3)
CAPTAIN
JAMES T. KIRK
COMMANDING OFFICER
05 0195
4)
STARSHIP U.S.S. ENTERPRISE UNITED FEDERATION OF PLANETS NCC-1701-A

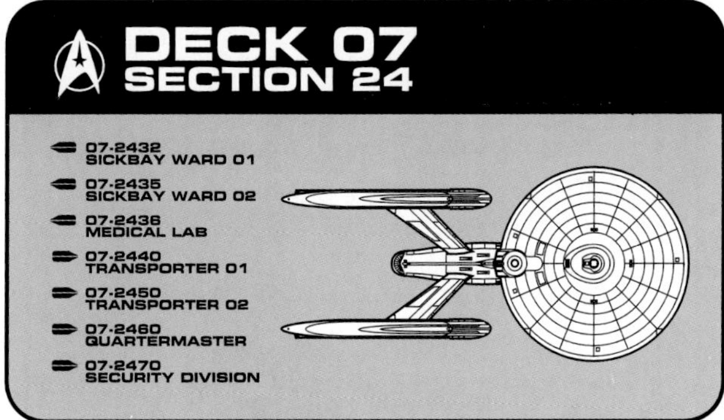

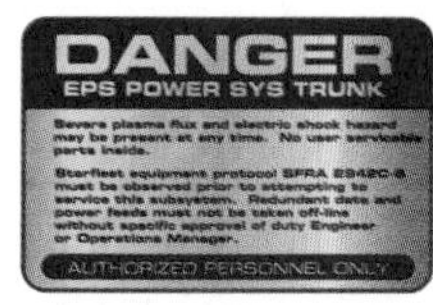

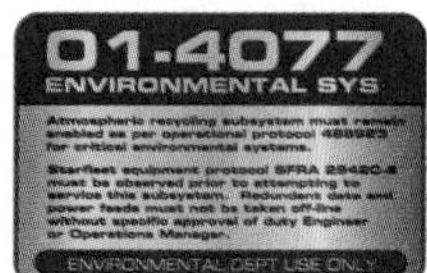

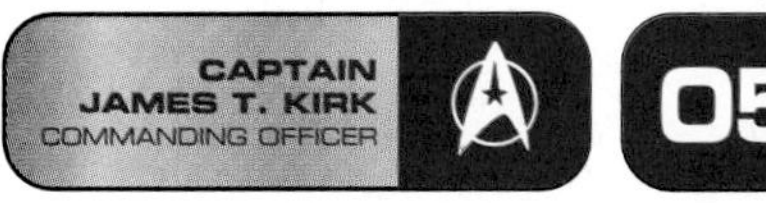

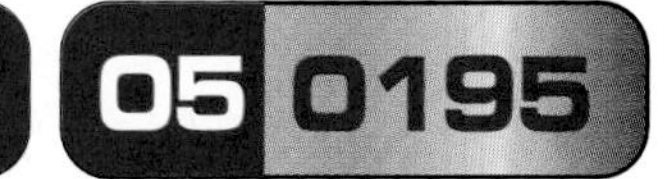

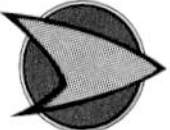

Typical signage (*STV-STVI*): 1) Directory sign. 2) Miscellaneous informational and caution signage. 3) Door sign. 4) Ship's exterior pennant.

---

1)
36 TURBOLIFT
08 3601 CAPTAIN JEAN-LUC PICARD
COMMANDING OFFICER
06 2054 PERSONNEL TRANSPORTER 3
2)
WELCOME TO STARBASE 74
STARFLEET OPERATIONAL SUPPORT SERVICES
3)
855 ACCESS PANEL 78-0067
REFER SERVICING TO QUALIFIED STARFLEET TECHNICIANS. NO USER-SERVICABLE PARTS INSIDE. REMEMBER, NO MATTER WHERE YOU GO, THERE YOU ARE.
954 ENGINEERING ACCESS ONLY
THREE HUNDRED THOUSAND KILOMETERS PER SECOND: IT'S NOT JUST A GOOD IDEA. IT'S THE LAW. YOUR ACTUAL MILEAGE MAY VARY, OF COURSE.
451 AUXILIARY SYSTEMS 32-2398
CAUTION: OBJECTS IN MIRROR ARE CLOSER THAN THEY APPEAR TO BE. A STITCH IN TIME SAVES NINE. IN SPACE, NO ONE CAN HEAR YOU SCREAM.
302 OPTICAL DATA NET SERVICE ACCESS
YOUR MISSION, SHOULD YOU CHOOSE TO ACCEPT IT, IS TO GO BOLDLY WHERE NO ONE HAS GONE BEFORE. THIS LABEL WILL SELF-DESTRUCT IN 5 SECONDS. GOOD LUCK, JIM.
4)
5)
NCC-74656

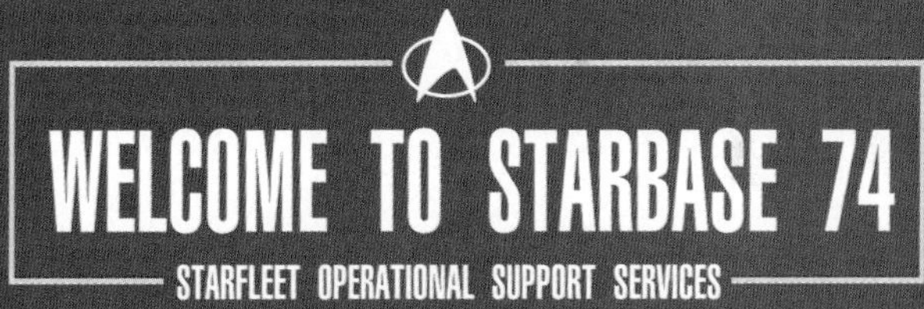

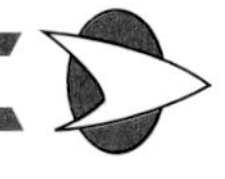

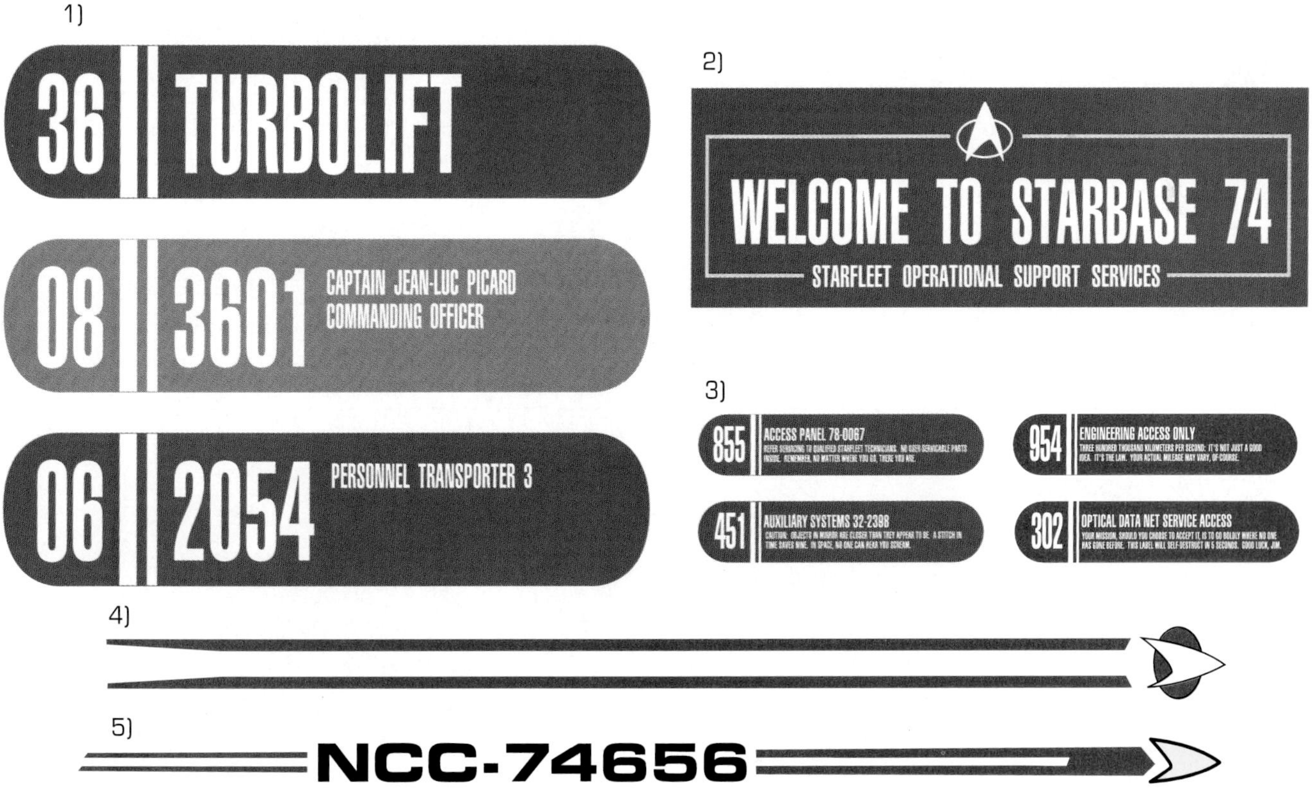

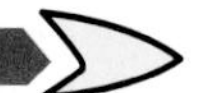

Typical signage (TNG, et al): 1) Door signs. The first two digits represent the deck number; the next four are the room number. 2) Starbase entry sign 3) Panel identification labels. The fine print on some of these labels, never legible on television, contained a few tiny "in-jokes." 4) Ship's exterior pennant (*Enterprise*-D). 5) Ship's exterior pennant (*Voyager*; similar style also used on *Defiant* and *Enterprise*-E).

Signage, other cultures.

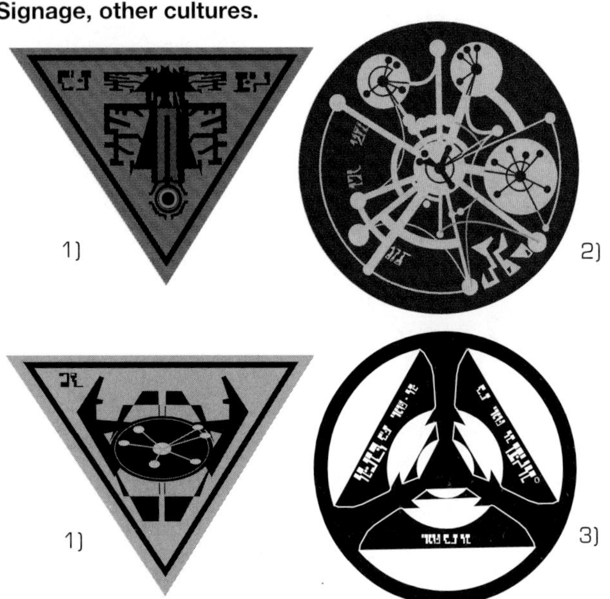

1) Cardassian systems junction signage. 2) Cardassian panel identification labels. 3) Cardassian airlock label.

Various shipping labels seen on *Star Trek: Deep Space Nine.*

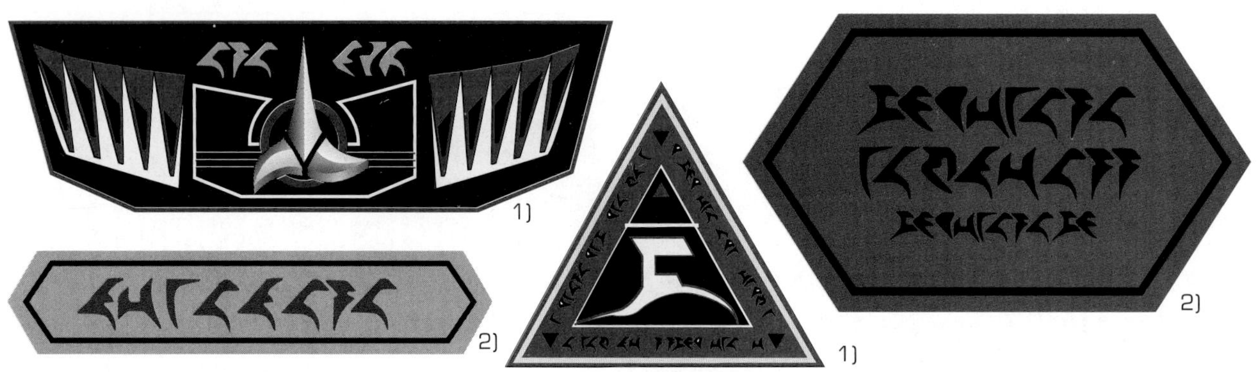

1) Klingon panel identification labels. 2) Miscellaneous Klingon informational signage.

Miscellaneous Romulan informational signage.

"Sins of the Father." *Next Generation* episode #65. Teleplay by Ronald D. Moore & W. Reed Moran. Based on a teleplay by Drew Deighan. Directed by Les Landau. Stardate 43685.2. *First aired in 1990. Worf returns to the Klingon Homeworld to defend his late father against charges of treason. Worf's story was later continued in "Reunion" (TNG) and "Redemption, Parts I and II" (TNG).* GUEST CAST: Charles Cooper as **Korrd, General**; Tony Todd as **Kurn**; Patrick Massett as **Duras**; Thelma Lee as **Kahlest**; Teddy Davis as Transporter tech. SEE: **Age of Ascension; caviar; *cha'DIch*; discommendation; Duras; First City; *ghojmok*; Great Hall; *ha'DIBah*; *Intrepid, U.S.S.*; Ja'rod; K'mpec; Kahlest; Khitomer massacre; Khitomer; Klingon Defense Force; Klingon High Council; Klingon Homeworld; Kurn; *kut'luch*; Lorgh; *Mek'ba*; Mogh; Officer Exchange Program; *pahtk*; *Qapla'*; replicator; *seloh*; Starbase 24; turn; Worf.**

Sipe, Ryan. Starfleet officer who was apparently killed by the extragalactic alien intelligence that attempted to infiltrate **Starfleet Command** in 2364. ("Conspiracy" [TNG]).

Sir Guy of Gisbourne. (Clive Revill). One of the legendary foes of the outlaw **Robin Hood** in Earth's old England. Some ancient tales hold that Sir Guy was in love with Robin's lady, the fair **Maid Marian**. Sir Guy appeared in a fantasy crafted for the *Enterprise*-D crew by **Q**. ("QPid" [TNG]). *Clive Revill also provided the voice of the galactic emperor in* The Empire Strikes Back.

Sirah. (Kay E. Kuter). Title given to the leader of a community on the planet **Bajor**. Many years ago, the villagers were fighting among themselves, and the first Sirah knew he must find a way to unite his people. That first Sirah used a small stone, a fragment from one of the **Orbs** from the **Celestial Temple**, to focus the villager's thoughts into the illusion of a terrible cloud creature called the ***Dal'Rok***. The *Dal'Rok* threatened the village, until the Sirah told stories of the strength and unity of the village, frightening away the evil force. This ritual was repeated every year after harvest, thereby providing the village with a common foe. The fact that the *Dal'Rok* was only an illusion was kept secret from the people and passed from Sirah to Sirah. ("The Storyteller" [DS9]). SEE: **Hovath**.

Sirco Ch'Ano. Trader on planet **Bajor.** Sirco swapped seven **tessipates** of land to **Nog** and **Jake Sisko** on stardate 46844 in exchange for 100 gross of **self-sealing stem bolts**. Sirco Ch'Ano had originally ordered the stem bolts from a Lissepean captain, but had to renege on the deal when he couldn't deliver the **latinum** as payment. ("Progress" [DS9]). SEE: **Noh-Jay Consortium.**

sirillium. A highly combustible and versatile energy source. Sirillium gas was found in certain types of nebulae. It could be used to boost deflector-shield efficiency and as a warp-plasma catalyst. In 2293, the crew of the *U.S.S. Excelsior* encountered the Azure Nebula, which contained sirillium. In 2293, to evade a Klingon battle cruiser, Captain Sulu ignited the sirillium in the Azure Nebula using a positron beam modulated to a subspace frequency. In 2373, the crew of the *Voyager* encountered a type-17 nebula that contained sirillium. ("Flashback" [VGR]).

Sirius. Star. Sirius was used by Sulu as a navigational reference when the original *Enterprise* was thrown across the galaxy in 2267 by the advanced civilization known as the **Metrons**. ("Arena" [TOS]). *Sirius is, of course, the Dog Star in Earth mythology.*

Sirol, Commander. (Michael Mack). Romulan officer in command of the *Warbird Terix*. In 2370 Sirol was in charge of a Romulan attempt to locate the ***U.S.S. Pegasus***, though he claimed his ship was conducting a study of **gaseous anomalies**. ("The *Pegasus*" [TNG]). *Michael Mack also played Ensign Hayes in* Star Trek Generations.

Sisko's. Restaurant located in the French Quarter of New Orleans, Louisiana on Earth. ("The Visitor" [DS9]). Sisko's was owned by **Joseph Sisko**, father to Ben Sisko, and featured an excellent menu of Creole cuisine. ("Homefront" [DS9]). (In an alternate future in which Ben Sisko was believed killed aboard the *Defiant* in 2372, the restaurant was the site of Jake Sisko's marriage to Korena in 2384. SEE: **Sisko, Jake**.) ("The Visitor" [DS9]).

Sisko, Benjamin (mirror). (Avery Brooks). In the **mirror universe**, a Terran who served under the direct command of the **Intendant** of **Terok Nor (mirror)**. Sisko commanded an **Alliance** ship, exacting duties from ships who traversed the Bajoran (mirror) sector, and returning those tributes to the Intendant. Sisko attributed his privileged Terran status to the fact that he "amused" the Intendant, but he knew he was still a slave. In 2370, he was persuaded by the presence of Kira Nerys and Julian Bashir to abandon his favored post and flee Alliance control to fight for human freedom. ("Crossover" [DS9]). The mirror Sisko became a leader of the **Terran resistance** against the Alliance. His abrasive personality offended many of his fellow rebels, as it had, in 2366, alienated his wife, **Jennifer Sisko (mirror)**. Benjamin Sisko (mirror) was killed in 2371 when his ship was attacked by Cardassian forces while Sisko was on a mission to persuade his ex-wife to abandon scientific work that she was doing for the **Alliance**. ("Through the Looking Glass" [DS9]).

Sisko, Benjamin. (Avery Brooks). Starfleet officer who commanded station **Deep Space 9** following the **Cardassian** withdrawal from **Bajor** in 2369. Shortly after his posting to Deep Space 9, Sisko made contact with the mysterious life-forms identified as Bajor's legendary **Prophets** in the Bajoran **Celestial Temple** located in the **Denorios Belt**. As a result, religious leader **Kai Opaka** indicated that Sisko was the **Emissary** promised by prophecy as the one who would save the **Bajoran** people. Sisko was uncomfortable with his role as Emissary, but felt obligated to respect Bajoran religious beliefs. ("Emissary" [DS9]).

Ben Sisko entered **Starfleet Academy** in 2350. For the first few weeks, he would beam back to his family home in New Orleans every night to have dinner with his parents. ("Homefront" [DS9]). During his sophomore year, Benjamin Sisko spent a field-study assignment on Starbase 137. ("The Ascent" [DS9]). Early in his Starfleet career, Ensign Sisko was mentored by **Curzon Dax**, a **Trill** who met Sisko at **Pelios Station** before the two served aboard the *U.S.S. Livingston*. ("Invasive

Procedures" [DS9]). Sisko later served aboard the *Starship Okinawa* under Captain Leyton (SEE: **Leyton, Admiral**). While Sisko's interests were in engineering, Leyton saw command potential in the young officer and promoted him to lieutenant commander, making him the ship's first officer. ("Homefront" [DS9], "Paradise Lost" [DS9]). Aboard the *Okinawa*, Sisko and Leyton fought in the war between the Federation and the **Tzenkethi**. ("The Adversary" [DS9]). Sisko served as executive officer with the rank of lieutenant commander aboard the ***U.S.S. Saratoga*** at the time of the ship's destruction in the battle of **Wolf 359**. ("Emissary" [DS9]). Sisko was subsequently assigned to the **Utopia Planitia Fleet Yards** on Mars, where he spent three years. ("Emissary" [DS9]). One of his projects at Utopia Planitia included design work on the experimental *Starship* ***Defiant***. ("*Defiant*" [DS9]). Sisko also worked on Earth, directing the construction of orbital habitats. ("Way of the Warrior" [DS9]). Sisko was subsequently promoted to commander and assigned to station **Deep Space 9**. ("Emissary" [DS9]). Among Sisko's staff at Deep Space 9 was Science Officer **Jadzia Dax**, a Trill whom he had once known as Curzon Dax. Sisko initially found it difficult to relate to his old friend in the body of a beautiful woman, but the two eventually came to renew their friendship. ("A Man Alone" [DS9], "Dax" [DS9]).

Commanding Deep Space 9 brought its share of difficult decisions, tempered with Sisko's personal experiences. He was profoundly affected by his encounter with the **Borg**. In 2370, when a **protouniverse** threatened the safety of his station, Sisko refused to arbitrarily destroy the miniature cosmos, because he felt that to do so would be to act with the same indifference the Borg had shown to the Federation. ("Playing God" [DS9]). Later that year, Sisko lost his friendship with academy classmate **Calvin Hudson** when Hudson joined the Maquis, fighting the Cardassians in violation of Federation law. ("The Maquis, Part I" [DS9]). In 2372, Sisko was temporarily appointed head of Starfleet security when a **Dominion** infiltration of Starfleet was feared. Sisko was instrumental in preventing an attempted coup by **Admiral Leyton**. ("Homefront" [DS9], "Paradise Lost" [DS9]).

Sisko's role as Emissary of the Bajoran people sometimes put him in a difficult position with regard to his duties as a Starfleet officer. In 2373, Sisko felt obligated to oppose Bajor's admission to the Federation. Sisko had experienced a vision, called ***pag'tem'far*** in the Bajoran language, that led him to believe that admission at that time would be unwise. The **Bajoran Chamber of Ministers** accepted Sisko's recommendation, angering the Federation government and Starfleet Command. ("Rapture" [DS9]).

In 2371, Sisko was abducted by **Miles O'Brien (mirror)** and taken to the **mirror universe** to help the **Terran rebellion**'s fight against the **Alliance**. Sisko was disconcerted to learn that the counterpart of his late wife, Jennifer, was still alive in the mirror universe. It was Sisko's difficult job to convince **Jennifer Sisko (mirror)** to abandon her work for the Alliance, and to persuade her to instead join the **Terran rebellion**. ("Through the Looking Glass" [DS9]).

Ben Sisko was a devoted family man who grew up in New Orleans on Earth. ("Family Business" [DS9], "Explorers" [DS9]). His father, **Joseph Sisko**, was a gourmet chef who ran a small bistro called **Sisko's** in the French Quarter of New Orleans. The elder Sisko insisted the family dine together, so that his "taste testers" could sample his new recipes. ("A Man Alone" [DS9], "The Visitor" [DS9]). Benjamin met Jennifer, his future wife, at Gilgo Beach on Earth, around 2353, just after Sisko's graduation from **Starfleet Academy**. ("Emissary" [DS9]). Ben and Jennifer subsequently married, and had a son, Jake, in 2355. ("Move Along Home" [DS9]). Ben and Jennifer served together aboard the *Starship* ***Saratoga***, until Jennifer's tragic death in the Battle of **Wolf 359** in early 2367. A single parent, Sisko raised their son, Jake, first at Utopia Planitia, then at station Deep Space 9. ("Emissary" [DS9]). Ben had a sister, **Judith Sisko** ("Homefront" [DS9]) who lived in Portland, Oregon, on Earth. ("Past Tense, Part I" [DS9]). After Jennifer's death, Sisko was reluctant to form another relationship. It was not until late 2371 that he took an interest in freighter captain **Kasidy Yates**. ("The Adversary" [DS9]). Sisko's relationship with Yates was put to the test in 2372 when it was discovered that she was a Maquis smuggler. He continued to have feelings for her despite her conviction for arms running. ("For the Cause" [DS9]).

One of Ben's favorite recreational activities was a holosuite program of Earth's famous **baseball** players, such as **Buck Bokai** (*pictured*), **Tris Speaker,** and **Ted Williams.** Using this program, Ben and his son, Jake, enjoyed playing with these greats. The program also allowed Ben to cheer his hero, Buck Bokai, in the sparsely attended 2042 World Series that spelled the end of professional baseball. ("If Wishes Were Horses" [DS9]). Ben was something of an aficionado of 21st-century **Earth** history ("Past Tense, Part I" [DS9]), and he enjoyed collecting ancient African artifacts. ("The Search, Part I" [DS9]). Sisko also enjoyed wrestling and was captain of the wrestling team at Starfleet Academy in 2351. ("Apocalypse Rising" [DS9]). One of Sisko's most remarkable recreational activities was his construction of a **Bajoran solar-sail vessel** of ancient design, in 2371. Along with Jake, Sisko piloted it to **Cardassia**, a dramatic demonstration of how ancient **Bajorans** accomplished the same feat some eight centuries ago. ("Explorers" [DS9]).

Sisko was an admirer of legendary starship Captain **James T. Kirk**. Sisko actually had a chance to meet Kirk when the *Defiant* traveled back in time to 2267, where he met Kirk aboard the original ***Starship Enterprise***. In a breach of Starfleet Regulation 157, Section III, Paragraph 18, Sisko even greeted Kirk and got his autograph. ("Trials and Tribble-ations" [DS9]).

Benjamin Sisko was promoted to the rank of captain on stardate 48959.1, in late 2371. ("The Adversary" [DS9]). Sisko was injured in a Jem'Hadar attack in early 2372 aboard the *Defiant*, during a trade conference with the **Karemma**. Sisko suffered a blow to his head, resulting in a concussion with subcranial bleeding. ("Starship Down" [DS9]).

(Ben Sisko was believed killed in early 2372 in an accident aboard the *Defiant*. In fact, Sisko had vanished from our time continuum, but reappeared periodically, somehow tied to his son, Jake. After several decades, Jake sacrificed himself to allow his father to return to the time of the accident, thereby excising this future timeline.) ("The Visitor" [DS9]). *Ben Sisko first appeared in "Emissary" (DS9).*

Sisko, Jake. (Cirroc Lofton). Son of **Benjamin Sisko** and **Jennifer Sisko**. Born in 2355, he lost his mother on the ***U.S.S. Saratoga*** during the battle of **Wolf 359** in 2367. Jake came to live on station **Deep Space 9** when his father took command of the facility in 2369. ("Emissary" [DS9]). On Deep Space 9, Jake befriended young **Nog**, with whom he created a fictitious company, the **Noh-Jay Consortium**, for their ingenious "business" dealings. ("Progress" [DS9]). Jake did well in his studies, and even tutored a young woman, **Mardah**, in entomology. Jake and Mardah, a **dabo girl** who worked at

Quark's bar, became attracted to each other, to the consternation of Ben Sisko. Jake enjoyed playing **dom-jot**, becoming quite skilled at the game. ("Playing God" [DS9, "The Abandoned" [DS9]).

Although Ben Sisko hoped that Jake would follow in his footsteps, becoming a Starfleet officer, Jake's passion was as a writer. ("The Abandoned" [DS9]). In 2370, Jake told his father he didn't want to attend **Starfleet Academy**. ("Shadowplay" [DS9]). Once Jake realized that he did not want to pursue a career in Starfleet, he began to flourish as a writer. He was accepted to the prestigious **Pennington School** on Earth in 2371, and was even offered a writing fellowship. Jake nevertheless deferred admission, remaining instead with his father on Deep Space 9. ("Explorers" [DS9]). Jake wrote his first novel in 2372, a semi-autobiographial work called ***Anslem***. Jake's writing was inspired by a woman named **Onaya**, who was in reality a noncorporeal life-form who literally lived on creative energy. Although Onaya's influence was potentially fatal, Jake's father recognized her threat to his son, and drove her away. ("The Muse" [DS9]). During the following year, Jake wrote a story called "Past Prologue." ("The Ascent" [DS9]).

In 2372, Jake traveled aboard the *Starship Defiant* to the Gamma Quadrant on a mission to observe a subspace inversion of the Bajoran wormhole. During the mission, his father was involved in an engine-room accident. (Sisko's apparent death was devastating to the young Jake, who never fully accepted the loss. In subsequent years, Benjamin Sisko would periodically reappear to Jake for a few minutes at a time. Jake, who had become a successful author with his books *Anslem* and ***Collected Stories***, became obsessed with learning what happened to his father. He abandoned his writing career and studied physics. In doing so, he estranged his wife, Korena. With the help of his old friends aboard the *Defiant*, Jake learned that in the accident, a subspace link had been created between him and his father. Periodically, the link would pull Ben Sisko forward into Jake's time, accounting for Ben's mysterious appearances. After several decades, Jake sacrificed his life at a critical moment so that his father could return to the past and avert the disastrous accident aboard the *Defiant*. In doing so, Jake excised this future timeline, so that his younger self could grow up without losing his father. In Jake's alternate future, by 2405, the Federation had abandoned station Deep Space 9 to Klingon control, while Bajor had entered into a mutual defense pact with Cardassia against the Klingons. Julian Bashir had a family and children; Nog had become a Starfleet captain; Morn owned Quark's bar; while Quark himself had retired to a small moon.) ("The Visitor" [DS9]).

In 2373, Jake accompanied Dr. Julian Bashir to planet **Ajilon Prime** to help at an emergency hospital during a Klingon attack. At Ajilon Prime, Jake Sisko experienced the horrors of war first-hand and learned of the fine line between courage and cowardice. ("Nor the Battle to the Strong" [DS9]). A few months later, Jake moved out of his father's quarters and became roommates with Starfleet Academy cadet **Nog**, who had returned to **Deep Space 9** for field-study duty. ("The Ascent" [DS9]). Jake sometimes babysat for Lieutenant **Vilix'pran**'s children. ("Business As Usual" [DS9]).

A younger Jake Sisko was played by Thomas Hobson for flashback scenes in "Emissary" (DS9). Older *Jake in "The Visitor" (DS9) was portrayed by Tony Todd, who also played Worf's brother, Kurn. Jake Sisko was first seen in "Emissary" (DS9).*

Sisko, Jennifer (mirror). (Felicia M. Bell). **Mirror universe** counterpart to Jennifer Sisko. This Jennifer did not die in the battle of **Wolf 359**, but instead continued her work as a scientist. She worked for the Alliance of the Cardassians and Klingons, trying to develop a **transpectral sensor array** that would enable the **Alliance** to find the **Terran resistance** in the **Badlands**. Professor Jennifer Sisko (mirror), who came from a privileged Terran family, believed her work for the Alliance would help prevent further loss of human life by ending the rebellion, which she believed to be futile. She and her husband, **Benjamin Sisko (mirror)**, separated in 2366. In 2371, **Benjamin Sisko** from our universe persuaded the mirror Jennifer Sisko to join the rebellion and abandon development of the sensor array. ("Through the Looking Glass" [DS9]). In 2372, Jennifer Sisko (mirror) abducted Jake Sisko, a ploy to persuade this universe's Benjamin Sisko to return to the mirror universe to help the **Terran resistance** complete the *Starship* ***Defiant*** **(mirror)** in time to fend off an impending attack by Alliance forces. While she was trying to get Jake safely back to his own universe, the mirror Jennifer Sisko was shot and mortally wounded by **Kira Nerys (mirror)**. At her deathbed, Benjamin and Jake Sisko again wept for a woman named Jennifer. ("Shattered Mirror" [DS9]).

Sisko, Jennifer. (Felicia Bell). Scientist. Wife to **Benjamin Sisko** and mother to **Jake Sisko**. Jennifer Sisko was killed on the ***U.S.S. Saratoga*** during the battle of **Wolf 359** in early 2367. Jennifer met her future husband on Gilgo Beach, shortly after Benjamin graduated from Starfleet Academy. ("Emissary" [DS9]).

Sisko, Joseph. (Brock Peters). Gourmet chef and proprietor of a Creole restaurant ("Explorers" [DS9]) called **Sisko's** in New Orleans on Earth. Joseph Sisko was the devoted father of several children, including Starfleet officer **Benjamin Sisko** and his sister Judith. Joseph taught his children the importance of family and how to cook. He was a headstrong man who in later years tended to neglect his health. He developed progressive atherosclerosis, eventually necessitating that he be given a new aorta. Sisko refused to comply in 2372 when security measures ordered by President **Jaresh-Inyo** required family members of key Starfleet officers to submit to **blood screening** tests. ("Homefront" [DS9]). *Brock Peters also played Admiral Cartwright in* Star Trek IV *and* Star Trek VI.

Sisko's restaurant sign.

Sisko, Judith. Sister of Starfleet officer Benjamin Sisko. ("Past Tense, Part I" [DS9]). Judith Sisko lived on Earth in Portland, Oregon, and like her mother, did not put enough cayenne pepper in her jambalaya. ("Homefront" [DS9]).

Sisko, Korena. (Galyn Görg). (In an alternate future in which Ben Sisko was believed killed aboard the *Defiant* in 2372, Jake Sisko married an artist named Korena. She and Jake were married in 2284 at Jake grandfather's restaurant in New Orleans on Earth. In that reality, Jake and Korena drifted apart when Jake went back to school to study subspace mechanics. SEE: **Sisko, Jake**.) ("The Visitor" [DS9]).

Sisters of Hope Infirmary. Charity hospital in 19th-century San Francisco on planet Earth. More than half of the victims of the time-traveling aliens from **Devidia II** came from this hospital. The crew of the *Enterprise*-D visited this infirmary in hopes of stopping the **Devidians**. ("Time's Arrow, Part II" [TNG]).

site-to-site transport. Also known as direct transport, the process whereby a transport subject is first beamed to the **transporter** from a remote location. However, instead of being materialized in the chamber, the subject is then transported directly to another location where it is materialized. For example, a critically injured patient might be beamed directly to sickbay instead of to the transporter room. Site-to-site transport is relatively costly in terms of energy usage, so it is used primarily for emergency situations. ("Brothers" [TNG], "The Game" [TNG], et al.). Site-to-site transport could also be initiated by a properly configured control **padd** at the destination. ("Non Sequitur" [VGR]). *During the original series, this procedure was considered to be extremely risky. ("Day of the Dove" [TOS]).*

Sito Jaxa. (Shannon Fill). A member of Starfleet Academy's **Nova Squadron** in 2368. Sito's craft was the first one struck during an accident that destroyed all five craft and killed one of the squadron members. ("The First Duty" [TNG]). SEE: **Kolvoord Starburst; Locarno, Cadet First Class Nicholas**. After the **Nova Squadron** incident, Sito was allowed to remain at the Academy, though it was extremely difficult for her. Following her graduation, she was assigned to the *Enterprise*-D. Sito was one of several ensigns considered for promotion in 2370. While aboard the *Enterprise*-D, Sito volunteered for a hazardous covert mission in which she accompanied **Joret Dal,** a Cardassian operative for the Federation, as he returned to Cardassian space. To get past the border patrols, Joret Dal posed as a bounty hunter, and Sito posed as his prisoner, a Bajoran terrorist. She was believed killed in an evacuation pod as she attempted to return to Federation space. ("Lower Decks" [TNG]). *Her given name was established in "Lower Decks" (TNG).*

Sixth Order. Division of the **Cardassian** military. **Gul Toran** served in the Sixth Order. ("Defiant" [DS9]).

skimmer. Vehicle used by the **Cardassians** for transportation on **Bajor** during the occupation. ("The Darkness and the Light" [DS9]).

"Skin of Evil." *Next Generation* episode #22. Teleplay by Joseph Stefano and Hannah Louise Shearer. Story by Joseph Stefano. Directed by Joseph L. Scanlan. Stardate 41601.3. *First aired in 1988. A malevolent life-form of pure evil traps a shuttlecraft and kills Tasha Yar. As a writer and producer, Joseph Stefano was responsible for the classic first season of* The Outer Limits *television series.* GUEST CAST: Mart McChesney as **Armus**; Ron Gans as **Armus,** voice of; Walker Boone as **Lynch**, **Leland T.**; Brad Zerbst as Nurse; Raymond Forchion as **Prieto**, **Lieutenant Ben**. SEE: **Armus; direct reticular stimulation; Lynch, Leland T.; Minnerly, Lieutenant; Mishiama wristlock; neural stimulator; norep; Prieto, Lieutenant Ben; Shuttlecraft 13; Swenson, Science Officer; Vagra II; Worf; Yar, Natasha; Zed Lapis Sector.**

Sklar. (Kelly Connell). Exo-geologist and colonist on a **Nezu** colony world in the Delta Quadrant. Sklar was also a traitor who assisted the **Etanian Order** in their attempted invasion of the planet. Sklar poisoned **Dr. Vatm** because he knew of the Etanian plan. Sklar died when he fell from a **mag-lev carriage**, hundreds of kilometers to the surface. ("Rise" [VGR]).

Skon. Son of Solkar. Father to **Sarek** of Vulcan; grandfather to **Spock**. *(Star Trek III: The Search for Spock).*

Skoran. (Michael G. Hagerty). Blacksmith of a village on planet **Barkon IV**. In 2370, Skoran fashioned some jewelry from metal fragments of unknown origin. He had obtained the fragments from a stranger named **Jayden**. Skoran did not realize that the fragments, pieces of a stray Federation probe, were dangerously radioactive. Nor did he realize that Jayden was actually a Starfleet officer named Data, who had been sent to recover the probe. Skoran and the **Barkonians** he sold the jewelry to developed radiation poisoning. Skoran blamed Jayden for bringing the illness to the village. He later led the attack that apparently killed Jayden. ("Thine Own Self" [TNG]). *Michael G. Hagerty also portrayed Larg in "Redemption, Part II" (TNG).*

Skrreea. Humanoid civilization that lived for some eight hundred years as slaves to the **T-Rogorans** in the Gamma Quadrant. When the T-Rogorans were conquered by the **Dominion** in 2370, some three million Skrreeas fled, eventually finding the Bajoran wormhole. Believing the wormhole to be the **Eye of the Universe** described in Skrreean legend, and believing planet Bajor to be **Kentanna**, their ancestral homeworld, the Skrreean refugees sought to colonize Bajor. Their application was rejected by the Bajoran provisional government, and the Skrreea later settled on planet **Draylon II**. ("Sanctuary" [DS9]). SEE: **Haneek.**

Sky Spirits. In the mythology of some Native American cultures on Earth, the Sky Spirits created the ancestors of the ancient **Rubber Tree People** more than a thousand generations ago. They led the humans across their planet to a new land where the people made their home. They gave these humans an extraordinary genetic gift, a strong sense of curiosity and of bold adventure, which served them well in their new home on what later became known as the American continents. The Sky Spirits were said to honor the land above all else. In 2372, **Chakotay**, himself a descendent of the Rubber Tree People, discovered the Sky Spirits on a planet in the Delta Quadrant. They possessed an extremely advanced technology that allowed them to cross vast interstellar distances. They even had a sophisticated cloaking technology and had the ability to control weather on a Class-M planet. ("Tattoo" [VGR]). SEE: **Inheritors**. *Richard Fancy played the Sky Spirits' descendent in "Tattoo."*

sleeper fungi. Common term for thallophytes that can be used in a poultice. ("Paradise" [DS9]).

sleeper ship. Spacecraft that used suspended animation to allow passengers and crew to hibernate during interstellar or other extended, usually slower-than-light travel. Sleeper ships fell into disuse by the year 2018 because of advances in sublight propusion. The ***S.S. Botany Bay*** was a sleeper ship. ("Space Seed" [TOS]). SEE: **cryosatellite; *T'Ong, I.K.S.***

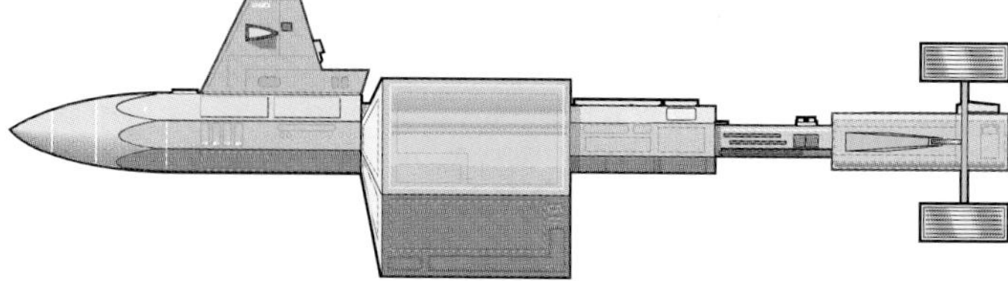

slingshot effect. Spaceflight maneuver in which a vessel closely approaches an astronomical body, using the body's gravitational field to provide additional speed. At warp speeds, the slingshot effect can propel a ship into a time warp. The slingshot effect was used to return the *Enterprise* to the 23rd century when the ship was accidentally sent to the year 1969 by near-collision with a **black star**. Also known as the **light-speed breakaway factor**. ("Tomorrow Is Yesterday" [TOS], "Assignment: Earth" [TOS], *Star Trek IV: The Voyage Home).*

slip. Form of **Ferengi** currency, a fraction of a bar of gold-pressed **latinum.** One bar of latinum was equal to two thousand slips. ("Body Parts" [DS9]).

Sloane, Lily. (Alfre Woodard). Twenty-first century aerospace engineer who worked with **Zefram Cochrane** to build the ***Phoenix***, the first ship from Earth to travel faster than light. Sloane and Cochrane built that ship largely from parts scrounged from abandoned military hardware left over from **World War III**. Sloane suffered radiation poisoning in a **Borg** attack that nearly prevented the launch of the *Phoenix*. She was later taken on-board the *Starship Enterprise*-E for treatment, where she again narrowly escaped death from the Borg. Sloane returned to Earth, where she took her place in history. *(Star Trek: First Contact).*

slug liver. Ferengi food. Slug liver is usually served raw. ("The Assignment" [DS9]).

Smiley. SEE: **O'Brien, Miles (mirror).**

Smith, Rebecca. Tactical officer assigned to the *Enterprise*-D, who joined the ship in 2370. She and Commander William Riker visited the ship's **arboretum**, when Riker accidentally rolled over into some **Cyprion cactus**. ("Genesis" [TNG]).

Smith, Yeoman. (Andrea Dromm). *Enterprise* crew member during the early days of Kirk's first five-year mission, circa 2265. ("Where No Man Has Gone Before" [TOS]). *Smith evidently left the* Enterprise *at about the same time that Janice Rand was assigned to the ship.*

Smithsonian Institution. Research institution founded at the bequest of scientist James Smithson, located in the city of Washington, D.C. on **Earth**. The Smithsonian was established in 1846 and comprised several museums and galleries, including the National Air and Space Museum. The Institution remained in existence into the 24th century. As a boy, future starship captain Jean-Luc Picard visited the Smithsonian and gazed in awe at the ***Phoenix***, the ship in which space pioneer **Zefram Cochrane** first flew at warp speed. *(Star Trek: First Contact). Paramount Pictures donated the 3.4-meter photographic miniature of the original* Starship Enterprise *to the Smithsonian Institution following the conclusion of the original* Star Trek *series. Other artifacts from the various* Star Trek *productions have been displayed at the National Air and Space Museum.*

snail juice. Ferengi beverage made from succulent molluskoids. Rom was fond of snail juice. ("Bar Association" [DS9], "Body Parts" [DS9]). He liked it with extra shells. ("The Ascent" [DS9]).

Snowden. Starfleet officer. Snowden served aboard the ***U.S.S. Okinawa*** while Benjamin Sisko was the vessel's executive officer. In 2372, Snowden and several other former *Okinawa* officers were reassigned by **Admiral Leyton** in preparation for his attempted coup of Earth's government. ("Paradise Lost" [DS9]).

so'wl'chu'. Klingon phrase that translates into "engage" or "activate." *(Star Trek III: The Search for Spock,* "Unification, Part I" [TNG]).

Sobi. (Judson Scott). A citizen of the planet **Brekka**, in charge of a shipment of narcotic **felicium** to be shipped to planet **Ornara**. Sobi was determined to maintain the exploitive relationship between Brekka and Ornara by concealing the narcotic nature of felicium from the **Ornarans**. ("Symbiosis" [TNG]). *Actor Judson Scott had previously played Joachim, Khan's protégé, in* Star Trek II: The Wrath of Khan.

Sobras. Planet in the Delta Quadrant. In 2372 a conference of Kazon first majes gathered at the request of *Voyager*'s Captain Kathryn Janeway and Trabe leader **Mabus** to discuss a peaceful end to hostilities. The peace conference was a trap engineered by Mabus. ("Alliances" [VGR]).

soccer. A form of Earth football in which a spherical ball is propelled toward the opponent's goal by kicking or by striking with the body or the head. The goalkeepers were the only players allowed to touch the ball with the hands or forearms. At the age of 13, **Worf** was the captain of his school soccer team on the farming community on **Gault**. ("Let He Who Is Without Sin..." [DS9]). SEE: **Mikel.**

Socrates. (469-399 BC). Greek philosopher from planet Earth. Socrates strove to understand the concept of self and the philosophical issues surrounding the self. In 2373, *Voyager*'s **Emergency Medical Hologram** incorporated segments of Socrates's personality into his personality-improvement project. ("Darkling" [VGR]).

sodium chloride. Common salt, one of the essential elements of life on Earth and other Class-M planets. Sodium chloride was of critical importance to the life-forms on planet **M-113**, and the last survivor of that planet's civilization was forced to kill **Nancy Crater** and several *Enterprise* crew personnel to obtain it. ("The Man Trap" [TOS]).

sodium pentothal. Proprietary name for a brand of thiopental sodium, a serum used as a truth-inducing drug on Earth in the 20th century. Sodium pentothal had no effect on Ferengi physiology. ("Little Green Men" [DS9]).

Soh-chlm. Klingon term for a legally appointed guardian, or surrogate mother. Citing her devotion to Alexander during a family crisis, Worf asked Counselor Troi to serve as Alexander's *Soh-chlm* in 2370. Troi gladly accepted. ("Parallels" [TNG]).

soil reclamators. Farm equipment developed by the Bajoran agricultural ministry. The reclamators allowed the Bajoran farmland, which had been poisoned by the Cardassians prior to their departure, to be detoxified and made fertile. These reclamators were in high demand, and in 2371 had been promised to a group of farmers in **Dahkur Province**. Following her appointment as acting First Minister, Kai **Winn** ordered the reclamators relocated to **Rakantha Province**. The order touched off a political struggle that nearly escalated into civil war. Her mismanagement of the incident led to Winn's withdrawal from that year's election for first minister. ("Shakaar" [DS9]). SEE: **Shakaar**.

"Sokath, his eyes uncovered!" A **Tamarian** metaphorical phrase referring to achieving sudden insight or understanding. ("Darmok" [TNG]).

Solais V. Class-M planet whose humanoid inhabitants had been at war for fifteen centuries until both sides sued for peace in 2365. The Solais requested the services of mediator **Riva**. By that time, Solais weapons technology had reached the point where laser warfare was being employed. Although he was not immediately successful in bringing peace to the Solais, Riva remained on the planet, hoping to teach both factions the use of sign language, and in doing so, to bring them to a common ground. ("Loud as a Whisper" [TNG]). In 2371, Captain **Kasidy Yates** hauled a load of duridium to Solais V. ("The Adversary" [DS9]).

solanagen-based entities. Life-forms that existed in a deep **subspace** domain. These humanoid entities accessed our own universe in 2369 when Geordi La Forge modified a sensor array, accidentally allowing the solanagen-based aliens to create a small pocket of their space inside ours. The life-forms forcibly abducted sleeping members of the *Enterprise*-D crew for medical testing until a **coherent graviton pulse** was used to close the spatial rupture. ("Schisms" [TNG]). *The entities were not given a formal name in the episode.*

solanagen. Molecular structure that can only exist in a **subspace** domain. The humanoid entities who abducted several *Enterprise*-D crew members in 2369 were solanagen-based life-forms. ("Schisms" [TNG]). SEE: **solanagen-based entities; tertiary subspace manifold; tetryon.**

solar neutrinos. Subatomic particles created by the fusion reactions in a star. Statistically, half of all solar neutrinos rotate in one direction, and half rotate the other, except under unusual conditions such as those created by Martus's gambling device in 2370. ("Rivals" [DS9]).

Solari. Star system of which planet **Solais V** is a part. ("Loud as a Whisper" [TNG]).

Solarion IV. Planet; site of a Federation colony, located in the Solarion system, near **Cardassian** space. In 2368, the Solarion IV colony was attacked and destroyed by forces claiming to be **Bajoran** terrorists. It was later found that the colony was attacked by Cardassian operatives trying to cause distrust between the Federation and the Bajorans. ("Ensign Ro" [TNG]).

solids. Term used by the **Founders** to refer to monoform non-**shape-shifters** like humanoids. Many years ago the solids, who feared the **changelings**, hunted, beat, and killed them. To this day the shape-shifters do not like or trust solids. ("The Search, Part II" [DS9]).

Solis, Lieutenant (J.G.) Orfil. (George de la Pena). Relief **flight controller** (conn) aboard the *Enterprise*-D. Solis assumed the conn when Geordi La Forge assumed command of the ship in Captain Picard's absence. ("The Arsenal of Freedom" [TNG]).

soliton wave. Nondispersing wavefront of subspace distortion. Soliton waves were studied as an experimental means of faster-than-light spacecraft propulsion by **Dr. Ja'Dar** of planet **Bilana III**. Planet-based soliton-wave generators created a nondispersing wavefront of subspace distortion, which a space vehicle could "ride" like a terrestrial surfboard. Although the system required an unwieldy planetary station on either end, it promised substantially higher propulsion efficiencies than those experienced by conventional starships. The first practical test of this technology was conducted by Dr. Ja'Dar in 2368 with assistance of personnel from the *Starship Enterprise*-D. The test involved a small unpiloted wave-rider vehicle that was sent from Bilana III to **Lemma II**, where a scattering field would dissipate the subspace soliton wave. The test was partially successful, although considerable difficulties were encountered in controlling and dispersing the wave. ("New Ground" [TNG]). *In 20th-century physics, solitons are waveforms that are nondispersing in fiber-optic transmissions.*

Solkar. Grandfather to **Sarek** of Vulcan, great-grandfather to **Spock**. Father to Skon. *(Star Trek III: The Search for Spock).*

Solok, DaiMon. (Lou Wagner). Ferengi smuggler who sometimes ran cargo to planet **Celtris III**. Captain Picard, Dr. Crusher, and Lieutenant Worf were able to procure passage to Celtris III on Solok's vessel on a covert Starfleet mission in 2369. ("Chain of Command, Part I" [TNG]). *Lou Wagner also played Krax in "The Nagus" (DS9).*

Solosos III. Class-M planet in the **Demilitarized Zone** that was the site of a **Maquis** colony. In 2373, in order to convince **Michael Eddington** to give himself up, Benjamin Sisko fired quantum torpedoes containing 50 kg of trilithium resin into the atmosphere of Solosos III, rendering the planet uninhabitable for the next 50 years. ("For the Uniform" [DS9]).

Somak. Starfleet Academy professor. Somak taught the Moral and Ethical Issues course, and she strongly advocated maintaining emotional distance between commanders and those under their command. Benjamin Sisko and Jadzia Dax both took Somak's class. ("The Ship" [DS9]).

somatophysical failure. In humanoid physiology, the collapse of all bodily systems. Captain Picard suffered massive somatophysical failure when he was physically separated from the emanations of the **Kataan probe** in 2368. ("The Inner Light" [TNG]).

Something for Breakfast. Play written by Dr. Beverly Crusher in 2369. Her manuscript for the play was lost in the main *Enterprise*-D computer system when an energy fluctuation in Data's neural net caused a peculiar malfunction in the computer's recreational programming data files. ("A Fistful of Datas" [TNG]). SEE: **Subroutine C-47**.

somnetic inducer. A small neural pad used to aid the induction of sleep in humanoids. Dr. Crusher prescribed a somnetic inducer for Geordi La Forge in late 2367 when a possible malfunction of his VISOR was suspected of causing insomnia. ("The Mind's Eye" [TNG]).

Sompek. Klingon emperor in ancient historic times. Sompek was responsible for conquering the city of **Tong Vey** in one of the most brutal battles in **Klingon** history. Ten thousand of Sompek's warriors laid siege to Tong Vey until the city surrendered, after which he ordered the city burned and all the inhabitants killed. ("Rules of Engagement" [DS9]).

Sonak, Commander. (Jon Rashad Kamal). Starfleet officer. Sonak was killed in a transporter malfunction while beaming up to the refurbished *Starship Enterprise*. Sonak, a Vulcan, would have served as science officer aboard that ship when it intercepted the **V'Ger** entity in 2271. *(Star Trek: The Motion Picture).*

***Sonchi* ceremony.** A Klingon ritual; part of the **Rite of Succession**. *Sonchi* translates as "he is dead." The *Sonchi* formally confirmed the death of a leader before his or her successor could be chosen, and involved jabbing the body with **Klingon painstiks** while issuing a verbal challenge. **K'mpec**'s *Sonchi* ceremony took place in 2367 aboard a Klingon spacecraft. ("Reunion" [TNG]).

"Song of the Sages." Epic poem from **Takarian** mythology that told of how the Great Sages would come from the sky to rule over the people as benevolent protectors for a time and then leave, going back to the sky after their work was done. ("False Profits" [VGR]).

Songi, Chairman. (Kim Hamilton). The planetary leader of **Gamelan V**. Songi was humanoid; her people were distinguished by beautiful facial tendrils. When high levels of radiation threatened her planet in 2367, she issued the general distress call that resulted in the *Enterprise*-D's arrival at her planet. ("Final Mission" [TNG]).

sonic disruptor. Handheld weapon used by civil authorities on planet **Eminiar VII**. ("A Taste of Armageddon" [TOS]). Similar weapons were used by Klingon warriors as well. SEE: **Klingon weapons; phase disruptor**.

sonic separator. Medical instrument. Dr. McCoy used a sonic separator to restore Spock's brain to his body on planet **Sigma Draconis VI** in 2268. ("Spock's Brain" [TOS]).

sonic shower. Personal hygiene device used for bathing aboard Federation starships in the 23rd century. *(Star Trek: The Motion Picture).* Sonic showers continued to be used into the 24th century. ("Resolutions" [VGR]).

sonodanite. Metallic alloy used in Federation shuttlecraft. ("Final Mission" [TNG]).

"Sons of Mogh." *Deep Space Nine* episode #87. Written by Ronald D. Moore. Directed by David Livingston. Stardate 49556.2. *First aired in 1996. Worf's brother Kurn, dishonored and cast out of Klingon society, arrives at Deep Space 9 requesting Worf's help to commit suicide.* GUEST CAST: Tony Todd as **Kurn**; Robert DoQui as **Noggra**; Dell Yount as **Tilikia**; Elliot Woods as Klingon officer. SEE: ***adanji*; Boslics; *Drovna, I.K.S.*; engram; Klingons; *Korinar, I.K.S.*; *koruts*; Kurn; *Mauk-to'Vor*; *mek'leth*; *mevak*; *movek*; Noggra; Rodek; Sorval, Commander; Tilikia; *Yukon, U.S.S.***

***soo-lak*.** Vulcan term referring to a third party who expresses a lack of interest, thereby trivializing that of another. ("Alter Ego" [VGR]).

Soong, Juliana. SEE: **Tainer, Dr. Juliana.**

Soong, Noonien. (Brent Spiner). Renowned cyberneticist, born in the late 23rd century, known as Earth's foremost robotics scientist. Soong's early achievements were overshadowed by his highly publicized failures when he tried to construct a **positronic brain**. Following that downfall, the reclusive Soong disappeared from public sight, traveling under an assumed name to the **Omicron Theta** colony, where he continued his work in secret. While on Omicron Theta, Dr. Soong met and married **Juliana O'Donnell**, who was one of the Omicron Theta colonists. With his wife's assistance, Soong developed a series of positronic androids. However, the first three "died" of positronic matrix failure. Perhaps his greatest success there was the creation of the humanoid androids **Data** and **Lore**. ("DataLore" [TNG]). Soong and Juliana escaped from Omicron Theta just as the colony was destroyed by the **Crystalline Entity**, leaving behind a dormant Data and the disassembled Lore. Soong's wife was injured in the escape. The Soongs were able to travel as far as **Terlina III**, where Juliana fell into a fatal coma. Unable to face the thought of living without the only woman he ever loved, Soong made an extremely advanced android replicate of her, and programmed it with Juliana's memories and personality. The android believed herself to actually be Juliana. Soong took great pains to ensure that she would never discover otherwise. Unfortunately, the android Juliana grew disenchanted with her husband and left him. ("Inheritance" [TNG]). Soong continued to work at his lab in seclusion. He broke this seclusion in 2367 when he commanded Data to come to his laboratory so that Soong could install a new chip in his creation, intended to give Data the ability to experience human emotions. Unfortunately, Lore also responded to Soong's summons, and Lore, jealous of Data, stole the chip. Soong died shortly thereafter. ("Brothers" [TNG]). Soong implanted a circuit into Data's base programming, intended to cause Data to dream when he reached a certain level of development. This circuit was prematurely activated in 2369 when Data experienced a severe plasma shock. Data's dreams included images of a young Dr. Soong as a blacksmith, forging a bird that represented Data himself. ("Birthright, Part I" [TNG]). *Soong was played by Brent Spiner, on the assumption that Data was made in his creator's image.* SEE: **Asimov, Isaac**.

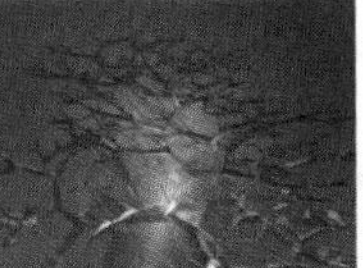

Soong-type android. Term used to describe artificial humanoid life-forms using designs developed by Dr. **Noonien Soong**. Soong-type androids have included **Data**, **Lore**, and **Lal**. ("The Offspring" [TNG]).

Sorad, Vedek. (Michael Durrell). Member of the **Vedek Assembly** on Bajor. He, along with **Minister Rozahn**, journeyed to Deep Space 9 in 2370 to inform **Haneek** that the **Skrreea**n request to settle on Bajor had been denied. ("Sanctuary" [DS9]).

Soral. Outstanding operatic tenor from the planet Vulcan. Soral performed the character of Rudolpho in **Puccini**'s *La Bohème* opposite **T'Penna**'s Mimi. To learn about opera, the *Voyager's* Emergency Medical Hologram studied recordings of *La Bohème* featuring Soral. ("The Swarm" [VGR]).

Soran, Dr. Tolian. (Malcolm McDowell). **El-Aurian** scientist whose wife and children were killed when the **Borg** destroyed the El-Aurian homeworld. Soran was among hundreds of refugees fleeing to Earth in 2293 aboard a convoy of El-Aurian transport ships, when the convoy collided with the **nexus** energy ribbon. Both ships were destroyed, but Soran and 46 others from the ***S.S. Lakul*** were rescued by the crew of the *Starship* ***Enterprise*-B**. Also rescued in the incident was fellow El-Aurian **Guinan**. As Soran was being rescued by transporter, he was briefly pulled into the nexus, where he experienced a powerful euphoria, and he subsequently became obsessed with returning to the nexus at any cost. The key, he found, was to find a way to force the nexus energy ribbon to travel through a planet, an unlikely occurrence given the vastness of interstellar space and the small size of planets. Soran worked for nearly a century, devising a horrific scheme to use **trilithium** explosions to destroy selected stars, thereby controlling the trajectory of the energy ribbon. He enlisted the aid of Klingon renegades **Lursa** and **B'Etor** to steal trilithium from a Romulan research facility. In exchange, Soran offered technical data on the use of trilithium for weapons applications. Soran's plan was discovered in 2371 when he destroyed the **Amargosa** star with a trilithium-laden probe launched from the **Amargosa Observatory**. *U.S.S.* ***Enterprise*-D** personnel intervened to prevent Soran from destroying a star in the **Veridian system**. Had Soran succeeded, the destruction of the star would have cost the lives of 230 million life-forms on planet **Veridian IV**. Former *Enterprise* Captain **James T. Kirk**, who had also been swept into the nexus in the *Lakul* rescue, played a critical role in stopping Soran, an effort that cost Kirk his life. Tolian Soran was killed when his trilithium probe launcher exploded on the surface of planet **Veridian III**. *(Star Trek Generations).*

Soren. (Melinda Culea). A **J'naii** pilot, part of a team that worked with *Enterprise*-D personnel to rescue a missing J'naii shuttle in 2368. During the rescue operation, Soren became romantically involved with Commander William Riker, thereby exhibiting female sexual behavior. Such gender-specific orientation was considered abhorrent to the J'naii culture, and Soren was subsequently arrested. Soren was subjected to **psychotectic** therapy, causing one to conform to the culturally acceptable androgynous norm. ("The Outcast" [TNG]). *The pronoun "one" is used here, as is proper to the J'naii culture when speaking of a member of this androgynous people, as opposed to the "she" or "he" pronouns often used in species with sexual differentiation.*

sorium. Explosive compound. Sorium was used in a Ferengi **locator bomb** intended to kill Quark when he served as **grand nagus** in 2369. ("The Nagus" [DS9]).

Sorm. (Nicholas Worth). Operative of the **Orion Syndicate**. **Draim** hired Sorm to go to Deep Space 9 and procure a data crystal from **Arissa** before killing her. Sorm killed **Tauvid Rem**. ("A Simple Investigation" [DS9]).

Sorval, Commander. Identity used by Worf in 2372 when he and his brother Kurn stole aboard the *I.K.S. Drovna* in search of the detonation codes for a Klingon minefield. ("Sons of Mogh" [DS9]).

SOS. Radio code signal for distress used on Earth in the 20th century to communicate a request for assistance. The letters SOS were encoded in an ancient telegraphy protocol known as Morse code. ("The 37's" [VGR]).

Soto. (Tom Morga). **Lethean** associate of Toral. At a tavern on Torna IV, Kor unwisely told the tale of the discovery of the true Shroud of the Sword. In 2372, Soto used his Lethean abilities to steal information from Kor's mind concerning the shroud. Soto accompanied Toral as he followed Kor on his quest for the Sword of Kahless, and was later killed by Kor. ("The Sword of Kahless" [DS9]). *Tom Morga previously played a Nausicaan in "Tapestry" [TNG]. Soto's name was not mentioned in dialog, but comes from the script.*

Sovak. (Max Grodénchik). Ferengi entrepreneur who sometimes worked with **Dr. Samuel Estragon** on less-than-ethical archaeological expeditions. Upon Estragon's death in 2366, Sovak paid Estragon's assistant, **Vash**, to steal Estragon's notes on the location of the ***Tox Uthat***. Vash used Sovak's money to conduct her own search for the fabled object, with Sovak trailing her. Besides coveting the *Uthat*, Sovak was also attracted to the beautiful Vash. ("Captain's Holiday" [TNG]). *Max Grodénchik later played Rom on* Star Trek: Deep Space Nine.

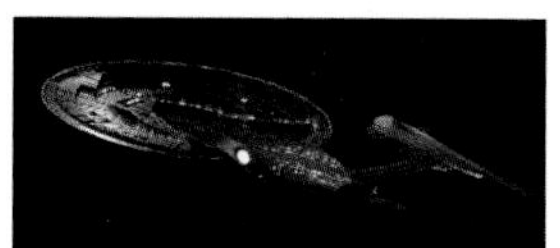

***Sovereign*-class starship.** Type of Federation spacecraft that in 2373 was the most advanced starship in Starfleet. *Sovereign*-class ships were almost 700 meters in length and were 24 decks thick. The ***U.S.S. Enterprise*-E**, launched in 2372 under the command of Captain Jean-Luc Picard, was a *Sovereign*-class vessel. *(Star Trek: First Contact). There is presumably also a* U.S.S. Sovereign*, which was the prototype for the class.*

Sowee TAH. Klingon phrase, a command to "decloak." ("The Way of the Warrior" [DS9]).

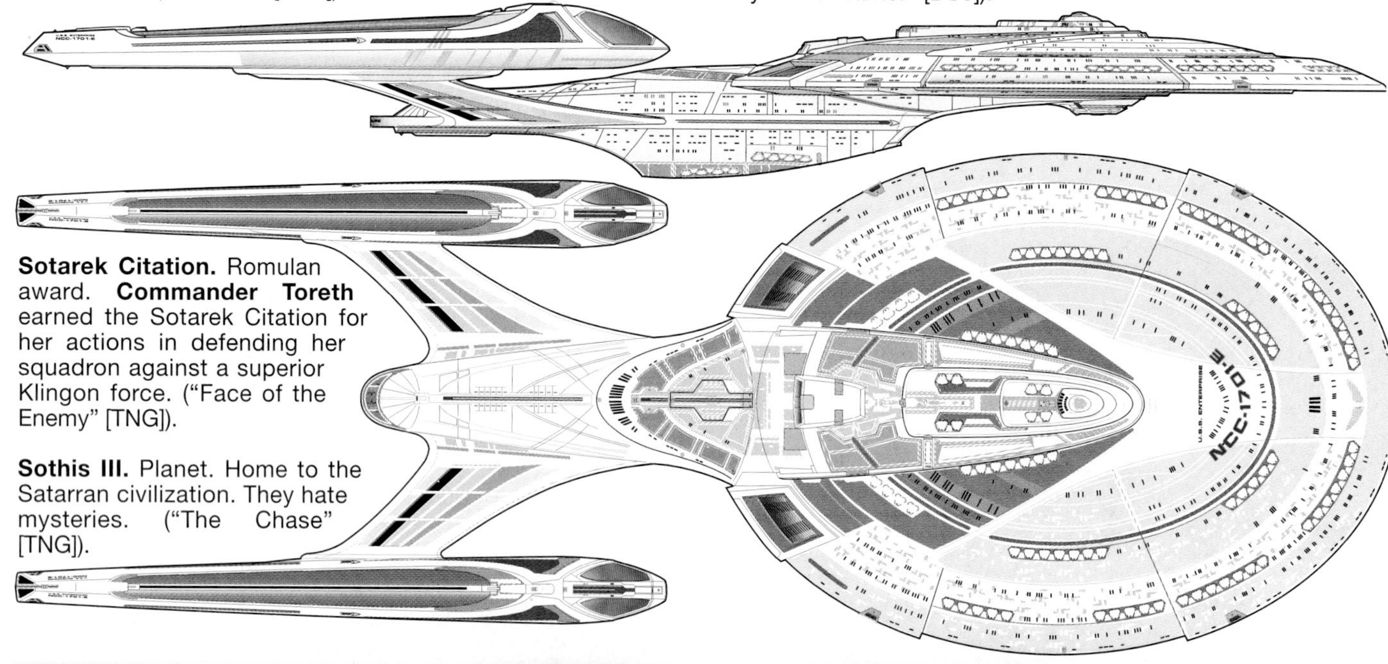

Sotarek Citation. Romulan award. **Commander Toreth** earned the Sotarek Citation for her actions in defending her squadron against a superior Klingon force. ("Face of the Enemy" [TNG]).

Sothis III. Planet. Home to the Satarran civilization. They hate mysteries. ("The Chase" [TNG]).

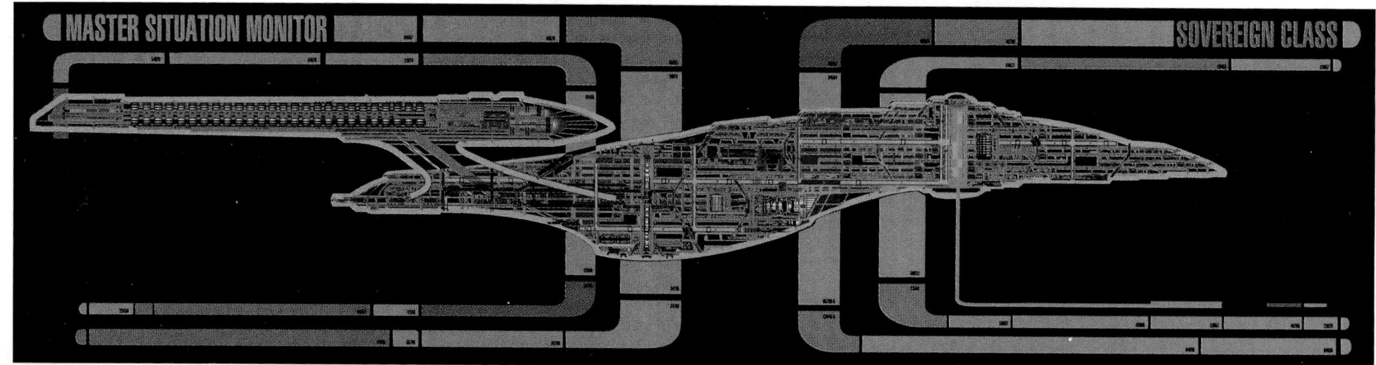

***Soyuz*-class starship.** A variant on the ***Miranda*-class** starship used by the Federation **Starfleet**. *Soyuz*-class ships featured an enlarged aft cargo and shuttlebay section, as well as several large outboard sensor pods. The *Soyuz* class was withdrawn from service by Starfleet in 2288. ("Cause and Effect" [TNG]). *It was originally hoped that a new design could be developed for the* Soyuz*-class* **U.S.S. Bozeman**, *but practical considerations dictated the reworking of the existing* Miranda*-class* **U.S.S. Reliant** *model originally built for* Star Trek II. *The modifications were designed by Greg Jein and Mike Okuda. The class was named for the Russian spacecraft that shuttled cosmonauts up to the Salyut and Mir space stations.*

"Space Seed." Original Series episode #24. Teleplay by Gene L. Coon and Carey Wilber. Story by Carey Wilber. Directed by Marc Daniels. Stardate 3141.9. *First aired in 1967. The* Enterprise *is commandeered by 20th-century genetic "superman" Khan Noonien Singh, who has survived for centuries aboard a "sleeper ship." This episode was the predecessor to the feature film* Star Trek II: The Wrath of Khan. GUEST CAST: Ricardo Montalban as **Khan**; Madlyn Rhue as **McGivers**, **Lieutenant Marla**; Blaisdell Makee as **Spinelli**, **Lieutenant**; Mark Tobin as **Joaquin**; Kathy Ahart as Crew woman; John Winston as Transporter technician; Joan Johnson as *Botany Bay* elite female guard; Bobby Bass as Guard; Barbara Baldavin as Baker, Angela; Joan Webster as Nurse; Jan Reddin, John Arndt, Crewmen; Gary Coombs as Kirk's stunt double; Chuck Couch as Kahn's stunt double. SEE: ***Botany Bay*, *S.S.*; Ceti Alpha V; DY-100; DY-500; decompression chamber; Eugenics Wars; Gamma 400 star system; Harrison; Joaquin; Kyle, Mr.; McGivers, Lieutenant Marla; McPherson; Milton; Otto; Rodriguez; Singh, Khan Noonien; sleeper ship; Spinelli, Lieutenant; Starbase 12; Thule**.

space door. Outer portal of an airlock or hangar deck that opens directly into space. ("Threshold" [VGR]).

space station. SEE: **Deep Space 9; Deep Space Station K-7; drydock; Earth Station McKinley; Lysian Central Command; Regula I; Spacedock**.

space warp. SEE: **subspace; warp drive**.

space-normal. Technical term describing slower-than-light (i.e. non-warp speed) travel. ("The *Galileo* Seven" [TOS]). SEE: **impulse drive**.

Spacedock. Massive station orbiting planet Earth, providing service facilities for Starfleet vessels. The *U.S.S. Enterprise* returned to Spacedock in 2285 following the battle with **Khan** in the **Mutara Nebula**. At the time, the ship was scheduled to be scrapped, but Kirk stole the *Enterprise* from Spacedock in his effort to rescue **Spock**. Also stationed at Spacedock at the time was the ***U.S.S. Excelsior***, undergoing tests of its experimental transwarp drive. *(Star Trek III: The Search for Spock). The Spacedock model was designed by David Carson and Nilo Rodis. It was built at ILM. The model was re-used more than once in* Star Trek: The Next Generation, *notably for Starbase 74 in "11001001" (TNG).* (In an alternate reality created by a **timestream**, the runabout ***U.S.S. Yellowstone*** was stolen from Spacedock in 2372 by Ensign **Harry Kim**, and **Tom Paris** stole the *Yellowstone* from Spacedock.) ("Non Sequitur" [VGR]). *The only shot of the Spacedock in "Non Sequitur" was of the doors, which were first seen as the Dyson Sphere doors from "Relics" (TNG).*

spatial interphase. Time-space phenomenon in which two or more dimensional planes briefly overlap and connect. The *Starship **Defiant*** disappeared into such a phenomenon in 2268, and *Enterprise* Captain James Kirk also became briefly trapped there while on a rescue mission. The interphase phenomenon also had debilitating effects on humanoid nervous systems and apparently caused the crew of the *Defiant* to mutiny and eventually kill each other. ("The Tholian Web" [TOS]).

spatial orientation systems. Subsystem of a holodeck computer, responsible for the attitude of objects in the holodeck environment. The spatial orientation systems aboard the *Enterprise*-D holodeck were suspected of malfunctioning in 2369 when holodeck characters began changing their dominant hands; that is, characters who were intended to be right-handed became left-handed and vice versa. ("Ship in a Bottle" [TNG]).

spatial orientation test. Holographic examination that was part of the entrance requirements for the **Starfleet Academy** preparatory program. ("Facets" [DS9]).

spatial scission. A divergence of **subspace** fields. Spatial scissions can cause a small region of space, and any matter in it, to be duplicated. A spatial scission in the Delta Quadrant caused the *Starship **Voyager*** to be duplicated in 2372. The commander of the duplicate *Voyager* ordered her ship destroyed so that the original ship would be safe. ("Deadlock" [VGR]).

spawn beetle. Insectoid life-form. Kes used spawn beetles to cross-pollinate vegetation in the airponics bay. ("Elogium" [VGR]).

Speaker, Tris. Famous Earth athlete who played **baseball** from 1907 to 1928. A holographic version of Speaker was available in a baseball holosuite program enjoyed by Jake and **Benjamin Sisko** on station Deep Space 9. ("If Wishes Were Horses" [DS9]). SEE: **Bokai, Buck**.

Spectral Analysis Department. *Enterprise-D* science department that studied the composition of stars and stellar phenomena. **Neela Daren** once wanted Spectral Analysis to have more time monitoring the **Borgolis Nebula**, but the sensor array was allocated to engineering. ("Lessons" [TNG]).

spectral line profile analysis. Astrophysics study, used in the science lab on station Deep Space 9. ("Playing God" [DS9]).

spectral rupture. Translated **Vhnori** term for subspace vacuole. ("Emanations" [VGR]). SEE: **subspace phenomena, subspace vacuole.**

"Spectre of the Gun." Original Series episode #56. Written by Lee Cronin. Directed by Vincent McEveety. Stardate 4385.3. *First aired in 1968. Kirk and company are trapped in a bizarre re-creation of the ancient American West and forced to fight in the gunfight at OK Corral. This was the first episode produced for the third season of the original Star Trek series. It was filmed under the title "The Last Gunfight," later changed to "Spectre of the Gun" during the editing process. Lee Cronin was the pen name for Gene L. Coon.* GUEST CAST: Ron Soble as **Earp**, **Wyatt**; Bonnie Beecher as **Sylvia**; Charles Maxwell as **Earp**, **Virgil**; Rex Holman as **Earp**, **Morgan**; Sam Gilman as **Holliday**, **Doc**; Charles Seel as Ed; Bill Zuckert as Behan, Johnny; Ed McCready as Barber; Abraham Sofaer as Melkotian voice; Gregg Palmer as Rancher; Richard Anthony as Rider; Gregory Reece, Paul Baxley, Bob Orrison, Men in bar; James Doohan as Melkotian buoy's voice; Mike Minor as Mask. SEE: **Claiborne, Billy; Clanton, Billy; Clanton, Ike; Earp, Morgan; Earp, Virgil; Earp, Wyatt; Ed; Holliday, Doc; McLowery, Frank; McLowery, Tom; Melkotians; OK Corral; Sylvia; Tombstone, Arizona; Vulcan mind-meld.**

Spectre. (Carel Struycken). Tall, menacing character with a stylized skull mask that inhabited the virtual reality created for the five hibernating survivors of the **Kohl settlement**. ("The Thaw" [VGR]). SEE: **Clown**. *Carel Struycken also portrayed Mr. Homn, Lwaxana Troi's manservant, in "Haven" (TNG) and "Ménage à Troi" (TNG).*

Spican flame gem. Pretty but common stone. Can be polished with Antarean glow water. A trader on **Deep Space Station K-7** was not interested in buying Spican flame gems from **Cyrano Jones** in 2267. ("The Trouble with Tribbles" [TOS]).

Spillane, Mickey. Pseudonym of **Earth** writer Frank Morrison (b. 1918), whose works included ***I, the Jury***, and *Survival:...Zero!* ("Profit and Loss" [DS9]). *Robert Justman was the assistant director on* Kiss Me Deadly, *a motion picture based upon Spillane's novel, directed by the famed Robert Aldrich.*

spinach juice. Beverage made from the succulent leaves of an Earth vegetable plant. Tom Paris and Kes both enjoyed spinach juice with a touch of pear. ("Eye of the Needle" [VGR]).

spinach, creamed. Earth dish made from a leafy vegetable mixed with butter and milk, creating a cream sauce. Tom Paris decided to buy creamed spinach with replicator rations from his **radiogenic sweepstakes** gambling scheme. ("Meld" [VGR]).

Spinelli, Lieutenant. (Blaisdell Makee). Crew member aboard the original *Starship Enterprise* in 2267. Kirk recorded a commendation for Spinelli when the bridge of the *Enterprise* was slowly deprived of life support during **Khan**'s takeover attempt. ("Space Seed" [TOS]). *Blaisdell Makee also played Mr. Singh in "The Changeling" (TOS).*

spiny lobe-fish. Type of meal served to Riker at the imaginary **Tilonus Institute for Mental Disorders**. The image of the spiny lobe-fish was generated while Riker was being brainwashed on planet **Tilonus IV** in 2369 and, like many of the elements of this delusional world, was unreal. ("Frame of Mind" [TNG]). SEE: ***Frame of Mind***.

Spitfire. Nickname for a small sublight combat aircraft employed by the British nation during Earth's second world war in the 1940s. Miles O'Brien piloted a Spitfire in his **Battle of Britain** holosuite simulation program. ("Accession" [DS9]).

Spith basil. Culinary spice native to the Delta Quadrant. ("Prototype" [VGR]).

Spock (mirror). (Leonard Nimoy). Science officer and second-in-command of the ***I.S.S. Enterprise*** in the **mirror universe**. The bearded first officer deduced the transposition of landing parties between universes and allowed the *U.S.S. Enterprise* landing party to return to their own universe. Knowing that one day Spock might be the captain of the *I.S.S. Enterprise*, Kirk planted seeds of doubt in Spock's mind about the fate of the evil empire he served, noting that Spock was a man of honor in both universes. ("Mirror, Mirror" [TOS]). Spock became the driving force to reform the **Terran Empire**, pressing for disarmament and peace. He found remarkable success, becoming the empire's commander-in-chief, and using that position to convince the brutal empire to change its ways. Unfortunately, Spock's reforms left the empire unable to resist outside attackers, and the empire soon fell to forces of the **Alliance**. ("Crossover" [DS9]).

"Spock's Brain." Original Series episode #61. Written by Lee Cronin. Directed by Marc Daniels. Stardate 5431.4. *First aired in 1968. A mysterious woman steals Spock's brain. Lee Cronin was the pen name of Gene L. Coon.* GUEST CAST: Marj Dusay as **Kara**; Majel Barrett as **Chapel, Christine**; James Daris as Creature; Sheila Leighton as **Luma**. SEE: **Controller; Eymorg; ion propulsion; Kara; Luma; Morg; Sigma Draconis III; Sigma Draconis IV; Sigma Draconis VI; Sigma Draconis; sonic separator; Teacher; trilaser connector.**

Spock, Dr. Benjamin McLane. Author, pediatrician, and social activist on 20th-century **Earth**. Benjamin Spock's best selling books on baby and child care shaped a generation's views on child rearing. Spock was also an outspoken opponent of the American military presence in a country known as Vietnam. Spock was among the names that *Voyager*'s **Emergency Medical Hologram** considered in 2371 when searching for a name to adopt as his own. ("Ex Post Facto" [VGR]). Star Trek *creator Gene Roddenberry insisted that the* Enterprise*'s Mr. Spock* was not *named after Benjamin Spock.*

Spock. (Leonard Nimoy). Science officer aboard the original *Starship* ***Enterprise*** under the command of Captain James T. Kirk. Born 2230 on planet **Vulcan**. His mother, **Amanda** Grayson, was a human schoolteacher from Earth, and his father, **Sarek**, was a diplomat from Vulcan. ("This Side of Paradise" [TOS], "Journey to Babel" [TOS]). As a result, he was torn between two worlds, the stern discipline of Vulcan logic and the emotionalism of his human side. The struggle to reconcile his two halves would torment him for much of his life. ("The Naked Time" [TOS]). Spock's Starfleet service number was S179-276 SP. As of 2267, he had earned the Vulcanian Scientific Legion of Honor, had been twice decorated by Starfleet Command ("Court Martial" [TOS]), and held an A7 computer expert classification. ("The Ultimate Computer" [TOS]). His blood type was T-negative. ("Journey to Babel" [TOS]).

Childhood and family: When he was five years old, Spock came home upset because Vulcan boys had tormented him, saying he wasn't really Vulcan. As a child, Spock had a pet **sehlat**, sort of a live Vulcan teddy bear. ("Journey to Babel" [TOS]). Spock was raised with an older half-brother, **Sybok**, until Sybok was ostracized from Vulcan society because he rejected the Vulcan dogma of pure logic. *(Gene Roddenberry considered the Sybok story to be apocryphal.)* Spock himself endured considerable antihuman prejudice on the part of many Vulcans, an experience that may have later made it easier for Spock to find a home in the interstellar community of Starfleet. *(Star Trek V: The Final Frontier).* At age seven, Spock was telepathically bonded with a young Vulcan girl named **T'Pring** (*pictured*). Less than a marriage, but more than a betrothal, the telepathic touch would draw the two together when the time was right after both came of age. ("Amok Time" [TOS]). Spock experienced ***Pon farr***, the powerful mating drive, in 2267, and he was compelled to return to Vulcan to claim T'Pring as his wife. T'Pring spurned Spock in favor of **Stonn**, freeing Spock. ("Amok Time" [TOS]). Spock's father, Sarek, had hoped his son would attend the **Vulcan Science Academy**, and was bitterly

disappointed when Spock instead chose to join Starfleet. Spock and his father had not spoken as father and son for 18 years when a medical emergency drew them together. ("Journey to Babel" [TOS]).

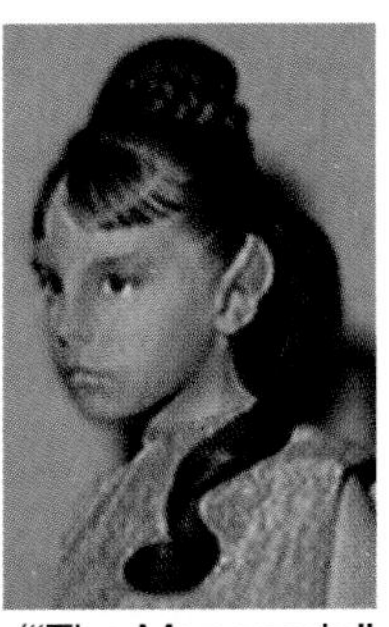

Aboard the *U.S.S. Enterprise*: Spock was the first Vulcan to enlist in the Federation **Starfleet**, and he distinguished himself greatly as science officer aboard the original ***U.S.S. Enterprise***. His logical Vulcan thought-patterns proved of tremendous value when Spock first served aboard the *Enterprise* during the command of Captain Christopher Pike. ("The Menagerie" [TOS]). *Spock said he worked with Pike for 11 years, 4 months, which suggests he was young enough when he first came aboard the* Enterprise *that he was probably still attending Starfleet Academy. Because of this, we speculate that Spock's first year on the* Enterprise *was as a cadet.* Under the command of James Kirk, Spock suffered infection by parasites on planet **Deneva** in 2267, an intensely painful experience. He survived the **Denevan neural parasites** after being exposed to intense electromagnetic radiation that drove the parasites from his body. Spock was briefly feared to have been blinded by the light, but it was later learned that his Vulcan **inner eyelid** had protected his vision. ("Operation—Annihilate!" [TOS]). Spock was critically wounded on Tyree's planet in 2267 with an ancient weapon known as a flintlock. He survived, using a Vulcan healing technique in which the mind concentrates on the injured organs. ("A Private Little War" [TOS]). Following the conclusion of Kirk's five-year mission, Spock retired from Starfleet, returning to Vulcan to pursue the ***Kolinahr*** discipline. Although he completed the training, intended to purge all remaining emotion, Spock nonetheless failed to achieve *Kolinahr* because his emotions were stirred by the **V'Ger** entity in 2271. *(Star Trek: The Motion Picture)*. Spock subsequently remained with Starfleet and was eventually promoted to *Enterprise* captain when that ship was assigned as a training vessel at Starfleet Academy.

Death and rebirth: Spock was killed in 2285 while saving the *Enterprise* from the detonation of the **Genesis Device** by **Khan Noonien Singh**. His body was consigned to space, but unknown to anyone at the time, his casket landed on the Genesis Planet *(Star Trek II: The Wrath of Khan).* Although believed dead at the time, Spock had, just prior to his death, mind-melded with McCoy. Spock had apparently intended for his friend to return Spock's ***katra*** to Vulcan in accordance with Vulcan custom. The presence of Spock's living spirit in McCoy's mind was later found to be an extraordinary opportunity to reunite Spock's body and spirit when his body was found to have been regenerated on the **Genesis Planet**. The ***fal-tor-pan*** (refusion) process was conducted at **Mount Seleya** on Vulcan, supervised by high priestess T'Lar. *(Star Trek III: The Search for Spock). Spock's younger selves in* Star Trek III *were played by Carl Steven, Vadia Potenza, Stephen Manley, and Joe W. Davis.* Later, Spock underwent several months of re-education, during which his mind was instructed in the Vulcan way, but his mother, Amanda, was concerned that he regain knowledge of his human heritage as well. Spock elected to return to Earth with his shipmates from the *Enterprise* to face charges stemming from Kirk's violation of Starfleet regulations in Spock's rescue. *(Star Trek IV: The Voyage Home).*

Later career: In later years, Spock's work became more diplomatic than scientific, even while he was still part of Starfleet. At the request of Ambassador Sarek, Spock served as Federation special envoy to the Klingon government in 2293, paving the way for the **Khitomer** peace accords with Chancellor **Azetbur**. *(Star Trek VI: The Undiscovered Country).* In 2368, Spock secretly traveled to **Romulus**, on a personal mission to further the cause of Romulan-Vulcan re-unification. Spock's disappearance caused great consternation among Federation authorities, and the *Enterprise*-D was dispatched to determine his whereabouts and intentions. Spock's contact on Romulus was **Senator Pardek**, who was believed to have met Spock during the Khitomer conference in 2293. Pardek was later learned to be an agent of the conservative Romulan government, seeking to use Spock's initiative to cover an attempted Romulan invasion of Vulcan. SEE: **Sela**. Following the attempted invasion, Spock chose to remain underground on Romulus in hopes of furthering the cause of re-unification. ("Unification, Parts I and II" [TNG]). Spock continued his activities in the Romulan underground, and in 2369 helped arrange the defection of Romulan **Vice-Proconsul M'ret** to the Federation. SEE: **N'Vek, Subcommander**. Spock indicated he believed the escape of M'ret would help establish an escape route for other Romulan dissidents who lived in fear for their lives. ("Face of the Enemy" [TNG]). Following the death of his father, Spock had one final, unexpected encounter with Sarek. Prior to his death, Sarek had mind-melded with **Jean-Luc Picard**, sharing with Picard his deepest emotions, unclouded by Vulcan logic. On Romulus, Picard allowed Spock to mind-meld with him, and Spock finally came to know of his father's love for him. ("Unification, Part II" [TNG]).

As far as we know, Spock remained on Romulus. In "Sarek" (TNG), Jean-Luc Picard noted that he had, years ago as a young lieutenant, attended the wedding of Sarek's son. Gene Roddenberry said he thought Picard was probably talking about Spock, but there is no direct evidence that Spock ever married. Picard did mention in "Unification, Part I" (TNG) that he had met Spock once before the episode: possibly at Spock's wedding? Spock's first appearance was in "The Cage" (TOS), the first pilot for the original Star Trek *series. Leonard Nimoy, under the pseudonym "Frank Force," provided the computer voice heard in the* Excelsior *elevator in* Star Trek III. *Nimoy's former assistant, Theresa E. Victor, played several roles in the* Star Trek *movies, including a bridge voice in* Star Trek II, *the* Enterprise *computer voice in* Star Trek III, *and an usher in the Federation Council in* Star Trek IV.

spoon head. Racist slang term used by some Bajorans to refer to Cardassians. ("Things Past" [DS9]).

spores, Omicron Ceti III. Symbiotic organism from planet Omicron Ceti III. These spores infested some of the Federation colonists on that planet in 2264. The spores thrived on **berthold rays**, offering the colonists protection from the otherwise-deadly radiation. The spores provided perfect health and extraordinary contentment to the host, but at the cost of intellectual stagnation. The *Enterprise* crew investigated the colony in 2267 and nearly all ship's personnel also became infected. Captain James Kirk discovered that strong negative or aggressive emotions could be used to drive the spores from their hosts, and used ultrasonic signals to create such irritation in his crew. ("This Side of Paradise" [TOS]). SEE: **Kalomi, Leila; Sandoval, Elias**.

sporocystian. Classification of **noncorporeal life**-forms native to another galaxy. Sporocystian life-forms are believed to exist at least partially in a **subspace** domain. Two sporocystian individuals from a group calling themselves the **Nacene** visited the Delta Quadrant of our galaxy a millennium ago. SEE: **Caretaker; Suspiria**. ("Cold Fire" [VGR])

Spot. Data's pet cat, Earth *Felis domesticus,* who lived with **Data** on the *Enterprise*-D. Spot was quite a gourmet, as **Data** created at least 221 different foods for her. ("Data's Day" [TNG]). A malfunction of the ship's replicator system resulting from an errant interface experiment in 2369 caused the ship's food slots to dispense cat food. ("A Fistful of Datas" [TNG]). SEE: **Subroutine C-47**. Commander Riker once agreed to care for Spot while Data was away at a conference for three days. Unfortunately, Spot did not care for Riker, and made her dislike evident. ("Timescape" [TNG]). In 2370, Geordi "borrowed" Spot in an attempt to see if he wanted to have his own cat. Geordi was less than satisfied with Spot's visit. Shortly after Spot's visit to Geordi's quarters, Data undertook to train his cat, also with less than satisfying results. While Spot's behavior continued unchanged, Geordi would note that Data's "training" was "coming along nicely." ("Force of Nature" [TNG]). The only person who Spot seemed to like was Lieutenant Barclay, who thought Spot was "a sweet little kitty." In 2370, Spot became pregnant. At the time, the father was undetermined, but Data intended to run a full DNA analysis of all 12 male cats on the ship to identify the sire. Spot also fell victim to the influence of **Barclay's Protomorphosis Syndrome**, apparently during the birth of her kittens. Spot devolved into a large **iguana**, but her kittens were unaffected. This led Data to devise a cure for the syndrome. ("Genesis" [TNG]). Spot survived the crash-landing of the *Enterprise*-D Saucer Module in 2371. Upon discovering Spot was unharmed, Data, under the influence of Soong's **emotion chip**, shed his first tears of joy. *(Star Trek Generations). Spot first appeared in "Data's Day," but didn't actually get a name until "In Theory" (TNG). In "Data's Day," Spot was a male Somali cat, but in later appearances, Data's friend somehow became a female orange tabby. We speculate that Spot may be a shape-shifter or an unfortunate victim of a transporter malfunction.*

spread pattern delta nine four. Experimental photon-torpedo firing pattern that was tested aboard the *Enterprise*-D in 2370. The test had less than spectacular results. ("Genesis" [TNG]).

spring wine. Intoxicating Bajoran beverage. ("Return to Grace" [DS9]).

springball. Sport played on **Bajor**. Kira Nerys played springball with her brothers while at the **Singha refugee camp** during the Cardassian occupation. While on Deep Space 9, Kira had Chief O'Brien create a holographic springball program for her. **Vedek Bareil** was also fond of the sport. ("Shadowplay" [DS9], "Life Support" [DS9]). Springball is a full-contact sport, similar to Earth handball, played on a court with a back wall that is marked to indicate goals and foul lines. The floor of the court is marked with foul lines as well. The court also has two unmarked side walls, and the back of the court is sometimes composed of a transparent force field, allowing spectators to view the game. The game is played with two people, the object being to try to hit the ball with a gloved hand so that it hits a clearly marked oval on the far wall without hitting the foul zones. The players can body check each other to prevent their opponent from making a shot, but punching and kicking are not allowed. Protective helmets are often worn. ("For the Cause" [DS9]). *Anthony Fredrickson designed the springball court.*

"Squire of Gothos, The." *Original Series* episode #18. Written by Paul Schneider. Directed by Don McDougall. Stardate 2124.5. *First aired in 1967. An incredibly powerful alien life-form torments the* Enterprise *crew, but is found to be simply a small child, playing with his toys. Many fans have noted the similarity between Trelane and Q, speculating that Trelane and his parents may have been members of the Q Continuum, although this has not actually been established in an episode. Paul Schneider also wrote "Balance of Terror" (TOS).* GUEST CAST: William Campbell as **Trelane**; Richard Carlyle as **Jaeger**, **Lieutenant Karl**; Michael Barrier as **DeSalle**, **Lieutenant**; Venita Wolf as **Ross**, **Yeoman Teresa**; Barbara Babcock as Mother's voice; James Doohan as Father's voice; Gary Coombs as Kirk's stunt double. SEE: **Beta VI; Bonaparte, Napoleon; DeSalle, Lieutenant; Gothos; Jaeger, Lieutenant Karl; noncorporeal life; Quadrant 904; Ross, Yeoman Teresa; Trelane.**

Ssestar. (John Durbin). Leader of the **Selay** delegation to the **Parliament** conference of 2364. ("Lonely Among Us" [TNG]).

Stacius Trade Guild. Organization in which **Zibalian** trader **Kivas Fajo** was a member. ("The Most Toys" [TNG]).

Stadi, Lieutenant. (Alicia Coppola). Starfleet officer assigned to the *U.S.S. Voyager* as conn. Stadi was fatally injured on the bridge during the ship's violent passage to the Delta Quadrant in 2371. ("Caretaker" [VGR]).

Stakoron II. Planet in the Gamma Quadrant. Stakoron II contains rich deposits of mizainite ore. Quark was to visit the planet in 2369, during his brief tenure as **grand nagus,** to negotiate for mining rights, but found it was part of a ruse devised by **Rom** and **Krax** to kill him. ("The Nagus" [DS9]).

standard orbit. Normal orbit assumed by a Federation starship above a Class-M planet. *The term "standard orbit" was used as an ingenious means of allowing the captain to give a technical-sounding command when the ship entered orbit, without having to bore the viewer with tedious details of orbital inclination, apogee, perigee, and orbital period. It was at one point thought that standard orbit would be synchronous, allowing the ship to remain stationary over a single point on a planet's surface, but a visual-effects shot of the ship, motionless over the planet, would not have been dynamic, thereby lacking dramatic value. Moving the ship was, therefore, a conscious decision by the show's producers. Even when the ship was required to "hover," some slight movement was shown so that the image wouldn't be static.*

Star Station India. Starfleet facility. *Enterprise*-D was en route for Star Station India on an urgent mission to rendezvous with a Starfleet courier but was diverted by a distress call from the *Starship* **Lantree**. ("Unnatural Selection" [TNG]).

Star Trek Generations. Story by Rick Berman and Ronald D. Moore & Brannon Braga. Screenplay by Ronald D. Moore & Brannon Braga. Directed by David Carson. Stardate 48650.1. *Original theatrical release date: 1994.*

Captain Jean-Luc Picard and Captain James Kirk meet in a time nexus and combine forces against a scientist who is jeopardizing the lives of millions of people. This was the seventh Star Trek *theatrical movie, and the first featuring the cast of* Star Trek: The Next Generation. *It also saw the appearance of the* Starship Enterprise-*B, the crash of the* Enterprise-*D, and the death of legendary Captain James T. Kirk.* CAST: Patrick Stewart as **Picard, Jean-Luc**; Jonathan Frakes as **Riker, William T.**; Brent Spiner as **Data**; LeVar Burton as **La Forge, Geordi**; Michael Dorn as **Worf**; Gates McFadden as **Crusher, Dr. Beverly**; Marina Sirtis as **Troi, Deanna**; Malcolm McDowell as **Soran, Dr. Tolian**; James Doohan as **Scott, Montgomery**; Walter Koenig as **Chekov, Pavel A.**; William Shatner as **Kirk, James T.**; Alan Ruck as **Harriman, Captain John**; Jacqueline Kim as **Sulu, Demora**; Jenette Goldstein as Science officer; Thomas Kopache as Com officer; Glenn Morshower as Navigator; Tim Russ as Lieutenant; Tommy Hinkley as Journalist; John Putch as Journalist; Christine Jansen as Journalist; Michael Mack as **Hayes, Ensign**; Dendrie Taylor as **Farrell, Lieutenant**; Patti Yasutake as **Ogawa, Nurse Alyssa**; Granville Ames as Transporter chief; Henry Marshall as Security officer; Brittany Parkyn as Girl with teddy bear; Majel Barrett as Computer voice; Barbara March as **Lursa**; Gwynyth Walsh as **B'Etor**; Rif Hutton as Klingon guard; Brian Thompson as Klingon helm; Marcy Goldman as El-Aurian survivor; Jim Krestalude as El-Aurian survivor; Judy Levitt as El-Aurian survivor; Kristopher Logan as El-Aurian survivor; Gwen Van Dam as El-Aurian survivor; Kim Braden as **Picard, Marie**; Christopher James Miller as **Picard, René**; Matthew Collins as Picard's kid; Mimi Collins as Picard's kid; Thomas Alexander Dekker as Picard's kid; Madison Eginton as Picard's kid; Olivia Hack as Picard's kid; Randy Hall, Michael Haynes, John Nowak, Bernie Pock, Don Pulford, Eric Stabenau, Pat Tallman, stunts; Bud Davis as Stunt coordinator. SEE: **Amargosa Observatory; Amargosa; antimatter containment; Antonia; B'Etor; Borg; *Bozeman, U.S.S.*; Breen; Butler; champagne; Chekov, Pavel A.; cloaking device, Klingon; Data; drydock; *Du'cha;* El-Aurian; emotion chip; *Enterprise*-B, *U.S.S.*; *Enterprise*-D, *U.S.S.*; *Enterprise*; *Farragut, U.S.S.*; Farrell, Lieutenant; Forcas III; Guinan; Harriman, Captain John; *Hawking, Shuttlecraft*; Hayes, Ensign; holodeck and holosuite programs; Kirk, James T.; Klingon bird-of-prey; Ktarian eggs; *Lakul, S.S.*; Lursa; Martian Colonies; nexus; Nobel Prize; Ogawa, Alyssa; Picard's photo album; Picard, Jean-Luc; Picard, Marie; Picard, René; Picard, Robert; Pluto; Riker, William T.; *Robert Fox, S.S.*; saucer separation; Scott, Montgomery; shields; Soran, Dr. Tolian; Spot; Stellar Cartography; Sulu, Demora; Sulu, Hikaru; temporal flux; Trafalgar, Battle of; trilithium; Veridian III; Veridian IV; Veridian system; VISOR; Worf.**

Star Trek II (series). *A proposed weekly* Star Trek *television series that would have been produced in 1977 and would have depicted a second five-year mission of the* Enterprise *under the command of James Kirk. (Note that this is* not *the same production as the feature film* Star Trek II: The Wrath of Khan.*) The* Star Trek II *series would have been aired on a new network owned by Paramount Pictures (much as was later done for* Star Trek: Voyager*), but the series was canceled shortly before it went into production. New characters on this show would have included Navigator Ilia (who would have been played by Persis Khambatta), Science Officer Xon (who would have been played by David Gautreaux), and Executive Officer Decker (who was still uncast at the time the series was canceled). The first episode, a two-hour made-for-television movie script entitled "In Thy Image," was rewritten, eventually becoming* Star Trek: The Motion Picture. *"In Thy Image" was itself based on a story outline entitled "Robots' Return," written by Gene Roddenberry around 1972 for his proposed CBS series* Genesis II. *Other scripts written for the aborted* Star Trek II *series included "The Child" and "Devil's Due," both of which were later rewritten to become episodes of* Star Trek: The Next Generation. *Also known as* Star Trek: Phase II.

Star Trek II: The Wrath of Khan. Screenplay by Jack B. Sowards. Story by Harve Bennett and Jack B. Sowards. Directed by Nicholas Meyer. Stardate 8130.3. *Original theatrical release date: 1982. Spock is killed when genetic superman Khan escapes from imprisonment on Ceti Alpha V, commandeers the* Starship Reliant*, and uses the secret Project Genesis to win revenge on James Kirk. The story is a sequel to "Space Seed" (TOS).* CAST: William Shatner as **Kirk, James T.**; Leonard Nimoy as **Spock**; DeForest Kelley as **McCoy, Dr. Leonard H.**; James Doohan as **Scott, Montgomery**; Walter Koenig as **Chekov, Pavel A.**; George Takei as **Sulu, Hikaru**; Nichelle Nichols as **Uhura**; Bibi Besch as **Marcus, Dr. Carol**; Merritt Butrick as **Marcus, Dr. David**; Paul Winfield as **Terrell, Captain Clark**; Kirstie Alley as **Saavik**; Ricardo Montalban as **Khan**; Ike Eisenmann as **Preston, Peter**; John Vargas as Jedda; John Winston as **Kyle, Mr.**; Paul Kent as **Beach, Commander**; Nicholas Guest as Cadet; Russell Takaki as Madison; Kevin Sullivan as March; Joel Marstan as Crew chief; Teresa E. Victor as Bridge voice; Dianne Harper, David Ruprecht, Radio voices; Marcy Vosburgh as Computer voice; Judson Scott as **Joaquim**; Steve Blalock, Janet Brady, Jim Burk, Diane Carter, Tony Cecere, Ann Chatterton, Gary Combs, Gilbert Combs, Jim Connors, Bill Couch, Sr. Bill Couch, Jr., Eddy Donno, John Eskobar, Allan Graf, Chuck Hicks, Tommy J. Huff, Hubie Kerns, Jr., Paula Moody, Tom Morga, Beth Nufer, Mary Peters, Ernest Robinson, John Robotham, Kim Washington, Mike Washlake, George Wilbur, stunts. SEE: **Altair VI; Beach, Mr.; Ceti Alpha V; Ceti Alpha VI; Ceti eel; chambers coil; Chekov, Pavel A.; dynoscanner; escape pod; Gamma Hydra; Genesis Device; gravitic mine; hyperchannel; Joachim; Khan Noonien Singh; Kirk, James T.; Klingon battle cruiser; Klingon Neutral Zone; *Kobayashi Maru* scenario; *Kobayashi Maru*; *K't'inga*-class battle cruiser; Kyle, Mr.; Marcus, Dr. Carol; Marcus, Dr. David; McGivers, Marla; Mutara Nebula; Mutara Sector; photon torpedo; planetary classification system; preanimate matter; prefix code; Preston, Peter; Project Genesis; Regula I Space Laboratory; Regula; *Reliant*, *U.S.S.*; retinal scan; Retnax V; Romulan ale; Saavik; Spock; Starfleet Academy; Starfleet Corps of Engineers; Starfleet General Orders and Regulations; *Tale of Two Cities, A*; *targ*; Terrell, Captain Clark.**

Star Trek III: The Search for Spock. Written by Harve Bennett. Directed by Leonard Nimoy. Stardate 8210.3. *Original theatrical release date: 1984. Kirk jeopardizes his career by stealing the* Enterprise *in an attempt to rescue Spock's body and soul.* CAST: William Shatner as **Kirk, James T.**; Leonard Nimoy as **Spock**; DeForest Kelley as **McCoy, Dr. Leonard H.**; James Doohan as **Scott, Montgomery**; George Takei as **Sulu, Hikaru**; Walter Koenig as **Chekov, Pavel A.**; Nichelle Nichols as **Uhura**; Mark Lenard as **Sarek**; Merritt Butrick as **Marcus, Dr. David**; Dame Judith Anderson as **T'Lar**; Robin Curtis as **Saavik**; Christopher Lloyd as **Kruge, Commander**; Phil Morris as Trainee Foster; Scott McGinnis as "Mr. Adventure"; Robert Hooks as **Morrow, Admiral**; Carl Steven as **Spock** age 9; Vadia Potenza as **Spock** age 13; Stephen Manley as **Spock** age 15; Joe W. Davis as **Spock** age 25; Paul Sorensen as Captain of the merchant spaceship; Cathie Shirriff as **Valkris**; Stephen Liska as Torg; John Larroquette as **Maltz**; Dave Cadiente as Klingon sergeant; Bob Cummings as Gunner #1; Branscombe Richmond as Gunner #2; Jeanne Mori as Helm *U.S.S. Grissom*; Mario Marcelino as Communications *U.S.S. Grissom*; Allan Miller as Alien in the bar; Sharon Thomas as Waitress in the bar; Conroy Gedeon as Civilian agent; James B. Sikking as **Styles, Captain**; Miguel Ferrer as First Officer of the *Excelsior*; Katherine Blum as Vulcan child; Gary Faga as Prison guard #1; Douglas Alan Shanklin as Prison guard #2; Grace Lee Whitney as Woman in cafeteria; Robin Kellick, Kimberly L. Ryusaki, Phil Weyland, Steve Blalock, stand-ins; Frank Welker as Spock screams (voice); Teresa E. Victor as *Enterprise* computer (voice); Harve Bennett as Flight recorder (voice); Judi Durand as Spacedock controller (voice); Frank Force as Elevator voice; The Loop Group as Background voices; John Meier as Stunt double for William Shatner; Al Jones as Stunt double for Christopher Lloyd; Steve Blalock, David Burton, Phil Chong, Eddy Donno, Kenny Endoso, Jon Halty, Chuck Hicks, Jeff Jensen, Don Charles McGovern, Tom Morga, Alan Oliney, Chuck Picerni, Jr., Danny Rogers, Frank James Sparks, David Zellitti, stunts; Ron Stein, R.A. Rondell, Stunt coordinators. SEE: **Altair water; cloaking device,**

Klingon; destruct sequence; *d'k tahg*; *Enterprise*, *U.S.S.*; Esteban, Captain J. T.; *Excelsior*, *U.S.S.*; *fal-tor-pan*; flight recorder; Genesis Planet; "Great Experiment, The"; *Grissom*, *U.S.S.*; *katra*; *kellicam*; Kirk, James T.; Klingon bird-of-prey; Kruge, Commander; lexorin; Maltz; Marcus, Dr. David; *Merchantman*; "Miracle Worker"; Morrow, Admiral; Mutara Sector; *Pon farr*; Project Genesis; protomatter; *Qapla'*; Saavik; Sarek; Seleya, Mount; Skon; *so'wl'chu'*; Solkar; Spacedock; Spock; Styles, Captain; T'Lar; terminium; "Tiny"; transwarp; Uhura; Valkris; warp factor.

Star Trek IV: The Voyage Home. Story by Leonard Nimoy and Harve Bennett. Screenplay by Steve Meerson & Peter Krikes and Harve Bennett & Nicholas Meyer. Directed by Leonard Nimoy. Stardate 8390. *Original theatrical release date: 1986. Kirk and company voyage back in time to San Francisco in 1986 to bring two humpback whales back to the future.* CAST: William Shatner as **Kirk, James T.**; Leonard Nimoy as **Spock**; DeForest Kelley as **McCoy, Dr. Leonard H.**; James Doohan as **Scott, Montgomery**; George Takei as **Sulu, Hikaru**; Walter Koenig as **Chekov, Pavel A.**; Nichelle Nichols as **Uhura**; Jane Wyatt as **Amanda**; Catherine Hicks as **Taylor, Dr. Gillian**; Mark Lenard as **Sarek**; Robin Curtis as **Saavik, Lt.**; Robert Ellenstein as **Federation president**; John Schuck as Klingon ambassador; Brock Peters as **Cartwright, Admiral**; Michael Snyder as Starfleet communications officer; Michael Berryman as Starfleet display officer; Mike Brislane as *Saratoga* science officer; Jane Wiedlin as Alien communications officer; Vijay Amritraj as Starship captain; Nick Ramus as *Saratoga* helmsman; Thaddeus Golas as Controller #1; Martin Pistone as Controller #2; Scott DeVenney as **Briggs, Bob**; Viola Stimpson as Lady in tour; Phil Rubenstein as 1st garbageman; John Miranda as 2nd garbageman; Joe Knowland as Antique store owner; Bob Sarlatte as Waiter; Everett Lee as Cafe owner; Richard Harder as Joe; Alex Henteloff as **Nichols, Dr.**; Tony Edwards as Pilot; Eve Smith as Elderly patient; Tom Mustin as Intern #1; Greg Karas as Intern #2; Raymond Singer as Young doctor; David Ellenstein as Doctor #1; Judy Levitt as Doctor #2; Teresa E. Victor as Usher; James Menges as Jogger; Kirk Thatcher as Punk on bus; Jeff Lester as FBI agent; Joe Lando as Shore patrolman; Newell Tarrant as CDO; Mike Timoney as Electronic technician; Jeffrey Martin as Electronic technician; 1st Sgt. Joseph Naradzay, USMC as Marine sergeant; 1st Lt. Donald W. Zautcke, USMC as Marine lieutenant; R. A. Rondell as Stunt coordinator; John Meier as Stunt double for William Shatner; Gregory Barnett as Stunt double for Leonard Nimoy; Steve M. Davidson, Clifford T. Fleming, Eddie Hice, Bennie E. Moore, Jr., Charles Picerni, Jr., Sharon Schaffer, Spike Silver, stunts. SEE: **Alameda; Amanda; Ambassador, Klingon; Andorians; Bering Sea; *Bounty*, *H.M.S.*; Briggs, Bob; Cartwright, Admiral; Cetacean Institute; *Challenger*; Chapel, Christine; Chekov, Pavel A.; dilithium; Earth; *Enterprise*, *U.S.S.* (aircraft carrier); *Enterprise*-A, *U.S.S.*; Federation Council; Federation president; George and Gracie; Huey 204; humpback whale; "I Hate You"; Kiri-kin-tha's First Law of Metaphysics; Kirk, James T.; Macintosh; *Megaptera Novaeangliae*; Mercy Hospital; Nichols, Dr.; Plexicorp; Probe, the; Rand, Janice; Robbins, Harold; Rogerson, Commander; Saavik; San Francisco; *Saratoga*, *U.S.S.*; Sarek; slingshot effect; Spock; Sulu, Hikaru; Susann, Jacqueline; Taylor, Dr. Gillian; Tellarites; T'plana-Hath; transparent aluminum; United Federation of Planets; whale song; yominium sulfide; *Yorktown*, *U.S.S.***

Star Trek V: The Final Frontier. Screenplay by David Loughery. Story by William Shatner, Harve Bennett, David Loughery. Directed by William Shatner. Stardate 8454.1. *Original theatrical release date: 1989. Spock's half-brother, Sybok, hijacks the* Enterprise*-A to pursue his visions of God at the center of the galaxy.* CAST: William Shatner as **Kirk, James T.**; Leonard Nimoy as **Spock**; DeForest Kelley as **McCoy, Dr. Leonard H.**; James Doohan as **Scott, Montgomery**; Walter Koenig as **Chekov, Pavel A.**; Nichelle Nichols as **Uhura**; George Takei as **Sulu, Hikaru**; David Warner as **Talbot, St. John**; Laurence Luckinbill as **Sybok**; Charles Cooper as **Korrd**; Cynthia Gouw as **Dar, Caithlin**; Todd Bryant as **Klaa, Captain**; Spice Williams as **Vixis**; Rex Holman as **J'Onn**; George Murdock as "God"; Jonathan Simpson as Young Sarek; Beverly Hart as High priestess; Steve Susskind as Pitchman; Harve Bennett as **Bennett, Admiral Robert**; Cynthia Blaise as **Amanda**; Bill Quinn as **McCoy, David**; Melanie Shatner as Yeoman; Glenn R. Wilder as Stunt coordinator; Don Pulford as Stunt double for William Shatner; Greg Barnett as Stunt double for Leonard Nimoy; Ken Bates as high fall stunts; David Burton, David Richard Ellis, Linda Fetters, James M. Halty, Eddie Hice, Thomas Huff, Joyce L. McNeal, Tom Morga, Frank Orsatti, Air Randell, Bruce Wayne Randall, R.A. Rondell, Tom Wetterman, Scott Wilder, Dick Ziker, stunts. SEE: **Amanda; beans; Bennett, Admiral Robert; *Copernicus*; Dar, Caithlin; Eden; El Capitan; *Enterprise*-A, *U.S.S.*; *Galileo* 5; Great Barrier, the; J'Onn; Kirk, James T.; Klaa, Captain; Korrd, General; Masefield, John; McCoy, David; McCoy, Leonard H.; "Moon Over Rigel VII"; "Moon's a Window to Heaven, The"; Nimbus III; Paradise City; *Pioneer 10*; *Qui'Tu*; Sarek; *Sha Ka Ree*; Spock; Sybok; Talbot, St. John; Vixis; *Vorta Vor*; Vulcan lute; Yosemite National Park.**

Star Trek VI: The Undiscovered Country. Story by Leonard Nimoy and Lawrence Konner & Mark Rosenthal. Screenplay by Nicholas Meyer & Denny Martin Flinn. Directed by Nicholas Meyer. Stardate 9521.6. *Original theatrical release date: 1991. An historic Klingon peace initiative is nearly thwarted when Klingon Chancellor Gorkon is assassinated, and Kirk and McCoy are wrongly convicted of his murder. This was intended as the last mission of the original* Enterprise *crew from the first* Star Trek *series, although individual cast members have since appeared in other films and episodes.* Star Trek VI *was released shortly after the death of* Star Trek *creator Gene Roddenberry, and the film opened with a simple title card reading: "Gene Roddenberry, 1921-1991."* CAST: William Shatner as **Kirk, James T.**; Leonard Nimoy as **Spock**; DeForest Kelley as **McCoy, Dr. Leonard H.**; James Doohan as **Scott, Montgomery**; Walter Koenig as **Chekov, Pavel A.**; Nichelle Nichols as **Uhura**; George Takei as **Sulu, Hikaru**; Kim Cattrall as **Valeris, Lt.**; Mark Lenard as **Sarek**; Grace Lee Whitney as **Rand, Janice**; Brock Peters as **Cartwright, Admiral**; Leon Russom as Chief In Command; Kurtwood Smith as **Federation president**; Christopher Plummer as **Chang, General**; Rosana DeSoto as **Azetbur**; David Warner as **Gorkon, Chancellor**; John Schuck as Klingon ambassador; Michael Dorn as Klingon defense attorney; Paul Rossilli as **Kerla, Brigadier**; Robert Easton as Klingon judge; Clifford Shegog as Klingon officer; W. Morgan Sheppard as Klingon commander; Brett Porter as Stec, General; Jeremy Roberts as *Excelsior* officer; Michael Bofshever as *Excelsior* engineer; Angelo Tiffe as *Excelsior* navigator; Boris Lee Krutonog as Lojur, Helmsman; Christian Slater as *Excelsior* communications officer; Iman as **Martia**; Tom Morga as Brute; Todd Bryant as Klingon translator; John Bloom as Behemoth alien; Jim Boeke as First Klingon general; Carlos Cestero as Munitions man; Edward Clements as Young crewman; Katie Jane Johnston as Martia as a child; Couglas Engalla as Prisoner at Rura Penthe; Matthias Hues as Second Klingon general; Darryl Henriques as **Nanclus**; David Orange as Sleepy Klingon; Judy Levitt as Military Aide; Shakti as ADC; Michael Snyder as **Dax**; Donald R. Pike as Stunt coordinator; Ed Anders, B.J. Baxley, Jeff Bornstein, Eddie Braun, Charlie Brewer, Hal Burton, Dorothy Ching-Davis, Brett Davidson, Marie Doest, Joe Farago, Sandy Free, Joy Hooper, Tom Huff, Jeff Imada, Jeffrey S. Jensen, Robert King, Scott Leva, Alan Marcus, Cole McKay, Eric Norris, Noon Orsatti, Deeana Pampena, Donald R. Pike, Gary T. Pike, Donald B. Pulford, Joycelyn Robinson, Danny Rogers, Don Ruffin, Spike Silver, Erik Stavenau, stunts. SEE: **Ambassador, Klingon; Azetbur; Beta Quadrant; bird-of-prey, Klingon; Burke, Yeoman; Camp Khitomer; Cartwright, Admiral; chameloid; chancellor; Chang, General; cloaking device, Klingon; Dax; dilithium; Earth; *Enterprise*-A, *U.S.S.*; *Excelsior*, *U.S.S.*; Federation president; Gorkon, Chancellor; gravitational unit; gravity boots; *Hamlet;* Kerla, Brigadier; Khitomer; Khitomer Accords; Kirk, James T.; Klaa, Captain; Klingon Empire; Klingon Homeworld; Klingons; Klingon Neutral Zone; *Kronos One*; Kronos; magnetic boots; Marcus, Dr. David; Martia; McCoy, Dr. Leonard H.; Morska; Nanclus; neutron radiation; Nixon, Richard M.; Operation Retrieve;**

Paris; plasma; Praxis; Qo'noS; Rand, Janice; Romulan ale; Rura Penthe; Samno, Yeoman; Sarek; Scott, Montgomery; Shakespeare, William; Spock; subspace phenomena; Sulu, Hikaru; *targ*; Tiberian bats; torpedo bay; "undiscovered country, the"; Uhura; United Federation of Planets; Valeris; Valtane, Dmitri; West, Colonel; Worf, Colonel.

Star Trek: Deep Space Nine (DS9). *Originally airing in 1993, the syndicated series about a group of Starfleet officers and Bajoran nationals on the former Cardassian space station,* **Deep Space 9**, *commanded by* **Benjamin Sisko**. *Created by Rick Berman and Michael Piller.* CAST: Avery Brooks as **Sisko, Benjamin**; René Auberjonois as **Odo**; Alexander Siddig as **Bashir, Dr. Julian**; Terry Farrell as **Dax, Jadzia**; Cirroc Lofton as **Sisko, Jake**; Colm Meaney as **O'Brien, Miles**; Armin Shimerman as **Quark**; Nana Visitor as **Kira Nerys**.

Star Trek: First Contact. Screenplay by Brannon Braga & Ronald D. Moore. Story by Rick Berman & Brannon Braga & Ronald D. Moore. Directed by Jonathan Frakes. Stardate 50893.5. *Original theatrical release date: 1996. The Borg travel into Earth's past to prevent Zefram Cochrane from inventing warp drive and making first contact with the Vulcans. This was the eighth* Star Trek *theatrical movie and the second to feature characters from* Star Trek: The Next Generation. *The movie marked the first appearance of the* Sovereign-*class* U.S.S. Enterprise-*E*. CAST: Patrick Stewart as **Picard**, **Jean-Luc**; Jonathan Frakes as **Riker**, **William T.**; Brent Spiner as **Data**; LeVar Burton as **La Forge**, **Geordi**; Michael Dorn as **Worf**; Gates McFadden as **Crusher**, **Beverly**; Marina Sirtis as **Troi**, **Deanna**; Alfre Woodard as **Lily**; James Cromwell as **Cochran**, **Zefram**; Alice Krige as **Borg queen**; Michael Horton as Security officer; Neal McDonough as **Hawk**, **Lieutenant**; Marnie McPhail as Eiger; Robert Picardo as **Emergency Medical Hologram**; Dwight Schultz as **Barclay**, **Reginald**; Adam Scott as *Defiant* conn officer; Jack Shearer as **Hayes, Admiral**; Eric Steinberg as **Porter**; Scott Strozier as Security officer; Patti Yasutake as **Ogawa, Nurse Alyssa**; Victor Bevine as Guard; David Cowgill as Guard; Scott Haven as Guard; Annette Helde as Guard; C.J. Bau as Bartender; Hillary Hayes as **Ruby**; Julie Morgan as Singer in nightclub; Ronald R. Rondell as Henchman; Don Stark as **Nicky the Nose**; Cully Fredricksen as Vulcan; Tamara Lee Krinsky as Townsperson; Don Fischer, Andrew Palmer, Robert L. Zachar, J. R. Horsting, Jon David Weigand, Heinrich James, Dan Woren, Borg; Ronald R. Rondell as Stunt coordinator; Kenny Alexander, Janet Brady, Chic Daniel, Eddy Donno, Tony Donno, Kenny Endoso, Christian Fletcher, Frankie Garbutt, Andy Gill, Gary Guercio, Jim Halty, Rosine Ace Hatem, Billy Hank Hooker, Buddy Joe Hooker, Maria Kelly, Jamie Keyser, Kim Robert Koscki, Joyce McNeal, Dustin Meier, Johnny C. Meier, Rita Minor, Jimmy Nickerson, John Nowak, Manny Perry, Steve Picerni, Danny Rogers, Jimmy Romano, Pat Romano, Peggy Lynn Ross, John Rottger, Craig Shuggart, Brian J. Williams, stunts; Joey Anaya, Jr., Billy Burton, Jr., Steve DeRelian, Andy Epper, Gary Epper, Tom Harper, Wayne King, Jr., Bob McGovern, Monty Rex Perlin, Tom Poster, stunt Borg. SEE: **Ahab, Captain; *Akira*-class starship; antiproton; Armstrong, Lake; autodestruct; Barclay, Reginald; Basic Warp Drive; Berlioz, Hector; Bizet, Georges; Borg queen; Borg ship; Borg sphere; Borg; *Bozeman, U.S.S.*; *Budapest, U.S.S.;* chronometric particles; Cochrane, Zefram; Data; Deep Space 5; *Defiant, U.S.S.*; dollar; Dyson; Earth; Eastern Coalition; ECON; Eddie; Eiger; Emergency Medical Hologram; emotion chip; *Endeavor, U.S.S.*; *Enterprise*-E, *U.S.S.*; first contact; fractal encryption; Gravett Island; Hawk, Lieutenant; Hayes, Admiral; Hill, Dixon; holodeck and holosuite programs: Dixon Hill; holodeck; hydroponics bay; interplexing beacon; Ivor Prime; La Forge, Geordi; Locutus of Borg; "Magic Carpet Ride"; *mek'leth*; *Moby-Dick*; Montana; moon; nanopolymer; navigational deflector; neuroprocessor; New Berlin; Nicki the Nose; *Norway*-class starship; ocular implant; Ogawa, Nurse Alyssa; *Phoenix*; Picard, Jean-Luc; plasma coolant; Porter, Paul; postatomic horror; quantum torpedoes; Romulan Neutral Zone; Ruby; security access code; Sloane, Lily; Smithsonian Institution; *Sovereign*-class starship; *Steamrunner*-class starship; Stellar Cartography; temporal vortex; tequila; theta radiation; *Thunderchild, U.S.S.;* Titan V rocket; titanium; Tycho City; Typhon sector; United Federation of Planets; VISOR; Vulcan ship; Vulcans; whiskey; Worf; World War III; *Yeager, U.S.S.;* Zefram Cochrane High School; zero-gravity combat training.**

Star Trek: The Motion Picture. Screenplay by Harold Livingston. Story by Alan Dean Foster. Directed by Robert Wise. Stardate 7412.6. *Original theatrical release date: 1979. Kirk reunites his original crew to save Earth from a powerful machine life-form called V'Ger.* CAST: William Shatner as **Kirk, James T.**; Leonard Nimoy as **Spock**; DeForest Kelley as **McCoy, Dr. Leonard H.**; James Doohan as **Scott, Montgomery**; George Takei as **Sulu, Hikaru**; Majel Barrett as **Chapel, Christine**; Walter Koenig as **Chekov, Pavel A.**; Nichelle Nichols as **Uhura**; Persis Khambatta as **Ilia**; Stephen Collins as **Decker, Willard**; Grace Lee Whitney as **Rand, Janice**; Marc Lenard as Klingon captain; Billy Van Zandt as Alien boy; Roger Aaron Brown as Episilon technician; Gary Faga as Airlock technician; David Gautreaux as **Branch, Commander**; John D. Gowans as Assistant to Rand; Howard Itzkowitz as Cargo deck ensign; Jon Rashad Kamal as **Sonak, Commander**; Marcy Lafferty as **DiFalco, Chief**; Michele Ameen Billy as Lieutenant; Terrence O'Connor as Ross, Chief; Michael Rougas as **Cleary**; Susan J. Sullivan as Woman; Ralph Brannen, Ralph Byers, Paula Crist, Iva Lane, Franklyn Seales, Momo Yashima, crew members; Jimmie Booth, Joel Kramer, Bill McTosh, Dave Moordigian, Tom Morga, Tony Rocco, Joel Schultz, Craig Thomas, Kingon crewman; Edna Glover, Norman Stuart, Paul Weber, **Vulcan Masters**; Joshua Gellegos as Security officer; Leslie C. Howard as Yeoman; Sayra Hummel, Junero Jennings, Technical assistant; Robert Bralver, William Couch, Keith L. Jensen, John Hugh McKnight, stunts. SEE: **AU; air tram; *Amar, I.K.S.*; Branch, Commander; *Columbia, U.S.S.*; carbon units; center seat; Chapel, Christine; Chekov, Pavel A.; Cleary; Creator; Decker, Willard; Delta IV; Deltans; DiFalco, Chief; drydock; *Enterprise, S.S.; Enterprise, Space Shuttle; Enterprise, U.S.S.*; Epsilon IX monitoring station; *I.K.S.*; Ilia; intermix formula; Jupiter; Kirk, James T.; *Kolinahr*; linguacode; McCoy, Leonard H.; maneuvering thrusters; NASA; Nogura, Admiral; Oath of Celibacy; orbital office complex; Probert, Commodore; Rand, Janice; rec deck; *Revere, U.S.S.*; San Francisco Yards; shuttle, Vulcan; Sonak, Commander; sonic shower; Spock; Starfleet Headquarters; thruster suit; travel pod; turboshaft; V'Ger; *Voyager VI*; Vulcan Master; warp drive; Work Bee; wormhole.**

Star Trek: The Next Generation (TNG). *Produced in 1987-1994, the made-for-syndication story of the* **Starship Enterprise-*D*** *under the command of Captain* **Jean-Luc Picard**. *The series ran for seven seasons, totalling 178 episodes. Following the conclusion of the series, the feature films* Star Trek Generations *and* Star Trek: First Contact *continued the adventures of these characters. Created by Gene Roddenberry.* CAST: Patrick Stewart as **Picard**, **Jean-Luc**; Jonathan Frakes as **Riker**, **William T.**; Brent Spiner as **Data**; LeVar Burton as **La Forge**, **Geordi**; Michael Dorn as **Worf**; Gates McFadden as **Crusher**, **Dr. Beverly**; Marina Sirtis as **Troi**, **Deanna**; Wil Wheaton as **Crusher, Wesley**; Denise Crosby as **Yar, Natasha**.

Star Trek: The Original Series (TOS). *The classic adventures of the first* **Starship Enterprise** *under the command of Captain* **James T. Kirk**. *The original* Star Trek *was created by Gene Roddenberry and ran for only three seasons, totaling 79 episodes that first aired on the NBC-TV network from 1966 to 1969.* Star Trek *became a pop culture icon when, instead of vanishing after its 1969 cancellation, it experienced a dramatic rebirth in syndication, becoming more popular than ever, spawning the* Star Trek *feature films and spinoff series.* CAST: William Shatner as **Kirk, James T.**; Leonard Nimoy as **Spock**; DeForest Kelley as **McCoy, Dr. Leonard H.**; James Doohan as **Scott, Montgomery**; George Takei as **Sulu, Hikaru**; Walter Koenig as **Chekov, Pavel A.**; Nichelle Nichols as **Uhura**; Majel Barrett as **Chapel, Christine**; Grace Lee Whitney as **Rand, Janice**.

Star Trek: Voyager (VGR). *Premiering in 1995 shortly after the end of* Star Trek: The Next Generation*,* Star Trek: Voyager *aired on the United Paramount Network and chronicled the adventures of Captain* ***Kathryn Janeway*** *and her crew aboard the* **Starship Voyager***, lost in the distant* ***Delta Quadrant****. Created by Rick Berman, Michael Piller, and Jeri Taylor.* CAST: Kate Mulgrew as **Janeway, Kathryn**; Robert Beltran as **Chakotay**; Roxann Biggs as **Torres, B'Elanna**; Jennifer Lien as **Kes**; Robert Duncan McNeill as **Paris, Thomas**; Ethan Phillips as **Neelix**; Robert Picardo as **Emergency Medical Hologram**; Tim Russ as **Tuvok**; Garrett Wang as **Kim, Harry**.

starbase. Any one of over five hundred command, scientific, strategic, service, and supply posts operated by the Federation **Starfleet**, located through-out Federation space and beyond. Many starbases are located on planetary surfaces, while others are space stations. SEE: **Deep Space 9**.

Starbase 2. Starfleet facility. Spock suggested Dr. Janice Lester should be taken to Starbase 2 for diagnosis of her medical condition, instead of to the Benecia Colony. ("Turnabout Intruder" [TOS]).

Starbase 4. Site where the *Enterprise* dropped off the children from the **Starnes Expedition** to planet **Triacus** in 2268. ("And the Children Shall Lead" [TOS]). A shuttlecraft was stolen by **Lokai** from Starbase 4 in 2268, two weeks before being recovered by the *Enterprise.* ("Let That Be Your Last Battlefield" [TOS]).

Starbase 6. Facility where the *U.S.S. Enterprise* crew was scheduled for rest and relaxation in 2268. Their vacation was cut short by an emergency call from Starfleet Command to divert to **Sector 39J** and investigate the disappearance of the *Starship* ***Intrepid****.* ("The Immunity Syndrome" [TOS]).

Starbase 9. The *Enterprise* was en route to Starbase 9 for resupply in 2267 when near-collision with a **black star** of high gravitational attraction propelled the ship into a time warp that sent the ship back to the year 1969. ("Tomorrow is Yesterday" [TOS]). Closest base to planet **Pyris VII**, which the *Enterprise* visited in 2267. ("Catspaw" [TOS]). SEE: **Korob; Sylvia.**

Starbase 10. Destination of the *Enterprise* after leaving **Deneva** in 2267. ("Operation: Annihilate!" [TOS]). **Commodore Stocker** was to assume command of Starbase 10 in 2267. ("The Deadly Years" [TOS]).

Starbase 11. Planetside facility. Commanded by **Commodore Stone** in 2267 when this base was the site of Kirk's court-martial for the death of **Commander Ben Finney**. ("Court Martial" [TOS]). The *Enterprise* later returned to Starbase 11, then under the command of **José Mendez**, when Spock abducted Captain **Christopher Pike** to live among the **Talosians**. ("The Menagerie, Parts I and II" [TOS]). *The beautiful matte painting of Starbase 11 in "Court Martial" was created by Albert Whitlock, Jr.*

Starbase 12. Command post in the Gamma 400 star system and where Kirk set course with the sleeper ship, ***S.S. Botany Bay***, in tow. ("Space Seed" [TOS]). It was the closest starbase to planet **Pollux IV**, which the *Enterprise* visited in 2267. ("Who Mourns for Adonais?" [TOS]). The base was evacuated for two days in late 2364, apparently because key Starfleet officials were under the control of the extragalactic alien intelligence that attempted to infiltrate Starfleet Command in that year. ("Conspiracy" [TNG]). The *Enterprise*-D was scheduled for a week's worth of maintenance overhaul there, following her mission on **Gemaris V** in 2366. ("Captain's Holiday" [TNG]). Starbase 12 was commanded by **Admiral Uttan Narsu** back in 2167, at the time the ***U.S.S. Essex*** was lost at planet **Mab-Bu VI**. ("Power Play" [TNG]).

Starbase 14. Facility that sent a message to the *Enterprise*-D in 2364 concerning the **Anchilles fever** outbreak on planet **Styris IV**. ("Code of Honor" [TNG]).

Starbase 23. Federation starbase, located very close to the Romulan Neutral Zone. Following her temporary removal from duty in 2369, Dr. Beverly Crusher was scheduled to arrive by shuttlecraft at Starbase 23. From there, she planned to take a transport to Earth. ("Suspicions" [TNG]). (In the anti-time reality created by the Q Continuum, Captain Picard sent word to Starbase 23 to check their personnel for the effects of **temporal reversion**.) ("All Good Things..." [TNG]).

Starbase 24. Starfleet facility near **Khitomer**. Young Worf's nursemaid, **Kahlest,** was taken there for treatment of her injuries following her rescue from Khitomer in 2346. ("Sins of the Father" [TNG], "Redemption, Part I" [TNG]).

Starbase 27. Facility to which Kirk was ordered to transport the surviving colonists from planet **Omicron Ceti III** in 2267. ("This Side of Paradise"[TOS]).

Starbase 36. The *Enterprise*-D was scheduled to stop at Starbase 36 in late 2367. Dr. Beverly Crusher suggested that Commander La Forge have his VISOR checked for malfunctions during the stopover there. ("The Mind's Eye" [TNG]).

Starbase 39-Sierra. Facility approximately 5 days' travel from the **Romulan Neutral Zone**. ("The Neutral Zone" [TNG]).

Starbase 41. **Arjin** traveled from Starbase 41 to station Deep Space 9 in order to meet his **field docent**, Jadzia Dax, in 2370.

He had met Dr. Julian Bashir on the transport from Starbase 41. ("Playing God" [DS9]).

Starbase 47. (In an alternate **quantum reality** visited by Worf in 2370, Starbase 47 was the object of covert surveillance by the Cardassians, who had reprogrammed the **Argus Array** to observe the starbase, as well as other Federation installations.) ("Parallels" [TNG]).

Starbase 63. Worf and Dax visited Starbase 63 just prior to stardate 50416. ("The Darkness and the Light" [DS9]).

Starbase 67. Counselor Troi and Commander La Forge were ordered by the **Ktarians** to travel to Starbase 67 to distribute the addictive **Ktarian game** to starships docked there. ("The Game" [TNG]).

Starbase 73. Facility at which the *Enterprise*-D received mission orders to investigate a distress signal detected from the **Ficus Sector**. Starbase 73 was commanded by **Admiral Moore**. ("Up the Long Ladder" [TNG]). **Worf** delivered his son, **Alexander Rozhenko**, to Starbase 73 in 2367. Worf's adoptive parents met them there, having agreed to accept custody of Alexander after the death of K'Ehleyr. ("Reunion" [TNG]).

Starbase 74. Massive orbital facility at planet Tarsas III. The *Enterprise*-D underwent a computer-systems upgrade there in 2364, although the operation was interrupted when a group of **Bynar** technicians attempted to hijack the ship to save their planet. Starbase 74 was commanded by **Commander Orfil Quinteros**. ("11001001" [TNG]). *Starbase 74 miniature shots were a partial re-use of some visual-effects elements originally shot for* Star Trek III *by Industrial Light and Magic. However, it's been pointed out that Starbase 74 must be a substantially larger structure than Spacedock as seen in* Star Trek III, *since the* Galaxy-*class* Enterprise-*D is a much larger ship than the original* Constitution-*class vessel. The shot of the* Enterprise-*D actually docked inside the station was a matte painting designed by Andy Probert.*

Starbase 82. Site where the *Enterprise*-D delivered a **Ktarian** vessel into Starfleet custody in 2368. ("The Game" [TNG]).

Starbase 83. The *Enterprise*-D traveled to Starbase 83 when Q returned the ship to Federation space after first contact with the **Borg**. ("Q Who?" [TNG]).

Starbase 84. Location where the *Enterprise*-D acquired a replacement warp core that had been infested by interphasic organisms. The core had been manufactured on planet **Thanatos VII,** where the **interphasic organisms** were attracted to the new interphasic-fusion manufacturing process. ("Phantasms" [TNG]). *The Starbase 84 miniature was a re-use of the Spacedock, originally created for* Star Trek III *by Industrial Light and Magic.*

Starbase 87. Intended destination of the *Enterprise*-D following its departure from **Boraal II**. ("Homeward" [TNG]).

Starbase 97. Starfleet facility commanded by Admiral Mitchell. Commander Calvin Hutchinson served for some time there, prior to his assignment to **Arkaria Base.** ("Starship Mine" [TNG]).

Starbase 103. Facility located a short distance from planet **Minos**. After ordering a saucer separation maneuver at Minos, Geordi La Forge instructed **Engineer Logan** to proceed to Starbase 103. ("The Arsenal of Freedom" [TNG]). *Of course, even if Starbase 103 was only a few light-years from Minos, it's unclear as to what purpose there might have been in heading toward the base, since the saucer section had no warp-drive capability.*

Starbase 105. Starfleet facility. (In the alternate history created when the ***Enterprise*-C** vanished from its "proper" time in 2344, Starbase 105 was a possible destination to which the *Enterprise*-C could have been escorted.) ("Yesterday's *Enterprise*" [TNG]).

Starbase 117. Site to which the *Enterprise*-D sent two members of the **Ferengi Trade Mission**, following their part in an accident that befell Kriosian **Ambassador Briam** in 2368. ("The Perfect Mate" [TNG]).

Starbase 118. Facility where the *Enterprise*-D picked up several new crew members in 2369. ("A Fistful of Datas" [TNG]).

Starbase 123. Starfleet facility that detected two *D'deridex*-class Romulan warbirds on an intercept course with **Tin Man** just prior to contact with that life-form in 2366. ("Tin Man" [TNG]).

Starbase 129. (In an alternate **quantum reality** visited by Worf in 2370, the *Enterprise*-D set course for Starbase 129 following significant damage to the secondary plasma conduits caused by an attacking Cardassian vessel.) ("Parallels" [TNG]).

Starbase 133. Site where the *Enterprise*-D docked in early 2367 for scheduled crew rotation. **Dr. Dalen Quaice** was posted at Starbase 133 prior to his retirement to his homeworld of Kenda II. ("Remember Me" [TNG]). The destination of the *Enterprise*-D after its mission at planet **Delta Rana IV**. ("The Survivors" [TNG]).

Starbase 137. During his sophomore year at the academy, Benjamin Sisko spent a field-study assignment on Starbase 137. ("The Ascent" [DS9]).

Starbase 152. The *Enterprise*-D traveled to Starbase 152 for inspection and repairs following contact with **Tin Man** in 2366. The *Enterprise*-D had been seriously damaged in that encounter. ("Tin Man" [TNG]).

Starbase 153. Facility from which special Federation Emissary **K'Ehleyr** was launched, inside of a modified class-8 probe, for a critical rendezvous with the *Enterprise*-D in 2365. ("The Emissary" [TNG]).

Starbase 157. Federation starbase that received a distress signal from the ***U.S.S. Lalo*** after it suffered an attack from a **Borg** vessel in 2366. ("The Best of Both Worlds, Part I" [TNG]).

Starbase 173. Space station facility located in Sector 23, near the **Romulan Neutral Zone**. Site of legal proceedings establishing the sentience of the android **Data**. Captain **Phillipa Louvois** served on Starbase 173. ("The Measure of a Man" [TNG]). Also at Starbase 173, engineering officer **Ensign Sonya Gomez** was among several new crew personnel transferred to the *Enterprise*-D. ("Q Who?" [TNG]). *Starbase 173 was a re-use of the* ***Regula 1*** *space station model originally seen in* Star Trek II: The Wrath of Khan.

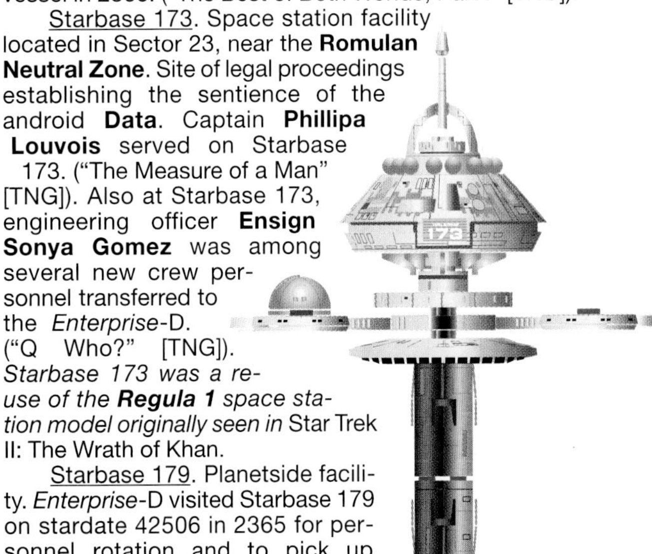

Starbase 179. Planetside facility. *Enterprise*-D visited Starbase 179 on stardate 42506 in 2365 for personnel rotation and to pick up Ensign **Mendon** as part of an **Officer Exchange Program**. ("A Matter of Honor" [TNG]).

Starbase 185. Facility that was nearest to the *Enterprise*-D after **Q** transported the vessel across the galaxy to **System J-25**. Data estimated the starbase was some two years, seven months away for the ship at maximum warp. ("Q Who?" [TNG]).

Starbase 200. Destination of the *Starship Enterprise* in 2267 when an unexplained time-warp distortion was encountered. This distortion caused complete disruption of normal magnetic and gravimetric fields in every quadrant of the galaxy. ("The Alternative Factor" [TOS]). SEE: **Lazarus**. *During the original* Star Trek *series, Starfleet supposedly had only 17 starbases. This was one of the few starbases in the original show that broke that rule.*

Starbase 201. Site where an orphaned Jem'Hadar child was to be taken in 2371. ("The Abandoned" [DS9]).

Starbase 211. The ***U.S.S. Phoenix*** was escorted by the *Enterprise*-D to Starbase 211 following **Captain Benjamin Maxwell**'s unauthorized attack in Cardassian space in 2367. ("The Wounded" [TNG]).

Starbase 212. Located near the Klingon border. Picard requested that Starbase 212 help search for a shuttlecraft missing from **Relay Station 47** in 2369. **Lieutenant Aquiel Uhnari** went there for reassignment after being cleared of criminal charges in that incident, found to have been caused by a **coalescent organism**. ("Aquiel" [TNG]).

Starbase 214. Facility where **Professor Berlinghoff Rasmussen** was deposited following his arrest in 2368. ("A Matter of Time" [TNG]).

Starbase 218. The *Enterprise*-D was en route to Starbase 218 in 2368 when it encountered the ancient **Kataan probe**. ("The Inner Light" [TNG]). In 2369, the *Enterprise-D* picked up new crew members at Starbase 218, including Lieutenant Commander **Neela Daren**. ("Lessons" [TNG]).

Starbase 219. Federation starbase commanded by **Admiral Nakamura**. In 2370, the starbase played host to the Annual Starfleet **Admiral's Banquet**. ("Phantasms" [TNG]).

Starbase 220. The *Enterprise*-D intended to tow the ill-fated ***Brattain*** to Starbase 220 when that ship was found disabled at a **Tyken's Rift**. Following its own escape from the Tyken's Rift, Data piloted the *Enterprise*-D to Starbase 220. ("Night Terrors" [TNG]).

Starbase 227. Destination of the *Enterprise*-D after returning the **psionic resonator** to the Security authorities on **Vulcan**. ("Gambit, Part II" [TNG]).

Starbase 231. Deanna Troi attended a class reunion there in 2370. ("Thine Own Self" [TNG]).

Starbase 234. Federation starbase from which Captain Jean-Luc Picard launched his armada to blockade Romulan forces covertly supplying the **Duras** family during the **Klingon civil war** in 2367-2368. Picard's task force was formed by commandeering all ships in the base's Spacedock, along with all ships within one day's travel of Starbase 234. ("Redemption, Part II" [TNG]). The *Enterprise*-D met **Admiral Brackett** at Starbase 234 before proceeding with an investigation into the disappearance of Ambassador **Spock** in 2368. ("Unification, Part I" [TNG]).

Starbase 247. Facility where Admiral **Erik Pressman** was held in 2370 to answer charges of violating the **Treaty of Algeron**. ("The *Pegasus*" [TNG]). (In the **anti-time future** created by the Q Continuum, **Admiral William T. Riker** was stationed at Starbase 247. The refitted *Enterprise*-D was deployed out of this Starbase, as it was serving as the Admiral's flagship.) ("All Good Things..." [TNG]).

Starbase 260. Destination of the *Enterprise*-D after its escape from the **Mar Oscura** Nebula in 2367. ("In Theory" [TNG]).

Starbase 295. The *Enterprise*-D headed to Starbase 295 after encountering the self-aware Borg in 2370. ("Descent, Part II" [TNG]).

Starbase 301. Federation starbase where the *Enterprise*-D traveled following a brief takeover by a **Satarran** operative. ("Conundrum" [TNG]).

Starbase 310. In 2370, Captain Picard met at Starbase 310 with **Admiral Nechayev** to discuss the new **Federation-Cardassian treaty** and the *Enterprise*-D's mission to planet **Dorvan V**. Wesley Crusher also came on-board during this stopover. ("Journey's End" [TNG]).

Starbase 313. Facility visited by the *Enterprise*-D in 2367. The ship picked up a shipment of scientific equipment to transport to the Guernica system. **Dr. Leah Brahms** also came on-board the *Enterprise*-D during this stopover. ("Galaxy's Child" [TNG]).

Starbase 324. Admiral **J. P. Hanson** returned to Starbase 324 after receiving confirmation of the encroachment of the **Borg** into Federation space. ("The Best of Both Worlds, Part I" [TNG]).

Starbase 328. The *Enterprise*-D picked up viral medicines for **Barson II** at Starbase 328. ("Eye of the Beholder" [TNG]).

Starbase 336. Station that detected an automated subspace-radio transmission in 2365 from the Klingon sleeper ship ***T'Ong***, a matter of great concern because the ship had been launched at a time when the Klingon Empire and the Federation were still at war. ("The Emissary" [TNG]).

Starbase 343. Following the completion of its mission with the **Acamarians**, the *Enterprise*-D went to Starbase 343 to take on medical supplies for the Alpha Leonis system. ("The Vengeance Factor" [TNG]).

Starbase 401. The Miles O'Brien replicant created by the **Paradas** contacted **Admiral Rollman** at Starbase 401. ("Whispers" [DS9]).

Starbase 416. Destination of the *Enterprise*-D after leaving **Ogus II** because of a medical emergency in 2367. ("Brothers" [TNG]).

Starbase 440. An **Ullian** delegation was to disembark the *Enterprise*-D at Starbase 440 in order to secure transportation to their homeworld. Captain Picard chose instead to deliver the Ullians to their world on the *Enterprise*-D. ("Violations" [TNG]).

Starbase 495. Destination of the the *Enterprise*-D after the attempted rescue at planet **Marijne VII** in 2370. ("Interface" [TNG]).

Starbase 514. The ***S.S. Vico*** was assigned out of Starbase 514 at the time of its destruction in 2368. ("Hero Worship" [TNG]).

Starbase 515. Planetside Starfleet facility located in the **Scylla Sector**, near the **Epsilon IX** Sector. Captain Picard and Wesley Crusher traveled there by shuttle in 2365, when Picard underwent a **cardiac replacement** procedure for his bionic heart, and Wesley took academy tests. ("Samaritan Snare" [TNG]). *The exterior of Starbase 515 was a re-use of the matte painting cityscape from "Angel One" (TNG).*

Starbase 621. The *Enterprise*-D delayed a scheduled stopover at Starbase 621 in order to assist the **Caldos colony** with its weather-control system. ("Sub Rosa" [TNG]).

Starbase 718. Location of an emergency conference that Picard attended in late 2364 to discuss the possibility of a new **Romulan** incursion. The meeting was triggered by the loss of communications with starbases and outposts near the Romulan Neutral Zone, although this was later believed to be due to Borg activity. This was shortly before the Romulans ended a 53-year period of isolationism that had begun in 2311. ("The Neutral Zone" [TNG]). *After this episode was made, it was decided that starbase numbers shouldn't go much higher than 500.*

Starbase Deep Space 9. SEE: **Deep Space 9**.

Starbase Earhart. Also known as Farspace Starbase Earhart. Starfleet facility where Ensign **Jean-Luc Picard** spent some time awaiting his first assignment after graduating from the academy. Picard picked a fight with three **Nausicaans** at the base's **Bonestell Recreation Facility**, and was nearly killed when one of them stabbed him through the heart. ("Samaritan Snare" [TNG], "Tapestry" [TNG]). *Named for aviation pioneer Amelia Earhart (1898-1937).*

Starbase G-6. Starfleet facility near planet Betazed from which Counselor Troi was able to visit her home via shuttlecraft. Starbase G-6 was also located near the **Sigma III Solar System**, which suffered a serious mining accident in 2364. ("Hide and "Q" [TNG]).

Starbase Lya III. Starfleet command base where **Admiral Haden** was stationed. Haden advised Jean-Luc Picard on the handling of the Romulan defector **Alidar Jarok** in 2366, although a two-hour transmission delay due to the distance to the Neutral Zone made it difficult for Haden to give timely advice. ("The Defector" [TNG]). The *Enterprise*-D headed to Starbase Lya III following its mission to **Angosia III.** ("The Hunted" [TNG]).

Starbase Montgomery. Planetside facility at which the *Enterprise*-D underwent engineering consultations on stardate 42686. ("The Icarus Factor" [TNG]).

Xendi Starbase 9. Site to which the ***U.S.S. Stargazer*** was towed after the *Enterprise*-D received the old vessel from the Ferengi in 2364. ("The Battle" [TNG]).

starboard. Ancient nautical term referring to the right side of a ship, as opposed to the port (left) side.

stardate. Timekeeping system used to provide a standard galactic temporal reference, compensating for relativistic time dilation, warp-speed displacement, and other peculiarities of interstellar space travel. *To those interested in the minutiae of stardate computation and a lot of other cool stuff about* Star Trek*, we shamelessly refer you to Appendix I in the 1996 edition of our book,* Star Trek Chronology: The History of the Future*, by Michael Okuda and Denise Okuda, also published by Pocket Books.*

stardrifter. Exotic beverage served at **Quark's bar**. One of Quark's customers ordered a stardrifter, which Quark tried to obtain from an unauthorized food replicator during the **aphasia virus** quarantine on Deep Space 9 in 2369. Kira Nerys once indulged, too. ("Babel" [DS9], "The Storyteller" [DS9]).

stardrive section. The secondary (engineering) hull and outboard warp nacelles of many types of Federation starships. ("Encounter at Farpoint, Part I" [TNG]). SEE: **Saucer Module**.

Starfleet Academy marathon. Much as in ancient Greece on Earth, a 40-kilometer footrace. In 2323, cadet **Jean-Luc Picard** became the only freshman ever to win the Starfleet Academy marathon, passing four upperclassmen on the last hill on planet Danula II. ("The Best of Both Worlds, Part II" [TNG]).

Starfleet Academy Preparatory Program. Six-week course designed to prepare prospective cadets for the **Starfleet Academy** entrance exam. Program admission is by testing only, and applicants are required to perform satisfactorily on a stress-reactions test, spatial-orientation test, and deductive-reasoning test. Testing for admission requires approximately four days. ("Facets" [DS9]).

Starfleet Academy. Training facility for Starfleet personnel ("Where No Man Has Gone Before" [TOS]) located at the Presidio of **San Francisco** on **Earth**. *(Star Trek II: The Wrath of Khan).* Established in 2161, the academy is a four-year institution. The motto of Starfleet Academy is "Ex astris, scientia," meaning "From the stars, knowledge." ("The First Duty" [TNG]). Non-Federation citizens require a letter of reference from a command-level Starfleet officer before they can take the academy entrance exam. When Nog applied for admission to the academy in 2371, Commander Benjamin Sisko wrote such a recommendation for him. ("Heart of Stone" [DS9]). In 2368, Captain Picard was asked to deliver the commencement address for that year's graduates. The occasion was marred by the loss of a cadet in an accident shortly before commencement. ("The First Duty" [TNG]). Academy cadets from the **Red Squad** became unwitting accomplices of Admiral Leyton's attempted coup of the Earth government in 2372. ("Homefront" [DS9], "Paradise Lost" [DS9]). SEE: **Academy Flight Range; Albert, Joshua; Boothby; Crusher, Wesley; Finnegan; Gill, John; Kirk, James T.; Kolvoord Starburst; Locarno, Cadet First Class Nicholas; Mitchell, Gary; Somak.** *The motto of Starfleet Academy is a paraphrase of "Ex luna scientia," the* Apollo 13 *motto, meaning "From the moon, knowledge." The* Apollo 13 *motto was, in turn, a paraphrase of "Ex tridens scientia," the motto of the United States Navy, meaning "From the sea, knowledge." The Starfleet Academy emblem is based on a design by Joe Senna. The academy campus grounds seen in "The First Duty" (TNG) were a combination of location filming at the Tillman Water Reclamation plant in Van Nuys and a matte painting by Illusion Arts, Inc. That building was also used (with a different matte painting) as part of Starfleet Command in "Homefront" (DS9).*

Starfleet battle simulation. SEE: **battle simulation, Starfleet.**

Starfleet Command. Operating authority for the interstellar scientific, exploratory, and defensive agency of the United Federation of Planets. ("Court Martial" [TOS]). The primary control hub was located in San Francisco on Earth, but other command facilities were located in various **starbases** throughout Federation space. Starfleet Command stayed in touch with its starships by means of a subspace radio communications network, but even with this faster-than-light medium, interstellar space is so vast that it was not uncommon for ships on the frontier to be out of touch. As a result, starship captains were frequently granted broad discretionary powers to interpret Federation policy in the absence of immediate instructions from Starfleet Command. *The term Starfleet Command was first used in the episode "Court Martial" (TOS). SEE:* ***United Earth Space Probe Agency****. Starfleet Command's fleet-operations center in San Francisco was seen in* Star Trek IV: The Voyage Home*. During that scene, Michael Snyder and Michael Berryman played Starfleet communications personnel. SEE:* ***Starfleet Headquarters****.*

Starfleet Corps of Engineers. Special projects division of Starfleet. The Starfleet Corps of Engineers was responsible for the construction of Dr. Marcus's underground laboratory complex at the asteroid **Regula** at which the second phase of **Project Genesis** was conducted. *(Star Trek II: The Wrath of Khan).* In an alternate reality created when his shuttle intersected a **timestream**, Ensign **Harry Kim** worked for the Corps of Engineers in 2372. He helped design a new runabout designated as a *Yellowstone*-class vessel. ("Non Sequitur" [VGR]). *"Non Sequitur" actually referred to it as the Starfleet Engineering Corps.*

Starfleet Cybernetics Journal. Scientific publication on artificial intelligence and advanced computer systems. Dr. Julian Bashir, upon meeting Data in 2369, hoped to author a paper for the journal on the phenomenon of Data's dreams. ("Birthright, Part I" [TNG]).

Starfleet Emergency Medical course. Instructional class offered to Starfleet personnel. It prepared them to render aid in many medical emergencies, including childbirth, should licensed personnel not be available. Worf's attendance in this course paid off when he assisted in the birth of **Molly O'Brien** in 2368. ("Disaster" [TNG]).

Starfleet engineering guidelines. SEE: **Starfleet General Orders and Regulations.**

Starfleet General Orders and Regulations. Starfleet maintained an extensive set of policies and procedures designed to guide the conduct of its missions and personnel.

General Order 1: The noninterference directive, prohibiting intervention in the normal development of any society. SEE: **Prime Directive**.

General Order 7: Forbids contact with planet **Talos IV**. As of 2267, the only death penalty left on the books. Spock was acquitted of violating this order after kidnapping **Christopher Pike** to live among the **Talosians**. ("The Menagerie, Parts I and II" [TOS]).

General Order 12: Requires adequate precautions be taken when being approached by a spacecraft with which contact has not been made. *(Star Trek II: The Wrath of Khan).*

General Order 15: Regulation that stated, in part, "No flag officer shall beam into a hazardous area without armed escort." Saavik reminded Kirk of General Order 15 before he beamed to the **Regula I Space Laboratory**. *(Star Trek II).*

General Order 24: A command to destroy the surface of a planet unless the order is countermanded within a specified period. Kirk invoked General Order 24 at planet **Eminiar VII** in an effort to force planetary authorities to enter peace talks with neighboring planet **Vendikar**. ("A Taste of Armageddon" [TOS]).

Order 104, Section B: Starfleet order that deals with chain of command. Commodore Matt Decker quoted regulation 104-B to Spock when taking command of the *Enterprise* in 2267. ("The Doomsday Machine" [TOS]).

Order 104, Section C: Starfleet regulation that states the **chief medical officer** may relieve a commander of duty if the commander is mentally or physically unfit. The physician would have to back up this claim with the results of a physical examination. ("The Doomsday Machine" [TOS]).

Regulation 46A: "If transmissions are being monitored during battle, no uncoded messages on an open channel." *(Star Trek II: The Wrath of Khan).*

Regulation 42/15: Engineering procedure relating to impulse engines, entitled "Pressure Variances in the Impulse Reaction Chamber Tank Storage." **Montgomery Scott** wrote this particular regulation for Starfleet, but many years later admitted that it was a wee bit conservative. ("Relics" [TNG]).

Regulation 157, Section III, Paragraph 18: Referring to time travel, "Starfleet officers shall take all necessary precautions to minimize any participation in historical events." ("Trials and Tribble-ations" [DS9]).

Away team guidelines: Specifically forbid the transport of unknown infectious agents onto a starship without first establishing containment and eradication protocols. ("Macrocosm" [VGR]).

Directive 101: Assures that an individual accused of a crime has the right to remain silent. In 2372, *Voyager* security Chief Tuvok informed confessed murderer **Lon Suder** that Starfleet Directive 101 freed him from answering questions concerning the crime. ("Meld" [VGR]).

Starfleet's **temporal displacement policy**: Prohibited time-traveling personnel from interfering in past time lines. ("Past Tense, Part I" [DS9]).

Starfleet engineering code: Required a secondary backup for mission-critical components, in case the primary backup fails. ("Destiny" [DS9]).

Starfleet Headquarters. Part of Starfleet Command, located in **San Francisco** on **Earth**. The facility includes a large aerial tram station. *(Star Trek: The Motion Picture).* An extragalactic intelligence of unknown origin attempted to gain control of Starfleet by placing neural parasites into the bodies of numerous officers at Starfleet Headquarters and elsewhere. This conspiracy was uncovered by **Admiral Norah Satie** ("The Drumhead" [TNG]), and was ended when Captain Picard and Commander Riker successfully destroyed the "mother" creature that inhabited the body of Commander **Dexter Remmick** ("Conspiracy" [TNG]). *Starfleet Headquarters was seen as several different matte paintings and miniature shots in* Star Trek: The Motion Picture, Star Trek IV: The Voyage Home, Star Trek VI: The Undiscovered Country, *and "Homefront" (DS9). The conference room interior scenes in* Star Trek VI *were filmed at the First Presbyterian Church of Hollywood, while the Starfleet Command grounds in "Homefront" were filmed at the Tillman Water Reclamation plant in Van Nuys, supplemented with a matte painting.*

Starfleet insignia. SEE: **insignia, Starfleet**.

Starfleet Medical Database. Computerized clearinghouse and archive of medical information available to Starfleet medical personnel. The database was also accessible by other Starfleet personnel, including **Reginald Barclay**. ("Genesis" [TNG]).

Starfleet Monitor Stations. Outposts located on the Federation border. In the alternate timeline created when the ***Enterprise*-C** vanished from its "proper" place in 2344, Starfleet Monitor Stations reported that Klingon battle cruisers were moving toward the *Enterprise*-D. ("Yesterday's *Enterprise*" [TNG]).

Starfleet temporal displacement policy. Starfleet doctrine intended to prevent interference in the flow of history by any time-traveling personnel. The policy prohibits any person transported into the past from doing anything that might alter the timeline. When a **transporter** accident deposited **Julian Bashir** on Earth in 2024, he lamented that Starfleet's temporal displacement policy prohibited him from preventing the deaths of hundreds of people in the **Bell Riots**. ("Past Tense, Part I" [DS9]).

Starfleet uniforms. SEE: **uniforms, Starfleet**.

Starfleet. Deep-space exploratory, scientific, diplomatic, and defensive agency of the **United Federation of Planets**. Starfleet was chartered by the Federation in 2161 with a mission to "boldly go where no man has gone before." The most visible part of the Starfleet is its interstellar **starships**. Additionally, Starfleet maintains a far-flung network of **starbases** to support deep-space operations. *Alas, there is no definitive list of all of Starfleet's ships or vessel types. The reason is that our producers need to keep the list somewhat vague in order to allow future episodes and movies to include both old and new ships as stories, not yet written, may require. (SEE:* ***starships*** *for a partial listing and some diagrams.)*

Stargazer, U.S.S. Federation starship, ***Constellation*** **class**, registry number NCC-2893. The *Stargazer* was under the command of Captain **Jean-Luc Picard** from 2333 to 2355 on a historic mission of deep-space exploration, prior to his assignment to the *Enterprise*-D. Lieutenant Jean-Luc Picard was a bridge officer on the *Stargazer* when its captain was killed. Picard took command of the bridge and was later offered command of the ship for his actions. ("Tapestry" [TNG]) During an exploratory mission to **Sector 21503**, the *Stargazer* was attacked by **Cardassian** forces and barely escaped. ("The Wounded" [TNG]). During Picard's command, the *Stargazer* visited planet **Chalna** in 2354. ("Allegiance" [TNG]). The starship was destroyed near the **Maxia**

Zeta star system by what was later learned to be a Ferengi vessel. Years later, the Ferengi Bok returned the hulk of the *Stargazer* to Picard as part of a plot to discredit Picard for what Bok believed to be Picard's part in Bok's son's death. ("The Battle" [TNG]). Following the loss of the *Stargazer* in 2355, Picard was court-martialed per standard Starfleet procedure, but cleared of wrongdoing. The prosecutor in the case was **Phillipa Louvois**, with whom Picard had been romantically involved. ("The Measure of a Man" [TNG]). SEE: ***Constellation*-class starship; Maxia, Battle of.** *The* Stargazer *was designed by Andrew Probert and Rick Sternbach. The miniature was built by Greg Jein. A smaller model of the* Stargazer *was on display in Captain Picard's ready room aboard the* Enterprise-*D. The* Stargazer *bridge was a redress of the Enterprise-D battle bridge. The dedication plaque on the* Stargazer *bridge bore the motto, devised by episode writer Herb Wright, "To bring light into the darkness."*

Starling, Henry. (Ed Begley, Jr.). Computer technology pioneer on 20th-century **Earth**, chief executive officer of the **Chronowerx** corporation. Starling was responsible for a remarkable number of major technological breakthroughs in Earth's computer industry, including the development of the first **isograted circuit** in 1969 and the **HyperPro PC** in 1996. It was not generally realized that Starling had, in 1967, accidentally discovered the wreckage of the ***Aeon***, a Federation **timeship** piloted by **Captain Braxton** that had crashed in the High Sierras in the 20th century. Starling used technology from the 29th-century vehicle as the basis for his remarkable breakthroughs. Starling spent much of his life in fear that someone from the future would return to his time to reclaim the timeship. He was thus well prepared when the *Starship Voyager* arrived in 1996. Starling was successful in thwarting *Voyager* personnel, even forcing the ship's **Emergency Medical Hologram** to be downloaded to the Earth's surface through the use of an **autonomous holoemitter** that was also based on 29th-century technology. Starling fled aboard the timeship and was killed by a photon torpedo fired from the *Voyager*. ("Future's End, Parts I and II" [VGR]). *The destruction of the timeship and the death of Starling apparently prevented the temporal explosion in the 29th century that had originally caused Braxton and the* Aeon *to go back into the past. It is nevertheless unclear what happened to the 20th-century events in the altered timeline. One might infer that all of Starling's "innovations" disappeared in the altered timeline. However, the holographic doctor's autonomous holoemitter did not disappear, suggesting that some effects of Braxton's 1967 crash remained, even in the altered timeline.*

Starnes Expedition. Party of Federation explorers led by **Professor Starnes**, sent to survey planet **Triacus** in 2268. An entity known as the **Gorgan** drove the adult members of the expedition to commit mass suicide by ingesting **cyalodin**. In the aftermath of the tragedy, the children, suffering from **lacunar amnesia**, were controlled by the Gorgan, who induced them to commandeer the *Starship Enterprise*. The children were later taken to Starbase 4. ("And the Children Shall Lead" [TOS]).

Starnes, Professor. (James Wellman). Leader of the **Starnes Expedition** to planet **Triacus** who was driven to suicide in 2268 by the evil **Gorgan**. Starnes was amazed how unaffected their children (including his son, **Tommy Starnes**) were by the increased level of anxiety from an unseen force that was influencing the adult members of the party. This anxiety, later found to be caused by the Gorgan, eventually culminated in the mass suicide of the adult members of the group. ("And the Children Shall Lead" [TOS]).

Starnes, Tommy. (Craig Hundley). One of the surviving children of the **Starnes Expedition** whose parents committed suicide on planet **Triacus** in 2268. In the aftermath of the tragedy, young Starnes was controlled by the **Gorgan**. ("And the Children Shall Lead" [TOS]). *Craig Hundley also played Peter Kirk in "Operation: Annihilate!" (TOS). Hundley became a musician who composed some incidental music for* Star Trek III: The Search for Spock.

"Starry Night." Famous 19th-century oil painting by Earth artist Vincent van Gogh (1853-1890). The painting was in the personal collection of **Zibalian** trader **Kivas Fajo**, at least until Fajo's collection was confiscated upon his arrest in 2366. ("The Most Toys" [TNG]).

stars. SEE: **planets, stars, and other celestial objects**.

"Starship Down." *Deep Space Nine* episode #79. Written by David Mack & John J. Ordover. Directed by Alexander Singer. Stardate 49263.5. *First aired in 1995. A trade agreement with the Karemma is threatened by the Jem'Hadar, who lure the* Defiant *into a huge planet's gaseous atmosphere for a deadly game of cat-and-mouse.* GUEST CAST: James Cromwell as **Hanok**; F.J. Rio as **Muniz**; Jay Baker as **Stevens**; Sara Mornell as **Carson**. SEE: **active-scan navigation; Badlands; baseball; Bolian currency; Boyce; Carson, Ensign; dabo; dualitic inverter; Emissary; Ferengi; Ferengi lobes; GSC; Festival of Lights; *Ha'mara*; Hanok; hot dog; Janklow; Jem'Hadar; Jo'kala; Jupiter; Karemma; Karemman fleece; Karemman vessel; *kava* root; Morn; Muniz, Enrique; ODN; planetary classification system; Sisko, Benjamin; Stevens; Tarkalian sheep herders; "Three brothers who went to Jo'kala, The."**

"Starship Mine." *Next Generation* episode #144. Written by Morgan Gendel. Directed by Cliff Bole. Stardate 46682.4. *First aired in 1993. Terrorists seize the* Enterprise-*D in an attempt to steal trilithium resin.* GUEST CAST: David Spielberg as **Hutchinson, Commander Calvin**; Marie Marshall as **Kelsey**; Tim Russ as **Devor**; Glenn Morshower as **Orton, Mr.**; Tom Nibley as **Neil**; Tim DeZarn as **Satler**; Patricia Tallman as **Kiros**; Arlee Reed as Waiter; Alan Altshuld as **Pomet**; Majel Barrett as Computer voice. SEE: **Arkaria Base; Arkarian water fowl; baryon particles; baryon sweep; Conklin, Captain; Devor; Edwell, Captain; field diverters; Gaspar VII; Hutchinson, Commander Calvin; Kelsey; Kiros; *Magellan*, *U.S.S.*; Mitchell, Admiral; Neil; optical transducer; ornithology; Orton, Mr.; Pomet; Remmler Array; saddle; Satler; security access code; Starbase 97; trilithium; Tyrellia.**

starships. Interstellar spacecraft capable of faster-than-light travel using **warp drive**. Perhaps the most famous starships in Federation history were the *Starships Enterprise*. SEE: **class; *Constitution*-class starship; *Excelsior*-class starship; *Galaxy*-class starship; *Miranda*-class starship; NCC; Starfleet.** SEE: Starship chart following pages.

stasis unit. Emergency medical device used aboard Federation starships. The device could hold a patient in a state of suspended animation until medical treatment could be rendered. ("Tapestry" [TNG], "Basics, Part II" [VGR]). A stasis unit could also be used to preserve the body of a deceased individual to prevent decay while awaiting burial. ("Innocence" [VGR]). In 2372, *Voyager's* Emergency Medical Hologram placed Captain Janeway and Commander Chakotay into stasis chambers while he searched for a cure to an insect-borne viral disease they had contracted. ("Resolutions" [VGR]).

Starship name	Registry	Class	Description	Episode or film
***Adelphi*, U.S.S.**	NCC-26849	*Ambassador*	Conducted disastrous first contact with planet **Ghorusda**	"Tin Man" (TNG)
***Agamemnon*, U.S.S.**	NCC-11638	*Apollo*	Part of the task force for the expected Borg invasion of 2369	"Descent" (TNG)
***Ahwahnee*, U.S.S.**	NCC-71620	*Cheyenne*	Lost in the battle of **Wolf 359**; named for North American native tribe	"Best of Both Worlds, Part II" (TNG)
***Ajax*, U.S.S.**	NCC-11574	*Apollo*	Corey Zweller's first ship assignment following his graduation; Kosinski tested experimental warp-drive upgrade in 2364	"Tapestry" (TNG), "Where No One Has Gone Before" (TNG), "Redemption, Part II" (TNG)
***Akagi*, U.S.S.**	NCC-62158	*Rigel*	Part of Picard's blockade armada in 2368	"Redemption, Part II" (TNG)
***Al-Batani*, U.S.S.**	NCC-42995	*Excelsior*	Janeway served as science officer under Captain Paris	"Caretaker" (VGR)
***Antares*, U.S.S.**	NCC-501	*Antares*	Science vessel; destroyed by **Charles Evans**	"Charlie X" (TOS)
***Appalachia*, U.S.S.**	NCC-52136	*Steamrunner*	Defended Earth against Borg incursion of 2373	*Star Trek: First Contact*
***Archon*, U.S.S.**	NCC-189	*Daedalus*	Early starship; lost at planet **Beta III** in 2167	"Return of the Archons" (TOS)
***Arcos*, U.S.S.**	NCC-6237	*Deneva*	Freighter ship; lost near planet **Turkana IV**	"Legacy" (TNG)
***Aries*, U.S.S.**	NCC-45167	*Renaissance*	Riker was offered command in 2365	"The Icarus Factor" (TNG), "Identity Crisis" (TNG)
***Armstrong*, U.S.S.**	NCC-57537	*Challenger*	Ambushed by Klingon battle group in 2373; named for *Apollo* 11 astronaut Neil Armstrong	"Apocalypse Rising" (DS9)
***Bellerephon*, U.S.S.**	NCC-62048	*Nebula*	Lost in the battle of **Wolf 359**; named for the ship from *Forbidden Planet*	"Emissary" (DS9)
***Berlin*, U.S.S.**	NCC-14232	*Excelsior*	Stationed near **Romulan Neutral Zone** in 2364	"Angel One" (TNG)
***Biko*, U.S.S.**	NCC-50331	*Olympic*	Scheduled to rendezvous with *Enterprise*-D on stardate 46271	"A Fistful of Datas" (TNG)
***Bonestell*, U.S.S.**	NCC-31600	*Oberth*	Lost in the battle of **Wolf 359**; named for astronomical artist Chesley Bonestell	"The Best of Both Worlds, Part II" (TNG)
***Bozeman*, U.S.S.**	NCC-1941	*Soyuz*	Caught in a temporal causality loop in 2278; escaped in 2368; named for the city of Bozeman, Montana	"Cause and Effect" (TNG), "All Good Things..." (TNG), *Star Trek: First Contact*
***Bradbury*, U.S.S.**	NX-72307	*Bradbury*	Transported Wesley Crusher to Starfleet	"Menage a Troi" (TNG)

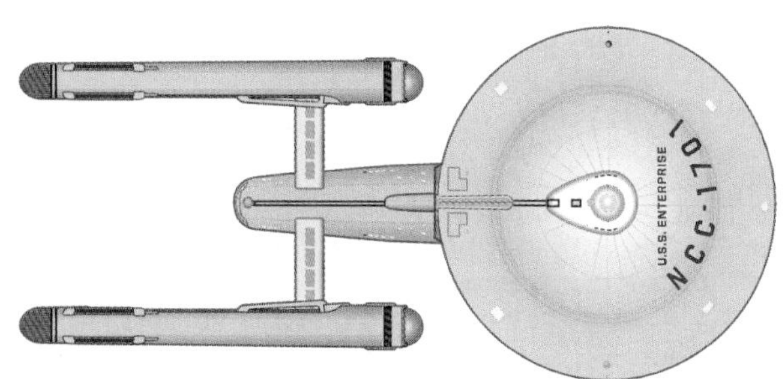

Constitution class (original configuration)

Sabre class

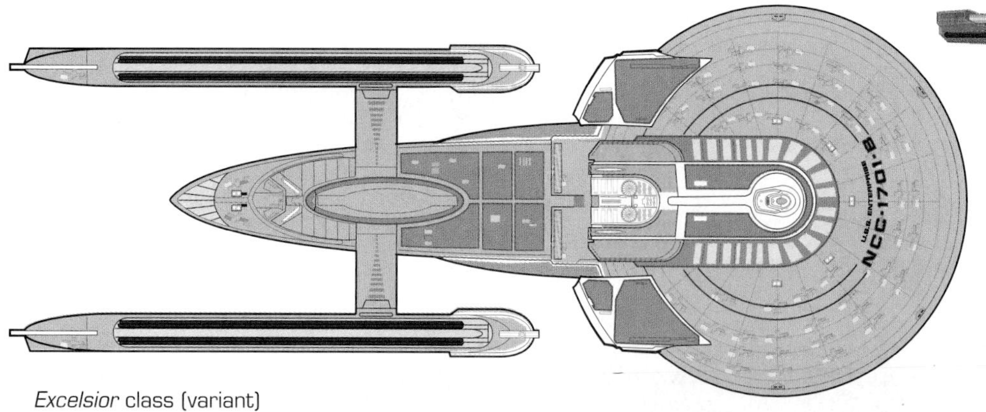

Excelsior class (variant)

Starship name	Registry	Class	Description	Episode or film
Brattain, U.S.S.	NCC-21166	*Miranda*	Trapped in a **Tyken's Rift** in 2367	"Night Terrors" (TNG)
Budapest, U.S.S.	NCC-64923	*Norway*	Defended Earth against Borg incursion of 2373	*Star Trek: First Contact*
Buran, U.S.S.	NCC-57580	*Challenger*	Lost in the battle of **Wolf 359**	"The Best of Both Worlds, Part II" (TNG)
Cairo, U.S.S.	NCC-42136	*Excelsior*	Commanded by Captain Edward Jellico	"Chain of Command, Part I" (TNG), "Preemptive Strike" (TNG)
Carolina, U.S.S.	NCC-160	*Daedalus*	Apparently sent emergency signal	"Friday's Child" (TOS)
Charleston, U.S.S.	NCC-42285	*Excelsior*	Transported 20th-century survivors back to Earth	"The Neutral Zone" (TNG)
Chekov, U.S.S.	NCC-53702	*Springfield*	Lost in the battle of **Wolf 359**; named for the noted Russian space explorer	"The Best of Both Worlds, Part II" (TNG)
Clement, U.S.S.	NCC-12537	*Apollo*	Scheduled to rendezvous with the *Enterprise*-D	"Lower Decks" (TNG)
Cochrane, U.S.S.	NCC-59318	*Oberth*	Transported Bashir to Deep Space 9; named for the inventer of warp drive	"Emissary" (DS9)
Columbia, U.S.S.	NCC-621	(unknown)	Ordered to rendezvous with *Revere*	*Star Trek: The Motion Picture*
Concord, U.S.S.	NCC-68711	*Freedom*	(In anti-time, deployed to Romulan Neutral Zone)	"All Good Things..." (TNG)
Constantinople, U.S.S.	NCC-34852	*Istanbul*	Suffered hull breach near **Gravesworld** in 2365	"The Schizoid Man" (TNG)
Constellation, U.S.S.	NCC-1974	*Constellation*	Transported Jem'Hadar to Starbase 201	"The Abandoned" (DS9)
Constellation, U.S.S.	NCC-1017	*Constitution*	Commanded by **Matt Decker;** destroyed in encounter with planet killer	"The Doomsday Machine" (TOS)
Constitution, U.S.S.	NCC-1700	*Constitution*	Class prototype ship for original *Starship Enterprise*; named for "Old Ironsides"	"Space Seed" (TOS)
Copernicus, U.S.S.	NCC- 623	*Oberth*	In space dock at the time the second *Enterprise* was launched	*Star Trek IV: The Voyage Home*
Crazy Horse, U.S.S.	NCC-50446	*Excelsior*	Part of task force 3 during expected Borg invasion of 2369	"The Pegasus" (TNG)
Crockett, U.S.S.	NCC- 38955	*Excelsior*	Transported Admiral Mitsuya to Deep Space 9	"Paradise" (DS9)
Defiant, U.S.S.	NCC-1764	*Constitution*	Lost in **spatial interphase**	"The Tholian Web" (TOS)
Defiant, U.S.S.	NX-74205	*Defiant*	Small, heavily armed prototype intended to defend against the Borg; assigned to station Deep Space 9	"The Search, Parts I & II (DS9), *Star Trek: Deep Space Nine, Star Trek: First Contact*
Denver, U.S.S.	NCC-54927	*Yorkshire*	Struck gravitic mine in 2368	"Ethics" (TNG)
Drake, U.S.S.	NCC-20381	*Wambundu*	Destroyed by ancient weapons system at **Minos**	"The Arsenal of Freedom" (TNG)
Drake, U.S.S.	NCC-70956	*Andromeda*	Ambushed by Klingon battle group in 2373	"Apocalypse Rising" (DS9)
Eagle, U.S.S.	NCC-956	*Constitution*	Potential participant in **Operation Retrieve**	*Star Trek VI: The Undiscovered Country*
Endeavor, U.S.S.	NCC-71805	*Nebula*	Served in Romulan blockade during Klingon civil war; part of armada that intercepted Borg ship	"Redemption, Part II" (TNG), "The Game" (TNG)
Enterprise, U.S.S.	NCC-1701	*Constitution*	First starship to bear the name; commanded by Captain **James T. Kirk**	*Star Trek: The Original Series, Star Trek: The Motion Picture, Star Trek II: The Wrath of Khan, Star Trek III: The Search for Spock*
Enterprise-A, U.S.S.	NCC-1701-A	*Constitution*	Second starship to bear the name; refit *Constitution*-class design	*Star Trek IV: The Voyage Home*
Enterprise-B, U.S.S.	NCC-1701-B	*Excelsior*	Launched in 2293 under the command of Captain **John Harriman**	*Star Trek Generations*
Enterprise-C, U.S.S.	NCC-1701-C	*Ambassador*	Lost and presumed destroyed near **Narendra III** in 2344 under command of **Rachel Garrett**	"Yesterday's Enterprise" (TNG)
Enterprise-D, U.S.S.	NCC-1701-D	*Galaxy*	Fifth starship to bear the name; commanded by Captain **Jean-Luc Picard**	*Star Trek: The Next Generation, Star Trek Generations*
Enterprise-E, U.S.S.	NCC-1701-E	*Sovereign*	Sixth starship to bear the name; launched in 2373 under command of **Jean-Luc Picard**	*Star Trek: First Contact*
Essex, U.S.S.	NCC-173	*Daedalus*	Lost in 2167 at planet **Mab-Bu VI**	"Power Play" (TNG)
Excalibur, U.S.S.	NCC-1664	*Constitution*	Seriously damaged in M-5 test in 2268	"The Ultimate Computer" (TOS)
Excalibur, U.S.S.	NCC-26517	*Ambassador*	Part of Romulan blockade in 2368	"Redemption, Part II" (TNG)
Excelsior, U.S.S.	NX-2000; (later NCC-2000)	*Excelsior*	Testbed for **transwarp** development project; later commanded by Captain **Hikaru Sulu**; prototype for *Excelsior*-class starships	*Star Trek III: The Search for Spock, Star Trek VI: The Undiscovered Country,* "Flashback" (VGR)
Exeter, U.S.S.	NCC-1672	*Constitution*	Crew killed by bacteriological warfare agent at Omega IV in 2268	"The Omega Glory" (TOS)
Exeter, U.S.S.	NCC-26531	*Ambassador*	Former posting of Tom Paris	"Non Sequitur" (VGR)

Starship name	Registry	Class	Description	Episode or film
***Farragut*, U.S.S.**	NCC-1647	*Constitution*	Kirk's first assignment after the academy	"Obsession" (TOS)
***Farragut*, U.S.S.**	NCC-60591	*Nebula*	Rescued crew of *Enterprise*-D at Veridian III in 2371; later destroyed near Ajilon Prime	*Star Trek Generations*, "Nor the Battle to the Strong" (DS9)
***Fearless*, U.S.S.**	NCC-4598	*Excelsior*	Testbed for Kosinski's experimental warp engine upgrades	"Where No One Has Gone Before" (TNG)
***Firebrand*, U.S.S.**	NCC-68723	*Freedom*	Lost in the battle of **Wolf 359**	"The Best of Both Worlds, Part II" (TNG)
***Fleming*, U.S.S.**	NCC-20316	*Wambundu*	Destroyed in Hekaras Corridor in 2370	"Force of Nature" (TNG)
***Gage*, U.S.S.**	NCC-11672	*Apollo*	Lost in the battle of **Wolf 359**	"Emissary" (DS9)
***Galaxy*, U.S.S.**	NCC-70637	*Galaxy*	Class prototype for fifth *Starship Enterprise*	*Star Trek: The Next Generation*
***Gandhi*, U.S.S.**	NCC-26632	*Ambassador*	**Thomas Riker** assigned to *Gandhi* in 2369	"Second Chances" (TNG)
***Ganges*, U.S.S.**	NCC-72454	*Danube*	Runabout assigned to Deep Space 9	"Past Prologue" (DS9), "Q-Less" (DS9), et al
***Gettysburg*, U.S.S.**	NCC-3890	*Constellation*	Last ship commanded by **Mark Jameson** before his promotion to admiral	"Too Short A Season" (TNG)
***Goddard*, U.S.S.**	NCC-59621	*Korolev*	Part of tachyon detection grid during Klingon civil war	"The Vengeance Factor" (TNG), "Redemption, Part II" (TNG)
***Gorkon*, U.S.S.**	NCC-40512	*Excelsior*	Admiral Nechayev's flagship in 2369	"Descent, Part I" (TNG)
***Grissom*, U.S.S.**	NCC-638	*Oberth*	Science vessel; destroyed at Genesis Planet	*Star Trek III: The Search for Spock*
***Grissom*, U.S.S.**	NCC-42857	*Excelsior*	Second Federation ship to bear the name	"The Most Toys" (TNG)
***Hathaway*, U.S.S.**	NCC-2593	*Constellation*	Participated in Starfleet battle simulation	"Peak Performance" (TNG)
***Havana*, U.S.S.**	NCC-34043	*Istanbul*	Scheduled to rendezvous with *Enterprise*-D in 2369	"Lessons" (TNG)
***Hera*, U.S.S.**	NCC-62006	*Nebula*	Commanded by Silva La Forge	"Interface" (TNG)
***Hermes*, U.S.S.**	NCC-10376	*Antares*	Served in armada during Klingon civil war	"Redemption, Part II" (TNG)
***Hood*, U.S.S.**	NCC-42296	*Excelsior*	Commanded by Robert DeSoto; Riker's posting prior to *Enterprise*-D	"Encounter at Farpoint" (TNG), "Tin Man" (TNG), et al

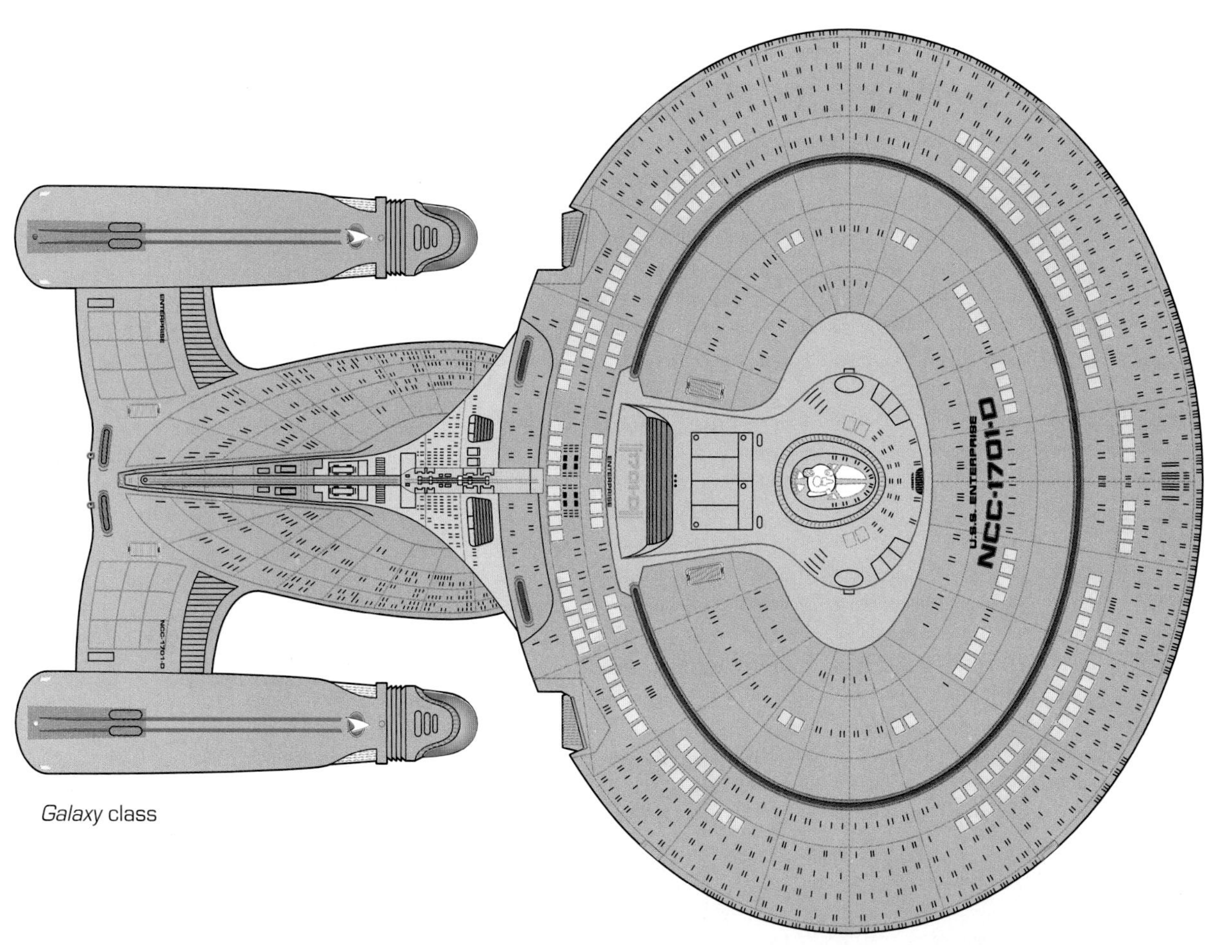

Galaxy class

Starship name	Registry	Class	Description	Episode or film
Hood, U.S.S.	NCC-1703	*Constitution*	Participated in M-5 multitronic computer test	"The Ultimate Computer" (TOS)
Horatio, U.S.S.	NCC-10532	*Ambassador*	Destroyed at **Dytallix B** in 2364	"Conspiracy" (TNG)
Horizon, U.S.S.	NCC-176	*Daedalus*	Lost in 2168 after visiting **Sigma Iotia II**	"A Piece of the Action" (TOS)
Hornet, U.S.S.	NCC-45231	*Renaissance*	Served in armada during Klingon civil war	"Redemption, Part II" (TNG)
Intrepid, U.S.S.	NCC-1631	*Constitution*	Destroyed by spaceborne amoeba in 2268	"Court Martial" (TOS), "The Immunity Syndrome" (TOS)
Intrepid, U.S.S.	NCC-38907	*Excelsior*	First ship to respond to distress calls after Khitomer massacre	"Sins of the Father" (TNG), "Family" (TNG)
Jenolen, U.S.S.	NCC-2010	*Sydney*	Transport ship lost in 2294 carrying **Montgomery Scott**	"Relics" (TNG)
Kearsarge, U.S.S.	NCC-57566	*Challenger*	Scheduled to rendezvous with *Enterprise*-D in 2370	"Firstborn" (TNG)
Kyushu, U.S.S.	NCC-65491	*New Orleans*	Lost in the battle of **Wolf 359**	"The Best of Both Worlds, Part II" (TNG)
LaSalle, U.S.S.	NCC-6203	*Deneva*	Reported radiation anomalies in 2367	"Reunion" (TNG)
Lakota, U.S.S.	NCC-42768	*Excelsior*	Tried to stop *Defiant* during Leyton's attempted coup in 2372	"Homefront" (DS9), "Paradise Lost" (DS9)
Lalo, U.S.S.	NCC-43837	*Mediterranean*	Detected Manheim's time/gravity experiments; believed lost in **Borg** attack	"We'll Always Have Paris" (TNG), "The Best of Both Worlds, Part I" (TNG)
Lantree, U.S.S.	NCC-1837	*Miranda*	Crew killed by genetically-engineered children	"Unnatural Selection" (TNG)
Lexington, U.S.S.	NCC-1709	*Constitution*	Commanded by Commodore **Robert Wesley**; participated in **M-5** tests	"The Ultimate Computer" (TOS)
Lexington, U.S.S.	NCC-14427	*Excelsior*	Transported medical supplies for Taranko colony	"Thine Own Self" (TNG)
Lexington, U.S.S.	NCC-61832	*Nebula*	Visited Deep Space 9 in 2371	"Explorers" (DS9)
Livingston, U.S.S.	NCC-34099	*Excelsior*	Benjamin Sisko and Curzon Dax once served aboard the *Livingston*	"Invasive Procedures" (DS9)
Magellan, U.S.S.	NCC-3069	*Constellation*	Commanded by Captain Conklin	"Starship Mine" (TNG)
Malinche, U.S.S.	NCC-38997	*Excelsior*	Attacked by **Maquis** forces	"For the Uniform" (DS9)
Maryland, U.S.S.	NCC-45109	*Renaissance*	Lost in the Gamma Quadrant	"In Purgatory's Shadow" (DS9)
Mekong, U.S.S.	NCC-72917	*Danube*	Runabout assigned to Deep Space 9	"The Maquis, Part II" (DS9), "Whispers" (DS9)

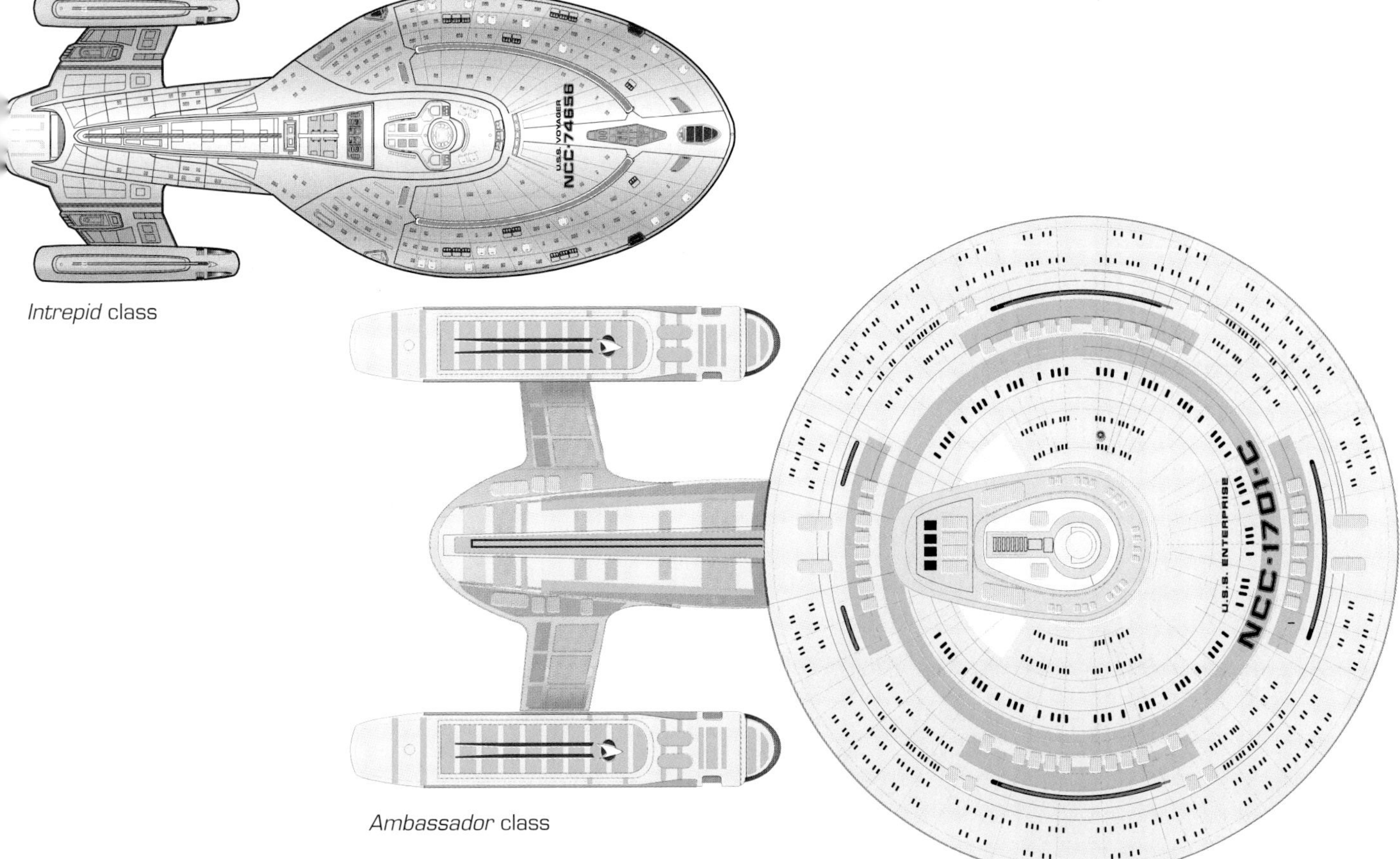

Intrepid class

Ambassador class

Starship name	Registry	Class	Description	Episode or film
***Melbourne*, U.S.S.**	NCC-62043	*Excelsior*	Lost in the battle of **Wolf 359**	"11001001" (TNG), "The Best of Both Worlds" (TNG), "Emissary" (DS9)
***Merrimack*, U.S.S.**	NCC-61827	*Nebula*	Transported Ambassador **Sarek** back to Vulcan in 2366	"Sarek" (TNG), "The Game" (TNG)
***Monitor*, U.S.S.**	NCC-61826	*Nebula*	Assigned to **Romulan Neutral Zone** in 2366	"The Defector" (TNG)
***Nobel*, U.S.S.**	NCC- 55012	*Olympic*	Searched for *U.S.S. Hera* in 2370	"Interface" (TNG)
***Odyssey*, U.S.S.**	NCC-71832	*Galaxy*	Destroyed by **Jem'Hadar** in 2370	"The Jem'Hadar" (DS9)
***Okinawa*, U.S.S.**	NCC-13958	*Excelsior*	Sisko's posting prior to *Saratoga*	"Homefront" (DS9), "Paradise Lost" (DS9)
***Orinoco*, U.S.S.**	NCC-72905	*Danube*	Runabout assigned to Deep Space 9; destroyed by Cardassian radicals	"The Siege" (DS9), "The Maquis, Part II" (DS9), "Whispers" (DS9)
***Pasteur*, U.S.S.**	NCC-58928	*Olympic*	(In anti-time future, a medical ship commanded by Beverly Crusher)	"All Good Things..." (TNG)
***Pegasus*, U.S.S.**	NCC-53847	*Oberth*	Destroyed during illegal test of Federation cloaking device; Riker's first posting	"The Pegasus" (TNG)
***Phoenix*, U.S.S.**	NCC-65420	*Nebula*	Commanded by Benjaman Maxwell; launched illegal offensive against Cardassians	"The Wounded" (TNG)
***Portland*, U.S.S.**	NCC-57418	*Chimera*	Searched for Odo and Garak in Algira sector	"The Die is Cast" (DS9)
***Potemkin*, U.S.S.**	NCC-1657	*Constitution*	Participated in **M-5** tests in 2268	"The Ultimate Computer" (TOS), "Turnabout Intruder" (TOS)
***Potemkin*, U.S.S.**	NCC-18253	*Excelsior*	Riker's early posting, prior to *Hood* and *Enterprise*-D	"Peak Performance" (TNG), "Second Chances" (TNG)
***Princeton*, U.S.S.**	NCC-59804	*Niagara*	Lost in the battle of **Wolf 359**	"The Best of Both Worlds, Part II" (TNG)
***Prokofiev*, U.S.S.**	NCC-68814	*Andromeda*	Dispatched to the **Demilitarized Zone** in 2370	"Tribunal" (DS9)
***Prometheus*, U.S.S.**	NCC-71201	*Nebula*	Participated in reignition of star Epsilon 119	"Second Sight" (DS9)
***Proxima*, U.S.S.**	NCC-61952	*Nebula*	Believed lost to **Dominion** forces	"In Purgatory's Shadow" (DS9)
***Raman*, U.S.S.**	NCC-59983	*Oberth*	Science vessel lost at **Marijne VII**	"Interface" (TNG)
***Reliant*, U.S.S.**	NCC-1864	*Miranda*	Participated in **Project Genesis**	*Star Trek II: The Wrath of Khan*
***Renegade*, U.S.S.**	NCC-63102	*New Orleans*	Met *Enterprise*-D at **Dytallix B**	"Conspiracy" (TNG)
***Republic*, U.S.S.**	NCC-1371	*Constitution*	Ensign Kirk's posting, along with Ben Finney	"Court Martial" (TOS)

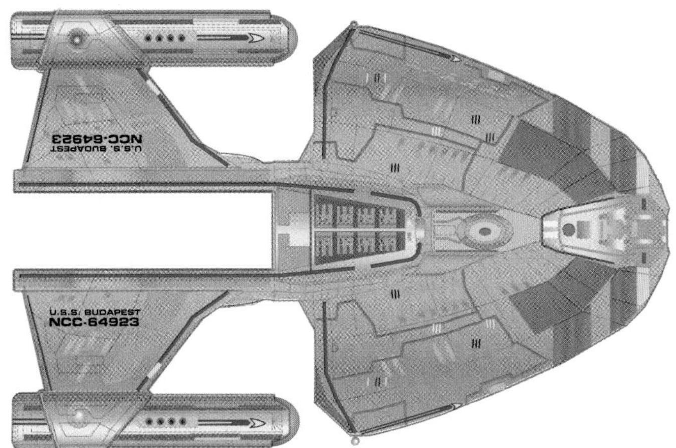

Norway class

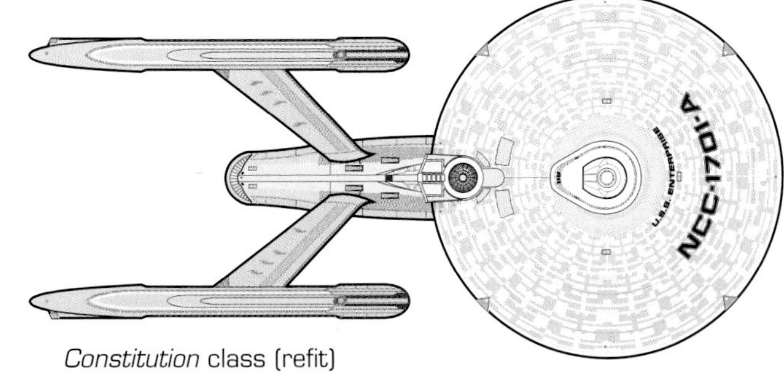

Constitution class (refit)

Starship name	Registry	Class	Description	Episode or film
Repulse, U.S.S.	NCC-2544	*Excelsior*	**Katherine Pulaski**'s posting prior to *Enterprise*-D	"The Child" (TNG), "Unnatural Selection" (TNG)
Revere, U.S.S.	NCC-595	(unknown)	Ordered to rendezvous with *U.S.S. Columbia*	*Star Trek: The Motion Picture*
Rio Grande, U.S.S.	NCC-72452	*Danube*	Runabout assigned to Deep Space 9	"Emissary" (DS9), et al
Roosevelt, U.S.S.	NCC-2573	*Excelsior*	Lost in the battle of **Wolf 359**; named for American president Theodore Roosevelt	"Unity" (VGR)
Rubicon, U.S.S.	NCC-72936	*Danube*	Runabout assigned to Deep Space 9	"Family Business" (DS9), "Hippocratic Oath"(DS9)
Rutledge, U.S.S.	NCC-57295	*New Orleans*	**Miles O'Brien**'s posting during the Cardassian war	"The Wounded" (TNG), "Paradise" (DS9)
Sarajevo, U.S.S.	NCC-38529	*Istanbul*	Believed lost to **Dominion** forces	"In Purgatory's Shadow" (DS9)
Saratoga, U.S.S.	NCC-1937	*Miranda*	Disabled by alien space probe in 2286	*Star Trek IV: The Voyage Home*
Saratoga, U.S.S.	NCC-31911	*Miranda*	Lost in the battle of **Wolf 359**	"Emissary" (DS9)
Stargazer, U.S.S.	NCC-2893	*Constellation*	Picard's former command; lost in the Battle of Maxia	"The Battle" (TNG), "Measure of a Man" (TNG), "Tapestry" (TNG)
Sutherland, U.S.S.	NCC-72015	*Nebula*	Commanded by Data during Picard's blockade of Romulan ships in 2368	"Redemption, Part II" (TNG)
T'Pau	NSP-17938	*Apollo*	Ship of Vulcan registry; decommissioned 2364	"Unification, Part I" (TNG)
Tecumseh, U.S.S.	NCC-14934	*Excelsior*	Participated in counterattack against Klingon forces in 2373	"Nor the Battle to the Strong" (DS9)
Thomas Paine, U.S.S.	NCC-65530	*New Orleans*	Met *Enterprise*-D at **Dytallix B** in 2364	"Conspiracy" (TNG)
Thunderchild, U.S.S.	NCC-63549	*Akira*	Defended sector 001 against **Borg** incursion of 2373	*Star Trek: First Contact*
Tian An Men, U.S.S.	NCC-21382	*Miranda*	Participated in Picard's blockade of Romulan ships in 2368	"Redemption, Part II" (TNG)
Tolstoy, U.S.S.	NCC-62095	*Rigel*	Lost in the battle of **Wolf 359**; named for Russian author Leo Tolstoy	"The Best of Both Worlds, Part II" (TNG)
Trieste, U.S.S.	NCC-37124	*Merced*	**Data**'s posting prior to *Enterprise*-D	"Clues" (TNG), "11001001" (TNG)
Tripoli, U.S.S.	NCC-19386	*Hokule'a*	Discovered **Data** at Omicron Theta colony in 2338	"Datalore" (TNG), "Unification, Part I" (TNG)
Tsiolkovsky, U.S.S.	NCC-53911	*Oberth*	Crew killed by Psi 2000 virus in 2364; named for Russian space pioneer Konstantin Tsiolkovsky	"The Naked Now" (TNG)
Ulysses, U.S.S.	NCC-66808	*Nebula*	Did scientific study in the Helsapont Nebula	"The Adversary" (DS9)
Valdemar, U.S.S.	NCC-26198	*Ambassador*	Dispatched to **Demilitarized Zone** in 2370	"Tribunal" (DS9)
Valiant, U.S.S.	NCC-1223	(unknown)	Destroyed at **Eminiar VII** in 2217	"A Taste of Armageddon" (TOS)
Venture, U.S.S.	NCC-71854	Galaxy	Led relief force to Deep Space 9 in 2372	"The Way of the Warrior" (DS9)
Vico, S.S.	NAR-18834	*Oberth*	Research vessel, lost in **Black Cluster**	"Hero Worship" (TNG)
Victory, U.S.S.	NCC-9754	*Constellation*	Geordi La Forge's posting prior to *Enterprise*-D	"Elementary, Dear Data" (TNG), "Identity Crisis" (TNG)
Volga, U.S.S.	NCC-73196	*Danube*	Runabout assigned to Deep Space 9	"Body Parts" (DS9)

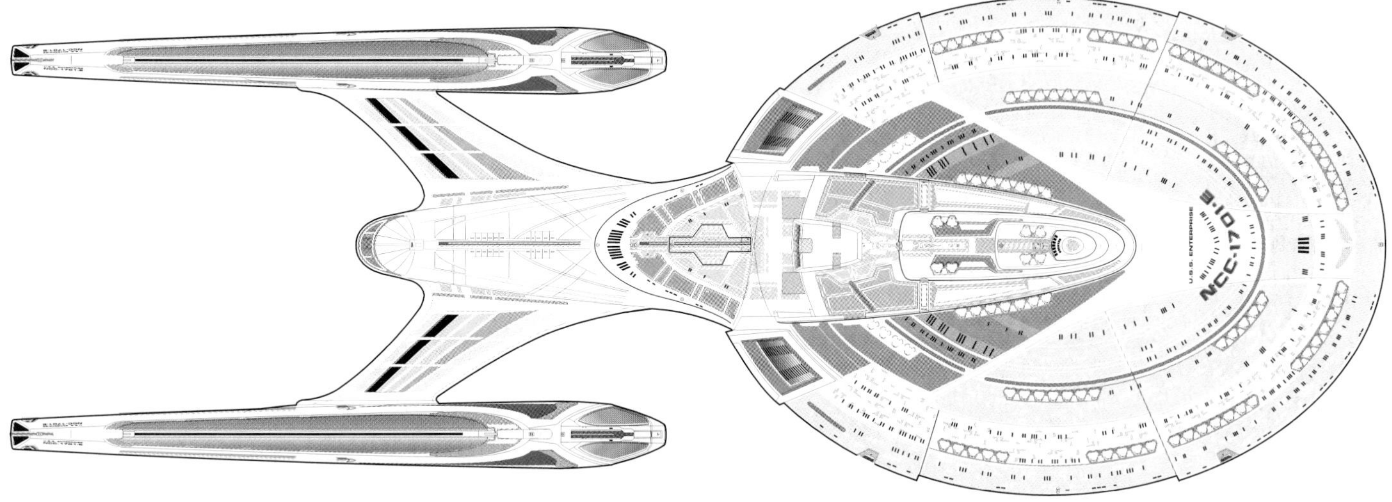

Sovereign class

Starship name	Registry	Class	Description	Episode or film
Voyager, U.S.S.	NCC-74656	*Intrepid*	Lost in **Delta Quadrant**	*Star Trek: Voyager*
Wellington, U.S.S.	NCC-28473	*Niagara*	Serviced at Starbase 74 in 2364; Ro's former posting	"11001001" (TNG), "Remember Me" (TNG), "Ensign Ro" (TNG)
Wyoming, U.S.S.	NCC-43730	*Mediterranean*	**Tuvok** served aboard *Wyoming* in 2349	"Flashback" (VGR)
Yamato, U.S.S.	NCC-71807	*Galaxy*	Destroyed by **Iconian** software weapon in 2365	"Where Silence Has Lease" (TNG), "Contagion" (TNG)
Yangtzee Kiang, U.S.S.	NCC-72453	*Danube*	Runabout assigned to Deep Space 9	"Emissary" (DS9), "Battle Lines" (DS9)
Yeager, U.S.S.	NCC-61947	*Saber*	Defended Sector 001 against **Borg** incursion	*Star Trek: First Contact*
Yellowstone, U.S.S.	NCC-70073	*Sequoia*	Transported **Melora Pazlar** to Deep Space 9	"Melora" (DS9)
Yellowstone, U.S.S.	NX-74751	*Yellowstone*	Prototype for advanced runabout	"Non Sequitur" (VGR)
Yorktown, U.S.S.	NCC-1717	*Constitution*	Scheduled to rendezvous with *Enterprise* in 2268	"Obsession" (TOS), *Star Trek IV: The Voyage Home*
Yorktown, U.S.S.	NCC-61137	*Zodiac*	(In anti-time future, ordered to make long-range sensor scans of Devron system)	"All Good Things..." (TNG)
Yosemite, U.S.S.	NCC-19002	*Oberth*	Science vessel; damaged while investigating plasma streamers	"Realm of Fear" (TNG)
Yukon, U.S.S.	NCC-74602	*Danube*	Runabout assigned to Deep Space 9	"Sons of Mogh" (DS9)
Zapata, U.S.S.	NCC-33184	*Surak*	Scheduled to rendezvous with *Enterprise*-D	"Menage a Troi" (TNG)
Zhukov, U.S.S.	NCC-26136	*Ambassador*	**Reginald Barclay** was assigned to *Zhukov* prior to *Enterprise*-D	"Hollow Pursuits" (TNG), "Data's Day" (TNG), "The Game" (TNG)

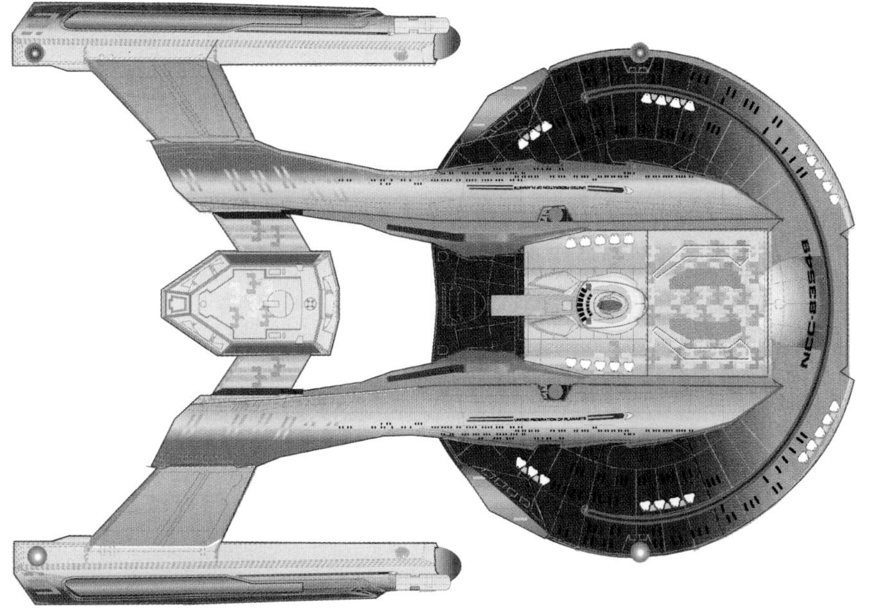

Akira class

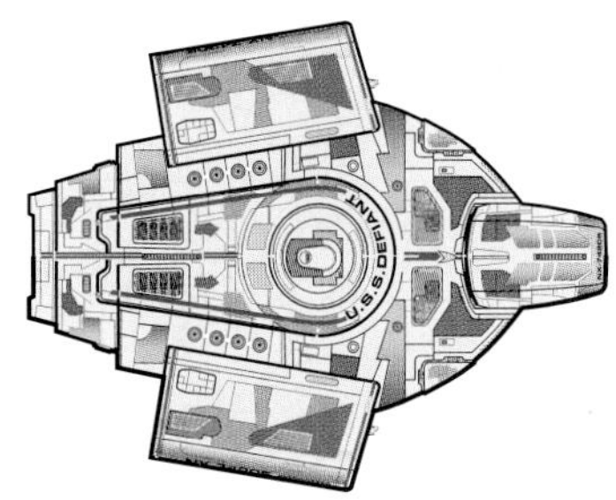

Defiant class

"State of Flux." *Voyager* episode #11. Teleplay by Chris Abbott. Story by Paul Robert Coyle. Directed by Robert Scheerer. Stardate 48658.2. *First aired in 1995. The* Voyager *crew learns that Ensign Seska is a Cardassian agent and that she has been secretly selling Federation replicator technology to the Kazons.* GUEST CAST: Martha Hackett as **Seska**; Josh Clark as **Carey**; Anthony DeLongis as **Culluh**, **Jal**; Majel Barrett as Computer voice. SEE: **bio-neural circuitry; bloodworms; Carey; Chakotay; Culluh; dermal regenerator; gin rummy; Jackson; *kaylo*; Kazon-Nistrim; Kazon; kelotane; *leola* root; masking circuitry; mushroom soup; neosorium composite; nucleonic radiation; Orkett's disease; pattern buffer; polaron; pyrocyte; Rakan folk songs; replicator; Seska; subspace bubble; *vakol* fish; *Voyager, U.S.S.***

static warp shell. A symmetrical **subspace bubble**, often toroidal or spherical in three-dimensional profile. A static warp shell cannot be used for warp-propulsion applications because warp drive requires an asymmetrical **warp field**. A static warp bubble was accidentally created in 2367 by Ensign Wesley Crusher aboard the *Enterprise*-D. Crusher had been working from Kosinski's warp-field equations, but something went wrong. Dr. Beverly Crusher was trapped inside the phenomenon, which became her own personal reality, shaped by her thoughts at the time the bubble was formed. Crusher had been thinking of lost friends, and her personal universe shrank until she was the only one left, demonstrating a link between consciousness and the physical universe. Crusher was recovered through the efforts of her son, with assistance from the Traveler. ("Remember Me" [TNG]). (In Q's **anti-time** realities, Data's plan to collapse the anti-time anomaly in the **Devron system** involved entering the anomaly and generating a large static warp shell inside. The shell acted as an artificial subspace barrier separating time from anti-time and collapsed the anomaly.) ("All Good Things..." [TNG]). A symmetrical (or static) subspace bubble could be generated around a person to permit survival in an environment high in ambient nucleonic radiation. In 2371, Ensign Seska used this technique in a failed attempt to retrieve a Federation replicator console that was on the bridge of a crippled Kazon vessel. ("State of Flux" [VGR]).

Station Lya IV. Space station. A trade stop for the ***Jovis***, following the kidnapping of Data by **Zibalian** trader **Kivas Fajo** in 2366. When queried by the *Enterprise*-D, Station Lya IV reported that the *Jovis* had been in orbit around the station for half a day. ("The Most Toys" [TNG]).

Station Nigala IV. Space station; destination of the *Enterprise*-D following its mission at **Bre'el IV** in 2366. ("Déjà Q" [TNG]).

Station Salem One. Site of an infamous sneak attack in which many Federation citizens were killed in a bloody preambie to war. ("The Enemy" [TNG]). *The adversary, the date, and the circumstances of this sneak attack were not established in the episode, although an early draft of "Family" (TNG) would have suggested that one of Wesley Crusher's ancestors was at Salem One.*

Statistical Mechanics. A mathematics class, required at Starfleet Academy. Cadet Wesley Crusher tutored **Joshua Albert** in Statistical Mechanics in 2368. ("The First Duty" [TNG]).

***Steamrunner*-class starship.** Type of Federation starship in use in the late 24th century. The *U.S.S. Appalachia* was a ship of the *Steamrunner* class. *(Star Trek: First Contact). The* Steamrunner-*class starship was designed by Alex Jaegar at ILM. It was rendered as a computer-generated visual effect.*

steelplast. Construction material used in the tunnel network beneath the capital city of planet **Mordan IV.** ("Too Short a Season" [TNG]).

Steinman analysis. Medical test noting individual specific data such as voice analysis and brain patterns. **Mira Romaine** was given a standard Steinman analysis while under the influence of the **Zetarians,** showing that her brain-wave patterns had been altered and now matched the patterns emitted by the aliens. ("The Lights of Zetar" [TOS]).

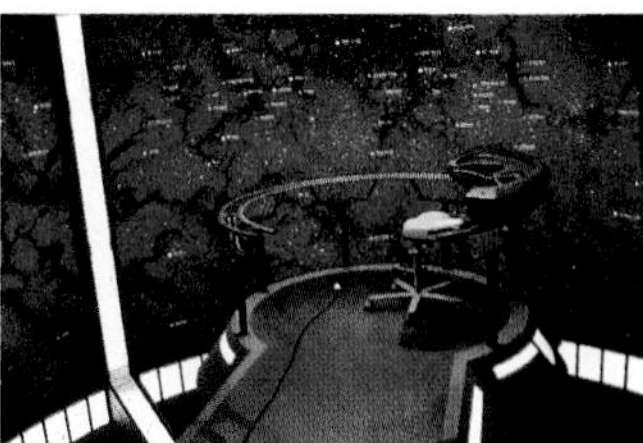

Stellar Cartography. Science department aboard Federation starships, dealing with star mapping. Lieutenant Commander **Neela Daren** headed the Stellar Cartography Department aboard the *Starship Enterprise*-D in 2369. ("Lessons" [TNG]). Stellar Cartography had a three-story map room that featured a large wraparound display screen. Captain Picard and Data used the map room to analyze **Dr. Tolian Soran**'s plan to control the trajectory of the nexus energy ribbon by destroying the star in the **Veridian system**. *(Star Trek Generations).* Stellar Cartography on a *Sovereign*-class vessel was located on Deck 11. *(Star Trek: First Contact).*

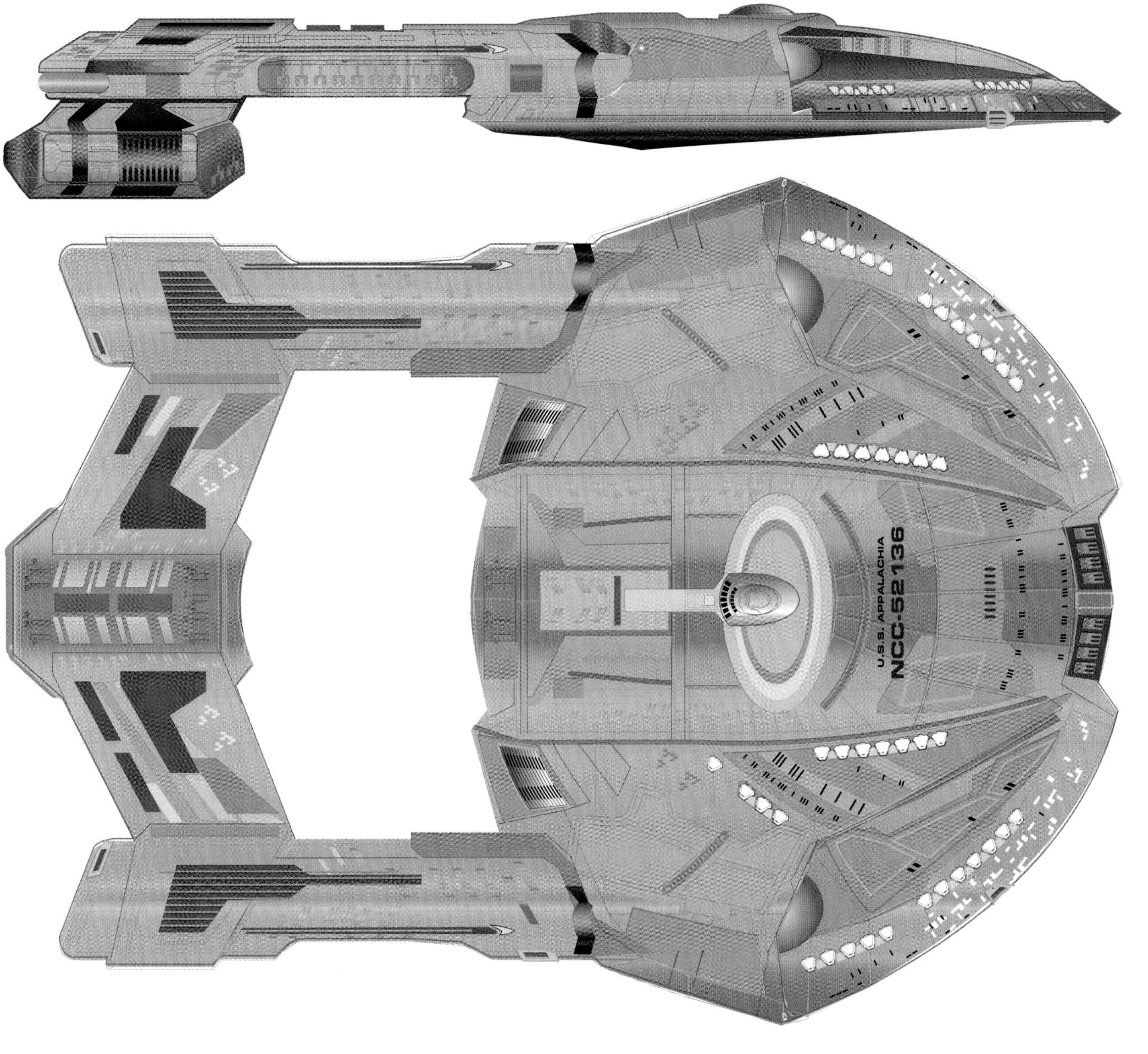

stellar core fragment. An extremely dense, massive piece of a disintegrated star, probably composed of **neutronium**. The *Enterprise*-D tracked such a fragment through the **Moab Sector** in 2368. SEE: **Genome Colony**. ("The Masterpiece Society" [TNG]).

Stephan. (Erick Weiss). Colonist on planet **Orellius**. ("Paradise" [DS9]). SEE: **Alixus.**

Stephan. A young soccer player who was the love of Beverly Crusher's life, when she was eight and he was 11. She dreamed that they would be married, but he never knew she existed. ("The Host" [TNG]). *At the time, Beverly's last name was Howard.*

Stevens. (Jay Baker). Noncommissioned Starfleet engineer assigned to station Deep Space 9. In 2372, Stevens was posted to engineering on the *U.S.S. Defiant* when the ship came under Jem'Hadar attack during a trade conference with the Karemma. ("Starship Down" [DS9]).

Stiles, Lieutenant. (Paul Comi). Navigator on the *U.S.S. Enterprise* during the **Romulan** incursion of 2266. Several members of Stiles's family had been lost during the Earth-Romulan conflicts of the previous century. ("Balance of Terror" [TOS]).

Sto-Vo-Kor. Klingon mythological place of the afterlife for the honored dead. The prophet **Kahless the Unforgettable** was said to await those who were worthy of *Sto-Vo-Kor.* ("Rightful Heir" [TNG]). SEE: ***Fek'lhr***.

Stocker, Commodore. (Charles Drake). Starfleet officer who assumed command of Starbase 10 in 2267. Stocker was transported to that post aboard the *Starship Enterprise.* While en route, several *Enterprise* personnel, including Captain Kirk, became ill with a radiation-induced hyperaccelerated aging disease. Fearing the imminent loss of these valuable officers, Stocker assumed command of the *Enterprise* and violated the **Romulan Neutral Zone** in an effort to reach Starbase 10's medical facilities more quickly. Stocker's action nearly triggered an interstellar incident. ("The Deadly Years" [TOS]). SEE: **corbomite**.

Stockholm Syndrome. In psychology, the tendency for hostages to sympathize with their captors after extended captivity. Dr. Crusher believed that **Jeremiah Rossa** might have exhibited Stockholm Syndrome after spending years with **Talarian** Captain **Endar**. ("Suddenly Human" [TNG]).

stokaline. Medication. McCoy gave stokaline to Spock after Spock put himself into a deep trance in an attempt to regain control of the *Enterprise* from the **Kelvans** in 2268. As a ruse, McCoy told the Kelvans that Spock suffered from **Rigelian Kassaba fever** and required the medication. ("By Any Other Name" [TOS]).

Stol. Cousin to **Quark**. Stol bought one of the items that **Vash** brought back from the Gamma Quadrant in 2369 for 105 bars of gold-pressed **latinum.** ("Q-Less" [DS9], "Family Business" [DS9]).

Stone of Gol. SEE: **Gol, Stone of.**

Stone, Commodore. (Percy Rodriguez). Commander of **Starbase 11** in 2267. Stone presided over the court-martial of Captain James Kirk for the apparent death of **Ben Finney** in that year. When circumstancial evidence implicated Kirk, Stone urged him to resign for the good of the service. Stone had commanded a starship earlier in his career. ("Court Martial" [TOS]). *Stone must have stepped down as commander of Starbase 11 shortly after Kirk's acquittal, since Stone had been replaced by Commodore José Mendez when the* Enterprise *returned to the base in the following episode, "The Menagerie, Part I" (TOS). Percy Rodriguez later played Primus Kimbridge in Gene Roddenberry's pilot movie,* Genesis II.

Stonn. (Lawrence Montaigne). Vulcan man who married **T'Pring** in 2267. T'Pring had been bonded to **Spock**, but she chose Stonn after Spock freed her for daring to challenge the wedding. Spock warned him that having may not be quite so good a thing as wanting. ("Amok Time" [TOS]). *Lawrence Montaigne also played the Romulan subcommander in "Balance of Terror" (TOS).*

Story of the Promise, The. Klingon gospel that tells of the pledge that prophet **Kahless the Unforgettable** gave the people of the homeworld. Kahless, who had united the homeworld to form the **Klingon Empire** and ruled with great wisdom, one day said it was time for him to depart. When the people begged him not to leave, Kahless said he was going ahead to ***Sto-Vo-Kor***, and promised to return one day. He pointed to a star in the heavens and told the people to look for him there "on that point of light." Klingon clerics later established a monastery on planet **Boreth**, orbiting that star, to await his return. ("Rightful Heir" [TNG]).

"Storyteller, The." *Deep Space Nine* episode #14. Teleplay by Kurt Michael Bensmiller and Ira Steven Behr. Story by Kurt Michael Bensmiller. Directed by David Livingston. Stardate 46729.1. *First aired in 1993. Chief O'Brien suddenly finds himself the spiritual leader of a Bajoran village.* GUEST CAST: Lawrence Monoson as **Hovath**; Kay E. Kuter as **Sirah**; Gina Phillips as **Varis Sul**; Jim Jansen as **Faren Kag**; Aron Eisenberg as **Nog**; Jordan Lund as **Woban**; Amy Benedict as Woman. SEE: **Bajorans; baseball; Bokai, Buck; Dal'Rok; Faren Kag; Ferengi Rules of Acquisition; Gamzian; Glyrhond; Hovath; *larish* pie; Navot; Odo; Paqu; Sirah; stardrifter; tetrarch; Trixian bubble juice; Varis Sul; Woban.**

Storyteller. SEE: **Sirah**.

straight nines. High-scoring move in **dom-jot**. The play is extremely difficult to achieve. ("Tapestry" [TNG]).

Straleb security ship. Vessel operated by the Straleb government. A Straleb security ship intercepted the *Starship Enterprise*-D shortly after stardate 42402, carrying Straleb Secretary **Kushell** and his entourage. ("The Outrageous Okona" [TNG]). *The miniature for this ship was designed by Rick Sternbach. The model was later modified for use in "The Hunted" (TNG).*

Straleb. Class-M planet, along with **Altec**, part of the Coalition of Madena. Although it was technically at peace with Altec, relations between the two planets had been strained to the point that an interplanetary incident was created when it was revealed that **Benzan** of Straleb had been engaged to **Yanar** of Altec in 2365. ("The Outrageous Okona" [TNG]).

strategema. Challenging holographic game of strategy and wills. Played by two contestants, the game involves manipulating circular icons on a three-dimensional grid to gain control of one's opponent's territory while defending your own. Riker once challenged **Zakdorn** strategist (and grand master strategema player) **Kolrami** to a game, and was defeated in only 23 moves. A later match between Kolrami and Data ended in Kolrami conceding defeat. Data later confided that his strategy had been to play not to win, but merely to maintain a tie until his opponent gave up. ("Peak Performance" [TNG]).

Strategic Operations Officer. Senior staff position on station Deep Space 9 added in 2372 and held by Lieutenant Commander **Worf**. The Strategic Ops Officer was assigned a new console in the station's **ops** center. ("The Way of the Warrior" [DS9]). The primary duty of Deep Space 9's Strategic Operations Officer was to coordinate all Starfleet activity in the Bajoran sector. ("Hippocratic Oath" [DS9]).

Stratos. Beautiful cloud city above the planet **Ardana**, believed to be the finest example of sustained antigravity elevation in the galaxy. Stratos was a study in the contrasts of Ardanan society: The Stratos city dwellers lived a life of leisure, while the **Troglytes**, who lived on the planet's surface, toiled under brutal conditions. By 2269, Troglyte activists, called **Disrupters**, were committing acts of terrorism and vandalism in the city to protest their plight. Their actions spurred the development of **filter masks** that were provided to the Troglyte miners to protect them from the harmful effects of the **zenite** gas found in the Ardanan mines. ("The Cloud Minders" [TOS]). *The model of the cloud city of Stratos was designed by original series art director Matt Jefferies, who also supervised the interior sets.*

stratospheric torpedoes. Starship-launched weapon designed to explode in a planet's atmosphere. In 2373, the **Maquis**, lead by **Michael Eddington**, used stratospheric torpedoes as the delivery system for cobalt diselenide, a biogenic weapon, against the Cardassian colonies on **Veloz Prime** and **Quatal Prime**. ("For the Uniform" [DS9]).

strawberries and cream. Traditional Earth breakfast food. Although limited to **ration packs**, Captain Janeway wished that she could have strawberries and cream for breakfast. ("Phage" [VGR]).

Strickler, Admiral. (Jack Shearer). High-ranking Starfleet official. Strickler stationed at Starfleet Headquarters in San Francisco, Earth, in 2372. In an alternate reality, Strickler presided over a meeting to discuss **Harry Kim**'s design for a prototype runabout, the ***U.S.S. Yellowstone***. ("Non Sequitur" [VGR]). *Jack Shearer also played Ruwon in "Visionary" (DS9) and Admiral Hayes in* Star Trek: First Contact.

strip. Form of Ferengi currency, a fraction of a bar of gold-pressed **latinum.** ("The Alternate" [DS9]). One bar of latinum was equal to 20 strips. ("Body Parts" [DS9]).

Strnad star system. Planetary system. The *Enterprise*-D delivered a party of Earth colonists to a planet in the Strnad system in 2364. The adjoining **Rubicun** star system contained another Class-M planet ruled by the Edo entity, who disapproved of the colonists living in the Strnad system. Because this location caused conflict to the **Edo god**, the colony was removed and transplanted elsewhere. ("Justice" [TNG]). *Named for* Star Trek: The Next Generation *production staff member Janet Strnad.*

Stroyerian. Spoken language. *U.S.S. Aries* First Officer Flaherty was fluent in Stroyerian, one of 40 languages that he spoke. ("The Icarus Factor" [TNG]).

structural breach. Break or hole in the hull of a starship. While attempting to escape from a **subspace rift** in 2370, the *Enterprise*-D came very close to suffering a structural breach. ("Force of Nature" [TNG]).

structural integrity field. Shaped force field used on Federation starships to supplement the mechanical strength of the ship's spaceframe. Without the structural integrity field, a starship would not be able to withstand the tremendous accelerations involved in spaceflight. During the *Enterprise*-D's contact with the **Tin Man** life-form in 2366, Chief Engineer La Forge diverted structural integrity power to strengthen the inner deflector grid, damaged in a Romulan attack. ("Tin Man" [TNG]).

strychnine. Alkaloid poison derived from the Earth plant *Strychnos nux vomica*. The poison also acts as a central-nervous-system stimulant, and in large doses causes convulsions and death. ("Ship in a Bottle" [TNG]).

Stubbs, Dr. Paul. (Ken Jenkins). Eminent astrophysicist. Stubbs came aboard the *Enterprise*-D in 2366 for transport to the **Kavis Alpha** Sector, where he was to conduct a neutronium-decay experiment. A complex individual, Stubbs had been regarded as something of a *wunderkind* in his youth, and the resulting social isolation left a lasting mark on him. His landmark experiment at Kavis Alpha was the culmination of over 20 years of work, but the launch of an instrument probe he called "the Egg" for the experiment was jeopardized with the unexpected evolution of sentient **nanites** on the *Enterprise*-D. Although Stubbs did not initially recognize the nanites as life-forms, they eventually agreed to cooperate with the execution of his experiment. Stubbs was an aficionado of the ancient game of **baseball,** and he was fond of daydreaming about the game's past glories, eschewing holographic re-creations in favor of his own imagination. ("Evolution" [TNG]).

stunstick. A meter-long, rodlike weapon that was used by cadre forces fighting for control of the **Turkana IV** colony. The weapon was capable of delivering a powerful electric shock to an opponent. **Ishara Yar** was injured by a stunstick during an away-team mission with members of the *Enterprise*-D crew in 2367. ("Legacy" [TNG]).

Sturgeon. *Enterprise* crew member. Sturgeon was killed on the surface of planet **M-113** by the salt vampire in 2266. ("The Man Trap" [TOS]). *Named for science-fiction writer Theodore Sturgeon, who wrote "Shore Leave" (TOS).*

Styles, Captain. (James B. Sikking). Commander of the *Starship **Excelsior*** during its initial trial runs in 2285. Styles unsuccessfully attempted to stop Kirk from stealing the *Enterprise* to reach the **Genesis Planet**. (*Star Trek III: The Search for Spock*). Styles was later succeeded by Captain **Hikaru Sulu**, who assumed command of the *Excelsior* when it entered service as a deep-space exploratory vessel in 2290. *(Star Trek VI: The Undiscovered Country).*

Styris IV. Planet. The population of Styris IV was threatened by deadly **Anchilles fever** in 2364. Deaths in the millions were averted by the availability of vaccine from planet **Ligon II**. ("Code of Honor" [TNG]).

styrolite. Clear plastic-like material used for biologic quarantine of potentially hazardous life-forms. A sheath of styrolite was used to encase a genetically engineered child from the **Darwin Genetic Research Station** when it was feared that the child might carry a dangerous disease organism. ("Unnatural Selection" [TNG]).

"Sub Rosa." *Next Generation* episode #166. Teleplay by Brannon Braga. Television story by Jeri Taylor. Based upon material by Jeanna F. Gallo. Directed by Jonathan Frakes. Stardate 47423.9. *First aired in 1994. After attending her grandmother's funeral, Beverly Crusher finds that she has inherited the family ghost.* Sub rosa *is a Latin term meaning "in secret". It is derived from the ancient practice of hanging a rose over a meeting as a symbol of secrecy.* GUEST CAST: Michael Keenan as **Maturin**; Shay Duffin as **Quint**, **Ned**; Duncan Regehr as **Ronin**; Ellen Albertini Dow as **Howard**, **Felisa**. SEE: **anaphasic life-form;**

caber toss; Caldos colony; camellia; Crusher, Beverly; deep tissue scan; ghost; Howard family candle; Howard, Felisa; Howard, Jessel; Maturin; Quint, Ned; Ronin; noncorporeal life; Selar, Dr.; Starbase 621; weather control system.

sub-nagus. Ferengi title for the official in charge of commerce in one district. Quark served under a sub-nagus during his youth. ("Playing God" [DS9]).

subatomic disruptor. Offensive weapon employed by the 29th-century *Timeship Aeon*. Subatomic disruptors cause the molecular structure of the target to come apart. ("Future's End, Part I" [VGR]).

subatomic particle shower. Potentially hazardous side effect of a near-critical warp-core **shock pulse**. ("Twisted" [VGR]).

subcutaneous transponder. SEE: **transponder, emergency**.

subdermal bioprobe. Small medical device that could be implanted just under a patient's skin, used to transmit biochemistry readings. ("Sacred Ground" [VGR]).

subdermal communicator. Small transmitter/receiver device implanted under the skin. **Benjamin Sisko** and **Miles O'Brien (mirror)** used subdermal communicators implanted behind their ears to keep in contact during their mission to recruit Professor **Jennifer Sisko (mirror)** to the side of the **Terran resistance**. ("Through the Looking Glass" [DS9]).

subhadar. A rank in the **Angosia**n military. **Roga Danar** earned the rank of subhadar twice during the **Tarsian War**. ("The Hunted" [TNG]).

subimpulse raider. Two-person interplanetary spacecraft used by the Bajoran resistance during the Cardassian occupation of Bajor. Deep Space 9 officers Kira and Dax used a subimpulse raider to reach Bajor during the attempted coup of 2370. The raider was hit by opposing weapons fire and crashed. ("The Siege" [DS9]).

sublight. Scientific term describing space-normal speeds, slower than *c*, the speed of light. Sublight speeds do not require **warp drive**, and are generally achieved using impulse power. As a result, sublight travel is subject to relativistic effects such as time dilation and Fitzgerald-Lorentz contraction. Sometimes referred to as space-normal travel. SEE: **impulse drive**.

submicron matrix transfer technology. Technique for replicating existing neural net pathways in a positronic brain into another positronic brain. This technology was introduced at a cybernetics conference in 2366, attended by Data, and led to Data's construction of his android daughter, **Lal**. ("The Offspring" [TNG]).

Subroutine C-47. Computer software on the *Enterprise*-D responsible for noncritical systems such as replicator selections and recreational programming. Subroutine C-47 was replaced by elements of Data's personal programming during an interface experiment in 2369. This caused malfunctions in food replicators, Captain Picard's music selections, and the holodeck program ***Ancient West.*** ("A Fistful of Datas" [TNG]). SEE: **Spot.**

subsonic transmitter. Electronic device used to generate audio signals of frequencies below the threshold of human hearing. Spock used a subsonic transmitter on planet **Omicron Ceti III** to drive the spores from the surviving colonists' bodies in 2267. The device broadcast an irritating frequency that was described as being like itching powder spread on the affected individuals. ("This Side of Paradise" [TOS]). SEE: **spores, Omicron Ceti III**.

Subspace Relay Station. SEE: **Relay Station 47**.

subspace bubble. SEE: **static warp shell**.

subspace inversion. Spectacular phenomenon in which subspace near a wormhole becomes fragmented. The Bajoran wormhole undergoes a subspace inversion every 50 years. In 2372 the staff of Deep Space 9 took the *Starship Defiant* to the Gamma Quadrant to observe the wormhole undergo this process. It was during that trip that an engine-room accident occurred that almost pulled Benjamin Sisko into subspace. SEE: **Sisko, Jake.** ("The Visitor" [DS9]).

subspace phenomena. SEE: **Exosia; infinite velocity, theory of; solanagen-based entities; tetryon; theta-band emissions; verteron; warp field**.

subspace compression. Phenomenon resulting from differential field-potential values in nearby portions of the same warp field. **Subspace** compression can cause different parts of an object to have different inertial densities, resulting in structural strain on the object. In severe cases, subspace compression can tear an object apart at the subatomic level. Depending on relative field symmetries, subspace compression can also cause numerous other, often unpredictable, side effects. ("Déjà Q" [TNG]).

subspace field distortions. Phenomena that generally indicate the presence of a warp-propulsion system. The **Cytherian** probe encountered by the *Enterprise*-D in 2367 did not create any detectable field distortions and its method of propulsion remained a mystery. ("The Nth Degree" [TNG]).

subspace funnel. Subspace link between two points in normal space. Geordi La Forge suggested that the **trionic initiators** in the ***U.S.S. Hera***'s **warp core** might have created a subspace funnel between her last reported position and **Marijne VII**. ("Interface" [TNG]).

subspace instabilities. Area of weakness in the fabric of normal space. Areas demonstrating subspace instabilities were more prone to **warp-field effect.** ("Force of Nature" [TNG]).

subspace interphase pocket. Localized section of space where subspace intrudes into normal space. In 2370, the runabout *Mekong* intercepted one such pocket and accidentally removed a rapidly expanding **protouniverse** from the area. ("Playing God" [DS9]).

subspace rift. The extrusion of subspace into normal space over a discernible event horizon. The cumulative exposure of warp-field energy to susceptible areas of space was thought to cause these rifts to form. ("Force of Nature" [TNG]).

subspace rupture. Huge swirling anomaly that draws surrounding matter into a central vortex. A subspace rupture was discovered in the Hanoli system in 2169 by a Vulcan ship. An elevated thoron reading near Deep Space 9 in 2369 was initially theorized by Dax to be a similar phenomenon, but this was later found to be incorrect. ("If Wishes Were Horses" [DS9]).

subspace shock wave. Powerful energy front generated by a massive energy discharge. A subspace shock wave was created when **Praxis**, a moon of the **Klingon Homeworld**, exploded in 2293, causing severe damage to the homeworld, as well as to the nearby *Starship* ***Excelsior***. *(Star Trek VI: The Undiscovered Country). The energy wave at the beginning of* Star Trek VI *was described as a subspace shock wave as a means of "explaining" how an explosion on Praxis could affect the* Excelsior, *which was presumably several light-years distant at the time, since a slower-than-light shock wave from a conventional explosion would have taken many years to bridge that distance. A subspace shock wave also provides some rationale for why such a powerful explosion failed to totally destroy the Klingon Homeworld.*

subspace transition rebound. Phenomenon associated with the use of folded-space transport devices such as those employed by the **Ansata** terrorists of planet **Rutia IV**. An adaptive subspace echogram was found to measure the rebound phenomenon with sufficient accuracy to locate the Ansata headquarters, despite the fact that folded-space transport was virtually undetectable with conventional sensors. ("The High Ground" [TNG]).

subspace vacuole. Short-lived interspatial passageway. Subspace vacuoles occurred naturally on the **Vhnori** homeworld, linking that planet to an area of space near a ringed planet in the Delta Quadrant. ("Emanations" [VGR]). SEE: **spectral rupture; Vhnori transference ritual**.

subspace technology. SEE: **Cochrane, Zefram; millicochrane; transwarp; trionic initiators; warp drive.**

subspace beacon. Signal capable of traversing **subspace**. The **combadges** worn by Starfleet personnel were capable of serving as subspace beacons. ("Time and Again" [VGR]).

subspace field inverter. Sophisticated equipment, not normally included in the inventory of a *Galaxy*-class starship. This device is capable of generating low levels of **eichner radiation**, which were found to stimulate growth of certain strains of deadly **plasma plague**. ("The Child" [TNG]).

subspace proximity detonator. Triggering mechanism employed by small explosive devices used in the **Koinonian** war a thousand years ago. Such a device, undetectable by a normal Starfleet tricorder, was responsible for the explosion that killed **Marla Aster** in 2366. ("The Bonding" [TNG]). Subspace proximity detonators were also used by the **Talarians** during the **Galen border conflicts** in the 2350s to booby-trap their ships. ("Suddenly Human" [TNG]).

subspace radio. Communications system using transmission of electromagnetic signals through a subspace medium rather than through normal relativistic space. The use of subspace radio permits communication across interstellar distances at speeds much greater than that of light, thereby significantly reducing the time lag associated with sending a conventional radio signal across such distances. Subspace communications can include voice, text, and/or visual data. Subspace radio was invented over a century after the development of the **warp drive**. News of the loss of the ***U.S.S. Horizon***, destroyed near planet Sigma Iotia II in 2168, prior to the invention of subspace radio, did not reach Federation space until 2268 because its distress call was sent by conventional radio. ("A Piece of the Action" [TOS]). Subspace communications within Federation space are made even more rapid by the use of a network of subspace relay stations, deep-space facilities that amplify, reroute, and retransmit subspace signals. ("Aquiel" [TNG]). SEE: **Relay Station 47**. An experimental subspace relay station, intended to permit communications through the Bajoran wormhole, was tested by a team of Cardassian, Bajoran, and Federation scientists in 2371. ("Destiny" [DS9]). Building a subspace transceiver was a common school project for children in science classes. ("Whispers" [DS9]).

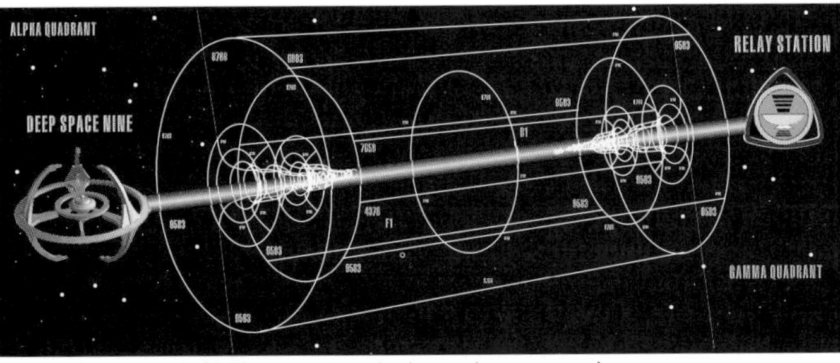

Bajoran wormhole: subspace relay

subspace resonator. Field manipulation device. The *Enterprise*-D supplied a subspace resonator to a disabled **Romulan science vessel** in 2368, enabling the Romulan ship to return home, albeit slowly. ("The Next Phase" [TNG]).

subspace shunt. Device used by the **Kobliad** criminal **Rao Vantika** to gain unauthorized control of computer systems such as those on Deep Space 9. Attached to a secondary system, the shunt could be used to bypass normal security lockouts. ("The Passenger" [DS9]).

subspace transponder. Device used to aid in the location of objects in space, such as ships or flight recorders. ("Dramatis Personae" [DS9]).

subspace transporter. Matter-energy teleportation system capable of transporting matter over several light-years, much further than possible with conventional **transporter** technology. A subspace transporter is capable of penetrating a starship's defensive **shields**. The process is dangerous, since in order to transport matter through subspace, it must be put in a very unstable state of **quantum flux**. The Federation abandoned its research in the field because it found the technology unreliable. Former DaiMon **Bok** used a subspace transporter in 2370 in a plot of revenge against Jean-Luc Picard. ("Bloodlines" [TNG]).

subspace. Spatial continuum with significantly different properties from our own, a fundamental part of **warp drive**. Warp-driven starships employ a subspace generator to create the asymmetrical spatial distortion necessary for the vessel to travel faster than the speed of light. Subspace is also used as a medium for subspace radio transmissions. SEE: **Cochrane, Zefram; subspace phenomena; subspace technology**. *Einstein's theories suggest that light-speed travel is impossible in our universe, so subspace and warp drive were "invented" by* Star Trek's *writers to explain how a starship might do it anyway. On the other hand,* ***Professor Stephen Hawking****, when visiting the* Enterprise-D *engine room at Paramount Pictures in 1993, said he was working on warp drive. We can hardly wait.*

Subytt freighter. Cargo vessel of Subytt registry. A Subytt freighter docked at station Deep Space 9 in 2370, smuggling defective **isolinear rods** to planet Bajor. Quark reported the situation to station Security Chief Odo, resulting in the arrest of three members of the freighter's crew. ("The Homecoming" [DS9]). SEE: **Ferengi Rules of Acquisition: #76**.

suck salt. To ingest sodium chloride in the form of a solid crystal stick. Considered to be a "nasty habit," conducive to health risks. ("Unification, Part II" [TNG]).

"Suddenly Human." *Next Generation* episode #76. Teleplay by John Whelpley & Jeri Taylor. Story by Ralph Phillips. Directed by Gabrielle Beaumont. Stardate 44143.7. *First aired in 1990. Picard tries to return an apparently abused child to his biological family.* GUEST CAST: Sherman Howard as **Endar**; Chad Allen as **Jono**; Barbara Townsend as **Rossa, Admiral Connaught**. SEE: **Age of Decision; *Alba Ra*; autosuture; *B'Nar*; banana split; Castal I; Endar; Galen border conflicts; Galen IV; high-energy X-ray laser; Jono; Merculite rockets; neutral particle weapons; *Q'Maire*; Rossa, Admiral Connaught; Rossa, Connor; Rossa, Jeremiah; Rossa, Moira; Sector 21947; Stockholm Syndrome; subspace technology; *t'stayan*; Talarian observation craft; Talarians; triangular envelopment; Woden Sector.**

Suder, Lon. (Brad Dourif). Crew member on the *Starship Voyager*, found guilty of murder in 2372. Suder had committed violent crimes years before, and attempts at treatment and rehabilitation had been unsuccessful. Suder had been a member of the Maquis, and had served with fellow *Voyager* crew members Chakotay and B'Elanna Torres during several skirmishes with Cardassian forces before coming onboard the Voyager in 2371, accepting an assignment as an engineer. In 2372, Suder murdered fellow *Voyager* engineer **Frank Darwin**. Although Betazoid, Suder felt no remorse for his crime and could not embody the emotions of others. *Voyager* Security Officer **Tuvok**, learning that Suder had committed violent crimes in the past, performed a **mind-meld** with Suder in hopes of finding reason for Suder's madness. Unfortunately, the only result was that Tuvok experienced a temporary, violent loss of emotional self-control. Suder was subsequently ordered to spend the rest of *Voyager*'s journey imprisoned in his quarters. ("Meld" [VGR]). While incarcerated, Suder became proficient at floriculture, an interest that he gained from his mind-meld with Tuvok. Suder even named a new hybrid orchid after Tuvok. Suder escaped imprisonment in late 2372 when **Kazon-Nistrim** forces captured the *Voyager*, and was the only organic *Voyager* crew member remaining on-board after the ship's crew was put off at planet **Hanon IV**. Suder was instrumental in helping to retake the ship from the Nistrim, but he was killed by a Kazon soldier while doing so. ("Basics, Parts I and II" [VGR]). *Brad Dourif also portrayed Piter De Vries, the mentat in the movie version of Frank Herbert's novel* Dune.

Sulan. (Brian Markinson). Chief surgeon of the **Vidiian Sodality**. He was a sympathetic man who sought to find a cure for the **phage**. In 2371, Sulan used a **genotron** to extract Klingon genetic information from **B'Elanna Torres** to produce a fully Klingon version of her, in hopes that the resulting Klingon individual would demonstrate resistance to the phage. In the process, a fully human Torres was also created. Sulan was attracted to the Klingon Torres, and after *Voyager* crew member **Peter Durst** was killed for organ harvesting, Sulan had Durst's face grafted onto his own in hopes that Torres would find it more pleasing. Sulan was so inured to the horrors of the **Vidiian** condition that he did not realize that a non-Vidiian would find that act repulsive. Nevertheless, Sulan's experiment was a success, demonstrating that Klingon physiology was resistant to the phage, paving the way for a possible cure based on an integration of Klingon genetic elements into Vidiian DNA. ("Faces" [VGR]). *Brian Markinson played both Sulan and Durst. He had previously played Vorin in "Homeward" (TNG).*

Sulu, Demora. (Jacqueline Kim). Helm officer of the *Starship* ***Enterprise*-B** at the time of the ship's launch in 2293, born 2271, the daughter of **Hikaru Sulu**. *(Star Trek Generations). Birth date assumes she was 22 years old at the time of the movie.*

Sulu (mirror). (George Takei). Lieutenant Sulu was security chief aboard the *I.S.S. Enterprise* in the **mirror universe**. ("Mirror, Mirror" [TOS])

Sulu, Hikaru. (George Takei). Helm officer aboard the original *Starship Enterprise* under the command of Captain James Kirk. Sulu, born in 2237 in San Francisco on Earth *(Star Trek IV: The Voyage Home),* was initially assigned as a physicist ("Where No Man Has Gone Before" [TOS]) aboard the *Enterprise* in 2265 ("The Deadly Years" [TOS]), but later transferred to the helm. ("The Corbomite Maneuver" [TOS]).

Sulu assumed command of the *Starship* ***Excelsior*** in 2290, and subsequently conducted a three-year scientific mission of cataloging gaseous planetary anomalies in the **Beta Quadrant**. Sulu and the *Excelsior* played a pivotal role in the historic **Khitomer** peace conference of 2293 by helping to protect the conference against Federation and Klingon forces seeking to disrupt the peace process. *(Star Trek VI: The Undiscovered Country).* During the incident, Sulu demonstrated his loyalty and courage when he risked his ship and his career by violating Starfleet orders and attempting a rescue of former shipmates **James T. Kirk** and **Leonard McCoy**. During the attempted rescue, Sulu narrowly escaped a Klingon patrol commanded by Captain **Kang** in the **Azure Nebula**. Sulu never entered the incident into his official log. ("Flashback" [VGR]).

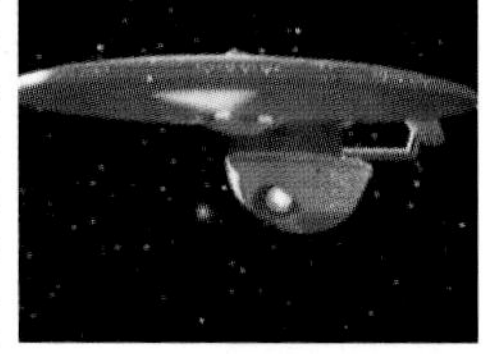

Sulu had a wide range of hobbies, including botany ("The Mantrap" [TOS]) and **fencing**. The latter interest surfaced when Sulu suffered the effects of the **Psi 2000 virus** in 2266, and Sulu threatened everyone in sight with a foil. ("The Naked Time" [TOS]). Old-style handguns were another of Sulu's hobbies, and he had always wanted a Police Special in his collection. ("Shore Leave" [TOS]).

Hikaru Sulu had a daughter, **Demora Sulu**, born in 2271. *(Star Trek Generations).*

Starfleet Command honored Sulu's contributions to space exploration by displaying his portrait in **Starfleet Headquarters** in San Francisco. ("Flashback" [VGR]).

"Tattoo" (VGR) establishes that a Captain Sulu, patrolling the Cardassian border, sponsored young ***Chakotay*** *for admission to Starfleet Academy around 2350. The episode does not make clear if this is Hikaru Sulu, who would have been around 113 years old at the time. (It could not have been Demora, since Chakotay referred to Sulu as "him.") "Encounter at Farpoint" (TNG) shows Admiral McCoy visiting the* Enterprise-D *at the age of 137, so 113 might not be out of the question.*

Sulu's first appearance was in "Where No Man Has Gone Before," in which he was the ship's physicist, but by "The Corbomite Maneuver" he had assumed his familiar post at the helm. A scene that was filmed for Star Trek II, *but not included in the final cut of the movie, would have shown that Sulu was about to assume command of the* Excelsior *at that time. A scene for* Star Trek IV *that was in the final draft of the script but not filmed would have had Sulu meeting a young boy in San Francisco who was Sulu's great-great-great-grandfather. Sulu's first name, Hikaru, was authorized by Gene Roddenberry in 1979, but was not used on film until* Star Trek VI: The Undiscovered Country.

Sun Tzu. Ancient Chinese philosopher whose writings on the art of warfare are still taught at Starfleet Academy. Among Sun Tzu's teachings was, "Know your enemy and know yourself, and victory will always be yours." ("The Last Outpost" [TNG]).

Suna. (Andrew Prine). Military official on planet **Tilonus IV.** Suna was seen as different characters by William Riker in a delusional world created in Riker's mind when he was brainwashed on that planet in 2369. Suna controlled the mind-conditioning equipment, and his image was projected as Lieutenant Suna aboard the *Enterprise*-D and as the administrator of the imaginary **Tilonus Institute for Mental Disorders**. ("Frame of Mind" [TNG]).

Sunad. (Charles Dennis). Commander of a **Zalkonian** warship. Sunad's ship was dispatched in 2366 to capture a fugitive Zalkonian named **John Doe**. Sunad, upon locating Doe aboard the *Enterprise*-D near the **Zeta Gelis** system, demanded Doe's extradition, alleging Doe to be an escaped criminal. It was later found that Doe was a member of a persecuted Zalkonian minority. ("Transfigurations" [TNG]). *Sunad was named for* Star Trek: The Next Generation *staff writer Richard Danus. (Spell it backward).*

Supera, Patterson. (Max Supera). Son of an *Enterprise*-D crew member. Patterson was one of the winners of the primary-school science fair held aboard the *Enterprise*-D in 2368. Young Patterson was also made an honorary officer in charge of radishes by Captain Picard. ("Disaster" [TNG]). SEE: **Flores, Marissa.** *Patterson's last name was not given in dialog, but was printed on the plaque that the kids gave the captain.*

supernova. A star, near the end of its life, that collapses due to hydrogen depletion, briefly igniting a violent fusion explosion of helium and other elements. The luminosity of a supernova can increase by a factor of hundreds of millions for a brief period. Supernovae are very rare, and only a few starship crews have ever witnessed one. The crew of the original *U.S.S. Enterprise* witnessed two, Minara in 2268 and Beta Niobe in 2269. An unusual number of supernovae exploded in 2373, a side effect of a civil war occurring in the **Q Continuum**. ("The Q and the Grey" [VGR]).

Supervisor 194. Code name for **Gary Seven** when he was assigned to **Earth** in 1968. ("Assignment: Earth" [TOS]).

Surak. (Barry Atwater). Father of the **Vulcan** philosophy, a man of peace and logic who helped lead his people out of a period of devastating wars, some two thousand years ago, when his people were ruled by violent passions. A replica of Surak was created by the **Excalbians** in 2269 as part of their attempt to study the human concept of "good" and "evil." ("The Savage Curtain" [TOS]). SEE: **Yarnek**. Surak led his people during what became known as the **Time of Awakening**; his philosophies of peace and logic helped prevent his people from being destroyed by the **Stone of Gol** in a terrible civil war. ("Gambit, Part II" [TNG]).

Sural. Former dictator of planet Sakura Prime. Sural was famous for having his rivals and parents beheaded. ("Dreadnought" [VGR]).

Surat, Jal. (John Gegenhuber). Leader of the **Kazon-Mostral** sect in 2372. ("Maneuvers" [VGR], "Alliances" [VGR]).

Surata IV. Class-M planet. Surata IV was surveyed by an *Enterprise*-D away team in 2365. During the away mission, **William T. Riker** was injured by contact with a native plant-form. He lost consciousness for several hours, but eventually recovered. ("Shades of Gray" [TNG]).

Surchid, Master. Leader of the first **Wadi** delegation to Deep Space 9 in 2369. **Falow** announced that he was the Master Surchid of the Wadi, and was supervisor of the **chula** game played at Quark's bar on Deep Space 9. ("Move Along Home" [DS9]).

surgical scrubber. Device employing an irradiating field, used in the 24th century to clean and disinfect a physician's hands prior to surgery. ("The Swarm" [VGR]).

Surjak. Former enemy of **Enabran Tain**. In 2373, **Garak** intimated that he was responsible for Surjak's death. ("In Purgatory's Shadow" [DS9]).

Surmak Ren. (Matthew Faison). Bajoran scientist who worked with noted geneticist **Dekon Elig**. Surmak Ren, a member of the Bajoran underground, and medical assistant to Dekon Elig, claimed to know little about the deadly aphasia virus created by Dekon. In 2369, while serving as chief administrator of the Ilvian Medical Complex, he was contacted when the virus was spreading throughout station Deep Space 9. When Surmak refused to cooperate, Kira kidnapped him to the station to help develop a cure. ("Babel" [DS9]). *The character was* not *named for anyone in Nickelodeon's animated series* Ren and Stimpy. *Heck, no.*

Surplus Depot Zed-15. Starfleet designation of the surplus depot located in orbit around planet **Qualor II**. The ***T'Pau*** was assigned to this depot in 2364, following its decommission. ("Unification, Part I" [TNG]).

surprise party. Traditional human ceremony in which a guest of honor is not made aware that the celebration will be taking place, until he or she arrives at said party. (In one **quantum reality** visited by Worf in 2370, his shipmates held a surprise party in honor of his birthday, mostly under the direction of Commander Riker, who "loves surprise parties.") ("Parallels" [TNG]). *It is important that the guest of honor not reveal that he or she was not at all surprised.*

"Survivors, The," *Next Generation* episode #51. Written by Michael Wagner. Directed by Les Landau. Stardate 43152.4. *First aired in 1989. The* Enterprise-D *investigates a lonely couple who are the sole survivors of a devastating attack that destroyed their colony.* GUEST CAST: John Anderson as **Uxbridge**, **Kevin**; Anne Haney as **Uxbridge**, **Rishon**. SEE: **Andorians; Delta Rana IV; Delta Rana star system; Douwd; Husnock ship; Husnock; New Martim Vaz; Starbase 133; Uxbridge, Kevin; Uxbridge, Rishon.**

Susann, Jacqueline. Popular 20th-century Earth novelist known for sensationalistic novels about that planet's rich and powerful. Spock read Susann's works during his study of Earth culture, and regarded her as one of the "giants" of human literature. *(Star Trek IV: The Voyage Home). Surely Spock's tongue was firmly planted in his cheek.*

"Suspicions." *Next Generation* episode #148. Written by Joe Menosky and Naren Shankar. Directed by Cliff Bole. Stardate 46830.1. *First aired in 1993. A scientist is murdered during a test of a new deflector-shield system.* GUEST CAST: Patti Yasutake as **Ogawa**, **Nurse Alyssa**; Tricia O'Neil as **Kurak**; Peter Slutsker as **Reyga**, **Dr.**; James Horan as **Jo'Bril**; John S. Ragin as **Christopher**, **Dr.**; Joan Stuart Morris as **T'Pan**, **Dr.**; Whoopi Goldberg as **Guinan**; Majel Barrett as Computer voice. SEE: **Altine Conference; baryon particles; Brooks, Admiral; Christopher, Dr.; Ferengi death rituals; Jo'Bril; *Justman, Shuttlecraft*; Kurak; metaphasic shield; plasma infuser; Reyga, Dr.; Selar, Dr.; Starbase 23; T'Pan, Dr.; Takarans; tennis elbow; tetryon particle; Vaytan; Vulcan Science Academy.**

Suspiria's Array. A space station in the **Delta Quadrant**, built by **Suspiria** in 2071. Similar to, but much smaller than, the Array built by the Caretaker near the Ocampa planet. Suspiria brought some 2,000 **Ocampa** people to her Array, where she made them her disciples, helping them to develop their psychokinetic powers so that they could join her in **Exosia**. ("Cold Fire" [VGR]). SEE: **Array; Tanis**.

Suspiria. (Lindsay Ridgeway). An extragalactic explorer who visited the **Ocampa** homeworld in the Delta Quadrant a millennium ago. After her people, the **Nacene**, accidentally devastated the ecosphere of the Ocampa planet, Suspiria was one of two of her people who remained behind to care for the Ocampa. Suspiria left the Ocampa planet and her mate, the **Caretaker**, around 2071, taking some two thousand Ocampa with her. She established a city in space, where she taught the Ocampa to develop their psychokinetic powers so that they could join her in the subspace domain known as **Exosia**. Suspiria was forced into Exosia in 2372 by the crew of the *Starship Voyager*. ("Cold Fire" [VGR]). SEE: **Suspiria's Array**. *Lindsay Ridgeway played the girl who represented Suspiria.*

Sutherland, U.S.S. Federation starship, *Nebula* class, Starfleet registry number NCC-72015. The *Sutherland* was commanded by Commander **Data** as part of Picard's armada to blockade the Romulan supply ships supplying the

Duras family forces during the **Klingon civil war** in 2367-2368. ("Redemption, Part II" [TNG]). *The* Sutherland *was a modification of the* Nebula-*class* ***U.S.S.* Phoenix**. *The upper sensor pod and supporting struts were changed for the* Sutherland. *The* Sutherland *was named for Horatio Hornblower's flagship in the classic C. S. Forester novels that served as one of Gene Roddenberry's original inspirations for* Star Trek.

Sutok. (Steve Kehela). Trader who frequented the **Nekrit Supply Depot** station in the Delta Quadrant. Sutok dealt in such contraband as **Rhuludian crystals**. Sutok was killed by Talaxian trader **Wixiban** during a failed narcotics deal in 2373. ("Fair Trade" [VGR]).

Sutter, Clara. (Noley Thornton). Daughter of *Enterprise*-D crew member **Daniel Sutter**. Because she had changed starships (and therefore homes) so many times in her young life, Clara invented an "invisible friend," **Isabella**, to keep her company. Clara was at first pleased, then frightened, when her imaginary companion suddenly became very real. ("Imaginary Friend" [TNG]). *Noley Thornton also played Taya in "Shadowplay" (DS9).*

Sutter, Ensign Daniel. (Jeff Allin). An *Enterprise*-D officer and part of the engineering staff. Sutter had served on several starships before his posting to the *Enterprise*-D in 2368. His daughter, **Clara Sutter**, lived with him. ("Imaginary Friend" [TNG]).

Suvin IV. Planet. Archaeologist Dr. Langford invited Captain Picard to join her in exploring the ruins at Suvin IV. ("Rascals" [TNG]).

"Swarm, The." *Voyager* episode #49. Written by Mike Sussman. Directed by Alexander Singer. Stardate 50252.3. *First aired in 1996.* Voyager *crosses into a section of space belonging to a mysterious culture that does not tolerate trespassers. The Doctor begins to suffer memory failure, prompting the crew to take drastic measures.* GUEST CAST: Carole Davis as **Diva**; Steven Houska as **Chardis**; Majel Barrett as Computer voice. SEE: **adaptive heuristic matrix; Bristow, Fred; Callas, Maria; Chardis; cortical analeptic; Emergency Medical Hologram; Freni, Mirella; gigaquad; holodeck and holosuite programs: hydrocortilene; interferometric pulse; Jupiter Station; Jupiter Station diagnostics; *La Bohème*; Lake Como; level-4 memory fragmentation; matrix overlay program; Mislen; multitronics; neuroelectric weapon; Nicoletti, Susan; "O soave fanciulla"; parrises squares; Pavarotti, Luciano; Pentangeli, Giuseppina; polaron; preganglionic fiber; Puccini, Giacomo; resonant particle wave; Soral; surgical scrubber; Swarm; T'Penna; Tabran monk; tachyon detection grid; universal translator; Zimmerman, Dr. Lewis.**

Swarm. A highly territorial civilization native to the Delta Quadrant. The Swarm employed neuroelectric weapons and thousands of small ships in swarmlike formations. They used sensor nets employing interlaced tachyon beams to monitor their borders. The universal translator aboard the *Voyager* had great difficulty in translating the language used by the Swarm. ("The Swarm" [VGR]).

swarm. Spaceborne life-form native to the Delta Quadrant. The swarm was a colony of about 2000 individuals that propelled themselves at speeds in excess of 3000 kilometers per second by means of flagellation. These creatures absorbed nutrients directly from space through their porous outer skin. One of the life-form's sexes was very large in relation to the opposite sex, comparable in size to a Federation starship. ("Elogium" [VGR]).

Swenson, Science Officer. *Enterprise*-D crew member. Swenson was scheduled to participate in a martial-arts competition aboard the ship just prior to Tasha Yar's death in 2364. ("Skin of Evil" [TNG]).

Swinn, Ensign. (Bahni Turpin). Starfleet officer assigned to the engineering section on the *U.S.S. Voyager*. ("Tuvix" [VGR], "Resolutions" [VGR]).

Switzer. A renowned Federation archaeologist who attended the annual symposium of the **Federation Archaeology Council** in 2367. ("QPid" [TNG]).

"Sword of Kahless, The." *Deep Space Nine* episode #81. Teleplay by Hans Beimler. Story by Richard Danus. Directed by LeVar Burton. No stardate given. *First aired in 1995. Kor sets out with Worf and Dax on a quest to find the mythical Sword of Kahless, which has been missing for a millennium.* GUEST CAST: John Colicos as **Kor**; Rick Pasqualone as **Toral**; Tom Morga as **Soto**. SEE: **Alvanian cave sloth; *bat'leth*; cave-rat; Degebian mountain goat; Hall of Heroes; Hur'q planet; Hur'q; Kahless the Unforgettable; Kang; Koloth; Kor; Korma Pass; Lethean; *Maj ram*; No'Mat; Sabak's armor; serpent of Xol; Shroud of the Sword; Soto; Sword of Kahless; T'nag; Toral; Torch of G'boj; Torna IV; Worf; Yridian brandy.**

Sword of Kahless. The first ***bat'leth*** forged by **Kahless the Unforgettable** around fifteen hundred years ago. In the centuries following Kahless's death, the sword became a sacred icon of the Klingon people, until it was taken by the **Hur'q** about one thousand years ago during their invasion of the Klingon Homeworld. The Sword of Kahless had been wrapped in a cloth that also became a revered object. After the disappearance of the sword, numerous fakes of the Shroud of the Sword emerged over the centuries. The true shroud was discovered by a Vulcan geological team, inspiring *Dahar* Master **Kor** to enlist the help of Jadzia Dax and Worf to set out on a quest for the legendary artifact in 2372. ("The Sword of Kahless" [DS9]). *Kor, Worf, and Dax actually found the Sword of*

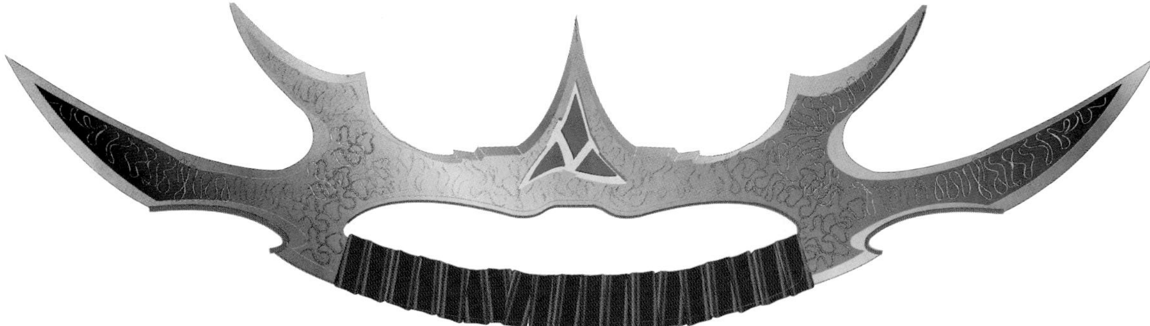

Kahless on a Hur'q planet in the Gamma Quadrant. Fearing that the sword would only serve to divide the Klingon Empire, they decided not to reveal its discovery. They left the ancient bat'leth *floating somewhere in free space, perhaps to be found in another thousand years. This entry reflects their wish that the sword remains lost for the time being.* SEE: **Toral.**

Sybo. (Pilar Seurat). Wife of Prefect **Jarvis** of planet **Argelius II**. Sybo was gifted with the Argelian power of empathic contact and attempted to learn who committed a series of brutal murders on her planet in 2267. Sybo was murdered by the noncorporeal entity who was the object of her investigation. SEE: **Redjac**. ("Wolf in the Fold" [TOS]).

Sybok. (Laurence Luckinbill). Son of **Sarek** of Vulcan and half-brother to **Spock**. Sybok was born in 2224 to Sarek and his first wife, a Vulcan princess. After the death of his mother, Sybok was raised with his half-brother, Spock. Even as a youth, Sybok was a rebel in the highly conformist Vulcan society, and he was eventually ostracized because he sought to find meaning in emotions as well as in logic. Sybok left his homeworld to pursue his visions of the mythical planet ***Sha Ka Ree***. Sybok did not realize that these visions had been implanted by a malevolent creature living near the center of the galaxy. This creature inspired Sybok to gather a group of followers at planet **Nimbus III** in 2287, then to hijack the *Starship Enterprise*-A to the planet it called *Sha Ka Ree*, in hopes of using the starship to gain its own freedom. Sybok perished at the planet he believed was *Sha Ka Ree*, having realized too late the malevolent nature of the entity there. *(Star Trek V: The Final Frontier).*

***Sydney*-class transport.** Small starship resembling a runabout. The *Jenolen*, lost in 2294 carrying **Montgomery Scott**, was a *Sydney*-class ship. ("Relics" [TNG]). Some *Sydney*-class ships were built without warp drive, intended for use as large shuttlecraft. *(Star Trek VI). The* Jenolen *miniature was a modification of a large shuttlecraft originally built for* Star Trek VI.

Sylleran Rift. Astronomical object. **Mikhal Traveler Zahir** wanted to explore the Sylleran Rift in 2373 with *Starship Voyager* crew member Kes. ("Darkling" [VGR]).

Sylvia. (Antoinette Bower). Extragalactic life-form who traveled to planet **Pyris VII** along with **Korob**, another from her world. Sylvia used a device called a **transmuter** to assume humanoid form when she captured personnel from the *Enterprise* in 2267. Unfamiliar with human existence, Sylvia became intoxicated with human senses and became cruel toward her captives. She and Korob died after the transmuter was destroyed. ("Catspaw" [TOS]).

Sylvia. (Bonnie Beecher). Woman who was infatuated with **Billy Claiborne** in the replica of **Tombstone, Arizona,** created by the **Melkotians** in 2268. Chekov was cast by the Melkotians in the role of Claiborne, but did not seem to mind Sylvia's attentions. ("Spectre of the Gun" [TOS]).

Symbalene blood burn. Virulent disease. Symbalene blood burn can kill an entire planetary population in a very short period of time. Nevertheless, the destruction of the **Malurian** civilization in 2267, caused by **Nomad**, was even more rapid than a plague of Symbalene blood burn. ("The Changeling" [TOS]).

symbiogenesis. A reproductive process in which organisms of two different species merge to form an offspring of a third, unique species. Symbiogenetic organisms are rare compared with species that employ sexual reproduction or parenthogenesis. A symbiogenetic orchid plant was the catalyst for the accidental merging of Tuvok and Neelix into **Tuvix** in 2372. ("Tuvix" [VGR]).

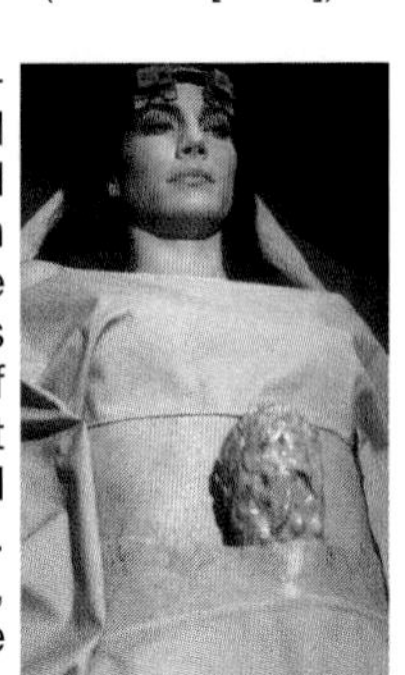

symbiont. A small, sightless, sessile intelligent life-form, one-half of the **Trill** joined species. Symbionts breed in underground chambers, known as the caves of Mak'ala, on the Trill homeworld. SEE: **Guardians**. While they remain in the pools there, the symbionts communicate with each other by means of a visible electric discharge. The placement of the symbionts was governed by the **Trill Symbiosis Commission**. ("Equilibrium" [DS9]). The symbiont lived within a humanoid host, gaining sustenance and mobility from the host. ("The Host" [TNG]). SEE: **Odan, Ambassador; Mak'ala, caves of.** The symbiont's intelligence is the dominant personality in the joined life-form, although the host's personality is reflected as well. Symbionts can have enormously long life spans and, upon the death of a host, can be transplanted into another. The resulting new joined life-form is considered to be another person, although it retains memories of previous joinings. ("Dax" [DS9]). Once a symbiont is removed, the host usually dies within hours. Improper joining of host and symbiont can cause psychological damage to both. ("Invasive Procedures" [DS9]). SEE: **Dax, Jadzia; Dax (symbiont)**.

Symbiosis Evaluation Board. Powerful assembly on planet **Trill** responsible for judging the suitability of Trill initiates for symbiosis. ("Invasive Procedures" [DS9]).

"Symbiosis." Next Generation episode #23. Teleplay by Robert Lewin and Richard Manning and Hans Beimler. Story by Robert Lewin. Directed by Win Phelps. No stardate given in episode. *First aired in 1988. The* Enterprise-*D discovers two planets, one of which is populated by a civilization of drug addicts, the other of which supplies their narcotics. This was actor Denise Crosby's last episode as Natasha Yar, even though it was filmed after "Skin of Evil" (TNG), in which Tasha dies. Denise Crosby can be seen breaking out of character and waving farewell at the end of "Symbiosis," just before the cargo bay door closes.* GUEST CAST: Judson Scott as **Sobi**; Merritt Butrick as **T'Jon**; Richard Lineback as **Romas**; Kimberly Farr as **Langor**. SEE: **Brekka; Brekkians; Delos; felicium; Langor; Ornara; Ornarans; Romas; *Sanction*; Sobi; T'Jon**.

symbols. *SEE following pages.*

synaptic induction. Technique in neurotherapy used for patients suffering from traumatic memory loss. Dr. Crusher attempted synaptic induction with the **Zalkonian** called **John Doe** in 2366, but because his neural nets did not conform to any known patterns, the therapy was ineffective. ("Transfigurations" [TNG]).

synaptic pattern displacement. Scientific term for the consciousness sharing used by **Vulcans** in a mind-meld or, in extreme cases, the transference of one's ***katra***. Dr. Julian Bashir was unaware that the technique could be performed by a non-Vulcan, although the **Kobliad** criminal **Rao Vantika** used something similar to place his consciousness into Bashir's mind in 2369. ("The Passenger" [DS9]). SEE: **Vulcan mind-meld**.

synaptic reconstruction. Surgery which neutralizes the synaptic pathways responsible for deviant behavior. While being

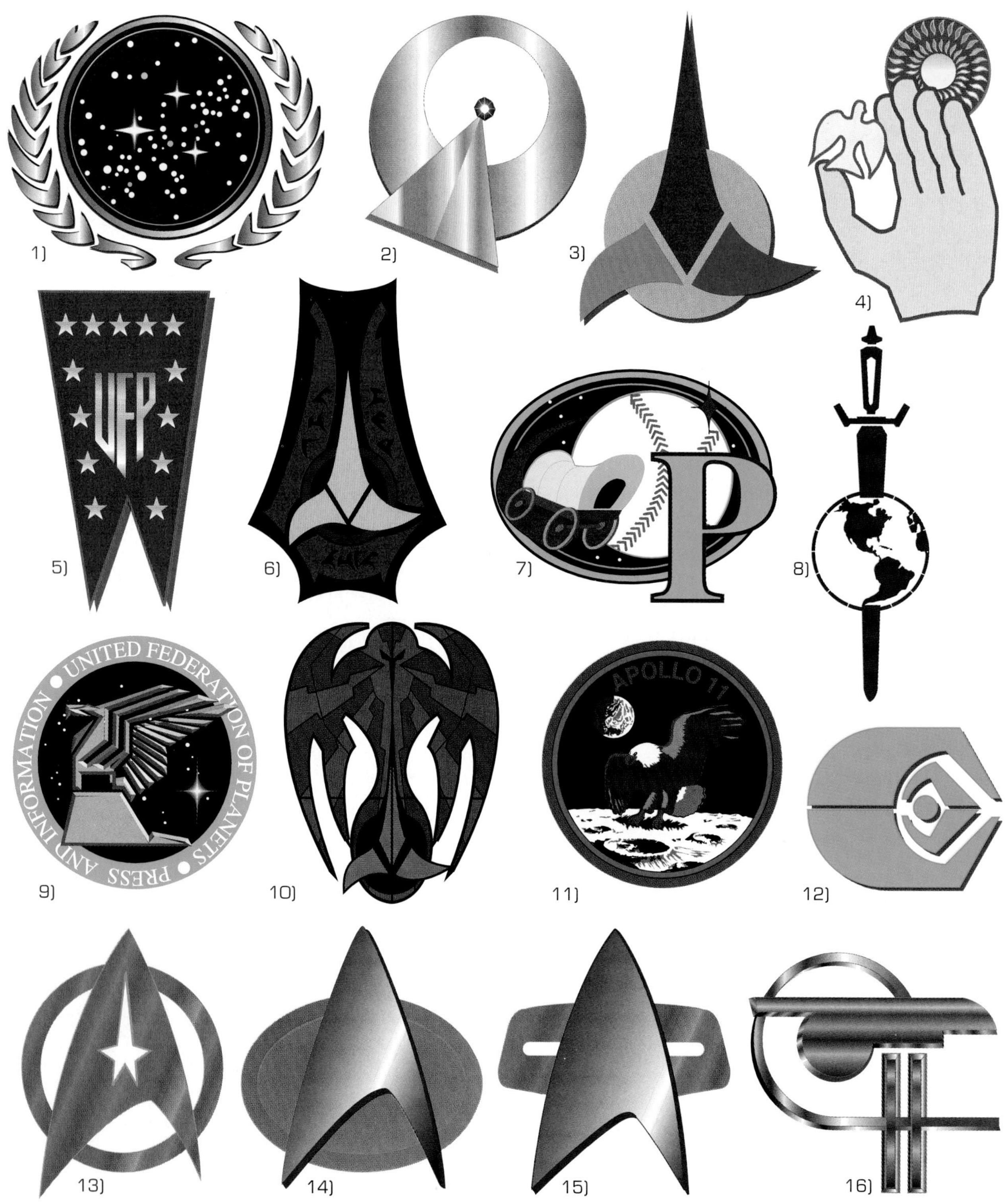

1) Great Seal of the United Federation of Planets. 2) Vulcan IDIC symbol. 3) Emblem of the Klingon Empire. 4) Symbol of the Tantalus V rehabilitation colony. 5) Early Federation pennant ("And the Children Shall Lead" [TOS]). 6) Klingon ceremonial banner. 7) Pike City Pioneers baseball team patch ("Family Business" [DS9]). 8) Mirror empire emblem ("Mirror, Mirror" [TOS]). 9) Seal of the Federation Press and Information Bureau (*Star Trek Generations*). 10) Symbol of the Cardassian-Klingon Alliance in the mirror universe ("Crossover" [DS9]). 11) *Apollo 11* mission patch. 12) Seal of the Ferengi alliance ("The Last Outpost" [TNG], et al). 13) Starfleet cadet emblem (*Star Trek II*, et al). 14) Starfleet insignia (Star Trek: The Next Generation). 15) Starfleet insignia (*Star Trek Generations*, et al). 16) Trill symbol. SEE: **Insignia and rank markings, Starfleet.**

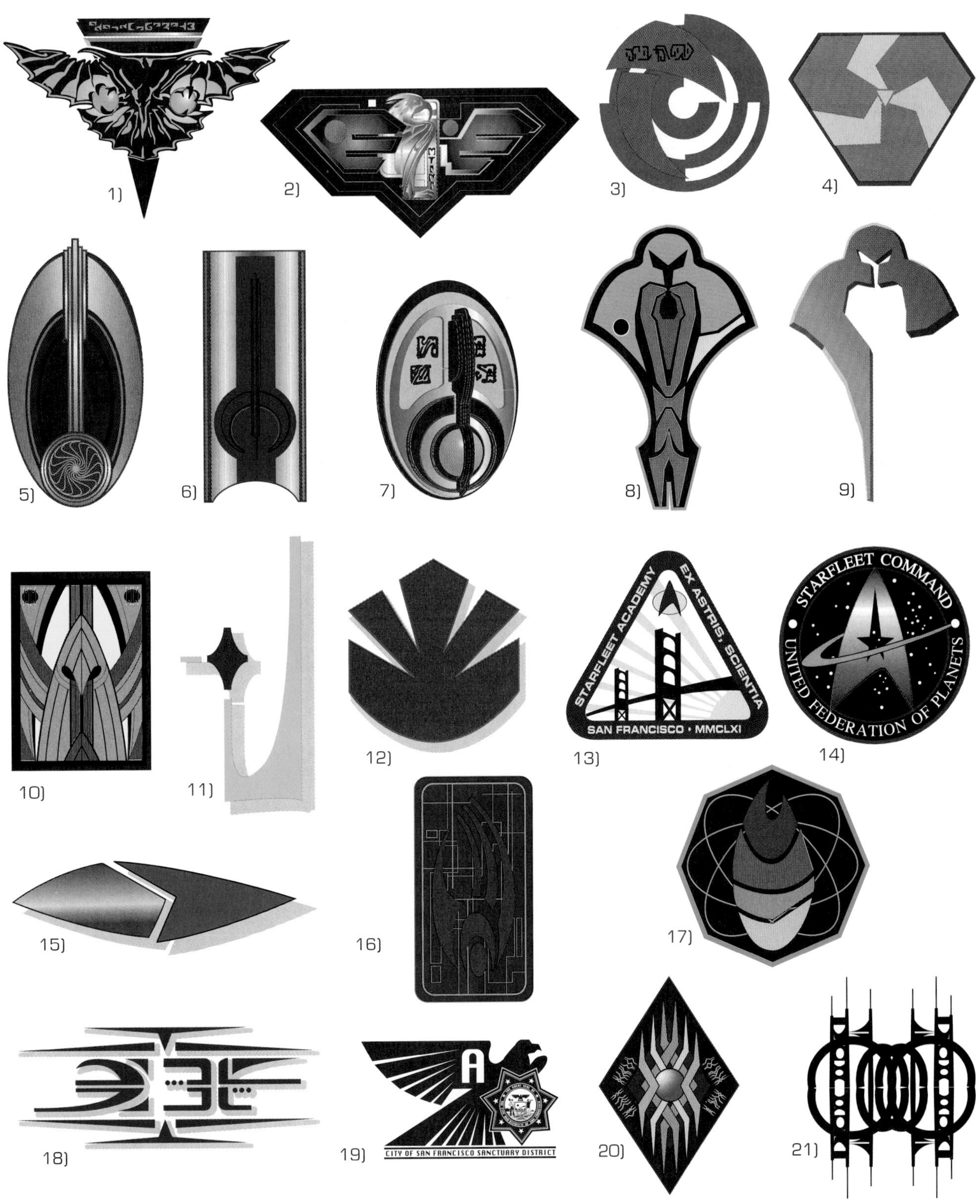

1) Emblem of the Romulan Star Empire. 2) Tal Shiar symbol. 3) Logo of the Iconians. 4) Symbol of the Providers of Triskelion. 5) Symbol of the Bajoran faith. 6) Bajoran military banner. 7) Bajoran religious plaque. 8) Symbol of the Cardassian Union. 9) Symbol of the Obsidian Order. 10) Logo of Quark's bar. 11) Symbol of the Dominion. 12) Maquis patch. 13) Starfleet Academy emblem. 14) Starfleet Command seal. 15) 29th-century Starfleet insignia, also used as the Chronowerx logo. 16) Symbol of the Borg. 17) Polaric ion power plant sign ("Time and Again" [VGR]). 18) Mark of the Kazon. 19) Sanctuary District emblem from Earth's 21st century. 20) Standard of the Vidiian Sodality. 21) Harvester symbol ("Armageddon Game" [DS9]).

brainwashed on planet **Tilonus IV**, Riker experienced a delusional world where he was an inmate at a mental hospital and was threatened with synaptic reconstruction to "correct" his "psychotic personality." ("Frame of Mind" [TNG]). SEE: ***Frame of Mind*; neurosomatic technique; Syrus, Dr.**

synaptic scanning. Technique developed by **Dr. Noonien Soong** which allowed for the transfer of human personality traits and memories into a positronic matrix, such as that used in an android's brain. Soong used this to transfer the identity of his wife Juliana into an android made in her image. ("Inheritance" [TNG]). *We speculate this may be a further development of engram transfers used by Dr. Richard Daystrom in "The Ultimate Computer" (TOS).*

synchronous orbit. Orbit about a planetary or other body such that the orbiting body remains above a fixed point. Also known as a geosynchronous orbit. ("Inheritance" [TNG]). SEE: **standard orbit**. *The commercial communication satellites used by Paramount Pictures for the distribution of the* Star Trek *television shows occupy synchronous orbits around planet Earth, a concept originally proposed by Arthur C. Clarke.*

synthale. Bajoran beverage served at **Quark's bar** at **Deep Space 9**. Quark didn't like the stuff, warning, "Don't ever trust an ale from a god-fearing people." ("Emissary" [DS9]). The beverage is a brilliant blue in color. ("Playing God" [DS9]).

synthehol. An alcohol substitute invented by the **Ferengi** that permits one to enjoy the intoxicating effects of alcoholic beverages without the deleterious consequences. **Robert Picard** believed that synthehol had ruined Jean-Luc's palate. Jean-Luc, however, felt it had heightened his appreciation for the fruits of genuine vineyards. ("Family" [TNG]). Captain **Montgomery Scott** easily distinguished between real Scotch and the synthehol-based substitute served in the Ten-Forward Lounge aboard the *Enterprise*-D. ("Relics" [TNG]).

***Synthococcus novae*.** Dangerous bacillus-strain organism, a by-product of modern technology. Although treatable, the deadly bacillus was regarded as a significant health hazard. **Dr. Sevrin** was a carrier of the disease but immune to it, passing it on to others yet remaining symptom-free. ("The Way to Eden" [TOS]).

Syrus, Dr. (David Selberg). Nonexistent physician at the imaginary **Tilonus Institute for Mental Disorders** who supposedly treated William Riker for a psychiatric malady on planet **Tilonus IV** in 2369. In reality, Dr. Syrus did not exist, but was projected into Riker's mind by political interrogation officers on planet Tilonus IV. They hoped to extract strategic information from the *Enterprise*-D first officer. ("Frame of Mind" [TNG]). *David Selberg also played Whalen in "The Big Goodbye" (TNG).*

System J-25. Star system some 7,000 light-years from Federation space. The sixth planet in the system, an inhabited Class M-world, was observed in 2365 to have large craterlike scars where roadway patterns indicated cities should have been. It was believed the damage was caused by the **Borg**. ("Q Who?" [TNG]). In late 2366, similar surface conditions were discovered on planet **Jouret IV** at the **New Providence colony**, indicating a Borg encroachment into Federation space. ("The Best of Both Worlds, Part I" [TNG]).

system 5 disruptors. SEE: **disruptors, system 5**.

T

T'Acog, I.K.S. Klingon cruiser, *K't'inga* class. The *T'Acog* was sent to return the criminals **Korris**, **Konmel**, and **Kunivas** to the **Klingon Homeworld** in 2364. The offenders managed to destroy the *T'Acog* and commandeered the **Talarian** freighter ***Batris***. ("Heart of Glory" [TNG]). *The T'Acog was a re-use of footage from* Star Trek: The Motion Picture.

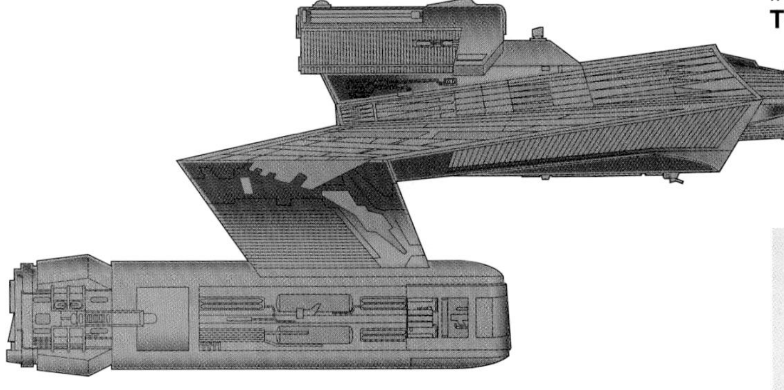

t'an. A metallic-crystal rod used when playing the Vulcan ***kal-toh*** puzzle. ("Alter Ego" [VGR]).

***T'gha* maneuver.** Illegal move in formal *bat'leth* competitions, involving a blow to the head. (The Worf of an alternate **quantum reality** felt a *T'gha* maneuver unfairly robbed him of his Champion Standing in the *bat'leth* competition on Forcas III.) ("Parallels" [TNG]).

***t'gla*.** Derogatory **Klingon** term. **T'Kar** called **Jadzia Dax** a mindless *t'gla* for not fighting harder to retain her symbiont. ("Invasive Procedures" [DS9]).

T'Jon. (Merritt Butrick). Captain of the **Ornaran** freighter ship ***Sanction***. Like all Ornarans of his time, T'Jon was addicted to a medicinal substance called **felicium** from the planet Brekka. The intellectual impairment caused by this addiction may have been responsible for his lack of understanding of the technical aspects of his ship's operation. ("Symbiosis" [TNG]). *Actor Merritt Butrick had played **David Marcus,** son of James Kirk, in* Star Trek II *and* Star Trek III.

T'Kar. (Tim Russ). Klingon mercenary hired by **Verad** to assist in Verad's plan to steal **Jadzia Dax**'s **Trill symbiont** in 2370 by taking over station **Deep Space 9**. ("Invasive Procedures" [DS9]). *Tim Russ also portrayed Devor in "Starship Mine" (TNG), an unnamed bridge officer in* Star Trek Generations, *and Tuvok on* Star Trek: Voyager.

T'Karath Sanctuary. Ancient catacombs located on planet **Vulcan**. It had been a stronghold for one of the political factions during the last Vulcan civil war, two millennia ago. **Tallera** and the other mercenaries were to deliver the pieces of the **Stone of Gol** to this location in 2370. ("Gambit, Part II" [TNG]).

T'Lani III. Planet whose population was destroyed by the **harvesters** during the war between the **T'Lani** and the **Kellerun**. ("Armageddon Game" [DS9]).

T'Lani munitions cruiser. Spacecraft. In 2370, a T'Lani cruiser was the site where the last of the deadly **harvester** nanobiogenic weapons were destroyed. This ship was more than a match for *Danube*-class Federation **runabout**s, both in speed and weaponry. ("Armageddon Game" [DS9]).

T'Lani Prime. Planet in the **T'Lani** star system. Following the end of the war with the Kellerun in 2370, a celebration was scheduled on T'Lani Prime to commemorate the destruction of the last **harvester** weapons. ("Armageddon Game" [DS9]).

T'Lani. Humanoid people who were at war with the **Kellerun** for centuries until finally reaching peace in 2370. The T'Lani suffered great losses during the war, including the entire population of planet **T'Lani III**, from the deadly **harvesters**. ("Armageddon Game" [DS9]).

T'Lar. (Dame Judith Anderson). Venerable **Vulcan** high priestess. T'Lar supervised the ***fal-tor-pan*** ceremony in which **Spock**'s body and living spirit were rejoined following his death in 2285. *(Star Trek III: The Search for Spock)*.

T'Lara. (Deborah Strang). Starfleet admiral. T'Lara of Vulcan presided over an extradition hearing on station Deep Space 9 in 2372 when Lieutenant Commander **Worf** was accused by Klingon authorities of firing on an unarmed transport spacecraft. ("Rules of Engagement" [DS9]).

T'lli Beta. Planet. T'lli Beta was the destination of the *Enterprise*-D when it encountered a school of **two-dimensional creatures** in 2367. ("The Loss" [TNG]). *T'lli Beta was named by episode writer Hilary Bader for her grandmother, Tillie Bader.*

t'lokan* schism.** In **Vulcan** physiology, a condition wherein a repressed memory causes physical brain damage. A *t'lokan* schism is the physical reaction to the battle between the conscious and the unconscious regarding the resurfacing of a traumatic memory. Vulcan psychocognitive research suggested that *t'lokan* schisms could be treated with a **mind-meld** between the patient and a family member, in an attempt to bring the repressed memory into the conscious mind. ("Flashback" [VGR]). SEE: ***pyllora.

T'Lor. Starfleet officer assigned to Deep Space 9. On stardate 50049.3, T'Lor was killed in a battle with the Jem'Hadar on Torga IV. ("The Ship" [DS9]). *Like Dr. Sevrin, T'Lor was from Tiburon.*

T'nag. Old enemy of Kang, Kor, and Koloth. The three legendary Klingon warriors once fought a glorious battle against T'nag and his army, emerging victorious against overwhelming odds. ("The Sword of Kahless" [DS9]).

T'Ong, I.K.S. Klingon deep-space exploratory cruiser, *K't'inga* class, launched in 2290 under the command of Captain **K'Temok**. Because of the extended nature of the mission, the entire crew spent most of the transit time in hibernation. The return of the ship to Klingon space in 2365 was a matter of concern because the ship had been launched in an era when the two respective governments were at war. It was feared that the crew of the *T'Ong* would believe that a state of war still existed, and that they might therefore attack the first Federation ship they encountered. Federation

Emissary **K'Ehleyr** helped avert such a crisis by working with *Enterprise*-D Security Chief Worf to gain command of the T'Ong before any hostilities could occur. ("The Emissary" [TNG]). *The* T'Ong *was a re-use of Klingon battle cruiser footage originally produced for* Star Trek: The Motion Picture.

T'Paal. SEE: **Tallera**.

T'Pan, Dr. (Joan Stuart-Morris). Director of the Vulcan Science Academy from 2354 to 2369. Dr. T'Pan was a pre-eminent expert in subspace morphology. She was invited aboard the *Enterprise*-D in 2369 to witness the test of a new **metaphasic shield** invented by **Dr. Reyga**. When Dr. Reyga was killed shortly after the test, Dr. T'Pan came under suspicion for his murder. ("Suspicions" [TNG])

T'Para. Learned **Vulcan** priestess who dwelt in the province of **Raal**. ("Innocence" [VGR]).

T'Pau. (Celia Lovsky). High-ranking **Vulcan** official. T'Pau, who was the only person ever to turn down a seat on the **Federation Council**, presided at Spock's near-wedding in 2267. ("Amok Time" [TOS]). In 2373, *Voyager*'s **Emergency Medical Hologram** incorporated segments of T'Pau's personality into his personality-improvement project. ("Darkling" [VGR]).

T'Pau. Vulcan spacecraft, registry number NSP-17938. The *T'Pau* was decommissioned in 2364 and assigned to the Starfleet surplus depot in orbit around planet **Qualor II**. In 2368, parts of the *T'Pau*'s navigational deflector array were discovered in the wreckage of a **Ferengi cargo shuttle**. Investigation of the unauthorized parts transfer led to the discovery that the *T'Pau* had been surreptitiously acquired by the Romulans. The ship was used to carry some two thousand Romulan troops during an attempted Romulan invasion of planet Vulcan in 2368. When the attempted invasion was exposed by Ambassador Spock, the Romulans destroyed the ship to avoid capture. ("Unification, Part I" [TNG]). *The ship was presumably named after the Vulcan dignitary from "Amok Time" (TOS).*

T'Pel, Ambassador. (Sierra Pecheur). False identity assumed by Romulan **Subcommander Selok** on an undercover mission in the Federation. As T'Pel, Selok posed as a Vulcan ambassador who was renowned as one of the Federation's most honored diplomats. In 2367, T'Pel was transported to the **Romulan Neutral Zone** aboard the *Enterprise*-D as part of a supposed Romulan peace initiative. T'Pel was apparently killed in a transporter accident while beaming over to the Romulan warbird ***Devoras***. It was later learned that her "death" was staged to cover her return to Romulan territory. ("Data's Day" [TNG]).

T'Pel. (Marva Hicks). Citizen of planet **Vulcan**, wife to Starfleet officer **Tuvok**. T'Pel had three sons and a daughter with Tuvok. After Tuvok was lost aboard the *Starship Voyager*, he once hallucinated that he was back home on Vulcan with T'Pel. ("Persistence of Vision" [VGR]). T'Pel married Tuvok after he entered ***Pon farr*** in 2304. ("Flashback" [VGR]).

T'Penna. Outstanding operatic soprano from the planet **Vulcan**. T'Penna performed Mimi in **Puccini's** *La Bohème* opposite **Soral**'s Rudolpho. To learn about opera, the *Voyager's* Emergency Medical Hologram studied recordings of *La Bohème* featuring T'Penna. ("The Swarm" [VGR]).

T'Pera. (Amy Traicoff). A holodeck character designed by Voyager's Emergency Medical Hologram, part of a therapy program intended to cure Ensign **Vorik** of the effects of ***Pon farr***. ("Blood Fever" [VGR]).

T'plana-Hath. Matron of **Vulcan** philosophy who said, "Logic is the cement of our civilization with which we ascend from chaos using reason as our guide." Spock successfully identified the quote during a memory test in 2286. *(Star Trek IV: The Voyage Home). According to Star Trek: First Contact cowriter Ronald D. Moore, the Vulcan ship that made first contact with humans on planet Earth in 2063 was the* T'plana-Hath, *although this was not established in actual dialog.*

T'Pring. (Arlene Martel). Vulcan woman who was telepathically bonded with **Spock** when they were both seven years old. At their marriage ceremony in 2267, she rejected Spock and selected Captain Kirk as her champion, forcing the two men to fight for her possession. She had chosen Kirk, knowing that Spock would release her for making the challenge and that Kirk would not want her, so that she would be free to choose **Stonn** as her consort. T'Pring explained that Spock had become something of a legend among her people, and that she did not wish to be the consort of a legend, preferring Stonn. ("Amok Time" [TOS]). SEE: ***Pon farr***. *T'Pring was the first Vulcan woman seen on* Star Trek*, and her name established the pattern that Vulcan women tend to have names beginning with the letter T.*

T'Rul, Subcommander. (Martha Hackett). Officer of the **Romulan Empire**. When the Romulan government loaned a **cloaking device** to Starfleet in 2371, T'Rul was assigned to operate and guard the device. ("The Search, Parts I and II" [DS9]). *Martha Hackett also portrayed Seska on* Star Trek: Voyager.

t'san s'at. A Vulcan process of eliminating emotions, *t'san s'at* is the intellectual deconstruction of emotional patterns. ("Alter Ego" [VGR]).

T'Shanik. (Tasia Valenza). One of three candidates who competed with Wesley Crusher for a single opening to Starfleet Academy at **Relva VII** in 2364. A female from Vulcana Regar, T'Shanik was a runner-up in the competition. ("Coming of Age" [TNG]).

t'stayan. A **Talarian** riding animal. *T'stayans* possessed six hooves and were reported to be very powerful animals. Talarian Captain **Endar** said his adopted son, **Jono**, had broken two ribs while riding one of these creatures. ("Suddenly Human" [TNG]).

T'su, Ensign Lian. (Julia Nickson). Relief-operations manager aboard the *Enterprise*-D. T'Su took **ops** when Data beamed down to planet **Minos** to investigate the disappearance of the ***Drake***. ("The Arsenal of Freedom" [TNG]). *Julia Nickson also played Cassandra in "Paradise" (DS9), and Catherine Sakai on* Babylon 5.

T'su, Tan. (Vladimir Velasco). Engineer of the Federation freighter ***Arcos***. T'su was forced to abandon his craft with the *Arcos* pilot when the *Arcos* suffered a warp-containment breach near planet **Turkana IV** in 2367. T'su, along with the pilot, was held prisoner by a group on Turkana IV until rescued by an away team from the *Enterprise*-D. ("Legacy" [TNG]).

T'Vis. Klingon warrior, son of Barot. In 2373, T'Vis was inducted by Chancellor Gowron into the **Order of the *Bat'leth***. ("Apocalypse Rising" [DS9]).

***T'Vran*.** Vulcan ship. The *T'Vran* offered assistance to a runabout from Deep Space 9 after a **Miradorn** vessel was destroyed in the **Chamra Nebula** in 2369. The *T'Vran* then transported **Rakhari** fugitive **Croden** and his daughter to the planet **Vulcan** to start new lives. ("Vortex" [DS9]).

T-9 energy converter. Sophisticated power device. A T-9 converter was stolen in 2364 by Ferengi agents from an automated Federation monitor post on planet **Gamma Tauri IV**. ("The Last Outpost" [TNG]).

T-cell stimulator. Medical treatment tool. The device increases the production of T-cells, a type of lymphocyte which enables humanoid bodies to fight infection. ("Identity Crisis" [TNG]).

T-cell. Type of white blood cell in humanoids that is responsible for identification of antigens and activation of certain immune cells. A dormant T-cell was responsible for Lieutenant **Reginald Barclay**'s contraction of **Urodelean flu** in 2370. Dr. Crusher administered a synthetic T-cell to enable him to fight the disease naturally. This activated Barclay's latent **introns**, and was responsible for the outbreak of **Barclay's Protomorphosis Syndrome** among the crew. ("Genesis" [TNG]). *Even though Dr. Crusher told Barclay the T-cell in his DNA was dormant, there are no T-cells in DNA. There is DNA in T-cells, which might be where the doctor got confused....*

T-negative. Rare **Vulcan** blood type. **Sarek** and his son **Spock** both had T-negative blood. Commander Spock served as the blood donor for his father's heart surgery aboard the *Enterprise* in 2267. ("Journey to Babel" [TOS])

T-Rogorans. Civilization located in the Gamma Quadrant. For eight hundred years, the T-Rogorans enslaved the **Skrreea**, until 2370, when the T-Rogorans were conquered by the **Dominion**. ("Sanctuary" [DS9]).

T-tauri type star system. System with a young star whose diameter oscillates as that star settles into a stable size. In 2367, the *Enterprise*-D encountered a T-tauri star system with a single Class-M planet in the **Ngame Nebula**. ("Clues" [TNG]).

Taar, DaiMon. (Mike Gomez). Commander of the **Ferengi Marauder** spacecraft that made first contact with the Federation in 2364. Taar's ship was believed responsible for stealing a Federation T-9 energy converter from **Gamma Tauri IV**. ("The Last Outpost" [TNG]).

Tabran monk. Member of a monastic order known for their very celibate lives. ("The Swarm" [VGR]).

tachyon detection grid. Technique for using a network of active tachyon beams to detect cloaked Romulan ships passing through the net. The grid, devised by Geordi La Forge, required about 20 starships in order to be tactically effective, and was successfully used in 2368 to detect a convoy of Romulan ships on a covert mission to supply the **Duras** family forces in the **Klingon civil war**. ("Redemption, Part II" [TNG]). In 2373, Klingon forces employed a tachyon detection grid to protect **Ty'Gokor**, the newly relocated site of Gowron's command center. ("Apocalypse Rising" [DS9]). SEE: **cloaking device, Romulan**. The Swarm of the Delta Quadrant used a tachyon detection grid to monitor the borders of their space. ("The Swarm" [VGR]).

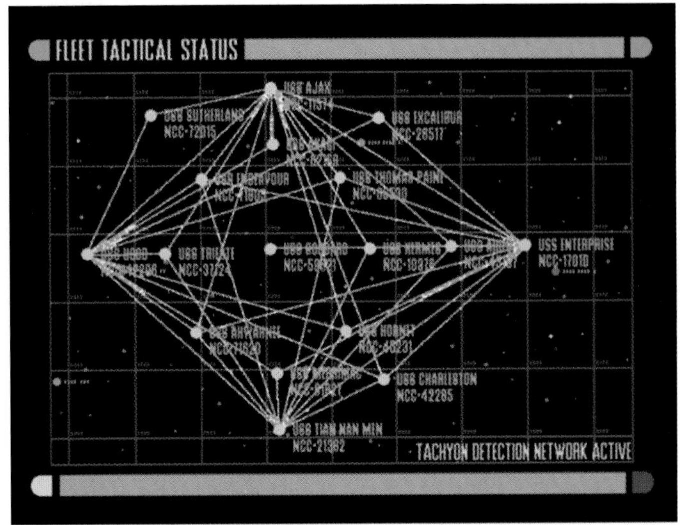

tachyon eddies. Interstellar currents of tachyon particles. Tachyon eddies in the **Denorios Belt** were believed responsible for sweeping ancient **Bajoran solar-sail vessel**s across interstellar distances some eight centuries ago. This phenomenon was demonstrated in 2371 when Benjamin Sisko built a replica of these ships and was swept at warp speeds to **Cardassia** by tachyon eddies. ("Explorers" [DS9]).

tachyon scan. Romulan vessels use tachyon scan sensor technology. ("The *Pegasus*" [TNG]). A tachyon sweep of a nebula can be used to detect cloaked vessels within. ("Flashback" [VGR]).

tachyon. Subatomic particle that can exist only at faster-than-light speeds. A tachyon cannot travel slower than light, just as many other particles cannot normally exceed the speed of light. Tachyons can be used to detect objects concealed by a **Romulan cloaking device**. ("Redemption, Part II" [TNG]). Romulan vessels use tachyon scan sensor technology. ("The *Pegasus*" [TNG]). A tachyon sweep of a nebula can be used to detect cloaked vessels within. ("Flashback" [VGR]). A tachyon burst can be used to disperse a temporal field. ("Coda" [VGR]).

Tagana. (Patricia Tallman). Health-care professional who worked at station Deep Space 9. Tagana was a nurse on duty in 2372 when **Jake Sisko** was treated for the deleterious effects of his association with **Onaya**. ("The Muse" [DS9]). *Patricia Tallman previously played Kiros in "Starship Mine" (TNG) and has made other appearances as a stunt performer on* Star Trek: The Next Generation *and* Deep Space Nine. *Tallman also played Lyta Alexander on* Babylon 5.

Tagas. A mythical land ruled by **Elamos the Magnificent**. ("Hero Worship" [TNG]).

Taggert, Captain. (J. Patrick McNamara). Commander of the *Starship* ***Repulse***. Former *Enterprise*-D Chief Medical Officer **Dr. Katherine Pulaski** served under Taggert aboard the *Repulse* prior to her assignment to the *Enterprise*-D. Taggert spoke highly of Pulaski, and once noted he would have even given her a shuttlecraft if it would have kept her aboard his ship. ("Unnatural Selection" [TNG]).

Tagra IV. Ecologically devastated planet in the Argolis Cluster. In 2369 the *Enterprise*-D traveled to Tagra IV to deliver much-needed supplies. ("True-Q" [TNG]). SEE: **baristatic filter; Amanda Rogers; Lote, Orn.**

Tagrans. Inhabitants of the planet **Tagra IV**. ("True-Q" [TNG]).

Taguan. Archaeological period on planet **Marlonia.** Picard once studied pottery from planet Marlonia that was very similar to early Taguan designs, but was probably closer to the Buranian period. ("Rascals" [TNG]).

Tagus III. A small planet, home to a glorious civilization some two billion years ago. Although the Taguans have long since disappeared, the planet has been the subject of 22,000 years of archaeological study. By 2367, despite 947 known excavations of the Taguan ruins, the civilization remained largely a mystery. The ruins of Tagus III were the subject of Captain **Jean-Luc Picard**'s keynote address to the **Federation Archaeological Council**'s annual symposium in 2367. ("QPid" [TNG]).

Tahiti Syndrome. Twentieth-century term for a human longing for a peaceful, idyllic natural setting when suffering from the stresses of modern life. McCoy noted Kirk's reaction upon observing the ancient Native American lifestyle on **Miramanee's planet**, commenting that overpressured leader types like starship captains often exhibited the Tahiti Syndrome. ("The Paradise Syndrome" [TOS]). *Not at all like the reactions of those who work on weekly science-fiction television shows....*

Tahna Los. (Jeffrey Nordling). **Bajoran** terrorist and member of the militant ***Kohn-Ma*** splinter group, who stopped at nothing to assure Bajor's independence from outside forces. In 2369, he tried unsuccessfully to destroy one side of the **wormhole** in hopes of minimizing Bajor's importance to the Federation and the Cardassians. ("Past Prologue" [DS9]).

tai chi. SEE: ***Mok'bara.***

Taibak. (John Fleck). Romulan scientist. Taibak developed a neural-control device in 2367 that, by using a direct access to the visual interface of Geordi La Forge's **VISOR**, permitted La Forge to be programmed to commit criminal acts. ("The Mind's Eye" [TNG]). SEE: **E-band emissions.**

tailor shop. Sartorial parlor on the **Promenade** of station **Deep Space 9**. The tailor shop location on the **Promenade** was run by exiled Cardassian Elim **Garak** (*pictured*). In 2371, Garak blew up his shop in an effort to enlist Odo's protection from **Retaya**, a Flaxian assassin hired by the **Tal Shiar**. ("Improbable Cause" [DS9]). *The choice of tailor as an occupation for Garak was the work of* Star Trek: Deep Space Nine *producer Peter Allan Fields, a tip of the hat to* The Man From U.N.C.L.E. *television series, in which Del Floria's tailor shop served as the secret entrance to U.N.C.L.E. headquarters. Fields was a writer on that show. The Promenade set featured a free-standing building-directory sign that listed (in very tiny print) Garak's shop, as well as a few never-seen places including the Banzai Institute, Milliways Restaurant, the Diet Smith Corporation, Spacely Sprockets, the Jupiter Mining Corporation, the Forbin Project, Pancho's Happy Bottom Riding Club, Tom Servo's Used Robots, Yoyodyne Propulsion Systems, and, of course, Del Floria's Tailor Shop.*

Tain, Enabran. (Paul Dooley). Former leader of the Cardassian **Obsidian Order**. Tain became head of that intelligence agency in

2348 and gained a reputation of being a hard, unforgiving man, who considered compassion to be a great weakness. When Tain retired from the powerful post in 2368, he was the only head of that agency to have survived long enough to be able to retire. When Tain's son, **Elim Garak**, also a member of the Obsidian Order, committed a serious misdeed, Tain had his own son exiled to station **Terok Nor**. Tain was forced to retire after the incident. ("The Wire" [DS9], "In Purgatory's Shadow" [DS9]). In 2371, Tain attempted a comeback by masterminding a joint operation between the Obsidian Order and the Romulan **Tal Shiar**, a first strike against the **Founders** of the **Dominion**. As part of his plan, Tain ordered the assassination of six of his former advisors, including Garak, who was the only one of the six to escape death. Tain subsequently invited Garak to join him in leading the attack. Tain's offensive was a major disaster, resulting in the loss of all 20 Cardassian and Romulan ships to a **Jem'Hadar** ambush in the **Omarion Nebula**. ("Improbable Cause" [DS9], "The Die is Cast" [DS9]). SEE: **Lovok, Colonel; Mila; Retaya.** Tain was believed killed in the incident, although he was actually captured and held at **Dominion internment camp 371**, on an asteroid in the Gamma Quadrant. While in captivity, Tain managed to secretly construct a subspace radio transmitter, which he used to alert his son, Garak, to the fact that he and others had survived the failed offensive and were being held by the Jem'Hadar. His health failing, Tain died in 2373 while Garak led a Starfleet mission to rescue the captives. On his deathbed, Tain told his son that he was proud of him. ("In Purgatory's Shadow" [DS9]). *Enabran Tain was first seen in "The Wire" (DS9). The set decorations in Tain's home, seen in "The Wire," included a barely seen replica of the Hovitos fertility idol from the opening scenes of* Raiders of the Lost Ark.

Tainer, Dr. Juliana. (Fionnula Flanagan). Human geologist who resided with her husband on planet **Atrea IV**. Mrs. Tainer was born Juliana O'Donnell, and was a colonist on **Omicron Theta** during the same period that **Dr. Noonien Soong** resided there in the 2330s. Juliana and Soong fell in love and, over the objections of Juliana's mother, secretly married on a trip to Mavala IV. Juliana assisted Soong in the development and construction of five positronic androids, the last two being **Lore** and **Data**. Juliana considered each of the androids as her children; the failure of the first four was very painful for her. The Soongs were nearing the final phases of Data's programming when Omicron Theta was attacked by the **Crystalline Entity**. Fearing that Data would behave as had his predecessor, Lore, Juliana

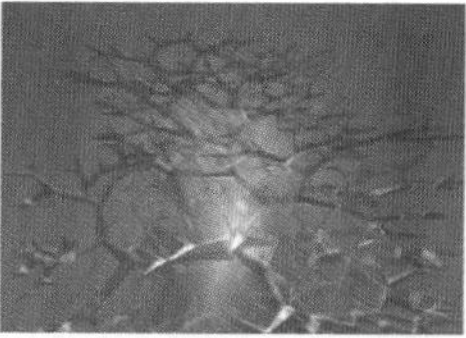

persuaded Soong to leave the android behind as they fled the Entity. The Soongs were able to travel as far as Terlina III, but Juliana had been injured by the Entity and became comatose. Unable to stand the thought of losing her, Soong created an extremely advanced android in her image and implanted the android with her memories. Following the human Juliana's death, Soong activated this new android. This android believed herself to be Juliana Soong and believed that she had just recovered from a serious accident. Soong went to great lengths to ensure that the android Juliana would not discover her true nature. He designed a feedback processor which sent out a false biosignal to fool sensor devices. He also programmed the android to shut down in the event that her design was discovered, so she would not discover the truth herself. For a time, Soong and his android creation were happy. But Juliana became unhappy with her life on Terlina III; eventually she left the planet and Soong. Sometime later Juliana met and married Dr. Pran Tainer, an Atrean geologist. Juliana followed her son, Data, and his accomplishments, until she was finally able to reunite with him at Atrea IV in 2370. Though Juliana's true nature was discovered by Data, he honored Soong's wishes and allowed Juliana to live out the remainder of her days believing she was human. ("Inheritance" [TNG]). *Fionnula Flanagan also portrayed Enina Tandro in "Dax" (DS9).*

Tainer, Dr. Pran. (William Lithgow). Atrean geologist who, along with his wife, **Juliana Tainer**, discovered the dangerous cooling in the magma of **Atrea IV** in 2370. Dr. Tainer worked with the crew of the *Enterprise*-D to reliquefy the core of his planet. ("Inheritance" [TNG])

Taitt, Ensign. (Alex Datcher). Bridge science officer aboard the *Enterprise*-D. Taitt was on duty during the encounter with the self-aware **Borg** in 2370. She did her **Starfleet Academy** senior honors thesis in solar dynamics. Taitt devised the plan that succesfully induced a solar-fusion eruption, destroying the enemy ship. ("Descent, Part II" [TNG]). SEE: **metaphasic shield.**

Tajor, Glinn. (Mic Rogers). Aide to **Gul Lemec** during talks aboard the *Starship Enterprise*-D in 2369. ("Chain of Command, Part I" [TNG]).

Tak Tak consul. (Albie Selznick). Commander of a **Tak Tak** spacecraft. In 2373, a Tak Tak consul was assigned to destroy a Garan mining colony to protect the system from a **macrovirus** invasion. ("Macrocosm" [VGR]).

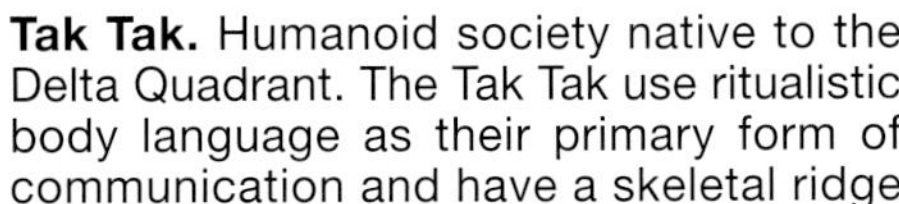

Tak Tak. Humanoid society native to the Delta Quadrant. The Tak Tak use ritualistic body language as their primary form of communication and have a skeletal ridge which protrudes from their forehead, around their nose, and into their chin. The Tak Tak had serious problems with **macrovirus** infestations, and by 2373, had a strict policy of destroying any infected ship or colony. Captain Janeway described them as one of the more unusual species encountered in the Delta Quadrant, and also as the most unforgiving people she had ever met. Captain Janeway unknowingly gave one of the worst insults possible to a Tak Tak by placing her hands on her hips during a negotiation meeting in 2373. ("Macrocosm" [VGR]).

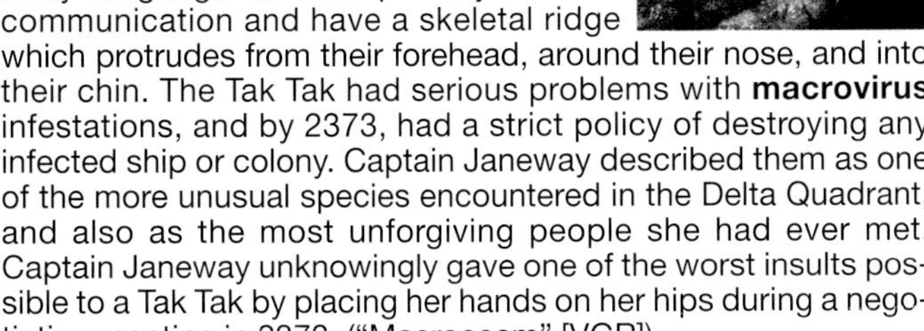

Takana root tea. Beverage found on a planet in the Teplan system located in the Gamma Quadrant. ("The Quickening" [DS9]).

Takar loggerhead eggs. Breakfast food. Served by Neelix. ("The Cloud" [VGR]).

Takar. Nation on a Class-M world in the Delta Quadrant. ("False Profits" [VGR]).

Takaran wildebeest. Noisy animal. ("Crossfire" [DS9]).

Takarans. Humanoid species whose members have vaguely reptilian features. Little was known about the Takarans until 2369, when *Enterprise*-D Chief Medical Officer Beverly Crusher was given an opportunity to autopsy a Takaran. Crusher discovered that the Takarans did not have organs in the traditional sense; rather, Takaran internal physiology was homogeneous throughout the body. This made the Takarans extremely difficult to injure or kill. Effective damage would have to be done on a cellular level. Crusher also discovered that Takarans were able to control the rate of their cellular physiology, allowing them to put themselves into a state resembling death. ("Suspicions" [TNG]). SEE: **Jo'Bril.**

Takarian bard. (Michael Ensign). Street poet on the **Takarian** homeworld who recited passages from the "Song of the Sages" in exchange for contributions. The bard wore an eye patch over one of his eyes for dramatic effect and sympathy. ("False Profits" [VGR]). *Michael Ensign previously portrayed Krola in "First Contact" (TNG) and Lojal in "The Forsaken" (DS9).*

Takarian mead. Alcoholic beverage made from the fermentation of honey and water. Takarian mead was served at Quark's bar on Deep Space 9. ("The Visitor" [DS9]).

Takarian merchant. (John Walter Davis). Takarian man who heartily embraced the profit-centered philosophy preached by the two Ferengi who posed as the Great Sages. ("False Profits" [VGR]).

Takarian sandal maker. (Alan Altshuld). Indigent craftsman and family man who lived in the poorest quarter of a city on the Takarian homeworld. He asked the **Great Sages** for some food and medicine, but they sold him a copy of the **Ferengi Rules of Acquisition** instead. ("False Profits" [VGR]). *Alan Altshuld previously played Pomet in "Starship Mine" (TNG) and Yaranek in "Gambit, Part I" (DS9).*

Takarian temple. Building in **Takar** erected to honor the **Great Sages**. The two Ferengi from the Alpha Quadrant who claimed to be the legendary Great Sages used the temple as their Divine Vault from their arrival in 2366 until their subsequent banishment in 2373 at the hands of the *Voyager* crew. ("False Profits" [VGR]).

Takarians. Humanoid pre-industrial bronze-age civilization that existed on a Class-M planet in the Delta Quadrant. Takarian mythology held that Great Sages would come from the sky to rule over the people as benevolent protectors. The Takarians had a flourishing society until two Ferengi from the Alpha Quadrant arrived in 2366 and pretended to be the Great Sages from ancient lore. The false demigods were banished by the *U.S.S. Voyager* crew in 2373. ("False Profits" [VGR]). SEE: **Arridor, Dr.**

***takeo* herbs.** Bajoran plants valued for their medicinal value. Dr. Julian Bashir prescribed *takeo* herbs for Kira Nerys in 2373 to help her swollen ankles during her pregnancy. ("Looking for *par'Mach* in All the Wrong Places" [DS9]).

***takka* berries.** Edible fruit originating on planet **Drayan II**. ("Innocence" [VGR]).

Takrit. Civilization in the Delta Quadrant. Takrit were mercenaries operating in the **Sobras** system. It was believed that the Takrit assisted the **Trabe** who plotted to assassinate a gathering of Kazon leaders on planet Sobras in 2372. ("Alliances" [VGR]).

Tal Shiar. Elite **Romulan** imperial intelligence service. The Tal Shiar was a secret, often brutal, sometimes extragovernmental agency that enforced loyalty among the Romulan citizenry and military. Tal Shiar agents carried broad discretionary powers and were able to overrule field military commanders with little fear of reprisal from government authorities. Some elements of Romulan society, including members of the military, felt the Tal Shiar's tactics to be unnecessarily brutal, but such opinions were rarely spoken publicly for fear of retribution that included the sudden "disappearance" of family members. Deanna Troi was coerced to assume the identity of Tal Shiar member **Major Rakal** as part of an elaborate plot to enable Romulan **Vice-Proconsul M'ret** to defect to the Federation. ("Face of the Enemy" [TNG]).

SEE: **N'Vek, Subcommander**. In 2371, the Tal Shiar joined forces with the Cardassian **Obsidian Order** to mount a pre-emptive first strike against the **Founders** of the **Dominion**. The joint operation involved secretly massing a fleet of 20 warships in the **Orias system** before attacking the **Founders' homeworld** in the **Omarion Nebula**. The fleet was ambushed by some 150 **Jem'Hadar** ships hiding in the nebula. The incident was a stunning defeat for the Tal Shiar, effectively eliminating the Tal Shiar as a viable force in interstellar politics and increasing the vulnerability of the **Romulan Star Empire** to external attack. The mission had been infiltrated by a Founder under the guise of a Romulan officer named **Colonel Lovok.** ("Improbable Cause" [DS9], "The Die is Cast" [DS9]). In 2373 it was learned that a few Romulan Tal Shiar members had survived the disastrous attack in the Omarion Nebula and were being held captive by the Jem'Hadar at **Dominion internment camp 371** on an asteroid in the Gamma Quadrant. ("In Purgatory's Shadow" [DS9]). *The Tal Shiar emblem, worn on the collar, was designed by Ricardo Delgado.*

tal-shaya**.** Ancient method of execution on Vulcan that was considered a merciful form of death. Pressure was applied to a specific portion of the victim's neck until it snapped, causing instantaneous death. *Tal-shaya* was used to murder Tellarite ambassador **Gav** prior to the **Babel Conference** of 2267 in an effort to cast suspicion upon the Vulcan ambassador. ("Journey to Babel" [TOS]).

Tal. (Jack Donner). Subcommander on the **Romulan battle cruiser** that captured the Federation starship *Enterprise* when the ship crossed the **Romulan Neutral Zone** in 2268 on a secret spy mission. ("The *Enterprise* Incident" [TOS]).

Talak'talan, Third. (Cress Williams). **Jem'Hadar** soldier. Third Talak'talan commanded a small force that captured Starfleet Commander Benjamin Sisko in 2370. Talak'talan personally delivered news of Sisko's capture to station Deep Space 9, along with news of the destruction of **New Bajor** and several Federation ships. ("The Jem'Hadar" [DS9]).

Talar. (Ronnie Clair Edwards). Healer and scientist in a village on planet **Barkon IV**. In 2370, Talar surmised incorrectly that Data was a member of a race of "icemen" who were believed to live in the **Vellorian mountains** on Barkon IV. She attempted to treat villagers who were suffering from radiation poisoning. ("Thine Own Self" [TNG]).

Talarian hook spider. Arachnid with half-meter-long legs. **Miles O'Brien**, who was afraid of spiders, had to get past 20 of these creatures when repairing an emitter array at the starbase on planet Zayra IV. ("Realm of Fear" [TNG]).

Talarian observation craft. A small vessel used as a training ship for young **Talarian** warriors. In 2367, the *Enterprise*-D discovered one of these craft adrift in **Sector 21947**. The craft had developed a serious radiation leak in its propulsion system, and Dr. Crusher's team evacuated the survivors, including a human youth named **Jono**, to the *Enterprise*-D. ("Suddenly Human" [TNG]). *The ship model was designed by Rick Sternbach and built by Greg Jein.*

Talarians. A humanoid species characterized by a distinctive hairless enlargement of the coronal area of the skull. Talarian society was patriarchal and encouraged warriorlike behavior. Talarians followed a rigid set of traditions and customs. ("Suddenly Human" [TNG]). SEE: **Endar; Galen border conflicts.** Former Cardassian agent **Garak** pointed out a Talarian as an example of someone who didn't rush through his meal. ("Improbable Cause" [DS9]). Talarians sometimes have bad reactions to ***raktajino***, causing them to become unruly. ("A Simple Investigation" [DS9]). *Talarians were mentioned in "Heart of Glory" (TNG), but not actually seen until "Suddenly Human." The Talarian seen in "Improbable Cause" (*pictured*), had a different appearance from those seen in "Suddenly Human."*

Talavian freighter. Cargo vessel of Talavian registry. On stardate 50416.2, **Silaran Prin** attached a **hunter probe** to a Talavian ship to get it close enough to **Deep Space 9.** ("The Darkness and the Light" [DS9]).

Talavians. Civilization. Captain Livara, a Romulan spy, posed as a Talavian smuggler operating in the Bajoran sector beginning in 2367. ("Things Past" [DS9]).

Talax. Inhabited Class-M planet in the Delta Quadrant. Homeworld to the **Talaxian** civilization, including **Neelix**. Talax has at least one moon, **Rinax**. ("Jetrel" [VGR]). The Talax system has three suns. ("Macrocosm" [VGR]).

Talaxian fighter. Small, highly-maneuverable combat craft used by **Talaxian** forces. Several Talaxian fighters, led by Commander **Paxim**, supported Lieutenant Tom Paris in retaking the *Voyager* from the Kazon-Nistrim in early 2373. ("Basics, Part II" [VGR]).

Talaxian tomato. Large pulpy edible berry cultivated as a vegetable, originating on planet Talax. ("Resolutions" [VGR]).

Talaxians. Humanoid civilization native to the planet **Talax** in the Delta Quadrant. The Talaxians surrendered to the **Haakonian Order** in 2356 after a decade-long war was ended by the deployment of the **metreon cascade**, a deadly weapon that killed over 300,000 Talaxians on **Rinax**. Talaxians who came in contact with

Talaxian in typical attire

Neelix's away uniform

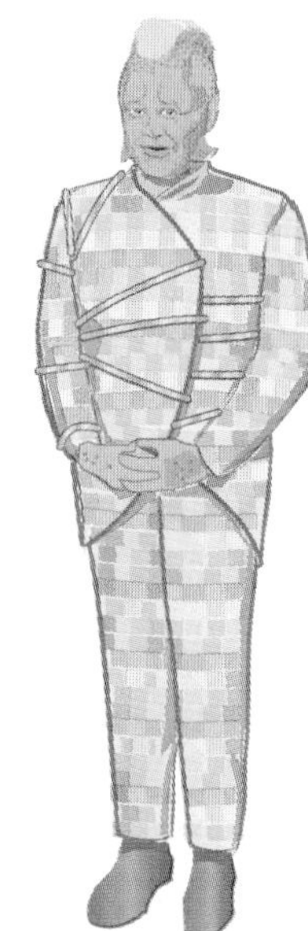

Talaxian in typical attire

the fallout from the metreon cascade suffered **metremia**, a deadly blood disease. ("Jetrel" [VGR]). The Talaxian respiratory system is directly linked to multiple points along the spinal column. ("Phage" [VGR]). It is a tradition in Talaxian society to share the history of a meal before eating. It was seen as a way of enhancing the culinary experience. ("Flashback" [VGR]). *Neelix was Talaxian.*

Talbot, St. John. (David Warner). Federation diplomatic representative to the **Paradise City** settlement on planet **Nimbus III**. *(Star Trek V: The Final Frontier). Actor David Warner later played the part of* **Chancellor Gorkon** *in* Star Trek VI: The Undiscovered Country *as well as the Cardassian* **Gul Madred** *in "Chain of Command, Part II" (TNG).*

talchok. Small two-tailed vermin indigenous to **Rinax**. Talchoks had sharp claws and fangs. ("Jetrel" [VGR]).

Tale of Two Cities, A. Novel written by terrestrial author Charles Dickens in 1859. The book was a historical story set during Earth's French Revolution. Spock gave Kirk an antique hardbound printed copy of *A Tale of Two Cities* as a birthday gift in 2285. *(Star Trek II: The Wrath of Khan).*

talent night. Evening entertainment program put on by **Neelix** aboard the *Voyager* on stardate 50518. The performances included a clarinet solo by Ensign **Harry Kim**, a reading of **Vulcan** poetry by Lieutenant **Tuvok**, and a ballet piece entitled "dying swan" performed by **Kathryn Janeway**. ("Coda" [VGR]).

talgonite. Ceramic substance, used in the construction of the **Kataan probe**. ("The Inner Light" [TNG]).

Tallera. (Robin Curtis). Agent of the **Vulcan isolationist movement** who infiltrated **Arctus Baran**'s mercenary crew in 2370. Tallera also claimed to be a member of the Vulcan **V'Shar** security agency, but this, too, was a cover to conceal her mission to acquire fragments of the ancient **Stone of Gol**, a **psionic resonator**, for the Vulcan isolationists. Tallera was captured and turned over to Vulcan **Security Minister Satok**. ("Gambit, Parts I and II" [TNG]). *Robin Curtis also portrayed Lieutenant Saavik in* Star Trek III and IV.

Tallonian crystals. Much sought-after crystals that were illegal to possess anywhere but on the Tallonian homeworld. The smuggler Regana Tosh attempted to sell a Tallonian crystal to Quark on station Deep Space 9 in 2372. ("Hippocratic Oath" [DS9]).

Talmadge, Captain. Commander of the ***Dorian***, a transport vessel. Talmadge's ship was attacked near planet **Rekag-Seronia** in 2369 while attempting to deliver **Ambassador Ves Alkar** to that planet in hopes of mediating peace there. ("Man of the People" [TNG]).

Talos IV. Class-M planet, formerly the home of a thriving, technologically advanced humanoid civilization. Thousands of centuries ago, a terrible nuclear war killed nearly all the planet's inhabitants and nearly rendered the planet itself uninhabitable. SEE: **Talosians**. The original *Enterprise* was the only Federation starship ever to visit the planet, although the survey vessel ***S.S. Columbia*** crashed there in 2236. As of 2266, contact with Talos IV was a violation of Starfleet **General Order 7**, a death penalty offense because of the immense and addictive power of the Talosians' illusion technology. ("The Cage," "The Menagerie, Parts I and II" [TOS]). SEE: **Pike, Christopher**.

Talos Star Group. Location of planet **Talos IV**. ("The Cage," "The Menagerie, Part I" [TOS]).

Talosians. Dominant humanoid life-form on planet **Talos IV**. The Talosians were nearly made extinct by nuclear war, and the few survivors clung to life underground, where they became dangerously dependent upon the illusion-creating technology developed by their ancestors. By the mid-23rd century, the Talosians resorted to capturing passing space travelers to serve as sources of illusions. A human woman named **Vina** was so captured in 2236 when her ship, the ***S.S. Columbia***, crashed on Talos IV. In 2254, the Talosians subsequently captured *Enterprise* captain **Christopher Pike** in the hope that he would establish a permanent human community with Vina, but Pike demonstrated that human resistance to captivity was so great as to make his people unsuitable subjects for their needs. Nevertheless, in 2266, the Talosians invited Pike to return to their world after an accident left him severely disabled. At Talos, illusions made it possible for Pike to live out the remainder of his life unfettered by the damage to his physical body. ("The Cage," "The Menagerie, Parts I and II" [TOS]). *Gene Roddenberry, while forced by production practicality to make the Talosians a humanoid species (so that they could be played by human actors), nevertheless took the imaginative step of casting women in the roles, while dubbing male voices for the characters.*

***talsa* root soup.** Soup native to the people of a planet in the Mokra Order. Caylem made *talsa* root soup for Kathryn Janeway. ("Resistance" [VGR]).

Taluno, Kai. Twenty-second century **Bajoran** religious leader who first discovered the **Bajoran wormhole**. A ship carrying Kai Taluno was damaged in the **Denorios Belt.** There, he claimed the heavens opened up and almost swallowed his ship. Bajoran religious faith holds that the phenomenon was the **Celestial Temple**, home of the Bajoran **Prophets**. ("Emissary" [DS9]).

Talura. (Charlie Curtis). Humanoid female. Talura was the companion of arms merchant **Hagath** during his trip to station Deep Space 9 in 2373. ("Business As Usual" [DS9]).

***Talvath*.** Romulan science vessel piloted by **Dr. Telek R'Mor**. The vessel was launched in 2349 on an extended mission. In 2351, Dr. R'Mor encountered a **micro-wormhole** in **Sector 1385** of the Alpha Quadrant. He communicated through it with the crew of the *Starship Voyager*, which was in the Delta Quadrant in 2371. ("Eye of the Needle" [VGR]). *We never saw the Talvath.*

Tamal. (Michael Canavan). **Maquis** member. Tamal operated the port tactical station on the bridge of the *U.S.S.* ***Defiant*** during **Thomas Riker**'s unauthorized mission to the Orias system in 2371. `("Defiant" [DS9]).

Tamar. (Alan Echevarria). Inhabitant of a planet in the Teplan system located in the Gamma Quadrant. Tamar suffered from a fatal disease known as the blight. In 2372, after sharing his last meal with family and friends, Tamar drank poison and died. SEE: **Teplan blight.** ("The Quickening" [DS9]).

Tamarian frost. A sweet beverage. Available in the Ten-Forward Lounge of the *Enterprise*-D. ("Hero Worship" [TNG]).

Tamarians. A humanoid civilization, first encountered by the Federation in 2268. The Tamarians were faintly reptilian in appearance, and their spoken language was based almost entirely on metaphors drawn from their culture's mythology. Early encounters between the Federation and the Tamarians were without incident, but the two societies were unable to communicate. A breakthrough finally came in 2368, when a Tamarian captain, **Dathon**, confined both himself and *Enterprise*-D Captain Picard on the surface of planet **El-Adrel IV**. ("Darmok" [TNG]).

Tambor Beta VI. White dwarf star. The **emergent life-form** created aboard the *Enterprise*-D in 2370 used a modified tractor beam to collect all the vertion particles from Tambor Beta VI. ("Emergence" [TNG]).

Tamen Sahsheer. SEE: **Sahsheer**.

Tamoon. (Jane Ross). **Drill thrall** on planet **Triskelion**. In 2268, Tamoon was responsible for training Chekov to fight in her **Provider**'s games. ("The Gamesters of Triskelion" [TOS]).

Tamura, Yeoman. (Miko Mayama). Crew member aboard the original *Starship Enterprise.* Tamura served on a landing party to planet **Eminiar VII** in 2267. ("A Taste of Armageddon" [TOS]).

Tan Ru*.** Space probe of unknown origin, programmed to gather and sterilize soil samples from distant planets as a precursor to colonization. While it drifted through space, *Tan Ru* collided with Earth probe ***Nomad and somehow merged with it. ("The Changeling" [TOS]).

Tanagra. SEE: **"Darmok and Jalad at Tanagra."**

Tanandra Bay. Ocean inlet located on planet **Ajilon Prime**. Tanandra Bay was the location of a Starfleet base. ("Nor the Battle to the Strong" [DS9]).

Tandro, Enina. (Fionnula Flanagan). Widow of the late **General Ardelon Tandro** of planet **Klaestron IV.** In 2369 her son, **Ilon Tandro,** accused **Jadzia Dax** of the murder of his father 30 years before. After Odo contacted her with news of the trial implicating Jadzia Dax, Enina came forward to confess that **Curzon Dax** was in bed with her at the time of a secret transmission implicating the Trill. She told Jadzia, in confidence, that her husband had betrayed his own people and the rebels had killed him. This fact had been kept secret in order to protect the memory of a man so cherished by his people. Dax had concealed this information out of Curzon's desire to protect Enina, even if it meant she would have been convicted of a murder Curzon did not commit. ("Dax" [DS9]).

Tandro, General Ardelon. Statesman from the planet **Klaestron IV** who was reportedly murdered in 2339 during a civil war on his planet. He became a national hero after his death, with statues of him erected all over the planet. Ardelon Tandro was good friends with Federation mediator **Curzon Dax**, but was unaware that his wife, **Enina Tandro**, was conducting a love affair with Dax. Thirty years later, when **Jadzia Dax** was accused of Tandro's murder, Dax refused to offer any defense, preferring to be found guilty rather than betray Enina. It was not until Enina came forward and admitted that she had been in bed with Curzon Dax at the time of a secret transmission that Dax was acquitted. Enina also spoke privately with Jadzia Dax, explaining that her late husband had betrayed his own people. The rebels had killed him for it, but that truth remained secret. ("Dax" [DS9]).

Tandro, Ilon. (Gregory Itzen). Head of the special diplomatic envoy from planet **Klaestron IV** who attempted to extradite Jadzia Dax from Deep Space 9 in 2369 for the murder of his father, **General Ardelon Tandro**. The general, who had been good friends with **Curzon Dax**, had been murdered 30 years before, but new evidence surfaced in 2369 implicating the Trill host. Tandro maintained that although Curzon Dax was gone, Jadzia Dax could be prosecuted for the murder of his father. The paramount question as to whether a **Trill** host was responsible for the symbiont's past lives was not addressed because the murder charge was laid to rest when Ardelon's widow, **Enina Tandro**, revealed that **Curzon Dax** was in bed with her at the time of the secret transmission that had been the source of the indictment. ("Dax" [DS9]).

Tango Sierra, Science Station. Orbital research facility. Dr. **Hester Dealt** worked at station Tango Sierra in 2365 to cure a deadly outbreak of **plasma plague** that had stricken the densely populated Rachelis system. ("The Child" [TNG]). *Science Station Tango Sierra was a re-use of the Regula I space station model seen in* Star Trek II. *Regula I was itself a modification of the orbital office-complex model originally built for* Star Trek: The Motion Picture.

Tango. Young **Christopher Pike**'s horse when he was growing up in **Mojave** on Earth. The **Talosians** created an illusory version of Tango when Pike was held captive on **Talos IV**. Tango was fond of sugar cubes. ("The Cage," "The Menagerie, Part II" [TOS]).

Tanis. (Gary Graham). One of **Suspiria**'s followers. Tanis lived on **Suspiria's Array**, where he worked to develop his latent Ocampa abilities in hopes of joining Suspiria in the **subspace** domain known as **Exosia**. Suspiria also helped Tanis and her other Ocampa followers to extend their lives. Tanis lived to over 14 years of age, nearly twice the normal life span for the Ocampa people. His father lived to be 20. Tanis was driven into Exosia, along with Suspiria, when Suspiria threatened the crew of the *Starship Voyager* in 2372. ("Cold Fire" [VGR]). *Gary Graham also played Sikes in the* Alien Nation *television series and made-for-television movies.*

Tantalus field. Covert anti-personnel weapon used by the alternate Captain Kirk in the **mirror universe** aboard the ***I.S.S. Enterprise*.** The Tantalus field was controlled from a small viewscreen located in the mirror Kirk's quarters and was used to eliminate enemies. The Tantalus field tracked its intended target, enabling the operator to vaporize the victim by remote control. ("Mirror, Mirror" [TOS]). SEE: **Kirk, James T. (mirror)**.

Tantalus V. Penal colony administered by **Dr. Simon Van Gelder** in 2266. Tantalus V was located on a distant planet and protected by a force field, preventing transporter use or other possible escape. Considerably advanced beyond early prisons, Tantalus V was more of a hospital for sick minds. One treatment developed there, a **neural neutralizer**, was found to have deadly effects on its patients. ("Dagger of the Mind" [TOS]). *Named for the Greek mythic figure who stole ambrosia from the tables of the gods, feeding it to mortals.*

Tanuga IV. Class-M planet. The late **Dr. Nel Apgar** attempted to develop a **Krieger-wave** converter at his laboratory near Tanuga IV. Apgar was killed when his space station exploded in 2366. ("A Matter of Perspective"[TNG]).

Tanugans. Humanoid civilization on planet **Tanuga IV**. Tanugans are distinguished by their prominent eyebrow and forehead ridges. The Tanugan system of justice held that the accused were guilty until proven innocent, which became a problem for *Enterprise*-D Commander **William Riker** when he was accused of the murder of Tanugan scientist **Dr. Nel Apgar** in 2366. ("A Matter of Perspective" [TNG]).

Tanzian flu. A medical condition whose symptoms included increased respiration rate, dilated pupils, and orange coloration of the ears. ("Parturition" [VGR]).

"Tapestry." Next Generation episode #141. Written by Ronald D. Moore. Directed by Les Landau. Stardate not given. First aired in 1993. A dying Picard relives his past, with the help of Q. Picard's flashback scenes with the Nausicaans at the Bonestell Facility dramatize an incident first mentioned in "Samaritan Snare" (TNG). GUEST CAST: Ned Vaughn as **Zweller, Cortin**; J. C. Brandy as **Batanides, Marta**; Clint Carmichael as **Nausicaans**; Rae Norman as Penny; John de Lancie as **Q**; Clive Church as **Picard, Maurice**; Marcus Nash as Young Picard; Majel Barrett as Computer voice. SEE: ***Ajax, U.S.S.*; barokie; Batanides, Marta; Bonestell Recreational Facility; compressed tetryon beam; dom-jot; Halloway, Captain Thomas; Lenarians; magnaspanner; Milika III; Morikin VII; Muroc, Penny; Narth, Captain; Nausicaans; Picard, Jean-Luc; Picard, Maurice; pulmonary support unit; Q; Selar, Dr.; Starbase Earhart; *Stargazer, U.S.S.*; stasis unit; straight nines; *undari*; Zweller, Cortin.**

Tarahong detention center. Penal settlement; institution where **Quark**'s cousin, **Barbo**, was incarcerated for selling defective warp drives to the Tarahong government. ("The Nagus" [DS9]).

Taranko colony. Federation settlement. In 2370, the Taranko colony required medical supplies urgently. The *Enterprise*-D picked up the supplies from the ***U.S.S. Lexington*** and then transported them to Taranko. ("Thine Own Self" [TNG]).

Tarbolde, Phineas. Poet on the Canopus Planet who wrote **"Nightingale Woman"** in 1996, considered to be one of the most passionate love sonnets written in the past few centuries. **Gary Mitchell** was able to quote the sonnet after exposure to the barrier at the edge of the galaxy. ("Where No Man Has Gone Before" [TOS]). Tarbolde's creativity was, in part, inspired by a noncorporeal entity known as **Onaya**, who was also responsible for the brevity of his life. ("The Muse" [DS9]).

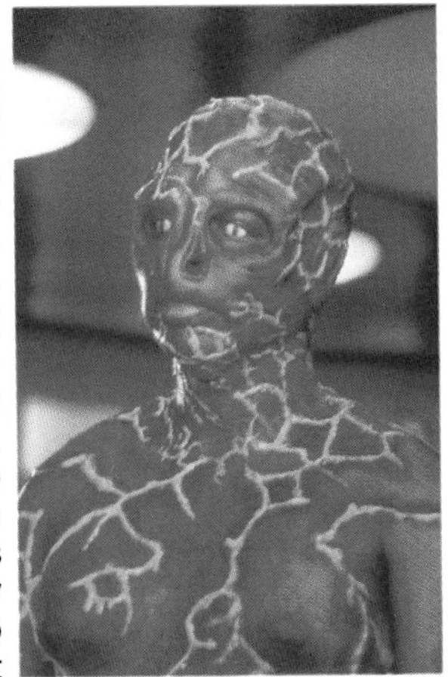

Tarchannen III. Class-M planet. Site of a Federation outpost. Tarchannen III was home to an unusual life-form that reproduced by planting a strand of DNA into a host body. The DNA strand would eventually take over the host body, causing it to metamorphose into a nonsentient reptilian humanoid. It is believed that all 49 members of the Tarchannen outpost suffered this fate in 2362 when contact was lost with the outpost. The ***U.S.S. Victory***, dispatched to investigate the outpost, sent an away team to the planet. Five years later, all five members of the away team were irresistibly compelled to return to the planet, apparently part of the metamorphosis process. Three members of the away team completed the metamorphosis and were irretrievably lost. The process was identified by Dr. Beverly Crusher in time to save former *Victory* away team members **Geordi La Forge** and **Susanna Leijten** from the same fate. *Enterprise*-D Captain Picard ordered warning beacons placed around Tarchannen III so the planet would not be revisited. ("Identity Crisis" [TNG]). *The transformed versions of the Tarchannen III creatures were played by popular Los Angeles area radio personalities Mark and Brian, who called themselves the Lizard Creatures from Hell.*

***Tarchee* cat.** Animal indigenous to the **Nechani** homeworld in the Delta Quadrant. *Tarchee* cats were known to be high strung and fussy. ("Sacred Ground" [VGR]).

***tardeth*.** Large and fearsome **Drayan** animal possessing copious amounts of hair. ("Innocence" [VGR]).

Tarella. Class-M planet that once supported humanoid life-forms. Years ago, a deadly biological weapon was created during a war between the inhabitants of two land masses. The resulting disease wiped out the planet's population. A few Tarellians escaped to other worlds, infecting those planets as well. The remaining Tarellians were hunted as plague carriers, and many were killed by people fearful of contamination. The last eight survivors of Tarella headed toward planet **Haven** in 2364. ("Haven" [TNG]).

Tarellians. Humanoid culture from planet **Tarella** that was nearly wiped out by a deadly biological weapon during the Tarellian wars. ("Haven" [TNG]).

Taresia. Class-M planet in the Delta Quadrant, homeworld of the **Taresians**. The planet was protected by a defensive **tachyon** grid projected by a series of satellites. ("Favorite Son" [VGR]).

Taresians. Technologically sophisticated, spacefaring, humanoid civilization in the Delta Quadrant. The Taresian population was ninety percent female because male children were very rare. To assure an adequate childbirth rate, the Taresians genetically engineered a retrovirus that they placed on several planets in the Delta Quadrant. The retrovirus was designed to alter the DNA of a male host's body, mutating it into a Taresian being. The retrovirus also imparted an instinctive urge to return to Taresia so that their bodies could be denucleated. ("Favorite Son" [VGR]).

***targ* scoop.** Device used on the front of Klingon ground-assault vehicles. *Targ* scoops prevented collisions with *targ* herds by emitting a high-frequency tone which dispersed the animals away from the vehicle's path. ("Elogium" [VGR]).

***targ*.** Furry piglike Klingon animal. **Worf** had a *targ* as a pet when he was young, and an illusory *targ* once appeared on the *Enterprise*-D bridge. ("Where No One Has Gone Before" [TNG]). The *targ* is regarded as a vicious and destructive animal. ("Crossfire" [DS9]). SEE: **heart of *targ*.** Targs are sometimes spotted. ("Favorite Son" [VGR]). *We wonder if either Commander Kruge's pet (in* Star Trek III: The Search for Spock) *or the jackal-like pet of the Klingon warden at the Rura Penthe prison* (Star Trek VI: The Undiscovered Country) *were also* targs. *The* targ *was actually a tame wild boar named Marilou who wore spikes for filming. While Marilou was not vicious or destructive, she exuded a powerful, pungent odor that clung, for weeks, to anyone unfortunate to have touched her, a fact to which Bob Justman can attest. Marilou also left a distinctive spot on the* Enterprise-D *bridge that remained on the set for the remainder of the first season of* Star Trek: The Next Generation. *Molly O'Brien had a stuffed* targ *toy in her quarters on Deep Space 9.*

targeting scanner. Sensor visual display device used for tactical applications. The targeting scanner at the helm station on the **bridge** of a *Constitution*-class starship was normally stowed in the console, automatically deploying when needed.

Targhee moonbeast. Life-form noted for its loud bray. The sound produced by a **Valtese horn** was said to resemble the moonbeast's call. ("The Perfect Mate" [TNG]).

tarin juice. Nutritious beverage consumed by the **Enarans** of the Delta Quadrant. ("Remember" [VGR]).

Taris Murn. J'naii shuttle vehicle that was lost inside an area of **null space** in the **J'naii** system in 2368. The *Taris Murn* had a crew of two, who, despite the loss of all electromagnetic power into the null space, remained alive long enough to be rescued by a shuttlecraft from the *Enterprise*-D. ("The Outcast" [TNG]). *The miniature of the* Taris Murn*, seen only briefly, was a re-use of the* **Nenebek** *model originally built for "Final Mission" (TNG).* SEE: ***Toron*-class shuttlecraft.**

Taris, Subcommander. (Carolyn Seymour). Commanding officer of the Romulan warbird ***Haakona***. ("Contagion" [TNG]). *Carolyn Seymour also played Commander Toreth in "Face of the Enemy" (TNG) and Mirasta Yale in "First Contact" (TNG). She also played* ***Mrs. Templeton****, the housekeeper in Janeway's gothic romance holo-novel.*

Tark. (Joseph Bernard). Father to **Kara**, the Argelian dancer. ("Wolf in the Fold" [TOS]).

Tarkalean condor. Large avian life-form. In 2373, when Odo pursued two Yridians who had been cheating at Quark's dabo tables, he momentarily forgot he was a solid and instinctively leapt after them, intending to change into a Tarkalean condor in flight. ("Nor the Battle to the Strong" [DS9]).

Tarkalean hawk. Predatory avian life-form. Odo took great pleasure in assuming the form of a Tarkalean hawk after he regained his shape-shifting abilities in 2373. ("The Begotten" [DS9]).

Tarkalean tea. Beverage. Dr. Julian Bashir enjoyed Tarkalean tea. ("Past Prologue" [DS9]). *Tarkalean tea was also mentioned in numerous other episodes, including "Cardassians" (DS9), "The Wire" (DS9) "Distant Voices" (DS9) and "Trials and Tribble-ations" (DS9).*

Tarkalian sheep herders. Livestock tenders. Tarkalian sheep herders fell on hard times in 2372, and Quark used this fact as an excuse to unfairly inflate prices charged to the Karemma. ("Starship Down" [DS9]).

Tarkan. Civilization in the Delta Quadrant. Ruthless and powerful, the Tarkan assimilate all intruders who dare to enter their area of space. ("Darkling" [VGR]).

Tarkannans. Civilization. Commander Chakotay participated in the Federation's **first contact** with the Tarkannans while on his first starship assignment. Males and females of the Tarkannan race use different styles of movement. Chakotay's gesture for "hello" was misinterpreted by the Tarkannans as a proposition to their ambassador. ("Innocence" [VGR]).

Tarkassian razorbeast. Animal that has a propensity for leaping about. Young **Guinan** tempted young **Ro** to start jumping on the bed like a Tarkassian razorbeast. ("Rascals" [TNG]). When Guinan was a child, a Tarkassian razorbeast was her imaginary friend; the creature protected her and made her feel safe. She described it as huge, covered with brown fur, and having enormous spiny wings. Guinan fondly recalled that it was very frightening, especially when it smiled. As Guinan grew older, the razorbeast faded away, leaving behind only the idea, but Guinan still talked to it occasionally. ("Imaginary Friend" [TNG]).

Tarmin. (David Sage). The head of an **Ullian** delegation of telepathic researchers. Tarmin was a researcher who described himself as an "archaeologist of the mind." He worked for years to compile a database of memories that would serve as a library for cultural research. Tarmin was briefly implicated in three cases of **telepathic memory invasion** rape that occurred on the *Starship Enterprise*-D in 2368. He was cleared when his son, **Jev**, was found to be guilty of the telepathic rapes. ("Violations" [TNG]).

Tarod IX. Planet near the **Romulan Neutral Zone**. Tarod IX was attacked by the **Borg** in 2364, although Romulan activity was initially suspected. ("The Neutral Zone" [TNG]).

Tarok. Class-M moon located in **Kazon-Ogla** space. Tarok was used by the Ogla to conduct training exercises. In 2372, ***Starship Voyager*** Commander **Chakotay** and Kazon **Kar** crash-landed on Tarok but were subsequently rescued. ("Initiations" [VGR]).

Tarquin Hill, The Master of. An artist of planet **Kurl**, the Master of Tarquin Hill lived some twelve thousand years ago. The Master of Tarquin Hill was so named by later archaeologists who have come to know and respect the visionary artistry and influence of his work, although his name has never been learned. ("The Chase" [TNG]). SEE: **Kurlan *naiskos***.

Tarrana. (Susan Christy). **Boraalan** native and daughter of **Kateras**. Tarrana was unbetrothed in 2370; her father hoped Worf, who Tarrana thought to be a **Boraalan seer**, would choose her as his wife. ("Homeward" [TNG]).

Tarsas III. Earthlike planet. **Starbase 74** orbits Tarsas III. ("11001001" [TNG]). *Of course, the reason Tarsas III was so Earthlike was that the Starbase 74 exterior visual effects shots were re-uses of the* ***Spacedock*** *scenes originally created for* Star Trek III: The Search for Spock*.*

Tarses, Crewman Simon. (Spencer Garrett). A native of the **Martian Colonies**, Crewman First Class Tarses was assigned as a medical technician aboard the *Enterprise*-D in 2366. Tarses was accused as a conspirator in the Romulan theft of *Enterprise*-D technical data in 2367. While Tarses was not guilty of the theft, he had lied on his Starfleet entrance papers, concealing the fact that his paternal grandfather was Romulan. When this fact was brought out during the conspiracy hearings, Tarses feared his career in Starfleet was over. ("The Drumhead" [TNG]).

Tarsian War. A conflict fought by the people of **Angosia III** in the mid-24th century. The **Angosian** government utilized extensive biochemical and psychological manipulation on their soldiers so that they might more effectively fight this war. ("The Hunted" [TNG]). SEE: **Danar, Roga**. *The episode does not make clear who the Angosians were fighting, or if it was a civil war.*

Tarsus IV. Location of an Earth colony that suffered a terrible famine in 2246 when an exotic fungus nearly destroyed the food supply. Colony governor **Kodos** declared martial law, and ordered half of the population, some four thousand colonists, put to death in order to insure the survival of the remainder. Although relief arrived, it was too late to prevent the executions. Kodos was believed dead following discovery of a burned body, but it was later learned that Kodos had escaped, living under the name **Anton Karidian** (*pictured*). Only nine eyewitnesses to the killings survived, among them **James Kirk**, **Kevin Riley**, and **Thomas Leighton**. ("The Conscience of the King" [TOS]).

Tartaran landscapes. Paintings. **Quark** had a collection of Tartaran landscapes in his quarters on Deep Space 9. Quark invited two voluptuous women—created from his imagination by unknown aliens from the Gamma Quadrant—to his quarters to view his collection of Tartaran landscapes. They seemed willing enough. ("If Wishes Were Horses" [DS9]).

Tartaras V. Planet; site where the ruins of the Rokai provincial capital were discovered in 2369. **Vash** decided to explore the ruins on Tartaras V instead of returning to Earth after her visit to Deep Space 9. ("Q-Less" [DS9]).

tartoc. Vegetation used as an ingredient in salads. ("Business As Usual" [DS9]).

Tarvokian pound cake. A dessert food. Lieutenant Worf made a Tarvokian pound cake to welcome Cadet Wesley Crusher back to the *Enterprise*-D in 2368. ("The Game" [TNG]).

Tarvokian powder cake. White dessert confection. Counselor Troi offered some Tarvokian powder cake to Ambassador **Loquel** while entertaining him aboard the *Enterprise*-D in 2370. ("Liaisons" [TNG]).

Tasha. SEE: **Yar, Natasha**.

taspar egg. The ova of a **Cardassian** fowl. Boiled taspar egg is considered a delicacy on Cardassia. Raw taspar egg, however, is considered extremely unappetizing. ("Chain of Command, Part II" [TNG]).

"Taste of Armageddon, A." Original Series episode #23. Teleplay by Robert Hamner and Gene L. Coon. Story by Robert Hamner. Directed by Joseph Pevney. Stardate 3192.1. *First aired in 1967. The* Enterprise *is caught in a bizarre interplanetary war fought entirely by computers, but with real deaths.* GUEST CAST: David Opatoshu as **Anan 7**; Gene Lyons as **Fox, Ambassador Robert**; Barbara Babcock as **Mea 3**; Miko Mayama as **Tamura, Yeoman**; David L. Ross as **Galloway, Lieutenant**; Sean Kenney as **DePaul, Lieutenant**; Robert Sampson as Sar 6; Frank da Vinci as Osborne, Lieutenant; Eddie Paskey, Bill Blackburn, Ron Veto, Frank Vinci, John Burnside, Eminiar guards and technicians; Majel Barrett as Computer voice, Malone as Ambassadorial secretary. SEE: **Anan 7; Cluster NGC 321; Code 710; DePaul, Lieutenant; Eminiar VII; Fox, Ambassador Robert; fusion bombs; Galloway, Lieutenant; Mea 3; Prime Directive; sonic disruptor; Starfleet General Orders and Regulations; Tamura, Yeoman; tricobalt explosive; *Valiant, U.S.S.*; Vendikar; Vulcan mind-meld.**

Tataglia. A noted concert violinist. **Data** programmed himself to emulate Tataglia's performance style for a Mozart concert in honor of Ambassador Sarek's visit to the *Enterprise*-D in 2366. ("Sarek" [TNG]).

"Tattoo." *Voyager* episode #25. Teleplay by Michael Piller. Story by Larry Brody. Directed by Alexander Singer. No stardate mentioned. *First aired in 1995. On a distant planet in the Delta Quadrant, Chakotay discovers his roots.* GUEST CAST: Henry Darrow as **Kolopak**; Richard Fancy as Alien; Douglas Spain as Young Chakotay; Nancy Hower as **Wildman, Samantha**; Richard Chaves as Chief; Joseph Palmas as **Antonio**; Majel Barrett as Computer voice. SEE: **antithoron radiation; Antonio; Baldoxic vinegar; *CHAH-mooz-ee*; Chakotay; Cypriprdium; Emergency Medical Hologram; Inheritors; Kolopak; Levodian flu; magnesite; medicine bundle; Neelix; polyferranide; Rubber Tree People; Sky Spirits; Sulu, Hikaru; Tuvok; Wildman, Samantha.**

Tau Alpha C. A very distant planet. Homeworld to the **Traveler**. Little is known about Tau Alpha C, except that its humanoid inhabitants are extremely advanced. ("Where No One Has Gone Before" [TNG]).

Tau Ceti III. Planet. Site where Jean-Luc Picard once met **Captain Rixx** some time prior to 2364. ("Conspiracy" [TNG]).

Tau Ceti Prime. First planet in the Tau Ceti star system. Tau Ceti Prime was the site of a tragic accident in 2358 that claimed the life of **Admiral Janeway**. ("Coda" [VGR]).

Tau Ceti. Star located some eight light-years from the Sol System. Site where a Romulan vessel was defeated by the *Enterprise* using the **Cochrane deceleration maneuver**. ("Whom Gods Destroy" [TOS]).

Tau Cygna V. Class-H world, desert-like, and bathed in hazardous **hyperonic radiation**. The planet was ceded to the **Sheliak Corporate** by the **Treaty of Armens** in 2255. A Federation colony was established there in the 2270s in violation of that agreement. The **Sheliak** demanded removal of the colony in 2366 under the terms of the treaty. ("The Ensigns of Command" [TNG]).

Taugan sector. Region of space containing several planets with ruins of **Romulan** origin, including **Calder II**, **Barradas III**, **Draken IV** and **Yadalla Prime.** ("Gambit, Parts I and II" [TNG]).

Taurik, Ensign. (Alexander Enberg). Starfleet officer assigned to the *Enterprise*-D. Taurik worked in engineering control and shared quarters with Ensign **Sam Lavelle**. Taurik was one of several ensigns being considered for promotion in 2370. ("Lower Decks" [TNG]).

Taurus II. Class-M planet. Site where the ***Shuttlecraft Galileo***, under the command of Mr. Spock, crashed in 2267. Shuttle crew members **Latimer** and **Gaetano** were killed by indigenous humanoid creatures on the planet. The humanoids were described as "huge, furry creatures" approximately four meters tall and possessing crude stone spears. ("The *Galileo* Seven" [TOS]). *Named for the constellation Taurus (the bull).*

Tauvid Rem. (Brant Cotton). Alias used by an Idanian intelligence agent. "Tauvid Rem" was sent to station Deep Space 9 to awaken **Arissa**, a sleeper agent, and give her a **data crystal** containing her memories. Tauvid Rem arrived on the station but before he could make contact with Arissa, he was killed by one of **Draim**'s men. ("A Simple Investigation" [DS9]).

Tava. (Sachi Parker). A physician on planet **Malcor III**. Tava helped care for William Riker, masquerading as **Rivas Jakara** at the **Sikla Medical Facility** in 2367. ("First Contact" [TNG]).

Tavela Minor. Federation planet. Dr. Crusher suggested Tavela Minor as a good place for **Alyssa Ogawa** to take a vacation with her new male friend. ("Imaginary Friend" [TNG]). *The episode script said "Telana," but Crusher clearly said "Tavela."*

Tavnians. Humanoid civilization. Tavnians had a patriarchal society that believed in strict separation of the sexes. According to Tavnian tradition, male infants were taken and raised by men, and girls were raised by women. Tavnian children were not told that the other sex exists until they were 16 years old. ("The Muse" [DS9]). SEE: **wedding**.

Taxco. (Constance Towers). **Arbazan** ambassador who visited **Deep Space 9** in 2369 on a fact-finding mission to the **wormhole**. Taxco initially expressed dissatisfaction with the accommodations on the station, but later softened when **Dr. Julian Bashir**'s quick thinking saved her life. ("The Forsaken" [DS9]).

Taya. (Noley Thornton). A **sentient holographic life-form**; in 2370, the ten-year-old granddaughter of **Rurigan**. She and all the other inhabitants of the settlement on **Yadera II**, except Rurigan, were living holograms. ("Shadowplay" [DS9]). *Noley Thornton also portrayed Clara Sutter in "Imaginary Friend" (TNG).*

Taylor, Dr. Gillian. (Catherine Hicks). Twentieth-century marine biologist and assistant director of the **Cetacean Institute** on Earth. Taylor supervised the care of **George and Gracie**, two **humpback whale**s living in captivity at the institute. She was distraught when the two whales had to be released into the open ocean, but she later traveled, with Kirk and the two humpbacks, to the 23rd century, where she earned a post on a science vessel. *(Star Trek IV: The Voyage Home).*

Taymon. (Patrick Fabian). Humanoid male who was lured to **Taresia** with a genetically engineered retrovirus. Taymon was a member of a merchant fleet in the Delta Quadrant. When there, the Taresian females convinced Taymon that he was a native of their world. In a ceremony, Taymon was joined to Malia. After the bonding ritual, Taymon died when a large number of his body's cells were denucleated to provide genetic material for conception. ("Favorite Son" [VGR]).

Tayna. (Juli Donald). Assistant to **Tanugan** scientist Dr. **Nel Apgar**. Tayna testified against Commander William Riker when Riker was accused of Apgar's murder in 2366. ("A Matter of Perspective" [TNG]).

Te'nari. One of the Bajoran ***D'jarra***s. The *Te'nari D'jarra* was considered below others, such as the *Ih'valla D'jarra.* ("Accession" [DS9]).

tea ceremony, Klingon. Klingon ritual in which two friends share a poisoned tea served on a tray decorated with simple flowers. The ceremony is test of bravery, a chance to share with a friend a look at one's mortality, and a reminder that death is an experienced best shared—like the tea. Worf shared a Klingon tea ceremony with Katherine Pulaski after she helped him save face by hiding the fact that he was suffering from a childhood disease. ("Up the Long Ladder" [TNG]).

tea. Beverage made with leaves from an Earth plant, soaked in boiling water. Captain **Hikaru Sulu** enjoyed having a cup of tea each morning on the bridge of the *Excelsior*. Ensign Tuvok prepared a Vulcan blend for him on one occasion in 2293. ("Flashback" [VGR]). SEE: **Earl Grey tea; tea ceremony, Klingon**.

Teacher. Helmetlike device used by the **Eymorg** women of planet **Sigma Draconis VI** to temporarily gain technical knowledge and skills. **Kara**, leader of the Eymorgs in 2268, used the Teacher to learn the advanced surgical techniques required to steal Spock's brain for use in the **Controller**. Dr. McCoy subsequently used the Teacher to obtain the skills necessary to return the brain to Spock's body. ("Spock's Brain" [TOS]).

Tears of the Prophet. SEE: **Orb.**

Tebok, Commander. (Marc Alaimo). Commanding officer of the **Romulan warbird** starship that crossed the **Romulan Neutral Zone** in 2364, ending the period of isolationism begun in 2311 after the **Tomed Incident**. Tebok was on a mission to investigate Federation knowledge of the destruction of several Romulan outposts in the area. Tebok entered into a limited agreement with Picard, consenting to share information about the cause of the outposts' destruction, later found to be due to the **Borg**. ("The Neutral Zone" [TNG]). *Marc Alaimo played several other roles, including **Gul Dukat** in* Star Trek: Deep Space Nine. SEE: **Badar N'D'D**.

technobabble. Complex technical jargon that seems unintelligible to the uninitiated. ("Parturition" [VGR]). *Technobabble is also a gag term sometimes used by* Star Trek *production personnel and* Star Trek *enthusiasts to refer to some of the more obfuscatory technical dialog on the show.*

Technology Future. Paper-based hardcopy periodical publication on 20th-century Earth. *Technology Future* dealt extensively with the extraordinary advances in computer technology that occured during that period. The December, 1995, issue of *Technology Future* featured a cover story on computer pioneer **Henry Starling**. ("Future's End, Part I" [VGR]).

tectonic plates. Major subdivisions of the crust of a Class-M planet, which meet in seams known as fault lines. By 2367, the ambitious **Atlantis Project** had not yet determined a way to relieve the pressure on Earth's tectonic plates as they built up the mantle to raise the ocean floor. ("Family" [TNG]).

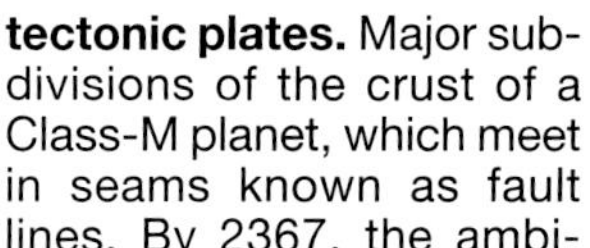

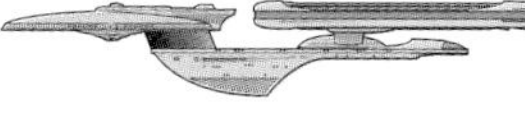

Tecumseh, U.S.S. Federation starship. In 2373, the *Tecumseh* and the *Starship* ***Rutledge*** were ordered to launch a counterattack against Klingon forces in the **Archanis** sector. The science officer of the *Tecumseh* was the husband of Dr. Kalandra. ("Nor the Battle to the Strong" [DS9]).

teddy bear. A stuffed toy bear, also a nickname for an animal species on planet Vulcan that has six-inch fangs and is not at all like its counterpart on Earth. ("Journey to Babel" [TOS]). SEE: **Kukalaka; sehlat.**

teer. Title given to the leader of the **Ten Tribes** on planet **Capella IV**. In 2267, High **Teer Akaar** was killed by rival **Maab**, who then claimed the title. ("Friday's Child" [TOS]). SEE: **Akaar, Leonard James**.

tekasite. Unstable material. In 2373 a changeling infiltrator posing as Dr. **Julian Bashir** hijacked the runabout *Yukon* and attempted to destroy the Bajoran sun with a **trilithium** explosive containing tekasite and **protomatter**. ("By Inferno's Light" [DS9]).

Tekoa. (Rosie Malek-Yonan). Engineer from planet Bajor assigned to the swing shift on Deep Space 9 in 2373. ("The Assignment" [DS9]).

Tel'Peh. Captain of the Klingon attack cruiser *Toh'Kaht*. ("Dramatis Personae" [DS9]). SEE: **Saltah'na energy spheres; Saltah'na; Hon'Tihl**.

Telak, Glinn. Cardassian officer aboard the warship ***Vetar*** under the command of **Gul Evek**. In 2370, Telak participated in the attempted removal of Federation colonists from planet **Dorvan V** after the Federation ceded the planet to the Cardassian Union. ("Journey's End" [TNG]). SEE: **Federation-Cardassian treaty**.

Telaka, Captain L. Isao. Commander of the *Starship* ***Lantree***. Telaka, among with the rest of his crew, was killed in 2365 after being exposed to the genetically engineered children from the **Darwin Genetic Research Station** on planet **Gagarin IV**. Although Telaka was the same age as Commander Riker, he died of premature old age caused by the children's deadly antibodies. ("Unnatural Selection" [TNG]).

Teldarian cruiser. Spacecraft. A Teldarian cruiser transported Geordi La Forge to the **Kriosian** system in late 2367 so he could rendezvous with the *Enterprise*-D. ("The Mind's Eye" [TNG]).

telegraph. Early telecommunication device from 19th-century Earth. The Excalbians' re-creation of President Abraham Lincoln was intrigued with 23rd-century technology, which permitted telegraphy to transmit voice information, as well as alphanumeric codes. ("The Savage Curtain" [TOS]). Worf used components from a telegraph machine connected to a Starfleet communicator pin to create a protective shield. Worf used the shield to protect himself when he, his son Alexander, and Counselor Troi were trapped in the malfunctioning holodeck program ***Ancient West***. ("A Fistful of Datas" [TNG]).

telekinetic suppression collar. Device used to inhibit the telekinetic ability of a telepath. Eris claimed that the **Jem'Hadar** had placed a telekinetic suppression collar on her so that she could not escape imprisonment. Quark's careful examination of the device revealed it to be little more than a complicated locking mechanism. This discovery helped uncover Eris's role as a **Dominion** agent. ("The Jem'Hadar" [DS9]).

telencephalon. Medical term for brain used on planet **Malcor III**. ("First Contact" [TNG]).

telepathic cortex. Lobe of the **Vulcan** brain responsible for telepathic functions. **Vulcan mind-meld**s are controlled through the telepathic cortex. ("Flashback" [VGR]).

telepathic memory invasion. A form of criminal assault found on the **Ullian** homeworld, the forced telepathic intrusion on an unwilling mind, usually inflicting painful memories on the victim. This crime of rape was thought to have been eradicated from the Ullian homeworld by social advances, but telepathic researcher **Jev** (*pictured*) was found to have committed several acts of telepathic memory invasion on several planets in 2368. ("Violations" [TNG]).

telepathic rape. SEE: **telepathic memory invasion**.

Teleris. Star cluster. **Q** invited **Vash** to visit Teleris, but she declined. ("Q-Less" [DS9]).

television. Form of mass-media entertainment popular on **Earth** in the late 20th and early 21st centuries. By the year 2040, it had fallen from popularity. *(Except, of course, for* Star Trek*).* ("The Neutral Zone" [TNG]).

Telfas Prime. Planet. Location of a mining community where *Starship Voyager*'s Commander Chakotay met Maquis **Kurt Bendera**. ("Alliances" [VGR]).

Tellarites. Civilization of sturdy humanoids with distinguished snouts and a propensity toward strong emotion. Tellarite ambassador **Gav** was among the delegates to the **Babel Conference** in 2267. ("Journey to Babel" [TOS]). In 2370, **Kono** escaped Deep Space 9 on a Tellarite vessel. ("Shadowplay" [DS9]). The helm officer who served under Captain Laporin was Tellarite. ("Apocalypse Rising" [DS9]). *Tellarites have also been seen in "Whom Gods Destroy" (TOS), and in the Federation Council chambers in* Star Trek IV.

Telle, Glinn. (Marco Rodriguez). Cardassian aide to **Gul Macet.** ("The Wounded" [TNG]). *Marco Rodriguez also played Captain Paul Rice in "The Arsenal of Freedom" (TNG).*

tellerium. Material used as an antimatter reaction-rate facilitator in the warp core of the *U.S.S. Voyager*. ("Resistance" [VGR]).

Tellun star system. Planetary system containing the planets **Elas** and **Troyius**. As of 2268, the two worlds had been at war with each other for many years, although it was hoped that a political marriage in that year would finally bring peace. ("Elaan of Troyius" [TOS]). SEE: **Elaan**.

Tellurian mint truffles. Chocolate candy. Tellurian mint truffles were among Keiko O'Brien's favorite sweets. ("The Assignment" [DS9]).

Tellurian spices. A valuable commodity. **Zibalian** trader **Kivas Fajo** offered Tellurian spices for sale to a group of Andorians in 2366. ("The Most Toys" [TNG]).

Telluridian synthale. A drink popular with the colonists on planet **Turkana IV**. The beverage was scarce enough to become a commodity worth stealing from opposing cadres. ("Legacy" [TNG]).

Telnorri. Counselor on station Deep Space 9. In 2372, Telnorri helped Miles O'Brien cope with the experience of memories that had been implanted by the **Argrathi** government. ("Hard Time" [DS9]).

Telok. (John Cothran, Jr.). In the **mirror universe**, a Klingon security officer at **Terok Nor (mirror)**. Prior to his posting on Terok Nor, Telok had served four years as the personal guard for the House of Duras. ("Crossover" [DS9]). *John Cothran, Jr. also played Nu'Daq in "The Chase" (TNG).*

Telurian plague. A terrible disease that was still incurable in the 2360s. ("A Matter of Time" [TNG]).

Teluridian IV. Planet in the Alpha Quadrant. Teluridian IV was the site of a battle between the Maquis and at least two Starfleet runabouts. In that battle, Chakotay and B'Elanna Torres fooled the runabouts into believing that their Maquis ship was damaged, then attacked when their enemies approached. ("Ex Post Facto" [VGR]).

Temarek. (Elkanah Burns). A **Gatherer** living on **Gamma Hromi II**. ("The Vengeance Factor" [TNG]).

Temecklian virus. Disease. There was an outbreak of Temecklian virus on Bajor in 2372. ("For the Cause" [DS9]).

Temo'Zuma. (Marshall Teague). Jem'Hadar soldier under the command of Goran'Agar. In 2372, Goran'Agar brought his crew to Bopak III because he believed that the planet could cure his men of their addiction to ketracel-white. ("Hippocratic Oath" [DS9]). *Temo'Zuma's name was not mentioned in dialog, but is from the script only.*

Tempest, The. Tragicomedy written in 1611 by noted Earth dramatist **William Shakespeare**. *Enterprise*-D officer Data created a holodeck program to stage Act V, Scene I of *The Tempest* in 2370 so that he could play the role of Prospero. ("Emergence" [TNG]). *The* Miranda-*class starship designation was named for Miranda, daughter of Prospero in this play.*

Temple of Akadar. SEE: **Akadar, Temple of**.

Temple of Commerce. SEE: **Tower of Commerce**.

Templeton, Mrs. (Carolyn Seymour). Holonovel character. Mrs. Templeton was the stern housekeeper for **Lord Burleigh** in Janeway's gothic romance story. ("Cathexis" [VGR]). When a **Bothan** invaded the *Voyager* in 2372, Janeway had a hallucination that Mrs. Templeton attacked her with a knife. ("Persistence of Vision" [VGR]). SEE: **Janeway Lambda-1.** *Carolyn Seymour also played* ***Subcommander Taris*** *in "Contagion" (TNG) and Commander Toreth in "Face of the Enemy" (TNG).*

Temporal Integrity Commission. Government agency of the United Federation of Planets in the 29th century. The commission was established to monitor the timestream and to dispatch **timeships** to investigate deviations from the normal flow of history. ("Future's End, Part II" [VGR]). *Presumably an outgrowth of Temporal Investigations.*

Temporal Investigations. SEE: **Federation Department of Temporal Investigations.**

Temporal Prime Directive. General order employed in the Federation of the 29th century that prohibited interference with the normal development of history. This included giving aid or information to inhabitants of previous eras, because such actions might influence future eras. ("Future's End, Part II" [VGR]).

temporal anomaly. Rift or hole in the space-time continuum, which allows for passage from one time period to another, or from one parallel reality to another. ("Parallels" [TNG]). SEE: **quantum fissure.** *Temporal anomalies have been the basis for many troubling situations in episodes such as "Time Squared" (TNG), "Yesterday's Enterprise" (TNG),"Cause and Effect" (TNG), "All Good Things..." (TNG), and "Past Tense" (DS9). While they make for interesting story situations, the technical details are often rather obscure.*

temporal causality loop. A disruption in the space-time continuum in which a localized fragment of time is repeated over and over again, ad infinitum. Minor variations are possible in successive iterations of a loop. The ***U.S.S. Bozeman*** was trapped in a temporal causality loop in 2278, emerging 90 years later in 2368. Just prior to the return of the *Bozeman*, the ***Enterprise*-D** was caught in the same causality loop, where it spent some 17.4 days. ("Cause and Effect" [TNG]).

temporal distortion. A disruption in the space-time continuum. The *Enterprise*-D's sensors detected a temporal distortion with the appearance of Professor **Berlinghoff Rasmussen**'s **time-travel pod** in 2368. ("A Matter of Time" [TNG]). A temporal disturbance in the space-time continuum can cause time within temporal fragments to pass at different rates than that of surrounding space. ("Timescape" [TNG]). SEE: **temporal rift**.

temporal explosion. Energetic disturbance in the space-time continuum. In one possible future, a massive temporal explosion occurred in the 29th century, destroying all of Earth's solar system. When evidence was discovered that the 24th-century starship *Voyager* was somehow responsible for this cataclysm, **Captain Braxton**, commanding the Federation timeship ***Aeon***, was dispatched to prevent the explosion. During the mission, the *Aeon* was accidentally sent to Earth's 20th century, where an individual named **Henry Starling** discovered Braxton's ship and was in fact responsible for triggering the 29th-century temporal explosion. The disaster was averted when the *Voyager* crew destroyed the timeship in 1996. ("Future's End, Parts I and II" [VGR]).

temporal flux. Phenomenon in which matter passes from one space-time continuum to another. Temporal flux can interfere with the operation of transporters if the object or person to be transported is in a state of temporal flux. *(Star Trek Generations).* SEE: **nexus**.

temporal narcosis. Delirium produced by exposure to a **temporal distortion** phenomenon. ("Timescape" [TNG]).

temporal reversion. Phenomenon that can occurred in proximity to an **anti-time** anomaly. Exposure could cause living cell structures to revert to earlier forms. In some cases this had the effect of causing old injuries to heal. This benefit was temporary, as prolonged exposure caused cells to coalesce and cease to function. ("All Good Things..." [TNG]).

temporal rift. Also known as a time displacement or a temporal distortion, a "hole in time." A temporal rift was created by a photon torpedo explosion in 2344, accidentally sending the *Starship* ***Enterprise*-C** some 22 years into the future. When that ship emerged in 2366, Commander Data noted the rift appeared to resemble a Kerr loop of superstring material. He noted that the rift was not stable and had no discernible event horizon. The rift remained stable long enough for the *Enterprise*-C to return to its proper place in history. ("Yesterday's *Enterprise*" [TNG]). SEE: **gravimetric fluctuations**. Federation timeships of the 29th century created artificial temporal rifts, using a graviton matrix, when they navigated through time. ("Future's End, Part I" [VGR]).

temporal signature. Property of matter that uniquely identifies the time period in which that matter belongs. ("The Visitor" [DS9]).

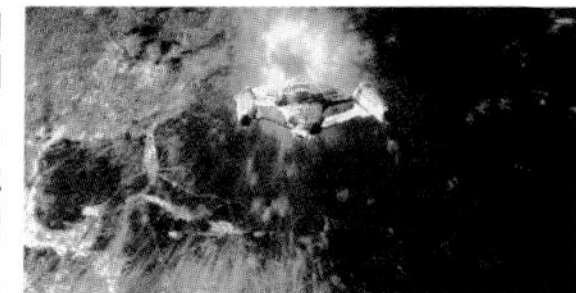

temporal vortex. Time-spanning conduit created by the controlled emission of **chronometric particle**s. In 2373, a **Borg sphere** created a temporal vortex and used it to travel into Earth's past to the year 2063, along with the *Starship Enterprise*-E. *(Star Trek: First Contact).*

Temtibi Lagoon. Body of water on the pleasure planet **Risa**. In 2373, **Arandis** was the chief facilitator for the entire Temtibi Lagoon. ("Let He Who Is Without Sin..." [DS9]).

Ten Tribes. Nation-state on planet **Capella IV**. The Ten Tribes were governed by a leader known as a high **teer**. The title was passed from father to son, except in cases of coup d'état. ("Friday's Child" [TOS]).

Ten-Forward Lounge. A large recreation room located on Deck 10 of the *Starship Enterprise*-D, on the front rim of the **Saucer Module**. Ten-Forward was enjoyed by most off-duty personnel, and served as the social center of the ship. Ten-Forward featured a bar, tended by **Guinan**, and numerous tables from which one could enjoy the spectacular vista offered by the windows looking out into space. ("The Child" [TNG]). Although a wide variety of exotic beverages were served in Ten-Forward, most of them used an ingredient called **synthehol**, an alcohol substitute that avoided some of the unpleasant side effects of alcoholic beverages. ("Relics" [TNG]). *Ten-Forward was built after the first season of* Star Trek: The Next Generation. *It was first seen in "The Child" (TNG), the first episode of the second season. The set has been re-dressed to serve as a theatre and a concert hall. In* Star Trek VI: The Undiscovered Country, *it even served as the office of the Federation Council president complete with a view of Paris out the windows. It was later*

revamped to serve as the mess hall aboard the Starship Voyager. *Also on* Voyager, *Ten-Forward's windows were recycled to serve as the windows in Janeway's ready room and in the briefing room.*

Tenarus cluster. Star system near Kazon territory in the Delta Quadrant. ("Basics, Part I" [VGR]).

tennis elbow. Twentieth-century Earth slang for radio-humeral bursitis: the inflammation of the muscles attached to the epicondyle of the humerus of the human forearm. The inflammation was caused by the stress of striking the ball with a racquet in the ancient sport of tennis. ("Suspicions" [TNG]).

tennis. Game played by striking a ball back and forth with racquets over a net stretched between two equal areas that together constitute a court. Captain Kathryn Janeway played tennis while she was in high school. She took up the game again in 2373 after 19 years of not playing. ("Future's End, Part I" [VGR]).

Teplan blight. Viral disease endemic to the humanoid population of a planet in the Teplan system, located in the Gamma Quadrant. Called simply "the blight" by the planet's inhabitants, the disease was introduced to the population in 2171 by the **Jem'Hadar** in retribution for the planet's having resisted **Dominion** control. The blight is characterized by spiderlike lesions that appear blue at birth but redden when death is imminent. Starfleet physician **Dr. Julian Bashir** was successful in developing a vaccine that eradicated the disease from unborn children, so that the next generation might be disease-free. ("The Quickening" [DS9]). SEE: **quicken; Trevean**.

Teplan system. Planetary system located in the Gamma Quadrant just outside **Dominion** space. In 2172, the inhabitants of one of the planets in the Teplan system resisted the Dominion, and for their defiance, a deadly plague called "the blight" was unleashed on their world. SEE: **Teplan blight.** For two centuries, the blight devastated Teplan society, causing untold suffering. In 2372, a Starfleet team led by **Dr. Julian Bashir** sought to develop a cure for the disease. Although Bashir could not find a cure, he was successful in developing a vaccine that was effective if administered before birth. ("The Quickening" [DS9]).

Mural of a Teplan city before the blight.

Tepo. (John Harmon). Minor leader on planet **Sigma Iotia II** in 2268. Tepo was transported to a meeting between the bosses of the planet attempting to arrange some type of cooperative government. ("A Piece of the Action" [TOS]). SEE: **Iotians.**

tequila. Alcoholic liquor distilled from products of the agave plant of Earth. Commander Deanna Troi was unfamiliar with tequila but drank some at the insistence of **Zefram Cochrane**. *(Star Trek: First Contact).*

terakine. Analgesic medication. Terakine was administered to Commander William Riker following an accident in *bat'leth* practice where he fractured a rib. ("The *Pegasus*" [TNG]).

terawatt. Measure of power, 10^{12} watts, or one trillion watts. ("A Matter of Time" [TNG]).

Terellian Death Syndrome. Disease whose symptoms include dizziness, blurred vision, palpitations, and stinging in the lower spine. The condition causes cellular decay, which can be reversed if caught early enough. In 2370, **Reginald Barclay** diagnosed himself as suffering from Terellian Death Syndrome. Fortunately, he was wrong. ("Genesis" [TNG]). SEE: **hypochondria**.

Terellian spices. Aromatic flavoring. **Anna** had some Terellian spices in her stores of a crashed **Terellian** freighter. She mixed them with a collection of ***coltayin* roots** to make soup. ("Liaisons" [TNG]).

Terellians. Species of four-armed sentient humanoids. A Terellian freighter that crashed on a planet near the Iyaaran homeworld was used as a shelter by **Anna** and by Captain Jean-Luc Picard. ("Liaisons" [TNG]).

Terikof Belt. Area within the **Badlands**, beyond the Moriya system in the Alpha Quadrant. The Terikof Belt contained a number of Class-M planetoids where the **Maquis** sometimes took refuge. ("Caretaker" [VGR]).

terikon particle decay. Energy signature used to identify archaeological artifacts. Captain Jean-Luc Picard used terikon particle delay to determine the authenticity of artifacts stolen by **Baran** in 2370 that were thought to be fragments of the **Stone of Gol**. ("Gambit, Parts I and II" [TNG]).

Terix. Imperial Romulan warbird under the command of **Sirol**. In 2370, the *Terix* was involved in a Romulan attempt to locate the *Starship* ***Pegasus***. ("The *Pegasus*" [TNG]). (In the **anti-time** reality created by the **Q Continuum**, the *Terix* was under the command of **Tomalak,** who was in command of a fleet of 30 Romulan vessels which had been deployed along the Romulan side of the Neutral Zone.) ("All Good Things..." [TNG]).

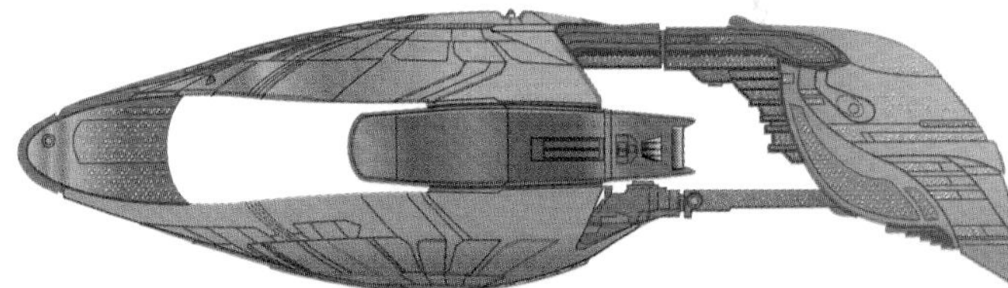

Terkim. Maternal uncle to **Guinan**. She referred to him as "kind of a family misfit...(a) bad influence." She also said he was the only one of her relatives with a sense of humor. ("Hollow Pursuits" [TNG]).

Terlina III. Planetary location of **Dr. Noonien Soong**'s laboratory. It was here that Soong and his wife **Juliana Soong** landed, following their escape from **Omicron Theta**. Juliana died shortly after their arrival, from injuries sustained in their escape from the **Crystalline Entity**. Following her death, Soong created her android double in his lab, as well as creating the **emotion chip** for Data. In 2367, Soong died in his laboratory. ("Inheritance" [TNG], "Brothers" [TNG]).

Terlina system. Location of planet **Terlina III**. ("Inheritance" [TNG]).

terminium. Metal alloy. Terminium was used in the casing of **photon torpedo**es. Spock's casket, located on the surface of the **Genesis Planet**, was composed of terminium. *(Star Trek III: The Search for Spock).*

terminus. Medical term for foot used on planet **Malcor III**. ("First Contact" [TNG]).

Terok Nor (mirror). In the **mirror universe**, an ore-processing station in orbit of the planet **Bajor (mirror)**. The station was also the **Alliance**'s command post for the Bajoran sector. It was operated by Alliance personnel, mostly Klingon and Cardassian, although the station **Intendant** in 2370 was a Bajoran national named **Kira Nerys (mirror)**. ("Crossover" [DS9], "Through the Looking Glass" [DS9]). By 2372, the **Terran resistance** had driven the Alliance from Terok Nor. A major breakthrough in the resistance struggle came with the construction of the *Starship* ***Defiant*** **(mirror)** at Terok Nor. With Benjamin Sisko's help, the Terrans were able to use the *Defiant (mirror)* to fend off an Alliance attack fleet led by Regent **Worf (mirror)**, allowing the Terrans to retain control of the station. ("Shattered Mirror" [DS9]).

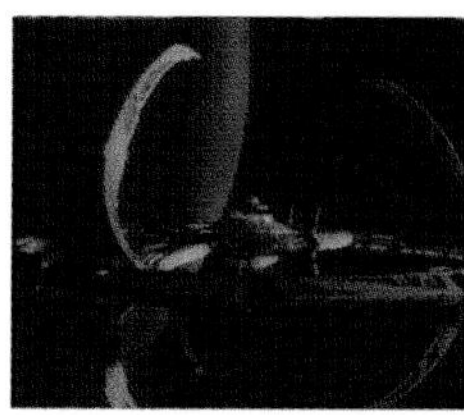

Terok Nor. Cardassian mining space station in **Bajoran** space. Terok Nor was the original **Cardassian** designation for the station that became known as **Deep Space 9**. ("Cardassians" [DS9]). Built in 2351 ("Babel" [DS9]), Terok Nor was commanded by **Gul Dukat** during the Cardassian occupation of planet Bajor. During the Cardassian occupation, Terok Nor's main function was to process raw **uridium** ore using the forced labor of Bajoran prisoners. When in full operation the station was capable of processing 20,000 tons of ore per day. ("Civil Defense" [DS9]). Bajorans assigned to the station were housed in community quarters. Only those Bajorans in favor with the Cardassian commanders had private quarters. ("Necessary Evil" [DS9]).

Teros, Nathaniel. SEE: **neuromuscular adaptation theory.**

Terosa Prime. Planet. **Nidell Seyetik** lost control of her **psychoprojective telepathic** abilities at Terosa Prime in 2367 due to deep emotional distress, nearly killing her. ("Second Sight" [DS9]).

Terraform Command. Federation administrative office responsible for overseeing **terraforming** projects. ("Home Soil" [TNG]).

terraforming. In engineering, terraforming refers to any of several very large-scale engineering and biological techniques in which uninhabitable planetary environments can be altered so that a planet can support life. The Federation enforces very strict regulations regarding terraforming, to protect any indigenous lifeforms that might be threatened by such projects. A terraforming project at **Velara III** was found to endanger indigenous life, and the project was discontinued. ("Home Soil" [TNG]). **Professor Gideon Seyetik** was responsible for several major terraforming efforts, including planets **Blue Horizon** and **New Halana**. ("Second Sight" [DS9]). SEE: **Project Genesis.**

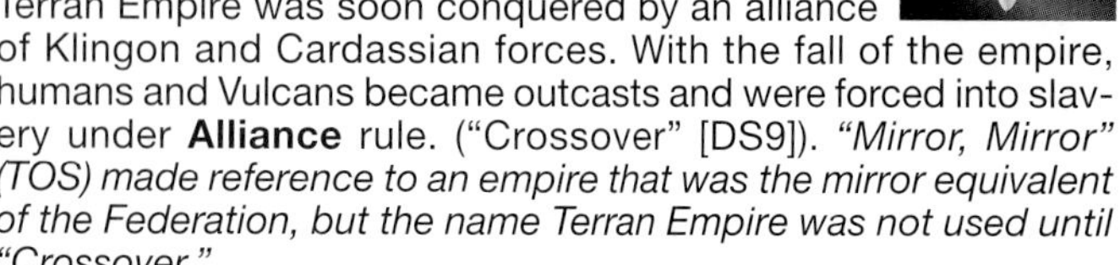

Terran Empire. In the **mirror universe**, the repressive interstellar government dominated by Terrans from the planet Earth. The empire ruled by terror, enforced by its fleet of starships. In 2267, members of the original *U.S.S. Enterprise* crew were accidentally transported to the mirror universe, and their brief presence had a profound effect on the Terran Empire. The visiting James Kirk convinced **Spock (mirror)** of the illogic of waiting for the inevitable collapse of the empire. Spock was successful in pressing for reforms, preaching peace and disarmament, eventually becoming the empire's commander-in-chief. Unfortunately, Spock's reforms left the empire unable to defend itself, and the Terran Empire was soon conquered by an alliance of Klingon and Cardassian forces. With the fall of the empire, humans and Vulcans became outcasts and were forced into slavery under **Alliance** rule. ("Crossover" [DS9]). *"Mirror, Mirror" (TOS) made reference to an empire that was the mirror equivalent of the Federation, but the name Terran Empire was not used until "Crossover."*

Terran resistance. In the **mirror universe**, a loosely-organized band of humans and friends who fought against the **Alliance** of the Klingon Empire and the Cardassian Union. The Terran resistance was formed in 2370 by **Benjamin Sisko (mirror)** after his escape from **Terok Nor (mirror)**. Others in the resistance included members of the **Ferengi**, the **Vulcans**, and the **Trill**. ("Through the Looking Glass" [DS9]). By 2372, the resistance was successful in driving the Alliance from station **Terok Nor (mirror)**. Another major stride was the construction of a new starship, the ***Defiant*** **(mirror)**, based on a ship of the same name from our universe. ("Shattered Mirror" [DS9]).

Terran. Term used in the **mirror universe** for humans. ("Crossover" [DS9]).

Terrell, Captain Clark. (Paul Winfield). Commander of the *Starship* ***Reliant***, Terrell died in 2285 while on a survey mission for **Project Genesis**. *(Star Trek II: The Wrath of Khan). Paul Winfield also played Captain Dathon in "Darmok" (TNG).*

Terrellian plague. Dangerously virulent disease. (In the **anti-time** reality created by the **Q Continuum**, during 2395 there was an outbreak of Terrellian plague on **Romulus**. The Klingons allowed Federation medical ships to cross the border, and the *U.S.S. Pasteur* used this outbreak as an excuse to enter the **Neutral Zone**.) ("All Good Things..." [TNG].)

Terrellians. Spacefaring civilization. In 2371, Nog arranged for himself and Jake to play **dom-jot** with a trio of Terrellians who had bragged about their prowess at the game. ("Life Support" [DS9]).

Tersa, Jal. (Larry Cedar). A member of the **Kazon-Pommar** sect in 2372. A acquaintance of Neelix, Tersa introduced the Kazon first majes during a peace conference arranged by *Starship Voyager* Captain Kathryn Janeway and **Trabe** leader **Mabus**. ("Alliances" [VGR]).

tertiary subspace manifold. Location of the **solanagen-based entities** in their subspace domain. ("Schisms" [TNG]). SEE: **coherent graviton pulse; tetryon.**

tesokine. Pharmaceutical. Dr. Julian Bashir gave Kira Nerys tesokine in 2372 so that the O'Briens' baby that she carried could metabolize Bajoran nutrients. ("Body Parts" [DS9]).

Tessen III. Federation planet. Tessen III was threatened by an asteroid in 2368. Intervention by the crew of the *Enterprise*-D saved the planet. The crew was able to destroy the asteroid in the planet's upper atmosphere by disrupting the core of the asteroid with a particle beam. ("Cost of Living" [TNG]). SEE: **nitrium metal parasites**.

tessipate. Unit of land area in the **Bajoran** system of measures. **Sirco Ch'Ano** sold **Nog** and **Jake Sisko** seven tessipates of land on planet **Bajor** in exchange for **self-sealing stem bolts**. ("Progress" [DS9]).

Tethys III. Green planet with a hydrogen-helium composition and a frozen helium core. ("Clues" [TNG]). *Data used library images of Tethys III to cover up for the Paxans' Class-M protoplanet.*

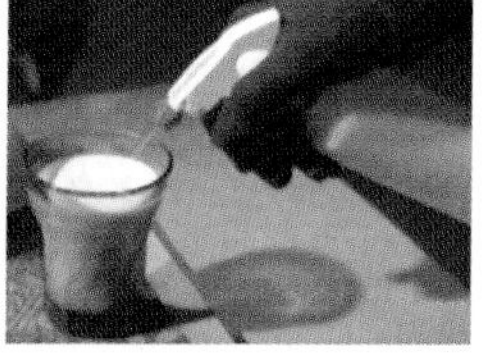

tetralubisol. A highly volatile liquid lubricant used aboard Federation starships. **Lenore Karidian** attempted to murder **Kevin Riley** by poisoning his glass of milk with tetralubisol. ("The Conscience of the King" [TOS]).

tetrarch. Title given to the leader of the **Paqu** people on planet Bajor. **Varis Sul** was tetrarch in 2369. ("The Storyteller" [DS9]).

tetryon. Subatomic particle that can exist only in **subspace** and is unstable in normal space. Tetryon emissions were found in the *Enterprise*-D cargo bay in 2369, sent by **solanagen-based aliens.** ("Schisms" [TNG]). The disruptor banks on a **Klingon bird-of-prey** could be modified to emit tetryon particles, to disable directed-energy weapons. ("Blood Oath" [DS9]). Tetryon particles are present near cloaked vessels. A tetryon compositor was a component of a Romulan **cloaking device**. ("The Die is Cast" [DS9]). In 2371, the **quantum singularity** powering a cloaked **Romulan warbird** in orbit around Deep Space 9 gave off tetryon emissions, allowing station personnel to track the otherwise undetectable ship. ("Visionary" [DS9]). The **Caretaker** used a coherent tetryon beam to survey spacecraft that he had abducted to the Delta Quadrant. ("Caretaker" [VGR]). A field of tetryons can be produced when a phased ionic pulse comes into contact with a **metaphasic shield**. Tetryon particles were detected in tissues from the pilot Jo'Bril, proving the field had been sabotaged during a test in 2369. ("Suspicions" [TNG]). Tetryon fields can also occur naturally and can be a hazard to warp-driven craft. An unusually intense field was located in the sector near the Hekaras system, making the **Hekaras Corridor** the only safe navigational route. In 2370, the crew of the *Enterprise*-D discovered that the areas where tetyron fields were dense were also susceptible to **warp field effect**, and their use had to be limited to essential travel only. The decay of tetryon particles causes an energy phenomenon known as tetryon radiation. Since tetryons can exist only in subspace, the presence of tetryon radiation can be indicative of an intrusion of subspace into normal space, i.e. the formation of a subspace rift. ("Force of Nature" [TNG]). Tetryon plasma emits multiflux gamma radiation, causing it to disrupt subspace. In an alternate reality, Ensign **Harry Kim** designed the runabout ***U.S.S. Yellowstone***, which was equipped with tetryon-plasma warp nacelles. ("Non Sequitur" [VGR]). Tetryon radiation in sufficient doses can be lethal to Founders and caused the death of a **changeling infant** in 2373. ("The Begotten" [DS9]).

thalamus. A portion of the humanoid brain, deep within the cerebral hemispheres. The thalamus relays bodily sensations to the cortex for interpretation. ("Violations" [TNG]).

Thalassa. (Diana Muldaur). One of three survivors from **Sargon's planet** after it was destroyed half a million years ago in a devastating war. Thalassa, who was the wife of **Sargon**, and a handful of other survivors of that war were placed into survival canisters, and three of them were revived in 2268 by the crew of the *Starship Enterprise*. Thalassa and the others temporarily occupied the bodies of **Dr. Ann Mulhall**, Kirk, and Spock, so that they could build android bodies for their intellects. But she eventually realized that the temptations to abuse her superior power inside a living body were too great, so she and her husband opted to face oblivion together. ("Return to Tomorrow" [TOS]).

Thalian chocolate mousse. A dessert made with cocoa from planet **Thalos VII**, where the beans are aged for four centuries. Wesley Crusher ordered a replicated dish of Thalian chocolate mouse for the lovely young **Salia** of planet **Daled IV**. ("The Dauphin" [TNG]).

thalmerite. Powerful chemical explosive compound. A thalmerite device was used to destroy the Klingon attack cruiser ***Toh'Kaht*** when its crew was under the influence of the **Saltah'na energy spheres** in 2369. (Dramatis Personae" [DS9]). The captain of a **Numiri** patrol ship released a shuttle when *U.S.S. Voyager* Captain Janeway told him it contained 40 tons of thalmerite. ("Ex Post Facto" [VGR]).

Thalos VII. Planet. Cocoa beans are aged on Thalos VII for four centuries, producing an incomparable confection. Wesley Crusher visited there once while aboard the *Enterprise*-D, and later recalled that it was one of his favorite planets. ("The Dauphin" [TNG]). SEE: **Thalian chocolate mousse**.

thanatologist. In the **Vhnori** culture, a scientist specializing in the study of death. Thanatologists also presided over **Vhnori transference rituals** in which death became the way to the **Next Emanation**. Dr. Neria and Dr. Ranora were thanatologists. ("Emanations" [VGR]).

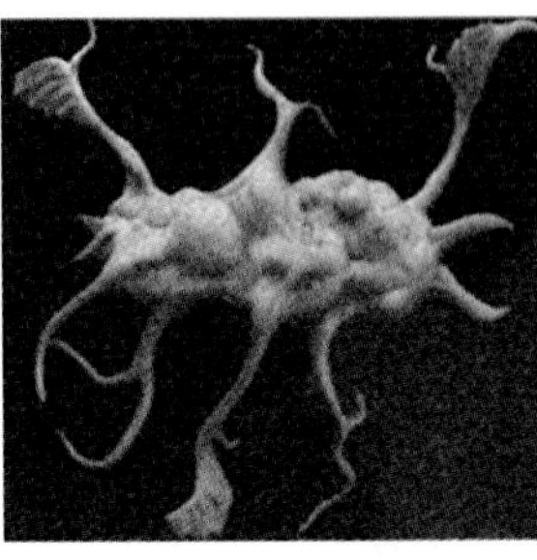

Thanatos VII. Planet. Site where a new interphasic fusion process was developed. The process was used to manufacture plasma-flow conduits. In 2370, the *Enterprise*-D received a plasma-flow conduit manufactured on this world as part of a new warp-core installation. Unfortunately, the manufacturing process attracted **interphasic organisms**, which infested the core, and later the crew of the ship. ("Phantasms" [TNG])

Thanksgiving. Traditional Earth holiday in which thanks are offered for life and its blessings. Thanksgiving was still celebrated aboard the *Enterprise* in 2266. The *Enterprise* chef was preparing hams for the crew's dinner, when **Charles Evans** used his **Thasian** powers to transmute them into real turkeys. ("Charlie X" [TOS]). *The voice of the befuddled* Enterprise *chef was provided by* Star Trek *creator Gene Roddenberry.*

Thann. (Willard Sage). One of the **Vians** who, in 2268, tested **Gem** to see if her people were worthy of being rescued from the impending nova of the star Minara. ("The Empath" [TOS]). *Note that the name "Thann" is from the episode script only and was not spoken in the aired episode.*

Thasians. Mysterious civilization from planet **Thasus**. The Thasians, **noncorporeal life-forms**, cared for young **Charles Evans** after his parents were killed in a transport crash. They gave him extraordinary telekinetic powers so he could survive, but those powers ultimately made him unable to function in human society, so the Thasians were forced to return him to Thasus after his rescue in 2266 by the crew of the science vessel ***Antares***. ("Charlie X" [TOS]).

Thasus. Planet, homeworld of the **Thasians**. Site of a transport vessel crash in 2252, in which all aboard were killed except for three-year-old **Charles Evans**. Unknown to the Federation at the time, Thasus was the home of a civilization of beings that had evolved beyond the need for physical bodies, existing as pure mental energy. ("Charlie X" [TOS]).

"That Which Survives." Original Series episode #69. Teleplay by John Meredyth Lucas. Story by Michael Richards. Directed by Herb Wallerstein. No stardate given in episode. *First aired in 1968.* Enterprise *crew members are stranded on a ghost planet and terrorized by the image of a beautiful woman, the only survivor of a tragic accident.* GUEST CAST: Lee Meriwether as **Losira**; Arthur Batanides as **D'Amato, Lieutenant**; Naomi Pollack as **Rahda, Lieutenant**; Booker Bradshaw as **M'Benga, Dr.**; Brad Forrest as Wyatt, Ensign; Kenneth Washington as **Watkins, John B.** SEE: **cellular disruption; D'Amato, Lieutenant; diburnium-osmium alloy; Kalandan outpost; Kalandans; Losira; M'Benga, Dr.; magnetic probe; matter/antimatter integrator; Rhada, Lieutenant; Sanchez, Dr.; warp drive; Watkins, John B.**

"Thaw, The." *Voyager* episode #39. Teleplay by Joe Menosky. Story by Richard Gadas. Directed by Marvin V. Rush. No stardate given. *First aired in 1996. Unable to revive a group of humanoids in a computer-generated hibernation, Kim and Torres allow themselves to enter their dream state, only to discover someone else is there—a malevolent clown who has no intention of letting them leave.* GUEST CAST: McKean Michael as **Clown**; Patty Maloney as Little woman, The; Carel Struycken as **Spectre**; Tony Carlin as

Kohl Physician; Shannon O'Hurley as **Kohl Programmer**; Tomas Kopachee as **Viorsa**. SEE: **Baytart, Pablo; Chulak; Clown; Galorndon Core; Kim, Harry; Kohl hibernation system; Kohl physician; Kohl programmer; Kohl settlement; Nicoletti, Susan; norepinephrine; recall subroutine; roller coaster; Spectre; Viorsa.**

Thei, Subcommander. (Anthony James). First officer of the **Romulan warbird** that crossed the Neutral Zone in 2364, serving under **Commander Tebok**. ("The Neutral Zone" [TNG]).

Thelev. (William O'Connell). A minor member of **Andorian** Ambassador **Shras**'s staff. Thelev was an **Orion** operative, surgically altered to appear Andorian, and planted in the ambassador's party to create havoc aboard the *Enterprise* on the way to the **Babel Conference** of 2267 in hopes of blocking the **Coridan** admission to the Federation. Thelev critically injured Captain Kirk and refused to disclose the identity of the intruder vessel firing upon the *Enterprise*. Thelev had orders to self-destruct, and died of a slow poison shortly after the intruder vessel also destroyed itself. ("Journey to Babel" [TOS]).

Thelka IV. Planet. Captain Picard discovered a particularly delicious dessert on Thelka IV. Picard re-created the dessert for **Neela Daren,** but the couple was unable to sample the delicacy, as duty called them away from dinner. ("Lessons" [TNG]).

Thelusian flu. An exotic but harmless rhinovirus. The first officer of the ***U.S.S. Lantree*** was treated for Thelusian flu two days before that ship made contact with the **Darwin Genetic Research Station** on planet Gagarin IV in 2365, but Dr. Pulaski ruled out the virus's having anything to do with the hyperaccelerated aging experienced by the *Lantree* crew after that contact. ("Unnatural Selection" [TNG]).

Theoretical Propulsion Group. Starfleet engineering design team based at the **Utopia Planitia Fleet Yards** on Mars. The Theoretical Propulsion Group was largely responsible for the development of the warp engines for the ***Galaxy*-class starships** in the early 2360s. **Dr. Leah Brahms** was a junior team member during that project. ("Booby Trap" [TNG]). By 2367, Brahms had been promoted to senior design engineer. ("Galaxy's Child" [TNG]).

theragen. Biochemical weapon used by the Klingon military, a nerve gas that is instantly lethal if used in pure form. Dr. McCoy prepared a diluted form of theragen mixed with alcohol to deaden certain nerve inputs to the brain in an effort to prevent madness in the *Enterprise* crew caused by exposure to **spatial interphase** in 2268. ("The Tholian Web" [TOS]).

thermal deflector. Protective force field. Used on planet **Bersallis III** to shield the Federation outpost from a **Bersallis firestorm**. ("Lessons" [TNG]). SEE: **Daren, Neela**.

thermal interferometry scanner. Device for measuring distances by comparing interference of thermal gradients. ("Imaginary Friend" [TNG]).

thermal inversion gradient. Atmospheric phenomenon in which a mass of warm air is trapped beneath a layer of cooler air. Thermal inversion gradients can give rise to **electrodynamic turbulence**. ("Innocence" [VGR]).

thermal stabilizers. Devices used in artificial planetary atmospheric control systems. Thermal stabilizers were employed as part of the **weather control matrix** developed for planet **Hekaras II**. ("Force of Nature" [TNG]).

thermal sweep. Directed-heat weapon used by the **Enarans** of the Delta Quadrant, which killed by vaporizing the target. ("Remember" [VGR]).

thermoconcrete. Construction material mostly made of silicon, used by Federation starship personnel to build emergency shelters. Dr. McCoy used thermoconcrete to heal the wounds inflicted on the **Horta** of planet **Janus VI** by Federation mining personnel in 2267. ("The Devil in the Dark" [TOS]).

thermologist. Scientist who studies the underground distribution of geologic heat. Thermologists were used in the energy transfer from **Jeraddo** to planet **Bajor**. ("Progress" [DS9]).

Thesia, Jewel of. A spectacular diamondlike gemstone, a national heritage of the planet **Straleb**. The Jewel of Thesia was believed to have been stolen by Captain **Thadiun Okona** in 2365. The jewel was later found to have been taken by **Benzan** of the Straleb as a pledge of marriage to **Yanar** of the planet **Altec**. ("The Outrageous Okona" [TNG]).

Theta 116. Star system. The eighth planet of the Theta 116 system was the final destination of the ill-fated ***Charybdis*** interstellar probe under the command of **Colonel Stephen Richey**. That planet, first explored by a Klingon expedition, had an atmosphere of nitrogen and methane. Surface temperatures averaged -291 Celsius, and the surface was swept with high winds and storms. ("The Royale" [TNG]). *Yes, we know that -291 Celsius is below absolute zero, and that such a temperature is therefore meaningless. Unfortunately, the show's technical consultants (including the authors of this Encyclopedia) missed this point of basic science, so now our mistake has been immortalized. *Sigh*.*

Theta Cygnus Prime. Planet in the Theta Cygnus system. ("Progress" [DS9]).

Theta Cygni XII. Planet. The population of Theta Cygni XII suffered mass insanity caused by the **Denevan neural parasites**. ("Operation—Annihilate!" [TOS]). *Theta Cygni was struck sometime between 2067 (when **Levinius V** was infested) and 2265 (when **Ingraham B** was attacked).*

Theta VII. Planet. Location of a colony that desperately required vaccines being transported by the ***U.S.S. Yorktown*** on stardate 3619. The *U.S.S. Enterprise* was unable to make a scheduled rendezvous with the *Yorktown* because of an encounter with the deadly **dikironium cloud creature**. After the cloud entity was destroyed, the *Enterprise* was able to transport the vaccines to the colony. ("Obsession" [TOS]).

theta designation. In the mirror universe, an **Alliance** classification given to **Terran** workers who had earned a certain degree of trust. Thetas were allowed to work unsupervised and were afforded certain privileges. **Miles O'Brien (mirror)** had a theta designation. ("Crossover" [DS9]).

theta flux distortion. Spatial phenomenon. The *Enterprise*-D's sensors were not designed to detect theta flux distortions. Such distortions can rupture warp cores if they grow large enough and come in contact with a ship. ("Emergence" [TNG]).

theta radiation. Hazardous form of ionizing energy. Theta radiation is deleterious to humanoids, but in moderate doses, its effects were treatable. In 2063 a Borg attack damaged Zefram Cochrane's warp ship, the *Phoenix*. It suffered damage to its throttle assembly, causing a theta radiation leak. *(Star Trek: First Contact).*

theta-band emissions. Subspace carrier waves often associated with background subspace radiation. In 2369, Starfleet Intelligence was led to believe that the Cardassians were utilizing theta-band emissions as a delivery system for a powerful **metagenic weapon**. Captain Picard, who had conducted extensive tests on theta-band emissions while in command of the *Stargazer*, was the only active Starfleet officer familiar with those systems. ("Chain of Command, Part I" [TNG]).

theta-matrix compositer. A component of the **warp drive** systems of recent Federation starships, including those of the *Galaxy* class. The device made dilithium recrystallization ten times more efficient than it was on ***Excelsior*-Class** starships. ("Family" [TNG]).

theta-xenon. Gaseous substance found in some nebulas. ("Flashback" [VGR]).

thialo. Term used at a decision point in the **Wadi** game of **chula**. Wadi leader **Falow** used it during the chula game with Quark on Deep Space 9 in 2369. *Thialo* meant that Quark had to choose which of the three remaining players—Kira, Dax, or Sisko—would be killed so that the others could continue their journey home. ("Move Along Home" [DS9]).

"Thine Own Self." *Next Generation* episode #168. Teleplay by Ronald D. Moore. Story by Christopher Hatton. Directed by Winrich Kolbe. Stardate 47611.2. *First aired in 1994. Data finds himself stranded on a planet with a pre-industrial society, and he has no memory of who he is or how he got there. Deanna Troi was promoted to full commander in this episode .* GUEST CAST: Ronnie Claire Edwards as **Talar**; Michael Rothhaar as **Garvin**; Kimberly Cullum as **Gia**; Michael G. Hagerty as **Skoran**; Andy Kossin as Apprentice; Richard Ortega-Miró as Rainer; Majel Barrett as Computer voice. SEE: **Barkon IV; Barkonians; Bridge Officer Examination, Starfleet; *dorak;* Garvin; Gia; Bridge Officer Exam, Starfleet; Jayden; *Lexington, U.S.S.*; *selton*; Skoran; Starbase 231; Talar; Taranko colony; Troi, Deanna; Vellorian mountains.**

"Things Past." *Deep Space Nine* episode #106. Written by Michael Taylor. Directed by LeVar Burton. No stardate given. *First aired in 1996. Sisko, Dax, Garak and Odo find themselves as condemned Bajorans on DS9 seven years in the past, during the Cardassian occupation.* GUEST CAST: Marc Alaimo as **Dukat**; Victor Bevine as **Belar**; Andrew Robinson as **Garak, Elim**; Kurtwood Smith as **Thrax**; Brenan Baird as Soldier; Louahn Lowe as **Okala**; Judi Durand as Station computer voice. SEE: **Belar; Brin Tusk; Dukat, Gul; Great Link; Ishan Chaye; Jillur Gueta; Kara Polos; Livara; *maraji* crystals; Marat Kobar; morphogenic enzyme; Musilla Province; Okala; plasma disruption; Rakantha Province; spoon head; Talavians; Thrax; Timor Landi; trinitrogen chloride.**

Third of Five. (Jonathan Del Arco). **Borg** designation for the individual Borg known to the *Enterprise*-D crew as **Hugh**. ("I, Borg" [TNG]).

"37's, The." *Voyager* episode #20. Written by Jeri Taylor & Brannon Braga. Directed by James L. Conway. Stardate 48975.1. *First aired in 1995. After following a distress signal to an alien planet, the crew discovers Amelia Earhart among eight humans preserved by cryogenics. This was the first episode of the second season. This is the first episode where* Voyager *lands on a planet. "The 37's" was the 20th episode produced during Star Trek: Voyager's first season, but was held back to be the first episode aired during the show's second season.* GUEST CAST: John Rubinstein as **Evansville**; David Graf as **Noonan**; Mel Winkler as **Hayes**; James Saito as **Nogami**; Sharon Lawrence as **Earhart, Amelia**. SEE: **Berlin, Karyn; blue alert; Briori; cryostasis chamber; Earhart, Amelia; Evansville, John; Ford pickup truck; fruit cocktail; gasoline; green beans; Hayes, Jack; Hoover, J. Edgar; hover car; Janeway, Kathryn; Jell-O; landing struts; Lockheed Electra; Mars; Martian Colonies; Nogami; Noonan, Fred; planetary classification system: Class-L; SOS; Thirty-Sevens; trinimbic interference; universal translator; *Voyager, U.S.S.***

Thirty-Sevens. Among the human colonists on the former **Briori** homeworld in the Delta Quadrant, the name given to some 300 humans who were kidnapped from **Earth** in 1937 and brought to the Briori planet. The Briori enslaved the Thirty-Sevens and their descendents, until the humans revolted against their captors. A few of the Thirty-Sevens survived for centuries, preserved in cryogenic stasis until they were revived by *Starship Voyager* personnel in late 2371. The descendents of the Thirty-Sevens included **John Evansville**. ("The 37's" [VGR]). SEE: **Earhart, Amelia** (*pictured*).

"This Side of Paradise." Original Series episode #25. Teleplay by D. C. Fontana. Story by Nathan Butler and D. C. Fontana. Directed by Ralph Senensky. Stardate 3417.3. *First aired in 1967. At a colony where alien spores provide total contentment, Mr. Spock finds happiness with a woman who once loved him. Nathan Butler was the pen name of science-fiction writer Jerry Sohl. His original story, entitled "Sandoval's Planet," was submitted in June, 1966. His next story treatment, two months later, was entitled "Power Play," as was his first-draft screenplay. Shortly thereafter, the script was assigned to D.C. Fontana, and was retitled "The Way of the Spores." On October 27, 1966, Bob Justman wrote a memo to Gene Roddenberry, objecting to the latest title. His memo concluded with: "This is probably the nicest thing I have said to you in weeks, and no doubt you are and will be eternally grateful for this, as it is one of the shortest memos I have ever written to you." Fontana's version was retitled "This Side of Paradise." In a later memo, Justman observed that Fontana's work was "[a]s usual, a shootable and well-constructed first draft from the mysterious D. C. Fontana." The script went into production on January 5, 1967 and has become regarded as pivotal in the development of the Spock character. The shot of Kirk entering the empty bridge of the* Enterprise *in this episode was later reused as the establishing shot for Scotty's holodeck re-creation of the bridge in "Relics" (TNG).* GUEST CAST: Jill Ireland as **Kalomi, Leila**; Frank Overton as **Sandoval, Elias**; Grant Woods as **Kelowitz, Lieutenant Commander**; Michael Barrier as **DeSalle, Lieutenant**; Dick Scotter as **Painter, Mr.**; Eddie Paskey as **Leslie, Mr.**; Bobby Bass as Crewman #2; Sean Morgan, John Lindesmith, Engineers; Fred Shue as Crewman; C. O'Brien as Kirk's stunt double; Bill Catching as Spock's stunt double. SEE: **Berengaria VII; berthold rays; DeSalle, Lieutenant; Kalomi, Leila; Kelowitz, Lieutenant Commander; Komack, Admiral; Leslie, Mr.; Omicron Ceti III; Painter, Mr.; Sandoval, Elias; Spock; spores, Omicron Ceti III; Starbase 27; subsonic transmitter.**

Tholian Assembly. Governing body of the **Tholian** people. ("The Tholian Web" [TOS]).

Tholian freighter. Cargo spacecraft of **Tholian** registry. In 2372, Kasidy Yates said that she was going to rendezvous with a Tholian freighter to transfer cargo. In fact, she actually met and transferred cargo to a Maquis raider vessel. ("For the Cause" [DS9]).

Tholian silk. A difficult-to-obtain fine fabric of **Tholian** origin. Benjamin Sisko got a Tholian silk scarf for Kasidy Yates in 2371 with the help of the Tholian ambassador, who owed him a favor. ("The Way of the Warrior" [DS9]).

"Tholian Web, The." Original Series episode #64. Written by Judy Burns and Chet Richards. Directed by Herb Wallerstein. Stardate 5693.2. *First aired in 1968. Kirk disappears and is presumed dead* *while Spock tries to keep the* Enterprise *from being the victim of a weblike alien weapon. The original script was an unsolicited submission entitled "In Essence Nothing," which Bob Justman read and recommended to producer Fred Freiberger. It was writer Judy Burns's first professional sale, leading to a lengthy writing career. Burns also teaches scriptwriting at UCLA and other schools and colleges.* GUEST CAST: Majel Barrett as **Chapel, Christine**; Sean Morgan as **O'Neil, Lieutenant**; Barbara Babcock as Tholians' voices. SEE: ***Defiant*, *U.S.S.*; environmental suit; Kirk, James T.; Loskene, Commander; spatial interphase; theragen; Tholian Assembly; Tholian web; Tholian; tri-ox compound.**

Tholian web. Energy field used by the **Tholians** to entrap a disabled enemy spacecraft. A tractor field is spun by two Tholian ships that remain outside of weapons range, encircling the target vessel. Upon completion of the web, the field is contracted, destroying the ship within. While attempting to rescue the ***U.S.S. Defiant*** in 2268, the *Enterprise* nearly fell victim to a Tholian web. ("The Tholian Web" [TOS]).

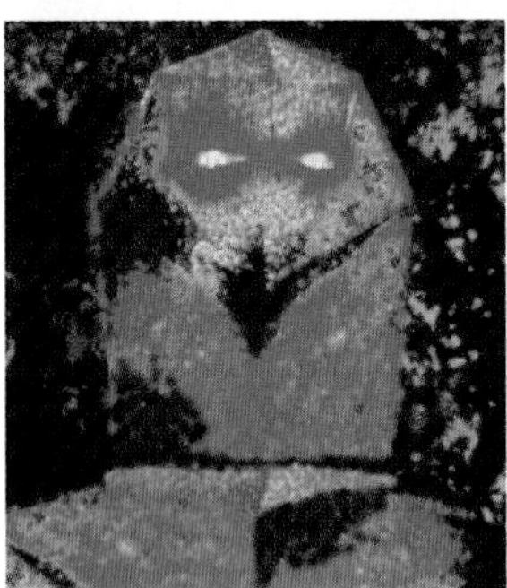

Tholians. Civilization known for its punctuality and highly territorial nature. The Tholians accused the *Starship Enterprise* of violating a territorial annex of the Tholian Assembly while on a rescue mission, when the ***U.S.S. Defiant*** was trapped in **interspace** in 2268. SEE: **Loskene, Commander.** ("The Tholian Web" [TOS]). The ongoing conflict with the Tholians flared up again in 2353 when the Tholians attacked and nearly destroyed a Federation starbase, with the loss of nearly all personnel. Civilian advisor **Kyle Riker** was the only survivor in the incident. ("The Icarus Factor" [TNG]). Conflict with the Tholians continued well into the 24th century, and simulated Tholian battles were part of the Starfleet Academy curriculum as recently as 2355, when William Riker was able to calculate a sensory blind spot in a simulated Tholian vessel, and use that to his advantage. ("Peak Performance" [TNG]). Tensions with the Tholians remained sufficiently high that Ambassador **K'Ehleyr**, in 2367, feared a Klingon civil war would eventually involve the Tholians ("Reunion" [TNG]), although diplomatic relations between the Tholians and the Federation were established. In 2371, a Tholian ambassador visited **Deep Space 9**. ("Life Support" [DS9]). Razka Karn, a petty criminal, had been in trouble with the Tholians. Because of this, he often sought refuge in the **Badlands**. ("Indiscretion" [DS9]). A Tholian observer was present at the ill-fated **Antwerp Conference** on Earth on stardate 49170.65. ("Homefront" [DS9]). *We've seen a Tholian in only one episode, "The Tholian Web" (TOS), and even that was just a few shots on the* Enterprise *main viewer. Those shots, which used visual effects and a puppet designed by Mike Minor, seemed to show the faceted head of Commander Loskene. It was not, however, made clear if that was indeed Loskene's head, or if it was simply a helmet. It was also not clear if Loskene's body below the viewer's frame was humanoid or something more exotic.*

Tholl, Kova. (Stephen Markle). A **Mizarian** national. Tholl was imprisoned with Captain Picard during an alien experiment on the nature of authority. Tholl described himself as "a simple public servant." ("Allegiance" [TNG]). SEE: **Haro, Mitena**.

Thomas Paine, U.S.S. Federation starship, *New Orleans* class, registry number NCC-65530, commanded by **Captain Rixx**. The *Thomas Paine* was one of the ships that met the *Enterprise*-D at planet **Dytallix B** when an alien intelligence attempted to take over Starfleet Command in 2364. ("Conspiracy" [TNG]). *The* Thomas Paine *was named for the American patriot and writer.*

Thompson, Yeoman Leslie. (Julie Cobb). Member of the *Enterprise* landing party that answered the distress call from the **Kelvans** in 2268. As a demonstration of their superior power, the Kelvans distilled Thompson into a small, dry duodecahedron made of her chemical components, then crushed the object, killing her instantly. ("By Any Other Name" [TOS]).

Thopok. (Phil Morris). Klingon warrior. Thopok was commander of the guard in the service of the Lady **Grilka** in 2373. Thopok was discharged from the House of Grilka with his honor intact after Quark defeated him in battle. ("Looking for *par'Mach* in All the Wrong Places" [DS9]). *Phil Morris also played a Starfleet cadet in Star Trek III. He is the son of Greg Morris, who portrayed Barney Collier in Paramount's* Mission: Impossible *series. Phil played Collier's son in Paramount's* Mission: Impossible 1988 *sequel series.*

thorium. Radioactive metal with an atomic number of 90. Thorium was used for fission power aboard **Terok Nor (mirror)**. ("Crossover" [DS9]). SEE: **thoron**.

Thorne, Ensign. An *Enterprise*-D crew member and part of the engineering staff. Thorne was injured when exposure to a dark-matter pocket in the **Mar Oscura** Nebula in late 2367 caused a cryogenic control conduit in the engineering section to explode. ("In Theory" [TNG]).

thoron. Radioactive isotope, a by-product of decaying **thorium**, also known as radon-220. Elevated thoron emissions near the **Denorios Belt** accompanied the appearance of unknown aliens from the **Gamma Quadrant** in 2369. ("If Wishes Were Horses" [DS9]). A high-energy thoron field was utilized on **Deep Space 9** to block sensor scans from an outside source. ("Emissary" [DS9]). Portable thoron generators were employed by Starfleet medical practitioners to treat radiation burns. They can also be used to block scans from Federation **tricorder** sensors. ("Basics, Part II" [VGR]). A Nechisti shrine on the Nechani homeworld gave off high levels of thoron radiation in addition to being surrounded by a powerful biogenic energy field. ("Sacred Ground" [VGR]). Thoron radiation was lethal to the **memory virus** discovered in 2373. ("Flashback" [VGR]). The Ilari people of the Delta Quadrant used thoron-rifle energy weapons. ("Warlord" [VGR]). In 2373, the *U.S.S. Voyager* 's Emergency Medical Hologram used a thoron-field pulse in an attempt to eliminate an alien presence that lodged itself in Kathryn Janeway's cerebral cortex following a near-fatal injury. ("Coda" [VGR]).

thought maker. A small spherical device of Ferengi manufacture designed to control neural activity in a humanoid brain. The

thought maker transmitted a low-level electromagnetic signal at its victim, enabling it to implant sensory experiences or trigger memories. The device was forbidden by the Ferengi government, but **DaiMon Bok** obtained two such devices in his attempt to exact revenge upon Captain Picard for the death of his son in the **Battle of Maxia**. ("The Battle" [TNG]).

thralls. SEE: **drill thralls.**

Thrax. (Kurtwood Smith). Cardassian officer who was in charge of security on the Promenade of station **Terok Nor** before **Odo** took over in 2367. ("Things Past" [DS9]). *Kurtwood Smith previously played the Federation president in* Star Trek VI: The Undiscovered Country.

"Three brothers who went to Jo'kala, The." Old Bajoran fable about three brothers who were *kava* farmers. They grew a huge *kava* root and sold it in the city of Jo'kala. After arguing over how to divide the proceeds, the three brothers finally decided that it would be best if they gave all the money away, and went back to their farm where they belonged. ("Starship Down" [DS9]).

three-dimensional chess. Multilevel version of the ancient terrestrial game of strategy and warfare. One popular version of this game uses a board with three 4x4 main boards, and a number of 2x2 secondary boards. Aboard the original *Starship Enterprise*, both Captain Kirk and Mr. Spock were accomplished three-dimensional-chess players. ("Where No Man Has Gone Before" [TOS]). Three-dimensional chess was the basis for a security code used on the original *Enterprise* to protect against the possibility of an imposter assuming the identity of a command crew member, especially over voice communications. As of stardate 5718, the code was "queen to queen's level 3," to which the required response was "queen to king's level 1." ("Whom Gods Destroy" [TOS]). The game was something of a Starfleet tradition and continued to find favor among the patrons of the **Ten-Forward Lounge** on the *Enterprise*-D. *The three-dimensional chess game in Ten-Forward was based on the game board built for the first* Star Trek *series, but close examination of some of the chess pieces might reveal a replica of the robot from* Lost in Space. *That game board has also been seen on Deep Space 9. No official rules were ever developed for this game, although ever-ingenious* Star Trek *fans have developed several sets of rules for themselves.*

"Threshold." *Voyager* episode #32. Teleplay by Brannon Braga. Story by Michael DeLuca. Directed by Alexander Singer. Stardate 49373.4. *First aired in 1996. Lieutenant Tom Paris becomes the first human to break the warp 10 speed barrier, causing Janeway and him to mutate into another stage of evolution. This episode marks the first explanation of the transwarp concept first mentioned in* Star Trek III, *and the first appearance of* Voyager's *small "speedboat" shuttlecraft.* GUEST CAST: Raphael Sbarge as **Jonas**; Mirron E. Willis as **Rettik**; Majel Barrett as Computer voice. SEE: **acidichloride; AMU; antiproton; Armstrong, Neil; *Cochrane, Shuttlecraft*; dark-matter nebula; dilithium; duranium; Emergency Medical Hologram; gigaquad; holodeck and holosuite programs: Transwarp flight; infinite velocity, theory of; Janeway, Kathryn; Jonas, Michael; Kalavian biscuits; Neelix; Paris delight; Paris, Thomas; parsec; pizza; Rettick; space door; Trabalian freighter; transwarp; tritanium; warp 10; Wright, Orville.**

"Through the Looking Glass." *Deep Space Nine* episode #66. Written by Ira Steven Behr & Robert Hewitt Wolfe. Directed by Winrich Kolbe. No stardate given. *First aired in 1995. Sisko returns to the mirror universe, where he must assume the identity of a rebel leader fighting for human freedom This episode was a sequel to "Crossover" (DS9) and "Mirror, Mirror" (TOS).* GUEST CAST: Andrew Robinson as **Garak, Elim**; Felecia M. Bell as **Sisko, Jennifer (mirror)**; Max Grodénchik as **Rom (mirror)**; Tim Russ as **Tuvok (mirror)**; John Patrick Hayden as Cardassian overseer; Dennis Madalone as Marauder. SEE: **Alliance; Badlands; Bashir, Julian (mirror); Dax, Jadzia (mirror); Garak (mirror); mirror universe; Morn; O'Brien, Miles (mirror); Rebel Raider ship; Rom (mirror); Sisko, Benjamin (mirror); Sisko, Jennifer (mirror); subdermal communicator; Terok Nor; Terran resistance; transpectral sensor array; Tuvok (mirror); vole; Vulcan lute.**

thruster suit. Protective garment designed to allow humanoid starship crew members to work in an airless environment. A thruster suit also incorporates a small propulsion unit to permit maneuvering in weightless conditions, intended for emergency evacuation. Spock used a thruster suit when he left the *Enterprise* to attempt a mind-meld with **V'Ger**. (*Star Trek: The Motion Picture*).

Thule. Crew member aboard the original *Starship Enterprise*. In 2267, Thule was trapped on the bridge during **Khan**'s takeover attempt. ("Space Seed" [TOS]).

Thunderchild, U.S.S. Federation starship, ***Akira*-class**, Starfleet registry number NCC-63549. The *Thunderchild* was among the ships defending Sector 001 against the Borg incursion of 2373. *(Star Trek: First Contact). Named for the* H.M.S. Thunderchild, *a fictional British warship from H.G. Wells's classic novel* The War of the Worlds.

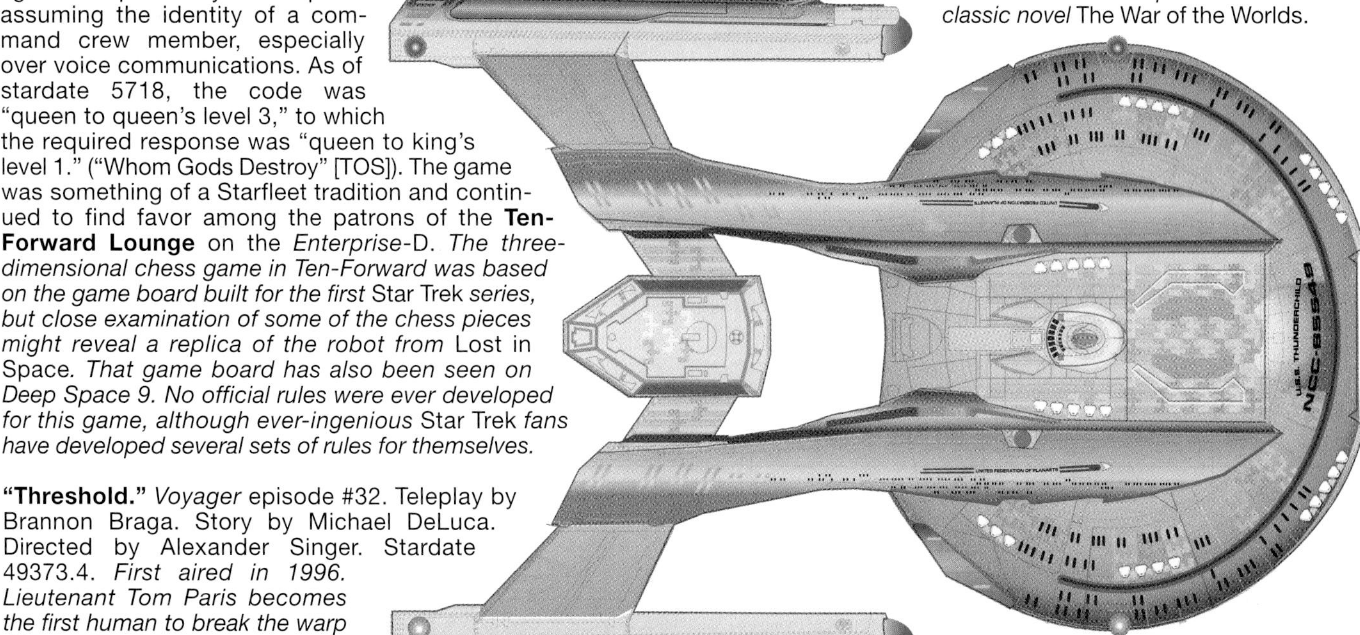

thymus. Organ in humanoid bodies, located anterior to the trachea. The thymus is responsible for producing lymphocytes, known as T-cells, which are part of humanoid immune systems. The alien DNA strand from Tarchannen III implanted in the members of the ***Victory*** away team was discovered residing in the thymus. Removal of the DNA strand allowed the victim to return to normal, providing some of the victim's original DNA remained. ("Identity Crisis" [TNG])

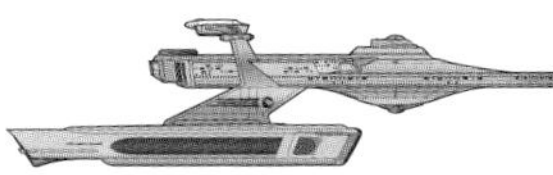

Tian An Men, U.S.S. Federation starship, *Miranda* class, Starfleet registry number NCC-21382. It served in Picard's armada to blockade Romulan supply ships supplying the **Duras** family forces during the **Klingon civil war** of 2367-2368. ("Redemption, Part II" [TNG]). *The* Tian An Men *was named in honor of the many who died in the cause of Chinese freedom, much as the present-day U.S. Navy had a* U.S.S. Lexington *whose name celebrates the first battle in the American war for independence.*

Tiberian bats. Avian life-forms known for sticking together. Spock compared some incriminating **gravity boots** as sticking to the guilty parties like a pair of Tiberian bats. (*Star Trek VI: The Undiscovered Country*).

Tiburon. Planet. **Dr. Sevrin** studied as a research engineer at Tiburon in the field of acoustics and communication. He was dismissed from Tiburon when he started the movement seeking the planet **Eden**, rejecting the advancements of the 23rd century. ("The Way to Eden" [TOS]). In the past, the infamous scientist **Zora** conducted brutal medical experiments on the body chemistry of people from Tiburon. ("The Savage Curtain" [TOS]).

Tieran. (Leigh J. McCluskey). Noted figure in **Ilari** politics. During the 22nd century, Tieran was a war hero and a brilliant leader. Tieran became Autarch of Ilari around 2173, bringing security and stability during a difficult time in Ilari history. However, in peacetime, Tieran became paranoid, and the Ilari people eventually ousted him. In 2373, Tieran was killed when his shuttle was attacked. Before he expired, Tieran used a special cortical implant to transfer his neural pattern into the mind of *Voyager* crew member Kes. He used Kes's body against her will in a bid to take over the Ilari government. Tieran's consciousness was destroyed when a team from the *Starship Voyager* was successful in rescuing Kes ("Warlord" [VGR]).

Tierna. (John Gegenhuber). Member of the **Kazon-Nistrim** sect. Tierna's body was booby-trapped in part of an elaborate scheme devised by **Jal Culluh** in 2372 to capture the *U.S.S. Voyager*. Tierna was brought aboard the *Voyager*, where he exploded, crippling the Federation ship. ("Basics, Part I" [VGR]). *John Gegenhuber also portrayed Kelat in "Maneuvers" (VGR) and "Alliances" (VGR).*

tiger. Large carniverous feline, native to planet Earth. Unwitting *Enterprise* crew members conjured up a Bengal tiger on the **amusement park planet** in 2267. ("Shore Leave" [TOS]). *A real elephant was also waiting in the wings, but the pachyderm never made it to the film.*

***Tika* cat.** Small animal known for its timidity. ("Faces" [VGR]).

Til'amin froth. Beverage. Served in the **Ten-forward Lounge** on the *Enterprise*-D. ("Eye of the Beholder" [TNG]).

Tilikia. (Dell Yount). Crew member on a Boslic freighter. ("Sons of Mogh" [DS9]). *Tilikia's name was not mentioned in dialog, but only appeared in the script.*

Tilonus Institute for Mental Disorders. Imaginary psychiatric hospital on planet **Tilonus IV** that only existed in the mind of William Riker when he was being interrogated on that planet in 2369. ("Frame of Mind" [TNG]).

Tilonus IV. Class-M planet, home to a humanoid civilization. The government of Tilonus IV was in a state of total anarchy when Commander William Riker attempted to rescue a Federation research team there in 2369. He was captured and subjected to neural manipulation in an attempt to extract tactical information from him. ("Frame of Mind" [TNG]). SEE: ***Frame of Mind;*** **Suna**.

"Time and Again." *Voyager* episode #4. Teleplay by David Kemper and Michael Piller. Story by David Kemper. Directed by Les Landau. No stardate given. First aired in 1995. *While investigating a planet destroyed by a global explosion, Captain Janeway and Tom Paris travel back in time, learning that they may have caused the disaster.* GUEST CAST: Nicholas Surovy as Makull; Joel Polis as Terla; Brady Bluhm as **Latika**; Ryan MacDonald as Shopkeeper; Steve Vaught as Officer; Jerry Spicer as Guard. SEE: **Chaltok IV; combadge; Delaney sisters; Drakina Forest dwellers; Kalto province; Kalton; Kes; Latika; Markov; nadion; Ny Terla; Paris, Admiral; Pe'Nar Makull, Polaric Test Ban Treaty; polaric ion energy; pre-warp civilization; Prime Directive; red dwarf; subspace technology; transtator; *Voyager, U.S.S.***

Time of Awakening. Period of **Vulcan** history, some two thousand years ago, when the Vulcan people began to reject their violent passions and to embrace peace and logic as a way of life. The **Stone of Gol** was believed destroyed during the Time of Awakening. ("Gambit, Part II" [TNG]). SEE: **Surak**.

"Time Squared." *Next Generation* episode #39. Teleplay by Maurice Hurley. Story by Kurt Michael Bensmiller. Directed by Joseph L. Scanlan. Stardate 42679.2. *First aired in 1989. A duplicate of Captain Picard from six hours in the future is found drifting in space, the aftermath of the destruction of the* Enterprise-D. *This episode was originally planned to be a lead-in to "Q Who?" (TNG). If this had been done, we would have learned that Q had been responsible for the unexplained time vortex in this episode. "Time Squared" marked the first appearance of the small two-person "shuttlepod" vehicle.* GUEST CAST: Diana Muldaur as **Pulaski**, **Dr. Katherine**; Colm Meaney as **O'Brien**, **Miles**. *SEE:* ***El-Baz, Shuttlepod*; Endicor system; energy vortex; Ennan VI; Owon eggs; Picard, Jean-Luc; Riker, William T.; shuttlepod**.

time portal. SEE: **atavachron; Guardian of Forever**.

timestream. A temporal inversion fold in the space-time matrix, timestreams weave throughout the galaxy and are home to intelligent life-forms. In 2372, when Ensign **Harry Kim**'s shuttlecraft intersected such a timestream, Kim found himself in an alternate reality. Kim was able to return to his reality by re-creating the conditions of the accident and flying back into the timestream. ("Non Sequitur" [VGR]). SEE: **Cosimo**.

"Time's Arrow, Part I." *Next Generation* episode #126. Teleplay by Joe Menosky and Michael Piller. Story by Joe Menosky. Directed by Les Landau. Stardate 45959.1. *First aired in 1992. Data goes back in time to 19th-century Earth, where he meets Mark Twain. This was the cliff-hanger ending to the fifth season.* GUEST CAST: Jerry Hardin as **Clemens**, **Samuel Langhorne**; Michael Aron as **London**, **Jack**; Barry Kivel as Doorman; Ken Thorley as Seaman; Sheldon P. Wolfchild as **Falling Hawk**, **Joe**; Jack Murdock as Beggar; Marc Alaimo as **La Rouque**, **Frederick**; Milt Tarver as Scientist; Whoopi Goldberg as **Guinan**; Michael Hungerford as Roughneck. SEE: **bitanium; cholera; Clemens, Samuel Langhorne; Colt Firearms; communicator; Data; Devidia II; Devidians; Exochemistry; Falling Hawk, Joe; Guinan; Hotel Brian; La Rouque, Frederick; LB10445; London, Jack; Marrab sector; microcentrum cell membrane; ophidian; phase conditioners; phase discriminator; pistol; Sector 001; seismic regulators; triolic waves; Twain, Mark; Tzartak aperitif.**

"Time's Arrow, Part II." *Next Generation* episode #127. Teleplay by Jeri Taylor. Story by Joe Menosky. Directed by Les Landau. Stardate 46001.3. *First aired in 1992. Picard and company return to the past to rescue Data and save Earth from invading aliens. This was the first episode of* Star Trek: The Next Generation*'s sixth season.* GUEST CAST: Jerry Hardin as **Clemens, Samuel Langhorne**; Pamela Kosh as **Carmichael, Mrs.**; William Boyett as Policeman; Michael Aron as **London, Jack**; James Gleason as **Apollinaire, Dr.**; Mary Stein as **Devidian nurse**; Alexander Enberg as Young reporter; Whoopi Goldberg as **Guinan**; Bill Cho Lee as Male patient; Majel Barrett as Computer voice. SEE: **Appollinaire, Dr.; Carmichael, Mrs.; Clemens, Samuel Langhorne; Data; Devidian nurse; Guinan; Halley's comet; Hotel Brian; London, Jack; *Midsummer's Night Dream, A*; neural depletion; ophidian; Presidio; Sisters of Hope Infirmary; Twain, Mark.**

time-travel pod. A 26th-century craft, five meters in length, constructed of plasticized tritanium mesh. Twenty-second-century **Professor Berlinghoff Rasmussen** traveled to the *Enterprise*-D in 2368 using one of these craft, which he had stolen from an unfortunate 26th-century traveler. ("A Matter of Time" [TNG]).

"Timescape." *Next Generation* episode #151. Written by Brannon Braga. Directed by Adam Nimoy. Stardate 46944.2. *First aired in 1993. The* Enterprise*-D and a Romulan ship are frozen in time, moments away from an explosion that will destroy both ships.* GUEST CAST: Michael Bofshever as Male Romulan and Alien male; John DeMita as Romulan; Joel Fredericks as Engineer. SEE: **artificial quantum singularity; black hole; emergency transporter armbands; mitosis; Mizan, Dr.; nitrogen narcosis; phase discriminator; plasma conversion sensor; plexing; quantum singularity life-form; Romulan warbird; runabout; Spot; temporal distortion; temporal narcosis; Vassbinder, Dr.; Wagner, Professor.**

timeship. Federation vehicle in use in the 29th century, capable of navigating through time using artificially generated temporal rifts. The *Timeship **Aeon,*** commanded by **Captain Braxton**, was one such vessel. ("Future's End, Part I and II" [VGR]).

Timicin, Dr. (David Ogden Stiers). A scientist and native of the planet **Kaelon II**. Timicin spent many years trying to develop a technique whereby the life of his world's dying sun might be extended. Timicin worked aboard the *Enterprise*-D in 2367 to conduct a test on his **helium fusion enhancement** process on a red giant star in the Praxillus system. Although the experiment failed, Timicin was prepared to return to Kaelon II for his **Resolution**, the end of his life under Kaelon tradition. But upon further review, Timicin became convinced that he could solve the problems and sought asylum aboard the *Enterprise*-D so he could continue his work. Timicin's requests provoked a diplomatic incident. Timicin withdrew his request for asylum and returned to Kaelon II, where his Resolution was carried out as planned. He was accompanied to the planet's surface by **Lwaxana Troi**. ("Half a Life" [TNG]). *One of the computer readouts studied by Timicin in engineering bore the numeric code 4077, a salute to David Ogden Stiers's work in the television series* M*A*S*H.

Timor Landi. Bajoran national. Timor was born in 2321, had a wife and two sons who lived in **Rakantha Province** on **Bajor**, and was a bookkeeper. In 2367, Timor Landi, along with Jillur Gueta and Ishan Chaye, was wrongly accused of attempting to assassinate **Gul Dukat** on station **Terok Nor**. The three were executed after a cursory investigation by **Odo**, Terok Nor's chief of security. ("Things Past" [DS9]).

Timor. (Nicholas Cascone). Member of the **Guardians**, who cared for the Trill symbionts in the **caves of Mak'ala** on the **Trill homeworld**. When **Jadzia Dax** fell ill in 2371, Timor believed her symptoms had something to do with one of the symbiont's previous hosts. ("Equilibrium" [DS9]).

Timothy. (Joshua Harris). A ten-year-old human boy who was the sole survivor of the research vessel ***S.S. Vico*** when it was destroyed by gravitational wavefronts in the Black Cluster in 2368. Timothy's mother was the ship's system engineer, and his father was the ship's second officer. Unable to deal with the overwhelming shock of his loss, Timothy chose to emulate Commander Data, who had rescued him from the *Vico*. As an android, Timothy would feel no fear or sadness and would not have to deal with the loss of his family. Timothy felt somehow responsible for the destruction of the *Vico*. He hid his sense of guilt by telling the crew of the *Enterprise*-D that the ship had been attacked by mysterious aliens. When Timothy finally came to terms with the loss of his family and friends, his recollections of events aboard the *Vico* were instrumental in helping the *Enterprise*-D escape the same fate. ("Hero Worship" [TNG]). *Timothy's last name was not given in the episode.* SEE: **Black Cluster.**

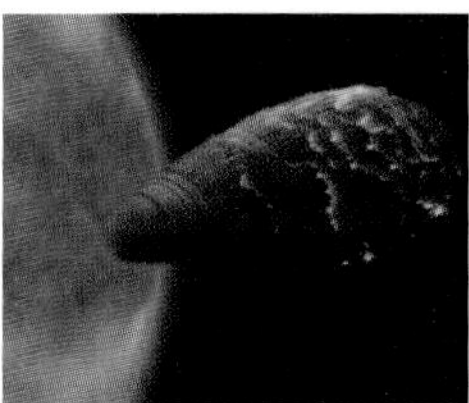

Tin Man. Starfleet designation for the living spacecraft discovered near the **Beta Stromgren** system in 2366 by the **Vega IX probe**. The Romulans intercepted the Vega IX transmissions and dispatched two *D'deridex*-class warbirds to capture it. Tin Man, which called itself **Gomtuu**, eluded capture, and departed into the unknown with **Tam Elbrun**. ("Tin Man" [TNG]).

"Tin Man." *Next Generation* episode #68. Written by Dennis Putman Bailey & David Bischoff. Directed by Robert Scheerer. Stardate 43779.3. *First aired in 1990. The* Enterprise*-D investigates a living spaceship that is dying of loneliness.* GUEST CAST: Michael Cavanaugh as **DeSoto, Captain Robert**; Peter Vogt as Romulan commander; Colm Meaney as **O'Brien, Miles**; Harry Groener as **Elbrun, Tam**. SEE: ***Adelphi, U.S.S.*; Beta Stromgren; Betazoids; Chandra V; *D'deridex*-class warbird; Darson, Captain; DeSoto, Captain Robert; Elbrun, Tam; first contact; Ghorusda Disaster; Gomtuu; Hayashi system; *Hood, U.S.S.*; linguacode; Starbase 123; Starbase 152; structural integrity field; Tin Man; Troi, Deanna; University of Betazed; Vega IX probe.**

tinghamut. A Vulcan children's toy. ("Apocalypse Rising" [DS9]).

"Tiny." Nickname that Sulu hated. *(Star Trek III: The Search for Spock). Don't call him "Tiny."*

Tiron. (Jeffrey Combs). Rich patron of **Quark's bar**. Tiron found **Kira Nerys** very attractive. When Kira, in 2371, failed to return his interest, Tiron commissioned a custom holosuite program from Quark that would create a holographic replica of Kira. Creation of such a replica without consent of the person being modeled was illegal, so Quark illicitly accessed the **Deep Space 9** personnel files to obtain information on Kira. Discovering this, Kira and Security Chief **Odo** altered the program, so that it placed Quark's head on Kira's body. After running this altered program, Tiron swore to ruin Quark. ("Meridian" [DS9]) *Jeffrey Combs also played Liquidator Brunt in "Bar Association" (DS9) and Body Parts (DS9) and Weyoun in "To the Death" (DS9)*

tissue mitigator. Medical instrument used in surgical procedures. ("Samaritan Snare" [TNG]).

Titan V rocket. Primitive space transport vehicle developed as an intercontinental ballistic missile by the government of the United States on Earth. In 2063, **Zefram Cochrane** used a Titan V rocket as the launch vehicle for his warp ship, the ***Phoenix***. The Titan V missile-launch complex used by Cochrane was located in Montana. *(Star Trek: First Contact). Cochrane's launch complex was filmed on location in Charlton Flats in California's Angeles Forest. The missile silo interior scenes were filmed at the Titan Missile Silo Museum in Tucson, Arizona. Although the rocket used for the missile silo scenes was a real United States Air Force Titan II, the film's art department labeled it as a Titan V, partially because the rocket engines were changed, but also because a real Titan II wouldn't have had the power to lift the* Phoenix *into orbit.*

Titan's Turn. Dangerous maneuver sometimes used by Starfleet shuttle pilots making the **Jovian run**. The procedure, banned by Starfleet, involves flying almost directly toward Titan, a moon of Saturn, then almost skimming Titan's atmosphere before turning sharply around the moon at 0.7*c*. **Geordi La Forge** was skilled at Titan's Turn during his days as a shuttle pilot, as was **Captain Edward Jellico**. ("Chain of Command, Part II" [TNG]).

Titan. The largest of Saturn's moons. Titan's diameter is half that of Earth's. Titan was used as an approach point for **Nova Squadron**'s maneuvers in 2368. ("The First Duty" [TNG]).

titanium. Dark gray metallic element, atomic number 22. Lightweight and very strong, titanium was used extensively in early spacecraft, such as Zefram Cochrane's ***Phoenix***. *(Star Trek: First Contact).*

Titus IV. Planet. **Miles O'Brien** almost stepped on a **Lycosa tarantula** on Titus IV. O'Brien kept the creature as a pet, naming her Christina. ("Realm of Fear" [TNG]).

Tixiplik, Plix. Criminal wanted in seven star systems for illegal weapons sales. Nog and Jake Sisko noticed a wanted poster of Tixiplik, a Reegrunion national, in Odo's security office on Deep Space 9 in 2370. ("Sanctuary" [DS9]).

TKL ration. The standard meal pack used aboard the *Enterprise*-D during the war with the Klingons in the alternate timeline created when the ***Enterprise*-C** vanished from its "proper" place in 2344. TKL rations were issued when replicators were on minimum power. ("Yesterday's *Enterprise*" [TNG]).

Tkon Empire. A defunct interstellar federation that flourished some six hundred thousand years ago. At its peak, the Tkon Empire had a population numbered in the trillions and was so powerful it was actually capable of moving planets. The Tkon were virtually wiped out when their sun went supernova, but a small number of outposts survived, including one at planet Delphi Ardu. The *Enterprise*-D encountered this outpost in 2364, making first contact with the Tkon, as well as with the **Ferengi**. ("The Last Outpost" [TNG]).

Tkon, ages of. As noted by the Tkon use of galactic motionary startime charts, the order of Tkon is as follows: Bastu, Cimi, Xora, Makto, Ozari, and Fendor. The central star of the Tkon Empire destabilized in the Age of Makto. ("The Last Outpost" [TNG]).

Tlhlngan jIH. In the **Klingon** culture, these words are part of an oath spoken between husband and wife in solemnizing their marriage. The words approximately translate to "I am a Klingon." ("The Emissary" [TNG]).

"To the Death." *Deep Space Nine* episode #96. Written by Ira Steven Behr & Robert Hewitt Wolfe. Directed by LeVar Burton. Stardate 49904.2. First aired in 1996. *After Deep Space 9 is attacked by renegade Jem'Hadar, Sisko uneasily accepts a Dominion proposal to join forces and destroy an Iconian gateway that would allow the renegades to conquer both Alpha and Gamma Quadrants.* GUEST CAST: Brian Thompson as **Toman'torax**; Scott Haven as **Virak'kara**; Jeffrey Combs as **Weyoun**; Clarence Williams III as **Omet'iklan**. SEE: **Ahjess; Bashir, Dr. Julian; Breen; Dax, Lela; Deep Space 9; Dominion; electroplasma system; Founders; Free Haven; Iconian gateway; Jem'Hadar; magnaton pulse; microfusion initiator; neutronium; O'Brien, Miles; O'Brien, Molly; Omet'iklan; psychographic profile; Ramirez; Toman'torax; Vandros IV; Virak'kara; Vorta; Weyoun; white.**

tobacco. Earth plant (*Nicotiana tabacum*) whose leaves, in ancient times, were smoked or chewed for a dangerously addictive drug known as nicotine. ("Little Green Men" [DS9]).

Toddman, Vice Admiral. (Leon Russom). Starfleet official assigned to Security. In 2371, Admiral Toddman ordered Commander **Benjamin Sisko** to put the ***U.S.S. Defiant*** on stand-by alert against possible Jem'Hadar attacks. ("The Die is Cast" [DS9]). SEE: **Eddington, Michael; Obsidian Order; Tal Shiar.**

Toff, Palor. (Nehemiah Persoff). Wealthy 24th-century collector and friend to **Zibalian** trader **Kivas Fajo**. Toff and Fajo were involved in a friendly rivalry over their respective collections. ("The Most Toys" [TNG]).

***Toffa* ale.** An alcoholic beverage popular in the Delta Quadrant. Wixiban and Neelix enjoyed *Toffa* ale at the **Nekrit Supply Depot**. ("Fair Trade" [VGR]).

Tog, DaiMon. (Frank Corsentino). Commander of the Ferengi Marauder vessel ***Krayton***. Tog attended the interstellar **Trade Agreements Conference** on **Betazed** in 2366. During the conference, he became enamored with **Lwaxana Troi** and abducted her, along with Commander Riker and Counselor Troi. Tog had hoped to persuade Lwaxana to use her telepathic powers to aid his business dealings. ("Ménage à Troi" [TNG]).

Toh'Kaht, I.K.S. Klingon ***Vor'cha*-class** attack cruiser that exploded in 2369 shortly after returning through the **Bajoran wormhole** from an exploratory mission into the **Gamma Quadrant**. The *Toh'Kaht* was the victim of telepathic energy spheres from the Saltah'na civilization. ("Dramatis Personae" [DS9]). SEE: **Hon'Tihl; Kee'Bhor; Saltah'na energy spheres; Tel'Peh.**

toh-maire. Volatile pockets of gas in the **Chamra Vortex**. When in the Nebula, being pursued by a **Miradorn** ship, **Odo** lured the attacking ship into a *toh-maire*, which destroyed the vessel when the *toh-maire* ignited. SEE: **Ah-Kel; Croden.** ("Vortex" [DS9]). In 2373, a runabout piloted by Worf and Garak encountered *toh-maire* gas pockets in a nebula in the Gamma Quadrant. ("In Purgatory's Shadow" [DS9]).

Tohvun III. Neutral planet located near the Federation-Cardassian border. ("Chain of Command, Part II" [TNG]).

tohzah. A Klingon expletive. **Alidar Jarok** used this term to insult Lieutenant Worf. ("The Defector" [TNG]).

tojal in *yamok* sauce. Cardassian delicacy, served as an appetizer. ("Destiny" [DS9]).

Tokath. (Alan Scarfe). **Romulan** officer who was reluctant to execute nearly a hundred Klingon prisoners after the infamous **Khitomer massacre** of 2346. Tokath sacrificed his military career to establish a secret prison camp in the **Carraya System** where these prisoners were allowed to live out their lives. At the camp, Tokath took a Klingon woman, **Gi'ral**, as his wife, and they had a daughter named **Ba'el**. The sanctity of Tokath's prison was nearly shattered in 2369 when **Worf** discovered its existence and tried to free the Klingon prisoners, not realizing that they had long ago grown to regard it as their home. Tokath allowed a compromise whereby several children of prisoners were allowed to leave, as long as they promised to keep the existence of the camp a secret. ("Birthright, Parts I and II" [TNG]). *Alan Scharfe also played Admiral Mendak in "Data's Day" (TNG).*

Tokyo Base. Starfleet facility. **Kyle Riker** developed the **Fuurinkazan battle strategies** at Tokyo Base. ("The Icarus Factor" [TNG]).

Tolena, Vedek. Bajoran candidate for **kai** in 2370. Kira Nerys teasingly told **Vedek Bareil** that she was thinking of voting for Vedek Tolena. ("Collaborator" [DS9]).

Tolstoy, U.S.S. Federation starship, ***Rigel* class**, Starfleet registry number NCC-62095. The *Tolstoy* was destroyed by the Borg at the battle of **Wolf 359** in 2367. ("The Best of Both Worlds, Part II" [TNG]). *The* Tolstoy *was named for the Russian author Leo Tolstoy, who wrote* War and Peace.

Tomalak. (Andreas Katsulas). Officer of the Romulan guard. Commander of the **Romulan warbird** that entered Federation space to retrieve the crew of the downed Romulan scoutship ***Pi*** in 2366. Tomalak denied that the scoutship was doing anything improper in Federation space, claiming that the *Pi* had suffered a navigational failure. ("The Enemy" [TNG]). Tomalak next encountered the *Enterprise*-D when the Federation ship illegally entered the Neutral Zone to investigate reports of a secret Romulan base at **Nelvana III**. The reports were a trick, and Tomalak had prepared a welcoming committee of two warbirds to attempt to capture the *Enterprise*-D. ("The Defector" [TNG]). A fantasy version of Tomalak was encountered by Riker in 2367 during a virtual reality engineered by **Barash** on **Alpha Onias III**. In this fantasy, Tomalak was a Romulan ambassador on a peace mission to the Federation. ("Future Imperfect" [TNG]). (In the **anti-time** reality created by the **Q Continuum**, Tomalak took command of the Romulan Warbird ***Terix***, which was one of more than 30 Romulan vessels amassed at the **Romulan Neutral Zone** on stardate 47988. The fleet was deployed in response to the **temporal anomaly** which formed in the **Devron system**.) ("All Good Things..." [TNG]). *Andreas Katsulas is also familiar to genre fans for his role as G'Kar, the Narn ambassador on* Babylon 5, *and for his portrayal of Newcomer Overseer Coolock on the* Alien Nation *television series.*

Toman'torax. (Brian Thompson). **Jem'Hadar** warrior. Toman'torax, who served as Second under the command of Omet'iklan, was part of the Jem'Hadar squad assigned to prevent a group of renegade Jem'Hadar from using an **Iconian gateway** in 2372. Omet'iklan killed Toman'torax for violating an order. ("To the Death" [DS9]). *Brian Thompson was also the Klingon second officer in "A Matter of Honor (TNG)."*

Tomar. (Robert Fortier). **Kelvan** who assisted in the capture of the *Enterprise* landing party in 2268 and forced the crew to set course for the **Andromeda Galaxy**. Aboard the *Enterprise*, Scotty got the Kelvan drunk in an attempt to make his humanoid side vulnerable. ("By Any Other Name" [TOS]). *It was to Tomar that Scotty uttered his famous line, "It's green."* SEE: **Aldebaran whiskey**.

tomato soup. Traditional Earth dish. The food replicators in the **mess hall** aboard the *U.S.S. Voyager* were programmed with 14 different varieties of tomato soup, including Bolian-style, with rice, with vegetables, and with pasta. Tom Paris preferred his tomato soup plain. ("Caretaker" [VGR]).

Tombstone, Arizona. Town in the ancient American West made famous by the gunfight at the **OK Corral** between lawmen led by **Wyatt Earp** and the gang led by **Ike Clanton** on October 26, 1881. A bizarre replica of the town was created by the Melkotians in 2268 as part of their plan for the death of Kirk and members of his *Enterprise* crew. ("Spectre of the Gun" [TOS]).

Tomed Incident. An encounter between the **Romulan Star Empire** and the **United Federation of Planets** in 2311. Thousands of Federation lives were lost in this incident, and the Romulans thereafter entered an extended period of isolationism, during which there was no contact at all between the two powers. The isolationist period lasted until 2364. ("The Neutral Zone" [TNG]). *Later episodes established several contacts between the Klingons and the Romulans between 2311 and 2364, even though this seems somewhat inconsistent with "The Neutral Zone."*

Tomlinson, Lieutenant Robert. (Stephen Mines). Phaser-control officer aboard the *U.S.S. Enterprise* during the Romulan incursion of 2266. Tomlinson had been engaged to marry fellow *Enterprise* crew member Angela Martine, but the wedding ceremony was interrupted by news of the Romulan attack. Tomlinson was later killed during the battle. ("Balance of Terror" [TOS]).

tomographic imaging scanner. Sensor scan which involves a series of narrow-beam X-rays to scan objects in a multiphasic mode. A tomographic imaging scanner was developed at the **Daystrom Institute** and was still in the theoretical stage in 2364. By 2370 the scanners were in general use aboard starships. (In Q's **anti-time** reality, Data used a tomographic imaging scanner to map the internal structure of the **temporal anomaly** discovered in the Devron system. From the results of the scan he concluded that the rift was created by the convergence of the three identical **inverse tachyon beams**, each originating from a different time period.) ("All Good Things..." [TNG]).

"Tomorrow Is Yesterday." Original Series episode #21. Written by D. C. Fontana. Directed by Michael O'Herlihy. Stardate

3113.2. *First aired in 1967. The* Enterprise *accidentally travels back in time to the 20th century, where it is sighted by the Air Force as a UFO. The episode does not make it clear exactly when in the 20th century the* Enterprise *was, but the radio reference to the first moon-landing mission to be launched "next Wednesday" would seem to place it about a week before July 16, 1969, when* Apollo 11 *was launched.* GUEST CAST: Roger Perry as **Christopher**, **Captain John**; Hal Lynch as **air police sergeant**; Richard Merrifield as **Webb**; John Winston as **Kyle, Mr.**; Ed Peck as **Fellini**, **Colonel**; Mark Dempsey as Air Force captain; Jim Spencer as Air policeman; Sherri Townsend as Crew woman; Majel Barrett as Computer voice. SEE: **air police sergeant; Alpha Centauri; *Apollo* 11; black star; Blackjack; Bluejay 4; Christopher, Captain John; Christopher, Colonel Shaun Geoffrey; Cygnet XIV; Earth-Saturn probe; *Enterprise*; Fellini, Colonel; food slot; Kyle, Mr.; moon; Omaha Air Base; slingshot effect; Starbase 9; Saturn; UFO; United Earth Space Probe Agency; Webb**.

Tong Vey. Klingon city destroyed in ancient times by the Emperor **Sompek**. ("Rules of Engagement" [DS9]).

Tongo Rad. (Victor Brandt). Son of the **Catullan** ambassador and one of **Dr. Sevrin**'s followers who came on-board the *Enterprise* in 2269 on a quest for **Eden**. ("The Way to Eden" [TOS]).

***tongo*.** Ferengi game of chance and strategy that involved cards and a roulette-type wheel. *Tongo* plays included acquire, confront, initiate, risk, and roll away. ("Playing God" [DS9]). Other possible moves included challenge, evade, retreat, and sell. ("Rules of Acquisition" [DS9]). Jadzia Dax was an accomplished player, as reflected by her winnings at the game. This was upsetting to some Ferengi players, who seemed uncomfortable at being bested by a female. ("Playing God" [DS9], "Meridian" [DS9]). Dax nevertheless lost two bars of **latinum** on stardate 50416 to three-time champion **Captain Ramirez**, whom she challenged to a no-limit game. ("The Darkness and the Light" [DS9]).

Tongo cards.

Tonkian homing beacon. Navigational device. Stolen Tonkian homing beacons were discovered in the **Gatherer** camp on **Gamma Hromi II**. ("The Vengeance Factor" [TNG]).

Tonsa, Vedek. Bajoran spiritual leader. Tonsa was an excellent springball player. Tonsa was present on Deep Space 9 in 2372 during First Minister Shakaar's visit to meet with Federation delegates. ("Crossfire" [DS9]).

"Too Short a Season." *Next Generation* episode #12. Teleplay by Michael Michaelian and D. C. Fontana. Story by Michael Michaelian. Directed by Rob Bowman. Stardate 41309.5. *First aired in 1988. An aging Starfleet officer attempts to make amends at a planet where he traded weapons for hostages, fueling a civil war that lasted for 40 years.* GUEST CAST: Clayton Rohner as **Jameson**, **Admiral Mark**; Marsha Hunt as **Jameson**, **Anne**; Michael Pataki as **Karnas**. SEE: **Cerebus II; *Gettysburg, U.S.S.*; Hawkins; Idini Star Cluster; Iverson's disease; Jameson, Admiral Mark; Jameson, Anne; Karnas; Mordan IV; Peretor; Persephone V; steelplast.**

tooth sharpener. Small motorized tool used to file teeth sharp. The **Ferengi** used tooth sharpeners to keep their teeth nicely pointed. ("Family Business" [DS9]). In 2372, when Nog sold his childhood belongings in preparation for going off to Starfleet, Worf was interested in buying his tooth sharpener. ("Little Green Men" [DS9]).

topaline. Rare mineral needed for colonial life-support systems. It is found in abundance on planet **Capella IV**. Mining rights for topaline were the focus of a power struggle on that planet between the High **Teer Akaar**, who favored granting topaline rights to the Federation, and political rival **Maab**, who felt the Klingons would offer a more advantageous agreement. ("Friday's Child" [TOS]).

Topin system. Star system in the **Demilitarized Zone**. The system contained an unstable protostar that generated significant levels of **magnetascopic interference**. Ro Laren used the Tropin system as cover when she conducted a **Maquis** raid on the *Starship Enterprise*-D in 2370. ("Preemptive Strike" [TNG]).

Toq. (Sterling Macer). Child of **Klingon** warriors captured by Romulans in 2346 at **Khitomer**. Raised at the secret Romulan prison camp in the **Carraya System**, Toq had little exposure to Klingon culture until Worf visited the camp in 2369. Inspired by Worf's teachings of Klingon culture, Toq left the camp with Worf in order to join mainstream Klingon society. In doing so, Toq promised to keep the existence of the camp a secret. ("Birthright, Parts I and II" [TNG]).

Tor Jolan. Bajoran composer. Deep Space 9 officer Julian Bashir enjoyed Tor's work. ("Crossover" [DS9]). SEE: **Boldaric masters.**

Tora Naprem. Bajoran woman who fell in love with **Gul Dukat** during the Cardassian occupation of Bajor. In 2353 Tora Naprem and Gul Dukat had a daughter, **Tora Ziyal**. In 2366, Dukat, fearful that public knowledge of his illicit relationship with a Bajoran woman could ruin his career, sent Tora Naprem and their daughter away aboard the *Ravinok* to live on planet **Lissepia**. Tora was killed when the *Ravinok* was attacked by Breen warships and crashed on **Dozaria** in 2366, but her daughter survived. ("Indiscretion" [DS9]).

Tora Ziyal. (Cyia Batten, Tracy Middendorf, Melanie Smith). Daughter of **Tora Naprem** and **Gul Dukat**, born in 2353. Ziyal and her mother were passengers on the Cardassian ship *Ravinok* when it was attacked by two Breen warships and crashed on **Dozaria** in 2366. Tora Ziyal survived the crash and was forced to labor in the Breen dilithium mines on Dozaria. She and several other crash survivors were rescued by Kira Nerys and Gul Dukat in 2372. Dukat brought Tora Ziyal home with him to Cardassia to live with his family. ("Indiscretion" [DS9]). Ziyal was promptly ostracized by Cardassian society, and went to live with her father aboard the Cardassian freighter ***Groumall***. She fought alongside the *Groumall's* crew as they commandeered K'Temang's bird-of-prey. When her father decided to became a resistance fighter against the Klingons, Ziyal wanted to join his crusade, but Kira convinced Dukat that his daughter would be better off living on **Deep Space 9**. ("Return to Grace" [DS9]). On the station, Ziyal found herself attracted to **Elim Garak**, the only other Cardassian residing on Deep Space 9. ("For the Cause" [DS9]). Dukat strongly disapproved of the relationship and later disowned Ziyal when she chose to remain on the station rather than return to Cardassia with her father. ("In Purgatory's Shadow" [DS9], "By Inferno's Light" [DS9]). *Tora Ziyal was portrayed by Cyia Batten* (pictured), *in "Indiscretion" (DS9) and "Return to Grace" (DS9). She was played by Tracy Middendorf in "For the Cause" (DS9) and was portrayed by Melanie Smith in "In Purgatory's Shadow" (DS9) and "By Inferno's Light" (DS9).*

Torad IV. Planet in the Gamma Quadrant. In 2372, Major Kira, Doctor Bashir, and Keiko O'Brien traveled to Torad IV for a three-day botanical survey. ("Body Parts" [DS9]).

Torak, Governor. (Wayne Grace). **Klingon** official in charge of border space near Sector 2520. Torak was reluctant to investigate Picard's charges that **Morag**, a Klingon officer, might have been responsible for the murder of **Lieutenant Keith Rocha** at **Relay Station 47** in 2369, but agreed to do so upon learning that Picard was Gowron's **Arbiter of Succession**. Torak was later able to prove Morag's innocence, but allowed Morag to be taken into Federation custody for theft of encoded data from Relay Station 47. ("Aquiel" [TNG]).

Torak. A mythical demonic figure in the Drellian culture. ("Devil's Due" [TNG]).

Toral. (J. D. Cullum; Rick Pasqualone). The illegitimate son of **Klingon High Council** member **Duras**. In 2367, Duras family members **Lursa** and **B'Etor** launched a bid for young Toral to succeed the late **K'Mpec** as chancellor of the council. ("Redemption, Part I" [TNG]). Jean-Luc Picard, as **Arbiter of Succession**, ruled that Toral was not entitled to his late father's council position, since Toral had not yet distinguished himself in the service of the empire. Following the victory of **Gowron** against Duras family forces in the **Klingon civil war** of 2367-2368, Toral's life was forfeit because his father and grandfather had wrongfully dishonored the family of Mogh. **Worf**, eldest son of **Mogh**, nevertheless declined to demand Toral's death, much to the surprise of Gowron and the council. ("Redemption, Parts I and II" [TNG]). In 2372, Toral learned of *Dahar* Master **Kor**'s quest for the legendary **Sword of Kahless**. Hoping to use the artifact for his own political gain, Toral followed Kor to a **Hur'q** planet in the Gamma Quadrant and tried to steal the sword. ("The Sword of Kahless" [DS9]). *Toral fell in battle with Kor and Worf, but it was not totally clear whether he was killed or not. J. D. Cullum played Toral in "Redemption, Parts I and II" (TNG), and Rick Pasqualone* (pictured)*, played the part in "The Sword of Kahless" (DS9).*

Toran, Gul. (Edward Wiley). Cardassian military officer. Toran was dispatched to Deep Space 9 in 2370 to deal with political dissidents **Natima Lang**, **Rekelen**, and **Hogue**. Toran was killed by his old political enemy, Garak, after Garak realized that murdering the dissidents would hurt Cardassia. ("Profit and Loss" [DS9]). *Edward Wiley also portrayed Vagh in "The Mind's Eye" (TNG). See next entry.*

Toran, Gul. Officer serving in the **Sixth Order** of the **Cardassian** military. Gul Toran was commander of border outpost 61 in the **Almatha sector** in 2371. ("Defiant" [DS9]). *There must have been at least two Gul Torans, since an officer of that name was killed in 2370 in "Profit and Loss" (DS9). See previous entry.*

Toran. (Michael Bofshever). Official with the Bajoran provisional government in 2369. Minister Toran was in charge of the project to tap energy from the Bajoran moon, **Jeraddo**. ("Progress" [DS9]). *Toran must be a popular name.*

toranium. Extremely strong metal used in Cardassian construction. Toranium was used in the corridors on station **Deep Space 9**. Standard phasers are ineffective at cutting through toranium inlays, and a **bipolar torch** is recommended. ("The Forsaken" [DS9]).

Torch of G'boj. Ancient artifact that was a sacred icon of the Klingon people. ("The Sword of Kahless" [DS9]).

Tore, Nellen. (Ann Shea). A native of Delb II and an aide to Starfleet **Admiral Norah Satie**. She was a constant presence at Satie's side, taking notes on everything that was said. ("The Drumhead" [TNG]).

Toreth, Commander. (Carolyn Seymour). Romulan officer in command of the Imperial Romulan warbird ***Khazara***. A career officer, Toreth was proud and efficient, but had little respect for the **Tal Shiar** intelligence service, which had been responsible for the murder of her father for political reasons. ("Face of the Enemy" [TNG]). SEE: **Taris, Subcommander**. *Carolyn Seymour also played **Mrs. Templeton**, the housekeeper in Janeway's gothic romance holonovel.*

Torga IV. Uninhabited Class-M planet in the Gamma Quadrant. Torga IV is rich in cormaline deposits. In early 2373, Deep Space 9 scientists conducted a mining survey of Torga IV. While they were there, a Jem'Hadar warship crashed on the planet. After a standoff against several Jem'Hadar warriors, the Deep Space 9 team claimed the warship and took it back to the station. ("The Ship" [DS9]). *The surface of Torga IV was filmed at a rock quarry north of Los Angeles.*

Torigan, Ensign. *Starship Enterprise*-D crew member. Torigan served at Tactical on the Gamma shift on stardate 46852. ("Rightful Heir" [TNG]).

Torin. (Norman Snow). Klingon high cleric who served at the monastery at **Boreth**. He was part of the plot to create the clone of **Kahless the Unforgettable** in 2369. ("Rightful Heir" [TNG]).

Torman V. Class-M planet. Captain Picard, Dr. Crusher, and Lieutenant Worf traveled to Torman V in 2369 to secure "discreet" transportation to planet **Celtris III** for a covert Starfleet mission. ("Chain of Command, Part I" [TNG]).

Tormolen, Joe. (Stewart Moss). *Enterprise* crew member, and part of the landing party assigned to investigate the deaths of the **Psi 2000** science team in 2266. Tormolen, under the influence of the **Psi 2000 virus**, became extremely depressed and committed suicide by stabbing himself with a dinner knife. His wound was not severe, and Dr. McCoy later expressed the opinion that Tormolen died because he just didn't want to live. ("The Naked Time" [TOS]). *Stewart Moss also played Hanar in "By Any Other Name" (TOS).*

Torna IV. Planet. In 2372, at a tavern on Torna IV, **Kor** unwisely bragged of the discovery of the Shroud of the Sword. His story was heard by **Toral**, who later interfered with Kor's quest to find the Sword of Kahless. ("The Sword of Kahless" [DS9]).

***Toron*-class shuttlecraft.** Type of small, short-range **Klingon** spacecraft . The shuttlecraft piloted by the **Koral** was of the *Toron* class. ("Gambit, Part II" [TNG]). *The* Toron*-class shuttle was a redress of the* Nenebek *from "Final Mission" (TNG), which leads one to wonder if all the various* Nenebek *re-uses were* Toron*-class ships.*

Torona IV. Planet; home of the reclusive insectoid civilization known as the **Jarada**. ("The Big Goodbye" [TNG]).

torpedo bay. Facility for preparation and launch of photon torpedo weapons. Located on Deck 13 of refit ***Constitution*-class** Federation starships. *(Star Trek VI: The Undiscovered Country).* The forward torpedo bay on ***Galaxy*-class** ships was located on Deck 25. **Lieutenant Jenna D'Sora** worked in the torpedo bay of the *Enterprise*-D. ("In Theory" [TNG]).

torpedo sustainer engine. A miniature matter/antimatter fuel cell that powers a sustainer coil so that a **photon torpedo** can maintain a warp field handed off from the torpedo launching tube. The sustainer engines allow a photon torpedo to remain at warp if launched at warp. The sustainer engines were modified for photon torpedoes used in **Dr. Timicin**'s daring **helium fusion enhancement** experiment in 2367. ("Half a Life" [TNG]).

Torres, B'Elanna. (Roxann Biggs). Former member of the **Maquis** resistance group who became chief engineer of the ***U.S.S. Voyager***. Half-**Klingon** and half-human, Torres had an aggressive personality and had much difficulty controlling her temper, which she attributed to her Klingon heritage. ("Caretaker" [VGR]). B'Elanna spent her early years with her parents at the Federation colony on planet **Kessik IV**. ("Faces" [VGR]). B'Elanna's human father left her and moved to Earth when she was five. She and her Klingon mother subsequently went to live on the **Klingon Homeworld**, but as a result, B'Elanna wasn't close to either of her parents. ("Eye of the Needle" [VGR]).

Torres attended **Starfleet Academy**, but dropped out in her second year because of difficulty with Starfleet discipline. ("Caretaker" [VGR]). She had been a member of the academy's decathlon team. ("Basics, Part II" [VGR]). Torres felt that her sometimes-turbulent stint at the academy was evidence that she was not Starfleet material, but at least one of her instructors, **Professor Chapman**, was so impressed with her original thinking that he recommended she be accepted if she ever sought re-admission to the academy ("Parallax" [VGR]). She later joined the Maquis and served under **Chakotay** aboard a Maquis ship, and became a member of the *Voyager* crew when her ship and the *Voyager* were stranded in the Delta Quadrant in 2371. ("Caretaker" [VGR]). While in the Maquis, Torres was a close friend of **Seska**, not suspecting that she was a Cardassian agent. ("Maneuvers" [VGR]).

After joining the crew of the *Voyager* she had a violent altercation with **Lieutenant Carey,** her superior officer in engineering. Nevertheless, Captain Janeway chose Torres over Carey to be the chief engineer of the *Voyager*. ("Parallax" [VGR]). On stardate 48784, Torres was captured by a **Vidiian** scientist who used a genotron to split her into two individuals, one fully human, the other completely Klingon. SEE: **Sulan**. Her Klingon self sacrificed her life so that her human half could live, and *Voyager*'s holographic doctor was subsequently successful in restoring her original genetic structure to her surviving half. The experience helped Torres realize the importance of each half to her personality. ("Faces" [VGR]). Torres once sought Chakotay's help in locating her **animal guide**. She didn't get along with her guide and tried to kill it. ("The Cloud" [VGR]). SEE: **vision quest**. When fellow *Voyager* crew member **Vorik** underwent the Vulcan ***Pon farr*** in 2373, he asked Torres to become his mate. Torres declined, but nevertheless experienced *Pon farr* herself, the result of a neurochemical imbalance introduced by Vorik. Torres subsequently attempted to mate with Tom Paris. ("Blood Fever" [VGR]).

Torres's first appearance was in "Caretaker" (VGR); in early episodes Roxann Biggs was credited as Roxann Biggs-Dawson.

Torres, Lieutenant. (Jimmy Ortega). **Flight control officer** (conn) aboard the *Enterprise*-D. Torres was frozen by **Q** during the Enterprise-D's first encounter with Q in 2364, although he later recovered. ("Encounter at Farpoint, Part I" [TNG]).

Torsus. One of the self-aware **Borg** discovered on **Ohniaka III** in late 2369. Torsus was killed by the *Enterprise*-D away team. ("Descent, Part I" [TNG]).

Torze-qua. A musical portion of the historic Kriosian **Ceremony of Reconciliation** held aboard the *Enterprise*-D in 2368. ("The Perfect Mate" [TNG]).

Toscat. (David Selburg). An elder **Ocampa** male. Toscat was one of those Ocampa who settled for being taken care of by the **Caretaker** and who no longer questioned that way of life. ("Caretaker" [VGR]). *David Selburg also played Whalen in "The Big Goodbye" (TNG) and Dr. Syrus in "Frame of Mind" (TNG).*

Tosin. (James Horan). A powerful member of the **Kolaati**. In exchange for their lives after a failed attempt to deliver narcotics to **Sutok**, Tosin demanded that Wix and Neelix bring him three grams of **warp plasma**. A massive explosion took place after one of his henchmen fired his weapon into a leaking warp-plasma field. Tosin and the remaining henchmen were taken into custody by **Bahrat** aboard the **Nekrit Expanse Supply Depot**. ("Fair Trade" [VGR]). *James Horan also played Jo'Bril in "Suspicions" (TNG), Lieutenant Barnaby in "Descent, Part II" (TNG), and Ikat'ika in "In Purgatory's Shadow" (DS9) and "By Inferno's Light" (DS9).*

Tosk. (Scott MacDonald). Reptilian humanoid who, in 2369, was the first being to visit Deep Space 9 from the **Gamma Quadrant**. The collective name Tosk stood for beings bred and trained to be tracked by the **Hunters**. Requiring only 17 minutes of sleep per rotation and storing liquid nutrients in plastic fibers throughout his body, Tosk was completely self-sufficient. Brought aboard the station after his craft was damaged, he formed a friendship with Chief Miles O'Brien. Hampered by a code of silence, Tosk could not communicate his role as the hunted, even when the Hunters descended upon the station to take him back to their planet in disgrace. O'Brien disobeyed orders and the **Prime Directive** by allowing Tosk to escape, thus continuing the hunt and fulfilling his friend's deepest wish: the chance to die with honor. ("Captive Pursuit" [DS9]). *Scott MacDonald also played N'Vek in "Face of the Enemy" (TNG), and Goran'Agar in "Hippocratic Oath" (DS9).*

touch-and-go downwarping. A maneuver in which a starship drops briefly out of warp into normal space, then quickly accelerates back to warp speed. The *Enterprise*-D used this technique to transport an away team to **Gravesworld** while en route to an emergency rendezvous with the ***U.S.S. Constantinople***. ("The Schizoid Man" [TNG]).

Touth, Caves of. Series of underground caverns on **Rinax**. **Neelix** and his sister **Alixia** used to go exploring in the Caves of Touth. ("Rise" [VGR]).

Tower of Commerce. Administrative center on the **Ferengi** homeworld where business activity for the entire **Ferengi Alliance** was regulated. The spire-topped Tower of Commerce, located in the **Sacred Marketplace**, was the tallest building in the Ferengi Alliance. ("Family Business" [DS9]). *Referred to as the Temple of Commerce in "Prophet Motive" (DS9).*

Towles. An *Enterprise*-D crew member, and part of the engineering staff. Towles was one of two engineers left at the command post set up on a remote planet during the **Borg** incursion of late 2369. The command post was used to coordinate the teams searching for Commander **Data**, following his disappearance. ("Descent, Part I" [TNG]).

Tox Uthat. A **quantum phase inhibitor** invented in the 27th century by scientist **Kal Dano**. The *Tox Uthat* was a palm-sized crystal capable of halting all nuclear reactions within a star. Fearing the device would be stolen, Dano fled to the 22nd century, where he hid the device on planet **Risa**. The *Uthat* became something of a holy grail to criminals from the 27th century who traveled back in time to find the object, and for 24th-century archaeologists, who believed that the legends of the *Uthat* had a basis in fact. These included Dr. Samuel Estragon, who spent half of his life in search of the *Uthat*. Upon his death in 2366, his assistant **Vash** was successful in finding the device on planet Risa, hidden in a ***Horga'hn*** statuette. Vash was not the only one interested in the *Uthat*; other parties included **Sovak** and two **Vorgon** criminals from the future. Jean-Luc Picard, vacationing on Risa at the time, destroyed the *Tox Uthat* to prevent it falling into unscrupulous hands. ("Captain's Holiday" [TNG]).

Tozhat Resettlement Center. Orphanage on planet **Bajor** where many Cardassian war orphans were cared for. **Rugal** was taken in 2362 to the Tozhat Resettlement Center. ("Cardassians" [DS9]).

Trabalian freighter. Cargo vessel of Trabalian registry. **Neelix** served for two years as an engineering assistant aboard a Trabalian freighter. ("Threshold" [VGR]).

Trabe police. Law enforcement agency of the **Trabe** people. The Trabe police were responsible for the persecution of members of the **Kazon** and encouraged their captives to fight amongst themselves. Eventually, the Kazon became a powerful fighting force and freed themselves from their captors in 2346. ("Alliances" [VGR]).

Trabe. Technologically advanced civilization in the Delta Quadrant. The Trabe had enslaved the **Kazon**, deliberately causing the Kazon sects to fight one another, making them easier to control. Finally, in 2346, **Jal Sankur** was successful in uniting the sects to overthrow their Trabe oppressors. One legacy of the Trabe control of the Kazon was the fact that the Kazon continued to use spacecraft of Trabe design for many years thereafter. ("Initiations" [VGR], "Maneuvers" [VGR]). The surviving Trabe wandered through space, pursued by the Kazon, who would not allow the Trabe to settle on a new planet. In 2372, Trabe leader **Mabus** convinced *Starship Voyager* Captain Kathryn Janeway to call a conference of the Kazon **first majes** to discuss a plan for peace. However, the conference proved to be a trap by the Trabe to kill the most powerful Kazons as an act of revenge. The attempt failed, deepening Kazon hatred against the Trabe. ("Alliances" [VGR]).

Tracey, Captain Ronald. (Morgan Woodward). Captain of the *Starship* ***Exeter*** who violated the **Prime Directive** at planet **Omega IV** in 2268. On Omega IV, Tracey believed he had discovered the secret to immortality, but later learned that he had only found the long-lived survivors of a terrible bacteriological war. Returning to his ship, Tracey brought back a deadly virus from that war that killed all of his crew. Tracey then became involved in an ancient struggle between the **Yangs** and **Kohms** on Omega IV, providing phaser weapons to that primitive civilization. Tracey was later taken into custody by *Starship Enterprise* personnel and charged with having violated the Prime Directive. ("The Omega Glory" [TOS]). *Morgan Woodward also played Dr. Simon Van Gelder in "Dagger of the Mind" (TOS).*

Tracken II. Class-M planet in the **Demilitarized Zone** that was the site of a **Maquis** colony. In 2373, in a bid to draw out **Michael Eddington**, Captain Benjamin Sisko threatened to scatter **trilithium** into the atmosphere of Tracken II and render it uninhabitable as he had done to **Solosos III**. The threat was effective, and Michael Eddington gave himself up to Federation authorities. ("For the Uniform" [DS9]).

tractor beam. A focused linear graviton force beam used to physically manipulate objects across short distances. Tractor beams were used by Federation starships and other space vehicles as a means of towing other vessels. Tractor beams were also used to provide short-range guidance for approaching or departing shuttlecraft.

Tracy, Lieutenant Karen. (Virginia Aldridge). *Starship Enterprise* medical technician. Tracy was to run a psychotricorder analysis on Montgomery Scott on planet **Argelius II** in 2267. She was killed by the alien entity, **Redjac**, just prior to the analysis. ("Wolf in the Fold" [TOS]).

Trade Agreements Conference. A biennial interstellar congress held on planet **Betazed**. The *Enterprise*-D was in attendance at the conference in 2366 and hosted the closing reception. ("Ménage à Troi" [TNG]).

Trafalgar, Battle of. Naval engagement of the Napoleonic Wars, fought on Earth in 1805, which established British naval supremacy for more than 100 years. One of **Jean-Luc Picard**'s ancestors fought at the Battle of Trafalgar. *(Star Trek Generations)*. SEE: **Nelson, Lord Horatio; *Victory, H.M.S.***

Trager. Cardassian ***Galor*-class warship**, with a crew of 600, commanded by **Gul Macet**. In 2367, the *Trager* attacked the *Enterprise*-D in retaliation for the ***U.S.S. Phoenix***'s attack on a Cardassian science station. The action by the *Phoenix* had been a violation of the 2366 peace treaty between the Federation and the **Cardassians**. ("The Wounded" [TNG]).

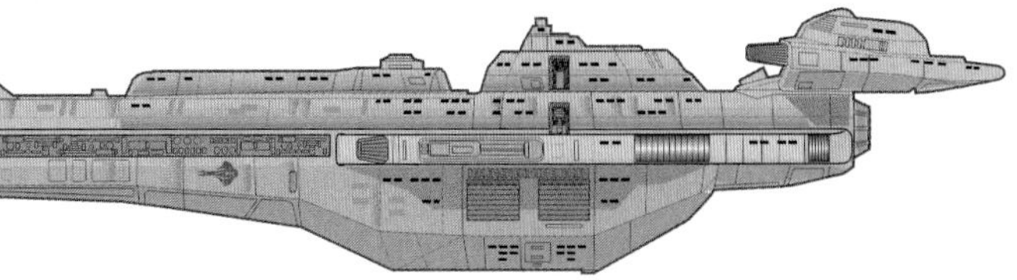

Traggle nectar. Beverage native to the Delta Quadrant, often served along with breakfast. ("Prototype" [VGR]).

Traidy. (John Durbin). Operative of the **Orion Syndicate**. Draim hired Traidy to go to Deep Space 9 and procure a **data crystal** from **Arissa** before killing her. ("A Simple Investigation" [DS9]).

trajector. Advanced technology developed by the people of **Sikaris**, permitting instantaneous **folded-space transport** across distances as great as 40,000 light-years. When the *Starship Voyager* visited Sikaris in 2371, *Voyager* personnel attempted to obtain trajector technology in hopes of speeding *Voyager*'s return to the Alpha Quadrant. Unfortunately, the Sikarian system was totally incompatible with Federation technology because of the use of antineutrinos as a catalyst in the space-folding process. ("Prime Factors." [VGR]). SEE: **Elway Theorem**.

Trajok. (Chris Nelson Norris). Jadzia Dax's friend. Trajok was her coach in **Galeo-Manada style wrestling**. ("Playing God" [DS9]).

Trakian ale. Drink. Riker was imbibing Trakian ale when Ensign **Sam Lavelle** tried to strike up a conversation at the bar in Ten-Forward. ("Lower Decks" [TNG]).

Trakor's Fourth Prophecy. Ancient text in the **Bajoran** religion. In the prophecy, Trakor stated that the **Emissary** would face a fiery trial and that he would be forced to make a difficult decision. ("Destiny" [DS9]).

Trakor's Third Prophecy. Ancient text in the **Bajoran** religion, written 3,000 years ago after Trakor first encountered the **Orb of Change**. His third prophecy predicted, "When the river wakes, stirred once more to **Janir**'s side, three vipers will return to their nest in the sky." Trakor added, "When the vipers try to peer through the temple gates, a sword will appear in the heavens, the temple will burn, and the gates will be cast open." This prophesy apparently came to pass in 2371, when three **silithium**-laden comet fragments ignited within the **Bajoran wormhole** (also known as the **Celestial Temple**), causing the wormhole to remain slightly open, shortly after the **Qui'al Dam** restored water to Janir city. ("Destiny" [DS9]). SEE: **Yarka.**

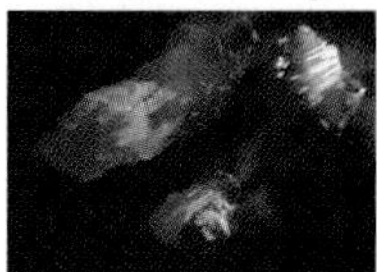

Trakor. Ancient **Bajoran** who encountered the **Orb of Change** 3,000 years ago and wrote several prophecies based on his visions. ("Destiny" [DS9]). SEE: **Trakor's Third Prophecy; Trakor's Fourth Prophecy**.

Tralesta. One of several clans of the **Acamarian** people. The Tralestas were all but wiped out in a massacre by their blood enemies, the **Lornak** clan, in 2286. One of the five surviving Tralestas, a woman named **Yuta**, underwent a biological alteration to slow her aging process so that she could exact revenge on the Lornaks. Over the next century, Yuta systematically tracked down and killed all the Lornaks with a genetically engineered **microvirus**. ("The Vengeance Factor" [TNG]).

Tranome Sar. Site of a battle between the Klingons and the Romulans. The father of an officer aboard the Klingon vessel ***Pagh*** was captured at Tranome Sar, but was not allowed to die. He later escaped and returned to the Klingon Homeworld, to await death in disgrace. ("A Matter of Honor" [TNG]).

"Transfigurations." *Next Generation* episode #73. Written by René Echevarria. Directed by Tom Benko. Stardate 43957.2. *First aired in 1990. Beverly Crusher saves a mysterious fugitive who is transforming into a noncorporeal energy being.* GUEST CAST: Mark LaMura as **Doe, John**; Charles Dennis as **Sunad**; Julie Warner as **Henshaw, Christi**; Colm Meaney as **O'Brien, Miles**; Patti Tippo as Temple, Nurse. SEE: **Crusher, Dr. Beverly; Doe, John; Henshaw, Christi; inaprovaline; motor assist bands; neurolink; noncorporeal life; O'Brien, Miles; protodynoplaser; Sunad; synaptic induction; Zalkon; Zalkonians; Zeta Gelis Cluster**.

transmuter. A thought-conversion device used by the extra-galactic life-forms **Korob** and **Sylvia**. The transmuter resembled a small wand, and served as a director or amplifier, converting their thoughts into physical matter or powerfully convincing images. Using the transmuter, Korob and Sylvia were able to create illusional humanoid forms for themselves, and were able to capture crew members from the *Starship Enterprise*. The transmuter was destroyed by Captain Kirk in order to permit himself and his crew to escape, whereupon Korob and Sylvia died. ("Catspaw" [TOS])

transparent aluminum. Optically clear, structurally rigid material used for construction in the 23rd century. Transparent aluminum was first devised in 1986 by Dr. **Nichols**, a scientist at **Plexicorp** in San Francisco. Nichols apparently had some assistance from time-traveling Starfleet personnel in making the invention. *(Star Trek IV: The Voyage Home).*

transpectral sensor array. Instrument that could theoretically penetrate the plasma storm interference of the **Badlands**. In the **mirror universe**, **Jennifer Sisko (mirror)** was building a transpectral sensor array to enable the **Alliance** to find the bases of the **Terran resistance** located in the Badlands. She abandoned development of the array after she was persuaded to join the rebellion by the Benjamin Sisko from our universe. ("Through the Looking Glass" [DS9]).

transponder, emergency. Small device designed to permit starship personnel to locate a landing party or away team member under emergency situations. Subcutaneous transponders made from **rubindium crystals** were injected into Kirk and Spock when they went to planet Ekos in 2267. ("Patterns of Force" [TOS]). Worf gave Riker a handheld emergency transponder when he was assigned to the Klingon ship *Pagh*. ("A Matter of Honor" [TNG]). Subspace transponders enabled personnel to be located across dimensional barriers. ("Emanations" [VGR]). In 2371 while investigating planet Avery III, subspace transponders were deployed to track the away team's movements. ("Faces" [VGR]). SEE: **boridium pellet.**

transport scrambler. Device that prevents transporters from functioning. Klingon forces used transport scramblers on Ajilon Prime to force the Federation to use easily-targeted hoppers to relocate troops. ("Nor the Battle to the Strong" [DS9]).

transport, near-warp. Term used to describe use of the transporter at relativistic speeds (near the speed of light). A somewhat disconcerting experience to those being transported. The *Enterprise*-D used this technique to transport an away team to Gravesworld while en route to an emergency rendezvous with the ***U.S.S. Constantinople***. ("The Schizoid Man" [TNG]).

Transporter Code 14. Command for an object to be dematerialized, then immediately rematerialized in a dissociated condition, effectively destroying the object. Captain Picard used Transporter Code 14 to destroy the fabled ***Tox Uthat*** at **Risa** in 2366. ("Captain's Holiday" [TNG]).

Transporter Theory. A class taught at Starfleet Academy. **Reginald Barclay** studied Transporter Theory under Dr. Olafson. ("Realm of Fear" [TNG]).

transporter carrier wave. A subspace signal through which a transporter beam is propagated. Romulan transporters, with minor adjustments, can reassemble the carrier wave of a Starfleet transporter. ("Data's Day" [TNG]).

transporter ID trace. A computer record maintained by a Federation starship's transporter system, recording the identity of all transport subjects. The transporter ID trace provided a useful means of verifying whether or not a person has actually been beamed. ("Unnatural Selection" [TNG], "Remember Me" [TNG]). Data and Dr. Beverly Crusher compared **Ambassador T'Pel's** transporter ID trace to her "remains," left on the transporter pad after her apparent death in 2367. The single-bit errors discovered by this comparison proved the remains were not those of the ambassador. ("Data's Day" [TNG]).

transporter psychosis. Rare medical disorder caused by a breakdown of neurochemical molecules during transport. Transporter psychosis was first diagnosed in 2209 by researchers on planet Delinia II. The condition affected the body's motor functions, as well as autonomic systems and higher brain functions. Victims were found to suffer from paranoid delusions, multi-infarct dementia, tactile and visual hallucinations, and psychogenic hysteria. Peripheral symptions included sleeplessness, accelerated heart rate, myopia, muscular spasms, and dehydration. The problem was eliminated around 2319 with the development of the multiplex **pattern buffer**. Lieutenant **Reginald Barclay**, suffering from acute fear of transporting, believed he might have been experiencing transporter psychosis. ("Realm of Fear" [TNG]).

transporter sensor log. Aboard Federation starships, a component of the transporter system that records transporter activity. In 2370, following the disappearance of Dr. Beverly Crusher and Captain Jean-Luc Picard during a routine transport, the transporter sensor log revealed an unusual concentration of **antigraviton** particles in the emitter coil. This led to the discovery that they had been kidnapped by the **Prytt**, who used a tractor beam to deflect the transporter beam into Prytt territory. ("Attached" [TNG]).

transporter shock. Rare phenomenon wherein a person experiences dizziness, headaches and disorientation after being transported. The effects of transporter shock wore off quickly, and this condition was usually the result of a transporter malfunction. ("Past Tense, Part I" [DS9]). SEE: **transporter psychosis**.

transporter targeting components. Aboard Federation starships, a subsystem of the **transporter** that is responsible for determining the exact coordinates of the materialization site. In 2370, following the disappearance of *Enterprise*-D Captain Jean-Luc Picard and Dr. Beverly Crusher during a routine transport, the targeting components were suspected as a possible cause, although later testing exonerated them. ("Attached" [TNG]).

transporter test article. A cylinder of **duranium** about one meter tall and 25 centimeters in diameter, used to test transporter performance by beaming the article away and then back to a transporter pad, or simply beaming it between pads. ("Hollow Pursuits" [TNG]). *The transporter test article prop was made from a Navy sonobuoy casing. The same shape was used for quite a number of props in* Star Trek: The Next Generation *and in the* Star Trek *movies.*

transporter, emergency. Short-range transporter aboard a starship used for evacuation purposes. The emergency transporters on the *Starship Voyager* had a range of less than ten kilometers. ("Future's End, Part I" [VGR]).

transporter. Matter-energy conversion device used to provide a convenient means of transportation. The transporter briefly converts an object or person into energy, beams that energy to another location, then reassembles the subject into its original form. ("The Cage" [TOS]). Transporters are unable to function when deflector shields are operational. ("Arena" [TOS]). Mark V and Mark VI transporters (which ceased being produced in 2356) were unsafe for the transport of unstable bio-matter. This problem was corrected in the more recent Mark VII units. ("Family Business" [DS9]). SEE: **annular confinement beam; autosequencers; beam; biofilter, transporter; emergency transporter armbands; food replicators; Heisenberg compensator; intraship beaming; ionizer, transporter; Kyle, Mr.; matter stream; molecular imaging scanner; O'Brien, Miles; pattern buffer; pattern enhancer; pattern lock; phase transition coils; phased matter; rematerialization subroutine; replicator; shuttle escape transporter; site-to-site transport; transport, near-warp; transporter carrier wave; transporter ID trace; transporter psychosis; transporter test article; Transporter Theory**. *The transporter was Gene Roddenberry's solution to the television production problem of how to get his characters from the starship down to a planet's surface. Landing a huge spaceship every week would have cost far too much for a television budget, but the transporter provided an ingenious means of getting the characters quickly (and inexpensively) into the midst of the action. Even though* Star Trek*'s visual effects budgets and techniques have improved to the point where a starship can occasionally land ("The 37s" [VGR]), the transporter still remains the landing system of choice.*

transtator. Key element of Federation technology, used in virtually every piece of Starfleet equipment. Dr. McCoy accidentally left his **communicator** behind on planet **Sigma Iotia II** in 2268, and it was believed possible that the **Iotians** would figure out how the transtator worked. ("A Piece of the Action" [TOS], "Trials and Tribble-ations" [DS9]). Even after the advent of **isolinear optical chip** and **bioneural gel pack** technology in the 24th century, transtator components continued to serve a critical role in Starfleet hardware. Harry Kim occasionally performed transtator assembly diagnostics on *Voyager*'s systems. ("Time and Again" [VGR]).

transwarp. In **subspace** physics, a velocity equalling warp 10, unattainable under normal **warp** theory. An object traveling at transwarp velocity would theoretically be moving infinitely fast, and would therefore in principle be occupying all points in the universe simultaneously. Controlling the point of exit from

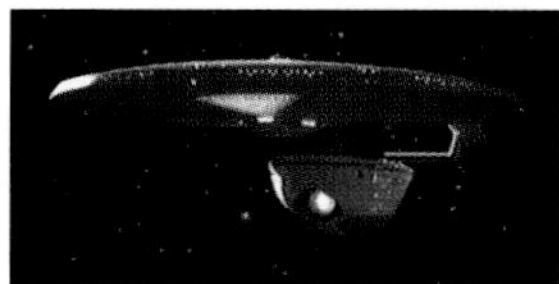

transwarp, and therefore the destination point in normal space, remains a significant unknown to Federation science. ("Threshold" [VGR]). The ***Starship Excelsior*** was launched in 2284 as a testbed for transwarp technology, although the experiment eventually proved a failure. *(Star Trek III: The Search for Spock).* It was not until 2372 that Lieutenant **Tom Paris**, aboard the *Shuttlecraft Cochrane*, became the first human to pilot a ship that could attain transwarp speeds. Unfortunately, transwarp velocity was shown to have extremely dangerous effects on living beings. ("Threshold" [VGR]). The **Borg**, however, had apparently solved these problems, because they used sophisticated transwarp conduits in 2369, allowing their ships to travel at least 20 times faster than normal warp-powered vessels. The Borg used their transwarp conduits to permit their ships to reach Federation space with little or no advance warning. ("Descent, Part I" [TNG]). Personnel aboard the Starship Enterprise-D devised a means to activate the Borg transwarp conduits, and used them to pursue a Borg ship. ("Descent, Part II" [TNG]).

tranya. Beverage served by **Balok** aboard the space vehicle ***Fesarius***. *Enterprise* Captain Kirk and officers McCoy and Bailey seemed to enjoy the stuff. ("The Corbomite Maneuver" [TOS]). Curzon Dax was also fond of the orange beverage, which he liked very cold. ("Facets" [DS9]). *(We like our* tranya *warm.)*

travel pod. Small shuttle vehicle used for inspection tours at Starfleet's orbital drydock facilities. Kirk and Scott rode to the *Enterprise* in a travel pod when the *Enterprise*'s transporters were not functional during the final preparations for the ship's departure to intercept the V'Ger entity in 2271. *(Star Trek: The Motion Picture,* also seen in *Star Trek II* and *Star Trek IV).*

Traveler. (Eric Menyuk). Humanoid from the distant planet **Tau Alpha C**. The Traveler possessed the ability to manipulate a previously unsuspected relationship among space, time, and thought, serving as a "lens," focusing the energies of thought in himself and others. Those energies could be translated into reality, although 24th-century science has yet to grasp these principles. He was a student of humanoid behavior, and sought passage on Federation ships as a means of observing humans, posing as an assistant to Starfleet propulsion specialist **Kosinski**. When the Traveler and Kosinski were aboard the *Enterprise*-D, a slight miscalculation caused the Traveler to send the ship first to Galaxy M-33, then an even greater extragalactic distance. During that time, the Traveler befriended young **Wesley Crusher** and encouraged Picard to support Crusher's unusual talents in mathematics, engineering, and science. ("Where No One Has Gone Before" [TNG]). The Traveler returned to the *Enterprise*-D in 2367 when a **static warp bubble**, accidentally created by Wesley Crusher from Kosinski's equations, trapped Dr. Beverly Crusher in an alternate reality. The Traveler helped Wesley use his mental abilities to establish the stable gateway through which Beverly was able to return, just before the bubble collapsed. ("Remember Me" [TNG]). SEE: **warp field**. In 2370, the Traveler assumed the identity of **Lakanta,** a colonist on **Dorvan V**. In this guise he introduced Wesley Crusher to the concept of the **vision quest**, and helped Wes to see that he had a future not only beyond Starfleet, but beyond human reality as we know it. The Traveler offered to be his guide in this new plane of existence. ("Journey's End" [TNG]). *Along with Brent Spiner, Eric Menyuk was one of the two finalists for the role of Data in* Star Trek: The Next Generation. *He was so impressive that producers Rick Berman and Bob Justman brought him back for this role.*

Travers, Commodore. Commander of Federation outpost on planet **Cestus III** in 2267 before it was destroyed by the **Gorns**. Travers was known for his hospitality, so Kirk and his senior officers from the *Enterprise* eagerly accepted an apparent invitation from Travers for dinner at the outpost, just before learning that nearly everyone on Cestus III had been killed in the Gorn attack. ("Arena" [TOS]).

Trazko. (Robert MacKenzie). Male associate of **Pallra**. She hired him to intervene with Quark when he attempted to obtain a list of Bajoran collaborators in 2370. Trazko shot Quark, severely injuring him. He later tried to kill Quark in the station infirmary, and was apprehended. ("Necessary Evil" [DS9]).

Treaty of Algeron. Peace accord established between the United Federation of Planets and the **Romulan Star Empire** following the Tomed Incident of 2311. The Treaty of Algeron reaffirmed the **Romulan Neutral Zone**, violation of which by either side without adequate notification would be considered an act of war. ("The Defector" [TNG]). The Treaty of Algeron also forbids the Federation from developing or using **cloaking device** technology in its spacecraft. ("The *Pegasus*" [TNG]). *The first edition of this Encyclopedia assumed that the treaty was signed after the Romulan war in 2160, but "The* Pegasus*" (TNG) makes it clear that it was signed after the Tomed Incident.*

Treaty of Alliance. Agreement between the **United Federation of Planets** and the **Klingon Empire** ending the war between the two powers. The pact allows for mutual aid and defense against aggressors, but forbids interference in the internal affairs of either government. ("Redemption, Part I" [TNG]). *It is not clear if this treaty was established during the* ***Khitomer*** *conference of 2293, after the* ***Narendra III*** *incident of 2344, after the Khitomer rescue in 2346, or at some other point not yet established in an episode or film.*

Treaty of Armens. SEE: **Armens, Treaty of.**

Trefayne. (David Hillary Hughes). Member of the **Council of Elders** on planet **Organia.** Trefayne telepathically voiced happenings outside the council chambers on planet **Organia** in 2267. ("Errand of Mercy" [TOS]).

Trelane. (William Campbell). Life-form of unknown origin and extraordinary powers. Trelane kidnapped several *Enterprise* crew members in 2267. A tall, dashing humanoid male in appearance, Trelane was actually a small child from a civilization of **noncorporeal life-forms**. With his ability to change matter to energy at will, he created the planet **Gothos** and manufactured an elaborate façade of a Gothic castle from Earth. Trelane patterned himself after an 18th-century Earth squire. He toyed with the *Enterprise* personnel, eventually forcing his parents to keep him from making any more planets until he could learn not to be cruel to inferior life-forms. ("The Squire of Gothos" [TOS]). SEE: **Q**. *Actor William Campbell also played Koloth in "The Trouble*

with Tribbles" (TOS) and "Blood Oath" (DS9). The voice of Trelane's mother was provided by Barbara Babcock, who also played Mea 3 in "A Taste of Armageddon" (TOS); the voice of Isis, the cat, in "Assignment: Earth" (TOS); the voice of Commander Loskene in "The Tholian Web" (TOS); and Philana in "Plato's Stepchildren" (TOS). James Doohan (Scotty) provided the voice of Trelane's father.

Trellan crepes. Dish of thin egg pancakes prepared with mushrooms and spices. Neelix often made Trellan crepes for Kes, since they were her favorite meal. ("Tuvix" [VGR]).

Trellan crocodile. Large reptilian animal known for its strength and potential destructive abilities. ("Crossfire" [DS9]).

Trent. (Leonard J. Crowfoot). A citizen on planet **Angel One** who worked in 2364 as an assistant to **Beata**, leader of the planet's governing council. Like most males on the planet, Trent was submissive to the authority of the ruling female class. ("Angel One" [TNG]). *Leonard Crowfoot also played the preliminary android version of Lal in "The Offspring" (TNG).*

Trentin Fala. (Jennifer Savidge). Unofficial member of the **Shakaar resistance cell,** she spent the **Bajoran** occupation cleaning floors in a **Cardassian** records office in **Dahkur Province**. Fala passed on vital information for years without getting caught. She was killed on stardate 50416.2 with a **remat detonator** while beaming aboard a **runabout.** It was an act of vengeance by **Silaran Prin,** who was disfigured in an attack years earlier by the Shakaar cell on the residence of Gul **Pirak**. She had passed on details showing how to defeat the security system. ("The Darkness and the Light" [DS9]).

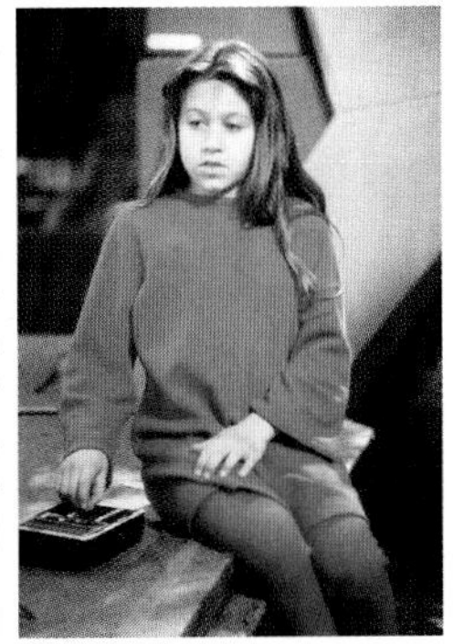

Tressa. (Tiffany Taubman). **Drayan** individual who, despite her advanced age of 96, looked and acted like what many other humanoid species would consider to be a young child. In 2372, Tressa and several other elder Drayans traveled to one of the Drayan moons in order to carry out their **final ritual**. Their shuttle crashed on the moon, and all of their **Attendants** died, leaving the elders alone. Lieutenant Tuvok, whose shuttle had also crashed there, comforted and took care of the easily confused Drayans. With Tuvok's help, Tressa faced her final ritual without fear, and she died of natural causes shortly thereafter. ("Innocence" [VGR]).

Trevean. (Michael Sarrazin). Inhabitant of a planet in the Teplan system located in the Gamma Quadrant. Trevean was a healer who helped people suffering from a planetwide disease known as the blight. When the disease reached terminal stage, Trevean prescribed a poison that ended the patient's life in dignity. Trevean was highly skeptical of Julian Bashir's efforts to develop a treatment for the blight, but delighted in Bashir's eventual success in finding a means to inoculate the next generation. SEE: **Teplan blight.** ("The Quickening" [DS9]).

tri-magnesite. Chemical that, combined with trevium, can produce an intensely bright light, rivaling that of a star. Tri-magnesite satellites were considered for use at planet **Deneva** in 2267 for eradication of the **Denevan neural parasites**, but a more limited spectrum of light was found to be preferable. ("Operation: Annihilate!" [TOS]). SEE: **ultraviolet satellite**.

tri-ox compound. Medication used to help a humanoid patient breathe more easily in a thin or oxygen-deprived atmosphere. When Kirk faced hand-to-hand combat with Spock on **Vulcan** in 2267, McCoy said he would administer tri-ox to Kirk to help him compensate for the thin Vulcan atmosphere. However, McCoy gave Kirk a neural paralyzer. ("Amok Time" [TOS]). *McCoy also administered tri-ox in "The Tholian Web" (TOS).* Lieutenant Tuvok administered a tri-ox compound in 2373 to the passengers of an orbital tether carriage. ("Rise" [VGR]).

Triacus. Class-M planet surveyed by the **Starnes Expedition** in 2268. The explorers unearthed an evil entity that drove the adult members of the colony to commit mass suicide. According to legend, Triacus was the home to a band of marauders who attacked the inhabitants of **Epsilon Indi**. After many centuries, the marauders were destroyed by those they had attempted to conquer. The legend also warned the essence of those destroyed would live again to do evil throughout the galaxy. ("And the Children Shall Lead" [TOS]). SEE: **Gorgan**.

triadium. Metallic compound. Triadium was a component of one of the artificial asteroids sent towards a **Nezu** colony world by the **Etanian Order**. ("Rise" [VGR]).

"Trials and Tribble-ations." *Deep Space Nine* episode #103. Teleplay by Ronald D. Moore & René Echevarria. Story by Ira Steven Behr & Hans Beimler & Robert Hewitt Wolfe. Based on "The Trouble With Tribbles" by David Gerrold. Directed by Jonathan West. No stardate given. *First aired in 1996. A special episode produced in celebration of* Star Trek's *30th anniversary. The crew of Deep Space 9 goes back in time, where they encounter Captain James T. Kirk and the original* Starship Enterprise *at Space Station K-7. Sisko and company must prevent a renegade Klingon agent from killing the legendary starship captain. "Trials and Tribble-ations" featured footage from "The Trouble With Tribbles" (TOS), plus visual effects and re-created sets that allowed characters from both shows to interact. David Gerrold, author of the original "Trouble With Tribbles," made a cameo appearance in this episode as a security guard in the corridors of the* Enterprise. *"Trials and Tribble-ations" was nominated for a Hugo Award for Best Dramatic Presentation at the 1997 World Science Fiction Convention.* GUEST CAST: Jack Blessing as **Dulmer**; James W. Jansen as **Lucsly**; Charlie Brill as **Darvin, Arne**; Leslie Ackerman as Waitress; Charles S. Chun as Engineer; Dierdre L. Imershien as **Watley, Lieutenant**. ACTORS APPEARING IN THE ORIGINAL *STAR TREK* EPISODE: William Shatner as **Kirk, James T.**; Leonard Nimoy as **Spock**; DeForest Kelley as **McCoy, Dr. Leonard H.**; James Doohan as **Scott, Montgomery**; Nichelle Nichols as **Uhura**; Walter Koenig as **Chekov, Pavel A**; Stanley Adams as **Jones, Cyrano**; Paul Baxley as **Freeman, Ensign**; Whit Bissell as **Lurry, Mr.**; Charlie Brill as **Darvin, Arne**; Michael Pataki as **Korax**; Guy Raymond as Trader/bartender; David Ross as Guard; William Schallert as **Baris, Nilz**. SEE: **Bashir, Julian; Cardassians; chroniton; Darvin, Arne; Dax, Emony; Deep Space Station K-7; Dulmer; duotronics; Elementary Temporal Mechanics; Federation Department of Temporal Investigations; fish juice; *Gr'oth, I.K.S.*; Hall of Warriors; kevas; Kirk, James T.; Klingons; Koloth; *Lexington, U.S.S.*; Lucsly; McCoy, Leonard H.; Orb of Time; Orb; predestination paradox; *raktajino*; sensors; Sisko, Benjamin; Starfleet General Orders and Regulations; Tarkalean tea; transtator; tribble; tricobalt explosive; tricorder; trillium; Waddle, Barry; Watley, Lieutenant.**

Trialus star system. Planetary system in the Gamma Quadrant. The ***Starship Defiant*** detected gravimetric distortions in the Trialus system on stardate 48423.2, shortly before planet **Meridian** appeared. ("Meridian" [DS9]).

triangular envelopment. A classic attack posture in which three spacecraft surround an enemy vessel at points describing the vertices of an equilateral triangle. Triangular envelopment was used by **Talarian** forces when threatening the *Enterprise*-D in 2367. ("Suddenly Human" [TNG]).

trianic energy beings. Noncorporeal life-forms. Trianic energy beings known as the **Komar** lived in a dark-matter nebula in the Delta Quadrant. ("Cathexis" [VGR]).

trianoline. Pharmaceutical sometimes prescribed for percussive injuries. ("Caretaker" [VGR]).

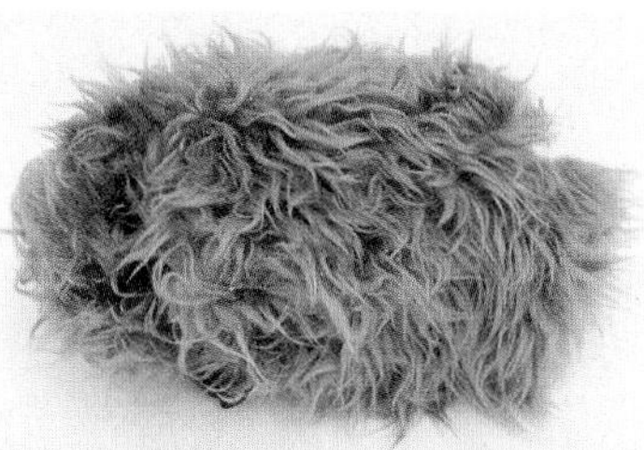

tribble. Soft, furry, warm-blooded animal. Tribbles were sold as pets by interstellar trader **Cyrano Jones**. Tribbles are hermaphroditic and capable of reproducing at prodigious rates, although they will stop breeding when food is withdrawn. Cyrano Jones gave a tribble to Lieutenant Uhura at **Deep Space Station K-7** in 2267. When Uhura returned to the *Enterprise* with her new pet, the tribble quickly multiplied until its offspring nearly overran the ship. Tribbles also multiplied on Station K-7, somehow finding their way into storage compartments containing a valuable grain called **quadrotriticale**. The grain had been poisoned by a Klingon spy, a fact revealed when many of the tribbles were found dead. The remaining tribbles on K-7 were presumably removed by Cyrano Jones, while Scotty beamed the tribbles from the *Enterprise* to the Klingon ship, where he expected them to be "no tribble at all." ("The Trouble with Tribbles" [TOS]). The **Klingons** considered tribbles to be an ecological menace, a plague to be wiped out. In the latter part of the 23rd century, hundreds of Klingon warriors were sent to track them down throughout the galaxy. An armada obliterated the tribble homeworld, and by the end of the 23rd century, tribbles were believed to have been eradicated. The extinction of the tribbles was reversed in 2373 when some live specimens were transported from the past aboard the *Starship Defiant* to **Deep Space 9**. ("Trials and Tribble-ations" [DS9]). *Tribbles were also seen in the bar visited by McCoy in* Star Trek III.

"Tribunal." *Deep Space Nine* episode #45. Written by Bill Dial. Directed by Avery Brooks. Stardate 47944.2. *First aired in 1994. O'Brien becomes a victim of the Cardassian court system, where the accused is always guilty.* GUEST CAST: Rosalind Chao as **O'Brien**, **Keiko**; Caroline Lagerfelt as **Makbar**; John Beck as **Boone**, **Raymond**; Richard Poe as **Evek**, **Gul**; Fritz Weaver as **Kovat**; Majel Barrett as Computer voice. SEE: **archon; Boone, Raymond; Cardassia; Cardassian Articles of Jurisprudence; Cardassian Bureau of Identification; Evek, Gul; *Hideki*-class Cardassian starship; Kovat; ladarium; Makbar; nestor; Odo; offender; *Prokofiev, U.S.S.;* public conservator; *Valdemar, U.S.S;* Volon III; weapons locker.**

triceron. An explosive compound. The bomb used to disrupt the ***Sonchi*** ceremony aboard **K'mpec**'s ship employed a triceron derivative. ("Reunion" [TNG]).

triclenidil. One of several chemicals used by the **Angosians** during the **Tarsian War** to "improve" their soldiers, making them more effective in combat. Unfortunately, the effects of many of these drugs were irreversible. ("The Hunted" [TNG]). SEE: **Danar, Roga**.

tricobalt explosive. Energy weapon in the war between planets **Vendikar** and **Eminiar VII** that ended in 2267. None of these devices were used for some five hundred years, but simulations of them were used in the computer war between the two planets. A mathematical attack launched by Vendikar on Eminiar VII in 2267 was based on a simulation of a tricobalt satellite. The original *Starship Enterprise* was declared a casualty of that attack. ("A Taste of Armageddon" [TOS]). Kathryn Janeway used several tricobalt devices to destroy the **Caretaker**'s **Array** in 2371, to prevent the Kazon-Ogla from gaining control of the station. ("Caretaker" [VGR]). **Arne Darvin**, in 2267, used a tiny tricobalt explosive device hidden in a **tribble** in an attempt to murder James Kirk. The bomb was discovered by Benjamin Sisko and Jadzia Dax, and it was beamed into space, where it exploded harmlessly. ("Trials and Tribble-ations" [DS9]).

tricorder operations manual. Instructional guide to Starfleet tricorders. ("Phage" [VGR]). *A detailed explanation of tricorder operations can be found in* Star Trek: The Next Generation Technical Manual *by Rick Sternbach and Michael Okuda*.

tricorder uplink. Information exchange transmission protocol used to send data between a tricorder in the field and a remote computer system or other tricorder. ("Future's End, Part II" [VGR]).

tricorder. Multipurpose scientific and technical instrument. Developed for **Starfleet**, the tricorder incorporated sensors, computers, and recorders in a convenient, portable form. ("The Naked Time" [TOS]). Several models of tricorders have been used by starship crews over the years. All of them have featured state-of-the-art sensing technology, and have been an essential part of starship missions and operations. Jadzia Dax was particularly fond of the classic design style of the 23rd-century tricorder, and she used to own one herself. ("Trials and Tribble-ations" [DS9]. Specialized tricorders are available for specific engineering, scientific, and medical applications. In 2366, standard-issue Starfleet tricorders were unable to detect subspace phenomena. ("The Bonding" [TNG]). They were also incapable of sensing neutrino emissions. ("The Enemy" [TNG]). The presence of **thoron** particles could interfere with a tricorder scan. The **Maquis** used to evade tricorder searches by using portable thoron generators. ("Basics, Part II" [VGR]). *The original series version of the tricorder was designed and built by Wah Chang. Some of the variations of this design used in the feature films were designed or built by Brick Price and Bill George. The tricorders in* Star Trek: The Next Generation, Star Trek: Deep Space Nine, *and* Star Trek: Voyager *were designed by Rick Sternbach.*

tricordrazine. A powerful neurostimulant drug usually administered subcutaneously by hypospray. Tricordrazine treatment was successfully used by Dr. Pulaski to stimulate neural activity in William Riker when he had suffered neural injury on an away mission at planet **Surata IV.** ("Shades of Gray" [TNG]). *Tricordrazine was presumably based on* ***cordrazine****, the drug that sent McCoy on a paranoid flight in "The City on the Edge of Forever" (TOS).*

tricyanate. A purple crystalline substance that occurs naturally on planet **Beta Agni II**. Toxic to humanoids, tricyanate contamination was found in the water supply of the Beta Agni II colony in 2366, an incident later found to have been engineered by **Zibalian** trader **Kivas Fajo**. ("The Most Toys" [TNG]).

Trieste, U.S.S. A *Merced*-class Federation starship, Starfleet registry number NCC-37124. The *Trieste* was stationed near Starbase 74 and was unable to render assistance when the *Enterprise*-D was hijacked by the **Bynars** in 2364. The *Trieste* was some 66 hours away at the time. ("11001001" [TNG]). Data served aboard the *Trieste* prior to his assignment to the *Enterprise*-D. During Data's tour of duty on the *Trieste*, the ship once fell through a wormhole. ("Clues" [TNG]). *The* Trieste *was named for the bathyscaphe in which oceanographer Jacques Piccard (for whom Captain Picard was named) explored Earth's Marianas Trench in the 1960s.*

trigemic vapors. Aerosolized particles of proteins and amino acids. The atmosphere of **Planet Hell** had high concentrations of trigemic vapors, which caused severe humanoid skin irritation. ("Parturition" [VGR]).

trilaser connector. Medical instrument. Dr. McCoy used a trilaser connector to restore Spock's brain to his body on planet **Sigma Draconis VI** in 2268. ("Spock's Brain" [TOS]).

trilithium. Exotic chemical compound that acts as a powerful nuclear inhibitor. A few kilograms of trilithium, delivered into

Tricorders.

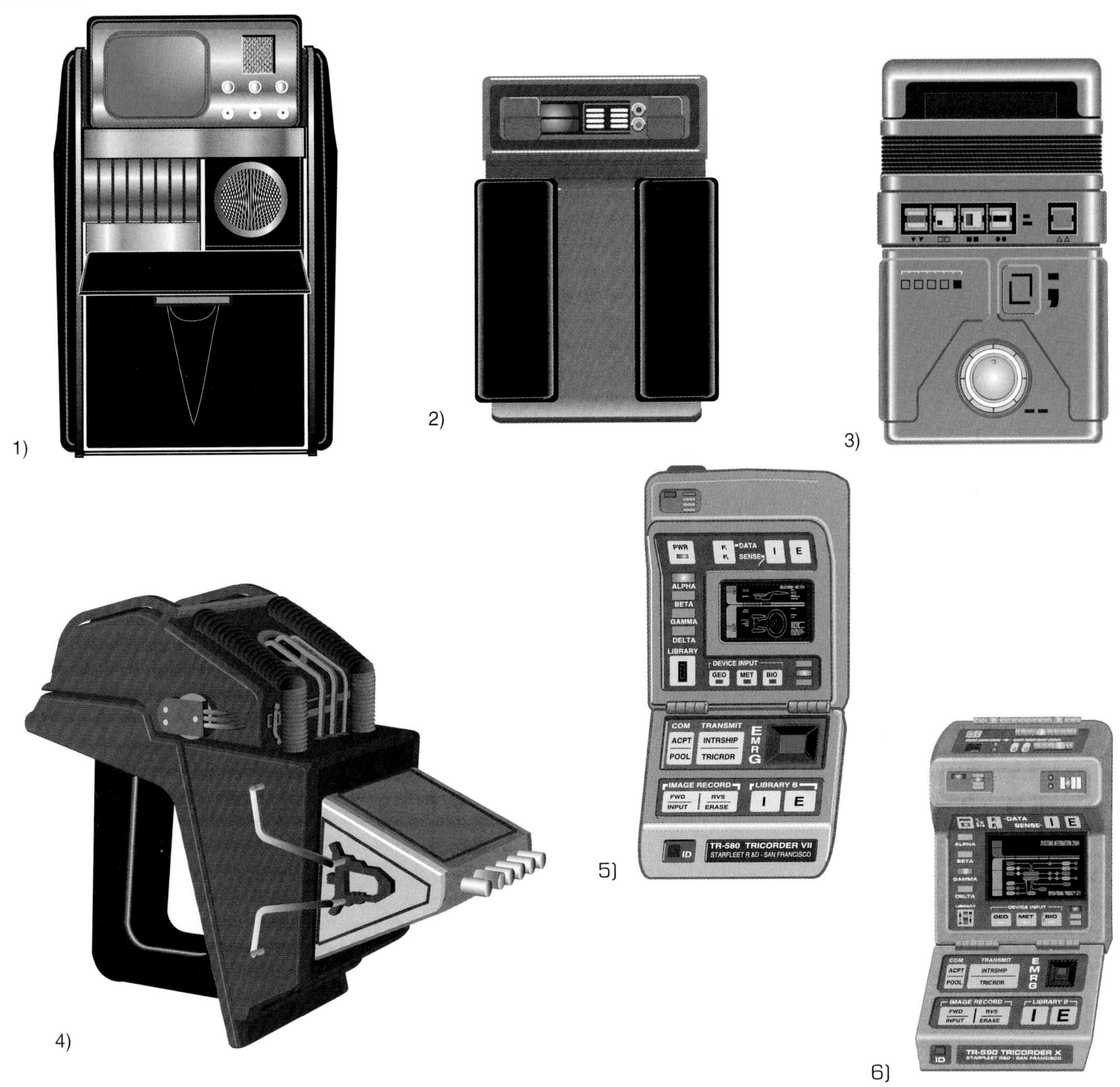

1) *Star Trek: The Original Series.* 2) *Star Trek: The Motion Picture.* 3) *Star Trek III: The Search for Spock.* 4) *Star Trek II: The Wrath of Khan.* 5) *Star Trek: The Next Generation.* 6) *Star Trek: Deep Space Nine, Star Trek: Voyager.*

the heart of a star, can generate a quantum implosion of sufficient force to halt all fusion reactions in the star. The resulting energy release would also destroy any planets in the star's system. Romulan scientists have studied trilithium, although as of 2371 no trilithium-based weapons had been reported. **Dr. Tolian Soran** stole quantities of trilithium from a Romulan research facility for use in his quest to return to the **nexus**. *(Star Trek Generations).* SEE: **Amargosa; Veridian system.** Trilithium resin is a highly toxic waste by-product created when **dilithium** is exposed to intense matter/antimatter reactions in a starship's warp engine core. The compound is extremely unstable and is generally regarded as useful only as an explosive. In 2369, a group of politically nonaligned terrorists sought to steal trilithium from the warp core of the *Enterprise*-D while the ship was docked at the **Remmler Array** at **Arkaria Base**. ("Starship Mine" [TNG]). Trilithium can be made from **paralithium.** On stardate 50156.2, a trilithium-based explosive device was used by the Delta Quadrant terrorist group known as Open Sky to bomb the Laktivia recreation facility on **Akritiri**, killing 47 off-duty patrollers. ("The Chute" [VGR]). In 2373, in order to convince **Michael Eddington** to give himself up, Benjamin Sisko fired quantum torpedoes containing 50 kilograms of trilithium resin into the atmosphere of **Solosos III**, a Maquis colony. This made the planet uninhabitable for at least 50 years. ("For the Uniform" [DS9]). In 2373, the changeling infiltrator who replaced Julian Bashir hijacked the *Yukon* in an attempted suicide mission to destroy the Bajoran sun with a trilithium explosive that also contained **tekasite** and **protomatter**. The *Defiant*, under the command of Kira Nerys, intercepted the *Yukon* and tractored it away from the sun. The trilithium explosive destroyed the *Yukon* and killed the changeling infiltrator. ("By Inferno's Light" [DS9]).

Trill homeworld. Class-M planet that is home to the joined species known as the **Trill.** ("Invasive Procedures" [DS9]). Interesting geological formations on the Trill homeworld include the Tenaran ice cliffs and the **caves of Mak'ala.** ("Equilibrium" [DS9]). The oceans on planet Trill are purple. ("Past Tense, Part I" [DS9]).

Trill Symbiosis Commission. Powerful Trill government body that oversees the testing, selection, and joining of **Trill** humanoid hosts with **symbionts**. The Symbiosis Commission maintained strict guidelines for those host candidates, as it was commonly believed that only one in a thousand Trill humanoids was capable of being **joined**, and to join an unsuitable host would result in rejection of the symbiont within a matter of days. ("Equilibrium" [DS9]). **Audrid Dax** was, at one time, head of the Symbiosis Commission. **Curzon Dax** also served on the Commission. ("Facets" [DS9]). *When **Jadzia Dax** fell ill in 2371, her friends learned that nearly half the Trill population was capable of being joined. This fact was concealed by the Symbiosis Commission for fear that the symbionts, available in limited numbers, would become commodities to be bought and sold. Dax's friends agreed to keep this secret in order to gain commission assistance to save her life.* SEE: **Dax, Joran.**

Trill. A joined species comprised of a humanoid **host** and a small vermiform **symbiont** that lives in an internal abdominal pocket of the host body. Most of the personality and memories of the Trill reside in the symbionts, which are extremely long-lived, although the host also contributes personality traits to the joined life-form. Upon the death of a host body, a Trill symbiont is usually transplanted into another host. ("The Host" [TNG]). For a joined Trill, nothing was more important than protecting the life of the symbiont. ("Rejoined" [DS9]).

Trill hosts enter voluntarily into their association with the symbiont, and in fact there is intense competition among potential hosts to determine who will be accorded this high honor. Only one Trill candidate in ten is chosen to be joined with a symbiont. The decision of who is to be allowed to be joined is the responsibility of the **Symbiosis Evaluation Board**. Improper joining is believed to cause damage to both host and symbiont. ("Invasive Procedures" [DS9]). SEE: **Trill Symbiosis Commission**. Children are directed by their parents towards becoming a host. While the influence of the **symbiont** is very strong, good host candidates can balance the influence of the symbiont with their own interests, and hence produce the best possible merge of the two personalities. ("Playing God" [DS9]).

Hosts are accepted into their mid-twenties. Once joined, the host and symbiont become biologically interdependent, and after 93 hours, neither can survive without the other. The resulting new joined life-form is considered to be another person, although it retains memories of previous joinings. ("The Host" [TNG], "Emissary" [DS9], "Dax" [DS9]). SEE: **Dax, Curzon; Dax, Jadzia** (*pictured*); **Kareel; Odan, Ambassador.** Despite the fact that a symbiont retains memories in subsequent joinings, Trill society very strongly disapproves of **reassociation** of subsequent hosts, in cases where previous hosts had been married. ("Rejoined" [DS9]). Trills' hands are naturally cold. Sometimes friendships with other species don't survive when the Trill moves to the next host. Trills are highly allergic to insect bites, as the toxins released interfere with the biochemical connections between the host and the symbiont. ("The Siege" [DS9]). Trill hosts sometimes have sexual feelings, but they do their best to rise above them, at least according to Jadzia Dax. ("A Man Alone" [DS9]). They do not have to uphold commitments of the previous hosts. ("Blood Oath" [DS9]). *Certain Trill symbionts can be severely damaged by beaming, which is why Odan insisted on using the shuttlecraft in "The Host" (TNG). Other Trills, including Jadzia Dax, don't seem to have the same problem.*

trillium 323. Mineral substance found on planet Caldonia. Negotiator **Devinoni Ral** arranged to acquire rights to the **Caldonians**' trillium 323 as part of the **Chrysalian** bid for the **Barzan wormhole** in 2366. ("The Price" [TNG]).

trillium. Gemstone traded on planet **Organia**. Spock posed as a trader dealing in kevas and trillium. ("Errand of Mercy [TOS]). **Arne Darvin**, in near-exile on Cardassia Prime in 2373, also posed as a dealer in trillium. ("Trials and Tribble-ations" (DS9).

trinimbic interference. Powerful energy disturbance in the upper atmosphere of a Class-L planet. Trinimbic interference can render sensors and transporters ineffective and can cause heavy atmospheric turbulence. ("The 37's" [VGR]).

trinitrogen chloride. Chemical. Trinitrogen chloride, also known as TNC, was used as a cleaning solution. TNC could also be used in some types of plasma grenades. The chambered plasma grenade used in an attempted assassination of Gul Dukat on station Terok Nor in 2367 contained TNC. ("Things Past" [DS9]).

triolic waves. By-product of an energy source employed by the beings on planet **Devidia II**. The energy source had deleterious effects on most living tissue, except for life-forms with **microcentrum cell membranes**. ("Time's Arrow, Part I" [TNG]).

Triona System. Star system located in a remote sector. The site of a Starfleet outpost to which **Lieutenant Keith Rocha** was assigned in 2369. While at the Triona System, Rocha was apparently killed by **coalescent organisms** that subsequently assumed his form. ("Aquiel" [TNG]).

trionic initiators. Component in starship **warp cores**. In rare circumstances, trionic initiators could create strange side-effects such as warp bubbles, subspace funnels, and other subspace deformations. ("Interface" [TNG]). SEE: **subspace phenomena; subspace technology**.

trionium. Chemical compound. Trionium was detected by *Enterprise*-D sensors in nebula **FGC-47**. ("Imaginary Friend" [TNG]).

tripamine. Biochemical substance. Tripamine can sometimes be detected as a residue in the cerebral cortex following a temporal shift. ("All Good Things..." [TNG]).

Tripoli, U.S.S. Federation starship, *Hokule'a* class, Starfleet registry number NCC-19386. The Tripoli was the ship that discovered the android **Data** at the remains of the Federation colony at **Omicron Theta** in 2338. The crew of the *Tripoli* activated Data, who later went on to become a member of Starfleet. ("Datalore" [TNG]). The *Tripoli* was decommissioned and was relegated to **Surplus Depot Zed-15** on planet **Qualor II**. In 2368, the *Tripoli* was stolen by Romulan operatives. ("Unification, Part I" [TNG]).

tripolymer composites. High-strength synthetic plastic compounds. Tripolymer composites were used in the construction of the android Data, who has about 24.6 kilograms of the material in his body. ("The Most Toys" [TNG]). Tripolymers are not electrically conductive. ("Disaster" [TNG]).

tripolymer plasma. Form of highly ionized matter used as a power source in the Automated Personnel Units built by the Pralor in the Delta Quadrant. ("Prototype" [VGR]).

triptacederin. Analgesic medication. Garak used triptacederin to combat the severe pain transmitted by his **cranial implant**. ("The Wire" [DS9]).

trisec. Measurement of time on planet **Triskelion**, approximately equal to three Earth seconds. ("The Gamesters of Triskelion" [TOS]).

Triskelion. Planet in the M24 Alpha, a trinary star system. The planet was ruled by three disembodied brains called **Providers**, who maintained a colony of humanoid slaves for gaming purposes. These slaves were freed in 2268. ("The Gamesters of Triskelion" [TOS]). SEE: **drill thralls**.

tritanium. Exotic metal alloy used in the construction of Federation spacecraft hulls. ("The Menagerie" [TOS], "Threshold" [VGR]).

tritium. Isotope of hydrogen with an atomic weight of 3. Low concentrations of tritium gas were used to trace particle flow to a dangerous **graviton field** buildup on station Deep Space 9 in 2369. Tritium gas is mildly radioactive and is hazardous when highly concentrated, but the amount used on the station was very small. ("Q-Less" [DS9]).

tritonium. Radioactive material. The Bajoran resistance used to carry subdermal implants of tritonium isotopes. In the event of capture, the implant could be tracked. ("Indiscretion" [DS9]).

Trixian bubble juice. Pink beverage. **Varis Sul** of **Paqu** ordered Trixian bubble juice at Quark's bar on Deep Space 9, then threw it in Quark's face after suffering a perceived insult. ("The Storyteller" [DS9]). Nog liked Trixian bubble juice. ("Prophet Motive" [DS9]).

Troglytes. Citizens of the planet **Ardana** who lived on the planet's surface, performing mining and other labor-intensive tasks that supported the privileged few who lived in the cloud city of Stratos. The Troglytes who worked in the mines were forced to breathe toxic **zenite** gas, resulting in impairment of mental processes. Troglyte political activists, known as **Disrupters**, forced the **Stratos** government in 2269 to recognize these hazardous working conditions and provide appropriate safety equipment. The Troglytes expressed an intent to win political and economic equality, as well. ("The Cloud Minders" [TOS])

Troi, Deanna. (Marina Sirtis). Counselor aboard the *U.S.S. Enterprise*-D under the command of Captain Jean-Luc Picard. ("Encounter at Farpoint" [TNG]). Daughter of **Lwaxana Troi** and **Ian Andrew Troi**, Deanna was betrothed to **Wyatt Miller** through the Betazoid custom of genetic bonding when they were both children. Deanna and Wyatt never married, though, because Wyatt chose to join the last surviving **Tarellians** in search of a cure for the Tarellian plague. ("Haven" [TNG]). When she was growing up, Deanna did not know that she had an older sister, **Kestra Troi**, who died when Deanna was only an infant. ("Dark Page" [TNG]).

Deanna's father used to read her heroic stories about the ancient American West on planet Earth, and she remained fond of these stories into her adulthood. ("A Fistful of Datas" [TNG]). SEE: ***Ancient West***; **Durango**. Troi studied psychology at the University of Betazed prior to her joining Starfleet. ("Tin Man" [TNG]).

While a psychology student on Betazed, Troi became romantically involved with Lieutenant **William T. Riker.** ("Ménage à Troi" [TNG]). Troi had hopes of a serious commitment between the two, but Riker's career plans took him away to an assignment aboard the ***U.S.S. Potemkin***. ("Encounter at Farpoint" [TNG], "Second Chances" [TNG]). Troi graduated from the academy (possibly having taken classes on Betazed) in 2359. ("Conundrum" [TNG]). Troi was once involuntarily impregnated by an unknown **noncorporeal life**-form. Troi named the child **Ian Andrew Troi**, after her late father. ("The Child" [TNG]).

(In an alternate **quantum reality** visited by Worf in 2370, Troi and Worf were married, and in another, the two were married and had two children. It was perhaps the knowledge that the two of them had a romantic relationship in other quantum universes that led Worf to pursue such a relationship in his own universe.) ("Parallels" [TNG]).

Troi suffered a brief loss of her empathic powers in 2367 from proximity to a newly discovered group of **two-dimensional creatures**. Although Troi found the loss disconcerting, she was pleased to discover that she could still function as ship's counselor without her Betazoid abilities. ("The Loss" [TNG]). Counselor Troi assumed temporary command of the *Enterprise*-D on stardate 45156 when the ship was disabled from collision with two **quantum filaments**. Troi, who held the rank of lieutenant commander, was the senior officer on the bridge at the time. ("Disaster" [TNG]). She later undertook the field training program for advancement to the rank of commander. She passed the **Bridge Officer Exam** and was promoted to full commander on stardate 47611. ("Thine Own Self" [TNG]).

Troi said she never met a chocolate she didn't like. ("The Price" [TNG], "The Game" [TNG]). In 2370, Troi was assigned as liaison officer for **Iyaaran** ambassador **Loquel**. Troi commented that the ambassador had tested even *her* limits for chocolate. ("Liaisons" [TNG]).

Deanna Troi was first seen in "Encounter at Farpoint" (TNG). Marina Sirtis originally auditioned for the part of Natasha Yar and was almost cast for the part, but Gene Roddenberry decided at the last moment to switch the roles of Yar and Troi between Sirtis and Denise Crosby.

Troi, Ian Andrew (II). (R. J. Williams, Zachary Benjamin). Son of *Enterprise*-D Counselor **Deanna Troi** after she was impregnated by a **noncorporeal life**-form entity in 2365. Ian Andrew appeared to have an identical genetic pattern to his half-human, half-Betazoid mother, but gestated and grew at a tremendously accelerated rate. The child was later found to be the effort of the energy lifeform to learn more about human life. Ian Andrew died at the apparent physiological age of about 8, but a chronological age of only a few days, when the energy entity learned it was emitting a form of radiation that seriously threatened the crew of the *Enterprise*. ("The Child" [TNG]).

Troi, Ian Andrew (senior). (Amick Byram). Human father of **Deanna Troi**, and husband to Betazoid Ambassador **Lwaxana Troi**. ("The Child" [TNG]). Ian Andrew Troi was a Starfleet officer who died when Deanna was seven. ("Dark Page" [TNG]).

Troi, Kestra. (Andreana Weiner). (2329-2336). Daughter of **Lwaxana** and **Ian Andrew Troi (senior)** and sister of Deanna Troi. Kestra Troi was born in 2329, a year after her parents' marriage. She died in a drowning accident when she was seven years old. Lwaxana blamed herself for her child's death and blocked the incident from her mind for over 30 years. As a result, Deanna Troi never learned that she had had an older sister until the memory resurfaced in her mother's mind in 2370. ("Dark Page" [TNG]). See: **Hedril**.

Troi, Lwaxana. (Majel Barrett). Ambassador for the government of **Betazed**, and **Deanna Troi**'s mother. Lwaxana Troi was daughter of the Fifth House, Holder of the Sacred Chalice of Rixx, Heir to the Holy Rings of Betazed. ("Haven" [TNG]). Lwaxana, a full Betazoid, married a Starfleet officer, **Ian Andrew Troi** ("The Child" [TNG]), and the couple had two children, Kestra and Deanna. Kestra died in 2336 in a swimming accident. Lwaxana suppressed the memory of her death until 2370. ("Dark Page" [TNG]). Her other daughter, Deanna Troi, became a Starfleet officer. Ian Troi died when Deanna was seven. ("Dark Page" [TNG]).

Lwaxana Troi became a full ambassador of Betazed in 2365, and represented her government at the **Pacifica** Conference in that year. At about that time, Troi entered what is known in Betazoid culture as **the phase**, during which a woman's sexuality matures and her sex drive quadruples. At one point during her phase, Troi had hoped to marry either Jean-Luc Picard or William Riker. ("Manhunt" [TNG]). In 2366, Troi was kidnapped by **DaiMon Tog** in an attempt to use her empathic powers for his personal gain. The ambassador was able to escape by convincing Tog that her "jealous lover" Picard would destroy Tog's ship if she was not returned. ("Ménage à Troi" [TNG]). Lwaxana became engaged to marry **Minister Campio** of planet **Kostolain** in 2368, but the wedding was canceled when Campio could not accept the traditional Betazoid custom of conducting the ceremony in the nude. ("Cost of Living" [TNG]). Something of a free spirit, Lwaxana enjoyed vacationing at the colorful **Parallax Colony** on planet **Shiralea VI**, where she was very fond of the mud baths. When she could not actually visit there, she indulged in a holodeck re-creation of the colony. ("Cost of Living" [TNG]).

Ambassador Troi paid an official visit to **Deep Space 9** in 2371 as the Betazoid representative to the **Bajoran Gratitude Festival**. Troi did not realize that she was suffering from **Zanthi fever**, which caused her to project amorous emotions onto several station personnel. ("Fascination" [DS9]). Lwaxana married a **Tavnian** man, **Jeyal**, in 2371, and subsequently became pregnant with his son. Troi rebelled against Tavnian tradition when she refused to acquiesce to Jeyal's wish to have her son taken from her at birth to be raised among men only. Troi returned to Deep Space 9, where she sought the protection of her friend, Odo. Lwaxana and Odo wed in a traditional Tavnian marriage ceremony, thereby nullifying Jeyal's claim upon his unborn son. Not wishing to further inconvenience Odo, Lwaxana returned to **Betazed** to have her child. ("The Muse" [DS9]). *Majel Barrett, the widow of* Star Trek *creator Gene Roddenberry, also played Number One in the first* Star Trek *pilot, "The Cage" (TOS), as well as Nurse Christine Chapel. Barrett also lent her voice to the* U.S.S. Enterprise *computer, the Companion ("Metamorphosis" [TOS]), and the Beta 5 computer ("Assignment: Earth" [TOS]). Lwaxana Troi's first appearance was in "Haven" (TNG). She also appeared in "The Forsaken" (DS9).*

trombone. Ancient Earth musical instrument enjoyed by William Riker on the *Enterprise*-D. Riker was an enthusiastic amateur musician who liked to practice during his off-duty hours. ("11001001" [TNG]). He also gave occasional performances to his crew mates in the Ten-Forward Lounge. William Riker gave his favorite trombone to his newly discovered twin, **Thomas Riker**, in 2369, just before Thomas transferred to the ***U.S.S. Gandhi***. ("Second Chances" [TNG]).

troposphere. Region of a **Class-M planet**'s atmosphere nearest the surface. ("Rise" [VGR]).

"Trouble With Tribbles, The." Original Series episode #42. Written by David Gerrold. Directed by Joseph Pevney. Stardate 4523.3. *First aired in 1967. Tribbles are unbelievably cute, but the trouble is that they reproduce at an amazing rate. "The Trouble With Tribbles" was nominated for a Hugo Award for Best Dramatic Presentation at the 1968 World Science Fiction Convention. In 1996, Paramount Pictures paid tribute to the 30th anniversary of* Star Trek *with a special episode of* Star Trek: Deep Space Nine, *entitled "Trials and Tribble-ations" (DS9), in which Ben Sisko and company went back in time to revisit the events of "The Trouble With Tribbles." "Trials and Tribble-ations" suggested that stardate 4523 was a Friday, mainly because the original episode had first aired on a Friday night in December, 1967.* GUEST CAST: William Schallert as **Baris, Nilz**; William Campbell as **Koloth, Captain**; Stanley Adams as **Jones, Cyrano**; Whit Bissell as **Lurry, Mr.**; Michael Pataki as **Korax**; Ed Reimers as Fitzpatrick, Admiral; Charlie Brill as **Darvin, Arne**; Paul Baxley as **Freeman, Ensign**; David L. Ross as Guard; Guy Raymond as Trader/bartender; Eddie Paskey as Security guard; Jay Jones as Scott's stunt double; Jerry Summers as Chekov's stunt double; Phip Adams as Korax's stunt double; Bob Miles, Bob Orrison, Dick Crockett, Richard Antoni, Klingon stunt doubles. SEE: **Antarian glow water; Baris, Nilz; Burke, John; Code 1 Emergency; credit; Darvin, Arne; Deep Space Station K-7; Denebian slime devil; Donatu V, Battle of; food slot; Freeman, Ensign; *Gr'oth, I.K.S.;* Jones, Cyrano; Klingonese; Koloth, Captain; Korax; Lurry, Mr.; Organian Peace Treaty; quadrotriticale; Regulan blood worms; Sherman's Planet; Spican flame gem; tribble.**

Troyians. Humanoid civilization from planet **Troyius.** The Troyians had been at war with the neighboring planet **Elas** for many years. A marriage between the ruler of Troyius and the **Dohlman** of Elas was arranged in 2268 as a means of bringing peace to the two worlds. ("Elaan of Troyius" [TOS]).

Troyius, Elaan of. SEE: **Elaan**.

Troyius. Class-M planet in the **Tellun star system**, homeworld to the **Troyian** people. Troyius was a plentiful source of naturally occurring **dilithium** crystals, making the planet of considerable strategic interest to the Klingon Empire in 2268. ("Elaan of Troyius" [TOS]).

Trudy series. Android model designed by Harry Mudd. ("I, Mudd" [TOS]).

True Way, The. A **Cardassian** separatist group opposed to the peace treaty between Cardassia and Bajor. The True Way blamed the Federation for Cardassia's economic and political troubles. In 2372 the True Way committed their first terrorist action in support of their beliefs by sabotaging the warp core of the Federation runabout *Orinoco*. ("Our Man Bashir" [DS9]). Within weeks, the group succeeded in assassinating two Bajoran officials. An operative of the True Way attempted to assassinate First Minister **Shakaar Edon** on Deep Space 9 in 2372 during his meetings with Federation delegates. ("Crossfire" [DS9]).

"True-Q." *Next Generation* episode #132. Written by René Echevarria. Directed by Robert Scheerer. Stardate 46192.3. *First aired in 1992. Q torments a young woman who doesn't realize she's a member of the Q Continuum.* GUEST CAST: Olivia d'Abo as **Rogers, Amanda**; John P. Connolly as **Lote, Orn**; John de Lancie as **Q**. SEE: **Argolis Cluster; baristatic filter; Bilaren system; Ogawa, Nurse Alyssa; Lote, Orn; Q Continuum; Q; Rogers, Amanda; Tagra IV; Tagrans; weather modification net.**

Truman, Harry S (1884-1972). Thirty-third President of the United States of America on **Earth**. Truman served as chief executive of the American nation from 1945 to 1953. When an extraterrestrial spacecraft of Ferengi origin was captured by American military forces near **Roswell**, New Mexico, in 1947, Truman ordered **General Rex Denning** to conduct a full investigation because of the potential threat to national security. ("Little Green Men" [DS9]).

tryoxene. Naturally-occurring material. Tryoxene was a component of one of the artificial asteroids sent towards a **Nezu** colony world by the **Etanian Order**. ("Rise" [VGR]).

tryptophan-lysine distillates. Medication. **Dr. Katherine Pulaski** prescribed tryptophanlysine distillates for treatment of a flu virus. She also prescribed generous doses of PCS—Pulaski's Chicken Soup. ("The Icarus Factor" [TNG]).

tsetse fly. Any of a group of small flies indigenous to the continent of Africa on Earth. The insect was noted for transmitting African sleeping sickness. ("Ship in a Bottle" [TNG]).

Tsingtao, Ray. (Brian Tochi). One of the surviving children of the **Starnes Expedition** whose parents committed suicide on planet **Triacus** in 2268. In the aftermath of the tragedy, young Tsingtao was controlled by the **Gorgan**. ("And the Children Shall Lead" [TOS]). *Many years after Brian Tochi's appearance as Ray Tsingtao in the Original Series, Tochi appeared as Ensign Peter Lin, an* Enterprise*-D crew member, in "Night Terrors" (TNG).*

***Tsiolkovsky*, U.S.S.** Federation science vessel, ***Oberth* class,** Starfleet registry NCC-53911. The *Tsiolkovsky* had been on a routine science mission monitoring the collapse of a red super giant star into a white dwarf in 2364 when the entire crew of 80 became infected with a variant of the **Psi 2000 virus**. All ship's personnel died from the effects of the virus. ("The Naked Now" [TNG]). *The* Tsiolkovsky *was named for Russian space pioneer Konstantin Tsiolkovsky. The ship miniature was a redress of the* **Grissom** *from* Star Trek III. *The dedication plaque for the ship bore a quote from Tsiolkovsky: "The Earth is the cradle of the mind, but one cannot remain in the cradle forever."*

tube grubs. Ferengi delicacy, worms eaten while the creatures are still alive. Tube grubs are best when served dank and musty. ("Family Business" [DS9]). The Ferengi **Zek** complimented Quark on the chilled tube grubs at a dinner given to honor the **grand nagus** on Deep Space 9 in 2369. ("The Nagus" [DS9]). Tube grubs were also served in Zek's honor when he visited the station in 2370. ("Rules of Acquisition" [DS9]). In 2372, Joseph Sisko considered offering Cajun-style tube grubs at **Sisko's**, his restaurant in New Orleans. ("Homefront" [DS9]).

Tula. (Brioni Farrel). Inhabitant of planet **Beta III** during the end of **Landru**'s rule in 2267. Tula, the daughter of **Reger**, was assaulted by **Bilar** during the **Red Hour**, a festival of uncontrolled violence and lust. ("Return of the Archons" [TOS]).

tulaberry wine. Beverage originating in the Gamma Quadrant. **Grand Nagus Zek** viewed the wine as a way to establish a Ferengi business presence in the Gamma Quadrant in 2370. ("Rules of Acquisition" [DS9]). Quark threatened **Ornithar** that the Ferengi would cease purchasing tulaberry wine from **Karemma** if Ornithar didn't help Sisko find the **Founders**. ("The Search, Part I" [DS9]). SEE: **Dosi**.

Tumak. (Andrew Koenig). **Skrreea**n youth, the son of Skrreean leader **Haneek**. Tumak was killed in 2370 during his people's search for a new home, after **Bajoran** authorities denied the Skrreean request to colonize on Bajor. Tumak became angry and piloted a spacecraft to Bajor, where it was destroyed by the Bajoran military. ("Sanctuary" [DS9]).

Tumek. (Joseph Ruskin). Trusted servant to the House of **Kozak**. Tumek oversaw the ***brek'tal* ritual** between **Kozak**'s widow, **Grilka**, and her new husband, **Quark**. ("The House of Quark" [DS9]). In 2373, Tumek traveled to Deep Space 9 with the Lady Grilka to attend to the affairs of her House. ("Looking for *par'Mach* in All the Wrong Places" [DS9]). *Joseph Ruskin also portrayed the master drill thrall, Galt, in "The Gamesters of Triskelion" (TOS) and the unseen informant in "Improbable Cause" (DS9).*

turboelevator. SEE: **turbolift**.

turbolift. Starfleet term for a high-speed elevator system used aboard Federation starships for intraship personnel transport. Turbolifts are controlled verbally, with a voice-recognition computer device that directs elevator movement both horizontally and vertically within the ship. Also called turboelevators. Access to the **bridge** of most Federation starships was via turbolift. ("Where No Man Has Gone Before" [TOS]). The old Cardassian station **Deep Space 9** was also equipped with turbolifts, although the system was somewhat antiquated by Federation standards. Turbolifts on Deep Space 9 had open-air cabs and were powered by multiphase alternating current. ("The Forsaken" [DS9]).

turboshaft. Aboard a Federation starship, a passageway, either horizontal or vertical, intended for use of the **turboelevator** system. *(Star Trek: The Motion Picture*; "Disaster" [TNG]).

Turkana IV. A Class-M planet, site of a failed Federation colony. The colonial government began to collapse in 2337, leaving dozens of rival factions fighting for control. Eventually, the colony's main city was destroyed, and the population was forced to move underground. In 2352, the remains of the Turkanian government broke off all diplomatic ties with the Federation. By the time the *Enterprise*-D visited the planet in 2367, the colony was largely controlled by two rival cadres, the **Coalition** and the **Alliance**; each controlled approximately one-half of the colony. Turkana IV was the birthplace of *Enterprise*-D Security Chief **Natasha Yar**, who was born there in 2337. Yar's younger sister, **Ishara Yar**, was born on Turkana IV in 2342. ("Legacy" [TNG]).

turn. English translation of the Klingon term for year, as in one turn (or revolution) of a planet around its sun. ("Sins of the Father" [TNG]).

"Turnabout Intruder." Original Series episode #79. Teleplay by Arthur H. Singer. Story by Gene Roddenberry. Directed by Herb Wallerstein. Stardate 5928.5. *First aired in 1969. Captain Kirk is kidnapped by a woman scientist who places her consciousness in his body, then traps his in hers. Arthur Singer was the story editor during* Star Trek's *third season. This was the last episode of the original* Star Trek *television series. Captain Picard's opening log reference to an "archaeological survey on Camus II" in "Legacy" (TNG) was intended as a tribute to this milestone in* Star Trek *history.* GUEST CAST: Sandra Smith and William Shatner as **Lester, Dr. Janice**; Harry Landers as **Coleman, Dr. Arthur**; Majel Barrett as **Chapel, Christine**; Barbara Baldavin as Lisa; David L. Ross as **Galloway, Lieutenant**; John Boyer as Guard; Roger Holloway as **Lemli, Mr.** SEE: **Benecia Colony; Beta Aurigae; Camus II; celebium; Coleman, Dr. Arthur; Kirk, James T.; Lemli, Mr.; Lester, Dr. Janice; life-energy transfer; *Potemkin*, U.S.S.; Robbiani dermal-optic test; Starbase 2.**

Turrel, Legate. (Andrew Prine). **Cardassian** politician and diplomat, one of the framers of the historic 2371 treaty between the **Bajorans** and the Cardassians. Turrel worked with **Vedek Bareil** for five months during initial negotiations for the accord. On stardate 48498, Turrel journeyed to **Deep Space 9** to meet with Kai **Winn** to finalize the discussions of the treaty. ("Life Support" [DS9]). *Andrew Prine previously played Suna in "Frame of Mind" (TNG).*

Tuvix. (Tom Wright). Sentient humanoid who was created in 2372 when a transporter accident merged *Voyager* crew members **Tuvok** and **Neelix** at the molecular level. The resulting individual possessed the memories and knowledge of both Neelix and Tuvok, but had a single consciousness. Tuvix, as the resulting individual became known, had an identity distinct from either Neelix or Tuvok. When a means was discovered of seperating Neelix and Tuvok into their original forms, Tuvix objected on the grounds that doing so would mean the end of his life as Tuvix. Voyager captain Janeway nevertheless ordered Tuvix to undergo the seperation on the grounds that doing so restored both Tuvok and Neelix to life. ("Tuvix" [VGR]). SEE: **symbiogenesis**.

"Tuvix." *Voyager* episode #40. Teleplay by Kenneth Biller. Story by Andrew Shepard Price & Mark Gaberman. Directed by Cliff Bole. Stardate 49655.2. *First aired in 1996. A transporter accident merges Tuvok and Neelix into a single person, Tuvix, who doesn't want to be separated again.* GUEST CAST: Tom Wright as **Tuvix**; Simon Billig as **Hogan**; Bahni Turpin as **Swinn**. SEE: **Andorian amoeba; barium; chloroplast; chrysanthemum; clematis; cytoplasmic protein; Emergency Medical Hologram; Hogan; Jupiter Station; lysosomal enzyme; molecular imaging scanner; Neelix; Ocampan prayer taper; radioisotope; sickbay; Swinn, Ensign; symbiogenesis; Trellan crepes; Tuvix; Tuvok; Vulcan dirge; X-rays.**

Tuvok (mirror). (Tim Russ). **Mirror universe** counterpart to **Tuvok**. The mirror Tuvok was not lost aboard the *Starship **Voyager***. Instead, he became a member of the **Terran resistance**, fighting against the oppressive **Alliance** of the Klingon Empire and the Cardassian Union. ("Through the Looking Glass" [DS9]). *Tim Russ's appearance on* Star Trek: Deep Space 9 *as Tuvok was the first cross-over of a* Voyager *character onto another* Star Trek *series.*

Tuvok orchid. Species of flowering plant created by Lon Suder late in 2372 using genetic splicing techniques. Suder named the new flower after his mentor, Lieutenant Tuvok. ("Basics, Part I" [VGR]).

Tuvok. (Tim Russ). Security officer on the *U.S.S. **Voyager***. ("Caretaker" [VGR]). Tuvok taught at the **Starfleet Academy** for 16 years. ("Learning Curve" [VGR]). He was married in 2304 ("Ex Post Facto" [VGR]) to **T'Pel.** ("Persistence of Vision" [VGR]). Tuvok and T'Pel had four children, three sons and a daughter. ("Elogium" [VGR]). At home on Vulcan, Tuvok was proficient at playing his **Vulcan lute**, a stringed musical instrument. ("Persistence of Vision" [VGR], "Innocence" [VGR]). He was skilled at horticulture, known for breeding prize Vulcan orchids. ("Tattoo" [VGR]).

Tuvok entered Starfleet Academy in 2289 at his parents' insistence. In 2293, he was assigned to the *U.S.S. **Excelsior*** as a junior science officer under the command of Captain **Hikaru Sulu**. Tuvok did not realize it at the time, but he became infected with a parasitic **memory virus** from fellow crew member **Dmitri Valtane**. Tuvok found it difficult to accept the multicultural environment of Starfleet, preferring the controlled discipline of his own Vulcan people. ("Flashback" [VGR]). Tuvok even spoke out against Captain **Spock**'s visionary proposal of an alliance between the Federation and the Klingon Empire. ("Alliances" [VGR]). Tuvok resigned from Starfleet shortly thereafter and returned to his homeworld to undergo the ***Kolinahr*** discipline. His studies were interrupted in 2304 when he underwent *Pon farr* and married **T'Pel**. After raising a family of his own, Tuvok appreciated his parents' motives for sending him to Starfleet. After a 51-year absence, Tuvok returned to Starfleet in 2349 and was assigned to the *U.S.S. Wyoming*. ("Flashback" [VGR]).

Tuvok was once stationed at the Jupiter Station some time prior to 2371. While there, he kept in contact with Kathryn Janeway by written letters. ("Tuvix" [VGR]). Tuvok taught archery science for several years at the Vulcan Institute of Defensive Arts. ("Basics, Part II" [VGR]).

In 2371, Tuvok went undercover and infiltrated the **Maquis**, ending up on Chakotay's ship. The Maquis ship and later the *Voyager* were abruptly transported to the **Delta Quadrant**, and Tuvok returned to his regular Starfleet duties. ("Caretaker" [VGR]). Tuvok, who had been Kathryn Janeway's tactical officer for many years, would ordinarily have been assigned to replace *Voyager's* first officer, who died in the first encounter with the **Caretaker**.

Janeway nevertheless elected to appoint **Chakotay** to that position in the interest of building trust with the new Maquis members of her crew. ("Twisted" [VGR]). In 2371, a member of the Komar species took control of Tuvok in an attempt to lead *Voyager* into a dark-matter nebula so that the Komar could extract the crew's neural energy. The attempt was not successful, and the alien left Tuvok's body. ("Cathexis" [VGR]). In 2372, Tuvok performed a **Vulcan mind-meld** with confessed murderer **Lon Suder**. The meld caused a neurochemical imbalance in Tuvok's brain, leading to a temporary, violent loss of emotional self-control. ("Meld" [VGR]). In 2372, Tuvok and Neelix were involved in a transporter accident that merged them at the molecular level, forming a new living being who adopted the name **Tuvix**. Tuvok did not exist during the two weeks that Tuvix lived. ("Tuvix" [VGR]).

Tuvok's first appearance was in "Caretaker" (VGR). Tim Russ previously portrayed Devor in "Starship Mine" (TNG), T'Kar in "Invasive Procedures" (DS9), and an unnamed lieutenant on the bridge of the Enterprise-B *in* Star Trek Generations. *(We were tempted to speculate that this officer might have been Tuvok, but you can see that Tim Russ wasn't wearing pointed ears in those scenes.) Russ was also a candidate for the role of Geordi La Forge in* Star Trek: The Next Generation.

tuwaly pie. Bajoran dessert. ("Shakaar" [DS9]).

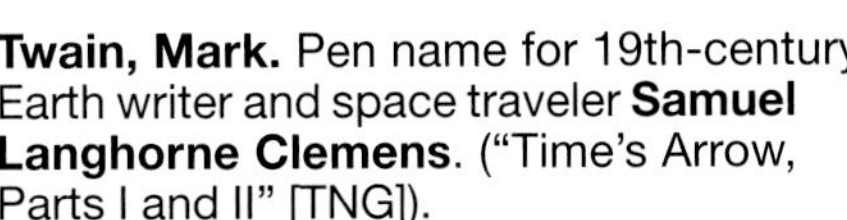

Twain, Mark. Pen name for 19th-century Earth writer and space traveler **Samuel Langhorne Clemens**. ("Time's Arrow, Parts I and II" [TNG]).

Twenty-First Street Mission. Institution in the city of New York on **Earth** during the Great Depression of the 1930s, managed by social worker **Edith Keeler**. The Twenty-First Street Mission provided food and shelter to the unfortunate victims of the economic downturn. ("The City on the Edge of Forever" [TOS]).

"Twisted." *Voyager* episode #19. Teleplay by Kenneth Biller. Story by Arnold Rudnick & Rich Hosek. Directed by Kim Friedman. No stardate given. *First aired in 1995. After encountering a distortion ring, the ship changes shape and is transformed into a changing labyrinth that stymies the crew's efforts to move between decks and causes crew members to disappear. Kes celebrates her second birthday in this episode.* GUEST CAST: Judy Geeson as **Sandrine**; Larry A. Hankin as **Gaunt Gary**; Tom Virtue as **Baxter, Lieutenant**; Terry Correll as Crew member. SEE: **accelerometer; Ayala, Lieutenant; Baxter, Lieutenant; distortion ring being; Gaunt Gary; gigaquad; Hargrove; holodeck and holosuite programs: Sandrine's; Jimbalian fudge; Kes; Kyoto, Ensign; *I'maki* nut; Nicoletti, Susan; photoplasma; Sandrine; shock pulse; subatomic particle shower; Tuvok.**

two-dimensional creatures. Life-forms from a two-dimensional continuum. A group of these creatures entered our continuum in 2367 and were discovered by scientists aboard the *Enterprise*-D. The creatures were described as resembling bioluminescent plankton, floating freely in interstellar space, much as fish swim in Earth's oceans. The presence of these life-forms also caused the temporary loss of Deanna Troi's empathic powers. The creatures, attempting to return to their own space through a **cosmic string fragment**, had apparently lost their way until *Enterprise*-D personnel used the ship's main deflector to generate the appropriate subspace harmonics to guide their return. ("The Loss" [TNG]).

two-headed Malgorian. Life-form reputed to be incapable of making up its mind about what it wants. Bajoran farmer **Mullibok** compared Major Kira Nerys to a two-headed Malgorian because she wanted to let her friend stay on **Jeraddo**, but her duty required an enforcement of the evacuation order. ("Progress" [DS9]).

Ty'Gokor. Fortified planetoid located in an asteroid field deep within Klingon space. Site of the **Hall of Warriors**. In 2372, Chancellor Gowron relocated Klingon military headquarters to Ty'Gokor. Early in 2373, Captain Benjamin Sisko and his men infiltrated the Hall of Warriors on Ty'Gokor and exposed General **Martok** as a changeling. ("Apocalypse Rising" [DS9]). *The armored space stations orbiting Ty'Gokor were designed by Anthony Fredrickson.*

Tycho City. Population center located on Earth's **moon**. On a clear day in the 24th century, you could see Tycho City from the surface of the Earth. *(Star Trek: First Contact).*

Tycho IV. Planet. Home to the spacefaring **dikironium cloud creature**. The ***U.S.S. Farragut*** lost 200 crew members fighting that entity in the Tycho system in 2257. Captain Kirk of the *Enterprise* destroyed the creature there in 2268. ("Obsession" [TOS]).

Tye, DaiMon. Ferengi entrepreneur. Odo once suggested that Tye was more devious than Quark. ("Civil Defense" [DS9]).

Tygarian freighter. SEE: ***Nanut.***

Tyken's Rift. A rare rupture in the fabric of space, undetectable by most sensors. Named for Bela Tyken, a Melthusian captain who first discovered the phenomenon, the rift effectively drained all energy from any space vehicle unlucky enough to fall into it. When Tyken found his ship trapped in the rift, he was able to escape by generating a massive energy burst using anicium and yurium, overloading the rift and allowing him to escape. In 2367, the ***U.S.S. Brattain*** and later the *U.S.S. Enterprise*-D were trapped in a Tyken's Rift. Both crews suffered severe **REM sleep** deprivation, a condition found to be caused by an alien intelligence also trapped in the rift. This intelligence was trying to communicate with the Starfleet vessels, in an effort to propose a cooperative effort that would enable all to escape. The realization that the aliens were trying to communicate came too late to save the crew of the *Brattain*, but the *Enterprise*-D was able to work with the aliens to generate an explosion large enough to rupture the rift and let both ships escape. ("Night Terrors" [TNG]).

Tyler, Ensign. (Gina Ravarra). Starfleet engineering officer. She was part of the engineering team aboard the *Enterprise*-D that installed a new warp core in 2370. Tyler had an obvious but unrequited crush on Geordi La Forge. ("Phantasms" [TNG]).

Tyler, Ensign. Starfleet officer assigned to station Deep Space 9. Ensign Tyler broke his leg in 2372. ("Rejoined" [DS9]).

Tyler, José. (Peter Duryea). Navigator on the original *Starship Enterprise* under the command of Captain Christopher Pike, circa 2254. ("The Cage," "The Menagerie, Parts I and II" [TOS]).

type-1 phaser; type-2 phaser; etc. SEE: **phaser type-1, phaser type-2, etc.**

Typhon Expanse. Region of space. Site where the ***U.S.S. Bozeman*** disappeared in 2278 into a **temporal causality loop**. A second Federation starship, the ***Enterprise*-D**, was also trapped in that causality loop near the Typhon Expanse for some 17.4 days in 2368. ("Cause and Effect" [TNG]).

Typhon sector. Region of Federation space. On stardate 50893, Admiral Hayes mobilized a fleet of starships in the Typhon sector to meet the **Borg** ship that entered Federation space on a heading for Earth. *(Star Trek: First Contact)*.

Tyree. (Michael Whitney). Leader of the primitive **hill people** of his planet. **James T. Kirk** met Tyree while commanding his first planetary survey mission in 2254. They became friends and were ceremonially made brothers. Tyree and Kirk met again in 2267 when the *Enterprise* visited the planet for scientific research. Upon learning that the Klingons were supplying the neighboring village people with **flintlock** weapons, Kirk tried to convince Tyree of the need to fight to protect his people. Tyree initially refused, but later accepted similar weapons after the villagers murdered his wife, **Nona**. In providing weapons to Tyree's hill people, the Federation was making a measured effort to maintain the balance of power on the planet. ("A Private Little War" [TOS]). *Tyree's planet was not given a name in the episode, although an unfilmed line in the script suggested it might have been Neural. Kirk was presumably serving aboard the* **U.S.S. Farragut** *(described as his first assignment after the academy in "Obsession" [TOS]) at the time of his first visit to Tyree's planet.*

Tyrellia. Federation planet, one of seven known inhabited worlds with no atmosphere at all. The planet also has no magnetic pole, one of only three such inhabited worlds. ("Starship Mine" [TNG]).

Tyrinean blade carving. A half-meter-high, transparent, cubist sculpture. **Lieutenant Jenna D'Sora** gave a Tyrinean blade carving to Data. It was her attempt to brighten up his quarters. ("In Theory" [TNG]).

Tyrus VIIA. Planet. Site where **Dr. Farallon** developed and tested an experimental **particle fountain** mining technique in 2369. The *Enterprise*-D assisted in the initial testing phase. ("The Quality of Life" [TNG]).

Tzartak aperitif. Specialty beverage. The drink was adjusted so that its vapor point was one half-degree below the body temperature of the patron who would be consuming it. The liquid would immediately evaporate upon contact with the drinker's tongue. The flavor of the beverage was carried entirely by the vapors. Guinan once served a Tzartak aperitif in the *Enterprise*-D's **Ten-Forward Lounge.** ("Time's Arrow, Part I" [TNG]).

Tzenketh. Planet that was the homeworld of the **Tzenkethi** civilization. Cardassian intelligence operative **Elim Garak** was once on Tzenketh, where he became trapped in a confined space when walls collapsed in on him. This triggered a severe attack of claustrophobia. ("By Inferno's Light" [DS9]).

Tzenkethi war. Conflict between the **United Federation of Planets** and the **Tzenkethi**. ("The Adversary" [DS9]). **Benjamin Sisko** fought in the Federation-Tzenkethi war while serving as executive officer of the ***Starship Okinawa*** under the command of Captain Leyton. ("Paradise Lost" [DS9]).

Tzenkethi. Civilization native to the Alpha Quadrant. The Tzenkethi were once at war with the United Federation of Planets. In 2371, a **Founder** posing as Ambassador Krajensky almost caused another **Tzenkethi war** when he seized control of the ***U.S.S. Defiant*** with the intent of attacking a Tzenkethi settlement. ("The Adversary" [DS9]).

U.S.S. Identifying prefix used as part of the names of Federation starships, as in ***U.S.S. Enterprise***. *Oddly enough, there is still some question as to what* U.S.S. *actually stands for. Captains Pike and Kirk identified the* Enterprise *as a United Space Ship, but it was also called a United Star Ship in other episodes. We assume that ships with an S.S. prefix are usually vessels of Federation registry, but not part of the Federation starfleet.*

Ubean prison. Rehabilitation facility under Ubean jurisdiction in the Delta Quadrant. **Wixiban** was incarcerated in a Ubean prison for a year for smuggling contraband. ("Fair Trade" [VGR]).

UESPA. SEE: **United Earth Space Probe Agency**.

Ufandi III. Planet; site where the *Enterprise*-D encountered an **Yridian freighter** carrying **magnesite ore** in 2370. ("Firstborn" [TNG]).

UFO. Twentieth-century Earth abbreviation for Unidentified Flying Object. The *Starship Enterprise* was detected as an unidentified flying object when it was observed in the atmosphere by the **Omaha Air Base** on Earth in the year 1969. ("Tomorrow Is Yesterday" [TOS]). When the *U.S.S. Voyager* visited Earth in 1996, it was similarly termed a UFO by the news media of the time, although some authorities dismissed it as a hoax. ("Future's End, Part II" [VGR]). SEE: ***Quark's Treasure***.

"Ugly Bags of Mostly Water." Term used by the crystalline **microbrain**s of planet **Velara III** to describe crew members of the *Enterprise*-D. Data noted that the term was an accurate description of humanoid life-forms, since they are composed of over 90 percent water. ("Home Soil" [TNG]).

UHC card. Official document that could serve as proof of identification in 21st-century **San Francisco** on **Earth**. ("Past Tense, Part I" [DS9]). *UHC probably stands for Universal Health Care.*

Uhlan. A junior rank in the **Romulan** guard. ("Unification, Part II" [TNG]).

Uhnari, Lieutenant Aquiel. (Renée Jones). Starfleet officer, formerly assigned to **Relay Station 47**. Uhnari served some nine months at that station in 2368-69, but was transferred after a tragic incident in which **Lieutenant Keith Rocha**, her fellow officer at the station, was discovered to have been killed by a **coalescent organism**. A communications technician, Uhnari was from **Halii** and missed her homeworld very much. Uhnari enjoyed reading gothic fiction and had a pet dog named Maura. During the investigation into Rocha's death, Uhnari became romantically involved with Geordi La Forge. Uhnari's last posting prior to Relay Station 47 had been on **Deriben V**. ("Aquiel" [TNG]).

Uhura. (Nichelle Nichols). Communications officer aboard the original *Starship Enterprise* under the command of Captain James Kirk. ("The Corbomite Maneuver" [TOS]). She was born in 2239; her name is derived from the Swahili word for "freedom." ("Is There in Truth No Beauty?" [TOS]). A highly skilled technician, Uhura was also a talented musician, and enjoyed serenading her fellow crew members with song. ("Charlie X" [TOS], "The Conscience of the King" [TOS], *Star Trek V: The Final Frontier).* Her memory was wiped clean in 2267 by the errant space probe ***Nomad***, requiring her to be re-educated. ("The Changeling" [TOS]). Following the re-assignment of the original *Enterprise* to Starfleet Academy in 2284, Uhura served at Starfleet Command on Earth. *(Star Trek III: The Search for Spock).* Uhura was scheduled to give a seminar at the academy in 2293, although she volunteered to return to her old post on the *Enterprise*-A at Kirk's request prior to the historic **Khitomer** conference. *(Star Trek VI: The Undiscovered Country.)* SEE: **"Beyond Antares"; "Moon's a Window to Heaven, The."** *Uhura's first appearance was in "The Corbomite Maneuver" (TOS).*

Ulani Belor. (Wendy Robie). Scientist who worked for the **Cardassian** Ministry of Science. In 2371, Ulani and her colleague, **Gilora Rejal,** worked with **Bajoran** scientists and Starfleet personnel at Deep Space 9 to test a **subspace radio** relay station. This experiment was intended to allow communication between the **Alpha** and **Gamma Quadrants** through the **Bajoran wormhole**. ("Destiny" [DS9]).

Ullians. A humanoid species of telepaths, characterized by skin involutions in the temporal area of their skulls. Though Ullians are able to read the minds of many other species, they themselves are unreadable by certain other telepathic groups, particularly **Betazoids**. Prior to the year 2068, Ullian society was plagued by violence, and cases of **telepathic memory invasion** rape were common among the population. But by the 21st century, the Ullians had evolved into a peaceful people, and such barbaric acts virtually disappeared. In the 2300s, certain members of the Ullian society received special training in the art of telepathic memory retrieval and were using that talent to amass a library of individual memories, not unlike a collection of oral histories. By 2368, Ullian historians had compiled memories from 11 planets, but research was delayed by the arrest of researcher **Jev** (*pictured*) for several cases of telepathic rape. ("Violations" [TNG]).

Ultima Thule. Planet. Site of a purification plant that produced weapons-grade **dolamide**. The **Valerians** supplied extremely pure dolamide, processed on Ultima Thule, to the Cardassians during the occupation of planet Bajor. (Dramatis Personae" [DS9]). SEE: ***Sherval Das***. *Ultima Thule was also the name of a planet in "Death's Other Domain," an episode of* Space: 1999. *The name is derived from a Greek term for the "end of the earth."*

"Ultimate Computer, The." Original Series episode #53. Teleplay by D. C. Fontana. Story by Laurence N. Wolfe. Directed by John Meredyth Lucas. Stardate 4729.4. *First aired in 1968. Famous scientist Richard Daystrom's latest invention is a new computer system that could replace James Kirk as captain of the* Enterprise. GUEST CAST: William Marshall as **Daystrom**, **Dr. Richard**; Sean Morgan as **Harper**, **Ensign**; Barry Russo as **Wesley**, **Commodore Robert**; James Doohan as Commodore Enwright's voice and as M-5 computer voice. SEE: **Alpha Carinae II; Carstairs, Ensign; *Constitution*-class starship; Daystrom Institute; Daystrom, Dr. Richard; Deep Space Station K-7; dunsel; duotronic; emergency manual monitor; engram; *Excalibur, U.S.S.*; Finagle's Folly; Harper, Ensign; Harris, Captain; *Hood, U.S.S.*; Kazanga; *Lexington, U.S.S.*; M-1 through M-4; M-5; multitronics; Nobel Prize; *Potemkin, U.S.S.*; Rawlens; Sakar; Spock; Wesley, Commodore Robert; *Woden*; Zee-Magnees Prize.**

ultrasonic generator. Device used to create high-frequency sonic energy. Some crystal structures can be shattered by using an ultrasonic generator to set up a sympathetic vibration. ("Heart of Stone" [DS9]).

ultraviolet satellite. Device capable of generating high levels of ultraviolet radiation. Two hundred ten ultraviolet satellites were used to irradiate the surface of planet **Deneva** in 2267 to eradicate the **Denevan neural parasites** that had infested the planet's population. ("Operation: Annihilate!" [TOS]).

ultritium. A powerful chemical explosive, virtually undetectable by transporter scanners. Large amounts of ultritium were found in the robes of the **Antedean** delegation to the **Pacifica** conference of 2365. It was subsequently learned that the Antedean delegates had planned to use the explosives to blow up the entire conference. ("Manhunt" [TNG]). Ultritium explosives were used by the crew of the Romulan scoutship ***Pi*** to destroy their ship at planet **Galorndon Core**, inside Federation space, in 2366. ("The Enemy" [TNG]). The **Jem'Hadar** used ultritium concussion shells for artillery bombardment. ("The Ship" [DS9]).The Dominion had once mined ultritium on an asteroid that was later converted into **Dominion internment camp 371**. ("In Purgatory's Shadow" [DS9]).

Ulysses, U.S.S. Federation starship, *Nebula* class, Starfleet registry number NCC-66808. In 2371, the *U.S.S. Ulysses,* commanded by Captain Entebe, studied protoplanetary masses in the Helaspont Nebula. ("The Adversary" [DS9]).

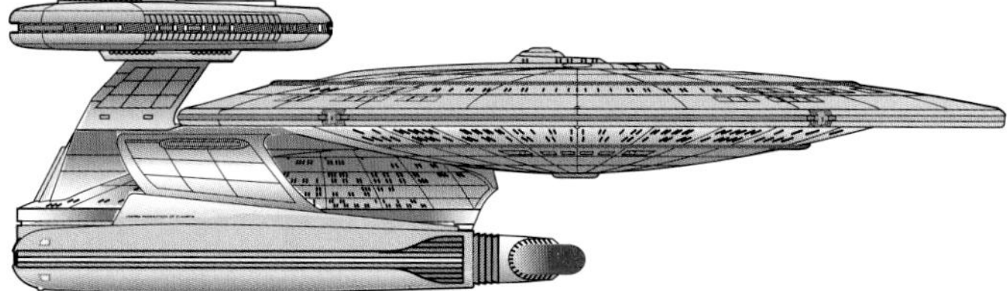

Ulysses. Classic novel written by Earth author James Joyce. Captain Picard took a copy with him on his vacation to **Risa** in 2366. ("Captain's Holiday" [TNG]).

Umani sector. Section of space. Jeyal's transport came from the Umani sector on its way to station Deep Space 9. ("The Muse" [DS9]).

Umbato, Lieutenant. An *Enterprise*-D crew member. Umbato broke two ribs during a holodeck exercise the night of the Ishikawa-O'Brien wedding. ("Data's Day" [TNG]).

umbilical port. A series of exterior connection plugs on the outer hull of a starship. When a ship was docked at a starbase or other support facility, umbilicals could be connected to the ship to provide an external supply of power, atmosphere, and other consumables to the ship. ("Remember Me" [TNG]).

Umoth VIII. Planet; location of a **Federation** colony in the **Demilitarized Zone**. In 2370, **Cardassian** sabotage caused 35 colonists on Umoth VIII to be hospitalized after eating from tainted public food replicators. ("The Maquis, Part II" [DS9]).

uncertainty principle. Concept in quantum mechanics postulated by Earth scientist Dr. Werner Heisenberg in 1927. The uncertainty principle states that increasing the accuracy of the measurement in one observable quantity also increases the uncertainty of knowledge of other quantities in the equation. In returning Worf to his correct **quantum reality**, an alternate Data was unsure at what time Worf would return, as the uncertainty principle made time a variable in his equations. ("Parallels" [TNG]). SEE: **Heisenberg compensators.**

Undalar. Location on planet **Bajor** noted for its spectacular cliffs. In 2372, while pregnant with her second child, Keiko O'Brien expressed an interest in rappelling down the cliffs of Undalar to get a fungus sample. Needless to say, Miles O'Brien was opposed to the idea. ("Body Parts" [DS9]).

undari. In the **Nausicaan** language, a word meaning "coward." ("Tapestry" [TNG]).

Underhill, Pell. Twenty-second-century physicist who theorized that a major disruption of the time-space continuity of an energy flow could be compensated for by trillions of small counterreactions. ("Clues" [TNG]).

"undiscovered country, the." In the literature of **Shakespeare**, the undiscovered country referred to the unknown future, at least according to **Chancellor Gorkon**, who toasted "the undiscovered country" at a diplomatic dinner prior to his abortive peace initiative in 2293. *(Star Trek VI: The Undiscovered Country). Gorkon was quoting from the famous "To be, or not to be" soliloquy in Shakespeare's* Hamlet, *Act III, Scene 1.*

Unefra III. Planet. Former **Obsidian Order** leader **Enabran Tain** lived on Unefra III after his retirement. ("Improbable Cause" [DS9]).

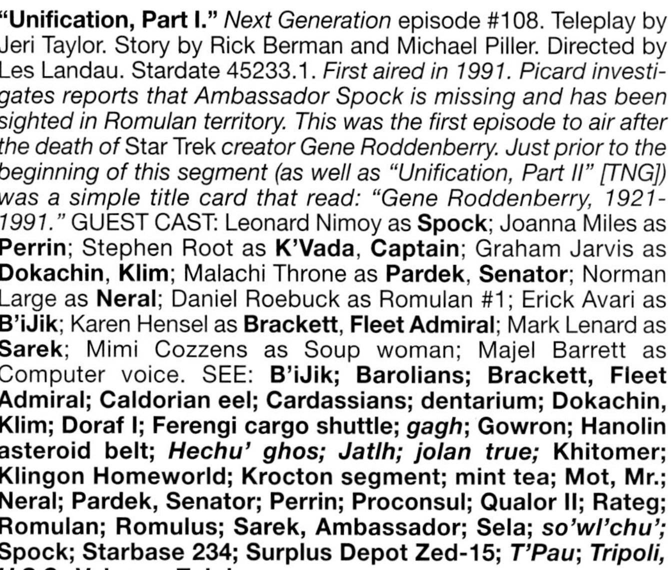

Unferth. (Christopher Neame). Character in the holonovel ***Beowulf***. Unferth was one of **King Hrothgar**'s courtiers; he voiced considerable objection to the appearance of *Voyager* crew members in Hrothgar's hall. ("Heroes and Demons" [VGR]).

"Unification, Part I." *Next Generation* episode #108. Teleplay by Jeri Taylor. Story by Rick Berman and Michael Piller. Directed by Les Landau. Stardate 45233.1. *First aired in 1991. Picard investigates reports that Ambassador Spock is missing and has been sighted in Romulan territory. This was the first episode to air after the death of* Star Trek *creator Gene Roddenberry. Just prior to the beginning of this segment (as well as "Unification, Part II" [TNG]) was a simple title card that read: "Gene Roddenberry, 1921-1991."* GUEST CAST: Leonard Nimoy as **Spock**; Joanna Miles as **Perrin**; Stephen Root as **K'Vada**, **Captain**; Graham Jarvis as **Dokachin**, **Klim**; Malachi Throne as **Pardek**, **Senator**; Norman Large as **Neral**; Daniel Roebuck as Romulan #1; Erick Avari as **B'iJik**; Karen Hensel as **Brackett**, **Fleet Admiral**; Mark Lenard as **Sarek**; Mimi Cozzens as Soup woman; Majel Barrett as Computer voice. SEE: **B'iJik; Barolians; Brackett, Fleet Admiral; Caldorian eel; Cardassians; dentarium; Dokachin, Klim; Doraf I; Ferengi cargo shuttle; *gagh*; Gowron; Hanolin asteroid belt; *Hechu' ghos; Jatlh; jolan true;* Khitomer; Klingon Homeworld; Krocton segment; mint tea; Mot, Mr.; Neral; Pardek, Senator; Perrin; Proconsul; Qualor II; Rateg; Romulan; Romulus; Sarek, Ambassador; Sela; *so'wl'chu';* Spock; Starbase 234; Surplus Depot Zed-15; *T'Pau*; *Tripoli, U.S.S.*; Vulcans; Zakdorn.**

"Unification, Part II." *Next Generation* episode #107. Teleplay by Michael Piller. Story by Rick Berman and Michael Piller. Directed by Cliff Bole. Stardate 45245.8. *First aired in 1991. Spock learns he's been a pawn in a Romulan plot to conquer his homeworld of Vulcan. This episode was actually filmed before "Unification, Part I" because of Leonard Nimoy's schedule. Spock's presence on Romulus would later be mentioned in "Face of the Enemy" [TNG], even though Spock himself wasn't seen in that episode.* GUEST CAST: Leonard Nimoy as **Spock**; Stephen Root as **K'Vada**, **Captain**; Malachi Throne as **Pardek**, **Senator**; Norman Large as **Neral**; Daniel Roebuck as Romulan #1; Bill Bastiana as **Omag**; Susan Fallender as Romulan #2; Denise Crosby as **Sela**; Vidal Peterson as **D'Tan**; Harriet Leider as **Amarie**. SEE: ***Aktuh and Melota*; Amarie; Andorian blues; Bardakian pronghorn moose; Barolian freighter; "cowboy diplomacy"; D'Tan; Dulisian IV; Galorndon Core; *jolan true*; Klingon opera; Krocton segment; K'Vada, Captain; "Melor Famagal"; Neral; Omag's girls; Omag; Pardek, Senator; Proconsul; progressive encryption lock; Romulan; Romulan Star Empire;**

Uniforms, Starfleet (TOS). 1) Duty uniform, female (pilot version). 2) Field jacket (pilot version). 3) Duty uniform, male (pilot version). *Spock's version of the pilot costume had snaps on his collar, evidently to make it easier to change his shirt without damaging his makeup.* 4) Commanding officer's wraparound (first season version). *This version was first seen in "The Enemy Within" (TOS), probably to make it easier to tell Kirk apart from his evil twin.* 5) Duty uniform, male (series version). 6) Duty uniform, female (series version).

7) Athletic wear, "Charlie X" (TOS). 8) Commanding officer's wraparound (second season version). 9) Commanding officer's duty uniform, female (series version). 10) Utility jumpsuit. *This was often worn by technicians and transporter operators.* 11) Dress uniform, "Court Martial" (TOS). 12) Medical tunic. *This was usually worn by Dr. McCoy.* *Costumes designed by William Ware Theiss.*

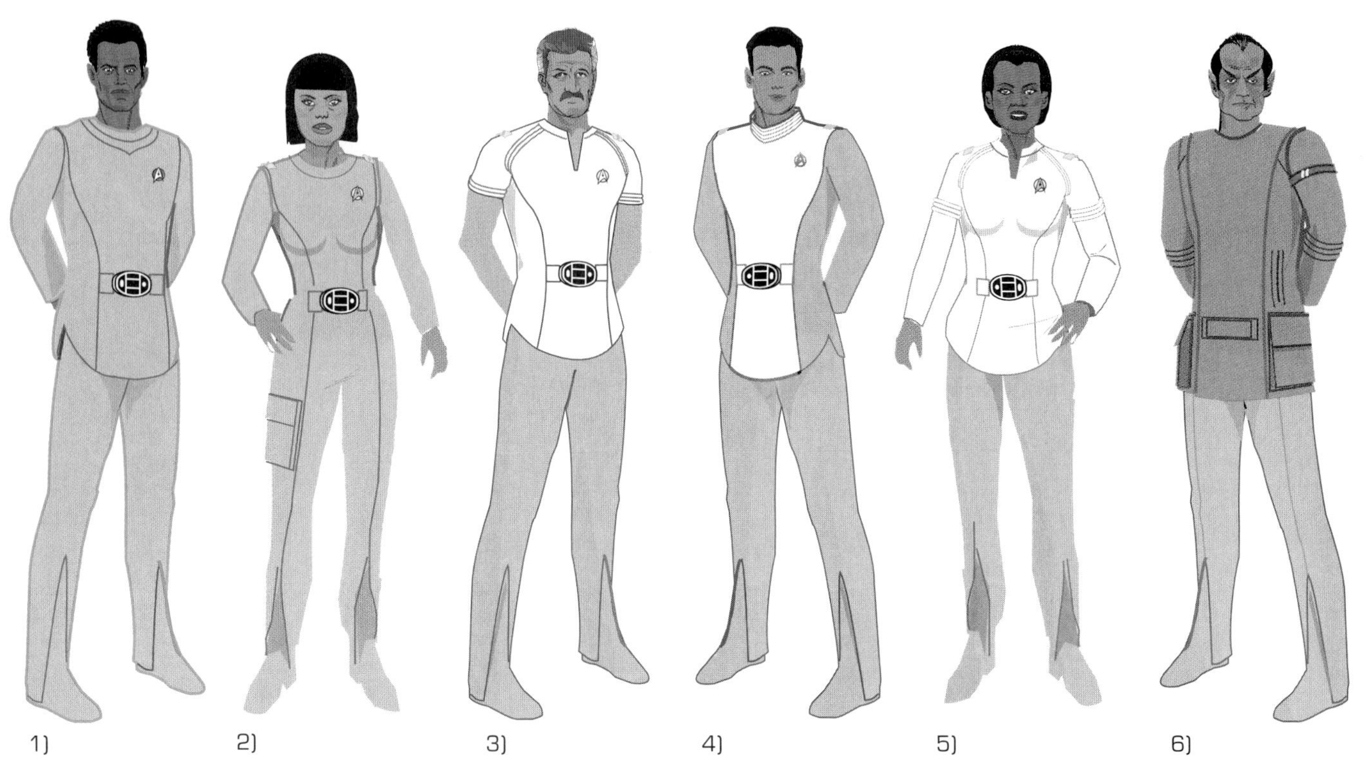

Uniforms, Starfleet (ST:TMP). 1) Duty uniform. 2) Utility jumpsuit. 3) Short-sleeve fatigue. 4) Admiral's uniform. 5) Long-sleeve fatigue. 6) Field jacket, used for landing party duty. Most of these uniforms were created for both male and female crew members. *Costumes designed by Robert Fletcher.*

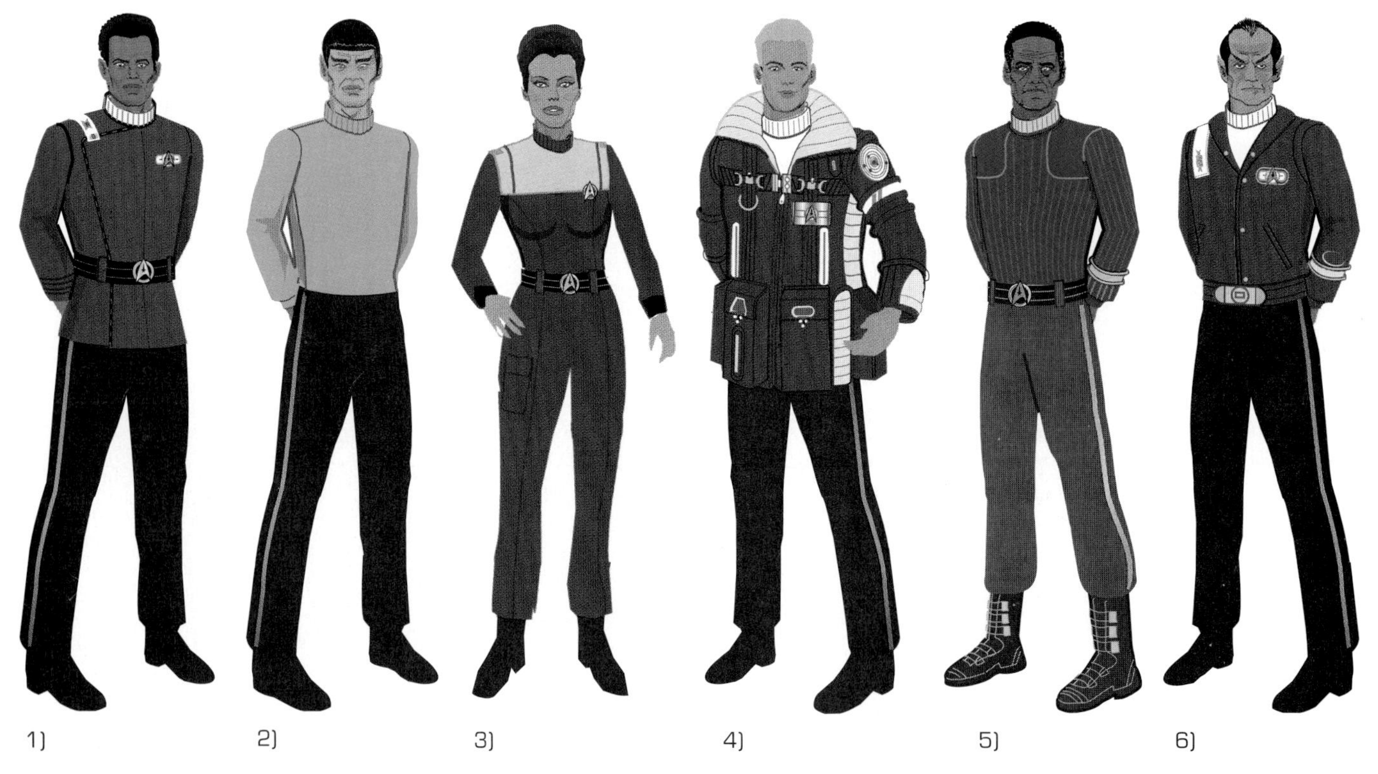

Uniforms, Starfleet (ST II). 1) Officer's duty uniform. 2) Duty uniform without jacket. 3) Cadet jumpsuit. 4) Field jacket. 5) Field duty (*STV*). 6) Officer's "bomber jacket" (*STV*). *These uniforms, originally designed for the second* Star Trek *movie, were used in all the subsequent original-series movies, and were featured in several episodes from* The Next Generation*-era as well. Costumes designed by Robert Fletcher, Nilo Rodis, and Dodie Shepherd.*

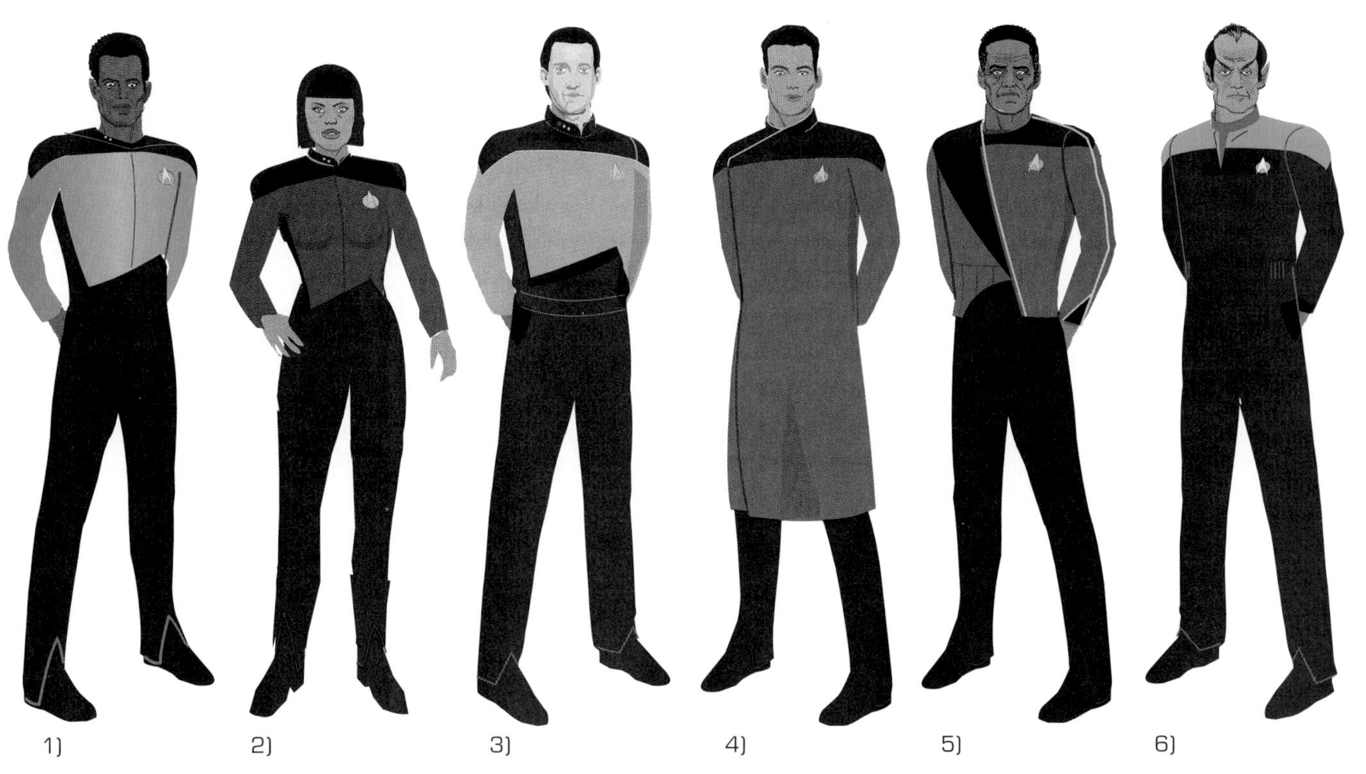

1) 2) 3) 4) 5) 6)

Uniforms, Starfleet (TNG, DS9, VGR, STG, ST:FC). 1) Duty uniform (TNG, first and second season). 2) Duty uniform, (TNG, third season). *The first season duty uniforms continued to be used, mostly for background crew.* 3) Duty uniform. *Unlike earlier versions, this costume featured a separate jacket, making it more comfortable for the actors to wear.* (TNG, third season). 4) Dress uniform (TNG, first season). 5) Admiral's uniform (TNG, first season). 6) Starfleet jumpsuit (*Star Trek Generations*, DS9 and VGR). *TNG Starfleet uniforms by William Ware Theiss, later versions by Bob Blackman.*

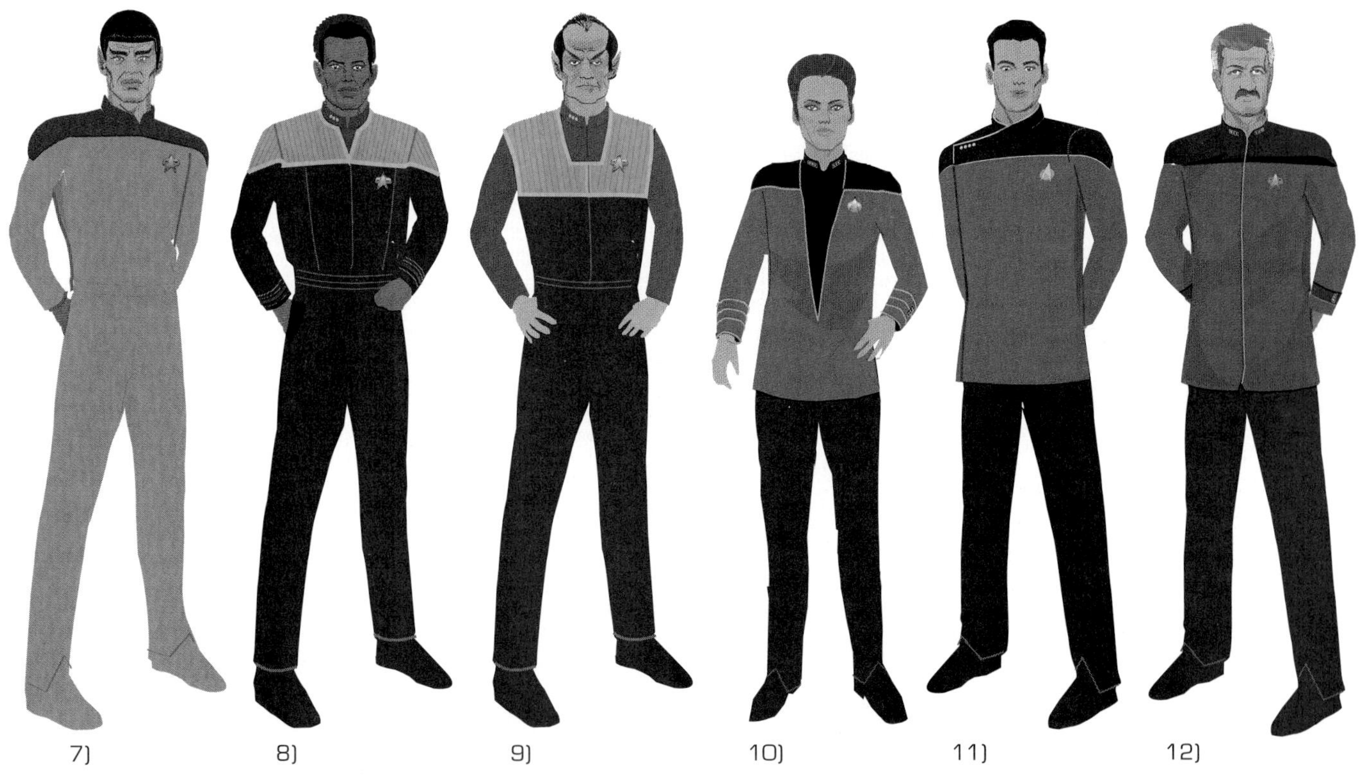

7) 8) 9) 10) 11) 12)

7) Cadet uniform (DS9, fourth season). *An earlier variation, with a black jumpsuit, was seen in "The First Duty" (TNG).* 8) Duty uniform (*Star Trek: First Contact*, DS9, fifth season). 9) Officer's vest (*ST:FC*). *Ben Sisko wore this occasionally, as well.* 10) Admiral's uniform (TNG, fifth season). 11) Dress uniform (TNG, sixth season). 12) Admiral's uniform (TNG, seventh season). *Starfleet costume variations by Bob Blackman.*

Romulus; Rutian archaeological vessel; Sela; Spock; suck salt; Uhlan; Vulcan nerve pinch; Vulcans.

Uniform Code of Justice. Federation legal guidelines governing the administration of justice. Chapter 4, article 12 granted a witness the right to make a statement before being questioned in a trial or hearing. ("The Drumhead" [TNG]). SEE: **Seventh Guarantee**.

uniforms, Starfleet. *A variety of Starfleet uniforms have been featured throughout the various incarnations of* Star Trek. *The original Starfleet uniforms were created by original* Star Trek *costume designer William Ware Theiss, who also designed the original version of the arrowhead-shaped Starfleet emblem. Theiss's work included the versions designed for the two pilot episodes, as well as the various black-collared costumes used during the series itself, and the dress uniforms. Starfleet uniforms seen in the first four* Star Trek *movies were designed by Robert Fletcher. The variations added in* Star Trek V *were designed by Nilo Rodis, and in* Star Trek VI *by Dodie Shepherd. Bill Theiss also designed the original versions of the uniforms for the first season of* Star Trek: The Next Generation, *while Robert Blackman and Durinda Rice Wood designed additional versions and modifications in subsequent seasons. Blackman also designed the Starfleet jumpsuits seen in* Star Trek: Deep Space Nine, Star Trek: Voyager, Star Trek Generations, *and* Star Trek: First Contact. SEE: Illustrations previous three pages, **insignia, Starfleet**.

United Earth Space Probe Agency. Early operating authority for the first *Starship Enterprise*. ("Charlie X" [TOS]). Kirk mentioned the UESPA to **Captain John Christopher** when Christopher asked if the *Enterprise* had been built by the Navy. Kirk answered that they were a combined service and that their authority was the United Earth Space Probe Agency. ("Tomorrow Is Yesterday" [TOS]). *The term United Earth Space Probe Agency was actually devised by story editor John D. F. Black early during the show's first season. It was only used a couple of times before being replaced with Starfleet by "Court Martial" (TOS). (It was once abbreviated as UESPA, pronounced YOU-SPAH). Later episodes have suggested that Starfleet existed even before the first pilot episode, and we assume that Starfleet existed as far back as 2161, when the Federation was founded.*

United Federation of Planets. An intersellar alliance of planetary governments and colonies, united for mutual trade, exploratory, scientific, cultural, diplomatic, and defensive endeavors, founded in 2161. ("The Outcast" [TNG]). In 2373, the Federation comprised more than 150 member planets, spread out across 8,000 light-years. *(Star Trek: First Contact).* Membership in the Federation was predicated on a number of factors, such as the existence of a unified planetary government.

("Attached" [TNG]). Similarly, under the Federation charter, caste-based discrimination is not permitted on member planets. ("Accession" [DS9]). Federation members include **Earth**, **Vulcan**, and numerous other planetary states. The Federation is governed by the **Federation Council**, composed of representatives from the various member planets, that meet in the city of **San Francisco** on Earth. The Council itself is led by the **Federation president**, whose office is in the city of Paris on planet Earth. *(Star Trek IV: The Voyage Home, Star Trek VI: The Undiscovered Country,* "Homefront" [DS9], and "Paradise Lost" [DS9]*).* The economic structure within the Federation made very little use of money in the 20th-century sense of the term. By the 24th century, the acquisition of wealth ceased to be the driving force in the lives of the majority of Federation citizens. ("The Neutral Zone" [TNG], *Star Trek: First Contact).*

Although the Federation and its Starfleet have done an extraordinary job of maintaining a generally peaceful climate in this part of the galaxy *(Star Trek II: The Wrath of Khan),* the Federation and its member planets have been involved in a number of armed conflicts over the years. Notable among these are the tensions with the **Klingon Empire** that lasted almost a century until the **Organian Peace Treaty** of 2267, and later the **Khitomer** conference of 2293. Still unresolved are conflicts with the **Romulan Star Empire** and the **Tholian Assembly**. The Federation was involved in a protracted, bitter war with the **Cardassians** that dated back to the 2350s. An uneasy peace treaty with the Cardassian Union was reached in 2366. ("The Wounded" [TNG]). Conflict with the Cardassians continued at lower levels for years. One particular hot spot was **Bajor**, after the end of Cardassian occupation of the planet in 2369, when the Federation took over operation of the old Cardassian mining station **Deep Space 9** in the Bajoran system near the newly discovered stable wormhole. ("Emissary" [DS9]). *There is no definitive list of members in the Federation, since the shows' writers need the freedom to invent new members as specific stories require. The 150-member figure was deliberately chosen to approximate the members in Earth's present United Nations.* SEE: **Constitution of the United Federation of Planets**.

United Nations, New. An organization of nation-states on planet Earth, formed during the 21st century. In 2036, the New United Nations declared that no Earth citizen could be made to answer for the crimes of their race or forebearers. The New United Nations had ceased to exist by the year 2079, in the aftermath of **World War III**. ("Encounter at Farpoint, Part I" [TNG]).

United States Constitution. Legal document providing the foundation for the representative democracy that formed the basis of the government of the **United States of America** on Earth. The United States Constitution provided for extensive protection of individual rights, including the right to face one's accuser. ("Court Martial" [TOS]). The **Yangs** of planet **Omega IV** adopted the United States Constitution and an American flag as symbols of their fight against their enemies the **Kohms**. ("The Omega Glory" [TOS]).

United States of America. Nation-state on planet Earth, founded in 1776, that world's first large-scale experiment in representational democratic government. The United States was responsible for many of Earth's early achievements in space exploration. The United States' flag of 2033 had 52 stars, a number that was maintained until 2079. ("The Royale" [TNG]). *It is not known if the United States ceased to exist*

in 2079 or if a 53rd state was added then. That year does appear to coincide with the end of the ***World War III*** *nuclear holocaust.*

units of measure. SEE: **AMU; AU; *baktun*; denkir; gigajoule; gigaquad; GSC; isoton; *kellicam; kellipate*; kilodyne; kiloquad; *kolem*; kph; melakol; MEV; microdyne; micron; millicochrane; onkian; parsec; Ritter scale; *selton*; terawatt; tessipate; trisec; roentgen; warp factor.**

"Unity." *Voyager* episode #59. Written by Kenneth Biller. Directed by Robert Duncan McNeill. Stardate 50614.2. First aired in 1997. *Chakotay discovers a colony of former Borg drones who assimilate him to save his life.* GUEST CAST: Lori Hallier as **Frazier, Riley**; Susan Patterson as **Kaplan, Ensign**; Ivar Brogger as **Orum**. SEE: **axonal amplifier; Borg; Borg collective; Chakotay; Farn; Frazier, Riley; holodeck and holosuite programs: hoverball; hoverball; Kaplan, Ensign; message buoy; Nekrit Expanse; neural transponder; Orum; Parein; *Roosevelt, U.S.S.***

universal translator. Device used to provide real-time two-way translation of spoken languages. It operated by sensing and comparing brain-wave frequencies, then selecting comparable concepts to use as a basis for translation. Kirk used a handheld universal translator to communicate with the life-form known as the **Companion** in 2267. ("Metamorphosis" TOS]). A software version of the universal translator was programmed into the *Enterprise*-D's main computer. This enabled real-time communications with such life-forms as the **nanites**. ("Evolution" [TNG]). The **combadges** worn by Starfleet personnel in the latter half of the 24th century incorporated miniature universal translators. ("The 37's" [VGR]). Even smaller versions of the universal translator could be inserted into the outer ear, providing unobtrusive operation. Such devices could, however, be disrupted by exposure to beta radiation. ("Little Green Men" [DS9]). The universal translator generally requires an adequate sample of a language in order to establish a translation matrix. ("Sanctuary" [DS9]). The universal translator aboard the *U.S.S. Voyager* had great difficulty in translating the language used by a mysterious civilization called the Swarm in 2373. ("The Swarm" [VGR]). *Actually, we figured that Paramount somehow managed to install universal translators in everyone's television receivers, which could also explain why so many of the galaxy's life-forms seem to be speaking English and other Earth languages.*

universe, parallel. SEE: **mirror universe**.

University of Betazed. Educational institution on planet Betazed; school at which **Deanna Troi** studied psychology prior to her joining Starfleet. As a student at the university, she helped care for **Tam Elbrun**. ("Tin Man" [TNG]).

"Unnatural Selection." *Next Generation* episode #33. Written by John Mason & Mike Gray. Directed by Paul Lynch. Stardate 42494.8. *First aired in 1989. Scientists who have genetically designed their children for superior immune systems find themselves aging incredibly quickly, the victims of that improved immunity.* GUEST CAST: Diana Muldaur as **Pulaski**, **Dr. Katherine**; Patricia Smith as **Kingsley**, **Dr. Sara**; Colm Meaney as **O'Brien**, **Miles**; J. Patrick McNamara as **Taggert**, **Captain**; Scott Trost as Ensign. SEE: **Darwin Genetic Research Station; Gagarin IV; Gamma 7 Sector; Kingsley, Dr. Sara; *Lantree, U.S.S.*; "Linear Models of Viral Propagation"; marker beacon; Pulaski, Dr. Katherine; quarantine transmitter; *Repulse, U.S.S.*; *Sakharov*, *Shuttlecraft*; security access code; Star Station India; styrolite; Taggert, Captain; Telaka, Captain L. Isao; Thelusian flu; transporter ID trace**.

"Up the Long Ladder." *Next Generation* episode #44. Written by Melinda M. Snodgrass. Directed by Winrich Kolbe. Stardate 42823.2. *First aired in 1989. Captain Picard must persuade two vastly dissimilar colonies, each doomed, that they can survive only by living together.* GUEST CAST: Diana Muldaur as **Pulaski**, **Dr. Katherine**; Barrie Ingham as **Odell**, **Danilo**; Jon De Vries as **Granger**, **Walter**; Rosalyn Landor as **Odell**, **Brenna**; Colm Meaney as **O'Brien**, **Miles**.SEE: **Bringloid V; Bringloidi; *chech'tluth*; clone; Dieghan, Liam; European Hegemony; Ficus Sector; firefighting; Granger, Walter; love poetry, Klingon; Mariposa; *Mariposa, S.S.*; Moore, Admiral; Neo-Transcendentalism; Odell, Brenna; Odell, Danilo; replicative fading; *rop'ngor*; Starbase 73; tea ceremony, Klingon; Vallis, Elizabeth; World War III; Yoshimitsu computers**.

uridium. Unstable mineral substance. Even in its raw form, uridium ore could explode if subjected to a strong electrical charge. Cardassian mining station **Terok Nor**, in orbit around planet **Bajor**, processed raw uridium ore using the forced labor of Bajoran prisoners during the Cardassian occupation of Bajor. ("Civil Defense" [DS9]). *We therefore assume that Bajor was a source of uridium ore, although it is not clear if there are any uridium deposits left after the Cardassian departure from Bajor.* The Cardassians used uridium alloy in their starship sensor arrays. ("Indiscretion" [DS9]).

Urodelean flu. Mild affliction with symptoms that include an imbalance in the **K-3 cell count**, increased intravascular pressure, and heightened electrophoretic activity. Most humans have a natural immunity against the disease. **Reginald Barclay** contracted Urodelean flu because the **T-cell** in his DNA that would normally fight off the infection was dormant. Dr. Beverly Crusher activated his dormant gene with a synthetic T-cell to help him fight off the flu. ("Genesis" [TNG]). *Well... T-cells are white blood cells, which definitely will not fit inside of genes. Actually, it probably should be the DNA in his T-cell.*

user code clearance. A password required to access the control systems of a starship. ("Hero Worship" [TNG]). SEE: **security access code.**

Ustard, Subcommander. Romulan officer who was killed in a transporter accident during the time that **Elim Garak** was a gardener at the **Cardassian Embassy on Romulus**. ("Broken Link" [DS9]).

GALAXY CLASS STARSHIP DEVELOPMENT PROJECT
UTOPIA PLANITIA STARFLEET YARDS, MARS

Utopia Planitia Fleet Yards. Starfleet shipyards in orbit around the planet **Mars** and on the surface of the planet. The *Enterprise*-D was built there. Members of the ***Galaxy*-Class Starship Development Project** team included Dr. **Leah Brahms** ("Booby Trap" [TNG]). The actual construction of the *Enterprise*-D was supervised by Commander **Orfil Quinteros**. ("11001001" [TNG]). Lieutenant Commander **Benjamin Sisko** was assigned to Utopia Planitia for some three years following the tragic death of his wife aboard the ***U.S.S. Saratoga*** in early 2367, prior to his assignment to station **Deep Space 9** in mid-2369. ("Emissary" [DS9]). While at Utopia Planitia, Sisko participated in the design of the new *Starship Defiant*, which was intended to help Starfleet defend against an anticipated **Borg** offensive. ("The Search, Part I" [DS9]). Starfleet records show that an accidental plasma discharge occurred while the *Enterprise*-D was being constructed in 2362, and three individuals were killed. In 2370 it was learned that Lieutenant **Walter J. Pierce** had murdered **Marla Finn** and her lover, then committed suicide. ("Eye of the Beholder" [TNG]). In an alternate **quantum reality** visited by Worf in 2370, some unknown entity was using the **Argus Array** to covertly survey the Utopia Planitia Fleet Yards. ("Parallels" [TNG]). SEE: **Martian Colonies**. *Part of the Utopia Planitia Fleet Yards on the surface of Mars was very briefly glimpsed as a view from deep space in "Parallels" (TNG), while Brahms's drafting room (presumably in the orbital part of the yards) was re-created in "Booby Trap" (TNG) and "Galaxy's Child" (TNG).*

Utopia Planitia. Location on planet **Mars** first explored by the automated space probe *Viking 2,* which soft-landed there on September 3, 1976, part of Earth's first attempt to employ spaceflight in the search for extraterrestrial life. It is also the site of the **Utopia Planitia Fleet Yards** where the ***Starship Enterprise*-D** was built in the mid-24th century. ("Booby Trap" [TNG]). **Tom Paris**'s idea of a perfect date was a visit to the hills overlooking Utopia Planitia on Mars, in a 1957-model **Chevy**. ("Lifesigns" [VGR]). *The city of Utopia Planitia in "Lifesigns" was a matte painting by Dan Curry, based on designs by Anthony Fredrickson and Doug Drexler. The fact that the* Enterprise-D *was supposed to have been built at Utopia Planitia was inscribed on the* ***dedication plaque*** *for the ship located on the main bridge. A copy of the dedication plaque was included in a CD-ROM collection of art and literature assembled by the Planetary Society and was launched toward the surface of Mars aboard the Russian* Mars '96 *space probe, although the probe never made it out of Earth orbit due to a launch vehicle malfunction.*

uttaberries. A blueberrylike fruit found on **Betazed**. Mr. Homn liked uttaberries. ("Ménage à Troi" [TNG]).

uttaberry crepes. Food. Benjamin Sisko ordered uttaberry crepes at Quark's bar on Deep Space 9. ("Armageddon Game" [DS9]).

Ux-Mal. Star system. A group of noncorporeal criminal life-forms were exiled from Ux-Mal to a moon of planet **Mab-Bu VI** during the 18th century. The criminals remained at Mab-Bu VI for four centuries before they made an unsuccessful attempt to escape aboard the *Starship* ***Essex*** in 2167. Two centuries later, they made a second attempt to escape their prison when the *Starship* ***Enterprise*-D** visited that moon. ("Power Play" [TNG]).

Uxbridge, Kevin. (John Anderson). Apparently the last survivor of the **Delta Rana IV** colony. Records showed him in 2366 to be an 85-year-old human botanist, but the crew of the *Enterprise*-D discovered him to be a **Douwd**, who had masqueraded as a human for more than 50 years. Uxbridge survived the **Husnock** attack at Delta Rana IV, and in retribution used his enormous powers to annihilate the entire Husnock race. Uxbridge later felt profound regret over his act of destruction and remained in self-imposed isolation on the planet, along with an image of his human wife, **Rishon Uxbridge**, who had perished in the Husnock attack. ("The Survivors" [TNG]).

Uxbridge, Rishon. (Anne Haney). Botanist and composer of tao-classical music; the wife of **Kevin Uxbridge**. She was 82 years old when she was killed in the **Husnock** attack on the **Delta Rana IV** colony. ("The Survivors" [TNG]). *Anne Haney later played a Bajoran judge in "Dax" (DS9).*

V'Ger. Contraction for "Voyager." A massive machine life-form built around **NASA**'s ancient ***Voyager VI*** space probe. *Voyager*, which launched from Earth in the late 20th century, had fallen into a black hole and emerged on the other side of the galaxy, near a planet of living machines. The inhabitants of the machine planet found the robot *Voyager VI* to be a kindred spirit, and gave it the ability to carry out what they believed to be *Voyager*'s prime directive: To learn all that is learnable, and to return that knowledge to its creator. Unfortunately, in doing so, they gave *Voyager*, now called V'Ger, the ability to destroy the objects being studied. Upon reaching Earth, where V'Ger believed its creator resided, V'Ger joined with **Willard Decker** and **Ilia**, and departed for parts unknown. *(Star Trek: The Motion Picture).*

V'sal. SEE: **Mot**.

V'Shar. Security arm of the **Vulcan** government. **Tallera** claimed to be a member of the V'Shar, but she was in fact an agent of the **Vulcan isolationist movement**. ("Gambit, Parts I and II" [TNG]).

Vaal. Sophisticated computer god-machine that controlled planet **Gamma Trianguli VI**. The inhabitants of the planet worshipped Vaal as a god, providing it with fuel. In exchange, Vaal provided an idyllic, Edenic environment. Vaal maintained a powerful planetary defense system that crippled the *Enterprise* when the ship orbited the planet in 2267. Vaal nearly destroyed the *Enterprise* before a barrage of phaser fire succeeded in destroying the computer. ("The Apple" [TOS]). SEE: **Akuta**.

Vaatrik. Bajoran national who ran the chemist's shop on **Terok Nor** during the Cardassian occupation of Bajor. Vaatrik was suspected of being a Cardassian collaborator. Vaatrik was killed in 2365 when he stumbled upon a Bajoran resistance member, **Kira Nerys**, who was searching his shop for a list of other Bajoran collaborators. Vaatrik's murder remained unsolved until 2370, when Kira admitted her part in his death to station Security Chief **Odo**. ("Necessary Evil" [DS9]). SEE: **Pallra.**

Vacca VI. Class-M Federation planet, located in the **Cabral sector**. Vacca VI was settled by the **Boraalans** in 2370. Vacca's surface conditions were slightly less favorable than the Boraalans were accustomed to. ("Homeward" [TNG]).

Vadosia. (Jack Shearer). Ambassador for the **Bolian** government. Vadosia visited **Deep Space 9** in 2369 on a fact-finding mission to the **Bajoran wormhole**. ("The Forsaken" [DS9]).

Vadris III. Planet. Natives of Vadris III think they're the only intelligent life in the universe. **Q** offered to take archaeologist **Vash** to Vadris III, but she declined. ("Q-Less" [DS9]).

Vagh. (Ed Wiley). A Klingon warrior and governor of the **Kriosian system**, a Klingon protectorate. When the Kriosian population under his control began to rebel and demand independence in 2367, Vagh accused the Federation of aiding their cause. The crew of the *Enterprise*-D was able to show that it was the Romulans who were supporting the rebels. Governor Vagh became the target of an assassination attempt by Geordi La Forge, acting under Romulan control. The Romulans hoped by having La Forge murder the governor, a rift would be formed in the alliance between the Federation and the Klingons. ("The Mind's Eye" [TNG]).

Vagra II. Planet in the Zed Lapis Sector. Now nearly deserted, Vagra II was the home to life-forms who left the planet to become creatures of dazzling beauty. In doing so, they left behind a creature called **Armus**, which still lives on the planet. *Enterprise*-D shuttlecraft 13 crashed there in 2364, and Security Chief **Natasha Yar** was killed there by Armus while on a rescue mission to the planet's surface. ("Skin of Evil" [TNG]).

vajhaq. Game played on the planet **Meridian**. ("Meridian" [DS9]).

Vak clover soup. Fine food. Quark served Vak clover soup to **Fallit Kot** during his stay on station Deep Space 9. ("Melora" [DS9]).

***vakol* fish.** Aquatic life-form from a planet in the Delta Quadrant. The *vakol* was able to enlarge itself much like an Earth puffer fish. ("State of Flux" [VGR]).

Valdemar, U.S.S. Federation starship, *Ambassador* class, Starfleet registy number NCC-26198. The *Valdemar* was dispatched to the border of the Federation-Cardassian **Demilitarized Zone** in 2370, following the arrest of Starfleet officer Miles O'Brien. ("Tribunal" [DS9]). *Probably named for Valdemar Poulsen, the inventor of the first tape recorder.*

Valek, Jal. (Johnny Martin). Leader of the **Kazon-Oglamar** sect in 2372. ("Maneuvers" [VGR], "Alliances" [VGR]).

valerian root tea. Beverage. A favorite of Deanna Troi. ("Second Chances" [TNG]).

Valerians. Civilization. The Valerians were believed to have supplied extremely pure weapons-grade **dolamide** to the **Cardassians** during the occupation of Bajor. When a Valerian transport vessel requested permission to dock at Deep Space 9 in 2369 for repairs, Major Kira Nerys asked that their request be denied because of their history with the Cardassians, but Commander Sisko refused. ("Dramatis Personae" [DS9]).

Valeris. (Kim Cattrall). Starfleet officer who was part of the conspiracy to assassinate Klingon **Chancellor Gorkon** in 2293. Valeris had been mentored by **Spock**, and was the first Vulcan to graduate at the top of her class at **Starfleet Academy**. Although fiercely logical, Valeris feared the changes that would be wrought when a new era of peace came upon the Federation. She was arrested at the Khitomer peace conference for her role in the assassination of Gorkon. *(Star Trek VI: The Undiscovered Country).*

Valiant, S.S. Early interstellar vessel that embarked on exploratory mission in 2065 and was lost when it was swept out of the galaxy, into the energy barrier. Shortly after contact with the barrier, at least one crew member mutated into a godlike being, forcing the ship's captain to order the *Valiant* destroyed to prevent the escape of the mutated crew member. ("Where No Man Has Gone Before" [TOS]). SEE: **barrier, galactic**.

Valiant, U.S.S. Federation starship that contacted planet **Eminiar VII** in 2217 and was destroyed. The *Valiant* was declared a casualty in the 500-year-old war between planets Eminiar VII and **Vendikar**. ("A Taste of Armageddon" [TOS]). *We assume this is a different ship from the* S.S. Valiant *that disappeared around 2065. We conjecture that the* Valiant *had a registry number of NCC-1223.*

Valjean. Fictional character, hero of **Victor Hugo**'s 1862 novel ***Les Misérables***. Valjean, guilty of a trivial offense, was relentlessly pursued by **Javert**, a police detective. *Les Misérables* was Maquis leader **Michael Eddington**'s favorite book, and he saw himself as a dashing, romantic figure, fighting the good fight just like Valjean. ("For the Uniform" [DS9]).

Valkris. (Cathie Shirriff). Klingon operative who obtained then-secret **Project Genesis** data from the Federation, providing it to the Klingon government. Valkris was killed by Klingon Commander **Kruge** because she had read the Genesis material, but her death was an honorable one. *(Star Trek III: The Search for Spock).*

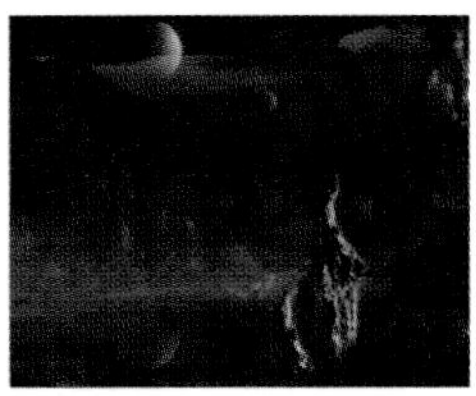

Valley of Chula. Scenic valley on planet **Romulus**. Data re-created the Valley of Chula on the *Enterprise*-D holodeck for the benefit of **Alidar Jarok**, but Jarok found the spectacular sight to be of little comfort. ("The Defector" [TNG]).

Valley. Area on planet **Beta III.** The *Enterprise* landing party claimed to be from the Valley. ("Return of the Archons" [TOS]).

Vallis, Elizabeth. One of five survivors of the crash of the ***S.S. Mariposa*** on the planet of the same name. Vallis and the other four survivors turned to cloning technology to populate their world. ("Up the Long Ladder" [TNG]).

Valo system. A solar system located in neutral space near the **Cardassian** border. Many **Bajorans** settled in the Valo system following the annexation of their homeworld by the Cardassians. Bajoran leader **Keeve Falor** resided in a settlement camp on the southern continent of Valo II. Another Bajoran leader, **Jaz Holza**, lived in a settlement camp on Valo III. The third moon of Valo I had a composition that made sensor readings impossible. The Bajoran terrorist leader **Orta** maintained a base on this moon. ("Ensign Ro" [TNG]).

Valt Minor. Star system neighboring **Krios**, which takes its name from Valt, one of the two brothers who once ruled a vast empire. Valt was at war for centuries with neighboring system Krios (named after Valt's brother), until the historic **Ceremony of Reconciliation** in 2368. ("The Perfect Mate" [TNG]).

Valtane, Dmitri. (Jeremy Roberts). Science officer aboard the ***U.S.S. Excelsior*** under the command of Captain Sulu in 2293. *(Star Trek VI: The Undiscovered Country).* Lieutenant Valtane did not realize that he was the host to a parasitic **memory virus** living in his brain. Valtane was killed in 2293 when the *Excelsior* fought several Klingon battle cruisers near the Azure Nebula. At the moment of his death, the memory virus migrated from Valtane to then-Ensign **Tuvok**. ("Flashback" [VGR]). *Jeremy Roberts portrayed Valtane in both* Star Trek VI: The Undiscovered Country *and "Flashback" (VGR). Some fans have noted an apparent error in "Flashback," in that Valtane was seen alive at the end of Star Trek VI, in contradiction of his death in "Flashback." We can only speculate that Valtane had a twin brother, or that Tuvok's memory wasn't quite perfect.*

Valtese horns. A musical instrument from the **Valt Minor** star system. Though the horns sounded like braying Targhee moonbeasts, they were said to soothe the nerves of Valtese males, at least according to the empathic metamorph Kamala. ("The Perfect Mate" [TNG]).

Valtese. Humanoid civilization inhabiting the star system of **Valt Minor**. ("The Perfect Mate" [TNG]). SEE: **Krios**.

Van Doren, Dr. Cardiologist who developed a **cardiac replacement** technique. Van Doren's procedures were used in the replacement of **Jean-Luc Picard**'s heart in 2327. By 2365, the mortality rate for the procedure had been reduced to 2.4 percent. ("Samaritan Snare" [TNG]).

Van Gelder, Dr. Simon. (Morgan Woodward). Director of the **Tantalus V** penal colony in 2266. Van Gelder became dangerously insane from testing an experimental **neural neutralizer** device, after which **Dr. Tristan Adams** took control of the colony, using the neural neutralizer to further his own goals. Van Gelder recovered and returned to his duties as director after Adams died from exposure to the neutralizer. ("Dagger of the Mind" [TOS]). *Actor Morgan Woodward would later portray Captain Ron Tracey in "The Omega Glory" (TOS).*

Van Mayter, Lieutenant. An *Enterprise*-D crew member and part of the engineering staff. Van Mayter was killed when she was caught in a section of the ship that phased out of existence when exposed to dark matter in the **Mar Oscura** Nebula in 2367. The phasing caused the lieutenant to be trapped in the deck itself. ("In Theory" [TNG]).

Vanderberg, Chief Engineer. (Ken Lynch). Leader of the **pergium** mining station on **Janus VI** in 2267. Vanderberg summoned the *Enterprise* when 50 of his men were mysteriously killed by an entity later learned to be an intelligent subterranean life-form known as the **Horta**. ("The Devil in the Dark" [TOS]).

Vandor IV. Planetoid in the Vandor star system; the location of **Dr. Paul Manheim**'s laboratory, where he conducted studies into the relationships between time and gravity. Manheim lived there with his wife, **Jenice Manheim**. ("We'll Always Have Paris" [TNG]).

Vandor star system. Remote binary system consisting of a B-class giant with an orbiting companion pulsar. Location of **Dr. Paul Manheim**'s laboratory. ("We'll Always Have Paris" [TNG]).

Vandros IV. Planet in the Gamma Quadrant where an ancient **Iconian gateway** was discovered by Dominion scientists in 2372. ("To the Death" [DS9]).

Vanna. (Charlene Polite). One of the leaders of the **Troglyte** underground on planet **Ardana**, known as the **Disrupters**, who won early reforms for the Troglyte working class in 2269. ("The Cloud Minders" [TOS]).

Vanoben transport. Spacecraft. A valuable, ornately carved sphere was stolen from a Vanoben transport in 2369. An item looking very much like this artifact was subsequently brought to Deep Space 9 by the **Miradorn** twins **Ah-Kel** and **Ro-Kel**, who were seeking a buyer for their prize. ("Vortex" [DS9]).

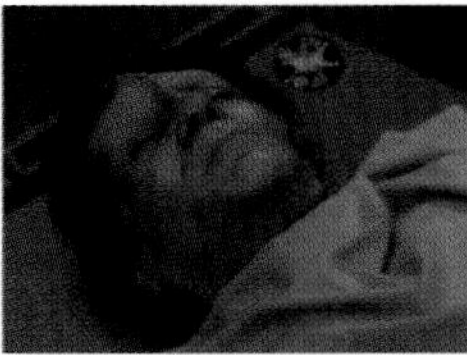

Vantika, Rao. (James Harper). **Kobliad** scientist and criminal who fled Kobliad authorities for 20 years before finally being killed on station Deep Space 9 in 2369. Vantika had been using illegal means to obtain **deuridium**, a substance needed to prolong his life, when he was captured by Kobliad security officer **Kajada**. Vantika transferred his consciousness to Dr. Julian Bashir, using a **microscopic generator** device, intending to escape in Bashir's body. His plan failed when Dax trapped Vantika's consciousness in an energy containment cell, then Kajada destroyed the cell. ("The Passenger" [DS9]).

Varani. (William Schallert). Renowned Bajoran musician who had performed at the **Jalanda Forum** before it was destroyed. After the Cardassian occupation, Varani was reduced to playing at such venues as Quark's bar on Deep Space 9. ("Sanctuary" [DS9]). *William Schallert also played Nilz Baris in "The Trouble with Tribbles" (TOS).*

Varaxian LM-7. A deadly biological weapon. ("Business As Usual" [DS9]).

Varel. (Susanna Thompson). Romulan officer. She was an assistant to Mirok during the testing of a **Romulan interphase** generator in 2368. ("The Next Phase" [TNG]).

Varis Sul. (Gina Phillips). Leader, or **tetrarch,** of the **Paqu** village on planet **Bajor**. Varis Sul came to Deep Space 9 in 2369 to negotiate land boundaries with representatives of the rival **Navot** village. Varis, who was only 15 years old at the time of the negotiations, had become the leader of the Paqu when her parents were killed by the **Cardassians**. While on the station, Varis became friends with **Nog** and **Jake Sisko**, who gave her the idea of turning the border dispute into an opportunity. She decided to compromise by offering free trade access to both sides of the river in exchange for giving the Navot back their land. ("The Storyteller" [DS9]). SEE: **Ferengi Rules of Acquisition; Glyrhond**.

Varley, Captain Donald. (Thalmus Rasulala). Friend to Jean-Luc Picard and commander of the ***U.S.S. Yamato*** at the time of its destruction in 2365. ("Contagion" [TNG]). *Two of Varley's officers, unseen but referred to on Varley's computer-screen logs, were Commander Steve Gerber and Lieutenant Commander Beth Woods, named for the episode's writers. Varley may have been named for noted s-f writer John Varley.*

varmeliate fiber. Foodstuff from the planet **Napinne.** Neelix brought some varmeliate fiber to the *Voyager* from Napinne. ("Learning Curve" [VGR]).

Varon-T disruptor. A small pistol, banned in the Federation. Only five of these devices were manufactured; **Zibalian** trader **Kivas Fajo** reportedly owned four of them. A vicious weapon, the Varon-T disrupted the body from the inside out, causing a slow and painful death. Fajo used one of the disruptors to kill his assistant, **Varria**, in 2366. ("The Most Toys" [TNG]).

Varria. (Jane Daly). Assistant to Zibalian trader **Kivas Fajo**. Varria came into Fajo's employ as a young adult and served him for 14 years, during which the amoral Fajo delighted at the gradual loss of her ideals. In 2366, when Fajo kidnapped Data, Varria attempted to help Data escape. Varria was murdered by Fajo during the escape attempt. ("The Most Toys" [TNG]).

Vash. (Jennifer Hetrick). Archaeologist and adventurer. Jean-Luc Picard first met Vash on the resort planet **Risa** in 2366. Vash, an attractive human female, had been an assistant to scientist **Dr. Samuel Estragon** as he searched for the fabled *Tox Uthat*. After Estragon's death, in 2366, Vash used his notes to locate the *Uthat*, buried on the resort planet of Risa. Vash had competitors in her search, including Estragon's ex-associate **Sovak** and two **Vorgon** criminals from the future. Picard, vacationing on Risa at the time, assisted Vash. Although the *Uthat* was later destroyed by Picard, he and Vash parted friends, after having become romantically involved during their adventure. ("Captain's Holiday" [TNG]). Vash returned to the *Enterprise*-D to attend a **Federation Archaeology Council** symposium held there in 2367. She was abducted, along with Picard and other *Enterprise*-D personnel, by **Q**, who cast them all into an elaborate recreation of Earth's ancient **Robin Hood** legends. Despite this, Vash later agreed to join Q in exploring unknown parts of the galaxy. ("QPid" [TNG]). She explored the Gamma Quadrant for two years with Q, but eventually left him to explore on her own. In 2369, Vash was discovered in the Gamma Quadrant by the runabout ***U.S.S. Ganges*** and brought back to Deep Space 9, bringing with her several artifacts from her travels. Vash attempted to raise money by auctioning some of her treasures at **Quark's bar**, but one of the artifacts contained a life-form from the Gamma Quadrant that generated a **graviton field** that nearly destroyed the station. Having been away from Earth for 12 years, Vash was tempted to accept an invitation from the **Daystrom Institute** to speak on her travels, but she ultimately declined. ("Q-Less" [DS9]).

vasokin. Experimental drug that can increase blood flow to a humanoid patient's organs. In 22 percent of cases on record as of 2371, vasokin had the side effect of causing severe damage to the subject's lungs, kidneys, heart, and even brain. In 2371 it was used to prolong the life of **Vedek Bareil** so he could continue peace negotiations with the Cardassians. ("Life Support" [DS9]).

Vassbinder, Dr. Federation scientist. Vassbinder spoke at a deep-space psychology seminar attended by members of the *Enterprise*-D crew in 2369. Vassbinder gave what Picard described as a "hypnotic" lecture on the ionization effect of warp nacelles before realizing he was supposed to be talking about psychology. ("Timescape" [TNG]). Wesley Crusher cited Vassbinder's research in disapproving of a warp relay upgrade which Geordi La Forge had installed on the *Enterprise*-D. ("Journey's End" [TNG]).

Vatm, Dr. (Tom Towles). Prominent **Nezu** astrophysicist. In 2373, Dr. Vatm learned that the asteroids that had been plaguing a Nezu colony world were artificial, and that they were sent by the **Etanian Order** as a prelude to invasion. Dr. Vatm secretly collected information about Etanian technology, discovering that one of the Nezu colonists was a traitor. The traitor was **Sklar**, who then poisoned Vatm to prevent any interference in the Etanian plan. ("Rise" [VGR]). *Tom Towles previously portrayed Hon'Tihl in "Dramatis Personae" (DS9).*

Vault of Eternal Destitution. In **Ferengi** mythology, the part of the afterlife reserved for those who have failed to earn a profit during their mortal lives. ("Little Green Men" [DS9]).

Vault of Tomorrow. Subterranean chamber on planet **Janus VI** where the **silicon-based life**-form known as the **Horta** kept the eggs from which would be born their next generation. Federation miners on Janus VI broke into the Vault of Tomorrow in 2267, thereby accidentally threatening the future of the Horta species. ("The Devil in the Dark" [TOS]).

Vaytan. Star with a superdense corona. Vaytan was chosen as the site for the first test of a new **metaphasic shield** device in 2369. ("Suspicions" [TNG]).

Vedek Assembly. Influential congress of 112 **Bajoran** spiritual leaders on planet **Bajor**. Among the members of the assembly in 2369 were **Vedek Bareil** (*pictured*) and Vedek **Winn**, two leading contenders to become the next **kai**, following the departure of **Kai Opaka**. Vedek Bareil told Commander Sisko he longed for the simplicity of his arboretum after listening to 112 vedeks speaking at once. ("In the Hands of the Prophets" [DS9]). In 2370, the **Bajoran Chamber of Ministers** and the **Vedek** Assembly denied a request from Skrreean refugees to colonize on planet Bajor. ("Sanctuary" [DS9]).

vedek. Title given to a **Bajoran** religious leader who was a member of the powerful **Vedek Assembly**. ("In the Hands of the Prophets" [DS9]).

Vega Colony. Federation settlement. The *U.S.S. Enterprise*, under the command of Captain Christopher Pike, was en route to the Vega Colony when it picked up a distress call from the ***S.S. Columbia*** in 2254. ("The Cage," "The Menagerie, Part I" [TOS]). *Vega is the brightest star in the constellation Lyra (the harp) as seen from Earth.*

Vega IX probe. A long-range automated Starfleet probe that was sent to record the collapse of **Beta Stromgren** in 2366. The probe discovered the living spacecraft code-named **Tin Man** in orbit of the star. ("Tin Man" [TNG]).

Vega-Omicron Sector. Region of space. Patrol assignment of the ***U.S.S. Aries*** at the time Riker declined the opportunity to command that ship in 2365. ("The Icarus Factor" [TNG]).

Vegan choriomeningitis. Rare and deadly disease. James Kirk almost died of Vegan choriomeningitis in his youth. The disease remained dormant in his bloodstream and in 2268 was used by people of planet Gideon to infect volunteers willing to die to solve their overpopulation crisis. Symptoms include high fever, pain in the extremities, delirium, and death if not treated within 24 hours. ("The Mark of Gideon" [TOS]).

vegetable bouillon. Clear soup made from plants. Captain Janeway liked vegetable bouillon. ("Eye of the Needle" [VGR]).

***VeK'tal* response.** A measure of Klingon physiological condition. ("Ethics" [TNG]).

Vek. Civilization. The Vek were at war with the Minnobian people in 2373. ("Business As Usual" [DS9]).

***veklava*.** Bajoran food. *Veklava* was served on Deep Space 9 in 2372 at the reception for the Trill science team led by Lenara Kahn. ("Rejoined" [DS9]).

Vekma. (Laura Drake). Klingon warrior, female; crew member aboard the Klingon vessel ***Pagh*** during Riker's tenure as first officer on that ship in 2365. Vekma had fun at Riker's expense, wondering out loud if Riker would have the stamina to endure a Klingon female. It is not known if she had the chance to satisfy her curiosity. ("A Matter of Honor" [TNG]). *Vekma was not identified by name in the episode; her name appears only in the script.*

Vekor. (Caitlin Brown). Member of the band of mercenaries led by **Arctus Baran.** She was present during the abduction of Commander Riker from **Barradas III.** Vekor joined in the mutiny against Baran, and was part of the mercenary landing party to Vulcan. She was killed there when **Tallera** activated the **psionic resonator**. ("Gambit, Parts I and II" [TNG]). *Caitlin Brown also played Ty Kajada in "The Passenger" (DS9), as well as Na'Toth, the Narn ambassadorial aide during the first season of* Babylon 5.

Vel. (James Parks). **Akritirian** freighter master and member of the terrorist group **Open Sky**. He had a younger sister, Piri. The explosive device used to bomb the **Laktivia** recreational facility in 2373 was produced aboard Vel's ship. ("The Chute" [VGR]).

Velara III. Non-Class-M planet that was the object of a **terraforming** project under the direction of **Kurt Mandl** in 2364.

Previously believed to be uninhabited, Velara III was discovered to be the home of subsurface crystalline life-forms called "**microbrains.**" Mandl attempted to conceal the existence of these life-forms because part of his project involved raising the water table on the planet, a move that would threaten the life-forms. Acting in self-defense, the microbrains seized control of the *Starship Enterprise*-D, and the planet was eventually quarantined by Federation order at the request of the microbrains. ("Home Soil" [TNG]).

Vellorian mountains. Mountain range on planet **Barkon IV**. There was a village located some distance from the mountains. Village healer **Talar** surmised incorrectly that Data was a member of a race of "icemen" who were believed to live in these mountains. ("Thine Own Self" [TNG]).

Velos VII Internment Camp. Cardassian prison camp. **Dr. Dekon Elig** was imprisoned at the Velos VII camp and was killed there in 2362 while trying to escape. ("Babel" [DS9]).

Veloz Prime. Class-M planet in the **Demilitarized Zone** on which the Federation maintained a colony. Cardassia took possession of Veloz Prime in 2370 with the signing of the Cardassian-Federation treaty, which placed the planet within Cardassian territory. In 2373, the Maquis, lead by Michael Eddington, used the biogenic agent cobalt diselenide as a biogenic weapon against the Cardassian colony on Veloz Prime. The Maquis intended to reclaim the planet, since cobalt diselenide was deadly only to Cardassians. ("For the Uniform" [DS9]).

Veltan sex idol. A rare objet d'art. Twenty-fourth century collector **Palor Toff** boasted of owning a Veltan sex idol; his friend **Kivas Fajo** claimed to own four. ("The Most Toys" [TNG]).

vendarite. Valuable mineral on planet **Ligos VII**. The renegade Ferengi who invaded the *Enterprise*-D in 2369 used the science team stationed on the planet as slave laborers to mine the vendarite. ("Rascals" [TNG]).

Vendikar. Planet in **Cluster NGC 321** that had been at war with its neighbor **Eminiar VII** for 500 years, ending in 2267. Vendikar was originally settled by people from Eminiar VII, but they turned against their homeworld. The two planets developed an agreement whereby they would conduct their war by computers only. Attacks would be launched mathematically, and those individuals designated as casualties would have 24 hours to report to disintegration chambers so that their deaths could be recorded. The arrangement lasted until 2267, when Captain Kirk broke the subspace radio link between the two worlds, forcing them to the bargaining table for peace talks. ("A Taste of Armageddon" [TOS]).

"Vengeance Factor, The." *Next Generation* episode #57. Written by Sam Rolfe. Directed by Timothy Bond. Stardate 43421.9. *First* *aired in 1989. A beautiful young woman is actually an old weapon of death whose mission is to exact revenge on a rival clan. The late Sam Rolfe developed* The Man From U.N.C.L.E. *television series in the early 1960s.* GUEST CAST: Lisa Wilcox as **Yuta**; Joey Aresco as **Brull**; Nancy Parsons as **Marouk**; Stephen Lee as **Chorgan**; Marc Lawrence as **Volnoth**; Elkanah Burns as **Temarek**. SEE: **Acamar III; Acamar system; Acamarians/ Gatherers; Artonian lasers; Brull; Chorgan; Gamma Hromi II; *Goddard, U.S.S.*; Hromi Cluster; Marouk; microvirus; noranium alloy; *parthas* à la Yuta; Penthor-Mul; Starbase 343; Temarek; Tonkian homing beacons; Tralesta; Volnoth; Yuta.**

Ventanian thimble. An archeological artifact from the Lapeongical period of Ventanian history. Captain Picard kept one on his ready-room desk. He was impressed that **Kamala**, the **empathic metamorph** from Krios, recognized it, just as she knew he would be. ("The Perfect Mate" [TNG]).

Ventax II. A Class-M planet that, a millennium ago, suffered from terrible wars and environmental havoc. According to Ventaxian legend, this dark age was ended by the Contract of Ardra, in which the mythic figure **Ardra** agreed to grant a thousand years of peace and prosperity in exchange for the population delivering itself into slavery at the end of the millennium. Federation anthropologist **Dr. Howard Clark** issued a distress call from Ventax II in 2367 when a con artist identifying herself as Ardra attempted to collect on that contract. First contact with the Ventaxians had been made in 2297 by a Klingon expedition. ("Devil's Due" [TNG]).

ventral impeller. Propulsion device mounted on the bottom of **Jem'Hadar warships**, presumably used for planetary landing and takeoff. ("The Ship" [DS9]).

Venture, U.S.S. Federation starship, *Galaxy* class, Starfleet registry number NCC-71854. The *U.S.S. Venture* was the lead ship in the relief force of starships sent by Starfleet in 2372 to help station Deep Space 9 deal with the Klingon invasion of Cardassian space. Admiral Hastur led the relief force and probably embarked on the *Venture.* ("The Way of the Warrior" [DS9]).

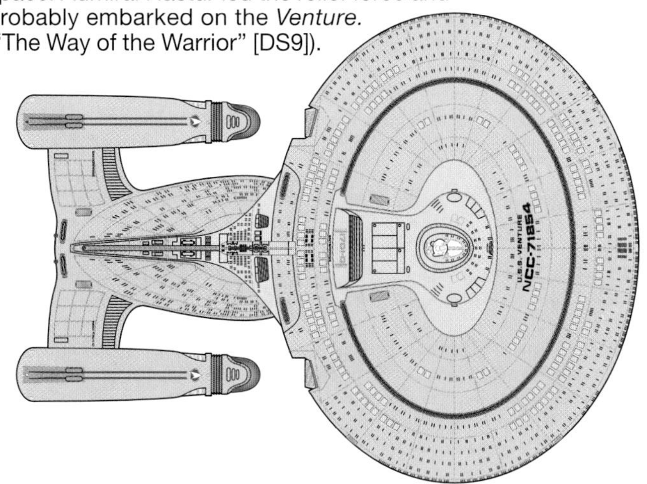

Venus drug. An illegal substance believed to make women more beautiful and men more handsome and attractive to the opposite sex. Although the drug appeared to be highly effective when used to enhance the appearance of Mudd's women, it was later noted that a placebo dose (consisting of inert gelatin) had a similar effect when ingested by **Eve McHuron**, suggesting that belief in oneself is still the most effective enhancement of all. ("Mudd's Women" [TOS]).

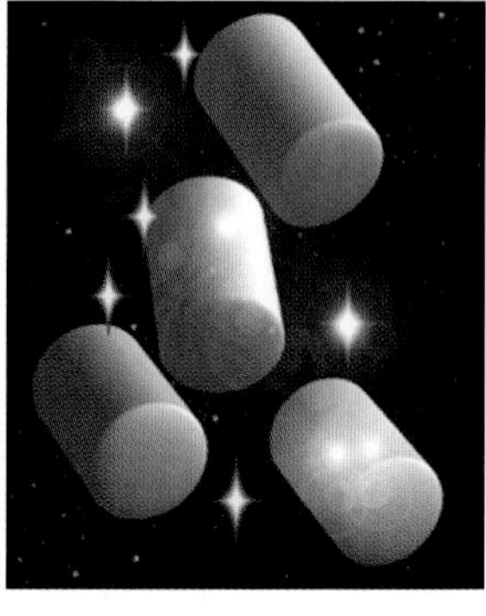

Venus. The second planet in the Sol system. In 2371 several **terraforming** stations were in operation on Venus. ("Past Tense, Part I" [DS9]). During Chakotay's first year at the academy, he trained as a pilot for a couple of months on Venus to learn how to handle atmospheric storms. ("Future's End, Part II" [VGR]).

Verad. (John Glover). **Trill** initiate whose application for joining with a Trill **symbiont** was rejected by the **Symbiosis Evaluation Board**. Although 90 percent of all initiates are similarly rejected, Verad refused to accept this decision and attempted to steal the **Dax** symbiont from **Jadzia Dax** in 2370. Verad was nearly successful in executing an elaborate scheme in which he employed **Klingon** mercenaries to commandeer station **Deep Space 9** and forced station medical personnel to surgically transfer the symbiont from Jadzia to himself. The surgical procedure was completed, but station personnel regained control of the facility and reversed the procedure before Jadzia suffered permanent injury. Verad had hoped to escape into the **Gamma Quadrant** with his companion, **Mareel**, but Mareel's realization that Verad Dax was not the same man she had earlier loved contributed to his downfall. Although the removal of the symbiont left Verad mentally incapacitated, Mareel said she would care for him for the rest of his life. ("Invasive Procedures" [DS9]).

Verath. Star system. A statue from the Verath system was auctioned off at Quark's bar by archaeologist **Vash** in 2369. Vash explained that the civilization of the Verathans reached its height 30,000 years ago and conducted trade to other systems through an interconnected communication network. ("Q-Less" [DS9]).

Veridian III. Uninhabited Class-M planet in the **Veridian system**. In 2371, the **nexus** energy ribbon passed very near to Veridian III. For this reason, **Dr. Tolian Soran** used Veridian III as the launch site for his **trilithium** probe, used in his unsuccessful attempt to extinguish the Veridian star. The Saucer Module of the *Starship* ***Enterprise*-D** crash-landed on the surface of Veridian III in the incident, which also claimed the life of former *Enterprise* Captain **James T. Kirk**. Captain Kirk is buried on a mountaintop on planet Veridian III. *(Star Trek Generations). The mountaintop scenes in* Star Trek Generations *were filmed at a location called the Valley of Fire, near Las Vegas, Nevada.*

Veridian IV. Class-M planet in the **Veridian system** which, in 2371, supported a pre-industrial humanoid society with a population of 230 million. *(Star Trek Generations).*

Veridian system. Star system with four planets orbiting the star Veridian. Two planets in the system, Veridian III and IV, were Class-M worlds. The **nexus** energy ribbon passed through the Veridian system in 2371. *(Star Trek Generations).*

Veridium Six. A slow-acting, cumulative poison. Veridium Six was used to kill Klingon High Council leader **K'mpec** in 2367. Administered in small doses in K'mpec's favorite wine, the poison had no antidote. ("Reunion" [TNG]).

Verillians. Sentient culture. In 2373, some Verillians were in the market for sophisticated weapons. They eventually made a deal with the **Metron Consortium**. ("Business As Usual" [DS9]).

vermicula. A food consisting of small wormlike animals, consumed by the humanoid inhabitants of planet **Antede III**. ("Manhunt" [TNG]).

vertazine. Medication used by Federation medical personnel to combat vertigo. ("Cause and Effect" [TNG], "Parallels" [TNG]).

verterium cortenide. Densified composite material composed of polysilicate verterium and monocrystal cortenum. The *U.S.S. Voyager*'s warp coils were made of verterium cortenide. ("Investigations" [VGR]).

verteron mine. Weapon designed by Hekaran scientists **Serova** and **Rabal**. These devices, which resembled signal buoys, were programmed to emit a massive **verteron** pulse when any ship approached. The pulse would effectively disable all the **subspace** systems of the affected ship. ("Force of Nature" [TNG]).

verteron. Subatomic particle associated with **subspace** phenomena. Artificially created verterons allow a vessel on impulse power to pass through the **Bajoran wormhole** unharmed. A class on the subject taught by **Keiko O'Brien** at her school on Deep Space 9 in 2369 explained this fact to her students, despite Vedek **Winn**'s objections that such a lesson might be considered blasphemy in the Bajoran religion. ("In the Hands of the Prophets" [DS9]). Verterons can block sensor operation, and were suggested as a possible method for disguising the hulk of the ***Pegasus*** from the Romulan sensors. ("The *Pegasus*" [TNG]). Within the Bajoran wormhole, concentrations of verterons formed verteron-nodes, appearing as spherical objects. They generally have no adverse effect on a ship passing through the wormhole, but verteron-node radiation caused resonance leakage and rapid expansion of a **protouniverse** being transported through the wormhole in 2370. ("Playing God" [DS9]). Verterons were detected from the **micro-wormhole** encountered by the *Starship Voyager* on stardate 48579. ("Eye of the Needle" [VGR]). SEE: **silithium**. The Delta Quadrant terminus of the Barzan wormhole disappeared in mid-2372, leaving behind a slight subspace instability. Ensign Harry Kim and Lieutenant B'Elanna Torres caused the Barzan wormhole to reappear by bombarding the subspace instability with verteron particles. ("False Profits" [VGR]).

Vertiform City. SEE: **emergent life-form holodeck sequence.**

vertion. Subatomic particle. The only natural source of vertion particles is white dwarf stars. The **emergent life-form** aboard the *Enterprise*-D in 2370 used vertion particles to construct a semiorganic artificial life-form. Chief Engineer Geordi La Forge was able to create vertions for the emergent life-form by detonating a modified photon torpedo in the **McPherson Nebula**. ("Emergence" [TNG]).

veruul. A Romulan expletive. Riker used this term to counter Alidar Jarok's insults to Lieutenant Worf. ("The Defector" [TNG]).

Veta, Admiral. Senior Starfleet officer. In 2373 Admiral Veta attended what would have been the signing ceremony for Bajor's entrance into the Federation, held at Deep Space 9. ("Rapture" [DS9]).

Vetar. Cardassian warship, ***Galor* class**, commanded by **Gul Evek**. The *Vetar* was present at planet **Dorvan V** in 2370 during Evek's mission to survey the planet. ("Journey's End" [TNG]). The *Vetar* was destroyed in 2371 when Evek's ship was destroyed in the **Badlands**. ("Caretaker" [VGR]).

Vhnori transference ritual. Ceremony in which a **Vhnori** person enters a **cenotaph** to end his or her life so that he or she can be sent to the **Next Emanation** through a **spectral rupture**. Some Vhnori came to doubt the validity of the transference ritual after Ensign Harry Kim appeared on their homeworld in 2371, apparently from the Next Emanation. ("Emanations" [VGR]).

Vhnori. Technologically sophisticated humanoid civilization. The Vhnori didn't believe in any kind of spirit in the manner common to many other humanoid cultures. The Vhnori sent their dead through **spectral ruptures** into the **Next Emanation** in a ceremony called a **Vhnori transference ritual**. They believed that in the afterlife they would reach a higher consciousness and be reunited with their dead relatives there. *Voyager* officer Harry Kim briefly visited the Vhnori homeworld in 2371 by means of a spectral rupture. Because the spectral rupture traversed an unknown distance, the actual location of the Vhnori homeworld remained a mystery; it may have been located in another galaxy, another time, or even another dimension. ("Emanations" [VGR]). SEE: **cenotaph; Ptera; thanatologist**.

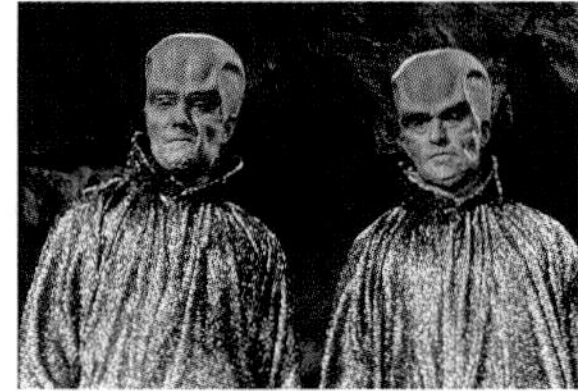

Vians. Advanced humanoid civilization of unknown origin. The Vians rendered aid to the **Minaran star system** in 2268 when the star went nova. Due to limited resources, the Vians had the ability to save the inhabitants of only one of the Minaran planets. The Vians therefore conducted an elaborate experiment to determine which planet's inhabitants would be saved. The extraordinary self-sacrifice of the **Minaran empath**, Gem, caused the Vians to choose to save **Gem**'s people. ("The Empath" [TOS]).

Vicarian razorback. Animal life-form; a vicious and dangerous beast. ("The Die is Cast" [DS9]).

Vico, S.S. Federation research vessel, *Oberth* class, registry number NAR-18834. In 2368, the *Vico* was assigned to explore the interior of the **Black Cluster**. Inside the cluster, the *Vico* encountered severe gravitational wavefronts that were amplified by the *Vico*'s shields, destroying the ship. There was only one survivor, a young boy named **Timothy**, who was rescued by the *Enterprise*-D. ("Hero Worship" [TNG]). *Because the* Vico *had an S.S. designation and it did not have an NCC registry prefix, we assume it was not a Starfleet vessel, even though it was of Federation registry.*

Victory, H.M.S. Ancient British sailing ship. The *H.M.S. Victory* was **Lord Horatio Nelson**'s (1758-1805) flagship during the **Battle of Trafalgar**, in which he was killed. Geordi La Forge built a large model of the oceangoing vessel as a gift for *Starship Victory* **Captain Zimbata**. ("Elementary, Dear Data" [TNG]). Prior to the **Borg** encounter of 2366-2367, Captain Jean-Luc Picard drew inspiration from Nelson's courage at Trafalgar. ("The Best of Both Worlds, Part I" [TNG]). *Geordi's* Victory *model still graces the late Gene Roddenberry's office in the home of his widow, Majel Barrett Roddenberry.*

Victory, U.S.S. Federation *Constellation*-class starship, registry number NCC-9754. Commanded by **Captain Zimbata**. Geordi La Forge served as an ensign aboard the *Victory* prior to his assignment to the *Enterprise*-D. ("Elementary, Dear Data" [TNG]). In 2362, a *Victory* away team was sent to the surface of planet **Tarchannen III** to investigate the disappearance of 49 Federation personnel. It was not realized at the time that all five members of that team (including Geordi La Forge) were infected with an alien DNA strand that would compel them to return to Tarchannen III five years later. ("Identity Crisis" [TNG]). *The* Victory *was a re-use of the* U.S.S. Stargazer *model originally built for "The Battle" (TNG).*

victurium alloy. Metal used in the structure of some space vehicles. The *Enterprise*-D transporters were unable to penetrate the large amount of alloy in the hull of the ***S.S. Vico***. ("Hero Worship" [TNG]).

Vidiian Sodality. Government of the Vidiian people in the Delta Quadrant. ("Phage" [VGR], "Faces" [VGR]).

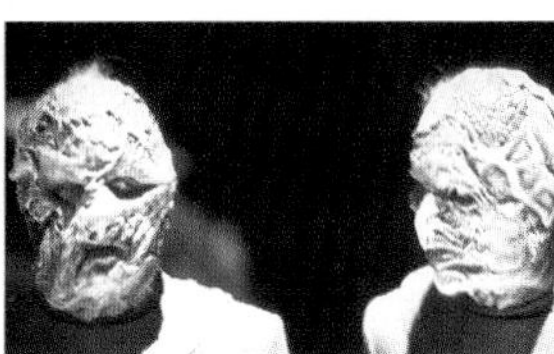

Vidiians. Humanoid species native to the **Delta Quadrant**. Once known as a society of educators, artists, and explorers, the Vidiians were stricken two millennia ago by a terrible disease known as the **phage**, which destroyed the organs of their bodies. The Vidiians survived only through the widespread use of organ transplantation to replace diseased body parts. Although Vidiians relied largely on transplants from dead bodies, their needs were so great that they captured individuals of other species to serve as involuntary organ donors. The **Vidiian Sodality** developed sophisticated medical technology to make extensive interspecies transplants possible. ("Phage" [VGR]). SEE: **Dereth; *honatta*; Motura; Neelix**. Because of the debilitating nature of the phage, the Vidiians often used healthy captives as slaves to perform hard labor, prior to killing them for organ harvesting. ("Faces" [VGR]). In 2372, Vidiian physician **Danara Pel** provided medical assistance to *Voyager* officers Janeway and Chakotay, saving their lives from an unknown viral disease. Unfortunately, other Vidiians took advantage of Pel's humanitarian mission to launch an attack on the *Voyager*. ("Resolutions" [VGR]). *Pictured symbol of Vidiian Sodality.*

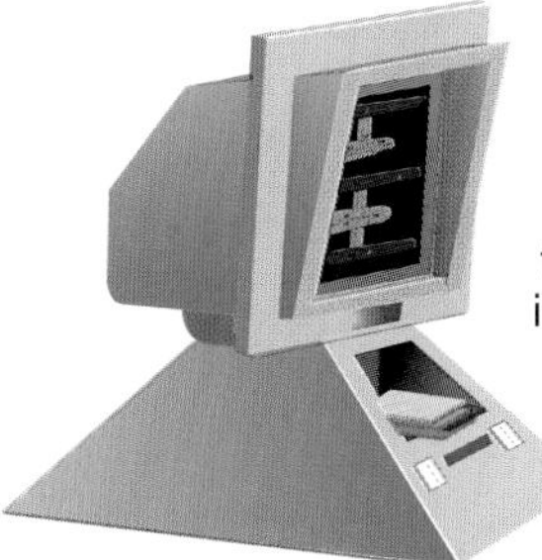

viewer. Generic term describing visual display screens used aboard Federation starships. Some viewers include holographic screen matrices, enabling them to display three-dimensional images. Viewers can be small desktop devices intended for personal use, or can be large wall-mounted units as in a main viewer on a starship's bridge.

Vigo, Jason. (Ken Olandt). Born in 2346 to **Miranda Vigo** and a Starfleet officer. Jason moved to **Camor V** with his mother in 2358. Life on Camor V proved difficult, and Jason was arrested by local authorities for several minor offenses. In 2370, former DaiMon **Bok** surreptitiously resequenced Jason's DNA to make it appear that Jason was the son of *Enterprise*-D Captain **Jean-Luc Picard**, who had in fact had an affair with Jason's mother in 2346. Bok planned to let Picard believe that he had a son, then planned to kill this long-lost offspring. Bok hoped this would gain revenge against Picard for Picard's role in the death of Bok's son in the **Battle of Maxia** in 2355. As a result of Bok's genetic tampering, Jason developed **Forrester-Trent Syndrome**, a treatable condition that provided evidence of Bok's plot. Bok's plan failed, and Jason returned to Camor V, having found not a father but perhaps a new friend. ("Bloodlines" [TNG]).

Vigo, Miranda. Mother of **Jason Vigo. Miranda** was born on **New Gaul** around 2320 and trained as a botanist. She had a brief but intense romantic relationship with **Jean-Luc Picard** in 2346 and although the couple planned to stay in touch, they never saw each other again. In 2346, Miranda had a son, Jason, by an unnamed Starfleet officer; the boy never learned the true identity of his father. In 2358, Miranda and her ten-year-old child moved to **Camor V**, where she cared for orphans left homeless from the Cardassian war. Although it was a difficult life, Miranda enjoyed tending crops and teaching the orphans to read and survive. Her untimely death came at the hands of two men on the streets of Camor V who killed her for the food she was carrying. ("Bloodlines" [TNG]). *We suspect that an early draft of "Bloodlines" may have intended Miranda to be a former member of Picard's crew aboard the* Stargazer*, since his weapons officer aboard that ship (seen in "The Battle" [TNG]) was named* ***Vigo****. We speculate that as the story was developed, the* Stargazer *connection was dropped, but the character name was not changed.*

Vigo. Weapons officer aboard the ***U.S.S. Stargazer*** during the **Battle of Maxia** in the year 2355 under the command of Captain Jean-Luc Picard. ("The Battle" [TNG]).

***viinerine*.** Traditional Romulan food. Troi, masquerading as a Romulan officer, misidentified another Romulan dish as *viinerine*, but managed to bluff her way out of the situation. ("Face of the Enemy" [TNG]).

Vilix'pran. Humanoid Starfleet officer on station **Deep Space 9**. In 2371, he held the rank of ensign and was expecting twins through a process called budding. ("Heart of Stone" [DS9]). By 2373, he held the rank of lieutenant and had six offspring, with more buds on the way. ("Apocalypse Rising" [DS9]). Vilix'pran's children had little wings. **Jake Sisko** sometimes babysat with them. ("Business As Usual" [DS9]).

Vilmor II. Planet in the Vilmoran system covered by dry ocean beds but little life. Billions of years ago, Vilmor II was covered by oceans full of life that had been seeded by ancient humanoids some four billion years ago. The genetic codes from fossils on Vilmor II provided the last pieces of an interstellar puzzle left behind by those humanoids in the genes of life on planets across the galaxy. ("The Chase" [TNG]). SEE: **humanoid life**.

Vin. (Dick Miller). Sergeant in the **Sanctuary District** Police in **San Francisco** on **Earth** in 2024. Vin was one of the hostages taken during the **Bell Riots**. ("Past Tense, Parts I and II" [DS9]). *Vin's last name was never given.*

Vina. (Susan Oliver). A crew member aboard the ***S.S. Columbia,*** and the only survivor of the expedition when it crashed on planet **Talos IV** in 2236. The **Talosians** cared for her and attempted to mend her wounds, but had no idea what a human being should look like. As a result, Vina was restored to health, but was severely disfigured. ("The Cage," "The Menagerie, Parts I and II" [TOS]).

Vinod. (Michael Buchman Silver). Son of **Orellius** colony leader **Alixus**. He assisted his mother in her plans to strand the colonists of the ***Santa Maria*** on planet Orellius . ("Paradise" [DS9]).

"Violations." *Next Generation* episode #112. Teleplay by Pamela Gray and Jeri Taylor. Story by Shari Goodhartz and T. Michael and Pamela Gray. Directed by Robert Wiemer. Stardate 45429.3. *First aired in 1992. A researcher visiting the* Enterprise-D *commits a number of brutal telepathic rapes.* GUEST CAST: Rosalind Chao as **O'Brien**, **Keiko**; Ben Lemon as **Jev**; David Sage as **Tarmin**; Rick Fitts as **Martin**, **Dr.**; Eve Brenner as **Inad**; Doug Wert as **Crusher**, **Jack**; Craig Benton as **Davis**, **Ensign**; Majel Barrett as Computer voice. SEE: **antimatter containment; Betazoids; Circassian cat; CPK levels; Crusher, Jack R.; Davis, Ensign; diencephalon; hippocampus; histamine; Hurada III; Inad; Iresine Syndrome; Japanese brush writing; Jev; Kaldra IV; Keller, Ensign; La Forge, Geordi; Martin, Dr.; Melina II; Nel system; O'Brien, Keiko; Obachan; Starbase 440; Tarmin; telepathic memory invasion; thalamus; Ullians.**

Viorsa. (Thomas Kopache). Planner and resident of the ill-fated **Kohl settlement** in the Delta Quadrant when their planet entered a period of severe glaciation. Viorsa was one of the five settlers who entered stasis in the **Kohl hibernation system** in order to wait until the glaciation ended. Their hibernation system malfunctioned, creating a malevolent **Clown** character out of the fear that existed in their collected consciousnesses. The Clown held them captive and killed three of them, including Viorsa, before the remaining two, the physician and the programmer, were rescued by the crew of the *Voyager* in 2372. ("The Thaw" [VGR]). *Thomas Kopache was previously seen as the Romulan Mirok in "The Next Phase" (TNG).*

Virak'kara. (Scott Haven) **Jem'Hadar** warrior. Virak'kara, who served under the command of Omet'iklan, was part of the Jem'Hadar squad assigned to prevent a group of renegade Jem'Hadar from using an **Iconian gateway** in 2372. ("To the Death" [DS9]).

virtual display. Personal visual display device used for command intelligence aboard **Jem'Hadar warships**. The display required the use of a headset, which created a visual image that only the wearer could see, so that others aboard the ship thus had no indication as to where the ship was heading. Virtual displays were provided for the Jem'Hadar First and the **Vorta** supervisor. ("The Ship" [DS9]).

visceral writing. Term used by famous writer Revalus, referring to writing with an actual pigment-based pen on real paper, allowing the artist to fully experience the sensation of creativity. ("The Muse" [DS9]).

vision quest. Self-examination technique, often a rite of puberty, practiced by some Native Americans, involving fasting, isolation, and the seeking of guidance from supernatural forces. Among the colonists of planet **Dorvan V**, an individual seeking a vision would go inside the **Habak** and light a fire. Eventually, the individual would enter a trancelike state and receive a vision, where he would receive guidance from the spirits. **Lakanta** claimed to have seen **Wesley Crusher** in one of his vision quests. Later, Wesley would see his father, **Jack Crusher**, in a vision quest of his own. ("Journey's End" [TNG]). Other Native Americans, including **Chakotay**, (*pictured*) used an ***akoonah*** to aid their vision quest. Chakotay helped Captain Janeway experience her own vision quest in search of her **animal guide**. ("The Cloud" [VGR]). SEE: **Torres, B'Elanna.**

"Visionary." *Deep Space Nine* episode #63. Teleplay by John Shirley. Story by Ethan H. Calk. Directed by Reza Badiyi. No stardate given. *First aired in 1995. While battling a case of radiation poisoning, O'Brien begins to timeshift into the future, where he sees himself killed—and the station destroyed.* GUEST CAST: Jack Shearer as **Ruwon**; Annette Helde as **Karina**; Ray Young as **Morka**; Bob Minor as **Bo'rak**; Dennis Madalone as **Atul**. SEE: **asinolyathin; Atul; basilar arterial scan; Bo'rak; darts; Davlos III; delta-series radioisotopes; hyronalin; Karina; Klingon Intelligence; Morka; quantum singularity; Quark's bar; replicator; Romulans; Ruwon; tetryon particles.**

"Visitor, The." *Deep Space Nine* episode #76. Written by Michael Taylor. Directed by David Livingston. No stardate given. *First aired in 1995. When a freak accident kills Ben Sisko aboard the* Defiant, *his son, Jake, spends the rest of his life searching for a way to reach across time and space to restore his beloved father to life. The future Starfleet uniforms in this episode were originally designed for "All Good Things..." (TNG). "The Visitor" was nominated for a Hugo Award for Best Dramatic Presentation at the 1996 World Science Fiction Convention.* GUEST CAST: Tony Todd as **Sisko, Jake** (older); Galyn Görg as **Sisko, Korena**; Aron Eisenberg as **Nog**; Rachel Robinson as **Melanie**; Majel Barrett as Computer voice. SEE: ***Anslem*; antimatter containment; Bajoran wormhole; Betar Prize; blackened redfish; *Collected Stories*; *Defiant, U.S.S.;* holodeck and holosuite programs; ion surfing; Melanie; Morn; New Orleans; Nog; Sisko's; Sisko, Benjamin; Sisko, Jake; Sisko, Korena; subspace inversion; Takarian mead; temporal signature.**

VISOR. Acronym for Visual Instrument and Sensory Organ Replacement. A remarkable piece of bioelectronic engineering that allowed **Geordi La Forge** to see, despite the fact that he was born blind. A slim device worn over the face like a pair of sunglasses, the VISOR permitted vision not only in visible light, but across much of the electromagnetic spectrum, including infrared and radio waves. The VISOR operates on a subspace field pulse. The VISOR, while giving La Forge better-than-normal sight, also caused him continuous pain. ("Encounter at Farpoint, Part II" [TNG]). A device called a **Visual Acuity Transmitter** was once used with Geordi's VISOR in an attempt to allow transmission of Geordi's visual perceptions, but the device proved unreliable and the images were extremely difficult to interpret. To the untrained eye, the VISOR output resembled a crazy collage of swirling colors and vague shapes. ("Heart of Glory" [TNG]). **Dr. Katherine Pulaski** once proposed to Geordi a surgical procedure which would have replaced his VISOR with optical implant devices offering nearly

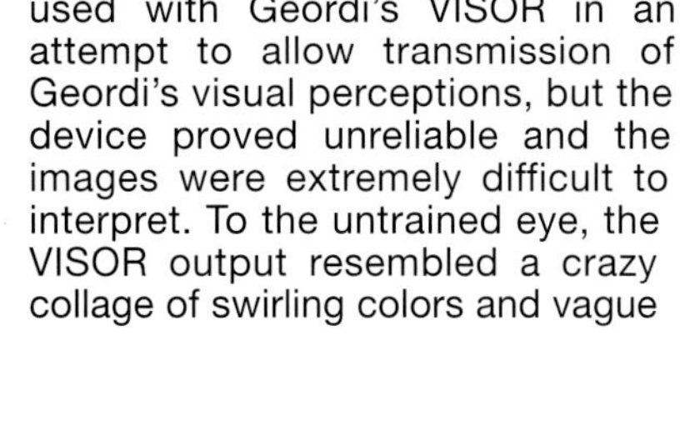

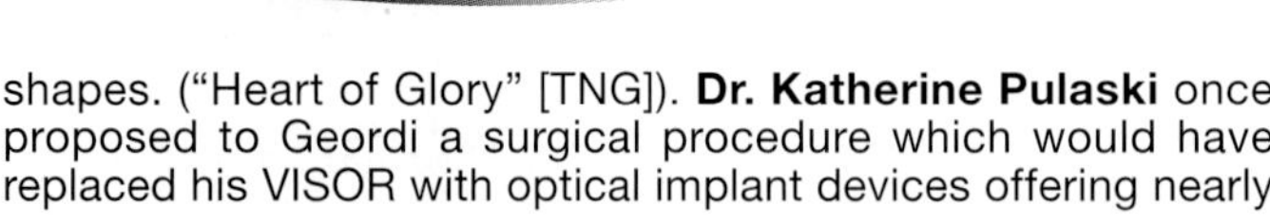

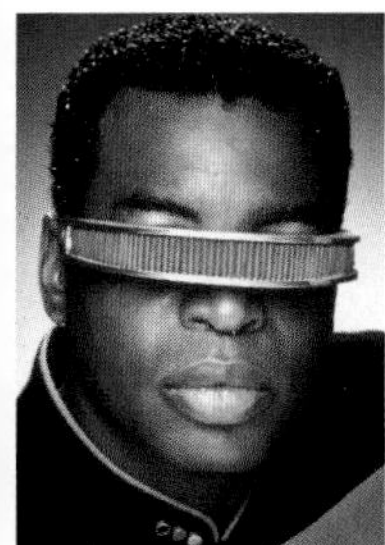

the same visual range. Geordi declined the opportunity. ("Loud as a Whisper" [TNG]). La Forge and Centurion **Bochra** linked La Forge's VISOR with a tricorder to form a device capable of detecting neutrino emissions, since a standard tricorder was incapable of detecting this phenomenon. This improvisation saved both men's lives because they were trapped on planet **Galorndon Core** at the time. ("The Enemy" [TNG]). SEE: **neural output pods**. La Forge's VISOR provided the Romulans with a unique opportunity to use his neural implants to provide direct input to his visual cortex, giving them the ability to program La Forge's mind to commit criminal acts. The Romulans tried unsuccessfully to use La Forge to murder Klingon governor **Vagh** in 2367 with this technique. ("The Mind's Eye" [TNG]). In 2370, when Worf encountered a **quantum anomaly**, the presence of Geordi's VISOR would cause Worf to shift from one reality to the next. As Worf arrived in a **quantum reality** where Geordi was killed, the cause of his shifting was discovered, and the Data of that reality was able to suggest a solution to the problem. ("Parallels" [TNG]). Geordi's VISOR was modified by **Dr. Tolian Soran** in 2371 when La Forge was held captive aboard a Klingon bird-of-prey. The modified VISOR transmitted visual information back to the Klingon ship, giving **Lursa** and **B'Etor** access to vital shield modulation data, making it possible for them to launch a devastating attack on the starship. *(Star Trek Generations).* By stardate 50893, LaForge had been given ocular implants to replace his VISOR. *(Star Trek: First Contact). Geordi's VISOR was modeled on a hair clip donated to the show by UCLA researcher Kiku Annon. Kiku's barette was sprayed with metallic gold paint and used as a prototype for the prop.*

Visual Acuity Transmitter. Small device that permitted the short-range transmission of visual images recorded by the **VISOR** worn by **Geordi La Forge**. This device was used when La Forge participated in a rescue mission to a crippled **Talarian** freighter in 2364, but the unit failed after a short time because the complexity of the signal exceeded the unit's ability to handle. The image displayed by the Visual Acuity Transmitter contained an enormous amount of information, but was difficult for an untrained human to view. ("Heart of Glory" [TNG]).

Vitarian wool underwear. Undergarment. According to Garak, Vitarian wool underwear was unsurpassed in keeping one warm. Garak sold some to Morn in 2372. ("The Way of the Warrior" [DS9]).

Viterian, Captain. (Lesley Kahn). Commander of the Kobheerian transport vessel ***Rak-Minunis***. ("Duet" [DS9]). An image of this Kobheerian captain was programmed into a **holo-filter** aboard the *U.S.S. Defiant* when the ship stopped on its way to Cardassia in 2371. ("Second Skin" [DS9]). *The exact footage of the Kobheerian captain from "Duet" (DS9) was re-used for the Kobheerian captain in "Second Skin," to save production time and money*.

Vixis. (Spice Williams). First officer of the Klingon bird-of-prey commanded by **Captain Klaa**. *(Star Trek V: The Final Frontier).*

Vlugta asteroid belt. Asteroid field in the Vlugtan star system. **Alsia** conned **Martus Mazur** out of 10,000 **isiks** by telling him she needed the money to commission a study on the effect of asteroid mining on intersystem navigation. ("Rivals" [DS9]).

Vlugtan star system. Location of Vlugta asteroid belt. ("Rivals" [DS9]).

Vodrey Nebula. Stellar cloud located near the Maranga star system. Science personnel from the *Starship Enterprise*-D studied the Vodrey Nebula on stardate 47779.4. ("Firstborn" [TNG]). *Named for* Star Trek *fan William F. Vodrey.*

voice-transit conductors. Telecommunications system used by the now-vanished civilization on planet **Kataan**. ("The Inner Light" [TNG]).

Vok'sha. Civilization from the planet Rakella Prime. The Vok'sha believe that hate is a beast that lives in the belly. Their greatest mythical hero is a man who ate stones for 23 days to kill the beast. He is revered as a saint. ("Heroes and Demons" [VGR]).

Volchok Prime. Planet. Ferengi entrepreneur Hoex bought out his rival Turot's controlling interest in a cargo port at Volchok Prime. ("The Nagus" [DS9]).

vole bellies. Commodity traded on the **Ferengi Futures Exchange**. In 2372, Quark traveled to Ferenginar to negotiate a vole belly deal and made a respectable 15 percent profit margin. ("Body Parts" [DS9]).

vole. Cardassian rodent. Significant numbers of rat-like voles remained on station **Deep Space 9** after the Cardassian withdrawal from the facility in 2369. Voles later became a serious problem, chewing through power conduits, apparently attracted to electromagnetic fields. When station personnel contacted the Cardassian Central Command for advice on eradicating these pests, **Gul Evek** sarcastically suggested that a Federation withdrawal from Bajor might solve the problem. ("Playing God" [DS9]). Vole fighting was a popular spectator sport among Cardassian gamblers. In 2371, Quark hoped to set up vole fights by renting the shop next to his bar. ("Destiny" [DS9]). Federation authorities considered vole fighting to be inhumane, and barred such games from station Deep Space 9, much to Quark's chagrin. ("Through the Looking Glass" [DS9]). *The vole was the invention of illustrator Ricardo Delgado and executive producer Ira Steven Behr. The creature itself was designed by makeup supervisor Michael Westmore.*

Volga, U.S.S. Starfleet *Danube*-class runabout assigned to Deep Space 9. Starfleet registry number NCC-73196. In 2372, Major Kira, Doctor Bashir, and Keiko O'Brien used the *Volga* to journey to Torad IV to conduct a three-day botanical survey. On the return trip, the ship encountered an asteroid field which overwhelmed the ship's deflectors. A large rock sideswiped the ship, and O'Brien was severely injured. ("Body Parts" [DS9]). The *Volga* was to have been used in the massive response to an anticipated Dominion invasion of the Alpha Quadrant in 2373. ("By Inferno's Light" [DS9]).

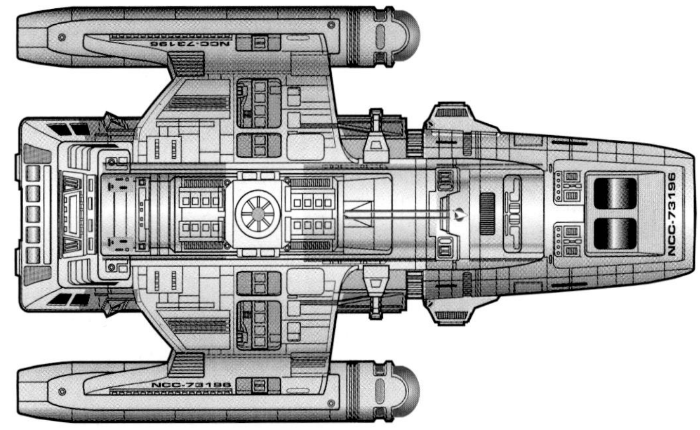

volleyball. Earth team sport played between two teams who use their hands to hit an inflated ball over a net that separates the two teams. Harry Kim enjoyed volleyball and had a holoprogram featuring the 2216 Olympic gold medal volleyball team. ("Warlord" [VGR]). Volleyball was also available in Neelix's **Polynesian resort** program. ("Alter Ego" [VGR]).

Volnar Colony. Settlement in the Bajor sector. One could buy a dozen assorted shapes of *Lobi* crystals for a Cardassian **lek** at the Volnar Colony. ("Caretaker" [VGR]).

Volnoth. (Marc Lawrence). Elderly **Gatherer** and member of the clan **Lornak**. Volnoth died suddenly during the negotiations on **Gamma Hromi II** in 2366. Investigation revealed him to have been murdered by **Yuta** in vengeance for the Lornaks' massacre of the **Tralesta** clan in 2286. ("The Vengeance Factor" [TNG]).

Volon II. Planet that was Federation territory, now in the Demilitarized Zone. Colonized by Federation citizens, including Maquis member **William Samuels**. ("The Maquis, Parts I and II" [DS9]).

Volon III. Planet; location of Federation colonies in the **Demilitarized Zone**. Leaders from each of the colonies in the Volon system would meet periodically on Volon III to discuss colonial matters. The **Maquis** also used the colony for a meeting place. ("The Maquis, Part II" [DS9]). The Cardassian spy altered to pass for **Raymond Boone** took up residence on Volon III and operated a **ladarium** mining sluice there in 2362. ("Tribunal" [DS9]).

***Voltaire*, *Shuttlepod*.** Shuttlepod #03, attached to the *Starship Enterprise*-D. Captain Picard piloted the *Voltaire*, using the shuttlepod to fly ahead of the *Enterprise*-D, guiding the starship out of the **Mar Oscura** Nebula in 2367. The *Voltaire* was destroyed, although Picard was beamed to safety. ("In Theory" [TNG]). *The* Voltaire *was named for the 18th-century French writer and philosopher.*

Volterra nebula. A stellar "nursery" in which proto-stars are in the process of coalescing from nebular material. The *Enterprise*-D conducted a survey mission in the Volterra nebula in 2369. ("The Chase" [TNG]).

***Vor'cha*-class attack cruiser.** SEE: **Klingon attack cruiser**.

Vorch-doh-baghk, Kahless! Translates as "All hail Kahless." The ritual greeting for the Klingon historical figure. ("Rightful Heir" [TNG]).

Vorgons. A humanoid civilization, capable of time travel. Two Vorgon criminals, **Ajur** and **Boratus**, traveled back some three hundred years from the 27th century to locate Jean-Luc Picard, in hopes of finding the powerful ***Tox Uthat***. Ajur and Boratus were thwarted when Picard destroyed the object to prevent it from falling into the wrong hands. ("Captain's Holiday" [TNG]).

Vorian pterodactyl. Large reptilian flying animal. ("The Ascent" [DS9]).

Vorik. (Alexander Enberg). Crew member aboard the *Starship Voyager*. ("Alter Ego" [VGR]). He assisted B'Elanna Torres with maintenance on the *Voyager's* plasma injectors during the ship's visit to the **Nekrit Expanse** in 2373. ("Fair Trade" [VGR]). Ensign Vorik spent summers exploring the Osana caverns, which involved some treacherous climbing. Vorik experienced ***Pon farr*** on stardate 50537, and attempted to mate with fellow *Voyager* crew member **B'Elanna Torres**. A brief physical contact between them initiated the Vulcan telepathic mating bond and caused her to suffer the same **neurochemical imbalance**. ("Blood Fever" [VGR]). Vorik's *Pon farr* ended when he fought Torres in the ritual ***Koon-ut-kal-if-fee***.

vorilium. Material. Vorilium is utilized in *Starship Voyager*'s engines. ("Darkling" [VGR]).

vorillium. Raw material needed by the crew of the *Voyager*. On stardate 50698, an away mission procured some vorillium from a planet in the Delta Quadrant. ("Favorite Son" [VGR]).

Vorin. (Brian Markinson). Inhabitant of the **Boraalan** village transported to the *Enterprise*-D holodeck by **Nikolai Rozhenko** in 2370. Vorin, who was the village chronicle, accidentally exited the holodeck and learned that he was aboard a starship, not in a cave on his homeworld. He was taken to sickbay, where an unsuccessful attempt was made to erase his memory of what he had seen. Captain Picard offered Vorin the choice of returning to his people, where he would be unable to tell them of the things he had seen, or remaining with the crew of the *Enterprise*-D. Unfortunately, Vorin was unable to make the choice. He was found dead shortly afterwards, having committed suicide. ("Homeward" [TNG]). SEE: **Boraalan chronicle**.

Vorlem, Gul. Cardassian military officer. A former enemy of **Enabran Tain**. In 2373, **Garak** intimated that he was responsible for Vorlem's death. ("In Purgatory's Shadow" [DS9]).

Vorn*, *I.K.S. Klingon bird-of-prey spacecraft that transported **Klingon High Council** member **Duras** to a rendezvous with the *Enterprise*-D in 2367. Duras was aboard the *Vorn* when Lieutenant **Worf** discovered that Duras had murdered **K'Ehleyr**. Worf, claiming the right of vengeance, killed Duras aboard the *Vorn*. ("Reunion" [TNG]).

Voroth Sea. Large body of water on the planet **Vulcan**. ("Innocence" [VGR]).

Vorta Vor. In Romulan mythology, the source of all creation. *(Star Trek V: The Final Frontier).* SEE: ***Sha Ka Ree***.

Vorta. Civilization from the **Gamma Quadrant** and member of the **Dominion**. The Vorta were the Dominion's representatives to the **Karemma**. The Vorta instructed the Karemma to direct all communications for the Dominion to an automated subspace relay outpost on Callinon VII. ("The Search, Parts I and II" [DS9]). SEE: **Borath**; **Eris**. The Vorta also controlled the deadly **Jem'Hadar** warriors on behalf of the **Founders**. To do this, the Vorta controlled supply of the drug **ketracel-white**, which the Jem'Hadar needed to survive. ("Hippocratic Oath" [DS9], "To the Death" [DS9]).

"Vortex." *Deep Space Nine* episode #12. Written by Sam Rolfe. Directed by Winrich Kolbe. No stardate given. *First aired in 1993. A fugitive bargains with Odo for his safety.* GUEST CAST: Cliff DeYoung as **Croden**; Randy Oglesby as **Ah-Kel**; Max Grodénchik as **Rom**; Gordon Clapp as Hadron; Kathleen Garrett as Vulcan officer; Leslie Engelberg as **Yareth**; Majel Barrett as

Computer voice. SEE: **Ah-Kel; Chamra Vortex; changeling; Croden; Exarch; *Ganges, U.S.S.*; Miradorn; Nehelik Province; Odo; Rakhar; Rakhari; Rigelian freighter; Ro-Kel; *T'Vran*; *toh-maire*; Vanoben transport; Yareth.**

Voval. (Eric Pierpoint). **Iyaaran** ambassador and a pilot. Voval flew the craft that was supposedly sent to transport Captain Jean-Luc Picard to the Iyaaran homeworld during the first Iyaaran diplomatic contact with the Federation in 2370. The spacecraft crashed en route, and Picard found himself marooned with a human woman, Anna. In truth, Anna was Voval, who had assumed her form in an attempt to learn firsthand of human intimacy and the emotion of love. ("Liaisons" [TNG]). *Eric Pierpoint is also familiar to genre fans for his portrayal of Newcomer police detective George Francisco in the television series* Alien Nation.

Voyager VI. Early automated interplanetary space probe launched from Earth in the late 1990s. Upon leaving the Sol System, *Voyager VI* fell into a black hole and emerged on the other side of the galaxy, near a planet of living machines. *(Star Trek: The Motion Picture).* SEE: **SETI greeting; V'Ger**. *Voyager I and II, actual space probes launched by NASA in the 1970s, were among the first to explore Jupiter, Saturn, and the outer Sol System. NASA's Jet Propulsion Laboratory, which managed the Voyager project, provided technical assistance during the making of* Star Trek: The Motion Picture *that included construction blueprints of the actual* Voyager *probes.*

***Voyager,* U.S.S.** Federation starship, *Intrepid* class, Starfleet registry number NCC-74656, commanded by Captain **Kathryn Janeway**. *Voyager* had a gross mass of 700,000 metric tons ("Phage" [VGR]) and was 15 decks thick. ("Caretaker" [VGR]). The ship had a complement of 38 photon torpedoes as of stardate 48546.2. ("The Cloud" [VGR]). *Voyager* had a crew complement of 141 and had a sustainable cruising velocity of warp factor 9.975. The ship featured improved computer systems in which some traditional optical processors were replaced with **bio-neural circuitry**. ("Caretaker" [VGR]). *Voyager* was also equipped with conventional isolinear optical circuits. ("Learning Curve" [VGR]). The **bridge** was located on Deck 1, while the **mess hall** was located one level down on Deck 2, Section 13. Deck 4 had cargo bay facilities. The **shuttlebay** was located on Deck 10, as were additional cargo bays. Environmental control was located on Deck 12. ("Macrocosm" [VGR]). *Voyager* had the capability of landing on the surface of a Class-M planet, then returning to space. ("The 37's" [VGR]). *The* Voyager's *landing in "The 37's" was the first time in* Star Trek *history that a starship soft-landed on a planet's surface and returned into space. The show traditionally avoided such a maneuver because of the expensive visual effects required for a spaceship landing, preferring instead to use the transporter; but by the time* Voyager *was in production, visual effects techniques (and budgets) had improved to the point where this was occasionally feasible.*

In 2371 the *Voyager* was violently propelled into the **Delta Quadrant** by a powerful **displacement wave** generated by the **Caretaker**. Stranded some 70,000 light-years from home, Captain Janeway invited the crew of a similarly stranded **Maquis** vessel to join the *Voyager* crew, and asked Maquis officer **Chakotay** to serve as her second-in-command. At the time *Voyager* was swept into the Delta Quadrant, it had been on a mission to pursue Chakotay's ship. ("Caretaker" [VGR]). *Voyager* lost contact with Starfleet on stardate 48307.5. ("Non Sequitur" [VGR]). Ironically, the mission to pursue Chakotay's Maquis ship was supposed to have lasted only three weeks. ("Elogium" [VGR]). In late 2371, the *Voyager* had a crew of 152. A minimum of 100 people was normally required to operate the vessel successfully. ("The 37's" [VGR]).

The *Starship Voyager* had no counselor aboard. ("The Cloud" [VGR]). Cabin 125-A on Deck 2 was originally designated as the captain's private dining room. Because power availability was limited after the ship was stranded in the Delta Quadrant, the crew adopted a system of replicator-usage rationing in order to conserve energy. As part of this effort, **Neelix** converted part of the **mess hall** into a makeshift kitchen, where he prepared a wide range of delicacies for the crew. ("Phage" [VGR]). *Voyager* had a **Stellar Cartography** Department. ("Time and Again" [VGR]). The **warp core** on *Voyager* was ejected on stardate 48734, when Chakotay sought to prevent the ship from entering a nebula inhabited by the **Komar**. The core was subsequently recovered and reinstalled. ("Cathexis" [VGR]). An exact duplicate of the *Voyager* was created by a **spatial scission** on stardate 49548.7 after the ship entered a plasma drift containing a subspace divergence field. In order to prevent her ship from being taken over by Vidiians, the Captain Janeway in command of the duplicate *Voyager* ordered it to self-destruct. ("Deadlock" [VGR]).

The Starship Voyager *was designed by series production designer Richard D. James and senior illustrator Rick Sternbach. The photographic miniature was built by Tony Meininger and photographed under the supervision of visual effects producer Dan Curry. Digital versions of the ship were also used for some computer-generated visual effects by Santa Barbara Studios, Digital Muse, and Foundation Imaging.*

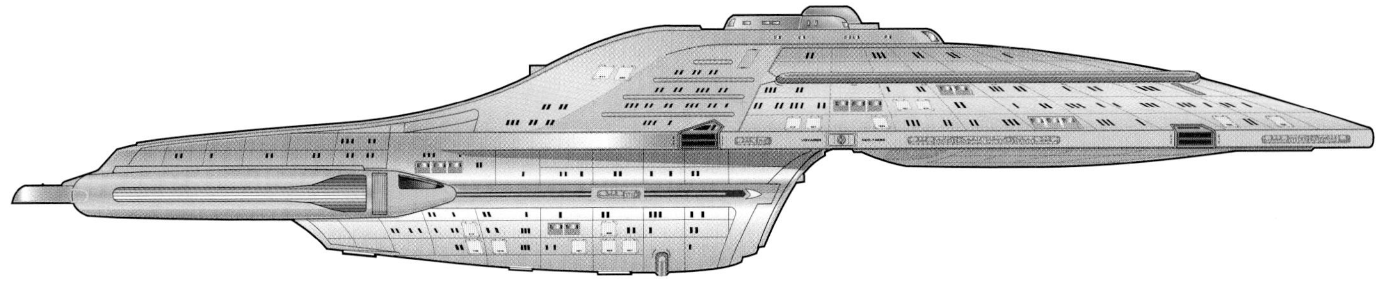

Vulcan Bill of Rights. Document that guarantees the fundamental personal freedoms of every Vulcan citizen. ("The Maquis, Part I" [DS9]).

Vulcan death grip. There is no such thing as a Vulcan death grip, but Spock claimed to have used it when he apparently killed Kirk during their spy mission aboard a Romulan vessel in 2268. The ruse allowed Kirk to escape back to the *Enterprise*. ("The *Enterprise* Incident" [TOS]).

Vulcan dirge. Traditional Vulcan funeral song. One Vulcan dirge starts, "O starless night of boundless black..." ("Tuvix" [VGR]).

Vulcan *favinit* plant. Foliage from planet **Vulcan**. In 2372, *Starship Voyager*'s Lieutenant Tuvok created a rare hybrid flower by grafting a *favinit* plant with a South American orchid from Earth. ("Alliances" [VGR]).

Vulcan harp. SEE: **Vulcan lute**.

Vulcan Institute of Defensive Arts. Learning institution located on Vulcan. Tuvok taught archery science for several years at the Vulcan Institute of Defensive Arts. ("Basics, Part II" [VGR]).

Vulcan isolationist movement. Small but growing group of separatists on **Vulcan** during the late 24th century. The isolationists believed that contact with alien civilizations had polluted their culture and destroyed Vulcan purity. They advocated the total isolation of Vulcan from the rest of the galaxy and the eradication of all alien influences from their planet. **Tallera** was a member of the isolationist group, who, in 2370, tried to reassemble the ancient **Stone of Gol** for use in furthering the movement's goals. ("Gambit, Part II" [TNG]).

Vulcan Love Slave Part II: The Revenge. Sexual fantasy holographic program. Quark obtained the program for his holosuites. ("Doctor Bashir, I Presume?" [DS9]).

Vulcan Love Slave. Romantic novel, at least according to Quark, who recommended the story to Odo in 2373. ("The Ascent" [DS9]).

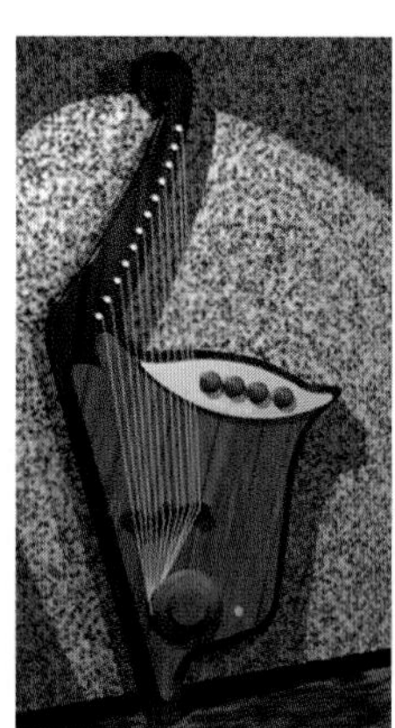

Vulcan lute. Stringed musical instrument from planet Vulcan. **Spock** enjoyed playing the harplike instrument during his off-duty hours. ("Charlie X" [TOS]). **Tuvok** owned a Vulcan lute, which he played at home. ("Persistence of Vision" [VGR], "Innocence" [VGR]). *The Vulcan lute was first seen in "Charlie X" (TOS), then later used in "The Conscience of the King" (TOS), in which Spock accompanied Uhura's song* ***"Beyond Antares,"*** *"Amok Time" (TOS); and "The Way to Eden" (TOS). A replica of the original prop, borrowed from Gene Roddenberry's office, was used in* Star Trek V: The Final Frontier. *A Vulcan lute was seen in the mirror Kira Nerys's quarters in "Through the Looking Glass" (DS9). That prop was loaned to the show from the collection of* Star Trek *graphic designer Doug Drexler. It was first referred to as a lute in "Persistence of Vision" (VGR). In "Innocence," Tuvok said his lute had five strings, but the actual prop had 12 strings.*

Vulcan Master. (Edna Glover, Paul Weber, Norman Stuart). Elder mentors who guided Vulcan aspirants through the arduous ***Kolinahr*** ritual. *(Star Trek: The Motion Picture).*

Vulcan mind-meld. An ancient Vulcan ritual in which two persons are telepathically linked, sharing each other's consciousness. To Vulcans, mind-melding is a deeply personal experience, providing an intense intimacy. ("Dagger of the Mind" [TOS]). Scientifically, the process is described as a **synaptic pattern displacement**. ("The Passenger" [DS9]). **Spock** used a mind-meld in 2266 to determine the truth of **Dr. Simon Van Gelder**'s

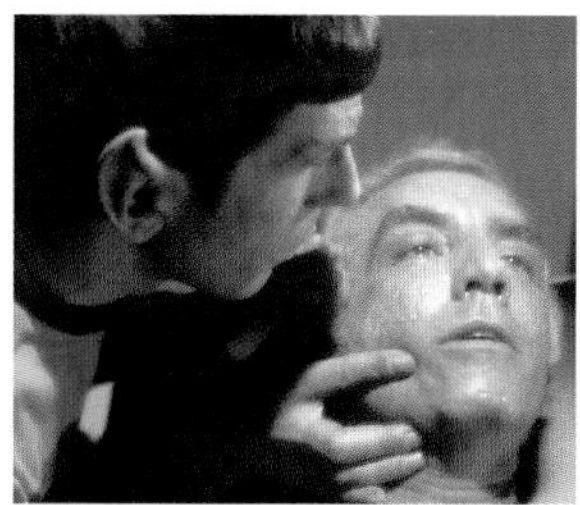

apparently wild claims that he was the director of the **Tantalus V** penal colony. ("Dagger of the Mind" [TOS]). Spock occasionally used his mind-melding skills to provide a telepathic distraction to an adversary, as at **Eminiar VII.** ("A Taste of Armageddon" [TOS]). Mind-melding can be performed with intelligences as diverse as humans, the robot space probe ***Nomad*** ("The Changeling"), the **Horta** ("The Devil in the Dark" [TOS]), and the **Kelvans.** When mind-melding with the Kelvan named **Kelinda**, Spock was able to glimpse the apparently humanoid creature's true form: an immense being with hundreds of tentacles. ("By Any Other Name" [TOS]).

A mind-meld was used to permit **Jean-Luc Picard** to provide emotional support to Ambassador **Sarek** in 2366 when the ambassador was suffering the debilitating effects of terminal **Bendii Syndrome**. Sarek benefited from the captain's emotional control, but Picard had to endure the fierce onslaught of the ambassador's unleashed emotions. ("Sarek" [TNG]). In 2370, **Sakonna** unsuccessfully tried to perform a mind-meld with **Gul Dukat** in an attempt to gather information for the **Maquis**. Dukat attributed his ability to resist the mind-meld to his Cardassian training. ("The Maquis, Part II" [DS9]).

The Vulcan mind-meld can be used so that one person can hone another's skill. In 2371, **Tuvok** proposed a mind-meld with Kes in hopes of focusing Kes's telepathic abilities. ("Cathexis" [VGR]). Tuvok used a Vulcan mind-meld on Tom Paris in 2371 to view the memories contained in Paris's Banean neuroimplant. Tuvok used these memories to determine that Paris did not kill Banean scientist Tolen Ren. ("Ex Post Facto" [VGR]). In 2372, Tuvok mind-melded with accused murder **Lon Suder**, causing a neurochemical imbalance in the mesiofrontal cortex of Tuvok's brain, unleashing uncontrollably violent emotions. ("Meld" [VGR]). *The Vulcan mind-meld was first used in "Dagger of the Mind" (TOS). Mind-melds were also performed in "The Paradise Syndrome" (TOS), "Spectre of the Gun" (TOS), "The Omega Glory" (TOS),* Star Trek: The Motion Picture, Star Trek II, Star Trek III, Star Trek VI, *and "Unification, Part II" (TNG).* SEE: ***katra.***

Vulcan mocha. Beverage, similar to **coffee**. **Harry Kim** enjoyed Vulcan mocha, extra sweet. ("Non Sequitur" [VGR]).

Vulcan mollusks. Fine food. Quark served Vulcan mollusks to **Fallit Kot** during his stay on station Deep Space 9. They are best when sautéed in Rhombolian butter. ("Melora" [DS9]).

Vulcan nerve pinch. A Vulcan technique in which finger pressure is applied to certain nerves at the base of the neck, instantly and nonviolently rendering that individual unconscious. Although the technique appears to work on nearly all humanoid species (and several nonhumanoids as well), few non-Vulcans have been able to master the nerve pinch. ("The Enemy Within" [TOS]). The Vulcan nerve pinch can cause trauma to the trapezius nerve bundle. ("Cathexis" [VGR]). **Spock** tried, unsuccessfully, to teach the nerve pinch to Kirk, but many years later, Data was able to master the technique. ("Unification, Part II" [TNG]). *The Famous Spock Nerve Pinch (as it became known to the show's production staff) was invented by actor Leonard Nimoy, who devised it because he thought Spock would not stoop to rendering an opponent unconscious with a karate chop.* SEE: **FSNP**.

Vulcan port. Intoxicating beverage. Quark offered Vulcan port to **Sakonna** when beginning business negotiations. Quark said the green drink was three centuries old and very expensive. ("The Maquis, Part I" [DS9]).

Vulcan restaurant. The Promenade of station Deep Space 9 featured a restaurant specializing in Vulcan cuisine. ("Indiscretion" [DS9]).

Vulcan Science Academy. Institute of higher learning on planet Vulcan. **Spock** chose to apply to Starfleet in 2249 rather than

Vulcan ship

stay on his homeworld and study at the academy. That decision was the cause of a rift between Spock and his father, **Sarek**, that lasted for 18 years. ("Journey to Babel" [TOS]). The director of the academy from 2354 to 2369 was subspace theoretician **Dr. T'Pan.** ("Suspicions" [TNG]).

Vulcan ship. Survey ship of Vulcan registry that was in the vicinity of Earth's solar system in 2063. On April 4, 2063, the ship passed through Earth's solar system at that same time that **Zefram Cochrane** made his first faster-than-light flight test in the ***Phoenix***. The Vulcan ship detected the *Phoenix's* warp signature and realized that humans had discovered warp drive. On the evening of the next day, the Vulcan ship touched down near Cochrane's launch site in Montana and made **first contact** with humankind. *(Star Trek: First Contact). The Vulcan survey ship was designed by John Eaves and rendered as a computer-generated image by Pacific Ocean Post.*

Vulcan spice tea. Hot beverage, available from replicators on the *U.S.S. Voyager.* ("Alliances" [VGR]).

Vulcan. Class-M planet, homeworld to the Vulcan people. Hot and arid, Vulcan is a member of the **United Federation of Planets**. Vulcan was the homeworld of **Spock** and **Sarek**. The planet has no moon. ("The Man Trap" [TOS]). There are wilderness preserves on Vulcan. ("Life Support" [DS9]). Centuries ago, Cardassian serialist poet **Iloja of Prim** spent time on Vulcan while he was in exile. ("Destiny" [DS9]). *The original* Starship Enterprise *visited Vulcan in "Amok Time" (TOS) and "Journey to Babel" (TOS). We also saw Vulcan (curiously with several moons—or at least nearby planets) in* Star Trek: The Motion Picture, *then again in* Star Trek III *and* Star Trek IV. *The* Enterprise-D *visited Vulcan in "Sarek" (TNG) and "Unification, Part I" (TNG).* SEE: **Fire Plains; Kir; Raal; Voroth Sea; Vulcans**.

Vulcana Regar. City on planet **Vulcan**, home to **T'Shanik**. ("Coming of Age" [TNG]).

Vulcanis. Alternate name for planet **Vulcan**. *Vulcanis was used in the first few episodes of the original* Star Trek *series before Spock's homeworld was changed to Vulcan.*

Vulcans. Humanoid species native to planet Vulcan. Vulcans were once a passionate, violent people whose civilization was

Vulcans.

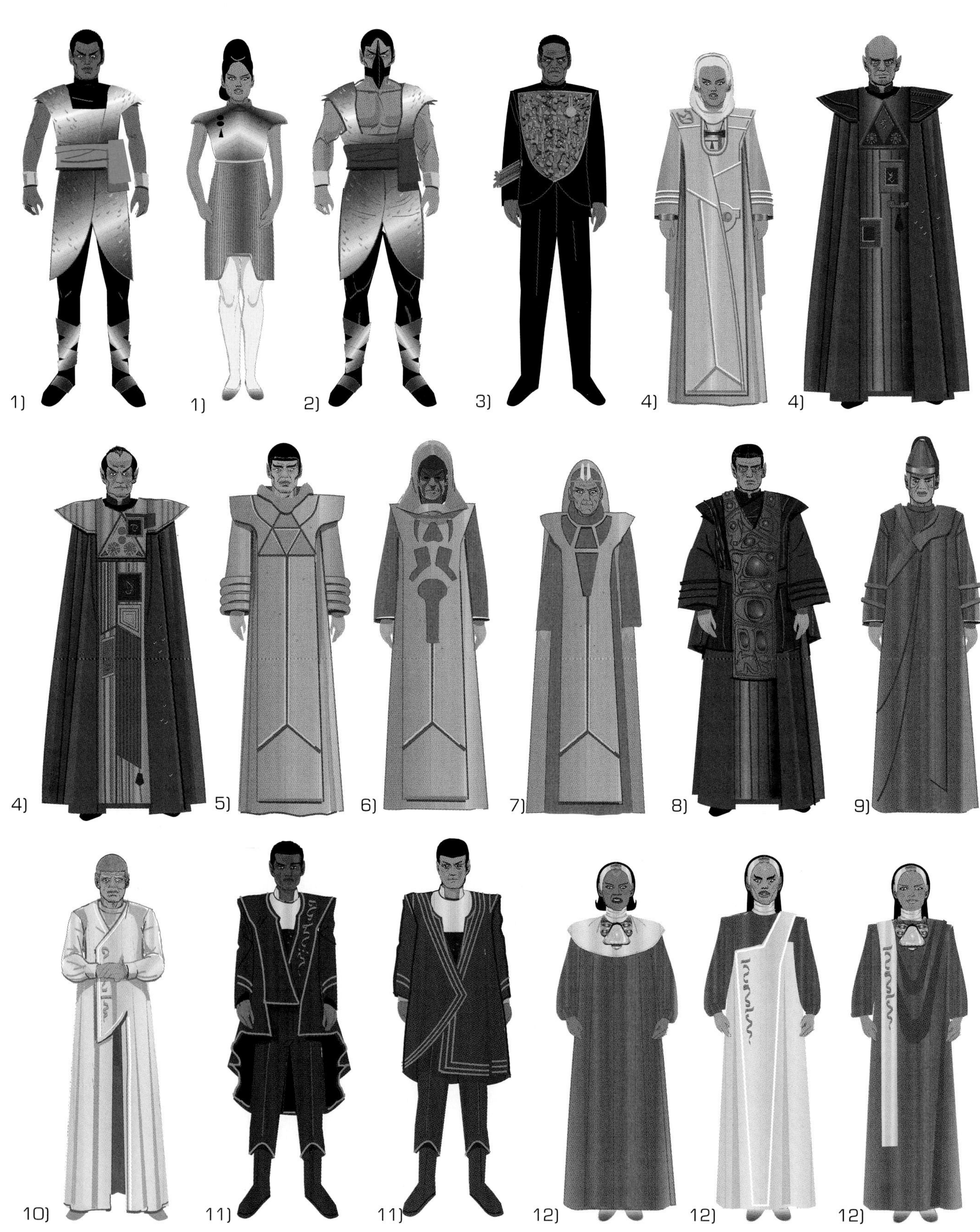

1) Ceremonial (TOS). 2) Ceremonial guard (TOS). 3) Diplomat (TOS). 4) Master (*ST:TMP*). 5) Monk (*ST III*). 6) Monk, variant (*ST III*). 7) High priestess (*ST III*). 8) Diplomat (*ST III*). 9) Monastery guard (*ST III*). 10) Diplomat (TNG). 11) Diplomatic aide (TNG). 12) Civilian (TNG).

torn by terrible wars. ("Let That Be Your Last Battlefield" [TOS], "All Our Yesterdays" [TOS]). The ancient philosopher **Surak**, revered as the father of Vulcan civilization, led his people some two thousand years ago to reject their emotions in favor of a philosophy that embraced pure logic. ("The Savage Curtain" [TOS]). This remarkable renaissance became known as the **Time of Awakening**. ("Gambit, Part II" [TNG]). Vulcan society is now based entirely on logic, and any trappings of emotion are considered to be socially unacceptable.

One group did not accept Surak's teachings and instead left Vulcan to found the warrior **Romulan Star Empire**. ("Unification, Part I" [TNG]). Their descendents and offshoots colonized many planets across the quadrant. ("Gambit, Part II" [TNG]). Tensions remained between the two peoples, and a century-long war once raged between the Vulcans and the Romulans. No one on either side realized that the war had been ignited by **Quinn**, a member of the **Q Continuum**. *We don't know when the war was, except that it was before 2072.* ("Death Wish" [VGR]). By the 24th century, however, a small number of Vulcan citizens sought reconciliation with their Romulan cousins, a movement supported by Ambassador **Spock**, as well as by members of a Romulan underground. ("Unification, Parts I and II" [TNG]).

In the distant past, Vulcans killed to win their mates. Even in the present, Vulcans revert to ancient mating rituals, apparently the price these people must pay for totally suppressing their natural emotions. When Vulcan children are about seven, their parents select a future mate, and the two children are joined in a ceremony that links them telepathically. When the two children come of age, they are compelled to join together for the marriage rituals. The time of mating, ***Pon farr***, is when the stoically logical Vulcans pay for their rigid control by experiencing a period of total emotional abandon. In Vulcan adults, *Pon farr* comes every seven years. ("Amok Time" [TOS]). SEE: ***Koon-ut-kal-if-fee;*** **wedding**. Vulcans who reach a certain infirmity with age sometimes practice ritual suicide. ("Death Wish" [VGR]).

Because planet Vulcan has a higher gravity than Earth, and its atmosphere is thinner, Vulcans in an Earth-normal environment demonstrate greater physical strength and more acute hearing than humans. The intensity of the Vulcan sun caused the Vulcans to evolve a secondary eyelid to protect the retina. This inner eyelid involuntarily closes when the eye is exposed to extremely intense light. Spock's **inner eyelid** protected him in 2267 against powerful light used in an experiment designed to eradicate the **Denevan neural parasite**. ("Operation: Annihilate!" [TOS]). A Vulcan's heart is where a human's liver is. When injured, Vulcans concentrate their strength, blood, and antibodies onto the injured organs by a type of self-induced hypnosis. ("A Private Little War" [TOS]). Vulcans have very different blood chemistry from **Bolians**. A blood transfusion from a Vulcan to a Bolian would be fatal for the Bolian. ("Prototype" [VGR]).

Certain elements of Vulcan prehistory suggest that the Vulcan race may have originated with colonists from another planet, possibly humanoids from **Sargon's planet** 500,000 years ago. ("Return to Tomorrow" [TOS]). Vulcans have telepathic capacity, as practiced in the **Vulcan mind-meld**. Although the telepathic ability is quite limited, Spock once felt the death screams of the 400 Vulcan crew members of the *Starship* ***Intrepid*** across interstellar distances. ("The Immunity Syndrome" [TOS]). Located in the mesiofrontal cortex of the Vulcan brain lies the psychosuppression system responsible for the cessation of emotions. On rare occasions, this area of the brain can be disrupted following a mind-meld with a violent individual. ("Meld" [VGR]).

Vulcans were the first extraterrestrials to be encountered by the people of planet Earth. On April 4, 2063, a Vulcan survey ship passed through Earth's solar system at that same time that **Zefram Cochrane** made his first faster-than-light spaceflight test in the ***Phoenix***. The Vulcan ship detected the *Phoenix's* warp signature and realized that humans had discovered warp drive. On the evening of the next day, the Vulcan ship touched down near Cochrane's launch site in Montana. On April 5, 2063, Vulcans made first contact with humankind. *(Star Trek: First Contact). The Vulcan who made first contact with Zefram Cochrane was played by Cully Fredricksen.*

SEE: ***fal-tor-pan*****; humanoid life;** ***katra*****;** ***Kolinahr*****;** ***Plak-tow*****;** ***plomeek*** **soup; Pon farr; Sarek; Spock; Stonn;** ***tal-shaya*****; T'Pau; T'Pring; T'plana-Hath; Vulcan isolationist movement; Vulcan nerve pinch.**

W-particle interference. Unusual phenomenon associated with gaps in normal space. Commander Data used ship's sensors to scan for W-particle interference to confirm the presence of gaps in normal space within the **Mar Oscura** in 2367. ("In Theory" [TNG]).

Waddle, Barry. Pseudonym adopted by former Klingon intelligence agent **Arne Darvin** when he posed as a human merchant dealing in **kevas** and **trillium**. ("Trials and Tribble-ations" [DS9]).

Wade, Dr. April. Physician from the University of Nairobi on **Earth**. Wade, who was born in 2264, was a nominee for the prestigious **Carrington Award** in 2368 and 2371. ("Prophet Motive" [DS9]).

Wadi. Humanoid civilization from the Gamma Quadrant. First encountered by a Vulcan ship in 2369. A Wadi diplomatic delegation was the first formal first contact from the **Gamma Quadrant** to visit the Alpha Quadrant through the **Bajoran wormhole**. Tall in stature, the Wadi were interested mostly in games and went straight to **Quark's bar** upon arriving at station Deep Space 9. When Quark cheated them at **dabo**, the leader of the Wadi, **Falow,** forced him to play an elaborate game they called **chula**. The stakes were high, and involved the involuntary participation of key members of the Deep Space 9 crew. ("Move Along Home" [DS9]).

Wagner, Professor. Scientist. Wagner was a speaker at the deep-space psychology seminar attended by members of the *Enterprise*-D crew in 2369. Counselor Troi spent a great deal of time at the professor's lecture, but later admitted she found it less than stimulating. ("Timescape" [TNG]).

Wagnor. (Andrew Bicknell). Spacecraft pilot with the Angosian government. Wagnor flew the Angosian police vessel commandeered by **Roga Danar** after his escape from the *Enterprise*-D in 2366. ("The Hunted" [TNG]).

Wainwright, Captain. (James G. MacDonald). United States Army Air Corps officer on mid-20th century Earth. Wainwright participated in the investigation of an extraterrestrial spacecraft discovered near **Roswell**, New Mexico, in 1947. Wainwright interrogated the occupants of the craft, being convinced that the Ferengi were invaders, and that they posed a serious threat to American national security. ("Little Green Men" [DS9]). SEE: ***Quark's Treasure***.

Wait, The. Literary work by the famous writer Revalus. ("The Muse" [DS9]).

Wallace, Darian. (Guy Vardaman). Starfleet officer who served at the **Utopia Planitia Fleet Yards** at the time the *Starship Enterprise*-D was under construction. ("Eye of the Beholder" [TNG]). Wallace was transferred to the *Enterprise*-D crew just prior to the ship's first mission under the command of Captain Picard in 2364. ("All Good Things..." [TNG]). Wallace was one of two officers left at the command post set up on a remote planet. The command post was used to coordinate the teams searching for Commander **Data**, following his disappearance in late 2369. ("Descent, Parts I & II" [TNG]). *Guy Vardaman was an extra and a stand-in through all seven seasons of* Star Trek: The Next Generation. *He could occasionally be seen as a background crew member, sometimes in engineering, as well as in Ten-Forward. As an engineering technician, he helped assemble Lore's parts in "Datalore" (TNG), and in command uniform, he flew the ship in "The Wounded" (TNG) and "The Hunted" (TNG). He did not have a last name until "Descent, Part I" (TNG), where he was a security officer. (Obviously, Wallace was a multitalented guy.) He finally got a first name in a computer screen display in "Eye of the Beholder" (TNG). Wallace was among the* Enterprise-*D crew members who first greeted Picard when the captain first boarded the ship in a flashback scene in "All Good Things..." (TNG), and he was among the last to evacuate the stardrive section just prior to the ship's crash in* Star Trek Generations. *He first appeared in "The Big Goodbye" (TNG). Guy Vardaman also worked occasionally as a photo-double for Data's hands (for extreme close-up shots of Data's fingers pressing buttons, for example), and appeared as a Klingon and a Romulan as well.*

Wallace, Dr. Janet. (Sarah Marshall). Expert in endocrinology. Dr. Wallace was aboard the original *Starship Enterprise* in 2267 when a radiation-induced hyper-accelerated aging disease struck several of the *Enterprise* crew members. She and James Kirk had been romantically involved in 2261, but decided to go their separate ways, pursuing different careers. She later met and married **Dr. Theodore Wallace**, a man 26 years her senior, when they were working on a project together on planet **Aldebaran** III. ("The Deadly Years"[TOS]). *An early draft of the script for* Star Trek II: The Wrath of Khan *had Janet Wallace as Kirk's long-lost lover in the role that eventually became Dr. Carol Marcus.*

Wallace, Dr. Theodore. Scientist. Husband to endocrinologist **Janet Wallace**. He met his wife on Aldebaran III, where the couple worked together until his death prior to 2267. ("The Deadly Years" [TOS]).

Walsh, Captain Leo Francis. Name assumed by **Harcourt Fenton Mudd** when he came on-board the *Enterprise* in 2266. According to Mr. Mudd, Leo Walsh was to be the captain on his transport vessel but suddenly died, making it necessary for Mudd to take charge. ("Mudd's Women" [TOS]).

Wanoni tracehound. Predatory animal that pursued its prey with enthusiastic vigor. **Odo** likened **Lwaxana Troi** to a Wanoni tracehound when she expressed interest in the **shape-shifter**. ("The Forsaken" [DS9]).

Wantsomore, Lady. Character in ***The Queen's Gambit*** holosuite program. In the scenario, Wantsomore was a beautiful socialite who was brainwashed to assassinate the Queen of England. ("A Simple Investigation" [DS9]).

warbird, Romulan. SEE: **Romulan warbird**.

wardroom. Conference room and lounge used by the senior staff of station **Deep Space 9.** Although the basic architecture was **Cardassian**, in early 2371 the wardroom was redecorated and furnished in the more comfortable, ergonomic **Federation** style. ("The Search, Parts I and II" [DS9]). *The wardroom was first seen in "The Search, Part I" (DS9).*

"Warlord"*.* *Voyager* episode #52. Teleplay by Lisa Klink. Story by Andrew Shepard Price & Mark Gaberman. Directed by David Livingston. Stardate 50348.1. *First aired in 1996. An egomaniacal tyrant named Tieran places his mind into the body of Kes, using her to overthrow his government.* GUEST CAST: Anthony Crivello as **Adin**; Brad Greenquist as **Demmas**; Galyn Görg as **Nori**; Charles Emmett as **Resh**; Karl Wiedergott as **Ameron**; Leigh J.

McCloskey as **Tieran**; Majel Barrett as Computer voice. SEE: **Adin; Ameron; Demmas; Denar; *Gallia* nectar; gamma radiation; holodeck and holosuite programs: Paxau resort, Volleyball; Ilari autarch; Ilari bioelectric microfibers; Ilari First Castallan; Ilari talisman; Ilari; Kes; lectrazine; Martin, Ensign; Neelix; Nori; *paraka* wings; Paxau resort; Rekarri starbursts; Resh; thoron; Tieran; volleyball; Yaro.**

warm milk with a dash of nutmeg. Traditional cure for insomnia, sometimes prescribed by *Enterprise*-D Chief Medical Officer Crusher. ("All Good Things..." [TNG]).

warning beacon. Transmitter intended to inform nearby space vehicles of a potential hazard. Warning beacons were placed around planet **Tarchannen III** in 2367 after it was discovered that one of the life-forms on the planet reproduced by mutating unsuspecting visitors. ("Identity Crisis" [TNG]).

warnog. Klingon ale. ("Rightful Heir" [TNG]).

warp 10. Under warp theory, an infinite velocity unattainable by normal warp drive technology. An object traveling at warp 10 would theoretically occupy all points in the universe simultaneously. ("Threshold" [VGR]). SEE: **infinite velocity, theory of; transwarp**.

warp 13. SEE: **anti-time (future); warp speed.**

warp core breach. SEE: **antimatter containment**.

warp core. SEE: **matter/antimatter reaction chamber**.

warp drive. Primary propulsion system used by most faster-than-light interstellar spacecraft. Warp drive systems used by Federation **starships** employ the controlled annihilation of matter and **antimatter** ("The Naked Time" [TOS]), regulated by **dilithium crystals**, to generate the tremendous power required to warp space and travel faster than light. Warp drive was invented in 2063 by noted scientist **Zefram Cochrane** (*pictured*) of Alpha Centauri. ("Metamorphosis" [TOS]). It is inadvisable to go to warp inside of a solar system because

exceeding the speed of light near a gravity well can be dangerous if the gravitational potentials are not precisely taken into account. (*Star Trek: The Motion Picture;* "By Inferno's Light" [DS9]). SEE: **antimatter containment; Cochrane distortion; dilithium; matter/antimatter reaction chamber; nacelle; subspace; subspace phenomena; subspace technology; transwarp; warp factor.** *For more detailed information regarding warp drive and other technical matters, please refer to the* Star Trek: The Next Generation Technical Manual *by Rick Sternbach and Michael Okuda, published by Pocket Books.*

warp factor. Unit of measure for faster-than-light warp velocities generated by **warp drive**. Warp factor one is c, the speed of light, while higher speeds are computed geometrically under one of two different formulae. The original *Constitution*-class *Starship Enterprise* had a cruising speed of warp factor 6, and could reach warp 8 only with significant danger to the ship itself. ("Arena" [TOS]). The ship nevertheless reached warp 11 in 2267 when modified by ***Nomad*** to increase engine efficiency by 57 percent. ("The Changeling" [TOS]). The **Kelvans** were also successful in modifying the ship's engines to reach warp 11. ("By Any Other Name" [TOS]). The ship reached warp 14.1 in 2268 when the warp engines were sabotoged by **Losira**. ("That Which Survives" [TOS]). In 2284, Starfleet conducted a series of unsuccessful tests on an experimental **transwarp** propulsion system that would have dramatically increased the speed of warp drive systems. (*Star Trek III: The Search for Spock*). By the 24th century, a new warp-factor scale was in use that employed an asymptotic curve, placing warp 10 as an infinite value. Under the new scale, the *Galaxy*-class *Enterprise*-D had a normal cruising speed of warp 6 (392 times light speed, about warp 7.3 under the old system), and a maximum normal velocity of warp 9.2 (about 1649 times light speed, equivalent to about warp 11.8 in the "old" system). In 2370, following the formation of a massive **subspace rift** within the **Hekaras Corridor,** the Federation Council agreed that the use of warp fields posed a significant threat to some areas of space. Therefore the Council decreed that some areas would be limited to essential travel only. Furthermore, the Council imposed a Federation-wide "speed limit" of warp 5, which could only be exceeded in times of extreme emergency. ("Force of Nature" [TNG]). Later advances in Federation warp drive technology permitted the use of speeds exceeding warp 5. One of the first ships to be so equipped was the *Intrepid*-class *U.S.S. Voyager*, whose variable-geometry warp drive **nacelles** prevented damage to the subspace continuum. ("Caretaker, Parts I and II" [VGR]). *The original* Star Trek *series occasionally had ships and other objects traveling at warp 10 or faster. At the beginning of* Star Trek: The Next Generation, *Gene Roddenberry said he wanted to change the warp-speed scale to put warp 10 at the absolute top of the scale. We therefore assume that the warp scale has been recalibrated so that all the speeds shown in the original show are "actually" less than warp 10. Interestingly, the original* Star Trek *series never established actual speeds for warp factors in any episode or movie, although the old warp factor cubed formula has come to be generally accepted. A temporary upper limit for warp speed travel was established in "Force of Nature" (TNG), when speeds exceeding warp 5 were found to cause dangerous damage to the space-time continuum. This speed limit was abandoned a couple of years later when it was assumed that newer Federation starships (like the* U.S.S. Voyager *and the new* Defiant*) had improved, environmentally friendly warp drive systems that did not cause damage to the spatial continuum. In the final televised episode of* The Next Generation, *both the* U.S.S. Pasteur *and the* Enterprise-*D were ordered to use "warp 13." This may yet another recalibration of the warp curve, although it is not clear if this will happen in the "real" Star Trek timeline, since that future was a fabrication of Q. It is also possible that this alludes to some kind of implementation of transwarp drive, as seen in "Threshold" (VGR).* SEE: chart on following page.

warp field coils. Toroidal structures within a starship's warp drive **nacelles** that, when bombarded by high energy plasma, actually form the subspace "bubble" in which the ship travels in warp. Exposure to a **verteron** pulse can overload field coils, causing **warp drive**, and all other subspace systems, to fail. ("Force of Nature" [TNG]). *Warp field coils were seen behind the nacelle control room in "Eye of the Beholder" (TNG).*

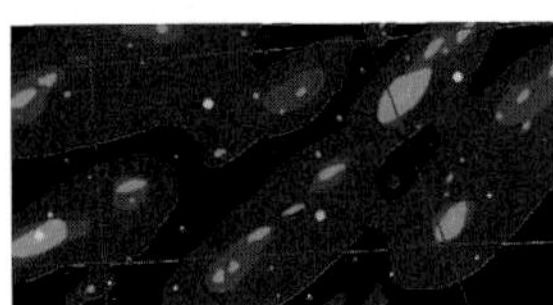

warp field effect. Cumulative damage to the structure of the subspace continuum caused by repeated exposure of an area to warp travel. Areas with already preexisting **subspace instability** were particularly sensitive to the effect. As the exposure to warp field energy increased, so did the chances of a subspace rupture. The warp field effect was particularly severe when warp factor 5 was exceeded. ("Force of Nature" [TNG]). SEE: **Hekaras Corridor; Serova, Dr**. Later advancements in Federation warp drive technology made it possible to employ high warp speeds without causing excessive damage to the subspace continuum. ("Caretaker, Parts I and II" [VGR]). SEE: **subspace phenomena; subspace technology.**

APPROXIMATE TIME TO TRAVEL

SPEED	Number of Kilometers per hour	Number of times speed of light	Earth to Moon 400,000 kilometers	Across Sol system 12 million kilometers	To nearby star 5 light-years	Across one sector 20 light-years	Across Federation 10,000 light-years	Across entire Galaxy 100,000 light-years	To nearby Galaxy 2,000,000 light-years	NOTES
Standard orbit	9600	< 0.00001 SUBLIGHT	42 hours	142 years	558,335 years	2 million years	1 billion years	11.17 Billion years	223 billion years	synchronous orbit around Class-M planet
Full impulse (1/4 light speed)	270 million	0.25 SUBLIGHT	5.38 seconds	44 hours	20 years	80 years	40,000 years	400,000 years	8 million years	normal maximum impulse speed
Warp factor 1	1 billion	1	1.34 seconds	11 hours	5 years	20 years	10,000 years	100,000 years	2 million years	Warp 1 = SPEED OF LIGHT
Warp factor 2	11 billion	10	0.13 seconds	1 hour	6 months	3 years	992 years	9,921 years	198,425 years	
Warp factor 3	42 billion	39	0.03 seconds	17 minutes	2 months	1 year	257 years	2,568 years	51,360 years	
Warp factor 4	109 billion	102	0.01 seconds	7 minutes	18 days	2 months	98 years	984 years	19,686 years	
Warp factor 5	229 billion	214	0.006291 seconds	3 minutes	9 days	1 month	47 years	468 years	9,357 years	
Warp factor 6	421 billion	392	0.003426 seconds	2 minutes	5 days	19 days	25 years	255 years	5,096 years	normal cruising speed of Federation starships
Warp factor 7	703 billion	656	0.002050 seconds	1 minute	3 days	11 days	15 years	152 years	3,048 years	
Warp factor 8	1.10 trillion	1,024	0.001313 seconds	39 seconds	2 days	7 days	10 years	98 years	1,953 years	
Warp factor 9	1.62 trillion	1,516	0.000887 seconds	26 seconds	1 day	5 days	7 years	66 years	1,319 years	
Warp factor 9.2	1.77 trillion	1,649	0.000816 seconds	24 seconds	1 day	4 days	6 years	61 years	1,213 years	normal maximum speed of Federation starships
Warp factor 9.6	2.05 trillion	1,909	0.000704 seconds	20 seconds	23 hours	4 days	5 years	52 years	1,048 years	
Warp factor 9.9	3.27 trillion	3,053	0.000440 seconds	13 seconds	14 hours	2 days	3 years	33 years	655 years	
Warp factor 9.99	8.48 trillion	7,912	0.000170 seconds	5 seconds	6 hours	22 hours	1 year	13 years	253 years	
Warp factor 9.9999	214 trillion	199,516	0.000007 seconds	0.2 seconds	13 minutes	53 minutes	18 days	6 months	10 years	subspace radio speed with booster relays
Warp factor 10	∞ <infinite>	∞ <infinite>	0	0	0	0	0	0	0	Warp 10 unattainable, except with transwarp

Use these estimates for comparison only—your actual mileage may vary.

warp field. The "bubble" of **subspace** in which a starship travels when using **warp drive**. A low-level warp field can have the effect of reducing the local **gravitational constant** within the field itself. This is because a subspace field resembles the time-space distortion of a gravitational field. The effect is that a low-level warp field can be used to temporarily reduce the apparent mass of an object (with relationship to the outside universe). This technique was used by Geordi La Forge in an unsuccessful attempt to prevent the moon of planet **Bre'el IV** from crashing into the planet in 2366. ("Déjà Q" [TNG]). O'Brien was able to use a low-level warp field to reduce the mass of Deep Space 9 sufficiently for the station's maneuvering thrusters to move the station to the **Denorios Belt** following the discovery of the Bajoran wormhole in 2369. ("Emissary" [DS9]). There is a link, not yet understood by science, between consciousness and the physical reality of subspace, as demonstrated by the **Traveler** in 2364. ("Where No One Has Gone Before" [TNG]). A nonpropulsive **static warp shell**, toroidal in shape, was accidentally created in 2367 by Ensign Wesley Crusher aboard the *Enterprise*-D. ("Remember Me" [TNG]). Warp field phase adjustments were used to suppress the subspace interference generated by a starship's warp engines. By adjusting the field phase of the Ferengi ship ***Krayton***, Commander Riker was able to send a surreptitious signal to the *Enterprise*-D when he was held captive on that ship in 2366. ("Ménage à Troi" [TNG]). SEE: **subspace phenomena; subspace technology**.

warp nacelle. SEE: **nacelle**.

warp particles. Subatomic matter created by a **warp field**, unstable under **space-normal** conditions. When the *Starship Voyager* was trapped in a type-4 **quantum singularity** in 2371, the crew saturated the event horizon with warp particles to find a subspace instability. ("Parallax" [VGR]).

warp plasma particles. Residual amounts of plasma created during a matter/antimatter reaction. It has been determined that discharging a phaser or disruptor weapon in the vicinity of warp plama particles will cause the particles to ignite. Transporter beams are also known to destabilize the plasma. **Tosin**, a member of the **Kolaati**, demanded that **Neelix** and **Wixiban** provide him with three grams of warp plasma to improve their engine efficiency. SEE: **matter/antimatter reaction chamber**. ("Fair Trade" [VGR]).

warp shadows. Energy phenomenon produced under certain conditions by warp-driven starships. Warp shadows have been known to cause sensor ghosts to appear on some types of sensors. Alliance ships in the mirror universe had sensors that were affected by warp shadows. ("Shattered Mirror" [DS9]).

Warren, Dr. Mary. (Lois Hall). Scientist assigned to the Federation anthropological field team on planet **Mintaka III**. Warren died from injuries she sustained in a failure of the anthropologists' "**duck blind**" in 2366. ("Who Watches the Watchers?" [TNG]).

Warrior/Adonis. (Leo Damian). A member of the interpretive Chorus of mediator **Riva** from planet **Ramatis III**. Each member of the Chorus represented a different part of Riva's personality. Warrior/Adonis represented passion, the libido, and the anarchy of lust. He also said he was the romantic and the definition of honor. ("Loud As a Whisper" [TNG]). SEE: **Scholar/Artist**; **Woman**.

Wasaka. (George Aguilar). Member of the tribal council of the **Dorvan V** colony in 2370. ("Journey's End" [TNG]).

Washburn. (Richard Compton). Engineering officer aboard the original *Starship Enterprise*. Washburn was part of the boarding party to the derelict ***U.S.S. Constellation*** in 2267. ("The Doomsday Machine" [TOS]). *Richard Compton went on to become a television director who directed "Haven" (TNG). By some amazing coincidence, Compton's first assistant director on "Haven" was Charles Washburn, who is himself a veteran of the original* Star Trek *series.*

watercress sandwiches. Finger food made with the leaves of the plant form *Rorippa Nasturtium-aquaticum*. They were typically served as part of a "high-tea" meal. ("Journey's End" [TNG]).

Watergate. Residential building on 20th-century planet **Earth**, site of a notorious political scandal that forced an American president to resign in disgrace. **Q** thought that the Watergate affair, like the Spanish Inquisition, gave ancient Earth more character than it had in the 24th century. ("Q-Less" [DS9]). SEE: **Nixon, Richard M**.

Watkins, John B. (Kenneth Washington). *Enterprise* engineer killed by **Losira**, near the **Kalandan outpost** in 2268. ("That Which Survives" [TOS]).

Watley, Lieutenant. (Dierdre L. Imershein). Starfleet officer aboard the original *Starship Enterprise* in 2267. Watley had transferred from the *U.S.S. Lexington* shortly before stardate 4523.3 and was in the medical/sciences department. **Julian Bashir** suspected that Watley might have been his great-grandmother. ("Trials and Tribble-ations" [DS9]). *Dierdre L. Imershein previously played Joval in "Captain's Holiday" (TNG).* SEE: **predestination paradox.**

Watley. (Patrick Egan). Starfleet engineer assigned to the swing shift on station Deep Space 9 in 2373. ("The Assignment" [DS9]). *Possibly a descendent of the Lieutenant Watley who served aboard the original* Starship Enterprise.

"Way of the Warrior, The, Parts I and II." *Deep Space Nine* episode #73 and 74. Written by Ira Steven Behr & Robert Hewitt Wolfe. Directed by James L. Conway. Stardate 49011.4. *First aired in 1995. The station is drawn into a conflict between the Klingons and the Cardassians, and Gowron dissolves of the treaty between the Klingons and the Federation. This two-hour first episode of the fourth season was produced as a made-for-TV movie, although in later airings it became two separate hour-long episodes. Worf joins the cast of* Star Trek: Deep Space Nine *in this episode and Dax and Bashir have received promotions.* GUEST CAST: Penny Johnson as **Yates, Kasidy**; Marc Alaimo as **Dukat**; Robert O'Reilly as **Gowron**; J. G. Hertzler as **Martok, General**; Obi Ndefo as **Drex**; Christopher Darga as **Kaybok**; William Dennis Hunt as **Huraga**; Andrew Robinson as **Garak, Elim**; Patricia Tallman as Weapons officer; Judi Durand as Station computer voice. SEE: **Betreka Nebula Incident; blood screening; Boreth; Cardassian Central Command; Cardassians; Cestus III;** ***CHEGH-chew jaj-VAM jaj-KAK; d'blok; d'k tahg;*** **Deep Space 9; Detapa Council; Drex; Dukat; Federation Council; Gaila; Garak; Gowron; Gramillion sand peas;** ***Grishnar*** **cat; Hastur, Admiral; holodeck and holosuite programs; Hoobishan Baths; Huraga;** ***In'Cha***; **Kahless the Unforgettable; Kaybok, Commander; Khitomer Accords; Klingon bloodwine; Klingon Empire; Lancelot, Sir;** ***M'Char***; **Malko; Martok, General;** ***Negh'Var***; **Nyberrite Alliance; Odo;** ***Prakesh***; **Quark; root beer; Rozhenko, Alexander; Sisko, Benjamin;** ***Sowee TAH***; **Strategic Operations Officer; Tholian silk;** ***Venture, U.S.S.***; **Vitarian wool underwear; Worf;** ***Xhosa***; ***yamok*** **sauce; Yates, Kasidy.**

"Way to Eden, The." Original Series episode #75. Teleplay by Arthur Heinemann. Story by Michael Richards and Arthur Heinemann. Directed by David Alexander. Stardate 5832.3. *First aired in 1969. The* Enterprise *is hijacked by a group of renegades* *who have rejected modern technological life to search for the mythical planet Eden. An early version of this episode, originally titled "Joanna," written by D. C. Fontana, was a love story between James Kirk and Joanna McCoy, daughter of* ***Dr. Leonard McCoy****. In the aired version, the Joanna character became Irina Galliulin, Chekov's love interest. Michael Richards is the pseudonym of D.C. Fontana.* GUEST CAST: Skip P. Homeier as **Sevrin**, **Dr. Thomas**; Charles Napier as **Adam**; Mary-Linda Rapelye as **Irina Galliulin**; Majel Barrett as **Chapel, Christine**; Victor Brandt as **Tongo Rad**; Elizabeth Rogers as **Palmer, Lieutenant**; Deborah Downey as Girl #1; Phyllis Douglas as Girl #2. SEE: **Adam; *Aurora*; auxiliary control; Catualla; Chekov, Pavel A.; Eden; *Galileo II*, *Shuttlecraft*; Herbert; Galliulin, Irina; One; Palmer, Lieutenant; Sevrin, Dr.; *Synthococcus novae*; Tiburon; Tongo Rad; Vulcan lute**.

"We'll Always Have Paris." *Next Generation* episode #24. Written by Deborah Dean Davis and Hannah Louise Shearer. Directed by Robert Becker. Stardate 41697.9. *First aired in 1988. While responding to a distress call from a noted scientist, Picard encounters a woman he once loved, now the wife of that scientist.* GUEST CAST: Michelle Phillips as **Manheim**, **Jenice**; Rod Loomis as **Manheim**, **Dr. Paul**; Isabel Lorca as **Gabrielle**; Dan Kern as **Dean**, **Lieutenant**; Jean-Paul Vignon as **Edourd**; Kally Ashmore as Francine; Lance Spellerberg as **Herbert, Transporter Chief**. SEE: **Blue Parrot Cafe; Cafe des Artistes; Coltar IV; Dean, Lieutenant; Edouard; fencing; Gabrielle; Herbert, Transporter Chief; Ilecom system; *Lalo*, *U.S.S.*; Manheim Effect; Manheim, Dr. Paul; Manheim, Jenice; Paris; Pegos Minor; Picard, Jean-Luc; Sarona VIII; Vandor IV; Vandor star system**.

weapons locker. Aboard a starship or space station, a storage facility for armaments. Twenty-four photon warheads were stolen from weapons locker #4 on Deep Space 9 on stardate 47944. While they were initially believed to have been stolen for the **Maquis**, further investigation revealed the theft to have been perpetrated by Cardassian agents, who hoped to use the warheads to discredit the Federation. ("Tribunal" [DS9]).

weather control matrix. Planet-wide system of substations that control atmospheric humidity, cloud patterns, thermal changes and the flow of wind currents. In 2370, the weather control system of **Caldos colony** malfunctioned, necessitating assistance from the *Enterprise*-D. The starship used a power transfer beam to one of the weather control substations to stabilize the system. A feedback loop developed, causing climatic changes aboard the ship, including the development of fog on the bridge. ("Sub Rosa" [TNG]). A weather control matrix was designed for planet **Hekaras II** following a gravitational shift that affected the planet's orbit and changed its climate. ("Force of Nature" [TNG]). Some weather control systems, such as the one installed at planet **Risa**, even helped maintain geologic stability. Risa's weather control system was sabotoged in 2373 by members of the **New Essentialists Movement**. ("Let He Who Is Without Sin..." [DS9]).

weather modification net. System used to detect and dissipate dangerous meteorological disturbances in a planetary atmosphere. A weather modification net did not detect the tornado that killed **Amanda Rogers**'s biological parents in Topeka, Kansas, on Earth. ("True-Q" [TNG]).

Webb, Danny. (Richard Lee Jackson). Son of **Michael Webb**. In 2024, Danny, his sister, and his parents were residents of **Sanctuary District** A in San Francisco on Earth. He and his father were involved in the **Bell Riots**. ("Past Tense, Parts I and II" [DS9]).

Webb, Michael. (Bill Smitrovich). **Earth** civil rights leader who was killed in the **Bell Riots** of 2024. Webb had worked as a plant manager of ChemTech Industries, until he lost his job and was forced to live in **Sanctuary District** A of the city of **San Francisco**. In the slang of the era, Michael Webb was called a **gimme**. In 2024, Webb and other District A residents organized a rally outside the **Processing Center** that exploded into what would later be called the Bell Riots. Webb was killed when government troops stormed the District on the orders of **Governor Chen**. ("Past Tense, Parts I and II" [DS9]).

Webb. (Richard Merrifield). Radar monitor technician with Earth's 20th-century United States Air Force in Omaha, Nebraska. Webb was on duty in July, 1969, when the *Starship Enterprise* was picked up as a UFO. The starship had been propelled back to 20th-century Earth and was low in the atmosphere when it was detected. ("Tomorrow Is Yesterday" [TOS]).

wedding. In many humanoid cultures, a ceremony celebrating the joining of two individuals into a family unit. Specific rituals vary widely.

Andorians. Marriage ceremonies among **Andorians** generally require groups of four people. ("Data's Day" [TNG]). *Unfortunately, the episode gives no further specifics about Andorian weddings, except for this one mention.*

Betazoids. On planet **Betazed**, children are often genetically bonded by their parents at a young age. When the children are older, they are expected to marry. The wedding ceremony itself is resplendent with ancient Betazoid culture, requiring the bride, the groom, and the guests to go naked, honoring the act of love being celebrated. ("Haven" [TNG], "Cost of Living" [TNG]).

Humans. Worf once observed that human bonding rituals "involve a great deal of talking and dancing and crying." ("Haven" [TNG]). Following the long-standing human tradition of a ship's captain officiating at weddings, *Enterprise* Captain Kirk conducted the Martine/Tomlinson wedding in 2266. Unfortunately, this wedding was interrupted by a Romulan attack. ("Balance of Terror" [TOS]). Wedding ceremonies held aboard the *Enterprise*-D included the wedding of **Keiko Ishikawa** and **Miles O'Brien** in 2367 ("Data's Day" [TNG]) and the Lwaxana Troi/Campio wedding of 2368 ("Cost of Living" [TNG]), though the latter wedding was not completed because the groom abruptly left the ceremony. There were also the 2364 nuptials planned for Deanna Troi and Wyatt Miller, but this ceremony was canceled after the groom left the ship. ("Haven" [TNG]). Among the Native American settlers on **Miramanee's planet**, the day on which a wedding was held was called a Joining Day ("The Paradise Syndrome" [TOS]).

Klingons. In one **Klingon** marriage ceremony, known simply as the Oath, wedding vows could be solemnized with the simple expression, ***Tlhingan jIH***, from the male, with an appropriate response by the female. ("The Emissary" [TNG]). SEE: ***jIH dok*; Oath, Klingon; divorce, Klingon.** Fracturing a clavicle on the wedding night is considered a blessing on the marriage. ("Blood Fever" [VGR]).

Tavnians. In a Tavnian wedding, the groom must stand before the bride and tell her why he wishes to marry her. Then, in front of his family and friends, he must proclaim his love for her, and convince her to accept him as her husband. However, anyone present at the ceremony who doubts the groom's sincerity may challenge the validity of the marriage. ("The Muse" [DS9]). SEE: **Jeyal**.

Vulcans. In the rigidly logical **Vulcan** culture, weddings can be a colorful display of ancient pageantry

and intense biological compulsion that harkens back to that people's ancient past. Vulcans take a mate once every seven years during the ***Pon farr*** (time of mating). A Vulcan who does not obey the mating urge may die. It is common for Vulcan parents to select mates for their children when a child reaches about seven years of age. Two children so selected are telepatically linked in a traditional ceremony. The linkage is less than a wedding, but more than a betrothal, and the two are drawn back together when they both come of age and enter the *Pon farr*. ("Amok Time" [TOS]).

Weld Ram, Dr. (Matt McKenzie). Bajoran scientist who accompanied **Dr. Mora Pol** on an expedition to a planet **L-S VI** in 2370. While the landing party searched for clues to Odo's origin, ground tremors opened fissures in the ground that released noxious gas. The gas seriously affected Dr. Weld, but he survived because of Dr. Bashir's efforts. ("The Alternate" [DS9]). *Dr. Weld's given name, Ram, was never mentioned in dialog and appeared only the script.*

Wellington*, *U.S.S. Federation starship, *Niagara* class, Starfleet registry number NCC-28473. The *Wellington* underwent a computer system upgrade by **Bynar** technicians at **Starbase 74** in 2364. ("11001001" [TNG]). The *Wellington* was in the vicinity of Starbase 123 in early 2367. It reported no unusual readings after a warp field experiment aboard the *Enterprise*-D by Wesley Crusher. ("Remember Me" [TNG]). Ensign **Ro Laren** served aboard the *Wellington* until she was held responsible for an incident in which eight people were killed on **Garon II** because of Ro's failure to obey orders. ("Ensign Ro" [TNG]).

Welsh rabbit. Traditional Earth cheese dish. Kathryn Janeway's grandfather prepared Welsh rabbit for her when she was a child. ("Death Wish" [VGR]).

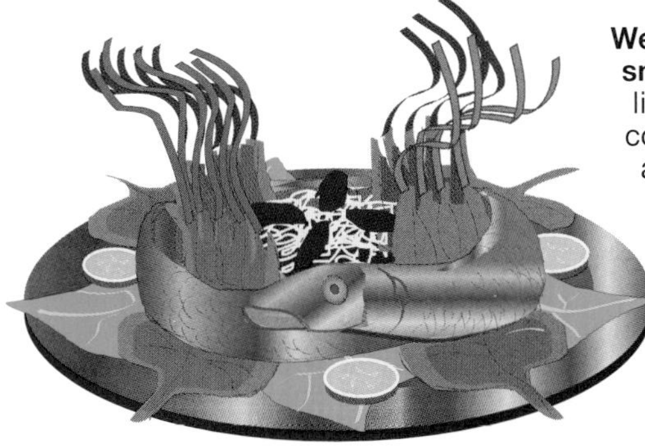

Wentlian condor snake. Serpentine life-form. Stuffed condor snake was a favorite dish of the **Regent of Palamar**. ("Business As Usual" [DS9]).

Wesley, Commodore Robert. (Barry Russo). Commander of the *Starship* ***Lexington*** in 2268 and officer in charge of the disastrous **M-5** computer tests. A friend of James Kirk's, Bob Wesley had the courage not to attack the *Enterprise* after the M-5 **multitronic** unit malfunctioned seriously. ("The Ultimate Computer" [TOS]). *Bob Wesley was named for* Star Trek *creator Gene Roddenberry, whose middle name was Wesley. Roddenberry used Robert Wesley as his pen name on his television scripts in the 1950s while he was still working for the Los Angeles Police Department. Barry Russo also played* ***Lieutenant Commander Giotto*** *in "The Devil in the Dark" (TOS).*

West, Colonel. (René Auberjonois). Starfleet officer who conspired with **Admiral Cartwright** and Klingon **General Chang** to obstruct **Chancellor Gorkon**'s peace initiatives in 2293. West was the trigger man who, disguised as a Klingon, unsuccessfully

attempted to assassinate the **Federation Council President** at the **Khitomer** conference. *(Star Trek VI: The Undiscovered Country).* SEE: **Operation Retrieve.** *Colonel West's scenes in* Star Trek VI *were cut prior to the theatrical release of that film, but they were restored in the videocassette and laserdisk versions. Actor Rene Auberjonois also played* ***Odo*** *in* Star Trek: Deep Space Nine.

Weyoun. (Jeffrey Combs). **Vorta** field supervisor who, in 2372, represented the **Dominion** during the joint **Jem'Hadar**-Federation mission to prevent renegade Jem'Hadar warriors from controlling an **Iconian gateway** on planet Vandros IV. Weyoun was killed by his Jem'Hadar First,**Omet'iklan**, for questioning their oath of loyalty to the **Founders**. ("To the Death" [DS9]). Prior to his death, Weyoun prepared a report about Captain Benjamin Sisko that was later read by the Vorta field operative **Kilana**. ("The Ship [DS9]). *Weyoun's clone returned in "Ties of Blood and Water" (DS9). Actor Jeffrey Combs also appeared as Ferengi Liquidator Brunt, and Tiron in "Meridian" (DS9).*

whale song. A beautiful, mournful sound produced by the **humpback whale**s of planet Earth. It is not known what purpose these songs serve, but it is believed by some scientists that they are a form of communication for these highly intelligent cetaceans. Whale song was also the medium of communication between humpback whales and an alien space probe of unknown origin. *(Star Trek IV: The Voyage Home).* SEE: **Probe, the.**

Whalen. (David Selburg). Literature historian and 20th-century specialist aboard *Enterprise*-D. Whalen was injured in a **Dixon Hill** holodeck simulation when the system was damaged by a **Jaradan** probe in 2364. ("The Big Goodbye" [TNG]). *David Selburg also played Dr. Syrus in "Frame of Mind" (TNG).*

"What Are Little Girls Made Of?" Original Series episode #10. Written by Robert Bloch. Directed by James Goldstone. Stardate 2712.4. *First broadcast in 1966. Nurse Chapel's long-lost fiancé is discovered, living in a "perfect" android body, on a planet controlled by incredibly sophisticated robots that destroyed the civilization there. James Goldstone also directed the second pilot episode, "Where No Man Has Gone Before" (TOS).* GUEST CAST: Michael Strong as **Korby**, **Dr. Roger**; Sherry Jackson as **Andrea**; Ted Cassidy as **Ruk**; Majel Barrett as **Chapel**, **Christine**; Harry Basch as **Brown**, **Dr.**; Vince Deadrick as **Matthews**; Budd Albright as **Rayburn**; Paul Baxley as Kirk's stunt double; Denver Matson as Rayburn's stunt double. SEE: **Andrea; android; archaeology; Brown, Dr.; Chapel, Christine; Earth Colony 2; Exo III; Kirk, George Samuel; Kirk, James T.; Korby, Dr. Roger; Matthews; Midos V; Old Ones; Rayburn; Ruk**.

Whatley, Admiral Charles. (Ernest Perry, Jr.). Starfleet senior officer. In 2373, Admiral Whatley led the delegation to Deep Space 9 that was to formally admit Bajor as a member of the Federation. ("Rapture" [DS9]).

Whatley, Kevin. Son of Starfleet Admiral Charles Whatley. ("Rapture" [DS9]).

"When the Bough Breaks." *Next Generation* episode #18. Written by Hannah Louise Shearer. Directed by Kim Manners. Stardate 41509.1. *First aired in 1988. An advanced civilization offers to trade scientific information in exchange for the children of* Enterprise-*D crew members.* GUEST CAST: Jerry Hardin as **Radue**; Brenda Strong as **Rashella**; Jandi Swanson as Katie; Paul Lambert as **Melian**; Ivy Bethune as **Duana**; Dierk Torsek as **Bernard, Dr. Harry, Sr.**; Michele Marsh as Leda; Dan Mason as **Accolan**; Philip N. Waller as **Bernard, Harry, Jr.**; Connie Danese as Toya; Jessica and Vanessa Bova as Alexandra. SEE: **Accolan; Aldea; Aldeans; Bernard, Dr. Harry, Sr.; Bernard, Harry, Jr.; calculus; cloaking device, Aldean; Custodian, The; Duana; Epsilon Mynos system; Melian; Neinman; ozone; Progenitors; Radue; Rashella; Xerxes VII; Zadar IV.**

"Where No Man Has Gone Before." *Original Series* episode #2. Written by Samuel A. Peeples. Directed by James Goldstone. Stardate 1312.4. *First aired in 1966. An energy barrier at the edge of the galaxy mutates Kirk's friend, Gary Mitchell, into a godlike being. This was the second pilot episode for the original* Star Trek *series. It was the first episode in which most of the regular original cast (including Captain Kirk) appear. Spock was, in fact, the only character to be carried over from the first pilot. The designs of the costumes and many sets were changed somewhat between this episode and "The Corbomite Maneuver" (TOS), the first regular series episode. "Where No Man Has Gone Before" prompted NBC to buy* Star Trek *as a weekly series.* GUEST CAST: Gary Lockwood as **Mitchell, Gary**; Sally Kellerman as **Dehner, Dr. Elizabeth**; Lloyd Haynes as Alden, Lieutenant; Andrea Dromm as **Smith, Yeoman**; Paul Carr as **Kelso, Lieutenant Lee**; Paul Fix as **Piper, Dr. Mark**; Hal Needham as Mitchell's stunt double; Eddie Paskey as **Leslie, Mr.**; Dick Crockett as Kirk's stunt double; Paul Baxley as Stunt double. SEE: **Aldebaran; barrier, galactic; Canopus Planet; Dehner, Dr. Elizabeth; Delta Vega; Dimorus; extrasensory perception; Kaferian apples; Kelso, Lieutenant Lee; Kirk, James T.; Leslie, Mr.; lithium cracking station; lithium crystals; Mitchell, Gary; "Nightingale Woman"; phaser rifle; Piper, Dr. Mark; recorder marker; Scott, Montgomery; sensors; Smith, Yeoman; Starfleet Academy; Sulu, Hikaru; Tarbolde, Phineas; three-dimensional chess; turbolift; *Valiant*, *S.S.***

"Where No One Has Gone Before." *Next Generation* episode #6. Written by Diane Duane & Michael Reaves. Directed by Rob Bowman. Stardate 41263.1. *First aired in 1987. A warp drive experiment gone awry sends the* Enterprise-*D into another galaxy. This episode was loosely based on Diane Duane's* Star Trek *novel,* The Wounded Sky. *This was the first appearance of the Traveler, who would be seen again in "Remember Me" (TNG) and "Journey's End" (TNG).* GUEST CAST: Stanley Kamel as **Kosinski**; Eric Menyuk as **Traveler**; Herta Ware as **Picard, Yvette Gessard**; Biff Yeager as **Argyle, Lieutenant Commander**; Charles Dayton as Crew member; Victoria Dillard as Ballerina.SEE: ***Ajax*, *U.S.S.*; Argyle, Lieutenant Commander; Crusher, Wesley; *Fearless*, *U.S.S*; Galaxy M33; intermix formula; Kosinski; Picard, Jean-Luc; Picard, Yvette Gessard; *targ*; Tau Alpha C; Traveler; warp field; Worf; Yar, Natasha.**

"Where Silence Has Lease." *Next Generation* episode #28. Written by Jack B. Sowards. Directed by Winrich Kolbe. Stardate 42193.6. *First aired in 1988. The* Enterprise-*D is trapped in a "hole in space" by a life-form named Nagilum trying to understand the concept of death. This episode was the first time we saw Worf's holodeck Klingon exercise program.* GUEST CAST: Diana Muldaur as **Pulaski, Dr. Katherine**; Earl Boen as **Nagilum**; Charles Douglass as Haskell; Colm Meaney as **O'Brien, Miles**. SEE: **autodestruct; calisthenics program, Klingon; Class 1 sensor probe; Cornelian star system; "hole in space"; Morgana Quadrant; Nagilum; noncorporeal life; *Yamato*, *U.S.S.***

whip, Ferengi. SEE: **Ferengi whip**.

whiskey. Alcoholic liquor made from the distillation of certain fermented grains. In the 2060s, whiskey was Zefram Cochrane's drink of choice, although he liked tequila, too. *(Star Trek: First Contact)*. Miles O'Brien enjoyed malt Irish whiskey at his surprise birthday party in 2373 on station Deep Space 9. ("The Assignment" [DS9]).

"Whispers." *Deep Space Nine* episode #34. Written by Paul Robert Coyle. Directed by Les Landau. Stardate 47552.1. *First aired in 1994. O'Brien suspects a conspiracy when he suddenly finds himself treated as an outcast.* GUEST CAST: Rosalind Chao as **O'Brien, Keiko**; Todd Waring as **DeCurtis, Ensign**; Susan Bay as **Rollman, Admiral;** Philip LeStrange as **Coutu**; Hana Hatae as **O'Brien, Molly**. SEE: **annual physicals; coffee; Coutu; DeCurtis, Ensign; emitter crystal; endive salad; Ferengi Rules of Acquisition; flan; fricandeau stew; Gupta, Admiral; *Mekong*, *U.S.S.*; O'Brien, Michael; O'Brien, Miles; Parada II; Parada IV; Parada system; Paradas; RF power conduit; *Rio Grande*, *U.S.S.*; , Rollman, Admiral; Starbase 401; subspace technology.**

White Rabbit. Fantasy character from Earth writer Lewis Carroll's book ***Alice in Wonderland.*** The White Rabbit was a sentient biped who was very late for an important date when he appeared to Dr. McCoy on the **amusement park planet**. McCoy had noted that the planet looked like something out of *Alice in Wonderland.* ("Shore Leave" [TOS]).

white rhinos. Extinct animal species from planet Earth. White rhinoceros were known by the zoological name *Ceratotherium simum.* The species was hunted to extinction in the 22nd century. ("New Ground" [TNG]). *Given the continued poaching of the rhinoceros, it is unfortunately very possible that this* Star Trek *prediction will come true much sooner than the 22nd century.*

white. Addictive drug, an isogenic enzyme also known as **ketracel-white**. Jem'Hadar soldiers were genetically engineered to be addicted to white, and the **Dominion** (through their agents, the **Vorta**), used this addiction to control the **Jem'Hadar**. White also provided nourishment, making it unnecessary for Jem'Hadar warriors to waste time on such things as eating. Vials of white were stored in an electronically-locked metal case carried by Vorta field operatives. ("To the Death" [DS9]).*Originally established in "The Abandoned" (DS9), it was first called "white" in "Hippocratic Oath" (DS9).*

"Who Mourns for Adonais?" Original Series episode #33. Written by Gilbert Ralston. Directed by Marc Daniels. Stardate 3468.1. *First aired in 1967. The* Enterprise *is captured by a powerful alien who was once worshipped on planet Earth as the Greek god Apollo. He wants the* Enterprise *crew as his new subjects, and one* Enterprise *crew member to love him.* GUEST CAST: Michael Forest as **Apollo**; Leslie Parrish as **Palamas, Lieutenant Carolyn**; John Winston as **Kyle, Lieutenant**; Jay Jones as Scott's stunt double. SEE: **A&A officer; Antos IV; Apollo; Beta Geminorum system; Chekov, Pavel A.; dryworm; gods, Greek; Kyle, Mr.; Palamas, Lieutenant Carolyn; Pollux IV; Pollux V; Starbase 12.**

"Who Watches the Watchers?" *Next Generation* episode #52. Written by Richard Manning & Hans Beimler. Directed by Robert Wiemer. Stardate 43173.5. *First aired in 1989. A cultural observervation team is accidentally discovered by a planet's native humanoids ,who decide that Captain Picard is their god.* GUEST CAST: Kathryn Leigh Scott as **Nuria**; Ray Wise as **Liko**; James Greene as **Barron, Dr.**; Pamala Segall as **Oji**; John McLiam as **Fento**; James McIntire as **Hali**; Lois Hall as **Warren, Dr. Mary**. SEE: **Barron, Dr.; duck blind; Fento; Hali; hologenerator; Liko; Mintaka III; Mintakan tapestry; Mintakans; Nuria; Oji; Palmer, Dr.; proto-Vulcan; Warren, Dr. Mary.**

"Whom Gods Destroy." Original Series episode #71. Teleplay by Lee Erwin. Story by Lee Erwin and Jerry Sohl. Directed by Herb Wallerstein. Stardate 5718.3. *First aired in 1969. Kirk and Spock are held captive in an insane asylum by a former Starfleet hero who wants to be ruler of the galaxy.* GUEST CAST: Steve Ihnat as **Garth of Izar**; Yvonne Craig as **Marta**; Richard Geary as Andorian; Gary Downey as Tellarite; Keye Luke as **Cory, Governor Donald**. SEE: **Antos IV; Axanar; cellular metamorphosis; Cochrane deceleration maneuver; Cory, Governor Donald; Elba II; environmental suits; fleet captain; Garth of Izar; Kirk, James T.; Marta; mutiny; Tau Ceti; three-dimensional chess.**

Wildman, Samantha. (Nancy Hower). Starfleet officer, a xenobiologist, assigned to the Science Department aboard the *Starship Voyager*. ("Elogium" [VGR]). Ensign Wildman was married, but her husband, a Ktarian man named Greskrendtregk ("Dreadnought" [VGR]), remained at station Deep Space 9 when the *Voyager* was swept into the Delta Quadrant. In 2372, Ensign Wildman learned that she was pregnant ("Elogium" [VGR]) with her first child. ("Tattoo" [VGR]). Wildman gave birth to her child on stardate 49548, at about the same time that *Voyager* was duplicated in an encounter with a **spatial scission**. Complications in delivery required the use of an emergency fetal transport procedure. The infant suffered from hemocythemia, and died shortly after birth, although the duplicate child aboard the duplicate *Voyager* was not so afflicted. The healthy baby was sent to Wildman shortly before that ship was destroyed. ("Deadlock" [VGR]). *We learned Wildman's first name in "Deadlock" (VGR). "Elogium" co-writer Jimmy Diggs named the character in honor of Samantha Wildman, a very special girl who lived in Florida. When tragedy struck, taking Samantha's life at the age of only seven, her parents donated Samantha's kidneys for transplantation, saving the life of Diggs's wife, Linnette. Diggs learned that the real Samantha loved animals, so he made her* Voyager *namesake the head of the ship's xenobiology department.*

Wilkins, Professor. Member of the **Starnes Expedition** to planet **Triacus** in 2268. ("And the Children Shall Lead" [TOS]).

Willemheld. Twenty-third-century Earth playwright. Bashir felt that Earth writers after Willemheld's time were too derivative of alien drama. ("The Die is Cast" [DS9]).

Williams, Ted. Famous **baseball** player who was an outfielder for the Boston Red Sox from 1939 to1960 on Earth. Williams twice won the Triple Crown and was elected to Baseball's Hall of Fame in 1966. A holographic version of Williams was available in a baseball **holosuite** program enjoyed by Jake and **Benjamin Sisko** on station Deep Space 9. ("If Wishes Were Horses" [DS9]). SEE: **Bokai, Buck**.

Wilson, Transporter Technician. (Garland Thompson). *Enterprise* crew member under the command of Captain James Kirk in 2266. Wilson surrendered his phaser pistol to a partial duplicate of Kirk created in a transporter malfunction. ("The Enemy Within" [TOS]).

Winchester. Brand name for a chemically-powered firearm used on 19th-century Earth. Deanna Troi's holodeck character, Durango, carried a Winchester in the program ***Ancient West.*** ("A Fistful of Datas" [TNG]).

"Wink of an Eye." Original Series episode #68. Teleplay by Arthur Heinemann. Story by Lee Cronin. Directed by Jud Taylor. Stardate 5710.5. *First aired in 1968. The* Enterprise *is commandeered by aliens who exist in a hyperaccelerated time frame. Lee Cronin was a pseudonym for Gene L. Coon.* GUEST CAST: Kathie Browne as **Deela**; Jason Evers as **Rael**; Majel Barrett as **Chapel, Christine**; Erik Holland as Ekor; Geoffrey Binney as Compton; Ed Hice, Richard Geary, Scalosians; Majel Barrett as Computer voice. SEE: **Compton; Deela; hyperacceleration; Rael; refrigeration unit; Scalos; Scalosians.**

Winn. (Louise Fletcher). Politically ambitious **Bajoran** religious leader who succeeded **Kai Opaka**, following Opaka's disappearance in 2369. ("In the Hands of the Prophets" [DS9]). During the Cardassian occupation, Winn spent five years in a Cardassian prison, where she endured numerous beatings for having taught the word of the Prophets. ("Rapture" [DS9]). While a member of the Vedek Assembly, Winn, a member of an orthodox order, engineered conflict on station Deep Space 9, claiming that the teaching of scientific theories on the origins of the **Bajoran wormhole** was inconsistent with Bajoran religious faith. Winn was, in fact, plotting to draw her political rival, **Vedek Bareil**, to the station, where Winn's co-conspirator attempted to assassinate him—an unsuccessful effort to eliminate Bareil as candidate for **kai**. ("In the Hands of the Prophets" [DS9]). SEE: **Neela**. Winn aggressively pursued the office, aligning herself with **Minister Jaro Essa**, who promised to make her the next kai, in return for her political endorsement of his bid to lead the government. ("The Circle" [DS9]). Continuing her quest, Winn uncovered evidence implicating her opponent, Vedek Bareil, in the infamous **Kendra Valley massacre**. Bareil withdrew his candidacy, and Winn was elected kai in 2370. ("The Collaborator" [DS9]). In 2371 Kai Winn surprised her political opponents when she concluded a historic peace accord with the Cardassians. Vedek Bareil, her former political rival, played a key role in negotiating the treaty and provided valuable advice to Winn during the final talks prior to signing. ("Life Support" [DS9]). SEE: **Turrel, Legate.** Later that year following the sudden death of **Bajoran First Minister Kalem**, Winn was appointed to fill the remainder of his term. Despite her ambitions, Winn was politically inexperienced, and shortly after her appointment, she touched off a political controversy over a pair of **soil reclamators**. Winn nearly escalated the minor incident into civil war, and her resulting loss of popularity forced her to withdraw from the upcoming election for the next term as first minister. ("Shakaar" [DS9]). In 2372, when **Akorem Laan** briefly assumed the role of **Emissary**, Kai Winn supported his view that Bajor should return to the traditional caste-based ***D'jarra*** system even if it meant giving up Federation membership. ("Accession" [DS9]). Winn had difficulty accepting **Benjamin Sisko**, a man from Earth, as the **Emissary**. Sisko's unexpected opposition to the Federation government in the matter of Bajor's admission to the Federation in 2373 helped her realize that he was, indeed, the one promised by ancient prophecy, a view further reinforced by Sisko's discovery of the sacred lost city of **B'hala**. Winn later said she was ashamed she had ever doubted he was the true Emissary. ("Rapture" [DS9]). *Winn's first appearance was in "In the Hands of the Prophets" [DS9]).*

"Wire, The." *Deep Space Nine* episode # 42. Written by Robert Hewitt Wolfe. Directed by Kim Friedman. No stardate given. First aired in 1994. *Garak suffers crippling pain, and it is discovered to be caused by a device planted in his brain by Cardassian intelligence.* GUEST CAST: Andrew Robinson as **Garak, Elim**; Jimmie F. Skaggs as **Boheeka**; Ann Gillespie as **Jabara**; Paul Dooley as **Tain, Enabran**. SEE: **Algorian mammoth; Arawath Colony, Bashir, Dr. Julian; Boheeka; cranial implant; Dax, Tobin; endorphins; Galipotans; Garak, Elim; hyperzine; I'danian spice pudding; *kanar*; Ledonia III; leukocyte; *Meditations on a Crimson Shadow*; *Never-ending Sacrifice, The*; Merak II; mycorrhizal fungus; Obsidian Order; postcentral gyrus; Preloc; Saurian brandy; Rigel IV; Tain, Enabran; Tarkalean tea; triptacederin.**

Wise Ones. Ancient civilization also known as the **Preservers**. ("The Paradise Syndrome" [TOS]).

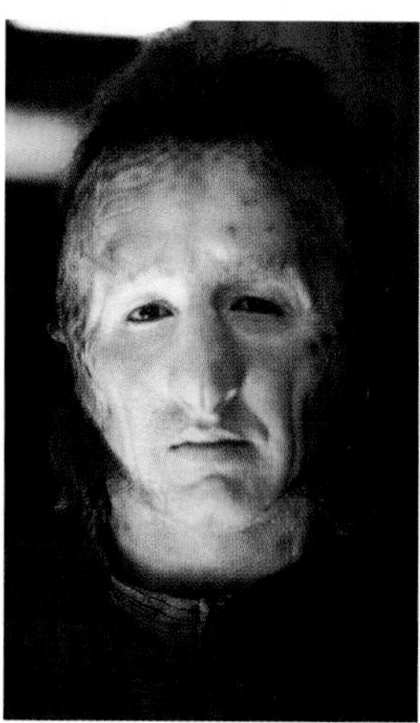

Wixiban. (James Nardini). Also known as Wix. A member of the Talaxian race, Wix is a long-time friend to Neelix. Wix spent one year in a Ubean prison for smuggling contraband. **Neelix** was also involved in this act, but escaped capture. While a prisoner in the Ubean prison, Wix was forced to eat worms to stay alive. He slept in a cell where vermin chewed on him all night, and he was punished terribly. Wix was forced to live aboard the Nekrit Expanse Supply Depot for three years after his ship was confiscated by the Station Manager, **Bahrat**. Wix conspired to smuggle illicit drugs aboard the station for delivery to the Kolaati. During a failed attempt to deliver the drugs, Wix killed the alien Sutok in self-defense using a Federation phaser. Upon confessing his crimes to Bahrat, Wix and Neelix helped capture Tosin and other members of the Kolaati. For his efforts, Bahrat returned Wix's shuttle, and he was allowed to go on his way, reportedly back to a **Talaxian colony**. ("Fair Trade" [VGR]).

Woban. (Jordan Lund). Leader of the **Navot** village on planet Bajor. Woban came to Deep Space 9 in 2369 to negotiate a land dispute with representatives of the rival **Paqu** nation. ("The Storyteller" [DS9]). See: **Glyrhond; Varis Sul**.

Woden Sector. Region of space. Site where the **Talarian** warship ***Q'Maire*** was located when it responded to a distress call from a **Talarian observation craft** in 2367. ("Suddenly Human" [TNG]). *The sector was named as an homage to the ship of the same name that was destroyed in "The Ultimate Computer" (TOS).*

Woden. Old-style ore freighter that was automated and carried no crew. The *Woden* was destroyed by the **M-5** mutitronic unit in 2268 when that experimental computer malfunctioned seriously. ("The Ultimate Computer" [TOS]). *The* Woden *was a re-use of the* S.S. Botany Bay *model from "Space Seed" (TOS).*

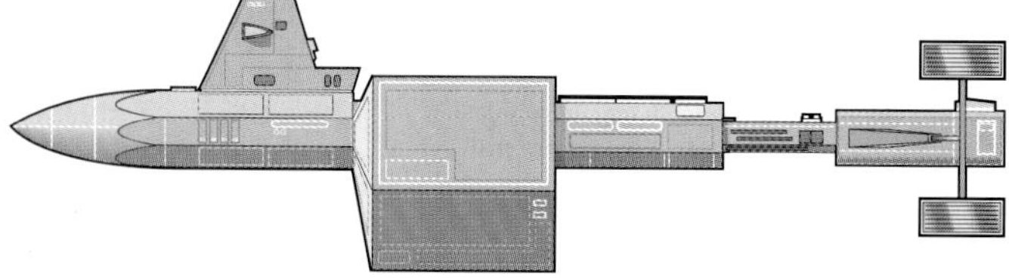

Wogneer creatures. Life-forms that lived in the Ordek Nebula. Captain Picard played a part in protecting them. ("Allegiance" [TNG]).

Wolf 359. Star located 7.8 light-years from Sol. Wolf 359 was the site of a terrible battle in which some 40 Federation starships tried in vain to prevent a Borg invasion of Earth in early 2367. Commanded by **Admiral J. P. Hanson**, the Starfleet armada was decimated by the Borg ship, resulting in the loss of 39 ships and 11,000 lives. Among the vessels lost were the *Starships* ***Tolstoy***, ***Kyushu***, ***Melbourne***, and ***Saratoga***. ("The Best of Both Worlds, Part II" [TNG]). *Casualty figures from "The Drumhead" (TNG).* Saratoga *established in "Emissary" (DS9). The aftermath of the battle of Wolf 359 was shown in "The Best of Both Worlds, Part II" (TNG), but three years after that episode was made, "Emissary" (DS9) had a dramatic flashback that showed some of the battle itself, in which* ***Ben Sisko****'s wife,* ***Jennifer Sisko****, was killed in the destruction of the* Saratoga. *Wolf 359 is a real star. Located 7.8 light-years away in the constellation Leo, it is the fourth-closest star to Earth.*

"Wolf in the Fold." Original Series episode #36. Written by Robert Bloch. Directed by Joseph Pevney. Stardate 3614.9. *First aired in 1967. Scotty is accused of murdering two women on a peaceful planet, but the culprit is an evil entity that was once known as Jack the Ripper.* GUEST CAST: John Fiedler as **Hengist, Mr.**; Charles Macaulay as **Jarvis**; Pilar Seurat as **Sybo**; Charles Dierkop as **Morla**; Joseph Bernard as **Tark**; Tania Lemani as **Kara**; John Winston as Transporter chief; Virginia Aldridge as **Tracy, Lieutenant Karen**; Judy McConnell as Tankris, Yeoman; Judi Sherven as Nurse; John Winston as Argelian bartender; Suzanne Lodge, Marlys Burdette, Serving girls; Majel Barrett as Computer voice; Paul Baxley as Hengist's stunt double. SEE: **Alpha Carinae V; Alpha Majoris I; Alpha Proxima II; Argelians; Argelius II; Argus River region; Beratis; Deneb II; drella; Hengist, Mr.; Jack the Ripper; Jarvis; Kara; Kesla; Martian Colonies; mellitus; Morla; *pi* (π); psychotricorder; Redjac; Rigel IV; Scott, Montgomery; Sybo; Tark; Tracy, Lieutenant Karen.**

Woman. (Marnie Mosiman). A member of the interpretive Chorus of mediator **Riva** from planet **Ramatis III**. Each member of the Chorus represented a different part of Riva's personality. Woman represented harmony, wisdom, and the balance that bound together passion and intellect. ("Loud as a Whisper" [TNG]). SEE: **Scholar/Artist**; **Warrior/Adonis**.

wompat. Animal often kept as a pet by **Cardassian** children. ("Chain of Command, Part II" [TNG]).

Woo, Dr. Professor at the **Daystrom Institute**. Benjamin Sisko told **Vash** that Professor Woo was especially eager for her to return to the institute to speak on her travels through the Gamma Quadrant. ("Q-Less" [DS9]).

Woodstock. Open-air music festival held near Bethel, New York, on Earth in 1969, attended by about 500,000 persons. Woodstock came to symbolize the solidarity of the generation of flower children, war protesters, and youth in general, and was the most publicized counterculture happening of the decade. It was not generally realized that a spotlight operator named **Maury Ginsberg**, with the assistance of a mysterious person named **Quinn**, prevented a sound-system malfunction that would have kept the concert from starting on time. ("Death Wish" [VGR]).

Worf (mirror). (Michael Dorn). The mirror universe Worf was Regent and leader of the **Alliance** of Cardassian and Klingon military forces. In 2372, he commanded an Alliance battle fleet on a mission to retake station **Terok Nor (mirror)** from the **Terran resistance**. The ***Defiant*** **(mirror)**, commanded by this universe's Captain Benjamin Sisko, successfully engaged the Alliance fleet with the help of a Rebel raider ship commanded by Julian Bashir (mirror). Rather than risk destruction, Worf (mirror) ordered the Alliance fleet home. ("Shattered Mirror" [DS9]).

Worf, Colonel. (Michael Dorn). Klingon official who unsuccessfully defended Kirk and McCoy in 2293 when the two Starfleet officers were placed on trial for the assassination of **Chancellor Gorkon**. *(Star Trek VI: The Undiscovered Country). Publicity materials for* Star Trek VI *(and the evidence of the character name and the actor) suggest that Colonel Worf was the grandfather of* Enterprise-D *security officer* ***Worf****, and father of* ***Mogh****.*

Worf. (Michael Dorn). The first **Klingon** warrior to serve in the Federation **Starfleet** and an influential figure in Klingon politics. ("Encounter at Farpoint, Part I" [TNG]).

Childhood and family. Worf, son of **Mogh**, was born on the **Klingon Homeworld** in 2340. ("Sins of the Father" [TNG]). As a young child, Worf was fond of his pet ***targ***. ("Where No One Has Gone Before" [TNG]). He accompanied his parents to the **Khitomer** outpost in 2346. Worf was orphaned later that year in the brutal **Khitomer massacre**, a Romulan attack in which 4,000 Klingons were killed. Worf was rescued by **Sergey Rozhenko**, a human crew member from the ***U.S.S. Intrepid***. Sergey and his wife, **Helena Rozhenko**, adopted Worf and raised him as their own son, because it was believed that Worf had no remaining family on the Homeworld. ("Sins of the Father" [TNG]). With his new family on the farm world of **Gault** ("Heart of Glory" [TNG]), and later on **Earth**, Worf found it difficult to fit into the alien world of humans and was a bit of a hellraiser. ("Family" [TNG]). In 2353, while living on Gault, Worf accidentally caused the death of a human boy named Mikel during a soccer match. During a championship game Mikel's and Worf's heads collided, breaking the human boy's neck. Worf felt responsible, and ever since that day, Worf practiced extreme restraint whenever dealing with humans, who were physically fragile compared to Klingons. ("Let He Who Is Without Sin..." [DS9]). Worf was raised along with an adoptive brother, **Nikolai Rozhenko**, the Rozhenkos' biological son. ("Homeward" [TNG]). For some reason, Worf's experiences on Earth never included drinking prune juice. When given a taste of it by Guinan in 2366, Worf pronounced it "a warrior's drink." ("Yesterday's *Enterprise*" [TNG]). Worf visited the homeworld as a boy, but he was shunned by his cousins for being too human. His parents once allowed him to visit **No'Mat**, where a vision of **Kahless the Unforgettable** appeared to Worf, telling him that he would do something no other Klingon had ever done. ("The Sword of Kahless" [DS9]). Nikolai entered **Starfleet Academy** at the same time as Worf, but later dropped out because he found Starfleet not to his liking. ("Heart of Glory" [TNG]). Worf's hobbies include building models of ancient Klingon ocean sailing vessels in a bottle, considered difficult handiwork. ("Peak Performance" [TNG]). Worf's adoptive parents remained close to him over the years, and made it a point to visit him in early 2367 when the *Enterprise*-D was docked at **Earth Station McKinley** for repairs. ("Family" [TNG]). Worf had a son, **Alexander Rozhenko**, in 2366, with Ambassador **K'Ehleyr**, with whom he had been romantically involved. When K'Ehleyr was murdered by Klingon high council member **Duras**, Alexander returned to Earth to be cared for by Sergey and Helena. ("Reunion" [TNG]).

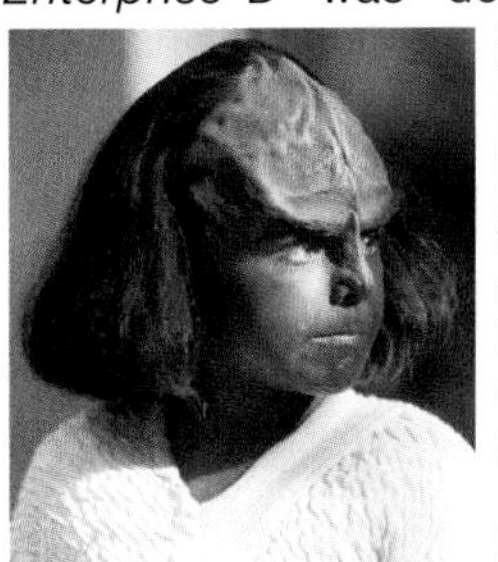

The first Klingon in Starfleet. Following his graduation from **Starfleet Academy** in 2361, Worf held the rank of lieutenant, junior grade, and served as flight control officer (conn) aboard the *U.S.S. Enterprise*-D. ("Encounter at Farpoint" [TNG]). *(There is a three-year period between his graduation and the start of* Star Trek: The Next Generation *that is still unaccounted for.)* Worf was promoted to acting chief of security and made a full lieutenant following the death of Lieutenant **Natasha Yar** at planet **Vagra II** in late 2364. ("Skin of Evil" [TNG]). Worf felt intense guilt when Lieutenant **Marla Aster** was accidentally killed on an away mission in 2366, orphaning her son **Jeremy Aster**. Worf later took Jeremy into his family through the Klingon ***R'uustai***, or bonding, ceremony. ("The Bonding" [TNG]).

In 2368, Worf's spinal column was shattered in an accident when several cargo containers collapsed onto him. Worf was left paralyzed, and his prognosis indicated little hope for a full recovery. In accordance with Klingon tradition, Worf refused medical treatment and opted for the ***Hegh'bat*** form of ritual suicide. He was dissuaded from taking his life when **Dr. Toby Russell** performed a dangerous experimental surgical procedure called **genetronic replication**, in which a new spinal column was generated to replace the damaged organ. The surgery was successful, in part because Klingon physiology includes redundancy for nearly all vital bodily functions. ("Ethics" [TNG]). SEE: ***brak'lul***.

Worf once investigated a claim that his father had not died at Khitomer, but was instead being held prisoner at a secret Romulan prison camp in the **Carraya System**. Although the report was false, Worf did indeed find a prison camp where survivors of the Khitomer massacre and their families were being held. At the camp, Worf fell in love with a half-Romulan, half-Klingon woman named **Ba'el**. Worf led some of the prisoners to freedom, but the majority (including Ba'el) chose to remain, regarding the Carraya prison as their home. ("Birthright, Parts I and II" [TNG]). *Worf and the freed prisoners all promised never to reveal the story of the prison camp at Carraya, so we assume neither Starfleet nor the Klingon government have knowledge of it.*

Worf was promoted to lieutenant commander in 2371 in a ceremony held on a holodeck representation of the 19th-century sailing frigate *Enterprise*. *(Star Trek Generations).* Following the destruction of the *Enterprise*-D, Worf returned to study for a year at the monastery on **Boreth** before he accepted an assignment to serve as strategic operations officer at station **Deep Space 9.** The promotion marked a change in career path for Worf, from operations to command. ("The Way of the Warrior" [DS9]). For some reason, Worf found living on the station uncomfortable, so he moved his residence from quarters in the station to a stateroom aboard the *U.S.S. Defiant*. ("Bar Association" [DS9]). Worf took advantage of time alone on the *Defiant* by playing Klingon opera very loudly on the ship's sound system. He particularly liked the singing of Barak-Kadan. ("Looking for *par'Mach* in All the Wrong Places" [DS9]).

In 2373, Worf found himself attracted to the Lady **Grilka** when she visited station Deep Space 9, although she prefered the company of Quark. Worf's interest in Grilka nearly blinded him to the attentions of **Jadzia Dax**, who had always had a fascination for things Klingon. It was not until the two shared a holosuite opera of **Kahless and Lukara** that Worf and Jadzia consummated their romantic relationship. ("Looking for *par'Mach* in All the Wrong Places" [DS9]). Worf commanded the *Starship Defiant* on stardate 50893 as part of the Starfleet armada that intercepted a **Borg** cube at Earth. After the Defiant was incapacitated in that battle, Worf and his crew were beamed aboard the ***Starship Enterprise*-E**, where Worf served as tactical officer for the remainder of the encounter. *(Star Trek: First Contact). He returned to the cast of* Star Trek: Deep Space Nine *the following week.*

In Klingon politics. Worf was thrust into high-level Klingon politics in 2366 when he discovered that he had a biological brother, **Kurn**. The **Klingon High Council** had ruled that their father, **Mogh,** had committed treason years ago at **Khitomer**. Worf and Kurn challenged this judgment, but found the High Council unwilling to hear evidence that the politically powerful **Duras** family had falsified the charges against Mogh. Although Worf was willing to die in the challenge to protect his family honor, he eventually chose to accept a humiliating discommendation rather than allow his brother to be killed. ("Sins of the Father" [TNG]). Worf later killed Duras for having murdered **K'Ehleyr**. ("Reunion" [TNG]). Worf was once again dragged into high-level Klingon politics in late 2367 and early 2368 when a challenge to **Gowron**'s reign by the Duras family triggered a **Klingon civil war**. Worf and Kurn agreed to support the Gowron regime in exchange for the rightful restoration of honor to the Mogh family. During the conflict, Worf was forced to resign his Starfleet commission because he would not otherwise be permitted to take sides in that internal political matter. ("Redemption, Parts I and II" [TNG]).

In 2369, Worf experienced a crisis of faith, and requested a leave of absence to visit the Klingon monastery on **Boreth**. While meditating to invoke visions of **Kahless the Unforgettable**, Worf met a very real vision of Kahless. It was discovered that this Kahless was in fact a clone of the original, created by the clerics of Boreth. At Worf's suggestion, and with the support of Chancellor Gowron, the new Kahless was installed as the ceremonial emperor of the Klingon people in 2369. ("Rightful Heir" [TNG]). Despite Worf's support of Gowron's regime, he refused to join in the Klingon invasion of Cardassia in 2372, an act of defiance for which Gowron ordered Worf's family removed from the High Council, his titles stripped, his land seized, making Worf *persona non grata* anywhere in the empire. ("The Way of the Warrior" [DS9]). Shortly thereafter, Worf became an pawn in a deception orchestrated by the Klingon government. Worf was accused of destroying a civilian transport ship and murdering 441 Klingon citizens. A hearing at Deep Space 9 revealed that government agents had faked the deaths by using the names of Klingon citizens who had died earlier in a crash on Galorda Prime. The Gowron regime had hoped to disgrace Worf, and to gain sympathy for the empire's plan to annex Cardassian territory. ("Rules of Engagement" [DS9]).

Worf's first appearance was in "Encounter at Farpoint" [TNG]). He was a regular during all seven seasons of Star Trek: The Next Generation, and subsequently became a series regular on Star Trek: Deep Space Nine beginning with "The Way of the Warrior" (DS9), the opening episode of that show's fourth season. The character was conceived by Gene Roddenberry and Bob Justman, who wanted a Klingon on the Enterprise-*D bridge as a reminder to the audience that today's enemies can become tomorrow's friends. Although Worf was originally intended to be little more than a costumed extra with elaborate makeup, he has since grown into one of the most complex and interesting of* Star Trek *characters.*

Work Bee. Small one-person extravehicular craft used for orbital construction and similar work. The Work Bee employed a modular design and could be equipped with robotic waldoes, or it could be used as a control cab for a cargo sled. *(Star Trek: The Motion Picture). The Work Bee was designed by Andrew Probert. The model was built at Magicam. Inc. The Work Bee model was later resurrected for an appearance in the fourth-season main titles of* Star Trek: Deep Space Nine.

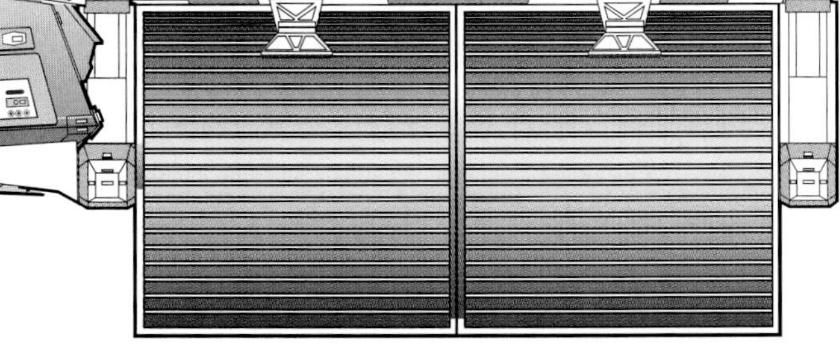

World Series. Championship **baseball** games formerly played each year on Earth. The World Series was once an event of planetary interest, but gradually declined in popularity until 2042, when only 300 spectators attended the last game of the final World Series, won by **Buck Bokai** of the **London Kings.** ("If Wishes Were Horses" [DS9]). SEE: **Newson, Eddie.**

World War III. A nuclear war that devastated much of Earth in 2053. ("Bread and Circuses" [TOS], *Star Trek: First Contact).* In the **postatomic horror** after this conflict, much of Earth reverted to a barbaric state, and legal systems were adopted that ended many individual rights, including the right to legal counsel. ("Encounter at Farpoint, Part I" [TNG]). Earth was still recovering from World War III in the early 22nd century. One philosopher of the time was Liam Dieghan, founder of the Neo-Transcendentalist movement. Dieghan advocated a return to a simpler life, one more in harmony with nature. ("Up the Long Ladder" [TNG]). SEE: **Eastern Coalition; Eugenics Wars.** *Spock, in "Bread and Circuses" (TOS), said that 37 million people had died in World War III, but* Star Trek: First Contact *gives the death toll at 600 million. It is not clear which figure should be regarded as "correct," although the Federation's records of this period have been described as "fragmentary."*

Wormhole Junction. Slang name for station **Deep Space 9**. ("Playing God" [DS9]).

wormhole aliens. SEE: **Prophets**.

wormhole, Bajoran. SEE: **Bajoran wormhole**.

wormhole. A subspace bridge (or tunnel) between two points in "normal" time and space. Most wormholes are extremely unstable, and their endpoints fluctuate widely across time and space. An improperly balanced warp-drive system can create an artificial wormhole that can pose a serious danger to the ship and its crew. *(Star Trek: The Motion Picture).* SEE: **Bajoran wormhole; Barzan wormhole; quantum fluctuations; *Trieste, U.S.S.***

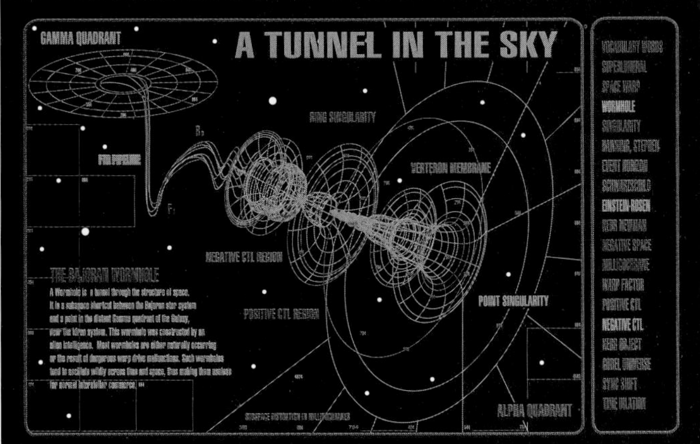

"Wounded, The." *Next Generation* episode #86. Teleplay by Jeri Taylor. Story by Stuart Charno & Sara Charno and Cy Chermax. Directed by Chip Chalmers. Stardate 44429.6. *First aired in 1991. A renegade Starfleet captain threatens the fragile peace between the Federation and the Cardassian Union. This episode introduces the Cardassians, a new group of adversaries for our Federation heroes that would appear frequently in* Star Trek: Deep Space Nine. GUEST CAST: Bob Gunton as **Maxwell, Captain Benjamin**; Rosalind Chao as **O'Brien, Keiko**; Marc Alaimo as **Macet, Gul**; Colm Meaney as **O'Brien, Miles**; Marco Rodriguez as **Telle, Glinn**; Tim Winters as **Daro, Glinn**; John Hancock as **Haden, Admiral**. SEE: **Cardassia; Cardassians; Cardies; coded transponder frequency; Cuellar system; Daro, Glinn; *Galor*-class Cardassian warship; glinn; gul; Haden, Admiral; *kanar*; Kayden, Will; Kelrabi system; Macet, Gul; Maxwell, Captain Benjamin; "Minstrel Boy, The"; *Nebula*-class starship; O'Brien, Miles; *Phoenix, U.S.S.*; plankton loaf; potato casserole; prefix code; *Rutledge, U.S.S.*; Sector 21503; Sector 21505; Setlik III; Starbase 211; *Stargazer, U.S.S.*; *Trager*; United Federation of Planets.**

Wrenn. (Raye Birke). Commander of the last **Tarellian** vessel carrying survivors of the Tarellian plague. Wrenn attempted to land his ship on planet **Haven** in 2364 when the physician **Wyatt Miller** joined his people in an effort to seek a cure for their disease. Father to **Ariana**. ("Haven" [TNG]).

Wright, Admiral. Starfleet officer assigned to **Earth** in 2371. ("Past Tense, Part I" [DS9]).

Wright, Orville. (1871-1948) Earth aviation pioneer. Co-inventor of that planet's first heavier-than-air aircraft (along with his brother, Wilbur Wright), and pilot of Earth's first airplane. ("Threshold" [VGR]).

Wrightwell, Commander. Starfleet officer and aide to Admiral **Alynna Nechayev**. Wrightwell provided Captain Jean-Luc Picard with information about Admiral Nechayev's dietary preferences. ("Journey's End" [TNG]).

Wrigley's Pleasure Planet. Planet. *Enterprise* crew member **Darnell** saw the last surviving **M-113 creature** in the form of a woman he had left behind on Wrigley's Pleasure Planet. ("The Man Trap" [TOS]).

Writ of Accountability. Legal document issued by the **Ferengi Commerce Authority** to individuals required to produce a detailed financial statement to the FCA. Presented as an ominous black scroll. ("Family Business" [DS9]).

written languages. SEE *illustration next page.*

Wu. (Lloyd Kino). **Kohm** inhabitant of planet **Omega IV**. At the time of the *Enterprise* visit to Omega IV in 2268, Wu was 462 years old. Wu's ancestors had survived a terrible biological war, and their descendants inherited powerful antibodies that protected against disease, prolonging life. ("The Omega Glory" [TOS]).

Wyoming, U.S.S. Federation starship. **Tuvok** served aboard the *Starship Wyoming* in 2349 after returning to Starfleet following an absence of 51 years. ("Flashback" [VGR]).

Written languages. Specimens of writing from several cultures. Note that in most cases we have deliberately refrained from developing a translation for written alien languages. The reason is that if the words or symbols have English equivalents, it is much more difficult to organize the patterns of the writing in an alien fashion. That is why most written alien languages on *Star Trek* don't have "normal" word groupings or paragraph blocks. For example, Ferengi is based on a branching flow chart, using lots of 60-degree angles, whereas ancient Vulcan seems to be based on some kinds of musical scales.

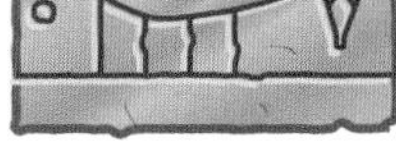

D'arsay pictographs

Ancient Vulcan

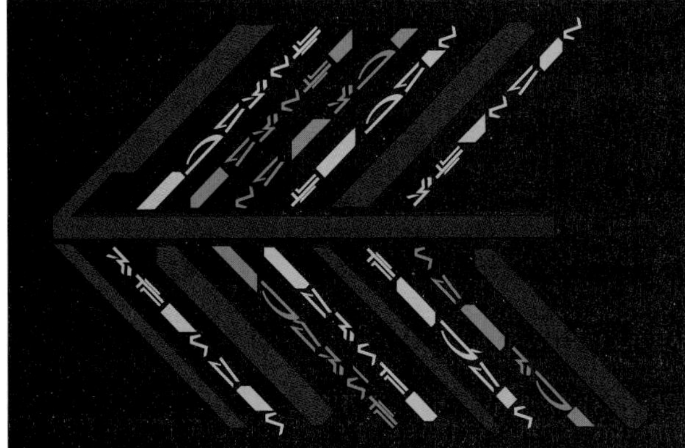

Kohl

Ferengi

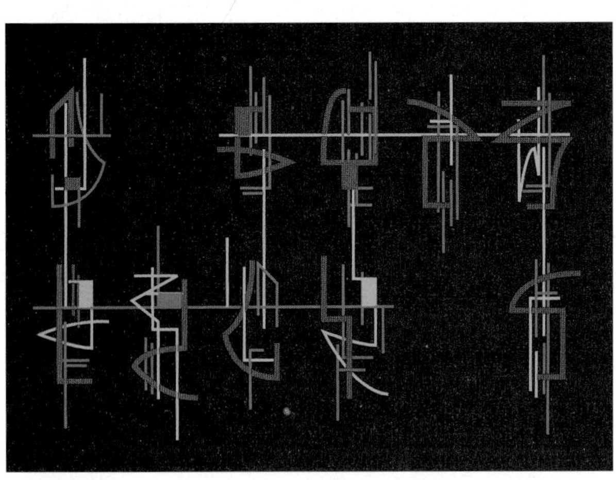

Banean

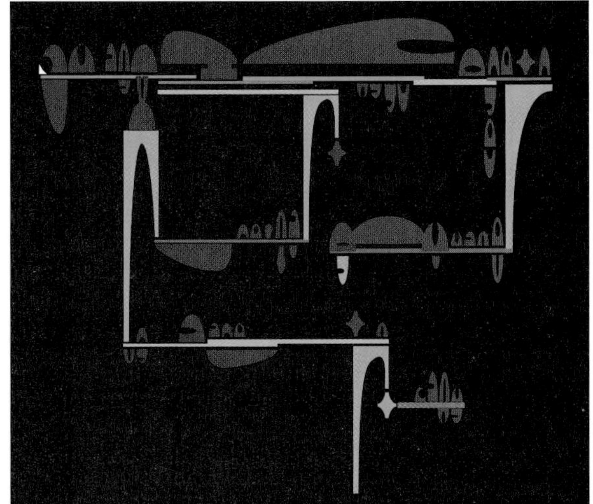

Jem'Hadar

Pralor

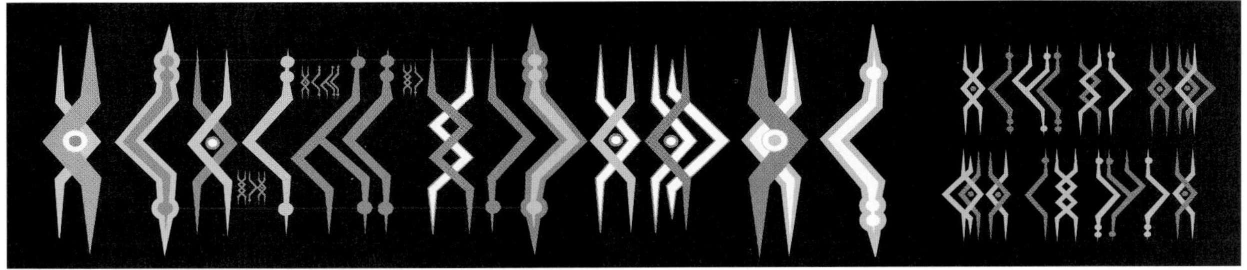
Vidiian

Klingon

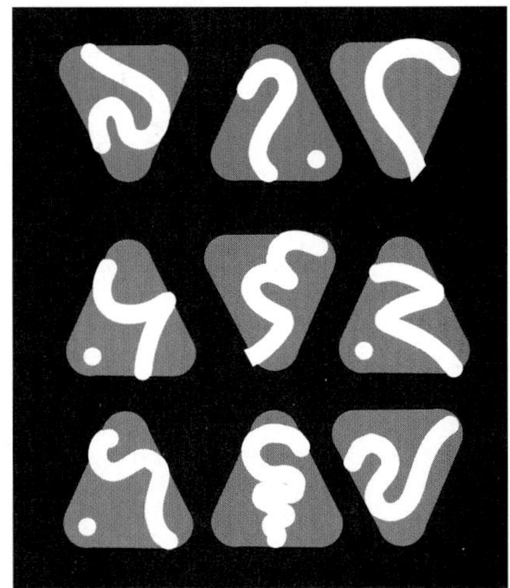
Trill

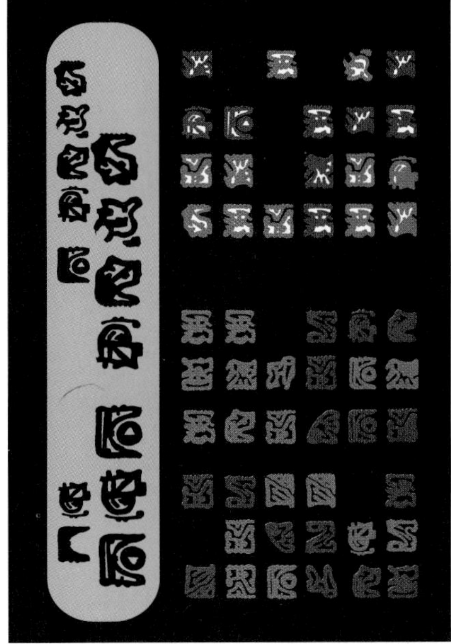
Bajoran

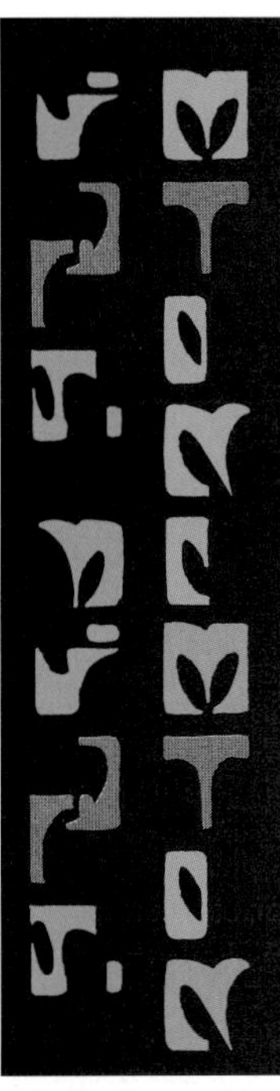
Romulan

Bahrat

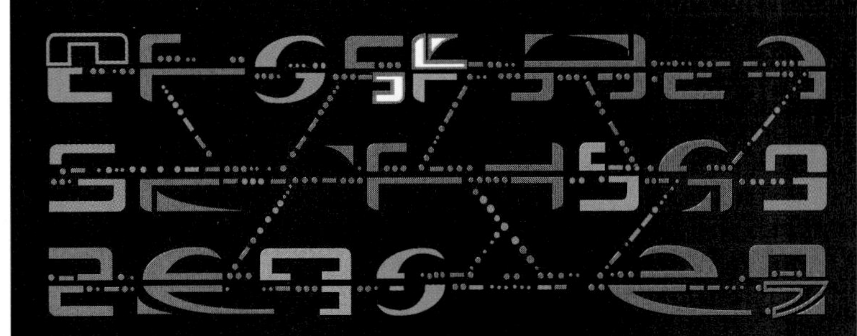
Kazon

X-rays. Energetic form of electromagnetic radiation with wavelengths between 10^{-11} to 10^{-9} meters. X-rays were used in early medical imaging scanners into the late 21st century. ("Tuvix" [VGR]).

Xanthras III. Planet. Destination of the *Enterprise*-D following its mission in the Gamma Erandi Nebula in 2366. The *Enterprise* was to rendezvous with the ***U.S.S. Zapata***. ("Ménage à Troi" [TNG]).

Xelo. Valet to **Lwaxana Troi** prior to Mr. **Homn**. Mrs. Troi said she terminated Xelo's employment because he was strongly attracted to her. ("Haven" [TNG]).

Xendi Sabu star system. Solar system. Site where the *Enterprise*-D rendezvoused with a Ferengi vessel in 2364 when **DaiMon Bok** offered Captain Picard the extraordinary gift of Picard's old vessel, the ***Stargazer***. ("The Battle" [TNG]). In 2370, a probe was sent from the Xendi Sabu system to the *Enterprise*-D which contained a series of threats against Picard. ("Bloodlines" [TNG]). SEE: **Vigo, Jason**. *The Xendi Sabu system was called the Xendi Kabu system in "Bloodlines" [TNG].*

Xendi Starbase 9. Federation starbase. Site where the ***U.S.S. Stargazer*** was towed after the *Enterprise*-D received the old vessel from the Ferengi in 2364. ("The Battle" [TNG]).

xenophobia. In psychology, a fear of or prejudice against beings outside of one's own race or social group. Xenophobia has played a part in many planetary and interplanetary conflicts, including the dispute between the peoples of **Kesprytt III**. ("Attached" [TNG]).

xenopolycythemia. Disease in humanoids characterized by an abnormal proliferation of red blood cells causing varied symptoms including weakness, fatigue, enlarged spleen, and pain in the extremities. **Dr. Leonard McCoy** was diagnosed with terminal xenopolycythemia in 2268. He was cured, thanks to advanced medical information from the spaceship ***Yonada.*** Prior to that time, xenopolycythemia was considered to be invariably fatal. ("For the World Is Hollow and I Have Touched the Sky" [TOS]).

Xepolites. Humanoid civilization. Like the **Lissepians**, the politically unaffiliated Xepolites served as covert intermediaries for the Cardassians, but unlike the Lissepians, Xepolite free traders have never been caught doing so. Xepolite ships had a maximum speed of warp 9.8, with hulls made of a sensor-reflective material. ("The Maquis, Part II" [DS9]). SEE: **Drofo Awa**.

Xerxes VII. Planet. Legend has it that a mythical land called Neinman may be found on Xerxes VII. ("When the Bough Breaks" [TNG]).

Xhosa. Small *Antares*-class cargo freighter owned by Petarian interests. In 2372, the *Xhosa* was commanded by Captain **Kasidy Yates**. The *Xhosa* was intercepted by the Klingon bird-of-prey *M'Char* on stardate 49011 during the Klingon offensive on Cardassia. The *Xhosa* was freed thanks to intervention by Sisko in command of the ***Defiant***. ("The Way of the Warrior" [DS9]). *The ship's name is pronounced "Zosha." The exterior of the* Xhosa *was a re-use of the* Batris, *first seen in "Heart of Glory" (TNG). The bridge interior, seen in "For the Cause" (DS9), featured control panel and instrument designs that were closely based on the panels designed for the original* Starship Enterprise *bridge.*

XO. Abbreviation for executive officer. ("Paradise Lost" [DS9]).

***xupta* tree.** Plant indigenous to planet **Orellius**. It produces an oil extract that is soothing to sore muscles. ("Paradise"[DS9]).

Y'Pora. (Peggy Roeder). Bajoran midwife. Y'Pora was present on Deep Space 9 in 2373 when Kira Nerys gave birth to Kirayoshi O'Brien. ("The Begotten" [DS9]).

Y'tem. Klingon **bird-of-prey** that was part of the combined Federation and Klingon fleet amassed at DS9 in 2373 to meet an anticipated Dominion invasion force. ("By Inferno's Light" [DS9]).

ya'nora kor. In **Klingon** culture, an accusation that a parent is unfit to raise a child. **K'mtar** charged Worf with *ya'nora kor* in 2370 when Worf refused to force his son Alexander to leave the *Enterprise*-D for the **Ogat Training Academy**. ("Firstborn" [TNG]).

Ya'Seem. Archaeological discovery first uncovered by the renowned scientist **M'Tell**. ("The Chase" [TNG]). *Unfortunately, the episode does not make clear what Ya'Seem is or why it was so important.*

Yadalla Prime. Planet in the **Taugus** sector that possessed archeological ruins of **Romulan** origin. This made the planet a potential target for **Arctus Baran**'s mercenaries in 2370. ("Gambit, Parts I and II" [TNG]).

Yadera II. Planet located in the **Gamma Quadrant.** Home to **Rurigan** after his homeworld, Yadera Prime, was conquered by the **Dominion** in 2340. With the aid of a **hologenerator**, Rurigan created an entire village population of **sentient holographic life-forms** on Yadera II. ("Shadowplay" [DS9]). *The painting used to represent the landscape of Yadera II was re-used later as the planet Ronara in "Preemptive Strike" (TNG).*

Yadera Prime. Planet located in the **Gamma Quadrant**. Yadera Prime was conquered by the **Dominion** in 2340. **Rurigan**, an inhabitant of Yadera Prime, became unhappy with life there, so he moved to **Yadera II** and created a holographic village full of people in which to live. ("Shadowplay" [DS9]).

Yaderans. Apparently humanoids on planet **Yadera II**, but actually **sentient holographic life-forms**. ("Shadowplay" [DS9]). SEE: **Rurigan**.

Yadozi Desert. A legendary dry environment. Odo compared the possibility of Dax being infatuated with Quark to the likelihood of finding a drink of water in the Yadozi Desert. ("A Man Alone" [DS9]).

Yale, Mirasta. (Carolyn Seymour). Minister of Science on planet **Malcor III**. Yale supervised her planet's development of warp-drive technology and was a strong advocate of her people's space exploration programs in 2367. Prior to the construction of the first warp-powered spacecraft, the discovery of a covert Federation presence on Malcor III led the conservative Malcorian government to delay the planet's space program. Yale chose to leave her planet and explore space aboard the *Enterprise*-D. ("First Contact" [TNG]). SEE: **first contact**. *Carolyn Seymour has played not only a Malcorian, but two Romulans. She portrayed Subcommander Taris in "Contagion" (TNG) and Commander Toreth in "Face of the Enemy" (TNG). She also played Mrs. Templeton, the housekeeper in Janeway's gothic romance holo-novel.*

Yallitians. Technologically sophisticated life-forms indigenous to the **Delta Quadrant**. Yallitians have three spinal cords. ("Phage" [VGR]).

Yalosians. Sentient life-forms. Yalosians breathe a mixture of nitrogen, benzene, and hydrogen fluoride, and were unable to perceive the red-orange part of the color spectrum. A Yalosian ambassador was scheduled to visit station Deep Space 9 in 2371. ("Improbable Cause" [DS9]).

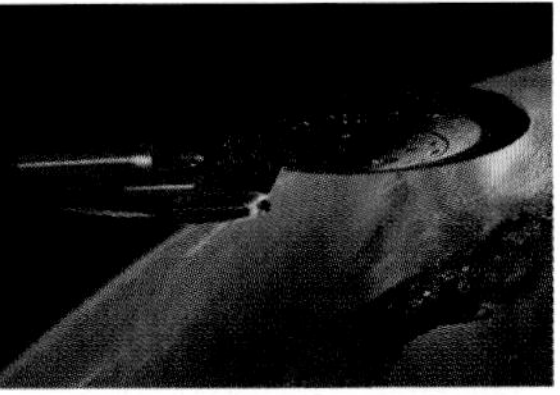

Yamato, U.S.S. *Galaxy*-class Federation starship commanded by **Captain Donald Varley**. Starfleet registry number NCC-71807. A sister ship of the *Enterprise*-D. ("Where Silence Has Lease" [TNG]). The *Yamato* was destroyed in 2365 by an ancient **Iconian** computer software weapon that caused the failure of the ship's antimatter containment system, resulting in the ship's explosion and the loss of all hands. The software weapon had also been responsible for a series of other malfunctions aboard the *Yamato*, including the failure of a shuttlebay force field. ("Contagion" [TNG]). *Although the* Yamato*'s registry number was established in "Contagion" to be NCC-71807, an earlier, incorrect number was given in "Where Silence Has Lease," when an illusory version of that ship was seen. An early draft for that episode gave the number as NCC-1305E, which didn't fit into the numbering scheme developed for starships in* The Next Generation. *Mike Okuda wrote a note to the producers, requesting the number be changed, but didn't send the memo because a later draft of that script dropped the reference to the* Yamato*'s registry number. Mike wasn't aware that an even-later draft of the script restored the scene and the incorrect number. By the time he found out (when he saw the completed episode on the air), he had already prepared the markings for the* U.S.S. Yamato *saucer, for the scene when that ship blew up in the episode "Contagion" (TNG), as well as the ship's log computer screens for that episode. Named for the Japanese World War II battleship. The dedication plaque for the bridge of the* Yamato *bore a motto from Thomas Jefferson: "I have sworn eternal hostility against every form of tyranny over the mind of man."*

***yamok* sauce**. Cardassian foodstuff and condiment. On stardate 46844, **Ferengi** entrepreneur **Quark** had 5,000 wrappages of *yamok* sauce, a considerable surplus since his **Cardassian** clientele had fallen off sharply when station **Deep Space 9** was taken over by Starfleet. Quark didn't know what to do with the stuff, so his nephew **Nog** used it in a business venture ("Progress" [DS9]). **Aamin Marritza** liked *yamok* sauce on his ***sem'hal* stew**. ("Duet" [DS9]). Chief O'Brien and Doctor Bashir enjoyed *yamok* sauce on Gramillion sand peas. ("The Way of the Warrior" [DS9]). Tora Ziyal liked it on asparagus. ("By Inferno's Light" [DS9]).

Yan-Isleth. Elite Klingon military unit known as the Brotherhood of the Sword; the personal security force of the chancellor of the Klingon Empire. ("Apocalypse Rising" [DS9]).

Yanar. (Rosalind Ingledew). Daughter of **Debin** from the planet **Altec**. Yanar had been secretly engaged to marry **Benzan** of Straleb, and nearly triggered a breakdown of the **Coalition of Madena** when she accepted the Jewel of Thesia from Benzan as a pledge of marriage. ("The Outrageous Okona" [TNG]).

Yangs. One of two ethnic groups on planet **Omega IV** who, centuries ago, fought a terrible bacteriological war. The few survivors of the conflict lived because they happened to have powerful natural immunity, and had extraordinarily long life spans. In 2268, Starfleet captain **Ronald Tracey** of the ***U.S.S. Exeter*** sided with the **Kohms**, ancient enemies of the Yangs, supplying the Kohms with phasers that proved devastating in their technologically primitive conflict. *Enterprise* personnel, investigating the disappearance of the *Exeter*, theorized that the Yangs were culturally similar to Earth's 20th-century "Yankees," based on their worship of such icons as the American flag and the United States' Constitution. ("The Omega Glory" [TOS]).

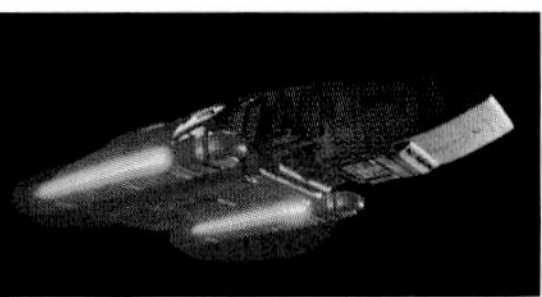

Yangtzee Kiang, U.S.S. Starfleet *Danube*-class **runabout**, registry number NCC-72453, one of three runabouts assigned to station **Deep Space 9**. ("Emissary" [DS9], "Past Prologue" [DS9]). The *Yangtzee Kiang* was destroyed in a crash on a penal-colony moon in the Gamma Quadrant. Bajoran religious leader **Kai Opaka** was killed in the crash, although artificial microbes in the moon's environment later restored her to life, for as long as she remained there. ("Battle Lines" [DS9]). The *Yangtzee Kiang* was replaced on Deep Space 9 by the *U.S.S. Orinoco*. ("The Siege" [DS9]).

Yankees. Professional **baseball** team on **Earth** in the 20th and 21st centuries. Sanctuary District Police Sergeant **Vin** thought that the 1999 Yankees were the best ball club he had ever seen. ("Past Tense, Part II" [DS9]).

Yar, Ishara. (Beth Toussaint). The younger sister of *Enterprise*-D Security Chief **Natasha Yar**. Born in the failed **Turkana IV** colony in 2342, Ishara was orphaned just after birth. Ishara was raised by her sister, Tasha, until she became a loyal member of the **Coalition** cadre, one of the factions fighting for control of the colony. When Natasha Yar left Turkana IV in 2352, Ishara chose to remain behind because she felt her cadre was her family. Ishara regarded her sister as a coward for leaving Turkana. When the *Enterprise*-D arrived at Turkana IV in 2367, Ishara acted as liaison between the *Enterprise*-D crew and the Coalition. The *Enterprise*-D crew, and Data in particular, were eager to accept her as a friend, but Ishara used this trust in an unsuccessful attempt to gain a tactical advantage over the rival **Alliance** cadre. ("Legacy" [TNG]). *Beth Toussaint also played Anna Sheridan in one episode of* Babylon 5, *although later appearances of that character were played by Melissa Gilbert.*

Yar, Natasha, (alternate). (Denise Crosby). In the alternate timeline created when the ***Enterprise*-C** vanished from its "proper" place in 2344 into a temporal rift, *Enterprise*-D Security Officer Tasha Yar did not die at planet **Vagra II** in 2364. Instead, she remained as security chief aboard that ship during a war between the Federation and the Klingons. The alternate Yar was on duty when the *Enterprise*-C emerged from a temporal rift, and she served as liaison between the two ships, working closely with **Lieutenant Richard Castillo**, with whom she became romantically involved. When it was learned that the *Enterprise*-C had to return to the past, the alternate Yar volunteered to return with that ship, despite the knowledge that the mission meant virtually certain death. ("Yesterday's *Enterprise*" [TNG]). No direct evidence survived of the existence of the alternate Yar (or the emergence of the *Enterprise*-C) after the return of the *Enterprise*-C to the past. However, in 2367, a Romulan operative named **Sela** began a series of covert operations against the Klingon government. Sela was apparently the child of Yar and a Romulan general who had captured the *Enterprise*-C bridge crew at **Narendra III**. The Romulan general agreed to spare the bridge crew if Yar agreed to become his consort. Sela was born a year later, in 2345. Sela claimed that the alternate Yar was killed trying to escape when Sela was four. ("Redemption, Part II" [TNG]).

Yar, Natasha. (Denise Crosby). *Enterprise*-D chief of security under the command of Captain **Jean-Luc Picard**. ("Encounter at Farpoint, Part I" [TNG]).

Ukrainian in descent, Yar was born on a failed Federation colony on planet **Turkana IV**. Her parents were killed when she was only five, and she spent much of her childhood in a bitter struggle for survival, evading marauding rape gangs and caring for her younger sister, **Ishara Yar**. One of the few "normal" aspects of her childhood was her ownership of a pet kitten that she protected. ("Where No One Has Gone Before" [TNG]). Tasha escaped from Turkana IV at the age of 15, choosing to join Starfleet. ("The Naked Now" [TNG]).

As a Starfleet officer, she impressed Captain Jean-Luc Picard with her courage in rescuing a wounded colonist, making her way through a Carnellian mine field. Thus, Picard requested that she be transferred to the *Enterprise*-D in early 2364. ("Legacy" [TNG]). *The Carnel backstory seems to imply that Yar met Captain Picard and joined the* Enterprise-D *crew after the ship was launched and was on patrol, but "All Good Things..." [TNG] makes it clear that Picard met Yar when she piloted the shuttlecraft that first took him to the ship just prior to his assuming command of the* Enterprise-D. While under the inhibition-stripping effects of the **Psi 2000 virus** in early 2364, Tasha apparently became intimate with fellow *Enterprise*-D crew member **Data**. ("The Naked Now" [TNG]).

Yar was killed in late 2364 while participating in a rescue mission on planet **Vagra II**. SEE: **Armus**. Tasha, knowing her line of work entailed considerable risk, left a holographic farewell to her comrades in which she thanked her shipmates for being part of her life. ("Skin of Evil" [TNG]). Data kept a small holographic portrait of Tasha, and he considered it one of his most precious personal possessions. ("The Measure of a Man" [TNG]).

*Tasha Yar was first seen in "Encounter at Farpoint" (TNG). Although her character died in "Skin of Evil" (TNG), we saw her holographic portrait in "The Measure of a Man" (TNG), and her alternate-timeline version (**SEE: Yar, Natasha [alternate]**) in "Yesterday's Enterprise" (TNG). She also appeared in "All Good Things..." (TNG). The alternate Tasha's daughter, **Sela**, was also played by Denise Crosby.*

Yareena. (Karole Selmon). Wealthy landowner and wife of leader **Lutan** on planet **Ligon II**. Yareena was nearly killed in ritual combat with *Enterprise*-D Security Chief Yar in 2364 when both became involved in a local power struggle. ("Code of Honor" [TNG]).

Yareth. (Leslie Engelberg). The daughter of the **Rakhari** fugitive **Croden**. When Croden was convicted of crimes against the Rakhari state, Croden hid Yareth in a stasis chamber on an asteroid in the **Chamra Vortex** so that she would not be executed with the rest of his family. She remained in stasis until 2369, when with the assistance of Odo, she was freed. ("Vortex" [DS9]).

Yarka. (Erick Avari). Former Bajoran **vedek**. In 2371, Yarka came to believe that **Trakor's Third Prophecy** predicted disaster as a result of the scientific project being undertaken at Deep Space 9 to place a **subspace radio** relay station in the Gamma Quadrant. Yarka ultimately realized that he had misinterpreted the prophecy. ("Destiny" [DS9]).

Yarnek. (Janos Prohaska, voice of Bart LaRue). Scientist from planet **Excalbia** who, in 2269, conducted an experiment to examine the human philosophies of "good" and "evil." The **Excalbians**, who appeared to be creatures of rock, created replicas of several historical figures falling into either category, placed them into a conflict, and then observed the results. Included among the combatants were *Enterprise* officers Kirk and Spock. Good eventually did triumph over evil, allowing the *Enterprise* to be set free, but Yarnek promised that other cultures would be tested in the same manner. ("The Savage Curtain" [TOS]). *Yarnek's name was never mentioned in the aired episode and was obtained from the script. Janos Prohaska also built and played the **Horta** in "Devil in the Dark" (TOS) and the **mugato** in "A Private Little War" (TOS). Bart LaRue supplied the voice of the **Guardian of Forever** in "City on the Edge of Forever" (TOS) and played the Roman television announcer in "Bread and Circuses" (TOS).*

Yaro. Geographical and administrative province on planet **Ilari**. Tieran had a number of supporters in Yaro Province. ("Warlord" [VGR]).

Yash-El, night blessing of. "Dream not of today." **Jean-Luc Picard** missed a question based on the night blessing of Yash-El on his final archaeology exam under **Professor Richard Galen**. ("The Chase" [TNG]).

Yates, Kasidy. (Penny Johnson). Civilian freighter captain who operated in the Bajor sector. Yates met **Benjamin Sisko** through his son, Jake, in 2371. ("Family Business" [DS9]). By early 2372, Kasidy Yates and Benjamin Sisko grew increasingly fond of each other, but often had difficulty finding time together owing to their busy schedules. Yates' freighter, the ***Xhosa***, was intercepted by the Klingon bird-of-prey *M'Char* in 2372 during the Klingon offensive on Cardassia. The *Xhosa* was freed thanks to intervention by Sisko in command of the ***Defiant***. ("The Way of the Warrior" [DS9]). Shortly thereafter, Yates accepted a position as a freighter captain with the Bajoran Ministry of Commerce. She was allowed to use her own ship, pick her own crew, and operate wholly within the Bajoran sector. In accepting the job, she intended to take up residence on station Deep Space 9. ("Indiscretion" [DS9]). Kasidy and Ben shared a love of **baseball** and enjoyed each other's company. Kasidy Yates's youngest brother was a colonist on **Cestus III**, and played for the **Pike City Pioneers**. ("Family Business" [DS9]). Yates was arrested by Starfleet in 2372 for smuggling weapons to the **Maquis**. ("For the Cause" [DS9]). Yates was convicted and sentenced to six months in a Federation prison. After serving her sentence, she returned to Deep Space 9 and took up residence there. ("Rapture" [DS9]). *Penny Johnson also portrayed Dobara in "Homeward" (TNG).*

Yattho. Beta Quadrant civilization. The Yattho are reputed to have the ability to predict the future. ("Before and After" [VGR]).

Yeager loop. An aerobatic maneuver executed by five single-pilot spacecraft. Starting in a Diamond Slot formation, the five ships would perform an Immelmann turn in concert. The Yeager loop was used as a demonstration of piloting prowess by cadets at **Starfleet Academy**. ("The First Duty" [TNG]). *Named for one of Chuck Yeager's most famous flight maneuvers, see next entry.*

Yeager, Chuck. Aircraft test pilot on planet Earth, the first human to fly faster than the speed of sound. Yeager accomplished this feat on October 14, 1947, in a rocket-powered craft called the *Glamorous Glennis*. Commander La Forge likened **Dr. Ja'Dar**'s revolutionary **soliton wave** rider experiment in 2368 to Yeager's historic achievement. ("New Ground" [TNG]).

Yeager, U.S.S. Federation starship, ***Saber*-class**, Starfleet registry number NCC-61947. The *Yeager* was among the ships defending Sector 001 against the **Borg** incursion of 2373. *(Star Trek: First Contact). Named for test pilot Chuck Yeager, the first human to fly faster than the speed of sound.*

Yellow Alert. A state of significantly increased readiness aboard Federation starships and other vessels. In the event of an actual or imminent emergency, the commanding officer can order the state of readiness increased even further to **Red Alert**

Yellowstone, U.S.S. Federation starship, *Sequoia* class, Starfleet registry number NCC-70073. The *Yellowstone* transported **Ensign Melora Pazlar** to station Deep Space 9 in 2370. ("Melora" [DS9]). *The Yellowstone was named after the United States' largest and oldest national park, which was established in 1872.*

Yellowstone, U.S.S. Prototype for an advanced Starfleet **runabout** spacecraft that employed **tetryon** plasma **warp nacelle**s. Starfleet registry number NX-74751. In an alternate reality, Ensign **Harry Kim** and Lieutenant **Laska** were key members of the *Yellowstone* design team in 2372. The craft lost antimatter containment and was destroyed when Kim was returning to his original reality. ("Non Sequitur" [VGR]).

Yeln. (Tony Papenfus) **Obsidian Order** agent. In 2371, Yeln planted false records that placed Kira Nerys at the **Elemspur Detention Center** during the Cardassian occupation of Bajor. ("Second Skin" [DS9]). ("Second Skin" [DS9]). SEE: **Ghemor, Legate**.

"Yesterday's *Enterprise*." *Next Generation* episode #63. Teleplay by Ira Steven Behr & Richard Manning & Hans Beimler & Ronald D. Moore. From a story by Trent Christopher Ganino & Eric Stillwell. Directed by David Carson. Stardate 43625.2. *First aired in 1990. A* Starship Enterprise *from the past emerges into the present, and the shape of time becomes badly distorted.* GUEST CAST: Denise Crosby as **Yar**, **Natasha (alternate)**; Christopher McDonald as **Castillo**, **Lieutenant Richard**; Tricia O'Neil as **Garrett**, **Captain Rachel**; Whoopi Goldberg as **Guinan**. SEE: ***Ambassador*-class starship; Archer IV (alternate); Archer IV; Castillo, Lieutenant Richard; class-1 probe; *Enterprise*-C, *U.S.S.*; Garrett, Captain Rachel; gravimetric fluctuations; Guinan; *K'Vort*-class battle cruisers; Klingon War (alternate); military log; Narendra III (alternate); Narendra III; prune juice; Romulans; Selar, Dr.; Starbase 105; Starfleet Monitor Stations; temporal rift; TKL ration; warbird, Romulan; Worf; Yar, Natasha (alternate).**

Yeto. (Steve Rankin). **Klingon** mercenary hired by **Verad** in 2370 for his plan to steal the **Dax** symbiont. ("Invasive Procedures" [DS9]). *Steve Rankin also played Patahk in "The Enemy" (TNG).*

Yigrish cream pie. Dessert. Available at the **Replimat** on station Deep Space 9. ("Distant Voices" [DS9]).

yIntagh. A Klingon expletive. ("Redemption, Part I" [TNG]).

Yiri, General. Former head of the Trelonian government. Yiri's political activities, including the assassination of his own brother, made for interesting lunchtime conversation. ("Profit and Loss" [DS9]). *Unfortunately, Garak and Bashir never did make it clear just when and where these political machinations took place.*

Yndar. Deputy in Deep Space 9's station security force. ("Apocalypse Rising" [DS9]).

Yog. (Colin Mitchell). Commander of a **Yridian freighter** spacecraft. In 2370, Yog received a shipment of **magnesite ore** from the Duras sisters, **Lursa** and **B'Etor**. ("Firstborn" [TNG]).

yominium sulfide. Chemical compound with the molecular formula $K_4Ym_3 (SO_7^3 Es_2)$. The makeup of this substance was a question in Spock's memory test during his reeducation in 2286. *(Star Trek IV: The Voyage Home). Yominium was the "invention" of* Star Trek IV *associate producer Kirk Thatcher, who named it for Leonard Nimoy (spell it backward). Yes, we know the formula is inconsistent with a sulfide. SEE:* ***"I Hate You."***

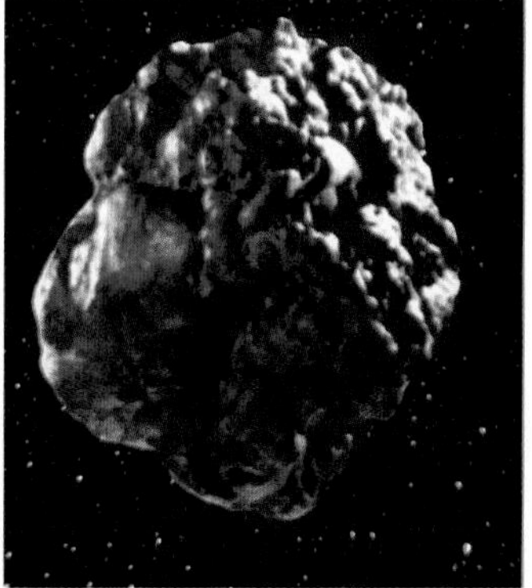

Yonada. Multigeneration spaceship built by the **Fabrini** civilization 10,000 years ago. *Yonada*, which was built inside a large asteroid, was a slower-than-light ship designed to transport part of the Fabrini civilization to a "promised world" when their home sun went nova ten millennia ago. ("For the World Is Hollow and I Have Touched the Sky" [TOS]). SEE: **Natira**. Yonada *was expected to reach its final destination in late 2269. Kirk promised McCoy that they would be there for the arrival, but since this would have been just after the end of the original* Star Trek *series, we do not know if they made it.*

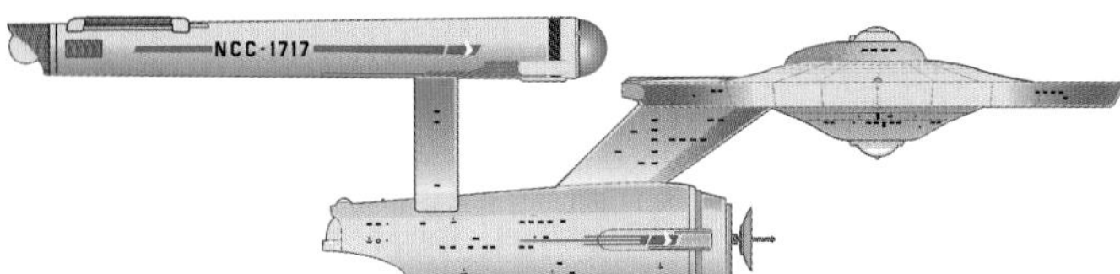

Yorktown*, *U.S.S. Federation starship, *Constitution* class, Starfleet registry number NCC-1717. The *Yorktown* was scheduled to rendezvous with the *Enterprise* in 2268 to transfer critically needed vaccines for planet **Theta VII**. The *Enterprise* was unable to make the rendezvous with the *Yorktown* until the investigation and destruction of the **dikironium cloud creature** was complete. ("Obsession" [TOS]). The *Yorktown* was disabled by an alien space probe approaching Earth in 2286. The ship's chief engineer rigged a makeshift solar sail to provide emergency power. *(Star Trek IV: The Voyage Home).* SEE: **Probe, the.** *Named for the American aircraft carrier that fought in the Pacific theater during World War II. The captain of the* Yorktown, *seen on a communications viewer in Starfleet Command, was played by Vijay Armitraj. His character's name, according to the script, was captain Joel Randolph. Also seen on one of the big Starfleet screens was* Go-Gos *singer (and* Star Trek *aficionado) Jane Wiedlin, who played an alien communications officer. According to the script, she was officer Trillya of the* Starship Shepard, *but this was not established in the final version of the film.* Yorktown *was the original name of* Star Trek*'s spaceship, before the ship was called* Enterprise, *from Gene Roddenberry's first draft of the series outline written in 1964. Roddenberry reportedly suggested that the second* Starship Enterprise, *NCC-1701-A, launched at the end of* Star Trek IV, *had previously been named the* Yorktown, *since it seems unlikely that Starfleet could have built an all-new ship so quickly. If this was the case, the* Yorktown *may have made it safely back to Earth and been repaired and renamed, or perhaps there was a newer, replacement* Yorktown *already under construction at the time of the probe crisis.*

Yorktown*, *U.S.S. Federation starship, *Zodiac* class, Starfleet registry number NCC-61137. (In the **anti-time** reality created by the **Q Continuum**, Admiral **William Riker** ordered the *Yorktown* to make long-range sensor sweeps of the **Devron system** in search of a **temporal anomaly**.) ("All Good Things..." [TNG]).

Yorktown*, *U.S.S. The second Federation starship to bear the name. **Tuvok**'s father served aboard the *Starship Yorktown* in 2293. ("Flashback" [VGR]).

Yoruba mask. Ancient African artifact from Earth. **Benjamin Sisko**'s collection of African art included a 2,000-year-old Yoruba mask. ("The Search, Part I" [DS9]).

Yosemite National Park. One of the most beautiful places on planet Earth, set aside as a nature preserve in 1890. Yosemite, located in northern California on the North American continent, was a favored shore-leave spot for Captain Kirk, and he was joined there by shipmates Spock and McCoy for a camping expedition in 2287. *(Star Trek V: The Final Frontier).*

Yosemite*, *U.S.S. Federation starship, ***Oberth* class**, registry number NCC-19002. The *Yosemite* was severely damaged while conducting a study of the **plasma streamer** between a binary star pair in the **Igo Sector** in 2369. During transport of plasma samples to the ship, **quasi-energy microbes** caused an explosion of a sample container, resulting in severe damage to the ship and the death of at least one crew member. ("Realm of Fear" [TNG]). *The ship was named for Yosemite National Park.*

Yoshimitsu computer. Electronic data-processing device. Some 225 Yoshimitsu computers were carried aboard the ***S.S. Mariposa*** when it set out for the **Ficus Sector** in 2123. ("Up the Long Ladder" [TNG]).

Yranac. (Alan Altshuld). **Yridian** trader. *Enterprise*-D personnel encountered Yranac in a bar on **Dessica II.** Yranac had witnessed the apparent death of Captain Picard there in 2370. Yranac was brought aboard the *Enterprise*-D for interrogation. ("Gambit, Part I" [TNG]). *Alan Altshuld also portrayed Pomet in "Starship Mine" (TNG).*

Yridian brandy. Alcoholic beverage. In 2372, Worf shared with Kor a bottle of Yridian brandy that he had been saving for a special occasion. ("The Sword of Kahless" [DS9]).

Yridian freighter. Cargo vessel of Yridian registry. An Yridian freighter commanded by **Yog** received a shipment of **magnesite ore** from the Duras sisters in 2370. ("Firstborn" [TNG]).

Yridian tea. Beverage. Deanna Troi enjoyed Yridian tea. ("Eye of the Beholder" [TNG]).

Yridian yak. Grazing animal known for its large size. ("Accession" [DS9]).

Yridians. Civilization of humanoids known as interstellar dealers of information. Yridian agents, working for Cardassian interests, were responsible for the murder of archaeologist **Richard Galen** in 2369, in an effort to steal his research data. The Romulans intercepted communications between the Yridians and the Cardassians, making the Romulans aware of the importance of Galen's work. ("The Chase" [TNG]). SEE: **humanoid life. Jaglom Shrek**, who sold **Worf** information about **Mogh**, was Yridian. ("Birthright, Part I" [TNG]). Yridian operatives were suspected of helping Cardassians transfer weapons into the Demilitarized Zone in late 2370. This claim was never proven. ("The Maquis, Part I" [DS9]). In 2371, **Garak** listed an unnamed Yridian national as someone who might want Garak dead. ("Improbable Cause" [DS9]).

Yukon*, *U.S.S. *Danube*-class runabout assigned to station Deep Space 9. Starfleet registry number NCC-74602. In 2372, Major Kira and Chief O'Brien used the *Yukon* to make an inspection tour of the Bajoran colonies along the Cardassian border. ("Sons of Mogh" [DS9]). The *Yukon* was destroyed by the *Starship Defiant* in 2373 when a changeling infiltrator hijacked it in an effort to destroy the Bajoran sun with a **trilithium** explosive. ("By Inferno's Light" [DS9]). *The* Yukon *replaced the runabout* Orinoco, *which was destroyed in "Our Man Bashir" (DS9). The* Yukon *was named after the river in Northwest Canada and central Alaska flowing 1,979 miles to the Bering Sea. The* Yukon *was destroyed in "By Inferno's Light" (DS9).*

Yuta. (Lisa Wilcox). An **Acamarian** and member of the clan **Tralesta**, she was Sovereign **Marouk**'s chef and chief food taster. Yuta was the last surviving member of the Acamarian Tralesta clan that had been massacred in 2286 by the rival **Lornak** clan. Though she appeared to be a woman in her twenties, her body had been altered to dramatically reduce her rate of aging so that she could exact revenge against the Lornaks. Her body was infused with a genetically engineered **microvirus** that was harmless to all except the members of the Lornak clan. Over the next century, Yuta was successful in murdering nearly all members of the Lornak clan by exposing them to this microvirus. Commander Riker was attracted to her, but after determining her true purpose, he was forced to kill her to prevent her from assassinating **Chorgan**, the Gatherer Leader and the last member of the Lornak clan. Yuta's victims included **Volnoth** and **Penthor-Mul.** ("The Vengeance Factor" [TNG]).

Yutan. (Gary Pillar). Member of the **hill people** tribe on **Tyree**'s planet. ("A Private Little War" [TOS]).

***zabathu*, Andorian.** An animal similar to terrestrial horse. Holographic simulations of this animal were available for riding on the *Enterprise*-D **holodeck**. ("Pen Pals" [TNG]).

Zabee nuts. Snack food prepared by Neelix for the crew of the *U.S.S. Voyager*. ("Investigations" [VGR]).

Zabo. (Steve Marlo). One of **Jojo Krako**'s henchmen on planet **Sigma Iotia II** in 2268. ("A Piece of the Action" [TOS]).

***zabo* meat.** Cardassian food. Keiko O'Brien served *zabo* meat to **Rugal** on Deep Space 9 in 2370. ("Cardassians" [DS9]).

Zadar IV. Planet on which oceanographer **Dr. Harry Bernard, Sr.,** once lived with his son prior to their residence aboard the *Enterprise*-D. ("When the Bough Breaks" [TNG]).

Zaheva, Captain Chantal. (Deborah Taylor). Commanding officer of the ***U.S.S. Brattain***. Zaheva died violently along with most of her crew when *Brattain* personnel suffered severe dream deprivation when the ship was trapped in a **Tyken's Rift** in 2367. ("Night Terrors" [TNG]).

Zahir. (David Lee Smith). Inhabitant of the Delta Quadrant; a member of the **Mikhal Travelers**. In 2373, Zahir assisted the *Starship Voyager* crew with information concerning space on their path to the Alpha Quadrant. During the encounters with *Voyager*, Zahir fell in love with Kes. Although he wanted Kes to join him in his travels, she reluctantly declined. ("Darkling" [VGR]).

Zakarian, Commander. Starfleet officer who taught a survival course at Starfleet Academy. Zakarian had a number of allergies, earning him the nickname "Sneezy." ("Caretaker" [VGR]).

Zakdorn. Humanoid civilization. **Sirna Kolrami** was Zakdorn ("Peak Performance" [TNG]), as was **Klim Dokachin**. ("Unification, Part I" [TNG]).

Zaldans. Humanoid race characterized by webbed hands. Zaldan cultural values reject human courtesy as a form of dishonesty, so the proper (and courteous) way to address a Zaldan is with brutal honesty. ("Coming of Age" [TNG]). SEE: **Rondon**.

Zalkon. Homeworld of the **Zalkonians**. The government of this plant claimed the **Zeta Gelis Cluster** as part of their space. ("Transfigurations" [TNG]).

Zalkonians. A humanoid race distinguished by multiple horizontal facial ridges. Sometime prior to 2366, a few members of the Zalkonian race began suffering from painful isoelectrical bursts and exhibiting strange mutations of their tissues. The Zalkonian government, fearful of these new beings, persecuted and attempted to kill everyone who experienced these mutations. One Zalkonian, who became known as **John Doe**, escaped his homeworld, and was successful in allowing the metamorphosis aboard the *Enterprise*-D in 2366, becoming the first of his race to transmute into a noncorporeal being. ("Transfigurations" [TNG]).

Zambrano, Battle of. Historic conflict on planet **Solais V**, location of which later became the site of peace talks mediated by **Riva** of planet **Ramatis III**. ("Loud as a Whisper" [TNG]). *The Battle of Zambrano, identified only in a computer graphic map seen on the bridge, was named for "Loud as a Whisper" writer Jacqueline Zambrano.*

Zan Periculi. Species of flower native to Lappa IV, a Ferengi world. **DaiMon Tog** presented some of these flowers to Lwaxana Troi. ("Ménage à Troi" [TNG]).

Zanthi fever. Viral condition that affects the empathic abilities of mature **Betazoids**. A patient suffering from Zanthi fever can involuntarily project emotions onto others. **Lwaxana Troi** contracted Zanthi fever in 2371 and caused several individuals at station Deep Space 9 to experience amorous emotions during the **Bajoran Gratitude Festival**. ("Fascination" [DS9]).

Zapata*, *U.S.S. Federation starship, *Surak* class, Starfleet registry number NCC-33814. The *Enterprise*-D was scheduled to meet the *Zapata* following the mission to the Gamma Erandi Nebula in 2366. ("Ménage à Troi" [TNG]).

Zarabeth. (Mariette Hartley). Citizen of planet **Sarpeidon** who was banished after two members of her family conspired to kill planetary leader **Zor Khan**. Zarabeth was sent some 5,000 years into her planet's past, into a brutal ice age, where she lived in total isolation. Her loneliness was broken only briefly when Spock and McCoy were accidentally sent into Sarpeidon's past by the **atavachron**, before returning to their present. While there, Spock became emotionally involved with Zarabeth, who loved him, too. ("All Our Yesterdays" [TOS]). *Mariette Hartley also played the mutant Lyra'a in Gene Roddenberry's pilot film,* Genesis II.

Zarale, Gul. Cardassian officer responsible for the massacre of six Bajoran villages during the occupation. Zarale was killed by **Li Nalas** at Sahving Valley on Bajor, and the story of his death became a heroic legend among Bajoran resistance fighters. ("The Homecoming" [DS9]).

***zark*.** Klingon riding animal, somewhat similar to an Earth horse. ("Pen Pals" [TNG]).

Zaterl emerald. A semi-mythical gemstone, reputed to be located in the ruins of Ligillium. Captain Picard offered to take **Ardra** there to try to convince her to accept arbitration in the matter of the **Contract of Ardra**. ("Devil's Due" [TNG]).

Zaynar. (J. Michael Flynn). An aide to Angosian prime minister **Nayrok**. ("The Hunted" [TNG]).

Zayra IV. Fourth planet in the Zayra star system. Location of a Federation starbase and home to the species of arachnid known as the **Talarian hook spider**. **Miles O'Brien** was called in to reroute an emitter array at a starbase on that planet, some time prior to his assignment to the *Enterprise*-D. ("Realm of Fear" [TNG]).

Zayra. (Edward Albert). Bajoran national who operated the Transit Aid center on station Deep Space 9. Zayra accused **Odo** of murdering **Ibudan** in 2369. Zayra incited others to form a lynch mob to harass the shape-shifter. ("A Man Alone" [DS9]).

Zed Lapis Sector. Region of space. Location of planet Vagra II. ("Skin of Evil" [TNG]).

Zee-Magnees Prize. Prestigeous scientific award. **Dr. Richard Daystrom** won the Zee-Magnees Prize for his invention of **duotronics** in 2243. Daystrom was only 24 years old at the time. ("The Ultimate Computer" [TOS]). *A framed certificate on the wall of **Dr. Ira Graves**'s laboratory in "The Schizoid Man" (TNG) indicated that Graves had also won the coveted award for his work in positronic neural networks, although the certificate wasn't clearly visible in the final cut of the episode.*

Zef'No. (Mike Genovese). Captain of the **Kressari** freighter, *Calondon*. Zef'No was responsible for the transfer of Cardassian supplied weapons to the Circle in 2370. ("The Circle" [DS9]). *Zef'No's name was not mentioned on air and is from the script.*

Zefram Cochrane High School. Secondary school named for the legendary inventor of warp drive. Geordi LaForge attended **Zefram Cochrane** High School from 2349 to 2353. *(Star Trek: First Contact).*

Zek. (Wallace Shawn). Leader of Ferengi commerce who served as **grand nagus**. Zek had enormous ears and carried a cane with a head carved in his likeness made from gold-pressed **latinum**. Zek convened a major trade conference on Deep Space 9 in 2369 to announce the appointment of his successor as grand nagus. Zek named Quark as his successor, and apparently died shortly thereafter. In fact, Zek's supposed death was a ruse intended to test the suitability of his son, **Krax**, to one day assume the mantle as nagus. Zek came out of hiding when he realized that his son was not as mercenary as Zek would have liked. Zek therefore decided not to retire at that time. ("The Nagus" [DS9]). Zek later recruited Quark to act as his negotiator to purchase **tulaberry wine** from the **Dosi** in the Gamma Quadrant, but it was a ploy by Zek to learn more about the mysterious **Dominion**, a powerful force in that region of space. ("Rules of Acquisition" [DS9]). Zek underwent a dramatic temporary personality change in 2371 after obtaining the Bajoran **Orb of Wisdom** and encountering the Bajoran **Prophets**. Zek had hoped that meeting the Prophets would help him learn enough about the future to make an inconceivable profit, but instead, the wormhole aliens found Zek's acquisitive nature offensive. They devolved Zek's personality to a time before the Ferengi people revered profit above all. While in this noncompetitive state, Zek rewrote all 285 **Ferengi Rules of Acquisition**, and formed the **Ferengi Benevolent Association**. Quark eventually convinced the wormhole entities to restore Zek to his former self. ("Prophet Motive" [DS9]). SEE: **Ferengi Rules of Acquisition, Revised**.

zenite. Rare mineral substance found on planet **Ardana.** Zenite was used to combat botanical plagues such as that which occurred on planet **Merak II** in 2269. Zenite is mined, and in its raw state produces hazardous zenite gas, which was found to impair mental functions in unprotected mine workers. ("The Cloud Minders" [TOS]). SEE: **filter masks; Troglytes.**

Zeon. Outer Class-M planet in star system M43 Alpha. The inhabitants of Zeon had simple interplanetary capabilities by the 23rd century. The Zeon people were victims of a campaign of genocide by the Nazi-style government on planet **Ekos** in 2268. ("Patterns of Force" [TOS]).

zero-grav tumbling. Form of performance art. Shakaar Edon invited Kira Nerys to watch a performance of zero-grav tumbling on the Promenade of Deep Space 9 in 2373. ("The Begotten" [DS9]).

zero-gravity combat training. Form of Starfleet training in which personnel practice hand-to-hand combat in micro-gravity environments. *(Star Trek: First Contact).*

Zeta Alpha II. Planet. Zeta Alpha II was the departure point of the ***U.S.S. Lalo***, just before that ship was lost to the **Borg** in 2366. ("The Best of Both Worlds, Part I" [TNG]).

Zeta Gelis Cluster. Region of space. The *Enterprise*-D charted the Zeta Gelis Cluster in 2366. While mapping this area, the crew discovered the **Zalkonian** known as **John Doe** on one of the planets there. The *Enterprise*-D continued to map the Zeta Gelis Cluster during the seven-week period of Doe's recovery. ("Transfigurations" [TNG]).

Zeta Gomal IV. Planet. Homeworld to the swarming moths that were the subject of *Enterprise*-D science fair winner **Jay Gordon**'s project in 2368. ("Disaster" [TNG]).

Zetar. Planet. All corporeal life on Zetar was destroyed millennia ago. ("The Lights of Zetar" [TOS]). SEE: **Zetarians.**

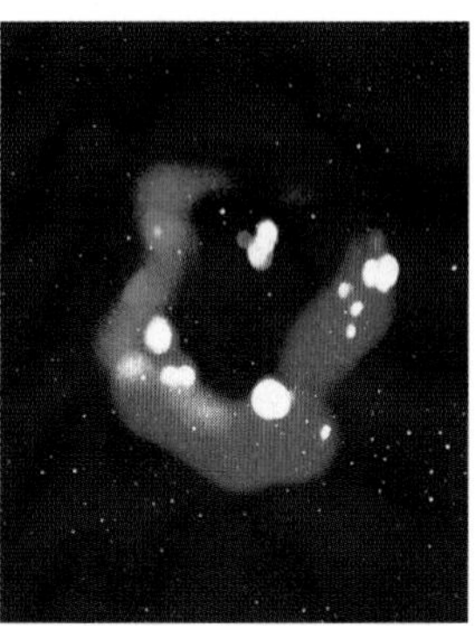

Zetarians. Mysterious **noncorporeal life**-forms, the last survivors of the planet **Zetar**. The Zetarians wandered through space for millennia, searching for a body in which they could live again. They thought they had found such a body when they discovered *Enterprise* crew member **Mira Romaine** in 2269. When Romaine's fellow crew members discovered that her mind had been invaded by the Zetarians and that she was in danger of losing her identity, Romaine was placed into a decompression chamber where the Zetarians were driven from her body. ("The Lights of Zetar" [TOS]).

zhian'tara. Trill rite of closure, a ceremony to allow a joined **Trill** to meet the **symbiont**'s previous hosts. The *zhian'tara* is accomplished by telepathically transferring the memories of each past host from the symbiont to a different friend, who embodies that host's personality for the length of the ceremony. The *zhian'tara* allows joined Trill insight into their past lives. **Jadzia Dax** underwent her *zhian'tara* in 2371, and her closest friends and fellow officers agreed to embody her previous hosts for the ceremony. ("Facets" [DS9]).

Zhukov, U.S.S. Federation starship, *Ambassador* class, Starfleet registry number NCC-62136. The ship was commanded by **Captain Gleason**. The *Zhukov* was **Reginald Barclay**'s assignment prior to his being transfered to the *Enterprise*-D in 2366. ("Hollow Pursuits" [TNG]). The starship met the *Enterprise*-D again in 2367 for the transfer of Federation ambassador **T'Pel**. ("Data's Day" [TNG]). The *Zhukov* transfered several science teams to the *Enterprise*-D in preparation for the *Enterprise*-D's mission at the **Phoenix Cluster** in 2368. ("The Game" [TNG]). *The* Zhukov *was named for Russian general Grigori Konstantinovich Zhukov (1896-1974).*

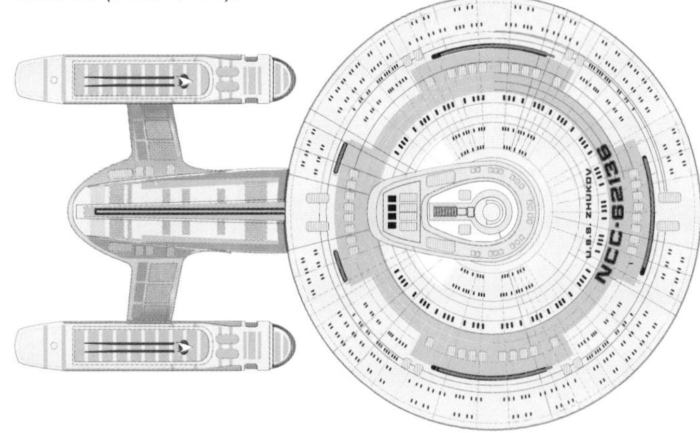

Zibalians. Life-forms, largely humanoid, with distinctive tattooing in the temporal areas of the face. Some Zibalians were traders, including the notorious **Kivas Fajo**. ("The Most Toys" [TNG]).

zilm'kach. Segmented orange foodstuff favored by Klingons. ("Melora" [DS9]).

Zimbata, Captain. Commander of the *Starship* ***Victory***. Geordi La Forge served under Zimbata aboard the *Victory* in 2363 prior to La Forge's assignment to the *Enterprise*-D. Geordi presented Zimbata with a gift of a model of the ancient sailing ship *Victory* in 2365. ("Elementary, Dear Data" [TNG]).

Zimmerman, Dr. SEE: **Emergency Medical Hologram**.

Zimmerman, Lewis. Starfleet technician assigned to the Holoprogramming Center at Starfleet's **Jupiter Station**. Dr. Lewis Zimmerman programmed the **Emergency Medical Hologram** on the *U.S.S. Voyager*; he also provided the model for the doctor's appearance. ("The Cloud" [VGR]). Former *Enterprise*-D crew member **Reginald Barclay** worked with Zimmerman on the EMH project. ("Projections" [VGR]). A holographic version of Zimmerman was featured in the EMH diagnostic program. ("The Swarm" [VGR]). By 2373, Zimmerman was the Director of Holographic Imaging and Programing at **Jupiter Station**. Zimmerman traveled to **Deep Space 9** after Starfleet selected **Julian Bashir** as the model for a new **Longterm Medical Holographic** program. As part of his preparation for the project, Zimmerman brought **Richard** and **Amsha Bashir**, Julian's parents, to the station, uncovering a terrible family secret. Zimmerman became smitten with dabo girl **Leeta**, who nearly left the station after he offered her the job of managing the cafe back on Jupiter Station. ("Doctor Bashir, I Presume?" [DS9]).

Zio. (Don McManus). Inmate of the **Akritirian prison satellite**. Zio arrived at the facility in 2367 and after a time he learned how to maintain his sanity despite the effects of the clamp. ("The Chute" [VGR]).

Ziyal. SEE: **Tora Ziyal**.

Zlangco. (Paul Collins). Leader of the **Nol-Ennis,** who fought his eternal enemies, the **Ennis**, on a penal-colony moon in the Gamma Quadrant. ("Battle Lines" [DS9]).

Zocal's Third Prophecy. Ancient text in the **Bajoran** religion written by Zocal after an encounter with an **Orb**. His third prophecy stated that only someone touched by the Prophets could find the ruins of the sacred lost city of **B'hala**. ("Rapture" [DS9]).

Zolan. (Dion Anderson) Humanoid who accompanied **Rugal** and **Proka Migdal** to station Deep Space 9 in 2370. Zolan told Dr. Julian Bashir that Proka mistreated Rugal because the boy was Cardassian. This unsubstantiated charge prompted Commander Benjamin Sisko to remove Rugal from his Bajoran father. ("Cardassians" [DS9]). *Zolan's name was never mentioned in the aired episode and only appeared in the script.*

Zor Khan. Tyrant on planet **Sarpeidon.** Zor Khan banished **Zarabeth** 5,000 years into the past because two of her kinsmen were involved in a conspiracy to kill him. ("All Our Yesterdays" [TOS]).

Zora. (Carol Daniels Derment). Notorious scientist who conducted cruel experiments of the body chemistries of living beings on the planet **Tiburon**. A replica of Zora was created by the inhabitants of planet **Excalbia** in 2269, part of their study of the human concepts of "good" and "evil." ("The Savage Curtain" [TOS]). SEE: **Yarnek**.

Zorn, Groppler. (Michael Bell). A leader of the **Bandi** people of planet **Deneb IV** in 2364. Zorn had participated in the capture of a spaceborne shape-shifting life-form, coercing it to assume the form of a starbase. ("Encounter at Farpoint, Parts I and II" [TNG]).

Zweller, Cortin. (Ned Vaughn). Aka Corey Zweller. Starfleet officer. Zweller was an academy friend of Ensign **Jean-Luc Picard**. Following their graduation from Starfleet Academy in 2327, Ensigns Corey Zweller, **Marta Batanides,** and Jean-Luc Picard were assigned to **Starbase Earhart** to await their first deep-space assignments. During this layover, Corey was challenged to a game of **dom-jot** by a **Nausicaan**, leading to a fight in which Picard was impaled by one of the Nausicaans and his heart was damaged beyond repair. Zweller was later assigned to the *Starship* ***Ajax***. ("Tapestry" [TNG]).

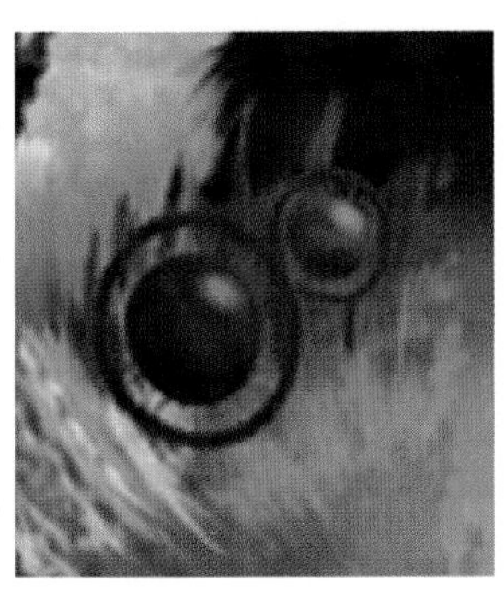

***zylo* eggs.** Life-form. Data chose *zylo* eggs as a subject for his first attempt at **painting**. *Pictured, painting by Rick Sternbach.* ("11001001" [TNG]).

Zyree. (Emilia Crow). **Dosi** negotiator. When **Inglatu** was unable to provide the Ferengi with 100,000 vats of **tulaberry wine** in 2370, Zyree offered to put Quark in touch with the **Karemma**, who would be able to deliver such quantities. ("Rules of Acquisition" [DS9]).

Zytchin III. Third planet in the Zytchin system. Captain Picard once spent a four-day vacation at Zytchin III. He told Dr. Crusher that he enjoyed his time there, but later said he had lied. ("Captain's Holiday" [TNG]).

ABOUT THE SUPPLEMENT

This special supplement to the 1997 edition of the *Star Trek Encyclopedia* includes several episodes from the 1996–1997 season of *Star Trek: Voyager* and *Star Trek: Deep Space Nine* that were not included in the 1997 edition. It includes the entirety of the 1997–1998 season of both shows, as well as the first few episodes of the 1998–1999 season. We have also snuck in a few datapoints from the final episodes of *Star Trek: Deep Space Nine* to indicate the fates of some of the principal characters. Please note, however, that we did not provide full coverage for these episodes. The supplement also includes material from *Star Trek: Insurrection*.

Entries tagged with an asterisk (*) are supplemental to entries in the 1997 edition of the *Encyclopedia*. In other words, you can find out more about the subject of an asterisked entry by looking under the same title in the main section of this book.

ablative armor.* Starship outer hull layer designed to vaporize under weapons fire, thereby dissipating energy and protecting the ship's interior. In 2374, the experimental prototype *Starship Prometheus* was equipped with ablative armor. ("Message in a Bottle" [VGR]).

accelerated critical neural pathway formation.* Illegal medical procedure intended to enhance the mental and physical abilities of a humanoid child. The Federation ban on DNA resequencing was based on the argument that if genetically enhanced people were allowed to compete freely, all parents would feel pressured to have their children enhanced so that they could keep up. ("Statistical Probabilities" [DS9]).

acrybite. Mined substance. Acrybite futures were traded on the Ferengi Futures Exchange. ("Ferengi Love Songs" [DS9]).

Adislo, Hars. (John Hostetter). Starfleet officer who served aboard the *Starship Enterprise*-E in 2375. Hars Adislo wrote a research paper on thermionic transconductance, which he presented at the Nel Bato Conference in 2374. (*Star Trek: Insurrection*).

Adventures of Captain Proton. SEE: ***Captain Proton, The Adventures of*; Proton, Captain.**

Adventures of Flotter, The. SEE: **Flotter, The Adventures of.**

"Afterimage." *Deep Space Nine* episode #153. Written by René Echevarria. Directed by Les Landau. No stardate given. *First aired in 1998. Ezri Dax struggles to win acceptance among Jadzia's old friends in general and with Worf in particular while Garak suffers from claustrophobia. Ezri Dax is promoted from ensign to lieutenant junior grade and becomes station counselor in this episode.* GUEST CAST: Andrew Robinson as **Garak, Elim**. SEE: **Alamo, Battle of the; Crockett, Davy; Dax, Emony; Dax, Ezri; Dax, Tobin; *Destiny, U.S.S.*; Fanalian toddy; Garak, Elim; holodeck and holosuite programs: Alamo, Battle of the; Ocean view; Kalandra Sector; kilm steak; Raymer, Captain; seamer; Seventh Fleet; Tain, Enabran; Talpet; Worf.**

Agrat-mot Nebula. Interstellar dust cloud located in B'omar space in the Delta Quadrant. The Agrat-mot Nebula was a key resource in the **B'omar Sovereignty**'s trade negotiations with the Nassordin. ("The Raven" [VGR]).

ahdar. Rank in the **Son'a** space service, approximately equivalent to a Starfleet commander. **Ru'afo** held the rank of ahdar in 2375. (*Star Trek: Insurrection*).

Akagi, U.S.S.* Federation starship. In 2374, the *Akagi* was a part of the Ninth Fleet headquartered at starbase Deep Space 9. ("You Are Cordially Invited" [DS9]).

Akira*-class starship. Type of space vehicle used by the Federation **Starfleet**. Several *Akira*-class vessels fought in the combined Alpha Quadrant fleet that invaded Cardassia in late 2374, and three were destroyed by Cardassian orbital weapon platforms at the Chin'toka System. ("Tears of the Prophets" [DS9]).

akoonah.* Device used by some Native Americans to focus their thoughts during a **vision quest** experience. **Chakotay** allowed Neelix to use his *akoonah* in 2374 when guiding Neelix through a vision quest. ("Mortal Coil" [VGR]). Later, Chakotay used it to assist him in entering a lucid dreaming state when *Voyager* was threatened by a **dream species**. ("Waking Moments" [VGR]).

Alamo, Battle of the. Historic military engagement waged at a Franciscan mission building in San Antonio, Texas, on the North American continent on Earth in 1836. Two hundred Texan volunteers, fighting for Texan independence against the nation of Mexico, defended the Alamo against an overwhelmingly superior Mexican military force for 13 days, but were eventually killed. Miles O'Brien suggested that the Battle of the Alamo might make a good holosuite program, but Bashir disagreed ("Wrongs Darker Than Death or Night" [DS9]) although by early 2375, the two were indeed planning such a simulation SEE: **Crockett, Davy.** ("Afterimage" [DS9]).

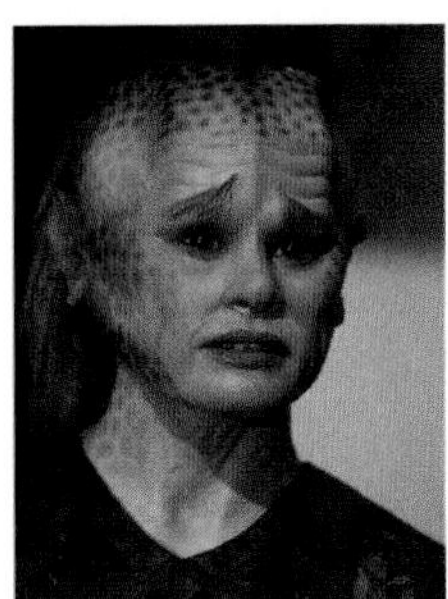

Alixia.* (Robin Stapler). Native of planet Talax. Sister to **Neelix**, Alixia died in the war with the **Haakonian Order**. Neelix missed Alixia very much, and he kept as a memento a necklace that had once belonged to her. ("Mortal Coil" [VGR]).

"All the Way." Popular mid-20th-century Earth song made famous by such singers as **Frank Sinatra** and **Vic Fontaine**. "All the Way" was Jadzia Dax's favorite song. After Jadzia's death in late 2374, Worf repeatedly instructed the holographic re-creation of Fontaine to sing the song, Worf's way of mourning his wife's passing. ("Image in the Sand" [DS9]).

Allied Forces. International military agency during **Earth**'s second world war of the 20th century. Consisting of armed forces from the **United States of America**, Great Britain, Canada, **France**, and the **Union of Soviet Socialist Republics**, the Allies were successful in defeating the Axis army, led by **Nazi Germany**. SEE: **World War II**. ("The Killing Game, Parts I and II" [VGR]).

Allos. (Jeff Austin). Delta Quadrant quantum scientist. In 2374, Allos created about 200 million **Omega molecules** in an attempt to help his resource-poor homeworld. ("The Omega Directive" [VGR]). *Jeff Austin previously played a Bolian in "The Adversary" (DS9).*

Almar. Romulan subcommander serving on the *Warbird* ***T'Met*** in 2374. ("Message in a Bottle" [VGR]).

almond pudding. A soft dessert made from milk, flavored with the fruit of the almond tree *Prunus amygdalus*. ("Unforgettable" [VGR]).

Alpha Centauri.* Star. Alpha Centauri is located near Betazed, Vulcan, Andor, Earth, and Tellar. ("In the Pale Moonlight" [DS9]).

Alpha Quadrant.* One quarter of the entire Milky Way Galaxy; the region in which most of the **United Federation of Planets**, including **Earth**, is located. The civilizations of the Alpha Quadrant faced a grave threat during the bitter and costly **Dominion** war of the 2370s. Numerous Alpha and Beta Quadrant powers, including the United Federation of Planets, the Klingon Empire, and the Romulan Star Empire banded together to prevent an invasion by the Founders of the Dominion.

Alpha-Hirogen. (Tiny Ron; Tony Todd; Danny Goldring). In **Hirogen** society, Alpha-Hirogen refers to the leader of a pack of Hirogen hunters. One such alpha *(played by Tiny Ron)* commanded a Hirogen ship and was in charge of a **Hirogen relay station**. ("Message in a Bottle" [VGR]). This particular alpha captured *Voyager* crew members Tuvok and Seven of Nine, hoping to claim them as valuable prizes of the hunt. ("Hunters" [VGR]). Another alpha believed Hirogen culture, which had

remained essentially unchanged for a millennium, to be in danger of stagnation. He feared that the ritual of the hunt had dominated his people so much that they were no longer growing or advancing. In 2374, he seized upon the discovery of Federation holodeck technology, proposing that his people could satisfy their need for the hunt through the use of holographic environments. He argued that this would allow his society to use its space travel resources for the technological and social advancement of the Hirogen people, instead of on increasingly unprofitable warfare. Although this alpha was killed during a simulated hunt, there were some indications that this radical idea might find acceptance among at least some of the Hirogen. SEE: **French Resistance; optronic datacore**. ("The Killing Game, Parts I and II." [VGR]). *Tiny Ron played the Alpha-Hirogen in "Message in a Bottle" and "Hunters," Tony Todd was another alpha in "Prey" (VGR), and* Danny Goldring (pictured) *was the alpha who hoped to use holodecks to create a new Hirogen society in "The Killing Game, Parts I and II."*

Alpha. Colloquial term used by the **Jem'Hadar** to refer to a Jem'Hadar soldier bred in the Alpha Quadrant during the Dominion war. The Alphas were created in 2374 to relieve a shortage of Jem'Hadar troops in that part of the galaxy after Starfleet forces blockaded the **Bajoran wormhole**. ("One Little Ship" [DS9]).

Alsuran Empire. Delta Quadrant civilization. In an alternate timeline, the Alsuran Empire was wiped out by the **Krenim temporal weapon ship**. ("Year of Hell, Part II" [VGR]).

Altair sandwich. Hearty meal served between two large slices of bread; favored by Julian Bashir. ("You Are Cordially Invited" [DS9]).

Aluura. (Symba Smith). Humanoid dabo girl at Quark's bar in 2374. She was very beautiful, and her excellent work record notwithstanding, Quark threatened to fire her if she did not gratify him with ***oo-mox***. She later decided that it might be fun at that. ("Profit and Lace" [DS9]).

alva. Small pale yellow fruit indigenous to Bajor. Alvas were unknown in the mirror universe. ("Resurrection" [DS9]).

Alzen. (Rosemary Forsyth). **Srivani** scientist. Alzen, along with about 50 other researchers, was part of a Srivani science team that secretly came aboard the Federation starship *Voyager* in 2374 to conduct invasive and dangerous medical tests on the ship's crew. ("Scientific Method" [VGR]). *Character's name is from the script and was not mentioned in dialog.*

Amanin. Psychiatrist. Amanin, from planet **Betazed**, developed a method of retrieving unconscious memories from a humanoid mind, utilizing a combination of sensory isolation and focused breathing. Such recovered memories were, however, found to sometimes be the product of unrelated stimuli and could therefore be wildly inaccurate if not corroborated by other evidence. In 2374, *Starship Voyager*'s **Emergency Medical Hologram** incorporated Ananim's memory reconstruction methods into his psychiatric routines. ("Retrospect" [VGR]).

Amaro. (Jeffrey King). Starfleet security officer stationed at Deep Space 9. Amaro attended Starfleet Academy with **Stolzoff**, and the two were good friends. In 2373, Amaro was part of a salvage team sent from DS9 to the abandoned Cardassian station **Empok Nor**. Amaro was killed at Empok Nor by former Cardassian security operative Elim Garak when Garak suffered from the effects of a powerful **psychotropic drug**. ("Empok Nor" [DS9]).

Amasov, Captain. Starfleet officer and commander of the *Nebula*-class ***U.S.S. Endeavour***. Captain Amasov faced the Borg in battle at **Wolf 359**, and his ship was the only one to survive the encounter. After the horrific massacre, Amasov said, "It is my opinion that the **Borg** are as close to pure evil as any race we've ever discovered." ("Scorpion, Part I" [VGR]). *Probably a tip of the hat to science-fiction writer Isaac Asimov.*

Amonak. One of the most sacred temples on the planet Vulcan. **T'Pel** traveled, along with her children, to the Temple of Amonak to ask the priests at the temple to say prayers for the return of her husband, Tuvok, from the Delta Quadrant. ("Hunters" [VGR]). *Probably named for* Star Trek: Deep Space Nine *special-effects supervisor Gary Monak.*

Amsterdam News. Paper-based hard-copy periodical publication on 20th-century Earth. *The Amsterdam News* was a newspaper published in New York, serving that city's African-American community. ("Far Beyond the Stars" [DS9]).

anaerobic metabolites. Chemical compounds used in biomedical research. In 2373 Nog procured two liters of such metabolites suspended in hydrosaline solution from Dr. Bashir to be traded to Dr. Giger for a 1951 Willie Mays baseball card for Captain Benjamin Sisko. ("In the Cards" [DS9]).

Andor. Homeworld of the **Andorian** civilization. On stardate 51597.2, Worf suggested a mountain-climbing expedition on Andor as a possible honeymoon destination, but his new bride, Jadzia, had other ideas. ("Change of Heart" [DS9]). Also known as Andoria, Andor is located near Betazed, Vulcan, Tellar, Earth, and Alpha Centauri. ("In the Pale Moonlight" [DS9]). Early in her Starfleet career, Lisa Cusak was assigned as an attaché to the Federation embassy on Andor. ("The Sound of Her Voice" [DS9]).

Andros III. Planet. Research scientist Dr. Bathkin was from Andros III. ("In the Cards" [DS9]).

anesthezine.* Fast-acting anesthetic aerosol. Anesthezine was among the emergency crowd-control measures available on board the ***Starship Prometheus***. ("Message in a Bottle" [VGR]).

anetrizine. Pharmaceutical used to anesthetize cranial nerves. ("The Gift" [VGR]).

Anij. (Donna Murphy). Member of the peaceful **Ba'ku** community. Anij was drawn to **Jean-Luc Picard** when he visited her world in 2375, and the two quickly formed a deep personal bond, despite her strong distrust of offlanders. Like most of her people, Anij had the ability to live in the moment to such a degree that time for them would slow to a crawl. To accomplish this, she entered a meditative state (*Star Trek: Insurrection*).

animazine. Stimulant drug. Animazine was used in 2374 on board the *Starship Voyager* to prevent crew members from falling prey to the **neurogenic field** generated by the **dream species**, although, like any such medication, its effectiveness was limited. ("Waking Moments" [VGR]).

Annorax (Kurtwood Smith). **Krenim** scientist who worked to develop a temporal weapon of mass destruction. In an alternate timeline, Annorax was one of the greatest mass murderers in the galaxy, rivaling even the Borg collective. In this alternate timeline, Annorax developed the **Krenim temporal weapon ship** and used it against the **Rilnar**, enemies of the Krenim. Unfortunately, Annorax had failed to adequately consider the complexities of **temporal mechanics**. The elimination of the Rilnar from history left his people susceptible to a deadly disease that left some 50 million Krenim dead, including his beloved wife. Annorax spent the next 200 years using his temporal weapon, trying to restore his people's original timeline, but each use brought further unpredicted side effects. In the process, he destroyed thousands of worlds, eliminating billions of innocent lives, but he was never able to entirely restore his people. The alternate Annorax was reunited with his wife when his ship was attacked by the Federation starship *Voyager*, causing a temporal incursion that removed the Krenim ship from the timeline. SEE: **Obrist.** ("Year of Hell, Parts I and II" [VGR]). *Kurtwood Smith played the Federation President in* Star Trek VI: The Undiscovered Country, *as well as Thrax in "Things Past" (DS9). Annorax was apparently named for Professor Pierre Aronnax, a character in Jules Verne's novel* 20,000 Leagues under the Sea. *(In "Year of Hell," Tom Paris compared Annorax to Captain Nemo, another character from Verne's novel.)*

anti-back flow valve. One-way check valve in the plasma vents of a starship, intended to prevent foreign matter from entering the ship through the vents. ("One Little Ship" [DS9]).

anticoagulant. Chemical that prevents the clotting of blood. **Jem'Hadar** weapons are designed to leave anticoagulants in the wounds they cause so that even grazing hits can result in massive blood loss. ("Change of Heart" [DS9]).

antigrav.* Gravity repulsion device. Antigrav thrusters were used by some Federation starships during the terminal phase of landing on a planetary surface, as well as for takeoff. ("Demon" [VGR]).

antigraviton.* Elementary particle, a quantum unit opposite to a **graviton**. The **self-replicating mines** used in the field blocking the Bajoran wormhole in 2374 were vulnerable to antigraviton beams that could isolate each, preventing them from duplicating. ("Behind the Lines" [DS9]).

antipsychotic. Psychotropic pharmaceutical used to reduce psychotic tendencies in sentient humanoid patients. ("One" [VGR]).

antithoron. Antimatter equivalent of radon-220. ("Hunters" [VGR]).

Archer, Valerie. (Kate Vernon). Starfleet officer. Commander Archer, whose parents were both starship officers, served at Starfleet Headquarters in 2375. A re-creation of Archer was part of a training facility created by **Species 8472** in the Delta Quadrant in 2375 in preparation for an intelligence-gathering program against the Federation. The replica of Archer, who was actually an 8472 individual, befriended Chakotay, finding him attractive despite the enormous differences in their species. ("In the Flesh" [VGR]).

Argala. Planet in the Delta Quadrant. Argala, which had an arctic tundra climate, was the home to a technologically sophisticated civilization. An Argala ship or space station was once captured by **Nyrian** operatives, using their translocation technology. ("Displaced" [VGR]).

Argolis Cluster.* Stellar group. Argolis contained many protostars. The cluster was the hiding place of a **Dominion** sensor array that provided a critical tactical advantage over the Federation Starfleet during the devastating Dominion war in 2374. The massive Dominion array was destroyed on stardate 51145 by the Federation starship *Defiant*, commanded by Lieutenant Commander Jadzia Dax. ("Behind the Lines" [DS9]). The Argolis Cluster was located near Betazed and the Kalandra Sector. ("The Reckoning" [DS9]).

arithrazine. Powerful pharmaceutical used to treat theta radiation poisoning. Starfleet regulations stipulate that a physician must be present whenever arithrazine is administered. In her preparations for executing the Omega Directive on stardate 51781, Captain Janeway required 20 milligrams of arithrazine to inoculate against theta radiation. ("The Omega Directive" [VGR]).

Armstrong Park. Open public square with grass and trees located in the city of New Orleans, Louisiana, on planet Earth. Named for 20th-century jazz great Louis Armstrong. The park, which was sometimes used for musical performances, was located not far from **Sisko's** restaurant. ("Image in the Sand" [DS9]).

Arritheans. Delta Quadrant civilization. Around stardate 51186, the crew of the *Voyager* had trade dealings with the Arritheans. ("Revulsion" [VGR]).

Artim. (Michael Welch). Inhabitant of the Ba'ku planet, born in 2363, son of Sojef. Artim had a **Ba'ku rhyl** as a pet who lived in his pocket. Artim befriended **Data** in 2375 during Dougherty's attempt to drive the Ba'ku people from their homeworld. (Star Trek: Insurrection).

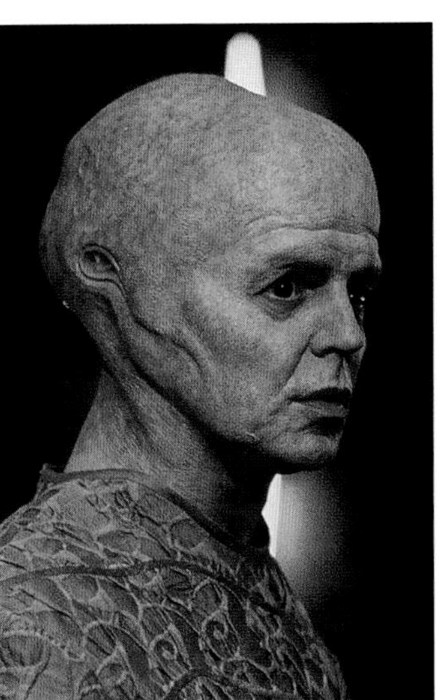

Arturis. (Ray Wise). Member of a Delta Quadrant species. Like many of his people, Arturis was a gifted linguist. When his people were assimilated by the **Borg** in 2374, Arturis reasoned that the Federation starship *Voyager*'s aid to the Borg against **Species 8472** was responsible. He believed that had *Voyager* not so allied themselves, the Borg would have been defeated by Species 8472, and his people would not have been assimilated. Seeking revenge, Arturis created an elaborate trap to convince the *Voyager* crew that Starfleet had sent an advanced starship, the ***U.S.S. Dauntless***, to rescue them. In fact, there was no Federation starship *Dauntless*; the vessel was a fake onto which Arturis hoped to trap the *Voyager* crew so that they could be sent into Borg space to be assimilated. The *Voyager* crew discovered the deception in time to escape Arturis's trap, but Arturis himself was assimilated when his ship entered Borg space. ("Hope and Fear" [VGR]). *Ray Wise previously played Liko in "Who Watches the Watchers?"* (TNG).

Ashmore, Ensign.* Starfleet officer; member of the *Starship Voyager* crew. On stardate 51501.4, Ashmore received a letter from home via a Starfleet transmission sent through a **Hirogen relay station**. ("Hunters" [VGR]). *There were obviously at least two Ashmores on* Voyager*: one, a woman seen in earlier episodes; and in later episodes (including "Retrospect" [VGR]), a male crew member.*

astral eddy. Spatial phenomenon occurring at the interfold between space and subspace. Astral eddies can involve massive discharges of plasmatic energy with temperature gradients of up to nine million kelvins. Such phenomena can be very violent and destructive to space vehicles. An astral eddy, intruding into normal space, was responsible for the destruction of a **Vostigye** space station on stardate 50836. ("Real Life" [VGR]).

Australian aborigines. Native inhabitants of Earth's Australian continent. Australian aboriginal tradition holds that their distant ancestors dreamed the universe into existence. Chakotay noted a parallel between the aboriginal creation myth and the **dream species** that invaded the *Starship Voyager* in 2374. ("Waking Moments" [VGR]).

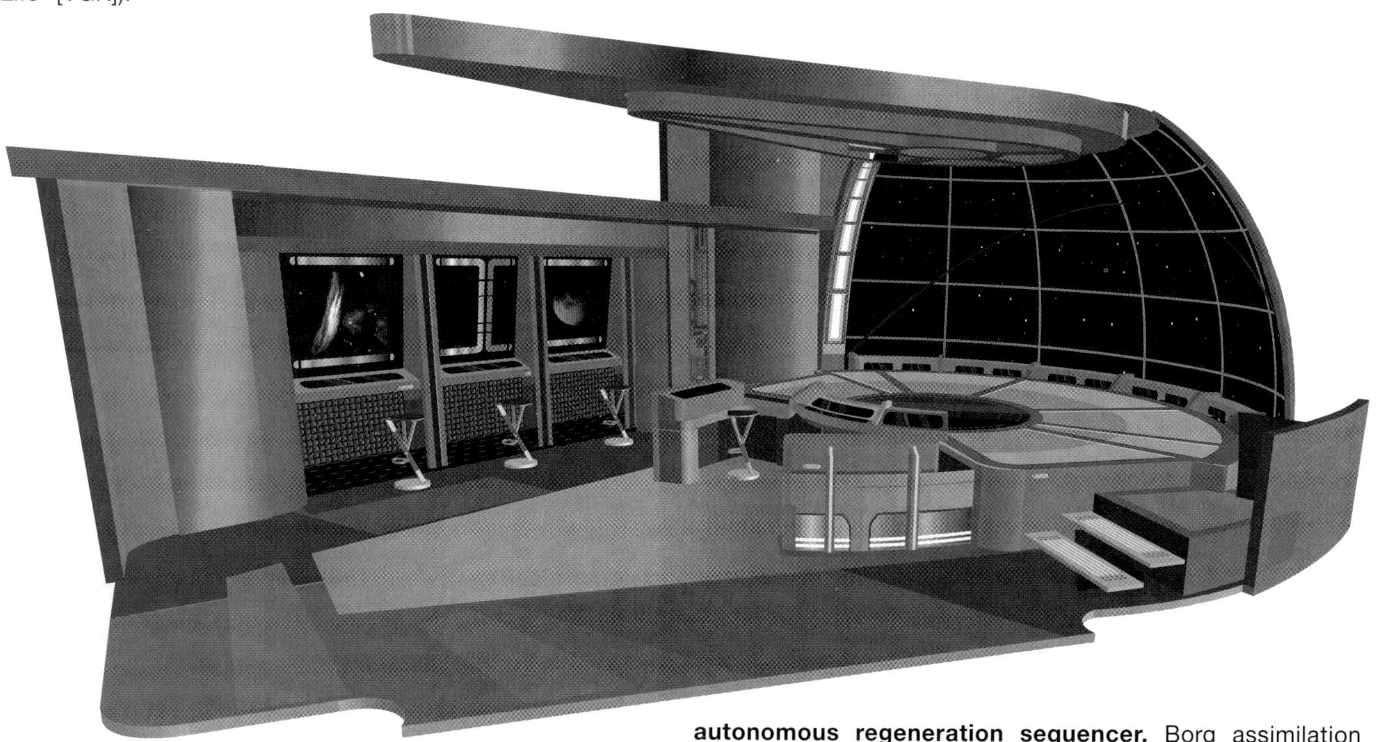

Astrometrics. Stellar cartographic laboratory aboard a Federation starship. Around stardate 51186, Ensign **Harry Kim** worked with **Seven of Nine** to design enhancements to *Voyager*'s Astrometrics Lab. ("Revulsion" [VGR]). The upgraded facility, now incorporating both Borg and Starfleet technology, was activated on stardate 51212. The Astrometrics Lab was utilized as a sophisticated navigational tool, calculating the starship's position relative to the center of the galaxy. ("Year of Hell, Parts I and II" [VGR]). *"Year of Hell" was the first episode to introduce the Astrometrics Lab.*

asymmetric encryption circuit. Data-processing component used in a Starfleet security protocol system. ("One Little Ship" [DS9]).

Athos IV. Small, fog-bound Class-M planetoid located in the Badlands. Athos IV was used as a base by the Maquis in 2373. ("Blaze of Glory" [DS9]).

Atoa, Lieutenant Manuele. (Sidney Liufau). Starfleet officer assigned to the *Starship Sutherland*. Lieutenant Atoa was a friend of Jadzia Dax, and he attended her prewedding party on station Deep Space 9 on stardate 51247. While at the party, Atoa performed a traditional Samoan fire knife dance. Atoa and Morn drank too much at the party and fell asleep on the floor, waking up and leaving late the next morning. ("You Are Cordially Invited" [DS9]).

auditory nerve nibble. Sexual technique of ***oo-mox*** devised to pleasure a Ferengi male by a very specific stimulation of his ears. ("Profit and Lace" [DS9]).

autonomous regeneration sequencer. Borg assimilation device. A regeneration sequencer used technology from **Species 259** that automatically replicated any Borg circuitry that was removed or disabled by non-Borg means. Autonomous regeneration sequencers were among the Borg hardware implanted into the *Starship Voyager* in 2374, making difficult their later removal by *Voyager* personnel. ("The Gift" [VGR]).

autosuture. Medical device used to close wounds. ("Soldiers of the Empire" [DS9]).

Avik, Commander. Officer of the **Benthan Guard**. In 2372, Commander Avik mistook Tom Paris for a thief who had stolen a prototype coaxial drive starship from Benthos IV. Avik attempted to take Paris into custody when the stolen ship entered the Kotaba Expanse. ("Vis à Vis" [VGR]).

axonol. Anesthetic aerosol. Axonol was among the emergency crowd-control anesthetics on board the ***Starship Prometheus.*** ("Message in a Bottle" [VGR]).

Ayala, Lieutenant.* Starfleet officer, crew member aboard the *Starship Voyager*. In early 2374, Ayala stood guard at the detention cell that held Borg drone Seven of Nine. ("The Gift" [VGR]). *Ayala was a lieutenant in earlier episodes, but was referred to as an ensign in "The Gift."*

B'Hala.* Ancient Bajoran city. The Temple of B'Hala was some 15,000 years old, built on ruins at least 10,000 years older. Archaeologists studying the deeper ruins in 2374 found an ancient stone inscribed with runes that prophesied the great spiritual conflict called the **Reckoning** (*pictured*). ("The Reckoning" [DS9]).

B'Moth, I.K.S. Klingon battle cruiser, *K't'inga*-class. The *I.K.S. B'Moth* was reported missing while on patrol near the Cardassian border in 2373. **General Martok**, in command of the *Bird-of-Prey Rotarran*, found the damaged hulk of the *B'Moth* and rescued the surviving 35 members of the crew. ("Soldiers of the Empire" [DS9]).

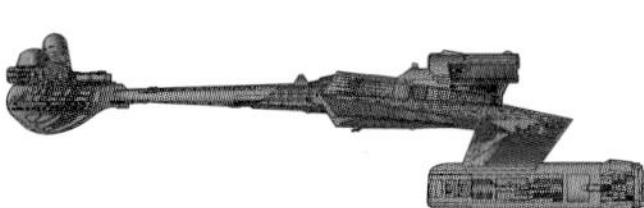

B'omar Sovereignty. Governing body of the **B'omar** people. ("The Raven" [VGR]).

B'omar. Technologically sophisticated humanoid civilization from the Delta Quadrant. In 2374 the B'omar government was willing to permit passage of the Federation starship *U.S.S. Voyager* through B'omar space, but imposed such severe limitations on the agreement that *Voyager* personnel elected to travel around the region instead. ("The Raven" [VGR]).

Br'er Rabbit. Fantasy character in the Uncle Remus stories by Earth writer Joel Chandler Harris, published in the early 1880s. The character was a clever rabbit who lived in a **briar patch** in a rural southern community in the American nation. (*Star Trek: Insurrection*).

Ba'ku planet. Class-M planet in the **Briar Patch** region of Federation space. Homeworld of **Ba'ku** and **Son'a** people. The planet was surrounded by an unusual ring system saturated with metaphasic radiation particles. Unknown to most offlanders, exposure to these particles had the effect of rejuvenating many humanoid life-forms, extending their life span for centuries. The Ba'ku planet had concentrations of **kelbonite** in its mountain ranges and had a number of subsurface hydrothermal caverns. In 2375, the world became a Federation protectorate after outlaw Starfleet officers attempted to drive off the rightful inhabitants in a bid to take possession of the planet. (*Star Trek: Insurrection*).

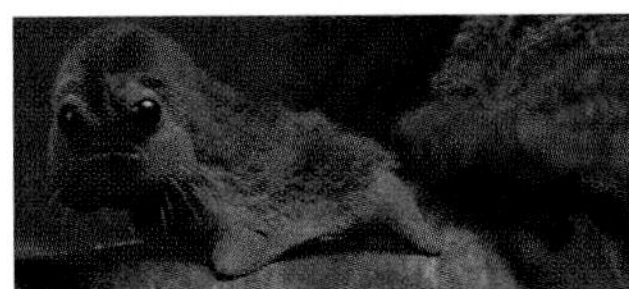

Ba'ku rhyl. Small animal life-form indigenous to the **Ba'ku planet**. **Artim** had a rhyl as a pet that he kept in his pocket. (*Star Trek: Insurrection*).

Ba'ku. Humanoid civilization from a planet in the **Briar Patch**. The Ba'ku originally came from a culture on the verge of destroying itself with technologically advanced weapons of war. In 2066, a small group left their homeworld, colonizing an isolated world in the Briar Patch. The surface of the new **Ba'ku planet** was bombarded with metaphasic particles that somehow reversed the effects of aging in many humanoid species. As a result, the Ba'ku now found themselves to be extremely long-lived and found that they had the time to devote themselves to art and craftsmanship. Ba'ku villagers, who numbered less than a thousand, formed an intensely insular community. Some Ba'ku, who chose to associate with offlanders, were banished from their homeworld after an unsuccessful bid to overthrow the Ba'ku leadership. In 2375, these outcasts, now known as the **Son'a**, allied themselves with some unscrupulous Federation officials in an attempt to remove the remaining inhabitants, so that the Son'a could return to the Ba'ku planet and reap the rejuvenating benefits of the metaphasic particles. Intervention by Captain Jean-Luc Picard of the Starship *Enterprise*-E was responsible for preventing the attempted abduction, and the *U.S.S. Ticonderoga* was dispatched to the Ba'ku homeworld in 2375 to facilitate the planet becoming a Federation protectorate. (*Star Trek: Insurrection*). *The beautiful Ba'ku village was built at Lake Sherwood, north of Los Angeles, under the direction of production designer Herman Zimmerman.*

baby wormhole. Alternate term for a **micro-wormhole**. ("Displaced" [VGR]).

Badlands.* Dangerous region of space. In 2374, around stardate 51597.2, covert Starfleet agent **Glinn Lasaran** beamed an encrypted transmission into the Badlands. Worf and Dax traveled there in the *Shenandoah* to receive his message. ("Change of Heart" [DS9]).

Baduviam tapestry. Multilayered textile art form usually used as a decorative wall hanging. ("Call to Arms" [DS9]).

Bajor.* Class-M planet, homeworld to the **Bajoran** people. The fourth moon of Bajor was called **Derna**. ("Image in the Sand" [DS9]).

Bajoran Council of Ministers. SEE: **Bajoran Chamber of Ministers.**

Bajoran Gratitude Festival.* Annual **Bajoran** holiday. At the request of the **Emissary**, the festival was held on station Deep Space 9 in 2374, despite the fact that the Federation was in the middle of the war with the Dominion. The traditional Bajoran greeting during the festival was "*Peldor joi!*" ("Tears of the Prophets" [DS9]).

Bajoran impulse ship.* Sublight military spacecraft of Bajoran registry. Colonel Kira Nerys used several impulse ships in a blockade of the Romulan fleet in the Bajor system in 2375. ("Shadows and Symbols" [DS9]).

Bajoran lilac. Variety of floriculture indigenous to planet Bajor. They were the favorite of **Kira Meru**, Kira Nerys's mother. ("Wrongs Darker Than Death or Night" [DS9]).

Bajoran shrimp. Small edible marine decapod indigenous to the green oceans of Bajor. ("You Are Cordially Invited" [DS9]).

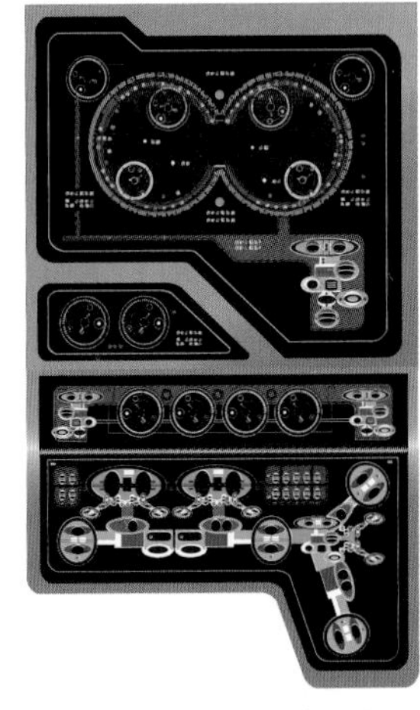

Control interface from a Bajoran impulse ship.

Bajoran wormhole.* Subspace passageway linking the Bajor sector of the Alpha Quadrant with the **Gamma Quadrant**. Millennia ago, the wormhole, known to the **Bajoran** people as the **Celestial**

Temple, was home to two forms of energy beings, later known as the Bajoran **Prophets** and the **Pah-wraiths**. The Pah-wraiths were banished from the wormhole to the fire caves of Bajor. ("The Reckoning" [DS9]). In late 2373, Starfleet personnel blockaded the Bajoran wormhole with a huge field of powerful **self-replicating mine**s in an attempt to deny use of the passage to **Dominion** forces. ("Call to Arms" [DS9]). The minefield resisted Cardassian efforts to deactivate it long enough to delay a massive Dominion incursion into the Alpha Quadrant. Once the minefield was disabled, Benjamin Sisko, the **Emissary**, appealed directly to the Prophets to intervene by destroying the invading Dominion fleet. ("Sacrifice of Angels" [DS9]). In late 2374, the wormhole sealed after a Pah-wraith carried by Gul Dukat merged with the Orb of Contemplation on Deep Space 9. ("Tears of the Prophets" [DS9]). The wormhole remained closed for several months until Sisko discovered the **Orb of the Emissary**. When Sisko opened the ark of the Orb, the Prophets returned to the wormhole. ("Shadows and Symbols" [DS9]).

Bajorans.* Civilization native to planet **Bajor**. Some five million Bajorans were killed by **Cardassian** forces during the occupation while **Gul Dukat** served as prefect of Bajor. ("Waltz" [DS9]).

Balancar Agricultural Consortium. International business alliance on planet **Balancar**. In 2374, the Balancar Agricultural Consortium faked a drought and stockpiled syrup of squill in order to drive up its price. ("The Magnificent Ferengi" [DS9]).

Balancar. Planet. Syrup of squill, a popular food topping, was made from the squill plant, which grew only on Balancar. ("The Magnificent Ferengi" [DS9]).

baldric. Traditional **Klingon** warrior's sash, often adorned with symbols of the warrior's House, or with other medals of valor. (*Star Trek: Insurrection*). *The Klingon sash was first seen on Kor's uniform in "Errand of Mercy" (TOS), but the term "baldric" was not used until* Star Trek: Insurrection.

balsamic vinaigrette. Salad dressing made with special vinegar. (*Star Trek: Insurrection*).

bamboo. Any of some 500 species of woody reedlike grass plants indigenous to Earth. The Starfleet Academy and Starfleet Headquarters grounds in San Francisco featured decorative plantings of bamboo. ("In the Flesh" [VGR]).

banana pancakes. Thin flat cakes made from batter fried in a pan, flavored with the yellow pulpy fruit of the banana plant, *Musa paradisiaca sapientum.* B'Elanna Torres, whose grandmother used to make banana pancakes for her, later recalled that they always put a smile on her face. ("Extreme Risk" [VGR]).

Bandee. Bajoran national who worked as a nurse in the Infirmary of Deep Space 9 in 2374. ("Inquisition" [DS9]).

barbecued shrimp. A dish of small edible marine decapods grilled over an open flame and served with a seasoned sauce. Barbecued shrimp was served at **Sisko's** restaurant in New Orleans on Earth. ("Image in the Sand" [DS9]).

Bareil Antos (mirror). (Philip Anglim). Petty thief and con man in the mirror universe. He was very different from his counterpart in our universe, the noted Bajoran cleric. The mirror Bareil was once involved with a woman named **Lisea** (mirror), whom he met at an Ilvian pleasure center. The two were together for five years until she was killed by a drunken Cardassian soldier. In 2374, as part of a plan with **Kira Nerys (mirror)**, he entered our universe to purloin a Bajoran Orb. He fell for Kira Nerys of our universe, who persuaded him to abandon his plan and return to his universe without the Orb. ("Resurrection" [DS9]).

Bareil, Vedek.* Bajoran religious and political figure. Bareil Antos had a strict routine that he never deviated from, eating only two meals of simple food a day. Antos used to say, "When you overindulge the body, you starve the soul." ("Resurrection" [DS9]).

Barrica. Site of a **Cardassian** base on planet **Setlik III** during the conflict with the Federation in 2347. While at Setlik III, **Miles O'Brien** led two dozen men against the Barrica encampment, driving out an entire regiment of Cardassian soldiers. ("Empok Nor" [DS9]).

barrowbug. Insect life indigenous to the planet Bajor. ("Ties of Blood and Water" [DS9]).

Baseball Hall of Fame. Museum and honorary society located in Cooperstown, New York, on Earth. The Baseball Hall of Fame was established in 1936 to commemorate the sport of **baseball** and its players. ("In the Cards" [DS9]).

baseball trading card. Twentieth century Earth popular art form. **Baseball** trading cards were small rectangular sheets of cardboard printed with colorful images of professional baseball players along with text and statistical data describing the player's performance. Baseball cards that survived into the 24th century were highly valued by collectors, including **Kivas Fajo** and Benjamin Sisko. ("In the Cards" [DS9]). SEE: **Bokai, Buck**; **Maris, Roger**; **Mays, Willie**.

baseball.* Ancient Earth team sport once popular in the American nation. Major League Baseball was one of the first professional sports in 20th-century America to break the racial barrier, providing an opportunity for African-American athletes to assert their status as equals in their society. ("Far Beyond the Stars" [DS9]). In baseball, it was traditional to commemorate a great game or a great player by inscribing one's name onto the ball used in the game, a practice known as autographing. The **Niners** baseball team honored their coach, **Benjamin Sisko**, by presenting him with an autographed baseball after their game with the *T'Kumbra* **Logicians** in early 2375. ("Take Me Out to the Holosuite" [DS9]). SEE: **batter; bunt; chewing gum; Fancy Dan; Giants; Hawkins, Willie; Logicians; Niners; strike; umpire.**

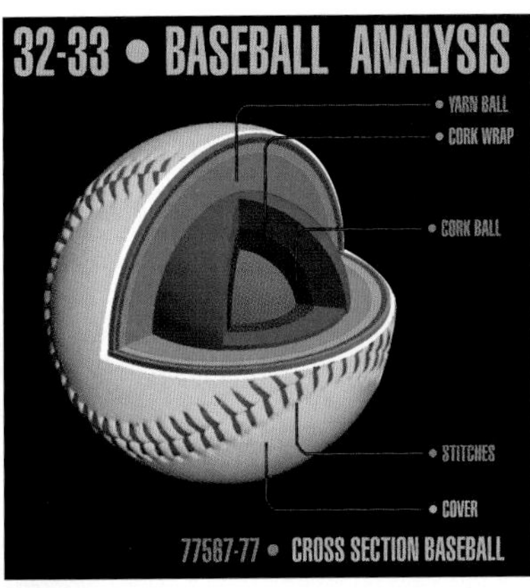

Bashir, Julian.* Starfleet chief medical officer assigned to station **Deep Space 9**. Julian Bashir was a distant relative of 15th-century Earth poet Singh el Bashir. Julian's genetic enhancements included mental ability, hand-eye coordination, reflexes, and vision. ("Statistical Probabilities" [DS9]). Bashir was kidnapped in 2374 by operatives of Starfleet's **Section 31**, a covert-operations unit of Starfleet Intelligence. Bashir demonstrated his loyalty to Starfleet and the Federation during extreme duress during tests imposed by Section 31 operatives. Bashir subsequently declined an invitation to become a part of the intelligence unit. ("Inquisition" [DS9]). Although Bashir was remarkably successful in keeping his genetically enhanced nature from interfering with his integration into normal society, it did serve as a barrier to his entering into a long-term romantic relationship. In 2375, he briefly hoped that his former patient, **Sarina Douglas**, who was herself genetically enhanced, might return the affection that he felt for her. ("Chrysalis" [DS9]). Bashir discovered that Section 31 had been responsible for developing and unleashing a deadly virus against the **Founders** of the Dominion. ("When it Rains..." [DS9]). Angered that a Federation agency would attempt to commit genocide, Bashir kidnapped Section 31 operative Luther **Sloan**, and forcibly obtained technical information about the virus from Sloan's brain. Using these data, Bashir developed a cure for the disease. ("Extreme Measures" [DS9]). Bashir's cure saved the Founders' race and was a major factor in the ending of the devastating Dominion war. Late in 2375, Julian Bashir became romantically involved with **Ezri Dax**. ("What You Leave Behind" [DS9]).

Bashir, Singh el. Fifteenth-century Earth poet. Bashir's work was later characterized by some scholars as ostensibly derivative. Singh el Bashir was a distant ancestor of Dr. Julian Bashir. ("Statistical Probabilities" [DS9]).

Basso Tromac. (David Bowe). Bajoran national who collaborated with the Cardassians during the occupation. While working for Prefect Gul Dukat, Basso procured several Bajoran comfort women from the Singha refugee camp for use aboard the Cardassian space station Terok Nor. ("Wrongs Darker Than Death or Night" [DS9]). *Given name (Tromac) is from the script.*

bat-LEH. Klingon term that meant "honor." ("Sons and Daughters" [DS9]).

bat. Nocturnal flying mammal with greatly elongated forelimbs and wings formed by skin stretched over long digits. A species of bat was indigenous to Bajor. ("The Reckoning" [DS9]).

Bathkin, Dr. Scientist from Andros III. Bathkin developed a controversial theory suggesting that humanoid immortality might be attained through the use of a device that kept the body's cells entertained. He believed that people died due to the monotonous routine of cellular metabolism literally boring the body's cells to death. Dr. Bathkin died in a 2358 shuttle accident before he could complete his work. Years later, in 2373, **Dr. Elias Giger** built a treatment chamber based on Bathkin's theories. SEE: **cellular regeneration and entertainment chamber.** ("In the Cards" [DS9]).

batter. Offensive player in the ancient Earth sport of **baseball**. The batter swung a club, called a bat, to intercept a thrown ball, attempting to redirect the trajectory of the ball as far as possible into the playing field. ("Take Me Out to the Holosuite" [DS9]).

battlefield trauma kit. Small packet of medical supplies used to dress wounds in the field. ("Call to Arms" [DS9]).

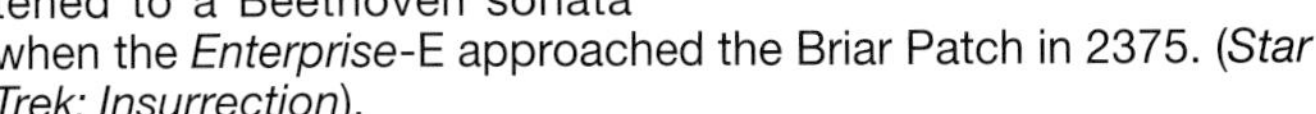

Beethoven, Ludwig van. (1770–1827). Noted composer of classical Earth music. Captain Jean-Luc Picard listened to a Beethoven sonata when the *Enterprise*-E approached the Briar Patch in 2375. (*Star Trek: Insurrection*).

"Behind the Lines." *Deep Space Nine* episode #128. Written by René Echevarria. Directed by LeVar Burton. Stardate 51145.3. *First aired in 1997. Sisko receives a promotion that takes him away from the* Defiant *and Odo's loyalties are tested by the arrival of the female shape-shifter. This episode was part of the story arc that concluded with "Sacrifice of Angels" (DS9).* GUEST CAST: Jeffrey Combs as **Weyoun**; Marc Alaimo as **Gul Dukat**; Max Grodénchik as **Rom**; Aron Eisenberg as **Nog**; Casey Biggs as **Damar**; Barry Jenner as **Ross, Admiral William**; Salome Jens as **Founder Leader.** SEE: **antigraviton; Argolis Cluster; Bennet, Captain; captain; Damar; Dax, Jadzia; Founder Leader; Founders; Great Link; Haj, Lieutenant; Kirby, Angie; Krim, Legate; Odo; phaser array power cell; Rom; Ross, Admiral William; Saurian brandy; self-replicating mine; Seventh Tactical Wing; starbase: 375.**

bekk. An enlisted rank of the **Klingon Defense Force**. Bekk Alexander Rozhenko served aboard the *Bird-of-Prey Rotarran* in 2374. ("Sons and Daughters" [DS9]).

Belle. (Lindsey Haun). Holographic character, the daughter of the *Starship Voyager*'s **Emergency Medical Hologram** in the **Doctor's family program Beta-Rho**. Belle was an outgoing and athletic girl who loved her father. During the course of the program, Belle sustained a serious cranial injury while playing **parrises squares**. Tragically, Belle died from her injuries, despite her father's best efforts to save her. ("Real Life" [VGR]). *Lindsey Haun previously played the holodeck character Beatrice Burleigh in "Cathexis" (VGR) and "Learning Curve" (VGR).*

bemonite. Metallic ore. Bemonite tends to inhibit energy propagation such as that employed in a transporter beam. ("Once Upon a Time" [VGR]).

Bennet, Captain. Starfleet officer. Bennet was adjutant to Admiral Ross, and in 2374 she was promoted to command Starfleet's Seventh Tactical Wing. ("Behind the Lines" [DS9]).

Benthan Guard. Security organization charged with maintaining order within the Benthan solar system. **Commander Avik** was an official of the Benthan Guard. ("Vis à Vis" [VGR]).

Benthans. Technologically sophisticated humanoid civilization from the Delta Quadrant. In 2374 Benthan scientists tested a prototype spacecraft that used a **coaxial warp drive** propulsion system. ("Vis à Vis" [VGR]).

Benthos IV. Planet in the Delta Quadrant, homeworld to the Benthans. ("Vis à Vis" [VGR]).

Benzar.* Planet. Shortly after entering the Dominion war on the side of the Federation and the Klingon Empire, Romulan forces forced the Dominion to retreat from the Benzar system. ("The Reckoning" [DS9]).

bergamot tea. Beverage made by infusion of the perennial herb *Monarda didyma*. Neelix drank bergamot tea when he had trouble sleeping in early 2375. ("Night" [VGR]).

Beta Quadrant.* One quarter of the Milky Way Galaxy. The *U.S.S. Olympia* embarked on an eight-year mission of long-range exploration of the Beta Quadrant in 2363, returning in 2371. ("The Sound of Her Voice" [DS9]).

beta matrix compositor. Main component of a **plasma distribution manifold** of Cardassian manufacture. Beta matrix compositors cannot be reproduced with **replicator** technology. Accordingly, when the beta matrix compositors on Deep Space 9 failed in 2373, it was deemed necessary to conduct a salvage mission to the abandoned station Empok Nor to obtain replacement units. ("Empok Nor" [DS9]).

Betazed.* Planet. Around stardate 51721 during the **Dominion** war, Betazed was captured by Dominion invasion forces. The Federation Tenth Fleet had been assigned to defend Betazed, but was caught out of position on a training exercise. Once Betazed had been captured, other nearby Federation systems and planets, including Vulcan, Tellar, Alpha Centauri, and Andor, were at risk of Dominion invasion. ("In the Pale Moonlight" [DS9]).

Beyond the Galactic Edge. Work of 21st-century literature by Hesterman. The Species 8472 replica of Valerie Archer found the book to offer insight into the complexities of human society. ("In the Flesh" [VGR])

Big Bang.* Explosion at the origin of the universe. Some Federation cosmologists theorized that the **Omega molecule** once existed in nature for an infinitesimal period of time at the moment of the Big Bang. Some have even postulated that Omega may have been the primal source of energy for the formation of the universe as we know it. ("The Omega Directive" [VGR]). Some scientists believe that the slowing of the universe's rate of expansion will eventually lead it to collapse back upon itself in some 60 to 70 trillion years. Whether or not this happens, and the time until it would happen, is determined by the total amount of matter in the universe, as well as by a value known as the cosmological constant, the measure of gravitational attraction created by a given mass. Some unconventional theorists have even proposed that a final collapse might be avoided through the use of an astronomically large number of powerful subspace generators to modify the cosmological constant on an intergalactic scale. SEE: **Jack.** ("Chrysalis" [DS9]).

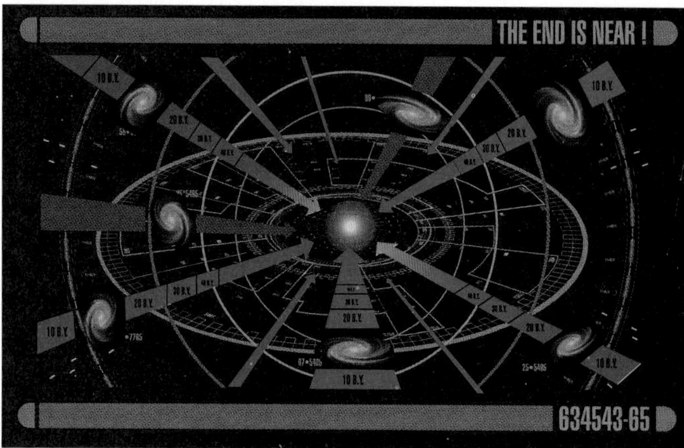

Schematic of possible "big crunch" at the end of the universe.

Bilby, Liam. (Nick Tate). Minor operative of the **Orion Syndicate**. Bilby operated out of Farius Prime and worked for Raimus, a very powerful member of that organization. Liam Bilby was a devoted family man who had a wife and two children who lived in New Sydney. In 2374, Bilby hired a technician named Connelly, who was in reality **Miles O'Brien**, an undercover agent for Starfleet. Bilby and O'Brien became friends, a move that ultimately cost Bilby his life during a syndicate attempt to assassinate the Klingon ambassador to Farius. Bilby undertook the assignment, even after O'Brien had warned him that authorities knew of the plot, because he feared that failure to follow through would result in brutal syndicate retribution against his family. Just before his death, Bilby asked Miles to care for his pet cat, **Chester**. ("Honor Among Thieves" [DS9]). SEE: **Bolias, Bank of.** *The character's first name is from the script. Nick Tate also portrayed Dirgo in "Final Mission" (TNG) as well as astronaut Alan Carter on* Space: 1999.

Billings, U.S.S. Federation starship. When future *Voyager* captain **Kathryn Janeway** had just earned the rank of commander early in her career, she served aboard the *Starship Billings*. Future *Voyager* security chief **Tuvok** also served on the *Billings* during that time. During her first year aboard, Janeway sent an away team to survey a volcanic moon. The shuttle was damaged by a magma eruption, and three crew members were severely injured. Janeway felt responsible for the incident, and the next day, she returned to the moon alone to complete the survey. She wanted the crew to know that their suffering had not been in vain. ("Night" [VGR]). *Named for the city in south central Montana.*

binary pulsar. Stellar formation of twin rapidly spinning neutron stars orbiting a common center of gravity. In 2374, the *Starship Voyager* encountered a binary pulsar in the Delta Quadrant and conducted a survey of the rare formation. ("Scientific Method" [VGR]).

bio-dart. Natural biological defense system of the **Voth** people in the Delta Quadrant. The Voth are able to shoot small darts from special orifices on their forearms. The darts deliver a fast-acting chemical that can temporarily render another individual unconscious. Chakotay was hit by a dart sent by scientist Tova Veer. ("Distant Origin" [VGR]).

biomimetic gel.* Hazardous substance. In a highly illegal operation, Benjamin Sisko arranged for 85 liters of biomimetic gel to be given to Garak to be traded for a special Cardassian **optolythic data rod** during the Dominion war. ("In the Pale Moonlight" [DS9]).

biomolecular warhead. Weapon developed for use against an incursion into this galaxy by **Species 8472** in early 2374. Biomolecular warheads were developed by the crew of the *Starship Voyager* in cooperation with Borg drone Seven of Nine. They were based on a Starfleet **photon torpedo**, customized to deliver a quantity of modified Borg **nanoprobe**s to a Species

8472 **bioship**. The nanoprobes were successful in destroying the organic elements of the bioships. ("Scorpion, Part II" [VGR]).

bioship. Warp-capable starship used by **Species 8472**. Bioships employed organic technology for most of their systems. Capable of operating in both their native **fluidic space** as well as in our space, bioships used a matter/**antimatter** reaction power source along with an electrodynamic fluid circulatory system. Bioships possessed extremely powerful energy weapons and were capable of rapid biological regeneration of damaged systems, making them nearly impervious to attack. Species 8472 used bioships in their incursion into our space in late 2373. ("Scorpion, Part I" [VGR]). The biological tissue composing the bioship structure was in many ways similar to that found in members of Species 8472. In early 2374, the crew of the *Voyager* destroyed several bioships by using Starfleet photon torpedoes with **biomolecular warheads** filled with Borg **nanoprobe**s modified to target Species 8472 cells at the genetic level. ("Scorpion, Part II" [VGR]). *The bioship exteriors were computer-generated renderings by Foundation Imaging.*

biosynthetic gland. Borg replacement for the original organic glands of an assimilated humanoid. ("The Gift" [VGR]).

bipolar flow junction. Conduit branch within the plasma guides of a starship warp propulsion system. ("One Little Ship" [DS9]).

blast shutters. Protective view port covers used on Starfleet ships such as runabouts. Blast shutters could be lowered in place to prevent damage from external objects or other hazards. ("One Little Ship" [DS9]).

"Blaze of Glory." *Deep Space Nine* episode #121. Written by Robert Hewitt Wolfe & Ira Steven Behr. Directed by Kim Friedman. No stardate given. *First aired in 1997. Sisko springs Michael Eddington from incarceration in hopes of stopping a final Maquis attack that could lead to a devastating Cardassian and Dominion reprisal. This episode concludes the storyline begun in "For the Cause" (DS9) and which continued in "For the Uniform" (DS9). Michael Eddington dies in this episode.* GUEST CAST: Kenneth Marshall as **Eddington, Michael**; J. G. Hertzler as **Martok, General**; Aron Eisenberg as **Nog**; Gretchen German as **Sullivan, Rebecca**. SEE: **Athos IV; carrot; class-4 cloak; curried chicken; decibel; *Defiant, U.S.S.*; Eddington, Michael; Hudson, Calvin; impulse flow regulator; *khi-GOSH*; Ligorian mastodon; loon; Maquis; Morn; rice; squid; Sullivan, Rebecca; tarragon; Vance.**

Bligh, Captain William. (1754–1817) Naval commander on planet Earth during the 18th century. Bligh was a British officer on Captain James Cook's second voyage around planet Earth in 1772–1775. Bligh was known for harsh discipline of his crew, and in 1789, the crew of the *H.M.S. Bounty* mutinied against him, setting him adrift in Earth's South Pacific Ocean. In an alternate timeline, Chakotay drew an analogy between Bligh and **Annorax**, commander of the **Krenim temporal weapon ship**, whose crew disapproved of his methods. ("Year of Hell, Part II" [VGR]).

blood pie. SEE: ***rokeg* blood pie.**

bloodwine.* Klingon beverage. Worf preferred bloodwine that was very young and very sweet. ("Change of Heart" [DS9]).

Boday, Captain.* Starfleet officer. Kira Nerys once declined Dax's suggestion that she have dinner with Boday, causing Dax to chide her friend for being unable to see past Boday's transparent skull. ("Resurrection" [DS9]).

Bolians.* Civilization. In 2373, the Bolian government authorized the Ferengi Gaming Commission to manage their gambling emporiums. ("Ferengi Love Songs" [DS9]). Many Bolians lived on Earth in the 24th century. ("Hope and Fear" [VGR]).

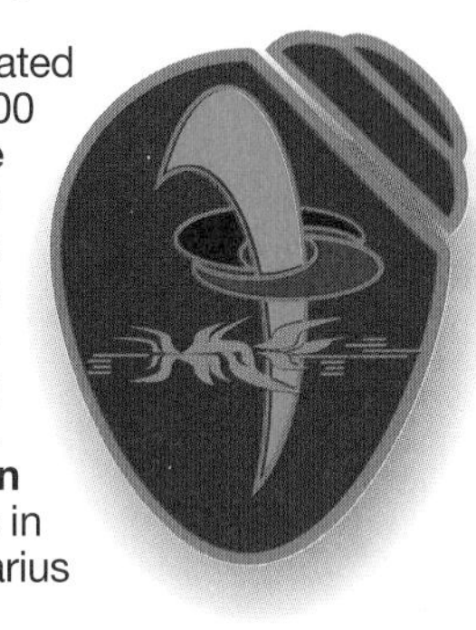

Bolias, Bank of. Financial institution located on Bolias. In 2365, **Morn** deposited 1,000 bars of **gold-pressed latinum** into the Bank of Bolias. The bars had been stolen from the Central Bank of Lissepia in the infamous **Lissepian Mother's Day Heist**. Morn removed all of the **latinum** from the bars before depositing them. ("Who Mourns for Morn?" [DS9]). **Liam Bilby**, an operative of the **Orion Syndicate**, robbed the Bank of Bolias in 2374 by using a combooth on planet Farius Prime. ("Honor Among Thieves" [DS9]).

Boothby.* Groundskeeper at **Starfleet Headquarters** and **Starfleet Academy** on Earth. Boothby began working at Starfleet in San Francisco in 2321; his career there spanned more than a half-century, during which his mentoring of numerous promising cadets belied his apparently humble role as groundskeeper. Some of those whom Boothby took under his wing included **Jean-Luc Picard**, Captain Lopez, Captain Richardson, **Valerie Archer**, and **Kathryn Janeway**. When Janeway was an academy cadet, groundskeeper Boothby used to give her fresh roses for her quarters. A re-creation of Boothby was part of a training facility created by **Species 8472** in the Delta Quadrant in 2375 in preparation for an extensive intelligence-gathering operation against the Federation. ("In the Flesh" [VGR]).

Boq'ta. (Andy Milder). Starfleet engineer assigned to Deep Space 9. In 2373, Boq'ta was part of a salvage team sent from DS9 to the abandoned Cardassian station **Empok Nor**. Boq'ta was killed at Empok Nor by a Cardassian soldier who was under the influence of a powerful **psychotropic drug**. ("Empok Nor" [DS9]).

Borg organelle. Tiny subcellular nanite that was introduced into a drone candidate by the **Borg** during assimilation. Organelles regulated cell functions in a Borg drone. ("The Gift" [VGR]).

Borg sphere.* Small **Borg** spacecraft, generally spherical in shape. The *U.S.S. Voyager* encountered a Borg sphere in the Delta Quadrant in early 2375. The sphere had been responding to a proximity transceiver signal transmitted by **One**, a Borg drone born on *Voyager*. When the Borg ship threatened to assimilate *Voyager* and its crew, One boarded the sphere. One, sacrificing himself for the *Voyager* crew, was successful in commandeering the Borg vessel and piloting it into a nearby protonebula, where the sphere exploded. ("Drone" [VGR]).

Borg.* Civilization of cybernetically enhanced beings. Borg space was vast, comprising thousands of solar systems in the **Delta Quadrant**. All Borg drones were linked together in a great collective through which information was shared; while each drone had access to the sum of Borg knowledge, retaining information useful to its specific role in the collective. ("The Omega Directive" [VGR]). The Borg, being a collective mind, had no lies and kept no secrets from each other. Deception was impossible because all thoughts were shared. ("Day of Honor" [VGR]). In the aftermath of the devastating battle at **Wolf 359** in 2367, Captain Amasov of the *Starship Endeavor*, wrote, "It is my opinion that the Borg are as close to pure evil as any race we've ever encountered."

Captain **Jean-Luc Picard** of the *Starship Enterprise*-D, who had been assimilated during the battle, wrote, "In their collective state, the Borg are utterly without mercy, driven by one will alone: the will to conquer. They are beyond reason, beyond redemption." The Borg invaded an extradimensional domain of **fluidic space** in 2373, seeking unsuccessfully to assimilate a life-form they had designated as **Species 8472**. The Borg attack triggered a swift retaliation strike by Species 8472 into our galaxy, using powerful biogenically engineered **bioship** technology against which the Borg had no defense. The Borg, unable to assimilate this adversary, was not able to gain detailed knowledge of 8472 technology. Fearful of being defeated by Species 8472, the Borg agreed to a deal with the commander of the *Starship Voyager*, permitting the Federation vessel safe passage through Borg space in exchange for assistance in developing **biomolecular warhead** technology using Borg **nanoprobe**s. A Borg drone, designated **Seven of Nine**, became separated from the collective during the development process for the weapon, and subsequently joined the *Voyager* crew. ("Scorpion, Parts I & II" [VGR]). SEE: **injection tubule.** The Borg experience with Species 8472 was unique. They were the only life-form to mount what the Borg considered to be true resistance to assimilation. ("Prey" [VGR]). Borg influence even extended to **Galactic Cluster 3**, where they assimilated the omnicordial life-forms known as **Species 259**. ("The Gift" [VGR]). The Borg do not assimilate all species they encounter, sometimes rejecting those that might detract from the Borg goal of perfection. The Borg gained the sum of knowledge and technology of each species they assimilated. From one such culture they gained a technique to use modified **nanoprobe**s to revive a drone (or other humanoid) that has been clinically dead for as long as 73 hours. ("Mortal Coil" [VGR]). The Borg had no religion in the sense common to many other cultures, but their pursuit of perfection led them to regard the immensely powerful **Omega molecule**, known to the Borg as Particle 010, with something approaching reverence. The collective believed it to exist in a flawless state, and was willing to go to any lengths to assimilate it. ("The Omega Directive" [VGR]). Borg drones do not experience fear, but individual drones, once separated from the collective, have been known to undergo severe anxiety when they are alone. ("One" [VGR]).

Borge, Victor. Twentieth-century Earth entertainer. Borge was a piano musician and comedian who specialized in one-person shows on radio and television. ("His Way" [DS9]).

boronite. Construction material used in the fabrication of **Vostigye** space stations. ("Real Life" [VGR]). Boronite, which is an extremely rare mined substance, is the only raw material known that could be used to create Omega molecules. ("The Omega Directive" [VGR]).

Borven, Glinn. Cardassian military officer, aide to Gul Trepar in 2373. ("Ties of Blood and Water" [DS9]).

Bradbury, Ray. Noted 20th-century Earth writer of fantasy and **science fiction**. Bradbury's work included nostalgic tales, poetry, and radio drama, as well as screenplays for **television** and motion pictures. Bradbury was noted for his ability to capture the bizarre, the grotesque, and the sentimental. Herbert Rossoff felt he would be in good company if his stories were published alongside those of Bradbury in ***Galaxy Science Fiction*** magazine. ("Far Beyond the Stars" [DS9]). *Ray Bradbury was a good friend of* Star Trek *creator Gene Roddenberry and was a speaker at Roddenberry's memorial service in 1991.*

***Bre'Nan* ritual.** Rite performed in preparation for a traditional Klingon **wedding**, in which the bride-to-be meets her prospective mother-in-law so that her intended's mother can pass judgment on her son's choice of a wife. **Jadzia Dax** nearly met her match when the Lady **Sirella** had doubts about Jadzia's suitability to join the House of Martok prior to Jadzia's wedding to Worf in 2374. ("You Are Cordially Invited" [DS9]).

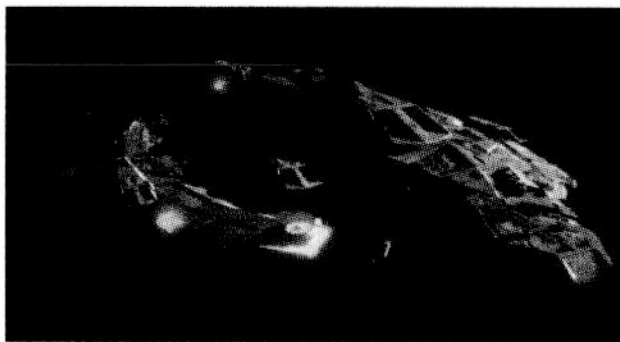

Breen.* Civilization. The Breen used spacecraft that employed biological technology. ("Scorpion, Part I" [VGR]). The Breen allied themselves with the **Dominion** during the Dominion war ("Strange Bedfellows" [DS9]) and launched a devastating attack against the city of **San Francisco** on Earth in late 2375. ("The Changing Face of Evil" [DS9]).

Briar Patch. Region of Federation space located in Sector 441. The Briar Patch was full of supernova remnants, false vacuum fluctuations, and low levels of metaphasic radiation from interstellar dust in the region. The space matter made it dangerous for a starship to travel through the area at speeds greater than one-third impulse for fear of overheating the ship's manifolds. Location of the **Ba'ku planet**. The region was whimsically named for the tangled hardwood shrub that featured prominently in the *Uncle Remus* stories by Joel Chandler Harris, published in 1880 and 1883. (*Star Trek: Insurrection*).

bridal auction. Traditional part of Ferengi **wedding** festivities. ("Call to Arms" [DS9]).

Brigette. (Roxann Dawson). Persona imposed upon **B'Elanna Torres** while under Hirogen **neural interface** control in the **French Resistance** holodeck program in late 2374. Brigette was a citizen of Earth's republic of France. Brigette had once been in love with an American soldier named **Bobby Davis**, but later conceived a child with an officer of the Nazi army, even while a member of the underground working to free her nation from the control of **Nazi Germany**. ("The Killing Game, Parts I and II" [VGR]).

British Intelligence. Security agency for the nation-state of Great Britain during the 20th century. During Earth's second world war, British Intelligence provided the government of Great Britain and its allies with data that proved critical in the defeat of **Nazi Germany**. SEE: **Allied Forces; World War II.** ("The Killing Game, Part I" [VGR]).

British Radio Network. Audio-based information broadcast agency operated by the government of Great Britain on Earth during that planet's 20th century. During Earth's second world war, the British Radio Network provided covert messages to operatives of the **French Resistance**, encoded into normal news broadcasts. SEE: **World War II**. ("The Killing Game, Part I" [VGR]).

Broik. A waiter employed at Quark's bar on station Deep Space 9. ("Who Mourns for Morn?" [DS9]).

Brone. (Michael Mahonen). Photometric projection of a **Vori** soldier, part of an elaborate mind-control technique used by the Vori military to conscript new soldiers. In the simulation, Brone was a tough, but fair-minded Vori defender and team leader of the Fourth Vori Defense Contingent. ("Nemesis" [VGR]).

Brooks, Ensign. (Sue Henley). Crew member on board ***U.S.S. Voyager***. (In an alternate timeline, Ensign Brooks was Seven of Nine's roommate.). ("Year of Hell, Part I" [VGR]).

Brota. (Brian Evaret Chandler). Inhabitant of the planet **Gaia** in an alternate timeline. In this alternate reality, Brota was the leader of a group of Gaians who chose to live their lives according to Klingon traditions, calling themselves the "Sons of Mogh." Brota ceased to exist in 2373 when his timeline vanished. ("Children of Time" [DS9]).

Brunt.* Official of the **Ferengi Commerce Authority**. In 2373, Brunt offered to restore Quark's license in exchange for assistance in disrupting the relationship between Grand Nagus **Zek** and Quark's mother, **Ishka**. Brunt's actions, which placed the financial stability of the entire Ferengi Alliance at risk, were part of an unsuccessful plot in which Brunt hoped to dethrone Zek in order to ascend to nagus. Disgraced, Brunt was relieved of his position as Liquidator. ("Ferengi Love Songs" [DS9]). Brunt redeemed himself in Zek's eyes the following year when he participated in the rescue mission that freed Ishka from Dominion captivity. ("The Magnificent Ferengi" [DS9]). This did not stop Brunt from continuing to maneuver to depose Zek several months later when Zek publicly embraced the radical policy of social and economic equality for Ferengi females. Brunt was even able to serve as acting grand nagus for several days until Zek was able to reconsolidate his position. ("Profit and Lace" [DS9]).

Bullock, Admiral. (Tucker Smallwood). Senior officer at Starfleet Headquarters in San Francisco on Earth. A re-creation of Bullock was part of a training facility created by Species 8472 in the Delta Quadrant in 2375 in preparation for an extensive intelligence-gathering operation against the Federation. ("In the Flesh" [VGR]).

bunt. In the ancient Earth sport of **baseball**, a bunt was an offensive play in which a **batter** hit a ball with a minimum of force so that its ballistic trajectory carried it only a short distance into the infield. Rom, a member of the Niners baseball team in 2375, was regarded by his coach as a master of the bunt. ("Take Me Out to the Holosuite" [DS9]).

burgundy. Alcoholic beverage made from fermented Earth grapes, a red or white wine originally made in the Burgundy region of **France** on Earth. In 2375, Paris suggested to Torres that they could celebrate progress during construction of the *Delta Flyer* by sharing a bottle of burgundy. ("Extreme Risk" [VGR]).

Bussard collector.* Large electromagnetic device located at the front of warp drive nacelles of some Federation starships, used to collect interstellar hydrogen for use as fuel. Commander William Riker used the *Enterprise*-E's Bussard ramscoop in 2375 when collecting metreon gas for the Riker Maneuver. (*Star Trek: Insurrection*).

Caatati. Humanoid civilization originating in the Delta Quadrant. The Caatati people were assimilated by the **Borg** in 2372, reducing a population of millions to a few thousand individuals who escaped in 27 ships. By 2374, living conditions for the survivors aboard the ships was threatened by severe food and supply shortages, as well as numerous systems breakdowns. The *Starship Voyager* encountered the Caatati fleet early in that year. *Voyager* captain, Janeway, granted them humanitarian aid in the form of food, medical supplies and **thorium** replication technology, which the Caatati had lost in their encounter with the Borg. ("Day of Honor" [VGR]).

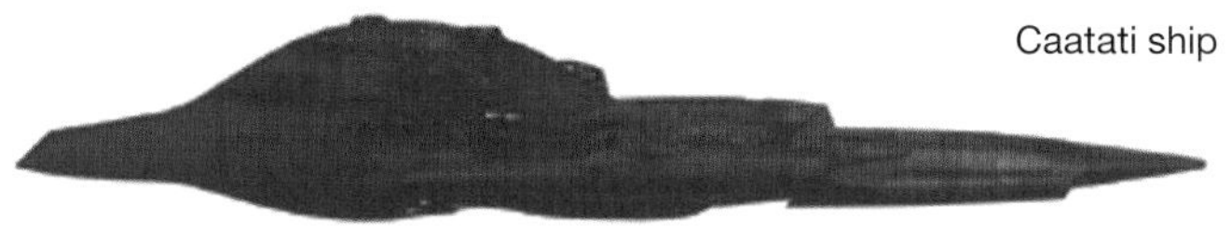

Caatati ship

Caesar salad. Earth vegetable dish made with romaine lettuce, lemon juice, egg, and anchovy dressing. ("His Way" [DS9]).

Cairo, U.S.S. Federation starship. The *Cairo* was lost and presumed destroyed in 2374 by **Dominion** forces while on patrol near the **Romulan Neutral Zone**. The ship had been under the command of Captain Leslie Wong at the time of its disappearance. ("In the Pale Moonlight" [DS9]).

Calandra Sector. Region of space within Federation territory. Around stardate 51721, the Dominion made a successful bid to take Betazed by staging an invasion from the Calandra Sector. ("In the Pale Moonlight" [DS9]).

"Call to Arms." *Deep Space Nine* episode #124. Written by Ira Steven Behr & Robert Hewitt Wolfe. Directed by Allan Kroeker. Stardate 50975.2. *First aired in 1997. The Federation mines the entrance to the wormhole to prevent further Dominion reinforcements from coming through. Gul Dukat, with Dominion support, attacks and takes over the station. Rom and Leeta get married, and Worf and Dax become engaged. This cliff-hanger marked the beginning of the Dominion war and was the last episode of the fifth season.* GUEST CAST: Andrew J. Robinson as **Garak, Elim**; Jeffrey Combs as **Weyoun**; Marc Alaimo as **Dukat, Gul**; Max Grodénchik as **Rom**; Aron Eisenberg as **Nog**; J. G. Hertzler as **Martok, General**; Chase Masterson as **Leeta**; Melanie Smith as **Tora Ziyal**; Casey Biggs as **Damar**. SEE: **Baduviam tapestry; Bajoran wormhole; battlefield trauma kit; bridal auction; coffee; Damar, Glinn; Dax, Jadzia; Deep Space 9; Dominion; Dukat, Gul; Federation News Service; Ferengi Rules of Acquisition; freedom of the press; latinum dance; Leeta; medkit; minefield; Miradorn; Promenade Merchants' Association; Rom; Romulans; self-replicating mine; Sisko, Benjamin; Sisko, Jake; Terok Nor; Tholian Assembly; Torros III; wedding: Ferengi; Worf.**

Camaro. Ancient wheeled, internal-combustion ground vehicle used on Earth during the 20th century. Considered by some to be emblematic of that culture's technology, the Camaro was manufactured by the Chevrolet Division of the General Motors Corporation of the United States of America and was widely used for subsonic surface transportation across land distances of many kilometers. A holographic replica of the 1969 version of the vehicle was the centerpiece of Lieutenant Tom Paris's recreational holodeck program, **Grease Monkey**. ("Vis à Vis" [VGR]).

Captain Proton, The Adventures of. Holodeck program, a **science-fiction** story in the style of low-budget noninteractive film serials produced on Earth in the 1930s. The Captain Proton stories reflected an early 20th-century futurist vision of the coming age of space exploration. The title character, **Captain Proton**, was a human space traveler who voyaged through his Sol System in a sublight **rocket ship**, defending his homeworld from a variety of extraterrestrial menaces including **Doctor Chaotica** and **Satan's Robot**. Proton was frequently accompanied on his exploits by his beautiful secretary, **Constance Goodheart** and best friend Buster. The holodeck program, devised by **Thomas Paris**, was designed to duplicate the look and feel of the 1930s serials, including the monochromatic image style and the simplistic special effects employed by motion pictures of the period. Naturally, Tom Paris usually played the title role. SEE: **Mines of Mercury**. ("Night" [VGR]). Paris was so enthusiastic about the Captain Proton program that he incorporated some 1930s-style aircraft instrumentation into the control systems of the ***Delta Flyer*** shuttlecraft, designed and built on the *Starship Voyager* in early 2375. ("Extreme Risk" [VGR]). *Captain Proton was first seen in "Night" (VGR).*

captain's yacht.* Luxury shuttle vehicle carried aboard some Federation starships for the exclusive use of the ship's commanding officer. The captain's yacht was berthed in a special docking port located on the underside of a ship's **Primary Hull**. Captain Jean-Luc Picard commandeered the *Cousteau*, the captain's yacht from the *Starship Enterprise*-E, in 2375 when he defended the **Ba'ku planet** in defiance of orders from Admiral Matthew Dougherty. The *Cousteau* was destroyed during the operation. (*Star Trek: Insurrection*). *The captain's yacht aboard the* Sovereign-*class* Starship Enterprise-*E was named* Cousteau, *in honor of the French oceanographer. The name, chosen by producer Rick Berman, was inscribed on a dedication plaque in the ship's cabin. The yacht was designed by Herman Zimmerman and John Eaves.*

captain. In an old Earth naval tradition, the title given to a person in command of a ship. The Federation granted the rank of captain to senior officers who commanded the Starfleet's powerful **starships**, although any officer holding the **center seat** of a spacecraft was properly addressed as "captain," regardless of that individual's actual service rank. Jadzia Dax was captain of the *Starship Defiant* while she commanded the ship in early 2374, even though she held the rank of lieutenant commander. ("Behind the Lines" [DS9]).

carbon 60. Isotope of the element carbon. Carbon 60 was used in the construction of **Vostigye** space stations. ("Real Life" [VGR]).

carburetor. Mechanical device used in ancient internal combustion engines to charge air with hydrocarbons to increase volatility. In 2374, Tom Paris suggested using a polaric modulator for an analogous purpose in a coaxial warp drive system by diluting the particle stream before it entered the coaxial drive. SEE: **Camaro**. ("Vis à Vis" [VGR]).

Cardassia.* Homeworld of the Cardassian people. By 2373, Cardassia hadn't signed an extradition treaty with either Bajor or the Federation. ("Ties of Blood and Water" [DS9]).

Cardassian Central Archives. Data repository for the Cardassian government. Kira Nerys of the Bajoran Militia earned sufficient notoriety in the eyes of the Cardassians that an entire section in the Central Archives was devoted to her. ("Ties of Blood and Water" [DS9]).

Cardassian Institute of Art. Higher learning center on Cardassia devoted to the fine arts. ("Sons and Daughters" [DS9]).

Cardassian Intelligence Bureau. Organization that replaced the **Obsidian Order** as the chief information gathering service for the Cardassian government under Gul Dukat during the Dominion alliance. ("Rocks and Shoals" [DS9]).

Cardassians.* Civilization. Cardassian forces were responsible for the death of over five million Bajorans while Gul Dukat served as prefect of Bajor during the occupation. ("Waltz" [DS9]). The Cardassian homeworld was occupied by the forces of the Dominion early in the Dominion war. Although the Cardassians started out as willing allies against the Alpha Quadrant forces led by the Federation, by late 2375 Cardassian public sentiment turned against the brutal Dominion government. In response, the Dominion leveled entire cities in an attempt to quash the rebellion. This triggered an even more massive uprising by Cardassian citizens and the Cardassian military led by Legate **Damar**, providing critical leverage for the Alpha Quadrant powers during the final, desperate hours of the Dominion war. Although the Cardassians won their freedom, the war exacted a toll of some 800 million Cardassian citizens massacred by the Dominion. ("What You Leave Behind" [DS9]).

cardiopulmonary reconstruction. Medical procedure for repairing the heart of a humanoid patient. ("Vis à Vis" [VGR]).

carrot. A long, reddish yellow, edible root of an umbelliferous Earth plant (*Daucus carota*). On a Starfleet runabout, replicator entree number 103 was curried chicken and rice with a side order of carrots. ("Blaze of Glory" [DS9]).

Casperia Prime. Planet, regarded as the vacation capital of the Horvian Cluster. Worf and Jadzia decided to spend their honeymoon there in 2374 because Jadzia wanted to go to a beautiful place where she could be pampered in luxury. ("Change of Heart" [DS9]). Julian Bashir was to have presented a paper at a Starfleet medical conference on Casperia Prime in 2374. ("Inquisition" [DS9]).

Cassie. (Penny Johnson). Twentieth-century Earth inhabitant who lived in New York city on the North American continent. Cassie worked as a waitress in a Harlem coffee shop. She was romantically involved with **Benny Russell** and hoped that the two would someday be married. ("Far Beyond the Stars" [DS9]). *Penny Johnson also played Kasidy Yates on* Star Trek: Deep Space Nine.

Cave Beyond Logic, A. Academic study of **Vulcan** philosophy as it relates to other cultures. Valerie Archer, or at least the Species 8472 version of her, studied *A Cave Beyond Logic: Vulcan Perspectives on Platonic Thought* in her quest to understand humanoid species in 2375. ("In the Flesh" [VGR]).

Caves of Kahless. Subterranean chambers located on the Klingon Homeworld. The Caves of Kahless were often used for traditional observances of the Klingon **Day of Honor**. In 2374, B'Elanna Torres and Tom Paris programmed a holodeck recreation of the caves so that she could observe the holiday. ("Day of Honor" [VGR]). SEE: **Kahless the Unforgettable**.

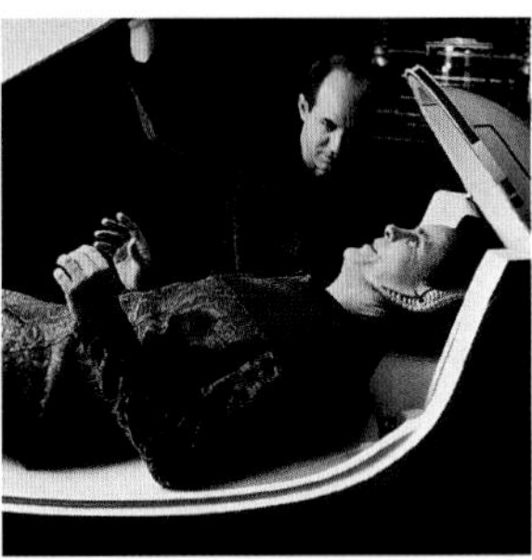

cellular regeneration and entertainment chamber. Experimental medical treatment device intended to make humanoid patients effectively immortal by keeping their cells entertained. Based on theories developed by **Dr. Bathkin** of Andros III, the controversial device was built by **Dr. Elias Giger**. Although Giger tested the chamber at Deep Space 9, he has not yet reported any results of his tests. ("In the Cards" [DS9]).

Central Bank of Lissepia. SEE: **Bolias, Bank of**

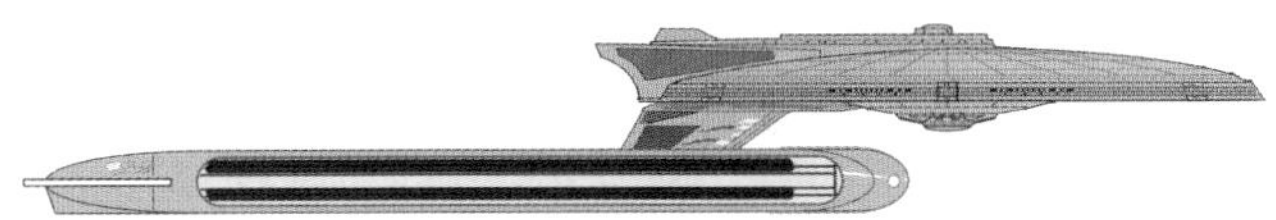

Centaur, U.S.S. Federation starship. The *Centaur* was commanded by Captain Charles Reynolds. In 2374 the *Centaur* encountered a **Jem'Hadar attack ship** commanded by Captain Benjamin Sisko and his crew on a secret mission deep inside Cardassian space. Not knowing that the ship was piloted by a Starfleet crew, Reynolds engaged the ship, causing it some damage. ("A Time to Stand" [DS9]). *The* Centaur *was named for the creature from Greek mythology that had the head and torso of a man joined to the body of a horse.*

Ch'Pok.* Warrior of the Klingon Empire. Ch'Pok had a son, **Katogh**, who served in the Klingon Defense Force. ("Sons and Daughters" [DS9]).

Ch'Targh. (Sam Zeller). Seasoned Klingon warrior who was helm officer of the *Bird-of-Prey* ***Rotarran*** under the command of General Martok in 2374 during the Dominion war. ("Sons and Daughters" [DS9]).

chadre kab. Yellow-colored culinary dish. Chadre kab could be prepared boiled, baked, stir-fried, or steamed. ("The Raven" [VGR]). Chadre kab was the first meal consumed by Seven of Nine, after returning to human society, aboard the *Starship Voyager*.

Chadwick. (Michael Harney). Operative of Starfleet Intelligence. In 2374, Chadwick investigated the Orion Syndicate, serving as a contact to Miles O'Brien when O'Brien worked undercover on planet Farius Prime. ("Honor Among Thieves" [DS9]).

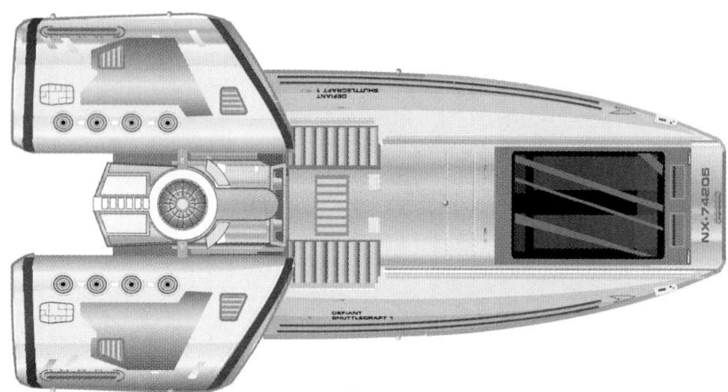

Chaffee*, Shuttlecraft.** Auxiliary craft attached to the Federation **starship *Defiant. ("The Sound of Her Voice" [DS9]). *The* Chaffee *was named for* Apollo 1 *astronaut Roger Chaffee and was designed by Doug Drexler.*

Chakotay.* (Robert Beltran). Former **Maquis** terrorist who joined the crew of the ***U.S.S. Voyager*** in 2371, serving as the ship's executive officer. Chakotay, who held the rank of commander in 2375, had Starfleet service number 47-alpha-612. ("In the Flesh" [VGR]). In 2374, Chakotay fell in love with **Kellin**, a Ramuran tracer. Although Ramuran defenses caused him (and his crewmates) to lose all memories of her shortly after her departure from *Voyager*, Chakotay took the precaution of writing down some of his memories, so that he might have some permanent record of their time together. ("Unforgettable" [VGR]).

Chamber of Opportunity. The office of the **grand nagus**, located forty flights up in the Tower of Commerce on **Ferenginar**, from which the entire **Ferengi Alliance** is controlled. ("Profit and Lace" [DS9]).

Chandler, Lieutenant. (Samantha Mudd). Starfleet officer assigned to the **Section 31** covert intelligence unit. In 2374, Chandler, along with Lieutenant Kagan and Director Sloan, conducted an elaborate holographic simulation designed to determine Julian Bashir's loyalty to the Federation, screening him for possible recruitment into Section 31. ("Inquisition" [DS9]).

"Change of Heart." *Deep Space Nine* episode #140. Written by Ronald D. Moore. Directed by David Livingston. Stardate 51597.2. *First aired in 1998. On a mission to extract an important defector from a Dominion base, Worf abandons his mission and risks his career to save his wife's life after she is wounded on a jungle planet.* GUEST CAST: Todd Waring as **Lasaran.** SEE: **Andor; anticoagulant; Badlands; bloodwine; Casperia Prime; full consortium; Horvian Cluster; Klingons; Lasaran, Glinn; Rozhenko, Nikolai; Rozhenko, Sergey; scotch; *Shenandoah, U.S.S.*; Soukara; *Sutherland, U.S.S.*; *tongo*; total monopoly; Trill; Ural Mountains; Vulcan's Forge; Worf.**

Chaotica, Doctor. (Martin Rayner). Menacing, villainous character in *The Adventures of Captain Proton* holodeck program. In the program, Doctor Chaotica was a megalomaniac extraterrestrial dictator who sought to enslave Earth's inhabitants. SEE: ***Captain Proton, The Adventures of.*** ("Night" [VGR]).

Chapman, Admiral. High-ranking Starfleet officer. ("Hope and Fear" [VGR]).

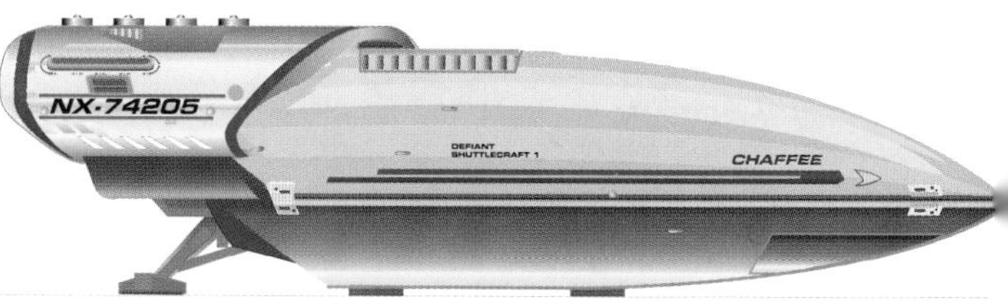

"Charge of the Light Brigade, The." Poem written by Alfred, Lord Tennyson in 1855, telling of heroism during a hopeless battle in ancient Earth history. Miles O'Brien and Julian Bashir recited part of it aboard the *Defiant* as they headed to Deep Space 9 to retake the station from the Dominion. ("Sacrifice of Angels" [DS9]).

Charlene. (Wendy Schaal). Holographic character, the wife of the *Starship Voyager*'s Emergency Medical Hologram in the **Doctor's family program Beta-Rho**. In the program, Charlene was the mother of two children, Jeffrey and Belle. ("Real Life" [VGR]).

Chateau Latour. Alcoholic beverage made from fermented Earth grapes, originating in the nation of **France** on Earth. Chateau Latour was available in the **Le Coeur de Lion** portion of the **French Resistance** holodeck program. ("The Killing Game, Part I" [VGR]).

chateaubriand. Aged tenderloin beef roast, served cooked. An Earth delicacy. ("His Way" [DS9]).

cherries jubilee. Earth dessert made with cherries flavored with liquors such as cognac and brandy, served flaming over vanilla-flavored ice cream. ("His Way" [DS9]).

Chester. Male long-haired cat, Earth *Felis domesticus*. Chester was the pet of Orion Syndicate operative **Liam Bilby**. When Bilby knew he was about to be killed in 2374, he asked his friend **Miles O'Brien** to take care of Chester. O'Brien subsequently took Chester back with him to station Deep Space 9, where Chester became the O'Brien family pet. ("Honor Among Thieves" [DS9]). Keiko O'Brien was not very fond of Chester. ("Time's Orphan" [DS9]).

chewing gum. Traditional Earth confection enjoyed as much for the pleasure of chewing as for its taste. Chewing gum was part of the culture surrounding the ancient game of **baseball**. When the Deep Space Niners played their epic game against the *T'Kumbra Logicians* in early 2375, Chief Miles O'Brien tried to get into the spirit of the game by replicating a pack of scotch-flavored chewing gum. ("Take Me Out to the Holosuite" [DS9]).

chief examiner. Senior officer of the Mari Constabulary law enforcement agency. In 2374 the Mari chief examiner was **Nimira**. ("Random Thoughts" [VGR]).

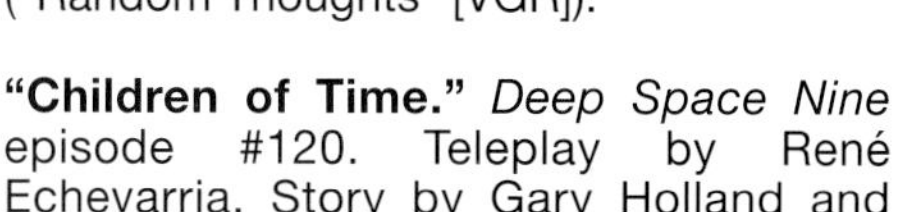

"Children of Time." *Deep Space Nine* episode #120. Teleplay by René Echevarria. Story by Gary Holland and Ethan H. Calk. Directed by Allan Kroeker. Stardate 50814.2. *First aired in 1997. Sisko and the* Defiant *crew must choose between the lives they have always known and the lives of their own descendants. In this episode, Kira learns that Odo loves her.* GUEST CAST: Jennifer Parsons as **O'Brien, Miranda**; Gary Frank as **Yedrin**; Brian Evaret Chandler as **Brota**; Marybeth Massett as **Parell**; Jesse Littlejohn as **Gabriel**; Doren Fein as **Molly**; Davida Williams as **Lisa**. SEE: **Brota; Dax, Yedrin; *Defiant, U.S.S.*; Gabriel; Gaia; Golian spa; Kenda shrine; keripate; Kira Nerys; Kirby, Angie; Lisa; Molly; neuropathway induction; O'Brien, Miranda; Odo; Parell; Pelios Station;**

Shakaar Edon; "Sons of Mogh, The;"; Tannenbaum, Ensign Rita; tessipate; torga; Torvin; yak bear; yelg melon.

Chile. Republic on the South American continent of planet Earth. ("Waking Moments" [VGR]).

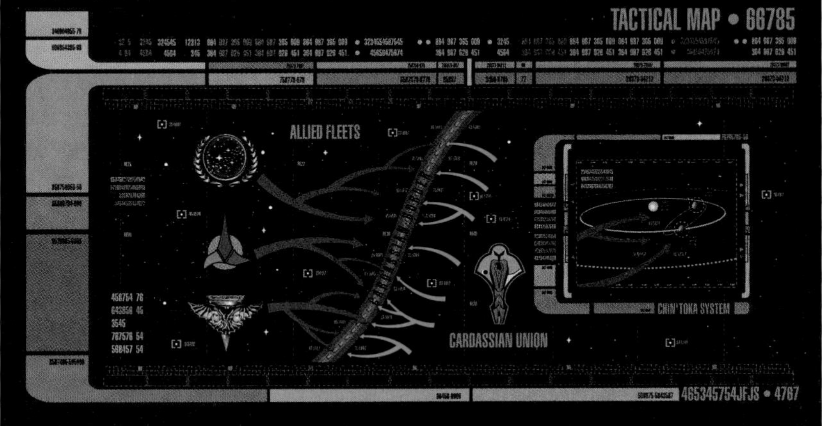

Historic battle for the Chin'toka System, 2374

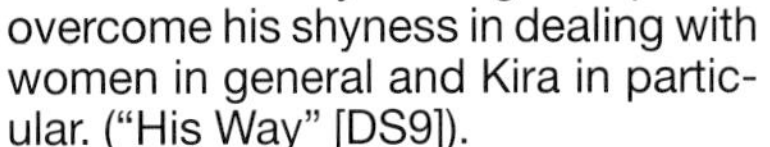

Chin'toka System. Strategically important planetary system that in late 2374 was held by the Dominion during their war with the Alpha Quadrant powers. The Chin'toka System was the site of a decisive battle in which Federation, Klingon, and Romulan forces destroyed a sophisticated Cardassian automated defense system, landing ground troops on Cardassian territory. ("Tears of the Prophets" [DS9]).

Christmas Carol, A. Popular novel written by Charles Dickens and published on Earth in 1843. The classic morality tale was the basis of a holodeck program employed by the *Enterprise*-D crew in 2367. ("Devil's Due" [TNG]). In 2374, the *Starship Voyager*'s Emergency Medical Hologram recommended that Seven of Nine should read *A Christmas Carol*, believing the book would help her better understand human society. ("The Omega Directive" [VGR]).

chromodynamic shield. Energy field. Chromodynamic shields could block the rejuvenating effects of metaphasic radiation found in the Briar Patch. (*Star Trek: Insurrection*).

chromoelectric force field. Protective energy shield. In 2374, **Entharan** arms dealer **Kovin** demonstrated the ability of a weapon to penetrate a chromoelectric force field to members of the *Starship Voyager*. ("Retrospect" [VGR]).

chromoelectric pulse. Energy discharge. In 2374, Lieutenant Tom Paris used a chromoelectric pulse to disrupt the coaxial drive of **Steth**'s ship. ("Vis à Vis" [VGR]).

chroniton torpedo.* Weapons system used by the **Krenim** Imperium. The use of chroniton technology made the torpedo able to pass unimpeded through conventional deflector shields. ("Year of Hell, Parts I & II" [VGR]). *The Krenim chroniton torpedo attack in "Year of Hell, Part I" had originally been intended as a tie-in to the attack foreshadowed in "Before and After" (VGR), where Kes attempted to deactivate the torpedo and was exposed to chroniton radiation. With the departure of actor Jennifer Lien, Seven of Nine was given that task in "Year of Hell."*

chroniton.* Elementary particle. Chroniton radiation is lethal to the life-forms living in the **Bajoran wormhole**. ("The Reckoning" [DS9]). Chroniton radiation was associated with the temporal incursion weaponry used by the **Krenim**. ("Year of Hell, Parts I and II" [VGR]).

"Chrysalis." Deep Space Nine episode #155. Written by René Echevarria. Directed by Jonathan West. *Jack and his genetically enhanced friends return to Deep Space 9, where Bashir is successful in helping the catatonic Sarina emerge to near normalcy, but her recovery is threatened when he falls in love with her. This episode continues the story of Jack and his friends first seen in "Statistical Probabilities" (DS9).* GUEST CAST: Tim Ransom as **Jack**; Hilary Shepard-Turner as **Lauren**; Michael Keenan as **Patrick**; Faith C. Salie as **Douglas, Sarina**; Aron Eisenberg as **Nog**; Randy Pflug as Security officer. SEE: **Bashir, Julian; Big Bang; Corgal Research Center; cosmological constant; Douglas, Sarina; *Farragut, U.S.S.*; Girani, Doctor; Jack; Lauren; Loews, Dr. Karen; neocortical probe; Patrick; tempura.**

Chrystal, Lola. (Nana Visitor). Holographic character, a 20th-century Earth singer, part of the **Vic Fontaine** holosuite program. Her repertoire included such songs as **"Fever."** Chrystal was designed by Vic to look exactly like **Kira Nerys** in hopes that Chrystal might help **Odo** overcome his shyness in dealing with women in general and Kira in particular. ("His Way" [DS9]).

Cinema Mystäre. Noninteractive analog motion picture projection auditorium in the city of **Sainte Claire** in the republic of **France** during the mid-20th century. In the **French Resistance** holodeck simulation, resistance fighters buried large quantities of munitions under the Cinema Mystäre for use in liberating their city from Nazi forces. ("The Killing Game, Part II" [VGR]).

city ship. SEE: **Voth city ship.**

clarinet.* Musical instrument. When the *Voyager* traveled through a spatial void in the Delta Quadrant in early 2375, **Harry Kim** wrote a concerto to play on his clarinet. Kim entitled the piece "Echoes of the Void." ("Night" [VGR]).

Clarus System.* Planetary group located near Ferenginar. ("Profit and Lace" [DS9]).

class-2 shuttlecraft. Starfleet designation for shuttles with small crew cabins and very limited amenities. Class-2 shuttles included shuttlecraft of types 6, 8, and 9. ("Drone" [VGR]).

class-3 probe. Autonomous free-flying remote data gathering device used by the Federation Starfleet. Class-3 probes were designed to have an extremely low sensor profile and emissions, making them suitable for use behind enemy lines. In 2374, the crew of the *U.S.S. Valiant* sent a class-3 probe to obtain intelligence information about a new Dominion battleship. ("*Valiant*" [DS9]).

class-4 cloak. Invisibility screen generator used by Klingon spacecraft. A few months before the Maquis were nearly wiped out in 2373, the Klingon government aided the Maquis in their fight against Cardassia by providing them with 30 class-4 cloaking devices. ("Blaze of Glory" [DS9]).

Class-Y planet. SEE: **planetary classification system: Class-Y**.

clone.* Technique for asexual reproduction by stimulating a single cell of an organism to reproduce into an offspring, genetically identical to the original. The **Vorta** used cloning technology to create replacement copies of useful individuals, including **Weyoun**. ("Ties of Blood and Water" [DS9]). Vorta cloning technology was delicate but normally very reliable, although defective clones occasionally occurred. In 2375, the Dominion believed that the sixth Weyoun clone was defective because he held the heretical view that the Founders' war with the Alpha Quadrant was wrong. ("Treachery, Faith, and the Great River" [DS9]).

Clyde. Mid-20th-century slang term for a person lacking up-to-date sophistication. ("His Way" [DS9]). SEE: **Harvey; square**.

coaxial warp drive. Starship propulsion system devised by **Benthan** scientists in 2374 that employs a folding-space technique, allowing a vessel to instantaneously travel across large distances. In 2374, the Benthans tested a prototype coaxial drive, finding it was prone to overload due to particle instabilities. ("Vis à Vis" [VGR]).

Cobum, Admiral. (Bart McCarthy). Senior Starfleet officer. In 2374, Cobum was one of the admirals who approved Captain Benjamin Sisko's daring plan to retake station Deep Space 9 from Dominion forces. Cobum was concerned that the plan would leave Earth vulnerable, but he nevertheless supported the action. ("Favor the Bold" [DS9]).

Cochrane, Shuttlecraft.* Shuttlecraft attached to the *Starship Voyager*. The *Cochrane* was nearly destroyed on a mission to investigate an **astral eddy** phenomenon on stardate 50836. ("Real Life" [VGR]). The *Cochrane*'s final flight was a mission to retrieve the *Voyager*'s warp core, which had been jettisoned during a systems emergency in early 2374. A Caatati spacecraft attempted to prevent the recovery by bombarding the *Cochrane* with a powerful antimatter pulse that destroyed the shuttlecraft. The crew survived by donning environmental suits and beaming themselves into space. ("Day of Honor" [VGR]).

coffee.* Traditional Earth beverage. Sisko liked his coffee served at exactly 60 °C (333 °K). ("Call to Arms" [DS9]). Chakotay preferred coffee hot, without cream or sugar. ("Scientific Method" [VGR]). Neelix occasionally brewed a particularly potent coffee blend containing firenuts. ("Mortal Coil" [VGR]).

coil spanner. Engineering tool. ("Empok Nor" [DS9]).

colliculi. A group of large cells near the midbrain section of a humanoid brain. A Borg implant in Seven of Nine's colliculi pressed against her trochlear nerve in early 2374, shortly after her separation from the collective, nearly sending her into fatal neural shock. ("The Gift" [VGR]).

Collins, Dorian. (Ashley Brianne McDonogh). Starfleet Academy cadet. In 2374, Collins and 34 other members of the elite **Red Squad** embarked on a three-month training cruise aboard the ***U.S.S. Valiant***, which was caught behind enemy lines when the Dominion war broke out. Dorian Collins, who was a native of **Tycho City** on Earth's **Moon**, was the only member of Red Squad to survive after the *Valiant* was destroyed when acting commander cadet, **Tim Watters,** unwisely ordered the ship to attack a massive Dominion battleship. ("*Valiant*" [DS9]). *Named for Apollo 11 astronaut Michael Collins.*

combooth. Colloquial term for a public communications terminal. Combooths were used for person-to-person audio and visual contact, as well as for data communications. Orion Syndicate operatives used a combooth on planet Farius Prime to rob the Bank of Bolias in 2374. ("Honor Among Thieves" [DS9]).

"Come Fly with Me." Popular 20th-century Earth song in which suborbital air travel was a metaphor for love, written by Sammy Cahn and James Van Heusen. The piece was performed by such notable entertainers as **Vic Fontaine** and **Frank Sinatra**. ("His Way" [DS9]).

comfort woman. Bajoran woman who was conscripted during the **Cardassian** occupation of **Bajor** to provide companionship and sexual services to Cardassian military officers at distant postings such as **Terok Nor**. Comfort women were given plenty of good food and luxurious clothes, and their families were given extra food and medicine, all extremely scarce for Bajoran nationals during the brutal years of the occupation. Other Bajorans of the period often viewed these women as enemy collaborators, but many comfort women, desperate about their families during the occupation, saw their services as the only way to ensure their families' survival. **Kira Meru**, mother to Kira Nerys, was a comfort woman for the infamous **Gul Dukat**. ("Wrongs Darker Than Death or Night" [DS9]).

"Concerning Flight." *Voyager* episode #79. Teleplay by Joe Menosky. Story by Jimmy Diggs & Joe Menosky. Directed by Jesús Salvador Treviño. Stardate 51386.4. *First aired in 1997. Small pirate ships raid the* Voyager. *Among the pirates' booty is the ship's computer core and the Leonardo da Vinci holographic program. This episode was the last appearance of John Rhys-Davies as the holographic Renaissance genius.* GUEST CAST: John Vargas as **Tau**; Don Pugsley as Alien visitor; John Rhys-Davies as **Leonardo da Vinci**; Doug Spearman as Alien buyer. SEE: **da Vinci, Leonardo; dispersion field; Florence; induction relay; main computer processor; Renaissance; security access code; Tau; translocator; transluminal processor.**

condition blue. SEE: **blue alert**

condition gray. SEE: **gray mode**.

Connelly. Name used by Miles O'Brien in 2374 when he worked as an undercover Starfleet operative on planet Farius Prime. ("Honor Among Thieves" [DS9]).

Constellation, U.S.S.* Federation starship. After the *Starship Honshu* was destroyed on stardate 51408.6, Starfleet assigned the *Constellation* and the *Defiant* to search for survivors in adjacent star systems. ("Waltz" [DS9]).

cordafin. Pharmaceutical used as a stimulant. Cadet Tim Watters abused cordafin in 2374 while serving as captain of the *U.S.S. Valiant*, possibly contributing to errors in judgment that led to the death of his crew and the destruction of the spacecraft. ("*Valiant*" [DS9]).

core matrix. Main component of a **Jem'Hadar attack ship**'s warp propulsion system. ("A Time to Stand" [DS9]).

Corgal Research Center. Scientific institution. **Sarina Douglas** began an internship at the Corgal Research Center in 2375, living with the family of a staff scientist there. ("Chrysalis" [DS9]).

Coridan.* Planet. On stardate 51474, a **Dominion** attack force led by Gelnon set its sights on the **dilithium**-rich Coridan planets. ("One Little Ship" [DS9]).

corn chowder. Rich, creamy Earth soup made with corn, potatoes, green and red peppers, and onions. ("The Sound of Her Voice" [DS9]).

Cortéz, U.S.S. Federation starship. The *Cortéz* was part of the task force commanded by Captain Sisko to retake station Deep Space 9 during the **Dominion** war in 2374. ("Favor the Bold," "Sacrifice of Angels" [DS9]). The *Cortéz* was reported missing and was presumed destroyed shortly after the retaking of station

Deep Space 9. At the time of its disappearance, the ship had been commanded by Captain Quentin Swofford. ("Far Beyond the Stars" [DS9]). *The ship was named for Hernán Cortéz, the Spanish conquistador who overthrew the Aztec empire and won Mexico for the crown of Spain.*

cosmological constant. In astrophysics, the cosmological constant is the measure of the intensity of gravitational attraction generated by a given quantity of matter. This exact value, as well as the total mass of all the matter in the universe, will determine the ultimate fate of the universe, whether it will continue to expand to the point of maximum entropy, or whether it will collapse upon itself trillions of years from now. SEE: **Big Bang; Jack**. ("Chrysalis" [DS9]).

***Cousteau*.** Captain's yacht carried aboard the *U.S.S. Enterprise*-E. The *Cousteau* was destroyed above the **Ba'ku planet** in 2375. (*Star Trek: Insurrection*).

Cox, Dr. Starfleet psychiatrist. Cox worked with Gul Dukat in 2374, while Dukat was held by Federation authorities. Cox encouraged Dukat to talk about his daughter Tora Ziyal whenever possible, since it was her death that brought on his mental instability during that period. ("Waltz" [DS9]).

crawfish étoufée. Cajun dish of fresh-water decapod crustaceans cooked in a seasoned sauce containing tomatoes, celery, onions, bell peppers, and garlic, and served over cooked rice. Crawfish étoufée was served in **Sisko's** New Orleans restaurant on Earth. ("Image in the Sand" [DS9]).

Cretaceous Period. Interval of geologic time that started 136 million years ago on **Earth** and lasted some 70 million years. Earth's dinosaurs became almost totally extinct at the end of the Cretaceous, with the notable exception of some **hadrosaurs**. ("Distant Origin" [VGR]).

Cretak, Senator. (Megan Cole). High-ranking official of the **Romulan Star Empire**. In early 2375, Cretak was a strong supporter of the Romulan alliance with the Federation and Klingon Empire against the **Dominion**. She worked with Starfleet admiral Ross, and the two had a good rapport. Nevertheless, Senator Cretak risked the alliance by deploying 7,000 plasma torpedoes at the hospital facility on the Bajoran moon Derna, much to the displeasure of the Bajoran government. ("Image in the Sand" [DS9]). Cretak refused Bajoran demands to remove the weapons from Bajoran space, but later backed down when the Federation Starfleet indicated it would support a blockade of Romulan shipments to Derna imposed by Colonel Kira Nerys. ("Shadows and Symbols" [DS9]). *Megan Cole previously played the J'naii Noor in "The Outcast" (TNG).*

Crockett, Davy. (1786–1836). Noted frontiersman and politician from the early history of the American nation on planet Earth. Crockett was killed in 1836, defending a fortress called the Alamo in the cause of Texan independence. In 2375, Miles O'Brien was to play the character of Crockett when he, Julian Bashir, and Odo participated in a holosuite re-creation of the historic battle. SEE: **Alamo, Battle of the.** ("Afterimage" [DS9]).

cruller. A small cake of sweetened dough, deep-fried in fat, popular on 20th-century Earth. Crullers were popular with the staff of *Incredible Tales* magazine. ("Far Beyond the Stars" [DS9]).

Culat, University of. Institute of higher learning. **Dr. Crell Moset** held the Chair of Exobiology at the University of Culat in 2371. ("Nothing Human" [VGR]).

Culhane, Ensign. Starfleet officer assigned to the *U.S.S. Voyager.* In 2374 Culhane stood watch on the bridge of the *Voyager*. ("Revulsion" [VGR]).

Curneth. (Michael Canavan). **Tracer** agent for the **Ramuran** government. Curneth retrieved Kellin in 2374 after Kellin fled her culture in hopes of finding a new life aboard *Voyager*. Curneth brought Kellin back to Ramura, erasing her memories of the outside world, as well as any memories or computer records of Kellin aboard the *Voyager*. ("Unforgettable" [VGR]). *Michael Canavan previously played Tamal in "Defiant" (DS9).*

curried chicken. A culinary Earth dish of chicken cooked in spicy sauce. On a Starfleet runabout, replicator entree number 103 was curried chicken and rice with a side order of carrots. ("Blaze of Glory" [DS9]).

Curtis, Lieutenant. (Breon Gorman). Starfleet officer. Curtis served as attaché to Admiral Matthew Dougherty in 2375. (*Star Trek: Insurrection*).

Cusak, Lisa. (Debra Wilson). Starfleet officer, born in 2320, who was captain of the ***U.S.S. Olympia***. Cusak commanded the *Olympia* on an eight-year mission of long-range exploration in the Beta Quadrant from 2363 to 2371. Cusak narrowly escaped death when the *Olympia* was destroyed while investigating a Class-L planet in the Rutharian sector in 2371. Cusak's escape pod landed on the surface of the planet, where she survived for several days before succumbing to carbon-dioxide poisoning. Prior to her death, she called for help, using **subspace radio**. Cusak's signal, distorted through an energy barrier surrounding the planet, was time-shifted three years into her future. The signal permitted her to communicate for several days with members of the *Starship Defiant* crew, who became friends with this woman from the past whom they never met. SEE: **Irish wake**. ("The Sound of Her Voice" [DS9]). *Cusak was never seen; only her voice was heard.*

Cuzar, Regent. (Peggy Miley). Dignitary with the Evoran delegation to the Federation. She attended a reception aboard the *U.S.S. Enterprise*-E in 2375. (*Star Trek: Insurrection*).

Cyrik Ocean. Large body of water located on a home planet of the Vaskan and Kyrian peoples. ("Living Witness" [VGR]).

cytoplasmic life-form. Sentient organism from the Delta Quadrant. Cytoplasmic life has multiple neocortices in the form of a series of nodes clustered along the primary nerve. They use these nodes to control their starships through the use of biochemical secretions. When injured, cytoplasmic life-forms can attach themselves to another life-form to supplement their damaged systems, like a life preserver. Federation scientists aboard the *Starship Voyager* found cytoplasmic life to be extremely unusual and were unable to communicate with an individual of that species, even with the aid of a universal translator. ("Nothing Human" [VGR]).

cytotoxic shock. Prostration of bodily function caused by high levels of cytotoxins. Cytotoxic shock in humanoid patients can be treated with inaprovaline. ("Nothing Human" [VGR]).

cytotoxin. Biochemical substance, a poisonous byproduct of cellular metabolism. Excessive levels of cytotoxins can lead to cytotoxic shock. ("Nothing Human" [VGR]).

da Vinci workshop program Janeway-7. Holodeck program featuring a re-creation of Earth Renaissance master **Leonardo da Vinci** in his workshop in Italy around the year 1502. *Voyager* captain **Kathryn Janeway** enjoyed the program, as it offered an opportunity for her to escape from the stresses of starship command while getting to know the historical figure who was one of her heroes. ("Scorpion, Parts I and II" [VGR]).

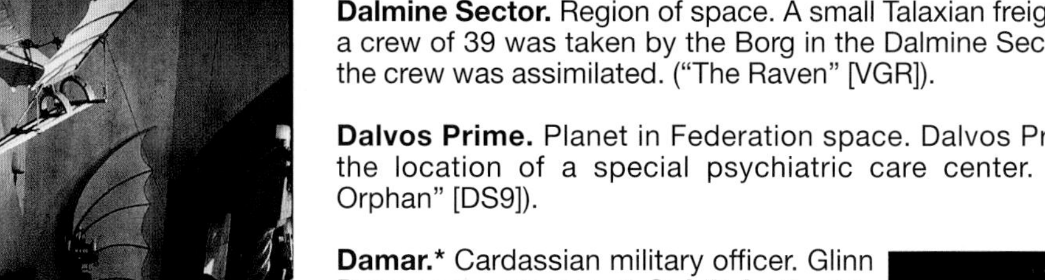

da Vinci, Leonardo. (John Rhys-Davies). Celebrated painter, draftsman, sculptor, architect, and scientist from Earth's **Renaissance** period. Leonardo da Vinci's genius, excelling in so many fields, epitomized the Renaissance ideal. He was generally believed to have lived from 1452 to 1519; historians were for centuries unaware that Leonardo was actually a man known as **Flint.** During his extraordinarily long life, Flint hid his nearly immortal nature by adopting many different identities, including Leonardo da Vinci. ("Requiem for Methuselah" [TOS]). Leonardo was a hero to *Voyager* captain **Kathryn Janeway**, who was a scientist by training. In late 2373, Janeway took the opportunity to work with da Vinci through the use of a **holodeck** re-creation of the master in his workshop as it may have existed in **Florence** around 1502. ("Scorpion, Parts I and II" [VGR]). The holographic version of da Vinci was stolen from *Voyager* on stardate 51386 by raider ships in the employ of a pirate named Tau in the Delta Quadrant. *Voyager* personnel were successful in recovering the holographic da Vinci, as well as several pieces of critical ship's equipment. In the process, the holographic Leonardo, working with Kathryn Janeway, was successful in building a heavier-than-air flying machine, a remarkable feat that even the original da Vinci had not been able to accomplish. ("Concerning Flight" [VGR]). *John Rhys-Davies also played Sallah in the motion picture* Raiders of the Lost Ark, *and Professor Maximillion Arturo in the television show* Sliders. *Leonardo's first appearance was in "Scorpion, Part I," and his last was in "Concerning Flight."*

Daelen. (Mary Elizabeth McGlynn; Dan Butler). Inhabitant of the Delta Quadrant. Daelen's genome was stolen by **Steth** sometime prior to stardate 51762. While in the body of a woman who was Steth's previous victim, Daelen caught up with his original body when it was occupied by Tom Paris. Paris and Daelen returned to *Voyager* and were able to compel Steth to return their bodies. ("Vis à Vis" [VGR]).

Dahkur Province.* Region of planet Bajor. Dahkur was a farming community. In the **mirror universe**, the hills of Dahkur were the site of several mining camps. ("Resurrection" [DS9]).

Daleth. (Rod Arrants). Vaskan ambassador. Daleth engaged in trade negotiations with Captain Kathryn Janeway in late 2374, just prior to the start of the **Great War** between the Vaskans and the Kyrians. Daleth's role in triggering the **Great War** was the topic of considerable disagreement by later scholars. ("Living Witness" [VGR]). *Rod Arrants previously played Rex in "Manhunt" (TNG).*

Dalmine Sector. Region of space. A small Talaxian freighter with a crew of 39 was taken by the Borg in the Dalmine Sector. All of the crew was assimilated. ("The Raven" [VGR]).

Dalvos Prime. Planet in Federation space. Dalvos Prime was the location of a special psychiatric care center. ("Time's Orphan" [DS9]).

Damar.* Cardassian military officer. Glinn Damar was present at **Gul Dukat**'s side when forces of the Cardassian and **Dominion** fleets recaptured station Deep Space 9 in 2373. ("Call to Arms" [DS9]). Around stardate 51145, Damar discovered a method of using an antigraviton beam to defeat the **self-replicating mine**s that blockaded the Bajoran wormhole. ("Behind the Lines" [DS9]). As Dukat's aide, Damar became concerned at Dukat's devotion to his daughter, **Tora Ziyal**, fearing that she might have loyalties to the Bajorans. Damar killed Ziyal in 2374 after hearing her confession that she had helped to sabotage the station's weapons systems. ("Sacrifice of Angels" [DS9]). By mid-2374, Damar had been promoted to **gul**, and he ruled Cardassia in place of Gul Dukat. ("Statistical Probabilities" [DS9]). The pressures of his responsibilities, as well as the untenable situation in which Damar found his people, led him to seek refuge in ***kanar***, an intoxicating beverage. ("Treachery, Faith, and the Great River" [DS9]). Damar soon realized that the Dominion cared nothing for the well-being of the Cardassian people. ("The Changing Face of Evil" [DS9]). He returned to his homeworld to rally his people to fight the Dominion. ("The Dogs of War" [DS9]). Damar was killed by Jem'Hadar forces during the final hours of the Dominion war, ironically fighting alongside former Bajoran terrorist **Kira Nerys**. ("What You Leave Behind" [DS9]). SEE: **Damar, Glinn** in main Encyclopedia.

Dammar. (Kenneth Tigar). **Nyrian** operative. Dammar was the first to be translocated to the *Voyager* in the Nyrian attempt to take over the ship on stardate 50912.4. ("Displaced" [VGR]).

Dark Time. Ten-year period in ancient **Klingon** history between the Second and Third Dynasties. The Dark Time was a period in which the empire was ruled by a council elected by the people. This was the first and only Klingon experiment in democratic government. The Dark Time began when General K'Trelan ended the Second Dynasty by assassinating Emperor Reclaw and the entire Imperial family. ("You Are Cordially Invited" [DS9]).

dark-matter nebula.* Interstellar dust or gas cloud that has no externally observable internal energy source. In 2374, a Jem'Hadar vessel commandeered by Captain Sisko and his staff was forced to take refuge in a dense dark-matter nebula in Cardassian space. The nebula contained a Class-M world that was not visible from outside the nebula. ("Rocks and Shoals" [DS9]).

Data.* Starfleet officer, the first artificial life-form to serve in the **Starfleet**. An android, Data did not breathe, and he could function underwater for extended periods of time. He was even able to alter his buoyancy so that he could walk underwater or float on the surface. His legs were 87.2 centimeters in length. Data's programming included a fail-safe that caused his ethical and moral subroutines to take over in the event that his cognitive functions were damaged. The fail-safe was designed to protect him against anyone who might try to take advantage of him in the event of severe memory loss. In 2375, Data served on a Federation sociology team, observing the **Ba'ku** homeworld, where he befriended a Ba'ku child named **Artim**. While there, he accidentally discovered a Son'a plot to conquer the Ba'ku planet. Data was fond of the works of **Gilbert and Sullivan**. (*Star Trek: Insurrection*).

Dauntless, U.S.S. Simulation of a Federation starship; a fraud fabricated by **Arturis** in 2374. Arturis had modified his own spacecraft to appear to be an experimental starship equipped with an innovative quantum slipstream drive system. Arturis had hoped to fool the crew of the *Starship Voyager* into believing that the *Dauntless* had been sent by Starfleet Command as a rescue ship. The ship was assimilated by the Borg after *Voyager* captain Janeway saw through the ruse. ("Hope and Fear" [VGR]). *The* Dauntless*'s fake registry number was NX-01A.*

Davis, Bobby. (Robert Duncan McNeill). Persona imposed upon **Thomas Paris** while under Hirogen **neural interface** control in the **French Resistance** holodeck program in late 2374. Davis was an officer with the American military, a lieutenant in the Fifth Armored Infantry of the **Allied Forces** in the war against **Nazi Germany** during Earth's 20th century. Davis visited the town of Sainte Claire prior to the war, where he fell in love with a beautiful French girl named **Brigette**. ("The Killing Game, Parts I and II" [VGR]).

Dax (symbiont).* The Dax symbiont was born in 2018. Dax was married six times as of 2374, twice as a groom, and three times as a bride. The first five ceremonies were conducted according to **Trill** custom, while the last was a Klingon wedding held at Deep Space 9. ("You Are Cordially Invited" [DS9]). Dax has had nine children, five as a mother and four as a father. ("Time's Orphan" [DS9]). The Jadzia host died in 2374 ("Tears of the Prophets" [DS9]) and the symbiont was subsequently transplanted to a new host, becoming **Ezri Dax**. ("Image in the Sand" [DS9]).

Dax, Audrid.* Fourth host to the **Dax symbiont**. Audrid loved to take walks in the woods. ("Shadows and Symbols" [DS9]).

Dax, Curzon.* Host to the **Dax symbiont** prior to Jadzia. Curzon Dax went on to negotiate the Khitomer Accords. Curzon never married. ("You Are Cordially Invited" [DS9]).

Dax, Emony.* Third host to the **Dax symbiont**. Emony was an Olympic gymnast ("Take Me Out to the Holosuite" [DS9]). She was an emotional individual ("Shadows and Symbols" [DS9]) who sometimes stood on her head to relax ("Afterimage" [DS9]).

Dax, Ezri. (Nicole deBoer). Ninth host of the **Dax** symbiont. ("Image in the Sand" [DS9]). Ensign Ezri Tigan was an assistant **counselor** aboard the *Starship Destiny* in late 2374 when the ship was assigned to transport the Dax symbiont back to **Trill**. En route, the medical condition of the symbiont took a turn for the worse, and it became necessary to implant it into the only Trill on the ship, Ensign Ezri Tigan. The newly joined Ezri Dax did her best to adjust to symbiotic life, despite the fact that she did not undergo the years of training and counseling normally required before joining. Also, she found that after joining, she tended to get queasy when traveling at warp speeds. ("Shadows and Symbols" [DS9]). Ezri had been right-handed, but became left-handed after her joining. At one point, she found joined life so difficult that she considered having the symbiont removed, but she soon found the inner strength necessary to adapt. Not only did she find she could still serve as an effective counselor, but she was promoted to the rank of lieutenant junior grade, and appointed as counselor for station **Deep Space 9**. Even so, she nearly declined the appointment out of respect for **Worf**'s discomfort at working in proximity to the new Dax host, until Worf indicated that he thought Jadzia would have wanted him to accept the new host. ("Afterimage" [DS9]). Ezri soon realized that she shared Jadzia's fondness for **Julian Bashir**. Ezri and Julian became romantically involved late in 2375. ("What You Leave Behind" [DS9]). *Nicole deBoer previously played Yuna in the* Mission: Genesis *television series. Ezri was first seen in "Image in the Sand," the first episode of* Star Trek: Deep Space Nine*'s seventh (and final) season.*

Dax, Jadzia.* Starfleet science officer assigned to station Deep Space 9. In late 2373, Worf and Jadzia became engaged to be married, just as the Dominion war was beginning. Jadzia, worried that Worf might welcome the glorious death that war might offer, insisted on the engagement so that Worf would have a good reason to keep himself alive. ("Call to Arms" [DS9]). Following the reassignment of Benjamin Sisko as Admiral Ross's adjutant in 2374, Dax served as captain of the *Starship Defiant*, conducting many hazardous missions against the Dominion. ("Behind the Lines" [DS9]). Jadzia's father's name was Kela. In 2374, on stardate 51247.5, Worf and Dax were married in a traditional Klingon **wedding** ceremony on Deep Space 9, at which time Dax was accepted into the House of Martok. ("You Are Cordially Invited" [DS9]). SEE: ***Bre'Nan* ritual.** Jadzia was deeply in love with Worf and hoped to raise a family with him. That dream was shattered in late 2374 when Dax was mortally wounded by a **Pah-wraith** inhabiting the body of **Gul Dukat**. Station medical personnel were successful in removing the Dax symbiont for transplantation, but Jadzia died shortly thereafter. ("Tears of the Prophets" [DS9]). Worf took Jadzia's death very hard. ("Image in the Sand" [DS9]). He found some measure of comfort in the fact that General Martok allowed him to command a dangerous mission to Monac IV, where he won a great victory in Jadzia's name, guaranteeing her entry into ***Sto-Vo-Kor***. ("Shadows and Symbols" [DS9]). *Jadzia Dax's last appearance was in "Tears of the Prophets."*

Dax, Tobin.* Second host to the **Dax symbiont**. Tobin had children, but he could never bring himself to discipline them, no matter what they did. Tobin was vegetarian. ("Afterimage" [DS9]).

Dax, Yedrin. (Gary Frank). Inhabitant of the planet **Gaia** in an alternate timeline. Yedrin Dax was descended from Jadzia Dax and Worf, who were stranded on Gaia in this timeline. Yedrin was the successor to Jadzia as host to the Dax symbiont. Yedrin ceased to exist in 2373 when the timeline vanished. ("Children of Time" [DS9]).

Day of Honor. Annual **Klingon** observance in which warriors test their honor by enduring a traditional ritual ordeal. During the Day of Honor, a warrior is expected to prepare by eating from the heart of a sanctified ***targ*** before drinking *mot'loch* from a **Grail of Kahless**. Next, the warrior must proclaim his or her battles during the past year before enduring such tests as the **Ritual of Twenty Painstiks**, combat with a ***bat'leth*** master, or a traverse of the sulfur lagoons of Gorath. **B'Elanna Torres** reluctantly agreed to observe the Day of Honor in 2374 in a holodeck re-creation of the Caves of Kahless, but she was unprepared for the demanding nature of the tests. ("Day of Honor" [VGR]). SEE: ***rokeg*** **blood pie.**

"Day of Honor." *Voyager* episode #72. Written by Jeri Taylor. Directed by Jesús Salvador Treviño. No stardate given. *First aired in 1997. Torres reluctantly observes the Klingon Day of Honor holiday and later finds herself floating stranded in deep space with Tom Paris, waiting to die when their environmental suits run out of oxygen. In this episode B'Elanna Torres admits that she loves Tom Paris.* GUEST CAST: Alexander Enberg as **Vorik;** Alan Altshuld as **Lumas;** Michael A. Krawic as **Rahmin;** Kevin P. Stillwell as **Moklor.** SEE: **Borg; Caatati; Caves of Kahless; *Cochrane, Shuttlecraft*; Day of Honor; environmental suit; Gorath; Grail of Kahless; holodeck and holosuite programs: Day of Honor; Lumas; matter/antimatter reaction chamber; Moklor; *mot'loch*; Nicoletti, Susan; painstik, Klingon; Paris, Thomas; Rahmin; Ritual of Twenty Painstiks; *rokeg* blood pie; security access code; space walk; Starfleet Academy; *targ*; thorium; Torres, B'Elanna; transwarp.**

de Neuf, Mademoiselle. (Jeri Ryan). Persona imposed upon **Seven of Nine** while under Hirogen **neural interface** control in the **French Resistance** holodeck program. Mademoiselle de Neuf was a beautiful singer in a French tavern who was also a member of the underground, fighting against the Nazi occupation of her homeland. de Neuf entertained audiences at **Le Coeur de Lion** with such period songs as "It Can't Be Wrong," "Moonlight Becomes You," and "That Old Black Magic." ("The Killing Game, Parts I and II" [VGR]). *Mademoiselle de Neuf translates as "Lady of Nine."*

decibel. Unit of measure for comparing sound intensity. One-tenth of a bel. Abbreviated dB. Sound above 140 dB can cause pain in the human ear. ("Blaze of Glory" [DS9]).

Decker. Engineer assigned to Deep Space 9 in 2373. ("In the Cards" [DS9]).

Decos Prime. Planet. In 2375, Decos Prime was the site of a Federation base. ("Treachery, Faith, and the Great River" [DS9]).

Deep Space 9.* Space station formerly known as Terok Nor. Deep Space 9 was constructed in 2346. ("Wrongs Darker Than Death or Night" [DS9]). *The earlier editions of this encyclopedia (as well as the* Star Trek Chronology*) gave the date for the station's construction as 2351, as inferred from "Babel" (DS9), but "Wrongs Darker Than Death or Night" (DS9) clearly established the date as 2346.* The station operated on a 26-hour-day cycle. ("Ties of Blood and Water" [DS9]). Late in 2373, the station once again became a focus of the escalating conflict with the Dominion. Benjamin Sisko, fearful that the Dominion was about to send a massive invasion fleet to the Alpha Quadrant, ordered the Bajoran wormhole to be blockaded with thousands of **self-replicating mine**s. Shortly thereafter, the Bajoran Chamber of Ministers, acting on advice from Sisko (as the Emissary to the Prophets), voted to sign a nonaggression pact with the Dominion. This forced the Bajoran government to expel all Starfleet personnel from Deep Space 9 and to turn the station to Dominion and Cardassian control. ("Call to Arms" [DS9]). The occupying forces focused on disabling the minefield so that Dominion reinforcements could be sent to the Alpha Quadrant through the Bajoran wormhole. The minefield remained active long enough for a Starfleet task force, commanded by Captain Benjamin Sisko, to break through Dominion lines and retake the station. The costly operation was made possible by direct intervention by the Prophets, who destroyed a large number of Dominion vessels in the wormhole. ("Sacrifice of Angels" [DS9]). Following the end of the Dominion war in 2375, Colonel **Kira Nerys** assumed command of the station, succeeding Starfleet officer Benjamin Sisko, who had left the linear realm to walk among the Bajoran Prophets. ("What You Leave Behind" [DS9]).

"Deep Space Nine." Unpublished **science-fiction** novella written in 1953 by Earth novelist **Benny Russell**. "Deep Space Nine" was the first in a series of compelling stories of a man named **Benjamin Sisko**, who commanded an alien space station on the edge of the final frontier. Science-fiction aficionado **Darlene Kursky** thought "Deep Space Nine" was the finest story she had read since **Robert Heinlein**'s ***The Puppet Masters***. Unfortunately, Russell's publishers feared the fact that the story featured a black man as its hero would make it unacceptable to mid-20th-century readers, so the story remained unpublished. ("Far Beyond the Stars" [DS9]). *Fortunately, Paramount Pictures had no such reservations in producing a television series with the same title.*

defender. Soldier in the **Vori** military in their war against the **Kradin**. ("Nemesis" [VGR]).

Defiant, U.S.S.* Federation starship assigned to starbase **Deep Space 9**. The *U.S.S. Defiant* had a class-7 warp drive ("One Little Ship" [DS9]), which was exceptionally powerful. Because of this, it could ionize nebular gases. This rendered the ship detectable in the **Badlands**, even when under cloak. ("Blaze of Glory" [DS9]). In 2373, the crew of the *Defiant* numbered about 50 people. The *Defiant* encountered a temporal anomaly at planet **Gaia**, creating an alternate timeline in which the ship was destroyed 200 years in the past, stranding the crew in the Gamma Quadrant. Although the timeline was excised, members of the *Defiant* crew did retain memory of the incident. ("Children of Time" [DS9]). The *Defiant* was destroyed by Breen forces in late 2375, just before the final battles of the Dominion war. ("The Changing Face of Evil" [DS9]). Several weeks later, when the *Defiant*-class *U.S.S. Sao Paulo* was assigned as a replacement to Deep Space 9, Admiral Ross granted special dispensation to Captain Benjamin Sisko to rename the new ship *U.S.S. Defiant*. ("The Dogs of War" [DS9]). The new *Defiant* played a pivotal role in the final battle of the Dominion war. ("What You Leave Behind" [DS9]).

Degora Street. Thoroughfare located in the industrial district on planet **Farius Prime**. ("Honor Among Thieves" [DS9]).

Dejaren. (Leland Orser). A holographic technician aboard a Serosian starship. Designated as an HD-25 isomorphic projection, Dejaren was assigned to perform hazardous tasks such as cleaning the reactor core and ejecting antimatter waste. Over time Dejaren began to experience a serious malfunction of his personality subroutines. He began to hate organic life-forms, becoming violently deranged. Around stardate 51186 he killed the vessel's six crew members. After experiencing problems in his holographic projection systems, he sent a distress call. *U.S.S. Voyager* personnel Torres and the Doctor responded to the call, but were forced to destroy Dejaren when he attacked both *Voyager* crew members. ("Revulsion" [VGR]). *Leland Orser previously played Gai in "Sanctuary" (DS9) and Colonel Lovok in "The Die is Cast" (DS9).*

Dell. Starfleet crew member assigned to the *U.S.S. Voyager*. In 2374, when Captain Janeway enlisted the ship's crew to help carry out the Omega Directive, Dell was assigned the task of recalibrating the ionic pressure seals of a harmonic resonance chamber. For the project, Seven of Nine designated Dell as "Three of Ten." ("The Omega Directive" [VGR]).

***Delta Flyer*.** Advanced shuttlecraft designed and built by the crew of the *U.S.S. Voyager* in early 2375. The *Delta Flyer* featured ultra-aerodynamic contours, retractable nacelles, parametallic hull plating, a tetraburnium alloy hull, unimatrix shielding, and Borg-inspired weapons systems including photonic missiles. ("Extreme Risk" [VGR]). The ship also employed **duranium** construction in its hull. ("Once Upon a Time" [VGR]). Thomas Paris, who was responsible for the basic design of the spacecraft, incorporated ancient control levers and meters from his Captain Proton holoprogram into the *Delta Flyer*'s pilot control console because he wanted to feel the ship he was piloting. Numerous other *Voyager* crew members collaborated on the *Flyer*'s design and construction. On its first mission, the shuttle entered the atmosphere of a gas giant planet on a mission to retrieve *Voyager*'s advanced multispatial probe. SEE: ***Captain Proton, The Adventures of*.** ("Extreme Risk" [VGR]). The *Delta Flyer* was seriously damaged during an ion storm when it was forced to make its first planetfall. The shuttle and its crew were trapped in a cavern under tons of rock, but both survived due to the robust construction techniques employed in the vessel. ("Once Upon a Time" [VGR]). *The* Delta Flyer *was designed by series production designer Richard James and senior illustrator Rick Sternbach.*

delta radiation.* Form of energy. Exposure to delta radiation can weaken such metals as viterium. ("*Valiant*" [DS9]).

Demon-Class planet. Informal name for a Class-Y world. SEE: **planetary classification system: Class-Y**. ("Demon" [VGR]).

"Demon." *Voyager* episode #92. Teleplay by Kenneth Biller. Story by Andre Bormanis. Directed by Anson Williams. No stardate given. *First aired in 1998. On a planet with an extremely hostile environment, the* Voyager *crew discovers a living liquid life-form that is evolving by creating exact copies of ship's personnel. Duplicates of the entire crew remain on the planet after the ship departs.* GUEST CAST: Alexander Enberg as **Vorik**; Susan Lewis as Transporter technician. SEE: **antigrav; Demon-class planet; dermalplast; deuterium; gray mode; Jirex; mimetic life-form; Nozawa; planetary classification system: Class-Y; thermionic radiation.**

Denevan crystals. Contraband material. It was a Federation crime to possess or sell Denevan crystals. In late 2374, Quark made a profit of 200 bars of latinum when he sold Denevan crystals to a Nausicaan entrepreneur. ("The Sound of Her Voice" [DS9]).

derada. Board game. Derada was a complex and subtle game of strategy played with eight pieces on each side on a board with sixteen spaces. Tom Paris and B'Elanna Torres played derada while traveling through the Void aboard the *Voyager* in 2375. ("Night" [VGR]).

dermalplast. Medical preparation used to treat chemical burns. ("Demon" [VGR]).

Derna. Planetoid. The fourth satellite orbiting the planet **Bajor**. In early 2375, Derna was uninhabited. During the **Dominion** war, the Bajoran Chamber of Ministers gave the Romulans permission to set up a hospital facility on Derna at the request of **Senator Cretak**. In addition to the hospital, however, the Romulans also deployed 7,000 plasma torpedoes on Derna, raising serious Bajoran questions about Romulan intentions. ("Image in the Sand" [DS9]). The Bajoran Militia subsequently blockaded Derna, preventing Romulan access to the planetoid until the Romulan government agreed to remove the weapons. ("Shadows and Symbols" [DS9]).

Destiny, U.S.S. Federation starship. In late 2374, shortly after the death of Jadzia Dax, the *Destiny* was assigned to transport the ailing Dax symbiont from Deep Space 9 back to Trill. Along the way, Dax took a turn for the worse. Ensign Ezri Tigan was the only Trill aboard the vessel, and became the new **Ezri Dax**. ("Shadows and Symbols" [DS9]). The *Destiny* returned to Deep Space 9 in early 2375 before joining the Seventh Fleet at Kalandra. Dax was to have rejoined the ship's crew but she opted instead to accept a posting to Deep Space 9. The *Destiny* was commanded by Captain Raymer. ("Afterimage" [DS9]). Destiny *is also the name of the United States' scientific lab module for the International Space Station.*

***deus ex machina*.** Latin for "god from the machine." *Deus ex machina* was a literary device used by some ancient Earth playwrights wherein, at the end of a play, characters would be helped out of their terrible plights by a god descending from the heavens. SEE: **"Dictates of Poetics."** ("Worse Case Scenario" [VGR]).

deuterium injector. Component of a Starfleet starship's warp propulsion system. ("One Little Ship" [DS9]).

"Dictates of Poetics." Essay by T'Hain of Vulcan, a guide to dramatic writing. "Dictates of Poetics" proffered that a character's actions must flow inexorably from his or her established traits. ("Worse Case Scenario" [VGR]).

dicyclic warp signature. Energy characteristic produced by the warp engines of **Hirogen** vessels, by which the ships could be identified by long-range sensors. ("Prey" [VGR]).

Diego, Captain. Starfleet officer. In 2374, Captain Diego commanded one of the Starfleet vessels that participated in the retaking of station Deep Space 9 from Dominion control in 2374. ("Sacrifice of Angels" [DS9]).

dilithium.* Crystalline substance used in warp propulsion systems aboard starships. **Metreon radiation**, even at very low levels, can cause a ship's dilithium matrix to collapse. ("The Sound of Her Voice" [DS9]). In 2374, the crew of the *Starship Voyager* negotiated with Vaskan representatives to obtain dilithium crystals in exchange for medical supplies. "Living Witness" [VGR]).

dilitus lobe. Structure of the **Voth** brain that was responsible for their sense of smell. Voth olfactory abilities were much more sensitive than that of many humanoid species. ("Distant Origin" [VGR]).

dinosaur. SEE: **hadrosaur; Voth.**

dispersion field. Energetic flux used to prevent the function of a transporter beam into a specific area. ("Concerning Flight" [VGR]).

"Displaced." *Voyager* episode #66. Written by Lisa Klink. Directed by Allan Kroeker. Stardate 50912.4. *First aired in 1997. One by one, the crew of the* Voyager *are replaced by invading Nyrians, with the crew being held captive in a habitat aboard a distant starship.* GUEST CAST: Mark L. Taylor as **Jarleth**; Nancy Youngblut as **Taleen**; James Noah as **Rislan**; Lawrence Rosenthal as **Molina, Ensign**. SEE: **Argala; baby wormhole; Dammar; Emergency Medical Hologram; holodeck and holosuite programs: *Bat'leth* combat workout; Jarleth; Klingons; Lang; Molina, Ensign; Nyria III; Nyrian vessel; Nyrians; Rislan; Starfleet Academy; *tal'oth*; Taleen; translocator; Tuvok.**

Distant Origin Theory. Controversial theory developed by **Voth** scientist **Forra Gegen** in 2363, hypothesizing that his people may have evolved on an unknown distant planet, migrating to the Delta Quadrant some 20 million years ago. Gegen uncovered strong evidence supporting his theory in 2373 with the discovery on planet **Hanon IV** of remains of a sentient being from a planet called **Earth** in the Alpha Quadrant. If true, this dramatic finding would have challenged **Voth Doctrine** that the Voth had originated in the Delta Quadrant. Although Gegen's evidence, based on comparative genetic data, was compelling, the Voth Ministry of Elders strongly disagreed. Gegen was accused of **heresy** and was forced to recant his beliefs. SEE: **hadrosaur; Hogan.** ("Distant Origin" [VGR]).

"Distant Origin." *Voyager* episode #65. Written by Brannon Braga & Joe Menosky. Directed by David Livingston. No stardate given. *First aired in 1997. An alien scientist contacts the* Voyager *to gain proof of his theory that his people descended from Earth's dinosaurs. No regular* Star Trek: Voyager *cast members were seen during the first 13 minutes of the show.* GUEST CAST: Henry Woronicz as **Gegen, Forra**; Marshall R. Teague as **Haluk**; Concetta Tomei as **Odala, Minister**; Christopher Liam Moore as **Veer, Tova**. SEE: **bio-dart; Cretaceous Period; dilitus lobe; Distant Origin Theory; Earth; eryops; Frola; Gegen, Forra; hadrosaur; Haluk; heresy; Hogan; Nekrit Supply Depot; Odala, Minister; portation; security access code; transwarp; vasodilation; Veer, Tova; Voth city ship; Voth Doctrine; Voth Ministry of Elders; Voth.**

DNA resequencing. SEE: **accelerated critical neural pathway formation.**

Doctor's family program Beta-Rho. Holodeck simulation program designed to allow the *Starship Voyager*'s **Emergency Medical Hologram** to experience the challenges of family life in humanoid society. In the program, the Doctor was married to a human woman named **Charlene**. The couple had two children, **Jeffrey** and **Belle**. The Doctor's initial version of the program portrayed all three characters as unrealistically idealized humans, but later the Doctor modified the family to more accurately resemble an actual family. He found the program unsettling but ultimately rewarding as he experienced the pain and joy of human life. ("Real Life" [VGR]).

Dominion battleship. Massive warship used by the Dominion in its war with the Alpha Quadrant powers. Cadet **Tim Watters**, in command of the ***U.S.S. Valiant*** in 2374, conducted a foolhardy attempt to destroy a Dominion battleship, resulting in his death and the loss of his ship and nearly his entire crew. ("*Valiant*" [DS9]).

Dominion.* Civilization in the **Gamma Quadrant**, ruled by the **Founders**. Once the Dominion established the alliance with the **Cardassians**, **Jem'Hadar** forces conducted a massive buildup of arms and spacecraft at Cardassia Prime throughout 2373. The Dominion incursion continued on diplomatic fronts as well, as the Vorta were successful in negotiating non jaggression pacts with the **Romulan Star Empire**, the Tholian Assembly, the Miradorn, and the **Bajorans**. The Federation, fearful that an invasion was imminent, established a minefield around the Bajoran wormhole, preventing further Dominion ship movement from the Gamma Quadrant. Dominion forces in the Alpha Quadrant responded by launching a massive assault on Federation starbase **Deep Space 9**. Simultaneously, Starfleet and Klingon forces launched a devastating strike against Dominion shipyards at Torros III. ("Call to Arms" [DS9]). Even with the Starfleet minefield blockading the wormhole, Dominion forces in the Alpha Quadrant inflicted extremely heavy casualties on the Federation and Klingon fleets through the early months of 2374. Perhaps the greatest Starfleet losses occurred at the Tyra system, where Jem'Hadar forces destroyed some 98 Federation vessels. ("A Time To Stand" [DS9]). The war continued badly for the Alpha Quadrant powers until later in that year when the Romulan Star Empire abrogated its nonaggression treaty with the Dominion. A massive assault by Federation, Klingon, and Romulan forces that captured the **Chin'toka System** from Cardassian control represented a major turning point in the war. SEE: **orbital weapon platform.** ("Tears of the Prophets" [DS9]). Nevertheless, aided by **Breen** forces and sophisticated Breen weaponry, the Dominion overwhelmed the Alpha Quadrant powers, despite the fact that a deadly virus was infecting the **Great Link**. ("The Changing Face of Evil" [DS9]). This biological weapon, a genetically engineered disease developed by the Federation's Section 31, nearly wiped out the Founders. ("When It Rains..." [DS9]). Despite an overwhelmingly powerful military force, the Dominion began to lose ground when the Alpha Quadrant powers developed the means to defend against Breen technology. ("Dogs of War" [DS9]). The Dominion, under the guidance of the **Founder Leader**, retreated to Cardassia Prime and adopted a siege strategy, hoping to hold off the Alpha Quadrant powers long enough to produce more ships and troops. Sensing Dominion vulnerability, the Alpha Quadrant powers launched a desperate final assault that overpowered the Dominion forces when the Cardassian military turned against the Founders. Nevertheless, the Founder Leader refused to surrender. She ordered all Dominion forces to fight to the death, leading the Alpha Quadrant leaders to anticipate an extremely high death toll. However, when **Odo** linked with her, curing her of the shapeshifter disease, his gesture of trust helped her understand that the Great Link could indeed live in peace with the solids of the galaxy. The Founder Leader subsequently ordered all Dominion forces to surrender. The Great Link itself was cured when Odo returned to his people after the end of the Dominion war. ("What You Leave Behind" [DS9]).

Don Carlo. Italian opera by Giuseppe Verdi, completed in 1867. The holographic doctor aboard *Voyager* enjoyed singing in a duet in a holodeck performance of *Don Carlo*. ("Night" [VGR]).

Donatu V.* Planet. The Klingon bird-of-prey *Rotarran* escorted a convoy to Donatu V in 2374 during the conflict between the Alpha Quadrant and the Dominion. ("Sons and Daughters" [DS9]).

Dorado. Starfleet officer aboard the *U.S.S. Voyager*. On stardate 51501.4, Dorado received a letter from her home via a Starfleet transmission sent through a **Hirogen relay station**. ("Hunters" [VGR]).

Dorala system. Region of space in the Alpha Quadrant. In 2374, during the Dominion war, General Martok dispatched three Klingon attack cruisers to bolster the defense perimeter around the Dorala system. ("The Reckoning" [DS9]).

Doran. Klingon warrior, daughter of W'mar. In 2374, Doran transferred from the *Vor'nak* to the *Rotarran*. ("Sons and Daughters" [DS9]).

Dougherty, Admiral Matthew. (Anthony Zerbe). High-ranking Starfleet officer. In 2375, Dougherty conspired with the Son'a to steal the Ba'ku planet from its inhabitants. Working with **Ahdar Ru'afo**, a **Son'a** official, Dougherty had hoped to harness an unusual metaphasic radiation particle field around the planet, so that the rejuvenating properties of the planet could be made available to all senior Starfleet and Federation officials. Dougherty planned to divert Federation attention from the planet so that he could use a **holoship** to remove the world's 600 inhabitants. Dougherty died on a Son'a ship after officers from the *Enterprise*-E were successful in stopping his plan. (*Star Trek: Insurrection*). *Anthony Zerbe played Matthias in the 1971 science-fiction film* The Omega Man, *which was based on* I Am Legend, *a story by Richard Matheson, who also wrote "The Enemy Within" (TOS).*

doughnut. A small, toroidally shaped pastry, cooked by deep frying in fat, popular on Earth as a breakfast or dessert food. ("Far Beyond the Stars" [DS9]).

Douglas, Sarina. (Faith C. Salie). Individual who, as a child, had been genetically altered through illegal **accelerated critical neural pathway formation**. Although the procedure was successful in enhancing Sarina's abilities, it made her emotionally withdrawn, almost to the point of catatonia, and she was institutionalized for most of her childhood and early adult life. Under the care of Starfleet psychiatrist Dr. Karen Loews, Sarina and three other genetically enhanced individuals traveled to starbase Deep Space 9 in 2374 to meet **Julian Bashir**. SEE: **Jack**. ("Statistical Probabilities" [DS9]). Bashir determined that her cataleptic condition was caused by a failure of her visual and auditory synapses to operate fast enough for her enhanced cerebral cortex. A risky experimental surgical procedure, conducted by Bashir, was successful in stimulating the growth of new synapses in her thalamus, restoring her ability to interact with other people. Douglas was released from the care of the institute, and she subsequently accepted a scientific internship at the Corgal Research Center. ("Chrysalis" [DS9]). *Sarina was first seen in "Statistical Probabilities," and got her last name in "Chrysalis."*

dream species. Telepathic humanoid civilization in the **Delta Quadrant**. These people lived in a cave and their consciousness existed only in a dream state. For centuries, the dream species had suffered attacks from a variety of outsiders they referred to as the waking species. In order to protect themselves, the dream species took refuge in underground caverns. They established an artificial **neurogenic field** surrounding their planet, causing intruders from any waking species to fall asleep. Once in the realm of sleep, the dream species could deal with such intruders on their own terms. In 2374 the *Starship Voyager* accidentally entered the dream species's neurogenic field, causing the crew to enter a state of **hyper-REM** sleep. The dream species held *Voyager* captive in their reality until Chakotay was able to enter a lucid dreaming state, confronting the humanoids and convincing them to dismantle the transmitter. ("Waking Moments" [VGR]).

drone. Small self-piloted flying devices used by the Son'a to track and pursue Ba'ku villagers in order to implant them with isolinear tags. Once a drone implanted a tag on a person, it would allow that person to be beamed up even in the presence of transporter inhibitors. (*Star Trek: Insurrection*).

"Drone." *Voyager* episode #96. Teleplay by Bryan Fuller and Brannon Braga & Joe Menosky. Story by Bryan Fuller and Harry Doc Kloor. Directed by Les Landau. No stardate given. *First aired in 1998. A new Borg drone is born when a transporter accident fuses nanoprobes from Seven of Nine and DNA from a* Voyager *crew member with the Doctor's 29th-century mobile emitter.* GUEST CAST: J. Paul Boehmer as **One;** Todd Babcock as **Mulchaey, Ensign;** Majel Barrett as Computer Voice. SEE: **Borg sphere; class-2 shuttlecraft; duranium; gravimetric shear; holo-imager; maturation chamber; mobile emitter; Mulchaey, Ensign; One; polydeutonic alloy; protonebula; proximity transceiver; Seven of Nine; *Voyager, U.S.S.***

Corbis

Du Bois, W.E.B. William Edward Burghardt Du Bois (1868–1963). Sociologist who led the fight for social and economic justice for the African-American population of the American nation on 20th-century Earth. Du Bois was one of the founders of the National Association for the Advancement of Colored People (NAACP). **Benny Russell** drew inspiration from Du Bois's work. ("Far Beyond the Stars" [DS9]).

duck blind.* In anthropological studies, a concealed observation post used for field studies of a native population. A Federation sociology team sent to observe the Ba'ku on their planet in 2375 set up a cloaked duck blind in a rock face overlooking the **Ba'ku** village. (*Star Trek: Insurrection*).

Dukat, Gul.* (Marc Alaimo). Cardassian military officer. Dukat returned to station **Deep Space 9**, redesignated as **Terok Nor**, in late 2373 when the Dominion took control of the station during the early days of the Dominion war. ("Call to Arms" [DS9]). Dukat was pleased when his daughter, **Tora Ziyal**, returned to the station to live with him, but he soon became fearful that she was rejecting her Cardassian heritage in favor of Bajoran influence. ("Sons and Daughters" [DS9]). Those fears were powerfully confirmed when Ziyal joined the Bajoran underground and was instrumental in the subsequent Dominion loss of the station to the Federation Starfleet. Nevertheless, Dukat loved his daughter and was devastated when she was killed by **Glinn Damar**. ("Sacrifice of Angels" [DS9]). Dukat, who was taken into Starfleet custody with the retaking of Deep Space 9, fell into deep depression after his daughter's death. He experienced severe hallucinations when he and Sisko were stranded together following the destruction of their Starfleet transport. It was during this period that Sisko learned that Dukat felt no remorse for the five million Bajoran people who were killed while he was prefect of **Bajor**. Dukat admitted that he believed Bajorans to be an inferior race and said he felt it was a mistake not to have killed all Bajorans. Early in his military career, shortly after his promotion to **glinn**, Dukat had served aboard the Cardassian vessel *Kornaire*. ("Waltz" [DS9]). Dukat attempted to regain his influence in the Cardassian military by employing an energy being known as a **Pah-wraith**, an enemy of the Bajoran Prophets. The Pah-wraith, working through Dukat's body, darkened the Bajoran **Orbs** and collapsed the wormhole. In the process, Dukat and the Pah-wraith also caused the death of **Jadzia Dax**. ("Tears of the Prophets" [DS9]). While serving as prefect of Bajor in 2346, Dukat enjoyed the companionship of a Bajoran **comfort woman** named **Kira Meru**. Kira, who was the mother of Kira Nerys, stayed with Dukat for about seven years until her death in 2353. ("Wrongs Darker Than Death or Night" [DS9]). *In "A Time to Stand" (DS9) we learned that Dukat's initials were S. G.* In 2375, Dukat became a follower of the evil **Pah-Wraith** known as **Kosst Amojan**. He disguised himself as a Bajoran national, calling himself Anjohl Tennan. He led Kai **Winn** to believe that he had been sent to her by the Prophets ("Til Death Do Us Part" [DS9]) Dukat manipulated Winn, feeding her resentment against Benjamin Sisko to weaken her faith in the Bajoran Prophets, eventually leading her to worship the Pah-wraiths. ("Strange Bedfellows" [DS9]). Dukat and Winn nearly succeeded in freeing the Pah-wraiths from the fire cave on Bajor. Neither Dukat nor the Pah-wraiths counted on the determination of the Emissary, who returned to Bajor to confront Kosst Amojan and returned all of the Pah-wraiths to the fire caves. Dukat became trapped with the Pah-wraiths and was believed destroyed. ("What You Leave Behind" [DS9]).

Dumah. (Mickey Cottrell). Representative of the **B'omar Sovereignty**. In 2374, Dumah and Gauman came aboard *Voyager* to negotiate a shortcut through their space. ("The Raven" [VGR]). *Mickey Cottrell previously played Chancellor Alrik in "The Perfect Mate" (TNG).*

Dunes. Luxury hotel and casino complex that was located in **Las Vegas** on Earth from the mid 1950s until 1993. **Vic Fontaine** was among the celebrities who dined at the Dunes. ("His Way" [DS9]).

Duran'Adar. Jem'Hadar sixth, who was part of a squad that commandeered the Federation starship *Defiant* on stardate 51474.2. ("One Little Ship" [DS9]).

duranium.* Metal alloy. *Voyager*'s hull was largely constructed from duranium alloy. ("Drone" [VGR]). Duranium was also used in the construction of the ***Delta Flyer***. ("Once Upon a Time" [VGR]).

dynamite. Chemical explosive developed on Earth by 19th-century scientist Alfred Nobel. Although intended by Nobel for industrial and construction applications, dynamite was used as a deadly weapon of war in such conflicts as Earth's **World War II**. ("The Killing Game, Part II" [VGR]).

ear-lift surgery. Cosmetic surgery performed on Ferengi to make their earlobes firmer. In 2374 Ishka traveled to Vulcan for cosmetic ear-lifting surgery to improve her looks. ("The Magnificent Ferengi" [DS9]).

Earth.* Third planet in the Sol system. Millions of years ago, Earth was dominated by a wide variety of reptilian life-forms, including those later known as dinosaurs. Most dinosaurs became extinct at the end of the Cretaceous Period some 60 million years ago. However, some hadrosaurs survived on an isolated land mass, where they evolved into an intelligent species that eventually became known as the **Voth**. Although the Voth homeland on Earth was eventually destroyed, the technologically advanced Voth had by that time developed spaceflight capability, and survived by traveling into space. They eventually settled in the Delta Quadrant of the galaxy, where they lost all records of their origin. SEE: **Distant Origin Theory**. ("Distant Origin" [VGR]). In the 24th century, Earth was home to many species such as Bolians, Vulcans, and Ktarians. ("Hope and Fear" [VGR]). Earth suffered a major attack by the **Breen** in 2375 when the Dominion war reached into the heart of Federation space. The city of San Francisco, headquarters for the Starfleet, suffered massive damage and loss of life in the attack. ("The Changing Face of Evil" [DS9]).

Eaton, Julius. (Alexander Siddig). Twentieth-century Earth writer of **science fiction** and fantasy. Eaton was a staff contributor to the pulp magazine ***Incredible Tales***. Eaton was married to Kay Eaton, a fellow writer. ("Far Beyond the Stars" [DS9]). *Alexander Siddig also played Dr. Julian Bashir on* Star Trek: Deep Space Nine*.*

Eaton, Kay. (Nana Visitor). Author who in 1953 wrote **science fiction** and fantasy stories for the pulp magazine ***Incredible Tales.*** Eaton resided in the Earth city of New York and was married to Julius Eaton and worked under the pen name of K.C. Hunter. Eaton used the sexually ambiguous pseudonym to conceal her gender because Earth society of that day did not give equal respect or equal pay to women writers. ("Far Beyond the Stars" [DS9]). *Nana Visitor also played Kira Nerys, although Kay did not have a wrinkled nose.*

"Echoes of the Void." Concerto written by **Harry Kim** aboard the *Starship Voyager* in 2375. Kim, who performed the piece on his clarinet, was inspired to write "Echoes of the Void" when the ship traveled through the seemingly endless expanse informally known as the **Void** in the Delta Quadrant. ("Night" [VGR]).

Eddington, Michael.* Starfleet officer who joined the Maquis terrorist group. Eddington married fellow Maquis member **Rebecca Sullivan** in 2373. Two weeks later, he was arrested by Starfleet authorities. He was released several months later when it was feared that Eddington's Maquis group had engineered a devastating missile attack against Cardassia Prime, an attack that could have drawn both the Cardassians and the Federation into an all-out war. Captain Benjamin Sisko transported Eddington to the **Badlands** to persuade him to provide information on the suspected sneak attack, but learned that there was in fact no attack in progress. The apparent attack was a fake engineered by Eddington's wife. Once in the Badlands, Eddington was killed by **Jem'Hadar** troops while helping Sisko evacuate the surviving members of Eddington's Maquis group from planet Athos IV. Rebecca Sullivan was among the survivors. ("Blaze of Glory" [DS9]).

Eelwasser. Brand name of a popular Ferengi beverage sold on Ferenginar and elsewhere. Eelwasser's chief competitor was **Slug-o-Cola**. ("Profit and Lace" [DS9]).

Eight-four-seven-two (8472), Species. SEE: **Species 8472**.

Einstein, Albert.* Theoretical physicist on 20th-century Earth. Einstein's work contributed significantly to the invention of deadly nuclear fission weapons by his people. Einstein regretted his role in developing the atomic bomb for the remainder of his life, despite the fact that its use was instrumental in ending Earth's devastating second world war in 1945. In 2374, Starfleet captain Kathryn Janeway, wrestling with the discovery of the incredibly destructive **Omega molecule**, came to understand how Einstein must have felt about the atomic bomb. ("The Omega Directive" [VGR]).

El Gatark. Region of space in Federation territory. El Gatark was held by enemy forces in 2374 during the **Dominion** war. ("*Valiant*" [DS9]).

Elder. In the **Jem'Hadar** culture, a title conveying great honor, bestowed upon a soldier who has survived to the advanced age of 20. ("To the Death" [DS9]). Ixtana'Rax was an Elder. ("One Little Ship" [DS9]).

electron resonance scanner. Medical imaging device. In 2374, the Doctor used an electron resonance scanner to help determine that genetic tags had been secretly placed in the crew by the Srivani. ("Scientific Method" [VGR]).

eliminator. In Ferengi society, an individual who earns his living by murdering people in exchange for payment. Eliminators are generally regarded by some as being psychopathic. **Leck** was an eliminator. ("The Magnificent Ferengi" [DS9]).

Ellison, Ralph. Twentieth-century Earth writer who won prominence with his first and only novel, *Invisible Man* (1952). The book was the powerful story of an African-American man who traveled from the southern region of his country to a northern community called Harlem, where he fought for social justice against racial discrimination, only to be ignored by those he'd hoped to help. **Benny Russell** drew inspiration from Ellison's work. ("Far Beyond the Stars" [DS9]).

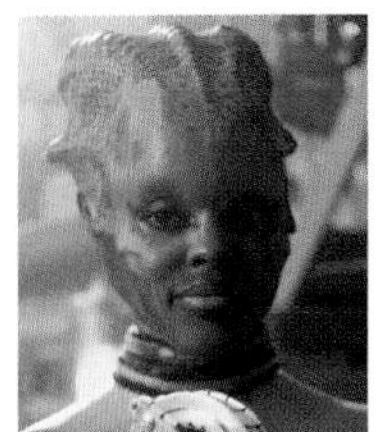

Ellora. Humanoid civilization. The Ellora were conquered early in the 24th century by the **Son'a**. By the late 24th century, the Ellora were integrated into Son'a society as a labor class. Elloran women were indentured as servants on Son'a spacecraft. (*Star Trek: Insurrection*).

Emck, Controller. (Ken Magee). Master of a **Malon** export vessel that operated in the eleventh gradient. Emck engaged in the highly profitable business of disposing of his nation's toxic antimatter waste products by dumping them into a region of space informally known as the **Void**. Unfortunately, this practice produced high levels of hazardous theta radiation, which was severely deleterious to **night beings** living in the Void. When Emck learned of this, he elected to continue dumping anyway, until he was forced to discontinue the practice by the Federation starship *Voyager*. ("Night" [VGR]).

Emergency Medical Hologram backup module. (Robert Picardo). Redundant EMH program unit carried by some Federation starships. The **Emergency Medical Hologram** backup module was intended to provide medical services for the ship's crew in the event that the main EMH program was damaged or destroyed. The EMH backup module from the Federation starship *Voyager* was stolen by followers of Tedran in the Delta Quadrant in late 2374. The module was subsequently lost for several centuries. **Kyrian** historian **Quarren** discovered the unit in 3074 under ruins in Kesef. Once reactivated, the backup holographic doctor served as an eyewitness to a critical period in ancient Kyrian history. Quarren and other Kyrian scholars were startled to learn that Kyrian assumptions about the 24th century were seriously mistaken. *Voyager*'s backup EMH later served the Kyrian and **Vaskan** people as Surgical Chancellor, a post he held for many years. Eventually, curious as to the fate of his friends on the *Starship Voyager*, whom he missed very much, the backup EMH took a small craft and set course for the Alpha Quadrant. ("Living Witness" [VGR]).

Emergency Medical Hologram-2 (Andy Dick). Experimental holographic program. EMH-2 was a prototype installed aboard the ***U.S.S. Prometheus*** in 2374 for field tests. When ***Starship Voyager***'s EMH arrived on the *Prometheus*, EMH-2 believed himself to be a more advanced hologram, but quickly realized that he needed help to defeat invading Romulans. ("Message in a Bottle" [VGR]).

Emergency Medical Hologram.* Chief medical officer aboard the *Starship Voyager*. *Voyager*'s EMH was activated on stardate 48315. ("Year of Hell, Part I" [VGR]). The Doctor strove continuously to improve himself and his ability to serve the *Voyager* crew. In one such effort in 2373, the Doctor devised a custom holodeck program to permit him to experience human family life. He found the program to be surprisingly profound, as he had not anticipated the depth of emotions triggered at the death of a family member. SEE: **Belle; Doctor's family program Beta-Rho.** ("Real Life" [VGR]). On stardate 50912, the EMH's optical sensors were reconfigured so he could see into the microwave range of the electromagnetic spectrum. ("Displaced" [VGR]). In 2374, the EMH traveled to the Alpha Quadrant and was successful in informing Starfleet Command of the fact that the *Voyager* had not been destroyed three years previously, but had in fact been pulled across the galaxy to the Delta Quadrant. Emergency Medical Hologram programs are not equipped with genitalia; however, the Doctor altered his program to allow for sexual relations. ("Message in a Bottle" [VGR]). *It is somewhat unclear with whom he had sex, but speculation might point to* ***Danara Pel*** *("Lifesigns" [VGR]).* The Doctor learned, however, that not all improvements were positive experiences. Around stardate 51658, using a new psychiatric subroutine, the Doctor recovered memories from Seven of Nine's mind that had apparently been repressed after a traumatic experience. This evidence, which appeared to implicate an **Entharan** trader of a serious crime, was later found to be erroneous, but resulted in the death of the trader. The Doctor later felt great remorse for his errors in the case, and *Voyager* captain Janeway expressed confidence that the experience would help him perform his duties with greater wisdom. ("Retrospect" [VGR]).

emitter stage. Component of a Federation **phaser** weapon. ("Soldiers of the Empire" [DS9]).

Emmanuel. Starfleet officer. Emmanuel was a crew member on board ***U.S.S. Voyager***. (In an alternate timeline, crewman Emmanuel was killed during a **Krenim** attack in 2374.) ("Year of Hell, Part I" [VGR]).

Empok Nor. Cardassian space station located in the Trivas system. Empok Nor, which was abandoned by the Cardassian military in 2372, was nearly identical in design to station **Terok Nor**. A team from **Deep Space 9** conducted a salvage mission to Empok Nor in 2373 to obtain abandoned Cardassian hardware for use on the former Terok Nor. As a precaution against such unauthorized intruders, three soldiers of the Cardassian First Order's Third Battalion were left behind in stasis to defend the station if need be. Their stasis chambers were programmed to revive them if station sensors detected an intruder. The soldiers were treated with powerful **psychotropic drug**s, giving them a heightened sense of paranoia toward outsiders, making them even more effective at defending the station. ("Empok Nor" [DS9]). SEE: **pattern scrambler**. Nearly a year later, a team of mercenaries led by **Quark** met at Empok Nor with a Dominion contingent for the purposes of a prisoner exchange. ("The Magnificent Ferengi" [DS9]). *Empok Nor and its interior sets were, of course, re-dresses of standing sets of station Deep Space 9.*

"Empok Nor." *Deep Space Nine* episode #122. Teleplay by Hans Beimler. Story by Bryan Fuller. Directed by Michael Vejar. No stardate given. *First aired in 1997. When Deep Space 9 suffers a severe shortage of Cardassian equipment, Sisko orders a salvage mission to an abandoned Cardassian space station, a duplicate of Deep Space 9. O'Brien, Garak, Nog, and a salvage team, stranded on the supposedly abandoned station, are hunted by soldiers left behind to guard the place. This episode marked the first use of Starfleet space suits in a television episode since the original* Star Trek *series. (The space suit costumes had been built for the feature film* Star Trek: First Contact.*)* GUEST CAST: Andrew Robinson as **Garak, Elim**; Aron Eisenberg as **Nog**; Marjean Holden as **Stolzoff**; Jeff King as **Amaro**; Tom Hodges as **Pechetti**; Andy Milder as **Boq'ta**; Tom Morga, Christopher Doyle as Cardassians. SEE: **Amaro; Barrica; beta matrix compositor; Boq'ta; coil spanner; Empok Nor; First Order; Garak, Elim; hyperspanner; kotra; O'Brien, Miles; pattern scrambler; Pechetti; plasma distribution manifold; psychotropic drug; Setlik III; Stolzoff; Third Battalion; Trivas system.**

Endeavour, U.S.S.* Federation starship. The *Endeavour* was commanded by Captain Amasov, and was the only starship to survive the disastrous encounter with the Borg at Wolf 359 in early 2367. ("Scorpion, Part I" [VGR]). *The* Endeavour *appears to have been the sole survivor of the battle of Wolf 359, although this was not explicitly established in any episode. We know that the* Endeavour *was still around in 2373 because it was part of the armada that met the Borg in* Star Trek: First Contact. *Nevertheless, Amasov's first-hand experiences with the Borg (from which Janeway read in "Scorpion, Part I") had to have been recorded before the* Voyager *departed from Deep Space 9 in 2371, which was before the Borg battle in* Star Trek: First Contact. *It therefore seems likely that the* Endeavour *(and Amasov) were also at Wolf 359 in 2367.*

engram transcriptor. Device used by the **Mari** Constabulary to record an individual's thoughts for later examination. ("Random Thoughts" [VGR]).

engramatic activity. Bioelectrical processes associated with the storage and retrieval of memories in an organic brain. In 2374, *Starship Voyager*'s **Emergency Medical Hologram** detected unusual engramatic activity in **Seven of Nine,** possibly indicating suppressed memories. ("Retrospect" [VGR]). SEE: **engram.**

engramatic dissociation. Psychological phenomenon in which a person with a sufficiently disciplined mind can compartmentalize contradictory information, believing one thing while doing another. **Section 31** operative Sloan accused Dr. Julian Bashir of being an unwitting Dominion spy, escaping detection through the use of engramatic dissociation. ("Inquisition" [DS9]).

engramatic purge. Medical procedure used to erase specific thoughts from a person's mind. The **Mari** government in the Delta Quadrant performed engramatic purges on criminals, believing the procedure to be a humane form of rehabilitation. ("Random Thoughts" [VGR]).

Entabans. Delta Quadrant civilization. The Entaban government was territorial, intolerant of ships entering their space. ("Vis à Vis" [VGR]).

Enterprise*-E, *U.S.S.* Federation starship, the sixth to bear the name. The *Enterprise*-E was equipped with a **captain's yacht**.

The *Enterprise*-E could be piloted manually with a joystick steering column located near the flight controller's console on the **bridge**. (*Star Trek: Insurrection*).

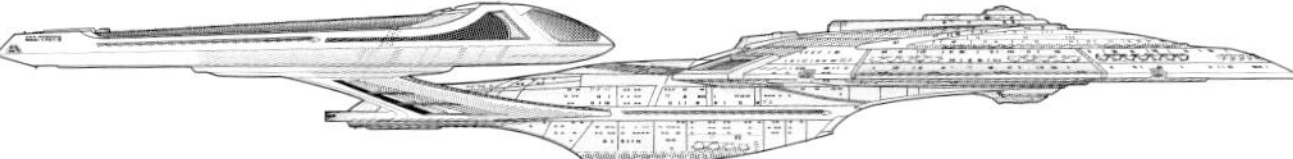

Entharan magistrate. (Adrian Sparks). Judiciary official of the Entharan government. In 2374, an Entharan magistrate ruled that sufficient evidence existed to investigate arms dealer **Kovin** for allegedly assaulting *Starship Voyager*'s crew member **Seven of Nine**. It was later learned that physical evidence in the case did not support a guilty verdict. ("Retrospect" [VGR]).

Entharans. Spacefaring civilization in the Delta Quadrant. The Entharan economy relies heavily on trade with neighboring cultures. In 2373, Entharan arms dealer **Kovin** was falsely accused of assaulting **Seven of Nine**, a crew member aboard the Federation starship *Voyager*. ("Retrospect" [VGR]).

environmental suit. Extravehicular personnel garment worn to permit a person to survive and work in space. Starfleet shuttlecraft sometimes carry environmental suits for emergency situations. ("Day of Honor" [VGR]).

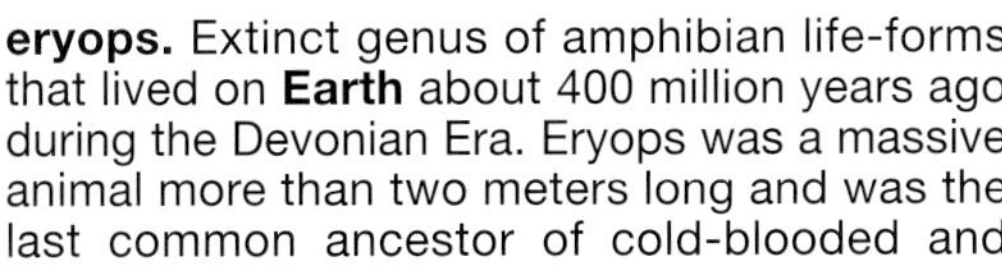

eryops. Extinct genus of amphibian life-forms that lived on **Earth** about 400 million years ago during the Devonian Era. Eryops was a massive animal more than two meters long and was the last common ancestor of cold-blooded and warm-blooded organisms on Earth. The eryops was also the common ancestor of humans and the **Voth**. SEE: **hadrosaur.** ("Distant Origin" [VGR]).

escape pod.* Small lifeboat that could be ejected from a starship or other space vehicle after a catastrophic accident. The crew of the ***U.S.S. Valiant*** abandoned ship in escape pods following a devastating encounter with a Dominion battleship in 2374. ("*Valiant*" [DS9]). In an alternate timeline, escape pods were used to evacuate all but senior officers from the badly damaged ***Starship Voyager*** during the encounter with the Krenim in 2374. ("Year of Hell, Part I" [VGR]).

eustachian tube rub. Sexual technique of ***oo-mox*** devised to pleasure a Ferengi male by a very specific stimulation of his ears. ("Profit and Lace" [DS9]).

Eventualists. A major movement in the art of sculpture. A post-eventualistic, pre-Matoian, bronze and triptin sculpture was sold at auction on station Deep Space 9 in late 2373. ("In the Cards" [DS9]).

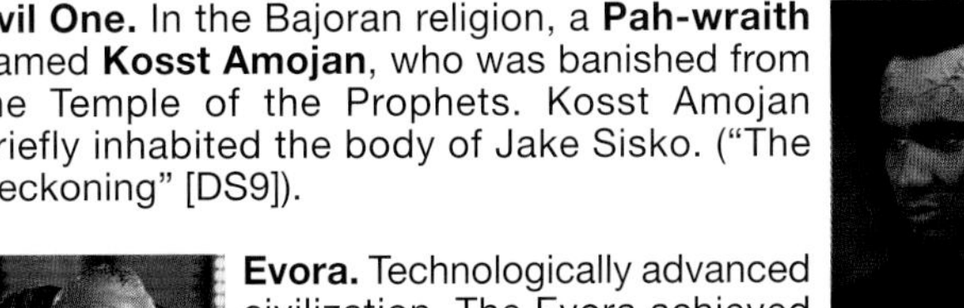

Evil One. In the Bajoran religion, a **Pah-wraith** named **Kosst Amojan**, who was banished from the Temple of the Prophets. Kosst Amojan briefly inhabited the body of Jake Sisko. ("The Reckoning" [DS9]).

Evora. Technologically advanced civilization. The Evora achieved interstellar travel capability in 2374 and were invited to become a Federation protectorate a year later. A diplomatic reception for an Evoran delegation was held aboard the *Starship Enterprise-E* in 2375. The Evora prefer a vegetarian diet. (*Star Trek: Insurrection*).

exatanium. Exotic metallic alloy. The fuselage of an experimental **Benthan** ship was made of exatanium. ("Vis à Vis" [VGR]).

Exeter, U.S.S.* Federation starship. In 2374, the *Exeter* was part of the Ninth Fleet headquartered at starbase Deep Space 9. ("You Are Cordially Invited" [DS9]).

exobiology.* Study of alien life. **Dr. Crell Moset** was a renowned expert in exobiology. ("Nothing Human" [VGR]).

exogenic field. Unstable energy field that can exist around a planet when unstable elements are present in the planet's core. Under certain conditions, exogenic fields can cause quantum reactions, producing high levels of hazardous subspace **metreon radiation**. ("The Sound of Her Voice" [DS9]).

"Extreme Risk." *Voyager* episode #97. Written by Kenneth Biller. Directed by Cliff Bole. No stardate given. *First aired in 1998. B'Elanna Torres wrestles with depression over the loss of her Maquis friends, while the* Voyager *crew builds a new shuttlecraft to retrieve a piece of valuable equipment from the atmosphere of a gas giant planet. In this episode, Torres uses the orbital skydiving outfit that was to have been used by Captain Kirk in the opening scenes of* Star Trek Generations. *This episode also marked the first appearance of the* Delta Flyer *shuttlecraft.* GUEST CAST: Hamilton Camp as **Vrelk, Controller;** Alexander Enberg as **Vorik;** Daniel Betances as shuttle pilot; Majel Barrett as Computer Voice. SEE: **banana pancakes; burgundy; *Captain Proton, The Adventures of; Delta Flyer*; holodeck and holosuite programs: orbital skydiving, Torres 2-1-6, Torres Zeta-1; immersion shield; kellinite; Li Paz; Malon export vessel; Malon shuttle; maple syrup; Meyer; multispatial probe; Nelson; orbital skydiving; Paris, Thomas; photonic missile; Sahreen; tetraburnium alloy; Torres, B'Elanna; Vorik; Vrelk, Controller.**

Fanalian toddy.* Alcoholic beverage. In early 2375, Julian Bashir and Ezri Dax shared Fanalian toddies at the Replimat on the Promenade of Deep Space 9 shortly after her arrival at the station. ("Afterimage" [DS9]).

Fancy Dan. In the jargon of the ancient Earth sport of **baseball**, Fancy Dan referred to the execution by a fielder of a play with an extra flourish in hopes of winning applause from the game's spectators. Ezri Dax executed a Fancy Dan during the epic holosuite game between the Deep Space **Niners** and the *T'Kumbra* **Logicians** in early 2375. ("Take Me Out to the Holosuite" [DS9]).

"Far Beyond the Stars." *Deep Space Nine* episode #138. Teleplay by Ira Steven Behr & Hans Beimler. Story by Marc Scott Zicree. Directed by Avery Brooks. No stardate given. *First aired in 1998. Sisko has a powerful Orb shadow experience, becoming a science-fiction writer who encounters the ugly reality of racism in 1953 America. The episode features appearances by several members of the regular* Star Trek: Deep Space Nine *cast playing other characters without their usual alien makeup*. GUEST CAST: Brock Peters as **Sisko, Joseph**/Preacher; Jeffrey Combs as **Weyoun**/Officer Kevin Mulkahey**;** Marc Alaimo as **Dukat, Gul**/Officer Burt Ryan; J. G. Hertzler as **Martok, General**/ **Rittenhouse, Roy;** Aron Eisenberg as **Nog**/Vendor; Penny Johnson as **Yates, Kasidy/Cassie.** SEE: ***Amsterdam News*; baseball; Bradbury, Ray; Cassie; *Cortéz, U.S.S.*; cruller; "Deep Space Nine"; doughnut; Du Bois, W.E.B.; Eaton, Julius; Eaton, Kay; Ellison, Ralph; frankfurter; *From Here to Eternity*; *Galaxy Science Fiction*; Giants; Gnome Press; Hawkins, Willie; Heinlein, Robert A.; Hughes, Langston; Hugo Award; Hunter, K.C.; Hurston, Zora Neale; *Incredible Tales*; Jimmy; Kursky, Darlene; Macklin, Albert; *Native Son*; Pabst, Douglas; *Puppet Masters, The*; Rittenhouse, Roy; rocket ship; Rossoff, Herbert; Russell, Benny; sauerkraut; science fiction; Sisko, Benjamin; Sisko, Joseph; steak and eggs; Sturgeon, Theodore; Swofford, Captain Quentin; Wells, H.G.; White Rose Redi-Tea; Wright, Richard.**

fare. Among members of the **Orion Syndicate**, a percentage of illicit profits paid to one's boss. ("Honor Among Thieves" [DS9]).

Farius Prime.* Planet. Farius Prime was the base of operations of **Raimus**, a powerful member of the **Orion Syndicate** criminal organization. **Liam Bilby** also resided on Farius Prime. ("Honor Among Thieves" [DS9]).

Farragut*, *U.S.S. Federation starship, *Excelsior* class. **Sarina Douglas** and her friends, **Patrick**, **Jack**, and **Lauren** traveled aboard the *Farragut* under false pretenses to station Deep Space 9 in early 2375. ("Chrysalis" [DS9]). *This was presumably the namesake of the* Farragut *on which Kirk served as a cadet ("Obsession" [TOS]), and perhaps also the* Nebula-*class ship seen in* Star Trek Generations *and destroyed in "Nor the Battle to the Strong" (DS9). "Chrysalis" did not explicitly establish this* Farragut *to be an* Excelsior-*class ship, but we did see such a ship at Deep Space 9 during the episode, so we are assuming that it was the* Farragut. *We speculate it was an older ship that had predated the* Nebula-*class vessel and had been decommissioned, but was pressed back into service during the Dominion war after the destruction of the* Nebula-*class ship.*

Farris, Karen. (Courtney Peldon). **Starfleet Academy** cadet. In 2374, Farris and 34 other members of the elite **Red Squad** embarked on a three-month training cruise aboard the ***U.S.S. Valiant***, which had been caught behind enemy lines when the Dominion war broke out. When the ship's senior officers were all killed in battle, cadet **Tim Watters** assumed command and assigned Farris as his executive officer. Farris and most of the crew were killed and the *Valiant* destroyed when Watters unwisely ordered the ship to attack a massive Dominion battleship. ("*Valiant*" [DS9]).

"Favor the Bold." *Deep Space Nine* episode #129. Written by Ira Steven Behr & Hans Beimler. Directed by Winrich Kolbe. No stardate given. *First aired in 1997. The Dominion prepares to take down the minefield that seals off the wormhole while Sisko assembles a fleet for a daring attempt to retake Deep Space 9. The story concluded in "Sacrifice of Angels" (DS9).* GUEST CAST: Andrew J. Robinson as **Garak, Elim**; Jeffrey Combs as **Weyoun**; Marc Alaimo as **Dukat, Gul**; Max Grodénchik as **Rom**; Aron Eisenberg as **Nog**; J. G. Hertzler as **Martok, General**; Melanie Smith as **Tora Ziyal**; Casey Biggs as **Damar**; Chase Masterson as **Leeta**; Barry Jenner as **Ross, Admiral William**; Salome Jens as **Founder Leader**; William Wellman, Jr. as Bajoran Officer; Bart McCarthy as **Admiral Cobum**; Ericka Klein as **Admiral Sitak**; Andrew Palmer as Jem'Hadar Soldier**.** SEE: **Cobum, Admiral; *Cortéz, U.S.S.*; Fifth Fleet; Gowron; Kotanka system; Morn; Ninth Fleet; Nog; Ross, Admiral William; *Sarek, U.S.S.*; Second Fleet; Sisko, Benjamin; Sitak, Admiral; Tammeron grain; Third Fleet; Vorta.**

Federation Medical Academy. School of medical instruction operated by the United Federation of Planets. ("Nothing Human" [VGR]).

Federation News Service. News reporting organization. In late 2373, **Jake Sisko** became an official correspondent for the Federation News Service. ("Call to Arms" [DS9]).

Felix. Friend of Julian Bashir. Felix designed the **Vic Fontaine** holosuite program. ("His Way" [DS9]).

Ferengi Bill of Opportunities. Important legal document that enumerated individual civil rights for **Ferengi** citizens. In 2374, Grand Nagus **Zek** added a new amendment to the Bill of Opportunities, recognizing the right of females to wear clothes. ("Profit and Lace" [DS9]).

Ferengi business license. Credential necessary for a Ferengi citizen to conduct business within the jurisdiction of the Ferengi Alliance. Loss of the license, which can be the result of a serious breach of business law, is tantamount to being ostracized from Ferengi society. Liquidator Brunt revoked **Quark**'s business license in 2372 when Quark broke a contract, but it was restored a year later. ("Ferengi Love Songs" [DS9]).

Ferengi Commerce Authority.* Agency of the Ferengi government. The FCA was governed by a board of 432 commissioners who have the power to elect the **grand nagus**. One very powerful and influential commissioner was **Nilva**, the chairman of **Slug-o-Cola**. ("Profit and Lace" [DS9]).

Ferengi Gaming Commission. Governmental body on Ferenginar that oversaw gambling enterprises. In 2373, the Bolian government gave permission to the Ferengi Gaming Commission to take over all of their gambling emporiums. ("Ferengi Love Songs" [DS9]).

"Ferengi Love Songs." *Deep Space Nine* episode #118. Written by Ira Steven Behr & Hans Beimler. Directed by Rene Auberjonois. No stardate given. *First aired in 1997. Quark's mother and the Grand Nagus Zek are in love, but the nefarious Brunt offers Quark his license back if he'll break up the couple. Rom and Leeta become engaged in this episode.* GUEST CAST: Cecily Adams as **Ishka**; Wallace Shawn as **Zek**; Tiny Ron as **Maihar'du;**

Jeffrey Combs as **Brunt**; Max Grodénchik as **Rom**; Chase Masterson as **Leeta**; Hamilton Camp as **Leck**. SEE: **acrybite; Bolians; Brunt; Ferengi business license; Ferengi Gaming Commission; Ferengi Rules of Acquisition: 94, 208, 229; Ferengi; First Clerk; Global Tongo Championships; Horran's 7th Prophecy; Igel, DaiMon; Ishka; jellied gree worms; jevonite; K'retok; Leck; Leeta; "Lobekins"; Marauder Mo; nagus, grand; Quark; Rom; security access code; slug steak; Smeet; *tongo*; Waiver of Property and Profit; wedding: Bajoran, Ferengi; Zek.**

Ferengi Rules of Acquisition.*
94th Rule: "Females and finances don't mix." ("Ferengi Love Songs" [DS9]).
98th Rule: "Every man has his price." ("In the Pale Moonlight" [DS9]).
168th Rule: "Whisper your way to success." ("Treachery, Faith, and the Great River" [DS9]).
190th Rule: "Hear all, trust nothing." ("Call to Arms" [DS9]).
208th Rule: "Sometimes, the only thing more dangerous than a question is an answer." ("Ferengi Love Songs" [DS9]).
229th Rule: "Latinum lasts longer than lust." ("Ferengi Love Songs" [DS9]).

Ferengi.* Civilization. Ferengi have deciduous childhood lobes that they lose as they grow older. A Ferengi's first set of ears are lost at a young age. The Ferengi believe that the universe is held together by the **Great Material Continuum**, also known as the Great River. They believe that each part of the universe has too much of one thing, but not enough of another, and it is through the continual flow of the Great River that wants and needs can be fulfilled, if one navigates the River with sufficient entrepreneurial skill. ("Treachery, Faith, and the Great River" [DS9]). The seeds of a profound revolution in Ferengi society were sown in 2373 when Grand Nagus **Zek** came to accept the guidance of a female, **Ishka**. While Ishka gave Zek sound financial advice that benefited the entire Ferengi Alliance, she also made no secret of her personal agenda to reform Ferengi law to grant equal rights to females. ("Ferengi Love Songs" [DS9]). Zek acted on this radical reform a year later when he amended the **Ferengi Bill of Opportunities** to grant females the right to wear clothes. Announcement of the amendment initially caused financial chaos throughout Ferengi society, nearly deposing Zek in the process. Stability and profitability returned when it became evident that equal economic opportunity for females resulted in the opening of exciting new markets for consumer goods. ("Profits and Lace" [DS9]).

Ferenginar.* Planet; homeworld of Ferengi society. Torrential rains, the smell of rotting vegetation, and the rivers of muck on Ferenginar are but a few of the things that many Ferengi find endearing about their homeworld. ("The Magnificent Ferengi" [DS9]).

"Fever." Popular 20th-century Earth musical composition telling of the early stages of a humanoid mating ritual. Written by Willie John and Eddie Cooley. **Lola Chrystal** sang "Fever" in the **Vic Fontaine** holosuite program. ("His Way" [DS9]).

Fifth Fleet. Task force of the Federation **Starfleet**. In 2374, elements of the Fifth Fleet joined a special large attack force commanded by Captain Benjamin Sisko to retake station Deep Space 9 from Dominion control. The Fifth Fleet had been previously assigned to combat duty along the Vulcan border. ("Favor the Bold" [DS9]).

Fiji. Island nation with a tropical climate located in the southern Pacific Ocean on planet Earth. In 2374, when Thomas Paris suggested creating a holodeck skiing program, B'Elanna Torres requested a warmer location such as Fiji. ("Waking Moments" [VGR]).

firenut. A dry, one-seeded fruit, consisting of an edible kernel in a woody shell. Neelix brewed a potent coffee blend containing firenuts. ("Mortal Coil" [VGR]).

First Clerk. Administrative official serving the **Ferengi** Alliance. The First Clerk was the personal financial assistant to the **grand nagus**. In 2373, Quark briefly held the position of First Clerk to Grand Nagus Zek. ("Ferengi Love Songs" [DS9]).

First Order. Cardassian military division. In 2372, three soldiers of the First Order's Third Battalion were given a massive dose of **psychotropic drug**s, placed in stasis tubes, and left on **Empok Nor** when the station was abandoned. The chambers were programmed to revive the soldiers when any unauthorized persons entered the abandoned station. ("Empok Nor" [DS9]).

Fitzpatrick. Starfleet officer aboard the *U.S.S. Voyager*. On stardate 51501.4, Fitzpatrick received a letter from his home via a Starfleet transmission sent through a **Hirogen relay station**. ("Hunters" [VGR]).

fleet liaison officer. Starfleet billet. In 2373, Lieutenant Commander Worf served as fleet liaison officer for Deep Space 9. ("Soldiers of the Empire" [DS9]).

Flith. (John Chandler). Member of the **Orion Syndicate** who worked for **Liam Bilby** on Farius Prime. Flith was killed in 2374 for the serious transgression of failing to pay his **fare** to the head boss. ("Honor Among Thieves" [DS9]).

Florence. City in the nation-state of Italy, located on the European continent of planet Earth. Florence was one of the centers of the remarkable explosion of art and science during the 14th through 17th centuries on Earth known as the **Renaissance**. One of Florence's most distinguished inhabitants during that period was **Leonardo da Vinci**. ("Concerning Flight" [VGR]).

Flotter, The Adventures of. Series of interactive holographic stories for children. The **Flotter** stories were set in the beautiful **Forest of Forever**, where a child met a variety of fanciful characters, each of which was a personification of some element or force of nature. The Flotter stories each taught children about those forces of nature through the behavior of the characters and how they responded to a child's actions. Children participating in the Flotter adventures were encouraged to develop deductive reasoning skills. For example, in one story when the character of Flotter disappeared, the character would not reappear until the participant realized that Flotter, who represented water, had evaporated. He would subsequently reappear when temperatures in the forest dropped low enough to allow water vapor to condense into rain. In another story, diverting a river, an apparent solution to an imminent dry spell, would actually flood the forest, causing giant mosquitoes to appear when the forest became a swamp. Some Flotter stories include "Flotter and the Tree Monster," "**Trevis** and the Terribly Twisted Trunk," and "Flotter, Trevis, and the **Ogre of Fire**." Naomi Wildman enjoyed the Flotter adventures when she was a child, as did future *Voyager* crew members Kathryn Janeway, Harry Kim, and Samantha Wildman. SEE: **Stinger**. ("Once Upon a Time" [VGR]).

Flotter. (Wallace Langham). Title character in the Adventures of Flotter holographic stories for children. Also known as Flotter T. Water III. The comical Flotter represented the element of water in the fanciful Forest of Forever. SEE: ***Flotter, The Adventures of.*** ("Once Upon a Time" [VGR]).

fluidic space. Spatial continuum filled with organic fluid matter, a dimension apart from our universe. This fluid space was the realm of **Species 8472**. In late 2373, while searching for species to assimilate, the **Borg** discovered the fluidic space that was home to Species 8472. The Borg found that Species 8472 had biogenically engineered technology that was superior to all other species yet known to them. The Borg attempted to assimilate them, but Species 8472 was resistant and instead pursued the Borg into our universe. ("Scorpion, Part II" [VGR]).

Fontaine, Vic. (James Darren). Twentieth-century Earth entertainer. Fontaine was a prominent singer who performed in the city of **Las Vegas** during the 1960s. Fontaine's contemporaries included such Earth celebrities as **Frank Sinatra** and **Dean Martin**. Among Fontaine's repertoire were such swing-era favorites as **"You're Nobody Till Somebody Loves You," "Come Fly with Me,"** and **"I've Got You under My Skin."** In 2374, an interactive re-creation of Fontaine was featured in a holosuite program created by Felix for his friend **Julian Bashir**. This remarkable simulation not only captured Fontaine's personality and sophisticated singing style, but was self-aware, giving him an attitude appropriate for the period. The Fontaine hologram was designed to be highly perceptive of the intricacies of interpersonal relationships. Both Bashir and **Odo** found his advice helpful in their respective love lives. Fontaine referred to himself (as well as to other holographic characters) as a "light bulb." ("His Way" [DS9]). Even Quark enjoyed Fontaine's brand of sophisticated music. ("Tears of the Prophets" [DS9]). Worf escaped into the world of Vic Fontaine in early 2375, shortly after the death of his wife, Jadzia. Worf spent many evenings in the holosuite simulation, repeatedly asking the holographic Vic to sing "All the Way," which was Jadzia's favorite song. ("Image in the Sand" [DS9]). *James Darren is well known to genre fans for his portrayal of Dr. Tony Newman in the 1966–67 television series* The Time Tunnel. *Darren also costarred with William Shatner in* T.J. Hooker. *Vic Fontaine was first seen in "His Way."*

footfall. Informal **Vori** unit of distance measure, about one meter. ("Nemesis" [VGR]).

Forest of Forever. Fanciful setting for the ***Adventures of Flotter*** stories for children. Within the beautiful Forest of Forever, such colorful characters as Flotter and Trevis dwelled. The Flotter stories emphasized the interrelationship of the various forces of nature, and the forest itself was nearly destroyed in a story entitled "Flotter, Trevis, and the Ogre of Fire." ("Once Upon a Time" [VGR]).

Fostossa virus. Disease organism. Fostossa virus was epidemic on Bajor during the Cardassian occupation, killing thousands of Bajorans. A cure for the disease was developed by **Dr. Crell Moset**, but only after extensive experimentation on Bajoran prisoners, resulting in the painful death of many of those unwilling subjects. ("Nothing Human" [VGR]).

Founder Leader.* Representative of the **Founders** of the **Dominion**. This individual became stranded in the Alpha Quadrant in early 2374 during the Dominion war. She visited Odo at Terok Nor, hoping to tempt him to return to his people. ("Behind the Lines" [DS9]). Although she linked extensively with Odo, she was disappointed when Odo chose to remain with the solids in the Alpha Quadrant. ("Sacrifice of Angels" [DS9]). The Founder Leader did not realize that in linking with Odo, she became infected with a deadly morphogenic virus that had been created by **Section 31** with the intent of wiping out the entire **Great Link**. ("Dogs of War" [DS9]). Despite the debilitating effects of the disease, the Founder Leader commanded the forces of the Dominion and its allies during the Dominion war. Even during the final days of the war, when the Alpha Quadrant powers had turned the tide against the Dominion, the Founder Leader refused to surrender, fearing that the Alpha powers would seek retribution against her people. She even ordered a brutal campaign of destruction against the Cardassian people when they began to rebel against Dominion rule. It was only after Odo linked with her one more time (in the process of curing her of the disease) that she believed that the Federation would not permit her people to be destroyed. The Founder Leader subsequently ordered the surrender of all Dominion forces, and later stood trial in a Federation court for her actions during the Dominion war. ("What You Leave Behind" [DS9]). *The Founder Leader was referred to as Female Shapeshifter in the scripts.*

Founders.* Civilization in the Gamma Quadrant, founders of the **Dominion**. Eons ago the Founders were solid beings, but they eventually evolved into shapeshifters. ("Behind the Lines" [DS9]). When the Founders ventured into space, they found themselves hated by nonshapeshifters, which the Founders called "solids." Eventually, the Founders enlisted the service of a people known as the **Vorta** to help them run the Dominion. The Vorta, who had been genetically engineered by the Founders, worshipped the Founders as gods. ("Treachery, Faith, and the Great River" [DS9]). While on their homeworld, the Founders preferred to exist in the **Great Link**, but they occasionally took other forms. The Founders don't use proper names when referring to each other because they don't consider themselves to be individuals. ("Behind the Lines" [DS9]). In early 2375, an epidemic befell the Founders, causing all in the Great Link to fall seriously ill. ("Treachery, Faith, and the Great River" [DS9]). The epidemic was caused by a morphogenic virus that was developed by the Federation's shadowy Section 31. ("When it Rains..." [DS9]). The genetically engineered disease was regarded as incurable and probably would have resulted in the extinction of the Founders if not for the efforts of Dr. Julian Bashir, who extracted information from the mind of a Section 31 operative, making a treatment possible. ("Extreme Measures" [DS9]). Nevertheless, the use of such a genocidal weapon reinforced Founder fears that they could never trust any solids. It was not until Odo returned to the Great Link at the end of the Dominion war that the Founders understood that peace was possible, despite the differences between them and the solids of the galaxy. ("What You Leave Behind" [DS9]).

Fourth Order.* Cardassian military unit. In 2373 **Gul Trepar** was the head of the Fourth Order. ("Ties of Blood and Water" [DS9]).

franc. Monetary unit used by the nation-state of **France** during the 20th century. ("The Killing Game, Part I" [VGR]).

France. Republic in the western portion of Earth's European continent. **Paris**, the capital city of France, is the location of the office of the President of the **United Federation of Planets**. (SEE: **Federation President**.) France was a major innovator in Earth society's culture and arts throughout much of history, and was a key contributor to Earth's **International Space Station** during the 20th and 21st century. France was also a pivotal battleground during that planet's second global war during the 20th century. SEE: **Allied Forces; French Resistance; World War II**. ("The Killing Game, Parts I and II" [VGR]).

Frane. (Bobby Burns). Inhabitant of the **Mari** homeworld. Frane, in violation of Mari law, was a habitual perpetrator of hostile mental images. He underwent years of neurogenic restructuring in an effort to cure him. In 2374, Frane, a telepath, stole a violent thought from visiting *Voyager* crew member B'Elanna Torres. Unable to handle the power of Torres's emotions, Frane committed an act of violence, nearly causing Torres to be punished under Mari law. SEE: **Guill**. ("Random Thoughts" [VGR]).

frankfurter. A smoked, often seasoned sausage, reddish in color, made with meat, popular on 20th-century Earth. Frankfurters were often served with **sauerkraut**. ("Far Beyond the Stars" [DS9]). SEE: **hot dog**.

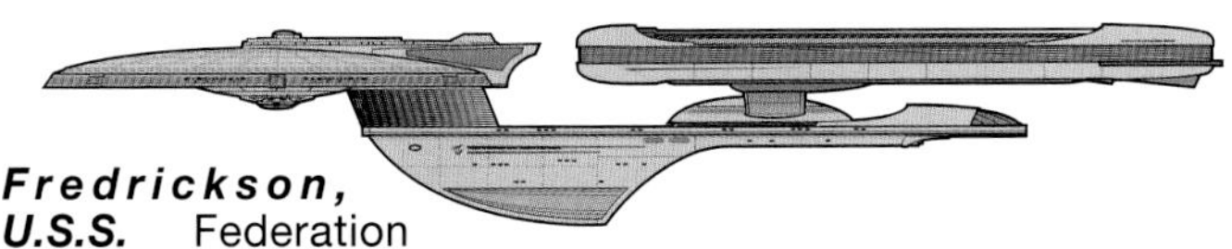

Fredrickson, U.S.S. Federation starship, *Excelsior*-class, registry number NCC-42111. The *Fredrickson* was one of several ships damaged in battle against forces of the Dominion in early 2374. ("A Time to Stand" [DS9]). *The ship was named for Anthony Fredrickson, a scenic artist on* Star Trek: Deep Space Nine.

freedom of the press. The right in a free society of the news media and the general citizenry to express opinions and to report news in any way they deem appropriate, without interference from the government. Even though some opinions and reports may be controversial, harmful, or simply wrong, freedom of the press is based on the belief that it is healthier for an educated adult citizenry to be exposed to as many viewpoints as possible so that they may make informed choices about their lives. The **United Federation of Planets** guarantees freedom of the press to its citizens, as did many ancient Earth civilizations. Other, less enlightened cultures sometimes believe it necessary to "protect" their citizenry from information that the government might find "dangerous," but such policies invariably encourage abuse and generally harm the society itself over the long term. Jake Sisko, a reporter for the Federation News Service, was startled to learn that the **Dominion** did not respect the freedom of the press. ("Call to Arms" [DS9]).

French Resistance. Holodeck simulation program. Re-creation of part of Earth's brutal second world war, set in the republic of **France** on the European continent. In the scenario, soldiers of **Nazi Germany** invaded France, forcing many French of the city of **Sainte Claire** to use covert means to fight against the occupying army. These French citizens included the owner and employees of **Le Coeur de Lion**, a tavern that served Nazi soldiers during the evening hours. The tavern was also a local headquarters for the underground during the day, from which resistance fighters later provided vital aid to liberation forces from the American army. **Hirogen** hunters, aboard the *Starship Voyager* in 2374, used the program to study human behavior. In this playing of the program, Klingon warrior characters from another holodeck simulation lent further assistance in freeing the French from the Nazis. SEE: **Allied Forces; de Neuf, Mademoiselle; Katrine; World War II.** ("The Killing Game, Parts I and II" [VGR]).

French toast. Earth breakfast dish of bread dipped in a batter of beaten eggs and fried. ("Real Life" [VGR]).

Frola. (Nina Minton). Young daughter of exobiologist **Forra Gegen**. Frola was interested in Tova Veer, her father's assistant. ("Distant Origin" [VGR]).

From Here to Eternity. Ancient motion picture produced on Earth in 1953 by Columbia Pictures. *From Here to Eternity* was a noninteractive entertainment film, the story of American military officers just prior to the beginning of Earth's second planetwide war. Many members of the viewing public preferred this type of reality-based story to the more imaginative fare offered by science fiction. Actor-singer **Frank Sinatra** won acclaim for his performance in this film. ("Far Beyond the Stars" [DS9]).

full consortium. In the game of ***tongo***, a high-value card hand. ("Change of Heart" [DS9]).

Gable, Clark * (1901–1960). Twentieth-century Earth entertainer, noted as an actor who played romantic lead characters in two-dimensional noninteractive motion pictures. In an alternate timeline, B'Elanna Torres and Harry Kim played a trivia game in which Torres incorrectly guessed that Gable had starred in the film *To Catch a Thief*. ("Year of Hell, Part I" [VGR]).

Gabriel. (Jesse Littlejohn). Inhabitant of the planet **Gaia** in an alternate timeline. Gabriel ceased to exist in 2373 when her timeline vanished. ("Children of Time" [DS9]).

gagh. * Klingon delicacy. *Gagh* is served frequently aboard Klingon warships. Crew members on such vessels have sometimes been known to grow tired of the lack of variety in shipboard cuisine when even *gagh* is served too often. ("Shadows and Symbols" [DS9]).

Gaia. Class-M planet in the Gamma Quadrant, fourth planet from its sun. Gaia was surrounded by an energy barrier that exhibited dangerous quantum fluctuations. These fluctuations were responsible for creation of an alternate timeline in which the *Starship Defiant* from the year 2373 crashed on the planet some 200 years in the past. *Defiant* crew member **Kira Nerys** died as a result of the crash. The surviving members of the *Defiant* crew, marooned on this distant world, established a colony that thrived for two centuries. By that time, some 8,000 descendants of the original *Defiant* crew lived there. One crew member, **Odo**, did survive that entire time, but always regretted deeply not having confessed his love for Kira. When the original *Defiant* returned to the planet, this alternate Odo caused the entire timeline, including himself and all inhabitants of the planet, to vanish so that the original Kira could live. ("Children of Time" [DS9]).

Gaila.* (Josh Pais). Ferengi entrepreneur, cousin to Quark. Gaila somehow escaped **General Nassuc**'s purification squad, but was ruined financially. He was even arrested for vagrancy on Thalos VI. In 2374, Gaila became part of the heroic mercenary team that effected **Ishka**'s rescue from the Dominion. ("The Magnificent Ferengi" [DS9]).

Gal'na. Ba'ku birth name of **Subahdar Gallatin**. Gal'na was born on the **Ba'ku planet**, but changed his name to Gallatin when he left his home to follow the ways of what his people called offlanders, becoming the **Son'a**. (*Star Trek: Insurrection*).

Galactic Cluster 3. Transmaterial energy plane intersecting 22 billion omnicordial life-forms. Galactic Cluster 3 was the realm of the technologically advanced sentient beings referred to by the Borg as **Species 259**. As of 2374, the only Starfleet data on Galactic Cluster 3 and its inhabitants were from former Borg drone Seven of Nine. ("The Gift" [VGR]).

Galaxy Science Fiction. Paper-based hard-copy periodical published on 20th-century Earth from 1950 through the 1980s. *Galaxy* specialized in **science fiction** stories, including those by several notable writers of the period. **Herbert Rossoff** felt he would be in good company should his writing be published in *Galaxy* alongside such notable authors as **Ray Bradbury**, **Robert A. Heinlein**, and **Theodore Sturgeon**. Heinlein's novel ***The Puppet Masters*** was serialized in *Galaxy* magazine in 1951. The publication was a competitor to ***Incredible Tales***. ("Far Beyond the Stars" [DS9]). *While* Galaxy *was a real magazine, the cover of the September 1953, issue as seen in "Far Beyond the Stars" featured artwork of a futuristic city that was actually a slightly modified version of a matte painting created by Albert Whitlock, Jr., in 1967 for "Court Martial" (TOS). Samuel Cogley was a character in that episode.*

Galaxy, U.S.S. * Federation starship, first vessel of her class, Starfleet registry number NCC-70637. The *U.S.S. Galaxy*, and four other ships of its class, fought in the combined fleet of allied Alpha Quadrant forces that invaded Cardassian space at the **Chin'toka System** in late 2374. The *Galaxy* was seriously damaged in the battle. ("Tears of the Prophets" [DS9]).

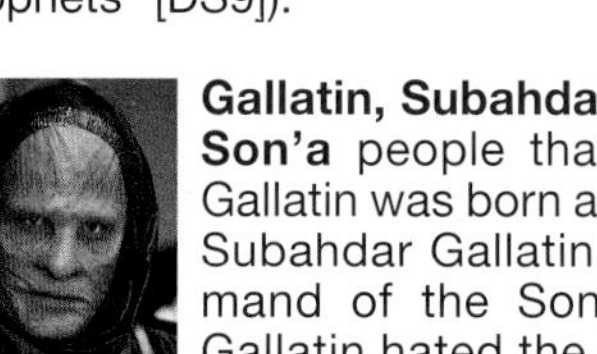

Gallatin, Subahdar. (Gregg Henry). Member of the **Son'a** people that left the **Ba'ku** around 2275. Gallatin was born as Gal'na on the **Ba'ku planet**. As Subahdar Gallatin, he served as second-in-command of the Son'a fleet under **Ahdar Ru'afo**. Gallatin hated the Ba'ku for banishing his people, but he was not willing to kill them. When Ru'afo planned to kill all the Ba'ku in order to take possession of the Ba'ku planet, Gallatin cooperated with Starfleet officers to prevent that from happening. (*Star Trek: Insurrection*).

Gamma. Colloquial term used by the **Jem'Hadar** to refer to a Jem'Hadar soldier bred in the Gamma Quadrant. The term was coined to distinguish them from **Alpha**s, who were bred in the Alpha Quadrant. All Jem'Hadar bred before 2374 weren't necessarily Gammas. ("One Little Ship" [DS9]).

Gand sector. Region of space in the Delta Quadrant. The **Borg** encountered a **Kazon** colony in the Gand sector. The Borg considered the Kazon unremarkable and thus did not assimilate them. ("Mortal Coil" [VGR]).

Gant. Ferengi national, cousin of Ensign Nog. Gant specialized in the selling of wines and spirits. In 2375, Gant helped Nog obtain sixteen cases of Klingon bloodwine vintage 2309. ("Treachery, Faith, and the Great River" [DS9]).

Gantt. (Rick Schatz). Member of the **Shakaar resistance cell** on Bajor, along with Kira Nerys. ("Ties of Blood and Water" [DS9]).

Garak, Elim.* Former member of the Cardassian **Obsidian Order** intelligence agency. In 2373, Garak was a member of a salvage team assigned to obtain badly needed engineering components from the abandoned Cardassian station **Empok Nor** for use on Deep Space 9. Garak was instrumental in helping the DS9 team avoid a variety of booby traps left behind on the station by the Cardassians. Unfortunately, one such trap involved a powerful **psychotropic drug** that affected Garak by amplifying his normal xenophobic tendencies so strongly that he killed a Starfleet officer before he could be subdued. ("Empok Nor" [DS9]). Garak demonstrated his considerable skill in

covert operations as well as his cold-blooded ruthlessness in 2374 when he worked with Benjamin Sisko on an extralegal operation to draw the Romulans into the war against the Dominion, an important turning point in the costly war. SEE: **Tolar, Grathon; Vreenak.** ("In the Pale Moonlight" [DS9]). Garak's father was Enabran Tain, former head of the Obsidian Order. When Garak was a child, his father sometimes locked him in a closet until the boy had learned his lesson. In later years, Garak wondered if this had caused his occasional bouts of severe claustrophobia. ("Afterimage" [DS9]). During the final, desperate days of the Dominion war, Garak returned to Cardassia Prime and, along with Damar and Kira, played an instrumental role in helping to rally Cardassian resistance against the Dominion. ("Dogs of War" [DS9]). After the final battle of the Dominion war was won, Garak remained on Cardassia to help rebuild his homeworld. ("What You Leave Behind" [DS9]).

Gatsby, Commander. Starfleet officer assigned to the ***U.S.S. Olympia***. Gatsby perished with the rest of the ship's company when the vessel was destroyed in orbit of the fourth planet in a star system in the Rutharian sector in 2371. ("The Sound of Her Voice" [DS9]).

Gauman. (Richard J. Zobel, Jr.). Representative of the **B'omar Sovereignty**. In 2374, Dumah and Gauman came aboard *Voyager* to negotiate a shortcut through their space. ("The Raven" [VGR]).

Gegen, Forra. (Henry Woronicz). **Voth** scientist in the field of exobiology and archaeology. Professor Gegen devised the **Distant Origin Theory**, a radical concept that suggested the Voth people had evolved on a planet in another part of the galaxy, migrating to Voth space in the **Delta Quadrant** about 20 million years ago. When Gegen found compelling evidence to support his theory in 2373, the Ministry of Elders accused him of **heresy** and forced him to recant his views. Gegen's assistant was **Tova Veer.** ("Distant Origin" [VGR]). *Henry Woronicz previously played the Klingon scientist J'Dan in "The Drumhead" (TNG).*

Gelnon. (Leland Crooke). **Vorta** official during the Dominion war. Gelnon was in charge of the Jem'Hadar detachment that captured the *Defiant* on stardate 51474.2. Gelnon proceeded to plan a Dominion attack on the dilithium-rich **Coridan** planets. ("One Little Ship" [DS9]).

genetic resequencing vector. Medical suspension formulated to shut down Borg nanoprobes as they emerge from dormancy. ("The Raven" [VGR]).

genome. Complete set of chromosomes imparting the genetic pattern of an individual. In 2374, several of *Starship Voyager*'s crew member **Seven of Nine**'s genomes were found on an instrument in **Kovin**'s lab. (Retrospect" [VGR]). On stardate 51762.4, the crew of the *Voyager* encountered Steth, a being capable of forcibly exchanging genomes with others. He employed this technique to trade bodies with his victims in order to adopt another person's identity. ("Vis à Vis" [VGR]).

Gentry, David. (Zach Galligan) Security officer at Starfleet Headquarters in San Francisco on Earth. Gentry's Starfleet service number was 99-Beta-3278. A re-creation of Ensign Gentry was part of a training facility created by **Species 8472** in the Delta Quadrant in 2375 in preparation for an intelligence-gathering program against the Federation. Study of the re-created Gentry by *Voyager* personnel suggested that Species 8472 was planning a massive invasion of the Alpha Quadrant. Although 8472's actual intent was merely to conduct intelligence gathering against a potential adversary, the re-created Gentry committed suicide rather than reveal more about his people's plans to *Voyager* personnel. ("In the Flesh" [VGR]).

Gettysburg, U.S.S.* Federation starship. The *Gettysburg* docked at station Deep Space 9 in early 2375 for maintenance. ("Treachery, Faith, and the Great River" [DS9]).

Ghemor, Legate.* Cardassian official. Legate Tekeny Ghemor entered the military when he was only 18. A year later he was one of 400 soldiers at the Kiessa monastery who conducted a brutal massacre in which 14 monks were murdered. Many years later, in 2373, Ghemor was diagnosed with Yarim Fel syndrome, a fatal condition. Having no surviving family, Ghemor regarded Kira as a surrogate daughter, and he decided to spend his last days with her on station Deep Space 9. Just prior to his death, Ghemor observed the Cardassian tradition of ***shri-tal,*** in which the dying give their secrets to their family to be used against their enemies. This inside data, provided to Kira, was regarded as an intelligence bonanza by Starfleet Command. Tekeny Ghemor was buried on Bajor, next to Kira Nerys's father, Kira Taban. ("Ties of Blood and Water" [DS9]).

Giants. Professional **baseball** team that played on Earth during the 20th and 21st centuries. **Willie Hawkins** played for the Giants in 1953 when they were based in New York. ("Far Beyond the Stars" [DS9]).

"Gift, The." *Voyager* episode #70. Written by Joe Menosky. Directed by Anson Williams. No stardate given. *First aired in 1997. Seven of Nine becomes a member of the* Voyager *crew. Kes undergoes a transformation into a powerful noncorporeal entity and hurls* Voyager *9,500 light-years closer to the Alpha Quadrant before departing. In this episode, the second of the fifth season, Kes leaves the cast of the show.* GUEST CAST: Jennifer Lien as **Kes.** SEE: **anetrizine; autonomous regeneration sequencer; Ayala, Lieutenant; biosynthetic gland; Borg organelle; Borg; colliculi; Galactic Cluster 3; Hansen, Annika; Kes; neuro sequencer; Omega Sector; omnicordial life-form; Seven of Nine; Species 259; Talaxian champagne; telesynaptic activity; Tendara Colony; trochlear nerve.**

Giger, Dr. Elias. (Brian Markinson). Research scientist. Giger was a student of Dr. Bathkin's controversial theories that immortality for humanoids might be achieved by keeping all the cells in the body properly entertained. To demonstrate Bathkin's concepts, Giger constructed a **cellular regeneration and entertainment chamber** at station Deep Space 9 in late 2373. While at Deep Space 9, Giger purchased at auction a lot of art objects, including an ancient **baseball trading card**. Giger bartered the card to Jake Sisko in exchange for supplies and equipment to complete construction of his cellular regeneration chamber. ("In the Cards" [DS9]). *Brian Markinson previously played Vorin in "Homeward" (TNG) and the Vidiian scientist Sulan and Lieutenant Peter Durst in "Faces" (VGR).*

Gilbert and Sullivan. Sir William Gilbert and Sir Arthur Sullivan. Noted 19th-century Earth writer-composers of comic operettas. Gilbert and Sullivan's works included *The **Pirates of Penzance*** ("Disaster" [TNG]) and ***H.M.S. Pinafore***. Their works survived into the 24th century, where they were still performed by such devotees as Jean-Luc Picard and Data. (*Star Trek: Insurrection*).

Ginger. (Cyndi Pass). Holographic character, a 1960s **Las Vegas** dancer in the **Vic Fontaine** program. Ginger once performed on the same stage as **Liberace**. She sometimes dated Vic. ("His Way" [DS9]).

Girani, Doctor. Physician assigned to station Deep Space 9 in 2375. ("Chrysalis" [DS9]).

Glintara Sector. Region of space located within Romulan territory. ("In the Pale Moonlight" [DS9]).

Global *Tongo* Championships. High-level ***tongo*** competition held annually on Ferenginar. The event featured various divisions, including a Golden Masters and a Female Division. Zek and Ishka met at the Global *Tongo* Championships in 2373. Grand Nagus Zek played in the Golden Masters' Division, which he had dominated for the past 26 years. ("Ferengi Love Songs" [DS9]).

Gnome Press. Publishing company on Earth during the 20th century specializing in hard-copy paper publications of **science-fiction** and fantasy stories. In 1953, Gnome Press published writer **Albert Macklin**'s first novel, a story about robots. ("Far Beyond the Stars" [DS9]). *In real life, Gnome Press published Isaac Asimov's early works, including* I, Robot.

Golana melon. Large round fruit of the gourd family found on the planet Golana. ("Time's Orphan" [DS9]).

Golana. Lush Class-M planet near Bajoran space. Golana was home to a technologically advanced civilization that vanished 1,000 years ago. Golana was later colonized by Bajorans around 2299. In 2374, while her family was picnicking on Golana, **Molly O'Brien** discovered an ancient time portal in a cave and fell through it. SEE: **Golanan time portal**. ("Time's Orphan" [DS9]).

Golanan time portal. Device created by the ancient Golanan civilization that created a passageway into the past or future. In 2374, while her family was picnicking on Golana, young Molly O'Brien (age eight) discovered a time portal in a cave. The child fell through the triangular mechanism, ending up 300 years in Golana's past, where she survived in the wilderness. After about ten years alone in the past, Molly returned briefly to 2374, but found herself unable to cope with human society. This version of Molly subsequently returned to ancient Golana, which she considered to be her home. In the process, she managed to return her eight-year-old self back to her parents' time. ("Time's Orphan" [DS9]).

Golanans. Technologically advanced civilization that lived on the planet Golana. The Golanans had sophisticated temporal technology. The entire Golanan civilization vanished one thousand years ago. ("Time's Orphan" [DS9]).

gold-pressed latinum. Form of the valuable liquid metal, latinum, suspended in ingots of gold. ("Who Mourns for Morn?" [DS9]).

gold. Element number 79, a soft, yellow metal, highly conductive, but resistant to chemical reactions and able to hold a lustrous surface finish. Symbol Au. Gold was used as a medium of monetary exchange in some primitive cultures, including those of old Earth. By the 24th century, gold was still a useful metal for industrial and decorative applications. Gold was also used as a medium for storing **latinum**, a highly valuable liquid metal. The combined form, used as currency in several cultures, was called gold-pressed latinum. ("Who Mourns for Morn?" [DS9]).

Golden Age of Bajor. An extended period of peace on **Bajor** predicted by **Shabren's Fifth Prophecy**. The Golden Age was prophesied to last a millennium and was to begin when **Kosst Amojan**, the Evil One, was destroyed. SEE: **Reckoning, the**. ("The Reckoning" [DS9]).

golf. An outdoor Earth game played on a large grassy field with a small resilient ball and a set of clubs. The object of the game is to direct the ball into a series of variously distributed holes using the smallest possible number of club strokes. Tom Paris and Harry Kim occasionally played golf aboard the *Starship Voyager*. ("Vis à Vis" [VGR]).

Golian spa. A resort that provided rest and relaxation facilities. ("Children of Time" [DS9]).

Golwat, Ensign.* Starfleet officer aboard the *U.S.S. Voyager*. On stardate 51501.4, Golwat received a letter from home in a Starfleet transmission received through a **Hirogen relay station**. ("Hunters" [VGR]).

Goodheart, Constance. (Kirsten Turner, Jeri Ryan). Character in *The Adventures of Captain Proton* holodeck program. Goodheart was **Captain Proton**'s media intermediary, a beautiful woman who often accompanied Proton on his heroic missions into space. On at least one occasion, Seven of Nine played Goodheart to Tom Paris's Captain Proton. ("Night" [VGR]). SEE: ***Captain Proton, The Adventures of.***

Gorath. Location in the Klingon Empire, site of unpleasant sulfur lagoons. Traversing these lagoons was often part of an ordeal designed to test a warrior's mettle as part of a traditional observance of the Klingon **Day of Honor**. ("Day of Honor" [VGR]).

gorch. Klingon pimple. (*Star Trek: Insurrection*).

Gordon, Ensign Paul. (Joseph Fuqua). Starfleet security officer who served under the command of Captain Sisko in 2374. Gordon was killed while serving on the crew of the commandeered Jem'Hadar vessel that crash-landed on a planet located in a **dark-matter nebula** in Cardassian space. ("Rocks and Shoals" [DS9]).

Goren system. Planetary system. In 2375, Starfleet Command requested that the *U.S.S. Enterprise*-E proceed to the Goren system to mediate a dispute. (*Star Trek: Insurrection*).

Gowron.* Klingon leader, head of his people's High Council. Despite initial reluctance, Gowron supported a bold Starfleet plan to retake station Deep Space 9 from **Dominion** control during the Dominion war in 2374. Gowron's warriors were crucial in this pivotal battle. ("Favor the Bold" [DS9]). As the Dominion war progressed, Gowron became concerned that the honors being given to field commander Martok might threaten Gowron's own political power base. Gowron soon moved to assume personal command of the Klingon forces. ("When it Rains..." [DS9]). Gowron, concerned more with consolidating his own power than with the welfare of his warriors, sent **General Martok** on a series of disastrous missions that seriously undermined the Alpha Quadrant powers' position in the final weeks of the Dominion war. Appalled at Gowron's squandering of Klingon lives and fearing the survival of the empire was in jeopardy, **Worf** finally took it upon himself to challenge Gowron for leadership of the high council. Worf killed Gowron in the ensuing *bat'leth* fight, but immediately relinquished the title of chancellor to Martok. ("Tacking into the Wind" [DS9]).

Grable, Betty. (1916–1973). Twentieth-century Earth entertainer. Grable was an actor, dancer, and singer who appeared in numerous motion pictures in the mid-20th century. Photographs of Grable, emphasizing her beautiful legs, were popular among soldiers of the American army during Earth's World War II. ("The Killing Game, Part II" [VGR]).

Graife. Bartender at a low-class tavern on planet Farius Prime. Graife's bar was frequented by **Liam Bilby** and his associates. Graife worked for Raimus, an operative of the **Orion Syndicate**. ("Honor Among Thieves" [DS9]).

Grail of Kahless. Sacred Klingon chalice that once belonged to **Kahless the Unforgettable**. Traditional observances of the Klingon **Day of Honor** often included drinking *mot'loch* from a replica of this icon. ("Day of Honor" [VGR]).

Grant, Cary. (1904–1986). Twentieth-century Earth entertainer, noted as an actor who played romantic lead characters in two-dimensional noninteractive motion pictures. Grant appeared in a variety of films including *To Catch a Thief* and *North by Northwest*. In an alternate timeline, B'Elanna Torres and Harry Kim played a trivia game in which one question concerned lead actor Grant in *To Catch a Thief*. ("Year of Hell, Part I" [VGR]).

***grapok* sauce.** Klingon condiment. ("Sons and Daughters" [DS9]).

gravimetric fluctuation.* Spatial distortion phenomenon. Gravimetric fluctuations can occur in proximity to a quantum singularity. ("Scorpion, Part I" [VGR]).

gravimetric shear. Deformation of a solid body by differential variations in a local gravitational field. ("Drone" [VGR]).

gravimetric torpedo. Sophisticated energy weapon. Captain Kathryn Janeway of the *U.S.S. Voyager* used a gravimetric torpedo on stardate 51781 to destroy about 200 million **Omega molecules**. ("The Omega Directive" [VGR]).

graviton stabilizer. Component in an artificial gravity generator. ("Treachery, Faith, and the Great River" [DS9]).

graviton.* Elementary particle, a quantum unit of gravitational force. An **interdimensional rift** can be created by directing a specifically modulated resonant graviton beam into space. ("Scorpion, Part II" [VGR]).

gray mode. Starship operational protocols designed for severe energy conservation. In gray mode, power to nonessential decks and systems was discontinued, and remaining systems were operated at 20 percent. *Voyager* entered gray mode in late 2374 when its supply of deuterium was almost exhausted. ("Demon" [VGR]).

***Gray's Anatomy*.** Classic medical reference textbook on the anatomical structure of humans from planet Earth. Written by Dr. Henry Gray, first published in noninteractive hard-copy form in 1858. ("Message in a Bottle" [VGR]).

Grease Monkey. Holographic program created by **Thomas Paris**. Set in the American nation on Earth's North American continent during the late 20th century, the program featured a re-creation of a personal vehicle maintenance and storage facility known in the vernacular as a "garage." In the garage was a wheeled land vehicle called a 1969 Chevrolet **Camaro**. Paris (and, evidently, inhabitants of the actual 20th century) derived enjoyment from adjusting the mechanical workings of the vehicle in hopes of increasing the power output of its internal combustion engine. The title refers to the tendency of one engaged in such work to become covered with a viscous fluid lubricant called grease. ("Vis à Vis" [VGR]).

Great Forest. Promised place of the afterlife in **Talaxian** mythology. The Great Forest was a beautiful place filled with sunlight where the departed will reunite with their ancestors and everyone who has ever loved them. At the heart of the Great Forest was the **Guiding Tree**. ("Mortal Coil" [VGR]).

Great Link.* A communal joining of the **Founders'** civilization in the Gamma Quadrant. In their common fluid form, the Link was a vast sea of undulating, viscous orange liquid. The purpose of the Link was not the exchange of information, but rather a merging of thought and form, as well as idea and sensation. While on their homeworld, the Founders preferred to exist in the Link, but they occasionally took other forms. ("Behind the Lines" [DS9]). In early 2375, a serious epidemic spread throughout the Great Link. ("Treachery, Faith, and the Great River" [DS9]). The disease, it was later learned, was a morphogenic virus intended to exterminate the entire Founder race. The Federation's shadowy Section 31 had deliberately infected Odo with the genocidal weapon, knowing that Odo would inadvertently spread the disease throughout the Great Link. ("When it Rains..." [DS9]). The genetically engineered disease was regarded as incurable and probably would have resulted in the extinction of the Founders if not for the efforts of Dr. Julian Bashir, who extracted information from the mind of a Section 31 operative, making a treatment possible. ("Extreme Measures" [DS9]). The Founders were cured shortly after the end of the Dominion war when Odo returned home to his people, spreading Bashir's cure throughout the Great Link. ("What You Leave Behind" [DS9]).

Great Material Continuum. In **Ferengi** mythology, the force that binds the universe together. The Ferengi people hold that each part of the universe is filled with too much of one thing and not enough of another. They believe the Great Continuum flows through them all like a mighty river, from "have" to "want" and back again, and if one navigates the river with grace and entrepreneurial skill, their ship would be filled with everything they desired. Also called the Great River. ("Treachery, Faith, and the Great River" [DS9]).

Great River. SEE: **Great Material Continuum.**

Great War. Armed conflict between the **Vaskan** and **Kyrian** peoples in the Delta Quadrant in 2374. Radical Kyrians, who had felt oppressed by the Vaskans for years, attacked the *U.S.S. Voyager* in 2374, while *Voyager* personnel were conducting trade negotiations with Vaskan ambassador Daleth. That event touched off armed conflict between the Vaskans and the Kyrians. Even after the end of the war, resentment and inequalities marred relations between the two cultures for centuries. Finally, in the late 31st century, historical evidence, in the form of the *Voyager*'s **Emergency Medical Hologram backup module**, became available. The evidence shed new light on the war's beginning, allowing the opening of a new dialog between the Kyrians and the Vaskans, leading in less than six years to a new era of harmony between the two former enemies. ("Living Witness" [VGR]).

grint hound. Four-legged Klingon animal. ("Time's Orphan" [DS9]).

groat. The grain of a cereal grass widely cultivated on Bajor and providing a flour used for baked goods such as bread and pastries. ("His Way" [DS9]).

groatcakes. Bajoran breakfast food. Leeta loved **syrup of squill** on her groatcakes. ("The Magnificent Ferengi" [DS9]).

Guiding Tree. In **Talaxian** mythology, a large, beautiful tree standing at the center of the Talaxian afterlife deep in the Great Forest. Talaxians believe the tree is there to help the dead find their way when they first arrive and it is the gathering place for all of one's ancestors and loved ones. ("Mortal Coil" [VGR]).

Guill. (Wayne Péré). Inhabitant of the **Mari** homeworld. Guill was a merchant who sold hardware at a marketplace. Guill, in violation of Mari law, also trafficked in illicit mental imagery. In 2374, Guill provoked visiting crew member B'Elanna Torres by bumping into **Frane**, an accomplice, provoking violent thoughts that Guill harvested for sale on the black market. ("Random Thoughts" [VGR]).

gumbo.* Traditional Earth dish, a featured item on the menu at **Sisko's** restaurant. Joseph Sisko's recipe for gumbo was perhaps his most closely guarded secret. ("Image in the Sand" [DS9]).

gyrodyne. Energy-producing device employed in **Jem'Hadar attack ships**. ("Rocks and Shoals" [DS9]).

H.M.S. Pinafore. Comic light opera by **Gilbert and Sullivan** of Earth, first performed in 1878 in the nation of England. The opera was the story of a naval captain's daughter falling in love with a common sailor on his ship. Jean-Luc Picard and Data rehearsed a planned production of *H.M.S. Pinafore* aboard the *Starship Enterprise*-E in 2375. (*Star Trek: Insurrection*).

hadrosaur. Reptilian life-form that evolved on **Earth** during the Cretaceous period. The hadrosaur was bipedal, stood about 1.5 meters tall, and had a pronounced crest on its head. Hadrosaurs and humans shared a common ancestor in the primitive amphibian eryops. After most dinosaurs on Earth vanished, the hadrosaurs continued to evolve on an isolated land mass, eventually becoming the sentient **Voth** species that lived in the Delta Quadrant of the galaxy. ("Distant Origin" [VGR]).

Hain. (Gregory Itzen). Former associate of **Morn** in the infamous Lissepian Mother's Day Heist. In 2365, Hain, Morn, Larell, Krit, and Nahsk robbed the Central Bank of Lissepia of 1,000 bars of **gold-pressed latinum** while the entire planet was celebrating Mother's Day. After the heist, Morn disappeared with all of the money, later staging his own apparent death in 2374, just as the statute of limitations on the case expired. Hain and his associates arrived separately on Deep Space 9 with different plans to get Morn's latinum. Hain claimed to be with **Lurian** security. The four were arrested for attempted murder by station security. ("Who Mourns for Morn?" [DS9]). SEE: **Lissepia, Central Bank of.** *Gregory Itzen also played Ilon Tandro in "Dax" (DS9).*

Haj, Lieutenant. Starfleet officer assigned to the conn aboard the *U.S.S. Defiant*. In 2374, Haj was injured during the *Defiant*'s mission to the Argolis Cluster. ("Behind the Lines" [DS9]).

Halb Daier. (Tim DeZarn). Member of the Bajoran resistance during the Cardassian occupation of Bajor. Halb was present on station **Terok Nor** when **Kira Meru** was brought aboard as a comfort woman. ("Wrongs Darker Than Death or Night" [DS9]). *Given name comes from the script. Tim DeZarn also played Haliz in "Initiations" (VGR) and Satler in "Starship Mine" (TNG).*

Haluk. (Marshall R. Teague). **Voth** security advisor to Minister Odala. ("Distant Origin" [VGR]). *Marshall R. Teague previously played the Jem'Hadar Temo'Zuma in "Hippocratic Oath" (DS9).*

Hamar. Mountain range on planet Qo'noS. *Var'Hama* candles were traditionally made with tallow from the shoulders of three *targ* captured in the Hamar mountains and sacrificed at dawn. ("You Are Cordially Invited" [DS9]).

Hammer, Mike. Fictional 20th-century Earth private detective from the Mike Hammer series of novels written by **Mickey Spillane**. In 2375, Odo recommended the Mike Hammer detective novel, *Kiss Me, Deadly*, to Kira Nerys. ("Shadows and Symbols" [DS9]).

Hanoran II. Planet. The *U.S.S. Enterprise-E* was scheduled to conduct an archeological mission to Hanoran II in 2375. Delays in the ship's arrival proved problematic because of the severity of the planet's monsoon season. (*Star Trek: Insurrection*).

Hansen, Annika. (Erica Lynne). Human child who was assimilated by the **Borg** collective, becoming the Borg drone designated **Seven of Nine**. Annika was born on stardate 25479 at the Tendara Colony, the daughter of two scientists. Her parents were explorers who preferred to work outside of large organized scientific institutions like the Federation Starfleet. ("The Gift" [VGR]). At age six, Annika traveled with her parents on a research mission aboard the ***U.S.S. Raven*** into the Delta Quadrant. In 2354, the *Raven* was boarded by the Borg, and the ship subsequently crashed on a Class-M planetoid orbiting the fifth planet of a yellow dwarf star. Annika and her family were assimilated into the Borg collective. ("The Raven" [VGR]).

Hansen, Erin. (Nikki Tyler, Laura Stepp [*pictured*]). Scientist who was believed to have been killed or assimilated in 2354 during a Borg attack on her research vessel, the ***U.S.S. Raven***. Dr. Hansen was mother to **Annika Hansen**, a child who was assimilated into the Borg collective, becoming the drone known as **Seven of Nine**. ("The Raven" [VGR]).

Hansen, Magnus. (David Anthony Marshall, Kirk Bailey [*pictured*]). Scientist who was father to the human child who became the Borg drone known as **Seven of Nine**. Hansen was believed to have been killed or assimilated in 2354 during a Borg attack on the research vessel ***U.S.S. Raven***. ("The Raven" [VGR]).

harmonic resonance chamber. Containment device designed by the Borg to hold and stabilize an **Omega molecule**. In 2374, on stardate 51781, Seven of Nine constructed a harmonic resonance chamber to contain the Omega molecules created in the Delta Quadrant by Dr. Allos. ("The Omega Directive" [VGR]).

Harvey. Mid-20th-century slang term for a person lacking up-to-date sophistication. ("His Way" [DS9]). SEE: **Clyde, square.**

***hasperat* soufflé.** Delicate dish made by baking blended *hasperat* in a deep pan. ("Sacrifice of Angels" [DS9]).

Hawkins, Willie. (Michael Dorn). Twentieth-century Earth professional **baseball** player. Hawkins played for the New York Giants baseball team in 1953. ("Far Beyond the Stars" [DS9]). *Michael Dorn also played Worf on* Star Trek: Deep Space Nine, *although Willie Hawkins did not have Klingon makeup.*

Hayes, Admiral.* (Jack Shearer). Senior Starfleet official. Admiral Hayes was a survivor of the **Borg** incursion of 2373. Around stardate 51501.4, Hayes sent an encrypted message to the *Starship Voyager*, expressing Starfleet's regret at not being able to help them return home, and containing data that Starfleet had collected about the Delta Quadrant. The message was sent via an ancient alien communications array and was included along with several personal letters to the *Voyager* crew from relatives and friends. ("Hope and Fear" [VGR]). SEE: **Hirogen relay station.** *Jack Shearer appeared as Hayes in* Star Trek: First Contact.

HD-25 maintenance unit. Holographic technician used aboard Serosian spacecraft in the Delta Quadrant. **Dejaren** was an HD-25 maintenance unit. ("Revulsion" [VGR]).

Heinlein, Robert A. (1907–1988). Twentieth-century Earth novelist. Heinlein was sometimes known as the "dean of **science fiction**" for his role in developing the genre as a sophisticated mode of literary expression. Heinlein's works included such stories as ***The Puppet Masters***, first published in ***Galaxy Science Fiction*** magazine. **Herbert Rossoff** felt he would be in good company if his stories were published alongside those of Heinlein. ("Far Beyond the Stars" [DS9]). *Many students of science fiction have regarded Heinlein's works as being a signifi-*

cant influence on Gene Roddenberry's development of the original Star Trek *television series.*

hematological scan. Medical diagnostic study of a patient's blood factors. ("Mortal Coil" [VGR]).

herbal tea. Hot Earth beverage made from aromatic plants such as chamomile. ("Unforgettable" [VGR]).

"Here's to the Losers." Popular 20th-century Earth musical composition that spoke of the challenges of attracting a suitable mate in humanoid society. The song was performed by such entertainers as **Vic Fontaine** and **Frank Sinatra**. The holographic re-creation of Fontaine sang it to Julian Bashir and Quark when the two were commiserating over their failure to win the romantic attentions of Jadzia Dax. ("Tears of the Prophets" [DS9]).

heresy. In some repressive societies, heresy is the crime of holding or expressing beliefs that might tend to challenge the authority of the established power structure in that society. In such societies, prosecution of heresy can be a means of silencing those who hold beliefs that those in power find objectionable. SEE: **Voth Doctrine**. ("Distant Origin" [VGR]).

Hesterman. Noted 21st-century author. Hesterman's works included *Beyond the Galactic Edge*. A replica of Starfleet officer Valerie Archer created by Species 8472 in 2375 found Hesterman's works to offer insight into the human species. ("In the Flesh" [VGR]).

heuristic subprocessor. Data-processing device used by Starfleet computing systems, such as those used to control a starship's dilithium articulation frame. ("One Little Ship" [DS9]).

hexadrin. Medication used in the treatment of Yarim Fel syndrome. ("Ties of Blood and Water" [DS9]).

Hickman, Ensign. Starfleet officer assigned to the Astrophysics section of the *U.S.S. Voyager*. Hickman sometimes did imitations of Captain Janeway's voice to amuse her fellow crew members. ("Scorpion, Part I" [VGR], "The Omega Directive" [VGR]).

Highway 1. Land roadway built along the Pacific coast of the North American continent on Earth during the 20th century. ("Vis à Vis" [VGR]).

Hippocratic Oath.* Traditional Earth code of ethics for physicians. The *Voyager*'s **Emergency Medical Hologram** provided emergency care for injured Romulan soldiers on board the ***U.S.S. Prometheus*** in 2374, noting that the Hippocratic Oath required him to render aid, even to the enemy. ("Message in a Bottle" [VGR]).

Hirogen medic. (Mark Metcalf). Hunter who participated in a takeover of the Federation starship *Voyager* in late 2374 in which an alpha used the ship's crew to simulate a variety of historic battles on the **holodeck**. This hunter was assigned to repair *Voyager* crew members who became injured or were killed during the simulations. SEE: **French Resistance**. ("The Killing Game, Parts I and II" [VGR]).

Hirogen relay station. Component of a far-flung communication network operated by the Hirogen in the Delta Quadrant; the series of network stations constructed by the **Hirogens** on the edge of the Delta Quadrant. In 2374 the *U.S.S. Voyager* established contact with the Hirogen relay stations, which enabled a holographic data stream to be sent to the ***Starship Prometheus*** located in the Alpha Quadrant. ("Message in a Bottle" [VGR]). SEE: **Alpha-Hirogen**. The relay system was built approximately 100,000 years ago, and individual stations relied on an extraordinary power technology using emissions from captured quantum singularities. The *Voyager* crew accessed the Hirogen relay system a second time several weeks later. By making a close approach to a relay station, they succeeded in downloading a message from Starfleet Command, as well as a number of personal messages addressed to members of the *Voyager* from family members and friends. ("Hunters" [VGR]).

Hirogen ship. Small but heavily armed cruiser spacecraft used by Hirogen hunters in the Delta Quadrant. Usually piloted by two hunters, these vessels were equipped with monotanium armor plating. ("Hunters" [VGR]). Hirogen ships had dicyclic warp signatures. ("Prey" [VGR]).

Hirogen SS Officer. (Mark Deakins). Persona assumed by a **Hirogen** hunter aboard the *Starship Voyager* in 2374 in the **French Resistance** holodeck simulation. In the simulation, the SS Officer was a military security operative in the army of **Nazi Germany**. ("The Killing Game, Parts I and II" [VGR]).

Hirogen. Spacefaring civilization in the Delta Quadrant. The Hirogen social structure is organized around packs of hunters, each led by a Hirogen designated as alpha. Status within each pack is determined by possession of prizes from hunts, usually body parts obtained from prey. Hirogen spacecraft roamed the Delta Quadrant, either alone or in small groups, seeking prey. By the 24th century, the nomadic Hirogen no longer identified any single planet as their homeworld. ("Hunters" [VGR], "Prey" [VGR]). SEE: **Alpha-Hirogen**. Hirogen culture requires a hunter to study his prey to understand its abilities, believing that such study is essential to prevent a hunter from becoming the hunted. ("The Killing Game, Parts I and II" [VGR]). The Hirogen civilization was not only ancient, but possessed extremely advanced technology. Some 100,000 years ago, they built a far-flung communications network throughout the Delta Quadrant that continued to operate into the 24th century. ("Message in a Bottle" [VGR]). SEE: **Hirogen relay station**. Yet by that time, Hirogen society put nearly all of its energy into increasingly unproductive hunts in increasingly exhausted territories, bringing cultural and scientific advancement to a near standstill. ("The Killing Game, Parts I and II" [VGR]).

"His Way" *Deep Space Nine* episode #144. Written by Ira Steven Behr & Hans Beimler. Directed by Allan Kroeker. No stardate given. *First aired in 1998. Odo receives lessons in love from a holographic 1960s lounge singer. Kira and Odo become romantically involved in this episode, which marked the first appearance of Vic Fontaine, who sang several Sinatra favorites. Nana Visitor, in the role of Lola Chrystal, sings "Fever."* GUEST CAST: James Darren as **Fontaine, Vic;** Debi A. Monahan as **Melissa;** Cyndi Pass as **Ginger**. SEE: **Borge, Victor; Caesar salad; chateaubriand; cherries jubilee; Chrystal, Lola; "Come Fly With Me"; Dunes; Felix; "Fever"; Fontaine, Vic; Ginger; groat; Harvey; holodeck and holosuite programs: Vic Fontaine; "I've Got You under My Skin"; Jessel, George; Kennedy, John F.; Kira Nerys; Las Vegas; Liberace; light bulb; Martin, Dean; Melissa; Odo; oysters Rockefeller; Sands; Sinatra, Frank; square; "They Can't Take That Away from Me"; Walker, Ensign; warp core breach; "You're Nobody Till Somebody Loves You"; Zevians.**

Hogan.* Starfleet officer who was killed in the Delta Quadrant while serving aboard the *Starship Voyager*. Hogan's skeletal remains were retrieved in late 2373 from Hanon IV by **Voth** archaeologist **Forra Gegen**, where they provided powerful evidence to support Gegen's **Distant Origin Theory**, suggesting that Voth and human people shared a common ancestor. ("Distant Origin" [VGR]).

Holna IV. Planet in the Kabrel system in the Alpha Quadrant. Holna IV had large deposits of **mizainite ore**. In peace talks with the Federation, the Dominion was willing to give up Holna IV for possession of the Kabrel system. ("Statistical Probabilities" [DS9]).

holo-imager.* Holographic-image recording device. The *Voyager*'s holographic Doctor used a holo-imager on a shuttle mission to investigate a protonebula in 2375. ("Drone" [VGR]). Chakotay used a holo-imager to photograph an elaborate re-creation of Starfleet Headquarters created by Species 8472 in 2375. ("In the Flesh" [VGR]).

holo-photographer. Profession in which one creates holographic images of items, persons, or locations. **Sarah Sisko** worked as a holo-photographer in Australia just prior to her death in 2336. ("Image in the Sand" [DS9]).

holodeck and holosuite programs*:

Alamo, Battle of the. Historic defense of the Alamo against overwhelming odds in the cause of Texan independence in 1836. ("Afterimage" [DS9]).

Ba'ku village. Designed to fool the **Ba'ku** into thinking they were on their homeworld while they were actually being abducted. (*Star Trek: Insurrection*).

baseball game. Twentieth-century ballpark, with or without spectators. SEE: **Niners**. ("Take Me Out to the Holosuite" [DS9]).

Bat'leth combat workout. Klingon workout program that featured combat using a *bat'leth*. ("Displaced" [VGR]; "Image in the Sand" [DS9]).

Captain Proton, The Adventures of. Science-fiction melodrama featuring the heroic **Captain Proton** and the maniacal **Doctor Chaotica**. ("Night" [VGR]).

Christmas Carol, A. The classic novel by Charles Dickens. ("The Omega Directive" [VGR]).

Crusades. Horrific religious warfare in ancient Europe. ("The Killing Game, Part I" [VGR]).

da Vinci workshop program Janeway-7. Workshop of the Renaissance genius around 1502. ("Scorpion, Part I" [VGR]).

Day of Honor. Traditional Klingon observance in the mystical **Caves of Kahless**. ("Day of Honor" [VGR]).

Doctor's family program Beta-Rho. Simulated human family created by *Voyager*'s holographic doctor. ("Real Life" [VGR]).

Don Carlo. The classic Italian opera by Giuseppe Verdi. ("Night" [VGR]).

Flotter, The Adventures of. Imaginative children's tales that teach the interrelationships of nature in the **Forest of Forever**. ("Once Upon a Time" [VGR]).

French Resistance. Underground fighting against soldiers of **Nazi Germany** in World War II. ("The Killing Game, Parts I and II" [VGR]).

Golf. Eighteen holes of green. ("Vis à Vis" [VGR]).

Grease Monkey. Program Paris Alpha-1. A 20th-century garage with a 1969 Chevrolet **Camaro**. ("Vis à Vis" [VGR]).

Insurrection Alpha. Training scenario to prepare for a possible **Maquis** mutiny on *Voyager*. ("Worse Case Scenario" [VGR]).

Kal'Hyah ritual. Klingon spiritual journey for a man and his closest friends before his wedding. ("You Are Cordially Invited" [DS9]).

Klingon battle. Vicious combat with the House of Mo'Kai. ("The Killing Game, Part I" [VGR]).

Ktarian moonrise. Romantic setting. ("Revulsion" [VGR]).

Medical Consultant. Simulation of exobiologist and war criminal Dr. **Crell Moset**. ("Nothing Human" [VGR]).

Ocean view. Wide-open outdoor vista intended to help Garak deal with claustrophobia. ("Afterimage" [DS9]).

orbital skydiving. Freefall from exospheric altitudes, then (hopefully) land safely on a planet surface. ("Extreme Risk" [VGR]).

Paris in 1928. One of the most romantic settings on the planet Earth. ("The Sound of Her Voice" [DS9]).

Section 31 test. Secret test of a Starfleet officer's loyalty to the Federation. ("Inquisition" [DS9]).

Socialization. Simulation of the *Voyager* crew to help **Seven of Nine** gain familiarity with social situations. ("One" [VGR]).

Son'a ship bridge. Used by Picard to trick Ru'afo so he wouldn't kill the Ba'ku. (*Star Trek: Insurrection*).

Torres 2-1-6. Brutal combat with Cardassian soldiers in dark caves. ("Extreme Risk" [VGR]).

Torres Zeta-1. Gruesome display of dead Maquis members. ("Extreme Risk" [VGR]).

Velocity. Game using phasers to control a small hovering puck. ("Hope and Fear" [VGR]).

Vic Fontaine. The prominent singer from the 1960s in his Las Vegas nightclub. ("His Way" [DS9]).

holodeck.* Holographic environment simulator. In 2374, the holodecks aboard the Federation starship *Voyager* were commandeered, along with the rest of the ship and its crew, by **Hirogen** hunters. The Hirogen, using neural interface devices, imprisoned the *Voyager* crew in a series of brutal simulations of ancient wars in an effort to study their behavior. ("The Killing Game, Parts I and II" [VGR]). SEE: **holodeck and holosuite programs.**

holoship. Starfleet spacecraft; a large, mobile, holographic environment simulator. Starfleet **admiral Matthew Dougherty** used a holoship in his attempt to gain control of the **Ba'ku planet** in 2375. Dougherty had hoped to use the holoship to create a duplicate of the **Ba'ku** inhabitants' village, so that they could be abducted without the knowledge of the Ba'ku. (*Star Trek: Insurrection*).

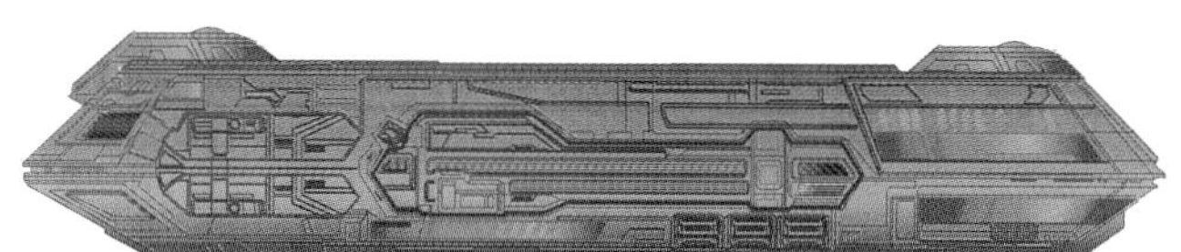

"Honor Among Thieves" *Deep Space Nine* episode #139. Teleplay by René Echevarria. Story by Philip Kim. Directed by Allan Eastman. No stardate given. *First aired in 1998. An undercover operation turns personal for O'Brien when he befriends his criminal contact. In this episode the O'Brien family adopts Chester the cat. O'Brien later investigated the disappearance of Bilby's widow in "Prodigal Daughter" (DS9).* GUEST CAST: Nick Tate as **Bilby, Liam**; Michael Harney as **Chadwick**; Carlos Carrasco as **Krole**; John Chandler as **Flith**; Leland Crooke as Vorta; Joseph Culp as **Raimus**; Brad Blaisdell as **Yint.** SEE: **Bilby, Liam; Bolias, Bank of; Chadwick; Chester; combooth; Connelly; Degora Street; fare; Farius Prime; Flith; Graife; Jinami Street; Krellans; Krole; New Sydney; nozala sandwich; O'Brien, Miles; Orion Syndicate; pets; Raimus; Risa; vilm sauce; Yint.**

Honshu, U.S.S. Federation starship, *Nebula* class. On stardate 51408.6, the *Honshu* was attacked and destroyed by a wing of Cardassian destroyers. Captain Benjamin Sisko and Gul Dukat, who were aboard the ship bound for a special hearing on Dukat's case on Starbase 621, managed to escape in a shuttlecraft. ("Waltz" [DS9]). *The* Honshu *was named for the largest of the islands of Japan.*

Hood, U.S.S.* Federation starship. The *Hood* fought in the combined fleet of allied Alpha Quadrant forces that invaded Cardassian space at the **Chin'toka System** in late 2374. ("Tears of the Prophets" [DS9]).

"Hope and Fear." *Voyager* episode #94. Teleplay by Brannon Braga & Joe Menosky. Story by Rick Berman & Brannon Braga & Joe Menosky. Directed by Winrich Kolbe. Stardate 51978.2. *First aired in 1998. The amazing discovery of a Federation starship to return the* Voyager *crew to Earth turns out to be a plot to win revenge against Janeway for having helped the Borg against Species 8472. In this last episode of* Voyager's *fourth season, the ship succeeds in moving another 300 light-years closer to home.* GUEST CAST: Ray Wise as **Arturis;** Jack Shearer as **Hayes, Admiral.** SEE: **Arturis; Bolians; Chapman, Admiral; *Dauntless, U.S.S.*; Earth; Hayes, Admiral; holodeck and holosuite programs: Velocity; Janeway, Kathryn; Ktarians; particle synthesis; quantum slipstream drive; recursion matrix; Seven of Nine; Species 116; transwarp; triaxilation; trinary syntax; velocity; *Voyager, U.S.S.*; xenon-based life-form.**

Hor-CHA, I.K.S. Klingon starship. At a replica of Starfleet Headquarters created by Species 8472 as a training facility for infiltration of the Alpha Quadrant, a re-creation of Commander Valerie Archer was assigned to the *Hor-CHA* as first officer in early 2375. ("In the Flesh" [VGR]).

Horran's Seventh Prophecy. Ancient text in the **Bajoran** religion. The prophecy began, "He will come to the palace, carrying a chalice overflowing with sweet, spring wine." ("Ferengi Love Songs" [DS9]).

Horvian Cluster. Stellar group; location of planet **Casperia Prime**. ("Change of Heart" [DS9]).

Hovas, Legate. High-ranking official in the Cardassian government. In early 2375 Legate Damar attended a dinner held in Hovas's honor. ("Shadows and Symbols" [DS9]).

hoverball.* Sport. Thomas Paris and Harry Kim enjoyed an occasional late-night game of hoverball. ("Waking Moments" [VGR]).

hovercraft. Vehicle that travels slightly above the ground, usually elevated by a cushion of air. In 2336, **Sarah Sisko** died in a hovercraft accident in Australia. ("Image in the Sand" [DS9]).

Hudson, Calvin.* Former Starfleet officer who joined the Maquis terrorist group. Hudson was killed in a skirmish with the Cardassians sometime between 2370 and 2373. ("Blaze of Glory" [DS9]).

Hughes, Langston. (1902–1967). Twentieth-century Earth poet and writer. Hughes was one of his world's foremost interpreters of the experience of African-Americans as a minority in the American nation. **Benny Russell** drew inspiration from Hughes's work. ("Far Beyond the Stars" [DS9]).

Hugo Award. Prize for excellence in **science fiction** presented annually at the World Science Fiction Convention on Earth. Named for pioneering 20th-century science-fiction magazine editor Hugo Gernsback, a Hugo Award was a **rocket ship**-shaped trophy. **Herbert Rossoff** won a Hugo Award in 1953. ("Far Beyond the Stars" [DS9]). *Episode cowriter (and executive producer) Ira Steven Behr said that one reason the episode was set in the year 1953 was because that was when the Hugos were first awarded. We infer that Rossoff won a Hugo because we saw him stuff a rocket ship–shaped Hugo trophy from his desk into his briefcase when he threatened to quit* Incredible Tales *magazine. (In reality, the Hugo for Best Novel of 1953 went to Alfred Bester for* The Demolished Man.*) Rossoff's Hugo actually belongs to* Star Trek *senior illustrator Rick Sternbach, who loaned it to the studio for the episode. Rick has won the coveted trophy twice in the "Best Professional Artist" category.* Star Trek *itself has been honored four times with Hugo Awards for "Best Dramatic Presentation." The first was in 1967 for "The Menagerie, Parts I and II" (TOS), then in 1968 for "City on the Edge of Forever" (TOS), in 1993 for "The Inner Light" (TNG), and most recently in 1995 for "All Good Things..." (TNG). Numerous other episodes have also been nominated for the prize.*

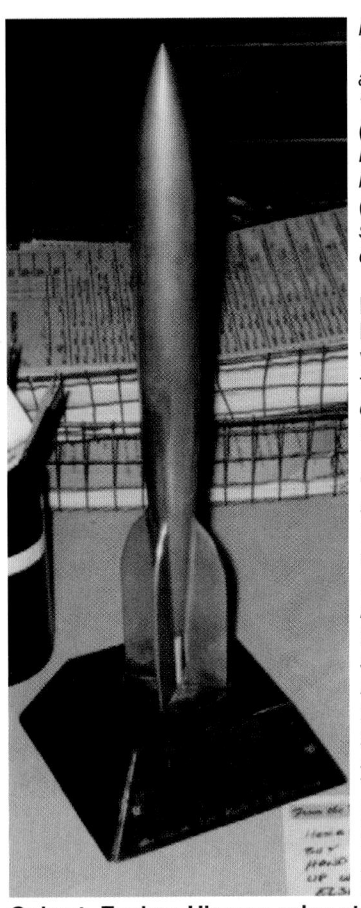

Hunter, K.C. Pen name used by author **Kay Eaton** when writing science fiction stories for the pulp magazine ***Incredible Tales*** in the 1950s. ("Far Beyond the Stars" [DS9]).

"Hunters." *Voyager* episode #83. Written by Jeri Taylor. Directed by David Livingston. Stardate 51501.4. *First aired in 1997. While* Voyager *extracts messages from home through the Hirogen relay system, the ship is attacked by Hirogen hunters. In one of the messages from home, Janeway learns that her ex-fiancé has since married someone else.* GUEST CAST: Tiny Ron as **Alpha-Hirogen;** Roger Morrissey as Beta-Hirogen**.** SEE: **Alpha-Hirogen; Amonak; antithoron; Ashmore, Ensign; Dorado; Fitzpatrick; Golwat, Ensign; Hirogen relay station; Hirogen ship; Hirogen; Janeway, Kathryn; Johnson, Mark; ketric; Kyoto, Ensign; Maquis; Molly; monotanium; Nicoletti, Susan; osteotomy; Paris, Admiral Owen; Paris, Thomas; Parsons, Ensign; polaron; quantum singularity; Sek; Species 5174; Sveta; T'Meni; T'Pel; Trayken beast; Tuvok; *Voyager, U.S.S.***

Hurston, Zora Neale. (1903–1960). Twentieth-century Earth folklorist and writer. Hurston was associated with the Harlem Renaissance, celebrating African-American culture in the voice of the rural South. **Benny Russell** drew inspiration from Hurston's work. ("Far Beyond the Stars" [DS9]).

hyper-REM. Abnormal neurological condition during sleep. In 2374, the crew of the ***Starship Voyager*** experienced a prolonged and agitated period of deep hyper-REM sleep initiated by a **dream species**. ("Waking Moments" [VGR]).

hyperspanner. General purpose engineering tool used by Starfleet personnel. ("Empok Nor" [DS9]).

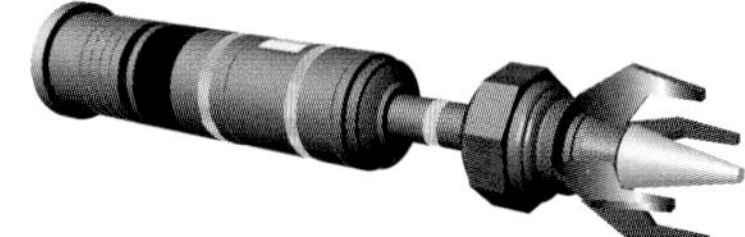

hypicate cream. Cosmetic product. In 2374, Ishka predicted that hypicate cream would be a source of great profit if marketed to newly franchised Ferengi females. ("Profit and Lace" [DS9]).

hypicate. Root that had many varied uses. Hypicate was used in certain medicines, diffractive optics, and even some beauty supplies. Ishka applied a hypicate cream twice a day to her head; she felt it made her skin smooth. ("The Magnificent Ferengi" [DS9]).

hyronalin.* Drug used to treat radiation poisoning. A combination of hyronalin and lectrazine helped to protect Tom Paris during a mission to investigate an astral eddy. ("Real Life" [VGR]).

"I've Got You under My Skin." Popular 20th-century Earth musical composition that spoke of the power of love in human society. Written by Cole Porter. The song was performed by such entertainers as **Vic Fontaine** and **Frank Sinatra**. ("His Way" [DS9]).

ice cream. Dessert food; a frozen blended mixture of dairy cream, flavoring, and sweetening. ("Sons and Daughters" [DS9]). Chakotay and Kellin had some ice cream aboard the *Starship Voyager* around stardate 51813. ("Unforgettable" [VGR]).

ideogram. Symbol used as a graphic representation of a single thought pictured. All forms of the Bajoran language, even versions found in ancient archaeologic sites, shared certain root ideograms, pictured. ("The Reckoning" [DS9]).

Igel, DaiMon. Ferengi entrepreneur. Igel asked Grand Nagus **Zek** for financial advice in 2373. ("Ferengi Love Songs" [DS9]).

Iliana.* Daughter of Cardassian intelligence official **Ghemor**. In 2373, Gul Dukat and Vorta operative Weyoun claimed that they knew the whereabouts of Iliana, an attempt to convince Ghemor to return to Cardassia. ("Ties of Blood and Water" [DS9]).

Ilvia*. City on Bajor. In the mirror universe, **Lisea** was from Ilvia. ("Resurrection" [DS9]).

"Image in the Sand." *Deep Space Nine* episode #151. Written by Ira Steven Behr & Hans Beimler. Directed by Les Landau. No stardate given. *First aired in 1998. Kira deals with a new Romulan presence on the station, while on Earth, Benjamin Sisko learns of an undiscovered Orb that may be the key to restoring the Prophets and the wormhole. This was the first episode of the seventh and final season of* Star Trek: Deep Space Nine. *It continued the storyline begun in "Tears of the Prophets" (DS9), which in turn was later continued in "Shadows and Symbols" (DS9). Nicole deBoer joined the cast as Ezri Dax in this episode, and Kira was promoted to colonel.* GUEST CAST: Aron Eisenberg as **Nog;** J. G. Hertzler as **Martok, General;** Casey Biggs as **Damar;** Megan Cole as **Cretak, Senator;** Brock Peters as **Sisko, Joseph;** Jeffrey Combs as **Weyoun;** Barry Jenner as **Ross, Admiral Michael;** James Darren as **Fontaine, Vic;** Johnny Moran as Bajoran man. SEE: **"All the Way"; Armstrong Park; Bajor; barbecued shrimp; crawfish étoufée; Cretak, Senator; Dax (symbiont); Dax, Ezri; Dax, Jadzia; Derna; gumbo; holodeck and holosuite programs: *Bat'leth* combat workout; holophotographer; hovercraft; Jackson Square; Kira Nerys; Martok, General; Monac IV; Orb of the Emissary; *osol* twist; Pah-wraith; plasma torpedo; Ross, Admiral William; Sisko's; Sisko, Benjamin; Sisko, Jake; Sisko, Joseph; Sisko, Sarah; *Sto-Vo-Kor*; trilithium; Tyree; Worf; Yaltar, Gul.**

immersion shield. Advanced deflector technique employing unimatrix shield technology. Devised by Tuvok, immersion shielding was first demonstrated on a multispatial probe built by the *Voyager* crew in early 2374. Immersion shielding was later used effectively on *Voyager*'s new ***Delta Flyer*** shuttlecraft. ("Extreme Risk" [VGR]).

impulse flow regulator. Component of a starship's propulsion system. A Maquis tactic to evade pursuers entailed realigning the flow regulators while the engines were operating. This dangerous technique allowed the plasma field behind the vessel to be detonated by the impulse exhaust. ("Blaze of Glory" [DS9]).

"In the Cards." *Deep Space Nine* episode #123. Teleplay by Ronald D. Moore. Story by Truly Barr Clark & Scott J. Neal. Directed by Michael Dorn. Stardate 50929.4. No stardate given. *First aired in 1997. Jake and Nog go to great lengths to procure an ancient baseball trading card for Benjamin Sisko in the hopes of raising his spirits. This was the first episode directed by actor Michael Dorn.* GUEST CAST: Jeffrey Combs as **Weyoun**; Brian Markinson as **Giger, Dr. Elias**; Aron Eisenberg as **Nog**; Chase Masterson as **Leeta**; Louise Fletcher as **Winn**. SEE: **anaerobic metabolites; Andros III; Baseball Hall of Fame; baseball trading card; Bathkin, Dr.; cellular regeneration and entertainment chamber; Decker; Eventualists; Giger, Dr. Elias; Kandra Vilk; Kukalaka; mandala; Martian Colonies; Matoian; Mays, Willie; money; neodymium power cell; Orb of Wisdom; polaron; *Tian An Men, U.S.S.*; velvet painting; Winn.**

"In the Flesh." *Voyager* episode #98. Written by Nick Sagan. Directed by David Livingston. No stardate given. *A perfect re-creation of Starfleet Headquarters, located deep in the Delta Quadrant, is a training camp from which Species 8472 may—or may not—be planning an invasion of the Federation.* GUEST CAST: Ray Walston as **Boothby**; Kate Vernon as **Archer, Valerie**; Tucker Smallwood as **Bullock, Admiral**; Zach Galligan as **Gentry, David**. SEE: **Archer, Valerie; bamboo; *Beyond the Galactic Edge*; Boothby; Bullock, Admiral; Cave Beyond Logic, A; Chakotay; Gentry, David; Hesterman; holo-imager; *Hor-CHA, I.K.S.*; *Intrepid, U.S.S.*; isodyne relay; Kim, Harry; Kinis; Klingon martini; Larson; Logistical Support; Night Owl; O'Halloran, Ensign; Orbital Flight Control; Paris, Admiral Owen; Quantum Cafe; Shaw, George Bernard; Species 8472; Starfleet brat; Starfleet General Orders and Regulations: Directive 010; Starfleet Headquarters; Terrasphere 8; Union of Soviet Socialist Republics.**

"In the Pale Moonlight." *Deep Space Nine* episode #143. Teleplay by Michael Taylor. Story by Peter Allan Fields. Directed by Victor Lobl. Stardate 51721.3. *First aired in 1998. Sisko compromises his personal ethics by committing illegal acts to draw the Romulans into the war against the Dominion in hopes of increasing the chances of the Federation's survival.* GUEST CAST: Andrew J. Robinson as **Garak, Elim;** Jeffrey Combs as **Weyoun;** Casey Biggs as **Damar;** Howard Shangraw as **Tolar, Grathon;** Stephen McHattie as **Vreenak.** SEE: **Alpha Centauri; Andor; Betazed; biomimetic gel; *Cairo, U.S.S.*; Calandra Sector; Ferengi Rules of Acquisition: 98; Garak, Elim; Glintara Sector; *kali-fal*; M'Pella; Neral; optolythic data rod; Romulan Neutral Zone; Romulan shuttle; Romulans; Sisko, Benjamin; Soukara; Tal Shiar; Tellar; Tenth Fleet; Tolar, Grathon; Vreenak; Vulcan; Whelan bitters; Wong, Captain Leslie.**

inaprovaline.* Cardiostimulatory pharmaceutical. In 2375, the *Voyager*'s holographic Doctor used 2 milligrams of inaprovaline to treat B'Elanna Torres for cytotoxic shock. ("Nothing Human" [VGR]).

Incredible Tales*.** Paper-based hard-copy periodical published in the city of New York on 20th-century Earth during the 1950s. *Incredible Tales* specialized in publishing **science-fiction** stories, including those by such notable writers as **Benny Russell**, **Albert Macklin**, **Julius Eaton**, **K.C. Hunter**, and **Hugo Award** winner **Herbert Rossoff**. The magazine was edited by **Douglas Pabst**, and **Roy Rittenhouse** was the illustrator. *Incredible Tales* was a competitor of ***Galaxy Science Fiction magazine. ("Far Beyond the Stars" [DS9]).

induction relay. Power transfer device used in Federation starship computers. ("Concerning Flight" [VGR]).

induction stabilizer. Engineering component aboard Jem'Hadar attack vessels. ("A Time to Stand" [DS9]).

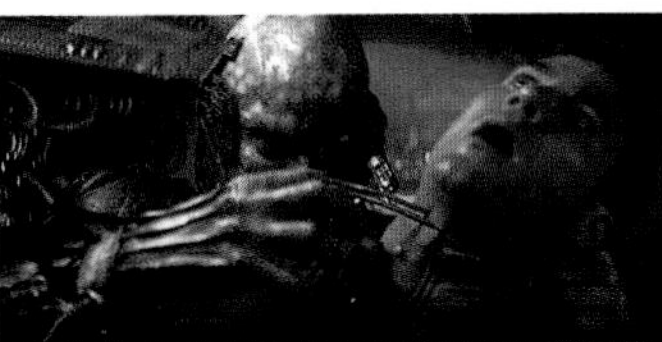

injection tubule. Borg implant, used in the **Borg** assimilation process. An injection tubule was a tiny, extendible dagger-like sharp tube located on the fingertips of a Borg drone. When extended, the device would inject Borg **nanoprobe**s into the body of the individual targeted for assimilation. In the bloodstream, the nanoprobes would assimilate the candidate into the Borg collective. ("Scorpion, Part I" [VGR]). *These were first seen in* Star Trek: First Contact.

"Inquisition." *Deep Space Nine* episode #142. Teleplay by Bradley Thompson & David Weddle. Directed by Michael Dorn. No stardate given. *First aired in 1998. Doctor Bashir is abducted by a secret Starfleet intelligence agency that employs extreme means to test his loyalty and, perhaps, to recruit him. This episode establishes the existence of the shadowy Section 31 intelligence agency.* GUEST CAST: William Sadler as **Sloan;** Jeffrey Combs as **Weyoun;** Samantha Mudd as **Chandler, Lieutenant;** Benjamin Brown as **Kagan, Lieutenant**. SEE: **Bandee; Bashir, Julian; Casperia Prime; Chandler, Lieutenant; engramatic dissociation; holodeck and holosuite programs: Section 31 test; Kagan, Lieutenant; kayak; *moba* jam; neurosynaptic relay; red leaf tea; scone; Section 31; Seventh Fleet; Sloan; starbase: 53; Starfleet General Orders and Regulations: Special Order 66715; Starfleet Intelligence; Starfleet Internal Affairs Department.**

Insurrection Alpha. Holodeck program, a tactical training scenario written by **Tuvok** in 2371 to prepare the *Starship Voyager*'s security staff for a possible **Maquis** attempt to commandeer the ship. The program began with Chakotay, as a disgruntled Maquis leader, recruiting members of the *Voyager* crew to side with him in a planned mutiny. The rebellion became violent and spread quickly throughout the ship. It was up to the holodeck participant to quell the rebellion without loss of life or damage to the ship. Tuvok began developing Insurrection Alpha shortly after the ship was swept into the Delta Quadrant, when he believed that the Maquis portion of the *Voyager* crew posed a real security threat. He did not complete the program because it soon became evident that former Maquis members and their Starfleet colleagues were working well together, so the threat of a mutiny was minimal. Tuvok had intended to delete the program, but evidently failed to do so. Two years later, several members of the *Voyager* crew accidentally discovered Insurrection Alpha, and ran it as a recreational holodeck program. Unfortunately, no one realized that Cardassian agent **Seska**, before her departure from *Voyager*, had modified the program so that a self-aware holographic replica of herself would both take control of the program and attempt to commandeer the ship itself. ("Worse Case Scenario" [VGR]).

intelligence officer. Starfleet billet. In 2373, Lieutenant Commander **Worf** served as intelligence officer for station Deep Space 9. ("Soldiers of the Empire" [DS9]).

interdimensional rift. Discontinuity in the fabric of space-time that can be a portal to other dimensions such as the **fluidic realm** of Species 8472. An interdimensional rift can be created by directing a specifically modulated resonant graviton beam into space. ("Scorpion, Part II" [VGR]).

interfold layer. Chaotic phenomenon that can form when a region of subspace intrudes into normal space. An interfold layer can cause **astral eddie**s. ("Real Life" [VGR]).

Internal Affairs. SEE: **Starfleet Internal Affairs Department.**

International Space Station. Orbital scientific outpost above planet **Earth** during the late 20th and early 21st centuries. The station, which was built and operated by several nation-states working together, including some that had previously been bitter enemies, represented a significant step in that planet's social evolution as well as its spaceflight capability. **Benjamin Sisko** displayed a model of an early version of Earth's International Space Station in his office on station Deep Space 9. *Ben Sisko's ISS model was provided by Majel Barrett Roddenberry, who presented it as a gift to the show. The* Star Trek: Deep Space Nine *art department made one tiny modification to the model. They changed the name on a model space shuttle, docked to the station, to bear the name* Enterprise, *even though the real shuttle* Enterprise *never flew in space.*

Intrepid, U.S.S. Federation starship. The *Intrepid* was assigned to patrol the Romulan Neutral Zone in early 2375. ("In the Flesh" [VGR]). *This was presumably the prototype for the* Intrepid *class of starships that included the* U.S.S. Voyager.

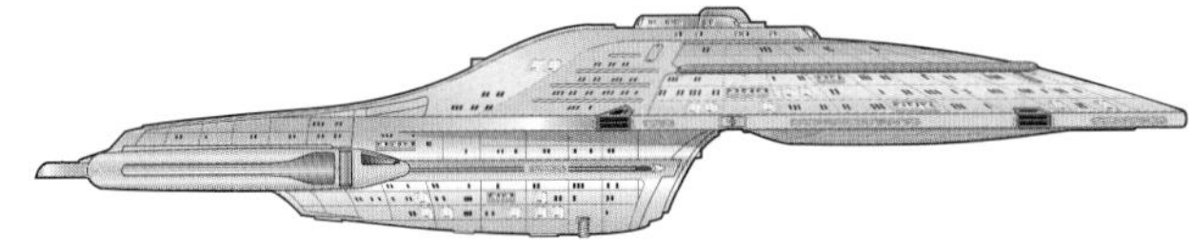

ion mallet. Equipment used in the sport of **parrises squares**. ("Real Life" [VGR]).

ion storm. Disruptive concentration of energetically charged particles. An ion storm caused serious damage to the *Delta Flyer* in 2375. ("Once Upon a Time" [VGR]).

Iponu. Temple on planet **Bajor**. The **Orb of Time** was kept at the Iponu temple. ("Wrongs Darker Than Death or Night" [DS9]).

Irish wake. In Earth culture from the nation of Ireland, an Irish wake is a ritual performed after an individual's death, in which the surviving family and friends gather to share memories and to celebrate the life of the deceased. In late 2374, members of the crew of the *Starship Defiant* held a wake for Captain **Lisa Cusak** on Deep Space 9. Although none of the *Defiant* crew had ever met Cusak, she had made such an impact on their lives that they wanted to honor her passing. Worf found the ritual to be almost Klingon in nature. ("The Sound of Her Voice" [DS9]).

Irtok System. Planetary group. Located near Ferenginar. ("Profit and Lace" [DS9]).

Ishka.* (Cecily Adams). Ferengi entrepreneur, mother of **Quark**. In 2373, Ishka and the Grand Nagus **Zek** became friends and were soon romantically involved. When she learned that Zek was suffering from a failing memory, Ishka worked behind the scenes to help Zek in his business dealings. When Liquidator **Brunt** learned of this development, he enlisted Quark in an unsuccessful effort to break up Ishka and Zek's relationship. As Zek's advisor, Ishka made no secret of her hope to reform Ferengi society to grant equal rights to females. ("Ferengi Love Songs" [DS9]). In 2374, Ishka, who was over 100 years old, traveled to Vulcan for cosmetic ear-lifting surgery to make her look younger. Her transport ship was captured by the Dominion. Ishka was subsequently rescued by a heroic mercenary team led by Quark with Rom and Nog. ("The Magnificent Ferengi" [DS9]). Ishka suffered a heart attack later that year, necessitating a new heart. Her convalescence came just as Zek had imposed remarkable reforms on Ferengi society, granting females the right to wear clothing. ("Profit and Lace" [DS9]). *Andrea Martin played Ishka in "Family Business" (DS9), while Cecily Adams portrayed the character in "Ferengi Love Songs" (DS9), "The Magnificent Ferengi" (DS9), and "Profit and Lace" (DS9).*

isodyne relay. Component of a Starfleet **tricorder**. ("In the Flesh" [VGR]).

isokinetic cannon. Weapon capable of penetrating shields of heavily armored vessels. In 2374, Entharan arms dealer **Kovin** demonstrated an isokinetic cannon to the crew of the *Starship Voyager*. ("Retrospect" [VGR]).

isolation suit. Starfleet garment equipped with a cloaking device, rendering the wearer unobservable. Isolation suits were used by Federation scientists for covert sociological studies such as those conducted at the Ba'ku planet in 2375. (*Star Trek: Insurrection*).

isolinear tag. Tiny transponder device permitting a tracking system to locate an object to which a tag has been attached. Starfleet personnel under the command of Admiral Dougherty used isolinear tags to locate and transport Ba'ku inhabitants in 2375, despite the fact that the Ba'ku had taken refuge in areas of high kelbonite concentrations. (*Star Trek: Insurrection*).

isolytic subspace weapon. Weapon of mass destruction. Isolytic subspace weapons were highly unpredictable and could cause dangerous tears in the subspace fabric. The Son'a used an isolytic subspace weapon against the *Enterprise*-E in 2375. Isolytic weapons were banned by the second Khitomer Accords. (*Star Trek: Insurrection*).

isomagnetic disintegrator. Large shoulder-mounted directed-energy weapon used by the Federation. Jean-Luc Picard brought isomagnetic disintegrators down to the Ba'ku homeworld in 2375 to use in preventing the planet's inhabitants from being forcibly removed by the Son'a. (*Star Trek: Insurrection*).

isomolecular scanner. Advanced medical diagnostic device. Federation starships were not routinely equipped with isomolecular scanners, even though they could be useful in the study of life-forms with very alien physiologies. ("Nothing Human" [VGR]).

isomorphic projection. Technical term for hologram used by the Serosians. **Dejaren** was an isomorphic projection. ("Revulsion" [VGR]).

isoton.* Unit of measure for mass. Also used to describe power of an explosive device. A class-6 Starfleet **photon torpedo** had an explosive yield of 200 isotons. Borg multikinetic neutronic mines were capable of generating a five-million-isoton explosion. ("Scorpion, Part II" [VGR]). Emck's **Malon export vessel** had a payload capacity of some 90 million isotons. ("Night" [VGR]). *Isoton, invented by* Star Trek *science consultant Andre Bormanis, is another one of those terms that we may never define precisely.*

"It Can't Be Wrong." Musical composition popular on 20th-century Earth, telling of romantic attraction between two humanoids. **Mademoiselle de Neuf** sang it in the **French Resistance** holodeck program. ("The Killing Game, Part I" [VGR]).

Ixtana'Rax. (Fritz Sperberg). **Jem'Hadar** second, part of a squad that captured the *U.S.S. Defiant* on stardate 51474.2. Ixtana'Rax was an Elder gamma Jem'Hadar and was wary of Captain Sisko; he cautioned First Kudak'Etan against using members of the *Defiant* crew to repair the ship's warp drive. Kudak'Etan didn't listen, and the ship was reclaimed by Sisko and his crew. Ixtana'Rax was killed in the conflict. ("One Little Ship" [DS9]).

Jack. (Tim Ransom). Individual who, as a child, had been genetically altered through illegal and unsuccessful **accelerated critical neural pathway formation**. Although the procedure had been intended to enhance Jack's abilities, it resulted in giving Jack an extremely aggressive personality, so much so that he could not easily fit into normal society, and he spent much of his life institutionalized. Jack was a nervous individual, but possessed great intelligence and physical coordination. Under the care of Starfleet psychiatrist Dr. Karen Loews, Jack and three other genetically enhanced individuals traveled to starbase Deep Space 9 in 2374 to meet **Julian Bashir**, who had also undergone genetic enhancement as a child. At Deep Space 9, Jack and his group made analytical projections about the Dominion war that Starfleet considered important. ("Statistical Probabilities" [DS9]). Despite (or because of) his difficulty in functioning in "normal" society, Jack was a brilliantly unconventional scientist and inventor. He devised a remarkable means of increasing the accuracy of a neocortical probe beyond the theoretical limits imposed by quantum physics, and even studied hypothetical means of averting the ultimate collapse of the universe. Jack returned to Deep Space 9 in 2375 to seek an unorthodox surgical procedure for **Sarina Douglas**. ("Chrysalis" [DS9]). SEE: **Big Bang; Lauren; Patrick**.

Jackson Square. Urban mall located in **New Orleans**, Louisiana, on Earth. In June 2331, Joseph Sisko met his first wife, Sarah, in Jackson Square. ("Image in the Sand" [DS9]).

jak'tahla. Klingon for the phase of growth in which an individual enters sexual maturity. *Jak'tahla* is often accompanied by mood swings, unusually aggressive tendencies, as well as ***gorches***. (*Star Trek: Insurrection*).

Janeway, Kathryn.* Starfleet officer, captain of the Federation starship ***Voyager***. Janeway was born on May 20 ("Year of Hell, Part I" [VGR]) in the state of Indiana on planet Earth. ("Hope and Fear" [VGR]). As a child, Janeway enjoyed ***The Adventures of Flotter*** children's holographic tales. ("Once Upon a Time" [VGR]). In late 2373, Janeway began spending personal time in a holodeck program, a re-creation of Renaissance master **Leonardo da Vinci**. Janeway, who was a scientist by training, enjoyed working with the historical figure, drawing inspiration from his unique perspective of science and the world in general. ("Scorpion, Parts I and II" [VGR]). Janeway had always regarded da Vinci as a hero and had even built models of some of his designs when she was a child. ("The Raven" [VGR]). Early in her Starfleet career, Janeway was a lieutenant on an away team mission during a **Cardassian** border dispute. Although Janeway and the other members of her team were later decorated by Starfleet for a military success, Janeway would later recall that she was most proud that she had helped to provide humanitarian medical aid to an injured Cardassian soldier, saving his life. ("Prey" [VGR]). In another instance, while serving aboard the ***U.S.S. Billings***, shortly after her promotion to commander, Janeway blamed herself for a shuttle accident in which three crew members were injured on a scientific mission. ("Night" [VGR]). Janeway completed her first starship command assignment in 2365. After returning from the mission, security specialist **Tuvok** criticized her in front of three Starfleet admirals for failing to observe proper tactical procedures during her voyage. It was Janeway's first meeting with Tuvok, and she would later agree that his criticisms were correct. ("Revulsion" [VGR]). Prior to the *Voyager*'s departure from Deep Space 9 in 2371, Janeway had been engaged to marry a man named **Mark Johnson**. After the ship was swept into the Delta Quadrant, she consciously avoided entering into a romantic relationship because of her commitment to Mark. In 2374, however, she was saddened when a message from Starfleet included a letter from Mark, in which he told of his marriage to a coworker. ("Hunters" [VGR]).

Jarleth. (Mark L. Taylor). Space traveler from the Delta Quadrant. Jarleth, whose homeworld had a desertlike environment, had been kidnapped by the **Nyrians**. ("Displaced" [VGR]).

Jeffrey. (Glenn Harris). Holographic character, the son of the *Starship Voyager*'s **Emergency Medical Hologram** in the **Doctor's family program Beta-Rho**. Jeffrey was originally created as an ideal son, but in a modified version of the program, he became a troublesome teenager, whose friends included two Klingon youths, much to the disapproval of Jeffrey's father. ("Real Life" [VGR]).

jellied gree worms. Ferengi delicacy. ("Ferengi Love Songs" [DS9]).

Jem'Hadar attack ship.* Warcraft of the **Dominion**. Jem'Hadar attack ships were vulnerable if attacked from directly above. The ship's shields were weakest at the dorsal field junctions, located on the upper hull. ("Treachery, Faith, and the Great River" [DS9]).

Jem'Hadar battleship. Large Dominion military spacecraft. In 2373, Gul Dukat and Weyoun took a Jem'Hadar battleship to station Deep Space 9 in hopes of intimidating Captain Sisko into releasing Cardassian dissident Legate Ghemor into Dominion custody. ("Ties of Blood and Water" [DS9]).

Jem'Hadar warship.* Military spacecraft of **Jem'Hadar** design. In early 2374, Benjamin Sisko and his staff used the captured Jem'Hadar attack ship on a covert mission to destroy a **ketracel-white** storage facility deep inside Cardassian space. The strike was the first major Starfleet victory in the Dominion war. ("A Time to Stand" [DS9]).

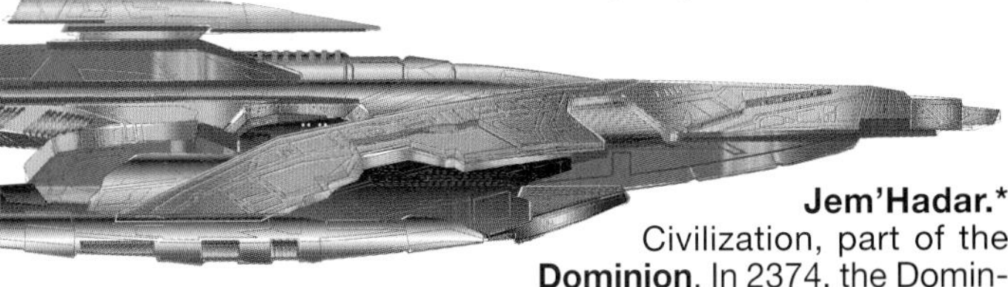

Jem'Hadar.* Civilization, part of the **Dominion**. In 2374, the Dominion began breeding Jem'Hadar soldiers in the **Alpha Quadrant**. The move was prompted by a shortage of Jem'Hadar caused by the Starfleet blockade of the Bajoran wormhole during the early days of the Dominion war. These Jem'Hadar, sometimes called "Alphas," were headstrong and arrogant, specifically engineered for effectiveness in battle in the Alpha Quadrant. ("One Little Ship" [DS9]). A major Jem'Hadar Alpha Quadrant victory occurred in early 2374 when a Jem'Hadar fleet inflicted 87 percent casualties on a massive Starfleet task force at the Tyra system. ("A Time to Stand" [DS9]). The Vorta feared that the Jem'Hadar would be uncontrollable without the use of the white, but the Vorta underestimated the loyalty and obedience of the Jem'Hadar. For example, in 2374, when **Keevan**, a Vorta supervisor, betrayed all the Jem'Hadar under his command, the Jem'Hadar soldiers knowingly and willingly went to their deaths because they believed that "Obedience brings victory" and that "Victory is life." ("Rocks and Shoals" [DS9]).

Jessel, George. (1898–1981). Twentieth-century Earth comedian, television personality, and movie actor. Entertainer **Vic Fontaine** was fond of quoting Jessel, who once made a dedication to "whatever makes you happy." ("His Way" [DS9]).

jevonite.* Mined substance. In 2373, the Ferengi Alliance sold its *lokar* bean investments, using the proceeds to buy jevonite. The move, engineered by Grand Nagus Zek, was regarded by observers as a brilliant financial stroke. ("Ferengi Love Songs" [DS9]).

JFK. SEE: **Kennedy, John F.**

Jimmy. (Cirroc Lofton). Inhabitant of 20th-century Earth. Jimmy lived on the streets of the city of New York, often running afoul of the law. Jimmy was killed by law-enforcement officials in 1953, a victim of unequal treatment under the law due to racist attitudes held by some individuals during that period. ("Far Beyond the Stars" [DS9]). *We didn't learn Jimmy's last name. Cirroc Lofton also played Jake Sisko on* Star Trek: Deep Space Nine.

Jinami Street. Small avenue in a low-rent residential district on planet **Farius Prime**. ("Honor Among Thieves" [DS9]).

Jirex. Greatest writer in the Talaxian canon. Neelix read parables from the *Selected Works of Jirex* every night before going to sleep. ("Demon" [VGR]).

Johnson, Mark.* Citizen of planet Earth. In 2371, Johnson was engaged to marry Starfleet officer **Kathryn Janeway**. Johnson was devastated when he heard that the *Voyager* had been lost in the **Badlands**. For a long time, he held out hope that the ship and its captain were safe. He eventually realized that he was clinging to a fantasy, and so began to live his life again. Finally, in early 2374, Mark Johnson married a woman who worked with him. Ironically, four months later, Johnson learned that his former fiancée was alive in the Delta Quadrant, struggling to return home aboard the *Voyager*. Mark wrote a letter to Janeway informing her of his marriage. The letter, transmitted along with many other personal messages to *Voyager* crew members, was received by *Voyager* in the Delta Quadrant by means of an ancient communications relay system. ("Hunters" [VGR]). *Mark's full name was not established until "Hunters," where it was readable on a padd. He is listed simply as "Mark" in the main section of this* Encyclopedia.

Jones, Lieutenant. (Randy James). Starfleet officer assigned to the security force on Deep Space 9. ("Time's Orphan" [DS9]).

Jungian therapy. Psychiatric treatment based on the theories of **Carl Gustav Jung**. In 2374, *Starship Voyager*'s **Emergency Medical Hologram** incorporated Jungian therapy into his psychiatric subroutine. (Retrospect" [VGR]).

K'Kath. (Chad Haywood). Holographic character, the friend of the **Emergency Medical Hologram**'s son, **Jeffrey**, in the **Doctor's family program Beta-Rho**. K'Kath and Larg, both Klingon youths, elected to invite the (simulated) human Jeffrey to go through a first bloodletting ceremony involving a *kut'luch* dagger. ("Real Life" [VGR]).

K'retok. Klingon warrior who served under General Martok aboard station Deep Space 9 in 2373. Martok disciplined K'retok by throwing him off a second-story balcony on the Promenade on station Deep Space 9. ("Ferengi Love Songs" [DS9]).

K'Trelan. Historic figure in **Klingon** history. K'Trelan killed Emperor Reclaw, ending the Second Dynasty and casting the empire into what later scholars called the **Dark Time**. In actuality, K'Trelan was responsible for an extraordinary ten-year period in which the empire was ruled by a representational democracy. ("You Are Cordially Invited" [DS9]).

Kabrel I. First planet in the binary Kabrel system. Source of trinucleic fungi. In 2374, the Dominion sought to control the Kabrel system because they wanted to break down the trinucleic fungi to make yridium bicantizine, an active ingredient in **ketracel-white**. ("Statistical Probabilities" [DS9]).

Kabrel II. Second planet in the Kabrel system. Kabrel II possessed some cormaline deposits. ("Statistical Probabilities" [DS9]).

Kagan, Lieutenant. (Benjamin Brown). Starfleet officer assigned to **Section 31**. In 2374, Kagan, along with Lieutenant Chandler and Deputy Director **Sloan**, participated in an elaborate holographic simulation designed to determine Julian Bashir's loyalty to Starfleet and to test him for possible membership in Section 31. ("Inquisition" [DS9]).

"Kahless and Lukara."* Klingon opera, considered to be the greatest romance of all time. Immediately after they were married, the royal couple was attacked and nearly killed by Molor's troops. This lead to the tradition of the *Ma'Stakas*, still observed in Klingon **wedding** ceremonies. ("You Are Cordially Invited" [DS9]).

Kal'Hyah. A mental and spiritual journey that a Klingon man and his friends traditionally share during the last four nights before his wedding. The ritual was made up of six trials: deprivation, blood, pain, sacrifice, anguish, and death. Filled with song and fellowship, the *Kal'Hyah* was difficult by human standards but exhilarating to Klingons. Worf celebrated his *Kal'Hyah* in a holosuite at Quark's bar in 2374. ("You Are Cordially Invited" [DS9]). SEE: **wedding: Klingon**.

kal-toh.* Vulcan game of logic and symmetry. In 2374, on stardate 51781, Tuvok and Kim had an all-night *kal-toh* match. Seven of Nine was exceptionally adept at the game because of her mastery of spatial harmonics. ("The Omega Directive" [VGR]).

Kalandra Sector. Region of space within Federation territory near Betazed and the Argolis Cluster. The Dominion gained control of the Kalandra Sector after it captured Betazed in 2374. ("The Reckoning" [DS9]). In early 2375, the Seventh Fleet launched a new offensive at Kalandra. The strike was based on intercepted Dominion communications, decoded by Garak, that the enemy was vulnerable there. ("Afterimage" [DS9]).

kali-fal. Pale blue-green **Romulan** beverage. According to Romulan connoisseurs, quality *kali-fal* has a powerful aroma that forcibly opens one's sinuses well before the first sip. Ben Sisko replicated the beverage for Senator Vreenak in 2374, but the replica lacked the powerful aroma. ("In the Pale Moonlight" [DS9]).

kanar.* Intoxicating **Cardassian** beverage, a viscous brown liquid. Gul **Damar** was quite fond of *kanar*, although his Vorta colleagues regarded this as a weakness. ("Treachery, Faith, and the Great River" [DS9]).

Kandra Vilk. Merchant who operated a Bajoran antiques and tapestries shop on the Promenade of Deep Space 9. She left two months prior to stardate 50929 to live in the **Coridan** system. ("In the Cards" [DS9]).

Kaplan, Ensign. Starfleet officer assigned to the *U.S.S. Voyager*. Kaplan occasionally played **golf** with Tom Paris and Harry Kim. ("Vis à Vis" [VGR]). *There were apparently two Ensign Kaplans on* Voyager, *since another officer with the same name, played by Susan Patterson, was killed in "Unity" (VGR).*

kar'takin. A short polearm with cleaverlike blades along one side. The *kar'takin* was a favored weapon of Jem'Hadar soldiers. ("Sons and Daughters" [DS9]).

Karana. Concubine who lived outside the imperial stables on the Klingon homeworld during the Second Klingon Dynasty. In modern times, the Lady **Sirella** of the House of Martok claimed her 23rd maternal grandmother was Shenara, daughter of the Emperor Reclaw. In actuality, however, Sirella's 23rd maternal grandmother was Karana. ("You Are Cordially Invited" [DS9]).

Karr, Commandant. (Mark Metcalf). Persona assumed by the **Alpha-Hirogen** who commandeered the *Starship Voyager* in 2374 in the **French Resistance** holodeck simulation. In the simulation, Karr was a military officer in the army of **Nazi Germany** who had once served under Field Marshall **Erwin Rommel**. ("The Killing Game, Parts I and II" [VGR]).

Karya. (Meghan Murphy). Photometric projection of a **Vori** civilian, part of an elaborate mind-control technique used by the Vori military to conscript new soldiers. In the simulation, Karya was a young girl who lived at the Larhana settlement with her grandfather, Penno. The destruction of Karya's village was calculated to induce the conscript to feel sympathy for the Vori cause against their **Kradin** enemies. ("Nemesis" [VGR]).

Katogh. Klingon warrior, son of **Ch'Pok**. In 2374 Katogh transferred from the *Vor'nak* to the *Rotarran*. ("Sons and Daughters" [DS9]).

Katrine. (Kate Mulgrew). Persona imposed upon **Kathryn Janeway** while under Hirogen **neural interface** control in the **French Resistance** holodeck program in late 2374. Katrine was a citizen of the republic of France who was a member of the underground who fought to free her nation from the control of **Nazi Germany**. Katrine owned **Le Coeur de Lion**, a small tavern in the city of Sainte Claire, at which Nazi officers dined at night, but which served as an underground headquarters during the day. ("The Killing Game, Parts I and II" [VGR]).

***kava* juice.** Beverage made from squeezing the roots of a Bajoran *kava* plant. Miles O'Brien and Julian Bashir liked fresh *kava* juice. They preferred the real thing to a replicated synthetic. ("You Are Cordially Invited" [DS9]).

***kava* nut.** Edible fruit of a Bajoran *kava* plant. *Kava* nuts were one of the few foods that the Vorta could really enjoy, given their very limited sense of taste. ("Treachery, Faith, and the Great River" [DS9]).

***kava* roll.** Small Bajoran bread. Kira liked *kava* rolls with her breakfast *raktajino*. ("Resurrection" [DS9]).

kayak. Small, highly maneuverable water craft originally used by the Inuit people of North America on Earth. Other cultures adopted the basic design for sport. **Miles O'Brien** enjoyed kayaking in holographic simulation programs, although he injured his shoulder many times while attempting to navigate his simulated craft through treacherous river rapids. ("Transfigurations" [TNG], "Heart of Stone" [DS9], "Shakaar" [DS9], "Inquisition" [DS9]).

Kazon.* Civilization in the Delta Quadrant. The Borg referred to the Kazon as Species 329. The Borg encountered a Kazon colony in the Gand sector but did not assimilate them because they considered them unworthy. ("Mortal Coil" [VGR]).

Keevan. (Christopher Shea). **Vorta** official. Keevan commanded a **Jem'Hadar** vessel that crashed on a planet in a dark-matter nebula in Cardassian space in 2374. Much of his crew's supply of **ketracel-white** was ruined in the crash. Believing that without the white he would lose control of his Jem'Hadar crew, Keevan betrayed them to a Starfleet team led by Captain Benjamin Sisko, offering to trade his survival for the lives of those under his command. The Jem'Hadar unit followed Keevan's orders and were killed in a hopeless firefight, even though they knew that their Vorta leader had betrayed them. Keevan was taken into custody as a Federation prisoner of war. ("Rocks and Shoals" [DS9]). Keevan was subsequently traded to Jem'Hadar authorities in a prisoner exchange that freed Ferengi citizen **Ishka** from Dominion captivity, although he was accidentally killed by Ferengi mercenaries before the trade could be completed. Keevan's dying words were, "I hate Ferengi." ("The Magnificent Ferengi" [DS9]).

Kela. Trill man, father of **Jadzia Dax**. ("You Are Cordially Invited" [DS9]).

kelbonite.* Refractory ore. Kelbonite interfered with Federation sensors and inhibited transporter operation. Kelbonite deposits are found on the Ba'ku homeworld. (*Star Trek: Insurrection*).

Kellin. (Virginia Madsen). **Ramuran** citizen who worked as a **tracer** and security operative for the Ramurans. In 2374, Kellin's duties took her to the Federation starship *Voyager*, which was passing through Ramuran space. Kellin fell in love with **Chakotay**, but because of Ramuran pheromones that induce memory erasure following all offworld contacts, neither Kellin nor Chakotay retained any memory of their relationship after her departure from *Voyager*. ("Unforgettable" [VGR]).

kellinite. Construction material. Sometime used to lend strength to spacecraft hulls. ("Extreme Risk" [VGR]).

Kelvans.* Civilization from the Andromeda Galaxy. In the past, Worf stood in battle with Kelvans who were twice his size. ("Time's Orphan" [DS9]).

Kenda shrine. Sacred temple on Bajor. On stardate 50814.2 Kira Nerys and Shakaar Edon ended their relationship after visiting the Kenda Shrine and being told that they were not meant to walk the same path. ("Children of Time" [DS9]).

Kendra Valley. Region on planet Bajor, site of the infamous Kendra Valley massacre. In 2374, near the time of the Reckoning, Kendra Valley experienced a devastating earthquake that left hundreds homeless. ("The Reckoning" [DS9]).

Kendren System. Planetary group. In 2374, near stardate 51762, Neelix gathered food samples from the fourth planet in the Kendren System for the crew of the *Starship Voyager*. ("Vis à Vis" [VGR]).

Corbis

Kennedy, John F. (1917–1963). Visionary 35th president of Earth's American nation. Kennedy was responsible for some of his people's remarkable social, economic, and scientific progress during the second half of the 20th century. He was instrumental in committing the **United States of America** to achieving the historic goal of landing the first humans on Earth's **moon** and returning them safely to their homeworld. Kennedy was a highly charismatic leader who was sometimes referred to by his initials, JFK. His many admirers included noted entertainer Vic Fontaine. ("His Way" [DS9]). SEE: **Apollo 11**.

Kepla Sector. Region of space in the Alpha Quadrant. In 2374, the *U.S.S. Valiant* was transiting the Kepla Sector when the Dominion war broke out. On the first day of the war, a Dominion invasion force swept through the sector and the starship was caught behind enemy lines. ("*Valiant*" [DS9]).

kerripate. Unit of land area in the Bajoran system of measures. A kerripate is a fraction of a tessipate. ("Children of Time" [DS9]).

Kes.* (Jennifer Lien). Member of the *Starship Voyager* crew. In early 2374, Kes's innate **Ocampa**n mental powers increased in strength, possibly stimulated by involuntary contact with **Species 8472**. ("Scorpion, Parts I and II" [VGR]). In the days that followed, she began to exhibit extraordinary telekinetic abilities and enhanced perception that enabled her to see beyond the subatomic level of matter. Her telepathic centers soon entered a state of hyperstimulation and her body briefly discorporated, almost killing **Neelix**, and causing serious damage to *Voyager* itself. At Kes's request, she was placed aboard a shuttlecraft and separated to a safe distance. Shortly thereafter, Kes transformed into a noncorporeal being of pure energy. Her final gift to her corporeal friends aboard *Voyager* was to teleport the ship and its crew some 9,500 light-years closer to the Alpha Quadrant. ("The Gift" [VGR]). *Jennifer Lien left the regular cast of* Star Trek: Voyager *at the end of the third season, but made two additional guest appearances at the beginning of the fourth season, in "Scorpion, Part II," and in "The Gift," which was her last.*

Kesef. Location on a home planet of the **Vaskan** and **Kyrian** peoples. In 3074, the *Starship Voyager*'s **Emergency Medical Hologram backup module** was found intact nine meters below ruins at Kesef. The module had been taken by followers of Tedran during a raid on *Voyager* in late 2374. ("Living Witness" [VGR]).

ketracel-white.* Drug used by the **Founders** to control their **Jem'Hadar** soldiers. Absence of regular white dosage resulted in severe withdrawal symptoms, including anxiety and severely violent behavior. **Vorta** supervisors feared that a depletion of white supplies would cause Jem'Hadar soldiers to turn into senselessly violent animals, but the Vorta underestimated the Jem'Hadar's capacity for duty and self-sacrifice. ("Rocks and Shoals" [DS9]). Dominion supplies of ketracel-white in the Alpha Quadrant began to run short in early 2374 due to a Starfleet blockade of the Bajoran wormhole. Supplies became even more limited when a Starfleet team commanded by Benjamin Sisko was successful in destroying a major ketracel-white storage facility on Torga IV. ("A Time to

Stand" [DS9]). Yridium bicantizine is an active ingredient in ketracel-white. SEE: **Kabrel I.** ("Statistical Probabilities" [DS9]). The **Son'a** produced quantities of the narcotic. (*Star Trek: Insurrection*).

ketric. Hirogen unit of length measurement, equal to several kilometers. ("Hunters" [VGR]).

Ketteract, Dr. Starfleet physicist who synthesized a single **Omega molecule** around 2274. He had hoped Omega would be the basis for an inexhaustible power source. The molecule destabilized, destroying a classified research station in the Lantaru Sector. Ketteract and 126 of the Federation's leading scientists were lost in the accident. SEE: **Omega Directive**. ("The Omega Directive" [VGR]).

khi-GOSH. Klingon term meaning "Let's go." ("Blaze of Glory" [DS9]).

Khitomer Accords.* Historic peace treaty between the **Klingon Empire** and the **United Federation of Planets**. Ambassador **Curzon Dax** represented the Federation in negotiations with the Klingon Empire for the Khitomer Accords in 2293. ("You Are Cordially Invited" [DS9]). The second Khitomer Accords banned subspace weapons, including isolytic burst weapons. (*Star Trek: Insurrection*).

Kiessa Monastery. Religious temple on planet Bajor. The Kiessa Monastery was the site of a brutal massacre in the mid-24th century when some 400 Cardassian soldiers raided the temple and burned it to the ground. Seventeen monks at Kiessa, who had been hiding weapons for the Bajoran resistance, were killed in the incident. ("Ties of Blood and Water" [DS9]).

"Killing Game, The, Part I." *Voyager* episode #86. Written by Brannon Braga & Joe Menosky. Directed by David Livingston. No stardate mentioned. *First aired in 1998. Hirogen hunters take over the* Starship Voyager *and use its crew in holographic simulations of battle.* GUEST CAST: Danny Goldring as **Alpha-Hirogen**; Mark Deakins as **Hirogen SS Officer**; Mark Metcalf as **Hirogen Medic**; J. Paul Boehmer as **Nazi Kapitan**; Paul S. Eckstein as Young Hirogen. SEE: **Allied Forces; Alpha-Hirogen; Brigette; British Intelligence; British Radio Network; Chateau Latour; Davis, Bobby; de Neuf, Mademoiselle; franc; France; French Resistance; Hirogen Medic; Hirogen SS Officer; Hirogen; holodeck and holosuite programs: Crusades, French Resistance, Klingon battle; holodeck; "It Can't Be Wrong"; Karr, Commandant; Katrine; Le Coeur de Lion; Master Race; Miller, Captain; "Moonlight Becomes You"; Nazi Germany; Nazi Kapitan; neural interface; Praxiteles; Reichsmark; Rommel, Erwin; safety protocol; Sainte Claire; Smith, Reginald; "That Old Black Magic"; Third Reich; United States of America; vacuum tube; *Voyager, U.S.S.;* World War II.**

"Killing Game, The, Part II." *Voyager* episode #87. Written by Brannon Braga and Joe Menosky. Directed by Victor Lobl. Stardate 51715.2. *First aired in 1998. Holographic warriors from the Hirogen World War II simulation overrun the* Voyager *and Janeway must work within the French Resistance program to regain control of her ship.* GUEST CAST: Danny Goldring as **Alpha-Hirogen**; Mark Deakins as **Hirogen SS Officer**; Mark Metcalf as **Hirogen Medic**; J. Paul Boehmer as **Nazi Kapitan**; Paul S. Eckstein as Young Hirogen; Peter Hendrixson as Klingon; Majel Barrett as Computer Voice. SEE: **Allied Forces; Alpha-Hirogen; Brigette; Cinema Mystère; Davis, Bobby; de Neuf, Mademoiselle; dynamite; France; French Resistance; Grable, Betty; Hirogen medic; Hirogen SS Officer; Hirogen; holodeck and holosuite programs: French Resistance; holodeck; Karr, Commandant; Katrine; Kraut; Le Coeur de Lion; machine gun; Master Race; Miller, Captain, Nazi Germany; Nazi Kapitan; neural interface; nucleonic charge; optronic data-core; RAF; Sainte Claire; swastika; Third Reich; United States of America; West, Mae; World War II.**

kilm steak. Grilled slice of kilm meat. ("Afterimage" [DS9]).

Kim, Harry.* Operations officer for the Federation starship *Voyager*. Kim was born in South Carolina on **Earth**, although he was raised elsewhere. He played **tennis** and **parisses squares**, but volleyball was his favorite sport. ("One" [VGR]). As a child, Kim was fond of ***The Adventures of Flotter*** holographic tales. ("Once Upon a Time" [VGR]). His father, who worked at Starfleet Command, was proud of his skill at the ancient Earth art of birdcalling. ("In the Flesh" [VGR]). Harry Kim enjoyed music, once composing a concerto that he dubbed "Echoes of the Void" for himself to perform on his clarinet. He also enjoyed indulging in holodeck programs with his friend, **Thomas Paris**. One favorite was ***The Adventures of Captain Proton***, in which Kim played a sidekick to Paris's heroic **Captain Proton**. ("Night" [VGR]). In early 2374 he was assigned to work with **Seven of Nine** to upgrade *Voyager*'s **Astrometrics** Lab. While their collaboration was highly productive, yielding a dramatically improved stellar cartographic capability for the ship, Kim found it somewhat uncomfortable to work in such close proximity with the former Borg drone, whom he found sexually attractive. ("Revulsion" [VGR]).

Kinis. Junior officer at Starfleet Headquarters in San Francisco on Earth. Kinis was an aide to Admiral Bullock. A re-creation of Kinis was part of a training facility created by Species 8472 in the Delta Quadrant in 2375 in preparation for infiltrating the Federation. ("In the Flesh" [VGR]).

Kira Meru. (Leslie Hope). Icon painter from Dahkur Province, and mother to Bajoran resistance fighter **Kira Nerys**. Kira Meru was the wife of **Kira Taban** and mother to their three children, Nerys, Reon, and Pohl. During the Cardassian occupation of her homeworld, Meru and her family were interned at the Singha refugee camp. In 2346, she was taken from Singha to become a **comfort woman** on space station **Terok Nor**. She caught the eye of Prefect **Gul Dukat** and was moved into his quarters. While on Terok Nor, she was befriended by a woman who, unbeknownst to Meru, was her daughter, Kira Nerys, who had traveled back in time from 2374 through the Orb of Time. The Kira family was given extra rations of food and medicine, which Taban believed was responsible for saving Meru's children from starvation. Meru became Dukat's lover, remaining with him for seven years until her death in 2353. Although many Bajorans viewed comfort women like Meru as collaborators with the hated Cardassians, Meru's husband, Taban, understood her sacrifice and never forgot his love for her. ("Wrongs Darker Than Death or Night" [DS9]). Kira Meru was born in 2314. ("Second Skin" [DS9]).

Kira Nerys (mirror).* Counterpart to Kira Nerys in the **mirror universe**. In 2374, the mirror Kira devised a plan with the mirror version of Bareil Antos to steal one of the Bajoran Orbs from our universe. The mirror Kira became jealous when the mirror Bareil became attracted to her counterpart in our universe, and was further angered when the mirror Bareil abandoned their plan. Both individuals subsequently returned to the mirror universe. SEE: **Bareil Antos (mirror).** ("Resurrection" [DS9]).

Kira Nerys.* Member of the Bajoran militia who served as liaison to the Federation Starfleet on space station Deep Space 9. Her father, **Kira Taban**, was a farmer who fought against the Cardassian occupation as part of the Bajoran resistance forces.

Nerys felt enormous guilt that she was not at her father's side when he died from wounds sustained in a Cardassian attack. She carried the guilt for years until finding a measure of absolution in 2373 when she stayed with **Legate Ghemor**, who regarded her as a surrogate daughter, during his final hours. ("Ties of Blood and Water" [DS9]). Kira's two brothers were named Kira Pohl and Kira Reon. Nerys never really knew **Kira Meru**, her mother, because she was three years old when her mother left. Her father, **Kira Taban**, always told Nerys that her mother died in the **Singha refugee camp**, a story that Nerys believed until 2374 when she used the **Orb of Time** to travel back to 2346. Nerys, in the past under an assumed name, met Meru, her mother, and was horrified to learn that Meru had served as a comfort woman for Cardassian troops and had become mistress to Gul Dukat. Feeling betrayed that her mother was a Cardassian collaborator, Nerys nearly allowed Meru to die in an assassination attempt on Dukat. Nerys saved her mother's life (and that of Dukat) when she learned that her father, **Kira Taban**, was able to find forgiveness for his wife, and that he loved her unconditionally despite what she had done. ("Wrongs Darker Than Death or Night" [DS9]). Kira was the only Bajoran official to remain behind on Deep Space 9—or Terok Nor—after the Federation withdrew from the facility in late 2373 at the beginning of the Dominion war. Kira believed that it was her duty to respect her government's instructions to work with the Dominion and Cardassian occupation forces. Kira's feelings changed dramatically in the aftermath of Vedek Yassim's dramatic suicide in early 2374, protesting the occupation. ("Rocks and Shoals" [DS9]). Kira's relationship with Shakaar lasted only a year, ending after a visit to the Kenda Shrine revealed that they were not meant to walk the same path. Shortly thereafter, she learned that **Odo** had been in love with her for years, but had hidden his feelings so as not to jeopardize their friendship. ("Children of Time" [DS9]). Odo found it difficult to express his feelings for her until several months later, when a self-aware hologram named **Vic Fontaine** brought the two together. ("His Way" [DS9]). Kira Nerys was promoted to the rank of colonel in the Bajoran Militia in early 2375. ("Image in the Sand" [DS9]). During the final days of the Dominion war in 2375, Kira once again became a resistance fighter, this time ironically leading the battle to liberate the Cardassian homeworld from Dominion occupation. For the purposes of this assignment, Kira accepted a Starfleet commission making it easier for her to work with **Damar** and other Cardassians. ("When It Rains..." [DS9]). After the end of the war, Kira was heartbroken when Odo felt compelled to leave her so that he could return to the **Great Link** of his people. Kira subsequently returned to station **Deep Space 9**, serving as its commander after the departure of Starfleet captain **Benjamin Sisko**. ("What You Leave Behind" [DS9]).

Kira Pohl. Son of Kira Taban and **Kira Meru**, brother of Nerys and Reon. Pohl was raised in the **Singha refugee camp** on Bajor and he was only two years old when his mother was taken from Singha to become Gul Dukat's mistress on Terok Nor. ("Wrongs Darker Than Death or Night" [DS9]).

Kira Reon. Son of Kira Taban and **Kira Meru**, brother of Nerys and Pohl. Like Nerys and Pohl, Reon was raised in the **Singha refugee camp**, where he suffered from serious malnutrition as a child. ("Wrongs Darker Than Death or Night" [DS9]).

Kira Taban. (Thomas Kopache). Farmer and member of the Bajoran resistance during the Cardassian occupation of his homeworld; father of Bajoran resistance fighter **Kira Nerys**. ("Ties of Blood and Water" [DS9]). Taban was married to **Kira Meru** and father to their three children: Nerys, Reon, and Pohl. After Meru was taken from the family to become a **comfort woman** for Cardassian officers in 2346, Taban raised their children alone at the **Singha refugee center**. Although the loss of his wife was horrifying to Taban, he never lost his love for her, telling their children that she was the bravest woman he had ever known. ("Wrongs Darker Than Death or Night" [DS9]). Taban died during the occupation from injuries received when Cardassians razed the Bajoran village where he lived. ("Ties of Blood and Water" [DS9]). *His given name was mentioned in the script only. Thomas Kopache previously played Mirok, a Romulan officer, in "The Next Phase" (TNG) and Viorsa in "The Thaw" (VGR).*

Kirby, Angie. Starfleet officer assigned to the *U.S.S. Defiant* in 2373. In an alternate reality, Ensign Kirby was among the *Defiant* crew members stranded 200 years in the past on the planet **Gaia**. With no hope of return, the alternate Kirby married Dr. Julian Bashir and had many descendants. The alternate Kirby ceased to exist when the timeline vanished, although the original individual continued to live in the original timeline. ("Children of Time" [DS9]). The original Julian Bashir was attracted to Kirby, and he tried to impress her with accounts of his bravery under fire during the *Defiant*'s mission to the Argolis Cluster. ("Behind the Lines" [DS9]).

Kiss Me, Deadly**.** Hard-boiled detective novel written by **Mickey Spillane** and published in 1952. The novel featured detective Mike Hammer, and in 2375, Odo recommended the novel to Kira Nerys. ("Shadows and Symbols" [DS9]).

Klingon death ritual.* Ceremonial acts performed upon the death of a Klingon. Warriors would sometimes follow the death howl with a recitation of a Klingon mourning chant: *neH taH Kronos. Hegh bat'lhqu Hoch nej maH. neH taH Kronos. yay je bat'lh manob Hegh.* Translated: "Only Kronos endures. All we can hope for is a glorious death. Only Kronos endures. In death there is victory and honor." Worf recited the chant upon the death of his wife, Jadzia Dax, in late 2374. ("Tears of the Prophets" [DS9]).

Klingon Defense Force.* Interstellar military agency of the Klingon Empire. In 2373, **Worf**, a Starfleet officer, was placed on detached service to the Klingon Defense Force in order to sign aboard the *Bird-of-Prey Rotarran* as first officer under **General Martok**. ("Soldiers of the Empire" [DS9]).

Klingon Empire.* Government of the Klingon people, founded 15 centuries ago by **Kahless the Unforgettable**.

Second Klingon Dynasty. Emperor Reclaw ruled the empire during this period, which ended when General **K'Trelan** assassinated Reclaw and his family. ("You Are Cordially Invited" [DS9])

Dark Time. Following the death of Reclaw was a ten-year period during which was conducted the first and only Klingon experiment in representational democracy. During what later became known as the Dark Time, the empire was ruled by an elected council. ("You Are Cordially Invited" [DS9])

Third Klingon Dynasty. Although the Reclaw dynasty had ended a decade earlier with the death of Emperor Reclaw, a new imperial family assumed leadership of the empire at the end of the Dark Time, taking on the names and titles of Reclaw's family to create the illusion of an unbroken royal line. ("You Are Cordially Invited" [DS9]).

Second Empire. A fleet of Klingon ships, sent by Chancellor Mow'ga, entered Breen space and was never heard from again. ("'Til Death Do Us Part" [DS9]).

K'mpec. The longest reign of the Klingon High Council in the history of the empire came to an end in 2367 when Chancellor K'mpec was murdered by political rival Duras. K'mpec was succeeded by Gowron. ("Reunion" [TNG]).

Gowron. Gowron's leadership of the high council came to an end in 2375 when a series of politically motivated decisions by Gowron cost the lives of numerous Klingon warriors during the final days of the Dominion war. Appalled by Gowron's squandering of warriors' lives, Worf slew Gowron in a *bat'leth* fight for honor. ("Tacking into the Wind" [DS9]).

Martok. Although Worf had earned the right to lead the high

council by killing Gowron, Worf stood aside to allow Martok to ascend to the chancellorship. ("Tacking into the Wind" [DS9]).

Klingon martini. Alcoholic beverage made with vermouth, gin, and a dash of Klingon bloodwine. Valerie Archer enjoyed Klingon martinis at the Quantum Cafe. ("In the Flesh" [VGR]).

Klingons.* Spacefaring civilization originating on planet Qo'noS. The social and military hierarchy of a Klingon spacecraft is very strict. A subordinate can challenge his superior only under extreme circumstances such as dereliction of duty, dishonorable conduct, or cowardice. It is traditional among Klingon warriors to sing songs of dedication and courage when going into battle ("Soldiers of the Empire" [DS9]). Klingon tradition also calls for an important event or battle to be commemorated by composing a poem. ("One Little Ship" [DS9]). Klingons are sensitive to extreme cold. ("Change of Heart" [DS9]; "Displaced" [VGR]). The Klingon people used incense, an ancient remedy believed to expel demons. They also used another kind of incense as a mental relaxant. ("Nothing Human" [VGR]).

kolar beast. Klingon animal. (*Star Trek: Insurrection*).

Koral. (James Greene). Bajoran monk engaged in theological research duties at the excavation site of the ancient city of B'Hala. In 2374, Koral discovered an artifact foretelling an epic conflict known as **the Reckoning**. Koral bore the religious title of ranjen. ("The Reckoning" [DS9]).

Kornaire. Cardassian vessel. Dukat served aboard the *Kornaire* shortly after he was promoted to the rank of glinn. ("Waltz" [DS9]).

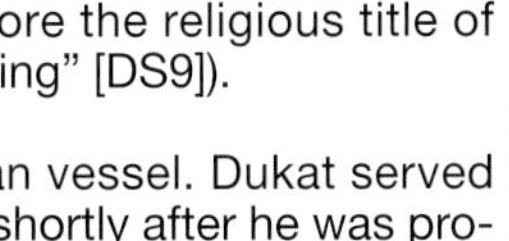

Kornan. (Rick Worthy). Klingon warrior, son of Shovak. In 2373, Kornan served as weapons officer aboard the *Bird-of-Prey* ***Rotarran***. Like much of the *Rotarran* crew, Kornan was discouraged and cynical until a victory under the command of **General Martok** restored his warrior's pride. ("Soldiers of the Empire" [DS9]). *Rick Worthy previously played Cravic Unit 122 and Pralor Unit 3947 in "Prototype" (VGR).*

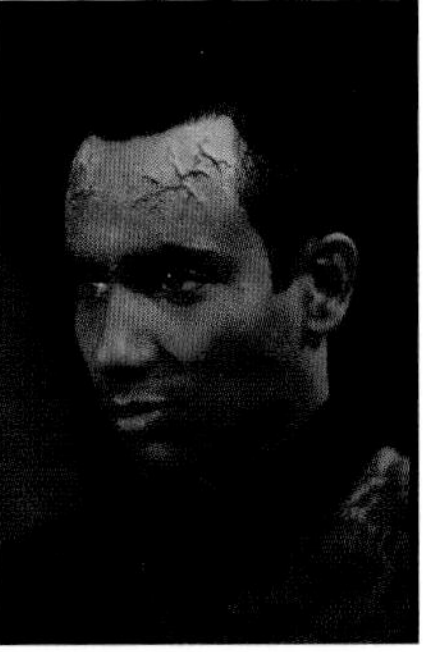

Kosst Amojan. In Bajoran religion, Kosst Amojan was the Evil One, a **Pah-wraith** banished long ago from the **Celestial Temple**. Kosst Amojan returned in 2374 to fight a Prophet in a prophesied conflict called the Reckoning. The Reckoning began on Deep Space 9 when Kosst Amojan occupied the body of Jake Sisko, opposing a Prophet who inhabited the body of Kira Nerys. The epic battle was interrupted when Kai **Winn** defied the will of the **Prophets** by releasing low levels of chroniton radiation onto the station, driving both energy beings away. ("The Reckoning" [DS9]). Several months later, when the Emissary discovered the long-lost **Orb of the Emissary**, Kosst Amojan and the other Pah-wraiths were once again banished. ("Shadows and Symbols" [DS9]). Shortly thereafter, Kosst Amojan recruited agents from the linear realm to aid him in his efforts to release the Pah-wraiths from their imprisonment in the **fire caves** on Bajor. These agents included **Gul Dukat**, who already hated the Bajoran people, ("'Til Death Do Us Part" [DS9]) and **Kai Winn**, whose lack of faith in the Prophets made it possible for her to be turned to evil. ("Strange Bedfellows" [DS9]). Although Kosst Amojan nearly succeeded in freeing the Pah-wraiths, he was defeated by **Benjamin Sisko**, the **Emissary** to the Bajoran Prophets. ("What You Leave Behind" [DS9]).

Kotaba Expanse. Region of space in the Delta Quadrant, near Benthan territory. ("Vis à Vis" [VGR]).

Kotanka system. Planetary group in the Alpha Quadrant. ("Favor the Bold" [DS9]).

Koth. Klingon warrior, son of Larna. In 2374 Koth transferred from the *Vor'nak* to the *Rotarran*. ("Sons and Daughters" [DS9]).

kotra. Traditional **Cardassian** game of strategy and decisive action. Kotra was played between two opponents using a variety of pieces on a game board. ("Empok Nor" [DS9]).

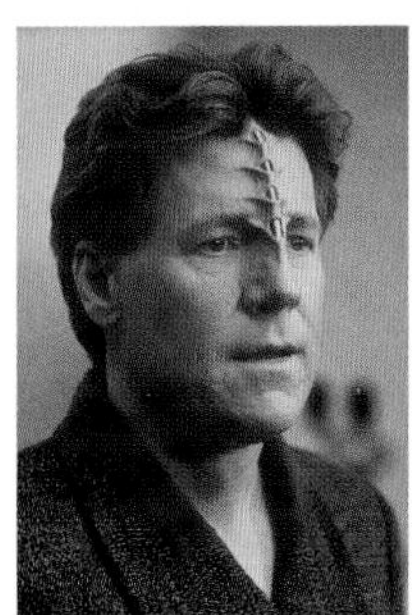

Kovin. (Michael Horton). Weapons dealer. Member of the **Entharan** civilization, Kovin negotiated for the sale of weapons to members of the *Starship Voyager* in 2374. During his trade negotiations, Kovin was accused of assaulting **Seven of Nine** and removing some of her Borg nanoprobes for weapons use. Entharan authorities agreed that sufficient evidence existed to investigate the charges, based on repressed memories recovered from Seven's mind. Further investigation yielded physical evidence suggesting the recovered memories were erroneous, but Kovin, fearing an unjust trial, died while fleeing Entharan authorities. ("Retrospect" [VGR]).

krada legs. Klingon culinary dish consisting of the broiled lower appendages of a small animal. Kira Nerys liked krada legs. ("The Sound of Her Voice" [DS9]).

Kradin. Sentient humanoid civilization that shared a Class-M world in the Delta Quadrant with the **Vori** people. The Kradin and the Vori declared war on each other around 2364. Each side characterized the other as inhuman beasts in an effort to manipulate their citizenry to support the war. In 2374, Kradin government officials helped the crew of the *Starship Voyager* to rescue Commander Chakotay, whose shuttlecraft had crashed on the Kradin homeworld. ("Nemesis" [VGR]).

Krady beast. Racist term used by the **Vori** in reference to a **Kradin** national. ("Nemesis" [VGR]).

Kraut. Racist term referring to citizens of the nation-state of **Nazi Germany** during Earth's 20th century. The term is a reference to a food called **sauerkraut**, popular in the German culture. ("The Killing Game, Part II" [VGR]).

Krellans. Civilization. Krellan food was popular on many worlds, including Farius Prime. ("Honor Among Thieves" [DS9]).

Krenim Imperium. Government of the **Krenim** people. ("Year of Hell, Parts I and II" [VGR]).

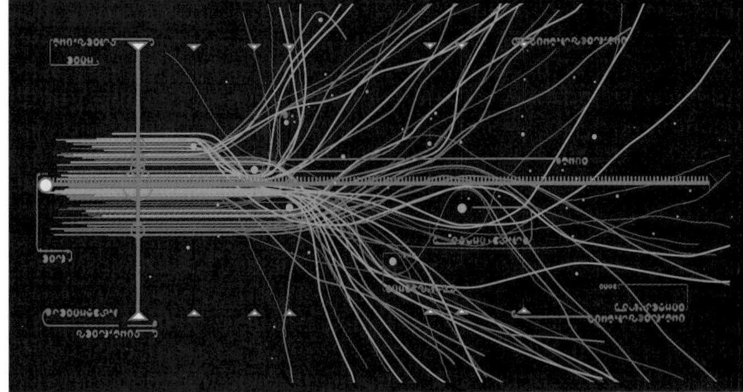

Krenim temporal weapon ship. In an alternate timeline, an incredibly powerful weapon of mass destruction. The ship created a focused temporal shock wave that actually removed an object from the continuum. Not only did the object disappear

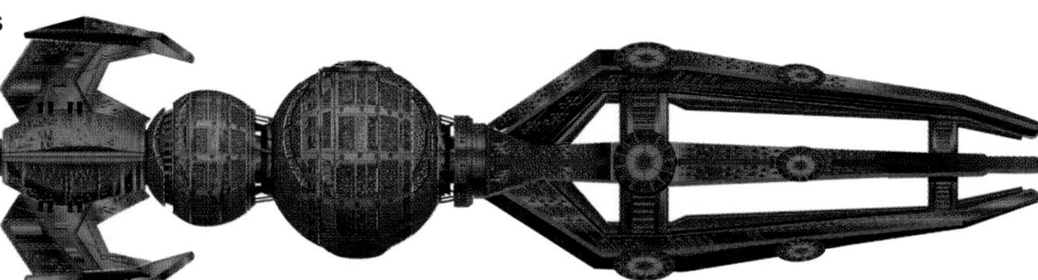

from history, but all effects of that object throughout the timeline also vanished. The ship operated in a state of temporal flux, outside normal space-time, so that it was immune not only to the effects of its temporal shock waves, but it was also impervious to most forms of attack. Devised and operated in the alternate reality by a **Krenim** scientist named **Annorax**, the temporal weapon was first used around 2174 against the **Rilnar** people. Unfortunately, Annorax failed to fully consider the complexities of **temporal mechanics** in using the weapon. The elimination of the Rilnar from history somehow made Annorax's people susceptible to a deadly disease that left some 50 million Krenim dead. Over the next two centuries, he used the temporal weapon repeatedly in a vain effort to somehow reverse the damage. In the process, Annorax erased thousands of inhabited worlds and billions of intelligent beings. Finally, in 2374, the Federation starship *Voyager*, in cooperation with several Delta Quadrant powers, destroyed the weapon ship. Ironically, the resulting temporal incursion erased the ship and its damage from the timeline. SEE: **Mawasi; Nihydron; Obrist.** ("Year of Hell, Parts I and II" [VGR]).

Krenim. Delta quadrant civilization. In certain alternate timelines, the Krenim did not exist or were a very minor power. In others, the Krenim were a major power in the Delta Quadrant. SEE: **Annorax; Krenim temporal weapon ship**. ("Year of Hell, Parts I and II" [VGR]).

Krim, Legate. Cardassian official. Krim paid a visit to station **Terok Nor** around stardate 51145. ("Behind the Lines" [DS9]).

Krit. (Brad Greenquist). Former associate of **Morn** in the infamous **Lissepian Mother's Day Heist**. In 2365, Hain, Morn, Larell, Krit, and his brother, Nahsk, robbed the Central Bank of Lissepia of 1,000 bars of **gold-pressed latinum** while the entire planet was celebrating Mother's Day. After the heist, Morn disappeared with all of the money, later staging his own apparent death in 2374, just as the statue of limitations expired on the case. Krit and his associates arrived separately on Deep Space 9 with different plans to get Morn's latinum. The four were arrested for attempted murder by station security. ("Who Mourns for Morn?" [DS9]). SEE: **Lissepia, Central Bank of.** *Brad Greenquist also played Demmas in "Warlord" (VGR).*

Krole. (Carlos Carrasco). Criminal who worked for **Liam Bilby** on Farius Prime. Krole had a dataport implant and was quite adept at using it to commit various larcenies. ("Honor Among Thieves" [DS9]). *Carlos Carrasco also played the Klingon D'Ghor in "House of Quark" (DS9), a Klingon officer in "Shattered Mirror" (DS9), and Bahrat in "Fair Trade" (VGR).*

Ktarian merlot. Alcoholic beverage. Similar to Earth's Saint-Émilion wines, it was made from the fermentation of black Ktarian grapes. Tom Paris and B'Elanna Torres enjoyed 2282 vintage Ktarian merlot on stardate 51244. ("Scientific Method" [VGR]).

Ktarians.* Civilization in the Alpha Quadrant. Ktarian children develop much faster than human children. **Naomi Wildman** was half Ktarian. ("Mortal Coil" [VGR]). Many Ktarians lived on Earth in the 24th century. ("Hope and Fear" [VGR]).

Kudak'Etan. (Scott Thompson Baker). Jem'Hadar first during the Dominion war. Kudak'Etan was in charge of a squad that commandeered the *Defiant* on stardate 51474. Kudak'Etan was an **Alpha** Jem'Hadar and felt he was superior to the **Gammas**. Kudak'Etan was killed in the conflict when Captain Sisko and his crew retook the ship. ("One Little Ship" [DS9]).

Kuiper belt. Disk-shaped region near the outer rim of some solar systems, generally located beyond the orbits of a system's planets. A Kuiper belt can contain many small icy bodies, some of which can become short-period comets. It can act as a reservoir for these bodies in the same way that an Oort cloud can act as a reservoir for the long-period comets. In 2375, Odo piloted the *Runabout Rio Grande* into a Kuiper belt to evade four Jem'Hadar attack ships. ("Treachery, Faith, and the Great River" [DS9]). *Named for the Dutch-born American astronomer Gerard Kuiper (1905–1973), best known for his study of the surface of Earth's Moon, his discovery of Miranda and Nereid, and his discovery of the atmosphere on Titan.*

Kukalaka.* Stuffed toy animal; **Julian Bashir**'s beloved teddy bear. While dating Bashir, Leeta became fond of Kukalaka and borrowed him. After their relationship ended, she neglected to return the cherished childhood toy. As a favor to Dr. Bashir, Nog procured the bear back from Leeta's quarters without her knowledge. ("In the Cards" [DS9]).

Kursky, Darlene. (Terry Farrell). Inhabitant of 20th-century Earth. Kursky worked as media intermediary to **Douglas Pabst**, editor of the 1950s pulp **science-fiction** magazine ***Incredible Tales***. Kursky was a fan of noted science-fiction writers **Robert A. Heinlein** and **Benny Russell**. ("Far Beyond the Stars" [DS9]). *Terry Farrell also played Jadzia Dax on* Star Trek: Deep Space Nine*, although Kursky did not have Trill spots.*

kut'luch. Klingon warrior's dagger. The *kut'luch* is used in a first bloodletting ritual that prepares one to become a warrior. ("Real Life" [VGR]).

Kyana Prime. Colony on the outskirts of **Krenim** space. Kyana Prime was home to **Annorax**, a Krenim scientist, and his family. In an alternate timeline, Kyana Prime was destroyed after Annorax's **Krenim temporal weapon ship** changed history. (Year of Hell, Parts I & II" [VGR]).

Kyoto, Ensign.* Starfleet officer aboard the *U.S.S. Voyager*. On stardate 51501, Kyoto received a letter from home in a Starfleet transmission received through a **Hirogen relay station**. ("Hunters" [VGR]).

Kyrian arbiter. (Marie Chambers). Thirty-first-century Kyrian scholar, member of the board responsible for evaluating historical evidence relating to the **Great War** between the Vaskan and Kyrian peoples. ("Living Witness" [VGR]).

Kyrian Heritage, Museum of. Center for historical study and education on the homeworld of the **Vaskan** and **Kyrian** peoples. The museum was founded by noted historian **Quarren**, who was its first curator. Museum displays included several artifacts from the Federation starship *Voyager*, which had been present in Kyrian space at the beginning of the Great War of 2374 between the Kyrians and the Vaskans. A major display in 3074 was an elaborate holographic re-creation of what Kyrian scholars incorrectly believed to be *Voyager*'s role in conspiring with Vaskan agents to commit atrocities against the Kyrian people. This revisionist history had the unfortunate effect of reinforcing racial tensions between the two peoples. In 3074, however, new historical evidence provided by the *Voyager*'s **Emergency Medical Hologram backup module** shed new light on the past, causing Kyrian scholars to re-examine their ancestors' role in the war. This extraordinary revelation was a major turning point in Kyrian history, and later was itself the subject of a display in the Museum of Kyrian Heritage. SEE: **Tedran.** ("Living Witness" [VGR]). *The set of the museum was later re-dressed as the Son'a body-sculpture facility in* Star Trek: Insurrection.

Kyrians. Technologically advanced humanoid Delta Quadrant civilization. The Kyrians felt oppressed by the **Vaskan** people, and in late 2374, radical Kyrians attacked the *U.S.S. Voyager* during trade negotiations with Vaskan Ambassador Daleth. That event touched off a **Great War** between the Vaskans and the Kyrians. Even after the war was over, Kyrian resentment against the Vaskans was strong. Kyrian educators taught that the war had been started by the *Voyager* crew, conspiring with Vaskan forces to commit atrocities against the Kyrian people. These beliefs persisted for some seven centuries until 3074, when newly discovered historical evidence revealed the revised Kyrian teachings to be incorrect. The new evidence opened the way to a new era of understanding between the Kyrians and their former enemies. SEE: **Emergency Medical Hologram backup module; Kyrian Heritage, Museum of; Tedran**. ("Living Witness" [VGR]).

La Forge, Geordi.* Chief engineer aboard the *Starship Enterprise*-E. The rejuvenating effects of the **Ba'ku planet** temporarily regenerated La Forge's optic nerves, eliminating his need for optic implants. He found "normal" sight limiting. (*Star Trek: Insurrection*).

La'voti V. Planet in the Delta Quadrant. The *U.S.S. Voyager* once visited La'voti V. ("Nothing Human" [VGR]).

Lamat'Ukan. (Christian Zimmerman). **Jem'Hadar** third during the **Dominion** war. Lamat'Ukan was part of a squad that commandeered the *Defiant* on stardate 51474. He was later taken prisoner by the *Defiant* crew and transferred to a Federation prisoner-of-war camp. ("One Little Ship" [DS9]).

Lang.* (Deborah Levin). Starfleet officer assigned to the *U.S.S. Voyager*. On stardate 50912.4, she became acting chief of security after Lieutenant Tuvok was abducted from the ship by **Nyrians**. ("Displaced" [VGR]). *Lang was also seen in "Blood Fever" (VGR).*

Lantaru Sector. Region of Federation space. Formerly the location of a classified research center. Around 2274, Starfleet physicist Dr. Ketteract synthesized a single **Omega molecule** at the station. The molecule destabilized, obliterating the research station and destroying subspace for several light-years in all directions. The damage to subspace made it impossible to create a stable warp field in the Lantaru Sector. ("The Omega Directive" [VGR]).

Larell. (Bridget Ann White). Former associate of **Morn** in the infamous Lissepian Mother's Day Heist. In 2365, Hain, Morn, Larell, Krit, and Nahsk robbed the Central Bank of Lissepia of 1,000 bars of **gold-pressed latinum** while the entire planet was celebrating Mother's Day. After the heist, Morn disappeared with all of the money, later staging his own apparent death in 2374, just as the statue of limitations expired on the case. Larell and her associates arrived separately on Deep Space 9 with different plans to get Morn's latinum. Larell, who posed as Morn's ex-wife, used her sexual charms on Quark, the heir to Morn's estate, a plan that was very nearly successful. The four conspirators were arrested for attempted murder by station security. ("Who Mourns for Morn?" [DS9]). SEE: **Lissepia, Central Bank of.**

Larg. (Stephen Ralston). Holographic character, the friend of the **Emergency Medical Hologram**'s son, **Jeffrey**, in the **Doctor's family program Beta-Rho**. Larg and K'Kath, both Klingon youths, elected to invite Jeffrey to go through a first bloodletting ceremony involving a *kut'luch* dagger. ("Real Life" [VGR]).

Larhana settlement. Photometric projection of a **Vori** village, part of an elaborate mind-control technique used by the Vori military to conscript new soldiers. In the simulation, the settlement's inhabitants were massacred by the **Kradin**, a horrific scene designed to induce the conscript soldiers to feel sympathy for the Vori cause against their Kradin enemies. ("Nemesis" [VGR]).

Larna. Klingon warrior, father of Koth. ("Sons and Daughters" [DS9]).

Larson. Junior officer at Starfleet Headquarters in San Francisco on Earth. Larson was assigned to the Federation Council deputy liaison officer in 2375. A re-creation of Larson was part of a training facility created by Species 8472 in the Delta Quadrant in 2375 in preparation for infiltrating the Federation. ("In the Flesh" [VGR]).

Las Vegas. Resort city on Earth's North American continent. Popular entertainer **Vic Fontaine** performed extensively in Las Vegas during the mid-20th century. ("His Way" [DS9]).

Lasaran, Glinn. (Todd Waring). Officer in the **Cardassian** military stationed on **Cardassia Prime** during the Dominion war. Lasaran was a covert Federation operative who passed important military intelligence data to Starfleet. In 2374, Dominion security began to suspect him, and he requested that Starfleet help him defect. On stardate 51597, Starfleet officers Worf and Jadzia Dax took the *Runabout Shenandoah* on a mission to extract him from the Dominion base on Soukara. Worf abandoned the mission after Dax was seriously injured. Lasaran was subsequently killed trying to reenter the base on Soukara. ("Change of Heart" [DS9]). *His rank is from the script. Todd Waring also portrayed Ensign DeCurtis in "Whispers" (DS9).*

lateral microbrace. Component of a starship's dilithium articulation frame. ("One Little Ship" [DS9]).

latinum dance. Traditional activity that is usually part of Ferengi **wedding** festivities. ("Call to Arms" [DS9]).

latinum.* Latinum was a valuable liquid metal, commonly stored in suspension in ingots of gold metal. **Gold-pressed latinum** was accepted as a medium of monetary exchange in many parts of the galaxy. Prolonged exposure to pure liquid latinum can be mildly toxic to some humanoid species. SEE: **Morn.** ("Who Mourns for Morn?" [DS9]).

Launching Pad. Bar located near the **Starfleet Academy** campus on Earth. As a cadet, Benjamin Sisko once made the mistake of debating logic with Solok, a fellow cadet of Vulcan heritage. ("Take Me Out to the Holosuite" [DS9]). SEE: **Quantum Cafe.**

Lauren. (Hilary Shepard-Turner). Individual who, as a child, had been genetically altered through illegal (and unsuccessful) **accelerated critical neural pathway formation.** Although the procedure had been intended to enhance Lauren's abilities, it resulted in giving her a dysfunctional personality that could not easily fit into normal society, and she spent much of her life institutionalized. Lauren possessed an intelligence far above average, and imagined herself as highly desirable to the opposite sex. Under the care of Starfleet psychiatrist Dr. Karen Loews, Lauren and three other genetically enhanced individuals traveled to starbase Deep Space 9 in 2374 to meet Julian Bashir. ("Statistical Probabilities" [DS9]). Lauren returned to Deep Space 9 a year later in hopes of gaining approval for an unorthodox surgical procedure for her friend **Sarina Douglas**. SEE: **Jack**. *Hilary Shepard played Hoya in "The Ship" (DS9).*

Le Coeur de Lion. Holographic environment in the **French Resistance** holodeck program, a re-creation of an ancient French tavern during Earth's second global war. Located in the municipality of **Sainte Claire**, Le Coeur de Lion was owned and operated by a woman named **Katrine**, who was an operative in the French underground, fighting against the Nazi occupation of her country. SEE: **de Neuf, Mademoiselle.** ("The Killing Game, Parts I and II" [VGR]). *The interior of Le Coeur de Lion incorporated parts of the Chez Sandrine bar set used earlier in the series.*

Leck. (Hamilton Camp). **Ferengi** entrepreneur. Leck visited Grand Nagus **Zek** for financial advice in 2373. ("Ferengi Love Songs" [DS9]). In 2374, Leck was part of the heroic team of mercenaries that effected the rescue of Ferengi citizen **Ishka** from the Dominion. Leck was particularly qualified for the mission because he was a professional **eliminator**, highly skilled at knife throwing. ("The Magnificent Ferengi" [DS9]).

Leeta.* Employee of Quark's bar. **Rom** and Leeta became engaged in 2373 ("Ferengi Love Songs" [DS9]) and were married on stardate 50975. The ceremony was performed by the Emissary, Benjamin Sisko, and was attended by Rom's son, **Nog**, and by Rom's brother, **Quark**. ("Call to Arms" [DS9]).

Legate's Crest of Valor. Prestigious Cardassian medal. **Dr. Crell Moset** received the Legate's Crest of Valor for his historic breakthrough development of a cure for the deadly **Fostossa virus**. ("Nothing Human" [VGR]).

leola* root. Vegetable. While experiencing **hyper-REM** sleep nightmares in 2374, Neelix dreamt of being boiled alive in a pot of *leola* root stew—a nightmare, despite the fact that his imaginary stew was perfectly seasoned. ("Waking Moments" [VGR]).

Leskit. (David Graf). Klingon warrior. Leskit served as pilot of the *Bird-of-Prey* ***Rotarran*** in 2373. Like much of the *Rotarran* crew, Leskit was discouraged and cynical until a victory under the command of **General Martok** restored his warrior's pride. ("Soldiers of the Empire" [DS9]). *David Graf previously played Fred Noonan in "The 37's" (VGR).*

Letant. (David Birney). Influential member of the **Romulan Senate**. In late 2374, Senator Letant headed a delegation to Deep Space 9, resulting in a Romulan decision to lend military support to the Federation and Klingon forces that were fighting against **Dominion** forces in defense of the Alpha Quadrant. ("Tears of the Prophets" [DS9]).

Li Paz. Member of the **Maquis** terrorist group. Li Paz was killed in 2374 when the rebels were eradicated by the Cardassians with the help of the Dominion. Future *Voyager* crew members B'Elanna Torres and Chakotay were also members of the same group. ("Extreme Risk" [VGR]).

Liberace. (1919–1987). Twentieth-century Earth entertainer. Liberace was a flamboyant pianist who was known for his outrageous attire. He frequently performed in **Las Vegas**. ("His Way" [DS9]).

library. Information storage and retrieval center. Traditionally, libraries are repositories of books, but they often contain sophisticated computer systems for research and study. The *Starship Enterprise*-E had a library to serve its crew and staff. (*Star Trek: Insurrection*).

light bulb. Vic Fontaine's slang term for a holographic character, a creation of computer-controlled photons and force fields. ("His Way" [DS9]).

Ligorian mastodon. Large stealthy animal. ("Blaze of Glory" [DS9]).

Limara'Son. (Paul S. Eckstein). Jem'Hadar soldier who was a crew member on an attack vessel commanded by **Keevan**. Limara'Son was killed in 2374 when Keevan betrayed all the Jem'Hadar soldiers under his command. ("Rocks and Shoals" [DS9]).

linguini with Bajoran shrimp. Seafood dish of extruded carbohydrate paste served with cooked marine decapods indigenous to Bajor. ("You Are Cordially Invited" [DS9]).

Linkasa. Klingon warrior. Father of **Sirella**. ("You Are Cordially Invited" [DS9]).

Lisa. (Davida Williams). Inhabitant of the planet **Gaia** in an alternate timeline. In this alternate reality, Lisa was a descendant of Jadzia Dax and Worf after the crew of the *U.S.S. Defiant* became marooned on Gaia in 2173. ("Children of Time" [DS9]).

Lisea (mirror). Bajoran woman who once worked at an Ilvian pleasure center on Bajor in the **mirror universe**. Lisea met **Bareil Antos (mirror)**, who taught her to become a thief, changing her life. She was deeply grateful for this, and the two stayed together for five years until she was killed by a drunken Cardassian soldier. ("Resurrection" [DS9]).

Lissepia, Central Bank of. Financial institution located on Lissepia. In 2365, the bank was robbed of 1,000 bars of **gold-pressed latinum** while the entire planet was celebrating a holiday. The heist, which was perpetrated by Hain, **Morn**, Larell, Krit, and Nahsk, was later called the Lissepian Mother's Day Heist. ("Who Mourns for Morn?" [DS9]).

Lissepian Mother's Day Heist. Notorious robbery of 1,000 bars of **gold-pressed latinum** from the Central Bank on Lissepia in 2365 during the planet's Mother's Day celebration. The case remained unsolved for years until 2374, when authorities learned that the heist had been perpetrated by Hain, **Morn**, Larell, Krit and Nahsk. After the robbery, Morn cheated his co-conspirators by stealing the latinum, then going into hiding until the statute of limitations had expired. ("Who Mourns for Morn?" [DS9]).

Livanian beet. Variety of aromatic succulent root of a biennial Livanian herb used as a vegetable. Morn sometimes shipped Livanian beets in his cargo ship. ("Who Mourns for Morn?" [DS9]).

"Living Witness." *Voyager* episode #91. Teleplay by Bryan Fuller and Brannon Braga & Joe Menosky. Story by Brannon Braga. Directed by Tim Russ. No stardate given. *First aired in 1998. Seven hundred years in the future, the holographic Doctor testifies as the sole witness in a war-crimes trial against the crew of the* Voyager. *First episode directed by actor Tim Russ.* GUEST CAST: Henry Woronicz as **Quarren**; Rod Arrants as **Daleth**; Craig Richard Nelson as **Vaskan Arbiter**; Marie Chambers as **Kyrian Arbiter**; Brian Fitzpatrick as **Tedran**; Morgan H. Margolis as Vaskan visitor; Mary Anne McGarry as **Tabris**; Timothy Davis-Reed as Kyrian spectator. SEE: **Cyrik Ocean; Daleth; dilithium; Emergency Medical Hologram backup module; Great War; Kesef; Kyrian arbiter; Kyrian Heritage, Museum of; Kyrians; photon grenade; Quarren; surgical chancellor; Tabris; Tedran; Vaskan arbiter; Vaskans.**

Lo-Tarik, Trajis. (Wade Williams). Imaginary person. Seven of Nine hallucinated Trajis when her Borg implants became affected by subnucleonic radiation while she piloted the *Voyager* alone through a nebula in late 2374. ("One" [VGR]).

"Lobekins." Ferengi term of endearment. Nickname used by **Ishka** to refer to Grand Nagus Zek. ("Ferengi Love Songs" [DS9]).

lobling. Term of affection applied to **Ferengi** children. ("Profit and Lace" [DS9]).

Loews, Dr. Karen. (Jeannetta Arnette). Starfleet psychiatrist. Loews's patients included four victims of unsuccessful **accelerated critical neural pathway formation**, who were cared for at a Federation institute. In an attempt to broaden their horizons and show them their potential, in 2374 Dr. Loews took her charges, **Sarina Douglas, Jack, Lauren**, and **Patrick**, to starbase Deep Space 9 in 2374 to meet Julian Bashir. ("Statistical Probabilities" [DS9]). In 2375, Loews, acting as Douglas's legal guardian, agreed to grant permission for a risky experimental surgical procedure developed by Bashir, which greatly improved Douglas's ability to respond to and communicate with the outside world. ("Chrysalis" [DS9]).

Logicians. Informal **baseball** team formed among the crew of the *Starship T'Kumbra* in early 2375.

T'Kumbra captain **Solok** organized the team specifically to challenge his former academy classmate Benjamin Sisko at station Deep Space 9. The Logicians defeated the **Niners** in a game held in one of the station's holosuites. ("Take Me Out to the Holosuite" [DS9]).

Logistical Support. Starfleet operational division responsible for matériel supply for spacecraft and ground-support facilities. The Logistics complex at Starfleet Headquarters was a security area. ("In the Flesh" [VGR]).

loon. Diving, fish-eating waterfowl indigenous to Earth. A monetary coin from the Earth nation of Canada featured an image of a loon. One such coin was an heirloom in Michael Eddington's family for over 200 years. ("Blaze of Glory" [DS9]).

Lorenzo, Al. Starfleet officer. Chief of operations on Decos Prime in 2375. Lorenzo had an unusual hobby, collecting holophotos of himself sitting behind the desks of famous Starfleet captains. Lorenzo often obtained these images by sneaking into their offices. In 2375, Lorenzo borrowed Captain Benjamin Sisko's desk from Ensign Nog in exchange for an induction modulation. Lorenzo's collection included photos of himself behind the desks of captains Jean-Luc Picard and Robert DeSoto. ("Treachery, Faith, and the Great River" [DS9]).

lucid dreaming. Form of self-hypnosis. Lucid dreaming is a technique that allows a subject to take control of dreams. In 2374, Chakotay used lucid dreaming to make contact with a **dream species**. ("Waking Moments" [VGR]).

Lumas. (Alan Altshuld). Representative of the **Caatati** people in 2374, when his people were in desperate need of supplies following a **Borg** attack. Lumas gratefully accepted a gift of supplies and food from the Federation starship *Voyager*, but later attempted to use force to coerce *Voyager* personnel to provide still more matériel. ("Day of Honor" [VGR]). *Alan Altshuld previously played Pomet in "Starship Mine" (TNG) and Yaranek in "Gambit, Part I" (TNG).*

Lumba. (Armin Shimerman). Temporary identity taken by Quark in 2374 when he was surgically transformed into a Ferengi female in an elaborate plan to help Grand Nagus Zek retain his office. "Lumba" caught the attentions of FCA Commissioner **Nilva**, despite the fact that she wore clothing. ("Profit and Lace" [DS9]).

Luna. Alternate name for the **Moon**, Earth's natural satellite. Dorian Collins, a native of the Moon, noted that a lunar native would never use the term "Luna." ("*Valiant*" [DS9]).

Lunar Schooner. Nickname referring to Federation citizens living on Earth's **Moon**. Jake Sisko used the term to describe **Dorian Collins**. ("*Valiant*" [DS9]).

Lupi. Favorite doll of Molly O'Brien. ("Time's Orphan" [DS9]).

Lurians. Humanoid civilization. **Morn**, a regular patron of Quark's bar, was Lurian. Lurians have two stomachs and multiple hearts. It is a Lurian custom to bring gifts of food and drink for the deceased at their funeral, so they will have something to sustain them in the afterlife. The Lurian homeworld is ruled by a monarchy. ("Who Mourns for Morn?" [DS9]). Lurians have four lungs. ("The Sound of Her Voice" [DS9]).

Lytasians. Civilization of sentient beings. Two hundred seventy-three Lytasians slaughtered ten lone Ferengi in the Battle of Prexnak, regarded by some scholars as the most important battle in Ferengi history. ("The Magnificent Ferengi" [DS9]).

M'Nea. Heroine in the Klingon novel *Woman Warriors at the River of Blood*. ("Real Life" [VGR]).

M'Pella. Employee of Quark's bar who worked as a **dabo girl** in 2374. ("In the Pale Moonlight" [DS9]).

Ma'Stakas. Ceremonial clubs, used in a Klingon **wedding** ritual. The participants in the groom's *Kal'Hyah* carry *Ma'Stakas* with them during their journey. In a traditional Klingon wedding, after the couple are pronounced married, they are symbolically attacked by the groomsmen, who wield *Ma'Stakas*. This tradition grew out of the story of **"Kahless and Lukara."** ("You Are Cordially Invited" [DS9]).

machine gun. Antipersonnel firearm used during the 20th century on planet Earth. A machine gun employed chemical explosive cartridges to propel a number of sublight projectiles fired in rapid succession at a target, often to deadly effect. Machine guns were used during Earth's **World War II**. ("The Killing Game, Part II" [VGR]).

Macklin, Albert. (Colm Meaney). Twentieth-century Earth writer who worked in 1953 for ***Incredible Tales*** magazine. Macklin specialized in **science-fiction** tales about robots and other futuristic machines. His first book was a novel about robots published by **Gnome Press**. He was also a fair bongo player. ("Far Beyond the Stars" [DS9]). *Macklin's fondness for playing bongo drums was loosely inspired by the late Nobel laureate physicist Richard Feynman. Colm Meaney also played O'Brien on* Star Trek: Deep Space Nine.

Madrat. Patron of Quark's bar. Madrat was injured when an adult version of Molly O'Brien felt threatened and attacked him with a broken bottle. Madrat, a Tarkalian national, recovered in the station infirmary, but filed charges against Molly anyway. SEE: **Golanan time portal.** ("Time's Orphan" [DS9]).

Magellan, U.S.S.* Federation starship. In 2374, the *Magellan* participated in the daring and costly mission to retake station Deep Space 9 from **Dominion** control, preventing a massive incursion of Dominion ships into the Alpha Quadrant. ("Sacrifice of Angels" [DS9]). *Named for explorer Ferdinand Magellan.*

magnetic plasma guide. Plasma containment coil, part of a starship's warp propulsion system. Magnetic plasma guides use powerful magnets to control the flow of the ionized plasma gas. ("One Little Ship" [DS9]).

magneton scan.* Sensor protocol. Kellin, a Ramuran tracer, used a magneton sweep to disrupt the **polarization cloak** used by a runaway in 2374, thereby rendering the escapee visible. ("Unforgettable" [VGR]).

"Magnificent Ferengi, The." *Deep Space Nine* episode #134. Written by Ira Steven Behr & Hans Beimler. Directed by Chip Chalmers. No stardate given. *First aired in 1997. Quark leads a Ferengi mission to rescue his mother from the Dominion. The episode continues "Ferengi Love Songs" (DS9), where we learned of the relationship between Ishka and Zek; "Rocks and Shoals" (DS9), in which Keevan was captured; and "Empok Nor" (DS9), in which we first saw station Empok Nor.* GUEST CAST: Jeffrey Combs as **Brunt**; Max Grodénchik as **Rom**; Aron Eisenberg as **Nog**; Cecily Adams as **Ishka**; Josh Pais as **Gaila**; Christopher Shea as **Keevan**; Hamilton Camp as **Leck**; Chase Masterson as **Leeta**; Iggy Pop as **Yelgrun.** SEE: **Balancar Agricultural Consortium; Balancar; Brunt; ear-lift surgery; eliminator; Empok Nor; Ferenginar; Gaila; groatcakes; hypicate; Ishka; Keevan; Leck; Lytasians; neural stimulator; Prexnak, Battle of; Quark; squill; syrup of squill; Thalos VI; Vorta; Yelgrun; Zek.**

mahk-cha. Klingon term meaning "engage." ("Soldiers of the Empire" [DS9]).

main computer processor. Central data-processing system on a Federation starship. The main processor of an *Intrepid*-class starship was capable of simultaneous access to 47 million data channels, and transluminal processing at a rate of 575 trillion calculation per nanosecond. The device could operate in temperature margins from 10 to 1,790 kelvins. The main computer core of the *Starship Voyager* was stolen by a pirate named Tau in the Delta Quadrant in 2374, although *Voyager* personnel were later able to recover the device. ("Concerning Flight" [VGR]).

maj-Kkah. Klingon term that meant "well done." ("Sons and Daughters" [DS9]).

Majestic, U.S.S. Federation starship, *Miranda* class. In 2374, the *Majestic* was destroyed in the daring—and costly—mission to retake station Deep Space 9 from Dominion control, preventing a massive incursion of Dominion ships into the Alpha Quadrant. ("Sacrifice of Angels" [DS9]).

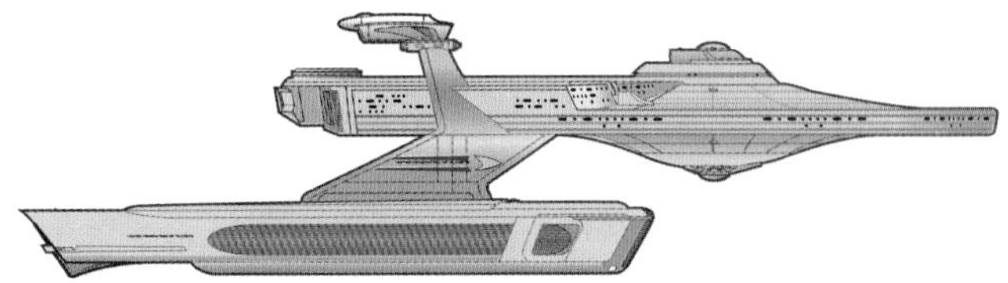

Malin. (Ted Barba). Inhabitant of the Mari homeworld in 2374. Malin bought illicit hostile mental imagery from **Guill** on the black market. ("Random Thoughts" [VGR]).

Malkothian spirits. Beverage distilled by the Alsuran Empire. In an alternate timeline, the **Krenim temporal weapon ship** eradicated all trace of the Alsuran Empire. In this reality, all that remained of that civilization was a bottle of Malkothian spirits. ("Year of Hell, Part II" [VGR]).

Malon export vessel. Large freighter spacecraft of Malon registry. A Malon export vessel commanded by **Controller Emck** was used to transport massive quantities of contaminated antimatter to a region of space informally known as the **Void** until early 2375. Export vessels typically had a capacity in excess of 90 million isotons. ("Night" [VGR], "Extreme Risk" [VGR]).

Malon shuttle. Small spacecraft specifically designed by the Malon to survive a trip into the atmosphere of a gas giant. Its hull was composed of tetraburnium alloys. ("Extreme Risk" [VGR]).

Malons. Technologically advanced civilization from the Delta Quadrant. The Malon economy employed an antimatter power generation system that yielded large quantities of toxic antimatter waste, which was jettisoned into a region of space informally known as the **Void**, through a spatial vortex. It was not generally realized that the Void was home to a sentient species of **night beings** who were being poisoned by theta radiation from the six billion isotons of toxic antimatter being dumped there every day. The practice ceased in 2374, when the Federation starship *Voyager* sealed the vortex, forcing the Malons to seek alternative energy technologies for their society. ("Night" [VGR]).

mambo. A traditional style of Earth dance set to syncopated, four-beat music. (*Star Trek: Insurrection*).

mandala. Small personal Bajoran prayer shrine. ("In the Cards" [DS9]).

manual steering column. Control device used to directly pilot a spacecraft through the use of a hand-operated joystick, generally reserved for emergency use in case of computer-systems failure. A manual steering column was located near the flight controller's station on the **bridge** of a *Sovereign*-class starship. (*Star Trek: Insurrection*).

Manzar colony. Federation settlement. The Manzar colony was located in the same sector as the Evora homeworld. In 2375, Lieutenant Commander Worf traveled to the colony to install a new defense perimeter. (*Star Trek: Insurrection*).

mapa bread. Bajoran baked food made from grain meal. ("You Are Cordially Invited" [DS9]).

maple syrup. The refined sweet sap of the Earth deciduous sugar maple tree, in liquid form. B'Elanna Torres enjoyed banana pancakes with maple syrup on the *Voyager* in 2375. ("Extreme Risk" [VGR]).

Maquis.* Terrorist organization of outlaw Starfleet officers and Federation colonists opposed to **Cardassian** occupation of former Federation territory ceded to the Cardassians. In 2373, the Maquis were almost completely wiped out by the Cardassian forces allied with the **Dominion**. The Maquis defeat came despite military aid from the Klingon government, which included some 30 class-4 cloaking devices. Only a few Maquis groups survived the Cardassian and Dominion attacks, including a handful of survivors of **Michael Eddington**'s team who were rescued from **Athos IV** ("Blaze of Glory" [DS9]), as well as members of **Chakotay**'s ship who joined the crew of the *Starship Voyager* in the Delta Quadrant. ("Hunters" [VGR]).

Marauder Mo™. A fictional adventure character popular with Ferengi male children in the mid-to-late 24th century. Toy figurines based on the character were also popular with Ferengi children during that period. As a child, Quark acquired several Marauder Mo figures that he kept into his adulthood. They appreciated in value as time passed, but would have been worth more had they been kept in their original packaging. ("Ferengi Love Songs" [DS9]). *As with any business investment, there is always some risk involved; not all Marauder Mo figures increase in value, some go down.*

Marcus, Dr. Carol.* Noted 23rd-century scientist who led the development of the Genesis Device. In 2374, Starfleet captain Kathryn Janeway, wrestling with the discovery of the incredibly destructive **Omega molecule**, said she understood how Marcus must have felt when the Genesis Device proved to be a powerful weapon. ("The Omega Directive" [VGR]).

Mari Constabulary. Law-enforcement agency of the Mari society in the Delta Quadrant. ("Random Thoughts" [VGR]).

Mari. Technologically advanced civilization of sentient humanoid telepaths in the Delta Quadrant. Mari society was once overrun by criminal violence. In the early 24th century, the government sought to eliminate violence by outlawing hostile thought, since in a telepathic society, such thought could lead directly to violent acts. By 2374, the incidence of reported violent crime had dropped to nearly zero, in large part due to laws subjecting those with violent thoughts to **engramatic purge**s and **neurogenic restructuring** to erase violent impulses from their brains. These laws had the unintended side effect of creating a thriving black market in illicit violent mental images. SEE: **Guill; Nimira; Talli**. ("Random Thoughts" [VGR]).

Mark. SEE: **Johnson, Mark**.

Marna. (Marilyn Fox). Photometric projection of a **Vori** civilian, part of an elaborate mind-control technique used by the Vori military to conscript new soldiers. In the simulation, Marna was a woman who lived at the Larhana Settlement. The destruction of Marna's village was calculated to induce the conscript to feel sympathy for the Vori cause against their **Kradin** enemies. ("Nemesis" [VGR]).

Martian Colonies.* Settlements on the fourth planet of the Sol system. The flag of the first Martian colonies was inspired by a velvet painting of an ancient bullfighter. ("In the Cards" [DS9]).

Corbis

Martin, Dean. (1917–1995). Twentieth-century Earth entertainer. Martin was a suave, sophisticated singer who also achieved wide success as a comedic actor. He frequently performed in **Las Vegas.** Singer **Vic Fontaine** said he was a friend of Dean Martin. ("His Way" [DS9]).

Martok degh, to-Duq degh, bat-LEH degh, mat-LEH degh. Klingon phrase that meant "Badge of Martok, badge of courage, badge of honor, badge of loyalty." ("Sons and Daughters" [DS9]).

Martok, General.* Klingon leader. In 2373, Martok assumed command of the *Bird-of-Prey* ***Rotarran*** in order to conduct a search for the missing battle cruiser *I.K.S. B'Moth*. During the mission, spacecraft first officer **Worf** was instrumental in defeating a Jem'Hadar ship and rescuing 35 warriors from the *B'Moth*'s crew. So impressed was Martok with Worf's actions that he made the son of Mogh a member of the House of Martok. ("Soldiers of the Empire" [DS9]). Martok even appointed Worf as first officer on a dangerous mission to Monac IV in early 2375 so that Worf could earn entry into *Sto-Vo-Kor* for his late wife, Jadzia. ("Image in the Sand" [DS9]). Martok enjoyed gambling. He was a shrewd judge of character and cared deeply about those under his command. In 2374, General Martok accepted Worf's son, **Alexander Rozhenko**, into the **House** of Martok, having already granted that honor to Worf himself. ("Sons and Daughters" [DS9]). Martok was married to **Sirella**, who then carried the title of Mistress of the House of Martok. Martok and Sirella had a number of children. On stardate 51247.5 Martok was promoted to supreme commander of the **Ninth Fleet**, stationed at Deep Space 9 to defend the strategically critical Bajor Sector against Dominion and Cardassian aggression. ("You Are Cordially Invited" [DS9]). Martok commanded the Klingon wing of the allied Alpha Quadrant fleet that successfully captured the **Chin'toka System** from Dominion control in 2374. ("Tears of the Prophets" [DS9]). Martok's battlefield acumen was critical in several victories by the Alpha Quadrant powers. Unfortunately, the resulting accolades caused Chancellor **Gowron** to fear that Martok might soon become a political rival for leadership of the high council. Gowron seized direct command of the Klingon military and ordered Martok to undertake a series of foolhardy combat engagements, resulting in terrible losses among Klingon forces. Martok was blamed for these costly defeats, but refused to question Gowron, even though he knew that Gowron had intended the missions to undermine Martok's image. After Gowron was killed by challenger Worf, Martok assumed the chancellorship when Worf declined to accept leadership of the council. ("Tacking into the Wind" [DS9]). *John Hertzler also appeared as the Vulcan captain of the* U.S.S. Saratoga *in "Emissary, Parts I and II" (DS9).*

Banner of the House of Martok

Master Race. Term used by the government of Earth's **Nazi Germany** nation during the 20th century to describe its citizens, which it held to be genetically superior to other members of the human species. The label was intended to rationalize brutal Nazi efforts to conquer the planet, as well as a horrific policy of genocide, practiced upon those the Nazis termed "degenerate." ("The Killing Game, Parts I and II" [VGR]).

***mat-LEH*.** Klingon term that meant "loyalty." ("Sons and Daughters" [DS9]).

Matoian. Noted sculptor whose work became a recognized style. A post-eventualistic, pre-Matoian bronze and triptin sculpture was sold at auction on station Deep Space 9 in late 2373. ("In the Cards" [DS9]).

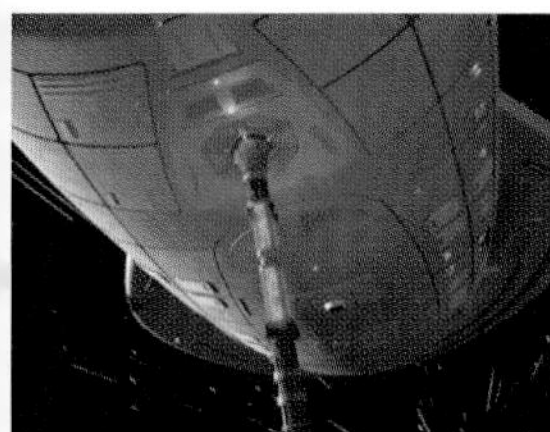

matter/antimatter reaction chamber.* Key component of a starship's **warp drive**, also known as a warp core. The warp core of the *Starship Voyager* became flooded with tachyons during an experimental attempt to create a transwarp conduit in early 2374. The emergency necessitated that the core be jettisoned, although it was later retrieved, repaired, and reinstalled. ("Day of Honor" [VGR]). The *Enterprise*-E ejected its warp core near the Ba'ku planet in 2375 when Son'a forces used isolytic weapons. (*Star Trek: Insurrection*). *An external view of a core ejection was seen* (pictured) *in "Day of Honor" (VGR).*

maturation chamber. Device used to nurture embryonic **Borg** drones until they are capable of independent biological operation. When a transporter malfunction fused Borg nanoprobes from Seven of Nine with the Doctor's mobile emitter in 2375, the resulting Borg construct formed a maturation chamber and cloned a drone within it based on DNA from a *Voyager* crew member. ("Drone" [VGR]).

Mavek. Cardassian junior officer assigned to the operations center of the Dominion-occupied station **Terok Nor** in 2374. ("Rocks and Shoals" [DS9]).

Mawasi. Civilization in the Delta Quadrant. In an alternate timeline, the Mawasi were allied with the ***Starship Voyager*** in 2375 to defeat the **Krenim temporal weapon ship**. ("Year of Hell, Part II" [VGR]).

maxilla. Jawbone; part of facial structure in humanoid anatomy. In 2374, *Voyager* crew member Seven of Nine struck weapons dealer **Kovin** in the premaxilla bone. ("Retrospect" [VGR]).

Mays, Willie. Twentieth-century American professional **baseball** player and member of the **Baseball Hall of Fame**. Mays played for the Giants and the New York Mets teams and was the first player besides Babe Ruth to hit more than 600 home runs in his career. In 2373, Jake Sisko went to great lengths to procure a mint condition 1951 rookie Willie Mays **baseball trading card** for his father, Benjamin Sisko. ("In the Cards" [DS9]).

McCauley, Ensign. Starfleet officer. McCauley participated in the covert sociological study of the Ba'ku in 2375. (*Star Trek: Insurrection*).

McConnell, Lieutenant. Starfleet officer assigned to the *U.S.S. Honshu*. McConnell was killed on stardate 51408 when the *Honshu* was attacked and destroyed by a wing of Cardassian spacecraft. During the battle, McConnell helped Gul Dukat carry a wounded Benjamin Sisko into a shuttlecraft. On their way, a piece of shrapnel hit McConnell in the head, killing him. ("Waltz" [DS9]).

McCoy, Dr. Leonard H.* Chief medical officer aboard the original ***Starship Enterprise*** under the command of Captain **James T. Kirk**. McCoy wrote a medical text entitled *Comparative Alien Physiology* that was considered a classic in medical literature into the 24th century. ("Message in a Bottle" [VGR]).

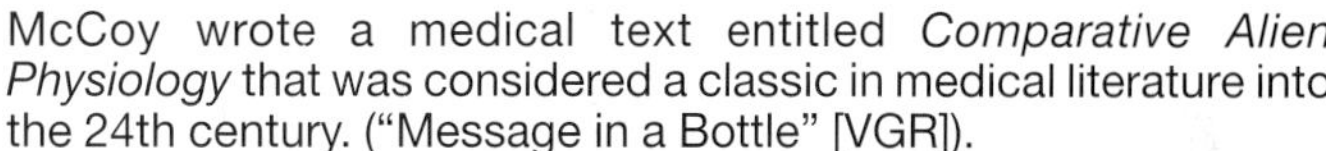

Medal of Valor, Christopher Pike. Starfleet commendation given to members who acquit themselves honorably in the service of others. Named for **Christopher Pike**, a commander of the first *Starship Enterprise,* who later served as fleet captain. In 2374, Captain **Benjamin Sisko** was awarded the Christopher Pike Medal of Valor for his leadership in the recapture of station Deep Space 9 from Dominion forces. ("Tears of the Prophets" [DS9]). Captain **Solok** of the *Starship T'Kumbra* was twice honored with the Pike Medal of Valor for his courageous service during the Dominion war. ("Take Me Out to the Holosuite" [DS9]).

medicine bundle.* A collection of personal items used in a Native American **vision quest** ritual. Neelix's experience with death on stardate 51449 compelled him to seek answers in a vision quest. In preparation, **Neelix** made a medicine bundle that contained a necklace that once belonged to his sister, Alixia; a dried flower from Kes's garden; and a sculpture of the Guiding Tree from Talaxian mythology. ("Mortal Coil" [VGR]).

medkit. Small Starfleet-issue satchel of equipment used in medical emergencies. A medkit contained a medical **tricorder**, a hypospray, a dermal regenerator, and a battlefield trauma kit. ("Call to Arms" [DS9]).

Melissa. (Debi A. Monahan). Holographic character, a 1960s Las Vegas dancer in the **Vic Fontaine** program. Melissa thought Odo was adorable. ("His Way" [DS9]).

Mercury. First planet in the Sol system. Orbiting Sol at a distance of some 58 million kilometers, with dayside temperatures of up to 430 celsius, Mercury is inhospitable to unprotected humanoid life. Imaginary mines on Mercury were fictional settings for some holodeck stories in *The Adventures of Captain Proton* series devised by Tom Paris. SEE: ***Captain Proton, The Adventures of***. ("Night" [VGR]).

"Message in a Bottle." *Voyager* episode #81. Teleplay by Lisa Klink. Story by Rick Williams. Directed by Nancy Malone. No stardate given. First aired in 1997. *An alien relay station allows* Starship Voyager's *Emergency Medical Hologram to beam to the Alpha Quadrant aboard the* U.S.S. Prometheus, *where he works with another hologram to defeat a party of Romulans. Starfleet Command learns for the first time that* Voyager *was not destroyed four years ago, but is in the Delta Quadrant, heading for home.* GUEST CAST: Judson Scott as **Rekar**; Valerie Wildman as **Nevala**; Andy Dick as **Emergency Medical Hologram-2**; Tiny Ron as **Alpha-Hirogen**; Majel Barrett as Computer Voice; Tony Sears as *Prometheus* officer. SEE: **ablative armor; Almar; anesthezine; axonol; Emergency Medical Hologram-2; Emergency Medical Hologram; *Gray's Anatomy*; Hippocratic Oath; Hirogen relay station; Hirogen; McCoy, Dr. Leonard H.; multivector assault mode; neurozine; Nevala; *Prometheus, U.S.S.*; Rekar; "Rodeo Red's Red Hot Rootin' Tootin' Chili"; Starfleet General Orders and Regulations: Security Protocol 28, Subsection D; *T'Met*; Terrellian plague; thrombic modulator; Torothka virus; *Voyager, U.S.S.***

metaphasic radiation. Energy form associated with subspace phenomena. Under certain conditions, exposure to metaphasic radiation particles can cause a cessation or even a reversal of biological processes associated with aging in many humanoid species. The ring system of the **Ba'ku planet** had high levels of metaphasic radiation, causing inhabitants on the planet to live for centuries. These effects were only observed on adults. (*Star Trek: Insurrection*).

metreon gas. Combustible form of plasma. The region of space known as the Briar Patch had pockets of high metreon gas content. (*Star Trek: Insurrection*). SEE: **Riker Maneuver**.

metreon radiation. Form of subspace energy. Metreon radiation can be created by certain quantum reactions such as those caused by an unstable exogenic field. Metreon radiation can cause the dilithium matrix of a starship's warp drive to collapse, resulting in loss of propulsion for the vessel. In 2371, an exogenic field surrounding a planet in a star system in the Rutharian sector was probed by the active sensors of the *U.S.S. Olympia*. This triggered a quantum reaction that liberated an enormous surge of metreon radiation that disabled the ship's engines, resulting in the loss of all hands. ("The Sound of Her Voice" [DS9]).

Meyer. Member of the **Maquis** terrorist group. Meyer was killed in 2374, when the rebels were eradicated by the Cardassians with the help of the Dominion. Future *Voyager* crew members B'Elanna Torres and Chakotay were also members of the same group. ("Extreme Risk" [VGR]).

micro-inducer. Precision electronic engineering tool. ("Scientific Method" [VGR]).

microsuture. Surgical technology for knitting tissue at the cellular level. ("Rocks and Shoals" [DS9]).

Mikah. Planet in the Delta Quadrant. The Federation starship *Voyager* visited Mikah in 2374. ("Unforgettable" [VGR]).

Miller, Captain. (Robert Beltran). Persona imposed upon **Chakotay** while under Hirogen **neural interface** control in the **French Resistance** holodeck program in late 2374. Miller was an officer with the American military, commanding the Fifth Armored Infantry of the **Allied Forces** in the war against **Nazi Germany** during Earth's 20th century. ("The Killing Game, Parts I and II" [VGR]).

mimetic life-form. Metallic liquid life-form that evolved as an abundant biomass on a **Class-Y planet** in the Delta Quadrant. The mimetic life-form was primarily composed of deuterium, hydrogen sulfate, dichromates, and protein molecules. In late 2374, the Federation starship *Voyager* visited the mimetic life-form's homeworld. When a mishap brought two of *Voyager*'s humanoid crew members into physical contact with the life-form, the nonsentient liquid life-form sampled the DNA of both individuals and somehow created near-perfect duplicates of them. The only difference was that the duplicates were perfectly adapted to live in the extreme environmental conditions normal to a Class-Y world. In creating the duplicates, the life-form gained sentience and realized that it did not wish to be alone. Other members of the *Voyager* crew therefore agreed to allow themselves to be duplicated by the life-form, which called itself "silver blood," allowing the duplicates to remain behind so that the silver blood would not need to be alone. ("Demon" [VGR]).

Mines of Mercury. Fictional setting in *The Adventures of Captain Proton* **holodeck** stories, an excavation site on the planet closest to Earth's sun, Sol. In those tales, **Doctor Chaotica**'s vanquished enemies toiled as slaves in the Mines of Mercury. ("Night" [VGR]).

Miradorn.* Civilization. In 2373, the Miradorn signed a nonaggression pact with the **Dominion**, affecting the balance of power in the Alpha Quadrant, a prelude to the devastating Dominion war. ("Call to Arms" [DS9]).

***Mithran*-class fighter.** Spacecraft developed by Benthan scientists in 2374. The vessel was intended to be the most advanced in the quadrant. Steth hoped to be able to be test pilot of the *Mithran*-class fighter. ("Vis à Vis" [VGR]).

mitochondria. Subcellular structure common in many carbon-based life-forms. Mitochondria are organelles that help to metabolize oxygen and nutrients. Naomi Wildman, learning cellular biology from *Voyager*'s Emergency Medical Hologram, referred to mitochondria as "the warp core of the cell." ("Once Upon a Time" [VGR]).

mizainite ore.* Mined substance. There were large mizainite deposits on planet Holna IV. Mizainite was used extensively by Dominion shipyards in the construction of warships. ("Statistical Probabilities" [DS9]).

***moba* jam.** Preserves made from the Bajoran *moba* fruit. One of Julian Bashir's favorite breakfasts included hot buttered scones with *moba* jam. ("Inquisition" [DS9]).

mobile emitter. A miniature holographic imaging projector used by Voyager's **Emergency Medical Hologram**, allowing him to operate in areas where holographic equipment has not been installed. The device, which employed 29th-century technology, was made from **polydeutonic alloy**. In 2375, a transporter malfunction aboard the *U.S.S. Voyager* fused Borg nanoprobes from Seven of Nine with the Doctor's mobile emitter, which developed into a device that produced a drone who named himself **One**. ("Drone" [VGR]). SEE: **autonomous holo-emitter**.

Moklor. (Kevin P. Stillwell). Holographic character, a Klingon warrior who was part of the **Day of Honor** program written by B'Elanna Torres and Tom Paris in 2374. ("Day of Honor" [VGR]).

Molina, Ensign. (Lawrence Rosenthal). Starfleet officer assigned to the security section of the *U.S.S. Voyager*. ("Displaced" [VGR]). *Molina's name is from the script, and he had no dialogue.*

Molly. (Doren Fein). Inhabitant of the planet **Gaia** in an alternate timeline. In this parallel reality, Molly was the great-great-great-great-great granddaughter of Chief Miles O'Brien and Ensign Rita Tannenbaum after the crew of the *U.S.S. Defiant* became marooned on Gaia in 2173. ("Children of Time" [DS9]).

Molly. Irish setter, pet of **Kathryn Janeway**. Molly was left in the care of Mark Johnson when Janeway disappeared and was presumed lost in 2371 on a mission into the Badlands. Molly had a litter of puppies shortly thereafter, and Mark gave them all away to good homes. ("Hunters" [VGR]).

Monac IV. Planet. Site of a Dominion orbital shipyard in 2375. General Martok undertook a mission to destroy the shipyards at Monac IV, inviting Worf to be his first officer on the mission. ("Image in the Sand" [DS9]). The shipyards were destroyed when a Klingon bird-of-prey, commanded by General Martok, performed a daring maneuver, skimming the surface of the Monac star, triggering a powerful solar flare that also destroyed several Jem'Hadar ships. ("Shadows and Symbols" [DS9]). *Probably named for* Star Trek: Deep Space 9 *special effects supervisor Gary Monak.*

money. In many cultures, a system of standardized units serving as a medium of exchange. By the 24th century, the Federation had abandoned currency-based economics in favor of a philosophy of self-enhancement. Many other cultures, including the Ferengi, nevertheless preferred other economic systems, including those of capitalism. ("In the Cards" [DS9]). SEE: **monetary units**.

monotanium. Metal alloy. Monotanium was used as armor plating on Hirogen spacecraft. Monotanium armor can scatter Federation-style weapons targeting beams, ("Hunters" [VGR]) although the metal could be susceptible to an isokinetic cannon of sufficient power. ("Retrospect" [VGR]).

***moolt* nectar.** Delicious beverage. An aged fruit compote served by Neelix at *Voyager*'s annual Prixin celebration was aged in *moolt* nectar. ("Mortal Coil" [VGR]).

Moon.* Earth's natural satellite. Dorian Collins was a native of Tycho City on the Moon. ("*Valiant*" [DS9]).

"Moonlight Becomes You." Twentieth-century song popular in western culture on planet Earth. Written by Johnny Burke and James van Heusen, the song tells of romantic images created by solar reflections from Earth's natural satellite. **Mademoiselle de Neuf** sang it in the **French Resistance** holodeck program. ("The Killing Game, Part I" [VGR]).

Morn.* (Mark Shepherd). Patron of **Quark's bar**. Morn made a living piloting his cargo freighter in the Bajor Sector until 2374. ("Who Mourns for Morn?" [DS9]). Morn was an excitable fellow. When Deep Space 9 faced imminent **Dominion** attack in 2373, Morn panicked and leaped up, hitting Quark with a barstool before running out of the bar screaming, "We're all doomed!" Morn ran to a Bajoran shrine, falling naked onto his knees, begging the Prophets for protection. He was arrested by station security shortly thereafter. ("Blaze of Glory" [DS9]). Later, when the Dominion seized control of communications from Terok Nor, Morn served as a courier of a vital message from the station's resistance cell to Captain Benjamin Sisko on Starbase 375. The message, which was hidden in a birthday present to Morn's mother, warned that the Dominion was about to dismantle the minefield blockading the Bajoran wormhole. ("Favor the Bold" [DS9]). Morn attended Jadzia Dax's prewedding party in 2374. He drank too much at the celebration and fell asleep on the floor, waking up late the next morning. ("You Are Cordially Invited" [DS9]). Morn had a checkered past. In 2365, he was one of the perpetrators of the infamous **Lissepian Mother's Day Heist**, along with Hain, Larell, Krit, and Nahsk. After the heist, Morn disappeared with the 1,000 bars of **gold-pressed latinum** that they had stolen from the Central Bank of Lissepia. Morn laid low for several years, living in the Bajor Sector on station Terok Nor, which later became known as Deep Space 9. After the statute of limitations expired on the case, Morn faked his own death by scuttling his ship during an ion storm, after which his co-conspirators were arrested while trying to find the missing latinum. The ingenious Morn had enlisted the unwitting aid of Quark, to whom he later paid 100 bricks' worth of latinum for his trouble. Morn's co-conspirators never knew that he had hidden the stolen latinum in his second stomach for the entire time since the robbery, a trick made possible by the fact that **Lurian**s have two stomachs. The only ill effect was that the liquid latinum had caused his hair to fall out. ("Who Mourns for Morn?" [DS9]). *Of course, the entire character of Morn was something of a gag devised by the show's producers: Despite the fact that he was continually referred to as talkative and excitable, we almost never actually* saw *him do anything except imbibe quietly at Quark's bar. In "Who Mourns For Morn?" Mark Shepherd (*sans *Morn makeup) appeared briefly as the bar patron that Quark encouraged to sit in Morn's vacated bar stool.*

"Mortal Coil." *Voyager* episode #80. Written by Bryan Fuller. Directed by Allan Kroeker. Stardate 51449.2. *First aired in 1997. After Neelix is killed in a shuttlecraft accident, Seven of Nine uses Borg technology to bring him back to life. Shaken by the experience, Neelix questions his assumptions about life and the promised afterlife.* GUEST CAST: Nancy Hower as **Wildman, Samantha**; Brooke Stephens as **Wildman, Naomi**; Robin Stapler as **Alixia.** SEE: ***akoonah*; Alixia; Borg; coffee; firenut; Gand sector; Great Forest; Guiding Tree; hematological scan; Kazon; Ktarians; *moolt* nectar; nanoprobe; Neelix; pizza; Prixin; protomatter nebula; protomatter; Seven of Nine; Species 149; Species 329; Talaxians; Talmouth, Dunes of; vision quest; Wildman, Samantha; Wildman, Naomi.**

Moset, Dr. Crell. (David Clennon). **Cardassian** physician, an expert in nonhuman exobiology. Dr. Moset was renowned for having developed a cure for the deadly Fostossa virus, although Moset's breakthrough came from extensive experimentation on Bajoran prisoners during the Cardassian occupation of **Bajor**. Many subjects suffered agonizing death or disfigurement as a result of Moset's work, which included the exposure of living patients to lethal **nadion** radiation and poisonous **polytrinic acid**. As of 2371, Dr. Crell Moset was the Chairman of Exobiology at the University of Culat. In 2375, the *Voyager* crew created a holographic simulation program, re-creating Moset's knowledge and personality in order to provide medical advice in treating crew member B'Elanna Torres, who was suffering from a cytoplasmic parasite. The program was an invaluable aid, but *Voyager*'s Emergency Medical Hologram, upon learning of the real Moset's practices, felt compelled by ethical considerations to delete the Moset program, along with all records of his monstrous research. ("Nothing Human" [VGR]). *David Clennon played NASA lunar geologist Lee Silver in the 1998 HBO miniseries* From the Earth to the Moon. *The real Dr. Silver worked with Farouk El-Baz (for whom a Starfleet shuttlecraft was named) during Project Apollo.*

mot'loch. Potent Klingon drink that was traditionally imbibed as part of a traditional observance of the Klingon **Day of Honor**. ("Day of Honor" [VGR]).

Mulchaey, Ensign. (Todd Babcock). Starfleet officer assigned to the engineering department of the *U.S.S. Voyager*. In 2375, a **transporter** malfunction fused Borg **nanoprobe**s from Seven of Nine with the Doctor's **mobile emitter.** The nanoprobes assimilated the emitter, which developed into a device that sampled Mulchaey's DNA, producing a Borg drone who later named himself **One**. ("Drone" [VGR]).

multidimensional transporter device. Electronic apparatus created in the **mirror universe** to allow passage to our universe through a **transporter** beam. ("Resurrection" [DS9]).

multikinetic neutronic mine. Borg weapon with an explosive yield of five million isotons. Multikinetic neutronic mines were favored by the Borg for use as a delivery system for **biomolecular warhead**s, but Starfleet torpedoes with class-6 and class-10 warheads were ultimately used carrying the nanoprobes that destroyed several Species 8472 **bioships** in early 2374. ("Scorpion, Part II" [VGR]).

multispatial probe. Autonomous remote sensing device built by the crew of the *Voyager* in 2375. The probe was equipped with Borg shielding technology that successfully protected the probe even when it ventured into the atmosphere of a gas giant. ("Extreme Risk" [VGR]).

multivector assault mode. Tactical capability built into the experimental Federation starship ***U.S.S. Prometheus***, giving the vessel the capability of separating into three distinct spacecraft. Each section was capable of independent operation with full weapons and navigational capability. One of the first uses of this technique occurred in 2374 during a test flight of the *Prometheus* in which Romulan forces had commandeered the ship. The Romulans were successful in using multivector attack

mode in disabling a pursuing *Nebula*-class vessel. ("Message in a Bottle" [VGR]).

Musashi, U.S.S. Federation starship. In 2375, Ensign Nog gave the *Musashi*'s crew an induction modulator in exchange for a phaser emitter. ("Treachery, Faith, and the Great River" [DS9]). *Named for the Japanese dreadnought that sunk in the Sibuyan Sea on October 25, 1944, during the Battle of Leyte Gulf.*

mushroom pilaf. Side dish of spiced rice and mushrooms prepared with a sauce. ("Real Life" [VGR]).

Mutara-class nebula. Type of interstellar gas cloud. *Voyager* encountered a Mutara-class nebula on stardate 51929. The nebula was at least 110 light-years across and was filled with subnucleonic radiation, extremely deleterious to organic tissue and starship systems. ("One" [VGR]).

Mylean. Humanoid civilization that occupied a region of space near **Talax** in the Delta Quadrant. Myleans resembled **Talaxians** but were covered in small dark-brown spots. Talaxians and Myleans are genetically compatible and sometimes intermarry. **Neelix**'s great-grandfather was Mylean. ("Scientific Method" [VGR]).

N'Garen. (Gabrielle Union). Klingon warrior, daughter of Tse'Dek. In 2374 N'Garen transferred from the *Vor'nak* to the *Bird-of-Prey Rotarran*. N'Garen stood watch on the bridge of the *Rotarran*. ("Sons and Daughters" [DS9]).

nadion.* Energetic subatomic particle. When searching for a cure for the deadly Fostossa virus, Dr. Crell Moset exposed the internal organs of living Bajoran prisoners to nadion radiation, killing his experimental subjects in less than a week. ("Nothing Human" [VGR]).

nagus, grand.* Ferengi master of commerce. The grand nagus was elected by the 432 commissioners of the powerful **Ferengi Commerce Authority**. The traditional office of the grand nagus was the Chamber of Opportunity, located on the 40th floor of the **Tower of Commerce** on Ferenginar. ("Profit and Lace" [DS9]). SEE: **Zek**. The office of grand nagus could be dangerous for the nagus himself, as it was many years ago for Grand Nagus Smeet, who became the only nagus ever to be assassinated. Smeet was killed along with his **first clerk** after a catastrophic drop in the Ferengi financial market. ("Ferengi Love Songs" [DS9]). **Rom**, brother of Quark, was appointed grand nagus by Zek in 2375, when Zek retired to live on Risa. ("Dogs of War" [DS9]).

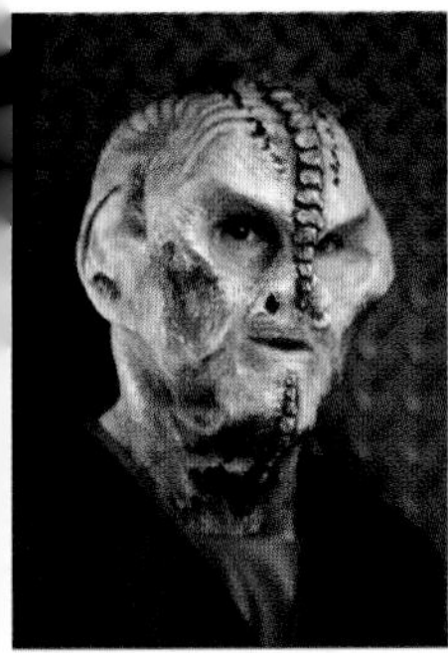

Nahsk. (Cyril O'Reilly). Former associate of **Morn** in the infamous **Lissepian Mother's Day Heist**. In 2365, Hain, Morn, Larell, Nahsk, and his brother, Krit, robbed the Central Bank of Lissepia of 1,000 bars of **gold-pressed latinum** while the entire planet was celebrating Mother's Day. After the heist, Morn disappeared with all of the money, later staging his own apparent death in 2374, just as the statute of limitations expired on the case. Nahsk and his associates arrived separately on Deep Space 9 with different plans to get Morn's latinum. The four were arrested for attempted murder by station security. ("Who Mourns for Morn?" [DS9]). SEE: **Lissepia, Central Bank of.**

Namon. (Nathan Anderson). Photometric projection of a **Vori** defender, part of an elaborate mind-control technique used by the Vori military to conscript new soldiers. In the simulation, Namon was a soldier, part of a Vori defense contingent under the command of team leader Brone. ("Nemesis" [VGR]).

Nane. Bajoran cleric who taught art at a university on Bajor. Vedek Nane instructed Tora Ziyal in 2374. ("Sons and Daughters" [DS9]).

nanoprobe. Submicroscopic robot used by the **Borg** in their assimilation process. Using an **injection tubule**, a Borg drone would inject a number of nanoprobes into the body of an individual targeted for assimilation. In the subject's bloodstream, the nanoprobes would attach to blood cells, taking over their functions, thereby spreading Borg technology throughout the body. ("Scorpion, Part I" [VGR]). The Borg could modify nanoprobes, programming them to reverse the effects of cellular necrosis in a dead humanoid body. The use of such nanoprobes could revive such a body up to 73 hours after the time of death. Former Borg drone **Seven of Nine** used this procedure on stardate 51449.2 to revive Neelix after he was killed in a shuttle accident. ("Mortal Coil" [VGR]). In late 2373, the *Voyager*'s Emergency Medical Hologram developed a technique to modify Borg nanoprobes to serve as a weapon against **Species 8472**. The innovative process involved reprogramming the devices to emit an electrochemical signature matching those of 8472 cells, allowing them to be absorbed without being rejected. The Borg, lacking sufficient understanding of Species 8472, indicated they would not assimilate the *Starship Voyager* in exchange for these modified nanoprobes. ("Scorpion, Part I" [VGR]). The crew of the *Voyager* was later successful in destroying several **bioships** by using photon torpedoes with **biomolecular warheads** filled with these modified Borg nanoprobes. ("Scorpion, Part II" [VGR]).

Napart Malor. Noted Cardassian artist who founded the Valonnan school on Cardassia. ("Sons and Daughters" [DS9]).

Nara, Lieutenant. Starfleet officer. Nara served aboard the *Starship Enterprise*-E in 2375 and stood watch at the tactical console on the bridge during the ship's conflict with two Son'a ships. (*Star Trek: Insurrection*).

narrative parameters file. Portion of a **holodeck** program defining characteristics of the scenario, including characters and their motivations and actions. ("Worse Case Scenario" [VGR]).

Nassordin. Delta Quadrant civilization that traded with the B'omar. ("The Raven" [VGR]).

***Native Son*.** Influential 20th-century Earth novel written by American author Richard Wright in 1940. *Native Son* was among the first books to protest the second-class social and economic status accorded African-Americans in American society during Earth's second World War. **Benny Russell** drew inspiration from *Native Son*. ("Far Beyond the Stars" [DS9]).

Nausicaans.* Humanoid space-faring society. In late 2374, Quark made a profit of 200 bars of gold-pressed latinum when he sold Denevan crystals to a Nausicaan entrepreneur. ("The Sound of Her Voice" [DS9]).

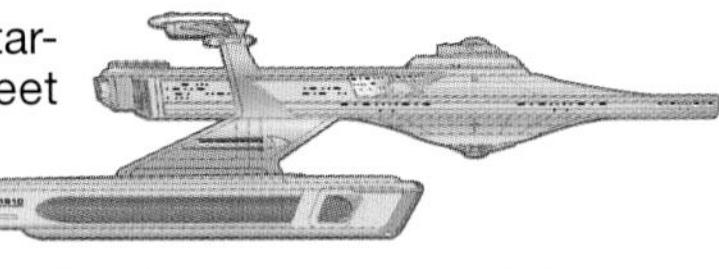

Nautilus, U.S.S. Federation starship, *Miranda* class, Starfleet registry number NCC-31910. The *Nautilus* fought in the combined fleet of allied Alpha Quadrant forces that invaded Cardassian space at the **Chin'toka System** in late 2374. ("Tears of the Prophets" [DS9]). *Named for the first submarine to reach the North Pole, as well as for **Captain Nemo**'s fictional vessel in Jules Verne's classic novel* 20,000 Leagues under the Sea. *The name was not in dialog, seen only* very *faintly on the ship's hull in visual-effects scenes.*

Nazi Germany. Nation during **Earth**'s early 20th century, a major aggressor in Earth's second global conflict during that century. The term "Nazi" was an abbreviation for "Nationalsozialistische Partei," or National Socialist Party. The Nazi government proclaimed its people to be a "**Master Race**," labeling others as corrupt and degenerate. Political strongman Adolf Hitler used this belief as justification for his brutal attempt to conquer the planet and to practice genocide on his enemies, one of the darkest chapters in Earth's history. SEE: **Allied Forces; French Resistance; World War II.** ("The Killing Game, Parts I and II" [VGR]). Some historians have noted that Nazi Germany's fascist government was among the most efficient ever devised by 20th-century humans. Some have even speculated on possible benefits of a more humane government based on similar principles. In one case, however, a large-scale test of this concept conducted on planet **Ekos** in violation of the **Prime Directive** by noted sociologist **John Gill** suggested that concentration of power by an isolated elite leadership inevitably leads to abuse. ("Patterns of Force" [TOS]).

Nazi Kapitan. (J. Paul Boehmer). Holographic character, part of the **French Resistance** holodeck program; a military officer in the army of **Nazi Germany**. The officer was the father of **Brigitte**'s child. ("The Killing Game, Parts I and II" [VGR]).

Neeley, Lieutenant Lisa. (Sarah MacDonnell). Starfleet security officer who served under the command of Captain Sisko in 2374. She was a member of the crew of the commandeered Jem'Hadar vessel that crash-landed on a planet located within a dark-matter nebula in Cardassian space. ("Rocks and Shoals" [DS9]).

Neelix.* Crew member aboard the Federation starship ***Voyager***. Neelix's great-grandfather was Mylean. ("Scientific Method" [VGR]). As a child, Neelix was orphaned in a war that also took the lives of his sisters. ("Once Upon a Time" [VGR]). Neelix was particularly close to his sister, Alixia, and he kept as a memento a necklace that once belonged to her. ("Mortal Coil" [VGR]). Neelix treasured a holographic image of Alixia, and would sometimes talk to the image when he was troubled. ("Once Upon a Time" [VGR]). Neelix was a good friend of young **Naomi Wildman**. He even enjoyed reading her bedtime stories and tucking her into bed at night. Neelix was killed in 2374 during a shuttle mission into a protomatter nebula on stardate 51449 when the craft was hit by an energy discharge. Seven of Nine used modified Borg **nanoprobe**s to bring Neelix back to life. Afterward, Neelix began to question his people's belief in the **Guiding Tree** at the center of the **Great Forest** of the afterlife in Talaxian beliefs. He was able to find a measure of peace through an **vision quest** that he experienced under Chakotay's guidance. ("Mortal Coil" [VGR]). When the *Voyager* traveled through a extensive spatial void in early 2375, the profound emptiness caused Neelix to suffer from **nihiliphobia**, the fear of nothingness, subjecting him to anxiety and panic attacks. ("Night" [VGR]).

Nekrit Supply Depot.* Space station in Nekrit space. Several months after the *Voyager*'s visit to the depot, a trader from the station provided information on the Federation ship to **Forra Gegen**, leading the noted Voth scientist to locate the *Voyager*, providing compelling evidence in support of his **Distant Origin Theory**. ("Distant Origin" [VGR]).

Nel Bato Conference. Scientific convention. Captain Jean-Luc Picard attended the Nel Bato Conference in 2374. (*Star Trek: Insurrection*).

Nelson. Member of the **Maquis** terrorist group. Nelson was killed in 2374 when the rebels were eradicated by the Cardassians with the help of the Dominion. Future *Voyager* crew members B'Elanna Torres and Chakotay were also members of the same group. ("Extreme Risk" [VGR]).

"Nemesis." *Voyager* episode #71. Written by Kenneth Biller. Directed by Alexander Singer. Stardate 51082.4. *First aired in 1997. Chakotay crash-lands in a planet's war zone and is rescued by one of the factions, but he is the victim of an elaborate campaign to make him hate the other side.* GUEST CAST: Michael Mahonen as **Brone**; Matt E. Levin as **Rafin**; Nathan Anderson as **Namon**; Peter Vogt as Commandant; Booth Colman as **Penno**; Meghan Murphy as **Karya**; Terrence Evans as **Treen**; Marilyn Fox as **Marna**; Pancho Demmings as Kradin Soldier. SEE: **Brone; defender; footfall; Karya; Kradin; Krady beast; Larhana settlement; Marna; Namon; omicron particles; Penno; photometric projection; Rafin; Treen; upturned; Vori language terms; Vori; Wayafter**.

Nemo, Captain. Character from the Earth **science-fiction** novel *20,000 Leagues under the Sea*, written in 1870 by futurist Jules Verne. Nemo was a reclusive technologist and undersea explorer who circumnavigated his planet in a ship called the *Nautilus*. In an alternate timeline, Thomas Paris compared Krenim scientist **Annorax** to Captain Nemo. ("Year of Hell, Part II" [VGR]). SEE: ***Nautilus, U.S.S.***

neocortex. Structure within some life-forms that perform the same function as the brain in humanoids. ("Nothing Human" [VGR]).

neocortical probe. Medical instrument capable of precision manipulation of neural proteins on an extremely small scale. The accuracy of the device was limited by the quantum nature of matter, but a remarkable redesign of the probe by Dr. Julian Bashir and his colleagues was responsible for increasing precision to the subatomic level, well beyond limits of conventional theory. ("Chrysalis" [DS9]).

neodymium power cell. Chemical energy storage device. In 2373, Jake Sisko and Nog procured a neodymium power cell from Chief O'Brien to be traded to Dr. Giger for a 1951 Willie Mays baseball trading card for Jake's father. ("In the Cards" [DS9]).

Neral.* Proconsul of the **Romulan Star Empire** during the late 24th century. One of Neral's most trusted advisors was Senator **Vreenak**. ("In the Pale Moonlight" [DS9]).

neural interface. Subdermal bioelectrical device, linking a humanoid neocortex to an external computer system. Used by the **Hirogen** to cause a humanoid subject to believe that a **holodeck** simulation was in fact real, subsuming the subject's real identity in favor of the identity of a **holodeck** character. ("The Killing Game, Parts I and II" [VGR]).

neural stimulator.* Medical instrument. In 2374, Nog used several neural stimulators to animate the corpse of **Keevan**, creating the illusion that Keevan was alive so that a prisoner exchange for Nog's grandmother, Ishka, could still take place. ("The Magnificent Ferengi" [DS9]).

neuro sequencer. Medical device used to stabilize the cerebral cortex. ("The Gift" [VGR]).

neurogenic field. Electrical energy generated by a humanoid brain. A **dream species** in the Delta Quadrant used an artificial neurogenic field as a defense mechanism to protect themselves against attack by outsiders that they called waking species. In 2374, this field caused members of the *Starship Voyager* crew to fall into a state of **hyper-REM** sleep. ("Waking Moments" [VGR]).

neurogenic restructuring. Invasive medical procedure used by **Mari** authorities, intended to permanently purge violent thoughts from a criminal's mind. The process was not entirely effective. ("Random Thoughts" [VGR]).

neurolytic emitter. Device used by **Ramuran** tracers to wipe memories of the outside world from the minds of runaways. Curneth wiped **Kellin**'s memories of Chakotay in 2374. As a result, she chose to return to Ramura rather than stay aboard *Voyager*. ("Unforgettable" [VGR]).

neuropathway induction. Medical procedure used to repair damaged neural pathways in a humanoid brain. Kira Nerys required neuropathway induction after she experienced an energy discharge on the bridge of the *Defiant* on stardate 50814, but the *Defiant*'s sickbay was not equipped for the procedure. ("Children of Time" [DS9]).

neuropeptide. Form of **cellular peptides** that are a main constituent of brain tissue in many organic life-forms. The bioships used by **Species 8472** used binary matrices laced with neuropeptides in the semiorganic computer systems of their **bioships**. ("Scorpion, Part I" [VGR]).

neuroregeneration. Medical technique sometimes effective in treating Yarim Fel Syndrome. ("Ties of Blood and Water" [DS9]).

neurosynaptic relay. Medical device used to record a subject's neuroelectric activity. Neurosynaptic relay data can be used as indication of the truthfulness of a subject's statements. ("Inquisition" [DS9]).

neurozine. Anesthetic aerosol. Neurozine was among the emergency crowd-control anesthetics on board the ***Starship Prometheus*** and was used to incapacitate **Romulan**s who had commandeered the ship in 2374. ("Message in a Bottle" [VGR]).

Nevala (Valerie Wildman). Romulan operative. Nevala assisted in commandeering the ***U.S.S. Prometheus*** in 2374. ("Message in a Bottle" [VGR]).

New Sydney. City on an Earth colony world. Liam Bilby's wife and two children lived in New Sydney, although he resided on Farius Prime. ("Honor Among Thieves" [DS9]).

Nicoletti, Susan.* (Christine Delgado). Starfleet officer, member of the *Starship Voyager* crew. In 2374, Nicoletti worked with Ensign Vorik to bring *Voyager*'s impulse engines back online after the ship's warp core was ejected. ("Day of Honor" [VGR]). On stardate 51501.4, Nicoletti received a letter from home in a Starfleet transmission received through a **Hirogen relay station**. ("Hunters" [VGR]).

Night Owl. Coffee shop on Market Street in the city of **San Francisco** on Earth. Kathryn Janeway was fond of the Night Owl when she was a cadet at **Starfleet Academy**. ("In the Flesh" [VGR]).

night beings. Technologically sophisticated humanoids indigenous to the region of the Delta Quadrant informally known as the **Void**. The night beings, who came to the Delta Quadrant millions of years ago, were nearly wiped out in the late 24th century by lethal theta radiation, the result of toxic antimatter dumping by **Malons**. ("Night" [VGR]).

night ships. Small maneuverable spacecraft used by the **night beings** in the Delta Quadrant The ships had dampening field generators and transporter technology. When Malon **Controller Emck**'s freighter blocked *Voyager*'s path through the spatial vortex leading from the **Void**, several night ships set upon the freighter and subdued it, allowing *Voyager* to destroy it and the vortex. ("Night" [VGR]).

"Night." *Voyager* episode #95. Written by Brannon Braga & Joe Menosky. Directed by David Livingston. Stardate 52081.2. *First aired in 1998. While traveling through a vast spatial void, the* Voyager *crew encounters the Malon, who are dumping dangerous radioactive waste into the void, killing the area's inhabitants.* GUEST CAST: Ken Magee as **Emck, Controller**; Steve Dennis as **night being;** Martin Rayner as **Chaotica, Doctor**; Kirsten Turner as **Goodheart, Constance**. SEE: **bergamot tea; *Billings, U.S.S.*; Captain Proton, *The Adventures of*; Chaotica, Doctor; clarinet; derada; *Don Carlo*; "Echoes of the Void"; Emck, Controller; Goodheart, Constance; holodeck and holosuite programs: *Captain Proton, The Adventures of, Don Carlo*; isoton; Janeway, Kathryn; Kim, Harry; Malon export vessel; Malons; Mercury; Mines of Mercury; Neelix; night beings; night ships; nihiliphobia; Novokovich gambit; Paris, Thomas; Proton, Captain; radiometric converter; rocket ship; Satan's Robot; "Satan's Robot Conquers the World;" theta radiation; Tuvok; Verdi, Giuseppe; Void.**

nihiliphobia. The fear of nothingness. Neelix suffered from nihiliphobia when the *Voyager* traveled through the profound emptiness of the region of space informally known as the **Void** in early 2375. Symptoms of nihiliphobia can include anxiety and even panic attacks leading to collapse. ("Night" [VGR]).

Nihydron. Civilization in the Delta Quadrant. In an alternate timeline, the Nihydron allied with the ***Starship Voyager*** in 2375 to defeat the **Krenim temporal weapon ship**. ("Year of Hell, Part II" [VGR]).

Nilva. (Henry Gibson). Ferengi entrepreneur. Nilva, who was chairman of the **Slug-o-Cola** company, was an influential commissioner of the powerful **Ferengi Commerce Authority**. Nilva was among those who opposed Grand Nagus **Zek**'s radical reforms of 2374 that granted Ferengi females the unprecedented right to wear clothing. Nilva was prepared to vote to depose Zek in favor of **Brunt**. Nilva reversed his stand, supporting Zek and his reforms after meeting with **Lumba**, a female financial advisor to Zek on station Deep Space 9. Lumba, who attracted Nilva's sexual interest, convinced him that granting equal rights to females would provide dramatically increased business opportunities. ("Profit and Lace" [DS9]). *Comedian Henry Gibson was a regular on the innovative television series* Laugh-In.

Nimira. (Gwynyth Walsh). High-ranking law-enforcement official of the **Mari Constabulary**. Nimira was proud of her society's efforts to rid itself of violent crime by outlawing violent thought. In 2374, Nimira conducted an investigation of violent thought, apparently committed by B'Elanna Torres, a crew member from the visiting Federation starship *Voyager*. Although evidence strongly implicated Torres, Nimira, working with *Voyager* security chief Tuvok, found that a Mari national was actually responsible. Nimira had not been aware that Mari laws prohibiting hostile thought had led to the creation of a thriving black market in illicit violent mental imagery. ("Random Thoughts" [VGR]). *Gwynyth Walsh previously played B'Etor in "Redemption, Parts I and II" (TNG), "Past Prologue" (DS9), "Firstborn" (TNG), and* Star Trek Generations.

Niners. Informal **baseball** team formed among officers and friends on station Deep Space 9 in early 2375. The Niners was organized by station commander **Benjamin Sisko** specifically to meet a challenge issued by the **Logicians** of the *Starship T'Kumbra*. The starting line-up for the Deep Space Niners was: Pitcher: Jake "The Slider" Sisko; catcher: Nog; first base: Worf, second base: Ben Sisko; third base: Kasidy Yates; shortstop: Kira Nerys; left field: Julian Bashir; center field: Ezri Dax; and right field: Leeta. Miles O'Brien served as first-base coach. Quark and Rom were pinch hitters. Although the Niners lost the game to the Logicians, they succeeded in allowing Ben Sisko to bask in the joy of his favorite sport. ("Take Me Out to the Holosuite" [DS9]). *The epic holosuite game between the Deep Space Niners and the* T'Kumbra *Logicians was filmed on location at Loyola Marymount University in Los Angeles.*

Ninth Fleet. Task force comprised of vessels from the Federation **Starfleet** and the **Klingon Defense Force** assigned to protect the strategically critical Bajor sector during the Dominion war in 2374. On stardate 51247, starbase Deep Space 9 was designated headquarters for the Ninth Fleet, and **General Martok** was promoted to supreme commander of the fleet. Ships assigned to the Ninth Fleet in 2374 included the *Akagi*, the *Exeter*, the *Potemkin*, and the *Sutherland*. ("You Are Cordially Invited" [DS9]). In 2374, elements of the Ninth Fleet joined a special large attack force commanded by Captain Benjamin Sisko to retake station Deep Space 9 from Dominion control. ("Favor the Bold" [DS9]).

Ninth Order. Cardassian military division. During the Cardassian occupation of Bajor, the Third Assault Group of the Ninth Order raided the **Dahkur Province**. ("Ties of Blood and Water" [DS9]).

Nog.* Starfleet officer, the first native of **Ferenginar** to serve in the Federation **Starfleet**. ("*Valiant*" [DS9]). Nog became an ensign through a battlefield commission during the Dominion war in 2374. He wore an engineering uniform. ("Favor the Bold" [DS9]). Around stardate 51825, Nog served as acting chief engineer of the ***U.S.S. Valiant*** in the final days before that ship's tragic end. ("*Valiant*" [DS9]). Nog was seriously injured, losing one of his legs during the **Dominion** war during a battle with the Jem'Hadar at station AR-558. ("The Siege of AR-558" [DS9]). Although he was fitted with a bionic replacement leg, the emotional scars of the horrors of combat took longer to heal. ("It's Only a Paper Moon" [DS9]). Nevertheless, Nog returned to duty in time for the final battles of the Dominion war, so impressing his superiors that Captain Benjamin Sisko, in one of his final actions before departing the linear domain, recommended Nog for a promotion to the rank of lieutenant. ("What You Leave Behind" [DS9]).

nonlinear dynamics. Technique for advanced statistical analysis modeling. Julian Bashir and three other genetically engineered individuals used nonlinear dynamics to run analyses of the war with the Dominion in order to make some predictions of probable outcomes. ("Statistical Probabilities" [DS9]). SEE: **Jack.**

Norpin falcon. Avian predator from Norpin that was widely known for having razor-keen reflexes. ("Sons and Daughters" [DS9]).

Northwest Passage. Informal name for a region of the Delta Quadrant in the midst of **Borg** space, through which the crew of the *Starship Voyager* had hoped to pass undetected by the Borg. Unfortunately, the *Voyager* crew discovered the Northwest Passage to be filled with intense gravimetric distortions caused by a string of quantum singularities. ("Scorpion, Part I" [VGR]). These distortions served as access ports to our universe through which **Species 8472** entered from their native fluid space, forcing *Voyager* to travel through Borg space instead. ("Scorpion, Part II" [VGR]).

"Nothing Human." *Voyager* episode #100. Written by Jeri Taylor. Story by Andre Bormanis. Directed by David Livingston. No stardate given. *First aired in 1998. When an alien parasite attaches itself to B'Elanna, the Doctor creates a holographic colleague to help remove it, but he later learns that his consultant was a Cardassian war criminal, whose medical knowledge was gained by horrific mistreatment of Bajoran war prisoners.* GUEST CAST: David Clennon as **Moset, Dr. Crell**; Jad Mager as **Tabor, Ensign**. SEE: **Culat, University of; cytoplasmic life-form; cytotoxic shock; cytotoxin; exobiology; Federation Medical Academy; Fostossa virus; holodeck and holosuite programs: Medical Consultant; inaprovaline; isomolecular scanner; Klingons; La'voti V; Legate's Crest of Valor; Moset, Dr. Crell; nadion; neocortex; Pala Mar; Paris, Thomas; polytrinic acid; rock and roll; stenophyl; Tabor, Ensign; triaxilation; universal translator.**

Novokovich gambit. Famous opening tactic in the game of **derada**, named for the master player Novokovich. ("Night" [VGR]).

nozala sandwich. A Krellan food. Krole enjoyed nozala sandwiches. ("Honor Among Thieves" [DS9]).

Nozawa. (John Tempoya). Starfleet officer assigned to the *Starship Voyager*. Nozawa was a transporter operator and was injured when dangerous atmospheric gases from a Class-Y planet were accidentally beamed aboard in 2374. ("Demon" [VGR]).

nucleonic charge. Hirogen explosive weapon. ("The Killing Game, Part II" [VGR]).

nutritional supplement 14-beta-7. Liquid food consumed by Seven of Nine. ("One" [VGR]).

Nyria III. Class-M planet in the Delta Quadrant. Nyria III has a very warm, arid climate and a much lower daytime light level than Earth. The **Nyrians** maintained a colony on Nyria III. ("Displaced" [VGR]).

Nyrian vessel. Immense starship used by the **Nyrians** in their acts of piracy against spacecraft and space stations belonging to other Delta Quadrant civilizations. The massive ship contained 94 different environmental biospheres, in which the crews of the stolen vessels could be incarcerated. The Nyrians took care to create remarkably accurate simulations of the various crews' homeworlds in an attempt to make their lives in captivity as pleasant as possible. ("Displaced" [VGR]).

Nyrians. Technologically advanced humanoid civilization from the Delta Quadrant. The Nyrians had advanced long-range transporter systems called **translocator**s that they used to abduct crews of passing spacecraft and nearby space stations. Using their translocators, they replaced the crews of those ships and stations with Nyrian personnel, thereby gaining control of those vessels. Despite these acts of piracy, the Nyrians considered themselves a benevolent people, and they went to considerable lengths to care for those whose ships they had stolen. In 2373, Nyrian operatives abducted the crew of the Federation starship *Voyager*. The captivity did not last long, for *Voyager* captain Janeway and her crew were successful in escaping from the **Nyrian vessel**. In the process, they persuaded the Nyrians to release the prisoners held in the other environments on the Nyrian ship. ("Displaced" [VGR]).

O'Brien, Miles.* Starfleet engineer who served aboard the *Starship Enterprise*-D before being transferred to space station **Deep Space 9**. While at **Setlik III**, O'Brien led two dozen troops against the Barrica encampment, successfully driving out an entire regiment of **Cardassian** soldiers. ("Empok Nor" [DS9]). In 2374, Miles secretly worked as an undercover operative for Starfleet on Farius Prime. O'Brien infiltrated an **Orion Syndicate** group believed to have ties to the Dominion. While O'Brien was successful in his mission, he deeply regretted that it resulted in the death of **Liam Bilby**, a syndicate member whom O'Brien had befriended. Just before Bilby's death, O'Brien promised to take care of Bilby's pet cat, **Chester**. Upon returning to Deep Space 9, Chester became the O'Brien family pet. ("Honor Among Thieves" [DS9]). After the Dominion war, Miles O'Brien accepted a professorship in engineering at the Starfleet Academy and moved to Earth, along with his family. ("What You Leave Behind" [DS9]).

O'Brien, Miranda. (Jennifer S. Parsons). Inhabitant of the planet **Gaia** in an alternate timeline. In this alternate reality, Miranda O'Brien was a descendant of Chief Miles O'Brien and Ensign Rita Tannenbaum. Miranda ceased to exist in 2373 when her timeline vanished. ("Children of Time" [DS9]). *Jennifer S. Parsons previously played an Ocampan nurse in "Caretaker" (VGR).*

O'Brien, Molly.* Daughter of Miles and Keiko O'Brien. Molly had a favorite doll named Lupi. ("Time's Orphan" [DS9]). In 2374, while on a picnic with her family, Molly fell through a time portal on the planet Golana. The eight-year-old child ended up 300 years in the past, where she managed to survive alone for ten years in the Golanan wilderness. Her parents were able to use the **Golanan time portal** to return her to 2374, but by that time this alternate Molly considered Golana to be her home, and she was unable to reintegrate into human society. The older Molly subsequently returned to Golana's past, where she was able to effect the return of her original eight-year-old self to her parents in 2374. ("Time's Orphan" [DS9]). *The eighteen-year-old alternate Molly in "Time's Orphan" (DS9) was played by Michelle Krusiec* (pictured).

O'Halloran, Ensign. Junior officer at Starfleet Headquarters in San Francisco on Earth. O'Halloran was a patron of the **Quantum Cafe** during after-duty hours. A re-creation of O'Halloran was part of a training facility created by **Species 8472** in the Delta Quadrant in 2375 in preparation for operations planned against the Federation. The replica of O'Halloran had occasional problems in retaining his human form. ("In the Flesh" [VGR]).

Obrist. (John Loprieno). Citizen of the **Krenim** Imperium. In an alternate timeline, Obrist was a senior officer on the **Krenim temporal weapon ship**. For two hundred years, Obrist carried out the orders of his commander, **Annorax**,to eradicate civilizations in an attempt to restore Krenim history. Obrist eventually became outraged at Annorax's use of mass murder to achieve his goals, and cooperated with officers from the Federation starship *Voyager* to stop Annorax and destroy the temporal weapon ship. ("Year of Hell, Parts I and II" [VGR]).

Odala, Minister. (Concetta Tomei). Leading member of the Ministry of Elders of the Voth people in 2373. Odala categorically condemned and ridiculed Professor Forra Gegen's **Distant Origin Theory** even after being presented with convincing proof. SEE: **heresy**. ("Distant Origin" [VGR]). *Concetta Tomei played Major Lila Garreau on the* China Beach *television series.*

Odo.* Chief of security at station Deep Space 9. Odo cared deeply for his friend, Kira Nerys, but for years he was reluctant to admit it to himself or to her for fear of jeopardizing their friendship. This was especially difficult for Odo when Kira, unaware of his feelings, would confide in him about her romantic relationships with Shakaar Edon and Vedek Bareil. Odo might never have revealed his feelings to Kira had not an alternate version of himself from another timeline forced the issue in late 2373. SEE: **Gaia**. ("Children of Time" [DS9]). Odo became gradually more open in his feelings toward Kira during the following months, although the relationship was threatened when he linked with the **Founder Leader** during the Dominion war. Odo found the temptations of the link to be so powerful that he inadvertently allowed Rom, a member of the resistance, to be captured by Cardassian authorities. ("Behind the Lines" [DS9]). Odo eventually chose to remain with his solid friends in the Alpha Quadrant. ("Sacrifice of Angels" [DS9]). Odo finally expressed his feelings to Kira in late 2374 after receiving encouragement and counsel from **Vic Fontaine**, an expert in affairs of the heart. ("His Way" [DS9]). Odo and Kira became romantically involved shortly thereafter, but their happiness was not to last. Unbeknownst to Odo, he had been infected with a deadly virus that had been created by **Section 31**. The covert Federation agency knew that Odo would pass the disease to all Founders through the **Great Link**. The genetically engineered disease eventually affected Odo ("When it Rains..." [DS9]). He would have died of the disease if not for the extraordinary efforts of Julian Bashir, who extracted information from the mind of Section 31 operative Sloan, making it possible to eradicate the virus. ("Extreme Measures" [DS9]). During the final hours of the terrible **Dominion** war, Odo linked with the **Founder Leader**, knowing that doing so would transmit Bashir's cure to her. Although Federation authorities had vehemently opposed such a link, Odo's act of trust made it possible for the Founder Leader to understand that her people could indeed live in peace with solids. This, in turn, prevented further bloodshed when she ordered the forces of the Dominion to end hostilities. The link had a second result. Odo came to realize that he must return to the Great Link, not only to cure his people, but to help them to understand that peace was possible with the solids of the galaxy. Sadly, in the process, Odo had to leave his beloved Kira. ("What You Leave Behind" [DS9]).

offlander. Term used by the **Ba'ku** people, referring to individuals from other worlds. (*Star Trek: Insurrection*).

Ogre of Fire. Holographic character in the ***Adventures of Flotter*** stories for children. The Ogre represented the force of fire, which could be terribly destructive to the beautiful Forest of Forever. ("Once Upon a Time" [VGR]).

Olmerak. Star system. Olmerak was the location of a Dominion base. In 2375, at least one squadron of Jem'Hadar attack ships was quartered there. ("Treachery, Faith, and the Great River" [DS9]).

Olympia, U.S.S. Federation starship. The *Olympia*, commanded by Captain **Lisa Cusak**, conducted an eight-year mission of deep space exploration in the Beta Quadrant from 2363 through 2371. En route back to Federation space, the ship investigated a planet in the Rutharian sector. The *Olympia* was crippled when its active sensor scans triggered a powerful quantum reaction in an exogenic energy field surrounding the planet, causing a surge of **metreon radiation**. The ship subsequently exploded with the eventual loss of all hands. ("The Sound of Her Voice" [DS9]). *Named for the region in western Peloponnesus on Earth that was the site of the ancient Olympic games.*

"Omega Directive, The." *Voyager* episode #89. Teleplay by Lisa Klink. Story by Jimmy Diggs & Steve J. Kay. Directed by Victor Lobl. Stardate 51781.2. *First aired in 1998. Captain Janeway leads* Voyager *on a mission to destroy a deadly, unstable substance that threatens the fabric of space.* GUEST CAST: Jeff Austin as **Allos**; Kevin McCorkle as Alien Captain. SEE: **Allos; arithrazine; Big Bang; Borg; boronite; *Christmas Carol, A*; Dell; Einstein, Albert; gravimetric torpedo; harmonic resonance chamber; Hickman, Ensign; *kal-toh*; Ketteract, Dr.; Lantaru Sector; Marcus, Dr. Carol; Omega Directive; Omega molecule; Particle 010; Prime Directive; protostar; security access code; Seven of Nine; Species 262; Species 263; subspace phenomena: subspace rupture; terahertz; theta radiation.**

Omega Directive. Classified Starfleet general order requiring the captain of a starship to notify Starfleet Command immediately upon detection of an **Omega molecule**. The directive authorizes the use of any and all means necessary to destroy an Omega molecule. The Omega Directive was deemed necessary because of the extreme power and the extreme threat to interstellar civilization posed by even a single Omega molecule. The Omega Directive even authorized a starship captain to violate the **Prime Directive** if necessary to erase knowledge of even the existence of Omega. ("The Omega Directive" [VGR]).

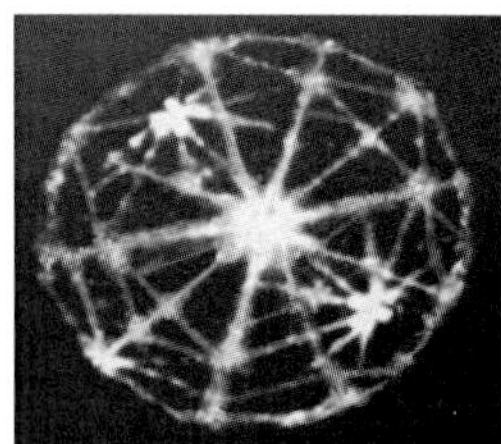

Omega molecule. Short-lived, highly unstable particle, believed to be the most powerful substance in the universe. Some cosmologists theorize that Omega existed in nature at the instant of the **Big Bang**, when the universe as we know it was born. An Omega molecule would be so energetic that even a few such particles could theoretically power an entire planet. A single Omega molecule was synthesized in the late 23rd century by **Dr. Ketteract**, a Federation scientist. The particle remained stable for only a fraction of a second before it exploded, destroying the research station and causing subspace ruptures extending across several light-years, making warp travel impossible in the region. Starfleet Command immediately realized that the use of even a few Omega molecules could effectively end spacefaring civilization as we know it. Starfleet not only banned research into Omega, but issued the Omega Directive, ordering the destruction of any Omega molecules and the suppression of any knowledge of the particle's existence. Other cultures did, however, have knowledge of Omega. The **Borg**, which referred to it as Particle 010, regarded Omega with near-reverence. The collective believed it to exist in a flawless state and was willing to go to any lengths to assimilate it. Another civilization in the Delta Quadrant was actually successful in synthesizing some 200 million Omega molecules in 2374, although *Starship Voyager* personnel destroyed the molecules before damage to the subspace continuum could result. ("The Omega Directive" [VGR]).

Omega Sector. Area of Federation space in the Alpha Quadrant. A remote outpost in the Omega Sector was the last known location of the two scientists who were the parents of Annika Hansen, the girl who would later become the Borg drone Seven of Nine. ("The Gift" [VGR]).

omicron particle.* Subatomic product of matter/antimatter reactions. In early 2374, Chakotay, on a survey mission in a shuttlecraft, detected omicron radiation in the atmosphere of a planet inhabited by the Vori and the Kradin peoples. ("Nemesis" [VGR]).

omnicordial life-form. Type of being that dwelled in Galactic Cluster 3. Species 259 was an omnicordal life-form. ("The Gift" [VGR]).

"Once Upon a Time." *Voyager* episode #99. Written by Michael Taylor. Directed by John Kretchmer. No stardate given. *Young Naomi Wildman loses herself in a holodeck fairy tale while her mother fights for her life on a distant planet.* GUEST CAST: Wallace Langham as **Flotter**; Justin Louis as **Trevis**; Scarlett Pomer as **Wildman, Naomi**; Nancy Hower as **Wildman, Samantha**. SEE: **bemonite; *Delta Flyer*; duranium; *Flotter, The Adventures of*; Flotter; Forest of Forever; holodeck and holosuite programs: *Flotter, The Adventures of*; ion storm; Janeway, Kathryn; Kim, Harry; mitochondria; Neelix; Ogre of Fire; Starfleet General Orders and Regulations: Regulation 476-9; Stinger; Trevis; Wildman, Naomi; Wildman, Samantha.**

"One Little Ship." *Deep Space Nine* episode #137. Written by David Weddle & Bradley Thompson. Directed by Allan Kroeker. Stardate 51474.2. First aired in 1998. When a runabout piloted by Dax, O'Brien, and Bashir is shrunken to just a few centimeters in length, the tiny ship and crew are Sisko's only hope as the Jem'Hadar overtake the *Defiant*. GUEST CAST: Aron Eisenberg as **Nog**; Scott Thompson Baker as **Kudak'Etan;** Fritz Sperberg as **Ixtana'Rax;** Leland Crooke as **Gelnon**; Christian Zimmerman as **Lamat'Ukan.** SEE: **Alpha; anti-back flow valve; asymmetric encryption circuit; bipolar flow junction; blast shutters; Coridan; *Defiant, U.S.S.*; Duran'Adar; Elder; Gamma; Gelnon; Ixtana'Rax; Jem'Hadar; Klingons; Kudak'Etan; Lamat'Ukan; lateral microbrace; magnetic plasma guide; rectilinear expansion module; *Rubicon, U.S.S.*; Seltan carnosaur; subspace phenomena: subspace compression; transwarp; warp drive, class-7.**

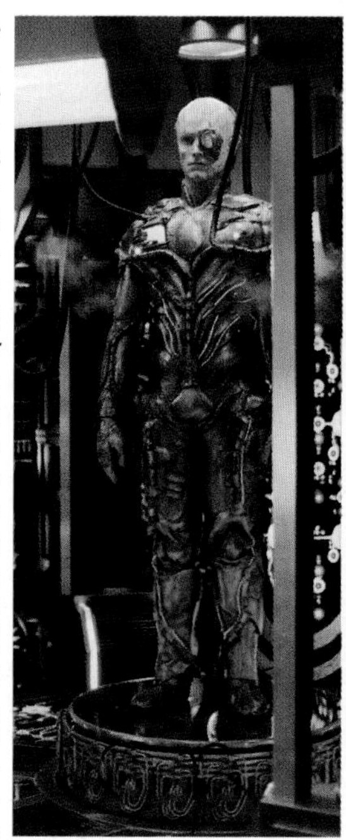

One. (J. Paul Boehmer). **Borg** drone that was created aboard the *U.S.S. Voyager* in early 2375. One was the accidental result of a transporter malfunction that fused Borg **nanoprobes** with the **Emergency Medical Hologram**'s mobile emitter. The combined device, responding to Borg assimilation protocols built into the nanoprobes, sampled **DNA** from **Ensign Mulchaey**, a member of the *Voyager* crew. The Borg device used Mulchaey's DNA to produce a humanoid drone. This drone incorporated extremely advanced technology assimilated from the Doctor's **mobile emitter**, which had originated in Earth's 29th century, several centuries in *Voyager*'s future. As a result, this drone was substantially more sophisticated than other Borg drones of the 24th century. He had reactive body armor, multidimensional adaptability, and internal transporter nodes. Being separated from the collective, he was curious about his Borg origins. At the same time, encouraged by Seven of Nine, who served as a role model, the drone came to accept the cultural values of the Federation Starfleet. He even chose the designation "One" for himself, emphasizing his individuality. By the time One accidentally summoned a nearby **Borg sphere** spacecraft, he had accepted the value of individual diversity to the point where he did not wish to be assimilated into the Borg collective. He transported to the Borg ship, destroying it to prevent assimilation of the *Voyager* and its crew. In the process, One became gravely injured, but subsequently refused medical treatment, allowing himself to die to prevent his advanced 29th-century technology from falling into Borg hands. ("Drone" [VGR]). *J. Paul Boehmer was previously seen as the Nazi Kapitan in "The Killing Game, Parts I and II" (VGR).*

"One." *Voyager* episode #93. Written by Jeri Taylor. Directed by Kenneth Biller. Stardate 51929.3. *First aired in 1998. While the* Voyager *crew seeks refuge in stasis, Seven of Nine must pilot the ship through a dangerous nebula while facing her greatest fear: being alone.* GUEST CAST: Wade Williams as **Lo-Tarik, Trajis;** Ron Ostrow as Borg drone. SEE: **antipsychotic; holodeck and holosuite programs; Kim, Harry; Lo-Tarik, Trajis; Mutara-class nebula; nutritional supplement 14-beta-7; Paris, Thomas Eugene; potato salad; stasis unit; subnucleonic radiation; Torres, B'Elanna.**

Oo-mox ***for Fun and Profit.*** Short instructional book that described the various techniques for performing *oo-mox* on a Ferengi male. ("Profit and Lace" [DS9]).

oo-mox.*** Ferengi sexual foreplay. Some *oo-mox* techniques include the tympanic tickle, the eustachian tube rub, and the infamous auditory canal nibble. ("Profit and Lace" [DS9]).

optolythic data rod. Recording medium used by the Cardassian government for official record keeping. Information could only be transcribed on a rod once, and then could not be altered. The rods were manufactured only as needed on Cardassia Prime and were almost impossible to obtain by outsiders. SEE: **Tolar, Grathon.** ("In the Pale Moonlight" [DS9]).

optronic datacore. A key element of holographic technology used in a Federation starship's **holodeck**. *Voyager* captain Kathryn Janeway gave an optronic datacore to a **Hirogen** hunter in 2374. Janeway hoped that the technology might someday help Hirogen society wean itself from expending its energies on wasteful hunts, so that it might return to cultural and scientific development. ("The Killing Game, Part II" [VGR]).

Orb of Contemplation. One of the sacred Orbs of the Bajoran people. In late 2374, the Orb of Contemplation was present on Deep Space 9 during the Bajoran Gratitude Festival. While at the station, a **Pah-wraith** carried by Gul Dukat merged with the Orb, causing all of the Orbs to go dark and sealing the **Bajoran wormhole**. ("Tears of the Prophets" [DS9]).

Orb of Prophecy.* One of the sacred Orbs of the Bajoran Prophets. In 2374 the Orb of Prophecy resided in the Bajoran shrine located on the Promenade of station Deep Space 9. Vedek Ossan permitted the mirror version of Bareil Antos, who had transported from the mirror universe, to have an Orb experience with the Orb of Prophecy, in which he saw a possible future with himself and Kira having a family on Bajor, although this was not to be. ("Resurrection" [DS9]).

Orb of the Emissary. One of the most mysterious of the Orbs of the **Prophets**. Existence of the Orb of the Emissary was not known even to the Bajorans until 2375. In that year, **Benjamin Sisko**, the **Emissary**, experienced a vision from the Prophets. Based on this vision and on an ancient Bajoran inscription on a locket once belonging to his mother, Benjamin Sisko mounted an expedition to seek the Orb of the Emissary. ("Image in the Sand" [DS9]). Sisko found the Orb, buried in the sand on planet **Tyree**. When he opened the ark containing the Orb, the Prophets returned to the Celestial Temple, the wormhole was restored along with the other Orbs, and the **Pah-wraiths** were once again banished. ("Shadows and Symbols" [DS9]).

Orb of Time.* One of the sacred Orbs of the Bajoran Prophets. The Orb of Time was kept at the Temple of Iponu on Bajor. In 2374, the Emissary intervened with temple officials to allow Kira Nerys to consult the Orb of Time to learn of her mother's fate during the occupation. ("Wrongs Darker Than Death or Night" [DS9]).

Orb of Wisdom.* One of the sacred Orbs of the Bajoran Prophets. Kai Winn consulted the Orb of Wisdom on stardate 50929, hoping for insight regarding whether Bajor should sign a nonaggression pact with the Dominion. The Orb provided her no answers, and she instead sought guidance from the Emissary. ("In the Cards" [DS9]).

Orb.* Energy artifact created by life-forms in the **Bajoran wormhole**, said to be gifts to the Bajoran people from the **Prophets**. It was said that the content of one's Orb experience was a deeply personal matter and was not meant to be shared with others. ("Resurrection" [DS9]). Orbs were traditionally stored in small, ornate vaults called arks. ("Shadows and Symbols" [DS9]).

Orbital Flight Control. Starfleet operational unit responsible for coordination and scheduling of spacecraft in the Sol sector. Starfleet officers Young and Reiskin were assigned to Orbital Flight Control in 2375, tasked with monitoring incoming vessels from the Bolian Sector. ("In the Flesh" [VGR]).

orbital skydiving. Sporting activity in which an individual, wearing a special protective suit, leaps from a spacecraft at orbital altitudes. The individual plunges hundreds of kilometers, soaring through atmospheric entry, before landing safely on the planet's surface. B'Elanna Torres engaged in simulated orbital skydiving in a *Voyager* **holodeck** with the **safety protocol**s disengaged. ("Extreme Risk" [VGR]). *The opening scenes of* Star Trek Generations *were originally planned to show Captain James Kirk engaging in orbital skydiving, but the scenes were cut from the final film. Kirk's protective suit was later modified for Torres to wear in "Extreme Risk" (VGR).*

orbital weapon platform. Powerful automated defense station developed by the **Cardassian** military for use during the **Dominion** war. The stations employed regenerative force fields for hull protection and were equipped with 1,000 plasma torpedoes. Power was supplied by subspace link from a central generator at a remote site, typically a nearby moon. A network of orbital weapons platforms were deployed in late 2374 to defend the **Chin'toka System**. Cardassian strategists had hoped that use of the platforms would permit reassignment of valuable warships to other systems, but allied Alpha Quadrant forces were able to destroy the devices, resulting in capture of the system by allied forces. ("Tears of the Prophets" [DS9]).

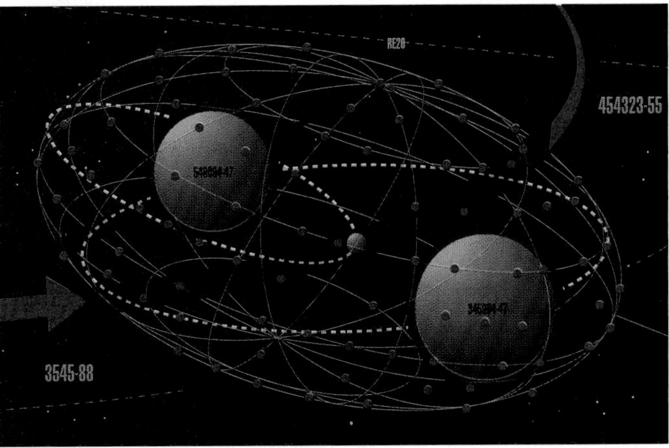

Deployment of Orbital Weapon Systems platforms at the Chin'toka System, 2374

Orion Syndicate.* Interstellar criminal organization. The Orion Syndicate had operatives on Farius Prime who, in 2374, worked with **Dominion** agents in an unsuccessful plan to assassinate the Klingon ambassador to that planet. Members of the Orion Syndicate were expected to pay a portion of their income, called a **fare**, to their superiors in the organization. The syndicate was extremely harsh toward anyone who betrayed it, and would go to almost any length to kill such a person. If that was not possible, the syndicate was known to kill that person's family. SEE: **Bilby, Liam; Raimus**. ("Honor Among Thieves" [DS9]).

Ortakin. (Scott Leva). Klingon warrior who was a young crew member aboard the *Bird-of-Prey* ***Rotarran*** in 2373. Like much of the *Rotarran* crew, Ortakin was discouraged and cynical until a victory under the command of **General Martok** restored his warrior's pride. ("Soldiers of the Empire" [DS9]).

***osol* twist.** Romulan confection with a distinctive tart flavor. ("Image in the Sand" [DS9]).

Ossan, Vedek. (John Towey). Bajoran spiritual leader who in 2374 presided over the Bajoran shrine located on the Promenade of station Deep Space 9. Ossan allowed Bareil Antos (mirror) to have an Orb experience with the Orb of Prophecy and Change. Ossan's decision to permit Bareil the experience may have been influenced by the fact that the mirror Bareil was physically identical to the late noted Bajoran vedek. ("Resurrection" [DS9]).

osteotomy. Surgical procedure in which all of an organism's bones are removed. The procedure, used by the **Hirogen** to remove body parts used as prizes of the hunt, is fatal to the victim. ("Hunters" [VGR]).

ovarian resequencing enzymes. Complex organic compounds used in a medical fertility treatment. In 2374, Dr. Julian Bashir used ovarian resequencing enzyme therapy to make it possible for Jadzia Dax and Worf to have a child. ("Tears of the Prophets" [DS9]).

oysters Rockefeller. Appetizer consisting of oysters baked in a rich spinach, scallion, anchovy, and garlic sauce. Named for a wealthy family on 20th-century Earth. ("His Way" [DS9]).

Pabst, Douglas. (Rene Auberjonois). Editor of the **science-fiction** pulp magazine ***Incredible Tales*** published in New York city on Earth in the 1950s. ("Far Beyond the Stars" [DS9]). *Rene Auberjonois also played Odo on* Star Trek: Deep Space Nine, *although Pabst did not have Odo's makeup.*

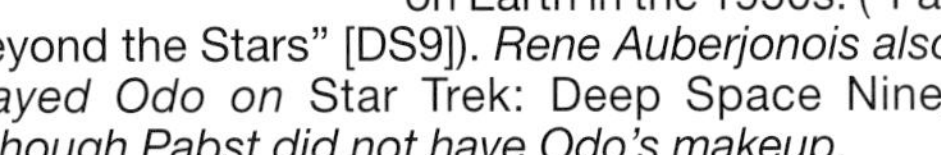

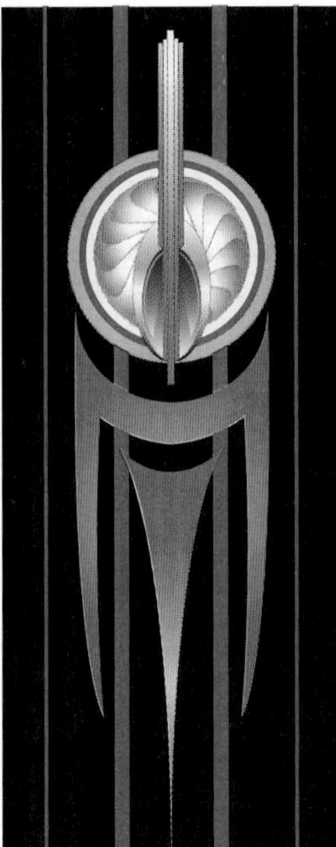

Pah-wraith.* Energy being native to the **Bajoran wormhole**, the Pah-wraiths were enemies of the Bajoran **Prophets**. **Kosst Amojan** was a Pah-wraith who was banished from the Celestial Temple. He returned in 2374 to fight a Prophet in the prophesied conflict called **the Reckoning**. SEE: **Shabren's Fifth Prophecy.** ("The Reckoning" [DS9]). Later that year, deposed Cardassian leader Gul Dukat summoned a Pah-wraith, causing all nine of the Orbs to go dark and the Bajoran wormhole to seal. Dukat and the Pah-wraith also caused the death of **Jadzia Dax**. ("Tears of the Prophets" [DS9]). Later, when Benjamin Sisko located the Orb of the Emissary, the Pah-wraiths tried to keep him from opening the Orb ark by subjecting him to an Orb-shadow vision. In the vision, Sisko once again saw himself as writer **Benny Russell**, but as Russell found the courage to write his story, Sisko found the will to open the Orb ark, restoring the Prophets and their wormhole. ("Shadows and Symbols" [DS9]). The disappearance of the Prophets in late 2374 triggered the emergence of a Bajoran cult worshipping the Pah-wraiths. The cult believed that the disappearance of the Prophets heralded a new era for Bajor, and they identified themselves by wearing red armbands. The cult of the Pah-wraiths had existed years earlier, but was long considered a joke, but their group became more popular after the Prophets disappeared at the end of 2374. A young member of the cult tried to kill Benjamin Sisko on Earth to prevent him from finding the Orb of the Emissary. ("Image in the Sand" [DS9]). The evil Kosst Amojan seduced **Gul Dukat** and Kai **Winn**, using them in an effort to free the Pah-wraiths from the fire caves on Bajor. ("Strange Bedfellows" [DS9]). Although Kosst Amojan nearly succeeded, he was stopped by the Emissary, who was able to imprison all of the Pah-wraiths in the fire caves. ("What You Leave Behind" [DS9]).

painstik, Klingon.* Ritual baton with electrical sparking grid on one end. The infamous Ritual of Twenty Painstiks was sometimes part of a traditional observance of the Klingon **Day of Honor**. ("Day of Honor" [VGR]).

Pala Mar. Location on the Delta Quadrant planet La'voti V. While visiting La'voti V on a mission, Lieutenant Tom Paris slipped into a fetid mud pit in Pala Mar. ("Nothing Human" [VGR]).

Par'tok. Klingon cargo vessel. ("Sons and Daughters" [DS9]).

parabolic thruster. Engineering component aboard Jem'Hadar attack vessels. ("A Time to Stand" [DS9]).

Parell. (Marybeth Massett). Inhabitant of the planet **Gaia** in an alternate timeline. In this reality, Parell lived with a group of Gaians who chose to live their lives according to Klingon tradition. Parell ceased to exist in 2373 when her timeline vanished. ("Children of Time" [DS9]).

Paris, Admiral Owen.* Senior Starfleet officer; father to *Voyager* crew member Thomas Paris. Owen Paris was an instructor at **Starfleet Academy** in San Francisco on Earth. ("In the Flesh" [VGR]). In 2374, the elder Paris sent a letter to his son in the Delta Quadrant, transmitted through the Hirogen relay system. The contents of the letter were not successfully retrieved from the relay station before the station was destroyed. ("Hunters" [VGR]). *We learned his first name in "Hunters" (VGR).*

Paris, Thomas.* Conn officer for the ***U.S.S. Voyager***. Among the *Voyager* crew in 2374, Tom Paris had the greatest amount of medical training (except for the holographic Doctor), and around stardate 51186, he was assigned additional duties as an assistant in the ship's sickbay. ("Revulsion" [VGR]). Paris harbored an attraction for crewmate **B'Elanna Torres**. She indicated no interest in him until an incident in early 2374, in which both were stranded in deep space with oxygen nearly exhausted, when she confessed her love for him. ("Day of Honor" [VGR]). During his youth, Tom Paris's relationship with his father was often strained, a situation that continued into his adulthood. ("Hunters" [VGR]). When he was 16 years old, he "borrowed" his father's shuttlecraft for a joyride. Unfortunately, a mishap sent the shuttle to the bottom of Lake Tahoe. ("Vis à Vis" [VGR]). Fortunately, he did better in early 2375, when he spearheaded the design and construction of the ***Delta Flyer*** shuttlecraft aboard the *Voyager*. ("Extreme Risk" [VGR]). Paris's interest in 20th-century American culture manifested itself in his peculiar choice in holodeck entertainment programs, ranging from **Grease Monkey** ("Vis à Vis" [VGR]) to ***The Adventures of Captain Proton***. ("Night" [VGR]). Paris also enjoyed a 20th-century music form known as "**rock and roll**." ("Nothing Human" [VGR]).

parrises squares.* Popular sport. An ion mallet was used in the game. ("Real Life" [VGR]). **M'Kota R'Cho** was the only Klingon athlete ever to play parrises squares. ("Year of Hell, Part I" [VGR]).

Parsons, Ensign. Officer aboard the *U.S.S. Voyager* in 2373. He had a microbial infection near stardate 50836. On stardate 51501, Parsons got a letter from home in a Starfleet transmission received through a **Hirogen relay station**. ("Hunters" [VGR]).

Particle 010. Borg designation for the **Omega molecule**. ("The Omega Directive" [VGR]).

particle synthesis. Advanced technology for replication of matter. Arturis's people were adept at the use of particle synthesis to create objects and environments. Particle synthesis was more sophisticated than the replicator systems used by the Federation Starfleet. ("Hope and Fear" [VGR]).

Parton. (Scott Hamm). **Starfleet Academy** cadet and member of **Red Squad**. In 2374, Parton was part of a training cruise aboard the ***U.S.S. Valiant***, which was caught behind enemy lines when the Dominion war broke out. Parton was killed when the *Valiant*'s acting commander, cadet **Tim Watters**, unwisely ordered the ship on a mission to take out a Dominion battleship. ("*Valiant*" [DS9]).

passive voice transitive. Grammatical sentence form used in the **Dominion** language. The passive voice transitive is used only when making a request, not a statement. ("Statistical Probabilities" [DS9]).

Patrick. (Michael Keenan). Individual who, as a child, had been genetically altered through illegal **accelerated critical neural pathway formation**. Although the procedure was successful in enhancing Patrick's abilities, it resulted in giving him a dysfunctional personality that could not easily fit into normal society. He was extremely intelligent and observant but socially immature, and spent most of his life institutionalized. Under the care of Starfleet psychiatrist Dr. Karen Loews, Patrick and three other genetically enhanced individuals traveled to starbase Deep Space 9 in 2374 to meet Julian Bashir. ("Statistical Probabilities" [DS9]). Patrick later returned to Deep Space 9, along with his friends, by impersonating a Starfleet admiral. ("Chrysalis" [DS9]). SEE: **Jack**. *Michael Keenan previously played Maturin in "Sub Rosa" (TNG) and King Hrothgar in "Heroes and Demons" (VGR).*

pattern scrambler. Device that causes a transporter beam to lose coherence upon rematerialization. Pattern scramblers had the effect of killing persons in transit quite unpleasantly. The Cardassians sometimes used pattern scramblers to prevent non-Cardassians from gaining unauthorized entry into stations such as **Empok Nor**. ("Empok Nor" [DS9]). A **remat detonator** was one type of pattern scrambler. ("The Darkness and the Light" [DS9]).

Pechetti. (Tom Hodges). Starfleet engineer assigned to Deep Space 9. As a hobby, Pechetti collected Cardassian military emblems and insignia. In 2373, Pechetti accompanied a salvage team from DS9 sent to the abandoned Cardassian station **Empok Nor** to get replacement engineering components. Pechetti was killed on Empok Nor by a Cardassian soldier who was left behind in stasis to guard the station against intruders. ("Empok Nor" [DS9]).

Pelios Station.* Federation facility. Benjamin Sisko once met a memorable woman there, but he later preferred Dax not remind him of the incident. ("Children of Time" [DS9]).

Pelosa system. Planetary system located in Sector 507. In 2375, the Dominion established a new ketracel-white storage facility in the Pelosa system. ("Treachery, Faith, and the Great River" [DS9]).

Penno. (Booth Colman). Photometric projection of a **Vori** civilian, part of an elaborate mind-control technique used by the Vori military to conscript new soldiers. In the simulation, Penno was a man who lived at the Larhana Settlement with his grandchild, Karya. Penno's death at the hand of **Kradin** soldiers was calculated to induce the conscript to feel sympathy for the Vori. ("Nemesis" [VGR]). *Booth Colman played Dr. Zaius in the 1974* Planet of the Apes *television series.*

Perim, Kell. (Stephanie Niznik). Starfleet officer. Ensign Perim served as bridge conn officer aboard the *Starship Enterprise*-E in 2375. (*Star Trek: Insurrection*).

phase variance. Characteristic of matter relating to its alignment within a dimensional plane. While aboard the *U.S.S. Voyager* to conduct secret experiments on the crew in 2374, **Srivani** researchers evaded detection by placing themselves slightly out of phase. They could be detected by setting internal sensors to a phase variance of 0.15. ("Scientific Method" [VGR]).

phaser array power cell. Disposable component of a starship's phaser array. These power cells were cylindrical and about a meter in length. During the Dominion war, Captain Benjamin Sisko maintained a tradition with his crew aboard the *Starship Defiant* of celebrating the completion of a combat mission by toasting the disposal of an exhausted phaser power cell. ("Behind the Lines" [DS9]).

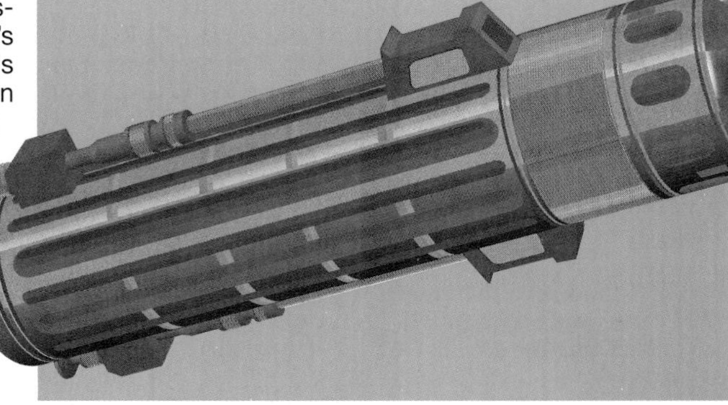

photometric projection. Holographic imaging technology employed by the Vori people. ("Nemesis" [VGR]).

photon grenade.* Short-range, variable-yield energy weapon that creates a powerful electromagnetic pulse. In 3074, **Vaskan** rioters used photon grenades in an attack on the Museum of Kyrian Heritage. ("Living Witness" [VGR]).

photon torpedo.* Starfleet weapon. Class-6 photon torpedoes had an explosive yield of 200 isotons. ("Scorpion, Part II" [VGR]).

photonic missile. Weapon of Borg design. Photonic missiles were installed aboard the *Delta Flyer*. ("Extreme Risk" [VGR]).

physiosensor. Component of a 24th-century Starfleet bio-bed. A physiosensor scanned a patient, providing medical personnel with a continuous display of the patient's vital signs. ("Vis à Vis" [VGR]).

Picard, Jean-Luc.* Captain of the fifth and sixth *Starships Enterprise*. Picard fell in love with **Anij**, a native of the **Ba'ku planet**, in 2375. When he learned of a plot by Admiral Matthew Dougherty and the **Son'a** to steal Anij's idyllic homeworld, Picard resigned his Starfleet commission and led the Ba'ku in resistance. Picard, aided by other members of the *Enterprise*-E crew, was successful in stopping the theft of the planet and was later reinstated as *Enterprise* commander. (*Star Trek: Insurrection*).

Pike, Christopher.* Twenty-third-century Starfleet officer; early captain of the first *Starship Enterprise*. The Christopher Pike Medal of Valor was named in his honor. SEE: **Medal of Valor, Christopher Pike**. ("Tears of the Prophets" [DS9]).

Pinar. (Shaun Bieniek). Bajoran national who was a deputy on Odo's security force on Deep Space 9. ("Time's Orphan" [DS9]).

pizza.* Earth food made from thin baked bread crust covered with toppings such as cheese, vegetables, and spiced meats. In 2374 Tom Paris asked Neelix to serve it at least once a week in the *Voyager*'s mess hall. ("Mortal Coil" [VGR]).

planetary classification system.*

Class-H planets can have an oxygen-argon atmosphere. ("Scorpion, Part II" [VGR]). *"The Ensigns of Command" (TNG) established that Class-H worlds can be bathed in lethal radiation.*

Class-L worlds have relatively high concentrations of atmospheric carbon dioxide, compared to a Class-M planet. Many humanoid species require the use of an oxygen supplement such as **tri-ox** compound in order to survive on many Class-L planets. ("The Sound of Her Voice" [DS9]). *"The 37s" (VGR) established that Class-L planets can also have oxygen-argon atmospheres.*

Class-Y planets, sometimes called Demon-Class worlds, are extremely inhospitable to humanoids. Surface temperatures can exceed 500 kelvins, with toxic atmospheres filled with thermionic radiation. It can be dangerous for a spaceship even to orbit a Class-Y planet. SEE: **mimetic life-form.** ("Demon" [VGR]).

plasma distribution manifold. Component of the power distribution network on a Cardassian space station. When station Deep Space 9's plasma distribution manifold failed in 2373, a salvage team was sent to Empok Nor, a station nearly identical in design to DS9, to get replacement components. ("Empok Nor" [DS9]).

plasma torpedo. Powerful weapon employed by the Romulan Star Empire. Romulan plasma torpedoes employed **trilithium** isotopes. Senator Cretak deployed 7,000 plasma torpedoes at the hospital facility on Derna, much to the displeasure of the Bajoran government and the Federation. ("Image in the Sand" [DS9]).

***pleeka* rind with grub meal.** Casserole made from foodstuffs found on a planet in the Delta Quadrant. Neelix prepared the dish for the *Voyager* crew, although it met with decidedly mixed reviews. ("Real Life" [VGR]). Harry Kim, however, liked the stuff and even occasionally ate it for breakfast. ("Scientific Method" [VGR]).

polarization cloak. Invisibility screen used by **Ramuran** officials to prevent detection of spacecraft or personnel. A polarization cloak can be disrupted by use of a magneton sweep. ("Unforgettable" [VGR]).

polaron.* Subatomic particle. Dr. Elias Giger's **cellular regeneration and entertainment chamber** used highly charged polaric particles in its functioning. ("In the Cards" [DS9]). The **Borg** sometimes employed polaron beams to scan other vessels. ("Scorpion, Part I" [VGR]). In 2374, Seven of Nine and Tuvok used a polaron pulse to stabilize the containment field around a quantum singularity used as a power source in an ancient Hirogen relay station. ("Hunters" [VGR]).

polydeutonic alloy. Advanced metallic material, the product of 29th-century science. The EMH's **mobile emitter** was composed of polydeutonic alloy. The Borg drone known as **One**, whose body included technology from the 29th-century emitter, had plating composed of polydeutonic alloy. ("Drone" [VGR]).

polyduranide.* Construction material. In 2374, Tom Paris and Harry Kim fabricated **golf** clubs made from polyduranide. ("Vis à Vis" [VGR]).

polytrinic acid. Corrosive chemical. During the Cardassian occupation of Bajor, Dr. **Crell Moset** exposed Bajoran prisoners to polytrinic acid to see how long it would take for their skin to heal. ("Nothing Human" [VGR]).

portation. Transporter technology used by the **Voth** in the Delta Quadrant. ("Distant Origin" [VGR]).

potato salad. Earth side dish made from cooked tubers mixed with pickles, mustard, and onions in a paste of egg whites and vegetable oil, usually served cold. ("One" [VGR]).

Potemkin*, U.S.S. Federation starship. In 2374 the *U.S.S. Potemkin* was part of the **Ninth Fleet** headquartered at starbase Deep Space 9, defending the Bajor Sector during the Dominion war. ("You Are Cordially Invited" [DS9]).

Praxiteles. Artist from the ancient Greek nation on Earth. The few surviving works of Praxiteles were among the art treasures looted by the army of **Nazi Germany** during Earth's World War II. ("The Killing Game, Part I" [VGR]).

prefire chamber. Component of a Federation **phaser** weapon. ("Soldiers of the Empire" [DS9]).

Prexnak, Battle of. The most important battle in Ferengi history, an engagement in which ten lone Ferengi stood against 273 Lytasians and were slaughtered, demonstrating their heroism in combat. ("The Magnificent Ferengi" [DS9]).

"Prey." *Voyager* episode #84. Written by Brannon Braga. Directed by Allan Eastman. Stardate 51652.3. *First aired in 1997. The* Voyager *crew rescues a wounded Hirogen hunter from his wrecked ship and later enlists his help when a member of Species 8472 threatens* Voyager. GUEST CAST: Clint Carmichael as Hirogen Hunter; Tony Todd as **Alpha-Hirogen**. SEE: **Alpha-Hirogen; Borg; dicyclic warp signature; Hirogen ship; Hirogen; Janeway, Kathryn; Seven of Nine; Species 8472.**

Prime Directive.* Starfleet General Order #1, prohibiting interference with other cultures. The threat to the galaxy posed by the existence of the **Omega molecule** was believed to be so great that the Prime Directive could be disregarded if necessary to carry out the **Omega Directive.** ("The Omega Directive" [VGR]).

Prixin. Annual **Talaxian** celebration of family. The crew of the *Starship Voyager* celebrated Prixin each year with a party. ("Mortal Coil" [VGR]).

"Profit and Lace." *Deep Space Nine* episode #147. Written by Ira Steven Behr & Hans Beimler. Directed by Alexander Siddig. No stardate given. *First aired in 1998. When Grand Nagus Zek is deposed, Quark poses as a female to help him regain his position against the schemes of brunt.* GUEST CAST: Henry Gibson as **Nilva;** Jeffrey Combs as **Brunt;** Max Grodénchik as **Rom;** Aron Eisenberg as **Nog;** Cecily Adams as **Ishka;** Chase Masterson as **Leeta;** Tiny Ron as **Maihar'du;** Sylvain Cecile as **Uri'lash;** Wallace Shawn as **Zek;** Symba Smith as **Aluura.** SEE: **Aluura; auditory nerve nibble; Brunt; Chamber of Opportunity; Clarus System; Eelwasser; eustachian tube rub; Ferengi Bill of Opportunities; Ferengi Commerce Authority; Ferengi; hypicate cream; Irtok System; Ishka; lobling; Lumba; Nilva; *oo-mox*; Oo-mox *for Fun and Profit*; Quark's bar; Quark; sex-change operation; Slug-o-Cola; snail steak; tympanic tickle; Uri'lash; Zek.**

progeria. Rare genetic disorder that caused premature aging in humanoid children. The disorder, which never affected adults, was eradicated by medical science around 2174. ("Scientific Method" [VGR]).

Promenade Merchants' Association. Organization of entrepreneurs and others doing business on the **Promenade** of Starbase **Deep Space 9**. Quark was the leader of the Promenade Merchants' Association. ("Call to Arms" [DS9]).

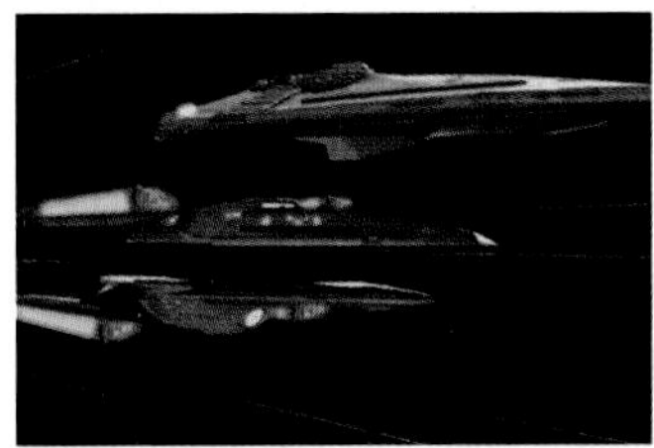

***Prometheus*, U.S.S.** Experimental prototype Starfleet vessel. The *Starship Prometheus*, registry number NX-59650, was designed for deep-space tactical assignments, the first starship of her class. The ship had regenerative shielding, **ablative armor**, and the ability to travel at warp 9.9, making it the fastest vessel in Starfleet. Holoemitters were installed throughout the ship, allowing the ship's holographic doctor, designated **Emergency Medical Hologram-2**, to operate in all crew areas. *Prometheus* was so specialized that only four people in all of Starfleet were trained to operate it. Perhaps the most innovative feature of the *Prometheus* was its ability to separate into three independent spacecraft, allowing it to employ a **multivector assault mode** during combat situations. During one of the ship's first test flights, a group of **Romulans** commandeered the starship, killing her crew. SEE: **Rekar.** While escaping Federation space, the Romulans used the ship's multivector assault capability to enable them to elude pursuit by a *Nebula*-class Federation starship. Control of the ship was regained by the on-board Emergency Medical Hologram with assistance from the holographic Doctor from the *Starship Voyager*. ("Message in a Bottle" [VGR]). *The* Prometheus *was designed by* Star Trek: Voyager *senior illustrator Rick Sternbach and rendered as a computer-generated image by Foundation Imaging. The* Prometheus *interiors were designed*

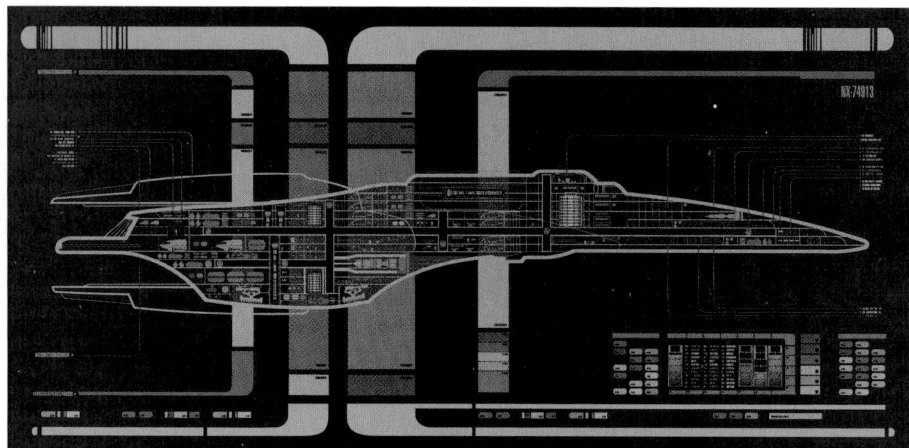

by series production designer Richard James, using re-dressed portions of the re-created Starship Excelsior *bridge that James had made for "Flashback" (VGR), as well as the* Voyager *sickbay in addition to new sets. Actor Tony Sears, who played the* Prometheus *officer killed by the Romulans, previously worked in the* Star Trek: Voyager *art department.*

Prophets.* Energy life-forms from the **Bajoran wormhole**, central figures in the Bajoran religion, also known as wormhole aliens. Although the Prophets considered themselves to be above corporeal matters, they acknowledged that they were "of Bajor." They also respected **Benjamin Sisko** sufficiently that they acceded to his request to intervene on behalf of the Bajoran people in 2374, destroying a massive Dominion invasion fleet in the wormhole before it could reach Bajoran space. ("Sacrifice of Angels" [DS9]). Shortly thereafter, the Prophets sent one of their number to station Deep Space 9 to battle an errant **Pah-wraith** in a long-prophesied conflict called the **Reckoning**. Kai **Winn** interfered before it could reach a conclusion. ("The Reckoning" [DS9]). The Prophets vanished after the wormhole was sealed in late 2374 ("Tears of the Prophets" [DS9]), but they returned several months later when the Emissary opened the ark containing the long-lost **Orb of the Emissary**. Sisko long wondered why the Prophets had chosen him as their Emissary. In fact, he was destined for the role from the time of his conception, which was brought about when a prophet possessed the human woman who would become his mother. This woman later gave birth to Benjamin Sisko. SEE: **Sisko, Sarah**. ("Shadows and Symbols" [DS9]). Benjamin Sisko fulfilled his destiny in late 2375, when he fought with agents of the Pah-wraith known as **Kosst Amojan** and succeeded in returning the Pah-wraiths to their prison in the fire caves on Bajor. Having fulfilled the destiny for which he was born, Benjamin Sisko left the linear domain of existence and entered the realm of the Celestial Temple. ("What You Leave Behind" [DS9]).

protomatter nebula. Interstellar dust cloud containing pockets of naturally occurring protomatter. On stardate 51449.2, the *U.S.S. Voyager* encountered a protomatter nebula in the Delta Quadrant. ("Mortal Coil" [VGR]).

protomatter.* Hazardous, energetic substance. Protomatter makes an effective, albeit unstable, source of energy. Neelix had experience handling protomatter, and he used to trade in it. On stardate 51449 the *Voyager* encountered a class-1 nebula containing pockets of protomatter. ("Mortal Coil" [VGR]).

proton weapon. Energetic charged-particle armament. **Ramuran** starships employed tightly focused proton-based beam weapons. ("Unforgettable" [VGR]).

Proton, Captain. Title character in *The Adventures of Captain Proton* holodeck program. By his own admission, Proton was a Spaceman First Class, Protector of Earth, and the Scourge of Intergalactic Evil. Tom Paris (who devised the stories) portrayed the heroic Captain Proton when he and Harry Kim ran the program in early 2375. SEE: ***Captain Proton, The Adventures of.*** ("Night" [VGR]).

protonebula. Newly forming interstellar dust cloud. The *U.S.S. Voyager* encountered a protonebula in the Delta Quadrant in early 2375. This protonebula was growing quickly, giving off plasma surges with intense internal gravimetric shear forces. ("Drone" [VGR]).

protostar.* Early development stage of a star. A type-6 protostar could theoretically be detonated to create a wormhole. ("The Omega Directive" [VGR]).

proximity transceiver. Borg device that permits the collective to locate a drone if it becomes separated from the collective. A drone's proximity transceiver is activated in the presence of another drone. Seven of Nine's transceiver was activated in early 2375 when a drone, later designated as **One**, was created on the *Starship Voyager*. One's transceiver later alerted a nearby Borg sphere to *Voyager*'s presence. ("Drone" [VGR]).

psychotropic drug. Any of a variety of pharmaceuticals intended to alter the psychological behavior of a patient. Powerful psychotropic drugs were sometimes used by the Cardassian military to amplify xenophobic tendencies in its soldiers. Such conditioning was performed on three soldiers stationed on the abandoned Cardassian station **Empok Nor** to defend the facility against intruders. ("Empok Nor" [DS9]). SEE: **Garak**.

Puppet Masters, The. Twentieth-century science-fiction novel written on Earth by **Robert Heinlein**, first published in 1951 by ***Galaxy Science Fiction*** magazine. *The Puppet Masters* was a tale of an extraterrestrial invasion of planet Earth. Darlene Kursky thought it was an even better story than **Benny Russell**'s "Deep Space Nine." ("Far Beyond the Stars" [DS9]).

Qay'be'. Klingon language phrase meaning "No problem." ("Real Life" [VGR]). *The expression was devised by Klingon language consultant Marc Okrand at the request of* Star Trek III *visual-effects supervisor Ken Ralston, and was subsequently incorporated into the Klingon lexicon. It became a catchphrase for Ralston and his ILM crew, whenever they faced an unexpected problem or a last-minute change of plans during the production of the movie. No matter how difficult the problem or how unusual the request might be, the proper warrior's response was a firm* Qay'be'*!*

qu'vatlh. Klingon animal noted for stubbornness, much as the Earth mule is. ("Sons and Daughters" [DS9]).

Quantum Cafe. Bar and nightclub near **Starfleet Headquarters** in **San Francisco**. ("In the Flesh" [VGR]). SEE: **Launching Pad**.

quantum singularity.* Spatial phenomenon. The immensely formidable beings known to the Borg as **Species 8472** used a string of quantum singularities in the Delta Quadrant to travel from their dimension to ours in late 2373. ("Scorpion, Part I" [VGR]). In early 2374, Seven of Nine opened an entrance to the **fluidic space** realm of Species 8472 by creating a quantum singularity with a resonant graviton beam. ("Scorpion, Part II" [VGR]). The ancient **Hirogen** people actually harvested tiny quantum singularities many thousands of years ago, using them to power a network of relay stations in the Delta Quadrant. The singularities generated almost four terawatts. ("Hunters" [VGR]).

quantum slipstream drive. Advanced warp propulsion technology, similar to Borg **transwarp** drive. Quantum slipstream drive was capable of speeds far greater than conventional warp drive, without using antimatter. The drive operated by routing energy from the quantum drive through deflector emitters to create a slipstream through subspace. The *Starship Voyager* crew experimented with quantum slipstream drive and were able to travel some 300 light-years closer to home before determining that instability during operation made it unsafe for use. They had based their design on a spacecraft operated by **Arturis**, which appeared to be a Federation starship. ("Hope and Fear" [VGR]). SEE: ***Dauntless, U.S.S.***

Quark's bar.* Business establishment on the **Promenade** of station **Deep Space 9**. The full name of Quark's business was Quark's Bar, Grill, Gaming House, and Holosuite Arcade. ("Profit and Lace" [DS9]).

Quark.* Owner of a bar on the **Promenade** of station **Deep Space 9**. Quark regained his Ferengi business license in 2373 in exchange for helping Brunt break up the relationship between his mother **Ishka** and the Grand Nagus **Zek**. Quark later got the two back together. ("Ferengi Love Songs" [DS9]). Quark became a reluctant war hero when he played a pivotal role in the dramatic Starfleet recapture of Deep Space 9 from Dominion control in 2374. Quark, along with **Tora Ziyal**, freed several resistance fighters from Dominion imprisonment, killing two Jem'Hadar soldiers in the process. ("Sacrifice of Angels" [DS9]). Later that year, Quark led a team of six Ferengi mercenaries who rescued his mother from Dominion captivity. ("The Magnificent Ferengi" [DS9]). Quark came to the rescue again in 2374 when he underwent a sex-change operation so that he could convince Commissioner **Nilva** of the wisdom of Zek's radical reforms that granted females the right to wear clothing. ("Profit and Lace" [DS9]). Quark was nevertheless rather conservative in his views of Ferengi politics and was opposed to many of Zek's more radical reforms. It was not surprising, therefore, that Quark was passed over by Zek in his search for a successor in 2375. While Quark's brother, Rom, became the new grand nagus ("Dogs of War" [DS9]), Quark himself remained on Deep Space 9, tending his bar and counting his profits. ("What You Leave Behind" [DS9]).

Quarren. (Henry Woronicz). Historian who founded the Museum of Kyrian Heritage and acted as its curator in 3074. Quarren created a dramatic holographic re-creation of the early days of the **Great War** between the **Kyrians** and the **Vaskans** in 2374. Quarren's re-creation, based on revisionist Kyrian historical records, erroneously taught that the crew of the Federation starship *Voyager* had conspired with Vaskan agents to commit atrocities against the Kyrian people. Quarren's discovery in 3074 of the ancient *Voyager* **Emergency Medical Hologram backup module** was instrumental in challenging this dogma, opening the way for a new era of harmony between the two former enemies. SEE: **Kyrian Heritage, Museum of.** ("Living Witness" [VGR]). *Henry Woronicz previously played Professor Forra Gegen in "Distant Origin" (VGR).*

Quen, Prylar. Bajoran monk during the time of the Cardassian occupation of Bajor. ("Ties of Blood and Water" [DS9]).

R'Cho, M'Kota. Athlete, the first and only **Klingon** to play **parrises squares**. During the **parrises squares** championship finals of 2342, a referee called a controversial penalty that angered M'Kota R'Cho. The furious player in turn strangled the referee. Harry Kim and B'Elanna Torres referred to M'Kota R'Cho in an alternate timeline while playing a game of trivia. ("Year of Hell, Part I" [VGR]). *Obviously, Harry and B'Elanna were speaking of* professional *parrises squares players, since Worf played the game in "11001001" (TNG).*

radiometric converter. Components of a Federation starship's energy by-product processing system. Radiometric converters were employed to purify reactants to eliminate any toxic waste. The converters also absorbed hazardous theta radiation, recycling it so that it could be used to power a variety of subsystems. ("Night" [VGR]).

RAF. Royal Air Force. Aerial military unit of the nation-state of Great Britain, a component of the **Allied Forces** in Earth's **World War II** during the 20th century. ("The Killing Game, Part II" [VGR]). SEE: **Spitfire.**

Rafin. (Matt E. Levin). Photometric projection of a **Vori** defender, part of an elaborate mind-control technique used by the Vori military to conscript new soldiers in their war against the **Kradin**. In the simulation, Rafin was an inexperienced Vori soldier under the command of team leader Brone. ("Nemesis" [VGR]).

Rahmin. (Michael A. Krawic). Representative of the Caatati people. Rahmin met with the crew of the *Voyager* in 2374 and requested humanitarian aid in the form of food, medical supplies, and thorium isotopes. ("Day of Honor" [VGR]). *Michael A. Krawic previously played William Patrick Samuels in "Maquis, Part I" (TNG).*

Raimus. (Joseph Culp). Powerful member of the notorious **Orion Syndicate**, based on **Farius Prime**. Raimus had dealings with the Dominion, and in 2374, he helped to organize an unsuccessful attempt to assassinate the Klingon ambassador to Farius Prime. The plot was thwarted when Starfleet Intelligence tipped off the Klingons about the planned attack. SEE: **Bilby, Liam.** ("Honor Among Thieves" [DS9]).

Rakantha Province.* Farming community on **Bajor**. In 2374, Rakantha experienced serious floods, destroying two-thirds of the region's wheat harvest. The flooding was interpreted as a sign of the coming of **the Reckoning**. ("The Reckoning" [DS9]).

Ram Izad. Civilization in the Delta Quadrant. In an alternate timeline, the Ram Izad species were eradicated by the **Krenim temporal weapon ship**. ("Year of Hell, Part II" [VGR]).

Ramirez, Captain. Starfleet officer; commander of the *Defiant*-class ***U.S.S. Valiant***. In 2374, the *Valiant* took a group of 35 cadets from Starfleet Academy's elite **Red Squad** on a training cruise. Ramirez was seriously wounded in a Cardassian attack near El Gatark that took the lives of the ship's entire senior staff. Ramirez managed to repair his ship, ensuring the immediate survival of his remaining crew, but died a day later of his injuries, ordering cadet **Tim Watters** to take command of his vessel. ("*Valiant*" [DS9]).

ramufta. Fancy culinary dish. Tora Ziyal prepared *ramufta* for a dinner in early 2374. ("Sons and Daughters" [DS9]).

Ramura. Planet located in the Delta Quadrant, homeworld of the technologically advanced **Ramurans**. ("Unforgettable" [VGR]).

Ramuran tracer ship. Small, heavily armed warp-capable spacecraft used by **tracer** units of the secretive Ramuran government. Tracer ships employed polarization cloaks and proton-based particle beam weapons. ("Unforgettable" [VGR]).

Ramurans. Technologically advanced humanoid civilization from the Delta Quadrant. Ramuran bodies produce a pheromone that blocks long-term memory engrams in other species, so that any encounter by a non-Ramuran is forgotten by the non-Ramuran within a matter of hours. The Ramurans were fearful of contact with other worlds. They enhanced their biochemical trait technologically to prevent detection, using means including computer viruses that would erase any record of contact with the Ramurans, as well as polarization cloaks that prevented detection of their ships. The Ramuran government did not allow any of its citizens to leave their society. The government employed enforcement agents called **tracer**s to track down any Ramuran who tried to escape, then to erase any memory or record of the Ramurans that might be retained by non-Ramurans. Kellin and Curneth were Ramuran tracers. ("Unforgettable" [VGR]).

"Random Thoughts." *Voyager* episode #78. Written by Kenneth Biller. Directed by Alexander Singer. No stardate given. *First aired in 1997. Shore leave on a planet of telepaths turns sour when the peaceful inhabitants arrest B'Elanna Torres for the crime of having violent thoughts.* GUEST CAST: Gwynyth Walsh as **Nimira**; Wayne Péré as **Guill**; Rebecca McFarland as **Talli**; Jeanette Miller as **Tembit**; Ted Barba as **Malin**; Bobby Burns as **Frane.** SEE: **chief examiner; engram transcriptor; engramatic purge; Frane; Guill; Malin; Mari Constabulary; Mari; neurogenic restructuring; Nimira; renn; talchok; Talli; Tembit; waterplum.**

ranjen. Title of religious honor bestowed upon **Bajoran** monks engaged in theological research duties. Archaeologist **Rakantha** held the largely symbolic title. ("The Reckoning" [DS9]).

Raven, U.S.S. Federation spacecraft, registry number NAR-32450. While on a science mission, the ship was attacked by the Borg in 2354 and crashed on a Class-M moon in the Delta Quadrant. All aboard were either killed or assimilated by the **Borg**, including two well-known Federation scientists and their young daughter. The girl, **Annika Hansen**, was assimilated by the Borg, becoming the drone designated as **Seven of Nine**. ("The Raven" [VGR]). *In "The Raven," the art department assumed that the* Raven *was a vessel of Federation registry, but not a ship of the Federation Starfleet; hence, the registry number (seen in the matte painting) did not have an NCC prefix. Later, "Dark Frontier" (VGR) made it clear that the ship was indeed a Starfleet vessel.*

"Raven, The." *Voyager* episode #74. Teleplay by Bryan Fuller. Story by Bryan Fuller and Harry Doc Kloor. Directed by LeVar Burton. No stardate given. *First aired in 1997. Following a Borg homing signal, Seven of Nine is drawn to the crash site of the ship on which as a child she and her parents were assimilated by the Borg.* GUEST CAST: Richard J. Zobel, Jr., as **Gauman**; Mickey Cottell as **Dumah**; David Anthony Marshall as **Hansen, Magnus**; Nikki Tyler as **Hansen, Erin**; Erica Lynne as **Hansen, Annika.** SEE: **Agrat-Mot Nebula; B'omar Sovereignty; B'omar; chadre kab; Dalmine Sector; Dumah; Gauman; genetic resequencing vector; Hansen, Annika; Hansen, Erin; Hansen, Magnus; Janeway, Kathryn; Nassordin; *Raven, U.S.S.*; raven; Seven of Nine; Species 218; Species 3259; Talaxians; tritanium.**

raven. Heavy-billed dark Earth bird (*Corvus corvidae*), indigenous to much of that world's northern hemisphere. In early 2374, Seven of Nine had flashbacks to her capture by the Borg when she was a child. In her flashbacks she saw images of a menacing black raven, probably symbolizing the terror that she felt, and which also alluded to the *U.S.S. Raven*, the vessel on which she was traveling at the time of her capture. ("The Raven" [VGR]).

Raymer, Captain. Starfleet officer. In 2375, Raymer commanded the *Starship Destiny*. ("Afterimage" [DS9]).

"Real Life." *Voyager* episode #64. Teleplay by Jeri Taylor. Story by Harry Doc Kloor. Directed by Anson Williams. Stardate

50836.2. *First aired in 1997. The Doctor creates a holographic family to help him experience life in a normal human society. Tom Paris takes a shuttlecraft to investigate an astral eddy.* GUEST CAST: Lindsey Haun as **Belle**; Wendy Schall as **Charlene**; Glenn Harris as **Jeffrey**; Chad Haywood as **K'Kath**; Stephen Ralston as **Larg**. SEE: **astral eddy; Belle; boronite; carbon 60; Charlene; *Cochrane, Shuttlecraft*; Doctor's family program Beta-Rho; Emergency Medical Hologram; French toast; holodeck and holosuite programs: Doctor's family program Beta-Rho; hyronalin; interfold layer; ion mallet; Jeffrey; K'Kath; *kut'luch*; Larg; M'Nea; mushroom pilaf; parrises squares; Parsons, Ensign; *pleeka* rind with grub meal; *Qay'be'*; Rorg; sarium; Vostigye; vulky; *Woman Warriors at the River of Blood*.**

Ancient text predicting The Reckoning.

Reckoning, The. Great spiritual battle between good and evil foretold 25,000 years ago in Bajoran prophesy. The prophesy began to unfold in 2374 when a **Prophet** emerged from the **Bajoran wormhole** and occupied the body of Kira Nerys on starbase Deep Space 9. A **Pah-wraith** known as **Kosst Amojan**, also from the wormhole, took possession of Jake Sisko, and the two waged battle. The two energy beings nearly destroyed the space station, but Starfleet officer Benjamin Sisko, the **Emissary**, had faith that the prophets would protect the Bajoran people. The Reckoning was averted when Kai **Winn** defied the will of the Prophets by exposing the two wormhole aliens to chroniton radiation, driving them away. ("The Reckoning" [DS9]). SEE: **Evil One; Shabren's Fifth Prophecy.**

"Reckoning, The." *Deep Space Nine* episode #145. Teleplay by David Weddle & Bradley Thompson. Story by Harry M. Werksman & Gabrielle Stanton. Directed by Jesús Salvador Treviño. No stardate given. *First aired in 1998. A Prophet chooses the station as the site for an epic clash with a Pah-wraith, and Sisko risks his son's life to fulfill his role as the Emissary.* GUEST CAST: James Greene as **Koral;** Louise Fletcher as **Winn.** SEE: **Argolis Cluster; B'Hala; Bajoran wormhole; bat; Benzar; chroniton; Dorala system; Evil One; Golden Age of Bajor; ideogram; Kalandra Sector; Kendra Valley; Koral; Kosst Amojan; Pah-wraith; Rakantha Province; ranjen; Reckoning, The; Romulans; Seventh Fleet; Shabren's Fifth Prophecy; Sybaron; Tamulna; Tibor Nebula; Vulcan; wheat; Winn.**

Reclaw. Last emperor of the **Second Klingon Dynasty**. The Second Dynasty ended when General **K'Trelan** assassinated Emperor Reclaw, plunging the Empire into the Dark Time. ("You Are Cordially Invited" [DS9]).

rectilinear expansion module. Data-processing device used by Starfleet computing systems such as those used in a starship's security protocol system. ("One Little Ship" [DS9]).

recursion matrix. Algorithmic construct that forms the cipher key to decrypting a coded data stream. ("Hope and Fear" [VGR]).

Red Squad.* Elite group of **Starfleet Academy** cadets. In early 2374, 35 members of Red Squad embarked on a three-month training cruise aboard the ***U.S.S. Valiant***. When the **Dominion** war broke out, the ship and all aboard were trapped behind enemy lines. Later, when the ship's commander and senior staff were all killed in a Cardassian attack, Red Squad cadet **Tim Watters** assumed command of the *Valiant*, in charge of a crew consisting entirely of Red Squad members. The charismatic Watters held his crew together behind enemy lines for eight months. Unfortunately, out of touch with his superiors, Watters led his crew on a foolhardy attack on a massive **Dominion battleship** on stardate 51825. The incident resulted in Watters's death, along with the death of most of his crew and the loss of his ship. The only member of Red Squad to survive the battle was **Dorian Collins**. ("*Valiant*" [DS9]).

red leaf tea.* Beverage. One of Julian Bashir's favorite breakfasts included hot buttered scones with *moba* jam and red leaf tea. ("Inquisition" [DS9]).

Reichsmark. Monetary unit used by the nation-state of **Nazi Germany** on Earth during the 20th century. ("The Killing Game, Part I" [VGR]).

Rekar. (Judson Scott). Romulan commander. Rekar commandeered the ***Starship Prometheus*** in 2374. ("Message in a Bottle" [VGR]). *Actor Judson Scott also played Joaquim in* Star Trek II: The Wrath of Kahn *and Sobi in "Symbiosis" (TNG).*

relay station. SEE: **Hirogen relay station.**

Remata'Klan. (Phil Morris). **Jem'Hadar** third who led the Jem'Hadar unit under the command of Vorta supervisor **Keevan** in early 2374. Remata'Klan was a man of honor, and although he knew that Keevan had betrayed the Jem'Hadar, Remata'Klan followed his orders and led the unit into a hopeless firefight with Captain Sisko and his crew. He and all his men perished in the battle. ("Rocks and Shoals" [DS9]). *Phil Morris previously played trainee Foster in* Star Trek III: The Search for Spock *and Thopok, a Klingon, in "Looking for* par'Mach *in All the Wrong Places" [DS9]. The son of actor Greg Morris, Phil also played Barney Collier's son in the 1988 series revival of* Mission: Impossible.

Renaissance. Literally, "rebirth." A remarkable period of **Earth** history during which the people of Europe experienced a rebirth of science, culture, and the arts. Beginning around the 14th century in the nation-state of Italy, the Renaissance spread across the European continent over the next three centuries. Painter, sculptor, engineer and scientist **Leonardo da Vinci** was one of the greatest products of the Renaissance. One of da Vinici's works was the Mona Lisa (pictured). ("Concerning Flight" [VGR]).

renn. Monetary unit used by the **Mari** people in the Delta Quadrant. ("Random Thoughts" [VGR]).

Republic, U.S.S.* Federation starship. After serving for decades in Starfleet, the *Starship Republic* became a cadet-training vessel, rarely venturing out of Earth's Sol system. ("*Valiant*" [DS9]). *The episode does not make it clear if this was the same ship that Kirk served on as a cadet, but episode writer Ronald D. Moore indicated he thought it probably was.*

Resket. (Chuck Magnus). **Ramuran** national. Resket fled from his homeworld in 2374 but was captured by **tracer** agents, who erased his memories of contact with the outside. ("Unforgettable" [VGR]). *Resket spoke no dialog.*

resonance emitter. Engineering component aboard Jem'Hadar attack vessels. ("A Time to Stand" [DS9]).

"Resurrection." *Deep Space Nine* episode #132. Written by René Echevarria. Directed by LeVar Burton. No stardate given. *First aired in 1997. The alternate-universe double of Bareil comes to the station to steal a Bajoran Orb.* GUEST CAST: John Towey as **Vedek Ossan**; Philip Anglim as **Bareil Antos (mirror).** SEE: **alva; Bareil Antos (mirror); Bareil, Vedek; Boday, Captain; Dahkur Province; Ilvia; *kava* roll; Kira Nerys (mirror); Lisea (mirror); multidimensional transporter device; Orb; Orb of Prophecy; Ossan, Vedek; security access code; Somata oil; Trag'tok, Dr.; Ventar system.**

"Retrospect" *Voyager* episode #85. Teleplay by Bryan Fuller & Lisa Klink. Story by Andrew Shepard Price & Mark Gaberman. Directed by Jesús Salvador Treviño. Stardate 51658.2. *First aired in 1998. Repressed memories from Seven of Nine seem to implicate a weapons dealer of having forcibly extracted Borg nanoprobes from Seven's body.* GUEST CAST: Michael Horton as **Koven**; Adrian Sparks as **Entharan Magistrate**; Michelle Agnew as Scharn. SEE: **Amanin; Ashmore, Ensign; chromoelectric force field; Emergency Medical Hologram; engramatic activity; Entharan magistrate; Entharans; genome; isokinetic cannon; Jungian therapy; Kovin; maxilla; monotanium; Seven of Nine; terawatt power particle beam rifle.**

"Revulsion." *Voyager* episode #73. Written by Lisa Klink. Directed by Kenneth Biller. Stardate 51186.2. *First aired in 1997. Torres and the Doctor lend aid to an alien holographic individual who proves to be violently deranged.* GUEST CAST: Leland Orser as **Dejaren.** SEE: **antimatter radiation; Arritheans; Astrometrics; Culhane, Ensign; Dejaren; HD-25 maintenance unit; holodeck and holosuite programs: Ktarian moonrise; isomorphic projection; Janeway, Kathryn; Kim, Harry; Paris, Thomas; Seros; Serosian ship; Spectrum; Tuvok; Vulcan tea.**

Reynolds, Charles. Starfleet officer and commander of the *U.S.S. Centaur*. In early 2374, during the Dominion war, Reynolds ordered the *Centaur* to attack a **Jem'Hadar warship** near the Cardassian border, unaware that the enemy vessel was piloted by his friend, Ben Sisko, on a covert Starfleet mission. ("A Time to Stand" [DS9]). Reynolds subsequently commanded a destroyer unit in the daring and costly mission to retake station Deep Space 9 from Dominion control, preventing a massive incursion of Dominion ships into the Alpha Quadrant. ("Sacrifice of Angels" [DS9]).

rice. The edible seeds of an annual Earth cereal grass (*Oryza sativa*), rich in carbohydrates. Aboard a Starfleet runabout, replicator entree number 103 was curried chicken and rice with a side order of carrots. ("Blaze of Glory" [DS9]).

Riker Maneuver. Informal name for a risky tactic employed by Commander William T. Riker during a battle with two Son'a ships in 2375. Riker used his ship's **Bussard collector** to collect volatile metreon gas, then expelled the gas at an enemy ship. When a Son'a fired on Riker's ship, the gas ignited, catching the enemy inside the explosion. (*Star Trek: Insurrection*).

Riker, William T.* Executive officer of the *Starships Enterprise*-D and -E under the command of Captain Jean-Luc Picard. In 2375, Will Riker and **Deanna Troi**, possibly influenced by the rejuvenating effects of the **Ba'ku planet**, renewed their romantic relationship. She preferred him clean-shaven, so he shaved off his beard for her. During the mission to the Ba'ku planet, Riker successfully defeated two Son'a vessels by executing a risky plan termed the **Riker Maneuver**. To carry out his tactic, Riker used the *Enterprise*-E's manual steering column to pilot the ship during a major systems outage. (*Star Trek: Insurrection*).

Rilnar. Civilization in the Delta Quadrant, enemies of the **Krenim** Imperium. In an alternate timeline, the Rilnar were the first people to be eliminated from history by **Annorax** through the use of the **Krenim temporal weapon ship**. In using the weapon, Annorax failed to consider possible side effects of such destruction. With the Rilnar no longer existing, Annorax's own people lost a critical genome and some 50 million Krenim fell victim to a previously benign disease. ("Year of Hell, Part II" [VGR]).

rippleberry. Small succulent fruit. Rippleberries were one of the few foods that the Vorta could really enjoy despite their limited sense of taste. ("Treachery, Faith, and the Great River" [DS9]).

Risa.* Resort planet. In 2373, the Starfleet officer in charge of the weather-control system on Risa was recruited by the **Orion Syndicate**. In exchange for money, this individual gave the syndicate classified information, compromising Starfleet security operations. ("Honor Among Thieves" [DS9]).

Rislan. (James Noah). **Nyrian** operative who participated in the Nyrian attempt to capture the Federation starship *Voyager* on stardate 50912.4. ("Displaced" [VGR]).

Rittenhouse, Roy. (J.G. Hertzler). Twentieth-century Earth **science-fiction** artist. Rittenhouse produced many imaginative paintings and illustrations of futuristic settings and alien planets published in ***Incredible Tales*** magazine during the 1950s. As was common for publications of that type, Rittenhouse would each month create a number of fanciful drawings that would serve as a basis for the magazine's writers to produce the stories for that month's issue. One such Rittenhouse sketch was a space station that served as an inspiration for **Benny Russell**'s unpublished novella, "Deep Space Nine." SEE: **rocket ship**. ("Far Beyond the Stars" [DS9]). *Rittenhouse's paintings and other* Incredible Tales *art seen in the magazine's office were created by John Eaves, Doug Drexler, Jim Van Over, Anthony Fredrickson, and Rick Sternbach. Some additional Rittenhouse sketches were by Matt Jefferies from the original* Star Trek *series. J.G. Hertzler also played General Martok on* Star Trek: Deep Space Nine*, although Rittenhouse did not have Klingon makeup.*

Ritual of Twenty Painstiks. Gauntlet of Klingon warriors wielding painstiks to test a warrior's mettle in observance of the **Day of Honor**. ("Day of Honor" [VGR]). SEE: **painstik, Klingon**.

Ro'tin. Ba'ku name for **Ahdar Ru'afo**. Ro'tin was born on the **Ba'ku planet**, but changed his name to Ru'afo when he left his home to follow the ways of what his people called offlanders, becoming the **Son'a**. (*Star Trek: Insurrection*).

rock and roll. Style of music popular on late 20th- and early 21st-century **Earth**. Rock and roll music found great favor with the youth-oriented culture of the planet, and was influenced by a broad range of that world's musical traditions, including blues, gospel, classical, African, Latin, country-and-western, and electronic music. Tom Paris, an aficionado of 20th-century American culture, was fond of rock and roll music. ("Nothing Human" [VGR]).

rocket ship. Any of numerous hypothetical designs for early impulse-powered orbital or interplanetary spacecraft as envisioned by **science-fiction** writers and other visionaries of 20th-century Earth. Fictional space hero **Captain Proton** flew a rocket ship in his imaginary exploits to defend planet Earth against the evil **Doctor Chaotica** and other extraterrestrial menaces. ("Night" [VGR]). The cover of ***Incredible Tales*** magazine often featured imaginative paintings of rocket ships on fanciful alien planets. ("Far Beyond the Stars" [DS9]).

"Rocks and Shoals." *Deep Space Nine* episode #126. Written by Ronald D. Moore. Directed by Michael Vejar. No stardate given. *First aired in 1997. Sisko and his crew's commandeered Jem'Hadar ship is forced to crash on a planet occupied by the crew of a Dominion ship that had earlier become stranded.* GUEST CAST: Andrew J. Robinson as **Garak, Elim**; Phil Morris as **Remata'Klan**; Christopher Shea as **Keevan**; Aron Eisenberg as **Nog**; Paul S. Eckstein as **Limara'Son**; Lilyan Chauvin as **Yassim, Vedek**; Sarah MacDonnell as **Neeley, Lieutenant Lisa**; Joseph Fuqua as **Gordon, Ensign Paul.** SEE: **Cardassian Intelligence Bureau; dark-matter nebula; Gordon, Ensign Paul; gyrodyne; Jem'Hadar; Keevan; ketracel-white; Kira Nerys; Limara'Son; Mavek; microsuture; Neeley, Lieutenant Lisa; Remata'Klan; shroud; Yak'Talon; Yassim, Vedek.**

"Rodeo Red's Red Hot Rootin' Tootin' Chili." Spicy bean and meat dish in a tomato sauce concocted by Neelix for the crew of the *Starship Voyager* in 2374 as an example of classic American Earth cuisine. One of the flavorings, jalapeño peppers, caused many who consumed the dish to report to sickbay with heartburn. ("Message in a Bottle" [VGR]).

rokeg* blood pie. Traditional Klingon dish. Many Klingon families serve blood pie on the **Day of Honor**. ("Day of Honor" [VGR]).

Rom.* Grand nagus of the **Ferengi Alliance** who once worked as a waste extraction engineer at station Deep Space 9. Rom and **Leeta** became engaged in 2373. Like any Ferengi, he expected his bride to sign the traditional **Waiver of Property and Profit**. When Leeta refused to agree to the waiver, Rom feared that she wanted to marry him only for his money. These fears were allayed when Leeta was still willing to marry Rom after he donated all of his profits to the Bajoran War Orphans Fund. ("Ferengi Love Songs" [DS9]). Rom and Leeta were married on stardate 50975. The ceremony was performed by the **Emissary**, Benjamin Sisko and was attended by **Nog** and **Quark**. ("Call to Arms" [DS9]). Rom was active in the Bajoran resistance against the Cardassian and Dominion occupation of Deep Space 9 during the Dominion war. He was arrested by Cardassian authorities on stardate 51145 while attempting to sabotage the station's deflector array. ("Behind the Lines" [DS9]). Rom was a technological genius. He invented the **self-replicating mine**s that prevented a major Dominion incursion into the Alpha Quadrant during the early days of the Dominion war. ("Call to Arms" [DS9]). Rom's technical brilliance was matched by considerable wisdom in societal matters. Unlike more conservative Ferengi citizens, Rom saw the sense in **Zek**'s radical social reforms for the long-term progress of Ferengi culture. It was this vision that Zek recognized in 2375 when he appointed Rom to succeed him as the next **grand nagus** of the Ferengi Alliance. ("Dogs of War" [DS9]).

Rommel, Erwin. (1891–1944). High-ranking officer of the military forces of **Nazi Germany** during Earth's 20th century. Rommel, who was regarded as a brilliant tactician, commanded Nazi forces occupying the nation of **France** during the later part of Earth's second world war. In the **French Resistance** holodeck program, the new commandant of Sainte Claire once served under Rommel. SEE: **World War II**. ("The Killing Game, Part I" [VGR]).

Romulan Neutral Zone.* Region of space between the **Romulan Star Empire** and the **United Federation of Planets**. During the early days of the Dominion war, the Romulan Neutral Zone was used by Dominion forces as a safe region for staging a series of devastating attacks on Federation territory, at least until the Romulan entry into the conflict. ("In the Pale Moonlight" [DS9]).

Romulan shuttle. Small short-range spacecraft of Romulan design. Senator **Vreenak** traveled to a secret meeting on station Deep Space 9 in 2374 aboard a Romulan shuttle. Vreenak's ship was later destroyed, apparently by Dominion operatives. ("In the Pale Moonlight" [DS9]). *The Romulan shuttle was designed by Doug Drexler. The miniature was built by Tony Meininger.*

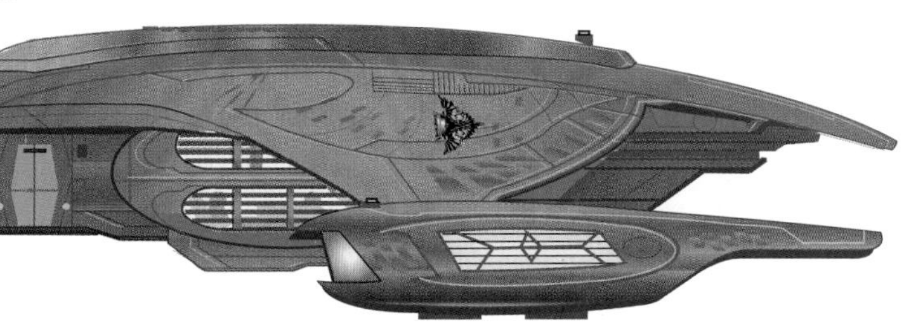

Romulans.* Civilization. In late 2373, the Romulans signed a nonaggression pact with the **Dominion**, significantly affecting the balance of power in the **Alpha Quadrant**. ("Call to Arms" [DS9]). The Romulans, nominally allies with the Dominion, remained uninvolved in the ensuing Dominion war while other major powers in the Alpha Quadrant suffered tremendous losses in the conflict. By late 2374, the Romulans entered the war against the Dominion after the **Tal Shiar** intelligence agency discovered evidence that the Dominion was planning to invade Romulan territory. Romulan authorities did not realize that the "evidence" had in fact been falsified by Benjamin Sisko and Elim Garak in a successful effort to persuade the Romulan government to reverse its decision to ally with the Dominion. SEE: **Vreenak.** ("In the Pale Moonlight" [DS9]). The Romulans were soon a significant force in the war, driving the Dominion from the Benzar system ("The Reckoning" [DS9]). Romulan forces also were instrumental in the dramatic Dominion defeat at the **Chin'toka System**. ("Tears of the Prophets" [DS9]).

Rorg. Male character in the Klingon novel *Woman Warriors at the River of Blood.* ("Real Life" [VGR]).

Ross, Admiral William. (Barry Jenner). Senior Starfleet officer. In early 2374, Admiral Ross transferred Benjamin Sisko from command of the *Defiant* to a desk job at Starbase 375. ("A Time to Stand" [DS9]). Ross promoted Sisko to serve as his adjutant after Captain Bennet, his previous adjutant, was promoted to command the Seventh Tactical Wing. ("Behind the Lines" [DS9]). Shortly thereafter, Ross supported a bold plan proposed by Sisko to retake station Deep Space 9 from Dominion control. ("Favor the Bold" [DS9]). Ross subsequently presented Sisko with the **Christopher Pike Medal of Valor** for the daring recapture of Deep Space 9. ("Tears of the Prophets" [DS9]). Ross had a good rapport with Romulan senator **Cretak**. ("Image in the Sand" [DS9]). Admiral Ross represented the United Federation of Planets at the signing ceremony, held on station Deep Space 9, that ended the terrible Dominion war in late 2375. ("What You Leave Behind" [DS9]). *Ross first appeared was in "A Time to Stand" [DS9] and got a first name in "Image in the Sand" (DS9).*

Rossoff, Herbert. (Armin Shimerman). Twentieth-century Earth writer and temperamental connoisseur of pastry products. Rossoff was a highly regarded writer of **science-fiction** stories for such publications as ***Incredible Tales*** in the 1950s. ("Far Beyond the Stars" [DS9]). SEE: **Hugo Award**. *Armin Shimerman also played Quark on* Star Trek: Deep Space Nine, *although Rossoff did not have Ferengi makeup.*

Rotarran, I.K.S. Klingon bird-of-prey. In 2373 the Klingon High Council gave **General Martok** command of the *Rotarran* to conduct a search for the battle cruiser *I.K.S. B'Moth*. When Martok took command, it had been seven months since the crew of the *Rotarran* had a victory, and crew morale was therefore low. Martok led the crew into battle with the Jem'Hadar, destroying a Jem'Hadar vessel. In doing so, the crew of the *Rotarran* rescued 35 survivors of the *B'Moth* and restored their pride as warriors. ("Soldiers of the Empire" [DS9]). The *Rotarran* was also one of the Klingon vessels authorized by Chancellor Gowron to lend assistance to the Starfleet task force that retook station Deep Space 9 from Dominion control in 2374. ("Sacrifice of Angels" [DS9]).

Rozhenko, Alexander.* (Marc Worden). Son of **Worf** and **K'Ehleyr.** Alexander felt resentment toward his father for, as he saw it, abandoning him to his grandparents. Alexander eventually grew dissatisfied with life on Earth and enlisted in the Klingon Defense Force. His grandparents were not pleased with Alexander's decision, but they supported him once he made it clear that this was what he wanted. Alexander was assigned to the *Bird-of-Prey* ***Rotarran***, where he served with his father during the Dominion war in 2374. Serving together was difficult for both Alexander and Worf, until Alexander agreed to join his father as a member of the House of **Martok** in a ceremony held aboard the *I.K.S. Rotarran*. ("Sons and Daughters" [DS9]). Alexander was subsequently transferred to the battle cruiser ***I.K.S. Ya'Vang.*** Alexander was honored when his father asked him to act as *Tawi'Yan* (sword bearer) at Worf's wedding to Jadzia Dax in 2374. Alexander spoke very little Klingonese. ("You Are Cordially Invited" [DS9]). *Alexander was played as a young adult by Marc Worden in "Sons and Daughters" (DS9) and "You Are Cordially Invited" (DS9).*

Rozhenko, Helena.* Earth citizen; mother to Worf and Nikolai; grandmother to Alexander Rozhenko. Although Alexander returned to Earth to live with his grandparents, he eventually decided to enlist in the Klingon Defense Force. Helena and Sergey Rozhenko weren't pleased with this idea, but they supported Alexander in his decision. ("Sons and Daughters" [DS9]).

Rozhenko, Nikolai.* Son of Sergey and **Helena Rozhenko**; adoptive brother of **Worf**. When Nikolai was a boy, his father used to take the two brothers on camping trips in the Ural Mountains of Earth. Every night they would listen to the wolves howling in the distance. Nikolai was afraid of them, but Worf would lie in his tent for hours just listening. ("Change of Heart" [DS9]).

Ru'afo, Ahdar. (F. Murray Abraham). Leader of the Son'a people from around 2275 to 2375. Ru'afo was born as **Ro'tin** on the **Ba'ku planet**, but changed his name to Ru'afo when he was exiled from his planet. In the years away from his homeworld and the rejuvenating effects of its metaphasic radiation field, Ru'afo gradually suffered the debilitating effects of aging. Rebuked in his efforts to return home, Ru'afo allied his people with a renegade Starfleet officer, **Admiral Matthew Dougherty**, who agreed to remove the Ba'ku people from their planet. In exchange, both the Son'a and the Federation would share in the benefit of the **metaphasic radiation**. Ru'afo's plan was halted by the crew of the *Starship Enterprise*-E, led by Captain Jean-Luc Picard. Ru'afo was killed aboard a Son'a particle-collection spacecraft that would have devastated the Ba'ku planet while harvesting metaphasic particles from the Ba'ku planet's ring system. (*Star Trek: Insurrection*). *F. Murray Abraham portrayed Antonio Salieri in the 1984 motion picture* Amadeus, *for which he won an Academy Award for best actor.*

Rubicon, U.S.S.* Starfleet **runabout** assigned to station Deep Space 9. On stardate 51474.2, the *Rubicon* was used to investigate a rare subspace compression anomaly discovered in Federation space. The runabout, piloted by Jadzia Dax, Julian Bashir, and Miles O'Brien, entered the phenomenon and were subjected to severe spatial distortions. The phenomenon miniaturized the ship, reducing the crew to the height of about one centimeter. This extraordinary condition enabled the *Rubicon* crew to play a pivotal role in recapturing the *Starship Defiant* from a Jem'Hadar squad. Later, re-entering the anomaly restored the *Rubicon* to normal size. ("One Little Ship" [DS9]).

Rukani. Technologically advanced Delta Quadrant civilization. The Rukani were featured in Insurrection Alpha, a holodeck training program written by Tuvok. ("Worse Case Scenario" [VGR]).

Russell, Benny. (Avery Brooks). Twentieth-century Earth writer. Russell specialized in works of **science fiction**, including several stories published in ***Incredible Tales*** magazine during the 1950s. Russell was a victim of the pervasive racism of the period, which caused him and other African-Americans to be treated as second-class citizens. One of Russell's finest works was a story of an astronaut named **Benjamin Sisko**, who commanded a space station in the far reaches of the galaxy. Russell was not able to get his story, entitled "Deep Space Nine," printed because the publisher of *Incredible Tales* feared the magazine's readership would not accept a story in which the hero was a black man. Russell took this rejection very hard, and subsequently suffered a nervous breakdown. ("Far Beyond the Stars" [DS9]). Russell was institutionalized, but his visions continued to haunt him. When his caregivers refused to give him paper or a typewriter, Russell found himself compelled to continue his stories by writing on the walls of his hospital ward. His psychiatrist, **Dr. Wykoff**, offered to release him if he would repudiate his stories by erasing them, but Russell refused. ("Shadows and Symbols" [DS9]). SEE: **Cassie; Pah-wraiths**. *Avery Brooks also played Ben Sisko on* Star Trek: Deep Space Nine.

Russol, Gul. Cardassian military officer. Russol, who was an informant to Deep Space 9 security chief Odo, was executed by the Cardassian Central Command in 2374. ("Treachery, Faith, and the Great River" [DS9]).

Rutharian sector. Region of space near the boundary of the Beta Quadrant. The *U.S.S. Olympia* was destroyed in orbit of the fourth planet in a star system in the Rutharian sector in 2371, with a loss of all hands. ("The Sound of Her Voice" [DS9]).

"Sacrifice of Angels." *Deep Space Nine* episode #130. Written by Ira Steven Behr & Hans Beimler. Directed by Allan Kroeker. No stardate given. *First aired in 1997. The minefield blocking the wormhole is brought down by the Dominion just as Sisko's fleet arrives and reclaims the station. This episode was the second of two parts, concluding the storyline begun in "Favor the Bold" (DS9). Tora Ziyal, Gul Dukat's daughter, is killed in this episode.* GUEST CAST: Andrew J. Robinson as **Garak, Elim**; Jeffrey Combs as **Weyoun**; Marc Alaimo as **Dukat, Gul**; Max Grodénchik as **Rom**; Aron Eisenberg as **Nog**; J. G. Hertzler as **Martok, General**; Melanie Smith as **Tora Ziyal**; Casey Biggs as **Damar**; Chase Masterson as **Leeta**; Salome Jens as **Founder Leader**; Darin Cooper as Cardassian officer. SEE: **Bajoran wormhole; *Charge of the Light Brigade, The*; *Cortéz, U.S.S.*; Damar, Glinn; Deep Space 9; Diego, Captain; Dukat; Founder Leader; *hasperat* soufflé; *Magellan, U.S.S.*; *Majestic, U.S.S.*; Odo; Prophets; Quark; Reynolds, Charles; *Rotarran, I.K.S.*; self-replicating mine; Sisko, Benjamin; *Sitak, U.S.S.*; Tora Ziyal; *Venture, U.S.S.***

safety protocol. Subroutine of some holographic environmental simulators (such as a **holodeck** or holosuite) designed to prevent the experience from injuring or killing the participant. ("Soldiers of the Empire" [DS9]). For example, in a simulated sword fight, the safety protocol might cause a holographic character's sword to disappear a few milliseconds before the sword penetrated the body of a participant. **Hirogen** hunters who commandeered the *Starship Voyager* and its holodecks in late 2374 operated a number of battle simulations with the safety protocols off, believing that to do otherwise would remove the sense of the hunt. ("The Killing Game, Part I" [VGR]). B'Elanna Torres, suffering from severe depression in early 2375 after learning of the death of nearly all her former Maquis associates, began running dangerous holodeck programs such as **orbital skydiving** with the safety protocols off. ("Extreme Risk" [VGR]).

Sahgi. (Michelle Horn). Bajoran national. As a young child, Sahgi celebrated the **Bajoran Gratitude Festival** on Deep Space 9 in 2374. While there she met the Emissary, Benjamin Sisko. ("Tears of the Prophets" [DS9]).

Sahreen. Member of the **Maquis** terrorist group. Sahreen was killed in 2374 when the rebels were eradicated by the Cardassians with the help of the Dominion. Future *Voyager* crew members B'Elanna Torres and Chakotay were also members of the same group. ("Extreme Risk" [VGR]).

Saint Moritz. Town in southeastern Switzerland located on planet Earth. Saint Moritz was site of the Winter Olympics games in 1928 and 1948. In 2374, Thomas Paris suggested he and B'Elanna Torres create a snow-skiing program located at Saint Moritz, but Torres said she preferred something a little warmer. ("Waking Moments" [VGR]).

Sainte Claire. City in the nation-state of **France** on planet Earth. During that planet's second world war of the 20th century, Sainte Claire was occupied by the army of **Nazi Germany**. An underground resistance organization fought against the Nazi occupation, later working with American troops to free the city. Sainte Claire was the setting of the **French Resistance** holodeck simulation program. ("The Killing Game, Parts I and II" [VGR]). *The streets of Sainte Claire were filmed on the "European street" backlot at Universal Studios in Los Angeles, suitably re-dressed by the* Star Trek: Voyager *art department.*

Samoa. Group of islands in the central Pacific Ocean on planet Earth. In 2374 when Thomas Paris suggested creating a holodeck skiing program, B'Elanna Torres requested a warmer location such as Samoa or Fiji. ("Waking Moments" [VGR]).

Sands. Luxury hotel and casino complex that was located in **Las Vegas** on Earth from December 15, 1952, through June 30, 1996. In 1958, noted singer **Vic Fontaine** played the Sands, where he caroused with celebrities of the era, including Frank Sinatra and Dean Martin. ("His Way" [DS9]).

Saratoga, U.S.S. Federation starship, replacement for the *Miranda*-class vessel destroyed in the battle of Wolf 359. In 2374, the *Saratoga* visited starbase Deep Space 9. ("Wrongs Darker Than Death or Night" [DS9]).

Sarek, U.S.S. Federation starship. The *Sarek* was part of the task force commanded by Captain Sisko to retake station Deep Space 9 from Dominion control during the Dominion war. ("Favor the Bold" [DS9]). *Named for the Vulcan ambassador.*

Sarina. SEE: **Douglas, Sarina.**

sarium. Material used in space-borne construction. **Vostigye** space stations employed sarium in their design. ("Real Life" [VGR]).

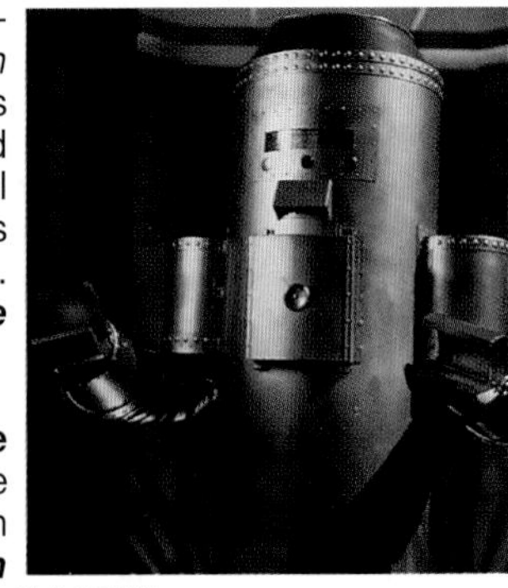

Satan's Robot. Holographic character in *The Adventures of Captain Proton* holodeck program. Satan's Robot was a fanciful humanoid robot controlled by the maniacal **Doctor Chaotica** in his nefarious plans to enslave Earth's inhabitants. SEE: ***Captain Proton, The Adventures of.*** ("Night" [VGR]).

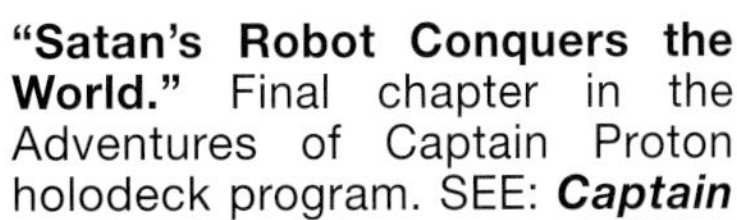

"Satan's Robot Conquers the World." Final chapter in the Adventures of Captain Proton holodeck program. SEE: ***Captain Proton, The Adventures of.*** ("Night" [VGR]).

sauerkraut. Shredded and salted cabbage fermented in its own juice, originating on the European continent of planet Earth. Sauerkraut was often served with **frankfurter**s. ("Far Beyond the Stars" [DS9]).

Saurian brandy.* Alcoholic beverage. While at Starbase 375 in early 2374, Nog obtained some to help the crew of the *Defiant* celebrate the completion of a combat mission against the Dominion. ("Behind the Lines" [DS9]). Saurian brandy was Benjamin Sisko's favorite drink. ("Treachery, Faith, and the Great River" [DS9]).

science fiction. Branch of literature and media dealing with the effects of science and technology on society. Science fiction was an important fixture of Earth's popular culture, providing entertainment that warned of potential dystopian futures, while helping to inspire humans to reach for the stars. ("Far Beyond the Stars" [DS9]). SEE: ***Captain Proton, The Adventures of*; Hugo Award; *Incredible Tales;* rocket ship**.

"Scientific Method." *Voyager* episode #75. Teleplay by Lisa Klink. Story by Sherry Klein & Harry Doc Kloor. Directed by David Livingston. Stardate 51244.3. *First aired in 1997. Undetectable alien scientists secretly conduct invasive and dangerous medical tests on the* Voyager *crew in the name of medical research.* GUEST CAST: Rosemary Forsyth as **Alzen**; Annette Helde as **Takar.** SEE: **Alzen; binary pulsar; coffee; electron resonance scanner; Ktarian merlot; micro-inducer; Mylean; Neelix; phase variance; *pleeka* rind with grub meal; progeria; scrambled eggs; Srivani; Takar.**

scone. A round Earth tea biscuit usually eaten with butter. Julian Bashir enjoyed hot buttered scones with *moba* jam and red leaf tea for breakfast. ("Inquisition" [DS9]).

"Scorpion, Part I." *Voyager* episode #68. Written by Brannon Braga & Joe Menosky. Directed by David Livingston. Stardate 50984.3. *First aired in 1997. Janeway forms an alliance with the Borg in hopes of fending off the attacks of the formidable Species 8472. Janeway's holographic re-creation of Leonardo da Vinci was first seen here. Jennifer Lien made her last regular appearance as Kes in this episode, although she would make two guest appearances at the beginning of the next season. "Scorpion, Part I," the last episode of the third season, was a cliff-hanger that was resolved in the opening episode of the fourth season.* GUEST CAST: John Rhys-Davies as **da Vinci, Leonardo.** SEE: **Amasov, Captain; bioship; Borg; Breen; da Vinci workshop program Janeway-7; da Vinci, Leonardo; *Endeavour, U.S.S.*; gravimetric fluctuation; Hickman, Ensign; holodeck and holosuite programs: da Vinci workshop program Janeway-7; injection tubule; Janeway, Kathryn; Kes; nanoprobe; neuropeptide; Northwest Passage; polaron; quantum singularity; scorpion; scudi; skeletal lock; Species 8472; *Voyager, U.S.S.*; Wolf 359.**

"Scorpion, Part II." *Voyager* episode #69. Written by Brannon Braga & Joe Menosky. Directed by Winrich Kolbe. Stardate 51003.7. *First aired in 1997. The* Voyager *crew fight off Species 8472 with the assistance of Seven of Nine, the Borg liaison to the* Voyager. *This episode was the first of* Star Trek: Voyager*'s fourth season and marked the first appearance of Seven of Nine.* GUEST CAST: Jennifer Lien as **Kes.** SEE: **biomolecular warhead; bioship; Borg; da Vinci workshop program Janeway-7; da Vinci, Leonardo; fluidic space; graviton; interdimensional rift; isoton; Janeway, Kathryn; Kes; multikinetic neutronic mine; nanoprobe; photon torpedo; planetary classification system: Class-H; scorpion; Seven of Nine; Species 8472; *Voyager, U.S.S.***

scorpion. Predatory arachnid life-form native to planet Earth. Commander Chakotay, questioning Captain Janeway's decision to enter into a truce with the Borg in late 2373, warned that the Borg might be like an Earth scorpion, unable to change its basic predatory nature, even when logic might dictate otherwise. ("Scorpion, Part I" [VGR]). Captain Janeway used "scorpion" as a code word to warn Chakotay of an attempt by **Seven of Nine** to take over the *Voyager* on stardate 51003.7. ("Scorpion, Part II" [VGR]).

scotch.* Alcoholic beverage. Miles O'Brien preferred single malt scotch that was made in the Scottish highlands on Earth. ("Change of Heart" [DS9]). O'Brien even used scotch as a flavoring in specially made chewing gum that he shared with Julian Bashir during a baseball game in 2375. ("Take Me Out to the Holosuite" [DS9]).

scout ship, Starfleet. Small spacecraft used by the Federation. In 2375, Data fled the Ba'ku planet in a scout ship after a Son'a-directed energy weapon caused his neural systems to malfunction. (*Star Trek: Insurrection*). *The interior of Data's scout ship was a redress of the* Shuttlecraft Cochrane *built for* Star Trek: Voyager.

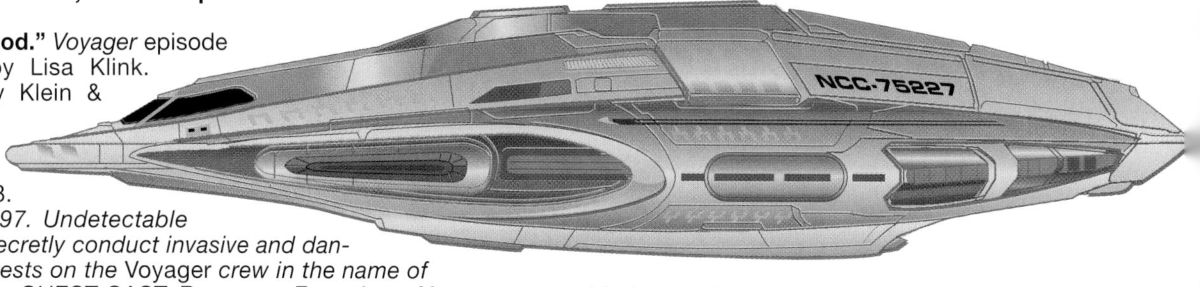

NCC-75227

scrambled eggs. Dish of beaten raw chicken eggs cooked in a pan. Neelix served scrambled eggs in the galley of the *Voyager*. ("Scientific Method" [VGR]).

scudi. Monetary unit used in the nation of Italy on Earth around the year 1502. ("Scorpion, Part I" [VGR]).

Sea of Clouds. Plain on Earth's **Moon**, impact site of the *Ranger VII* instrumented space probe in July 1964. Lunar resident Dorian Collins used to enjoy hiking out with her father across the Sea of Clouds to watch the sun come up. ("*Valiant*" [DS9]).

seamer. Small hand-held device used to bond fabrics by joining them along a line. Garak used a seamer in his tailor shop on Deep Space 9. ("Afterimage" [DS9]).

Second Fleet. Task force of the Federation **Starfleet**. In 2374, elements of the Second Fleet joined a special large attack force commanded by Captain Benjamin Sisko to retake station Deep Space 9 from Dominion control. ("Favor the Bold" [DS9]).

Second Klingon Dynasty. Period in Klingon history in which Emperor **Reclaw** ruled the empire. The Second Dynasty ended when General **K'Trelan** assassinated Emperor Reclaw and his family and plunged the empire into the Dark Time. ("You Are Cordially Invited" [DS9]).

Section 31. Secretive covert operations unit of the **Starfleet Intelligence** division. Established under the Starfleet charter, Section 31 was responsible for searching out and identifying extraordinary dangers to the Federation. Section 31 was also responsible for dealing with such threats, and did so quietly, often employing extralegal techniques. Starfleet Section 31 was in many ways similar to the Romulan **Tal Shiar** or the Cardassian **Obsidian Order**. In 2374, Section 31 operatives invited Dr. Julian Bashir to join the agency. ("Inquisition" [DS9]). Section 31 was responsible for developing and unleashing a deadly biological weapon against the Founders of the Dominion. ("When it Rains" [DS9]). This deliberate attempt at genocide nearly succeeded until Dr. Julian Bashir discovered a cure to the virus by forcibly invading the mind of Sloan. ("Extreme Measures" [DS9]).

sector.*

Sector 441. Stellar region in Federation space containing the **Briar Patch** and the **Ba'ku planet**. (*Star Trek: Insurrection*).

Sector 507. Region of space containing the Pelosa system. In 2375, the Dominion established a new ketracel-white storage facility in the Pelosa system. ("Treachery, Faith, and the Great River" [DS9]).

security access code.* Personal verbal passcode. Benjamin Sisko: "Sisko A-4-7-1." ("Blaze of Glory" [DS9]). "Sisko 7-1-green." ("Resurrection" [DS9]). Grand Nagus Zek: "3-7-4/1-5-6." ("Ferengi Love Songs" [DS9]). Kathryn Janeway: "Janeway pi-1-1-0." ("Concerning Flight" [VGR]). "Janeway 1-1-5-3-red: clearance level 10." ("The Omega Directive" [VGR]). Tom Paris: "Alpha

2-4-9." ("Distant Origin" [VGR]). Tuvok: "4-7-7-4." ("Worse Case Scenario" [VGR]). Seska: "Zeta-one." ("Worse Case Scenario" [VGR]). B'Elanna Torres: "Torres omega-phi-9-3." ("Day of Honor" [VGR]). Ahdar Ru'afo used "Delta-2-1." (*Star Trek: Insurrection*).

Sek. Son of **T'Pel** and Starfleet officer **Tuvok**. Between 2371 and 2374, Sek entered *Pon farr*, mated, and had a daughter, **T'Meni**, named for Tuvok's mother. ("Hunters" [VGR]).

self-replicating mine. Free-floating explosive device incorporating a replicator subsystem; invented by Rom at the beginning of the **Dominion** war. A field of self-replicating mines was extremely difficult to deactivate because any mines that were destroyed would immediately be replaced by duplicates. Starfleet personnel used self-replicating mines to blockade the **Bajoran wormhole** against a feared Dominion invasion in late 2373. ("Call to Arms" [DS9]). The mines were extremely effective at preventing further Dominion incursions into the Alpha Quadrant, although the Dominion already had substantial assets deployed in Cardassian space. Unfortunately, Cardassian technicians were able to develop a means of using antigraviton beams to render the mines' replicators ineffective. ("Behind the Lines" [DS9]). The minefield nevertheless remained operational long enough to delay a massive Dominion incursion, allowing Starfleet forces to retake Deep Space 9. ("Sacrifice of Angels" [DS9]). *Emmy Award–nominated* Star Trek: Deep Space Nine *set decorator Laura Richarz used large plastic drums originally sold as garden composters as the basis for Starfleet's self-replicating mines.*

Seltan carnosaur. Immense reptilian behemoth on the order of 300 meters tall. ("One Little Ship" [DS9]).

Sentinel, U.S.S. Federation starship. In 2375, Ensign Nog gave the *Sentinel*'s crew a phaser emitter in exchange for a graviton stabilizer. ("Treachery, Faith, and the Great River" [DS9]).

Seros. Planet in the Delta Quadrant. Seros was the homeworld to a civilization of technologically sophisticated humanoids. ("Revulsion" [VGR]).

Serosian ship. Small spacecraft of Serosian registry. A Serosian ship with a crew of six left Seros in mid-2373. The crew was murdered by **Dejaren**, the ship's HD-25 maintenance unit, who had experienced a serious malfunction. ("Revulsion" [VGR]).

Seska.* Undercover Cardassian operative who became a member of the *Voyager* crew. In 2371, shortly before leaving the ship, Seska discovered the existence of **Insurrection Alpha,** a holodeck training program. Seska rewrote the scenario to act as a trap to anyone who reopened the program's narrative parameters file. On stardate 50953.4, Tuvok and Tom Paris were ensnared in Seska's modified version of Insurrection Alpha until Captain Janeway was successful in reprogramming portions of the scenario. ("Worse Case Scenario" [VGR]).

Setlik III.* Planet. While at Setlik III in 2347, Miles O'Brien led two dozen men against the Barrica encampment, driving out an entire Cardassian regiment. ("Empok Nor" [DS9]).

Seven of Nine. (Jeri Ryan). **Borg** drone who left the collective and joined the crew of the Federation ***Starship Voyager*** in early 2374. ("Scorpion, Part II" [VGR]). Seven of Nine, who was Tertiary Adjunct of Unimatrix Zero One, was born a human female named **Annika Hansen** in 2348 at the Tendara colony on stardate 25479. Annika's parents, Erin Hansen and Magnus Hansen, were noted scientists who were last seen in the Omega Sector in 2356, having departed from station Deep Space 4 aboard the science vessel *Raven* on an expedition to the Delta Quadrant. The *Raven* encountered a Borg ship in B'omar space and crashed on a Class-M moon. Annika's parents were presumed killed or assimilated by the Borg in the incident, and Annika was assimilated at the age of six. ("The Raven" [VGR]). Seven of Nine was assigned as Borg liaison to Starfleet captain **Kathryn Janeway** in early 2374 when the collective formed an uneasy alliance with Janeway to defeat Species 8472. Seven was the only drone from her cube to survive the encounter that saw her ship destroyed when it attempted to assimilate *Voyager*. ("Scorpion, Part II" [VGR]). Thus separated from the collective, Seven's human physiology reasserted itself, and *Voyager* personnel removed most of Seven's Borg implants to increase her chances of survival. The use of dermaplastic grafts and follicle stimulation even gave her a nearly normal human appearance. ("The Gift" [VGR]). Having spent most of her life as a Borg drone, Seven of Nine did not at first consider herself to be human, objecting strongly to losing her Borg identity against her will. Her *Voyager* shipmates, including Captain Janeway, were nevertheless committed to helping her make what proved to be a difficult return to human society and to the alien concept of freedom. ("The Raven" [VGR]). At one point, she disobeyed a direct order from Janeway, believing disobedience to be in the best interests of the ship and crew. Seven found it frustrating to be punished for this action, after having been encouraged to exert her individuality. ("Prey" [VGR]). Human emotions such as anger and remorse also proved uncomfortable for her, as when she incorrectly believed herself to have been attacked by an Entharan weapons dealer on stardate 51658. ("Retrospect" [VGR]). Nevertheless, by late 2374, she found the thought of being

reassimilated by the Borg collective to be unappealing. ("Hope and Fear" [VGR]). Seven did not lose all of her Borg values, however. She shared the Borg sense of wonder at the discovery of **Omega molecule**s on stardate 51781. ("The Omega Directive" [VGR]). In early 2375, she found herself serving as a role model to a new Borg drone, designated **One**. Seven was successful in communicating her newfound personal values to One, including the sense of pride in individuality; she was saddened when One died. ("Drone" [VGR]). *Seven of Nine's first appearance was in "Scorpion, Part II" (VGR) when Jeri Ryan joined the* Voyager *cast at the beginning of the show's fourth season.*

Seventh Fleet. Federation **Starfleet** task force. In early 2374 the Seventh Fleet of the Federation engaged **Dominion** forces at the Tyra system. Of the 112 ships originally in the Seventh Fleet, only 14 survived the encounter at the Tyra system. ("A Time to Stand" [DS9], "Inquisition" [DS9]). The Seventh Fleet suffered further losses while assigned to protect Vulcan by intercepting Dominion forces at the Tibor Nebula. Nearly half of the fleet's remaining forces were lost en route at Sybaron. ("The Reckoning" [DS9]). In early 2375, the Seventh Fleet grouped at Kalandra to launch a new offensive based on information that the enemy was vulnerable there. ("Afterimage" [DS9]).

Seventh Tactical Wing. Fleet of Federation starships commanded by Captain Bennet. The Seventh Tactical Wing was formed in 2374 to fight in the war against the Dominion. ("Behind the Lines" [DS9]).

sex-change operation. Medical procedure performed to transform the physical characteristics of a person's body so that he or she may pass for another sex. In 2374, Quark was surgically transformed into a Ferengi female in an elaborate plan to convince powerful Ferengi Commerce Authority commissioner Nilva that Zek should be reinstated as Nagus. ("Profit and Lace" [DS9]).

Shabren's Fifth Prophecy. Ancient text in the **Bajoran** religion written after Shabren encountered an Orb of the **Prophets**. His fifth prophecy stated that if the **Evil One** is destroyed, it will bring about a thousand years of peace. This was to be the rebirth of **Bajor**, a Golden Age. ("The Reckoning" [DS9]).

"Shadows and Symbols." *Deep Space Nine* episode #152. Written by Ira Steven Behr & Hans Beimler. Directed by Allan Kroeker. Stardate 52152.6. *First aired in 1998. Ezri Dax accompanies the Siskos on an expedition to find the Orb of the Emissary, and Worf takes part in a dangerous mission to ensure Jadzia's entrance into the Klingon afterlife. Meanwhile, Kira single-handedly blockades the Romulan fleet to force them to remove weapons from one of Bajor's moons.* GUEST CAST: Jeffrey Combs as **Weyoun;** Brock Peters as **Sisko, Joseph;** Casey Biggs as **Damar/Wykoff, Dr.;** Megan Cole as **Cretak, Senator;** J. G. Hertzler as **Martok, General;** Barry Jenner as **Ross, Admiral;** Aron Eisenberg as **Nog;** Deborah Lacey as **Sisko, Sarah;** Lori Lively as **Siana;** Cuanhtemoc Sanchez as Bajoran crewman. SEE: **Bajoran impulse ship; Bajoran wormhole; Cretak, Senator; Dax, Audrid; Dax, Emony; Dax, Ezri; Dax, Jadzia; Derna; *Destiny, U.S.S.*; *gagh*; Hammer, Mike; Hovas, Legate; *Kiss Me, Deadly*; Kosst Amojan; Monac IV; Orb of the Emissary; Orb; Pah-wraiths; Prophets; Russell, Benny; Siana; Sisko, Sarah; solar plasma ejection; Spillane, Mickey; Tyree; water pack; Worf; Wykoff, Dr.**

Shakaar Edon.* Political leader on planet Bajor. Shakaar's relationship with Kira ended in 2373 after a visit to the Kenda shrine on Bajor revealed that they were not meant to walk the same path. ("Children of Time" [DS9]).

Shaw, George Bernard. (1856–1950). Playwright, journalist, and social critic from the nation of Great Britain on 19th- and 20th-century **Earth**. Valerie Archer had a book of Shaw's collected works in her quarters at Starfleet Headquarters in 2375. ("In the Flesh" [VGR]).

Shelby, Captain. Federation officer in command of the *U.S.S. Sutherland* in 2374. Jadzia Dax was a good friend of Captain Shelby. Captain Shelby owed Jadzia Dax a favor and so gave *Sutherland* crew member Lieutenant Atoa the day off to attend Dax's pre-wedding party on Deep Space 9. ("You Are Cordially Invited" [DS9]).

Shenandoah, U.S.S. Starfleet **runabout**, *Danube* class, assigned to starbase Deep Space 9. In 2374, on stardate 51597.2, Lieutenant Commanders Worf and Jadzia Dax took the *Shenandoah* on a mission to extract a Cardassian defector from the Dominion base on planet Soukara. The mission was a failure. ("Change of Heart" [DS9]). On stardate 51825, Ensign Nog and Jake Sisko took the *Shenandoah* from Starbase 257 on a mission to deliver an official diplomatic message to Grand Nagus Zek on Ferenginar. En route the vessel was attacked by Jem'Hadar fighters. The crew abandoned ship and were rescued by the ***Starship Valiant***. ("*Valiant*" [DS9]).

Shenara. Daughter of **Emperor Reclaw** of the **Second Klingon Dynasty**. In the traditional telling of the chronicle of the women in Sirella's family in modern times, Shenara was held to be Sirella's 23rd maternal grandmother. The actual 23rd maternal grandmother of Sirella was Karana, a concubine who had lived outside the imperial stables. ("You Are Cordially Invited" [DS9]).

Shepard, Riley Aldrin.* (David Drew Gallagher). Starfleet cadet, member of the elite **Red Squad**. In 2374, Shepard participated in a training cruise aboard the *U.S.S. Valiant,* which was caught behind enemy lines when the Dominion war broke out. When the ship's senior officers were killed in battle, cadet **Tim Watters** assumed command, assigning Shepard to the **conn**. Shepard and most of the crew were killed when Watters unwisely ordered an attack on a massive Dominion battleship. ("*Valiant*" [DS9]).

ShirKahr, U.S.S. Federation starship, *Miranda* class, Starfleet registry number NCC-31905. The *ShirKahr* fought in the combined fleet of allied Alpha Quadrant forces that invaded Cardassian space at the **Chin'toka System** in late 2374 and was destroyed by **orbital weapon platform**s employed by the Dominion. ("Tears of the Prophets" [DS9]). *Named for the Vulcan*

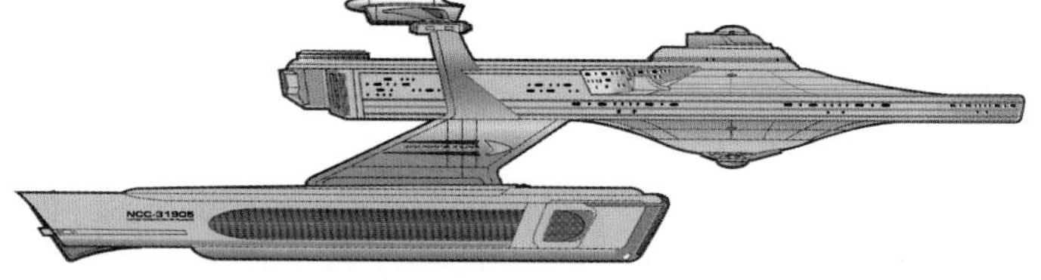

city that, in the animated episode "Yesteryear," was Spock's hometown. The name was not in dialog, seen only very faintly on the ship's hull in visual-effects scenes.

shri-tal. Cardassian tradition in which a dying person gives their secrets to their family to be used against their enemies. In 2373, **Legate Ghemor** observed *shri-tal* by revealing many Cardassian state secrets to Bajoran Militia officer **Kira Nerys**. Ghemor, who was secretly a member of the Cardassian underground movement, regarded Kira as something of a surrogate daughter, and therefore provided this intelligence bonanza to Bajoran and Starfleet authorities as a way to continue his fight against the Cardassian government. ("Ties of Blood and Water" [DS9]).

shroud. Personnel cloaking technology used by the **Jem'Hadar**. ("Rocks and Shoals" [DS9]).

Siana. (Lori Lively). Cardassian woman. Damar met Siana at a dinner in 2375 honoring Legate Hovas. Damar found Siana attractive. ("Shadows and Symbols" [DS9]).

Silven surprise. Beverage served at Quark's bar. ("*Valiant*" [DS9]).

silver blood. SEE: **mimetic life-form.**

"Simple Investigation, A." *Deep Space Nine* episode #115. Written by René Echevarria. Directed by John Kretchmer. No stardate given. *First aired in 1997. Odo falls in love with a mysterious woman visiting the station who turns out to be an undercover intelligence agent with no memory of her true identity.* GUEST CAST: Dey Young as **Arissa**; Nicholas Worth as **Sorm**; Brant Cotton as **Tauvid Rem**; John Durbin as **Traidy**; Randy Mulkey as Idanian #2. SEE: **Arissa; data crystal; dataport; Draim; Dunlap, Nigel; encryption lockout; Falcon; Finnea Prime; holodeck and holosuite programs: *Queen's Gambit, The*; Idanians; net-girl; Odo; Orion Syndicate; *Queen's Gambit, The*; *raktajino*; Risean tapestries; Sorm; Talarians; Tauvid Rem; Traidy; Wantsomore, Lady.** *Note: These cross-referenced items can all be found in the main body of the encyclopedia. This master entry for this episode was inadvertently omitted from the main body, so it is being printed here, in the addendum.*

Corbis

Sinatra, Frank. (1915–1998). Twentieth-century Earth entertainer. Sinatra described himself as a sophisticated "saloon singer" who defined the term "swingin'." Sinatra, who was arguably the greatest performer of American popular song, frequently sang in **Las Vegas** and also achieved wide success as a motion-picture actor. Singer **Vic Fontaine** said he was a friend of Sinatra's. ("His Way" [DS9]). SEE: ***From Here To Eternity.*** *Frank Sinatra's music was a source of inspiration to members of the* Star Trek: Deep Space Nine *graphics department.*

Singha refugee camp.* Internment facility for Bajoran nationals during the Cardassian occupation of Bajor. In 2346, Kira Meru, wife of a Bajoran farmer, was taken from her family at the camp to become a **comfort woman** on space station Terok Nor. ("Wrongs Darker Than Death or Night" [DS9]).

Sirella. (Shannon Cochran). Mistress of the House of Martok, wife of **General Martok**, daughter of Linkasa, and mother to the general's children. A confident, regal woman of strong convictions, Sirella was also a mercurial, arrogant, and prideful warrior. Sirella journeyed to Deep Space 9 on stardate 51247.5 to judge Jadzia Dax's worthiness to join the House of Martok. Sirella performed the marriage ceremony on the station and then welcomed Jadzia Dax as her daughter. ("You Are Cordially Invited" [DS9]). SEE: **Karana.** *Shannon Cochran previously played Kalita in "Preemptive Strike" (TNG) and "Defiant" (DS9).*

Sisko's.* Cajun restaurant in the city of **New Orleans** on Earth, owned by **Joseph Sisko**. Located near Armstrong Park. Known for Joseph's gumbo. **Benjamin Sisko** spent three months at Sisko's in early 2375 while he sought to adjust to the deaths he had witnessed in the Dominion war, including the loss of his friend, Jadzia Dax. During that time, Ben spent many hours entertaining diners with his heartfelt piano playing. ("Image in the Sand" [DS9]).

Sisko, Benjamin.* Starfleet officer and **Emissary** to the Bajoran **Prophets**. Ben Sisko, son of **Joseph Sisko** and **Sarah Sisko**, was born in 2332. ("Image in the Sand" [DS9]). In addition to excelling as an explorer, diplomat, and leader, one of Sisko's personal passions was the ancient Earth game of **baseball**, an interest he shared with **Kasidy Yates**. SEE: **Niners.** ("Take Me Out to the Holosuite" [DS9]). Perhaps Benjamin Sisko's greatest challenge was the **Dominion** war, which began in late 2373. In his role of the Emissary to the Bajoran people, Sisko felt compelled to recommend that the Bajoran government sign a nonaggression treaty with the **Dominion**, despite Starfleet objections. Shortly thereafter, Sisko and all other Starfleet personnel were ordered to abandon station **Deep Space 9**, and the facility was returned to Cardassian control. ("Call to Arms" [DS9]). Sisko was subsequently stationed at **Starbase 375**. He was assigned to a covert mission to pilot a captured Dominion spacecraft into Cardassian space to destroy a Dominion ketracel-white storage facility, the first major Starfleet victory in the brutal Dominion war. ("A Time to Stand" [DS9]). Sisko subsequently led a daring offensive into Dominion territory to recapture station Deep Space 9 in a successful effort to prevent a huge Dominion fleet from invading the **Alpha Quadrant**. Sisko's role as the Emissary was of unexpected value when he was able to convince the Prophets to intervene on behalf of the Bajoran people to destroy the Dominion fleet in the wormhole. ("Sacrifice of Angels" [DS9]). During the following months, Starfleet casualties in the conflict reached horrific proportions, prompting Sisko to believe that survival of the Federation depended on persuading the **Romulan** government to enter the war against the Dominion. Sisko, with the assistance of **Elim Garak**, effected the Romulan entry by falsifying evidence that the Dominion was planning to invade Romulan territory. Sisko regretted his illegal acts in the operation that cost at least two lives, but he firmly believed it necessary to the survival of not only the Federation, but the Klingon and Romulan empires as well. SEE: **Vreenak.** ("In the Pale Moonlight" [DS9]). Over the years Sisko grew to love Bajor. He began to think of it as a paradise and said that he hoped to make a home there someday. ("Favor the Bold" [DS9]). In the midst of the Dominion war, Sisko experienced an intense **Orb-shadow** vision, becoming a science-fiction magazine writer on Earth during the 1950s. Sisko, as author **Benny Russell**, wrote a remarkable novella about a future space station commander named Ben Sisko. Neither Sisko nor Russell was entirely sure of who was the dreamer, and who was the dream. ("Far Beyond the Stars" [DS9]). Sisko was honored with the Christopher Pike Medal of Valor for his role in the recapture of Deep Space 9 from Dominion control. He was subsequently instrumental in planning the daring attack on Cardassian forces that liberated the **Chin'toka System** from Dominion control. During that battle, his close friend **Jadzia Dax** was killed by Gul Dukat and a Pah-wraith. Sisko, who had seen the death of literally thousands during the terrible war, found it difficult to endure yet one more death, and he took a leave to return to Earth to visit his father. ("Tears of the Prophets" [DS9]). Sisko spent three months on Earth until a vision from the Prophets sent him to planet **Tyree** to search for the heretofore-unknown **Orb of the Emissary**. Sisko's search was made more urgent by the fact that his vision also contained the image of a mysterious woman named **Sarah Sisko**, whom Ben's father, Joseph, revealed was Ben's real mother. ("Image in the Sand" [DS9]). Sarah had in fact been controlled by a Bajoran prophet who had seen to it that Benjamin was born to become the Bajoran Emissary. When Benjamin became engaged to Kasidy Yates in 2375, the Sarah prophet warned him that he would know nothing but sorrow if he married Kasidy. Although Sisko took the prophet's warning seriously, he nevertheless married Kasidy in a quiet civil ceremony held aboard station Deep Space 9. ("'Til Death Do Us Part" [DS9]). Ben Sisko's remaining weeks as a corporeal human were dominated by the conclusion of the Dominion war. Shortly after the surrender of the Dominion, Benjamin Sisko returned to the **fire caves** on Bajor to confront **Kosst Amojan**. The evil **Pah-wraith** had seduced both Kai **Winn** and **Gul Dukat**, but neither was able to prevent Sisko from trapping the Pah-wraiths in the fire caves, thus ensuring the survival of not only the Bajoran people, but the Prophets themselves. His destiny fulfilled, Benjamin Sisko left the realm of linear existence and became one with the Bajoran Prophets. ("What You Leave Behind" [DS9]).

Sisko, Jake.* Son of Starfleet officer and Bajoran religious figure **Benjamin Sisko**. In late 2373 Jake Sisko became an official correspondent for the **Federation News Service**. He reported on events on station Deep Space 9 during the **Dominion** war, even risking his life by remaining on the station after the Federation withdrew from the facility. ("Call to Arms" [DS9]). Jake later sold a book of stories about life on Deep Space 9 under Dominion rule to the Federation News Service. ("You Are Cordially Invited" [DS9]). Jake and his grandfather, Joseph, accompanied Ben Sisko on an expedition to **Tyree** in early 2375 to find the **Orb of the Emissary**. ("Image in the Sand" [DS9]).

Sisko, Joseph.* Owner of a restaurant in the city of **New Orleans** on Earth; father of Benjamin Sisko. In June 2331, Joseph Sisko met a woman named Sarah at Jackson Square in New Orleans. The two fell in love and were married in August 2331. **Sarah Sisko** gave birth to Benjamin in 2332. Their marriage of two years ended when Sarah left her husband Joseph two days after Ben's first birthday in 2333. Joseph looked for her for years, finally learning that she had died in 2336. Joseph later remarried, but he never told his son, Benjamin, about his mother's true identity. Joseph told Ben that his second wife was Ben's mother. ("Image in the Sand" [DS9]). In 2374, Joseph left Earth for the first time. He journeyed to station Deep Space 9 to visit his son Benjamin and his grandson, Jake. ("Far Beyond the Stars" [DS9]).

Sisko, Sarah. (Deborah Lacey). Mother of Benjamin Sisko, former wife of Joseph Sisko. ("Image in the Sand" [DS9]). In 2331, Sarah had been possessed by a Bajoran **Prophet** to ensure that she would marry Joseph Sisko and that she would have a son. That son, Benjamin, was destined to be the Emissary. The Prophet left her when Ben was one year old. Sarah Sisko then left Joseph because she hadn't chosen him in the first place. ("Shadows and Symbols" [DS9]). Sarah subsequently became a holo-photographer in Australia. She died in a hovercraft accident in 2336. ("Image in the Sand" [DS9]). The Sarah prophet cared for Benjamin and in late 2375 tried to warn him that his plan to marry Kasidy Yates would bring him sorrow. ("'Til Death Do Us Part" [DS9]).

Sitak, Admiral. (Ericka Klein). Senior Starfleet officer. In 2374, Sitak was one of the admirals who approved Captain Benjamin Sisko's daring plan to retake station Deep Space 9 from Dominion forces. ("Favor the Bold" [DS9]). *Sitak was Vulcan.*

Sitak, U.S.S. Federation starship, *Miranda* class. In 2374, the *Sitak* was destroyed in the daring—and costly—mission to retake station Deep Space 9 from Dominion control, preventing a massive incursion of Dominion ships into the Alpha Quadrant. ("Sacrifice of Angels" [DS9]).

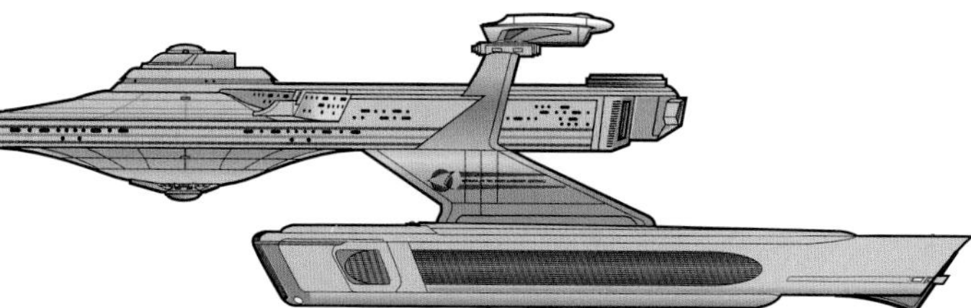

skeletal lock. Unorthodox technique for **transporter** operation improvised by B'Elanna Torres in 2373. Torres, unable to establish a transporter lock by conventional means, was able to use sensors to scan for the minerals in the transport subjects' bodies. ("Scorpion, Part I" [VGR]).

skimmer. Military vehicle used by the Cardassian military during the occupation of Bajor. ("Ties of Blood and Water" [DS9]).

Sloan. (William Sadler). Highly placed operative in **Section 31**, the covert operations department of Starfleet Intelligence. In 2374, Sloan led a team of agents of Section 31 that set up an elaborate holographic simulation designed to determine Julian Bashir's loyalty to Starfleet. Sloan was impressed by Bashir and invited him to become an agent for Section 31. ("Inquisition" [DS9]). Sloan was instrumental in the development and use of a genocidal disease virus intended to wipe out the Founders of the Dominion. ("When it Rains..." [DS9]). Luther Sloan committed suicide in late 2375, in an unsuccessful attempt to prevent Julian Bashir from forcibly extracting technical information about the virus from Sloan's brain. ("Extreme Measures" [DS9]).

slug steak. Culinary dish popular on the Ferengi homeworld. Ishka enjoyed slug steaks. ("Ferengi Love Songs" [DS9]).

Slug-o-Cola. Lime-green beverage that was very popular on Ferenginar. Made with 43 percent live algae, Slug-o-Cola was known by its traditional advertising slogan proclaiming it to be, "The slimiest cola in the galaxy." The Slug-o-Cola company was run by **Nilva**, a powerful commissioner with the Ferengi Commerce Authority. In 2374, in an effort to take advantage of profit opportunities in the rapidly developing market of female consumers, Nilva considered a new slogan that would remind women that drinking his product would, "Keep your teeth a sparkling shade of green." Slug-o-Cola's chief competitor was **Eelwasser**. ("Profit and Lace" [DS9]).

Smeet. Former **grand nagus** of the **Ferengi** Alliance. Smeet was the only nagus to be assassinated while in office. He and his first clerk were killed after a huge plummet in the Ferengi financial market. ("Ferengi Love Songs" [DS9]). *We don't know when Smeet served as nagus, although it was before Zek's term.*

Smith, Reginald. News reporter for the British Radio Network on Earth during that planet's second world war. ("The Killing Game, Part I" [VGR]).

snail steak. Grilled slices of succulent molluskoids much favored by the Ferengi. ("Profit and Lace" [DS9]).

Sojef. (Daniel Hugh Kelly). Community leader on the **Ba'ku planet** in 2375. Sojef didn't want his son Artim to get too interested in Data because his people shunned advanced technology. (*Star Trek: Insurrection*). *Actor Daniel Hugh Kelly also played astronaut Eugene (Gene) Cernan, commander of Apollo 17 and lunar module pilot on Apollo 10, in the 1998 HBO miniseries* From the Earth to the Moon.

solar plasma ejection. Prominence of superheated ionized gas projecting hundreds of millions of kilometers away from the surface of a star. In 2375, General Martok, piloting a Klingon bird-of-prey, skimmed the surface of the star Monac, firing an electromagnetic pulse, creating a solar plasma ejection. The prominence vaporized a Dominion orbital shipyard in the Monac system, along with several Jem'Hadar attack ships. ("Shadows and Symbols" [DS9]).

"Soldiers of the Empire." *Deep Space Nine* episode #119. Written by Ronald D. Moore. Directed by LeVar Burton. No stardate given. *First aired in 1997. On a mission for the Klingon Empire, Worf realizes that his friend General Martok may no longer be fit to lead.* GUEST CAST: J.G. Hertzler as **Martok, General**; David Graf as **Leskit**; Rick Worthy as **Kornan**; Sandra Nelson as **Tavana**; Scott Leva as **Ortakin**; Aron Eisenberg as **Nog**. SEE: **autosuture; *B'Moth, I.K.S.*; emitter stage; fleet liaison officer; intelligence officer; Klingon Defense Force; Klingons; Kornan; Leskit; *mahk-cha*; Martok, General; Ortakin; prefire chamber; *Rotarran, I.K.S.*; safety protocol; stewed bok-rat liver; Tavana; Tong Beak Nebula; *tova'dok*; Warrior's Anthem; Worf.**

Solis, Vedek. Bajoran spiritual leader. In late 2374, Solis was detained briefly for violation of regulations prohibiting fund-raising on the Promenade of station Deep Space 9 without a license. ("Tears of the Prophets" [DS9]).

Solok. (Greg Wagrowsky). Starfleet officer. Captain of the Federation starship ***U.S.S. T'Kumbra*** in 2375. Solok, who attended Starfleet Academy with **Benjamin Sisko**, took considerable pleasure in what he felt to be the superior nature of his Vulcan heritage over those of his classmates. Solok, displaying uncharacteristic pride, went out of his way to conduct such demonstrations throughout his Starfleet career. When Solok's ship put into port at Deep Space 9 in early 2375, Solok organized a baseball team from his crew, in hopes of beating Ben Sisko at Sisko's favorite sport. Solok's team, the **Logicians**, beat the Deep Space **Niners** in a game held on the station's holodeck, leaving Solok puzzled at the joy exhibited by Sisko and his team over the simple pleasure of the sport. ("Take Me Out to the Holosuite" [DS9]).

Somata oil. Lubricant often warmed and used in massages. ("Resurrection" [DS9]).

Son'a body enhancement facility. Area aboard a **Son'a ship** where the chronically discohesive physiognomies of Son'a individuals received elaborate surgical facial and body rejuvenation therapies. (*Star Trek: Insurrection*). *The body enhancement facility set was a re-dress of the Museum of Kyrian Heritage set built for "Living Witness" (VGR).*

Son'a collector ship. Specialized science spacecraft constructed for the purpose of collecting **metaphasic radiation** particles from the ring structure of the **Ba'ku planet** in 2375. Ahdar Ru'afo was killed when the collector's autodestruct systems were engaged. (*Star Trek: Insurrection*).

Son'a Command. Operational authority for Son'a spaceflight operations. (*Star Trek: Insurrection*).

Son'a ship. Warp-driven spacecraft used by the Son'a. Son'a ships confronted the *Sovereign*-class *Enterprise*-E in 2375 at the Ba'ku planet in the Briar Patch. (*Star Trek: Insurrection*). *The Son'a ships were designed by illustrator John Eaves under the direction of production designer Herman Zimmerman. (See following page)*

Son'a shuttle. Small spacecraft capable of atmospheric flight. Son'a shuttles were capable of launching autonomously piloted isolinear-tag implanting drones. (*Star Trek: Insurrection*).

Son'a. Spacefaring humanoid civilization. The Son'a were a nomadic and largely hedonistic people who lived in opulence and coveted such material objects as jewels and precious metals. They were originally from the **Ba'ku planet**, but joined with offlanders around 2275 in an unsuccessful bid to take control of the idyllic **Ba'ku** society. The Ba'ku elders banished the renegades, who later called themselves the Son'a. In 2325, the Son'a conquered and enslaved the **Tarlac** and **Ellora** peoples. By 2375, genetic anomalies prevented the Son'a from procreation. They used genetic manipulation and other cosmetic techniques to extend life and physical appearance, but they knew they were

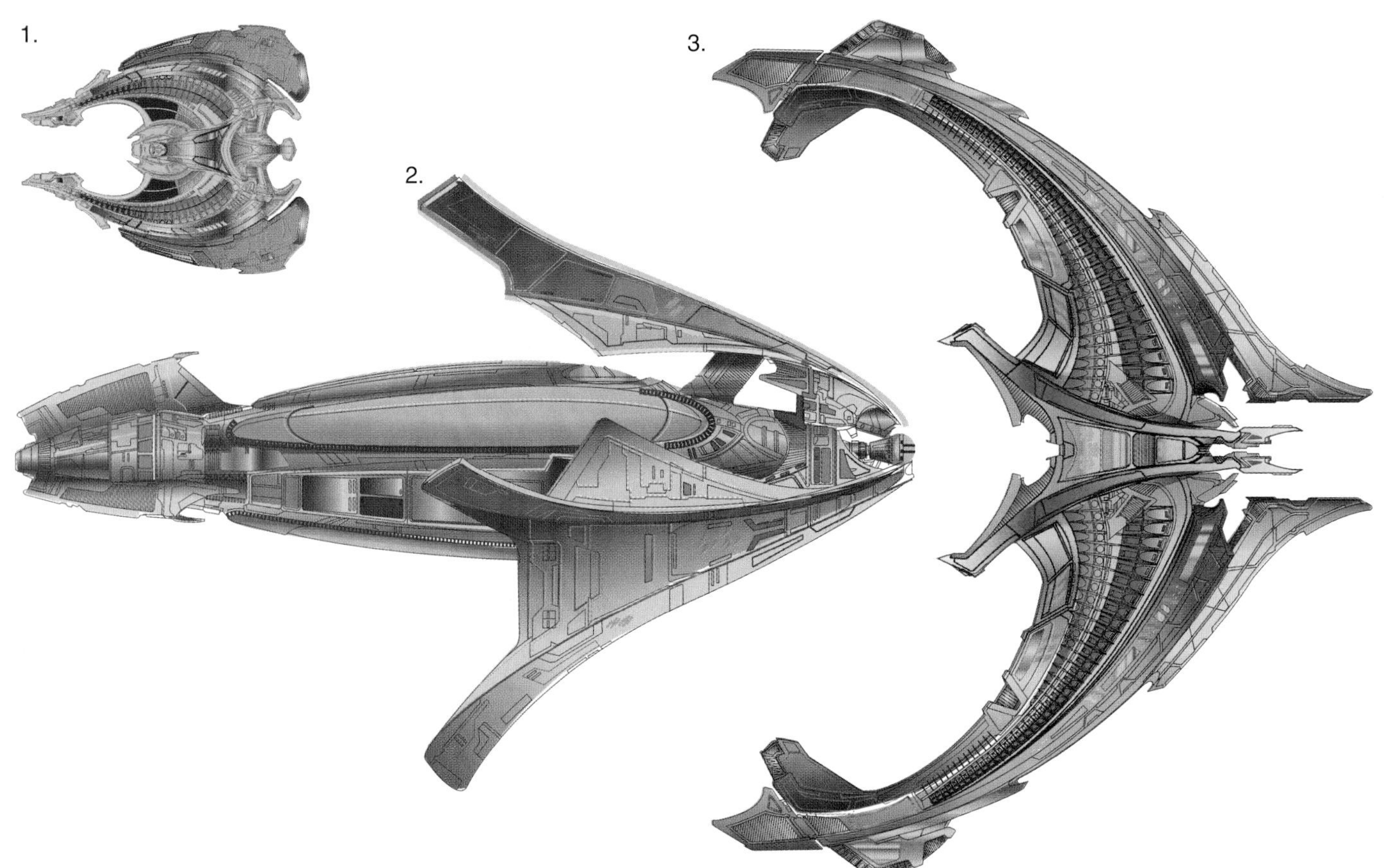

Son'a spacecraft. 1) Son'a scout ship; capable of atmospheric flight. 2) Son'a collector ship; designed to harvest metaphasic particles. 3) Son'a ship; designed for both science and tactical operations. *Not to scale.*

a dying society. In a desperate second attempt to take control of their old homeworld, the Son'a, led by **Ahdar Ru'afo**, allied themselves in 2375 with renegade Starfleet officer **Admiral Matthew Dougherty**. Ru'afo and Dougherty had hoped to abduct the entire Ba'ku population, some 600 individuals, without their knowledge by using a holoship, clearing the Ba'ku planet for Son'a use. After Captain Jean-Luc Picard of the *Starship Enterprise*-E stopped Ru'afo's plan, at least some of the surviving Son'a found themselves cautiously accepted back into Ba'ku society. (*Star Trek: Insurrection*).

"Sons and Daughters." *Deep Space Nine* episode #127. Written by Bradley Thompson & David Weddle. Directed by Jesús Salvador Treviño. No stardate given. *Alexander turns up as one of the crew of Martok's ship while Worf acts as first officer. Tora Ziyal returns to the station. This episode marked the first appearance of Alexander on* Deep Space Nine *and the first appearance of Marc Worden as an adult Alexander* GUEST CAST: Marc Worden as **Rozhenko, Alexander**; Marc Alaimo as **Gul Dukat**; J. G. Hertzler as **Martok, General**; Melanie Smith as **Tora Ziyal**; Casey Biggs as **Damar**; Sam Zeller as **Ch'Targh**; Gabrielle Union as **N'Garen.** SEE: ***bat-LEH;*** **bekk; Cardassian Institute of Art; Ch'Pok; Ch'Targh; Donatu V; Doran; Dukat, Gul;** ***grapok*** **sauce; ice cream;** ***kar'takin*****; Katogh; Koth; Larna;** ***maj-Kkah*****;** ***Martok degh, to-Duq degh, bat-LEH degh, mat-LEH degh;*** **Martok, General;** ***mat-LEH*****; N'Garen; Nane; Napart Malor; Norpin falcon;** ***Par'tok*****;** ***qu'vatlh; ramufta*****;** ***Rotarran, I.K.S.*****; Rozhenko, Alexander; Rozhenko, Helena; Tanas, General;** ***to-Duq*****; Topek; Tora Ziyal; Tse'Dek; Valonnan school;** ***Vor'nak*****;** ***wachk ihw, wachk kkor-duh*****; wedding: Klingon; Worf;** ***yih-Ghom-HAH.***

"Sons of Mogh, The." Inhabitants of the planet **Gaia** in an alternate timeline. In this alternate reality, the Sons of Mogh was a group of Gaians who chose to live their lives according to Klingon warrior tradition. They revered the memory of Worf, a Klingon warrior who served aboard the *Starship Defiant*. Some of the Sons of Mogh were actually descended from Worf. ("Children of Time" [DS9]).

Soukara. Planet in Cardassian space that was the location of a **Dominion** base. On stardate 51597.2, Lieutenant Commanders Worf and Jadzia Dax took the *Runabout Shenandoah* to Soukara on a mission to extract Starfleet operative **Glinn Lasaran**. The mission was a failure and Lasaran was killed on Soukara. ("Change of Heart" [DS9]). In late 2374, **Vreenak** of the Romulan Senate made a trip to the Dominion base on Soukara for a diplomatic meeting with Weyoun. ("In the Pale Moonlight" [DS9]).

"Sound of Her Voice, The." *Deep Space Nine* episode #149. Teleplay by Ronald D. Moore. Story by Pam Pietroforte. Directed by Winrich Kolbe. Stardate 51948.3. *First aired in 1998. Sisko and the crew of the* Defiant *race to save an unseen Starfleet captain stranded alone on an oxygen-starved planet. This episode provides a (brief) glimpse of the* Defiant *shuttlebay.* GUEST CAST: Debra Wilson as the voice of **Cusak, Captain Lisa**; Penny Johnson as **Yates, Kasidy.** SEE: **Andor; Beta Quadrant;** ***Chaffee, Shuttlecraft*****; corn chowder; Cusak, Lisa; Denevan crystals; dilithium; exogenic field; Gatsby, Commander; holodeck and holosuite programs: Paris in 1928; Irish wake; krada legs; Lurians; metreon radiation; Nausicaans;** ***Olympia, U.S.S.*****; planetary classification system: Class-L; Rutharian sector; tri-ox compound; Vega; Yates, Kasidy.**

soy meal. Food of ground beans from the Earth plant *Glycine max.* Soy meal could be moistened, formed into patties, and served fried. ("Unforgettable" [VGR]).

space walk. To leave the artificial environment of a spacecraft, entering the microgravity vacuum of deep space. Space walks are often performed for exterior maintenance on a space vehicle or for scientific and exploratory missions. Most humanoid species require the use of an **environmental suit** during such extravehicular activities. ("Day of Honor" [VGR]).

Species 116. Borg designation for a technologically sophisticated humanoid civilization from the Delta Quadrant. They were gifted linguists, with some individuals knowing several thousand languages. Centuries ago, the Borg first tried to assimilate Species 116, but they outwitted and eluded them until 2374, when the Borg assimilated all but about 20,000 individuals. **Arturis** was a member of Species 116 who had escaped assimilation. ("Hope and Fear" [VGR]).

Species 149. Borg designation for a technologically sophisticated civilization possessing advanced medical science. The Borg assimilated Species 149, obtaining from them a technique that allowed reactivation of "dead" Borg drones by using modified nanoprobes. ("Mortal Coil" [VGR]).

Species 218. Borg designation for **Talaxians**. ("The Raven" [VGR]).

Species 259. Borg designation for a technologically advanced omnicordial life-form that inhabited Galactic cluster 3. The Borg assimilated Species 259 and gained a pattern-duplication design from them that they incorporated into their **autonomous regeneration sequencers**. ("The Gift" [VGR]).

Species 262. A primitive Delta Quadrant civilization assimilated by the Borg around 2145. The **Borg** took an interest in Species 262's mythology, which mentioned a powerful substance that could burn the sky. The substance may have been the **Omega molecule**. ("The Omega Directive" [VGR]).

Species 263. A Delta Quadrant civilization, regarded as primitive by the Borg. Species 263 believed that the **Omega molecule** was a drop of blood from their creator. ("The Omega Directive" [VGR]).

Species 329. Borg designation for the **Kazon** people. ("Mortal Coil" [VGR]).

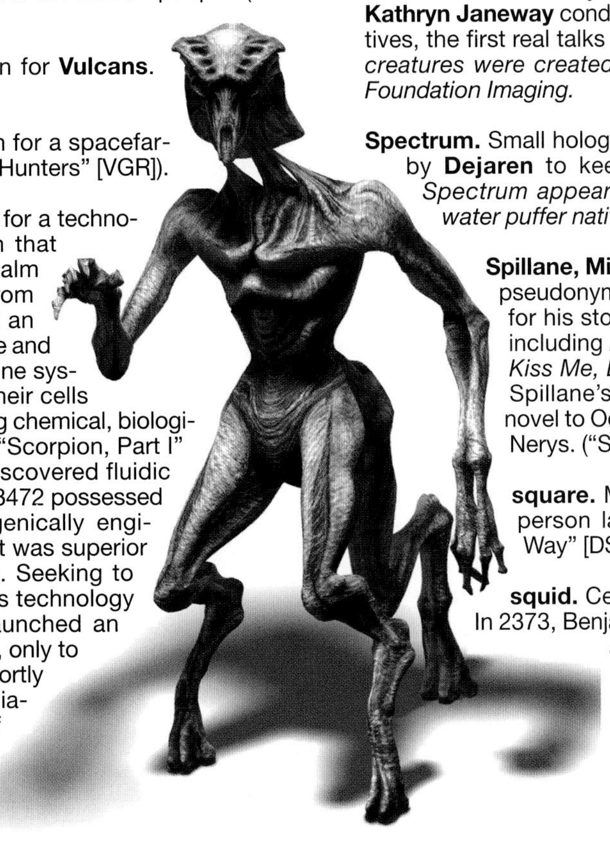

Species 3259. Borg designation for **Vulcans**. ("The Raven" [VGR]).

Species 5174. Borg designation for a spacefaring Delta Quadrant civilization. ("Hunters" [VGR]).

Species 8472. Borg designation for a technologically sophisticated life-form that existed in a **fluidic space** realm located in a dimension apart from our universe. Species 8472 had an extremely dense genetic structure and an extraordinarily powerful immune system. Anything that penetrated their cells was instantly destroyed, including chemical, biological, or technological intruders. ("Scorpion, Part I" [VGR]). In late 2373 the **Borg** discovered fluidic space and learned that Species 8472 possessed organic spacecraft and a biogenically engineered weapons technology that was superior to anything known to the Borg. Seeking to assimilate this civilization and its technology into the collective, the Borg launched an attack on the fluidic space realm, only to be repulsed by Species 8472. Shortly thereafter, 8472 launched a retaliatory strike, sending hundreds of powerful **bioships** into the Delta Quadrant with the goal of eliminating all life-forms from the galaxy. The 8472 assault was halted when the Borg obtained **nanoprobe** weapons technology from the crew of the ***Starship Voyager***, a weapons system against which Species 8472 had no effective defense at the time. ("Scorpion, Part II" [VGR]). One 8472 ship was sufficiently damaged in the battle that it was not able to return home to flu-

idic space. This lone vessel was pursued by **Hirogen** hunters, and its crew killed, despite an effort by the crew of the *Starship Voyager* to lend humanitarian assistance to the last surviving 8472 individual. ("Prey" [VGR]). The Species 8472 hostility toward the humanoid societies of the **Milky Way Galaxy** was evidently the result of *Voyager*'s alliance with the Borg in 2374. Fearing that the Alpha Quadrant powers were planning a devastating attack into fluidic space, Species 8472 sought to better prepare itself by gathering detailed intelligence on Starfleet operations and humanoid societies. To do so, Species 8472 constructed a series of elaborate re-creations of key Alpha Quadrant locales, including **Starfleet Headquarters**, for the purposes of training 8472 operatives to infiltrate Federation society. This training was considered necessary because of the alien biology, culture, and values of the humanoid societies. For example, Species 8472 saw literature, art, and music as alien concepts. They considered humanoid genetics to be impure and felt deeply threatened by the violent tendencies of many humanoid cultures. They even found the nonfluidic spatial environment difficult to deal with. Some of Species 8472's fears were allayed in 2375 when *Starship Voyager* captain **Kathryn Janeway** conducted negotiations with 8472 representatives, the first real talks between the two cultures. *Species 8472 creatures were created as computer-generated renderings by Foundation Imaging.*

Spectrum. Small holographic character, a pet fish programmed by **Dejaren** to keep him company. ("Revulsion" [VGR]). *Spectrum appeared to be a spiny porcupine fish, a salt water puffer native to Earth's tropical seas.*

Spillane, Mickey.* Popular 20th-century Earth writer, pseudonym for Frank Morrison. Spillane was known for his stories of fictional detective Mike Hammer, including ***I, the Jury*** ("Profit and Loss" [DS9]) and *Kiss Me, Deadly*. Miles O'Brien, who was a fan of Spillane's work, recommended a Mike Hammer novel to Odo, who in turn recommended one to Kira Nerys. ("Shadows and Symbols" [DS9]).

square. Mid-20th century Earth slang term for a person lacking up-to-date sophistication. ("His Way" [DS9]). SEE: **Clyde, Harvey.**

squid. Cephalopod life-form indigenous to Earth. In 2373, Benjamin Sisko prepared a meal of squid with a sauce of puréed tube grubs. Squid was Nog's favorite Earth food. ("Blaze of Glory" [DS9]).

squill. Plant which grew only on the planet Balancar. Syrup of squill was made from this plant. ("The Magnificent Ferengi" [DS9]).

Srivani. Technologically advanced civilization of androgynous humanoids. The Srivani had submolecular technology well beyond that of the Federation in the late 24th century. Around stardate 51244, about 50 Srivani scientists, including Alzen and Takar, conducted a series of invasive medical tests on the crew of the Federation starship *Voyager* without the knowledge or consent of the experimental subjects. These tests involved genetic markers that caused severe mutations, some of which proved lethal. The Srivani, who went to considerable lengths to avoid detection, claimed their data were to be used to help cure physical and psychological disorders that afflicted millions of people, but the *Voyager* crew refused to consent to the tests. Once the Srivanian activity was discovered, *Voyager* captain Janeway purposefully steered her ship into a binary pulsar to force them off of her ship. ("Scientific Method" [VGR]). *The name of these people is from the script only and was not mentioned in dialog.*

Star Trek: Insurrection. Screenplay by Michael Piller. Story by Rick Berman & Michael Piller. Directed by Jonathan Frakes. No stardate given. *Original theatrical release date: 1998. Picard and the crew of the* Enterprise-*E defy the Federation by preventing a peace-loving people from being forcibly relocated from a planet that possesses remarkable rejuvenating properties. This was the ninth* Star Trek *theatrical movie, the third featuring the* Star Trek: The Next Generation *cast, and the second film directed by Jonathan Frakes.* CAST: Patrick Stewart as **Picard, Jean-Luc**; Jonathan Frakes as **Riker, William T.**; Brent Spiner as **Data**; LeVar Burton as **La Forge, Geordi**; Michael Dorn as **Worf**; Gates McFadden as **Crusher, Beverly**; Marina Sirtis as **Troi, Deanna**; F. Murray Abraham as **Ru'afo, Ahdar**; Donna Murphy as **Anij**; Anthony Zerbe as **Dougherty, Admiral Matthew**; Gregg Henry as **Gallatin**; Daniel Hugh Kelly as **Sojef**; Michael Welch as **Artim**; Mark Deakins as **Tournel**; Stephanie Niznik as **Perim, Kell**; Michael Horton as Daniels; Bruce French as Son'a Officer #1; Breon Gorman as **Curtis, Lieutenant**; John Hostetter as **Adislo, Hars**; Rick Worthy as Elloran Officer #1; D. Elliot Woods as Starfleet Officer; Jennifer Tung as Female Ensign; Raye Birk as Son'a Doctor; Peggy Miley as **Cuzar, Regent**; Claudette Nevens as Son'a Officer #2, Greg Poland as Elloran Officer #2; Kenneth Lane Edwards as Ensign; Joseph Ruskin as Son'a Officer #3; Zachary Williams as Ba'ku Child; McKenzie Westmore as Ba'ku Woman; Rick Avery as Stunt Coordinator; Stunt Players: Chris Antonucci, Jane Austin, Brian Avery, Joni Avery, Mike Avery, Gary Baxley, Hunter Baxley, Chris Howell, Richard L. Blackwell, Steve Blalock, Joey Box, Eddie Braun, Tony Brubaker, Zane Cassidy, Lauro Chartrand, Eliza Coleman, Scott Allan Cook, Mondy Cox, Charlie Croughwell, Joshua Croughwell, Phil Culotta, Mark DeAlessandro, Mark Donaldson, Christopher Doyle, Kiante Elam, Eurlyhne Epper-Woldman, Corey Eubanks, Tabby Hanson, Jeffrey S. Jensen, Julius LeFlore, Steven Lambert, Irvin E. Lewis, Clint Lilley, Kurt Lott, Diana R. Lupo, Eddie Mathews, Buck McDancer, Sonia Jo McDancer, James Minor, John Nowak, Chris O'Hara, Ian Quinn, T.J. Rigby, Denise Lynne Roberts, Robby Robinson, Spiro Razatos, Dennis Scott, Michelle Sebek, Paul Sklar, Mike Smith, Jeff Smolek, Monica Staggs, Warren A. Stevens, Tim Trella, Mark Wagner, Jennifer Watson, Gary Wayton, Webster Whinery, Brian J. Williams, Darlene Williams, Eddie Yansik. SEE: **Adislo, Hars; ahdar; Anij; Artim; Br'er Rabbit; Ba'ku planet; Ba'ku rhyl; Ba'ku; baldric; balsamic vinaigrette; Beethoven, Ludwig van; Briar Patch; Bussard collector; captain's yacht; chromodynamic shield; *Cousteau*; Curtis, Lieutenant; Cuzar, Regent; Data; Dougherty, Admiral Matthew; drone; duck blind; Ellora; *Enterprise*-E, *U.S.S.*; Evora; Gal'na; Gallatin, Subahdar; Gilbert and Sullivan; *gorch*; Goren system; *H.M.S. Pinafore*; Hanoran II; holodeck and holosuite programs: Ba'ku village, Son'a ship bridge; holoship; isolation suit; isolinear tag; isolytic subspace weapon; isomagnetic disintegrator; *jak'tahla*; kelbonite; ketracel-white; Khitomer Accords; kolar beast; La Forge, Geordi; library; mambo; manual steering column; Manzar colony; matter/antimatter reaction chamber; McCauley, Ensign; metaphasic radiation; metreon gas; Nara, Lieutenant; Nel Bato Conference; offlander; Perim, Kell; Picard, Jean-Luc; Riker Maneuver; Riker, William T.; Ro'tin; Ru'afo, Ahdar; scout ship, Starfleet; Sector: 441; security access code; Sojef; Son'a body enhancement facility; Son'a collector ship; Son'a Command; Son'a ship; Son'a shuttle; Son'a; subahdar; subspace phenomena: subspace tear; subspace technology: subspace weapon; tachyon; Tarlac; tetryon pulse launcher; thermolytic reaction; *Ticonderoga, U.S.S.*; torque sensor; Tournel; transporter inhibitor; Troi, Deanna; ultritium; Worf.**

starbase.*

Starbase 53. Federation station. In 2374, Section 31 operatives told Julian Bashir that he was to be taken to Starbase 53 for questioning. ("Inquisition" [DS9]).

Starbase 257. Point of departure for the *Runabout Shenandoah* prior to a diplomatic mission to Ferenginar. ("*Valiant*" [DS9]).

Starbase 375. Station located near Cardassian space. In early 2374, Admiral Ross transferred Benjamin Sisko from command of the *Defiant* to a desk job at starbase 375. A Jem'Hadar warship, captured in 2373, was held at Starbase 375 and refurbished for use in a covert Starfleet mission against the Dominion in early 2374. ("A Time to Stand" [DS9], "Behind the Lines" [DS9]). *Starbase 375 was a re-use of the Regula I Space Laboratory model first seen in* Star Trek II: The Wrath of Kahn.

Starbase 621. Station where a special jury was to have been convened for arraignment of Gul Dukat on war crimes charges in 2374. ("Waltz" [DS9]).

Starfleet Academy.* Training college for Starfleet personnel. The required curriculum at the academy included survival classes. ("Displaced" [VGR]). Third-year requirements included a six-week course of actual **space walk**s so that cadets could become used to extravehicular activity. ("Day of Honor" [VGR]). Also offered was a class in **temporal mechanics**. ("Year of Hell, Part II" [VGR]). The Launching Pad was a favorite watering hole for cadets after class. ("Take Me Out to the Holosuite" [DS9]).

Starfleet brat. Slang term for a child whose parents are both career Starfleet officers, and who grew up aboard Starfleet spacecraft or at Starfleet facilities. Valerie Archer described herself as a Starfleet brat. ("In the Flesh" [VGR]).

Starfleet General Orders and Regulations*:

Directive 010. "Before engaging alien species in battle...any and all attempts to make first contact and achieve a nonmilitary solution must be made." ("In the Flesh" [VGR]).

Omega Directive. Requires the captain of a starship to notify Starfleet Command immediately upon detection of an **Omega molecule** and authorizes use of any means necessary to destroy it, even at the cost of violating the **Prime Directive**. ("The Omega Directive" [VGR]).

Regulation 121, Section A. Authorizes the **chief medical officer** of a starship to relieve the **captain** of command if the captain is mentally or emotionally unfit. ("Year of Hell, Part II" [VGR]).

Regulation 476-9. "All away teams must report to the bridge at least once every 24 hours." ("Once Upon a Time" [VGR]).

Security Protocol 28, Subsection D. In the event of hostile takeover of a starship, the **Emergency Medical Hologram** is to deactivate and wait for rescue. ("Message in a Bottle" [VGR]).

Special Order 66715. Grants the **Starfleet Internal Affairs Department** authority to neutralize security threats to the Federation by whatever means necessary. ("Inquisition" [DS9]).

Starfleet Headquarters.* Part of **Starfleet Command** in the San Francisco area of Earth's North American continent. Located near the Federation Council building, Starfleet Headquarters included an Astrophysics center and the Starfleet Medical Complex. The officers' club at Starfleet Headquarters was the Quantum Cafe. There was also a Vulcan nightclub just around the corner from headquarters. **Boothby** was the groundskeeper (and sage) for Starfleet Headquarters throughout much of the 24th century. **Species 8472** created an incredibly detailed replica of Starfleet Headquarters, including its inhabitants, as part of its preparations for an intelligence-gathering program against the Federation in 2375. ("In the Flesh" [VGR]). Starfleet Headquarters was seriously damaged in an attack by Breen forces during the Dominion war in late 2375. ("The Changing Face of Evil" [DS9]). *Starfleet Headquarters exteriors in "In the Flesh" were filmed at the Tillman Water Reclamation plant in Van Nuys, California.*

Starfleet Intelligence. Branch of the **Starfleet** tasked with keeping the Federation Council and Starfleet Command informed of activities by alien powers affecting the interests of the **United Federation of Planets**. Perhaps the least-known part of Starfleet Intelligence was the **Section 31** covert intelligence unit, which operated independently, without direct executive oversight, to identify and neutralize serious threats to the Federation. ("Inquisition" [DS9]).

Starfleet Internal Affairs Department. Unit of the Federation **Starfleet** responsible for investigating allegations of wrongdoing by Starfleet personnel. Internal Affairs reported directly to the **Federation Council**. Operatives of the **Section 31** covert-intelligence unit represented themselves as being part of Internal Affairs in 2374 when investigating Julian Bashir. ("Inquisition" [DS9]).

Starfleet News Service. SEE: **Federation News Service**.

Starfleet.* Interstellar exploratory, defensive, and scientific agency of the **United Federation of Planets**. The Federation Starfleet suffered tremendous losses during the terrible **Dominion** war, in which the Federation allied itself with numerous other **Alpha Quadrant** powers to repel a devastating invasion by the Dominion of the **Gamma Quadrant**. ("What You Leave Behind" [DS9]).

stasis unit.* Emergency medical equipment designed to hold a humanoid patient in a state of suspended animation. On stardate 51929, nearly the entire crew of the *Starship Voyager* entered stasis units for approximately four weeks so that they could survive exposure to intense subnucleonic radiation while the ship crossed a Mutara-class nebula. ("One" [VGR]).

"Statistical Probabilities." *Deep Space Nine* episode #133. Teleplay by René Echevarria. Story by Pam Pietroforte. Directed by Anson Williams. No stardate given. *First aired in 1997. Genetically engineered savants under Bashir's supervision predict doom for the Federation. Jack and his friends later returned in "Chrysalis" (DS9).* GUEST CAST: Jeffrey Combs as **Weyoun**; Tim Ransom as **Jack**; Jeannetta Arnette as **Loews, Dr. Karen**; Hilary Shepard-Turner as **Lauren**; Michael Keenan as **Patrick**; Casey Biggs as **Damar**; Faith C. Salie as **Douglas, Sarina.** SEE: **accelerated critical neural pathway formation; Bashir, Julian; Bashir, Singh el; Damar; Douglas, Sarina; Holna IV; Jack; Kabrel I; Kabrel II; ketracel-white; Lauren; Loews, Dr. Karen; mizainite ore; nonlinear dynamics; passive voice transitive; Patrick; yridium bicantizine.**

steak and eggs. Breakfast dish of the flesh of an Earth bovine broiled or grilled, served with cooked chicken eggs. ("Far Beyond the Stars" [DS9]).

steak with mushrooms. Traditional Earth meal made with a slice of the flesh of an adult Earth bovine broiled or grilled and served with mushrooms. ("You Are Cordially Invited" [DS9]).

stenophyl. Pharmaceutical that can be used to treat anaphylactic shock in cytoplasmic life-forms. ("Nothing Human" [VGR]).

Steth. (Dan Butler). Unscrupulous being capable of selective DNA exchange. Steth was able to absorb the DNA of an unwitting victim and deposit his current genetic material into that victim. Steth did this in order to switch bodies with his victims and then to assume their identity for a time. In 2374, on stardate 51762.4, Steth took over Tom Paris's body, stranding him in an experimental coaxial drive vessel. When threatened with discovery, Steth took over Kathryn Janeway's body. Tom Paris and **Daelen**, another victim, joined forces and captured Steth, forcing him to return all involved to their rightful bodies. ("Vis à Vis" [VGR]). *We never learned Steth's true appearance. Steth occupied several bodies and so was played variously by Dan Butler, Mary Elizabeth McGlynn (pictured), Robert Duncan McNeill, and Kate Mulgrew.*

stewed bok-rat liver. Klingon dish. Stewed bok-rat liver was served aboard the *Bird-of-Prey Rotarran*. ("Soldiers of the Empire" [DS9]).

Stinger. Holographic character in the popular ***Adventures of Flotter*** stories for children. Stinger was a huge mosquito who lived in the Forest of Forever. Kathryn Janeway, at the age of six, met Stinger after she accidentally flooded the entire forest in one of the Flotter stories. ("Once Upon a Time" [VGR]).

Sto-Vo-Kor*. Klingon place of the afterlife for the honored dead. According to traditional **Klingon** beliefs, to gain entry into *Sto-Vo-Kor*, a warrior must have eaten the heart of an enemy and have died in glorious battle. Otherwise, entry might be gained after death if a glorious victory was dedicated to the name of the fallen warrior. **Worf**, concerned that his wife, Jadzia, had not died in combat, volunteered for a dangerous mission to Monac IV under the command of General Martok in hopes of winning her entry to *Sto-Vo-Kor*. In this endeavor, Worf was joined by his friends (*pictured*), who offered to partake in this Klingon ritual. ("Image in the Sand" [DS9]).

Stolzoff. (Marjean Holden). Starfleet security officer. Stolzoff was assigned to Deep Space 9 along with her friend, **Amaro**, with whom she had attended Starfleet Academy. In 2373, Stolzoff was killed while participating in a salvage operation on the abandoned Cardassian station Empok Nor. Stolzoff was killed by a Cardassian soldier who was under the influence of powerful **psychotropic drugs**. ("Empok Nor" [DS9]).

Strickler, Ensign. Starfleet officer. Ensign Strickler was a crew member aboard ***U.S.S. Voyager***. In an alternate timeline, Strickler was killed during a **Krenim** attack. ("Year of Hell, Part I" [VGR]).

strike. In the ancient Earth sport of **baseball**, a strike is a play in which a **batter** swings, but fails to hit a ball pitched to him or her. A strike could also be called if a batter fails to attempt to hit a pitched ball and the ball was judged by the **umpire** to be within a "strike zone." ("Take Me Out to the Holosuite" [DS9]).

Sturgeon, Theodore. Twentieth-century Earth writer. Sturgeon was highly regarded for his imaginative **science-fiction** short stories and novels, as well as his work for the field of television. **Herbert**

Rossoff felt he would be in good company if his stories were published alongside those of Sturgeon in ***Galaxy Science Fiction*** magazine. ("Far Beyond the Stars" [DS9]). *Ted Sturgeon also wrote the* Star Trek *episodes "Shore Leave" (TOS) and "Amok Time" (TOS).*

subahdar. Rank in the **Son'a** space fleet service, approximately equivalent to a Starfleet lieutenant commander. Gallatin held the rank of subahdar. (*Star Trek: Insurrection*).

subnucleonic radiation. Energetic subatomic particles. Subnucleonic radiation was extremely harmful to organic tissue, as well as to many types of equipment found aboard a Federation starship. The *U.S.S. Voyager* crossed a Mutara-class nebula on stardate 51929.3, exposing the ship and crew to hazardous levels of subnucleonic radiation. ("One" [VGR]).

subspace phenomena*

subspace compression. A rare, naturally occurring subspace compression anomaly discovered in Federation space in 2374 was found to reduce the physical size of objects that entered the anomaly. It was hoped that study of the phenomenon might lead to better understanding of the creation of transwarp corridors. SEE: ***Rubicon, U.S.S.*** ("One Little Ship" [DS9]).

subspace rupture. Destruction of the subspace continuum caused by an **Omega molecule**. ("The Omega Directive" [VGR]).

subspace tear. Discontinuity allowing subspace to spill into normal space. A subspace tear can be caused by an isolytic subspace weapon. (*Star Trek: Insurrection*).

subspace technology* subspace weapon. Weapons that directly affect subspace are extremely dangerous and unpredictable. They have been banned by the second Khitomer Accords. Isolytic burst weapons are subspace weapons. (*Star Trek: Insurrection*).

Sullivan, Rebecca. (Gretchen German). Member of the outlaw **Maquis** resistance organization who fought against Cardassian encroachment on Federation territory. Sullivan married fellow Maquis member **Michael Eddington** in 2373, shortly before he was arrested by Federation authorities. Sullivan, along with other Maquis operatives on planet Athos IV, caused Starfleet officials to believe that Maquis operatives had launched a massive missile attack against Cardassia Prime. The incident prompted fears that the Federation and the Cardassians might be plunged into an all-out war. Starfleet released Eddington in an effort to avert the nonexistent attack. Eddington was killed at Athos IV while rescuing Sullivan and other Maquis operatives from a Jem'Hadar assault. ("Blaze of Glory" [DS9]).

supernova. Beverage served at Quark's bar. ("*Valiant*" [DS9]).

surgical chancellor. Position of great respect and importance within the **Vaskan** and **Kyrian** society of the 31st century. The **Emergency Medical Hologram backup module** from the *U.S.S. Voyager* served as surgical chancellor for many years. ("Living Witness" [VGR]).

Sutherland, U.S.S.* Federation starship. In 2374 the *Sutherland*, under the command of Captain Shelby, was a part of the **Ninth Fleet** headquartered at station Deep Space 9. **Lieutenant Manuele Atoa** was part of the ship's crew in 2374. ("You Are Cordially Invited" [DS9]). The *Sutherland* was due to visit Deep Space 9 one day after stardate 51597.2. ("Change of Heart" [DS9]).

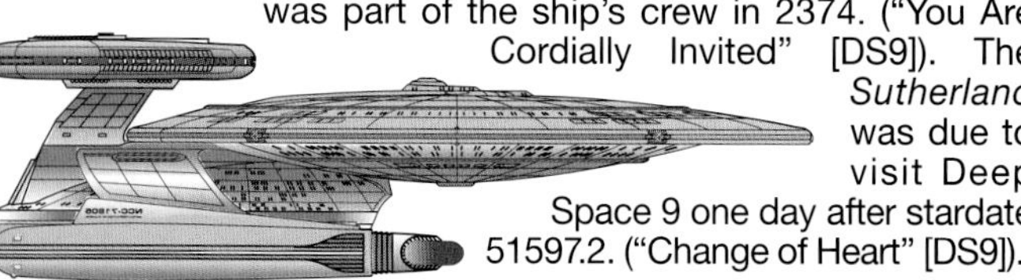

Sveta. Former member of the **Maquis** terrorist organization. Sveta was responsible for recruiting **Chakotay** into the Maquis. Sveta was being held in a Federation prison in 2374 and was one of the very few Maquis who escaped death at the hands of the Cardassians. Sveta, who was also a friend of B'Elanna Torres, wrote a letter to Chakotay, transmitted to *Voyager* through the Hirogen relay system, informing him of the tragic turn of events. ("Hunters" [VGR]).

swastika. Ancient Earth symbol for good luck, employed as a national emblem by the government of **Nazi Germany** during the mid-20th century. ("The Killing Game, Part II" [VGR]).

Swofford, Captain Quentin. Starfleet officer. Swofford commanded the *Starship Cortez* and was presumed killed when his ship disappeared in 2374. Years prior to his death, Swofford was introduced to his future wife by his good friend Benjamin Sisko. ("Far Beyond the Stars" [DS9]).

Sybaron. Star system in the Alpha Quadrant. Location where in 2374 Starfleet's Seventh Fleet met enemy forces and suffered heavy losses that reduced them to half strength during the **Dominion** war. ("The Reckoning" [DS9]).

symmetric warp field. Uniformly shaped subspace bubble that is incompatible with warp propulsion. In 2374, on stardate 51762.4, Tom Paris employed a symmetric warp field to contain the unstable coaxial core of an experimental Benthan ship. ("Vis à Vis" [VGR]).

syrup of squill. Delicious red topping made from the squill plant. The syrup was very popular and was used on such foods as groatcakes. Squill grew only on the planet **Balancar**. Syrup of squill was in short supply in the Alpha Quadrant from early 2373 into the following year. ("The Magnificent Ferengi" [DS9]).

T'Hain. Noted Vulcan literary scholar who wrote "Dictates of Poetics." T'Hain believed that a character's actions must flow inexorably from his or her established traits. ("Worse Case Scenario" [VGR]).

T'Kumbra, U.S.S. Federation starship, *Nebula* class. Commanded by Captain **Solok**, the *T'Kumbra* served on the front lines of the **Dominion** war. In early 2375, the vessel put in to station Deep Space 9 for repairs including an overhaul of the ship's warp core and upgrades to the inertial damper systems. While at the station, several members of the ship's crew indulged Solok's desire to challenge his former classmate, Benjamin Sisko, to the ancient Earth sport of baseball. The *T'Kumbra* team, composed entirely of **Vulcan** nationals, called themselves the **Logicians**. ("Take Me Out to the Holosuite" [DS9]).

T'Meni. Mother of Starfleet officer **Tuvok**. Tuvok's son, **Sek**, had a daughter who was named for T'Meni. ("Hunters" [VGR]).

T'Met. Romulan warbird. In 2374, the *T'Met* participated in an unsuccessful attempt to steal an experimental prototype Starfleet vessel, ***U.S.S. Prometheus.*** ("Message in a Bottle" [VGR]).

T'Pel.* Wife to Starfleet officer **Tuvok**. T'Pel continued to raise their children after Tuvok's disappearance aboard the *Starship Voyager* in 2371. In Tuvok's absence, T'Pel became a grandmother when her eldest son, **Sek**, had a daughter named **T'Meni**. In 2374, T'Pel learned that she had not been widowed when *Voyager* disappeared. She took her children to the temple at **Amonak,** where she asked the priests to pray for her husband's return. ("Hunters" [VGR]).

Tabor, Ensign. (Jad Mager). *Starship Voyager* crew member. Once a member of the **Maquis**, Tabor later served in *Voyager*'s engineering department. As a child on Bajor during the occupation, Tabor witnessed brutal medical experiments on his relatives, conducted by Cardassian researcher **Dr. Crell Moset**. Tabor's brother and grandfather died horribly during Moset's tests. Years later, in 2375, Ensign Tabor attempted to resign his commission in protest against the use by *Voyager* crew members of Moset's medical research, although his request was denied by Commander Chakotay. ("Nothing Human" [VGR]).

Tabris. (Mary Anne McGarry). Museum curator on the Vaskan/Kyrian home planet in the 33rd century. She was proud that their two peoples found a respect for their divergent cultures and traditions and lived in harmony. SEE: **Kyrian Heritage, Museum of**. ("Living Witness" [VGR]). *The character's name is from the script.*

tachyon.* Subatomic particle that exists only at faster-than-light speeds. A tachyon burst fired at a ship's deflector shields could permit a transporter beam to pass through the shield by forcing the ship's crew to reset the shield harmonics, momentarily allowing a transporter beam to penetrate. (*Star Trek: Insurrection*).

Tahiti. Island in the southern Pacific Ocean on planet Earth. In 2374 when Thomas Paris suggested spending time in a holodeck skiing program, B'Elanna Torres requested a warmer location, such as Tahiti. ("Waking Moments" [VGR]).

Tahoe, Lake. Inland body of water located in the Sierra Nevada mountains of North America on planet Earth. When he was 16 years old, Tom Paris took his father's shuttle on an unauthorized flight. In the course of the trip, the ship's relays were ruined and the shuttle ended up at the bottom of Lake Tahoe. ("Vis à Vis" [VGR]).

Tain, Enabran.* Former head of the Cardassian **Obsidian Order** intelligence agency. Father to **Elim Garak**. When his son misbehaved as a child, Tain locked him in a closet until he learned his lesson. ("Afterimage" [DS9]).

Takar. (Annette Helde). **Srivani** scientist. Takar, along with about 50 other researchers, was part of a Srivani science team that secretly came aboard the Federation starship *Voyager* in 2374 to conduct invasive and dangerous medical tests on the ship's crew. ("Scientific Method" [VGR]). *Annette Helde previously portrayed Karina in "Visionary" (DS9) and a Starfleet guard in* Star Trek: First Contact. *Character's name is from the script and was not mentioned in dialog.*

"Take Me Out to the Holosuite." *Deep Space Nine* episode #154. Written by Ronald D. Moore. Directed by Chip Chalmers. No stardate given. First aired in 1998. *Benjamin Sisko settles a score with his old academy nemesis with a game of baseball on the station's holosuite.* GUEST CAST: Greg Wagrowsky as **Solok**; Penny Johnson as **Yates, Kasidy**; Chase Masterson as **Leeta**; Max Grodénchik as **Rom**; Aron Eisenberg as **Nog**. SEE: **baseball; batter; bunt; chewing gum; Dax, Emony; Fancy Dan; holodeck and holosuite programs: baseball game; Launching Pad; Logicians; Medal of Valor, Christopher Pike; Niners; Sisko, Benjamin; Solok; Starfleet Academy; strike; *T'Kumbra, U.S.S.*; umpire; Yates, Kasidy.**

Tal Shiar.* Romulan intelligence agency. Senator **Vreenak** was vice chairman of the Tal Shiar until his death in 2374. ("In the Pale Moonlight" [DS9]).

tal'oth. A Vulcan ritual that required a young adult to survive for four months in the Vulcan desert with a ritual blade as their only possession. While on Vulcan, Tuvok took part in the ritual of *tal'oth*. ("Displaced" [VGR]). *The* tal'oth *appears to be similar to young Spock's* Kahs-wan *ordeal, seen in the animated episode "Yesteryear," first aired in 1973.*

Talaxian champagne. Alcoholic beverage made from fermented moon-ripened Talaxian fruit. Talaxian champagne was Kes's favorite beverage. ("The Gift" [VGR]).

Talaxians.* Civilization. Each year, the Talaxian people observe a holiday they call **Prixin**, a celebration of their families. The Talaxian people traditionally mourn their dead for a full week in a burial ceremony. Many Talaxians believe that upon death they will go to a beautiful place called the **Great Forest**. ("Mortal Coil" [VGR]). SEE: **Guiding Tree.**

talchok.* Talaxian animal. Talchok musk was used to make a cologne used by some Talaxian men. ("Random Thoughts" [VGR]).

Taleen. (Nancy Youngblut). Crew member of a Nyrian vessel in 2373. Taleen participated in the Nyrian attempt to resettle the crew of the *Starship Voyager* in 2373. ("Displaced" [VGR]).

Talli. (Rebecca McFarland). Grocery vendor on the **Mari** homeworld. In 2374, Talli befriended Neelix, a crew member from the visiting *Starship Voyager*. Talli was killed shortly thereafter, the result of an errant hostile thought stolen by **Guill**, a dealer in illegal violent mental images. SEE: **Tembit**. ("Random Thoughts" [VGR]).

Talmouth, Dunes of. Scenic location on planet Talax. Neelix and his sister, Alixia, once made an expedition to the Dunes of Talmouth. ("Mortal Coil" [VGR]).

Talpet. Deputy of the Bajoran security force aboard station Deep Space 9 in 2375. ("Afterimage" [DS9]).

Tammeron grain. Agricultural product used by the Cardassians. ("Favor the Bold" [DS9]).

Tamulna. Province on planet **Bajor**. In 2374, **Tamulna** was struck by a powerful tornado, an incident that was interpreted by some as a sign of the coming of **the Reckoning**. ("The Reckoning" [DS9]).

Tanas, General. Klingon warrior in command of the *Vor'cha*-class Klingon attack cruiser *Vor'nak*. In 2374, Tanas provided several new crew members for General Martok's ship, the *Rotarran*. ("Sons and Daughters" [DS9]).

Tannenbaum, Ensign Rita. Starfleet officer assigned to the engineering section of the *U.S.S. Defiant* in 2373. In an alternate reality, Tannenbaum was among the *Defiant* crew members stranded in the past on the planet Gaia. In this alternate reality Tannenbaum married Miles O'Brien ten years after the crash, and the two had several children. The alternate Tannenbaum ceased to exist when the timeline vanished, although the original individual continued to live in the original timeline. ("Children of Time" [DS9]).

targ*. Klingon animal. Traditional Klingon weddings include a ritual *targ* sacrifice followed by the wedding feast. ("A Time to Stand" [DS9]). Tallow made from *targ* shoulders is used to make proper *var'Hama* candles. ("You Are Cordially Invited" [DS9]). Observance of the Klingon **Day of Honor** included the eating of the heart of a sanctified *targ*. ("Day of Honor" [VGR]).

Tarlac. Humanoid civilization. The Tarlac were conquered early in the 24th century by the **Son'a**. By the late 24th century, the Tarlac were integrated into Son'a society as a labor class. Tarlac women were indentured as servants on Son'a spacecraft. (*Star Trek: Insurrection*).

tarragon. Earth seasoning made from the aromatic leaves of a European perennial plant (*Artemisia dracunculus*). ("Blaze of Glory" [DS9]).

Tatalia, Maria. Starfleet officer. Tatalia was wounded in action in the Dominion war near stardate 51721.3. She was a friend of Jadzia Dax. ("In the Pale Moonlight" [DS9]).

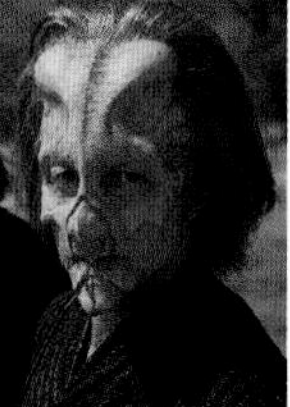

Tau. (John Vargas). Strong-arm ruler of the seventh province on the northern continent on a Class-M planet in the Delta Quadrant. He employed small, fast starships to swarm around visiting ships and steal technologically advanced equipment by using special high-energy translocators. Tau would later sell these devices to the highest bidder. Tau stole several pieces of valuable equipment including a **main computer processor** from the Federation starship *Voyager* in 2374, although *Voyager* personnel were later successful in recovering their property. Among the stolen items was the Doctor's mobile holographic emitter, as well as an intelligent software entity, a holographic character modeled on **Leonardo da Vinci**. ("Concerning Flight" [VGR]). *John Vargas also played Jedda in* Star Trek II: The Wrath of Kahn.

Tavana. (Sandra Nelson). Klingon warrior. Tavana served as engineering officer aboard the *Bird-of-Prey* ***Rotarran*** in 2373. Like much of the *Rotarran* crew, Tavana was discouraged and cynical until a victory under the command of **General Martok** restored her warrior's pride. ("Soldiers of the Empire" [DS9]). *Sandra Nelson previously played Marayna in "Alter Ego" (VGR).*

***Tawi'Yan*.** Klingon term meaning "sword-bearer." In a Klingon **wedding**, the *Tawi'Yan* is similar to the best man in a human wedding. Alexander Rozhenko acted as the *Tawi'Yan* in his father Worf's wedding to Jadzia Dax in 2374. ("You Are Cordially Invited" [DS9]).

"Tears of the Prophets." *Deep Space Nine* episode #150. Written by Ira Steven Behr & Hans Beimler. Directed by Allan Kroeker. No stardate given. *First aired in 1998. The tide begins to turn in the Dominion war as a combined Federation, Klingon, and Romulan fleet makes a daring assault on Cardassian territory. Jadzia Dax dies in this episode, which was the last of the sixth season.* GUEST CAST: Andrew J. Robinson as **Garak, Elim**; Jeffrey Combs as **Weyoun**; Marc Alaimo as **Dukat, Gul**; David Birney as **Letant**; J. G. Hertzler as **Martok, General**; Aron Eisenberg as **Nog**; Casey Biggs as **Damar**; Barry Jenner as **Ross, Admiral William**; James Darren as **Fontaine, Vic**; Michelle Horn as **Sahgi**; Bob Kirsh as Glinn. SEE: ***Akira*-class starship; Bajoran Gratitude Festival; Bajoran wormhole; Chin'toka System; Dax (symbiont); Dax, Jadzia; Dukat, Gul; Fontaine, Vic; *Galaxy, U.S.S.*; "Here's to the Losers"; Klingon death ritual; Letant; Martok, General; Medal of Valor, Christopher Pike; *Nautilus, U.S.S.*; Orb of Contemplation; orbital weapon platform; ovarian resequencing enzymes; Pah-wraith; Pike, Christopher; Prophets; Romulans; Ross, Admiral William; Sahgi; *ShirKahr, U.S.S.*; Sisko, Benjamin; Solis, Vedek; *Valley Forge, U.S.S.*; *Venture, U.S.S.*; Worf.**

Tedran. (Brian Fitzpatrick). Radical **Kyrian** leader who lead an attack against the Federation starship *Voyager* during **Vaskan** ambassador Daleth's visit to the ship in late 2374. Tedran and a small group of his people boarded the starship and proceeded to seize technology and hostages. Tedran was eventually caught and was killed by Daleth. In the 31st century, Kyrian society mistakenly believed Tedran to have been a noble martyr to his people instead of the angry suspicious man that he was. ("Living Witness" [VGR]).

telesynaptic activity. Neural electrical impulses in the telepathic areas of the brains of some humanoid species. ("The Gift" [VGR]).

Tellar. Planet, homeworld to the Tellarite civilization. Tellar is located near Betazed, Vulcan, Andor, and Alpha Centauri. ("In the Pale Moonlight" [DS9]).

Tembit. (Jeanette Miller). Inhabitant of the **Mari** homeworld. Tembit occasionally purchased illegal violent thought images from the planet's black market. In 2374, an errant hostile image stolen from B'Elanna Torres's mind by **Guill** ended up in Tembit's mind, causing her to be seized by a wave of emotion that led her to stab a young woman, **Talli**, to death. ("Random Thoughts" [VGR]).

Tempasa. Population center on planet **Bajor**. ("Ties of Blood and Water" [DS9]).

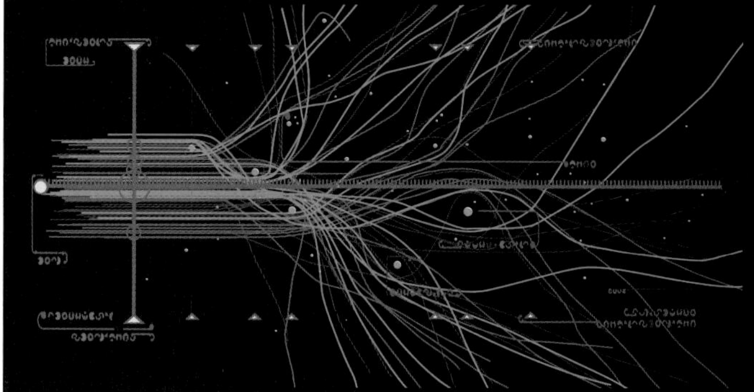

temporal mechanics. Study of time, its processes, and consequences of its change. Temporal mechanics is an enormously complex subject because of the infinitely complex interrelationships between each object in a time continuum. Krenim scientist **Annorax** studied temporal mechanics for two centuries in hopes of developing mathematical models that would let him use a **Krenim temporal weapon ship** to restore the Krenim timeline. **Professor Vassbinder** taught a class on temporal mechanics at **Starfleet Academy**. ("Year of Hell, Parts I and II" [VGR]).

temporal weapon. SEE: **Krenim temporal weapon ship.**

tempura. Earth food, traditional to Japanese culture, consisting of vegetables and seafood fried in a light batter. Keiko O'Brien sometimes prepared tempura for family meals. ("Chrysalis" [DS9]).

Tendara Colony. Federation planet. Annika Hansen, the girl who became the Borg drone Seven of Nine, was born at the Tendara Colony on stardate 25479. ("The Gift" [VGR]).

Tenth Fleet. Tactical group of Federation starships formed during the war with the Dominion. In 2374, the Tenth Fleet was assigned to defend Betazed and was unfortunately caught out of position on a training exercise when the planet was captured by a Dominion fleet. ("In the Pale Moonlight" [DS9]).

terahertz. Measure of frequency, one trillion cycles per second. ("The Omega Directive" [VGR]).

terawatt power particle beam rifle. Powerful energy weapon. In 2374, **Entharan** arms dealer Kovin attempted to sell a terawatt power particle beam rifle to the crew of the *Starship Voyager*. (Retrospect" [VGR]).

termination implant. Small device inserted into the brain stems of all **Vorta** that allowed them to commit suicide in the event that they were ever captured by an enemy. When triggered via physical manipulation, the implant causes the Vorta individual to die within minutes, somewhat painfully. The sixth **Weyoun** clone used his termination implant to kill himself in 2375. ("Treachery, Faith, and the Great River" [DS9]).

Terok Nor.* Cardassian space station that later became known as **Deep Space 9**. The station became operational in 2346. ("Wrongs Darker Than Death or Night" [DS9]). *The earlier editions of this encyclopedia (as well as the* Star Trek Chronology*) gave the date for the station's construction as 2351, as inferred from "Babel" (DS9), but "Wrongs Darker Than Death or Night" (DS9) clearly established the date as 2346.* The name Terok Nor came back into use in 2374 when Deep Space 9 was returned to Cardassian control during the Dominion war. ("Call to Arms" [DS9]).

Terrasphere 8. Species 8472 facility located in the Delta Quadrant. Terrasphere 8 contained an elaborate re-creation of the Federation's Starfleet Command complex in the city of San Francisco on Earth. The purpose of the re-creation was to permit Species 8472 operatives to familiarize themselves with Earth so they could infiltrate the planet on covert-intelligence missions. The re-creation included not only much of Starfleet Headquarters, but part of the surrounding city of San Francisco, including the Quantum Cafe. ("In the Flesh" [VGR]).

Terrellian plague.* Dangerous disease. After Neelix served a meal that he called **"Rodeo Red's Red Hot Rootin' Tootin' Chili"** for the crew of the *Starship Voyager* in 2374, he feared that his customers might be suffering from Terrellian plague, but medical testing determined that they only had ordinary heartburn. ("Message in a Bottle" [VGR]).

tessipate.* Bajoran unit of land measure. Tessipates were subdivided into kerripates. ("Children of Time" [DS9]).

tetraburnium alloy. Construction material used in the fabrication of spacecraft hulls. Tetraburnium alloys were stronger than titanium. The *Delta Flyer* and a Malon shuttle both had tetraburnium alloy hulls. ("Extreme Risk" [VGR]).

tetryon pulse launcher. Powerful weapon used by the Federation. Jean-Luc Picard brought tetryon pulse launchers down to the Ba'ku homeworld in 2375 to use in preventing the planet's inhabitants from being forcibly removed by the Son'a. (*Star Trek: Insurrection*).

Thalos VI. Planet. Gaila was arrested for vagrancy on Thalos VI. ("The Magnificent Ferengi" [DS9]).

"That Old Black Magic." Musical composition popular on 20th-century Earth, telling of the mysterious power of humanoid love to defy logical analysis. **Mademoiselle de Neuf** sang it in the **French Resistance** holodeck program. ("The Killing Game, Part I" [VGR]).

thermionic radiation. Hazardous energy form. Thermionic radiation is present in the atmosphere of a Class-Y planet. ("Demon" [VGR]).

thermolytic reaction. Energetic release of metaphasic radiation. The Son'a planned to use massive thermolytic reactions to plunder the Ba'ku planet's ring structure of its rejuvenating metaphasic radiation. (*Star Trek: Insurrection*).

theta radiation.* Hazardous energy. Theta radiation can be produced by an **Omega molecule**. Arithrazine was prescribed to treat cases of theta-radiation poisoning. ("The Omega Directive" [VGR]). Industrial waste in the form of contaminated antimatter created by **Malon** energy production was responsible for dangerous levels of theta radiation in the region of space informally known as the **Void**. ("Night" [VGR]).

"They Can't Take That Away from Me." Popular 20th-century Earth song performed by such notable entertainers as **Vic Fontaine** and **Frank Sinatra**, written by George and Ira Gershwin. Odo became fond of humming the piece after performing on stage with Vic Fontaine in a holosuite program. ("His Way" [DS9]).

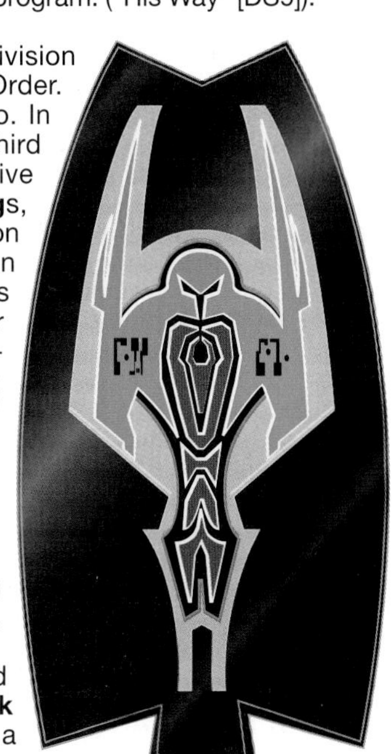

Third Battalion. Military subdivision of the **Cardassian** First Order. "Death to All" was their motto. In 2372, three soldiers of the Third Battalion were given a massive dose of **psychotropic drugs**, placed in stasis tubes, and left on **Empok Nor** when the station was abandoned. The chambers revived the soldiers a year later when sensors detected intruders on the station. ("Empok Nor" [DS9]). *Tom Morga and Chris Doyle played the soldiers.*

Third Fleet. Task force of the Federation **Starfleet**. In 2374, the Third Fleet was assigned to defend Earth from Dominion forces. ("Favor the Bold" [DS9]).

Third Klingon Dynasty. Period in Klingon history after the **Dark Time**. During the third dynasty a new imperial family was set up, members of which assumed the names and titles of Emperor **Reclaw**'s family to create the illusion of an unbroken royal line. ("You Are Cordially Invited" [DS9]).

Third Reich. Alternate name for the government of **Nazi Germany** during Earth's **World War II**. ("The Killing Game, Parts I and II" [VGR]).

Tholian Assembly.* Civilization in the Alpha Quadrant. In 2373 the Tholian Assembly signed a nonaggression pact with the **Dominion**, affecting the balance of power in the quadrant, a prelude to the devastating Dominion war. ("Call to Arms" [DS9]).

thorium. Radioactive metal element, atomic number 90. Thorium isotopes, when subjected to neutron bombardment, can yield fissile uranium isotopes, valuable for nuclear fuel. **Caatati** technology was dependent on thorium isotopes. When the Borg assimilated the Caatati in late 2372, the survivors lost their ability to produce the metal until 2374, when *Voyager* crew member Seven of Nine provided the technology to them. ("Day of Honor" [VGR]).

thrombic modulator. Medical instrument used to assist in blood coagulation. In 2374, on board the ***U.S.S. Prometheus***, the **Emergency Medical Hologram-2** requested a thrombic modulator while treating an injured Romulan soldier. ("Message in a Bottle" [VGR]).

Tian An Men, U.S.S.* Federation starship named for those on Earth who lost their lives in the name of Chinese freedom. The *Tian An Men* was lost near the Cardassian border in late 2373, around stardate 50929, and was presumed destroyed by Dominion forces. ("In the Cards" [DS9]).

Tibor Nebula. Interstellar dust cloud in Federation space, located near planet **Vulcan**. In 2374, during the **Dominion** war, Starfleet assigned its Seventh Fleet to protect Vulcan from attack by intercepting a Dominion fleet at the Tibor Nebula. ("The Reckoning" [DS9]).

Ticonderoga, U.S.S. Federation starship. The *Ticonderoga* reported to the Ba'ku homeworld in 2375 to facilitate the planet becoming a Federation protectorate. (*Star Trek: Insurrection*). *Named to honor the capture of Fort Ticonderoga on May 10, 1775, by Ethan Allen and the Green Mountain Boys.*

"Ties of Blood and Water." *Deep Space Nine* episode #117. Teleplay by Robert Hewitt Wolfe. Story by Edmund Newton & Robbin L. Slocum. Directed by Avery Brooks. Stardate 50712.5. *First aired in 1997. Kira comforts Legate Ghemor, who comes to the station to die and tell her his Cardassian secrets. This episode was a sequel to "Second Skin" (DS9).* GUEST CAST: Lawrence Pressman as **Ghemor, Legate**; Marc Alaimo as **Dukat, Gul**; Jeffrey Combs as **Weyoun**; Thomas Kopache as **Kira Taban**; Rick Schatz as **Gantt**; William Lucking as Furel. SEE: **barrowbug; Borven, Glinn; Cardassia; Cardassian Central Archives; clone; Deep Space 9; Fourth Order; Gantt; Ghemor, Legate; hexadrin; Iliana; Jem'Hadar battleship; Kiessa Monastery; Kira Nerys; Kira Taban; neuroregeneration; Ninth Order; Quen, Prylar; *shri-tal*; skimmer; Tempasa; Trepar, Gul; triptacedrine; voraxna; Vorta; Weyoun; Yarim Fel syndrome; "Yoshi."**

"Time to Stand, A." *Deep Space Nine* episode #125. Written by Ira Steven Behr & Hans Beimler. Directed by Allan Kroeker. No stardate given. *First aired in 1997. Sisko and his crew embark on a secret mission in a captured Jem'Hadar warship. This was a direct continuation of "Call To Arms" (DS9), the last episode of the fifth season, and was the first of a multiepisode arc that told the story of the Dominion war.* GUEST CAST: Andrew J. Robinson as **Garak, Elim**; Jeffrey Combs as **Weyoun**; Marc Alaimo as **Dukat, Gul**; Aron Eisenberg as **Nog**; J. G. Hertzler as **Martok, General**; Casey Biggs as **Damar**; Barry Jenner as **Ross, Admiral William**; Brock Peters as **Sisko, Joseph.** SEE: ***Centaur, U.S.S.*; core matrix; Dominion; Dukat, Gul; *Fredrickson, U.S.S.*; induction stabilizer; Jem'Hadar; Jem'Hadar warship; ketracel-white; parabolic thruster; resonance emitter; Reynolds, Charles; Ross, Admiral William; Seventh Fleet; Sisko, Benjamin; starbase: 375; *targ*; Tyra system; ultritium; wedding: Klingon.**

"Time's Orphan." *Deep Space Nine* episode #148. Teleplay by Bradley Thompson & David Weddle. Story by Joe Menosky. Directed by Allan Kroeker. No stardate given. *First aired in 1998. An accidental fall through a time portal turns O'Brien's eight-year-old daughter into a wild, dangerously unsocialized eighteen-year-old.* GUEST CAST: Rosalind Chao as **O'Brien, Keiko**; Michelle Krusiec as **O'Brien, Molly** (adult); Hana Hatae as **Molly O'Brien**; Shaun Bieniek as **Pinar**; Randy James as **Jones, Lieutenant.** SEE: **Chester; Dalvos Prime; Dax (symbiont); Golana melon; Golana; Golanan time portal; Golanans; grint hound; Jones, Lieutenant; Kelvans; Lupi; Madrat; O'Brien, Molly; Pinar.**

Titanic. Earth-based ocean vessel that sank on its maiden voyage in 1912, killing over 1,200 humans. In an alternate timeline, Thomas Paris used the technologically innovative *Titanic* as a model for special transverse bulkheads he designed to strengthen the Federation starship *Voyager*. ("Year of Hell, Part I" [VGR]). *Former* Star Trek *visual-effects supervisor Robert Legato won an Academy Award for his work on the 1997 motion picture* Titanic.

to-Duq. Klingon term that means "courage." ("Sons and Daughters" [DS9]).

Tolar, Grathon. (Howard Shangraw). Individual who was known as an expert forger of holographic records. In 2374, **Elim Garak** and **Benjamin Sisko** employed Grathon Tolar's services to prepare a **optolythic data rod** containing holographic records falsified to make it appear that the Dominion was about to invade Romulan territory. After making the recording, Garak killed Tolar to prevent him from revealing the details of the covert operation. ("In the Pale Moonlight" [DS9]).

Tong Beak Nebula. Interstellar dust cloud located near the Cardassian/Federation border. In 2373 the Dominion operated Jem'Hadar ships in the nebula. ("Soldiers of the Empire" [DS9]).

tongo*. Ferengi card game. In *tongo*, a full consortium was usually a winning hand, but could be beaten by a total monopoly. Possible actions by a player included options to buy, index the margin, and leverage the buy-in. **Quark** was a very good player. One month before stardate 51597, Quark began a remarkable winning streak that stretched for more than 207 straight *tongo* victories. ("Change of Heart" [DS9]). A **Global *Tongo* Championship** is held each year on Ferenginar. ("Ferengi Love Songs" [DS9]).

Topek. Bajoran vedek who was also a renowned artist. ("Sons and Daughters" [DS9]).

Tora Ziyal.* (Melanie Smith). Daughter of **Gul Dukat** and **Tora Naprem.** With assistance from her friend **Kira Nerys**, Ziyal moved to Bajor, where she attended the university. On Bajor, she discovered that she was interested in art, a talent she developed under Vedek Nane. The director of the Cardassian Institute of Art was impressed enough with her work to include her work in an exhibition of new artists. Ziyal found she did not fit in on Bajor because she carried the stigma of being the daughter of the infamous Dukat, and subsequently returned to live with her father on station Terok Nor (formerly Deep Space 9). ("Sons and Daughters" [DS9]). She loved her father, but felt deeply betrayed by the atrocities he had committed against the **Bajoran** people. Ziyal ultimately sided with the Bajoran resistance, working with Quark to provide vital assistance in Benjamin Sisko's daring mission that retook the station from Dominion control, preventing a massive Dominion incursion into the Alpha Quadrant. Ziyal was subsequently murdered by Glinn **Damar**. She died in her father's arms. ("Sacrifice of Angels" [DS9]).

torga. Animal indigenous to planet **Gaia**. Torga were used as riding animals. ("Children of Time" [DS9]).

Torothka virus. Disease. Symptoms include stomach cramps and skin rash. In 2374, while aboard the ***U.S.S. Prometheus***, *Starship Voyager*'s Emergency Medical Hologram warned the invading Romulans they may have been exposed to Torothka virus. ("Message in a Bottle" [VGR]). *Of course, it is possible the Doctor just made up the virus as a ruse to gain access to* Prometheus *bridge controls.*

Torres, B'Elanna.* Chief engineer aboard the *Starship Voyager* and former member of the **Maquis** terrorist group. Torres joined the Maquis after group member (and future *Voyager* crewmate) **Chakotay** saved her life. ("One" [VGR]). When Voyager received a number of personal messages from Starfleet in late 2374, Torres was shocked to learn that virtually all of her friends from the Maquis had been murdered by Cardassian forces. Torres subsequently went into a period of severe depression, during which she sometimes ran hazardous holodeck programs such as **orbital skydiving** with the **safety protocol**s disengaged. ("Extreme Risk" [VGR]). Torres was uncomfortable with **Klingon** tradition, but decided to respect that part of her heritage in 2374 when she reluctantly agreed to observe the Klingon **Day of Honor**. Torres also had difficulty with close interpersonal relationships, finding it easier to keep people at arm's length. This changed on that Day of Honor when, stranded in space, believing herself to have only seconds of breathable oxygen remaining, she professed her love for **Tom Paris**. ("Day of Honor" [VGR]). *Roxann Dawson was previously credited as Roxann Biggs and Roxann Biggs-Dawson.*

Torros III. Planet in Cardassian space. In 2373 the Dominion built a shipyard on Torros III, but Federation forces destroyed it around stardate 50975. ("Call to Arms" [DS9]).

Toruk-DOH. A particularly vile Klingon curse. ("You Are Cordially Invited" [DS9]).

Torvin. Inhabitant of the planet **Gaia** in an alternate timeline. In this alternate reality, Torvin was a descendant of Jadzia Dax and Worf. ("Children of Time" [DS9]).

total monopoly. In the game of ***tongo***, a high-value hand of cards. A total monopoly beats a full consortium. ("Change of Heart" [DS9]).

Tournel. (Mark Deakins). Village leader within the Ba'ku community. (*Star Trek: Insurrection*). *Mark Deakins was previously seen as the Hirogen SS Officer in "The Killing Game, Parts I and II" (VGR).*

tova'dok. Klingon term for a moment of clarity shared between two warriors on the field of battle. In *tova'dok,* much was said without the need for words. ("Soldiers of the Empire" [DS9]).

tracer. Agents of the **Ramuran** government tasked with tracking down any Ramurans who try to leave their world. Upon being captured, Tracers would use a **neurolytic emitter** to erase memories of the outside world from the runaways. **Kellin** and **Curneth** were tracers. ("Unforgettable" [VGR]).

Trag'tok, Dr. Physician. Trag'tok was an acquaintance of Kira Nerys and Jadzia Dax. In 2374, Dax suggested to Kira that she should ask him to dinner, but for some reason Kira was bothered by the fact that he had three eyes. ("Resurrection" [DS9]).

Trakian ale.* Beverage. In 2374, while aboard *Voyager* in the form of Tom Paris, the genome thief Steth drank replicated Trakian ale. ("Vis à Vis" [VGR]).

translocator. Nyrian device used to transport persons and objects instantly across distances as great as ten light-years. The **Nyrian** translocator operated by creating a powerful spatial distortion field around the object being transported. The distortion field also created a surge of **polaron** particles. The device was a key part of Nyrian efforts to abduct the crews of passing starships. ("Displaced" [VGR]). Raider ships in the employ of Tau used translocator devices to steal high-tech equipment from the *Voyager*. ("Concerning Flight" [VGR]).

transluminal processor. Computer computational unit incorporating incredibly fast processing capability. Federation starship computers employ transluminal processors. SEE: **main computer processor**. ("Concerning Flight" [VGR]).

transporter inhibitor. Device that generates an energy field, preventing the operation of a transporter in an area of several square meters. (*Star Trek: Insurrection*).

transwarp.* Advanced propulsion technology. In 2374 a rare **subspace** compression phenomenon was discovered in Federation space. It was hoped that the study of the anomaly could provide Starfleet with the key to the creation of transwarp conduits. ("One Little Ship" [DS9]). During the same year, with the help of Seven of Nine, the crew of the *Starship Voyager* attempted unsuccessfully to create a transwarp conduit. The *Voyager*'s warp engines were nearly destroyed in the attempt. ("Day of Honor" [VGR]). The **Voth** people in the Delta Quadrant used a form of transwarp propulsion for their space vehicles. Voth transwarp was superior to 24th-century Starfleet warp drive technology. ("Distant Origin" [VGR]). SEE: **subspace phenomena: subspace compression.** Borg transwarp technology was very similar to the **quantum slipstream drive** used by Arturis's people. ("Hope and Fear" [VGR]).

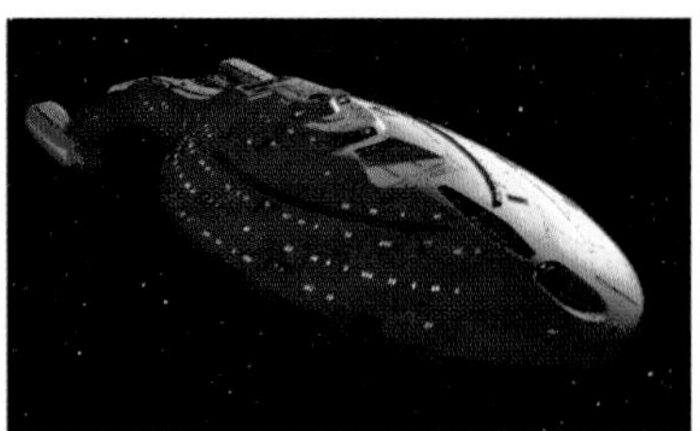

traumatic stress syndrome. Mental illness. Traumatic stress syndrome is a reaction to an extreme crisis and may cause symptoms of irritability, sleeplessness, obsessive thoughts, and reckless behavior. In an alternate timeline, the *Voyager*'s Emergency Medical Hologram relieved Captain Kathryn Janeway after she exhibited signs of traumatic stress syndrome during the extended **Krenim** altercation of 2374–2375. ("Year of Hell, Part II" [VGR]).

Trayken beast. Large and very powerful life-form. ("Hunters" [VGR]).

"Treachery, Faith, and the Great River." *Deep Space Nine* episode #156. Teleplay by David Weddle & Bradley Thompson and Ira Steven Behr & Hans Beimler. Story by Philip Kim. Directed by Steve Posey. No stardate given. *First aired in 1998. Weyoun defects from the Dominion, and Nog makes elaborate trades to obtain a vital component for the* Defiant. GUEST CAST: Jeffrey Combs as **Weyoun**; Casey Biggs as **Damar**; J. G. Hertzler as **Martok, General**; Aron Eisenberg as **Nog**; Max Grodénchik as **Rom**; Salome Jens as **Female Shape-shifter.** SEE: **clone; Damar; Decos Prime; Ferengi Rules of Acquisition: 168th Rule; Ferengi; Founders; Gant; *Gettysburg, U.S.S.*; graviton stabilizer; Great Link; Great Material Continuum; Jem'Hadar attack ship; *kanar*; *kava* nut; Kuiper belt; Lorenzo, Al; *Musashi, U.S.S.*; Olmerak; Pelosa system; *Rio Grande, U.S.S.*; rippleberry; Russol, Gul; Saurian brandy; sector: 507; *Sentinel, U.S.S.*; termination implant; Vorta; Weyoun; Willoughby, Chief Edgar.**

Treen. (Terrence Evans). **Kradin** government official. In 2374, Ambassador Treen assisted the crew of the *Starship Voyager* to locate Commander Chakotay and rescue him from the **Vori** military. ("Nemesis" [VGR]). *Terrence Evans previously played Baltrim in "Progress" (DS9) and Proka Migdal in "Cardassians" (DS9).*

Trepar, Gul. Cardassian military officer. Trepar commanded the Fourth Order in 2373. Trepar, who was a bitter rival of **Gul Dukat**, outranked Dukat before the Cardassians allied themselves with the Dominion. ("Ties of Blood and Water" [DS9]).

Trevis. (Justin Louis). One of the lead characters in The Adventures of Flotter holographic stories for children. Trevis was an embodiment of tree life in the fanciful Forest of Forever. In one of the stories, Trevis was dependent on his friend, Flotter T. Watter, an example of how the Flotter stories taught the interdependence of the various forces of nature. ("Once Upon a Time" [VGR]).

tri-ox compound.* Medication. Humanoids can compensate for high levels of carbon dioxide in the atmosphere of a Class-L planet by taking injections of tri-ox compound. Recommended dosage for an adult human is 15 milliliters every four hours. Tri-ox compound allowed Captain **Lisa Cusak** to survive in a Class-L planet's atmosphere for several days. ("The Sound of Her Voice" [DS9]).

triage. In emergency medicine, when medical resources are limited during a disaster, triage refers to dividing the injured into three groups. The first is those who are so severely injured that they will die regardless of treatment. The second is those whose lives are not immediately imperiled by their injuries. The third is those who can be saved by immediate medical attention. The purpose of triage is to allocate scarce medical resources to save the greatest number of lives. In an alternate timeline, *Voyager*'s Emergency Medical Hologram reminded Tom Paris that the rules of triage prevented him from spending too much time with any one patient, even if it was someone with whom he was emotionally involved. ("Year of Hell, Part I" [VGR]).

triaxilation. Complex mathematical process. A recursion matrix can be extracted from an encrypted data stream using triaxilation techniques. ("Hope and Fear" [VGR]). The species of sentient cytoplasmic beings encountered by the crew of the *Voyager* in 2375 employed triaxilating sound patterns containing over 10,000 separate sound patterns for vocal communication, although a universal translator could not decipher the language. ("Nothing Human" [VGR]).

trilithium.* Highly energetic, toxic substance. Trilithium isotopes are used in Romulan plasma torpedoes. ("Image in the Sand" [DS9]).

Trill.* Joined species. Trills are more sensitive to extreme heat than many humanoids. ("Change of Heart" [DS9]).

trinary syntax. Rules for the arrangement and meaning of tokens employed in complex computational languages such as Starfleet encryption protocols. ("Hope and Fear" [VGR]).

trioxin. Medication used to treat severe lung damage. ("Year of Hell, Part II" [VGR]).

triptacedrine. Pharmaceutical used to alleviate pain. Triptacedrine was given to Legate Ghemor in 2373 to help him with the pain of Yarim Fel syndrome. ("Ties of Blood and Water" [DS9]).

triptin. Material sometimes used in three-dimensional art. A post-eventualistic, pre-Matoian sculpture made from bronze and triptin was sold at auction on station Deep Space 9 in late 2373. ("In the Cards" [DS9]).

tritanium.* Alloy used in spacecraft construction. The hull of the *U.S.S. Raven* was composed of tritanium. ("The Raven" [VGR]).

Trivas system. Planetary system in Cardassian space. The Trivas system was the location of **Empok Nor**, a Cardassian space station abandoned in 2372. ("Empok Nor" [DS9]).

trochlear nerve. Pulley-shaped bundle of neurons in a humanoid brain. A Borg implant in Seven of Nine's colliculi pressed against her trochlear nerve in early 2374, shortly after her separation from the collective, nearly sending her into fatal neural shock. ("The Gift" [VGR]).

Troi, Deanna.* Counselor aboard the *U.S.S. Enterprise*-D and *Enterprise*-E under the command of Captain Jean-Luc Picard. In 2375, while serving together on the *Enterprise*-E, Deanna and Will Riker discovered they still shared an affection for each other, and the two renewed their romantic relationship. (*Star Trek: Insurrection*).

Tse'Dek. Klingon warrior, father of N'Garen. ("Sons and Daughters" [DS9]).

Tuvok.* Security officer on the *Starship Voyager*. While on **Vulcan**, Tuvok once took part in the ritual of *tal'oth*, in which he had to survive in the Vulcan desert for four months with a ritual blade as his only possession. ("Displaced" [VGR]). Tuvok first met **Kathryn Janeway** in 2365 when he criticized her in front of three Starfleet admirals for failing to observe proper tactical procedures during her first command. ("Revulsion" [VGR]). Tuvok also served with Janeway aboard the ***U.S.S. Billings***. ("Night" [VGR]). In 2374, around stardate 51186, Tuvok was promoted to the rank of lieutenant commander. ("Revulsion" [VGR]). On stardate 51501, Tuvok received a letter from his wife, **T'Pel**, in a Starfleet transmission received through a **Hirogen relay station**. In the letter, Tuvok learned that he had become a grandfather. The grandchild was named T'Meni, after Tuvok's mother. ("Hunters" [VGR]).

Tycho City.* Settlement on Earth's **Moon**. Cadet **Dorian Collins** was from Tycho City. ("*Valiant*" [DS9]).

tympanic tickle. Sexual technique of ***oo-mox*** devised to pleasure a Ferengi male by a delicate stimulation of his ears. ("Profit and Lace" [DS9]).

Tyra system. Planetary system. Site of a devastating Starfleet defeat in early 2374 during the Dominion war. Out of some 112 Starfleet vessels in the battle, Jem'Hadar forces destroyed 98, leaving only 14 surviving ships. ("A Time to Stand" [DS9]).

Tyree. Class-M planet in Federation space. In 2375, the Prophets of Bajor sent a vision to Benjamin Sisko in which he found a woman's face in the sand on the planet Tyree. Sisko later mounted an expedition to Tyree to seek the **Orb of the Emissary**. ("Image in the Sand" [DS9]). Benjamin Sisko—assisted by his father, Joseph; his son, Jake; and Ezri Dax—were successful in finding the Orb of the Emissary buried in the sand on Tyree. When Ben opened the ark holding the Orb, the Prophets returned to the Celestial Temple, restored the wormhole to operation, and banished the Pah-wraiths once again. ("Shadows and Symbols" [DS9]).

ultritium.* Chemical explosive. During the Cardassian occupation of Bajor, the Bajoran resistance had access to ultritium resin, which they used for terrorist actions, such as an attempt to assassinate Gul Dukat in 2346 at station Terok Nor. ("Wrongs Darker Than Death or Night" [DS9]). Benjamin Sisko's crew used a bomb containing 90 isotons of enriched ultritium to destroy a ketracel-white storage and distribution facility deep within Cardassian space in early 2374. ("A Time to Stand" [DS9]). Jean-Luc Picard brought ultritium explosives down to the Ba'ku homeworld in 2375 to use in preventing the planet's inhabitants from being forcibly removed by the Son'a. (*Star Trek: Insurrection*).

umpire. In the ancient Earth sport of **baseball**, an umpire was a referee, responsible for interpreting rules as they applied to a specific game. In baseball, touching the umpire is grounds for ejecting a player from the game. Odo served as umpire in the baseball game between the **Logicians** and the **Niners** in early 2375, when he had to enforce that rule twice. ("Take Me Out to the Holosuite" [DS9]).

"Unforgettable." *Voyager* episode #90. Written by Greg Elliot & Michael Perricone. Directed by Andrew J. Robinson. Stardate 51813.4. *First aired in 1998. Chakotay is captivated by a beautiful woman who claims they've met before, but she is from a planet whose people cannot be remembered by outsiders.* GUEST CAST: Virginia Madsen as **Kellin**; Michael Canavan as **Curneth;** Chuck Magnus as **Resket**. SEE: **almond pudding; Chakotay; Curneth; herbal tea; ice cream; Kellin; magneton scan; Mikah; neurolytic emitter; polarization cloak; proton weapon; Ramura; Ramuran tracer ship; Ramurans; Resket; soy meal; tracer.**

Union of Soviet Socialist Republics. Nation-state on 20th-century **Earth**, a bold attempt to provide its working people with the economic benefits of a communal society without arbitrary class stratification. Although the experiment proved unsuccessful, the Soviet Union was responsible for Earth's first voyages into space, including the historic flight of Yuri Gagarin on the *Vostok I* spacecraft in 1961 and the remarkable *Mir* orbital station in the 1980s and 1990s. The Soviet Union was often at political and military odds with the **United States of America**, and the Soviet government expended considerable energy to gather intelligence data on the American republic, even going so far as to construct replicas of American cities where Soviet **secret agent**s could be trained to infiltrate American society. *U.S.S. Voyager* captain Kathryn Janeway observed that Species 8472 had done much the same thing in 2375 when they created a duplicate of Starfleet Headquarters in the Delta Quadrant. SEE: **Terrasphere 8.** ("In the Flesh" [VGR]). *The dedication plaque for the* U.S.S. Tsiolkovsky, *seen briefly in "The Naked Now" (TNG), indicated that the ship had been built at the Baikonur Cosmodrome in the U.S.S.R. The plaque, made in 1987, failed to anticipate the collapse of the Soviet Union just a few years later, but was intended to commemorate the extraordinary achievements of the Russian people in the exploration of space, as well as the pioneering vision of Russian theoretician Konstantin Tsiolkovsky.*

United Federation of Planets. * Interstellar alliance located mostly in the **Alpha Quadrant** of the galaxy. The late 24th century was a time of great adversity for the Federation. After having survived assaults by the Borg, the Federation allied itself with other Alpha Quadrant powers to defend itself in a costly, brutal war against an invasion by the **Dominion** of the Gamma Quadrant. ("What You Leave Behind" [DS9]).

United States of America.* Republic on planet **Earth**, founded in 1776. The American nation was a major participant in the planet's brutal second world war during the 20th century, providing military strength to the **Allied Forces** in such operations as the liberation of France from Nazi Germany. ("The Killing Game, Parts I and II" [VGR]). SEE: **Allied Forces; Apollo 11; French Resistance; Kennedy, John F.; World War II**.

universal translator.* Sophisticated computer device capable of real-time conversion of a given language into nearly any other language. The universal translator was incapable, however, of translating a spoken language that employed sound **triaxilation**, used by a cytoplasmic species encountered by the *Starship Voyager* in 2375. ("Nothing Human" [VGR]).

upturned. The **Vori** and the **Kradin** people believed that after they died their spirits would descend to the afterlife, which they called the gloried Wayafter, but only if their bodies were lying face down. The greatest desecration to the Vori or Kradin dead was to "upturn" the body, so that the deceased could not go to the Wayafter. During their extended war, the Vori and the Kradin accused each other of dishonoring each other's dead in this fashion. ("Nemesis" [VGR]).

Ural Mountains. Spectacular geological feature in Russia on Earth. When Worf was a boy, his father used to take him and his brother, Nikolai, on camping trips in the Ural Mountains. ("Change of Heart" [DS9]).

Uri'lash. (Sylvain Cecile). Tall humanoid who acted as a traditional Hupyrian servant to **Brunt** during the brief time in 2374 when Brunt was acting grand nagus of Ferenginar. ("Profit and Lace" [DS9]).

vacuum tube. Ancient electronic component consisting of an evacuated glass envelope containing a heated cathode, often used to amplify a faint electrical signal. Found in 20th-century amplitude-modulation radio receivers such as those used by the French Resistance during World War II. ("The Killing Game, Part I" [VGR]). SEE: **mnemonic memory circuit**.

Valiant*, U.S.S.** Federation starship, ***Defiant class, Starfleet registry number NCC-74210. In 2374, the *Valiant*, under the command of **Captain Ramirez**, undertook a training voyage to circumnavigate the Federation with a crew consisting of cadets from Starfleet Academy's **Red Squad**. The ship was caught behind enemy lines when the **Dominion** war broke out. Shortly thereafter, Ramirez and the entire senior staff were killed in a battle with a Cardassian battle cruiser near El Gatark. Cadet **Tim Watters** subsequently assumed command of the vessel, continuing the *Valiant*'s mission for nearly eight months with a crew consisting entirely of Red Squad members. Under Watters's command, the *Valiant* was destroyed and nearly the entire crew killed on stardate 51825.4 when Watters took the ship on an impossible mission to single-handedly destroy a massive **Dominion battleship**. ("*Valiant*" [DS9]). Valiant *was an early name considered for the ship that later became the* Defiant *on* Star Trek: Deep Space Nine. *At another point, it was also thought that the* Defiant *might be designated as a* Valiant-*class ship, until "The Search, Part I" (DS9) made it clear that the* Defiant *was the first ship of her class, making it (and the* Valiant*) a* Defiant-*class ship. Some early production illustrations have been published that erroneously designate the* Defiant *as a* Valiant-*class vessel.*

"*Valiant*." *Deep Space Nine* episode #146. Written by Ronald D. Moore. Directed by Michael Vejar. Stardate 51825.4. *First aired in 1998. Nog and Jake are rescued by a starship run by elite academy cadets who take their duty dangerously too far.* GUEST CAST: Aron Eisenberg as **Nog;** Paul Popowich as **Watters, Tim;** Courtney Peldon as **Farris, Karen;** David Drew Gallagher as **Shepard, Riley Aldrin;** Ashley Brianne McDonogh as **Collins, Dorian;** Scott Hamm as **Parton.** SEE: **class-3 probe; Collins, Dorian; cordafin; delta radiation; Dominion battleship; El Gatark; escape pod; Farris, Karen; Kepla Sector; Luna; Lunar Schooner; Moon; Nog; Parton; Ramirez, Captain; Red Squad; *Republic, U.S.S.*; Sea of Clouds; *Shenandoah, U.S.S.*; Shepard, Riley Aldrin; Silven surprise; Sisko, Jake; supernova; Tycho City; *Valiant, U.S.S.*; viterium; Watters, Tim.**

***Valley Forge*, U.S.S.** Federation starship, *Excelsior*-class, Starfleet registry number NCC-43305. The *Valley Forge* fought in the combined fleet of allied Alpha Quadrant forces that invaded Cardassian space at the **Chin'toka System** in late 2374. ("Tears of the Prophets" [DS9]). *The name was not in dialog, seen only* very *faintly on the ship's hull in visual effects scenes. Named for the site in Pennsylvania where General George Washington's troops spent a bitter winter during the American Revolutionary War.*

Valonnan school. Style of Cardassian minimalist art founded by noted artist Napart Malor. Gul Dukat thought his daughter, **Tora Ziyal**, had a style reminiscent of the Valonnan school. ("Sons and Daughters" [DS9]).

Vance. Shuttle pilot and member of Michael Eddington's **Maquis** cell. Vance was killed in 2373 by the Jem'Hadar on Athos IV. ("Blaze of Glory" [DS9]).

***var'Hama* candle.** Primitive light source employing chemical combustion of animal fat; used in some Klingon ceremonies. *Var'Hama* candles are often displayed by a bride-to-be to welcome the female head of her intended's house prior to the wedding. Traditionally, to make the candles three *targ* are captured in the Hamar Mountains and sacrificed at dawn. The shoulders of the *targ* are boiled into tallow and hand-molded for two days into *var'Hama* candles. The lady **Sirella** was a connoisseur of such things and could easily distinguish a genuine *var'Hama* from a replicated fake. ("You Are Cordially Invited" [DS9]).

Vaskan arbiter. (Craig Richard Nelson). Thirty-first-century Vaskan scholar, member of the board responsible for evaluating historical evidence relating to the **Great War** between the Vaskan and Kyrian peoples. ("Living Witness" [VGR]).

Vaskans. Technologically advanced humanoid Delta Quadrant civilization. The Vaskans lived in a society along with the **Kyrian** people. The Kyrians felt themselves oppressed by the Vaskans, and in late 2374, radical Kyrians attacked the *U.S.S. Voyager* during trade negotiations with Vaskan ambassador Daleth. That event touched off a **Great War** between the Vaskans and the Kyrians. Tensions and inequalities between the Vaskans and Kyrians existed well into the 31st century, but by 3080 the two peoples lived in harmony. SEE: **Kyrian Heritage, Museum of**. ("Living Witness" [VGR]).

vasodilation. Medical term referring to a state in a vascular lifeform in which the blood vessels are temporarily enlarged, allowing a higher rate of blood flow through the circulatory system. In the Voth species, vasodilation is also a form of nonverbal communication in which much about another individual's emotional state can be gleaned from the shade of their skin. The Voth used vasodilation during courtship. ("Distant Origin" [VGR]).

Vassbinder, Professor.* Multidisciplinary scientist. Vassbinder also taught a class on **temporal mechanics** at the Starfleet Academy. Chakotay failed Vassbinder's temporal mechanics class. ("Year of Hell, Part II" [VGR]).

Veer, Tova. (Christopher Liam Moore). Scientist and member of the **Voth** archeology circle in 2373. Veer was the assistant to Professor **Forra Gegen** and was a supporter of the controversial **Distant Origin Theory**. The Ministry of Elders, fearful of the social ramifications should the Distant Origin Theory be widely known, compelled Veer to denounce Professor Gegen and the theory. ("Distant Origin" [VGR]).

Vega. Star, also called Alpha Lyrae, located 26.5 light-years from the Sol system. In late 2374 during the war with the Dominion, the *Starship Defiant* escorted a convoy designated PQ-1 to the Vegan system. ("The Sound of Her Voice" [DS9]).

velocity. An athletic game in which two opponents use hand phasers to control the flight of a hovering disk. Each player strove to avoid being hit by a disk by shooting it and sending it back toward their opponent. It was a fast-paced, physical game, with both players in constant motion. A complete game consisted of ten rounds. *Voyager* crew members enjoyed velocity on a holodeck playing field. ("Hope and Fear" [VGR]).

velvet painting. Art form in which acrylic paints were applied over a canvas covered with black velvet fabric. A 20th-century velvet painting of an Earth bullfighter was sold at auction on Deep Space 9 in late 2373. A similar image had been the inspiration for the first flag of the Martian Colonies. ("In the Cards" [DS9]).

Ventar system. Planetary system in the Alpha Quadrant. ("Resurrection" [DS9]).

Venture, U.S.S.* Federation starship. In 2374, the *Venture* participated in the daring and costly mission to retake station Deep Space 9 from Dominion control, preventing a massive incursion of Dominion ships into the Alpha Quadrant. ("Sacrifice of Angels" [DS9]). The *U.S.S. Venture* and four *Galaxy*-class ships fought in the combined fleet of allied Alpha Quadrant forces that invaded Cardassian space at the **Chin'toka System** in late 2374. ("Tears of the Prophets" [DS9]).

Verdi, Giuseppe. (1813–1901). Operatic composer from the nation of Italy on Earth, noted composer of several operas including *Rigoletto* and *Don Carlo*. In 2375, the holographic doctor aboard the *Voyager* practiced singing an operatic duet from Verdi's *Don Carlo*. ("Night" [VGR]).

vilm sauce. Condiment used on nozala sandwiches. ("Honor Among Thieves" [DS9]).

"Vis à Vis." *Voyager* episode #88. Written by Robert J. Doherty. Directed by Jesús Salvador Treviño. Stardate 51762.4. *First aired in 1998.* Voyager *crew members are victimized by a being capable of forcibly exchanging genomes with others in order to steal their appearance and identities.* GUEST CAST: Dan Butler as **Steth;** Mary Elizabeth McGlynn as **Daelen.** SEE: **Avik, Commander; Benthan Guard; Benthans; Benthos IV; Camaro; carburetor; cardiopulmonary reconstruction; chromoelectric pulse; coaxial warp drive; Daelen; Entabans; exatanium; genome; golf; Highway 1; holodeck and holosuite programs: Golf, Grease Monkey; Kaplan, Ensign; Kendren System; Kotaba Expanse; *Mithran*-class fighter; Paris, Thomas; physiosensor; polyduranide; Steth; subatomic dilution; symmetric warp field; Tahoe, Lake; Trakian ale.**

vision quest.* Ritual for focusing one's thoughts inward, observed by some of Earth's Native American cultures. **Neelix**'s experience with death on stardate 51449 compelled him to seek answers in a vision quest with **Chakotay**'s guidance. ("Mortal Coil" [VGR]).

viterium. Metal alloy. Exposure to delta radiation greatly weakens viterium, which is normally strong and resilient. A Dominion battleship encountered by the *U.S.S. Valiant* on stardate 51825 used viterium support braces in its antimatter storage system. ("*Valiant*" [DS9]).

Void. Informal name of a vast expanse in the Delta Quadrant bereft of any star systems. The Void, which was home to a civilization of technologically advanced **night beings**, was over 2,500 light-years across. The Void and its inhabitants were exposed for years to hazardous **theta radiation** caused by dumping of hazardous antimatter waste by **Malon** freighters. This practice was ended in 2375 when the Federation starship *Voyager*, crossing through the Void at the time, destroyed a spatial vortex that had been used as a conduit for the toxic waste dumping. ("Night" [VGR]).

Vor'nak. *Vor'cha*-class Klingon attack cruiser commanded by General Tanas. In early 2374, the *Vor'nak* rendezvoused with the *Rotarran* to transfer five crew replacements to the *Rotarran*. ("Sons and Daughters" [DS9]).

voraxna. Poison deadly to Cardassians. Gul Dukat sent a bottle of ***kanar***, heavily laced with voraxna, to **Legate Ghemor** in 2373 in an attempt to kill him before Ghemor could reveal Cardassian state secrets to Kira Nerys. ("Ties of Blood and Water" [DS9]).

Vori language terms. backwalk. To retreat. before. Used as a noun. A past event was said to have taken place "in the before." blossom. Flower. brightly greeted. To be made welcome. clash. Battle or war. clasher. Soldier. cluster. A group of people, or as a verb, to gather. colors. Clothing as a designation of one's national affiliation, Vori or Kradin. covering. Clothing. **defender.** Member of the Vori military. drill. To train. fastwalk. To run. fathom. To understand. **footfall.** Informal unit of distance measure, about one meter. fume. Poison gas. glimpse. Eye, or as a verb, to see. gray. Adjective meaning elderly. **Krady beast.** Racist term for a Kradin national. little likely. Improbable. mark. A specific location or a target. much another. Very different. nemesis. Enemy, the Kradin. Kradin nationals also referred to the Vori as the nemesis. new light. Morning. novice. Newly enlisted member of the Vori Defense Contingent. now. Used as a noun. An event in the present was said to be happening "in the now." nullify. To kill. old light. Evening. plantings. Farmland or crops. rages. Anger. sharp. To be smart. sly. To conceal oneself. soonafter. The near future. An impending event was said to be in the soonafter. sphere. Planet. tellings. Instruction or advice. top low and glimpses wide. "Keep your head down and your eyes open." trembles. Fear. To have the trembles was to be afraid. trunks. Forest. **upturned.** To be desecrated in death. **Wayafter.** The afterlife. A dead person was said to be in the Wayafter. *We assume, of course, that these are English translations of the Vori language, revealing the limitations of the universal translator.* ("Nemesis" [VGR]).

Vori. Sentient humanoid civilization that shared a Class-M world in the Delta Quadrant with the **Kradin** people. The Vori and the Kradin declared war on each other around 2364. Each side characterized the other as inhuman beasts, to motivate their citizenry to support the war. The Vori, finding it difficult to recruit new soldiers, conscripted their own people and offworlders through sophisticated mind-control techniques. A new conscript would be subjected to elaborate psychometric projections and psychotropic manipulation, causing the conscript to believe he was in the company of Vori guerrillas. In the course of the mind-control simulation, the conscript would be led to feel an emotional bonding with his fellow defenders. The conscript would then be made to feel anger when those defenders were brutally killed by the Kradin and outrage when the Kradin (apparently) massacred the inhabitants of a Vori village. In 2374, Commander Chakotay was so conscripted after crash-landing his shuttle on their world. SEE: **Vori language terms.** ("Nemesis" [VGR]).

Vorik.* (Alexander Enberg). Starfleet officer who served in the engineering department of the *Starship Voyager*. Vorik was a member of the development team that designed and built the *Delta Flyer* shuttlecraft in early 2375. ("Extreme Risk" [VGR]). *Alexander Enberg previously portrayed the similarly named Ensign Taurik in "Lower Decks" (TNG).*

Vorta.* Humanoid species, part of the **Dominion** in the Gamma Quadrant. Aeons ago, the Vorta were small, timid apelike forest dwellers who lived in hollowed-out trees. One day, a family of Vorta hid a shape-shifter who was fleeing from a mob of angry "solids." So grateful was the shape-shifter that he promised the Vorta that they would one day be transformed into powerful beings and that they would become an important part of an interstellar empire. The shape-shifters, later known as the **Founders**, made good on this promise when they genetically engineered the Vorta to assist them in ruling the Dominion. This engineering included a compulsion to worship the Founders as gods. ("Treachery, Faith, and the Great River" [DS9]). The Vorta reproduce by cloning and use the technique to achieve a sort of immortality. Vorta are immune to most forms of poison. ("Ties of Blood and Water" [DS9]). Since the Vorta were genetically engineered by the Founders, they have only the skills and abilities deemed by the Founders to be necessary for their assigned role in the Dominion. For example, the Vorta were not given an aesthetic sense and are tone-deaf. They have very good hearing but poor eyesight. ("Favor the Bold" [DS9]). They have a very limited sense of taste. *Kava* nuts and rippleberries are the only foods that they really enjoy. ("Treachery, Faith, and the Great River" [DS9]). Vorta are expected to kill themselves if captured by enemies of the Dominion by using a **termination implant**. ("The Magnificent Ferengi" [DS9], "Treachery, Faith, and the Great River" [DS9]).

Vostigye. Delta Quadrant civilization. The crew of the *U.S.S. Voyager* made long-range communications contact with Vostigye scientists in 2373. Unfortunately, a scheduled rendezvous with a Vostigye science space station failed to happen because the station was destroyed by an **astral eddy** just prior to stardate 50836.2. ("Real Life" [VGR]).

Voth city ship. Huge spacefaring **Voth** metropolis measuring approximately eleven kilometers in length. The ship, which used a sophisticated **transwarp** propulsion system, was large and powerful enough to capture the Federation starship *Voyager* and to hold it within its structure. ("Distant Origin" [VGR]).

Voth Doctrine. In the **Voth** culture, the belief that the Voth were the first sentient beings to evolve in their part of the galaxy. Much of Voth culture, including their belief in the legitimacy of their rule of their region of the Delta Quadrant, followed directly from Voth Doctrine. As a result, the Voth government had a strong tendency to try to suppress any opinions or findings that might tend to examine or question these beliefs. An example was the strong government reaction to the **Distant Origin Theory** in 2373. SEE: **heresy**. ("Distant Origin" [VGR]).

Voth Ministry of Elders. Governing body within the Voth society. The Ministry oversaw matters of the state, especially those issues dealing with interpretation and challenges to **Voth Doctrine**. Minister Odala was the head of the Ministry of Elders in 2373. Odala, fearful of the social ramifications should the **Distant Origin Theory** be widely known, censured Professor **Forra Gegen** and forced him to renounce his belief in the theory. ("Distant Origin" [VGR]).

Voth. Technologically sophisticated reptilian civilization from the Delta Quadrant. Although Voth Doctrine holds that the Voth evolved as the first sentient life-forms in their part of the galaxy, the Voth were actually descended from Earth's dinosaurs, some of whom migrated into space millions of years ago. The Voth settled in the Delta Quadrant some 20 million years ago, and all memory of their original homeworld has long since been lost. ("Distant Origin" [VGR]). SEE: **Distant Origin Theory; Gegen, Forra; hadrosaur; Ministry of Elders; transwarp.**

Voyager, U.S.S.* Federation starship lost in the Delta Quadrant in 2371. The ship's hull was primarily composed of duranium alloy. ("Drone" [VGR]). The ship was equipped with two holodecks. ("The Killing Game, Part I" (VGR)]. In early 2374 the ship's inventory included 32 class-6 photon torpedoes. ("Scorpion, Part II" [VGR]). Shortly after the *Voyager* arrived in the Delta Quadrant, ship's security chief **Tuvok** considered the merging of the *Voyager*'s crew with **Chakotay**'s Maquis members to be a possible security risk. Tuvok went so far as to begin work on a holodeck program, entitled **Insurrection Alpha,** to train junior security personnel to deal with a possible **Maquis** uprising. ("Worse Case Scenario" [VGR]). The *Voyager* traveled through **Borg** space in late 2373 and early 2374. Passage through this hostile region was possible because of a risky truce negotiated by Captain Janeway in which the Borg agreed not to assimilate *Voyager* in exchange for assistance in defending against an invasion by the extradimensional life-form known as **Species 8472**. Borg drones, temporarily aboard *Voyager* as part of the exchange agreement, installed a significant amount of Borg technology into the vessel's systems, some of which was deemed useful and permitted to remain, even after the conclusion of the operation. ("Scorpion, Parts I and II" [VGR]). In 2374, an alternate timeline was created in which the *U.S.S. Voyager* was pursued for an entire year by a **Krenim temporal weapon ship**. The alternate *Voyager* was destroyed in a collision with the Krenim ship, triggering a massive temporal incursion that restored the original timeline. ("Year of Hell, Parts I and II" [VGR]). Starfleet Command believed the *Voyager* to have been destroyed in the Badlands in 2371. It was not until 2374, when the ship's **Emergency Medical Hologram** was transported to the ***Starship Prometheus*** by means of a **Hirogen relay station**, that Starfleet authorities learned that the ship and crew had survived and that they were striving to return home from the distant Delta Quadrant. ("Message in a Bottle" [VGR]). Starfleet sent a message in response through the Hirogen relay, but only some of the data were successfully received by *Voyager*. Those data included several personal messages from family and friends of *Voyager* crew members. ("Hunters" [VGR]). The data also included an encrypted message from Admiral Hayes, acknowledging Starfleet's awareness that *Voyager* had survived, but expressing regret that Starfleet knew of no way to bring *Voyager* home any faster. ("Hope and Fear" [VGR]).

Vreenak. (Stephen McHattie). **Romulan** senator, elected in 2360. Vreenak was secretary of the War Plans Council and vice chairman of the **Tal Shiar** and was also one of Proconsul **Neral**'s most trusted advisors. Vreenak negotiated a nonaggression pact with the **Dominion** in 2373 and was one of the most ardently pro-Dominion voices in the senate. In 2374, while returning home from a meeting with the Dominion on Soukara, Senator Vreenak's **Romulan shuttle** was destroyed by a bomb. Investigating the incident, the Tal Shiar concluded that Vreenak had been assassinated by Dominion agents seeking to destroy evidence of an impending Dominion invasion of Romulan territory. The Romulan government subsequently abrogated the nonaggression treaty, entering the war against the Dominion. SEE: **Tolar, Grathon.** ("In the Pale Moonlight" [DS9]).

Vrelk, Controller. (Hamilton Camp). Master of a **Malon export vessel**. In 2375, Vrelk's crew constructed a special purpose shuttle to venture into the atmosphere of a gas giant in an attempt to steal *Voyager*'s advanced probe, but *Voyager*'s new shuttle, the *Delta Flyer*, beat them to it. ("Extreme Risk" [VGR]). *Hamilton Camp has also played Leck in "Ferengi Love Songs" (DS9) and "The Magnificent Ferengi" (DS9).*

Vulcan tea. Beverage originating on Vulcan made from aromatic plant leaves steeped in hot water. Lieutenant Commander Tuvok occasionally drank Vulcan tea aboard the *Voyager*. ("Revulsion" [VGR]).

Vulcan's Forge. Formidable range of mountains on planet **Vulcan**. On stardate 51597.2, Worf suggested a two-week hiking trip across Vulcan's Forge as a possible honeymoon destination, but his new bride, Jadzia Dax, rejected the idea. ("Change of Heart" [DS9]).

Vulcan.* Planet. Vulcan is located near Betazed, Andor, Tellar, and Alpha Centauri. ("In the Pale Moonlight" [DS9]). Starfleet's **Seventh Fleet** suffered heavy losses while protecting Vulcan during the Dominion war in late 2374. ("The Reckoning" [DS9]).

vulky. Derogatory slang adjective term meaning "uninteresting," with racist overtones, derived from the word Vulcan. ("Real Life" [VGR]).

wachk ihw, wachk kkor-duh. Klingon phrase that meant "one blood, one house." ("Sons and Daughters" [DS9]).

Waiver of Property and Profit. Ferengi legal document to which females are expected to agree before marriage. The W. P. and P., as it is sometime called, states that in the event that the marriage ends, the female relinquishes claim to her husband's estate. When **Rom** and **Leeta** became engaged in 2373, Leeta refused to sign a Waiver of Property and Profit. ("Ferengi Love Songs" [DS9]).

"Waking Moments." *Voyager* episode #82. Written by Andre Bormanis. Directed by Alexander Singer. Stardate 51471.3. First aired in 1997. *The* Starship Voyager *falls prey to a dream species that attacks the crew in their sleep.* GUEST CAST: Mark Colson as Dream Alien; Jennifer Gundy as Ensign; Majel Barrett as Computer Voice. SEE: ***akoonah*; animazine; Australian aborigines; Chile; dream species; Fiji; hoverball; hyper-REM; *leola* root; lucid dreaming; neurogenic field; Saint Moritz; Samoa; Tahiti; waking species.**

waking species. Term used by the Delta Quadrant **dream species** for their enemies who did not live in a hyper-REM state. ("Waking Moments" [VGR]).

Walker, Ensign. Starfleet officer assigned to Deep Space 9. In 2374, Julian Bashir asked Walker to dinner three times, but she turned him down until his fourth invitation, which he made using advice he had received from **Vic Fontaine**. ("His Way" [DS9]).

"Waltz." *Deep Space Nine* episode #135. Written by Ronald D. Moore. Directed by Rene Auberjonois. Stardate 51408.6. *First aired in 1997. Gul Dukat, suffering from delusions after the death of his daughter, reveals his true evil nature when he and Benjamin Sisko are marooned on a planet together.* GUEST CAST: Jeffrey Combs as **Weyoun**; Marc Alaimo as **Dukat, Gul**; Casey Biggs as **Damar.** SEE: **Bajorans; Cardassians; *Constellation, U.S.S.*; Cox, Dr.; Dukat, Gul; *Honshu, U.S.S.*; *Kornaire*; McConnell, Lieutenant; starbase: 621.**

warp core breach. Potent alcoholic beverage available at Quark's bar. A warp core breach was usually served in a very large glass goblet. ("His Way" [DS9]).

warp core. SEE: **matter/antimatter reaction chamber**.

warp drive, class-7. Model of warp drive system used aboard the *Starship Defiant*. ("One Little Ship" [DS9]).

Warrior's Anthem. Klingon battle song that was often sung by warriors as they went into battle. ("Soldiers of the Empire" [DS9]).

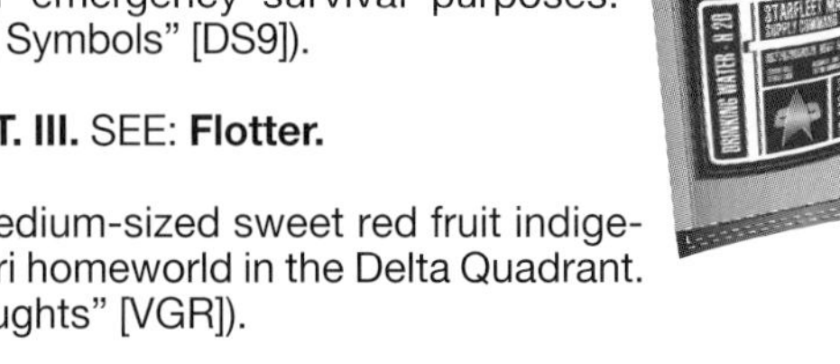

water pack. Starfleet issue package containing approximately 250 milliliters of drinking water, normally used for emergency survival purposes. ("Shadows and Symbols" [DS9]).

Water, Flotter T. III. SEE: **Flotter.**

waterplum. Medium-sized sweet red fruit indigenous to the Mari homeworld in the Delta Quadrant. ("Random Thoughts" [VGR]).

Watters, Tim. (Paul Popowich). Starfleet Academy cadet. In 2374, Watters and 34 other members of the elite Red Squad embarked on a training cruise aboard the ***U.S.S. Valiant*** under the command of **Captain Ramirez**. The ship became caught behind enemy lines when the Dominion war broke out and the senior officers were killed in battle. Before he died, Ramirez turned command over to cadet Tim Watters. Acting Commander Watters defied the odds and kept the ship intact for eight months in Dominion-held territory. Watters was a charismatic leader and the rest of the elite group of cadets followed him loyally, failing to see serious errors in Watters's judgment. On stardate 51825.4, he and most of his crew were killed and the *Valiant* destroyed when Watters took the ship on an impossible mission to single-handedly destroy a massive **Dominion battleship**. SEE: **cordafin.** ("*Valiant*" [DS9]).

Wayafter. In the **Vori** and **Kradin** cultures, the concept of the afterlife. A dead person was turned to face the ground so that his spirit could descend to the Wayafter. The greatest desecration to the Vori or Kradin dead was to "upturn" the body, so that the deceased could not go to the Wayafter. During their extended war, the Vori and the Kradin accused each other of dishonoring each other's dead in this fashion. ("Nemesis" [VGR]).

wedding*.

Bajoran. Traditional Bajoran weddings are conducted in accordance with ancient texts including Horran's Seventh Prophecy, which starts, "He will come to the palace, carrying a chalice overflowing with sweet spring wine." ("Ferengi Love Songs" [DS9]).

Ferengi. Ferengi females are expected to sign a document known as a **Waiver of Property and Profit** before they are allowed to enter into a marriage contract. ("Ferengi Love Songs" [DS9]). Traditional Ferengi weddings include a bridal auction and a latinum dance. The bride and all other females are naked at the ceremony. ("Call to Arms" [DS9]).

Klingon. During the last four days before his wedding, a Klingon groom, accompanied by his closest male friends, traditionally experiences the mental and spiritual journey called ***Kal'Hyah***. The Mistress of the groom's house tests the prospective bride by having her perform several rituals, which must be accomplished in strict adherence with tradition. The Mistress of the House often performs the actual ceremony, and she has the authority to reject the bride and call off the wedding if she so chooses. The ceremony recounts the stirring tale of how the Klingon gods forged the first two Klingon hearts from fire and steel and how the first couple joined forces and slew the gods. ("You Are Cordially Invited" [DS9]). SEE: ***Ma'Stakas*; *Tawi'Yan*; *var'Hama* candles.** After the vows were exchanged, the bride would present her ***d'k tahg*** to the head of the groom's family as a formal request that she be accepted into the groom's **House**. ("Sons and Daughters" [DS9]). Traditional Klingon weddings include a ritual *targ* sacrifice followed by the wedding feast. ("A Time to Stand" [DS9]).

Corbis

Wells, H. G. (1866–1946). Writer and futurist from 19th- and 20th-century Earth. Herbert George Wells wrote **science fiction** novels including *The Time Machine* (1895), *The Invisible Man* (1897), and *The War of the Worlds* (1898). Julius Eaton thought that Wells would not have approved of instant tea. ("Far Beyond the Stars" [DS9]).

West, Mae. (1892–1980). Twentieth-century Earth entertainer. Noted for her work in early motion pictures, West played outrageously sexy characters and was famous for her double entendres. She enjoyed popular success for appearances in several movies produced by Paramount Pictures. ("The Killing Game, Part II" [VGR]).

Weyoun.* Vorta operative. In keeping with normal Vorta practice, Weyoun was actually a series of clones of the original Weyoun progenitor. The fourth Weyoun clone was killed in 2372. His successor, the fifth Weyoun, became the chief **Dominion** liaison to the Cardassian government led by Gul Dukat in 2373. ("Ties of Blood and Water" [DS9]). The fifth Weyoun was killed in a suspicious transporter accident in early 2375. The sixth Weyoun, possibly a defective clone, felt that the Dominion war was wrong, and he attempted to defect to Odo. When the Dominion learned of this, a new Weyoun was cloned. This seventh Weyoun sent a squadron of Jem'Hadar ships to attack the runabout carrying the sixth Weyoun and Odo. The sixth Weyoun killed himself to prevent harm from befalling Odo. ("Treachery, Faith, and the Great River" [DS9]). The last two Weyoun clones served as aides to the Founder Leader during the final days of the Dominion war, ("Strange Bedfellows" [DS9]) carrying out the Founders' campaign of terror against the occupied Cardassian people. The last Weyoun was killed by Garak during the final hours of the war. ("What You Leave Behind" [DS9]).

wheat. The grain of a cereal grass widely cultivated as a food source by many humanoid cultures. A form of wheat was cultivated on planet **Bajor**. ("The Reckoning" [DS9]). SEE: **quadrotriticale**.

Whelan bitters. Alcoholic beverage containing bitter herbs. ("In the Pale Moonlight" [DS9]).

White Rose Redi-Tea. Brand name of a tea beverage available on Earth in the mid-20th century. The product was a dry powder that could be dissolved in water, instantly producing a reasonable facsimile of tea without the time or effort of brewing. Kay Eaton saw White Rose Redi-Tea as a symbol of the coming benefits of advancing technology, but Julius Eaton thought that anyone from the nation of England would find it appalling. ("Far Beyond the Stars" [DS9]).

"Who Mourns for Morn?" *Deep Space Nine* episode #136. Written by Mark Gehred-O'Connell. Directed by Victor Lobl. No stardate given. *First aired in 1997. When Morn fakes his death, Quark inherits a fortune and a group of claims to the estate, Despite this all, Morn still doesn't utter a word.* GUEST CAST: Gregory Itzin as **Hain**; Brad Greenquist as **Krit**; Bridget Ann White as **Larell**; Cyril O'Reilly as **Nahsk**; Mark Shepherd as **Morn**. SEE: **Bolias, Bank of; Broik; gold-pressed latinum; gold; Hain; Krit; Larell; latinum; Lissepia, Central Bank of; Lissepian Mother's Day Heist; Livanian beet; Lurians; Morn; Nahsk.**

Wildman, Naomi. (Brooke Stephens; Scarlett Pomer). Daughter of *Voyager* crew member **Samantha Wildman**, Naomi was the first child to be born on the *Starship Voyager* after it was lost in the Delta Quadrant. Naomi grew very quickly, owing to her **Ktarian** heritage, and by the age of two, she was the size and intelligence of a four-year-old human child. **Neelix** was a good friend to Samantha and her daughter and would often tuck Naomi into bed when the child feared that there were monsters in her room. Naomi especially liked when Neelix told her stories of the **Great Forest**. ("Mortal Coil" [VGR]). Naomi was an extremely bright child. She enjoyed the classic children's holographic stories, ***The Adventures of Flotter***. ("Once Upon a Time" [VGR]). *Brooke Stephens played Naomi in "Mortal Coil," while Scarlett Pomer assumed the role in "Once Upon a Time."*)

Wildman, Samantha.* (Nancy Hower). Starfleet officer who served aboard the *Starship Voyager*. Ensign Wildman named her daughter Naomi. ("Mortal Coil" [VGR]). Wildman was seriously injured in early 2375 while participating in a scientific mission aboard the *Delta Flyer* shuttlecraft. ("Once Upon a Time" [VGR]).

Willoughby, Chief Edgar. Starfleet quartermaster for the Bajor sector in 2375. Willoughby was fond of Gamzian wine. He had a wife, Cynthia, as well as a daughter, Melissa, born in 2367, and a son, Edgar, Jr., who was born in 2370. ("Treachery, Faith, and the Great River" [DS9]). *This character may have been named as an homage to the classic 1960* Twilight Zone *episode, "A Stop at Willoughby," starring James Daly.*

Winn.* Ambitious Bajoran religious and political leader who betrayed her people by allying herself with the evil **Pah-wraiths**. In late 2373, Winn supported a startling **Dominion** proposal for a nonaggression pact with **Bajor**. Although Federation officials strongly opposed the move, Winn felt that a treaty with the Dominion might help assure her planet's survival in the event of a Dominion invasion through the wormhole. ("In the Cards" [DS9]). Winn was uncomfortable with the fact that **Benjamin Sisko**, a non-Bajoran, had such an important role in Bajoran affairs as the **Emissary** to the Prophets. These feelings motivated her in 2374 to interfere with the will of the **Prophets**, when she interrupted **the Reckoning**, an epic battle between good and evil foretold by ancient prophesy. Ironically, the non-Bajoran Sisko demonstrated greater faith in Bajor's gods than did Winn. ("The Reckoning" [DS9]). By late 2375, Winn bitterly resented the fact that Benjamin Sisko, a non-Bajoran, played such a major part in her religion, and she was thus an easy target for manipulation when **Gul Dukat** disguised himself as a Bajoran farmer. Winn was willingly seduced by Dukat, an agent of the evil **Pah-wraith** known as **Kosst Amojan**, who skillfully fed Winn's hatred and her ambition, turning her against the Prophets. ("'Til Death Do Us Part" [DS9], "Strange Bedfellows" [DS9]). Winn schemed with Dukat to release the Pah-wraiths from the **fire caves** of Bajor ("The Changing Face of Evil" [DS9]). Although she nearly succeeded in unleashing all of the Pah-wraiths, Winn had a last-minute change of heart. She sacrificed herself so that the Emissary could permanently seal the Pah-wraiths in the fire caves, thereby ensuring the survival of not only the Bajoran people, but the Prophets themselves. ("What You Leave Behind" [DS9]) *"'Til Death Do Us Part" (DS9) established her given name as Adami.*

Wolf 359.* Star. The only Federation starship to survive the disastrous battle with the **Borg** at Wolf 359 in 2367 was the *Nebula*-class ***U.S.S. Endeavour***. ("Scorpion, Part I" [VGR]).

Woman Warriors at the River of Blood. Klingon romance novel. B'Elanna Torres read this novel in 2373, causing Tom Paris to speculate about the possibility of a romantic relationship between the two. ("Real Life" [VGR]).

Wong, Captain Leslie. Starfleet officer and captain of the *U.S.S. Cairo*. She taught at the academy in 2361 during Jadzia Dax's second year. Wong was presumed killed in 2374, when the *Cairo* disappeared and was believed destroyed ("In the Pale Moonlight" [DS9]).

Worf.* The first **Klingon** warrior to serve in the Federation **Starfleet**. When Worf was a boy growing up in Russia ("Image in the Sand" [DS9]), his father used to take him and his brother Nikolai on camping trips in the Ural Mountains. Every night they would listen to the wolves howling in the distance. Nikolai was afraid of them, but Worf would lie in his tent for hours just listening. Worf would later recall that he secretly felt the urge to strip off his clothes and run into the night to live in the forest as something wild. SEE: **Rozhenko, Nikolai**. ("Change of Heart" [DS9]). During the Dominion war, Worf served aboard the *Bird-of-Prey* ***Rotarran*** under **General Martok**. So pleased was Martok with Worf that he

made Worf a member of the House of Martok. ("Soldiers of the Empire" [DS9]). In late 2373, Worf and Jadzia became engaged to be married. ("Call to Arms" [DS9]). Worf never felt fully comfortable with his son, Alexander, and the two became further estranged when Alexander went to live with Worf's parents on Earth. Worf reacted angrily when Alexander subsequently joined the Klingon Defense Force and the two served together aboard the bird-of-prey ***I.K.S. Rotarran***, but the two began to heal their relationship when Alexander agreed to join his father as a member of the House of Martok. ("Sons and Daughters" [DS9]). Ever since he was a boy, Worf had always wanted a traditional Klingon wedding, possibly as a way of compensating for the fact that he was raised in human society. In 2374, on stardate 51247, Worf got his wish when he and Dax were married in a traditional Klingon ceremony on Deep Space 9. In the ceremony, his son Alexander was Worf's *Tawi'Yan*, or sword bearer. ("You Are Cordially Invited" [DS9]). On stardate 51597.2, Worf commanded a mission into Dominion territory to extract a vital Starfleet operative from possible Dominion capture. The mission was a failure when the informant was killed by Jem'Hadar forces after Worf chose to care for his wife, who had been critically wounded, instead of making the rendezvous with the informant. SEE: **Lasaran, Glinn**. Captain Sisko subsequently entered another serious reprimand in Worf's record after the incident, meaning that Worf had little chance of ever being granted a command of his own by Starfleet. ("Change of Heart" [DS9]). Worf was deeply in love with Jadzia, but his dream of raising a family with her was shattered in 2374 when Jadzia was tragically killed by a Pah-wraith inhabiting the body of Gul Dukat. ("Tears of the Prophets" [DS9]). After her death, Worf worried that Jadzia had not died in battle, and might therefore be denied entry to ***Sto-Vo-Kor*** in the afterlife. ("Image in the Sand" [DS9]). He therefore volunteered for a dangerous mission, dedicating the glorious victory to her name so that she might have a place among the honored dead. In this effort, Worf was assisted by his friends Julian Bashir, Miles O'Brien, and Quark, who also risked their lives to honor Jadzia. ("Shadows and Symbols" [DS9]). Upon his return, however, Worf was faced with an unexpected challenge: the emotionally difficult task of meeting the new host to the Dax symbiont. Worf's discomfort was so great that **Ezri Dax** nearly refused a posting to Deep Space 9 out of respect for Worf's feelings. She agreed to stay only after Worf indicated that he believed Jadzia would have wanted him to accept her as the new host. ("Afterimage" [DS9]). In 2375, Worf briefly rejoined the crew of the *Enterprise*-E to prevent the Ba'ku people from being forcibly removed from their homeworld by the Son'a. (*Star Trek: Insurrection*). During the final weeks of the **Dominion** war, Worf became appalled that Chancellor **Gowron** was squandering the lives of Klingon warriors in pursuit of personal political gain. Worf urged the chancellor to reconsider his strategies, but was rebuffed. Soon, Worf realized that Gowron's politically motivated decisions threatened the survival of the empire itself. Worf challenged and slew Gowron in a *bat'leth* fight for honor, and in so doing, earned the right to lead the high council. Nevertheless, Worf believed that the interests of his people would be best served with Martok leading the empire, so Worf stood aside and Martok became chancellor. ("Tacking into the Wind" [DS9]). After the Dominion war, Worf became the Federation ambassador to **Qo'noS**. ("What You Leave Behind" [DS9]).

World War II. Global conflict on planet **Earth** from 1939 to 1945 in which a group of nations called the Axis sought to gain planetary dominance over other nations that called themselves the Allies. The **Hirogen**, studying Earth violence in 2374, were fascinated with World War II and used it as a basis for a holodeck simulation to examine human behavior. SEE: **Allied Forces; Einstein, Albert; French Resistance; Nazi Germany; United States of America.** ("The Killing Game, Parts I and II" [VGR]).

"Worse Case Scenario." *Voyager* episode #67. Written by Kenneth Biller. Directed by Alexander Singer. Stardate 50953.4. *First aired in 1997. The crew discovers a secret holographic program depicting Seska and the Maquis leading an insurrection aboard* Voyager, *and Tuvok and Paris become trapped in it. Seska returns in this episode, even though she's only a hologram.* GUEST CAST: Martha Hackett as **Seska**. SEE: ***deus ex machina*; "Dictates of Poetics"; holodeck and holosuite programs: Insurrection Alpha; Insurrection Alpha; narrative parameters file; Rukani; security access code; Seska; T'Hain; *Voyager, U.S.S.***

Wright, Richard. (1908–1960). Twentieth-century Earth author. Through his influential novel, *Native Son*, Wright was among the first writers to protest the second-class economic and social status accorded to African-Americans in American society. Science-fiction writer **Benny Russell** drew inspiration from Wright's work. ("Far Beyond the Stars" [DS9]).

Corbis

"Wrongs Darker Than Death or Night." *Deep Space Nine* episode #141. Written by Ira Steven Behr & Hans Beimler. Directed by Jonathan West. No stardate given. *First aired in 1998. Kira goes back in time to learn that her mother was a "comfort woman" who had a relationship with Gul Dukat during the occupation.* GUEST CAST: Leslie Hope as **Kira Meru**; Marc Alaimo as **Dukat, Gul**; David Bowe as **Basso Tromac**; Wayne Grace as Legate; Tim deZarn as **Halb Daier**; Thomas Kopache as **Kira Taban**; John Marzelli as Scavenger; Marc Marosi as Gul. SEE: **Alamo, Battle of the; Bajoran lilac; Basso Tromac; comfort woman; Deep Space 9; Dukat, Gul; Halb Daier; Iponu; Kira Meru; Kira Nerys; Kira Pohl; Kira Reon; Kira Taban; Orb of Time; *Saratoga, U.S.S.*; Singha refugee camp; Terok Nor; ultritium.**

Wykoff, Dr. (Casey Biggs). Psychiatrist on Earth's North American continent during the mid-20th century. Wykoff was assigned to the case of writer **Benny Russell** when Russell was incarcerated for believing too strongly in the reality of a **science-fiction** story he had written. Russell's story had been a continuation of his novella, **"Deep Space Nine."** In this new adventure, Ben Sisko had voyaged to a planet called Tyree in search of a relic called the Orb of the Emissary. Wykoff urged Russell to repudiate his visions by erasing what he had written, but Russell refused. ("Shadows and Symbols" [DS9]). *Casey Biggs also played Damar.*

xenon-based life-form. Biological forms whose organic chemistry is based on the gaseous element xenon, rather than the more common element, carbon. The crew of the *Starship Voyager* encountered xenon-based sentient beings on a trade mission on stardate 51978.2. ("Hope and Fear" [VGR]).

Y

Ya'Vang, I.K.S. Klingon battle cruiser. The *Ya'Vang* took heavy losses in 2374 during the Dominion war. Several of the *Rotarran* crew, including Alexander Rozhenko, transferred to the *Ya'Vang*. ("You Are Cordially Invited" [DS9]).

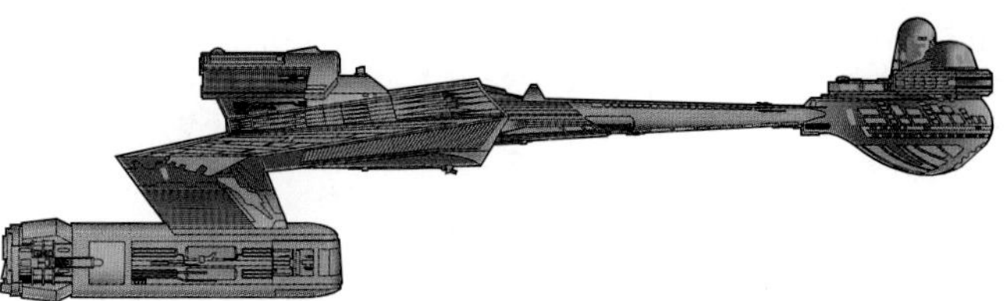

yak bear. Large carnivorous animal indigenous to the planet Gaia. ("Children of Time" [DS9]).

Yak'Talon. Jem'Hadar soldier who was part of the crew of an attack vessel commanded by **Keevan**. Yak'Talon and all the other Jem'Hadar were killed in a firefight with Captain Benjamin Sisko and his crew on a planet in a dark matter nebula in Cardassian space. ("Rocks and Shoals" [DS9]).

Yaltar, Gul. Cardassian officer. Yaltar served in the Third Order. ("Image in the Sand" [DS9]).

Yarim Fel syndrome. Terminal disease affecting Cardassians. The malady attacks the organ systems of the body and causes great pain. **Legate Ghemor** died of Yarim Fel syndrome in 2373. ("Ties of Blood and Water" [DS9]).

Yassim, Vedek. (Lilyan Chauvin). Bajoran cleric. Yassim was a woman of great personal convictions. Vedek Yassim martyred herself by committing suicide on station Deep Space 9's Promenade in protest of the **Dominion** occupation of her homeworld. The demonstration had a profound impact on **Kira Nerys**, who saw Yassim's death as pivotal in her decision to oppose the Dominion. ("Rocks and Shoals" [DS9]).

Yates, Kasidy.* Freighter captain. Yates normally operated as an independent contractor, but once acted as convoy liaison officer for Starfleet aboard the *Defiant* during the Dominion war in late 2374. Yates was romantically involved with Starfleet officer **Benjamin Sisko**. ("The Sound of Her Voice" [DS9]). SEE: **Cassie**. In early 2375, Yates took advantage of a lull in her shipping schedule to spend a couple of weeks with Sisko at Deep Space 9, where she joined the Deep Space **Niners**, an informal **baseball** team, playing third base. ("Take Me Out to the Holosuite" [DS9]). Kasidy Shameeka Yates married Benjamin Lafayette Sisko in a quiet ceremony aboard station Deep Space 9 in late 2375. ("'Til Death Do Us Part" [DS9]). Kasidy became pregnant with Benjamin's child ("Dogs of War" [DS9]), but sadly, Benjamin departed the linear realm before he could see the child born. ("What You Leave Behind" [DS9]).

"Year of Hell, Part I." *Voyager* episode #76. Written by Brannon Braga & Joe Menosky. Directed by Allan Kroeker. Stardate 51212.3. First aired in 1997. *The* Starship Voyager *is nearly destroyed by a megalomaniac who uses time itself as a weapon to eradicate all trace of his enemies, obliterating entire civilizations in the process.* GUEST CAST: Kurtwood Smith as **Annorax**; John Loprieno as **Obrist**; Peter Slutsker as Krenim commandant; Rick Fitts as **Zahl official**; Sue Henley as **Ensign Brooks**. Deborah Levin as **Lang**. SEE: **Annorax; Astrometrics Lab; Brooks, Ensign; chroniton torpedo; chroniton; Emergency Medical Hologram; Emmanuel; escape pod; Gable, Clark; Grant, Cary; Janeway, Kathryn; Krenim Imperium; Krenim temporal weapon ship; Krenim; Kyana Prime; Obrist; parrises squares; R'Cho, M'Kota; Strickler, Ensign; *Titanic*; *Voyager, U.S.S.*; Zahl official; Zahl.**

"Year of Hell, Part II." *Voyager* episode #77. Written by Brannon Braga & Joe Menosky. Directed by Mike Vejar. Stardate 51212.3. First aired in 1997. *Janeway struggles to keep her ship and crew together despite months of pounding from the Krenim temporal weapon ship.* GUEST CAST: Kurtwood Smith as **Annorax**; John Loprieno as **Obrist**; Peter Slutsker as Krenim commandant; Lise Simms as Annorax's wife. SEE: **Alsuran Empire; Annorax; Astrometrics; Bligh, Captain William; chroniton torpedo; chroniton; escape pod; Janeway, Kathryn; Krenim Imperium; Krenim temporal weapon ship; Krenim; Kyana Prime; Malkothian spirits; Mawasi; Nemo, Captain; Nihydron; Obrist; Ram Izad; Rilnar; Starfleet General Orders and Regulations: Regulation 121, Section A; temporal mechanics; traumatic stress syndrome; trioxin; Vassbinder, Professor; *Voyager, U.S.S.***

yelg melon. Type of large juicy edible fruit indigenous to Gaia. ("Children of Time" [DS9]).

Yelgrun. (Iggy Pop). Vorta official. Yelgrun traveled to Empok Nor in 2374 for a prisoner exchange in which Ferengi citizen Ishka was to be traded for Vorta officer **Keevan**. The exchange did not go as planned, and Yelgrun was captured by Quark and his rescue team. ("The Magnificent Ferengi" [DS9]). *Yelgrun was played by Iggy Pop, the popular rock musician.*

yih-Ghom-HAH. Klingon term that meant "dismissed." ("Sons and Daughters" [DS9]).

Yint. (Brad Blaisdell). Arms dealer on Farius Prime. Yint sold three defective Klingon disruptor rifles to **Orion Syndicate** operative **Liam Bilby** in 2374. Yint was killed for his error in judgment. ("Honor Among Thieves" [DS9]).

"Yoshi." Nickname for **Kirayoshi O'Brien**. ("Ties of Blood and Water" [DS9]).

"You Are Cordially Invited." *Deep Space Nine* episode #131. Written by Ronald D. Moore. Directed by David Livingston. Stardate 51247.5. *First aired in 1997. Worf's plans for a traditional Klingon wedding are threatened when Martok's wife refuses to accept Dax into their family. Worf and Dax get married in this episode, and we learn that Dax is 356 years old as of 2374.* GUEST CAST: J. G. Hertzler as **Martok, General**; Marc Worden as **Rozhenko, Alexander**; Shannon Cochran as **Sirella**; Chase Masterson as **Leeta**; Aron Eisenberg as **Nog**; Max Grodénchik as **Rom**; Sidney Liufau as **Atoa, Lieutenant Manuele.** SEE: ***Akagi, U.S.S.*; Altair sandwich; Atoa, Lieutenant Manuele; Bajoran shrimp; *Bre'Nan* ritual; Dark Time; Dax (symbiont); Dax, Curzon; Dax, Jadzia; *Exeter, U.S.S.*; Hamar; holodeck and holosuite programs: *Kal'Hyah* ritual; K'Trelan; "Kahless and Lukara"; *Kal'Hyah*; Karana; *kava* juice; Kela; Khitomer Accords; Klingon Empire; linguini with Bajoran shrimp; Linkasa; *Ma'Stakas*; mapa bread; Martok, General; Morn; Ninth Fleet; *Potemkin, U.S.S.*; Reclaw; Rozhenko, Alexander; Second Klingon Dynasty; Shelby, Captain; Shenara; Sirella; Sisko, Jake; steak with mushrooms; *Sutherland, U.S.S.*; *targ*; *Tawi'Yan*; Third Klingon Dynasty; *Toruk-DOH*; *var'Hama* candle; wedding: Klingon; Worf; *Ya'Vang, I.K.S.***

"You're Nobody Till Somebody Loves You." Twentieth-century Earth musical composition written by R. Morgan, L. Stock, and J. Cavanaugh. The song, which extolled the importance of having a romantic relationship in one's life, was popularized by such entertainers as **Vic Fontaine** and **Frank Sinatra**. ("His Way" [DS9]).

yridium bicantizine. Chemical compound, an active ingredient in **ketracel-white**. In 2374, the Dominion sought to control the Kabrel system because a planet there was a source of trinucleic fungi, which could be used to produce yridium bicantizine. ("Statistical Probabilities" [DS9]).

Z

Zahl official. (Rick Fitts). Representative of the **Zahl** government. ("Year of Hell, Part I" [VGR]).

Zahl. Delta quadrant civilization. In an alternate timeline, the Zahl civilization was completely eradicated in 2374 by the **Krenim temporal weapon ship**. "Year of Hell, Part I" [VGR]).

Zek.* Former grand nagus of the Ferengi Alliance. ("The Dogs of War" [DS9]). Zek was an excellent *tongo* player, winning the Global *Tongo* Championships for 27 years straight. In 2373, Zek met **Ishka,** and the two fell in love. About that time, Zek had began to suffer from a failing memory. Ishka learned of this and worked behind the scenes to help him in his business dealings. ("Ferengi Love Songs" [DS9]). In 2374, Zek let Ishka travel to **Vulcan** to receive cosmetic ear-lifting surgery to improve her looks, despite Ferengi laws that prohibited females from traveling off planet. When her transport ship was captured by the Dominion, Zek offered a reward of 50 bars of gold-pressed latinum for her safe return. ("The Magnificent Ferengi" [DS9]). Zek was aware of Ishka's hopes to reform Ferengi society to grant equal rights to females. ("Ferengi Love Songs" [DS9]). While Zek was something of a traditionalist, he ultimately saw the wisdom of Ishka's position and in 2374 imposed a radical amendment to the **Ferengi Bill of Opportunities**, granting for the first time to females the right to wear clothing. The reaction to Zek's reforms was swift and dramatic. Financial chaos erupted throughout the alliance as soon as fully clothed females began appearing in public. In the tumult, Zek was temporarily deposed as grand nagus by Brunt, until Zek and Quark were successful in convincing FCA Commissioner **Nilva** that equal rights for women would open tremendous new opportunities for profit. ("Profit and Lace" [DS9]). Zek's far-reaching social vision extended to the levying of a progressive income tax on all business, even including bribes. He used the resulting revenues to fund new social programs including wage subsidies for the poor, retirement benefits for the aged, and health care. He even instituted a representative legislature known as the Congress of Economic Advisors that was empowered to enact or reject the proclamations of the nagus. Grand Nagus Zek retired to Risa in late 2375. He appointed **Rom** as his successor. ("The Dogs of War" [DS9])."

Zevians. Civilization. In 2374, Zevian authorities requested information on a smuggling ring from the security office at Deep Space 9. ("His Way" [DS9]).

APPENDICES

FEDERATION STARSHIPS & SHIPS OF EARTH REGISTRY

Ships shown to approximate scale.

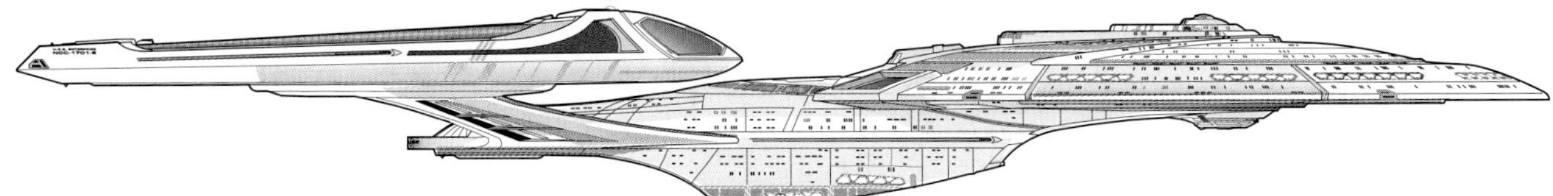

Sovereign-class starship, *U.S.S Enterprise*-E (*Star Trek:First Contact*).

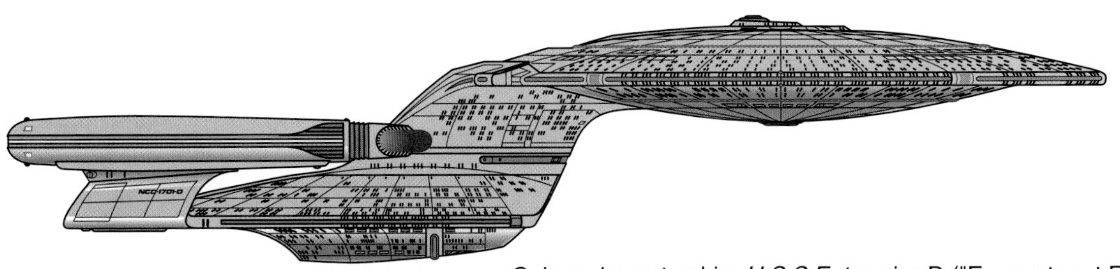

Galaxy-class starship, *U.S.S Enterprise*-D ("Encounter at Farpoint" [TNG]).

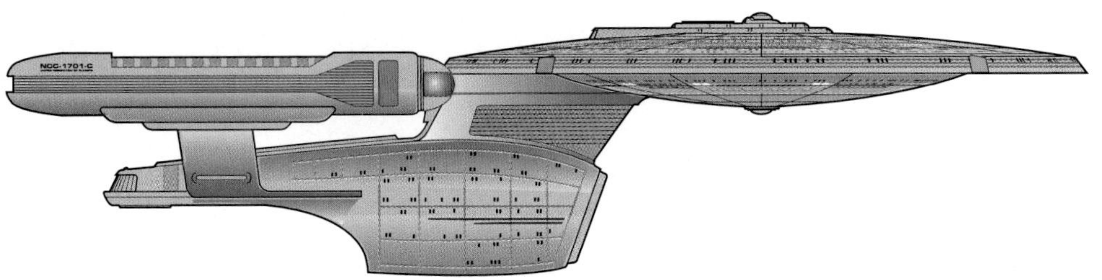

Ambassador-class starship, *U.S.S Enterprise*-C ("Yesterdays Enterprise" [TNG]).

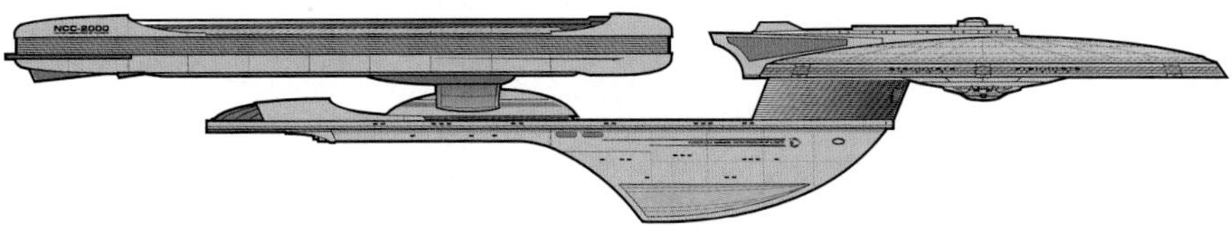

Excelsior-class starship, *U.S.S Excelsior* (*Star Trek III: The Search for Spock*).

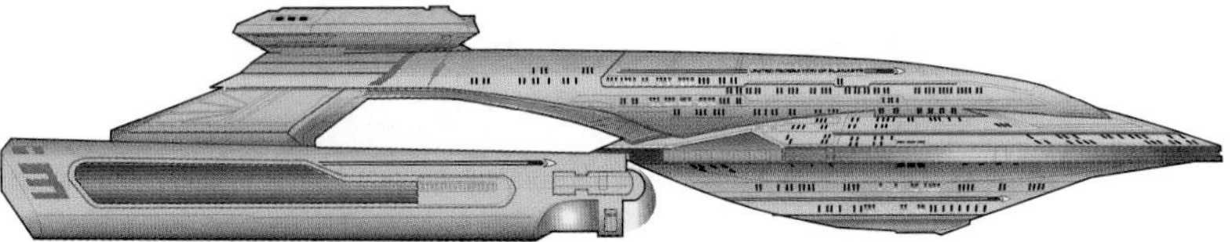

Akira-class starship, *U.S.S. Thunderchild* (*Star Trek:First Contact*).

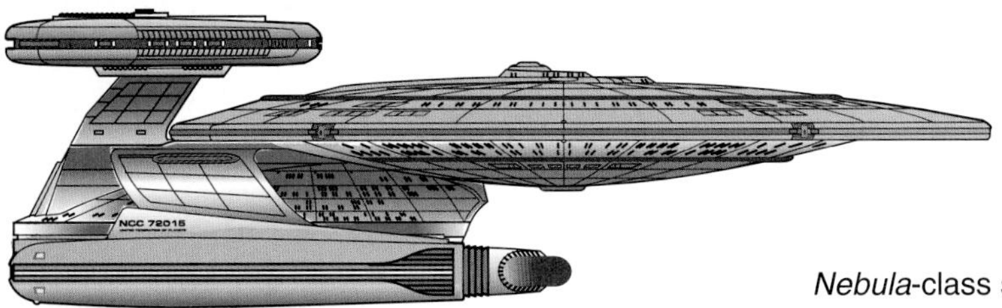

Nebula-class starship, *U.S.S. Phoenix* ("The Wounded" [TNG]).

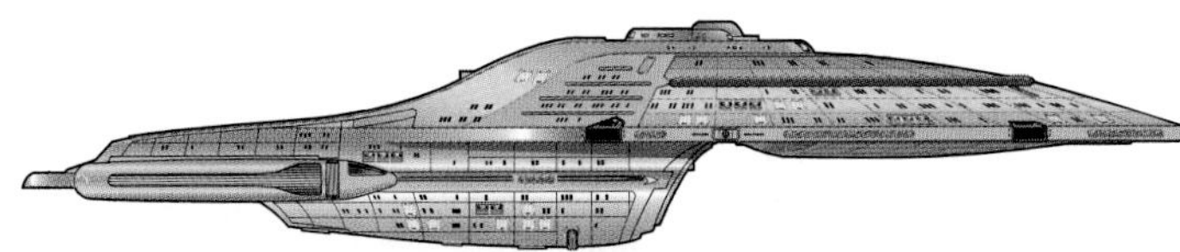

Intrepid-class starship, *U.S.S. Voyager* ("Caretaker, Part I" [VGR]).

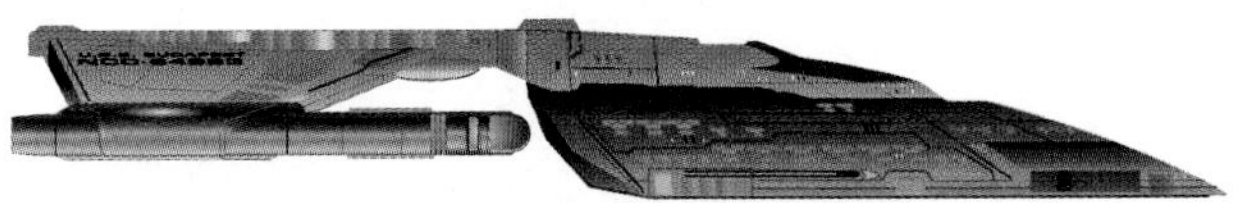

Norway-class starship, *U.S.S. Budapest* (*Star Trek:First Contact*).

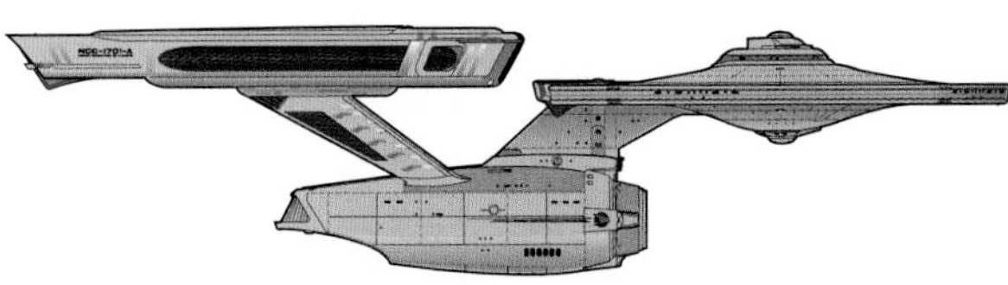

Constitution-class starship (refit), *U.S.S. Enterprise* (*Star Trek:The Motion Picture*).

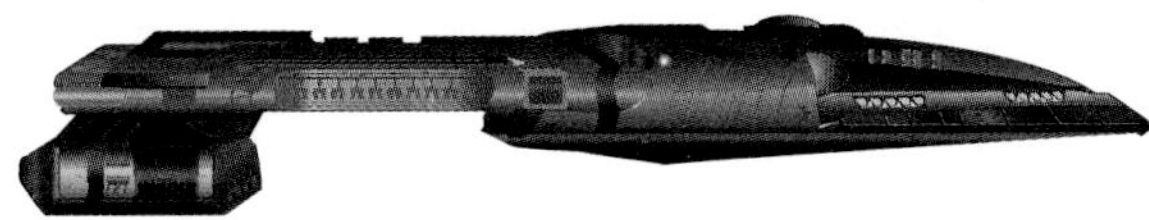

Steamrunner-class starship, *U.S.S. Appalachia* (*Star Trek:First Contact*).

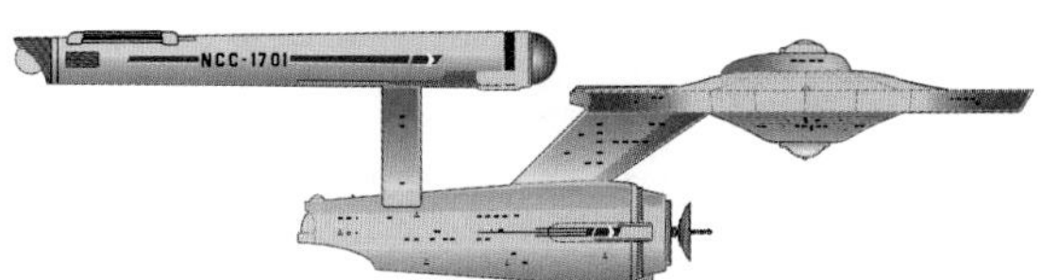

Constitution-class starship (original configuration), *U.S.S. Enterprise* (TOS).

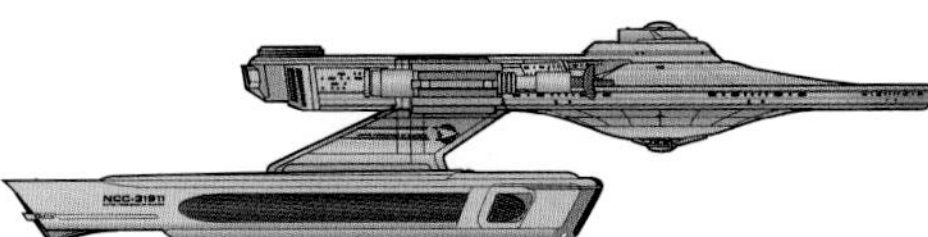

Miranda-class starship (variant), *U.S.S Saratoga* ("Emissary, Part I" [DS9]).

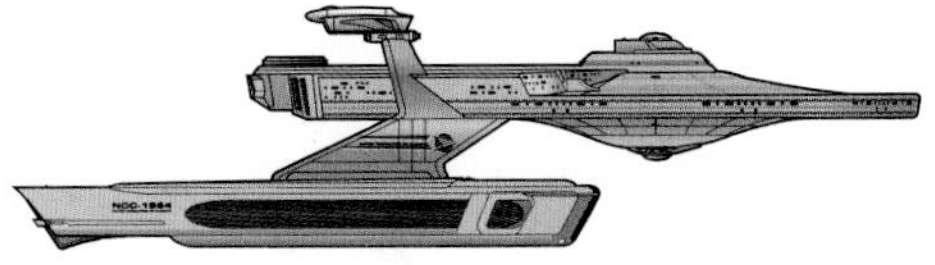

Miranda-class starship (original configuration), *U.S.S. Reliant* (*Star Trek II: The Wrath of Khan*).

Prototype warp ship, the *Phoenix* (*Star Trek:First Contact*).

Saturn V launch vehicle, *Apollo 11*.

S.S. Valiant (conjectural design).

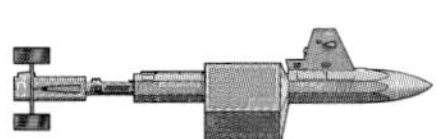

DY-100-class sleeper ship, *S.S. Botany Bay* ("Space Seed" [TOS]).

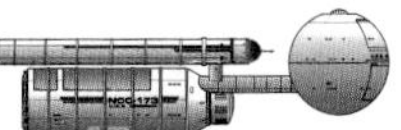

Daedalus-class starship (conjectural design).

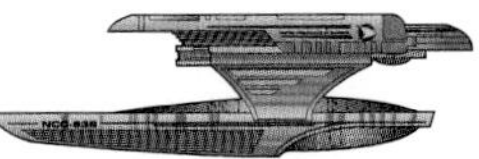

Oberth-class starship, *U.S.S. Grissom* (*Star Trek III: The Search for Spock*).

Defiant-class starship, *U.S.S. Defiant* ("The Search, Part I" [DS9]).

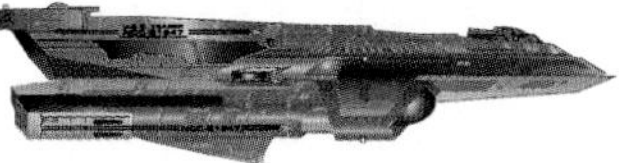

Saber-class starship, *U.S.S.Yeager* (*Star Trek:First Contact*).

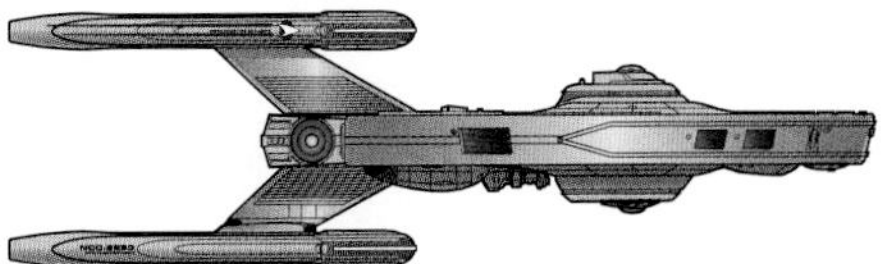

Constellation-class starship, *U.S.S. Stargazer* ("The Battle" [TNG]).

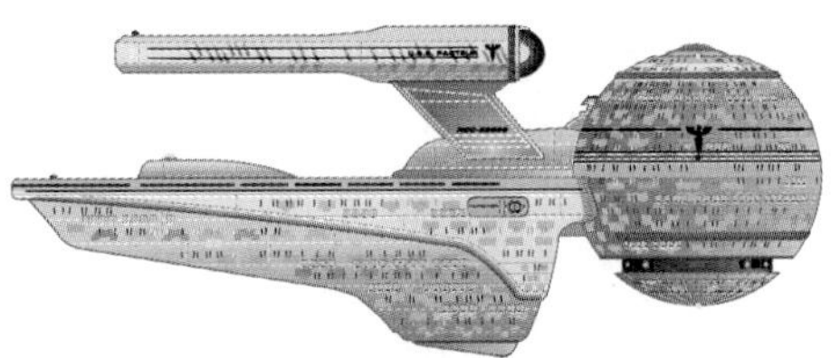

Olympic-class starship (anti-time future), *U.S.S. Pasteur* ("All Good Things..." [TNG]).

SHIPS OF THE GALAXY

Ships shown to approximate scale except the Kazon warship and Romulan warbird, which are shown at a smaller scale (see size relation chart at the bottom of the page).

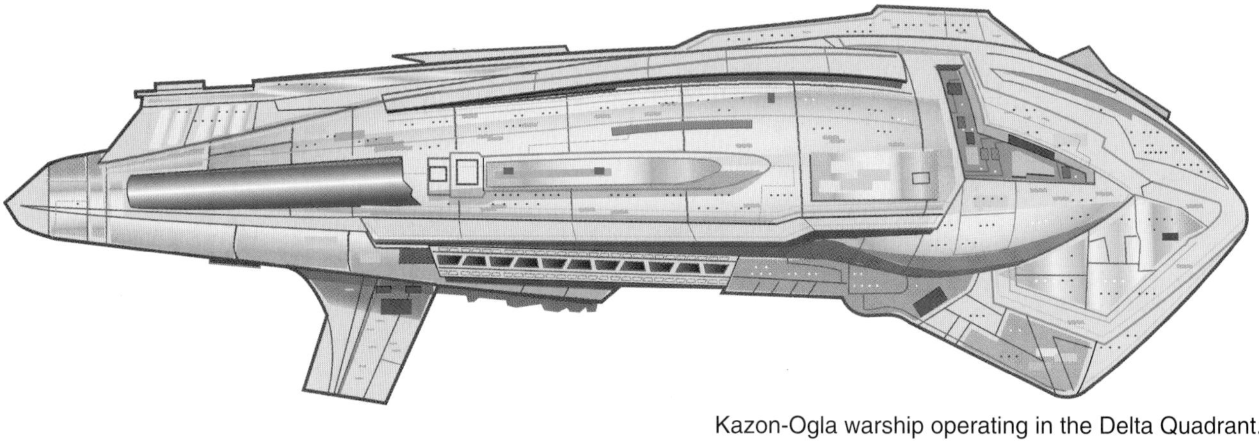

Kazon-Ogla warship operating in the Delta Quadrant.

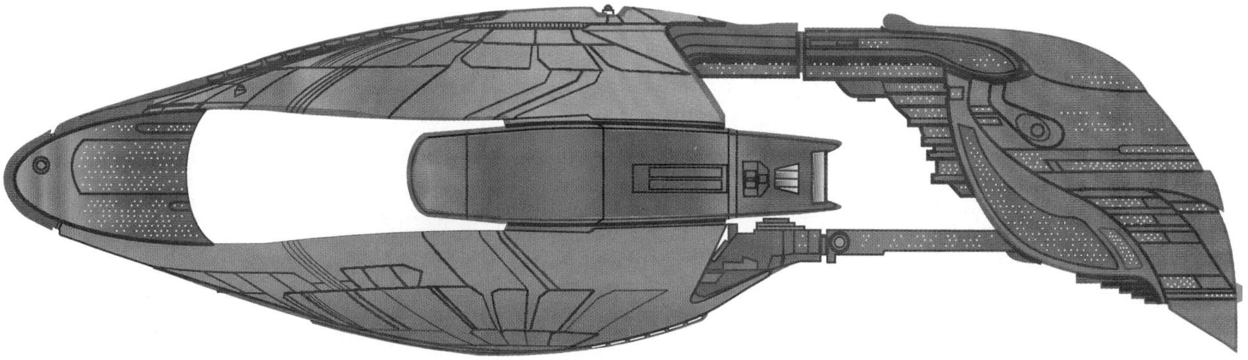

D'deridex-class, Romulan warbird.

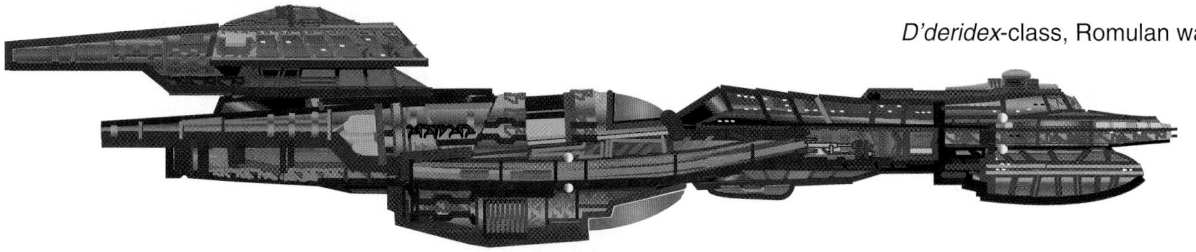

Negh'Var-class warship, flagship of the Klingon Defense Force. A variation of this class warship was first seen in "All Good Things..." (TNG).

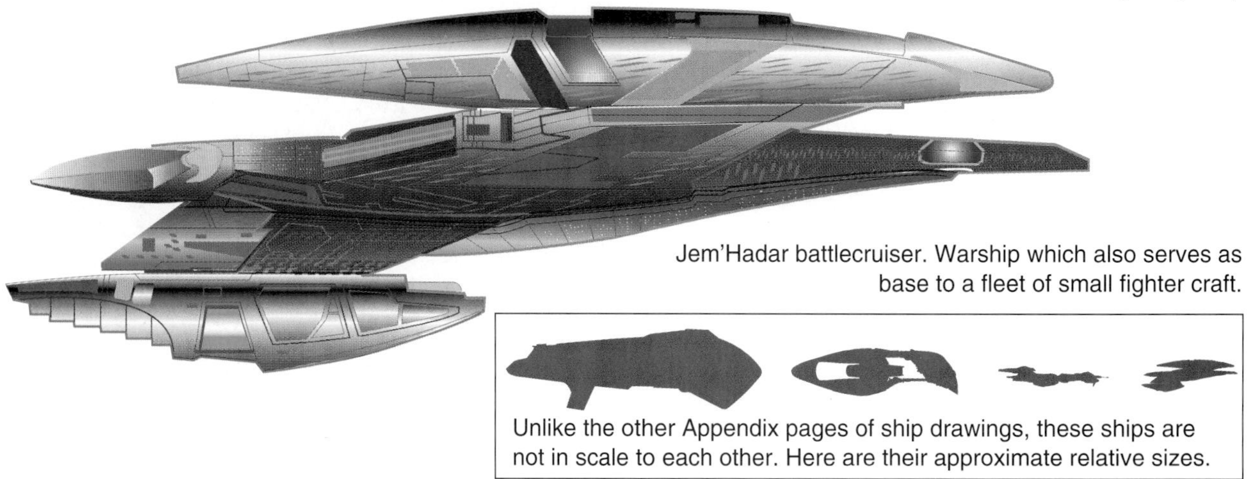

Jem'Hadar battlecruiser. Warship which also serves as base to a fleet of small fighter craft.

Unlike the other Appendix pages of ship drawings, these ships are not in scale to each other. Here are their approximate relative sizes.

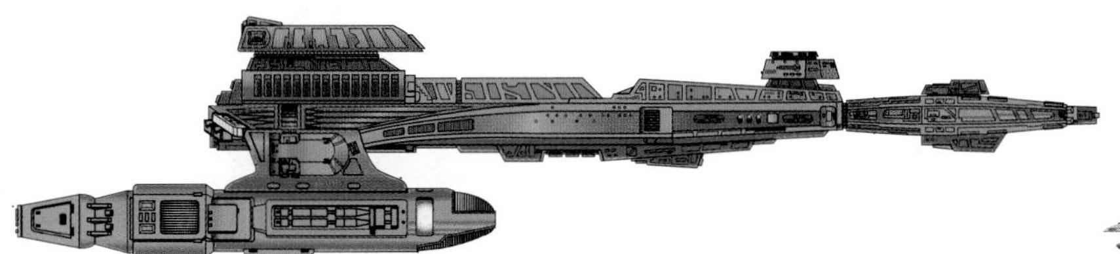

Klingon *Vor'cha*-class attack cruiser ("Reunion" [TNG]).

Jem'Hadar attack ship ("The Jem'Hadar" [DS9]).

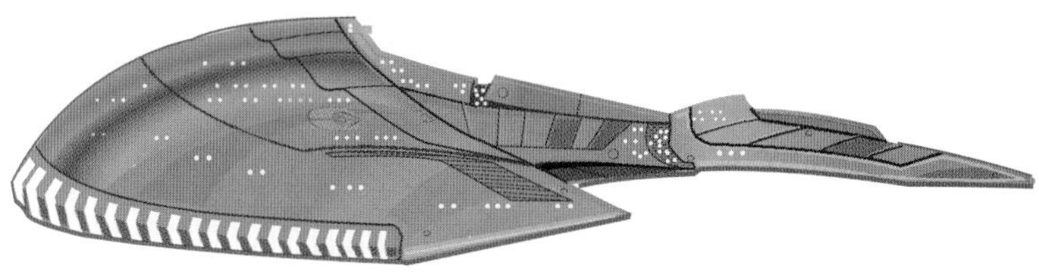

Ferengi *D'Kora*-class marauder ("The Last Outpost" [TNG]).

Vulcan survey ship (ST:FC).

Vulcan shuttle (ST:TMP).

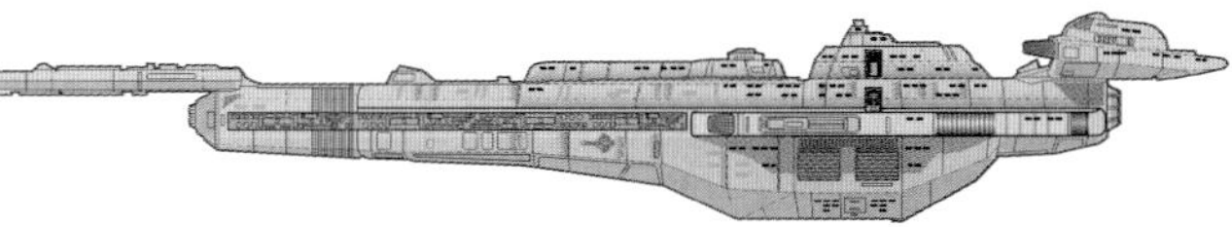

Cardassian *Galor*-class warship ("The Wounded" [TNG]).

Romulan scout ship. ("The Defector" [TNG]).

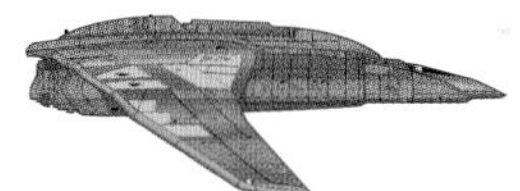

Bajoran assault vessel ("The Siege" [DS9]).

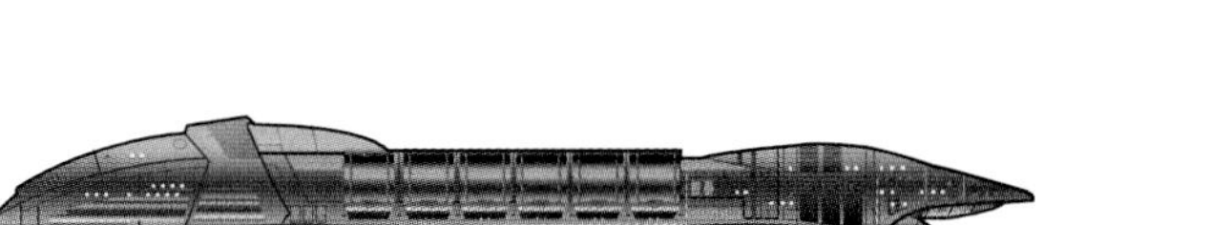

Karemman vessel ("Starship Down" [DS9]).

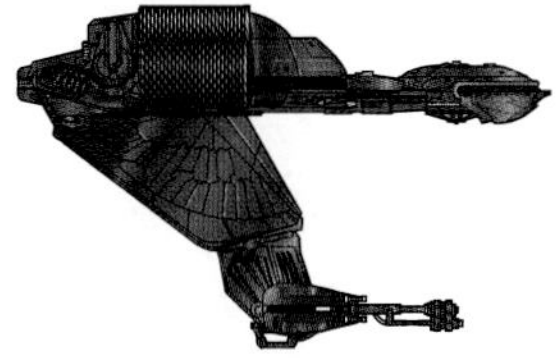

Klingon *K'Vort*-class bird-of-prey (STIII).

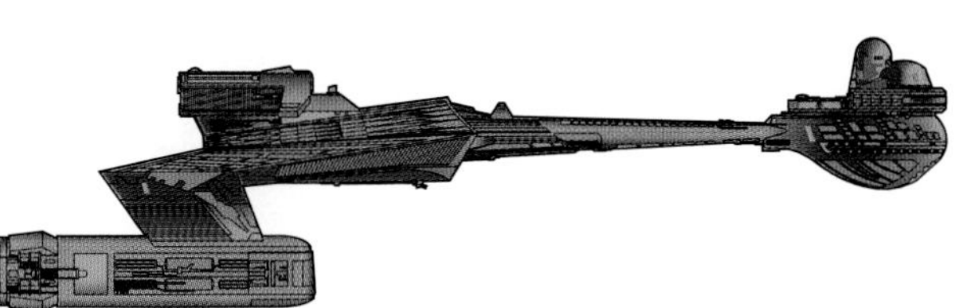

Klingon *K'Tinga*-class battle cruiser (ST:TMP).

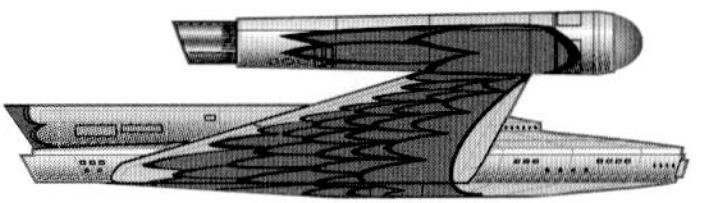

Romulan bird-of-prey. ("Balance of Terror" [TOS]).

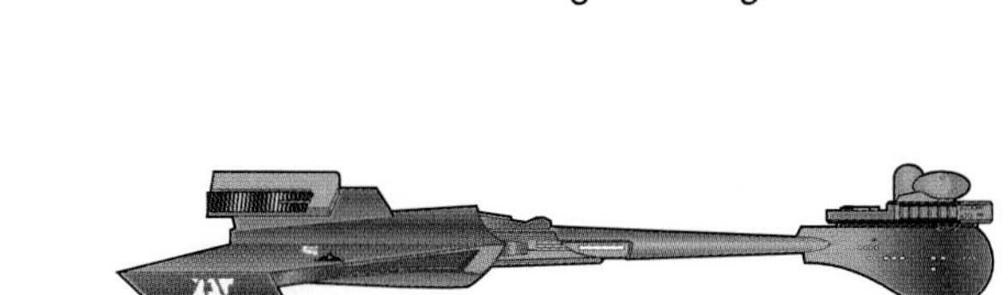

Klingon D-7 battle cruiser ("Elaan Troyius" [TOS]).

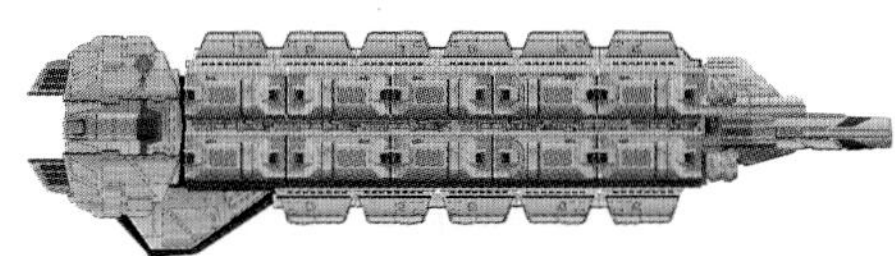

Cardassian military freighter ("Return to Grace" [DS9]).

HISTORICAL EVENTS IN THE *STAR TREK* UNIVERSE

This timeline is drawn from the *Star Trek Chronology: The History of the Future* by Denise Okuda and Michael Okuda, published by Pocket Books. For further historical information, as well as for information on how this timeline was derived, we refer you to the *Chronology.*

1957: First artificial satellite is launched from Earth. *Sputnik I* is orbited by the Soviet Union, marking the dawn of Earth's Space Age.

1969: Neil Armstrong becomes the first human to walk on Earth's moon, proclaiming the historic *Apollo* 11 flight to be "one small step for [a] man, one giant leap for mankind."

Computer pioneer Henry Starling introduces the first isograted circuit, spurring the beginning of Earth's microcomputer revolution.

1992: The Eugenics Wars begin when a group of genetically bred "supermen" seize control of one-quarter of Earth, plunging the planet into a terrible conflict. (Fortunately, Los Angeles is spared destruction.)

1996: Eugenics Wars end. The genetic tyrants are overthrown. One "superman," Khan Noonien Singh, escapes into space aboard the *S.S. Botany Bay.*

Earth scientists announce discovery of a possible microfossil from Mars, the first physical evidence of life from another world.

2018: The Dax symbiont is born on Trill.

2026: Joe DiMaggio's hitting record is broken by Buck Bokai, a shortstop from the London Kings.

2053: Earth is devastated by World War III.

2063: Warp drive is invented by Zefram Cochrane. The development of the faster-than-light drive is a crucial milestone in human history.

A day after Cochrane's first warp flight, a Vulcan spacecraft lands on Earth, humankind's first official contact with an extraterrestrial intelligence.

2065: *S.S. Valiant* is lost near the edge of the galaxy.

2079: Earth continues to recover from the postatomic horror, a recovery spawned by Cochrane's flight.

2117: Zefram Cochrane disappears and is believed dead.

2156: Romulan Wars begin between Earth forces and the Romulan Star Empire.

2160: Romulan Wars ended by the Battle of Cheron. The Romulan Neutral Zone is established.

2161: The United Federation of Planets is incorporated.

Starfleet is established with a charter "to boldly go where no man has gone before."

2165: Sarek of Vulcan is born.

2218: First contact with the Klingon Empire. The incident is a disaster, leading to nearly a century of hostilities between the Klingons and the Federation.

2222: Montgomery Scott is born.

2227: Leonard H. McCoy is born.

2230: Spock is born on Vulcan, son of Sarek and Amanda.

2233: James T. Kirk is born in Iowa on Earth.

2237: Hikaru Sulu is born in San Francisco on Earth.

2239: Uhura is born on Earth.

2243: Dr. Richard Daystrom invents duotronics, the basis for the computer systems used aboard the *Enterprise*.

2245: The first *Starship Enterprise*, NCC-1701, is launched. Captain Robert April commands the ship's first five-year mission of exploration.

Pavel A. Chekov is born.

2249: Spock enters Starfleet Academy.

2250: Kirk enrolls in Starfleet Academy. As a cadet, he serves aboard the *U.S.S. Republic*.

2251: Christopher Pike assumes command of the *Starship Enterprise*. He heads two five-year missions of exploration into the unknown.

2252: Spock, a cadet at Starfleet Academy, begins serving aboard the *Enterprise* under Captain Pike.

2253: Spock graduates from Starfleet Academy.

2254: Kirk graduates from Starfleet Academy, the only cadet ever to beat the infamous "no-win" *Kobayashi Maru* training scenario. Kirk is assigned to *U.S.S. Farragut*.

Starship Enterprise at planet Talos IV.

2261: David Marcus, son of James Kirk and Carol Marcus, is born.

2264: James T. Kirk begins historic five-year mission in command of the *Starship Enterprise*.

Tuvok is born.

2266: **First season of the original *Star Trek* series.** (Continues into 2267.)

Romulan forces violate the Neutral Zone for the first time in over a century.

Captain Christopher Pike, severely injured in a training accident, returns to Talos IV to live.

2267: *S.S. Botany Bay*, Khan's sleeper ship, is discovered adrift near the Mutara Sector. Khan and his followers are exiled to planet Ceti Alpha V.

Relations with the Klingon Empire deteriorate; open warfare is averted by establishment of the Organian Peace Treaty.

Second season of the original *Star Trek* series. (Continues into 2268.)

Spock returns to his homeworld to take T'Pring as his bride, but he is spurned in favor of Stonn.

Coridan is admitted to the Federation after the Babel Conference.

2268: Third season of the original *Star Trek* series. (Continues into 2269.)

Romulan/Klingon alliance established, permitting the exchange of spacecraft designs and military technology, including the cloaking device.

Kirk and Spock arrested by Romulan authorities on a covert mission to steal an improved Romulan cloaking device.

2269: Kirk's five-year mission ends. *Enterprise* returns to Spacedock for major upgrade.

Kirk promoted to admiral, Spock and McCoy retire from Starfleet.

2271: *Star Trek: The Motion Picture*

Enterprise successfully defends Earth from V'Ger probe. Spock and McCoy return to Starfleet.

2284: Spock becomes an instructor at Starfleet Academy. *U.S.S. Enterprise* assigned to training duty at the Acad-emy.

2285: *Star Trek II: The Wrath of Khan.*

Khan escapes from Ceti Alpha V, hijacks *U.S.S. Reliant,* tries to steal Project Genesis.

Spock dies defending the *Enterprise*.

Star Trek III: The Search for Spock.

Original *Starship Enterprise* destroyed as Kirk and crew rescue Spock's body, which is later reunited with his katra.

Spock is reborn on Genesis Planet.

2286: *Star Trek IV: The Voyage Home.*

Kirk and company save Earth from an alien probe by bringing two humpback whales to the 23rd century.

U.S.S. Enterprise-A, the second starship to bear the name, is launched. Kirk demoted from admiral to captain, and placed in command of the new ship.

2287: *Star Trek V: The Final Frontier.*

Starship Enterprise-A is hijacked by Spock's half-brother, Sybok, who pursues his visions of God.

2290: Hikaru Sulu promoted to captain of the *Starship Excelsior*.

2293: *Star Trek VI: The Undiscovered Country.*

Klingon moon Praxis explodes, crippling the Klingon economy, forcing the Khitomer peace accords.

Starship Enterprise-A retired.

***Star Trek Generations*.**

Starship Enterprise-B launched under the command of Captain John Harriman. Captain James T. Kirk reported killed on the maiden voyage of the ship.

2295: Captain Scott retires, is missing en route to the Norpin Colony aboard the *U.S.S. Jenolen*.

2298: Tuvok resigns from Starfleet.

2305: Jean-Luc Picard is born.

2311: The Tomed Incident. The Romulans enter an extended period of isolationism that lasts until 2364.

2324: Beverly Howard, the future Beverly Crusher, is born.

2327: Jean-Luc Picard graduates from Starfleet Academy.

2328: Cardassian Union annexes Bajor.

2332: Benjamin Sisko is born on Earth.

2333: Jean-Luc Picard assumes command of the *U.S.S. Stargazer*.

2335: William T. Riker is born in Valdez, Alaska, on Earth.

2336: Deanna Troi is born on Betazed.

2337: Natasha Yar is born on Turkana IV.

2338: Data is discovered on planet Omicron Theta.

2340: Worf is born on the Klingon Homeworld.

2341: Jadzia is born on Trill. Julian Bashir is born.

2343: Kira Nerys is born on Bajor.

2344: *Starship Enterprise*-C is destroyed at Narendra III.

2346: Worf's parents are killed by Romulans at the Khitomer massacre. Worf is adopted by a human Starfleet officer, Sergey Rozhenko.

Terok Nor, a mining space station, is built by the Cardassians during their occupation of Bajor.

2348: Annika Hansen, the future Seven of Nine, is born.

2349: Harry Kim is born.

2353: Chakotay enters Starfleet Academy.

2355: *U.S.S. Stargazer* is nearly destroyed in the Battle of Maxia.

Jake Sisko is born.

2357: Riker graduates from Starfleet Academy. His first assignment is the ill-fated *U.S.S. Pegasus*.

2361: Riker, now aboard the *Starship Potemkin*, participates in a rescue mission at planet Nervala IV. A transporter malfunction creates an exact duplicate of Riker, trapped at Nervala IV.

2363: *Starship Enterprise*-D, the fifth starship to bear the name, is launched under the command of Jean-Luc Picard.

William Riker serves as executive officer aboard the *U.S.S. Hood* prior to his assignment to the *Enterprise*-D.

2364: First season of *Star Trek: The Next Generation*.

First known contact with the Ferengi. First contact with Q.

Natasha Yar is killed at planet Vagra II.

2365: Second season of *Star Trek: The Next Generation*.

Dr. Katherine Pulaski serves as *Enterprise*-D chief medical officer.

First known contact with the Borg.

2366: Third season of *Star Trek: The Next Generation*

Enterprise-C briefly enters this time from the past.

Worf accepts discommendation for acts his late father did not commit against the Klingon Empire.

Captain Jean-Luc Picard is captured by the Borg, becoming Locutus of Borg.

2367: Fourth season of *Star Trek: The Next Generation*.

Thirty-nine starships destroyed by the Borg in the battle of Wolf 359.

Alexander Rozhenko, son of Worf and K'Ehleyr, is born.

Wesley Crusher is accepted to Starfleet Academy.

Jean-Luc Picard serves as arbiter of succession to determine the new leader of the Klingon High Council.

2368: Fifth season of *Star Trek: The Next Generation*.

Duras family attempts to seize control of the Klingon High Council, plunging the empire into a brief civil war.

Ambassador Spock is sighted on Romulus, supporting reunification of the Romulan and Vulcan peoples.

Ambassador Sarek of Vulcan dies at age 203.

Wesley Crusher admits to participating in a cover-up of a fatal accident at Starfleet Academy and is held back for a year.

2369: Sixth season of *Star Trek: The Next Generation*; First season of *Star Trek: Deep Space Nine*

Montgomery Scott is discovered alive, suspended in a transporter beam aboard the *U.S.S. Jenolen*.

Cardassians withdraw claim to Bajor. Federation Starfleet assumes control of station Deep Space 9 at the request of the Bajoran provisional government.

Benjamin Sisko assigned to command Deep Space 9. First stable wormhole discovered near planet Bajor.

Kai Opaka is killed in the Gamma Quadrant, triggering power struggle to determine her successor.

2370: Seventh season of *Star Trek: The Next Generation*, Second season of *Star Trek: Deep Space Nine*.

A religious extremist group called the Circle attempts to overthrow the Bajoran provisional government.

Kes is born on the Ocampa homeworld.

A clone of the legendary Kahless the Unforgettable is ruled the rightful heir to the throne, becoming the new emperor of the Klingon Empire.

Wesley Crusher goes off with the Traveler to explore other dimensions.

Humanity survives annihilation in a test devised by Q to determine if the human mind can encompass new ideas.

Dominion invasion of Alpha Quadrant feared.

2371: Third season of *Star Trek: Deep Space Nine*. First season of *Star Trek Voyager*.

Starship Defiant assigned to Deep Space 9.

Starship Voyager lost in the badlands.

***Star Trek Generations*.**

Legendary captain James T. Kirk emerges from nexus, killed at Veridian III.

Starship Enterprise-D destroyed at Veridian III.

2372: Fourth season of *Star Trek: Deep Space Nine*. Second season of *Star Trek Voyager*.

Amelia Earhart discovered alive in Delta Quadrant.

Klingon Empire dissolves Khitomer accords, attacks Cardassia. Worf assigned to Deep Space 9.

Tom Paris becomes first human to break transwarp barrier.

Starship Enterprise-E launched under command of Jean-Luc Picard.

2373: Fifth season of *Star Trek: Deep Space Nine*. Third season of *Star Trek Voyager*.

Voyager leaves Kazon space, enters Nekrit Expanse, encounters Borg Collective. Kes evolves into the next level of Ocampa existence.

Cardassian Union forms alliance with the Dominion, threatening stability of the Alpha Quadrant.

***Star Trek: First Contact*.**

Starship Enterprise-E helps to repel major Borg offensive in Sol sector.

2374: Sixth season of *Star Trek: Deep Space Nine*. Fourth season of *Star Trek Voyager*.

Federation embroiled in large-scale war with the Dominion. Worf marries Jadzia Dax, who is later killed by Gul Dukat.

Voyager threatened by Species 8472. Former Borg drone Seven of Nine joins the *Voyager* crew. *Voyager* succeeds in contacting Starfleet Command through the use of a Hirogen relay system, making authorities aware for the first time that the *Voyager* crew is alive and well in the Delta Quadrant.

2375: Seventh season of *Star Trek: Deep Space Nine*. Fifth season of *Star Trek Voyager*.

Voyager crew builds new Delta Flyer shuttlecraft.

Ezri Dax becomes the latest host for the Dax symbiont.

Dominion war ends as Odo returns to the Great Link.

Benjamin Sisko leaves the linear realm and becomes one of the Bajoran Prophets, Kira Nerys assumes command of station Deep Space 9 as Rom becomes the next Grand Nagus of the Ferengi Alliance.

***Star Trek: Insurrection*.**

Starship Enterprise-E prevents an illegal attempt to relocate inhabitants of the Ba'ku planet.

TIMELINE OF *STAR TREK* PRODUCTION

Early 1960s: Ex-police officer and noted Western writer Gene Roddenberry begins developing ideas for a new adventure television series. One of his concepts involves a 19th-century dirigible á la Jules Verne. His ideas eventually evolve into *Star Trek*, which Roddenberry refers to as "Wagon Train to the Stars."

1964: Roddenberry submits a series proposal for *Star Trek* to MGM, where he receives the first of several rejections. Conventional wisdom in the television industry holds that science fiction is too expensive and too difficult to produce.

Desilu Studios agrees to develop *Star Trek*, and signs Roddenberry to a development deal. Desilu attempts to sell the series concept to CBS, which initially expresses interest, but instead develops a series called *Lost in Space*. The NBC network agrees to fund the *Star Trek* pilot, featuring a script written by Gene Roddenberry.

"The Cage" (TOS) is filmed with Jeffrey Hunter in the part of *Enterprise* captain Christopher Pike.

1965: The completed episode is delivered to NBC, which subsequently rejects the pilot.

NBC makes the highly unusual move of ordering a second pilot episode, requesting that several changes be made in the *Star Trek* format. Among these is the elimination of a woman second-in-command and the alien Mr. Spock. Roddenberry accedes to the first request, but refuses on the second. NBC also requests that the series be more solidly action-adventure based. Three new scripts are developed for the second pilot. These include "Mudd's Women," "The Omega Glory," and "Where No Man Has Gone Before."

"Where No Man Has Gone Before" (TOS) is filmed with William Shatner in the role of Captain James T. Kirk. Leonard Nimoy as Mr. Spock is the only character retained from the first pilot episode.

1966: NBC accepts the second *Star Trek* pilot episode and places the show in its upcoming Fall schedule. Production begins on the first regular episode, entitled "The Corbomite Maneuver" (TOS).

September 8: The first episode of *Star Trek* airs on the NBC television network. The episode is "The Man Trap" (TOS), which was actually the fifth segment filmed.

1967: Desilu Studios and Paramount Pictures are acquired by Gulf & Western Industries, which combines the two facilities under the Paramount name.

Star Trek is renewed for a second season by NBC. Although the show is far from a ratings hit, it develops a loyal viewership.

1968: Prompted by low ratings, NBC cancels *Star Trek* at the end of the second season. An extraordinary outburst of fan support, including a massive letter-writing campaign spearheaded by Bjo Trimble, results in the network being deluged by letters. NBC bows to viewer pressure and makes an on-air announcement that *Star Trek* is renewed for a third year.

In the aftermath of the dramatic renewal announcement, NBC schedules *Star Trek's* third year for Friday nights at 10:00, considered at the time to be a "death slot" because of low viewership potential. Roddenberry subsequently resigns as show producer (retaining the title of executive producer) and Fred Freiberger produces *Star Trek's* third season.

1969: *Star Trek* is canceled after its third season, ironically at almost the same time as Neil Armstrong becomes the first human to walk on the moon. The last episode to be produced and aired is "Turnabout Intruder" (TOS).

Star Trek returns immediately to television in syndicated reruns around the country, frequently in more favorable time slots than it had during its original network run. This extensive exposure wins many new viewers for *Star Trek*.

1972: *Star Trek's* popularity continues to grow, and the first *Star Trek* convention is held in New York. The organizers expect a couple of hundred attendees, but are surprised to find the final count exceeds 3,000. NBC considers a *Star Trek* revival, possibly as a television movie, although this project never comes to fruition.

1973: An animated version of *Star Trek* airs on NBC, produced by Filmation Associates. Gene Roddenberry and D.C. Fontana are both actively involved in writing and producing the series, which runs for some 22 half-hour episodes. Original series actors contribute their voice talents to the Emmy Award–winning show.

1976: Paramount attempts to develop a low-budget feature-film version of *Star Trek*. Numerous big-name writers are invited to pitch story ideas, but nothing comes of the project, although *James Bond* production designer Ken Adam and *Star Wars* illustrator Ralph McQuarrie are engaged to design a new version of the *Enterprise*.

NASA unveils the prototype of its new space shuttle. This first reusable spaceship is named *Enterprise*, in honor of *Star Trek's* starship.

1977: Paramount announces plans to produce a new weekly series entitled *Star Trek II* for syndication, bypassing the existing networks. This show (also known as *Star Trek: Phase II*) would be the flagship of a studio attempt to create a new network, much as was done years later with UPN and *Star Trek: Voyager*. This proposed *Star Trek II* series would feature the adventures of a second five-year mission of the *Enterprise* under the command of Captain Kirk. All of the original series actors agree to return, except for Leonard Nimoy, whose character is slated to be replaced by a full-Vulcan officer named Xon.

1978: Spurred by the unprecedented success of *Star Wars*, as well as lackluster interest in Paramount's network project, the studio cancels *Star Trek II* just two weeks before the scheduled start of principal photography. Instead, Paramount announces plans to expand the first episode into a major feature film to be directed by Robert Wise. In a surprise last-minute move, Leonard Nimoy agrees to return as Mr. Spock.

1979: *Star Trek: The Motion Picture* is released. The film is a resounding financial success, although fan and critical reaction is mixed.

1980: Based on the success of *Star Trek: The Motion Picture*, a second *Star Trek* feature is placed in development under the supervision of Harve Bennett. The project eventually becomes *Star Trek II: The Wrath of Khan,* a sequel to "Space Seed" (TOS). Some members of the *Star Trek* fan community react negatively to plans for the film to feature the death of Spock.

1982: *Star Trek II: The Wrath of Khan,* directed by Nicholas Meyer, is released to critical and financial success. Just prior to release, the film's ending is modified slightly to make Spock's death more ambiguous, leaving the door open for his return in a sequel.

Shortly after *Star Trek II's* release, Leonard Nimoy indicates a willingness to return for such a sequel, and plans are announced for *Star Trek III* to be directed by Nimoy.

1984: *Star Trek III: The Search for Spock* is released, featuring the return of Spock from the dead and the destruction of the original *Starship Enterprise*.

1986: *Star Trek IV: The Voyage Home* is released. Leonard Nimoy also directs this story of time travel back to the 20th century.

As *Star Trek* celebrates its 20th anniversary, Paramount announces plans to produce a new syndicated series entitled *Star Trek: The Next Generation*, to be produced by Gene Roddenberry, featuring an all-new cast. Roddenberry recruits original series veterans Bob Justman, Eddie Milkis, Dorothy Fontana, David Gerrold, and John Dwyer to get the new show underway.

1987: *Star Trek: The Next Generation* debuts as a syndicated weekly series featuring Patrick Stewart as Captain Jean-Luc Picard aboard the *Starship Enterprise*-D. Although Roddenberry is actively involved in the show's early production, he later steps back into a more supervisory role, leaving day-to-day operations in the hands of Rick Berman. Bob Justman retires after completion of post-production on the 1987–1988 season.

1988: William Shatner takes a turn at directing the fifth feature, *Star Trek V: The Final Frontier*.

Star Trek: The Next Generation is renewed for a second season. Whoopi Goldberg joins the *Star Trek* cast as Guinan, and Diana Muldaur plays *Enterprise*-D chief medical officer Katherine Pulaski.

1989: Gates McFadden returns to the *Star Trek* cast as Dr. Beverly Crusher at the beginning of the show's third season.

1990: *Star Trek: The Next Generation* is renewed for an unprecedented fourth season. Wil Wheaton, as Wesley Crusher, departs the *Star Trek* cast midway through the year. The last segment of the season, "Redemption, Part I" (TNG), is the show's 100th episode.

1991: Gene Roddenberry dies at the age of 70, shortly after the 25th anniversary of his creation, which has become more popular than ever.

Star Trek VI: The Undiscovered Country is released, touted as the final voyage of the original crew.

1993: A new *Star Trek* series entitled *Star Trek: Deep Space Nine* premieres, featuring Avery Brooks as Commander Benjamin Sisko in charge of station Deep Space 9. The show is created by Rick Berman and Michael Piller.

1994: *Star Trek: The Next Generation* concludes its run after seven seasons and 178 episodes.

The seventh *Star Trek* movie, *Star Trek Generations*, is directed by David Carson, featuring the death of Captain James T. Kirk and the destruction of the *Starship Enterprise*-D.

1995: *Star Trek: Voyager* premieres on the new United Paramount Network. Starring Kate Mulgrew as Captain Kathryn Janeway, the show is created by Rick Berman, Michael Piller, and Jeri Taylor.

Michael Dorn joins the cast of *Star Trek: Deep Space Nine* as Worf.

1996: *Star Trek* celebrates its thirtieth anniversary with "Trials and Tribble-ations" (DS9), a special episode of *Star Trek: Deep Space Nine* revisiting James Kirk and his crew aboard the original *Starship Enterprise*, and with a special episode of *Star Trek: Voyager* entitled "Flashback" (VGR), featuring the adventures of Captain Sulu commanding the *Starship Excelsior*.

The eighth feature film, *Star Trek: First Contact*, directed by Jonathan Frakes, is released, with Captain Jean-Luc Picard and crew aboard an all-new *Starship Enterprise*-E.

1997: Jennifer Lien leaves the cast of *Star Trek: Voyager*. She is replaced by Jeri Ryan as Seven of Nine.

1998: *Star Trek: Insurrection*, the ninth *Star Trek* movie, is directed by Jonathan Frakes, the second adventure aboard the *Enterprise*-E, and the third with the *Star Trek: The Next Generation* cast.

Terry Farrell departs *Star Trek: Deep Space Nine* as her character is killed at the end of the sixth season. Nicole deBoer joins the cast as Ezri, the new host of the Dax symbiont.

Paramount Pictures launches *Star Trek: The Experience* at the Las Vegas Hilton.

1999: *Star Trek: Deep Space Nine* concludes its seventh and final year of production.

And the adventure continues....

WRITER AND DIRECTOR CREDITS

The authors of this book wish to acknowledge the writers and directors of the *Star Trek* television episodes and motion pictures, from whose work this volume has been compiled. Episodes are listed in production order, not in aired sequence. Episodes are also listed alphabetically by title in the main body of the Encyclopedia. See the Introduction for notes on converting these episode numbers into Desilu and Paramount's internal production numbers.

Star Trek: The Original Series Year 1 (originally aired 1966–67)

1. "The Cage." Written by Gene Roddenberry. Directed by Robert Butler.
2. "Where No Man Has Gone Before." Written by Samuel A. Peeples. Directed by James Goldstone.
3. "The Corbomite Maneuver." Written by Jerry Sohl. Directed by Joseph Sargent.
4. "Mudd's Women." Teleplay by Stephen Kandel. Story by Gene Roddenberry. Directed by Harvey Hart.
5. "The Enemy Within." Written by Richard Matheson. Directed by Leo Penn.
6. "The Man Trap." Written by George Clayton Johnson. Directed by Marc Daniels.
7. "The Naked Time." Written by John D. F. Black. Directed by Marc Daniels.
8. "Charlie X." Teleplay by D. C. Fontana. Story by Gene Roddenberry. Directed by Lawrence Dobkin.
9. "Balance of Terror." Written by Paul Schneider. Directed by Vincent McEveety.
10. "What Are Little Girls Made Of?" Written by Robert Bloch. Directed by James Goldstone.
11. "Dagger of the Mind." Written by S. Bar-David. Directed by Vincent McEveety.
12. "Miri." Written by Adrian Spies. Directed by Vincent McEveety.
13. "The Conscience of the King." Written by Barry Trivers. Directed by Gerd Osward.
14. "The Galileo Seven." Teleplay by Oliver Crawford and S. Bar-David. Story by Oliver Crawford. Directed by Robert Gist.
15. "Court Martial." Teleplay by Don M. Mankiewicz and Steven W. Carabatsos. Story by Don M. Mankiewicz. Directed by Marc Daniels.
16. "The Menagerie, Parts I and II." Written by Gene Roddenberry. Directed by Marc Daniels.
17. "Shore Leave." Written by Theodore Sturgeon. Directed by Robert Sparr.
18. "The Squire of Gothos." Written by Paul Schneider. Directed by Don McDougall.
19. "Arena." Teleplay by Gene L. Coon. Story by Fredric Brown. Directed by Joseph Pevney.
20. "The Alternative Factor." Written by Don Ingalls. Directed by Gerd Oswald.
21. "Tomorrow Is Yesterday." Written by D. C. Fontana. Directed by Michael O'Herlihy.
22. "The Return of the Archons." Teleplay by Boris Sobelman. Story by Gene Roddenberry. Directed by Joseph Pevney.
23. "A Taste of Armageddon." Teleplay by Robert Hamner and Gene L. Coon. Story by Robert Hamner. Directed by Joseph Pevney.
24. "Space Seed." Teleplay by Gene L. Coon and Carey Wilber. Story by Carey Wilber. Directed by Marc Daniels.
25. "This Side of Paradise." Teleplay by D. C. Fontana. Story by Nathan Butler and D. C. Fontana. Directed by Ralph Senensky.
26. "The Devil in the Dark." Written by Gene L. Coon. Directed by Joseph Pevney.
27. "Errand of Mercy." Written by Gene L. Coon. Directed by John Newland.
28. "The City on the Edge of Forever." Written by Harlan Ellison. Directed by Joseph Pevney.
29. "Operation: Annihilate!" Written by Steven W. Carabatsos. Directed by Herschel Daugherty.

Star Trek: The Original Series Year 2 (originally aired 1967–68)

30. "Catspaw." Written by Robert Bloch. Directed by Joseph Pevney.
31. "Metamorphosis." Written by Gene L. Coon. Directed by Ralph Senensky.
32. "Friday's Child." Written by D. C. Fontana. Directed by Joseph Pevney.
33. "Who Mourns for Adonais?" Written by Gilbert Ralston. Directed by Marc Daniels.
34. "Amok Time." Written by Theodore Sturgeon. Directed by Joseph Pevney.
35. "The Doomsday Machine." Written by Norman Spinrad. Directed by Marc Daniels.
36. "Wolf in the Fold." Written by Robert Bloch. Directed by Joseph Pevney.
37. "The Changeling." Written by John Meredyth Lucas. Directed by Marc Daniels.
38. "The Apple." Written by Max Ehrlich. Directed by Joseph Pevney.
39. "Mirror, Mirror." Written by Jerome Bixby. Directed by Marc Daniels.
40. "The Deadly Years." Written by David P. Harmon. Directed by Joseph Pevney.
41. "I, Mudd." Written by Stephen Kandel. Directed by Marc Daniels.
42. "The Trouble with Tribbles." Written by David Gerrold. Directed by Joseph Pevney.
43. "Bread and Circuses." Written by Gene Roddenberry and Gene L. Coon. Directed by Ralph Senensky.
44. "Journey to Babel." Written by D. C. Fontana. Directed by Joseph Pevney.
45. "A Private Little War." Teleplay by Gene Roddenberry. Story by Jud Crucis. Directed by Marc Daniels.
46. "The Gamesters of Triskelion." Written by Margaret Armen. Directed by Gene Nelson.
47. "Obsession." Written by Art Wallace. Directed by Ralph Senensky.
48. "The Immunity Syndrome." Written by Robert Sabaroff. Directed by Joseph Pevney.

49. "A Piece of the Action." Teleplay by David P. Harmon and Gene L. Coon. Story by David P. Harmon. Directed by James Komack.

50. "By Any Other Name." Teleplay by D. C. Fontana and Jerome Bixby. Story by Jerome Bixby. Directed by Marc Daniels.

51. "Return to Tomorrow." Written by John Kingsbridge. Directed by Ralph Senensky.

52. "Patterns of Force." Written by John Meredyth Lucas. Directed by Vincent McEveety.

53. "The Ultimate Computer." Teleplay by D. C. Fontana. Story by Laurence N. Wolfe. Directed by John Meredyth Lucas.

54. The Omega Glory." Written by Gene Roddenberry. Directed by Vincent McEveety.

55. "Assignment Earth." Teleplay by Art Wallace. Story by Gene Roddenberry and Art Wallace. Directed by Marc Daniels.

Star Trek: The Original Series Year 3 (originally aired 1968–69)

56. "Spectre of the Gun." Written by Lee Cronin. Directed by Vincent McEveety.

57. "Elaan of Troyius." Written by John Meredyth Lucas. Directed by John Meredyth Lucas.

58. "The Paradise Syndrome." Written by Margaret Armen. Directed by Jud Taylor.

59. "The *Enterprise* Incident." Written by D. C. Fontana. Directed by John Meredyth Lucas.

60. "And the Children Shall Lead." Written by Edward J. Lakso. Directed by Marvin Chomsky.

61. "Spock's Brain." Written by Lee Cronin. Directed by Marc Daniels.

62. "Is There in Truth No Beauty?" Written by Jean Lisette Aroeste. Directed by Ralph Senensky.

63. "The Empath." Written by Joyce Muskat. Directed by John Erman.

64. "The Tholian Web." Written by Judy Burns and Chet Richards. Directed by Herb Wallerstein.

65. "For the World Is Hollow and I Have Touched the Sky." Written by Rik Vollaerts. Directed by Tony Leader.

66. "Day of the Dove." Written by Jerome Bixby. Directed by Marvin Chomsky.

67. "Plato's Stepchildren." Written by Meyer Dolinsky. Directed by David Alexander.

68. "Wink of an Eye." Teleplay by Arthur Heinemann. Story by Lee Cronin. Directed by Jud Taylor.

69. "That Which Survives." Teleplay by John Meredyth Lucas. Story by Michael Richards. Directed by Herb Wallerstein.

70. "Let That Be Your Last Battlefield." Teleplay by Oliver Crawford. Story by Lee Cronin. Directed by Jud Taylor.

71. "Whom Gods Destroy." Teleplay by Lee Erwin. Story by Lee Erwin and Jerry Sohl. Directed by Herb Wallerstein.

72. "The Mark of Gideon." Written by George F. Slavin and Stanley Adams. Directed by Jud Taylor.

73. "The Lights of Zetar." Written by Jeremy Tarcher and Shari Lewis. Directed by Herb Kenwith.

74. "The Cloud Minders." Teleplay by Margaret Armen. Story by David Gerrold and Oliver Crawford. Directed by Jud Taylor.

75. "The Way to Eden." Teleplay by Arthur Heinemann. Story by Michael Richards and Arthur Heinemann. Directed by David Alexander.

76. "Requiem for Methuselah." Written by Jerome Bixby. Directed by Murray Golden.

77. "The Savage Curtain." Teleplay by Gene Roddenberry and Arthur Heinemann. Story by Gene Roddenberry. Directed by Herschel Daugherty.

78. "All Our Yesterdays." Written by Jean Lisette Aroeste. Directed by Marvin Chomsky.

79. "Turnabout Intruder." Teleplay by Arthur H. Singer. Story by Gene Roddenberry. Directed by Herb Wallerstein.

Star Trek movies (originally released 1979–96)

1. *Star Trek: The Motion Picture.* Screenplay by Harold Livingston. Story by Alan Dean Foster. Directed by Robert Wise.

2. *Star Trek II: The Wrath of Khan.* Screenplay by Jack B. Sowards. Story by Harve Bennett and Jack B. Sowards. Directed by Nicholas Meyer.

3. *Star Trek III: The Search for Spock.* Written by Harve Bennett. Directed by Leonard Nimoy.

4. *Star Trek IV: The Voyage Home.* Story by Leonard Nimoy and Harve Bennett. Screenplay by Steve Meerson & Peter Krikes and Harve Bennett & Nicholas Meyer. Directed by Leonard Nimoy.

5. *Star Trek V: The Final Frontier.* Story by William Shatner & Harve Bennett & David Loughery. Screenplay by David Loughery. Directed by William Shatner.

6. *Star Trek VI: The Undiscovered Country*. Story by Leonard Nimoy and Nicholas Meyer & Denny Martin Flinn. Screenplay by Nicholas Meyer & Denny Martin Flinn. Directed by Nicholas Meyer.

7. *Star Trek Generations*. Story by Rick Berman & Ronald D. Moore & Brannon Braga. Screenplay by Ronald D. Moore & Brannon Braga. Directed by David Carson.

8. *Star Trek: First Contact*. Story by Rick Berman & Brannon Braga & Ronald D. Moore. Screenplay by Brannon Braga & Ronald D. Moore. Directed by Jonathan Frakes.

9. *Star Trek: Insurrection*. Screenplay by Michael Piller. Story by Rick Berman & Michael Piller. Directed by Jonathan Frakes.

Star Trek: The Next Generation Year 1 (first aired 1987–88)

1. "Encounter at Farpoint, Part I." Written by D. C. Fontana and Gene Roddenberry. Directed by Corey Allen.

2. "Encounter at Farpoint, Part II." Written by D. C. Fontana and Gene Roddenberry. Directed by Corey Allen.

3. "The Naked Now." Teleplay by J. Michael Bingham. Story by John D. F. Black and J. Michael Bingham. Directed by Paul Lynch.

4. "Code of Honor." Written by Katharyn Powers & Michael Baron. Directed by Russ Mayberry.

5. "Haven." Teleplay by Tracy Tormé. Story by Tracy Tormé & Lan Okun. Directed by Richard Compton.

6. "Where No One Has Gone Before." Written by Diane Duane & Michael Reaves. Directed by Robert Bowman.

7. "The Last Outpost." Teleplay by Herbert Wright. Story by Richard Krzemien. Directed by Richard Colla.

8. "Lonely Among Us." Teleplay by D. C. Fontana. Story by Michael Halperin. Directed by Cliff Bole.

9. "Justice." Teleplay by Worley Thorne. Story by Ralph Wills and Worley Thorne. Directed by James L. Conway.

10. "The Battle." Teleplay by Herbert Wright. Story by Larry Forrester. Directed by Robert Bowman.

11. "Hide and Q." Teleplay by C. J. Holland and Gene Roddenberry. Story by C. J. Holland. Directed by Cliff Bole.

12. "Too Short a Season." Teleplay by Michael Michaelian and D. C. Fontana. Story by Michael Michaelian. Directed by Robert Bowman.

13. "The Big Goodbye." Written by Tracy Tormé. Directed by Joseph L. Scanlan.

14. "Datalore." Teleplay by Robert Lewin and Gene Roddenberry. Story by Robert Lewin and Maurice Hurley. Directed by Robert Bowman.

15. "Angel One." Written by Patrick Barry. Directed by Michael Rhodes.

16. "11001001." Written by Maurice Hurley & Robert Lewin. Directed by Paul Lynch.

17. "Home Soil." Teleplay by Robert Sabaroff. Story by Karl Guers & Ralph Sanchez and Robert Sabaroff. Directed by Corey Allen.

18. "When the Bough Breaks." Written by Hannah Louise Shearer. Directed by Kim Manners.

19. "Coming of Age." Written by Sandy Fries. Directed by Mike Vejar.

20. "Heart of Glory." Teleplay by Maurice Hurley. Story by Maurice Hurley and Herbert Wright & D. C. Fontana. Directed by Robert Bowman.

21. "The Arsenal of Freedom." Teleplay by Richard Manning & Hans Beimler. Story by Maurice Hurley & Robert Lewin. Directed by Les Landau.

22. "Skin of Evil." Teleplay by Joseph Stefano and Hannah Louise Shearer. Story by Joseph Stefano. Directed by Joseph L. Scanlan.

23. "Symbiosis." Teleplay by Robert Lewin and Richard Manning and Hans Beimler. Story by Robert Lewin. Directed by Win Phelps.

24. "We'll Always Have Paris." Written by Deborah Dean Davis and Hannah Louise Shearer. Directed by Robert Becker.

25. "Conspiracy." Teleplay by Tracy Tormé. Story by Robert Sabaroff. Directed by Cliff Bole.

26. "The Neutral Zone." Television story & teleplay by Maurice Hurley. From a story by Deborah McIntyre & Mona Glee. Directed by James Conway.

Star Trek: The Next Generation Year 2 (first aired 1988–89)

27. "The Child." Written by Jaron Summers & Jon Povill and Maurice Hurley. Directed by Robert Bowman.

28. "Where Silence Has Lease." Written by Jack B. Sowards. Directed by Winrich Kolbe.

29. "Elementary, Dear Data." Written by Brian Alan Lane. Directed by Robert Bowman.

30. "The Outrageous Okona." Teleplay by Burton Armus. Story by Les Menchen & Lance Dickson and David Landsberg. Directed by Robert Becker.

31. "The Schizoid Man." Teleplay by Tracy Tormé. Story by Richard Manning & Hans Beimler. Directed by Les Landau.

32. "Loud as a Whisper." Written by Jacqueline Zambrano. Directed by Larry Shaw.

33. "Unnatural Selection." Written by John Mason & Mike Gray. Directed by Paul Lynch.

34. "A Matter of Honor." Teleplay by Burton Armus. Story by Wanda M. Haight & Gregory Amos and Burton Armus. Directed by Robert Bowman.

35. "The Measure of a Man." Written by Melinda M. Snodgrass. Directed by Robert Scheerer.

36. "The Dauphin." Written by Scott Rubenstein & Leonard Mlodinow. Directed by Robert Bowman.

37. "Contagion." Written by Steve Gerber & Beth Woods. Directed by Joseph I. Scanlan.

38. "The Royale." Written by Keith Mills. Directed by Cliff Bole.

39. "Time Squared." Teleplay by Maurice Hurley. Story by Kurt Michael Bensmiller. Directed by Joseph L. Scanlan.

40. "The Icarus Factor." Teleplay by David Assael and Robert L. McCullough. Story by David Assael. Directed by Robert Iscove.

41. "Pen Pals." Teleplay by Melinda M. Snodgrass. Story by Hannah Louise Shearer. Directed by Winrich Kolbe.

42. "Q Who?" Written by Maurice Hurley. Directed by Robert Bowman.

43. "Samaritan Snare." Written by Robert L. McCullough. Directed by Les Landau.

44. "Up the Long Ladder." Written by Melinda M. Snodgrass. Directed by Winrich Kolbe.

45. "Manhunt." Written by Terry Devereaux. Directed by Robert Bowman.

46. "The Emissary." Television story and teleplay by Richard Manning & Hans Beimler. Based on an unpublished story by Thomas H. Calder. Directed by Cliff Bole.

47. "Peak Performance." Written by David Kemper. Directed by Robert Scheerer.

48. "Shades of Gray." Teleplay by Maurice Hurley and Richard Manning & Hans Beimler. Story by Maurice Hurley. Directed by Robert Bowman.

Star Trek: The Next Generation Year 3 (first aired 1989–90)

49. "The Ensigns of Command." Written by Melinda M. Snodgrass. Directed by Cliff Bole.

50. "Evolution." Teleplay by Michael Piller. Story by Michael Piller and Michael Wagner. Directed by Winrich Kolbe.

51. "The Survivors." Written by Michael Wagner. Directed by Les Landau.

52. "Who Watches the Watchers?" Written by Richard Manning & Hans Beimler. Directed by Robert Wiemer.

53. "The Bonding." Written by Ronald D. Moore. Directed by Winrich Kolbe.

54. "Booby Trap." Teleplay by Ron Roman and Michael Piller & Richard Danus. Story by Michael Wagner & Ron Roman. Directed by Gabrielle Beaumont.

55. "The Enemy." Written by David Kemper and Michael Piller. Directed by David Carson.

56. "The Price." Written by Hannah Louise Shearer. Directed by Robert Scheerer.

57. "The Vengeance Factor." Written by Sam Rolfe. Directed by Timothy Bond.

58. "The Defector." Written by Ronald D. Moore. Directed by Robert Scheerer.

59. "The Hunted." Written by Robin Bernheim. Directed by Cliff Bole.

60. "The High Ground." Written by Melinda M. Snodgrass. Directed by Gabrielle Beaumont.

61. "Deja Q." Written by Richard Danus. Directed by Les Landau.

62. "A Matter of Perspective." Written by Ed Zuckerman. Directed by Cliff Bole.

63. "Yesterday's *Enterprise*." Teleplay by Ira Steven Behr & Richard Manning & Hans Beimler & Ronald D. Moore. From a story by Trent Christopher Ganino & Eric A. Stillwell. Directed by David Carson.

64. "The Offspring." Written by René Echevarria. Directed by Jonathan Frakes.

65. "Sins of the Father." Teleplay by Ronald D. Moore & W. Reed Moran. Based on a teleplay by Drew Deighan. Directed by Les Landau.

66. "Allegiance." Written by Richard Manning & Hans Beimler. Directed by Winrich Kolbe.

67. "Captain's Holiday." Written by Ira Steven Behr. Directed by Chip Chalmers.

68. "Tin Man." Written by Dennis Putman Bailey & David Bischoff. Directed by Robert Scheerer.

69. "Hollow Pursuits." Written by Sally Caves. Directed by Cliff Bole.

70. "The Most Toys." Written by Shari Goodhartz. Directed by Tim Bond.

71. "Sarek." Television story and teleplay by Peter S. Beagle. From an unpublished story by Marc Cushman & Jake Jacobs. Directed by Les Landau.

72. "Menage à Troi." Written by Fred Bronson & Susan Sackett. Directed by Robert Legato.

73. "Transfigurations." Written by Rene Echevarria. Directed by Tom Benko.

74. "The Best of Both Worlds, Part I." Written by Michael Piller. Directed by Cliff Bole.

Star Trek: The Next Generation Year 4 (first aired 1990–91)

75. "The Best of Both Worlds, Part II." Written by Michael Piller. Directed by Cliff Bole.

76. "Suddenly Human." Teleplay by John Whelpley & Jeri Taylor. Story by Ralph Phillips. Directed by Gabrielle Beaumont.

77. "Brothers." Written by Rick Berman. Directed by Robert Bowman.

78. "Family." Written by Ronald D. Moore. Directed by Les Landau.

79. "Remember Me." Written by Lee Sheldon. Directed by Cliff Bole.

80. "Legacy." Written by Joe Menosky. Directed by Robert Scheerer.

81. "Reunion." Teleplay by Thomas Perry & Jo Perry and Ronald D. Moore & Brannon Braga. Story by Drew Deighan and Thomas Perry & Jo Perry. Directed by Jonathan Frakes.

82. "Future Imperfect." Written by J. Larry Carroll & David Bennett Carren. Directed by Les Landau.

83. "Final Mission." Teleplay by Kasey Arnold-Ince and Jeri Taylor. Story by Kasey Arnold-Ince. Directed by Corey Allen.

84. "The Loss." Teleplay by Hilary J. Bader and Alan J. Alder & Vanessa Greene. Story by Hilary J. Bader. Directed by Chip Chalmers.

85. "Data's Day." Teleplay by Harold Apter and Ronald D. Moore. Story by Harold Apter. Directed by Robert Wiemer.

86. "The Wounded." Teleplay by Jeri Taylor. Story by Stuart Charno & Sara Charno and Cy Chermax. Directed by Chip Chalmers.

87. "Devil's Due." Teleplay by Philip LaZebnik. Story by Philip LaZebnik and William Douglas Lansford. Directed by Tom Benko.

88. "Clues." Teleplay by Bruce D. Arthurs and Joe Menosky. Story by Bruce D. Arthurs. Directed by Les Landau.

89. "First Contact." Teleplay by Dennis Russell Bailey & David Bischoff and Joe Menosky & Ronald D. Moore and Michael Piller. Story by Marc Scott Zicree. Directed by Cliff Bole.

90. "Galaxy's Child." Teleplay by Maurice Hurley. Story by Thomas Kartozian. Directed by Winrich Kolbe.

91. "Night Terrors." Teleplay by Pamela Douglas and Jeri Taylor. Story by Sheri Goodhartz. Directed by Les Landau.

92. "Identity Crisis." Teleplay by Brannon Braga. Based on a story by Timothy De Haas. Directed by Winrich Kolbe.

93. "The Nth Degree." Written by Joe Menosky. Directed by Robert Legato.

94. "QPid." Teleplay by Ira Steven Behr. Story by Randee Russell and Ira Steven Behr. Directed by Cliff Bole.

95. "The Drumhead." Written by Jeri Taylor. Directed by Jonathan Frakes.

96. "Half a Life." Teleplay by Peter Allan Fields. Story by Ted Roberts and Peter Allan Fields. Directed by Les Landau.

97. "The Host." Written by Michel Horvat. Directed by Marvin Rush.

98. "The Mind's Eye." Teleplay by René Echevarria. Story by Ken Schafer and René Echevarria. Directed by David Livingston.

99. "In Theory." Written by Joe Menosky & Ronald D. Moore. Directed by Patrick Stewart.

100. "Redemption, Part I." Written by Ronald D. Moore. Directed by Cliff Bole.

Star Trek: The Next Generation Year 5 (first aired 1991–92)

101. "Redemption, Part II." Written by Ronald D. Moore. Directed by David Carson.

102. "Darmok." Teleplay by Joe Menosky. Story by Philip LaZebnik and Joe Menosky. Directed by Winrich Kolbe.

103. "Ensign Ro." Teleplay by Michael Piller. Story by Rick Berman and Michael Piller. Directed by Les Landau.

104. "Silicon Avatar." Teleplay by Jeri Taylor. From a story by Lawrence V. Conley. Directed by Cliff Bole.

105. "Disaster." Teleplay by Ronald D. Moore. Story by Ron Jarvis & Philip A. Scorza. Directed by Gabrielle Beaumont.

106. "The Game." Teleplay by Brannon Braga. Story by Susan Sackett & Fred Bronson and Brannon Braga. Directed by Corey Allen.

107. "Unification, Part I." Teleplay by Jeri Taylor. Story by Rick Berman and Michael Piller. Directed by Les Landau.

108. "Unification, Part II." Teleplay by Michael Piller. Story by Rick Berman and Michael Piller. Directed by Cliff Bole.

109. "A Matter of Time." Written by Rick Berman. Directed by Paul Lynch.

110. "New Ground." Teleplay by Grant Rosenberg. Story by Sara Charno and Stuart Charno. Directed by Robert Scheerer.

111. "Hero Worship." Teleplay by Joe Menosky. Story by Hilary J. Bader. Directed by Patrick Stewart.

112. "Violations." Teleplay by Pamela Gray and Jeri Taylor. Story by Shari Good-hartz and T. Michael and Pamela Gray. Directed by Robert Wiemer.

113. "The Masterpiece Society." Teleplay by Adam Belanoff and Michael Piller. Story by James Kahn and Adam Belanoff. Directed by Winrich Kolbe.

114. "Conundrum." Teleplay by Barry Schkolnick. Story by Paul Schiffer. Directed by Les Landau.

115. "Power Play." Teleplay by Rene Balcer and Herbert J. Wright & Brannon Braga. Story by Paul Reuben and Maurice Hurley. Directed by David Livingston.

116. "Ethics." Teleplay by Ronald D. Moore. Story by Sara Charno & Stuart Charno. Directed by Chip Chalmers.

117. "The Outcast." Written by Jeri Taylor. Directed by Robert Scheerer.

118. "Cause and Effect." Written by Brannon Braga. Directed by Jonathan Frakes.

119. "The First Duty." Written by Ronald D. Moore & Naren Shankar. Directed by Paul Lynch.

120. "Cost of Living." Written by Peter Allan Fields. Directed by Winrich Kolbe.

121. "The Perfect Mate." Teleplay by Gary Perconte and Michael Piller. Story by René Echevarria and Gary Perconte. Directed by Cliff Bole.

122. "Imaginary Friend." Teleplay by Edith Swensen and Brannon Braga. Story by Jean Louise Matthias & Ronald Wilkerson and Richard Fliegel. Directed by Gabrielle Beaumont.

123. "I, Borg." Written by René Echevarria. Directed by Robert Lederman.

124. "The Next Phase." Written by Ronald D. Moore. Directed by David Carson.

125. "The Inner Light." Teleplay by Morgan Gendel and Peter Allan Fields. Story by Morgan Gendel. Directed by Peter Lauritson.

126. "Time's Arrow, Part I." Teleplay by Joe Menosky and Michael Piller. Story by Joe Menosky. Directed by Les Landau.

***Star Trek: The Next Generation* Year 6 (first aired 1992–93)**

127. "Time's Arrow, Part II." Teleplay by Jeri Taylor. Story by Joe Menosky. Directed by Les Landau.

128. "Realm of Fear." Written by Brannon Braga. Directed by Cliff Bole.

129. "Man of the People." Written by Frank Abatemarco. Directed by Winrich Kolbe.

130. "Relics." Written by Ronald D. Moore. Directed by Alexander Singer.

131. "Schisms." Teleplay by Brannon Braga. Story by Jean Louise Matthias & Ron Wilkerson. Directed by Robert Wiemer.

132. "True-Q." Written by René Echevarria. Directed by Robert Scheerer.

133. "Rascals." Teleplay by Allison Hock. Story by Ward Botsford & Diana Dru Botsford and Michael Piller. Directed by Adam Nimoy.

134. "A Fistful of Datas." Teleplay by Robert Hewitt Wolfe and Brannon Braga. Story by Robert Hewitt Wolfe. Directed by Patrick Stewart.

135. "The Quality of Life." Written by Naren Shankar. Directed by Jonathan Frakes.

136. "Chain of Command, Part I." Teleplay by Ronald D. Moore. Story by Frank Abatemarco. Directed by Robert Scheerer.

137. "Chain of Command, Part II." Written by Frank Abatemarco. Directed by Les Landau.

138. "Ship in a Bottle." Written by Rene Echevarria. Directed by Alexander Singer.

139. "Aquiel." Teleplay by Brannon Braga & Ronald D. Moore. Story by Jeri Taylor. Directed by Cliff Bole.

140. "Face of the Enemy." Teleplay by Naren Shankar. Story by René Echevarria. Directed by Gabrielle Beaumont.

141. "Tapestry." Written by Ronald D. Moore. Directed by Les Landau.

142. "Birthright, Part I." Written by Brannon Braga. Directed by Winrich Kolbe.

143. "Birthright, Part II." Written by René Echevarria. Directed by Dan Curry.

144. "Starship Mine." Written by Morgan Gendel. Directed by Cliff Bole.

145. "Lessons." Written by Ronald Wilkerson & Jean Louise Matthias. Directed by Robert Wiemer.

146. "The Chase." Story by Ronald D. Moore & Joe Menosky. Teleplay by Joe Menosky. Directed by Jonathan Frakes.

147. "Frame of Mind." Written by Brannon Braga. Directed by James L. Conway.

148. "Suspicions." Written by Joe Menosky and Naren Shankar. Directed by Cliff Bole.

149. "Rightful Heir." Teleplay by Ronald D. Moore. Story by James E. Brooks. Directed by Winrich Kolbe.

150. "Second Chances." Story by Michael A. Medlock. Teleplay by René Echevarria. Directed by LeVar Burton.

151. "Timescape." Written by Brannon Braga. Directed by Adam Nimoy.

152. "Descent, Part I." Story by Jeri Taylor. Teleplay by Ronald D. Moore. Directed by Alexander Singer.

***Star Trek: The Next Generation* Year 7 (first aired 1993–94)**

153. "Descent, Part II." Written by René Echevarria. Directed by Alexander Singer.

154. "Liaisons." Teleplay by Jeanne Carrigan Fauci. Story by Roger Eschbacher & Jaq Greenspan. Directed by Cliff Bole.

155. "Interface." Written by Joe Menosky. Directed by Robert Wiemer.

156. "Gambit, Part I." Teleplay by Naren Shankar. Story by Christopher Hatton and Naren Shankar. Directed by Peter Lauritson.

157. "Gambit, Part II." Teleplay by Ronald D. Moore. Story by Naren Shankar. Directed by Alexander Singer.

158. "Phantasms." Written by Brannon Braga. Directed by Patrick Stewart.

159. "Dark Page." Written by Hilary J. Bader. Directed by Les Landau.

160. "Attached." Written by Nicholas Sagan. Directed by Jonathan Frakes.

161. "Force of Nature." Written by Naren Shankar. Directed by Robert Lederman.

162. "Inheritance." Teleplay by Dan Koeppel and René Echevarria. Story by Dan Koeppel. Directed by Robert Scheerer.

163. "Parallels." Written by Brannon Braga. Directed by Robert Wiemer.

164. "The Pegasus." Written by Ronald D. Moore. Directed by LeVar Burton.

165. "Homeward." Teleplay by Naren Shankar. Television story by Spike Steingasser. Based on material by William N. Stape. Directed by Alexander Singer.

166. "Sub Rosa." Teleplay by Brannon Braga. Television story by Jeri Taylor. Based upon material by Jeanna F. Gallo. Directed by Jonathan Frakes.

167. "Lower Decks." Teleplay by René Echevarria. Story by Ronald Wilkerson & Jean Louise Matthias. Directed by Gabrielle Beaumont.

168. "Thine Own Self." Teleplay by Ronald D. Moore. Story by Christopher Hatton. Directed by Winrich Kolbe.

169. "Masks." Written by Joe Menosky. Directed by Robert Weimer.

170. "Eye of the Beholder." Teleplay by René Echevarria. Story by Brannon Braga. Directed by Cliff Bole.

171. "Genesis." Written by Brannon Braga. Directed by Gates McFadden.

172. "Journey's End." Written by Ronald D. Moore. Directed by Corey Allen.

173. "First Born." Teleplay by René Echevarria. Story by Mark Kalbfeld. Directed by Jonathan West.

174. "Bloodlines." Written by Nicholas Sagan. Directed by Jonathan West.

175. "Emergence." Teleplay by Joe Menosky. Story by Brannon Braga. Directed by Cliff Bole.

176. "Preemptive Strike." Teleplay by René Echevarria. Story by Naren Shankar. Directed by Patrick Stewart.

177. "All Good Things... Part I." Written by Ronald D. Moore and Brannon Braga. Directed by Winrich Kolbe.

178. "All Good Things... Part II." Written by Ronald D. Moore and Brannon Braga. Directed by Winrich Kolbe.

Star Trek: Deep Space Nine Year 1 (first aired 1992–1993)

1. "Emissary, Part I." Teleplay by Michael Piller. Story by Rick Berman and Michael Piller. Directed by David Carson.

2. "Emissary, Part II." Teleplay by Michael Piller. Story by Rick Berman and Michael Piller. Directed by David Carson.

3. "A Man Alone." Teleplay by Michael Piller. Story by Gerald Sanford and Michael Piller. Directed by Paul Lynch.

4. "Past Prologue." Written by Kathryn Powers. Directed by Winrich Kolbe.

5. "Babel." Teleplay by Michael McGreevey and Naren Shankar. Story by Sally Caves and Ira Steven Behr. Directed by Paul Lynch.

6. "Captive Pursuit." Teleplay by Jill Sherman Donner and Michael Piller. Story by Jill Sherman Donner. Directed by Corey Allen.

7. "Q-Less." Teleplay by Robert Hewitt Wolfe. Story by Hannah Louise Shearer. Directed by Paul Lynch.

8. "Dax." Teleplay by D. C. Fontana and Peter Allan Fields. Story by Peter Allan Fields. Directed by David Carson.

9. "The Passenger." Teleplay by Morgan Gendel and Robert Hewitt Wolfe & Michael Piller. Story by Morgan Gendel. Directed by Paul Lynch.

10. "Move Along Home." Teleplay by Frederick Rappaport and Lisa Rich & Jeanne Carrigan-Fauci. Story by Michael Piller. Directed by David Carson.

11. "The Nagus." Teleplay by Ira Steven Behr. Story by David Livingston. Directed by David Livingston.

12. "Vortex." Written by Sam Rolfe. Directed by Winrich Kolbe.

13. "Battle Lines." Teleplay by Richard Danus and Evan Carlos Somers. Story by Hilary Bader. Directed by Paul Lynch.

14. "The Storyteller." Teleplay by Kurt Michael Bensmiller and Ira Steven Behr. Story by Kurt Michael Bensmiller. Directed by David Livingston.

15. "Progress." Written by Peter Allan Fields. Directed by Les Landau.

16. "If Wishes Were Horses." Teleplay by Neil McCue Crawford & William L. Crawford and Michael Piller. Story by Neil McCue Crawford & William L. Crawford. Directed by Robert Legato.

17. "The Forsaken." Teleplay by Don Carlos Dunaway and Michael Piller. Story by Jim Trombetta. Directed by Les Landau.

18. "Dramatis Personae." Written by Joe Menosky. Directed by Cliff Bole.

19. "Duet." Teleplay by Peter Allan Fields. Story by Lisa Rich & Jeanne Carrigan-Fauci. Directed by James L. Conway.

20. "In the Hands of the Prophets." Written by Robert Hewitt Wolfe. Directed by David Livingston.

Star Trek: Deep Space Nine Year 2 (first aired 1993–94)

21. "The Homecoming." Teleplay by Ira Steven Behr. Story by Jeri Taylor and Ira Steven Behr. Directed by Winrich Kolbe.

22. "The Circle." Written by Peter Allan Fields. Directed by Corey Allen.

23. "The Siege." Written by Michael Piller. Directed by Winrich Kolbe.

24. "Invasive Procedures." Teleplay by John Whelpley and Robert Hewitt Wolfe. Story by John Whelpley. Directed by Les Landau.

25. "Cardassians." Teleplay by James Crocker. Story by Gene Wolande & John Wright. Directed by Cliff Bole.

26. "Melora." Teleplay by Evan Carlos Somers and Steven Baum and Michael Piller & James Crocker. Story by Evan Carlos Somers. Directed by Winrich Kolbe.

27. "Rules of Acquisition." Teleplay by Ira Steven Behr. Story by Hilary Bader. Directed by David Livingston.

28. "Necessary Evil." Written by Peter Allan Fields. Directed by James L. Conway.

29. "Second Sight" Teleplay by Mark Gehred-O'Connel and Ira Steven Behr & Robert Hewitt Wolfe. Story by Mark Gehred-O'Connel. Directed by Alexander Singer.

30. "Sanctuary." Teleplay by Frederick Rappaport. Story by Gabe Essoe & Kelley Miles. Directed by Les Landau.

31. "Rivals." Teleplay by Joe Menosky. Story by Jim Trombetta and Michael Piller. Directed by David Livingston.

32. "The Alternate." Teleplay by Bill Dial. Story by Jim Trombetta and Bill Dial. Directed by David Carson.

33. "Armageddon Game." Written by Morgan Gendel. Directed by Winrich Kolbe.

34. "Whispers." Written by Paul Robert Coyle. Directed by Les Landau.

35. "Paradise." Teleplay by Jeff King and Richard Manning & Hans Beimler. Story by Jim Trombetta and James Crocker. Directed by Corey Allen.

36. "Shadowplay." Written by Robert Hewitt Wolfe. Directed by Robert Scheerer.

37. "Playing God." Story by Jim Trombetta. Teleplay by Jim Trombetta and Michael Piller. Directed by David Livingston.

38. "Profit and Loss." Written by Flip Kobler & Cindy Marcus. Directed by Robert Wiemer.

39. "Blood Oath." Television story and teleplay by Peter Allan Fields. Directed by Winrich Kolbe.

40. "The Maquis, Part I." Teleplay by James Crocker. Story by Rick Berman & Michael Piller & Jeri Taylor and James Crocker. Directed by David Livingston.

41. "The Maquis, Part II." Teleplay by Ira Steven Behr. Story by Rick Berman & Michael Piller & Jeri Taylor and Ira Steven Behr. Directed by Corey Allen.

42. "The Wire." Written by Robert Hewitt Wolfe. Directed by Kim Friedman.

43. "Crossover." Teleplay by Peter Allan Fields & Michael Piller. Story by Peter Allan Fields. Directed by David Livingston.

44. "The Collaborator." Teleplay by Gary Holland and Ira Steven Behr & Robert Hewitt Wolfe. Story by Gary Holland. Directed by Cliff Bole.

45. "Tribunal." Written by Bill Dial. Directed by Avery Brooks.

46. "The Jem'Hadar." Written by Ira Steven Behr. Directed by Kim Friedman.

Star Trek: Deep Space Nine Year 3 (first aired 1994–95)

47. "The Search, Part I." Teleplay by Ronald D. Moore. Story by Ira Steven Behr & Robert Hewitt Wolfe. Directed by Kim Friedman.

48. "The Search, Part II." Teleplay by Ira Steven Behr. Story by Ira Steven Behr & Robert Hewitt Wolfe. Directed by Jonathan Frakes.

49. "The House of Quark." Story by Tom Benko. Teleplay by Ronald D. Moore. Directed by Les Landau.

50. "Equilibrium." Story by Christopher Teague. Teleplay by René Echevarria. Directed by Cliff Bole.

51. "Second Skin." Written by Robert Hewitt Wolfe. Directed by Les Landau.

52. "The Abandoned." Written by D. Thomas Maio & Steve Warnek. Directed by Avery Brooks.

53. "Civil Defense." Written by Mike Krohn. Directed by Reza Badiyi.

54. "Meridian." Teleplay by Mark Gehred-O'Connel. Story by Hilary Bader and Evan Carlos Somers. Directed by Jonathan Frakes.

55. "Defiant." Written by Ronald D. Moore. Directed by Cliff Bole.

56. "Fascination." Teleplay by Philip LaZebnik. Story by Ira Steven Behr & James Crocker. Directed by Avery Brooks.

57. "Past Tense, Part I." Teleplay by Robert Hewitt Wolfe. Story by Ira Steven Behr & Robert Hewitt Wolfe. Directed by Reza Badiyi.

58. "Past Tense, Part II." Teleplay by Ira Steven Behr & René Echevarria. Story by Ira Steven Behr & Robert Hewitt Wolfe. Directed by Jonathan Frakes.

59. "Life Support." Teleplay by Ronald D. Moore. Story by Christian Ford & Roger Soffer. Directed by Reza Badiyi.

60. "Heart of Stone." Written by Ira Steven Behr & Robert Hewitt Wolfe. Directed by Alexander Singer.

61. "Destiny." Written by David S. Cohen & Martin A. Winer. Directed by Les Landau.

62. "Prophet Motive." Written by Ira Steven Behr & Robert Hewitt Wolfe. Directed by Rene Auberjonois.

63. "Visionary." Teleplay by John Shirley. Story by Ethan H. Calk. Directed by Reza Badiyi.

64. "Distant Voices." Teleplay by Ira Steven Behr & Robert Hewitt Wolfe. Story by Joe Menosky. Directed by Alexander Singer.

65. "Improbable Cause." Teleplay by René Echevarria. Story by Robert Lederman & David R. Long. Directed by Avery Brooks.

66. "Through the Looking Glass." Written by Ira Steven Behr & Robert Hewitt Wolfe. Directed by Winrich Kolbe.

67. "The Die is Cast." Written by Ronald D. Moore. Directed by David Livingston.

68. "Explorers." Written by René Echevarria. Story by Hilary Bader. Directed by Cliff Bole.

69. "Family Business." Written by Ira Steven Behr & Robert Hewitt Wolfe. Directed by Rene Auberjonois.

70. "Shakaar." Written by Gordon Dawson. Directed by Jonathan West.

71. "Facets." Written by René Echevarria. Directed by Cliff Bole.

72. "The Adversary." Written by Ira Steven Behr & Robert Hewitt Wolfe. Directed by Alexander Singer.

Star Trek: Deep Space Nine Year 4 (first aired 1995–96)

73. "The Way of the Warrior, Part I." Written by Ira Steven Behr & Robert Hewitt Wolfe. Directed by James L. Conway.

74. "The Way of the Warrior, Part II." Written by Ira Steven Behr & Robert Hewitt Wolfe. Directed by James L. Conway.

75. "Hippocratic Oath." Teleplay by Lisa Klink. Story by Nicholas Corea and Lisa Klink. Directed by Rene Auberjonois.

76. "The Visitor." Written by Michael Taylor. Directed by David Livingston.

77. "Indiscretion." Teleplay by Nicholas Corea. Story by Toni Marberry & Jack Treviño. Directed by LeVar Burton.

78. "Rejoined." Teleplay by Ronald D. Moore & René Echevarria. Story by René Echeverria. Directed by Avery Brooks.

79. "Starship Down." Written by David Mack & John J. Ordover. Directed by Alexander Singer.

80. "Little Green Men." Teleplay by Ira Steven Behr & Robert Hewitt Wolfe. Story by Toni Marberry & Jack Treviño.

81. "The Sword of Kahless." Teleplay by Hans Beimler. Story by Richard Danus. Directed by LeVar Burton.

82. "Our Man Bashir." Teleplay by Ronald D. Moore. Story by Robert Gillian. Directed by Winrich Kolbe.

83. "Homefront." Written by Ira Steven Behr & Robert Hewitt Wolfe. Directed by David Livingston.

84. "Paradise Lost." Teleplay by Ira Steven Behr & Robert Hewitt Wolfe. Story by Ronald D. Moore. Directed by Reza Badiyi.

85. "Crossfire." Written by René Echevarria. Directed by Les Landau.

86. "Return to Grace." Teleplay by Hans Beimler. Story by Tom Benko. Directed by Jonathan West.

87. "Sons of Mogh." Written by Ronald D. Moore. Directed by David Livingston.

88. "The Bar Association." Teleplay by Robert Hewitt Wolfe and Ira Steven Behr. Story by Barbara J. Lee & Jenifer A. Lee. Directed by LeVar Burton.

89. "Accession." Written by Jane Espenson. Directed by Les Landau.

90. "Rules of Engagement." Story by Bradley Thompson & David Weddle. Teleplay by Ronald D. Moore. Directed by LeVar Burton.

91. "Hard Time." Story by Daniel Keys Moran & Lynn Barker. Teleplay by Robert Hewitt Wolfe. Directed by Alexander Singer.

92. "Shattered Mirror." Written by Ira Steven Behr & Hans Beimler. Directed by James L. Conway.

93. "The Muse." Teleplay by René Echevarria. Story by René Echevarria & Majel Barrett Roddenberry. Directed by David Livingston.

94. "For the Cause." Teleplay by Ronald D. Moore. Story by Mark Gehred-O'Connel. Directed by James L. Conway.

95. "The Quickening." Written by Naren Shankar. Directed by Rene Auberjonois.

96. "To the Death." Written by Ira Steven Behr & Robert Hewitt Wolfe. Directed by LeVar Burton.

97. "Body Parts." Teleplay by Hans Beimler. Story by Louis P. De Santis & Robert J. Bolivar. Directed by Avery Brooks.

98. "Broken Link." Teleplay by Robert Hewitt Wolfe & Ira Steven Behr. Story by George Brozak. Directed by Les Landau.

Star Trek: Deep Space Nine Year 5 (first aired 1996–97)

99. "Apocalypse Rising." Written by Ira Steven Behr & Robert Hewitt Wolfe. Directed by James L. Conway.

100. "The Ship." Teleplay by Hans Beimler. Story by Pam Wigginton & Richard Carson. Directed by Kim Friedman.

101. "Looking for *par'Mach* in All the Wrong Places." Written by Ronald D. Moore. Directed by Andrew J. Robinson.

102. "Nor the Battle to the Strong." Teleplay by René Echevarria. Story by Brice R. Parker. Directed by Kim Friedman.

103. "Trials and Tribble-ations." Teleplay by Ronald D. Moore & René Echevarria. Story by Ira Steven Behr & Hans Beimler & Robert Hewitt Wolfe. Directed by Jonathan West.

104. "The Assignment." Teleplay by David Weddle & Bradley Thompson. Story by David R. Long & Robert Lederman. Directed by Allan Kroeker.

105. "Let He Who Is Without Sin..." Written by Robert Hewitt Wolfe & Ira Steven Behr. Directed by Rene Auberjonois.

106. "Things Past." Written by Michael Taylor. Directed by LeVar Burton.

107. "The Ascent" Written by Ira Steven Behr & Robert Hewitt Wolfe. Directed by Alan Kroeker.

108. "Rapture." Teleplay by Hans Beimler. Story by L. J. Strom. Directed by Jonathan West.

109. "The Darkness and the Light." Teleplay by Ronald D. Moore. Story by Bryan Fuller. Directed by Michael Vejar.

110. "The Begotten." Written by René Echevarria. Directed by Jesús Salvador Treviño.

111. "For the Uniform." Written by Peter Allan Fields. Directed by Victor Lobl.

112. "In Purgatory's Shadow." Written by Robert Hewitt Wolfe & Ira Steven Behr. Directed by Gabrielle Beaumont.

113. "By Inferno's Light." Written by Ira Steven Behr & Robert Hewitt Wolfe. Directed by Les Landau.

114. "Doctor Bashir, I Presume?" Teleplay by Ronald D. Moore. Story by Jimmy Diggs. Directed by David Livingston.

115. "A Simple Investigation." Written by René Echevarria. Directed by John Kretchmer.

116. "Business As Usual." Written by Bradley Thompson & David Weddle. Directed by Siddig El Fadil.

117. "Ties of Blood and Water." Teleplay by Robert Hewitt Wolfe. Story by Edmund Newton & Robbin L. Slocum. Directed by Avery Brooks.

118. "Ferengi Love Songs." Written by Ira Steven Behr & Hans Beimler. Directed by Rene Auberjonois.

119. "Soldiers of the Empire." Written by Ronald D. Moore. Directed by LeVar Burton.

120. "Children of Time." Teleplay by René Echevarria. Story by Gary Holland and Ethan H. Calk. Directed by Allan Kroeker.

121. "Blaze of Glory." Written by Robert Hewitt Wolfe & Ira Steven Behr. Directed by Kim Friedman.

122. "Empok Nor." Teleplay by Hans Beimler. Story by Bryan Fuller. Directed by Michael Vejar.

123. "In the Cards." Teleplay by Ronald D. Moore. Story by Truly Barr Clark & Scott J. Neal. Directed by Michael Dorn.

124. "Call to Arms." Written by Ira Steven Behr & Robert Hewitt Wolfe. Directed by Allan Kroeker.

Star Trek: Deep Space Nine Year 6 (First aired 1997–98)

125. "A Time to Stand." Written by Ira Steven Behr & Hans Beimler. Directed by Allan Kroeker.

126. "Rocks and Shoals." Written by Ronald D. Moore. Directed by Michael Vejar.

127. "Sons and Daughters." Written by Bradley Thompson & David Weddle. Directed by Jesús Salvador Treviño.

128. "Behind the Lines." Written by René Echevarria. Directed by LeVar Burton.

129. "Favor the Bold." Written by Ira Steven Behr & Hans Beimler. Directed by Winrich Kolbe.

130. "Sacrifice of Angels." Written by Ira Steven Behr & Hans Beimler. Directed by Allan Kroeker.

131. "You Are Cordially Invited." Written by Ronald D. Moore. Directed by David Livingston.

132. "Resurrection." Written by René Echevarria. Directed by LeVar Burton.

133. "Statistical Probabilities." Teleplay by René Echevarria. Story by Pam Pietroforte. Directed by Anson Williams.

134. "The Magnificent Ferengi." Written by Ira Steven Behr & Hans Beimler. Directed by Chip Chalmers.

135. "Waltz." Written by Ronald D. Moore. Directed by Rene Auberjonois.

136. "Who Mourns for Morn?" Written by Mark Gehred-O'Connell. Directed by Victor Lobl.

137. "One Little Ship." Written by David Weddle & Bradley Thompson. Directed by Allan Kroeker.

138. "Far Beyond the Stars." Teleplay by Ira Steven Behr & Hans Beimler. Story by Marc Scott Zicree. Directed by Avery Brooks.

139. "Honor Among Thieves." Teleplay by René Echevarria. Story by Philip Kim. Directed by Allan Eastman.

140. "Change of Heart." Written by Ronald D. Moore. Directed by David Livingston.

141. "Wrongs Darker Than Death or Night." Written by Ira Steven Behr & Hans Beimler. Directed by Jonathan West.

142. "Inquisition." Teleplay by Bradley Thompson & David Weddle. Directed by Michael Dorn.

143. "In the Pale Moonlight." Teleplay by Michael Taylor. Story by Peter Allan Fields. Directed by Victor Lobl.

144. "His Way" Written by Ira Steven Behr & Hans Beimler. Directed by Allan Kroeker.

145. "The Reckoning." Teleplay by David Weddle & Bradley Thompson. Story by Harry M. Werksman & Gabrielle Stanton. Directed by Jesús Salvador Treviño.

146. "*Valiant*." Written by Ronald D. Moore. Directed by Michael Vejar.

147. "Profit and Lace." Written by Ira Steven Behr & Hans Beimler. Directed by Alexander Siddig.

148. "Time's Orphan." Teleplay by Bradley Thompson & David Weddle. Story by Joe Menosky. Directed by Allan Kroeker.

149. "The Sound of Her Voice." Teleplay by Ronald D. Moore. Story by Pam Pietroforte. Directed by Winrich Kolbe.

150. "Tears of the Prophets." Written by Ira Steven Behr & Hans Beimler. Directed by Allan Kroeker.

Star Trek: Deep Space Nine Year 7 (First aired 1998–99)

151. "Image in the Sand." Written by Ira Steven Behr & Hans Beimler. Directed by Les Landau.

152. "Shadows and Symbols." Written by Ira Steven Behr & Hans Beimler. Directed by Allan Kroeker.

153. "Afterimage." Written by René Echevarria. Directed by Les Landau.

154. "Take Me Out to the Holosuite." Written by Ronald D. Moore. Directed by Chip Chalmers.

155. "Chrysalis." Written by René Echevarria. Directed by Jonathan West.

156. "Treachery, Faith, and the Great River." Teleplay by David Weddle & Bradley Thompson. Story by Philip Kim. Directed by Steve Posey.

157. "Once More into the Breach." Written by Ronald D. Moore. Directed by Allan Kroeker.

158. "The Siege of AR-558." Written by Ira Steven Behr & Hans Beimler. Directed by Winrich Kolbe.

159. "Covenant." Written by René Echevarria. Directed by John Kretchmer.

160. "It's Only a Paper Moon." Teleplay by Ronald D. Moore. Story by David Mack & John J. Ordover. Directed by Anson Williams.

161. "Prodigal Daughter." Written by Bradley Thompson & David Weddle. Directed by Victor Lobl.

162. "Emperor's New Cloak." Written by Ira Steven Behr & Hans Beimler. Directed by LeVar Burton.

163. "Field of Fire." Written by Robert Hewitt Wolfe. Directed by Tony Dow.

164. "Chimera." Written by René Echevarria. Directed by Steve Posey.

165. "*Inter Arma Enim Silent Leges*." Written by Ronald D. Moore. Directed by David Livingston.

166. "Badda-bing Badda-bang." Written by Ira Steven Behr & Hans Beimler. Directed by Mike Vejar.

167. "Penumbra." Written by René Echevarria. Directed by Steve Posey.

168. "'Til Death Us Do Part." Written by David Weddle & Bradley Thompson. Directed by Winrich Kolbe.

169. "Strange Bedfellows." Written by Ronald D. Moore. Directed by Rene Auberjonois.

170. "The Changing Face of Evil." Written by Ira Steven Behr & Hans Beimler. Directed by Mike Vejar.

171. "When it Rains..." Teleplay by René Echevarria. Story by René Echevarria & Spike Steingasser. Directed by Michael Dorn.

172. "Tacking into the Wind." Written by Ronald D. Moore. Directed by Mike Vejar.

173. "Extreme Measures." Written by Bradley Thompson & David Weddle. Directed by Steve Posey.

174. "The Dogs of War." Teleplay by René Echevarria & Ronald D. Moore. Story by Peter Allan Fields. Directed by Avery Brooks.

175. "What You Leave Behind, Part I." Written by Ira Steven Behr & Hans Beimler. Directed by Allan Kroeker.

176. "What You Leave Behind, Part II." Written by Ira Steven Behr & Hans Beimler. Directed by Allan Kroeker.

Star Trek: Voyager Year 1 (first aired in 1995)

1. "Caretaker, Part I." Teleplay by Michael Piller & Jeri Taylor. Story by Rick Berman & Michael Piller & Jeri Taylor. Directed by Winrich Kolbe.

2. "Caretaker, Part II." Teleplay by Michael Piller & Jeri Taylor. Story by Rick Berman & Michael Piller & Jeri Taylor. Directed by Winrich Kolbe.

3. "Parallax." Teleplay by Brannon Braga. Story by Jim Trombetta. Directed by Kim Friedman.

4. "Time and Again." Teleplay by David Kemper and Michael Piller. Story by David Kemper. Directed by Les Landau.

5. "Phage." Teleplay by Skye Dent and Brannon Braga. Story by Timothy De Haas. Directed by Winrich Kolbe.

6. "The Cloud." Teleplay by Tom Szollosi and Michael Piller. Story by Brannon Braga. Directed by David Livingston.

7. "Eye of the Needle." Teleplay by Bill Dial and Jeri Taylor. Story by Hilary Bader. Directed by Winrich Kolbe.

8. "Ex Post Facto." Teleplay by Evan Carlos Somers and Michael Piller. Story by Evan Carlos Somers. Directed by LeVar Burton.

9. "Emanations." Written by Brannon Braga. Directed by David Livingston.

10. "Prime Factors." Teleplay by Michael Perricone and Greg Elliot. Story by David R. George III & Eric Stillwell. Directed by Les Landau.

11. "State of Flux." Teleplay by Chris Abbott. Story by Paul Robert Coyle. Directed by Robert Scheerer.

12. "Heroes and Demons." Written by Naren Shankar. Directed by Les Landau.

13. "Cathexis." Teleplay by Brannon Braga. Story by Brannon Braga & Joe Menosky. Directed by Kim Friedman.

14. "Faces." Teleplay by Kenneth Biller. Story by Jonathan Glassner and Kenneth Biller. Directed by Winrich Kolbe.

15. "Jetrel." Teleplay by Jack Klein & Karen Klein and Kenneth Biller. Story by James Thomton & Scott Nimerfro. Directed by Kim Friedman.

16. "Learning Curve." Written by Ronald Wilkerson & Jean Louise Matthias. Directed by David Livingston.

Star Trek: Voyager Year 2 (first aired 1995–96)

17. "Projections." Written by Brannon Braga. Directed by Jonathan Frakes.

18. "Elogium." Teleplay by Kenneth Biller and Jeri Taylor. Story by Jimmy Diggs & Steve J. Kay. Directed by Winrich Kolbe.

19. "Twisted." Teleplay by Kenneth Biller. Story by Arnold Rudnick & Rich Hosek. Directed by Kim Friedman.

20. "The 37's." Written by Jeri Taylor & Brannon Braga. Directed by James L. Conway.

21. "Initiations." Written by Kenneth Biller. Directed by Winrich Kolbe.

22. "Non Sequitur." Written by Brannon Braga. Directed by David Livingston.

23. "Parturition." Written by Tom Szollosi. Directed by Jonathan Frakes.

24. "Persistence of Vision." Written by Jeri Taylor. Directed by James L. Conway.

25. "Tattoo." Teleplay by Michael Piller. Story by Larry Brody. Directed by Alexander Singer.

26. "Cold Fire." Teleplay by Brannon Braga. Story by Anthony Williams. Directed by Cliff Bole

27. "Maneuvers." Written by Kenneth Biller. Directed by David Livingston.

28. "Resistance." Teleplay by Lisa Klink. Story by Michael Jan Friedman & Kevin J. Ryan. Directed by Winrich Kolbe.

29. "Prototype." Written by Nicholas Corea. Directed by Jonathan Frakes.

30. "Death Wish." Teleplay by Michael Piller. Story by Shawn Piller. Directed by James L. Conway.

31. "Alliances." Written by Jeri Taylor. Directed by Les Landau.

32. "Threshold." Teleplay by Brannon Braga. Story by Michael DeLuca. Directed by Alexander Singer.

33. "Meld." Teleplay by Michael Piller. Story by Michael Sussman. Directed by Cliff Bole.

34. "Dreadnought." Written by Gary Holland. Directed by LeVar Buron.

35. "Lifesigns." Written by Kenneth Biller. Directed by Cliff Bole.

36. "Investigations." Teleplay by Jeri Taylor. Story by Jeff Schnaufer & Ed Bond. Directed by Les Landau.

37. "Deadlock." Written by Brannon Braga. Directed by David Livingston.

38. "Innocence." Teleplay by Lisa Klink. Story by Anthony Williams. Directed by James L. Conway.

39. "The Thaw." Teleplay by Joe Menosky. Story by Richard Gadas. Directed by Marvin V. Rush.

40. "Tuvix." Teleplay by Kenneth Biller. Story by Andrew Shepard Price & Mark Gaberman. Directed by Cliff Bole.

41. "Resolutions." Written by Jeri Taylor. Directed by Alexander Singer.

42. "Basics, Part I." Written by Michael Piller. Directed by Winrich Kolbe.

Star Trek: Voyager Year 3 (first aired 1996–97)

43. "Sacred Ground." Teleplay by Lisa Klink. Story by Geo Cameron. Directed by Robert Duncan McNeill.

44. "False Profits." Teleplay by Joe Menosky. Story by George A. Brozak. Directed by Cliff Bole.

45. "Flashback." Written by Brannon Braga. Directed by David Livingston.

46. "Basics, Part II." Written by Michael Piller. Directed by Winrich Kolbe.

47. "The Chute." Teleplay by Kenneth Biller. Story by Clayvon C. Harris. Directed by Les Landau.

48. "Remember." Teleplay by Lisa Klink. Story by Brannon Braga & Joe Menosky. Directed by Winrich Kolbe.

49. "The Swarm." Written by Mike Sussman. Directed by Alexander Singer.

50. "Future's End, Part I." Written by Brannon Braga & Joe Menosky. Directed by David Livingston.

51. "Future's End, Part II." Written by Brannon Braga & Joe Menosky. Directed by Cliff Bole.

52. "Warlord." Teleplay by Lisa Klink. Story by Andrew Shepard Price & Mark Gaberman. Directed by David Livingston.

53. "The Q and the Grey." Teleplay by Kenneth Biller. Story by Shawn Piller. Directed by Cliff Bole.

54. "Macrocosm." Written by Brannon Braga. Directed by Alexander Singer.

55. "Alter Ego." Written by Joe Menosky. Directed by Robert Picardo.

56. "Fair Trade." Teleplay by André Bormanis. Story by Ronald Wilkerson & Jean Louise Matthias. Directed by Jesus Salvador Treviño.

57. "Blood Fever." Written by Lisa Klink. Directed by Andrew Robinson.

58. "Coda." Written by Jeri Taylor. Directed by Nancy Malone.

59. "Unity." Written by Kenneth Biller. Directed by Robert Duncan McNeill.

60. "Rise." Teleplay by Brannon Braga. Story by Jimmy Diggs. Directed by Robert Scheerer.

61. "Darkling." Teleplay by Joe Menosky. Story by Brannon Braga & Joe Menosky. Directed by Alexander Singer.

62. "Favorite Son." Written by Lisa Klink. Directed by Marvin V. Rush.

63. "Before and After." Written by Kenneth Biller. Directed by Allan Kroeker.

64. "Real Life." Teleplay by Jeri Taylor. Story by Harry Doc Kloor. Directed by Anson Williams.

65. "Distant Origin." Written by Brannon Braga & Joe Menosky. Directed by David Livingston.

66. "Displaced." Written by Lisa Klink. Directed by Allan Kroeker.

67. "Worse Case Scenario." Written by Kenneth Biller. Directed by Alexander Singer.

68. "Scorpion, Part I." Written by Brannon Braga & Joe Menosky. Directed by David Livingston.

Star Trek: Voyager Year 4 (First aired 1997–98)

69. "Scorpion, Part II." Written by Brannon Braga & Joe Menosky. Directed by Winrich Kolbe.

70. "The Gift." Written by Joe Menosky. Directed by Anson Williams.

71. "Nemesis." Written by Kenneth Biller. Directed by Alexander Singer.

72. "Day of Honor." Written by Jeri Taylor. Directed by Jesús Salvador Treviño.

73. "Revulsion." Written by Lisa Klink. Directed by Kenneth Biller.

74. "The Raven." Teleplay by Bryan Fuller. Story by Bryan Fuller and Harry Doc Kloor. Directed by LeVar Burton.

75. "Scientific Method." Teleplay by Lisa Klink. Story by Sherry Klein & Harry Doc Kloor. Directed by David Livingston.

76. "Year of Hell, Part I." Written by Brannon Braga & Joe Menosky. Directed by Allan Kroeker.

77. "Year of Hell, Part II." Written by Brannon Braga & Joe Menosky. Directed by Mike Vejar.

78. "Random Thoughts." Written by Kenneth Biller. Directed by Alexander Singer.

79. "Concerning Flight." Teleplay by Joe Menosky. Story by Jimmy Diggs & Joe Menosky. Directed by Jesús Salvador Treviño.

80. "Mortal Coil." Written by Bryan Fuller. Directed by Allan Kroeker.

81. "Message in a Bottle." Teleplay by Lisa Klink. Story by Rick Williams. Directed by Nancy Malone.

82. "Waking Moments." Written by Andre Bormanis. Directed by Alexander Singer.

83. "Hunters." Written by Jeri Taylor. Directed by David Livingston.

84. "Prey." Written by Brannon Braga. Directed by Allan Eastman.

85. "Retrospect" Teleplay by Bryan Fuller & Lisa Klink. Story by Andrew Shepard Price & Mark Gaberman. Directed by Jesús Salvador Treviño.

86. "The Killing Game, Part I." Written by Brannon Braga & Joe Menosky. Directed by David Livingston.

87. "The Killing Game, Part II." Written by Brannon Braga & Joe Menosky. Directed by Victor Lobl.

88. "Vis à Vis." Written by Robert J. Doherty. Directed by Jesús Salvador Treviño.

89. "The Omega Directive." Teleplay by Lisa Klink. Story by Jimmy Diggs & Steve J. Kay. Directed by Victor Lobl.

90. "Unforgettable." Written by Greg Elliot & Michael Perricone. Directed by Andrew J. Robinson.

91. "Living Witness." Teleplay by Bryan Fuller and Brannon Braga & Joe Menosky. Story by Brannon Braga. Directed by Tim Russ.

92. "Demon." Teleplay by Kenneth Biller. Story by Andre Bormanis. Directed by Anson Williams.

93. "One." Written by Jeri Taylor. Directed by Kenneth Biller.

94. "Hope and Fear." Teleplay by Brannon Braga & Joe Menosky. Story by Rick Berman & Brannon Braga & Joe Menosky. Directed by Winrich Kolbe.

Star Trek: Voyager Year 5 (First aired 1998-99)

95. "Night." Written by Brannon Braga & Joe Menosky. Directed by David Livingston.

96. "Drone." Teleplay by Bryan Fuller and Brannon Braga & Joe Menosky. Story by Bryan Fuller and Harry Doc Kloor. Directed by Les Landau.

97. "Extreme Risk." Written by Kenneth Biller. Directed by Cliff Bole.

98. "In the Flesh." Written by Nick Sagan. Directed by David Livingston.

99. "Once Upon a Time." Written by Michael Taylor. Directed by John Kretchmer.

100. "Nothing Human." Written by Jeri Taylor. Directed by David Livingston.

101. "Timeless." Teleplay by Brannon Braga & Joe Menosky. Story by Rick Berman & Brannon Braga & Joe Menosky. Directed by LeVar Burton.

102. "Thirty Days." Teleplay by Kenneth Biller. Story by Scott Miller. Directed by Winrich Kolbe.

103. "Infinite Regress." Teleplay by Robert J. Doherty. Story by Robert J. Doherty and Jimmy Diggs. Directed by David Livingston.

104. "The Refugee." Written by Michael Taylor. Directed by Les Landau.

105. "Gravity." Teleplay by Nick Sagan & Bryan Fuller. Story by Jimmy Diggs and Bryan Fuller & Nick Sagan. Directed by Terry Windell.

106. "Latent Image." Teleplay by Joe Menosky. Story by Eileen Connors and Brannon Braga & Joe Menosky. Directed by Mike Vejar.

107. "Bride of Chaotica." Teleplay by Bryan Fuller & Michael Taylor. Story by Bryan Fuller. Directed by Allan Kroeker.

108. "The Fight." Teleplay by Joe Menosky. Story by Michael Taylor. Directed by Winrich Kolbe.

109. "Bliss." Teleplay by Robert J. Doherty. Story by Bill Prady. Directed by Cliff Bole.

110. "The Disease." Teleplay by Michael Taylor. Story by Kenneth Biller. Directed by David Livingston.

111. "Dark Frontier, Part I." Written by Brannon Braga & Joe Menosky. Directed by Cliff Bole.

112. "Dark Frontier, Part II." Written by Brannon Braga & Joe Menosky. Directed by Terry Windell.

113. "Course: Oblivion." Teleplay by Bryan Fuller & Nick Sagan. Story by Bryan Fuller. Directed by Anson Williams.

114. "Think Tank." Teleplay by Michael Taylor. Story by Rick Berman & Brannon Braga. Directed by Terrence O'Hara.

115. "Juggernaut." Teleplay by Bryan Fuller & Nick Sagan and Kenneth Biller. Story by Bryan Fuller. Directed by Allan Kroeker.

116. "Someone to Watch Over Me." Teleplay by Michael Taylor. Story by Brannon Braga. Directed by Robert Duncan McNeill.

117. "11:59." Teleplay by Joe Menosky. Story by Brannon Braga & Joe Menosky. Directed by David Livingston.

118. "Relativity." Teleplay by Bryan Fuller & Nick Sagan & Michael Taylor. Story by Nick Sagan. Directed by Allan Eastman.

119. "Warhead." Teleplay by Michael Taylor & Kenneth Biller. Story by Brannon Braga. Directed by John Kretchmer.

120. "Equinox." Teleplay by Brannon Braga & Joe Menosky. Story by Rick Berman & Brannon Braga & Joe Menosky. Directed by David Livingston.

CAST

NOTE: Character names in **boldface** correspond with listings in the main body of the encyclopedia, where more information on those characters (including episode titles) can generally be found. Characters not in boldface do not have corresponding entries, so episode-title information is given for these.

Abbott, Jon: **Ayelborne**
Abraham, F. Murray: **Ru'afo, Ahdar**
Acker, Sharon: **Odona**
Ackerman, Leslie: Waitress, "Trials And Tribble-ations" (DS9)
Adams, Cecily: **Ishka**
Adams, Marc: Hamlet, "Conscience of the King, The" (TOS)
Adams, Mary Kay: **Grilka**
Adams, Phil: Flint's stunt double, "Requiem for Methuselah" (TOS); Kirk's stunt double, "Savage Curtain, The" (TOS); Korax's stunt double, "Trouble with Tribbles, The" (TOS)
Adams, Stanley: **Jones**, **Cyrano**
Agnew, Michelle: Scharn, "Retrospect" (VGR)
Aguilar, Christopher: **Kim, Andrew**
Aguilar, George: **Wasaka**
Ahart, Kathy: Crew woman, "Space Seed" (TOS)
Alaimo, Marc: **Badar N'D'D; Dukat**; **La Rouque**, **Frederick**; **Macet**, **Gul**; Romulan #1, "Neutral Zone, The" (TNG); **Tebok, Commander**; Officer Burt Ryan, "Far Beyond the Stars" (DS9)
Albert, Edward: **Zayra**
Albright, Budd: **Rayburn**
Aldrich, Rhonda: **Madeline**
Aldridge, Virginia: **Tracy**, **Lieutenant Karen**
Alexander, Elle: Female guard, "Nor the Battle to the Strong" (DS9)
Alexander, Kenny: Stunt, *ST:FC*
Allen, Chad: **Jono**
Allen, George E.: Engineer #1, "Devil in the Dark, The" (TOS)
Allen, Richard: **Kentor**
Alley, Kirstie: **Saavik**
Allin, Jeff: **Sutter**, **Ensign Daniel**
Allport, Carolyn: **Bradley**, **Jessica**
Altshuld, Alan: **Pomet**; Sandal maker, "False Profits" (VGR); **Yranac; Lumas**
Ames, Granville: Transporter chief, *STG*
Amick, Mädchen: Teenage girl, "Dauphin, The" (TNG)
Amodeo, Luigi: Gigolo, The, "Cloud, The" (VGR)
Anaya, Jr., Joey: Stunt Borg, *ST:FC*
Anders, Ed: Stunts, *ST6*
Anderson, Barbara: **Karidian**, **Lenore**
Anderson, Dame Judith: **T'Lar**
Anderson, Dion: **Zolan**
Anderson, Erich: **MacDuff**, **Commander Keiran**
Anderson, John: **Uxbridge**, **Kevin**
Anderson, Michael John: **Rumpelstiltskin**
Anderson, Nathan: **Namon**
Anderson, Sam: Assistant manager, "Royale, The" (TNG)
Anderson, Steven: **Nilrem**
Andes, Keith: **Akuta**
Andre, Benita: **Anara**
Andrece, Alyce: **Alice series #1-250**
Andrece, Rhae: **Alice series #251-500**
Andrews, Tige: **Kras**
Anglim, Philip: **Bareil**, **Vedek; Bareil, Antos (mirror)**
Ansara, Michael: **Jeyal**; **Kang**
Anthony, Larry: Transporter chief, "Man Trap, The" (TOS)
Anthony, Richard: Rider, "Spectre of the Gun" & "Dagger of the Mind"(TOS)
Antoni, Richard: Klingon stunt double, "Trouble with Tribbles, The" (TOS)
Antonio, Lou: **Lokai**
Antonucci, Chris: Stunts, *ST:I*
Arenberg, Lee: **Bok**, **DaiMon**; **Gral**; **Prak**, **DaiMon**
Aresco, Joey: **Brull**
Argiro, Vinny: Hitman, "Emergence" (TNG)
Armagnal, Gary: **McNary**
Armitraj, Vijay: Starship captain, *ST4*
Armor, Gene: Bajoran bureaucrat, "Emissary" (DS9)
Armstrong, Dave: Kartan, "Operation: Annihilate!" (TOS)
Armstrong, Vaughn: **Danar, Gul**; **Korris**, **Captain**; **Telek**
Arndt, John: Crewman, "Space Seed" (TOS); Fields, Engineer, "Balance of Terror" (TOS); First crewman, "Dagger of the Mind" (TOS); Security guard #2, "Miri" (TOS)
Arnemann, Dawn: **Gladstone**, **Miss**
Arnett, Cameron: **Mandel**, **Ensign**
Arnette, Jeannetta: **Loews, Dr. Karen**
Aron, Michael: **London**, **Jack**
Arrants, Rod: **Rex; Daleth**
Ashbrook, Daphne: **Pazlar**, **Melora**
Ashmore, Kally: Francine, "We'll Always Have Paris" (TNG)
Astar, Shay: **Isabella**
Atienza, Frank: Kohm villager, "Omega Glory, The" (TOS)
Atwater, Barry: **Surak**
Auberjonois, Rene: **Odo; West, Colonel; Pabst, Douglas**
Austin, Jane: Stunts, *ST:I*
Austin, Jeff: **Allos;** Bolian, "Adversary, The" (DS9)
Austin, Karen: **Kalandra**
Avari, Erick: **B'iJik**; **Yarka**
Avery, Brian: Stunts, *ST:I*
Avery, Joni: Stunts, *ST:I*
Avery, Mike: Stunts, *ST:I*
Avery, Rick: Stunt Coordinator, *ST:I*
Ayres, Jerry: O'Herlihy, Lieutenant, "Arena" (TOS); **Rizzo**, **Ensign**

Babcock, Barbara: Exceiver computer voice and Isis's voice, "Assignment: Earth" (TOS); **Mea 3**; Mother's voice, "Squire of Gothos, The" (TOS); **Philana**; Tholians' voices, "Tholian Web, The" (TOS); Zetar voices, "Lights of Zetar, The" (TOS)
Babcock, Todd: **Mulchaey, Ensign**
Bader, Dietrich: Tactical crewman, "Emissary, The" (TNG)
Badie, Mina: Security officer, "Paradise Lost" (DS9)
Baer, Parley: Old man #1, "Sacred Ground" (VGR)
Bailey, Kirk: **Hansen, Magnus**
Bailous, Michael H.: Jem'Hadar #1, "Hippocratic Oath" (DS9)
Baird, Brenan: Soldier, "Things Past" (DS9)
Baker, Becky Ann: **Nechisti guide**
Baker, Bob: Beauregard puppeteer, "Man Trap, The" (TOS)
Baker, Jay: **Stevens**
Baker, Scott Thompson: **Kudak'Etan**
Bakey, Ed: First fop, "All Our Yesterdays" (TOS)
Bakke, Brenda: **Rivan**
Bal, Jeanne: **Crater**, **Nancy**
Baldavin, Barbara: Baker, Angela, "Space Seed" (TOS); Lisa, "Turnabout Intruder" (TOS); **Martine**, **Ensign Angela**
Balver, Robert: Yeoman, "Is There in Truth No Beauty?" (TOS)
Banes, Lisa: **Renhol**, **Dr.**
Banks, Emily: **Barrows**, **Tonia**
Banks, Jonathan: **Shel-La**, **Golin**
Barba, Ted: **Malin**
Barker: Talosian female, "Cage, The" (TOS)
Barlow, Jennifer: Gibson, Ensign, "Dauphin, The" (TNG)
Barnett, Gregory: Stunt double for Leonard Nimoy, *ST4, ST5*
Barrett, Majel: **Chapel**, **Christine**; Narrator, "Cold Fire" (VGR); **Troi**, **Lwaxana.** Voice of the **Companion**, "Metamorphosis" (TOS); Computer voice; SEE also: Hudec, M. Leigh.
Barrett, Stan: Jailer, The, "All Our Yesterdays" (TOS)
Barrier, Michael: **DeSalle**, **Lieutenant**; Guard #1, "City on the Edge of Forever, The" (TOS)
Barry, Carolyne: Female engineer, "Home Soil" (TNG)
Bartels, Ivor: Young Klingon, "Apocalypse Rising" (DS9)
Basch, Harry: **Brown**, **Dr.**
Bass, Bob: Chekov's boy #1, "Mirror, Mirror" (TOS); Engineer stunt double, "I, Mudd" (TOS); Crewman #2, "This Side of Paradise" (TOS); Guard, "Space Seed" (TOS); Klingon guard, "Errand of Mercy" (TOS); Scott's stunt double, "City on the Edge of Forever, The" (TOS)
Bastiani, Bill: **Omag**
Batanides, Arthur: **D'Amato**, **Lieutenant**
Bates, Ken: High fall stunts, *ST5*

Batten, Cyia: **Tora Ziyal**
Bau, C.J.: Bartender, *ST:FC*
Bauer, Robert: **Kunivas**
Baxley, B.J.: Stunts, *ST6*
Baxley, Gary: Stunts, *ST:I*
Baxley, Hunter: Stunts, *ST:I*
Baxley, Paul: Black Knight, "Shore Leave" (TOS); First trooper, "Patterns of Force" (TOS); **Freeman**, **Ensign**; Hengist's stunt double, "Wolf in the Fold" (TOS); Kirk's and Apella's stunt double, "Private Little War, A" (TOS); Kirk's stunt double, "What Are Little Girls Made Of?" (TOS); McCoy's stunt double, "Empath, The" (TOS); McKinley, Crewman, "Assignment: Earth" (TOS); Man in bar, "Spectre of the Gun" (TOS); Native stunt double, "Apple, The" (TOS); Patrol leader, "Private Little War, A" (TOS); Policeman and McCoy's stunt double, "Bread and Circuses" (TOS); Stunt double, "Where No Man Has Gone Before" (TOS)
Bay, Susan: **Rollman**, **Admiral**
Bayle, Hayne: Ten-Forward crew, "Offspring, The" (TNG)
Baylor, Hal: Policeman, "City on the Edge of Forever, The" (TOS)
Beacham, Stephanie: **Barthalomew, Countess Regina; Westphalen, Dr. Kristin**
Bearnard, Arthur: **Apella**
Beatty, Bruce: **Ben**
Beck, Charles: Elasian guard #2, "Elaan of Troyius" (TOS)
Beck, John: **Boone**, **Raymond**
Becker, James G.: Ten-Forward crew, "Offspring, The" (TNG)
Beecher, Bonnie: **Sylvia**
Beecroft, Gregory: **Mickey D**
Beggs, Hagan: **Hansen**, **Mr.**
Begley, Jr., Ed: **Starling**, **Henry**
Behar, Eli: Therapist, "Dagger of the Mind" (TOS)
Belgrey, Thomas: Crew member, "Realm of Fear" (TNG)
Bell, Felecia M.: **Sisko**, **Jennifer**; **Sisko**, **Jennifer (mirror)**
Bell, Michael: **Borum**; **Drofo Awa;** Xepolite captain, "Maquis, The, Part II" (DS9); **Zorn**, **Groppler**
Bellah, John: Crewman I, "Charlie X" (TOS); Laughing crewman, "Naked Time, The" (TOS)
Belli, Caesar: **O'Connel**, **Steve**
Belli, Melvin: **Gorgan**
Beltran, Robert: **Chakotay**
Benedict, Amy: Woman, "Storyteller, The" (DS9)
Benjamin, Zachary: **Troi**, **Ian Andrew (II)**
Bennett, Fran: **Shanthi**, **Fleet Admiral**
Bennett, Harve: Flight recorder voice, *ST3*; **Bennett, Admiral Robert**
Bennett, John Lendale: **Bell**, **Gabriel**; **Kozak**; Towering Klingon, "Apocalypse Rising" (DS9)
Benton, Craig: **Davis**, **Ensign**
Benzali, Daniel: Surgeon, "Samaritan Snare" (TNG)
Bergere, Lee: **Lincoln**, **Abraham**
Bergmann, Alan: **Lal**
Berkoff, Steven: **Hagath**
Bernard, Joseph: **Tark**
Bernsen, Corbin: **Q2**
Berryman, Michael: **Rixx**, **Captain**; Starfleet communication officer, *ST4*
Besch, Bibi: **Marcus**, **Dr. Carol**
Betances, Daniel: Shuttle pilot, "Extreme Risk" (VGR)
Bethune, Ivy: **Duana**
Bevine, Victor: **Belar**; Guard, *ST:FC*
Bevis, Leslie: **Boslic freighter captain**; **Rionoj**
Beymer, Richard: **Li Nalas**
Bicknell, Andrew: **Wagnor**
Bieniek, Shaun: **Pinar**
Biggs, Casey: **Damar, Glinn; Wykoff, Dr.**
Biggs, Roxann: **Torres, B'Elanna**
Bikel, Theodore: **Rozhenko**, **Sergey**
Billig, Simon: **Hogan**
Billings, Earl: **Henry**, **Admiral Thomas**
Billy, Michele Ameen: Lieutenant, *ST:TMP*
Bin-Al-Hussein, HRH Abdullah: Medical technician, "Investigations" (VGR)
Binney, Geoffrey: Compton, "Wink of an Eye" (TOS)
Birk, Raye: **Wrenn**; Son'a Doctor, *ST:I*
Birkin, David Tristen: **Picard**, **Rene**; Picard, Jean-Luc (child), "Rascals" (TNG)
Birney, David: **Letant**
Bissell, Whit: **Lurry**, **Mr.**
Black, James: Helmsman, "Shattered Mirror" (DS9)
Blackburn, Bill: Eminiar guard and technician, "Taste of Armageddon" (TOS); Hadley, Lieutenant, "Piece of the Action, A" (TOS); Security guard, "Alternative Factor, The" (TOS) and "Is There in Truth No Beauty?" (TOS); Trooper, "Patterns of Force" (TOS); White Rabbit, "Shore Leave" (TOS).
Blackwell, Richard L.: Stunts, *ST:I*
Blaisdel, Makee: **Singh**, **Mr.**
Blaisdell, Brad: **Yint**
Blaise, Cynthia: **Amanda**
Blake, Geoffrey: **Arjin**
Blalock, Steve: Stunts, *ST2*, *ST3*, *ST:I*
Blanton, Arell: **Dickerson**, **Lieutenant**
Blessing, Jack: **Dulmer**
Bloom, John: Behemoth alien, *ST6*
Bluhm, Brady: **Latika**
Blum, Katherine: Vulcan child, *ST3*
Bochman, George: Crewman, "Corbomite Maneuver, The" (TOS)
Boehmer, J. Paul: **One; Nazi Kapitan**
Boeke, Jim: First Klingon general, *ST6*
Boen, Earl: **Nagilum**
Bofshever, Michael: *Excelsior* engineer, *ST6*; Male Romulan and Alien male, "Timescape" (TNG); **Toran**
Bohn, Bruce: **Ishan**
Bolder, Cal: **Keel**
Bolender, Bill: **Albino**, **the**
Bonne, Shirley: **Ruth**
Bonney, Gail: Second witch, "Catspaw" (TOS)
Bonsall, Brian: **Rozhenko**, **Alexander**
Boone, Walker: **Lynch**, **Leland T.**
Booth, Jimmie: Klingon crew member, *ST:TMP*
Borelli, Emilio: **Frool**
Bornstein, Jeff: Stunt, *ST6*
Boryer, Lucy: **Janeway**, **Ensign**
Bosson, Barbara: **Roana**
Bouchet, Barbara: **Kelinda**
Bova, Jessica and Vanessa: Alexandra, "When The Bough Breaks" (TNG)
Bowe, David: **Basso Tromac**
Bower, Antoinette: **Sylvia**
Box, Joey: Stunts, *ST:I*
Boyer, John: Guard, "Turnabout Intruder" (TOS)
Boyer, Katy: Zero One, "11001001" (TNG)
Boyett, William: **Bell**, **Lieutenant Dan**; Policeman, "Time's Arrow, Part II" (TNG)
Braden, Kim: **Brooks**, **Ensign Janet**; **Picard, Marie**.
Bradshaw, Brooker: **M'Benga**, **Dr.**
Brady, Janet: Stunt, *ST2, ST:FC*
Bralver, Robert: **Grant**; Stunt, *ST:TMP*
Bramhall, Mark: **Nador**, **Gul**
Bramley, William: Policeman, "Bread and Circuses" (TOS)
Brandt, Victor: **Tongo Rad**; Watson, "Elaan of Troyius" (TOS)
Brandt, Walker: **Hajar**, **Cadet Second Class Jean**
Brandy, J. C.: **Batanides**, **Marta**
Brannen, Ralph: Crew member, *ST:TMP*
Braun, Eddie: Stunt, *ST6; ST:I*
Brenner, Eve: **Inad**; **Mirell**, **Jora**
Brewer, Charlie: Stunt, *ST6*
Brian, David: **Gill**, **John**
Brickhouse, Marci: **Luvsitt, Mona**
Brill, Charlie: **Darvin**, **Arne**
Brislane, Mike: *Saratoga* science officer, *ST4*
Brocco, Peter: Claymare, "Errand of Mercy" (TOS)
Brocksmith, Roy: **Kolrami**, **Sirna**; Razka, "Indiscretion" (DS9)
Brogger, Ivar: **Orum**
Brookes, Jacqueline: **Brand**, **Admiral**
Brooks, Alison: **Chilton**, **Ensign Nell**
Brooks, Avery: **Sisko, Benjamin; Russell, Benny**
Brooks, Joel: **Falow**
Brooks, Lee: Aphasia victim, "Babel" (DS9)
Brooks, Stephen: **Garrovick**, **Ensign**
Brophy, Brian: **Maddox**, **Commander Bruce**
Brown, Benjamin: **Kagan, Lieutenant**
Brown, Caitlin: **Kajada**, **Ty**; **Vekor**
Brown, Georgia: **Rozhenko**, **Helena**
Brown, Henry: Numiri captain, "Ex Post Facto" (VGR)
Brown, Jeb: Ensign, "Nor the Battle to the Strong" (DS9)
Brown, Marcia: Alice, "Shore Leave" (TOS)
Brown, Mark Robert: Linden, Don, "And the Children Shall Lead" (TOS)
Brown, Robert: **Lazarus**
Brown, Roger Aaron: Episilon technician, *ST:TMP*
Brown, Ron: Drummer, "11001001" (TNG)
Brown, Wren T.: Transporter pilot, "Manhunt" (TNG)
Browne, Kathie: **Deela**
Brubaker, Tony: Stunts, *ST:I*
Bruck, Karl: King Duncan, "Conscience of the King, The" (TOS)
Bry, Ellen: **Farallon**, **Dr.**
Bryant, Clara: **Chandra**
Bryant, Todd: **Klaa**, **Captain**; Klingon translator, *ST6*
Bryant, Ursaline: **Scott**, **Tryla**

Buckland, Marc: Waiter, "High Ground, The" (TNG)
Budaska, Robert: Burly Klingon, "Apocalypse Rising" (DS9)
Buktenica, Ray: **Deyos**
Bullock, Gary: **Goth**
Bundy, Brooke: **MacDougal**, **Sarah**
Buonomo, John: Orderly, "Requiem for Methuselah" (TOS)
Burdette, Marlys: Krako's gun moll, "Piece of the Action, A" (TOS); Serving girl, "Wolf in the Fold" (TOS)
Burk, Jim: Stunt, *ST2*
Burke, Billy: **Ari**
Burke, Michael Reilly: **Hogue**; **Goval**
Burke, Ron: Native stunt double, "Apple, The" (TOS)
Burns, Bobby: **Frane**
Burns, Elkanah: **Temarek**
Burns, Tim: Russ, "Doomsday Machine, The" (TOS)
Burnside, John: Eminiar guard/technician, "Taste of Armageddon" (TOS)
Burton, David: Stunt, *ST3*, *ST5*
Burton, Hal: Stunts, *ST6*
Burton, Jr., Billy: Stunt Borg, *ST:FC*
Burton, LeVar: **Alan-a-Dale; La Forge, Geordi**
Butler, Dan: **Steth**
Butler, Megan: Lieutenant, "Emissary" (DS9)
Butrick, Merritt: **Marcus**, **Dr. David**; **T'Jon**
Byers, Ralph: Crew member, *ST:TMP*
Byram, Amick: **Hickman**, **Lieutenant Paul**; **Troi**, **Ian Andrew (senior)**
Byram, Cassandra: Conn officer "Emissary" (DS9)
Byrd, Carl: **Shea**, **Lieutenant**

Cadiente, Dave: Klingon sergeant, *ST3*
Cadiente, Jeff: **Loran, Jal**
Cadora, Eric: Customer, "Business as Usual" (DS9)
Calenti, Vince: Security guard, "Alter-native Factor, The" (TOS)
Callan, Cecile: **Ptera**
Callan, K: **Alsia**
Calomee, Gloria: Crew woman, "Corbomite Maneuver, The" (TOS)
Cameron, Laura: Bajoran woman, "Q-Less" (DS9)
Camp, Hamilton: **Vrelk, Controller; Leck**
Campbell, William: **Koloth, Captain**; **Okona**, **Thadiun; Trelane**
Canada, Ron: **Benbeck**, **Martin**; **Ch'Pok**
Canavan, Michael: **Tamal; Curneth**
Canon, Peter: Gestapo lieutenant, "Patterns of Force" (TOS)
Cansino, Richard: **Garin, Dr.**
Cappola, Alicia: **Stadi**, **Lieutenant**
Carhart, Timothy: **Hobson**, **Lieutenant Commander Christopher**
Cariou, Len: **Janeway, Admiral**
Carlin, Amanda: Kobb, "Maquis, The, Part I" (DS9)
Carlin, Tony: **Kohl physician**
Carlson, Katrina: Bajoran officer, "Siege, The" (DS9)
Carlyle, Richard: **Jaeger**, **Lieutenant Karl**
Carmel, Roger C.: **Mudd**, **Harcourt Fenton**
Carmichael, Clint: **Nausicaan**; Hirogen hunter, "Prey" (VGR)
Carpenter, David: **Onara**
Carr, Darleen: **E'Tyshra**
Carr, John: Security guard, "Shore Leave" (TOS)
Carr, Kevin: Bajoran, "Life Support" (DS9)
Carr, Paul: **Kelso, Lieutenant Lee**
Carrasco, Carlos: **Bahrat**; **D'Ghor**; **Krole**; Klingon officer, "Shattered Mirror" (DS9)
Carroll, Christopher: **Benil**, **Gul**; **Alben, Captain**
Carson, Darwyn: Romulan, "Improbable Cause" (DS9)
Carson, Fred: First Denevan, "Operation: Annihilate!" (TOS)
Carter, Diane: Stunt, *ST2*
Carter, Mitch David: Swat leader, "Past Tense, Part II" (DS9)
Caruso, Anthony: **Oxmyx**, **Bela**
Carver, Stephen James: Helmsman, "Redemption II" (TNG); **Ibudan**; Tayar, "Descent" (TNG)
Cascone, Nicholas: **Davies**, **Ensign**; **Timor**
Casey, Bernie: **Hudson**, **Calvin**
Cassel, Seymour: **Dealt, Lieutenant Commander Hester**
Cassidy, Martin: Male villager, "Shadowplay" (DS9)
Cassidy, Ted: **Balok** (voice of puppet); **Ruk**
Cassidy, Zane: Stunts, *ST:I*
Catching, Bill: Lazarus' stunt double, "Alternative Factor, The" (TOS); Lincoln's stunt double, "Savage Curtain, The" (TOS); Spock's stunt double, "This Side of Paradise" (TOS); Surak's stunt double, "Savage Curtain, The" (TOS)
Cathey, Reg E.: **Morag**
Catron, Jerry: Montgomery, Security Guard, "Doomsday Machine, The" (TOS); Second Denevan, "Operation: Annihilate!" (TOS)
Cattrall, Kim: **Valeris**, **Lt.**
Cavanaugh, Michael: **DeSoto**, **Captain Robert**
Cavens, Al: Second fop, "All Our Yesterdays" (TOS)
Cavett, Jon: Guard, "Devil in the Dark, The" (TOS)
Cecere, Tony: Stunt, *ST2*
Cecile, Sylvain: **Uri'lash**
Cedar, Larry: **Nydom**, **Dr.**; **Tersa, Jal**
Cervera, Jr, Jorge: Bandito, "Fistful of Datas, A" (TNG)
Cestero, Carlos: Munitions man, *ST6*
Chadwick, Robert: Romulan scanner operator, "Balance of Terror" (TOS)
Chalfy, Dylan: Head officer, "Homefront" (DS9)
Chambers, Marie: **Kryian Arbiter**
Champion, Michael: **Boratus**
Chandler, Brian Evaret: **Brota**
Chandler, Estee: **Mirren**, **Oliana**
Chandler, Jefrey Alan: Guardian, "Facets" (DS9); **Garan**, **Hatil**
Chandler, John: **Flith**
Chao, Rosalind: **O'Brien, Keiko**
Chapman, Lanei: **Rager**, **Ensign**
Chartrand, Lauro: Stunts, *ST:I*
Chatterton, Ann: Stunts, *ST2*
Chauvin, Lilyan: **Yassim, Vedek**
Chaves, Richard: Chief, "Tattoo" (VGR)
Ching-Davis, Dorothy: Stunt, *ST6*
Chong, Phil: Stunt, *ST3*
Christian, David: **Martin, Ensign**
Christie: Hood, "Piece of the Action, A" (TOS)
Christopher, Dennis: **Borath**
Christopher, Robin: **Neela**
Christy, Susan: **Tarrana**
Chun, Charles S.: Engineer, "Trials and Tribble-ations" (DS9)
Church, Clive: **Picard**, **Maurice**
Cignoni, Diana: Dabo girl, "Emissary" (DS9) and "Man Alone, A" (DS9)
Cirigliano, John: **Ranora, Dr.**
Clapp, Gordon: Hadron, "Vortex" (DS9)
Clark, Bobby: Chekov's boy #2, "Mirror, Mirror" (TOS); Native stunt double, "Apple, The" (TOS); Stunt double, "Return of the Archons" (TOS)
Clark, Josh: **Carey, Lieutenant**; Conn, "Justice" (TNG)
Clarke, Christopher: **Byron, Lord**
Clements, Edward: Young crewman, *ST6*
Clendenin, Bob: Vidiian surgeon, "Deadlock" (VGR)
Clennon, David: **Moset, Dr. Crell**
Clow, Chuck: Kirk's stunt double, "Court Martial" (TOS) & "Friday's Child" (TOS)
Cobb, Julie: **Thompson**, **Yeoman Leslie**
Coburn, David: **Brower**, **Ensign**
Cochran, Shannon: **Kalita; Sirella**
Cockrum, Dennis: Alien captain, "Face of the Enemy" (TNG)
Coe, George: **Durken**, **Chancellor Avel**
Coffey, Gordon: Romulan soldier, "*Enterprise* Incident, The" (TOS)
Cogan, Rhodie: First witch, "Catspaw" (TOS)
Cole, Megan: **Noor; Cretak, Senator**
Coleman, Eliza: Stunts, *ST:I*
Colicos, John: **Kor**
Collins, Christopher: Head guard, "Blood Oath" (DS9); **Kargan**, **Captain**; **Pakled captain**; **Durg**
Collins, Joan: **Keeler**, **Edith**
Collins, Matthew: Picard's child, *STG*
Collins, Mimi: Picard's child, *STG*
Collins, Paul: **Zlangco**
Collins, Rickey D'Shon: **Eric**
Collins, Sheldon: Tough kid, "Piece of the Action, A" (TOS)
Collins, Stephen: **Decker**, **Willard**
Collison, Frank: **Dolak**, **Gul**
Colman, Booth: **Penno**
Colson, Mark: Dream alien, "Waking Moments" (VGR)
Combs, David Q.: 1st mediator, "Justice" (TNG)
Combs, Gary: Stunt, *ST2*
Combs, Gilbert: Stunt, *ST2*
Combs, Jeffrey: **Brunt**; **Tiron**; **Weyoun**; **Mulkahey, Officer Kevin**
Comi, Paul: **Stiles**, **Lieutenant**
Compton, Richard: Romulan technical officer, "*Enterprise* Incident, The" (TOS); **Washburn**
Conley, Sharon: **Jomat Luson**
Connolly, John P.: **Lote, Orn**
Connors, Jim: Stunt, *ST2*
Conrad, Bart: **Kransnowsky**
Conrad, Christian R.: **Dunbar**
Conrad, Christian: **Brilgar**
Conte: Hood, "Piece of the Action, A" (TOS)

Conway, Kevin: **Kahless the Unforgettable**
Cook, Jr., Elisha: **Cogley**, **Samuel T.**
Cook, Scott Allan: Stunts, *ST:I*
Coombs, Gary: Clark, Bobby, "Arena" (TOS); Kirk's stunt double, "Squire of Gothos, The" (TOS) & "Alternative Factor, The" (TOS) & "Space Seed" (TOS), & "Operation: Annihilate!" (TOS); Klingon guard, "Errand of Mercy" (TOS); Latimer stunt double, "Galileo Seven, The" (TOS)
Cooper, Charles: **K'mpec**; **Korrd, General**
Cooper, Darin: Cardassian officer, "Sacrifice of Angels" (DS9)
Copage, John: Elliot, "Doomsday Machine, The" (TOS)
Coppola, Alicia: **Stadi, Lieutenant**
Corbett, Glenn: **Cochrane**, **Zefram**
Corbett, Michael: **Rabal**, **Dr.**
Cord, Erik: Thug, "Big Goodbye, The" (TNG)
Corey, Jeff: **Plasus**
Correll, Terry: Crew member, "Twisted" (VGR); Crew member, "Elogium" (VGR)
Corsentino, Frank: **Bok**, **DaiMon**; **Tog**, **DaiMon**
Costanza, Robert: **Bender**, **Slade**
Costello, Ward: **Quinn**, **Admiral Gregory**
Coster, Nicholas: **Haftel**, **Admiral**
Cotran, John: **Telok**; **Nu'Daq**
Cotton, Brant: **Tauvid Rem**
Cottrell, Mickey: **Alrik**, **Chancellor; Dumah**
Couch, Chuck: Khan's stunt double, "Space Seed" (TOS)
Couch, Jr., Bill: Stunt, *ST2*
Couch, Sr., Bill: Stunt, *ST2*
Couch, William: Stunt, *ST:TMP*
Courtney, Chuck: Davod, "Patterns of Force" (TOS)
Cousins, Brian: **Crosis**; **Parem**
Cowgill, David: Guard, *ST:FC;* Hanonian, "Basics, Part II" (VGR)
Cox, Mondy: Stunts, *ST:I*
Cox, Nikki: **Sarjenka**
Cox, Richard: **Finn**, **Kyril**
Cox, Ronny: **Jellico**, **Captain Edward**
Cozzens, Mimi: Soup woman, "Unification, Part I" (TNG)
Craig, Yvonne: **Marta**
Crawford, John: **Ferris**, **Galactic High Commissioner**
Creaghan, Dennis: **Louis**
Crist, Paula: Crew member, *ST:TMP*
Crivello, Anthony: **Adin**
Crockett, Dick: Andorian thrall, "Gamesters of Triskelion, The" (TOS); Kirk's stunt double, "Where No Man Has Gone Before" (TOS); Klingon stunt double, "Trouble with Tribbles, The" (TOS)
Crombie, Peter: **Fallit Kot**
Cromwell, James: **Cochrane**, **Zefram**; **Hanok**; **Nayrok**; **Shrek**, **Jaglom**
Cronin, Patrick: **Erko**
Crooke, Leland: Vorta, "Honor Among Thieves" (DS9); **Gelnon**
Crosby, Denise: **Sela**; **Yar**, **Natasha**
Crosby, Mary: **Lang, Natima**
Croughwell, Charlie: Stunts, *ST:I*
Croughwell, Joshua: Stunts, *ST:I*
Crow, Emilia: **Zyree**
Crowfoot, Leonard J.: **Lal; Trent**
Crowley, David L.: Workman, "Phantasms" (TNG)
Culea, Melinda: **Soren**
Cullen, Brett: **Deral**
Cullum, J. D.: **Toral**
Cullum, Kimberly: **Gia**
Culotta, Phil: Stunts, *ST:I*
Culp, Joseph: **Raimus**
Cummings, Bob: Gunner #1, *ST3*
Cumpsty, Michael: **Burleigh**, **Lord**
Cupo, Patrick: Bajoran man, "Man Alone, A" (DS9)
Curry, Dan: **Dekon Elig**
Curtis, Billy: Little copper ambassador, "Journey to Babel" (TOS)
Curtis, Charlie: **Talura**
Curtis, Keene: Old man #2, "Sacred Ground" (VGR)
Curtis, Kelly: **Sarda**, **Miss**
Curtis, Robin: **Saavik, Lt.**; **Tallera**
Curtis, Tom: **Corrigan**
Curtis-Brown, Robert: **Hazar**, **General**

D'Abo, Olivia: **Rogers**, **Amanda**
D'Arcy, Tracey: Young woman, "Cost of Living" (TNG)
Da Vinci, Bud: Crewman, "Naked Time, The" (TOS) & "Lights of Zetar, The" (TOS)
da Vinci, Frank: Brent, Lieutenant, "Naked Time, The" (TOS); Guard, "Mudd's Women" (TOS); Osborne, Lieutenant, "Taste of Armageddon" (TOS); Security guard, "Charlie X" (TOS)
Dalton, Lezlie: **Drea**
Daly, James: **Flint**
Daly, Jane: **Varria**
Damas, Bertila: **Sakonna**
Damian, Leo: **Warrior/Adonis**
Damon, Gabriel: **Aster**, **Jeremy**
Danek, Michael: Singer, "Firstborn" (TNG)
Danese, Connie: Toya, "When The Bough Breaks" (TNG)
Dang, Timothy: Main bridge security, "Encounter at Farpoint" (TNG)
Daniel, Chic: Stunt, *ST:FC*
Daniels, Jerry: **Marple**
Dante, Michael: **Maab**
Danziger, Cory: **Potts**, **Jake**
Darby, Kim: **Miri**
Darga, Christopher: **Kaybok**
Daris, James: Creature, "Spock's Brain" (TOS)
Darren, James: **Fontaine, Vic**
Darrow, Henry: **Savar**, **Admiral**; **Kolopak**
Datcher, Alex: **Taitt**, **Ensign**
David, Troy: Maston, Larry, "Conscience of the King, The" (TOS)
Davidson, Brett: Stunt, *ST6*
Davidson, Steve M.: Stunt, *ST4*
Davies, Stephen: **Arak'Taral**; **Nakahn**; Tactical officer, "Emissary" (DS9)
Davis, Bud: Stunt coordinator, *STG*
Davis, Carole: **Pentangeli, Giuseppina**
Davis, Daniel: **Moriarty**, **Professor James**
Davis, Joe W.: **Spock**, age 25
Davis, John Walter: **Takarian merchant**
Davis, Teddy: Transporter tech, "Sins Of The Father" (TNG)
Davis, Walter: Klingon soldier, "Errand of Mercy" (TOS); Romulan crewman, "Balance of Terror" (TOS); Therapist, "Dagger of the Mind" (TOS)
Davis-Reed, Timothy: Kryan spectator, "Living Witness" (VGR)
Davison, Bruce: **Jareth**
Dawson, Roxann: **Torres, B'Elanna**
Dayton, Charles: Crew member, "Where No One Has Gone Before" (TNG)
De Lugo, Winston: Timothy, "Court Martial" (TOS)
De Young, Cliff: **Croden**
de la Pena, George: **Solis**, **Lieutenant (J.G.) Orfil**
de Lancie, John: **Lord High Sheriff of Nottingham**; **Q**
de Sousa, Noel: **Gandhi, Mahatma**
de Vries, Jon: **Granger**, **Wilson**
Deadrick, Vince: Decker's stunt double, "Doomsday Machine, The" (TOS); Finnegan's stunt double, "Shore Leave" (TOS); **Matthews**; McCoy's stunt double, "Mirror, Mirror" (TOS); Native stunt double, "Apple, The" (TOS); Norman's stunt double, "I, Mudd" (TOS); Romulan crewman, "Balance of Terror" (TOS); Security guard, "Is There in Truth No Beauty?" (TOS)
Deakins, Mark: **Hirogen SS Officer; Tournel**
DeAlessandro, Mark: Stunts, *ST:I*
Dean, Robertson: Pilot, "Face of the Enemy" (TNG)
deBoer, Nicole: **Dax, Ezri**
Deer, Richard: Fitzgerald, Admiral, "Mark of Gideon, The" (TOS)
DeHorter, Zora: Risian woman, "Let He Who Is Without Sin" (DS9)
Dekker, Thomas: Picard's child, *STG*; **Burleigh**, **Henry**
Del Arco, Jonathan: **Hugh**; **Third of Five**
Delano, Lee: **Kalo**
Delgado, Christine: **Ashmore, Ensign; Nicoletti, Susan**
DeLongis, Anthony: **Culluh**, **Jal**
Demetral, Chris: **Barash**
DeMita, John: Romulan, "Timescape" (TNG)
Demmings, Pancho: Kradin Soldier, "Nemesis" (VGR)
Dempsey, Mark: Air force captain, "Tomorrow Is Yesterday" (TOS)
Demyan, Lincoln: Lipton, Sergeant, "Assignment: Earth" (TOS)
Denberg, Susan: **Magda**
Dengel, Jake: Mordoc, "Last Outpost, The" (TNG)
Denis, William: **Mendrossen**, **Ki**
Dennehy, Elizabeth: **Shelby**, **Lieutenant Commander**
Dennis, Charles: **Sunad**
Dennis, Peter: **Newton**, **Isaac**
Dennis, Steve: **night being**
Denver, Maryesther: Third witch, "Catspaw" (TOS)
DeRelian, Steve: Stunt Borg, *ST:FC*
Derment, Carol Daniels: **Zora**
Derr, Richard: **Barstow**, **Commodore**
Desai, Shelly: **V'Sal**
DeSoto, Rosana: **Azetbur**
DeVenney, Scott: **Briggs**, **Bob**
DeZarn, Tim: **Haliz**; **Satler; Halb Daier**

Dial, Dick: **Kaplan**, **Lieutenant**; Kirk's stunt double, "Arena" (TOS); Sam, "Devil in the Dark, The" (TOS); Stunt double, "Immunity Syndrome, The" (TOS); Technician #2, "And the Children Shall Lead" (TOS); Warrior's stunt double, "Friday's Child" (TOS)
Diaunté: Jem'Hadar guard, "Search, The, Part II" (DS9)
Dick, Andy: **EMH-2**
Dierkop, Charles: **Morla**
Dillard, Victoria: Ballerina, "Where No One Has Gone Before" (TNG)
Dimitin, Nick: **Nausicaan**
Diol, Susan: **Davila, Carmen**; **Pel, Denara**
Dobkin, Larry: **Kell**
Doest, Marie: Stunt, *ST6*
Dohrmann, Angela: **Ricky**
Donahue, Elinor: **Hedford, Commissioner Nancy**
Donald, Juli: **Tayna**
Donald, Juliana: **Emi**
Donaldson, Mark: Stunts, *ST:I*
Donner, Jack: **Tal**
Donno, Eddy: Stunt, *ST2*, *ST3*, *ST:FC*
Donno, Tony: Stunt, *ST:FC*
Doohan, James: Commodore Enwright's voice, "Ultimate Computer, The" (TOS); Father's voice, "Squire of Gothos, The" (TOS); M-5 computer voice, "Ultimate Computer, The" (TOS); Melkotian buoy's voice, "Spectre of the Gun" (TOS); **Sargon**, voice of; **Scott, Montgomery**; Voice of the **Oracle**
Dooley, Paul: **Tain, Enabran**
DoQui, Robert: **Noggra**
Dorman, John: **Holem Lenaris**
Dorn, Michael: **Worf; Duchamps; Worf, Colonel; Hawkins, Willie**
Douglas, Phyllis: Girl #2, "Way to Eden, The" (TOS); **Mears, Yeoman**
Douglass, Charles: Haskell, "Where Silence Has Lease" (TNG)
Dourif, Brad: **Suder, Lon**
Dow, Ellen Albertini: **Howard, Felisa**
Downey, Deborah: Girl #1, "Way to Eden, The" (TOS)
Downey, Gary: Tellarite, "Whom Gods Destroy" (TOS)
Downing, J.: **Kelso, Chief**
Doyle, Chris: Jem'Hadar officer, "Search, The, Part II" (DS9); Cardassian, "Empok Nor" (DS9); stunts, *ST:I*
Drake, Charles: **Stocker, Commodore**
Drake, Laura: **Vekma**
Dromm, Andrea: **Smith, Yeoman**
DuBois, Marta: **Ardra**
Ducheau, Christin: Crewman, "Naked Time, The" (TOS)
Duffin, Shay: **Quint, Ned**
Dugan, Mike: Rigel VII warrior, "Cage, The" (TOS)
Duncan, Lee: Evans, "Elaan of Troyius" (TOS)
Dunham, Brett: Security chief, "Menagerie, The (Parts I & II)" (TOS)
Dunn, Michael: **Alexander**
Dunst, Kirsten: **Hedril**
Durand, Judi: Computer voice, DS9; Spacedock controller voice, *ST3*
Durbin, John: **Lemec, Gul**; **Ssestar; Traidy**
Durock, Dick: Elasian guard #1, "Elaan of Troyius" (TOS)
Durrell, Michael: **Sorad, Vedek**
Duryea, Peter: **Tyler, José**
Dusay, Marj: **Kara**
Dweck, Jon and Scott: Boys who stole phasers, "Miri" (TOS)
Dynarski, Gene: **Childress, Ben**; Krodak, "Mark of Gideon, The" (TOS); **Quinteros, Commander Orfil**

Easton, Robert: Klingon judge, *ST6*
Echevarria, Alan: Patient, "Quickening, The" (DS9); **Tamar**
Eckstein, Paul S.: Young Hirogen, "Killing Game, The, Part I" (VGR); **Limara'Son**
Ede, George: Poet, "Cost of Living" (TNG)
Edmiston, Walker: Space Central voice, "Amok Time" (TOS)
Edwards, Jennifer: **Kyle, Ms.**
Edwards, Kenneth Lane: Ensign, *ST:I*
Edwards, Paddi: **Anya**
Edwards, Ronnie Claire: **Talar**
Edwards, Tony: Pilot, *ST4*
Egan, Patrick: **Watley**
Eggar, Samantha: **Picard, Marie**
Eginton, Madison: Picard's child, *STG*
Eiding, Paul: **Loquel**
Einspahr, Steven: Teacher, "Hero Worship" (TNG)
Eisenberg, Aron: **Nog; Kar**; Vendor, "Far Beyond the Stars" (DS9)
Eisenmann, Ike: **Preston, Peter**
Eitner, Don: Kirk's stunt double, "Enemy Within, The" (TOS); Navigator, "Charlie X" (TOS)
El Fadil, Siddig (aka Siddig, Alexander): **Bashir, Dr. Julian; Eaton, Julius**
El Guindi: **Bashir, Amsha**
El Razzac, Abdul Salaam: Bass player, "11001001" (TNG)
Elam, Kiante: Stunts, *ST:I*
Elder, Judyann: **Ballard, Lieutenant**
Elias, Lou: 1st Technician, "And the Children Shall Lead" (TOS); Troglyte, "Cloud Minders, The" (TOS)
Ellenstein, David: Doctor #1, *ST4*
Ellenstein, Robert: **Federation Council President**; **Miller, Steven**
Elliott, Biff: **Schmitter**
Elliott, Kay: **Mudd, Stella**
Ellis, David Richard: Stunt, *ST5*
Emmett, Charles: **Resh**
Enberg, Alexander: **Taurik, Ensign**; **Vorik**; Young reporter, "Time's Arrow, Part II" (TNG)
Endoso, Kenny: Stunt, *ST3, ST:FC*
Engalla, Couglas: Prisoner at Rura Penthe, *ST6*
Engelberg, Leslie: **Yareth**
Ensign, Michael: **Krola**; **Lojal; Takarian bard**
Epper, Andy: Stunt Borg, *ST:FC*
Epper, Gary: Stunt Borg, *ST:FC*
Epper, Tony: Drunken Klingon, "Apocalypse Rising" (DS9)
Epper-Woldman, Eurlyhne: Stunts, *ST:I*
Eppers, Gary: Surak's stunt double, "Savage Curtain, The" (TOS)
Epperson, Van: Bajoran clerk, "Q-Less" (DS9)
Erb, Stephanie: **Liva**
Erickson, Mark: **Piersall, Lieutenant**
Erskine, David: Bandi shopkeeper "Encounter at Farpoint" (TNG)
Erwin, Bill: **Quaice**, **Dr. Dalen**
Erwin, Libby: Technician, "Lights of Zetar The" (TOS)
Eskobar, John: Stunt, *ST2*
Esten, Charles: **Dathan**; **Divok**
Eubanks, Corey: Stunts, *ST:I*
Eugene, Michael: Fairman vendor, "In the Hands of the Prophets" (DS9)
Evans, Richard: **Isak**
Evans, Steven John: Guard, "Maquis, The, Part I" (DS9)
Evans, Terrence: **Baltrim**; **Proka Migdal; Treen**
Evers, Jason: **Rael**
Ewing, Diana: **Droxine**

Fabian, Patrick: **Taymon**
Faga, Gary: Airlock technician, *ST:TMP*; Prison guard #1, *ST3*
Faison, Matthew: **Surmak, Ren**
Fallender, Susan: Romulan #2, "Unification II" (TNG)
Fancy, Richard: Alien, "Tattoo" (VGR); **Satelk, Captain**
Farago, Joe: Stunt, *ST6*
Farley, James: **Lang, Lieutenant**
Farley, Keythe: Vidiian #2, "Deadlock" (VGR)
Farley, Morgan: **Hacom**; Old Yang scholar, "Omega Glory, The" (TOS)
Farr, Kimberly: **Langor**
Farrel, Brioni: **Tula**
Farrell, Geraldine: **Galis Blin**
Farrell, Terry: **Dax, Jadzia; Bare, Professor Honey; Kursky, Darlene**
Farwell, Jonathan: **Keel, Walker**
Fass, Bob: Scotty's stunt double, "Catspaw" (TOS)
Feder, Todd: Federation male, "Babel" (DS9)
Fega, Russ: **Paxim**
Fein, Doren: **Molly**
Ferdin, Pamelyn: **Janowski, Mary**
Ferguson, Jessie Lawerence: **Lutan**
Ferguson, Lynnda: Doran, "Emissary" (DS9)
Ferrer, Miguel: First officer of the *Excelsior*, *ST3*
Ferro, Carlos: **Dern, Ensign**
Fetters, Linda: Stunt, *ST5*
Fiedler, John: **Hengist, Commissioner**
Fields, Jimmy: Cloud Guard #2, "Cloud Minders, The" (TOS)
Fill, Shannon: **Sito Jaxa**
Fiordellisi, Angelina: Kaminer, "Schisms" (TNG)
Fischer, Don: Borg, *ST:FC;* Jem'Hadar guard, "By Inferno's Light" (DS9)
Fiske, Michael: **Garan miner**
Fitts, Rick: **Martin, Dr.; Zahl official**
Fitzpatrick, Brian: **Tedran**
Fix, Paul: **Piper, Dr. Mark**
Flanagan, Fionnula: **Tainer, Dr. Juliana**; **Tandro, Enina**
Flanagan, Kellie: Blonde girl, "Miri" (TOS)
Fleck, John: **Ornithar**; **Taibak**
Fleetwood, Mick: Antedean dignitary, "Manhunt" (TNG)
Fleming, Clifford T.: Stunt, *ST4*
Fletcher, Christian: Stunt, *ST:FC*
Fletcher, Louise: **Winn**
Flores, Erika: **Flores, Marissa**

Flynn, J. Michael: **Zaynar**
Forbes, Michelle: **Dara**; **Ro Laren**
Force, Frank: Elevator voice, *ST3*
Forchion, Raymond: **Prieto**, **Lieutenant Ben**
Forest, Michael: **Apollo**
Forester, Nichole: Dabo girl, "Distant Voices" (DS9)
Forrest, Brad: Wyatt, Ensign, "That Which Survives" (TOS)
Forsyth, Rosemary: **Alzen**
Fortier, Robert: **Tomar**
Foster, Carey: Crew stuntman, "Alternative Factor, The" (TOS)
Foster, Meg: **Onaya**
Foster, Stacie: **Bartel**, **Engineer**
Fox, Marilyn: **Marna**
Foxworth, Jerry: Security guard, "Mudd's Women" (TOS)
Foxworth, Robert: **Leyton, Admiral**
Frakes, Jonathan: **Jakara, Rivas; Riker, Thomas**; **Riker**, **William T.**
Francis, John H.: Science crew member, "Sarek" (TNG)
Frank, Gary: **Dax, Yedrin**
Frankfather, William: Male shape-shifter, "Search, The, Part II" (DS9)
Frankham, David: **Marvick**, **Laurence**
Franklin, Shiela: **Felton**, **Ensign**
Franklyn-Robbins, John: **Macias**
Fredericks, Joel: Engineer, "Timescape" (TNG)
Fredericksen, Cully: Alien #1, **Dereth;** "Phage" (VGR); Vulcan, *ST:FC*
Free, Sandy: Stunt, *ST6*
French, Bruce: **Genestra**, **Sabin**; Ocampa doctor, "Caretaker" (VGR); Son'a Officer, *ST:I*
French, Susan: **Maylor**, **Sev**
Frewer, Matt: **Rasmussen**, **Berlinghoff**
Friedman, Mal: **Hendorff**, **Ensign**
Froman, David: **K'nera**
Fuqua, Joseph: **Gordon, Ensign Paul**

Gabriel, John: Crewman, "Corbomite Maneuver, The" (TOS)
Gage, Ben: **Akaar**, **Teer**
Gallagher, David Drew: **Shepard, Riley Aldrin**
Gallagher, Megan: **Garland**; **Mareel**
Galligan, Zach: **Gentry, David**
Gammell, Robin: **Mauric**, **Ambassador**
Gans, Ron: Armus, voice of, "Skin of Evil" (TNG)
Ganthier, Dan: **Lavelle**, **Sam**
Garbutt, Frankie: Stunt, *ST:FC*
Garcia, Leo: Bellboy, "Royale, The" (TNG)
Garion, Buddy: Hood, "Piece of the Action, A" (TOS)
Garner, Shay: Scientist, "Matter of Time, A" (TNG)
Garon, Richard: **Bennet**, **Ensign**
Garr, Roderick: **Regana Tosh**
Garr, Teri: **Lincoln**, **Roberta**
Garrett, Donna: Vanna's stunt double, "Cloud Minders, The" (TOS)
Garrett, John: Lieutenant, "Loud as a Whisper" (TNG)
Garrett, Joy: **Meyers**, **Annie**
Garrett, Kathleen: Vulcan officer, "Vortex" (DS9)
Garrett, Ralph: Marvick's stunt double, "Is There in Truth No Beauty?" (TOS); Troglyte stunt double, "Cloud Minders, The" (TOS)
Garrett, Spencer: **Tarses**, **Crewman Simon**
Gates, Barbara: Astrochemist, "Changeling, The" (TOS)
Gatti, Jennifer: **Ba'el**; **Libby**
Gautreaux, David: **Branch**, **Commander**
Geary, Richard: Andorian, "Whom Gods Destroy" (TOS); Cloud City sentinel #1, "Cloud Minders, The" (TOS); Salish's stunt double, "Paradise Syndrome, The" (TOS); Scalosian, "Wink of an Eye" (TOS)
Gedeon, Conroy: Civilian agent, *ST3*
Geer, Ellen: **Marr**, **Dr. Kila**
Geeson, Judy: **Sandrine**
Gegenhuber, John: **Surat**, **Jal; Tierna.**
Gehring, Ted: Second policeman, "Assignment: Earth" (TOS)
Gellegos, Joshua: Security officer, *ST:TMP*
Genovese, Mike: Desk sergeant, "Big Goodbye, The" (TNG); **Zef'No**
Gentile, Robert: Romulan technician, "*Enterprise* Incident, The" (TOS)
George, Brian: **Bashir, Richard**
George, Victoria: **Haines**, **Ensign**
German, Gretchen: **Sullivan, Rebecca**
Gerrit, Graham: **Quinn**; Hunter, "Captive Pursuit" (DS9)
Gerrold, David: *Enterprise* crew member, *ST:TMP*; Security guard, "Trials and Tribble-ations" (DS9)
Gevedon, Stephen: Klingon #1, "Crossover" (DS9)
Giambalvo, Louis: **Cosimo**
Gianasi, Rick: Gigolo, "Lifesigns" (VGR)
Gibbs, Alan: Stunt double, "Is There in Truth No Beauty?" (TOS)
Gibney, Susan: **Benteen, Erika**; **Brahms**, **Dr. Leah**
Gibson, Henry: **Nilva**
Gierasch, Stefan: **Moseley**, **Hal**
Gilbert, Richard: Hill, Bosus, "Descent" (TNG)
Gill, Andy: Stunt, *ST:FC*
Gillespie, Ann H.: **Hildebrandt**
Gillespie, Anne H.: Bajoran nurse, "Distant Voices" (DS9); **Jabara**; Nurse, "Life Support" (DS9)
Gilman, C.: Knight in armor, "Emergence" (TNG)
Gilman, Sam: **Holliday**, **Doc**
Gimpel, Sharon: M-113 creature, "Man Trap, The" (TOS)
Ginsberg, Maury: **Ginsberg, Maury**
Glass, Seamon: **Benton**
Gleason, James: **Apollinaire**, **Dr.**
Glover, Edna: **Vulcan Master**
Glover, John: **Verad**
Golas, Thaddeus: Controller #1, *ST4*
Goldberg, Whoopi: **Guinan**
Goldman, Marcy: El-Aurian survivor, *STG*
Goldring, Danny: **Burke; Kell**, **Legate; Alpha-Hirogen**
Goldstein, Jenette: Science officer, *STG*
Gomez, Mike: **Lurin**, **DaiMon**; Tarr, DaiMon, "Last Outpost, The" (TNG)
Gonzales, Armando: Spock's Flamenco dance double, "Plato's Stepchildren" (TOS)
Goodwin, Jim: **Farrell**, **Lieutenant John**
Goodwin, Laurel: **Colt**, **Yeoman J.M.**
Gordon, Barry: **Nava**
Görg, Galyn: **Sisko, Korena**; **Nori**
Gorman, Breon: **Curtis, Lieutenant**
Gorshin, Frank: **Bele**
Goslins, Martin: **Satok**, **Security Minister**
Gotell, Walter: **Mandl**, **Kurt**
Gouw, Cynthia: **Dar**, **Caithlin**
Gowans, John D.: Assistant to Rand, *ST:TMP*
Graas, John Christian: **Gordon**, **Jay**
Grace, April: **Hubbell**, **Chief**; Transporter chief, "Emissary" (DS9)
Grace, Wayne: **Torak**, **Governor**; Legate, "Wrongs Darker than Death or Night" (DS9)
Graf, Allan: Stunt, *ST2*
Graf, David: **Noonan, Fred; Leskit**
Graf, Kathryn: Bajoran man, "Man Alone, A" (DS9)
Graham, Gary: **Tanis**
Grammer, Kelsey: **Bateson**, **Captain Morgan**
Grando, Sandra: 2nd officer, "Jem'Hadar, The" (DS9)
Graves, David Michael: 2nd Edo boy, "Justice" (TNG)
Gray, Bruce: **Chekote**, **Admiral**
Greay, Dick: Security guard, "Is There in Truth No Beauty?" (TOS)
Green, Gilbert: S.S. Major, "Patterns of Force" (TOS)
Green, Mel: Secretary, "Family Business" (DS9)
Greene, James: **Barron**, **Dr.; Koral**
Greenquist, Brad: **Demmas; Krit**
Gregory, James: **Adams**, **Dr. Tristam**
Gregory, Steven: **Kurland**, **Jake**
Grey, Joel: **Caylem**
Grodénchik, Max: Ferengi pit boss, "Emissary" (DS9); **Par Lenor**; **Rom**; **Sovak**
Groener, Harry: **Elbrun**, **Tam**; **Nechani magistrate**,
Groves, Robin: Hatil's wife, "Emanations" (VGR)
Grudt, Mona: **Graham**, **Ensign**
Gruz, K.: **Bendera, Kurt**
Gruzal, Jim: Don Juan, "Shore Leave" (TOS)
Guercio, Gary: Stunt, *ST:FC*
Guerra, Castulo: **Mendoza**, **Dr.**
Guerrero, Evelyn: Young female ensign, "Encounter at Farpoint" (TNG)
Guest, Nicholas: Cadet, *ST2*
Guidera, Anthony: Cardassian, "Circle, The" (DS9)
Guillory, Bennett: Medical big shot, "Prophet Motive" (DS9)
Guinan, Francis: **Kray**, **Minister**
Gundy, Jennifer: Ensign, "Waking Moments" (VGR)
Gunning, Charles: Miner #3, "Perfect Mate, The" (TNG)
Gunton, Bob: **Maxwell**, **Captain Benjamin**
Guttman, Ronald: **Labin, Gathorel**

Hack, Olivia: Picard's kid, *STG*
Hackett, Martha: **Seska**; **T'Rul**, **Subcommander**
Hagen, Molly: **Eris**
Hagerty, Michael G.: **Larg**; **Skoran**
Haggerty, Dylan: **Epran**
Haig, Sid: First lawgiver, "Return of the Archons" (TOS)

Hale, Richard: **Goro**
Hall, Albert: **Galek Sar**
Hall, Anthony: **Bailey, Lieutenant David**
Hall, Kevin Peter: **Leyor**
Hall, Lois: **Warren, Dr. Mary**
Hall, Randy: Stunt, *STG*
Hallier, Lori: **Frazier, Riley**
Halligan, Tim: **Farrakk**
Halsted, Christopher: 1st Learner, "Cost of Living" (TNG)
Halty, James M.: Stunt, *ST5*
Halty, Jim: Stunt, *ST:FC*
Halty, Jon: Stunt, *ST3*
Hamilton, Kim: **Songi, Chairman**
Hamm, Scott: **Parton**
Hancock, John: **Haden, Admiral**
Haney, Anne: Bajoran judge, "Dax" (DS9); **Renora; Uxbridge, Rishon**
Hankin, Larry A.: **Gaunt Gary**
Hanson, Tabby: Stunts, *ST:I*
Harder, Richard: Joe, *ST4*
Hardin, Jerry: **Clemens, Samuel Langhorne; Neria, Dr.; Radue**
Harewood, Nancy: **Nara, Lieutenant**
Harmon, John: Rodent, "City on the Edge of Forever, The" (TOS); **Tepo**
Harney, Michael: **Chadwick**
Harper, Dianne: Radio voice, *ST2*
Harper, James: **Vantika, Rao**
Harper, Robert: **Lathal Bine**
Harper, Tom: Stunt Borg, *ST:FC*
Harris, Estelle: Old woman, "Sacred Ground" (VGR)
Harris, Glenn: **Jeffrey**
Harris, Joshua: **Timothy**
Harris, Michael: **Byleth**
Harris, Rachel: **Martis**
Harrison, Gracie: **Raymond,Clare**
Hart, Beverly: High priestess, *ST5*
Hartley, Mariette: **Zarabeth**
Hartman, Ena: Crew woman, "Corbomite Maneuver, The" (TOS)
Hatae, Hana: **O'Brien, Molly**
Hatcher, Teri: **Robinson, B. G.**
Hatem, Rosine Ace: Stunt, *ST:FC*
Haun, Lindsey: **Burleigh, Beatrice; Belle**
Haven, Scott: Guard, *ST:FC*; Kazon, "Basics, Part II" (VGR) ; **Virak'kara**
Hawkes, Andrew: **Amat'igan**
Hawking, Professor Stephen: **Hawking, Dr. Stephen William**
Hayashi, Henry: Male guest, "Past Tense, Part I" (DS9)
Hayden, John Patrick: Cardassian overseer, "Through The Looking Glass" (DS9)
Hayenga, Jeffery: **Orta**
Hayes, Hillary: Ruby, *ST:FC*
Haymer, Johnny: Constable, "All Our Yesterdays" (TOS)
Haynes, Lloyd: Alden, Lieutenant, "Where No Man Has Gone Before" (TOS)
Haynes, Michael: Stunts, *STG*
Hays, Kathryn: **Gem**
Haywood, Chad: **K'Kath**
Healy, Christine: **Rakal, Seltin**
Hearn, George: **Berel**
Hecht, Gina: **Apgar, Mauna**
Held, Christopher: **Lindstrom**
Helde, Annette: Guard, *ST:FC*; **Karina; Takar**
Heller, Chip: Warrior #2, "Loud As A Whisper" (TNG)
Henderson, Albert: **Cos**
Hendra, Jessica: **Dejar**
Hendrixson, Peter: Klingon, "The Killing Game, Part II" (VGR)
Henley, Sue: **Brooks, Ensign**
Hennings, Sam: **Ramsey**
Henriques, Darryl: **Nanclus; Portal**
Henry, Gregg: **Gallatin**
Hensel, Karen: **Brackett, Fleet Admiral; Deela**
Henteloff, Alex: **Nichols, Dr.**
Herd, Richard: **L'Kor**
Herron, Robert: Crewman in gym, "Charlie X" (TOS); **Kahless;** Kirk's stunt double and stunt double captain, "Menagerie, The Parts I and II" (TOS); Pike's stunt double & stunt captain, "Cage, The" (TOS)
Hertzler, J.G.: **Martok, General; Rittenhouse, Roy**
Hertzler, John Noah: Vulcan captain, "Emissary" (DS9)
Hetrick, Jennifer: **Maid Marian; Vash**
Hice, Ed: Scalosian, "Wink of an Eye" (TOS)
Hice, Eddie: Stunt, *ST4*, *ST5*
Hicks, Catherine: **Taylor, Dr. Gillian**
Hicks, Chuck: Military officer, "Encounter at Farpoint" (TNG); Stunts, *ST2*, *ST3*
Hicks, Marva: **T'Pel**
Hill, Marianne: **Noel, Dr. Helen**
Hillyer, Sharyn: Girl #2, "Piece of the Action, A" (TOS)
Hines, Grainger: **Gosheven**
Hinkley, Brent: Militiaman, "Future's End, Part II" (VGR)
Hinkley, Tommy: Journalist, *STG*
Hiroyuki, Cary: Balliff, Mandarin, "Encounter at Farpoint, Parts I and II" (TNG)
Hobson, Thomas: Young Jake, "Emissary" (DS9)
Hochwald, Bari: **Lense, Dr. Elizabeth**
Hodges, Tom: **Pechetti**
Hodgin, Hugh: **Prototype** and **6263**
Hoffman, Elizabeth: **Bhavani, Premier**
Holden, Marjean: **Stolzoff**
Holland, Erik: Ekor, "Wink of an Eye" (TOS)
Holloway, Roger: **Lemli, Mr.**
Holly, Patty: Female guest, "Past Tense, Part I" (DS9)
Holman, Rex: **Earp, Morgan; J'Onn**
Holton, Mark: Bolian, "Nor the Battle to the Strong" (DS9)
Homeier, Skip: **Melakon; Sevrin, Dr. Thomas**
Hooker, Billy Hank: Stunt, *ST:FC*
Hooker, Buddy Joe: Stunt, *ST:FC*
Hooks, Robert: **Morrow, Admiral**
Hooper, Joy: Stunt, *ST6*
Hope, Leslie: **Kira Meru**
Hopkins, Kaitlin: **Kilana**
Horan, James: **Barnaby, Lieutenant; Jo'Bril; Tosin; Ikat'ika**
Horgan, Patrick: **Eneg**
Horn, Michelle: **Sahgi**
Horsting, J.R.: Borg, *ST:FC*
Horton, Michael: **Koven**; Security officer, *ST:FC;* Daniels, *ST:I*
Hostetter, John: **Adislo, Hars**
Hotton, Donald: Monk #1, "Emissary" (DS9)
Houska, Steven: **Chardis**
Howard, Clint: **Balok; Grady**
Howard, Leslie C.: Yeoman, *ST:TMP*
Howard, Sherman: **Endar**; Syvar, "Shakaar" (DS9)
Howard, Susan: **Mara**
Howard, Vince: Uhura's crewman, "Man Trap, The" (TOS)
Howden, Mike: Romulan guard, "Enterprise Incident, The" (TOS); Rowe, Lieutenant, "Catspaw" (TOS)
Howell, Chris: Stunts, *ST:I*
Hower, Nancy: **Wildman, Samantha**
Hoyt, Clegg: *Pitcairn* transporter chief, "Cage, The" (TOS)
Hoyt, John: **Boyce, Dr. Phillip**
Hubbard, Jamie: **Salia**
Hubbell, J.P.: Ensign, "Man of the People" (TNG)
Huddleston, David: Conductor, "Emergence" (TNG)
Hudec, M. Leigh (aka Barrett, Majel) **Number One.**
Hues, Matthias: Second Klingon general *ST6*
Huff, Thomas: Stunt, *ST5*
Huff, Tom: Stunt, *ST6*
Huff, Tommy J.: Stunt, *ST2*
Hughes, David Hillary: **Trefayne**
Hughes, Wendy: **Daren, Neela**
Hummel, Sayra: Technical assistant *ST:TMP*
Humphrey, Mark: **Lito**
Hundley, Craig: **Kirk, Peter; Starnes, Tommy**
Hungerford, Michael: Roughneck, "Time's Arrow, Part I" (TNG)
Hunt, Marsha: **Jameson, Anne**
Hunt, William Dennis: **Huraga**
Hunter, Jeffrey: **Pike, Christopher**
Hupp, Jana Marie: **Monroe, Lieutenant; Pavlick, Ensign**
Hurley, Craig: **Peeples, Ensign**
Hurley, Diane M.: Woman, "Game, The" (TNG)
Hurst, David: **Hodin**
Hutchinson, Harry: Trooper, "Shakaar" (DS9)
Hutton, Rif: Klingon guard, *STG*
Hyde, Bruce: **Riley, Kevin Thomas**
Hyman, Charles B.: **Konmel, Lieutenant**

Ihnat, Steve: **Garth of Izar**
Imada, Jeff: Stunts, *ST6*
Iman: **Martia**
Imershien, Dierdre L.: **Joval; Watley, Lieutenant**
Ingham, Barrie: **Odell, Danilo**
Ingledew, Rosalind: **Yanar**
Ireland, Jill: **Kalomi, Leila**
Ito, Robert: **Chang, Tac Officer**
Itzen, Gregory: **Tandro, Ilon; Hain**
Itzkowitz, Howard: Cargo deck ensign, *ST:TMP*
Ivar, Stan: **Mark**

Jace, Michael: 1st officer, "Jem'Hadar, The" (DS9)
Jackson, Richard Lee: **Webb, Danny**
Jackson, Sherry: **Andrea**
Jackson, Tom: **Anthwara**
Jacobson, Jill: **Aroya**; Vanessa, "Royale, The" (TNG)
Jaeck, Scott: Administrator, "Inner Light, The" (TNG); **Cavit, Lieutenant Commander**

James, Anthony: **Thei, Subcommander**
James, Heinrich: Borg, *ST:FC*
James, Randy: **Jones, Lieutenant**
Janes, Loren: Kirk's stunt double, "Charlie X" (TOS); Norman's stunt double, "I, Mudd" (TOS)
Jansen, Christine: Journalist, *STG*
Jansen, James W.: **Faren Kag**; **Lucsly**
Janssen, Famke: **Kamala**
Jarvis, Graham: **Dokachin**, **Klim**
Jason, Harvey: **Leech**, **Felix**
Jay, Tony: **Campio**, **Minister**
Jean, Brenda: **Berlin, Karyn**
Jemison, Dr. Mae: **Palmer**, **Lieutenant**
Jenkins, Ken: **Stubbs**, **Dr. Paul**
Jenner, Barry: **Ross, Admiral William**
Jennings, Junero: Technical assistant, *ST:TMP*
Jens, Salome: **Founder Leader**; Humanoid, "Chase, The" (TNG)
Jensen, Jeff: Stunt, *ST3*
Jensen, Jeffrey S.: Stunt, *ST6; ST:I*
Jensen, Keith L.: Stunt, *ST:TMP*
Jenson, Roy: **Cloud William**
Jewell, Lois: **Drusilla**
Jochim, Anthony: Survivor #3, "Cage, The" (TOS)
Johnson, Alexandra: One Zero, "11001001" (TNG)
Johnson, Bob: Provider voice #1, "Gamesters of Triskelion, The" (TOS)
Johnson, Eric David: **Daggin**
Johnson, Georgann: **Gromek**, **Admiral**
Johnson, Joan: *Botany Bay* elite female guard, "Space Seed" (TOS)
Johnson, Julie: Landon's stunt double, "Apple, The" (TOS)
Johnson, Penny: **Yates**, **Kasidy; Dobara**; **Cassie**
Johnson, Robert C.: 1st Talosian's voice, "Cage, The" (TOS)
Johnston, Chris: Vidiian #1, "Deadlock" (VGR)
Johnston, Katie Jane: Martia as a child, *ST6*
Jones, Al: Stunt double for Christopher Lloyd, *ST3*
Jones, Isis: Guinan (child), "Rascals" (TNG)
Jones, Jay: Crew stunt double, "And the Children Shall Lead" (TOS); Kirk's stunt double, "Empath, The" (TOS); **Mallory**, **Lieutenant**; Mirt, "Piece of the Action, A" (TOS); Prisoner #1, "Cloud Minders, The" (TOS); Scott's stunt double, "Who Mourns for Adonais?" (TOS) & "Trouble with Tribbles, The" (TOS); Stunt double, "Immunity Syndrome, The" (TOS)
Jones, Jim: **Jackson;** Kras's stunt double, "Friday's Child" (TOS); McCoy's stunt double, "Catspaw" (TOS)
Jones, Judith: Edo girl, "Justice" (TNG)
Jones, Morgan: Nesvig, Colonel, "Assignment: Earth" (TOS)
Jones, Renée: **Uhnari**, **Lieutenant Aquiel**
Jordan, Leslie: **Kol**
Judd, Ashley: **Lefler**, **Ensign Robin**
Jung, Nathan: **Genghis Khan**

Kahn, Lesley: **Viterian, Captain**
Kaine, Nancy: **Sanric**
Kamal, Jon Rashad: **Sonak**, **Commander**
Kamel, Stanley: **Kosinski**
Kaminar, Lisa: **Lillias**
Karas, Greg: Intern #2, *ST4*
Karen, Anna: Woman, "All Our Yesterdays" (TOS)
Kasdorf, Lenore: **Lorin**, **Security Minister**
Katarina, Anna: Valeda, "Haven" (TNG)
Kates, Bernard: **Freud**, **Dr. Sigmund**
Katsulas, Andreas: **Tomalak**
Katz, Cindy: Yteppa, "Second Skin" (DS9)
Kava, Caroline: **Russell**, **Dr. Toby**
Kavovit, Andrew: **Kirby**
Keane, Kerrie: **Devos**, **Alexana**
Keefer, Don: Cromwell, Mr., "Assignment: Earth" (TOS)
Keenan, Michael: **Hrothgar**, **King**; **Maturin; Patrick**
Kehela, Steve: **Sutok**
Kehler, Jack: **Jaheel**, **Captain**
Keith, Brian: **Mullibok**
Kelleher, Tim: **Gaines, Lieutenant**, "All Good Things..." (TNG)
Keller, Dore: Crew member, "Child, The" (TNG)
Kellerman, Sally: **Dehner**, **Dr. Elizabeth**
Kellett, Pete: **Farrell (mirror)**
Kelley, DeForest: **McCoy**, **Dr. Leonard H.**
Kelly, Daniel Hugh: **Sojef**
Kelly, Irene: Sirah, "Omega Glory, The" (TOS)
Kelly, Maria: Stunt, *ST:FC*
Kelvin, Max: **Achilles**
Kemp, Jeremy: **Picard**, **Robert**
Kenney, Sean: **DePaul**, **Lieutenant**; Pike, Captain (Injured), "Menagerie, The Parts I and II" (TOS)
Kent, Paul: **Beach**, **Commander**
Kepros, Nicholas: **Movar**
Kerbeck, Robert: Cardassian soldier, "Defiant" (DS9)
Kern, Dan: **Dean**, **Lieutenant**; **Kellan**
Kerns, Jr., Hubie: Stunt, *ST2*
Kerr, Patrick: Bothan, "Persistence of Vision" (VGR)
Keyser, Jamie: Stunt, *ST:FC*
Khambatta, Persis: **Ilia**
Kiely, Mark: **Lasca**, **Lieutenant**
Kiley, Richard: **Seyetik**, **Professor Gideon**
Kilpatrick, Patrick: **Razik**
Kim, Jacqueline: **Sulu, Demora**
Kimborough, Matthew: Alien high roller, "Abandoned, The" (DS9)
King, Bobby C.: Security chief, "Paradise Lost" (DS9)
King, Caroline Junko: O'Brien, Keiko (child), "Rascals" (TNG)
King, Jeff: **Amaro**
King, Jr., Wayne: Stunt Borg, *ST:FC*
King, Robert: Stunts, *ST4, ST6*
Kingsley, Danitza: **Ariana**
Kino, Lloyd: **Wu**
Kirkland, Kelli: **Rinna**
Kirsh, Bob: Glinn, "Tears of the Prophets" (DS9)
Kivel, Barry: Doorman, "Time's Arrow, Part I" (TNG)
Klein, Ericka: **Admiral Sitak**
Klunis, Tom: **Lamonay, S.**
Knepper, Rob: **Miller**, **Wyatt**
Knickerbocker, Thomas: Gunman, "Clues" (TNG)
Knight, William: Amorous crewman, "Naked Time, The" (TOS)
Knight, Wyatt: Technician #2, "Coming of Age" (TNG)
Knowland, Joe: Antique store owner, *ST4*
Koch, Kenny: Kissing crewman, "The Naked Now" (TNG)
Koenig, Andrew: **Tumak**
Koenig, Walter: **Chekov**, **Pavel A.**
Kohnert, Mary: **Allenby**, **Ensign Tess**
Kopache, Thomas: Com officer, *STG*; Engineer, "Emergence" (TNG); **Mirok**; **Viorsa; Kira Taban**
Kopyc, Frank: Bolian aide, "Let He Who Is Without Sin" (DS9)
Koscki, Kim Robert: Stunt, *ST:FC*
Kosh, Pamela: **Carmichael**, **Mrs.**; **Jessel**
Kossin, Andy: Apprentice, "Thine Own Self" (TNG)
Kovack, Michael: **Tyree**
Kovack, Nancy: **Nona**
Kowal, Jon: **Gossett**, **Herm**
Kramer, Joel: Klingon crew member, *ST:TMP*
Krawic, Michael A.: **Samuels**, **William Patrick; Rahmin**
Krestalude, Jim: El-Aurian survivor, *STG*
Krige, Alice: **Borg queen**
Krinsky, Tamara Lee: Townsperson, *ST:FC*
Krusiec, Michelle: **O'Brien, Molly**
Krutonog, Boris: Helmsman, "Flashback" (VGR); Lojur, Helmsman, *ST6*
Kusatsu, Clyde: **Nakamura**, **Admiral**
Kuter, Kay E.: **Sirah**

La Rue, Bart: Announcer, "Bread and Circuses" (TOS); Guardian voice, "City on the Edge of Forever, The" (TOS); Newscaster, "Patterns of Force" (TOS); **Yarnek**, voice of
LaBelle, Rob: **Kafar**
LaCamara, Carlos: **Retaya**
Lacey, Deborah: **Sisko, Sarah**
Lafferty, Marcy: **DiFalco**, **Chief**
Lagerfelt, Caroline: **Makbar**
Laird, Lamont: Indian boy, "Paradise Syndrome, The" (TOS)
Lambert, Paul: **Clark, Dr. Howard; Melian**
Lambert, Steven: Stunts, *ST:I*
Lamey, Thad: Devil monster, "Devil's Due" (TNG)
LaMura, Mark: **Doe**, **John**
Lander, David L.: Tactician, "Peak Performance" (TNG)
Landers, Harry: **Coleman**, **Dr. Arthur**
Lando, Joe: Shore patrolman, *ST4*
Landor, Rosalyn: **Odell**, **Brenna**
Landry, Karen: **Ajur**
Lane, Iva: Crew member, *ST:TMP*; Zero Zero, "11001001" (TNG)
Lang, Charley: **Duffy**, **Lieutenant**
Langham, Wallace: **Flotter**
Langton, Basil: **Banjo man**; **Caretaker**
Lansing, Robert: **Seven**, **Gary**
Large, Norman: **Maques**; **Neral**; Lissepian captain, "Duet" (DS9); Ocampa, "Cold Fire" (VGR)
Larroquette, John: **Maltz**
Lashly, James: **Kopf**, **Ensign**; **Primmin**, **Lieutenant George**
Laskey: Trooper, "Patterns of Force" (TOS)
Lauden, Jay: **Liator**
Lauritson, Peter: **Raymond, Thomas**
Lauter, Ed: **Albert**, **Lieutenant Commander**
Lavin, Richard: 2nd mediator, "Justice" (TNG); Warrior #1, "Loud as a Whisper" (TNG)

Lawrence, Marc: **Volnoth**
Lawrence, Mittie: Crew woman, "Corbomite Maneuver, The" (TOS)
Lawrence, Sharon: **Earhart, Amelia**
le Gault, Lance: **K'Temoc**
LeBeauf, Sabrina: **Giusti, Ensign**
Lee, Bill Cho: Male patient, "Time's Arrow, Part II" (TNG)
Lee, Everett: Cafe owner, *ST4*
Lee, Stephen: Bartender, "Gambit, Part I" (TNG); **Chorgan**
Lee, Thelma: **Kahlest**
LeFlore, Julius: Stunts, *ST:I*
Legarde, Tom and Ted: Herman series, "I, Mudd" (TOS)
Leider, Harriet: **Amarie**
Leigh, Steven Vincent: **Reese, Lieutenant**
Leighton, Sheila: **Luma**
Lemani, Tania: **Kara**
Lemon, Ben: **Jev**
Lenard, Marc: Klingon captain, *ST:TMP*; **Romulan commander**; **Sarek**
Leone, Maria: Ten-Forward crew, "Offspring, The" (TNG)
Leong, Page: **Anaya, Ensign April**
Leonhardt, Nora: **Finn, Marla E.**
Lessing, Arnold: Carlisle, Lieutenant, & voice of Security guard #1, "Changeling, The" (TOS)
Lester, Jeff: FBI agent, *ST4*
Lester, Loren: Attendant, "Quickening, The" (DS9)
Lester, Terry: **Haron, Jal**
LeStrange, Philip: **Coutu**
Leva, Scott: Stunts, *ST6;* **Ortakin**
Leverington, Shelby: **Brossmer, Chief**
Levin, Deborah: **Lang**
Levin, Matt E.: **Rafin**
Levitt, Judy: Doctor #2, *ST4*; El-Aurian survivor, *STG*; Military aide, *ST6*
Lewis, Irvin E.: Stunts, *ST:I*
Lewis, Susan: Transporter technician, "Demon" (VGR)
Libertini, Richard: **Akorem Laan**
Lien, Jennifer: **Kes**
Lifford, Tina: **Lee**
Lilley, Clint: Stunts, *ST:I*
Lindesmith, John: Engineer, "Paradise Syndrome, The" (TOS) &"This Side of Paradise" (TOS); Helmsman, "Charlie X" (TOS)
Lindsey, Elizabeth: **Kim, Luisa**
Lineback, Richard: **Peers, Selin**; **Romas**
Linville, Joanne: **Romulan commander**
Lippe, Jonathan: Crewman, "Corbomite Maneuver, The" (TOS)
Liska, Stephen: Torg, *ST3*
Lithgow, William: **Tainer, Dr. Pran**
Littlejohn, Jesse: **Gabriel**
Liufau, Sidney: **Atoa, Lieutenant Manuele**
Lively, Lori: **Siana**
Lloyd, Christopher: **Kruge, Commander**
Lloyd, Norman: **Galen, Professor Richard**
Locher, Felix: **Johnson, Robert**
Lockwood, Gary: **Mitchell, Gary**
Lodge, Suzanne: Serving girl, "Wolf in the Fold" (TOS)
Loesch, Roger: Male Romulan, "By Inferno's Light" (DS9)
Loftin, Carey: Truck driver, "City on the Edge of Forever, The" (TOS)
Lofton, Cirroc: **Sisko, Jake**; **Jimmy**
Logan, Kristopher: El-Aurian survivor, *STG*
Loken, Kristanna S.: **Malia**
Long, Ed: **Midro**
Long, Heather: **Omag's girl**
Loomis, Rod: **Manheim, Dr. Paul**
Lopez, Perry: **Rodriguez, Lieutenant Esteban**
Loprieno, John: **Obrist**
Lorca, Isabel: **Gabrielle**
Lord, Lisa: Nurse, "Nor the Battle to the Strong" (DS9)
Lormer, Jon: **Haskins, Dr. Theodore**; Old man, "For the World Is Hollow and I Have Touched the Sky" (TOS); Tamar, "Return of the Archons" (TOS)
Loseth, Eva: **Riska**
Lott, Kurt: Stunts, *ST:I*
Lou, Cindy: *Enterprise* nurse, "Return to Tomorrow" (TOS)
Louden, Jay: **Liator**
Louis, Justin: **Trevis**
Lounibos, Tim: **Kwan, Daniel L.**
Lovsky, Celia: **T'Pau**
Lowe, Louahn: **Okala**
Lucia, Charles O.: **Mabus**
Lucia, Chip: **Alkar, Ambassador Ves**
Luckinbill, Laurence: **Sybok**
Lucking, William: **Furel**
Luke, Keye: **Cory, Governor Donald**
Lum, Benjamin W.S.: **Shimoda, Jim**
Luna, Barbara: **Moreau, Marlena (mirror)**
Lund, Jordan: **Kulge**; **Woban**
Lundin, Victor: Klingon Lieutenant #1, "Errand of Mercy" (TOS)
Lupo, Diana R.: Stunts, *ST:I*
Lupo, Tom: Security guard, "Alternative Factor, The" (TOS)
Lustig, Aaron: Doctor, "Ex Post Facto" (VGR)
Luz, Franc: **Odan, Ambassador**
Lynch, Barry: **DeSeve, Ensign Stefan**
Lynch, Hal: **air police sergeant**
Lynch, Ken: **Vanderberg, Chief Engineer**
Lynch, Richard: **Baran, Arctus**
Lynne, Erica: **Hansen, Annika**
Lyon, Bob: Villager stunt double, "Private Little War, A" (TOS)
Lyons, Gene: **Fox, Ambassador Robert**

Ma, Tzi: **biomolecular physiologist**
Macaulay, Charles: **Jarvis**; **Landru**
MacDonald, James G.: **Wainwright, Captain**
MacDonald, Ryan: Shopkeeper, "Time and Again" (VGR)
MacDonald, Scott: **Goran'Agar**; **N'Vek, Subcommander**; **Rollins**; **Tosk**
MacDonnell, Sarah: **Neeley, Lieutenant Lisa**
Macer, Sterling: **Toq**
Macht, Stephen: **Krim, General**
Mack, Michael: **Hayes, Ensign**; **Sirol, Commander**
MacKenzie, Robert: **Trazko**
MacLachlan, Janet: **Masters, Lieutenant**
MacNeal, Catherine: **Henley, Mariah**
Madalone, Dennis: **Atul**; Guard, "Shattered Mirror" (DS9); **Hendrick, Chief;** Marauder, "Crossover" (DS9) & "Through The Looking Glass" (DS9); Ramos, "Heart of Glory" (TNG); Transporter technician "Identity Crisis" (TNG)
Madden, Edward: Geologist, "Cage, The" (TOS); **Fisher, Geological Technician**
Madsen, Virginia: **Kellin**
Maffei, Buck: Creature, "Galileo Seven The" (TOS)
Magee, Ken: **Emck, Controller**; Klingon monster, "Devil's Due" (TNG)
Mager, Jed: **Tabor, Ensign**
Magnus, Chuck: **Resket**
Maguire, Michael L.: **Benaren**
Mahonen, Michael: **Brone**
Makee, Blaisdell: **Spinelli, Lieutenant**
Malek-Yonan, Rosie: **Tekoa**
Malone: Ambassadorial secretary, "Taste of Armageddon" (TOS)
Maloney, Patty: Little woman, The, "Thaw, The" (VGR)
Manard, Biff: Ruffian, "Elementary, Dear Data" (TNG)
Mandan, Robert: **Pa'Dar, Kotran**
Mandell, Johnny: Sulu's boy, "Mirror, Mirror" (TOS)
Manley, Stephen: **Spock** age 15
Marcelino, Mario: Communications *U.S.S. Grissom*, *ST3*
March, Barbara: **Lursa**
Marcus, Alan: Stunts, *ST6*
Marcus, Trula M.: Female villager, "Shadowplay" (DS9)
Marcuse, Theo: **Korob**
Margolis, Heide: **Norva**
Margolis, Mark: **Apgar, Dr. Nel**
Margolis, Morgan H.: Vaskan visitor, "Living Witness" (VGR)
Mariya, Lily: Ops officer, "Emissary, The" (DS9)
Markham, Monte: **Fullerton, Pascal**
Markinson, Brian: **Durst, Peter**; **Sulan**; **Vorin; Giger, Dr. Elias**
Markle, Stephen: **Tholl, Kova**
Marko, Peter: **Gaetano, Lieutenant**
Marlo, Steve: **Zabo**
Marlow, Scott: **Keeve Falor**
Marosi, Marc: Gul, "Wrongs Darker Than Death or Night" (DS9)
Mars, Bruce: Crewman, "Corbomite Maneuver, The" (TOS); **Finnegan**; First policeman, "Assignment: Earth" (TOS)
Mars, Kenneth: **Colyus**
Marsden, Jason: **Grimp**
Marsh, Michele: Leda, "When the Bough Breaks" (TNG)
Marshall, David Anthony: **Hansen, Magnus**
Marshall, Don: **Boma, Lieutenant**
Marshall, Henry: Security officer, *STG*
Marshall, Joan: **Shaw, Areel**
Marshall, Kenneth: **Eddington, Michael**
Marshall, Marie: **Kelsey**
Marshall, Sarah: **Wallace, Dr. Janet**
Marshall, William: **Daystrom, Dr. Richard**
Marstan, Joel: Crew chief, *ST2*
Martel, Arlene: **T'Pring**
Martin, Andrea: **Ishka**
Martin, Jeffrey: Electronic technician, *ST4*
Martin, Johnny: **Valek, Jal**
Martin, Meade: Engineer, "Changeling, The" (TOS)
Martin, Nan: **Miller, Victoria**
Martinez, Benito: **Salazar**

Marzelli, John: Scavenger, "Wrongs Darker Than Death or Night" (DS9)
Mason, Dan: **Accolan**
Massett, Marybeth: **Parell**
Massett, Patrick: **Duras**
Massey, Athena: **Jessen**
Massey, Eve H. **Mirell, Jora**
Masterson, Chase: **Leeta**
Mathews, Eddie: Stunts, *ST:I*
Matson, Denver: Rayburn's stunt double, "What Are Little Girls Made Of?" (TOS)
Matthew, Eric: 1st Edo boy, "Justice" (TNG)
Matthew, Stephen: Garvin, Ensign, "All Good Things..." (TNG)
Maurer, Ralph: **Bilar**; S.S. Lieutenant, "Patterns of Force" (TOS)
Maurishka, Zahra: Yeoman, "Operation: Annihilate!" (TOS)
Maxwell, Charles: **Earp**, **Virgil**
May, Deborah: **Haneek**; **Lyris**
Mayama, Miko: **Tamura**, **Yeoman**
McBride, Jeff Magnus: **Belar, Joran**
McBroom, Amanda: **Louvois**, **Captain Phillipa**
McCabe, Angelo: Crew member, "Schisms" (TNG)
McCarthy, Bart: **Admiral Cobum**
McCarthy, Jeff: **Danar**, **Roga**; Human doctor, "Caretaker" (VGR)
McCarthy, Julianna: **Mila**
McChesney, Mart: **Armus**; Sheliak, "Ensigns of Command, The" (TNG)
McCleister, Tom: Kolos, "Q-Less" (DS9)
McCloy, Johanna: **Calloway**, **Maddy**
McCluskey, Leigh J.: **Tieran**
McConnell, Judy: Tankris, Yeoman, "Wolf in the Fold" (TOS)
McCorkle, Kevin: Alien Captain, "The Omega Directive" (VGR)
McCormack, J. Patrick: **Bennett, Rear Admiral**
McCormick, Carolyn: **Minuet**
McCoy, Matt: **Ral**, **Devinoni**
McCready, Ed: Barber, "Spectre of the Gun" (TOS); Boy creature, "Miri" (TOS); Carter, Dr., "Omega Glory, The" (TOS); Inmate, "Dagger of the Mind" (TOS); S. S. Trooper, "Patterns of Force" (TOS)
McCusker, Mary: Nurse, "Evolution" (TNG)
McDancer, Buck: Stunts, *ST:I*
McDancer, Sonia Jo: Stunts, *ST:I*
McDermott, Kevin: Alien batter, "Emissary" (DS9)
McDonald, Christopher: **Castillo**, **Lieutenant Richard**
McDonogh, Ashley Brianne: **Collins, Dorian**
McDonough, Neal: **Hawk**, **Lieutenant**
McDowell, Malcolm: **Soran**, **Dr. Tolian**
McElroy, Scott: Guard, "Darkness and the Light, The" (DS9)
McEveety, Steven: Redheaded boy, "Miri" (TOS)
McFadden, Gates: **Crusher**, **Dr. Beverly**
McFarland, Rebecca: **Talli**
McGarry, Mary Anne: **Tabris**
McGinnis, Scott: "Mr. Adventure," *ST3*
McGlynn, Elizabeth: **Daelen**
McGonagle, Richard: **Ja'Dar**, **Dr.**
McGovern, Bob: Stunt Borg, *ST:FC*
McGovern, Don Charles: Stunts, *ST3*
McGowan, Oliver: **Caretaker**
McGrath, Derek: **Chell**
McGuire, Betty: **Rozahn**, **Minister**
McHattie, Stephen: **Vreenak**
McIntire, James: **Hali**
McIntosh: Hood, "Piece of the Action, A" (TOS)
McKane, Brendan: Technician #1, "Coming of Age" (TNG)
McKay, Cole: Stunts, *ST6*
McKean, Michael: **Clown**
McKee, Robin: **Ren**, **Lidell**
McKenzie, Matt: **Weld Ram**, **Dr.**
McKnight, John Hugh: Stunt, *ST:TMP*
McLiam, John: **Fento**
McManus, Don: **Zio**
McNally, Kelli Ann: One One, "11001001" (TNG)
McNally, Terrence: **B'tardat**
McNamara, J. Patrick: **Taggert**, **Captain**
McNeal, Joyce L.: Stunt, *ST5*
McNeal, Joyce: Stunt, *ST:FC*
McNeill, Robert Duncan: **Locarno**, **Cadet First Class Nicholas; Paris, Thomas**
McNulty, Patricia: **Lawton**, **Yeoman Tina**
McPhail, Marnie: **Alcia**; Eiger, *ST:FC*
McPherson, Patricia: **Ariel**
McTosh, Bill: Klingon crew member, *ST:TMP*
Meader, William: **Lindstrom**
Meaney, Colm: **O'Brien**, **Miles; Macklin, Albert**
Megna, John: Little boy, "Miri" (TOS)
Meier, Dustin: Stunt, *ST:FC*
Meier, John: Stunt double for William Shatner, *ST3*, *ST4*
Meier, Johnny C.: Stunt, *ST:FC*
Mell, Joseph: Earth trader, "Cage, The" (TOS)
Melton, Troy: Finney's stunt double, "Court Martial" (TOS); Genghis Khan's stunt double, "Savage Curtain, The" (TOS)
Mendell, Lorine: **Giddings, Dianna**
Menges, James: Jogger, *ST4*
Menyuk, Eric: **Traveler**
Meriwether, Lee: **Losira**
Merrifield, Richard: **Webb**
Merrill, Todd: Gleason, "Future Imperfect" (TNG)
Merson, Richard: Pie man, "Elementary, Dear Data" (TNG)
Meseroll, Kenneth: **McDowell**, **Ensign**
Metcalf, Mark: **Hirogen Medic**
Metzler, Jim: **Brynner**, **Christopher**
Michael, Christopher: Helm officer, "Rules of Engagement" (DS9); Man #1, "Legacy" (TNG)
Michaels, D.: Flapper, "Emergence" (TNG)
Michaels, Janna: Young Kes, "Before and After" (VGR)
Middendorf, Tracy: **Ziyal**
Milder, Andy: **Boq'ta**
Miles, Bob: Cloud City sentinel #2, "Cloud Minders, The" (TOS); Klingon stunt double, "Trouble with Tribbles, The" (TOS); McCoy's stunt double, "Miri" (TOS)
Miles, Joanna: **Perrin**
Miley, Peggy: **Cuzar, Regent**
Military, Frank: **Coleridge**, **Biddle "B.C."**
Miller, Allan: Alien in the bar, *ST3*
Miller, Christopher James: **Picard, René**
Miller, Dick: Vendor, "Big Goodbye, The" (TNG); **Vin**
Miller, Jeanette: **Tembit**
Mines, Stephen: **Tomlinson**, **Lieutenant Robert**
Minor, Bob: **Bo'rak**
Minor, James: Stunts, *ST:I*
Minor, Mike: Mask, "Spectre of the Gun" (TOS)
Minor, Rita: Stunt, *ST:FC*
Minton, Nina: **Frola**
Miranda, John: 2nd garbageman, *ST4*
Mirault, Donald: **Hayne**
Mirich, Ernie: Waiter, "Relics" (TNG)
Mitchell, Colin: **Yog**
Mitchell, Dallas: Nellis, Tom, "Charlie X" (TOS)
Mitchell, James X.: **Josephs**, **Lieutenant**
Moffat, Katherine: **Jol**, **Etana; Pallra**
Monaghan, Marjorie: **Freya**
Monahan, Debi A.: **Melissa**
Moncure, Lisa: Latia, "Quickening, The" (DS9)
Mondy, Bill: Jakin, "Armageddon Game" (DS9)
Monoson, Lawrence: **Hovath**
Montaigne, Lawrence: **Decius**; **Stonn**
Montalban, Ricardo: **Khan**
Montgomery, Karen: **Beata**
Moody, Paula: Stunts, *ST2*
Moordigian, Dave: Klingon crew member, *ST:TMP*
Moore, Allan Dean: Wounded crew member, "Frame of Mind" (TNG)
Moore, Christopher Liam: **Veer, Tova**
Moore, Jr., Bennie E.: Stunts, *ST4*
Moosekian, Duke: **Gillespie**, **Chief**
Moran, Johnny: Bajoran man, "Image in the Sand" (DS9)
Morga, Tom: Brute, The, *ST6*; Jem'Hadar soldier, "Search, The, Part II" (DS9); Klingon crewman, *ST:TMP*; **Minnis**; **Soto**; Nausicaan, "Tapestry" (TNG); Stunts, *ST2*, *ST3*, *ST5;* Cardassian, *"Empok Nor" (DS9)*
Morgan, Julie: Singer in nightclub, *ST:FC*
Morgan, Rosemary: **Piri**
Morgan, Sean: Engineer, "Paradise Syndrome, The" (TOS) & "This Side of Paradise" (TOS); **Harper**, **Ensign**; **O'Neil**, **Lieutenant**
Mori, Jeanne: Helm, *U.S.S. Grissom*, *ST3*
Mornell, Sara: **Carson**
Morocco, Beans: **Rib**
Morris, Leslie: **Reginold**
Morris, Phil: Black boy in army helmet, "Miri" (TOS); Foster, Trainee, *ST3*; **Thopok; Remata'Klan**
Morrison, Kenny: **Gerron**
Morrissey, Roger: Beta-Hirogen, "Hunters" (VGR)
Morrow, Byron: **Komack**, **Admiral**; Westervliet, Admiral, "For the World Is Hollow and I Have Touched the Sky" (TOS)
Morshower, Glenn: Guard #1, "Resistance" (VGR); **Burke**, **Lieutenant**; Navigator, *STG*; **Orton**, **Mr.**
Morton, Jim: **Einstein**, **Albert**
Morton, Mickey: **Kloog**
Moser, Diane: Ten-Forward crew, "Offspring, The" (TNG)
Mosiman, Marnie: Woman, "Loud as a Whisper" (TNG)
Moss, Arnold: **Karidian**, **Anton**
Moss, Stewart: Crewman, "Corbomite

Maneuver, The" (TOS); **Hanar; Tormolen, Joe**
Mowry, Tahj D.: **Corin**
Mudd, Samantha: **Chandler, Lieutenant**
Mudie, Leonard: Survivor #2, "Cage, The" (TOS)
Muldaur, Diana: **Jones, Dr. Miranda; Mulhall, Dr. Ann; Pulaski, Dr. Katherine; Thalassa**
Mulgrew, Kate: **Janeway, Kathryn**
Mulkey, Randy: Idanian #2, "A Simple Investigation" (DS9)
Mulroney, Kieran: **Benzan**
Munson, Warren: **Holt, Admiral Marcus; Paris, Admiral**
Muramoto, Betty: Scientist, "Déjà Q" (TNG)
Murdock, George: "God," *ST5*; **Hanson, Admiral J.P.**
Murdock, Jack: Beggar, "Time's Arrow, Part I" (TNG)
Murdock, Kermit: Prosecutor, "All Our Yesterdays" (TOS)
Murphy, Donna: **Anij**
Murphy, Meghan: **Karya**
Murray, Clayton: Militiaman, "Future's End, Part II" (VGR)
Mustin, Tom: Intern #1, *ST4*

Naff, Lycia: **Gomez, Ensign Sonya**
Nagler, Morgan: Kid #1, "Rascals" (TNG)
Nakauchi, Paul: Tygarian officer, "Homecoming, The" (DS9)
Nalder, Reggie: **Shras**
Nalee, Elaine: Injured woman, "Hide and Q" (TNG)
Napier, Charles: **Adam; Denning, General Rex**
Naradzay, 1st Sgt. Joseph, USMC: Marine sergeant, *ST4*
Nardini, James: **Wixiban**
Nash, Jennifer: **Meribor**
Nash, Marcus: Young Picard, "Tapestry" (TNG)
Ndefo, Obi: **Drex**
Neale, Leslie: Nagel, Ensign, "Peak Performance" (TNG)
Neame, Christopher: **Unferth**
Needham, Hal: Mitchell's stunt double, "Where No Man Has Gone Before" (TOS)
Needles, David Paul: Miner #1, "Perfect Mate, The" (TNG)
Nelson, Carolyn: Arkins, Doris, "Deadly Years, The" (TOS)
Nelson, Craig Richard: **Krag; Vaskan Arbiter**
Nelson, John: Medical technician, "Schisms" (TNG)
Nelson, Sandra: **Marayna; Tavana**
Neptune, Peter: Aron, "Dauphin, The" (TNG)
Neuwirth, Bebe: **Lanel**
Nevens, Claudette: Son'a Officer #2, *ST:I*
Neville, John: **Newton, Isaac**
Newman, Andrew Hill: **Otel, Jaret**
Newman, William: **Kalin, Trose**
Newmar, Julie: **Eleen**
Nibley, Tom: **Neil**
Nicholas, Hassan: Jem'Hadar boy, "Abandoned, The" (DS9)
Nichols, Nichelle: **Uhura**
Nickerson, Jimmy: Stunt, *ST:FC*
Nickson, Julia: **Cassandra; T'su, Ensign Lian**
Nimoy, Leonard: **Spock**
Nims, Shair: **Sayana**
Niznik, Stephanie: **Perim, Kell**
Noah, James: **Pren, Dr. Hanor; Rislan**
Nogulich, Natalia: **Necheyev, Alynna**
Noland, Valora: **Daras**
Nordling, Jeffrey: **Tahna Los**
Norman, Rae: Penny, "Tapestry" (TNG)
Norris, Chris Nelson: **Trajok**
Norris, Eric: Stunts, *ST6*
Norwick, Natalie: **Leighton, Martha**
Novak, Frank: Businessman, "Babel" (DS9)
Nowak, John: Stunt, *ST:FC*; Stunts, *STG*, *ST:I*
Nufer, Beth: Stunts, *ST2*
Nuyen, France: **Elaan**

O'Brien, C.: Kirk's stunt double, "This Side of Paradise" (TOS)
O'Brien, Gary: Crew member, "Elogium" (VGR)
O'Brien, Joycelyn: **Haro, Mitena**
O'Brien, Shana: **Omag's girl**
O'Connell, William: **Thelev**
O'Connor, Terrence: Ross, Chief, *ST:TMP*
O'Connor, Tim: **Briam, Ambassador**
O'Donnell, Annie: **Keena**
O'Farrell, Conor: Carlson
O'Hanlon, Jr., George: Transporter chief, "Future Imperfect" (TNG)
O'Hara, Chris: Stunts, *ST:I*
O'Herlihy, Gavin: **Jabin**
O'Hurley, Shannon: **Kohl programmer**
O'Neil, Tricia: **Garrett, Captain Rachel; Korinas; Kurak**
O'Quinn, Terry: **Pressman, Erik**
O'Reilly, Cyril: **Nahsk**
O'Reilly, Robert: **Gowron**
Ogelsby, Randy: **Ah-Kel; Silaran, Prin**
Oglesby, Thomas: **Scholar/Artist**
Olandt, Ken: **Vigo, Jason**
Oliney, Alan: Stunts, *ST3*
Oliver, David: Young humanoid man, "Cost of Living" (TNG)
Oliver, Susan: **Vina**
Olson, Heather L.: **Orra, Jil**
Opatoshu, David: **Anan 7**
Oppenheimer, Alan: **Keogh, Captain; Koroth**
Orange, David: Sleepy Klingon, *ST6*
Orend, Jack R.: Human, "Crossover" (DS9)
Orrison, Bob: Engineer stunt double, "I, Mudd" (TOS); Klingon stunt double, "Trouble with Tribbles, The" (TOS); McCoy's and Village stunt double, "Private Little War, A" (TOS); Men in bar, "Spectre of the Gun" (TOS); Policeman, guard, "Bread and Circuses" (TOS); Spock's stunt double, "Savage Curtain, The" (TOS)
Orsatti, Frank: Stunt, *ST5*
Orsatti, Noon: Stunts, *ST6*
Orser, Leland: Gai, "Sanctuary" (DS9); **Lovok, Colonel; Dejaren**
Ortega, Jimmy: **Torres, Lieutenant**
Ortega-Miró, Richard: Rainer, "Thine Own Self" (TNG)
Orth-Pallavicini, Nicole: **Kareel**
Ostrow, Ron: Borg Drone, "One" (VGR)
Overton, Frank: **Sandoval, Elias**

Pais, Josh: **Gaila**
Palmas, Joseph: **Antonio**
Palmer, Andrew: Borg, *ST:FC;* Jem'Hadar soldier, "Favor the Bold" (DS9)
Palmer, Charles: Vulcan litter bearer, "Amok Time" (TOS)
Palmer, Gregg: Rancher, "Spectre of the Gun" (TOS)
Pampena, Deeana: Stunts, *ST6*
Papenfuss, Tony: **Yeln**
Parker, Sachi: **Tava**
Parks, Charles: **Eblan**
Parks, James: **Trotta; Vel**
Parkyn, Brittany: Girl with teddy bear, *STG*
Parlen, Megan: Ro Laren (child), "Rascals" (TNG)
Parr, Stephen: Valerian, "Dramatis Personae" (DS9)
Parrish, Julie: Piper, Miss, "Menagerie, The Parts I and II" (TOS)
Parrish, Leslie: **Palamas, Lieutenant Carolyn**
Parros, Peter: Tactics officer, "Matter Of Honor, A" (TNG)
Parsons, Jennifer: Ocampa nurse, "Caretaker" (VGR); **Miranda**
Parsons, Nancy: **Marouk**
Parton, Regina: Nona's stunt double, "Private Little War, A" (TOS)
Partridge, Derek: Dionyd, "Plato's Stepchildren" (TOS)
Paskey, Eddie: Conners, "Enemy Within, The" (TOS) & "Mudd's Women" (TOS); Eminiar guard/technician, "Taste of Armageddon" (TOS); **Leslie, Mr.**; Ryan, Lieutenant, "Naked Time, The" (TOS); Security guard, "Devil in the Dark, The" (TOS), "Return to Tomorrow" (TOS) & "Trouble with Tribbles, The" (TOS); Transporter chief, "Operation: Annihilate!" (TOS)
Pasqualone, Rick: **Toral**
Pass, Cyndi: **Ginger**
Pataki, Michael: **Karnas; Korax**
Paton, Angela: Adah Reh, Aunt, "Caretaker" (VGR)
Patrick, Christian: Transporter chief, "Alternative Factor, The" (TOS)
Patrick, Randal: Crew member #1, "Evolution" (TNG)
Patterson, Susan: **Kaplan, Ensign**
Paz, Joe: Vulcan litter bearer, "Amok Time" (TOS)
Pecheur, Sierra: **T'Pel, Ambassador**
Peck, Ed: **Fellini, Colonel**
Peek, Russ: Vulcan executioner, "Amok Time" (TOS)
Peldon, Courtney: **Farris, Karen**
Penn, Edward: **Kateras**
Péré, Wayne: **Guill**
Perkins, Gil: Stunt slave, "Bread and Circuses" (TOS)
Perkins, Jack: Master of the Games, "Bread and Circuses" (TOS)
Perlin, Monty Rex: Stunt Borg, *ST:FC*
Perna, David: McCoy's stunt double, "City on the Edge of Forever, The" (TOS);

Spock's stunt double, "Amok Time" (TOS) & "Private Little War, A" (TOS)
Perrin, Vic: **Balok** (Clint Howard's voice); Gorn's voice, and Metron's voice, "Arena" (TOS); Tharn, "Mirror, Mirror" (TOS); voice of **Nomad**
Perry, Jr., Ernest: **Whatley, Admiral Charles**
Perry, Manny: Stunt, *ST:FC*
Perry, Roger: **Christopher**, **Captain John**
Persoff, Nehemiah: **Toff**, **Palor**
Peters, Brock: **Cartwright**, **Admiral**; **Sisko, Joseph**,
Peters, Mary: Stunt, *ST2*
Peterson, Vidal: **D'Tan**; **Rugal**
Pettiet, Christopher: Boy, "High Ground, The" (TNG)
Pettyjohn, Angelique: **Shahna**
Pflug, Randy: Guard, "Dramatis Personae" (DS9), Security officer, "Chrysalis" (DS9)
Phillips, Ethan: **Neelix; Farek, Dr.**; Maître d', *ST: FC*
Phillips, Gina: **Varis Sul**
Phillips, Michelle: **Manheim**, **Jenice**
Phillips, Robert: Space officer (Orion), "Cage, The" (TOS)
Picardo, Robert: **Emergency Medical Hologram**; **Zimmerman, Lewis**
Picerni, Jr., Charles: Stunt, *ST3*, *ST4*
Picerni, Steve: Stunt, *ST:FC*
Pierpoint, Eric: **Voval**; **Sanders, Captain**
Pietz, Amy: **Rhodes**, **Sandra**
Pike, Donald R.: Stunt coordinator, *ST6*
Pike, Gary T.: Stunts, *ST6*
Pillar, Gary: **Yutan**
Pillsbury, Garth: Prisoner, "Cloud Minders, The" (TOS); Wilson, "Mirror, Mirror" (TOS)
Pine, Phillip: **Green**, **Colonel**
Pine, Robert: **Liria**
Pinson, Allen: Spock's stunt double, "Bread and Circuses" (TOS)
Piscopo, Joe: **Comic, The**
Pistone, Martin: Controller #2, *ST4*
Plakson, Suzie: **Q female**; **K'Ehleyr**; **Selar**, **Dr.**
Plana, Tony: **Amaros**
Plummer, Christopher: **Chang**, **General**
Plunkett, Maryann: **Leijten**, **Susanna**
Pock, Bernie: Stunts, *STG*
Poe, Richard: Cardassian officer, "Playing God" (DS9); **Evek**, **Gul**
Poland, Greg: Elloran Officer #2, *ST:I*
Polis, Joel: Terla, "Time and Again" (VGR)
Polite, Charlene: **Vanna**
Pollard, Michael J.: **Jahn**
Pollock, Naomi: Indian woman, "Paradise Syndrome, The" (TOS); **Rahda**, **Lieutenant**
Pomer, Scarlett: **Wildman, Naomi**
Pop, Iggy: **Yelgrun**
Popowich, Paul: **Watters, Tim**
Porter, Brett: Stec, General, *ST6*
Poster, Tom: Stunt Borg, *ST:FC*
Potenza, Vadia: **Spock,** age 13
Potts, Cliff: **Kennelly**, **Admiral**
Powell, Susan: **Aster**, **Lieutenant Marla**
Powell-Blair, William: Cardassian officer, "Emissary" (DS9)
Prendergast, Gerard: **Bensen**, **Bjorn**
Presnell, Harve: **Q colonel**
Pressman, Lawrence: **Ghemor**, **Legate**; **Krajensky, Ambassador**.
Prine, Andrew: **Suna**; **Turrel**, **Legate**
Prisco, Thomas: **Heler**
Prohaska, Janos: Anthropoid ape and Humanoid bird, "Cage, The" (TOS); **Horta**; **mugato**; **Yarnek**, costumed
Prokop, Paul: Guard, "Mirror, Mirror" (TOS)
Proscia, Ray: Vidiian commander, "Deadlock" (VGR)
Prosky, John: **Brathaw**
Pruitt, Jeff: Ensign, "Dramatis Personae" (DS9)
Pugsley, Don: Alien visitor, "Concerning Flight" (VGR)
Pulford, Don: Stunt double for William Shatner, *ST5*; Stunts, *STG*; Stunts, *ST6*
Putch, John: Journalist, *STG*; **Mendon**, **Ensign**; **Mordock**
Pyne, Francine: Blonde Nancy (Nancy III), "Man Trap, The" (TOS)
Pyper-Ferguson, John: **Hollander**, **Eli**
Pysirr, Geoff: **Hanjuan**

Quinn, Bill: **McCoy, David**
Quinn, Ian: Stunts, *ST:I*

Ragin, John S.: **Christopher**, **Dr.**
Ralston, Stephen: **Larg**
Ramsay, Anne Elizabeth: **Clancy**, **Assistant Engineer**
Ramsey, Logan: **Marcus**, **Claudius**
Ramus, Nick: *Saratoga* helmsman, *ST4*
Randall, Bruce Wayne: Stunts, *ST5*
Randell, Air: Stunts, *ST5*
Rankin, Steve: Cardassian officer, "Emissary" (DS9); **Patahk**; **Yeto**
Ransom, Tim: **Jack**
Rapelye, Mary-Linda: **Galliulin**, **Irina**
Rappaport, Stephen B.: **Motura**
Rasulala, Thalmus: **Varley**, **Captain Donald**
Ravarra, Gina: **Tyler**, **Ensign**
Rawlings, Alice: **Finney**, **Jamie**
Raymond, Guy: Trader/bartender, "Trouble with Tribbles, The" (TOS)
Raymone, Kirk: Cloud Guard #1, "Cloud Minders, The" (TOS); Duur, "Friday's Child" (TOS)
Rayne, Sarah: **Elani**
Rayner, Martin: **Chaotica, Doctor**
Raz, Kavi: **Singh**, **Lieutenant Commander**
Razatos, Spiro: Stunts, *ST:I*
Reason, Rhodes: **Flavius**
Rector, Jeff: Alien #2, "Allegiance" (TNG)
Rector, Jerry: Alien #1, "Allegiance" (TNG)
Reddin, Ian: Security guard, "Menagerie, The Parts I and II" (TOS)
Reddin, Jan: Crewman, "Space Seed" (TOS)
Reddington, Tina: Girl, "Remember" (VGR)
Reece, Gregory: Man in bar, "Spectre of the Gun" (TOS)
Reed, Arlee: Hayseed, "Emergence" (TNG); Waiter, "Starship Mine" (TNG)
Reed, Margaret: **Serova**, **Dr.**
Regehr, Duncan: **Ronin**; **Shakaar Edon**
Reid, Ryan: Transporter technician, "Power Play" (TNG)
Reilly, Don: **Dal**, **Joret**
Reimers, Ed: Fitzpatrick, Admiral, "Trouble with Tribbles, The" (TOS)
Reinhardt, Ray: **Aaron, Admiral**; **Ren**, **Tolan**
Remsen, Bert: **Kubus Oak**
Renan, David: Conn "The Naked Now" (TNG)
Revill, Clive: **Sir Guy of Gisbourne**
Rhue, Madlyn: **McGivers**, **Lieutenant Marla**
Rhys-Davies, John: **da Vinci, Leonardo**
Richardson, Salli Elise: **Fenna**; **Seyetik**, **Nidell**
Richman, Peter Mark: **Offenhouse, Ralph**; Branscombe: Gunner #2, *ST3*
Riddle, Larry: Officer, "Alternative Factor, The" (TOS)
Rider, Michael: Security guard, "Reunion" (TNG); Transporter chief, "Code of Honor" (TNG), "Haven" (TNG) & "Naked Now, The" (TNG)
Ridgeway, Lindsay: **Suspiria**
Riele, Richard: **Batai**
Rigby, T.J.: Stunts, *ST:I*
Rignack, Roger: Miner #2, "Perfect Mate, The" (TNG)
Rio, F.J.: **Muniz**
Riordan, Robert: First guard, "Progress" (DS9); **Rondon**
Rippy, Leon: **Clemonds, Sonny**
Rivers, Victor: **Altovar**
Rizzoli, Tony: **Kainon**
Roarke, Adam: Garrison, C.P.O., and First crewman, "Cage, The" (TOS)
Roberts, Davis: Lewis, "Devil in the Dark, The" (TOS); **Ozaba**
Roberts, Denise Lynne: Stunts, *ST:I*
Roberts, Jeremy: **Valtane, Dmitri**
Roberts, Jerry: **Meso'Clan**
Robie, Wendy: **Ulani Belor**
Robinson, Andrew J.: **Garak**, **Elim**
Robinson, Bumper: Teenage Jem'Hadar, "Abandoned, The" (DS9)
Robinson, Ernest: Stunt, *ST2*
Robinson, Jay: **Petri**
Robinson, Joyce: **Gates, Ensign**
Robinson, Joycelyn: Stunt, *ST6*
Robinson, Rachel: **Melanie**
Robinson, Robby: Stunts, *ST:I*
Robotham, John: Stunts, *ST2*
Rocco, Tony: Klingon crew member, *ST:TMP*
Roccuzzo, Mario: **Malencon**, **Arthur**
Roche, Eugene: **Brel**, **Jor**
Roddenberry, Darlene: Dirty-faced girl in flowered dress, "Miri" (TOS)
Roddenberry, Dawn: Little blond girl, "Miri" (TOS)
Roddenberry, Gene: Galley chef's voice, "Charlie X" (TOS)
Roddenberry, Majel Barrett: SEE: Barrett, Majel.
Rodrigo, Al: **Bernardo**
Rodriguez, Marco: **Rice**, **Captain Paul**; **Telle**, **Glinn**
Rodriguez, Percy: **Stone**, **Commodore**
Roe, Matt: **Latha Mabrin**
Roebuck, Daniel: Romulan #1, "Unification (Parts I and II)" (TNG)
Roeder, Peggy: **Y'Pora**
Rogers, Danny: Stunt, *ST3*, *ST6*, *ST:FC*
Rogers, Elizabeth: **Palmer**, **Lieutenant**; Companion's voice, "Metamorphosis" (TOS)
Rogers, Mic: **Tajor, Glinn**

Rohner, Clayton: **Jameson, Admiral Mark**
Rolston, Mark: **Pierce, Walter J.**
Romano, Jimmy: Stunt, *ST:FC*
Romano, Pat: Stunt, *ST:FC*
Romero, Ned: Krell, "Private Little War, A" (TOS); **Lakanta**
Ron, Tiny: **Maihar'du; Alpha-Hirogen**
Rondell, R. A.: Stunt coordinator, *ST4*, *ST5*
Rondell, Ronald R.: Henchman and Stunt coordinator, *ST:FC*
Root, Stephen: **K'Vada, Captain**
Rose, Christine: **Gi'ral**
Rose, Margot: **Eline**; **Rinn**
Rose, Michael: **Niles**
Rosemond, Nedra: Uhura's stunt double, "Mirror, Mirror" (TOS)
Rosenthal, Lawrence: **Molina, Ensign**
Ross, David: **Galloway, Lieutenant**; Guard, "Return of the Archons" (TOS) & "Trouble with Tribbles, The" (TOS); **Johnson, Lieutenant**; Security guard #1, "Miri" (TOS); Transporter chief, "Galileo Seven, The" (TOS)
Ross, Jane: **Tamoon**
Ross, Peggy Lynn: Stunt, *ST:FC*
Rossilli, Paul: **Kerla**
Rothhaar, Michael: **Garvin**
Rottger, John: Stunt, *ST:FC*
Rougas, Michael: **Cleary**
Rowe, Douglas: **Debin**
Rowe, Stephen: Chanting monk, "Emissary" (DS9)
Royal, Allan G.: **Braxton**
Rubenstein, Phil: 1st garbageman, *ST4*
Rubinek, Saul: **Fajo, Kivas**
Rubinstein, John: **Evansville**
Ruck, Alan: **Harriman, Captain John**
Ruffin, Don: Stunts, *ST6*
Ruginis, Vyto: **Logan, Chief Enigneer**
Ruprecht, David: Radio voice, *ST2*
Ruskin, Joseph: **Galt**; Informant, "Improbable Cause" (DS9); **Tumek**; Son'a Officer #3, *ST:I*
Russ, Tim: **Tuvok**; **Devor**; Lieutenant, *STG*; **T'Kar**
Russell, Mauri: Vulcan bell carrier and Vulcan litter bearer, "Amok Time" (TOS)
Russo, Barry: **Giotto, Lieutenant Commander**; **Wesley, Commodore Robert**
Russom, Leon: Chief in command, *ST6*; **Toddman, Vice Admiral**
Ryan, Jeri: **Seven of Nine**
Ryan, Mitchell: **Riker, Kyle**
Ryan, Tim: **Otner, Dr. Bejal**
Rydbeck, Whitney: **Alans**
Ryder, Alfred: **Crater, Professor**
Ryder, Richard: Bajoran deputy, "Past Prologue" (DS9); Bajoran deputy, "Babel" (DS9)
Ryen, Adam: **Potts, Willie**

Sadler, William: **Sloan**
Sage, David: **Tarmin**
Sage, Willard: **Thann**
Saito, James: **Nogami**
Salaam, Abdul: El Razzac bass player, "11001001" (TNG)
Sale, Irene: Dr. Noel's stunt double, "Dagger of the Mind" (TOS); Louise and Female creature, "Miri" (TOS); Teller's stunt double, "Shore Leave" (TOS)
Salie, Faith C.: **Douglas, Sarina**
Salinger, Diane: **Lupaza**
Salvato, Laura Jane: **Gia**
Sampson, Robert: Sar 6, "Taste of Armageddon" (TOS)
Sanchez, Cuanhtemoc: Bajoran crewman, "Shadows and Symbols" (DS9)
Sandor, Steve: **Lars**
Sarandon, Chris: **Mazur, Martus**
Sargent, William: **Leighton, Dr. Thomas**
Sarlatte, Bob: Waiter, *ST4*
Sarrazin, Michael: **Trevean**
Savidge, Jennifer: **Trentin Fala**
Saviola, Camille: **Opaka, Kai**
Savoye, Dugan: Man, "Eye of the Beholder" (TNG)
Sawaya, George: **Humbolt, Chief**, "Menagerie, The Parts I and II" (TOS); Second soldier, "Errand of Mercy" (TOS)
Saxe, Carl: Korob's stunt double, "Catspaw" (TOS)
Sayre, Jill: Marta, "Abandoned, The" (DS9)
Sbarge, Raphael: **Jonas**
Scarabelli, Michele: **D'Sora, Lieutenant Jenna**
Scarfe, Alan: **Augris**; **Mendak, Admiral; Tokath**
Scarry, Rick: **Jarth**
Schaffer, Sharon: Stunt, *ST4*
Schall, Wendy: **Charlene**
Schallert, William: **Baris, Nilz**; **Varani**
Scharf, Sabrina: **Miramanee**
Schatz, Rick: **Gantt**
Schenker, Wendy: Romulan pilot, "Die Is Cast, The" (DS9)
Schenkkan, Robert: **Remmick, Dexter**
Schiavelli, Vincent: **Peddler**, **Minosian**
Schmidt, Folkert: Doctor, "Contagion" (TNG)
Schmidt, Georgia: 1st Talosian, "Cage, The" (TOS)
Schoener, Reiner: **Esoqq**
Schuck, John: Klingon ambassador, *ST4* & *ST6*; **Parn**
Schultz, Armand: **Dalby, Kenneth**
Schultz, Dwight: **Barclay, Reginald**
Schultz, Joel: Klingon crew member, *ST:TMP*
Scoggins, Tracy: **Gilora Rejal**
Scott, Adam: *Defiant* conn officer, *ST:FC*
Scott, Dennis: Stunts, *ST:I*
Scott, Judson: **Joaquim; Sobi; Rekar**
Scott, Kathryn Leigh: **Nuria**
Scott, Renara: Admiral, "Realm of Fear" (TNG)
Scott, Ted: Eraclitus, "Plato's Stepchildren" (TOS)
Scott, Walter: Cloud guard, "Cloud Minders, The" (TOS)
Scotter, Dick: **Painter, Mr.**
Seago, Howie: **Riva**
Seales, Franklyn: Crew member, *ST:TMP*
Sears, Tony: *Prometheus* officer, "Message in a Bottle" (VGR)
Sebastian, Tom: Warrior, "Shore Leave" (TOS)
Sebek, Michelle: Stunts, *ST:I*
Seel, Charles: Ed, "Spectre of the Gun (TOS)
Seeley, Eileen: **McKenzie**, **Ard'rian**
Segall, Pamala: **Oji**
Selburg, David: **Syrus, Dr.**; **Toscat Whalen**
Selmon, Karole: **Yareena**
Selsby, Harv: Security guard, "Cloud Minders, The" (TOS)
Selznick, Albie: Juggler, "Cost of Living" (TNG); **Tak Tak consul**
Serena, Sande: 2nd Talosian, "Cage, The" (TOS)
Server, Eric: Peace officer, "Circle, The" (DS9)
Seurat, Pilar: **Sybo**
Seymour, Carolyn: **Taris, Subcommander**; **Templeton, Mrs.**; **Toreth Commander, Yale, Mirasta**
Shaffer, Nicholas: Cowl, "Sanctuary" (DS9)
Shakti: ADC, *ST6*
Shangraw, Howard: **Tolar, Grathon**
Shanklin, Douglas Alan: Prison guard #2, *ST3*
Sharp, Eric: Map vendor, "Fair Trade" (VGR)
Shatner, Lizabeth: Blonde girl in red-striped dress, "Miri" (TOS)
Shatner, Melanie: Brunette in black lace dress, "Miri" (TOS); Yeoman, *ST5*
Shatner, William: **Kirk, James T.**; **Lester, Dr. Janice**; Sam Kirk's body, "Operation: Annihilate!" (TOS); **Sargon**, Body of
Shawn, Wallace: **Zek, Grand Nagus**
Shayne, Cari: **Eliann**
Shea, Ann: **Tore, Nellen**
Shea, Christopher: **Keevan**
Shearer, Jack: **Hayes, Admiral**; **Ruwon**; **Strickler, Admiral**; **Vadosia**
Shearman, Alan: **Lestrade, Inspector**
Shegog, Clifford: Klingon officer, *ST6*
Sheldon, Jack: Piano player, "11001001" (TNG)
Shelyne, Carole: **Metron**
Shepard, Hilary: **Hoya**
Shepard-Turner: **Lauren**
Shepherd, Jim: Thelev's stunt double, "Journey to Babel" (TOS)
Shepherd, Mark: **Morn**
Sheppard, W. Morgan: **Graves, Dr. Ira**; Klingon commander, *ST6*
Sherven, Judi: Nurse, "Wolf in the Fold" (TOS)
Shimerman, Armin: **Quark**; **Bractor**; **Letek**; **Lumba**; **Rossoff, Herbert**
Shirriff, Cathie: **Valkris**
Shor, Dan: **Arridor, Dr.**
Shue, Fred: Crewman, "This Side of Paradise" (TOS)
Shuggart, Craig: Stunt, *ST:FC*
Shull, John Kenton: **K'Temang**; **Molor**; Security officer, "Shakaar" (DS9); Kazon, "Basics, Part II." (VGR)
Shutan, Jan: **Romaine, Lieutenant Mira**
Siddig, Alexander (aka El Fadil, Siddig): **Bashir, Dr. Julian**; **Eaton, Julius**
Sierra, Gregory: **Entek**
Sikking, James B.: **Styles, Captain**
Silver, Michael Buchman: **Vinod**
Silver, Spike: Stunts, *ST4*, *ST6*
Silverman, Sarah: **Robinson, Rain**
Simmons, Jean: **Satie, Admiral Norah**
Simms, Lise: Annorax's wife, "Year of Hell, Part II" (VGR)

Simpson, Jonathan: Young Sarek, *ST5*
Sims, Keely: Farmer's daughter, "Caretaker" (VGR)
Sinclair, Madge: Captain, *U.S.S. Saratoga, ST4;* **La Forge, Silva**
Singer, Raymond: Young doctor, *ST4*
Singh, Reginald Lal: Chandra, Captian, "Court Martial" (TOS)
Sirtis, Marina: **Troi, Deanna**
Sisti, Michelan: Tol, "Bloodlines" (TNG)
Sisto, Rocco: **Sakkath**
Skaggs, Jimmie F.: **Boheeka**
Sklar, Paul: Stunts, *ST:I*
Slack, Ben: **K'Tal**
Slater, Christian: *Excelsior* communications officer, *ST6*
Slickner, Roy: Villageer stunt double, "Private Little War, A" (TOS)
Sloyan, James: **Jarok, Alidar**; **Jetrel, Dr. Ma'Bor**; **K'Mtar**; **Mora Pol, Dr.**
Slutsker, Peter: **Birta, DaiMon**; **Nibor**; **Reyga, Dr.**; Krenim commandant, "Year of Hell, Parts I and II" (VGR)
Smallwood, Tucker: **Bullock, Admiral**
Smith, David Lee: **Zahir**
Smith, Eve: Elderly patient, *ST4*
Smith, Frank Owen: **Dax, Curzon**
Smith, Fred G.: Policeman, "High Ground, The" (TNG)
Smith, Greg "Christopher": Male guard, "Nor the Battle to the Strong" (DS9)
Smith, K. L.: Klingon, "Elaan of Troyius" (TOS)
Smith, Kurtwood: **Federation President; Thrax; Annorax**
Smith, Melanie: **Tora Ziyal**
Smith, Michael Bailey: Hanonian, "Basics, Part II" (VGR)
Smith, Mike: Stunts, *ST:I*
Smith, Patricia: **Kingsley, Dr. Sara**
Smith, Sandra: **Lester, Dr. Janice**
Smith, Symba: **Aluura**
Smithers, William: **Merrick, R.M.**
Smitrovich, Bill: **Webb, Michael**
Smolek, Jeff: Stunts, *ST:I*
Snetow, Joel: **Jasad, Gul**
Snow, Norman: **Torin**
Snyder, John: **Bochra, Centurion**; **Conor, Aaron**
Snyder, Michael: **Dax**; **Morta**; **Qol**; Starfleet communications officer, *ST4*
Soble, Ron: **Earp, Wyatt**
Sofaer, Abraham: Melkotian voice, "Spectre of the Gun" (TOS); Thasian, "Charlie X" (TOS)
Solari, Rudy: **Salish**
Sorel, Louise: **Kapec, Rayna**
Sorel, Ted: **Kaval**
Sorensen, Paul: Captain of the merchantship, *ST3*
Sorenson, Cindy: Furry animal, "Dauphin, The" (TNG)
Sorvino, Paul: **Rozhenko, Nikolai**
Soul, David: **Makora**
Spain, Douglas: Young Chakotay, "Tattoo" (VGR)
Sparber, Herschel: **Jaresh-Inyo**
Sparks, Adrian: **Entharan Magistrate**
Sparks, Dana: Williams, "Contagion" (TNG)
Sparks, Frank James: Stunt, *ST3*
Spearman, Doug: Alien buyer, "Concerning Flight" (VGR)
Spellerberg, Lance: **Herbert, Transporter Chief**
Spencer, Jim: Air policeman, "Tomorrow Is Yesterday" (TOS)
Sperberg, Fritz: **Ixtana'Rax**
Spicer, Jerry: Guard, "Time and Again" (VGR)
Spielberg, David: **Hutchinson, Commander Calvin**
Spiner, Brent: **Data**; **Lore**; **Soong, Noonien**
Spound, Michael: **Lorrum**
Sroka, Jerry: **Laxeth**
Stabenau, Eric: Stunts, *STG*
Staggs, Monica: Stunts, *ST:I*
Stapler, Robin: **Alixia**
Stark, Don: **Ashrok**; Nicky the Nose, *ST:FC*
Statier, Mary: Edith's stunt double, "City on the Edge of Forever, The" (TOS)
Staton, Joe: Servant, "QPid" (TNG)
Stauber, Carrie: Female Romulan, "By Inferno's Light" (DS9)
Stavenau, Erik: Stunt, *ST6*
Steele, Karen: **McHuron, Eve**
Steele, Tom: Crew stuntmen, "Alternative Factor, The" (TOS); Stunt slave, "Bread and Circuses" (TOS)
Stein, Mary: **Devidian nurse**
Stein, Ron: Stunt coordinator, *ST3*
Steinberg, Eric: **Porter, Paul**
Stellrecht, Skip: Engineering crewman, "The Naked Now" (TNG)
Stephens, Brooke: **Wildman, Naomi**
Stepp, Laura: **Hansen, Erin**
Steuer, Jon: **Rozhenko, Alexander**
Steven, Carl: **Spock** age 9
Stevens, J.C.: Kes aide, "Attached" (TNG)
Stevens, Warren A.: Stunts, *ST:I*
Stevens, Warren: **Rojan**
Stewart, Charles J.: **Ramart, Captain**
Stewart, Daniel: **Batai** (young)
Stewart, Patrick: **Picard, Jean-Luc; Kamin**
Stiers, David Ogden: **Timicin, Dr.**
Stillwell, Kevin P.: **Moklor**
Stimpson, Viola: Lady in tour, *ST4*
Strang, Deborah: **T'Lara**
Stratton, Albert: **Kushell**
Strickland, Gail: **Alixus**
Strong, Brenda: **Rashella**
Strong, Michael: **Korby, Dr. Roger**
Strozier, Scott: Security officer, *ST:FC*
Struycken, Carel: **Homn**; **Spectre**
Stuart, Eric: Stairway guard, "Past Tense, Part I" (DS9)
Stuart, Norman: **Vulcan Master**
Stuart-Morris, Joan : **T'Pan, Dr.**
Suhor, Yvonne: **Eudana**
Sullivan, Kevin: March, *ST2*
Sullivan, Liam: **Parmen**
Sullivan, Susan J.: Woman, *ST:TMP*
Summers, Jerry: Chekov's stunt double, "Trouble with Tribbles, The" (TOS); Green's stunt double, "Savage Curtain, The" (TOS)
Supera, Max: **Supera, Patterson**
Surovy, Nicholas: **Pe'Nar Makull**
Susskind, Steve: Pitchman, *ST5*
Swanson, Jandi: Katie, "When the Bough Breaks" (TNG)
Swedberg, Heidi: **Rekelen**
Swetow, Joel: **Gorta; Jasad, Gul**
Swift, Joan: **Kirk, Aurelan**
Swink, Kitty: Vayna, "Sanctuary" (DS9)
Symonds, Robert: **Porta, Vedek**
Takaki, Russell: Madison, *ST2*
Takei, George: **Sulu, Hikaru**
Talbert, Woody: Crewman, "Naked Time, The" (TOS)
Tallman, Patricia: **Kiros**; Stunt, *STG;* **Tagana;** Weapons officer, "Way of the Warrior, The" (DS9)
Tarbuck, Barbara: **Leka, Governor Trion**
Tarrant, Newell: CDO, *ST4*
Tarver, Milt: Scientist, "Time's Arrow, Part I" (TNG)
Tate, Nick: **Dirgo; Bilby, Liam**
Tatro, Richard: **Norman**
Taubman, Tiffany: **Tressa**
Tayback, Victor: **Krako, Jojo**
Taylor, Deborah: Zaheva, "Night Terrors" (TNG)
Taylor, Dendrie: **Farrell, Lieutenant**
Taylor, Keith: Jahn's friend, "Miri" (TOS)
Taylor, Mark L.: **Haritath; Jarleth**
Taylor, Ron: Klingon chef, "Melora" (DS9); Klingon host, "Playing God" (DS9)
Teague, Marshall: **Temo'Zuma; Haluk**
Templeman, S. A.: Bates, "Defector, The" (TNG)
Tempoya, John: **Nozawa**
Tentindo, Charles: **Jimenez**
Thatcher, Kirk: Punk on bus, *ST4*
Thatcher, Torin: **Marphon**
Thomas, Craig: Klingon crew member, *ST:TMP*
Thomas, Freyda: **Alenis Grem**
Thomas, Jr., William: **Santos**
Thomas, Sharon: Waitress in the bar, *ST3*
Thompson, Brian: **Klag**; Klingon helm, *STG*; **Toman'torax; Inglatu**; Klingon second officer, "A Matter of Honor" (TNG)
Thompson, Garland: 2nd Crewman, "Charlie X" (TOS); **Wilson, Transporter Technician**
Thompson, Scott: **Goss, DaiMon**
Thompson, Susanna: **Jaya; Kahn, Dr. Lenara**; **Varel**
Thor, Cameron: **Narik**
Thorley, Ken: **Mot**; Seaman, "Time's Arrow, Part I" (TNG)
Thorne, Dyanne: First girl, "Piece of the Action, A" (TOS)
Thornton, Maureen and Colleen: **Barbara series**
Thornton, Noley: **Sutter, Clara**; **Taya**
Thorson, Linda: **Ocett, Gul**
Thrett, Maggie: **Ruth**
Throne, Malachi: Keeper's voice, "Cage, The" (TOS); **Mendez, Commodore José**; **Pardek, Senator**
Tierney, Lawrence: **Redblock, Cyrus**; **Regent of Palamar**
Tiffe, Angelo: *Excelsior* navigator, *ST6*
Tigar, Kenneth: **Dammar**
Timoney, Mike: Electronic technician, *ST4*
Tinapp, Barton: Talaxian, "Faces" (VGR)
Tippo, Patti: Temple, Nurse, "Transfigurations" (TNG)
Tobey, Kenneth: **Rurigan**
Tobin, Mark: **Joaquin**; Klingon, "Day of the Dove" (TOS)
Tochi, Brian: **Lin, Ensign Peter**; **Tsingtao, Ray**
Todd, Hallie: **Lal**
Todd, Shay: Holowoman, "Alter Ego" (VGR)

Todd, Tony: **Kurn**; Sisko, Jake (older), "Visitor, The" (DS9); **Alpha-Hirogen**
Todoroff, Tom: **Darod**
Tomei, Concetta: **Odala, Minister**
Tompkins, Paul: **Brevelle, Ensign**
Torsek, Dierk: **Bernard**, **Dr. Harry, Sr.**
Toussaint, Beth: **Yar**, **Ishara**
Towers, Constance: **Taxco**
Towers, Robert: **Rata**
Towey, John: **Ossan, Vedek**
Towles, Tom: **Hon'Tihl**; **Vatm, Dr.**
Townes, Harry: **Reger**
Townsend, Barbara: **Rossa**, **Admiral Connaught**
Townsend, Sherri: Crew woman, "Tomorrow Is Yesterday" (TOS)
Toyota, Vic: Sulu's stunt double, "Catspaw" (TOS)
Tracy, Dennis: Man in gray flannel suit, "Emergence" (TNG)
Traicoff, Amy: **T'Pera**
Trainor, Saxon: **Larson**, **Lieutenant Linda**
Trella, Tim: **Palmer, Dr.**; stunts, *ST:I*
Trost, Scott: Bajoran officer, "Man Alone, A" (DS9); Ensign, "Unnatural Selection" (TNG); Shipley, Lieutenant, "Schisms" (TNG)
Trotta, Ed: **Pit**
Troupe, Tom: Harold, Lieutenant, "Arena" (TOS)
True, Garrison: Crewman guard #1, "Man Trap, The" (TOS)
Tsu, Irene: Harry's mother, "Favorite Son" (VGR)
Tubert, Marcello: **Jared**, **Acost**
Tung, Jennifer: Female Ensign, *ST:I*
Turner, Kirsten: **Goodheart, Constance**
Turpin, Bahni: **Swinn, Ensign**
Tyler, Nikki: **Hansen, Erin**

Udy, Hêlen: **Pel**
Union, Gabrielle: **N'Garen**

Valenza, Tasia: **T'Shanik**
Valk, Blair: Risian woman, "Let He Who Is Without Sin" (DS9)
Van Dam, Gwen: El-Aurian survivor, *STG*
Van Valkenburgh, Deborah: **Preston**, **Detective**
Van Zandt, Billy: Alien boy, *ST:TMP*
Vandenecker, Beau: Sam, "Charlie X" (TOS)
Vardaman, Guy: **Wallace, Darian**
Vargas, John: Jedda, *ST2;* **Tau**
Vassey, Liz: **Kristin**
Vaughn, Ned: **Zweller**, **Cortin**
Vaughn, Reese: **Latimer**, **Lieutenant**
Vaught, Steve: Officer, "Time and Again" (VGR)
Vawter, Nancy: **Blackwell**, **Admiral Margaret**
Velasco, Vladimir: **T'su**, **Tan**
Venton, Harley: **Collins, Ensign; Hutchinson**, **Transporter Chief**
Vereen, Ben: **La Forge**, **Doctor Edward M.**
Vernon, Harvey: **Belar, Yolad**
Vernon, Kate: **Archer, Valerie**
Veto, Ron: Eminiar guard and technician, "Taste of Armageddon" (TOS); Security guard, "Alternative Factor, The" (TOS)
Vickery, John: **Hagen**, **Andrus**
Victor, Theresa E.: Bridge voice, *ST2*; *Enterprise* computer voice, *ST3*; Usher, *ST4*
Vignon, Jean-Paul: **Edouard**
Villard, Tom: **Bek**, **Prylar**
Vince, Frank: **Daily, Jon (voice)**
Vinci, Frank: Crew stuntman, "Alternative Factor, The" (TOS); Eminiar guard and technician, "Taste of Armageddon" (TOS); Kirk's stunt double, "Catspaw" (TOS); Spock's stunt double, "Galileo Seven, The" (TOS); Stunt double, "Cage, The" (TOS); Vulcan bell carrier, "Amok Time" (TOS)
Vinovich, Steve: **Joseph**
Virgo, Jr., Peter: **Lumo**
Virtue, Tom: **Baxter**, **Lieutenant**
Visitor, Nana: **Kira Nerys; Eaton, Kay; Comananov, Anastasia; Chrystal, Lola**
Vogt, Peter: Romulan commander, "Tin Man" (TNG); "Man Alone, A" (DS9); Commandant, "Nemesis" (VGR)
Von Franckenstein, Clement: Gentleman, "Ship in a Bottle" (TNG)
Voorhies, Lark: **Leanne**
Vosburgh, Marcy: Computer voice, *ST2*

Wagner, Lou: **Krax; Solok, DaiMon**
Wagner, Mark: Stunts, *ST:I*
Wagrowsky, Greg: **Solok**
Walberg, Garry: **Hansen**, **Commander**
Walker, Jr., Robert: **Evans**, **Charles**
Wallace, Basil: Klingon guard #1, "Reunion" (TNG)
Wallace, George D.: Simon, Admiral, "Man of the People" (TNG)
Wallace, William A.: Crusher, Wes (25 years old), "Hide and Q" (TNG)
Waller, Philip N.: **Bernard**, **Harry, Jr.**
Walsh, Gwynyth: **B'Etor; Nimira**
Walston, Ray: **Boothby**
Walter, Tracey: **Berik**; Kayron, "Last Outpost, The" (TNG)
Walters, Marvin: Troglyte, "Cloud Minders, The" (TOS)
Wang, Garrett: **Kim, Harry**
Warburton, John: **Centurion**
Ware, Herta: **Picard, Yvette Gessard**
Warhit, Doug: **Kazago**
Waring, Todd: **DeCurtis**, **Ensign; Lasaran**
Warner, David: **Gorkon**, **Chancellor**; **Madred**, **Gul**; **Talbot**, **St. John**
Warner, Julie: **Henshaw**, **Christi**
Washburn, Beverly: **Galway**, **Arlene**
Washington, Kenneth: **Watkins, John B.**
Washington, Kim: Stunt, *ST2*
Washlake, Mike: Stunt, *ST2*
Wasson, Craig: **Ee'Char**
Wasson, Susanne: **Lethe**
Watkins, James Louis: **Hagon**
Watson, Bruce: **Green**, **Crewman**
Watson, Jennifer: Stunts, *ST:I*
Wayton, Gary: Stunts, *ST:I*
Weaver, Fritz: **Kovat**
Webb, Richard: **Finney**, **Ben**
Weber, Barbara: Dancing woman, "Return of the Archons" (TOS)
Weber, Paul: **Vulcan Master**
Weber, Steven: **Day**, **Colonel**
Webster, Derek: Sanders, Lieutenant, "Gambit, Part I" (TNG)
Webster, Joan: Nurse, "Space Seed (TOS)
Weigand, Jon David: Borg, *ST:FC*
Weiner, Andreana: **Troi**, **Kestra**
Weiss, Erick: Crew member, "Conundrum" (TNG); Kane, Ensign, "Relics" (TNG); **Stephan**
Welch, Michael: **Artim**
Welker, Frank: Spock screams (voice), *ST3*
Wellman, James: **Starnes**, **Professor**
Wellman, Jr., William: Bajoran officer, "Favor the Bold" (DS9)
Werntz, Gary: **Mavek**
Wert, Doug: **Crusher**, **Jack**
Westmore, McKenzie: Ba'ku Woman, *ST:I*
Weston, Brad: **Appel**, **Ed**
Wetterman, Tom: Stunts, *ST5*
Wheaton, Wil: **Crusher**, **Wesley**
Wheeler, Ellen: **Ekoria**
Wheeler, John: **Gav**
Whinery, Webster: Stunts, *ST:I*
White, Bridget Ann: **Larell**
White, Callan: **Krite**
White, Diz: Prostitute, "Elementary, Dear Data" (TNG)
White, Logan: **Batai** (young)
White, Peter: **Sharat**
Whiting, Arch: Assistant engineering officer, "Alternative Factor, The" (TOS)
Whitman, Parker: Cardassian officer, "Emissary" (DS9)
Whitney, Grace Lee: **Rand**, **Janice**; Woman in cafeteria, *ST3*
Whitney, Michael: **Tyree**
Whittaker, S.: Gunslinger, "Emergence" (TNG)
Wiedergott, Karl: **Ameron**
Wiedlin, Jane: Alien communications officer, *ST4*
Wiggins, Barry: Policeman, "Future's End" (VGR); Jem'Hadar officer, "By Inferno's Light" (DS9)
Wilbur, George: Stunts, *ST2*
Wilcox, Lisa: **Yuta**
Wilder, Glenn R.: Stunt coordinator, *ST5*
Wilder, Scott: Stunts, *ST5*
Wildman, Valerie: **Nevala**
Wiley, Edward: **Toran**, **Gul**; **Vagh**
Williams III, Clarence: **Omet'iklan**
Williams, Barbara: **Anna**
Williams, Brian J.: Stunt, *ST:FC; ST:I*
Williams, Cress: **Talak'talan**, **Third**
Williams, Darlene: Stunts, *ST:I*
Williams, Davida: **Lisa**
Williams, Justin: **Jarvin**
Williams, R.J.: **Troi**, **Ian Andrew (II)**
Williams, Spice: **Vixis**
Williams, Vanessa: **Arandis**
Williams, Wade: **Lo-Tarik**, **Trajis**
Williams, Zachary: Ba'ku child, *ST:I*
Williamson, Fred: Anka, "Cloud Minders, The" (TOS)
Willingham, Noble: Texas, "Royale, The" (TNG)
Willis, Marron E.: Klingon guard #2, "Reunion" (TNG); **Rettik**
Willrich, Rudolph: Bollan, Commandant, "Paradise Lost" (DS9); **Grax**, **Reittan**
Wilson, Debra: **Cusak, Captain Lisa**

Wilson, Tamara and Starr: **Maisie series**
Windom, William: **Decker**, **Commodore Matt**
Winfield, Paul: **Dathon**; **Terrell**, **Captain Clark**
Wingreen, Jason: **Linke**, **Dr.**
Winkler, Mel: **Hayes, Jack**
Winslow, Pamela: **McKnight**, **Ensign**
Winston, John: Argelian bartender, "Wolf in the Fold" (TOS); Computer voice, "Mirror, Mirror" (TOS); **Kyle**, **Mr.**; Transporter chief, "City on the Edge of Forever, The" (TOS) & "Wolf in the Fold" (TOS); Transporter technician, "Space Seed" (TOS)
Winters, Tim: **Daro**, **Glinn**
Wintersole, William: **Abrom**
Wirt, Kathleen: Aphasia victim, "Babel" (DS9)
Wise, Ray: **Liko; Arturis**
Wolf, Venita: **Ross**, **Yeoman Teresa**
Wolfchild, Sheldon P.: **Falling Hawk**, **Joe**
Wolfe, Ian: **Atoz**, **Mr.**; **Septimus**
Wong, Nancy: Personnel officer, "Court Martial" (TOS)
Wood, Laura: **Johnson**, **Elaine**; Old lady, "Charlie X" (TOS)
Woodard, Alfre: **Sloane, Lily**
Woods, Barbara Alyn: **Brianon**, **Kareen**
Woods, D. Elliot: Klingon officer, "Sons of Mogh" (DS9); Starfleet officer, *ST:I*
Woods, Grant: **Kelowitz**, **Lieutenant Commander**
Woodville, Kate: **Natira**
Woodward, Morgan: **Tracey**, **Captain Ronald**; **Van Gelder**, **Dr. Simon**
Worden, Marc: **Rozhenko, Alexander**
Woren, Dan: Borg, *ST:FC*
Woronicz, Henry: **J'Dan; Gegen, Forra; Quarren**
Worth, Nicholas: **Lissepian captain**; **Sorm**
Worthy, James: **Koral**
Worthy, Rick: **Cravic 122** and **3947; Kornan;** Elloran Officer #1, *ST:I*
Wright, Bruce: **Sarish**
Wright, Gary: Vulcan litter bearer, "Amok Time" (TOS)
Wright, Tom: **Tuvix**
Wyatt, Al: Lazarus's stunt doubles, "Alternative Factor, The" (TOS)
Wyatt, Jane: **Amanda**
Wyllie, Meg: **Keeper, The**

Yansik, Eddie: Stunts, *ST:I*
Yarnall, Celeste: **Landon**, **Yeoman Martha**
Yashima, Momo: Crew member, *ST:TMP*
Yasutake, Patti: **Ogawa**, **Nurse Alyssa**
Yeager, Biff: **Argyle**, **Lieutenant Commander**
Young, Dey: **Bates**, **Hannah**; **Arissa**
Young, Keone: **Bokai**, **Buck**
Young, Melissa: **Caprice**
Young, Ray: **Morka**
Young, Tony: **Kryton**
Youngblut, Nancy: **Taleen**
Yount, Dell: **Tilikia**
Yulin, Harris: **Marritza**, **Aamin**

Zacapa, Daniel: **Garcia**, **Henry**
Zachar, Robert L.: Borg, *STFC*; Head guard, "Apocalypse Rising" (DS9)
Zandarski, Grace: **Latara, Ensign**.
Zanuck, D.: Flapper, "Emergence" (TNG)
Zaslow, Michael: **Darnell**, **Crewman**; **Jordan**, **Ensign**
Zautcke, 1st Lt. Donald W., USMC: Marine lieutenant, *ST4*
Zeller, Sam: **Ch'Targh**
Zellitti, David: Stunt, *ST3*
Zenga, Bo: **Asoth**
Zerbe, Anthony: **Dougherty, Admiral Matthew**
Zerbst, Brad: Medical technician, "Justice" (TNG); Nurse, "Heart of Glory" (TNG) & "Skin Of Evil" (TNG)
Ziesmer, Jillian: Asha, "Cardassians" (DS9)
Ziker, Dick: Stunt, *ST5*
Zimmerman, Christian: **Lamat'Ukan**
Zobel, Jr., Richard J.: **Gauman**
Zuckert, Bill: Behan, Johnny, "Spectre of the Gun" (TOS)

PRODUCTION PERSONNEL

This is a list of production personnel and contractors from the *Star Trek* television episodes and feature films who have received on screen credit for their work. It should be noted that even though this is an imposing list, there are even more people who have made significant contributions to these projects who, for reasons of screen time, don't get credited, and therefore aren't listed here. This unfortunately, includes a lot of regular production crew personnel who work (or have worked) full-time on these projects. Suffice it to say that it takes a lot of hard work from a *lot* of people to make the *Star Trek* universe come to life.

Abaravich, Patric J.: Asst chief lighting tech, *ST:I*
Abascal, Paul: Add'l hairstylist, *ST3*
Abascal, Silvia: Hair stylist, *ST3, ST4*
Abatemarco, Frank: Superv prod-writer, *TNG*
Abbott, Chris: Writer, *VGR*
Acosta, Tom: Greensperson, *ST:I*
Acquistapace, Romolo: Gaffer, *ST2*
Adams, Stanley: Writer, *TOS*
Adamson, Joe: DGA Trainee, *ST4*
Adelman, Ruth: Sound editor, *TNG*, *DS9*, *VGR*
Aerotech, Inc.: Rocket propulsion, *STG*
Affonso, Barbara: Chief modelmaker, *ST:FC*
Agalsoff, John: Cable person, *ST:FC*
Agalsoff, Greg: Boom operator, *VGR*
Agha, Alia Alemeida: Visual effects coord, *STG;* Prod asst, *ST6*
Agriculture, Dept of, Inyo National Forest: Thanks to, *ST:I*
Ahern, Terry: Craft service, *ST2, DS9*
Aiello, Jaremy: Borg key sculptor, *ST:FC*
Ainsworth, Alfred: Video playback operator, *ST:I*
Akela Crane: Special thanks, *STG*
Alagna, John: Senior optical layout, *ST5*
Alaska Film Commission: Special thanks, *ST6*
Alaska Helicopter Company: Special thanks, *ST6*
Alba, Frederick G.: Visual effects assoc, *TNG*, *VGR*
Albright, Larry: Photographic props and miniatures, *ST:TMP, TNG, DS9*
Albucher, Aaron M.: Art dept prod asst, *ST6*
Alder, Alan J.: Writer, *TNG*
Alexander, David: Dir, *TOS*
Alexander, Dick: Mechanical design, *ST:TMP*
Alexander, Gary: Re-recording mixer, *ST5*
Alexander, Jan: Special makeup artist, *ST5*
Alexander, Janice R.: Hair stylist, *ST6*
Alexander, Jim: Sound mixer, *ST2*
Alexander, Jon: Optical camera operator, *ST6*
Alexander, Tim: Digital compositor, *ST:FC*
Alias/Wavefront Technologies: Software support, *ST:I*
Allan, Denny: Horse wrangler, *STG*
Allen, Corey: Dir, *TNG, DS9;* Writer, *TNG*
Allwine, Wayne, MPSE: Sound effects editor, *ST5*
Alonzo, John A., ASC: Dir of photography, *STG*
Alton, Andrea Moore: Writer, *DS9*
Amblin Imaging: Computer generated effects, *VGR*
Ambrose, Miles: Electrical tech, *ST5*
American Humane Association: Animal action supervision, *ST:FC*, *ST:I*
Amos, Gregory: Writer, *TNG*
Amundson, Peter: Effects editor, *ST2*
Anderson, Daryl: Optical effects, *TOS*
Anderson, Erik: First camera asst, *TOS*
Anderson, James: Set security, *VGR*
Anderson, Mark: Modelmaker, *STG*
Anderson, Richard L.: Superv sound editor, *ST:TMP*
Anderson, Rick: Modelmaker, *ST:FC;* Whale mechanical designer, *ST4*
Anderson, Scott: Computer graphics animator, *ST6*
Andrew-Tunstall, Brian: Hair stylist, *DS9*
Andrews, Bunny: Music editor, *ST6*
Andrews, Susan Kelly: Digital rotoscope and paint, *ST:FC*
Angelson, Eric: Visual effects coord, *ST5*
Apogee, Inc.: Photographic effects sequences, *ST:TMP*
Apperson, Mike: Labor foreperson, *ST6*
Apple Computer Company: Special thanks, *ST4, ST5*
Apter, Harold: Writer, *TNG*
Arakelian, Deborah: Asst to the prods, *ST2*; Prod asst, *ST3*
Argus, Camille: Wardrobe superv, *DS9*, *VGR;* Costumer, *TNG*, *STG*
Arizona State Film Commission: Thanks for assistance, *ST:FC*
Arko, Elisabeth: I/O support, *ST:I*
Arlen, Harold: Music, *ST3*
Armen, Margaret: Writer, *TOS*
Arms, Barbara: Asst choreographer, *ST3*
Armstorff, Roland: Prod asst, *ST6*
Armstrong, Brian: First asst photographer, *ST:I*
Armstrong, Eric: Computer graphics animator, *ST6*
Armus, Burton: Prod-writer, *TNG*
Arnesson, Joakim: Digital effects artist, *ST:FC*
Arnold, Richard: Research consultant, *TNG*
Arnold-Ince, Kasey: Writer, *TNG*
Aroeste, Jean Lisette: Writer, *TOS*
Aron, Joel: Computer graphics artist, *STG*
Arp, Thomas J.: Construction coord, *DS9*, *STG, ST:FC*, *ST:I*
Arroyo Seco Ranger District: Thanks for assistance, *ST:FC*
Arroyo, Sam "I Am": Craft service, *ST:I*
Arthurs, Bruce D.: Writer, *TNG*
Asano-Myers, Karen: Hair stylist, *VGR*
Aschkynazo, Caleb: Digital editorial coord, *ST:FC*
Asimov, Isaac: Special science consultant, *ST:TMP*
Asmen, Bill: Camera operator, *DS9*
Assael, David: Writer, *TNG*
Assmus, Carl: Grip, *STG*
Assocs & Ferren: Special visual effects prod, *ST5*
Atlantic Records and Tapes: Original soundtrack album, *ST2*
Atmajian, Jeff: Orchestrations, *ST:FC*
Au, Keneth: Lead compositor, *ST:I*
Aubel, Joe: Art dir, *ST4*
Auberjonois, Rene: Dir, *DS9*
Austin, Jean: Hair styles, *TOS*
Austin, Scott: Recordist, *ST5*
Ayer, Edward A.: Special effects, *ST2*

B/G Engineering: Optical and mechanical consultant, *ST:TMP*
Baber, Keith: Chief rigging electrician *ST6*
Babin, John D.: Rigging grip, *ST:FC*
Bachelin, Franz: Art dir, *TOS*
Bacho, Jr., Thomas D.: Borg crew, *ST:FC*
Backauskas, Michael: Visual effects superv, *TNG;* Visual effects coord, *DS9, VGR;* Special editorial, *ST:TMP*
Badami, Robert: Music editor, *ST2*, *ST3*
Baden, Shawn: Scenic artist, *ST:FC*
Baden, Sigfried C.: Recorder, *TOS*
Bader, Hilary J.: Writer, *TNG*, *DS9*, *VGR*
Badiyi, Reza: Dir, *DS9*
Baer, Rhonda: Location mgr, *ST6*
Bagdadi, Suzan: Hair designer, *VGR*
Baiardi, Valerie: Effects animator, *ST5*
Bailey, Bob: Visual effects superv, *DS9*
Bailey, Charlie: Modelmaker, *STG*
Bailey, Dennis Putman: Writer, *TNG*
Bailey, Dennis Russell: Writer, *TNG*
Bailey, Robert D.: Visual effects superv, *VGR*
Baillargeon, Paul: Music, *DS9*, *VGR*
Baker, Don: Photographic effects cameraman, *ST:TMP*
Baker, Gordan: Animation effects animator, *ST6*
Balcer, Rene: Writer, *TNG*
Baldo, Mark: Digital animation superv, *ST:I*
Baldwin, Bill: Asst ADR editor, *ST:I*
Ballas, James E., ACE: Film editor, *TOS*
Banks, Bobbi: ADR editor, *ST6*
Bar-David, S: Writer, *TOS*
Barbee, Chuck: Photographic effects cameraman, *ST:TMP*
Barbee, Stewart: Camera operator, *ST2*
Barberio, Philip: Visual effects superv, *TNG*, *VGR;* Visual effects series coord, *TNG*, *DS9;* Photographic effects cameraman, *ST:TMP*
Barbier, Larry: Still photographer, *TOS*
Barcroft, Lloyd: First company grip, *ST:FC*, *ST:I*
Bard, Dale: Tech advisor, *ST5*
Bard, Patrick: Grip, *ST:I*
Barker, Lynn: Writer, *DS9*
Barnes, Sheila: Prod office coord, *ST6*
Baron, Bob: ADR mixer, *ST6*, *STG, ST:FC*, *ST:I*
Baron, Michael: Writer, *TNG*
Barr, Bill: Key grip, *ST:FC*

Barraza, Alex: Rigging first company grip, *ST:I*
Barrett, Tom: Visual effects editor, *ST:I*
Barron, Craig: Visual effects superv, *ST:FC;* Superv matte photographer, *ST4, ST6;* Matte camera superv, *ST3*; Matte photography asst, *ST2*
Barron, Eddie: Hair stylist, *TNG*
Barron, Tom: Motion control system design (Image G), *TNG, DS9, VGR*
Barry, Kevin F.: Prod asst, *ST4*
Barry, Patricia: Asst prod, *ST5*
Barry, Patrick: Writer, *TNG*
Bartholomew, David: Photographic effects editorial, *ST:TMP*
Bartle, John: Editor, *STG*
Bartlett, Ron: Foley editor, *ST5*
Barton, Mary Ann: Casting, *ST3*
Base Gamma Electronic Systems: Special thanks, *ST5*
Baskin, Daryl: Editor, *TNG, VGR*
Bates, Ken: Highest descender fall recorded in the United States, *ST5*
Bauer, Joe: Visual effects superv, *TNG, VGR*; Visual effects coord, *TNG*
Bauer, Mike: Digital effects artist, *ST:FC*
Baum, Nick: Computer engineering, *ST5*
Baum, Steven: Writer, *DS9*
Baxter, Deborah: Assistance to photographic effects, *ST:TMP*
Baxter, Michael: 2nd asst dir, *DS9*
Bayard, Richard J.: Construction coord, *DS9, ST4, ST5, ST6*
Bayard, Ted: Prod asst, *ST:I*
Bayliss, James: Set designer, *ST4*
Beach, Dugan: Computer graphics tech asst, *ST:FC*
Beagle, Peter S.: Writer, *TNG*
Beaird, Ben: First company grip, *ST6*
Bean, Randall K.: Scanning, *ST6*
Bear, Jack: Wardrobe, *ST:TMP*
Beasley, David: Effects props and miniatures, *ST:TMP*
Beaumont, Gabrielle: Dir, *TNG, DS9*
Beazlie, Kimon: Wardrobe, *ST2*
Bechtold, Lisze: Animation and graphics, *ST:TMP*
Beck, Don: Produced promotion commercials, *DS9, TNG*
Beck, Mat: Electronic design, *ST:TMP*
Beck, Richard: Asst property master, *ST6*
Beck, William: Modelmaker, *ST3*
Becker, Martin: Special effects, *ST2*
Becker, Robert: Dir, *TNG*
Beeler, Kathleen: Digital compositor, *ST:FC;* Rotoscope artist, *ST6*
Behr, Ira Steven: Exec prod-writer, *DS9;* Prod-writer, *TNG;* Thanks for assistance, *ST:FC*
Beichman, Dr. Charles A.: Scientific advisor, *ST5*
Beimler, Hans: Superv prod-writer, *DS9;* Co-prod-exec script consultant-story editor-writer, *TNG*
Bekoff, Matt: Set designer, *DS9*
Belanoff, Adam: Writer, *TNG*
Bell, Bruce E.: Sound editor, *ST6*
Bell, David: Music, *DS9, VGR*
Bell, John: Storyboard artist, *ST4*
Bell, Jr., Cliff: Loop editor, *ST2*
Bellis, Richard: Music, *DS9*
Belt, Bill: Property person, *STG*
Benavente, Michael J.: Sound effects editor, *ST4, ST5*
Benefiel, Mona Thal: Asst to Mr. Trumbull, *ST:TMP*
Benko, Tom, ACE: Dir-editor, *TNG;* Editor-writer, *DS9;* Editor, *VGR*
Bennes, Adam: Effects tech, *ST:FC*
Bennett, Christopher E.: Apprentice film editor, *ST5*
Bennett, Dennis: Digital compositor, *ST:I*
Bennett, Harve: Exec prod-writer, *ST2;* Prod-writer, *ST3, ST4, ST5*
Bennett, Yudi: First asst dir, *STG*
Bensmiller, Kurt Michael: Writer, *TNG, DS9*
Bentkowski, Pamela: Superv foley editor, *STG, ST:FC;* Foley editor, *ST3*
Bentley, Gary F.: Special effects, *ST2*
Bento, Scott: Prod intern, *ST6*
Berger, Lee: Senior staff (VIFX), *ST:I*
Berger, Peter E., ACE: Editor, *ST4, ST5, STG, ST:I*
Berger, Richard: Set designer, *ST4*
Bergeron, Elza: Casting, *ST3*
Bergin, Jil-Sheree: Visual effects coord, *ST6*
Bergman, Charlene: Asst to Mr. Bennett, *ST5*
Bergman, Christopher D.: Lead compositor, *ST:I*
Bergman, Cliff: Construction foreperson, *ST6*
Berlatsky, David: Editor, *TNG*
Berlioz, Hector: "Vallon Sonore" from Les Troyens, *ST:FC*
Berman, Rick: Creator-exec prod-writer *DS9, VGR;* Exec prod-writer, *TNG;* Prod-writer, *STG, ST:FC, ST:I*
Bernard, Alan, CAS: Sound mixer, *TNG, VGR*
Bernay, S.J. Casey: Scenic artist, *VGR;* (This appendix compiled by)
Berndt-Shackelford, Bethany: Digital paint artist, *ST:FC*
Bernheim, Robin: Writer, *TNG*
Berry, David: Optical line-up, *ST3;* Optical printer operator, *ST2*
Berry, Greg: Set designer, *VGR*
Bertazzon, Kevin Adunio: 3D animator, *ST:I*
Berti, Thane: Photographic effects photography, *ST:TMP*
Bertino, Thomas: Rotoscope superv, *ST6*
Berton, John: Computer graphics animator, *ST6*
Bettcher, Al: Camera operator, *ST:TMP*
Bettis, John: Music, *ST5*
Betts, Benjamin A.: Video playback operator, *VGR;* Video engineer, *ST:FC;* superv video engineer, *ST:I*
Betts, James H.: Prod painter, *ST5*
Betts, Tom: Set designer, *DS9*
Beyer, Earl: Scanning operator, *ST:FC*
Beyers, John: Asst chief lighting techs, *ST6*
Biagio, Chuck: Best boy grip, *ST:FC*
Biddiscombe, Carl F.: Set decorator, *TOS*
Biggins, Joe: Visual effects camera asst, *STG*
Biggs, Judy: Prod asst, *ST5*
Biklian, Andrea: Negative line-up, *ST:FC*
Biller, Kenneth: Prod-exec story editor-writer-dir, *VGR*
Billinger, III, George J.: Camera operator/steadicam, *STG*
Bilog, Michael: Asst accountant, *ST:I*
Bingham, J. Michael.: Writer, *TNG*
Binion, Earl: Set security, *DS9*
Binyon, Jr., Claude: Asst dir, *TOS*
Birdsong, Odi: Optical scanning dept prod asst, *ST:FC*
Birmelin, Bruce: Still photographer, *ST2, ST4, ST5*
Birnie, Cameron: Set designer, *ST3*
Bischoff, David: Writer, *TNG*
Bishop, Bruce: Effects props and miniatures, *ST:TMP*
Bissell, Jim: Special thanks, *ST5*
Bissett, Russ: Driver captain, *TOS*
Bixby, Alison Gail: Key costumer, *TNG*
Bixby, Jerome: Writer, *TOS*
Black, Donald T.: Special effects asst, *ST:FC, ST:I*
Black, John D. F.: Assoc prod-story editor-writer, *TOS;* Writer, *TNG*
Blackman, Robert: Costume designer, *TNG, DS9, VGR, STG*; Starfleet uniforms designer, *ST:FC, ST:I*
Blanchard, Malcolm: Computer database management, *ST2*
Blangsted, Else: Superv music editor, *ST4*
Blau Prince, Patricia: ILM senior staff, *ST:FC;* Exec in charge of prod, *STG*
Blevins, Cha: Key costumer, *TNG*
Bloch, Lisa A.: Prod asst, *STG*
Bloch, Robert: Writer, *TOS*
Blom, Harry: Borg crew, *ST:FC*
Blue Sky/VIFX: Visual effects by, *ST:I*
Blymyer, Michael: Lighting tech, *ST:I*
Blymyer, Patrick R.: Chief lighting tech, *ST:FC, ST:I*
Board, Timothy: Add'l editing, *ST:FC*
Boccio, Frank Del: First asst photographer, *ST6*
Bogart, Rodney: Computer graphics software, *ST:FC*
Boisseau, Solange Schwalbe: Foley editor, *ST5*
Bole, Cliff: Dir, *TNG, DS9, VGR*
Bolger, Cosmos: Photographic effects photography, *ST:TMP*
Bolivar, Robert J.: Writer, *DS9*
Bonchune, Rob: CGI supervisor, *VGR*
Bond, Ed: Writer, *VGR*
Bond, Timothy: Dir, *TNG*
Bonnem, Christine: Location mgr, *STG*
Bono, Jerry: Key costumer, *TNG, DS9*
Bookout, Tom: Grip, *VGR*
Borden, Destiny: Asst editor, *ST4;* asst sound editor, *ST5*
Bordonaro, Rita: Hair stylist, *TNG*
Borggrebe-Taylor, Patti: Key costumer, *DS9*
Bormanis, Andre: Science consultant, *TNG, DS9;* Science consultant-writer, *VGR;* Technical consultant, *ST:FC, ST:I*
Bornstein, Bob: Music preparation, *ST6, STG, ST:FC*
Bosché, Mary Ellen: Key costumer, *TNG, DS9*
Boston University: Geometric designs, *ST:TMP*
Botnick, Bruce: Music recorded and mixed by, *ST:FC, ST:I;* Music scoring mixer, *ST5*
Botsford, Diana Dru: Writer, *TNG*
Botsford, Ward: Writer, *TNG*
Bouchez, Kevin: Visual effects animator, *DS9, VGR*

Boule, Cliff: Tactical displays, *ST6*
Bousman, Tracy: Asst art dir, *TOS*
Bowen, Steve: Digital compositor, *STG*; colorist, *TNG, DS9, VGR*
Bowles, Buddy: Chief lighting tech, *TNG*
Bowman, Robert: Dir, *TNG*
Bowman, Virginia: 3D digital artist, *ST:I*
Boyce, Todd: Computer graphics animator, *ST:FC*
Boyle, Kimberly: Secretary to Mr. Bennett, *ST5*
Brady, Dale: Creature creation, *ST4*
Braga, Brannon: Exec prod, superv prod-writer, *VGR;* Co-prod-story editor-writer, *TNG;* Writer, *STG, ST:FC*
Braggs, Steve: Digital effects artist, *ST:FC*
Brame, Bill: Film editor, *TOS*
Branit, Bruce: CGI supervisor, *VGR*
Brauer, Fred: Special effects, *ST2*
Braun, Werner: Climbing rigger, *ST5*
Brazil Fabrication & Design: Miniatures, *DS9*
Breedlove, Norman: Special effects asst, *TOS*
Brennan, Barbara: Computer graphics artist, *STG*
Brennan, Joseph F.: Boom operator, *STG, ST:FC, ST:I*
Brenneis, Marty: Model electronics, *ST2*
Brenner, Faye: Script superv, *ST6*
Bresin, Marty: Mechanical special effects, *ST:TMP*
Breton, Brooke: Assoc prod, *ST4, ST5, ST6;* Postprod superv, *TNG*
Brevick, Noel: Digital matte, *ST:FC*
Brewer, Jeff: Modelmaker, *ST:FC*
Brian, Bob: Craft service, *TOS*
Bridwell, Jim: Climbing rigger, *ST5*
Briggs, Jack: Property master, *TOS*
Brittenham, Lee Ann: Hair stylist, *DS9, ST:FC, ST:I*
Bro, Anthony: Set Designer, *DS9;* Prod asst, *ST:FC*
Brockliss, Anthony: Asst art dir, *ST5*
Brockman, Melissa: Digital effects prod, *ST:I*
Brodsky, Steve: Transportation captain, *STG*
Brodt, Dale: Digital prod mgr, *ST:FC*
Brody, Larry: Writer, *VGR*
Bronner, Robin: DGA trainee, *ST:FC*
Bronson, Dan: Wardrobe, *ST3;* Men's wardrobe, *ST4*
Bronson, Fred: Writer, *TNG*
Bronson, John D.: Men's wardrobe, *ST5*
Brooker, Mike: 2nd company grip, *ST4*
Brooks, Avery: Dir, *DS9*
Brooks, James E.: Writer, *TNG*
Brooks, Rolland M.: Art dir, *TOS*
Brookshire, Rebeca R.: Asst to Mr. Winter, *ST4, ST5, ST6*
Broussard, Al: Effects props and miniatures, *ST:TMP*
Brown, Edward R., ASC: Dir of photography, *TNG*
Brown, Fredric: Writer, *TOS*
Brown, Judi: Script superv, *DS9, STG, ST:FC, ST:I*
Brown, Leah P.: Costumer, *ST:FC*
Brown, Mark A.: Senior staff (VIFX), *ST:I*
Brown, Randy: Digital compositor, *ST:I*
Brown, Stewart: Precision printer, optical unit, *ST5*
Brownfield, Dick: Special effects, *TNG, VGR*
Brozak, George A.: Writer, *DS9, VGR*
Brozsek, Bela: Digital effects, *ST:I*
Bruce Hill Prods: Ultra high speed camera, *ST2*
Bruce Schluter Design, Inc.: Main titles, *ST:FC*
Bruce, David: Animation stand camera operator, *ST5*
Bruce, Raul A.: Boom operator, *ST3*
Bryant, Belinda: Makeup artist, *ST:FC, ST:I*
Bryant, Elijah: Set dresser, *ST:FC*
Bryant, Thomas R.: Visual effects editor, *ST6*; Asst film editor, *ST4*
Brzezinski, Carol: Digital post superv, *ST:FC*
Buck, Mary V.: Casting, *ST2*
Buckley, James: On set dresser, *ST:FC, ST:I*; Asst property master, *ST6*
Buckner, Adam: Visual effects coord, *DS9*
Budd, George: Special sound effects, *ST4*
Budgett, Cheryl: Compositing superv, *ST:I*
Buhmiller, Todd W.: Prod asst, *ST:FC*
Burbank Studios, The: Video playback and displays, *ST3;* Video displays, *ST2*
Bureau of Land Management: Special thanks, *ST5*
Burgess, Randy: First company grip, *VGR*
Burke, Johnny: Music, *ST:FC*
Burkett, Deena: Animation and graphics, *ST:TMP*
Burman Studio, The: Special makeup appliances, *ST3*
Burman, Ellis: Special makeup artist, *ST5;* makeup artist, *ST:I*
Burman, Sonny: Makeup artist, *DS9, ST:FC*
Burnam, Burt "Skip": 2nd asst dir, *ST5*
Burns, Judy: Writer, *TOS*
Burrow, Cathy: Digital rotoscope & paint, *ST:FC*
Burton, LeVar: Dir, *TNG, DS9, VGR*
Bush, Robin Michel: Wardrobe, *ST2*
Bussan, Mark: Makeup artist, *DS9, ST:FC, ST:I*
Bustamante, Alexi: Borg crew, *ST:FC*
Butler, Don: Digital compositor, *ST:FC;* Computer graphics artist, *STG*
Butler, Nathan: Writer, *TOS*
Butler, Robert: Dir, *TOS*
Butz, Richard: Key costumer, *TNG*
Bystrom, Joel: 2nd company grip (2nd unit), *ST:I*

Cabot, Zayra: Prod assoc, *TNG, VGR*
Cadrette, Kirk: Computer animator, *ST:FC*
Caine, Dick: Computer systems engineer, *STG*
Calder, Thomas H.: Writer, *TNG*
Caldwell, Scott: Asst film editor, *ST6*
Calhoun, Philip: Set dresser, *ST:FC*
California Film Commission: Special thanks, *ST5*
Calk, Ethan H.: Writer, *DS9*
Callery, Sean P.: Sound editor, *DS9;* Sound effects editor, *STG*
Calvet, Camille: Makeup artist, *DS9, ST:FC*
Camacho, Ernie: Assoc digital compositor, *STG*
Cameron, B.C.: First asst dir, *DS9*
Cameron, Geo: Writer, *VGR*
Campbell, Bob: Gaffer, *TOS*
Campbell, Deborah L.: Prod asst, *ST5*
Campbell, Glenn: Photographic effects photography, *ST:TMP*
Campbell, M. Kathryn: Special editorial, *ST:TMP*
Campbell, Pauline: Seamstress, *TOS*
Canamar, Kevin A.: First aid, *ST:FC*
Canamar, Valerie: Asst to Mr. Westmore, *ST:I*
Canavan, Jeff W.: Add'l editing, *ST:I*
Cancienne, Bill: Asst property master, *STG*
Candrella, Joe: First asst dir-2nd asst dir, *DS9*
Cane, Mark: Photographic effects grip, *ST:TMP*
Cannom, Greg: Jackal mastiff creation, *ST6*
Cantamessa, Gene S., CAS: Prod sound, *ST6;* Sound mixer, *ST3, ST4*
Cantamessa, Steve G.: Boom operator, *ST4, ST6*
Cantrell, Greg: Rigging chief lighting tech, *ST:FC, ST:I*
Capitol Records: Original soundtrack album, *ST3*
Caplan, Phil: Camera operator, *ST5*
Caple, Scott: Animator, *ST2*
Capra, III, Frank: 2nd asst dir, *ST4*
Carabatsos, Steven W.: Script consultant-writer, *TOS*
Carl Zeiss, Inc., Electron Microscopy & Image Processing Equipment: Special thanks, *ST5*
Carmichael, Robert: Dir, *ST5*
Carol-Schwary, Susan: Hair designer, *TNG*
Carpenter, Loren: Computer graphics, *ST2*
Carren, David Bennett: Story editor-writer, *TNG*
Carrigan-Fauci, Jeanne: Writer, *DS9*
Carroll, J. Larry: Story editor-writer, *TNG*
Carroll, John M.: Propmaker foreperson, *ST:FC;* Construction foreperson, *ST:I; DS9*
Carroll, John: Online editor, *TNG*
Carson, David: Dir, *DS9, TNG, STG*
Carson, David: Visual effects art dir, *ST3*
Carson, Jo: Asst camera person, *ST4*
Carter, Richard: Asst to the prod, *TOS*
Carter, Rick: Asst to exec prod, *TOS*
Case, Jeff: Dolly grip, *ST6*
Casey, Sean: Whale mold superv, *ST4;* Modelmaker, *ST2, ST3*
Cash, Don: Makeup artist, *TOS*
Casner, Barbara: Asst prod office coord, *ST:FC*
Casny, Gloria: Hair stylist, *DS9*
Cason, Rick: Writer, *DS9*
Castro, Elizabeth: Visual effects coordinator-visual effects asst editor, *VGR*
Cates, Jonathan: Asst film editor, *STG*
Catmull, Ed: Computer graphics, *ST2*
Catmull, Hazel: Hair stylist, *ST5*
Caton, Craig: Creature creation, *ST4*
Causey, Thomas D.: Sound mixer, *STG, ST:FC, ST:I*
Cavarretta, James: Recordists, *ST6*
Caves, Sally: Writer, *TNG, DS9*
Cenex casting: Extras casting, *ST:FC, ST:I*
Central Casting: Extras casting, *ST6, STG, ST:FC, ST:I*

Cervantes, Max: Special props, *TNG*
Cetrone, Clete F.: Propmaker foreperson, *ST:FC*; Construction foreperson, *ST:I*
Chalmers, Chip: Dir-first asst dir, *TNG;* Dir, *DS9*
Chaloukian, Dale: Sound editor, *VGR*
Chamberlain, Amanda: Key costumer, *TNG*; Costumer, *TNG*, *ST:I*
Chamberlain, David: Model maker, *TNG, DS9, VGR*
Chambers, Monique K.: Postprod coord, *DS9, VGR*; Asst to Mr. Lauritson, *ST:I*
Chandler Group, The: Pyrotechnic effects photography, *ST:I*
Chang, Wah Min: Special props and design, *TOS*
Chaplin, Chris: Computer graphics technical asst, *STG*
Chapman, Michael: Key costumer, *DS9*
Chapman: Cranes and dollies by, *ST:FC*
Chapnick, Morris: Asst to prod, *TOS*
Charno, Sara: Writer, *TNG*
Charno, Stuart: Writer, *TNG*
Charnock, Ed: Paint foreperson, *TNG, ST4*; Paint foreman, *ST3*
Chattaway, Jay: Music, *TNG*, *DS9*, *VGR*
Chauvin, Eric: Matte painting, *VGR, DS9*
Chefalo, Darlis: Hair stylist, *DS9*
Chen, Joseph: Set medic, *ST:I*
Chermax, Cy: Writer, *TNG*
Chess, Joe, SOC: Camera operator, *TNG*, *DS9*, *VGR*
Chichester, John: Set designer, *VGR*
Chielens, Martin X.: Asst film editor, *ST3*
Chilberg, II, John E.: Art dir, *ST3*
Childers, Adrienne: Costumer, *ST6*
Childers, Dave: Stage tech, *ST2*
Childress, Wade: Camera operator, *ST6;* Equipment coord, *ST2*
Chin, Brian: Modelmaker, *ST2*
Ching, Merllyn: Animation and graphics, *ST:TMP*
Chitty, Patrick A.: Borg crew, *ST:FC*
Cho, Albert: First asst dir (2nd unit), *ST:I*
Chomsky, Marvin: Dir, *TOS*
Chostner, Terry: Still photography superv, *ST3;* Still photographer, *ST2*
Chrisoulas, Bob: Optical laboratory tech, *ST2*
Christenberry, Ian: Lighting tech, *ST6*, *ST:I*
Christensen, Eric: Modelmaker, *ST4*
Chronister, Richard: Special effects asst, *TNG, VGR, ST:I*
Chung, Kyeng-Im: Digital effects artist, *ST:FC*
Cimity, Barbara: Tactical displays, *ST6*
Cimityart: Tactical displays, *ST6*
Cinema Research Corp.: Photographic effects, *TOS;* Opticals, *ST6;* Titles and addl opticals by, *ST:I*
Cinema Vehicle Services: Thanks for assistance, *ST:FC*
CIS Hollywood: Digital visual effects, *STG* ; Special video compositing, *TNG*, *DS9*, *VGR*; Rear screen projection compositing, *ST6;* Addl 2D/3D graphics, *ST:I*
City of Pasadena: Special thanks, *STG*
Claborn, Buckie: System administrator, *ST:I*
Clark, Donald: Optical camera operator, *ST3, ST4*, *ST6;* Optical printer operator, *ST2*
Clark, Gary A.: Prod painter, *ST6; STG;* Paint foreperson, *ST5, ST:FC*
Clark, Jeffrey: Sound effects editor, *ST:FC*, *ST:I*
Clark, Larry E.: Construction foreperson, *STG*, *ST:I*
Clark, Larry: Paint foreperson, *ST:I*
Clark, Patrick: Boom, *ST2*
Clark, Paul: Greensperson, *STG*
Clark, Truly Barr: Writer, *DS9*
Clarke, Ken: First aid, *ST6*
Claude, Vic: Craft service, *TOS*
Clavadetscher, Charlie: Effects camera operator, *ST6*
Clayton, John: Construction foreperson, *TNG*
Claytor, James: Set designer, *DS9*
Clee, Mona: Writer, *TNG*
Clemans, Jerry, CAS: Re-recording mixer, *TNG*
Clemente, Paul Michael: Model unit coord, *ST5*
Cline, Jeff: 2nd asst dir, *TNG*
Codon-Tharp, Caryl: Hair stylist, *DS9*
Codron, Arthur J.: Visual effects asst editor, *TNG*; Visual effects asst editor-visual effects coord, *VGR*
Cohen, David S.: Writer, *DS9*
Cohen, Manie: Prod asst, *STG*
Cohen, Richard: Computer graphics animator, *ST6*
Coia, Henry S.: Prod painter, *ST6*
Cole, Harold: Stage tech, *ST2*
Cole, Lee: Graphic designer, *ST2;* Graphics, *ST:TMP*; Set designer, *DS9, VGR*
Cole, Pat: Computer graphics, *ST2*
Coleman, Rob: Computer graphics artist, *ST5*
Colin, Stephanie: Key costumer, *DS9*
Colla, Richard: Dir, *TNG*
Collier, David: Prod asst, *ST:I*
Collins, James: Prod asst, *ST5*
Collins, William "Tex": First aid, *ST:FC*
Collis, Jack T.: Prod designer, *ST4*
Colombini, Cara: Postprod coord, *DS9*, *VGR*
Colón, Rafael F.: Digital compositor, *ST:I*
Colwell, Joe: Borg crew, *ST:FC*
Communication Arts, Inc.: Titles, *ST:TMP*
Composite Image Systems: Special video compositing, *TNG*
Compton, Richard: Dir-writer, *TNG*
Computer Graphics Laboratory, University of California, San Francisco: Molecular Computer Graphics, *ST2*
Comstock, Samuel: Animation superv, *ST2*
Coniglio, John: Asst film editor, *STG*
Conkey, Jackie: Asst to prod, *TOS*
Conley, Lawrence V.: Writer, *TNG*
Connole, Tom: 2nd camera asst, *ST2*
Connolly, Laura: Hair stylist, *TNG*, *VGR*, *STG*
Connors, Eileen: Writer, *VGR*
Conti, Walt: Whale design and project superv, *ST4*
Contreras, Armando: 2nd company grip, *ST:FC*, *ST:I*
Contreras, Tino: Rigging 2nd company grip, *ST:FC*
Conway, James L.: Dir, *TNG*, *DS9*, *VGR*
Cook, Daniel: Grip, *ST6*
Cook, Richard J.: Digital coord, *ST:FC*
Cook, Rob: Computer graphics, *ST2*
Coon, Gene L.: Producer-writer, *TOS*
Cooper, "Big" Ed: Best boy, *ST3*
Cooper, Marc: Digital effects artist, *ST:FC*
Cooperman, Jack, ASC: Underwater dir of photography, *ST4*
Coppoly, Charles: Electrician, *TOS*
Corcoran-Woods, Phyllis: Key costumer, *DS9*
Corea, Nicholas: Writer, *DS9*, *VGR*
Corey, Matthew: Writer, *TNG*
Cornish, Selena: Assoc digital compositor, *STG*
Correll, Charles, ASC,: Dir of photography, *ST3*
Corvino, Ken: Systems support specialist, *STG*
Corwin, Richard: Dialogue editor, *STG*, *ST:FC*, *ST:I*
Cotter, Ed: Film librarian, *TOS*
Couch, Bill: Stunt coord, *ST2*
Coughlin, Kerwin: Casting, *TOS*
Couk, Anne: First asst sound editor, *ST:I*; asst sound editor, *ST:FC*
Coulson, Catherine: First camera asst, *ST2*
Courage, Alexander: Theme from *Star Trek* television series, *ST:TMP, ST2, ST3, ST4, ST5, ST6, STG, ST:FC, ST:I;* Music, *ST4, ST5, ST6, STG, ST:FC;* Orchestrations, *ST:FC*, *ST:I;* Theme music, music composed and conducted, *TOS;* Main title theme, *TNG*
Coursey, Susan: Asst to Mr. Ferren, *ST5*
Couture, Stephane: Computer animator, *ST:FC*
Covington, Barbara: Asst to prod, *DS9*
Cowan, Elrene: Animation and graphics, *ST:TMP*
Cowitt, Leo: Electrician, *TOS*
Cox, Betsy: Digital compositor, *ST:FC*, *ST:I*
Cox, Don: Photographic effects cameraman, *ST:TMP*
Coyle, Paul Robert: Writer, *DS9*, *VGR*
Craig, Harrison: Model maker, *ST:I*
Craig, John R.: Asst prod auditor, *ST4*
Cramer, Douglas S.: Exec vice-president in charge of prod, *TOS*
Cranham, Tom: Prod illustrator, *ST:TMP*
Crawford, David: Digital compositor, *ST:FC*, *ST:I*
Crawford, Leland: Hair stylist, *TNG*, *DS9*
Crawford, Nell McCue: Writer, *DS9*
Crawford, Oliver: Writer, *TOS*
Crawford, Shirley: Hair stylist, *TNG*
Crawford, William L.: Writer, *DS9*
Cremin, Kevin: DGA trainee, *ST:TMP*
Cremona, Rosemary: 2nd asst dir, *ST:FC*, *ST:I*
Criscione, Tony: Asst prod auditor, *ST5*
Critters of the Cinema: Cat, *STG*
Crocker, James: Superv prod-writer, *DS9*
Crockett, Bob: Alaska liaison, *ST6*
Cronin, Lee: Writer, *TOS*
Cronn, Richard: Chief lighting tech, *TNG*
Crosman, Peter: Animation effects animator, *ST6*
Crowley, Nathan: Set designer, *DS9*
Crucis, Jud: Writer, *TOS*
Crum, Eugene: Special effects foreper-

son, *ST:FC*, *ST:I;* Asst special effects, *ST6*, *STG*
Crump, Chris: Effects props and miniatures, *ST:TMP*
CST Entertainment, Inc.: Colorization, *VGR*
Culhane, Christopher: Asst to prods, *VGR*
Culina, Victor: Lead man, *TOS*
Cullum, Phillip: Mechanical fabrication, *ST5*
Cummins, Michael: Modelmaker, *STG*
Curd, Geneva: Cutter and fitter, *TOS*
Curda, Gregory J.: Foley mixer, *ST5*, *ST6*
Currey, Gail: ILM senior staff, *ST:FC;* Computer graphics prod superv, *ST6*
Curry, Dan: Dir-visual effects prod, *TNG;* Visual effects prod-main title design *DS9*, *VGR;* Main title design, *STG;* Title design, *ST4;* Thanks for assistance, *ST:FC*, *ST:I*
Curtis, Greg: Special effects foreperson, *ST:FC;* Special effects asst, *STG*
Curtis, Scott: Foley editor, *ST:FC*
Cushman, Marc: Writer, *TNG*
Cushner, Joshua: Motion control programmer, *DS9*, *VGR*
Cusick, Shaun: Modeler/creature designer, *ST:I*
Cybulski, John: Asst chief rigging electrician, *ST6*

D'Agosta, Joseph: Casting, *TOS*
D'Alessandro, Gloria: Dialogue editor, *STG*
D'Amico, Andrea: Digital visual effects prod, *ST:FC*
D'Angelo, Dick: Swing person, *DS9*
Dabney, Keith, Asst editor, *VGR*
Dahm, Carolyn M.: Asst to Mr. Williams, *STG*
Dalton, Dirk: Sound effects creation, *ST:TMP*
Danchick, Roy: Special thanks, *ST4*
Dandib, Daniel: Asst film editor, *ST6*
Daniel, John: CGI artist, *VGR*
Daniels, Carl W.: Prod mixer-sound mixer, *TOS*
Daniels, Marc: Dir, *TOS*
Danus, Richard: Writer-exec story editor, *TNG*; Writer, *DS9*
Darcy, Virginia, CHS: Hair styles, *TOS*
Darensbourg, Eric: Prod asst, *ST:FC*
Datin, Richard C.: Model maker, *TOS*
Daugherty, Herschel: Dir, *TOS*
Daulton, Peter: Camera operator, *ST4;* Asst cameraman, *ST3;* Motion control camera operator, *ST6*
Dave Archer studios: Special thanks, *ST6*
Davey, Doug, CAS: Re-recording mixer, *TNG*, *DS9*, *VGR*
Davidson, Howard: Transportation co-captain, *ST2*
Davidson, Julian: Music coord, *TOS*
Davis, Brian C.: 3D animator, *ST:I*
Davis, C. Marie: Visual effects prod, *STG*
Davis, Capt. Walter: Acknowledgment, *ST4*
Davis, Don: Music, *TNG*
Davis, Jay: Animator, *ST2*
Davis, Larry M.: 2nd asst dir, *TNG*
Davis, Maril: Prod associate-asst to prods, *DS9*, *VGR*; Asst to Mr. Berman, *ST:I*
Davis, Richard: Modelmaker, *ST3*
Davis, Sharon: Set designer, *DS9*, *ST:I*
Davis, Sir Colin: "Vallon Sonore" from Les Troyens, conductor, *ST:FC*
Davis, Zack: ADR editor, *ST:FC*, *ST:I*
Dawkins, Johnny: Story editor, *TNG*
Dawn, Jeff: Makeup artist, *ST4*, *ST5*
Dawn, Robert: Makeup artist, *TOS*
Dawn, Wes: Makeup artist, *ST3*, *ST4*, *ST5*
Dawson, Bob: Special effects superv, *ST2*, *ST3*
Dawson, Gordon: Writer, *DS9*
Day, Gordon L., CAS: Re-recording mixer, *TOS*
De Crescent, Sandy: Orchestra contractor, *ST:FC*, *ST:I*
De Graff, Monty: Editor, *TNG*
De Haas, Timothy: Writer, *TNG*, *VGR*
De Moraes, Lisa: Asst editor, *TNG*, *VGR*
de Graf/Wahrman, Inc.: Special thanks, *ST5*
de la Garza, Bob: Swing person, *VGR*
de los Santos-Geary, Gloria: Digital compositor, *ST:I*
de Muth, Charles Ray: Costumer, *ST:FC*
de Sousa, Mark E. A.: 3D animator, *ST:I*
Dean Davis, Deborah: Writer, *TNG*
Dean, Doug: First asst dir, *TNG*
Dean, Kris: Special electronics, *ST:TMP*
Deane, Howard S., ACE: Editor, *TNG*
Debney, John: Music, *DS9*, *TNG*
DeCesare, Sara: VFX prod coord, *ST:I*
Defeo, Mike: Modeler/creature designer, *ST:I*
DeGaetano, Al: Construction coord, *ST2*
DeGaetano, Dave: Construction coord, *DS9*
Deighan, Drew: Writer, *TNG*
Del Rio, Elena: Costume superv, *STG*
Delara, A.Y. Dexter: Visual effects coord, *DS9*, *ST:I*
Delgado, Ricardo: Illustrator, *DS9*, *ST:FC*
della Santina, Robert: Coordinating prod-unit prod mgr, *DS9*
DeLuca, Michael: Writer, *VGR*
Deluxe: Color by, *STG*, *ST:FC*, *ST:I*
DeMeritt, Michael: 2nd asst dir, *VGR*
Demkowicz, Krystyna: Visual effects prod, *ST:FC;* Exec project management, *ST6*
Demolski, Berny: Electrician, *ST:FC*
Demolski, Richard: Stage, *ST6*
DeMorrio, Rebecca: Hair stylist, *DS9*
Denali Prods, Inc.: Provided, *ST5*
Denault, Craig: Camera operator, *ST2*
Denove, Thomas F.: Dir of photography, *TNG*
Dent, Skye: Writer, *VGR*
Denton Vacuum, Inc.: Special thanks, *ST5*
Denver, Patrick: Model shop foreperson, *ST:I*
Deoudes, Mitch: Digital effects artist, *ST:FC*
Dept. of Defense and the Dept. of the Air Force: Acknowledgment, *ST:FC*
Dept. of Defense, Philip M. Strub: Acknowledgment, *ST:FC*
Dept. of the Navy and the Dept. of Defense: Acknowledgment, *ST4*
DeRuelle, Gene: Asst dir, *TOS*
DeSantis, Louis P.: Writer, *DS9*
DeSart, Monique: Add'l hairstylist, *ST4*
DeScenna, Linda: Set decorator, *ST:TMP*
deSoria, Charles: First camera asst, *TOS*
deVally, Ray: Asst editor, *TOS*
Devereaux, Terry: Writer, *TNG*
DeVito, Matthew: Electrician, *TOS*
DeWalt, Tom: 2D digital artist, *ST:I*
Dewe, Bryan: Mechanical engineer, *ST:FC*
Dial, Bill: Writer, *DS9*, *VGR*
Diamos, Angela: Animation and graphics *ST:TMP*
Dianda, Joseph: 2nd company grip, *STG*
Diaz, Alex: Borg crew, *ST:FC*
Diaz, Suzanne: Makeup artist, *VGR*
Dickman, Dan: Special thanks, *STG*
Dickson, Jim: Add'l photography, *ST:TMP*
Dickson, Lance: Writer, *TNG*
Didjurgis, Cy: Animation and graphics, *ST:TMP*
Diepenbrock, Bob: Modelmaker, *ST2*
Diggs, James: Prod painter, *ST:I*
Diggs, Jimmy: Writer, *DS9*, *VGR*
DiGiovanni, Rick: Lead person, *DS9*
Digital Equipment Corporation: Medical computer displays, *ST:TMP*
Digital Magic: Digital optical effects-computer generated imagery, *VGR;* Video optical effects, *TNG*, *DS9*
Digital Muse: Computer generated effects, *DS9*, *VGR*
Dismukes, Charles: Apprentice asst dir, *TOS*
Ditmars, Ivan: Brahms paraphrase for "Requiem for Methuselah," *TOS*
Dittert, Les: Optical superv, *ST6*
Dobkin, Lawrence: Dir, *TOS*
Dochterman, Daren: Illustrator, *VGR*
Doherty, Robert J.: Writer-asst to prods, *VGR*
Dolan, William K. (Bill): Lead person, *ST:FC*, *STG*, *ST:I*; property person, *ST4*
Dolby Stereo: Stereo digital sound, *STG;* Surround sound, *TNG;* Sound, *ST:TMP*, *ST2*, *ST3*, *ST4*, *ST5*, *ST6*
Dolby: In selected theatres, *ST:I*
Dolinsky, Meyer: Writer, *TOS*
Dollé, Shirley: Hair designer, *DS9*
Donner, Jill Sherman: Writer, *DS9*
Donovan, Giovanni: Modelmaker, *STG*, *ST:FC*
Dooley, Doug: Senior animator, *ST:I*
Doran, Jeff: Digital compositor, *ST:FC*
Doran, Jeffrey: Optical camera operator, *ST6*
Dorn, Aaron: Transportation, *TOS*
Dorn, Brian Van: Borg crew, *ST:FC*
Dorn, Michael: Dir, *DS9*
Dorney, Dennis: Photographic effects photography, *ST:TMP*
Dorney, Roger: Superv of optical photography, *ST:TMP*
Dornisch, William P.: Editor, *ST2*
Dorsett, Tommy: Visual effects editor, *ST:I*
Dorton, Louise: Art dir-set designer, *VGR;* Set designer, *ST6*
Doublin, Tony: Miniatures, *VGR*
Doud, Ross: Set decorator, *TOS*
Douglas, Pamela: Writer, *TNG*
Dova, Dick: First company grip, *STG;* Stage tech, *ST2*, *ST4*
Dow, Donald: Effects dir of photography, *ST4;* Visual effects cameraman, *ST3;* Effects cameraman, *ST2*
Dow, Jim: Miniatures, *ST:TMP*
Dow, Richard: Dolly grip, *ST4*
Dow, Tony: Dir, *DS9*

Down, Tim: Special thanks, *ST5*
Downer, John: Art dept prod asst, *ST6*
Doyle, A. Conan: Sherlock Holmes characters created by, used by arrangement with Jean Conan Doyle, *TNG*
Dranitzke, David: Plate coord, *ST:FC*
Drapanas, Wendy: Scenic artist, *TNG, VGR*
Drapkin, David: Animation stand camera operator, model unit, *ST5*
Drapkin, Rachel A.: Model unit mgr, model unit, *ST5*
Drayman, Charles Evan: Costumer, *TNG*
Drexler, Doug: Scenic artist/space hero: *DS9, STG, ST:FC, ST:I*; Makeup artist, *TNG*
Drury, Joe: 2nd costumer, *TOS*
dts: Digital sound, *STG, ST:I*
Duane, Diane: Writer, *TNG*
Dubbs, Joe: Computer animation and tactical display, *ST5*
Duchowny, Roger: 2nd asst dir, *TOS*
Duff, Tom: Computer graphics, *ST2*
Dufva, Kenneth: Foley artist, *ST5, ST6, STG, ST:FC*
Duignan, Patricia Rose: Prod superv, *ST2*
Dukes, Larry: Driver, *DS9*
Dunagan, George: Asst chief lighting tech, *ST:I*
Dunaway, Don Carlos: Writer, *DS9*
Duncan, John: Modelmaker, *ST:FC*
Duning, George: Music composed and conducted, *TOS*
Dunn, John: Sound effects editor, *ST5*
Dupont, Lex: Asst photographer, *ST5*
Dupont, Tom: Paramedic, *ST5*
Durand International: Special thanks, *ST6*
Durling, Jeff: Lighting tech, *ST6*
Duron, Gus: Avid editor, *ST:I*
Dutton, Bob: Property person, *STG*
Dutton, Nan, CSA: Original casting, *VGR*
Dutton, Syd: Borg matte painting, *ST:FC;* matte paintings, *ST5, TNG, DS9, VGR*
Duval, Huey: Property person, *ST4*
Dwyer, John M.: Set decorator, *TOS, TNG, ST4, ST5, STG, ST:FC, ST:I*
Dyer, Wilson: Sound editor, *TNG*
Dykstra, Janet: Assistance to photographic effects, *ST:TMP*
Dykstra, John: Superv, special photographic effects-photographic effects superv, *ST:TMP*

Earl, Janet: 24-frame video displays, *ST6*
Eastman Kodak Film: Printed on, *ST:FC, ST:I*
Eastman, Allan: Dir, *VGR, DS9*
Eaves, John: Senior illustrator, *DS9;* Illustrator, *ST:FC, STG, ST:I*
Ebert, Clarence: 2nd company grip, *ST3*
Eby, Douglas: Photographic effects cameraman, *ST:TMP*
Echevarria, René: Prod-writer-cosuperv prod, *DS9;* Exec story editor-writer, *TNG*
Eckton, Teresa: Sound effects editor, *ST2*
Edds, Hank, SMA: Makeup artist, *TNG*
Eddy, Selwyn, III: Digital matchmover, *ST:FC;* Camera operator, *ST4;* Optical camera operator, *ST6;* Visual effects cameraman, *ST3;* Asst camera operator, *ST2*
Edge of Etiquette: Music, *ST4*
Editel/LA: Optical compositing-editing facilities, *DS9*
Edlund, Richard: Optical effects, *TOS*
Edmonson, Mike: Special effects asst, *ST5*
Edwards, Jackie: Asst to Mr. Stewart, *STG, ST:FC, ST:I*
Edwards, Tim: Transportation captain, *ST:FC*
Effects Unlimited: Photographic effects, *TOS*
EFILM: Digital film recording, *STG*
Efros, Mel: Unit prod mgr-co-prod, *ST5;* unit prod mgr, *ST4*
Egan, Edward: Unit publicist, *ST2*
Eguia, Charles C.: Asst property master, *ST2*
Ehle, Thom: Dolby stereo consultant, *ST6*
Ehrlich, Max: Writer, *TOS*
Eichholz, Bernhard: Borg crew, *ST:FC*
Eidelman, Cliff: Music composer and conductor, *ST6*
Eidelman, Robin K.: Asst music editor, *ST6*
Eisenstein, Kathryn S.: Original casting, *VGR*
Eisner, Carol: Asst to the prods, *TNG*
Ekker, Leslie: Animation and graphics, *ST:TMP*
El Fadil, Siddig: Dir, *DS9*
Elder, Marie: Asst auditor, *ST:FC;* Asst prod auditor, *ST5*
Elek, Katalin: Special makeup artist, *ST5*
Elias, Carolyn L.: Hair stylist, *STG*
Elias, Richard: 2nd company grip (2nd unit), *ST:I*
Elkins, Judy: Visual effects coord, *DS9;* Animator, *ST2*
Ellentuck, Kinnereth: Film librarian, *ST5*
Elliott, Don: Special effects, *ST4*
Elliott, Greg: Writer, *VGR*
Ellis, John: Photographic effects cameraman, *ST:TMP;* Optical printer operator, *ST2*
Ellis, Michael: Optical processing, *ST6;* Scanning operator, *STG*
Ellison, Harlan: Writer, *TOS*
Elsen, Kate: Digital rotoscope & paint, *ST:FC*
Elswitt, Robert: Photographic effects photography, *ST:TMP*
Elwood, Gregory: Digital compositor, *ST:I*
Embree, Thom: Lighting tech, *ST6, ST:I*
Embrey, Chuck: Photographic effects gaffer, *ST:TMP*
Emmons, Anastasia: Asst visual effects editor, *ST:FC*
Eng, Ron: Sound effects editor, *ST:I*
Engalla, Wendy: Casting assoc, *ST6*
England, Jason: Asst sound editor, *ST:I*
English, Russ: Set security, *DS9*
Epic Records: Original soundtrack album, *ST5*
Erdmann, Terry: Unit publicist, *ST5*
Eriksen, Nathan: Digital record operator, *ST:I*
Erland, John: Effects props and miniatures, *ST:TMP*
Erman, John: Dir, *TOS*
Erwin, Lee: Writer, *TOS*
Eschbacher, Roger: Writer, *TNG*
Espenson, Jane: Writer, *DS9*
Espinoza, Richard: 2nd asst dir, *ST2*
Essoe, Gabe: Writer, *DS9*
Estes, Ken: Video playback, *DS9*
Ettleman, Lee: Effects props and miniatures, *ST:TMP*
Evan Drayman, Charles: Costumer, *TNG*
Evangelatos, Peter G.: Special effects, *ST2, ST3*
Evans & Sutherland Digistar System: Starfield effects, *ST2*
Evans & Sutherland Picture System: Tactical displays, *ST2*
Evans, Andy: Special effects asst, *ST:FC*
Evans, Chris: Chief digital matte artist, *ST:FC;* Matte painting superv, *ST4,* Matte artist, *ST3, ST2*
Evans, Jim: Coord, *ST5*
Everton, Deborah: Costume designer, *ST:FC*

Faerman, Michael: Prod exec, *ST5*
Falesitch, Steffan: Sound editor, *DS9*
Falkengren, Jon A.: Dolly grip, *ST5, ST3*
Fambry, Bob: Painter, *DS9*
Fante, John V.: Dir of photography, *ST6;* camera operator, *ST4*
Farrar, Scott: Visual effects superv, *ST6;* Visual effects cameraman, *ST3;* Effects cameraman, *ST2;* Photographic effects photography, *ST:TMP*
Farrell, J. P.: Co-prod-superv prod-superv editor, *DS9;* Co-prod-superv editor, *VGR;* Superv editor, *TNG*
Fasal, John Paul: Special sound effects, *ST6*
Fatjo, Lolita: Preprod coord, *DS9, VGR;* Preprod assoc, *TNG;* Prod assoc, *ST:FC*
Fattibene, Mark: 3D digital artist, *ST:I*
Fauci, Jeanne Carrigan: Writer, *TNG*
Fearing, Jr., Roger: Asst sound editor, *ST:FC, ST:I*
Fearing, Tammy: Foley editor, *ST:FC, ST:I*
Fechtman, Robert: Set designer, *STG*
Feemster, Randy: Camera operator, *ST:FC*
Fegan, Jack: Asst editor, *TOS*
Feightner, Bill: Tech superv, *STG*
Fein, David Lee: Foley artist, *ST5, ST6, STG, ST:FC*
Feinberg, Irving A.: Property master, *TOS*
Feldman, Glen: Asst property master, *ST:FC*
Ferguson, Carolyn: Hair stylist, *TNG*
Ferguson, Ellen: Rotoscope artist, *ST4*
Ferguson, Mary Jane: Script superv, *ST2*
Ferguson, Perry: Asst art dir, *TOS*
Fernandes, Kristine: Postprod superv-prod assoc, *DS9;* Asst to Mr. Berman, *STG* Prod assoc, *TNG, VGR*
Fernandez, Mary Jo: Asst to Mr. Shatner, *ST5, ST6*
Fernandez, Robert: Music scoring mixer, *STG*
Fernley, Robert: Optical processing, *ST6*
Ferraro, Ralph: Orchestrations, *ST4*
Ferren, Bran: Visual effects, *ST5*
Fesh, William J.: Borg crew, *ST:FC*
Feuerstein, Allen: Creature creation, *ST4*
Ficarra, Glenn: Motion control rigger, *DS9, VGR*

Fielding, Jerry: Music composed and conducted, *TOS*
Fields, Peter Allan: Prod-writer, *DS9;* Exec script consultant-writer, *TNG*
Film Effects of Hollywood: Photographic effects, *TOS*
Fink, Mike: Effects props and miniatures, *ST:TMP*
Finks, Wilbur: Swing person, *DS9*
Finley, III, Bobby: Stage tech, *ST2*
Finley, Eugene: Add'l sound effects, *ST2*
Finley, Jr., Robert: Pyrotech, *ST4*; Stage, *ST6*
Finnerman, Jerry: Dir of photography, *TOS;* 2nd unit photography, *DS9*
Finnerty, Daniel F.: Asst editor, *ST3*
Fischer, Lorraine: Asst to prods, *VGR*
Fisher, Brian: CGI artist, *VGR*
Fitzgerald, Edward G.: Leadperson, *ST6*
Fitzgerald, Kim: Prod assoc, *TNG*, *DS9*, *VGR*
Fitzsimmons, Patrick: Superv stage tech, *STG;* Stage tech, *ST2*
Fiyalko, Terri: Sound effects editor, *ST:I*
Flanagan, Gina A.: Senior sketch artist, *ST:FC*
Flanderka, Dennis: Grip, *ST6*
Fleck, Jerry: First asst dir, *TNG*, *VGR*, *ST:FC*, *ST:I*
Fletcher, Robert: Costume designer, *ST:TMP, ST2, ST3, ST4*
Flick, Christopher: Foley editor, *ST:I*; asst editor, *ST4*
Flick, Stephen Hunter, MPSE: Sound effects editor, *ST4;* Sound editor, *ST:TMP*
Fliegel, Richard: Writer, *TNG*
Flinn, Denny Martin: Writer, *ST6*
Foam Tec, Inc.: Planet interior/exterior, snow and ice scenery, *ST6*
Fog, Stephen: Special electronics, *ST:TMP*
Foley, John, ACE: Film editor, *TOS*
Fong, Steve: Senior Inferno compositor, *DS9, VGR*
Fontana, D. C.: Assoc prod-writer, *TNG;* Script consultant-writer, *TOS;* Writer, *DS9*
Ford, Christian: Writer, *DS9*
Foreman, Jon: Chief modelmaker, *STG*, *ST:FC;* Modelmaker, *ST6*
Forher, Lenny: Assoc digital compositor, *STG*
Forrest-Chambers, Sue: Makeup artist, *TNG*
Forrester, Larry: Writer, *TNG*
Fortina, Carl: Orchestra contractor, *STG*, *ST6*
Fortmuller, Gail: First asst dir, *DS9*
Fortmuller, George: 2nd asst dir, *ST5*
Fortune, Bruce D.: Asst editor, *ST3*
Foster, Alan Dean: Writer, *ST:TMP*
Foster, Frank.: Asst special effects, *DS9*, *ST6, ST5*
Fought, Deb: Digital rotoscope & paint, *ST:FC*
Foundation Imaging: Computer generated effects, *VGR*
Four (4)MC Sound Services: Post prod sound, *DS9, VGR*
Four Media Company: Editing facilities, *DS9, VGR*
Fowler, Harold: First aid, *STG*
Fox, Douglas I.: Property master, *STG*
Fox, Tony: Transportation captain, *ST6*
Foy, Richard: Titles, *ST:TMP*
Frakes, Jonathan: Dir, *TNG*, *DS9*, *VGR*, *ST:FC*, *ST:I*
Francis, Al: Dir of photography, *TOS*
Francis, Bob: Electrical tech, *ST5*
Frank, Rob: Asst location manager, *ST:I*
Frankel, Scott: Computer graphics artist, *STG;* Digital compositor, *ST:FC*
Frankenheimer, Leslie: Set decorator, *VGR*
Frankley, Cameron: Superv sound editor, *ST:FC*, *ST:I*
Franklin, Warren: General mgr, ILM, *ST4;* Prod superv, *ST3;* Prod coord, *ST2*
Frasco, Gerald J.: Asst prod coord, *STG*
Frazee, Donald L.: Special effects asst, *STG;* Asst special effects, *ST6*, *ST:I;* Special effects foreperson, *ST:FC*
Frazee, Logan: Special effects asst, *STG*, *ST:FC*, *ST:I;* Asst special effects, *ST6*
Frazee, Terry D.: Special effects superv, *ST6, STG;* Special effects coord, *ST:FC*, *ST:I*
Fredrickson, Anthony: Scenic artist, *DS9*, *STG, ST:FC*, *ST:I*
Freedle, Sam: Unit prod mgr, *TNG*
Freeman, Meg: Digital effects painter, *ST:I*
Freiberger, Fred: Producer, *TOS*
French, Edward: Special alien makeup creation, *ST6*
Fried, Gerald: Music composed and conducted, *TOS*
Friedlich, Buffee: Art dept prod asst, *ST6*
Friedman, Diane: Asst location mgr, *STG*
Friedman, Kim: Dir, *DS9*, *VGR*
Friedman, Michael Jan: Writer, *VGR*
Friedman, Michael: Lead man, *ST2*
Friedrick, Eva Marie: Asst to Mr. Shatner, *ST5*
Friedstand, Robert: Photographic effects photography, *ST:TMP*
Fries, Sandy: Writer, *TNG*
Frith, John: Electrical tech, *ST5*
Fucci, Marva: Asst sound editor, *ST6*
Fucci, Thomas: Sound editor, *ST6*
Fukai, Arlene: First asst dir, *VGR;* 2nd asst dir, *TNG;* 2nd 2nd asst dir, *STG*
Fukuchi, Primrose Y.: Asst auditor, *ST:FC*
Fulcrum Studios LLC: Addl 2D/3D graphics, *ST:I*
Fuller, Bryan: Story editor, *VGR*; Writer, *DS9, VGR*
Fulmer, Joseph: Effects rigger, *STG*
Fulmer, Michael: Modelmaker, *ST2*, *ST3*

Gaberman, Mark: Writer, *VGR*
Gabl, Rosi: Sketch artist, *ST:I*
Gadas, Richard: Writer, *VGR*
Gadette, Jerry: Standby painter, *ST4*
Gaeta, John: Chief lighting tech, model unit, *ST5*
Gaines, Bob: Climbing double for William Shatner, *ST5*
Gair, Gordon: Lead man, *TOS*
Gala Catering: Catering, *ST:I*
Gallo, Jeanna F.: Writer, *TNG*
Galloway, Craig: Asst editor, *DS9*
Galloway, Ron: Swing gang, *ST3*
Galvan, David R.: Prod painter, *ST:FC*
Gambetta, George: Senior scanning operator, *ST:FC;* Scanning, *ST6*
Ganino, Trent Christopher: Writer, *TNG*
Garber, Jake: Makeup artist, *ST:FC*
Garden, David: 2nd asst photographer *ST:I*
Garlington, Joe: Effects props and miniatures, *ST:TMP*
Garretson, Katy E.: 2nd asst dir, *ST6*
Garrett, James A.: Asst editor, *VGR*
Garutso, Karen: Prod asst, *ST:FC*
Garza, Ernest: Visual consultant, *ST:TMP*
Gates, Dean: Makeup artist, *DS9*
Gauger, Laurie: Asst prod office coord, *ST6*
Gausche, Steve: First company grip, *TNG*, *DS9*
Gauvreau, Andy: 3D animator, *ST:I*
Gawley, Steve: Chief modelmaker, *STG;* Superv modelmaker, *ST2*, *ST3*
Gaynor, Larry: Digital artist, *STG*
Gazdik, John: Camera asst, *ST:FC*
Gehr, Rocky: Special effects, *ST3*
Gehred-O'Connel, Mark: Writer, *DS9*
Gehring, Bo: Computer motion control system for miniatures, *ST:TMP*
Geideman, Tim: Optical laboratory tech, *ST2;* Lab tech, *ST4;* Optical line-up, *STG*; Negative line-up, *ST:FC*
Gendel, Morgan: Writer, *TNG*, *DS9*
Genne, Michael: Asst cameraman, *ST:TMP*
Genovese, Cosmo: Script superv, *TNG*, *DS9*, *VGR*
Gentile, Mary Beth: Asst to Mr. Winter, *ST6*
Gentle Jungle: Animals by, *ST:I*
George Randle Co: Mechanical designs, *ST:TMP*
George, Bruno: Photographic effects cameraman, *ST:TMP*
George, Christopher: Photographic effects photography, *ST:TMP*
George, III, David R.: Writer, *VGR*
George, Gary: Digital record out manager, *ST:I*
George, William: Visual effects art dir, *ST6;* Add'l spacecraft design, *ST3;* Modelmaker, *ST:TMP, ST2;* Art consultant, *ST:FC;* Visual effects art dir, *STG*
Gerard, Pete: Effects props and miniatures, *ST:TMP*
Gerber, Steve: Writer, *TNG*
Gerken, Jim: Computer animation and tactical displays, *ST4, ST5*
German, Jennifer: Digital compositor, *ST:FC*, *ST:I*
Gernand, Brian: Chief modelmaker, *STG;* Modelmaker, *ST6*
Gerrety, Patrick M.: Borg crew, *ST:FC*
Gerrity, Christopher T.: First asst dir, *ST6*
Gerrold, David: Writer, *TOS*; Program consultant, *TNG*
Gerzevitz, Michael: Chief lighting tech, *ST5*
Gian, Michael G.: Swing gang, *ST2*
Giardino-Zych, Marilyn: Script superv, *DS9*
Giarratana, Deborah: Senior staff (VIFX), *ST:I*
Gibb, Jim: Sound boom, *TOS*
Gibbens, Marcy Stoeven: Asst sound editor, *ST6*
Gibbs, David: Aerial coord, *ST:I*
Gibbs, R. Harrison: Prod asst, *ST6*

Gibson, Robert: Asst location manager, *ST:I*
Gilbert, Donna Barrett: Hair stylist, *ST5*
Gilbert, William S.: "A British Tar" from *H.M.S. Pinafore* by, *ST:I*
Gilberti, Ray: Asst cameraman, *ST3, ST4*
Gillian, Robert: Asst prod assoc, *ST:FC;* Writer, *DS9*
Gilligan, Rick: Effects props and miniatures, *ST:TMP*
Gilman, John: Special electronics, *ST:TMP*
Gilmore, Dean: Sound mixer, *TNG*
Gilson, Fulton Greg: Transportation captain, *ST:I*
Gioffre, Rocco: Add'l matte paintings, *ST:TMP*
Giovannetti, Bart: Computer graphics sequence superv, *STG*
Gist, Robert: Dir, *TOS*
Gitlin, Alan: First asst photographer, *STG*
Glaser, Jan, CSA,: Casting assoc, *ST6*
Glass, Jr., Robert W.: Re-recording mixer, *ST3*
Glass, Leora: Asst to photographic effects, *ST:TMP*
Glasser, Norm: Chief lighting tech, *ST3*
Glassner, Jonathan: Writer, *VGR*
Gleason, Mike: Visual effects editor, *ST4, ST:FC*
Glen Glenn Sound Co.: Sound, *TOS, ST2, ST3*
Glick, Michael S.: Asst dir, *TOS*
Glockner-Ferrari, Debbie of the Humpback Whale Fund: Special thanks, *ST4*
Glover, Kristin R.: Camera operator, *ST6*
Gluck, Daniel: Set designer, *ST4, ST2*
Gluckstern, Cheryl: Postprod coord-visual effects assoc, *DS9, VGR;* Prod assoc, *TNG;* Asst to Mr. Lauritson, *STG*
GNP Crescendo Records: Soundtrack album, *STG, ST:FC, ST:I*
Gobruegge, Les D.: Set designer, *TNG, ST:FC*
Gocke, Bill: Sound mixer, *TNG, DS9*
Gold, David: Photographic effects gaffer, *ST:TMP*
Goldberg, Joyce: Asst to Mr. Yuricich, *ST:TMP*
Goldberg, Lisa: Digital producer, *ST:I*
Golden, Murray: Dir, *TOS*
Golden, Philip: Assistance to photographic effects, *ST:TMP*
Goldfarb, David: Add'l 2nd asst dir, *ST:FC, ST:I*
Goldman, Jeremy: Digital effects artist, *ST:FC*
Goldsmith, Jerry: Theme from *ST:TMP* , orchestra conducted by, *ST:FC, ST:I;* Music, *ST5, ST:TMP, ST:FC, ST:I;* Main title theme, *TNG;* Theme, *VGR*
Goldsmith, Joel: Add'l music, *ST:FC;* Sound effects creation, *ST:TMP*
Goldstein, David: 2nd asst photographer, *STG*
Goldstein, Libby: Casting asst, *VGR*
Goldstone, James: Dir, *TOS*
Gomes, Rob: Prod asst, *ST:I*
Gonzales, Phil: Photographic effects photography, *ST:TMP*
Goodale, Scott: Construction foreman, *ST3*
Goodhartz, Shari: Writer, *TNG*
Goodman, Elisa: Casting assoc, *TNG*
Goodnight, Jim: Special electronics, *ST:TMP*
Goodson, John: Model superv, *STG;* Model project superv, *ST:FC;* Modelmaker, *ST6*
Goold, Louis: Optical layout, *ST5*
Gordon, Antoinette: Set designer, *ST5*
Gordon, Ralph: Optical superv, *ST4;* Optical line-up, *ST2, ST3*
Gordon, Suzanne: Publicity, *ST:TMP*
Gorman, Ben: Klingon and Vulcan prosthetics, *ST5*
Gorman, Ned: Prod asst, *ST4*
Gorsuch, Stephanie: Prod asst, *ST:FC*
Gosiewski, Phil: Camera operator, *ST5*
Gowdy, Lloyd: Asst chief lighting tech, *ST4*
Graffeo, Charles M.: Set decorator, *ST2*
Graffeo, John: Swing gang, *ST2*
Grafton, Abbot: Optical and mechanical consultant, *ST:TMP*
Grahn, Dale: Color timer, *ST6*
Grand, Robert: Unit prod mgr, *STG*
Gravenor, Charlotte A.: Hair stylist, *VGR*
Graves, John: Effects camera operator, *ST6*
Graves, Michael R.: 2nd grip, *TOS*
Gravett, Jacques: Asst editor, *VGR*
Gray's Harbor Historical Seaport Authority and the *Lady Washington*: Special thanks, *STG*
Gray, Pamela: Writer, *TNG*
Gray, T. Michael: Prod-writer, *TNG*
Greeley, Jeffrey P.: First asst photographer, *STG*
Green, Al: Camera operator, *TOS*
Green, Caroleen: Digital matte artist, *ST:FC;* Matte artist, *ST4*
Green, Christopher: Animation effects animator, *ST6*
Green, Dr. Richard H.: Tech advisor, *ST2, ST3*
Green, Les: Asst editor, *TOS*
Greene, Vanessa: Writer, *TNG*
Greenspan, Jaq: Writer, *TNG*
Greenwood, Ronald E.: Property master, *ST4;* Asst property, *ST3*
Greenwood, Timothy: Negative cutter/projectionist, *ST6;* Projectionist, *ST:FC*
Gregg, Kris: Effects props and miniatures, *ST:TMP*
Gregory Jein, Inc.: Miniatures, *DS9;* New spacecraft models designer, *ST5*
Grevera, John J.: Swing person, *VGR*
Griffin, James S.: First asst dir, *VGR*
Griffith, Gene: Key grip, *ST2*
Griffith, Robert E.: First company grip, *STG*
Grigsby, Matthew K.: Payroll accounting, *ST:I*
Grindstaff, Douglas H.: Sound editor-sound effects editor-asst film editor, *TOS*
Griswold, Carol Lee: Prod asst, *ST6*
Gross, John: CGI producer, *VGR*
Grower, Janet: Prod support, *ST:I*
Grower, John: Effects superv, *STG, ST:I*
Guaglione, Eric: Animation superv, *STG*
Guers, Karl: Writer, *TNG*
Guinta, Dawn: Computer imaging superv, *STG*
Gundelfinger, Alan: Optical consultant, *ST:TMP*
Gutman, David: Digital compositor, *ST:I*
Guttierez, Rick: Effects props and miniatures, *ST:TMP*

Haas, Christine: Prod office coord, *ST:I*
Haboush, Jeffrey J.: Re-recording mixer, *ST6*
Hagedorn, Jim: Optical camera operator, *ST4*
Haggar, John A.: Visual effects editor, *ST:FC* ; Asst film editor, *ST2, ST3, ST5*
Haggar, Terry P.: Color timer, *ST3, STG*
Haight, Wanda M.: Writer, *TNG*
Haire, Chris, CAS: Re-recording mixer, *TNG, DS9, VGR*
Haire, Steven: Climbing rigger, *ST5*
Hall, Cecelia: Superv sound editor, *ST2, ST3;* Sound editor, *ST:TMP*
Hall, Darrell: Music editor, *ST:I*
Hall, Deborah: Key costumer, *TNG*
Hall, Greg: Costumer, *ST6*
Hall, Ken: Superv music editor, *ST:I;* music editor, *ST5, ST:TMP, ST:FC, ST:I*
Hall, Nelson: Modelmaker, *STG;* Optical processing, *ST6*
Haller, Ernest, ASC: Dir of photography, *TOS*
Haller, Scott G. G.: Sound effects editor, *ST:FC;* Asst sound editor, *STG*
Halperin, Michael: Writer, *TNG*
Hamilton, Jr., Lumas: Hair stylist, *ST:I*
Hamilton, Jr., Warren MPSE: Sound effects editor, *ST4, ST5*
Hamner, Robert: Writer, *TOS*
Hanable, Brian: Compositor, *ST:I*
Haney, Mike: Recordist, *ST6*
Hanks, David: Digital matchmover, *ST:FC;* Motion control camera asst, *ST6;* Asst cameraman, *ST3*
Hanley, John W.: Film editor, *TOS*
Hanley, Sean: ADR editor, *ST3;* Dialogue editor, *ST:TMP*
Hanna, Steve: Animal trainer, *ST:I*
Hannigan, Rick: Optical painting, *ST6*
Hansard, Sr., Donald: Process coord, *ST4*
Hansard: Process compositing, *ST6*
Hanson, Kurt: Scenic artist, *ST:I*
Hardberger, David: Photographic effects cameraman, *ST:TMP;* Asst camera operator, *ST2*
Harders, Robert: Roto artist, *ST:I*
Harding, Alan: Photographic effects cameraman, *ST:TMP*
Harker, Gregory: Senior animation stand photographer, *ST5*
Harlan, Robin: Foley artist, *ST:FC, ST:I*
Harman, Lynn: Transportation captain, *ST3*
Harmon, David P.: Writer, *TOS*
Harmon, II, John W.: Dolly grip, *STG*
Harper, Catherine: Foley artist, *ST:I*
Harper, Dennis: Key grip, *ST3*
Harrington, Neil: Starfield and tactical displays, *ST2*
Harris, Andrew: 3D digital artist, *ST:I*
Harris, Barbara: Voice casting, *ST4, ST5, ST6, STG, ST:FC, ST:I;* Voice-over casting, *ST3*
Harris, Clayvon C.: Writer, *VGR*
Harris, David: Greensperson, *ST:I*
Harris, Eugene: Asst art dir, *TOS*

Harris, Leon: Art dir, *ST:TMP*
Harris, Linda: Animation and graphics, *ST:TMP*
Harrison, Eric: Men's wardrobe superv, *ST4*
Harrison, Matthew: Foley editor, *ST6*
Harstedt, Jeffrey: Video coord, *ST6*
Hart, Clyde: 2nd company grip, *ST6*
Hart, Harvey: Dir, *TOS*
Hartley, Richard: Asst chief lighting tech, *ST5*
Hartwell, Chester: Equipment mgr, *ST5*
Harvey, Brian: Prod asst, *ST:I*
Harvey, Geoff "Hoaf": 3D animator, *ST:I*
Harvey, Ken: Key costumer, *TOS*
Harvey, T. Ashley: Sound editor, *DS9, VGR*
Harvie, Ray: Storyboard artist, *ST:I*
Haskin, Byron: Assoc prod, *TOS*
Hatch, Wilbur: Music consultant, *TOS*
Hatton, Christopher: Writer, *TNG*
Haughton, Stanford G.: Sound mixer, *TOS*
Hausman, Matthew: 3D animator, *ST:I*
Haver, Dorene: Digital compositor, *ST:FC*
Hawkins, William P.: Set designer, *ST:FC*
Haydn, Franz J.: String Quartet in D Major, Opus 64, No. 5, "The Lark" by, *ST:I*
Haye, Jack: Modelmaker, *ST6*
Hayes, Brad: CGI supervisor, *VGR*
Hayes, Jack: Orchestrations, *ST2*
Haymore, June Abston: Makeup artist, *TNG, STG*
Haynes, Monica: Starfleet uniform costumer, *ST:I*
Hays, Sanja Milkovic: Costume designer, *ST:I*
Heath, Bill: Postprod exec, *TOS*
Heileson, Vincent R.: Prod auditor, *ST:FC*
Heindel, Toby: Camera operator, *ST4;* Asst cameraman, *ST3*
Heindel, Todd: Lab tech, *ST4*
Heinemann, Arthur: Writer, *TOS*
Heinz, Christine: Key costumer, *ST6, ST:FC*
Heller, John: Inferno artist, *ST:I*
Hellstrom, Robert: Asst to prod, *TOS*
Helman, Pablo: Sabre compositing artist, *ST:FC*
Helmer, Riche: Effects props and miniatures, *ST:TMP*
Hemphill, Doug M.: Sound effects recordist, *ST4;* Re-recording mixer, *ST5*
Hendershot, Matt: Digital effects artist, *ST:FC*
Henrikson, Jim: Music editor, *TOS*
Henriques, III, Edouard: Special makeup artist, *ST5*
Henry, Agnes G.: Wardrobe superv, *ST2;* Women's wardrobe superv, *ST3;* Wardrobe, *ST:TMP*
Henry, Linda: Optical effects line up, *ST6*
Herbertson, Scott: Set Designer, *DS9*
Herbick, Michael: Re-recording mixer, *ST6, ST:I*
Hernandez, Adam: Apprentice editor, *ST:I*
Hernandez, Dawn: Postprod coord, *TNG, DS9*
Heron, Dave: Key rigging tech, *STG*
Heron, Geoff: Key pyrotech, *ST:FC;* Effects rigger, *STG*
Hershman, Brent Lon: Asst to Ms. Breton, *ST6*
Hetos, Phil: Color timer, *ST:I*
Heuer, Ellen: Foley, *ST3, ST4*
Hickey, Megan: Prod asst, *STG*
High, Ron E., SOC: Camera operator, *VGR*
Hilkene, Michael: Sound effects editor, *ST2*
Hill, George Roy: Grip, *TOS*
Hill, Robert: Asst cameraman, *ST3;* Asst camera operator, *ST2;* Plate camera asst, *ST6*; Visual effects camera asst, *ST:FC*
Hinkle, Jack: Photographic effects editorial, *ST:TMP*
Hiroshima: Music, *ST5*
Hirsh, Edward: Prod mgr, *ST4;* Stage mgr, *STG;* Stage tech, *ST2*
Hladececk, Joel: Motion control camera, *ST6*
Hoag, Grant: Film editor, *TOS*
Hock, Allison: Writer, *TNG*
Hockridge, John: First asst dir, *ST3*
Hodges, Joseph: Set designer, *DS9*
Hoerter, Dennis: Motion control facility superv, *TNG, DS9, VGR*
Hofacre, Michael: Apprentice editor, *ST6*
Hoffman, Bob: Unit publicist, *ST6*
Hoffman, Matthew A.: Key costumer, *TNG, VGR;* Costumer, *STG*
Hoffman, Tina: Makeup artist, *VGR*
Hoffmeister, Edward: Visual effects asst editor, *DS9*
Hohman, R. J.: Special effects, *DS9*
Holder, Paul: Asst colorist, *DS9, VGR*
Holland, C. J.: Writer, *TNG*
Holland, Diane: Digital effects prod, *ST:I*
Holland, Gary: Writer, *DS9*
Hollander, Jesse: Lighting effects specialist, *ST:I*
Hollander, Richard: Computer animation and tactical displays, *ST4;* Electronic and mechanical design, *ST:TMP*; Senior staff (VIFX), *ST:I*
Hollister, Robert: Photographic effects photography, *ST:TMP*
Hollister, Tom: Photographic effects photography, *ST:TMP*
Hollowach, Mike: Set dresser, *ST:I*
Hollywood Armor: Wardrobe accessories, *ST3*
Holzman, Ethan: Asst sound editor, *ST:I*
Home on the Range: Catering, *STG, ST:I*
Homsher, Thomas R.: Special effects, *ST3*
Hooper, Carl: Computer graphics animator, *ST:FC*
Hooper, Greg: Set designer, *VGR*
Hope, Clint: Special projects superv, *ST5*
Horch, Steve: Special props, *TNG, DS9, VGR*
Hormann, Uel: Digital compositor, *ST:I*
Horn, Steve: Asst colorist, *TNG, DS9, VGR*
Horner, James: Composer, *ST2, ST3*
Hornick, Daniel: Modeling, *ST:I*
Hornstein, Ellen J.: Asst to Mr. Frakes, *ST:I*; Prod asst, *ST:FC*
Hornstein, Martin: Exec prod-unit prod mgr, *ST:FC, ST:I;* Co-prod, *ST6*
Horowitz, Ron: ADR editor, *ST3*
Horton, John: Acknowledgment, *ST4*
Horvat, Michel: Writer, *TNG*
Hosek, Rich: Writer, *VGR*
Hotaki, Mari: Visual effects coord, *DS9*
Houston, Sandy: Rotoscope artist, *ST6*
Howard A. Anderson Co.: Photographic effects, *TOS*
Howard, Adam: Digital visual effects superv, *ST:FC*
Howard, Bill: Hair stylist, *TNG*
Howard, Caleb J.: R&D superv, *ST:I*
Howard, Frank: Sound editor, *ST6*
Howard, Jennifer Ann: Digital compositor, *ST:I*
Howard, Larry: Gaffer, *ST:TMP*
Howard, Merri D.: Prod-cosuperv prod, *VGR*; Line prod-unit prod mgr-first asst dir, *TNG;* Thanks for assistance, *ST:FC, ST:I*
Howarth, Alan S.: Sound effects creation, *ST:TMP;* Special sound effects, *ST2, ST3, ST4, ST5, ST6*
Howe, Ross: 2nd boom, *TOS*
Howell, Carmon H.: First company grip, *ST5*
Howie, Wade: Computer graphics animator, *ST6*
Hoy, William: Editor, *TNG;* Film editor, *ST6*
Hubbard, Joe: Asst art dir, *ST4*
Hubbell, Don: Rigging 2nd company grip, *ST:I*
Huddleston, Gary: Camera operator, *DS9*
Hudson, David J.: Re-recording mixer, *ST2, ST3, ST4*
Hudson, Tony: Whale operator/puppeteer, *ST4*
Hudson, Tripp: Prod coord, *STG*
Hughlett, James: Set dresser, *ST:I*
Huizing, Timothy P.: Borg dept head, *ST:FC*
Hulett, Don L.: Property master, *ST5, ST6*
Hulett, Kurt V.: Property master, *ST5*
Hundley, Craig: Music, *ST3*
Hunsaker, Jack: Music editor, *TOS*
Hunt, Jeremy: CGI artist, *VGR*
Hunter, Peg: Optical lineup, *ST4, ST6;* Computer graphics artist, *STG*
Hunter/Gratzner Industries, Inc.: Pyrotechnic miniatures, *ST:I*
Hurley, Maurice: Co-exec prod-writer, *TNG*
Hutzel, Gary: Visual effects superv, *TNG, DS9*
Huxley, Craig: Music, *ST4*
Hydrel: Special thanks, *ST6*
Hyman, Barry: Titles and opticals, *ST5*

Ichikawa, Cindy M.: Prod superv, *ST:I*, asst prod office coord, *ST:FC*
Ignaszewski, Jay: Visual effects editor, *ST3*
Iguchi, Fred: Special electronics, *ST:TMP*
Illusion Arts, Inc.: Matte paintings, *DS9, VGR, ST5, STG;* Borg matte painting, *ST:FC*
ILM Computer Graphics: Time travel, *ST4*
ILM stage crew: Stage techs, *ST3*
Image "G": Motion control photography, *TNG, DS9, VGR*
Industrial Light & Magic: Co-produced by-visual effects prod, *ST4;* Special visual effects prod, *ST2, ST3;* Special visual effects, *TNG, ST6, STG;* Special visual animation and visual effects, *ST:FC;* Stock optical recomposites, *ST5*
Ingalls, Don: Writer, *TOS*
International Alliance of Theatrical Stage Employees (IATSE): *TOS, TNG; DS9; VGR; ST:TMP, ST2, ST3, ST4, ST5, ST6, STG, ST:FC, ST:I*
International Scientific Instruments, Inc.: Special thanks, *ST5*

ppolito, Joseph A.: Superv dialogue editor, *STG*
rving, Conrad: First asst dir, *DS9*
scove, Robert: Dir, *TNG*
vanjack, Dennis C.: Standby painter, *ST3*
verson, Karen: Makeup artist, *DS9*
vins, Anthony "Max": Digital superv, *ST:I*
vins, Christopher: Digital compositor, *ST:I*

Jack Daniels: Special thanks, *ST5*
Jackson, Celine: Digital film I/O, *ST:FC*
Jackson, Doug: Sound effects editor, *ST:FC*
Jacobs, Jake: Writer, *TNG*
Jacobson, Joni: Creative superv computer imaging, *STG*
Jacobson, Phil: Asst chief lighting tech, *DS9*
Jacoby, Al: Asst props, *TOS*
Jaeger, Alex: Visual effects art dir, *ST:FC*
Jaffe, Steven-Charles: Prod, *ST6;* 2nd unit dir, *ST6*
James, John: Photographic effects project mgr *ST:TMP*
James, Richard D.: Prod designer, *TNG*, *VGR*
James, Tom: 2nd grip, *ST2*
Jarel, Don: Photographic effects cameraman, *ST:TMP*
Jaros, Julie: 3D digital artist, *ST:I*
Jarvis, Ron: Writer, *TNG*
Jefferies, John: Set designer, *TOS*
Jefferies, Walter M. "Matt": Prod designer-art dir, *TOS*
Jein, Greg: Miniatures, *ST:TMP, TNG, DS9, VGR,* Special props, *ST6*; model maker, *ST:I*
Jencks, Nancy: Dirt removal, *ST:FC*
Jenkins, Adam: Re-recording mixer, *STG*
Jenkins, Chris: Re-recording mixer, *ST5, STG*
Jennings, Joseph R.: Prod designer, *ST2;* Art dir, *ST:TMP*
Jennings, Mark R.: Cable person, *ST6*; Utility, *ST4*
Jensen, Erik: Visual effects coord, *ST4*
Jensen, Gary L.: Crane operator, *ST2*
Jensen, Stuart: Casting, *ST3*
Jerrell, Brad: Key grip/lighting tech, *ST:FC;* Stage tech, *ST4*
Jet Propulsion Laboratory, Pasadena: Special thanks, *ST5;* Acknowledgment, *ST2*
Jewell, Austen: Unit prod mgr, *ST2*
Jo Ann Kane Music Service: Music preparation, *ST:I*
Joanou, Phil: Special visual consultant, *ST:TMP*
Johnson, Clinton O.: Helicopter camera operator, *ST6*
Johnson, George Clayton: Writer, *TOS*
Johnson, Greg: Borg project foreperson, *ST:FC*
Johnson, Jack: Prod illustrator, *ST:TMP*
Johnson, Jon E., MPSE: Sound effects editor, *STG*
Johnson, Keith: Optical camera operator, *ST6*
Johnson, Ken: Sound effects recordist, *ST5*
Johnson, Normal: Costumer, *TNG*
Johnson, Paul: Electronic design, *ST:TMP*; Physical prod technologist, *ST:I*
Johnson, Ralph: Chief lighting tech, *DS9*
Johnson, Randy: Matte photography, *ST4*
Johnson, Rodger: Title design, *ST2*
Johnson, Tom: Add'l sound effects, *ST3*
Johnson, Troy: Climbing rigger, *ST5*
Johnson, Wendell: Prod asst, *ST5*
Johnston, Ann M.: Asst to Mr. Shepherd, *ST:TMP*
Johnston, Martha E.: Set designer, *ST:FC*
Jones, Albert: Special effects asst, *TOS*
Jones, Bruce: Visual effects prod, *STG, ST:I*
Jones, Curtis B.: Propmaker foreperson, *ST:FC;* Construction foreperson, *ST:I*
Jones, Dean Carl: Makeup artist, *DS9, ST:I*
Jones, Don: Recorder, *TOS*
Jones, Doug: Negative superv, *ST:FC*
Jones, Ed: Optical line-up, *ST2*
Jones, Proctor: Assistance to photographic effects, *ST:TMP*
Jones, Ron: Music, *TNG*
Jones, Sue: Visual effects coord, *DS9*
Jones, Thomas B.: Craft services, *ST4, ST5*
Jones, Tim: Hair stylist, *TNG*
Jordan, Paul: Electrical engineering, *ST5*
Jorgensen, Kris: Costumer, *TNG*
Josselyn, John: Scenic artist, *ST:FC*
Joyce, Michael: Effects props and miniatures, *ST:TMP*
Joyce, Sean: Matte artist, *ST4*
Juday, Penny: Art dept coord, *ST:FC, ST:I;* Prod asst, *STG*
Julian, Heidi: Prod coord, *DS9;* Postprod assoc, *TNG*
Justman, Robert H.: Superv prod-consulting prod, *TNG;* Prod-assoc prod-asst dir, *TOS*

Kacic-Alesic, Zoran: Computer graphics software developer, *STG*
Kaelin, Michael: Video support, *ST:I*
Kafity, Suhail F.: Sound editor, *ST6*
Kaftan, Nicola: Animation and graphics, *ST:TMP*
Kahn, James: Writer, *TNG*
Kail, James: Makeup artist, *ST3*
Kalbfeld, Mark: Writer, *TNG*
Kalosh, Brenda: 2nd asst dir, *TNG*
Kandel, Stephen: Writer, *TOS*
Kaplan, Sol: Music composed and conducted, *TOS*
Karpman, David: Optical line up, *ST6*
Kartozian, Thomas: Writer, *TNG*
Katz, Aaron: 24-frame video displays, *ST6*
Katz, David: 24-frame video displays, *ST6*
Katz, Michael: Lighting tech, *ST6*
Kaufman, Jason: Modelmaker, *TNG, DS9, VGR*
Kay, John: Music, *ST:FC*
Kay, Steve J.: Writer, *VGR*
Kaye, Alan S.: Set designer, *DS9, ST6, ST:I*
Kaye, Pam: Prod accountant, *ST6*
Keath, Jack: Loop editor, *ST2*
Keats, Hazel: Hair styles, *TOS*
Keck, Annitta H.: Thanks for assistance, *ST:FC*
Keefer, Jim: Animator, *ST2*
Keeler, Ira: Modelmaker, *ST3, ST:FC*
Kehl, Judd, Camera operator, *VGR*
Kehoe, Patrick: First asst dir, *ST4*
Kellam DeForest Research: Research, *TOS*
Keller, Frank P., ACE: Film editor, *TOS*
Keller, Jack: Recordist, *ST:I*
Keller, Michael James: 2nd asst dir, *DS9*
Kelley, Gene: Construction coord, *ST:TMP*
Kelley, Severine: Prod coord, *ST:I*
Kelley, Terry: Editor, *DS9*
Kellough, Michael: Set construction, *ST5*
Kelly, Denny: Photographic effects editorial, *ST:TMP*
Kelly, Dick: Camera operator, *TOS*
Kelly, Rob A.: Asst to Mr. Westmore, *ST:I*
Kemper, David: Writer, *TNG, VGR*
Kendall, Deborah: Effects props and miniatures, *ST:TMP*
Kenney, William J.: Casting, *TOS*
Kent, Debra: 2nd asst dir, *DS9*
Kenwith, Herb: Dir, *TOS*
Keppler, Rolf John: Special makeup artist, *ST5*
Keppler, Werner: Makeup artist, *TNG, ST2*
Kern County Board of Trade: Special thanks, *STG*
Kessler, Adrienne: Hair stylist, *DS9*
Kidd, William: Add'l orchestrations, *ST6*
Kilburn, Scott: 3D digital artist, *ST:I*
Kilkenny, John: Visual effects prod, *ST:I*
Killey, Bill: Camera operator, *ST5*
Kim, Jennifer Jung: Texture painter, *ST:I*
Kim, Philip: Writer-asst to prod, *DS9*
Kimball, John: Animation and graphics, *ST:TMP*
Kimberlin, Bill: Chief visual effects editor, *ST3*
Kimble, Greg: Digital optical superv, *ST:FC, ST:I*; Photographic effects photography, *ST:TMP*
King, Jeff: Writer, *DS9*
King, Linda A.: Set designer, *ST:FC;* Prod asst, *STG*
Kingsbridge, John: Writer, *TOS*
Kinwald, Ron: 2nd asst dir, *TNG*
Kissel, Gil, Asst dir, *TOS*
Kite, Richard: Cable person, *STG, ST:I*
Klein, Jack: Writer, *VGR*
Klein, Karen: Writer, *VGR*
Klein, Steve: Photographic effects editorial, *ST:TMP*
Kline, John: Sound effects editor, *ST2*
Kline, Mark: Photographic effects grip, *ST:TMP*
Kline, Martin: Prod illustrator, *ST:TMP*
Kline, Richard H., ASC: Dir of photography, *ST:TMP*
Klink, Lisa: Exec story editor-writer, *VGR;* Writer, *DS9*
Kloor, Harry Doc: Writer, *VGR*
Knapp, Douglas H., SOC: Dir of photography-camera operator, *VGR*
Knoll, John: Visual effects superv, *STG, ST:FC;* Computer animation, *DS9*
Knoller, Wendy: Postprod superv, *TNG*
Knowlton, Kim: Animator, *ST2*
Knox, R.D.: Chief lighting tech, *TNG, DS9*
Kobayashi, Alan: Scenic artist, *TNG, STG, ST:I*
Kobler, Flip: Writer, *DS9*
Kobold, Jerry: Lead man, *ST3*
Kochoff, Kristina: Prod assoc, *VGR*
Koczera, Peter: Digital compositor/artist, *STG*

Koefoed, Christopher L.: Asst editor, *ST2*
Koeppel, Dan: Writer, *TNG*
Koeppel, David A.: Asst editor, *DS9, VGR*
Koester, Thomas: Animation and graphics, *ST:TMP*
Kohut, Bob: Mechanical fabrication, *ST5*
Kolbe, Winrich: Dir, *TNG, DS9, VGR*
Kolhweck, Clifford: Music editor, *ST:FC*
Komack, James: Dir, *TOS*
Konner, Lawrence: Writer, *ST6*
Konwicka, Maria: 2D artist, *ST5*
Kopelman, Mitch: Digital effects superv, *ST:I*
Korda, Nicholas: ADR editor, *ST4, STG*
Koslowsky, Jon: Editor, *TNG*
Kozachic, Pete: Asst cameraperson, *ST4*
Kozikowski, Greg: Video engineer, *ST:I*
Kracke, Don: Title design, *ST2*
Kraft, Inc: Special thanks, *ST5*
Krainin, Deborah L.: Asst to Mr. Jaffe, *ST6*
Kramer, Daniel: Computer graphics animator, *ST:FC*
Kraus, Paul: Modelmaker, *ST4*
Krepela, Neil: Matte photography, *ST2*
Kretchmer, John: Dir, *DS9*
Kriegler, Richard: Art dir, *ST:I*
Krikes, Peter: Writer, *ST4*
Kroeker, Allan: Dir, *DS9, VGR*
Krohn, Mike: Writer, *DS9*
Krosskove, Kris, SOC: Dir of photography-camera operator, *TNG, DS9*
Krzemien, Richard: Writer, *TNG*
Kucera, Valerie Mickaelian: Prod coord, *ST5*
Kuehn, Bradley: Optical photography superv, *ST6*
Kunz, Carol: Wardrobe superv-key costumer, *TNG, DS9;* Wardrobe superv, *VGR*
Kuramoto, Dan: Prod Music, *ST5*
Kuran, Peter: Visual Concept Engineering, Inc., add'l optical effects, *ST5*
Kurtz, Don: Effects props and miniatures, *ST:TMP*
Kurtz, Susan: Dialog editor, *ST:I*
Kutchaver, Kevin: Animation effects, *ST6*

La Cava, Lily: Script superv, *ST3, ST4*
La Fave, Michael: 3D animator, *ST:I*
LaBounta, Henry: Computer graphics artist, *STG*
Laiken, Milt: Optical consultant, *ST:TMP*
Lakso, Edward J.: Writer, *TOS*
Lam, Garrett E.: Digital compositor, *ST:I*
Lama, Christopher: Rigging asst chief lighting tech, *ST:FC, ST:I*
Lambdin, Susanne: Writer, *TNG*
Lampson, Barbara: Hair stylist, *TNG*
Landaker, Alan: Chief engineer, *ST2, ST3, ST4*
Landaker, Gregg: Re-recording mixer, *ST:TMP*
Landaker, Hal: Video superv, *ST2, ST3, ST4*
Landau, Les: Dir, *DS9, VGR;* Dir-first asst dir, *TNG*
Landsberg, David: Writer, *TNG*
Lane, Brian Alan: Writer, *TNG*
Lang, Charles: Chief rigging electrician, *ST6*
Lang, Mary Etta: Women's wardrobe, *ST4;* Wardrobe, *ST:TMP*
Lang-Matz, Laura: Visual effects coord-visual effects assoc, *DS9*
Langer, Irene: Female costumer, *TOS*
Langham, Charles: Best boy, *ST2*
Langridge, Dr. Robert: Molecular computer graphics, *ST2*
Lansford, William Douglas: Writer, *TNG*
Lanteri, Michael: Special effects superv, *ST4*
Lapham, Richard: Music editor, *TOS*
Larson, Lance: Asst property master, *ST:I*
LaSalandra, John, SME: Music editor, *TNG*
Laser Media Rentals: Laser, *TNG*
Laszlo, Andrew, ASC: Dir of photography, *ST5*
Later, Adria: Studio teacher, *ST:I*
Laughlin, Bob: Paint foreperson, *VGR*
Laughlin, Jim: Electrician, *TOS*
Laurienzo, Lance: Asst sound editor, *STG*
Lauritson, Peter: Consulting prod-prod-dir, *TNG;* Consulting prod-superv prod, *DS9;* Superv prod, *VGR;* Coprod, *STG;* Coprod-2nd unit dir, *ST:FC, ST:I;* Assoc prod, *TNG*
Law, Lin: Photographic effects cameraman, *ST:TMP*
Lawerence, Paul: 2nd asst dir, *DS9*
Lawler, Michael: Photographic effects cameraman, *ST:TMP*
Lay, Tom: Illustrator, *ST3*
LaZebnik, Philip: Writer, *TNG, DS9*
Le Ber, Susan: Purchasing agent, *ST5*
Le Blanc, Deidre: Animation and graphics, *ST:TMP*
Le Pre, Gus: Hair stylist, *TNG*
Leader, Tony: Dir, *TOS*
Leaper, Angela: Electronic editor, *ST:FC*
Learned, Alison: Visual effects editor, *ST:I*
Leasure, Frank "Ferb": Construction foreperson, *ST:FC*; General foreperson, *ST:I*
Leben, Mike: Motion control programmer, *DS9, VGR*
Lebowitz, Adam (Mojo): CGI supervisor, *VGR*
Leckman, Tad: Digital matte, *ST:FC*
Lederman, Robert: Dir-editor, *TNG;* Editor, *VGR;* Editor-writer, *DS9*
Lee, Barbara J.: Writer, *DS9*
Lee, Don: Special video compositing, *TNG*; Digital compositing superv, *STG*
Lee, Erik: 3D animator, *ST:I*
Lee, Hyun Sean: Inferno artist, *ST:I*
Lee, James Do Young: Digital compositor, *ST:I*
Lee, Jenifer A.: Writer, *DS9*
Lee, Jennifer: Optical line up, *ST6*
Lee, Norma: Hair designer, *DS9*
Lee, Robin: Asst visual effects editor, *ST6*
Legato, Robert: Dir-visual effects superv, *TNG, DS9*
Leichliter, Otto: Computer engineering, *ST5*
Lemont, Lee: ADR editor, *STG*
Lenihan, Kathryn: Animator, *ST2*
Leonetti, John: Dir of photography (2nd unit), *ST:I*
Leonetti, Matthew F. ASC: Dir of photography, *ST:FC; ST:I*
Lesser, Veronica E.: 2D artist, *ST5*
Letteri, Joe: Computer graphics animator, *ST6*
Leveque, John: Sound effects editor, *ST3*
Levi Strauss & Co., Special thanks, *ST5*
Levitt, Len: Key costumer, *DS9*
Levy, Don: Unit publicist, *STG*
Lew, Stewart W.: Computer graphics artist, *STG*
Lewin, Robert: Co-prod-writer, *TNG*
Lewis, Shari: Writer, *TOS*
Leyden, Robin: Special electronics *ST:TMP*
Lichtwardt, Ellen: Animation superv, *ST4*
Liedtka, Scott: Senior technical superv, *ST:I*
Likowski, James: Foley editor, *STG*
Lilly, Jack F.: Sound mixer, *TOS*
Lim, James: Optical camera operator, *ST3*
Lin, Jeff: 3D animator, *ST:I*
Lindemoen, Burton: 2nd company grip, *ST5*
Lingard, Carlton Scott: Special effects asst, *ST:FC, ST:I;* Asst special effects, *ST6*
Linn, James: Wardrobe superv, *ST2;* Men's wardrobe superv, *ST4*
Lippman, Stuart: Script superv, *DS9*
Lipshultz, Andrew: Unit publicist, *ST4*
Lipsky, Stephanie: Key costumer, *DS9*
Litt, Robert J.: Re-recording mixer, *ST:I*
Littleton, Kenneth: Digital compositor, *ST:FC, ST:I*
Littleton, Lawrence: Digital compositor, *ST:FC, ST:I*
Livingston, Carlyle: Miniature effects superv, *ST:I*
Livingston, David: Superv prod-dir, *VGR;* Superv prod-dir-unit prod mgr, *TNG;* Superv prod-dir-writer, *DS9*
Livingston, Harold: Screenplay, *ST:TMP*
Lloyd, Gene: Cable man, *TOS*
Lloyd, Oliver: 2D digital artist, *ST:I*
Lloyd, Peter: Storyboards, *ST:I*
Lobl, Victor: Dir, *DS9, VGR*
Loeffler, John: Asst editor, *TOS*
Logan, Bruce: Add'l photography, *ST:TMP*
Logan, Karen: Prod support, *ST6*
Lombardi, David: CGI supervisor, *VGR*
Lombardi, Joe: Special effects, *TOS*
London, Keith: Model support, *ST:FC*
Long, David R.: Writer, *DS9*
Long, Roy: Construction coordinator, *TOS*
Longbotham, Brian: Prod kinetic lighting effects, *ST:TMP*
Longo, Joe: Property master, *TNG, DS9, ST2, ST3*
Look, Bradley M.: Makeup artist, *ST:FC, ST:I, VGR*
Lord, Liz: Digital compositor, *ST:I*
Lorente, Ross: Stage, *ST6*
Los Alamos National Laboratory: Add'l computer graphics, *ST2*
Losso, Ernest A: Casting, *TOS*
Lotito, Joe: Prod asst, *ST6*
Loughery, David: Writer, *ST5*
Lowery-Johnson, Junie, CSA: Casting, *TNG, DS9, VGR, STG, ST:FC, ST:I*
Lucas, John Meredyth: Prod-dir-writer, *TOS*
Luckenbach, David: Camera operator, *ST:FC, ST:I*
Luckey, Angie: Asst sound editor, *ST5*
Luckoff, Nancy: Computer graphics resource mgr, *ST:FC;* Prod asst, *ST6*
Lupica, Francisco: Sound effects creation, *ST:TMP*
Lurie, Darren: 3D digital artist, *ST:I*
Ly, Vinh: Computer system administrator, *STG*

Lynch, Margaret: Prod asst, *STG*
Lynch, Michael: Modelmaker, *STG*
Lynch, Paul: Dir, *TNG*, *DS9*
Lynn, Jr., Harvey P: Science consultant, *TOS*
Lyons, Robert: Motion control camera operator, *ST5*

Mabin, Anthony: Inferno artist, *ST:I*
Mack, David: Writer, *DS9*
MacKenzie, Michael: Equipment engineering superv, *ST3*
Mackey, Amanda: Casting, *ST4*
MacKinnon, James: Makeup artist, *ST:FC*
Macpartland, Ladd: Asst visual effects editor, *ST:FC*
Macsems, Bill: Property master, *ST:I*
Madalone, Dennis: Stunt coord, *TNG*, *DS9*, *VGR*
Madera County Film Commission: Special thanks, *ST5*
Magdaleno, Jim: Junior illustrator-scenic artist, *VGR;* Scenic artist, *TNG*
Magicam, Inc.: Model manufacture, *ST:TMP*
Magliochetti, Al: Animation effects, *ST6*
Maier, Jodie: Digital matchmover, *ST:FC*
Maio, D. Thomas: Writer, *DS9*
Major League Baseball Properties, Inc.: Trademark licensing, *DS9*
Makau, Margaret: Wardrobe mistress, *TOS*
Makhart, Larry: Video playback operator, *STG*
Malcolm, Paul: Makeup artist, *TOS*
Maldonado, Phil: Key costumer, *TNG*
Malone, Nancy: Dir, *VGR*
Maloney, Greg: Digital compositor, *ST:FC*
Maltese, Daniel E.: Set designer, *ST2*
Maltzahn, Karey: Visual effects editor, *STG*
Malyn, Shari: Animation effects coord, *ST6*
Mammoth Lakes Film Commission: Thanks to, *ST:I*
Mandel, Geoff: Scenic artist, *ST:I*; graphics prod asst, *STG*
Mangini, Mark: Music-sound effects, *ST4;* Sound effects, *ST5*
Mangini, Tim: Foley editor, *ST4*
Manis, Brian: Prod asst, *STG*
Mankiewicz, Don M.: Writer, *TOS*
Mann, Jeff: ILM senior staff, *ST:FC;* Model shop superv, *ST4;* Modelmaker, *ST2*, *ST3*
Mann, Louis: Set designer, *TNG*
Mann, Michael: Location mgr, *ST4*, *ST5*
Mannell, Cleo: Key costumer, *DS9*
Manners, Kelly A.: Unit prod mgr, *TNG*
Manners, Kim: Dir, *TNG*
Manning, Kal: Chief lighting tech, *ST4*
Manning, Patrick: Tailor, *TOS*
Manning, Richard: Co-prod-story editor-writer, *TNG;* Writer, *DS9*
Maples, Paul: Motion control programmer, *DS9*, *VGR*
Marberry, Toni: Writer, *DS9*
March, Marvin: Set decorator, *TOS*
Marcus, Cindy: Writer, *DS9*
Marine Detachment, *U.S.S. Ranger:* Acknowledgment, *ST4*
Mark Ferrari of the Humpback Whale Fund: Special thanks, *ST4*
Mark, Steve: Photographic effects editorial, *ST:TMP*
Markart, Larry: Video playback operator, *VGR*, *ST:FC*
Markham, Joseph R.: Key costumer, *ST6;* Men's wardrobe, *ST4*, *ST5;* Wardrobe, *ST2*, *ST3*
Marks, Elliott S.: Still photographer, *STG*, *ST:FC*, *ST:I*
Marks, Kim: Dir of photography, *STG*
Marsden, Guy: Visual consultant, *ST:TMP*
Marsh, Clay: Photographic effects cameraman, *ST:TMP*
Marshall, David: Music editor, *ST4*
Marshall, Drain: Electrician, *TOS*
Marshall, Tim: Asst chief lighting tech, *ST:FC*
Marston, Joel: Dialogue coach, *ST3*
Martin, James: Illustrator, *DS9*, *VGR*
Martin, Victoria: Foley editor, *ST6*
Martinez, Pete: 24-frame video displays, *ST6*
Martinez, Terri: Postprod superv, *DS9;* Postprod assoc-asst to the prods, *TNG*
Marvin, Courtenay: Asst sound editor, *ST:FC*
Maschwitz, Stu: Digital effects artist, *ST:FC*
Maser, Elaine: Costume superv, *ST6*
Mashimo, Fumi: Digital animator, *ST:FC*
Maslow, Steve: Re-recording mixer, *ST:TMP*
Mason, John: Prod-writer, *TNG*
Masteran, Jacklin: Hair stylist, *DS9*
Masters, Todd: Borg design superv, *ST:FC*
Matakovich, Jeff: Photo chemical composites, *STG*
Mather, Bill: Digital matte artist, *STG*
Matherly, David: Borg dept head, *ST:FC*
Matheson, John H.: Construction foreperson, *ST4*, *ST5*
Matheson, Richard: Writer, *TOS*
Mathias, Nelson: Electrician, *TOS*
Matiosian, Mace: Superv sound editor, *TNG*, *DS9*
Matlovshy, Alisa: 2nd asst dir, *DS9*
Matlovsky, Samuel: Music composed and conducted, *TOS*
Matte World Digital: Digital matte paintings, *ST:FC*
Matte World: Matte painting effects, *ST6*
Mattey, Ray: Mechanical special effects, *ST:TMP*
Matthews Studios Electronics, Inc.: Nettman Camera Remote Systems, *STG*
Matthias, Jean Louise: Writer, *TNG*, *VGR*
Matthies, Tina: Prod asst, *ST6*
Matz, Laura: Visual effects assoc, *DS9*
May, Mike: First asst photographer, *STG*
May, Mike: Lead man, TOS
Mayberry, Russ: Dir-writer, *TNG*
Mayer, Michael L.: Art dir, *VGR*
Mayhugh, Scott: 2nd company grip, *STG*
Mayne, Robert D.: Transportation coord, *ST3*, *ST:TMP*
Maytum, Chuch: Extras casting, *ST6*
MCA compact discs and cassettes: Soundtrack album, *ST6*
McAllister, Steve: Starfield and tactical displays, *ST2*
McArdle, Pat: First asst photographer, *STG*
McArdle, Patrick: Asst cameraman, *ST3*
McAteer, Vivian: Hair designer, *TNG*
McBee, Chris: Hair stylist, *ST:FC*
McCall, Robert: Prod illustrator, *ST:TMP*
McCann, Stephanie: 2D digital artist, *ST:I*
McCardle, Paul: Wardrobe, *TOS*
McCarthy, Dennis: Costumer, *ST:I*
McCarthy, Dennis: Orchestrations-orchestra conducted-Music, *STG;* Music, *TNG*, *VGR*; Music-main title theme, *DS9*
McCarthy, Ralph H.: Best boy, *TOS*
McCauley, Danny: Asst dir, *ST:TMP*
McCleod, John: Stage tech, *ST2*; Stunt rigger, *ST5*
McClung, Pat: Effects props and miniatures, *ST:TMP*
McCoy, James L.: Makeup artist, *ST2*, *ST3*, *ST4*
McCrae, Susan: Prod asst, *ST5*
McCrail, Charles Reynolds, RADM: Acknowledgment, *ST4*
McCue, David: Optical camera operator, *ST4*; photographic effects cameraman, *ST:TMP*
McCulloch, Cameron: Sound mixer, *TOS*
McCulloch, Mary: Computer graphics artist, *STG*
McCullough, Robert L.: Prod-writer, *TNG*
McCune, Grant: Miniatures superv, *ST:TMP*
McCurdy, Heather: Prod asst, *ST:FC*
McCusker, Michael: Asst to Mr. Meyer, *ST6*
McDonald, Dave: ADR recordist, *ST:I*
McDonald, Jr., Stewart D.: Utility sound tech, *ST5*
McDonough, Michael: Add'l sound design by, *ST:I*
McDougall, Don: Dir, *TOS*
McDuffee, Mike: Transportation coord, *ST2*
McElhatton, Russ: Photographic effects photography, *ST:TMP*
McEveety, Vincent: Dir, *TOS*
McFadden, Gates: Dir-choreographer, *TNG*
McGough, David: Key costumer, *TNG*
McGovern, Bill: 2nd camera asst, *TOS*
McGovern, Michael: Visual effects editor, *ST6*, *STG*, *ST:FC*
McGrath, Jeff: Computer animation and tactical display, *ST5*
McGrath, Roberto: Still lab tech, *ST2*
McGreevey, Michael: Writer, *DS9*
McIlvain, Randy: Art dir, *DS9*
McIntyre, Deborah: Writer, *TNG*
McKane, Frank: Asst chief lighting tech, *ST4*
McKay, Shawn: Hair stylist, *VGR*
McKenzie, Mark: Orchestrations, *ST6*, *STG*
McKenzie, Richard Frank: Set designer, *ST5*, *TNG*
McKinley, Roni: Visual effects prod, *STG*
McKinney, Mimi: Asst to Mr. Dykstra, *ST:TMP*
McKnight, Scott: Blue screen rigging electrician, *STG;* Lighting tech, *ST:I*
McLaughlin, Raymond A.: Transportation coord, *ST5;* Transportation captain, *ST4*
McManus, Brian: Makeup artist for Mr. Shatner, *ST6*, *STG*
McMillen, Mike: Effects props and miniatures, *ST:TMP*
McMurray, Greg: Special electronics, *ST:TMP*
McNalley, Tim: Makeup artist, *TOS*
McNamara, Scott: Modelmaker, *STG*
McNaughton, Brandon: Digital compositor, *ST:FC*, *ST:I*
McNeill, Robert Duncan: Dir, *VGR*

McQuarrie, Ralph: Visual consultant, *ST4*
McRitchie, Greig: Orchestrations, *ST3*
McWilliams, Kimalyn: Prod asst, *ST:I*
Meade, Syd: Prod illustrator, *ST:TMP*
Medina, Greg: Construction coord, *DS9*
Medlock, Michael A.: Writer, *TNG*
Meehan, Michael: Location mgr, *ST4*
Meek, Rusty: Asst dir, *TOS*
Meerson, Steve: Screenplay by, *ST4*
Mees, Jim: Set decorator, *TNG, VGR*
Mei, David V.: Senior modelmaker, model unit, *ST5*
Meier, Barb: Animator, *ST6*
Meinardus, Dick: First asst photographer, *ST5*
Meininger, Mariane: Model shop coord, *TNG, DS9, VGR*
Meininger, Tony: Miniatures, *TNG, DS9, VGR*
Melichar, Jeff: Set security, *ST2*
Melkonian, Nadim: Climbing rigger, *ST5*
Menchen, Les: Writer, *TNG*
Mendoza, Sammy: Propmaker foreperson, *ST:FC;* Construction foreperson, *ST:I*
Menosky, Joe: Co-prod-exec story editor-writer, *TNG;* Prod-writer-superv prod, *VGR;* Writer, *DS9*
Mercer, Johnny: Music, *ST3*
Meredith, Ron: Asst sound editor, *ST:I*
Merhoff, Don: Best boy, *TOS*
Merhoff, George H.: Gaffer, *TOS*
Merkovich, Matt: CGI supervisor, *VGR*
Merrick, Jean: Wardrobe, *ST3*
Merritt, Sonny: Costumer, *ST:FC*
Metcalfe, Mel: Re-recording mixer, *ST2, ST4*
Metoyer, Robert J.: First asst dir, *TNG*
Metrocolor: Color by, *ST:TMP*
Meyer, Nicholas: Dir-writer, *ST6;* Dir, *ST2;* Writer, *ST4*
Meyers, Jr., Donald E.: Special effects asst, *STG;* Special effects foreperson: *ST:FC*
Miarecki, Ed: Modelmaker, *ST:FC*
Michael, T.: Writer, *TNG*
Michaelian, Michael: Writer, *TNG*
Michaels, Mickey S.: Set decorator, *DS9, ST6*
Micheli, Amanda: Optical scanning dept. coord, *ST:FC*
Michelson, Harold: Prod designer, *ST:TMP*
Mickelberry, Nancy: Set designer, *ST:FC, ST:I*
Middleton, Mike: Special visual consultant, *ST:TMP*
Milch, Tony: Sound effects editor, *ST:FC*
Miles, Kelley: Writer, *DS9*
Milkis, Edward K.: Assoc prod-asst to prod, *TOS*
Millar, Bill: Photographic effects project manager, *ST:TMP*
Miller, Alvah J.: Electronic design, *ST:TMP*
Miller, Dean: Climbing rigger, *ST5*
Miller, F. Hudson: Superv sound editor, *ST6*
Miller, Linda: Computer animation and tactical display, *ST5*
Miller, Mark: Whale operator/puppeteer, *ST4*
Miller, Patricia: Hair stylist, *TNG, VGR, STG*
Miller, Paul: Video playback operator, *ST:I ;* Utility, *VGR*
Miller, Richard: Modelmaker, *ST6, STG*
Miller, Robert W.: Borg crew, *ST:FC*
Miller, Scott: Writer, *VGR*
Millerburg, John: Animation and graphics, *ST:TMP*
Milliken, Mike: Color timer, *ST:FC*
Mills, Brian: First company grip, *TNG*
Mills, Keith: Writer, *TNG*
Mills, Michael J.: Makeup superv, *ST6;* Special makeup artist, *ST5*
Mills, Ryan: 2D digital artist, *ST:I*
Min, Michael: Computer graphics technical asst, *STG*
Minor, Michael: Art dir, *ST2;* Prod illustrator, *ST:TMP*
Minster, Barbara: Hair stylist, *VGR, ST:TMP*
Mirano, Virgil: Visual consultant, *ST:TMP*
Mistovich, Mike: Asst to prods, *DS9*
Mitchell, Jim: Computer graphics animator, *ST6*
Mitchell, Rick: Asst film editor, *ST:TMP*
Mitchell, Todd: Scanning operator, *ST:FC*
Mlodinow, Leonard: Story editor-writer, *TNG*
Moc, Peter: Operator, *STG*
Moc, Richard: Tech superv, *STG*
Modern Film Effects: Add'l optical effects, *ST2*
Modern Sound: Postprod sound, *TNG, DS9, VGR*
Moehnke, T.E.: Superv stage tech, *ST2*
Moehnke, Ted: Miniature pyrotechnics and fire effects, *ST3*
Mohagen, Craig: Stage, *ST6*
Mohammed, Theresa Repola: Negative cutter, *ST6, STG, ST:FC, ST:I*
Molatore, Terry: Rotoscope artist, *ST6*
Molin, Steve: Digital effects artist, *ST:FC*
Mollicone, Anthony: Rigging first company grip, *ST:FC*
Monak, Gary: Special effects, *DS9*
Monak, Richard: Special effects asst, *ST:I*
Monat, Sarah: Foley artist, *ST:FC, ST:I*
Mongovan, Jack: Rotoscope artist, *ST6*
Monroe, Steve: Construction foreperson, *TNG*
Monster Cable: Special thanks, *ST5*
Montemayor, Gloria: Hair stylist, *VGR*
Monterey Bay Aquarium, Monterey, California: Special thanks, *ST4*
Montgomery, Amanda: Computer graphics resource asst, *ST:FC*
Moore, Bruce: Asst craft service, *ST:FC*
Moore, Don: Prod illustrator, *ST:TMP*
Moore, Eric: Props, model unit, *ST5*
Moore, Mark: Visual effects art dir, *ST6;* Concept designer, *STG*
Moore, Michael: Hair stylist, *TNG*
Moore, Mike: Special props, *TNG, DS9, VGR*
Moore, Robert M.: Costumer, *ST6*
Moore, Ronald B.: Visual effects superv, *TNG, VGR, STG*
Moore, Ronald D.: Co-executive prod-writer, *DS9;* Prod-exec story editor-writer, *TNG* ; Writer, *STG, ST:FC;*
Moore, Sue: Women's wardrobe, *ST5*
Moore, Thomas: Prod asst, *ST:I*
Moore, Wade: Music, *ST:FC*
Morales, Zeke: VFX editor, *ST:I*
Moran, Daniel Keys: Writer, *DS9*
Moran, Tim: Special effects, *ST4*
Moran, W. Reed: Writer, *TNG*
Moreau, Harry: Animation effects *ST:TMP;* Title design, *ST4*
Moreau, Linda: Animation and graphics *ST:TMP*
Morehead, Jack; Superintendent, Yosemite National Park Services: Special thanks, *ST5*
Moreland, Ron: CGI superv, *ST:I* Animator, *STG*
Moreno, David: Sound effects recordist, *ST5*
Moreve, Rushton: "Magic Carpet Ride" by, *ST:FC*
Morey, Robert: First asst photographer, *ST6*
Morey, Steve: Propmaker foreperson, *ST:FC*
Morgan, Connie: Animation and graphics, *ST:TMP*
Morgan, Julie: Music, *ST:FC*
Morgan, Kristine: Borg prod coord, *ST:FC*
Morgan, Max: Photographic effects cameraman, *ST:TMP*
Morgan, Robert: Craft service, *ST3*
Morgan, Tim: Electric gaffer, *ST:FC*
Morgan: Script superv, *DS9*
Morris, Jim: ILM president, *STG;* ILM senior staff, *ST:FC*
Morris, Joe: Rigger, *ST6*
Morris, Thaine: Pyrotechnics, *ST2*
Morrisey, Robert: Asst sound editor, *ST:FC*
Morrison, Richard, CAS: Re-recording mixer, *TNG, DS9, VGR*
Morse, Mary Kay: Makeup artist, *ST:FC, ST:I*
Morss, Dylan: Prod asst, *ST:I*
Morton, Arthur: Orchestrations, *ST:TMP, ST5, ST:FC*
Morton, David: Stage, *ST6*
Morton, Josh: Special electronics, *ST:TMP*
Mosko, Gilbert A.: Makeup artist, *TNG, VGR, ST6, STG, ST:FC*
Mossler, Helen, CAS: Casting exec, *TNG, DS9, VGR*
Moudakis, Pat: Swing person-asst property, *DS9*
Movie Magic: Add'l optical effects, *ST3*
Movielab: Color, *ST2, ST3*
Mozart, Wolfgang A.: String Quartet in B-Flat, Opus 10, No. 3, "The Hunt" by, *ST:I*
MPAA: *ST:TMP, ST2, ST3, ST4, ST5, SG6, STG, ST:FC, ST:I*
Mudgett, Danny: Digital compositor, *STG*
Mueller, Ellen: Rotoscope artist, *ST6*
Mullen, Charles: Animation superv, *ST3*
Mullendore, Joseph: Music composed and conducted, *TOS*
Mumford, Andrew: Digital compositor/artist, *STG*
Munoz, Dan: Prod support, *ST:I*
Munoz, Gloria: Borg crew, *ST:FC*
Munoz, Jose: Prod asst, *ST:I*
Murietta, Al: Costumer, *TOS*
Murphy, David: Electrician, *ST:FC*
Murphy, George: Assoc visual effects superv, *ST:FC*
Murray, Alan: Sound editor, *ST:TMP*
Muskat, Joyce: Writer, *TOS*
Musso, Joseph: Illustrator, *ST:FC*
Myers, Donald E.: Asst special effects, *ST6*

Myers, Duncan: Optical laboratory tech, *ST2*
Myers, Jr., Donald E.: Special effects foreperson, *ST:FC*
Myers, Kenny: Makeup dept head, *ST6;* Special makeup design, *ST5*
Myers, Mike: Special electronics, *ST:TMP*
Myers, Pat: Digital effects artist, *ST:FC;* Computer graphics artist, *STG*

Nabisco: Special thanks, *ST4*
Nakada, Ken: Digital compositing, *ST:FC*
Napoli, Anatonia: Writer, *TNG*
Nardino, Gary: Exec prod, *ST3*
Narita, Hiro: Dir of photography, *ST6*
Nash, Erik: Special visual consultant, *ST:TMP;* Motion control photography, *TNG*
Nash, Gerald: Optical and mechanical consultant, *ST:TMP*
Nash-Morgan, Genieve: Makeup artist, *ST:I*
Nathan, Ron: Photographic effects photography, *ST:TMP*
Nathanson, Seth: Electrical engineering, *ST5*
National Aeronautics and Space Admini-stration: Acknowledgment, *ST2*, *ST:TMP*
Natividad, Edwin: Illustrator, *ST:I*
Nauke, Daniel: Fabricator, model unit, *ST5*
Neal, Candace: Hair designer, *DS9;* Hair stylist, *TNG*
Neal, John: Scoring mixer, *ST:TMP*
Neal, Scott J.: Writer, *DS9*
Neale, Michael: Location manager, *ST:I*
Negron, David: Prod illustrator, *ST:TMP*
Neill, Ve: Makeup artist, *ST:TMP*
Neilson, Gina: Prod coord, *ST4*
Nellis, Barbara L.: Computer graphics artist, *STG*
Nelson, Dan: Effects tech, *ST:FC*
Nelson, Gene: Dir, *TOS*
Nelson, Greg: Makeup artist, *VGR*
Nelson, Lori J.: Optical coord, *ST4*
Nelson, Wayne: Transportation coord, *ST:FC*, *ST:I*
Nemeck, Janet: Asst prod assoc, *ST:FC*
Neskoromny, Andrew: Art dir, *TNG*, *VGR;* Set designer, *ST5*
Nesterowicz, John: Asst property, *VGR*
Nethercutt, Davy: Inferno compositor, *DS9*, *VGR*
Neufeld, Glenn: Visual effects superv, *DS9*
Neuss, Wendy: Prod, *VGR;* Co-prod-post-prod superv, *TNG;* Thanks for assistance, *ST:FC*
Nevada Film Commission: Special thanks, *STG*
Neville, Jerry: Swing person, *DS9*
New Directions: "Dreams Begin Responsibilities," *STG*
New York Zoological Society: Special thanks, *ST4*
Newland, John: Dir, *TOS*
Newland, Kenneth: Transportation captain, *ST:FC*, *ST:I*
Newlin-Mazaraki, Robert: Prod asst, *ST:FC*
Newman, Craig: Tactical displays, *ST6*
Newton, Edmund: Writer, *DS9*
Nicastro, Christian: Asst modeler, *DS9*, *VGR*
Nicholson, Bruce: Optical photography superv, *ST2*
Nicholson, Sam: Prod kinetic lighting effects, *ST:TMP;* Add'l special lighting effects, *ST2*
Nimerfro, Scott: Writer, *VGR*
Nimoy, Adam: Dir, *TNG*; Asst to Mr. Meyer, *ST6*
Nimoy, Leonard: Exec prod-writer, *ST6;* Dir-writer, *ST4;* Dir, *ST3*
Nimoy, Nancy: Creature creation, *ST4*
Nishino, Kenneth: First asst photographer, *ST4*, *ST5*
Noble, Cameron: Motion control camera, *ST:FC*
Nocifora, April: Postprod coord, *DS9*
Nolan, Don: Optical layout, optical unit, *ST5*
Noland, Bob: Color timer, *ST3*
Nolin, Gary: Head of physical production, *ST:I*
Nollman, Eugene C.: Set designer, *ST6*
Nordquist, Kerry: Still lab tech, *ST2*
Norman, Eric: Asst to prod, *VGR*; Prod asst, *ST:I*
Norman, Phill: Main title design, *ST:I*
Norman, Viviane: Hair stylist, *VGR*
Normand, Josée: Hair designer, *DS9*, *VGR;* Hair stylist, *TNG*
Norwood, Phillip: Effects animator, *ST3*
November, Mary: Asst film editor, *STG*
Novocom, Inc.: Computer animation and tactical display, *ST4*, *ST5*
Nowell, David, SOC,: Camera operator, *ST3*
Nushawg, Christopher S.: Set designer, *ST:I*
Nuzzo, William: Craft service *ST6*,, *STG*, *ST:FC*
Nygren, Donald O.: Chief lighting tech, *ST5*

O'Byrne, Luke: Prod coord, *ST:FC*
O'Connell, Carol A.: Hair stylists, *ST6;* Add'l hairstylist, *ST3*, *ST4*
O'Connell, Dan: Foley, *ST3*, *ST4*
O'Connor, FX: Pyrotechnic effects, *ST:I*
O'Halloran, Michael: Asst to prods, *VGR*
O'Hara, Terrence: Dir, *VGR*
O'Hara, Katie: Tactical displays, *ST6*
O'Hea, Frank: Standby painter, *VGR*
O'Herlihy, Michael: Dir, *TOS*
O'Keefe, Jennie: DGA trainee, *ST:I*
O'Neill, Sandy: Unit publicist, *ST:I*
O'Neill, Kate: Visual effects camera asst, *STG;* Motion control camera asst, *ST6*
Oakden, Frank: Cable man, *TOS*
Oehler, Gregory: Digital artist, *STG*
Oehlke, Paul: Camera asst, *ST6*
Ogle, Charles A.: Accountant, *ST:TMP*
Okrand, Marc: Alien language creation, *ST3;* Vulcan translation, *ST2;* Klingon dialogue consultant, *ST5;* Klingon language specialist, *ST6*
Okuda, Denise Lynn: Scenic artist-video superv, *ST:FC*, *ST:I;* Scenic artist, *DS9*, *ST6;* *STG;* Video coord, *VGR*
Okuda, Michael: Scenic art superv/tech consultant, *TNG*, *DS9*, *VGR*, *ST:FC*, *ST:I;* Scenic art consultant, *VGR*, *DS9;* Scenic art superv, *STG;* Graphic designer, *ST6;* Computer animation and tactical displays, *ST4;* Scenic artist, *TNG*, *ST5*
Okun, Lan: Writer, *TNG*
Olague, Michael: Visual effects chief lighting tech, *STG;* Stage tech, *ST4*
Olin, Lisa J.: Asst to Mr. Frakes, *ST:FC*
Oliver, John E.: Music, *ST:FC*
Olsen, Paul: Animation and graphics, *ST:TMP*
Olson, Jeff: Visual effects prod, *ST:FC;* Model dept superv, *STG*
Omnibus Video, Inc.: Instrumentation displays computer animation, *ST3*
Oppenheimer, Mark: First asst dir (2nd unit), *ST:I*
Orbison, Roy: Music, *ST:FC*
Ordaz, Frank: Matte artist, *ST2*, *ST3*, *ST4*
Ordover, John J.: Writer, *DS9*
Oster, Steve: Prod-cosuperv prod, *DS9;* Thanks for assistance, *ST:FC*, *ST:I*
Ostroff, Maggie: Asst sound editor, *ST6*
Oswald, Gerd: Dir, *TOS*
Overbeck, Bob: Special effects, *TOS*
Overdiek, Diane: Prod coord, *TNG*, *VGR*
Overton, Mark: Boom operator, *DS9*
Overton, Todd: Utility, *DS9*
Overton, Tom: Sound mixer, *ST:TMP*
Owen, David: Still photo, *ST:FC*
Owens, Mike: Asst camera operator, *ST2*
Ozols-Graham, Venita: First asst dir, *DS9*

P., John: Special sound effects, *ST5*
Pacific Data Images: Add'l digital compositing, *ST6*
Pacific Ocean Post Digital Film Group: Digital visual effects, *ST:FC;* Computer generated imagery-digital optical effects, *VGR*; Video optical effects, *DS9*
Pacific Title/Mirage: Titles and addl opticals by, *ST:I*
Pacific Title: Titles and opticals, *STG*; Add'l optical effects, *ST:FC*
Page, David: Costumer, *TNG*
Pahk, Tom: Effects props and miniatures, *ST:TMP*
Paige, Marvin: Casting, *ST:TMP*
Paisley, James A.: Prod manager, *TOS*
Palinski, Maurice: Key costumer, *TNG*, *DS9*
Palmer, David: Texture painter, *ST:I*
Palmer, R. J.: Sound editor, *ST6*
Panavision: Filmed in, *ST:TMP*, *ST2*, *ST3*, *ST4*, *ST5*, *ST6*, *STG*, *ST:FC*, *ST:I;* Panaflex cameras, cameras and lenses, *TNG*, *DS9*, *VGR*
Panek, Jeri: Starfield and tactical displays, *ST2*
Pangrazio, Michael: Matte artist superv, *ST6;* Matte painting superv, *ST3*
Paramount Pictures Scoring Stage M: Score recorded and mixed, *ST:FC*, *ST:I;* Music score recorded at, *STG*
Paramount Pictures: Digital sound editing, *STG*, *ST:FC*, *ST:I*
Parish, Billy: Asst property master, *ST:I*
Parker, Brice R.: Writer, *DS9*
Parker, Edward M.: Set decorator, *TOS*
Parker, Norman E.: 2nd asst, 2nd camera, *ST3*
Parker, Robert: Special thanks, *ST5*
Parks, Michael: 3D digital artist, *ST:I*
Parrish, Frank: 2nd asst photographer, *ST6*
Parsons, Leslie: Art dir, *VGR*
Parsons, Jr., Linsdley: Exec in charge of prod, *ST:TMP*

Pasquale, Joe: Computer graphics animator, *ST6*
Patterson, Andrew: ADR editor, *ST5*
Patterson, Richard: Digital superv, *ST:FC*
Payne, Jeffrey R.: Foley editor, *STG*; dialog editor, *ST:I*
Payne, Roger: Special thanks, *ST4*
Pearce, Joan: Research, *TOS, TNG, DS9, VGR*
Pearson, Tim L.: Prod auditor, *STG*; prod accountant, *ST:I*
Peck, Terry: Asst effects editor, *ST4*
Pederson, Steve: Re-recording mixers, *ST:FC*
Pedigo, Tom: Set decorator, *TNG, ST3*
Peed, Mike: Photographic effects photography, *ST:TMP*
Peeples, Samuel A.: Writer, *TOS*
Peets, William: Chief lighting tech, *DS9, VGR*
Peiny, Arnaud: Grip, *ST6*
Penn, Leo: Dir, *TOS*
Penner, Dick: Music, *ST:FC*
Pennington, Don: Miniatures, *VGR*
Perconte, Gary: Writer, *TNG*
Perricone, Michael: Writer, *VGR*
Perry, Bert: Electrician, *TOS*
Perry, Jo: Writer, *TNG*
Perry, Thomas: Writer, *TNG*
Perry, Tom: Re-recording mixers, *ST:FC*
Peter, Kuran: VCE photographic effects, *ST6*
Peter, Stolz: Stage tech, *ST2*
Peterman, Don, ASC: Dir of photography, *ST4*
Peterman, Jay: 2nd asst photographer, *ST4*
Peterman, Keith: Camera operator, *ST4, ST5*
Peters, Gregg: Assoc prod-unit prod mgr-asst dir, *TOS*
Petersen, Dennis K.: Special effects, *ST3*
Peterson, Alan: Modelmaker, *ST6*
Peterson, Lorne: Chief modelmaker, *STG*
Peterson, Lowell: Camera operator, *TNG*
Peterson, Mark: Computer animation and tactical displays, *ST4*
Peterson, Michael: Digital compositor, *ST:FC*
Petrie, Don: Prod auditor, *ST5*
Petrulli-Heskes, Rebecca: Rotoscope artist, *ST6*
Petterson, David: Digital record operator, *ST:I*
Pettijohn, Sonny: Asst sound editor, *ST5*
Pevney, Joseph: Dir, *TOS*
Pfaltzgraff: Special thanks, *ST6*
Pfeil, David Oliver: Main title design and computer illustration, *ST6*
Phelan, Walter T.: Borg crew, *ST:FC*
Phelps, Raymond A.: Men's wardrobe, *ST5*
Phelps, Win: Dir, *TNG*
Philip Edgerly Agency, The: Special artwork provided, *STG*
Phillips, Deborah: Asst VFX editor, *ST:I*
Phillips, Fred B., SMA: Makeup artist, *TOS, ST:TMP*
Phillips, Janna: Makeup artist, *TNG, DS9, ST:TMP*
Phillips, Jonathan: Apprentice sound editor, *ST6*
Phillips, Ralph: Writer, *TNG*
Phillips, William F.: Assoc prod, *ST2*
Picardo, Robert: Dir, *VGR*
Pickrell, Gregory: Asst art dir, *TNG*
Pierce, Greg: Animation and graphics, *ST:TMP*
Pierce, Jeff: Digital film I/O, Vision Art, *ST:FC*
Pietroforte, Pam: Writer, *DS9*
Piller, Michael: Creator-creative consultant-exec prod-writer, *VGR, DS9;* Exec prod-writer, *TNG*; writer-coprod, *ST:I*
Piller, Shawn: Writer, *TNG, VGR*
Pima Air and Space Museum and Titan Missile Museum: Thanks for assistance, *ST:FC*
Pine, Ed: Unit publicist, *ST3*
Piner, John: Photographic effects projectionist, *ST:TMP*
Pines, Joshua: Film scanning/recording superv, *ST:FC;* Scanning superv, *STG;* Scanning, *ST6*
Pinkos, Joe: Property person, *STG*
Pinney, Clay: Special effects, *ST4*
Pipes, Ron: Klingon and Vulcan prosthetics, *ST5*
Pitone, Anthony: Digital tech asst, *ST:FC*
Pixar Animation Studios: Software support, *ST:I*
Playback Technologies: Thanks for assistance, *ST:FC, ST:I*
Plunkett, Sean: Climbing rigger, *ST5*
Pock, Bernie: Stunt rigger, *ST5*
Polaroid Corporation: Tech assistance, *ST:TMP*
Polkinghorne, George: Mechanical design, *ST:TMP*
Pollaro, Lisa L.: Digital compositor, *ST:I*
Pono, Anthony: Dolly grip, *TOS*
Pooler, Jerry: Photographic effects cameraman, *ST:TMP*
Poor, Robert D.: Computer graphics, *ST2*
POP Film & POP Animation: Visual effects by, *ST:I*
POP Television: Visual effects compositing, *DS9*
Porter, Terry: Re-recording mixer, *ST4*
Porter, Thomas: Computer graphics, *ST2*
Posell, Jonathan: Asst editor, *DS9*
Posey, Steve: Dir, *DS9*
Pospisil, John: Special sound effects, *ST4*
Post Group. The: Digital composites, *STG;* Video optical effects, *TNG*
Potts, Terri: coprod-assoc prod-postprod superv, *DS9*
Poungpeth, Chalermpon "Yo": Animator, *STG*
Povill, Jon: Assoc prod, *ST:TMP;* Writer, *TNG*
Powell, Dave: Key costumer, *TNG*
Powell, Ellen: Hair stylist, *ST:I*
Powell, Tom: Electrician, *TOS*
Powers, Kathryn: Writer, *TNG, DS9*
Prady, Bill: Writer, *VGR*
Precision Machine: Mechanical designs, *ST:TMP*
Prendergast, Bonnie: Script superv, *ST:TMP*
Presock, Buz: Prod asst, *ST:I*
Price, Andrew Shepard: Writer, *VGR*
Price, Brick: Modelmaker, *TOS*
Price, Lynn: Construction coord, *ST3*
Price, Samuel: Special effects asst, *ST:FC, ST:I*
Price, Travis: Matte painter, *ST:I*
Prime Computer, Inc.: Computer graphics, *TNG*
Princton Gamma-tech: Special thanks, *ST5*
Pritchett, Darrell: Mechanical special effects, *ST:TMP*
Probert, Andrew: Consulting senior illustrator, *TNG;* Prod illustrator, *ST:TMP*
Prohaska, Janos: Special props and design, *TOS*
Proton: Special thanks, *ST6*
Public Missiles Ltd.: Special thanks, *STG*
Puga, Donnie: General paint foreperson, *DS9*
Purcell, William: Special effects, *ST2*
Purser, Tom: Construction foreperson, *TNG, VGR, ST:I*

Quinn, Thomas: Motion control support, model unit, *ST5*
Quist, Gerald: Makeup artist, *TNG, ST6*

Rabjohn, Richard E.: Editor, *DS9*
Race, Louis: First asst dir, *DS9*
Rader, George: Head grip, *TOS*
Rader, Scott: Digital visual effects superv, *ST:FC*
Radley, Elizabeth: Video and computer superv, *ST:FC;* Video consultant, *DS9, VGR, STG*
Raff, Robert H.: Music editor, *TOS*
Raitano, A.J.: Motion control rigger, *DS9, VGR*
Ralke, Cliff: Dolly grip, *TOS*
Ralston, Gilbert: Writer, *TOS*
Ralston, Kenneth: Superv of visual effects, *ST3, ST4;* Special visual effects superv, *ST2*
Ramirez, David: Editor, *TNG, DS9*
Ramirez, Jonathan Paul: Asst editor, *DS9*
Ramsay, John: Effects props and miniatures, *ST:TMP*
Ramsay, Todd: Editor, *ST:TMP*
Randall, Corky: Wrangler, *ST5*
Ranger, U.S.S., Officers and men of: Acknowledgment, *ST4*
Rao, Krishna: Camera operator, *STG*
Rao, Raman: Chief lighting tech, *ST6*
Raoul, MPSE: dialogue editor, *STG*
Rapp, Edward Lee: Motion control and animation prod, model unit, *ST5*
Rapp, Paulette, Asst to prod, *TOS*
Rappaport, Frederick: Writer, *DS9*
Raring, Bob: Color timer, *ST4, ST5*
Rauh, Dick: Effects animation superv, optical unit, *ST5*
Rawlins, Lex: Photographic effects photography, *ST:TMP*
Rawlins, Phil: Unit prod mgr, *ST:TMP;* Asst dir, *TOS*
Ray, Charles: Stage, *ST6*
Reade, Gertrude: Hair styles, *TOS*
Reardon, Craig: Makeup artist, *DS9*
Reaves, Michael: Writer, *TNG*
Record Plant Scoring: Music recorded at, *ST5;* Scoring, *ST4*
Reding, Steven: Effects camera operator, *ST6*
Reebok International, Ltd.: Special thanks, *ST5*
Reed, Chris: Modelmaker, *STG*

Reeder, Andrew: Asst art dir, *DS9*
Reel People, Inc.: Negative cutting, *ST4, ST5*
Reeves, William: Computer graphics, *ST2*
Regne, Claudia: Borg crew, *ST:FC*
Reilly, Ed: Best boy, *ST3*
Reilly, Garet: Costume supervisor, *ST:I*
Rendich, Travis G.: Apprentice editor, *ST:FC*
Rendu, Carolyn: Rotoscope artist, *ST6*
Renfro, James R.: Lighting tech, *STG*
Repola, Arthur: Superv effects editor, *ST2*
Repola, Patrick: Optical camera operator, *ST6*
Resch, Ron: Geometric designs, *ST:TMP*
Rescher, Gayne, ASC: Dir of photography, *ST2*
Resnick, Laurie: Rotoscope artist, *DS9, VGR*
Reuben, Paul: Writer, *TNG*
Revo, Inc.: Special thanks, *ST5*
Rhodaback, Gary: Effects props and miniatures, *ST:TMP*
Rhodes, Matt: Software development, *ST:I*
Rhodes, Michael: Dir, *TNG*
Rhythm & Hues, Inc.: Computer animation *TNG, DS9*
Rich, Lisa: Writer, *TNG, DS9*
Richard Snell Designs, Inc.: Klingon and Vulcan prosthetics creation, *ST5, ST6;* Creature creation, *ST4*
Richards, Chet: Writer, *TOS*
Richards, Michael: Writer, *TOS*
Richards, Preston: Negative cutter/projectionist, *ST6*
Richardson, Andree: Asst to Mr. Coon, *TOS*
Richardson, Paul Bruce: Sound effects editor, *ST3*
Richarz, Laura, SDSA: Set decorator, *DS9*
Riddle, Cynthia: DGA Trainee, *ST3*
Riddle, Jay: Computer graphics superv, *ST6;* Animation camera operator, *ST4*
Rider, Jim: Motion control programmer, *DS9, VGR*
Riedel, Jack: Senior motion control photographer, model unit, *ST5*
Riley, Bobbi Lynn: CGI coordinator, *VGR*
Rimbey, Gary: Special thanks, *STG*
Rioux, Robert: 3D modeler, *ST:I*
Ritchie, Gary: Recordists, *ST6*
Rivera, Edwin: Compositing superv, *ST:I*
Rivera, Miguel: Sound editor, *TNG, DS9, VGR*
Rivera, Paul: Digital compositing superv, *ST:FC*
Rivera, Will: Animator, *STG*
Robert Abel and Assocs, Inc.: Special visual effects conception and design, *ST:TMP*
Roberts, Eric: Video playback operator, *ST:I*
Roberts, Lori M.: First asst accountant, *ST:I*
Roberts, Randy: Editor, *TNG*
Roberts, Ted: Writer, *TNG*
Robertson, Barry: Technical supervisor, *ST:I*
Robinson, Andrew J.: Dir, *DS9, VGR*
Robinson, Jonathan B.: Digital compositor, *ST:I*
Roby, Mike: Color wedging, *ST:I*
Roccuzzo, Michael: Construction accountang, *ST:I*
Rockler, Aaron H.: Labor foreperson, *STG, ST:FC, ST:I* ; *DS9*
Rockow, Jill: Makeup artist, *DS9*
Roda, Ha Ngan Thi: 3D animator, *ST:I*
Rodahl, Mark: Digital superv, *ST:I*
Roddenberry, Gene: Creator-exec prod-writer, *TOS, TNG;* Prod, *ST:TMP;* Exec consultant, *ST2, ST3, ST4, ST5;* Theme from *Star Trek* television series, *ST:TMP; Star Trek* movies, *DS9,* and *VGR* are based on *Star Trek* created by
Roddenberry, Majel Barrett: Writer, *DS9*
Rode, Donald R.: Film editor, *TOS*
Rodis, Nilo: Art dir-costume designer, *ST5;* Art dir, *ST6;* Asst art dir, *ST4;* Visual effects art dir, *ST3, ST4*
Roesler, David: Key costumer, *TNG;* Costumer, *STG*
Rohland, James: Makeup artist, *ST:I, VGR*
Rolfe, Sam: Writer, *TNG, DS9*
Roman, Ron: Writer, *TNG*
Romanis, George: Music, *TNG*
Romano, Pete: Underwater whale photography, *ST4*
Romans, Penny: Choreographer, *TOS*
Romero, Ceasar: Inferno artist, *ST:I*
Ronci, Barbara: Hair stylist, *ST:FC*
Ronne, David, CAS: Sound mixer, *ST5*
Roose, Ronald: Editor, *ST6*
Rose, Joshua D.: Digital prod, *ST:FC*
Rosenberg, Grant: Writer, *TNG*
Rosenberg, Marty: Visual effects dir of photography, *ST:FC;* Asst cameraperson, *ST4*
Rosenfeld, Wendy: Postprod superv, *TNG*
Rosenfeldt, Tomàs: 3D animator, *ST:I*
Rosenman, Leonard and The Yellowjackets: Add'l musical score, *ST4*
Rosenman, Leonard: Music, *ST4*
Rosenstein, Ira Stanley: Location mgr, *ST:FC*
Rosenthal, Mark: Writer, *ST6*
Ross, Chris: Effects and miniatures, *ST:TMP*
Ross, Stephen J.: Prod, *ST5*
Ross, Susan: Modelmaker, *ST6*
Ross, William: Orchestrations, *STG*
Rosseter, Thomas: Digital compositor, *ST:FC;* Optical line up, *ST6, ST2*
Rossi, April: Postprod superv, *DS9, VGR;* Asst to Mr. Lauritson, *ST:FC*
Rossi, David: Postprod coord, *ST:FC;* Prod assoc, *TNG, DS9, VGR, ST:I*
Roth, Clifford: Special effects asst, *TOS*
Roth, Jeff: Casting asst, *ST:FC*
Rothbart, Jonathan: Digital animatic artist, *ST:FC*
Rothwell, John: Publicity, *ST:TMP*
Rourke Engineering: Mechanical designs, *ST:TMP*
Roux-Lough, Brigette: Asst to Mr. Bennett, *ST4*
Rowe, Rick: Construction grip, *ST:I*
Rowe, Stephen M.: Music editor, *DS9, STG*
Rowohlt, Robert: Senior optical photographer, optical unit, *ST5*
Rubenstein, Scott: Story editor-writer, *TNG*
Ruberg, Elden E., CAS: Re-recording mixer, *TOS*
Rubin, Dick: Prop master, *ST:TMP*
Rubinstein, Sylvia: Asst to Mr. Bennett, *ST3, ST4*
Rudnick, Arnold: Writer, *VGR*
Rudnyk, Marian: Roto artist, *ST:I*
Rugg, Jim: Special effects, *TOS*
Rush, Marvin V., ASC: Dir of photography, *TNG, VGR;* Dir of photography, *DS9*
Russ, Tim: Dir, *VGR*
Russell, Bill: Climbing rigger, *ST5*
Russell, Blake: Set designer, *ST3*
Russell, Greg P., CAS: Re-recording mixers, *ST6*
Russell, Paul Francis: Special effects asst, *ST:I*
Russell, Randee: Writer, *TNG*
Russell, Scott: Construction accounting asst, *ST6*
Russo, Charlie: Swing gang, *ST3*
Rutter, George A.: Script superv, *TOS*
Ryan, Jim: Computer programmer, *STG*
Ryan, Kevin J.: Writer, *VGR*
Rygiel, Jim: Visual effects superv, *ST:I*
Ryland Davies and The Orchestra and Chorus of the Royal Opera House, Covent Garden: "Vallon Sonore" from Les Troyens, performed by, *ST:FC*

Sabaroff, Robert: Writer, *TOS, TNG*
Sabre, Richard: Hair designer-hair superv, *TNG;* Hair stylist, *DS9*
Sackett, Susan: Prod assoc-writer, *TNG;* Asst to Mr. Roddenberry, *ST:TMP, ST4, ST5*
Sackman, Gerry.: Music editor, *TNG, DS9, VGR*
Saenz, Patrice D.: Digital matchmover, *ST:FC*
Sagan, Nicholas: Story editor, *VGR*; Writer, *TNG, VGR*
Saindon, Eric: Modeling, *ST:I*
Salerno, Nino: Tactical displays, *ST6*
Sallin, Robert: Prod, *ST2*
Samec, Kathi: Systems mgr, *STG, ST:I*
Samish, Peter: Set designer, *DS9*
Sampson, Jim: Asst property master, *ST:I*
Samuels, Brian: 3D animator, *ST:I*
Sanchez, Jorge: 2nd asst photographer, *STG*
Sanchez, Ralph: Writer, *TNG*
Sander, Rick: Digital effects, *ST:I*
Sanders, John: Digital record operator, *ST:I*
Sanders, Steve: Modelmaker, *ST2*
Sandler, Jeffrey L., MPSE: Sound effects editor, *STG*
Sanford, Gerald: Writer, *DS9*
Santa Barbara Film Commission: Thanks to, *ST:I*
Santa Barbara Studios: Special visual effects, *STG, ST:I;* Computer generated imagery-main title design, *VGR*
Santantonia, Kim: Hair stylist, *TNG*
Santiago, David: 3D animator, *ST:I*
Santoni, Mark: First asst photographer, *ST:FC, ST:I*
Santoni, Paul: 2nd asst photographer, *ST:FC*
Santy, Michael: Asst camera operator, *ST2*
Sardanis, Steve: Set designer, *TOS*
Sargent, Joseph: Dir, *TOS*
Sasgen, Joseph C.: Asst special effects, *DS9, ST6, ST5*
Sass, Steve: Electronic design, *ST:TMP*

Sater, Gerald L. "Jerry": Transportation coord, *ST6*
Satterfield, Stewart: Transportation captain, *TNG*, *DS9*, *VGR;* Transportation coord, *ST4*
Saunders, Lt. Lee: Acknowledgment, *ST4*
Sawicki, Marc: Matte photographer, *ST5*
Sawyer, Tom: Dolly grip, *ST3*
Scalzo, John: Rigging electrician, *ST:I*
Scanlan, Joseph L.: Dir, *TNG*
Scanlan, Tim: Postprod superv, *VGR*
Schaeffer, Bill: Roto artist, *ST:I*
Schafer, Ken: Writer, *TNG*
Schawb, Debbie: Asst to Mr. Schoenbrun, *ST3*
Scheerer, Robert: Dir, *TNG*, *DS9*, *VGR*
Scheideman, Elaine: Costume superv, *TNG*
Schertzinger, Victor: Music, *ST3*
Schick, Elliot: Asst dir, *TOS*
Schiffer, Paul: Writer, *TNG*
Schkolnick, Barry: Writer, *TNG*
Schlag, John: Computer graphics superv, *STG*
Schlichting, Paul F.: DGA trainee, *ST5*
Schmidt, Heidi: Digital tech asst, *ST:FC*
Schnaufer, Jeff: Writer, *VGR*
Schneider, Paul: Writer, *TOS*
Schnitzer, Chris: Motion control rigger, *DS9, VGR*
Schoenbrun, Michael P.: Unit prod mgr, *ST3*
Schoengarth, Bruce: Film editor, *TOS*
Schor, Leslie: Digital effects coord, *ST:I*
Schulkey, Curt: Sound effects editor, *ST2*
Schultz, Alan: Dolly grip, *ST:I*
Schultz, Dennis: Effects props and miniatures, *ST:TMP*
Schulz, Norman: Special effects asst, *TOS*
Schulze, Robert: Optical photographer, optical unit, *ST5*
Schuyler, John: Boom operator, *ST5*
Schwab, Deborah L.: Prod office coord, *ST:FC*
Schwalbe, Solange: Foley editor, *ST4*
Schwarcz, Bobbie: Casting asst, *ST:I*
Schwartz, Delmore: Special thanks, *STG*
Schwartz, Gregory: Still photographer, *ST6*
Schwartz, James: Electrician, *TOS*
Schwiebert, Chris: Camera operator, *TOS*
Scollard, Christopher: Digital effects prod, *ST:I*
Scorza, Philip A.: Writer, *TNG*
Scott, David: Effects props and miniatures, *ST:TMP*
Scott, L. J.: Writer, *TNG*
Scott, Michael, SOC: 2nd camera operator, *ST3*
SDDS-Sony Dynamic Digital Sound: In selected theatres, *ST:I*
Sears, Tony: Art dept prod asst, *VGR*
Seawright, Dennis B.: 2nd asst photographer, *ST5*
Seay, Jonathan: Photographic effects photography, *ST:TMP*
Secretary of the Air Force Office of Public Affairs Western Region: Acknowledgment, *ST:FC*
Segulin, Tim: Optical effects line up, *ST6*
Seibert, Carl: CG producer, *ST:I*
Seiden, Alex: Visual effects co-superv, *STG;* Computer graphics animator, *ST6*
Seifert, Dieter: Mechanical designs, *ST:TMP*
Seirafi, Ziad: Visual effects coord, *VGR*
Sellmer, Richard: Apprentice editor, *ST6*
Selzer, James: Asst location mgr, *ST:FC*
Sena, Sandra: Prod assoc, *DS9*, *VGR*
Senensky, Ralph: Dir, *TOS*
Senevirante, Gihan "Sandy": Rigging electrician, *ST:I*
Sepulveda, Alfredo R.: 2nd asst cameraman, *ST3*
Sepulveda, Fernando: Lead person, *VGR*
Serafine, Frank: Sound effects creation, *ST:TMP;* Special sound effects, *ST3*
Seron, Ori: Asst to Mr. Nimoy, *ST4*
Sertin, Charles: Property person, *ST4*
Server, Mark S.: Recordist, *ST2*
Severy, Cleo: Key costumer, *DS9*
Shaffer, Gary: Casting asst, *TOS*
Shaffer, Kendell: Visual effects coord, *DS9*
Shankar, Naren: Story editor-science consultant-writer, *TNG;* Writer, *VGR*
Shannon, John: Still photographer, *ST3*
Shapiro, Leonard "Tiger": 2nd asst dir, *TOS*
Sharp Electronics Corporation USA & Japan: TFT LCD color monitors by, *STG*
Shatner, William: Dir-writer, *ST5*
Shaw, Larry: Dir, *TNG*
Shaw, Sarah: Costume superv, *ST:FC*
Shea, John F.: Borg crew, *ST:FC*
Shea, Shannon: Creature creation, *ST4*
Shearer, Hannah Louise: Exec story editor-writer, *TNG;* Writer, *DS9*
Sheinberg, Noel: Optical coord, model unit, *ST5*
Sheldon, Lee: Prod-writer, *TNG*
Sheldon, Mindy: Asst prod accountant, *ST6*
Shelly, James: General mgr, Assocs & Ferren, *ST5*
Shelton, Kai: Special effects asst, *ST:I*
Shepard, Bill, CSA: Casting, *ST5;* Casting administrator, *ST4*
Shepard, Cecil: Boom operator, *TOS*
Shepard, Dodie: Costume designer, *ST6;* Costume superv, *ST5*
Shepherd, Robert: Photographic effects project mgr, *ST:TMP*
Sherman, Brad: Re-recording mixers, *ST:FC*
Sherwin, Jill: Asst to prods, *DS9*
Shine, Kathy: Travel arrangements, *ST2*
Shipley, Walter: Climbing rigger, *ST5*
Shirley, John: Writer, *DS9*
Shock, Hudson: Compositing superv, *ST:I*
Shockwave Entertainment: Special thanks, *STG*
Shomer, Amy: Prod asst, *ST:I*
Short, Robert: Effects props and miniatures, *ST:TMP*
Shostrom, Mark: Makeup artist, *VGR*
Shourt, Bill: Mechanical design, *ST:TMP*
Shourt, John: Prod illustrator, *ST:TMP*
Shreve, Leo: Film editor, *TOS*
Shugrue, Michael: Video engineer, *ST:I*
Shugrue, Robert F.: Editor, *ST3*
Shull, Kimberley: Key Costumer, *VGR*
Shultz, Alan: Dolly grip, *ST:FC*
Shumaker, Dan: Computer graphics tech asst, *ST:FC*
Shurtleff, Tut: Assistance to photographic effects, *ST:TMP*
Sibley, Paul: Climbing rigger, *ST5*
Sickles, Karen: CGI coordinator, *VGR*
Siegel, Tom: Key costumer, *VGR*, *STG*
Signorelli, Phil: Key costumer, *TNG*
Silfka, Richard King: Mold maker, *TNG*
Silicon Graphics, Inc.: Hardware support *ST:I*
Silver, Andrew: Preview music editor, *ST:I*
Silverberg, Daniel: 2nd asst dir, *STG*
Silvestri, Alan: "Makeover Mambo" by, *ST:I*
Simmons, Adele G.: First asst dir, *TNG*, *VGR*
Simmons, Charmaine Nash: Costumer, *TNG*
Simon, Bruce A.: Unit prod mgr-first asst dir, *TNG*
Simpson, Russ: Miniatures, *ST:TMP*
Sims, Alan: Property master, *TNG*, *VGR*
Singer, Alexander: Dir, *TNG*, *DS9*, *VGR*
Singer, Arthur H.: Story consultant-writer, *TOS*
Singer, Randy: Foley mixer, *STG, ST:FC*, *ST:I*
Singleton, Dick: Effects props and miniatures, *ST:TMP*
Siracusa, Jim: Sound effects editor, *ST2*
Sireika, David: 2nd company grip, *VGR*
Slater, Mary Jo, CSA: Casting, *ST6*
Slavin, George F.: Writer, *TOS*
Slifka, Richard King: Model maker, *TNG*, *DS9, VGR, ST:I*
Slocum, Robbin: Prod assoc, *DS9*
Slocum, Steve: Photographic effects photography, *ST:TMP*
Small, Thomas: Superv foley editor, *ST:I*; asst sound editor, *STG*
Smallberries, John: Orbital ergonomics, *ST:I*
Smiley, Richard: Effects props and miniatures, *ST:TMP*
Smith, Alvy Ray: Computer graphics, *ST2*
Smith, Daryl: Asst chief lighting tech (2nd unit), *ST:I*
Smith, Doug: Asst digital effects artist, *ST:FC;* Photographic effects cameraman, *ST:TMP*
Smith, Emile: CGI animator, *VGR*
Smith, Glenn: Aerial coord, *ST:I*
Smith, Gregory W.: First asst photographer, *STG*
Smith, Gregory: Music, *DS9*
Smith, Heather: Prod coord, *ST:FC*
Smith, Herb: 2nd grip, *TOS*
Smith, Keith: Dir of photography, *TOS*
Smith, Kenneth F.: Optical superv, *ST:FC;* Optical photography superv, *ST3;* Optical camera operator, *ST6;* Optical printer operator, *ST2*
Smith, Kim: Chief modelmaker, *ST:FC;* Modelmaker, *ST6, STG*
Smith, Mark: Re-recording mixer, *STG*
Smith, Nora Jeanne: Special editorial, *ST:TMP*
Smith, Pete: Art dir, *ST4*
Smith, Ronald W.: Hair stylist, *DS9*
Smith, Susan: Prod asst, *ST4*
Smith, Sylvia T.: Asst to prod, *TOS*
Smith, Tom: General mgr, ILM, *ST2*, *ST3*
Smothers, Heidi: Prod coord, *DS9*
Smothers, Waverly: 2nd company grip, *ST4*

Smutko, Al: Construction coord, *TNG*, *VGR*
Smythe, Doug: Computer graphics artist, *STG*
Snodgrass, Melinda M.: Exec script consultant-story editor-writer, *TNG*
Snow, Ben: Computer graphics artist, *STG*
Snowden, Tom: Optical layout, optical unit, *ST5*
Snyder, William E., ASE: Dir of photography, *TOS*
Sobelman, Boris: Writer, *TOS*
Soffer, Roger: Writer, *DS9*
Sohl, Jerry: Writer, *TOS*
Sokoloff, Elaine: Art studio paintings, *TNG*
Sokolsky, Ivan "Bing": Add'l photography, *ST:FC;* Dir of photography (2nd unit), *ST:I*
Soldo, Chris: First asst dir, *STG*
Soloman, Gerald: Hair stylist, *DS9*
Solow, Bruce Allen: First asst dir, *TNG*
Solow, Herbert F.: Exec in charge of prod, *TOS*
Somers, Evan Carlos: Writer, *DS9*, *VGR*
Sommers, Tony: Modelmaker, *STG*
Sonheim, Carol: Animal trainer, *ST:I*
Sony Corp of America: Computer monitors, *TNG*
Sorbel, Bob: Key grip, *ST:TMP;* First company grip, *TNG*, *DS9*, *VGR*
Sorce, Marsha: Recordist, *ST:I*
Sorokin, Joseph G.: Sound editor, *TOS*
Sosalla, David: Visual effects superv, *ST:I;* Creature superv, *ST3;* Effects props and miniatures, *ST:TMP*
Southcott, Tim: Camera asst, *TOS*
Sowards, Jack B.: Writer, *TNG*, *ST2*
Sparr, Robert: Dir, *TOS*
Speckman, Gary: Set designer, *TNG*, *VGR*
Spence, David: Sound effects editor, *ST5*
Spies, Adrian: Writer, *TOS*
Spinrad, Norman: Writer, *TOS*
Spohn, Stuart: Chief lighting tech, *STG*
Sprocket Systems: Add'l sound effects, *ST3*
Spurlock, Robert: Special effects, *ST4;* Effects props and miniatures, *ST:TMP*
Squadron, Seth: Prod asst, *ST:FC*
Squires, Scott: Photographic effects cameraman, *ST:TMP*
St. Clair, David M.: Operator, *STG*
Stafford, Fred: ADR editor, *ST6*
Stairs, Lt. Sandra: Acknowledgment, *ST4*
Stanton, Gabrielle: Writer, *DS9*
Stape, William N.: Writer, *TNG*
Starr, Christa: Computer graphics tech asst, *ST:FC*
State of California, State Lands Commissions: Special thanks, *ST5*
State of Nevada Dept of Conservation and Natural Resources: Special thanks, *STG*
Steele, Russell Alan: Prod asst, *ST6*
Stefano, Joseph: Writer, *TNG*
Steiner, Armin: Music scoring mixer, *ST6*
Steiner, Fred: Music composed and conducted, *TOS;* Music, *TNG*
Steinert, Kim: Asst prod office coord, *ST:I*
Steingasser, Spike: Writer, *TNG*
Steinhauer, Bob: Apprentice asst dir, *TOS*
Stel, Tim: Stage manager, Image G, *TNG, VGR, DS9*
Stephens, David J.: R&D superv, *ST:I*
Stepic, Irene: Costumer, *ST:I*
Steppenwolf: Music, *ST:FC*
Sternbach, Rick: Senior illustrator/tech consultant, *TNG*, *DS9*, *VGR;* Illustrator, *ST:TMP, ST5, ST:FC*
Sterry, Calvin: First company grip, *ST4*
Stetson, Mark: Effects props and miniatures, *ST:TMP*
Stevens, Richard M.: 2nd asst photographer, *ST6*
Stewart, Bryan: Writer, *TNG*
Stewart, Dave: Photographic effects dir of photography, *ST:TMP*
Stewart, Eddie: Precision printer, optical unit, *ST5*
Stewart, Harry: Special effects, *ST2*
Stewart, Patrick: Dir, *TNG*; assoc prod, *ST:I*
Stich, Eric: Electrical engineering, live action effects unit, *ST5*
Stich, William B., ACE: Editor, *DS9*
Stillman, Chris: Digital matte, *ST:FC*
Stillman, John: Computer graphics prod asst, *STG*
Stillwell, Eric A.: Writer-researcher-pre-prod assoc, *TNG;* Writer-prod assoc, *VGR*; prod assoc, *ST:I*
Stillwell, Mary: Asst to prod, *TOS*
Stimson, Mark: Asst special effects, *TNG*, *VGR*
Stipes, David: Visual effects superv, *TNG*, *DS9*, *VGR*
Stokes/Kohne Assocs, Inc.: "Entity" and "Soliton Wave" animation sequences, *TNG*
Stone, David, MPSE: Sound effects editor, *ST4*
Stone, Jack: Makeup artist, *TOS*
Stone, Joseph J.: Set decorator, *TOS*
Stotler, Simon: Prod asst, *ST:FC*
Stout, Janet: Costume superv, *TNG*
Stradling, Bob: Asst photographer, *ST5*
Strangis, Greg: Creative consultant, *TNG*
Strasburg, Heidi: Costumer, *ST:FC*
Straus, James Satoru: Animation superv, *ST:I*
Strayframes: Instrumentation displays computer animation, *ST3*
Stringer, Ken: 2nd asst dir, *ST3*
Strom, L. J.: Writer, *DS9*
Stromberg, Robert: Matte artist, *ST:FC; DS9, VGR*
Stromquist, Eben: Modelmaker, *ST6*
Sturgeon, Theodore: Writer, *TOS*
Subramaniam, Babu: First asst dir, *TNG*
Suhr, Randy: 2nd 2nd asst dir, *ST6*
Sullivan, Arthur: "A British Tar" from *H.M.S .Pinafore* by, *ST:I*
Sullivan, Becky, MPSE: Superv ADR editor, *STG*
Sullivan, John: Photographic effects cameraman, *ST:TMP*
Sullivan, Michael: Model photography design and lighting, *ST5*
Summers, Jaron: Writer, *TNG*
Sunley, Ed: Costume superv, *TNG*
Surma, Ron, CSA: Casting, *TNG*, *DS9*, *VGR*, *STG*, *ST:FC*, *ST:I*
Suskin, Mitch: Visual effects superv, *VGR*
Susman, Barton M.: Lead person, *ST4*, *ST5*
Sussman, Michael: Writer, *VGR*
Sutherland Computer Corporation: Computer equipment, *ST:TMP*
Sutherland, Duncan: Camera engineer, *STG*
Swanek, Dick: Optical superv, optical unit, *ST5*
Swann, Monte: 24-frame video displays, *ST6*
Swanson, Robert L.: Film editor, *TOS*
Swarthe, Robert: Special animation effects, *ST:TMP*
Sweeney, Michael: Photographic effects photography, *ST:TMP*
Sweeney, Patrick: Add'l visual effects photography, *ST:FC;* Visual effects camera operator, *STG;* Motion control camera operator, *ST6;* Camera operator, *ST4*
Sweeney, Rob: First asst climbing photographer, *ST5*
Sweet, Larry: First company grip (2nd unit), *ST:I*
Swensen, Edith: Writer, *TNG*
Swenson, Eric: Effects camera operator, *ST6*
Swett, Dave: Camera dept coord, *ST:I*
Sylte: Payroll superv, *STG*
Sylvester, Cory: Borg crew, *ST:FC*
Sylvester, Mark: Software support, *ST:I*
Symbolics, Inc., graphics division: Instrumentation displays computer animation, *ST3*
Szakmeister, Michael: Superv dialogue editor, *ST:FC*, *ST:I*
Szollosi, Tom: Writer, *VGR*

Tabacco, Michael: Modelmaker, *ST5*
Tade, Paul: Sound editor, *DS9*
Tahmizian, Jivan: Sound editor, *DS9*
Takahasi, Wes Ford: Animation superv, *ST6*
Takemura, David: Visual effects superv, *DS9, VGR, ST:FC;* Visual effects coord, *TNG*
Takeuchi, Peter: Visual effects prod, *ST6*
Talley, Tom: Construction foreperson, *ST:I; DS9*
Tan, Ka Yaw: CGI artist, *VGR*
Tan, Lawrence: Digital modeler, *ST:FC;* Model shop superv, *ST6;* Chief modelmaker, *ST4, STG;* Modelmaker, *ST2*
Tango, Jesse: Lighting tech, *STG*, *ST:I*
Tarcher, Jeremy: Writer, *TOS*
Tayir, Andre: Choreographer, *ST3*
Taylor, Bill, ASC: Borg matte painting, *ST:FC*
Taylor, Brenda: Prod asst, *ST:FC*
Taylor, Chad: Sabre compositing artist, *ST:FC*
Taylor, Dione: Hair stylist, *ST2*
Taylor, Jeri: Creator-exec prod-writer-creative consultant, *VGR;* Exec prod-writer, *TNG;* Writer, *DS9;* Special thanks, *STG;* Thanks for assistance, *ST:FC*
Taylor, Jud: Dir, *TOS*
Taylor, Michael: Writer, *DS9, VGR*
Taylor, Richard: RA&A designs, *ST:TMP*
Teague, Christopher: Writer, *DS9*
Tebeau, Scott D.: Borg dept head, *ST:FC*
Tebeau, Shanna: Borg crew, *ST:FC*

Technicolor: Color by, *ST4, ST5, ST6*
Templeman, Kirk: Key costumer, *TOS*
Terrian, Anita: Secretary, *ST:TMP*
Terry, Ken: First asst film editor, *ST:I*
Teska, John: CGI animator, *VGR*
Texier, Eric: Digital effects artist, *ST:FC*
Thatcher, Kirk: Assoc prod-music, *ST4*
Theisen, Ginger: Visual effects coords, *STG*
Theiss, William Ware: Costumes creation; exec consultant-original Starfleet uniforms, *TNG;* Costume creation, *TOS*
Theren, Paul: Digital modeler, *ST6, ST:FC*
Thom, Randy: Add'l sound effects, *ST3*
Thomas, Bob: Photographic effects photography, *ST:TMP*
Thomas, Cari: Visual effects coord, *DS9;* Scenic artist, *TNG, ST5*
Thomas, Jamie: Key costumer, *VGR;* Costumer, *STG*
Thompson, Bradley: Story editor-writer, *DS9*
Thompson, Greg: Asst sound editor, *ST6*
Thompson, Jr., John: 2nd grip, *TOS*
Thompson, Kimberley: Key costumer, *TNG*
Thompson, Rick: Effects props and miniatures, *ST:TMP*
Thompson, Robert D.: 3D animator, *ST:I*
Thoms, Wil: Asst special effects, *TNG, VGR*
Thomton, James: Writer, *VGR*
Thorin, Jeffrey S.: 2nd asst photographer, *ST5*
Thornberg, Sara: Prod coord, *DS9*
Thorne, Worley: Writer, *TNG*
Thornton, Randy D.: Asst film editor, *ST:TMP*
Thornton, Ron: CGI producer, *VGR*
Thorson, Robert Cecil: Prod auditor, *ST4*
Ticotin, David A.: 2nd 2nd asst dir, *ST:FC*
Tidwell, Wayne: Video assist, *ST:FC, ST:I*
Tieman, Debbie: Asst prod auditor, *STG;* Asst prod accountant, *ST6*
Tierney, Joy: Seamstress, *TOS*
Tillinger, Harrison: Special effects asst, *TOS*
Tinta, Paul: Asst sound editor, *ST:I*
Tipton, Brian: Special effects, *ST4*
Tistone, Anthony: Electrician, *TOS*
To, Lam Van: Computer graphics tech asst, *ST:FC*
Todd A-O Studios: Sound, *STG*
Todd A-O/GlenGlenn Studios: Sound, *ST4, ST5*
Todd Masters Co.: Borg effects creation, *ST:FC*
Todd, Ryan: 3D digital artist, *ST:I*
Tom, Robert: Digital paint artist, *ST:FC*
Tomita, Masanobu "Tomi": Sound effects editor, *STG;* Sound editor, *TNG;* Superv sound effects editor, *VGR*
Tooke, Peterson: Motion control stage mgr, *ST5*
Tooley, Suzie Vissotzky: Computer graphics prod mgr, *ST:FC*
Tordjmann, Fabien: Film editor, *TOS*
Tormé, Tracy: Creative consultant-exec story editor-writer, *TNG*
Torres, Robert A.: First asst cameraman, *ST3*
Toussieng, Yolanda: Superv hair stylist, *ST:I;* hair designer, *TNG;* Key hairstylist, *ST:FC*
Townsend, Nancy P.: 2nd 2nd asst dir, *ST:I*
Trapp, Kaye: Asst property master, *ST4*
Travis, Debbie: Costumer, *ST:I*
Traxel, Mel: Still photographer, *ST:TMP*
Tremblay, Susan: 2D superv, model unit, *ST5*
Treviño, Jack: Writer, *DS9*
Treviño, Jesús Salvador: Dir, *DS9, VGR*
Treweek, Laurence: Computer graphics artist, *STG*
Trifkovic, Dragisa: 2D digital artist, *ST:I*
Trimble, Bjo: Rock collection by, *ST2*
Tripi, Alicia: Hair stylist, *DS9*
Trivers, Barry: Writer, *TOS*
Trombetta, Jim: Writer, *DS9, VGR*
Trotter, Morgan: Digital compositor, *ST:FC*
Trotti, David: 2nd asst dir, *TNG;* DGA trainee, *ST6*
Trumbull, Don: Mechanical design, *ST:TMP*
Trumbull, Douglas: Dir, special photographic effects, *ST:TMP*
Tsujimoto, Guy: Sound editor, *TNG, DS9*
Tucker, David: Optical painting, *ST6*
Tucker, Steve: Editor, *TNG, DS9*
Tugendhaft, Barry R.: Greensperson, *ST:FC*
Tumen, Marion: Script superv, *ST5*
Turner, Dennis: Computer graphics sequence superv, *ST:FC;* Computer graphics artist, *STG*
Turner, Kyle: Asst to Tom Smith, *ST2*
Turner, Patrick: Plate camera operator, *ST6*
Turner, Paul: Effects props and miniatures, *ST:TMP*
Turner, Susan: Effects props and miniatures, *ST:TMP*
Tuskes, Alan: Borg crew, *ST:FC*
Twentieth Century Fox: Music score recorded at, *ST6*
Tyson, Elliot: Re-recording mixer, *ST:I*
Tyus, Pernell Youngblood: Camera operator *VGR, STG*

U.S. Coast Guard, Long Beach: Acknowledgment, *ST4*
U.S. Coast Guard, San Francisco: Acknowledgment, *ST4*
U.S. Forest Service: Special thanks, *STG*
Uesugi, Yusei: Digital matte artist, *STG*
Ullman, Stephen: Camera operator/B cam, *ST:I*
Ulrich, Robert, MPSE: Superv ADR editor, *ST:FC, ST:I*
Unger, Penny, Asst to prod, *TOS*
United States Marine Corp Air/Ground Combat Center, 29 Palms, California: Special thanks, *ST3*
Unitel Video: Editing facilities, *TNG, DS9, VGR*
Unsinn, Jim: Video playback, *DS9;* 24-frame video displays, *ST6*
Unsinn, III, Joseph A.: Video playback superv, *STG;* Video playback operator, *DS9*
USDA Forest Service, Angeles National Forest: Thanks for assistance, *ST:FC*

Valdez, III, Frank X.: Asst chief lighting tech, *STG, ST:FC*; Lighting tech, *ST:I*
Valencia, Danny: Hair stylist, *ST:FC*
Valencia, Rick: Transportation captain, *ST2*
Valentine, Joe: Camera operator, *ST5*
Valley of Fire State Park: Special thanks, *STG*
Vallone, John: Art dir, *ST:TMP*
Van Auken, Pat: Effects props effects grip, *ST:TMP*
Van Heusen, James: Music, *ST:FC*
Van Over, James E.: Scenic artist, *DS9, VGR, ST:FC, ST:I;* Special thanks, *STG*
Van Slyke, David F.: Sound effects editor, *ST:FC*
Van Thillo, Wim: Modelmaker, *ST6*
Vandenecker, Tony: Special effects, *ST3*
Vanderveer Photo Effects: Photographic effects, *TOS*
Vargo, Mark: Optical printer operator, *ST2*
Varney, Bill: Superv re-recording mixer, *ST:TMP*
Varney, Shaun: Add'l sound design by, *ST:I*
Vaughn, Bruce: Asst photographer, live action effects unit, *ST5*
Vaughn, Lisa: Optical scanning coord, *ST6*
Vecchio, Faith: Hair stylist, *DS9*
Vecchitto, Bruce: Optical superv, *STG;* Optical lineup, *ST4*
Veilleux, Gaston: Transportation coord, *STG;* Transportation captain, *ST5*
Veilleux, Jim: Special visual effects superv, *ST2*
Vejar, Michael: Dir, *TNG, DS9*
Velasquez, David: Key costumer, *TNG*
Velazquez, Dawn: Coprod-assoc prod-postprod superv, *VGR;* Postprod coord, *TNG, DS9;* Asst to Mr. Lauritson, *STG*
Veneziano, Sandy L.: Art dir, *TNG, STG;* Asst art dir, *ST5*
Ventresco, Michael: Senior effects animator, optical unit, *ST5*
Venuto, A. J.: Borg crew, *ST:FC*
Vermont, Laurie: Prod coord, *ST3*
Vernon, Billy: Script superv, *TOS*
Vesely, Lila: 3D digital artist, *ST:I*
Vetter, John: Film loader, *ST:I*
Victor, Teresa E.: Asst to Mr. Nimoy, *ST3*
Video Image: 24-frame video displays, *ST6*; Computer animation and tactical displays, *ST4*
Viespi, Wayne: Grip, *ST:I*
VIFX: Computer animation segments, *DS9*
Vignes, Valentine: Asst model wrangler, model unit, *ST5*
Vill, Kerry A.: Prod asst, *ST:FC*
Villasenor, Paul: Visual effects asst editor, *VGR*
Villaseor, George C.: Asst film editor, *ST4, ST5*
Vision Art Design & Animation: Computer animation, *DS9, VGR*
Vision Art: Digital visual effects, *ST:FC*
Visual Concept Engineering: Add'l animation, *ST2*
Vitolla, Pat: Grip: *VGR*
Voegler, Charles: Video playback operator, *ST:I*
Voightlander, Bill: ADR editor, *ST5*
Vollaerts, Rik: Writer, *TOS*
Von Puttkamer, Jesco: Special science advisor, *ST:TMP*

Voss, Ron: Labor foreperson, *VGR*
Vreeland, Russell: 2nd asst dir, *TOS*

Waddy, Colin: Sound editor, *ST:TMP*
Wade, Brian: Creature creation, *ST4;* Klingon and Vulcan prosthetics, *ST5*
Wagner, Dianne: Set designer, *STG*
Wagner, Michael: Writer, *TNG*
Wallace, Art: Writer, *TOS*
Wallace, Brian: Set security, *ST6*
Wallach, Peter: Motion control & animation superv, model unit, *ST5*
Wallerstein, Herb: Dir, *TOS*
Wallin, Dan, Record Plant Scoring: Scoring mixer, *ST2, ST3, ST4*
Walters, Bruce: Effects camera superv, *ST6;* Animation camera operator, *ST4;* Effects animator, *ST3*
Walters, Ron: Makeup artist, *ST6*
Walton, Steve: Modelmaker, *STG*
Walvoord, Dave: Senior lighting effects specialist, *ST:I*
Walzer, Andrea: Script superv, *ST6*
Wam!Net, Inc.: Hardware support, *ST:I*
Ward, J. D.: Recordist, *ST5*
Ward, Lazard: Set security, *TNG, VGR*
Warnaar, Brad: Orchestrations, *STG*
Warnek, Steve: Writer, *DS9*
Warren, Gene: Special designs (props), *TOS*
Wash, John: Computer animation and tactical displays, *ST4*
Washburn, Charles: 2nd asst dir, *TOS*; 1st asst dir, *TNG*
Wassel, Liz: 2D artist, model unit, *ST5*
Wassel. Mike: Matte artist, *ST:FC*
Waterhouse, Abram: Co-costume designer, *TNG, DS9*
Watson, Brent: Starfield and tactical displays, *ST2*
Watters, II, George: Superv sound editor, *ST6;* Sound editor, *ST:TMP, ST2, ST3*
Wax, Jerry: Set dresser, *ST:FC, ST:I*
Weathers, Michael: Chief lighting tech (2nd unit), *ST:I*
Weaver, Andra: Costumer, *TOS*
Webb, Alan D.: Process projection support, *ST5*
Webb, E. Gedney: Music, *TNG*
Webber, Don: Effects props and miniatures, *ST:TMP*
Weber, R. Stephen: Makeup artist, *ST:FC*
Webster, Brett: Asst to photographic effects, *ST:TMP*
Webster, Ron: Computer engineering, *ST5*
Weddle, David: Story editor-writer, *DS9*
Weed, Howie: Modelmaker, *ST6, STG*
Weeks, Gary: Effects props and miniatures, *ST:TMP*
Weeks, Randy: Tactical displays, *ST6*
Weinstein, Howard: Special thanks, *ST4*
Weis, Michael: Tech advisor, *ST5*
Weldon, Alex: Mechanical special effects, *ST:TMP*
Weldon, Michael D.: First asst photographer, *ST:FC*
Welke, Stephen: Postprod superv, *VGR*
Wells, Richard D.: First asst dir, *TNG, DS9*
Wendell, Mark: CGI superv, *ST:I;* Animator, *STG*
Wensel, Brian: Prod accountant, *ST6*
Werksman, Harry M.: Writer, *DS9*
Wescam, Inc.: Wescam provided by, *ST:FC*
Wesley, Ken: Digital effects artist, *ST:FC*
West, Jonathan, ASC: Dir-dir of photography, *TNG, DS9*
West, Ray, CAS: Re-recording mixer, *ST2, ST3*
Westerfield, Karen J.: Makeup artist, *DS9*
Westheimer Company: Titles and opticals, *ST5;* Add'l optical effects, *ST4;* Photographic effects, *TOS*
Westmore, June: Makeup artist, *ST:FC, ST:I*
Westmore, II, Michael: Editor, *DS9;* Asst editor, *TNG;* Prosthetic electronics, *TNG;* Electronic appliances, *ST:FC*
Westmore, Michael: Makeup design and superv, *TNG, DS9, VGR, ST:FC, ST:I ;* Special makeup effects design and supervision, *STG*
Westmore, Monty: Makeup artist, *ST:FC, ST:I*
Westmore, Pat: Hair styles, *TOS*
Weston, Tom: Photographer, live action effects unit, *ST5*
Wetmore, Evans: Electronic and mechanical design, *ST:TMP*
Whalen, Shawn: 2nd company grip, *ST:I*
Wheeler, Charles F., ASC: Add'l photography, *ST:TMP*
Wheeler, Don: Effects props and miniatures, *ST:TMP*
Wheeler, John W., ACE: Film editor, *ST:FC*
Wheeler, Scott: Makeup artist, *VGR, ST:FC, ST:I*
Whelan, Shawn: 2nd company grip, *ST:FC*
Whelpley, John: Writer, *TNG, DS9*
Whipple, Don: Dolly grip, *TOS, ST2*
Whisnant, John D.: Optical line up, *ST6*
White, Dana: Model maker, *TNG*
White, Jack: 2nd company grip, *DS9*
White, Linle: Hair stylist, *DS9*
White, Lisa P.: Writer, TNG
White, Lisa: Location mgr, *TNG, DS9, VGR*
Whitfield, Rick: Video coord, *ST3*
Whitley, Brian: First asst dir, *DS9*
Whitlock, Albert: Matte paintings, *TOS*
Whittaker, David A., MPSE: Sound effects editor, *ST5*
Wiatr, Bob: Compositor, *ST:I*
Widin, Bernard A.: Prod superv, *TOS*
Wiemer, Robert: Dir, *TNG, DS9*
Wigginton, Pam: Writer, *DS9*
Wilber, Carey: Writer, *TOS*
Wilbur, Todd: 3D animator, *ST:I*
Wilcox, Kelly: 3D digital artist, *ST:I*
Wilder, Brad: Makeup artist, *ST:I*
Wildfire, LA: Ultraviolet effect and lighting, *ST6; TNG*
Wiley, Charles: Modelmaker, *ST6*
Wilhoite, Lance: Compositor, *ST:I*
Wilkerson, Ronald: Writer, *TNG, VGR*
Wilkinson, Frost: Photographer, *ST5*
Wilkinson, Ronald R.: Art dir, *ST:FC, ST:I;* Set designer, *DS9, ST5, ST6, STG*
Williams, Anson: Dir, *DS9, VGR*
Williams, Anthony: Writer, *VGR*
Williams, Bernie: Exec prod-unit prod mgr, *STG*
Williams, Edward L.: Visual effects series coord, *DS9;* Visual effects coord, *TNG;* Visual effects superv, *VGR*
Williams, Eric: Sound editor, *DS9*
Williams, Georgina: Hair stylist, *TNG*
Williams, Kerry Dean: Sound effects editor, *ST:FC, ST:I*
Williams, Larry: Asst VFX editor, *ST:I*
Williams, Michael: Prod asst, *STG*
Willis, Mike: Scanning operator, *ST5*
Wills, Ralph: Writer, *TNG*
Wilson, Dean: Property master, *ST:FC*
Wilson, Mitch: Senior color timer, optical unit, *ST5*
Wilson, Victoria: Asst to Mr. Carson, *STG*
Wiltz, Murphy: Best boy, *ST2*
Wilzbach, Greg: Animation and graphics, *ST:TMP*
Windell, Terry: Dir, *VGR*
Winer, Martin A.: Writer, *DS9*
Wingo, Derik: Borg crew, *ST:FC*
Winiger, Ralph Allen: Special effects asst, *ST:FC, ST:I*
Winter, Ralph: Exec prod, *ST4, ST5;* Prod, *ST6;* Assoc prod, *ST3*
Winter, Robin: 2nd asst dir, *DS9*
Wise, Douglas E.: First asst dir, *ST2, ST4, ST5, ST6;* 2nd asst dir, *ST:TMP*
Wise, Rob: Asst cameraman, *ST:TMP*
Wise, Robert: Dir, *ST:TMP*
Wisner, Ken: Mechanical engineering, live action effects unit, *ST5*
Wistrom, Bill: Superv sound editor, *TNG, DS9, VGR;* Thanks for assistance, *ST:FC*
Witherspoon, Wayne: Addl 2nd asst dir, *ST:I*
Witt, Vicki: Asst editor, *ST2;* Photographic effects editorial, *ST:TMP*
Witthans, Bill: Dolly grip, *DS9*
Witters, David J.: 3D digital artist, *ST:I*
Wolande, Gene: Writer, *DS9*
Wolf, Butch: Foley editor, *ST6*
Wolfe, Lawerence N.: Writer, *TOS*
Wolfe, Robert Hewitt: Prod-exec story editor-writer, *DS9;* Writer, *TNG*
Wolff, Debra: Optical line up, *ST6*
Wolpa, Jack: Men's wardrobe superv, *ST3*
Wolvington, James W.: Superv sound editor, *STG, ST:FC, ST:I;* Superv sound editor-superv sound effects editor, *TNG, DS9, VGR*
Wonderworks: Miniatures, *VGR*
Wood, Durinda Rice: Costume designer, *TNG*
Wood, Eugene: Visual effects coord-asst editor, *VGR;* Asst editor, *DS9*
Wood, Jonathan: Digital effects, *ST:I*
Wood, Kelley: Prod coord, *STG*
Wood, Michael L.: Special effects superv, *ST5*
Wood, Natalie, Makeup artist, *VGR*
Woods, Beth: Writer, *TNG*
Woods, Jack: Sound editor, *ST6;* Sound effects editor, *ST3*
Wooten, Diane E.: Photographic effects photography, *ST:TMP*
Wordes, Smith: Choreographer, *ST:FC*
Work, Christi: Key costumer, *ST:I*
Workman, Jimmy: Prod asst, *ST:I*
Worman, Alex: Unit publicist, *ST:FC*
Worsdale, Lt. Col. Thomas R.: Acknowledgment, *ST:FC*
Wright, Edmond: Grip, *DS9*
Wright, Herbert J.: Prod-writer, *TNG*
Wright, James: Dolby sound consultant, *ST:I*

Wright, John D.: Rigging electrician, *ST:I*
Wright, John: Writer, *DS9*
Wright, Michelle: Prod superv, *STG*
Wrinkle, Sharon: Prod accountant, *ST:I*

Yacobian, Brad: Line prod-unit prod mgr, *VGR;* Unit prod mgr-first asst dir, *TNG*
Yale, Dan: Sound editor, *TNG*, *DS9*
Yeatman, Hoyt: Photographic effects cameraman, *ST:TMP*
Yerxa, Alison: Animation and graphics, *ST:TMP*; Art dept superv, *ST:I*
Yeung, Tsz "Gee": Digital effects, *ST:I*
Yosemite National Park Services: Special thanks, *ST5*
Yoshimura, Jesse: Prod asst, *ST:I*
Yost, Jeffery: Computer graphics software, *ST:FC*
Young, John: Loader, *ST:FC*
Younger, Larry: Compositing asst, *DS9, VGR*
Yuricich, Matthew: Matte paintings, *ST:TMP*
Yuricich, Richard: Prod, special photographic effects-effects dir of photography, *ST:TMP*
Yurosek, Dennis: Orchestrations, *STG*

Zabit, Heidi: Digital rotoscope and paint, *ST:FC*
Zach, Tim: Decals and graphics, model unit, *ST5*
Zambrano, Jacqueline: Writer, *TNG*
Zapata, Joy A.: Hair designer-hair stylist, *TNG;* Key hair stylist, *STG*
Zargarpour, Habib: Computer graphics superv/animator, *ST:FC;* Computer graphics artist, *STG*
Zicree, Marc Scott: Writer, *TNG, DS9*
Zietlow, Jacqueline: VCE administration, *ST6*
Zimmerman, Chad: Visual effects assoc, *VGR*; Asst to prods, *DS9, VGR*
Zimmerman, Fritz: Set designer, *DS9*
Zimmerman, Harry: 2nd asst photographer, *ST:I*
Zimmerman, Herman: Prod designer-visual consultant, *DS9;* Prod designer-original set design, *TNG;* Prod designer, *ST5*, *ST6*, *STG, ST:FC*, *ST:I*
Zimmerman, Thomas: Borg crew, *ST:FC*
Zoller, Debbie: Makeup artist, *STG*
Zuberano, Maurice: Prod illustrator, *ST:TMP*
Zuckerman, Ed: Writer, *TNG*
Zurawski, George: On-set dresser, *DS9*
Zutavern, Louis J.: Modelmaker, *TNG, DS9, VGR*

BIBLIOGRAPHY

Alexander, David: *Star Trek Creator, the Authorized Biography of Gene Roddenberry* (Roc Books, 1994). In-depth biography of *Star Trek*'s creator.

Asherman, Allan: *The Making of Star Trek II* (Pocket Books, 1982). Interviews with key production personnel and the cast of the second feature film.

Asherman, Allan: *The Star Trek Compendium* (Pocket Books, rev. ed. 1993). Episode-by-episode guide to the original *Star Trek* series and feature films.

Asherman, Allan: *The Star Trek Interview Book* (Pocket Books, 1988). Interviews with cast and key creative personnel from the original *Star Trek* television series and feature films.

Bormanis, Andre: *Star Trek Science Logs* (Pocket Books, 1998). Science in the *Star Trek* universe, by the show's science consultant.

Chaikin, Andrew: *A Man on the Moon: The Voyages of the Apollo Astronauts* (Viking, 1994; Penguin 1998). An account of those who participated in one of the greatest adventures in human history.

Clarke, Arthur C.: *Profiles of the Future* (Bantam Books, 1958). Clarke's classic exploration into the limits of technology; arguably the source of inspiration for some of *Star Trek*'s future science.

Dillard, J.M.: *Star Trek: Where No One Has Gone Before, A History in Pictures* (Pocket Books, rev. ed. 1996). A photographic history of *Star Trek* from the original series to *Star Trek: Voyager*. Introduction by William Shatner.

Dillard, J.M. and Eaves, John: *Star Trek Sketchbook: The Movies* (Pocket Books, 1997). The art of *Star Trek Generations* and *Star Trek: First Contact*.

Erdmann, Terry J.: *Star Trek Action!* (Pocket Books, 1998). Lavish photo essay of the making of two minutes of finished film from *Star Trek: Deep Space Nine*, *Star Trek: Voyager*, and *Star Trek: Insurrection*.

Erdmann, Terry J.: *The Secrets of Star Trek: Insurrection* (Pocket Books, 1998). Behind the scenes of the ninth *Star Trek* movie.

Gerrold, David: *The Trouble with Tribbles* (Ballantine Books, 1974). Gerrold's experiences in the writing and production of the classic Original Series episode.

Gerrold, David: *The World of Star Trek* (Ballantine Books, 1974; rev. ed. Bluejay Books, 1984). Overview of the original *Star Trek* phenomenon by one of the writers of the original *Star Trek* series.

Johnson, Shane: *Mr. Scott's Guide to the Enterprise* (Pocket Books, 1987). Technical information on the refurbished ship from the first few *Star Trek* movies.

Koenig, Walter: *Chekov's Enterprise: A Personal Journal of the Making of Star Trek: The Motion Picture* (Pocket Books, 1980; Intergalactic Press, 1991). Anecdotes from the actor's personal diary.

Krauss, Lawrence M.: *The Physics of Star Trek* (Basic Books, 1995). Real science as seen through the *Star Trek* universe. Introduction by Stephen W. Hawking.

Nemecek, Larry: *Star Trek: The Next Generation Companion* (Pocket Books, rev. ed. 1995). Episode-by-episode guide to the series.

Okrand, Marc: *The Klingon Dictionary* (Pocket Books, 1985). Authentic reference to the spoken Klingon language by the linguist who invented it for the films and television shows.

Okuda, Michael and Okuda, Denise: *Star Trek Chronology: The History of the Future* (Pocket Books, rev. ed. 1996). A definitive timeline of the *Star Trek* universe.

Poe, Stephen: *A Vision of the Future: Star Trek: Voyager* (Pocket Books, 1997). Behind the scenes of *Star Trek: Voyager*.

Reeves-Stevens, Judith and Garfield: *The Art of Star Trek* (Pocket Books, 1995). An extensive collection of art from all incarnations of *Star Trek*. Introduction by Herman Zimmerman.

Reeves-Stevens, Judith and Garfield: *The Making of Star Trek: Deep Space Nine* (Pocket Books, 1994). Behind the scenes of *Star Trek: Deep Space Nine*.

Reeves-Stevens, Judith and Garfield: *Star Trek Phase II* (Pocket Books, 1997). The making of the *Star Trek* sequel series that was *almost* produced in 1977.

Reeves-Stevens, Judith and Garfield: *Star Trek: The Next Generation—The Continuing Mission* (Pocket Books, 1997). Behind the scenes of *Star Trek: The Next Generation*.

Sackett, Susan and Roddenberry, Gene: *The Making of Star Trek: The Motion Picture* (Pocket Books, 1980). Behind the scenes of the first feature film.

Sagan, Carl: *Pale Blue Dot: A Vision of the Human Future in Space* (Random House, 1994). Present-day adventures of the exploration of interplanetary space and a look into the future.

Shatner, William with Kreski, Chris: *Star Trek Memories* (HarperCollins, 1993). Anecdotes from the making of the original series.

Shatner, William with Kreski, Chris: *Star Trek Movie Memories* (HarperCollins, 1994). Anecdotes from the making of the *Star Trek* feature films.

Sherwin, Jill: *Quotable Star Trek* (Pocket Books, 1999). Wit and wisdom from the final frontier.

Solow, Herbert F. and Justman, Robert H: *Inside Star Trek, The Real Story* (Pocket Books, 1996). Insightful, authoritative history of the original *Star Trek* series by two of the key figures who made it happen.

Solow, Herbert F. and Solow, Yvonne F.: *Star Trek Sketchbook: The Original Series* (Pocket Books, 1997). Features the works of such luminaries as Matt Jefferies, William Ware Theiss, Fred Phillips, and Wah Chang.

Sternbach, Rick and Okuda, Michael: *Star Trek: The Next Generation Technical Manual* (Pocket Books, 1991). Just about everything you ever wanted to know about the inner workings of the *Starship Enterprise*-D, in far more technical detail than you *ever* wanted to know it. Introduction by Gene Roddenberry.

Sternbach, Rick: *Star Trek: The Next Generation U.S.S. Enterprise NCC-1701-D Blueprints* (Pocket Books, 1996). Detailed deck plans of the *Galaxy*-class *U.S.S. Enterprise*-D. Introduction by Robert H. Justman.

Stine, G. Harry: *Living in Space, A Handbook for Work an Exploration Stations Beyond the Earth's Atmosphere* (M Evans and Company, 1997). Cool stuff we'll need to d before we can get around to building starships.

Toffler, Alvin: *Future Shock* (Random House, 1970). Toffler's classic treatise on the impact of technology and acceleratin change on our society.

Trimble, Bjo: *On the Good Ship Enterprise, My 15 Years With Sta Trek* (Donning Company, 1982). Trimble's adventures in an around *Star Trek* production, fandom, and conventions.

Trimble, Bjo: *The Star Trek Concordance* (Citadel Press, rev. ed. 1995). Trimble's updated reference to the first *Star Tre* series, the movies, and the animated *Star Trek*.

Whitfield, Stephen E. and Roddenberry, Gene: *The Making of Sta Trek* (Ballantine Books, 1968). Behind the scenes of the firs *Star Trek* television series.

Zimmerman, Herman and Sternbach, Rick and Drexler, Doug: *Star Trek: Deep Space Nine Technical Manual* (Pocke Books 1998). The technical details of our favorite deep space station as well as lots of Starfleet hardware. Introduction by Ira Steven Behr, with an afterword by Ronald D. Moore.

Zubrin, Robert and Wagner, Richard: *The Case for Mars, The Plan to Settle the Red Planet and Why We Must* (Simon & Schuster, 1997). Ingenious proposal for a voyage to Mars using mostly existing technology, and a look at the benefits of such an enterprise.

ABOUT THE AUTHORS

Michael Okuda is the scenic art supervisor for *Star Trek: Voyager.* He is responsible for that show's control panels, signage, alien written languages, computer readout animation, and other strange things. Michael worked on all seven years of *Star Trek: The Next Generation* and *Star Trek: Deep Space Nine*. His other credits include six *Star Trek* feature films, *The Flash, The Human Target,* and the never-seen American version of *Red Dwarf.*

Along with Rick Sternbach, Michael serves as a technical consultant to the writing staff of *Star Trek* and is coauthor of the *Star Trek: The Next Generation Technical Manual* book and CD-ROM. Michael grew up in Hawai'i, where he graduated from Roosevelt High School and earned a BA in communications from the University of Hawai'i at Manoa. He is a member of IATSE Local 816 (Scenic, Title and Graphic Artists) and is a member of the American Civil Liberties Union. Mike is a proponent of science education and he *really* wants to be the first graphic artist in space.

Denise Okuda's credits include *Star Trek: Deep Space Nine, Star Trek: Insurrection, Star Trek: First Contact, Star Trek Generations, Star Trek VI: The Undiscovered Country,* and promotional work for 20th-Century Fox's cult classic, *The Adventures of Buckaroo Banzai: Across the Eighth Dimension.* Taking advantage of her degree in nursing, Denise has occasionally served as a medical consultant to the writing staff of *Star Trek.* Her hobbies include tropical fish and frequent trips to Yosemite National Park. She is active in supporting environmental causes and is an ardent fan of the Green Bay Packers.

Denise currently works as a video supervisor for *Star Trek: Voyager.* Along with her husband, Michael, Denise is a coauthor of the *Star Trek Chronology: The History of the Future,* an associate producer on Simon & Schuster Interactive's *Star Trek Omnipedia* and the *Captain's Chair* CD-ROM, and a consultant on *Buckaroo Banzai: Ancient Secrets & New Mysteries*. Denise lives in Los Angeles, California, with her husband and their dogs, Molly and Tranya.

Doug Drexler (illustrator) is an Academy Award®–winning makeup artist who always wanted to be a graphic designer. He did graphics on all seven years of *Star Trek: Deep Space Nine*, where he had the time of his life. His other *Star Trek* credits include makeup work for *Star Trek: The Next Generation* and graphics for *Star Trek Generations* and *Star Trek: First Contact*. Doug, who is a fan of the late, great Frank Sinatra, says the biggest thrill in his career was helping to re-create the classic original *Starship Enterprise* for the *Star Trek: Deep Space Nine* episode, "Trials and Tribble-ations." Doug designed illustrations and diagrams for *The Star Trek Encyclopedia* and is a coauthor of the *Star Trek: Deep Space Nine Technical Manual*.

Margaret Clark (photo editor, not shown) is an executive editor for Pocket Books' *Star Trek* publishing program. Before joining Pocket Books, Margaret worked as an editor at various publishers, specializing in illustrated works. The books she edited were honored on three separate occasions with gold medals from the Society of Illustrators. Margaret, who grew up on Long Island where the Apollo Lunar Module was built, was responsible for the massive task of selecting the photos used in this tome. To quote the authors, "Better you doing it than us."

Authors' photography by Robbie Robinson.